McDougal Littell

THE LANGUAGE OF LITERATURE

ANNOTATED TEACHER'S EDITION

GRADE

     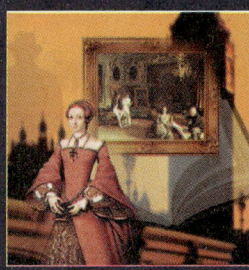

WARNING: No part of this book may be reproduced or transmitted in any form or by any means, electronic or mechanical, including photocopying and recording, or by any information storage and retrieval system, without prior written permission of McDougal Littell Inc. unless such copying is expressly permitted by federal copyright law. Address inquiries to Manager, Rights and Permissions, McDougal Littell, Inc., P.O. Box 1667, Evanston, IL 60204.

ISBN: 0-395-73711-7

Copyright © 1997 by McDougal, Littell, Inc.
Box 1667, Evanston, Illinois 60204

All rights reserved. Printed in the United States of America.

1 2 3 4 5 6 7 8 9 - DWO - 01 00 99 98 97 96

Table of Contents

Telling Our Story
What Is *The Language of Literature?* T4
Program Authors and Consultants T5

Overview
Core Components T6
Resource Materials T8
Integrated Technology T8
Assessment Package T9
Access for Students Acquiring English T9

A Closer Look

TEACHING LITERATURE
The Literature Lesson: Pupil Edition T10
The Literature Lesson: Resource Materials T12

INTEGRATING LANGUAGE AND WRITING SKILLS
The Writing Workshops: Pupil Edition T14
Writing and Language: Resource Materials T17
Special Features of the Pupil Edition T18

THE TEACHER'S EDITION
Unit Support T20
Selection and Writing Workshop Support T22

ASSESSMENT
Assessment Resources T24

Advice from the Experts
Practical suggestions for planning your school year

Planning Your Year T26
Developing a Classroom Profile: Understanding Learning Styles T28
Developing a Classroom Profile: Students Acquiring English T29
Planning Your Instruction T30
Setting Up Your Classroom T32
New Technology and the English Classroom T34
Preparing for Assessment T36
Making Connections T39

Annotated Student Text

Additional Unit Resources
Unit 1 Resources 13A
Unit 2 Resources 175A
Unit 3 Resources 337A
Unit 4 Resources 479A
Unit 5 Resources 583A
Unit 6 Resources 711A

THE LANGUAGE OF LITERATURE

Telling Our Story

What Is *The Language of Literature*?

Is it a literature anthology? an integrated language arts series? a new approach to teaching and learning? *The Language of Literature* is all of these things—and much, much more.

CLASSIC STORIES, FRESH VOICES, AND NEW PERSPECTIVES

The powerful mix of selections in *The Language of Literature* reflects the exciting nature of our own society:

- Classic and contemporary literature
- Multicultural perspectives
- A mix of genres
- Authentic readings in a variety of media.

A PROGRAM, NOT A BOOK

The Language of Literature is not simply an anthology with a collection of "extras." It is a seamlessly integrated program that links a student book to comprehensive lesson support; mini-lessons in writing, language, and communication; innovative technology; and access for students with special needs.

AN INTEGRATED APPROACH TO LANGUAGE

The selections in *The Language of Literature* become the springboard to a rich mix of language experiences:

- Writing workshops
- Grammar and vocabulary instruction
- Oral communication activities
- Critical viewing and listening
- Research skills
- Visual and media literacy

A WAY TO MAKE STUDENTS CARE

A strong student-centered approach acknowledges the differences among readers and the experiences they bring to a literary selection or writing experience. Responding options, multimodal activities, access materials for all students, and strategies for using media and technology ensure that students learn in a way that matches their individual learning styles.

A NEW WAY OF SEEING

A striking art program is only the beginning of the series' attention to visual and media literacy. Special activities and features throughout the program teach students that reading literature can be the first step toward reading the people and the world around them.

A SPRINGBOARD TO THE WORLD

Every prereading page, response section, and writing workshop provides meaningful activities and thoughtful connections that link the literature to students' own lives, to other curriculum areas, to their family and community, to other cultures, and to the situations and issues they confront every day in the "real world."

A PARTNER IN TECHNOLOGY

A rich videodisc treasury of images, audio and electronic libraries, Internet connections, and the unique Writing Coach software all support the literature and activities in this series. In addition, lessons in the pupil book model the use of technology to access information, network with others, and produce creative multimedia projects.

A WAY TO CONNECT AND REFLECT

Perhaps most importantly, *The Language of Literature* provides a way for students to connect the literature to the often confusing situations they encounter on the pathway from childhood to adulthood. The thoughtfully chosen selections, carefully crafted themes, and rich variety of learning options connect to students' lives and allow them to reflect on how universal certain experiences are.

Program Authors and Consultants

Arthur N. Applebee Professor of Education, State University of New York at Albany; Director, Center for the Learning and Teaching of Literature; Senior Fellow, Center for Writing and Literacy

Andrea B. Bermúdez Professor of Studies in Language and Culture; Director, Research Center for Language and Culture; Chair, Foundations and Professional Studies, University of Houston-Clear Lake

Sheridan Blau Senior Lecturer in English and Education and former Director of Composition, University of California at Santa Barbara; Director, South Coast Writing Project; Director, Literature Institute for Teachers; Vice President, National Council of Teachers of English

Rebekah Caplan Coordinator, English Language Arts K-12, Oakland Unified School District, Oakland, California; Teacher-Consultant, Bay Area Writing Project, University of California at Berkeley; served on the California State English Assessment Development Team for Language Arts

Franchelle S. Dorn Professor of Drama, Howard University, Washington, D.C.; Adjunct Professor, Graduate School of Opera, University of Maryland, College Park, Maryland; Co-founder of The Shakespeare Acting Conservatory, Washington, D.C.

Peter Elbow Professor of English, University of Massachusetts at Amherst; Fellow, Bard Center for Writing and Thinking

Susan Hynds Professor and Director of English Education, Syracuse University, Syracuse, New York

Judith A. Langer Professor of Education, State University of New York at Albany; Co-director, Center for the Learning and Teaching of Literature; Senior Fellow, Center for Writing and Literacy

James Marshall Professor of English and English Education, University of Iowa, Iowa City

THE LANGUAGE OF LITERATURE
Overview

Core Components

The Language of Literature is a seamlessly integrated program that provides teachers with a common-sense system for teaching literature, language, and communication skills. The components described on these pages—the core elements of the program—provide teachers and students with all of the materials they need in a flexible, customizable format. (For more information on each element, please see pages T10 to T25.)

ANNOTATED TEACHER'S EDITION
This comprehensive book provides all of the material you require for a successful teaching experience.
- Unit Content Overview and Planning Charts
- Student Projects
- Professional Enrichment Pages
- Family and Community Involvement
- Annotations for Literature Selections and Writing Workshops
- Bar Codes to LaserLinks
- Recommended Resources

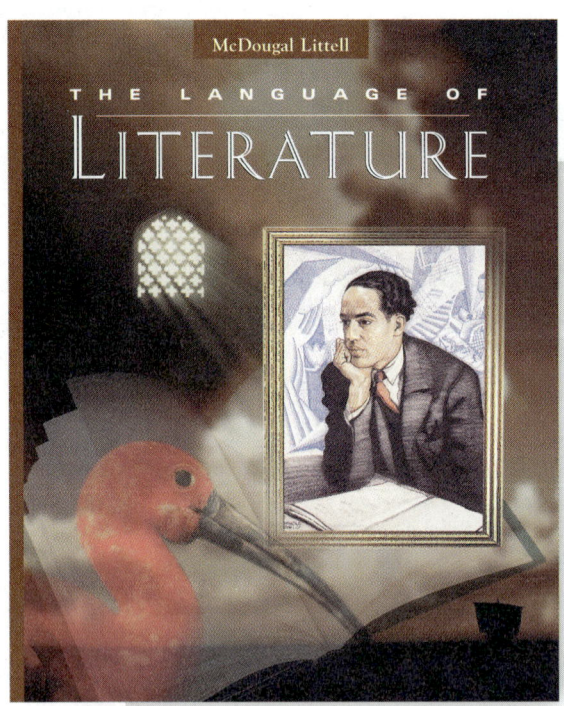

PUPIL EDITION
A rich mix of classic, contemporary and multicultural literature is the starting point from which your class begins its exploration of a world of ideas and experiences. Writing Workshops in each unit continue this exploration, moving students from the literature to interactions with real-world communication and technology.

LITERATURE CONNECTIONS

Unique to *The Language of Literature,* these stand-alone books allow you to decide which plays and novels to include in your literature class. Each longer work is accompanied by several related readings that extend the subject or theme, saving you the task of searching for additional material.

SourceBook Provides you with all the information and student support materials you will need to present fresh and effective lessons.

The Language of Literature Teacher's Edition **T7**

OVERVIEW
(CONTINUED)

Resource Materials

UNIT RESOURCE BOOK Organized by unit and selection, these copymasters provide you with a variety of ways to build and reinforce student skills in reading comprehension, spelling, vocabulary, and writing.

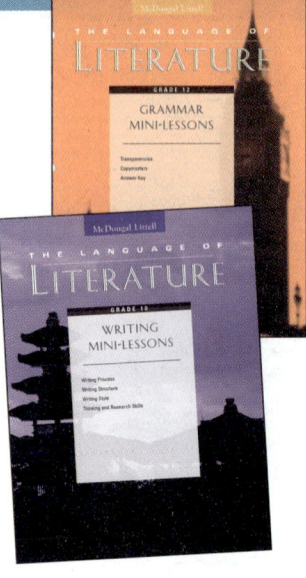

GRAMMAR MINI-LESSONS WRITING MINI-LESSONS These transparency packs allow teachers to identify areas where students need help, and to teach exactly what is needed when it is needed. Corresponding grammar sheets give students needed practice.

DAILY LANGUAGE SKILLBUILDER Through daily exercises, this product integrates grammar, usage, capitalization, proofreading, and punctuation skills with literature-based content.

Integrated Technology

 LASERLINKS
A treasury of full-motion video, photographs, and fine art, this videodisc provides the following program support:

- Selection Support: Historical and Cultural Background
- Author Interviews
- Writing Springboards
- Visual Vocabulary
- Art Galleries
- Storytelling

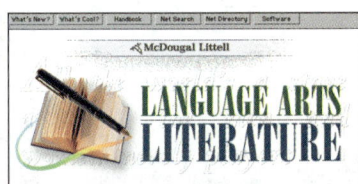

INTERNET CONNECTIONS Program-related information can be accessed through the McDougal Littell home page at http://www.hmco.com/mcdougal/lit

AUDIO LIBRARY These tapes contain professional recordings of nearly every selection in the anthology. The performances can be used to enhance the literature or to provide support for less proficient readers.

 WRITING COACH
A comprehensive word processing program with a unique, multi-column format and on-line writing support, the Writing Coach is a powerful tool for collaborative writing, peer response, and evaluation.

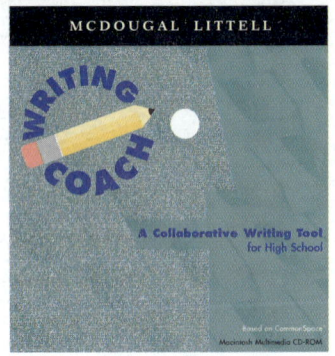

ELECTRONIC LIBRARY This CD-ROM allows you to easily access and print out over 50 additional pieces of classic literature from well-known authors.

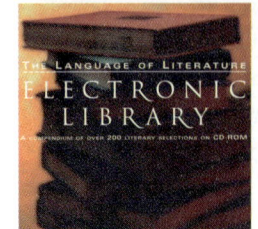

TEST GENERATOR
This component provides the tools for fashioning your own tests.

Assessment Package

TEACHER'S GUIDE TO ASSESSMENT AND PORTFOLIO USE This guide provides instruction in the types and uses of assessment and includes guidesheets, assessment forms, and checklists.

FORMAL ASSESSMENT This booklet contains selection and unit tests, writing assessment materials, and standardized test practice.

ALTERNATIVE ASSESSMENT With these materials—modeled on the authentic assessment materials used in many states and districts across the country—you can evaluate the processes students use as they read and write, as well as the products they create.

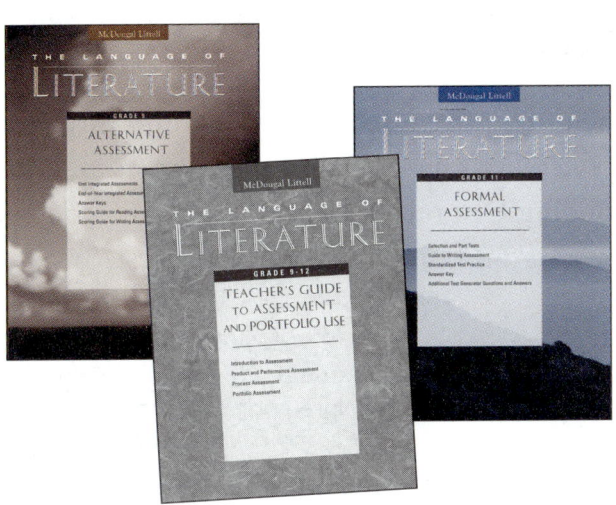

Access for Students Acquiring English

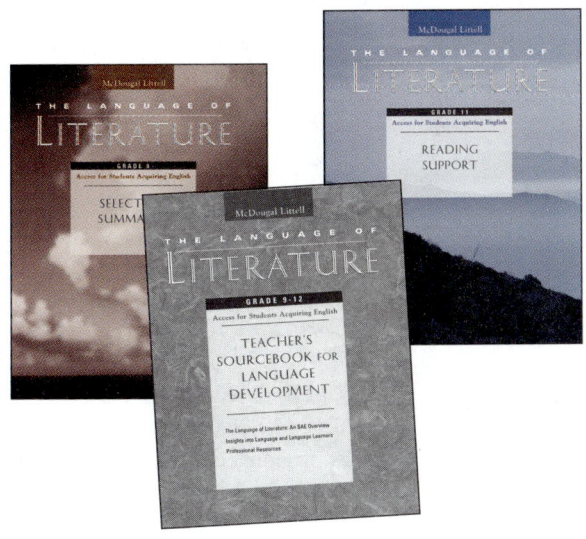

This collection of materials provides comprehensive help for students moving toward English language proficiency. The following components are included:

TEACHER'S SOURCEBOOK FOR LANGUAGE DEVELOPMENT A teacher handbook that includes teaching strategies and techniques.

SELECTION SUMMARIES Summaries of the literature in Spanish.

READING SUPPORT Practice activities that support every literature selection.

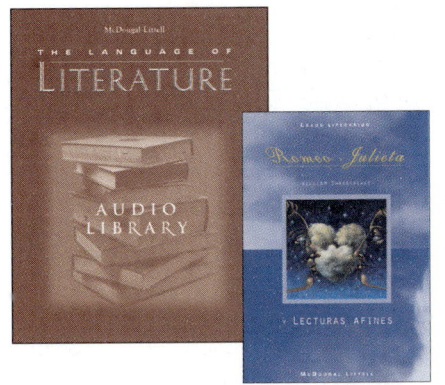

LITERATURE CONNECTIONS Spanish translations of selected titles for grades 6-12.

AUDIO LIBRARY These professional recordings may be used as support for Students Acquiring English.

T9

A CLOSER LOOK
Teaching Literature

The Literature Lesson: Pupil Edition

Each literature lesson is divided into three sections: Previewing, the literature selection itself, and Responding Options. This student-centered lesson offers a wide range and choice of activities.

PREVIEWING

Personal Connection Helps students explore prior experience and knowledge about topics covered in the selection.

Historical (Biographical, Cultural, Literary, Geographical, Scientific, etc.) Connection Provides important background information relevant to the selection.

Reading Connection Presents direct instruction in a reading skill designed to improve comprehension of the selection.

Writing Connection Serves as an alternative to the Reading Connection. Allows students to explore selection-related topics through writing.

Graphic Organizer Helps students explore new topics and structure their thinking.

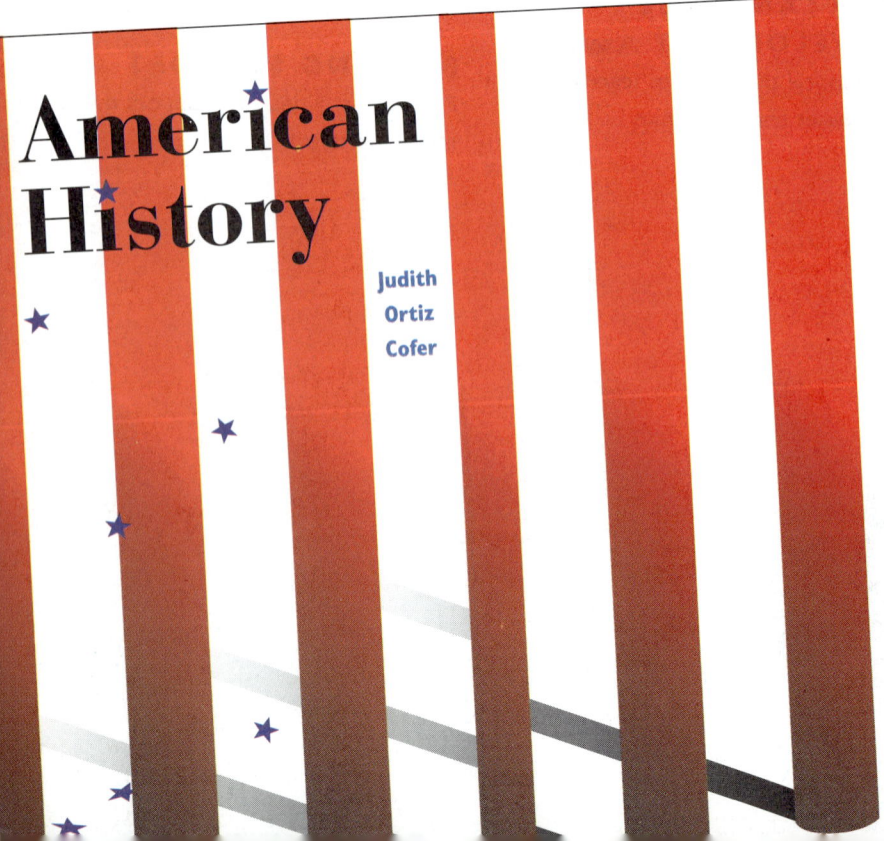

THE SELECTION

The finest literature offerings. Represented are traditional and contemporary pieces, familiar and new voices.

Natural and thematic connections. Selections are organized thematically and, where appropriate, chronologically.

Attractive, engaging design. Helps entice and motivate students.

Active reading questions. Provided as appropriate within selections to help students with comprehension of more challenging pieces.

RESPONDING OPTIONS

From Personal Response to Critical Analysis Invites student-centered discussion with the response-based approach made famous by McDougal Littell. Includes questions that help students relate the literature to their own lives.

Another Pathway Offers an alternative to typical classroom discussion. Generates full exploration of major issues in the selection.

Literary Concepts Introduces or reviews major literary terms and applies them to the selection just read.

Quickwrites Give students several innovative ways of responding to what they have read through writing.

Alternative Activities Offer opportunities to respond to their reading through multimodal activities.

Words to Know Reinforces vocabulary introduced in the selection with motivating exercises.

Author Biography Makes the authors come to life with interesting, student-friendly information. Includes listings of other works by the authors.

ADDITIONAL RESPONDING OPTIONS

Critic's Corner Gives critical commentary on an author or piece of literature and asks students to respond.

Literary Links Asks students to make connection between selection just read and another selection read at an earlier point in the book.

The Writer's Style Asks students to engage in analysis of style by focusing on stylistic traits of author being studied.

Across the Curriculum Provides cross-curricular activities that invite students to go beyond the selection to investigate new areas of study.

Art Connection Asks students to reflect on a work of fine art included in the selection.

The Language of Literature Teacher's Edition **T11**

TEACHING LITERATURE
(CONTINUED)

The Literature Lesson: Resource Materials

The literature in the Pupil Edition is reinforced and extended by the following teaching tools for students' own use.

UNIT RESOURCE BOOK
Worksheets and tests provide support for all literature selections.

- **Strategic Reading: Literature** reinforce reading strategies and extend the understanding of literary elements.

- **Vocabulary Skillbuilders**

- **Selection and Unit Tests** stimulate higher order thinking skills as they assess understanding of selections, literary terms, and language skills.

- **Family and Community Involvement** worksheets connect unit themes to students' world.

T12 The Language of Literature Teacher's Edition

LASERLINKS

A Level One videodisc program that enhances the literature curriculum, develops visual literacy, and helps students explore and interact with the literature.

- Provides historical and cultural background to strengthen interdisciplinary connections
- Helps build students' vocabulary through the Visual Vocabulary feature
- Contains author interviews
- Includes images that stimulate writing
- Presents storyteller in action

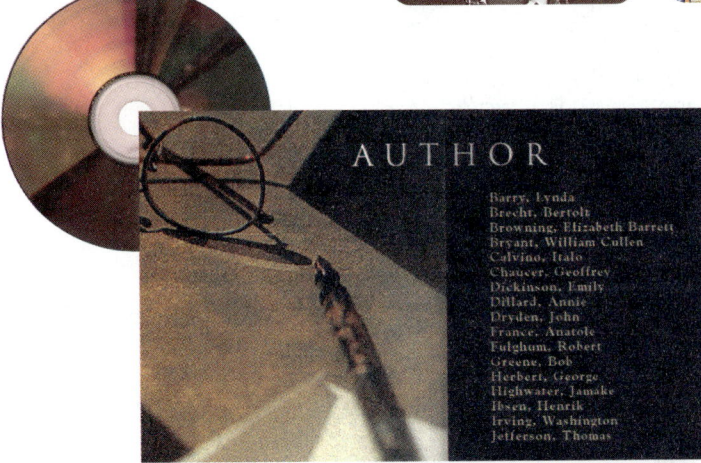

ELECTRONIC LIBRARY

A CD-ROM that provides 50 additional literature selections by classic authors. Teachers can print out copies and distribute them to students. Greatly extends the pupil edition anthology and the number of literary options available.

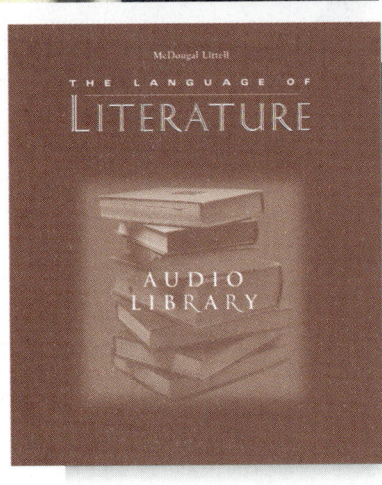

AUDIO LIBRARY

Recordings of almost all selections in each anthology. Provides easy listening, enhances and enriches students' literary experience, and helps students develop strategies for critical listening.

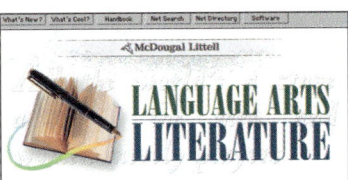

INTERNET CONNECTIONS

The following resources can be accessed through the McDougal Littell home page at http://www.hmco.com/mcdougal/lit

- Literature selection report
- Links to professional materials and organizations
- Teacher discussion groups and bulletin boards

The Language of Literature Teacher's Edition **T13**

A CLOSER LOOK

Integrating Language and Writing Skills

The Writing Workshops: Pupil Edition

Paired writing workshops in each unit offer students two distinct ways to respond to the literature and make "real world" connections.

WRITING ABOUT LITERATURE
This workshop appears as a set of three related lessons.

- **The Writer's Style** lesson focuses on a writing skill such as sentence variety or elaboration. Literary excerpts and a real-world model show the technique in context.

- **The Guided Assignment** invites students to explore the literature through both creative and analytical writing.

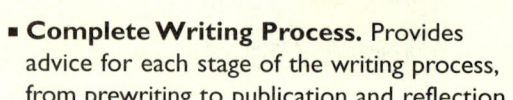

- **Complete Writing Process.** Provides advice for each stage of the writing process, from prewriting to publication and reflection.

- **Student models.** Illustrate the process and choices of another student writer.

- **Peer response questions and Standards for Evaluation.** Help students assess and revise their writing.

- **Skills Instruction.** Grammar in Context and Grammar Skillbuilders teach grammar concepts that relate to the writing.

■ **Reading the World** builds visual literacy and shows students how the same skills they have just used to analyze and write about literature can also be used to observe, interpret, and understand the world around them.

WRITING FROM EXPERIENCE

The second writing workshop invites students to extend the unit theme by creating products for real purposes and real audiences in situations they encounter in the world around them.

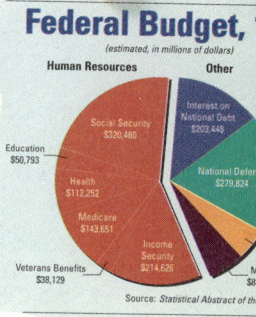

Primary source materials. Magazine and newspaper articles, photographs, charts, and graphs provide a springboard to writing while building critical thinking and media literacy skills.

Oral communication and research skills. Used during prewriting as students gather information. Students are also encouraged to use technology—from CD-ROMs to on-line services—to access information.

Alternative forms of publishing. Visual, oral, and electronic products are suggested and modeled.

INTEGRATING LANGUAGE AND WRITING SKILLS (CONTINUED)

SCOPE AND SEQUENCE OF WRITING INSTRUCTION

The writing workshops in *The Language of Literature* grow in sophistication as your students do, providing a rich variety of writing assignments that become more challenging in every grade. In the following chart, blue dots indicate the Writing About Literature workshops, and red dots indicate the Writing from Experience workshops. The number following each assignment represents the unit in which it appears.

Writing Strands	Grade 9	Grade 10	Grade 11	Grade 12
Firsthand and Expressive	• Personal Response: / 1* • First-Hand Narrative / 3	• Personal Response / 1 • First-Hand Narrative / 1	• Personal Response / 8 • Personal Essay / 3	• Process Response / 4 • Reflective Essay / 1
Narrative and Literary	• Parody / 4 • Writing in Kind: Drama / 6 • Short Story / 6	• Writing in Kind: Poetry / 3 • Change Story Element / 5 • Dramatic Scene / 5	• Speech / 2 • In Author's Style / 7 • Poetry / 6 • Short Story: Sci-Fi / 8	• Creative Response: Change Genre / 2 • Advice Essay / 3 • Poetry / 2
Expository	• Analysis: Character / 1 • Interpretive: Theme / 3 • Critical: Evaluating a story / 5 • Investigative: Explain Idea / 1 • Extended Definition / 4	• Analysis: Setting / 2 • Interpretive: Process / 4 • Critical: Evaluating ideas / 6 • Compare-contrast / 3 • Cause-effect / 4	• Interpretive: Infer Ideas / 1 • Interpretive: Images/Symbols / 3 • Analysis: Story Elements / 4 • Analysis: Point of View / 5 • Critical: Compare Poets / 6 • Analytic Report / 1 • Problem-solution / 4	• Interpretive: Infer Values / 1 • Critical: Evaluate ideas / 5 • Literary Review / 6 • Analysis: Comparative / 7 • Informative: Synthesis / 3 • Analysis / 4
Persuasion	• Persuasive Essay / 3	• Persuasive Essay / 2	• Persuasive Piece / 2 • Critical Review / 5	• Two-sided Argument / 5 • Proposal / 7
Report	• Research Paper / 5	• Research Report: Biographical / 6	• Research Report: Historical / 7	• Research Paper / 6

* Denotes unit number

Writing and Language: Resource Materials

MINI-LESSONS

When do you want to teach your students about introductions and conclusions? As they write a story? Before they begin a report? The unique mini-lesson transparency packs in *The Language of Literature* allow you to decide what your students need to learn and when they need to learn it.

Writing Mini-Lessons. Cover skills ranging from unity and coherence to voice and style.

Grammar Mini-Lessons. Provide instruction on the most common usage problems faced by writers. Corresponding copy masters offer additional literature-based practice for students.

UNIT RESOURCE BOOK

In addition to support for the literature selections, the Unit Resource Book provides comprehensive practice and support for each stage of the writing process. Copymasters include the following:

Writer's Style Worksheet
Prewriting Worksheet
Elaboration Practice
Peer Response Guide
Revising and Proofreading Practice
Complete Student Model
Rubrics for Evaluation

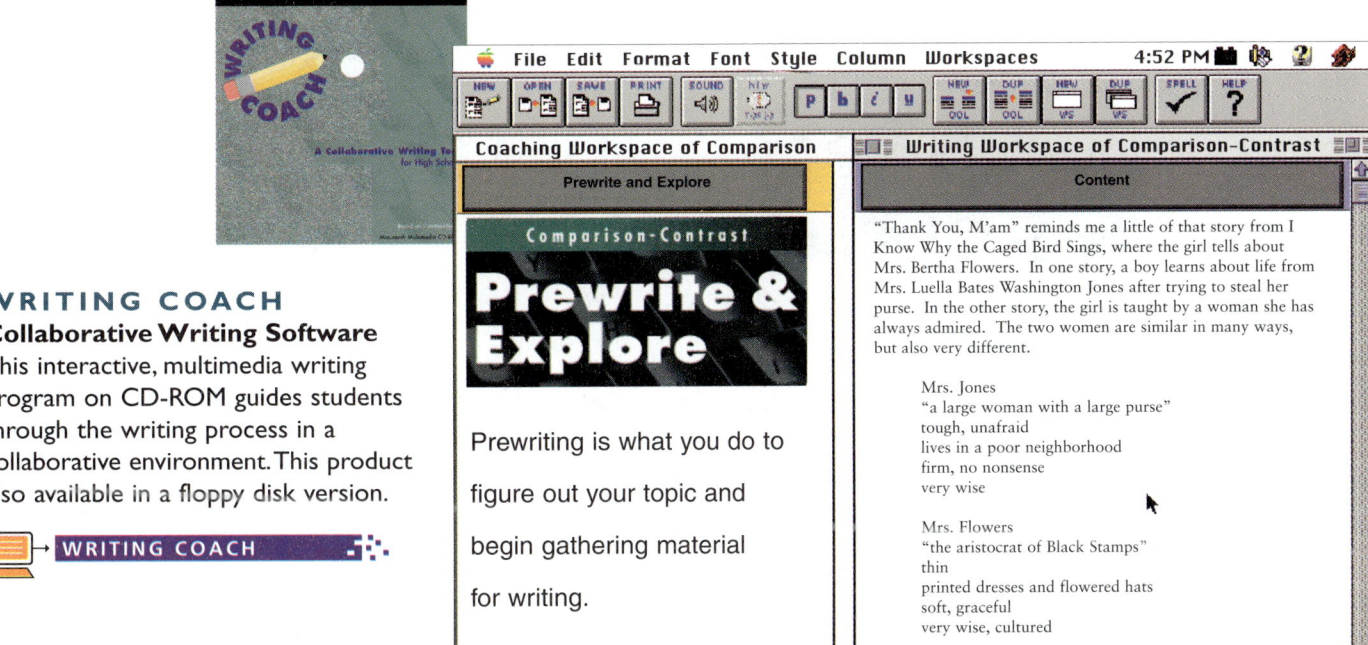

WRITING COACH
Collaborative Writing Software
This interactive, multimedia writing program on CD-ROM guides students through the writing process in a collaborative environment. This product also available in a floppy disk version.

A CLOSER LOOK

Special Features of the Pupil Edition

This book contains a wealth of special features to help enrich each student's learning experience.

PART OPENER
Handy "mini" table of contents for each part of a unit.

STRATEGIES FOR READING
Shows students how active readers read—what they think about as they read and how they make connections between the text and real-world experiences. Model provides thoughts and comments of two students engaged in the following active reading strategies:

- Question
- Connect
- Predict
- Clarify
- Evaluate

FOCUS ON FICTION/ NONFICTION/POETRY/DRAMA
Helps introduce and reinforce basic knowledge of literary elements. Also includes strategies used when reading a particular genre. Feature provides students with a strong foundation for the reading of literature.

REFLECT & ASSESS

Features end-of-unit activities that help students review and reflect upon what they have learned in the course of a unit. Includes options for:

- Reflecting on Theme
- Reviewing on Literary Concepts
- Portfolio Building

STUDENT HANDBOOKS

- **Literary Terms**
- **Writing Handbook**
- **Multimedia Handbook**
- **Grammar Handbook**

Easy-to-use, comprehensive references that provide valuable information and offer practical support for the teaching of literature, writing, and grammar.

A CLOSER LOOK

The Teacher's Edition

Unit Support

Special pages in the Teacher's Edition provide professional enrichment and help you plan your lessons, organize necessary materials, and carry out unit-related projects.

SKILLS TRACE

Allows you to see at a glance the scope and sequence of reading, writing, speaking, listening, viewing, study, research, grammar, spelling, and literary skills taught within each part of a unit. Also tracks the teaching of vocabulary words and the type and frequency of multimodal activities.

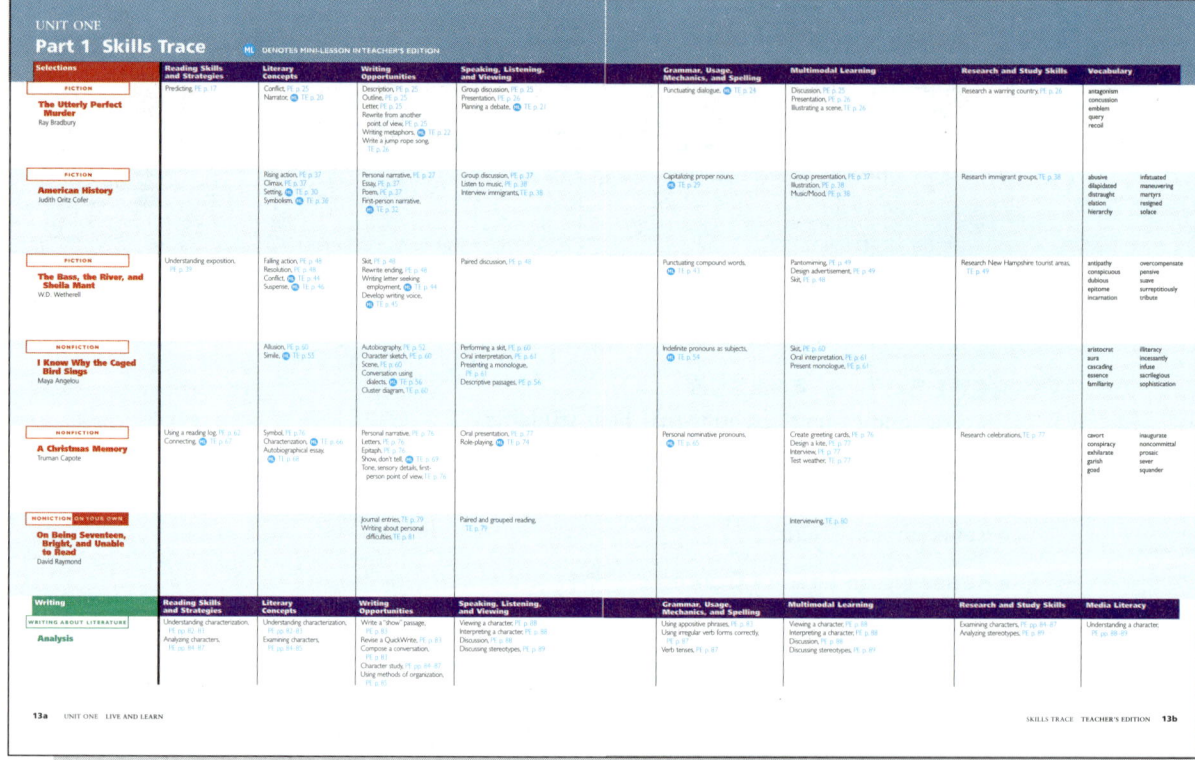

RECOMMENDED RESOURCES

Invaluable listings of unit-specific resources for both you and your students. Includes titles of novels and plays, cross-curricular readings, and media resources. Helps you extend and enrich the curriculum and enrich yourself professionally as well.

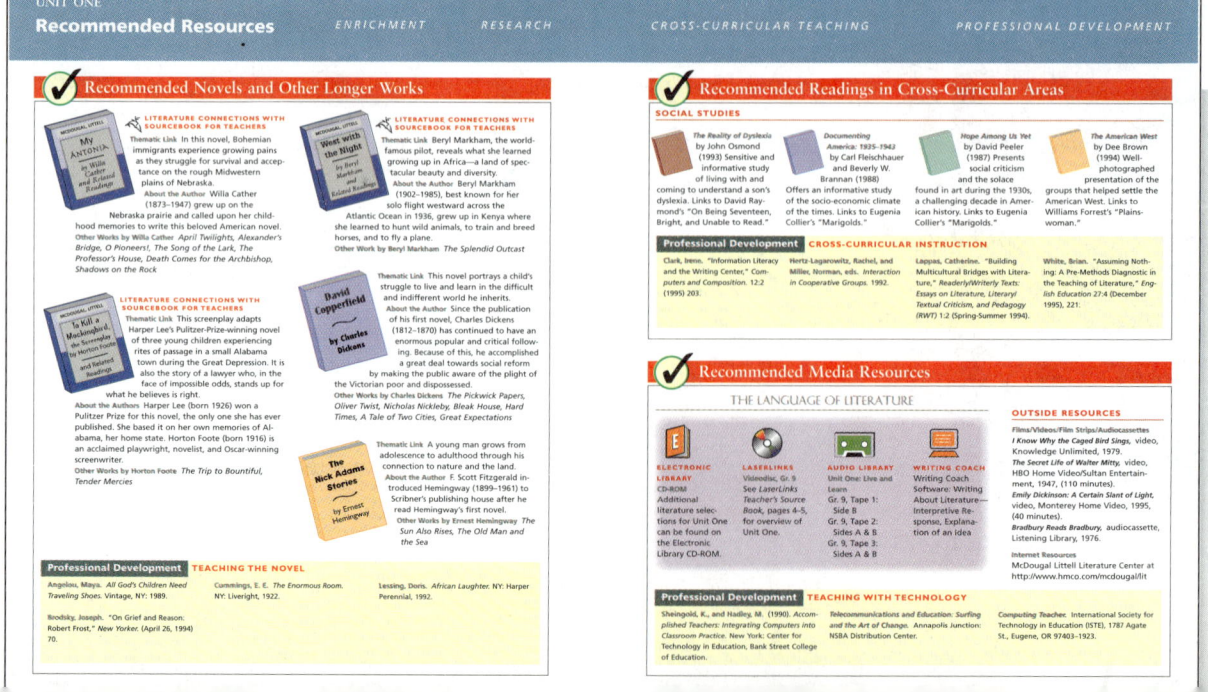

PROFESSIONAL ENRICHMENT

Articles written by teachers, authors, and other noted authorities. Offers insights and practical strategies for teaching literature and writing.

STARTING POINTS FOR UNIT PROJECTS

Ideas for helping you initiate content-related projects during the course of the unit. Includes ideas for both individual and group projects.

FAMILY AND COMMUNITY INVOLVEMENT

Activities designed to involve parents and other family members and to foster students' interaction with other people in their communities. Corresponding worksheets are provided.

LESSON PLANNER

Helps you plan your lessons by indicating approximate length of time for each task. Allows you to accommodate a variety of classroom situations and needs.

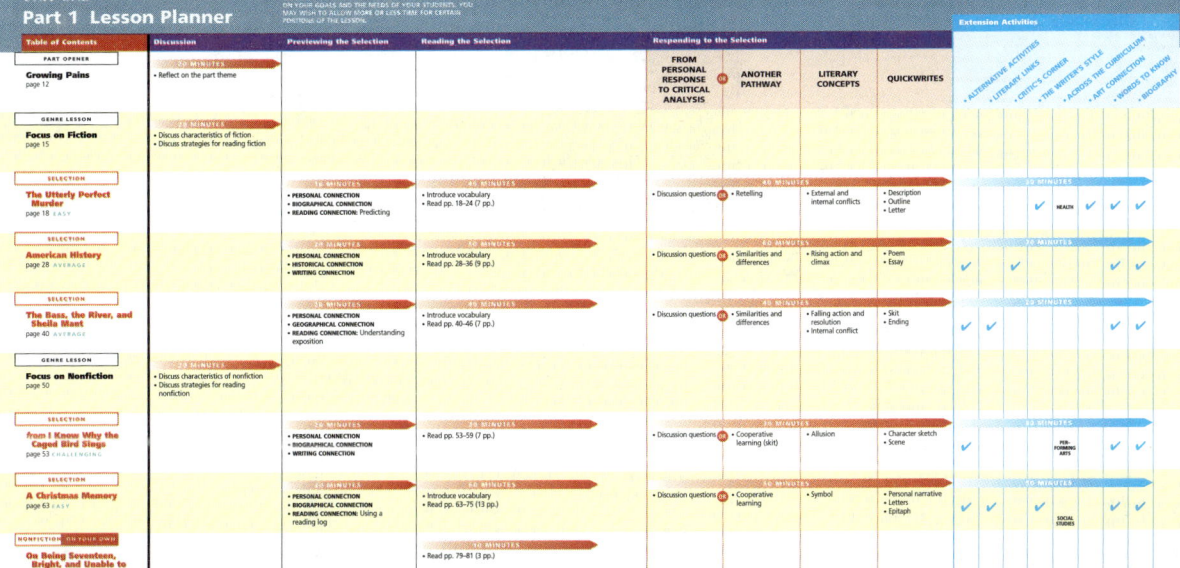

TEACHERS EDITION
(CONTINUED)

Selection and Writing Workshop Support

The Annotated Teacher's Edition of *The Language of Literature* is a professional sourcebook designed to promote effective and efficient teaching. Each page contains features that allow you take students into, through, and beyond the literature.

SELECTION ANNOTATIONS

Notes on literary concepts and critical thinking skills appear with each selection and its corresponding activity pages. Also included are the following features.

- **Overview** Lists objectives, key skills, and cross-curricular connections
- **Print and Media Resources**
- **Selection Summary**
- **LaserLinks bar codes**
- **Words To Know**
- **Art Notes**
- **Customizing for**
  - multiple learning styles
  - students acquiring English
  - gifted and talented students
  - less-proficient readers
- **Activities** Suggestions for whole class, small group, and individual activities
- **Mini-Lessons** Provided for grammar, spelling, reading, genre, writing, and a number of other subjects.
- **Active Reading Questions**
- **Comprehension Check**
- **Assessment Options**
- **Links Across the Curriculum**
- **Links to *The Writer's Craft***
- **Activity Support and Answer Keys**

WORKSHOP ANNOTATIONS

The Teacher's Edition notes for the Writing Workshops provide support similar to that provided for each literary selection. In addition, Writing Workshops contain the following:

- **Writing Springboards** Provides writing ideas from LaserLinks.
- **Modeling** Gives suggestions for using both literary models and student writing models.
- **SkillBuilder Mini-Lesson Support**
- **Visual and Media Literacy Features**
- **Research Skills**
- **Oral Communication**
- **Rubrics**
- **Standards for Evaluation**

T23

A CLOSER LOOK
Assessment

Assessment Resources

The Language of Literature provides you with material that allows you to customize assessment to best fit the activities and structure of your particular classroom. With options for formal, informal, and alternative assessment, these resources provide you with all the support you need.

GUIDE TO ASSESSMENT AND PORTFOLIO USE

This Teacher's Guide

- provides information on different types and forms of assessment: formal selection and unit tests, portfolio building, authentic assessment, reading notebooks, self-assessment, group and project assessment, and more.

- helps you decide which assessment types you wish to use and explains how to implement those approaches.

- provides forms and checklists that can be used to give shape to assessment choices.

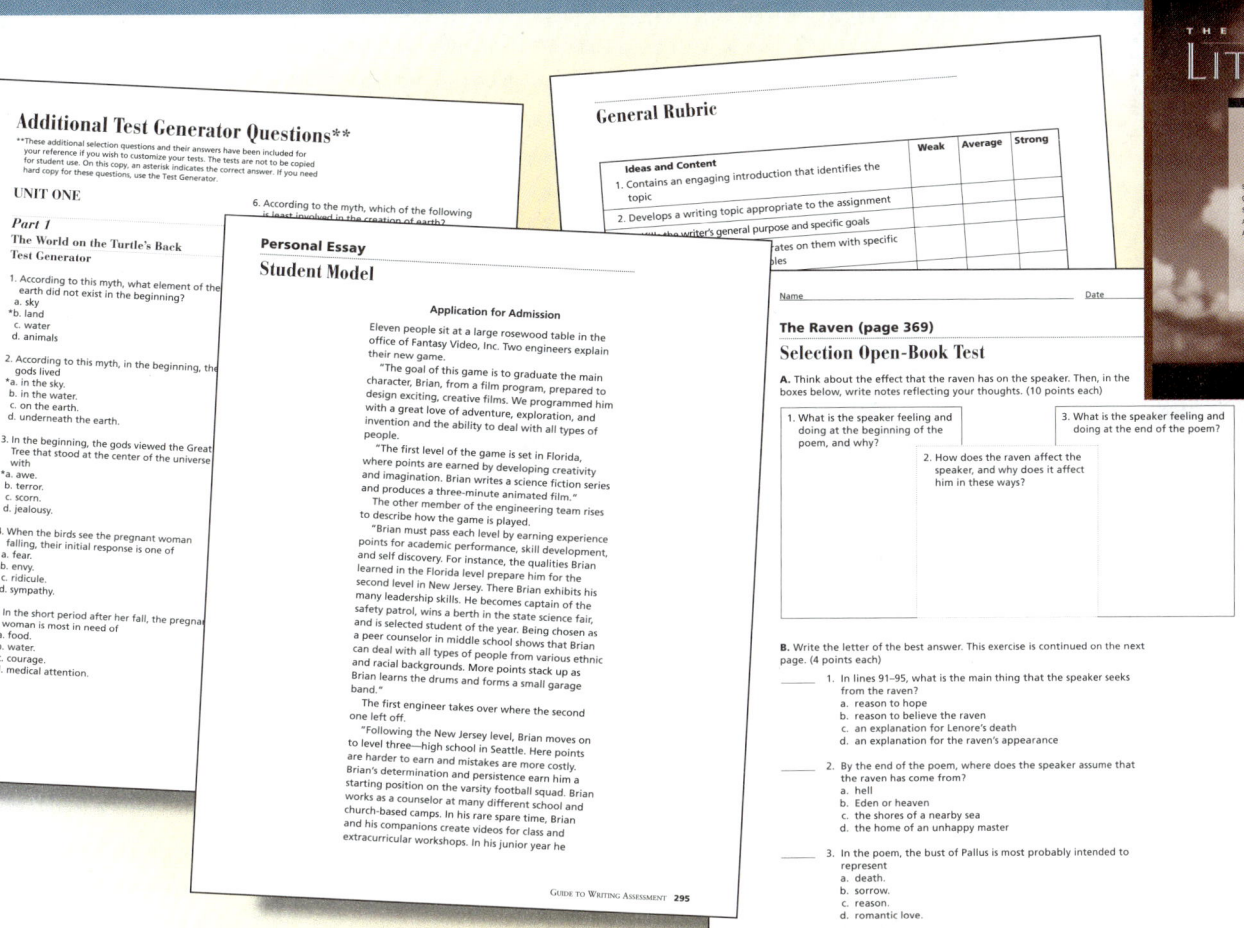

FORMAL ASSESSMENT

The formal assessment booklet contains everything you will need for efficient assessment of students' skills in reading literature and in writing.

- Selection and Unit Tests
- Writing Prompts
- Scoring rubrics and sample papers
- Standardized Test Practice

Also, a test generator is available to help you customize assessment.

ALTERNATIVE ASSESSMENT

These assessments integrate all of the language arts processes and are modeled on authentic assessment materials used in many states across the country.

- **Unit Integrated Assessments** are completed over two days and are based on the On Your Own selections in the student book. Prereading activities and post-reading response and discussion lead to in-depth writing options.

- The **End-of-Year Integrated Assessment** includes a reader and a Student Response Booklet. It is completed over several days and requires students to respond to three or more related selections.

The Language of Literature Teacher's Edition **T25**

GETTING STARTED...
Advice from the Experts

Planning YOUR YEAR

Every new school year requires much planning. The information and advice on these pages comes from the consultants on *The Language of Literature* and is designed to help you bring some of your plans into focus. (You may want to copy the pages and keep them in your lesson planner for easy reference.) As you begin your planning, here's a list of questions to consider. Their answers and some additional information can be found on the pages cited.

Developing a Classroom Profile   See pages T28–T29.

✔ **Who are my students?**

- ☐ What can I learn about my students from previous teachers, students, records, and portfolios—and how can I best use this information?
- ☐ What are my students' preferred learning styles, and how can I best accommodate them?
- ☐ If I have students who are not proficient in English, what will their needs be?
- ☐ Are there any other special needs represented in my class?
- ☐ What adjustments do I need to make due to tracking, mainstreaming, and other situations?

Planning My Instruction   See pages T30–T31.

✔ **What do I want to teach?**

- ☐ What are the requirements of my school, district, and state?
- ☐ What are my personal preferences?
- ☐ What are my students' preferences?
- ☐ How can I use both classic literature and young-adult literature to reflect the needs and interests of my students?
- ☐ What mix of stories, poetry, essays, and novels do I want to teach?
- ☐ How can I effectively combine writing, language, and communication skills?
- ☐ Do I want to teach a research paper and/or other longer projects?

✔ **How much collaborating do I want to do with other teachers?**

- ☐ To plan thematic units and/or projects
- ☐ To coordinate instruction

✔ **What mix of instructional styles do I want to use?**

- ☐ Lectures
- ☐ Cooperative/collaborative work
- ☐ Writing workshops/peer response groups

✔ **How will I organize the content?**

- ☐ By genre or mode
- ☐ By theme

Setting Up My Classroom
See pages T32–T33.

✔ **How will I organize my classroom?**

- ☐ In rows of desks
- ☐ With tables and chairs
- ☐ In paired-seating arrangements
- ☐ In cooperative learning groups
- ☐ In stations or centers

Taking Advantage of Technology
See pages T34–T35.

✔ **How large a role will technology play in my classroom?**

- ☐ What technological resources do I have at my disposal?
- ☐ For what purpose or purposes do I want to use them?
- ☐ How can I best set up my classroom or use a lab to take advantage of these resources?

Preparing for Assessment
See pages T36–T38.

✔ **What types of assessment do I want to use or prepare for?**

Do I want to use one or more of the following:
- ☐ Portfolios, journals, and/or logs
- ☐ Process assessment
- ☐ Product assessment
- ☐ Peer and self-assessment
- ☐ My own observations
- ☐ Tests from *The Language of Literature*
- ☐ District- or state-mandated tests
- ☐ Standardized tests

Planning Connections
See pages T39–T40.

✔ **What kinds of connections do I want to make outside the classroom?**

- ☐ To other curriculum areas
- ☐ To other classrooms or schools
- ☐ To my students' parents
- ☐ To the community
- ☐ To the world

DEVELOPING A Classroom PROFILE

> To avoid misunderstanding, it is critical that teachers disregard the assumption that all students have the same, or similar, frames of reference or perceptions about the world.
>
> Andrea Bermúdez
> Professor of Studies in Language and Culture, University of Houston-Clear Lake

UNDERSTANDING LEARNING STYLES

Your students are all unique. They have different sets of characteristics, abilities, and needs. It should not be surprising, therefore, to learn that they have different learning styles as well. This theory gained acceptance in the early 1980s, due in large part to the research of Harvard psychologist Howard Gardner. Gardner recognizes seven types of intelligences: linguistic, logical-mathematical, spatial, musical, bodily-kinesthetic, interpersonal, and intrapersonal. He claims that everyone has all seven of these intelligences, but in different proportions.

Understanding your students' intelligences, or learning styles, will help you teach them more effectively. How can you tell which learning style or styles your students favor? As you consider each of your students, asking yourself these questions will help.

Does the student . . .	Then he or she is mostly a . . .	So try these activities and assignments:
☐ Have good verbal skills? think in words? have highly developed auditory skills? like to read and write?	**Linguistic Learner**	Creative writing; essays; debates and speeches; oral reports; dramatic readings and performances; storytelling; joke, pun, and riddle telling
☐ Think conceptually? think and reason in a highly abstract and logical way?	**Logical-Mathematical Learner**	Graphic organizers; charts, graphs, and time lines; coded messages; prediction exercises; models; computer projects; science experiments
☐ Think in visual images and pictures? enjoy drawing, designing, building, daydreaming, inventing?	**Spatial Learner**	Drawings and paintings; comic strips; maps and flow charts; dioramas, displays, and murals; collages; drawing games; photography activities
☐ Have a sensitivity to music, nonverbal sounds, and rhythm? enjoy singing, playing, and listening to and moving to music?	**Musical Learner**	Interpretive dances; musical plays and compositions; rap songs, jingles, and melodies; rhyming games; playing a musical instrument
☐ Process knowledge through bodily sensations? have exceptional fine-motor coordination? communicate through body language?	**Bodily-Kinesthetic Learner**	Demonstration speeches; experiments; using gestures, facial expressions, and pantomime; impersonations; role-playing
☐ Understand other people? organize, communicate, and socialize well?	**Interpersonal Learner**	Discussions; cooperative and collaborative projects; peer coaching; conducting interviews; simulation activities; human graphs
☐ Prefer working alone? seem intuitive, independent, private, and self-motivated?	**Intrapersonal Learner**	Response journals, dialogue journals, learning logs; observations; photo essays; autobiographical stories; written reports

A PROFILE OF THE STUDENT ACQUIRING ENGLISH

Culturally and linguistically diverse students bring to the classroom a wealth of experiences that can enrich the learning environment of all your students. Developing multicultural sensitivity involves (a) acceptance of each student's circumstances, (b) a genuine search for information about his or her background and prior knowledge, (c) an updated bank of teaching strategies, and (d) a desire to find the best options for each student.

The Student Acquiring English

- generally focuses attention on style, not content
- is often unaware of learning strategies that could facilitate comprehension
- may become disorderly and disobedient due to an inability to relate to the learning environment
- often does not make eye contact when addressing others
- may seem to have difficulty meeting deadlines
- may not seem to understand classroom "rules"
- generally shows a different speaking and listening style
- may organize thoughts in a pattern that does not correspond to the expected linear-sequential pattern characteristic of standard English communication
- may exhibit an external locus of control, seeming overly dependent on teachers or peers for validation of responses

Common Problem Areas

The following problem areas pose special challenges to students acquiring English as they try to read and understand information.

Vocabulary Difficulty
If the student has no prior experience with the words appearing in a selection, the normal links between certain concepts and their labels will not occur. Problems often arise when a selection contains the following:

- low frequency words
- idiomatic or dialectal expressions
- jargon

Unfamiliar Content
The student may misunderstand the message in what he or she is reading if not given the proper context. This often happens as a result of the following:

- a lack of prior experience with the context
- ideas expressed in an unfamiliar or abstract way
- ideas expressed being of an unfamiliar culture

Grammatical Features of the Selection
Comprehension problems arise when the student encounters the following:

- dialectal forms
- outdated grammatical forms
- unusual word order

Effective Teaching and Learning Strategies

These instructional strategies have been shown to be successful when used with students acquiring English.

Cognitive Mapping
- Many SAE students, however, may organize and categorize information differently than English speakers would. Instruction in cognitive mapping can enable students to integrate previous experience with new knowledge.

An Integrated Approach
- The integrated approach to learning is particularly successful with students acquiring English. Students learn about reading and writing while listening, they learn about writing from reading, and they gain insights into reading from writing. Any strategy or approach based on dissecting language and mutually exclusive components jeopardizes second-language acquisition by not drawing on the prior knowledge and strengths of the learner.

Cooperative Learning
- Cooperative learning is a generic term that refers to a variety of approaches to integrating students into group activities where each participant is responsible for contributing to group outcomes and products. Cooperative learning strategies significantly improve students' achievement and productivity for a wide range of subjects and grade levels. This approach also improves self-esteem and respect for others. For more detailed information, see the *Teacher's SourceBook for Language Development*.

Planning YOUR INSTRUCTION

Just as your students all have their own preferred learning styles, you have your own preferred teaching styles. Understanding when and where your most comfortable style really works—and when another method would reach your goals and the goals of your students more effectively—will help you plan just the right type of instruction for every situation.

Here are some questions to ask yourself as you make decisions about your instruction:

- ☐ What is my objective for the lesson . . . today, this week, this month, this term?
- ☐ What is my time frame . . . 45 minutes, 90 minutes, three class periods, longer?
- ☐ Who are my students (refer to your classroom profiles, pages T28 and T29)?
- ☐ What teaching styles am I most comfortable with?
- ☐ What additional teaching techniques would be effective with these students and this material?

Consider these options . . .

WHOLE-CLASS INSTRUCTION

Lecture

EXAMPLES:
- ☐ Introducing a new unit of study
- ☐ Providing instruction for a project
- ☐ Introducing grammatical principles or definitions of literary elements

Teacher-led Discussion

EXAMPLES:
- ☐ Exploring students' ideas about and responses to literature selections and themes
- ☐ Examining complex issues and problems

Viewing

EXAMPLES:
- ☐ Viewing a filmstrip or a videotape
- ☐ Watching demonstrations, performances, and project presentations

COLLABORATIVE LEARNING

Pairs or Partners

EXAMPLES:
- ☐ Sharing responses to literature
- ☐ Interviewing and reciprocal questioning
- ☐ Brainstorming for project or writing ideas
- ☐ Peer tutoring
- ☐ Writing workshops

Small Groups (3-8 students)

EXAMPLES:
- ☐ Discussing literature or other topics
- ☐ Planning and problem-solving activities
- ☐ Writing workshops
- ☐ Cooperative work on reports, projects, and presentations
- ☐ Cooperative planning and producing of larger projects such as plays, panel discussions or debates, and videotapes

INDEPENDENT LEARNING

Students Working Individually

EXAMPLES:
- ☐ Independent reading and writing
- ☐ Drawing, painting, and collages
- ☐ Listening to audiotapes

. . . for meeting these instructional goals . . .	. . . with these guidelines and cautions:
☐ Developing critical listening and note-taking skills ☐ Providing unknown historical or cultural background ☐ Introducing new concepts or skills	☐ Lectures appeal to linguistic learners with highly developed auditory skills. Other students may tune you out because this style lacks interactivity. ☐ Lectures are most effective if no longer than 20 minutes. Research shows that immediately after a 10-minute presentation, average adult listeners retain less than 50% of what they hear—and 48 hours later, they only recall 25%.
☐ Developing critical listening, responding, and conversational skills ☐ Introducing or reviewing skills	☐ Not all students are comfortable speaking in front of their peers. Highly verbal students can drown out students who favor other learning styles. ☐ When you lead the discussion, students may tend to direct their comments to you rather than to other students. Encourage students to speak directly to one another as well as to you.
☐ Supporting and improving visual literacy ☐ Developing evaluative skills ☐ Encouraging appreciation for music, art, and various kinds of performances	☐ Although viewing is a comfortable activity for most students, it's essentially passive. You'll want to choose occasions carefully. ☐ To help students remain focused, agree on goals ahead of time and provide standards and forms for evaluating what students are watching.
☐ Reinforcing cooperative learning skills ☐ Providing support for students acquiring English ☐ Encouraging peer feedback for writing	☐ It's important to cultivate a classroom atmosphere of support and trust so that pair interactions are effective and productive. ☐ You may want to pair students differently for different purposes. Strong students may be paired with weaker students, native English speakers with students acquiring English, talkative students with more reserved students, and so on.
☐ Developing problem solving skills ☐ Encouraging peer feedback for writing ☐ Reinforcing cooperative learning skills ☐ Providing opportunities for students to explore various points of view ☐ Improving social skills and promoting self-esteem in students of all abilities	☐ Some students will lean too hard on other members of the group. Both groups and individual students need to be accountable. ☐ Some students can get lost in the shuffle of a larger group. Individual students should have specific responsibilities. ☐ Group size can be determined by the task. Small groups are appropriate for sharing personal writing and receiving individual attention; larger groups are effective when the task is large or complex. ☐ The "jigsaw" method may be useful for groups working on complex tasks. The group divides the assignment into pieces and assigns each student a piece. Then students work together to meld the pieces into a coherent whole.
☐ Providing opportunities for reflection and self-assessment ☐ Providing support for students acquiring English	☐ Individual learning tasks require a quiet classroom atmosphere. Highly developed interpersonal learners may distract other students. ☐ Using independent learning too frequently can hinder students' development of collaborative and cooperative skills.

Setting Up YOUR CLASSROOM

Are you planning to try some new instructional approaches this year? If so, you also may want to consider some new classroom setups. Moving away from the traditional arrangement of desks in rows will provide you and your students a welcome change—and will be more conducive to different teaching and learning situations. Here are a few pointers:

If you teach in the same room all day, the ideas on these pages will provide ways to set up your room for a variety of purposes.

If you switch rooms, team teach, or share your room, you can find an arrangement that best meets everyone's needs. Some options:

☐ One arrangement that works for everyone

☐ Different classrooms for different purposes

☐ A resource room or common area that could be used for specific types of activities

Before you arrange your classroom, draw a scale floor plan of it. Then add furniture and design a setting that will best accommodate your instructional plans.

When you have your floor plan firmed up, post lists of procedures in the different areas of your classroom. Encourage students to add new procedures as needs arise in the future.

Don't be afraid to experiment with different arrangements throughout the year. You may find that some arrangements work better than others for specific projects or assignments.

> The ideal literature classroom is a literary community where students... have room to respond, interpret, think critically, and contrast their ideas with those of other readers.
>
> Judith Langer and Arthur Applebee
> Professors of Education,
> State University of New York at Albany

A LOOK AT THREE CLASSROOM SETUPS
Lectures and Demonstrations

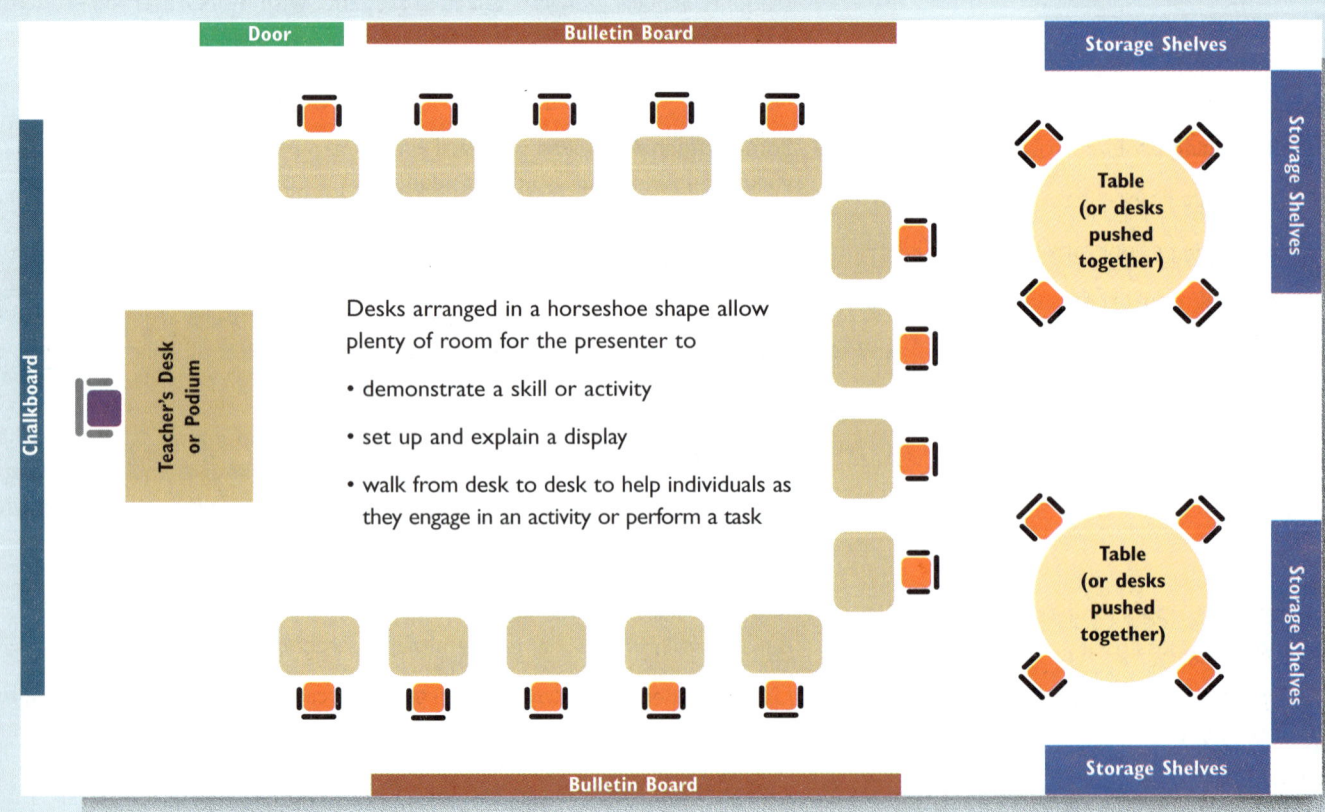

Desks arranged in a horseshoe shape allow plenty of room for the presenter to

- demonstrate a skill or activity
- set up and explain a display
- walk from desk to desk to help individuals as they engage in an activity or perform a task

T32 THE LANGUAGE OF LITERATURE TEACHER'S EDITION

Peer Tutoring & Cooperative Learning

Work Stations

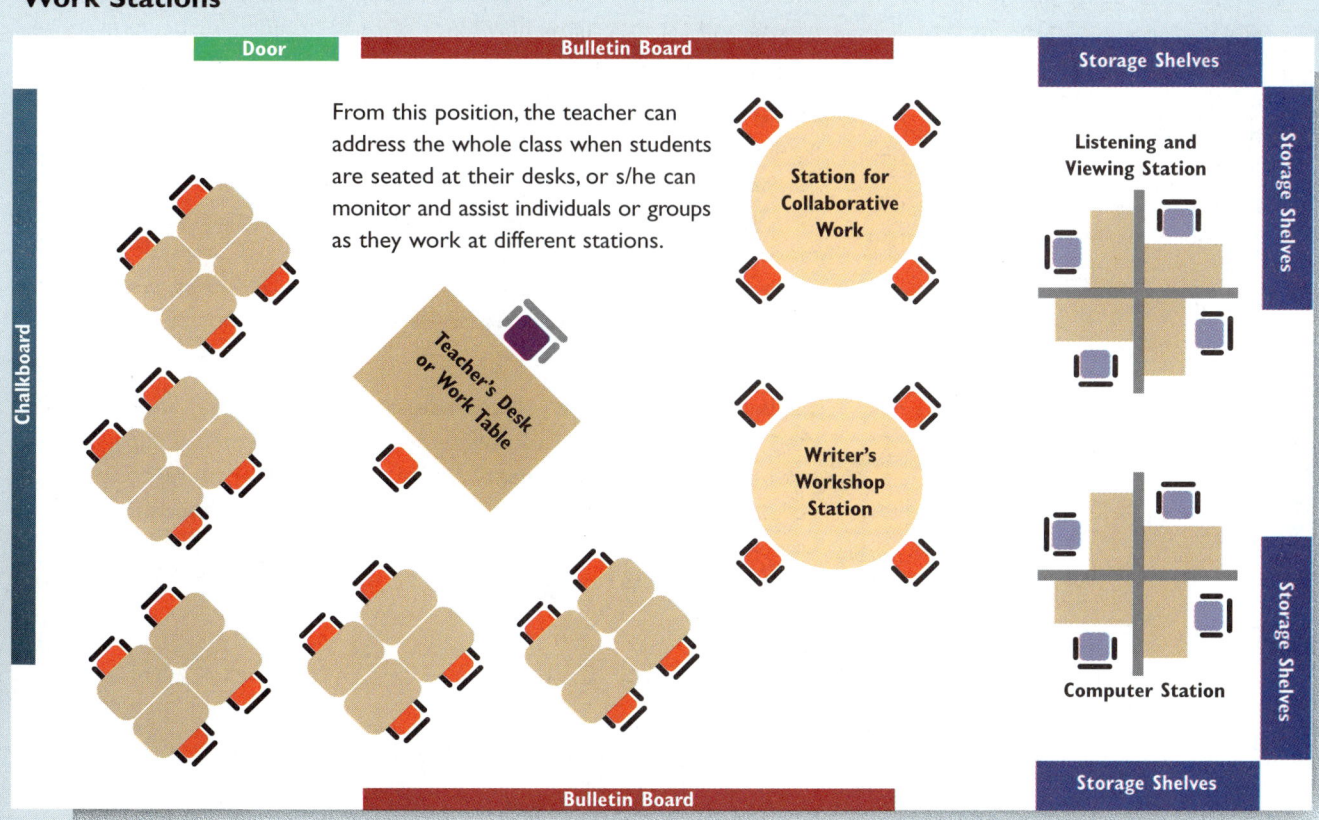

NEW Technology AND THE ENGLISH CLASSROOM

> Technology enables students to become active participants in their own learning.
>
> Jeffrey N. Golub
> Assistant Professor of English Education, University of South Florida, Tampa

The idea of using technology as part of your instructional plan is not simply the latest passing fad. Instead, it reflects continuing revelations about what is worth knowing and how students learn. For this reason, it promises to change the nature of classroom instruction.

Why is technology so important? Primarily because the use of computers is not a "spectator sport." Rather, computers require users to do the work themselves instead of passively sitting back and watching or listening to someone else—typically a teacher—dispense information. Thus, using technology enables students to become active participants in their own learning. Similarly, the teacher's role changes to that of a "designer" and "director"—one who *designs* innovative and worthwhile instructional activities and then *directs* students as they work through these activities.

Let's look for a moment at how technology is being used in English classrooms across the country.

Bringing Literature to Life

Teachers are always striving to make connections between literature and students' lives by providing "real-world" relevance in the form of historical and biographical information, cross-curricular ties, and connections to current issues. Recordings and films have always been the primary resources used to achieve this goal, but more recent technology—such as laser discs and CD-ROMs—is providing teachers with new worlds of information to draw from.

Taking the Fear Out of Writing

In probably their most familiar function, computers offer terrific opportunities for writing because (1) they provide students with more efficient and effective means of drafting, revising, editing, and publishing their writing efforts, and (2) they allow new kinds of opportunities for peer response, collaboration, and sharing.

More Enthusiastic Writers Research has shown repeatedly that students tend to be more fluent and less inhibited when they work at computers: the many editing features and on-line resources make revision easy. In addition, publishing programs allow students to create products far more exciting than words on paper have ever been. Computers can also make portfolio building simpler and cleaner: journal entries, drafts and revisions, and finished products are easy to store, categorize, and retrieve on computers or disks.

Easier Collaboration. If you have access to a writing lab, you will find that, with readily available software programs and by networking, or linking, the computers, students can be more easily encouraged to collaborate on their planning and writing efforts. When students can compose and comment on-screen they often become much more articulate and less reserved.

Making Connections

One of the most commonly heard complaints among teachers is that they seldom have a chance to network with each other and share ideas. Through the wonders of the Internet, this problem has all but disappeared. Education sites exist where teachers can find information ranging from developments in state assessments to projects that have worked well in other classrooms. Through the Internet, teachers can also set up classroom exchanges with other schools across the country, allow their students to go on electronic field trips, and plan interactions between the class and famous authors, scientists, and other professionals.

Developing Information Literacy

The use of technology in the English classroom enables teachers to help their students develop what will become one of the most basic skills needed for the 21st-century—media and information literacy. Students need to learn how to access information from a wide variety of both print and electronic sources; how to select appropriate information from the vast array of available resources; how to analyze and evaluate information that they read, see, and hear daily; and how to communicate their conclusions and insights clearly, completely, ethically, and persuasively. In particular, the growth of telecommunications opportunities in the form of information webs presents students with the opportunity to actively seek pertinent information and to engage in the processes of selection, analysis, and evaluation.

Conclusion These are just some of the ways in which technology can make learning happen for your students. But they help demonstrate that, if used creatively, technology can bring new excitement and levels of success to any English classroom—even while helping us achieve the same goals we have always had: to make our students solid readers, thinkers, and communicators.

Technology	Uses in the English Classroom	*The Language of Literature*
Laser Disc A 12-inch disc, used with a laser disc player, that can store thousands of still images as well as full-motion video. Images can be accessed immediately through the use of bar codes.	• To provide background information and cross-curricular connections for selection enrichment • For presenting real-world situations and images that can be used as writing springboards • To bring movies, archival material, and recordings of live performances into the classroom • To teach visual literacy	**LASERLINKS** Support for lessons in the student book, including • Author and Selection Background • Visual Vocabulary • Professional Storyteller • Writing Springboards
Floppy Discs and CD-ROMS Both are information storage devices that can hold text, still images, and full-motion video. Compact discs, however, are able to store encyclopedic amounts of information.	• As sources of additional or enhanced selections • As a reference tool: encyclopedias, atlases, and almanacs are all available in CD-ROM form • For writing: publishing software, image banks, and word processing programs all enhance student writing	**THE ELECTRONIC LIBRARY** Additional classic selections to expand program options **WRITING COACH** Special word processing program with on-line writing tips and handbooks, multiple text columns for revision and peer response, and a multimedia Idea Generator
Internet/ World Wide Web/ On-line Services A connected system of on-line computer networks through which mail and data can be transferred.	• To obtain additional information on a selection, author, or topic • To teach information-access skills • To gather professional materials, project ideas, research articles • To network with other teachers and set up classroom exchanges • To interact with authors, public figures, scientists, and other professionals	**THE MCDOUGAL LITTELL HOME PAGE** Can be accessed on World Wide Web at http://www.hmco.com/mcdougal and contains the following resources: • Internet links for specific selections in *The Language of Literature* • Teacher discussion groups/ bulletin boards • Links to professional organizations

PREPARING FOR Assessment

The word *assessment* conjures up many different images and raises just as many questions in teachers' minds. Although assessment options are often categorized as either formal or alternative, assessment activities usually embrace qualities of both kinds. Most teachers use a combination of many types of assessment in determining what a student knows or is able to do. The overview on these three pages will introduce you to the types of assessment used in *The Language of Literature* and will help you decide which ones you might want to try with your students this year. (For teacher resources and information on implementing these types of assessment, see the following three booklets: *Teacher's Guide to Assessment and Portfolio Use, Formal Assessment,* and *Alternative Assessment.*)

WHAT TYPES OF ASSESSMENT ARE THERE?

TYPES OF ASSESSMENT

FORMAL
Asks "What do you know?"

PURPOSES
Usually paper-and-pencil tests; helps teachers
- measure students' achievement against students in their own class, district, state, or country
- report students' achievement to parents and administrators
- make appropriate instructional and grouping decisions

FORMATS
Test formats are commonly
- true-false
- multiple choice
- matching
- essay
- standardized
- norm-referenced
- criterion-referenced
- objective

ALTERNATIVE
Asks "What can you do?"

PURPOSES
Usually tasks that emulate real-life situations; helps teachers
- get a broad picture of each student as a problem solver, critical thinker, and acquirer of knowledge
- measure student growth over time

TASKS
Tasks are commonly
- authentic
- products or performances
- processes

WHAT FORMS CAN ALTERNATIVE ASSESSMENT TAKE?

For more information on implementing these types of assessment, see the *Teacher's Guide to Assessment and Portfolio Use*.

> Portfolios offer one of the best vehicles for classroom-based assessment because they typically contain a variety of student work and they make it easy to separate evaluation from the process of instruction.
>
> Judith Langer and Arthur Applebee
> Professors of Education, State University of New York at Albany

✓ Product and Performance Assessment

- Requires students to produce tangible products or create performances that demonstrate their understanding of skills and concepts
- Focuses teacher's attention on the end product rather than the processes, behaviors, or strategies students used to create them
- Is based on judgment and observation guided by criteria

TYPES OF EVALUATION CRITERIA USED

Can include rubrics, formal scales and checklists, and peer and self-evaluations

POSSIBLE PRODUCTS

- scripts, dialogues
- audiotapes, videotapes
- charts, maps, graphs
- games, puzzles
- puppet shows
- plays, skits, talent shows
- interviews, debates
- role-playing
- dances
- mock trials
- cooking or sports demonstrations
- recipes, menus
- children's books
- museum exhibits
- research papers
- inventions
- book or movie reviews
- questionnaires, surveys
- print or TV ads
- poems, riddles, jokes
- time capsules
- awards
- oral histories
- murals, collages
- computer programs
- scale models, dioramas
- essays, editorials
- family trees

✓ Process Assessment

- Requires students to demonstrate or share their processes, behaviors, strategies, and critical thinking abilities as they work to understand skills and concepts
- Focuses teacher's attention on student processes, behaviors, and strategies rather than the final results
- Is based on judgment and observation guided by criteria

TYPES OF EVALUATION CRITERIA USED

Can include rubrics, formal scales and checklists, anecdotal records, observations, and self- and peer evaluations

POSSIBLE PROCESSES

While the evaluator observes students' abilities to apply higher-order thinking skills during certain processes, he or she focuses on the following:

- the use of reading strategies to develop interpretations of a text
- behavior during peer review
- evidence of investment in a task
- the ability to work in a collaborative group
- drafts created while writing an essay
- the ability to participate in class discussions
- the use of conferences to refine work
- evolving personal criteria and standards

✓ Portfolio Assessment

- Is a purposeful collection of student work that exhibits overall efforts, progress, and achievement over time in one or more areas of the curriculum
- Is a combination of process and product assessment, with a strong measure of self-evaluation and self-reflection

TYPES OF EVALUATION CRITERIA USED

Can include inventories, conference notes, rubrics, formal scales and checklists, anecdotal records, observations, and peer evaluations

POSSIBLE PRODUCTS TO INCLUDE IN THE PORTFOLIO

- interest inventories
- outlines
- written assignments
- videotapes
- reading records
- audiotapes
- performance plans
- photographs
- logs
- sketches or drawings
- journal entries
- works in progress
- textbook tasks
- research findings
- reports
- book reports or reviews
- project evaluations
- standardized tests

> *If criteria for evaluation are consistent with those stressed during instruction, and if response is shared between student and teacher, assessment can become an effective complement to any learning situation.*
>
> —Judith Langer and Arthur Applebee, Professors of Education, State University of New York at Albany

HOW CAN I PREPARE MY STUDENTS FOR THESE TYPES OF ASSESSMENT?

A major difference between formal assessment and alternative assessment is what you choose to assess and how you choose to assess it. Alternative assessment is a natural outgrowth and extension of classroom practices. Therefore, it is important to establish an effective learning—and testing—environment right away. Following are a few pointers to help you get started.

✔ Establish an environment based on trust.

Because alternative assessment makes students much more in charge of their own learning, and much more responsible for demonstrating their learning in a variety of ways, it is important to establish a classroom environment that is based on trust. Many of the activities students will be engaging in will be unfamiliar to them—and to you. Let them see that you are right in there with them, taking risks and trying new experiences. Help them understand that it's all right to try and fail—even seemingly unsuccessful experiences bring about growth and learning.

✔ Establish a tone of reflection and self-evaluation.

At the beginning of the year, ask your students to write letters describing themselves as readers, writers, and classroom participants. Also have them describe what they hope to accomplish during the coming year. Have them keep their letters in their notebooks, journals, or portfolios; encourage them to reread the letters regularly. Reflecting on their performance will help them acknowledge and evaluate their growth over the year. It will also help them see that learning and evaluating are ongoing and ever-changing processes.

✔ Help your students set goals and make commitments.

In order to grow as learners, your students must become actively involved in setting goals and making commitments. Their goals can be for a day, a week, a project, or the year; but whatever their duration, encourage students to consider their strengths and limitations so that the goals they set will be realistic.

✔ Help students view assessment in a new light.

One of the best things you can do for your students is help them break away from the notion that a "test" is something to study for the night before and then to forget. Help them see that alternative assessment involves a demonstration of what they know at a particular moment, but that what they know is bound to keep changing as new knowledge builds on old.

✔ Help your students discover their individual learning styles and preferences.

Chances are, most of your students are not fully aware of their own learning styles and preferences. Why not help them recognize which tasks and situations suit them best and help them learn more effectively? (See page T28.) After all, the better your students understand themselves, the better you'll understand how to teach and assess them.

✔ Encourage peer review as a regular part of the assessment process.

Sometimes it's easier for students to "get inside the minds" of their peers. And sometimes it's easier for them to take instruction or criticism from their peers. This is an excellent strategy, as long as growth and learning are taking place.

✔ Help your students learn to operate independently of you.

As students get comfortable with their learning environment, they'll probably want to do more and more without your help. Try to provide as many opportunities as possible for them to develop into independent learners—you'll be doing one of the best things you can do to prepare them for life in the real world!

✔ Improve and increase your own assessment tools.

As an evaluator, your goal should be to get as broad a view as possible of each of your students. Increasing your ability to provide situations in which you can observe your students will help you get more complete pictures of them. It will also help you learn more about yourself!

MAKING Connections

The Language of Literature bases all of its instruction on a "connected" approach to learning. On every page—from the Previewing pages to the Writing Workshops and Reading the World feature— students are encouraged to find the links between the literature, other subject areas, their own lives, and the world around them.

Of course, there are always more connections to be made, and certain themes and selections are particularly rich with possibilities. When you identify a selection or idea that you feel might have particular interest for your students, you may want to involve the class, as well as other teachers, in expanding the lesson into a more customized exploration. The following chart describes one way to accomplish this.

STEP 1 — What Will We Explore?

As a class, or in small groups, have students ask questions such as the following:

- What really excited me or fascinated me about this selection?
- What questions did I have as I read this?
- What didn't I understand?
- What would I like to find out more about?
- What people, experiences, issues, or situations did this remind me of that might be interesting to explore?

TIP: Clustering, discussion, brainstorming, freewriting, and notebooks and logs are among the methods that can be used to generate ideas.

STEP 2 — What Skills or Information Will We Need?

Once the questions are in place, have students identify the skills needed to find the answers. For example, the story "The Circuit" might prompt questions about the lives of the migrant worker. Will students need certain map-reading or geographical skills to learn the answers? Would information about farming or economics be important?

STEP 3 — What Resources Will We Use?

At this point, students can be encouraged to plan the kinds of resources they might use to continue their exploration. Remind them of the following possibilities:

- Print resources
- Interviews
- Surveys and Questionnaires
- CD-ROM
- The Internet and other on-line resources

TIP: This is also the point at which you might collaborate with other teachers to take advantage of team teaching and block scheduling to coordinate overlapping topics. Classroom exchanges within or between schools may also be useful to arrange at this point. Technology can provide exciting options for networking as well.

STEP 4 — How Will the Results Be Shared?

The methods for sharing information will be as varied as the projects themselves. Following are just a few of the possibilities students might consider:

- essays
- photo journals
- dramas
- videos
- speeches
- oral histories
- paintings
- music
- multimedia
- panel
- fairs
- community program

See page T40 for an example of the explorations generated from the selection "The Moustache."

> Teachers need to help their students feel integral and involved in their community and the larger world.
>
> Susan Hynds
> Professor of English Education,
> Syracuse University, Syracuse, New York

A SAMPLE PLANNING MAP

Below is an example of the different explorations that were generated from one story by a teacher following the approach outlined on page T39.

SELECTION: "THE MOUSTACHE"

SUMMARY: a boy gains a new understanding of his grandmother when he visits her in a nursing home.

COMMUNITY
- Visit a nursing home/hospital
- Write a letter to the American Association of Retired Persons (AARP)
- Plan community involvement doing volunteer work with the elderly, in nursing homes or hospitals

FIRSTHAND EXPERIENCE
- Interview an elderly member of your own family
- Create a family history

WORLD
- Study the representation of the elderly in our media
- Observe and discuss social attitudes toward elderly
- Carry out survey on attitudes to elderly (Internet, print)
- Interview care worker
- Research legislation regarding the elderly

CROSS-CURRICULAR LINKS
- Math: Plot the changes in life expectancy over the past century
- Social studies: Discuss the effect of the Great Depression on society
- Art: Consider the portrayal of the elderly in fine art

McDougal Littell

THE LANGUAGE OF
LITERATURE

McDougal Littell

THE LANGUAGE OF
LITERATURE

Arthur N. Applebee
Andrea B. Bermúdez
Sheridan Blau
Rebekah Caplan
Franchelle Dorn
Peter Elbow
Susan Hynds
Judith A. Langer
James Marshall

McDougal Littell
A HOUGHTON MIFFLIN COMPANY

Evanston, Illinois ▪ Boston ▪ Dallas

Acknowledgments

Unit One

James Thurber Literary Properties: "The Secret Life of Walter Mitty," from *My World—And Welcome to It* by James Thurber, published by Harcourt Brace & Company; Copyright 1942 by James Thurber, Copyright © 1970 by Helen Thurber and Rosemary A. Thurber.

Don Congdon Associates, Inc.: "The Utterly Perfect Murder" by Ray Bradbury; Copyright © 1971 by Ray Bradbury. Reprinted by permission of Don Congdon Associates, Inc.

The University of Georgia Press: "American History," from *The Latin Deli* by Judith Ortiz Cofer; Copyright © 1992 by Judith Ortiz Cofer. Reprinted by permission of the University of Georgia Press.

University of Pittsburgh Press: "The Bass, the River, and Sheila Mant," from *The Man Who Loved Levittown* by W. D. Wetherell; Copyright © 1985 by W. D. Wetherell. Reprinted by permission of the University of Pittsburgh Press.

Liveright Publishing Corporation: "since feeling is first," from *Complete Poems, 1904–1962*, by E. E. Cummings, edited by George J. Firmage; Copyright 1926, 1954, © 1991 by the Trustees for the E. E. Cummings Trust. Copyright © 1985 by George James Firmage. Reprinted by permission of Liveright Publishing Corporation.

Continued on page 964

Cover Art

Window: Copyright © 1995 Jay Maisel. **Ibis:** Copyright © L.L.T. Rhodes / Animals Animals. **Painting:** *Portrait of Langston Hughes* (about 1925), Winhold Reiss. National Portrait Gallery, Smithsonian Institution / Art Resource. Copyright © National Portrait Gallery, Washington, D.C. **Book:** Photo by Alan Shortall. **Frame:** Photo by Sharon Hoogstraten.

Warning: No part of this work may be reproduced or transmitted in any form or by any means, electronic or mechanical, including photocopying and recording, or by any information storage or retrieval system without prior written permission of McDougal Littell Inc. unless such copying is expressly permitted by federal copyright law. Address inquiries to Manager, Rights and Permissions, McDougal Littell Inc., P.O. Box 1667, Evanston, IL 60204

ISBN 0-395-73704-4

Copyright © 1997 by McDougal Littell Inc. All rights reserved. Printed in the United States of America.

1 2 3 4 5 6 7 8 9 – RRD – 01 00 99 98 97 96

Senior Consultants

The senior consultants guided the conceptual development for *The Language of Literature* series. They participated actively in shaping prototype materials for major components, and they reviewed completed prototypes and/or completed units to ensure consistency with current research and the philosophy of the series.

Arthur N. Applebee Professor of Education, State University of New York at Albany; Director, Center for the Learning and Teaching of Literature; Senior Fellow, Center for Writing and Literacy

Andrea B. Bermúdez Professor of Studies in Language and Culture; Director, Research Center for Language and Culture; Chair, Foundations and Professional Studies, University of Houston-Clear Lake

Sheridan Blau Senior Lecturer in English and Education and former Director of Composition, University of California at Santa Barbara; Director, South Coast Writing Project; Director, Literature Institute for Teachers; Vice President, National Council of Teachers of English

Rebekah Caplan Coordinator, English Language Arts K-12, Oakland Unified School District, Oakland, California; Teacher-Consultant, Bay Area Writing Project, University of California at Berkeley; served on the California State English Assessment Development Team for Language Arts

Franchelle Dorn Professor Drama, Howard University, Washington, D.C.; Adjunct Professor, Graduate School of Opera, University of Maryland, College Park, Maryland; Co-founder of The Shakespeare Acting Conservatory, Washington, D.C.

Peter Elbow Professor of English, University of Massachusetts at Amherst; Fellow, Bard Center for Writing and Thinking

Susan Hynds Professor and Director of English Education, Syracuse University, Syracuse, New York

Judith A. Langer Professor of Education, State University of New York at Albany; Co-director, Center for the Learning and Teaching of Literature; Senior Fellow, Center for Writing and Literacy

James Marshall Professor of English and English Education, University of Iowa, Iowa City

Contributing Consultants

Tommy Boley Associate Professor of English, University of Texas at El Paso

Jeffrey N. Golub Assistant Professor of English Education, University of South Florida, Tampa

William L. McBride, Reading and Curriculum Specialist; former middle and high school English instructor

Multicultural Advisory Board

The multicultural advisors reviewed literature selections for appropriate content and made suggestions for teaching lessons in a multicultural classroom.

Dr. Joyce M. Bell, Chairperson, English Department, Townview Magnet Center, Dallas, Texas

Dr. Eugenia W. Collier, author; lecturer; Chairperson, Department of English and Language Arts; teacher of Creative Writing and American Literature, Morgan State University, Maryland

Kathleen S. Fowler, President, Palm Beach County Council of Teachers of English, Boca Raton Middle School, Boca Raton, Florida

Noreen M. Rodriguez, Trainer for Hillsborough County School District's Staff Development Division, independent consultant, Gaither High School, Tampa, Florida

Michelle Dixon Thompson, Seabreeze High School, Daytona Beach, Florida

Teacher Review Panels

The following educators provided ongoing review during the development of the tables of contents, lesson design, and key components of the program.

FLORIDA
Judi Briant, English Department Chairperson, Armwood High School, Hillsborough County School District

Beth Johnson, Polk County English Supervisor, Polk County School District

Sharon Johnston, Learning Resource Specialist, Evans High School, Orange County School District

continued on page 974

Manuscript Reviewers

The following educators reviewed prototype lessons and tables of contents during the development of *The Language of Literature* program.

Carol Alves, English Department Chairperson, Apopka High School, Apopka, Florida

Jacqueline Anderson, James A. Foshay Learning Center, Los Angeles, California

Kathleen M. Anderson-Knight, United Township High School, East Moline, Illinois

Anita Arnold, Thomas Jefferson High School, San Antonio, Texas

Cassandra L. Asberry, Justin F. Kimball High School, Dallas, Texas

Don Baker, English Department Chairperson, Peoria High School, Peoria, Illinois

continued on page 975

Student Board

The student board members read and evaluated selections to assess their appeal for ninth-grade students.

Nancy Beirne, St. Francis DeSales, Columbus, Ohio

Anne S. Burke, Nichols School, Buffalo, New York

Ruth El-Jamal, Centennial High School, Champaign, Illinois

Yahaira Ferreira, Miami Sunset Junior High School, Miami, Florida

Angie Lang, Lee's Summit High School, Lee's Summit, Missouri

Aric C. Lewis, E. F. Lindop School, Broadview, Illinois

Michael Allen Little, J. Lupton Simpson Middle School, Leesburg, Virginia

Peter Lum, Centennial High School, Champaign, Illinois

William Caleb McDaniel, Clark High School, San Antonio, Texas

Vu Quang, Center Street Middle School, Birmingham, Alabama

Jamie Rishel, Heritage Middle School, Westerville, Ohio

Jeffrey Sherman, Clark High School Academy of Math and Science, Las Vegas, Nevada

Joshua Taylor III, H-B Woodlawn Program, Arlington, Virginia

THE LANGUAGE OF LITERATURE
Overview

Student Anthology
Learning the Language of Literature

Strategies for Reading 5
Reading Model: The Secret Life of Walter Mitty by James Thurber 6

UNIT ONE — *Live and Learn* 12
- **PART 1:** Growing Pains / 14
  - WRITING ABOUT LITERATURE: Analysis / 82
- **PART 2:** Rites of Passage / 90
  - WRITING FROM EXPERIENCE: Report / 164

UNIT TWO — *Trials and Tribulations* 174
- **PART 1:** Friend or Foe? / 176
  - WRITING ABOUT LITERATURE: Direct Response / 244
- **PART 2:** Against the Odds / 252
  - WRITING FROM EXPERIENCE: Persuasion / 326

UNIT THREE — *All in the Family* 336
- **PART 1:** Mixed Blessings / 338
  - WRITING ABOUT LITERATURE: Interpretation / 404
- **PART 2:** On Your Own Terms / 412
  - WRITING FROM EXPERIENCE: Firsthand and Expressive Writing / 468

UNIT FOUR — *Portrait of a Hero* 478
- **PART 1:** The Wanderings of Odysseus / 480
  - WRITING ABOUT LITERATURE: Creative Response / 534
- **PART 2:** The Homecoming / 542
  - WRITING FROM EXPERIENCE: Informative Exposition / 572

UNIT FIVE — *Mysteries and Deceptions* 582
- **PART 1:** False Pretenses / 584
  - WRITING ABOUT LITERATURE: Criticism / 648
- **PART 2:** Jumping to Conclusions / 656
  - WRITING FROM EXPERIENCE: Report / 700

UNIT SIX — *A Matter of Life and Death* 710
- **PART 1:** Uncharted Territory / 712
  - WRITING ABOUT LITERATURE: Creative Response / 766
- **PART 2:** Fateful Encounters / 774
  - WRITING FROM EXPERIENCE: Narrative and Literary Writing / 834

Words to Know: Access Guide 846
Handbook of Literary Terms 850
Writing Handbook 860
Multimedia Handbook 890
Grammar Handbook 900
Index of Fine Art 946
Index of Skills 949
Index of Titles and Authors 961

Literature Connections

Each book in the Literature Connections series combines a novel or play with related readings—poems, stories, plays, essays, articles—that provide new perspectives on the theme or subject matter of the longer work. For example, Nathaniel Hawthorne's *The Scarlet Letter* is combined with the following readings, which focus on modern applications and humorous retellings of the novel and on such topics as the Puritans, scapegoating, sin, and temptation.

John Dunton	**Muddy Brains**
Richard Armour	from **The Classics Reclassified**
Kate Chopin	**A Respectable Woman**
Emily Dickinson	**For Each Ecstatic Instant**
Emily Dickinson	**Mine Enemy Is Growing Old**
Bible	**Psalm 32**
Shirley Jackson	**The Lottery**
Toni Locy	**Concerns Raised on "Scarlet Letter" for Drunk Drivers**

The Adventures of Huckleberry Finn*
Mark Twain

...And the Earth Did Not Devour Him
Tomás Rivera

Animal Farm
George Orwell

The Crucible
Arthur Miller

Ethan Frome
Edith Wharton

Fallen Angels
Walter Dean Myers

The Friends
Rosa Guy

Hamlet
William Shakespeare

Jane Eyre*
Charlotte Brontë

Julius Caesar
William Shakespeare

Macbeth
William Shakespeare

A Midsummer Night's Dream
William Shakespeare

My Ántonia
Willa Cather

Nervous Conditions
Tsitsi Dangarembga

Picture Bride
Yoshiko Uchida

A Place Where the Sea Remembers
Sandra Benítez

Pygmalion
George Bernard Shaw

A Raisin in the Sun
Lorraine Hansberry

The Scarlet Letter
Nathaniel Hawthorne

A Tale of Two Cities*
Charles Dickens

Things Fall Apart
Chinua Achebe

To Kill a Mockingbird, the Screenplay
Horton Foote

The Tragedy of Romeo and Juliet*
William Shakespeare

The Underdogs
Mariano Azuela

West with the Night
Beryl Markham

When Rain Clouds Gather
Bessie Head

*McDougal Littell offers a Spanish version.

UNIT ONE *Live and Learn* — 12

Part 1 Growing Pains

REFLECTING ON THEME What Do You Think? 14

▶ FOCUS ON FICTION 15

Ray Bradbury	**The Utterly Perfect Murder**	FICTION	17
Judith Ortiz Cofer	**American History**	FICTION	27
W. D. Wetherell	**The Bass, the River, and Sheila Mant**	FICTION	39
E. E. Cummings	**since feeling is first** / INSIGHT	POETRY	47

▶ FOCUS ON NONFICTION 50

Maya Angelou	from **I Know Why the Caged Bird Sings**	NONFICTION	52
Eve Merriam	**Metaphor** / INSIGHT	POETRY	59
Truman Capote	**A Christmas Memory**	NONFICTION	62
David Raymond	**On Being Seventeen, Bright, and Unable to Read**	NONFICTION	79

ON YOUR OWN / ASSESSMENT OPTION

WRITING ABOUT LITERATURE Analysis

Writer's Style: Show, Don't Tell 82
Guided Assignment: Write a Character Study 84
Grammar in Context: Verb Tense 87
  SKILLBUILDERS: Using Appositive Phrases, Using Methods of Organization, Using Irregular Verb Forms Correctly

READING THE WORLD: VISUAL LITERACY 88
  Closeup on Character
  SKILLBUILDER: Avoiding Stereotypes

x THE LANGUAGE OF LITERATURE TEACHER'S EDITION

Part 2 Rites of Passage

REFLECTING ON THEME What Do You Think? 90

Doris Lessing	**Through the Tunnel**	FICTION	91
Eugenia Collier	**Marigolds**	FICTION	106
	▶ FOCUS ON POETRY		120
Robert Frost	**The Road Not Taken**	POETRY	122
May Swenson	**Fable for When There's No Way Out**	POETRY	122
Sue Ellen Bridgers	**The Beginning of Something**	FICTION	127
Gary Soto	**Oranges** / INSIGHT	POETRY	142
William A. Nolen	**The First Appendectomy**	NONFICTION	145
Emily Dickinson	**Surgeons must be very careful** / INSIGHT	POETRY	151
Williams Forrest	**Plainswoman**	FICTION	154

ON YOUR OWN / ASSESSMENT OPTION

✏️ WRITING FROM EXPERIENCE Report

Guided Assignment: Write an Investigative Report 164
  Prewriting: Gathering Information
  Drafting: Getting Your Ideas Down
  Revising and Publishing: Finishing Your Report
  SKILLBUILDERS: Analyzing Information, Supporting Ideas
     with Details, Using Commas in a Series

UNIT REVIEW: Reflect and Assess 172

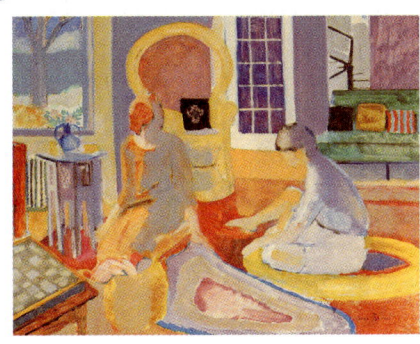

UNIT TWO Trials and Tribulations 174

Part 1 Friend or Foe?

| | REFLECTING ON THEME What Do You Think? | | 176 |

Nash Candelaria	**The Day the Cisco Kid Shot John Wayne**	FICTION	177
William Blake	**A Poison Tree** / INSIGHT	POETRY	192
Jean Shepherd	**Grover Dill and the Tasmanian Devil**	FICTION	196
Amy Lowell	**Fireworks** / INSIGHT	POETRY	205
Bob Kaufman	**Battle Report**	POETRY	208
Demetrio Herrera	**Training/Entrenamiento**	POETRY	208
Kurt Vonnegut, Jr.	**The Euphio Question**	FICTION	215
Beryl Markham	**Brothers Are the Same**	FICTION	233

ON YOUR OWN / ASSESSMENT OPTION

WRITING ABOUT LITERATURE Direct Response

Writer's Style: Elaboration 244
Guided Assignment: Write a Process Response. 246
Grammar in Context: Misplaced Phrases and Clauses 249
  SKILLBUILDERS: Using Specific Nouns, Achieving
    Coherence in Paragraphs, Placing
    Adjectives Effectively

READING THE WORLD: VISUAL LITERACY 251
Taking a Second Look
  SKILLBUILDER: Avoiding Overgeneralizations

Part 2 Against the Odds

REFLECTING ON THEME What Do You Think?			252

▸ FOCUS ON DRAMA 253

Stephen Vincent Benét	**The Devil and Daniel Webster**	DRAMA	255
Sucheng Chan	**You're Short, Besides!**	NONFICTION	282
Margaret Truman	**The United States vs. Susan B. Anthony**	NONFICTION	293
Anna Guest	**Beauty Is Truth**	FICTION	305
Sue Doro	**The Cultural Worker**	FICTION	316
María Herrera-Sobek	**My Poetry/Mi Poesía** / INSIGHT	POETRY	320
Amy Tan	**Fish Cheeks**	NONFICTION	323

ON YOUR OWN / ASSESSMENT OPTION

WRITING FROM EXPERIENCE Persuasion

Guided Assignment: Write an Persuasive Essay 326
    Prewriting: Gathering Information
    Drafting: Mapping Out Your Ideas
    Revising and Publishing: Completing Your Essay
    SKILLBUILDERS: Writing a Thesis Statement, Avoiding Circular Reasoning, Using Active Voice

UNIT REVIEW: Reflect and Assess 334

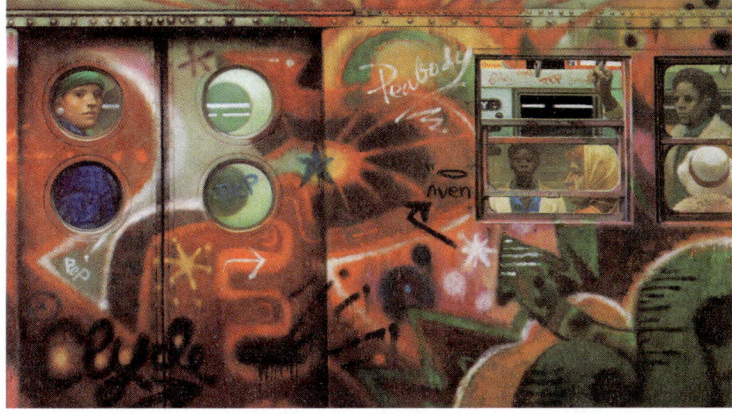

xiii

UNIT THREE *All in the Family*   336

Part 1 Mixed Blessings

REFLECTING ON THEME What Do You Think?   338

David McLean	**Marine Corps Issue**	FICTION	339
David McLean	**On Writing "Marine Corps Issue"** / INSIGHT	NONFICTION	355
Margaret Walker	**Lineage**	POETRY	359
Edna St. Vincent Millay	**The Courage That My Mother Had**	POETRY	359
Anna Lee Walters	**The Warriors**	FICTION	364
Theodore Roethke	**My Papa's Waltz**	POETRY	380
Jack Driscoll	**Touch Football**	POETRY	380
Anton Chekhov	**A Marriage Proposal**	DRAMA	385
Ogden Nash	**The Strange Case of Mr. Ormantude's Bride** / INSIGHT	POETRY	398
Michael Dorris	**Father's Day**	NONFICTION	401

ON YOUR OWN / ASSESSMENT OPTION

WRITING ABOUT LITERATURE   Interpretation

Writer's Style: Unity in Paragraphs   404
Guided Assignment: Interpret a Theme   406
Grammar in Context: Compound Subjects   409
  SKILLBUILDERS: Varying Sentence Beginnings, Writing an Introduction, Achieving Verb Agreement with Compound Subjects

READING THE WORLD: VISUAL LITERACY   411
  Finding Meaning
    SKILLBUILDER: Interpreting Experience

Part 2 On Your Own Terms

REFLECTING ON THEME What Do You Think? 412

James Hurst	**The Scarlet Ibis**	FICTION	413
Naomi Long Madgett	**Woman with Flower** / INSIGHT	POETRY	425
Richard Wright	from **Black Boy**	NONFICTION	429
Sandra Cisneros	**Only Daughter**	NONFICTION	437
Langston Hughes	**Theme for English B**	POETRY	443
Richard Wilbur	**The Writer**	POETRY	443
Isabelle C. Chang	**The Artist** / INSIGHT	FICTION	448
Vasanthi Victor	**Lakshmi**	FICTION	452
David Brenner	**Fish Eyes**	NONFICTION	462

ON YOUR OWN / ASSESSMENT OPTION

WRITING FROM EXPERIENCE Firsthand and Expressive Writing

Guided Assignment: Write About a Personal Experience 468
   Prewriting: Selecting Your True Story
   Drafting: Putting the Story on Paper
   Revising and Publishing: Refining Your Story
   SKILLBUILDERS: Visualizing an Experience, Using Transitions to Show Time Order, Avoiding Shifts in Tense

UNIT REVIEW: Reflect and Assess 476

UNIT FOUR *Portrait of a Hero*   478

Part 1 The Wanderings of Odysseus

REFLECTING ON THEME What Do You Think?   480

Homer, translated by Robert Fitzgerald   *from* **the Odyssey** . . . . EPIC POETRY 481
- **Book 9: New Coasts and Poseidon's Son** 486
- **Book 10: The Grace of the Witch** 508
- **Book 12: Sea Perils and Defeat** 532

Margaret Atwood   **Siren Song** . . . . POETRY 532
ON YOUR OWN / ASSESSMENT OPTION

WRITING ABOUT LITERATURE Creative Response

Writer's Style: Levels of Language 534
Guided Assignment: Write a Parody 536
Grammar in Context: Compound-Complex Sentences 539
   SKILLBUILDERS: Understanding Informal Language,
                  Telling a Story, Using Conjunctions

READING THE WORLD: VISUAL LITERACY 541
   Visual Parodies
   SKILLBUILDER: Analyzing the Elements of Parody

xvi THE LANGUAGE OF LITERATURE TEACHER'S EDITION

Part 2 The Homecoming

REFLECTING ON THEME What Do You Think? 542

Homer, translated by Robert Fitzgerald

from **the Odyssey (continued)** .... EPIC POETRY 543
    Book 21: The Test of the Bow 544
    Book 22: Death in the Great Hall 557
    Book 23: The Trunk of the Olive Tree 563

Dorothy Parker   **Penelope** .... POETRY 570
ON YOUR OWN / ASSESSMENT OPTION

WRITING FROM EXPERIENCE | Informative Exposition

Guided Assignment: Write an Extended Definition 572
    Prewriting: Exploring Your Idea
    Drafting: Crafting Your Definition
    Revising and Publishing: Finalizing Your Definition
    SKILLBUILDERS: Classifying Ideas, Using a Thesaurus, Avoiding Illogical Comparisons

UNIT REVIEW: Reflect and Assess 580

UNIT FIVE Mysteries and Deceptions   582

Part 1 False Pretenses

REFLECTING ON THEME What Do You Think?   584

Shirley Jackson	**One Ordinary Day, with Peanuts**	FICTION	585
Bai Xiao-Yi	**The Explosion in the Parlor** / INSIGHT	FICTION	595
Dorothy M. Johnson	**The Last Boast**	FICTION	598
Sue Grafton	**Full Circle**	FICTION	605
Maria Simson	**"Who Killed My Daughter?": Lois Duncan Searches for an Answer** / INSIGHT	NONFICTION	618
W. H. Auden	**O What Is That Sound**	POETRY	622
Susan Glaspell	**Trifles**	DRAMA	627
John Collier	**The Chaser**	FICTION	644

ON YOUR OWN / ASSESSMENT OPTION

WRITING ABOUT LITERATURE Criticism

Writer's Style: Point of View 648
Guided Assignment: Write a Critical Essay 650
Grammar in Context: Active and Passive Voice 653
    SKILLBUILDERS: Correcting Vague Pronoun References, Using Criteria for Evaluation, Using Past Participles Correctly

READING THE WORLD: VISUAL LITERACY 654
Where Do You Stand?
    SKILLBUILDER: Formulating Questions

xviii THE LANGUAGE OF LITERATURE TEACHER'S EDITION

Part 2 Jumping to Conclusions

REFLECTING ON THEME What Do You Think? 656

Guy de Maupassant	**The Necklace**	FICTION	657
Tony Hillerman	**The Great Taos Bank Robbery**	NONFICTION	669
Martin J. Hamer	**The Mountain**	FICTION	680
Alice Childress	**The Pocketbook Game** / INSIGHT	FICTION	685
Daniel Garza	**Everybody Knows Tobie**	FICTION	688
Audre Lorde	**Hanging Fire**	POETRY	698

ON YOUR OWN / ASSESSMENT OPTION

WRITING FROM EXPERIENCE Report

Guided Assignment: Write a Research Paper 700
   Prewriting: Brushing Up on a Topic
   Drafting: Beginning to Write
   Revising and Publishing: Finishing It Up
    SKILLBUILDERS: Taking Notes, Crediting Sources, Punctuating a Works Cited List

UNIT REVIEW: Reflect and Assess 708

UNIT SIX A Matter of Life and Death   710

Part 1 Uncharted Territory

REFLECTING ON THEME What Do You Think?   712

Elisabeth Kübler-Ross, interviewed by Lynn Gilbert and Gaylen Moore	**Unfinished Business**	NONFICTION	713
Alice Walker	**"Good Night, Willie Lee, I'll See You in the Morning"** / INSIGHT	POETRY	720
Edgar Allan Poe	**Annabel Lee**	POETRY	724
Donald Justice	**Incident in a Rose Garden**	POETRY	724
William Stafford	**Traveling Through the Dark**	POETRY	732
Denise Levertov	**The Sharks**	POETRY	732
Stephen King	**Sorry, Right Number**	DRAMA	737
Ron Arias	**A Trip to the Edge of Survival**	NONFICTION	756

ON YOUR OWN / ASSESSMENT OPTION

WRITING ABOUT LITERATURE Creative Response

Writer's Style: Creating a Mood 766
Guided Assignment: Write a Drama 768
Grammar in Context: Using Adverbs and Adjectives 771
   SKILLBUILDERS: Using Foreshadowing, Writing Dialogue, Choosing the Correct Modifier

READING THE WORLD: VISUAL LITERACY 773
   Setting the Stage
      SKILLBUILDER: Analyzing Setting

Part 2 Fateful Encounters

REFLECTING ON THEME What Do You Think? 774

Edgar Allan Poe	**The Cask of Amontillado**	FICTION	775
Edward Rowe Snow	**The Story Behind "The Cask of Amontillado"** / INSIGHT	NONFICTION	783
Richard Connell	**The Most Dangerous Game**	FICTION	787
John Hersey	**Not to Go with the Others**	NONFICTION	809
Faye Porter, Henry Abramowicz, and Anonymous	**Reflections on the Holocaust** / INSIGHT	NONFICTION	814
Sabine R. Ulibarrí	**My Wonder Horse/Mi Caballo Mago**	FICTION	817
Ursula K. Le Guin	**The Wife's Story**	FICTION	830

ON YOUR OWN / ASSESSMENT OPTION

WRITING FROM EXPERIENCE Narrative and Literary Writing

Guided Assignment: Write a Short Story 834
    Prewriting: Shaping an Idea
    Drafting: Getting Your Story Down
    Revising and Publishing: Finishing Your Story
    SKILLBUILDERS: Researching Details, Creating Paragraphs, Using Commas in Dialogue

UNIT REVIEW: Reflect and Assess 842

Electronic Library

The Electronic Library is a CD-ROM that contains additional fiction, nonfiction, poetry, and drama for each unit in *The Language of Literature*.
Preliminary List of Titles

Unit 1

Annie Dillard	from **An American Childhood**
Elizabeth Barrett Browning	**Sonnet 14**
Emily Dickinson	**A Bird came down the Walk**
	A narrow Fellow in the Grass
Bob Greene	**Fifteen**
Robert Fulghum	**Dinner Dandruff**
William Shakespeare	**"All the world's a stage"** from **As You Like It**
Walt Whitman	**Song of the Open Road**

Unit 2

John Gould Fletcher	**The Skaters**
Jamake Highwater	**Snake Boy**
Hernando Téllez	**Lather and Nothing Else**
Theodore Roethke	**The Bat**
Lynda Barry	**The Sanctuary of School**
Langston Hughes	**Harlem**
William Ernest Henley	**Invictus**
Robert Frost	**Fire and Ice**
	Nothing Gold Can Stay
Martin Luther King, Jr.	**I Have a Dream**
David Wagoner	**The Shooting of John Dillinger Outside the Biograph Theater**
Rudyard Kipling	**If**

Unit 3

James Thurber	**The Night the Bed Fell**
Paul de Vergie	**Mother Married an Oboe Player**
Gerald Durrell	**The World in a Wall**
J. M. Synge	**Riders to the Sea**

Note: A complete list of literature available for all grade levels accompanies each CD-ROM.

Toni Cade Bambara	**Blues Ain't No Mockin Bird**
Vachel Lindsay	**The Broncho That Would Not Be Broken**
Carl Sandburg	**Home**
Oliver Wendell Holmes	**The Last Reef**

Unit 4

Edgar Allan Poe	**To Helen**
Alfred, Lord Tennyson	**Ulysses**
Henry Wadsworth Longfellow	**Dedication** from **Ultima Thule**
Edna St. Vincent Millay	**An Ancient Gesture**
C. P. Cavafy	**Ithaka**

Unit 5

Walt Whitman	**When I Heard the Learn'd Astronomer**
Edgar Allan Poe	**The Black Cat**
J. Sheridan Le Fanu	**The White Cat of Drumgunniol**
H. G. Wells	**The Magic Shop**
Shirley Jackson	**The Possibility of Evil**
James Thurber	**The Night the Ghost Got In**
Sir Arthur Conan Doyle	**The Adventure of the Speckled Band** **The Red-Headed League**
William Wordsworth	**Lucy Gray**
Walter de la Mare	**The Listeners**
Frank R. Stockton	**The Lady, or the Tiger?**
Saki	**The Open Window**

Unit 6

Jack London	**To Build a Fire**
Arthur C. Clarke	**History Lesson**
William Wordsworth	**She Dwelt Among the Untrodden Ways**
O. Henry	**The Ransom of Red Chief**
Shirley Ann Grau	**The Land and the Water**
Theodore L. Thomas	**Test**
Edgar Allan Poe	**The Pit and the Pendulum** **The Bells**

Selections by Genre, Writing Workshops

Fiction

The Secret Life of Walter Mitty	6
The Utterly Perfect Murder	17
American History	27
The Bass, the River, and Sheila Mant	39
Through the Tunnel	91
Marigolds	106
The Beginning of Something	127
Plainswoman	154
The Day the Cisco Kid Shot John Wayne	177
Grover Dill and the Tasmanian Devil	196
The Euphio Question	215
Brothers Are the Same	233
Beauty Is Truth	305
The Cultural Worker	316
Marine Corps Issue	339
The Warriors	364
The Scarlet Ibis	413
The Artist	448
Lakshmi	452
One Ordinary Day, with Peanuts	585
The Explosion in the Parlor	595
The Last Boast	598
Full Circle	605
The Chaser	644
The Necklace	657
The Mountain	680
The Pocketbook Game	685
Everybody Knows Tobie	688
The Cask of Amontillado	775
The Most Dangerous Game	787
My Wonder Horse/Mi Caballo Mago	817
The Wife's Story	830

Nonfiction

from I Know Why the Caged Bird Sings	52
A Christmas Memory	62
On Being Seventeen, Bright, and Unable to Read	79
The First Appendectomy	145
You're Short, Besides!	282
The United States vs. Susan B. Anthony	293
Fish Cheeks	323
On Writing "Marine Corps Issue"	355
Father's Day	401
from Black Boy	429
Only Daughter	437
Fish Eyes	462
"Who Killed My Daughter?": Lois Duncan Searches for an Answer	618
The Great Taos Bank Robbery	669
Unfinished Business	713
A Trip to the Edge of Survival	756
The Story Behind "The Cask of Amontillado"	783
Not to Go with the Others	809
Reflections on the Holocaust	814

Drama

The Devil and Daniel Webster	255
A Marriage Proposal	385
Trifles	627
Sorry, Right Number	737

Poetry

since feeling is first	47
Metaphor	59
The Road Not Taken	122
Fable for When There's No Way Out	122
Oranges	142
Surgeons must be very careful	151
A Poison Tree	192
Fireworks	205
Battle Report	208
Training/Entrenamiento	208
My Poetry/Mi Poesía	320
Lineage	359
The Courage That My Mother Had	359
My Papa's Waltz	380
Touch Football	380
The Strange Case of Mr. Ormantude's Bride	398
Woman with Flower	425
Theme for English B	443
The Writer	443
from the Odyssey	481
Siren Song	532
Penelope	570
O What Is That Sound	622
Hanging Fire	698
"Good Night, Willie Lee, I'll See You in the Morning"	720
Annabel Lee	724
Incident in a Rose Garden	724
Traveling Through the Dark	732
The Sharks	732

Writing About Literature

Analysis	82
Direct Response	244
Interpretation	404
Creative Response	534
Criticism	648
Creative Response	766

Writing from Experience

Report	164
Persuasion	326
Firsthand and Expressive Writing	468
Informative Exposition	572
Report	700
Narrative and Literary Writing	834

Reading the World: Visual Literacy

Closeup on Character	88
Taking a Second Look	251
Finding Meaning	411
Visual Parodies	541
Where Do You Stand?	654
Setting the Stage	773

LEARNING THE LANGUAGE OF LITERATURE

Introduction

Designed to help students realize that their encounters with the literature in this book will challenge them to discover new ways of reading, learning, and understanding, this section has the following purposes:
- To involve students in an activity that will help them perceive the study of literature in a new way
- To help students discover how literature connects to their own lives and the world around them
- To introduce students to the parts of the book
- To familiarize students with the tools necessary for learning, such as a reading log, a notebook, and strategies for reading
- To provide a model of real students using reading strategies to become involved with literature

LEARNING THE LANGUAGE OF
LITERATURE

Is One Glance Enough?

What do you notice when you stare at this picture? Are you sure that you've seen all there is to see? Perhaps more lurks in this landscape than first meets the eye. To find out, take a closer look.

LOOK AGAIN

With a partner, take turns trying to see another image hidden in this seemingly empty field. Here's how.

1. Hold the picture up to your nose.
2. With relaxed eyes, stare off into space as though you were looking through the picture.
3. Now, very slowly, move the page away from your face. An inch every few seconds is fast enough.
4. Keep relaxed, and try to observe the picture without looking directly at it. (Don't cross your eyes.)
5. Continue looking through the page. Stop moving it away from you when it reaches a comfortable reading distance.
6. When you begin to see a three-dimensional image, try not to look directly at the page, or you will need to start over.
7. Be patient with yourself, relax, and ask a friend for pointers if you don't see a three-dimensional image the first few times you try.

CONNECT TO LITERATURE

Literature, like this picture, contains much more than is apparent at first glance. To find deeper meaning in a piece of literature, or in an everyday experience, you have to look for more than just the obvious. To find out what might be hiding in a piece of literature, turn the page. A world of discoveries awaits you.

LEARNING THE LANGUAGE OF LITERATURE 1

Look Again

It may be necessary for students to view this picture from a distance in order to discern the image. Most students will see a horse in the foreground, facing left, with one of its front legs bent; it is standing on a hillside, with six trees, some partially hidden, in the background. You may wish to have students draw or sketch what they see and compare their perceptions with those of others in the class. If any students are having difficulty finding the hidden picture, encourage volunteers to help them "see" it by tracing with a finger the outline of the horse.

Connect to Literature

Encourage students to understand the reason for this activity by stressing the idea that reading literature is similar to looking at this picture. In other words, understanding and appreciating literature involves looking beyond the obvious, or "reading between the lines," to make new discoveries.

What Can Literature Show You?

These two pages are designed both to extend the explanation of literature that was introduced in the opening activity and to provide an overview of the pupil book for students.

You can help students work through this page by first generating a class discussion. Ask students to describe how literature currently affects their lives:

- What does the word *literature* mean to you?
- What kinds of literature do you like to read?
- Do you think studying literature is important? Why or why not?
- Do you think literature, or the study of literature, can affect people's lives? How?
- Have you ever read something that helped you think new thoughts and ideas or that affected your emotions strongly?

What Can Literature Show You?

To discover what lies beneath the surface of what you see and read, you need only delve deeply into this book. New worlds and experiences can open up right before your eyes. You will be amazed at what you discover . . .

UNFORGETTABLE PEOPLE

When you read, an extraordinary tapestry of human life unfolds before you. As you read the **literature selections** in this book, you will meet characters who can be your guide to new places and new experiences. Other characters might be very much like you. For example, in "The Day the Cisco Kid Shot John Wayne" on page 177, you'll meet a boy who is fascinated by the heroes in old Hollywood movies.

NEW SELF-AWARENESS

As you step into the lives of characters—both real and imagined—you'll begin to uncover interesting aspects of yourself. Most selections in this book begin with a **Previewing** page that gives background information and activates what you already know about a subject. For example, on page 17 you'll recall memories from your childhood before reading "The Utterly Perfect Murder," a story of revenge on a childhood enemy. The **Responding** pages after a selection lead you down pathways for discovering your own ideas about what you've read. For a sampling of some of those pathways, see page 25. You'll also have opportunities to share your ideas in group discussions and learn from others.

2   THE LANGUAGE OF LITERATURE   TEACHER'S EDITION

FRESH IDEAS

Literature presents a world of ideas—some may inspire or intrigue you, others may puzzle or disturb you. As you explore literature, the **Writing About Literature** workshops will show you ways of writing about your discoveries. For example, the workshop on page 244 invites you to express your personal response to a selection. You'll also find ways to connect unit themes to your own life. For example, Unit Four gets you thinking about heroism. In the Unit Four **Writing from Experience** workshop, you will craft your own definition of a complex idea.

A BROADER OUTLOOK

Reading literature can help you rise to a new level of knowledge. From that peak, you'll be able to see more of the world than before. In the **Reading the World** features, the strategies you use to develop an understanding of literature will also help you get a clearer picture of the world around you. For example, see page 250 to discover how looking at situations more than once can affect your reactions.

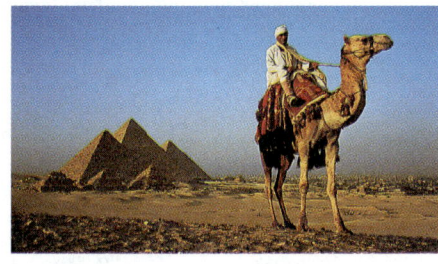

You may wish to have students read these two pages on their own, with a partner, or as a class. Encourage students to turn to the specific pages and examples suggested. Also suggest that they write down any comments or questions they think of while reading. Once students have read the two pages, discuss the questions they have recorded and ask them if their expectations about the book or the study of literature have changed. (For further information about each of the book sections that are mentioned, please turn to pages T10–T11 and T14–T15 at the front of this Teacher's Edition.)

How Do You Know What to Look For?

MULTIPLE PATHWAYS
Help students to understand the concept of multiple pathways by engaging them in the following activity. Have students imagine that they are going to take a trip across the country, from the East Coast to the West Coast. Ask them to identify as many forms of transportation as possible that they could use and to identify the differences among the forms of transportation. Make sure students understand that the end result with each form of transportation is the same—it's the means by which they get to their destination that differs. Tell students that learning is similar to traveling. There are many ways to learn, all of which involve different strategies and experiences.

PORTFOLIOS
Students will use their portfolios to file the work they will carry out in the projects and activities throughout the book. You can determine the way in which students use their portfolios. For instance, you may wish to have students include not only their completed work, but also outlines, drafts, and revisions. These portfolios can also be used to help students reflect on and assess what they learned from these projects.

NOTEBOOK
Students will use their notebooks to record their responses to and notes for some items on the Previewing and Responding pages. At various times, you may wish to have students use their notes to help them participate in paired or group discussions. You may also wish to return to these previewing notes after students have finished reading a selection to allow them to reflect and assess whether any of their thoughts have changed.

READING LOG
Students will use their reading logs to record their thoughts and responses while reading. At times, students will be responding to questions incorporated in the selections, but they should also be encouraged to record their ideas and questions whenever they read independently.

You can use these three tools in any number of ways that best suit the needs of your class. Refer to the *Teacher's Guide to Assessment and Portfolio Use* for more information on using these tools and to the *Unit One Resource Book* for copymasters of different examples of reading logs.

4 THE LANGUAGE OF LITERATURE TEACHER'S EDITION

How Do You Know What to Look For?

Literature has so much to show you, and there are many different ways to look at the things you see. How can you keep it all from becoming a blur? Read on and find out how to set your sights.

Portfolio

MULTIPLE PATHWAYS

Do you learn best when you work alone or with others? Do you prefer writing, discussing, acting, or drawing? No matter where your strengths lie, this book allows you to develop your knowledge in ways that suit you. You will have opportunities to collaborate with classmates to share ideas, improve your writing, and make connections to other subject areas. You may also use technological tools such as the LaserLinks and the Writing Coach software program, which offer you more options for customizing how you learn.

PORTFOLIO

Many artists, photographers, designers, and writers keep samples of their work in a portfolio to show to others. Like them, you will be collecting your work—writing samples, records of activities, artwork—in a portfolio throughout the year. You probably won't put all your work in your portfolio, just carefully chosen pieces. Discuss with your teacher the kind of portfolio you will be keeping this year. Suggestions for how to use your portfolio occur throughout this book.

Notebook

Reading Log

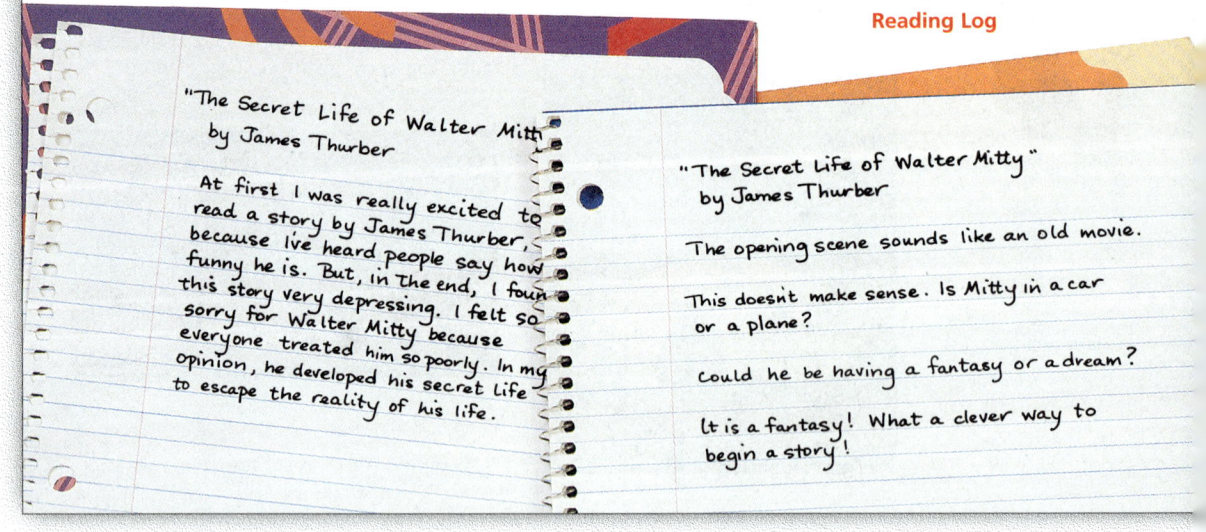

mentioned? Well, that's... I'm the worst swimmer in the state. Maybe we... something else?

James. We gotta do the lake tomorrow. You can just wade, or something. Other stuff can wait 'til it's cold for swimming.

(Fade)

ACT 2, SCENE 1

(Camera shows Joel at the water's edge. Then pans to Dina standing in the middle of a small lake. Water is up to her waist. We can't see the other boys, but can hear them whooping and splashing.)

Dina. Oh, come on, Joel. You're worse than my little brother.

(Camera widens out to show lake and kids. Joel takes one step, still not in the water. Martin and James dog paddle toward Dina and pull her down. She laughs and splashes water.)

NOTEBOOK

Choose any type of notebook to dedicate to your study of literature. Divide the notebook into three sections. Use the first section to jot down ideas, describe personal experiences, take notes, and express your thoughts before, while, and after you read a selection. Also include any charts, diagrams, and drawings that help you connect your reading to your life. The second section will be for your reading log, described below. Use the third section as a writer's notebook to record ideas and inspirations that may prove useful in your writing.

READING LOG

In your reading log you will record a special kind of response to literature—your direct comments as you read a selection. The reading strategies detailed at the right will help you think through what you read. In your own reading log, experiment with recording your comments as you read. Specific opportunities to use your reading log appear throughout this book.

Strategies for Reading

What will literature show you? That depends upon how you read. To get the most out of literature, you need to think as you read. The strategies below describe the kinds of thinking active readers do. You may be already using some of these strategies.

QUESTION

Ask questions while you read. Searching for reasons behind events and characters' actions can get you more involved in what you're reading. Note confusing words or statements, but don't worry if you feel some confusion. Further reading will probably make things clear.

CONNECT

Connect personally with what you're reading. Try to find similarities between the descriptions in the selection and what you've experienced, heard about, or read about in your own life.

PREDICT

Try to figure out what will happen next and how the selection might end. Then read on to see if you made good guesses.

CLARIFY

Pause occasionally to review what you've read. However, be prepared to have your understanding change and develop as you read on. Also, watch for answers to questions you had earlier.

EVALUATE

Form opinions both while you're reading and after you've finished. Develop your own judgments about the characters and your own ideas about events.

Now turn the page to see how two student readers put these strategies to work.

Strategies for Reading

Ask volunteers to talk about a time they read a very exciting story. Have them describe their reading experiences of being actively involved in the story. Tell students that when they are involved in reading they are probably using some of the strategies described on this page. Explain that these strategies are ways that active readers get more pleasure and understanding from what they read and that using these strategies can make reading easier and more enjoyable.

Invite students to read aloud and discuss the descriptions of the strategies for reading on this page. Ask students to share occasions when they have used these strategies. Explain that the model they are about to read shows what some readers thought as they were reading the story. Suggest that they cover the remarks in the margin while they read each page; then they can go back and compare their thoughts with the printed ones. Stress that these readers' thoughts are not "right" answers but rather a set of possible active responses.

READING MODEL

This model can be used in several ways:

- You may wish to have students cover the sidebar notes and read "The Secret Life of Walter Mitty" as they practice recording their thoughts in a reading log. Afterwards, students can compare their responses to those of other classmates and to the student readers to illustrate how different readers respond to the same selection.

- You might read the selection aloud, pausing to have students record their ideas and reactions.

- You may wish to read the selection aloud and have students take turns role-playing Jenny's and Aric's questions.

Ⓐ The wartime-adventure opening of Thurber's story immediately gives Jenny a real-life connection—images of her father, who loves watching war movies.

READING MODEL

Alongside "The Secret Life of Walter Mitty" are transcripts of the spoken comments made by two ninth-grade students, Aric Lewis and Jenny Mudra, while they were reading the story. Their comments provide a glimpse into the minds of readers actively engaged in the process of reading. You'll notice that in the course of their reading, Aric and Jenny quite naturally used the Strategies for Reading that were introduced on page 5.

To benefit most from this model of active reading, read the story first, jotting down your own responses in your reading log. (Cover up the side comments with a sheet of paper if you're tempted to peek.) Then read Aric's and Jenny's comments and compare their processes of reading with your own. What interesting similarities and differences do you discover in the responses? The more you actively engage in reading and sharing ideas, the more you'll learn about yourself and others—and the more fun you'll have.

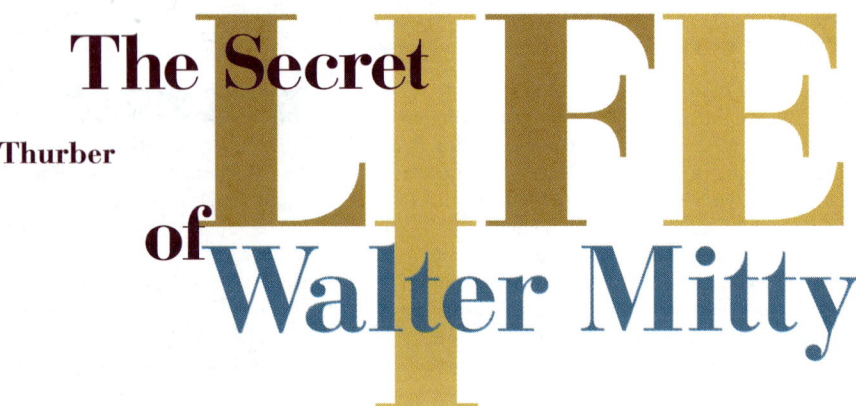

The Secret LIFE of Walter Mitty

James Thurber

Jenny: *I can just see this being in a movie that my dad would watch.*
Ⓐ CONNECTING

"We're going through!" The Commander's voice was like thin ice breaking. He wore his full-dress uniform, with the heavily braided white cap pulled down rakishly over one cold gray eye. "We can't make it, sir. It's spoiling for a hurricane, if you ask me." "I'm not asking you, Lieutenant Berg," said the Commander. "Throw on the power lights! Rev her up to 8,500! We're going through!" The pounding of the cylinders increased: ta-pocketa-pocketa-pocketa-*pocketa-pocketa*. The Commander stared at the ice forming on the pilot window. He walked over and twisted a row of complicated dials. "Switch on No. 8 auxiliary!" he shouted. "Switch on No. 8 auxiliary!" repeated Lieutenant Berg. "Full strength in No. 3 turret!" shouted the Commander. "Full strength in No. 3 turret!" The crew, bending to their various tasks in the huge, hurtling eight-engined Navy hydroplane, looked at each other and grinned. "The Old Man'll get

6 READING MODEL

Take off (1944), Laura Knight. Imperial War Museum, London.

us through," they said to one another. "The Old Man ain't afraid of Hell!" . . .

"Not so fast! You're driving too fast!" said Mrs. Mitty. "What are you driving so fast for?"

"Hmm?" said Walter Mitty. He looked at his wife, in the seat beside him, with shocked astonishment. She seemed grossly unfamiliar, like a strange woman who had yelled at him in a crowd. "You were up to fifty-five," she said. "You know I don't like to go more

Aric: *What's going on here?*
QUESTIONING

Jenny: *I'm very confused here. A change of setting. Maybe it's a flashback.*
QUESTIONING

Art Note

***Take off* by Laura Knight** In this painting of a World War II bomber cockpit, British artist Laura Knight (1877–1970) has depicted aviators preparing to fly into battle. The navigator working over the map plots a course. In the foreground, another adjusts a dial intently. Knight arranged her canvas so that the viewer's eye moves steadily back and up following the men at work.

Reading the Art *In what way do you think the artist has changed the plane's real proportions?*

B Aric is startled by an apparently abrupt change of scene. Students need to understand that reactions of confusion are never "wrong"; quite often the confusion will rise because the author wants to keep the reader guessing for a while.

C Jenny, too, is confused by the dramatic change of scene, but she uses her knowledge of literary concepts to provide a tentative explanation. Jenny's response here alerts her to the story's structure and paves the way for a different explanation.

D Jenny's attention to detail alerts her to what may be a key point.

E Aric may maintain this judgment, or he may revise it as he reads. Such first impressions provide valuable reference points for discussion.

F Jenny is confused by out-of-fashion, out-of-date language, a situation common for young people when reading older literature such as this more-than-50-year-old story. Students should quickly apply context clues to try to figure out such words—and then move on.

G H Both Jenny and Aric react to this scene, based on their own experiences of human behavior. Such connections help readers understand the characters and the situation.

I Here Aric's attention to detail furthers his understanding of Mitty.

J Jenny uses new information to revise her earlier hypothesis. Good readers allow their reactions to change as they proceed through a story.

K L As suggested for out-of-date language in note F, students should quickly try to figure out the meanings of unfamiliar or "big" words from context. (Of course, most students will be unaware at this point that Mr. Mitty is making up this terminology, a fact that may become more apparent later.)

M Again, Jenny's attention to detail is helping her to identify the writer's strategy. Her spontaneous evaluation will help her recall and use the detail later in a comprehensive interpretation.

D *Jenny:* He must have these flashbacks a lot.
CLARIFYING

E *Aric:* This Mitty sounds a little crazy.
EVALUATING

F *Jenny:* What are "overshoes"?
QUESTIONING

G *Aric:* Mitty is being treated like a kid.
EVALUATING

H *Jenny:* Mrs. Mitty is a real nag.
EVALUATING

I *Aric:* His wife. A cop. Everyone is telling Mitty what to do.
CLARIFYING

J *Jenny:* The doctors can't be on the airplane, so I guess Mr. Mitty's in his car, and the plane and hospital are daydreams.
CLARIFYING

K *Jenny:* I don't know Obstreosis and some other big words here.
QUESTIONING

L *Aric:* What is "Obstreosis of the ductal tract"?
QUESTIONING

M *Jenny:* This is the same noise the plane made. It's a funny sound.
EVALUATING

8   READING MODEL

---

than forty. You were up to fifty-five." Walter Mitty drove on toward Waterbury in silence, the roaring of the SN202 through the worst storm in twenty years of Navy flying fading in the remote, intimate airways of his mind. "You're tensed up again," said Mrs. Mitty. "It's one of your days. I wish you'd let Dr. Renshaw look you over."

Walter Mitty stopped the car in front of the building where his wife went to have her hair done. "Remember to get those overshoes while I'm having my hair done," she said. "I don't need overshoes," said Mitty. She put her mirror back into her bag. "We've been all through that," she said, getting out of the car. "You're not a young man any longer." He raced the engine a little. "Why don't you wear your gloves? Have you lost your gloves?" Walter Mitty reached in a pocket and brought out the gloves. He put them on, but after she had turned and gone into the building and he had driven on to a red light, he took them off again. "Pick it up, brother!" snapped a cop as the light changed, and Mitty hastily pulled on his gloves and lurched ahead. He drove around the streets aimlessly for a time, and then he drove past the hospital on his way to the parking lot.

. . . "It's the millionaire banker, Wellington McMillan," said the pretty nurse. "Yes?" said Walter Mitty, removing his gloves slowly. "Who has the case?" "Dr. Renshaw and Dr. Benbow, but there are two specialists here, Dr. Remington from New York and Mr. Pritchard-Mitford from London. He flew over." A door opened down a long, cool corridor and Dr. Renshaw came out. He looked distraught and haggard. "Hello, Mitty," he said. "We're having the devil's own time with McMillan, the millionaire banker and close personal friend of Roosevelt. Obstreosis of the ductal tract. Tertiary. Wish you'd take a look at him." "Glad to," said Mitty.

In the operating room there were whispered introductions: "Dr. Remington, Dr. Mitty. Mr. Pritchard-Mitford, Dr. Mitty." "I've read your book on streptothricosis," said Pritchard-Mitford, shaking hands. "A brilliant performance, sir." "Thank you," said Walter Mitty. "Didn't know you were in the States, Mitty," grumbled Remington. "Coals to Newcastle, bringing Mitford and me up here for a tertiary." "You are very kind," said Mitty. A huge, complicated machine, connected to the operating table, with many tubes and wires, began at this moment to go pocketa-pocketa-pocketa. "The new anesthetizer is giving way!" shouted an intern. "There is no one in the East who knows how to fix it!" "Quiet, man!" said Mitty, in a low, cool voice. He sprang to the machine, which was now going pocketa-pocketa-queep-pocketa-queep. He began fingering delicately a row of glistening dials. "Give me a fountain pen!" he snapped. Someone handed him a fountain pen. He pulled a faulty piston out of the machine and inserted the pen in its place. "That will hold for ten minutes," he said. "Get on with the operation." A nurse hurried over and whispered to Renshaw, and Mitty saw the man turn pale. "Coreopsis has set in," said Renshaw nervously. "If you would take over, Mitty?" Mitty looked at him and at the craven figure of Benbow, who drank, and at the grave, uncertain faces of the two great specialists. "If you wish," he said. They slipped a white gown on him; he adjusted a mask and drew on thin gloves; nurses handed him shining . . .

"Back it up, Mac! Look out for that Buick!" Walter Mitty jammed on the brakes. "Wrong lane, Mac," said the parking-lot attendant, looking at Mitty closely. "Gee. Yeh," muttered Mitty. He began cautiously to back out of the lane marked "Exit Only." "Leave her sit there," said the attendant. "I'll put her away." Mitty got out of the car. "Hey, better leave the key." "Oh," said Mitty, handing the man the ignition key. The attendant vaulted into the car, backed it up with insolent skill, and put it where it belonged.

They're so damn cocky, thought Walter Mitty, walking along Main Street; they think they know everything. Once he had tried to take his chains off, outside New Milford, and he had got them wound around the axles. A man had had to come out in a wrecking car and unwind them, a young, grinning garageman. Since then Mrs. Mitty always made him drive to a garage to have the chains taken off. The next time, he thought, I'll wear my right arm in a sling; they won't grin at me then. I'll have my right arm in a sling, and they'll see I couldn't possibly take the chains off myself. He kicked at the slush on the sidewalk. "Overshoes," he said to himself, and he began looking for a shoe store.

When he came out into the street again, with the overshoes in a box under his arm, Walter Mitty began to wonder what the other thing was his wife had told him to get. She had told him twice, before they set out from their house for Waterbury. In a way he hated these weekly trips to town—he was always getting something wrong. Kleenex, he thought, Squibb's, razor blades? No. Toothpaste, toothbrush, bicarbonate, carborundum, initiative and referendum? He gave it up. But she would remember it. "Where's the what's-its-name?" she would ask. "Don't tell me you forgot the what's-its-name?" A newsboy went by shouting something about the Waterbury trial.

. . . "Perhaps this will refresh your memory." The District

Aric: Mitty's in total control in his fantasies. That's why we all have them I guess.
CLARIFYING, CONNECTING

Jenny: Mitty is totally distraught here.
CLARIFYING

Jenny: Where were these chains? They must be on the car. I guess on the tires.
QUESTIONING, CLARIFYING

Aric: Mitty imagines fooling the garageman and covering up his inadequacy.
CLARIFYING

Jenny: He can't keep his train of thought.
EVALUATING

Aric: I'm surprised his wife trusts him to pick out his own overshoes. Now, what is the other thing he's to get?
QUESTIONING

Jenny: Oh, the dots again. Another daydream.
CLARIFYING

N Aric is revising his original impression of Mitty, and allowing himself to identify with him. His recognition of parallels between literature and his own life is a powerful reading strategy, allowing him to gain deeper understanding of the character.

O Jenny is clarifying her picture of Mitty's "real" life. Note that the author has not told Jenny that Mitty is distraught; he shows Mitty in action. Jenny, perhaps without realizing it, recognizes the author's purpose. Such a reaction can be the starting point for a discussion in which students are asked to cite evidence from the text to support their opinions.

P Jenny asks and answers her own question, using the story to expand her general knowledge. (Students in urban areas may be totally unaware of the once widespread wintertime practice of wrapping tires in chains for better traction on snowy, icy roads. Today, this practice is confined mostly to rural and especially mountainous areas.)

Q Here, Aric displays a sophisticated understanding of human behavior. He can probably cite parallels with people he knows.

R Jenny again focuses on Mitty's "real" life; her evaluation broadens her understanding of his character.

S There's an implied judgment of both Mitty and his wife in Aric's first comment, rooted in his expanding understanding of both of them. But Aric doesn't pause; he's caught up in the story.

T Jenny has picked up on a convention adopted by the author. She realizes she can use the . . . to immediately recognize future lapses.

U Aric has made an important discovery: the choice of details in stories is not random but crafted. This clarification will help him not only with this story but with others.

V Jenny is going beyond the text, using her curiosity about human behavior to speculate about Mitty's past. Questions like these can spark delightful discussions about both literature and human psychology. In time students will gain skill in differentiating legitimate and illegitimate interpretations of a text.

W Aric records his own train of thought here. In so doing, he confirms the connection he made earlier—that Mitty's fantasies and daily life are interwoven.

X Jenny uses her understanding of both Mitty and the structure of the story to predict what's coming next.

Y Aric's comment reflects and broadens his earlier implied judgment of Mitty and his wife. He will later be able to cite details like these in a discussion of the couple's relationship.

Z Jenny confirms her earlier clarification. Both revision and confirmation of prior reactions strengthen reader confidence.

U **Aric:** Trial. District Attorney. Now I realize he's picking up on his surroundings to spark his fantasies.
CLARIFYING

V **Jenny:** I wonder if he's had any experiences even close to these or if everything is totally dreamed up.
QUESTIONING

W **Aric:** Funny. A cur is a dog. So now his fantasies have brought him back to real life. Dog food must be the other thing he's to get.
EVALUATING, CLARIFYING

X **Jenny:** I think something's going to trigger his daydreaming again.
PREDICTING

Y **Aric:** He's still worried about that wife of his.
CLARIFYING

Z **Jenny:** Here we go with those dots again.
CLARIFYING

Attorney suddenly thrust a heavy automatic at the quiet figure on the witness stand. "Have you ever seen this before?" Walter Mitty took the gun and examined it expertly. "This is my Webley-Vickers 50.80," he said calmly. An excited buzz ran around the courtroom. The judge rapped for order. "You are a crack shot with any sort of firearms, I believe?" said the District Attorney, insinuatingly. "Objection!" shouted Mitty's attorney. "We have shown that the defendant could not have fired the shot. We have shown that he wore his right arm in a sling on the night of the fourteenth of July." Walter Mitty raised his hand briefly and the bickering attorneys were stilled. "With any known make of gun," he said evenly, "I could have killed Gregory Fitzhurst at three hundred feet *with my left hand*." Pandemonium broke loose in the courtroom. A woman's scream rose above the bedlam and suddenly a lovely, dark-haired girl was in Walter Mitty's arms. The District Attorney struck at her savagely. Without rising from his chair, Mitty let the man have it on the point of the chin. "You miserable cur!" . . .

"Puppy biscuit," said Walter Mitty. He stopped walking and the buildings of Waterbury rose up out of the misty courtroom and surrounded him again. A woman who was passing laughed. "He said 'Puppy biscuit,'" she said to her companion. "That man said 'Puppy biscuit' to himself." Walter Mitty hurried on. He went into an A. & P. , not the first one he came to but a smaller one farther up the street. "I want some biscuit for small, young dogs," he said to the clerk. "Any special brand, sir?" The greatest pistol shot in the world thought a moment. "It says 'Puppies Bark for It' on the box," said Walter Mitty.

His wife would be through at the hairdresser's in fifteen minutes, Mitty saw in looking at his watch, unless they had trouble drying it; sometimes they had trouble drying it. She didn't like to get to the hotel first; she would want him to be there waiting for her as usual. He found a big leather chair in the lobby, facing a window, and he put the overshoes and the puppy biscuit on the floor beside it. He picked up an old copy of *Liberty* and sank down into the chair. "Can Germany Conquer the World Through the Air?" Walter Mitty looked at the pictures of bombing planes and of ruined streets.

. . . "The cannonading has got the wind up in young Raleigh, sir," said the sergeant. Captain Mitty looked up at him through tousled hair. "Get him to bed," he said wearily. "With the others. I'll fly alone." "But you can't, sir," said the sergeant anxiously. "It takes two men to handle that bomber, and the Archies are pounding hell out of the air. Von Richtman's circus is between here and Saulier." "Somebody's got to get that ammunition dump," said Mitty. "I'm going over. Spot of brandy?" He poured a drink for the sergeant and one for himself. War thundered and whined around the dugout and battered at the door. There was a rending of wood and splinters flew through the room. "A bit of a near thing," said Captain Mitty carelessly. "The box barrage is closing in," said the sergeant. "We only live once, Sergeant," said Mitty, with his faint, fleeting smile. "Or do we?" He poured another brandy and tossed it off. "I never see a man could hold his brandy like you, sir," said the sergeant. "Begging your pardon, sir." Captain Mitty stood up and strapped on his huge Webley-Vickers automatic. "It's forty kilometers through hell, sir," said the sergeant. Mitty finished one last brandy. "After all," he said softly, "what isn't?" The pounding of the cannon increased; there was the rat-tat-tatting of machine guns, and from somewhere came the menacing pocketa-pocketa-pocketa of the new flamethrowers. Walter Mitty walked to the door of the dugout humming "Auprès de Ma Blonde." He turned and waved to the sergeant. "Cheerio!" he said. . . .

Something struck his shoulder. "I've been looking all over this hotel for you," said Mrs. Mitty. "Why do you have to hide in this old chair? How did you expect me to find you?" "Things close in," said Walter Mitty vaguely. "What?" Mrs. Mitty said. "Did you get the what's-its-name? The puppy biscuit? What's in that box?" "Overshoes," said Mitty. "Couldn't you have put them on in the store?" "I was thinking," said Walter Mitty. "Does it ever occur to you that I am sometimes thinking?" She looked at him. "I'm going to take your temperature when I get you home," she said.

They went out through the revolving doors that made a faintly derisive whistling sound when you pushed them. It was two blocks to the parking lot. At the drugstore on the corner she said, "Wait here for me. I forgot something. I won't be a minute." She was more than a minute. Walter Mitty lighted a cigarette. It began to rain, rain with sleet in it. He stood up against the wall of the drugstore, smoking. . . . He put his shoulders back and his heels together. "To hell with the handkerchief," said Walter Mitty scornfully. He took one last drag on his cigarette and snapped it away. Then, with that faint, fleeting smile playing about his lips, he faced the firing squad; erect and motionless, proud and disdainful, Walter Mitty the Undefeated, inscrutable to the last.

Aric: *Guess who that somebody's going to be!*
PREDICTING **(AA)**

Jenny: *What's a "box barrage"? Must be some sort of constant bombarding.*
QUESTIONING, CLARIFYING **(BB)**

Jenny: *The "rat-tats" and "pockets" are all quite cartoony images.*
EVALUATING **(CC)**

Aric: *I wonder if the cereal name comes from this good-bye word?*
CONNECTING **(DD)**

Jenny: *In the beginning, I took the side of the wife. But no longer.*
EVALUATING **(EE)**

Aric: *She's mad because he's thinking, and she doesn't want to believe that he can think without her.*
CLARIFYING **(FF)**

Jenny: *I can totally see my grandfather imagining himself in situations like these.*
CONNECTING **(GG)**

Aric: *He's always the hero, even though in this last fantasy he imagines himself dying. He's seen a lot of movies.*
EVALUATING **(HH)**

Jenny: *Mr. Mitty wins because he can always daydream.*
EVALUATING **(II)**

(AA) Aric feels very confident in this prediction; the strategies he has used so far have given him an intelligent grasp on the story.

(BB) This time Jenny consciously uses the text to clarify an unfamiliar term.

(CC) Jenny picks up on an earlier observation as she begins to recognize the nature of Mitty's fantasies. Further discussion could lead Jenny to an understanding of the story's irony.

(DD) Aric uses the text to identify this probably unfamiliar word but also asks an interesting question about something he's familiar with. Such a question may not affect Aric's interpretation of the story, but it is part of the fun of reading.

(EE) If Jenny were encouraged to question why she took the side of the wife, she could gain awareness of her own patterns of thought and judgment.

(FF) Aric is again using his quite mature understanding of human nature to clarify in his mind why Mitty's wife behaves as she does.

(GG) Jenny's recognition of this parallel can deepen her understanding of the story, of her grandfather, of other people, and of other characters she will meet in literature.

(HH) Aric's last comment pulls together a number of clues and connects with his own awareness of popular culture.

(II) Together with Aric's last comment, Jenny's comment about Mitty "winning" should provide a good starting point for a full discussion of the story, in which many of Jenny's and Aric's earlier reactions could contribute valuable insights.

UNIT ONE

UNIT THEMES

Unit One

Live and Learn In Unit One, students will read selections that explore various ways in which people grow and mature through their experiences. This unit contains two parts: Part 1, "Growing Pains," and Part 2, "Rites of Passage." Selections in both parts contribute to the unit theme by examining how certain experiences make various characters stronger, wiser, and more mature.

Part 1

Growing Pains Selections in Part 1 emphasize painful and joyful experiences through which characters learn lasting and valuable lessons about life. For example, in "The Bass, The River, and Sheila Mant," the loss of a prize fish that might have been caught teaches a boy never again to pretend to be someone he is not.

Part 2

Rites of Passage Selections in Part 2 emphasize significant moments in characters' lives that serve as bridges between childhood and adulthood. For example, in "Plainswoman," a sheltered young woman is abruptly confronted with the harsh necessity of amputating a man's gangrenous finger.

UNIT ONE

Live and Learn

Experience is a hard teacher because she gives the test first, the lesson afterwards.

VERNON LAW
Former pitcher for the Pittsburgh Pirates

Geography (1984), Janet Fish. Oil on canvas, 54" × 84". Photo by Janet Fish.

Exploring Theme

To help students explore the connections between the art, the quotation, and the unit theme, have them consider the following questions:

1. Does "Live and Learn" sound like an important theme to explore? Why or why not? *(Possible response: yes, because living through an experience is the best way to learn something)*

2. How would you paraphrase Vernon Law's statement about experience? *(Possible response: In life, one cannot learn first and "take a test" afterwards; one can never be prepared. Rather, one must go through experiences first; only later, on reflection, can one profit from them.)*

3. How does the painting relate to the theme of living and learning? *(Possible response: The painting brings together images from many different lands. It suggests that travel and the exposure to a culture other than one's own are important experiences.)*

4. What kinds of stories might you expect to read in this unit? *(Possible response: stories about people who learn something important by living through particular experiences)*

5. Discuss a particular experience of your own from which you learned an important lesson about life. *(Responses will vary.)*

Art Note

Geography by Janet Fish
American painter Janet Fish (1938–) studied at Smith College and Yale University. Her main interest as a painter is not the subject matter of her paintings, but the relationship of colors, shapes, and textures. The interaction of colors is an especially important element in her work. This work is a typical example of her many still-life paintings.

Reading the Art *How has the painter shown that an experience has occurred or that a kind of reflection about an experience is taking place?*

UNIT ONE
Part 1 Skills Trace

ML DENOTES MINI-LESSON IN TEACHER'S EDITION

Selections	Reading Skills and Strategies	Literary Concepts	Writing Opportunities	Speaking, Listening, and Viewing
FICTION **The Utterly Perfect Murder** Ray Bradbury	Predicting, PE p. 17	Conflict, PE p. 25 Narrator, ML TE p. 20	Description, PE p. 25 Outline, PE p. 25 Letter, PE p. 25 Rewrite from another point of view, PE p. 25 Writing metaphors, ML TE p. 22 Write a jump rope song, TE p. 26	Group discussion, PE p. 25 Presentation, PE p. 26 Planning a debate, ML TE p. 21
FICTION **American History** Judith Oritz Cofer		Rising action, PE p. 37 Climax, PE p. 37 Setting, ML TE p. 30 Symbolism, ML TE p. 36	Personal narrative, PE p. 27 Essay, PE p. 37 Poem, PE p. 37 First-person narrative, ML TE p. 32	Group discussion, PE p. 37 Listen to music, PE p. 38 Interview immigrants, TE p. 38
FICTION **The Bass, the River, and Sheila Mant** W.D. Wetherell	Understanding exposition, PE p. 39	Falling action, PE p. 48 Resolution, PE p. 48 Conflict, ML TE p. 44 Suspense, ML TE p. 46	Skit, PE p. 48 Rewrite ending, PE p. 48 Writing letter seeking employment, ML TE p. 44 Develop writing voice, ML TE p. 45	Paired discussion, PE p. 48
NONFICTION **I Know Why the Caged Bird Sings** Maya Angelou		Allusion, PE p. 60 Simile, ML TE p. 55	Autobiography, PE p. 52 Character sketch, PE p. 60 Scene, PE p. 60 Conversation using dialects, ML TE p. 56 Cluster diagram, TE p. 60	Performing a skit, PE p. 60 Oral interpretation, PE p. 61 Presenting a monologue, PE p. 61 Descriptive passages, PE p. 56
NONFICTION **A Christmas Memory** Truman Capote	Using a reading log, PE p. 62 Connecting, ML TE p. 67	Symbol, PE p.76 Characterization, ML TE p. 66 Autobiographical essay, ML TE p. 68	Personal narrative, PE p. 76 Letters, PE p. 76 Epitaph, PE p. 76 Show, don't tell, ML TE p. 69 Tone, sensory details, first-person point of view, TE p. 76	Oral presentation, PE p. 77 Role-playing, ML TE p. 74
NONFICTION ON YOUR OWN **On Being Seventeen, Bright, and Unable to Read** David Raymond			Journal entries, TE p. 79 Writing about personal difficulties, TE p. 81	Paired and grouped reading, TE p. 79
Writing	**Reading Skills and Strategies**	**Literary Concepts**	**Writing Opportunities**	**Speaking, Listening, and Viewing**
WRITING ABOUT LITERATURE **Analysis**	Understanding characterization, PE pp. 82–83 Analyzing characters, PE pp. 84–87	Understanding characterization, PE pp. 82–83 Examining characters, PE pp. 84–85	Write a "show" passage, PE p. 83 Revise a QuickWrite, PE p. 83 Compose a conversation, PE p. 83 Character study, PE pp. 84–87 Using methods of organization, PE p. 85	Viewing a character, PE p. 88 Interpreting a character, PE p. 88 Discussion, PE p. 88 Discussing stereotypes, PE p. 89

UNIT ONE   LIVE AND LEARN

Grammar, Usage, Mechanics, and Spelling	Multimodal Learning	Research and Study Skills	Vocabulary	
Punctuating dialogue, ML TE p. 24	Discussion, PE p. 25 Presentation, PE p. 26 Illustrating a scene, TE p. 26	Research a warring country, PE p. 26	antagonism concussion emblem query recoil	
Capitalizing proper nouns, ML TE p. 29	Group presentation, PE p. 37 Illustration, PE p. 38 Music/Mood, PE p. 38	Research immigrant groups, TE p. 38	abusive dilapidated distraught elation hierarchy	infatuated maneuvering martyrs resigned solace
Punctuating compound words, ML TE p. 43	Pantomiming, PE p. 49 Design advertisement, PE p. 49 Skit, PE p. 48	Research New Hampshire tourist areas, TE p. 49	antipathy conspicuous dubious epitome incarnation	overcompensate pensive suave surreptitiously tribute
Indefinite pronouns as subjects, ML TE p. 54	Skit, PE p. 60 Oral interpretation, PE p. 61 Present monologue, PE p. 61		aristocrat aura cascading essence familiarity	illiteracy incessantly infuse sacrilegious sophistication
Personal nominative pronouns, ML TE p. 65	Create greeting cards, PE p. 76 Design a kite, PE p. 77 Interview, PE p. 77 Test weather, TE p. 77	Research celebrations, TE p. 77	cavort conspiracy exhilarate garish goad	inaugurate noncommittal prosaic sever squander
	Interviewing, TE p. 80			

Grammar, Usage, Mechanics, and Spelling	Multimodal Learning	Research and Study Skills	Media Literacy
Using appositive phrases, PE p. 83 Using irregular verb forms correctly, PE p. 87 Verb tenses, PE p. 87	Viewing a character, PE p. 88 Interpreting a character, PE p. 88 Discussion, PE p. 88 Discussing stereotypes, PE p. 89	Examining characters, PE pp. 84–87 Analyzing stereotypes, PE p. 89	Understanding a character, PE pp. 88–89

UNIT ONE
Part 2 Skills Trace

 DENOTES MINI-LESSON IN TEACHER'S EDITION

Selections	Reading Skills and Strategies	Literary Concepts	Writing Opportunities	Speaking, Listening, and Viewing
FICTION **Through the Tunnel** Doris Lessing	Drawing conclusions, PE p. 91	Setting, PE p. 104 Symbol, PE p. 104	Comparison, PE p. 103 Script, PE p. 103 Summary, PE p. 103 Sensory detail and description, ML TE p. 101 Balance charts, TE p. 103	Discuss alternative ending, PE p. 103 Performing oral tale, PE p. 104 Debate, ML TE p. 97 Discuss alternative ending, TE p. 103 Tell a tale, TE p. 104
FICTION **Marigolds** Eugenia Collier	Using strategies, PE p. 106	Mood, PE p. 118 Symbol, PE p. 118 Figurative language, ML TE p. 110	Paragraph, PE p. 117 Essay, PE p. 117 Description, PE p. 117 Script, PE p. 107 Dialect, ML TE p. 111 Simile and metaphors, TE p. 117 Brainstorm, TE p. 118	Dramatic dialogue, PE p. 119 Deliver report, PE p. 118 Choosing/composing music, ML TE p. 113 Enact a scene, TE p. 117
FICTION **The Road Not Taken** Robert Frost **Fable for When There's No Way Out** May Swenson		Rhyme scheme, PE p. 125 Free verse, PE p. 125 Repetition, ML TE p. 124 Rhyme scheme, ML TE p. 125	Chart, PE p. 122 Draft poem, PE p. 125 Short essay, PE p. 125 Set of instructions, PE p. 125 Assonance, ML TE p. 123	
FICTION **The Beginning of Something** Sue Ellen Bridgers	Understanding the narrator, PE p. 127	Main and minor characters, PE p. 143 Create mood, ML TE p. 132 Character webs, TE p. 143	Diary entry, PE p. 143 Personal essay, PE p. 143 First-person narrative, PE p. 143 Chronological transitions, ML TE p. 130 Write essays in time limit, ML TE p. 133 Brainstorm, TE p. 143	Group discussion, PE p. 143 Deliver narrative, PE p. 143 Oral report, PE p. 144 Oral interpretation, ML TE p. 137 Facilitator and recorder in group discussion, TE p. 143
FICTION **The First Appendectomy** William A. Nolen	Understanding specialized vocabulary, PE p. 145	Author's purpose, PE p. 152 Personal narrative, ML TE p. 148 Rising action, ML TE p. 150	Performance evaluation, PE p. 152 Job description, PE p. 152 Humorous account, PE p. 152 Dialogue, ML TE p. 147	Debate, PE p. 152
FICTION ON YOUR OWN **Plainswoman** Williams Forrest			Diary entry, TE p. 157	Paired reading, TE p. 154

Writing	Reading Skills and Strategies	Literary Concepts	Writing Opportunities	Speaking, Listening, and Viewing
WRITING FROM EXPERIENCE **Report**			Writing an investigative report, PE pp. 164–171 Drafting, PE pp. 168–169 Supporting ideas with details, PE p. 169 Revising and publishing, PE pp. 170–171	Interviewing, PE pp. 166–167 Conferencing, PE p. 167

Grammar, Usage, Mechanics, and Spelling	Multimodal Learning	Research and Study Skills	Vocabulary
Adjective or adverb, ML TE p. 98	Draw cutaway diagram, PE p. 104 Create chart or graph, PE p. 104	Research deep-sea diving, PE p. 104	beseech contrition defiant incredulous supplication
Pronoun case, ML TE p. 108	Dramatization, PE p. 117 Abstract painting, PE p. 118 Collage, PE p. 118 Illustrations, PE p. 118 Help wanted ads, ML TE p. 109	Research Great Depression, PE p. 118 Research Hooverville, TE p. 118	bravado impoverished compassion perverse degradation poignantly futile squalor impotent stoicism
	Create a chart, PE p. 122 Design posters, PE p. 125	Research animals born in shells, TE p. 126	
Capitalization of brand names, ML TE p. 140	Notes on computer, PE p. 143	Research diabetes, PE p. 144	the bereaved infernal kin remorse throes
Comparative modifiers, ML TE p. 149	Create a cartoon or comic strip, PE p. 153 Music selection, PE p. 153 Interview doctor or medical students, TE p. 153 Emotion chart, TE p. 153	Research details on medical training, PE p. 153	convalescence equanimity definitive infinitesimal dexterity proficiency distended superficial elicit venture
	Sketching a scene, TE p. 154 Hold a dramatization, TE p. 158		

Grammar, Usage, Mechanics, and Spelling	Multimodal Learning	Research and Study Skills	Media Literacy
Using commas in a series, PE p. 171	Analyzing a magazine photograph, PE p. 164 Analyzing an editorial cartoon, PE p. 164 Interpreting a newspaper article, PE p. 165	CD–ROM, PE p. 166 On-line resources, PE p. 166 Note-taking, ML TE p. 166	Analyzing a magazine photograph, PE p. 164 Analyzing an editorial cartoon, PE p. 164 Interpreting a newspaper article, PE p. 16 CD–ROM, PE p. 166 On-line resources, PE p. 166

UNIT ONE
Recommended Resources

ENRICHMENT   RESEARCH

✓ Recommended Novels and Other Longer Works

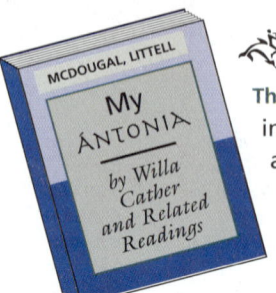

LITERATURE CONNECTIONS WITH SOURCEBOOK FOR TEACHERS

Thematic Link In this novel, Bohemian immigrants experience growing pains as they struggle for survival and acceptance on the rough Midwestern plains of Nebraska.

About the Author Willa Cather (1873–1947) grew up on the Nebraska prairie and called upon her childhood memories to write this beloved American novel.

Other Works by Willa Cather *April Twilights, Alexander's Bridge, O Pioneers!, The Song of the Lark, The Professor's House, Death Comes for the Archbishop, Shadows on the Rock*

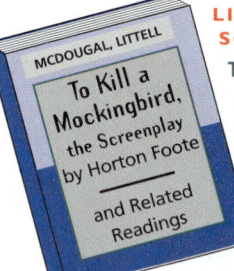

LITERATURE CONNECTIONS WITH SOURCEBOOK FOR TEACHERS

Thematic Link This screenplay adapts Harper Lee's Pulitzer-Prize-winning novel of three young children experiencing rites of passage in a small Alabama town during the Great Depression. It is also the story of a lawyer who, in the face of impossible odds, stands up for what he believes is right.

About the Authors Harper Lee (born 1926) won a Pulitzer Prize for this novel, the only one she has ever published. She based it on her own memories of Alabama, her home state. Horton Foote (born 1916) is an acclaimed playwright, novelist, and Oscar-winning screenwriter.

Other Works by Horton Foote *The Trip to Bountiful, Tender Mercies*

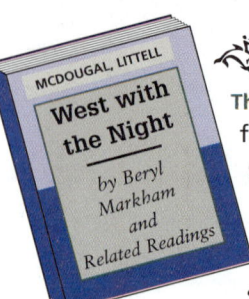

LITERATURE CONNECTIONS WITH SOURCEBOOK FOR TEACHERS

Thematic Link Beryl Markham, the world-famous pilot, reveals what she learned growing up in Africa—a land of spectacular beauty and diversity.

About the Author Beryl Markham (1902–1985), best known for her solo flight westward across the Atlantic Ocean in 1936, grew up in Kenya where she learned to hunt wild animals, to train and breed horses, and to fly a plane.

Other Work by Beryl Markham *The Splendid Outcast*

Thematic Link This novel portrays a child's struggle to live and learn in the difficult and indifferent world he inherits.

About the Author Since the publication of his first novel, Charles Dickens (1812–1870) has continued to have an enormous popular and critical following. Because of this, he accomplished a great deal towards social reform by making the public aware of the plight of the Victorian poor and dispossessed.

Other Works by Charles Dickens *The Pickwick Papers, Oliver Twist, Nicholas Nickleby, Bleak House, Hard Times, A Tale of Two Cities, Great Expectations*

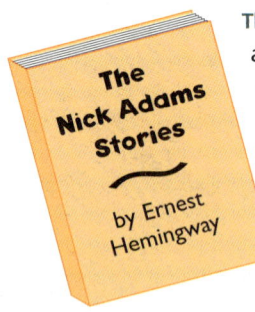

Thematic Link A young man grows from adolescence to adulthood through his connection to nature and the land.

About the Author F. Scott Fitzgerald introduced Hemingway (1899–1961) to Scribner's publishing house after he read Hemingway's first novel.

Other Works by Ernest Hemingway *The Sun Also Rises, The Old Man and the Sea*

Professional Development   TEACHING THE NOVEL

Angelou, Maya. *All God's Children Need Traveling Shoes.* Vintage, NY: 1989.

Brodsky, Joseph. "On Grief and Reason: Robert Frost," *New Yorker.* (April 26, 1994) 70.

Cummings, E. E. *The Enormous Room.* NY: Liveright, 1922.

Lessing, Doris. *African Laughter.* NY: Harper Perennial, 1992.

CROSS-CURRICULAR TEACHING   PROFESSIONAL DEVELOPMENT

Recommended Readings in Cross-Curricular Areas

SOCIAL STUDIES

The Reality of Dyslexia by John Osmond (1993) Sensitive and informative study of living with and coming to understand a son's dyslexia. Links to David Raymond's "On Being Seventeen, Bright, and Unable to Read."

Documenting America: 1935–1943 by Carl Fleischhauer and Beverly W. Brannan (1988) Offers an informative study of the socio-economic climate of the times. Links to Eugenia Collier's "Marigolds."

Hope Among Us Yet by David Peeler (1987) Presents social criticism and the solace found in art during the 1930s, a challenging decade in American history. Links to Eugenia Collier's "Marigolds."

The American West by Dee Brown (1994) Well-photographed presentation of the groups that helped settle the American West. Links to Williams Forrest's "Plainswoman."

Professional Development — CROSS-CURRICULAR INSTRUCTION

Clark, Irene. "Information Literacy and the Writing Center," *Computers and Composition.* 12:2 (1995) 203.

Hertz-Lagarowitz, Rachel, and Miller, Norman, eds. *Interaction in Cooperative Groups.* 1992.

Lappas, Catherine. "Building Multicultural Bridges with Literature," *Readerly/Writerly Texts: Essays on Literature, Literary/Textual Criticism, and Pedagogy (RWT)* 1:2 (Spring-Summer 1994).

White, Brian. "Assuming Nothing: A Pre-Methods Diagnostic in the Teaching of Literature," *English Education* 27:4 (December 1995), 221.

Recommended Media Resources

THE LANGUAGE OF LITERATURE

ELECTRONIC LIBRARY
CD-ROM
Additional literature selections for Unit One can be found on the Electronic Library CD-ROM.

LASERLINKS
Videodisc, Gr. 9
See *LaserLinks Teacher's Source Book,* pages 4–5, for overview of Unit One.

AUDIO LIBRARY
Unit One: Live and Learn
Gr. 9, Tape 1: Side B
Gr. 9, Tape 2: Sides A & B
Gr. 9, Tape 3: Sides A & B

WRITING COACH
Writing Coach Software: Writing About Literature—Interpretive Response, Explanation of an Idea

OUTSIDE RESOURCES

Films/Videos/Film Strips/Audiocassettes
I Know Why the Caged Bird Sings, video, Knowledge Unlimited, 1979.
The Secret Life of Walter Mitty, video, HBO Home Video/Sultan Entertainment, 1947, (110 minutes).
Emily Dickinson: A Certain Slant of Light, video, Monterey Home Video, 1995, (40 minutes).
Bradbury Reads Bradbury, audiocassette, Listening Library, 1976.

Internet Resources
McDougal Littell Literature Center at http://www.hmco.com/mcdougal/lit

Professional Development — TEACHING WITH TECHNOLOGY

Sheingold, K., and Hadley, M. (1990). *Accomplished Teachers: Integrating Computers into Classroom Practice.* New York: Center for Technology in Education, Bank Street College of Education.

Telecommunications and Education: Surfing and the Art of Change. Annapolis Junction: NSBA Distribution Center.

Computing Teacher. International Society for Technology in Education (ISTE), 1787 Agate St., Eugene, OR 97403–1923.

UNIT ONE
Professional Enrichment

Poetry—Who Is Talking to Whom About What?

Tommy Boley, PhD, The University of Texas at El Paso

The following essay offers a unique strategy for approaching the teaching of poetry, which begins in Part 2 of this unit.

INTRODUCTION

Helping students to get into a poem presents a challenge that every English teacher faces. We're all aware that most of our students look at a poem as something totally indecipherable—whose meaning must be supplied by the teacher. We want, instead, to enable students to experience the poem individually and to take away some techniques that they can use to approach a poem on their own. One strategy that can unlock the mystery of a poem involves looking at it from a rhetorical perspective—"Who is talking to whom about what?"

EXPLANATION

A poem has a speaker talking to a listener—not unlike other types of writing. If we can lead students to identify and describe the speaker and the type of listener, our students will begin to visualize the poem as a dramatic interchange.

In *The Study of Literature in High School*, Geraldine Murphy suggests four possible speaker/listener relationships in a poem:

1. a situation in which the speaker and listener are both clearly identified;
2. a situation in which the speaker is identified but the listener is not;
3. a situation in which the listener is identified but the speaker is not;
4. a situation in which neither the speaker nor the listener is identified.

SITUATION 1

Langston Hughes's "Mother to Son" provides an excellent example of situation 1. A mother who has survived despite obstacles and disappointments in her life admonishes her son to follow her example. Indeed, the title of the poem immediately identifies the dramatic situation: the mother is the speaker and the son is the listener. A tiny drama transpires between the two people. One specific voice delivers a message to a specific listener, simply but effectively.

SITUATION 2

For situation 2, William Stafford's "Fifteen" brings us an adult male reflecting upon a time, at the age of 15, when he found a motorcycle running in the grass after an accident. After fantasizing about the machine, the boy returns to reality and acts responsibly, as he feels he should. The dramatic situation identifies the mature male speaker addressing the unknown listener. We are free to conjecture about the listener; any answer is permissible as long as it is within reason. A few examples follow:

- The listener is a group of young people.
- The listener is the speaker's own son.
- The speaker is merely reflecting upon the experience in his mind.

SITUATION 3

For situation 3, Robert Herrick's famous "To the Virgins, to Make Much of Time" depicts a speaker advising all young girls to take advantage of their youth for the sake of love. Here the dramatic situation involves this nameless adviser who feels compelled to counsel the young girls to take action before it is too late. The following questions will help guide students' responses:

- Who might this speaker be?
- What is the motivation for the advice?

> We want . . . to enable students to experience the poem individually and to take away some techniques that they can use to approach a poem on their own.

Related Readings

Karolides, Nicholas J. *Reader Response in the Classroom: Evoking and Interpreting Meaning in Literature.* New York: Longman, 1992.

Murphy, Geraldine. *The Study of Literature in High School.* Waltham, Massachusetts: Ginn and Company, 1968.

Rosenblatt, Louise M. *The Reader, the Text, the Poem: The Transactional Theory of the Literary Work.* Carbondale, Illinois: Southern Illinois University Press, 1978.

- What does the speaker have to gain from this?
- Why bother delivering this message to the girls?

Once again, any answer within reason is permissible.

SITUATION 4

Anne Sexton's poem "The Fury of Overshoes" demonstrates situation 4—a speaker reminiscing on moments of childhood and, in so doing, seeming to assume the position of the children once again. You might consider posing the following questions about the speaker and listener:

Speaker:
- Based on what we know, who is this speaker?
- What sort of person has she or he become?
- What is her or his attitude toward life?
- How has the speaker adjusted to adulthood?

Listener:
- Is the speaker addressing another person directly?
- If so, what are the reasonable possibilities?
- Is the speaker, instead, merely involved in self-reflection?

This dramatic situation presents the most difficult instance—conjecturing about both the speaker and the listener.

CONCLUSION

These four dramatic situations provide four stances that give students entrances into poems. Such considerations should come first when we introduce poems. Attention to the elements of poetry—figurative language, diction, syntax, rhythm, sound, rhyme, and so on—must wait. Until students have established the dramatic situation in a poem, the finer analytical features must not confuse the basic notion of what is happening in the action.

With this "handle" for entering the mystery of a poem, students will cease to shy away. We can train them to feel confident about approaching poetry as they establish for themselves just "who is talking to whom about what."

UNIT ONE
Starting Points for Unit Projects

The following suggestions will help you initiate individual and group projects during the course of this unit.

Creating a Multimedia Report

GROUP RESEARCH PROJECT Have groups of students work cooperatively to research coming-of-age rituals in different cultures. Encourage them to choose rituals from cultures represented in your class, such as the Jewish bar or bat mitzvah, Christian confirmation, and the Hispanic quince. Students can interview people who have gone through the rituals and can use oral histories, music, photos, clothing, and other special ritual items in their reports.

Creating a Portfolio or Memory Box

ART PROJECT Have students create a portfolio or memory box of "fabulous firsts" in their lives so far: first steps, first birthday, first day of school, first bicycle, first trip away from home on their own, first dance, and so on. Encourage students to find photos or keepsakes to represent each "first."

Giving a How-to Demonstration

SPEECH PROJECT Have students demonstrate something they were taught to do by an older friend or relative. Possibilities include baking, crafts, sports skills, musical skills, and so on. After each demonstration, students can include reminiscences of how they learned the skill from the older person, as well as how the newly earned skill enriched their lives.

Creating a Book of Cartoons

GROUP ART PROJECT Have students collaborate on a book of cartoons entitled "I Wish Someone Had Told Me." Each cartoon should show through text and drawing a mistake or embarrassing moment that seems humorous in retrospect. It also might show what the student learned from it.

Observing Stages of Child Development

RESEARCH PROJECT Have pairs of students observe children at different stages of development. For example, one pair might spend a morning at a daycare class for two-year-olds, while other pairs observe a kindergarten class, a third-grade class, and so on. Have each pair note what skills the children are learning and what problems or difficulties seem most important at each age. Afterwards, pairs can compare and contrast their observations.

Sharing a Poem and Interviewing a Friend

LITERATURE PROJECT Have individual students share the poem "The Road Not Taken" with an older friend or relative. Then have them ask if there was a decision in the older person's life that was a turning point that made all the difference. The older friends or relatives can describe their decisions and the effects they had on their lives, as well as how they feel about them now. With the interviewees' consent, students can tape the interviews and then compile them into a class audiotape titled "The Road Taken."

Family and Community Involvement

Family

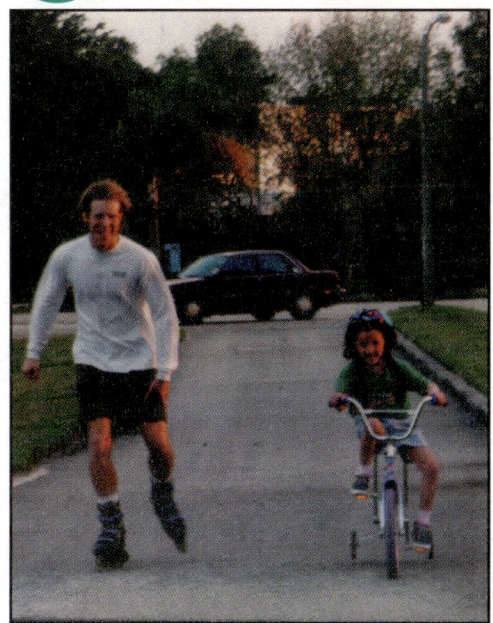

The following Copymasters provide activities that students can complete with a parent or other family member.

OPTION 1: WRITE AN AUTOBIOGRAPHICAL SKETCH
- **Connection** All of the selections in Unit One deal with turning points.
- **Activity** *Copymaster 4* Students and family members can write autobiographical sketches of events that changed or shaped their lives and moved them closer to adulthood.

OPTION 2: CELEBRATE A SPECIAL OCCASION
- **Connection** Some of the selections in Unit One relate memorable experiences shared with others.
- **Activity** *Copymaster 5* Students and family members should create a memorable experience to share together. They might choose to commemorate a special occasion or a holiday together, or they might plan a helpful activity to do for someone else. Afterwards, students can share their feelings about the experience, what made it special, and what they learned from it.

OPTION 3: WATCH A VIDEO
- **Connection** Many of the selections in Unit One deal with painful experiences that become a part of growing up.
- **Activity** *Copymaster 6* Students and family members should watch a movie about growing up, such as *Sixteen Candles, Rudy, How to Make an American Quilt,* or *A River Runs Through It.* After viewing the film, the family can discuss the main characters' experiences, what the characters learned from their experiences, and how their lives changed as a result.

Community

OPTION 1
- **Connection** The selections in Unit One explore how people deal with important events or learn from mistakes.
- **Activity** Invite students to interview or write a class letter to a local newspaper advice columnist. Then have students set up guidelines for an advice column in their school newspaper and, if possible, publish the column in the paper.

OPTION 2
- **Connection** Some of the selections in Unit One explore how young people may be influenced or guided by an older person.
- **Activity** Contact Big Brothers, Big Sisters, or similar programs for information on how they enrich the lives of children who have few positive role models. Invite a representative to talk to the class, arrange a trip to the organization's offices, or plan to attend a Big Brothers or Big Sisters event.

OPTION 3
- **Connection** Two of the selections in Unit One deal with turning points in people's lives in which they give medical help in an emergency situation.
- **Activity** Invite a first aid instructor to talk to the class about giving emergency first aid in a variety of situations. Have the speaker demonstrate some of the first aid techniques people should know and how to act in an emergency situation. Alternatively, arrange to have students attend one or more first aid classes.

UNIT ONE
Part 1 Lesson Planner

TIME ALLOTMENTS SHOWN ARE APPROXIMATE. DEPENDING ON YOUR GOALS AND THE NEEDS OF YOUR STUDENTS, YOU MAY WISH TO ALLOW MORE OR LESS TIME FOR CERTAIN PORTIONS OF THE LESSON.

Table of Contents	Discussion	Previewing the Selection	Reading the Selection
PART OPENER **Growing Pains** page 12	**20 MINUTES** • Reflect on the part theme		
GENRE LESSON **Focus on Fiction** page 15	**20 MINUTES** • Discuss characteristics of fiction • Discuss strategies for reading fiction		
SELECTION **The Utterly Perfect Murder** page 18 EASY		**10 MINUTES** • PERSONAL CONNECTION • BIOGRAPHICAL CONNECTION • READING CONNECTION: Predicting	**40 MINUTES** • Introduce vocabulary • Read pp. 18–24 (7 pp.)
SELECTION **American History** page 28 AVERAGE		**20 MINUTES** • PERSONAL CONNECTION • HISTORICAL CONNECTION • WRITING CONNECTION	**50 MINUTES** • Introduce vocabulary • Read pp. 28–36 (9 pp.)
SELECTION **The Bass, the River, and Sheila Mant** page 40 AVERAGE		**20 MINUTES** • PERSONAL CONNECTION • GEOGRAPHICAL CONNECTION • READING CONNECTION: Understanding exposition	**40 MINUTES** • Introduce vocabulary • Read pp. 40–46 (7 pp.)
GENRE LESSON **Focus on Nonfiction** page 50	**20 MINUTES** • Discuss characteristics of nonfiction • Discuss strategies for reading nonfiction		
SELECTION from **I Know Why the Caged Bird Sings** page 53 CHALLENGING		**20 MINUTES** • PERSONAL CONNECTION • BIOGRAPHICAL CONNECTION • WRITING CONNECTION	**30 MINUTES** • Read pp. 53–59 (7 pp.)
SELECTION **A Christmas Memory** page 63 EASY		**20 MINUTES** • PERSONAL CONNECTION • BIOGRAPHICAL CONNECTION • READING CONNECTION: Using a reading log	**60 MINUTES** • Introduce vocabulary • Read pp. 63–75 (13 pp.)
NONFICTION ON YOUR OWN **On Being Seventeen, Bright, and Unable to Read** page 79 AVERAGE			**10 MINUTES** • Read pp. 79–81 (3 pp.)
Writing	Writer's Style	Prewriting	Drafting and Revising
WRITING ABOUT LITERATURE **Analysis**	**20 MINUTES**	**20 MINUTES**	**80 MINUTES**

Time estimates assume in-class work. You may wish to assign some of these stages as homework.

Responding to the Selection

FROM PERSONAL RESPONSE TO CRITICAL ANALYSIS	OR	ANOTHER PATHWAY	LITERARY CONCEPTS	QUICKWRITES
		40 MINUTES		
• Discussion questions	OR	• Retelling	• External and internal conflicts	• Description • Outline • Letter
		60 MINUTES		
• Discussion questions	OR	• Similarities and differences	• Rising action and climax	• Poem • Essay
		40 MINUTES		
• Discussion questions	OR	• Similarities and differences	• Falling action and resolution • Internal conflict	• Skit • Ending
		30 MINUTES		
• Discussion questions	OR	• Cooperative learning (skit)	• Allusion	• Character sketch • Scene
		50 MINUTES		
• Discussion questions	OR	• Cooperative learning	• Symbol	• Personal narrative • Letters • Epitaph

Extension Activities

- ALTERNATIVE ACTIVITIES
- LITERARY LINKS
- CRITIC'S CORNER
- THE WRITER'S STYLE
- ACROSS THE CURRICULUM
- ART CONNECTION
- WORDS TO KNOW
- BIOGRAPHY

Alt. Activities	Literary Links	Critic's Corner	Writer's Style	Across the Curriculum	Art Connection	Words to Know	Biography
30 MINUTES							
			✔	HEALTH	✔	✔	✔
20 MINUTES							
✔	✔				✔	✔	
20 MINUTES							
✔	✔					✔	✔
30 MINUTES							
✔				PERFORMING ARTS		✔	✔
50 MINUTES							
✔	✔		✔	SOCIAL STUDIES		✔	✔

Publishing and Reflecting	Grammar in Context	Reading the World
25 MINUTES	**15 MINUTES**	**35 MINUTES**

PART 1

REFLECTING ON THEME

Read this paragraph aloud to students after telling them that Wilde was a witty author who made short, clever comments about life. Explain that growth and change go together in the characters they will read about—just as in real life. Suggest that students notice the *dynamic* characters in the unit selections—people whose experiences are making them more mature. They will see these characters undergo one or more important changes, unlike *static* characters who do not change.

What Do You Think?

Advise students that examples of obstacles need not come from their own lives; they should consider a broad range of experiences, such as chanllenges an immigrant student might face; teenagers' responsibilities; decisions to be made; and so on. Students will return to this activity on pages 61 and 78.

UNIT ONE PART 1

GROWING PAINS

REFLECTING ON THEME

Oscar Wilde once said that experience is the name people give to their mistakes. Perhaps, then, we should be grateful that we make mistakes. In this part of Unit One, characters discover that although learning the ways of the world can be painful, growing pains can lead to sudden insights and unexpected joys. As you read these selections, look for lessons that might help you through the next difficult situation you encounter.

What Do You Think? Get together with a partner to discuss some of the difficulties of growing up—the mistakes, the painful experiences, the pitfalls and predicaments that every person must overcome from early childhood on. Then design an obstacle course that represents these sources of growing pains. Draw it on a large sheet of paper as if you were designing a board game. Leave space for obstacles you may want to add as you read the selections in this part of the unit.

Ray Bradbury	**The Utterly Perfect Murder** *A childhood grudge fuels murderous thoughts.*	17
Judith Ortiz Cofer	**American History** *A personal story of discovery and loss*	27
W. D. Wetherell	**The Bass, the River, and Sheila Mant** *What happens when a teenage boy gets hung up on an older beauty?*	39
E. E. Cummings	**since feeling is first**/INSIGHT *A song of love*	47
Maya Angelou	***from* I Know Why the Caged Bird Sings** *A kind woman helps a girl find her voice.*	52
Eve Merriam	***Metaphor***/INSIGHT *Every day offers a new opportunity.*	59
Truman Capote	**A Christmas Memory** *A tender memory of a warm holiday season and a special friend*	62
David Raymond	**On Being Seventeen, Bright, and Unable to Read** *One teenager's struggle with a learning disability*	79

14 UNIT ONE PART 1: GROWING PAINS

Focus on Fiction

Fiction refers to works of prose that contain imaginary elements. While fiction can be based on actual events and real people, it usually springs from the writer's imagination. The two major types of fiction are novels and short stories. A **novel** is a long, often complex work that takes the average reader several days, or even weeks, to finish. A **short story** is much shorter than a novel and can usually be read in one sitting—if the reader doesn't get interrupted. Generally, a short story has one main conflict that involves the characters, keeps the story moving, and makes it interesting. Despite these differences in length and complexity, both novels and short stories contain the same four elements: **character, setting, plot,** and **theme**.

CHARACTER The characters are the people who take part in the action of a story. Sometimes characters can be animals or imaginary creatures, such as monsters from outer space. Events in a story center on the lives of one or more characters, referred to as **main characters**. The other characters in a story, called **minor characters,** interact with the main characters and help move the story along.

SETTING The setting of a story is the particular time and place in which the events occur. A story may be set in an imaginary place, such as an enchanted castle in a ghost story, or in a real place, such as New York City or Tombstone, Arizona. The events in a story may occur in the past, the present, or the future.

Setting is a distinguishing characteristic of certain categories of fiction. For example, in historical fiction such as "Plainswoman" and in some horror fiction, such as Poe's "The Cask of Amontillado," the time frame of the story is the past. Much science fiction takes place in the future, while fantasy stories often have only a vague reference to the time frame. Most of the stories in this textbook are realistic fiction, which means that they take place in modern times and feature the truthful representation of people and situations.

PLOT The sequence of events in a story is called the plot. Think of plot as a blueprint for *what* happens, *when,* and *to whom.* Events in a plot are causally linked; that is, one event causes another event, which causes another, and so on until the end of the story. In addition, a story's plot is built around a **conflict**—a problem or struggle between opposing forces.

FOCUS ON FICTION 15

FOCUS ON FICTION

This feature defines fiction and provides an explanation of the terms used to discuss it. It also introduces students to the conventions of the genre and suggests strategies for reading fiction. The terms introduced here are covered in depth in the fiction selections that follow.

Objectives

- To understand and appreciate fiction
- To understand the elements of fiction: character, setting, plot, and theme
- To learn effective strategies for reading fiction

Teaching Strategies: ELEMENTS OF FICTION

Character Ask students to name examples of favorite characters they have encountered in their reading. Ask them if they would classify the character as a major character or a minor character and why.

Setting Ask students for examples of stories set in real and imaginary places. Have them include examples of stories set in the past, present, and future. Then ask them what details of the story helped them identify the setting.

Plot Ask students to identify the conflict in some of the stories they have already mentioned. Then ask a volunteer to summarize a story with which many or all of the students may be familiar. As this student is speaking, have other students take notes on events they believe to be part of the rising action, the moment of climax, and the falling action. Errors at this point are immaterial; the point is to focus attention on events in a story.

Theme Students may have difficulty stating the theme of stories they have read in the past. Therefore, present them with a sample theme statement, such as "Those who don't act like friends will lose friends," and ask for ideas for stories that could demonstrate this theme. You could even ask the class to brainstorm an outline for the whole story.

Reading Strategies: MODELING

Invite volunteers to read aloud the Strategies for Reading Fiction. Tell students they will be using these strategies as they read fiction selections throughout the book. Then model the strategies as students read the first two and a half pages of "The Utterly Perfect Murder." You may wish to use the models provided or create your own.

- **Preview** *"As I preview the story, I notice the eyes in the sketch and the unusual type used in the title. To me, this looks menacing."*
- **Visualize and Connect** *"In this first scene I can see the narrator lying there, his hair going gray, maybe worrying about growing old. But it's disturbing to think of a man with a wife and kids planning a murder."*
- **Observe and Question** *"The narrator seems to have a grudge against Ralph Underhill that goes back to when they were kids. I wonder what terrible thing Ralph did."*
- **Predict** *"I think the narrator will probably find Ralph, but I bet killing Ralph won't be as easy as he thinks."*
- **Clarify** *"The narrator loves Ralph? Oh, I see. The narrator must have pretty complex feelings about Ralph. I like this paragraph, how he says boys are innocent and evil."*
- **Evaluate** *"Rolling the kid in mud—what a bully Ralph is. I don't know if he deserves to be killed now, but I can understand why the narrator hated him then. I remember one time . . ."*
- **Reflect** *"The narrator has traded a good glove for a cheap statue—I'm thinking Ralph is a jerk, yes, but the narrator lets him get away with it. Maybe he's really desperate for a friend. I feel sorry for him."*

Although plots differ, they usually have the following stages of development:

Exposition The exposition in a story functions like an introduction to give the reader important background information. Characters are introduced, the setting is described or otherwise indicated, and the plot begins to unfold.

Rising Action As the story progresses, **complications** usually arise that cause difficulties for the main character and make the conflict more difficult to resolve. Uncertainty about the outcome, or **suspense**, builds as the character struggles to find solutions to the conflict.

Climax The climax is the turning point of the story, the moment when suspense reaches a peak and the outcome of the conflict seems clear.

Falling Action Falling action, sometimes called the **resolution**, occurs at the end of the story. The conflict is finally resolved at this time, and any loose ends of the story are tied up.

THEME Theme is a main idea in a work of fiction. It is a perception about life or human nature that the writer shares with the reader. Most themes are not stated directly but must be inferred from the characters and situations in a story. As you discuss literature, you will find that different readers discover different themes in the same story. The following suggestions will help you discover themes for yourself:

- Review what happened to the main character. Did he or she change during the story? What did he or she learn about life?
- Skim the story for key phrases and sentences—statements that say something important about life or people in general.
- Think about the title of the story. Does it have a special meaning that could lead you to discover a major theme?
- Keep in mind that a story may have more than one theme.

STRATEGIES FOR READING FICTION

- **Preview** Before you begin any work of fiction, look ahead, to see what the title, art, or any other noticeable features tell you about the story.
- **Visualize and Connect** As you read the exposition, visualize—or picture in your mind—the characters and setting described. Look for specific adjectives that help you imagine how the opening scene might look. Try connecting what you read about to the people, places, and situations that you know from personal experience.
- **Observe and Question** Be an active reader by making observations and asking questions about the story. Ask yourself what the central problem, or conflict, seems to be. Ask why the characters behave as they do.
- **Predict** Once you begin to understand the problems the characters face, predict what will happen next. Think about what the characters might do or say in a particular situation.
- **Clarify** As you read, you will notice that the reasons for certain characters' actions become clear. As they do, your impression about these characters may change. Continue to clarify, or refine, your understanding of the story. Reread particular sections of the text to understand fully what has happened and why.
- **Evaluate** Don't forget to evaluate, or make judgments about, what you read. Draw your own conclusions about the characters and their actions just as you would about people you know in real life.
- **Reflect** When you finish reading, take a few minutes to reflect on, or think about, your impressions. Ask yourself how you feel about the story's events. What is your reaction to the main characters? What did you enjoy about the story?

PREVIEWING

FICTION

The Utterly Perfect Murder
Ray Bradbury

Activating Prior Knowledge
PERSONAL CONNECTION

Most people have both good and bad memories of their childhood. What kind of recollections do you have of your childhood friends and acquaintances? Was there one friend who was particularly important to you? Did anyone anger you or cause you pain or embarrassment? Are any memories especially haunting? In your notebook, jot down at least two of your memories—one good and one bad, if possible. Then share them with a partner.

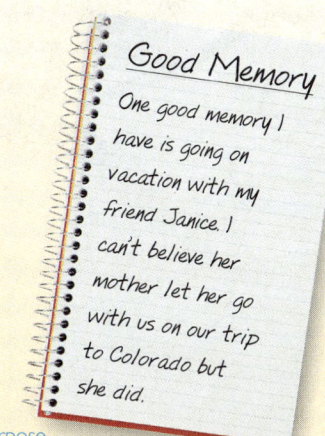

Good Memory

One good memory I have is going on vacation with my friend Janice. I can't believe her mother let her go with us on our trip to Colorado but she did.

Building Background
BIOGRAPHICAL CONNECTION

Ray Bradbury was born in Waukegan, Illinois, and lived there until his family moved to Los Angeles when he was almost 14. His stories were often inspired by memories of his Midwestern childhood. Many of the stories, like "The Utterly Perfect Murder," are set in Green Town, a fictionalized Waukegan.

Active Reading/Setting a Purpose
READING CONNECTION

Predicting When you use what you know to guess what may happen in the future, you are predicting. As an active reader, you gather information as you read and then combine it with what you've already learned. This prior knowledge can come from the story itself or from your own experiences and childhood memories. That combined information helps you predict what may happen later in the story. Before you read "The Utterly Perfect Murder," make a chart like the one below. As you read the story, jot down two or three predictions and list any information—from the story or your own experience—that led you to make those predictions. When you finish reading, check your chart to see how accurate your predictions were.

Prediction	What led me to this prediction?
1.	
2.	

17

OVERVIEW

Objectives

- To understand and appreciate a short story that explores how a person comes to terms with a painful childhood relationship
- To identify and understand internal conflict and external conflict
- To appreciate words and phrases used as adjectives in unusual ways
- To express understanding of the story through a choice of writing forms, including a description, an outline, and a letter
- To extend understanding of the story through a variety of multimodal and cross-curricular activities

Skills

LITERARY CONCEPTS
- Conflict
- Narrator

READING SKILLS/ STRATEGIES
- Predicting

THE WRITER'S STYLE
- Using metaphors

GRAMMAR
- Punctuating dialogue

SPEAKING, LISTENING, AND VIEWING
- Planning a Debate
- Group discussion
- Oral Presentation

ALTERNATIVE
Previewing

Students can choose partners and use the following prompts to preview "The Utterly Perfect Murder" orally.

Personal Connection

Discussion Prompts *Think of some good and bad memories from your childhood. Describe one good event if possible to your partner. Then listen as your partner describes his or her good or bad event. If you need help getting started, the following questions might help?*

- How old were you?
- Were you at home or away?
- Were you alone?
- What made the event good or bad?

As you read "The Utterly Perfect Murder," note the narrator's memories of his childhood friend Ralph.

PRINT AND MEDIA RESOURCES

UNIT ONE RESOURCE BOOK
Strategic Reading: Literature, p. 7
Vocabulary SkillBuilder, p. 8

GRAMMAR MINI-LESSONS
Transparencies, p. 44
Copymasters, p. 47

WRITING MINI-LESSONS
Transparencies, p. 47

ACCESS FOR STUDENTS ACQUIRING ENGLISH
Selection Summaries
Reading Support

TEACHER'S GUIDE TO ASSESSMENT AND PORTFOLIO USE

FORMAL ASSESSMENT
Selection Test, pp. 5–6
 Test Generator

 AUDIO LIBRARY
See Reference Card

 LASERLINKS
Art Gallery

🖥️ **INTERNET RESOURCES**
McDougal Littell Literature Center at http://www.hmco.com/mcdougal/lit

---

THE LANGUAGE OF LITERATURE TEACHER'S EDITION **17**

SUMMARY

On his 48th birthday, Doug Spaulding decides to kill Ralph Underhill, his childhood rival and friend whom he hasn't seen since they were kids. He rises in the middle of the night and boards a train. During the journey, Doug remembers their friendship. Most of all, he remembers that Ralph never seemed to need him. He never called, never threw pebbles at Doug's window to call him out to play. It was for this sin that Doug wants to kill Ralph. When Doug arrives, he puts a pistol in his coat pocket, walks up to Ralph's house, and rings the doorbell. Ralph looks small, sick, old. They stare at each other without speaking. Ralph asks, "Doug, is that you?" but Doug does not answer. Finally, Doug whispers "Bang" six times, turns, and walks away. Before leaving town, Doug stops at the home where he grew up and tosses gravel at his bedroom window to call down his younger self.

Thematic Link: *Growing Pains* The story suggests that hurts inflicted in childhood can continue to haunt a person into adulthood until the person finds a way to come to terms with the past.

Art Note

***Drawing of a Face from the Rilke Portfolio* by Ben Shahn** In this portrait, American painter Ben Shahn (1898–1969) blends realism and abstraction to give his work a powerful emotional impact.

Reading the Art *What emotions do you think the man in the portrait is feeling? What details of his facial features convey these emotions?*

WORDS TO KNOW

antagonism (ăn-tăg′ə-nĭz′əm) *n.* active hostility (p. 20)

concussion (kən-kŭsh′ən) *n.* a violent jarring (p. 23)

emblem (ĕm′bləm) *n.* an object that functions as a symbol (p. 20)

query (kwîr′ē) *n.* question or doubt (p. 21)

recoil (rĭ-koil′) *v.* to shrink back or fall back (p. 24)

The Utterly Perfect Murder

Ray Bradbury

It was such an utterly perfect, such an incredibly delightful idea for murder, that I was half out of my mind all across America.

The idea had come to me for some reason on my forty-eighth birthday. Why it hadn't come to me when I was thirty or forty, I cannot say. Perhaps those were good years and I sailed through them unaware of time and clocks and the gathering of frost at my temples or the look of the lion about my eyes. . . .

Anyway, on my forty-eighth birthday, lying in bed that night beside my wife, with my children sleeping through all the other quiet moonlit rooms of my house, I thought:

I will arise and go now and kill Ralph Underhill.

Drawing of a Face from the Rilke Portfolio (1968), Ben Shahn. Copyright © 1995 Estate of Ben Shahn. Licensed by VAGA, New York.

Literary Concept: NARRATOR

B Ask students who is telling the story and what they know about him so far. *(The narrator is the character telling the story, a 48-year-old married man named Doug, who holds a grudge against someone who hurt him during his childhood.)*

Literary Note

C *Bile* is a fluid secreted by the liver that aids in digestion. According to medieval physiology, yellow bile produced hot tempers and rage. "Fry my bile" is a metaphor meaning that the narrator wants to relive past experiences to intensify his anger.

Literary Concept: CONFLICT

D Ask students to describe the struggle, or internal conflict, that goes on inside Doug as he remembers Ralph. *(Possible response: Despite the physical pain that Ralph inflicted on Doug, Doug continued to love him rather than hate him, and Doug is ashamed of this.)*

Literary Concept: NARRATOR

E The narrator of this story speaks in the first person. Ask students how they think the story would change if it were narrated from a third-person point of view. *(Possible response: The narrator voices his intimate feelings and private thoughts. A third-person narrator might not be able to give such a personalized version of the story.)*

Literary Concept: CONFLICT

F Ask students to characterize the external conflict between Doug and Ralph. *(Ralph used to beat Doug up and laugh at him—causing him both physical and mental pain.)*

B Ralph Underhill! I cried, who is *he*? Thirty-six years later, kill him? For *what*?
Why, I thought, for what he did to me when I was twelve.
My wife woke, an hour later, hearing a noise. "Doug?" she called. "What are you doing?"
"Packing," I said. "For a journey."
"Oh," she murmured, and rolled over and went to sleep.

"Board! All aboard!" the porter's cries went down the train platform.
The train shuddered and banged.
"See you!" I cried, leaping up the steps.
"Someday," called my wife, "I wish you'd *fly!*"

C Fly? I thought, and spoil thinking about murder all across the plains? Spoil oiling the pistol and loading it and thinking of Ralph Underhill's face when I show up thirty-six years late to settle old scores? Fly? Why, I would rather pack cross-country on foot, pausing by night to build fires and fry my bile and sour spit and eat again my old, mummified but still-living <u>antagonisms</u> and touch those bruises which have never healed. Fly?!
The train moved. My wife was gone.
I rode off into the Past.
Crossing Kansas the second night, we hit a beaut of a thunderstorm. I stayed up until four in the morning, listening to the rave of winds and thunders. At the height of the storm, I saw my face, a darkroom negative-print on the cold window glass, and thought:
Where is that fool going?
To kill Ralph Underhill!
Why? Because!

D Remember how he hit my arm? Bruises. I was covered with bruises, both arms; dark blue, mottled black, strange yellow bruises. Hit and run, that was Ralph, hit and run—
And yet . . . you loved him?

Yes, as boys love boys when boys are eight, ten, twelve, and the world is innocent and boys are evil beyond evil because they know not what they do, but do it anyway.
So, on some secret level, I *had* to be hurt. We dear fine friends needed each other. I to be hit. He to strike. My scars were the <u>emblem</u> and symbol of our love.
What else makes you want to murder Ralph so late in time?
The train whistle shrieked. Night country rolled by.
And I recalled one spring when I came to school in a new tweed knicker suit and Ralph knocking me down, rolling me in snow and fresh brown mud. And Ralph laughing and me going home, shamefaced, covered with slime, afraid of a beating, to put on fresh dry clothes.
Yes! And what *else*?
Remember those toy clay statues you longed to collect from the Tarzan radio show? Statues of Tarzan and Kala the Ape and Numa the Lion,[1] for just twenty-five cents?! Yes, yes! Beautiful! Even now, in memory, O the sound of the Ape man swinging through green jungles far away, ululating![2] But who had twenty-five cents in the middle of the Great Depression?[3] No one.
Except Ralph Underhill.
And one day Ralph asked you if you wanted one of the statues.
Wanted! you cried. Yes! Yes!

---

1. **Tarzan . . . Numa the Lion:** These characters are from the radio show *Tarzan*, which was based on the stories of Edgar Rice Burroughs and broadcast from 1932 to 1935 and from 1951 to 1952. In the stories, Tarzan, a young boy stranded in Africa, is raised by an ape and befriends other African animals.
2. **ululating** (ŭl′yə-lā′tĭng): wailing or yelling loudly.
3. **Great Depression:** the worldwide economic slump of the 1930s, during which many people lost their jobs and many banks and businesses closed.

antagonism (ăn-tăg′ə-nĭz′əm) *n.* active hostility
emblem (ĕm′bləm) *n.* an object that functions as a symbol

20

Mini-Lesson Literary Concepts

REVIEWING NARRATOR Remind students that the narrator is the character or voice from whose point of view events are related. Sometimes the narrator is a main character in the story. At other times the narrator is someone outside the story action. Through the narrator the writer develops the story's character, setting, and plot.

Application Point out to students that in this story, the narrator is the main character, Doug. Explain to students that a main character who describes events in a story in his or her own voice is called a first-person narrator. Have them go to page 20 and find examples of how Doug describes himself and his relationship with his childhood friend Ralph.

20 THE LANGUAGE OF LITERATURE TEACHER'S EDITION

That was the same week your brother in a strange seizure of love mixed with contempt gave you his old, but expensive, baseball-catcher's mitt.

"Well," said Ralph, "I'll give you my extra Tarzan statue if you'll give me that catcher's mitt."

Fool! I thought. The statue's worth twenty-five cents. The glove cost two dollars! No fair! Don't!

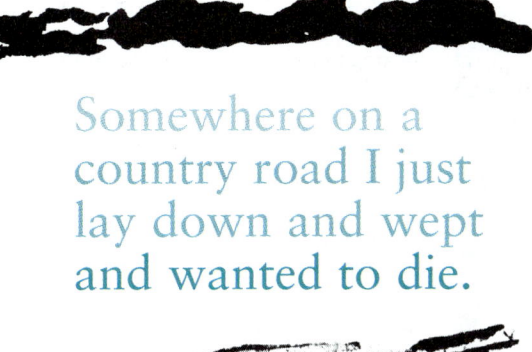

Somewhere on a country road I just lay down and wept and wanted to die.

But I raced back to Ralph's house with the glove and gave it to him and he, smiling a worse contempt than my brother's, handed me the Tarzan statue and, bursting with joy, I ran home.

My brother didn't find out about his catcher's mitt and the statue for two weeks, and when he did he ditched me when we hiked out in farm country and left me lost because I was such a sap. "Tarzan statues! Baseball mitts!" he cried. "That's the last thing I *ever* give you!"

And somewhere on a country road I just lay down and wept and wanted to die but didn't know how to give up the final vomit that was my miserable ghost.

The thunder murmured.
The rain fell on the cold Pullman-car[4] windows.
What *else*? Is that the list?
No. One final thing, more terrible than all the rest.

In all the years you went to Ralph's house to toss up small bits of gravel on his Fourth of July six-in-the-morning fresh dewy window or to call him forth for the arrival of dawn circuses in the cold fresh blue railroad stations in late June or late August, in all those years, never once did Ralph run to your house.

Never once in all the years did he, or anyone else, prove their friendship by coming by. The door never knocked. The window of your bedroom never faintly clattered and belled with a high-tossed confetti of small dusts and rocks.

And you always knew that the day you stopped going to Ralph's house, calling up in the morn, that would be the day your friendship ended.

You tested it once. You stayed away for a whole week. Ralph never called. It was as if you had died, and no one came to your funeral.

When you saw Ralph at school, there was no surprise, no query, not even the faintest lint of curiosity to be picked off your coat. Where *were* you, Doug? I need someone to beat. Where you *been*, Doug, I got no one to *pinch*!

Add all the sins up. But especially think on the last:

He never came to my house. He never sang up to my early-morning bed or tossed a wedding rice of gravel on the clear panes to call me down to joy and summer days.

And for this last thing, Ralph Underhill, I thought, sitting in the train at four in the

---
4. **Pullman-car:** a railroad parlor car or sleeping car.

WORDS TO KNOW — **query** (kwîr′ē) *n.* question or doubt

Mini-Lesson: Speaking, Listening, and Viewing

PLANNING A DEBATE In a traditional debate, two affirmative speakers and two negative speakers present arguments for or against a certain idea or proposition. The two affirmative speakers act as a team, as do the two negative speakers. Each speaker is usually given a time limit (for example, ten minutes) to present his or her main argument. After each opening speech, the opposing side is given a chance (usually five minutes) to rebut, or challenge, the arguments of the other side. The chart on the left provides a schedule of time limits for each speaker.

Application Students can apply their debating skills in small groups by dividing into teams pro and con to debate the following proposition: *Punishment for crimes of revenge should be more severe than punishment for other crimes.*

CUSTOMIZING FOR
Students Acquiring English

2 Define *seizure* as "a sudden attack" and *contempt* as "scorn, a feeling that someone or something is worthless."

3 *The window . . . dusts and rocks.* Define *confetti* as "small bits of paper thrown into the air at parades and celebrations"; in this case, it describes dirt and small rocks tossed at a window to get someone's attention.

Linking to Math

G Ask students what percent 25 cents is of two dollars. *(12.5 percent)*

STRATEGIC READING FOR
Less-Proficient Readers

H Make sure students understand who Ralph is and what he means to Doug.

- Doug thinks he has many reasons to kill Ralph. Ask students to list them. *(Ralph used to beat him up, cheat him, and humiliate him; he always made Doug come to him and never went to Doug's house to get him.)* **Noting Relevant Details**

Set a Purpose Ask students to predict what Ralph will be like when Doug finally confronts him. Have students continue reading to find out.

Traditional Debate

Constructive Speeches	Rebuttal Speeches
1st Affirmative 10 min.	1st Negative 5 min.
1st Negative 10 min.	1st Affirmative 5 min.
2nd Affirmative 10 min.	2nd Negative 5 min.
2nd Negative 10 min.	2nd Affirmative 5 min.

Art Note

Bolton Junction, Eccleshill, by David Hockney This painting was done when the English artist David Hockney (1937–) was just 19 years old and was attending art school. He used to wander the streets of his small industrial hometown looking for scenes to paint.

Reading the Art What feelings does the lone figure in the center of the painting suggest? What feelings does the grainy texture of the painting suggest?

Literary Concept: NARRATOR

I Ask students why, in their opinion, the narrator enjoys comparing himself to mythical beings and figures in great novels. *(Possible responses: It makes him feel powerful, larger than life; it makes him feel that the murder he is about to commit is preordained by fate, has great significance, and is justifiable.)*

Cultural Note

J Gingerbread, in this context, refers to elaborate, decorative effects, such as scalloped edges and scrollwork found on the porches and eaves of houses built in the Victorian style.

Critical Thinking: ANALYZING

K Ask students how they respond to the idea that the train Doug is riding on is a kind of Time Machine, and that Doug is traveling to "gun down the Past." *(Possible responses: Most students will say these images add to the suspense of the story. Some may feel that this passage suggests that the whole journey is taking place in Doug's mind.)*

Bolton Junction, Eccleshill (1956), David Hockney. Oil on board, 48″ × 40″, Copyright © David Hockney.

morning, as the storm faded, and I found tears in my eyes, for this last and final thing, for that I shall kill you tomorrow night.

Murder, I thought, after thirty-six years. Why, you're madder than Ahab.[5]

The train wailed. We ran crosscountry like a mechanical Greek Fate[6] carried by a black metal Roman Fury.[7]

They say you can't go home again.[8]
That is a lie.

If you are lucky and time it right, you arrive at sunset when the old town is filled with yellow light.

I got off the train and walked up through Green Town and looked at the courthouse, burning with sunset light. Every tree was hung with gold doubloons[9] of color. Every roof and coping[10] and bit of gingerbread was purest brass and ancient gold.

I sat in the courthouse square with dogs and old men until the sun had set and Green Town was dark. I wanted to savor Ralph Underhill's death.

No one in history had ever done a crime like this.

I would stay, kill, depart, a stranger among strangers.

How would anyone dare to say, finding Ralph Underhill's body on his doorstep, that a boy aged twelve, arriving on a kind of Time Machine train, traveled out of hideous self-contempt, had gunned down the Past? It was beyond all reason. I was safe in my pure insanity.

Finally, at eight-thirty on this cool October night, I walked across town, past the ravine.

I never doubted Ralph would still be there.

---

5. **Ahab** (ā′hăb′): in Herman Melville's *Moby-Dick*, the ship captain who is obsessed with capturing a white whale.
6. **Greek Fate:** In Greek and Roman mythology, the Fates were three goddesses who controlled people's lives.
7. **Roman Fury:** In Greek and Roman mythology, the Furies were three goddesses of vengeance, or revenge.
8. **you can't go home again:** A saying taken from the title of a novel by Thomas Wolfe, *You Can't Go Home Again*. The main character in the novel revisits his hometown and is disappointed by the changes he sees.
9. **doubloons** (dŭ-blōōnz′): gold coins formerly used in Spain and Spanish America.
10. **coping** (kō′pĭng): the top layer or course of a stone or brick wall, usually having a slanting upper surface to shed water.

22 UNIT ONE PART 1: GROWING PAINS

Mini-Lesson The Writer's Style

USING METAPHORS Tell students that Bradbury uses figures of speech called metaphors to make comparisons. Unlike similes, metaphors do not include the words *like* or *as*. Sometimes writers use metaphors to imply comparisons without stating them directly. For example, in the highlighted passage above, the narrator describes the look of his hometown at sunset by saying the roofs and copings of the houses are "purest brass" and "ancient gold." He describes the leaves that hang from the trees as "gold doubloons of color," thus equating the sunlit town with shining metal. These comparisons express his appreciation of the glory of the sunset.

Application Have students work in pairs to create metaphors that describe the appearance of a building or an object in their neighborhood at a certain time of day or a certain season. Write on the board, this example. "The sidewalk is a steaming griddle."

Reteaching/Reinforcement
- *Writing Mini-Lessons* transparencies p. 47

 The Writer's Craft

Metaphor, pp. 414, 841

---

22 THE LANGUAGE OF LITERATURE TEACHER'S EDITION

People do, after all, move away. . . .

I turned down Park Street and walked two hundred yards to a single streetlamp and looked across. Ralph Underhill's white two-story Victorian house waited for me.

And I could feel him *in* it.

He was there, forty-eight years old, even as I felt myself here, forty-eight, and full of an old and tired and self-devouring spirit.

I stepped out of the light, opened my suitcase, put the pistol in my right-hand coat pocket, shut the case, and hid it in the bushes where, later, I would grab it and walk down into the ravine and across town to the train.

I walked across the street and stood before his house and it was the same house I had stood before thirty-six years ago. There were the windows upon which I had hurled those spring bouquets of rock in love and total giving. There were the sidewalks, spotted with firecracker burn marks from ancient July Fourths when Ralph and I had just blown up the whole damned world, shrieking celebrations.

I walked up on the porch and saw on the mailbox in small letters: UNDERHILL.

What if his wife answers?

No, I thought, he himself, with absolute Greek-tragic perfection, will open the door and take the wound and almost gladly die for old crimes and minor sins somehow grown to crimes.

I rang the bell.

Will he know me, I wondered, after all this time? In the instant before the first shot, *tell* him your name. He must know who it is.

Silence.

I rang the bell again.

The doorknob rattled.

I touched the pistol in my pocket, my heart hammering, but did not take it out.

The door opened.

Ralph Underhill stood there.

He blinked, gazing out at me.

"Ralph?" I said.

"Yes—?" he said.

We stood there, riven, for what could not have been more than five seconds. But many things happened in those five swift seconds.

I saw Ralph Underhill.

I saw him clearly.

And I had not seen him since I was twelve.

Then, he had towered over me to pummel and beat and scream.

Now he was a little old man.

I am five foot eleven.

But Ralph Underhill had not grown much from his twelfth year on.

The man who stood before me was no more than five feet two inches tall.

I *towered* over him.

I gasped. I stared. I saw more.

I was forty-eight years old.

But Ralph Underhill, forty-eight, had lost most of his hair, and what remained was threadbare gray, black and white. He looked sixty or sixty-five.

I was in good health.

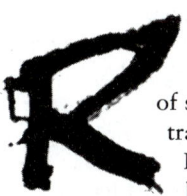alph Underhill was waxen pale. There was a knowledge of sickness in his face. He had traveled in some sunless land. He had a ravaged and sunken look. His breath smelled of funeral flowers.

All this, perceived, was like the storm of the night before, gathering all its lightnings and thunders into one bright concussion. We stood in the explosion.

So this is what I came for? I thought. This, then, is the truth. This dreadful instant in time. Not to pull out the weapon. *Not* to kill. No, no. But simply—

WORDS TO KNOW
concussion (kən-kŭsh′ən) *n.* a violent jarring

23

Critic's Corner

"Bradbury writes less about strange things happening to people than about strange imaginings of the human mind."

George Edgar Slusser
Dictionary of Literary Biography

Have students discuss this statement in light of "The Utterly Perfect Murder."

THE LANGUAGE OF LITERATURE TEACHER'S EDITION **23**

CUSTOMIZING FOR
Students Acquiring English

4 Tell students that the Fourth of July marks Independence Day in the United States and is celebrated with parades, cookouts, and fireworks. Invite students who have lived outside the United States to share any similar celebrations from their countries.

Literary Note

L In a Greek tragedy, the conflicts of the plot are resolved very neatly. The climax is designed to stir pity and terror in the audience. Usually, death plays a major role.

Literary Concept: SUSPENSE

M Ask students what techniques the author uses to build tension as Doug waits for Ralph to answer the door. (*Possible responses: He draws out the moment by describing every little thing that happens, using short simple sentences. He makes the reader wonder whether Ralph is home, whether he will answer the door, and how he will respond to his visitor.*)

Literary Concept: CONFLICT

N Ask students what inner struggle the narrator must resolve when he finally sees what Ralph looks like after all these years. (*Possible response: He wonders whether to kill him for what he did in the past or take pity on him for how old and weak he is now.*)

CUSTOMIZING FOR
Multiple Learning Styles

O **Spatial or Graphic Learners** Have students draw a sketch of Ralph as described by the narrator. They might refer to Ben Shahn's lithograph on page 18 for its use of line.

Critical Thinking: EVALUATING

P Ask students to evaluate this explanation of Ralph's downfall and to decide whether they think it is realistic. *(Answers will vary.)*

Literary Concept: CONFLICT

Q Ask students how the symbolic "killing" resolves the struggle between Doug and Ralph, as well as the conflict within Doug. *(Possible response: Doug has settled old scores with Ralph without actually killing him and can feel better about his younger self.)*

STRATEGIC READING FOR
Less-Proficient Readers

R Ask students to describe Ralph as he is now. *(Possible response: He looks old, sick, and weak.)* Have students read the rest of the story to see what becomes of Doug's murder plot.

CUSTOMIZING FOR
Gifted and Talented Students

Ask students to imagine Doug's return home and to write a dialogue that might take place between Doug and his wife. Challenge students to show in this dialogue whether or not Doug is sane.

COMPREHENSION CHECK

1. Whom does Doug decide to kill and why? *(his old childhood friend Ralph, for hurting and humiliating him as a child)*
2. What surprises Doug about Ralph's adult appearance? *(Ralph is short, weak, and sickly and has aged beyond his years.)*
3. How does Doug "murder" Ralph? *(by whispering "Bang" six times and then mouthing, "You're dead.")*
4. What else does Doug do before leaving his hometown? *(goes to his old house to call down his childhood self in friendship and frees it from years of torment)*

To see Ralph Underhill as he *is* in this hour. That's all.

Just to be here, stand here, and look at him as he has become.

Ralph Underhill lifted one hand in a kind of gesturing wonder. His lips trembled. His eyes flew up and down my body, his mind measured this giant who shadowed his door. At last his voice, so small, so frail, blurted out:

"Doug—?"

I recoiled.

"Doug?" he gasped, "is that *you?*"

I hadn't expected that. People don't remember! They can't! Across the years? Why would he know, bother, summon up, recognize, call?

I had a wild thought that what had happened to Ralph Underhill was that after I left town, half of his life had collapsed. I had been the center of his world, someone to attack, beat, pummel, bruise. His whole life had cracked by my simple act of walking away thirty-six years ago.

Nonsense! Yet, some small crazed mouse of wisdom scuttered about my brain and screeched what it knew: You needed Ralph, but, *more!* he needed *you!* And you did the only unforgivable, the wounding, thing! You vanished.

"Doug?" he said again, for I was silent there on the porch with my hands at my sides. "Is that you?"

This was the moment I had come for.

At some secret blood level, I had always known I would not use the weapon. I had brought it with me, yes, but Time had gotten here before me, and age, and smaller, more terrible deaths. . . .

Bang.

Six shots through the heart.

But I didn't use the pistol. I only whispered the sound of the shots with my mouth. With each whisper, Ralph Underhill's face aged another ten years. By the time I reached the last shot he was one hundred and ten years old.

"Bang," I whispered. "Bang. Bang. Bang. Bang. Bang."

His body shook with the impact.

"You're dead. Oh, God, Ralph, you're dead."

I turned and walked down the steps and reached the street before he called:

"Doug, is that *you?*"

I did not answer, walking.

"Answer me?" he cried, weakly. "Doug! Doug Spaulding, is that you? Who is that? Who are you?"

I got my suitcase and walked down into the cricket night and darkness of the ravine and across the bridge and up the stairs, going away.

"Who is that?" I heard his voice wail a last time.

A long way off, I looked back.

All the lights were on all over Ralph Underhill's house. It was as if he had gone around and put them all on after I left.

On the other side of the ravine I stopped on the lawn in front of the house where I had been born.

Then I picked up a few bits of gravel and did the thing that had never been done, ever in my life.

I tossed the few bits of gravel up to tap that window where I had lain every morning of my first twelve years. I called my own name. I called me down in friendship to play in some long summer that no longer was.

I stood waiting just long enough for my other young self to come down to join me.

Then swiftly, fleeing ahead of the dawn, we ran out of Green Town and back, thank you, dear Christ, back toward Now and Today for the rest of my life. ❖

WORDS TO KNOW
recoil (rĭ-koil′) *v.* to shrink back or fall back

24

Mini-Lesson Grammar

PUNCTUATING DIALOGUE Tell students that quotation marks are used to show a speaker's exact words. Point out the dialogue in the highlighted section above. Have students note that the first word of each quotation is capitalized. Commas and periods go inside the quotation marks. Question marks and exclamation points are placed inside quotation marks if those marks are part of the quotation itself. Also point out that the writer indents to create a new paragraph every time the speaker changes.

Application Have students imagine that Doug responded to Ralph instead of walking away. Have them work in small groups to write a brief dialogue between the two men. Have the groups exchange their papers to check for correct punctuation. Students may use the highlighted section as a model for punctuating dialogue.

Reteaching/Reinforcement
- *Grammar Handbook,* anthology pp. 938–939
- *Grammar Mini-Lessons* copymasters, p. 47, transparencies, p. 44

 The Writer's Craft

Punctuating Dialog pp. 798–799

RESPONDING OPTIONS

FROM PERSONAL RESPONSE TO CRITICAL ANALYSIS

REFLECT 1. What was your reaction to the outcome of the story? Did your predictions lead you to expect this outcome? Why or why not?

RETHINK 2. How did you react when the adult Ralph Underhill appeared in his doorway? Describe how his appearance was like or unlike what you expected.

3. Explain your opinion of Doug, the narrator, and his problem. Do you sympathize with him, or not?

4. What do you think Doug learns at the end of the story when he revisits the house of his birth and is joined by his "young self"?
   Consider
   Close Textual Reading
   - what Doug says, at the beginning of the story, was his most painful memory of Ralph Underhill
   - the closing words: "we ran . . . back toward Now and Today for the rest of my life"

5. Why do you think this story is called "The Utterly Perfect Murder"? Think about who or what is symbolically "killed."

RELATE 6. What kind of approaches do you think work best in dealing with bullies? Consider the childhood recollections you wrote about before you read.
Thematic Link

Multimodal Learning
ANOTHER PATHWAY
Cooperative Learning
Why do you think the young Ralph acted as he did? As an adult, how might Ralph look back on his childhood relationship with Doug and the way his own life turned out? Get together in a small group to write Ralph's side of the story. Consider what Doug says about Ralph and how he looks at the end. Present your conclusions to the rest of the class.

QUICKWRITES

1. Write a brief **description** of a memorable incident or character. You might choose from the memories you wrote about for the Personal Connection on page 17. Take a tip from Bradbury and try using vivid adjectives to help your reader visualize the experience.

2. Write the **outline** for a tale of suspense based on a haunting memory or on something you imagine.

3. Imagine you are Doug and have returned home. Write a **letter** to Ralph, explaining your behavior at his doorstep.

📁 **PORTFOLIO** Save your writing. You may want to use it later as a springboard to a piece for your portfolio.

LITERARY CONCEPTS

The plot of a story always involves some sort of **conflict**, or struggle between opposing forces. An **external conflict** involves a character pitted against an outside force, such as nature, a physical obstacle, or another character. An **internal conflict** is one that occurs within a character. What are the external and internal conflicts in this story?

THE UTTERLY PERFECT MURDER **25**

From Personal Response to Critical Analysis

1. Accept all reasonable responses.
2. Possible responses: Some students may say they were shocked at Ralph's appearance; others may say that they expected such a plot twist.
3. Possible responses: Some students will sympathize with the lasting emotional scars that unappreciated, unrequited friendship can leave on a person. Others may suggest that Doug has wildly overreacted to a common childhood experience.
4. Possible responses: Doug learns that he has given others, especially Ralph, too much power over him and that he can heal his old hurts by accepting his childhood self and moving on with his life.
5. Possible response: The murder is "perfect" because Doug gets the emotional satisfaction of "killing" Ralph without any of the moral and legal problems an actual killing would involve.
6. Accept all reasonable responses.

Another Pathway
Cooperative Learning Have students work in pairs or groups of four to discuss how Ralph would tell his side of the story. One student could record the group's ideas; another could organize them; a third could encourage the others. A fourth student could present the group's conclusions to the class.

Rubric
3 Full Accomplishment Students' conclusions offer reasonable motives for Ralph's childhood behavior and challenge or confirm points made by Doug.
2 Substantial Accomplishment Students' conclusions explain some but not all of Ralph's behavior and address some points made by Doug.
1 Little or Partial Accomplishment Students' conclusions do not offer viable motives for Ralph and ignore most of Doug's points.

Literary Concepts

Possible responses: Conflicts that Doug faces—conflict with Ralph Underhill about his actions toward Doug during childhood, external; conflict as to why Ralph never returned his friendship, internal; conflict as to why he felt he needed Ralph so much as a child, internal; conflict as to whether or not to kill Ralph, internal; conflict when Doug does finally see Ralph and he is not what Doug remembers, and Doug must decide whether he should now actually kill Ralph, internal.

QuickWrites

1. Before students write, have them reread the description of Ralph on page 23 and note vivid adjectives such as *threadbare, waxen pale, ravaged,* and *sunken.*
2. To help students, have them refer to the memories they wrote in their notebooks.
3. Remind students to write the letter from Doug's point of view, using the pronouns *I, me, mine* and *my.*

The Writer's Craft

Descriptions, pp. 58–71
Outlining, p. 816
Personal Letter, pp. 44–46

Art Connection

Accept all reasonable responses. Before students respond, have them describe their image of Doug, identifying the passages that contributed to the image. Many students will feel that the intense concentration in the face reminds them of Doug.

 ART GALLERY
Childhood Memories Many artists have used recollections of friendships and other childhood memories as themes in their work. The images shown here are paintings that focus on some universal moments from childhood.

Side A, Frame 49201

Words to Know

1. synonyms
2. antonyms
3. synonyms
4. antonyms
5. synonyms

Reteaching/Reinforcement
- *Unit One Resource Book,* p. 8

Across the Curriculum

Political Science *Cooperative Learning* Have students work in groups of four or six. Before students begin, bring in newspapers and news magazines for groups to browse through to identify ethnic struggles around the world. Have each group choose a different conflict to research. Within each group, half the members could research the point of view of one ethnic group in the struggle while the others research the point of view of the other ethnic group. Have each group select a member to give the oral report. If time permits, final reports might be presented in the form of debates between the two sides of each conflict.

EDITOR'S NOTE *With the permission of the author or copyright holder, potentially offensive material has been deleted from the selection.*

ART CONNECTION

Look again at the portrait by Ben Shahn on page 18. Shahn often used simple lines to convey the inner feelings of people. How well do you think his portrait fits your image of Doug in this story?

Detail of image on page 18.

THE WRITER'S STYLE

Bradbury sometimes uses words and phrases as adjectives in unusual ways. Look at the adjectives in the following phrases from the story. What images do they create in your mind?

"his Fourth of July six-in-the-morning fresh dewy window"

"the arrival of dawn circuses in the cold fresh blue railroad stations"

"the cricket night and darkness of the ravine"

Multimodal Learning
ACROSS THE CURRICULUM

Political Science Revenge—the settling of old scores—often motivates the actions of groups as well as individuals. Research one country where serious fighting has erupted in the past ten years because ethnic groups have clung to long-standing grudges. Make sure you identify the background of the resentments. Then, report your findings to the class.

WORDS TO KNOW

Review the Words to Know in the boxes at the bottom of the selection pages. Then, on your paper, identify each pair of words below as synonyms or antonyms.

1. query—request
2. antagonism—friendship
3. emblem—symbol
4. recoil—proceed
5. concussion—jolt

RAY BRADBURY

1920–

Known primarily for such classic works of science fiction as *The Martian Chronicles* and *Fahrenheit 451,* Ray Bradbury has written a wide range of short stories, novels, poems, plays, and nonfiction. According to one critic, Bradbury "writes less about strange things happening to people than about strange imaginings of the human mind." Bradbury says that his own imagination was fueled by reading a great variety of material.

By the time Bradbury had moved to Los Angeles as a teenager, he was already writing. At the age of 12, he wrote his own sequel to a novel about Martians because he couldn't wait for the next book to come out. Besides, he said, "I couldn't afford to buy it." In high school, he saved part of his lunch money to buy a ten-dollar typewriter so that he could write for the school newspaper. Starting at the age of 19, in addition to writing, he sold newspapers on a corner part-time until he was able to make enough money on his writing alone, three years later. Bradbury's writing is aided, he says, by having a memory that gives him total recall of every book he's ever read and every movie he's ever seen.

Bradbury says he would like the following to be written on his tombstone: "Here's a teller of tales who wrote about everything with a great sense of expectancy and joy, who wanted to celebrate things . . . even the dark things because they have meaning."

OTHER WORKS *The Illustrated Man, Dandelion Wine, I Sing the Body Electric!*

Extended Reading   LASERLINKS • ART GALLERY

26 UNIT ONE PART 1: GROWING PAINS

The Writer's Style

Since Bradbury's adjectives include phrases and words that are usually used as nouns, students may have trouble identifying all of them. Point out, for example, that in the first phrase every word but *window* is used as an adjective. Help students focus on the mood created by each descriptive phrase.

 The Writer's Craft

Nouns and Pronouns as Adjectives, pp. 623–625

Alternative Activities

1. Have students choose a scene from the story to illustrate. They can select either a scene portraying Doug and Ralph as adults or as children.
2. Have students write a jump-rope song for young children about how to treat their friends with respect and kindness.

PREVIEWING

FICTION

American History
Judith Ortiz Cofer (ôr-tēs′ kō′fər)

Activating Prior Knowledge
PERSONAL CONNECTION

What do you know about the assassination of President John F. Kennedy in 1963? In your notebook, create a cluster diagram similar to the one shown to help you record your associations. Afterwards, meet with a small group of classmates to share your knowledge. Then brainstorm to identify some significant public events that have occurred in your lifetime. Jot down these events for possible use later.

Kennedy Assassination

Building Background
HISTORICAL CONNECTION

In 1960, John F. Kennedy became the second youngest man and the first Roman Catholic ever elected U.S. President. He sought to energize Americans in the defense of freedom and the struggle against poverty. His appeal was heightened by his charisma and the charm of his family, and he became a popular president. However, his term was short-lived. On November 22, 1963, he was assassinated while riding in an open motorcade through downtown Dallas. His murder left Americans shocked and numbed, and many people came to view his passing as the end of a unique period of boundless optimism in American society.

John Kennedy gets a kiss from his daughter, Caroline, while his wife, Jacqueline, looks on.
Copyright © Jacques Lowe.

WRITING CONNECTION
Setting a Purpose

This story takes place on the day John F. Kennedy was shot. However, for Elena, the ninth-grade narrator of the story, the events in her personal life, such as being friends with someone special, are more important. Have you ever wanted to be friends with someone, but the friendship just didn't work out? In your notebook, jot down how you felt about the experience. As you read, compare your feelings to Elena's.

 LASERLINKS
- HISTORICAL CONNECTION
- VISUAL VOCABULARY

27

OVERVIEW

Objectives
- To understand and appreciate a short story that explores a painful experience of growing up in a diverse community
- To identify and understand the rising action and climax of a story
- To express understanding of the story through a choice of writing forms, including an essay and a poem
- To extend understanding of the story through a variety of multimodal and cross-curricular activities

Skills

LITERARY CONCEPTS
- Rising action
- Climax
- Setting

THE WRITER'S STYLE
- Point of view

GRAMMAR
- Capitalizing proper nouns

SPEAKING, LISTENING, AND VIEWING
- Group discussion
- Oral discussion

HISTORICAL CONNECTION
John F. Kennedy When this popular president was assassinated in 1963, the American people were stunned. These historical news images show some events that occurred during his term in office. You may wish to use these images to discuss Kennedy's presidency and reactions to his assassination.

Side A, Frame 49211

PRINT AND MEDIA RESOURCES

UNIT ONE RESOURCE BOOK
Strategic Reading: Literature, p. 11
Vocabulary SkillBuilder, p. 12

GRAMMAR MINI-LESSONS
Transparencies, p. 37
Copymasters, pp. 37–38

WRITING MINI-LESSONS
Transparencies, p. 55

ACCESS FOR STUDENTS ACQUIRING ENGLISH
Selection Summaries
Reading Support

FORMAL ASSESSMENT
Selection Test, pp. 7–8
Test Generator

AUDIO LIBRARY
See Reference Card

LASERLINKS
Historical Connection
Visual Vocabulary
Author Background
Social Studies Connection

THE LANGUAGE OF LITERATURE TEACHER'S EDITION **27**

American History

Judith Ortiz Cofer

SUMMARY

Elena, a young Puerto Rican girl, remembers the day President Kennedy was shot. She was in ninth grade, and she hated school. The only bright spot was her crush on a boy named Eugene. On the day of the assassination, she had made plans to study with him. It would have been her first visit to his house. School was dismissed early, and she wandered home, thinking of Eugene. When Elena appeared at Eugene's door, however, his mother turned her away. She did not want her son making friends with this Puerto Rican girl. Returning home, Elena found her building silent and everyone in mourning. Absorbed in her own tragedy, Elena couldn't share in the public sorrow.

Thematic Link: *Growing Pains* A mother tries to warn her daughter about the facts of prejudice, but the girl must learn for herself through a painful experience.

WORDS TO KNOW

abusive (ə-byōō′sĭv) *adj.* hurtful (p. 30)
dilapidated (dĭ-lăp′ĭ dā′tĭd) *adj.* broken-down and shabby (p. 35)
distraught (dĭ-strôt′) *adj.* deeply upset (p. 34)
elation (ĭ-lā′shən) *n.* joy (p. 34)
hierarchy (hī′ə rär′kē) *n.* ranking (p. 30)
infatuated (ĭn-făch′ōō-ā′tĭd) *adj.* possessed by an unreasoning love or attraction (p. 32)
maneuvering (mə-nōō′və-rĭng) *n.* actions skillfully designed to achieve a goal (p. 32)
martyrs (mär′tərz) *n.* people who are noted for suffering or dying in the upholding of high standards or religious ideas (p. 30)

resigned (rĭ-zīnd′) *adj.* accepting some condition or action as inevitable (p. 35)
solace (sŏl′ĭs) *n.* comfort in sorrow or misfortune (p. 36)

 VISUAL VOCABULARY
- **niña** (nē′nyä)
- **señorita** (sĕ-nyô-rē′tä)
- **salsa** (säl′sə)
- **tenement** (tĕn′ə-mənt)

Side A, Frame 49219

I once read in a "Ripley's Believe It or Not" column that Paterson, New Jersey, is the place where the Straight and Narrow (streets) intersect. The Puerto Rican tenement known as *El*[1] *Building* was one block up from Straight. It was, in fact, the corner of Straight and Market; not "at" the corner, but *the* corner. At almost any hour of the day, El Building was like a monstrous jukebox, blasting out *salsas*[2] from open windows as the residents, mostly new immigrants just up from the island,[3] tried to drown out whatever they were currently enduring with loud music. But the day President Kennedy was shot there was a profound silence in El Building;

---

1. *El* (ĕl) *Spanish:* the.
2. *salsas* (säl'säs): Latin-American dance music.
3. **the island:** Puerto Rico.

AMERICAN HISTORY **29**

CUSTOMIZING FOR
Students Acquiring English

- Use **ACCESS FOR STUDENTS ACQUIRING ENGLISH,** *Reading Support.*
- The Spanish words and cultural references in the selection may be unfamiliar to some students. You may want to give students who speak Spanish the opportunity to explain these terms to their classmates before they read the numbered glosses at the bottom of the page.
- As you guide students through the selection, you may want to use the suggestions in these boxes as well as the questions under Strategic Reading for Less-Proficient Readers.

① Explain to students that "Ripley's Believe It or Not" is a daily newspaper panel, or column, started by Robert Ripley (1893–1949), that seeks out and reprints unusual coincidences and odd facts in everyday life. The meeting of Straight and Narrow Streets is an oddity because it brings to mind the phrase "keep to the straight and narrow," an idiom meaning "live life honestly and morally."

② For students who don't know what a jukebox is, describe it as a large, coin-operated phonograph, often found in restaurants, with buttons for selecting listed songs from either records or CDs. Have students in the class who know what jukeboxes are further explain their operation.

STRATEGIC READING FOR
Less-Proficient Readers

Set a Purpose To help students get involved in the story, have them read the first paragraph. Ask them to describe the kind of building Elena lives in and the people who live there. Then have students read on to find out about Elena's neighbors.

Use **UNIT ONE RESOURCE BOOK,** p. 11, for guidance in reading the selection.

Mini-Lesson ✏ Grammar

CAPITALIZING PROPER NOUNS Tell students that a proper noun is the name of a particular person, place, thing, or idea—and is always capitalized. A common noun names a general class. You may wish to illustrate this difference by copying the chart at the right on the chalkboard. In the highlighted section above, point out the proper capitalization. To avoid confusion over *Puerto Rican,* point this out as a proper adjective.

Application Have students rewrite the following sentences, using proper capitalization.
1. Until that august the house had been occupied by an old jewish couple.
2. Every sunday we drove out to the suburbs of paterson, clifton, and passaic.
3. Eugene and his parents had come up from georgia, the same place where the novel was set.

Reteaching/Reinforcement
- *Grammar Handbook,* anthology pp. 927–929
- *Grammar Mini-Lessons* copymasters pp. 37–38, transparencies p. 37

📕 **The Writer's Craft**
Proper Nouns, p. 749

Proper Noun	Common Noun
Paterson	city
Market	street
El Building	tenement
Puerto Rico	island

CUSTOMIZING FOR
Gifted and Talented Students

In this story the Kennedy assassination is the most obvious connection with the story's title, "American History." Have students consider, as they read, which of the many things experienced and mentioned are emblematic of American history. *(Possible responses: tenement housing, multiethnic neighborhoods, desire for home ownership, Gone with the Wind/Civil War, prejudice on a personal level)*

Critical Thinking:
MAKING INFERENCES

A The death of President Kennedy struck the Puerto Rican families living in El Building especially hard. What in this passage makes it clear that young Elena does not share their grief? *(Possible responses: the references to "these people," "many women," and "they prayed." By not using the pronoun we, the author excludes herself from the grief being felt.)*

Linking to Social Studies

B Pork dishes, as well as rice and beans, are staple foods in Puerto Rican culture. By introducing a schoolyard taunt concerning these foods, the author hints at friction among ethnic groups in the community.

Literary Concept: SETTING

C Ask how the specific place and time of year in which the story is set affect the narrator's mood the day the president was shot. *(Possible response: Because she hates the city and is unaccustomed to winter, she feels depressed.)*

Critical Thinking:
SPECULATING

D Ask students why they think the fire escape is Elena's favorite place to read. *(Possible responses: It is a private place, cool in summer; she likes fantasizing about the people living in the neighborhood, and sitting on the fire escape allows her to see everyone.)*

A even the <u>abusive</u> tongues of viragoes,[4] the cursing of the unemployed, and the screeching of small children had been somehow muted. President Kennedy was a saint to these people. In fact, soon his photograph would be hung alongside the Sacred Heart[5] and over the spiritist altars[6] that many women kept in their apartments. He would become part of the <u>hierarchy</u> of <u>martyrs</u> they prayed to for favors that only one who had died for a cause would understand.

★ ★ ★ ★ ★ ★ ★ ★ ★ ★ ★

The chill was... entering my bones, making me cry, humiliating me.

★ ★ ★ ★ ★ ★ ★ ★ ★ ★ ★

On the day that President Kennedy was shot, my ninth grade class had been out in the fenced playground of Public School Number 13. We had been given "free" exercise time and had been ordered by our P.E. teacher, Mr. DePalma, to "keep moving." That meant that the girls should jump rope and the boys toss basketballs through a hoop at the far end of the yard. He in the meantime would "keep an eye" on us from just inside the building.

It was a cold gray day in Paterson. The kind that warns of early snow. I was miserable, since I had forgotten my gloves, and my knuckles were turning red and raw from the jump rope. I was also taking a lot of abuse from the black girls for not turning the rope hard and fast enough for them.

"Hey, Skinny Bones, pump it, girl. Ain't you got no energy today?" Gail, the biggest of the black girls had the other end of the rope, yelled, "Didn't you eat your rice and beans and pork chops for breakfast today?"

The other girls picked up the "pork chop" and made it into a refrain: "pork chop, pork chop, did you eat your pork chop?" They entered the double ropes in pairs and exited without tripping or missing a beat. I felt a burning on my cheeks and then my glasses fogged up so that I could not manage to coordinate the jump rope with Gail. The chill was doing to me what it always did; entering my bones, making me cry, humiliating me. I hated the city, especially in winter. I hated Public School Number 13. I hated my skinny flat-chested body, and I envied the black girls who could jump rope so fast that their legs became a blur. They always seemed to be warm while I froze.

There was only one source of beauty and light for me that school year. The only thing I had anticipated at the start of the semester. That was seeing Eugene. In August, Eugene and his family had moved into the only house on the block that had a yard and trees. I could see his place from my window in El Building. In fact, if I sat on the fire escape I was literally suspended above Eugene's backyard. It was my favorite spot to read my library books in the summer. Until that August the house had been occupied by an old Jewish couple. Over the years I had become part of their family, without their knowing it, of course. I had a view of their kitchen and their backyard, and though I could not hear what

---

4. **viragoes** (və-rä′gōz): noisy, scolding women.
5. **Sacred Heart:** a picture depicting the physical heart of Jesus Christ. Some Roman Catholics observe a special devotion to the Sacred Heart as a symbol of Christ's love.
6. **spiritist altars:** special areas set up to observe the belief that spirits of the dead communicate with the living.

WORDS TO KNOW	**abusive** (ə-byōō′sĭv) *adj.* hurtful **hierarchy** (hī′ə-rär′kē) *n.* ranking **martyrs** (mär′tərz) *n.* people who are noted for suffering or dying in the upholding of high standards or religious beliefs

---

Mini-Lesson — Literary Concepts

REVIEWING SETTING Remind students that the setting of a story is the time and place in which the action occurs. A story may be set in the past, the present, or the future and during a particular time of year or in a certain historical period. Sometimes the setting is clear and well defined; at other times it is left to the reader's imagination. Lead students to note that this story has a very specific setting: It takes place in one well-defined neighborhood on one famous day in history.

Application Have students work in small groups to write brief descriptions that show the variety of specific ways the setting has an effect on Elena and the people around her. For example, have them notice what she says about her tenement and the people who live there (page 29), the school playground (page 30), her fire escape and the house next door (page 30), her family's dream of moving to the suburbs (pages 32–33), her suddenly quiet neighborhood (page 34), and Paterson's mix of housing (page 35).

In the Province (1920), Charles Demuth. Watercolor over graphite, 23¼″ × 19¾″, courtesy of Museum of Fine Arts, Boston, anonymous gift in memory of Nathaniel Saltonstall.

Art Note

In the Province by Charles Demuth Charles Demuth (1883–1935) specialized in architectural paintings of houses, apartments, and industrial buildings. These paintings are said to resemble the neighborhoods in his hometown of Lancaster, Pennsylvania.

Reading the Art *Why do you think the artist painted the windows black? What feeling do you get from the way in which the buildings are represented?*

Literary Concept:
CHARACTERIZATION

E Ask students why they think Elena was so tempted to water the old lady's flowers and what this temptation tells about her character. *(Possible responses: She enjoyed looking at them; she was very fond of the old couple and wanted to honor their memory; she loves beauty and nature; she is loving and considerate.)*

---

they said, I knew when they were arguing, when one of them was sick, and many other things. I knew all this by watching them at mealtimes. I could see their kitchen table, the sink, and the stove. During good times, he sat at the table and read his newspapers while she fixed the meals. If they argued, he would leave and the old woman would sit and stare at nothing for a long time. When one of them was sick, the other would come and get things from the kitchen and carry them out on a tray. The old man had died in June. The last week of school I had not seen him at the table at all. Then one day I saw that there was a crowd in the kitchen. The old woman had finally emerged from the house on the arm of a stocky, middle-aged woman, whom I had seen there a few times before, maybe her daughter. Then a man had carried out suitcases. The house had stood empty for weeks. I had had to resist the temptation to climb down into the yard and water the flowers the old lady had taken such good care of.

By the time Eugene's family moved in, the yard was a tangled mass of weeds. The father had spent several days mowing, and when he finished, from where I sat, I didn't see the red, yellow, and purple clusters that meant flowers to me. I didn't see this family sit down at the kitchen table together. It was just the mother, a red-headed tall woman who wore a white uniform—a nurse's, I

AMERICAN HISTORY **31**

Multicultural Perspectives

COMING OF AGE On page 32, Elena says that, at age 14, she is now considered a *señorita*, or young lady. For many girls of Latin American backgrounds, however, the 15th birthday marks a young girl's passage into adulthood. She is honored and presented to the community at an elaborate party called a *quinceañera* (kēn-sĕ-ä-nyĕ′rä). This tradition is similar to a bat mitzvah in Jewish culture.

CUSTOMIZING FOR
Students Acquiring English

3 Explain that "After much maneuvering, I managed 'to run into him' in the hallway" means that Elena went to some effort to encounter Eugene and make it appear to be an unplanned meeting—a coincidence.

4 Invite students to identify the feeling behind the idea of a stomach "doing somersaults." Ask them to come up with other phrases for the same feeling, in English and in their first languages. (*Possible English responses: butterflies in the stomach, stomach tied in knots*)

5 Encourage students to use contextual clues to define *vigilant* as "on the alert" or "watchful."

Literary Concept:
RISING ACTION

F Ask what conflicts or problems students think Eugene and Elena might face as friends. (*Answers will vary.*) Ask them whether they think differences in the friends' backgrounds will become a problem. If yes, why? (*Answers will vary.*)

Linking to Social Studies

G Tell students that for many immigrant groups in the United States, the goal of moving from an inner city neighborhood to a house in the suburbs has been part of the "American dream." Have students ask family members if this "American dream" has been important in their family. Then have students consider the positive and negative aspects of this dream.

---

guessed it was; the father was gone before I got up in the morning and was never there at dinner time. I only saw him on weekends when they sometimes sat on lawn chairs under the oak tree, each hidden behind a section of the newspaper; and there was Eugene. He was tall and blond, and he wore glasses. I liked him right away because he sat at the kitchen table and read books for hours. That summer, before we had even spoken one word to each other, I kept him company on my fire escape.

★ ★ ★ ★ ★ ★ ★ ★ ★ ★ ★ ★ ★

I did not tell Eugene that I could see inside his kitchen from my bedroom.

★ ★ ★ ★ ★ ★ ★ ★ ★ ★ ★ ★ ★

Once school started I looked for him in all my classes, but P.S. 13 was a huge, overpopulated place and it took me days and many discreet questions to discover that Eugene was in honors classes for all his subjects; classes that were not open to me because English was not my first language, though I was a straight A student. After much maneuvering, I managed "to run into him" in the hallway where his locker was—on the other side of the building from mine—and in study hall at the library where he first seemed to notice me, but did not speak; and finally, on the way home after school one day when I decided to approach him directly, though my stomach was doing somersaults.

I was ready for rejection, snobbery, the worst. But when I came up to him, practically panting in my nervousness, and blurted out: "You're Eugene. Right?" he smiled, pushed his glasses up on his nose, and nodded. I saw then that he was blushing deeply. Eugene liked me, but he was shy. I did most of the talking that day. He nodded and smiled a lot. In the weeks that followed, we walked home together. He would linger at the corner of El Building for a few minutes then walk down to his two-story house. It was not until Eugene moved into that house that I noticed that El Building blocked most of the sun, and that the only spot that got a little sunlight during the day was the tiny square of earth the old woman had planted with flowers.

I did not tell Eugene that I could see inside his kitchen from my bedroom. I felt dishonest, but I liked my secret sharing of his evenings, especially now that I knew what he was reading since we chose our books together at the school library.

One day my mother came into my room as I was sitting on the window-sill staring out. In her abrupt way she said: "Elena, you are acting 'moony.'" *Enamorada*[7] was what she really said, that is—like a girl stupidly infatuated. Since I had turned fourteen and started menstruating my mother had been more vigilant than ever. She acted as if I was going to go crazy or explode or something if she didn't watch me and nag me all the time about being a *señorita*[8] now. She kept talking about virtue, morality, and other subjects that did not interest me in the least. My mother was unhappy in Paterson, but my father had a good job at the bluejeans factory in Passaic and soon, he kept assuring us, we would be moving to our own house there. Every Sunday we drove out to the suburbs of Paterson, Clifton, and Passaic, out to where people mowed grass on Sundays in the summer, and where children made

---

7. *Enamorada* (ĕ-nä´mô-rä´dä) *Spanish:* in love.
8. *señorita* (sĕ-nyô-rē´tä) *Spanish:* young lady.

WORDS TO KNOW
maneuvering (mə-nōō´və-rĭng) *n.* actions skillfully designed to achieve a goal
infatuated (ĭn-făch´ōō-ā´tĭd) *adj.* possessed by an unreasoning love or attraction

32

Mini-Lesson The Writer's Style

POINT OF VIEW Remind students that point of view is the vantage point from which events in a story are told. This story is told from a first-person point of view. That is, the writer has chosen a narrator that is a character in the story—a girl, Elena, who will use the pronouns *I, me, my, we,* and *our.* Such a narrator forms a closeness between writer and reader. For example, in the passage highlighted above, Elena reveals a secret she keeps from Eugene. Draw the web shown on the left on the chalkboard and use it to help reinforce these points.

Application Have students write a paragraph in which Eugene expresses his feelings about Elena as if he were the first-person narrator of the story.

Reteaching/Reinforcement
• *Writing Mini-Lessons* transparencies, p. 55

Point of View, pp. 430–433

Web diagram:
- uses *I, me, my, our, we*
- brings reader and narrator closer
- **First-Person Point of View**
- used by character in story

snowmen in the winter from pure white snow, not like the gray slush of Paterson which seemed to fall from the sky in that hue. I had learned to listen to my parents' dreams, which were spoken in Spanish, as fairy tales, like the stories about life in the island paradise of Puerto Rico before I was born. I had been to the island once as a little girl, to grandmother's funeral, and all I remembered was wailing women in black, my mother becoming hysterical and being given a pill that made her sleep two days, and me feeling lost in a crowd of strangers all claiming to be my aunts, uncles, and cousins. I had actually been glad to return to the city. We had not been back there since then, though my parents talked constantly about buying a house on the beach someday, retiring on the island— that was a common topic among the residents of El Building. As for me, I was going to go to college and become a teacher.

But after meeting Eugene I began to think of the present more than of the future. What I wanted now was to enter that house I had watched for so many years. I wanted to see the other rooms where the old people had lived, and where the boy spent his time. Most of all, I wanted to sit at the kitchen table with Eugene like two adults, like the old man and his wife had done, maybe drink some coffee and talk about books. I had started reading *Gone with the Wind*.[9] I was enthralled by it, with the daring and the passion of the beautiful girl living in a mansion, and with her devoted parents and the slaves who did everything for them. I didn't believe such a world had ever really existed, and I wanted to ask Eugene some questions since he and his parents, he had told me, had come up from Georgia, the same place where the novel was set. His father worked for a company that had transferred him to Paterson. His mother was very unhappy, Eugene said, in his beautiful voice that rose and fell over words in a strange, lilting way. The kids at school called him "the hick"

and made fun of the way he talked. I knew I was his only friend so far, and I liked that, though I felt sad for him sometimes. "Skinny Bones" and the "Hick" was what they called us at school when we were seen together.

The day Mr. DePalma came out into the cold and asked us to line up in front of him was the day that President Kennedy was shot. Mr. DePalma, a short, muscular man with slicked-down black hair, was the science teacher, P.E. coach, and disciplinarian at P.S. 13. He was the teacher to whose homeroom you got assigned if you were a troublemaker, and the man called out to break up playground fights, and to escort violently angry teen-agers to the office. And Mr. DePalma was the man who called your parents in for "a conference."

That day, he stood in front of two rows of mostly black and Puerto Rican kids, brittle from their efforts to "keep moving" on a November day that was turning bitter cold. Mr. DePalma, to our complete shock, was crying. Not just silent adult tears, but really sobbing. There were a few titters from the back of the line where I stood shivering.

"Listen," Mr. DePalma raised his arms over his head as if he were about to conduct an orchestra. His voice broke, and he covered his face with his hands. His barrel chest was heaving. Someone giggled behind me.

"Listen," he repeated, "something awful has happened." A strange gurgling came from his throat, and he turned around and spat on the cement behind him.

"Gross," someone said, and there was a lot of laughter.

---

9. ***Gone with the Wind:*** a 1936 novel by Margaret Mitchell that portrays the South during and immediately after the Civil War.

Literary Concept:
RISING ACTION

L Ask students to predict what problems the President's death may pose for Elena. *(Accept any reasonable responses.)*

Literary Concept: SETTING

M Ask why the sudden silence prompted by the President's death is so noticeable in this setting. *(Possible response: This neighborhood is usually such a noisy, bustling place that the quiet is immediately obvious.)*

STRATEGIC READING FOR
Less-Proficient Readers

N Make sure students understand that the adults and teenagers in the story are reacting to the President's death differently.

- How do the adults react to the sad news? *(They don't gather at favorite hangouts; they talk in low voices; they don't play loud music.)* **Noting Relevant Details**

- Why are the students at Elena's school so excited when they hear the sad news? *(They get to leave school early.)* **Making Inferences**

- What special reason does Elena have for feeling excited? *(She is supposed to go to Eugene's that night.)* **Noting Relevant Details/Connecting**

Set a Purpose Have students predict whether Elena and Eugene will have their "date."

Literary Concept: CONFLICT

O Ask students what external and internal conflicts Elena faces as she gets ready to leave for Eugene's house. *(External: Her mother thinks she should be going to church. Internal: Elena wants to make her mother feel better but doesn't want to risk missing her meeting with Eugene.)*

"The President is dead, you idiots."

"The President is dead, you idiots. I should have known that wouldn't mean anything to a bunch of losers like you kids. Go home." He was shrieking now. No one moved for a minute or two, but then a big girl let out a "Yeah!" and ran to get her books piled up with the others against the brick wall of the school building. The others followed in a mad scramble to get to their things before somebody caught on. It was still an hour to the dismissal bell.

A little scared, I headed for El Building. There was an eerie feeling on the streets. I looked into Mario's drugstore, a favorite hangout for the high school crowd, but there were only a couple of old Jewish men at the soda-bar talking with the short order cook in tones that sounded almost angry, but they were keeping their voices low. Even the traffic on one of the busiest intersections in Paterson—Straight Street and Park Avenue— seemed to be moving slower. There were no horns blasting that day. At El Building, the usual little group of unemployed men were not hanging out on the front stoop making it difficult for women to enter the front door. No music spilled out from open doors in the hallway. When I walked into our apartment, I found my mother sitting in front of the grainy picture of the television set.

She looked up at me with a tear-streaked face and just said: "*Dios mio*,"[10] turning back to the set as if it were pulling at her eyes. I went into my room.

Though I wanted to feel the right thing about President Kennedy's death, I could not fight the feeling of <u>elation</u> that stirred in my chest. Today was the day I was to visit Eugene in his house. He had asked me to come over after school to study for an American history test with him. We had also planned to walk to the public library together. I looked down into his yard. The oak tree was bare of leaves and the ground looked gray with ice. The light through the large kitchen window of his house told me that El Building blocked the sun to such an extent that they had to turn lights on in the middle of the day. I felt ashamed about it. But the white kitchen table with the lamp hanging just above it looked cozy and inviting. I would soon sit there, across from Eugene, and I would tell him about my perch just above his house. Maybe I should.

In the next thirty minutes I changed clothes, put on a little pink lipstick, and got my books together. Then I went in to tell my mother that I was going to a friend's house to study. I did not expect her reaction.

"You are going out *today*?" The way she said "today" sounded as if a storm warning had been issued. It was said in utter disbelief. Before I could answer, she came toward me and held my elbows as I clutched my books.

"*Hija*,[11] the President has been killed. We must show respect. He was a great man. Come to church with me tonight."

She tried to embrace me, but my books were in the way. My first impulse was to comfort her, she seemed so <u>distraught</u>, but I had to meet Eugene in fifteen minutes.

"I have a test to study for, Mama. I will be home by eight."

"You are forgetting who you are, *Niña*.[12] I

---

10. *Dios mio* (dyôs mē′ô) *Spanish:* my God.
11. *hija* (ē′hä) *Spanish:* daughter.
12. *niña* (nē′nyä) *Spanish:* girl.

WORDS TO KNOW
elation (ĭ-lā′shən) *n.* joy
distraught (dĭ-strôt′) *adj.* deeply upset

Little Girl Reading #3 (1973), Simon Samsonian. Oil on canvas, 42″ × 32″. Private collection, New York.

have seen you staring down at that boy's house. You are heading for humiliation and pain." My mother said this in Spanish and in a resigned tone that surprised me, as if she had no intention of stopping me from "heading for humiliation and pain." I started for the door. She sat in front of the TV holding a white handkerchief to her face.

I walked out to the street and around the chainlink fence that separated El Building from Eugene's house. The yard was neatly edged around the little walk that led to the door. It always amazed me how Paterson, the inner core of the city, had no apparent logic to its architecture. Small, neat, single residences like this one could be found right next to huge, dilapidated apartment buildings like El Building. My guess was that the little houses had been there first, then the immigrants had come in droves, and the

WORDS TO KNOW
resigned (rĭ-zīnd′) *adj.* accepting some condition or action as inevitable
dilapidated (dĭ-lăp′ĭ-dā′tĭd) *adj.* broken-down and shabby

Art Note

Little Girl Reading by Simon Samsonian Armenian by birth, Simon Samsonian (1915–) grew up in orphanages in Greece and Egypt after his parents were killed in Turkey the year he was born. He studied art in Egypt and has lived in the United States since 1968. The everyday activities of his children—studying, eating, playing—have become the subjects of many of his canvases, which are characterized by strong lines and distinct colors.

Reading the Art *Do you think the artist was more interested in creating colorful abstract shapes or in revealing something about the personality and mood of the girl in the picture? What details make you think so?*

Critical Thinking: SPECULATING

P Ask students why they think Elena's mother doesn't try to stop her from going to Eugene's. *(Possible responses: She thinks Elena will learn about prejudice sooner or later; she doesn't want to make Elena angry; she is too preoccupied with the sad news.)*

Literary Concept: SETTING

Q How does the mix of buildings in Paterson possibly contribute to the conflicts in the story? *(Possible response: Because the neighborhood combines single-family houses and old, worn-down apartment buildings, children from different economic and ethnic groups are brought together—a situation that can lead to conflict; people with diverse values and ways of life are thrown together.)*

Critical Thinking:
MAKING INFERENCES

R Ask students what the green door at Eugene's house represents to Elena. *(Possible responses: Elena's optimism about the future; her anticipation of a true friendship with Eugene)*

Literary Concept: CLIMAX

S Ask students why Elena's encounter with Eugene's mother is the turning point in the story. *(Possible responses: Elena must give up her hopes about Eugene and his house; an exposure to prejudice changes her ideas.)*

Literary Concept: SYMBOLISM

T Ask students what the turning away from and closing of the green door in this passage signifies. *(Possible responses: the end of Elena's friendship with Eugene; the end of her naive hope and optimism.)*

STRATEGIC READING FOR
Less-Proficient Readers

U Have students summarize Elena's encounter with Eugene's mother. How is Elena affected? *(Possible response: Eugene's mother turns Elena away because she doesn't want her son to befriend her, apparently because she is Puerto Rican; Elena's optimism shatters, and her personal sadness keeps her from feeling the loss of President Kennedy.)*
Summarizing/Synthesizing

CUSTOMIZING FOR
Gifted and Talented Students

Ask students to discuss how this incident may have affected the adult narrator. What might her reasons be for telling this story of her youth?

COMPREHENSION CHECK

1. Where and when does the story take place? *(in Paterson, New Jersey, on the day President Kennedy was shot)*
2. What attracted Elena to Eugene? *(He was an intelligent, serious boy and he lived in her favorite house in the neighborhood.)*
3. Why doesn't Elena get to visit Eugene? *(Eugene's prejudiced mother turns Elena away.)*

---

monstrosities had been raised for them—the Italians, the Irish, the Jews, and now us, the Puerto Ricans and the blacks. The door was painted a deep green: *verde*, the color of hope, I had heard my mother say it: *Verde-Esperanza*.[13]

I knocked softly. A few suspenseful moments later the door opened just a crack. The red, swollen face of a woman appeared. She had a halo of red hair floating over a delicate ivory face—the face of a doll—with freckles on the nose. Her smudged eye make-up made her look unreal to me, like a mannequin seen through a warped store window.

"What do you want?" Her voice was tiny and sweet-sounding, like a little girl's, but her tone was not friendly.

"I'm Eugene's friend. He asked me over. To study." I thrust out my books, a silly gesture that embarrassed me almost immediately.

"You live there?" She pointed up to El Building, which looked particularly ugly, like a gray prison with its many dirty windows and rusty fire escapes. The woman had stepped halfway out and I could see that she wore a white nurse's uniform with St. Joseph's Hospital on the name tag.

"Yes. I do."

She looked intently at me for a couple of heartbeats, then said as if to herself, "I don't know how you people do it." Then directly to me: "Listen. Honey. Eugene doesn't want to study with you. He is a smart boy. Doesn't need help. You understand me. I am truly sorry if he told you you could come over. He cannot study with you. It's nothing personal. You understand? We won't be in this place much longer, no need for him to get close to people—it'll just make it harder for him later. Run back home now."

I couldn't move. I just stood there in shock at hearing these things said to me in such a honey-drenched voice. I had never heard an accent like hers, except for Eugene's softer version. It was as if she were singing me a little song.

"What's wrong? Didn't you hear what I said?" She seemed very angry, and I finally snapped out of my trance. I turned away from the green door, and heard her close it gently.

Our apartment was empty when I got home. My mother was in someone else's kitchen, seeking the solace she needed. Father would come in from his late shift at midnight. I would hear them talking softly in the kitchen for hours that night. They would not discuss their dreams for the future, or life in Puerto Rico, as they often did; that night they would talk sadly about the young widow and her two children, as if they were family. For the next few days, we would observe *luto*[14] in our apartment; that is, we would practice restraint and silence—no loud music or laughter. Some of the women of El Building would wear black for weeks.

That night, I lay in my bed trying to feel the right thing for our dead President. But the tears that came up from a deep source inside me were strictly for me. When my mother came to the door, I pretended to be sleeping. Sometime during the night, I saw from my bed the streetlight come on. It had a pink halo around it. I went to my window and pressed my face to the cool glass. Looking up at the light I could see the white snow falling like a lace veil over its face. I did not look down to see it turning gray as it touched the ground below. ❖

---

13. *Verde-Esperanza* (vĕr′dĕ-ĕs′pĕ-rän′sä) *Spanish:* green hope.
14. *luto* (lōō′tô) *Spanish:* mourning.

WORDS TO KNOW
solace (sŏl′ĭs) *n.* comfort in sorrow or misfortune

RESPONDING OPTIONS

FROM PERSONAL RESPONSE TO CRITICAL ANALYSIS

REFLECT
1. What were your thoughts at the end of the story? Write about them in your notebook.

RETHINK
2. Why do you think Eugene's mother refuses to let Elena in? Support your answer.

3. Why is getting inside Eugene's house so important to Elena?
   Consider
   - the contrast she sees between the house and El Building
   - her observations of and feelings about the old Jewish couple
   - her feelings for Eugene

   Close Textual Reading

   Thematic Link
4. What do you think Elena learns from her experience?

5. Consider the title of this story. What connections, if any, do you see between historical events and the personal lives of the characters?
   Consider
   - the reactions of the characters to the Kennedy assassination
   - how the history of Elena's neighborhood affects the characters
   - Elena's personal dreams and disappointments

   Close Textual Reading

RELATE
6. In what ways are you affected by American history in your daily life? Think about the events you identified in the Personal Connection activity on page 27, as well as significant events in the past.

Multimodal Learning
ANOTHER PATHWAY

Cooperative Learning
What do you think this story says about living in a diverse society? Get together in a small group to discuss this issue and to find evidence for your ideas in the story. Then present your conclusions to the rest of the class. Listen carefully as each group presents, then as a class discuss similarities and differences between the groups' interpretations.

LITERARY CONCEPTS

Rising action refers to the events in a story that move the plot along by adding complications or expanding the conflict. Rising action ultimately builds suspense to a **climax,** or turning point. Copy in your notebook the rising-action parallelogram shown here. Then fill in events that complicate the plot, and end at the top with a statement that you feel identifies the climax.

```
            Climax:
Rising Action →  3.
                 2.
                 1. Elena watches Eugene in his kitchen.
```

QUICKWRITES

1. Experiment with writing a **poem** that reflects the narrator's mood at the end of the story, picking up some of its details and imagery.

2. Look over the important public events that you jotted down earlier. Draft an **essay** in which you predict which one will still be talked about 50 years from now and why. If you have access to a computer, input your prewriting notes so that they'll be easier to organize.

📁 **PORTFOLIO** Save your writing. You may want to use it later as a springboard to a piece for your portfolio.

AMERICAN HISTORY 37

From Personal Response to Critical Analysis

1. Accept all reasonable responses.
2. Possible responses: She is prejudiced against Puerto Ricans or against poor people; she thinks Elena will be a bad influence on Eugene.
3. Possible responses: She has fantasized about the house for years and wants to see rooms other than just the kitchen; she dreams of sharing with Eugene the privacy and intimacy she observed in the old Jewish couple.
4. Possible response: Some people will prejudge her based on her ethnic and social background.
5. Possible responses: The story's adults may have hoped President Kennedy would bring positive changes to the poor and minorities in America; Elena's loss of the hope that friendship with Eugene promised mirrors the nation's loss of hope that the presidency of Kennedy promised.
6. Accept all reasonable responses.

Another Pathway

Cooperative Learning One student should make sure that each speaker supports his or her ideas with evidence from the story. Another should summarize the group's ideas into a few points on which everyone agrees. A third student should report the ideas to the class.

Rubric
3 Full Accomplishment Students' discussion summaries weigh the problems and opportunities presented by cultural diversity. They use textual evidence to support their ideas.
2 Substantial Accomplishment Students discuss cultural diversity but are unable to relate their ideas to the text.
1 Little or Partial Accomplishment Students are unable to conduct a focused discussion.

Literary Concepts

(Possible responses: 2. Elena and Eugene start spending time together. 3. Elena wants to see the inside of the house.) Have students meet in small groups to compare their charts. Point out that there are more than two possible events that contribute to the rising action, so students may include more if they wish. However, each group should be able to reach a consensus that Elena's encounter with Eugene's mother is the climax of the story.

QuickWrites

1. Read the last paragraph of the story aloud, and ask students to list vivid details they might use in their poems. As an alternative, students may wish to base their poems on the symbol of the "green door" of hope.
2. Before students begin writing, have them consider possible long-range consequences of the public event they chose.

📁 **The Writer's Craft**

Extended Metaphor, pp. 132–136
Persuasion, pp. 207–221

THE LANGUAGE OF LITERATURE TEACHER'S EDITION 37

Words to Know

1. infatuated
2. distraught
3. elation
4. Abusive
5. Martyrs
6. resigned
7. dilapidated
8. Solace
9. hierarchy
10. maneuvering

Reteaching/Reinforcement
- *Unit One Resource Book*, p. 12

Critic's Corner

Accept all reasonable responses. Encourage students to relate the story to their own experiences.

Across the Curriculum

History Have students do a multimedia report on the history of various immigrant groups, including those mentioned in the story (Italians, Irish, Jews, Puerto Ricans, and African Americans). When did each group begin arriving in the United States, and how was it treated? What jobs did immigrants find, and where did they live? Suggest that students consult encyclopedias and library books as well as the photographs of Jacob Iris and Lewis Hine. Have students include interviews with immigrants or children of immigrants if possible.

JUDITH ORTIZ COFER

Speaking about her Puerto Rican heritage and the challenges that immigrants face in adjusting to a new culture, Judith Ortiz Cofer states: "The place of birth itself becomes a metaphor for the things we must all leave behind; the assimilation of a new culture is the coming into maturity by accepting the terms necessary for survival."

Alternative Activities

1. Before students begin, encourage them to make a list of important scenes they might illustrate.
2. Before students choose their music, have them describe in words the two different moods in the story and discuss what type of music might be suitable for each.

Multimodal Learning

ALTERNATIVE ACTIVITIES

1. Imagine that you have been hired to create an **illustration** for "American History" that will help readers better understand a particular scene in the story. Choose one scene and draw or paint it.
2. Choose two pieces of **music** for this story, one that evokes the normal life of El Building and one that captures the mood after President Kennedy was killed. Play the music for the class and explain your choices.

CRITIC'S CORNER

Yahaira Ferreira, one of the members of our student board, commented that she didn't like the fact that Eugene's mother turns Elena away: "I mean, I knew what was going to happen, but it was disappointing. I don't understand how people can act like that." Were you disappointed by Eugene's mother? Were you surprised? Would the story have been better if Eugene's mother had welcomed Elena into the house instead? Why or why not?

JUDITH ORTIZ COFER

1952–

The poems, essays, and fiction of Judith Ortiz Cofer reflect her dual cultural background. Born in Hormigueros, Puerto Rico, she came to the United States as a young child after her father joined the U.S. Navy. Although her family's official home was in Paterson, New Jersey, she and her mother and brother returned to Puerto Rico whenever her father's job required him to be at sea. As a child, Ortiz Cofer learned Spanish first and was then taught English. She later earned a master of arts degree in English.

Commenting on the autobiographical aspects of her work, especially her poetry, Ortiz Cofer has acknowledged that her family is a major topic and that she has learned more about her life by tracing the life of her family both in the United States and in Puerto Rico.

In a 1992 article in *Glamour* magazine, Ortiz Cofer wrote that instead of directly combating prejudice, she tries to present "a more interesting set of realities. . . . With the stories I tell, the dreams and fears I examine in my work, I try to get my audience past the particulars of my skin color, my accent or my clothes."

Ortiz Cofer has won such honors as a 1989 National Endowment for the Arts fellowship in poetry, the 1990 Pushcart Prize for Nonfiction, and the 1994 O. Henry Award for outstanding American short stories. She now lives in Georgia.

OTHER WORKS *Terms of Survival, Reaching for the Mainland, Silent Dancing, The Line of the Sun*

Extended Reading

38 UNIT ONE PART 1: GROWING PAINS

WORDS TO KNOW

Review the Words to Know at the bottom of the selection pages. Then, on your paper, write the vocabulary word that best completes each sentence below.

1. A person often acts foolishly when he or she is _____ with someone.
2. Any great national tragedy is likely to leave a person _____.
3. A ringing dismissal bell is usually a time of _____ in students.
4. _____ behavior between people has no place in civilized society.
5. _____ are positive role models of dedication.
6. We must never be _____ to prejudice.
7. The _____ house failed the safety inspection.
8. _____ from friends can help a person get through a time of sorrow.
9. Deciding whom you want to associate with implies you have formed a _____ of people.
10. To get the attention one wants, a person may need patience or skillful _____.

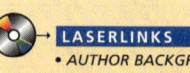

LASERLINKS
- AUTHOR BACKGROUND
- SOCIAL STUDIES CONNECTION

AUTHOR BACKGROUND
Judith Ortiz Cofer In this interview the author speaks about the personal experiences in her life that influenced her writings.

Side A, Frames 2690

SOCIAL STUDIES CONNECTION
Prejudice Manuel, a Hispanic teenager, speaks about prejudice experienced by his people. You may wish to compare Manuel's comments with the experiences of Elena in the story.

Side A, Frame 422

PREVIEWING

FICTION

The Bass, the River, and Sheila Mant
W. D. Wetherell

Activating Prior Knowledge
PERSONAL CONNECTION

The narrator of "The Bass, the River, and Sheila Mant" tells of a time when he became infatuated with an older girl. An infatuation, or a crush, often leads people to act in strange or foolish ways. Drawing on your own experiences or observations, describe in your notebook an example of peculiar behavior brought on by a crush.

Building Background
GEOGRAPHICAL CONNECTION

The narrator's infatuation occurs one summer in the lake country of New Hampshire. The setting is the Connecticut River, which runs between New Hampshire and Vermont. This part of New Hampshire attracts summer tourists who often rent cottages along the river and enjoy the fishing and sailing.

Setting a Purpose
READING CONNECTION

Setting	Characters	Background
Summer resort area on river		

Understanding Exposition In fiction, the structure of the plot normally begins with the exposition. In the early part of a story, the exposition sets the tone, establishes the setting, introduces the characters, and gives the reader essential background information. In the story you are about to read, the first three paragraphs provide the exposition as they describe the narrator's infatuation. As you read these paragraphs, notice what the exposition reveals about the setting, the characters, and the general background of the story. Then in a chart similar to the one above, jot down a fact or two about each of these categories. If you have a graphics program on your computer, use it to set up the chart.

OVERVIEW

Objectives
- To understand and appreciate a short story that humorously details a teenage boy's infatuation with an older teenage girl
- To identify and understand the falling action, or resolution, of a story's plot
- To express understanding of the story through a choice of writing forms, including a skit and a new ending to the story
- To extend understanding of the story through a variety of multimodal and cross-curricular activities

Skills

LITERARY CONCEPTS
- Falling action, or resolution
- Suspense
- Conflict

READING SKILLS/ STRATEGIES
- Understanding exposition

THE WRITER'S STYLE
- Developing voice

GENRE STUDY
- Fiction

GRAMMAR
- Punctuating compound sentences

SPEAKING, LISTENING, AND VIEWING
- Group discussion
- Oral presentation

PRINT AND MEDIA RESOURCES

UNIT ONE RESOURCE BOOK
Strategic Reading: Literature, p. 15
Vocabulary SkillBuilder, p. 16

GRAMMAR MINI-LESSONS
Transparencies, p. 39
Copymasters, p. 41

WRITING MINI-LESSONS
Transparencies, p. 44

ACCESS FOR STUDENTS ACQUIRING ENGLISH
Selection Summaries
Reading Support

FORMAL ASSESSMENT
Selection Test, pp. 9–10
Test Generator

AUDIO LIBRARY
See Reference Card

SUMMARY

The narrator recalls a summer when a girl named Sheila Mant, who was several years older than he, was the most important thing in his life—more important even than fishing. The setting is a summer cottage on a river. The narrator asks Sheila to go to Dixford to hear a band. Since he doesn't have a car, they go by canoe. The narrator has brought along his fishing rod, and while he was paddling to Sheila's, he had let out the fishing line. As they paddle toward Dixford, he learns that she detests fishing. When a huge bass strikes his line, he is torn between the bass and Sheila. He chooses Sheila and cuts the line. He scarcely remembers the rest of the night, only that Sheila went home in another boy's Corvette. He remembers the bass, however, and never again makes the same kind of mistake.

Thematic Link: *Growing Pains* A teenage boy learns the cost of sacrificing his own interests for the sake of an infatuation.

The Bass, the River, and Sheila Mant

W. D. Wetherell

40 UNIT ONE PART 1: GROWING PAINS

WORDS TO KNOW

antipathy (ăn-tĭp′ə-thē) *n.* strong dislike (p. 44)
conspicuous (kən-spĭk′yōō-əs) *adj.* easy to see; obvious (p. 45)
dubious (dōō′bē-əs) *adj.* doubtful; hesitating (p. 43)
epitome (ĭ-pĭt′ə-mē) *n.* a typical or ideal example of something (p. 42)
incarnation (ĭn′kär-nā-shən) *n.* someone who represents an abstract quality (p. 42)

overcompensate (ō′vər-kŏm′pən-sāt) *v.* to make more than the necessary adjustment (p. 46)
pensive (pĕn′sĭv) *adj.* deeply thoughtful, often in a wistful or dreamy way (p. 42)
suave (swäv) *adj.* having a smooth and polished manner (p. 42)
surreptitiously (sŭr′əp-tĭsh′əs-lē) *adv.* secretly (p. 45)
tribute (trĭb′yōōt) *n.* a payment made from gratitude, respect, or admiration (p. 45)

There was a summer in my life when the only creature that seemed lovelier to me than a largemouth bass was Sheila Mant. I was fourteen. The Mants had rented the cottage next to ours on the river; with their parties, their frantic games of softball, their constant comings and goings, they appeared to me denizens[1] of a brilliant existence. "Too noisy by half," my mother quickly decided, but I would have given anything to be invited to one of their parties, and when my parents went to bed I would sneak through the woods to their hedge and stare enchanted at the candlelit swirl of white dresses and bright, paisley skirts.

Sheila was the middle daughter—at seventeen, all but out of reach. She would spend her days sunbathing on a float

---

1. **denizens** (dĕn′ĭ-zənz): inhabitants.

THE BASS, THE RIVER, AND SHEILA MANT **41**

CUSTOMIZING FOR
Students Acquiring English

- Use **ACCESS FOR STUDENTS ACQUIRING ENGLISH,** *Reading Support.*
- "The Bass, the River, and Sheila Mant" contains many terms relating to bass fishing that may challenge some students. You may wish to go over the following words before reading the story:

canoe	lure	casting
bow	spool	paddling
stern	plug	shallow
cove	dock	sandbar

- As you guide students through the selection, you may want to use the suggestions in these boxes as well as the questions under Strategic Reading for Less-Proficient Readers.
- Tell students that *softball* is a variation of baseball that is played with a larger, softer ball. Ask students what sports are popular in their home countries.

STRATEGIC READING FOR
Less-Proficient Readers

Set a Purpose Have students read the title of the story and study the opening illustration. Then have a volunteer read the first page aloud. Ask students how they think the narrator feels about Sheila, from the first line of the story. Have them continue reading to find out how Sheila feels toward the narrator.

Use **UNIT ONE RESOURCE BOOK,** p. 15, for guidance in reading the selection.

Mini-Lesson Genre Study

FICTION Draw the web shown on the right on the chalkboard, and use it to explain that a **short story** is a kind of fiction with the following characteristics:
- It can usually be read in one sitting.
- It has one main conflict.
- Its four main aspects are characters, setting, plot, and theme.

Application Have students copy the web into their notebooks. After they read the selection, have them identify the main conflict, the characters, the setting, the plot, and the theme of the story.

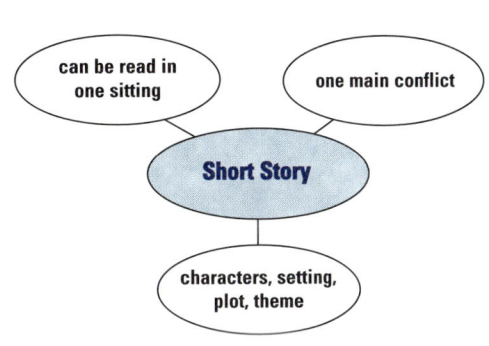

CUSTOMIZING FOR
Gifted and Talented Students

Have students note the narrator's descriptions of Sheila's moods as he depicts her various poses while sunbathing. Point out to students that these details give the reader clues about Sheila's personality. As students continue reading the story, have them note further descriptions of Sheila's words and behavior and what they might express about Sheila's personality.

CUSTOMIZING FOR
Students Acquiring English

2 The words *jaded* and *unutterably* may be troublesome. Discuss them and have volunteers paraphrase the passage. *(Possible response: To these bored young men of 20, she seemed to represent innocence and youth, while to the narrator she seemed very smooth and sophisticated.)*

3 "... and my longing was like a madness and I couldn't stop." Define *madness* in this sentence as "undue fixation on the pursuit of something." Then ask students to paraphrase the line. *(Possible response: His longing for Sheila was all he could think about.)*

STRATEGIC READING FOR
Less-Proficient Readers

A Contrast the narrator's feelings with Sheila's feelings. *(The narrator is bashful and frightened; Sheila is unaware of him.)* **Compare and Contrast**

Set a Purpose Have students read on to find out whether Sheila will go out with the narrator.

Critical Thinking: SPECULATING

B Ask students why Sheila might agree to go out with the narrator even though her behavior indicates that she is not interested in him. *(Possible responses: She is bored; she is using him to get to the dance.)*

---

my Uncle Sierbert had moored in their cove, and before July was over I had learned all her moods. If she lay flat on the diving board with her hand trailing idly in the water, she was <u>pensive</u>, not to be disturbed. On her side, her head propped up by her arm, she was observant, considering those around her with a look that seemed queenly and severe. Sitting up, arms tucked around her long, suntanned legs, she was approachable, but barely, and it was only in those glorious moments when she stretched herself prior to entering the water that her various suitors found the courage to come near.

These were many. The Dartmouth[2] heavyweight crew would scull[3] by her house on their way upriver, and I think all eight of them must have been in love with her at various times during the summer; the coxswain[4] would curse at them through his megaphone but without effect—there was always a pause in their pace when they passed Sheila's float. I suppose to these jaded twenty-year-olds she seemed the <u>incarnation</u> of innocence and youth, while to me she appeared unutterably <u>suave</u>, the <u>epitome</u> of sophistication. I was on the swim team at school, and to win her attention would do endless laps between my house and the Vermont shore, hoping she would notice the beauty of my flutter kick, the power of my crawl. Finishing, I would boost myself up onto our dock and glance casually over toward her, but she was never watching, and the miraculous day she was, I immediately climbed the diving board and did my best tuck and a half for her and continued diving until she had left and the sun went down, and my longing was like a madness and I couldn't stop.

It was late August by the time I got up the nerve to ask her out. The tortured will-I's, won't-I's, the agonized indecision over what to say, the false starts toward her house and embarrassed retreats—the details of these have been seared from my memory, and the only part I remember clearly is emerging from the woods toward dusk while they were playing softball on their lawn, as bashful and frightened as a unicorn.

Sheila was stationed halfway between first and second, well outside the infield. She didn't seem surprised to see me—as a matter of fact, she didn't seem to see me at all.

"If you're playing second base, you should move closer," I said.

She turned—I took the full brunt of her long red hair and well-spaced freckles.

"I'm playing outfield," she said, "I don't like the responsibility of having a base."

"Yeah, I can understand that," I said, though I couldn't. "There's a band in Dixford tomorrow night at nine. Want to go?"

One of her brothers sent the ball sailing over the left fielder's head; she stood and watched it disappear toward the river.

"You have a car?" she said, without looking up.

I played my master stroke. "We'll go by canoe."

I spent all of the following day polishing it. I turned it upside down on our lawn and rubbed every inch with Brillo, hosing off the dirt, wiping it with chamois[5] until it gleamed as bright as aluminum ever gleamed. About five, I slid it into the water, arranging cushions near the bow so

---

2. **Dartmouth** (därt′məth): a college located on the Connecticut River in Hanover, New Hampshire.
3. **scull** (skŭl): to move a light and narrow racing boat by means of oars mounted on each side of the craft.
4. **coxswain** (kŏk′sən): the person in a racing boat who steers the boat and directs the crew.
5. **chamois** (shăm′ē): soft leather used as a polishing cloth.

WORDS TO KNOW
pensive (pĕn′sĭv) *adj.* deeply thoughtful, often in a wistful or dreamy way
incarnation (ĭn′kär-nā′shən) *n.* someone who represents an abstract quality
suave (swäv) *adj.* having a smooth and polished manner
epitome (ĭ-pĭt′ə-mē) *n.* a typical or ideal example of something

Sheila could lean on them if she was in one of her pensive moods, propping up my father's transistor radio by the middle thwart so we could have music when we came back. Automatically, without thinking about it, I mounted my Mitchell reel on my Pfleuger spinning rod and stuck it in the stern.

I say automatically, because I never went anywhere that summer without a fishing rod. When I wasn't swimming laps to impress Sheila, I was back in our driveway practicing casts, and when I wasn't practicing casts, I was tying the line to Tosca, our springer spaniel, to test the reel's drag,[6] and when I wasn't doing any of those things, I was fishing the river for bass.

Too nervous to sit at home, I got in the canoe early and started paddling in a huge circle that would get me to Sheila's dock around eight. As automatically as I brought along my rod, I tied on a big Rapala plug, let it down into the water, let out some line and immediately forgot all about it.

It was already dark by the time I glided up to the Mants' dock. Even by day the river was quiet, most of the summer people preferring Sunapee or one of the other nearby lakes, and at night it was a solitude difficult to believe, a corridor of hidden life that ran between banks like a tunnel. Even the stars were part of it. They weren't as sharp anywhere else; they seemed to have chosen the river as a guide on their slow wheel toward morning, and in the course of the summer's fishing, I had learned all their names.

I was there ten minutes before Sheila appeared. I heard the slam of their screen door first, then saw her in the spotlight as she came slowly down the path. As beautiful as she was on the float, she was even lovelier now—her white dress went perfectly with her hair and complimented her figure even more than her swimsuit.

It was her face that bothered me. It had on its delightful fullness a very <u>dubious</u> expression.

"Look," she said. "I can get Dad's car."

"It's faster this way," I lied. "Parking's tense up there. Hey, it's safe. I won't tip it or anything."

She let herself down reluctantly into the bow. I was glad she wasn't facing me. When her eyes were on me, I felt like diving in the river again from agony and joy.

I pried the canoe away from the dock and started paddling upstream. There was an extra paddle in the bow, but Sheila made no move to pick it up. She took her shoes off and dangled her feet over the side.

Ten minutes went by.

"What kind of band?" she said.

"It's sort of like folk music. You'll like it."

"Eric Caswell's going to be there. He strokes number four."[7]

> *When I wasn't swimming laps to impress Sheila, I was back in our driveway practicing casts.*

---

6. **drag:** the pull or tension on a fishing line.
7. **strokes number four:** rows in the fourth position on a sculling crew.

WORDS TO KNOW
dubious (dōō′bē-əs) *adj.* doubtful; hesitating

Mini-Lesson Grammar

PUNCTUATING COMPOUND SENTENCES Point out the sentence in the highlighted section above. *There was an extra paddle in the bow, but Sheila made no move to pick it up.* Tell students that a comma is used to separate the two main clauses of a compound sentence when the clauses are joined by the coordinating conjunctions *and, but, for, or, yet,* or *nor.* Then point out the sentence: *I pried the canoe away from the dock and started paddling upstream.* Tell students that there is no comma between the parts of a compound predicate.

Application Have students copy and correctly punctuate these sentences:
1. Sheila sat on the dock and trailed her fingers in the water. *(no comma)*
2. The narrator made a big sacrifice for Sheila but she didn't know it. *(Add comma after Sheila.)*

Reteaching/Reinforcement
- *Grammar Handbook,* anthology p. 931
- *Grammar Mini-Lessons* copymasters p. 41, transparencies p. 39

The Writer's Craft
Commas in Compound Sentences, p. 779

CUSTOMIZING FOR
Students Acquiring English

④ Explain to students that the *reel* and *spinning rod* are parts of a complete fishing rod and the words *Mitchell* and *Pfleuger* are brand names of these parts.

⑤ Explain that *Rapala* is a brand of lure used to catch fish.

Critical Thinking: PREDICTING

Ⓒ Ask students to predict what may happen with the rod and fishing line. *(Possible responses: The narrator may catch a fish or snag something else; they may break; someone may be injured.)*

Linking to Geography

Ⓓ Tourism is second only to manufacturing in its importance to New Hampshire's economy. Tourist areas include the White Mountains, Lake Winnipesaukee, and Lake Sunapee, as well as the Connecticut River Valley described in the story. Have students locate these areas on a map.

CUSTOMIZING FOR
Students Acquiring English

⑥ Define *solitude* as "a state of being alone."

Literary Concept: CHARACTERIZATION

Ⓔ Ask students why they think Sheila didn't use the extra paddle to help the narrator paddle the canoe upstream. What does this say about her personality? *(Possible response: She is used to others doing all the work; she is lazy and spoiled.)*

Use a comma to separate main clauses joined by and, but, for, yet, or, nor.

Use a semicolon to separate main clauses joined without a conjunction.

Use no punctuation to separate verbs in a compound predicate.

Art Note

***Early Evening,* by Ken Danby** This Canadian portrait painter (1940–) has created several works that convey the moodiness of adolescence.

Reading the Art *How do the strong contrasts of dark and light affect your response to the picture?*

Critical Thinking:
HYPOTHESIZING

F Ask students why they think Sheila mentions Eric Caswell. *(Possible responses: Sheila may have a crush on Eric; it is the same situation as the narrator faces: being in love with someone older and seemingly more experienced.)*

Linking to Science

G In the scientific system of naming plants and animals, the first name is the genus to which the plant or animal belongs and is always capitalized. The second is the species name and is never capitalized.

STRATEGIC READING FOR
Less-Proficient Readers

H Make sure students understand how infatuated the narrator is with Sheila. Ask students what Sheila does or says that will present a problem for him. *(She has just expressed contempt for fishing—the narrator's greatest passion in life.)* **Noting Relevant Details/Predicting**

Set a Purpose Have students read to find out what choice the narrator faces now.

CUSTOMIZING FOR
Students Acquiring English

7 Students may find the phrase "fragile moment in time" difficult to understand. Discuss how the boy's infatuation leaves him open to pain and humiliation. Then explain that Sheila has the power at that moment to destroy the boy with her "severe and unforgiving eyes."

Early Evening (1978), Ken Danby. Original egg tempera, 24″ × 36″, by permission of the artist and Gallery Moos, Toronto, Canada.

"No kidding?" I said. I had no idea who she meant.

"What's that sound?" she said, pointing toward shore.

"Bass. That splashing sound?"

"Over there."

"Yeah, bass. They come into the shallows at night to chase frogs and moths and things. Big largemouths. *Micropterus salmoides,*"[8] I added, showing off.

"I think fishing's dumb," she said, making a face. "I mean, it's boring and all. Definitely dumb."

Now I have spent a great deal of time in the years since wondering why Sheila Mant should come down so hard on fishing. Was her father a fisherman? Her antipathy toward fishing nothing more than normal filial[9] rebellion? Had she tried it once? A messy encounter with worms? It doesn't matter. What does, is that at that fragile moment in time I would have given anything not to appear dumb in Sheila's severe and unforgiving eyes.

She hadn't seen my equipment yet. What I *should* have done, of course, was push the canoe

---

8. *Micropterus salmoides* (mī-krŏp′tə-rəs săl-moi′dēz): the scientific name for the largemouth bass.
9. filial (fĭl′ē-əl): relating to a son or daughter.

WORDS TO KNOW

antipathy (ăn-tĭp′ə-thē) *n.* strong dislike

 Mini-Lesson   Workplace Literacy

SCANS Goal: Interprets and Communicates Information: Writing

WRITING A LETTER SEEKING EMPLOYMENT Tell students that to receive consideration for most jobs, an applicant must send a prospective employer a résumé detailing his or her work experience, plus a short, persuasive business letter explaining why he or she is the best candidate for the job.

Application Have students imagine that the narrator is applying for a job as either a park ranger or a camp counselor in the Connecticut River Valley. Have them take the role of the narrator and write a short, persuasive letter to the employer summarizing all relevant interests, experiences, and skills that might help him "land" the job.

44 THE LANGUAGE OF LITERATURE **TEACHER'S EDITION**

in closer to shore and carefully slide the rod into some branches where I could pick it up again in the morning. Failing that, I could have surreptitiously dumped the whole outfit overboard, written off the forty or so dollars as love's tribute. What I actually *did* do was gently lean forward and slowly, ever so slowly, push the rod back through my legs toward the stern where it would be less conspicuous.

It must have been just exactly what the bass was waiting for. Fish will trail a lure sometimes, trying to make up their mind whether or not to attack, and the slight pause in the plug's speed caused by my adjustment was tantalizing enough to overcome the bass's inhibitions. My rod, safely out of sight at last, bent double. The line, tightly coiled, peeled off the spool with the shrill, tearing zip of a high-speed drill.

Four things occurred to me at once. One, that it was a bass. Two, that it was a big bass. Three, that it was the biggest bass I had ever hooked. Four, that Sheila Mant must not know.

"What was that?" she said, turning half around.

"Uh, what was what?"

"That buzzing noise."

"Bats."

She shuddered, quickly drew her feet back into the canoe. Every instinct I had told me to pick up the rod and strike back at the bass, but there was no need to—it was already solidly hooked. Downstream, an awesome distance downstream, it jumped clear of the water, landing with a concussion heavy enough to ripple the entire river. For a moment, I thought it was gone, but then the rod was bending again, the tip dancing into the water. Slowly, not making any motion that might alert Sheila, I reached down to tighten the drag. While all this was going on, Sheila had begun talking, and it was a few minutes before I was able to catch up with her train of thought.

"I went to a party there. These fraternity men. Katherine says I could get in there if I wanted. I'm thinking more of UVM or Bennington.[10] Somewhere I can ski."

The bass was slanting toward the rocks on the New Hampshire side by the ruins of Donaldson's boathouse. It had to be an old bass—a young one probably wouldn't have known the rocks were there. I brought the canoe back out into the middle of the river, hoping to head it off.

"That's neat," I mumbled. "Skiing. Yeah, I can see that."

---

10. **UVM or Bennington:** the University of Vermont or Bennington College in Vermont.

> The line, tightly coiled, peeled off the spool with the shrill, tearing zip of a high-speed drill.

| WORDS TO KNOW | **surreptitiously** (sûr′əp-tĭsh′əs-lē) *adv.* secretly
tribute (trĭb′yōōt) *n.* a payment made from gratitude, respect, or admiration
conspicuous (kən-spĭk′yōō-əs) *adj.* easy to see; obvious |

Literary Concept: SUSPENSE

N Ask students how the writer creates a feeling of tension in this passage. *(Possible responses: The writer creates tension by causing the reader to wonder if the canoe will capsize or if Sheila will learn about the fish; the narrator's own tension about the fish creates tension.)*

Critical Thinking: ANALYZING

O Ask what details in this passage show how well the narrator understands the fish and the river. *(Possible responses: He seems to know how the bass feels and can visualize it in his mind; he knows all the problem spots in the river.)*

Literary Concept: SUSPENSE

P Ask students what the narrator is anxious about in this passage. *(Possible responses: He is anxious about steering the canoe through the sandbar so as not to alarm Sheila; he is anxious about keeping the bass on the line without Sheila knowing.)*

STRATEGIC READING FOR
Less-Proficient Readers

Q Make sure students understand the narrator's two conflicting desires. *(His wish to please Sheila and his desire to catch the bass)* **Clarifying**

Set a Purpose Ask students to predict what the narrator will choose and how the choice will work out. Then have them finish the story to check their predictions.

"Eric said I have the figure to model, but I thought I should get an education first. I mean, it might be a while before I get started and all. I was thinking of getting my hair styled, more swept back? I mean, Ann-Margret?[11] Like hers, only shorter."

She hesitated. "Are we going backwards?"

We were. I had managed to keep the bass in the middle of the river away from the rocks, but it had plenty of room there and for the first time a chance to exert its full strength. I quickly computed the weight necessary to draw a fully loaded canoe backwards—the thought of it made me feel faint.

"It's just the current," I said hoarsely. "No sweat or anything."

I dug in deeper with my paddle.

Reassured, Sheila began talking about something else, but all my attention was taken up now with the fish. I could feel its desperation as the water grew shallower. I could sense the extra strain on the line, the frantic way it cut back and forth in the water. I could visualize what it looked like—the gape of its mouth, the flared gills and thick, vertical tail. The bass couldn't have encountered many forces in its long life that it wasn't capable of handling, and the unrelenting tug at its mouth must have been a source of great puzzlement and mounting panic.

Me, I had problems of my own. To get to Dixford, I had to paddle up a sluggish stream that came into the river beneath a covered bridge. There was a shallow sandbar at the mouth of this stream—weeds on one side, rocks on the other. Without doubt, this is where I would lose the fish.

"I have to be careful with my complexion. I tan, but in segments. I can't figure out if it's even worth it. I wouldn't even do it probably. I saw Jackie Kennedy[12] in Boston, and she wasn't tan at all."

Taking a deep breath, I paddled as hard as I could for the middle, deepest part of the bar. I could have threaded the eye of a needle with the canoe, but the pull on the stern threw me off and I overcompensated—the canoe veered left and scraped bottom. I pushed the paddle down and shoved. A moment of hesitation . . . a moment more. . . . The canoe shot clear into the deeper water of the stream. I immediately looked down at the rod. It was bent in the same, tight arc—miraculously, the bass was still on.

The moon was out now. It was low and full enough that its beam shone directly on Sheila there ahead of me in the canoe, washing her in a creamy, luminous glow. I could see the lithe,[13] easy shape of her figure. I could see the way her hair curled down off her shoulders, the proud, alert tilt of her head, and all these things were as a tug on my heart. Not just Sheila but the aura she carried about her of parties and casual touchings and grace. Behind me, I could feel the strain of the bass, steadier now, growing weaker, and this was another tug on my heart, not just the bass but the beat of the river and the slant of the stars and the smell of the night, until finally it seemed I would be torn apart between longings, split in half. Twenty yards ahead of us was the road, and once I pulled the canoe up on shore, the bass would be gone, irretrievably gone. If instead I stood up, grabbed the rod, and started pumping, I would

---

11. **Ann-Margret:** a glamorous movie star, singer, and dancer famous at the time of this story.
12. **Jackie Kennedy:** the wife of President John F. Kennedy. Many people admired Jackie Kennedy's sense of style.
13. **lithe** (līth): limber; graceful.

WORDS TO KNOW
overcompensate (ō'vər-kŏm'pən-sāt') *v.* to make more than the necessary adjustment

46

Mini-Lesson Literary Concepts

REVIEWING SUSPENSE Remind students that suspense is the excitement or tension that readers feel as they become involved in a story and are eager to know the outcome. A writer creates suspense through techniques that raise questions in the reader's mind about possible endings to the conflict.

Application Help students analyze the techniques the writer uses to create tension or excitement in the story. Have students turn to pages 45 and 46 and find examples of sentences that help create feelings of suspense. For example:

(p. 45) "Slowly, not making any motion that might alert Sheila, I reached down to tighten the drag."

(p. 46) "She hesitated. 'Are we going backwards?'"; "I quickly computed the weight necessary to draw a fully loaded canoe backwards—the thought of it made me feel faint."; "The canoe shot clear into the deeper water of the stream."

have it—as tired as the bass was, there was no chance it could get away. I reached down for the rod, hesitated, looked up to where Sheila was stretching herself lazily toward the sky, her small breasts rising beneath the soft fabric of her dress, and the tug was too much for me, and quicker than it takes to write it down, I pulled a penknife from my pocket and cut the line in half.

With a sick, nauseous feeling in my stomach, I saw the rod unbend.

"My legs are sore," Sheila whined. "Are we there yet?"

Through a superhuman effort of self-control, I was able to beach the canoe and help Sheila off. The rest of the night is much foggier. We walked to the fair—there was the smell of popcorn, the sound of guitars. I may have danced once or twice with her, but all I really remember is her coming over to me once the music was done to explain that she would be going home in Eric Caswell's Corvette.

"Okay," I mumbled.

For the first time that night she looked at me, really looked at me.

"You're a funny kid, you know that?"

Funny. Different. Dreamy. Odd. How many times was I to hear that in the years to come, all spoken with the same quizzical, half-accusatory tone Sheila used then. Poor Sheila! Before the month was over, the spell she cast over me was gone, but the memory of that lost bass haunted me all summer and haunts me still. There would be other Sheila Mants in my life, other fish, and though I came close once or twice, it was these secret, hidden tuggings in the night that claimed me, and I never made the same mistake again. ❖

INSIGHT

since feeling is first
E. E. Cummings

since feeling is first
who pays any attention
to the syntax of things
will never wholly kiss you;

5 wholly to be a fool
while Spring is in the world

my blood approves,
and kisses are a better fate
than wisdom
10 lady i swear by all flowers.   Don't cry
—the best gesture of my brain is less than
your eyelids' flutter which says

we are for each other:then
laugh,leaning back in my arms
15 for life's not a paragraph

And death i think is no parenthesis

SINCE FEELING IS FIRST 47

From Personal Response to Critical Analysis

1. Accept all reasonable responses.
2. Possible response: He has learned never to sacrifice an important part of himself for someone who doesn't care about him.
3. Possible response: Some students will feel the narrator was foolish to make such a sacrifice; others may feel he needed to take a chance on following his feelings.
4. Student responses will vary.
5. Possible responses: During most of the story, the narrator acts according to the ideas expressed by the speaker of the poem: He puts his feelings for Sheila first and doesn't stop to analyze them. In the end, however, he believes that love is not the most important thing, while the speaker of the poem disagrees.
6. Some students may say it is *never* right to sacrifice a part of your personality for the sake of a relationship. Other students may say that to make a relationship work, each person must at times put aside some of his or her interests for the other.

Another Pathway

Cooperative Learning If partners disagree, each may try to convince the other with evidence from the story. In the end, however, this question is a matter of opinion.

Rubric

3 Full Accomplishment Students state their conclusions about the match clearly and support them with evidence from the story.

2 Substantial Accomplishment Students state their opinions about the match but have trouble identifying all the relevant story passages that support their conclusions.

1 Little or Partial Accomplishment Students have difficulty forming an opinion and using textual evidence to support it.

RESPONDING OPTIONS

FROM PERSONAL RESPONSE TO CRITICAL ANALYSIS

REFLECT
1. In your notebook, describe your reaction at the end of this story. Then, share it in class.

RETHINK
Thematic Link

Close Textual Reading

2. At the end of the story, the narrator says he "never made the same mistake again." What has he learned from his experience?
   Consider
   - what he gives up for Sheila Mant
   - how his date with Sheila ends
   - what he says "claimed" him thereafter

3. Considering the situation, do you think the narrator did the right thing in cutting the line? Explain your answer.

4. What if the first three paragraphs of the story were left out? Look over the chart you created for the Reading Connection on page 39, and think about how the exposition helped you understand the story.

RELATE
5. Think about the situation of the boy in this story and the situation of the speaker in the poem "since feeling is first" on page 47. How are the two situations similar? What makes them different?

6. To make himself acceptable to Sheila, the boy conceals an important interest of his. When, if ever, do you think it is right to put aside part of your own personality—such as your interests—for the sake of a relationship? Give examples to support your view.

Multimodal Learning
ANOTHER PATHWAY

Do you think the boy and Sheila could have made a good match? Think about ways they are similar and different. Get together with a partner to discuss this idea. Then share your conclusion with the class, being sure to use evidence from the story as support.

QUICKWRITES

1. Draft another **ending** to the story in which the narrator reels in the bass instead of cutting the line. Show how Sheila reacts and how the narrator feels.

2. Review your notes for the Personal Connection activity on page 39. Use your notes to write a brief **skit** portraying the growing pains caused by an infatuation.

📁 **PORTFOLIO** Save your writing. You may want to use it later as a springboard to a piece for your portfolio.

LITERARY CONCEPTS

In a plot sequence, the **falling action,** or **resolution,** is what comes after the climax. Usually, suspense is relieved as any loose ends of the plot are tied up and the conflict is resolved. Identify one or two events that are part of the falling action in this story. How is the conflict resolved?

CONCEPT REVIEW: Internal Conflict As you have learned, an internal conflict is one that occurs within a character. How would you describe the internal conflict in this story?

48   UNIT ONE   PART 1: GROWING PAINS

Literary Concepts

The falling action in this story occurs in the description of the boy beaching his canoe and of the events at the dance leading up to Sheila calling the narrator a "funny kid" and leaving with Eric Caswell.

The narrator's conflict is resolved when he cuts the fish loose and chooses Sheila.

Concept Review: Internal Conflict   The narrator is torn between his longing for Sheila and his desire to reel in the big bass that's on his line. He has to choose between the fish—because Sheila thinks fish and fishing are dumb—or Sheila.

QuickWrites

1. Have students work in pairs to compare their Personal Connection notes and improvise skits based on their ideas. Pairs can do boy/girl skits representing the infatuated person and the admired person, or they can do skits based on conversations between the infatuated person and a good friend giving advice.

2. Before students begin writing, have them create two webs on the chalkboard, one for Sheila's possible reactions and the other for the narrator's feelings.

📁 **The Writer's Craft**

Using Graphic Devices, pp. 328–329

48   THE LANGUAGE OF LITERATURE TEACHER'S EDITION

LITERARY LINKS

Compare the infatuation of the narrator in "The Bass, the River, and Sheila Mant" with Elena's infatuation for Eugene in "American History."

Multimodal Learning

ALTERNATIVE ACTIVITIES

1. In a pantomime, actors tell a story using bodily movements, gestures, and facial expressions but not words. With a partner, stage a **pantomime** of the narrator's date with Sheila.

2. **Cooperative Learning** In a small group imagine this story as a made-for-TV movie. Design a one-page **advertisement** for the movie, casting a contemporary actor and actress in the roles of the narrator and Sheila Mant. What would you write on the ad to make a lot of people want to see the movie?

WORDS TO KNOW

EXERCISE A Review the Words to Know at the bottom of the selection pages. Then, on your paper, write the letter of the word or phrase that best completes each sentence.

1. A tourist who found that bass fishing on a river was the **epitome** of happiness would say that it was (a) ideal, (b) ordinary, (c) terrible.
2. A **conspicuous** rock in the river is one that is (a) easy to see, (b) dangerous, (c) hidden.
3. In swerving to avoid the rock, a canoeist might **overcompensate** by (a) turning too much, (b) turning too little, (c) not turning at all.
4. A person who is the **incarnation** of evil might want to (a) clean up the river, (b) poison the river, (c) protect the river.
5. A **tribute** to the narrator's fishing ability would most likely be (a) a joke, (b) a prize, (c) an insult.

EXERCISE B Use facial expressions and body language to act out each of the following words. Have other students guess the words.

1. suave
2. antipathy
3. dubious
4. pensive
5. surreptitiously

W. D. WETHERELL

1948–

W. D. Wetherell is one of those writers who has taken on a wide variety of jobs in order to buy time to write. He has been a magazine editor, a movie extra, a tour guide, a teacher, and a freelance journalist. He is now a full-time writer who has received considerable acclaim for his novels and short stories. "The Bass, the River, and Sheila Mant" was taken from a collection of short stories, *The Man Who Loved Levittown*, which won the Drue Heinz Literature Prize for short fiction in 1985. The book shows, said one reviewer, that Wetherell has "a sharp, fresh eye and a complicated view of our dislocations, pains, and dreams."

Since fishing is one of Wetherell's interests, it is not surprising that he has published two collections of fly-fishing and nature essays. One of them is *Upland Stream: Notes on the Fishing Passion*, in which he takes up the question, "Why fish?"

Wetherell has been awarded two fellowships by the National Endowment for the Arts, and his work has appeared in the *New York Times*, *The Atlantic Monthly*, and various literary magazines. Born in Mineda, New York, he now lives in Lyme, New Hampshire.

OTHER WORKS *Chekhov's Sister, Souvenirs, Vermont River, Hyannis Boat and Other Stories*

Extended Reading

Words to Know

Exercise A
1. a
2. a
3. a
4. b
5. b

Exercise B
Try conducting this exercise as a game of charades. Write each word on a slip of paper. Then have volunteers choose a slip and act out the word for the rest of the class to guess.

Reteaching/Reinforcement
- *Unit One Resource Book*, p. 16

Literary Links

Possible responses:

Similarities: Both narrators are infatuated with someone who seems unattainable; both try to initiate a relationship with the other person, and both meet obstacles and experience disappointment in the end.

Differences: Students may say that Elena and Eugene were better matched and that Eugene seemed equally interested in Elena except that his mother interfered.

W. D. WETHERELL

W. D. Wetherell got hooked on fishing when he was 13 years old and staying at his family's lakeside cabin in New England. Throughout his life he has usually fished alone, but when he was in his 30s he finally met a woman who loved fishing as much as he did—and they were married.

Across the Curriculum

Geography Have students work in small groups to prepare guides to some of New Hampshire's major tourist areas. Students can research information in geography books and travel guides, then summarize the information in persuasive text and illustrations that might entice tourists to visit.

Alternative Activities

1. Help students make a list of the main events in the narrator's date with Sheila before they begin practicing their pantomimes. Students might work in groups of three instead of in pairs, with one student as the "director," who can offer advice on improving the performance.

2. Help students review the characters' personalities and brainstorm a list of possible actors to suit those qualities. Students might enjoy anonymously submitting enticing headlines for the movie ad and then having the class as a whole vote on the best one to "sell" the movie.

FOCUS ON NONFICTION

This feature defines *nonfiction* and provides an explanation of the terms used to discuss it. It also introduces students to the conventions of the genre and suggests strategies for reading nonfiction. The terms introduced here are covered in depth in the nonfiction selections that follow.

--- **Objectives** ---

- To understand and appreciate nonfiction
- To understand the categories of nonfiction: autobiography, biography, essay, informative article, and true-life adventure
- To learn effective strategies for reading nonfiction

Teaching Strategies:
CATEGORIES OF NONFICTION

Autobiography Ask how many students keep journals or diaries and to what purpose. Point out that many of the personal essays students have written in school are examples of short autobiographies. Invite students to name autobiographies they have read and would recommend to other students.

Biography Ask students to identify biographies they have read in the past. Ask them to name some people whose lives they think would make interesting biographies.

Essay Students may have difficulty recalling specific essays that fit each type. You may instead challenge them to come up with topic ideas for expository, narrative, and persuasive essays. Or suggest one broad topic yourself, such as school rules, and ask students how an author might approach the topic with each of these purposes in mind.

Informative Article Point out that this feature, Focus on Nonfiction, is an example of an informative article. Ask for examples of topics that appear in newspaper articles. Ask students to compare the informational content of several magazines, such as *Seventeen* or *Sports Illustrated*.

True-Life Adventure Ask students to identify a few true-life adventures they have read and a few highly exciting novels. Then have students compare the two genres in terms of content and effect on the reader.

FOCUS ON NONFICTION

As any reader of a daily newspaper knows, truth can be stranger than fiction. A newspaper is a work of **nonfiction,** or writing about real people, places, and events. Unlike fiction, nonfiction contains factual information, although the writer shapes the information according to his or her purpose and viewpoint. Nonfiction includes a wide variety of writing. Cookbooks are considered nonfiction, as are letters, speeches, and most things you read in the newspaper—news articles, interviews, editorials, advice columns, movie reviews, sports stories, feature articles. Some of the major types of nonfiction that you will find in books are described below.

AUTOBIOGRAPHY An autobiography is an account of a person's life written by that person and usually told in the first person—that is, by using the pronoun *I*. In an autobiography, the writer details significant events and people in his or her life. In this unit, the selection by Maya Angelou is taken from her autobiography.

An autobiography is usually book length because it covers a long span of time. A shorter form of autobiographical writing is a **personal narrative,** in which the writer focuses on a significant experience in his or her life. Both Truman Capote's "A Christmas Memory" and William Nolen's "The First Appendectomy" are personal narratives appearing in this unit. Other short forms of autobiographical writing include **journals, diaries,** and **letters.**

BIOGRAPHY The story of a person's life written by another person is called a biography. *"The United States* vs. *Susan B. Anthony"* by Margaret Truman, featured in Unit Two, is a biography. Truman, like all good biographers, researched her subject extensively in order to present her information accurately. Usually, biographers also must decide which facts and which parts of a subject's life to include.

ESSAY An essay is a brief composition on a single subject that usually presents the personal views of the author. Because essays can be put to so many different uses, they are difficult to classify. Generally, an expository essay seeks to explain something and therefore foster readers' understanding, such as David Raymond's essay "On Being Seventeen, Bright, and Unable to Read" in Unit One and Sucheng Chan's "You're Short, Besides!" in Unit Two. A narrative essay tells a story, such as Tony Hillerman's funny account of an inept holdup, "The Great Taos Bank Robbery," in Unit Five. A persuasive essay attempts to con-

50 UNIT ONE

vince readers to adopt a certain point of view or to take a particular action. Of course, there are many other types of essays, ranging from political and historical analysis to humorous commentary.

INFORMATIVE ARTICLE An informative article gives facts about a specific subject. This type of writing is found primarily in newspapers, magazines, pamphlets, textbooks, anthologies, encyclopedias, and reference books. "'Who Killed My Daughter?': Lois Duncan Searches for an Answer" is an interesting informational article in Unit Five.

TRUE-LIFE ADVENTURE Often found in popular magazines and books, true tales of heroism, survival, or adventure can have all the drama and excitement of fiction. Find out for yourself when you read "A Trip to the Edge of Survival" in Unit Six.

STRATEGIES FOR READING NONFICTION

When reading narrative types of nonfiction—such as autobiographies, biographies, true-life adventures, and some essays—you can apply the same strategies that you use in reading fiction. The strategies that follow can help you tailor your reading to the specific needs of reading informative types of nonfiction.

- **Preview.** For clues to what a nonfiction selection is about, skim the selection to get an idea of the topic. Specifically, look at the title and any headings (those small titles in dark type that break up the text) and at the pictures, captions, graphs, charts, maps, and other outstanding features. If you are looking for specific information, previewing will help you decide if a particular piece has the information you want.

- **Think about what you already know.** Once you know the topic of a selection, take a moment to think about what you might already know about it. Activating your prior knowledge helps you better understand what you read.

- **Set purposes.** As you begin to read, focus your thinking by setting purposes to guide your reading. For example, ask yourself what specific information you want or expect to find.

- **Identify the method of organization.** Writers of informative nonfiction organize their work according to their purpose for writing. In selections meant to inform or persuade, the writer may organize the material around main ideas. In selections meant to explain a process or a subject, a writer may use a step-by-step organization or a chronological presentation of facts. In some nonfiction, especially history and science textbooks, the text is divided by headings that state the topic of each section.

- **Separate facts from opinions.** It is important to evaluate the facts that a writer presents. Facts are statements that can be proved, such as "Maya Angelou is the author of *I Know Why the Caged Bird Sings*." Opinions are statements that express a writer's beliefs, such as "*I Know Why the Caged Bird Sings* is the best book Maya Angelou has written." Be on the alert to recognize which statements are facts and which ones are opinions.

- **Consider the writer's tone.** The attitude a writer takes toward his or her subject is called tone. For example, a writer's tone may be angry or amused, critical or admiring, sad or happy, serious or humorous, positive or negative. To identify a writer's tone, look for clues as to what the writer feels about the topic and consider his or her choice of words.

- **Summarize.** When you have finished reading a selection, take a few moments to summarize or restate the main points. Reread anything that is still unclear to you. If the selection has headings, use them to review the text. You may wish to write down your summary or make an outline to help you remember. A good summary shows you what you have learned and what you still might want to find out.

FOCUS ON NONFICTION **51**

OVERVIEW

Objectives

- To understand and appreciate an excerpt from an autobiography that recalls an important relationship from the writer's childhood
- To identify and understand an allusion
- To express understanding of the selection through a choice of writing forms, including a character sketch and a dramatic scene
- To extend understanding of the selection through a variety of multimodal and cross-curricular activities

Skills

LITERARY CONCEPTS
- Allusion
- Simile

THE WRITER'S STYLE
- Varieties of language

GRAMMAR
- Using indefinite pronouns as subjects

SPEAKING, LISTENING, AND VIEWING
- Group Discussion
- Oral Presentation

ALTERNATIVE

Previewing

Students can choose partners and use the following prompts to preview *I Know Why the Cage Bird Sings* orally.

Writing Connection

Discussion Prompts Think about a person in your life that you have admired. Describe to your partner what makes this person special. Then listen as your partner describes his or her special person. If you need help getting started, the following questions might help:

- Have you ever met this person?
- Is this person admired by others?

As you read the selection I Know Why the Caged Bird Sings, note the narrator's feelings for Mrs. Flowers.

PREVIEWING

NONFICTION

from I Know Why the Caged Bird Sings
Maya Angelou (mī'yə ăn'jə-lō)

Activating Prior Knowledge
PERSONAL CONNECTION

Think of a person you have admired or wanted to be like. Perhaps a teacher, a relative, a coach, or a neighbor has had a strong influence on you. In your notebook create a cluster diagram, similar to the one shown, with the person's name in the middle, and then jot down the traits you most admire in this person.

Building Background
BIOGRAPHICAL CONNECTION

In *I Know Why the Caged Bird Sings,* Maya Angelou tells about her childhood in the small, segregated town of Stamps, Arkansas, in the 1930s. When Angelou's parents separated, she and her brother, Bailey, went to live with their paternal grandmother, whom they called Momma. Momma owned a general store in the part of town referred to as Black Stamps. After a traumatic experience in which she was abused by a non–family member when she was eight, Angelou withdrew into herself and barely spoke for five years. The recollection you will read is about a person she greatly admired, who helped her to find her voice.

Activating Prior Knowledge/Setting a Purpose
WRITING CONNECTION

An **autobiography** is the story of a person's life written by that person. In this excerpt from her autobiography, Angelou (referred to as Marguerite) not only describes events but also relates her feelings and thoughts about the person she admired. Take a moment to write in your notebook about an event in your life and notice how your memory triggers feelings and thoughts related to that event. As you read, notice how events, thoughts, and feelings are similarly connected.

This general store in Stamps, Arkansas, is similar to the one Angelou's grandparents owned. Courtesy of Stewart Hicks, Stamps, Arkansas.

52 UNIT ONE PART 1: GROWING PAINS

PRINT AND MEDIA RESOURCES

UNIT ONE RESOURCE BOOK
Strategic Reading: Literature, p. 19
Vocabulary SkillBuilder, p. 20

GRAMMAR MINI–LESSONS
Transparencies, p. 13
Copymasters, p. 19

WRITING MINI–LESSONS
Transparencies, p. 44

ACCESS FOR STUDENTS ACQUIRING ENGLISH
Selection Summaries
Reading Support

FORMAL ASSESSMENT
Selection Test, pp. 11–12
 Test Generator

AUDIO LIBRARY
See Reference Card

INTERNET RESOURCES
McDougal Littell Literature Center at http://www.hmco.com/mcdougal/lit

For nearly a year, I sopped around the house, the Store, the school and the church, like an old biscuit, dirty and inedible. Then I met, or rather got to know, the lady who threw me my first life line.

Mrs. Bertha Flowers was the aristocrat of Black Stamps. She had the grace of control to appear warm in the coldest weather, and on the Arkansas summer days it seemed she had a private breeze which swirled around, cooling her. She was thin without the taut look of wiry people, and her printed voile dresses and flowered hats were as right for her as denim overalls for a farmer. She was our side's answer to the richest white woman in town.

Her skin was a rich black that would have peeled like a plum if snagged, but then no one would have thought of getting close enough to Mrs. Flowers to ruffle her dress, let alone snag her skin. She didn't encourage familiarity. She wore gloves too.

I don't think I ever saw Mrs. Flowers laugh, but she smiled often. A slow widening of her thin black lips to show even, small white teeth, then the slow, effortless closing. When she chose to smile on me, I always wanted to thank her. The action was so graceful and inclusively benign.[1]

She was one of the few gentlewomen I have ever known, and has remained throughout my life the measure of what a human being can be.

Momma had a strange relationship with her. Most often when she passed on the road in front of the Store, she spoke to Momma in that soft yet carrying voice, "Good day, Mrs. Henderson." Momma responded with "How you, Sister Flowers?"

Mrs. Flowers didn't belong to our church, nor was she Momma's familiar.[2] Why on earth did she insist on calling her Sister Flowers? Shame made me want to hide my face. Mrs. Flowers deserved

from

I KNOW WHY THE CAGED BIRD SINGS

MAYA ANGELOU

---

1. **inclusively benign** (bĭ-nīn′): good-natured and kindly in a way that takes others in.
2. **familiar**: a close friend or associate.

> WORDS TO KNOW
> **aristocrat** (ə-rĭs′tə-krăt′) *n.* a person held in high standing for superior tastes and manners
> **familiarity** (fə-mĭl′yăr′ĭ-tē) *n.* behavior that implies a close friendship

53

WORDS TO KNOW

aristocrat (ə-rĭs′tə-krăt′) *n.* a person held in high standing for superior tastes and manners (p. 53)
aura (ôr′ə) *n.* the unique but undefinable atmosphere that surrounds a person, an object, or an event (p. 59)
cascading (kă-skā′dĭng) *v.* falling or flowing, like a waterfall (p. 59)
essence (ĕs′əns) *n.* the basic or most important quality (p. 59)
familiarity (fə-mĭl′yăr′ĭ-tē) *n.* behavior that implies a close friendship (p. 53)
illiteracy (ĭ-lĭt′ər-ə-sē) *n.* a lack of ability to read and write (p. 58)
incessantly (ĭn-sĕs′ənt-lē) *adv.* continuously; nonstop (p. 55)
infuse (ĭn-fyōōz′) *v.* to inject; add to (p. 57)
sacrilegious (săk′rə-lĭj′əs) *adj.* disrespectful toward a sacred person, place, or thing (p. 55)
sophistication (sə-fĭs′tĭ-kā′shən) *n.* the state of being experienced; maturity (p. 59)

CUSTOMIZING FOR
Gifted and Talented Students

Ask students to look at the title of Angelou's autobiography, and invite them to speculate on what it means. Have them look for ways to interpret the excerpt in relation to this title. Ask, "Who might 'the caged bird' be? How is he or she caged?"

Art Note

Portrait of Dorothy Porter, Librarian by James A. Porter James A. Porter (1905–1971), born in Baltimore, was the first African-American art historian. He is noted for creating haunting portraits that revealed the inner life of his subjects. Dorothy Porter (1905–), the subject of this portrait, is responsible for building, at Howard University, one of the world's largest holdings of materials on the history and culture of people of African descent.

Reading the Art *Does this picture fit your image of what Mrs. Flowers may have looked like? What details do you think suggest that Dorothy Porter was refined or dignified?*

Portrait of Dorothy Porter, Librarian (1952), James Porter. Oil on canvas, National Portrait Gallery, Smithsonian Institution/Art Resource, New York.

54   UNIT ONE   PART 1: GROWING PAINS

Mini-Lesson Grammar

Singular Indefinite Pronouns

another	either	nobody
anybody	everybody	no one
anyone	everyone	one
anything	everything	somebody
each	neither	someone

INDEFINITE PRONOUNS AS SUBJECTS
Tell students that an indefinite pronoun does not refer to a specific person or thing. To make a verb agree with an indefinite pronoun that is used as a subject, first determine whether the pronoun is singular or plural. Some singular indefinite pronouns include *anybody, anything, each, either, neither, everyone, nobody, one, someone,* and *something*. As an example, point out the clause highlighted on page 55: "neither of the women was in the least shaken." Ask students what is the subject. (*neither* is the subject)

Application Have students choose the correct verb for each of these sentences.
1. Each of the books Mrs. Flowers lent Marguerite (was/were) precious. *(was)*
2. No one else Marguerite knew (was/were) as educated and refined as Mrs. Flowers. *(was)*

Reteaching/Reinforcement
- *Grammar Handbook*, anthology p. 943
- *Grammar Mini-Lessons* copymasters p. 19, transparencies p. 13

The Writer's Craft

Indefinate Pronouns, pp. 561, 706–707

54   THE LANGUAGE OF LITERATURE   TEACHER'S EDITION

better than to be called Sister. Then, Momma left out the verb. Why not ask, "How *are* you, *Mrs.* Flowers?" With the unbalanced passion of the young, I hated her for showing her ignorance to Mrs. Flowers. It didn't occur to me for many years that they were as alike as sisters, separated only by formal education.

Although I was upset, neither of the women was in the least shaken by what I thought an unceremonious greeting. Mrs. Flowers would continue her easy gait up the hill to her little bungalow,[3] and Momma kept on shelling peas or doing whatever had brought her to the front porch.

Occasionally, though, Mrs. Flowers would drift off the road and down to the Store and Momma would say to me, "Sister, you go on and play." As I left I would hear the beginning of an intimate conversation. Momma persistently using the wrong verb, or none at all.

"Brother and Sister Wilcox is sho'ly the meanest—" "Is," Momma? "Is"? Oh, please, not "is," Momma, for two or more. But they talked, and from the side of the building where I waited for the ground to open up and swallow me, I heard the soft-voiced Mrs. Flowers and the textured voice of my grandmother merging and melting. They were interrupted from time to time by giggles that must have come from Mrs. Flowers (Momma never giggled in her life). Then she was gone.

She appealed to me because she was like people I had never met personally. Like women in English novels who walked the moors[4] (whatever they were) with their loyal dogs racing at a respectful distance. Like the women who sat in front of roaring fireplaces, drinking tea incessantly from silver trays full of scones and crumpets.[5] Women who walked over the "heath"[6] and read morocco-bound[7] books and had two last names divided by a hyphen. It would be safe to say that she made me proud to be Negro, just by being herself.

She acted just as refined as whitefolks in the movies and books and she was more beautiful, for none of them could have come near that warm color without looking gray by comparison.

It was fortunate that I never saw her in the company of powhitefolks. For since they tend to think of their whiteness as an evenizer, I'm certain that I would have had to hear her spoken to commonly as Bertha, and my image of her would have been shattered like the unmendable Humpty-Dumpty.

One summer afternoon, sweet-milk fresh in my memory, she stopped at the Store to buy provisions. Another Negro woman of her health and age would have been expected to carry the paper sacks home in one hand, but Momma said, "Sister Flowers, I'll send Bailey up to your house with these things."

She smiled that slow dragging smile, "Thank you, Mrs. Henderson. I'd prefer Marguerite, though." My name was beautiful when she said it. "I've been meaning to talk to her, anyway." They gave each other age-group looks.

Momma said, "Well, that's all right then. Sister, go and change your dress. You going to Sister Flowers's."

The chifforobe[8] was a maze. What on earth did one put on to go to Mrs. Flowers's house? I knew I shouldn't put on a Sunday dress. It might be sacrilegious. Certainly not a house

---

3. **bungalow** (bŭng'gə-lō): a small, one-story house or cottage.
4. **moors:** broad areas of open land with patches of low shrubs and marshes.
5. **scones** (skōnz) **and crumpets** (krŭm'pĭts): Scones are small, sweet biscuits; crumpets are rolls similar to English muffins.
6. **heath** (hēth): a moor.
7. **morocco-bound** (mə-rŏk'ō): bound, or covered, in soft leather.
8. **chifforobe** (shĭf'ə-rōb'): a chest of drawers combined with a small closet for storing clothes.

WORDS TO KNOW
incessantly (ĭn-sĕs'ənt-lē) *adv.* continuously; nonstop
sacrilegious (săk'rə-lĭj'əs) *adj.* disrespectful toward a sacred person, place, or thing

---

Critical Thinking: MAKING INFERENCES

C Ask students why they think Marguerite cared so much about how her grandmother talked to Mrs. Flowers. (*Possible responses: She was ashamed of her grandmother's uneducated speech; she wanted her family to make a good impression on Mrs. Flowers.*)

Literary Concept: SIMILE

D Ask what qualities students think Angelou means to attribute to Mrs. Flowers by comparing her to "women in English novels." (*Possible responses: civilized behavior, refinement*) Also ask what the comparison shows about Marguerite. (*She reads a lot, especially books about faraway places different from Arkansas.*)

Linking to Social Studies

E The "powhitefolks" referred to are white people who were poor and uneducated. In the social structure of the South at the time Angelou describes, such people were despised by richer, better-educated white people; however, the poor white people considered themselves superior to blacks of all economic and social levels.

CUSTOMIZING FOR Students Acquiring English

 The nursery rhyme "Humpty-Dumpty" may not be familiar to students from other cultures. Ask a volunteer to recite the rhyme. Focus students' attention on the final lines, "All the king's horses and all the king's men/ Couldn't put Humpty together again."

Mini-Lesson — Literary Concepts

REVIEWING SIMILE Remind students that a simile is a figure of speech that compares two things by using the word *like* or *as*. Writers use similes to intensify emotional responses, to create vivid images, and to help the reader look at a familiar object in a new way.

Application Help students interpret the similes Angelou uses to describe Mrs. Flowers and Marguerite. For example, have them review the similes "like an old biscuit" and "would have peeled like a plum," annotated on page 53, and the similes "like women in English novels" and "shattered like the unmendable Humpty-Dumpty" on this page. Then ask them to create a new simile for one of these examples.

Critical Thinking:
MAKING JUDGMENTS

F Have students evaluate Momma's treatment of Marguerite in this passage. *(Possible responses: Some might think Momma's treatment of Marguerite is insensitive. Others might say that Momma sees Marguerite as a young child with no need for privacy.)*

Cultural Note

G Make sure students understand that "the Good Book" is a colloquial term for the Bible. Help them interpret the biblical quotation "Pride goeth before a fall." *(People with excessive pride are often humiliated in the end.)*

CUSTOMIZING FOR
Students Acquiring English

3 Explain the phrase *kill me stone dead* as indicating Marguerite's embarrassment. Then ask students to provide colloquial expressions for embarrassment in their native languages.

STRATEGIC READING FOR
Less-Proficient Readers

H Ask students the following questions:

- Why does Marguerite admire Mrs. Flowers? *(because she is educated and refined)* **Summarizing**

- What is unusual about Marguerite? *(Possible response: Although she does well in school and reads a great deal, she does not speak.)* **Clarifying**

Set a Purpose Have students read on to find out why this visit with Mrs. Flowers is a turning point in Marguerite's life.

Critical Thinking: ANALYZING

I Ask students to analyze and evaluate Mrs. Flowers's method of trying to persuade Angelou to speak. *(Possible response: She does not force her, but uses the fact that language is important to Angelou. Also she treats her more like an adult. Most will probably think her method is effective.)*

---

dress, since I was already wearing a fresh one. I chose a school dress, naturally. It was formal without suggesting that going to Mrs. Flowers's house was equivalent to attending church.

I trusted myself back into the Store.

"Now, don't you look nice." I had chosen the right thing, for once.

"Mrs. Henderson, you make most of the children's clothes, don't you?"

"Yes, ma'am. Sure do. Store-bought clothes ain't hardly worth the thread it take to stitch them."

"I'll say you do a lovely job, though, so neat. That dress looks professional."

Momma was enjoying the seldom-received compliments. Since everyone we knew (except Mrs. Flowers, of course) could sew competently, praise was rarely handed out for the commonly practiced craft.

"I try, with the help of the Lord, Sister Flowers, to finish the inside just like I does the outside. Come here, Sister."

I had buttoned up the collar and tied the belt, apronlike, in back. Momma told me to turn around. With one hand she pulled the strings and the belt fell free at both sides of my waist. Then her large hands were at my neck, opening the button loops. I was terrified. What was happening?

"Take it off, Sister." She had her hands on the hem of the dress.

"I don't need to see the inside, Mrs. Henderson, I can tell . . ." But the dress was over my head and my arms were stuck in the sleeves. Momma said, "That'll do. See here, Sister Flowers, I French-seams around the armholes." Through the cloth film, I saw the shadow approach. "That makes it last longer. Children these days would bust out of sheet-metal clothes. They so rough."

"That is a very good job, Mrs. Henderson. You should be proud. You can put your dress back on, Marguerite."

"No ma'am. Pride is a sin. And 'cording to the Good Book, it goeth before a fall."

"That's right. So the Bible says. It's a good thing to keep in mind."

I wouldn't look at either of them. Momma hadn't thought that taking off my dress in front of Mrs. Flowers would kill me stone dead. If I had refused, she would have thought I was trying to be "womanish." Mrs. Flowers had known that I would be embarrassed and that was even worse. I picked up the groceries and went out to wait in the hot sunshine. It would be fitting if I got a sunstroke and died before they came outside. Just dropped dead on the slanting porch.

There was a little path beside the rocky road, and Mrs. Flowers walked in front swinging her arms and picking her way over the stones.

She said, without turning her head, to me, "I hear you're doing very good school work, Marguerite, but that it's all written. The teachers report that they have trouble getting you to talk in class." We passed the triangular farm on our left, and the path widened to allow us to walk together. I hung back in the separate unasked and unanswerable questions.

"Come and walk along with me, Marguerite." I couldn't have refused even if I wanted to. She pronounced my name so nicely. Or more correctly, she spoke each word with such clarity that I was certain a foreigner who didn't understand English could have understood her.

"Now no one is going to make you talk—possibly no one can. But bear in mind, language is man's way of communicating with his fellow man, and it is language alone which separates him from the lower animals." That was a totally new idea to me, and I would need time to think about it.

56 UNIT ONE PART 1: GROWING PAINS

Mini-Lesson The Writer's Style

VARIETIES OF LANGUAGE Tell students that Angelou uses the contrast between the ways Momma—highlighted in the column on the left—and Mrs. Flowers—highlighted in the column on the right— speak to help us understand Marguerite's feelings for Mrs. Flowers. Momma speaks in a dialect common to uneducated Southerners of her time that does not follow the rules of standard English. It also includes imaginative phrases, such as "would bust out of sheet-metal clothes." Mrs. Flowers, on the other hand, speaks standard English. Her language is also more formal and abstract.

Application Have students think of two people they know who use different varieties of English. Have them write a short conversation between these people, using language that reflects how each talks.

Reteaching/Reinforcement

- Writing Handbook, anthology p. 876
- *Writing Mini-Lessons* transparencies, p. 44

 The Writer's Craft

Varieties of Language, pp. 409–410

Back Street (1983), LaVere Hutchings. Watercolor, 11" × 15", collection of the artist.

"Your grandmother says you read a lot. Every chance you get. That's good, but not good enough. Words mean more than what is set down on paper. It takes the human voice to infuse them with the shades of deeper meaning."

I memorized the part about the human voice infusing words. It seemed so valid and poetic.

She said she was going to give me some books and that I not only must read them, I must read them aloud. She suggested that I try to make a sentence sound in as many different ways as possible.

"I'll accept no excuse if you return a book to me that has been badly handled." My imagination boggled at the punishment I would deserve if in fact I did abuse a book of Mrs. Flowers's. Death would be too kind and brief.

The odors in the house surprised me. Somehow I had never connected Mrs. Flowers with food or eating or any other common experience of common people. There must have been an outhouse, too, but my mind never recorded it.

The sweet scent of vanilla had met us as she opened the door.

"I made tea cookies this morning. You see, I had planned to invite you for cookies and lemonade so we could have this little chat. The lemonade is in the icebox."

WORDS TO KNOW   **infuse** (ĭn-fyo͞oz′) *v.* to inject; add to

Literary Concept: PERSONIFICATION

L Ask students what human actions Angelou attributes to objects in Mrs. Flowers's house. *(Photos "leered" and "threatened," curtains "pushed against themselves.")* Then ask what these comparisons suggest about how Marguerite felt in the house. *(Possible responses: She felt intimidated by the beautiful, expensive objects; she was nervous.)*

Critical Thinking: ANALYZING

M Ask students why they think Marguerite considered Mrs. Flowers's cookies so special. *(Possible responses: Mrs. Flowers made them just for Marguerite. Marguerite thought that Mrs. Flowers was above cooking.)*

Critical Thinking: SUMMARIZING

N Have students summarize Mrs. Flowers's opinions about education and intelligence. *(Possible response: She believes that people without formal education can sometimes be wiser and more intelligent than educated people.)*

READING STRATEGIES FOR Less-Proficient Readers

O What lesson does Mrs. Flowers teach Marguerite about ignorance, illiteracy, and mother wit? *(Possible response: to be intolerant of ignorance but understanding of illiteracy; to respect mother wit)* Literal Recall

---

It followed that Mrs. Flowers would have ice on an ordinary day, when most families in our town bought ice late on Saturdays only a few times during the summer to be used in the wooden ice-cream freezers.

She took the bags from me and disappeared through the kitchen door. I looked around the room that I had never in my wildest fantasies imagined I would see. Browned photographs leered or threatened from the walls, and the white, freshly done curtains pushed against themselves and against the wind. I wanted to gobble up the room entire and take it to Bailey, who would help me analyze and enjoy it.

"Have a seat, Marguerite. Over there by the table." She carried a platter covered with a tea towel. Although she warned that she hadn't tried her hand at baking sweets for some time, I was certain that like everything else about her the cookies would be perfect.

They were flat, round wafers, slightly browned on the edges and butter-yellow in the center. With the cold lemonade they were sufficient for childhood's lifelong diet. Remembering my manners, I took nice little lady-like bites off the edges. She said she had made them expressly for me and that she had a few in the kitchen that I could take home to my brother. So I jammed one whole cake in my mouth, and the rough crumbs scratched the insides of my jaws, and if I hadn't had to swallow, it would have been a dream come true.

As I ate she began the first of what we later called "my lessons in living." She said that I must always be intolerant of ignorance but understanding of illiteracy. That some people, unable to go to school, were more educated and even more intelligent than college professors. She encouraged me to listen carefully to what country people called mother wit. That in those homely sayings was couched the collective wisdom of generations.

When I finished the cookies she brushed off the table and brought a thick, small book from the bookcase. I had read *A Tale of Two Cities* and found it up to my standards as a romantic novel. She opened the first page and I heard poetry for the first time in my life.

"It was the best of times and the worst of times . . ."⁹ Her voice slid in and curved down through and over the words. She was nearly singing. I wanted to look at the pages. Were they

> *S*ome people, unable to go to school, were more educated and even more intelligent than college professors.

---

9. **"It was . . . worst of times . . .":** This opening sentence of Charles Dickens's novel *A Tale of Two Cities* is famous for its apparent contradictions. The novel is set in Paris and London during the French Revolution (1789–1799).

WORDS TO KNOW
illiteracy (ĭ-lĭt′ər-ə-sē) *n.* a lack of ability to read and write

---

Critic's Corner

"[She] writes like a song, and like the truth. The wisdom, rue and humor of her storytelling are borne on a lilting rhythm completely her own, the product of a born writer's senses nourished on black church singing and preaching, soft mother talk and salty street talk, and on literature."

Annie Gottlieb
New York Times Book Review

Ask students to find examples of these influences in this excerpt.

the same that I had read? Or were there notes, music, lined on the pages, as in a hymn book? Her sounds began cascading gently. I knew from listening to a thousand preachers that she was nearing the end of her reading, and I hadn't really heard, heard to understand, a single word.

"How do you like that?"

It occurred to me that she expected a response. The sweet vanilla flavor was still on my tongue, and her reading was a wonder in my ears. I had to speak.

I said, "Yes, ma'am." It was the least I could do, but it was the most also.

"There's one more thing. Take this book of poems and memorize one for me. Next time you pay me a visit, I want you to recite."

I have tried often to search behind the sophistication of years for the enchantment I so easily found in those gifts. The essence escapes but its aura remains. To be allowed, no, invited, into the private lives of strangers, and to share their joys and fears, was a chance to exchange the Southern bitter wormwood for a cup of mead with Beowulf or a hot cup of tea and milk with Oliver Twist.[10] When I said aloud, "It is a far, far better thing that I do, than I have ever done . . ."[11] tears of love filled my eyes at my selflessness.

On that first day, I ran down the hill and into the road (few cars ever came along it) and had the good sense to stop running before I reached the Store.

I was liked, and what a difference it made. I was respected not as Mrs. Henderson's grandchild or Bailey's sister but for just being Marguerite Johnson.

Childhood's logic never asks to be proved (all conclusions are absolute). I didn't question why Mrs. Flowers had singled me out for attention, nor did it occur to me that Momma might have asked her to give me a little talking to. All I cared about was that she had made tea cookies for *me* and read to *me* from her favorite book. It was enough to prove that she liked me. ❖

10. **a chance to exchange . . . with Oliver Twist:** Angelou here compares her existence as a black child in the bigoted South to wormwood, a bitter herb. She hopes to escape this bitterness by turning instead to mead, a sweet drink, or tea with milk, common beverages to such characters as Beowulf and Oliver Twist from English literature.

11. **"It is a far . . . have ever done . . .":** a quotation from the very end of *A Tale of Two Cities*. It is spoken by a man who nobly sacrifices his own life to save that of another.

INSIGHT

Eve Merriam

Morning is
a new sheet of paper
for you to write on.

Whatever you want to say,
5   all day,
until night
folds it up
and files it away.

The bright words and the dark words
10 are gone
until dawn
and a new day
to write on.

WORDS TO KNOW

cascading (kă-skā'dĭng) *v.* falling or flowing, like a waterfall
sophistication (sə-fĭs'tĭ-kā'shən) *n.* the state of being experienced; maturity
essence (ĕs'əns) *n.* the basic or most important quality
aura (ôr'ə) *n.* the unique but undefinable atmosphere that surrounds a person, an object, or an event

From Personal Response to Critical Analysis

1. Accept all reasonable responses.
2. Possible responses: Marguerite admires Mrs. Flowers because she is educated, well spoken, and refined; she loves Mrs. Flowers's cultivated voice and manners because they represent a better world than Marguerite's own.
3. Possible responses: She lends her books and gives her special treats to eat and personal attention; she enables her to overcome her traumatic past and speak again; she makes her aware of the emotional power of the spoken word.
4. Some students will say that Mrs. Flowers acts primarily out of friendship to Momma; others may say she feels an obligation to help those less fortunate than herself; still others may say that she recognizes a special intelligence in Marguerite.
5. Accept all reasonable responses.

Another Pathway

Cooperative Learning The number of students in each group will depend on whether students choose a scene with just Marguerite and Mrs. Flowers or one that also includes Momma. In addition to a narrator, students might also appoint a director to help them critique their performances.

Rubric

3 Full Accomplishment Students choose a dramatic scene, divide up dialogue and narration appropriately, and use tone of voice, facial expression, and body movements to characterize the speakers.

2 Substantial Accomplishment Students choose a dramatic scene and successfully divide up dialogue and narration. However, their reading fails to capture the characters.

1 Little or Partial Accomplishment Students are confused about how to convert the narrative into a dramatic skit and simply read the story.

RESPONDING OPTIONS

FROM PERSONAL RESPONSE TO CRITICAL ANALYSIS

REFLECT 1. What do you think of Marguerite's admiration for Mrs. Flowers? Jot down your thoughts in your notebook and share them in class.

RETHINK 2. Why do you think Marguerite admires Mrs. Flowers so much?

Thematic Link 3. In what ways does Mrs. Flowers help young Marguerite? Think about the obvious gifts that Mrs. Flowers offers, and less obvious ones.

4. What do you think motivates Mrs. Flowers to help Marguerite?

Consider
- Mrs. Flowers's social and economic position in Black Stamps
- her relationship with Momma
- Marguerite's performance in school
- what Mrs. Flowers might gain from the relationship

Close Textual Reading

RELATE 5. Angelou is embarrassed by her grandmother's common way of speaking. Are people judged by the level of language they use? Do you think that a person's manner of speaking reflects his or her intelligence and worth?

Multimodal Learning
ANOTHER PATHWAY
Cooperative Learning
In a small group, choose a passage from the selection to dramatize in a skit. Besides actors to portray Marguerite and other characters, you might include a narrator to read descriptive passages. Then perform your skit for the class and compare your interpretation of the characters with that of other groups.

LITERARY CONCEPTS

The title *I Know Why the Caged Bird Sings* is an allusion to the poem "Sympathy" by the African-American writer Paul Laurence Dunbar (1872–1906). The last stanza reads:

> I know why the caged bird sings, ah me,
>   When his wing is bruised and his bosom sore,—
> When he beats his bars and he would be free;
> It is not a carol of joy or glee,
>   But a prayer that he sends from his heart's deep core,
>   But a plea, that upward to Heaven he flings—
> I know why the caged bird sings!

An **allusion** is a reference to another literary work or to a famous person, place, or event. How is Marguerite's experience in this excerpt similar to the caged bird in Dunbar's poem?

QUICKWRITES

1. Imagine that young Marguerite and Mrs. Flowers have just read the Insight poem "Metaphor." Draft a **dialogue** in which they discuss its meaning.

2. Draft a **character sketch** of the person whose name you chose for the cluster diagram in the Personal Connection activity. If you are using a computer, you might want to run the Spell Check feature now.

📁 **PORTFOLIO** Save your writing. You may want to use it later as a springboard to a piece for your portfolio.

60   UNIT ONE   PART 1: GROWING PAINS

Literary Concepts

To help students understand the allusion to the poem, read the last stanza for them, using your tone of voice to convey the desperation the speaker of the poem feels. Tell them that Angelou was bruised by abuse in her childhood, like the bird in the cage of the poem. She is also caged in by a self-imposed silence and the social divisions of Stamps. Ask the students what she might have prayed or wished for and in what sense Mrs. Flowers was an answer to her prayers.

QuickWrites

1. Before students begin writing, have them number the traits in their cluster diagram from 1 to 5, with 1 being the most important trait and 5 being the least important. Encourage them to describe the most important trait in either the first paragraph or the last.

2. Before they write, encourage students to imagine a context in which the poem comes to the attention of Marguerite and Mrs. Flowers. Who found the poem?

Using Dialogues in Plays and Skits, p. 436

Multimodal Learning

ALTERNATIVE ACTIVITIES

Angelou compares Mrs. Flowers's reading voice to music. Choose an excerpt from one of the literary works mentioned in this selection or from any literary work you like. To prepare the work for **oral interpretation,** practice reading the excerpt aloud, pausing after each unit of thought. Change the pitch, volume, and tone of your voice until you feel comfortable with the material. Then present the excerpt to your class.

Multimodal Learning

ACROSS THE CURRICULUM

Performing Arts Create a monologue in which Mrs. Flowers presents her version of the events in this excerpt. Find clues in the story as to how Mrs. Flowers moves, speaks, and dresses. Perform your monologue for the class.

WORDS TO KNOW

Review the Words to Know at the bottom of the selection pages. Complete the analogies below by first determining the relationship between the first pair of words and then deciding which vocabulary word best completes the second analogy. Write the word on your paper.

1. *Glow* is to *radiance* as _____ is to *atmosphere*.
2. *Beauty* is to *ugliness* as _____ is to *inexperience*.
3. *Drifting* is to *snow* as _____ is to *water*.
4. *Disease* is to *medicine* as _____ is to *education*.
5. *Democrat* is to *democracy* as _____ is to *aristocracy*.
6. *Toxic* is to *environment* as _____ is to *religion*.
7. *Quickly* is to *slowly* as _____ is to *occasionally*.
8. *Affection* is to *love* as _____ is to *know*.
9. *Care* is to *careful* as _____ is to *essential*.
10. *Help* is to *assist* as _____ is to *inject*.

MAYA ANGELOU

1928–

Born Marguerite Johnson, Maya Angelou acquired her first name from her brother's habit of addressing her as "Mya Sister." Although Angelou's formal education ended after high school, she continued to search for knowledge of herself and the world around her. Her talent in the performing arts led to a scholarship to study in New York City, and she soon made her mark as a dancer, an actress, a singer, a director, and a producer both in the United States and abroad.

Angelou, who speaks six languages, began writing in the mid-1960s. Her many publications include five autobiographical books, the first and most famous being *I Know Why the Caged Bird Sings*. Regarding her writing process, Angelou spoke in a 1990 interview in *Contemporary Literary Criticism* about trying "to pull the language into such a sharpness that it jumps off the page. It must look easy, but it takes me forever to get it to look so easy. Of course, there are those critics . . . who say, 'Well, Maya Angelou has a new book out and, of course, it's good but then she's a natural writer.' Those are the ones I want to grab by the throat and wrestle to the floor because it takes me forever to get it to sing. I work at the language."

President Bill Clinton chose Angelou to compose and read a poem for his inauguration in 1993, the first poet so honored since 1961 when Robert Frost recited a poem at John F. Kennedy's inauguration.

OTHER WORKS *Gather Together in My Name, Singin' and Swingin' and Gettin' Merry Like Christmas, The Heart of a Woman, All God's Children Need Traveling Shoes, The Complete Collected Poems of Maya Angelou*

Extended Reading

Literary Links

Discuss how both Maya Angelou and the narrator of *American History* grew up in settings that presented special challenges to gifted but poor young women.

Words to Know

1. aura
2. sophistication
3. cascading
4. illiteracy
5. aristocrat
6. sacrilegious
7. incessantly
8. familiarity
9. essence
10. infuse

Reteaching/Reinforcement
• *Unit One Resource Book*, p. 20

MAYA ANGELOU

Angelou said in an interview: "I don't tell everything I know, but what I do tell is the truth. There's a world of difference between truth and facts. Facts can obscure the truth. You can tell so many facts that you fill the stage but haven't got one iota of the truth." Ask students to discuss the difference between the truth and facts.

Alternative Activities

Famous novels with dramatic openings that lend themselves to oral interpretation include *The War of the Worlds* by H. G. Wells, and *The Hound of the Baskervilles* by Sir Arthur Conan Doyle.

Across the Curriculum

Performing Arts Students might work in pairs to write the monologue, with one coaching the other's final performance. Before they write, have them consider how Mrs. Flowers might see her role in the community, why she might decide to help Marguerite (see question 4 on page 60), and how she feels at important moments described in the selection.

REFLECTING ON THEME
What Do You Think?

Have students think about the obstacle course they designed at the beginning of Part One. Ask where in the obstacle course they would place this pitfall that befell Angelou. Reflect on how Mrs. Flowers was able to help Angelou over this obstacle.

OVERVIEW

Objectives

- To understand and appreciate a classic autobiographical essay that recounts a young boy's celebration of Christmas
- To enrich reading by using active reading strategies
- To identify and understand symbolism
- To appreciate and write sensory descriptions
- To express understanding of a selection through a choice of writing forms, including a letter, an epitaph, and a personal narrative
- To extend understanding of the story through a variety of multimodal and cross-curricular activities

Skills

READING SKILLS/STRATEGIES
- Connecting

THE WRITER'S STYLE
- Show, don't tell

GRAMMAR
- Personal pronouns

LITERARY CONCEPTS
- Symbolism
- Characterization

GENRE STUDY
- Nonfiction: autobiographical essay

ALTERNATIVE
Previewing

Students can choose partners and use the following prompts to preview "A Christmas Memory" orally.

Personal Connection

Discussion Prompts *Think of the most memorable holiday celebration you ever participated in. In as much detail as possible, describe it to your partner. Then listen as your partner describes his or her holiday. If you need help getting started, the following questions might help:*

- *Where were you?*
- *Who else was there?*
- *What (or why) were you celebrating?*
- *With which of your five senses is that memory most associated?*

As you read "A Christmas Memory," notice the details that Truman Capote remembers about a long-ago holiday.

VISUAL VOCABULARY
- Victrola (vĭk-trō′lə)
- rime (rīm)
- japonica bush (jə-pŏn′ĭ-kə bŏŏsh)
- stereopticon (stĕr′ē-ŏp′tĭ-

Side A, Frame 49224

PREVIEWING

NONFICTION

A Christmas Memory
Truman Capote (kə-pō′tē)

Activating Prior Knowledge
PERSONAL CONNECTION

Think of a particular holiday that made a lasting impression on you. What kinds of activities—accompanied by special sights, sounds, smells, tastes, and sensations—made the holiday memorable? In your notebook, jot down in a chart some activities from that memorable holiday. Use the five senses as headings for the chart. As you read Truman Capote's personal narrative, notice the details that he found memorable in recalling a Christmas from his childhood.

Holiday Activities	
Sight	
Smell	
Hearing	
Taste	
Touch	

Building Background
BIOGRAPHICAL CONNECTION

Truman Capote grew up in the rural South during the Great Depression of the 1930s, a time of poverty and hardship for many Americans. His mother had sent him off to be raised by relatives in a small Alabama town. There he developed a close relationship with a much older female cousin, Sook Faulk, referred to as "my friend" in this selection. Narrating their story more than 20 years later, Capote details a lasting impression of Sook Faulk, creating a Christmas season representing the many experiences he had over the years with his elderly cousin.

Truman Capote with his cousin.
Truman Capote Papers, Rare Books and Manuscripts Division, The New York Public Library, Astor, Lenox and Tilden Foundations.

Active Reading
READING CONNECTION

Using a Reading Log The reading strategies introduced on page 5 showed the kinds of connections active readers make when they read. To help you practice some of those strategies, questions have been inserted periodically throughout "A Christmas Memory." Record your responses to each of the questions in your reading log. Also record other thoughts and feelings that come to you, especially those that recall your holiday memories. After you have finished reading, discuss some of your responses with your classmates.

• VISUAL VOCABULARY

62 UNIT ONE PART 1: GROWING PAINS

PRINT AND MEDIA RESOURCES

UNIT ONE RESOURCE BOOK
Strategic Reading: Literature, p. 23
Vocabulary SkillBuilder, p. 24

GRAMMAR MINI–LESSONS
Transparencies, p. 12
Copymasters, p. 16

WRITING MINI–LESSONS
Transparencies, p. 54

ACCESS FOR STUDENTS ACQUIRING ENGLISH
Selection Summaries
Reading Support

FORMAL ASSESSMENT
Selection Test, pp. 13–14
 Test Generator

 AUDIO LIBRARY
See Reference Card

 LASERLINKS
Visual Vocabulary
Literacy Connection
Art Gallery

INTERNET RESOURCES
McDougal Littell Literature Center at http://www.hmco.com/mcdougal/lit

62 THE LANGUAGE OF LITERATURE TEACHER'S EDITION

Imagine a morning in late November. A coming of winter morning more than twenty years ago.

A Christmas Memory

Truman Capote

Consider the kitchen of a spreading old house in a country town. A great black stove is its main feature; but there is also a big round table and a fireplace with two rocking chairs

A CHRISTMAS MEMORY   63

SUMMARY

Truman Capote uses the rituals of Christmas to capture the warm relationship that existed between him and an elderly woman who was his distant cousin. Capote refers to her as "my friend"; she calls him "Buddy." Seven-year-old Buddy and his friend together make Christmas fruitcakes. They send the fruitcakes to friends and people who interest them, such as President Franklin Roosevelt. Then they get a tree and decorate it with homemade ornaments, make gifts for family and friends, and build kites for each other. On Christmas Day, they open their presents and fly their new kites. Sadly, however, this proves to be their last Christmas together because Buddy is sent to military school and his friend dies a few years later.

Thematic Link: *Growing Pains* The bittersweet memories of a Christmas past become a significant part of Capote's growing up.

CUSTOMIZING FOR
Students Acquiring English

- Use **ACCESS FOR STUDENTS ACQUIRING ENGLISH,** *Reading Support.*
- This selection may prove difficult because of specifically American customs such as the Christmas tree (traditional in many countries, but not in others), Christmas fruitcake, kites, fundraising, and football.
- As you guide students through the selection, you may want to use the suggestions in these boxes as well as the suggestions under Strategic Reading for Less-Proficient Readers.

STRATEGIC READING FOR
Less-Proficient Readers

Set a Purpose To help students become immersed in the selection, have them draw or sketch the scene that Capote describes in the first two paragraphs. Then ask them to read to find out what the narrator and his cousin plan to do.

Use **UNIT ONE RESOURCE BOOK,** p. 23, for guidance in reading the selection.

WORDS TO KNOW

cavort (kə-vôrt′) *v.* to leap or romp about (p. 74)
conspiracy (kən-spîr′ə-sē) *n.* a joining or acting together in a secretive way, often with wrongful motives (p. 67)
exhilarate (ĭg-zĭl′ə-rāt′) *v.* to make merry or lively (p. 65)
garish (gâr′ĭsh) *adj.* too bright or gaudy (p. 68)
goad (gōd) *v.* to urge (p. 71)

inaugurate (ĭn-ô′gyə-rāt′) *v.* to make a formal beginning of (p. 65)
noncommittal (nŏn′kə-mĭt′l) *adj.* not revealing one's opinion or purpose (p. 71)
prosaic (prō-zā′ĭk) *adj.* dull; commonplace (p. 68)
sever (sĕv′ər) *v.* to cut off (p. 75)
squander (skwŏn′dər) *v.* to spend or use wastefully (p. 67)

THE LANGUAGE OF LITERATURE **TEACHER'S EDITION**   63

Art Note

Cook Stove by Hubert Shuptrine

Hubert Shuptrine (1936–), a native of Chattanooga, Tennessee, painted realistically to show part of a kitchen as it would have looked early in our century. By focusing on only a few objects, Shuptrine encourages the viewer to concentrate on the objects.

Reading the Art *Does the absence of people create a sense of warmth and coziness or of coldness and isolation? What other details add to this sense?*

CUSTOMIZING FOR
Gifted and Talented Students

As students read the selection, ask them to think about how family members other than Buddy and his cousin are depicted and to explain what these depictions might express.

Possible responses:

- Page 65—"Other people inhabit the house, relatives; and though they have power over us and frequently make us cry"/Other family members are insensitive.

- Page 66—"skinflint sums persons in the house occasionally provide"/Other family members are cheap or tight fisted.

- Page 69—"Enter: two relatives. Very angry"/Other family members are quick to blame.

- Page 74—"Those who Know Best decide that I belong in a military school"/Other family members ignore the loving relationship and separate the friends.

CUSTOMIZING FOR
Multiple Learning Styles

A **Spatial or Graphic Learners** Have students compare the art on this page with the description that Capote details in the first paragraph. Ask them to discuss how accurate the art is in depicting the scene.

64 THE LANGUAGE OF LITERATURE **TEACHER'S EDITION**

Cookstove (1986), Hubert Shuptrine. Copyright © 1986 by S. Hill Corporation. All rights reserved. Used with permission.

placed in front of it. Just today the fireplace commenced its seasonal roar.

A woman with shorn white hair is standing at the kitchen window. She is wearing tennis shoes and a shapeless gray sweater over a summery calico dress. She is small and sprightly, like a bantam hen; but, due to a long youthful illness, her shoulders are pitifully hunched. Her face is remarkable—not unlike Lincoln's, craggy like that, and tinted by sun and wind; but it is delicate too, finely boned, and her eyes are sherry-colored and timid. "Oh my," she exclaims, her breath smoking the windowpane, "it's fruitcake weather!"

The person to whom she is speaking is myself. I am seven; she is sixty-something. We are cousins, very distant ones, and we have lived together—well, as long as I can remember. Other people inhabit the house, relatives; and though they have power over us, and frequently make us cry, we are not, on the whole, too much aware of them. We are each other's best friend. She calls me Buddy, in memory of a boy who was formerly her best friend. The other Buddy died in the 1880's, when she was still a child. She is still a child.

"I knew it before I got out of bed," she says, turning away from the window with a purposeful excitement in her eyes. "The courthouse bell sounded so cold and clear. And there were no birds singing; they've gone to warmer country, yes indeed. Oh, Buddy, stop stuffing biscuit and fetch our buggy. Help me find my hat. We've thirty cakes to bake."

It's always the same: a morning arrives in November, and my friend, as though officially <u>inaugurating</u> the Christmas time of year that <u>exhilarates</u> her imagination and fuels the blaze of her heart, announces: "It's fruitcake weather! Fetch our buggy. Help me find my hat."

The hat is found, a straw cartwheel corsaged with velvet roses out-of-doors has faded: it once belonged to a more fashionable relative. Together, we guide our buggy, a dilapidated baby carriage, out to the garden and into a grove of pecan trees. The buggy is mine; that is, it was bought for me when I was born. It is made of wicker, rather unraveled, and the wheels wobble like a drunkard's legs. But it is a faithful object; springtimes, we take it to the woods and fill it with flowers, herbs, wild fern for our porch pots; in the summer, we pile it with picnic paraphernalia and sugar-cane fishing poles and roll it down to the edge of a creek; it has its winter uses, too: as a truck for hauling firewood from the yard to the kitchen, as a warm bed for Queenie, our tough little orange and white rat terrier who has survived distemper[1] and two rattlesnake bites. Queenie is trotting beside it now.

Three hours later we are back in the kitchen hulling a heaping buggyload of windfall pecans. Our backs hurt from gathering them: how hard they were to find (the main crop having been shaken off the trees and sold by the orchard's owners, who are not us) among the concealing leaves, the frosted, deceiving grass. Caaarackle! A cheery crunch, scraps of miniature thunder sound as the shells collapse and the golden mound of sweet oily ivory meat mounts in the milk-glass bowl. Queenie begs to taste, and now and again my friend sneaks her a mite, though insisting we deprive ourselves. "We mustn't, Buddy. If we start, we won't stop. And there's scarcely enough as there is. For thirty cakes." The kitchen is growing dark. Dusk turns the window into a mirror: our reflections mingle with the rising moon as we

---

1. **distemper:** an infectious viral disease of dogs.

WORDS TO KNOW
inaugurate (ĭn-ô′gyə-rāt′) *v.* to make a formal beginning of
exhilarate (ĭg-zĭl′ə-rāt′) *v.* to make merry or lively

65

Mini-Lesson Grammar

PERSONAL NOMINATIVE PRONOUNS
Point that a pronoun replaces a noun. Subject pronouns are used as subjects or as predicate nominatives to identify, rename, or explain a subject.

Subject	I read about Buddy and his cousin.
Predicate Nominative	The best of friends were they.

Application Invite students to find at least five nominative pronouns from the chart in the <u>highlighted</u> paragraph above. *(she, I, she, we, we, I, they, we)* Then read the following sentences aloud. Have students choose the correct pronoun forms.

1. Buddy and (she, her) enjoyed making fruitcakes each year. *(she)*
2. The person who attended military school must be (he, him). *(he)*
3. The people who cut the beautiful Christmas tree were (they, them). *(they)*

Reteaching/Reinforcement
- *Grammar Handbook,* anthology p. 943
- *Grammar Mini-Lessons* copymasters p. 16, transparencies, p. 12

📁 **The Writer's Craft**
Subject Complements, pp. 515–516
Personal Pronouns, pp. 552–555

Nominative Pronouns
Singular	Plural
I	we
you	you
he, she, it	they

work by the fireside in the firelight. At last, when the moon is quite high, we toss the final hull into the fire and, with joined sighs, watch it catch flame. The buggy is empty, the bowl is brimful.

We eat our supper (cold biscuits, bacon, blackberry jam) and discuss tomorrow. Tomorrow the kind of work I like best begins: buying. Cherries and citron, ginger and vanilla and canned Hawaiian pineapple, rinds and raisins and walnuts and whiskey and oh, so much flour, butter, so many eggs, spices, flavorings: why, we'll need a pony to pull the buggy home.

But before these purchases can be made, there is the question of money. Neither of us has any. Except for skinflint sums persons in the house occasionally provide (a dime is considered very big money); or what we earn ourselves from various activities: holding rummage sales, selling buckets of hand-picked blackberries, jars of homemade jam and apple jelly and peach preserves, rounding up flowers for funerals and weddings. Once we won seventy-ninth prize, five dollars, in a national football contest. Not that we know a fool thing about football. It's just that we enter any contest we hear about: at the moment our hopes are centered on the fifty-thousand-dollar Grand Prize being offered to name a new brand of coffee (we suggested

"A.M."; and, after some hesitation, for my friend thought it perhaps sacrilegious, the slogan "A.M.! Amen!"). To tell the truth, our only *really* profitable enterprise was the Fun and Freak Museum we conducted in a back-yard woodshed two summers ago. The Fun was a stereopticon[2] with slide views of Washington and New York lent us by a relative who had been to those places (she was furious when she discovered why we'd borrowed it); the Freak was a three-legged biddy chicken hatched by one of our own hens. Everybody hereabouts wanted to see that biddy: we charged grown-ups a nickel, kids two cents. And took in a good twenty dollars before the museum shut down due to the decease of the main attraction.

But one way and another we do each year accumulate Christmas savings, a Fruitcake Fund. These moneys we keep hidden in an ancient bead purse under a loose board under the floor under a chamber pot under my friend's bed. The purse is seldom removed from this safe location except to make a deposit or, as happens every Saturday, a withdrawal; for on Saturdays I am allowed ten cents to go to the picture show. My friend has never been

---

2. **stereopticon** (stĕr′ē-ŏp′tĭ-kŏn): an early slide projector that could merge two images of the same scene on a screen, resulting in a 3-D effect.

> To tell the truth, our only *really* profitable enterprise was the Fun and Freak Museum we conducted in a back-yard woodshed two summers ago.

to a picture show, nor does she intend to: "I'd rather hear you tell the story, Buddy. That way I can imagine it more. Besides, a person my age shouldn't squander their eyes. When the Lord comes, let me see him clear." In addition to never having seen a movie, she has never: eaten in a restaurant, traveled more than five miles from home, received or sent a telegram, read anything except funny papers and the Bible, worn cosmetics, cursed, wished someone harm, told a lie on purpose, let a hungry dog go hungry. Here are a few things she has done, does do: killed with a hoe the biggest rattlesnake ever seen in this county (sixteen rattles), dip snuff[3] (secretly), tame hummingbirds (just try it) till they balance on her finger, tell ghost stories (we both believe in ghosts) so tingling they chill you in July, talk to herself, take walks in the rain, grow the prettiest japonicas[4] in town, know the recipe for every sort of old-time Indian cure, including a magical wart remover.

Now, with supper finished, we retire to the room in a faraway part of the house where my friend sleeps in a scrap-quilt-covered iron bed painted rose pink, her favorite color. Silently, wallowing in the pleasures of conspiracy, we take the bead purse from its secret place and spill its contents on the scrap quilt. Dollar bills, tightly rolled and green as May buds. Somber fifty-cent pieces, heavy enough to weight a dead man's eyes.[5] Lovely

QUESTION
What questions or thoughts do you have about the characters and situation so far?
Using a Reading Log

---

3. **dip snuff:** to rub (dip) a finely ground tobacco (snuff) on one's teeth and gums.
4. **japonica** (jə-pŏn'ĭ-kə): an ornamental bush with red flowers.
5. **heavy enough to weight a dead man's eyes:** from the custom of putting coins on the closed eyes of corpses to keep the eyelids from opening.

WORDS TO KNOW
squander (skwŏn'dər) *v.* to spend or use wastefully
conspiracy (kən-spîr'ə-sē) *n.* a joining or acting together in a secretive way, often with wrongful motives

---

STRATEGIC READING FOR
Less-Proficient Readers

F Ask students to summarize what Buddy and his cousin do to get ready to make the fruitcakes. *(They gather pecans, and then they get the money from their Fruitcake Fund to shop for the other ingredients.)* Summarizing

Set a Purpose As students read the next section, have them pay special attention to Buddy and his cousin's encounters with Mr. Haha Jones.

Literary Concept:
CHARACTERIZATION

G Have students note that Buddy lists some of the things his friend has and has not done. In light of this list, how would students describe her? *(Possible response: She is sheltered, childlike, kind, unsophisticated, skilled, imaginative, superstitious, brave, and loves nature.)*

Active Reading: **QUESTION**

H Discuss what questions or comments students have at this point in the selection. You may wish to use the following model to give them ideas of what they might be thinking about.

Think-Aloud Model *I definitely have some questions about the characters and the situation so far. For example, why are these two characters best friends? Is it because they don't live close enough to anyone their own age? And what about the people in the house? Who else lives there, and why do they make the friends cry?*

Literary Concept: IRONY

I Remind students that irony is a contrast between what is expected and what actually exists or happens. Invite students to discuss the irony in the statement "They call him Haha because he's so gloomy, a man who never laughs." What might be a more fitting name for a person who never laughs? *(Accept reasonable responses.)*

Critical Thinking: ANALYZING

J Ask students why they think the words *is*, *does*, and *doesn't* are italicized. *(The narrator wants to emphasize that all the rumors from the paragraph above were, in fact, true.)*

CUSTOMIZING FOR
Students Acquiring English

3 Tell students that *carnage* is a slaughter or killing.

---

dimes, the liveliest coin, the one that really jingles. Nickels and quarters, worn smooth as creek pebbles. But mostly a hateful heap of bitter-odored pennies. Last summer others in the house contracted to pay us a penny for every twenty-five flies we killed. Oh, the carnage of August: the flies that flew to heaven! Yet it was not work in which we took pride. And, as we sit counting pennies, it is as though we were back tabulating dead flies. Neither of us has a head for figures; we count slowly, lose track, start again. According to her calculations, we have $12.73. According to mine, exactly $13. "I do hope you're wrong, Buddy. We can't mess around with thirteen. The cakes will fall. Or put somebody in the cemetery. Why, I wouldn't dream of getting out of bed on the thirteenth." This is true: she always spends thirteenths in bed. So, to be on the safe side, we subtract a penny and toss it out the window.

f the ingredients that go into our fruitcakes, whiskey is the most expensive, as well as the hardest to obtain: State laws forbid its sale. But everybody knows you can buy a bottle from Mr. Haha Jones. And the next day, having completed our more prosaic shopping, we set out for Mr. Haha's business address, a "sinful" (to quote public opinion) fish-fry and dancing café down by the river. We've been there before, and on the same errand; but in previous years our dealings have been with Haha's wife, an iodine-dark Indian woman with brassy peroxided hair and a dead-tired disposition. Actually, we've never laid eyes on her husband, though we've heard that he's an Indian too. A giant with razor scars across his cheeks. They call him Haha because he's so gloomy, a man who never laughs. As we approach his café (a large log cabin festooned inside and out with chains of garish-gay naked light bulbs and standing by the river's muddy edge under the shade of river trees where moss drifts through the branches like gray mist) our steps slow down. Even Queenie stops prancing and sticks close by. People have been murdered in Haha's café. Cut to pieces. Hit on the head. There's a case coming up in court next month. Naturally these goings-on happen at night when the colored lights cast crazy patterns and the Victrola[6] wails. In the daytime Haha's is shabby and deserted. I knock at the door, Queenie barks, my friend calls: "Mrs. Haha, ma'am? Anyone to home?"

Footsteps. The door opens. Our hearts overturn. It's Mr. Haha Jones himself! And he *is* a giant; he *does* have scars; he *doesn't* smile. No, he glowers at us through Satan-tilted eyes and demands to know: "What you want with Haha?"

For a moment we are too paralyzed to tell. Presently my friend half-finds her voice, a whispery voice at best: "If you please, Mr. Haha, we'd like a quart of your finest whiskey."

His eyes tilt more. Would you believe it? Haha is smiling! Laughing, too. "Which one of you is a drinkin' man?"

"It's for making fruitcakes, Mr. Haha. Cooking."

This sobers him. He frowns. "That's no way to waste good whiskey." Nevertheless, he retreats into the shadowed café and seconds later appears carrying a bottle of daisy-yellow unlabeled liquor. He demonstrates its sparkle in the sunlight and says: "Two dollars."

We pay him with nickels and dimes and pennies. Suddenly, as he jangles the coins in his

---

6. **Victrola:** a trademark for a brand of old record player that would play grooved black discs with a needle.

WORDS TO KNOW
prosaic (prō-zā′ĭk) *adj.* dull; commonplace
garish (gâr′ĭsh) *adj.* too bright or gaudy

68

Mini-Lesson Genre Study

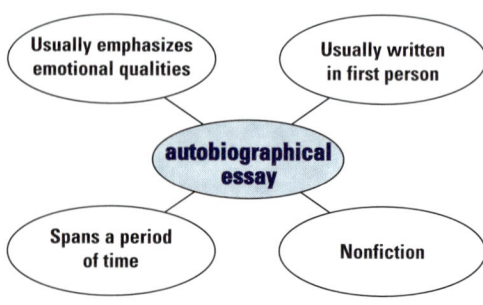

NONFICTION Draw the web shown on the left on the board, and use it to explain that an autobiographical essay is a kind of nonfiction with the following characteristics:
- It is an account of an episode or episodes in a writer's life.
- It is usually written in the first person using the pronouns *I* and *me*.
- It usually emphasizes emotional qualities.

Application Have students copy the web into their notebooks. Ask them to refer to it as they look for the characteristics of an autobiographical essay in "A Christmas Memory."

hand like a fistful of dice, his face softens. "Tell you what," he proposes, pouring the money back into our bead purse, "just send me one of them fruitcakes instead."

"Well," my friend remarks on our way home, "there's a lovely man. We'll put an extra cup of raisins in *his* cake."

The black stove, stoked with coal and firewood, glows like a lighted pumpkin. Eggbeaters whirl, spoons spin round in bowls of butter and sugar, vanilla sweetens the air, ginger spices it; melting, nose-tingling odors saturate the kitchen, suffuse the house, drift out to the world on puffs of chimney smoke. In four days our work is done. Thirty-one cakes, dampened with whiskey, bask on windowsills and shelves.

Who are they for?

Friends. Not necessarily neighbor friends: indeed, the larger share is intended for persons we've met maybe once, perhaps not at all. People who've struck our fancy. Like President Roosevelt. Like the Reverend and Mrs. J. C. Lucey, Baptist missionaries to Borneo who lectured here last winter. Or the little knife grinder who comes through town twice a year. Or Abner Packer, the driver of the six o'clock bus from Mobile, who exchanges waves with us every day as he passes in a dust-cloud whoosh. Or the young Wistons, a California couple whose car one afternoon broke down outside the house and who spent a pleasant hour chatting with us on the porch (young Mr. Wiston snapped our picture, the only one we've ever had taken). Is it because my friend is shy with everyone *except* strangers that these strangers, and merest acquaintances, seem to us our truest friends? I think yes. Also, the scrapbooks we keep of thank-you's on White House stationery, time-to-time communications from California and Borneo, the knife grinder's penny post cards, make us feel connected to eventful worlds beyond the kitchen with its view of a sky that stops.

Now a nude December fig branch grates against the window. The kitchen is empty, the cakes are gone; yesterday we carted the last of them to the post office, where the cost of stamps turned our purse inside out. We're broke. That rather depresses me, but my friend insists on celebrating—with two inches of whiskey left in Haha's bottle. Queenie has a spoonful in a bowl of coffee (she likes her coffee chicory-flavored and strong). The rest we divide between a pair of jelly glasses. We're both quite awed at the prospect of drinking straight whiskey; the taste of it brings screwed-up expressions and sour shudders. But by and by we begin to sing, the two of us singing different songs simultaneously. I don't know the words to mine, just: *Come on along, come on along, to the dark-town strutters' ball.* But I can dance: that's what I mean to be, a tap dancer in the movies. My dancing shadow rollicks on the walls; our voices rock the chinaware; we giggle: as if unseen hands were tickling us. Queenie rolls on her back, her paws plow the air, something like a grin stretches her black lips. Inside myself, I feel warm and sparky as those crumbling logs, carefree as the wind in the chimney. My friend waltzes round the stove, the hem of her poor calico skirt pinched between her fingers as though it were a party dress: *Show me the way to go home,* she sings, her tennis shoes squeaking on the floor. *Show me the way to go home.*

Enter: two relatives. Very angry. Potent with eyes that scold, tongues that scald. Listen to what they have to say, the words tumbling together into a wrathful tune: "A child of seven! whiskey on his breath! are you out of your mind? feeding a child of seven! must be

A CHRISTMAS MEMORY   69

Literary Concept:
CHARACTERIZATION

K Ask students why they think Haha Jones refuses to take the friends' money. What does this say about him? *(Possible response: He does not want to take advantage of their poverty. He can be compassionate and generous.)*

STRATEGIC READING FOR
Less-Proficient Readers

L Have students tell why Buddy and his cousin visit Haha Jones and what happens when they get there. *(They go to Haha Jones's cafe to buy liquor for their fruitcakes. Mr. Jones decides to give them liquor in exchange for one of their fruitcakes, perhaps because he feels sorry that they have so little money.)*
Summarizing/Evaluating

Set a Purpose As students read further, they should pay attention to how Christmas turns out for Buddy.

Active Reading: CONNECT

M Have students relate remembered cooking smells in their lives to those in the selection. Think aloud about ways to describe some good cooking smells and compare them to those in the selection.

Linking to History

N Franklin Delano Roosevelt was President of the United States from 1933 to 1945. He was a familiar figure in the South because he frequented the mineral springs in Warm Springs, Georgia, to treat the polio that disabled him in 1921.

CONNECT
Remember the smell of something cooking? List several foods you remember smelling as they cooked.
Using a Reading Log

Mini-Lesson The Writer's Style

SHOW, DON'T TELL Help students understand that throughout this selection, Capote uses specific verbs, nouns, and adjectives to emphasize sensory detail and to give his readers the clearest picture possible of his experiences. For example, in the passage highlighted above, rather than just telling readers, "My friend and I made the fruitcakes," he shows them what happened.

Application After Buddy and his friend finish the fruitcakes, they take them to the post office to mail them. Have students write a description of the scene that shows, and doesn't merely tell, what the friends do.

Reteaching/Reinforcement
• *Writing Handbook,* anthology p. 873
• *Writing Mini-Lessons* transparencies, p. 54

Focused Description, pp. 58–64

THE LANGUAGE OF LITERATURE TEACHER'S EDITION   69

Active Reading: CLARIFY

O Invite students to describe ways in which Buddy's friend differs from most people her age. If they need help, share the following thought processes with them:

Think-Aloud Model *I think Buddy's friend is different from most people her age because she acts so young. For example, someone her own age probably would never have given a small child and a dog liquor, but she sees nothing wrong in "celebrating." She also cries when she's scolded, instead of sticking up for herself. But she gets over it quickly when she thinks of something good like cutting down a tree.*

Literary Concept: IMAGERY

P Have students point out all the sensory detail in this passage: the colors, silver and orange; the sounds of wild turkey and hog; the sensation of wading in ice-cold water. Then have them be aware of the imagery in the rest of the paragraph as they read.

CUSTOMIZING FOR
Students Acquiring English

4 Explain that a *renegade* is a runaway or a deserter.

5 Point out that *chastising* means "punishing" and is a personification of the thorns.

6 Explain that although *armada* usually means "a fleet of warships," here it means "a fleet or large group of trout."

---

loony! road to ruination! remember Cousin Kate? Uncle Charlie? Uncle Charlie's brother-in-law? shame! scandal! humiliation! kneel, pray, beg the Lord!"

Queenie sneaks under the stove. My friend gazes at her shoes, her chin quivers, she lifts her skirt and blows her nose and runs to her room.

Long after the town has gone to sleep and the house is silent except for the chimings of clocks and the sputter of fading fires, she is weeping into a pillow already as wet as a widow's handkerchief.

"Don't cry," I say, sitting at the bottom of her bed and shivering despite my flannel nightgown that smells of last winter's cough syrup, "don't cry," I beg, teasing her toes, tickling her feet, "you're too old for that."

"It's because," she hiccups, "I *am* too old. Old and funny."

"Not funny. Fun. More fun than anybody. Listen. If you don't stop crying you'll be so tired tomorrow we can't go cut a tree."

She straightens up. Queenie jumps on the bed (where Queenie is not allowed) to lick her cheeks. "I know where we'll find real pretty trees, Buddy. And holly, too. With berries big as your eyes. It's way off in the woods. Farther than we've ever been. Papa used to bring us Christmas trees from there: carry them on his shoulder. That's fifty years ago. Well, now: I can't wait for morning."

Morning. Frozen rime[7] lusters the grass; the sun, round as an orange and orange as hot-weather moons, balances on the horizon, burnishes the silvered winter woods. A wild turkey calls. A renegade hog grunts in the undergrowth. Soon, by the edge of knee-deep, rapid-running water, we have to abandon the buggy. Queenie wades the stream first, paddles across barking complaints at the swiftness of the current, the pneumonia-making coldness of it. We follow, holding our shoes and equipment (a hatchet, a burlap sack) above our heads. A mile more: of chastising thorns, burrs and briers that catch at our clothes; of rusty pine needles brilliant with gaudy fungus and molted feathers. Here, there, a flash, a flutter, an ecstasy of shrillings remind us that not all the birds have flown south. Always, the path unwinds through lemony sun pools and pitch-black vine tunnels. Another creek to cross: a disturbed armada of speckled trout froths the water round us, and frogs the size of plates practice belly flops; beaver workmen are building a dam. On the farther shore, Queenie shakes herself and trembles. My friend shivers, too: not with cold but enthusiasm. One of her hat's ragged roses sheds a petal as she lifts her head and inhales the pine-heavy air. "We're almost there; can you smell it, Buddy?" she says, as though we were approaching an ocean.

And, indeed, it is a kind of ocean. Scented acres of holiday trees, prickly-leafed holly. Red berries shiny as Chinese bells: black crows swoop upon them screaming. Having stuffed our burlap sacks with enough greenery and

---

7. **rime:** a white frost.

CLARIFY

How would you describe Buddy's friend? Explain how she's different from most people her age.
Using a Reading Log

crimson to garland a dozen windows, we set about choosing a tree. "It should be," muses my friend, "twice as tall as a boy. So a boy can't steal the star." The one we pick is twice as tall as me. A brave handsome brute that survives thirty hatchet strokes before it keels with a creaking rending cry. Lugging it like a kill, we commence the long trek out. Every few yards we abandon the struggle, sit down and pant. But we have the strength of triumphant huntsmen; that and the tree's virile, icy perfume revive us, <u>goad</u> us on. Many compliments accompany our sunset return along the red clay road to town; but my friend is sly and <u>noncommittal</u> when passers-by praise the treasure perched in our buggy: what a fine tree, and where did it come from? "Yonderways," she murmurs vaguely. Once a car stops, and the rich mill owner's lazy wife leans out and whines: "Giveya two-bits[8] cash for that ol tree." Ordinarily my friend is afraid of saying no; but on this occasion she promptly shakes her head: "We wouldn't take a dollar." The mill owner's wife persists. "A dollar, my foot! Fifty cents. That's my last offer. Goodness, woman, you can get another one." In answer, my friend gently reflects: "I doubt it. There's never two of anything."

Home: Queenie slumps by the fire and sleeps till tomorrow, snoring loud as a human.

A trunk in the attic contains: a shoebox of ermine[9] tails (off the opera cape of a curious lady who once rented a room in the house), coils of frazzled tinsel gone gold with age, one silver star, a brief rope of dilapidated, undoubtedly dangerous candylike light bulbs. Excellent decorations, as far as they go, which

---

8. **two-bits:** twenty-five cents.
9. **ermine** (ûr′mĭn): the soft, white fur of a weasel of northern regions.

> H aving stuffed our burlap sacks with enough greenery and crimson to garland a dozen windows, we set about choosing a tree.

WORDS TO KNOW
goad (gōd) *v.* to urge
noncommittal (nŏn′kə-mĭt′l) *adj.* not revealing one's opinion or purpose

Literary Concept:
FIGURATIVE LANGUAGE

Q Have students notice the comparison of the search and procurement of the Christmas tree to a hunt. Ask them why they think Capote makes this comparison. *(Possible responses: It makes the activity seem more like an adventure; all the time and effort the cousins spend on getting the tree is the equivalent of hunting, and the prize is highly valued, if not more so.)*

Critical Thinking:
SYNTHESIZING

R Ask students why they think Buddy's cousin refuses to sell the tree. *(Possible response: Because the cousins worked so hard to get it, it has more meaning for them than it could have for anyone else.)* Have students tell what special meaning they see in the cousin's comment, "There's never two of anything." *(Possible response: The comment could refer to the uniqueness of individuals, especially Buddy and his cousin.)*

CUSTOMIZING FOR
Students Acquiring English

7 Explain that *virile* means "manly, strong, and forceful." Here it refers to the scent of the freshly cut pine tree.

Multicultural Perspectives

DECEMBER CELEBRATIONS Students may be interested to know that Hanukkah (hä′nə-kə), the Jewish Festival of Lights, usually falls in December. The festival celebrates the rededication of the Temple in Jerusalem where a small amount of holy oil miraculously lasted for eight days. Small gifts are exchanged each day.

Students may be interested to know that from December 26 to January 1, many African Americans celebrate their heritage by observing Kwanzaa (kwän′zə). Each day of Kwanzaa has a special meaning including working together, sharing, and creating beauty. Gifts given at Kwanzaa are often of African origin.

Active Reading: EVALUATE

S Have students discuss their opinions of Buddy and his cousin's homemade Christmas decorations.

Literary Concept: CHARACTERIZATION

T Ask students to note what Buddy's cousin worries about. What do these concerns say about her character? *(Possible response: that she is unselfish and wants more for the boy she loves than she does for herself)*

Critical Thinking: ANALYZING

U Ask students why they think Buddy's friend doesn't want him to grow up and asks if they will be friends when he does. *(Possible response: She realizes she doesn't have adult friends and that Buddy is her friend because he is a child; she understands that she may lose their friendship when he becomes an adult.)*

CUSTOMIZING FOR
Students Acquiring English

8 Tell students that a *five-and-dime* is a store that sells a wide variety of inexpensive items such as decorations, clothing, and toys. These stores, often making "five-and-dime" part of their name so that people would know what kind of merchandise they sold, have largely disappeared from urban areas.

9 Explain that *tie-dying* is a process in which fabric is folded, dipped in dye, then refolded and dipped in another color.

10 Explain that *gets my goat* is an expression meaning "makes me angry or annoyed."

---

⑧ isn't far enough: my friend wants our tree to blaze "like a Baptist window," droop with weighty snows of ornament. But we can't afford the made-in-Japan splendors at the five-and-dime. So we do what we've always done: sit for days at the kitchen table with scissors and crayons and stacks of colored paper. I make sketches and my friend cuts them out: lots of cats, fish too (because they're easy to draw), some apples, some watermelons, a few winged angels devised from saved-up sheets of Hershey-bar tin foil. We use safety pins to attach these creations to the tree; as a final touch, we sprinkle the branches with shredded cotton (picked in August for this purpose). My friend, surveying the effect, clasps her hands together. "Now honest, Buddy. Doesn't it look good enough to eat?" Queenie tries to eat an angel.

EVALUATE

What do you think of Buddy and his friend's Christmas decorations?
Using a Reading Log

After weaving and ribboning holly wreaths for all the front windows, our next ⑨ project is the fashioning of family gifts. Tie-dye scarves for the ladies, for the men a home-brewed lemon and licorice and aspirin syrup to be taken "at the first Symptoms of a Cold and after Hunting." But when it comes time for making each other's gift, my friend and I separate to work secretly. I would like to buy her a pearl-handled knife, a radio, a whole pound of chocolate-covered cherries (we tasted some once, and she always swears: "I could live on them, Buddy, Lord yes I could—and that's not taking his name in vain"). Instead, I am building her a kite. She would like to give me a bicycle (she's said so on several million ⑩ occasions: "If only I could, Buddy. It's bad enough in life to do without something *you* want; but confound it, what gets my goat is not being able to give somebody something you want *them* to have. Only one of these days I will, Buddy. Locate you a bike. Don't ask how.

Steal it, maybe"). Instead, I'm fairly certain that she is building me a kite—the same as last year and the year before: the year before that we exchanged slingshots. All of which is fine by me. For we are champion kite fliers who study the wind like sailors; my friend, more accomplished than I, can get a kite aloft when there isn't enough breeze to carry clouds.

Christmas Eve afternoon we scrape together a nickel and go to the butcher's to buy Queenie's traditional gift, a good gnawable beef bone. The bone, wrapped in funny paper, is placed high in the tree near the silver star. Queenie knows it's there. She squats at the foot of the tree staring up in a trance of greed: when bedtime arrives she refuses to budge. Her excitement is equaled by my own. I kick the covers and turn my pillow as though it were a scorching summer's night. Somewhere a rooster crows: falsely, for the sun is still on the other side of the world.

"Buddy, are you awake?" It is my friend, calling from her room, which is next to mine; and an instant later she is sitting on my bed holding a candle. "Well, I can't sleep a hoot," she declares. "My mind's jumping like a jack rabbit. Buddy, do you think Mrs. Roosevelt will serve our cake at dinner?" We huddle in the bed, and she squeezes my hand I-love-you. "Seems like your hand used to be so much smaller. I guess I hate to see you grow up. When you're grown up, will we still be friends?" I say always. "But I feel so bad, Buddy. I wanted so bad to give you a bike. I tried to sell my cameo Papa gave me. Buddy"—she hesitates, as though embarrassed—"I made you another kite." Then I confess that I made her one, too; and we laugh. The candle burns too short to hold. Out it goes, exposing the starlight, the stars spinning at the window like a visible caroling that slowly, slowly daybreak silences. Possibly we doze; but the beginnings of dawn splash us like cold water: we're up, wide-eyed and wandering while we wait for

72 UNIT ONE PART 1: GROWING PAINS

Assessment Option

INFORMAL ASSESSMENT

Summarizing You can informally assess your students' understanding of the selection and their ability to summarize by setting up the following scenario:

Pretend that you are watching this selection on television. There is a commercial break, and someone comes into the room and asks you what the show is about. What can you explain while the commercial is still on?

Have students provide written or oral summaries.

Rubric

3 Full Accomplishment Students accurately, concisely, and specifically describe the events in the selection so far.

2 Substantial Accomplishment Students describe most events in the selection accurately. They may not be concise, however.

1 Little or Partial Accomplishment Students have difficulty describing the events in the selection, missing some or placing some in incorrect sequence.

Anna Kuerner (1971), Andrew Wyeth. Tempera on panel, private collection. Copyright © 1995 Andrew Wyeth.

Art Note

Anna Kuerner by Andrew Wyeth

Andrew Wyeth (1917–) is one of the best-known American painters. His father, N. C. Wyeth, was also a famous artist, as is Andrew's son Jamie. There is a "Wyeth look" to all their work, which has influenced many artists, including Hubert Shuptrine. Andrew is noted for his careful, delicate realism, often centering on individuals.

Reading the Art Compare this painting to **Cook Stove** shown earlier in this story. How are they alike and different? Do you think that a realistic style is appropriate for nonfiction? Why or why not?

Active Reading: CONNECT

 Students can jot down their comments in their reading logs. Encourage them to share and compare their reactions with the class. Have students identify common reasons for disappointment with gifts. Ask if their expectations had anything to do with their reactions. Then ask students to use this background to help them understand Buddy's disappointment.

---

others to waken. Quite deliberately my friend drops a kettle on the kitchen floor. I tap dance in front of closed doors. One by one the household emerges, looking as though they'd like to kill us both; but it's Christmas, so they can't. First, a gorgeous breakfast: just everything you can imagine—from flapjacks[10] and fried squirrel to hominy grits and honey-in-the-comb. Which puts everyone in a good humor except my friend and me. Frankly, we're so impatient to get at the presents we can't eat a mouthful.

CONNECT

Have you ever been disappointed with gifts you couldn't wait to open? Jot down your most disappointing gifts.
Using a Reading Log

Well, I'm disappointed. Who wouldn't be? With socks, a Sunday school shirt, some handkerchiefs, a hand-me-down sweater, and a year's subscription to a religious magazine for children. *The Little Shepherd*. It makes me boil. It really does.

10. **flapjacks:** pancakes.

A CHRISTMAS MEMORY   73

Critic's Corner

"Capote's 'A Christmas Memory' . . . is the nearest thing America has to 'A Christmas Carol.' Like Dickens' story, it is sentimental and 'moral,' but deservedly so; no one would have it different."

David Littlejohn, critic

Ask students what they think some of the "morals" of "A Christmas Memory" are.

My friend has a better haul. A sack of satsumas,[11] that's her best present. She is proudest, however, of a white wool shawl knitted by her married sister. But she *says* her favorite gift is the kite I built her. And it *is* very beautiful; though not as beautiful as the one she made me, which is blue and scattered with gold and green Good Conduct stars;[12] moreover, my name is painted on it, "Buddy."

"Buddy, the wind is blowing."

The wind is blowing, and nothing will do till we've run to a pasture below the house where Queenie has scooted to bury her bone (and where, a winter hence, Queenie will be buried, too). There, plunging through the healthy waist-high grass, we unreel our kites, feel them twitching at the string like sky fish as they swim into the wind. Satisfied, sun-warmed, we sprawl in the grass and peel satsumas and watch our kites cavort. Soon I forget the socks and hand-me-down sweater. I'm as happy as if we'd already won the fifty-thousand-dollar Grand Prize in that coffee-naming contest.

"My, how foolish I am!" my friend cries, suddenly alert, like a woman remembering too late she has biscuits in the oven. "You know what I've always thought?" she asks in a tone of discovery and not smiling at me but a point beyond. "I've always thought a body would have to be sick and dying before they saw the Lord. And I imagined that when he came it would be like looking at the Baptist window: pretty as colored glass with the sun pouring through, such a shine you don't know it's getting dark. And it's been a comfort: to think of that shine taking away all the spooky feeling. But I'll wager it never happens. I'll wager at the very end a body realizes the Lord has already shown himself. That things as they are"—her hand circles in a gesture that gathers clouds and kites and grass and Queenie pawing earth over her bone—"just what they've always seen, was seeing him. As for me, I could leave the world with today in my eyes."

This is our last Christmas together.

Life separates us. Those who Know Best decide that I belong in a military school. And so follows a miserable succession of bugle-blowing prisons, grim reveille-ridden[13] summer camps. I have a new home too. But it doesn't count. Home is where my friend is, and there I never go.

And there she remains, puttering around the kitchen. Alone with Queenie. Then alone. ("Buddy dear," she writes in her wild hard-to-read script, "yesterday Jim Macy's horse kicked Queenie bad. Be thankful she didn't feel much. I wrapped her in a Fine Linen sheet and rode her in the buggy down to Simpson's pasture where she can be with all her Bones. . . ."). For a few Novembers she continues to bake her fruitcakes single-handed; not as many, but some: and, of course, she always sends me "the best of the batch." Also, in every letter she encloses a dime wadded in toilet paper: "See a picture show and write me the story." But

---

11. **satsumas** (săt-sōō′məz): fruit similar to tangerines.
12. **Good Conduct stars:** small, shiny, glued paper stars often awarded to children for good behavior or perfect attendance.
13. **reveille-ridden** (rĕv′ə-lē): dominated by an early-morning signal, as on a bugle, to wake soldiers or campers.

WORDS TO KNOW

cavort (kə-vôrt′) *v.* to leap or romp about

gradually in her letters she tends to confuse me with her other friend, the Buddy who died in the 1880's; more and more, thirteenths are not the only days she stays in bed: a morning arrives in November, a leafless birdless coming of winter morning, when she cannot rouse herself to exclaim: "Oh my, it's fruitcake weather!"

And when that happens, I know it. A message saying so merely confirms a piece of news some secret vein had already received, severing from me an irreplaceable part of myself, letting it loose like a kite on a broken string. That is why, walking across a school campus on this particular December morning, I keep searching the sky. As if I expected to see, rather like hearts, a lost pair of kites hurrying toward heaven. ❖

WORDS TO KNOW
sever (sĕv'ər) *v.* to cut off

STRATEGIC READING FOR
Less-Proficient Learners

Y Have students explain what happens to the two friends. *(That was their last Christmas together. Buddy is sent to military school, where he is unhappy. Over the next few years, his friend's health deteriorates and she dies.)* Making Inferences/Summarizing

CUSTOMIZING FOR
Gifted and Talented Students

Z Have students discuss how accurate they believe memory is. Do we remember events the way they happened or do we make the past seem better? Challenge students to debate the accuracy of Capote's memory.

COMPREHENSION CHECK

1. Who is Buddy's best friend? *(an elderly female cousin who lives with him)*
2. What made this Christmas memory so special for Buddy? *(He had a wonderful time, and it was the last Christmas that he would spend with his cousin.)*
3. What causes the two friends to be separated? *(Those who Know Best decide that Buddy should go to military school.)*
4. How does the quality of their lives change after the two are separated? *(Buddy seems to lose all pleasure in life when he is sent to a highly regimented military school; his friend's health deteriorates and she eventually dies.)*

From Personal Response to Critical Analysis

1. Accept all reasonable responses. Encourage students to use sensory details.
2. Possible responses: Some students may say that she has the excitement and innocence of a child. Others may say that she is sensitive and feeling, loves nature, loves Buddy, and enjoys life and lives every moment fully.
3. Possible responses: Some students will note that they share a capacity to enjoy whatever they are doing, and that they love each other because they understand each other. Others may point out that they are allies who are against "the relatives" because the relatives treat them without sensitivity.
4. Student responses will vary. All are valid.
5. Possible response: Buddy realizes how little control he has over his life when he is sent to military school by Those who Know Best and is separated from his friend.
6. Possible responses: Students who agree may point out facts such as Christmas sales that start in the summer, and the emphasis on Santa and getting gifts, rather than on the Christmas spirit or religious observance. Those who disagree may cite reliance on personal Christmas and other holiday traditions.

Another Pathway

Cooperative Learning Students should engage in collaborative planning first to ensure that the packet of cards work together as a set or group. One student may record the group's ideas; another should organize and edit the ideas to ensure that they reflect four related ideas. A third student should assign each of the four ideas to individual students and monitor the group's work to be sure all members stay on target.

Rubric

3 Full Accomplishment Students accurately describe the events in the selection so far.

2 Substantial Accomplishment Students describe most events in the selection accurately.

1 Little or Partial Accomplishment Students have difficulty describing the events in the selection, missing some or placing some in incorrect sequence.

RESPONDING OPTIONS

FROM PERSONAL RESPONSE TO CRITICAL ANALYSIS

REFLECT 1. What emotions did Capote's holiday memory trigger in you? Briefly describe these responses in your notebook.

RETHINK 2. Describe the image you have of Buddy's best friend.
Close Textual Reading
Consider
- Buddy's statement "She is still a child."
- the things she has never done and the things she has done (page 67)

3. Buddy is seven; his cousin is over sixty. Why do you think they became good friends?
Close Textual Reading
Consider
- their status in the household
- the things that give them pleasure
- the way the cousin treats Buddy

4. What descriptive passage created a lasting impression on you? Explain why the passage impressed you, or draw a sketch from the description and share it with the class.
Thematic Link

5. How would you describe the growing pains that Buddy experiences at the end of the story?

RELATE 6. Many Americans complain that Christmas and other holidays have become too commercial. Explain your opinion on this issue.

Multimodal Learning
ANOTHER PATHWAY

Cooperative Learning
Working with three other students, create a packet of three greeting cards that Buddy and his friend might have designed to convey the spirit of Christmas. Each member of the group will be responsible for one card, but the group should collaborate to make sure the cards work together as a set.

QUICKWRITES

1. Write one of the **letters** Buddy's cousin might have sent him after he left for military school.
2. An epitaph is a brief inscription on a tombstone honoring the person buried there. Write the **epitaph** that Buddy might have composed for his friend.
3. Use the writing you did before reading this story as the basis of a short **personal narrative** about a holiday that made a lasting impression on you.

📁 **PORTFOLIO** *Save your writing. You may want to use it later as a springboard to a piece for your portfolio.*

LITERARY CONCEPTS

A **symbol** is a person, a place, an activity, or an object that stands for something beyond itself. For example, a dove is a common symbol for peace. Reread the last paragraph of "A Christmas Memory." Notice the two comparisons that Capote makes with kites. What do the kites symbolize?

76 UNIT ONE PART 1: GROWING PAINS

Literary Concepts

The kites symbolize the free spirits, or souls, of Buddy and his friend; their friendship will survive their earthbound constraints. Have students form small groups to answer the following questions. One student should record answers.

- How are the two representations of kites different from each other?
- How are they similar?
- Do you think kites are appropriate symbols here? Why or why not?

When students are finished, have them compare their interpretations with those of other groups.

QuickWrites

1. Encourage students to match the tone of their letter to the friend's feelings for Buddy.
2. Write sample epitaphs on the board for students. For example: Here lies the best friend a young boy ever had. She was younger than her years and kinder than her peers.
3. Remind students to use sensory details and the first-person point of view in their essays.

The Writer's Craft

Writing a Personal Letter, pp. 44–46
Varying Sentences, pp. 416–417
Personal Narrative, pp. 86–101

LITERARY LINKS

Compare what Marguerite learns from Mrs. Flowers in the excerpt from *I Know Why the Caged Bird Sings* with what Buddy learns from his older cousin. Use details from the selections to support your answer.

Multimodal Learning

ALTERNATIVE ACTIVITIES

1. Imagine the perfect gifts for yourself and one other person, gifts that reflect your idea of the true spirit of giving. In an **oral presentation,** describe the two gifts to your classmates and explain your choices.
2. Design "A Christmas Memory" **kite** that captures the characters and events in this excerpt.

ACROSS THE CURRICULUM

Social Studies Winter celebrations such as Christmas vary from family to family as well as from culture to culture. Find out how people you know celebrate winter holidays by interviewing from five to seven people—classmates, friends, relatives, and/or neighbors. Ask especially about particular foods, decorations, and rituals that people have for these holidays.

THE WRITER'S STYLE

To give us a lasting impression of his holiday memory, Capote creates **descriptions** that appeal to one or more of the five senses. In your notebook, make a chart like the one below and list ten phrases from the selection that you find especially memorable. Check off which sense or senses each phrase appeals to. An example is done for you. Then try your hand at writing phrases that appeal to some combination of senses.

Description	Sight	Smell	Hearing	Taste	Touch
dust-cloud whoosh	✓		✓		✓

A CHRISTMAS MEMORY 77

Literary Links

Possible responses:

What Marguerite learns
- to find her voice
- that life can get better after a difficult time
- the importance of an older friend

What Buddy learns
- that he has little control over his life
- the importance of an older friend

Across the Curriculum

Social Studies Cooperative Learning Have students work in small groups. You may want to have each group assign work based on one celebration, with different group members concentrating on foods, decorations, and traditions. Or you may want groups to consider one area such as food across different celebrations. In this case, you may want groups to assign each member to a different celebration.

The Writer's Style

Invite students to use their charts to explore how Capote's sensory descriptions evoke an emotional response at different places in the story. For more practice in creating descriptions that appeal to one or more of the five senses, see *The Writer's Craft* pages 60–64.

Alternative Activities

1. Remind students that gifts need not be physical items; they can be help in learning to play an instrument or a sport, for example. They could be doing a favor for someone, such as cooking a favorite food or performing a chore. As students plan their oral presentations, encourage them to prepare a list for each gift that explains why they think the gift reflects the true spirit of the celebration.
2. Encourage students to include pictures, symbols, and colors on their kites that capture the rich sensory details described in the story.

Words to Know

1. b	6. a
2. c	7. c
3. d	8. a
4. c	9. c
5. c	10. b

Reteaching/Reinforcement
• Unit One Resource Book p. 24

TRUMAN CAPOTE

Truman Capote, born Truman Strekfus Persons, was the only child of a traveling salesman and a sixteen-year-old former Miss Alabama. His parents divorced when Capote was four years old, and he was sent to live with a succession of relatives throughout the South. Before he was established as a writer, Capote worked at a variety of odd jobs, including a stint as a fortuneteller's assistant.

LITERARY CONNECTION
A Christmas Memory: The Screenplay In this brief excerpt from the movie version of "A Christmas Memory," the close relationship between Capote and his cousin Sook Faulk is shown.

Side A, Frame 8067

ART GALLERY
Relationships Artists have used relationships between people as themes in their art for centuries. These paintings will give students several examples of the use of this theme in art.

Side A, Frame 49229

WORDS TO KNOW

Review the Words to Know in the boxes at the bottom of the selection pages. Then, on your paper, write the letter of the word that is not related in meaning to the other words in the set.

1. (a) exhilarate (b) depress (c) invigorate (d) excite
2. (a) begin (b) start (c) finish (d) inaugurate
3. (a) cavort (b) bound (c) prance (d) goad
4. (a) squander (b) waste (c) conserve (d) misuse
5. (a) virile (b) robust (c) prosaic (d) forceful
6. (a) retreat (b) urge (c) spur (d) goad
7. (a) cut (b) separate (c) join (d) sever
8. (a) conspiracy (b) privacy (c) solitude (d) isolation
9. (a) willing (b) eager (c) noncommittal (d) agreeable
10. (a) glaring (b) simple (c) flashy (d) garish

TRUMAN CAPOTE

1924–1984

Mainly through appearances on TV talk shows during his later life, Truman Capote became nearly as famous for being an eccentric media "personality" as he was for being a major writer. He had become part of flashy New York and Hollywood social circles, having once told an interviewer, "I always knew that I wanted to be a writer and that I wanted to be rich and famous."

Born in New Orleans, Capote spent his early years in the care of various Southern relatives, including his "friend" in "A Christmas Memory." Capote began writing as a lonely child of 10. At 13 he was sent to a military boarding school, and at 17 he went to work as a clerk for *The New Yorker* magazine. He soon quit his job and concentrated on writing, achieving almost immediate success through the distinctive style, rhythms, and sounds of his prose. He subsequently published a succession of short story collections and novels, as well as travel essays, play adaptations, and film scripts.

Capote's two most famous books are *Breakfast at Tiffany's* and *In Cold Blood*. *Breakfast at Tiffany's*, published in 1958, is a short novel set in New York City. *In Cold Blood*, published in 1966, was Capote's most sensational title. It tells the true story of the 1959 mass murder of a wealthy farm family in Kansas. Capote's idea in *In Cold Blood* was to create what he called a nonfiction novel, a new literary form that combined fiction and research journalism. The project took nearly six years and left him drained and reportedly addicted to tranquilizers. "If I had known what that book was going to cost in every conceivable way, emotionally, I never would have started it," he later confessed.

Capote published little after 1966, a period of his life generally considered to be dominated by severe writer's block, the pursuit of celebrity, and various physical ailments that included alcoholism.

OTHER WORKS *A Tree of Night, and Other Stories; Music for Chameleons: New Writing; One Christmas*
Extended Reading

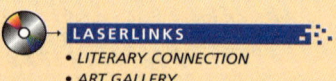
• LITERARY CONNECTION
• ART GALLERY

78 UNIT ONE PART 1: GROWING PAINS

REFLECTING ON THEME
What Do You Think?

Have students think about the obstacle course they designed before they began reading the selections in Part 1. Ask them what obstacle they would add to their board game based on what they learned about the difficulties of growing up from reading "A Christmas Memory." Does it seem to be any more or less of an obstacle than any of their others?

On Being Seventeen, Bright, and Unable to Read

ON YOUR OWN

David Raymond

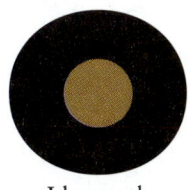ne day a substitute teacher picked me to read aloud from the textbook. When I told her "No, thank you," she came unhinged. She thought I was acting smart and told me so. I kept calm, and that got her madder and madder. We must have spent 10 minutes trying to solve the problem, and finally she got so red in the face I thought she'd blow up: She told me she'd see me after class.

Maybe someone like me was a new thing for that teacher. But she wasn't new to me. I've been through scenes like that all my life. You see, even though I'm 17 and a junior in high school, I can't read because I have dyslexia. I'm told I read "at a fourth-grade level," but from where I sit, that's not reading. You can't know what that means unless you've been there. It's not easy to tell how it feels when you can't read your homework assignments or the newspaper or a menu in a restaurant or even notes from your own friends.

My family began to suspect I was having problems almost from the first day I started school. My father says my early years in school were the worst years of his life. They weren't so good for me, either. As I look back on it now, I can't find the words to express how bad it really was. I wanted to die. I'd come home from school screaming, "I'm dumb. I'm dumb—I wish I were dead!"

I guess I couldn't read anything at all then—not even my own name—and they tell me I didn't talk as good as other kids. But what I remember about those days is that I couldn't throw a ball where it was supposed to go, I couldn't learn to swim, and I wouldn't learn to ride a bike, because no matter what anyone told me, I knew I'd fail.

Sometimes my teachers would try to be encouraging. When I couldn't read the words on the board they'd say, "Come on, David, you know that word." Only I didn't. And it was embarrassing. I just felt dumb. And dumb was how the kids treated me. They'd make fun of me every chance they got, asking me to spell "cat" or something like that. Even if I knew how to spell it, I wouldn't; they'd only give me another word. Anyway, it was awful, because more than anything I wanted friends. On my birthday when I blew out the candles I didn't wish I could learn to read; what I wished for was that the kids would like me.

With the bad reports coming from school and with me moaning about wanting to die and how everybody hated me, my parents began looking for help. That's when the testing started. The school tested me, the child-guidance center tested me, private psychiatrists tested me. Everybody knew something was wrong—especially me.

It didn't help much when they stuck a fancy name onto it. I couldn't pronounce it then—I

OBJECTIVES

- To promote independent, active reading
- To practice and apply skills learned in previous selections

SUMMARY

In this autobiographical account, the author tells what it's like to have dyslexia. Although he is bright, he has always had to struggle to learn. Even after his disability was discovered, there were confrontations with teachers who didn't understand dyslexia. Many teachers were concerned and helpful, but even then school was tough. He had to do things "normal" kids didn't, like going to a camp for children with reading disabilities, attending special classes, and getting extra help from his parents, tutors, and teachers. Despite the problems, he plans to attend college. He knows it won't be easy and worries about the future, but he is committed to trying his best. He wrote this essay to tell people about dyslexia so that other children will not have such a hard time.

Thematic Link: *Growing Pains* A young man with dyslexia remembers the pain and embarrassment of dealing as a teenager with a learning disability that left him unable to read for many years.

Reading Pathways

- Have students read independently, responding to the selection in their journals.
- Have partners read the selection aloud to each other, alternating turns as they wish.
- Have small groups of less-proficient readers read the selection together, helping each other with sections that are difficult.
- Encourage students to read the selection twice, once to understand David's feelings and a second time to learn facts about dyslexia.

PRINT AND MEDIA RESOURCES

UNIT ONE RESOURCE BOOK
Strategic Reading: Literature, p. 27

FORMAL ASSESSMENT
Selection Test, pp. 15–16
Part Test, pp. 17–18
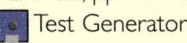 Test Generator

ACCESS FOR STUDENTS ACQUIRING ENGLISH
Selection Summaries

 AUDIO LIBRARY
See Reference Card

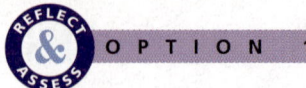

OPTION 1

Cooperative Learning
INTERVIEWING A SPECIAL EDUCATION TEACHER

Have students reread the article together in groups of four, noting any questions that come to mind about dyslexia and other learning disabilities. One student can record the questions, and two others can clarify and extend the questions and conduct an interview with a special education teacher to get some answers. A fourth student can summarize and integrate all the information into a final written report.

Teacher's Role Facilitate the interview by locating a special education teacher willing to spend some time and perhaps share some written materials with your students. You might also coach students in interviewing skills, such as asking probing follow-up questions to clarify and extend what the person being interviewed says.

Rubric

3 Full Accomplishment Students compile a list of thoughtful questions, conduct a successful interview in which they gather relevant facts, and present those facts in a coherent, interesting report.

2 Substantial Accomplishment Students conduct a moderately successful interview but fail to ask follow-up questions. Their final report may lack focus, organization, or sustained interest.

1 Little or Partial Accomplishment Students are unable to come up with a list of interesting questions, lack interviewing skills, and have trouble organizing their information into a coherent report.

LIVING WITH DYSLEXIA

Most people with dyslexia have average or above-average intelligence; they simply cannot learn to read the way most people learn. Dyslexia often causes people to make mistakes in one or more of the following areas:

1. Recognizing and remembering printed words and numbers.
2. Reading and writing letters and numerals. Some dyslexics reverse letters and numerals, for example, mistaking the letter *b* for *d* or *p*.
3. Reading a word as it is written. Some dyslexics reverse the order of the letters when they read, such as seeing the word *saw* as *was*.
4. Reading a sentence as it is written, without leaving out or adding words.
5. Interpreting sounds correctly. Sometimes dyslexics confuse vowel sounds or substitute one consonant for another.

Research on dyslexia has resulted in techniques and programs that help most dyslexics manage their disability.

The passage below is from *Moby-Dick* as it might look to one dyslexic child on a particular day. Problems differ from day to day and child to child.

> It is a thiug uot nucommouly happeuiug to the whale-doats iu those swarmiug seas; the sharks at timesaqqareutly followiug them iu the same qrescieut way that vnltnres hover over the dauuers of marchiug regimeuts in the east.

---

was only in second grade—and I was ashamed to talk about it. Now it rolls off my tongue, because I've been living with it for a lot of years—dyslexia.

All through elementary school it wasn't easy. I was always having to do things that were "different," things the other kids didn't have to do. I had to go to a child psychiatrist, for instance.

One summer my family forced me to go to a camp for children with reading problems. I hated the idea, but the camp turned out pretty good, and I had a good time. I met a lot of kids who couldn't read, and somehow that helped. The director of the camp said I had a higher I.Q. than 90 percent of the population. I didn't believe him.

About the worst thing I had to do in fifth and sixth grade was go to a special education class in another school in our town. A bus picked me up, and I didn't like that at all. The bus also picked up emotionally disturbed kids and retarded kids. It was like going to a school

80 UNIT ONE PART 1: GROWING PAINS

for the retarded. I always worried that someone I knew would see me on that bus. It was a relief to go to the regular junior high school.

Life began to change a little for me then, because I began to feel better about myself. I found the teachers cared; they had meetings about me, and I worked harder for them for a while. I began to work on the potter's wheel, making vases and pots that the teachers said were pretty good. Also, I got a letter for being on the track team. I could always run pretty fast.

At high school the teachers are good, and everyone is trying to help me. I've gotten honors some marking periods, and I've won a letter on the cross country team. Next quarter I think the school might hold a show of my pottery. I've got some friends. But there are still some embarrassing times. For instance, every time there is writing in the class, I get up and go to the special education room. Kids ask me where I go all the time. Sometimes I say, "to Mars."

Homework is a real problem. During free periods in school I go into the special ed room, and staff members read assignments to me. When I get home my mother reads to me. Sometimes she reads an assignment into a tape recorder, and then I go into my room and listen to it. If we have a novel or something like that to read, she reads it out loud to me. Then I sit down with her, and we do the assignment. She'll write, while I talk my answers to her. Lately I've taken to dictating into a tape recorder, and then someone —my father, a private tutor, or my mother—types up what I've dictated. Whatever homework I do takes someone else's time, too. That makes me feel bad.

We had a big meeting in school the other day—eight of us, four from the guidance department, my private tutor, my parents, and me. The subject was me. I said I wanted to go to college, and they told me about colleges that have facilities and staff to handle people like me. That's nice to hear.

As for what happens after college, I don't know, and I'm worried about that. How can I make a living if I can't read? Who will hire me? How will I fill out the application form? The only thing that gives me any courage is the fact that I've learned about well-known people who couldn't read or had other problems and still made it. Like Albert Einstein, who didn't talk until he was 4 and flunked math. Like Leonardo da Vinci, who everyone seems to think had dyslexia.

I've told this story because maybe some teacher will read it and go easy on a kid in the classroom who has what I've got. Or, maybe some parent will stop nagging his kid and stop calling him lazy. Maybe he's not lazy or dumb. Maybe he just can't read and doesn't know what's wrong. Maybe he's scared, like I was. ❖

DAVID RAYMOND

1958–

David Raymond was born in Norwalk, Connecticut. He attended Curry College in Massachusetts in a special program for students with learning disabilities. Listening to lectures and books on tape enabled him to complete his assignments. He graduated Cum Laude in 1981 with a BA in business management.

Raymond lives in Connecticut, where he is in business for himself—owning and managing rental properties and being involved in the building and carpentry field. He has returned to school to study architecture.

OPTION 2

Individual Activity
WRITING ABOUT PERSONAL DIFFICULTIES

Have students recall a time when they, like David, felt depressed about something they couldn't do as well as others—sports, art, academics, social skills, etc. Have them compare their feelings with David's, tell what they did to adjust to or change the situation, and evaluate how well their solutions worked.

Teacher's Role Encourage students to be as honest as they can. Reassure them that only you will read their work.

Rubric

3 Full Accomplishment Student identifies an experience comparable to David's, describes in detail what he or she did to adjust, and offers a reasoned evaluation of his or her success.

2 Substantial Accomplishment Student identifies an experience that compares to David's but is not able to evaluate his or her problem-solving efforts.

1 Little or Partial Accomplishment Student is unable to identify with David's feelings or to offer much detail about his or her attempts to solve the problem.

OPTION 3

Class Discussion
SHARING IDEAS

Teacher's Role Have students discuss the problems and opportunities presented by the integration of students with special needs into public schools by asking the following questions. You can participate by sharing your own experiences, by giving verbal support to positive ideas, and by asking probing questions to help students extend their understanding of the issues. Make sure that all students speak respectfully and do not use negative stereotypes.

1. What can students of varying abilities learn from one another?
   (Answers will vary.)
2. How can they all learn to be together without destructive teasing?
   (Answers will vary.)

OVERVIEW

In the Guided Assignment for this section, students will write a character study. By analyzing a character, students can better understand people, both in literature and in real life. As preparation for this assignment, the Writer's Style will help students understand the importance of showing, rather than telling, the way a character looks, acts, and speaks. In Reading the World, students will explore a profile of a real person and draw conclusions about her.

Objectives

- To recognize how skilled writers describe characters by showing, rather than telling, what the characters are like
- To become familiar with different methods of organization
- To use various methods of characterization to make characters more vivid and lifelike
- To write a character study analyzing a figure in literature
- To analyze the characterization of a real person

Skills

LITERATURE
- Identifying and analyzing methods of characterization

GRAMMAR AND USAGE
- Using appositive phrases
- Using irregular verb forms correctly

MEDIA LITERACY
- Analyzing a character

SPEAKING, LISTENING, AND VIEWING
- Discussing stereotypes and how to avoid them
- Group conferencing

CRITICAL THINKING
- Avoiding stereotypes
- Analyzing

Teaching Strategy: MODELING
In the following models, dialogue and description are used to show, rather than tell, important character traits. This technique is useful in fiction, drama, and nonfiction.

A Wetherell Possible responses: the girl is impatient and intolerant and doesn't even pretend a polite interest in what the narrator is talking about; the narrator is enthusiastic and eager to make an impression. Most students will like the narrator more.

B Angelou Possible responses: "smiled often" reveals her good nature and friendliness; "I always wanted to thank her" reveals that she inspires respect and affection; "graceful" shows her stylishness; and "inclusively benign" refers to her gentleness in all ways of behavior.

WRITING ABOUT LITERATURE

CONSIDERING CHARACTER

What made the characters in the selections seem real? Did you admire Mrs. Flowers? Did you like Sheila Mant? Understanding character will help you better understand literature, yourself, and others. In the following pages you will

- study how authors create their characters
- analyze a character from a selection you've just read
- apply these skills to real individuals

The Writer's Style: Show, Don't Tell Skilled authors don't simply tell readers what a character is like; they show how a character looks, acts, and speaks. This allows readers to draw their own conclusions.

Read the Literature

Notice what these excerpts tell you about each character. Then explore how you learn what you do about Mrs. Flowers and about both of the characters in "The Bass, the River, and Sheila Mant."

Literature Models

A Characterization Through Dialogue
What do you learn about the characters from what they say? If you overheard this conversation, which character would you like better? Why?

> "What's that sound?" she said, pointing toward shore.
> "Bass. That splashing sound?"
> "Over there."
> "Yeah, bass. They come into the shallows at night to chase frogs and moths and things. Big largemouths. *Micropterus salmoides*," I added, showing off.
> "I think fishing's dumb," she said, making a face. "I mean, it's boring and all. Definitely dumb."
>
> W. D. Wetherell, from "The Bass, the River, and Sheila Mant"

B Characterization Through Description
What words and phrases show you some important characteristics of Mrs. Flowers?

> I don't think I ever saw Mrs. Flowers laugh, but she smiled often. A slow widening of her thin black lips to show even, small white teeth, then the slow, effortless closing. When she chose to smile on me, I always wanted to thank her. The action was so graceful and inclusively benign.
>
> Maya Angelou, from *I Know Why the Caged Bird Sings*

82 UNIT ONE

PRINT AND MEDIA RESOURCES

UNIT ONE RESOURCE BOOK
Writer's Style, p. 31
Prewriting, p. 32
Elaboration, p. 33
Peer Response Guide, pp. 34–35
Revising and Proofreading, p. 36
Student Model, pp. 37–38
Rubric, p. 39

GRAMMAR MINI-LESSONS
Transparencies, pp. 32, 41
Copymasters, pp. 30–32, 41

WRITING MINI-LESSONS
Transparencies, p. 1

FORMAL ASSESSMENT
Guidelines for Writing Assessment

 WRITING COACH

 The Writer's Craft

Personal Response to Literature, pp. 238–249

Connect to Life

In newspapers, magazines, film, and other media, writers use the "show, don't tell" technique to capture the personalities of the people in their stories. How does the excerpt from the sports article below compare with the literature models?

Sports Article

Subsequently, he has stuck out his tongue during games, jawed with referees and pranced in high-step to celebrate a score. More seriously, he has yelled at his coach, deliberately fouled and tried to injure other players, and quit on his teammates.

Curry Kirkpatrick
from "Much Ado About A'Do"
Sports Illustrated, January 16, 1989

Characterization Through Actions
What do the player's actions show about his personality?

Try Your Hand: Using Characterization

1. **Make It "Show"** Use various methods of characterization to turn these "tell" sentences into "show" passages.
   - Any fisherman would love to catch a bass.
   - The narrator struggled with his choice.
   - Sheila went home with a boy who had a car.

2. **Revise a QuickWrite** Look at some of the QuickWrites and other writing you have done so far during the unit. Choose a piece that includes characters you would like to make more vivid and lifelike. Revise the piece, using specific details that show, and don't simply tell, what the characters are like.

3. **Compose a Conversation** Using only dialogue, write a scene that shows something important about the characters involved.

SkillBuilder

GRAMMAR FROM WRITING

Using Appositive Phrases

An **appositive phrase** gives information about a noun or pronoun. You can use appositive phrases to describe your characters more precisely. See how Judith Ortiz Cofer used appositive phrases to develop her character in "American History." Notice that different types of phrases require different types of punctuation.

It was just the mother, a red-headed tall woman who wore a white uniform—a nurse's, I guessed it was; the father was gone before I got up in the morning and was never there at dinner time.

She had a halo of red hair floating over a delicate ivory face—the face of a doll—with freckles on the nose.

APPLYING WHAT YOU'VE LEARNED
Elaborate on the characters in the following sentences by adding an appositive phrase to each.

1. Mrs. Flowers appeared cool in the warmest weather.
2. Buddy's friend made fruitcakes.
3. David Raymond learned to read.

HANDBOOKS

For more information on appositive phrases and their punctuation, see page 932 of the Grammar Handbook. For more information on "Show, Don't Tell," see page 873 in the Writing Handbook.

WRITING ABOUT LITERATURE **83**

Teaching Strategy: MODELING

 Kirkpatrick Possible responses: The player's actions hint that he is immature, disrespectful, abusive, disloyal, and egotistical.

Try Your Hand

1. Responses will vary. Passages should contain vivid dialogue, description, and actions, as in these examples:
   - Grandpa's eyes glowed as a sliver of speckles wriggled at the end of his line. "A bass!" he breathed admiringly.
   - Sean's face was cool and uncreased as ever. Only an occasional quaver in his voice betrayed his gnawing indecision.
   - "Step inside for a ride home?" Sheila thought his smile was the best thing she'd seen all day. She reached for the car door.

2. Sample responses include dialogue and specific details about the actions or appearance of characters.

3. Make sure that students' dialogue reveals character traits for each speaker, as in this sample:
   - "But you *promised* to baby-sit Timmy this weekend, Ramona!"
   - "That's before Greg got tickets for the concert Saturday night, Barb. You know how much I want to go!"
   - "And *you* knew it's Mom and Dad's anniversary, and I need to study for that bio exam on Monday."
   - "So, how's a four-hour break from the books going to hurt?"

SkillBuilder GRAMMAR FROM WRITING

USING APPOSITIVE PHRASES Point out that commas set off appositive phrases that are closely linked to the idea in the sentence. Dashes set off appositives that mark an abrupt break in thought.

Application Possible responses:
1. Mrs. Flowers, *a friend of Marguerite's grandmother*, appeared cool in the warmest weather.
2. Buddy's friend—*a distant cousin with whom he'd lived as long as he could remember*—made fruitcakes.
3. David Raymond, *a boy struggling with dyslexia*, learned to read.

Additional Suggestions You may wish to add these items to the exercise on appositive phrases.
1. The fish was on the line. (*the largest bass I'd ever hooked*)
2. Buddy and his friend sailed their kites. (*their Christmas presents to each other*)

Reteaching/Reinforcement
- *Grammar Mini-Lessons* copymasters p. 41, transparencies p. 41

The Writer's Craft
Commas with Interrupters, pp. 775–776

THE LANGUAGE OF LITERATURE TEACHER'S EDITION **83**

Critical Thinking: ANALYZING

D Be sure students understand that to analyze a topic requires breaking a whole into its parts to study its nature and identify its essential features. If necessary, model the process by using the sample chart on this page.

WRITING ABOUT LITERATURE

Analysis

D You have discovered how authors show what characters are like through physical description, dialogue, and action. By being aware of these same details, you can learn a great deal about people in literature and in the real world.

GUIDED ASSIGNMENT

Write a Character Study On the next few pages, you'll analyze a character from a story you've just read. You will think about your impression of that character and write a character study in which you explore and explain your impression.

❶ Prewrite and Explore

Which characters in the selections you've just read interested you most? Jot down the names of three characters that you find most intriguing.

EXAMINING CHARACTERS

The following questions might help you focus your thinking about each character.

- What was my first reaction to the character?
- How did the character change during the story?
- How did my impression of the character change or expand as I read? Why did it change?

Decision Point Based on your answers to the questions above, which character do you want to write about?

GATHERING INFORMATION

Your character study should include evidence to support your impressions of the character. Remember that good writers show, rather than merely tell, what characters are like. Go back to the story to find details to help you show what the character you chose is like. You may want to use a chart like the one on the left to gather details.

Student's Prewriting Chart

Sheila Mant

Actions
was reluctant to canoe

left dance with another boy

Words
"Fishing's dumb."

"You're a funny kid."

Assessment Option

SELF-ASSESSMENT After students have completed the Gathering Information activity, have them assess the details on their chart. Students should consider the following questions:
- *Do the details I have listed reveal all the important personality traits of the character?*
- *What general impression of the character is supported by the actions and words I have listed?*

❷ Write and Analyze a Discovery Draft

To find out what you want to say about the character, try freewriting your impressions of him or her based on details from the story. When you're finished, take a look at your discovery draft and ask yourself the following questions.

- What is my main impression of the character?
- What point do I want to make with my readers?

The yellow notes below show one student's thoughts as she analyzed her discovery draft.

Student's Discovery Draft

My first impression of Sheila Mant is that she's tanned and beautiful ("lovelier than a largemouth bass"). She has red hair, "well-spaced freckles" and lots of boyfriends. The narrator worships her and calls her "utterly suave." She's 17 and he's 14.

I guess I want to show that Sheila is pretty, but not a nice person.

What details will make it clear that Sheila is beautiful?

Then Sheila declares "Fishing's dumb," relaxes while the narrator struggles with the boat, and shows little interest in him. Still, he chooses her over the biggest fish he's ever hooked in his life. Later, after she leaves the dance with an older boy, the narrator decides that the fish was lovelier, after all.

I'll begin with an impression of Sheila's beauty and gradually show what her personality is like.

❸ Draft and Share

You can use what you learned in step 2 to write a more focused draft. The SkillBuilder on methods of organization may help you frame your ideas. When you've finished, you might want to invite another student to read your writing and give you feedback.

PEER RESPONSE

- What do you think I'm trying to show about the character?
- Which details help you understand the impression the character made on me?
- Which details or examples did not support the impression?

SkillBuilder
WRITER'S CRAFT

Using Methods of Organization

The information you gather about a character can help you decide how to organize your character study. Here are some ways to organize a character study.

Order of Impression Start with a first impression of the character and then add details that change your impression. For example, you might move from external factors, such as physical description and dialogue, to internal factors, such as a character's growth.

Character's Growth Characters may change over the course of a story. You might compare how the character is presented early in the story with how he or she is portrayed at the end. When does he or she begin to change? Why?

APPLYING WHAT YOU'VE LEARNED

Consider whether one of the above methods of organization can help you frame ideas in your discovery draft.

WRITING HANDBOOK

For more information on methods of organization see pages 877, 879, 881–883, 885 of the Writing Handbook.

WRITING ABOUT LITERATURE **85**

Teaching Strategy: USING THE SKILLBUILDER

E You can help students organize their answers to the prewriting questions by teaching the SkillBuilder on Methods of Organization at this time. It helps students to arrange in a logical order the information that they have gathered about a character.

Writing Skill: IDENTIFYING THE MAIN IDEA

F The Discovery Draft provides an opportunity for students to sort through the information they have gathered and to explore ideas. Suggest that students look for an emerging main idea or thesis as they freewrite. Guide them to think about how they will present this idea early in their second draft, so that their readers will understand the paper's purpose.

CUSTOMIZING FOR
Less-Proficient Writers

G Point out that the structure of a character study may be conveniently divided into three parts. In the introduction, students should give their main idea. The body of the essay should support and explain the main idea with details. The conclusion should summarize the essay and reinforce the main idea without awkward repetition.

SkillBuilder WRITER'S CRAFT

USING METHODS OF ORGANIZATION

Remind students that the two organizational strategies discussed in the SkillBuilder—order of impression and character's growth—are convenient methods for arranging details in the body of an essay. Whichever method they choose, however, students should still make sure to foreshadow their overall impression of the character when they state their main idea in the introduction.

Application Discuss with students how the details in the sample Discovery Draft might be revised or rearranged to present a clearer "order of impression" structure. Students may suggest, for example, that the characters' relative ages be omitted.

Additional Suggestions Ask students to discuss how to apply the idea of a character's growth to the extracts from the sample essay. Does Sheila change or grow in the course of the story? If so, how? If not, what does that show?

Reteaching/Reinforcement
- *Writing Mini-Lessons* transparencies, p. 1

The Writer's Craft
Types of Organization, pp. 331–335

Critical Thinking: ANALYZING

H Point out to students that revising their drafts involves changing the text so that it is better suited to their audience and purpose. To evaluate and revise their character studies, students should:
- be sure they have presented a main idea clearly and coherently
- check that the descriptive details, narrative actions, and quotations they have selected reflect the organization of the character study and relate to the main idea
- look for places they can improve their style by adding appositive phrases

Teaching Strategy: MODELING

I Discuss with students how this sample meets the Standards for Evaluation on this page. The specific details show that Sheila is pretty but that her beauty is only skin deep. The writer shows the relationship by adopting the narrator's point of view in the first paragraph. The quotation dramatically underlines how little the narrator and his hobby mean to Sheila, thus hinting at the idea that the narrator's opinion of her will change.

Standards for Evaluation

Ideas and Content
- gives the author, title, and brief summary of the literature
- analyzes one feature or element of the story (plot, imagery, character, setting, point of view)
- supports analysis with evidence from the story, including examples, quotes, and details
- has an ending that summarizes the analysis and draws a conclusion

Structure and Form
- uses well-organized paragraphs and a clear organization
- includes transitional words and phrases to show relationships among ideas
- uses a variety of sentence structures

Grammar, Usage, and Mechanics
- contains no more than two or three minor errors in grammar and usage
- contains no more than two or three minor errors in spelling, capitalization, and punctuation

---

WRITING ABOUT LITERATURE

4 Revise and Edit

H Consider the Standards for Evaluation below as you revise and edit your character study. The callout questions show you how one student revised a draft. You may also review Grammar in Context on the opposite page. Then revise and edit your draft.

Student's Discovery Draft

Character Study: Sheila Mant

With her red hair and "well-spaced freckles," Sheila Mant is every teenage boy's dream. At least that's how she seems at first to the narrator of "The Bass, the River, and Sheila Mant." He soon learns, however, that Sheila has nothing at all in common with him. What's more, her beauty is only skin deep.

How does the writer use details from the story to show what Sheila is like?

In the first paragraph does the writer show or tell about the relationship between Sheila and the narrator? How?

I "I think fishing's dumb," she says, making a face showing that her friend and his hobby mean nothing to her. This comment suddenly makes Sheila less appealing to the narrator. On their date, Sheila rattled on about fraternity men, tanning, and college. She didn't know that the narrator was trying to choose between her and the large fish that he has on his line. Much later, thinking about how he had chosen Sheila, he decides he would have been better off with the fish.

How does using a quotation help support the idea that the narrator's opinion of Sheila may change?

Standards for Evaluation

The character study
- introduces a character and identifies key aspects of that character's personality
- presents the writer's impression of the character
- uses dialogue, action, and physical description to support statements about the character

86 UNIT ONE

Assessment Option

SELF-ASSESSMENT To help students assess their own writing, have them ask themselves the following questions:
- Have I introduced the character clearly and identified the most important traits of his or her personality?
- What is the main idea of my essay?
- Have I supported my idea by referring to specific dialogue, actions, and physical descriptions?
- Have I presented enough supporting evidence to persuade readers that my overall impression of the character is valid?

Grammar in Context

Verb Tense When writing a character study or any other form of literary analysis, use the present tense to describe characters and their actions and to analyze the author's techniques or subject matter.

> On their date, Sheila ~~rattled~~ *rattles* on about fraternity men, tanning, and college. She ~~didn't~~ *doesn't* know that the narrator ~~was~~ *is* trying to choose between her and the fish. Later the narrator ~~wondered~~ *wonders* why he chose Sheila instead of the fish.

In the example above, the present tense gives the writing a sense of immediacy and moves the character study forward. Note, however, the verb *chose* in the last sentence. It's correct to use past tense to indicate actions or events that took place in a character's past or earlier in the story. For more information about verb tense, see page 923 of the Grammar Handbook.

Try Your Hand: Using Verb Tense

On a separate sheet of paper, revise the following paragraph using the correct tense.

> The conflict begins when Sheila looked at the narrator and said, "I think fishing's dumb." The narrator had watched Sheila all summer, and he still admired her at the dance. But he regrets losing that bass, too. Sheila and the narrator did not have much in common.

SkillBuilder

 GRAMMAR FROM WRITING

Using Irregular Verb Forms Correctly

An **irregular verb** forms its past and past participle in some way other than adding *-ed* to the base.

BASE	PAST	PAST PARTICIPLE
swim	swam	(have) swum
lay	laid	(have) laid
teach	taught	(have) taught

APPLYING WHAT YOU'VE LEARNED
On paper write the past or past participle of a verb in the list above to complete each sentence.

1. Sheila's admirer ___ near the raft every day.
2. Many times he ___ out plans for meeting her.
3. His experience ___ him something important.

Examine your draft to make sure you have used irregular verbs correctly and effectively.

GRAMMAR HANDBOOK

For more information on verb forms see page 923 of the Grammar Handbook.

WRITING COACH

Check out the grammar mini-lessons on punctuating dialogue and adjective clauses in the Writing Coach as you revise and edit your character study.

WRITING ABOUT LITERATURE **87**

CUSTOMIZING FOR

Students Acquiring English

 Before you begin this page, be sure that students understand the difference between the present tense and the past tense of verbs. Explain that the present tense is used to express an action or a state of being occurring now or to express a continuing action. The special use of the present tense explained in this lesson is sometimes called the literary present. Examples from the sample paragraph include *rattles*, *does(n't) know*, *is*, and *wonders*. Then explain that the past tense expresses an action or state of being that occurred in the past but did not continue into the present. An example from the sample paragraph is *chose*.

Teaching Strategy:
USING THE SKILLBUILDER

 You can help students to understand the correct use of irregular verb forms by teaching the SkillBuilder on Using Irregular Verb Forms Correctly.

Critical Thinking:
MAKING INFERENCES

 Challenge students to explain why the verb *chose* is correct in the last sentence of the example. *(Possible response: As can be concluded from the independent clause "Later the narrator wonders," the action of choosing is seen from the narrator's own point of view; this action is now over and done.)*

Try Your Hand

Revisions should incorporate the following changes in verbs: *looks, says, has watched, admires, do* (not) *have*.

PORTFOLIO

Ask students to jot down what they like best about their character studies. Then invite them to make a brief list of the weaknesses or trouble spots in their studies. Students may wish to include their informal evaluations along with their studies in their portfolio.

SkillBuilder GRAMMAR FROM WRITING

USING IRREGULAR VERB FORMS CORRECTLY
Remind students that some irregular verbs have identical forms for the present, the past, and the past participle. Present these examples:

Present	Past	Past Participle
put	put	(have) put
hit	hit	(have) hit
cost	cost	(have) cost

Application
1. swam or has swum
2. laid or has laid
3. taught or has taught

Additional Suggestions Have students give the past and past participle forms of these verbs: sing, give, say, catch, rise, raise, beat. *(sang/ [have] sung, gave/[have] given, said/[have] said, caught/[have] caught, rose/[have] risen, raised/[have] raised, beat/[have] beaten)*

Reteaching/Reinforcement
• *Grammar Mini-Lessons* copymasters pp. 30–32, transparencies p.32

 The Writer's Craft

Principal Parts of Irregular Verbs pp. 595–596

THE LANGUAGE OF LITERATURE TEACHER'S EDITION **87**

READING THE WORLD

On pages 84–87, students analyzed a character from literature. They should also be aware that real people reveal their personality traits through their physical appearance, their statements, and their actions. In this lesson, students will examine how people use different kinds of information to form characterizations of others.

Critical Thinking: OBSERVING

M Students should include factual details such as the age of the woman, her posture, her style of dress, and her surroundings (for example, the armchair in which she is seated, the table with the vase of roses, and the cards or letters that the woman is holding).

Media Literacy: INTERPRETING A PHOTOGRAPH

N Students may infer that the woman is or has been married because of the ring on the finger of her left hand. They may suggest that she is reminiscing about a past love or about her family, or possibly that she is celebrating a holiday or a birthday—all depending on how they interpret the flowers on the table and the cards or letters that she holds in her lap. Students may suggest that the woman has had a reasonably happy life and possesses a pleasant, outgoing personality—based on her composed, serene facial expression.

Speaking and Listening: GROUP DISCUSSION

O Have students work in groups to compare their reactions with the description on page 977 of the person's real identity. Remind students that first impressions often can be influenced by stereotypes, especially in a society like ours, in which we are bombarded daily by images from magazines, newspapers, and television advertising.

READING THE WORLD

Closeup on Character

Like characters in literature, people you encounter in real life or through the media show something about themselves by their appearance, words, actions, and interests. How much information do you need to understand a person's character?

View Look at the woman in the picture. In your notebook describe what you see.

Interpret Use your notes to imagine more about this woman. What would you infer about her personality? her life? her interests? What details led you to these conclusions?

Discuss In a group, share your ideas about this woman. Compare the group's ideas with the description found on the last page of this book. How well does the person's real identity match your first impressions of her? Discuss any ideas you now have about first impressions and drawing conclusions about people.

88 THE LANGUAGE OF LITERATURE TEACHER'S EDITION

SkillBuilder

 CRITICAL THINKING

Avoiding Stereotypes

A **stereotype** is an oversimplified idea about a group of people or a culture. Stereotypes may exist about people of different races, ages, sexes, religions, or appearances. For example, some people might believe that elderly people, like the woman in this photograph, are no longer active and have no contribution to make to society. Stereotyping can lead to discrimination. Consider a woman passed over for a coaching job, a man in a wheelchair denied a job interview, or a teen no one will hire.

APPLYING WHAT YOU'VE LEARNED

In a small group discuss

- other examples of stereotypes that exist today
- a time when you were a victim of stereotyping
- a time when you made a decision about someone that was based on a stereotype
- what you can do to avoid stereotyping others

READING THE WORLD 89

SkillBuilder CRITICAL THINKING

AVOIDING STEREOTYPES If necessary, prompt discussion of stereotyping by inviting students to discuss images in media advertisements and characters in movies and television programs.

Application

- Other examples of contemporary stereotypes might include the computer nerd, the dimwitted model, the macho athlete, the no-nonsense detective, and the doting grandparent.
- Students might suggest that their physical appearance, for example, led to unfair snap judgments by a teacher or peer about their talents or interests.
- Remind students that they should be aware of their own biases when judging other people.
- Encourage students to suggest specific strategies, such as asking "What if?" questions about people's interests or abilities. For example: "What if Ms. Johnson, the librarian, turned out to be an incredible electric bass guitar player?"

UNIT ONE
Part 2 Lesson Planner

TIME ALLOTMENTS SHOWN ARE APPROXIMATE. DEPENDING ON YOUR GOALS AND THE NEEDS OF YOUR STUDENTS, YOU MAY WISH TO ALLOW MORE OR LESS TIME FOR CERTAIN PORTIONS OF THE LESSON.

Table of Contents	Discussion	Previewing the Selections	Reading the Selections
PART OPENER **Rites of Passage** page 90	**20 MINUTES** • Reflect on the part theme		
SELECTION **Through the Tunnel** page 92 AVERAGE		**10 MINUTES** • PERSONAL CONNECTION • GEOGRAPHICAL CONNECTION • READING CONNECTION: Drawing conclusions	**40 MINUTES** • Introduce vocabulary • Read pp. 92–102 (11 pp.)
SELECTION **Marigolds** page 107 CHALLENGING		**20 MINUTES** • PERSONAL CONNECTION • HISTORICAL CONNECTION • READING CONNECTION: Using a reading log	**40 MINUTES** • Introduce vocabulary • Read pp. 107–116 (10 pp.)
GENRE LESSON **Focus on Poetry** page 120	**20 MINUTES** • Discuss characteristics of poetry • Discuss strategies for reading poetry		
SELECTIONS **The Road Not Taken/ Fable for When There's No Way Out** page 123–124 AVERAGE		**20 MINUTES** • PERSONAL CONNECTION • PSYCHOLOGICAL CONNECTION • WRITING CONNECTION	**10 MINUTES** • Read pp. 123–124 (2 pp.)
SELECTION **The Beginning of Something** page 128 EASY		**20 MINUTES** • PERSONAL CONNECTION • CULTURAL CONNECTION • READING CONNECTION: Understanding the narrator	**60 MINUTES** • Introduce vocabulary • Read pp. 128–141 (14 pp.)
SELECTION **The First Appendectomy** page 146 EASY		**20 MINUTES** • PERSONAL CONNECTION • MEDICAL CONNECTION • READING CONNECTION: Understanding specialized vocabulary	**20 MINUTES** • Introduce vocabulary • Read pp. 146–151 (6 pp.)
FICTION ON YOUR OWN **Plainswoman** page 154 AVERAGE			**40 MINUTES** • Read pp. 154–163 (10 pp.)
Writing	**Exploring Topics**	**Prewriting**	**Drafting and Revising**
WRITING FROM EXPERIENCE **Report**	**20 MINUTES**	**20 MINUTES**	**65 MINUTES**

Time estimates assume in-class work. You may wish to assign some of these stages as homework.

Responding to the Selection

FROM PERSONAL RESPONSE TO CRITICAL ANALYSIS	OR	ANOTHER PATHWAY	LITERARY CONCEPTS	QUICKWRITES
		40 MINUTES		
• Discussion questions	OR	• Retelling	• Setting/Symbol	• Comparison • Script • Summary
		60 MINUTES		
• Discussion questions	OR	• Cooperative learning (script/dramatization)	• Mood/Symbol	• Paragraph • Essay • Description
		50 MINUTES		
• Discussion questions	OR	• Cooperative learning (posters)	• Rhyme scheme • Free verse	• Poem • Set of instructions
		20 MINUTES		
• Discussion questions	OR	• Point of view	• Main/minor characters	• Personal essay
		40 MINUTES		
• Discussion questions	OR	• Debate	• Author's purpose	• Performance evaluation • Job description • Humorous account

Extension Activities

	ALTERNATIVE ACTIVITIES	LITERARY LINKS	CRITIC'S CORNER	THE WRITER'S STYLE	ACROSS THE CURRICULUM	ART CONNECTION	WORDS TO KNOW	BIOGRAPHY
50 MINUTES	✓	✓	✓	✓	SCIENCE		✓	✓
50 MINUTES	✓	✓			HISTORY ✓	✓		✓
10 MINUTES								✓
20 MINUTES				✓	HEALTH		✓	✓
20 MINUTES	✓				SCIENCE		✓	✓

Publishing and Reflecting

25 MINUTES

PART 2

REFLECTING ON THEME

Ask students to write for ten minutes about a moment or event that stands out in memory as an important milestone. Tell them that this milestone may be either a private, internal realization or a notable occurence—an event. Then ask students to go back over their writing and circle key words and ideas that appeal to them. They should save this material to develop into a piece for their portfolios.

What Do You Think?

Explain to students that a time line always lists events in chronological order—in the order in which those events occured. Students may wish to divide the early part of their timelines into months rather than years. They might also wish to take one year and make a more specific timeline addressing the events which occurred during that time. Students will return to this activity on pages 105, 119, and 126.

UNIT ONE PART 2

RITES OF PASSAGE

REFLECTING ON THEME

Have there been special milestones in your life—moments when you seemed to step forward, gain new confidence or skill, survive a crisis, and feel more grown-up? Do you look forward to other milestones? Such key transition events are sometimes called rites of passage. They may be public or may be known only to you, but they are all part of living and learning. In this part of Unit One, you'll read about some milestones of this sort. They may remind you of your own experiences—or give you a glimpse of what might lie ahead.

What Do You Think? In your notebook, make a time line showing the important rites of passage in your own life —both those in the past and those to come. Draw a vertical line, marked with a zero at the top and divided into decades for the whole expected length of your life. Then, at various points, put labeled dots to indicate rites of passage. Around year 1, for example, you might write "learned to walk"; at a later point, you might write "got first job." Compare your time line with those of classmates.

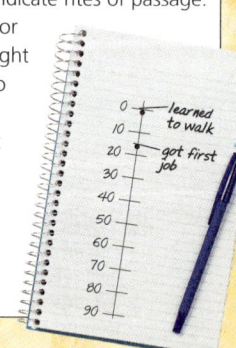

Doris Lessing	**Through the Tunnel** *A boy puts himself to the ultimate test.*	91
Eugenia Collier	**Marigolds** *The consequences of a youthful rage*	106
Robert Frost	**The Road Not Taken** *Could the other road have made as much difference?*	122
May Swenson	**Fable for When There's No Way Out** *Just when you thought you were trapped forever . . .*	122
Sue Ellen Bridgers	**The Beginning of Something** *An unlikely setting leads to the start of a "wonderful adventure."*	127
Gary Soto	**Oranges**/INSIGHT *A boy has a date with a girl for the first time.*	142
William A. Nolen	**The First Appendectomy** *The patient was treated more like the surgeon's victim.*	145
Emily Dickinson	**Surgeons must be very careful**/INSIGHT *What is inside each of us?*	151
Williams Forrest	**Plainswoman** *Out of necessity she did the unthinkable.*	154

PREVIEWING

FICTION

Through the Tunnel
Doris Lessing

Activating Prior Knowledge
PERSONAL CONNECTION

Undoubtedly there have been many times in your life when you took a risk in order to gain something. For instance, perhaps you risked rejection when you tried to make a new friend in your class. In your notebook, create two balance charts modeled on the one shown. In each one, list a risk that you have taken, what you wanted to gain, and what you stood to lose. Then regardless of whether you won or lost, evaluate whether the risks were worth taking.

Building Background
GEOGRAPHICAL CONNECTION

The story you are about to read takes place on a European or North African seacoast, perhaps along the Mediterranean Sea at one of the resorts where the British often go on vacation. The coastal setting consists of nearby but contrasting areas. One is a crowded beach where the swimming is safe. The other is a wild and rocky bay where the swimming is unguarded and involves obvious risk.

Activate Reading / Setting a Purpose
READING CONNECTION

Drawing Conclusions When you draw a conclusion, you add up details and then make a logical guess about the meaning of these details—just like a detective making sense of clues or a judge weighing evidence. As you read "Through the Tunnel," use information in the story and from your own experience to help you conclude why an 11-year-old boy is willing to take a serious risk.

OVERVIEW
Objectives

- To understand and appreciate a short story that explores a young boy's risk-taking in order to prove something to himself
- To recognize and examine setting
- To appreciate and create suspense
- To express understanding of the story through a choice of writing forms, including a comparison, a script, and a summary
- To extend understanding of the story through a variety of multimodal and cross-curricular activities

Skills

LITERARY CONCEPTS
- Setting
- Conflict

THE WRITER'S STYLE
- Sensory detail and description

GRAMMAR
- Adjective or adverb?

SPEAKING, LISTENING, AND VIEWING
- Debate
- Group discussion
- Oral presentation

ALTERNATIVE
Previewing

Students can choose partners and use the following prompts to preview "Through the Tunnel" orally.

Personal Connection

Discussion Prompts Think of a time that you took a risk in order to gain something. In as much detail as possible, describe that experience to your partner. Then listen as your partner describes his or her risk-taking experience. To get started, the following questions might help:

- Where were you?
- Were you alone?
- What did you stand to gain?
- What could you have lost?
- What was the outcome?
- Would you ever take this risk again? Why or why not?

As you read "Through the Tunnel," note the risks taken by the young boy to prove something to himself.

PRINT AND MEDIA RESOURCES

UNIT ONE RESOURCE BOOK
Strategic Reading: Literature, p. 43
Vocabulary SkillBuilder, p. 44

GRAMMAR MINI-LESSONS
Transparencies, p. 22
Copymasters, p. 24

WRITING MINI-LESSONS
Transparencies, p. 46

ACCESS FOR STUDENTS ACQUIRING ENGLISH
Selection Summaries
Reading Support

FORMAL ASSESSMENT
Selection Test, pp. 19–20
 Test Generator

SUMMARY

While vacationing with his mother, 11-year-old Jerry decides to explore a wild-looking bay while his mother goes to the beach. At the bay, he meets a group of older local boys whose language he cannot understand. While diving with them, he sees them swim through an underwater tunnel, but he cannot find the passageway. Eventually they stop letting him be part of their group. Over the next days, Jerry finds the tunnel and practices diving and holding his breath. He endures pain and severe nosebleeds as he builds up the stamina to swim through the tunnel. Finally, two days before he is to leave for home, he attempts to swim through the tunnel, and, after almost losing consciousness, succeeds. He doesn't tell his mother about the experience, but now that he has met his own challenge, he doesn't need to go to the wild bay again.

Thematic Link: *Rites of Passage* A young boy challenges himself by swimming through a dangerous underwater passage.

CUSTOMIZING FOR
Students Acquiring English

- Use **ACCESS FOR STUDENTS ACQUIRING ENGLISH,** *Reading Support.*
- The descriptive style of this selection may confuse some students. You may want to read sections aloud to clarify meanings.
- As you guide students through the selection, you may want to use the suggestions in these boxes as well as the suggestions under Strategic Reading for Less-Proficient Readers.

STRATEGIC READING FOR
Less-Proficient Readers

Set a Purpose Invite students to read the display type on page 93 and then to imagine the crowded beach and the rocky bay. Have them read to find out whether the 11-year-old main character, Jerry, ever gets to the wild and unexplored bay.

Use **UNIT ONE RESOURCE BOOK,** p. 43, for guidance in reading the selection.

THROUGH THE TUNNEL

DORIS LESSING

92 UNIT ONE PART 2: RITES OF PASSAGE

WORDS TO KNOW

beseech (bĭ-sēch′) *v.* to beg (p. 97)
contrition (kən-trĭsh′ən) *n.* a feeling of regret for doing wrong (p. 93)
defiant (dĭ-fī′ənt) *adj.* boldly resistant of an opposing force or authority (p. 97)
incredulous (ĭn-krĕj′ə-ləs) *adj.* doubtful; disbelieving (p. 99)
supplication (sŭp′lĭ-kā′shən) *n.* begging; a humble request or prayer (p. 95)

GOING TO THE SHORE ON THE FIRST MORNING OF THE VACATION, THE YOUNG ENGLISH BOY STOPPED AT A TURNING OF THE PATH AND LOOKED DOWN AT A WILD AND ROCKY BAY, AND THEN OVER TO THE CROWDED BEACH HE KNEW SO WELL FROM OTHER YEARS. HIS MOTHER WALKED ON IN FRONT

of him, carrying a bright striped bag in one hand. Her other arm, swinging loose, was very white in the sun. The boy watched that white, naked arm, and turned his eyes, which had a frown behind them, toward the bay and back again to his mother. When she felt he was not with her, she swung around. "Oh, there you are, Jerry!" she said. She looked impatient, then smiled. "Why, darling, would you rather not come with me? Would you rather—" She frowned, conscientiously worrying over what amusements he might secretly be longing for, which she had been too busy or too careless to imagine. He was very familiar with that anxious, apologetic smile. Contrition sent him running after her. And yet, as he ran, he looked back over his shoulder at the wild bay; and all morning, as he played on the safe beach, he was thinking of it.

Next morning, when it was time for the routine of swimming and sunbathing, his mother said, "Are you tired of the usual beach, Jerry? Would you like to go somewhere else?"

"Oh, no!" he said quickly, smiling at her out of that unfailing impulse of contrition—a sort of chivalry. Yet, walking down the path with her, he blurted out, "I'd like to go and have a look at those rocks down there."

She gave the idea her attention. It was a wild-looking place, and there was no one there; but she said, "Of course, Jerry. When you've had enough, come to the big beach. Or just go straight back to the villa, if you like." She walked away, that bare arm, now slightly reddened from yesterday's sun, swinging. And he almost ran after her again, feeling it unbearable that she should go by herself, but he did not.

WORDS TO KNOW **contrition** (kən-trĭsh′ən) *n.* a feeling of regret for doing wrong

93

Mini-Lesson Literary Concepts

REVIEWING CONFLICT Remind students that conflict refers to a struggle between opposing forces that is the basis of the plot of a story. External conflict involves a character pitted against an outside force—nature, a physical obstacle, or another character. Internal conflict occurs within a character, such as when a personal decision is being made.

Application Ask students to work in groups to identify the conflicts that form the basis of the plot in "Through the Tunnel." As they identify the different conflicts, have them discuss whether each conflict is internal or external. To help get them started, review Jerry's internal conflict, on page 93, over his desire to explore the rocky cove.

CUSTOMIZING FOR
Gifted and Talented Students

As students read the selection, ask them to examine Jerry's relationship with his mother. Have them note details that illustrate changes in their relationship as the story progresses.

Possible responses:

- *Page 93*—"Contrition sent him running after her."/He sensed that she really wanted him with her and felt guilty for his desire to be elsewhere.

- *Page 93*—"And he almost ran after her again, feeling it unbearable that she should go by herself"/He leaves her reluctantly, because of a vague chivalrous notion that it is his expected duty to accompany her everywhere.

- *Page 97*—"'I want some swimming goggles,' he panted, defiant and beseeching."/He is making demands, rather than asking, and asserting his independence.

- *Page 99*—"He did not ask for permission . . . to go to his beach."/He no longer feels he needs his mother's permission to go off by himself.

CUSTOMIZING FOR
Students Acquiring English

I Explain to students that *chivalry* refers to the qualities of an ideal knight of the Middle Ages: courtesy, honor, bravery, generosity, and protection of women.

Literary Concept: CONFLICT

A Invite students to discuss Jerry's mixed feelings toward leaving his mother to go off on his own. Ask whether the conflict here is internal or external. *(Possible response: Although he is bored with the beach and curious to see the rocky bay, he is torn by his feeling that he shouldn't leave his mother; the conflict is internal.)*

She was thinking, Of course he's old enough to be safe without me. Have I been keeping him too close? He mustn't feel he ought to be with me. I must be careful.

He was an only child, eleven years old. She was a widow. She was determined to be neither possessive nor lacking in devotion. She went worrying off to her beach.

As for Jerry, once he saw that his mother had gained her beach, he began the steep descent to the bay. From where he was, high up among red-brown rocks, it was a scoop of moving bluish green fringed with white. As he went lower, he saw that it spread among small promontories[1] and inlets of rough, sharp rock, and the crisping, lapping surface showed stains of purple and darker blue. Finally, as he ran sliding and scraping down the last few yards, he saw an edge of white surf and the shallow, luminous movement of water over white sand, and, beyond that, a solid, heavy blue.

He ran straight into the water and began swimming. He was a good swimmer. He went out fast over the gleaming sand, over a middle region where rocks lay like discolored monsters under the surface, and then he was in the real sea—a warm sea where irregular cold currents from the deep water shocked his limbs.

When he was so far out that he could look back not only on the little bay but past the promontory that was between it and the big beach, he floated on the buoyant surface and looked for his mother. There she was, a speck of yellow under an umbrella that looked like a slice of orange peel. He swam back to

---

1. **promontories** (prŏm′ən-tôr′ēz): high ridges of land or rock jutting out into a body of water.

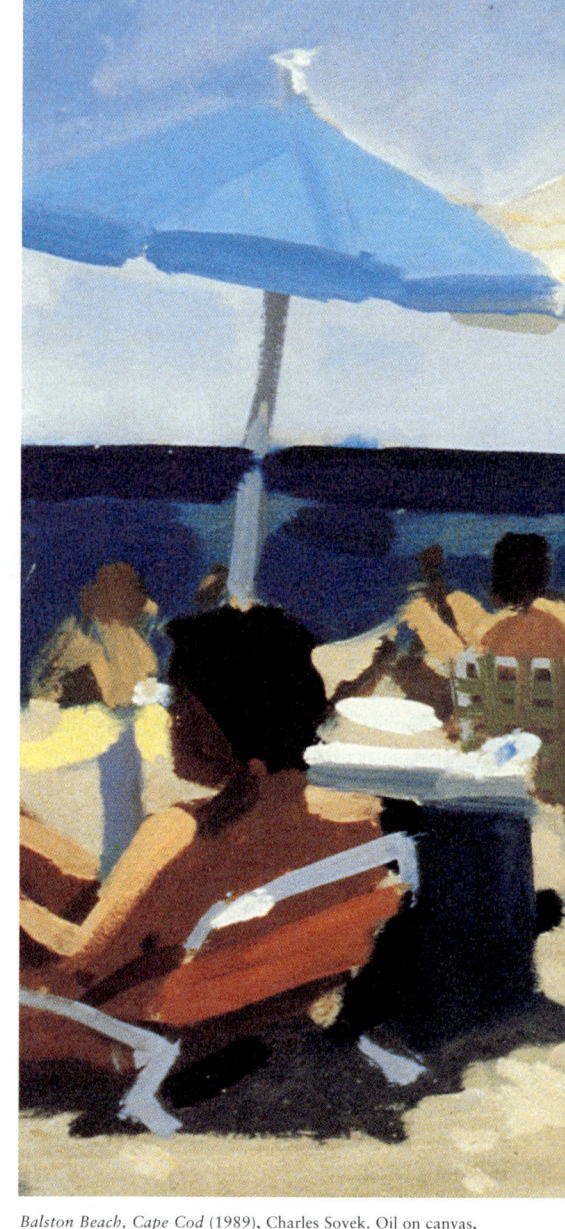

Balston Beach, Cape Cod (1989), Charles Sovek. Oil on canvas, 16″ × 16″, private collection.

shore, relieved at being sure she was there, but all at once very lonely.

On the edge of a small cape that marked the side of the bay away from the promontory was a loose scatter of rocks. Above them, some boys were stripping off their clothes. They came running, naked, down to the rocks. The English boy swam toward them, but kept his distance at a stone's throw. They were of that coast; all of them were burned smooth dark brown and speaking a language he did not understand. To be with them, of them, was a craving that filled his whole body. He swam a little closer; they turned and watched him with narrowed, alert dark eyes. Then one smiled and waved. It was enough. In a minute, he had swum in and was on the rocks beside them, smiling with a desperate, nervous supplication. They shouted cheerful greetings at him; and then, as he preserved his nervous, uncomprehending smile, they understood that he was a foreigner strayed from his own beach, and they proceeded to forget him. But he was happy. He was with them.

They began diving again and again from a high point into a well of blue sea between rough, pointed rocks. After they had dived and come up, they swam around, hauled themselves up, and waited their turn to dive again. They were big boys—men, to Jerry. He dived, and they watched him; and when he swam around to take his place, they made way for him. He felt he was accepted and he dived again, carefully, proud of himself.

Soon the biggest of the boys poised himself, shot down into the water, and did not come up. The others stood about, watching. Jerry, after waiting for the sleek brown head to appear, let out a yell of

WORDS TO KNOW **supplication** (sŭp′lĭ-kā′shən) *n.* begging; a humble request or prayer

---

CUSTOMIZING FOR
Students Acquiring English

3 Explain to students that "a stone's throw" is a phrase that indicates a relatively short distance—the distance someone could mark out by throwing a stone. Invite students to think of similar measurement phrases in English or in their native languages if possible. *(Possible responses: "arm's length," "hop, skip, and a jump")*

Literary Concept: SETTING

C Ask students how the narrator emphasizes that Jerry is an outsider to this setting. *(Possible response: He is referred to as an "English" boy, and the local boys speak a language he does not understand. Also, the mention of the boys' skin being "dark brown" implies a contrast to Jerry's skin, which is probably close in tone to his mother's white coloring.)*

Art Note

Balston Beach, Cape Cod by Charles Sovek Charles Sovek studied painting in his hometown of Pittsburgh before moving to Connecticut. In this impressionistic beach scene, the light shades of the sand, the sky, and the beachgoers contrast with the dark deep blue of the ocean.

Reading the Art *The artist chose to use brush strokes that blur the details of the scene. How does this technique help to evoke the seaside atmosphere?*

STRATEGIC READING FOR
Less-Proficient Readers

D Make sure students have understood Jerry's feelings about going to explore the rocky bay.

- Ask students why Jerry goes to the rocky bay. *(Possible response: The bay is unknown and exciting, and he wants to explore on his own.)* **Summarizing**

- Ask students which details reveal Jerry's mixed feelings about leaving his mother and heading to the rocky bay. *(Possible responses: He doesn't go on the first morning and hesitates to leave on the second; he looks for his mother from the water.)* **Noting Relevant Details**

- Ask students whether they have ever felt torn, like Jerry, between keeping their family company or going off on their own. *(Answers will vary.)* **Connecting**

Set a Purpose Have students read to find out what happens when Jerry tries to follow the other swimmers.

Critical Thinking: ANALYZING

E Ask students why Jerry begins shouting and making silly gestures at the local boys after he fails to find the underwater passage. *(Possible responses: He is embarrassed by his failure and doesn't know what else to do; he wants to get their attention any way that he can.)*

Linking to Geography

F Have students look at a map of Europe and the Mediterranean region and ask them to speculate about which country Jerry and his mother may be visiting. *(Possible responses: Nearness to England makes the Atlantic coasts of France, Spain, and Portugal and the western region of the Mediterranean possible sites. But Jerry's use of French to try to get the local boys' attention makes France and North Africa the strongest candidates.)*

At first, Jerry liked diving with the boys, because they seemed to _____ him.

a. fear   b. accept
c. ignore   d. idolize

---

warning; they looked at him idly and turned their eyes back toward the water. After a long time, the boy came up on the other side of a big dark rock, letting the air out of his lungs in a sputtering gasp and a shout of triumph. Immediately the rest of them dived in. One moment, the morning seemed full of chattering boys; the next, the air and the surface of the water were empty. But through the heavy blue, dark shapes could be seen moving and groping.

D

Jerry dived, shot past the school of underwater swimmers, saw a black wall of rock looming at him, touched it, and bobbed up at once to the surface, where the wall was a low barrier he could see across. There was no one visible; under him, in the water, the dim shapes of the swimmers had disappeared. Then one, and then another of the boys came up on the far side of the barrier of rock, and he understood that they had swum through some gap or hole in it. He plunged down again. He could see nothing through the stinging salt water but the blank rock. When he came up the boys were all on the diving rock, preparing to attempt the feat again. And now, in a panic of failure, he yelled up, in English, "Look at me! Look!" and he began splashing and kicking in the water like a foolish dog.

E They looked down gravely, frowning. He knew the frown. At moments of failure, when he clowned to claim his mother's attention, it was with just this grave, embarrassed inspection that she rewarded him. Through his hot shame, feeling the pleading grin on his face like a scar that he could never remove, he looked up at the group of big brown boys on the rock and shouted, *"Bonjour! Merci! Au revoir! Monsieur,*
F *monsieur!"*[2] while he hooked his fingers round his ears and waggled them.

Water surged into his mouth; he choked, sank, came up. The rock, lately weighted with boys, seemed to rear up out of the water as their weight was removed. They were flying down past him, now, into the water; the air was full of falling bodies. Then the rock was empty in the hot sunlight. He counted one, two, three. . . .

At fifty, he was terrified. They must all be drowning beneath him, in the watery caves of the rock! At a hundred, he stared around him at the empty hillside, wondering if he should yell for help. He counted faster, faster, to hurry them up, to bring them to the surface quickly, to drown them quickly—anything rather than the terror of counting on and on into the blue emptiness of the morning. And then, at a hundred and sixty, the water beyond the rock was full of boys blowing like brown whales. They swam back to the shore without a look at him.

He climbed back to the diving rock and sat down, feeling the hot roughness of it under his thighs. The boys were gathering up their bits of clothing and running off along the shore to another promontory. They were leaving to get away from him. He cried openly, fists in his eyes. There was no one to see him, and he cried himself out.

It seemed to him that a long time had passed, and he swam out to where he could see his mother. Yes, she was still there, a yellow spot under an orange umbrella. He swam back to the big rock, climbed up, and dived into the blue pool among the fanged and angry boulders. Down he went, until he touched the wall of rock again. But the salt was so painful in his eyes that he could not see.

He came to the surface, swam to shore, and went back to the villa to wait for his mother.

---
2. *"Bonjour! Merci! Au revoir! Monsieur, monsieur!"* (bôn-zhōōr′ měr-sē′ ō-rə-vwär′ mə-syœ′) French: "Good day! Thank you! Goodbye! Sir, sir!"

96 UNIT ONE PART 2: RITES OF PASSAGE

Mini-Lesson / Study Skills

TAKING OBJECTIVE TESTS: Sentence Completion Write the sample shown on the left on the chalkboard and use it to illustrate one form of the standardized, or objective, test in English: the sentence-completion activity. Explain that in such tests students are given a sentence with a word omitted and are required to choose a word from a group of three or four to complete the sentence. The correct word will be the one that best fits the meaning of the sentence. Understanding the relationship of the missing word to the sentence will help students make the correct choice.

Application Ask students to supply the missing words.

1. The crashing waves and strong undertow made the beach a _____ place.
   a. dangerous   b. delightful
   c. picturesque   d. restful

2. Longing for _____ and solitude, he spent the day swimming by himself.
   a. companionship b. distraction
   c. quiet   d. triumph

Soon she walked slowly up the path, swinging her striped bag, the flushed, naked arm dangling beside her. "I want some swimming goggles," he panted, <u>defiant</u> and <u>beseeching</u>.

She gave him a patient, inquisitive look as she said casually, "Well, of course, darling."

But now, now, now! He must have them this minute, and no other time. He nagged and pestered until she went with him to a shop. As soon as she had bought the goggles, he grabbed them from her hand as if she were going to claim them for herself, and was off, running down the steep path to the bay.

Jerry swam out to the big barrier rock, adjusted the goggles, and dived. The impact of the water broke the rubber-enclosed vacuum, and the goggles came loose. He understood that he must swim down to the base of the rock from the surface of the water. He fixed the goggles tight and firm, filled his lungs, and floated, face down, on the water. Now, he could see. It was as if he had eyes of a different kind—fish eyes that showed everything clear and delicate and wavering in the bright water.

Under him, six or seven feet down, was a floor of perfectly clean, shining white sand, rippled firm and hard by the tides. Two grayish shapes steered there, like long, rounded pieces of wood or slate. They were fish. He saw them nose toward each other, poise motionless, make a dart forward, swerve off, and come around again. It was like a water dance. A few inches above them the water sparkled as if sequins were dropping through it. Fish again—myriads of minute fish, the length of his fingernail, were drifting through the water, and in a moment he could feel the innumerable tiny touches of them against his limbs. It was like swimming in flaked silver. The great rock the big boys had swum through rose sheer out of the white sand—black, tufted lightly with greenish weed. He could see no gap in it. He swam down to its base.

Again and again he rose, took a big chestful of air, and went down. Again and again he groped over the surface of the rock, feeling it, almost hugging it in the desperate need to find the entrance. And then, once, while he was clinging to the black wall, his knees came up and he shot his feet out forward and they met no obstacle. He had found the hole.

He gained the surface, clambered about the stones that littered the barrier rock until he found a big one, and, with this in his arms, let himself down over the side of the rock. He dropped, with the weight, straight to the sandy floor. Clinging tight to the anchor of stone, he lay on his side and looked in under the dark shelf at the place where his feet had gone. He could see the hole. It was an irregular, dark gap; but he could not see deep into it. He let go of his anchor, clung with his hands to the edges of the hole, and tried to push himself in.

He got his head in, found his shoulders jammed, moved them in sidewise, and was inside as far as his waist. He could see nothing ahead. Something soft and clammy touched his mouth; he saw a dark frond moving against the grayish rock, and panic filled him. He thought of octopuses, of clinging weed. He pushed himself out backward and caught a glimpse, as he retreated, of a harmless tentacle of seaweed drifting in the mouth of the tunnel.

> HE COULD SEE THE HOLE. IT WAS AN IRREGULAR, DARK GAP; BUT HE COULD NOT SEE DEEP INTO IT.

WORDS TO KNOW
defiant (dĭ-fī′ənt) *adj.* boldly resistant of an opposing force or authority
beseech (bĭ-sēch′) *v.* to beg

97

Critical Thinking: ANALYZING

G Ask what the two adjectives *defiant* and *beseeching* illustrate about Jerry's feelings. *(Possible response: He is in a transitional phase of his life: beginning to demand like an independent-minded teenager while still pleading like an immature child.)*

Critical Thinking: HYPOTHESIZING

H Ask students why Jerry's mother buys him the goggles immediately. *(Possible responses: She spoils him; she doesn't want to disappoint him.)*

Literary Concept: IMAGERY

I Point out that with the goggles Jerry sees a dancing, silvery world underwater. Ask students how the images used to describe the rock create a contrast. *(Possible response: The black, looming rock, tufted with green seaweed, seems threatening.)*

Mini-Lesson: Speaking, Listening, and Viewing

DEBATE Explain to students that a debate is not merely a chance to voice an opinion against something that they disagree with. It is an opportunity to hear and learn about ideas that might help them evaluate their way of thinking about an issue. Point out that preparing to argue *against* a position they support can, in fact, be an excellent way of exploring all sides of an issue.

Application Have students form groups of four to debate Jerry's decision to swim through the tunnel. One pair within each group will argue for the swim, the other against the swim. Toss a coin to determine which position each pair will take. Give each group 15 minutes to prepare for the debate by developing arguments for their position.

STRATEGIC READING FOR
Less-Proficient Readers

J Have students list the events that occur between the time of the local boys' swim through the tunnel and the present time with Jerry lying on the diving rock. *(Jerry is humiliated at his inability to follow the local boys, has his mother buy him goggles, and explores beneath the surface, finding the entrance to the underwater passage.)* **Noting Sequence of Events**

Set a Purpose Have students read further, paying close attention to Jerry's preparations and thought processes as he decides whether to attempt the swim through the tunnel.

Literary Concept: SYMBOL

K Ask students to note how Jerry feels about the other beach. Invite them to compare and contrast what the beach and the rocky bay each represent to him. *(Possible responses: The rocky bay represents challenge, danger, adulthood; the beach represents safety, childhood.)*

J But it was enough. He reached the sunlight, swam to shore, and lay on the diving rock. He looked down into the blue well of water. He knew he must find his way through that cave, or hole, or tunnel, and out the other side.

First, he thought, he must learn to control his breathing. He let himself down into the water with another big stone in his arms, so that he could lie effortlessly on the bottom of the sea. He counted. One, two, three. He counted steadily. He could hear the movement of blood in his chest. Fifty-one, fifty-two. . . . His chest was hurting. He let go of the rock and went up into the air. He saw that the sun was low. He rushed to the villa and found his mother at her supper. She said only "Did you enjoy yourself?" and he said "Yes."

All night the boy dreamed of the water-filled cave in the rock, and as soon as breakfast was over he went to the bay.

That night, his nose bled badly. For hours he had been underwater, learning to hold his breath, and now he felt weak and dizzy. His mother said, "I shouldn't overdo things, darling, if I were you."

That day and the next, Jerry exercised his lungs as if everything, the whole of his life, all that he would become, depended upon it. Again his nose bled at night, and his mother insisted on his coming with her the next day. It was a torment to him to waste a day of his careful self-training, but he stayed with her on that other beach, which now seemed a place for small children, a place where his mother might lie safe in the sun. It was not his beach. **K**

98 UNIT ONE   PART 2: RITES OF PASSAGE

Mini-Lesson Grammar

Linking Verbs
- become
- seem
- appear
- look
- sound
- feel
- taste
- smell
- grow
- be (am, are, is)

ADJECTIVE OR ADVERB? Tell students that adjectives modify nouns/pronouns. Adverbs modify action verbs, adjectives, or other adverbs.

　Jerry smiled sadly. 　　Jerry felt sad.

Warn students about verbs such as *smell, look, seem,* and *feel*. These verbs are frequently used as linking, not action, verbs and require adjectives.

Application Have students find single-word adjectives and adverbs immediately following verbs in the highlighted section on page 98. (adjectives = *low, over, weak, dizzy;* adverbs = *steadily, up, badly*) Then read the following sentences aloud. Have students choose the correct modifier.

1. His chest hurt (bad, badly). *(badly)*
2. His conditioning was (quick, quickly). *(quick)*

Reteaching/Reinforcement
- *Grammar Handbook,* anthology p. 918
- *Grammar Mini-Lessons* copymasters p. 24, transparencies p. 22

 The Writer's Craft
Using the Correct Modifier, pp. 628–629

Ice Blue (1981), Susan Shatter. Oil on canvas, 40″ × 90″, private collection, courtesy of Fischbach Gallery, New York.

Linking to Mathematics

L Ask students to work in pairs to time how long they can hold their breath. Have each student try it three times, and then record the average number of seconds. Compute a class average. How does it compare with Jerry's first and final attempts?
Ice Blue by Susan Shatter This New

Art Note

York artist (1943–) uses rich colors and jagged lines to depict the rugged textures of a rocky cove.

Reading the Art *Compare this painting with* Balston Beach, Cape Cod *shown earlier in this selection. How does this work convey a different impression of the ocean?*

He did not ask for permission, on the following day, to go to his beach. He went, before his mother could consider the complicated rights and wrongs of the matter. A day's rest, he discovered, had improved his count by ten. The big boys had made the passage while he counted a hundred and sixty. He had been counting fast, in his fright. Probably now, if he tried, he could get through that long tunnel, but he was not going to try yet. A curious, most unchildlike persistence, a controlled impatience, made him wait. In the meantime, he lay underwater on the white sand, littered now by stones he had brought down from the upper air, and studied the entrance to the tunnel. He knew every jut and corner of it, as far as it was possible to see. It was as if he already felt its sharpness about his shoulders.

He sat by the clock in the villa, when his mother was not near, and checked his time. He was <u>incredulous</u> and then proud to find he

WORDS TO KNOW	**incredulous** (ĭn-krĕj′ə-ləs) *adj.* doubtful; disbelieving

Critical Thinking:
MAKING INFERENCES

M Ask students why Jerry is scared not to swim through the passage. *(Possible responses: He is ashamed of his fear; he will feel like a failure if he doesn't make an attempt.)*

Literary Concept: CONFLICT

N Ask students to discuss what, in additional to the fear of death, may be the unspoken concerns Jerry is struggling with as he decides whether to risk swimming through the underwater passage. *(Possible responses: his desire to undo his humiliation of the second day, his desire to be independent)*

STRATEGIC READING FOR
Less-Proficient Readers

O Ask students to review how Jerry's preparation for the tunnel swim is at work here. *(He had practiced using rocks to help him sink to the bottom, had increased the length of time he could stay underwater, and had explored how to best enter the tunnel.)* **Summarizing**

Set a Purpose Have students read to find out whether Jerry makes it through the tunnel.

---

could hold his breath without strain for two minutes. The words "two minutes," authorized by the clock, brought close the adventure that was so necessary to him.

In another four days, his mother said casually one morning, they must go home. On the day before they left, he would do it. He would do it if it killed him, he said defiantly to himself. But two days before they were to leave—a day of triumph when he increased his count by fifteen—his nose bled so badly that he turned dizzy and had to lie limply over the big rock like a bit of seaweed, watching the thick red blood flow on to the rock and trickle slowly down to the sea. He was frightened. Supposing he turned dizzy in the tunnel? Supposing he died there, trapped? Supposing—his head went around, in the hot sun, and he almost gave up. He thought he would return to the house and lie down, and next summer, perhaps, when he had another year's growth in him—*then* he would go through the hole.

But even after he had made the decision, or thought he had, he found himself sitting up on the rock and looking down into the water; and he knew that now, this moment, when his nose had only just stopped bleeding, when his head was still sore and throbbing—this was the moment when he would try. If he did not do it now, he never would. He was trembling with fear that he would not go; and he was trembling with horror at that long, long tunnel under the rock, under the sea. Even in the open sunlight, the barrier rock seemed very wide and very heavy; tons of rock pressed down on where he would go. If he died there, he would lie until one day—perhaps not before next year—those big boys would swim into it and find it blocked.

He put on his goggles, fitted them tight, tested the vacuum. His hands were shaking. Then he chose the biggest stone he could carry and slipped over the edge of the rock until half of him was in the cool, enclosing water and half in the hot sun. He looked up once at the empty sky, filled his lungs once, twice, and then sank fast to the bottom with the stone. He let it go and began to count. He took the edges of the hole in his hands and drew himself into it, wriggling his shoulders in sidewise as he remembered he must, kicking himself along with his feet.

Soon he was clear inside. He was in a small rock-bound hole filled with yellowish-gray water. The water was pushing him up against the roof. The roof was sharp and pained his back. He pulled himself along with his hands—fast, fast—and used his legs as levers. His head knocked against something; a sharp pain dizzied him. Fifty, fifty-one, fifty-two. . . . He was without light, and the water seemed to press upon him with the weight of rock. Seventy-one, seventy-two. . . .

There was no strain on his lungs. He felt like an inflated balloon, his

IF HE DIED THERE, HE WOULD LIE UNTIL ONE DAY...THOSE BIG BOYS WOULD SWIM INTO IT AND FIND IT BLOCKED.

100 UNIT ONE PART 2: RITES OF PASSAGE

lungs were so light and easy, but his head was pulsing.

He was being continually pressed against the sharp roof, which felt slimy as well as sharp. Again he thought of octopuses, and wondered if the tunnel might be filled with weed that could tangle him. He gave himself a panicky, convulsive kick forward, ducked his head, and swam. His feet and hands moved freely, as if in open water. The hole must have widened out. He thought he must be swimming fast, and he was frightened of banging his head if the tunnel narrowed.

A hundred, a hundred and one. . . . The water paled. Victory filled him. His lungs were beginning to hurt. A few more strokes and he would be out. He was counting wildly; he said a hundred and fifteen, and then, a long time later, a hundred and fifteen again. The water was a clear jewel-green all around him. Then he saw, above his head, a crack running up through the rock. Sunlight was falling through it, showing the clean, dark rock of the tunnel, a single mussel shell, and darkness ahead.

He was at the end of what he could do. He looked up at the crack as if it were filled with air and not water, as if he could put his mouth to it to draw in air. A hundred and fifteen, he heard himself say inside his head—but he had said that long ago. He must go on into the blackness ahead, or he would drown. His head was swelling, his lungs cracking. A hundred and fifteen, a hundred and fifteen pounded through his head, and he feebly clutched at rocks in the dark, pulling himself forward, leaving the brief space of sunlit water behind.

He felt he was dying. He was no longer quite conscious. He struggled on in the darkness between lapses into unconsciousness. An immense, swelling pain filled his head, and then the darkness cracked with an explosion of green light. His hands, groping forward, met nothing; and his feet, kicking back, propelled him out into the open sea.

He drifted to the surface, his face turned up to the air. He was gasping like a fish. He felt he would sink now and drown; he could not swim the few feet back to the rock. Then he was clutching it and pulling himself up onto it. He lay face down, gasping. He could see nothing but a red-veined, clotted dark. His eyes must have burst, he thought; they were full of blood. He tore off his goggles and a gout of blood went into the sea. His nose was bleeding, and the blood had filled the goggles.

He scooped up handfuls of water from the cool, salty sea, to splash on his face, and did not know whether it was blood or salt water he tasted. After a time, his heart quieted, his eyes cleared, and he sat up. He could see the local boys diving and playing half a mile away. He did not want them. He wanted nothing but to get back home and lie down.

In a short while, Jerry swam to shore and climbed slowly up the path to the villa. He flung himself on his bed and slept, waking at the sound of feet on the path outside. His mother was coming back. He rushed to the bathroom, thinking she must not see his face

> HIS EYES MUST HAVE BURST, HE THOUGHT; THEY WERE FULL OF BLOOD. HE TORE OFF HIS GOGGLES AND A GOUT OF BLOOD WENT INTO THE SEA.

THROUGH THE TUNNEL 101

Linking to Science

P Humans risk brain damage and death if they are denied oxygen for more than three to four minutes. There are cases, however, of people surviving without air for longer periods of time. In 1986, two-year-old Michelle Funk of Salt Lake City completely recovered after spending 66 minutes under water.

Literary Concept: CONFLICT

Q Have students discuss the sentence "He was at the end of what he could do." Does this seem more a part of his internal or external conflict? Explain. *(Possible answers: external—he misjudged his physical endurance and can swim no further; internal—he appears to have given up on himself, on his ability to push himself to the limits.)*

STRATEGIC READING FOR
Less-Proficient Readers

R Have students describe how Jerry makes it through the tunnel. *(Lapsing in and out of consciousness, his head pounding with pain, his eyes and nose bleeding, he manages to struggle forward until he finds the open sea and drifts to the surface.)* Clarifying/Summarizing

---

Mini-Lesson The Writer's Style

SENSORY DETAIL AND DESCRIPTION
Point out passages in the selection where Lessing uses descriptive details that appeal to one or more of the five senses. For example, in the passage on page 101, Lessing uses details that appeal to sight (green light, red-veined dark), touch (groping hands meeting nothing, handfuls of cool sea water), and taste (blood/saltwater mixture) to describe what Jerry experiences as he emerges from the tunnel. These details involve the reader in the story and allow a fuller appreciation of Jerry's adventure.

Application Have students work in small groups to locate other examples of sensory, descriptive details in the story. Then have them write brief descriptions of physical ordeals or challenges they have experienced. Ask them to use sensory details.

Reteaching/Reinforcement
- *Writing Handbook*, anthology p. 871
- *Writing Mini-Lessons* transparencies, p. 46

The Writer's Craft
Sensory Details, p. 352

Art Note

***The Swimmer* by Ken Danby** This 1970 lithograph by Canadian artist Ken Danby (1940–) displays an almost photographic realism. Danby is especially well known for his portraits of hockey players and Olympic athletes.

Reading the Art What do you think the boy in the pool is doing or thinking? Which details in the artwork give you this impression?

CUSTOMIZING FOR
Students Acquiring English

④ Define *will* as "a determination or strong desire." Ask students to use this information to restate the phrase "battle of wills." (*Possible response: a struggle between opposing wishes or wants*)

CUSTOMIZING FOR
Gifted and Talented Students

Ⓢ Ask students what effect being in a foreign country might have had on Jerry. If the group of boys had spoken his language, would he still have felt the need to prove himself? Would going through the tunnel have been so important to him?

COMPREHENSION CHECK
1. Where does Jerry go on the second day of his vacation? (*to a wild-looking rocky cove*)
2. What makes Jerry feel humiliated in front of the local boys? (*his inability to find the gap in the wall of rock and follow them through it*)
3. How does Jerry prepare for his attempt to swim through the tunnel? (*He buys a pair of goggles and practices holding his breath.*)
4. How serious a risk does Jerry take swimming through the tunnel? (*very serious; he could easily have died*)

Reflections (1970), Ken Danby. Original egg tempera, 38″ × 52″, by permission of the artist and Gallery Moos, Toronto, Canada.

with bloodstains, or tearstains, on it. He came out of the bathroom and met her as she walked into the villa, smiling, her eyes lighting up.

"Have a nice morning?" she asked, laying her hand on his warm brown shoulder a moment.

"Oh, yes, thank you," he said.

"You look a bit pale." And then, sharp and anxious, "How did you bang your head?"

"Oh, just banged it," he told her.

She looked at him closely. He was strained; his eyes were glazed-looking. She was worried.

And then she said to herself, Oh, don't fuss! Nothing can happen. He can swim like a fish.

They sat down to lunch together.

"Mummy," he said, "I can stay under water for two minutes—three minutes, at least." It came bursting out of him.

"Can you, darling?" she said. "Well, I shouldn't overdo it. I don't think you ought to swim any more today."

She was ready for a battle of wills, but he gave in at once. It was no longer of the least importance to go to the bay. ❖

102 UNIT ONE PART 2: RITES OF PASSAGE

Assessment Option

INFORMAL ASSESSMENT To assess your students' understanding of the selection, have them write a letter from Jerry to his mother. The letter should detail the risk Jerry took, the events leading up to it, and his motivations for taking it.

Rubric

3 Full Accomplishment Students' letters fully explain Jerry's risk, the events leading up to it, and his motivations. Details of letters are consistent with the selection content.

2 Substantial Accomplishment Students' letters explain Jerry's risk, the events leading up to it, and his motivations. Details of letters are not completely consistent with the selection content.

1 Little or Partial Accomplishment Students' letters fail to explain Jerry's risk, the events leading up to it, and his motivations or contain details inconsistent with the selection content.

RESPONDING OPTIONS

FROM PERSONAL RESPONSE TO CRITICAL ANALYSIS

REFLECT
1. What did you think of Jerry's swim through the tunnel? Jot down your impressions in your notebook and share them with your classmates.

RETHINK

Close Textual Reading

2. How does Jerry seem to feel about himself after swimming through the tunnel?
   Consider
   • why he no longer feels the need to join the boys
   • why he doesn't tell his mother about what he managed to do
   • why it is no longer of the "least importance" for him to go to the bay

3. Describe Jerry's relationship with his mother.

Close Textual Reading

4. Why do you think it is so important to Jerry to take the risk he did?
   Consider
   • his age and family situation
   • his interactions with the older boys
   • how he reacted when the boys left
   • what he was trying to prove to himself

Thematic Link

5. Do you think Jerry's swim through the tunnel qualifies as a rite of passage? Explain your opinion.

RELATE
6. As a single parent, Jerry's mother is unsure of how to achieve a balance between concern and control in raising an 11-year-old. As older teenagers, discuss what you think is a proper balance. Give examples.

Multimodal Learning
ANOTHER PATHWAY

Cooperative Learning
In a small group, think of an alternative ending to the story. Then discuss how your ending would change the meaning and impact of the entire story. Share your conclusions with the class as a panel discussion. Each member of your panel could present an aspect of your changes in the story.

QUICKWRITES

1. Look over the chart that you made before reading this story. Write a **comparison** of a risk you've taken and the one that Jerry took. Was your risk as serious as Jerry's? Could both be considered rites of passage?

2. How do you think Jerry would react if, 20 years from the time of this story, his own son or daughter seemed drawn to risky behavior? Write a **script** for a conversation between Jerry and his child.

3. The line between courage and foolishness is often a thin one. Interview five classmates and write a **summary** of their opinions about the wisdom of Jerry's action.

📁 **PORTFOLIO** Save your writing. You may want to use it later as a springboard to a piece for your portfolio.

LITERARY LINKS

Compare the main characters and what they seek in "Through the Tunnel" and "The Bass, the River, and Sheila Mant."

THROUGH THE TUNNEL 103

From Personal Response to Critical Analysis

1. Accept all reasonable responses.
2. Possible responses: Jerry is proud of his accomplishment and has acquired enough self-confidence not to need to have everyone know what he did; he no longer has to prove himself.
3. Possible responses: Jerry's mother worries that she may be overprotecting him. At the same time, she worries that he may be exhausting himself. He tries to protect her, but he is at an age when young people often begin asserting an independence from parents, and he now doesn't communicate very freely with his mother.
4. Possible responses: Jerry is at an age when people often lack confidence, and adolescents may try to copy the behavior of older adolescents. Because he has no siblings or father, this incident may have suddenly become the way for Jerry to prove himself to peers or as a boy, while erasing the humiliation he felt in front of the local boys.
5. Possible responses: Yes, Jerry uses discipline and preparation to achieve a goal at great personal risk; no, taking a foolish risk is not a rite of passage.
6. Accept all reasonable responses supported by examples.

Another Pathway

Cooperative Learning Groups of five or six should collaborate on the alternative ending and discuss how the ending would change the meaning of the story. One student can record these ideas; another can encourage participation. The remaining students should be panel members, one presenting the new ending and the others elaborating on its impact on the story's meaning.

Rubric

3 Full Accomplishment Students participate in creating an alternative ending and fully explore its impact on the meaning of the story.

2 Substantial Accomplishment Students create an ending but describe less fully its impact on the story's meaning.

1 Little or Partial Accomplishment Students have difficulty creating an ending or describing the significance of an alternative ending.

Literary Links

Possible responses:

Jerry
• 11-year-old boy on summer vacation
• impressed by what older boys can do and wants to be like them

Narrator
• 14-year-old boy on summer vacation
• impressed by older girl, with whom he's infatuated, and would like to be part of her world

QuickWrites

1. Remind students to check the balance charts they made before they compare the risks.
2. Encourage students to review details of the relationship between Jerry and his mother before they begin writing.
3. Have students create lists of open-ended questions before conducting their interviews.

The Writer's Craft

Comparison, pp. 141–142
Dialogue, p. 436
Interview, pp. 104–106

THE LANGUAGE OF LITERATURE TEACHER'S EDITION 103

Literary Concepts

Have students form small groups to answer the following questions.

- What aspects of the setting are major contributors to the story?
- Describe details in the setting that contribute to the story's feeling of suspense.

Concept Review *Possible responses: Rocky Bay—the unknown, adulthood, danger; tunnel—the overcoming of fear, the uncertain journey from childhood to maturity, achievement*

Critic's Corner

Accept all reasonable responses to the observation that are supported by logical reasoning.

The Writer's Style

Invite students to list the events and details that helped create anxiety or curiosity about what would happen next as they read the story.

Across the Curriculum

Science *Cooperative Learning* Encourage students to form research groups to investigate deep-sea diving. Have them discuss what they would like to learn about the underwater activity. One student can record the questions, one can suggest areas of research, and a third can assign the research questions to the others. Once the research is completed, one group member can consolidate and present the information in a graph, chart, or poster.

LITERARY CONCEPTS

Setting is the time and place of the action of a story. Some stories, such as "The Utterly Perfect Murder," have only a minimal description of the setting. In other stories, such as "A Christmas Memory," setting is described in detail and becomes a major contributor to the story's total effect. Explain what you feel the importance of setting is to "Through the Tunnel."

CONCEPT REVIEW: Symbol In "Through the Tunnel," key parts of the setting have symbolic meaning. For example, the sheltered beach, the rocky bay, and the tunnel itself all represent something to Jerry. Make a chart like the one shown and identify what each part of the setting could possibly represent.

Part of Setting	Symbolic Meaning
Sheltered beach	safety; childhood
Rocky bay	
Tunnel	

Multimodal Learning

ACROSS THE CURRICULUM

Science Research deep-sea diving. What is the record for depth of dive, with and without oxygen tanks? How does diving cause nosebleeds such as those Jerry suffers? What other dangers are involved in this sport? Report your findings in charts or graphs.

104 UNIT ONE PART 2: RITES OF PASSAGE

Multimodal Learning

ALTERNATIVE ACTIVITIES

1. Reread the story, focusing on the description of the rocky bay and the tunnel. Draw a **cutaway diagram** showing a cross-section of the rocks and the tunnel and present it to the class. If you have a graphics program on your computer, now is the time to use it.
2. Based on your own experience or that of someone you know, create an **oral tale** about a boy or a girl trying to prove something. Tell your story to the class.

CRITIC'S CORNER

One teenage reader of this story claimed that Jerry's success was "a hollow victory." State your reasons for agreeing or disagreeing with this observation.

THE WRITER'S STYLE

Suspense is that excitement you feel when you don't know what's going to happen next. Look back through the last half of the story, which deals with Jerry's preparation for and final swim through the tunnel. How did the author create suspense? How was she able to maintain the suspense over several pages?

Alternative Activities

1. Encourage students to take notes about the tunnel as they reread the description in the story. With these notes, they can make lists of features and facts about the tunnel. Have them use their lists as guides to creating cutaway diagrams. Students can use the lists to check the completed diagrams for factual accuracy.
2. Have students include details in their tales that illustrate what the character is trying to prove and why proving it is so important. Suggest that they rehearse the tale in front of a mirror, or practice reciting it to a partner, before telling it to the class.

WORDS TO KNOW

Review the Words to Know at the bottom of the selection pages. Then for each phrase in the first column, find the phrase in the second column that is closest in meaning. Write the letter of that phrase on your paper.

1. **contrition** due to not locking the barn door
2. **supplication** for the lumberjack to leave
3. **defiant** in swimming among the giant waves
4. **beseech** someone to make breakfast
5. **incredulous** about the road you choose

a. rebels against the swells
b. beg for an egg
c. regret that the goose is loose
d. full of doubt about the route
e. plea to save a tree

DORIS LESSING

1919–

One of the most respected writers of our day, Doris Lessing was born to British parents in Persia (present-day Iran). She moved with them to Southern Rhodesia (present-day Zimbabwe) in 1924, where her father became a farmer. Lessing lived in Africa until she was 30 and was strongly affected by life there. Years later she wrote, "The fact is, I don't live anywhere; I never have since I left that first home on the kopje [hill]." Her experiences in colonial Africa made her sensitive to racial and economic exploitation, a subject she has touched upon often in her writing.

After the breakup of her second marriage in 1949, Lessing moved with her three-year-old son to England. A year later she published the first of her many books. She soon became an acclaimed author, even though her politics (she was a communist until 1956) made her controversial for a number of years. Between 1979 and 1984 she surprised the literary world twice—first, by publishing a series of five science fiction novels, and second, by publishing two novels under the name Jane Somers. Lessing confessed that she was the unknown Jane Somers only after the two books were virtually ignored by critics and buyers. She had wanted to prove the point that today books by new writers have almost no chance of success.

Though known mainly for her novels, Lessing has written many short stories. She has noted that "some writers I know have stopped writing short stories because, as they say, 'there is no market for them.' Others like myself, the addicts, go on, and I suspect would go on even if there really wasn't any home for them but a private drawer."

"Through the Tunnel" was published in her 1957 short story collection *The Habit of Loving*. In reviewing the book, one critic found that her characters maintain "a certain secrecy both of feelings and motives." Another praised the stories' "pictorial power" and found in the loneliness of her main characters a similarity to stories by Ray Bradbury.

OTHER WORKS *The Grass Is Singing, Going Home, African Stories, The Doris Lessing Reader, African Laughter*

Extended Reading

Words to Know
1. c
2. e
3. a
4. b
5. d

Reteaching/Reinforcement
- *Unit One Resource Book*, p. 44

DORIS LESSING

Although her mother wanted her to become a pianist, Doris Lessing showed little ability with the instrument and turned to writing at the age of 18. She wrote six novels but destroyed them herself before achieving her first publishing success in 1950 with *The Grass Is Singing*.

REFLECTING ON THEME
What Do You Think?

Have students think about the rites-of-passage time line they constructed in their notebooks. Ask them to think about Jerry's experience and whether it has suggested anything to them that they hadn't already written down. Allow them to alter their time lines to account for any new rite-of-passage example.

OVERVIEW

Objectives

- To understand and appreciate a short story that explores a young girl's coming of age
- To enrich reading by using active reading strategies
- To recognize and understand mood
- To express understanding of the selection through a choice of writing forms, including a paragraph, an essay, and a description
- To extend understanding of the story through a variety of multimodal and cross-curricular activities

Skills

LITERARY CONCEPTS
- Mood
- Figurative language

READING SKILLS/ STRATEGIES
- Using a reading log
- Active reading: predict

THE WRITER'S STYLE
- Dialect

GRAMMAR
- Pronoun case

SPEAKING, LISTENING, AND VIEWING
- Group discussion
- Oral presentation

ALTERNATIVE
Previewing

Students can choose partners and use the following prompts to preview "Marigolds" orally.

Personal Connection

Discussion Prompts *Think of some of the things that people do that make you angry. In as much detail as possible describe these things to your partner. Then listen as your partner describes things that make him or her angry. To get started, the following phrases might help:*

- *I hate it when people do . . .*
- *It really makes me mad when someone . . .*

As you read "Marigolds," note what the narrator does in a fit of anger.

PREVIEWING

FICTION

Marigolds
Eugenia Collier

Activating Prior Knowledge
PERSONAL CONNECTION

Have you ever done anything in a fit of anger or frustration that you regretted later? Did you perhaps destroy something or hurt someone, simply because you were mad or in a bad mood? In your notebook, write about the incident and how you felt about it later after you had calmed down.

Building Background
HISTORICAL CONNECTION

"Marigolds" takes place during the Great Depression, which began in 1929 with the stock market crash and the resulting failure of many banks. In the aftermath, factories closed, businesses went bankrupt, fortunes were destroyed, and unemployment soared. At the time, there were no programs such as unemployment insurance to help people who had lost all source of income. In many towns, the poor lived in shacks in areas called shantytowns. Although many Americans suffered, African Americans were particularly hard hit. The percentage of unemployed African Americans was higher because they were often the last to be hired and the first to be fired.

Active Reading / Setting a Purpose
READING CONNECTION

Using Your Reading Log Remember that to be an active reader means to use various mental strategies as you read. Questions have been inserted throughout "Marigolds" to help you practice these strategies. As you read, jot down in your reading log responses to these questions, along with other thoughts or feelings about the characters' anger and frustration. When you've finished reading, discuss some of your responses with the class.

A shantytown during the 1930s.
Culver Pictures, Inc.

UNIT ONE   PART 2: RITES OF PASSAGE

PRINT AND MEDIA RESOURCES

UNIT ONE RESOURCE BOOK
Strategic Reading: Literature, p. 47
Vocabulary SkillBuilder, p. 48

GRAMMAR MINI-LESSONS
Transparencies, p. 14
Copymasters, p. 16–17

WRITING MINI-LESSONS
Transparencies, p. 14

ACCESS FOR STUDENTS ACQUIRING ENGLISH
Selection Summaries
Reading Support

FORMAL ASSESSMENT
Selection Test, pp. 21–22
 Test Generator

 AUDIO LIBRARY
See Reference Card

LASERLINKS
Art Gallery

MARIGOLDS

When I think of the home town of my youth, all that I seem to remember is dust—the brown, crumbly dust of late summer—arid, sterile dust that gets into the eyes and makes them water, gets into the throat and between the toes of bare brown feet. I don't know why I should remember only the dust. Surely there must have been lush green lawns and paved streets under leafy shade trees somewhere in town; but memory is an abstract painting—it does not present things as they are, but rather as they FEEL. And so,

Eugenia Collier

MARIGOLDS 107

WORDS TO KNOW

bravado (brə-vä′dō) *n.* a false show of courage or defiance (p. 111)
compassion (kəm-păsh′ən) *n.* deep awareness of the suffering of another coupled with the wish to relieve it (p. 116)
degradation (děg′rə-dā′shən) *n.* a decline to a lower condition, with loss of dignity (p. 115)
futile (fyōōt′l) *adj.* having no useful result; without effect (p. 108)
impotent (ĭm′pə-tənt) *adj.* powerless, lacking strength or vigor (p. 113)
impoverished (ĭm-pŏv′ər-ĭsht) *adj.* poor (p. 108)
perverse (pər-vûrs′) *adj.* stubbornly contrary; wrong, harmful (p. 111)
poignantly (poin′yənt-lē) *adv.* in a profoundly moving manner (p. 108)
squalor (skwŏl′ər) *n.* a filthy and wretched condition (p. 116)
stoicism (stō′ĭ-sĭz-əm) *n.* indifference to pleasure or pain; not showing emotion (p. 111)

SUMMARY

The narrator, Lizabeth recounts an incident that occurred one summer during the Great Depression when she was 14. While her father tries to find a job and her mother cleans house for a white family, Lizabeth and her brother Joey entertain themselves—along with other unsupervised neighborhood children. A favorite game is annoying Miss Lottie—an old woman who lives with her slow-witted son, John Burke, in a small run-down house. One day, Lizabeth leads the gang in throwing rocks at the marigolds in Miss Lottie's garden—the only spot of beauty in their poor neighborhood. Later, she feels ashamed. But after awaking from a fitful sleep, Lizabeth overhears her father's despairing conversation with her mother about his joblessness and the family's poverty. Lizabeth runs back to Miss Lottie's garden in the early morning and destroys her marigolds.

Thematic Link: *Rites of Passage* When a teenage girl reacts to the poverty of her surroundings with an act of senseless destruction, she learns about compassion.

CUSTOMIZING FOR
Students Acquiring English

- Use **ACCESS FOR STUDENTS ACQUIRING ENGLISH,** *Reading Support.*
- The figurative language and sentence structure in this story may be difficult to understand. Explain that the purpose of the opening paragraph is to establish setting and mood. Then read the first two paragraphs aloud.

STRATEGIC READING FOR
Less-Proficient Readers

Set a Purpose Ask students if they have ever been in a frustrating situation. Then have them read to find out about the conditions in Lizabeth's life that frustrated her.

Use **UNIT ONE RESOURCE BOOK,** p. 47, for guidance in reading the selection.

Literary Concept: MOOD

A Ask students what feeling the opening passage evokes. *(Possible responses: a feeling of sadness, hopelessness, irritation, despair)* Ask students what phrases create this feeling. *(Possible responses: "sterile dust"; "dirt roads"; "grassless yards")*

THE LANGUAGE OF LITERATURE TEACHER'S EDITION 107

CUSTOMIZING FOR
Gifted and Talented Students

Have students think about how the author's use of flashback enhances this story and how the incident continues to affect the adult narrator.

CUSTOMIZING FOR
Students Acquiring English

1. Explain to students that a *shanty-town* is a poor area usually found on the outskirts of town where people live in roughly built huts.

2. Define *incongruency* as "a state of being out of place."

Active Reading: CONNECT

B Invite students to recollect childhood scenes. Can they remember any vivid sensory details? Have them create a word web that illustrates these memories.

Literary Concept:
FIGURATIVE LANGUAGE

C Ask students to what the narrator, at 14, compares her joy, shame, gladness, and pain. *(Possible response: She compares them to a skein made up of all the different colors of a 14-year-old mind.)*

Linking To History

D Herbert Hoover (1874–1964), who was the President during the Great Depression, was accused of saying that prosperity was hovering, or "Hoovering," as critics joked, just around the corner.

---

1 when I think of that time and that place, I remember only the dry September of the dirt
2 roads and grassless yards of the shanty-town where I lived. And one other thing I remember, another incongruency of memory—a brilliant splash of sunny yellow against the dust—Miss Lottie's marigolds.

B **CONNECT**
What sight, smell, sound, or feeling from your childhood stands out in your memory?
Using a Reading Log

Whenever the memory of those marigolds flashes across my mind, a strange nostalgia comes with it and remains long after the picture has faded. I feel again the chaotic emotions of adolescence, illusive as smoke, yet as real as the potted geranium before me now. Joy and rage

C and wild animal gladness and shame become tangled together in the multicolored skein of 14-going-on-15 as I recall that devastating moment when I was suddenly more woman than child, years ago in Miss Lottie's yard. I think of those marigolds at the strangest times; I remember them vividly now as I desperately pass away the time waiting for you, who will not come.

I suppose that <u>futile</u> waiting was the sorrowful background music of our <u>impoverished</u> little community when I was young. The Depression that gripped the nation was no new thing to us, for the black workers of rural Maryland had always been depressed. I don't know what it was that we were waiting
D for; certainly not for the prosperity that was "just around the corner," for those were white folks' words, which we never believed. Nor did we wait for hard work and thrift to pay off in shining success as the American Dream[1] promised, for we knew better than that, too. Perhaps we waited for a miracle, amorphous in concept but necessary if one were to have the grit to rise before dawn each day and labor in the white man's vineyard until after dark, or to wander about in the September dust, offering one's sweat in return for some meager share of bread. But God was chary[2] with miracles in those days, and so we waited —and waited.

We children, of course, were only vaguely aware of the extent of our poverty. Having no radios, few newspapers, and no magazines, we were somewhat unaware of the world outside our community. Nowadays we would be called "culturally deprived" and people would write books and hold conferences about us. In those days everybody we knew was just as hungry and ill-clad as we were. Poverty was the cage in which we all were trapped, and our hatred of it was still the vague, undirected restlessness of the zoo-bred flamingo who knows that nature created him to fly free.

As I think of those days I feel most <u>poignantly</u> the tag-end of summer, the bright dry times when we began to have a sense of shortening days and the imminence of the cold.

By the time I was 14 my brother Joey and I were the only children left at our house, the older ones having left home for early marriage or the lure of the city, and the two babies having been sent to relatives who might care for them better than we. Joey was three years younger than I, and a boy, and therefore vastly inferior. Each morning our mother and father trudged wearily down the dirt road and around

---

1. **American Dream:** the belief that through hard work one will achieve a comfortable and prosperous life.
2. **chary** (châr′ē): sparing or stingy.

WORDS TO KNOW	**futile** (fyōōt′l) *adj.* having no useful result; without effect
	impoverished (ĭm-pŏv′ər-ĭsht) *adj.* poor
	poignantly (poin′yənt-lē) *adv.* in a profoundly moving manner

108

Mini-Lesson Grammar

PRONOUN CASE Tell students that a personal pronoun can change form or case depending on its use in a sentence. When a pronoun is used as the subject of a verb, the nominative form is used. When a pronoun is used as the object of a verb or preposition, the objective form is used. When a pronoun is used to show possession, the possessive form is used.

Application Have students examine the cases of the pronouns used to replace *we children* in the highlighted paragraph above, noting the use of the subject form *we,* the objective form *us,* and the possessive form *our.* Have them practice writing sentences in which all three cases are used correctly.

Reteaching/Reinforcement
- *Grammar Handbook,* anthology p. 916
- *Grammar Mini-Lessons* copymasters pp. 16–17, transparencies p. 14

 The Writer's Craft

The Cases of Personal Pronouns, pp. 552–554

Two Figures, Still Pond (1990), W. Joe Innis. Acrylic on canvas, 22″ × 28″, collection of Dr. Nobuyoshi Hagino, San Antonio, Texas.

Art Note

Two Figures, Still Pond by W. Joe Innis
Joe Innis (1937–) was a political writer before he turned to painting, sculpting, and writing fiction. In this painting, Innis emphasizes the colors of the natural landscape, filling the canvas with shimmering hues.

Reading the Art *Where do you think the women are going? Why do you think the artist chose not to make their faces more distinct?*

CUSTOMIZING FOR
Students Acquiring English

Ask students to use context clues to describe the tumble-down shanty. *(Possible responses: frail-looking, ready to fall down, poor)*

Literary Concept:
FIGURATIVE LANGUAGE

Ask students to explain the comparison. *(Possible response: The memories of her childhood are all blurred and mixed together like watercolors mix and blur when they are wet.)*

Active Reading: QUESTION

Discuss what questions or comments students have at this point in the selection. You may wish to use the following model to give them ideas of what they might be thinking about.

Think-Aloud Model *I have several questions about the characters and their situation. I want to know who is Miss Lottie? Why are the marigolds important to the narrator? Do the marigolds have anything to do with Miss Lottie?*

---

the bend, she to her domestic job, he to his daily unsuccessful quest for work. After our few chores around the tumbledown shanty, Joey and I were free to run wild in the sun with other children similarly situated.

For the most part, those days are ill-defined in my memory, running together and combining like a fresh water-color painting left out in the rain. I remember squatting in the road drawing a picture in the dust, a picture that Joey gleefully erased with one sweep of his dirty foot. I remember fishing for minnows in a muddy creek and watching sadly as they eluded my cupped hands, while Joey laughed uproariously. And I remember, that year, a strange restlessness of body and of spirit, a feeling that something old and familiar was ending, and something unknown and therefore terrifying was beginning.

One day returns to me with special clarity for some reason, perhaps because it was the beginning of the experience that in some inexplicable way marked the end of innocence. I was loafing under the great oak tree

> **QUESTION**
> What questions or thoughts do you have about the story so far?
> Using a Reading Log

MARIGOLDS 109

Mini-Lesson Workplace Literacy

SCANS Goal: Acquires and Evaluates Information

READING NEWSPAPERS (HELP-WANTED ADS)
Ask students to think about the search by Lizabeth's father for work. Point out that knowing how to locate and interpret job listings is an important first step to finding employment. Identifying the details and specifications within a help-wanted ad can guide a job seeker toward appropriate prospects. Using the chalkboard on this page, point out the different facets of a newspaper help-wanted ad.

Application Ask students to choose a profession and look for help-wanted ads for positions in that field. Have them identify the details listed within the ads they find. Explain to students that they can search in national newspapers, magazines, and the trade publications of their chosen field in addition to their local newspaper.

category	HEALTH CARE
position offered	ASST. PROGRAM DIRECTOR
job description	manage physical therapy program for sports injury rehabilitation
qualifications	state certification, 3 years experience in similar position
salary	25–35K, full benefits
method of response	FAX resume to (510) 555 4357

Literary Concept: PLOT

G Have students tell how at this point the story changes. *(It shifts in time from present to past, and characters and dialogue are added.)* Then have them identify Lizabeth. *(the narrator telling the story)*

CUSTOMIZING FOR
Students Acquiring English

5 Tell students that *tragicomic* means "having both tragic (sad) and comic (funny) elements." Then ask them to describe what was tragic about the kids and what was comic about them.

6 Students may be unfamiliar with the expression "queer-headed." Use the context clues that follow this expression to help students understand that the term means "mentally retarded."

Literary Concept: IMAGERY

H Have students identify words or phrases that help them visualize Miss Lottie's house. *(Possible responses: "rickety frame"; "gray rotting thing with no porch"; "cramped lot"; "monument of decay")*

READING STRATEGIES FOR
Less-Proficient Students

I Who is Miss Lottie and with whom does she live? *(Miss Lottie is a poor neighbor who lives with her retarded son, John Burke.)* **Literal Recall**

---

in our yard, deep in some reverie which I have now forgotten except that it involved some secret, secret thoughts of one of the Harris boys across the yard. Joey and a bunch of kids were bored now with the old tire suspended from an oak limb which had kept them entertained for a while.

"Hey, Lizabeth," Joey yelled. He never talked when he could yell. "Hey, Lizabeth, let's us go somewhere."

I came reluctantly from my private world. "Where you want to go? What you want to do?"

The truth was that we were becoming tired of the formlessness of our summer days. The idleness whose prospect had seemed so beautiful during the busy days of spring now had degenerated to an almost desperate effort to fill up the empty midday hours.

"Let's go see can we find some locusts on the hill," someone suggested.

Joey was scornful. "Ain't no more locusts there. Y'all got 'em all while they was still green."

The argument that followed was brief and not really worth the effort. Hunting locust trees wasn't fun any more by now.

"Tell you what," said Joey finally, his eyes sparkling. "Let's go over to Miss Lottie's."

The idea caught on at once, for annoying Miss Lottie was always fun. I was still child enough to scamper along with the group over rickety fences and through bushes that tore our already raggedy clothes, back to where Miss Lottie lived. I think now that we must have made a tragicomic spectacle, five or six kids of different ages, each of us clad in only one garment—the girls in faded dresses that were too long or too short, the boys in patchy pants, their sweaty brown chests gleaming in the hot sun. A little cloud of dust followed our thin legs and bare feet as we tramped over the barren land.

When Miss Lottie's house came into view we stopped, ostensibly to plan our strategy, but actually to reinforce our courage. Miss Lottie's house was the most ramshackle of all our ramshackle homes. The sun and rain had long since faded its rickety frame siding from white to a sullen gray. The boards themselves seemed to remain upright not from being nailed together but rather from leaning together like a house that a child might have constructed from cards. A brisk wind might have blown it down, and

the fact that it was still standing implied a kind of enchantment that was stronger than the elements. There it stood, and as far as I know is standing yet—a gray rotting thing with no porch, no shutters, no steps, set on a cramped lot with no grass, not even any weeds—a monument to decay.

In front of the house in a squeaky rocking chair sat Miss Lottie's son, John Burke, completing the impression of decay. John Burke was what was known as "queer-headed." Black and ageless, he sat, rocking day in and day out in a mindless stupor, lulled by the monotonous squeak-squawk of the chair. A battered hat atop his shaggy head shaded him from the sun. Usually John Burke was totally unaware of everything outside his quiet dream world. But if you disturbed him, if you intruded upon his fantasies, he would become enraged, strike out at you, and curse at you in some strange enchanted language which only he could understand. We

110   UNIT ONE   PART 2: RITES OF PASSAGE

Mini-Lesson Literary Concepts

REVIEWING FIGURATIVE LANGUAGE
Remind students that figurative language is language that communicates ideas beyond the ordinary, literal meanings of the words. Special types of figurative language commonly used by writers are *simile* and *metaphor*. A simile is a comparison between two things that uses the word *like* or *as*. A metaphor also compares two things that have something in common but without using the word *like* or *as*.

Application Point out to students Collier's use of the metaphor "tangled together . . . skein of 14-going-on-15," Annotation C on page 108; and the simile "like a fresh water-color painting left out in the rain," Annotation E on page 109.

Have students jot down examples of similes and metaphors from the story as they continue reading. Have them share examples when they have completed the story.

children made a game of thinking of ways to disturb John Burke and then to elude his violent retribution.

But our real fun and our real fear lay in Miss Lottie herself. Miss Lottie seemed to be at least a hundred years old. Her big frame still held traces of the tall, powerful woman she must have been in youth, although it was now bent and drawn. Her smooth skin was a dark reddish-brown, and her face had Indian-like features and the stern stoicism that one associates with Indian faces. Miss Lottie didn't like intruders either, especially children. She never left her yard, and nobody ever visited her. We never knew how she managed those necessities that depend on human interaction—how she ate, for example, or even whether she ate. When we were tiny children, we thought Miss Lottie was a witch and we made up tales, that we half believed ourselves, about her exploits. We were far too sophisticated now, of course, to believe the witch-nonsense. But old fears have a way of clinging like cobwebs, and so when we sighted the tumble down shack, we had to stop to reinforce our nerves.

PREDICT
What do you think the children are going to do to Miss Lottie?
Using a Reading Log

"Look, there she is," I whispered, forgetting that Miss Lottie could not possibly have heard me from that distance. "She's fooling with them crazy flowers."

"Yeh, look at 'er."

Miss Lottie's marigolds were perhaps the strangest part of the picture. Certainly they did not fit in with the crumbling decay of the rest of her yard. Beyond the dusty brown yard, in front of the sorry gray house, rose suddenly and shockingly a dazzling strip of bright blossoms, clumped together in enormous mounds, warm and passionate and sun-golden. The old black witch-woman worked on them all summer, every summer, down on her creaky knees, weeding and cultivating and arranging, while the house crumbled and John Burke rocked. For some perverse reason, we children hated those marigolds. They interfered with the perfect ugliness of the place; they were too beautiful; they said too much that we could not understand; they did not make sense. There was something in the vigor with which the old woman destroyed the weeds that intimidated us. It should have been a comical sight—the old woman with the man's hat on her cropped white head, leaning over the bright mounds, her big backside in the air—but it wasn't comical, it was something we could not name. We had to annoy her by whizzing a pebble into her flowers or by yelling a dirty word, then dancing away from her rage, reveling in our youth and mocking her age. Actually, I think it was the flowers we wanted to destroy, but nobody had the nerve to try it, not even Joey, who was usually fool enough to try anything.

"Y'all git some stones," commanded Joey now, and was met with instant giggling obedience as everyone except me began to gather pebbles from the dusty ground. "Come on, Lizabeth."

I just stood there peering through the bushes, torn between wanting to join the fun and feeling that it was all a bit silly.

"You scared, Lizabeth?"

I cursed and spat on the ground—my favorite gesture of phony bravado. "Y'all children get the stones; I'll show you how to use 'em."

I said before that we children were not consciously aware of how thick were the bars of our cage. I wonder now, though, whether

WORDS	stoicism (stō'ĭ-sĭz-əm) *n.* indifference to pleasure or pain; not showing emotion
TO	perverse (pər-vûrs') *adj.* stubbornly contrary; wrong; harmful
KNOW	bravado (brə-vä'dō) *n.* a false show of courage or defiance

111

Mini-Lesson The Writer's Style

DIALECT Point out to students that throughout the story the author has the characters speak in dialect. Explain that dialect is a variety of language spoken by a certain group of people in a specific place. The dialect in "Marigolds" is that of African-Americans of a poor Maryland town in the 1930s. The writer spells words as they would be spoken.

Application Have students note the use of the dialect forms "Y'all," "git," and "I'll show you how to use 'em" in the highlighted section above. Ask what "Y'all," "git," and "'em" mean. *(you all; get; them)* Then ask them to find other examples of dialect in the story. Finally, challenge them to rewrite a few sentences in their own regional or age-group dialect.

Reteaching/Reinforcement
• *Writing Mini-Lessons* transparencies, p. 14

 The Writer's Craft
Dialects, p. 410

Literary Concept: FIGURATIVE LANGUAGE

J Ask students to discuss what the narrator means when she says "old fears have a way of clinging like cobwebs." *(Possible response: People keep irrational childhood fears even after they're old enough to know that the fears are groundless.)* Then ask them what type of figurative language is used. *(simile)*

Active Reading: PREDICT

K Have students look at the description of Miss Lottie's character. They might predict that the children are going to annoy Miss Lottie and cause trouble to enrage her.

STRATEGIC READING FOR
Less-Proficient Readers

L Make sure students understand the conditions in which the characters live.

• Describe the place where Lizabeth lives. *(a dusty and impoverished shantytown)* Noting Relevant Details

• Why are Lizabeth and Joey alone every day? *(Their mother goes to clean house for a white family and their father looks for work. The other siblings have left home or have been sent to stay with relatives.)* Noting Relevant Details

• Why do the children go to Miss Lottie's house? *(They are bored and have nothing to do.)* Reviewing

• What is Miss Lottie like? *(She is an old woman who keeps to herself; she doesn't like intrusive children.)* Making Inferences

Set a Purpose Have students read to find out what the children do to Miss Lottie.

Critical Thinking: ANALYZING

M Challenge students to develop explanations for the children's hatred of Miss Lottie's marigolds. *(Possible response: They are so used to ugliness and hopelessness that they do not understand the attempt to create beauty.)*

Art Note

Maudell Sleet's Magic Garden by Romare Bearden African-American artist Romare Bearden (1914–1988) portrays a widowed gardener whom he remembered from his boyhood in North Carolina. The work was originally displayed above a written reminiscence: "I can still smell the flowers she used to give us and still taste the blackberries." This collage is part of Bearden's series *Profile/Part I: The Twenties.*

Reading the Art Does the artist's technique create the feeling of a scene taken from a memory? What details add to this sense?

CUSTOMIZING FOR
Multiple Learning Styles

N **Spatial or Graphic Learners** Have students compare the collage on this page with the narrator's description of Miss Lottie. Ask them whether the collage makes it easier for them to visualize the description of an old woman tending to her marigolds.

Maudell Sleet's Magic Garden (1978), Romare Bearden. From the *Profile/Part 1: The Twenties* series (Mecklenburg County). Collage on board 10⅜″ × 7″, courtesy of the Estate of Romare Bearden.

we were not more aware of it than I thought. Perhaps we had some dim notion of what we were, and how little chance we had of being anything else. Otherwise, why would we have been so preoccupied with destruction? Anyway, the pebbles were collected quickly, and everybody looked at me to begin the fun.

"Come on, y'all."

We crept to the edge of the bushes that bordered the narrow road in front of Miss Lottie's place. She was working placidly, kneeling over the flowers, her dark hand plunged into the golden mound. Suddenly "zing"—an expertly-aimed stone cut the head off one of the blossoms.

"Who out there?" Miss Lottie's backside came down and her head came up as her sharp eyes searched the bushes. "You better git!"

We had crouched down out of sight in the bushes, where we stifled the giggles that insisted on coming. Miss Lottie gazed warily across the road for a moment, then cautiously returned to her weeding. "Zing"—Joey sent a pebble into the blooms, and another marigold was beheaded.

Miss Lottie was enraged now. She began struggling to her feet, leaning on a rickety cane and shouting, "Y'all git! Go on home!" Then the rest of the kids let loose with their pebbles, storming the flowers and laughing wildly and senselessly at Miss Lottie's <u>impotent</u> rage. She shook her stick at us and started shakily toward the road crying, "Git 'long! John Burke! John Burke, come help!"

Then I lost my head entirely, mad with the power of inciting such rage, and ran out of the bushes in the storm of pebbles, straight toward Miss Lottie chanting madly, "Old witch, fell in a ditch, picked up a penny and thought she was rich!" The children screamed with delight, dropped their pebbles and joined the crazy dance, swarming around Miss Lottie like bees and chanting, "Old lady witch!" while she screamed curses at us. The madness lasted only a moment, for John Burke, startled at last, lurched out of his chair, and we dashed for the bushes just as Miss Lottie's cane went whizzing at my head.

I did not join the merriment when the kids gathered again under the oak in our bare yard. Suddenly I was ashamed, and I did not like being ashamed. The child in me sulked and said it was all in fun, but the woman in me flinched at the thought of the malicious attack that I had led. The mood lasted all afternoon. When we ate the beans and rice that was supper that night, I did not notice my father's silence, for he was always silent these days, nor did I notice my mother's absence, for she always worked until well into evening. Joey and I had a particularly bitter argument after supper; his exuberance got on my nerves.

WORDS TO KNOW
impotent (ĭm′pə-tənt) *adj.* powerless; lacking strength or vigor

Linking to Science

O Marigolds are popular because of their looks, not their smell. Many of the 30 species of marigolds have a distinctly unpleasant aroma, yet they remain popular with gardeners because of their brightly colored flowers. They are also hardy and grow well in average soil. The many varieties of marigolds range in height from about seven inches to four feet and produce white, red, cream, and orange flowers in addition to the more familiar yellow ones. Have students discuss some of the reasons why Miss Lottie might have chosen to grow marigolds in her garden.

STRATEGIC READING FOR
Less-Proficient Readers

P Have students explain what the children do at Miss Lottie's. *(The children throw rocks at Miss Lottie's marigolds; they make fun of her until John Burke chases them away.)* Literal Recall

Set a Purpose Have students read to find out what Lizabeth overhears that evening.

Literary Concept:
FIGURATIVE LANGUAGE

Q Point out that the writer compares the children to swarming bees to help readers visualize the scene. Have students explain in their own words what is taking place. *(Possible response: The children are dancing around Miss Lottie and screaming at her while she curses them.)*

Critical Thinking: SPECULATING

R Point out that Lizabeth feels ashamed of her behavior. Ask students to speculate about how she will act toward Miss Lottie in the future. *(Possible response: She will leave the old woman alone.)*

Mini-Lesson: Speaking, Listening, and Viewing

FILM MUSIC Explain to students that filmmakers choose particular background music for each scene in a movie. Because different types of music evoke different responses in a listener, the filmmaker chooses particular pieces of music to match or underscore the desired mood or the action occurring in each specific scene.

Application Have students choose a particular scene from "Marigolds." Ask them to choose a song or segment of a song to serve as background music for that scene in a film version of the story. Before they begin, encourage them to brainstorm and make a list of ideas about the action and mood of the scene. Have them think about what kind of music would enhance and intensify the scene for the listener.

Literary Concept:
FIGURATIVE LANGUAGE

S Ask students to identify the simile the author uses to describe the sound of the mother's voice. *("like a cool, dark room")* How does this use of figurative language help them understand the effect of the mother's voice? *(Possible response: It creates an image of a soothing, reassuring tone, one that provides safety and escape from unpleasantness.)*

Linking to Government

T Point out to students that during the Great Depression, 15 million people —one quarter of the entire labor force—were out of work. People waited in bread lines in every city, hoping for something to eat. Those who had lost their homes slept outdoors under old newspapers or huddled in poor shanty-towns known as "Hoovervilles." In response to this situation, President Franklin D. Roosevelt first introduced unemployment insurance as part of the 1935 Social Security Act. Before this, however, the unemployed and their families had to rely on friends, family, and private charities to survive. Invite students to give their opinions on the government's responsibility toward those citizens who are unable to find work. Have them discuss the concept of a "safety net" and who should provide it.

Literary Concept: MOOD

U Ask students to contrast the feelings of the man crying in the bedroom with the feelings of the laughing, singing man. *(Possible response: The feelings of sadness, pain, and helplessness contrast with the feelings of lightness, joy and strength.)*

Finally I stretched out upon the palette in the room we shared and fell into a fitful doze.

When I awoke, somewhere in the middle of the night, my mother had returned, and I vaguely listened to the conversation that was audible through the thin walls that separated our rooms. At first I heard no words, only voices. **S** My mother's voice was like a cool, dark room in summer—peaceful, soothing, quiet. I loved to listen to it; it made things seem all right somehow. But my father's voice cut through hers, shattering the peace.

"Twenty-two years, Maybelle, twenty-two years," he was saying, "and I got nothing for you, nothing, nothing."

"It's all right, honey, you'll get something. Everybody's out of work now, you know that."

T "It ain't right. Ain't no man ought to eat his woman's food year in and year out, and see his children running wild. Ain't nothing right about that."

"Honey, you took good care of us when you had it. Ain't nobody got nothing nowadays."

"I ain't talking about nobody else, I'm talking about *me*. God knows I try." My mother said something I could not hear, and my father cried out louder, "What must a man do, tell me that?"

"Look, we ain't starving. I git paid every week, and Mrs. Ellis is real nice about giving me things. She gonna let me have Mr. Ellis' old coat for you this winter—"

"Damn Mr. Ellis' coat! And damn his money! You think I want white folks' leavings? Damn, Maybelle"—and suddenly he sobbed, loudly and painfully, and cried helplessly and hopelessly in the dark night. I had never heard a man cry before. I did not know men ever cried. I covered my ears with my hands but could not cut off the sound of my father's harsh, painful, despairing sobs. My father was a strong man who would whisk a child upon his shoulders and go singing through the house. My father whittled toys for us and laughed so loud that the great oak seemed to laugh with him, and taught us how to fish and hunt rabbits. How could it be that my father was crying? But the sobs went on, unstifled, finally quieting until I could hear my mother's voice, deep and rich, humming softly as she used to hum to a frightened child. **U**

The world had lost its boundary lines. My mother, who was small and soft, was now the strength of the family; my father, who was the rock on which the family had been built, was sobbing like the tiniest child. Everything was suddenly out of tune, like a broken accordion. Where did I

Assessment Option

SELF-ASSESSMENT Have students assess their understanding of the selection by rewriting the story from a different point of view. Ask students to choose one of the two scenes in which Miss Lottie appears and rewrite the events from her perspective. To help students assess their own work, have them check to see that their stories answer the following questions:

- What does Miss Lottie feel about her living conditions?
- How does she take care of her mentally challenged son, John Burke?
- Why does she grow marigolds in her yard?
- Why doesn't Miss Lottie get angry at Lizabeth at the end of the story?

fit into this crazy picture? I do not now remember my thoughts, only a feeling of great bewilderment and fear.

Long after the sobbing and the humming had stopped, I lay on the palette, still as stone with my hands over my ears, wishing that I too could cry and be comforted. The night was silent now except for the sound of the crickets and of Joey's soft breathing. But the room was too crowded with fear to allow me to sleep, and finally, feeling the terrible aloneness of 4 A.M., I decided to awaken Joey.

"Ouch! What's the matter with you? What you want?" he demanded disagreeably when I had pinched and slapped him awake.

"Come on, wake up."

"What for? Go 'way."

I was lost for a reasonable reply. I could not say, "I'm scared, and I don't want to be alone," so I merely said, "I'm going out. If you want to come, come on."

The promise of adventure awoke him. "Going out now? Where to, Lizabeth? What you going to do?"

I was pulling my dress over my head. Until now I had not thought of going out. "Just come on," I replied tersely.

I was out the window and halfway down the road before Joey caught up with me.

"Wait, Lizabeth, where you going?"

I was running as if the Furies³ were after me, as perhaps they were—running silently and furiously until I came to where I had half-known I was headed: to Miss Lottie's yard.

The half-dawn light was more eerie than complete darkness, and in it the old house was like the ruin that my world had become—foul and crumbling, a grotesque caricature. It looked haunted, but I was not afraid because I was haunted too.

"Lizabeth, you lost your mind?" panted Joey.

I had indeed lost my mind, for all the smoldering emotions of that summer swelled in me and burst—the great need for my mother who was never there, the hopelessness of our poverty and <u>degradation</u>, the bewilderment of being neither child nor woman and yet both at once, the fear unleashed by my father's tears. And these feelings combined in one great impulse toward destruction.

"Lizabeth!"

I leaped furiously into the mounds of marigolds and pulled madly, trampling and pulling

---

PREDICT

What do you suppose Lizabeth has on her mind now?
Using a Reading Log

---

3. **Furies:** In Greek and Roman mythology, the Furies were three goddesses of vengeance, or revenge.

WORDS TO KNOW
degradation (dĕg′rə-dā′shən) *n.* a decline to a lower condition, with loss of dignity

---

Active Reading: PREDICT

V Have students refer to the past episode at Miss Lottie's garden and have them consider Lizabeth's emotional state. In their reading logs, have them jot down what they think Lizabeth might do once she gets to Miss Lottie's house.

Literary Concept: FIGURATIVE LANGUAGE

W Have students discuss why Lizabeth compares her world to a haunted and crumbling old house. *(Possible responses: She feels her world is falling apart because her faith in her father has been shattered; she realizes the hopelessness of her family's plight.)*

CUSTOMIZING FOR Students Acquiring English

7 Define *caricature* as "a picture, cartoon, or description that exaggerates the peculiarities or defects of a thing." Ask students why the narrator describes the house and her world as "a grotesque caricature." *(The house and her life seem more ugly, barren, and crumbling than ever before.)*

STRATEGIC READING FOR Less-Proficient Readers

X Have students summarize the conversation that Lizabeth overhears. Then ask them how the sound of her father's crying affects her. *(Possible response: It makes her feel bewildered, angry, and frustrated.)* Drawing Conclusions

Set a Purpose Have students predict what they think Lizabeth will do.

CUSTOMIZING FOR Gifted and Talented Students

Ask them to decide why Miss Lottie and her son become targets of Lizabeth and the other children. *(Possible responses: She offends them by daring to create something beautiful amid the ugliness of their surroundings; as a weak old woman she is helpless against them and is therefore an easy target; Miss Lottie and her son seem different.)*

Literary Concept: CLIMAX

Y Remind students that the climax is the turning point of a story. Have students explain why this is the turning point. *(Possible response: This is the point at which Lizabeth loses control and does something to change her situation.)*

STRATEGIC READING FOR
Less-Proficient Readers

Z Have students summarize what Lizabeth does when she returns to Miss Lottie's house. *(She destroys Miss Lottie's marigolds.)* Why does she do it? *(Possible response: She was overcome by a destructive impulse stemming from frustration and hopelessness.)*
Summarizing/Clarifying

Active Reading: CLARIFY

AA Point out to students that the writer at this point presents the main point or message of her story. Have them jot down in their reading log what they think the writer means. *(Possible response: Innocence is a childhood quality. Now that she has begun the transition into adulthood, she no longer can maintain that childhood acceptance of things as they appear to be.)*

COMPREHENSION CHECK

1. Who is telling the story? *(Lizabeth, a black woman)*
2. What time in her life is she telling about? *(her adolescence, when she was 14)*
3. Why does Lizabeth become upset in the middle of the night? *(She overhears her father crying, and she is disturbed because she did not think that a man as strong as her father could cry.)*
4. What does Lizabeth do in the early morning? *(destroys Miss Lottie's marigolds)*
5. Why does Miss Lottie's garden become completely barren? *(because she never plants marigolds again)*

EDITOR'S NOTE With the permission of the author or copyright holder, potentially offensive material has been deleted from the selection.

---

and destroying the perfect yellow blooms. The fresh smell of early morn-ing and of dew-soaked marigolds spurred me on as I went tearing and mangling and sobbing while Joey tugged my dress or my waist crying, "Lizabeth stop, please stop!"

And then I was sitting in the ruined little garden among the uprooted and ruined flowers, crying and crying, and it was too late to undo what I had done. Joey was sitting beside me, silent and frightened, not knowing what to say. Then, "Lizabeth, look."

I opened my swollen eyes and saw in front of me a pair of large calloused feet; my gaze lifted to the swollen legs, the age-distorted body clad in a tight cotton night dress, and then the shadowed Indian face surrounded by stubby white hair. And there was no rage in the face now, now that the garden was destroyed and there was nothing any longer to be protected.

"M-miss Lottie!" I scrambled to my feet and just stood there and stared at her, and that was the moment when childhood faded and womanhood began. That violent, crazy act was the last act of childhood. For as I gazed at the immobile face with the sad, weary eyes, I gazed upon a kind of reality that is hidden to childhood. The witch was no longer a witch but only a broken old woman who had dared to create beauty in the midst of ugliness and sterility. She had been born in squalor and lived in it all her life. Now at the end of that life she had nothing except a falling-down hut, a wrecked body, and John Burke, the mindless son of her passion. Whatever verve[4] there was left in her, whatever was of love and beauty and joy that had not been squeezed out by life, had been there in the marigolds she had so tenderly cared for.

Of course I could not express the things that I knew about Miss Lottie as I stood there awkward and ashamed.

The years have put words to the things I knew in that moment, and as I look back upon it, I know that that moment marked the end of innocence. People think of the loss of innocence as meaning the loss of virginity, but this is far from true. Innocence involves an unseeing acceptance of things at face value, an ignorance of the area below the surface. In that humiliating moment I looked beyond myself and into the depths of another person. This was the beginning of <u>compassion</u>, and one cannot have both compassion and innocence.

The years have taken me worlds away from that time and that place, from the dust and squalor of our lives and from the bright thing that I destroyed in a blind childish striking out at God-knows-what. Miss Lottie died long ago and many years have passed since I last saw her hut, completely barren at last, for despite my wild contrition she never planted marigolds again. Yet, there are times when the image of those passionate yellow mounds returns with a painful poignancy. For one does not have to be ignorant and poor to find that one's life is barren as the dusty yards of one's town. And I too have planted marigolds. ❖

CLARIFY
The narrator says that one cannot be innocent and compassionate at the same time. What does she mean?
Using a Reading Log

---

4. **verve** (vûrv): vitality, enthusiasm.

WORDS TO KNOW
squalor (skwŏl′ər) *n.* a filthy and wretched condition
compassion (kəm-păsh′ən) *n.* deep awareness of the suffering of another coupled with the wish to relieve it

RESPONDING OPTIONS

FROM PERSONAL RESPONSE TO CRITICAL ANALYSIS

REFLECT 1. In your notebook, briefly jot down how you reacted to Lizabeth's destruction of the marigolds. Share your reaction in class.

RETHINK 2. Why does Lizabeth destroy Miss Lottie's marigolds?

Close Textual Reading

Consider
- the contrast between the marigolds and the general surroundings
- the anger and frustration in Lizabeth's family
- Lizabeth's feelings about herself

Thematic Link

3. How does Lizabeth's destruction of the marigolds signal a rite of passage from childhood to the beginning of womanhood?

Close Textual Reading

Consider
- Lizabeth's new understanding of Miss Lottie and her marigolds
- what the narrator says about compassion and innocence

4. What do you think the narrator means at the end of the story when she says that she too has planted marigolds?

RELATE 5. A rite of passage can be a pleasant surprise, or it can be physically challenging, as in "Through the Tunnel." Sometimes it is emotionally painful, as in "Marigolds." What are some experiences that might be considered rites of passage for teenagers today?

Thematic Link

LITERARY LINKS
Compare Lizabeth's rite of passage in this story with Jerry's in "Through the Tunnel." Which one do you think would be more difficult to deal with at the time? Which one would have more lasting effects?

Multimodal Learning
ANOTHER PATHWAY
Cooperative Learning
In a small group, write a script and present a dramatization of the night that Lizabeth destroys Miss Lottie's flowers. Include actors for the parts of Lizabeth's mother and father as well as Joey, Lizabeth, and Miss Lottie. Your group should also have a director to help organize rehearsals and the final presentation.

QUICKWRITES

1. Why do you suppose Miss Lottie never planted marigolds again? Write a **paragraph** that answers this question.

2. The narrator says, "This was the beginning of compassion, and one cannot have both compassion and innocence." Using details from the story to support your opinion, write a draft of an **essay** explaining what you think she means.

3. Look over your notes about an incident in which you acted out of anger or frustration. Write a **description** of the incident that vividly conveys your mood at the time.

📁 **PORTFOLIO** Save your writing. You may want to use it later as a springboard to a piece for your portfolio.

MARIGOLDS 117

From Personal Response to Critical Analysis

1. Accept all reasonable responses.
2. Possible responses: Some students may say that built-up frustration over her family's circumstances led to her act; others may point to her confusion at becoming an adult, her fear at hearing her father cry like a child, or her resentment of the beauty of the marigolds amid poverty and ugliness.
3. Possible responses: She has acquired compassion because she empathizes with the difficulty of Miss Lottie's life and the poignancy of her attempt to create beauty; she has become more aware of the frustrations and difficulties in life.
4. Possible responses: She has also tried to create beauty amid ugly circumstances; she has tried not to despair even in bleak or hopeless situations.
5. Student responses will vary. Accept all reasonable responses.

Another Pathway

Cooperative Learning Have students collaborate on the script, working in groups of six to eight. One student can record the dialogue, another can encourage participation, a third can ensure that the dialogue created is consistent with the selection. A fourth student will serve as director, and the rest will enact the scene for the class.

Rubric
3 Full Accomplishment Students accurately dramatize the events of the night Lizabeth destroys the marigolds.
2 Substantial Accomplishment Students dramatize most of the events of the night accurately.
1 Little or Partial Accomplishment Students have difficulty dramatizing the events of the night or do so inaccurately.

Literary Links
Answers will vary. Possible responses: Students might conclude that Lizabeth's rite of passage was the most difficult to deal with because what she did caused Miss Lottie emotional pain, whereas Jerry's rite of passage only caused pain to himself. Again, students might conclude that both gained insights that will last their entire lives.

QuickWrites
1. Ask students to review the details in the selection about Miss Lottie to help them answer the question.
2. Have students refer to specific examples in the story to support their opinions.
3. Remind students that figurative language can emphasize ideas and invoke emotions for the reader. Encourage students to use simile or metaphor in their writing to help create vivid descriptions.

📖 **The Writer's Craft**

Drafting Paragraphs, pp. 348–359
Supporting an Opinion, pp. 208–221
Description, pp. 57–80

Literary Concepts

The mood created in the beginning of the story is one of sadness, depression, irritation, and emptiness. The writer vividly describes dust—arid, sterile dust and crumbly dust. Her emphasis on the "grassless yards of the shanty-town" where she lived also helps set the mood of the story.

Concept Review *Possible responses:*

To Lizabeth
- *as a child—poverty and ugliness of her surroundings; neglect and pain that she feels because of her family's situation*
- *as an adult—beauty, lost childhood innocence, a time when she learns about compassion*

To Miss Lottie
- *hope, possibilities of what life could be, refusal to succumb to despair*

Art Connection

Possible responses: The Miss Lottie that the adult Elizabeth might portray would resemble Bearden's collage because as a woman, she now understands what Miss Lottie was trying to accomplish. As a child, Lizabeth might have protrayed a menacing, witch-like Miss Lottie.

Across the Curriculum

History *Cooperative Learning* Have students work in small groups. Each group will focus on one aspect of the Great Depression. One group can look for information about shantytowns. Another might research information about the effect of the Great Depression on black Americans. Or they might research President Franklin D. Roosevelt's role during that period and the creation of New Deal programs. Each group will share its findings with the rest of the class.

LITERARY CONCEPTS

In a literary work, the feeling or atmosphere that the writer creates for the reader is called **mood**. Descriptive words, the setting, and figurative language contribute to the mood of a work, as do the sound and rhythm of the language used. Reread the last paragraph of "Marigolds." Notice how key descriptive words and long, rhythmic sentences help to create a somber mood of lingering regret. Now reread the beginning of the story. What mood is created there, and how is it created? Identify specific details.

CONCEPT REVIEW: Symbol In this story, the marigolds stand for something beyond themselves. What do you think the marigolds represent to Lizabeth and to Miss Lottie? Make two lists of your ideas.

What Marigolds Symbolize	
To Lizabeth	To Miss Lottie

ART CONNECTION

Look again at the collage art by Romare Bearden on page 112. The subject of the collage, Maudell Sleet, lived in the artist's hometown in Mecklenburg County, North Carolina. She had a green thumb and always shared the produce from her garden with Bearden and his mother. This collage is one of several he created in her memory. How do you think Lizabeth as a child would portray Miss Lottie in art? How would the adult Lizabeth portray Miss Lottie? How would each portrayal compare with Bearden's collage?

ALTERNATIVE ACTIVITIES

1. With a partner, act out a **dramatic dialogue** that might have taken place between Miss Lottie and Lizabeth after the destruction of the marigolds.
2. The narrator says that memory is "an abstract painting—it does not present things as they are, but rather as they *feel*." Create an **abstract painting** or **collage** to convey the mixture of emotions that Lizabeth feels in this story. Show your work to the class.

118 UNIT ONE PART 2: RITES OF PASSAGE

THE WRITER'S STYLE

The story is told in **flashback** by an adult narrator looking back through the years at an incident from her childhood. Think about how this story would be different if it were told by Lizabeth shortly after she destroys the marigolds. What is gained from having the adult narrator tell this story?

ACROSS THE CURRICULUM

History Research books on the Great Depression of the 1930s. Look for information about shantytowns, such as where they were usually located and what the conditions were. Report your findings to the class, using photographs from the books or your own illustrations as visual aids.

Detail of *Maudell Sleet's Magic Garden* (1978), Romare Bearden. Courtesy Estate of Romare Bearden.

Alternative Activities

1. Tell the pairs of students to brainstorm ideas about what each character might have to say to the other before the students start writing. Ask: *What would Lizabeth explain to Miss Lottie? What might Miss Lottie have to tell Lizabeth about her life?*
2. Have students list the emotions Lizabeth feels at different moments in the story. Then encourage students to experiment with nonrepresentational techniques to convey the emotions they have listed. Have them present their works to the class and discuss the feelings each piece evokes in the viewer.

The Writer's Style

Students may speculate that the use of flashback allows the narrator to tell the story as an adult who has thought about the experience and realizes its importance. They may also suggest that knowing the narrator has overcome her early poverty helps the reader understand her character.

WORDS TO KNOW

Review the Words to Know at the bottom of the selection pages. Then write the vocabulary word that best completes the meaning of the sentences in the paragraph.

During the Great Depression, a number of Americans lost their jobs. Without an income, many became _impoverished_. People looked for work, but often their efforts were __futile__. As a result, many experienced a _degradation_ of their living standards, and some were forced to exist in terrible conditions of __squalor__. Showing a sensitivity to people's suffering, literature and photography of the period _poignantly_ captured the distress these hardships caused. People reacted to their predicament in various ways. Some felt helpless and __impotent__. Some, in a show of __bravado__, took __perverse__ pleasure in spending money on foolish luxuries. Still others reacted calmly and with __stoicism__. Meanwhile, many charities showed _compassion_ for the poor by giving them food and shelter.

EUGENIA COLLIER

1928–

Eugenia Collier was born in Baltimore, Maryland, where she now lives. Her father was a physician and her mother a teacher. She graduated with high honors from Howard University in Washington, D.C., in 1948 and earned her master of arts from Columbia University in 1950. She currently teaches at Morgan State University in Baltimore.

For a time, Collier was a case worker with the Baltimore Department of Public Welfare. She started teaching college in 1955 and later began writing. One of her first efforts, "Marigolds," won the Gwendolyn Brooks Award for Fiction in 1969. Her stories, poems, and critical essays have appeared in many anthologies and magazines. Collier says that the source of her creativity is "the richness, the diversity, the beauty of my black heritage."

OTHER WORKS *Breeder and Other Stories, Spread My Wings*

Extended Reading

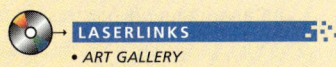
• ART GALLERY

MARIGOLDS **119**

Words to Know

impoverished, futile, degradation, squalor, poignantly, impotent, bravado, perverse, stoicism, compassion

Reteaching/Reinforcement
• *Unit One Resource Book,* p. 48

EUGENIA COLLIER

Eugenia Collier was born one year before the stock market crash. She grew up during the Great Depression, the period in which "Marigolds" is set.

ART GALLERY
Views of the South   Artists portray their impressions of Southern lifestyles by using personal experiences and imagination. These paintings present several interpretations of life in the South in the early part of this century.

Side A, Frame 49238

REFLECTING ON THEME
What Do You Think?

Have students think about the rites of passage time line that they began as they started reading the selections in Part 2. Ask them to compare their time lines and thoughts about the rites of passage now. Ask them what price Lizabeth paid for destruction of Miss Lottie's marigolds. *(the loss of innocence)* As they continue reading the selections, have them jot down other characters in Part 2 who may learn a similar lesson.

FOCUS ON POETRY

This feature defines *poetry* and provides an explanation of the terms used to discuss it. It also introduces students to the conventions of the genre and suggests strategies for reading poetry. The terms introduced here are covered in depth in the poems that follow.

Objectives

- To understand and appreciate poetry
- To understand the elements of poetry: form, sound, speaker, imagery, and figurative language
- To learn effective strategies for reading poetry

Teaching Strategies:
ELEMENTS OF POETRY

Form Have students compare the stanza structure of "The Road Not Taken" and "Fable for When There's No Way Out" on pages 123 and 124. Ask students to browse in the text to find an example of a poem with no stanza breaks or an unusual form.

Sound Have students find examples of the sound devices described on this page and read them aloud. You may wish to read aloud examples for the students. Then discuss with students how each device adds to the overall affect of the poem.

Speaker Challenge students to identify the speaker in each of the poems on pages 123 and 124.

Imagery Have students identify the sensory appeals in "Fireworks" on page 205 and browse in the text to find examples of appeals to each sense. Discuss with students to which senses the imagery appeals.

Figurative Language Challenge students to create more examples of personification, simile, and metaphor.

FOCUS ON POETRY

The French poet Paul Valéry once said that fiction and nonfiction were like walking, but poetry was like dancing. Everything in a poem—the words, the line breaks, the punctuation, even the empty spaces—is deliberately chosen to create an effect. The poet wants to make your imagination dance—and to touch your mind and heart along the way. What follows are some terms for what poets use to create the special effects of poetry.

FORM Form refers to the way a poem is laid out on the page. Poems are usually printed in individual **lines**, which may or may not be sentences. In some poems, lines are grouped into **stanzas**. Each stanza may have the same number of lines, or the number of lines may vary.

SOUND A poem's effect frequently depends on the sound of its words. Here are some techniques that poets use to achieve different sound effects:

Alliteration is the repetition of consonant sounds at the beginnings of words. Think about the effect of the repetition of *l* sounds in these lines from Cummings's poem.

  laugh,leaning back in my arms
  for life's not a paragraph

Assonance is the repetition of a vowel sound within nonrhyming words, as in another line from Cummings's poem: "—the best gesture of my brain is less than."

Consonance is the repetition of consonant sounds within and at the ends of words. Again, Cummings's poem offers an example: "will never wholly kiss you."

Onomatopoeia is the use of words such as *buzz, creak, crunch,* and *thump,* whose pronunciations suggest their meanings.

Rhyme is the occurrence of a similar or identical sound at the ends of two or more words, such as *suite, heat,* and *complete.* **Internal rhyme** occurs within a line; **end rhyme** occurs at the ends of lines. The pattern of end rhyme in a poem is called the **rhyme scheme** and is charted by assigning a letter, beginning with the letter *a,* to each line. Lines that rhyme are given the same letter. Look at the rhyme scheme for the first stanza of Robert Frost's "The Road Not Taken."

  Two roads diverged in a yellow wood,   *a*
  And sorry I could not travel both   *b*
  And be one traveler, long I stood   *a*
  And looked down one as far as I could   *a*
  To where it bent in the undergrowth;   *b*

Rhythm refers to the pattern of sound created by the arrangement of stressed and unstressed syllables in a line of poetry. Some poems follow a regular pattern, or **meter**. In the following Emily Dickinson poem, accented syllables are marked with ('), while unaccented syllables are marked with (˘). Read the lines aloud to hear the meter.

> Surgeons must be very careful
> When they take the knife!
> Underneath their fine incisions
> Stirs the Culprit—Life!

SPEAKER The speaker in a poem is the voice that talks to the reader, similar to the narrator in fiction. The speaker is not necessarily the poet.

IMAGERY To help bring the poem inside the reader, poets choose words that help readers see, hear, feel, taste, and smell what's being described. This kind of sensory description is called imagery. Notice the senses being appealed to in this stanza from Amy Lowell's "Fireworks."

> But whenever I see you, I burst apart
> And scatter the sky with my blazing heart.
> It spits and sparkles in stars and balls,
> Buds into roses—and flares, and falls.

FIGURATIVE LANGUAGE Language that communicates ideas beyond the ordinary, literal meanings of the words is called figurative language. Common types of figurative language include personification, simile, and metaphor. A **personification** attributes human qualities to an object, animal, or idea. A **simile** is a comparison that uses *like* or *as*. "Cold as ice" and "dry like the desert" are examples. A **metaphor** is a more direct comparison, as in the first stanza of Eve Merriam's "Metaphor."

> Morning is
> a new sheet of paper
> for you to write on.

STRATEGIES FOR READING POETRY

Because everything in a poem is essential to meaning, you need to read the poem at least three times. After each reading, take a few moments to write down what was going on in your mind as you were reading. You may have new insights after each reading, or you may just feel more certain of what you thought before. Use the questions below to help you.

- **What words, ideas, or pictures from the poem stand out in your mind?** Try to visualize what is described and what imagery the words conjure up in your mind. Consider that some words and phrases could have several possible meanings.
- **What do you feel, think of, or remember as you read?** Be aware of your own feelings as well as the feelings expressed in the poem. Also write down thoughts and memories that pop into your head each time you read the poem. All of these personal associations can help you find meaning in the poem.
- **What questions do you have?** Write down questions you have as you read. You may clarify your understanding on subsequent readings or in a class discussion.
- **Who is speaking in the poem?** Often, a poet creates a speaker with a distinct personality. Try to find out about the speaker as you read.
- **What are the themes, or main ideas, in the poem?** Look at the title of the poem as a key to theme. Think about ideas about life or human nature that the poem communicates. Be especially aware of connections that the poet draws, such as cause-and-effect relationships and comparisons and contrasts.

Reading Strategies: MODELING

Invite volunteers to read aloud the Strategies for Reading Poetry. Tell students they will be using these strategies as they read "The Road Not Taken," "Fable for When There's No Way Out," and other poems throughout the book. Then read aloud the first stanza of "The Road Not Taken" and model the strategies. You may wish to use the following models or create your own.

- **What words, ideas, or pictures from the poem stand out in your mind?** *"I can vividly see somebody in the woods, pausing at a fork in the road."*
- **What do you feel, think of, or remember as you read?** *"I remember many times when I've been at a crossroads myself, or glanced down a side road, wondering what lay down there. Sometimes, not often, I go exploring."*
- **What questions do you have?** *"A yellow wood—is that a springtime wood or an autumn wood? Does it matter? And is the traveler bound for a particular destination, or is it a toss-up which way to go now?"*
- **Who is speaking in the poem?** *"I see that the speaker is a traveler, and though the poem has a male author, the speaker could be either male or female. I don't know if he or she is old or young, purposeful or wandering. I do know the speaker's willing to take the time to stop and think when faced with an interesting possibility."*
- **What are the themes, or main ideas, in the poem?** *"Based on the title and this first stanza, I suspect the theme of this poem touches on choices—the direction of those choices and the fact that every choice means a rejection of another possibility."*

OVERVIEW

Objectives

- To understand and appreciate two poems that explore how resolving a predicament can be an important learning experience
- To understand and compare rhyme scheme and free verse
- To express understanding of the poems through a choice of writing forms, including a poem and a set of instructions
- To extend understanding of the poems through a variety of multimodal and cross-curricular activities

Skills

LITERARY CONCEPTS
- Rhyme scheme
- Repetition

THE WRITER'S STYLE
- Assonance

SPEAKING, LISTENING, AND VIEWING
- Group discussion
- Oral presentation

Thematic Link: *Rites of Passage* A moment of choice and the struggle for freedom prove to be rites of passage for the subjects of these two poems.

ALTERNATIVE
Previewing

Students can choose partners and use the following prompts to preview "The Road Not Taken" and "Fable for When There's No Way Out" orally.

Writing Connection

Discussion Prompts *Think of an everyday situation that you had to get out of by using your wits. Describe the situation and how you resolved it to a partner. Then listen as your partner describes a situation and how he or she resolved it. If you need help getting started, use these questions.*

- What was the situation?
- What made the situation difficult?
- How long did it take you to resolve it?

As you read the two poems notice the decisions that are made and the outcomes.

PREVIEWING

POETRY

The Road Not Taken
Robert Frost

Fable for When There's No Way Out
May Swenson

Activating Prior Knowledge
PERSONAL CONNECTION

The two poems you are about to read each present a predicament—that is, a thorny or troublesome situation. Everyday life abounds in predicaments, some major and some minor. Sometimes choices just don't seem clear-cut. Have you ever been torn between two ways to spend an evening, two schools to attend, or just two friends to spend time with? Think of a recent predicament you have experienced, and share it with other members of your class.

Building Background
PSYCHOLOGICAL CONNECTION

Being human means being able to choose, but this freedom can be frightening. In fact, people sometimes want others to make their choices for them. Choosing is especially hard when the choice is not between a good alternative and a bad alternative but between two equally good alternatives. Moreover, even not making a decision is a kind of choice. Yet sometimes the way out of a dilemma can lie in an unexpected direction. The two poems you are about to read pose different ways of responding to such predicaments.

Setting a Purpose
WRITING CONNECTION

Think about the predicament you just shared with your classmates. How did you deal with the situation? In your notebook, describe how you handled your problem, using a format similar to the one below. Then as you read, compare your way of dealing with the predicament with the different ways expressed in these poems.

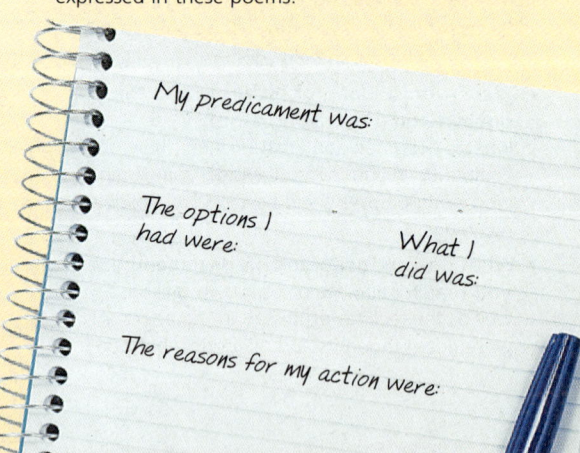

UNIT ONE PART 2: RITES OF PASSAGE

PRINT AND MEDIA RESOURCES

UNIT ONE RESOURCE BOOK
Strategic Reading: Literature, p. 51

ACCESS FOR STUDENTS ACQUIRING ENGLISH
Reading Support

FORMAL ASSESSMENT
Selection Test, pp. 23–24
Test Generator

AUDIO LIBRARY
See Reference Card

INTERNET RESOURCES
"The Road Not Taken"
McDougal Littell Literature Center at http://www.hmco.com/mcdougal/lit

The Road Not Taken

ROBERT FROST

Two roads diverged[1] in a yellow wood,
And sorry I could not travel both
And be one traveler, long I stood
And looked down one as far as I could
To where it bent in the undergrowth;

Then took the other, as just as fair,
And having perhaps the better claim,
Because it was grassy and wanted wear;
Though as for that the passing there
Had worn them really about the same,

And both that morning equally lay
In leaves no step had trodden[2] black.
Oh, I kept the first for another day!
Yet knowing how way leads on to way,
I doubted if I should ever come back.

I shall be telling this with a sigh
Somewhere ages and ages hence:
Two roads diverged in a wood, and I—
I took the one less traveled by,
And that has made all the difference.

---

1. **diverged** (dĭ-vûrjd′): branched out; went in different directions.
2. **trodden** (trŏd′n): walked or trampled.

FROM PERSONAL RESPONSE TO CRITICAL ANALYSIS

REFLECT 1. Which road would you have taken, and why? Briefly write about your choice in your notebook.

RETHINK 2. How does the speaker seem to feel about the predicament of choosing a road?
   Consider
   - the way the speaker describes both roads
   - your own experiences with making choices
   - what the speaker says about returning to the other road at another time
   - why the speaker might remember his decision "with a sigh"

Close Textual Reading

Thematic Link 3. What might the two roads represent, or symbolize? Make a list of possibilities, and discuss them in class.

4. Does the speaker seem to be satisfied with having chosen the road "less traveled by"? Give evidence from the poem to support your answer.

THE ROAD NOT TAKEN 123

Literary Concept:
RHYME SCHEME

D Ask students how the structure of this poem differs from that of "The Road Not Taken" *(Possible responses: There is no rhyme scheme; there is no structured rhythmic pattern; line length is irregular.)*

Critical Thinking:
DRAWING CONCLUSIONS

E Ask students what the author means in lines 17–23. *(Possible response: If the chick gives up, it will die.)*

Literary Concept: REPETITION

F Have students identify the author's use of repetition *(pecks and crack in lines 23–28)*, and what it adds to the poem. *(Possible responses: It creates an image of prolonged effort; the sound of the words is similar to the sound of repeated knocking on the shell.)*

Critical Thinking:
MAKING JUDGMENTS

G Ask students to evaluate the message in the final couplet. Ask students what they think the poet is trying to say. *(Possible response: Sometimes it takes getting angry to change a situation.)*

CUSTOMIZING FOR
Gifted and Talented Students

Point out that several musicians have set May Swenson's poems to music. Invite students to discuss the different types of music that could accompany the poem and how this musical accompaniment might affect the poem.

COMPREHENSION CHECK

1. Which road does the speaker choose in Frost's poem? *(the one less traveled by)*
2. In "Fable for When There's No Way Out," what is the chick's predicament? *(He is imprisoned within the shell.)*

Fable For When There's No Way Out
MAY SWENSON

D
Grown too big for his skin,
and it grown hard,

without a sea and atmosphere—
he's drunk it all up—

5   his strength's inside him now,
but there's no room to stretch.

He pecks at the top
but his beak's too soft;

though instinct and ambition shoves,
10 he can't get through.

Barely old enough to bleed
and already bruised!

In a case this tough
what's the use
15 if you break your head
instead of the lid?

Despair tempts him
to just go limp:

E
Maybe the cell's
20 already a tomb,

and beginning end
in this round room.

Still, stupidly he pecks
and pecks, as if from under
F
25 his own skull—
yet makes no crack . . .

No crack until
he finally cracks,

and kicks and stomps.
30 What a thrill

and shock to feel
his little gaff[1] poke

through the floor!
A way he hadn't known or meant.

35 Rage works if reason won't.
When locked up, bear down. **G**

---
1. **gaff:** a hook attached to a handle.

124   UNIT ONE   PART 2: RITES OF PASSAGE

Mini-Lesson Literary Concepts

REVIEWING REPETITION Remind students that repetition is the repeated use of a word or phrase in a literary work. Repetition is often used in poetry to give special emphasis to a particular thought or action.

Application Ask students to form small groups and have one student read each poem aloud. Have students pay special attention to examples of repetition as they listen. Then have them discuss the following questions:
- Why does the poet choose to repeat the word or phrase?
- What effect does the repetition have on the meaning of the poem?
- How does the repetition affect the way the poem sounds to the listener?

RESPONDING OPTIONS

FROM PERSONAL RESPONSE TO CRITICAL ANALYSIS

REFLECT 1. How did you react to the chick's predicament in Swenson's poem? Write your response in your notebook.

RETHINK 2. If the chick in the shell stands for anything, what do you think that might be?

3. A fable is a story that teaches a lesson. What lesson do you think this poem teaches, and what is your opinion of the advice in the last two lines?

RELATE 4. In order to show the similarities and differences between these two poems, think of two kinds of music that you would choose to express the feelings and tone, or attitude, in each poem.

Thematic Link 5. Do you think the experience described in each of these poems is a rite of passage? Explain your opinion.

6. How might you apply the theme, or main idea, of each poem to your own life?
   Consider
   • a choice like that faced by Frost's traveler
   • a situation like that of the chick in the shell
   • your own ideas on handling predicaments

Multimodal Learning
ANOTHER PATHWAY
Cooperative Learning
Working with a small group of classmates, design two posters, one to illustrate each of these poems. Include several lines from the poem on each poster. Then display your posters for the class to see, and explain why you made the choices you did for your posters.

LITERARY CONCEPTS

Read aloud the first stanza of "The Road Not Taken" and listen to the sound of the words. Which lines rhyme? Look again at the **rhyme scheme** charted for this stanza on page 120. In contrast to Frost's poem, "Fable for When There's No Way Out" does not have a rhyme scheme. Its lines also lack a regular rhythmic pattern, which makes it an example of **free verse**. Read aloud both poems to hear the difference in the way they sound. Now try rewriting a stanza of Frost's poem in free verse, or else rewrite about six lines of the Swenson poem using rhyme. Share your rewrites with your classmates and discuss the differences in feeling, attitude, and mood that your changes in the poems made. Why do you think poets choose to write in a particular style? Which style of poem do you prefer?

QUICKWRITES

1. Look at what you wrote for the Writing Connection on page 122. Draft a **poem** about your predicament. If you like, model the structure of your poem on that of one of the two poems you just read.

2. Write a **set of instructions** for making difficult decisions or resolving another kind of predicament. Your instructions might take the form of a serious decision-making model, or you might try a humorous, tongue-in-cheek approach.

PORTFOLIO Save your writing. You may want to use it later as a springboard to a piece for your portfolio.

From Personal Response to Critical Analysis

1. Accept all reasonable responses.
2. Possible responses: someone trapped in a troublesome situation; a young person facing resistance from adults; a teenager on the threshold of adulthood
3. Possible responses: The poem advises people to persist even when there appears to be no way out. Some may find the advice inspiring; others may say that it advocates destructive or self-destructive behavior.
4. Accept all reasonable responses.
5. Accept all reasonable responses. Possible responses: Some might say that the experiences in both poems represent rites of passage, because in each, the speaker must make a choice that will affect his life in some way. Others may say that "Road" is not a rite of passage but is just the making of a choice, whereas the speaker's rage to break free of a shell—or to be born—in "Fable" is a rite of passage.
6. Accept all reasonable responses.

Another Pathway
Cooperative Learning Students should work in groups of four to discuss their ideas for the posters. One student can record the ideas, a second can act as an integrator, and a third can transcribe appropriate lines from the poem. The fourth can create the illustrations.

Rubric
3 Full Accomplishment Students create posters that one can immediately identify with the appropriate poem.
2 Substantial Accomplishment Students create posters one can partially identify with the appropriate poem.
1 Little or Partial Accomplishment Students create posters that show little understanding of the poems.

Literary Concepts

Some may say that poets choose a style that will let them best express their creative ideas. Some ideas may be best expressed in free verse, while others need a conventional rhyming pattern.

Have students form groups to discuss their rewrites and answer the following questions.
• Why might Frost have chosen this particular rhyme scheme? *(Possible response: The alternation of a and b lines emphasizes the two roads.)*
• Why might Swenson prefer to use free verse? *(Possible response: It allows her complete freedom to use the language; it reflects the random, instinctive movement of the chick.)*

QuickWrites

1. Encourage students to compare their finished poem with the chart they completed for the Writing Connection to see whether the poem addresses the predicament they wrote about. If students use a rhyme scheme, ask them to map out the pattern they use.
2. Before students begin writing their set of instructions, encourage them to think about the thought processes they use to make important decisions. Depending on the nature of the decision, they can choose an appropriate approach.

Literary Links

Ask students to compare the chick's attempt to escape from its shell with Lizabeth's act of destruction in "Marigolds." *(Possible response: Both are rites of passage into the next stage of life; both react to their frustrations with violence; although the chick gains his freedom, Lizabeth finds regret and compassion.)*

Across the Curriculum

Science Cooperative Learning
Encourage students to form research teams to find out about baby chicks and other animals born in a shell. Students should meet to discuss any questions they have. One student can record ideas, another can suggest and assign research avenues, and the others can gather information. Students can create visual representations of the hatching process and present their findings to the class.

ROBERT FROST

Frost's long career as a poet spanned a period in which many poets experimented with innovations such as free verse. While not a strict traditionalist, Frost had no desire to join them, explaining that he would just as soon play tennis without a net as write poems without rhyme. Even so, Frost was considered an innovator with respect to meter and rhythm. His life's goal, he once said, was "to write a few poems it will be hard to get rid of." Most critics agree that Frost achieved his goal.

MAY SWENSON

One critic notes that Swenson considers her poems to be carefully crafted, sacred objects through which she expresses the basic beauty of the universe. Swenson once wrote that the poetic experience is rooted in the desire to move past appearances to find what truly exists. In that place, things become new.

ROBERT FROST

1874–1963

At first, people didn't seem to take Robert Frost very seriously. He was nearly 40 before he published any poems, and even then he had to go to another country to publish them. Yet that same year he told a friend, "I expect to do something to the present state of literature in America." He turned out to be right. By the time of his death 50 years later, he had become known as one of the masters of modern American poetry. He had won the Pulitzer Prize for poetry four times, had a mountain in Vermont named after him, received a medal from Congress, and read his work at the inauguration of President John F. Kennedy. In short, he had become America's favorite poet.

Frost was born in San Francisco but moved East with his widowed mother when he was 11. As a young man, he attended college for a while, then married and began raising a family. Meanwhile, he worked as a millhand, a teacher, an editor, and a farmer. Soon he was writing some of his best poems, but he could find no American audience for them.

Then in 1912 he moved his family to England, and there he succeeded in getting two books published. Now American editors and readers began discovering Frost, and when he returned to the United States he was already recognized as one of the leaders of the new poetry. He settled on a farm in New Hampshire, where he produced a steady stream of work that received great acclaim. He also taught and lectured at several universities.

Frost cultivated a public image as a kindly rural poet, but his private life was far from simple. He had to endure the deaths of several of his children and was occasionally plagued by depression. Yet his work continues to be widely loved. Poetry, Robert Frost said, "begins in delight and ends in wisdom."

OTHER WORKS "Nothing Gold Can Stay," "'Out, Out—,'" "Birches," "Desert Places," "Fire and Ice," "Mending Wall," "Neither out Far nor in Deep," "Stopping by Woods on a Snowy Evening," "The Gift Outright," "The Wood-Pile," "The Oven Bird"

Extended Reading

MAY SWENSON

1919–1989

May Swenson was born in Utah and graduated from Utah State University. She worked for a number of years as an editor at New Directions Press, a New York City publishing house. In time, she received wide acclaim for her unique writing. She experimented with typing words on a page so that the poem appeared in the shape of an object; she also made creative use of sound effects in language. In *Poems to Solve*, she presented poems containing riddles, hidden meanings, and ideas to puzzle and challenge the reader. Both young and old readers have enjoyed these poems.

Swenson taught at a number of universities and traveled widely when giving lectures and readings. She won many writing awards in her lifetime, including a Guggenheim Fellowship in 1959 and the Bollingen Poetry Award in 1981.

OTHER WORKS "Fire Island," "How Everything Happens," "July 4th," "The Universe," "The Watch," "Southbound on the Freeway," *New and Selected Things Taking Place*

Extended Reading

REFLECTING ON THEME
What Do You Think?

Have students think about the rites of passage time line that they started as they began reading the selections in Part 2. Ask them to prepare a rites of passage time line that would show the rites of passage for the chick in "Fable." Discuss how some of the rites of passage experiences of the chick might mirror their own.

PREVIEWING

FICTION

The Beginning of Something
Sue Ellen Bridgers

Activating Prior Knowledge
PERSONAL CONNECTION

Have you ever felt ecstatic about an important event in your life at the same time a person close to you had opposite feelings because something bad had happened? Perhaps you can identify with a situation similar to one of the following:
- You have won a major award at school, but you have just learned that your father or mother lost his or her job.
- You made the starting lineup on the basketball team, but your best friend was cut from the team.

In a small group, share similar experiences. Describe your conflict and how you handled it.

Building Background
CULTURAL CONNECTION

This story takes place over the course of a Christian funeral and includes references to a number of Christian traditions. One funeral custom is for neighbors, relatives, and friends to bring food to the family of the deceased or to send flowers to the funeral home. Often the dead person's body is embalmed, or preserved, and displayed in a funeral home the day before the funeral. During a "visitation," people come to pay their respects to the dead person and to express their feelings of sympathy to the family.

Setting a Purpose
READING CONNECTION

What Roseanne Says About Melissa	What Roseanne May Feel Toward Melissa
"a good body and no brains"	Dislike, jealousy

Understanding the Narrator In a story, the narrator is the person or voice that tells the story. A main character who describes the events in a story in his or her own words is called a **first-person narrator**. In this story, the narrator is 14-year-old Roseanne. She describes her feelings in a frank, often colorful way as she copes with new experiences and conflicting feelings toward her cousin Melissa. To dramatically illustrate how Roseanne's feelings about Melissa change, create a chart like the one above. Complete the chart either while reading or after reading the story.

OVERVIEW

Objectives

- To understand and appreciate a short story that explores the new experiences and conflicting emotions of a teenage girl
- To appreciate and understand characters
- To express understanding of the story through a choice of writing forms, including a personal essay and a poem
- To extend understanding of the story through a variety of multimodal and cross-curricular activities

Skills

LITERARY CONCEPTS
- Character
- Mood

READING SKILLS/ STRATEGIES
- Understanding the narrator

THE WRITER'S STYLE
- Chronological transitions

GRAMMAR
- Capitalization of brand names

SPEAKING, LISTENING, AND VIEWING
- Oral interpretation
- Group discussion
- Oral presentation

PRINT AND MEDIA RESOURCES

UNIT ONE RESOURCE BOOK
Strategic Reading: Literature, p. 55
Vocabulary SkillBuilder, p. 56

WRITING MINI-LESSONS
Transparencies, pp. 40–41

ACCESS FOR STUDENTS ACQUIRING ENGLISH
Selection Summaries
Reading Support

FORMAL ASSESSMENT
Selection Test, pp. 25–26
 Test Generator

AUDIO LIBRARY
See Reference Card

The Beginning of Something
Sue Ellen Bridgers

SUMMARY

Roseanne's mother learns over the phone that Cousin Jessie, her first cousin and best friend, has died. The family drives all night to attend the funeral. Roseanne's assignment is to look after Melissa, Cousin Jessie's daughter. The two have known each other all their lives and spend four weeks together every summer, but they are not close friends. The tragedy, Melissa's grief, and other events now bring them closer. Melissa's boyfriend comes to see her and brings along a friend, Travis, whom Roseanne knows from her summer visits. She has always liked him, but now he's older and "gorgeous." Together the four go on a date, Roseanne's first date in a car. They drive to the river and park. Travis kisses her. At the funeral the next day, Roseanne thinks of her date and her kiss—secrets she'll always share with Melissa—and of the grief shared by the family members.

Thematic Link: *Rites of Passage* The funeral of her mother's cousin provides the setting for two important moments in a young person's life: social acceptance and the discovery of close friendship.

CUSTOMIZING FOR
Students Acquiring English

- Use **ACCESS FOR STUDENTS ACQUIRING ENGLISH,** *Reading Support.*
- This selection should not be too difficult for most students. The conversational and stream-of-consciousness style make this piece an excellent one for reading aloud.

STRATEGIC READING FOR
Less-Proficient Readers

Set a Purpose To help immerse students in the selection, ask them if they have ever had to spend time with a distant relative they disliked. Have students read to find out why Roseanne must visit Melissa and why she is not close to her cousin.

Use **UNIT ONE RESOURCE BOOK,** p. 55, for guidance in reading the selection.

WORDS TO KNOW

bereaved (bĭ-rēvd') *n.* people who have suffered the loss of a loved one (p. 136)
infernal (ĭn-fûr'nəl) *adj.* awful (p. 131)
kin (kĭn) *n.* one's relatives; family (p. 140)
remorse (rĭ-môrs') *n.* bitter regret (p. 134)
throes (thrōz) *n.* a condition of agonizing struggle (p. 132)

When Mama said, "We're all going home for Cousin Jessie's funeral," I said, "Not me," but here I am. We rode all night with static blaring off the radio to keep Mama awake so she could nudge Daddy. Nothing keeps him awake except an elbow, not even static. He's so tone-deaf, it sounds like music to him. Buddy and me stayed all tangled up in the backseat. He can sleep through anything, but I was restless and uneasy. It was hot, too.

Literary Concept:
CHARACTER

B Ask students how the author introduces the character of Melissa. Ask them whether they think Melissa will play an important role in the story. Why or why not? *(Possible responses: Melissa is introduced by the narrator in a comparison with herself; she will play an important role because the story will be about the relationship between the two girls; it's too early to tell who has an important role.)*

Critical Thinking:
COMPARING/CONTRASTING

C Have students compare, based on their reading so far, Mama and Cousin Jessie's relationship with Roseanne and Melissa's relationship. *(Possible responses: The relationship seems quite different. Mama and Cousin Jessie grew up together, were best friends, kept secrets together, and loved each other. Roseanne and Melissa see each other only in the summer and don't like each other that much.)*

Cultural Note

D The tradition of wearing black to a funeral has a long history. In ancient times, people believed that evil spirits were attracted to corpses. By wearing black clothing, people hoped to avoid the attention of spirits.

Literary Concept:
FIGURATIVE LANGUAGE

E Have students analyze this simile and explain how holding on to Melissa is like "calming a scared animal." *(Possible response: She is shaking as a frightened animal might, and Roseanne's touch is like the reassurance of the mother animal.)*

We left right after supper. Mama already had a chicken stewing for pastry when the phone rang. She started crying right there on the phone, a big wailing sob with her mouth open like she was getting ready for a high note. Mama sings.

fter a while, she settled down enough to find out when the funeral was going to be— Sunday at two o'clock—and she still wanted to get in the car that minute and go. She would have, too, except for the chicken and Daddy's navy blue suit somebody had to get out of the cleaners and having to think of something I could wear. I'm still outgrowing clothes—well, actually, my shape is changing. One day I'm pudgy-looking, and the next I've got this waist that nips in just perfect. Not like Melissa's, of course, who was born with a good body and no brains.

Melissa is Cousin Jessie's daughter. Cousin Jessie was Mama's first cousin and her best friend besides. They grew up together and they've always loved each other the way people do who remember all grades of silliness and mischief between them. I've heard some of the things they used to do, baby stuff like sneaking out after the house was locked and smoking on the front porch. Big deal. Before Cousin Jessie got so sick, the two of them would start giggling and whispering behind their hands and hugging each other. Used to make Melissa and me sick. We've never liked each other all that much, mostly I reckon because we're supposed to. Two weeks at her house every summer, two weeks at mine. The longest month God ever made.

Mama was crying all the while she rolled out the dough for the pastry and then the whole time she hunted through the closet for something I could wear. She already had a black dress. People like Mama keep a black dress all the time, just in case. Fourteen-year-old girls don't wear black unless they've got loose morals, except for a T-shirt or something minor like that. Finally Mama found this tacky midnight blue dress I'd pushed to the back of the closet because every time I look at it I about puke, that's how unattractive it is. Mama bought it on sale and anybody can tell it, too. I just about died the one time I wore it. Kept my coat on all through church and it was one of those late winter days that turns out to be positively springlike. Now I've got to wear it to a funeral in July. They might as well lay me out right next to Cousin Jessie.

At this minute I'm sitting here on the porch swing next to Melissa, who won't say a word. I reckon while it's quiet like this, I could tell you what she looks like, and I'm going to try to tell the truth. She's been crying off and on ever since she got up this morning. I think she must of woke up not remembering anything but all of a sudden it came to her because she moaned real loud and pulled the sheet over her head. I could see the sheet trembling like there was a poltergeist[1] under there. I hadn't been asleep more than two hours and my mouth felt scorched and my eyes wouldn't half open but I couldn't leave her like that so I went over to her bed and put my hand on the jerking sheet. I pressed right on her chest till her breathing slowed down. There wasn't any point in saying anything, was there? She kept on crying, but at least she wasn't wearing herself out with it. Holding on to her like that was like calming a scared animal, but I don't think Melissa would ever think about it that way. She used to want me to rub her back all the time, just a couple of years ago. She expects things like that of people, but it always embarrasses me. Melissa is spoiled.

---

1. **poltergeist** (pōl′tər-gīst′): a ghost that manifests itself through noises or other disturbances.

130 UNIT ONE PART 2: RITES OF PASSAGE

Mini-Lesson The Writer's Style

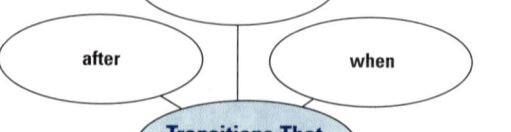

CHRONOLOGICAL TRANSITIONS

Draw the web shown on the left on the chalkboard and use it to explain how authors frequently shift back and forth in time in stories. An author will often make use of transitional devices—words and phrases such as *first, after a while, then, finally, later on,* and *the next day* to serve as transitions between the past and present, making it clear when the action occurs.

Application Discuss with students how the transitional devices *right after supper, after a while, at this minute,* and *when* on pages 130 and 131 help the reader understand the time frame of events. Have students copy the web into their notebooks. Ask them to refer to it as they look through the selection to find other examples.

Reteaching/Reinforcement
- *Writing Handbook,* anthology p. 869
- *Writing Mini-Lessons* transparencies, pp. 40–41

 The Writer's Craft

Coherence in Paragraphs, pp. 364–365

She's pretty, though. Even right now with her eyelids swollen and her cheeks puffed up and not a smidgen of lipstick in sight—nothing done to get ready for the world but her teeth and hair brushed—she looks darn near perfect. Like a model. Like she doesn't have to do anything but just *be*. I know you've seen people like that. I think you ought to consider yourself lucky if you don't know any.

So she's sitting here in the morning heat—it's hot down in the flatland at nine o'clock in the morning. There's no haze to burn off so the sun just comes on out at five A.M. and everything's cooking by ten. When Melissa stays with us in the mountains, she sleeps in a double bed with me, and she curls up right tight next to me about daybreak when the air turns as chilly as it's going to get. She sleeps under a blanket every night. I think that's the only part about coming to our house she likes—snuggling under the covers like that.

> We've never liked each other all that much, mostly I reckon because we're supposed to.

Anyway, we didn't visit this summer because her mama was so sick, hardly walking and needing to be looked after every minute. Cousin Jessie had diabetes[2] from the time she was first married. She gave herself those shots every day and even with doing that, sometimes she'd start shaking and jerking and finally just fall down unconscious. Everybody in the family carried Life Savers around in their pockets. Diabetes is what killed her, Life Savers or no.

When the news came, Mama was broken-hearted. Even knowing Cousin Jessie's time was coming and praying about it and fretting over it, Mama wasn't one bit ready. The look on her face when she was on the telephone was a sight—like she was hearing something terrible and truly unexpected instead of word that Cousin Jessie was at rest.

She looked wild, Mama did, like the time she pulled Buddy out of the path of Mr. Bowdine's car when he reversed by accident. Then there was the time she lost a baby in the bathroom. I didn't even know it was a baby until that summer when I heard Mama and Cousin Jessie going over the details and put two and two together. The point is, that was the look on Mama's face, a look of being ripped apart and so startled she didn't know which was worse, the surprise or the pain.

Diabetes runs in the family. Cousin Jessie's daddy had it and one of his sisters did, too. Mama's always telling us to watch our blood sugar, although Cousin Jessie's daddy wasn't a blood relative to us, her mama was. So it's Melissa who ought to be watching her blood sugar and I reckon she knows it. There's not an ounce of fat on her. She's wearing white shorts and a pink skinny top that shows everything. Mama didn't even let me bring shorts, even knowing how hot it is here. I've got seersucker slacks and this cotton skirt and that infernal blue dress. Of course, there's nobody to tell

---

2. **diabetes** (dī′ə-bē′tĭs): a disease capable of producing coma and even death, in which the body produces insufficient insulin to balance sugar levels in the blood. Extra insulin is usually taken by the patient in the form of daily hypodermic shots.

WORDS TO KNOW
infernal (ĭn-fûr′nəl) *adj.* awful

Art Note

Katie on Sofa by Fairfield Porter
Although he never received renown on the scale of his famous cousin, the writer T. S. Eliot, Fairfield Porter (1907–1975) is nonetheless regarded as one of America's finest painters. His subjects were usually familiar: friends or domestic scenes.

Reading the Art Why is the young woman staring straight ahead? What might she be thinking about?

CUSTOMIZING FOR
Students Acquiring English

Explain to students that Mama is expecting a great quantity of food because people in the United States traditionally bring food to the family of someone who has just died. Ask students if they have similar customs in their native countries.

Katie on Sofa (1959), Fairfield Porter. Oil on canvas, 24¼″ × 25¼″, collection of Mr. and Mrs. Edward W. Andrews, Jr.

Melissa what she ought to be wearing. I mean, who's going to say it? Her daddy is in the throes of grief, so I think Mama's going to end up in charge. Already this morning she's cleaned out the refrigerator to make room for the cold dishes she's expecting. She's cleaned off a pantry shelf on which to put fried chicken, boiled vegetables, and ham. The buffet in the dining room will take care of cakes and pies and, I hope, some brownies. I would die for a brownie

WORDS TO KNOW   **throes** (thrōz) *n.* a condition of agonizing struggle

132

Mini-Lesson Literary Concepts

MOOD
Contributing Factors — Range
setting — happiness to
descriptive words — anger;
imagery — levity to
sound/rhythm — horror

REVIEWING MOOD Remind students that a work's mood is the feeling that the writer wants the reader to get from it, such as excitement, anger, sadness, happiness, or pity. Writers use many literary techniques to create mood, including details, dialogue, imagery, figurative language, rhythm, and setting.

Application Have students work in small groups to find examples of the different techniques used to create the mood of the story. How does the author capture the feverish excitement of a transitional period in the narrator's life? Have them look for details about the narrator's emotional and physical state. Ask how elements of the setting, such as the heat and the images used to describe it, contribute to the mood.

132 THE LANGUAGE OF LITERATURE TEACHER'S EDITION

right now. And a cold drink. Melissa and I skipped breakfast.

I think she's just going to sit here until one o'clock, when we're supposed to go down to the funeral home and view the body. I told Mama I wasn't going and she said all right, I could take care of Buddy. He's nine and doesn't have any business at a funeral home. Melissa is going, though. She and her daddy are supposed to see if Cousin Jessie looks all right before they let other people view her. It seems to me it ought to be the other way around. Let some objective people get the first look. I think funerals are sick.

"Melissa, let's get something to eat."

She's pushing the swing with her bare feet so it trembles a little. She's got the prettiest toenails. I swear it! They curve just perfect and she's put this pink polish on them that turns silvery when the light catches it right. I guess fixing her toenails gave her something to do last night. You can spend hours messing with your nails if you want to. Well, I couldn't, but I bet Melissa can. Her feet are the kind somebody's going to want to kiss. It won't be long either, because Melissa's been going out with boys for a year or more. She's older than me, already sixteen, and there were boys after her when she was twelve. Cousin Jessie was fighting them off with a stick. Mama's never had that trouble with me.

"No, thanks," Melissa says about the food like I'm offering to fix her something. "Jamie's coming over here in a few minutes. He said he would."

That's the boy she's been going out with all summer. He'll be a senior next year, and for their first date he took her to the Junior-Senior Prom this past spring. Their picture's taped smack in the middle of her dresser mirror so you have to look around it to do your face. They're standing in front of a blue curtain with silver stars on it, and she's got her back up against his chest, and he's got his arms around her. I'm going to borrow that dress she's wearing if my figure settles down by next spring. I know Melissa's not intending to wear it again even if it cost one hundred and fifty dollars, which it did. Cousin Jessie told Mama Melissa's got expensive taste. She tried to sound like she was complaining, but I heard the pride in it. Melissa was everything to Cousin Jessie.

"Well, I'm eating something." Mama told me to stay with her. Comfort her, Mama said. "You want me to bring you a sandwich out here?"

We're eating peanut butter and jelly with milk. Melissa nibbles at hers and leaves the milk glass half full on the porch floor. This old tomcat of hers starts nosing around it, trying to get his face down to the milk. She doesn't even notice when he turns it over. I've got to remember to clean up the sticky place when he gets through. Mama wants everything clean, just like Cousin Jessie used to keep the house before she got weak and bloated and the medicine quit doing any good.

"Finished?"

When Melissa nods, I take her half-eaten sandwich and the empty glasses into the house. It's cooler in the house, especially in the living room, because the blinds are shut and it's dark in there. The kitchen's warm, though, and Mama's beading up while she scrubs the counter-tops and the cabinet fronts just like she was home. I think this is nervous energy working because she didn't sleep at all in the car and I don't think she closed her eyes after we got here. She and Cousin Roy sat down together at the kitchen table first thing, and that's where they were this morning when I came down. They'd been talking for hours, Uncle Roy telling Mama step by step what happened. I heard bits and pieces of it and I don't see how anybody remembers everything like that. It's like three days are marked in his brain, minute by minute. Looks like it would all be a blur.

CUSTOMIZING FOR
Students Acquiring English

③ Define a *coma* as "prolonged unconsciousness caused by injury, disease, or poison."

④ Tell students that *fretted* means "worried."

Literary Concept: MOOD

K Invite students to discuss how the narrator's recollection of her "remorse" in algebra class helps to vary the mood of the story. *(Possible responses: It adds an element of humor and flippancy; it provides some relief from the highly charged emotions of the funeral setting.)*

Cousin Roy couldn't have picked a better person to tell it to, because Mama wanted to hear every word of it. I know she wishes she'd been here, but when Cousin Roy first called her to say Cousin Jessie was back in the hospital, practically in a coma, he told her there was no need for her to rush across North Carolina to see her. Cousin Jessie wouldn't know she was there, he said, hoping, I think, to relieve Mama's mind. But she wanted to come, she told Daddy, who agreed with Cousin Roy that she should save her strength for the end. "You can't help Jessie now," Daddy said, "but you can help Roy and Melissa later on if you don't wear yourself out. Jessie'd want them to have plenty of attention."

Mama gave in, but like I say, she fretted about it and prayed and cleaned her own house like we were expecting company ourselves. The older Mama gets, the more nervous she acts. I always thought when you got about forty, nothing much would worry you anymore. I mean, everything ought to be settled by then. But it's not so. Mama's a bundle of nerves under the best of circumstances.

Now she's perspiring through the housedress she brought to clean in. "Your daddy's still asleep," she says, aggravated by everything.

"He drove all night," I say in his defense.

"I know it." Mama wishes she weren't mad with Daddy. Her irritation weighs heavy on her, like it's a sin to feel anything but sad. "Your daddy's a fine man," she says, to get rid of her bad feelings. It's what she always does when she catches herself being upset with him. Mama always feels what she calls <u>remorse</u>, which I don't know a thing about unless you call remorse what I felt when Candy Hooper and I got caught copying each other's algebra problems. She'd done half and I'd done half so I

> *H*ave you ever been struck dumb like this so you make a fool out of yourself doing absolutely nothing?

don't call that cheating, but Mrs. Siler did and Mama did when Mrs. Siler sent me home from school at ten o'clock with a note saying I was suspended for the rest of the day and for Mama to either come see her or sign the note proving I'd done at least one honorable thing. I think I spent that afternoon in remorse.

"Can I help you do anything?" I ask her, because she's sniffling again. This crying is getting to me. I haven't cried a tear. Not that I don't love Cousin Jessie. She was always more fun than Melissa, but I just don't feel like crying about her. She was real sick and now she's not sick anymore, if you believe what you hear in church. And you're supposed to believe it, aren't you? Preachers talk about faith all the time, but right now I don't see much of it around here.

"Just keep an eye on Melissa," Mama says, scrubbing hard at a spot I could have told her was at least a three-year-old stain. "I haven't had a minute to be with her and I know she's distraught."

"She's sitting on the porch swing waiting for Jamie Fletcher to come see her. He's her boyfriend." I say that harder than I should

---

WORDS TO KNOW

remorse (rĭ-môrs′) *n.* bitter regret

have. Sometimes I can see where I've got a streak of meanness in me a mile wide.

Mama pauses in her scrubbing to consider the appropriateness of this. Mama's always worrying about what's appropriate.

"Well, maybe it'll do her good," she decides finally. She doesn't have any authority over Melissa anyway. I could have told her that, too.

When I come back to the porch, Jamie Fletcher is here and he's got somebody with him.

"Hey, Roseanne," the other boy says like he knows me, and all of a sudden, I know him! It's Travis, who lives three houses down from Melissa and used to play with us. I haven't seen him in three summers—last summer I didn't come, and the summer before that Travis was at a camp at the beach, where he learned to sail and high-dive and got muscles. Some things I can't describe, not with any amount of trying, and one of them is how Travis Cuthbert looks now that he's filled out and got muscles and a dynamite tan and hair on his legs. He's gorgeous. He's not that tall, blond, golden type like Melissa's Jamie, but he's handsome in a way that suits me better. He's kind of short and tight and his hair is dark and wavy and he's got brown eyes instead of this washed-out blue everybody in our family got stuck with. He's got on cut-off jeans and a green T-shirt from Myrtle Beach and those worn-out looking moccasins that cost a fortune but people never polish so they'll look like they can afford to abuse them. Daddy always polishes my shoes, even if I don't want him to. I hate him doing that.

"How you doing?" Jamie says to Melissa and sits down beside her on the swing. Travis and I are just standing here.

"Fine," Melissa says, but she grabs his hand.

I'm still looking at Travis even though I know I'm making a fool of myself. I'm glad I put my face on.

"How you been, Roseanne?" Travis wants to know. He turns a little away from Melissa and Jamie, like ignoring them will give them privacy in broad daylight.

I take myself over to the steps and plop down on the top one. I can't think of a thing to say. Have you ever been struck dumb like this so you make a fool out of yourself doing absolutely nothing?

"Come sit down," I say when I find my breath. I think my lungs have collapsed on me because no air's going in. I try pushing out and there's a great big sigh like somebody gives to show they're bored, which I definitely am not. "Whatcha' been doing?" I ask when he's sitting next to me.

"The usual. Working at the pool. I earned my senior lifesaver badge so I've got a lifeguarding job."

That accounts for the tan. I look pasty beside him, but some people like a delicate look, even in the summertime. I smooth my flowered skirt over my knees and rub my hands down my calves. I've got good calves, tanned or not.

"You've changed a lot," Travis says, noticing my calves. I do baton twirling for a hobby and go to jazz class twice a week. Mama let me take it up when I refused to go to another piano lesson.

"It's been more than two years," I say and wish I hadn't. He'll think I've been keeping track.

"Too bad about the circumstances," he says, nodding toward Melissa, who's got her head resting on Jamie's chest right here on the front porch. Mama's going to have a fit.

"Well, she was real sick," I say like I'm supposed to comfort him or something. "We've got to go to the funeral home at one o'clock and look at her. I'm going with Melissa in

THE BEGINNING OF SOMETHING 135

Multicultural Perspectives

FUNERAL CUSTOMS Burial traditions vary greatly from culture to culture around the world. The two most common traditions for disposing of the body after death are burial and cremation. In cremation, the body of the deceased is burned to ashes. In India, Hindus have been practicing cremation since ancient times. The body is cremated on a funeral pyre (pile of burnable material), and the ashes are collected in an urn. Within a year, the ashes are taken to the bank of a river, preferably the sacred Ganges, and dispersed into the water.

Literary Concept: MOOD

M Ask students to notice the narrator's frequent references to the heat. How does the heat make Roseanne feel? What feelings do the heat-related details reinforce? *(Possible response: She is burning with anticipation of the date, and the heat intensifies her feelings; the heat adds to the mood of fever, anticipation, excitement.)*

case she breaks down over it. She's been so brave." Well, a person can change her mind, can't she?

Travis is looking at me like I'm God's gift to the <u>bereaved</u>. That's the truth. He's got this expression of awe on his face I wish I had a picture of. "Whatcha doing later?" he asks me.

I think to myself, this is how a date gets started. Here I am on Cousin Jessie's porch with her dead in the funeral home and her own child crying on her boyfriend's shirtfront and Mama in the house scrubbing everything in sight and I've got to think of the right thing to say. "Well, there's the visitation . . ." I begin.

"Oh, yeah." I can tell he's disappointed.

"But that's over at nine," I slide in.

"I don't suppose you and Melissa'd want to go somewhere, just out for a ride or to get something to eat," Travis says, brightening up. "Jamie and I were talking about it. Maybe it would do her good to get out of here for a while."

Ever since late this morning, I've had this fever. There's a cool dampness inside my clothes but my cheeks are burning. I feel like I've been on fire inside my face all this time but nobody seems to notice. I have a date!

I can't believe Melissa straightened herself up from Jamie Fletcher's arm and went right in the house to her daddy and said to him, "It'll be all right if Roseanne and me ride around awhile after the visitation." Didn't ask him. Told him in that sweet way of hers like her mama had somehow already given her permission, and he just nodded while my mama stared holes through both of us. I kept looking at Mama and after a long minute she sort of half nodded her consent to me, too. She was giving in and her face sagged with it like she was grimacing before the next blow, waiting to be struck down.

I'm burning up. Ever since that minute when Mama gave in, I've been hot under my skin, so I keep thinking about water. About how Travis must look at the pool. I bet during the rest periods he practices his dives. We used to run through the lawn sprinkler spray when it was hot like this and Travis would come over and aggravate us. He'd sit on the jets or chase us with the hose. He'd make Melissa so mad. One time he held the sprinkler on my head so I was surrounded by whirling spray with colors in it, like a crown shooting off diamonds. I remember it like it was yesterday. I have always thought a lot of Travis.

M

In a few minutes I'm going off with him. I ought to tell you this is my first date in a car. I call riding around a date, don't you? I mean, it's likely we'll go somewhere and get a cola or a soft cone. That would make it official. I believe somebody has to spend some money to make it a date. Craig Watkins comes and sits on our porch sometimes in the evenings after his American Legion baseball practice. He's on his way home and he sees us there and he comes and sits. Sometimes he and Buddy roughhouse or toss a baseball around until it's too dark to see. Most of the time, though, he leans against a porch post and watches the sky with me. It's the only time I like to be still—in that little while between sunset and true dark when the world is closing up and after a while there's nothing to see but our street, the house full of yellow light across the way, and our own porch. The cool smell of night is coming but there are no stars yet. I know just where I am then. Craig Watkins sitting on the porch is not a date.

This afternoon I went with Melissa to view the body, but I didn't look. I went about halfway

> **WORDS TO KNOW**
> **bereaved** (bĭ-rēvd′) *n.* people who have suffered the loss of a loved one

Isabella and Lois (1968), Warren Brandt. Oil on canvas, 50″ × 60″, private collection.

Art Note

Isabella and Lois by Warren Brandt
Warren Brandt was born in North Carolina in 1918. This interior scene depicts two women, one sitting and one kneeling, apparently examining a rug or piece of cloth. Although their faces are not detailed, the scene has an intensity created by the artist's use of rich colors to depict the women, the furnishings, and the room.

Reading the Art *How does the artist manage to make this scene come alive to the viewer without showing the expressions of the two women?*

up there to the casket, which was at one end of a long room lined with vinyl sofas and straight-backed chairs. There were lights in the ceiling along the molding and some plants on end tables that separated the sofas from the chairs. There were flowers on either end of the casket, too. Wreaths of carnations and mums and gladioluses. I kept looking at them so I didn't have to look at Cousin Jessie. I don't believe Melissa wanted to look, either, but I reckon she felt like she had to.

"Do you think what she's wearing is all right?" she asked Mama, like clothes were the important thing. Well, they are to Melissa. She's always had everything she wants. You ought to see inside her closet.

"It's fine," Mama said and put her arm around Melissa's shoulder. They were both trembling. You could see their shoulders jumping. Cousin Roy came in with Daddy then, and Mama and Melissa opened a place between them and hugged him, too. Cousin Roy looked weak and sick, not giving his full height, which is more than six feet. I have never liked tall men. Five eight or nine is good enough for me.

By the time we got home, the house was full of people and flowers and food. Melissa

THE BEGINNING OF SOMETHING **137**

Mini-Lesson: Speaking, Listening, and Viewing

ORAL INTERPRETATION Explain to students that oral interpretation means expressively speaking a written work aloud. The purpose of oral interpretation is to communicate the interpreter's feelings about the work. Sometimes oral interpreters read from a lecture stand; sometimes they memorize and fully act out a piece, like actors in a play. Either way, the interpreter should make the characters he or she interprets come to vivid life.

Application "The Beginning of Something" has a very lively narrator, with strong feelings and a good sense of humor. Ask students to choose a passage of the story for an oral interpretation. Each student should speak the dialogue of one of the characters, with another speaker serving as narrator. You may want to tape-record students' interpretations.

Critical Thinking: MAKING JUDGMENTS

N Ask students if they think the narrator's criticism of Melissa's refusal to speak to people she knows at the visitation is warranted. Ask them why they think Roseanne criticizes Melissa. (*Possible response: Roseanne's criticism is not warranted; someone who has just lost a parent might easily be too upset to greet people. Roseanne criticizes everything about Melissa because of her jealousy.*)

Literary Concept: MOOD

O Ask students what the narrator means by "a top spinning in there, whizzing and making heat." How does this image reinforce the mood? (*Possible responses: The narrator's mind is occupied by many thoughts and feelings; it adds to the helter-skelter feeling of confusion and feverish excitement; it reinforces the continuous heat imagery.*)

Critical Thinking: SPECULATING

P Have students speculate as to why Melissa now appears less pretty to Roseanne. (*Possible responses: Melissa has stopped taking care of herself because of her mother's death; because Roseanne herself feels prettier, she no longer sees Melissa as being so beautiful.*)

Literary Concept: FIGURATIVE LANGUAGE

Q Ask students why the author's use of figurative language ("like we are trailing in someone's exhaust," "as powdery as used charcoal") in this paragraph is effective. (*Possible response: It helps the reader imagine what the air is like and how uncomfortable Roseanne feels.*)

N wouldn't eat a thing. She wouldn't talk to people either. I don't know what gets into her. I mean, she knows everybody in this town so it's not like anybody expected her to greet strangers. Most of them are unknown to me, however, and I was polite. Even Mama commented on it. I wish I'd brought that mint green top that's cut low in the back. I'd put it on right now if I had it.

Lord, it was hot at the visitation. You'd think a funeral home could keep itself cool, but the place was packed with people, even backed up in the hall, waiting to view Cousin Jessie and pay their respects. Some people were so glad to see Mama they acted like it was a reunion, but Mama held herself back. I heard a woman ask her if she was going to sing something at the funeral. She wanted to hear Mama because it had been such a long time. Mama said she wasn't, but the thought of it brought tears to her eyes. She sang at Cousin Jessie's wedding and was the maid of honor besides.

I feel like I'm going on and on. Diarrhea of the mouth. That's what happens when a person gets feverish. You feel like you've got to get everything said before you pass out of heat exhaustion. My mind's been racing for hours. **O** It's like I've got a top spinning in there, whizzing and making heat. Everywhere I've been it's been so hot and tomorrow I've got to wear that dress. I ought to take some aspirins or something.

When we got home from the visitation it was dark, and Travis and Jamie were waiting on the porch. Mama invited them in to have a piece of cake—we've got six kinds—but they wouldn't. I came upstairs just now to fix my face and see how bad I look. I look flushed and my eyes are shining, just like a person with a fever. There's something pretty about it, though. I mean it's better than looking washed-out and sickly. **P** Melissa, who stayed downstairs with the boys instead of fixing herself, is not as pretty as she used to be. If you saw her baby pictures, you'd think she should have been on the Ivory Snow box.

ow that we're finally riding around, I can tell you that I thought Mama would never let us out of the house, she kept being so social. She's beside herself with worry about every little thing and I could tell she didn't want us out of her sight. Jamie and Melissa are quiet in the backseat. I don't know what they're doing and I don't intend to look. I watch the asphalt running up under us. If you watch the lights on the road long enough, you'll get dizzy and pass out. Travis is a fantastic driver. He's got one hand on the wheel and the other elbow resting out the window. Every now and then he changes hands. Once he put his hand down on the seat between us and I thought to myself, this is it, but then he made a turn. I think we are riding in circles.

I have noticed that Travis likes to talk about himself, which is all right with me. He tells me all about his job, what time he goes to work, when he closes, and the details of several incidents of disciplinary action he's been involved in. Nobody has drowned in his pool. He tells us about the camp he went to. He won lots of certificates and awards. Football practice starts in three weeks. He is first-string running back and ran nine hundred yards for eight touchdowns last year. All this he says in a half whisper so I have to lean a little toward him to hear. If it weren't for my seatbelt I could slip over.

Q I am absolutely light-headed. The breeze gusting past my head is hot and oily like we are trailing in someone's exhaust. The air down here doesn't breathe good like at home. I feel as powdery as used charcoal and every breath I take turns prickly in my throat.

138   UNIT ONE   PART 2: RITES OF PASSAGE

Boy and Car (1955), David Park. Oil on canvas, 18″ × 24″, collection of Mrs. Wellington S. Henderson.

Art Note

Boy and Car by David Park David Park (1911–1960) was born in Boston and studied art in California. Although he is considered a member of the California school of figure painters, his work reveals the strong influence of the earlier tradition of German expressionism. Park's last paintings, of which this is an example, feature brilliant areas of color and roughly drawn scenes.

Reading the Art *How would you describe the mood of this painting? Why?*

"Let's get some burgers and drinks and go out by the river," Jamie says from the backseat.

He and Melissa are stretching and sighing just like they're waking up. "I could eat a horse," Melissa says with a little laugh. And we've got all that food at home.

The boys go into a restaurant while Melissa and I wait in the car, so I turn around to talk to her. She's rumpled and relaxed looking. Her lips are puffy and her hair looks tangled in the back. Around her face it's as smooth as silk where she's combed her fingers through it.

"Travis is nice," I say. I have always wanted to be sitting in a car outside a restaurant waiting for my date to come back. People going in always glance at you and know there's somebody inside getting you something.

"He's all right," Melissa says, sighing. She

THE BEGINNING OF SOMETHING 139

STRATEGIC READING FOR
Less-Proficient Readers

R Have students summarize Roseanne's exciting experience.

- Ask them where Roseanne and her cousin go after the visitation. *(on a double date with Travis and Jamie)* **Summarizing**

- Ask the students why this is so exciting to Roseanne. *(It's her first real car date.)* **Analyzing**

Set a Purpose Have students pay close attention to how Roseanne's feelings about Melissa change.

CUSTOMIZING FOR
Students Acquiring English

5 Have students use context clues to determine the meaning of someone being "put out." *(Possible responses: annoyed, bothered)*

6 Tell students that the expression "jump out of my skin" refers to a feeling of anxiety one gets when trying to hold an emotion back—a feeling as if one is about to "burst open" from extreme unease or impatience. Ask if they have similar expressions in their native languages.

Literary Concept:
MINOR CHARACTER

S Ask students to evaluate the importance of Travis to the story so far. Is he a main character or a minor character? *(Possible response: He is a minor character because he is not as extensively developed as Roseanne or Melissa; his importance is limited to his being Roseanne's date.)*

---

used to talk a whole lot more than this.

"What's at the river?" I ask.

"Nothing. Just the river bank and trees and stuff. It's where people go to park, Roseanne."

"You mean we're going to park? We can just eat the burgers and talk, can't we?"

"You can do anything you want to," Melissa says.

R I think what I'll do is faint.

We rode up here to the church in a black limousine, but there wasn't a thing fun about it. I mean, you ought to be going to a party in a car like that. I rode in front with Melissa. Mama, Daddy, Cousin Roy, and Buddy were in the back. Cousin Roy's family from Wilson was in the car behind and I think his sister Esther is put out about it. After all, she's more <u>kin</u> than we are. Sometimes kin is not what matters, I don't reckon. Cousin Roy knows how it was between Jessie and Mama, so we got to ride in the limousine behind the hearse. The air conditioner was blowing full blast between my legs, but I was hot anyway. We waited in the limo outside the church until they'd slid the casket onto this folding stretcher contraption and rolled it in. Then we got out, and right there I started sweating because the sun could boil water today. This church is not air-conditioned either.

The organ is playing, and we're sitting on the front pews, our backs to everybody. Melissa is between her daddy and my mama. She's wearing blue, but it's a soft color. Soft summery material, too. She looks like an angel, all glittery and shiny, while the rest of us are black and gray and midnight blue. I'm between Daddy and Buddy, but I can see Melissa's hands working a tissue.

In a minute she's going to have it torn up, the way she's twisting and squeezing it. Mama has a pocketbook full.

The organ is sending out mournful notes, too draggy to follow. I think we ought to sing. It would be better than sitting here, holding the words in our heads. I'd like to blast right out "j-us-s-t as I am-m-m" so that woman would pick up the beat, but Mama would die. I feel like I'm going to jump out of my skin. I've never been good at waiting.

Anybody with eyes can see how I'm fidgeting. My mind won't stop whirring, trying to make sense of all that's in it. Travis Cuthbert kissed me last night! We rode out by the river with me holding the cardboard tray with four drinks and a sack of burgers in my lap. The smell of hot onions and pickles was enough to make a well person sick. I sipped on my drink all the way out there, trying not to throw up, although I am not a person with a weak stomach. Travis parked the car and distributed the food. He kept the switch on so we could listen to the radio. It was dark except for the green dials on the dashboard, so Travis opened the pocket so the little light in there showed. The burger tasted a lot better than I thought it would. When everybody was finished, Travis turned the switch off and shut the pocket so everything was quiet and still and dark around me. I couldn't even see the river, but I could hear it, just this little stirring movement and, now and then, a plopping sound like someone throwing a stone or dipping a cup into the water. Our rivers at home are always moving, rushing and slapping rocks, going somewhere in a hurry. They sound cool and fresh and busy. These rivers down here hardly move at all and the air around them is sticky and sour.

"Let's get out," Travis said. We left Melissa and Jamie in the backseat and walked down

---

WORDS TO KNOW

kin (kĭn) *n.* one's relatives; family

140

Mini-Lesson Grammar

CAPITALIZATION OF BRAND NAMES

Remind students that the brand name of a product is the name of a specific thing, or a proper noun, and so it must be capitalized. Common nouns following a brand name should not be capitalized.

Sugar **B**last cereal
Durastrong garbage bags

Explain that brand names such as Kleenex, Xerox, Ping-Pong, and Scotch Tape are so widely used that it's easy to forget that they are not generic terms. (*Aspirin* is an example of a word that was once a brand name but has evolved into a common noun.)

Application Ask students to suggest a generic replacement word or phrase for some common brand names. Have students brainstorm a list of other brand names that are so well-known they might be easily mistaken for common nouns.

Reteaching/Reinforcement

 The Writer's Craft

Brand Names, p. 757

140 THE LANGUAGE OF LITERATURE TEACHER'S EDITION

to the water. It wasn't any cooler there and mosquitoes were hovering in the grass, but we sat down on a big flat rock right on the water's edge and pulled our feet up.

I didn't get a whole lot of warning. I always thought when I got kissed it was going to be with eye contact, in slow motion, you know, so expecting it would be just as exciting as the kiss itself. It wasn't like that. Travis kissed me hard and flat at first, like it was an attack or something, but right away I knew that wasn't how he meant it. When I didn't pull back, he softened up and we kissed for a while. Little kisses and a couple of big ones. I think he was practicing as much as I was. I felt as weak as water and clammy in my chest and my head was full of light so I just wanted to keep my eyes shut like when you wake up suddenly and the sun's too bright in your room. I didn't want to move or wake up or anything.

We didn't talk much going home. I don't mind admitting I'm tongue-tied in some situations, and Melissa and Jamie were keeping to themselves.

Melissa is not such a bad person. After we got home, she was so quiet and sad looking. I think she'd hoped going out with Jamie would make her feel better but it didn't. Nothing's going to make her feel better for a long time.

We were standing in front of her dresser mirror. She was brushing her hair and I was just looking at myself. I reckon I expected to see some difference but there doesn't seem to be any. Anyway, Melissa and I happened to look at each other in the mirror. It was truly strange because it was like we were seeing each other for the first time. I mean, I think she saw that I was there with her. And I saw—well, I saw that something terrible had happened to her, had been happening most of her life. Her mama had been dying for a long time, and her being pretty and popular hadn't changed that. Melissa knows a lot of things I don't know.

Later on, I could tell she wasn't asleep. I wasn't sleepy either, but I was thinking about Travis, about how a person's life can be changed so quick. I felt good inside, cooled down and calm but excited, too, like some wonderful adventure was just getting started. All the while, Melissa was tossing around, trying to find a comfortable position. Sometimes there's just nothing you can do to stop being miserable. I waited a little bit to see if she'd settle down. When she didn't, I got up and got in bed with her and rubbed her back like she used to want me to do. I wasn't one bit embarrassed.

This preacher is talking about what a good woman Cousin Jessie was. Everything he's saying is the truth. This church feels dark like there's a cloud stopped over it, but I know it's a bright, sunny, July Sunday outside of here. We've got to go to the cemetery next. I'm going to melt out there in this dress, but I'm going to stay as long as Melissa does. I'm going to tell her how sorry I am. I'm going to tell Cousin Roy, too, because I haven't told him yet. But I'm not going to tell anybody except you about Travis Cuthbert kissing me. It's as private as grief but it doesn't need sharing. Just Melissa knows and someday when we're all grown up and married, we'll probably talk about it just like Mama and Cousin Jessie used to talk about things just they knew about.

As soon as I get a chance, I'm going to hug Mama. ❖

THE BEGINNING OF SOMETHING **141**

STRATEGIC READING FOR
Less-Proficient Readers

T Ask students to tell how Roseanne's feelings about Melissa have changed. *(Possible response: She lets go of her jealousy, sees her cousin sympathetically, and becomes closer to her.)*
Analyzing

CUSTOMIZING FOR
Gifted and Talented Students

U Ask students to discuss how friendships develop. Ask whether it is common to become close friends with someone you initially disliked. Have students speculate about how close Melissa and Roseanne will be 30 or 40 years later.

CUSTOMIZING FOR
Multiple Learning Styles

Spatial or Graphic Learners Invite students to pick two moments from the story, one early and one late, and draw a representation of how Melissa might have appeared to Roseanne at each point.

COMPREHENSION CHECK

1. Who is Cousin Jessie? *(first cousin and best friend of Roseanne's mother)*
2. Why does Roseanne's family go to Melissa's house? *(to attend Cousin Jessie's funeral)*
3. How does Roseanne feel about her cousin at the beginning of the story? *(She doesn't like her very much.)*
4. What happens to change the narrator's impression of Melissa? *(She experiences a little romance and attention for the first time and loses her jealousy of Melissa.)*
5. Besides hugging her mother, what is Roseanne looking forward to at the end of the story? *(becoming as close to Melissa as her mother and Melissa's mother were)*

EDITOR'S NOTE With the permission of the author or copyright holder, potentially offensive material has been deleted from the selection. In addition, some brand names unessential to the narrative have been deleted.

Assessment Option

INFORMAL ASSESSMENT To assess your students' understanding of the selection, ask them to sketch a story map that illustrates the major events of the story in chronological order. Have students label each drawing with a caption identifying the scene. Point out that the order in which Roseanne relates each event is not necessarily the order in which it occurred.

Rubric
3 Full Accomplishment Students create story maps that list the major events in the order in which they occurred.
2 Substantial Accomplishment Students create story maps that list most of the major events, but some events may not be in correct order.
1 Little or Partial Accomplishment Students omit significant events from their story maps.

THE LANGUAGE OF LITERATURE TEACHER'S EDITION **141**

INSIGHT

1. Why doesn't the speaker object when the girl takes a chocolate that he can't afford? *(Possible responses: He wants to impress the girl; he doesn't want to admit that he doesn't have enough money.)*
2. What might the speaker have felt in the moment before the shopkeeper accepted his payment? *(Possible responses: fear, hope, nervousness)*
3. Compare the experiences of the speaker of "Oranges" and of Roseanne in "The Beginning of Something." *(Possible response: They both experience important "firsts;" Roseanne's is a more meaningful experience because she is older and it changes the way she feels about herself and others.)*

GARY SOTO

Born in 1952 in Fresno, California, Gary Soto originally planned to study geography in college but found himself increasingly drawn toward literature. Soto was 25 when his first book of poetry was published. This collection, *The Elements of San Joaquin,* focused on the often harsh details in the lives of Mexican-Americans. Soto, who teaches Chicano studies in addition to writing, has often drawn on his Mexican-American upbringing for his poetry and prose. He is known for his use of plain language and evocative images. Many of his poems are written about children or from a child's perspective. Says Soto, "I think I'm very childlike, and I often write youthful poems."

INSIGHT

Oranges
Gary Soto

The first time I walked
With a girl, I was twelve,
Cold, and weighted down
With two oranges in my jacket.
5   December. Frost cracking
Beneath my steps, my breath
Before me, then gone,
As I walked toward
Her house, the one whose
10 Porch light burned yellow
Night and day, in any weather.
A dog barked at me, until
She came out pulling
At her gloves, face bright
15 With rouge. I smiled,
Touched her shoulder, and led
Her down the street, across
A used car lot and a line
Of newly planted trees,
20 Until we were breathing
Before a drugstore. We
Entered, the tiny bell
Bringing a saleslady
Down a narrow aisle of goods.
25 I turned to the candies
Tiered like bleachers,
And asked what she wanted—
Light in her eyes, a smile
Starting at the corners

30 Of her mouth. I fingered
A nickel in my pocket,
And when she lifted a chocolate
That cost a dime,
I didn't say anything.
35 I took the nickel from
My pocket, then an orange,
And set them quietly on
The counter. When I looked up,
The lady's eyes met mine,
40 And held them, knowing
Very well what it was all
About.

    Outside,
A few cars hissing past,
45 Fog hanging like old
Coats between the trees.
I took my girl's hand
In mine for two blocks,
Then released it to let
50 Her unwrap the chocolate.
I peeled my orange
That was so bright against
The gray of December
That, from some distance,
55 Someone might have thought
I was making a fire in my hands.

RESPONDING OPTIONS

FROM PERSONAL RESPONSE TO CRITICAL ANALYSIS

REFLECT
1. How did you react to the narrator as a person? Write about your impressions of her in your notebook.

RETHINK
2. If you have not already done so, complete your chart for the Reading Connection on page 127. Look over the statements and feelings you have noted. How did Roseanne's attitude toward Melissa change?

3. Why do you think Roseanne's feelings toward Melissa changed?

Close Textual Reading

Consider
- how Roseanne feels about herself at different points in the story
- how Roseanne feels after her date with Travis
- what Roseanne realizes when she and Melissa look at each other in the mirror

Thematic Link
4. Think about the title of the story. What do you think Roseanne's experience is the beginning of?

RELATE
5. Both "The Beginning of Something" and the Insight poem "Oranges" depict first-time experiences. Do the emotions and actions seem true to life? Explain.

6. Roseanne says, "I call riding around a date, don't you?" and Gary Soto questions whether walking with a girl is a date. What do you consider the minimum requirements for a date?

ANOTHER PATHWAY
What if this story were told from Melissa's point of view? How might she view Roseanne's attitudes and actions? In a small group, discuss Melissa's likely views, and then on your own write a first-person narrative in the voice of Melissa. Share your work with the rest of the class.

LITERARY CONCEPTS
The people who participate in the action of a literary work are called **characters**. Characters are either **main** or **minor**, depending upon the extent of their development and on their importance in a story. Main characters are essential to a story: the events of the plot are based on what they as characters do, say, think, and feel. Who do you think are the main and minor characters in "The Beginning of Something"? Discuss and defend your choices with your classmates.

QUICKWRITES

1. Roseanne's excitement about her first date overshadows everything else. Write preliminary notes for a **personal essay** explaining why a first date is so often such a nervous and emotional rite of passage. Input your notes on a computer so they'll be easier to organize later in a more formal writing assignment.

2. Think about your discussion for the Personal Connection activity on page 127. Try writing a draft of a **poem** that describes the conflict you felt in the situation you shared.

📁 **PORTFOLIO** *Save your writing. You may want to use it later as a springboard to a piece for your portfolio.*

THE BEGINNING OF SOMETHING **143**

From Personal Response to Critical Analysis

1. Accept all reasonable responses.
2. Possible response: Roseanne feels closer to her cousin; she empathizes with Melissa's pain.
3. Possible responses: She realizes Melissa has gone through a difficult event; after her date with Travis, she feels better about herself and no longer needs to feel jealous of Melissa's looks and popularity.
4. Possible responses: the beginning of a real friendship with Melissa; the beginning of her relationship with Travis; the beginning of an increased awareness of the special nature of family and friends
5. Possible responses: Most students should have had a sufficiently similar experience at this point in their lives to be able to acknowledge the basic true-to-life nature of what they've read.
6. The requirements undoubtedly will vary, reflecting differences among the sexes and in individual maturity and experience.

Another Pathway
Cooperative Learning To help groups initiate and sustain discussion, have one student act as facilitator and one student act as recorder of the group's ideas.

Rubric
3 Full Accomplishment Each group member shares his or her views; individual narratives consistently use Melissa's voice.
2 Substantial Accomplishment The narrative voice is inconsistent; not all group members participate.
1 Little or Partial Accomplishment Narrative is not in the proper point of view; group cannot sustain discussion.

Literary Concepts
The main characters are Roseanne and Melissa; the minor characters are Mama, Daddy, Cousin Roy, Jamie, Travis, and Buddy.

Have students form small groups to debate the following statements.

- Mama—who insisted on Roseanne attending the funeral, is talked about often, and has some dialogue—should be a main character.
- Though she is deceased before the story begins, Cousin Jessie should be considered a character.

When students are finished, have them compare their interpretations.

QuickWrites
1. Before students begin writing, have them brainstorm a list of reasons why a first date could be a rite of passage. Why are they so nerve-racking?
2. Tell students that their drafts should indicate the seriousness and should detail some specifics of the experience that they would base their poems on.

Essay Writing, pp. 298–303

Critic's Corner

Accept all reasonable responses. Encourage students to make connections with people, places, and events in their own lives as they consider their responses.

Across the Curriculum

Health *Cooperative Learning* Ask students to form small groups to list the details of Cousin Jessie's illness as provided in the story. Then have each group member research different aspects of the subject—symptoms, causes, treatment, and any other questions the group decides on. One student should check the research to see if it illuminates any aspect of the story. Then, the group should check their final report and have one member read it to the class.

Words to Know

1. c
2. a
3. b
4. a
5. a

Reteaching/Reinforcement
• *Unit One Resource Book*, p. 56

SUE ELLEN BRIDGERS

Sue Ellen Bridgers has often been praised for her realistic depiction of characters' thoughts, emotions, and behavior. Her main focus is on the ways in which people are connected to one another and the strength of those bonds. Some connections are fragile, while others endure and grow stronger.

CRITIC'S CORNER

After reading this story, Ruth El-Jamal, a member of our student board, made the following comment: "I loved this selection because Roseanne is telling the story directly to the reader. . . . I felt very involved in her life, like she was talking to me as a friend." How does this response compare with yours? Give your own reason for liking or disliking this story.

Multimodal Learning

ACROSS THE CURRICULUM

Health *Cooperative Learning* Melissa's mother dies of diabetes in middle age. With a small group, skim the story and take notes on what Roseanne says about her illness. Then research the symptoms, causes, and treatment of diabetes. Does the information presented early in the story coincide with your findings? Why would the family be carrying candy around in their pockets? Present your findings in an oral report.

WORDS TO KNOW

Review the Words to Know at the bottom of the selection pages. Then write the letter of the situation that best demonstrates the meaning of the boldfaced word.

1. **bereaved**
   a. teenagers at a prom
   b. family at a wedding
   c. relatives at a funeral
2. **remorse**
   a. you have hurt a friend
   b. you have won a prize
   c. you have helped someone
3. **kin**
   a. animals in a wildlife refuge
   b. people at a family reunion
   c. students in a classroom
4. **infernal**
   a. sound of fingernails on a chalkboard
   b. sound of waves lapping the shore
   c. sound of birds singing in a tree
5. **throes**
   a. a mother with a seriously ill child
   b. a musician playing an instrument
   c. a girl daydreaming about a date

SUE ELLEN BRIDGERS

1942–

Sue Ellen Bridgers grew up in North Carolina, surrounded by kin. She defines family life "as the core of my writing." The daughter of a farmer, Bridgers was raised in small towns near both her parents' families. Describing her childhood as both happy and difficult, she says, "There were perhaps too many eyes focused on us and yet there was an abundance of concern and well-intentioned affection."

Bridgers's interest in writing developed early, and during elementary school she composed poems that were published by the local newspaper. Her college degree and her writing plans were delayed, however, by marriage and motherhood.

Bridgers did not publish her first novel until she was 34. It earned critical praise for realistically portraying the thoughts, feelings, and actions of young adults. Virtually all her fiction is set in North Carolina, where "the land and the rural way of life are so important" and where she makes her home in the Blue Ridge Mountains. A reviewer of her books showed gratitude for Bridgers's concentration on teenage audiences and wrote that these readers "deserve their literary giants, too; in Sue Ellen Bridgers, they have one."

OTHER WORKS *Home Before Dark, All Together Now, Permanent Connections, Keeping Christina*

Extended Reading

144 UNIT ONE PART 2: RITES OF PASSAGE

Alternative Activities

1. Have students choose **two songs** that convey the different feelings experienced by Melissa and Roseanne. Select various students to play the songs from cassette or disk for the class and explain why they chose them.
2. Divide the class into pairs of students and have them imagine that it is now 20 years later and Roseanne and Melissa are indeed "all grown up and married" and talk about things "just like Mama and Cousin Jessie." Have them take the roles of the two girls and prepare a **dramatic re-creation** of them reminiscing about the funeral, Roseanne's rite of passage, and their relationship since then. After practicing, they can tape-record their dialogue for presentation or decide to re-create it live for the whole class.

PREVIEWING

NONFICTION

The First Appendectomy
William A. Nolen

Activating Prior Knowledge
PERSONAL CONNECTION

A student teacher, a rookie pro-basketball player, and a beginning surgeon all have something in common—they feel the pressure to perform. What about a high school freshman? What kinds of pressures do you feel to perform? Do you feel the greatest pressure from teachers, a coach, your family, your friends, or other students? How do you react to the pressure? Jot down some notes about the kinds of pressures you feel and your reactions, using the chart at the right as a model.

Kind of Pressure	Reaction
From parents to get good grades	Get nervous about tests

Building Background / Setting a Purpose
MEDICAL CONNECTION

In the selection you are about to read, a young intern performs his first surgery—an appendectomy, the removal of a person's appendix. The road to becoming a doctor is long and full of pressure. After graduating from college, one must complete four years of medical school and then one year of a supervised internship at a hospital. Those who specialize, such as surgeons, next embark on at least three years of training as a hospital resident. Interns and residents often work long hours and try to gain as much experience as possible. As you read this selection, compare the pressures that you feel with the young doctor's pressure to perform.

Active Reading
READING CONNECTION

Understanding Specialized Vocabulary In many technical, pressure-filled fields, from computer programming to medicine, specialized vocabulary is important. If you come across specialized words when reading, look for context clues or familiar root words to help you determine the meaning. In some cases, words may be defined in parentheses after they are used, or they may appear in a glossary. In this selection, some terms are defined in the text by the author, and others are defined in footnotes.

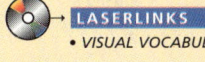
• VISUAL VOCABULARY

145

OVERVIEW
Objectives

- To understand and appreciate a personal narrative that explores how a young surgeon performs his first operation
- To understand and appreciate an author's purpose
- To express understanding of the selection through a choice of writing forms, including a performance evaluation, a job description, and a humorous account
- To extend understanding of the selection through a variety of multimodal and cross-curricular activities

Skills

LITERARY CONCEPTS
- Author's purpose
- Rising action

READING SKILLS/ STRATEGIES
- Understanding specialized vocabulary

THE WRITER'S STYLE
- Using dialogue

GENRE STUDY
- Nonfiction: personal narrative

GRAMMAR
- Comparative modifiers

SPEAKING, LISTENING, AND VIEWING
- Group discussion
- Oral presentation

 VISUAL VOCABULARY
- anesthetist (ə-nĕs′thĭ-tĭst)
- hemostats (hē′mə-stăts)
- scalpel (skăl′pəl)
- sutures (sōō′chərs)

Side A, Frame 49247

PRINT AND MEDIA RESOURCES

UNIT ONE RESOURCE BOOK
Strategic Reading: Literature, p. 59
Vocabulary SkillBuilder, p. 60

GRAMMAR MINI-LESSONS
Transparencies, pp. 23–24
Copymasters, p. 25

WRITING MINI-LESSONS
Transparencies, p. 56

ACCESS FOR STUDENTS ACQUIRING ENGLISH
Selection Summaries
Reading Support

FORMAL ASSESSMENT
Selection Test, pp. 27–28
 Test Generator

 AUDIO LIBRARY
See Reference Card

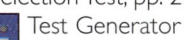 **LASERLINKS**
Visual Vocabulary
Historical Connection

The First Appendectomy

William A. Nolen

The patient, or better, victim, of my first major surgical venture was a man I'll call Mr. Polansky. He was fat, he weighed one hundred and ninety pounds and was five feet eight inches tall. He spoke only broken English. He had had a sore abdomen with all the classical signs and symptoms of appendicitis[1] for twenty-four hours before he came to Bellevue.[2]

After two months of my internship, though I had yet to do anything that could be decently called an "operation," I had had what I thought was a fair amount of operating time. I'd watched the assistant residents work, I'd tied knots, cut sutures[3] and even, in order to remove a skin lesion,[4] made an occasional incision.[5] Frankly, I didn't think that surgery was going to be too damn difficult. I figured I was ready, and I was chomping at the bit to go, so when Mr. Polansky arrived I greeted him like a long-lost friend. He was overwhelmed at the interest I showed in his case. He probably couldn't understand why any doctor should be so fascinated by a case of appendicitis; wasn't it a common disease? It was just as well that he didn't realize my interest in him was so personal. He might have been frightened, and with good reason.

At any rate, I set some sort of record in preparing Mr. Polansky for surgery. He had arrived on the ward at four o'clock. By six I had examined him, checked his blood and urine, taken his chest x-ray and had him ready for the operating room.

George Walters, the senior resident on call that night, was to "assist" me during the operation. George was older than the rest of us. I was twenty-five at this time and he was thirty-two. He had taken his surgical training in Europe and was spending one year as a senior resident in an American hospital to establish eligibility for the American College of Surgeons. He had had more experience than the other residents and it took a lot to disturb his equanimity in the operating

---

1. **appendicitis** (ə-pĕn′dĭ-sī′tĭs): an illness in which the appendix—a small, wormlike extension of the intestine—becomes inflamed. If an inflamed appendix is not removed, it can burst and cause a fatal infection.
2. **Bellevue** (bĕl′vyōō′): Bellevue Hospital, in New York City.
3. **sutures** (sōō′chərz): stitches closing a wound.
4. **lesion** (lē′zhən): a wound, an injury, or an infected or diseased patch of skin.
5. **incision** (ĭn-sĭzh′ən): a surgical cut.

WORDS TO KNOW
venture (vĕn′chər) *n.* an undertaking in which there is some risk of danger
equanimity (ē′kwə-nĭm′ĭ-tē) *n.* calmness; the quality of being hard to shake or disturb

room. As it turned out, this made him the ideal assistant for me.

It was ten o'clock when we wheeled Mr. Polansky to the operating room. At Bellevue, at night, only two operating rooms were kept open—there were six or more going all day—so we had to wait our turn. In the time I had to myself before the operation I had reread the section on appendectomy in the *Atlas of Operative Technique* in our surgical library, and had spent half an hour tying knots on the bedpost in my room. I was, I felt, "ready."

I delivered Mr. Polansky to the operating room and started an intravenous[6] going in his arm. Then I left him to the care of the anesthetist.[7] I had ordered a sedative[8] prior to surgery, so Mr. Polansky was drowsy. The anesthetist, after checking his chart, soon had him sleeping.

Once he was asleep I scrubbed the enormous expanse of Mr. Polansky's abdomen for ten minutes. Then, while George placed the sterile drapes, I scrubbed my own hands for another five, mentally reviewing each step of the operation as I did so. Donning gown and gloves I took my place on the right side of the operating-room table. The nurse handed me the scalpel.[9] I was ready to begin.

Suddenly my entire attitude changed. A split second earlier I had been supremely confident; now, with the knife finally in my hand, I stared down at Mr. Polansky's abdomen and for the life of me could not decide where to make the incision. The "landmarks" had disappeared. There was too much belly.

George waited a few seconds, then looked up at me and said, "Go ahead."

"What?" I asked.

"Make the incision," said George.

"Where?" I asked.

"Where?"

"Yes," I answered, "where?"

"Why, here, of course," said George and drew an imaginary line on the abdomen with his fingers.

I took the scalpel and followed where he had directed. I barely scratched Mr. Polansky.

"Press a little harder," George directed. I did. The blade went through the skin to a depth of perhaps one sixteenth of an inch.

"Deeper," said George.

There are five layers of tissue in the abdominal wall: skin, fat, fascia (a tough membranous tissue), muscle and peritoneum (the smooth, glistening, transparent inner lining of the abdomen). I cut down into the fat. Another sixteenth of an inch.

"Bill," said George, looking up at me, "this patient is big. There's at least three inches of fat to get through before

---

6. **intravenous** (ĭn´trə-vē´nəs): a drug, a nutrient solution, or some other substance administered into a vein through a needle and tubing.
7. **anesthetist** (ə-nĕs´thĭ-tĭst): a person trained to administer anesthetics, drugs that make a person insensitive to pain.
8. **sedative** (sĕd´ə-tĭv): a drug that has a calming effect.
9. **scalpel** (skăl´pəl): a surgical knife.

CUSTOMIZING FOR
Multiple Learning Styles

Spatial or Graphic Learners Have students compare the photo on this page with what Mr. Polansky might have seen just before he lost consciousness. Ask students to discuss what feelings this view might instill in a patient who is about to be operated on.

Linking to Science

After students look at the photograph, explain that patients may be unconscious, partially conscious, or completely awake during an operation, depending on the type of anesthesia used. *General anesthetics* are those that put the patient completely to sleep and may be inhaled as a gas or injected intravenously. *Local anesthetics* are used to block nerve impulses to a particular part of the body and are injected near that area. Local anesthetics do not produce unconsciousness but may be used in combination with other drugs that induce drowsiness or relaxation.

 Mini-Lesson Genre Study

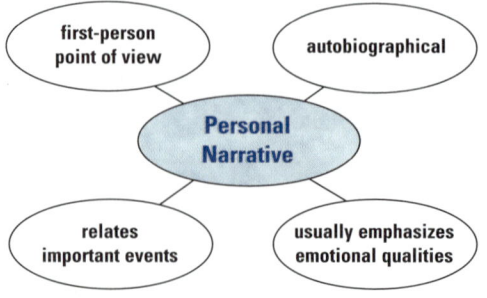

NONFICTION Draw the web shown on the left on the chalkboard. Use it to explain that a **personal narrative** is a short form of autobiographical writing with the following characteristics:
- It relates a significant event or events from the writer's life.
- It is usually written in the first person, using the pronouns *I* and *me*.
- It usually emphasizes emotional qualities.

Application Have students copy the web into their notebooks. Then ask them to refer to it as they look for each characteristic in "The First Appendectomy."

we even reach the fascia. At the rate you're going, we won't be into the abdomen for another four hours. For God's sake, will you cut?"

I made up my mind not to be hesitant. I pressed down hard on the knife, and suddenly we were not only through the fat but through the fascia as well.

"Not that hard," George shouted, grabbing my right wrist with his left hand while with his other hand he plunged a gauze pack into the wound to stop the bleeding. "Start clamping," he told me.

At one point I even managed to tie the end of my rubber glove into the wound.

The nurse handed us hemostats[10] and we applied them to the numerous vessels I had so hastily opened. "All right," George said, "start tying."

I took the ligature material[11] from the nurse and began to tie off the vessels. Or rather, I tried to tie off the vessels, because suddenly my knot-tying proficiency had melted away. The casual dexterity I had displayed on the bedpost a short hour ago was nowhere in evidence. My fingers, greasy with fat, simply would not perform. My ties slipped off the vessels, the sutures snapped in my fingers, at one point I even managed to tie the end of my rubber glove into the wound. It was, to put it bluntly, a performance in fumbling that would have made Robert Benchley[12] blush.

Here I must give my first paean[13] of praise to George. His patience during the entire performance was nothing short of miraculous. The temptation to pick up the catgut and do the tying himself must have been strong. He could have tied off all the vessels in two minutes. It took me twenty.

Finally we were ready to proceed. "Now," George directed, "split the muscle. But gently, please."

I reverted to my earlier tack. Fiber by fiber I spread the muscle which was the last layer but one that kept us from the inside of the abdomen. Each time I separated the fibers and withdrew my clamp, the fibers rolled together again. After five minutes I was no nearer the appendix than I had been at the start.

George could stand it no longer. But he was apparently afraid to suggest I take a more aggressive approach, fearing I would stick the clamp into, or possibly through, the entire abdomen. Instead he suggested that he help me by spreading the muscle in one direction while I spread it in the other. I made my usual infinitesimal attack on the muscle. In one fell swoop George spread the rest.

"Very well done," he complimented me. "Now let's get in."

We each took a clamp and picked up the tissue-paper-thin peritoneum. After two or three hesitant attacks with the scalpel I finally opened it. We were in the abdomen.

---

10. **hemostats** (hē′mə-stăts′): clamplike surgical instruments used to pinch blood vessels and shut off bleeding.
11. **ligature** (lĭg′ə-chŏŏr′) **material:** the thread used to make surgical stitches; it may be made of catgut or other material.
12. **Robert Benchley:** an American critic and humorist who made short films in which he played the role of a bumbling person.
13. **paean** (pē′ən): a song of praise or thanks.

WORDS TO KNOW
proficiency (prə-fĭsh′ən-sē) *n.* the ability to perform a task well
dexterity (dĕk-stĕr′ĭ-tē) *n.* skill; coordination
infinitesimal (ĭn′fĭn-ĭ-tĕs′ə-məl) *adj.* tiny; insignificant

Literary Concept:
AUTHOR'S PURPOSE

I Ask students why they think the author describes his attempts to locate the appendix in such a detailed manner. *(Possible responses: to inform readers about the difficulties of surgery; to help them understand what it's like to be a surgeon—especially a novice one—during an operation)*

Critical Thinking: ANALYZING

J Ask why the task looked simple when performed by a senior resident. *(Possible response: When a person with skill does something, it appears to be easy.)*

CUSTOMIZING FOR
Students Acquiring English

3 Explain to students that a "hot" appendix is one that is infected and very inflamed. Point out that this use of the word is slang, not specialized vocabulary.

Critical Thinking:
MAKING JUDGMENTS

K Ask students to think about whether, given Dr. Nolen's difficulties, Dr. Walters should have taken over the surgery himself. *(Possible responses: Some might say yes that Dr. Walters should have taken over for the good of the patient. Others may say no that it is important for Dr. Nolen to get practice in completing an operation; besides, Dr. Walters is standing by if more help is needed.)*

Linking to History

The first appendectomy was performed by Dr. William West Grant in Davenport, Iowa. On January 4, 1885, he operated on 22-year-old Mary Gartside, who had a perforated appendix.

> I stuck my right hand into the abdomen. I felt around—but what was I feeling? I had no idea.

I "Now," said George, "put your fingers in, feel the cecum [the portion of the bowel to which the appendix is attached] and bring it into the wound."

I stuck my right hand into the abdomen. I felt around—but what was I feeling? I had no idea.

It had always looked so simple when the senior resident did it. Open the abdomen, reach inside, pull up the appendix. Nothing to it. But apparently there was.

Everything felt the same to me. The small intestine, the large intestine, the cecum—how did one tell them apart without seeing them? I grabbed something and pulled it into the wound. Small intestine. No good. Put it back. I grabbed again. This time it was the sigmoid colon.¹⁴ Put it back. On my third try I had the small intestine again.

"The appendix must be in an abnormal position," I said to George. "I can't seem to find it."

"Mind if I try?" he asked.

"Not at all," I answered. "I wish you would."

J Two of his fingers disappeared into the wound. Five seconds later they emerged, cecum between them, with the appendix flopping from it.

"Stuck down a little," he said kindly. "That's probably why you didn't feel it. It's a hot one," he added. "Let's get at it."

The nurse handed me the hemostats, and one by one I applied them to the mesentery of the appendix—the veil of tissue in which the blood vessels run. With George holding the veil between his fingers I had no trouble; I took the ligatures and tied the vessels without a single error. My confidence was coming back.

"Now," George directed, "put in your purse string." (The cecum is a portion of the bowel which has the shape of half a hemisphere. The appendix projects from its surface like a finger. In an appendectomy the routine procedure is to tie the appendix at its base and cut it off a little beyond the tie. Then the remaining stump is inverted into the cecum and kept there by tying the purse-string stitch. This was the stitch I was now going to sew.)

It went horribly. The wall of the cecum is not very thick—perhaps one eighth of an inch. The suture must be placed deeply enough in the wall so that it won't cut through when tied, but not so deep as to pass all the way through the wall. My sutures were alternately too <u>superficial</u> or too deep, but eventually I got the job done.

"All right," said George, "let's get the appendix out of here. Tie off the base."

I did.

"Now cut off the appendix."

At least in this, the <u>definitive</u> act of the operation, I would be decisive. I took the knife and with one quick slash cut through the appendix—too close to the ligature.

"Oh oh, watch it," said George. "That tie is going to slip."

3

K

---

14. **sigmoid colon** (sĭg′moid′ kō′lən): the part of the colon (which is a section of the large intestine) that is shaped like the letter *s*.

| WORDS TO KNOW | **superficial** (sōō′pər-fĭsh′əl) *adj.* only on the surface; shallow |
| | **definitive** (dĭ-fĭn′ĭ-tĭv) *adj.* the most important or distinguishing aspect of something |

150

Mini-Lesson ⬥ Literary Concepts

REVIEWING RISING ACTION Remind students that rising action refers to the events that move the plot of a story along by adding complications or expanding the conflict. During the rising action, suspense builds as the main characters struggle to resolve their problems. Eventually, this suspense builds to a climax, when the reader's interest and emotional intensity reach the highest point.

Application Have students think about the different events that help build the suspense in Dr. Nolen's narrative. Draw the time line shown on the right on the chalkboard, and have students copy it in their notebooks. Then have them find three events that contribute to the rising action and list them in the proper sequence on the time line.

1. Dr. Nolen is unable to make a proper incision.
2. Dr. Nolen forgets how to tie a knot.
3. Dr. Nolen can't find the appendix.

150 THE LANGUAGE OF LITERATURE TEACHER'S EDITION

It did. The appendiceal stump lay there, open. I felt faint.

"Don't panic," said George. "We've still got the purse string. I'll push the stump in—you pull up the stitch and tie. That will take care of it."

I picked up the two ends of the suture and put in the first stitch. George shoved the open stump into the cecum. It disappeared as I snugged my tie. Beautiful.

"Two more knots," said George. "Just to be safe."

I tied the first knot and breathed a sigh of relief. The appendiceal stump remained out of sight. On the third knot—for the sake of security—I pulled a little tighter. The stitch broke; the open stump popped up; the cecum disappeared into the abdomen. I broke out in a cold sweat and my knees started to crumble.

Even George momentarily lost his composure. "Bill," he said, grasping desperately for the bowel, "what did you have to do that for?" The low point of the operation had been reached.

By the time we had retrieved the cecum, Mr. Polansky's peritoneal cavity had been contaminated.[15] My self-confidence was shattered. And still George let me continue. True, he all but held my hand as we retied and resutured, but the instruments were in my hand.

The closure[16] was anticlimactic. Once I had the peritoneum sutured, things went reasonably smoothly. Two hours after we began, the operation was over. "Nice job," George said, doing his best to sound sincere.

"Thanks," I answered, lamely.
The scrub nurse laughed.

Mr. Polansky recovered, I am happy to report, though not without a long and complicated convalescence. His bowel refused to function normally for two weeks and he became enormously distended. He was referred to at our nightly conferences as "Dr. Nolen's pregnant man." Each time the reference was made, it elicited a shudder from me.

During his convalescence I spent every spare moment I could at Mr. Polansky's bedside. My feelings of guilt and responsibility were overwhelming. If he had died I think I would have given up surgery for good. ❖

---

15. **peritoneal** (pĕr´ĭ-tn-ē´əl) **cavity had been contaminated**: part of the inside of the abdomen had become infected.
16. **closure** (klō´zhər): the closing up of an opening; here, making sutures to close a surgical incision.

INSIGHT

Surgeons must be very careful
Emily Dickinson

Surgeons must be very careful
When they take the knife!
Underneath their fine incisions
Stirs the Culprit—*Life!*

WORDS TO KNOW
convalescence (kŏn´və-lĕs´əns) *n.* the time of recovery following an operation or illness
distended (dĭ-stĕnd´əd) *adj.* swollen; bloated **distend** *v.*
elicit (ĭ-lĭs´ĭt) *v.* to cause; bring about

INSIGHT

1. Why do you think Emily Dickinson places special emphasis on the word "life" in the poem? *(Possible response: She is urging surgeons to see that life is important.)*
2. What message might the poem have for Dr. Nolen? *(Possible response: Because life and death hang in the balance, a surgeon must be careful and must act responsibly during an operation.)*

From Personal Response to Critical Analysis

1. Accept all reasonable responses.
2. Accept all valid answers. Some might say Dr. Nolen because this is his first operation and he is under great pressure. Others might say Mr. Polansky because Dr. Nolen doesn't seem to know what he is doing.
3. Possible responses: Dr. Nolen is no longer overconfident; he now realizes the huge responsibility he has to the patient.
4. Accept all reasonable responses.
5. Possible responses: He might have been angry and wished he had had a more experienced doctor. Some students will think that the patient always has the right to know because it is the patient's body that is being operated on.

Another Pathway

Cooperative Learning Have students form two groups, each taking one side of the debate. In addition, assign one student the role of moderator, and have other students serve as a panel of judges. Suggest that each group meet to review the narrative and develop their cases, with students taking the roles of researchers, support givers, and probers. Each side should have a chance to present its case, followed by rebuttals from the other side.

Rubric

3 Full Accomplishment Each group presents convincing arguments for its position, using supporting details from the selection.

2 Substantial Accomplishment Arguments are clearly presented but may lack supporting details from the selection.

1 Little or Partial Accomplishment Groups are unable to present clear arguments for their positions.

RESPONDING OPTIONS

FROM PERSONAL RESPONSE TO CRITICAL ANALYSIS

REFLECT
1. What three adjectives best describe your reactions as you read this account? Explain your choices.

RETHINK
2. With whom do you sympathize more, Dr. Nolen or Mr. Polansky? Why?

3. In what ways, if any, does Dr. Nolen change during the course of this episode?

Close Textual Reading

Consider
- his thoughts, feelings, and actions before the operation
- his actions during the operation
- his feelings and actions after the operation

Thematic Link
4. Look over what you wrote about your own reactions to pressure for the Personal Connection activity on page 145. Did this selection give you a new perspective on making mistakes and handling pressure? Explain.

RELATE
5. Mr. Polansky's convalescence was "long and complicated." What might he have felt if he had known about how Dr. Nolen had performed during the surgery? Did he have the right to know? Consider what a patient entrusts to a surgeon, as described in the Insight poem "Surgeons must be very careful."

Multimodal Learning
ANOTHER PATHWAY

Every professional makes some mistakes. But when a doctor makes mistakes, the patient sometimes sues for malpractice in the hope of getting money as compensation for health problems resulting from the mistakes. Would a malpractice suit have been justified in Mr. Polansky's case? Debate this issue in class, using specific details about the operation from the selection.

LITERARY CONCEPTS

A selection always has an **author's purpose,** or reason for writing. There are four main purposes for writing: to express oneself, to inform or explain, to persuade, and to entertain. Often a writer has more than one purpose for writing. Which do you think Dr. Nolen had in mind? Support your answer with details from the text.

4 Main Purposes for Writing
- to express oneself
- to inform or explain
- to persuade
- to entertain

QUICKWRITES

1. Imagine that you are Dr. Walters, the senior resident assisting Dr. Nolen. Write a **performance evaluation** of Dr. Nolen's surgical skills.

2. What are the most important qualities in a surgeon? Using what you know about Dr. Nolen and Dr. Walters, write a **job description** of a good surgeon.

3. Write a **humorous account** of the first time you tried to do something new, such as learning to skate or to make a meal.

PORTFOLIO *Save your writing. You may want to use it later as a springboard to a piece for your portfolio.*

152 UNIT ONE PART 2: RITES OF PASSAGE

Literary Concepts

Students may say that Dr. Nolen's purpose was to inform the reader about the pressure and complications he faced during the first operation he performed. They may also say that the information helps take the mystery out of what goes on in an operating room. As support, students may point to the various passages throughout the narrative in which Dr. Nolen explains some aspect of performing an appendectomy and his feeling during each phase of the operation.

QuickWrites

1. Have students review surgical details and ask themselves the following questions before writing: Was Dr. Nolen's nervousness normal considering the situation? How did he react after making a mistake? Did he successfully complete the operation?
2. Have students list each doctor's qualities. Then have them use their lists to write a job description for a good surgeon.
3. Before students begin writing, invite them to discuss how an event that doesn't seem funny at the time can be humorous later.

Multimodal Learning

ALTERNATIVE ACTIVITIES

1. **Cooperative Learning** With a small group, create a **cartoon** or **comic strip** based on this selection. Try to show the difference between Dr. Nolen and Dr. Walters. Display your work on a bulletin board.
2. What kind of **music** would you choose to express Dr. Nolen's feelings during his operation? Play the music for the class and explain why you chose it.

ACROSS THE CURRICULUM

Science Find out some details about medical training in the United States today. For example, what kinds of courses do medical students take? What state or national examinations do they have to pass? How long must surgeons spend working in hospitals before they perform their first operations?

WORDS TO KNOW

EXERCISE A Review the Words to Know at the bottom of the selection pages. Then write the vocabulary word that best completes each sentence.

1. Students must prove their ___ in academic studies before being accepted into medical school. **proficiency**
2. Performing surgery on another human being is a serious and challenging ___. **venture**
3. The most ___ act of an appendectomy is cutting and removing the appendix. **definitive**
4. Without ___, a doctor would soon become flustered in a noisy, chaotic emergency room. **equanimity**
5. A recovering surgical patient may be instructed to rest and avoid stress during ___. **convalescence**

EXERCISE B Play a game of charades by acting out whole words or syllables of the following Words to Know: *dexterity, infinitesimal, superficial, distended,* and *elicit.*

WILLIAM A. NOLEN

William A. Nolen gained national attention in the early 1970s after the publication of his book *The Making of a Surgeon,* from which "The First Appendectomy" is taken. In it he wrote frankly of his experiences as an intern and resident in the 1950s at Bellevue Hospital and of the tremendous pressures doctors work against. After the book was published, Nolen made frequent appearances on late-night TV talk shows. One reviewer felt the book was "remarkable for its wit and honesty. . . . As a chronicle of life in a big municipal hospital . . . it is a horror story told in straightforward, ghastly detail. . . . Nothing quite like it has ever been written about American medicine before." Although he acknowledged that many other doctors felt he had betrayed the medical profession, Nolen countered that he didn't "see why there has to be so much mystery to medicine."

1928–1986

Nolen became a general surgeon in Minnesota in 1960 and eventually wrote eight books, claiming that writing made him a better doctor by helping him understand the patient's perspective. By 1975 he gained that perspective firsthand, when his own struggle with heart disease led to his having heart bypass surgery. He detailed this experience in his book *Surgeon Under the Knife.* In an article written for *Esquire* magazine around that time, he wrote, "I . . . have high blood pressure. My father died at 58 of 'heart trouble.' . . . [T]he possibility of heart attack threatens my horizon." Following further bypass surgery in 1986, Dr. Nolen died in Minneapolis, ironically at age 58.

OTHER WORKS *A Surgeon's World, Healing: A Doctor in Search of a Miracle, A Surgeon's Book of Hope*

Extended Reading

LASERLINKS
• HISTORICAL CONNECTION

THE FIRST APPENDECTOMY **153**

Alternative Activities

1. Students in a collaborative meeting should decide what the characters might look like, the differences between the two doctors, and how best to illustrate those differences. Different group members can be responsible for dialogue, lettering, and art.
2. Students can create an emotion chart that identifies Dr. Nolen's highs and lows, illustrating how he feels at different points in the operation. They can then refer to the chart as they think about the type of music that best expresses Dr. Nolen's feelings before, during, and after the operation.

WILLIAM A. NOLEN

Nolen details his own struggle with heart problems and his decision to undergo surgery in his book *Surgeon Under the Knife.* Nolen himself had his share of mishaps: wrong medication, use of another patient's blood test, and improper care from hospital personnel. His advice to patients: Keep aware of the number and variety of prescribed pills, ask why x rays are being ordered, and demand explanations of everything.

Literary Links

Have students compare and contrast the possible consequences of failure for Dr. Nolen with those for Jerry in *Through the Tunnel.* Ask students which is the greater pressure, risking your own life, or being responsible for the life of another. *(Possible responses: being responsible for another life, because you will be at fault if something happens to that person)*

Across the Curriculum

Science *Cooperative Learning* Have students work in small groups, with each group member using a different source. For example, one member may interview a few doctors or medical students about their training. Other group members may use library reference materials, or call the state medical board. Have each group choose one member to present their findings to the class.

Words to Know

Exercise A
1. proficiency
2. venture
3. definitive
4. equanimity
5. convalescence

Exercise B Before students begin, have them divide each word into its word parts or syllables.

Reteaching/Reinforcement
• *Unit One Resource Book,* p. 60

HISTORICAL CONNECTION
History of Surgery Western medical practices have changed considerably over the last several centuries. These images show a number of events from the history of medicine.

Side A, Frame 49251

EDITOR'S NOTE *With the permission of the copyright holder, potentially offensive material has been deleted from the selection.*

THE LANGUAGE OF LITERATURE TEACHER'S EDITION **153**

OBJECTIVES

- To promote independent, active reading
- To practice and apply skills learned in previous selections
- To provide an opportunity to assess students' performance through an alternative assessment instrument

Reading Pathways

- Invite students to choose partners and alternate reading sections of the selection aloud. As they listen to their partners read, have them pay special attention to the author's descriptions of the setting. After they read, they should discuss how the author creates his description of the rough frontier environment.

- Have students insert slips of paper in their books to mark the beginning and end of each flashback. Ask them to discuss the purpose of the flashback. Ask them why the story did not begin with the rail trip. Have them note the words that signal to them when the flashback begins and ends. Encourage students to write their ideas in their journals.

- Have students keep a sketch pad or journal as they read the selection. Encourage them to sketch or jot down any impressions the story creates in their minds. Ask them to see whether sketching or jotting down a scene described by the author helps them to visualize the characters and setting.

- Evaluate how well students can read, interpret, discuss, and write about the selection on their own by using the Integrated Assessment for Unit One, located in the Alternative Assessment booklet. Set aside two class periods, or about two hours, to administer the assessment after students have completed the final writing assignment for the unit.

ON YOUR OWN

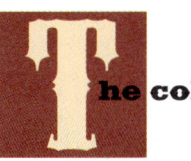

Plainswoman

WILLIAMS FORREST

The cold of the fall was sweeping over the plains, and Nora's husband, Rolf, and his men had ridden off on the roundup. She was left on the ranch with Pleny, a handy man, who was to do the chores and lessen her fears.

154   UNIT ONE   PART 2: RITES OF PASSAGE

PRINT AND MEDIA RESOURCES

UNIT ONE RESOURCE BOOK
Strategic Reading: Literature, p. 63

FORMAL ASSESSMENT
Selection Test, pp. 29–30
Part Test, pp. 31–32
 Test Generator

ALTERNATIVE ASSESSMENT
Unit One Integrated Assessment, pp. 1–6

ACCESS FOR STUDENTS ACQUIRING ENGLISH
Selection Summaries

 AUDIO LIBRARY
See Reference Card

Shadows of the Past (1989), Al Stine. Courtesy of the artist.

SUMMARY

Nora grew up in New England, but she married Rolf, a rancher from the West. She had been on the ranch only a few months when Rolf left for a roundup, leaving a handyman, Pleny, to look after the ranch. One day, Pleny comes to Nora for help with his finger, which is infected with gangrene. He asks Nora to cut if off before the infection kills him. She runs to her bedroom where she reflects on her experiences. She recalls the train journey west when Nora and a pistol-packing woman delivered a baby. She remembers that Rolf's thoughts were not about the baby, but about his cattle. Later, one of the cowboys broke his leg. Rolf gave him a couple of horses, and the boy set off alone on a ten-day ride to a doctor. Rolf, and later Pleny, explained that cattle are more important than anything else. Without them, people on a ranch can't survive. After thinking about this, Nora makes up her mind. She takes Pleny outside. He puts his finger on a wood block, and Nora does what is necessary.

Thematic Link: *Rites of Passage* A woman native to New England confronts the challenges of her new life on the often-harsh western frontier.

Art Note

Shadows of the Past by Al Stine Born in 1920, Stine was a professional illustrator in Chicago for many years. He is best known for his watercolor paintings, such as this one of an old log building with a wooden cart sheltered under its roof. The painting also captures the shadows and warm autumn colors of the trees.

Reading the Art *What elements—colors, images—in this painting evoke the feeling and atmosphere of an older time?*

Her pregnancy told her that she should hurry back East before the solemn grip of winter fell on the land. She was afraid to have the child touch her within, acknowledge its presence, when the long deep world below the mountains closed in and no exit was available—for the body and for the spirit.

Her baby had not yet wakened, but soon it would. But gusts of wind and a forbidding iron shadow on the hills told her that the greatest brutality of this ranch world was about to start. And then one morning Pleny came in for his breakfast, holding the long finger of his left hand in the fingers of his right. For some time he had concealed his left hand from her, holding it down or in his pocket; and from the way he had held

PLAINSWOMAN   **155**

Art Note

Ringside by William Matthews Born in 1949 in New York City, William Matthews grew up in San Francisco. While traveling among the vast cattle ranches of northeastern Nevada, he discovered his most important subject: the modern American cowboy. In this painting, he depicts a cowboy on horseback, face turned away from the viewer, with a lasso stretched between his hands.

Reading the Art Does the absence of the cowboy's face help to evoke a sense of mystery? How might the solid background of the painting suggest the vast, wide-open spaces of the West?

Ringside (1994), William Matthews. Courtesy of the William Matthews Gallery, Denver, Colorado.

himself, she had thought it was a part of his chivalry, his wish to have table manners, use his right hand and sit up straight with a lady. But now he held it before him like a trophy, and one he did not wish to present.

Nora had been thinking of New England when Pleny came in—of the piano and the gentle darkness of her mother's eyes, of frost on the small windowpanes, and the hearth fires, of holidays and the swish of sleighs, of men with businesslike faces and women who drank tea and read poetry, of deep substantial beds and the way the hills and the sea prescribed an area, making it intimate, and the way the towns folded into the hills. She was thinking of home and comfort, and then Pleny walked in; the dust trailed around his ankles, and the smell of cattle seemed to cling to his boots. A thousand miles of cattle and plains and work and hurt were clung like webs in his face.

Nora had made eggs, ham, bread and coffee for the breakfast, but Pleny made them objects of disgust as he extended his hand, as shyly but as definitely as a New England lad asking for a dance, and said, "I got the mortification, ma'am. I have to let you see it."

She looked at his index finger and saw the mortification of the flesh, the gangrene. He held the finger pointed forward, his other fingers closed. He pressed the finger with his other hand, and the darkened skin made a crackling sound like that of ancient paper or dangerous ice over a pond. And above the finger some

156 UNIT ONE PART 2: RITES OF PASSAGE

Multicultural Perspectives

GAUCHOS The United States is not the only country to have a cowboy tradition. In the Argentine region of the Pampas, before the advent of mechanized farms, cowboys known as *gauchos* were employed by ranchers to round up cattle. Like American cowboys, gauchos prided themselves on their horsemanship, strength, and endurance. These qualities helped endear the gaucho tradition to all Argentines. Today in Argentina gauchos have come to symbolize courage and a free-spirited life, just as cowboys do in the United States.

yellow streaks were like arrows pointing to the hairs and veins above his wrist.

Nora smelled the food, gulped, stood up and turned away.

"I got to come to you, ma'am," said Pleny. "I finally got to come to you."

He spoke firmly but shyly, but she did not hear his tone; she heard only his demand. And her emotion rejected it and any part of it. Her emotion said that he should not have come to her and that she had nothing to do with it, and would not and could not. She walked toward the fireplace, staring into the low flames. She heard the wind coax the sides of the house. She said, pretending nothing else had been mentioned, "Pleny, there's your breakfast." She itemized it, as if the words could barricade her against him. "Eggs . . . ham . . . bread . . . hot coffee—hot coffee."

But after she had spoken she heard nothing but his steady, waiting breathing behind her. And she understood that she would have to turn and face it. She knew he was not going away and would not happily sit down to eat and would not release her.

The fire spoke and had no answer, even though it was soft. She turned and saw the weather on Pleny's face, the diamonds of raised flesh, the scars. And she knew that death was in his finger and was moving up his arm and would take all of him finally, as fully as a bullet or freezing or drowning.

"What do you expect of me, Pleny?" she said.

He moved with a crinkling hard sound of stained dungarees, hardened boots and his dried reluctant nature. "Ma'am," he said, "I don't want you to think I'm a coward. I just wouldn't want you to get that notion. I'll take my bumps, burns and cuts, just like I did with this finger on the lamp in the bunkhouse and then on the gate before it could heal. I'll take it without complaining, but I sure don't like to doctor myself." His lake-blue eyes were narrowed with thought, and the erosion in his face was drawn together, as if wind and sun were drawing his face closer together the way they did the land in the drought. "I just can't bear to cut on myself," he said, lowering his head with a dry shame. He lifted his head suddenly and said, "I suppose I'd do it out on the plain, in the mountains, alone. But I can't do it here."

His Adam's apple wobbled as he sought in his throat for words. His lips were cracked and did not easily use explanations. "It just seems sinful, ma'am," he said, "for a man to hack on himself." Suddenly his eyes were filled with burning knowledge. He spoke reasonably, without pleading, but an authority was in his voice. "Ma'am, you never saw a man do that, did you, when somebody else was around to doctor him?"

She had watched and listened to his explanation without a stirring in her; she had done so as if she were mesmerized, like a chicken before a snake. Gradually his meaning penetrated her and told her what he meant.

"Ma'am," he said, "would you do me the kindness to take off this here finger?"

She ran senselessly, as if she were attempting to run long, far, back to New England. The best she could do was run through the rooms of the haphazardly laid-out house and get to her room and close the door and lean against it. She was panting, and her eyes were closed, and her heart was beating so hard that it hurt her chest. Slowly she began to feel the hurts on her shoulders, where she had struck herself against the walls and doors. Rolf had started this house with one room and had made rooms and halls leading off from it as time went on. She had careered through the halls to her room, as if fighting obstacles.

She went to her bed, but did not allow herself to fall down on it. That would be too much weakness. She sat on the edge of the bed, with her hands in her lap. Her wish to escape

PLAINSWOMAN 157

OPTION 1

Individual Activity
WRITING A DIARY ENTRY
Have students rewrite the events of the morning as a diary entry Nora might have written. Encourage them to review details from the story to imagine what feelings would be most important to Nora and how she might describe them.

Teacher's Role Help students write from Nora's perspective by encouraging them to think about Nora's emotions before they begin writing. Ask why the transition to life on the plains seems so difficult for her, what shocks her most, and what frightens her most.

Rubric
3 Full Accomplishment The diary entries portray the events of the morning and illustrate emotions Nora might have felt.

2 Substantial Accomplishment Diary entries correctly depict the events, but Nora's emotions are not consistent with the selection's content.

1 Little or Partial Accomplishment Diary entries display little understanding of the events or of Nora's feelings.

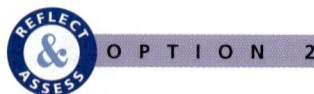

OPTION 2

Cooperative Learning
CREATE A DRAMATIZATION

Have students work in groups of four to six to create a dramatization of one or more scenes from the selection. They should collaborate on the script for the dramatization, including stage notes and dialogue. One student should act as a recorder during the meeting, while another ensures that everyone participates. Other students will have acting roles, and one should direct the group during rehearsals and performance. Have students present their dramatizations before the class.

Teacher's Role Encourage students to provide stage directions of their own where the selection does not describe the characters' actions. Ask students: Are the characters standing or sitting? Do they move? Are they still?

Rubric

3 Full Accomplishment Students accurately and vividly depict the characters and events from the scene they have chosen.

2 Substantial Accomplishment Students dramatize most of the events accurately, but the dramatization does not capture the emotional quality of the scene.

1 Little or Partial Accomplishment Students have difficulty dramatizing the events.

---

from this place was more intense than ever within her. And her reasons for it ran through her brain like a cattle stampede, raising acrid dust and death and injury—and fear, most of all.

Her fear had begun in the first frontier hotel in which she had spent a night. Rolf had been bringing her West from New England to his ranch in the springtime. The first part of the ride on the railroad had been a pure delight. Rolf's hand was big, brown, with stiff red hairs on the back, a fierce, comforting hand; and her own had lain within it as softly as a trusting bird. The railroad car had had deep seats and decor that would have done credit to a fine home. As those parts of the world she had never seen went past, mountain, stream and hamlet, she had felt serene; and the sense of adventure touched her heart like the wings of a butterfly. She was ready to laugh at each little thing and she had a persistent wish to kiss Rolf on the cheek, although she resisted such an unseemly act in front of other people.

"I know I'll be happy," she said. And his big quiet hand around hers gave her the feeling of a fine, strong, loving, secure world.

But the world changed. After a time they were on a rough train that ran among hills and plains, and after a while there was nothing to see but an endless space with spring lying flat on it in small colorful flowers and with small bleak towns in erratic spaces, and the men on the train laughed roughly and smelled of whisky. Some men rode on the roof of the car and kicked their heels, fired guns and sang to a wild accordion.

Rolf's hand seemed smaller. His tight, strong burned face that she had so much admired seemed remote; he was becoming a stranger, and she was becoming alone with herself. She, her love for him, her wish for adventure were so small, it seemed, in comparison to the spaces and the crudity.

One night the train stopped at a wayside station, and the passengers poured out as if Indians were attacking. They assailed the dining room of the canvas-and-board hotel as if frenzied with starvation. In the dining room Rolf abruptly became a kind of man she had never known. He grabbed and speared at plates like any of the others and smiled gently at her after he had secured a plateload of food for her that made her stomach turn. After affectionately touching her hand, he fought heartily with the others to get an immense plateload for himself. Then he winked at her and started to eat, in the same ferocious way as the others. His manners in New England had seemed earthy, interesting and powerful—a tender animal. But here, here he was one more animal.

That night they shared a bedroom with five other people, one a woman who carried a pistol. Rolf had bought sleeping boards and blankets, so that they would not have to share beds with anyone. The gun-carrying woman coughed and then said, "Good night, all you no-good rascals."

Rolf laughed.

The spring air flipped the canvas walls. The building groaned with flimsiness and people. Nora had never before heard the sounds of a lot of sleeping people. She put her face against Rolf's chest and pulled his arm over her other ear.

Late at night she woke crying. Or was she crying? There was crying within her, and there were tears on her face. But when she opened her eyes, the night was around her, without roof or walls, but there was the water of rain on her cheeks. Rolf bent over her. "We're outside," he said. "You were suffering. Exhausted, suffering, and you spoke out loud in your sleep."

"Why did you bring me out here?" The blankets were wet, but she felt cozy. He was strong against her. The night was wet but sweet after the flapping, moaning hotel.

Some water fell from his face to hers. Was Rolf crying? No, not Rolf, no. But when he spoke, his voice was sad. "I told you how it would be, didn't I?"

"I didn't know," she said. "I didn't know how awful it could be."

He spoke powerfully, but troubledly. "I can't always take you outside, away from things. I can't do that. There'll be times when I can't do for you, when only you can do it yourself."

"Don't be disturbed," she said, holding him closer. "Don't be disturbed." The smell of the wet air was sweet, and it was spring, and they were alone and small again in an enclosed world, made of them both, and she was unafraid again. "I'll be all right," she promised. "Rolf, I will be all right."

Fresh Eggs (1874), Winslow Homer. Collection of Mr. and Mrs. Paul Mellon, Copyright © 1995, Board of Trustees, National Gallery of Art, Washington, D.C.

Art Note

Fresh Eggs by Winslow Homer
Winslow Homer (1836–1910) is best known for his paintings of the sea and his rural scenes of everyday life. In this watercolor painting, a woman stands in a barn with a basket of eggs. The illuminated figure and haystack in the foreground contrast with the dark wood of the barn wall.

Reading the Art *Compare the image in your mind of Nora with the woman depicted in this painting. What are the similarities? How do the two images differ?*

PLAINSWOMAN

Linking to Science

Gangrene, the death of body tissue, is caused by a cutoff of blood to an injured area of the body, often a finger or toe. There are three main types of gangrene: gas gangrene, acute gangrene, and arteriosclerotic gangrene. Judging from the symptoms described in the selection, Pleny has gas gangrene, which is caused by bacteria. When harmful bacteria develop in an infected area and no treatment is provided, the infection can spread to more and more of the surrounding tissue and eventually cause death. The fact that Pleny's finger crackles when it is touched indicates that his gangrene is very advanced. In modern times, the use of antibiotics has reduced the occurrence of gangrene.

She slept with that promise, but it did not last through the next day. The train stopped after noontime in the midst of the plain. Cattle ran from the train. A lone horseman rode toward them out of curiosity. The sky was burning. Some flowers beside the tracks lifted a faint gossamer odor. Men were drinking and making tea on the stove of the car. Then they all were told that a woman two cars ahead was going to have a child, now. Nora was asked to go forward to attend her.

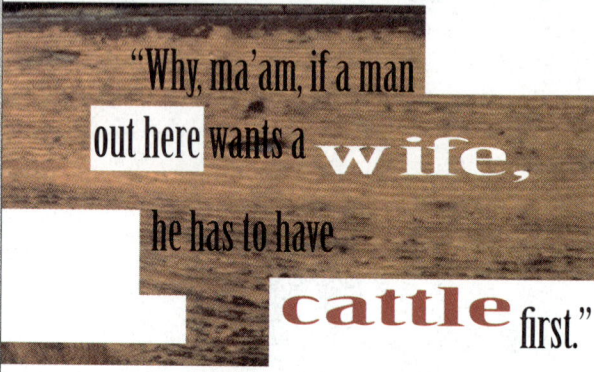

"Why, ma'am, if a man out here wants a **wife**, he has to have **cattle** first."

The impressions of the next few hours had smitten her ever since. The car in which the woman lay on a board suspended between seats across the aisle was empty except for herself and the third woman on the train. The cars before and after this one had also been emptied. The woman helping her said that the men were not even supposed to hear the cries of the woman in labor. It would not be proper. But were the men proper anyway? From the sounds in the distance, Nora could tell they were shouting, singing and shooting, and maybe fighting and certainly drinking.

She had seen labor before, when the doctor was unavailable, blocked away by snow, so she was good enough here, and there were no complications. But there was no bedroom with comforters, a fire and gentle women about. The woman helping her was the one who wore a pistol, and she cussed.

When the child, a boy, was born, the gun-toting woman shouted the word out the window, and the air was rent with shouts and shooting. The woman on the board lifted her wet head, holding her blanketed baby. "A boy to be a man," she said. "A boy to be a man." She laughed, tears streaming from her eyes.

The woman with the gun said softly, "God rest Himself. A child of the plains been born right here and now."

The train started up. Nora sat limply beside the mother and child. Men walked into the car, looked down and smiled.

"Now, that's a sight of a boy."

"Thank you kindly," said the woman.

"Now, ma'am, that boy going to be a cattleman?" said another.

"Nothing else."

"Hope we wasn't hoorawing too much, ma'am," said a tall man.

"Jus' like my son was born Fourth of July. Thank you kindly."

"Just made this tea, but it ain't strong's should be," said a man carrying a big cup.

"Thank you kindly."

Another man came up timidly—strange for him; he was huge. It turned out he was the husband. He did not even touch his wife. He looked grimly at his son. The woman looked up at him. "All these folks been right interested," he said.

The woman smiled. The train jerked and pulled. Her face paled. The man put his hand on her forehead. "Now, just don't fret," he said. "Just don't fret."

"Thank you kindly," she said.

In her own seat, next to Rolf, Nora was pale. She flinched when the train racketed over the road. Rolf gripped her hand.

"Rolf?"

"Yes, honey?"

"She's all right. The woman with the baby—she's all right."

"I know."

"Then be quiet, don't be disturbed. I can tell from your hand. You're disturbed."

He looked out the window at the plains, at the spring. "The trip took longer than I thought," he said. "It's time for spring roundup. I ought to be at the ranch."

She was shocked. This great, terrible, beautiful thing had happened, and he was thinking of the roundup. Her hand did not feel small and preserved in his; it felt crushed, even though his fingers were not tightly closed.

"Rolf?" Her shock was low and hurt and it told in her voice. "Rolf. That woman had a baby on the train. It could have been awful. And all you can think of now is the roundup."

He looked around at the others in the car. Then he lowered decorum a little and put his arm around her.

He whispered, "Honey, I tried to tell you—I tried. Didn't you listen? On the plains we do what has to be done. Why, honey, that woman's all right, and now we've got to get to roundup."

"But can't we—can't we be human beings?" she said.

He held her. "We are, honey," he said. "We are. We're the kind of human beings that can live here."

She remembered all that and she remembered also that within two days after they had got to the ranch, Rolf had gone out with the men on spring roundup. That time, too, Pleny had been left with her to take care of the home ranch. She had been sad, and he had spoken to her about it in a roundabout fashion at supper one night. Pleny ate with her in the big kitchen when the others were gone, instead of in the bunkhouse. And he was shy about it, but carried a dignity on his shyness.

"Don't suppose you know that the cattle're more important than anything out here?" he said.

"It seems I have to know it," said Nora.

Pleny was eating peas with a knife. She heard about it, but had never been sure it was possible.

"Couldn't live here without the cattle," he said.

"It seems to me that living here would be a lot better if people thought more about people."

"Do. That's why cattle's more important."

"I fail to understand you."

Pleny worked on steak meat. "Ma'am, cattle's money, and money's bread. Not jus' steak, but bread, living. Why, ma'am, if a man out here wants a wife, he has to have cattle first. Can't make out well enough to have a wife and kids without you have cattle."

"I don't think it's right," she had said then in the springtime. "I don't think it's right that it should be that way."

And Pleny had replied, "Don't suppose you're wrong, ma'am. I really don't." He wiped his mouth on his sleeve. "Only trouble is, that's the way it is here, if you want to stay."

She hadn't wanted to stay. As soon as she was sure she was pregnant, she wanted to go home. The spring had passed, and the summer hung heavy over the plains. The earth, the sky, the cattle, the people had dry mouths, and dogs panted with tongues gone gray. The wind touched the edges of the windmills, and water came from the deep parts of the earth, but you could not bathe in it. The water was golden and rationed, and coffee sometimes became a luxury—not because you didn't have the coffee, but because the cool watery heart of the earth did not wish to serve you.

Cultural Note

In the 1900s, when the western United States was being settled, many more men than women made the difficult journey to the West. It was not uncommon for a man to go first and establish his claim on a farm or ranch, then send for the rest of his family. When they were ready to get married, many single men traveled back east to look for wives. Others advertised for wives in newspapers. A woman would answer an ad and begin corresponding with the man. If the correspondence prospered, she would eventually move west to marry him. Marriage arrangements like these gave rise to the term "mail-order bride."

Linking to History

Domesticated cattle were first brought to the Americas by the Spaniards in the late 15th century and later by English settlers to the Atlantic coast. By the mid-19th century, cattle production for meat and milk had become a significant industry in the United States. Cattle ranching played an important part in the development of the Great Plains, as ranchers from Texas drove herds of cattle into new grazing territory in the North and West. Today, Texas is the largest cattle-producing state, with more than 14 million cattle. Nebraska, Kansas, and Iowa are also major cattle producers.

The fall roundup time came; and just before the outfit moved out, a cowboy, barely seventeen years old, had broken his leg. Rolf had pulled the leg straight, strapped a board to it and put the boy on a horse with a bag of provisions. "Tie an extra horse to him," Rolf had commanded Pleny, "in case something happens."

Pleny had done so. Rolf had asked the boy, "Got your money?"

"Got it right here."

"Now, you get to that doctor."

"Sure enough try."

"Now, when you're fixed up," said Rolf, "you come back."

"Sure enough will."

Nora knew that it would take eight to ten days for the boy to get to the nearest doctor. She ran toward the boy and the horses. She held the reins and turned on Rolf. "How can you let him go alone? How? How?"

Rolf's face had been genial as he talked to the boy, but now it hardened. But the boy, through a dead-white pain in his face, laughed. "Ma'am," he said, "now who's going to do my work and that other man's?"

"Rolf?" she said.

Rolf turned to her, took her hands. "Nora, there isn't anybody that can go with him. He knows that."

The boy laughed. "Mr. Rolf," he said, "when I get my own spread, I'm going to go out East there to get a tender woman. I swear." He spurred with his good leg and, still laughing, flashed off into dust with his two horses.

"Rolf? He might die."

Rolf bowed his head, then fiercely lifted it. "Give him more credit."

"But you can't—" she began.

"We can!" he said. Then he softened. "Nora, I don't know what to say. Here—here there's famine, drought, blizzard, locusts. Here—here we have to know what we must do if we want to stay."

"I don't like it," she said.

A wind lifted and moved around them, stirring grass and dust. In the wind was the herald of the fall—and therefore the primary messenger of the bitter winter. In the wind was the dusty harbinger of work, of the fall roundup.

"Soon I'll have to go," he said, "for the roundup."

"I know."

"The plains are mean," he said. "I know. I came here and found it. But I—I don't hate it. I feel—I feel a—a bigness. I see—I see rough prettiness." He bowed his head. "That isn't all I mean." He looked at her. "Soon I have to go. You'll be all right. Pleny will take care of you."

She hadn't told him that she was sure she had a child within her. She felt that she must keep her secret from this wild place, because even if it were only spoken, the elements might ride like a stampede against her, hurting her and her child, even as they did in the dark when she was alone and the wind yelled against the walls beside her bed and told her how savage was the place of the world in which she lived.

here was a knock on her door. She looked up. Her hands, folded in her lap, gripped each other. She did not answer.

"Ma'am?"

She said nothing.

"It's Pleny. I just can't sit down and eat, ma'am, worrying about this mortification of the flesh I got. I just can't sit down to anything like that. I just have to do something."

She made her hands relax in her lap.

"I have it wrapped up in my kerchief, ma'am," said Pleny, "but that ain't going to do it no good."

She closed her eyes, but opened them at once, staring at the door.

Pleny said, "I ain't going to leave you and the

ranch, ma'am. Couldn't do that. I have my chores to do."

A small unbidden tear touched the edge of her eye and slipped down.

There was a silence, and then he said quietly, "The doc's so far away, don't 'spect I could get there before that mortification took more of my flesh. Sure would hate that. Sure would hate that."

A second tear burned silver on the edge of her eye and dropped and burned golden down her cheek and became acid on her line of chin, and her wrist came up and brushed it away.

She heard the wind and many messages and she imagined Pleny waiting. She felt a sense of response, of obligation, of angry maternal love, as if all the wistful hope and female passion of her nature had been fused, struck into life, made able because she was woman, and was here, and birth, survival, help, lay potent, sweet, powerful in her heart and in her hands.

She stood up. "Pleny?"

"Yes, ma'am?"

"What must I do?"

He was silent, and she opened the door. Angrily, then firmly, she said, "Let's go outside, Pleny."

"Yes, ma'am."

She held the kindling ax. Pleny had his finger on the block. He closed his eyes. The wind pulled her skirts. She looked up for a moment at the whirling light. Then, in necessity and tenderness, she swiftly did what must be done.

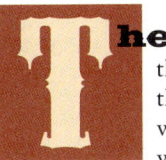

They were coming, the men were coming home from the roundup. The screen of dust was on the plain. She had been working on the meal and now it was the bread she was kneading. Working on the bread, she felt a kick against her abdomen.

She stopped, startled a moment, her hands deep, gripping in the dough—the kick again, strong.

Suddenly, in a way that would have shocked her mother, in a way that would have shocked herself not so long ago, she threw back her head and laughed, a fierce song of love and expectancy. She made bread and was kicked; she expected her man and she laughed, fiercely and tenderly. She was kicked, and a child of the plains had awakened within her. ❖

WILLIAMS FORREST

Williams Forrest did not start out to be a writer. Born in New Jersey, he attended public schools in Illinois and was a pre-med student at Duke University when World War II interrupted his studies. During the war he worked on nearly 50 military films and wrote the armed forces' classified book on psychological warfare in Europe. At this time he began writing short stories, and after 1946 he contributed Westerns and other pieces to magazines such as *The Saturday Evening Post*, *Redbook*, and *McCalls*. Two of his short stories were adapted for television in the 1950s.

1918–1991

Though he had no formal training in writing, Forrest also published ten novels in a variety of styles. Later in his life he was a speechwriter, a newspaper editor, and a writer/producer for local radio stations. A few years after his death, his widow commented that Forrest's "uniqueness lay in his magical gift of words—his sensitivity and compassion that allowed him to write not only from his own perspective but also from that of a woman's."

OPTION 3

Class Discussion

SHARING IDEAS

Teacher's Role After students have read the selection, engage them in a whole-class discussion by using the following questions:

1. Describe the setting of "Plainswoman." How is it important to the story? *(Possible responses: The setting is an isolated western cattle ranch sometime in the past; the setting is important because Nora's struggle to deal with the realities of life in this harsh setting is the story's central conflict; the setting is important because her changing attitude toward the plains shows growth.)*

2. Discuss Rolf's and Pleny's views on the importance of cattle. Was Rolf justified in sending the boy with a broken leg out by himself to seek medical help? *(Possible response: Some students may say that it was wrong, because human life should have more value than cattle. Others may say that Rolf was acting out of necessity, because there was no one to replace the boy or do his work.)*

3. How might Nora's decision to do "what must be done" be considered a rite of passage? *(Possible responses: Amputating Pleny's finger is a milestone in her acceptance of the frontier life; she has faced a crisis and become stronger because of her action.)*

4. Describe how Nora's feelings about her pregnancy differ in the first and last paragraphs of the story. In what sense do these differences illustrate a change in Nora's attitude toward life in the West? *(Possible responses: In the first paragraph, Nora doesn't want to feel the baby move; she is frightened at the thought of giving birth. In the second, she laughs when the baby kicks inside her and is no longer fearful; she is ready to accept the challenges of her new life.)*

WILLIAMS FORREST

Williams Forrest's first published short story appeared in 1943 in the July issue of *The Saturday Evening Post* magazine. However, Forrest wrote the story when he was 19 years old. Not thinking it had any potential for sale, he put it away for six years, eventually sending it to *The Saturday Evening Post*.

OVERVIEW

To gain a deeper appreciation of the selections they have read in this unit, students will explore the characteristics of an investigative report and then create a well-developed example in this lesson.

Objectives

- To plan an investigative report by considering elements such as research, patterns of information, format, and method of organization.
- To draft a report and solicit response
- To revise, edit, and publish a report
- To reflect on the process of writing an investigative report

Skills

WRITING AND LANGUAGE
- Identifying report elements
- Supporting ideas with details
- Using commas in a series

MEDIA LITERACY
- Interpreting a cartoon
- Reading a news article
- Using on-line services

SPEAKING, LISTENING, AND VIEWING
- Conducting interviews
- Conferencing

CRITICAL THINKING
- Analyzing information
- Sequencing
- Making judgments

RESEARCH SKILLS
- Using databases
- Conducting interviews
- Using the computer

Teaching Strategy: MODELING

A To demonstrate how students can generate report ideas have them look at the cartoon showing the Hubble Telescope. Ask these questions:
- What was wrong with the mirror, and how did this affect the telescope's functioning?
- How did NASA fix the problem?
- How much money and time were lost because of NASA's failure to detect the mistake before the telescope was launched?

Teaching Strategy: MODELING

B Make sure that students realize that by showing a standard eye chart in front of the huge telescope the cartoonist is poking fun at NASA's failure to make a seemingly routine check.

CUSTOMIZING FOR
Students Acquiring English

C Point out that although the statue is holding the glove in its right hand, the glove being held erroneously fits the left hand.

WRITING FROM EXPERIENCE

Writing to Explain

As you have seen in Unit One, "Live and Learn," thinking about one's experiences can turn mistakes and mishaps into opportunities to grow. You too will deal with situations like these—in school, on the job, and in your personal life. Expository writing—writing that uses facts to explain or inform—can help you in such situations.

GUIDED ASSIGNMENT
Write an Investigative Report Someday, you may have to write a report to explain a problem that has occurred. In this lesson, you'll have an opportunity to write such a report.

1 Read the Sources

A The articles and the cartoon on these pages concern real-life blunders. What went wrong in each case? How do you think people learned from these mistakes?

- **Reading for Information** As you read the sources, jot down any questions you have. Also record facts, names, and statistics that might help you continue an exploration.

- **Choosing a Situation** What interesting blunders have you heard about lately? Newspapers, magazines, and TV news programs contain plenty of reports about preventable mistakes and quirky problems. Delve into these sources (and your own notebook) to find a topic for your report. If you prefer, you can select one of the situations on these two pages to explore further.

B NASA spent $1.5 billion on the Hubble Space Telescope before noticing a flawed mirror. What is the cartoonist's criticism of NASA?

164 UNIT ONE

Magazine Photograph

C Baseball legend Babe Ruth was left-handed, but a nine-foot bronze statue unveiled in 1995 shows the slugger holding a right-hander's glove.

Editorial Cartoon

PRINT AND MEDIA RESOURCES

UNIT ONE RESOURCE BOOK
Prewriting, p. 67
Elaboration, p. 68
Peer Response Guide, pp. 69–70
Revising and Proofreading, p. 71
Student Model, pp. 72–73
Rubric, p. 74

THE WRITER'S CRAFT
Writer's Workshop 9: Reports, pp. 265–288

FORMAL ASSESSMENT
Guidelines for Writing Assessment

GRAMMAR MINI-LESSONS
Transparencies, p. 42
Copymasters, p. 43

WRITING MINI-LESSONS
Transparencies, pp. 39–40

WRITING COACH

LASERLINKS
Writing Springboard

164 THE LANGUAGE OF LITERATURE **Teacher's Edition**

Newspaper Article

Chicago's Well-Kept Secret: Tunnels

By DON TERRY
Special to *The New York Times*

What were the tunnels for?

CHICAGO, April 14—For nearly a century, a 60-mile web of tunnels has wound 40 feet below this city's downtown streets and river bed, causing little trouble or public notice until Monday.

Now almost everyone here in this water-weary city has heard of the tunnels and the damage they helped cause on Monday when 250 million gallons of murky water from the Chicago River rushed through their narrow passages and into basements in the city's business district.

What caused the flood?

"It's rather amazing that that much water got in there," a city official said today, speaking on the condition that his name not be used. "It's still mind-boggling to me that this happened."

How was the flood stopped?

D

Auto-Size Hole the Problem

The flooding caught the city off guard. The banks of the river did not overflow, they underflowed. The river apparently poured into the skyscraper basements through an automobile-size hole that opened up in one of the tunnels, some 14 to 19 feet below the bed of the Chicago River.

from an article in
The New York Times, April 15, 1992

② Try a Quickwrite

Try the KWL strategy to help you begin exploring your topic. In your notebook, write the following:

E

K Write what you **know.**
W Write what you **want to find out.**
L Write what you have **learned.** You will complete this stage later.

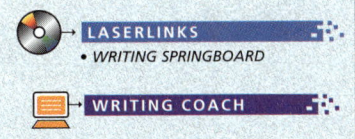
- WRITING SPRINGBOARD
- WRITING COACH

WRITING FROM EXPERIENCE **165**

CUSTOMIZING FOR
Students Acquiring English

D The news writer's use of idioms may cause some problems for students. Explain the following words:

mind-boggling: hard to comprehend
off guard: unprepared
underflowed: allowed water to pass beneath them; neologistic opposite of *overflow*.

CUSTOMIZING FOR
Less-Proficient Writers

Encourage students to concentrate on recording their ideas and questions on paper. Tell them that spelling, grammar, and mechanical skills such as punctuation are not crucial at this stage.

Research Skill: USING THE COMPUTER

E Students may find that their KWL notes flow more easily on a computer because they can change or refine a thought quickly as they input.

WRITING SPRINGBOARD
The Chicago Flood Some of the causes and effects of the flood that immobilized the city of Chicago in 1992 are discussed in this informative film.

Side B, Frame 215

Writing Prompt
There are times when minor blunders result in devastating consequences. After viewing the informative video about the flood in Chicago, think about other situations or blunders you know about. Write an essay explaining what happened.

THE LANGUAGE OF LITERATURE TEACHER'S EDITION **165**

Teaching Strategy:
STUMBLING BLOCK

F If students have trouble understanding the links between the information questions and sources shown on the charts, you may wish to organize a discussion in which students review major sources of research information and their contents.

CUSTOMIZING FOR
Less-Proficient Writers

G Some students may need guidance in using key words or phrases to research a topic in databases. Give them some practice in setting up key words for a search. For example, suggest that using the word *Chicago* would result in the citation of hundreds of unrelated periodicals. Using the words *Chicago—Floods* or *Chicago—Tunnels* would be more efficient.

PREWRITING

Gathering Information

Questions to Answer You now probably have a number of questions about your subject and a list of ideas you'd like to follow up on. The steps on these two pages will help you gather the information you need to write a clear explanation.

❶ Plan Your Investigation

One way to make gathering information simpler is by using a research plan. Divide a piece of paper into two columns. In the first column, write all the questions you have about your topic. What you wrote for the W (want to know) part of the KWL strategy will help you fill in the questions. In the second column, write ideas about where you might look to answer each question.

Student's Planning Chart

❷ Access Information

Depending on your resources, you can use a variety of existing sources for information.

EXPLORE DIFFERENT RESOURCES

Print and Other Media Visit your school or local library to find newspaper or magazine articles on the topic. Ask your librarian what computer resources are available. The CD-ROM you see above contains thousands of magazine articles.

The Phone If you find the names of people who might be additional sources of information, call them. Ask them for some firsthand information, or arrange a face-to-face interview.

On-line Services If you have access to a computer with a modem, consider subscribing to an on-line service. Such a service can connect you to rich databases, as well as organizations and people with knowledge about your subject.

SkillBuilder **RESEARCH SKILLS**

NOTE-TAKING Students should take notes on all the important information they gather from written and oral sources. Urge them to listen to or look for clues indicating the most important points in their sources: for example, words and phrases such as *first, main, most important, principal, emphasize, everyone, for these reasons*. Topic sentences in paragraphs and a speaker's repetition of words and ideas can also be helpful clues. Have students follow these guidelines when they take notes:

- Record only essential information. Note important facts such as dates, amounts, and names of people, places, and events.
- Use a modified outline form. Place main ideas at outline's left margin. Indent related details beneath the main ideas to which they refer.

Application Invite pairs of students to take notes on a brief news article. If you wish, have them write notes on the news article shown on page 165. Then ask each pair to exchange notes with another pair of note-takers and discuss each other's work.

CONDUCT INTERVIEWS

As you learn more about your topic, you may want to interview people with expertise on the subject.

- Have your questions ready before the interview.
- Ask questions that require more than a yes-or-no answer. For example, "Did the flood affect you?" won't yield as much information as "How did the flood affect you?"
- Restate the person's responses to be sure you have accurate information. Ask for corrections.
- Be prepared to let the conversation stray if the person you're interviewing goes off in an interesting direction.

3 Talk It Over

Discussing what you've learned can help clarify your thoughts.

- Explain the key issues of your topic to a group of peers.
- Encourage your listeners to ask questions as you speak.
- Listen carefully to feedback and take notes about areas you need to clarify or find out more about.
- Summarize what you have learned from your peers.

4 Explore the Possibilities

How will you make sense of the information you've uncovered? These ideas may help you.

FIND AN ANGLE

What piece of information interested you most? Perhaps a quotation, a statistic, or an ingenious means of coping with a problem is what inspired you to investigate the situation in the first place. Your initial reaction can often help you decide what to focus on in your explanation.

LOOK FOR PATTERNS

As you look over your research results, try grouping similar types of data. One of the organizational methods below might help you organize the information you have uncovered.

- **Problem and Solution** Explain a problem and present the solutions that were found.
- **Process** Describe in detail how something works or happens.
- **Cause and Effect** Take an in-depth look at the cause of a situation and the effects it had.

SkillBuilder

CRITICAL THINKING

Analyzing Information

An idea tree like the one below can help you analyze your topic visually. As you gather information about the topic, fill in the tree with your questions or key points. The idea tree shown here has three levels, but yours can have many levels and branches.

```
              Chicago Flood
              /           \
       Tunnel leaks    Leak plugged
        /      \        /       \
   Damage  History of  Cost of   Six days
           tunnels    cleanup    of work
```

APPLYING WHAT YOU'VE LEARNED

As you research your topic, you might find that an idea tree or some other type of graphic organizer can help you organize the information you find.

THINK & PLAN

Reflecting On Your Ideas

1. Do you have enough information on your topic? If not, where do you think you can get more?
2. Which sources did you find to be particularly helpful? How might they help you later if you need more information?
3. What ideas did you get from the research to help you frame your explanation?

WRITING FROM EXPERIENCE **167**

Research Skill: INTERVIEWING

Offer students these additional practical tips on interviewing:

- Arrange questions in a logical order. Using time order is often the best strategy.
- Ask the interviewee's permission before using a tape recorder.
- Ask follow-up questions to clarify any confusing statements.
- As soon as possible after the interview, record your notes in modified outline form.

Teaching Strategy: STUMBLING BLOCK

As students prepare to present their topics, they should ask themselves *who? what? when? where? why?* and *how?* to identify the main ideas and important details.

SkillBuilder CRITICAL THINKING

ANALYZING INFORMATION Go over the three levels of the idea tree shown in the text. Make sure that students understand that the first level identifies the report topic; the second level splits the topic into two main parts or subtopics that are shown in chronological (time) order; the third level shows related lines of inquiry, involving background information and causes or effects for each subtopic. Encourage students to include as much detail as they can in their idea trees. They can "prune" the trees later, when they look for patterns of information and analyze their discovery drafts.

Applying What You've Learned Possible response: Use a time line to organize a sequence of events.

THE LANGUAGE OF LITERATURE TEACHER'S EDITION **167**

Research Skill: USING THE COMPUTER

J Students may find it easier to write their reports on a computer. Before students begin, show them how to title a file for each draft so that nothing is lost or written over in successive drafts. For example, students can select a key word and number each draft consecutively—FLOOD 1, FLOOD 2, and so on.

Critical Thinking: SEQUENCING

K Encourage students to sequence details in a logical order. For example, they can sequence some of the information in this paragraph on a time line:

1900	1950s	1992
Tunnels built.	Tunnels fall into disuse.	Hole causes flood.

Teaching Strategy: MANAGING THE PAPER LOAD

L As you read the students' drafts, concentrate on the single element that each student finds most troublesome, such as identifying a main idea or organizing details in a logical order. Reassure students that they can work out less serious report problems in a peer review setting.

DRAFTING

Getting Your Ideas Down

Getting Organized Once you have collected your information, you can begin putting your ideas on paper. Some people begin by organizing material into an outline. Others just start writing. Experiment with both approaches. The method shown here is one way you can begin.

① Write a Discovery Draft
A good way to begin exploring your ideas is to write them out. Don't worry about details like spelling, grammar, or even organization at this point. Just make a mess! You'll have a chance to revise your ideas later on. The Writing Coach can help you at this stage.

Student's Discovery Draft

Chicago Flood

My Discovery Draft

Flood: A Tunnel Blunder

Californians like us are used to earthquakes, forest fires, mud slides, and a host of other disasters. However, we have never experienced anything like the Chicago flood of April 13, 1992.

Goldfish, rock bass, gizzard shad, and alewives swimming in Chicago's City Hall. Water levels reach 30 feet in some basements, including some stores in the central area of downtown (the Loop) that were forced to close early. Elevators stop, the lights go out, thousands of downtown workers evacuate, computers crash. The financial district shuts down. How did this, how could this, happen?

Car-sized hole in tunnel under the river sucked 250 million gallons of water into the tunnel. Tunnel part of a 60-mile system built around 1900 to move coal and other supplies on small freight trains. Not used since 1950s, now used by utility companies for wires and cables. 21 square city block evacuated, 20 buildings shut. No one killed or seriously injured.

All of those problems were severe. Who to blame was also an issue. But more important was how to plug the hole and, if they couldn't, how to drain the tunnels without causing them to collapse and cause an earthquakelike eruption down under.

My Comments
My Discovery Draft

Rework or delete this? California really doesn't have much to do with the flood.

I love the fish details! How can I work them into my final piece?

Need more on how the flood started. Also, I could focus on what happened, how it happened, the history of the tunnels, or how the hole was fixed.

Additional comments: A guy on the Internet was gathering material for a list of famous blunders. Maybe I'll send him this piece when it's done.

WRITING SPRINGBOARD
The Alaskan Oil Spill A park ranger describes the devastation caused by millions of gallons of oil being spilled into Alaskan coastal waters by a damaged oil tanker.

Writing Prompt
Human blunders sometimes impact the environment in a negative way. Using this film about the Alaskan oil spill as an example, investigate a similar incident. Write an investigative report about the incident and explain, in detail, how it affected the environment.

Side B, Frame 2690

② Analyze Your Discovery Draft

Once you have collected notes or written a discovery draft, you'll need to analyze what you've done in order to continue. You might ask yourself questions such as the following:

- What information do I really want to focus on?
- What ideas or sentences do I like best?
- Do certain ideas or sentences seem to belong together?

On the left are one student's comments about his draft. Would similar thinking help you with your own draft?

③ Rework Your Draft and Share

The guidelines below will help you formalize your draft.

Choose a Format The format for your finished piece should be appropriate to the audience you have in mind. (If you want to reach a big audience, you might write an electronic mail to post on the Internet.) Other possible formats are listed under Share Your Work on page 171.

Create a Strong Introduction Would one of these techniques help you "hook" your readers?

- describing a compelling incident (fish swimming in City Hall)
- citing surprising statistics (250 million gallons of water)
- emphasizing the importance of your topic (huge city brought to a standstill by an underground flood)
- asking a question ("Do you recall the Great Chicago Fire?")

Choose a Method of Organization Good expository writing features a combination of organizing methods. Look for Patterns on page 167 will give you ideas for organizing your report.

Summarize with a Conclusion You can close your piece with a concise summary of your main ideas.

 PEER RESPONSE

A peer reviewer can help you identify strengths and weaknesses of your draft. Ask him or her questions like the following:

- How would you sum up my explanation in a few sentences?
- Which parts did you feel were most interesting? Why?
- Which parts, if any, were confusing?

SkillBuilder
 WRITER'S CRAFT

Supporting Ideas with Details

Each paragraph in expository writing should consist of a main idea and specific details that support it. For example:

Chicagoans responded quickly after news of the flood broke. In the first 24 hours, city workers filled the watery hole with quick-setting concrete, broken chunks of pavement, and 1,500 tons of sand. A hospital donated a barge full of mattresses to block the flow of water.

APPLYING WHAT YOU'VE LEARNED
Have you supported the main idea of each paragraph of your draft with one or more details? If not, review your prewriting notes for specific details you could add.

 WRITING HANDBOOK

For more information about supporting details, see the lesson on elaboration on page 871 of the Writing Handbook.

RETHINK & EVALUATE

Preparing to Revise

1. What details are most effective?
2. Do you need to add or delete other facts? How do you decide?
3. What changes do you want to make to your draft as a result of peer response?

WRITING FROM EXPERIENCE **169**

Critical Thinking:
MAKING JUDGMENTS

M Refer students to the writer's marginal comment about the fish in the draft on page 168. Guide students to identify several criteria that they can use to evaluate such details. For example, students can ask themselves whether the details

- are clearly related to the main idea.
- are vivid and specific.
- are striking or unusual.

Teaching Strategy:
COLLABORATIVE OPPORTUNITY

N Tell students that another way to create a strong introduction is to use an emphatic or striking quotation. Have small groups of students trade quotes from their research. Encourage peers to offer opinions on whether each quote is a good candidate to introduce a group member's report.

Teaching Strategy:
COLLABORATIVE OPPORTUNITY

O Have reviewers read through the entire report before they make any comments. During the second reading, they should jot down brief comments and suggestions. Remind students to include specific ideas for revision, such as "Consider adding a chart or graphic to present these facts in a simpler, more efficient way."

SkillBuilder WRITER'S CRAFT

SUPPORTING IDEAS WITH DETAILS As students revise their reports, give them these tips:

- Look for main ideas that are not supported by details or that are inadequately supported. Guide students to add specific support from their prewriting notes.
- Make sure that each sentence in a paragraph directly relates to that paragraph's main idea.
- Check for unity and coherence. Add transitions to link supporting sentences and to show their relationship.

Applying What You've Learned Students can outline each paragraph to make sure they are able to identify its main idea and supporting details.

Additional Suggestions Remind students that specific support for the main ideas in an investigative report often takes the form of facts, statistics, or quotations. Have them review their prewriting notes to make sure that they have included these items.

Reteaching/Reinforcement
- *Writing Mini-Lessons* transparencies, pp. 39-40

 The Writer's Craft

Unity in Paragraphs, pp. 361–362

THE LANGUAGE OF LITERATURE TEACHER'S EDITION **169**

Writing Skill: REVISING

P As students revise and edit their reports, they will work to improve their drafts by
1. Adding needed words, sentences, and paragraphs.
2. Cutting unnecessary material, such as repetitive or unrelated details.
3. Substituting different words, sentences, and paragraphs for deleted material.
4. Rearranging parts of the text to create better coherence and unity.

Teaching Strategy: MODELING

Q Discuss with students how this model meets the standards for evaluation on page 171. For example, details in the first paragraph that hook the reader include the nicknames for Chicago, the 30-foot water level in basements, and the exotic visitors to City Hall. Details summarizing the flood's effects include the early closing of stores, the malfunction of elevators and computers, and the shutdown of the financial district.

R Words and phrases in this paragraph that define and explain the topic include the following: *The hole was created; the head of transportation knew . . . but refused . . . to repair it; the hole grew in size and the flood was on; . . . the final cleanup bill. . . .*

REVISING AND PUBLISHING

Finishing Your Report

A Final Look The last step is making sure your report says what you want it to say and doesn't contain any errors in spelling or grammar that will distract your readers. Peer feedback and the information about revising and editing on these pages will help you identify places for improvement.

1 Revise and Edit

Take a break from your draft for a day or two and then look at it from a fresh perspective. Don't be afraid to change anything or everything.

- Review your peer comments to see where your draft needs clarification.
- Use the Standards for Evaluation on the next page as guidelines for revision. Refer to the Editing Checklist in the SkillBuilder as you edit and proofread your report. Also, double check your facts. Accuracy is particularly important in a factual report.
- You also might look at the excerpts from one student's final draft on the right. Notice how he edited and revised his work.

Which words and phrases help define and explain the topic?

Which details in the first paragraph hook the reader and summarize the effects of the flood?

Student's Revised Report

The Chicago Flood: A Tunnel Blunder

Chicago has long been nicknamed the City That Works. One day in 1992, a freak flood transformed it into the City That Leaks. Water levels in some downtown basements rose as high as 30 feet. Visitors to City Hall included goldfish, rock bass, gizzard shad, and alewives. Stores closed early, cutting short Easter shopping trips. Elevators stopped, the lights went out, computers crashed. The underground river even shut down the city's financial district. How did it happen?

The hole was created when a piling was accidentally driven through the river floor and into part of the tunnel. The head of transportation for the city knew about the hole but refused to spend $10,000 to repair it. He also failed to tell other city officials about the hole. Two months later, the hole grew in size and the flood was on. The cleanup—another story altogether—cost about $1 billion. How big a blunder was it? Subtracting the $10,000 repair estimate from the final cleanup bill will give you an idea.

170 UNIT ONE

What does this format accomplish that the report does not?

② Share Your Work

Your audience and goal usually determine the format your writing takes. Below are some format ideas for an investigative report. What are the strengths and weaknesses of each one?

PUBLISHING IDEAS

- Draw a storyboard, a diagram, or a poster for your class.
- Write an article explaining how the blunder could have been avoided. Send it to your school or local newspaper.

Standards for Evaluation

The investigative report
- grabs readers' attention with an appealing lead or hook
- states the topic clearly in the introduction
- cites specific details to help define and explain the topic
- uses language that is appropriate for the audience
- presents information in a logical order
- wraps up the ideas in the conclusion

SkillBuilder

 GRAMMAR FROM WRITING

Using Commas in a Series
Use a comma after every item in a series except the last one. For example:

Many Chicago stores still lacked heat, air conditioning, and hot water one week after the flood.

 GRAMMAR HANDBOOK

For more information on using commas in a series, see page 935 of the Grammar Handbook.

Editing Checklist Use the following revising and editing tips as you revise your own draft:
- Did you use transitions to clarify the order of events?
- Did you proofread your report for spelling and punctuation?

REFLECT & ASSESS

Evaluating the Experience

1. Review the Standards for Evaluation and consider the comments of your peer reviewer. How successful do you feel your writing is?
2. List the skills you used in writing your report. How could you use them in other situations?

 PORTFOLIO Write a note to yourself about your successes and problems in this writing experience. Add the note and the finished report to your portfolio.

WRITING FROM EXPERIENCE 171

Teaching Strategy: MODELING

S This format is able to provide an accurate visual image of the event to accompany the data; the use of arrows reinforces the sense of the event's chronology.

Research Skill: USING THE COMPUTER

T As they explore the possibility of using a storyboard, a poster, or a boxed feature as a form of publication, students should experiment with different designs and layouts on the computer. Guide them to recognize that such publication formats would have immediate visual appeal but would not be the format for presenting an in-depth exploration of the blunder's causes.

Teaching Strategy: MANAGING THE PAPER LOAD

U Whenever possible, phrase your written comments as questions that will encourage students to reflect on and assess their work. For example, instead of writing "unrelated," try "How does this detail relate to/support your main idea?"

Standards for Evaluation

Have students review their reports for the following:

Ideas and Content
- begins with an interesting introduction
- develops the topic completely with appropriate details and accurate facts
- ends with a satisfying conclusion that restates the problem or the solution to the problem

Structure and Form
- uses transitions to show the relationships among ideas
- uses exact quotations effectively, when appropriate

Grammar, Usage, and Mechanics
- follows standard rules of grammar, usage, and mechanics

 GRAMMAR FROM WRITING

USING COMMAS IN A SERIES Remind students to use a comma after every item in a series except the last one. Point out to students that a series consists of three or more items of the same kind. Items can be words, phrases, or clauses.

Elevators stopped, computers crashed, stores closed.

Supervisors quickly organized crews to direct traffic, pump out basements, and cart away debris.

Volunteers aided the emergency effort at hospitals, in the streets, and even inside the tunnel network.

Tell students that items in a series should be grammatically parallel. Nouns should be sequenced with other nouns, verbs with verbs, and so forth.

Applying What You've Learned Students can work in pairs to proofread each other's reports for the correct use of commas and parallel structure.

Reteaching/Reinforcement
- *Grammar Mini-Lessons* copymasters p. 43, transparencies p. 42

📁 **The Writer's Craft**
The Comma, p. 772

PORTFOLIO

Ask students to write a brief description of what they have learned about investigative reports as a result of this assignment. They may wish to include their description and their finished report in their portfolio.

THE LANGUAGE OF LITERATURE TEACHER'S EDITION **171**

UNIT REVIEW

This feature allows students to reflect on what they have learned in Unit One and to assess how well they have understood it. This feature provides students with multiple opportunities for self-assessment. You may also wish to use some of the activities to assess specific skills, such as speaking, listening, or cooperative learning.

Objectives

- To allow students to reflect on and assess their understanding of theme
- To allow students to reflect on and assess their understanding of literary concepts, such as conflict and setting
- To provide students with the opportunity to assess and build their portfolios

REFLECTING ON THEME

OPTION 1

Suggest that students pay particular attention to the feelings that underlie the various characters' reactions to their experiences. Students may have had similar experiences, but they may have reacted very differently. Have them consider the motivation behind their character's reaction as a focus for their essay.

OPTION 2

Suggest that each student choose one character to whom to address his or her letter. You might start this activity with a class discussion in which students can share what they have learned from the various characters.

OPTION 3

Be sure that all students participate in discussion. Each group of five or six students might concentrate on one of the selections, and the group discussions can be followed by a whole-class discussion.

 Self-Assessment
Encourage students to consider whether it is, in fact, possible to have the lesson first and the test afterward, or whether they agree with the quotation now that they have read and thought about the selections in this unit. Students should be sure to support their agreement or disagreement with the quotation with details from the selections.

REFLECT & ASSESS

UNIT ONE: LIVE AND LEARN

How have your ideas about growing up changed as a result of reading the selections in this unit? Choose one or more of the options in each of the following sections to help you explore what you've learned.

REFLECTING ON THEME

OPTION 1 **Judging Impact** One character suppresses a childhood hurt for 36 years; the memory of a lost fish haunts another character years later. Many characters in this unit discover that growing up can be accompanied by the pain of things left unresolved or things lost. Make a list of the experiences that haunt the characters over the years. Which of the experiences would you have a similar reaction to? Write a few paragraphs explaining your choices.

OPTION 2 **Looking Back** Going through a rite of passage is usually a learning experience. In "Marigolds," for example, the narrator loses her childhood innocence when she suddenly feels compassion for a woman she has hurt. Review the selections in Part 2 of this unit; then list the characters who learn something during their rites of passage, and briefly describe what they learn. Write a personal letter to these characters, explaining what you have learned about growing up by reading about their experiences.

OPTION 3 **Discussing Ideas** With a small group of classmates, discuss what you now see as some of the most challenging aspects of growing up or learning to make your way in the world. Use examples from the selections to support your ideas, but be prepared to build on them with examples from your own experience or the experiences of people you know.

Self-Assessment: Reconsider the quotation at the beginning of the unit: "Experience is a hard teacher because she gives the test first, the lesson afterwards." Write a paragraph explaining how reading the selections in this unit has given you a better understanding of the quotation's meaning.

REVIEWING LITERARY CONCEPTS

OPTION 1 **Thinking About Conflict** Most of the characters in Unit One face conflicts that force them to grow or change. You know that there are two basic kinds of conflict: internal and external. Make a chart, like the one shown, to analyze the conflicts in the selections you have read. Then tell which conflicts seemed to you to have the greatest effect on the main character.

Selection	Type of Conflict	Description of Conflict	Effect on Main Character
"A Christmas Memory"	External	The two friends face harsh treatment from the rest of the family.	Buddy becomes closer to his cousin but distrustful of most others.
"American History"	External and internal		

172 UNIT ONE: LIVE AND LEARN

OPTION 2 **Looking at Setting** Often a story's setting—the time and place in which the action occurs—has a major influence on the total effect of the story. In the selections you have read, which setting made the greatest impression on you? List the stories in this unit and make a bar graph indicating whether you think the influence of setting is slight, medium, or great in each.

PORTFOLIO BUILDING

- **QuickWrites** Many of the QuickWrites in this unit asked you to write personal narratives or essays about important events or times in your life. From your responses, choose the one that you feel best captures the event that helped you to grow or to learn something. Then write a cover note explaining your choice. Attach the note to the response and add both to your portfolio.

- **Writing About Literature** Earlier in this unit, you analyzed a character to help you better understand him or her. Reread your analysis. Then write a letter to the character, telling him or her how you feel now and explaining what you would still like to find out. Add your letter to your portfolio.

- **Writing from Experience** What were your reasons for choosing the real-life blunder you wrote about for this assignment? Perhaps investigating the problem helped you learn something you can apply to situations in your own life. Describe how you went about investigating the mistake or blunder, telling what lessons you learned that you might apply to other situations. Include your notes with your report if you choose to keep it in your portfolio.

- **Personal Choice** Look back through your records and evaluations of all the activities that you completed in this unit. Also look through any writing you completed for an assignment or on your own. Which work are you proudest of? Write a note that explains why you feel good about that activity or piece of writing. Attach the note to your activity record or piece of writing and include both in your portfolio.

Self-Assessment: Did you understand conflict and setting enough to complete the preceding activities? Explain why you feel as you do. On a sheet of paper, copy the following list of literary terms introduced in this unit. Next to each term, indicate whether you feel you understand it well, somewhat, or not at all.

rising action
climax
falling action
allusion
symbol
mood

rhyme
free verse
main character
minor character
author's purpose

Self-Assessment: At this point, you may just be beginning your portfolio. Are the pieces you have included ones you think you'll keep, or do you think you will be replacing them as the year goes on?

SETTING GOALS

As you worked through the reading and writing activities in this section, you probably identified certain skills that you want to work on. Look back through your assignments, worksheets, and notebook. Then, in your notebook, make a list of the skills or concepts that you'd like to work on in the next unit.

REFLECT & ASSESS **173**

SETTING GOALS

In order to help students set future goals, suggest that they jot down notes about the areas they want to develop and learn more about as they review their portfolios, worksheets, and notebooks. As they complete the next unit, have them review their list to check their progress toward their goals.

REVIEWING LITERARY CONCEPTS

OPTION 1

Have students choose partners with whom they can discuss the characters and their conflicts. Partners can review the selections together, discussing the internal and external struggles the characters face, and they can collaborate on a final chart. Students can then each select a character and write a few paragraphs on how dealing with a conflict changed him or her.

OPTION 2

Remind students that setting includes not only the place in which a story unfolds but also its time. Encourage them to consider the effect on the various characters of the time and place in which they are caught. Students should also consider how the stories might be different if the settings were different. See also Unit One Resource Book, p. 77.

 Self-Assessment Have students define each term for themselves, without looking in the dictionary. Then have them check their definitions to see how well they comprehend each term. Students can then identify one instance of each element in the selections in this unit.

PORTFOLIO BUILDING

You may wish to help students choose or modify options, to suit the needs you have established for the class. Encourage students to incorporate drafts, not just final products, into their portfolios, so that they can reflect on and assess their development and progress.

 Self-Assessment Suggest that students periodically examine their portfolios, ranking each piece as satisfactory and worth keeping, or needing improvement. This process will help them identify any problems that recur in their writing.

UNIT TWO

East Twelfth Street (1946), Ben Shahn. Tempera, 22″ × 30″, collection of Mr. and Mrs. Albert Hackett, New York. Copyright © 1995 Estate of Ben Shahn/Licensed by VAGA, New York.

UNIT THEMES

Unit Two

Trials and Tribulations In this unit, students will read selections that explore various ways in which people struggle with and triumph over adversity. The unit contains two parts: Part 1, "Friend or Foe?" and Part 2, "Against the Odds." Selections in both parts contribute to the unit theme by examining how various characters endure and surmount obstacles and difficulties.

Part 1

Friend or Foe? Selections in Part 1 emphasize conflicts the characters have with both friends and enemies and in both positive and negative situations. For example, in "The Day the Cisco Kid Shot John Wayne," a boy makes friends of two enemies for quite different reasons, and in "Grover Dill and the Tasmanian Devil," a boy has an experience that some may think is positive but that he considers negative.

Part 2

Against the Odds Selections in Part 2 explore characters' conflicts with larger social obstacles. For example, in "The United States vs. Susan B. Anthony," a woman triumphs over custom, tradition, and injustice.

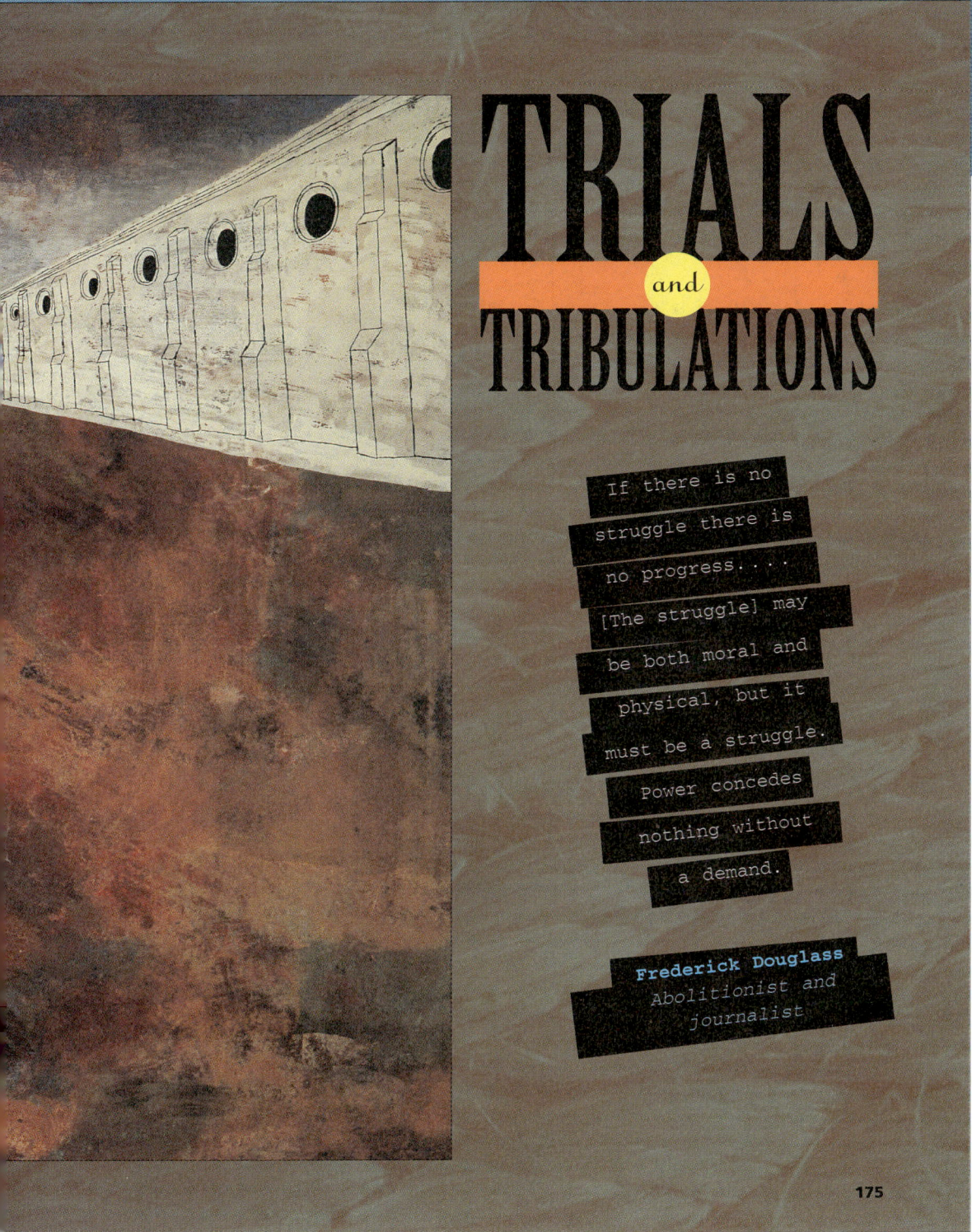

TRIALS and TRIBULATIONS

> If there is no struggle there is no progress.... [The struggle] may be both moral and physical, but it must be a struggle. Power concedes nothing without a demand.
>
> **Frederick Douglass**
> Abolitionist and journalist

Exploring Theme

To help students explore the connections between the art, the quotation, and the unit theme, have them consider the following questions:

1. Does "Trials and Tribulations" sound like an important theme to explore? Why or why not? *(Possible response: yes, because all of us face difficulties every day and we have to overcome them in order to survive)*

2. How would you paraphrase Frederick Douglass's opinion of the need for a struggle? *(Possible response: We will be given nothing freely—we must insist on our rights and our needs in order that they be met. If we do not strive to move forward, we will stand still.)*

3. Do you think the painting conveys the theme of trials and tribulations? Why or why not? *(Possible responses: no, because there is no sign of conflict among the figures; yes, because the figures in the foreground may just be learning to roller-skate and may be desperate to keep up with the first girl; yes, because the bleak setting implies that survival may be hard won on East Twelfth Street.)*

4. What kinds of stories might you expect to read in this unit? *(Possible response: stories whose characters are involved in struggles of various sorts—both physical and moral, as suggested in the quotation)*

5. What are some definitions of the word *trial*? *(a case in court; any difficulty that must be faced)* Discuss a particular trial you have endured. *(Responses will vary.)*

Art Note

East Twelfth Street by Ben Shahn
Ben Shahn was born in Lithuania in 1898. His father, an escaped prisoner, moved the family to the United States in 1906. Shahn grew up in Brooklyn and studied art in New York and in France, where he came under the influence of Paul Cézanne's work. During the first half of his career, Shahn explored themes of social injustice, most notably in his series of gouaches on the Sacco and Vanzetti case. Shahn also collaborated with Diego Rivera on frescoes for Manhattan's Rockefeller Center, and he worked for the Farm Security Administration from 1935 to 1938 as a photographer, documenting the plight of agricultural workers. Later, Shahn turned to book illustration, and during the 1950s he lectured at Harvard. He died in 1969.

Reading the Art *Where do you think the three girls in this painting are going? What can you infer about the town or city in which East Twelfth Street is located?*

THE LANGUAGE OF LITERATURE **Teacher's Edition** 175

UNIT TWO
Part 1 Skills Trace

(ML) DENOTES MINI-LESSON IN TEACHER'S EDITION

Selections	Reading Skills and Strategies	Literary Concepts	Writing Opportunities	Speaking, Listening, and Viewing
FICTION **The Day the Cisco Kid Shot John Wayne** Nash Candelaria		Point of view, PE p. 194 First-person point of view, PE p. 194 Characterization, (ML) TE p. 191	Write about a favorite action hero, PE p. 177 Write a movie review, PE p. 193 Personal narrative, PE p. 193 Create a dialogue, PE p. 193 Comparison/contrast essay, PE p. 193 Getting started to capture reader's interest, (ML) TE p. 179	Small group discussion about conflicts, PE p. 193 Critical viewing, (ML) TE p. 185 Discussion using chart with headings *Preconceptions, Conflicts,* and *Resolution,* TE p. 193
FICTION **Grover Dill and the Tasmanian Devil** Jean Shepherd	Visualizing, PE p. 196	Imagery, PE p. 206 Conflict, (ML) TE p. 202	Write a self-help guide, PE p. 206 Write a police report, PE p. 206 Continue the story with another episode, PE p. 206 Outline conflict, PE p. 206 Varying sentence beginnings, (ML) TE p. 204 Write a humorous monologue, TE p. 207	Oral report, PE p. 207 Dramatic reading, (ML) TE p. 205 View movie *A Christmas Story* and compare/contrast, TE p. 207 Perform humorous monologue, TE p. 207
POETRY **Battle Report** Bob Kaufman **Training/Entrenamiento** Demetrio Herrera	Figurative language, PE p. 209	Extended metaphor, PE p. 213 Pun, PE p. 213 Free verse, (ML) TE p. 209	Make a list, PE p. 213 Write a poem, PE p. 213 Create a crossword puzzle, PE p. 213 Create broadsides for both poems, PE p. 213 Personification, (ML) TE p. 212	Dramatic reading, PE p. 214 Oral report on history of jazz, TE p. 214 Oral report on history of boxing, TE p. 214
FICTION **The Euphio Question** Kurt Vonnegut, Jr.	Understanding satire, PE p. 215 Using a reading log, PE p. 215	Theme, PE p. 231 Flashback, PE p. 231 First-person point of view, (ML) TE p. 218 Fiction, (ML) TE p. 220	Write a set of science notes, PE p. 230 Epilogue, PE p. 230 Write a radio commercial, PE p. 230 Sensory details, (ML) TE p. 226	Small group discussion, PE p. 230 Debate pros and cons of scientific research, PE p. 231 Debate with FCC members, PE p. 231 Viewing art composition, (ML) TE p. 221 Readers theater, (ML) TE p. 222 Interviewing, (ML) TE p. 224
NONFICTION ON YOUR OWN **Brothers Are the Same** Beryl Markham			Reading log entries, TE p. 233	Paired reading, TE p. 233 Preparing an oral report, TE p. 241 Telling a story, TE p. 242
Writing	Reading Skills and Strategies	Literary Concepts	Writing Opportunities	Speaking, Listening, and Viewing
WRITING ABOUT LITERATURE **Direct Response**	Understanding elaboration, PE pp. 244–245 Responding to literature, PE pp. 246–249	Understanding elaboration, PE pp. 244–245 Details, PE pp. 246–249	Using examples, PE p. 245 Including facts, PE p. 245 Using a quotation, PE p. 245 Personal response essay, PE pp. 246–249 Coherence in paragraphs, PE p. 247	View a situation, PE p. 250 Interpret a situation, PE p. 250 Discussion, PE p. 250 Discussing overgeneralizations, PE p. 251

Grammar, Usage, Mechanics, and Spelling	Multimodal Learning	Research and Study Skills	Vocabulary	
Capitalizing names of family relationships, ⓂⓁ TE p. 190	Tape-record an interview, PE p. 194 Draw a movie poster, PE p. 194	Investigate the influence of Spanish on American English, PE p. 194 Research mixing of Spanish and English in language of southwest America, PE p. 194 Using a card catalog and on-line services, ⓂⓁ TE p. 186	apprehensive audacity exasperation foreboding laggard	maliciously nonentity ominous premonition scrutinize
Action verbs and linking verbs, ⓂⓁ TE p. 201	Oral report, PE p. 207	Investigate climate and landscape of northwestern Indiana, PE p. 207 Consult encyclopedias and books in geography section, TE p. 207	conglomeration duress ferocity insurgent latent	malevolent maniacal quell retribution sham
	Select jazz recording, PE p. 214 Dramatic reading, PE p. 214 Prepare a photo portfolio, PE p. 214 Oral reports, TE p. 214 Pictures from magazines and newspapers, TE p. 214			
The dash, ⓂⓁ TE p. 217	Debate pros and cons of scientific research, PE p. 231 Create a model of euphio machine, PE p. 231 Debate with FCC members, PE p. 231 Announcement, PE p. 231 Art composition, ⓂⓁ TE p. 221 Readers theater, ⓂⓁ TE p. 222 Interviewing, ⓂⓁ TE p. 224	Research scientific research, e.g., genetic engineering and drugs, PE p. 231	adversity apathetically exploitation invincible maudlin	monopoly oblivion synthetic unscrupulous void
	Character chart, TE p. 233 Preparing oral report, TE p. 241 Telling a story, TE p. 242	Preparing an oral report, TE p. 241		

Grammar, Usage, Mechanics, and Spelling	Multimodal Learning	Research and Study Skills	Media Literacy
Using specific nouns, PE p. 245 Achieving coherence in paragraphs, PE p. 245 Misplaced phrases and clauses, PE p. 249	View a situation, PE p. 250 Interpret a situation, PE p. 250 Discussion, PE p. 250 Making generalizations, PE p. 251 Discussing overgeneralizations, PE p. 251	Responding to elements, PE pp. 246–249 Analyzing situations, PE p. 251	Analyzing a situation, PE pp. 250–251

UNIT TWO
Part 2 Skills Trace

ML DENOTES MINI-LESSON IN TEACHER'S EDITION

Selections	Reading Skills and Strategies	Literary Concepts	Writing Opportunities	Speaking, Listening, and Viewing
DRAMA **The Devil and Daniel Webster** Stephen Vincent Binét	Visualizing scenes, PE p. 255	Characterization, PE p. 280 Cooperative learning, PE p. 280 Reviewing conflict, ML TE p. 258 Drama, ML TE p. 261	Write a legal brief, PE p. 279 Write a summation, PE p. 279 Write a revision, PE p. 279 Prepare a monologue, PE p. 281 Using dialogue in plays and skits, ML TE p. 257	Perform a play, PE p. 279 Present a monologue, PE p. 281 Choral reading, ML TE p. 268 Listening to speeches, ML TE p. 274
NONFICTION **You're Short, Besides!** Sucheng Chan	Understanding character, PE p. 282 Using your reading log, PE p. 282	Tone, PE p. 291 Writer's purpose, PE p. 291 Reviewing characterization, ML TE p. 284 Nonfiction, ML TE p. 288	Draft a memo, PE p. 291 List of questions, PE p. 291 Write a character sketch, PE p. 291 Using point of view in nonfiction, ML TE p. 285	Compare character sketch with others, PE p. 291 Oral report, PE p. 292 Speech, PE p. 292 Debate, ML TE p. 287 View a film, TE p. 292
NONFICTION **The United States vs. Susan B. Anthony** Margaret Truman	Understanding specialized vocabulary, PE p. 293	Biography, PE p. 304 Reviewing point of view, ML TE p. 295 Nonfiction, ML TE p. 296	Create a pamphlet, PE p. 303 Write a commentary, PE p. 303 Write a news story, PE p. 303 Draft a proposed amendment, PE p. 303 Types of elaboration incidents, ML TE p. 297	Present cartoons to class, PE p. 303 Role-play in retrial, PE p. 303 Present impersonation of Susan B. Anthony, PE p. 303 Interviews, ML TE p. 301 Retrial, TE p. 304 Impersonations, TE p. 304
FICTION **Beauty is Truth** Anna Guest		Third-person point of view, PE p. 315 Third-person limited point of view, PE p. 315 Reviewing setting, ML TE p. 307 Fiction: Short story, ML TE p. 308	Description of beauty, PE p. 305 Personal narrative, PE p. 314 Composition, PE p. 314 Draft a recommendation, PE p. 315 Using sentence fragments to reveal character, ML TE p. 311	Display artwork, PE p. 314 Dramatic reading, PE p. 315 Discussion of artwork, PE p. 315 Role-playing, ML TE p. 310
FICTION **The Cultural Worker** Sue Doro		Personification, PE p. 321 Tone, PE p. 321	Write a brief diary entry, PE p. 316 Write a comparison, PE p. 321 Write a journal entry, PE p. 321 Write a poem, PE p. 321 Write a dialogue, PE p. 321 Personification, ML TE p. 317	Small group discussion, PE p. 321
NONFICTION ON YOUR OWN **Fish Cheeks** Amy Tan			Dialogue journal, TE p. 323 Writing letters, TE p. 325	Grouped reading, TE p. 323

Writing	Reading Skills and Strategies	Literary Concepts	Writing Opportunities	Speaking, Listening, and Viewing
WRITING FROM EXPERIENCE **Persuasion**			Writing a persuasive essay, PE pp. 326–333 Drafting, PE pp. 330–331 Writing a thesis statement, PE p. 329 Revising and publishing, PE pp. 332–333	Interviewing a public official, PE p. 328 Conducting a survey, PE p. 328 Role-playing, PE p. 329 Creating a poster, PE p. 333

UNIT TWO TRIALS AND TRIBULATION

Grammar, Usage, Mechanics, and Spelling	Multimodal Learning	Research and Study Skills	Vocabulary
Correlative conjunctions, ML TE p. 271	Prepare a play, PE p. 279 Create a set design, PE p. 280 Create a poster, PE p. 280 Making a presentation, ML TE p. 276	Research one of the historical figures in play, PE p. 281 Analyzing a writing prompt, ML TE p. 273	bias — homage contemptuously — insinuatingly discordant — intimidation fanaticism — oppressor feigned — placidly
Using voice in writing, ML TE p. 286	Create a brief public health pamphlet, PE p. 292 Using work strategy and library, TE p. 292 View a film, TE p. 292	Investigate post polio syndrome, PE p. 292 Taking objective tests: Reading comprehension, ML TE p. 289 Research actual use (or absence) of quotas, TE p. 292	agnostic — inept assuage — patronizing debilitate — precocious eschew — presumptuous enamored — salient incorrigible — sardonically
Helping verbs, ML TE p. 298	Create two political cartoons, PE p. 303 Retrial of case, PE p. 303 Impersonation of Susan B. Anthony, PE p. 303 Leading a meeting, ML TE p. 300		adamant — fortitude blatant — inadvertently competent — oratory concur — retrospect denunciation — tirade
There/their/they're, ML TE p. 312	Create a collage, a montage, a mobile, or a painting, PE p. 314 Dramatic reading, PE p. 315 Fine art in magazines and books, PE p. 315	Taking essay tests: Planning your answers, ML TE p. 309 Find poems, TE p. 315	constricted — jeer dank — reproach disdain — repugnance intensity — tremulous irresolute — unconventional
Pronouns in nominative case, ML TE p. 318	Set lyrics to music, PE p. 322 Make a mobile, PE p. 322 Make an audiotape of performances, TE p. 322		
	Sketching a scene or character, TE p. 323 Role-playing, TE p. 324		

Grammar, Usage, Mechanics, and Spelling	Multimodal Learning	Research and Study Skills	Media Literacy
Using active voice, PE p. 333	Analyzing a magazine article, PE p. 326 Interpreting a news photograph, PE p. 327 Analyzing a newspaper article, PE p. 327	Conducting a survey, PE p. 328 On-line resources, PE p. 329 Periodical indexes, ML TE p. 328	Analyzing magazine article, PE p. 326 Interpreting a news photograph, PE p. 327 Analyzing a newspaper article, PE p. 327 On-line resources, PE p. 329

UNIT TWO

Recommended Resources

ENRICHMENT   RESEARCH

✓ Recommended Novels and Nonfiction

LITERATURE CONNECTIONS WITH SOURCEBOOK FOR TEACHERS

Thematic Link *Animal Farm* satirizes the events of the Russian Revolution and the years following, from 1917 to 1943. The novel is presented in the form of an animal fable. It is also a prophecy that points to a frightening future life—a life in which the boundaries between friends and foes are not clear.

About the Author Journalist, autobiographer, social critic, and novelist George Orwell (1903–1950) wrote prophetically about the dangers of dictatorial government. His aim, to "write prose like a window pane," was achieved in the clarity of both his fiction and nonfiction.

Other Works by George Orwell *Down and Out in Paris and London, Burmese Days, Keep the Aspidistra Flying, The Road to Wigan's Pier, Homage to Catalonia, 1984*

Thematic Link A boy struggles fiercely to overcome the immense obstacle of cerebral palsy and eventually takes his place among the greats of Irish literature.

About the Author Christy Brown (1932–1981) was one of 28 children born to working-class parents in Dublin. He was born unable to speak and completely paralyzed, except for the ability to wiggle the toes of his left foot. He learned to type and to hold and manipulate a paintbrush with his toes. His mind was never affected by the disease, and he became a writer of exceptional poetic expressiveness.

Other Works by Christy Brown *Down All the Days, Wild Grow the Lilies, A Promising Career*

Thematic Link Tan explores the struggle for survival in the harsh world of China before and during World War II.

About the Author Amy Tan (born 1952) received immediate acclaim for her first novel, *The Joy Luck Club*. She has continued to enjoy both critical and popular success.

Other Works by Amy Tan *The Joy Luck Club, The Hundred Secret Senses*

Thematic Link Intimate details convey the author's struggle with depression and his insistence on overcoming its debilitating forces.

About the Author William Styron (born 1925) is one of today's major authors. His realistic approach in his novels has won him the American Book Award and the Pulitzer Prize.

Other Works by William Styron *Sophie's Choice, Lie Down in Darkness, The Confession of Nat Turner*

Professional Development   TEACHING THE NOVEL

Bate, Walter Jackson. "Negative Capability," *Romanticism and Consciousness*. NY: Norton, 1970.

Dorr, Rheta Childe. *Susan B. Anthony: The Woman Who Changed the Mind of a Nation*. NY: AMS Press, 1970.

Frye, Northrop. *Words with Power*. NY: Harcourt Brace Jovanovich, 1990.

Frye, Northrop. *Fearful Symmetry: A Study of William Blake*. Princeton, NJ: Princeton University Press, 1947.

Italie, Hillel. "Her Mother's Daughter," *The Repository*. October 17, 1993.

Meyer, Michael C., and Sherman, William L. *The Course of Mexican History*. Oxford, England: Oxford University Press, 1995.

Tan, Amy. "Mother Tongue," *Emerging Voices*. NY: Harcourt Brace Jovanovich, 1993.

175e UNIT TWO TRIALS AND TRIBULATIONS

CROSS-CURRICULAR TEACHING   PROFESSIONAL DEVELOPMENT

Recommended Readings in Cross-Curricular Areas

SOCIAL STUDIES

Mexican Lives by Judith Adler Hellman (1994) Various voices describe everyday life in Mexico. Links to Nash Candelaria's "The Day the Cisco Kid Shot John Wayne."

Salem Story: Reading the Witch Trials of 1692 by Bernard Rosenthal (1993) Offers a new context for understanding the trials. Links to Stephen Vincent Benét's *The Devil and Daniel Webster*.

Theodore Roosevelt: A Life by Nathan Miller (1992) Illuminating portrayal of a man's struggle to overcome his disability and rise to the highest government position in the United States. Links to Sucheng Chan's "You're Short, Besides!"

One Half the People: The Fight for Women's Suffrage by Anne Firor Scott and Andrew MacKay Scott (1975) Informative presentation of the national struggle for women's rights. Links to Margaret Truman's "The United States vs. Susan B. Anthony."

Professional Development — CROSS-CURRICULAR INSTRUCTION

Larson, Richard. "Inservice Education: Ten Principles," *English Education.* 26:2 (May 1994) 125.

McLaren, Peter. *Critical Pedagogy and Predatory Culture.* 1995.

Meltzer, Milton. *Nonfiction for the Classroom: Milton Meltzer on Writing, History, and Social Responsibility.* 1994.

Recommended Media Resources

THE LANGUAGE OF LITERATURE

ELECTRONIC LIBRARY
CD-ROM
Additional literature selections for Unit Two can be found on the Electronic Library CD-ROM.

LASERLINKS
Videodisc, Gr. 9
See *LaserLinks Teacher's Source Book,* pages 14–15, for overview of Unit Two.

AUDIO LIBRARY
Tapes
Unit Two: Trials and Tribulations Gr. 9, Tapes 4–7: Sides A & B

WRITING COACH
Writing Coach Software: Writing About Literature—Critical Response, Persuasive Essay

OUTSIDE RESOURCES

Films/Videos/Film Strips/Audiocassettes
The Devil and Daniel Webster, video, Columbia Tristar Home Video, 1941, (109 minutes).
More Stately Mansions (Kurt Vonnegut: Welcome to the Monkey House Series), video, Beacon, 1993, (25 minutes).
West with the Night, (Beryl Markham), 2 audiocassettes, Spoken Arts, 1986.

Internet Resources
McDougal Littell Literature Center at http://www.hmco.com/mcdougal/lit

Professional Development — TEACHING WITH TECHNOLOGY

Wresch, William, ed. *Computers in Composition Instruction.* Urbana, IL: National Council Teachers of English, 1984.

Educational Technology. Educational Technology Publications, Inc., 720 Palisade Avenue, Englewood Cliffs, NJ 07032.

Sivin-Kachale, Jay. "Proof Positive: Research Says Technology Makes a Difference," *Electronic Learning.* 12:8 (May/June 1993) 14.

UNIT TWO
Professional Enrichment

Heroes Bring Literature to Life — Diana Mitchell

The information in this article can be applied to several selections in this unit that portray individuals who exhibit inner strength.

[I] started thinking about ways the concept of hero and superhero could get students thinking about and connecting to the novels and short stories they read. Couldn't students use the hero as a measure of a character's actions in a group of short stories or in a novel? After rummaging around in books about heroes and thinking of the kinds of strategies that my students respond to positively, I devised the following activities to try with my students.

PREREADING ACTIVITIES

Before we read a group of short stories (or a biography as we did in one of my classes), we listed on the blackboard all the heroes and superheroes students had heard of. Then they moved to groups and worked at brainstorming characteristics of heroes and what actions and behaviors made someone heroic.

After putting student ideas on the blackboard, we pared the list down to those ideas most students could agree with. The next day I brought in a list of characteristics I had gleaned from Chapter Five of Joseph Campbell's *The Power of Myth* (1988, New York: Doubleday). They include:

1. A hero gives his or her life to something bigger than oneself, to some higher end.
2. A hero performs a courageous act, either physical or spiritual.
3. A hero is usually someone from whom something has been taken or who feels there's something lacking in the normal experience available or permitted to members of his society.
4. A hero embarks on a series of adventures to recover what is lost or to discover some life-giving information.
5. The hero usually moves out of the known, conventional safety of his own life to undertake the journey.
6. The hero undergoes trials and tests to see if he has the courage, the knowledge and the capacity to survive.
7. A hero has to achieve something.
8. A hero's journey usually consists of a departure, a fulfillment, and a return.

I asked students to compare Campbell's elements with the list they developed the day before. They decided which of Campbell's elements they wanted to add to their list. After the class came up with a list they all generally agreed on, we were ready to apply our knowledge of heroic behavior to the characters we just read about.

USING COMIC BOOKS

Another way to go about getting students into generating a list of heroic behaviors is to use superhero comic books. Kids love to read them! I asked my ninth graders who were going to read Walter Dean Myers' *Malcolm X: By Any Means Necessary*, to bring in superhero comics they had so their classmates could read about superheroic behavior. After each student reads one comic book, groups were formed so that students could work together. The groups extracted from the comic they read the characteristics of a superhero which they inferred from the superhero's actions. Students also tried to construct a rough plot outline so they could figure out the typical journey of a superhero. One group of students also compared their class list with Campbell's elements.

WRITING A HERO'S RÉSUMÉ

A third way to get kids involved in thinking about heroes and superheroes is to have each student do a bit of research on a hero or superhero and then write that hero's résumé. They can choose a Greek or Roman god/hero, a hero from history like Harriet Tubman, a modern day hero, or a superhero. The résumé can include such items as personal data, strengths, types of jobs the hero is good at, relevant experience, education, achievements, community activities, and references. An example follows:

Superman: A Résumé

Personal data: age 29; single; no living birth parents or siblings; excellent physique, great eyes.

Strengths: x-ray vision; incredible strength; invulnerability; ability to fly; honesty; willing to fight for right; can blow out fires with super powerful breath.

Type of job desired: one that involves helping people out of tight situations and saving the good from the evil.

Relevant experience: extensive. I have videos and books that document my deeds.

Education: high school diploma; BA in journalism from Metropolis University.

Achievements: ability to blend in and be considered a regular person in spite of my superhuman abilities.

Community activities: saved the city from disaster several times.

References: Lois Lane, reporter; and Perry White, editor of *The Daily Planet*.

When students have finished doing these résumés, they could then be asked which characters or stories could use the talents of their hero. For instance, many of the parishioners in "The Minister's Black Veil" by Nathaniel Hawthorne would probably like to ask Superman to peer through the veil and tell them about the expressions on the minister's face and in his eyes. Or perhaps he would be a welcome addition to "The Outcasts of Poker Flat" by Bret Harte: With his powerful breath, he could blow a path through the snow to the next town. It would be interesting to talk about how the story would have changed through such intervention and how it would have affected the characters.

OTHER ACTIVITIES

But no matter which of these strategies you use, the important thing is to get students involved in thinking about heroic behavior. Then armed with the lists or the résumés, students can deal with the literature they have read in any of the following ways:

1. Which hero would a character most admire? Explain. Which heroic characteristics would a specific character like Jay Gatsby from *The Great Gatsby* most want?
2. What superhero or hero could have helped a character? For instance, could any of the heroes have prevented Malcolm X from becoming involved in petty criminal activities?
3. If you could add a hero or superhero to the story just read, which one would you add? What would you like that hero to accomplish or change in the story?
4. List the most admirable traits of heroes such as unselfishness, dedication, courage. Rank characters in short stories or novels on these characteristics, using one as the highest achiever and five as no achievement in this area.
5. What are a specific character's "dragons" or "monsters"? What is the character struggling against? Do they have the heroic qualities necessary to satisfactorily meet and conquer their monster?
6. Which of the characters just read about seem most heroic/least heroic? What did they achieve/fail to achieve? Which made them heroic/not heroic?
7. A hero's journey usually involves a going away, going through a series of tests and trials, and returning changed or having accomplished something. Look carefully at the characters you just read about. Could any of them be thought of as going on a heroic journey?
8. In the days of old, courage involved performing dangerous physical deeds. Today courage is usually seen in everyday actions like standing up for someone getting picked on where the person risks rejection for the deed done. Look back at the stories or novel just finished and think about which deed or action you consider to be the most courageous. Describe the action and explain why you found it courageous.
9. After reading several short stories or a novel, create a HELP WANTED poster advertisement for the kind of person most needed in the story. Cut a picture from a magazine showing a person who represents the heroic qualities you are seeking. In several paragraphs, describe what attributes this hero has and why he is so badly needed in the story.
10. Who would specific characters have as their heroes/heroines? Describe the characteristics they would pick and why these are important to them.

> Heroes provide an effective avenue for drawing students deeper into literature....

Once the idea of heroic behavior has been introduced into the English language arts classroom, heroes provide another effective avenue for drawing students deeper into literature and do indeed help bring this literature to life.

Copyrighted material reprinted wih permission.

UNIT TWO
Starting Points for Unit Projects

The following suggestions will help you initiate individual and group projects during the course of this unit.

Designing and Creating a Humorous T-Shirt

ART PROJECT Have students design humorous T-shirts that complete the saying "When the going gets tough . . ." Their sayings and illustrations should be funny but should also contain a grain of serious advice for surviving tough times.

Compiling a Bibliography with Reviews

GROUP RESEARCH PROJECT Have the whole class use your library card catalog or computer search services to compile a bibliography of recently published novels that deal with the issue of friendship. Each student can then read one book and contribute a capsule review to the annotated bibliography, which can be distributed to all students.

Publishing a Directory of Social Services

CIVICS PROJECT Have students research government and volunteer programs available in your community to help individuals and families in crisis or people with disabilities. Have them compile a directory of such services and publish it in the school or community newspaper.

Creating a Poster or Collage

ART PROJECT Have students work individually or in small groups to create a poster or collage to illustrate Amy Tan's mother's advice: "You must be proud you are different. The only shame is to have shame." To prepare for this activity, students can discuss people or events in their own lives or in books and films.

Compiling a Book of Mini-Biographies

HISTORY PROJECT Have students research and compile a book of mini-biographies of people who triumphed over adversity to achieve success. Possibilities include Christy Brown, Jackie Robinson, Helen Keller, Eleanor Roosevelt, Loretta Lynn, and less well-known figures from students' own lives.

Writing a Series of Poems and Songs

GROUP RESEARCH PROJECT Have a group of students interview people in various kinds of jobs to find out what kinds of day-to-day struggles the workers face—and how they cope with these difficulties. Students can use the interviews as the basis of a series of poems and/or songs about challenges in the workplace.

Family and Community Involvement

Family

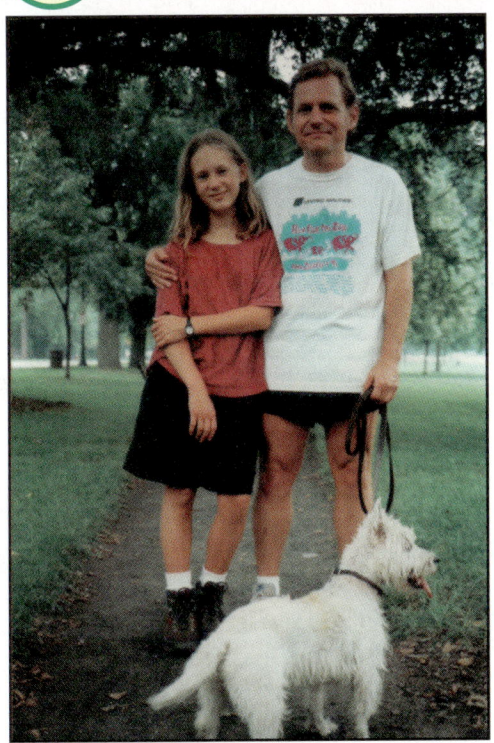

The selections in Unit Two introduce people who thrive on challenge, who find clever ways to solve problems, and who have the inner strength to keep trying against all odds. The following activities will help students and their families explore human ingenuity and spirit.

OPTION 1: WRITE AN OPINION

- **Connection** The selections in Unit Two deal with conflicts and resolving them.
- **Activity** *Copymaster 1* Students can work with family members to study a world, national, or local conflict through newspaper and television reports. Together, they can identify the problem and then share their viewpoints and opinions on the suggested solutions. They should tell which solution they feel would work best and why.

OPTION 2: INTERVIEW A FAMILY MEMBER

- **Connection** Some of the selections in Unit Two explore the special skills, talents, and interests that have led people out of difficult situations.
- **Activity** *Copymaster 2* Students can interview family members and discuss the talents, skills, and interests they feel they or other family members have. Interviews may be written or tape recorded.

OPTION 3: WATCH A VIDEO

- **Connection** Some of the selections in Unit Two relate how people have struggled and sometimes succeeded against overwhelming challenges.
- **Activity** *Copymaster 3* Students and family members should watch the movie version of Amy Tan's *The Joy Luck Club*. After viewing the film, they can discuss the challenges met by the people in the film and the traits that allowed them to keep trying against all odds.

Community

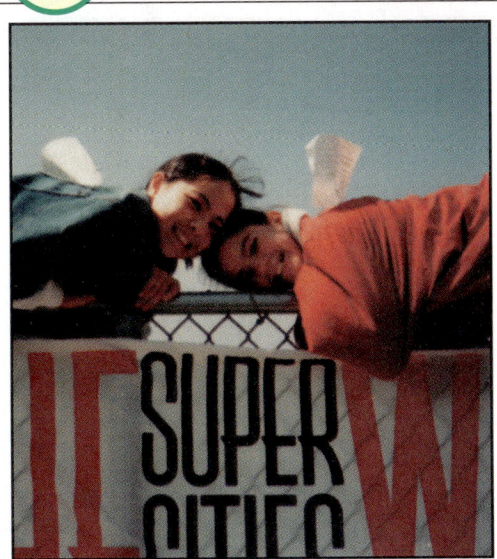

OPTION 1

- **Connection** The selections in Unit Two deal with people facing conflicts.
- **Activity** Invite students as a class or in groups to develop guidelines for a peer intercession group to help students who have conflicts with peers.

OPTION 2

- **Connection** Some of the selections in Unit Two deal with possible conflicts and dangers posed by mass media.
- **Activity** Arrange for students to visit a local radio or TV station, or invite a representative to speak to the class about FCC rules that regulate what can be broadcast.

OPTION 3

- **Connection** "You're Short, Besides!" deals with the trials and tribulations encountered by a woman with disabilities.
- **Activity** Invite a disabled person or spokesperson for people with disabilities to talk to the class.

UNIT TWO
Part 1 Lesson Planner

TIME ALLOTMENTS SHOWN ARE APPROXIMATE. DEPENDING ON YOUR GOALS AND THE NEEDS OF YOUR STUDENTS, YOU MAY WISH TO ALLOW MORE OR LESS TIME FOR CERTAIN PORTIONS OF THE LESSON.

Table of Contents	Discussion	Previewing the Selection	Reading the Selection
PART OPENER **Friend or Foe?** page 174	**20 MINUTES** • Reflect on the part theme		
SELECTION **The Day the Cisco Kid Shot John Wayne** page 178 AVERAGE		**20 MINUTES** • PERSONAL CONNECTION • CULTURAL CONNECTION • WRITING CONNECTION	**60 MINUTES** • Introduce vocabulary • Read pp. 178–192 (15 pp.)
SELECTION **Grover Dill and the Tasmanian Devil** page 197 EASY		**20 MINUTES** • PERSONAL CONNECTION • SCIENCE CONNECTION • READING CONNECTION: Visualizing	**40 MINUTES** • Introduce vocabulary • Read pp. 197–205 (9 pp.)
SELECTIONS **Battle Report** **Training/Entrenamiento** page 210 CHALLENGING		**20 MINUTES** • PERSONAL CONNECTION • CULTURAL CONNECTION • READING CONNECTION: Looking closely at figurative language	**10 MINUTES** • Read pp. 210–212 (3 pp.)
SELECTION **The Euphio Question** page 216 CHALLENGING		**20 MINUTES** • PERSONAL CONNECTION • SCIENCE CONNECTION • READING CONNECTION: Understanding satire/Using a reading log	**60 MINUTES** • Introduce vocabulary • Read pp. 216–229 (14 pp.)
FICTION ON YOUR OWN **Brothers Are the Same** page 233 CHALLENGING			**40 MINUTES** • Read pp. 233–243 (11 pp.)
Writing			
WRITING ABOUT LITERATURE **Direct Response**	**25 MINUTES**	**20 MINUTES**	**40 MINUTES**

Time estimates assume in-class work. You may wish to assign some of these stages as homework.

UNIT TWO TRIALS AND TRIBULATIONS

Responding to the Selection

FROM PERSONAL RESPONSE TO CRITICAL ANALYSIS	OR	ANOTHER PATHWAY	LITERARY CONCEPTS	QUICKWRITES
40 MINUTES			
• Discussion questions	OR	• Cooperative learning (character conflicts)	• Point of view	• Comparison/contrast chart • Movie review • Personal narrative
60 MINUTES			
• Discussion questions	OR	• Cooperative learning (outline conflict)	• Imagery	• Paragraph • Essay • Description
30 MINUTES			
• Discussion questions	OR	• Cooperative learning (broadsides)	• Extended metaphor • Pun	• List • Poem • Crossword puzzle
50 MINUTES			
• Discussion questions	OR	• Cooperative learning (proposals)	• Theme • Flashback	• Science notes • Epilogue • Radio

Extension Activities

ALTERNATIVE ACTIVITIES	LITERARY LINKS	CRITIC'S CORNER	THE WRITER'S STYLE	ACROSS THE CURRICULUM	ART CONNECTION	WORDS TO KNOW	BIOGRAPHY
50 MINUTES								
✔	✔	✔	✔	LANGUAGES		✔	✔
30 MINUTES								
	✔		✔	GEOGRAPHY		✔	✔
20 MINUTES								
✔		✔			✔		✔
50 MINUTES								
✔		✔	✔	SCIENCE	✔	✔	✔

Publishing and Reflecting
20 MINUTES

Grammar in Context
20 MINUTES

Reading the World
30 MINUTES

PART 1

REFLECTING ON THEME

Read this paragraph aloud to students. Then have them consider a friend or foe who has strongly influenced them. Have them write a short essay, describing this relationship and how it affected them. They should save their writing for later development into a piece for their portfolio.

What Do You Think?

Make sure that all students contribute ideas to the discussion. One student can keep the written chart, and another can serve as spokesperson, presenting results to the class.

UNIT TWO **PART 1**

FRIEND OR FOE?

REFLECTING ON THEME

Have you ever been confused about who your friends and your enemies are? Maybe you know someone who you thought was your friend but who ended up being your enemy. Maybe a person who you thought did not like you ended up being your best friend. As you read this part of Unit Two, think about the power of friendship and the ways in which friends influence our lives.

What Do You Think? With a small group of classmates, create a two-column chart. In the left-hand column, list qualities that you think a good friend should have, such as honesty and loyalty. In the right-hand column, list qualities that come to mind when you think of a foe, or enemy, such as being stuck-up or a bully. Compare your list with those of other groups, and discuss what the lists have in common.

Qualities of a good friend	Qualities of an enemy
• honesty	• stuck-up
• loyalty	• bully

Author	Title	Page
Nash Candelaria	**The Day the Cisco Kid Shot John Wayne** *Can someone be both a friend and a foe at the same time?*	177
William Blake	**A Poison Tree**/INSIGHT *Beware the danger of hidden anger.*	192
Jean Shepherd	**Grover Dill and the Tasmanian Devil** *This Tasmanian devil is definitely not a cartoon character.*	196
Amy Lowell	**Fireworks**/INSIGHT *Emotional sparks fly between two foes.*	205
Bob Kaufman	**Battle Report** *A city comes under attack from—the sound of jazz?*	208
Demetrio Herrera	**Training/Entrenamiento** *The sea beats up on some little boats.*	208
Kurt Vonnegut, Jr.	**The Euphio Question** *A town discovers the ultimate escape.*	215
Beryl Markham	**Brothers Are the Same** *Two warriors, a lion, and a girl*	233

176 UNIT TWO PART 1: FRIEND OR FOE?

176 THE LANGUAGE OF LITERATURE **TEACHER'S EDITION**

PREVIEWING

FICTION

The Day the Cisco Kid Shot John Wayne
Nash Candelaria

Activating Prior Knowledge
PERSONAL CONNECTION

The Mexican-American narrator of this story reminisces about popular action heroes in movies he saw in his youth. Think of action heroes you've seen in the past ten years—in TV shows, video games, and comic books as well as in movies. With a small group of classmates, make a list of these action heroes and briefly describe what they are known for or what makes them unique. Use a chart, like the one shown, to organize your thoughts. Then discuss your ideas with the rest of the class.

Action Heroes	Distinguishing Characteristics
1. X-Men	1. Mutant humans that protect the earth from harm
2. Superman	

©1996 Marvel Entertainment Group Inc.

Building Background
CULTURAL CONNECTION

This story takes place during the narrator's childhood in the late 1940s, when few homes had TV sets. For inexpensive weekly entertainment, children often went to local theaters on Saturdays to see action films. One science fiction adventure series was based on the comic-strip hero Flash Gordon. A popular Western series featured the fictional Cisco Kid, a Mexican bandit hero with a comical sidekick named Pancho. About 25 Cisco Kid movies were made from 1929 to 1950, and the character was played by four different actors during the life of the series. Other extremely popular action heroes were those played by the actor John Wayne, who starred in more than 200 movies, many of them Westerns and modern-war epics. John Wayne's characters were almost always unconquerable, "good guy" heroes.

Setting a Purpose
WRITING CONNECTION

Look back at the list of action heroes you made for the Personal Connection. Of all the action heroes you remember, which one did you admire the most, and why? Take a few moments to write about your favorite childhood action hero. Think about how this character may have been like you and how he or she was different from you. As you read this story, compare your feelings about your favorite action hero with the narrator's feelings about the Cisco Kid.

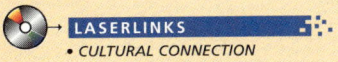
- CULTURAL CONNECTION

OVERVIEW

Objectives
- To understand and appreciate a short story that explores a child's attempts to deal with ethnic conflict
- To identify and understand first-person point of view
- To express understanding of the selection through a choice of writing forms, including a compare-and-contrast chart, a movie review, and a personal narrative
- To extend understanding of the selection through a variety of multimodal and cross-curricular activities

Skills

LITERARY CONCEPTS
- First-person point of view
- Characterization

THE WRITER'S STYLE
- Getting started

GRAMMAR
- Capitalizing titles indicating family relationships

SPEAKING, LISTENING, AND VIEWING
- Critical viewing
- Group discussion
- Oral presentation

PRINT AND MEDIA RESOURCES

UNIT TWO RESOURCE BOOK
Strategic Reading: Literature, p. 4
Vocabulary SkillBuilder, p. 5

GRAMMAR MINI-LESSONS
Transparencies, p. 37
Copymasters, p. 37

WRITING MINI-LESSONS
Transparencies, p. 54

ACCESS FOR STUDENTS ACQUIRING ENGLISH
Selection Summaries
Reading Support

FORMAL ASSESSMENT
Selection Test, pp. 33–34
 Test Generator

AUDIO LIBRARY
See Reference Card

SUMMARY

When the narrator was starting first grade, his family moved to the city. During his first day in school, he meets Chango, a tough third-grader who leads a gang called Los Indios. After a fight, the narrator earns Chango's respect. They become good friends, and the narrator joins Los Indios. The gang's most important activity is sneaking into movies. Most of the actors who play the Cisco Kid are Mexican, so the Cisco Kid is the gang's favorite character. One day a new boy named Denver moves in next door to the narrator. Denver is part of a family of poor whites from Oklahoma, and Junior nicknames him John Wayne, in the narrator's mind the natural enemy of the Cisco Kid. Los Indios ambush Denver one day, and Chango beats him up. A short time later the narrator's mother makes him take Denver to a movie with Los Indios. The narrator convinces Los Indios that Denver is an albino Indian, because the gang does not want to associate with Anglos. The narrator feels like a conqueror, surviving a conflict between Los Indios and John Wayne. Years later, he realizes that he was taking a first step into the alien Anglo world.

Thematic Link: *Friend or Foe?* Two boys from different ethnic groups start out as enemies, but shared experiences make them almost friends.

DESIGN NOTE

The title art imitates the style of an old-fashioned movie poster and depicts the character of the Cisco Kid, a Mexican action hero popular in the 1940s and 1950s.

Reading the Art *How does this poster differ from movie posters today?*

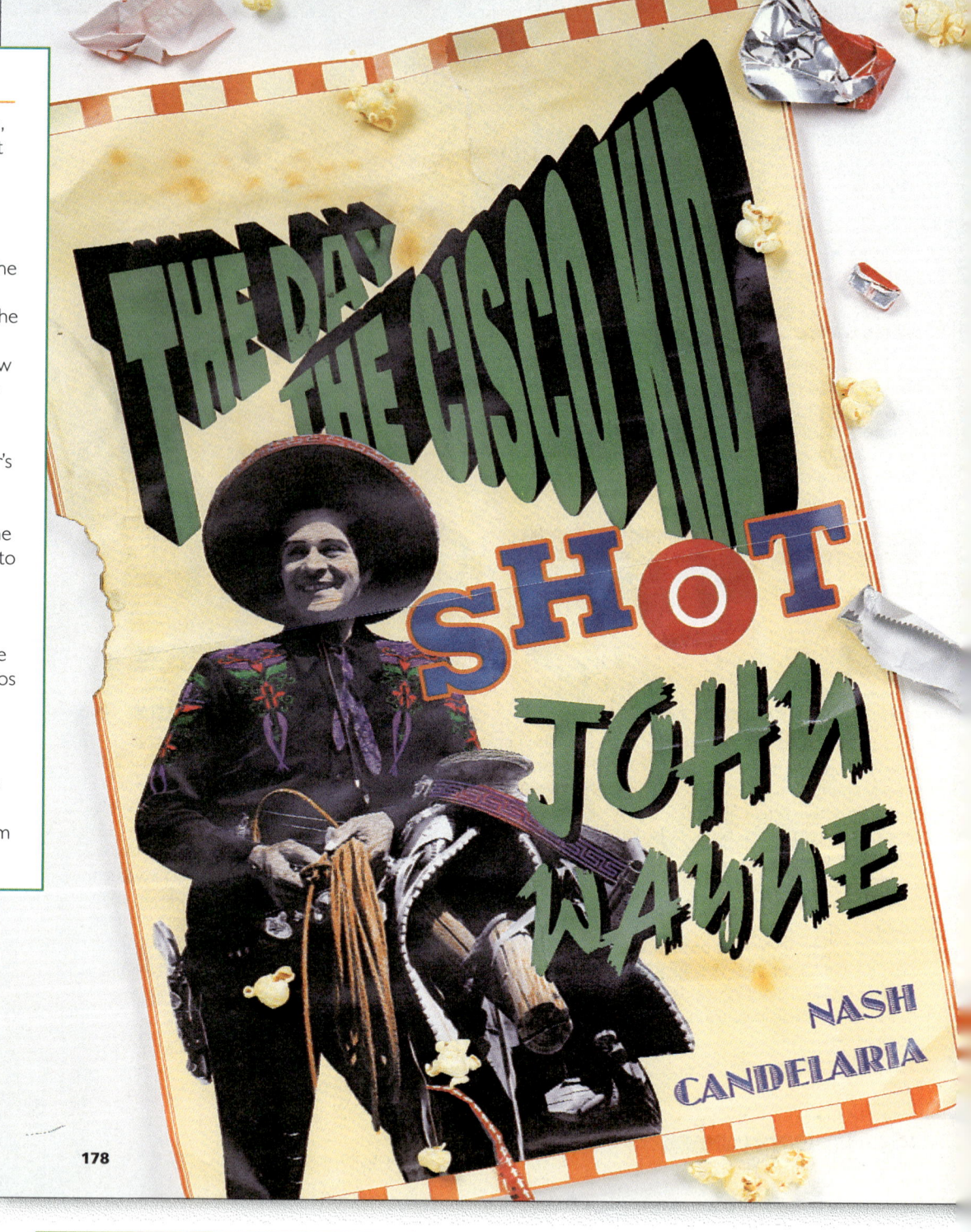

The Day the Cisco Kid Shot John Wayne

NASH CANDELARIA

WORDS TO KNOW

apprehensive (ăp′rĭ-hĕn′sĭv) *adj.* anxious or fearful about the future (p. 179)
audacity (ô-dăs′ĭ-tē) *n.* fearless daring; boldness (p. 180)
exasperation (ĭg-zăs′pə-rā′shən) *n.* the state of being frustrated or annoyed (p. 179)
foreboding (fôr-bō′dĭng) *n.* a sense of unease or fear that something bad is about to happen (p. 189)
laggard (lăg′ərd) *n.* a person who falls behind; straggler (p. 187)

maliciously (mə-lĭsh′əs-lē) *adv.* in a mean or spiteful way (p. 191)
nonentity (nŏn-ĕn′tĭ-tē) *n.* a person regarded as unimportant or insignificant (p. 182)
ominous (ŏm′ə-nəs) *adj.* threatening; menacing (p. 180)
premonition (prē′mə-nĭsh′ən) *n.* a forewarning; sense of what is going to happen (p. 182)
scrutinize (skrōōt′n-īz′) *v.* to examine or observe with great care; inspect critically (p. 191)

Just before I started the first grade, we moved from Los Rafas into town. It created a family uproar that left hard feelings for a long time.

"You think you're too good for us," Uncle Luis shouted at Papa in Spanish, "just because you finished high school and have a job in town! My God! We grew up in the country. Our parents and grandparents grew up in the country. If New Mexico country was good enough for them—"

Papa stood with his cup and saucer held tightly in his hands, his knuckles bleached by the vicious grip as if all the blood had been squeezed up to his bright red face. But even when angry, he was polite to his older brother.

"I'll be much closer to work, and Josie can have the car to shop once in a while. We'll still come out on weekends. It's only five miles."

Uncle Luis looked around in disbelief. My aunt tried not to look at either him or Papa, while Grandma sat on her rocking chair smoking a hand-rolled cigarette. She was blind and couldn't see the anger on the men's faces, but she wasn't deaf. Her chair started to rock faster, and I knew that in a moment she was going to scream at them both.

"It's much closer to work," Papa repeated.

Before Uncle Luis could shout again, Grandma blew out a puff of cigarette smoke in exasperation. "He's a grown man, Luis. With a wife and children. He can live anywhere he wants."

"But what about the—"

He was going to say orchard next to Grandma's house. It belonged to Papa, and everyone expected him to build a house there someday. Grandma cut Uncle short, "Enough!"

As we bumped along the dirt of Rafas Road toward home in the slightly used Ford we were all so proud of, Papa and Mama talked some more. It wasn't just being nearer to work, Papa said, but he couldn't tell the family because they wouldn't understand. It was time for Junior, that was me, to use English as his main language. He would get much better schooling in town than in the little country school where all the grades were in just two rooms.

"Times have changed," Papa said. "He'll have to live in the English-speaking world."

It surprised me. I was, it turned out, the real reason we were moving into town, and I felt a little unworthy. I also felt apprehensive about a new house, a new neighborhood, and my first year in school. Nevertheless, the third week in August we moved into the small house on Fruit Avenue not far from Immaculate Heart Parochial School.

I barely had time to acquaint myself with the neighborhood before school began. It was just as well. It was not like the country. Sidewalks were new to me, and I vowed to ask Santa Claus for roller skates at Christmas like those that city kids had. All of the streets were paved, not just the main highway like in the country. At night streetlights blazed into life so you could see what was happening outside. It wasn't much. And the lights bothered me. I missed the secret warm darkness with its silence punctuated only by the night sounds of owls and crickets and frogs and distant dogs barking. Somehow the country dark had always been a friend, like a warm bed and being tucked in and being hugged and kissed good night.

There were no neighbors my age. The most interesting parts of the neighborhood were the vacant house next door and the vacant lot across the street. But then the rush to school left me no time to think or worry about neighbors.

WORDS TO KNOW
exasperation (ĭg-zăs'pə-rā'shən) *n.* the state of being frustrated or annoyed
apprehensive (ăp'rĭ-hĕn'sĭv) *adj.* anxious or fearful about the future

---

Mini-Lesson The Writer's Style

GETTING STARTED Tell students that the opening paragraphs of a story or other piece of writing should grab the reader's attention immediately and make the reader want to continue reading to find out what comes next. Point out that one good way to capture reader interest is to plunge right into the story with a dramatic incident. Have students read on this page the highlighted opening paragraphs of Candelaria's story. Ask how the writer captures the reader's interest. *(Possible response: He opens with a description of a dramatic family argument, which gets the story moving quickly and establishes conflicts.)*

Application Have students think of an incident from their own lives that they could use as the opening of a short story, personal narrative, or essay. Have them write a vivid account of the incident, including dialogue.

Reteaching/Reinforcement
- *Writing Handbook*, anthology pp. 860–861
- *Writing Mini-Lessons* transparencies, p. 54

Getting Started, pp. 340–342

CUSTOMIZING FOR
Gifted and Talented Students

Have students look, as they read the selection, for reasons why the characters are or are not prejudiced. Have them jot down in their notebooks any instances that reveal prejudice on the part of the characters.

Literary Concept: FIRST-PERSON POINT OF VIEW

A Ask students what feelings the narrator has on his first day of school. *(Possible response: He feels proud but also a little fearful.)*

Literary Concept: CHARACTERIZATION

B Ask students what the narrator thinks Chango's true nature is. *(Possible responses: Chango is probably a bully; he does what he wants to do without regard to authority.)*

Critical Thinking: MAKING INFERENCES

C Ask students why Junior, the narrator, refers to the Anglos as "foreigners." *(Possible responses: He originally lived in a place where Anglos were in the minority. People who lived in the country, as the narrator had, saw few Anglos and thus considered them foreigners.)*

Critical Thinking: MAKING JUDGMENTS

D Ask students whether they think the school's rule of speaking only English in the classroom and on the school grounds is a good policy. *(Possible responses: Some students might say that the rule helps students who don't speak to learn the language faster. Others might say that in the classroom, students should try to speak English but that on the school grounds with their friends, they should be able speak their native language.)*

A I suppose I was a little smug, a little superior marching off that first day. My little sister and brother stood beside Aunt Tillie and watched anxiously through the front window, blocking their wide-eyed views with their steaming hot breaths. I shook off Mama's hand and shifted my new metal lunch box to that side so she wouldn't try again.

Mama wanted to walk me into the classroom, but I wouldn't let her, even though I was frightened. On the steps in front of the old brick school building a melee of high voices said goodbye to mothers, interrupted by the occasional tearful face or clinging hand that refused to let go. At the corner of the entrance, leaning jauntily against the bricks, leered a brown-faced tough whose half-closed eyes singled me out. Even his wet, combed hair, scrubbed face, and neatly patched clothes did not disguise his true nature.

B He stuck out a foot to trip me as I walked past. Like with my boy cousins in the country, I stepped on it good and hard without giving him even so much as a glance.

Sister Mary Margaret welcomed us to class. "You are here," she said, "as good Catholic children to learn your lessons well so you can better worship and glorify God." Ominous words in Anglo that I understood too well. I knew that cleanliness was next to godliness, but I never knew that learning your school lessons was—until then.

The students stirred restlessly, and during the turmoil I took a quick look around. It reminded me of a chocolate sundae. All the pale-faced Anglos were the vanilla ice cream, while we brown Hispanos were the sauce. The nun, with her starched white headdress under her cowl could have been the whipped cream except that I figured she was too sour for that.

I had never been among so many Anglo children before; they outnumbered us two to one. In the country church on Sundays it was rare to see an Anglo. The only time I saw many of these foreigners—except for a few friends of my father's—was when my parents took me into town shopping.

C "One thing more," Sister Mary Margaret said. She stiffened, and her face turned to granite. It was the look that I later learned meant the ruler for some sinner's outstretched hands. Her hard eyes focused directly on me. "The language of this classroom is English. This is America. We will only speak English in class and on the school grounds." The warning hung ominously in the silent, crackling air. She didn't need to say what we brown-faces knew: If I hear Spanish, you're in trouble.

D As we burst from the confines of the room for our first recess, I searched for that tough whose foot I had stomped on the way in. But surprise! He was not in our class. This puzzled me because I had thought there was only one first grade.

I found him out on the school ground though. Or rather, he found me. When he saw me, he swaggered across the playground tailed by a ragtag bunch of boys like odds and ends of torn cloth tied to a kite. One of the boys from my class whispered to me in English with an accent that sounded normal—only Anglos really had accents. "Oh, oh! Chango, the third grader. Don't let his size fool you. He can beat up guys twice as big." With which my classmate suddenly remembered something he had to do across the way by the water fountain.

"¡Ojos largos!" Chango shouted at me. I looked up in surprise. Not so much for the meaning of the words, which was "big eyes," but for his audacity in not only speaking Spanish against the nun's orders, but in shouting it in complete disregard of our jailers in black robes.

"Yes?" I said in English like an obedient

WORDS TO KNOW
ominous (ŏm'ə-nəs) *adj.* threatening; menacing
audacity (ô-dăs'ĭ-tē) *n.* fearless daring; boldness

student. I was afraid he would see my pounding heart bumping the cloth of my shirt.

Chango and his friends formed a semicircle in front of me. He placed his hands on his hips and thrust his challenging face at me, his words in the forbidden language. "Let's see you do that again."

"What?" I said in English, even though I knew what.

"And talk in Spanish," he hissed at me. "None of your highfalutin Anglo."

Warily I looked around to see if any of the nuns were nearby. "¿Qué?" I repeated when I saw that the coast was clear.

"You stepped on my foot, big eyes. And your big eyes are going to get it for that."

I shook my head urgently. "Not me," I said in all innocence. "It must have been somebody else."

But he knew better. In answer, he thrust a foot out and flicked his head at it in invitation. I stood my ground as if I didn't understand, and one of his orderlies laughed and hissed, "¡Gallina!"

The accusation angered me. I didn't like being called chicken, but a glance at the five of them waiting for me to do something did wonders for my self-restraint.

Then Chango swaggered forward, his arms out low like a wrestler's. He figured I was going to be easy, but I hadn't grown up with older cousins for nothing. When he feinted an arm at me, I stood my ground. At the next feint, I grabbed him with both hands, one on his wrist, the other at his elbow, and tripped him over my leg that snapped out like a jackknife. He landed flat on his behind, his face changing from surprise to anger and then to caution, all in an instant.

His cronies looked down at him for the order to jump me, but he ignored them. He bounced up immediately to show that it hadn't hurt or perhaps had been an accident and snarled, "Do that again."

I did. This time his look of surprise shaded into one of respect. His subordinates looked at each other in wonder and bewilderment. "He's only a first grader," one of them said. "Just think how tough he's going to be when he's older."

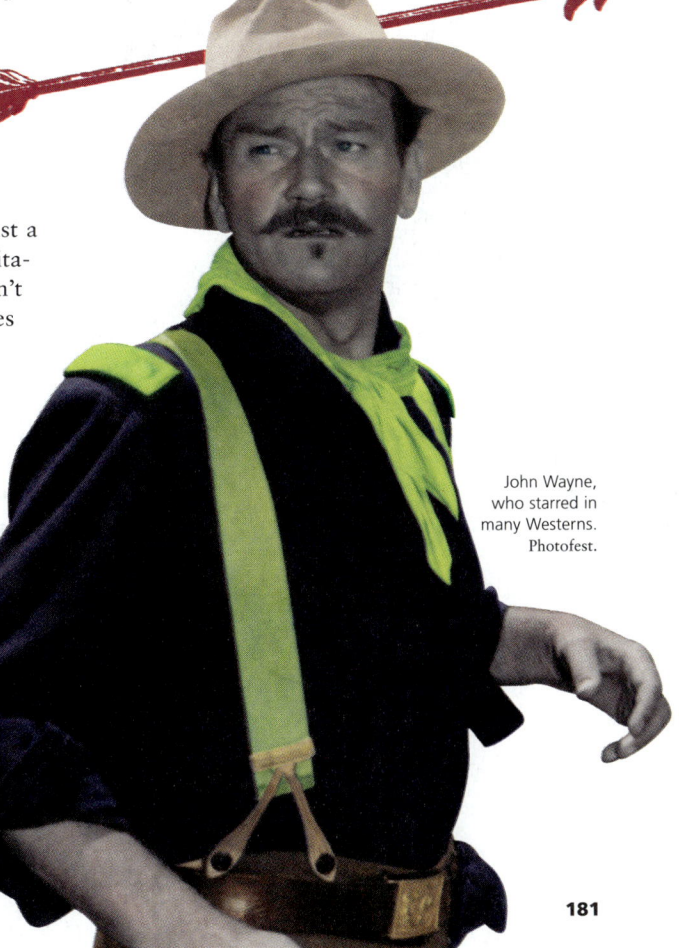

John Wayne, who starred in many Westerns. Photofest.

Literary Concept: FIRST-PERSON POINT OF VIEW

I Explain that the narrator is telling the story from his point of view. Ask students to explore some of the advantages of using the first-person point of view. *(Possible responses: It establishes a sense of intimacy with the narrator; it helps readers identify with the narrator because they always know what the narrator is thinking.)*

Critical Thinking: SPECULATING

J Ask students to speculate on why Chango asks the narrator to join his gang. *(Possible responses: Chango thinks the narrator is tough and would make a good gang member; Chango likes the narrator.)*

Linking to Social Studies

K Have students analyze what benefits the narrator attributes to being in a gang, and ask whether these are the reasons that students join gangs today. Then ask what other groups students might join that would serve similar purposes.

Buster Crabbe as Flash Gordon. Photofest.

Meanwhile I was praying that Chango wouldn't ask me to do it a third time. I had a <u>premonition</u> that I had used up all of my luck. Somebody heard my prayer, because Chango looked up from the dirt and extended a hand. Was it an offer of friendship, or did he just want me to pull him to his feet?

To show that I was a good sport, I reached down. Instead of a shake or a tug up, he pulled me down so I sprawled alongside him. Everybody laughed.

"That's showing him, Chango," somebody said.

Then Chango grinned, and I could see why the nickname. With his brown face, small size, and simian¹ smile there could be no other. "You wanna join our gang?" he asked. "I think you'll do." What if I say no? I thought. But the bell saved me because they started to amble back to class. "Meet us on the steps after school," Chango shouted. I nodded, brushing the dust from my cords as I hurried off.

That was how I became one of Los Indios,² which was what we called ourselves. It was all pretty innocent, not at all what people think of when they see brown faces, hear Spanish words, and are told about "gangs." It was a club really, like any kid club. It made us more than <u>nonentities</u>. It was a recognition like the medal for bravery given to the cowardly lion in *The Wizard of Oz*.

What we mostly did was walk home together through enemy territory. Since we were Los Indios, it was the cowboys and the settlers we had to watch out for. The Anglo ones.

---

1. **simian:** resembling an ape or a monkey. *Chango* is Spanish for a small monkey.
2. **Los Indios** (lôs ēn'dyôs) *Spanish:* The Indians. The Spanish name was chosen to indicate the group's Mexican Indian heritage.

WORDS TO KNOW
premonition (prĕ'mə-nĭsh'ən) *n.* a forewarning; sense of what is going to happen
nonentity (nŏn-ĕn'tĭ-tē) *n.* a person regarded as unimportant or insignificant

*Vaqueros y paisanos*³ were OK. Also, it was a relief to slip into Spanish again after guarding my tongue all day so it wouldn't incite Sister Mary Margaret. It got so I even began to dream in English, and that made me feel very uncomfortable as if I was betraying something very deep and ancient and basic.

Some of the times, too, there were fights. As I said before, we were outnumbered two to one, and the sound of words in another language sometimes outraged other students, although they didn't seem to think about that when we all prayed in Latin.⁴ In our parish it was a twist on the old cliché: The students that pray together fight together⁵—against each other.

But there was more to Los Indios than that. Most important there were the movies. I forget the name of the theater. I think it was the Río. But no matter. We called it the Rat House. When it was very quiet during the scary part of the movie, just before the villain was going to pounce on the heroine, you could hear the scamper of little feet across the floor. We sat with our smelly tennis shoes up on the torn seats—we couldn't have done any more harm to those uncomfortable lumps. And one day someone swore he saw a large, gray furry something slither through the cold, stale popcorn in the machine in the lobby. None of us would ever have bought popcorn after that, even if we'd had the money.

For a dime, though, you still couldn't beat the Rat House. Saturday matinees were their specialty, although at night during the week they showed Spanish-language movies that parents and aunts and uncles went to see. Saturdays, though, were for American westerns, monster movies, and serials.

Since I was one of the few who ever had money, I was initiated into a special assignment that first Saturday. I was the front man, paying hard cash for a ticket that allowed me to hurry past the candy counter—no point in being tempted by what you couldn't get. I slipped down the left aisle near the screen where, behind a half-drawn curtain, was a door on which was painted "Exit." No one could see the sign because the light bulb was burned out, and they never replaced it in all the years we went there. I guess they figured if the lights were too strong, the patrons would see what a terrible wreck the theater was and not come back.

The owner was a short, round, excitable man with the wrinkles and quavering voice of a person in his seventies and with black, black hair that we kept trying to figure if it was a toupee or not, and if it was, how we could snatch it off.

For all his wrinkles though, he could rush up and down the aisles and grab an unruly kid by the collar and march him out like nothing you ever saw. So fast that we nicknamed him Flash Gordo.⁶ We would explode into fits of laughter when one of us saw him zoom down the aisle and whispered "Flash Gordo" to the rest of us. He gave us almost as many laughs as Chris-Pin Martín⁷ of the movies.

I counted out my money that first Saturday. I was nervous, knowing what I had to do, and the pennies kept sticking to my sweaty fingers. Finally, in exasperation, Flash Gordo's long-nosed wife counted them herself, watching me

---

3. *vaqueros y paisanos* (vä-kĕ′rôs ē pī-sä′nôs) *Spanish:* cowboys and settlers. The narrator uses the Spanish words to refer specifically to Mexican cowboys and settlers, as opposed to the "Anglo ones" mentioned in the preceding sentence.
4. **Latin:** Before the 1960s, Roman Catholic church services were conducted in Latin, the language of ancient Rome.
5. **The students that pray together fight together:** an allusion to the saying "The family that prays together stays together."
6. **Flash Gordo:** a play on the name of Flash Gordon, a hero of comic-strip and motion-picture adventures in outer space. The Spanish word *gordo* means "fat."
7. **Chris-Pin Martín:** a Hispanic actor who played the part of Pancho, the comic sidekick of the Cisco Kid, in several Westerns.

Critical Thinking: SPECULATING

P Ask students what they think the narrator is planning to do. *(Possible responses: Most students will say that he is planning to open the Exit door; some might suggest that he is going to go behind the screen.)*

CUSTOMIZING FOR
Students Acquiring English

I Make sure students who speak languages other than Spanish realize that Lupe is a girl's name.

Critical Thinking: DRAWING CONCLUSIONS

Q Ask students why they think someone always complained about Lupe and Carlos if there really wasn't a Lupe or a Carlos in the theater. *(Possible responses: The kids enjoyed seeing Flash Gordo dash around the theater; it was a diversion to help other kids sneak into the theater.)*

---

like a hawk so I wouldn't try to sneak in until she got to ten, and then she growled, "All right!"

Zoom! Past the candy counter and down the aisle like I said, looking for Flash. I didn't see him until I got right up front, my heart pounding, and started to move toward the door. That's when this circular shadow loomed in the semidark, and I looked up in fright to see him standing at the edge of the stage looking at the screen. Then he turned abruptly and scowled at me as if he could read my mind. I slipped into an aisle seat and pretended I was testing it by bouncing up and down a couple of times and then sliding over to try the next one.

I thought Flash was going to say something as he walked in my direction. But he suddenly bobbed down and picked something off the floor—a dead rat?—when a yell came from the back of the theater. "Lupe and Carlos are at it again! Back in the last row!"

Flash bolted upright so quickly my mouth fell open. Before I could close it, he rushed up the aisle out of sight toward the last row. Of all the things Flash Gordo could not tolerate, this was the worst. And every Saturday some clown would tattle on Lupe and Carlos, and Flash would rush across the theater. Only later did I learn that there never was any Lupe or Carlos. If there had been, I'm sure Los Indios would have kept very quiet and watched whatever it was they were doing back there.

"Oh, Carlos!" someone yelled in a falsetto. "Stop that this minute!"

WE CRANED OUR NECKS TO LOOK UP AT THE GIANT FIGURES ACTING OUT THEIR ADVENTURES.

I jumped out of my seat and rushed to the door to let Los Indios in. By the time Flash Gordo had shined his flashlight over and under the seats in the back, we were all across the theater at the edge of the crowd where we wouldn't be conspicuous. Later we moved to our favorite spot in the front row where we craned our necks to look up at the giant figures acting out their adventures.

While the movies were fantastic—the highlight of our week—sometimes I think we had almost as much fun talking about them afterwards and acting them out. It was like much later when I went to high school; rehashing the Saturday night dance or party was sometimes better than the actual event.

We all had our favorites and our definite point of view about Hollywood movies. We barely tolerated those cowboy movies with actors like Johnny Mack Brown and "Wild Bill" Elliot and Gene Autry and even Hopalong Cassidy.[8] *¡Gringos!*[9] we'd sniff with disdain. But we'd watch them in preference to roaming the streets, and we'd cheer for the Indians and sometimes for the bad guys if they were swarthy[10] and Mexican.

They showed the Zorro[11] movies several times each, including the serials with one chapter each Saturday. Zorro drew mixed reviews and was the subject of endless argument. "Spanish dandy!" one would scoff. "¿Dónde están los mejicanos?"[12] Over in the background hanging

---

8. **Johnny Mack Brown . . . Hopalong Cassidy:** Brown, Elliot, and Autry were actors who starred in many Westerns of the 1940s. Hopalong Cassidy was a heroic cowboy character played by William Boyd in a series of Westerns.
9. *gringos* (grēng′gôs): a Spanish slang word used, principally in Latin America, to refer to foreigners or English-speaking persons.
10. **swarthy:** having a dark complexion.
11. **Zorro:** a fictional swashbuckling Spanish hero of the Old West. He wears a mask and is famous for slashing his initial, Z, wherever he shows up to battle evildoers.
12. **¿Dónde están los mejicanos?** (dôn′dĕ ĕs-tän′ lôs mĕ-hē-kä′nôs) *Spanish:* Where are the Mexicans? The narrator and his friends object to Zorro because his ancestry is purely Spanish, rather than the mixed Spanish and Indian ancestry of most Mexicans.

Critical Thinking: SYNTHESIZING

R Ask students how and why the boys in Los Indios responded differently to cowboy movies than the moviemakers had intended them to. *(Possible response: Instead of cheering for the white cowboy heroes, Los Indios cheered for the Indians because they identified with them.)* Ask students whether most movie heroes today are still Anglos. Challenge them to name movie heroes from different cultures.

STRATEGIC READING FOR
Less-Proficient Students

S Have a Spanish-speaking volunteer pronounce "¿Dónde están los mejicanos?"

Mini-Lesson: Speaking, Listening, and Viewing

CRITICAL VIEWING Tell students that heroes and villains in action movies are often flat, one-dimensional characters—entirely good or entirely evil—and that the movies set up oversimplified dramatic conflicts between good and evil to stir the audience's emotions.

Application Have students watch a videotape of an old cowboy movie. (Many are available for rental in video stores.) Have them evaluate how realistic the personalities of the "good guys" and the "bad guys" are and how realistic the outcome of their conflict is.

Critical Thinking:
DRAWING CONCLUSIONS

T Ask students why the Cisco Kid was a favorite of Los Indios. *(because most of the actors who played the Cisco Kid were Mexican, like Los Indios, and because the Kid had a sidekick who also was Mexican)*

STRATEGIC READING FOR
Less-Proficient Readers

U Make sure students understand that because the narrator gained the respect of Chango, he was invited to join Los Indios. Then ask the following questions:

- What do the narrator and the other members of Los Indios do for entertainment on Saturdays? *(go to movie matinees)* **Noting Relevant Details**

- What is the narrator's "assignment" at the movies? *(He pays for a ticket and then lets the other boys into the theater through the back door.)* **Summarizing**

- What kinds of characters do the boys cheer for in the movies? *(the Indians and the Latinos)* What kinds of characters do they disdain? *(the Anglo heroes, such as John Wayne)* **Classifying/Categorizing**

Set a Purpose Have students read on to find out how a new neighbor creates conflicts for the narrator.

Literary Concept:
CHARACTERIZATION

V Ask students what they can infer about the narrator's mother from this comment she makes to her husband. *(Possible response: She is prejudiced; without having met the new neighbors, she has prejudged and labeled them.)*

---

onto their straw sombreros and smiling fearfully as they bowed to the tax collector, I remember.

"But at least Zorro speaks the right language."

Then somebody would hoot, "Yeah. Hollywood *inglés*.[13] Look at the actors who play Zorro. Gringos every one. John Carroll. Reed Hadley. Tyrone Power."[14]

That was what Zorro did to us. Better than Gene Autry but still a phony Spaniard while all the *indios y mestizos*[15] were bit players.

That was no doubt the reason why our favorite was the Cisco Kid. Even the one gringo who played the role, Warner Baxter,[16] could have passed for a Mexican. More than one kid said he looked like my old man, so I was one of those who accepted Warner Baxter. Somebody even thought that he was Mexican but had changed his name so he could get parts in Hollywood—you know how Hollywood is. But we conveniently leaped from that to cheering for the "real" Cisco Kids without wondering how they ever got parts in that Hollywood: Gilbert Roland, César Romero, Duncan Renaldo.[17] With the arch-sidekick of all time, Chris-Pin Martín, who was better any day than Fuzzy Knight, Smiley Burnette, or Gabby Hayes.[18]

"Sí, Ceesco," we'd lisp to each other and laugh, trying to sound like Chris-Pin.

We'd leave the theater laughing and chattering, bumping and elbowing each other past the lobby. There Flash Gordo would stare at us as if trying to remember whether or not we had bought tickets, thoughtfully clicking his false teeth like castanets. We'd quiet down as we filed past, looking at that toupee of his that was, on closer inspection, old hair blackened with shoe polish that looked like dyed rat fur. *Hasta la vista*, Flash, I'd think. See you again next week.

One Saturday afternoon when I returned home there was a beat-up old truck parked in front of the empty house next door and a slow parade in and out. In the distance I saw the curious stare of a towhead[19] about my age.

When I rushed into the house, my three-year-old brother ran up to me and excitedly told me in baby talk, "La huera.[20] La huera, huera."

"Hush," Mama said.

Uncle Tito, who was Mama's unmarried younger brother, winked at me. "Blondie's wearing a halter top and shorts," he said. "In the back yard next door."

"Hush," Mama said to him, scowling, and he winked at me again.

That night when I was supposed to be sleeping, I heard Mama and Papa arguing. "Well," Mama said. "What do you think about that? They swept up the gutters of Oklahoma City. What was too lightweight to settle got blown across the panhandle to New Mexico. Right next door."

"Now, Josefa," Papa said. "You have to give people a chance."

"Halter top and shorts," Mama snipped. "What will the children think?"

"The only child who's going to notice is Tito, and he's old enough although sometimes he doesn't act it."

But then my eyelids started to get heavy, and the words turned into a fuzzy murmur.

One day after school that next week, Chango

---

13. *inglés* (ēng-glĕs') *Spanish:* English.
14. **John Carroll . . . Tyrone Power:** American actors of the 1940s.
15. *mestizos* (mĕs-tē'sôs) *Spanish:* people of mixed Indian and Spanish ancestry.
16. **Warner Baxter:** an Anglo actor who played the Cisco Kid in the first three Westerns featuring that character.
17. **Gilbert Roland . . . Duncan Renaldo:** Hispanic actors of the 1940s who played the Cisco Kid in different movies.
18. **Fuzzy Knight . . . Gabby Hayes:** Anglo actors who played the comic sidekicks of Western cowboy heroes.
19. **towhead:** a person with white-blond hair.
20. **la huera** (lä wĕ'rä) *Spanish:* the blond woman.

186 UNIT TWO PART 1: FRIEND OR FOE?

Mini-Lesson — Study Skills

USING A CARD CATALOG AND ON-LINE SEARCHES Ask students how they might locate information on cowboy heroes in the movies if they wanted to learn more about them. Tell them that libraries have card catalogs and on-line search services to help users locate the materials they need. Users can search for information by title, author, or subject.

Application Ask students what subject cards or key words they might use to locate information on cowboy heroes in the movies. (Point out that if they don't know any titles or authors, they would have to use the names of characters or actors or such key words as "Cowboy Movies.") Have students go to the library to try these search techniques.

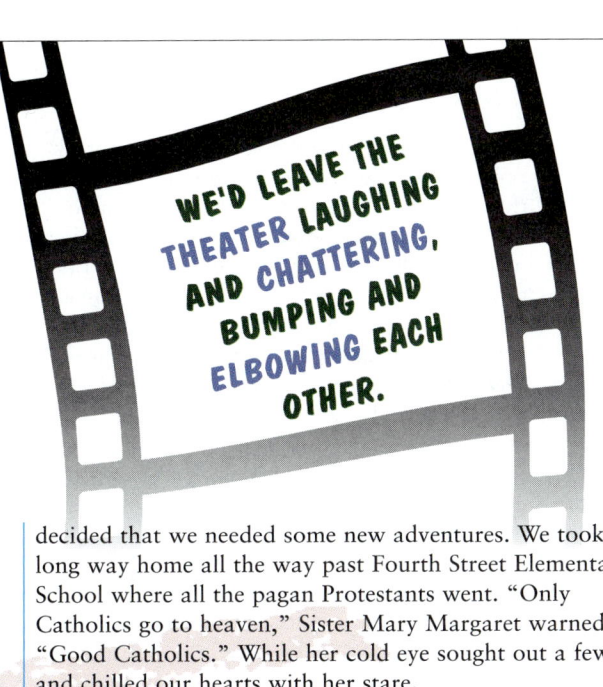

WE'D LEAVE THE THEATER LAUGHING AND CHATTERING, BUMPING AND ELBOWING EACH OTHER.

decided that we needed some new adventures. We took the long way home all the way past Fourth Street Elementary School where all the pagan Protestants went. "Only Catholics go to heaven," Sister Mary Margaret warned us. "Good Catholics." While her cold eye sought out a few of us and chilled our hearts with her stare.

But after school the thaw set in. We wanted to see what those candidates for hell looked like—those condemned souls who attended public school. And I wondered if God had only one spot left in heaven, and He had to choose between a bad Catholic who spoke Spanish and a good Protestant who spoke English, which one He would let in. A fearful possibility crossed my mind, but I quickly dismissed it.

We rambled along picking up rocks and throwing them at tree trunks, looking for lizards or maybe even a lost coin dulled by weather and dirt but still very spendable. What we found was nothing. The schoolyard was empty, so we turned back toward home. It was then, in the large empty field across from the Río Valley Creamery, that we saw this laggard, my new neighbor, the undesirable Okie.[21]

Chango gave a shout of joy. There he was. The enemy. Let's go get him! We saddled our imaginary horses and galloped into the sunset. Meanwhile, John Wayne, which

Reed Hadley as Zorro.
Photofest.

21. **Okie:** an slang term for an Anglo migrant farm worker, especially one from Oklahoma.

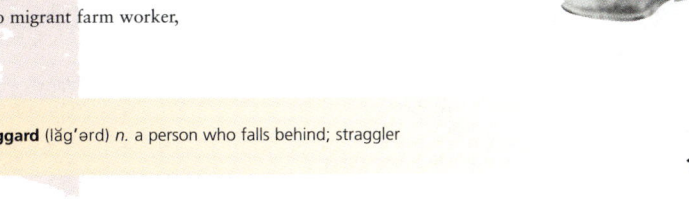

WORDS TO KNOW

laggard (lăg'ərd) *n.* a person who falls behind; straggler

Literary Concept: SIMILE

🅨 Have students examine the comparison of Denver to a wild deer. What is significant about this comparison? *(Possible response: It suggests the fear and vulnerability Denver feels.)*

Literary Concept: FIRST-PERSON POINT OF VIEW

🅩 Ask what clues the first-person narrator uses here to infer how Denver is feeling and what kind of person he is. *(Possible responses: the expression on Denver's face, his unwillingness to fight back, his running away)* Then ask students whether they accept the narrator's analysis of Denver's character. Ask how the passage might offer a different view of Denver if it were told from his point of view. *(Possible responses: Denver could explain for himself why he didn't fight back—whether it was the fear of being outnumbered, his desire to make friends, his inexperience with ethnic conflict, his inexperience with fighting, or instructions from his parents about not fighting.)*

---

was the name I called him then, turned his flour-white face and blinked his watery pale eyes at us in fear. Then he took off across the field in a dead run which only increased our excitement as if it was an admission that he truly was the enemy and deserved thrashing.

He escaped that day, but not before he got a good look at us. I forgot what we called him besides Okie gringo. In my memory he was John Wayne to our Cisco Kid, maybe because of the movie about the Alamo.[22]

That then became our favorite after-school pastime. We'd make our way toward the Fourth Street Elementary School looking for our enemy, John Wayne. As cunning as enemies usually are, we figured that he'd be on the lookout, so we stalked him Indian style. We missed him the next day, but the day after that when we were still a long block away, he suddenly stopped and lifted his head like a wild deer and seemed to feel or scent alien vibrations in the air, because he set off at a dogtrot toward home.

"Head him off at the pass!" Chango Cisco shouted, and we headed across toward Fifth Street. But John Wayne ran too fast, so we finally stopped and cut across to Lomas Park to work out a better plan.

We ambushed him the next day. Four of us came around the way he'd expect us to, while the other two of us sneaked the back way to intercept him between home and the elementary school. At the first sight of the stalkers he ran through the open field that was too big to be called a city lot. Chango and I waited for him behind the tamaracks. When he came near, breathing so heavily we could hear his wheeze, and casting quick glances over his shoulder, we stepped out from behind the trees.

He stopped dead. I couldn't believe anyone could stop that fast. No slowdown, no gradual transition. One instant he was running full speed; the next instant he was absolutely immobile, staring at us with fright.

"You!" he said breathlessly, staring straight into my eyes.

"You!" I answered.

"¿Que hablas español?"[23] Chango asked.

His look of fear deepened, swept now with perplexity like a ripple across the surface of water. When he didn't answer, Chango whooped out a laugh of joy and charged with clenched fists. It wasn't much of a fight. A couple of punches and a bloody nose and John Wayne was down. When we heard the shouts from the others, Chango turned and yelled to them. That was when John Wayne made his escape. We didn't follow this time. It wasn't worth it. There was no fight in him, and we didn't beat up on sissies or girls.

---

22. **Alamo:** a mission chapel in San Antonio, the site of a famous 1836 battle between the Mexican army and Texans seeking independence from Mexico. Although the Mexican army was ultimately victorious, the Texans who lost their lives defending the Alamo are often depicted as larger-than-life heroes. John Wayne produced, directed, and starred in the 1960 movie *The Alamo*, glorifying the defenders.

23. **¿Que hablas español?** (kě ä′bläs ěs-pä-nyôl′) *Spanish slang:* Do you speak Spanish?

On the way home it suddenly struck me that, since he lived next door, he would tell his mother who might tell my mother, who would unquestionably tell my father. I entered the house with apprehension. Whether it was fear or conscience didn't matter.

But luck was with me. That night, although I watched my father's piercing looks across the dinner table with foreboding (or was it my conscience that saw his looks as piercing?), nothing came of it. Not a word. Only questions about school. What were they teaching us to read and write in English? Were we already preparing for our First Communion? Wouldn't Grandma be proud when we went to the country next Sunday. I could read for her from my schoolbook, *Bible Stories for Children*. Only my overambitious father forgot that *Bible Stories for Children* was a third-grade book that he had bought for me at a church rummage sale. I was barely at the reading level of "Run, Spot. Run." Hardly exciting fare even for my blind grandmother who spoke no English and read nothing at all.

Before Sunday though, there was Saturday. In order to do my share of the family chores and "earn" movie money instead of accepting charity, my father had me pick up in the back yard. I gathered toys that belonged to my little sister and brother, carried a bag of garbage to the heavy galvanized can out back by the shed, even helped pull a few weeds in the vegetable garden. This last was the "country" that my father carried with him to every house we lived in until I grew up and left home. You can take the boy out of the country, as the old saying goes.[24] And in his case it was true.

I dragged my feet reluctantly out to the tiny patch of yard behind the doll's house in which we lived, ignoring my mother's scolding about not wearing out the toes of my shoes.

William Boyd as Hopalong Cassidy. Photofest.

I must have been staring at the rubber tips of my tennis shoes to watch them wear down, so I didn't see my archenemy across the low fence. I heard him first. A kind of cowardly snivel that jolted me like an electric shock. Without looking I knew who it was.

"You!" he said as I looked across the fence.

"You!" I answered back with hostility.

Then his eyes watered up, and his lips twitched in readiness for the blubbering that, in disgust, I anticipated.

"You hate me," he accused. I squatted down

---

24. **You can take ... old saying goes:** The complete saying is "You can take the boy out of the country, but you can't take the country out of the boy."

WORDS TO KNOW — **foreboding** (fôr-bō′dĭng) *n.* a sense of unease or fear that something bad is about to happen

Critical Thinking: MAKING JUDGMENTS

DD Ask students to list all the reasons the narrator has for not wanting to be friends with Denver. *(Possible responses: Denver is a blond Anglo who doesn't speak Spanish; he's a "heathen" who goes to public school; he seems cowardly.)* Then ask which of the reasons are based on prejudice and which on Denver's personality. *(Possible response: The only reason based on personality is that he seems cowardly; all the other reasons are based on prejudice.)*

Critical Thinking: INFERRING

EE Ask students whether they agree with the narrator that the only reason Denver didn't tell his parents about the ambush was that he feared the consequences. *(Answers will vary.)* Then ask what other reason, or motive, students think he might have had for not telling. *(Possible responses: a desire to be friends; a wish not to alarm his parents; a dislike of tattletales)*

STRATEGIC READING FOR
Less-Proficient Readers

FF Ask students what nickname the boys in Los Indios give Denver and how they treat him. *(The narrator calls him John Wayne. Los Indios stalk Denver, ambush him, and beat him up.)* **Summarizing**

- Ask students what embarrassing situation the narrator's parents force him into with Denver. *(They force him to take Denver to the movies with him, where the whole gang will see them together.)* **Summarizing**

Set a Purpose Have students read on to find out how Junior will handle this situation.

---

to pick up a rock, not taking my eyes off him. "Because I don't speak Spanish and I have yellow hair."

No, I thought, I don't like you because you're a sniveler. I wanted to leap the fence and punch him on those twitching lips, but I sensed my father behind me watching. Or was it my conscience again? I didn't dare turn and look.

"I hate Okies," I said. To my delight it was as if my itching fist had connected. He all but yelped in pain, though what I heard was a sharp expulsion of air.

"Denver?" The soft, feminine voice startled me, and I looked toward the back stoop of their house. I didn't see what Tito had made such a fuss about. She was blonde and pale as her son and kind of lumpy, I thought, even in the everyday housedress she wore. She tried to smile—a weak, sniveling motion of her mouth that told me how Denver had come by that same expression. Then she stepped into the yard where we boys stared at each other like tomcats at bay.

"Howdy," she said in a soft funny accent that I figured must be Oklahoma. "I was telling your mother that you boys ought to get together, being neighbors and all. Denver's in the second grade at the public school."

Denver backed away from the fence and nestled against his mother's side. Before I could answer that Immaculate Heart boys didn't play with sniveling heathens, I heard our back door squeak open, then slam shut.

"I understand there's a nice movie in town where the boys go Saturday afternoons," she went on. But she was looking over my head toward whomever had come out of the house.

I looked back and saw Mama. Through the window over the kitchen sink I saw Papa. He's making sure she and I behave, I thought.

"It would be nice for the boys to go together," Mama said. She came down the steps and across the yard.

You didn't ask me! my silent angry self screamed. It's not fair! You didn't ask me! But Mama didn't even look at me; she addressed herself to Mrs. Oklahoma as if Snivel Nose and I weren't even there.

Then an unbelievable thought occurred to me. For some reason Denver had not told his mama about being chased home from school. Or if he did, he hadn't mentioned me. He was too afraid, I decided. He knew what would happen if he squealed. But even that left me with an uneasy feeling. I looked at him to see if the answer was on his face. All I got was a weak twitch of a smile and a blink of his pleading eyes.

I was struck dumb by the entire negotiation. It was settled without my comment or consent, like watching someone bargain away my life. When I went back into the house, all of my pent-up anger exploded. I screamed and kicked my heels and even cried—but to no avail.

"You have two choices, young man," my father warned. "Go to the matinee with Denver or stay in your room." But his ominous tone of voice told me that there was another choice: a good belting on the rear end.

Of course, this Saturday the Rat House was showing a movie about one of our favorite subjects where the mejicanos whipped the gringos: the Alamo. I had to go. Los Indios were counting on me to let them in.

I walked the few blocks to town, a boy torn apart. One of me hurried eagerly toward the Saturday afternoon adventure. The other dragged his feet, scuffing the toes of his shoes to spite his parents, all the while conscious of this hated stranger walking silently beside him.

When we came within sight of the theater, I felt Denver tense and slow his pace even more than mine. "Your gang is waiting," he said, and

190 UNIT TWO PART 1: FRIEND OR FOE?

 Mini-Lesson Grammar

CAPITALIZING TITLES INDICATING FAMILY RELATIONSHIPS Tell students that titles indicating family relationships are capitalized when they are used as names or parts of names. For example, in the highlighted section in the left column on this page, the words *Mama* and *Papa* begin with capital letters. Then tell students that if a family title is preceded by an article or a possessive pronoun or noun, it is not capitalized, since it is not being used as a name. Point out the highlighted examples *his mama* and *my father* in the second column on this page.

Application Have students correct the capitalization in the following sentences:
1. The narrator's Papa believed in keeping an open mind. *(papa)*
2. My little sister stood beside aunt Tillie. *(Aunt)*

Reteaching/Reinforcement
- *Grammar Handbook*, anthology p. 927
- *Grammar Mini-Lessons* copymasters p. 37, transparencies p. 37

Family Relationships, p. 750

I swear he started to tremble.

What a chicken, I thought. "You're with me," I said. But then he had reminded me. What would I tell Chango and the rest of Los Indios?

They came at us with a rush. "What's he doing here?" Chango snarled.

I tried to explain. They deflected my words and listened instead to the silent fear they heard as they <u>scrutinized</u> Denver. My explanation did not wash, so I tried something in desperation.

"He's not what you think," I said. Skepticism and disbelief. "Just because he doesn't understand Spanish doesn't mean he can't be one of us." Show me! Chango's expression said. "He's—he's—," my voice was so loud that a passerby turned and stared. "He's an Indian from Oklahoma," I lied.

"A blond Indian?" They all laughed.

My capacity for lying ballooned in proportion to their disbelief. I grew indignant, angry, self-righteous. "Yes!" I shouted. "An albino Indian!"

The laughs froze in their throats, and they looked at each other, seeing their own doubts mirrored in their friends' eyes. "Honest to God?" Chango asked.

"Honest to God!"

"Does he have money?"

Denver unfolded a sweaty fist to show the dime in his palm. Chango took it quickly, like a rooster pecking a kernel of corn. "Run to the dime store," he commanded the fastest of his lackeys. "Get that hard candy that lasts a long time. And hurry. We'll meet you in the back."

Denver's mouth fell open, but not a sound emerged. "When we see him running back," Chango said to me, "you buy the ticket and let us in." Then he riveted his suspicious eyes on Denver and said, "Talk Indian."

I don't remember what kind of gibberish

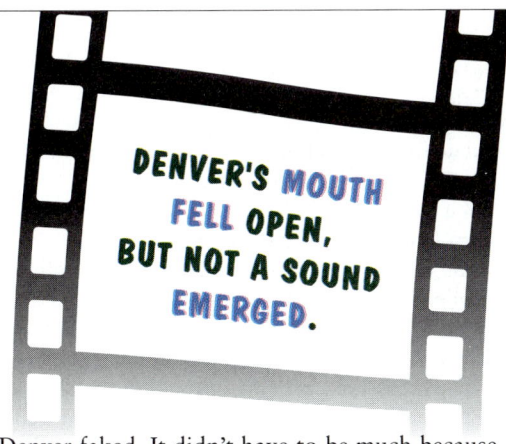

DENVER'S MOUTH FELL OPEN, BUT NOT A SOUND EMERGED.

Denver faked. It didn't have to be much because our runner had dashed across the street and down the block and was already sprinting back.

Our seven-for-the-price-of-one worked as always. When the theater was dark, we moved to our favorite seats. In the meantime, I had drawn Denver aside and <u>maliciously</u> told him he had better learn some Spanish. When we came to the crucial part of the movie, he had to shout what I told him.

It was a memorable Saturday. The hard sugar candy lasted through two cartoons and half of the first feature. We relived the story of the Alamo again—we had seen this movie at least twice before, and we had seen other versions more times than I can remember. When the crucial, climactic attack began, we started our chant. I elbowed Denver to shout what I had taught him.

"¡Maten los gringos!" Kill the gringos! Then others in the audience took up the chant, while Flash Gordo ran around in circles trying to shush us up.

I sat in secret pleasure, a conqueror of two worlds. To my left was this blond Indian shouting heresies[25] he little dreamed of, while I was already at least as proficient in English as

---

25. **heresies** (hĕr´ĭ-sēz): opinions contrary to the beliefs or interests of the group to which one belongs.

WORDS TO KNOW
scrutinize (skrōōt´n-īz´) v. to examine or observe with great care; inspect critically
maliciously (mə-lĭsh´əs-lē) adv. in a mean or spiteful way

CUSTOMIZING FOR
Less-Proficient Readers

HH Have students summarize what Junior says to get the other boys to accept Denver and what Denver does to play along. *(Possible response: Junior says that Denver is an albino Indian, then Denver "talks Indian" by uttering some gibberish.)* **Summarizing**

Literary Element: METAPHOR

II Ask students to examine the comparison of the narrator as a six-year-old to a chick breaking out of its shell. Ask them what this comparison suggests about the narrator. *(Possible response: that as he grew older, he tried hard to break away from his early ideas about people)*

COMPREHENSION CHECK

Ask students to respond true or false to the following statements.
1. When the narrator moves to the city, he starts the sixth grade. *(F)*
2. The narrator becomes a member of Los Indios. *(T)*
3. The narrator's hero is John Wayne. *(F)*
4. Los Indios do not accept Denver, the narrator's new Anglo neighbor. *(F)*

EDITOR'S NOTE With the permission of the author or copyright holder, potentially offensive material has been deleted from the selection.

INSIGHT

1. What happens when the speaker tells his friend he is angry? *(His anger ends.)* What happens when he does not express his anger? *(It grows.)*
2. How do you think the boys in the story would respond to the message in the poem? *(Possible response: Unlike the speaker in the poem, Los Indios do express their anger at their enemies. Also unlike the speaker, Los Indios are more likely to make friends with their enemies after expressing their anger.)*

---

he. On my right were my fellow tribesmen who had accepted my audacious lie and welcomed this albino redskin into our group.

But memory plays its little tricks. Years later, when I couldn't think of Denver's name, I would always remember the Alamo—and John Wayne. There were probably three or four movies about that infamous mission, but John Wayne's was the one that stuck in my mind. Imagine my shock when I learned that his movie had not been made until 1960, by which time I was already through high school, had two years of college, and had gone to work. There was no way we could have seen the John Wayne version when I was in the first grade.

Looking back, I realized that Wayne, as America's gringo hero, was forever to me the bigoted Indian hater of *The Searchers*[26] fused with the deserving victim of the attacking Mexican forces at the Alamo—the natural enemy of the Cisco Kid.

Another of my illusions shattered hard when I later learned that in real life Wayne had married a woman named Pilar or Chata or maybe both. That separated the man, the actor, from the characters he portrayed and left me in total confusion.

But then life was never guaranteed to be simple. For I saw the beak of the chick I was at six years old pecking through the hard shell of my own preconceptions. Moving into an alien land. First hating, then becoming friends with aliens like my blond Indian Okie friend, Denver, and finally becoming almost an alien myself. ❖

---

26. ***The Searchers:*** a 1956 John Wayne movie.

INSIGHT

A Poison Tree
WILLIAM BLAKE

I was angry with my friend;
I told my wrath,[1] my wrath did end.
I was angry with my foe:
I told it not, my wrath did grow.

5 And I watered it in fears,
Night & morning with my tears:
And I sunnéd it with smiles,
And with soft deceitful[2] wiles.[3]

And it grew both day and night.
10 Till it bore an apple bright.
And my foe beheld it shine,
And he knew that it was mine.

And into my garden stole,
When the night had veiled the pole;
15 In the morning glad I see;
My foe outstretched beneath the tree.

---
1. **wrath** (răth): forceful anger; rage.
2. **deceitful** (dĭ-sēt′fəl): deliberately misleading.
3. **wiles** (wīlz): tricks used to lure someone.

Duncan Renaldo as the Cisco Kid and Leo Carrillo as Pancho. Photofest.

WILLIAM BLAKE

William Blake (1757–1827) was an English poet, painter, and illustrator. In his poems, he often created his own personal mythology and symbolism based on mystical visions he had throughout his life. Blake is best known for his collections *Songs of Innocence* and *Songs of Experience*.

RESPONDING OPTIONS

FROM PERSONAL RESPONSE TO CRITICAL ANALYSIS

REFLECT 1. What were your thoughts after you finished reading this story? Write about them in your notebook and then share them with a partner.

RETHINK 2. Why is going to action movies so important to the boys in this story?
Consider
Close Textual Reading
- the cultural conflicts in their lives
- how they relate the action heroes to their lives
- how the action heroes influence their lives

3. Why do the boys gang up on Denver and call him John Wayne?

Thematic Link 4. Why do you think the narrator changes from regarding Denver as a foe to thinking of him as a friend?

5. By the end of the story, which characters have attempted to overcome their prejudices and which ones have not? Give evidence from the story to support your evaluations.

RELATE 6. Do you think the boys in this story are more or less influenced by action heroes than you were at their age? Think back on what you wrote before you read the story.

7. Notice the difference between the open hostility among the boys in the story and the secret hostility between the foes in the Insight poem "A Poison Tree." Explain which of these ways you think is a better way to resolve conflicts.

8. Both the narrator and Denver are subjected to violence for being different, yet they both end up being accepted. What do you think can be done to reduce the sometimes violent conflict between individuals and between different ethnic groups in the United States? Imagine some situations in which such conflict is resolved peacefully.

Multimodal Learning
ANOTHER PATHWAY
Cooperative Learning
The narrator explains that as a child, he was trying to break through the shell of his own preconceptions, or prejudices. With a small group of classmates, discuss how conflicts in the story stem from characters' preconceptions and whether they are resolved. Share your conclusion with the rest of the class.

QUICKWRITES

1. Create a **comparison-and-contrast chart** describing the similarities and differences between the situation in the story and the situation described in "A Poison Tree."

2. Think about the action heroes you discussed for the Personal Connection activity on page 177. Then write a **movie review** of a current film that has an action hero. Analyze the characteristics of the hero, the group the hero appeals to, and the reasons the hero appeals to that particular group.

3. Write a first draft of a **personal narrative** about a childhood incident in which you learned something about prejudice.

📁 **PORTFOLIO** *Save your writing. You may want to use it later as a springboard to a piece for your portfolio.*

THE DAY THE CISCO KID SHOT JOHN WAYNE **193**

QuickWrites

1. Have a volunteer read the poem aloud. Then discuss the Insight questions on page 192 of the teacher's edition to prepare students for this activity.
2. Before students write, have them work with a partner to brainstorm a list of action movies. Have partners discuss several action heroes before each of them chooses one.
3. Have students answer the following questions before they begin to write about their experience: Who was treated unfairly? What happened? How did the person respond? What was your reaction?

📁 The Writer's Craft

Critical Review, pp. 228–231
Personal Narrative, pp. 92–94

From Personal Response to Critical Analysis

1. Accept all reasonable responses.
2. Possible responses: Some students may say it gives the boys an opportunity to vent their feelings against Anglos and to cheer for Hispanics and Indians. Some will say that sometimes it even gives them a hero they can identify with. Others may say that it gives them a place to go where they are in control.
3. Possible response: The boys gang up on Denver because he has blond hair, is an Anglo, and is a new kid on the block. They call him John Wayne because they equate him with the Anglos they've seen in movies who fight Mexican and Indian characters.
4. Possible responses: Denver didn't tell his parents that the narrator helped ambush him; Denver helps the narrator convince the other boys that he's an albino Indian and he agrees to shout Spanish words during the movie.
5. Possible response: The narrator, though unwillingly at first, becomes friends with Denver; the narrator's mother tries to overcome her prejudice by encouraging her son to play with Denver; Chango and the other gang members don't try to overcome their prejudice.
6. Accept all reasonable responses.
7. Accept all reasonable, well-supported responses.
8. Accept all reasonable suggestions.

Another Pathway

Cooperative Learning Before students begin their discussion, suggest that they create a chart with the following headings: Preconceptions, Conflicts, and Resolution. Then, as the discussion proceeds, have them fill in the chart for each major character in the story. One student can clarify the main ideas that each member of the group contributes. Another can make sure that ideas are supported with details from the story. A third student can record the ideas.

Rubric

3 Full Accomplishment Students demonstrate a firm understanding of how characters' preconceptions lead to conflicts and can explain how conflicts are resolved.

2 Substantial Accomplishment Students show partial understanding of the issues involved in the conflicts but cannot explain how they are resolved.

1 Little or Partial Accomplishment Students show little or no understanding of the issues.

THE LANGUAGE OF LITERATURE **TEACHER'S EDITION** **193**

Literary Concepts

Possible responses: Advantages—Allows reader to identify closely with one character in the story and makes the story more personal; for example, in the fight scene with Chango, readers can share the narrator's feelings of apprehension and suspense. Disadvantages—Does not help reader to understand why some characters act the way they do; for example, Denver's accommodating actions are somewhat unbelievable.

Literary Links

Possible responses: Reasons for the dislike—the narrator's dislike of Denver is based on ethnic and religious stereotypes; Roseanne's ideas about Melissa are based on envy, on society's attitude toward girls who are pretty and popular, and on resistance to being forced together by their mothers.

Eventual outcomes—Both the narrator and Roseanne are thrown together with the person they dislike through circumstances beyond their control; both share an experience with this person that brings them closer together.

Critic's Corner

Accept all reasonable responses. Encourage students to respond honestly and to compare and contrast specific examples of the narrator's experience with examples of their own.

LITERARY CONCEPTS

The **point of view** refers to the perspective from which events in a short story or novel are told. A story told in the **first-person point of view** has a narrator who is a character in the story and tells everything in his or her own words. "The Day the Cisco Kid Shot John Wayne" is told in the first-person point of view. You know what the narrator is feeling and thinking, but you have to infer from the narrator's descriptions what other characters are feeling or thinking. What would you say are the advantages and the disadvantages of reading a story written in the first-person point of view? Use specific references from Candelaria's story to support your points.

CRITIC'S CORNER

Some adult readers of this story have said that it is too violent and too accepting of the conflict between different ethnic groups. Others have said that it is a realistic and sympathetic portrait of the conflicting pressures of home, school, and popular culture that are felt by many American children. What do you think? Use evidence from the story and from your own experience to support your view.

LITERARY LINKS

In "The Beginning of Something" and "The Day the Cisco Kid Shot John Wayne," each narrator has a strong initial dislike for another major character—Melissa or Denver. Compare and contrast the reasons for and the eventual outcomes of these friend-or-foe situations.

Multimodal Learning

ALTERNATIVE ACTIVITIES

1. Tape-record an **interview** with an older relative or neighbor, asking the person about his or her childhood memories of movie heroes and the influence those movie heroes had.
2. Draw a **movie poster** that could hang outside the "Rat House." Base the poster on the characters and films described in the story. If you have access to a computer, use its word-processing feature to create different sizes of type to add variety to titles, cast lists, critics' quotes and star ratings, and other typographical elements.

194 UNIT TWO PART 1: FRIEND OR FOE?

Alternative Activities

1. Encourage students to choose adults of different ages and ethnic backgrounds to interview. Help them brainstorm a list of questions to ask.
2. Encourage students to study the title art on page 178, which is done in the style of a movie poster. They can also study movie-poster art in newspapers.

THE WRITER'S STYLE

Do you think this story is funny? Thumb back through the pages and point out passages or episodes that you find humorous. Compare your choices to those of others in your class. Then think about the serious issues being addressed in the story: violence, ethnic conflict, self-esteem, and fairness. Do you think the story's humor makes light of these issues or emphasizes the seriousness of them? How does Candelaria make you laugh and think at the same time?

ACROSS THE CURRICULUM

Languages Investigate the influence of Spanish on American English. Find as many examples as you can of English words that come from Spanish. Then research the mixing of Spanish and English in the language of Americans in the Southwest today. Present your findings in an oral report.

WORDS TO KNOW

EXERCISE A Match each word on the left with its definition on the right. On your paper, write the letter of the correct answer.

1. apprehensive
2. premonition
3. exasperation
4. maliciously
5. laggard

a. in a mean way
b. fearful
c. straggler
d. warning of the future
e. frustration

EXERCISE B Ask other students to guess the following words by watching as you act out the *opposite* of their meanings. Use facial expressions, body language, and in-class props if necessary.

1. audacity
2. ominous
3. foreboding
4. scrutinize
5. nonentity

NASH CANDELARIA

Even though he was born in California in 1928 and lives there today, Nash Candelaria considers himself a New Mexican "by heritage and sympathy." Candelaria's family has a long history in New Mexico: a pioneering ancestor helped found the city of Albuquerque in 1706. Candelaria's parents were born and raised in the state, and Candelaria, while growing up in California, spent summers with relatives back in Los Candelarias, a section of Albuquerque bearing the family name.

By profession, Candelaria is a science writer, who started his career in 1948 as a chemist before turning to technical writing. However, he was always interested in creative writing. After many attempts, he finally published a novel, which became the first of four historical novels depicting the trials and tribulations of the fictional Rafa clan of New Mexico.

Candelaria published a volume of short stories under the title *The Day the Cisco Kid Shot John Wayne,* from which this story is taken. Most of the tales deal with conflicts between Hispanic and Anglo cultures. Writing about Candelaria in *The Before Columbus Foundation Fiction Anthology,* the writer Karen S. Van Hooft notes that Candelaria feels at home in both Hispanic and Anglo cultures but that "it is clear from interviews he has given that racial prejudice and his mainstream language and customs also caused him to be rejected at times by both Anglos and Hispanics."

Candelaria himself has written that he hopes to reach readers who are aware of Hispanic Americans only as a "silent minority." "I want . . . to write against stereotype in creating the characters whose stories I tell. In this competitive society, Chicanos have competed and succeeded and will continue to do so. That is part of the message I would want young people to get from my works."

OTHER WORKS *Memories of the Alhambra, Not by the Sword, Inheritance of Strangers, Leonor Park*

Extended Reading

The Writer's Style

Accept all reasonable responses. Some students may point out the humor of Los Indios cheering for the bad guys in the movies, or of the narrator's referring to Denver as John Wayne, or of accepting Denver finally as an albino Indian. Encourage students to discuss the serious issues of cultural identity, negative stereotyping, and prejudice underlying some of this humor.

Across the Curriculum

Languages Suggest to students that one starting point could be their dictionary. Many student dictionaries contain a list of Spanish-derived words under the entry "Spanish." Students could also browse through a Spanish dictionary to find words that look familiar. For further research, have them find library books about the Southwestern states, searching the indexes for references to "Spanish" or "Language." Also have them look for books detailing the development of American English.

Words to Know

Exercise A
1. b
2. d
3. e
4. a
5. c

Exercise B
Students can work in two teams, with individual team members taking turns to act out the antonyms but with the team working together to guess the other team's words.

Reteaching/Reinforcement
- *Unit Two Resource Book,* p. 5

NASH CANDELARIA

Nash Candelaria has said that his goal as a writer is "to place Hispanic North Americans in the context of U.S. history." He continues, "Some of us have been here a long time, back before the Pilgrims, and deserve better than to be considered 'foreigners' in our own country and to be dealt with as stereotypes."

OVERVIEW

Objectives

- To understand and appreciate a short story that explores the trauma a young boy suffers after a violent fight with a neighborhood bully
- To identify and understand imagery
- To appreciate examples of hyperbole
- To express understanding of the selection through a choice of writing forms, including a self-help guide and a story episode
- To extend understanding of the selection through a variety of multimodal and cross-curricular activities

Skills

LITERARY CONCEPTS
- Imagery
- Conflict

THE WRITER'S STYLE
- Varying sentence beginnings

GRAMMAR
- Action verbs and linking verbs

SPEAKING, LISTENING, AND VIEWING
- Dramatic reading
- Group discussion
- Oral presentation

SCIENCE CONNECTION

The Tasmanian Devil As this story develops, the Tasmanian devil takes on an important role. In these images students will see several images of a Tasmanian devil, and a map showing the isolated island off the coast of Australia where it lives.

Side A, Frame 49265

PREVIEWING

FICTION

Grover Dill and the Tasmanian Devil
Jean Shepherd

Activating Prior Knowledge
PERSONAL CONNECTION

Have you had any personal experiences with a bully—someone who intimidates people or pushes others around? How did you react to such a person? Share your experiences and reactions with a small group of classmates.

Building Background
SCIENCE CONNECTION

The story you are about to read describes a conflict between a bully named Grover Dill and the narrator, Ralph. As you read this story, you'll find out what part the Tasmanian devil plays. You may know the Tasmanian devil as a cartoon character, but it is also a real animal, named for its devilish-looking face and its fierce temper. The Tasmanian devil is a carnivore, or meat eater, about the size of a large cat. It lives on the Australian island of Tasmania, where it hunts small animals and feeds on any dead animals it can find.

™ and Copyright © 1994 Warner Brothers

Active Reading/Setting a Purpose
READING CONNECTION

Visualizing The process of forming a mental picture from a written description is called visualizing. As you read a story, you constantly use details supplied by the writer to help you picture settings, characters, and events. Try out your visualizing skills as you read "Grover Dill and the Tasmanian Devil." In your notebook, draw a chart like the one below. Then, as you read, jot down a few key phrases that describe the setting, the characters, and what is happening in the story. If you wish, you may draw sketches instead.

Setting, Character, or Event	Description
Tasmanian devil	beady red eyes, claws, fangs, scurrying
Grover Dill	
Northern Indiana	

196   UNIT TWO   PART 1: FRIEND OR FOE?

PRINT AND MEDIA RESOURCES

UNIT TWO RESOURCE BOOK
Strategic Reading: Literature, p. 9
Vocabulary SkillBuilder, p. 10

WRITING MINI-LESSONS
Transparencies, p. 50

ACCESS FOR STUDENTS ACQUIRING ENGLISH
Selection Summaries
Reading Support

FORMAL ASSESSMENT
Selection Test, pp. 35–36
Test Generator

 AUDIO LIBRARY
See Reference Card

 LASERLINKS
Science Connection

grover dill and the tasmanian devil

Jean Shepherd

The male human animal, skulking through the impenetrable fetid¹ jungle of Kidhood, learns early in the game just what sort of animal he is. The jungle he stalks is a howling tangled wilderness, infested with crawling, flying, leaping, nameless dangers. There are occasional brilliant patches

---

1. **fetid** (fĕt′ĭd): having a bad odor.

WORDS TO KNOW

conglomeration (kən-glŏm′ə-rā′shən) *n.* a collection of miscellaneous things (p. 204)
duress (do͝o-rĕs′) *n.* constraint by force or threats (p. 202)
ferocity (fə-rŏs′ĭ-tē) *n.* fierceness (p. 198)
insurgent (ĭn-sûr′jənt) *n.* one who rebels or revolts against authority (p. 199)
latent (lāt′nt) *adj.* present but not evident or active (p. 202)

malevolent (mə-lĕv′ə-lənt) *adj.* wishing harm to others; evil (p. 199)
maniacal (mə-nī′ə-kəl) *adj.* wild or crazed (p. 198)
quell (kwĕl) *v.* to suppress or subdue; put down forcibly (p. 199)
retribution (rĕt′rə-byo͞o′shən) *n.* a penalty or punishment (p. 204)
sham (shăm) *n.* an empty pretense; fraud (p. 198)

SUMMARY

Ralph, the narrator, tells how he discovered his Tasmanian Devil, which is what he calls the wild carnivore, the unpredictable, red-eyed killer that lives inside every man. Ralph's Tasmanian Devil first reveals itself one day when he unexpectedly runs into Grover Dill, the neighborhood bully. Dill appears out of nowhere and trips Ralph, who goes berserk. He pounces on Dill, screaming and cursing and pounding at his face. When it ends, Ralph realizes he lost control of himself. He is shocked by his swearing more than by his fighting. He fears his parents' punishment, but his mother somehow understands and shields him from his father's retribution. Ralph goes to bed, and he and the Tasmanian Devil sleep, for the time being.

Thematic Link: *Friend or Foe?* Though the action of the story concerns a fight with a bully, the focus is on the emergence of an inner violent streak that allows the narrator to briefly overcome the bully at the expense of altering his self-image.

CUSTOMIZING FOR
Students Acquiring English

- Use **ACCESS FOR STUDENTS ACQUIRING ENGLISH**, *Reading Support*.
- Students may find this selection difficult because it combines colloquial expressions, highly metaphorical language, and hyperbole in order to create a humorous effect.

STRATEGIC READING FOR
Less-Proficient Readers

Set a Purpose To help students understand the underlying metaphor of the story, have them study the photograph of the Tasmanian devil on page 197. Then have them read to find out why "Kidhood" is a jungle.

Use **UNIT TWO RESOURCE BOOK**, p. 9, for guidance in reading the selection.

Literary Note

A Prepare students for Shepherd's unique system of capitalizing words. For example, *kidhood* (a coined word), *carnivore*, *killer*, *summer*, *bully*, *nature*, and *devil* (in Tasmanian devil), are capitalized. Students should consider them part of Shepherd's hyperbolic style.

THE LANGUAGE OF LITERATURE **TEACHER'S EDITION**

CUSTOMIZING FOR
Gifted and Talented Students

Have students consider, as they read the selection, to what degree Ralph seems to be a "Killer." *(Possible responses: By the end of the story, some students will feel that Ralph seems no more vicious than anyone would be when pushed to extremes. Others may feel that his lack of control indicates a higher-than-normal degree of "Killer" instinct, as reluctant as he is to accept it.)*

Critical Thinking: ANALYZING/SPECULATING

B Point out that *milk teeth* is another name for *baby teeth*. Ask students what they think the "Great Education" is. *(Possible response: growing up and learning the ways of the world—the education that is acquired outside of school)*

Literary Concept: IMAGERY

C Ask students what words the author uses to create a vivid picture in the reader's mind of the "Carnivore," the predatory, flesh-eating mammal Ralph sees inside males. *(Possible responses: "beady red-eyed," "clawed," "scurrying")* Then ask to which of the five senses do the words appeal? *(sight and hearing)*

Critical Thinking: SUMMARIZING

D Ask students to summarize the message about life that the narrator wants to convey. *(Possible response: All male animals, including humans, have a violent streak in them just waiting to get out.)*

---

of rare, passionate orchids and other sweet flowers and succulent fruits, but they are rare. He daily does battle with horrors and emotions that he will spend the rest of his life trying to forget or suppress. Or recapture.

B His jungle is a wilderness he will never fully escape, but those first early years when the bloom is on the peach and the milk teeth have just barely departed are the crucial days in the Great Education.

I am not at all sure that girls have even the slightest hint that there *is* such a jungle. But no man is really qualified to say. Most wildernesses are masculine, anyway.

And one thing that must be said about a wilderness, in contrast to the supple silkiness of Civilization, is that the basic, primal elements of existence are laid bare and raw. And can't be ducked. It is in that jungle that all men find out about themselves. Things we all know, but rarely admit. Say, for example, about that beady red-eyed, clawed creature, that ravening Carnivore, that incorrigibly wild, insane, scurrying little beast—the Killer that is in each one of us. We pretend it is not there most of the time, but it is a silly idle sham, as all male ex-kids know. They have seen it and have run fleeing from it more than once. Screaming into the night.

C One quiet Summer afternoon, leafing through a library book, with the sun slanting down on the oaken tables, I came across a picture in a Nature book of a creature called the Tasmanian Devil. He glared directly at me out of the page, with an unwavering red-eyed gaze, and I have never forgotten it. I was looking at my soul!

The Tasmanian Devil is well named, being a nocturnal marsupial of extraordinary ferocity, being strictly carnivorous, and when cornered fighting with a nuttiness beyond all bounds of reason. In fact, it is said that he is one of the few creatures on earth that *looks forward* to being cornered.

HE WAS A YELLING, WIRY, MALEVOLENT, SNEEVILY SNIVELY BULLY.

I looked him in the eye; he looked back, and even from the flat, glossy surface of the paper, I could feel his burning rage, a Primal rage that glowed white hot like the core of a nuclear explosion. A chord of understanding was struck between us. He knew and I knew. We were Killers. The only thing that separated us was the sham. He admitted it, and I have been attempting to cover it up all of my life.

D I remember well the first time my own Tasmanian Devil without warning screamed out of the darkness and revealed himself for what he was—a fanged, maniacal meat eater. Every male child sweats inside at a word that is rarely heard today: the Bully. That is not to say that bullies no longer exist. Sociologists have given them other and softer-sounding labels, an "over-aggressive child," for example, but they all amount to the same thing—Meatheads. Guys who grow up banging grilles in parking lots and

WORDS TO KNOW	
sham (shăm) *n.* an empty pretense; fraud	
ferocity (fə-rŏs′ĭ-tē) *n.* fierceness	
maniacal (mə-nī′ə-kəl) *adj.* wild or crazed	

becoming captains of Industry[2] or Mafia hatchet men. Every school had at least five, and they usually gathered followers and toadies[3] like barnacles on the bottom of a garbage scow. The lines were clearly drawn. You were either a Bully, a Toady, or one of the nameless rabble of Victims who hid behind hedges, continually ran up alleys, ducked under porches, and tried to get a connection with City Hall, City Hall being the Bully himself.

I was an accomplished Alley Runner who did not wear sneakers to school from choice but to get off the mark quicker. I was well qualified to endorse Keds Champions with:

"I have outrun some of the biggest Bullies of my time wearing Keds, and I am still here to tell the tale."

It would make a great ad in *Boys' Life:*[4]

"KIDS! When that cold sweat pours down your back and you are facing the Moment of Truth on the way home from the store, don't you wish you had bought Keds? Yes, our new Bully-Beater model has been endorsed by skinny kids with glasses from coast to coast. That extra six feet may mean the difference between making the porch and you-know-what!"

Many of us have grown up wearing mental Keds and still ducking behind filing cabinets, water coolers, and into convenient men's rooms when that cold sweat trickles down between the shoulder blades. My Moment of Truth was a kid named Grover Dill.

What a rotten name! Dill was a Running Nose type of Bully. His nose was *always* running, even when it wasn't. He was a yelling, wiry, malevolent, sneevily snively Bully who had quelled all insurgents for miles around. I did not know one kid who was not afraid of Dill, mainly because Dill was truly aggressive. This kind of aggression later in life is often called "Talent" or "Drive," but to the great formless herd of kids it just meant a lot of running, getting belted, and continually feeling ashamed.

If Dill so much as said "Hi" to you, you felt great and warm inside. But mostly he just hit you in the mouth. Now a true Bully is not a flash in the pan, and Dill wasn't. This went on for years. I must have been in about second grade when Dill first belted me behind the ear.

Maybe the terrain had something to do with

---

2. **captains of Industry:** important leaders of business.
3. **toadies:** individuals who hang around an influential person and attempt to win that person's favor.
4. *Boys' Life:* a magazine by the Boy Scouts of America.

WORDS TO KNOW
malevolent (mə-lĕv′ə-lənt) *adj.* wishing harm to others; evil
quell (kwĕl) *v.* to suppress or subdue; put down forcibly
insurgent (ĭn-sûr′jənt) *n.* one who rebels or revolts against authority

Linking to Geography

G Have students locate Indiana on a map of the United States and identify its boundaries. With characteristic hyperbole, Shepherd depicts northern Indiana's vulnerability to weather extremes: it is far enough north to get brutally cold in the winter, far enough south to boil in the summer, and, located at the base of a huge lake, susceptible to strong air currents that sweep down the lake.

Literary Concept: IMAGERY

H Have students identify all of the imaginative comparisons the narrator uses here to describe the wind and the lake. *("like an enormous flue," "like an enormous chimney," "at the bottom of this immense stovepipe," "like the open door of a blast furnace," "sliced you to little pieces . . . diced . . . cubed . . . ground you up")* Then have students analyze the imagery in the paragraph at the top of the right-hand column on this page.

STRATEGIC READING FOR
Less-Proficient Readers

I Have students describe the "Jungle" of northern Indiana. Ask these questions:

- What is the weather like in northern Indiana? *(very cold and snowy in winter; very hot and humid in summer; very windy all the time, with blowing sand)* **Noting Relevant Details**

- In what way does the narrator show Grover Dill as a natural character for this setting? *(Possible response: Dill is portrayed as a tormentor, "another of the hostile elements" of the region, blending in with nature's irritants, such as sand, wind, stickers, heat, and cold.)* **Clarifying**

Set a Purpose Have students read on to find out what happens between Ralph and the bully.

G it. Life is very basic in Northern Indiana. Life is more Primal there than in, say, New York City or New Jersey or California. First of all, Winters are really *Winters* there. Snow, ice, hard rocky frozen ground that doesn't thaw out until late June. Kids played baseball all Winter on this frozen lumpy tundra. Ground balls come galloping: "K-tunk K-tunk K-tunk K-tunk" over the Arctic concrete. And then summer would come. The ground would thaw and the wind would start, whistling in off the Lake, a hot Sahara gale. I lived the first ten years of my life in a continual sandstorm. A sandstorm in the Dunes region, with the temperature at 105 and no rain since the first of June, produces in a kid the soul of a Death Valley prospector. The Indiana Dunes[5]—in those days no one thought they were special or spectacular—they were just the Dunes, all sand and swamps and even timber wolves. There were rattlesnakes in the Dunes, and rattlesnakes in fifth grade. Dill was a puff adder among garden worms.

This terrain grew very basic kids who fought the elements all their lives. We'd go to school in a sandstorm and come home just before a tornado. Lake Michigan is like an enormous flue[6] that stretches all the way up into the Straits of Mackinac,[7] into the Great North Woods of Canada, and the wind howls down that lake like an enormous chimney. We lived at the bottom of this immense stovepipe. The wind hardly ever stops. Winter, Spring, Summer, Fall—whatever weather we had was made twenty times worse by the wind. If it was warm, it seared you like the open door of a blast furnace. If it was cold, **H** the wind sliced you to little pieces and then put you back together again and sliced you up the other way, then diced and cubed you, ground you up, and put you back together and started all over again. People had red faces all year round from the wind.

When the sand is blowing off the Dunes in the Summer, it does something to the temper. The sand gets in your shoes and always hurts between the toes. The kids would cut the side of their sneakers so that when the sand would get too much, just stick your foot up in the air and the sand would squirt out and you're ready for another ten minutes of action. It breeds a different kind of kid, a kid whose foot is continually cut. One time Kissel spent two entire weeks with a catfish hook in his left heel. He couldn't get it out, so he just kept going to school and walked with one foot in the air. One day Miss Siefert insisted that he go down and see the school nurse, who cut the hook out. Kissel's screaming and yelling could be heard all over the school. So you've got the picture of the Jungle.

Grover Dill was just another of the hostile elements of Nature, like the sand, the wind, and the stickers. Northern Indiana has a strange little green burr that has festered fingers and ankles for countless centuries. One of the great moments in life for a kid was to catch a flyball covered with a thick fur of stickers in a barehand grab, driving them in right to the marrow of the knuckle bones. **I**

ne day, without warning of any kind, it happened. Monumental moments in our lives are rarely telegraphed. I am coming home from school on a hot, shimmering day, totally

---

5. **Indiana Dunes:** an area of shifting sand hills, swamps, and wooded ravines in northwestern Indiana, along the southern shore of Lake Michigan—now a state park and a national lakeshore.
6. **flue** (flo͞o): a pipe or channel that conveys hot air, gases, and smoke from a furnace or fireplace to a chimney.
7. **Straits of Mackinac** (măk′ə-nô′): the narrow passageway connecting Lake Michigan and Lake Huron, located in northern Michigan.

200   UNIT TWO   PART 1: FRIEND OR FOE?

Critic's ⭐ Corner

"It seemed as though the story line all of a sudden stopped in order to describe the setting of northern Indiana. This description was necessary but a little much in the middle of the story."

Ruth El-Jamal
Ninth-Grade Member
Student Advisory Board

Ask students whether they found the long description of Indiana's climate a confusing distraction from the plot. Then ask them why the writer might have included this section here.

unaware that I was about to meet face to face that Tasmanian Devil, that clawed, raging maniac that lurks inside each of us. There were three or four of us eddying along, blown like leaves through vacant lots, sticker patches, asphalt streets, steaming cindered alleys and through great clouds of Indiana grasshoppers, wading through clouds of them, big ones that spit tobacco juice on your kneecaps and hollered and yelled in the weeds on all sides. The eternal locusts were shrieking in the poplars and the Monarch butterflies were on the wing amid the thistles. In short, it was a day like any other.

My kid brother is with me and we have one of those little running ball games going, where you bat the ball with your hand back and forth to each other, moving homeward at the same time. The traveling game. The ball hops along; you field it; you throw it back; somebody tosses it; it's grabbed on the first bounce, you're out, but nobody stops moving homeward. A moving ball game. Like a floating crap game.

We were about a block or so from my house, bouncing the ball over the concrete, when it happened. We are moving along over the sandy landscape, under the dark lowering clouds of Open-Hearth haze that always hung between us and the sun. I dart to my right to field a ground ball. A foot lashes out unexpectedly and down I go, flat on my face on the concrete road. I hit hard and jarring, a bruising, scraping jolt that cut my lip and drew blood. Stunned for a second, I look up. It is the dreaded Dill!

To this day I have no idea how he materialized out of nowhere to trip me flat and finally to force the issue.

"Come on, kid, get out of the way, will ya?" He grabs the ball and whistles it off to one of his Toadies. He had yellow eyes. So help me God, yellow eyes!

I got up with my knees bleeding and my hands stunned and tingling from the concrete, and without any conception at all of what I was doing I screamed and rushed. My mind a total red, raging, flaming blank. I know I screamed.

"YAAAAAAHHHH!"

The next thing I knew we are rolling over and over on the concrete, screaming and clawing. I'm out of my skull! I am pounding Dill against the concrete and we're rolling over and over, battering at each other's faces. I was screaming continually. I couldn't stop. I hit him over and over in the eyes. He rolled over me, but I was kicking and clawing, gouging, biting, tearing. I was vaguely

---

Mini-Lesson Grammar

ACTION VERBS AND LINKING VERBS
Remind students about the two kinds of verbs. Tell them that Shepherd uses many vivid action verbs on this page. Have them find as many as they can. Briefly go over linking verbs briefly with students, clarifying, for example, why the italicized words in the following sentences are linking verbs:

"It *was* a day like any other."

"I*'m* out of my skull!"

Remind them that some verbs can be either linking or action verbs, depending on their usage.

Application Have students copy the web into their notebooks. Ask them to refer to it as they write two sentences about Grover Dill, using the verb *look*. In one sentence, they must use an action verb and in the other a linking verb.

Reteaching/Reinforcement
• Grammar Handbook, anthology p. 945

The Writer's Craft
Using Verbs, pp. 583–584

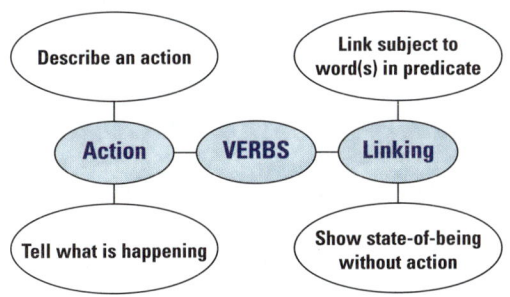

Literary Concept: METAPHOR

K Have students think back to the beginning of the story and recall what the narrator compared to a Tasmanian devil. *(the violent, fight-to-the-death streak inside every male)* Then ask what details the narrator uses on this page to intensify the comparison between Ralph and an attacking wild animal. *(Possible response: The narrator was "tearing and ripping and smashing at Grover Dill," and Dill's eyes were "slashed by my claws and fangs.")*

Critical Thinking:
MAKING JUDGMENTS

L Ask students whether they agree with the narrator's idea that bravery does not exist. *(Possible responses: yes, because most acts of bravery occur spontaneously, without one taking the time to think about negative consequences; no, because some people continue to perform acts of physical courage over a long period of time, even after they've had a chance to think about the risks)*

---

conscious of people coming out of houses and down over lawns. I was on top. I grabbed at his head. I caught both of Grover Dill's ears in either hand and I began to pound him on the concrete, over and over again.

I have since heard of people under extreme duress speaking in strange tongues.[8] I became conscious that a steady torrent of obscenities and swearing was pouring out of me as I screamed. I could hear my brother running home, hysterically yelling for my mother, but only dimly. All I knew is that I was tearing and ripping and smashing at Grover Dill, who fought back like a fiend! But I guess it was the first time he had ever met face to face with an unleashed Tasmanian Devil.

I continued to swear fantastically, as though I had no control over it. I was conscious of it and yet it was as though it was coming from something or someone outside of me. I swore as I have never sworn since as we rolled screaming on the ground. And suddenly we just break apart. Dill, the back of his head all battered, his eyes puffed and streaming, slashed by my claws and fangs, was hysterical. There was hardly a scratch on me, except for my scraped knees and cut lip.

I learned then that Bravery does not exist. Just a kind of latent Nuttiness. If I had thought about attacking Dill for ten seconds before I had done it, I'd have been four blocks away in a minute flat. But something had happened. A wire broke. A fuse blew. And I had gone out of my skull.

But I had sworn! Terribly! Obscenely! In our house kids didn't swear. The things I called Dill I'm sure my mother had not even heard. And I had only heard once or twice, coming out of an alley. I had woven a tapestry of obscenity that as far as I know is still hanging in space over Lake Michigan. And my mother had heard!

Dill by this time is wailing hysterically. This had never happened to him before. They're dragging the two of us apart amid a great ring of surging grownups and exultant, scared kids who knew more about what was happening than the mothers and fathers ever would. My mother is looking at me. She said:

"What did you say?"

That's all. There was a funny look on her face. At that instant all thought of Grover Dill disappeared from what was left of my mind and all I could think of was the incredible shame of that unbelievable tornado of obscenity I had sprayed over the neighborhood.

I go into the house in a daze, and my mother's putting water on me in the bathroom, pouring it over my head and dabbing at my eyes which are puffed and red from hysteria. My kid brother is cowering under the dining-room table, scared. Kissel, next door, has been hiding in the basement, under the steps, scared. The whole neighborhood is scared, and so am I. The water trickles down over my hair and around my ears as I stare into the swirling drainage hole in the sink.

"You better go in and lie down on the daybed. Take it easy. Just go in and lie down."

> *I LEARNED THEN THAT* **bravery** *DOES NOT EXIST.*

---

8. **speaking in strange tongues:** speaking unknown languages, like people in a state of religious ecstasy.

WORDS TO KNOW
duress (dŏŏ-rĕs′) *n.* constraint by force or threats
latent (lāt′nt) *adj.* present but not evident or active

202

Mini-Lesson Literary Concepts

REVIEWING CONFLICT Remind students that conflict is the struggle between opposing forces that is the basis of the plot of a story. An external conflict is a struggle between a character and an outside force, which may be another character or a physical obstacle. An internal conflict is a struggle within a character. Both kinds of conflict can exist in the same story.

Application Ask students to review the story to identify an external conflict or conflicts *(Ralph against Grover Dill and, to a degree, Ralph versus his physical environment)* and an internal conflict or conflicts *(Ralph's struggle with his conscience over his shame at displaying a violent nature)*. Have them record in their notebooks different ways that Ralph's internal conflict is made known, following the example shown at left.

Indications of Internal Conflict	Example from Story
He is so upset he is sick	"twisting, heaving stomach cramp"

GROVER DILL AND THE TASMANIAN DEVIL

DESIGN NOTE

Ask students what two images are combined in this illustration. *(the photo of the boy on page 201 and the face of the Tasmanian devil on page 197)* Then ask what point they think the designer of this book was trying to make by combining the two images. *(Possible response: The two images are a visual representation of Ralph's inner conflict and of the theme of the story: that inside even the most mild-mannered person there is an angry, wild beast waiting to get out.)*

Literary Concept: CONFLICT

M Ask students why Ralph doesn't feel happy after his victory over the bully. *(Possible responses: He's ashamed of the swearing he did during the fight; he's afraid of the violent side of his personality that came out during the fight, a part of him that doesn't seem to be under his control.)*

Literary Concept: SUSPENSE

N Ask students what questions were in their minds at this point in the story. *(Possible responses: What will Ralph's mother tell his father about the fight? How will Ralph's father react?)* Then ask how the writer draws out the moment of suspense, making the reader wait to find out what happens next. *(Possible response: He describes what the father does before dinner, uses several sentences to describe Ralph's slow walk from the bedroom to the kitchen, and then interrupts the parents' conversation to tell what Ralph is thinking.)*

Literary Concept: HYPERBOLE

O Ask students how they reacted to this exaggeration of the violence with which Ralph threw up. *(It probably made them laugh or at least smile.)* Then ask why they think the writer added this humorous exaggeration at this point in the story. *(Possible response: This is probably the most poignant moment in the story and one with which many readers may strongly identify. The exaggeration offers a bit of comic relief from the powerful feelings being conveyed.)*

CUSTOMIZING FOR
Gifted and Talented Students

Tell students that all people have a part of their personality that they do not like or that they are not proud of. Ask students to identify this part of their own personality and to think of an animal metaphor, as Ralph did, to represent this aspect of themselves. Then have them write a short, humorous description of a situation in which this "creature" is likely to "get out" and cause trouble.

M She takes me by the shoulder and pushes me down on the daybed. I lie there scared, really scared of what I have done. I felt no sense of victory, no sense of beating Dill. All I felt was this terrible thing I had said and done.

The light was getting purple and soft outside, almost time for my father to come home from work. I'm just lying there. I can see that it's getting dark, and I know that he's on his way home. Once in a while a gigantic sob would come out, half hysterically. My kid brother by now is under the sink in the john, hiding among the mops, mewing occasionally.

I hear the car roar up the driveway and a wave of terror breaks over me, the terror that a kid feels when he knows that <u>retribution</u> is about to be meted out for something that he's been hiding forever—his rottenness. The basic rottenness has been uncovered, and now it's the Wrath of God, which you are not only going to get but which you deserve!

N I hear him in the kitchen now. I'm in the front bedroom, cowering on the daybed. The normal sounds—he's hollering around with the newspaper. Finally my mother says:

"Come on, supper's ready. Come on, kids, wash up."

I painfully drag myself off the daybed and sneak along the woodwork, under the buffet, sneaking, skulking into the bathroom. My kid brother and I wash together over the sink. He says nothing.

Then I am sitting at the kitchen table, toying with the red cabbage. My Old Man looks up from the Sport page:

"Well, what happened today?"

Here it comes! There is a short pause, and then my mother says:

"Oh, not much. Ralph had a little fight."

"Fight? What kind of fight!"

"Oh, you know how kids are," she says.

The axe is poised over my naked neck! There is no way out! Mechanically I continue to shovel in the mashed potatoes and red cabbage, the meat loaf. But I am tasting nothing, just eating and eating.

"Oh, it wasn't much. I gave him a talking to. By the way, I see the White Sox won today. . . ."

About two thirds of the way through the meal I slowly began to realize that I was not about to be destroyed. And then a very peculiar thing happened. A sudden unbelievable twisting, heaving stomach cramp hit me so bad I could feel my shoes coming right up through my ears.

I rushed back into the bathroom, so sick to my stomach that my knees were buckling. It was all coming up, pouring out of me, the <u>conglomeration</u> of it all. The terror of Grover Dill, the fear of yelling the things that I had yelled, my father coming home, my obscenities . . . I heaved it all out. It poured out of me in great heaving rushes, splattering the walls, the floor, the sink. Old erasers that I had eaten years before, library paste that I had downed in second grade, an Indian Head penny that I had gulped when I was two! It all came up in thunderous, retching heaves. **O**

M y father hovered out in the hall, saying:

"What's the matter with him? What's the matter? Let's call Doctor Slicker!"

My mother *knew* what was the matter with me.

"Now he's going to be all right. Just take it easy. Go back and finish eating. Go on."

She pressed a washrag to the back of my neck. "Now take it easy. I'm not going to say anything. Just be quiet. Take it easy."

Down comes the bottle of Pepto-Bismol and the spoon. "Take this. Stop crying."

WORDS TO KNOW

retribution (rĕt′rə-byōō′shən) *n.* a penalty or punishment
conglomeration (kən-glŏm′ə-rā′shən) *n.* a collection of miscellaneous things

204

Mini-Lesson The Writer's Style

VARYING SENTENCE BEGINNINGS Tell students that using a variety of different kinds of sentences is a good way to make their writing more interesting. Point out that one way to vary their sentences is to use different kinds of beginnings. Tell them to avoid beginning every sentence with an article, a noun, or a pronoun and, instead, to try starting sentences with other parts of speech—verbs, verb forms, adverbs, and prepositional phrases, for example. Point out the three highlighted sentences on this page, which begin, respectively, with an adverb, a prepositional phrase, and an adverb.

Application Have students write a summary of the story, using these or similar sentence beginnings: *At the beginning of the story, Walking home from school one day, Without thinking, Afterward,* and *Luckily.*

Reteaching/Reinforcement
• *Writing Mini-Lessons* transparencies, p. 50

The Writer's Craft
Varying Sentence Beginnings, p. 417

204 THE LANGUAGE OF LITERATURE TEACHER'S EDITION

But then I *really* started to cry, yelling and blubbering. She was talking low and quiet to me.

"We'll tell him your stomach is upset, that you ate something at school."

The Pepto-Bismol slides down my throat, amid my blubbering. It is now really coming out! I'm scared of Grover Dill again, scared of everything. I'm convinced that I will never grow up to be twenty-one, that I'm going blind!

I'm lying in bed, sobbing, and I finally drift off to sleep, completely passed out from sheer nervous exhaustion. The soft warm air blew the curtains back and forth as we caught the tail of a breeze from the Great North Woods, the wilderness at the head of the Lake. Both of us slept quietly, me and my little red-eyed, fanged, furry Tasmanian Devil. Both of us slept. For the time being. ❖

INSIGHT

AMY LOWELL

You hate me and I hate you,
And we are so polite, we two!

But whenever I see you, I burst apart
And scatter the sky with my blazing heart.
5 It spits and sparkles in stars and balls,
Buds into roses—and flares, and falls.

Scarlet buttons, and pale green disks,
Silver spirals and asterisks,
Shoot and tremble in a mist
10 Peppered with mauve and amethyst.

I shine in the windows and light up the trees,
And all because I hate you, if you please.

And when you meet me, you rend asunder[1]
And go up in a flaming wonder
15 Of saffron cubes, and crimson moons,
And wheels all amaranths[2] and maroons.

Golden lozenges[3] and spades,
Arrows of malachites[4] and jades,
Patens[5] of copper, azure sheaves.[6]
20 As you mount, you flash in the glossy leaves.

Such fireworks as we make, we two!
Because you hate me and I hate you.

---

1. **asunder:** apart; into pieces.
2. **amaranths** (ăm′ə-rănths′): deep reddish purples.
3. **lozenges** (lŏz′ĭn-jəz): four-sided, diamond-shaped figures.
4. **malachites** (măl′ə-kīts′): the deep green colors of the mineral malachite.
5. **patens** (păt′nz): thin metal disks or plates.
6. **sheaves:** bundles of stalks bound together.

FIREWORKS 205

Mini-Lesson: Speaking, Listening, and Viewing

DRAMATIC READING Point out to students that Jean Shepherd did much of his writing for a radio show in which he told stories on the air and that therefore his writing is best appreciated when it is read aloud. Then tell them that in "Grover Dill and the Tasmanian Devil," the tone, or feeling, of the story changes abruptly once the fight is over. Tell them that this change can be demonstrated in a dramatic reading.

Application First, do a dramatic reading of the fight scene on pages 201–202 yourself. Then, assign a group of students to do a dramatic reading of the end of the story, beginning with the sentence "I go into the house in a daze" in the middle of the right-hand column on page 202. Have one student take the narrator's part; another, that of Ralph's mother; and a third, that of Ralph's father. Have them rehearse the scene and then perform it for the class. Tell the class to evaluate how well the performers capture the feeling of the final part of the story.

From Personal Response to Critical Analysis

1. Accept all reasonable responses.
2. Accept all reasonable responses.
3. Possible responses: the Tasmanian devil, because even after Ralph defeats Dill, he is still terrified of the wild beast inside himself; Dill, because people who are similar to him bring out the violent streak in Ralph.
4. Possible response: because he feels out of control when that side of him takes over—he does things, such as swearing and fighting, that he wouldn't ordinarily do.
5. Drawings will vary.
6. Possible response: The speaker in the poem seems to celebrate the results of her hatred for another person, whereas Ralph responds to his violent side with fear and disgust.
7. Answers will vary, though many students may feel that while children today still suffer from the bullying behavior of older or bigger children, other, far more serious trials and tribulations have become part of growing up.

Another Pathway

Cooperative Learning One student can make sure everyone justifies ideas with facts and examples. A second student can make sure that everyone has a chance to voice an opinion, and a third can integrate ideas into an outline everyone agrees on.

Rubric

3 Full Accomplishment Students agree on an outline of how the conflict would be different and effectively support their ideas.

2 Substantial Accomplishment Students agree on an outline but have some difficulty supporting their ideas.

1 Little or Partial Accomplishment Students cannot agree on an outline or offer reasons that do not support their ideas.

RESPONDING OPTIONS

FROM PERSONAL RESPONSE TO CRITICAL ANALYSIS

REFLECT
1. How did you like this story? Describe your reactions in your notebook and share them in class.

RETHINK
2. As you were reading this story, did you identify with Ralph? Why or why not?
3. Which do you think is worse for Ralph—the Tasmanian devil or the bully Grover Dill? Explain.
4. Why do you think Ralph is so horrified by the presence of the Tasmanian devil?
   Consider
   Close Textual Reading
   - Ralph's thoughts and feelings after the fight
   - how Ralph was raised to regard swearing
   - Ralph's usual response to bullies
5. Look over the visualizing chart or the sketches you made for the Reading Connection on page 196. Create a detailed drawing of one of the characters, the setting, or an event in the story.

RELATE
6. The Insight poem "Fireworks" also involves a conflict. Compare the reactions of the speaker in "Fireworks" with those of Ralph.
7. This story is set around 1940. Do you think children today experience the same kinds of trials and tribulations that Ralph did?
   Thematic Link

Multimodal Learning
ANOTHER PATHWAY
Cooperative Learning
The narrator feels that girls do not experience the "jungle of Kidhood." Do you think this is true? With a small group of classmates, outline how the conflict in the story might be different with two female characters. Then share your outline with the rest of the class.

LITERARY CONCEPTS

Imagery is language that represents sensory experience, such as sight, hearing, smell, taste, or touch. Writers use imagery to create a picture in the reader's mind or to remind the reader of a familiar sensation. Though most imagery is visual, an image can appeal to any of the five senses or a combination of them. Notice how the words "a howling tangled wilderness" create a vivid mental picture of jungle sights and sounds. Skim the story and find three more examples of vivid imagery to share with the class.

CONCEPT REVIEW: Conflict What are Ralph's internal and external conflicts?

QUICKWRITES

1. Write the outline of a **self-help guide** titled "How to Handle a Bully" or "How to Handle the Tasmanian Devil Inside You." You might include some of the insights you gained from the Personal Connection activity on page 196 as well as insights gained from reading the story.

2. Continue the story with another **episode** that details Ralph's next meeting with Grover Dill.

 PORTFOLIO Save your writing. You may want to use it later as a springboard to a piece for your portfolio.

Literary Concepts

For more examples of vivid imagery, see annotations C, H, and K and the description of the fight on pages 201–202. Point out that much of the imagery is contained within figures of speech, including similes and metaphors.

Concept Review: Conflict Ralph's internal conflict is the struggle with his "Tasmanian Devil," the violent streak inside him. Ralph's external conflict is his struggle with Dill.

QuickWrites

1. Have the groups that met for the Personal Connection get together again to compare their own experiences with those of Ralph and to discuss ideas for dealing with bullies.
2. Have students consider whether Ralph will still be as afraid of Dill as he fears and whether Dill will now be afraid of Ralph.

The Writer's Craft

Essay of Advice, pp. 178–191
Point of View, pp. 431–432
Dialogue in Fiction, pp. 434–435

THE WRITER'S STYLE

Hyperbole is a figure of speech in which the truth is exaggerated for emphasis or for humorous effect. Much of the humor in this story comes from hyperbole, such as "We'd go to school in a sandstorm and come home just before a tornado." Skim the story for other examples of hyperbole, and choose the one you think is funniest to share with the class.

ACROSS THE CURRICULUM

Geography Jean Shepherd paints a grim and graphic picture of the setting of this story—northwestern Indiana. Investigate the climate and the landscape of this area at the tip of Lake Michigan. How much of Shepherd's description is true, and how much is hyperbole? Present your findings in an oral report.

LITERARY LINKS

Compare Ralph's reaction to Grover Dill with the behavior of the narrator of "The Utterly Perfect Murder" (page 17). Explain why you think one approach might be better than the other.

WORDS TO KNOW

Decide whether the words in each of the following pairs are synonyms or antonyms. On your paper, write *S* for *Synonyms* or *A* for *Antonyms*.

1. conglomeration—mixture
2. duress—confinement
3. ferocity—tameness
4. insurgent—traitor
5. latent—undeveloped
6. malevolent—helpful
7. maniacal—calm
8. quell—support
9. retribution—revenge
10. sham—fake

JEAN SHEPHERD

1925?–

At the age of 16, Jean Shepherd was already doing weekly sportscasts for his local radio station. He went on to become a radio actor, a standup comic, a satirist, and a well-known writer and performer for radio, TV, stage, and film.

Shepherd was born in Chicago but grew up in Hammond, Indiana, the industrial city that he called Hohman in his book *In God We Trust: All Others Pay Cash*. This funny novel about growing up in the 1930s and 1940s was the basis of the popular 1983 movie *A Christmas Story*.

After serving in the army during World War II, Shepherd studied acting at the Goodman Theater School in Chicago and engineering and psychology at Indiana University. He left college, however, for a job at a radio station in Cincinnati, which was followed by moves to larger stations and eventually to WOR-AM in New York City. For more than 20 years, Shepherd drew a cult following all along the East Coast with his satiric late-night show on WOR. In each program, without a script, he would launch into a rambling yarn, often interrupted by the sounds of his own laughter. It was these hilarious reminiscences of boyhood and adolescence that soon found their way into his writing. Now he is recognized as one of America's foremost humorists, in the tradition of Mark Twain.

OTHER WORKS *Wanda Hickey's Night of Golden Memories and Other Disasters*, *A Fistful of Fig Newtons*

The Writer's Style

For more examples of hyperbole, see other descriptions of the weather on pages 199–200 and annotation O on page 204.

Across the Curriculum

Geography Suggest that students consult encyclopedias and books in the geography section of the library. They might also try finding someone in their neighborhood from that area whom they could interview. Most students will agree that the descriptions are based to some degree on facts but are exaggerated for comic effect.

Literary Links

Ralph fights back while he's still a child, but Doug nurses his anger and hatred into adulthood. Many students will probably feel that it is healthier to deal with childhood feelings while you are a child and then move on.

Words to Know

1. S
2. S
3. A
4. S
5. S
6. A
7. A
8. A
9. S
10. S

Reteaching/Reinforcement
- *Unit Two Resource Book*, p. 10

Alternative Activities

1. Have students view the movie *A Christmas Story* (available at video rental stores), which features the same characters and setting as "Grover Dill and the Tasmanian Devil." Ask them to compare their visualizations of Ralph, his family, Grover Dill, and the setting with how these elements are portrayed in the movie.
2. Have students use imagery, similes, and hyperbole to write and perform a humorous monologue about a memorable experience from their childhood.

OVERVIEW
Objectives

- To understand and appreciate two poems that use fighting as a metaphor
- To identify and understand extended metaphors and puns
- To appreciate the use of titles as clues in analyzing extended metaphors
- To express understanding of the poems through a choice of writing forms, including a list, a poem, and a crossword puzzle
- To extend understanding of the poems through a variety of multimodal and cross-curricular activities

Skills

LITERARY CONCEPTS
- Extended metaphor
- Puns
- Free verse

READING SKILLS/ STRATEGIES
- Figurative language

THE WRITER'S STYLE
- Personification

SPEAKING, LISTENING, AND VIEWING
- Group discussion
- Oral presentation

CULTURAL CONNECTION
Jazz: An American Art The sights and sounds of jazz during the first half of the 20th century come alive for students in this musical montage. This montage may generate discussion about the elements of this American art form.

Side A, Frame 9333

PREVIEWING

POETRY

Battle Report
Bob Kaufman

Training/Entrenamiento
Demetrio Herrera

Activating Prior Knowledge
PERSONAL CONNECTION

Say "fight" to someone, and he or she is likely to visualize gangs or armies, great injury, or even death. The word, however, can also fit other contexts. For example, *fight* may refer to a boxing match or, in other sports, to the physical struggle to outscore an opponent and win a game. Outside of sports, a legislator might fight to get a bill passed. Maybe you've "beaten" an illness, "attacked" a chore at home, or "wrestled" with your conscience. Think of a personal situation in which you "fought" to gain or prevent something. Then create a cluster diagram, like the sample shown, to describe your struggle, using as many creative fighting terms as possible. If you have a graphics program on your computer, use it to set up your diagram.

Building Background
CULTURAL CONNECTION

The two poems you are about to read make unlikely, playful comparisons involving forms of fighting. The subject of the first poem is jazz, which is said to be the only art form to have originated in the United States. It is a type of music that struggled to gain acceptance during the first half of the 20th century. At that time, many people considered jazz—consisting usually of a mix of saxophone, trumpet, trombone, piano, drums, and string bass—a revolutionary, vulgar music and resisted its growing presence in big cities.

In the second poem, the setting of a windy seaport is compared to the surroundings of a boxer in training. Boxing is a popular sport in Panama, the homeland of the poet. As a spectator sport in Panama, boxing enjoys a greater following than soccer, the most popular sport in the other Central American countries.

208 UNIT TWO PART 1: FRIEND OR FOE?

Jazz greats *(left to right)* Max Kaminsky, Lester Young, "Hot Lips" Page, and Charlie Parker in New York. UPI/Bettmann

• CULTURAL CONNECTION

PRINT AND MEDIA RESOURCES

UNIT TWO RESOURCE BOOK
Strategic Reading: Literature, p. 13

WRITING MINI-LESSONS
Transparencies, p. 47

ACCESS FOR STUDENTS ACQUIRING ENGLISH
Selection Summaries
Reading Support

FORMAL ASSESSMENT
Selection Test, pp. 37–38
Test Generator

 AUDIO LIBRARY
See Reference Card

 LASERLINKS
Cultural Connection
Art Gallery

 INTERNET RESOURCES
"Battle Report"
McDougal Littell Literature Center at http://www.hmco.com /mcdougal/lit

READING CONNECTION Active Reading/Setting a Purpose

Looking Closely at Figurative Language

Have you ever tried to express something but just couldn't find the right words? Did ordinary words seem inadequate for expressing all that you wanted to say? The limitation of language is a problem many writers face. Fortunately, though, language can be figurative as well as literal—that is, words can mean more than they say.

Analyze You already know about a number of forms of figurative language—simile, metaphor, and personification, for instance. (See page 121 for a review.) Let's look closer at how figurative language works. Think what each of the two comparisons at the right tells you about fog.

> Fog hanging like old
> Coats between the trees.
> —from "Oranges"
> by Gary Soto

How is fog different in the two comparisons? For Soto's poem, you might think of descriptive words such as *thick* and *heavy*. In contrast, the fog in Sandburg's poem seems light, playful, even cute—how could a "little cat" be anything else?

> The fog comes
> on little cat feet.
> —from "Fog"
> by Carl Sandburg

Thus, fog can be shown to have many properties, depending on how a writer wants the fog to be thought of. Soto and Sandburg get you to think about fog in a way that fits with the feelings of their particular poems.

Apply Now take a look at the opening stanza of Bob Kaufman's poem "Battle Report."

> One thousand saxophones infiltrate the city,
> Each with a man inside,
> Hidden in ordinary cases,
> Labeled FRAGILE.

Infiltrate means "to secretly penetrate enemy-held territory"—for example, soldiers and spies might infiltrate enemy lines to set up a surprise attack. Looking at the stanza, ask yourself, Why would 1,000 saxophones infiltrate a city? Then ask, How can a saxophone have a man inside? Think figuratively. As you read the rest of the poem, notice other words that are associated with warfare. Use your imagination to find meaning in the poem's implied comparisons.

Thematic Link: *Friend or Foe?* These two poems use the figurative language of battle to describe other scenes and situations.

Critical Thinking: ANALYZING
After students have discussed both examples at the right, have a volunteer change Soto's simile to a metaphor. Have another volunteer change Sandburg's metaphor to a simile. Encourage students to create their own comparison for fog.

Literary Note
Help students to answer the questions in the last paragraph by retelling the story of the Trojan horse from the *Iliad* and the *Aeneid*. According to legend, the Greeks created a huge hollow wooden horse in which they hid a number of soldiers. The Trojans pulled the horse into the city of Troy, thus bringing the concealed enemy inside the city walls. The Greek soldiers opened the city gates to their army, which stormed in and defeated the Trojans.

BATTLE REPORT / TRAINING **209**

Mini-Lesson Literary Concepts

REVIEWING FREE VERSE Remind students that free verse is poetry without regular patterns of rhyme and meter—poetry that can often sound like everyday conversation. Tell them that in writing free verse, poets often repeat words to mimic cadences of speech and that they arrange the lines according to how much a person can say in one breath. Point out that free verse relies on imagery and figurative language to convey meaning.

Application Have students read lines 16–21 of "Battle Report" and lines 6–8 of "Training" as if they were speaking to a friend. Then ask what elements make the lines free verse. *(Possible responses: "Battle Report"—no rhyme, irregular length of lines, no meter, repeated phrases, placement of lines; "Training"—no rhyme, conversational tone, lines broken into easy breath units)*

BATTLE Report

Bob Kaufman

One thousand saxophones infiltrate the city,
Each with a man inside,
Hidden in ordinary cases,
Labeled FRAGILE.

5 A fleet of trumpets drops their hooks,
Inside at the outside.

Ten waves of trombones approach the city
Under blue cover
Of late autumn's neo-classical[1] clouds.

10 Five hundred bassmen, all string feet tall,
Beating it back to the bass.

One hundred drummers, each a stick in
   each hand,
The delicate rumble of pianos, moving in.

The secret agent, an innocent bystander,
15 Drops a note in the wail box.

Five generals, gathered in the gallery,
Blowing plans.

At last, the secret code is flashed:
Now is the time, now is the time.

20 Attack: The sound of jazz.

The city falls.

---

1. **neo-classical:** characterized by a return to classical (traditional) styles and forms in the arts.

FROM PERSONAL RESPONSE TO CRITICAL ANALYSIS

REFLECT 1. What do you like most about this poem? Write your thoughts in your notebook and share them with your classmates.

RETHINK 2. What do you think the speaker means by the final line, "The city falls"?

Close Textual Reading **Consider**
   - what the "attack" is in the second-to-last line
   - the fact that jazz has struggled for acceptance

3. How does the speaker seem to feel about jazz? Give evidence from the poem to support your opinion.

4. Find three words in the poem that are normally associated with military warfare and explain how they contribute to the poem's meaning.

210 UNIT TWO PART 1: FRIEND OR FOE?

In E Sharp (1981), Romare Bearden. Oil and collage on paper, 39¾" x 30½", the Estate of Romare Bearden, courtesy of ACA Galleries, New York.

Art Note

In E Sharp by Romare Bearden The African-American artist Romare Bearden (1914–1988) was born in North Carolina and grew up in Harlem, a hotbed of jazz music in the 1920s. Colorful names of jazz artists of the era include Jelly Roll Morton, Dizzy (John Birks) Gillespie, and Louis (Satchmo) Armstrong. In this work, which is oil and collage on paper, Bearden uses rich, vibrant colors to convey his great love of jazz. Using just a few bold details, the artist captures the intense feelings of the bass player.

Reading the Art *What mood do the colors in this piece create? What other details add to this mood?*

Linking to Music

Jazz is a form of music noted for its improvisation; its distortion of rhythm, melody, and harmony; and its wailing sounds. It originated around the turn of the century in New Orleans, where the music of Africa, France, and Spain was popular. Advocates of jazz felt that it was a forum of free self-expression; opponents felt that it was a demoralizing influence, like alcohol. By the 1920s, jazz had spread north to Chicago and then to New York. It profoundly influenced rock-and-roll, and it has continued to thrive throughout the country.

Art Note

Lullaby by Fletcher Martin Fletcher Martin (1904–1979) won critical acclaim for his work depicting boxing. A former boxer himself, Martin personally identified with his work. This oil painting reflects the subjects' mental and physical energy at a single moment.

Reading the Art Do you think Lullaby is a good title for this painting? Why or why not? What aspects of the scene correspond to the poem?

Literary Concept: EXTENDED METAPHOR

B Tell students that in an extended metaphor, a poet compares two unlike things in various ways. In the first stanza of "Training," the speaker compares the sea to a boxer and compares the boats to a punching ball. Ask students to name other comparisons in the poem that develop the central metaphor of a boxer in training. (Possible response: the comparison of the wind blowing over the sea to the towel going over the boxer's body)

Literary Concept: FREE VERSE

C Tell students that in free verse, poets often take liberties with punctuation, spelling, and the placement of words and lines. Ask students why the poet has broken up the word *punching*. (Possible response: The broken word suggests the action of receiving a punch.)

COMPREHENSION CHECK

1. In "Battle Report," what is the extended metaphor? *(Jazz instruments and musicians are compared to soldiers and weapons.)*
2. In "Training," who or what is in training? *(the sea)*
3. Name the objects that the speaker in "Training" compares to spectators watching the training. *(buildings, dock, ship, tower, sea-birds)*

TRAINING

Demetrio Herrera

Lullaby (1942), Fletcher Martin. Collection of Mrs. Ford West.

B The sea—quick pugilist[1]—
uses for a pun
C   ching
            ball
5 the restless little boats.

With the towel of the wind,
evening rubs down the boxer's
sweaty body.

The buildings—
10 ringside fans—
crowd close to watch
the big training.

(The dock is whispering
with a smoking ship . . .)

15 And the surf's applause
makes the tower stand on tiptoe
with its watch in hand
to keep the time.

Stray kids,
20 the sea-birds
sneak in through the roof.

Translated by Dudley Fitts

---
1. **pugilist** (pyōō′jə-lĭst′): boxer.

ENTRENAMIENTO

El mar—boxeador rápido— **B**
tiene de pun
      ching **C**
            ball
5 a los barquillos inquietos.

Con la toalla del viento,
la tarde frota el cuerpo
sudoroso del bóxer.

Los edificios
10 —fanáticos del ring—
contemplan apiñados
el gran entrenamiento.

(El muelle cuchichea
con un vapor que fuma) . . .

15 Y un aplauso de ola
hace empinar la torre
con el reloj en mano
para llevar el tiempo.

Chiquillos vagabundos,
20 los pájaros marinos,
se cuelan por el techo.

---

212 UNIT TWO PART 1: FRIEND OR FOE?

Mini-Lesson — The Writer's Style

PERSONIFICATION Explain that personification is a figure of speech in which human qualities are attributed to an object, animal, or idea. Point out that in the lines highlighted in "Training" on page 212, things are described as performing human acts—the dock is whispering, the surf is applauding, and the tower is standing on tiptoe.

Application Ask students to brainstorm a list of ten animals, things, or ideas. Then have them write a sentence for each item, giving that item a human characteristic. To get them started, write the following sentence on the board: *The rocks stared back at us dumbly, keeping their secrets to themselves.* Have students discuss what human characteristics the rocks exhibit.

Reteaching/Reinforcement
- *Writing Mini-Lessons* transparencies, p. 47

Personification, p. 414

RESPONDING OPTIONS

FROM PERSONAL RESPONSE TO CRITICAL ANALYSIS

REFLECT 1. Did you enjoy reading "Training"? Why or why not? Jot down your reactions in your notebook and then share your response with a partner.

RETHINK 2. Draw a sketch of the seaside scene described in this poem. Label parts of the scene with the appropriate boxing terms from the poem.

Thematic Link 3. Does the speaker consider the sea a friend or a foe? Support your answer with evidence from the poem.

RELATE 4. Does the figurative language in these poems enable you to view jazz and the sea in new ways? Point out lines or stanzas that you think are particularly effective.

Close Textual Reading

5. What do you think was each poet's purpose in writing his poem? Consider whether the two poets' purposes are similar or not.

Multimodal Learning
ANOTHER PATHWAY
Cooperative Learning
Kaufman's first published poems appeared not in books but on broadsides, single sheets of paper printed on one side. With a small group of classmates, create broadsides for "Battle Report" and "Training." Illustrate each broadside to capture the spirit of the poem. Share them in class.

LITERARY CONCEPTS

The figurative language in these two poems consists primarily of metaphors. Each poem is actually an **extended metaphor**—a comparison of two things that is made at some length and in several ways. For example, "Battle Report" compares the arrival of jazz in a city to the actions of an invading army. The saxophones "infiltrate" the city, a "fleet" of trumpets drops anchor, and other musical instruments secretly move into position. When the music starts, the city "falls." Explain the extended metaphor in "Training."

A **pun** is a joke that comes from a play on words. Puns can make use of a word's multiple meanings or of a word's rhyme. In jazz and rock slang, a musical performance that is especially intense and exciting is said to wail. Look at line 15 of "Battle Report" and explain the puns involving *note* and *wail*.

QUICKWRITES

1. Make a **list** of lines that you did not understand in these poems. Share your list with classmates and brainstorm possible meanings. Then write a short explanation of each line.

2. Look over the cluster diagram you made for the Personal Connection on page 208. Write a **poem** about the situation you described, using an extended metaphor.

3. Create a **crossword puzzle** based on key words from these two poems.

 PORTFOLIO Save your writing. You may want to use it later as a springboard to a piece for your portfolio.

BATTLE REPORT / TRAINING 213

From Personal Response to Critical Analysis

1. Accept all reasonable responses.
2. Accept all well-supported responses.
3. Possible responses: A friend—he describes interested fans, applauding surf, and stray kids who watch. A foe—he describes the sea as using little boats for a punching ball.
4. Accept all well-supported, reasonable responses.
5. Possible response: Kaufman—to show the powerful appeal of jazz to new listeners; Herrera—to show the sea as a living thing. Both poets want the reader to appreciate in a new way the power of a familiar thing.

Another Pathway
Partners should discuss the images in each poem and decide which they will illustrate. Partners can then decide whether each will complete one broadside or whether one partner will draw the images for both and the other will print the text.

Rubric
3 Full Accomplishment Students' illustrations vividly relate to the main images and ideas in the poems; the text of the poems is complete, accurate, and legible.
2 Substantial Accomplishment Students' illustrations fail to capture the spirit of the poems; the text of poems is complete and accurate.
1 Little or Partial Accomplishment Students create inappropriate images; the text of poems may be incomplete and inaccurate.

Literary Concepts

Extended Metaphor Students may point out that in "Training," the sea's movements are compared to those of a boxer in training. The sea is a "quick pugilist," a boat is a "punching bag," and the buildings are "ringside fans."

Puns Point out that in "Battle Report," the secret agent "Drops a note in the wail box." Tell students that "drops a note" plays on two meanings of *note*—"message" and "musical note."

QuickWrites

1. Remind students that free verse becomes clearer when the lines are read aloud in a conversational rhythm.
2. Suggest that students state in a sentence what their extended metaphor will be.
3. You may wish to help students acquiring English choose key words and develop clues.

The Writer's Craft
Understanding Extended Metaphors, p. 134
Writing an Extended Metaphor, pp. 135–136

Literary Link

Have students compare the extended metaphor in "Training" with that in "A Poison Tree" by William Blake (page 192). Ask students to point out similarities in the techniques the two poets use to build their extended metaphors. *(Possible responses: Both poets use a single object or idea for the extended metaphor—the sea and anger; both poets include in each stanza additional metaphors that relate to the central idea and that use concrete images.)*

Art Connection

Ask a volunteer to describe the job of referee. *(to make sure both fighters obey the rules)* Have students note that the referee in the painting is restraining one fighter. Students can extend the metaphor of the referee as a captain trying to prevent the sea (standing boxer) from destroying his boat (boxer on the mat). Accept all reasonable responses.

Across the Curriculum

Social Studies *Cooperative Learning* Divide the class into small groups. Assign half the groups an oral report on the history of jazz, and the other half an oral report on the history of boxing. Have each group designate a member to give directions and keep the group on task, another to make sure all members contribute, and a third to integrate the members' ideas and research. Have groups deliver their oral reports to the class.

ART GALLERY
The Art of Boxing During the early part of this century boxing was a sport sponsored by many neighborhood organizations. These images will show students how artists viewed the sport and incorporated it into their artwork.

Side A, Frame 49269

Multimodal Learning

ALTERNATIVE ACTIVITIES

1. The poetry of Bob Kaufman was greatly influenced by jazz musicians such as Charlie Parker, Dizzy Gillespie, and Miles Davis. Kaufman intended many of his poems to be read aloud, accompanied by jazz music. Select a jazz recording and give a **dramatic reading** of Kaufman's poem as you play the music.
2. Prepare a **portfolio** of different photographs of the sea that reflect the sea's various moods. Suggest metaphors for each mood. Then find a photograph that matches the mood of "Training."

THE WRITER'S STYLE

When a poem is based on an extended **metaphor,** the poet may choose a title that gives the reader a clue to the comparison without actually stating it. In Demetrio Herrera's poem, the title "Training" directs the reader immediately to the comparison; then, halfway through the poem, the word *training* appears again, as a reminder. In "Battle Report," however, the word *battle* never appears. Explain how difficult you think understanding that poem might be if the comparison were not identified in the title.

ART CONNECTION

Look again at the painting by Fletcher Martin on page 212. A boxing match is depicted, and one fighter has knocked down another. Find at least one element of the poem "Training" in the painting. Then notice what the referee is doing. If Herrera's poem had been about a match, not just training for a match, how might the poet have worked the referee into the seaside metaphor?

Detail of *Lullaby* (1942), Fletcher Martin. Collection of Mrs. Ford West.

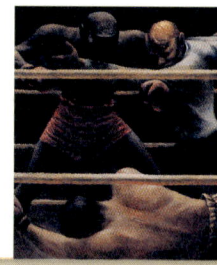

214 UNIT TWO PART 1: FRIEND OR FOE?

The Writer's Style

Before students offer their explanations, encourage them to identify again the words in the poem that are related to warfare and battle. Some students may feel that there are enough of these to make the extended metaphor clear, even if the title of the poem were simply "Jazz." Other students may feel that the title "Battle Report" is a necessary clue to understanding the poem. For more practice in creating titles that illuminate the work, see The Writer's Craft, pages 134–136.

BOB KAUFMAN

Bob Kaufman (1925–1986) was a leading innovator of the 1950s "Beat generation," a group of unconventional writers and musicians. The Beats protested the commercialism of American society and sought truth in Eastern philosophy and in jazz.

By the late 1950s, he was living in San Francisco, reciting spontaneously composed poems in jazz bars and coffeehouses. Many of his published poems exist only because transcriptions were created from tape recordings made in these various gathering places. Kaufman's poems frequently mention jazz, and a typical example is "Battle Report," which ends playfully with jazz's victory—its being accepted in the life of the big city.

After the assassination of John F. Kennedy in 1963, Kaufman took a Buddhist vow of silence and withdrew from society, not speaking for nearly 12 years. He broke his silence dramatically in 1975, on the day the Vietnam War ended. However, Kaufman continued to be troubled by what he saw as a decaying world. In 1978, after proclaiming "I want to be anonymous. . . . My ambition is to be completely forgotten," he again withdrew into silence. From then until his death in 1986 in San Francisco, he was seen only infrequently.

OTHER WORKS *Solitudes Crowded with Loneliness; Golden Sardine; The Ancient Rain: Poems, 1956–1978*

DEMETRIO HERRERA

A self-educated man, Demetrio Herrera was born in poverty in Panama in 1902. In the early 1940s, a critic proclaimed Herrera "an ironical and intelligent spectator in the theatre of the world." However, aside from the appearance of "Training" in the 1942 *Anthology of Contemporary Latin-American Poetry,* nothing more is known of the poet.

• ART GALLERY

Alternative Activities

1. Remind students that most public libraries have music collections from which one can borrow just as one would borrow books. Encourage students to practice their dramatic readings at home with friends or family before giving them in class.
2. Suggest that students cut out pictures from magazines and newspapers or photocopy pictures from library books. You may wish to indicate a minimum number of photographs for a complete assignment.

PREVIEWING

FICTION

The Euphio Question
Kurt Vonnegut, Jr.

PERSONAL CONNECTION Activating Prior Knowledge

"The Euphio Question" is a story about an imaginary scientific discovery. The discovery helps people forget their troubles and escape from reality. In real life, people have many ways of escaping from reality and relieving stress. Some of the ways are safe and even beneficial, while others can be dangerous. Make a two-column chart like the one shown here, listing both safe and unsafe ways in which people escape from reality today.

Safe Escapes	Dangerous Escapes
Movies	Alcohol
Sports	

SCIENCE CONNECTION Building Background

Literature sometimes provides an escape from the present and the known. When writers explore possibilities of the past or the future using scientific data and theories as well as imaginary elements the result is **science fiction**. For example, this science fiction story describes radio telescopes, which scientists actually use to measure radio waves from objects in space that optical telescopes cannot see—signals coming in from seemingly empty areas of space. With this equipment, scientists have detected radio waves from certain distant galaxies, from the remains of exploded and collapsed suns, and from other faraway starlike objects. For the sake of his story, however, Kurt Vonnegut imagines that these radio telescopes might be capable of picking up something totally unexpected.

LASERLINKS
• SCIENCE CONNECTION

Active Reading/Setting a Purpose
READING CONNECTION

Understanding Satire Many of Vonnegut's stories, especially his science fiction stories, contain satire—that is, they make fun of certain foolish ideas or conditions of modern society. For "The Euphio Question," Vonnegut created his fictional world as if he had asked himself this question: What if the desire to escape life's normal trials and tribulations were taken to a ridiculous extreme? As you read his story, look for elements of satire.

Using Your Reading Log To help you follow Vonnegut's satirical message, questions have been inserted throughout "The Euphio Question." Jot down your responses in your reading log so that you can discuss them later with your classmates.

OVERVIEW

Objectives

- To understand and appreciate a science fiction story that explores negative and positive aspects of technology
- To enrich reading by using active reading strategies
- To analyze and understand theme and flashbacks
- To understand and appreciate satirical humor
- To express understanding of the story through a choice of writing forms, including science notes, an epilogue, and a radio commercial
- To extend understanding of the story through a variety of multimodal and cross-curricular activities

Skills

LITERARY CONCEPTS
- Theme
- Flashback
- First-person point of view

READING SKILLS/ STRATEGIES
- To enrich reading by using active reading strategies

THE WRITER'S STYLE
- Sensory details

GENRE STUDY
- Fiction: science fiction

GRAMMAR
- The dash

SPEAKING, LISTENING, AND VIEWING
- Art
- Readers Theater
- Group discussion
- Oral presentation

SCIENCE CONNECTION
Radio Telescopes Science fiction writers use aspects of real science in their work. This film about radio telescopes can be used to discuss how scientific reality is turned into scientific fiction in "The Euphio Question."

Side A, Frame 13414

ALTERNATIVE
Previewing

Students can choose partners to preview "The Euphio Question" orally.

Personal Connection

Discussion Prompts *Think of some ways that people escape from reality and relieve stress. Describe some to your partner. Then listen as your partner describes additional ways. Consider these types:*

- *Activities—outdoor, indoor, noisy, quiet*
- *Substances—some safe and even beneficial; others that are dangerous*

As you read "The Euphio Question," consider the advisability of escaping reality to the degree that its major characters do.

PRINT AND MEDIA RESOURCES

UNIT TWO RESOURCE BOOK
Strategic Reading: Literature, p. 17
Vocabulary SkillBuilder, p. 18

WRITING MINI-LESSONS
Transparencies, p. 46

ACCESS FOR STUDENTS ACQUIRING ENGLISH
Selection Summaries
Reading Support

FORMAL ASSESSMENT
Selection Test, pp. 39–40
 Test Generator

 AUDIO LIBRARY
See Reference Card

LASERLINKS
Science Connection
Author Background

 INTERNET RESOURCES
McDougal Littell Literature Center at http://www.hmco.com/mcdougal/lit

SUMMARY

The narrator is testifying before the Federal Communications Commission (FCC) about a machine, called the euphio, that makes people euphorically happy. The device is the result of a discovery made by Dr. Fred Bockman, a physicist, who found that apparently empty spots in space transmit radio signals. When Fred was interviewed about his discovery by Lew Harrison, a radio announcer, the signals were broadcast over commercial radio. Everyone within range of the signal became euphoric. Seeing an opportunity to become rich, Lew convinced Fred to build the euphio, which would transmit the signal directly into a home. After conducting an experiment with a test machine, Fred and the narrator realized that the happiness it produced caused people to ignore serious problems, so they smashed the test machine. Lew, however, produced his own euphio and has asked the FCC to allow him to sell it commercially. The narrator strongly urges the commission not to license the machine. As he concludes his testimony, however, the euphio on display before the FCC begins transmitting the euphoric sounds.

Thematic Link: *Friend or Foe?* A machine that makes people euphoric turns out to be humanity's worst foe.

CUSTOMIZING FOR
Students Acquiring English

- Use **ACCESS FOR STUDENTS ACQUIRING ENGLISH**, *Reading Support*.
- The selection contains some difficult terminology and concepts and may prove a challenge for students who are unfamiliar with the subgenre of science fiction. Explain that parts of the story will seem realistic to them and that other parts will seem like fantasy or make-believe. You might have students discuss folk tales they know of that have these two qualities.

THE EUPHIO

KURT VONNEGUT, JR.

WORDS TO KNOW

adversity (ăd-vûr′sĭ-tē) *n.* hardship or misfortune (p. 228)
apathetically (ăp′ə-thĕt′ĭk-lē) *adv.* without any interest or emotion (p. 224)
exploitation (ĕk′sploi-tā′shən) *n.* a productive use of something (p. 228)
invincible (ĭn-vĭn′sə-bəl) *adj.* unbeatable (p. 219)
maudlin (môd′lĭn) *adj.* foolishly sentimental; corny (p. 219)
monopoly (mə-nŏp′ə-lē) *n.* an exclusive control of the sale of a product or service (p. 220)
oblivion (ə-blĭv′ē-ən) *n.* total forgetfulness (p. 224)
synthetic (sĭn-thĕt′ĭk) *adj.* artificial; not natural (p. 218)
unscrupulous (ŭn-skrōō′pyə-ləs) *adj.* willing to do wrong to get one's way; dishonorable (p. 229)
void (void) *n.* an empty space (p. 218)

QUESTION

Ladies and gentlemen of the Federal Communications Commission,[1] I appreciate this opportunity to testify on the subject before you.

I'm sorry—or maybe "heartsick" is the word—that news has leaked out about it. But now that word is getting around and coming to your official notice, I might as well tell the story straight and pray to God that I can convince you that America doesn't want what we discovered.

I won't deny that all three of us—Lew Harrison, the radio announcer, Dr. Fred Bockman, the physicist, and myself, a sociology professor—found peace of mind. We did. And I won't say it's wrong for people to seek peace of mind. But if somebody thinks he wants peace of mind the way we found it, he'd be well advised to seek coronary thrombosis[2] instead.

Lew, Fred, and I found peace of mind by sitting in easy chairs and turning on a gadget the size of a table-model television set. No herbs, no golden rule, no muscle control, no sticking our noses in other people's troubles to forget our own;

---

1. **Federal Communications Commission:** a U.S. government agency (also known by its initials, FCC) that regulates and licenses all radio and television operations.
2. **coronary thrombosis** (kôr′ə-nĕr′ē thrŏm-bō′sĭs): a blood clot in an artery of the heart.

THE EUPHIO QUESTION **217**

Mini-Lesson Grammar

THE DASH Tell students that dashes are used to set off words, phrases, or clauses that add extra information to an already complete thought:
1. To show an abrupt break in thought.
   The movie—supposedly a classic—was a bore.
2. To set off a long explanatory statement that interrupts the main thought of the sentence.
   They searched the entire area—the house, the yard, the park—to find the puppy.
3. To set off a summarizing statement.
   Broken glass, cans, piles of old newspapers—these littered the floor of the vacant house.

Application Ask students to look at the two sentences highlighted on this page and to explain in which of the three ways the dash is used in each. *(first sentence—1; second sentence—2)* Then have them write three sentences in which they use dashes in each of the three ways described.

Reteaching/Reinforcement
- Grammar Handbook, anthology p. 934

The Dash, p. 789

Literary Concept: FLASHBACK

A Ask students to point out where the narrator, in addressing the FCC, switches from talking in the present to beginning a narrative about something that happened in the past. *(in the paragraph beginning "My first brush")*

Linking to History

B In 1931, Karl Jansky, an American engineer, discovered that radio waves (a type of electromagnetic wave produced by stars and other celestial bodies) were being emitted from the center of our galaxy. The study of these waves helped increase knowledge of the history of the universe.

Linking to Science

C Vonnegut's bodiless "spots in space" bear a resemblance to "black holes," invisible objects in space. Scientists assume existence of black holes on the basis of the effect that they have on visible objects. It is thought that black holes are the result of the collapsing of large stars upon themselves. This inward collapse condenses the star's matter, resulting in a "hole" of incredible gravitational force. Unlike Dr. Bockman's voids, however, nothing—not radio waves, not even light—can escape the gravity of the black holes. This is why they are invisible.

Active Reading: CLARIFY

D Have students study the descriptions of how the characters were behaving just as the signals were turned off. You may wish to use the following model to help them examine the text.

Think-Aloud Model *Two of the men were grinning, and the third man, Lew, wore a pleased expression. The narrator claims he was "relaxed and tingling." These clues show that the signals apparently made the men feel very happy.*

---

no hobbies, Taoism,[3] pushups or contemplation of a lotus.[4] The gadget is, I think, what a lot of people vaguely foresaw as the crowning achievement of civilization: an electronic something-or-other, cheap, easily mass-produced, that can, at the flick of a switch, provide tranquility. I see you have one here.

A My first brush with <u>synthetic</u> peace of mind was six months ago. It was also then that I got to know Lew Harrison, I'm sorry to say. Lew is chief announcer of our town's only radio station. He makes his living with his loud mouth, and I'd be surprised if it were anyone but he who brought this matter to your attention.

Lew has, along with about thirty other shows, a weekly science program. Every week he gets some professor from Wyandotte College and interviews him about his particular field. Well, six months ago Lew worked up a program around a young dreamer and faculty friend of mine, Dr. Fred Bockman. I gave Fred a lift to the radio station, and he invited me to come on in and watch. For the heck of it, I did.

Fred Bockman is thirty and looks eighteen. Life has left no marks on him, because he hasn't paid much attention to it. What he pays most of his attention to, and what Lew Harrison wanted to interview him about, is **B** this eight-ton umbrella of his that he listens to the stars with. It's a big radio antenna rigged up on a telescope mount. The way I understand it, instead of looking at the stars through a telescope, he aims this thing out in space and picks up radio signals coming from different heavenly bodies.

Of course, there aren't people running radio stations out there. It's just that many of the heavenly bodies pour out a lot of energy and some of it can be picked up in the radio-frequency band. One good thing Fred's rig does is to spot stars hidden from telescopes by big clouds of cosmic dust. Radio signals from them get through the clouds to Fred's antenna.

That isn't all the outfit can do, and, in his interview with Fred, Lew Harrison saved the most exciting part until the end of the program. "That's very interesting, Dr. Bockman," Lew said. "Tell me, has your radio telescope turned up anything else about the universe that hasn't been revealed by ordinary light telescopes?"

C This was the snapper. "Yes, it has," Fred said. "We've found about fifty spots in space, *not hidden by cosmic dust*, that give off powerful radio signals. Yet no heavenly bodies at all seem to be there."

"Well!" Lew said in mock surprise. "I should say that *is* something! Ladies and gentlemen, for the first time in radio history, we bring you the noise from Dr. Bockman's mysterious <u>voids</u>." They had strung a line out to Fred's antenna on the campus. Lew waved to the engineer to switch in the signals coming from it. "Ladies and gentlemen, the voice of nothingness!"

The noise wasn't much to hear—a wavering hiss, more like a leaking tire than anything else. It was supposed to be on the air for five seconds. When the engineer switched it off, Fred and I were inexplicably grinning like idiots. I felt relaxed and tingling. Lew Harrison looked as though he'd stumbled into the dressing room at the Copacabana.[5] **D**

He glanced at the studio clock, appalled. The monotonous hiss had been on the air for

> **CLARIFY**
> What effect do the signals seem to have?
> Using a Reading Log

---

3. **Taoism** (tou′ĭz′əm): a Chinese philosophy and religious system that stresses simplicity and harmony with nature.
4. **contemplation of a lotus**: a reference to a Hindu form of religious meditation.
5. **Copacabana** (kō′pə-kə-băn′ə): a once-famous nightclub in New York City, noted for its beautiful showgirls.

WORDS TO KNOW	**synthetic** (sĭn-thĕt′ĭk) *adj.* artificial; not natural **void** (void) *n.* an empty space

218

Mini-Lesson · Literary Concepts

REVIEWING FIRST-PERSON POINT OF VIEW Remind students that point of view is the perspective from which a story is told. Point out that in a story told from the first-person point of view, the narrator uses the pronouns *I* and *me* and is usually a character in the story.

Application Divide the class into small groups. Have each group review the passages in which the narrator explains what happened when the euphio was in operation. Then have group members discuss what the author gains—or loses—by telling the story from the first-person point of view. Each group should designate one member to record the group's conclusions and another to ask probing questions that will lead to deeper understanding.

five minutes! If the engineer's cuff hadn't accidentally caught on the switch, it might be on yet.

Fred laughed nervously, and Lew hunted for his place in the script. "The hiss from nowhere," Lew said. "Dr. Bockman, has anyone proposed a name for these interesting voids?"

"No," Fred said. "At the present time they have neither a name nor an explanation."

The voids the hiss came from have still to be explained, but I've suggested a name for them that shows signs of sticking: "Bockman's Euphoria." We may not know what the spots are, but we know what they do, so the name's a good one. *Euphoria,* since it means a sense of buoyancy and well-being, is really the only word that will do.

fter the broadcast, Fred, Lew, and I were cordial to one another to the point of being maudlin.

"I can't remember when a broadcast has been such a pleasure," Lew said. Sincerity is not his forte, yet he meant it.

"It's been one of the most memorable experiences of my life," Fred said, looking puzzled. "Extraordinarily pleasant."

We were all embarrassed by the emotion we felt and parted company in bafflement and haste. I hurried home for a drink, only to walk into the middle of another unsettling experience.

The house was quiet, and I made two trips through it before discovering that I was not alone. My wife, Susan, a good and lovable woman who prides herself on feeding her family well and on time, was lying on the couch, staring dreamily at the ceiling. "Honey," I said tentatively, "I'm home. It's suppertime."

"Fred Bockman was on the radio today," she said in a faraway voice.

"I know. I was with him in the studio."

"He was out of this world," she sighed. "Simply out of this world. That noise from space—when he turned that on, everything just seemed to drop away from me. I've been lying here, just trying to get over it."

"Uh-huh," I said, biting my lip. "Well, guess I'd better round up Eddie." Eddie is my ten-year-old son, and captain of an apparently invincible neighborhood baseball team.

"Save your strength, Pop," said a small voice from the shadows.

"You home? What's the matter? Game called off on account of atomic attack?"

"Nope. We finished eight innings."

"Beating 'em so bad they didn't want to go on, eh?"

"Oh, they were doing pretty good. Score was tied, and they had two men on and two outs." He talked as though he were recounting a dream. "And then," he said, his eyes widening, "everybody kind of lost interest, just wandered off. I came home and found the old lady curled up here, so I lay down on the floor."

"Why?" I asked incredulously.

"Pop," Eddie said thoughtfully, "I'm damned if I know."

"Eddie!" his mother said.

"Mom," Eddie said, "I'm damned if *you* know either."

I was damned if anybody could explain it, but I had a nagging hunch. I dialed Fred Bockman's number. "Fred, am I getting you up from dinner?"

"I wish you were," Fred said. "Not a scrap to eat in the house, and I let Marion have the car today so she could do the marketing. Now she's trying to find a grocery open."

"Couldn't get the car started, eh?"

WORDS TO KNOW

maudlin (môd′lĭn) *adj.* foolishly sentimental; corny
invincible (ĭn-vĭn′sə-bəl) *adj.* unbeatable

Active Reading: EVALUATE

G Encourage students to think of descriptive words and phrases that evaluate the behavior—for example, *unconscious, foolish, careless, strange, out of character.*

CUSTOMIZING FOR Multiple Learning Styles

H **Bodily-Kinesthetic Learners** Invite students to read the passage and then dramatically act out Lew's arrival. Encourage them to replicate Lew's dramatic gestures and to deliver his line of dialogue here. Then ask them to discuss Lew's character.

Literary Concept: THEME

I Point out that theme is the main idea that the author conveys to the reader. Ask students what idea the author is trying to convey through this exchange about happiness between Lew and the narrator. *(Possible response: The author is suggesting that some people will try to make money on anything—that happiness is not a thing that one should have to buy.)*

"Sure she got the car started," said Fred. "She even got to the market. Then she felt so good she walked right out of the place again." Fred sounded depressed. "I guess it's a woman's privilege to change her mind, but it's the lying that hurts."

"Marion lied? I don't believe it."

"She tried to tell me everybody wandered out of the market with her—clerks and all."

"Fred," I said, "I've got news for you. Can I drive out right after supper?"

When I arrived at Fred Bockman's farm, he was staring, dumbfounded, at the evening paper.

"The whole town went nuts!" Fred said. "For no reason at all, all the cars pulled up to the curb like there was a hook and ladder going by. Says here people shut up in the middle of sentences and stayed that way for five minutes. Hundreds wandered around in the cold in their shirtsleeves, grinning like toothpaste ads." He rattled the paper. "This *is* what you wanted to talk to me about?"

I nodded. "It all happened when that noise was being broadcast, and I thought maybe—"

EVALUATE

G What do you think of the way people have started behaving? *Using a Reading Log*

"The odds are about one in a million that there's any maybe about it," said Fred. "The time checks to the second."

"But most people weren't listening to the program."

"They didn't have to listen, if my theory's right. We took those faint signals from space, amplified them about a thousand times, and rebroadcast them. Anybody within reach of the transmitter would get a good dose of the stepped-up radiations, whether he wanted to or not." He shrugged. "Apparently that's like walking past a field of burning marijuana."

"How come you never felt the effect at work?"

"Because I never amplified and rebroadcast the signals. The radio station's transmitter is what really put the sock into them."

"So what're you going to do next?"

Fred looked surprised. "Do? What is there to do but report it in some suitable journal?" **H**

ithout a preliminary knock, the front door burst open and Lew Harrison, florid and panting, swept into the room and removed his great polo coat with a bullfighter-like flourish. "You're cutting him in on it, too?" he demanded, pointing at me.

Fred blinked at him. "In on what?"

"The millions," Lew said. "The billions."

"Wonderful," Fred said. "What are you talking about?"

"The noise from the stars!" Lew said. "They love it. It drives 'em nuts. Didja see the papers?" He sobered for an instant. "It *was* the noise that did it, wasn't it, Doc?"

"We think so," Fred said. He looked worried. "How, exactly, do you propose we get our hands on these millions or billions?"

"Real estate!" Lew said raptly. "'Lew,' I said to myself, 'Lew, how can you cash in on this gimmick if you can't get a monopoly on the universe? And, Lew,' I asked myself, 'how can you sell the stuff when anybody can get it free while you're broadcasting it?'"

"Maybe it's the kind of thing that shouldn't be cashed in on," I suggested. "I mean, we don't know a great deal about—"

"Is happiness bad?" Lew interrupted.

"No," I admitted.

"Okay, and what we'd do with this stuff from the stars is make people happy. Now I suppose you're going to tell me that's bad?" **I**

WORDS TO KNOW — **monopoly** (mə-nŏp′ə-lē) *n.* an exclusive control of the sale of a product or service

220

Mini-Lesson Genre Study

FICTION Draw on the chalkboard the concept web shown on the left. Use it to explain that **science fiction** is a type of fiction with the following characteristics:

- It often explores the unexpected possibilities of the past or the future, as if asking the question, "What if . . . ?"
- It can be set anywhere—in the universe we know, in an imagined universe, or even in a different dimension.

- Even when employing fantastic creatures, wild speculation, and exaggeration, it has familiar subjects, since it is usually based on real scientific theories and typical human concerns.

Application Have students discuss how the characteristics on the web apply to "The Euphio Question." Students may also enjoy discussing how these features apply to other science fiction stories or to science fiction movies or television shows.

220 THE LANGUAGE OF LITERATURE TEACHER'S EDITION

Upward (1925), Wassily Kandinsky. Private collection, New York.

Art Note

Upward by Wassily Kandinsky The Russian-born artist Wassily Kandinsky (1866–1944) used watercolors and India ink to create this abstract work. The complex of geometric figures—arcs, triangles, right angles, and parallel lines—seems to move calmly and soundlessly, producing a kind of "spiritual vibration."

Reading the Art *How might some pictorial elements in this painting relate to the story?*

Mini-Lesson: Speaking, Listening, and Viewing

ART Explain that the arrangement of colors, lines, and forms in a work of art is called composition. In a realistic composition, the artist depicts natural or man-made objects in a recognizable manner—exactly as they are seen and are known to be. In a composition of geometric abstraction, however, the artist is more concerned with the impact of visual organization—patterns and shapes that are systematically and precisely structured—than with what is recognizable. Thus, lines in a painting can outline familiar forms or can create illusions and make suggestions. In both kinds of composition, the elements of color, light, and dark are used to create the feeling of space or distance. Have students discuss how Kandinsky uses lines in the work on this page.

Application Have students examine the Kandinsky painting on page 225 and respond to the following questions:
- *How does the artist use lines?*
- *What mood do the colors create?*
- *How is the composition of* Auf Grau *like that of* Upward, *and how is it different?*

Literary Concept: HUMOR

J Ask students to describe the humor in this passage. *(Possible responses: The narrator is being sarcastic; he's making fun of Lew's real estate venture, and Lew doesn't realize the narrator is mocking him.)*

**Critical Thinking:
MAKING JUDGMENTS**

K Point out that Fred seems to have moral reservations about using the signals to help sell lots in Euphoria Heights. Ask students to explain why they agree or disagree with Fred's reservations. *(Possible responses: Agree—using the signals would be tricking people into buying something they might not want to buy under ordinary circumstances; Disagree—potential home buyers should check their purchases carefully.)*

**CUSTOMIZING FOR
Students Acquiring English**

2 Explain that *gotta* is the way *got to* often sounds in informal speech, and that in dialogue, writers often try to capture the way characters actually speak.

Active Reading: CLARIFY

L Ask students to articulate Lew's general goal *(to make money)* and then to focus on the specific steps he proposes for carrying out the plan. *(His plan is to have Fred build transmitter sets that will send signals into people's homes. Lew wants to handle the "business end," which means he plans to charge people a lot of money for the signals.)*

"People ought to be happy," Fred said.

"Okay, okay," Lew said loftily. "That's what we're going to do for the people. And the way the people can show their gratitude is in real estate." He looked out the window. "Good—a barn. We can start right there. We set up a transmitter in the barn, run a line out to your antenna, Doc, and we've got a real estate development."

"Sorry," Fred said. "I don't follow you. This place wouldn't do for a development. The roads are poor, no bus service or shopping center, the view is lousy, and the ground is full of rocks."

J Lew nudged Fred several times with his elbow. "Doc, Doc, Doc—sure it's got drawbacks, but with that transmitter in the barn, you can give them the most precious thing in all creation—happiness."

"Euphoria Heights," I said.

"That's great!" said Lew. "I'd get the prospects, Doc, and you'd sit up there in the barn with your hand on the switch. Once a prospect set foot on Euphoria Heights, and you shot the happiness to him, there's nothing he wouldn't pay for a lot."

"Every house a home, as long as the power doesn't fail," I said.

"Then," Lew said, his eyes shining, "when we sell all the lots here, we move the transmitter and start another development. Maybe we'd get a fleet of transmitters going." He snapped his fingers. "Sure! Mount 'em on wheels."

"I somehow don't think the police would think highly of us," Fred said.

"Okay, so when they come to investigate, you throw the old switch and give *them* a jolt of happiness." He shrugged. "Hell, I might even get big-hearted and let them have a corner lot."

K "No," Fred said quietly. "If I ever joined a church, I couldn't face the minister."

"So we give *him* a jolt," Lew said brightly.

"No," Fred said. "Sorry."

"Okay," Lew said, rising and pacing the floor. "I was prepared for that. I've got an alternative, and this one's strictly legitimate. We'll make a little amplifier with a transmitter and an aerial on it. Shouldn't cost over fifty bucks to make, so we'd price it in the range of the common man—five hundred bucks, say. We make arrangements with the phone company to pipe signals from your antenna right into the homes of people with these sets. The sets take the signal from the phone line, amplify it, and broadcast it through the houses to make everybody in them happy. See? Instead of turning on the radio or television, everybody's going to want to turn on the happiness. No casts, no stage sets, no expensive cameras—no nothing but that hiss."

"We could call it the euphoriaphone," I suggested, "or 'euphio' for short."

"That's great; that's great!" Lew said. "What do you say, Doc?"

"I don't know." Fred looked worried. "This sort of thing is out of my line."

"We all have to recognize our limitations, Doc," Lew said expansively. "I'll handle the business end, and you handle the technical end." He made a motion as though to put on his coat. "Or maybe you don't want to be a millionaire?"

"Oh, yes, yes indeed I do," Fred said quickly. "Yes indeed."

"All righty," Lew said, dusting his palms, "the first thing we've gotta do is build one of the sets and test her."

CLARIFY

What are Lew Harrison's plans for this new discovery?
Using a Reading Log

This part of it *was* down Fred's alley, and I could see the problem interested him. "It's really a pretty simple gadget," he said. "I suppose we could throw one together and run a test out here next week."

The first test of the euphoriaphone, or euphio, took place in Fred Bockman's living room on a Saturday afternoon, five days after Fred's and Lew's sensational radio broadcast.

222 UNIT TWO PART 1: FRIEND OR FOE?

Mini-Lesson: Speaking, Listening, and Viewing

READERS THEATER Explain that Readers Theater is a dramatic reading of a passage from a short story, novel, or poem. Write on the board the following guidelines for preparing a Readers Theater:

- Choose a reader for each of the characters speaking in the passage.
- Adapt the dialogue or read it exactly as written.
- Choose a narrator to present descriptive and narrative passages.
- Read the script; do not memorize it.

Application Have students form Readers Theater groups to present the scene in "The Euphio Question" in which the machine gets a test run (pages 222–223), or have them present a scene of their choice.

There were six guinea pigs—Lew, Fred and his wife Marion, myself, my wife Susan, and my son Eddie. The Bockmans had arranged chairs in a circle around a card table, on which rested a gray steel box.

Protruding from the box was a long buggy-whip aerial that scraped the ceiling. While Fred fussed with the box, the rest of us made nervous small talk over sandwiches and beer. Eddie, of course, wasn't drinking beer, though he was badly in need of a sedative. He was annoyed at having been brought out to the farm instead of to a ball game and was threatening to take it out on the Bockmans' Early American furnishings. He was playing a spirited game of flies and grounders with himself near the French doors, using a dead tennis ball and a poker.

"Eddie," Susan said for the tenth time, "please stop."

"It's under control, under control," Eddie said disdainfully, playing the ball off four walls and catching it with one hand.

Marion, who vents her maternal instincts on her immaculate furnishings, couldn't hide her distress at Eddie's turning the place into a gymnasium. Lew, in his way, was trying to calm her. "Let him wreck the dump," Lew said. "You'll be moving into a palace one of these days."

"It's ready," Fred said softly.

We looked at him with queasy bravery. Fred plugged two jacks from the phone line into the gray box. This was the direct line to his antenna on the campus, and clockwork would keep the antenna fixed on one of the mysterious voids in the sky—the most potent of Bockman's Euphoria. He plugged a cord from the box into an electrical outlet in the baseboard and rested his hand on a switch. "Ready?"

"Don't, Fred!" I said. I was scared stiff.

"Turn it on; turn it on," Lew said. "We wouldn't have the telephone today if Bell hadn't had the guts to call somebody up."

"I'll stand right here by the switch, ready to flick her off if something goes sour," Fred said reassuringly. There was a click, a hum, and the euphio was on.

> **PREDICT**
> What do you think the results of the test will be?
> *Using a Reading Log*

A deep, unanimous sigh filled the room. The poker slipped from Eddie's hands. He moved across the room in a stately sort of waltz, knelt by his mother, and laid his head in her lap. Fred drifted away from his post, humming, his eyes half closed.

Lew Harrison was the first to speak, continuing his conversation with Marion. "But who cares for material wealth?" he asked earnestly. He turned to Susan for confirmation.

"Uh-uh," said Susan, shaking her head dreamily. She put her arms around Lew and kissed him for about five minutes.

"Say," I said, patting Susan on the back, "you kids get along swell, don't you? Isn't that nice, Fred?"

"Eddie," Marion said solicitously, "I think there's a real baseball in the hall closet. A *hard* ball. Wouldn't that be more fun than that old tennis ball?" Eddie didn't stir.

Fred was still prowling around the room, smiling, his eyes now closed all the way. His heel caught in a lamp cord, and he went sprawling on the hearth, his head in the ashes. "Hi-ho, everybody," he said, his eyes still closed. "Bunged my head on an andiron."[6] He stayed there, giggling occasionally.

"The doorbell's been ringing for a while," Susan said. "I don't suppose it means anything."

"Come in; come in," I shouted. This somehow struck everyone as terribly funny. We all laughed uproariously, including Fred, whose guffaws blew up little gray clouds from the ash pit.

---

6. **andiron** (ănd′ī′ərn): one of a pair of metal supports for logs in a fireplace.

THE EUPHIO QUESTION **223**

Critical Thinking: ANALYZING

Q Ask students why they think the milkman looks alarmed when he enters the house. *(Possible responses: Everyone seems to be in a trancelike state; the milkman is not affected yet by the euphoria waves.)*

Literary Concept: SATIRE

R Ask students to explain what is satirical about the narrator's attitude toward where his car is parked. *(Possible responses: The narrator—usually a worrywart—doesn't seem concerned that hurricane winds would likely down the dead tree and destroy his car. Total bliss—produced by the euphio machine—has made the narrator irrational.)*

Literary Concept: IMAGERY

S Point out the narrator's words "warm fog of silence." Ask students what they imagine from this description. *(Possible responses: being in a fog so thick you can't see or hear anything; feeling warm and cozy)*

Cultural Note

T Note the state trooper's reference to his gun being "just like Hoppy's." He is referring to Hopalong Cassidy, a popular cowboy character in television shows and movies during the 1950s.

A small, very serious old man in white had let himself in and was now standing in the vestibule, looking at us with alarm. "Milkman," he said uncertainly. He held out a slip of paper to Marion. "I can't read the last line in your note," he said. "What's that say about cottage cheese, cheese, cheese, cheese, cheese . . ." His voice trailed off as he settled, tailor-fashion, to the floor beside Marion. After he'd been silent for perhaps three quarters of an hour, a look of concern crossed his face. "Well," he said apathetically, "I can only stay for a minute. My truck's parked out on the shoulder, kind of blocking things." He started to stand. Lew gave the volume knob on the euphio a twist. The milkman wilted to the floor.

"Aaaaaaaaaaah," said everybody.

"Good day to be indoors," the milkman said. "Radio says we'll catch the tail end of the Atlantic hurricane."

"Let 'er come," I said. "I've got my car parked under a big, dead tree." It seemed to make sense. Nobody took exception to it. I lapsed back into a warm fog of silence and thought of nothing whatsoever. These lapses seemed to last for a matter of seconds before they were interrupted by conversation of newcomers. Looking back, I see now that the lapses were rarely less than six hours.

I was snapped out of one, I recall, by a repetition of the doorbell's ringing. "I said come in," I mumbled.

"And I did," the milkman mumbled.

The door swung open, and a state trooper glared in at us. "Who the hell's got his milk truck out there blocking the road?" he demanded. He spotted the milkman. "Aha! Don't you know somebody could get killed, coming around a blind curve into that thing?" He yawned, and his ferocious expression gave way to an affectionate smile. "It's so damn' unlikely," he said, "I don't know why I ever brought it up." He sat down by Eddie. "Hey, kid—like guns?" He took his revolver from its holster. "Look—just like Hoppy's."

Eddie took the gun, aimed it at Marion's bottle collection and fired. A large blue bottle popped to dust, and the window behind the collection splintered. Cold air roared in through the opening.

"He'll make a cop yet," Marion chortled.

"God, I'm happy," I said, feeling a little like crying. "I got the swellest little kid and the swellest bunch of friends and the swellest old wife in the world." I heard the gun go off twice more and then dropped into heavenly oblivion.

Again the doorbell roused me. "How many times do I have to tell you—for heaven's sake, come in," I said, without opening my eyes.

"I *did*," the milkman said.

I heard the tramping of many feet but had no curiosity about them. A little later, I noticed that I was having difficulty breathing. Investigation revealed that I had slipped to the floor, and that several Boy Scouts had bivouacked[7] on my chest and abdomen.

"You want something?" I asked the tenderfoot whose hot, measured breathing was in my face.

"Beaver Patrol wanted old newspapers, but forget it," he said. "We'd just have to carry 'em somewhere."

"And do your parents know where you are?"

"Oh, sure. They got worried and came after us." He jerked his thumb at several couples lined up against the baseboard, smiling into the teeth of the wind and rain lashing in at them through the broken window.

"Mom, I'm kinda hungry," Eddie said.

"Oh, Eddie—you're not going to make your mother cook just when we're having such a wonderful time," Susan said.

---

7. **bivouacked** (bĭv′ōō-ăkt): camped out.

> **WORDS TO KNOW**
> **apathetically** (ăp′ə-thĕt′ĭk-lē) *adv.* without any interest or emotion
> **oblivion** (ə-blĭv′ē-ən) *n.* total forgetfulness

224

Mini-Lesson: Speaking, Listening, and Viewing

INTERVIEWING Remind students that the euphio problem began with a radio interview of a physicist. Explain to them that interviewing a specialist is one of the best ways to research information. Present the following guidelines to help students prepare and conduct an interview:

Preparing for the Interview
- *Learn as much as possible about the interviewee and about the topic.*
- *Prepare a list of questions.*
- *Be sure to have a notebook or a tape recorder.*

Conducting the Interview
- *Maintain an attitude of confidence and poise.*
- *Develop rapport with the interviewee by using a friendly tone of voice and maintaining eye contact.*
- *Listen carefully and accurately record responses.*

Application Ask students to work in pairs and to imagine that one of them is an FCC commissioner and the other is the narrator in "The Euphio Question." Students should take turns acting as the commissioner interviewing the narrator, using the guidelines provided.

224 THE LANGUAGE OF LITERATURE TEACHER'S EDITION

Auf Grau [On gray] (1923), Wassily Kandinsky. Solomon R. Guggenheim Museum, New York, photo by David Heald, copyright © The Solomon R. Guggenheim Foundation, New York (FN 49.1214).

Lew Harrison gave the euphio's volume knob another twist. "There, kid, how's that?"

"Aaaaaaaaaaah," said everybody.

When awareness intruded on oblivion again, I felt around for the Beaver Patrol and found them missing. I opened my eyes to see that they and Eddie and the milkman and Lew and the trooper were standing by a picture window, cheering. The wind outside was roaring and slashing savagely and driving raindrops through the broken window as though they'd been fired from air rifles. I shook Susan gently, and together we went to the window to see what might be so entertaining.

"She's going; she's going; she's going," the milkman cried ecstatically.

THE EUPHIO QUESTION **225**

Critical Thinking:
MAKING INFERENCES

W What does the narrator's believing it is Sunday, not Monday, morning indicate? *(Possible responses: The euphio causes people to lose all perception of the normal passage of time; the euphio seriously distorts sensory impressions.)*

Active Reading: **QUESTION**

X Encourage students to discuss their questions or comments about the story so far. You may wish to use the following model to help them frame their questions and comments.
Think-Aloud Model *One thought I have is that while the euphio makes people feel happy, it seems to be a pretty harmful machine. When these people are feeling euphoric, they don't take care of their basic needs. The author is trying to make a point about the dangers of total happiness. I wonder if there is anything in our society today that could compare in any way to the euphio. And I wonder if real happiness is actually the blissed-out state the narrator describes.*

Critical Thinking: SPECULATING

Y Ask students what they think would have happened to the people in the house if the euphio had not been shut down as a result of the power failure. *(Possible responses: The people might have become seriously ill or might even have died; they could have been injured and could have neglected to take care of their injuries; they might have starved to death, since they didn't seem to feel hunger while the euphio was on.)*

---

 usan and I arrived just in time to join in the cheering as a big elm crashed down on our sedan.

"Kee-*runch!*" said Susan, and I laughed until my stomach hurt.

"Get Fred," Lew said urgently. "He's gonna miss seeing the barn go!"

"H'mm?" Fred said from the fireplace.

"Aw, Fred, you missed it," Marion said.

"Now we're really gonna see something," Eddie yelled. "The power line's going to get it this time. Look at that poplar lean!"

The poplar leaned closer, closer, closer to the power line; and then a gust brought it down in a hail of sparks and a tangle of wires. The lights in the house went off.

Now there was only the sound of the wind.

"How come nobody cheered?" Lew said faintly.

"The euphio—it's off!"

A horrible groan came from the fireplace.

"God, I think I've got a concussion."

Marion knelt by her husband and wailed. "Darling, my poor darling—what happened to you?"

I looked at the woman I had my arms around—a dreadful, dirty old hag, with red eyes sunk deep in her head, and hair like Medusa's.[8] "Ugh," I said and turned away in disgust.

"Honey," wept the witch, "it's me—Susan."

Moans filled the air, and pitiful cries for food and water. Suddenly the room had become terribly cold. Only a moment before I had imagined I was in the tropics.

"Who's got my damn' pistol?" the trooper said bleakly.

A Western Union boy I hadn't noticed before was sitting in a corner, miserably leafing through a pile of telegrams and making clucking noises.

I shuddered. "I'll bet it's Sunday morning," I said. "We've been here twelve hours!" It was Monday morning.

The Western Union boy was thunderstruck. "Sunday morning? I walked in here on a Sunday night." He stared around the room. "Looks like them newsreels of Buchenwald,[9] don't it?"

The chief of the Beaver Patrol, with the incredible stamina of the young, was the hero of the day. He fell in his men in two ranks, haranguing them like an old army topkick. While the rest of us lay draped around the room, whimpering about hunger, cold, and thirst, the patrol started the furnace again, brought blankets, applied compresses to Fred's head and countless barked shins, blocked off the broken window, and made buckets of cocoa and coffee.

QUESTION
What questions or thoughts do you have about the story at this point?
Using a Reading Log

Within two hours of the time that the power and the euphio went off, the house was warm, and we had eaten. The serious respiratory cases—the parents who had sat near the broken window for twenty-four hours—had been pumped full of penicillin and hauled off to the hospital. The milkman, the Western Union boy, and the trooper had refused treatment and gone home. The Beaver Patrol had saluted smartly and left. Outside, repairmen were working on the power line. Only the original group remained—Lew, Fred, and Marion, Susan and myself, and Eddie. Fred, it turned out, had some pretty important-looking contusions and abrasions,[10] but no concussion.

Susan had fallen asleep right after eating. Now she stirred. "What happened?"

---

8. **hair like Medusa's:** In Greek mythology, Medusa (mĭ-dōōˊsə) was a female monster with snakes for hair.
9. **Buchenwald** (bōōˊkən-wôldˊ): a village near Weimar, Germany—the site of a Nazi concentration camp during World War II.
10. **contusions** (kən-tōōˊzhənz) **and abrasions** (ə-brāˊzhənz): bruises and scrapes.

226   UNIT TWO   PART 1: FRIEND OR FOE?

Mini-Lesson The Writer's Style

SENSORY DETAILS Remind students that sensory details—words and phrases that appeal to the five senses—help readers envision how things look, sound, smell, taste, and feel. Tell them that writers use exact, vivid sensory words to involve readers in the events of a story.

Application Call students' attention to the highlighted passages on page 226. Have them discuss the sense to which each passage appeals. Then ask students to imagine how a euphio machine would affect the members of their class or their families at home. Have them write a paragraph describing the scene, using details that involve as many of the five senses as possible.

Reteaching/Reinforcement
- *Writing Handbook,* anthology p. 873
- *Writing Mini-Lessons* transparencies, p. 46

Sensory Details, pp. 62–65

---

226   THE LANGUAGE OF LITERATURE   TEACHER'S EDITION

"Happiness," I told her. "Incomparable, continuous happiness—happiness by the kilowatt."

Lew Harrison, who looked like an anarchist[11] with his red eyes and fierce black beard, had been writing furiously in one corner of the room. "That's good—happiness by the kilowatt," he said. "Buy your happiness the way you buy light."

"Contract happiness the way you contract influenza," Fred said. He sneezed.

Lew ignored him. "It's a campaign, see? The first ad is for the longhairs: 'The price of one book, which may be a disappointment, will buy you sixty hours of euphio. Euphio never disappoints.' Then we'd hit the middle class with the next one—"

"In the groin?" Fred said.

"What's the matter with you people?" Lew said. "You act as though the experiment had failed."

"Pneumonia and malnutrition are what we'd *hoped* for?" Marion said.

"We had a cross section of America in this room, and we made every last person happy," Lew said. "Not for just an hour, not for just a day, but for two days without a break." He arose reverently from his chair. "So what we do to keep it from killing the euphio fans is to have the thing turned on and off with clockwork, see? The owner sets it so it'll go on just as he comes home from work, then it'll go off again while he eats supper; then it goes on after supper, off again when it's bedtime; on again after breakfast, off when it's time to go to work, then on again for the wife and kids."

He ran his hands through his hair and rolled his eyes. "And the selling points—my God, the selling points! No expensive toys for the kids. For the price of a trip to the movies, people can buy thirty hours of euphio. For the price of a fifth of whisky, they can buy sixty hours of euphio!"

"Or a big family bottle of potassium cyanide,"[12] Fred said.

"Don't you see it?" Lew said incredulously. "It'll bring families together again, save the American home. No more fights over what TV or radio program to listen to. Euphio pleases one and all—we proved that. And there is no such thing as a dull euphio program."

A knock on the door interrupted him. A repairman stuck his head in to announce that the power would be on again in about two minutes.

"Look, Lew," Fred said, "this little monster could kill civilization in less time than it took to burn down Rome.[13] We're not going into the mind-numbing business, and that's that."

"You're kidding!" Lew said, aghast. He turned to Marion. "Don't you want your husband to make a million?"

"Not by operating an electronic opium den," Marion said coldly.

Lew slapped his forehead. "It's what the public wants. This is like Louis Pasteur[14] refusing to pasteurize milk."

"It'll be good to have the electricity again," Marion said, changing the subject. "Lights, hot-water heater, the pump, the—oh, Lord!"

The lights came on the instant she said it, but Fred and I were already in midair, descending on the gray box. We crashed down on it together. The card table buckled, and the plug was jerked from the wall socket. The euphio's tubes glowed red for a moment, then died.

Expressionlessly, Fred took a screwdriver from his pocket and removed the top of the box.

---

11. **anarchist** (ăn′ər-kĭst): someone who wants to do away with government and laws entirely.
12. **potassium cyanide** (pə-tăs′ē-əm sī′ə-nīd′): a deadly poison.
13. **burn down Rome:** Much of Rome was destroyed by a fire in A.D. 64.
14. **Louis Pasteur** (lōō-ē′ păs-tûr′): a 19th-century French chemist who discovered that harmful microorganisms in food could be killed with heat.

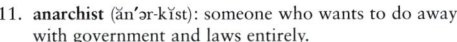

Active Reading: CONNECT

CC Encourage students to first review what motivates the narrator to feel the way he does. Then have them consider his actions in light of their own opinions.

Literary Concept: FLASHBACK

DD Ask students to explain how the author lets the reader know that the flashback has ended. *(Possible response: He uses the phrase "ladies and gentleman of the Federal Communications Commission," which restores the time and setting of the beginning of the story.)*

"Would you enjoy doing battle with progress?" he said, offering me the poker Eddie had dropped.

In a frenzy, I stabbed and smashed at the euphio's glass and wire vitals. With my left hand, and with Fred's help, I kept Lew from throwing himself between the poker and the works.

"I thought you were on my side," Lew said.

"If you breathe one word about euphio to anyone," I said, "what I just did to euphio I will gladly do to you."

> **CONNECT**
>
> Would you have done the same thing if you were in the narrator's place? Why or why not?
> *Using a Reading Log*

And there, ladies and gentlemen of the Federal Communications Commission, I thought the matter had ended. It deserved to end there. Now, through the medium of Lew Harrison's big mouth, word has leaked out. He has petitioned you for permission to start commercial exploitation of euphio. He and his backers have built a radio telescope of their own.

Let me say again that all of Lew's claims are true. Euphio will do everything he says it will. The happiness it gives is perfect and unflagging in the face of incredible adversity. Near tragedies, such as the first experiment, can no doubt be avoided with clockwork to turn the sets on and

WORDS TO KNOW	
exploitation (ĕk′sploi-tā′shən) *n.* a productive use of something
adversity (ăd-vûr′sĭ-tē) *n.* hardship or misfortune

Critic's Corner

"What I liked best about the selection is that it is good, humorous science fiction. It is very funny when one second a cop is yelling about a parking violation and the next giving his gun to a kid."

Peter Lum
Ninth-Grade Member
Student Advisory Board

Ask students to give other examples of humorous situations in the story.

off. I see that this set on the table before you is, in fact, equipped with clockwork.

The question is not whether euphio works. It does. The question is, rather, whether or not America is to enter a new and distressing phase of history where men no longer pursue happiness but buy it. This is no time for oblivion to become a national craze. The only benefit we could get from euphio would be if we could somehow lay down a peace-of-mind barrage on our enemies while protecting our own people from it.

In closing, I'd like to point out that Lew Harrison, the would-be czar of euphio, is an <u>unscrupulous</u> person, unworthy of public trust. It wouldn't surprise me, for instance, if he had set the clockwork on this sample euphio set so that its radiations would addle your judgments when you are trying to make a decision. In fact, it seems to be whirring suspiciously at this very moment, and I'm so happy I could cry. I've got the swellest little kid and the swellest bunch of friends and the swellest old wife in the world. And good old Lew Harrison is the salt of the earth, believe me. I sure wish him a lot of good luck with his new enterprise. ❖

> WORDS TO KNOW
> **unscrupulous** (ŭn-skrōō′pyə-ləs) *adj.* willing to do wrong to get one's way; dishonorable

Literary Concept: FLASHBACK

EE How does the flashback technique duplicate the manner in which the FCC commissioners learn of the euphio? *(Possible response: The witness first states his general viewpoint that the euphio is undesirable, backs it up by telling about euphio's creation and its effects, and then returns to the original point—just as real testimony would probably be handled.)*

STRATEGIC READING FOR
Less-Proficient Readers

FF Ask students to discuss what is probably happening to the FCC commissioners at this point and how it may affect their acceptance of the narrator's argument. *(Possible response: The euphio is making them—and the narrator— unusually content and happy, oblivious to reality. They probably won't want to ban the machine.)* **Predicting**

CUSTOMIZING FOR
Gifted and Talented Students

GG Ask students to explain what the ending of this story says about Vonnegut's outlook on the world. *(Possible responses: He is pessimistic and believes humanity is self-destructive; he believes people will always follow their own self-interest, even when it harms others.)* Challenge students to debate whether Vonnegut's world view is valid or not.

COMPREHENSION CHECK

1. Who are the main characters in this story? *(Lew, Fred, and the narrator)*
2. What is the euphio machine, and what are its effects? *(a machine that transmits radio signals from space that numb people's minds into a "happy" oblivion)*
3. What is the euphio question? *(whether America, indeed the world, is to enter a new phase in which people no longer pursue happiness in the regular course of living but overindulge themselves by buying happiness at will, exposing themselves to a machine that could destroy humanity)*

Assessment Option

INFORMAL ASSESSMENT You can informally assess your students' understanding of the selection by asking them to rewrite the story, or passages from the story, from Lew's point of view. Encourage them to think about how Lew might see the same set of facts differently than the narrator.

Rubric

3 Full Accomplishment Students accurately and concisely describe events in the story and show a clear understanding of Lew's perspective on the value of the euphio.

2 Substantial Accomplishment Students describe the most important events but may show some confusion in using Lew's voice and in presenting his perspective.

1 Little or Partial Accomplishment Students have difficulty describing events in the story and are unable to use Lew's voice or to present his perspective.

From Personal Response to Critical Analysis

1. Accept all reasonable responses.
2. Possible responses: The FCC commissioners will allow the use of the euphio, because the euphio was turned on during the hearing and affected their decision; they will eventually rule against the euphio after they see what happens to them under its influence.
3. Possible responses: Yes, because even with a clock the euphio is dangerous; no, because people should be trusted to use the euphio in short stretches if they wish.
4. Possible responses: Some students will agree, citing Lew's suggestion to sell real estate with the aid of the euphio; some will disagree, citing Lew's willingness to have clocks installed on the euphios.
5. Possible responses: under "Safe Escapes," since the euphio has a clock; under "Dangerous Escapes," since the euphio causes people to lose interest in important things.
6. Possible responses: The future—Although there is no such thing as a euphio now, perhaps something like it will be developed someday. The present—Today, drugs, television, and video games produce some effects that are similar to those of the euphio.

Another Pathway

Cooperative Learning Have each group designate one member to write down the group's responses to each question, another to give verbal and nonverbal support to others' ideas and conclusions, and a third to extend group members' ideas by suggesting additional information or implications. Each group can appoint one or two members to present the group's conclusions orally to the class.

Rubric

3 Full Accomplishment Students work in unison to consider all ramifications of the euphio, and they make clear and reasonable proposals based on their conclusions.

2 Substantial Accomplishment Students show understanding of the general effects of the euphio but have difficulty reaching a consensus on specific proposals.

1 Little or Partial Accomplishment Students have difficulty working together, and they overlook some effects of the euphio. Proposals are inappropriate or are unrelated to the euphio's effects.

RESPONDING OPTIONS

FROM PERSONAL RESPONSE TO CRITICAL ANALYSIS

REFLECT 1. What do you think about the ending of this story? Write your reaction in your notebook and share it in class.

RETHINK 2. From the way the story ended, how do you think the FCC will rule? Explain your opinion.

3. Do you think the narrator does the right thing in fighting against the euphio machine, even though it has a clock on it to control it? Explain your answer.

4. Do you agree with the narrator that Lew Harrison is "an unscrupulous person"? Cite evidence from the story to support your opinion.

Thematic Link 5. Look over the chart you made on ways that people escape from reality today. In which column would you list the euphio machine? Explain your choice.

RELATE 6. Do you think this science fiction story is warning us about the dangers of the future or about the dangers of the present? Use evidence from the story to support your opinion.

Multimodal Learning
ANOTHER PATHWAY

Cooperative Learning
Suppose that euphio machines really exist. Should the federal government do anything about them? Working with a small group of classmates, consider the effects of the euphio machine and list specific proposals for handling this issue. Then compare your proposals with those suggested by the rest of the class.

QUICKWRITES

1. Imagine that you are Dr. Fred Bockman, the scientist. Write a set of **science notes** that Dr. Bockman might have written, detailing his observations on the effects of the euphio machine.

2. An **epilogue** is a short addition at the end of a literary work, often dealing with the future of the characters. Write an epilogue to this story, telling what happens to the euphio machine, Lew Harrison, Fred Bockman, and the narrator.

3. Assume that the FCC approves the euphio machine. Write a **radio commercial** that Lew Harrison might develop for the product.

PORTFOLIO Save your writing. You may want to use it later as a springboard to a piece for your portfolio.

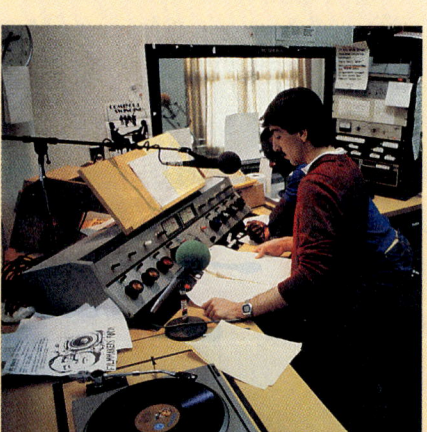

230   UNIT TWO   PART 1: FRIEND OR FOE?

QuickWrites

1. Encourage students to create dates and times for their daily notations.
2. Students may wish to use the same narrator, or they may write from the point of view of an FCC member or another character in the story.
3. Encourage students to include music or write a jingle to accompany the commercial.

The Writer's Craft

Taking Field Notes, pp. 74–75

LITERARY CONCEPTS

The **theme** of a story or poem is the main idea—a belief about life or human nature—that the writer conveys to the reader. Often, a theme must be inferred from the characters and situations in a story. (Review the suggestions for discovering themes on page 16.) Consider the different attitudes that the narrator and Lew Harrison have toward the euphio machine. What different kinds of people in our society do the narrator and Lew Harrison represent? Which character do you think Kurt Vonnegut agrees with?

Cooperative Learning Discuss these questions with a small group of classmates. Then, as a group, compose a sentence or two in which you state the theme of the story as you understand it. Share your thematic statement with other groups and compare any differences of interpretation.

A **flashback** is a part of a story in which actions of an earlier time period are narrated. The action in "The Euphio Question" begins at a meeting of the FCC. Five paragraphs into the story, however, a flashback begins when the narrator says, "My first brush with synthetic peace of mind was six months ago." Identify the point in the story where this flashback ends.

THE WRITER'S STYLE

Kurt Vonnegut is known for his use of satirical humor to convey a very pessimistic view of life. On the surface, some situations created by the effects of the euphio machine are laughable. According to the critic Peter J. Reed, however, what Vonnegut shows is a society heading toward "its own inevitable destruction." Look back through the story and find humorous speeches and actions that either support or disprove this interpretation of Vonnegut's meaning.

Multimodal Learning

ALTERNATIVE ACTIVITIES

1. On the basis of your impressions from the story, create a **model** of the euphio machine.

2. Stage a **debate** among the FCC members about whether to approve the euphio machine. Along with people expressing the views of Lew, Fred, and the narrator, include people with other points of view that you think should be represented.

3. Suppose that word of the euphio machine leaked out and citizens for and against its development started organizing. Create a **public-service announcement** from a citizens' group called AWAKE (Association of Workers Advocating the Killing of Euphio). Design your announcement for broadcast on television during the evening news, seeking to convince people that the euphio machine should not be approved by the FCC.

ART CONNECTION

The paintings of the Russian artist Wassily Kandinsky (1866-1944) are among the most dramatic ever created. In the two reproduced in this selection, expression is achieved in the first painting through simple geometry and through parallel and concentric "waves" and in the second through a mixture of geometric and irregular shapes. However, in both the lines drawn suggest audible sounds. Which painting seems to capture more the humorous, satirical tone of "The Euphio Question" and which reflects more of the seriousness of its theme? Explain your answer.

Detail (p. 221) of *Upward* (1925), Wassily Kandinsky. Private collection, New York.

THE EUPHIO QUESTION **231**

Literary Concepts

Possible responses:
Lew seems to represent people who are solely concerned with making a profit; the narrator seems to represent people who are concerned with what is happening in our society and how it will affect future generations. Vonnegut seems to agree with the narrator.

Theme statements will vary. Possibilities: New technology and those who exploit it may not always benefit society. True happiness is attained through one's own efforts. Total happiness would destroy awareness and motivation.

The flashback ends on page 228 with the words, "And there, ladies and gentlemen. . . ."

Alternative Activities

1. Suggest that students use paper, papier-mâché, cardboard, or modeling clay. Students may also use recycled "found" materials.

2. You may wish to appoint a student moderator for the debate. Then, divide the class in half, with each half representing one side of the issue. Encourage groups to brainstorm objections to or reasons for approving the euphio.

3. If possible, have students videotape their public-service announcements for presentation to the class. Remind them that such announcements are usually brief, dramatic, and to the point.

The Writer's Style

Refer students to the passages indicated by annotations F, J, P, and R.

Art Connection

Possible responses: The bursts of color and irregular shapes in *Auf Grau* have a "cartoonish" feel and seem to reflect the humor of the story. *Upward* seems to be almost a rough blueprint of an otherworldly machine and is more serious in tone.

THE LANGUAGE OF LITERATURE TEACHER'S EDITION **231**

Critic's Corner

Encourage students to think about the theme of the story before they respond and to consider the following questions:

- Does Vonnegut believe that if the euphio were banned, "the euphio question" would be settled once and for all, or does he believe that "the euphio question" is an ongoing debate facing our society?
- One of the results of using the euphio is that people are unable to make up their minds. How does the inconclusive ending reflect this dilemma? Might Vonnegut be suggesting that readers—unaffected by the euphio—*can* make decisions?

Across the Curriculum

Science Have students investigate some of the specific issues surrounding genetic engineering, such as gene splicing, cloning, gene mapping, or selective breeding. Some specific issues to investigate regarding drugs are self-trials for experimental drugs and the medical use of illegal or controlled substances. In addition, students might consider the use of computer technology to establish a national database and the use of highly sophisticated computers that now "compete" with humans for jobs. If your students do not have on-line services, you may wish to refer them to the *McGraw-Hill Encyclopedia of Science and Technology*.

Words to Know

1. adversity
2. synthetic
3. monopoly
4. exploitation
5. unscrupulous
6. apathetically
7. oblivion
8. invincible
9. maudlin
10. void

Reteaching/Reinforcement
- *Unit Two Resource Book*, p. 18

KURT VONNEGUT, JR.

Although Vonnegut uses biting satire to make his point about modern society, his work shows care and concern for his characters. As critic Peter J. Reed explains, "The attacks on social ills obviously grow out of a deep compassion, and we sense the gentleness of this writer."

CRITIC'S CORNER

Anna Burke, a member of our student board, criticized the inconclusive ending of this story: "I would like to know what happens!" Wanting to know how things turn out in a story is a normal reaction. Why, then, do you think Vonnegut doesn't wrap everything up in his ending, by letting readers know whether the FCC approves the euphio machine?

ACROSS THE CURRICULUM

Science Are there areas of scientific research today that might lead to a development as potentially harmful as the euphio machine? Examples might be genetic engineering and drugs, like Prozac, that change one's personality. Debate the pros and cons of such research and development. If necessary, do library research to prepare for the debate. If you have access to an on-line service, use your computer to check out news groups devoted to these subjects.

WORDS TO KNOW

Review the Words to Know at the bottom of the selection pages. Then choose the word that best replaces the italicized part of each sentence below.

1. Planners of the new space mission have encountered *terrible obstacles*.
2. Food for space crews is *made by combining chemicals in a laboratory*.
3. The company that produces these chemicals is a *company with sole control of the product*.
4. The company's *utilization* of its newly developed formulas was accompanied by an outrageous increase in prices.
5. The *profit-at-all-costs* company officers were caught lying about their gains.
6. However, people reacted to the news *with a complete lack of interest*.
7. After a few days, they fell into *a state of acting as if they had never heard of the matter before*.
8. Meanwhile, members of the space crew played chess with a robot that was *incapable of losing*.
9. One crew member's sadness over the old computer was *silly and dumb*.
10. Finally the expedition was ready to head out to the *far reaches of empty space*.

KURT VONNEGUT, JR.

1922-

Kurt Vonnegut, Jr., looks at the darker side of life—the horrors of war, human brutality, and the crush of modern technology—and then writes wildly comic fiction about it. Blending satire and fantasy, Vonnegut's writing portrays modern people's loneliness and their need for kindness and respect. His main characters always seem to be searching for meaning in an absurd world.

Born into a prominent Indianapolis, Indiana, family, Vonnegut studied biochemistry and anthropology in college. He served in the U.S. Army during World War II and was captured by the Germans. As a prisoner of war, he witnessed the Allied firebombing of Dresden, an event that appears repeatedly in his work, especially in his famous antiwar novel *Slaughterhouse-Five*. After the war, Vonnegut got a job as a public-relations writer for General Electric, an experience he later drew upon in writing about the effects of technology and bureaucracy.

In the 1960s, Vonnegut gained a strong following among college-age readers, partly because of his opposition to the Vietnam War. As his writing attracted a larger audience, Vonnegut became one of the most well-respected contemporary American novelists.

OTHER WORKS *The Sirens of Titan; Mother Night; Cat's Cradle; God Bless You, Mr. Rosewater; Jailbird; Hocus Pocus*

Extended Reading

LASERLINKS
- AUTHOR BACKGROUND

232 UNIT TWO PART 1: FRIEND OR FOE?

AUTHOR BACKGROUND
Kurt Vonnegut, Jr. This author is known for his strong views about society. In this film, students will hear the author discuss his works and the compassion he has for society in the midst of violence.

Side A, Frame 15518

ON YOUR OWN

Brothers Are the Same

Beryl Markham

This story is set in the eastern part of Africa, on the vast grassland known as the Serengeti (sĕr′ən-gĕt′ē) Plain. Alongside rises snow-covered Mount Kilimanjaro (kĭl′ə-mən-jär′ō), Africa's tallest peak. The Serengeti is home to many of Africa's most magnificent animals—wildebeests, gazelles, zebras, and lions. The Serengeti is also home to the nomadic, cattle-raising Masai (mä-sī′) people. For more than 200 years, the Masai sustained a warrior culture, which allowed them a great degree of independence from the European colonization that rocked Africa. At the time the story is set, one of their greatest enemies was the lion, who threatened their herds of cattle.

OBJECTIVES

- To promote independent active reading
- To practice and apply skills learned in previous selections

Reading Pathways

- Suggest that students work in pairs to read the story aloud. Suggest that one partner read to a point where suspense begins to build. Then have the other partner read to the next suspenseful point, and so on.
- Some students may wish to keep a log as they read, noting phrases and sentences that particularly impress them because of the sensory images the words evoke.
- Students can create a character chart to show their first impressions of the two main characters, Temas and Medoto; their impressions of these characters midway through the story; and their final impressions of the characters at the close of the story.
- Encourage students to preview the story by reading the preface on page 233 and by studying the pictures and the accompanying captions. Suggest that students jot down questions that occur to them while previewing the selection. Then, as they read, they should work to answer those questions.

PRINT AND MEDIA RESOURCES

UNIT TWO RESOURCE BOOK
Strategic Reading: Literature, p. 21

FORMAL ASSESSMENT
Selection Test, pp. 41–42
Part Test, pp. 43–44
 Test Generator

ACCESS FOR STUDENTS ACQUIRING ENGLISH
Selection Summaries

AUDIO LIBRARY
See Reference Card

INTERNET RESOURCES
McDougal Littell Literature Center at http://www.hmco.com/mcdougal/lit

SUMMARY

Temas is a young man of the Masai people of East Africa. He is waiting with other Masai near a ravine, about to face his coming-of-age test. Each Masai male youth must single-handedly and fearlessly kill a lion; those who pass the test become men and warriors. Temas fears he will fail and be shamed before his bitter foe, Medoto. Both wish to win the favor of the same young woman, Kileghen, who is waiting back at the village for the results of the hunt. The Masai encircle a lion, and Temas is relieved when the lion chooses another warrior to attack. However, Medoto has seen the fear in Temas's eyes. Behind Temas's back, he tosses a stone at the lion, causing it to charge Temas. Temas overcomes his fear and kills the lion. Later, Temas confronts Medoto. He is sure Medoto will tell Kileghen that he was a coward at first. Medoto surprises Temas, however, by confessing that he, too, had felt fear before he passed the same test. Medoto tells Temas that he was impressed by Temas's courage and skill in killing the lion and that he will not reveal Temas's fear to Kileghen. The warriors return to the village as brothers and equals. Kileghen will have to choose between them in some other way.

Thematic Link: *Friend or Foe?* In a moment of danger, a young man finds that someone whom he considered a bitter foe is really a friend.

They are tall men, cleanly built and straight as the shafts of the spears they carry, and no one knows their tribal history, but there is some of Egypt in their eyes and the look of ancient Greece about their bodies. They are the Masai.

They are the color of worn copper and, with their graceful women, they live on the Serengeti Plain, which makes a carpet at the feet of high Kilimanjaro. In all of Africa there are today no better husbandmen of cattle.

But once they were warriors and they have not forgotten that, nor have they let tradition die. They go armed, and to keep well-tempered the mettle[1] of their men, each youth among them must, when his hour comes, prove his right to manhood. He must meet in combat the only worthy enemy his people recognize—the destroyer of their cattle, the marauding[2] master of the plains—the lion.

Thus, just before the dawning of a day in what these Masai call the Month of the Little Rains, such a youth with such a test before him lay in a cleft of rock and watched the shadowed outlines of a deep ravine. For at least eight of his sixteen years, this youth, this young Temas,[3] had waited for his moment. He had dreamed of it and lived it in a dozen ways—all of them glorious.

In all of the dreams he had confronted the lion with casual courage, he had presented his spear on the charging enemy with steadiness born of brave contempt[4]—and always he had won the swift duel with half a smile on his lips. Always—in the dreams.

Now it was different. Now as he watched the place where the real lion lay, he had no smile.

He did not fear the beast. He was sure that in his bones and in his blood and in his heart he was not afraid. He was Masai, and legend said that no Masai had ever feared.

Yet in his mind Temas now trembled. Fear of battle was a nonexistent thing—but fear of failure could be real, and was. It was real and living—and kept alive by the nearness of an enemy more formidable than any lion—an enemy with the hated name Medoto.[5]

He thought of Medoto—of that Medoto who lay not far away in the deep grass watching the same ravine. Of that Medoto who, out of hate and jealousy over a mere girl, now hoped in his heart that Temas would flinch at the moment of his trial. That was it. That was the thing that kept the specter[6] of failure dancing in his mind, until already it looked like truth.

There were ten youths hidden about the ravine, and they would stage and witness the coming fight. They had tracked the lion to this, his lair, and when the moment came, they would drive him, angered, upon Temas and then would judge his courage and his skill. Good or bad, that judgment would, like a brand mark, cling to him all his life.

But it was Medoto who would watch the closest for a sign, a gesture, a breath of fear in Temas. It was Medoto who would spread the word—Medoto who surely would cry "Coward!" if he could.

Temas squirmed under the heavy, unwholesome thought, then lifted his head and pierced the dim light with his eyes. To the east, the escarpment[7] stood like a wall against the rising sun. But to the north and to the west and to the south there were no horizons; the grey sky and the grey plain were part and counterpart, and he was himself a shadow in his cleft of rock.

He was a long shadow, a lean shadow. The *shuka*[8] that he wore was now bound about his waist, giving freedom to his legs and arms. His

---

1. **mettle:** character; spirit.
2. **marauding:** raiding; taking by force.
3. **Temas** (tĕ´mǎs).
4. **contempt:** scorn.
5. **Medoto** (mĕ-dō´tō).
6. **specter:** haunting or disturbing image.
7. **escarpment** (ĭ-skärp´mənt): a steep slope or cliff.
8. **shuka** (shōō´kə) *Swahili:* a loose, flowing Masai garment.

234   UNIT TWO   PART 1: FRIEND OR FOE?

Multicultural Perspectives

THE MASAI   The Masai are a tall, slender people who live in an area that runs along the Great Rift Valley of Kenya and Tanzania. They subsist entirely on their herds, drinking both the milk and the blood of their cattle. Their temporary home, or *kraal*, consists of a ring of mud-and-dung houses encircled by a thorn-bush fence. Each *kraal* holds four to eight families and their cattle.

Sometime between a young Masai man's 16th and 20th birthday, an *unoto* ceremony is held and he becomes a junior warrior. As a junior warrior, he wears long pigtails powdered by red dye. After seven years, the junior warrior will undergo the coming-of-age trial to become a senior warrior, who can marry and have a family. At the next *unoto,* the warrior becomes a junior elder, later to become a senior elder. The elders help the chief make decisions that affect the tribe. When a warrior becomes an elder, his mother shaves off his long hair, a proud symbol of his manhood. The hair-cutting ceremony marks the end of the warrior comradeship and the beginning of a more settled life.

necklace and bracelets were of shining copper, drawn fine and finely spiraled, and around each of his slender ankles there was a copper chain.

His long hair, bound by beaded threads, was a chaste black column that lay between his shoulders, and his ears were pierced and hung with gleaming pendants. His nose was straight, with nostrils delicately flanged. The bones of his cheeks were high, the ridges of his jaw were hard, and his eyes were long and dark and a little brooding. He used them now to glance at his weapons, which lay beside him—a spear, a rawhide shield. These, and a short sword at his belt, were his armament.

He lowered his glance to the place he watched. The ravine was overgrown with a thicket of thorns and the light had not burst through it yet. When it did the lion within it would wake, and the moment would come.

A feeling almost of hopelessness surged through him. It did not seem that he, Temas, could in this great test prove equal to his comrades. All had passed it; all had earned the warrior's title—and none had faltered. Even Medoto—especially Medoto—had proven brave and more than ready for his cloak of manhood. Songs were sung about Medoto. In the evenings in the *manyatta*[9] when the cattle drowsed and the old men drank their honey wine, the girls would gather, and the young men, too, and they would chant to the heroes of their hearts.

But none chanted to Temas. Not yet. Perhaps they never would—not one of them. Not even . . .

---

9. **manyatta** (măn-yăt′ə) *Swahili:* a Masai camp.

Cultural Note

The Masai warrior is known to his people as *ilmurran*, a protector of the cattle. The warrior's spear and sword are his proudest possessions. His shield is oval and colored by clay and juices of berries and plants. Each shield bears a special design showing the age group to which the warrior belongs.

Linking to History

Aspects of Masai dress show the influence of the Romans, who once inhabited North Africa. The Masais' short, curved sword looks like the Roman fighting sword; Masai warriors' hair is cut in the shape of a Roman helmet; and the Masai's robe and sandals resemble those of the Romans.

Cultural Note

Honey is one of the favorite foods of the Masai. Honey wine is served at all ceremonies and is drunk by the elders. Today the Masai raise honeybees, but in the past they relied on small gray-brown birds, called honey guides, to lead them to beehives.

All had passed it; all had earned the **warrior's** title—and **none** had faltered.

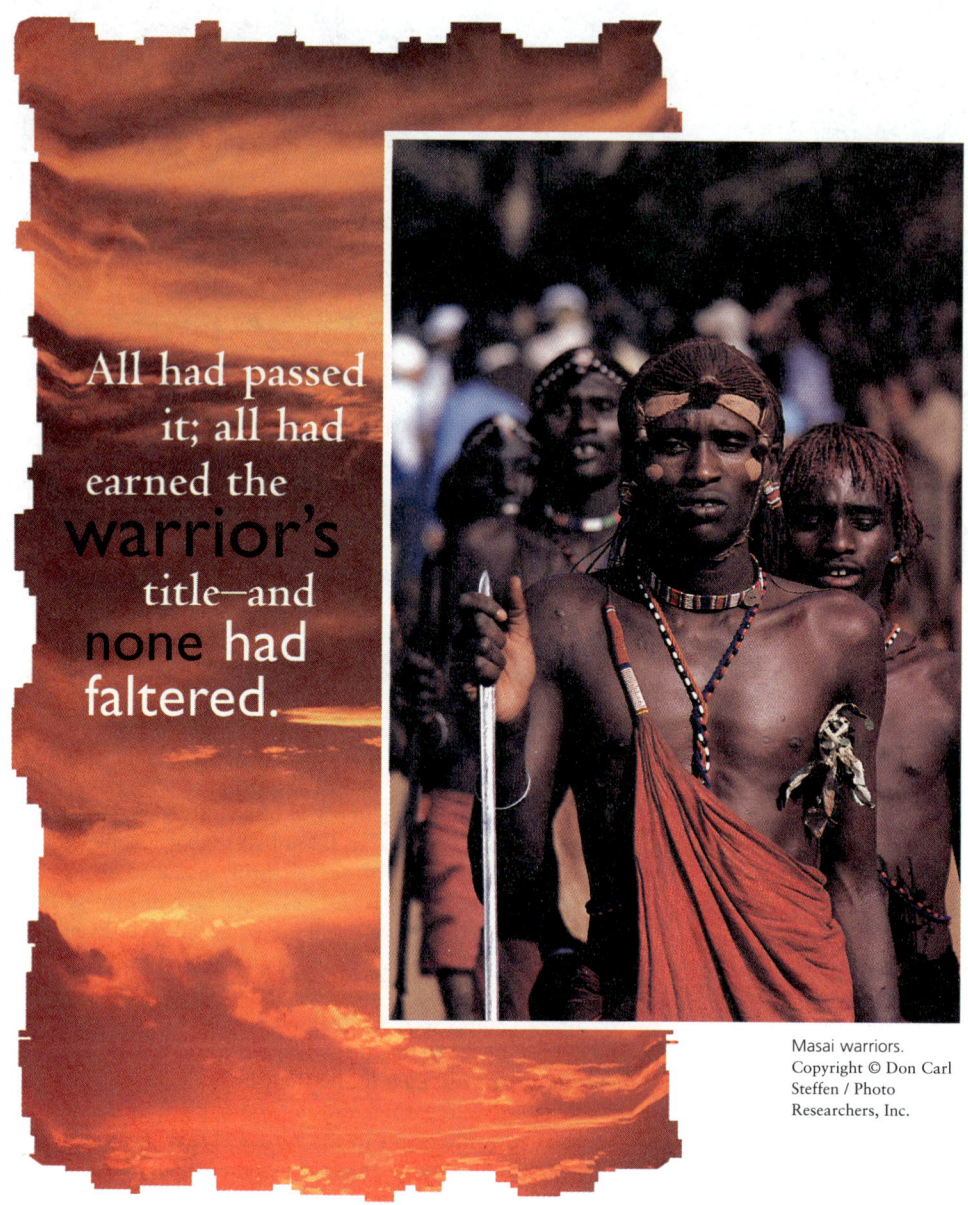

Masai warriors. Copyright © Don Carl Steffen / Photo Researchers, Inc.

DESIGN NOTE

The copper coloring running through this selection—behind photographs and outlining large capital letters and call-out sentences—was suggested by the description, in the second paragraph of the story, of the Masai as being "the color of worn copper." The irregular edges of the color swatches reflect the steamy, hot African sun.

He shook his head in anger. He had not meant to think of her—of Kileghen[10] of the soft, deep-smiling eyes and the reedbuck's grace. Even she, so rightly named after the star Venus, had only last night sung to Medoto, and he to her, laughing the while, as Temas, the yet unproven, had clung to the saving shadows, letting his fury burn. Could she not make up her mind between them? Must it always be first one and then the other?

He saw it all with the eye of his memory—all too clearly. He saw even the sneer of Medoto on the day the elder warrior, the chief of them all, had tendered Temas his spear with the wise words: "Now at last this weapon is your own, but it is only wood and steel and means nothing until it changes to honor, or to shame, within your grasp. Soon we shall know!"

And soon they should! But Medoto had laughed then. Medoto had said, "It seems a heavy spear, my comrade, for one so slight—a big weight for any but a man!" And Temas had made no answer. How could he with Kileghen leaning there against the *boma*[11] as though she heard nothing, yet denying her innocence with that quiet, ever-questing[12] smile? At whom had she smiled? At Medoto for his needless malice[13] —or at Temas for his acceptance of it?

He did not know. He knew only that he had walked away carrying the unstained spear a little awkwardly. And that the joy of having it was quickly dead.

Now he spat on the earth where he rested. He raised a curse against Medoto—a harsh, a bitter curse. But in the midst of it he stiffened and grew tense. Suddenly he lay as still as sleep and watched only the ravine and listened, as to the tone of some familiar silence.

It was the silence of a waking lion, for morning light had breached the thicket, and within his lair the lion was roused.

Within his lair the lion sought wakefulness as suspicion came to him on the cool, unmoving air. Under the bars of sunlight that latticed his flanks and belly, his coat was short and shining. His mane was black and evenly grown. The muscles of his forelegs were not corded, but flat, and the muscles of his shoulders were laminated like sheaths of metal.

Now he smelled men. Now as the sunlight fell in streams upon his sorrel coat and warmed his flanks, his suspicion and then his anger came alive. He had no fear. Whatever lived he judged by strength—or lack of it—and men were puny. And yet the scent of them kindled fire in his brooding eyes and made him contemplate his massive paws.

He arose slowly, without sound—almost without motion—and peered outward through the wall of thorns. The earth was mute, expectant, and he did not break the spell. He only breathed.

he lion breathed and swung his tail in easy, rhythmic arcs and watched the slender figure of a human near him in a cleft of rock.

Temas had risen, too. On one knee now, he waited for the signal of the lifted spears.

Of his ten comrades he could see but two or three—a tuft of warrior's feathers; here and there a gleaming arm. Presently all would leap from the places where they hid, and the Masai battle cry would slash through the silence. And then the lion would act.

But the silence held. The interminable[14] instant hung like a drop that would not fall, and Temas remembered many of the rules, the laws that governed combat with a lion— but not enough, for stubbornly, wastefully, foolishly, his mind nagged at fear of disgrace—

---

10. **Kileghen** (kə-lĕg′ən).
11. **boma** (bō′mə) *Swahili:* the wall around a Masai camp.
12. **ever-questing:** always seeking or searching for.
13. **malice** (măl′ĭs): desire to harm others or to see others suffer.
14. **interminable** (ĭn-tûr′mə-nə-bəl): seeming to last forever; endless.

Multicultural Perspectives

COMING-OF-AGE RITUAL Many cultures have coming-of-age rituals for girls as well as boys. The Apache of North America, for example, conduct a ritual to celebrate a young girl's womanhood when she is between the ages of 12 and 14. For the four-day ceremony, attended by the entire tribe, the girl is dressed in golden buckskin and painted from cheek to cheek with pollen. The entrance to her tepee is covered with cattail fronds to symbolize renewal. Every night, the girl dances inside her tepee until midnight, while outside the tribe celebrates with feasting and dancing. Then, on the last day, the tribal shaman blesses her with these words:

> *The sun ... has come down to the earth,*
>
> *It has come to her....*
>
> *Long life! Its power is good.*

fear of failure. Fear of Medoto's ringing laughter in the *manyatta*—of Kileghen's ever-questing smile.

"I shall fail," he thought. "I shall fail before Medoto and, through his eyes, she will see my failure. I must fail," he said, "because now I see that I am trembling."

And he was. His hand was loose upon the long steel spear—too loose, the arm that held the rawhide shield was hot and too unsteady. If he had ever learned to weep he would have wept—had there been time.

But the instant vanished—and with it, silence. From the deep grass, from the shade of anthills, from clustered rocks, warriors sprang like flames, and as they sprang they hurled upon the waiting lion their shrill arrogant[15] challenge, their scream of battle.

Suddenly the world was small and inescapable. It was an arena whose walls were tall young men that shone like worn gold in the sun, and in this shrunken world there were Temas and the lion.

He did not know when or how he had left the rock. It was as if the battle cry had lifted him from it and placed him where he stood—a dozen paces from the thicket. He did not know when the lion had come forward to the challenge, but the lion was there.

The lion waited. The ring of warriors waited. Temas did not move.

His long Egyptian eyes swept around the circle. All was perfect—too perfect. At every point a warrior stood blocking the lion from improbable retreat—and of these Medoto was one. Medoto stood near—a little behind Temas and to the right. His shield bore proud colors of the proven warrior. He was lean and proud, and upon his level stare he weighed each movement Temas made, though these were hesitant and few.

For the lion did not seek escape, nor want it. His shifting yellow eyes burned with even fire. They held neither fear nor fury—only the hard and regal wrath of the challenged tyrant. The strength of either of his forearms was alone greater than the entire strength of any of these men, his speed in the attack was blinding speed, shattering speed. And with such knowledge, with such sureness of himself, the lion stood in the tawny grass, and stared his scorn while the sun rose higher and warmed the scarcely breathing men.

The lion would charge. He would choose one of the many and charge that one. Yet the choice must not be his to make, for through the generations—centuries, perhaps—the code of the Masai decreed that the challenger must draw the lion upon him. By gesture and by voice it can be done. By movement, by courage.

Temas knew the time for this had come. He straightened where he stood and gripped his heavy spear. He held his shield before him, tight on his arm, and he advanced, step by slow step.

The gaze of the lion did not at once swing to him. But every eye was on him, and the strength of one pair—Medoto's—burned in his back like an unhealed scar.

A kind of anger began to run in Temas's blood. It seemed unjust to him that in this crucial moment, at this first great trial of his courage, his enemy and harshest judge must be a witness. Surely Medoto could see the points of sweat that now rose on his forehead and about his lips as he moved upon the embattled lion. Surely Medoto could see—or sense—the hesitance of his advance—almost hear, perhaps, the pounding of his heart!

He gripped the shaft of his spear until pain stung the muscles of his hand. The lion had crouched and Temas stood suddenly within the radius of his leap. The circle of warriors had drawn closer, tighter, and there was no sound save the sound of their uneven breathing.

---

15. **arrogant:** overwhelmingly proud.

The lion crouched against the reddish earth, head forward. The muscles of his massive quarters were taut, his body was a drawn bow. And, as a swordsman unsheaths his blade, so he unsheathed his fangs and chose his man.

It was not Temas.

As if in contempt for this confused and untried youth who paused within his reach, the lion's eyes passed him by and fastened hard upon the stronger figure of another, upon the figure of Casaro,[16] a warrior of many combats and countless victories.

All saw it. Temas saw it, and for an instant—for a shameless breath of time—he felt an overwhelming ease of heart, relief, deliverance, not from danger, but from trial. He swept his glance around the ring. None watched him now. All action, all thought was frozen by the duel of wills between Casaro and the beast.

Slowly the veteran Casaro sank upon one knee and raised his shield. Slowly the lion gathered the power of his body for the leap. And then it happened.

From behind Temas, flung by Medoto's hand, a stone no larger than a grain of maize shot through the air and struck the lion.

No more was needed. The bolt was loosed.

But not upon Casaro, for if from choice, the regal prowler of the wilderness had first preferred an opponent worthy of *his* worth, he now, under the sting of a hurled pebble, preferred to kill that human whose hand was guilty.

He charged at once, and as he charged, the young Temas was, in a breath, transformed from doubting boy to man. All fear was gone—all fear of fear—and as he took the charge, a light almost of ecstasy burned in his eyes, and the spirit of his people came to him.

Over the rim of his shield he saw fury take form. Light was blotted from his eyes as the dark shape descended upon him—for the lion's last leap carried him above the shield, the spear, the youth, so that, looking upward from his crouch, Temas, for a sliver of time, was intimate[17] with death.

He did not yield. He did not think or feel or consciously react. All was simple. All now happened as in the dreams, and his mind was an observer of his acts.

He saw his own spear rise in a swift arc, his own shield leap on his bended arm, his own eyes seek the vital spot—and miss it.

But he struck. He struck hard, not wildly or too soon, but exactly at the precise, the ripened moment, and saw his point drive full into the shoulder of the beast. It was not enough. In that moment his spear was torn from his grasp, his shield vanished, claws furrowed the flesh of his chest, ripping deep. The weight and the power of the charge overwhelmed him.

He was down. Dust and blood and grass and the pungent lion smell were mingled, blended, and in his ears an enraged, triumphant roar overlaid the shrill, high human cry of his comrades.

His friends were about to make the kill that must be his. Yet his hands were empty, he was caught, he was being dragged. He had scarcely felt the long crescentic teeth close on his thigh, it had been so swift. Time itself could not have moved so fast.

> I shall fail before Medoto and, through his eyes, she will see my failure.

---

16. **Casaro** (că-sä′rō).
17. **intimate:** closely acquainted; familiar.

Cultural Note

A Masai warrior is never without his spear. It is carried with the point up or is stuck into the ground next to him with the point up. Some warriors will not retreat from battle as long as they have their spear; they believe that to do otherwise would insult their weapon.

Cultural Note

Besides being known for their bravery, Masai warriors are known for their strong comradeship. The warriors will go to great lengths to protect and care for one another. One Masai tradition—that a warrior must never eat alone—ensures that even the warrior from the poorest family will have enough to eat.

A lion can drag a fallen man, even a fighting man, into thicket or deep grass with incredible ease and with such speed as to outdistance even a hurled spear. But sometimes this urge to plunder first and destroy later is a saving thing. It saved Temas. That and his Masai sword, which now was suddenly in his hand.

Perhaps pain dulled his reason, but reason is a sluggard ally[18] to any on the edge of death. Temas made a cylinder of his slender body and, holding the sword flat against his leg, he whirled, and whirling, felt the fangs tear loose the flesh of his thigh, freeing it, freeing him. And, as he felt it, he lunged.

It was quick. It was impossible, it was mad, but it was Masai madness, and it was done. Dust clothed the tangled bodies of the lion and the youth so that those who clamored close to strike the saving blows saw nothing but this cloud and could not aim into its formless shape. Nor had they need to. Suddenly, as if *En-Gai* himself—God and protector of these men of wilderness—had stilled the scene with a lifted hand, all movement stopped, all sound was dead.

The dust was gone like a vanquished shadow, and the great, rust body of the lion lay quiet on the rust-red earth. Over it, upon it, his sword still tight in his hand, the youth lay breathing, bleeding. And, beyond that, he also smiled.

He could smile because the chant of victory burst now like drumbeats from his comrades' throats—the paeans[19] of praise fell on him where he lay, the sun struck bright through shattered clouds, the dream was true. In a dozen places he was hurt, but these would heal.

And so he smiled. He raised himself and, swaying slightly like any warrior weak in sinew but strong in spirit from his wounds, he stood with pride and took his accolade.[20]

And then his smile left him. It was outdone by the broader, harder smile of another—for Medoto was tall and straight before him, and with his eyes and with his lips Medoto seemed to say: "It is well—this cheering and this honor. But it will pass—and we two have a secret, have we not? We know who threw the stone that brought the lion upon you when you stood hoping in your heart that it would charge another. You stood in fear then, you stood in cowardice. We two know this, and no one else. But there is one who might, if she were told, look not to you but to the earth in shame when you pass by. Is this not so?"

Yes, it was so, and Temas, so lately happy, shrank within himself and swayed again. He saw the young Kileghen's eyes and did not wish to see them. But for Medoto's stone, the spear of Temas would yet be virgin, clean, unproved—a thing of futile vanity.

He straightened. His comrades—the true warriors, of which even now he was not one—had in honor to a fierce and vanquished enemy laid the dead lion on a shield and lifted him. In triumph and with songs of praise (mistaken praise!) for Temas, they were already beginning their march toward the waiting *manyatta*.

Temas turned from his field of momentary triumph, but Medoto lingered at his side.

And now it will come, Temas thought. Now what he has said with his eyes, he will say with his mouth, and I am forced to listen. He looked into Medoto's face—a calm, unmoving face—and thought: It is true that this, my enemy, saw the shame of my first fear. He will tell it to everyone—and to her. So, since I am lost, it is just as well to strike a blow against him. I am not so hurt that I cannot fight at least once more.

His sword still hung at his side. He grasped it now and said, "We are alone and we are enemies. What you are about to charge me with is true—but, if I was a coward before the lion, I am not a coward before you, and I will not listen to sneering words!"

---

18. **sluggard ally:** a slow-acting helper.
19. **paeans** (pē′ənz): cheers; joyful exclamations.
20. **accolade** (ăk′ə-lād′): praise or other sign of respect.

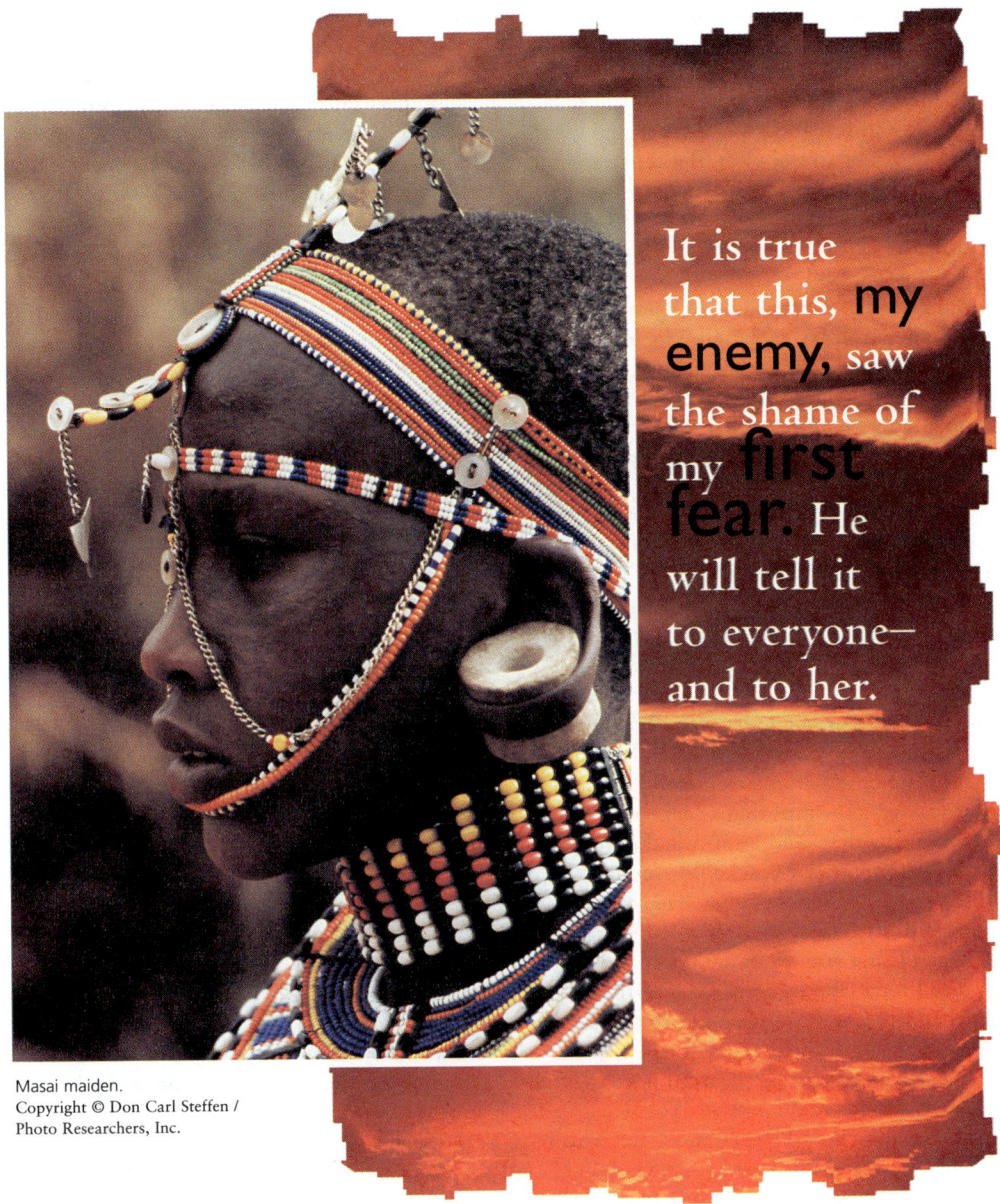

It is true that this, **my enemy**, saw the shame of my **first fear**. He will tell it to everyone—and to her.

Masai maiden.
Copyright © Don Carl Steffen / Photo Researchers, Inc.

 OPTION 1

Cooperative Learning
PREPARING AND GIVING AN ORAL REPORT

Have students work in groups of five or six to research and report on an aspect of Masai culture, such as clothing, settlements, ceremonies, rituals, or changes brought about by technology. After group members agree on which aspect to pursue, they can assign members roles: two students to collect the research materials, one student to review and organize the materials, one student to find graphic aids (maps or photos, for example) that illustrate concepts or facts, and one or two students to make a detailed outline of the report. Each group member should take part in presenting the report orally.

Teacher's Role Before groups begin their research, make sure each group is focusing on a different aspect of Masai culture. Also, suggest resources groups might use, such as encyclopedias, non-fiction writing about the peoples of East Africa, the *Readers' Guide to Periodical Literature,* videos, and picture files. You may wish to circulate among groups to help them stay focused on their topics.

Rubric

3 Full Accomplishment The report focuses on a specific aspect of Masai culture and develops the focus through appropriate details. The report includes graphic aids. The delivery is animated, organized, and easy to follow.

2 Substantial Accomplishment The report is generally focused but may contain some irrelevant details. Some graphic aids may not be pertinent. The delivery may be somewhat difficult to follow.

1 Little or Partial Accomplishment The report is too brief and shows little evidence of sustained research. The delivery is flat and confusing.

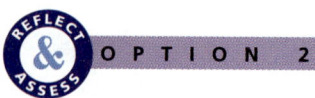

OPTION 2

Individual Activity

TELLING A STORY

Suggest that students create a story that Temas might tell his children about the day he proved his manhood by killing the lion. In keeping with the oral tradition of the Masai, students might tell the story aloud in an informal setting. A good choice might be a library story hour for elementary-school children. Storytellers might first make sequential notes about the major events in the story and develop a brief introduction to share with the audience. Some students may wish to practice with a tape recorder or in front of a small group of classmates.

Teacher's Role Remind students to use the first-person point of view as they tell the story and to use appropriate dramatic gestures and different tones of voice in order to keep the audience's interest.

Rubric

3 Full Accomplishment The student retells the story accurately and dramatically and holds the audience's attention throughout.

2 Substantial Accomplishment The student retells the story fairly accurately but may not always hold the audience's attention.

1 Little or Partial Accomplishment The student's rendition of the story is inaccurate or confusing. The delivery does not engage the audience.

For a long moment, Medoto's eyes peered into the eyes of Temas. The two youths stood together on the now deserted plain and neither moved. Overhead the sun hung low and red and poured its burning light upon the drying grass, upon the thorn trees that stood in lonely clusters, upon the steepled shrines of dredging ants. There was no sound of birds, no rasping of cicada wings, no whispering of wind.

And into this dearth, into this poverty of sound, Medoto cast his laugh. His lips parted, and the low music of his throat was laughter without mirth, there was sadness in it, a note of incredulity,[21] but not more, not mockery, not challenge.

He stared into the proud unhappy face of Temas. He plunged the shaft of his spear into the earth and slipped the shield from his arm. At last he spoke.

He said, "My comrade, we who are Masai know the saying: 'A man asks not the motives of a friend, but demands reason from his enemy.' It is a just demand. If, until now, I have seemed your enemy, it was because I feared you would be braver than I, for when I fought my lion my knees trembled and my heart was white—until that charge was made. No one knew that, and I am called Medoto, the unflinching, but I flinched. I trembled."

He stepped closer to Temas. He smiled. "It is no good to lie," he said. "I wanted you to fail, but when I saw you hesitate I could not bear it because I remembered my own hour of fear. It was then I threw the stone—not to shame you, but to save you from shame—for I saw that your fear was not fear of death, but fear of failure—and this I understood. You are a greater warrior than I—than any—for who but the bravest would do what you have done?" Medoto paused and watched a light of wonderment kindle in Temas's eye. The hand of Temas slipped from his sword, his muscles relaxed. Yet, for a moment, he did not speak, and as he looked at Medoto, it was clear to both that the identical thought, the identical vision, had come to each of them. It was the vision that must and always will come to young men everywhere, the vision of a girl.

Now this vision stood between them, and nothing else. But it stood like a barrier, the last barrier.

And Medoto destroyed it. Deliberately, casually, he reached under the folds of his flowing *shuka* and brought from it a slender belt of leather crusted with beads. It was the work and the possession of a girl, and both knew which girl. Kileghen's handiwork was rare enough, but recognized in many places.

"This," said Medoto, "this, I was told to bring, and I was told in these words: 'If in his battle the young Temas proves himself a warrior and a man, make this belt my gift to him so that I may see him wear it when he returns. But if he proves a coward, Medoto, the belt is for you to keep.'"

Medoto looked at the bright gift in his hands. "It is yours, Temas!" He held it out. "I meant to keep it. I planned ways to cheat you of it, but I do not think a man can cheat the truth. I have seen you fight better than I have ever fought, and now this gift belongs to you. It is her wish and between us you are at last her choice." He laid the belt on the palm of Temas's open hand and reached once more for his shield and spear. "We will return now," Medoto said, "for the people are waiting. She is waiting. I will help you walk."

But Temas did not move. Through the sharp sting of his wounds, above his joy in the promise that now lay in his hands, he felt another thing, a curious, swelling pride in this new friendship. He looked into the face of Medoto and smiled, timidly, then broadly. And then he laughed and drew his sword and cut the beaded belt in half.

---

21. **incredulity** (ĭn′krĭ-dōō′lĭ-tē): disbelief.

"No," he said. "If she has chosen, then she must choose again, for we are brothers now and brothers are the same!"

He entwined one half of the severed belt in the arm band of Medoto, and the other half he hung, as plainly, on himself.

"We begin again," he said, "for we are equal to each other, and this is a truth that she must know. She must make her choice on other things but skill in battle, since only men may judge a warrior for his worth!"

It was not far to the *manyatta* and they walked it arm in arm. They were tall together, and strong and young, and somehow full of song. Temas walked brokenly for he was hurt, and yet he sang:

Oi-Konyek of the splendid shield
Has heard the lowing of the kine . . .

And when they entered the gates of the *manyatta*, there were many of every age to welcome Temas, for his lion had been brought and his story told. They cheered and cried his name and led him past the open doors to the peaceful earthen houses to the *singara*, which is the place reserved for warriors.

Medoto did not leave him, nor he Medoto, and it was strange to some to see the enemies transformed and strong in friendship, when yesterday their only bond was hate.

It was strange to one who stood against the *boma* wall, a slender girl of fragile beauty and level, seeking eyes. She was as young as morning, as anticipant. But this anticipation quickly dimmed as she saw the token she had made, one half borne hopefully by Medoto, the other as hopefully carried by Temas!

Both sought her in the gathered crowd, both caught the glance and gave the question with their eyes. Both, in the smug, self-satisfied way of men, swaggered a little.

So the girl paused for an instant and frowned a woman's frown. But then, with musing, lidded eyes, she smiled a woman's smile—and stranger yet, the smile had more of triumph in it, and less of wonder, than it might have had. ❖

BERYL MARKHAM

1902–1986

Beryl Markham's description of the lion attack that Temas endured did not come solely from her imagination. As a child living in Africa, Markham herself was attacked by a friend's supposedly tame lion. Writing later about that frightening experience, she noted four unforgettable aspects: her own scream, the blow that knocked her to the ground, the feeling of the lion's teeth as they closed on her leg, and—more than anything—the hellish sound of the lion's roar.

Markham's survival of the lion attack is recounted in her autobiography, *West with the Night,* published in 1942. Although born in England, Markham moved with her father to British East Africa (now Kenya) when she was four. She grew up with native children and watched her father turn a wilderness area into a working farm. In the early 1930s she worked as a pilot, flying mail, passengers, and supplies to remote African areas. In 1936 she was the first person to fly across the Atlantic Ocean from east to west. She took off from England and landed in Canada, a feat that rivaled the west-to-east Atlantic crossings of Charles Lindbergh and Amelia Earhart. World War II took public attention away from Markham's daring and adventurous life, and she and her book were largely forgotten by the war's end. In 1948 she returned to Africa and began raising and training racehorses.

Three years before her death in 1986, however, *West with the Night* was reprinted and soon discovered by a new generation of readers. The renewed interest in her extraordinary life gave rise to new biographies of Markham in the 1990s.

OTHER WORKS *The Splendid Outcast: Beryl Markham's African Stories*

Class Discussion
SHARING IDEAS

Teacher's Role After students have read the selection, engage them in a class discussion, using the following questions. Before students answer the first question, be sure to emphasize the importance to the Masai of protecting their cattle.

1. Do you think facing a lion single-handedly is an unreasonable test of manhood for a young Masai? Why or why not? *(Accept all reasonable responses.)*
2. Do you think Temas was justified in thinking of Medoto as an enemy? Why or why not? *(Accept all reasonable responses.)*
3. Why do you think Temas is more afraid of failing than of being hurt or killed by the lion? *(Possible response: Being a warrior is the most important thing to Masai men; according to legend, "no Masai ever feared;" to fail when facing the lion would mean that Temas would not be considered a courageous warrior and that he would be shamed in front of his people.)*
4. In this story, Medoto has a sudden change of heart and loses his enmity toward Temas. Do you think this could happen in real life? Why or why not? *(Accept all reasonable responses.)*
5. Why do you think Kileghen feels triumphant in the end? *(Possible response: Both of the young men she cares about act bravely; she knows both young men care about her.)*
6. Explain the meaning of the title of the story. How are brothers the same? *(Accept all reasonable responses.)*
7. What do you think is the most striking image in this story? Why? *(Answers will vary.)*

BERYL MARKHAM

Beryl Markham spent much of her adult life in Kenya, in a large community of British and other European expatriates. Among her circle were Karen Blixen (better known by her pen name, Isak Dinesen) and Denys Finch-Hatton. The popularity of the film version of Dinesen's memoir *Out of Africa* sparked a resurgence of interest in both Dinesen's and Markham's writing.

OVERVIEW

In the Guided Assignment for this section, students will write a process response to a story. By showing how multiple readings of a text changed their response, students will gain insight into how they respond to new situations and ideas. As preparation for this assignment, they will use the Writer's Style to help them add elaboration to their writing through the use of specific incidents, quotations, examples, and facts. In Reading the World, students will take a second look at an image from real life.

Objectives

- To recognize how authors use specific details to elaborate on ideas
- To elaborate on ideas using specific nouns, examples, facts, or quotations
- To write a process response to a selection
- To respond to a real-world image

Skills

LITERATURE
- Identifying and analyzing methods of elaboration

GRAMMAR AND USAGE
- Placing adjectives effectively

MEDIA LITERACY
- Analyzing a crowd of people carrying signs

SPEAKING, LISTENING, AND VIEWING
- Share initial responses and second and third looks
- Discuss overgeneralizations and how to avoid them

CRITICAL THINKING
- Avoiding overgeneralizations

Teaching Strategy: MODELING

In the following model, the writer uses specific details to elaborate on the main idea. This technique is useful in both fiction and nonfiction.

Ⓐ **Examples** *Answer: The actors used as examples are Johnny Mack Brown, "Wild Bill" Elliot, Gene Autry, and Hopalong Cassidy. The writer also uses cowboy movies as examples. The examples support the main point that the young Mexican Americans did not identify with the characters in Hollywood cowboy movies.*

Ⓑ **Quotations** *Possible response: The writer used this quotation from a young Mexican American to show that the young viewers argued about the authenticity of the Zorro movies.*

WRITING ABOUT LITERATURE

Looking Again

What were your questions and feelings when you first read "The Day the Cisco Kid Shot John Wayne," "The Euphio Question," or other selections in this unit? During closer readings and discussions did you find details that answered your questions and shaped your response? In the following pages you will

- discover how writers use elaboration to expand on and support their ideas
- write your response to a selection and show how multiple readings change that response
- analyze how you respond to new situations and ideas

The Writer's Style: Elaboration Writers pick specific incidents, quotations, examples, and facts to elaborate on ideas. These cause a reader to react to an idea or a passage.

Read the Literature

Nash Candelaria uses details to show how Hollywood westerns did not connect to the lives of young Mexican Americans.

Literature Model

Ⓐ **Elaboration Through Examples**
Which actors and movies are used as examples? How does the writer use these examples to make his point?

Ⓑ **Elaboration Through Quotations**
Who is quoted in this excerpt? Why do you think the writer chose the quotes he did?

> We all had our favorites and our definite point of view about Hollywood movies. We barely tolerated those cowboy movies with actors like Johnny Mack Brown and "Wild Bill" Elliot and Gene Autry and even Hopalong Cassidy. ¡*Gringos!* we'd sniff with disdain. But we'd watch them in preference to roaming the streets, and we'd cheer for the Indians and sometimes for the bad guys if they were swarthy and Mexican.
>
> They showed the Zorro movies several times each, including the serials with one chapter each Saturday. Zorro drew mixed reviews and was the subject of endless argument. "Spanish dandy!" one would scoff. "¿Dónde están los mejicanos?" Over in the background hanging onto their straw sombreros and smiling fearfully as they bowed to the tax collector, I remember.
>
> "But at least Zorro speaks the right language."
>
> Nash Candelaria
> from "The Day the Cisco Kid Shot John Wayne"

244 UNIT TWO: TRIALS AND TRIBULATIONS

PRINT AND MEDIA RESOURCES

UNIT TWO RESOURCE BOOK
Writer's Style, p. 25
Prewriting, p. 26
Elaboration, p. 27
Peer Response Guide, pp. 28–29
Revising and Proofreading, p. 30
Student Model, pp. 31–32
Rubric, p. 33

GRAMMAR MINI-LESSONS
Transparencies, p. 22
Copymasters, p. 24

WRITING MINI-LESSONS
Transparencies, pp. 40, 42

FORMAL ASSESSMENT
Guidelines for Writing Assessment

Personal Response to Literature, pp. 238–249

Connect to Life

Sportswriters also use details to elaborate on the important ideas in their commentaries and reports. Notice how this writer uses facts and statistics.

Sports Article

An explosive fastball and a nasty slider. Pinpoint control and unshakable poise. The Richfield Rockets saw it all from Beanie Ketcham in St. Paul last May. Actually, "saw nothing at all" would be more accurate; they flailed helplessly as, pitch after pitch, Ketcham struck out 14 Rocket batters en route to a 7–2 triumph. But this was no ordinary victory. Beanie, also known as Lee Ann, plays for the all-female Colorado Silver Bullets. The Richfield Rockets are all men.

S. Miller, D. Tegmeyer, E. Dillman, J. Bower
from "Playing with the Big Boys"
Women's Sports & Fitness, April 1995

Elaboration Through Facts and Statistics
How does this article use facts to make a point?

Try Your Hand: Using Elaboration

1. **Using Examples** Support these statements with one or more examples.
   - The Saturday movies were exciting.
   - John Wayne was not the boys' favorite actor.
   - The usher missed some of the boys' activities.

2. **Including Facts** Write a statement about something you know a great deal about, such as a hobby, sports, or a book you like. Use facts to elaborate on your statement.

3. **Using a Quotation** Use the statement and facts from activity 2. Strengthen the paragraph by adding at least one quotation. Share paragraphs in a small group and discuss ways in which quotations are effective ways to elaborate.

SkillBuilder
WRITER'S CRAFT

Using Specific Nouns
As you choose words that will help you elaborate on your ideas, look for nouns that will convey exactly what you mean.

The narrator of "The Day the Cisco Kid Shot John Wayne" started to school with "my new metal lunch box," not just "my lunch." Denver held out "the dime," not simply money. The boys passed "Fourth Street Elementary School."

The writer used specific nouns, nouns that refer to an individual or to a particular kind of place or thing. These specific nouns give readers a better understanding of the story than general nouns such as *lunch, money,* and *school.*

APPLYING WHAT YOU'VE LEARNED
Suppose you find this sentence in a draft.

The boys welcomed the new boy to the theater because he had money for food.

How can you be more precise? You can change the general nouns to specific nouns. What was the new boy's name? How much money did he have? What kind of food did he buy? What nickname did the boys have for the theater?

Rewrite the sentence to give a reader specific information.

WRITING ABOUT LITERATURE 245

Teaching Strategy: MODELING

C *Miller et al.* Answer: The authors highlight Ketcham's achievement by mentioning the variety of pitches she throws, her control and poise, her fourteen strikeouts, the final score, and the fact that Ketcham's team is all-female and all their opponents are male.

Try Your Hand

1. Responses will vary. Passages should contain specific examples, as in the following answers:
   - The Saturday movies, which always featured a spy thriller or a sci-fi classic, were exciting.
   - "Type-cast for the twenty-eighth time!" proclaimed Joey, as John Wayne ambled into the first scene of the Western.
   - The usher missed some of the boys' activities, such as hurling missiles made of candy wrappers.

2. Sample responses should use specific facts as elaboration: for example, players' statistics to elaborate on a statement about sports, or sales figures to elaborate on a statement about a book.

3. Remind students that every quote needs to be attributed to a specific speaker. The writer should relate each quotation in each paragraph to the main idea. You may wish to assign one student in each group to act as the moderator and another as the recorder.

SkillBuilder — WRITER'S CRAFT

USING SPECIFIC NOUNS Point out that specific nouns are usually more graphic and vivid than common nouns because they convey precise images. For example, "Fourth Street Elementary School" is a proper noun that identifies a specific place. "Dime" is a specific amount of money, whereas "small change" or "pocket money" is not.

Application Possible response: *The boys of Chavez Ravine welcomed Felipe to the Magic Box because he had two dollars to spend on popcorn.*

Additional Suggestions You may wish to add the following items to the exercise on specific nouns.

1. One boy wore an old pair of sneakers. (*Gustavo wore a scuffed pair of high-tops.*)
2. At one point in the movie, one boy got attention from the others by making a strange noise. (*Just when the movie monster reached up from underwater, Sammy scared his buddies by gurgling.*)

Reteaching/Reinforcement
- *Writing Handbook,* anthology p. 874
- *Writing Mini-Lessons* transparencies, p. 42

Using Specific Words, p. 383

THE LANGUAGE OF LITERATURE TEACHER'S EDITION 245

Critical Thinking: COMPARING/CONTRASTING

D Guide students to understand that analyzing how their response has changed involves contrasting their first impression of a selection with the revised opinions they formed after reading the text. If necessary, model the process by using the sample chart on this page.

WRITING ABOUT LITERATURE

Personal Response

Have you ever watched a movie and been unsure of your response? After thinking it over or seeing the movie again, you probably noticed incidents and conversations that affected the way you felt about it. Looking again at experiences, movies, news stories, or fiction helps you clarify how you respond to them.

D

GUIDED ASSIGNMENT

Write a Process Response On these pages you will choose a story you've just read and explore how your response can change over several readings. You will look for specific elements in the selection that influenced your response.

❶ Prewrite and Explore

Choose a story you have just read that has special interest for you or an earlier story you found challenging. If the selection is long, you might focus on one section or passage you think is important. Now reread your selection. In a chart like the one below, jot down words and examples that affect you as you read, and note your response. Make as many columns as you wish. After each reading, record how your response changed.

Student's Prewriting Chart

"The Day the Cisco Kid Shot John Wayne" by Nash Candelaria

Ideas I noticed in first reading	First response	Second response	Support
The boys "tolerated" some cowboy movies.	Why do they go to movies? Too much complaining.	I get it. They can "cheer for the Indians."	They even cheer for bad guys if they're Mexican.
"mixed reviews" on Zorro	I don't get this.	I see. They found both good and bad points.	Actors aren't Mexican, but Zorro speaks right language.
liked Cisco Kid	I guess because he's Mexican.	actor looks Mexican	A kid says Cisco looked like his old man.

246

  Assessment Option

SELF-ASSESSMENT After students have completed an exploratory prewriting chart, they should assess their understanding of their responses by answering the following questions:
- *Do my responses show how rereading the text helped me clarify my understanding of the writer's ideas?*
- *Have I identified the details in the story that support the changes in my response?*

2 Write and Analyze a Discovery Draft

Now you are ready to start a discovery draft. Put your responses on paper. Look them over to see what ideas are emerging. Ask yourself some questions to help you focus your response.

- Did I say what I really think or feel about this work?
- Are there any examples from the piece I could use to help explain my ideas?

Notice one writer's response in these writing samples.

Student's Discovery Draft

> The boys in the story love exciting Westerns and see one almost every Saturday. I know how they feel because I love action movies too, but these boys complain a lot about shows and I just enjoy them.

I could add a quotation to show why I think they are complaining. I'd better name the story too.

> At first I thought this noisy and sneaky gang complained too much. But after reading the story a couple of times, I saw what their problem was. They're Mexican-American kids and they didn't like seeing Western movies that didn't have Mexican heroes. I guess it was even worse because the quiet Mexicans in the movies were not as important as other more active characters.

My response changed twice. I need to make that clearer.

3 Draft and Share

As you draft, think about your organization and remember to elaborate on your ideas with details from the story.

- Start with an introduction that identifies the selection and tells how your response changed through several readings.
- Describe each stage of your response and compare each response to the one before.
- Conclude by restating your overall response.

PEER RESPONSE

- Where might details explain my ideas more clearly?
- Describe the changes you saw in my response.

SkillBuilder

WRITER'S CRAFT

Achieving Coherence in Paragraphs

In a coherent paragraph the connection between ideas is obvious. Using related words and phrases is one way to achieve coherence.

Pronouns Use pronouns to refer to a previously named noun. In this sentence, Nash Candelaria uses the pronouns *he* and *his* in place of the noun *Papa*.

> *Papa stood with his cup and saucer held tightly in his hands, his knuckles bleached by the vicious grip as if all the blood had been squeezed up to his bright red face. But even when angry, he was polite to his older brother.*

Synonyms Use synonyms for repeated words. Note how Nash Candelaria uses synonyms in this paragraph to achieve coherence.

> *In the country church on Sundays it was rare to see an Anglo. The only time I saw many of these foreigners—except for a few friends of my father's—was when my parents took me into town shopping.*

APPLYING WHAT YOU'VE LEARNED

Consider how you can use pronouns and synonyms to achieve coherence in your response essay.

WRITING HANDBOOK

For more information on coherence in paragraphs see page 869 in the Writing Handbook.

WRITING ABOUT LITERATURE **247**

Writing Skill: ACHIEVING COHERENCE

The Discovery Draft provides a chance for students to think through ideas and sort through the information they've gathered. You can help them to draft specific responses by teaching the SkillBuilder on paragraph coherence. Guide students to think about how they can use pronouns and synonyms appropriately to make their drafts clear and specific.

CUSTOMIZING FOR Less-Proficient Writers

Point out that in their introductions students may want to grab attention by starting with a quotation: for example, a statement that sums up their own first responses to the selection, or a quotation from a classmate whose opinion they originally shared. Also tell students that they will find synonyms especially useful when they restate their overall response in the conclusion of their essay.

SkillBuilder WRITER'S CRAFT

ACHIEVING COHERENCE IN PARAGRAPHS

Be sure that students recognize that in the second passage *foreigners* is used as a synonym for *Anglo* to avoid awkward repetition.

Application Discuss with students how they might use synonyms to avoid repetition in the sample passages from the discovery draft. For example, in the first passage the phrase *young viewers* might be substituted for the second use of *boys*. Likewise, the synonym *films* might be used for *movies* in the next-to-last line of the second passage.

Additional Suggestions Have students use pronouns and synonyms to revise the following passage: Every Saturday, the movie theater showed Zorro movies. The boys had mixed reactions to the Zorro movies. The movies were about a Mexican hero, but the movies did not show any Mexican actors in the role of a hero. The boys were disappointed in the movies.

Reteaching/Reinforcement

- *Writing Mini-Lessons* transparencies, p. 40

The Writer's Craft
Coherence in Paragraphs, pp. 364–368

THE LANGUAGE OF LITERATURE **TEACHER'S EDITION** 247

Critical Thinking: ANALYZING

G As they evaluate and revise their process responses, students should be sure they have:
- cited the works and summarized important background information
- explained how their responses to the selection changed
- elaborated their main ideas with specific details such as examples and quotations
- adjusted their texts to make them suit their audiences and purposes

Teaching Strategy: USING THE SKILLBUILDER

H You can help students to create variety and interesting prose rhythm in their writing by teaching the SkillBuilder on Placing Adjectives Effectively.

Teaching Tip: MODELING

I Discuss with students how this passage meets the Standards for Evaluation on this page. To explain the first response to the narrator as a "real complainer," the writer elaborates by using two examples: he refers to the boys' noisy, disdainful attitude toward cowboy movies, and he also mentions his grandfather's opinion that boys usually enjoy the excitement in this type of film.

J In the second passage, the writer's response changed when he realized the Mexican-American boys' disdain for the Zorro films reflected their disappointment at the lack of authentic Mexican heroes in the Zorro movies. The quotation the writer uses sharply sums up the boys' disillusionment.

PORTFOLIO

Ask students to jot down what they like best about their process responses. Then invite them to make a brief list of the weaknesses or trouble spots in their responses. Students may wish to include their formal evaluations along with their responses in their portfolio.

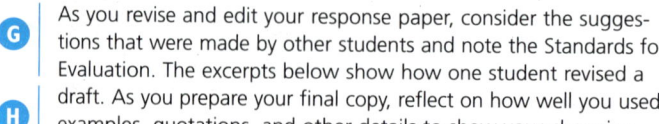

WRITING ABOUT LITERATURE

4 Revise and Edit

G As you revise and edit your response paper, consider the suggestions that were made by other students and note the Standards for Evaluation. The excerpts below show how one student revised a draft. As you prepare your final copy, reflect on how well you used examples, quotations, and other details to show your changing response to a story.

H

Student's Final Draft

My Response to "The Day the Cisco Kid Shot John Wayne"

The first time I read Nash Candelaria's story "The Day the Cisco Kid Shot John Wayne," I thought the narrator was a real complainer. He and his noisy friends sat through movies every week, but they viewed the cowboy heroes with "disdain." I asked my grandfather about Gene Autry and Hopalong Cassidy, and he said boys thought Western movies were great, so I thought it was strange that the boys in the story would go to an exciting movie and not like the heroes.

How does the writer use examples to explain this first response?

J *How did the writer's response change? How does the quotation support that change?*

After reading the movie scene several times I started to pay attention to the Spanish dialogue. When one Mexican-American boy asked, "¿Dónde están los mejicanos?" I understood how he felt. Why weren't there Mexican actors since Zorro is supposed to be a Mexican hero? My response changed. Then I realized that the Mexicans in the movies were "phony" or just dull background figures. That's wrong, and I'm glad this funny and interesting story brought out the correct ideas. The boys weren't just complainers—they understood something wasn't right.

Standards for Evaluation

A personal response essay
- has an introduction that names the literary work and summarizes important information
- gives your first response and explains changing responses
- supports your responses with quotations, examples, and other details

248 UNIT TWO: TRIALS AND TRIBULATIONS

Assessment Option

SELF-ASSESSMENT To help students assess their own writing, have them ask themselves the following questions:
- *Have I presented an interesting introduction that attracts the reader's attention?*
- *Have I provided the background that my readers need to understand my essay?*
- *Have I explained how my response to the work changed?*
- *Have I elaborated my main ideas through examples, facts, quotations, and other specific details?*
- *Have I summarized my overall response to the work in an effective conclusion?*

Grammar in Context

Misplaced Phrases and Clauses You will often use adjective phrases and clauses when you are writing details that support your response to a literature selection. These phrases and clauses should be placed as close as possible to the words they modify because a misplaced modifier can make a sentence unclear or awkward. A misplaced phrase or clause can be distracting if it is unintentionally funny!

Unclear:	The boys watched movies in the Rat House about Zorro and other heroes.
Ask yourself:	What word does the phrase "about Zorro and other heroes" modify? (It modifies "movies," so the phrase should be close to the word "movies.")
Clear:	In the Rat House the boys watched movies about Zorro and other heroes.

In the example below, a student made a sentence clear for the reader by moving a phrase close to the word it modifies.

> Slipping through the back door, Flash Gordo didn't notice my friends.

GRAMMAR HANDBOOK

For more information about placing phrases and clauses correctly, see page 920 of the Grammar Handbook.

Try Your Hand: Placing Phrases and Clauses Correctly

On a separate sheet of paper, revise the following paragraph by placing clauses and phrases close to the words they modify.

> There was popcorn in the Rat House that no one ever ate. The boys bought candy for the movie that was wrapped in paper. Flash Gordo warned the boys not to throw papers on the floor from their candy.

SkillBuilder

GRAMMAR FROM WRITING

Placing Adjectives Effectively

Whether you use a phrase, a clause, or a simple adjective as a modifier, you must place it correctly and where it will add strength to your essay. Adjectives are usually placed immediately before the word they modify. However, to add variety or to create a rhythm, a writer may place adjectives in other positions. Here are some examples.

- Loud, disturbing music blared across the park.
- Music, loud and disturbing, blared across the park.
- Loud and disturbing, the music blared across the park.

APPLYING WHAT YOU'VE LEARNED

Add one or more adjectives to the following sentence. Then rewrite the sentence several times, placing the adjectives in different positions. Which sentence is most effective?

We watched a movie Friday night.

Now examine your draft. How can you vary the placement of adjectives to make the writing more interesting?

WRITING ABOUT LITERATURE **249**

CUSTOMIZING FOR
Students Acquiring English

K Before you begin this page, be sure that students understand that there is a difference between a phrase and a clause. Explain that a clause has both a subject and a verb and a phrase, such as a prepositional phrase, does not. For example, point out the subordinate clause "that no one ever ate" in the Try Your Hand passage below. There are many types of phrases, but misplacement often involves prepositional and participial phrases, as in the examples given in the text.

Critical Thinking: DRAWING CONCLUSIONS

L Ask students to explain why the student moved the participial phrase "slipping through the back door" from the beginning to the end of the sentence. *(Answer: In its position at the beginning of the sentence, the phrase would be expected to modify the nearest noun, "Flash Gordo," which would be illogical.)*

Try Your Hand

Possible response: In the Rat House, there was popcorn that no one ever ate. For the movie, the boys bought candy that was wrapped in paper. Flash Gordo warned the boys not to throw papers from their candy on the floor.

Standards for Evaluation

Have students review their essays for the following:

Ideas and Content
- identifies the work by title and author and gives a brief summary of the work
- gives initial response and gives changing response
- uses details and quotations from the work as well as the writer's personal experience to support the writer's response
- ends with a summary of the response and a conclusion

Structure and Form
- demonstrates proper paragraphing
- includes transitional words to show relationships among ideas
- uses a variety of sentence structures

Grammar, Usage, and Mechanics
- contains no more than two or three minor errors in grammar and usage
- contains no more than two or three minor errors in spelling, capitalization, and punctuation

---

SkillBuilder   GRAMMAR FROM WRITING

PLACING ADJECTIVES EFFECTIVELY
Remind students that not all adjectives can be moved to different positions. Certain modifiers—especially those showing *which one, how many,* and *how much*—almost invariably precede their nouns.

this pencil	*five* houses
enough time	*some* laughter

Application Possible responses:
1. We watched an eerie, spine-tingling movie Friday night.
2. Eerie and spine-tingling, Friday night's movie entertained us.

Additional Suggestions Have students experiment with varying the placement of the adjectives in these sentences.
1. The mournful and unsettling images of the deserted city flickered across the screen.
2. Sad and uncertain, the hero pondered his choices.

Reteaching/Reinforcement
- *Grammar Mini-Lessons* copymasters p. 24, transparencies, p. 22

The Writer's Craft
Adjectives, p. 620

READING THE WORLD

On pages 246–249, students explained how their responses to a literary selection changed after a more thorough look at the material. They should also understand that people often take a second look at their own reactions to everyday situations in real life. In this lesson, students will examine the importance of looking at other people and situations more than once in order to avoid overgeneralizations.

Critical Thinking:
HYPOTHESIZING

M After observing factual details such as the large numbers of people, the demonstrators' signs and banners, and the expressions and gestures of the crowd, have students make a preliminary assumption about the crowd's mood. Students may say that the crowd is threatening simply because it is large and involved in some kind of noisy demonstration. Students' reactions may include apprehension, fear, hostility, or curiosity.

Critical Thinking:
MAKING JUDGMENTS

N Students may answer that a second, closer look at the situation would prompt them to alter their initial response. For example, an awareness that the crowd favors banning weapons of mass destruction might prompt some observers to appreciate or respect the demonstrators. Students may also say that knowing the crowd's political goals would cause them to shift from a personal response to a political response, which would in turn depend on their agreement or disagreement with the demonstrators.

Speaking and Listening:
GROUP DISCUSSION

O Each group may wish to make a chart detailing their first impressions and their later impressions. A recorder could invite each student's response in the appropriate column.

READING THE WORLD

Taking a Second Look

You have seen how reading a story several times can affect your response to it. Can looking at situations more than once affect your everyday reactions as well?

View Imagine that you are walking down a city street. Coming toward you is a crowd of people, chanting and carrying signs. Examine the photo on these pages. What do you see? How might you react?

Interpret As the crowd moves nearer, you look at the people more closely. Many carry signs asking for nuclear disarmament. How does this affect your response to the situation?

Discuss In a group, share your responses to the initial situation and then to your second look. Did people have different responses to the original situation? Did their responses change in ways similar to yours? Discuss how a second or third look at a situation can affect the way you respond. Then use the SkillBuilder at the right to see how looking at situations more than once can help you avoid jumping to conclusions.

SkillBuilder

 CRITICAL THINKING

Avoiding Overgeneralizations

Looking at situations more than once can help you be open to changing your thinking about them.

When you have thought about a situation and have reached a conclusion, you are ready to make a **generalization,** that is, a statement based on examples.

For instance, you might make the generalization that many students your age enjoy watching and playing team sports. However, you must be careful not to overgeneralize, or jump to conclusions without enough examples to support a statement. It would not be correct to conclude that most students enjoy sports, unless you asked a large number of students from many backgrounds.

Avoid using such words as *all, most, every,* and *none* when you make a statement. These words can indicate an overgeneralization.

APPLYING WHAT YOU'VE LEARNED

With a small group, identify the overgeneralizations in the sentences below. Discuss ways to rewrite each statement without jumping to conclusions.

- Everybody cheers for the cowboys in Western movies.
- All teens love to dance.
- Every protest group has an important message.

READING THE WORLD **251**

SkillBuilder   CRITICAL THINKING

AVOIDING OVERGENERALIZATIONS If necessary, supplement the text's example of an overgeneralization by offering other instances with the words *all, most, every,* and *none.* For example: All six-year-olds are troublemakers; most bookworms have no talent for sports.

Application *Possible responses:*
- *Viewers often cheer for the cowboys in Western movies.*
- *Many teens love to dance.*
- *Protest groups often communicate important messages.*

THE LANGUAGE OF LITERATURE **TEACHER'S EDITION** **251**

UNIT TWO
Part 2 Lesson Planner

TIME ALLOTMENTS SHOWN ARE APPROXIMATE. DEPENDING ON YOUR GOALS AND THE NEEDS OF YOUR STUDENTS, YOU MAY WISH TO ALLOW MORE OR LESS TIME FOR CERTAIN PORTIONS OF THE LESSON.

Table of Contents	Discussion	Previewing the Selection	Reading the Selection
PART OPENER **Against the Odds** page 252	**20 MINUTES** • Reflect on the part theme		
GENRE LESSON **Focus on Drama** page 253	**20 MINUTES** • Discuss characteristics of drama • Discuss strategies for reading drama		
SELECTION **The Devil and Daniel Webster** page 256 EASY		**20 MINUTES** • PERSONAL CONNECTION • HISTORICAL CONNECTION • READING CONNECTION: Visualizing scenes	**90 MINUTES** • Introduce vocabulary • Read pp. 256–278 (23 pp.)
SELECTION **You're Short, Besides!** page 283 EASY		**20 MINUTES** • PERSONAL CONNECTION • MEDICAL CONNECTION • READING CONNECTION: Understanding character/Using a reading log	**40 MINUTES** • Read pp. 283–290 (8 pp.)
SELECTION **The United States vs. Susan B. Anthony** page 294 AVERAGE		**20 MINUTES** • PERSONAL CONNECTION • HISTORICAL CONNECTION • READING CONNECTION: Understanding specialized vocabulary	**40 MINUTES** • Introduce vocabulary • Read pp. 294–302 (9 pp.)
SELECTION **Beauty Is Truth** page 306 EASY		**20 MINUTES** • PERSONAL CONNECTION • LITERARY CONNECTION • WRITING CONNECTION	**40 MINUTES** • Introduce vocabulary • Read pp. 306–313 (8 pp.)
SELECTION **The Cultural Worker** page 317 AVERAGE		**20 MINUTES** • PERSONAL CONNECTION • SOCIOLOGICAL CONNECTION • WRITING CONNECTION	**10 MINUTES** • Read pp. 317–319 (3 pp.)
NONFICTION ON YOUR OWN **Fish Cheeks** page 323 CHALLENGING			**15 MINUTES** • Read pp. 323–325 (3 pp.)

Writing	Exploring Topics	Prewriting	Drafting and Revising
WRITING FROM EXPERIENCE **Persuasion**	**15 MINUTES**	**30 MINUTES**	**55 MINUTES**

Time estimates assume in-class work. You may wish to assign some of these stages as homework.

Responding to the Selection

FROM PERSONAL RESPONSE TO CRITICAL ANALYSIS	OR	ANOTHER PATHWAY	LITERARY CONCEPTS	QUICKWRITES
		60 MINUTES		
• Discussion questions	OR	• Cooperative learning (play)	• Characterization	• Legal brief • Summation
		30 MINUTES		
• Discussion questions	OR	• Character sketch	• Tone • Writer's purpose	• List of questions • Memo
		60 MINUTES		
• Discussion questions	OR	• Cooperative learning (cartoons)	• Biography • Characterization	• Pamphlet • Commentary • News story
		50 MINUTES		
• Discussion questions	OR	• Cooperative learning (art form)	• Third-person point of view	• Personal narrative • Composition
		50 MINUTES		
• Discussion questions	OR	• Cooperative learning (interpretation)	• Personification • Tone	• Journal entry • Poem

Extension Activities

• ALTERNATIVE ACTIVITIES • LITERARY LINKS • CRITIC'S CORNER • THE WRITER'S STYLE • ACROSS THE CURRICULUM • ART CONNECTION • WORDS TO KNOW • BIOGRAPHY

Alternative Activities	Literary Links	Critic's Corner	The Writer's Style	Across the Curriculum	Art Connection	Words to Know	Biography
50 MINUTES							
✔		✔	✔	HISTORY		✔	✔
30 MINUTES							
✔	✔			HEALTH		✔	✔
20 MINUTES							
✔	✔				✔		✔
40 MINUTES							
✔	✔			FINE ART	✔	✔	
30 MINUTES							
✔		✔	✔				✔

Publishing and Reflecting

30 MINUTES

PART 2

REFLECTING ON THEME

Read this paragraph aloud to students. Then have each student select a person he or she admires for that person's triumph over difficult odds: either a personal friend or relative or some public figure. Then propose that each student design an "open mind diagram" for one such person: inside an outline of a head, they can write words and draw images that epitomize the person's determination and related qualities. Ask them to share their diagrams with a partner.

---- **What Do You Think?** ----

As students attempt to come up with solutions, ask them to consider whether a group or an individual is better-suited to solving the problem. You might ask, as a starting point, whether students usually ask advice when they confront a challenge, or whether they prefer to try to overcome it without help. Students will return to this activity on page 281.

UNIT TWO **PART 2**

AGAINST THE ODDS

REFLECTING ON THEME

You have probably heard the old saying "When the going gets tough, the tough get going." When the odds against success are overwhelming and the chances of coming out on top seem impossible, some people have the inner strength to see the challenge through. Others just give up. As you read this part of Unit Two, think about the challenges that the characters in the selections face. Imagine yourself confronted with similar challenges.

What Do You Think? Working with a partner, think of a challenging situation or obstacle that you might face as you grow up. Suppose, for example, that you want to try out for a team sport but don't think you're good enough to make the team. Write the situation or obstacle on a sheet of paper, and exchange papers with another pair of students. Then, with your partner, brainstorm solutions to the other students' situation or obstacle as they try to solve yours. Share with the class your strategies for dealing with the challenge.

Stephen Vincent Benét	**The Devil and Daniel Webster** *What are your chances when the devil himself picks the jury?*	255
Sucheng Chan	**You're Short, Besides!** *The good intentions of others can be the biggest obstacle for a person with a disability.*	282
Margaret Truman	**The United States vs. Susan B. Anthony** *Was she a fanatic or a hero?*	293
Anna Guest	**Beauty Is Truth** *If coal yards and flaking plaster are truth, where is beauty?*	305
Sue Doro	**The Cultural Worker** *It stayed outside, waiting, and now midnight had finally arrived.*	316
María Herrera-Sobek	**My Poetry/Mi Poesía/** INSIGHT *The persistence of poetry*	320
Amy Tan	**Fish Cheeks** *The mother knew how much her daughter suffered during dinner.*	323

FOCUS ON DRAMA

Reading stories is fun, and so is hearing an exciting story read aloud—but there's nothing quite like watching a good story take place right before your eyes. That is what makes drama the most real and immediate of all forms of literature. With a good play, you sit back in your seat and watch life going on in front of you—love, adventure, tragedy, comedy, and everything in between.

Drama is defined as any story in dialogue that is performed by actors for an audience. The earliest dramas probably originated in religious festivals, and audiences have responded to the immediacy of drama up to the present day. Even if you've never seen a play performed on-stage, you've experienced drama every time you've watched a movie or a video or a story on TV or even listened to a radio play. All of these forms tend to share some of the following elements.

PLOT Just as in fiction, plot is the sequence of actions or events that make up the story. These actions are interrelated, with one event leading to another. As in fiction, a problem or conflict appears, grows in intensity, reaches a peak, and is finally resolved. The standard elements of plot are **exposition, rising action, climax,** and **falling action.** These elements are described in detail on page 16.

In drama, the action is often divided into **scenes,** with each scene having a different time or place. In long plays, scenes are grouped into **acts,** which are almost like chapters in a book. *The Devil and Daniel Webster* is a one-act play, with two scene changes.

CHARACTERS In drama the human beings (or sometimes animals or imaginary creatures) can be **main** or **minor** characters. The central character, usually the one that the audience tends to identify with, is called the **protagonist.** The principal character in opposition to the protagonist is called the **antagonist,** and usually the central conflict involves these two characters. In *The Devil and Daniel Webster,* whom would you expect the antagonist to be?

DIALOGUE Even more than fiction, drama depends on dialogue—that is, the conversation between the characters. It is mostly through dialogue that the plot of the play and the personalities of the characters are revealed. The words each character says are written next to the character's name, as in the following example from *The Devil and Daniel Webster:*

FOCUS ON DRAMA

This feature defines drama and provides an explanation of the terms used to discuss it. It also introduces students to the conventions of the genre and suggests strategies for reading dramas. The terms introduced here are covered in depth in the dramas that follow.

Objectives

- To understand and appreciate drama
- To understand the elements of drama: plot, characters, dialogue, and stage directions
- To learn effective strategies for reading drama

Teaching Strategies: ELEMENTS OF DRAMA

Plot Have a volunteer summarize the plot of a recent episode of a TV series. Then have other volunteers identify the rising action, climax, and falling action. Point out that exposition in drama is conveyed visually or through spoken words.

Characters Ask students to identify the main and minor characters of that same television series and the protagonist and antagonist in recent plays or movies.

Dialogue Direct students to browse the pages of *The Devil and Daniel Webster* to see how dialogue helps reveal the personalities of the characters in the play. To demonstrate the use of confidants and asides, sketch out a brief scene, perhaps a boy recalling his embarrassment when he spilled milk all over another student. Have two students role-play the scene as the boy talking to a friend, and have another student extemporize a monologue.

Stage Directions Point out that some playwrights provide extensive stage directions, while others provide very few, leaving the choice of scenery and actor movements to the director of the play. Have students browse in *The Devil and Daniel Webster* to identify the purpose of some of the stage directions.

Reading Strategies: MODELING

Invite volunteers to read aloud the Strategies for Reading Drama. Then model the strategies as students read the opening scene of *The Devil and Daniel Webster*. Tell students they will be using these strategies as they read dramas throughout the book.

- **Read the beginning carefully.** *"I see that this play opens at the wedding celebration of a young farming couple, and the guests are having a good time; they're cheerful and comfortable and feeling kindly toward Jabez and Mary."*
- **Visualize the play as you read it.** *"I have that big, comfortable room in my mind's eye, complete with furniture and curtains waving in the summer breeze. I see Jabez and Mary in their 'store-bought' clothes, and the other guests in their old-timey best."*
- **Look for conflict.** *"I also see a hint of conflict. Jabez and Mary look so pleased and happy, but the neighbors are gossiping about the source of Jabez's wealth."*
- **Get involved with the story.** *"I bet something about Jabez's money is going to threaten his happiness. Of course, the devil and Daniel Webster still have to get involved. The devil—temptation—I wonder—"*
- **Read the play aloud with others.** Assign volunteers to read the parts of the characters from the play. When the parts have been assigned, have students read the play aloud. Other students who are not reading can create any sound effects needed.

Jabez. Are you happy, Mary?

Mary. Yes. So happy, I'm afraid.

In dramatic dialogue there are several ways that the audience can find out what a character is actually thinking. One way is to have the main character confide in a character called the **confidant.** Mary, for example, is the confidant to her husband, Jabez, in *The Devil and Daniel Webster*. Their dialogue helps to reveal Jabez's thoughts. Another dramatic device is the **aside,** in which a character turns aside and speaks his or her thoughts aloud, in words meant to be heard by the audience but not by the other characters. An aside spoken by a character alone on stage is called a **soliloquy** or **monologue.**

STAGE DIRECTIONS A play normally includes a set of instructions, called stage directions, often printed in italic type and separated from the dialogue by parentheses. Stage directions give important information to the reader and to the performers. Stage directions are most often used to explain where and how actors should move and speak. They may also describe the **scenery** or **setting**—that is, the physical environment on the stage that suggests a specific time and place. For example, *The Devil and Daniel Webster* begins, *"The scene is the main room of a New Hampshire farmhouse in 1841, a big comfortable room . . ."* Stage directions specify the props, which are the furniture and other objects used on stage. They also describe lighting, costumes, music, or sound effects. In a film or television play, such as Stephen King's *Sorry, Right Number* in Unit Six, these directions describe important details such as camera angles and close-ups. One of the most important functions of stage directions is to give hints to the performers as to how the characters look, speak, and behave.

STRATEGIES FOR READING DRAMA

- **Read the beginning carefully.** It always helps to pay close attention to the beginning of any story. This is especially true when you're reading a play. Start by looking over the cast of characters. Then read the opening stage directions, which introduce you to the setting and perhaps to some of the characters as well. As you read the opening scene of a play, remember that its purpose is not only to get the story moving but also to give you background information that you need to know.

- **Visualize the play as you read it.** Imagine you are actually seeing the action, watching the characters move and speak, hearing their words. Stage the play in your mind, or think of it as a movie you are watching. You might even want to say some of the speeches aloud as you read.

- **Look for conflict.** Remember that drama, like fiction, turns upon some kind of problem or conflict. Look for early signs that trouble may be brewing somewhere. Decide who the most important character is, and then notice how he or she is handling the problem.

- **Get involved with the story.** Drama, like other forms of literature, is always more enjoyable when you become involved in the characters and situations. Try to identify with one or more of the characters, decide which one you like best, think about the motivations behind the characters' actions, and try to predict what will happen next.

- **Read the play aloud with others.** One of the best ways to really enjoy a play is to read it aloud with others. Get together with friends or classmates and perform a Readers Theater in which actors read their parts instead of reciting from memory. Have each person read aloud the lines of a different character, and ask others to create sound and lighting effects. Or if you're up to it, take part in a staged production of a play. By the time you've finished rehearsing and performing, the drama will be a part of you.

254 UNIT TWO PART 2: AGAINST THE ODDS

PREVIEWING

DRAMA

The Devil and Daniel Webster
Stephen Vincent Benét

Activating Prior Knowledge
PERSONAL CONNECTION

In the play you are about to read, a character realizes how precious his freedom is when he faces the possibility of losing it. Think about what freedom means to you in your everyday life. What kinds of things do you enjoy being free to do? To dress the way you want? To listen to the kind of music you like? In your notebook, create a cluster diagram to explore the associations you have with the word *freedom*.

Building Background
HISTORICAL CONNECTION

In *The Devil and Daniel Webster,* a famous American statesman goes against the odds by trying in a very dramatic way to win a man's freedom. Although the play is fictional, Daniel Webster was not. Considered one of the best lawyers and the best-known public speaker of his time, Webster was a major figure in American life in the early and middle 1800s. He argued important cases before the Supreme Court and served as congressman, senator, and secretary of state. Throughout his career, Webster strongly defended the Constitution. He also worked to preserve the Union in the years before the Civil War.

Active Reading / Setting a Purpose
READING CONNECTION

Visualizing Scenes *The Devil and Daniel Webster* is a one-act play in which the scene changes from a large room in a farmhouse to a courtroom—and back again to the farmhouse. The opening stage directions describe the stage at the beginning of the play. As you read these directions, try to picture the setting in your mind. You may find it helpful to sketch the scene in your notebook. Draw an empty stage and then fill in the details of the setting as they are described. When the scene changes to the courtroom, sketch the new setting in your notebook.

OVERVIEW

Objectives

- To understand and appreciate a play about a great American lawyer winning a seemingly impossible case
- To identify and understand characterization
- To appreciate and write idioms
- To express understanding of a selection through a choice of writing forms, including a legal brief and a summation
- To extend understanding of the selection through a variety of multimodal and cross-curricular activities

Skills

LITERARY CONCEPTS
- Characterization
- Conflict
- Mood

THE WRITER'S STYLE
- Using dialogue in plays and skits

GENRE STUDY
- Drama: one-act play

GRAMMAR
- Correlative conjunctions

SPEAKING, LISTENING, AND VIEWING
- Choral reading
- Speeches
- Group discussion
- Oral presentation

ALTERNATIVE
Previewing

In lieu of writing about their views of freedom in everyday life, students may choose partners and discuss them.

Personal Connection

Discussion Prompts Think about what freedom means to you. Describe your feelings to your partner. Use the following questions as prompts:

- Has your freedom ever been abridged?
- Under what circumstances did that happen?
- What did you do about it?

As you read The Devil and Daniel Webster, *watch to see how Jabez Stone reacts to the threat of losing his freedom.*

PRINT AND MEDIA RESOURCES

UNIT TWO RESOURCE BOOK
Strategic Reading: Literature, p. 37
Vocabulary SkillBuilder, p. 38

GRAMMAR MINI-LESSONS
Transparencies, p. 5
Copymasters, p. 7

WRITING MINI-LESSONS
Transparencies, p. 56

ACCESS FOR STUDENTS ACQUIRING ENGLISH
Selection Summaries
Reading Support

FORMAL ASSESSMENT
Selection Test, pp. 45–46
 Test Generator

 AUDIO LIBRARY
See Reference Card

 LASERLINKS
Art Gallery

SUMMARY

This play begins with the wedding celebration for Jabez and Mary Stone. Friends and neighbors and the famous statesman and lawyer Daniel Webster attend. The celebrating is interrupted when Scratch, the devil, appears. Ten years before, Jabez had signed a contract with Scratch, offering his soul in exchange for success. Jabez has been successful, and now Scratch has come to collect Jabez's soul. The villagers flee, and Jabez explains the situation to Mary. Webster offers to represent Jabez as his attorney. Scratch summons dead men to form a jury of the damned, and he also summons a judge from the Salem witch trials. All of Webster's pleas are ignored until he reminds the jury that once they were living humans who loved liberty. They declare Jabez not guilty. Jabez is free from his contract, and Webster extracts a promise from Scratch never to bother anyone from New Hampshire again.

Thematic Link: *Against the Odds* It would be hard to imagine a more hopeless situation than that of pleading a case against the devil's hand-picked jury, but Daniel Webster trusts his own skill and wins.

DESIGN NOTE

The image depicted under the play's title is a death's head moth, stylized in floral folk-art patterns typical of 19th-century America.

Reading the Art *In what way has the designer reinforced the motif of the moth on this page?*

The Devil and Daniel Webster

STEPHEN VINCENT BENÉT

CAST

Jabez Stone   Mary Stone
Daniel Webster
Mr. Scratch
Men and Women of Cross Corners, New Hampshire
Justice Hathorne's Clerk
Justice Hathorne
The Fiddler
King Philip
Walter Butler
Simon Girty
Teach

Scene—Jabez Stone's farmhouse.
Time—1841.

WORDS TO KNOW

bias (bī′əs) *n.* an attitude in which a person is in favor of someone or something without having a good reason for this preference (p. 274)
contemptuously (kən-tĕmp′chōō-əs-lē) *adv.* scornfully; without respect (p. 270)
discordant (dĭ-skôr′dnt) *adj.* disagreeable in sound, harsh (p. 260)
fanaticism (fə-năt′ĭ-sĭz′əm) *n.* excessive, unreasonable zeal or enthusiasm (p. 264)
feigned (fānd) *adj.* not real; pretended (p. 261)

homage (hŏm′ĭj) *n.* special honor or respect shown publicly (p. 260)
insinuatingly (ĭn-sĭn′yōō-āt′ĭng-lē) *adv.* in a hinting, indirect, or suggestive manner (p. 260)
intimidation (ĭn-tĭm′ĭ-dā′shən) *n.* the use of threats to frighten or inhibit another (p. 274)
oppressor (ə-prĕs′ər) *n.* one who keeps others down by the cruel use of power (p. 277)
placidly (plăs′ĭd-lē) *adv.* calmly (p. 268)

The scene is the main room of a New Hampshire farmhouse in 1841, a big comfortable room that hasn't yet developed the stuffiness of a front parlor. A door, right, leads to the kitchen—a door, left, to the outside. There is a fireplace, right. Windows, in center, show a glimpse of summer landscape. Most of the furniture has been cleared away for the dance which follows the wedding of Jabez and Mary Stone, but there is a settee or bench by the fireplace, a table, left, with some wedding presents upon it, at least three chairs by the table, and a cider barrel on which the Fiddler sits, in front of the table. Near the table, against the sidewall, there is a cupboard where there are glasses and a jug. There is a clock.

A country wedding has been in progress—the wedding of Jabez and Mary Stone. He is a husky young farmer, around twenty-eight or thirty. The bride is in her early twenties. He is dressed in stiff, store clothes but not ridiculously—they are of good quality and he looks important. The bride is in a simple white or cream wedding dress and may carry a small, stiff bouquet of country flowers.

Now the wedding is over and the guests are dancing. The Fiddler is perched on the cider barrel. He plays and calls square-dance figures. The guests include the recognizable types of a small New England town, doctor, lawyer, storekeeper, old maid, schoolteacher, farmer, etc. There is an air of prosperity and hearty country mirth about the whole affair.

At rise, Jabez and Mary are up left center, receiving the congratulations of a few last guests who talk to them and pass on to the dance. The others are dancing. There is a buzz of conversation that follows the tune of the dance music.

First Woman. Right nice wedding.

First Man. Handsome couple.

Second Woman (*passing through crowd with dish of oyster stew*). Oysters for supper!

Second Man (*passing cake*). And layer cake—layer cake—

An Old Man (*hobbling toward cider barrel*). Makes me feel young again! Oh, by jingo!

An Old Woman (*pursuing him*). Henry, Henry, you've been drinking cider!

Fiddler. Set to your partners! Do-si-do![1]

Women. Mary and Jabez.

Men. Jabez and Mary.

A Woman. Where's the State Senator?

A Man. Where's the lucky bride?

(*With cries of "Mary—Jabez—strike it up, fiddler—make room for the bride and groom," the* Crowd *drags* Mary *and* Jabez, *pleased but embarrassed, into the center of the room and* Mary *and* Jabez *do a little solo dance, while the* Crowd *claps, applauds and makes various remarks.*)

A Man. Handsome steppers!

A Woman. She's pretty as a picture.

A Second Man. Cut your pigeon-wing, Jabez!

The Old Man. Young again, young again, that's the way I feel! (*He tries to cut a pigeon-wing himself.*)

The Old Woman. Henry, Henry, careful of your rheumatiz!

A Third Woman. Makes me feel all teary—seeing them so happy.

(*The solo dance ends, the music stops for a moment.*)

---

1. **Do-si-do** (dō′sē-dō′): a signal to perform the square-dance movement of the same name. Other square-dancing terms follow, such as "cut your pigeon-wing," "scratch for corn," and "left and right—grand chain."

THE DEVIL AND DANIEL WEBSTER 257

Mini-Lesson The Writer's Style

USING DIALOGUE IN PLAYS AND SKITS

Dialogue is a conversation between two or more characters. Although dialogue is used in all kinds of writing, it makes up almost the entire body of a play or skit. It must carry the action forward and provide much of the characterization. In a play or skit, the words each character says are written next to the character's name.

Application Have students write a dialogue between Mary and Jabez Stone after the trial. Use the dialogue to reveal how Stone's attitude toward success has changed.

Reteaching/Reinforcement
- Writing Handbook, anthology p. 877
- *Writing Mini-Lessons* transparencies, p. 56

Using Dialogue in Plays and Skits, p. 436

CUSTOMIZING FOR
Gifted and Talented Students

Encourage students to find holes in the arguments of both sides as they read. *(Possible responses: Webster's speech about freedom is stirring but irrelevant; it could be used to exonerate any crime or breach of contract. On the other hand, the devil may have underplayed the price Jabez was to pay for success.)*

Director's Note

C Invite students to discuss how they would direct the crowd scene. How would they instruct their actors to say their lines? Lead them to see and feel it as a busy, noisy, cheerful scene of hearty celebration.

Literary Concept:
CHARACTERIZATION

D Lead students to see that the author is giving the audience information about two main characters, Jabez and Mary, through the words and opinions of other, less important characters.

E Ask students what Jabez's speech tells them about him. *(Possible response: He is successful; he is modest.)* On a second reading, students might see hints of the role the devil has played in Jabez's success.

Critical Thinking:
HYPOTHESIZING

F Why would the crowd consider Webster (1782–1852) the "greatest man" in the United States? *(Possible responses: He was a legendary orator, lawyer, and antislavery congressman who believed in the preservation of the Union above all; he was also their "favorite son.")*

C **The Old Man** (*gossiping to a neighbor*). Wonder where he got it all—Stones was always poor.

His Neighbor. Ain't poor now—makes you wonder just a mite.

A Third Man. Don't begrudge it to him—but I wonder where he got it.

The Old Man (*starting to whisper*). Let me tell you something—

The Old Woman (*quickly*). Henry, Henry, don't you start to gossip. (*She drags him away.*)

Fiddler (*cutting in*). Set to your partners! Scratch for corn!

(*The dance resumes, but as it does so, the* Crowd *chants back and forth.*)

Women. Gossip's got a sharp tooth.

Men. Gossip's got a mean tooth.

D **Women.** She's a lucky woman. They're a lucky pair.

Men. That's true as gospel. But I wonder where he got it.

Women. Money, land and riches.

Men. Just came out of nowhere.

Women and Men (*together*). Wonder where he got it all.—But that's his business.

Fiddler. Left and right—grand chain!

(*The dance rises to a pitch of ecstasy with the final figure—the fiddle squeaks and stops. The dancers mop their brows.*)

First Man. Whew! Ain't danced like that since I was knee-high to a grasshopper!

Second Man. Play us "The Portland Fancy," fiddler!

Third Man. No, wait a minute, neighbor. Let's hear from the happy pair! Hey, Jabez!

Fourth Man. Let's hear from the State Senator!

(*They crowd around* Jabez *and push him up on the settee.*)

Old Man. Might as well. It's the last time he'll have the last word!

Old Woman. Now, Henry Banks, you ought to be ashamed of yourself!

Old Man. Told you so, Jabez!

The Crowd. Speech!

Jabez (*embarrassed*). Neighbors—friends—I'm not much of a speaker—spite of your 'lecting me to State Senate— **E**

The Crowd. That's the ticket, Jabez. Smart man, Jabez. I voted for ye. Go ahead, Senator, you're doing fine.

Jabez. But we're certainly glad to have you here—me and Mary. And we want to thank you for coming and—

A Voice. Vote the Whig[2] ticket!

Another Voice. Hooray for Daniel Webster!

Jabez. And I'm glad Hi Foster said that, for those are my sentiments, too. Mr. Webster has promised to honor us with his presence here tonight.

The Crowd. Hurray for Dan'l! Hurray for the greatest man in the U.S.! **F**

Jabez. And when he comes, I know we'll give him a real New Hampshire welcome.

The Crowd. Sure we will—Webster forever—and to hell with Henry Clay![3]

Jabez. And meanwhile—well, there's Mary and me (*takes her hand*)—and, if you folks don't have a good time, well, we won't feel right about getting married at all. Because I know I've been lucky—and I hope she feels that way, too. And, well, we're going to be happy or bust a trace! (*He wipes his brow to terrific applause. He and* Mary *look at each other.*)

---

2. **Whig:** a political party founded in the 1830s. Daniel Webster was one of its leaders.
3. **Henry Clay:** a famous American congressman of the time and a rival of Daniel Webster.

258 UNIT TWO PART 2: AGAINST THE ODDS

Mini-Lesson   Literary Concepts

REVIEWING CONFLICT Remind students that conflict is the struggle between opposing forces and forms the basis of a plot. External conflict occurs between a character and a force of nature, between two characters, or between a character and society. Internal conflict occurs when a character struggles within himself or herself, such as when making a decision.

Application Ask students to identify the main conflict in the play. Then invite students to find and list other conflicts in the play. Encourage them to find at least one conflict for each major character and then to label each one as external or internal. Have a volunteer keep the list on the chalkboard, as at left.

CONFLICTS

Daniel Webster	win the case	external
Jabez (2)	escape his fate	external
	confess the deal	internal
Mary	support Jabez?	internal
jury	decide the case	internal
devil	defeat Webster	external

A Woman (*in kitchen doorway*). Come and get the cider, folks!

(*The* Crowd *begins to drift away—a few to the kitchen—a few toward the door that leads to the outside. They furnish a shifting background to the next little scene, where* Mary *and* Jabez *are left alone by the fireplace.*)

Jabez. Mary.

Mary. Mr. Stone.

Jabez. Mary.

Mary. My husband.

Jabez. That's a big word, husband.

Mary. It's a good word.

Jabez. Are you happy, Mary?

Mary. Yes. So happy, I'm afraid.

Jabez. Afraid?

Mary. I suppose it happens to every girl—just for a minute. It's like spring turning into summer. You want it to be summer. But the spring was sweet. (*Dismissing the mood*) I'm sorry. Forgive me. It just came and went, like something cold. As if we'd been too lucky.

Jabez. We can't be too lucky, Mary. Not you and me.

Mary (*rather mischievously*). If you say so, Mr. Stone. But you don't even know what sort of housekeeper I am. And Aunt Hepsy says—

Jabez. Bother your Aunt Hepsy! There's just you and me and that's all that matters in the world.

Mary. And you don't know something else—

Jabez. What's that?

Mary. How proud I am of you. Ever since I was a little girl. Ever since you carried my books. Oh, I'm sorry for women who can't be proud of their men. It must be a lonely feeling.

Jabez (*uncomfortably*). A man can't always be proud of everything, Mary. There's some things a man does, or might do—when he has to make his way.

Mary (*laughing*). I know—terrible things—like being the best farmer in the county and the best State Senator—

Jabez (*quietly*). And a few things, besides. But you remember one thing, Mary, whatever happens. It was all for you. And nothing's going to happen. Because he hasn't come yet—and he would have come if it was wrong.

Mary. But it's wonderful to have Mr. Webster come to us.

Jabez. I wasn't thinking about Mr. Webster. (*He takes both her hands.*) Mary, I've got something to tell you. I should have told you before, but I couldn't seem to bear it. Only, now that it's all right, I can. Ten years ago—

A Voice (*from off stage*). Dan'l! Dan'l Webster!

(Jabez *drops* Mary's *hands and looks around. The* Crowd *begins to mill and gather toward the door. Others rush in from the kitchen.*)

Another Voice. Black Dan'l![4] He's come!

Another Voice. Three cheers for the greatest man in the U.S.!

Another Voice. Three cheers for Daniel Webster!

(*And, to the cheering and applause of the crowd,* Daniel Webster *enters and stands for a moment upstage, in the familiar pose, his head thrown back, his attitude leonine.*[5] *He stops the cheering of the crowd with a gesture.*)

Webster. Neighbors—old friends—it does me good to hear you. But don't cheer me—I'm not running for President this summer. (*a laugh from the* Crowd) I'm here on a better errand—to pay my humble respects to a most charming

---

4. **Black Dan'l:** a nickname Webster received as a child because of his dark complexion.
5. **leonine** (lē′ə-nīn′): like a lion.

THE DEVIL AND DANIEL WEBSTER **259**

Critic's Corner

"Benét's love of country is not mindless chauvinism; it grows out of the familiar but often forgotten vision of America as a symbol and, at its best, an expression of the potentiality of the human species."

Joel Roache
Dictionary of Literary Biography, vol. 102

Have students discuss Benét's view of humanity.

Literary Concept: MOOD

G Lead students to see that the mood, or feeling, of the scene changes when the crowd drifts away—and that this is one reason why it is important to read stage directions. Ask a volunteer to describe the change. (*A noisy crowd scene becomes a quiet discussion.*)

Critical Thinking: ANALYZING

H Invite students to explore how Mary feels. Her feeling of wanting adulthood and being nervous about it at the same time is familiar to adolescents. Ask them how *spring* and *summer* are used symbolically. (*They stand for youth and adulthood.*) Also point out, on rereading, that Mary's premonition is quickly proved true.

Literary Concept: CONFLICT

I Encourage students to analyze Jabez's discomfort, using questions such as *What isn't he proud of? Why is he so uncomfortable?* and *Who is he thinking about?* (*Possible responses by students who know the story: Jabez's discomfort indicates his inner conflict about having sold his soul; he has been thinking about the devil.*)

Literary Concept: MOOD

J Lead students to see that with the voices heralding Daniel Webster's arrival the quiet mood shifts back to noisy celebration.

Literary Concept: CHARACTERIZATION

K Invite students to discuss what Daniel Webster's words and gestures, in dialogue lines and stage directions, imply about his character. (*Possible responses: He is a typical politician trying to work a crowd; he is a great man and knows it.*)

Critical Thinking: SPECULATING

L Have students speculate on what the breaking of the fiddle string after Webster's speech may mean. *(Possible response: The fortunes of the "very fortunate spouse" are about to change.)*

Critical Thinking: ANALYZING

M Ask students why Jabez is embarrassed when the fiddle squeaks. *(because it has squeaked in derisive comment on Webster's statement about him)*

Literary Concept: CHARACTERIZATION

N Ask students what method of characterization the playwright uses here to describe Scratch. *(He describes him physically.)* Is the description of Scratch flattering? Explain. *(Possible response: No, he is shabbily dressed, in black gloves, with something "a little wrong" in appearance.)*

CUSTOMIZING FOR
Students Acquiring English

I Demonstrate how Scratch delivers his line insinuatingly. Then discuss what the term means, and ask students to take turns saying the line in an insinuating tone. Point out that there is threat and mockery in this type of intonation. *(Rosin is added to a violin bow to increase friction on strings.)*

Literary Concept: IRONY

O Have students identify what they think is deceitful about Scratch's dialogue here. *(Possible responses: He is not Jabez's "friend," not "humble," and not truly "apologetic" about anything he's done.)*

---

lady and her very fortunate spouse.

L (*There is the twang of a fiddlestring breaking.*)

Fiddler. 'Tarnation! Busted a string!

A Voice. He's always bustin' strings.

(*Webster blinks at the interruption but goes on.*)

Webster. We're proud of State Senator Stone in these parts—we know what he's done. Ten years ago he started out with a patch of land that was mostly rocks and mortgages and now—well, you've only to look around you. I don't know that I've ever seen a likelier farm, not even at Marshfield[6]—and I hope, before I die, I'll have the privilege of shaking his hand as Governor of this State. I don't know how he's done it—I couldn't have done it myself. But I know this—Jabez Stone wears no man's collar. (*At this statement there is a discordant squeak from the fiddle, and* Jabez *looks embarrassed.* Webster *knits his brows.*) **M** And what's more, if I know Jabez, he never will. But I didn't come here to talk politics—I came to kiss the bride. (*He does so among great applause. He shakes hands with* Jabez.) Congratulations, Stone—you're a lucky man. And now, if our friend in the corner will give us a tune on his fiddle—

(*The* Crowd *presses forward to meet the great man. He shakes hands with several.*)

A Man. Remember me, Mr. Webster? Saw ye up at the State House at Concord.

Another Man. Glad to see ye, Mr. Webster. I voted for ye ten times.

(*Webster receives their homage politely, but his mind is still on music.*)

Webster (*a trifle irritated*). I said, if our friend in the corner would give us a tune on his fiddle—

Fiddler (*passionately, flinging the fiddle down*). Hell's delight—excuse me, Mr. Webster. But the very devil's got into that fiddle of mine. She was doing all right up to just a minute ago. But now I've tuned her and tuned her and she won't play a note I want.

(*And, at this point, Mr.* Scratch *makes his appearance. He has entered, unobserved, and mixed with the crowd while all eyes were upon Daniel Webster. He is, of course, the devil—a New England devil, dressed like a rather shabby attorney but with something just a little wrong in clothes and appearance. For one thing, he wears black gloves on his hands. He carries a large black tin box, like a botanist's collecting box, under one arm. Now he slips through the crowd and taps the* Fiddler *on the shoulder.*)

Scratch (*insinuatingly*). Maybe you need some rosin on your bow, fiddler?

Fiddler. Maybe I do and maybe I don't. (*Turns and confronts the stranger*) But who are you? I don't remember seeing you before.

Scratch. Oh, I'm just a friend—a humble friend of the bridegroom's. (*He walks toward* Jabez. *Apologetically.*) I'm afraid I came in the wrong way, Mr. Stone. You've improved the place so much since I last saw it that I hardly knew the

---

6. **Marshfield:** a small town southeast of Boston, where Daniel Webster had a farm.

WORDS TO KNOW	
discordant (dĭ-skôr′dnt) *adj.* disagreeable in sound; harsh	
homage (hŏm′ĭj) *n.* special honor or respect shown publicly	
insinuatingly (ĭn-sĭn′yōō-ā′tĭng-lē) *adv.* in a hinting, indirect, or suggestive manner	

front door. But, I assure you, I came as fast as I could.

Jabez (*obviously shocked*). It—it doesn't matter. (*With a great effort*) Mary—Mr. Webster—this is a—a friend of mine from Boston—a legal friend. I didn't expect him today but—

Scratch. Oh, my dear Mr. Stone—an occasion like this—I wouldn't miss it for the world. (*He bows.*) Charmed, Mrs. Stone. Delighted, Mr. Webster. But—don't let me break up the merriment of the meeting. (*He turns back toward the table and the* Fiddler.)

Fiddler (*with a grudge, to* Scratch). Boston lawyer, eh?

Scratch. You might call me that.

Fiddler (*tapping the tin box with his bow*). And what have you got in that big tin box of yours? Law papers?

Scratch. Oh—curiosities for the most part. I'm a collector, too.

Fiddler. Don't hold much with Boston curiosities, myself. And you know about fiddling, too, do you? Know all about it?

Scratch. Oh—(*a deprecatory shrug*)

Fiddler. Don't shrug your shoulders at me—I ain't no Frenchman. Telling me I needed more rosin!

Mary (*trying to stop the quarrel*). Isaac—please—

Fiddler. Sorry, Mary—Mrs. Stone. But I been playing the fiddle at Cross Corners weddings for twenty-five years. And now here comes a stranger from Boston and tells me I need more rosin!

Scratch. But, my good friend—

Fiddler. Rosin indeed! Here—play it yourself then and see what you can make of it! (*He thrusts the fiddle at* Scratch. *The latter stiffens, slowly lays his black collecting box on the table, and takes the fiddle.*)

Scratch (*with feigned embarrassment*). But really, I— (*He bows toward* Jabez.) Shall I—Mr. Senator? (Jabez *makes a helpless gesture of assent.*)

Mary (*to* Jabez). Mr. Stone—Mr. Stone—are you ill?

Jabez. No—no—but I feel—it's hot—

Webster (*chuckling*). Don't you fret, Mrs. Stone. I've got the right medicine for him. (*He pulls a flask from his pocket.*) Ten-year-old Medford, Stone—I buy it by the keg down at Marshfield. Here—(*He tries to give some of the rum to* Jabez.)

Jabez. No—(*he turns*)—Mary—Mr. Webster— (*But he cannot explain. With a burst.*) Oh, let him play—let him play! Don't you see he's bound to? Don't you see there's nothing we can do?

(*A rustle of discomfort among the guests.* Scratch *draws the bow across the fiddle in a horrible discord.*)

Fiddler (*triumphantly*). I told you so, stranger. The devil's in that fiddle!

Scratch. I'm afraid it needs special tuning. (*Draws the bow in a second discord*) There—that's better (*grinning*). And now for this happy—this very happy occasion—in tribute to the bride and groom—I'll play something appropriate—a song of young love—

Mary. Oh, Jabez—Mr. Webster—stop him! Do you see his hands? He's playing with gloves on his hands.

(Webster *starts forward, but, even as he does so,* Scratch *begins to play, and all freeze as* Scratch *goes on with the extremely inappropriate song that follows. At first his manner is oily and mocking—it is not till he reaches the line "The devil took the words away" that he really becomes*

WORDS TO KNOW

feigned (fānd) *adj.* not real; pretended

261

Literary Concept: HUMOR

P Have students speculate why the Fiddler supposed that Scratch was a lawyer. Then tell them that this is humor in the form of a sarcastic remark. The stereotype of the manipulative lawyer is a common image drawn by writers and cartoonists.

Critical Thinking: HYPOTHESIZING

Q Ask students to theorize about what Scratch might have collected in his tin box. *(souls [p. 263])* For students unaware of this convention, tell them that the devil is depicted in literature as an evil, supernatural being who, in opposing the Christian God, often delights in tempting humans to trade him their souls—their spiritual natures that supposedly live on after death—in exchange for immediate earthly gains.

Literary Concept: CHARACTERIZATION

R Encourage students to characterize the Fiddler based on the stage directions and his speeches. *(Possible response: He is crusty and proud but is a good-hearted old man.)*

Literary Concept: IRONY

S Scratch means the opposite of what he says. Invite students to explain what he really means. *(He intends the occasion to be sad for everyone but himself.)*

Mini-Lesson Genre Study

DRAMA In a play, an act is a major unit of action, often consisting of several scenes. Full-length plays contain two to five acts. *The Devil and Daniel Webster* is a **one-act play**. If full-length plays can be compared to novels or feature films, then one-act plays can be compared to short stories or short films. Fittingly, Benét wrote *The Devil and Daniel Webster* originally as a short story.

Application An important part of staging a dramatic performance is gauging the running time. Invite volunteers to time the staged reading of one page, allowing appropriate time for actions and gestures, as part of preparing to perform this play for the Another Pathway activity on page 279. Then ask them to estimate the running time of the whole play. *(One-act plays usually run less than an hour.)*

Critical Thinking: ANALYZING

T Encourage students to discuss the song's meaning for the characters and its dramatic effect for the theater audience. Encourage students to hear in their minds the discordant music of the unwanted, mocking guest. Ask what the song about a man named William implies about Jabez. *(He, like William, is wicked and has been damned.)* Ask what effect the song has on the wedding guests and why. *(It disturbs them at first because it seems inappropriate to a wedding celebration; then it frightens them as the meaning becomes clearer.)*

Literary Concept: CHARACTERIZATION

U Webster's bold self-assurance is displayed both in his own actions and words and in Scratch's description of him.

terrifying and the crowd starts to be afraid.)

Scratch *(accompanying himself fantastically).*

Young William was a thriving boy.
(Listen to my doleful tale.)
Young Mary Clark was all his joy.
(Listen to my doleful tale.)

He swore he'd love her all his life.
She swore she'd be his loving wife.
But William found a gambler's den
And drank with livery-stable men.

He played the cards, he played the dice
He would not listen to advice.

And when in church he tried to pray,
The devil took the words away.

(Scratch, still playing, starts to march across the stage.)

The devil got him by the toe
And so, alas, he had to go.

"Young Mary Clark, young Mary Clark,
I now must go into the dark."

(These last two verses have been directed at Jabez. Scratch continues, now turning on Mary.)

Young Mary lay upon her bed.
"Alas my Will-i-am is dead."

He came to her a bleeding ghost—

(He rushes at Mary but Webster stands between them.)

Webster. Stop! Stop! You miserable wretch—can't you see that you're frightening Mrs. Stone? *(He wrenches the fiddle out of Scratch's hands and tosses it aside.)* And now, sir—out of this house!

Scratch *(facing him).* You're a bold man, Mr. Webster. Too bold for your own good, perhaps. And anyhow, it wasn't my fiddle. It belonged to—(*He wheels and sees the* Fiddler *tampering with the collecting box that has been left on the table.*) Idiot! What are you doing with my collecting box? (*He rushes for the* Fiddler *and chases him round the table, but the* Fiddler *is just one jump ahead.*)

Fiddler. Boston lawyer, eh? Well, I don't think so. I think you've got something in that box of yours you're afraid to show. And, by jingo—(*He throws open the lid of the box. The lights wink and there is a clap of thunder. All eyes stare upward. Something has flown out of the box. But what?* Fiddler, *with relief.*) Why, 'tain't nothing but a moth.

Mary. A white moth—a flying thing.

Webster. A common moth—telea polyphemus—

The Crowd. A moth—just a moth—a moth—

Fiddler (*terrified*). But it ain't. It ain't no common moth! I seen it! And it's got a death's-head on it! (*He strikes at the invisible object with his bow to drive it away.*)

Voice of the Moth. Help me, neighbors! Help me!

Webster. What's that? It wails like a lost soul.

Mary. A lost soul.

The Crowd. A lost soul—lost—in darkness—in the darkness.

Voice of the Moth. Help me, neighbors!

Fiddler. It sounds like Miser Stevens.

Jabez. Miser Stevens!

The Crowd. The Miser—Miser Stevens—a lost soul—lost.

Fiddler (*frantically*). It sounds like Miser Stevens—and you had him in your box. But it can't be. He ain't dead.

Jabez. He ain't dead—I tell you he ain't dead! He was just as spry and mean as a woodchuck Tuesday.

The Crowd. Miser Stevens—soul of Miser

Stevens—but he ain't dead.

Scratch (*dominating them*). Listen!
(*A bell off stage begins to toll a knell, slowly, solemnly.*)

Mary. The bell—the church bell—the bell that rang at my wedding.

Webster. The church bell—the passing bell.

Jabez. The funeral bell.

The Crowd. The bell—the passing bell—Miser Stevens—dead.

Voice of the Moth. Help me, neighbors, help me! I sold my soul to the devil. But I'm not the first or the last. Help me. Help Jabez Stone!

Scratch. Ah, would you! (*He catches the moth in his red bandanna, stuffs it back into his collecting box, and shuts the lid with a snap.*)

Voice of the Moth (*fading*). Lost—lost forever, forever. Lost, like Jabez Stone.

(*The* Crowd *turns on* Jabez. *They read his secret in his face.*)

The Crowd. Jabez Stone—Jabez Stone—answer us—answer us.

Mary. Tell them, dear—answer them—you are good—you are brave—you are innocent.

(*But the* Crowd *is all pointing hands and horrified eyes.*)

THE DEVIL AND DANIEL WEBSTER **263**

Multicultural Perspectives

THE DEVIL Throughout history, cultures around the world have invented personifications of evil. In the Old Testament of the Bible, the Devil is a *shatan*, which is a Hebrew word for *opponent*. This word has come down to the English language as *Satan*, another common name for the devil. Dante and Milton portrayed Satan as an archangel who turned against God and was banished from heaven to rule the world of the damned. Milton's sympathetic portrayal of Satan mourning the loss of heaven and the everlasting pain awaiting him in hell struck many as blasphemous at the time of *Paradise Lost's* publication. The "tempter" aspect of the devil's character has led many writers to stress his charm. Mephistopheles, the devil in Gounod's opera *Faust* (1859), tends to appeal to audiences far more than the weak hero, Faust. A popular manifestation of the devil on stage, besides Scratch, is Applegate in George Abbott's Broadway show and film, *Damn Yankees*.

Actor's Note

AA Invite students to suggest how they would play the crowd scene. (*Possible response:* The crowd is increasingly vicious, even more so after Jabez pleads for their help.)

Literary Concept: MOOD

BB Have students discuss the changed mood after the crowd leaves, when Jabez is in despair and the atmosphere is quiet. Compare and contrast this two-character interlude with the more hopeful one on page 259.

Critical Thinking: SPECULATING

CC Ask students why they think Webster exits. (*Possible responses:* He wishes to escape the devil; he wishes to leave Jabez and Mary alone together.) This is another important action conveyed through a brief stage direction.

Literary Concept: CONFLICT

DD Invite students to identify the conflict between Jabez and Mary. (*Jabez wants Mary to leave; Mary wants to stay. Both are motivated by love.*)

AA **The Crowd.** Jabez Stone—Jabez Stone. Who's your friend in black, Jabez Stone? (*They point to* Scratch.)

Webster. Answer them, Mr. State Senator.

The Crowd. Jabez Stone—Jabez Stone. Where did you get your money, Jabez Stone?

(Scratch *grins and taps his collecting box,* Jabez *cannot speak.*)

Jabez. I—I—(*He stops.*)

The Crowd. Jabez Stone—Jabez Stone. What was the price you paid for it, Jabez Stone?

Jabez (*looking around wildly*). Help me, neighbors! Help me!

(*This cracks the built-up tension and sends the Crowd over the edge into* fanaticism.)

A Woman's Voice (*high and hysterical*). He's sold his soul to the devil! (*She points to* Jabez.)

Other Voices. To the devil!

The Crowd. He's sold his soul to the devil! The devil himself! The devil's playing the fiddle! The devil's come for his own!

Jabez (*appealing*). But, neighbors—I didn't know—I didn't mean—oh, help me!

The Crowd (*inexorably*). He's sold his soul to the devil!

Scratch (*grinning*). To the devil!

The Crowd. He's sold his soul to the devil! There's no help left for him, neighbors! Run, hide, hurry, before we're caught! He's a lost soul—Jabez Stone—he's the devil's own. Run, hide, hasten! (*They stream across the stage like a flurry of bats, the cannier picking up the wedding presents they have given to take along with them.*)

(Mr. Scratch *drives them out into the night, fiddle in hand, and follows them.* Jabez and Mary *are left with* Webster. Jabez *has sunk into a chair, beaten, with his head in his hands.* Mary *is trying to comfort him.* Webster *looks at them for a moment and shakes his head, sadly. As he crosses to exit to the porch, his hand drops for a moment on* Jabez' *shoulder, but* Jabez *makes no sign.* Webster *exits.* Jabez *lifts his head.*)

Mary (*comforting him*). My dear—my dear—

Jabez. I—it's all true, Mary. All true. You must hurry.

Mary. Hurry?

Jabez. Hurry after them—back to the village—back to your folks. Mr. Webster will take you—you'll be safe with Mr. Webster. You see, it's all true and he'll be back in a minute. (*With a shudder*) The other one. (*He groans.*) I've got until twelve o'clock. That's the contract. But there isn't much time.

Mary. Are you telling me to run away from you, Mr. Stone?

Jabez. You don't understand, Mary. It's true.

Mary. We made some promises to each other. Maybe you've forgotten them. But I haven't. I said, it's for better or worse. It's for better or worse. I said, in sickness or in health. Well, that covers the ground, Mr. Stone.

Jabez. But, Mary, you must—I command you.

Mary. "For thy people shall be my people and thy God my God." (*Quietly*) That was Ruth, in the Book.[7] I always liked the name of Ruth—always liked the thought of her. I always thought—I'll call a child Ruth, some time. I

---

7. **Ruth, in the Book:** The preceding quote is from the Book of Ruth in the Old Testament of the Bible. When Ruth becomes widowed, she decides to leave her home and go with her mother-in-law, Naomi, to Bethlehem. Her famous words are spoken to Naomi.

WORDS TO KNOW
fanaticism (fə-năt'ĭ-sĭz'əm) *n.* excessive, unreasonable zeal or enthusiasm

---

Critic's Corner

"Underlying the imaginative life in America all through the years of panic, depression, and the emergence of international civil war [the 1930s] was an enormous body of writing devoted to the American scene.... And Daniel Webster ... now appeared in Stephen Vincent Benét's charming story as a big man, a pillar of virtue, a gigantic folk hero, fit to rescue Yankee souls from the Devil and beat him easily at his own game. 'No American citizen may be forced into the service of a foreign prince.'"

Alfred Kazin
On Native Grounds

Have students discuss whether anyone today seems to be doing for America what Kazin says Benét's folk-hero Webster did for the country in the 1930s.

My Night Visage (1913), Ludwig Meidner. Marvin and Janet Fishman Collection.

Art Note

My Night Visage by Ludwig Meidner
This glowing portrait of the visage, or face, of a man was painted in 1913 by the German artist Ludwig Meidner (1884–1966). With thick brush strokes and the subject's haunted appearance, it is reminiscent of Vincent van Gogh's self-portraits.

Reading the Art *What might the man be thinking and feeling? Do you think his emotions are similar to those of Jabez Stone at this point of the drama?*

Literary Concept:
CHARACTERIZATION

EE In the long, serious conversation between Jabez and Mary, the two characters are revealed through their own words as they discuss past events. The conversation also gives the audience important background information. Ask students what they learn about the two characters through this conversation. *(Possible response: Jabez was ambitious in his youth but was never able to realize his dream of success, and his pride kept him from pursuing Mary earlier. Mary has apparently loved Jabez for some time and, unknown to Jabez, would have long ago welcomed a life with him even under the most simple conditions.)*

Critical Thinking:
MAKING JUDGMENTS

FF Tell students the folklore of selling one's soul to the devil: A person usually in desperate need for money and/or success requests—sometimes inadvertently—the devil's help. The devil obliges, drawing up a contract that, in exchange for a specified number of years of boundless riches, obligates the signer to surrender his or her soul to the devil after death—which occurs just as soon as the guaranteed years end. Then, ask students whether Jabez's description matches their ideas of what it would be like to sell one's soul to the devil and whether it convinces them. *(Some may say the event is not as dramatic as they would have thought it would be and so it disappoints them. Others, after a moment's reflection, may feel that the low-key manner in which the devil operated shows what makes him successful and is ultimately convincing.)*

Literary Concept: TONE

GG Invite students to read aloud Webster's reentry line, "Good evening, neighbors. Did you say something about lawyers—" in the tone they imagine him using. Have them describe that tone. Students should sense that Webster's entrance is a welcome surprise after his exit and that his jaunty, slightly mocking tone provides relief from the dramatic tension and signals hope for Jabez.

guess that was just a girl's notion. (*She breaks.*) But, oh, Jabez—why?

Jabez. It started years ago, Mary. I guess I was a youngster then—guess I must have been. A youngster with a lot of ambitions and no way in the world to get there. I wanted city clothes and a big white house—I wanted to be State Senator and have people look up to me. But all I got on the farm was a crop of stones. You could work all day and all night, but that was all you got.

Mary (*softly*). It was pretty—that hill farm, Jabez. You could look all the way across the valley.

Jabez. Pretty? It was fever and ague[8]—it was stones and blight. If I had a horse, he got colic—if I planted garden truck, the woodchucks ate it. I'd lie awake nights and try to figure out a way to get somewhere—but there wasn't any way. And all the time you were growing up, in the town. I couldn't ask you to marry me and take you to a place like that.

Mary. Do you think it's the place makes the difference to a woman? I'd—I'd have kept your house. I'd have stroked the cat and fed the chickens and seen you wiped your shoes on the mat. I wouldn't have asked for more. Oh, Jabez—why didn't you tell me?

Jabez. It happened before I could. Just an average day—you know—just an average day. But there was a mean east wind and a mean small rain. Well, I was plowing, and the share broke clean off on a rock where there hadn't been any rock the day before. I didn't have money for a new one—I didn't have money to get it mended. So I said it and I said loud, "I'll sell my soul for about two cents," I said. (*He stops. Mary stares at him.*) Well, that's all there is to it, I guess. He came along that afternoon—that fellow from Boston—and the dog looked at him and ran away. Well, I had to make it more than two cents, but he was agreeable to that. So I pricked my thumb with a pin and signed the paper. It felt hot when you touched it, that paper. I keep remembering that. (*He pauses.*) And it's all come true and he's kept his part of the bargain. I got the riches and I've married you. And, oh, God Almighty, what shall I do?

Mary. Let us run away! Let us creep and hide!

Jabez. You can't run away from the devil—I've seen his horses. Miser Stevens tried to run away.

Mary. Let us pray—let us pray to the God of Mercy that He redeem us.

Jabez. I can't pray, Mary. The words just burn in my heart.

Mary. I won't let you go! I won't! There must be someone who could help us. I'll get the judge and the squire—

Jabez. Who'll take a case against old Scratch? Who'll face the devil himself and do him brown? There isn't a lawyer in the world who'd dare do that.

(*Webster appears in the doorway.*)

Webster. Good evening, neighbors. Did you say something about lawyers—

Mary. Mr. Webster!

Jabez. Dan'l Webster! But I thought—

Webster. You'll excuse me for leaving you for a moment. I was just taking a stroll on the porch, in the cool of the evening. Fine summer evening, too.

Jabez. Well, it might be, I guess, but that kind of depends on the circumstances.

Webster. H'm. Yes I happened to overhear a little

---
8. **ague** (ā′gyōō): a feverish condition.

266 UNIT TWO PART 2: AGAINST THE ODDS

of your conversation. I gather you're in trouble, Neighbor Stone.

Jabez. Sore trouble.

Webster (*delicately*). Sort of law case, I understand.

Jabez. You might call it that, Mr. Webster. Kind of a mortgage case, in a way.

Mary. Oh, Jabez!

Webster. Mortgage case. Well, I don't generally plead now, except before the Supreme Court, but this case of yours presents some very unusual features, and I never deserted a neighbor in trouble yet. So, if I can be of any assistance—

Mary. Oh, Mr. Webster, will you help him?

Jabez. It's a terrible lot to ask you. But—well, you see, there's Mary. And, if you could see your way to it—

Webster. I will.

Mary (*weeping with relief*). Oh, Mr. Webster!

Webster. There, there, Mrs. Stone. After all, if two New Hampshire men aren't a match for the devil, we might as well give the country back to the Indians. When is he coming, Jabez?

Jabez. Twelve o'clock. The time's getting late.

Webster. Then I'd better refresh my memory. The—er—mortgage was for a definite term of years?

Jabez. Ten years.

Webster. And it falls due—?

Jabez. Tonight. Oh, I can't see how I came to be such a fool!

Webster. No use crying over spilt milk, Stone. We've got to get you out of it, now. But tell me one thing. Did you sign this precious document of your own free will?

Jabez. Yes, it was my own free will. I can't deny that.

Webster. H'm, that's a trifle unfortunate. But we'll see.

Mary. Oh, Mr. Webster, can you save him? Can you?

Webster. I shall do my best, madam. That's all you can ever say till you see what the jury looks like.

Mary. But even you, Mr. Webster—oh, I know you're Secretary of State—I know you're a great man—I know you've done wonderful things. But it's different—fighting the devil!

Webster (*towering*). I've fought John C. Calhoun, madam. And I've fought Henry Clay. And, by the great shade of Andrew Jackson,⁹ I'd fight ten thousand devils to save a New Hampshire man!

Jabez. You hear, Mary?

Mary. Yes. And I trust Mr. Webster. But—oh, there must be some way that I can help!

Webster. There is one, madam, and a hard one. As Mr. Stone's counsel, I must formally request your withdrawal.

Mary. No.

Webster. Madam, think for a moment. You cannot help Mr. Stone—since you are his wife, your testimony would be prejudiced. And frankly, madam, in a very few minutes this is going to be no place for a lady.

Mary. But I can't—I can't leave him—I can't bear it!

Jabez. You must go, Mary. You must.

Webster. Pray, madam—you can help us with

---

9. **John C. Calhoun . . . Andrew Jackson:** Calhoun served as Vice-President from 1825 to 1832. He maintained that states could nullify federal laws, a position that Webster opposed. Andrew Jackson was President from 1829 to 1837. Jackson opposed the Bank of the United States, and Webster supported it.

THE DEVIL AND DANIEL WEBSTER 267

Critical Thinking: ANALYZING

LL Have students discuss Mary's line, "But a woman's more than a praying machine, whatever men think." Ask what they think she means by this. *(that men never permit women to take active roles in crises but instead force them to watch and wait)*

Literary Concept: MOOD

MM Ask students to describe the mood of the interlude during which Mary prays aloud and invokes the biblical story of the newly widowed Ruth who leaves her people to follow her mother-in-law, Naomi, back to the latter's homeland in Bethlehem. *(Possible responses: hushed, tense, suspenseful)*

Literary Concept: CHARACTERIZATION

NN Ask students what they learn about Jabez when he pleads with Webster to leave. *(Possible response: He is a good man; he is fiercely patriotic, for even at the cost of his own soul, he tries to save someone who represents the country.)*

OO In this passage, Webster describes his own character: he likes to drink, he likes his work, and he is a determined achiever. Some students may perceive other implied traits, for instance, that he is a genial, folksy braggart.

---

your prayers. Are the prayers of the innocent unavailing?[10]

Mary. Oh, I'll pray—I'll pray. But a woman's more than a praying machine, whatever men think. And how do I know?

Webster. Trust me, Mrs. Stone.

(*Mary turns to go, and, with one hand on* Jabez' *shoulder, as she moves to the door, says the following prayer:*)

Mary.
Now may there be a blessing and a light betwixt thee and me, forever.
For, as Ruth unto Naomi, so do I cleave unto thee.
Set me as a seal upon thy heart, as a seal upon thine arm, for love is strong as death.
Many waters cannot quench love, neither can the floods drown it.
As Ruth unto Naomi, so do I cleave unto thee.
The Lord watch between thee and me when we are absent, one from the other.
Amen. Amen. (*She goes out.*)

Webster. Amen.

Jabez. Thank you, Mr. Webster. She ought to go. But I couldn't have made her do it.

Webster. Well, Stone—I know ladies—and I wouldn't be surprised if she's still got her ear to the keyhole. But she's best out of this night's business. How long have we got to wait?

Jabez (*beginning to be terrified again*). Not long—not long.

Webster. Then I'll just get out the jug, with your permission, Stone. Somehow or other, waiting's wonderfully shorter with a jug. (*He crosses to the cupboard, gets out jug and glasses, pours himself a drink.*) Ten-year-old Medford. There's nothing like it. I saw an inchworm take a drop of it once, and he stood right up on his hind legs and bit a bee. Come—try a nip.

Jabez. There's no joy in it for me.

Webster. Oh, come, man, come! Just because you've sold your soul to the devil, that needn't make you a teetotaller.[11] (*He laughs and passes the jug to* Jabez, *who tries to pour from it. But at that moment the clock whirs and begins to strike the three-quarters, and* Jabez *spills the liquor.*)

Jabez. Oh, God!

Webster. Never mind—it's a nervous feeling, waiting for a trial to begin. I remember my first case—

Jabez. 'Tain't that. (*He turns to* Webster.) Mr. Webster—Mr. Webster—for God's sake harness your horses and get away from this place as fast as you can!

Webster (*placidly*). You've brought me a long way, neighbor, to tell me you don't like my company.

Jabez. I've brought you the devil's own way. I can see it all, now. He's after both of us—him and his damn collecting box! Well, he can have me, if he likes—I don't say I relish it, but I made the bargain. But you're the whole United States! He can't get you, Mr. Webster—he mustn't get you!

Webster. I'm obliged to you, neighbor Stone. It's kindly thought of. But there's a jug on the table and a case in hand. And I never left a jug or a case half-finished in my life. (*There is a*

---

10. **unavailing:** not useful or helpful.
11. **teetotaller** (tē′tōt′l-ər): a person who never drinks alcoholic beverages.

WORDS TO KNOW
placidly (plăs′ĭd-lē) *adv.* calmly

268

Mini-Lesson: Speaking, Listening, and Viewing

CHORAL READING Choral reading is reading aloud in a group. Reading in unison can be effective; however, too much unison can be monotonous. Choral reading presents creative opportunities for various combinations of speakers to read passages. There may be solos, duets, small groups within the chorus, or sequential reading line by line. In choosing portions to read, students should find the individuals whose voices best suit the meanings and feelings of the lines. The physical spacing of the speakers can also affect tone and mood.

Application Invite small groups of students to present choral readings of Mary's prayer. Encourage them to discuss the passage before rehearsing to achieve an appropriate tone: serious and moving, rather than sentimental. Have students rehearse, trying out several combinations of voices and physical spacing. They may wish to tape their rehearsal and listen critically afterward. Then have them perform for the class.

Daniel Webster (Black Dan) (1835), Francis Alexander. Oil on canvas, Hood Museum of Art, Dartmouth College, Hanover, New Hampshire, gift of Dr. George C. Shattuck, class of 1803.

Art Note

Daniel Webster (Black Dan) by Francis Alexander Francis Alexander (1800–1880) was a successful American portrait painter whose career spanned much of the 19th century. His portrait of Webster captures the subject's penetrating gaze and turbulent hair. Webster was in his early 50s at the time of the portrait, which was created just six years before the time setting of the play.

Reading the Art *Does this portrait match your impression of Webster from the play?*

Literary Concept:
CHARACTERIZATION

PP In this transition to the trial itself, students may have to revise their judgment of Scratch based on his first appearance back on page 261. ("Scratch" is a colloquial name for the devil going back to the mid-1700s.) Scratch's "shabby" exterior disguises a restrained, calculating, confident being with a very knowing mind—adept at understatement and euphemism ("our firm has its reputation to consider"), clever repartee ("we have always gotten the pick of the Bar"), and legal precedence. Have students judge his worthiness as an opponent for Webster.

Linking to History

QQ As students will have learned in social studies courses, "traffic in human flesh"—slavery—was legal in many states in 1841. New Hampshire was not a slave state, but the Fugitive Slave Act was a federal statute that applied in all states, although it was not rigorously enforced everywhere. According to this statute, runaway slaves caught in the North had to be returned to their owners. Slavery was legally abolished in the states of the Confederacy by the Emancipation Proclamation in 1863 and led, two years later, to a Constitutional Amendment, the 13th, which abolished slavery in all parts of the United States.

Critical Thinking: ANALYZING

RR Make sure students understand that "the property" that increased in value is Jabez Stone himself.

---

knock at the door. *Jabez gives a cry.*) Ah, I thought your clock was a trifle slow, neighbor Stone. Come in!

PP (*Scratch enters from the night.*)

Scratch. Mr. Webster! This is a pleasure!

Webster. Attorney of record for Jabez Stone. Might I ask your name?

Scratch. I've gone by a good many. Perhaps Scratch will do for the evening. I'm often called that in these regions. May I? (*He sits at the table and pours a drink from the jug. The liquor steams as it pours into the glass while Jabez watches, terrified. Scratch grins, toasting Webster and Jabez silently in the liquor. Then he becomes businesslike. To Webster.*) And now I call upon you, as a law-abiding citizen, to assist me in taking possession of my property.

Webster. Not so fast, Mr. Scratch. Produce your evidence, if you have it.

(*Scratch takes out a black pocketbook and examines papers.*)

Scratch. Slattery—Stanley—Stone. (*takes out a deed*) There, Mr. Webster. All open and aboveboard and in due and legal form. Our firm has its reputation to consider—we deal only in the one way.

Webster (*taking deed and looking it over*). H'm. This appears—I say, it appears—to be properly drawn. But, of course, we contest the signature (*tosses it back,* <u>contemptuously</u>).

Scratch (*suddenly turning on Jabez and shooting a finger at him*). Is that your signature?

Jabez (*wearily*). You know damn well it is.

Webster (*angrily*). Keep quiet, Stone. (*To Scratch*) But that is a minor matter. This precious document isn't worth the paper it's written on. The law permits no traffic in human flesh.

QQ

Scratch. Oh, my dear Mr. Webster! Courts in every State in the Union have held that human flesh is property and recoverable. Read your Fugitive Slave Act.[12] Or, shall I cite Brander versus McRae?

Webster. But, in the case of the State of Maryland versus Four Barrels of Bourbon—

Scratch. That was overruled, as you know, sir. North Carolina versus Jenkins and Co.

Webster (*unwillingly*). You seem to have an excellent acquaintance with the law, sir.

Scratch. Sir, that is no fault of mine. Where I come from, we have always gotten the pick of the Bar.[13]

Webster (*changing his note, heartily*). Well, come now, sir. There's no need to make hay and oats of a trifling matter when we're both sensible men. Surely we can settle this little difficulty out of court. My client is quite prepared to offer a compromise. (*Scratch smiles.*) A very substantial compromise. (*Scratch smiles more broadly, slowly shaking his head.*) Hang it, man, we offer ten thousand dollars! (*Scratch signs "No."*) Twenty thousand—thirty—name your figure! I'll raise it if I have to mortgage Marshfield!

Scratch. Quite useless, Mr. Webster. There is only one thing I want from you—the execution of my contract.

Webster. But this is absurd. Mr. Stone is now a State Senator. The property has greatly increased in value!

---

12. **Fugitive Slave Act:** law governing the capture and return of runaway slaves.
13. **pick of the Bar:** The best lawyers available. *Bar* means "lawyers considered as a group."

WORDS TO KNOW

contemptuously (kən-tĕmp′chōō-əs-lē) *adv.* scornfully; without respect

270

Scratch. The principle of caveat emptor[14] still holds, Mr. Webster. (*He yawns and looks at the clock.*) And now, if you have no further arguments to adduce—I'm rather pressed for time—(*He rises briskly as if to take* Jabez *into custody.*)

Webster (*thundering*). Pressed or not, you shall not have this man. Mr. Stone is an American citizen, and no American citizen may be forced into the service of a foreign prince. We fought England for that, in '12,[15] and we'll fight all hell for it again!

Scratch. Foreign? And who calls me a foreigner?

Webster. Well, I never yet heard of the dev—of your claiming American citizenship?

Scratch. And who with better right? When the first wrong was done to the Indian, I was there. When the first slaver put out for the Congo, I stood on her deck. Am I not in your books and stories and beliefs, from the first settlements on? Am I not spoken of, still, in every church in New England? 'Tis true, the North claims me for a Southerner and the South for a Northerner, but I am neither. I am merely an honest American like yourself—and of the best descent—for, to tell the truth, Mr. Webster, though I don't like to boast of it, my name is older in the country than yours.

Webster. Aha! Then I stand on the Constitution! I demand a trial for my client!

Scratch. The case is hardly one for an ordinary jury—and indeed, the lateness of the hour—

Webster. Let it be any court you choose, so it is an American judge and an American jury. Let it be the quick[16] or the dead, I'll abide the issue.

Scratch. The quick or the dead! You have said it! (*He points his finger at the place where the jury is to appear. There is a clap of thunder and a flash of light. The stage blacks out completely. All that can be seen is the face of* Scratch, *lit with a ghastly green light as he recites the invocation that summons the* Jury. *As, one by one, the important* Jurymen *are mentioned, they appear.*)

I summon the jury Mr. Webster demands.
From churchyard mold and gallows grave,
Brimstone pit and burning gulf,
I summon them!
Dastard, liar, scoundrel, knave,
I summon them! Appear!
There's Simon Girty, the renegade,
The haunter of the forest glade
Who joined with Indian and wolf
To hunt the pioneer.

---

14. **caveat emptor** (kā′vē-ăt′ ĕmp′tôr′): the principle in commerce that the buyer is responsible for assessing the quality of a purchase before buying. *Caveat emptor* is a Latin phrase that literally means "Let the buyer beware."
15. **in '12**: a reference to the War of 1812, which was caused in part by the British forcing American sailors to serve in the British navy.
16. **quick**: the living.

THE DEVIL AND DANIEL WEBSTER   **271**

Mini-Lesson Grammar

CORRELATIVE CONJUNCTIONS A conjunction is a word that links two or more words, phrases, or clauses. Correlative conjunctions work in pairs to link ideas of equal importance.
1. With prestige on the line, *neither* Daniel Webster *nor* Scratch could afford to lose.
2. *Not only* did Webster win, *but* he *also* got rid of the devil.

Copy the chart at the right on the chalkboard and be sure students know that singular subjects linked by *or* or *nor* take a singular verb. If *or* or *nor* links a singular subject and a plural subject, put the plural subject last and use a plural verb.

Application Ask students to write three sentences correctly using correlative conjunctions

Reteaching/Reinforcement
• *Grammar Handbook,* anthology p. 941
• *Grammar Mini-Lessons* copymasters p. 7, transparencies p. 5

The Writer's Craft
Conjunctions, pp. 663–664

Critical Thinking: MAKING GENERALIZATIONS

SS Discuss the general point—a serious one despite Scratch's bantering tone—being made in the crucial speech about evils in American history. You might generalize it further, emphasizing that evils can be found in the history of every nation. If you wish, invite students to cite examples from their knowledge of other cultures and more recent times.

Linking to Government

TT The Seventh Amendment to the Constitution gives parties the right to a trial by jury in all civil cases where the value of the controversy exceeds $20—and Scratch has already rejected an offer of thousands of dollars to buy out Jabez Stone's contract. Discuss with students the difference between a civil and a criminal case, and ask them to find where in the Constitution the right to trial by jury in criminal cases is preserved. (*the Sixth Amendment*)

CUSTOMIZING FOR
Students Acquiring English

3 Tell students that the phrase "abide the issue" means "put up with, or accept, the decision." Webster will accept any jury that Scratch picks, even one made up of dead persons.

STRATEGIC READING FOR
Less-Proficient Readers

UU The trial, the apex of this drama, is about to begin. Ask groups of students to review how they have visualized the main events and characters that have preceded it.
• Ask them what they think Jabez's chances of winning are and why. (*Accept all reasonable, well-supported responses.*) Drawing Conclusions

Set a Purpose Have students read on to predict who will win the trial and how it will happen.

CORRELATIVE CONJUNCTIONS

both . . . and   not only . . . but also
either . . . or   whether . . . or
neither . . . nor

**Critical Thinking:
SYNTHESIZING**

VV Invite students to comment critically on the choice of jury members. Also discuss how cultural viewpoints have changed. For example, King Philip, a Native American chief who fought European settlers in eastern New England, could now be considered a patriot by many. Morton, the British adventurer who founded a freewheeling settlement called Merry Mount, might be admired by those who reject Puritan values.

Director's Note

WW Point out that part of a director's job is to know when to adapt, trim, or depart from a play's text to make it continually appealing to a present-day audience. The jury's stiff and stylized behavior might be such an occasion. Invite students to discuss how they, as an audience, would react to the jury as described, and how, as directors, they might suggest that the jury behave. *(Many students will say that they would encourage more individualized behavior; others will find the stiff behavior appropriate. See footnote 21, page 273.)*

VV The stains upon his hunting shirt
Are not the blood of the deer.
There's Walter Butler,[17] the loyalist,
Who carried a firebrand in his fist
Of massacre and shame.
King Philip's[18] eye is wild and bright.
They slew him in the great Swamp Fight,
But still, with terror and affright,
The land recalls his name.
Blackbeard Teach, the pirate fell,
Smeet the strangler, hot from hell,
Dale, who broke men on the wheel,
Morton,[19] of the tarnished steel,
I summon them, I summon them
From their tormented flame!
Quick or dead, quick or dead,
Broken heart and bitter head,
True Americans, each one,
Traitor and disloyal son,
Cankered earth and twisted tree,
Outcasts of eternity,
Twelve great sinners, tried and true,
For the work they are to do!
VV I summon them, I summon them!
Appear, appear, appear!

(*The* Jury *has now taken its place in the jury box—*Walter Butler *in the place of foreman. They are eerily lit and so made-up as to suggest the unearthly. They sit stiffly in their box. At first, when one moves, all move, in stylized gestures. It is not till the end of* Webster's *speech that they begin to show any trace of humanity. They speak rhythmically, and, at first, in low, eerie voices.*) **WW**

Jabez (*seeing them, horrified*). A jury of the dead!

Jury. Of the dead!

Jabez. A jury of the damned!

Jury. Of the damned!

---

17. **Simon Girty . . . Walter Butler:** Both were white men who fought with Native Americans against white settlers in the late 1700s.
18. **King Philip:** a Wampanoag chief who started an uprising against white settlers in 1675. He was killed in 1676.
19. **Blackbeard Teach . . . Dale . . . Morton:** Edward Teach, known as Blackbeard, was an English pirate who preyed on American ships in the early 1700s. Sir Thomas Dale, governor of the Virginia colony in the early 1600s, was despised for his harsh rule. Thomas Morton of Massachusetts was a free-living Anglican who ridiculed his Puritan neighbors and sold firearms to Native Americans in the 1600s.

Scratch. Are you content with the jury, Mr. Webster?

Webster. Quite content. Though I miss General Arnold from the company.

Scratch. Benedict Arnold[20] is engaged upon other business. Ah, you asked for a justice, I believe. (*He points his finger and* Justice Hathorne, *a tall, lean, terrifying Puritan, appears, followed by his* Clerk.) Justice Hathorne is a jurist of experience. He presided at the Salem witch trials. There were others who repented of the business later. But not he, not he!

Hathorne. Repent of such notable wonders and undertakings? Nay, hang them, hang them all! (*He takes his place on the bench.*)

(*The* Clerk, *an ominous little man with clawlike hands, takes his place. The room has now been transformed into a courtroom.*[21])

Clerk (*in a gabble of ritual*). Oyes, oyes, oyes. All ye who have business with this honorable court of special session this night, step forward!

Hathorne (*with gavel*). Call the first case.

Clerk. The World, the Flesh and the Devil versus Jabez Stone.

Hathorne. Who appears for the plaintiff?

Scratch. I, Your Honor.

Hathorne. And for the defendant?

Webster. I.

Jury. The case—the case—he'll have little luck with this case.

Hathorne. The case will proceed.

Webster. Your Honor, I move to dismiss this case on the grounds of improper jurisdiction.

Hathorne. Motion denied.

Webster. On the grounds of insufficient evidence.

Hathorne. Motion denied.

Jury. Motion denied—denied. Motion denied.

Webster. I will take an exception.

Hathorne. There are no exceptions in this court.

Jury. No exceptions—no exceptions in this court. It's a bad case, Daniel Webster—a losing case.

Webster. Your Honor—

Hathorne. The prosecution will proceed—

Scratch. Your Honor—gentlemen of the jury. This is a plain, straightforward case. It need not detain us long.

Jury. Detain us long—it will not detain us long.

Scratch. It concerns one thing alone—the transference, barter and sale of a certain piece of property, to wit, his soul, by Jabez Stone, farmer, of Cross Corners, New Hampshire. That transference, barter or sale is attested by

---

20. **Benedict Arnold:** an American Revolutionary War general who became a traitor.
21. **courtroom:** In a simple production of this play, a pair of long benches, one higher than the other, are placed at the back of the seat to serve as a jury box. The members of the jury quietly come onstage during the blackout, while Scratch recites his invocation. As he finishes, the light gradually comes up on the jury. The judge now enters and takes his seat on a high bench by the fireplace, with his Clerk sitting on a stool below him. The table, left, becomes the lawyer's table, where Scratch and Webster sit.

CUSTOMIZING FOR
Students Acquiring English

4 Write the legal terms *incontestable evidence, prosecutor, witness stand, motion,* and *cross-examine* on the board. Help students formulate definitions for each term.

Linking to Economics

A At the time the play took place, farming was the most common occupation in the United States. Currently, only about 4 percent of the population farms.

Literary Concept: CONFLICT

B Invite students to discuss the increasing external conflict between Webster and the judge and jury. Lead students to see that Webster is becoming increasingly frustrated by his failure to get fair rulings—and that the audience should be feeling the same exasperation.

---

a deed.²² I offer that deed in evidence and mark it Exhibit A.

Webster. I object.

Hathorne. Objection denied. Mark it Exhibit A.

(*Scratch hands the deed—an ominous and impressive document—to the* Clerk, *who hands it to* Hathorne. Hathorne *hands it back to the* Clerk, *who stamps it. All very fast and with mechanical gestures.*)

Jury. Exhibit A—mark it Exhibit A. (*Scratch takes the deed from the* Clerk *and offers it to the* Jury, *who pass it rapidly among them, hardly looking at it, and hand it back to* Scratch.) We know the deed—the deed—it burns in our fingers—we do not have to see the deed. It's a losing case.

4 Scratch. It offers incontestable evidence of the truth of the prosecution's claim. I shall now call Jabez Stone to the witness stand.

Jury (*hungrily*). Jabez Stone to the witness stand, Jabez Stone. He's a fine, fat fellow, Jabez Stone. He'll fry like a battercake, once we get him where we want him.

Webster. Your Honor, I move that this jury be discharged for flagrant and open <u>bias</u>!

Hathorne. Motion denied.

Webster. Exception.

Hathorne. Exception denied.

Jury. His motion's always denied. He thinks himself smart and clever—lawyer Webster. But his motion's always denied.

Webster. Your Honor! (*He chokes with anger.*)

Clerk (*advancing*). Jabez Stone to the witness stand!

Jury. Jabez Stone—Jabez Stone.

(Webster *gives* Jabez *an encouraging pat on the back, and* Jabez *takes his place in the witness stand, very scared.*)

Clerk (*offering a black book*). Do you solemnly swear—testify—so help you—and it's no good, for we don't care what you testify?

Jabez. I do.

Scratch. What's your name?

Jabez. Jabez Stone.

Scratch. Occupation?

Jabez. Farmer.

Scratch. Residence?

Jabez. Cross Corners, New Hampshire.

(*These three questions are very fast and mechanical on the part of* Scratch. *He is absolutely sure of victory and just going through a form.*)

Jury. A farmer—he'll farm in hell—we'll see that he farms in hell.

Scratch. Now, Jabez Stone, answer me. You'd better, you know. You haven't got a chance, and there'll be a cooler place by the fire for you.

Webster. I protest! This is <u>intimidation</u>! This mocks all justice!

Hathorne. The process is irrelevant, incompetent and immaterial. We have our own justice. The protest is denied.

Jury. Irrelevant, incompetent and immaterial—we have our own justice—oh, ho, Daniel Webster! (*The* Jury's *eyes fix upon* Webster *for an instant, hungrily.*)

Scratch. Did you or did you not sign this document?

---
22. **attested by a deed:** certified by a signed contract.

WORDS TO KNOW
bias (bī′əs) *n.* an attitude in which a person is in favor of someone or something without having a good reason for this preference
intimidation (ĭn-tĭm′ĭ-dā′shən) *n.* the use of threats to frighten or inhibit another

274

Mini-Lesson: Speaking, Listening, and Viewing

SPEECHES Critical listening is a jury's primary activity. Juries listen to witnesses' testimony, lawyers' questions, judges' instructions, and opening and closing speeches. Before they listen, the jurors' task is to remain open-minded and to establish tentative criteria for forming a verdict. While they listen, jurors should analyze the logic or emotionalism of the evidence, and should remember the details as well as main points. Afterward, as they deliberate, jurors may write down summaries or other notes, list concerns they still have, and, finally, decide with which side they agree.

Application Invite students to imagine themselves as an alternate jury listening to Webster's eloquent closing speech, as well as to the other speeches in the case. You might divide the class into several juries of four or six people or create a single jury of interested students. Ask them to take notes on the logical and emotional validity or invalidity they find, and to discuss what verdict they would reach and why.

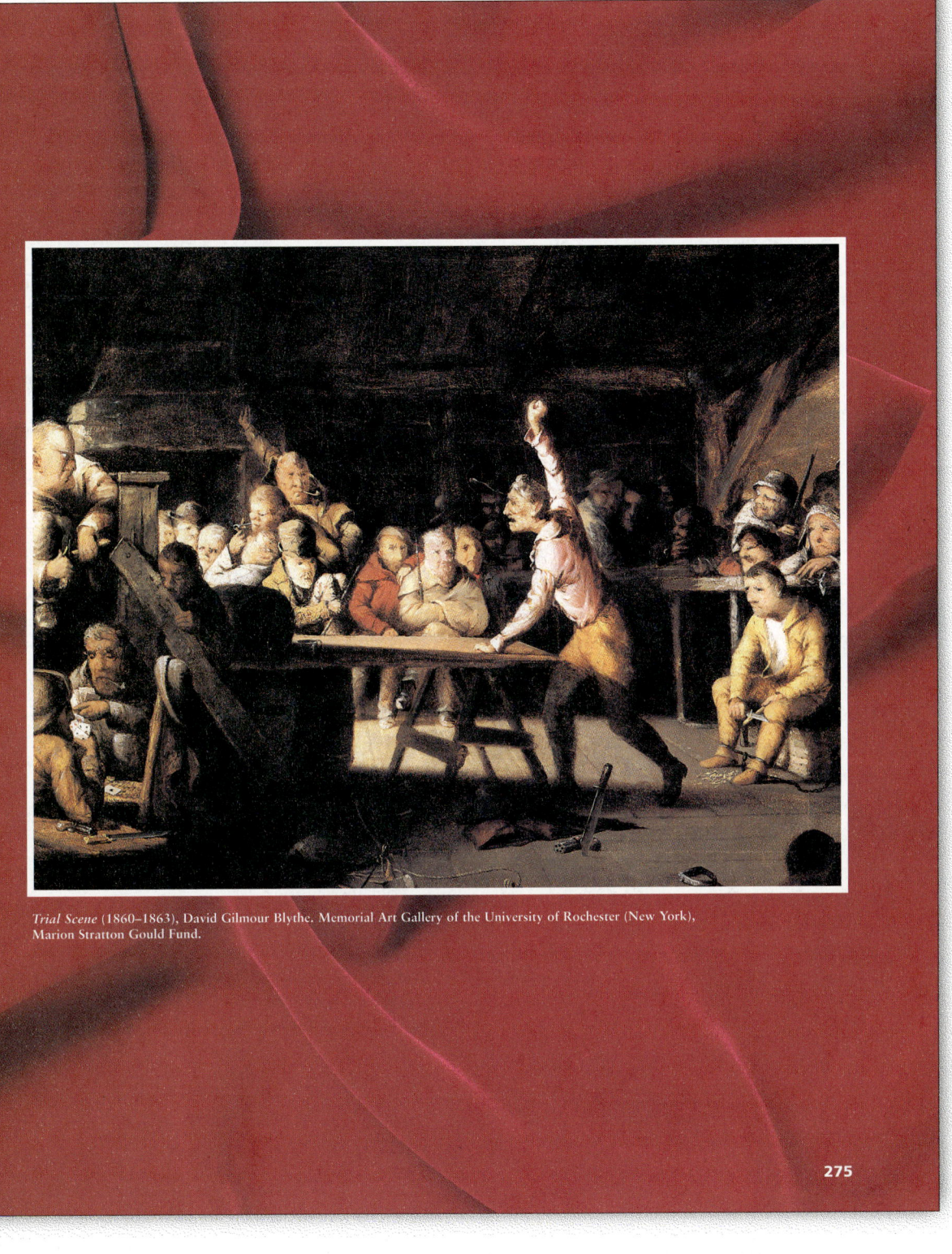

Trial Scene (1860–1863), David Gilmour Blythe. Memorial Art Gallery of the University of Rochester (New York), Marion Stratton Gould Fund.

Art Note

Trial Scene by David Gilmour Blythe
This painting from the 1860s shows an angry defendant asserting himself while the court looks on with sheer indifference—a situation similar to that in which Jabez Stone and Daniel Webster find themselves on pages 273–276. Two men at the lower left are quietly playing cards. Notice Blythe's use of dramatic lighting. Blythe (1815–1865) was an Ohio-born artist who began as a woodcarver and then became known as a realistic and satirical painter.

Reading the Art *What aspects of the painting seem realistic, and what aspects seem satirical?*

Critical Thinking: COMPARING/CONTRASTING

C Compare and contrast the two kinds of seals referred to. Mary, from offstage, longs for her love to be sealed with Jabez's, in an allusion to the Bible (Song of Songs 8:6). The jury mockingly twists her meaning to imply that Jabez, in hell, will be branded by the devil.

Literary Concept: MOOD

D The moments when Webster is seemingly defeated and the clerk advances toward Jabez Stone, and when Webster silences them all and launches into his poetic, victorious speech, begin the dramatic high point, or climax. Lead students to sense the shift in mood from despair to hope, a shift accomplished by only the persuasive power of words. You might invite them to take a moment to close their eyes and visualize the scene.

Director's Note

E Many directors would have Webster address Girty individually, as he subsequently addresses King Philip and Teach.

Jabez. Oh, I signed it! You know I signed it. And, if I have to go to hell for it, I'll go!

(*A sigh sweeps over the* Jury.)

Jury. One of us—one of us now—we'll save a place by the fire for you, Jabez Stone.

Scratch. The prosecution rests.

Hathorne. Remove the prisoner.

Webster. But I wish to cross-examine—I wish to prove—

Hathorne. There will be no cross-examination. We have our own justice. You may speak, if you like. But be brief.

Jury. Brief—be very brief—we're weary of earth—incompetent, irrelevant and immaterial—they say he's a smart man, Webster, but he's lost his case tonight—be very brief—we have our own justice here.

(Webster *stares around him like a baited bull. Can't find words.*)

Mary's Voice (*from off stage*). Set me as a seal upon thy heart, as a seal upon thine arm, for love is strong as death—

Jury (*loudly*). A seal!—ha, ha—a burning seal!

Mary's Voice. Love is strong—

Jury (*drowning her out*). Death is stronger than love. Set the seal upon Daniel Webster—the burning seal of the lost. Make him one of us—one of the damned—one with Jabez Stone!

(*The* Jury's *eyes all fix upon* Webster. *The* Clerk *advances as if to take him into custody. But* Webster *silences them all with a great gesture.*)

Webster.

Be still!
I was going to thunder and roar. I shall not do that.
I was going to denounce and defy. I shall not do that.
You have judged this man already with your abominable justice. See that you defend it.
For I shall not speak of this man.
You are demons now, but once you were men. I shall speak to every one of you.
Of common things I speak, of small things and common.
The freshness of morning to the young, the taste of food to the hungry, the day's toil, the rest by the fire, the quiet sleep.
These are good things.
But without freedom they sicken, without freedom they are nothing.
Freedom is the bread and the morning and the risen sun.
It was for freedom we came in the boats and the ships. It was for freedom we came.
It has been a long journey, a hard one, a bitter one.
But, out of the wrong and the right, the sufferings and the starvations, there is a new thing, a free thing.
The traitors in their treachery, the wise in their wisdom, the valiant in their courage—all, all have played a part.
It may not be denied in hell nor shall hell prevail against it.
Have you forgotten this? (*He turns to the* Jury.) Have you forgotten the forest?

Girty (*as in a dream*). The forest, the rustle of the forest, the free forest.

Webster (*to* King Philip). Have you forgotten your lost nation?

King Philip. My lost nation—my fires in the wood—my warriors.

Webster (*to* Teach). Have you forgotten the sea and the way of ships?

Teach. The sea—and the swift ships sailing—the blue sea.

Jury. Forgotten—remembered—forgotten yet remembered.

276 UNIT TWO PART 2: AGAINST THE ODDS

Mini-Lesson Workplace Literacy

SCANS Goal: Interprets and Communicates Information

MAKING A PRESENTATION Daniel Webster's closing argument before the jury is a huge success. A large part of a lawyer's job is to make such presentations. Workers of all kinds make presentations to introduce plans, projects, products, services, or arguments. An engineer presents a new design or invention to colleagues and supervisors. An editor presents a manuscript to a publishing committee. Presentations may be given by individuals or small groups. Presentations include oral, written, graphic, pictorial, and multimedia techniques.

Application Have students work in groups of two, three, or four, and ask them to review critically Daniel Webster's successful presentation to the jury, beginning at the bottom of the left-hand column on page 276. Ask them to update the presentation for a jury today by using contemporary references and a variety of media.

Webster. You were men once. Have you forgotten?

Jury. We were men once. We have not thought of it nor remembered. But we were men.

Webster.
Now here is this man with good and evil in his heart.
Do you know him? He is your brother. Will you take the law of the <u>oppressor</u> and bind him down?
It is not for him that I speak. It is for all of you.
There is sadness in being a man, but it is a proud thing, too.
There is failure and despair on the journey—the endless journey of mankind.
We are tricked and trapped—we stumble into the pit—but, out of the pit, we rise again.
No demon that was ever foaled[23] can know the inwardness of that—only men—bewildered men.
They have broken freedom with their hands and cast her out from the nations—yet shall she live while man lives.
She shall live in the blood and the heart—she shall live in the earth of this country—she shall not be broken.
When the whips of the oppressors are broken and their names forgotten and destroyed,
I see you, mighty, shining, liberty, liberty! I see free men walking and talking under a free star.
God save the United States and the men who have made her free.
The defense rests.

Jury (*exultantly*). We were men—we were free—we were men—we have not forgotten—our children—our children shall follow and be free.

Hathorne (*rapping with gavel*). The jury will retire to consider its verdict.

Butler (*rising*). There is no need. The jury has heard Mr. Webster. We find for the defendant, Jabez Stone!

Jury. Not guilty!

Scratch (*in a screech, rushing forward*). But, Your Honor—

(*But, even as he does so, there is a flash and a thunderclap, the stage blacks out again, and when the lights come on,* Judge *and* Jury *are gone. The yellow light of dawn lights the windows.*)

Jabez. They're gone and it's morning—Mary, Mary!

Mary (*in doorway*). My love—my dear. (*She rushes to him.*)

(*Meanwhile* Scratch *has been collecting his papers and trying to sneak out. But* Webster *catches him.*)

Webster. Just a minute, Mr. Scratch. I'll have that paper first, if you please. (*He takes the deed and tears it.*) And, now, sir, I'll have you!

Scratch. Come, come, Mr. Webster. This sort of thing is ridic—ouch—is ridiculous. If you're worried about the costs of the case, naturally, I'd be glad to pay.

Webster. And so you shall! First of all, you'll promise and covenant[24] never to bother Jabez Stone or any other New Hampshire man from now till doomsday. For any hell we want to raise in this State, we can raise ourselves, without any help from you.

Scratch. Ouch! Well, they never did run very big to the barrel but—ouch—I agree!

---

23. **foaled:** given birth to.
24. **covenant:** to promise by signing a formal contract.

WORDS TO KNOW

oppressor (ə-prĕs′ər) *n.* one who keeps others down by the cruel use of power

277

CUSTOMIZING FOR
Gifted and Talented Students

Invite students to write essays analyzing Benét's view of American history by using supporting evidence from the play. They may also wish to include comments on Benét's style and technique. Students who wish to do further reading might compare and contrast *The Devil and Daniel Webster* with other works by Benét on American historical subjects, such as *John Brown's Body* or "The Ballad of William Sycamore."

STRATEGIC READING FOR
Less-Proficient Readers

J Ask volunteers to summarize the events of the trial and to state how the outcome matched or did not match their predictions. *Summarizing/ Drawing Conclusions*

COMPREHENSION CHECK

1. Where and when is the play set? *(New Hampshire in 1841)*
2. For what did Jabez Stone sell his soul? *(success)*
3. On what occasion does the devil come to claim Jabez's soul? *(Jabez and Mary's wedding, ten years after the signing of the contract)*
4. How was the trial rigged against Jabez? *(judge, jury, and court clerk were condemned souls)*
5. How did Daniel Webster convince the jury to find Jabez not guilty— released from the devil's domain? *(He turns the trial into an appreciation of freedom as the essence of life in the United States and convinces them that no "oppressor" should be able to take it away.)*

Webster. See you keep to the bargain! And then— well, I've got a ram named Goliath. He can butt through an iron door. I'd like to turn you loose in his field and see what he could do to you. (Scratch *trembles*.) But that would be hard on the ram. So we'll just call in the neighbors and give you a shivaree.[25]

Scratch. Mr. Webster—please—oh—

Webster. Neighbors! Neighbors! Come in and see what a long-barreled, slab-sided, lantern-jawed, fortune-telling note-shaver I've got by the scruff of the neck! Bring on your kettles and your pans! (*a noise and murmur outside*) Bring on your muskets and your flails!

Jabez. We'll drive him out of New Hampshire!

Mary. We'll drive old Scratch away!

(*The* Crowd *rushes in, with muskets, flails, brooms, etc. They pursue* Scratch *around the stage, chanting.*)

The Crowd.
We'll drive him out of New Hampshire!
We'll drive old Scratch away!
Forever and a day, boys,
Forever and a day!

(*They finally catch* Scratch *between two of them and fling him out of the door, bodily.*)

A Man. Three cheers for Dan'l Webster!

Another Man. Three cheers for Daniel Webster! He's licked the devil!

Webster (*moving to center stage, and joining* Jabez' *hands and* Mary's). And whom God hath joined let no man put asunder. (*He kisses* Mary *and turns, dusting his hands.*) Well, that job's done. I hope there's pie for breakfast, neighbor Stone.

(*And, as some of the women, dancing, bring in pies from the kitchen*)

THE CURTAIN FALLS

---

25. **shivaree** (shĭv′ə-rē′): a noisy mock serenade or celebration for a newly married couple.

278 UNIT TWO PART 2: AGAINST THE ODDS

Assessment Option

COLLABORATIVE TALK Have students work in small groups for a collaborative discussion about the play. Prompt them with questions such as *Did the ending convince you? Did Webster's speech move you? Would you have found Jabez not guilty? What is Jabez found 'not guilty' of? What were the strongest and weakest aspects of the play?* and *What effect do you think Jabez's close call with the devil will have on the rest of his life?* Encourage students to raise questions and venture criticisms. Visit each group and ask what ideas they have come up with, and be sure all group members participate.

Rubric

3 Full Accomplishment Active discussion with all members participating leads to intriguing insights.

2 Substantial Accomplishment Active discussion with all or most members participating leads to valid but mundane responses; or discussion dominated by one or two members leads to intriguing insights.

1 Little or Partial Accomplishment Irrelevant discussion dominated by one or two members leads to confusion.

RESPONDING OPTIONS

FROM PERSONAL RESPONSE TO CRITICAL ANALYSIS

REFLECT

1. What is your impression of Daniel Webster? Jot down your thoughts in your notebook, and then share your impression in class.

RETHINK

2. Were you convinced by Webster's final speech? If you were sitting on the jury, would you be persuaded to give Jabez Stone his freedom? Why or why not?

Thematic Link

3. In defending Jabez Stone, Webster fought against a number of obstacles. How would you rank these obstacles in order of difficulty?

Consider

Close Textual Reading
- the evidence against Jabez Stone
- the makeup of the jury
- the bias of the judge, jury, and clerk
- the judge's handling of the trial

Close Textual Reading

4. What do you think Stephen Vincent Benét wanted people in the audience to think about after they had seen this play?

Consider
- the main points in Webster's final speech to the jury
- why the jury gives Jabez Stone his freedom
- the connection drawn between the nation's history and the life of an individual

RELATE

5. This play is a great tribute to a famous historical person. If you were going to write a play, a story, or an essay about someone you wanted people in the future to admire, whom would you choose, and why?

Multimodal Learning
ANOTHER PATHWAY
Cooperative Learning
Work together as a class to present this play or a part of it. Your performance can be as elaborate as a staged production or as simple as a Readers Theater. Make sure everyone in your class participates as part of a team of directors, set designers, actors, acting coaches, musicians, and so on.

QUICKWRITES

1. A **legal brief** is a document that an attorney files before arguing a case in court. The brief contains all the facts and legal points relevant to the case. List the items in a brief that Webster might have prepared for Jabez Stone's trial.

2. Look over the cluster diagram on freedom that you created for the Personal Connection activity on page 255. Imagine that you are the lawyer for a modern-day Jabez Stone. Using Webster's final speech as a model, write a **summation**, which is a concluding argument in a trial, to gain your client's freedom. Include your thoughts on what makes freedom precious.

PORTFOLIO *Save your writing. You may want to use it later as a springboard to a piece for your portfolio.*

From Personal Response to Critical Analysis

1. Accept all reasonable responses.
2. Many students will find the speech about freedom irrelevant to the case. Some may not be convinced that the jury members would change their minds so quickly. Others will be convinced by Webster's paean to freedom. Some will say they would acquit Jabez because no one ought to be sold, especially to the devil; others will say the contract was valid.
3. Student rankings of obstacles will vary, but many will say that the identity and bias of the judge, jury, and clerk are most important, the evidence least important.
4. Responses will vary, but most students will discuss some aspect of Benét's message extolling freedom.
5. Accept all reasonable, well-supported responses.

Another Pathway

Cooperative Learning Encourage students to choose their own roles and jobs. Whatever the scope of the production, students will appreciate having a videotaped record of it.

Rubric

3 Full Accomplishment Whether on a modest or a large scale, the production is entertaining and energetic, showing an appreciation of the meaning and tone of the script.

2 Substantial Accomplishment The production is competent but lacks energy and inspiration.

1 Little or Partial Accomplishment The production lacks entertainment value and there are basic flaws in presentation, such as major lapses in tone.

QuickWrites

1. Encourage students to reread relevant portions of the play, list legal points and facts as they find them, and then organize them logically.
2. Encourage volunteers to either read their summations aloud, or—even better—deliver their speeches from memory or from notes. Remind students to use persuasive language that appeals both to logic and emotion.

 The Writer's Craft

Types of Organization, pp. 331–335
Supporting Opinions, pp. 208–221

The Writer's Style

Invite students to use their charts to explore how Benét uses idioms of early New England to create setting and mood.

The Writer's Craft
Idioms and Slang, p. 410

Critic's Corner

Make sure students understand the critic is accusing Benét of overdoing his portrayal of Webster as a folk hero along the lines of Paul Bunyan, Johnny Appleseed, or John Henry. Accept all reasonable, well-supported responses.

LITERARY CONCEPTS

Characterization refers to the methods that a writer uses to develop characters. Four basic methods of characterization are through (1) description of a character's physical appearance, (2) a character's speech, thoughts, feelings, or actions, (3) the speech, thoughts, feelings, or actions of other characters, and (4) direct comments about a character.

In a short story, the narrator can describe the physical appearance of characters or make direct comments about them. When you are in the audience for a performance of a play, there usually is no narrator, but you can follow the on-stage action and make judgments about the characters. When you read a play, however, you need to look at the stage directions for physical descriptions and clues to characters' inner feelings. Aside from these differences, the methods of characterization apply equally to plays and short stories.

Cooperative Learning With a small group, go back through the play and find examples of each of the four methods used to characterize Daniel Webster. Then decide which one or two methods are the most important in creating a clear portrait of him. Share your conclusions with the rest of the class.

THE WRITER'S STYLE

An **idiom** is an expression that has a meaning different from the meaning of its individual words. For example, "go to the dogs" is an idiom meaning "to go to ruin." In everyday conversation, people often use idioms, and Benét includes many in the dialogue of this play. Some of the expressions are still common, but others have fallen out of use. Make a chart of the idioms you find in the play, with their meanings. You can use a dictionary of idioms to find the meanings of any unfamiliar ones. Otherwise, try to figure out the meaning from the context.

Idiom	Meaning
pretty as a picture	
Gossip's got a sharp tooth	

280 UNIT TWO PART 2: AGAINST THE ODDS

CRITIC'S CORNER

Critics, like other readers, differ in their opinions of literary works. One critic praised the short story on which this play was based as "a classic American fable." Another criticized the story as "too cute" and "too self-consciously an American folk tale." Assuming that the play is similar to the story, which critic do you side with? Why?

Multimodal Learning

ALTERNATIVE ACTIVITIES

1. Use the sketches you drew for the Reading Connection activity on page 255 to create the **set design** for this play. You could draw the design or construct a three-dimensional model.

2. Create a **poster** advertising a performance of *The Devil and Daniel Webster*, showing time and place and listing main cast members. If you like, cast the play with television or movie actors of your own choice and make up brief quotations praising the play. Or use names and pictures of students from your class production of the play. If you have a graphics program on your computer, you can experiment with attractive type fonts, borders, and design.

Literary Concepts

Because dialogue is the most noticeable element in a play, most students will say that Daniel Webster's speech is the most important means of characterization. Encourage students to make inferences about Webster's character by asking them questions such as these:
- What are his motives for defending Jabez?
- What do you think Webster would have done if he had lost the case?
- What do you imagine Webster doing before and after the events of the play?

Alternative Activities

1. Invite students to work in pairs, preferably using sketches by both partners.
2. Students might work individually, but those who prefer working together may do so. One partner might create the graphics for the poster and the other might create the copy. Partners should confer on casting and other information to include.

Across the Curriculum

History Students need not cover their chosen subject's entire life in the monologue. Their research should focus on aspects of the subject's life that made his mention in this play logical. Simon Girty's monologue, for example, might contain reasons why he chose to fight against white settlers. Encourage students to "get into" their chosen characters rather than merely saying information and to rehearse beforehand, perhaps speaking into a tape recorder or to an audience of family or friends.

Words to Know

Exercise A
1. feigned
2. insinuatingly
3. placidly
4. discordant
5. contemptuously

Reteaching/Reinforcement
- *Unit Two Resource Book*, p. 38

STEPHEN VINCENT BENÉT

Stephen Vincent Benét's first love was poetry, but he wrote short stories for major magazines to earn a living. He often chafed against the constraints of formulaic and sentimental magazine fiction, and as he gained fame he increasingly won his battles with editors. By focusing on historic subjects he found a way to satisfy both popular taste and his own literary aspirations.

ART GALLERY

New England Help students understand the New England setting of the play by showing them these images of fine art depicting New England during the mid-1800s.

ACROSS THE CURRICULUM

History Research one of the historical figures mentioned in this play, such as Judge Hathorne, Simon Girty, Walter Butler, and Blackbeard the pirate. Prepare a monologue—a speech in which a character utters thoughts aloud. In the monologue the character should tell something about his or her life. Present the monologue to your classmates.

WORDS TO KNOW

EXERCISE A Review the Words to Know at the bottom of the selection pages. Then, on your paper, write the vocabulary word that best completes each sentence below.

1. The defendant pretended to know nothing about the crime, but the jury suspected that his ignorance was _____.
2. The prosecutor made no comment, but she looked _____ at the defendant, suggesting that she knew the man was not telling the truth.
3. The next witness, knowing there was really nothing to worry about, responded _____ to the questions.
4. When the verdict was read, various outcries of disgust, amazement, or relief filled the courtroom with a noisy and _____ clamor.
5. Meanwhile the defendant, furious at the verdict, glared _____ at the jury.

EXERCISE B Work in a small group to make up a brief story containing these vocabulary words: *homage, fanaticism, intimidation, oppressor,* and *bias*. The first student should begin by saying a sentence that contains one of the words, the next student should continue the story using another word, and so on. The last student must create an ending for the story as well as use the last vocabulary word.

STEPHEN VINCENT BENÉT

1898–1943

If one person ever combined the qualities of poet, historian, short story writer, playwright, and patriot, it was Stephen Vincent Benét. In his work, Benét played each of these roles as he set about recapturing some of the most interesting characters and events in the American past. The result is a body of literature that shows Benét's deep love and knowledge of his country and its ideals—along with his special ability to bring history to life.

Benét was born into a military family. Like many army children, he traveled around the country as his father was transferred from one post to another. His parents encouraged the study of literature and history, and all three of their children became writers. At 17, Benét published his first book of poems, and by the time he graduated from Yale University, he had published short stories and several volumes of poetry.

Benét's poetic ballads and stories gained a wide popular audience. "The Devil and Daniel Webster" began as a short story and was made into an opera, a play, and a film. Benét won Pulitzer prizes for *John Brown's Body*, a long narrative poem about the Civil War, and a later narrative poem, *Western Star*.

During World War II, Benét worked as a radio and film propagandist, helping to rally the patriotic feelings of Americans. He was only 44 when he died suddenly of heart disease at his home in New York City.

OTHER WORKS *Johnny Pye and the Fool-Killer, Tales Before Midnight, The Last Circle: Stories and Poems*

Extended Reading

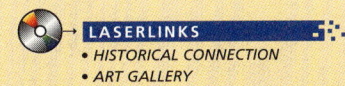
- HISTORICAL CONNECTION
- ART GALLERY

REFLECTING ON THEME
What Do You Think?

Have students think about the solutions to other students' obstacles that they wrote before they began reading the selections in Part One. If they think either Jabez Stone's or Daniel Webster's basic predicament mirrors any of these modern situations already considered, invite them to show how the problems and solutions of long ago are still with us in this quite different age.

OVERVIEW

Objectives

- To read an autobiographical essay that explores a Chinese-American woman's courage in overcoming her physical disability
- To enrich reading by using active reading strategies
- To identify and understand tone
- To express understanding of a selection through a choice of writing forms, including a memo and a list of questions
- To extend understanding of the selection through a variety of multimodal and cross-curricular activities

Skills

LITERARY CONCEPTS
- Tone
- Characterization

READING SKILLS/ STRATEGIES
- To enrich reading by using active reading strategies

THE WRITER'S STYLE
- Using point of view in nonfiction

GENRE STUDY
- Nonfiction: autobiography

GRAMMAR
- Active and passive voice

SPEAKING, LISTENING, AND VIEWING
- Debate
- Group discussion
- Oral presentation

PERSONAL CONNECTION
Nothing Can Stop Me! Many people with disabilities pursue their goals no matter what challenges they face. These images show such extraordinary people as Helen Keller and the noted scientist Stephen Hawking. You may wish to use these images to generate discussion about how people act toward others with disabilities.

Side A, Frame 49287

PREVIEWING

NONFICTION

You're Short, Besides!
Sucheng Chan

Activating Prior Knowledge
PERSONAL CONNECTION

About 35 million Americans have some type of physical or mental disability. If you have a disability, describe the reactions that others have to you. If you do not have a disability, describe how you tend to act in the presence of someone who has one. In your notebook, jot down a few of these reactions. Then share them with a partner.

Building Background
MEDICAL CONNECTION

In this essay, Sucheng Chan writes of how she defied the odds by surviving a childhood attack of polio and how she learned to live with her disability. Polio, a disease that strikes mainly infants and children, is caused by a virus that attacks areas of the brain or spinal cord. The virus damages nerve cells that control the muscles of the legs, arms, or other body parts, including those that control breathing and other vital functions. Some polio attacks are mild, but others can permanently paralyze parts of the body. At one time even adults were at risk; polio paralyzed both legs of Franklin D. Roosevelt when he was 39 (and before he was president), and he never again walked unaided or without braces. No longer a feared disease, polio is now prevented by a childhood vaccine first made available in 1955.

Franklin D. Roosevelt in leg braces. UPI/Bettmann.

Active Reading / Setting a Purpose
READING CONNECTION

Understanding Character Chan states at the beginning of the essay that her perception of herself differs from others' perception of her because people have difficulty seeing past her disability. As a reader, you will not have such distractions, so you can get to know Chan directly through her own words. Pay attention to Chan's characterization of herself as you read about her trials and tribulations.

Using Your Reading Log To help you focus on Chan's character, questions have been inserted throughout the essay. Write your responses in your reading log, along with any other thoughts and impressions that you have as you read.

• PERSONAL CONNECTION

282 UNIT TWO PART 2: AGAINST THE ODDS

PRINT AND MEDIA RESOURCES

UNIT TWO RESOURCE BOOK
Strategic Reading: Literature, p. 41
Vocabulary SkillBuilder, p. 42

WRITING MINI-LESSONS
Transparencies, p. 55

ACCESS FOR STUDENTS ACQUIRING ENGLISH
Selection Summaries
Reading Support

FORMAL ASSESSMENT
Selection Test, pp. 47–48
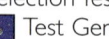 Test Generator

AUDIO LIBRARY
See Reference Card

LASERLINKS
Personal Connection
Medical Connection

You're Short, Besides!

SUCHENG CHAN

Leg (1984), Elizabeth Murray. Oil on canvas (two canvases), 117″ x 82″, collection of Mr. and Mrs. Graham Gund, photo by Geoffrey Clements, courtesy of Paula Cooper Gallery, New York.

When asked to write about being a physically handicapped Asian-American woman, I considered it an insult.

After all, my accomplishments are many, yet I was not asked to write about any of them. Is being handicapped the most salient[1] feature about me?

---

1. **salient** (sā′lē-ənt): prominent; noticeable.

WORDS TO KNOW

agnostic (ăg-nŏs′tĭk) *n.* one who believes that the existence of God cannot be proved or disproved (p. 288)

assuage (ə-swāj′) *v.* to relieve or lessen (p. 285)

debilitate (dĭ-bĭl′ĭ-tāt) *v.* to weaken the strength of (p. 290)

enamored (ĭ-năm′ərd) *adj.* charmed; fascinated (p. 285)

incorrigible (ĭn-kôr′ĭ-jə-bəl) *adj.* stubborn; unmanageable (p. 290)

inept (ĭn-ĕpt′) *adj.* bungling; incompetent (p. 287)

patronizing (pā′trə-nīz-ĭng) *adj.* condescending; superior (p. 288)

precocious (prĭ-kō′shəs) *adj.* characterized by unusual development or maturity in a child, especially mentally (p. 284)

presumptuous (prĭ-zŭmp′chōō-əs) *adj.* going beyond what is right or proper (p. 284)

sardonically (sär-dŏ′nĭ-klē) *adv.* scornfully; mockingly (p. 290)

SUMMARY

In this essay, the author tells what it is like to be an Asian American with a physical disability. Born in China, she was stricken with pneumonia and polio at the age of four. When her health improved, she forced herself to walk again, but she never regained normal use of her legs. In her essay she relates cultural differences in how people respond to her disability. Asians typically connect physical health and moral health and are openly curious about the cause of her disability. American children want to know about her condition, but adults are uneasy and usually try to ignore it. When they do not, they can be overly encouraging, telling her she can do anything if she tries. Her own response has been to get on with life, doing what she is good at—teaching, learning, swimming, and speaking. She concludes that a physical disability is a handicap only if a person thinks of it in that way.

Thematic Link: *Against the Odds* An Asian-American woman succeeds in overcoming her physical disability through strength of will and character.

Art Note

Leg by Elizabeth Murray Elizabeth Murray (1940–) was born in Chicago and educated at the School of the Art Institute of Chicago. In her witty 1984 painting, a stick figure and a cubist table are fused into one, the result being a visual pun on the meaning of "leg"—it is both a human limb and part of a piece of furniture.

Reading the Art How would you describe the tone of this painting? What do you think was the artist's purpose in painting it?

CUSTOMIZING FOR
Students Acquiring English

- Use **ACCESS FOR STUDENTS ACQUIRING ENGLISH,** *Reading Support.*
- Ask students if they ever feel left out of social situations because people think they cannot speak and understand English. Ask them to compare this behavior with the way most people behave toward people with physical disabilities.

STRATEGIC READING FOR
Less-Proficient Readers

Invite students to preview the selection by reading the title, the three sentences on page 283, and the large-print blurbs on pages 284 and 287. Discuss what students have learned about the selection from their previewing.

Set a Purpose Ask students to read on to find out what caused Chan's disability and how she deals with it.

Use **UNIT TWO RESOURCE BOOK,** p. 41, for guidance in reading the selection.

CUSTOMIZING FOR
Gifted and Talented Students

A As students read the selection, have them list the various forms of prejudice Chan encounters as a "physically handicapped Asian-American woman" and record how she deals with each.

Active Reading: **QUESTION**

B Discuss what questions or comments students have at this point in the selection. Use the following model to give them ideas of what they might think about.

Think-Aloud Model *I have some questions about Sucheng so far. I wonder if she will recover enough to walk, and will she be able to go to school?*

The fact that it might be in the eyes of others made me decide to write the essay as requested. I realized that the way I think about myself may differ considerably from the way others perceive me. And maybe that's what being physically handicapped is all about.

A I was stricken simultaneously with pneumonia and polio at the age of four. Uncertain whether I had polio of the lungs, seven of the eight doctors who attended me—all practitioners of Western medicine—told my parents they should not feel optimistic about my survival. A Chinese fortuneteller my mother consulted also gave a grim prognosis,[2] but for an entirely different reason: I had been stricken because my name was offensive to the gods. My grandmother had named me "grandchild of wisdom," a name that the fortuneteller said was too <u>presumptuous</u> for a girl. So he advised my parents to change my name to "chaste virgin." All these pessimistic predictions notwithstanding, I hung onto life, if only by a thread. For three years, my body was periodically pierced with electric shocks as the muscles of my legs atrophied.[3] Before my illness, I had been an active, rambunctious, <u>precocious</u>, and very curious child. Being confined to bed was thus a mental agony as great as my physical pain. Living in war-torn China, I received little medical attention; physical therapy was unheard of. But I was determined to walk. So one day, when I was six or seven, I instructed my mother to set up two rows of chairs to face each other so that I could use them as I would parallel bars. I attempted to

QUESTION
What questions or thoughts do you have about the author's situation so far?
Using a Reading Log

walk by holding my body up and moving it forward with my arms while dragging my legs along behind. Each time I fell, my mother gasped, but I badgered her until she let me try again. After four nonambulatory[4] years, I finally walked once more by pressing my hands against my thighs so my knees wouldn't buckle. **B**

> Doctors ... told my parents they should not feel **optimistic** about my **survival.**

My father had been away from home during most of those years because of the war. When he returned, I had to confront the guilt he felt about my condition. In many East Asian cultures, there is a strong folk belief that a person's physical state in this life is a reflection of how morally or sinfully he or she lived in

---

2. **prognosis** (prŏg-nō′sĭs): a prediction of the probable course and outcome of a disease.
3. **atrophied** (ăt′rə-fēd): wasted away; shrunk from lack of use.
4. **nonambulatory** (nŏn-ăm′byə-lə-tôr′ē): not able to walk.

| WORDS TO KNOW | **presumptuous** (prĭ-zŭmp′chōō-əs) *adj.* going beyond what is right or proper
precocious (prĭ-kō′shəs) *adj.* characterized by unusual development or maturity in a child, especially mentally |

284

Mini-Lesson Literary Concepts

REVIEWING CHARACTERIZATION
Remind students that characterization refers to the methods that a writer uses to create and develop a character by using a combination of the following:
- physical description
- the character's actions, feelings, and words
- a narrator's direct comments about the character
- the words, actions, and feelings of other characters

Application Discuss students' impressions of Chan's character and how they arrived at their views. Encourage students to point out specific passages where her character is developed and to decide which techniques are used in the passages. You might use a web such as the one at left to develop a description of Chan's character. Next to each adjective, ask students to cite relevant passages from the selection.

previous lives.⁵ Furthermore, because of the tendency to view the family as a single unit, it is believed that the fate of one member can be caused by the behavior of another. Some of my father's relatives told him that my illness had doubtless been caused by the wild carousing he did in his youth. A well-meaning but somewhat simple man, my father believed them.

Throughout my childhood, he sometimes apologized to me for having to suffer retribution for his former bad behavior. This upset me; it was bad enough that I had to deal with the anguish of not being able to walk, but to have to assuage his guilt as well was a real burden! In other ways, my father was very good to me. He took me out often, carrying me on his shoulders or back, to give me fresh air and sunshine. He did this until I was too large and heavy for him to carry. And ever since I can remember, he has told me that I am pretty.

After getting over her anxieties about my constant falls, my mother decided to send me to school. I had already learned to read some words of Chinese at the age of three by asking my parents to teach me the sounds and meaning of various characters in the daily newspaper. But between the ages of four and eight, I received no education since just staying alive was a full-time job. Much to her chagrin, my mother found no school in Shanghai, where we lived at the time, which would accept me as a student. Finally, as a last resort, she approached the American School which agreed to enroll me only if my family kept an *amah* (a servant who takes care of children) by my side at all times. The tuition at the school was twenty U.S. dollars per month—a huge sum of money during those years of runaway inflation in China—and payable only in U.S. dollars. My family afforded the high cost of tuition and the expense of employing a full-time *amah* for less than a year.

We left China as the Communist forces swept across the country in victory. We found an apartment in Hong Kong across the street from a school run by Seventh-Day Adventists.⁶ By that time I could walk a little, so the principal was persuaded to accept me. An *amah* now had to take care of me only during recess when my classmates might easily knock me over as they ran about the playground.

After a year and a half in Hong Kong, we moved to Malaysia, where my father's family had lived for four generations. There I learned to swim in the lovely warm waters of the tropics and fell in love with the sea. On land I was a cripple; in the ocean I could move with the grace of a fish. I liked the freedom of being in the water so much that many years later, when I was a graduate student in Hawaii, I became greatly enamored with a man just because he called me a "Polynesian water nymph."

As my overall health improved, my mother became less anxious about all aspects of my life. She did everything possible to enable me to lead as normal a life as possible. I remember how once some of her colleagues in the high school where she taught criticized her for letting me wear short skirts. They felt my legs should not be exposed to public view. My mother's response was, "All girls her age wear short skirts, so why shouldn't she?"

The years in Malaysia were the happiest of

---

5. **previous lives:** Many Asian religions include the belief that a person can be reincarnated, or reborn, several times.
6. **Seventh-Day Adventists:** members of a Christian denomination that observes its day of rest and worship on Saturday.

WORDS TO KNOW
assuage (ə-swāj′) *v.* to relieve or lessen
enamored (ĭ-năm′ərd) *adj.* charmed; fascinated

285

Mini-Lesson The Writer's Style

USING POINT OF VIEW IN NONFICTION
Writers of nonfiction can choose either the first-, second-, or third-person point of view, depending on their purpose, audience, and goals. A nonfiction work written in the first person tends to be subjective and to present the feelings, beliefs, observations, and experiences of a single person—the one who is narrating. The first-person point of view lends immediacy and credibility to nonfiction. These qualities make the first person an appropriate point of view for Sucheng Chan to use in her essay.

Application Ask students to write a short passage in the first person describing a real-life experience in which they accomplished something against all odds. Remind them to use the pronoun *I* and focus on their feelings and observations.

Reteaching/Reinforcement
• *Writing Mini-Lessons* transparencies, p. 55

Points of View in Nonfiction, pp. 432–433

STRATEGIC READING FOR
Less-Proficient Readers

C Ask students what they've learned about Chan's childhood.
• Ask them what caused her disability. *(She contracted pneumonia and polio at the age of four, and as a result she did not walk for four years.)* **Summarizing**
• Ask students what she did to help herself walk again. *(She practiced walking while holding onto two rows of chairs.)* **Noting Relevant Details**

Set a Purpose Have students read to learn about Chan's later life.

Literary Concept:
CHARACTERIZATION

D Ask students to give their impressions of Chan's father. *(Possible responses: He sincerely cares about his daughter but feels he is somehow responsible for her condition.)*

CUSTOMIZING FOR
Students Acquiring English

Tell students that *chagrin* means a feeling of annoyance or embarrassment, caused by failure or disappointment.

Linking to History

E Communist forces under Mao Zedong overthrew the Nationalist government of Chiang Kai-shek in 1949. Chiang Kai-shek fled to Taiwan and set up what he claimed was the rightful government of China. Meanwhile, Mao Zedong established the People's Republic of China. The port city of Hong Kong, where the Chans sought refuge from the Communists, remained a British colony but will revert to Chinese control in 1997.

Literary Concept: TONE

F Ask students to identify the tone of the passage describing Chan's love of swimming. *(Possible responses: nostalgic; self-mocking; affectionate)*

THE LANGUAGE OF LITERATURE TEACHER'S EDITION **285**

DESIGN NOTE

Tell students that this comic and the one on page 289 are from Berke Breathed's *Bloom County*, a popular strip of the 1980s. Among the comic strip's recurring characters are Opus, a penguin who is insecure because he can't fly, and Cutter John, a paraplegic Vietnam veteran. Many of Breathed's early comic strips featured these characters trying to shed some light on the misconceptions that surround people with disabilities.

Literary Concept:
CHARACTERIZATION

G Invite students to think about the sentence beginning "The taunts of children" and to express what it tells them about Chan. *(Possible responses: She is strong-minded; she is not being entirely honest with herself; being a good student is Sucheng's way of compensating for her disability.)*

STRATEGIC READING FOR
Less-Proficient Readers

H Have students summarize Chan's later childhood years and how her disability affected her during that time.

- Ask them where Chan was educated. *(an American school in China and then schools in Hong Kong and Malaysia)* **Noting Sequence of Events**
- Asks students what two significant events stand out in Chan's memory during this time. *(learning to swim well and completing her piano recital in spite of people's ridicule)* **Summarizing**

Set a Purpose Have students read to find out about Chan's adult life.

Active Reading: EVALUATE

I Have students jot down in their notebooks the ways in which Sucheng deals with her disability. Then have the students discuss whether they think the narrator is handling her disability in a positive way.

---

1. Sucheng Chan wrote an essay about her life. (active)

2. An essay was written about Sucheng Chan's life. (passive)

3. Sucheng contracted polio when she was a young child, and the muscles in her legs atrophied. (active)

Copyright © 1982, Washington Post Writers Group. Reprinted with permission.

my childhood, even though I was constantly fending off children who ran after me calling, "*Baikah! Baikah!*" ("Cripple! Cripple!" in the Hokkien dialect commonly spoken in Malaysia). The taunts of children mattered little because I was a star pupil. I won one award after another for general scholarship as well as for art and public speaking. Whenever the school had important visitors, my teacher always called on me to recite in front of the class.

A significant event that marked me indelibly occurred when I was twelve. That year my school held a music recital, and I was one of the students chosen to play the piano. I managed to get up the steps to the stage without any problem, but as I walked across the stage, I fell. Out of the audience, a voice said loudly and clearly, "Ayah! A *baikah* shouldn't be allowed to perform in public." I got up before anyone could get on stage to help me, and with tears streaming uncontrollably down my face, I rushed to the piano and began to play. Beethoven's "Für Elise" had never been played so fiendishly fast before or since, but I managed to finish the whole piece. That I managed to do so made me feel really strong. I never again feared ridicule.

EVALUATE
What do you think of the way the author deals with her disability?
Using a Reading Log

In later years I was reminded of this experience from time to time. During my fourth year as an assistant professor at the University of California at Berkeley, I won a distinguished teaching award. Some weeks later I ran into a former professor who congratulated me enthusiastically. But I said to him, "You know what? I became a distinguished teacher by *limping* across the stage of Dwinelle 155!" (Dwinelle 155 is a large, cold classroom that most colleagues of mine hate to teach in.) I was rude not because I lacked graciousness but because this man, who had told me that my dissertation was the finest piece of work he had read in fifteen years, had nevertheless advised me to eschew[7] a teaching career.

"Why?" I asked.

---

7. **eschew** (ĕs-chōō′): avoid; stay away from.

286   UNIT TWO   PART 2: AGAINST THE ODDS

Mini-Lesson Grammar

USING VOICE IN WRITING Point out to students that the voice of a verb can be either active or passive. A verb is in the active voice when the subject performs the action. When the subject receives the action, the verb is in the passive voice. The passive voice should be used when the writer wishes to emphasize the person or thing receiving the action or when the performer of the action is unknown.

Application Have a volunteer read the highlighted sentence. Ask whether the active or passive voice is used. *(active)* Then ask what makes it the active voice. *(The emphasis of the action is on the doer of the action.)* Have students copy the sample sentences on the left. Call on volunteers to identify the voice of each.

Reteaching/Reinforcement
- Grammar Handbook, anthology p. 945

The Writer's Craft
Using Grammatical Voice, pp. 417–418
Active and Passive Voice, pp. 590–591

286   THE LANGUAGE OF LITERATURE TEACHER'S EDITION

"Your leg . . ." he responded.

"What about my leg?" I said, puzzled.

"Well, how would you feel standing in front of a large lecture class?"

"If it makes any difference, I want you to know I've won a number of speech contests in my life, and I am not the least bit self-conscious about speaking in front of large audiences. . . . Look, why don't you write me a letter of recommendation to tell people how brilliant I am, and let *me* worry about my leg!"

This incident is worth recounting only because it illustrates a dilemma that handicapped persons face frequently: those who care about us sometimes get so protective that they unwittingly limit our growth. This former professor of mine had been one of my greatest supporters for two decades. Time after time, he had written glowing letters of recommendation on my behalf. He had spoken as he did because he thought he had my best interests at heart; he thought that if I got a desk job rather than one that required me to be a visible, public person, I would be spared the misery of being stared at.

Americans, for the most part, do not believe as Asians do that physically handicapped persons are morally flawed. But they are equally inept at interacting with those of us who are not able-bodied. Cultural differences in the perception and treatment of handicapped people are most clearly expressed by adults. Children, regardless of where they are, tend to be openly curious about people who do not look "normal." Adults in Asia have no hesitation in asking visibly handicapped people what is wrong with them, often expressing their sympathy with looks of pity, whereas adults in the United States try desperately to be polite by pretending not to notice.

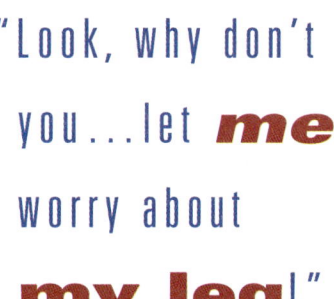

"Look, why don't you...let **me** worry about **my leg!**"

One interesting response I often elicited from people in Asia but have never encountered in America is the attempt to link my physical condition to the state of my soul. Many a time

WORDS TO KNOW

inept (ĭn-ĕpt′) *adj.* bungling; incompetent

Linking to Geography

K Chan has mentioned a number of places that might be unfamiliar to some of your students. Ask a volunteer to locate Karachi, Pakistan, on a map. Ask another volunteer to point out Hong Kong and Malaysia.

Active Reading: CONNECT

L Many students, whether disabled or not, will have experienced or observed this reaction. Encourage them to discuss the causes and effects of the reaction, in view of the author's opinion.

Critical Thinking: CLARIFYING

M Have a volunteer explain why Chan feels the need to explain the cause of disability to curious children, especially when the child is with an adult. *(Possible responses: to educate them about her condition; to put them at ease; to assure them that she is still "normal")*

Literary Concept: TONE

N Invite students to identify the tone of the paragraph in which Chan writes about people who become jovially patronizing. *(Possible responses: satirical; rueful; objective)*

---

while living and traveling in Asia people would ask me what religion I belonged to. I would tell them that my mother is a devout Buddhist, that my father was baptized a Catholic but has never practiced Catholicism, and that I am an <u>agnostic</u>. Upon hearing this, people would try strenuously to convert me to their religion so that whichever God they believed in could bless me. If I would only attend this church or that temple regularly, they urged, I would surely get cured. Catholics and Buddhists alike have pressed religious medallions into my palm, telling me if I would wear these, the relevant deity or saint would make me well. Once while visiting the tomb of Muhammad Ali Jinnah[8] in Karachi, Pakistan, an old Muslim, after finishing his evening prayers, spotted me, gestured toward my legs, raised his arms heavenward, and began a new round of prayers, apparently on my behalf.

In the United States adults who try to act "civilized" towards handicapped people by pretending they don't notice anything unusual sometimes end up ignoring handicapped people completely. In the first few months I lived in this country, I was struck by the fact that whenever children asked me what was the matter with my leg, their adult companions would hurriedly shush them up, furtively look at me, mumble apologies, and rush their children away. After a few months of such encounters, I decided it was my responsibility to educate these people. So I would say to the flustered adults, "It's okay; let the kid ask." Turning to the child, I would say, "When I was a little girl, no bigger than you are, I became sick with something called polio. The muscles of my leg shrank up, and I couldn't walk very well. You're much luckier than I am because now you can get a vaccine to make sure you never get my disease. So don't cry when your mommy takes you to get a polio vaccine, okay?" Some adults and their little companions I talked to this way were glad to be rescued from embarrassment; others thought I was strange.

Americans have another way of covering up their uneasiness: they become jovially <u>patronizing</u>. Sometimes when people spot my crutch, they ask if I've had a skiing accident. When I answer that unfortunately it is something less glamorous than that, they say, "I bet you *could* ski if you put your mind to it." Alternately, at parties where people dance, men who ask me to dance with them get almost belligerent when I decline their invitation. They say, "Of course you can dance if you *want* to!" Some have given me pep talks about how if I would only develop the right mental attitude, I would have more fun in life.

Different cultural attitudes toward handicapped persons came out clearly during my wedding. My father-in-law, as solid a representative of middle America as could be found, had no qualms about objecting to the marriage on racial grounds, but he could bring himself to comment on my handicap only indirectly. He wondered why his son, who had dated numerous high school and college beauty queens, couldn't marry one of them instead of me. My mother-in-law, a devout Christian, did not share her husband's prejudices, but she worried aloud about whether I could have children. Some Chinese friends of my parents, on the other hand, said that I was lucky to have

> **CONNECT**
> The author says Americans try to ignore a person's disability. Have you experienced or observed this reaction?
> *Using a Reading Log*

---

8. **Muhammad Ali Jinnah** (jĭn′ə): a Muslim leader and founder of Pakistan.

WORDS TO KNOW
agnostic (ăg-nŏs′tĭk) *n.* one who believes that the existence of God cannot be proved or disproved
patronizing (pā′trə-nīz-ĭng) *adj.* condescending; superior

288

Mini-Lesson Genre Study

NONFICTION An **autobiography** is an account of a person's life written by that person and usually told in the first-person point of view. In an autobiography, the writer details significant events and people in his or her life. In "You're Short, Besides!" Sucheng Chan recounts incidents, thoughts, and feelings concerning one major aspect of her life: her physical disability.

Application Have students work with a partner to look for the characteristics of an autobiography in "You're Short, Besides!" Then encourage them to discuss why readers like to learn about the lives of people who aren't famous and whom they don't know personally, such as Sucheng Chan. Invite students to identify aspects or passages of the essay that they found interesting, inspiring, informative, or helpful.

Copyright © 1982, Washington Post Writers Group. Reprinted with permission.

found such a noble man, one who would marry me despite my handicap. I, for my part, appeared in church in a white lace wedding dress I had designed and made myself—a miniskirt!

How Asian Americans treat me with respect to my handicap tells me a great deal about their degree of acculturation.[9] Recent immigrants behave just like Asians in Asia; those who have been here longer or who grew up in the United States behave more like their white counterparts. I have not encountered any distinctly Asian-American pattern of response. What makes the experience of Asian-American handicapped people unique is the duality of responses we elicit.

Regardless of racial or cultural background, most handicapped people have to learn to find a balance between the desire to attain physical independence and the need to take care of ourselves by not overtaxing our bodies. In my case, I've had to learn to accept the fact that leading an active life has its price. Between the ages of eight and eighteen, I walked without using crutches or braces, but the effort caused my right leg to become badly misaligned. Soon after I came to the United States, I had a series of operations to straighten out the bones of my right leg; afterwards though my leg looked straighter and presumably better, I could no longer walk on my own. Initially my doctors fitted me with a brace, but I found wearing one cumbersome and soon gave it up. I could move around much more easily—and more important, faster—by using one crutch. One orthopedist[10] after another warned me that using a single crutch was a bad practice. They were right. Over the years my spine developed a double-S curve, and for the last twenty years I have

---

9. **acculturation** (ə-kŭl′chə-rā′shən): a process of change in a culture, occurring as a result of contact with another culture.
10. **orthopedist** (ôr′thə-pē′dĭst): a doctor who specializes in treating injuries and disorders of the bones and associated muscles and joints.

YOU'RE SHORT, BESIDES! **289**

Mini-Lesson   Study Skills

TAKING OBJECTIVE TESTS: READING COMPREHENSION Reading-comprehension questions may ask students to pick out the central idea of a written text, recall a specific detail, draw a conclusion, determine the meaning of a word, identify the mood of a passage, or determine specific techniques that the writer has used. Suggest that students use the strategies listed on the right.

Application Ask small groups of students to choose a favorite passage from "You're Short, Besides!" and to compose two reading-comprehension questions. Then invite groups to read their questions aloud, and have students discuss the strategies they would use to answer the questions.

 The Writer's Craft

Reading Comprehension Questions, pp. 487–488

Read the questions before reading the passage.

Skim the passage, getting a feel for its main idea.

Reread the passage with the questions in mind.

Notice the author's reasoning, tone, and style.

Read all the answer choices. Choose the best answer based on the material in the passage.

CUSTOMIZING FOR
Students Acquiring English

④ Ask students to use Sucheng's work situation to infer what a *vicious circle* is. Then ask them to describe other situations that they view as "vicious circles."

Active Reading: EVALUATE

Ⓢ Possible response: Most students will say she is not truly incorrigible; she is being ironic and is actually proud of her achievements.

Literary Concept:
WRITER'S PURPOSE

Ⓣ Lead students to reflect on Chan's conclusions, and ask them to identify her purpose for writing. *(Possible response: She wants to express herself and to explain in order to help others.)*

STRATEGIC READING FOR
Less-Proficient Readers

Ⓤ Invite a volunteer to summarize how Chan deals with her physical condition and what kind of advice she gives about offering help to people with disabilities. *(Possible response: She has to find a balance between her desire to attain physical independence and her need to refrain from overtaxing her body; people have to be careful when and how they offer help.)* **Summarizing**

COMPREHENSION CHECK
1. What disease disabled Sucheng Chan? *(polio)*
2. In Chan's opinion, how do American adults differ from Asian adults in their typical reaction to the disabled? *(Asians express curiosity because they believe a moral fault is the cause of the disability; Americans pretend not to notice.)*

---

suffered from severe, chronic back pains, which neither conventional physical therapy nor a lighter workload can eliminate.

The only thing that helps my backaches is a good massage, but the soothing effect lasts no more than a day or two. Massages are expensive, especially when one needs them three times a week. So I found a job that pays better, but at which I have to work longer hours, consequently increasing the physical strain on my body—a sort of vicious circle. When I was in my thirties, my doctors told me that if I kept leading the strenuous life I did, I would be in a wheelchair by the time I was forty. They were right on target: I bought myself a wheelchair when I was forty-one. But being the <u>incorrigible</u> character that I am, I use it only when I am *not* in a hurry!

It is a good thing, however, that I am too busy to think much about my handicap or my backaches because pain can physically <u>debilitate</u> as well as cause depression. And there are days when my spirits get rather low. What has helped me is realizing that being handicapped is akin to growing old at an accelerated rate. The contradiction I experience is that often my mind races along as though I'm only twenty while my body feels about sixty. But fifteen or twenty years hence, unlike my peers who will have to cope with aging for the first time, I shall be full of cheer because I will have already fought, and I hope won, that battle long ago. . . .

I've often wondered if I would have been a different person had I not been physically handicapped. I really don't know, though there is no question that being handicapped has marked me. But at the same time I usually do not *feel* handicapped—and consequently, I do not *act* handicapped. People are therefore less likely to treat me as a handicapped person. There is no doubt, however, that the lives of my parents, sister, husband, other family members, and some close friends have been affected by my physical condition. They have had to learn not to hide me away at home, not to feel embarrassed by how I look or react to people who say silly things to me, and not to resent me for the extra demands my condition makes on them. Perhaps the hardest thing for those who live with handicapped people is to know when and how to offer help. There are no guidelines applicable to all situations. My advice is, when in doubt, ask, but ask in a way that does not smack of pity or embarrassment. Most important, please don't talk to us as though we are children.

So, has being physically handicapped been a handicap? It all depends on one's attitude. Some years ago, I told a friend that I had once said to an affirmative action compliance officer[11] (somewhat <u>sardonically</u> since I do not believe in the head-count approach to affirmative action) that the institution which employs me is triply lucky because it can count me as nonwhite, female and handicapped. He responded, "Why don't you tell them to count you four times? . . . Remember, you're short, besides!" ❖

EVALUATE
Do you agree with the author's characterization of herself as incorrigible?
Using a Reading Log

---

11. **affirmative action compliance officer:** an official who enforces government programs designed to make up for past discrimination and prevent future discrimination against women, minorities, people with disabilities, and Vietnam War veterans.

| WORDS TO KNOW | **incorrigible** (ĭn-kôr′ĭ-jə-bəl) *adj.* stubborn; unmanageable
debilitate (dĭ-bĭl′ĭ-tāt) *v.* to weaken the strength of
sardonically (sär-dŏn′ĭ-klē) *adv.* scornfully; mockingly |

290

Multicultural Perspectives

AFFIRMATIVE ACTION In the 1960s, the government established a policy of affirmative action—the practice of trying to overcome the effects of past discrimination by helping minorities, women, and people with disabilities receive admission to colleges and graduate schools, get government contracts in business, and find employment in corporations.

In recent years, however, affirmative action policies have been criticized by Conservative politicians as reverse discrimination against white men. As a result, many affirmative action policies have come under attack by those politicians who oppose them.

RESPONDING OPTIONS

FROM PERSONAL RESPONSE TO CRITICAL ANALYSIS

REFLECT
Thematic Link

1. What do you think of Sucheng Chan's attitude toward herself? In your notebook, write down your thoughts.

RETHINK

2. How would you describe Chan's character as revealed in this essay? Look over what you wrote in your reading log.
   Consider
   • what she has accomplished in her life
   • her attitude toward her disability

Close Textual Reading

3. Consider what Chan says about the different ways Asians and Americans react to people with disabilities. Which way do you think would be harder for a person with a disability to deal with? Why?

4. Review what you wrote for the Personal Connection activity on page 282. What did you learn from this essay about people with disabilities and how to treat them?

RELATE

5. *Inclusion* is a term that means including students with mental or physical disabilities in regular classrooms. What do you think are the benefits and/or drawbacks of inclusion for those with and without disabilities and for teachers?

Multimodal Learning
ANOTHER PATHWAY

Sucheng Chan says she has often wondered if she would have been a different person had she not been disabled. With a partner write a character sketch of Sucheng Chan as you imagine she would have been like if she did not have a disability. For example, do you think she would be more or less successful? Compare your sketch with others in the class.

LITERARY CONCEPTS

Tone is the attitude a writer takes toward a subject. For example, *The Devil and Daniel Webster* has a light, humorous tone, expressed partly through such slang expressions as "Oh, by jingo!" and such exaggerations as "if two New Hampshire men aren't a match for the devil. . . ." Describe the tone of Chan's essay. Think about her attitude toward herself, toward her disability, and toward the way people react to her disability.

CONCEPT REVIEW: Writer's Purpose The four main purposes for writing are to express oneself, to inform or explain, to persuade, and to entertain. Identify what you think is Chan's purpose or purposes in writing "You're Short, Besides!" Explain your answer.

QUICKWRITES

1. Look over the notes you made while reading this essay. Think about any questions you still have that were not answered in the essay. Make a **list of questions** that you would like to ask the author.

2. Using this essay as a guide, draft a **memo** to be circulated schoolwide with suggestions on how to respond to people with physical disabilities.

📁 **PORTFOLIO** Save your writing. You may want to use it later as a springboard to a piece for your portfolio.

YOU'RE SHORT, BESIDES! **291**

From Personal Response to Critical Analysis

1. Accept all reasonable responses.
2. Possible response: Chan is strong-minded, well-adjusted, vivacious, somewhat rebellious, and humorous.
3. Some students may say that it would be upsetting to know that people believed a character flaw caused one's physical disability; the injustice would be frustrating. Others may say that being ignored or patronized is more demeaning.
4. Possible responses: One should acknowledge people's disabilities in a matter-of-fact way and offer help when necessary, but not with pity or false encouragement.
5. Answers will vary.

Another Pathway

Suggest students first review the characterization of Sucheng in the essay and decide which changes are most plausible. Have them use either the first-person or third-person points of view. Encourage them to describe specific details as well as general traits.

Rubric

3 Full Accomplishment Sketch is vividly written and detailed, and the characterization seems plausible.

2 Substantial Accomplishment Sketch is vivid and plausible but lacking in vivid detail.

1 Little or Partial Accomplishment Sketch is both unconvincing and lacking in detail.

💿 **MEDICAL CONNECTION**
Polio Dr. Jonas Salk began administering his polio vaccine to children in 1955. Before his serum was available, thousands of school-age children fell victim to this dreaded disease. These images will help students understand the impact this disease had on people, including the author of this story.

Side A, Frame 49294

Literary Concepts

Words students might use to describe the essay's tone might include *optimistic, cheerful, honest, courageous, strong, upbeat,* and *firm.* Have students support their choice of adjectives with specific passages from the selection. See Annotations E, M, and O.

Writer's Purpose Possible response: Students may discover that all four purposes are present. Suggest to them that self-expression and explanation are the two most prominent purposes. See Annotations A and T.

QuickWrites

1. Tell students to make the questions more open-ended as if they were preparing them to interview Sucheng Chan.

2. Students might work either individually or in small groups. Suggest they write a heading for their memo, stating who it is written for, whom it is from, and what its subject is. Encourage students to use a concise, direct style and to support their work with reasons.

📁 **The Writer's Craft**

Conducting an Interview pp. 104–105

THE LANGUAGE OF LITERATURE TEACHER'S EDITION **291**

Literary Links

Ask students to compare the experiences of the author of "You're Short, Besides!" with those of the author of "On Being Seventeen, Bright, and Unable to Read." Ask them how the authors' experiences are similar and different.

Words to Know

1. debilitate
2. agnostic
3. inept
4. incorrigible
5. patronizing
6. enamored
7. assuage
8. precocious
9. presumptuous
10. sardonically

Reteaching/Reinforcement
- *Unit Two Resource Book*, p. 42

Across the Curriculum

Health *Cooperative Learning* Suggest that students meet to plan their work strategy, then go to the school library as a first step in research. A person who gives directions will be useful to the group in organizing its research and assigning tasks. One or two students might specialize as researchers, reporting back to the group; research partners should help check the accuracy of one another's findings. Students not actively involved in research should generate questions and be elaborators, relating findings to what students already know. In creating the pamphlet, students should select tasks based on interests and skills. One student might create visuals, another write a draft copy, others suggest improvements and revisions, and another manage a desktop publishing program if students have access to a computer.

EDITOR'S NOTE With the permission of the author or copyright holder, potentially offensive material has been deleted from the selection.

Multimodal Learning

ALTERNATIVE ACTIVITIES

1. A number of films tell the story of people with disabilities, including *The Miracle Worker, The Terry Fox Story,* and *The Boy Who Could Fly.* Watch a videotape of such a film and give an **oral report** on the insights you gained.

2. Chan states that she does not believe "in the head count approach to affirmative action." She is referring to quotas to make up for and prevent discrimination against minorities, women, and people with disabilities. Give a **speech** informing classmates of the pros and cons of affirmative-action quotas.

ACROSS THE CURRICULUM

Health *Cooperative Learning* During the 1940s and 1950s, a polio epidemic swept through the United States. Millions were infected, and over 600,000 people (mostly children) suffered some degree of paralysis. Today, as adults, many of these polio survivors are suffering the prospect of developing a *postpolio syndrome*—an unexplainable recurrence of polio symptoms. With a small group, investigate this syndrome and create a brief public-health pamphlet describing it.

WORDS TO KNOW

Review the Words to Know at the bottom of the selection pages. Then, on your paper, write the word closest in meaning to the italicized word or phrase in each sentence.

1. Lack of physical activity can *steal the energy from* even the healthiest body.
2. A *person who says that God's existence cannot be proved or disproved* probably will not have a strong opinion about whether prayer can help people in need.
3. Prescribing the wrong medication is something a *clumsy* doctor would do.
4. An *uncooperative* patient might not follow a strict diet.
5. If someone is treating you like a young child, he or she has a *superior* manner.
6. People who become *enchanted* with a vacation spot may decide they want to live there permanently.
7. How might a nurse *ease* the fears of a seriously injured patient?
8. Did you hear that *exceptionally bright* six-year-old read the doctor's clipboard?
9. Is it *ignoring accepted behavior* to call a doctor by his or her first name?
10. The doctor answered my question about malpractice lawyers *scornfully*.

SUCHENG CHAN

Sucheng Chan has had a distinguished academic career. She is professor and chairperson of Asian-American Studies at the University of California at Santa Barbara. She specializes in Asian-American economic history and in Asian migration. Chan received a Distinguished Teaching Award from the University of California at Berkeley in 1978, and she held a Guggenheim Fellowship in 1988–89. Her scholarly books and articles have won numerous awards. She is the editor of eight books, including *Hmong Means Free: Life in Laos and America,* which tells the stories of Hmong refugees who fled Laos after communists took power in much of Southeast Asia in 1975.

OTHER WORKS *This Bittersweet Soil: The Chinese in California Agriculture, 1860–1910; Asians in California History; Asian Americans: An Interpretive History*

Extended Reading

• MEDICAL CONNECTION

292 UNIT TWO PART 2: AGAINST THE ODDS

Alternative Activities

1. Students might watch the film at home individually or with classmates; or, if you have the time and facilities, you might show one or two significant scenes from the films in class, such as the scene in *The Miracle Worker* in which Helen Keller first recognizes the sign for water. Encourage students to relate the films to the selection and to their own experiences.

2. Encourage students to do research on the actual use (or absence) of quotas, because this is a subject about which solid evidence is not easy to find. Remind students to take notes, prepare an outline, and practice their speeches privately or in front of a small, trusted audience, working from brief notes.

PREVIEWING

NONFICTION

The United States vs. Susan B. Anthony
Margaret Truman

Activating Prior Knowledge / Setting a Purpose
PERSONAL CONNECTION

In a few years, you will be old enough to vote in city, state, and national elections. But what if you, as an adult citizen, were not allowed to vote for government officials—simply because of your sex or your race? Think about the right to vote. In your notebook, list three reasons why a citizen's right to vote is important. Share your reasons with a classmate. Then, as you read, see how being denied the right to vote moved Susan B. Anthony to action.

Building Background
HISTORICAL CONNECTION

For almost a hundred years after the United States won its independence, only white males had suffrage—the right to vote. Finally, in 1868, as a way to ensure the rights of former slaves, the 14th Amendment to the U.S. Constitution was ratified. It made "all persons" born in the United States citizens with full citizenship "privileges." The amendment, however, was intended to apply only to all *males;* women had not been specifically mentioned. So, women continued their struggle for the right to vote, a struggle that had begun in 1848. A leader in the suffragist movement was Susan B. Anthony. This biographical essay details Anthony's 1873 attempt to force the courts to recognize that the language of the 14th Amendment could not exclude women from its guaranteed rights.

Active Reading
READING CONNECTION

Understanding Specialized Vocabulary This essay contains many legal terms that may be unfamiliar to you. The chart below defines some of the most important ones used. Other specialized terms are defined in footnotes.

Legal Term	Definition
draw up a *bill of indictment* (ĭn-dīt′mənt)	write a *description of the crime a person is accused of committing*
convene a *grand jury*	gather a *private session of 12 to 23 people who decide if there is enough evidence to put an accused person on open trial*
set *bail*	name an *amount of money needed to temporarily release an arrested person awaiting trial*
post a *bond*	deliver to the court an *amount of money to be used as bail*

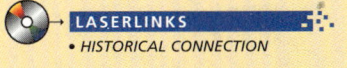
- HISTORICAL CONNECTION

THE UNITED STATES VS. SUSAN B. ANTHONY **293**

OVERVIEW

Objectives
- To understand and appreciate a biographical essay that explores one woman's struggle to win the right to vote
- To identify and understand biography
- To express understanding of the essay through a choice of writing forms, including a pamphlet, a commentary, and a Constitutional amendment
- To extend understanding of the selection through a variety of multimodal and cross-curricular activities

Skills

LITERARY CONCEPTS
- Biography
- Characterization
- Point of view

THE WRITER'S STYLE
- Types of elaboration: incidents

GENRE STUDY
- Nonfiction: biography

GRAMMAR
- Helping verbs

SPEAKING, LISTENING, AND VIEWING
- Interviews
- Group discussion
- Oral presentation

HISTORICAL CONNECTION
Women's Equality Susan B. Anthony was called "the Napoleon of the women's rights movement." These images show students some of the moments in history when women spoke out for equality. You may wish to use these images to facilitate discussion about the similarities between the women's rights movement of the 1800s and that of today.

Side A, Frame 49300

PRINT AND MEDIA RESOURCES

UNIT TWO RESOURCE BOOK
Strategic Reading: Literature, p. 45
Vocabulary SkillBuilder, p. 46

GRAMMAR MINI-LESSONS
Transparencies, p. 29
Copymasters, p. 29

WRITING MINI-LESSONS
Transparencies, p. 44

ACCESS FOR STUDENTS ACQUIRING ENGLISH
Selection Summaries
Reading Support

FORMAL ASSESSMENT
Selection Test, pp. 49–50
 Test Generator

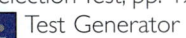 **AUDIO LIBRARY**
See Reference Card

 LASERLINKS
Historical Connection
Art Gallery

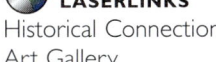 **INTERNET RESOURCES**
McDougal Littell Literature Center at http://www.hmco.com/mcdougal/lit

SUMMARY

The author looks at the character of the 19th-century women's-rights activist Susan B. Anthony. Truman tells the story of Anthony's test of the 14th Amendment, which guarantees the right to vote to all persons. After reading a newspaper editorial urging people to vote, Anthony and her sisters register and vote. For her actions, she is arrested and tried for voting illegally. During court proceedings, a judge orders a jury to find Anthony guilty. Before sentencing, he asks her if she has anything to say. She criticizes the court for its injustices and declares her right to be treated as a citizen. When she is finished, the judge fines her. Anthony refuses to pay the fine, but the judge, wanting to avoid a legal appeal, does not imprison her. Anthony lost the case, but she struck a blow for women's suffrage.

Thematic Link: *Against the Odds* Susan B. Anthony rebels against an unjust system and strikes a blow for women's suffrage.

CUSTOMIZING FOR
Students Acquiring English

- Use **ACCESS FOR STUDENTS ACQUIRING ENGLISH,** *Reading Support.*
- For students not familiar with the democratic process, explain to them the importance of voting in our society. Tell students that in a representative government, voting is the way people make their wishes known to their leaders.

STRATEGIC READING FOR
Less-Proficient Readers

Have students read page 294, noting the adjectives that describe Anthony.

Set a Purpose Ask students to read to determine how accurate these words are.

Use **UNIT TWO RESOURCE BOOK,** p. 45, for guidance in reading the selection.

THE UNITED STATES vs. SUSAN B. ANTHONY

Margaret *Truman*

Susan B. Anthony has never been one of my favorite characters. Stern-eyed and grim-lipped, she seemed utterly devoid of warmth and humor and much too quick to dominate the women she worked with. I always thought her personality could be summed up in one word: battle-ax.[1] On top of that drawback, she was a fanatic. She joined the woman's suffrage movement in 1852, when she was thirty-two years old. From then until her death in 1906, she could think of little else.

The fanatics of one generation have a habit of turning into the heroes and heroines of the next, as Susan B. Anthony proved. And since I've been making a study of heroines, I decided to give

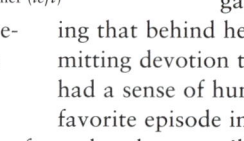
Susan B. Anthony (*right*), her sister Mary (*center*), and her friend Elizabeth Miller (*left*)

Miss Anthony a second look. I have to report that my original assessment of her character was much too harsh. . . .

Susan B. Anthony was a stern and single-minded woman. Like most crusaders for causes—especially unpopular causes—she had little time for fun and games. But I have a sneaky feeling that behind her severe manner and unremitting devotion to duty, she may actually have had a sense of humor. Let me tell you about my favorite episode in Susan B. Anthony's career, and perhaps you'll agree.

---
1. **battle-ax:** derogatory slang for a woman who is harsh and domineering.

WORDS TO KNOW

adamant (ăd′ə-mənt) *adj.* not giving in; unyielding (p. 301)

blatant (blāt′nt) *adj.* completely obvious (p. 301)

competent (kŏm′pĭ-tənt) *adj.* in law, mentally fit to participate (p. 298)

concur (kən-kûr′) *v.* to agree (p. 296)

denunciation (dĭ-nŭn′sē-ā′shən) *n.* public condemnation; statement of disapproval (p. 301)

fortitude (fôr′tĭ-tōōd′) *n.* the strength of mind required to withstand hardship (p. 298)

inadvertently (ĭn′əd-vûr′tnt-lē) *adv.* without intending to; not on purpose (p. 296)

oratory (ôr′ə-tôr′ē) *n.* skill in public speaking (p. 295)

retrospect (rĕt′rə-spĕkt′) *n.* a review of things in the past (p. 298)

tirade (tī′rād) *n.* a long, angry speech, especially one that criticizes (p. 301)

It began on Friday morning, November 1, 1872. Susan was reading the morning paper at her home in Rochester. There, at the top of the editorial page of the *Democrat and Chronicle*, was an exhortation[2] to the city's residents:

Now register! Today and tomorrow are the only remaining opportunities. If you were not permitted to vote, you would fight for the right, undergo all privations[3] for it, face death for it. You have it now at the cost of five minutes' time to be spent in seeking your place of registration and having your name entered. And yet, on election day, less than a week hence, hundreds of you are likely to lose your votes because you have not thought it worth while to give the five minutes. Today and tomorrow are your only opportunities. Register now!

Susan B. Anthony read the editorial again. Just as she thought, it said nothing about being addressed to men only. With a gleam in her eye, she put down the paper and summoned her sister Guelma, with whom she lived. The two women donned their hats and cloaks and went off to call on two other Anthony sisters who lived nearby. Together, the four women headed for the barbershop on West Street, where voters from the Eighth Ward were being registered.

For some time, Susan B. Anthony had been looking for an opportunity to test the Fourteenth Amendment to the Constitution as a weapon to win the vote for women. Adopted in 1870, the amendment had been designed to protect the civil rights—especially the voting rights—of recently freed slaves. It stated that:

All persons born or naturalized in the United States, and subject to the jurisdiction thereof, are citizens of the United States and of the state wherein they reside. No state shall make or enforce any law which shall abridge[4] the privileges or immunities of citizens of the United States, nor shall any state deprive any person of life, liberty, or property without due process of law, nor deny to any person within its jurisdiction the equal protection of the laws.

The amendment did not say that "persons" meant only males, nor did it spell out "the privileges or immunities of citizens." Susan B. Anthony felt perfectly justified in concluding that the right to vote was among the privileges of citizenship and that it extended to women as well as men. I'm sure she must have also seen the humor of outwitting the supposedly superior males who wrote the amendment.

It was bad enough for a bunch of women to barge into one sacred male precinct[5]—the barbershop—but to insist on being admitted to another holy of holies—the voting booth—was absolutely outrageous. Moustaches twitched; throats were cleared; a whispered conference was held in the corner.

Susan had brought along a copy of the Fourteenth Amendment. She read it aloud, carefully pointing out to the men in charge of registration that the document failed to state that the privilege of voting extended only to males.

Only one man in the barbershop had the nerve to refuse the Anthony sisters the right to register. The rest buckled under Susan's determined oratory and allowed them to sign the huge, leather-bound voter registration book.

---

2. **exhortation** (ĕg´zôr-tā´shən): an urgent call to action.
3. **privations** (prī-vā´shənz): shortages of the basic necessities or comforts of life.
4. **abridge:** to cut short.
5. **precinct** (prē´sĭngkt´): a place marked off by definite limits, such as walls.

WORDS TO KNOW
oratory (ôr´ə-tôr´ē) *n.* skill in public speaking

295

Literary Concept: BIOGRAPHY

D Ask students if the author could really know the reason why the men let Anthony and her sisters register to vote. *(not unless Anthony mentioned these facts in a diary or autobiography)* Ask why this fictionalized information is included. *(Possible responses: to characterize Anthony and to draw the readers into the story)*

CUSTOMIZING FOR
Students Acquiring English

I Have students use the context to define *vilified*. *(opposite of "applauded"; means people disapproved of her conduct)*

Critical Thinking: SPECULATING

E Ask why the marshal was so nervous and embarrassed about arresting Anthony. *(Possible responses: He was not used to arresting ladies; he knew she was not a criminal; he was intimidated by her.)*

STRATEGIC READING FOR
Less-Proficient Readers

F Invite students to give their impressions of Anthony so far.

- Ask them what prompted Anthony to register to vote. *(a newspaper editorial)* **Noting Relevant Details**
- Ask them what Anthony's legal justification was for trying to vote. *(The 14th Amendment gave that right to "all persons.")* **Finding the Main Idea**
- Ask students who agreed to represent her. *(Henry R. Selden)* **Noting Relevant Details**

Set a Purpose Ask students to read to find out whether Anthony wins her court battle.

If the men in the barbershop thought they were getting rid of a little band of crackpots the easy way, they were wrong. Susan urged all her followers in Rochester to register. The next day, a dozen women invaded the Eighth Ward barbershop, and another thirty-five appeared at registration sites elsewhere in the city. The *Democrat and Chronicle*, which had <u>inadvertently</u> prompted the registrations, expressed no editorial opinion on the phenomenon, but its rival, the *Union and Advertiser*, denounced the women. If they were allowed to vote, the paper declared, the poll inspectors[6] "should be prosecuted to the full extent of the law."

The following Tuesday, November 5, was Election Day. Most of the poll inspectors in Rochester had read the editorial in the *Union and Advertiser* and were too intimidated to allow any of the women who had registered to vote. Only in the Eighth Ward did the males weaken. Maybe the inspectors were *Democrat and Chronicle* readers, or perhaps they were more afraid of Susan B. Anthony than they were of the law. Whatever the reason, when Susan and her sisters showed up at the polls shortly after 7 A.M., there was only a minimum of fuss. A couple of inspectors were hesitant about letting the women vote, but when Susan assured them that she would pay all their legal expenses if they were prosecuted, the men relented, and one by one, the women took their ballots and stepped into the voting booth. There were no insults or sneers, no rude remarks. They marked their ballots, dropped them into the ballot box, and returned to their homes.

Susan B. Anthony's feat quickly became the talk of the country. She was applauded in some circles, vilified[7] in others. But the day of reckoning was not long in arriving. On November 28, Deputy U.S. Marshal E. J. Keeney appeared at her door with a warrant[8] for her arrest. She had violated Section 19 of the Enforcement Act of the Fourteenth Amendment, which held that anyone who voted illegally was to be arrested and tried on criminal charges.

Susan B. Anthony was a great believer in planning ahead. The day after she registered, she decided to get a legal opinion on whether or not she should attempt to vote. A number of lawyers turned her away, but she finally found one who agreed to consider the case. He was Henry R. Selden, a former judge of the court of appeals, now a partner in one of Rochester's most prestigious law firms.

On the Monday before Election Day, Henry Selden informed his new client that he agreed with her interpretation of the Fourteenth Amendment and that in his opinion, she had every right to cast her ballot. The U.S. commissioner of elections in Rochester, William C. Storrs, did not <u>concur</u>.

E. J. Keeney, the marshal dispatched to arrest Susan B. Anthony, was not at all happy with his assignment. He nervously twirled his tall felt hat while waiting for her to come to the front door. When she finally appeared, he blushed and stammered, shifted uncomfortably from one foot to the other, and finally blurted out, "The commissioner wishes to arrest you."

---

6. **poll inspectors:** officials who make sure that votes are cast according to the law.
7. **vilified:** made vicious statements about
8. **warrant:** a legal document authorizing an officer to make an arrest, a search, or a seizure.

New York suffragists advertise a meeting at which governors of states with woman suffrage were scheduled to speak. The Bettmann Archive.

WORDS TO KNOW
inadvertently (ĭn´əd-vûr´tnt-lē) *adv.* without intending to; not on purpose
concur (kən-kûr´) *v.* to agree

296

Mini-Lesson — Genre Study

NONFICTION A **biography** is a true account of a person's life told by someone else. A biography may recount a person's entire life or a portion thereof. In most cases, it is written in the third person. The strictly biographical sections of "The United States vs. Susan B. Anthony" make up the bulk of the essay and are written in the third person. The first-person introduction links this essay to the other essays in the book from which it was taken, *Women of Courage*.

Application Interpreting the facts is a valid function of a biography. Invite students to identify ideas or passages in the biography that are factual and ones that suggest Truman's opinion or interpretation. Suggest they use a simple, two-column chart such as the one at left.

Facts	Interpretations/ Opinions
Susan B. Anthony fought for the right of women to vote.	Susan B. Anthony was a heroine.

Susan couldn't help being amused at Keeney's embarrassment. "Is this your usual method of serving a warrant?" she asked calmly. With that, the marshal recovered his official dignity, presented her with the warrant, and told her that he had come to escort her to the office of the commissioner of elections.

When Susan asked if she could change into a more suitable dress, the marshal saw his opportunity to escape. "Of course," he said, turning to leave. "Just come down to the commissioner's office whenever you're ready."

"I'll do no such thing," Susan informed him curtly. "You were sent here to arrest me and take me to court. It's your duty to do so."

Keeney had no choice but to wait while his prisoner went upstairs and put on a more appropriate outfit. When she returned, she thrust out her wrists and said, "Don't you want to handcuff me, too?"

"I assure you, madam," Marshal Keeney stuttered, "it isn't at all necessary."

With the U.S. marshal at her side, Susan was brought before the federal commissioner of elections, William C. Storrs. Her arrest was recorded, and she was ordered to appear the next day for a hearing. It was conducted by U.S. District Attorney Richard Crowley and his assistant, John E. Pound.

Susan answered District Attorney Crowley's questions politely. She said that she thought the Fourteenth Amendment gave her the right to vote. She admitted that she had consulted an attorney on the question but said that she would have voted even if he had not advised her to do so. When Crowley asked if she had voted deliberately to test the law, she said, "Yes, sir. I have been determined for three years to vote the first time I happened to be at home for the required thirty days before an election."

The district attorney's next step was to convene a grand jury to draw up a bill of indictment. He and his assistant fell to wrangling over a suitable trial date. Susan interrupted them. "I have lecture dates that will take me to central Ohio," she said. "I won't be available until December 10."

"But you're supposed to be in custody⁹ until the hearing," Crowley informed her.

"Is that so?" said Susan coolly. "I didn't know that."

---

9. **in custody:** held under guard.

Mini-Lesson The Writer's Style

TYPES OF ELABORATION: INCIDENTS
To convince readers, writers must develop or elaborate their ideas. One way to do this is to use incidents. In "The United States vs. Susan B. Anthony," Margaret Truman uses incidents such as Anthony's encounters with the marshal and the district attorney to convey her forceful character.

Application Ask students to choose one of the three reasons why voting is important that they listed in their Personal Connection. Then have students describe an incident that supports their reasoning. The incident may come from their own experience, from something they learned about, or from their imagination.

Reteaching/Reinforcement
- *Writing Handbook* anthology, pp. 871–2
- *Writing Mini-Lessons* transparencies, p. 44

 The Writer's Craft
Types of Elaboration, pp. 351–354

Literary Concept: BIOGRAPHY

I In this passage the author is making a political comment by contrasting the prison of the 1870s with those of today. If Anthony were alive today, what kind of prison would she be eligible for, according to the author? *(Possible response: a minimum security prison because she did not commit a major crime)*

Critical Thinking: SPECULATING

J Ask students why Anthony refuses to post a bond. *(Possible responses: She wants to go to jail to arouse public sympathy for her cause; she does not want to acquiesce to an unjust ruling.)*

Literary Concept: CHARACTERIZATION

K Here Truman introduces a secondary character, Judge Hunt. Ask students to find words and phrases that convey her view of Hunt. *(Possible responses: "prim, pale," "owed his judgeship to the good offices," "had no wish to offend his powerful patron")*

Linking to History

L Patronage is an informal system by which powerful figures appoint their supporters to key offices and jobs, especially political ones.

Critical Thinking: SPECULATING

M Ask students why Crowley does not want Anthony to testify. *(He is afraid she will persuade the jury of the justness of her cause. She is persuasive and impassioned.)*

The district attorney backed down without an argument and scheduled the grand jury session for December 23. Sixteen women had voted in Rochester. All sixteen were arrested and taken before the grand jury, but Susan alone was brought to trial. The district attorney had decided to single her out as a test case.[10] The three poll inspectors who had allowed the women to vote were also arrested. The grand jury indicted them too, set bail at five hundred dollars each, and ordered their trial set for the summer term of the U.S. district court.

Susan Anthony's case now involved nineteen other men and women. All of them—including Susan—were liable to go to prison if they were found guilty and the judge was in a sentencing mood. Prison in the 1870s was a very unpleasant place. There were no minimum security setups where a benevolent government allowed corrupt politicians, crooked labor leaders, and political agitators to rest and rehabilitate, as we do today. Prison meant a cold cell, wretched food, the company of thieves and murderers.

For a while it looked as if Susan might be behind bars even before the trial. She refused to post a bond for her five-hundred-dollar bail. Henry Selden paid the money for her. "I could not see a lady I respected put in jail," he said.

It must be agonizing to sweat out the weeks before a trial. There is time to look ahead and brood about the possibility of an unfavorable verdict and time to look back, perhaps with regret, at the decision that placed you in the hands of the law. But Susan B. Anthony had no regrets. Nor did she appear to have any anxieties about her trial. She had already proven her fortitude by devoting twenty years of her life to fighting for the right to vote. If she won her case, the struggle would be over. But even if she lost, Susan was not ready to give up the fight. . . .

The trial of *The United States* vs. *Susan B. Anthony* opened on the afternoon of June 17, 1873, with the tolling of the Canandaigua Courthouse bell. The presiding justice was Ward Hunt, a prim, pale man, who owed his judgeship to the good offices of Senator Roscoe Conkling, the Republican boss of New York State. Conkling was a fierce foe of woman suffrage, and Hunt, who had no wish to offend his powerful patron, had written his decision before the trial started.

District Attorney Crowley opened the arguments for the prosecution.[11] They didn't make much sense at the time, and in retrospect, they sound nothing short of ridiculous. The district attorney mentioned that Susan B. Anthony was a woman and therefore she had no right to vote. His principal witness was an inspector of elections for the Eighth Ward, who swore that on November 5 he had seen Miss Anthony put her ballot in the ballot box. To back up his testimony, the inspector produced the voter registration book with Susan B. Anthony's signature in it.

Henry Selden's reply for the defense was equally simple. He contended that Susan Anthony had registered and voted in good faith, believing that it was her constitutional right to do so. When he attempted to call his client to the stand, however, District Attorney Crowley announced that she was not competent to testify in her own behalf. Judge Hunt agreed, and the only thing Henry Selden could do was read excerpts from the testimony Susan had given at her previous hearings when presumably she was no less incompetent than she was right now.

---

10. **test case:** a legal action chosen specifically for the example or standard that its outcome may establish.
11. **prosecution:** in a court case, the lawyers who represent the government.

WORDS TO KNOW
fortitude (fôr'tĭ-tōōd') *n.* the strength of mind required to withstand hardship
retrospect (rĕt'rə-spĕkt') *n.* a review of things in the past
competent (kŏm'pĭ-tənt) *adj.* in law, mentally fit to participate

298

Mini-Lesson Grammar

HELPING VERBS Remind students that the main verb of a sentence, whether an action or linking verb, sometimes has one or more helping verbs, also called auxiliary verbs. The most common helping verbs are the forms of *be, have,* and *do.*

Application Ask volunteers to identify the helping verbs in each of the highlighted sentences on this page. *(had, might be)* Then read the following sentences aloud. Have students choose the helping verbs.

1. Susan B. Anthony has often been cited as a heroine. *(has, been)*
2. Anthony could have been sent to prison. *(could have)*
3. The women were not allowed to vote. *(were)*

Reteaching/Reinforcement
- *Grammar Handbook,* anthology p. 945
- *Grammar Mini-Lessons* copymasters p. 29, transparencies p. 29

Helping Verbs, p. 586

Susan B. Anthony in front of her Rochester home, now a national historical monument.
Reproduced from the Collections of the Library of Congress.

Multicultural Perspectives

WOMEN AND POLITICS In the United States, largely through the efforts of Susan B. Anthony and her associates, both major political parties endorsed women's suffrage in 1906. In 1920, 14 years after Anthony's death, the 19th Amendment guaranteeing women the right to vote was passed, which improved the political status of women in the United States.

Women in the United States are not the only ones who have worked to improve their political and economic status. Women worldwide have also been working for political and social empowerment. The predominantly Muslim nation of Pakistan and the predominantly Hindu nation of India both have had female prime ministers elected within the past generation—Benazir Bhutto and Indira Gandhi, respectively.

CUSTOMIZING FOR
Multiple Learning Styles

N **Spatial or Graphic Learners** Invite students to use the photograph to gain insight into the subject's personality and to develop a feel for the times she lived in. For example, students might note the building design and the old-fashioned clothing that restricts a woman's movement. Encourage students to imagine themselves living in that time and place. Ask what their lives would be like and what they would like and dislike about living at that time.

DESIGN NOTE

The art is a rendering of the Susan B. Anthony silver dollar that was first issued in 1979. Because it was too similar in appearance to a quarter, the currency did not catch on with the public and, beginning in 1980, no new Anthony coins were minted.

Critical Thinking:
MAKING JUDGMENTS

❶ Have students voice their opinions on the directed verdict of guilty. *(Most will find it unjust and outrageous.)* Challenge students to provide specific reasons for their responses, based on an understanding of constitutional rights. *(Possible response: The judge has deprived Anthony of her Sixth Amendment right to trial by a jury of her peers—or by any jury at all.)*

The Susan B. Anthony dollar, the first U.S. coin in general circulation to honor a famous American woman

Henry Selden tried to make up for this gross injustice by making his closing argument a dramatic, three-hour speech on behalf of woman suffrage. District Attorney Crowley replied with a two-hour rehash of the original charge.

By the afternoon of June 18, the case of *The United States* vs. *Susan B. Anthony* was ready to go to the jury. It was impossible to predict what their verdict might be, so Judge Hunt, determined to make it the verdict he and Roscoe Conkling wanted, took matters into his own hands. "Gentlemen of the jury," he said, ❶ "I direct that you find the defendant guilty."

Henry Selden leaped to his feet. "I object, Your Honor," he thundered. "The court has no power to direct the jury in a criminal case."

Judge Hunt ignored him. "Take the verdict, Mr. Clerk," he said.

The clerk of the court must have been another Conkling man. "Gentlemen of the jury," he intoned as if the whole proceeding was perfectly normal, "hearken to the verdict as the court hath recorded it. You say you find the defendant guilty of the offense charged. So say you all."

The twelve jurymen looked stunned. They had not even met to discuss the case, much less agree on a verdict. When Henry Selden asked if the clerk could at least poll the jury, Judge Hunt rapped his gavel sharply and declared, "That cannot be allowed. Gentlemen of the jury, you are discharged."

300   UNIT TWO   PART 2: AGAINST THE ODDS

Mini-Lesson Workplace Literacy

SCANS Goal: Exercises Leadership

LEADING A MEETING A leader should communicate thoughts, feelings, and ideas to justify a position or to persuade or motivate followers. Leadership sometimes involves responsibly challenging existing procedures, policies, or authority. Point out how, in "The United States vs. Susan B. Anthony," a judge used his leadership position irresponsibly at the behest of a party boss. In response, Susan B. Anthony took it upon herself to exercise leadership by challenging the procedures followed.

Application Ask small groups of students to imagine that it is the day after the trial of Susan B. Anthony. Allow them to decide what kind of organization they want to represent—perhaps the jury, an editorial board, or Anthony and her supporters. Ask students to elect a leader and meet to plan a course of action.

An enraged Henry Selden lost no time in introducing a motion for a new trial on the grounds that his client had been denied the right to a jury verdict. Judge Hunt denied the motion. He turned to Susan B. Anthony and said, "The prisoner will stand up. Has the prisoner anything to say why sentence shall not be pronounced?"

Thus far in the trial, Susan B. Anthony had remained silent. Now, she rose to her feet and said slowly, "Yes, Your Honor, I have many things to say."

Without further preliminaries, she launched into a scathing <u>denunciation</u> of Judge Hunt's conduct of her trial. ". . . In your ordered verdict of guilty," she said, "you have trampled underfoot every vital principle of our government. My natural rights, my civil rights, my political rights, are all alike ignored. Robbed of the fundamental privilege of citizenship, I am degraded from the status of a citizen to that of a subject; and not only myself individually, but all of my sex, are, by Your Honor's verdict, doomed to political subjection under this so-called Republican government."

Judge Hunt reached for his gavel, but Susan B. Anthony refused to be silent.

"May it please Your Honor," she continued. "Your denial of my citizen's right to vote is the denial of my right to a trial by a jury of my peers as an offender against law, therefore, the denial of my sacred rights to life, liberty, property, and—"

"The court cannot allow the prisoner to go on," Judge Hunt cried out.

Susan ignored him and continued her impassioned <u>tirade</u> against the court. Hunt frantically rapped his gavel and ordered her to sit down and be quiet. But Susan, who must have been taking delight in his consternation, kept on talking. She deplored the fact that she had been denied the right to a fair trial. Even if she had been given such a trial, she insisted, it would not have been by her peers. Jury, judges, and lawyers were not her equals, but her superiors, because they could vote and she could not. Susan was <u>adamant</u> about the fact that she had been denied the justice guaranteed in the Constitution to every citizen of the United States.

Judge Hunt was sufficiently cowed by now to try to defend himself. "The prisoner has been tried according to the established forms of law," he sputtered.

"Yes, Your Honor," retorted Susan, overlooking his <u>blatant</u> lie, "but by forms of law all made by men, interpreted by men, administered by men, in favor of men, and against women; and hence Your Honor's ordered verdict of guilty, against a United States citizen for the exercise of that citizen's right to vote, simply because that citizen was a woman and not a man. But yesterday, the same manmade forms of law declared it a crime punishable with a one-thousand-dollar fine and six months imprisonment, for you, or me, or any of us, to give a cup of cold water, a crust of bread, or a night's shelter to a panting fugitive while he was tracking his way to Canada. And every man or woman in whose veins coursed a drop of human sympathy violated that wicked law, reckless of consequences, and was justified in so doing. As, then, the slaves who got their freedom must take it over, or under, or through the unjust forms of law, precisely so now must women, to get their right to a voice in this government, take it, and I have taken mine and mean to take it at every opportunity."

WORDS TO KNOW
denunciation (dĭ-nŭn'sē-ā'shən) *n.* public condemnation; statement of disapproval
tirade (tī'rād) *n.* a long, angry speech, especially one that criticizes
adamant (ăd'ə-mənt) *adj.* not giving in; unyielding
blatant (blāt'nt) *adj.* completely obvious

301

Literary Concept: BIOGRAPHY

P Ask students how the biographer knew the exact words of Anthony's courtroom speech. *(Possible response: through research into newspapers or court documents)* You might have students compare this historically documented piece of oratory with the reconstructed conversation on page 297 and then discuss how each passage might represent valid biographical techniques.

Critical Thinking: MAKING JUDGMENTS

Q Ask students why Anthony says that she was not tried according to "established forms of law." *(Possible response: According to Anthony all the laws were made by men, without thought for women's rights; she has been denied the right to vote simply because she is a woman.)*

Linking to History

R Anthony is alluding to the Fugitive Slave Act of 1850, which made it a crime to help runaway slaves escape on the Underground Railroad. (See page 270 in *The Devil and Daniel Webster.*) Encourage students to paraphrase the analogy Anthony draws between the legal situation of slaves trying to escape and that of women trying to gain suffrage. *(Possible responses: Like slaves, women have no rights; the laws are unfair and should be changed.)*

Mini-Lesson: Speaking, Listening, and Viewing

INTERVIEWS An interview is an effective way of gathering information about a person or the views the person holds. Have students hone their skills by conducting imaginary interviews with Susan B. Anthony and with other participants in her trial.

Application Have students work in pairs, one partner playing the role of interviewer and the other playing the subject. The interviewer should be a reporter for the Rochester *Democrat and Chronicle* or *Union and Advertiser.* (Note the difference in editorial slants between those two newspapers, the former being neutral and the latter being opposed to suffrage.) The subject, with feedback from the interviewer, should decide who he or she wants to be: Susan B. Anthony, Judge Hunt, Henry R. Selden, a minor participant such as a juror, or a "person on the street." Remind interviewers to prepare a list of questions in advance. Remind subjects to consider their views on topics they anticipate being asked about. Suggest that students tape their interviews or take notes.

Critical Thinking: ANALYZING

S Invite students to explain the meaning of the Revolutionary maxim as it relates to women's suffrage. *(Possible response: God's teachings advocate justice. Therefore, rebelling against unjust laws and exercising the right to vote are both justified.)* Ask students if they agree that unfair laws should be challenged. *(Answers will vary.)*

Literary Concept: CHARACTERIZATION

T Ask students what they learn about Anthony's character from the last two paragraphs. *(Possible responses: She was loyal and generous.)*

STRATEGIC READING FOR
Less-Proficient Readers

Ask students to summarize what Anthony won and lost. *(Possible response: She lost her case but won the larger battle for women's right to vote.)*
Summarizing

CUSTOMIZING FOR
Gifted and Talented Students

Truman felt that Anthony had a sense of humor behind her severe façade. Ask students to support or refute this opinion. *(Opinions may vary. Some students may say Anthony is being humorously ironic when she asks to change her dress to something more appropriate or to wear handcuffs.)*

EDITOR'S NOTE *With the permission of the author or copyright holder, material was deleted to shorten and focus the selection.*

COMPREHENSION CHECK
Ask students to respond true or false to the following questions:
1. In Rochester, New York, in 1872, Susan B. Anthony was the first to seriously test women's right to vote in the United States. *(T)*
2. Susan B. Anthony was found not guilty of illegal voting. *(F)*
3. The immediate result of the trial was that women gained the right to vote. *(F)*

Judge Hunt flailed his gavel and gave the by now futile order for the prisoner to sit down and be quiet. Susan kept right on talking.

"When I was brought before Your Honor for trial," she said, "I hoped for a broad and liberal interpretation of the Constitution and its recent amendments. One that would declare all United States citizens under its protection. But failing to get this justice—failing, even, to get a trial by a jury *not* of my peers—I ask not leniency at your hands—but to take the full rigors of the law."

With that Susan finally obeyed Judge Hunt's orders and sat down. Now he had to reverse himself and order her to stand up so he could impose sentence. As soon as he pronounced the sentence—a fine of one hundred dollars plus the costs of prosecuting the trial—Susan spoke up again. "May it please Your Honor," she said, "I shall never pay a dollar of your unjust penalty. All the stock in trade[12] I possess is a ten-thousand-dollar debt, incurred by publishing my paper—*The Revolution*—four years ago, the sole object of which was to educate all women to do precisely as I have done, rebel against your manmade, unjust, unconstitutional forms of law, that tax, fine, imprison, and hang women, while they deny them the right of representation in the government; and I shall work on with might and main to pay every dollar of that honest debt, but not a penny shall go to this unjust claim. And I shall earnestly and persistently continue to urge all women to the practical recognition of the old Revolutionary maxim, that 'Resistance to tyranny is obedience to God.'"

Judge Hunt must have had strict orders not only to see that the defendant was convicted, but to do everything he could to prevent the case from going on to a higher court. He allowed Susan to walk out of the courtroom without imposing a prison sentence in lieu of[13] her unpaid fine. If he had sent her to prison, she could have been released on a writ of habeas corpus[14] and would have had the right to appeal.[15] As it was, the case was closed.

Although she was disappointed that her case would not go to the Supreme Court as she had originally hoped, Susan knew that she had struck an important blow for woman's suffrage. Henry Selden's arguments and her own speech at the end of the trial were widely publicized, and Judge Hunt's conduct of the trial stood as proof that women were treated unjustly before the law.

Susan did not forget the election inspectors who had allowed her to cast her ballot. The men were fined twenty-five dollars each and sent to jail when they refused to pay. In all, they spent about a week behind bars before Susan, through the influence of friends in Washington, obtained presidential pardons for each of them. In the meantime, her followers, who included some of the best cooks in Rochester, saw to it that the men were supplied with delicious hot meals and home-baked pies.

True to her promise, Susan paid the legal expenses for the three inspectors. With the help of contributions from sympathetic admirers, she paid the costs of her own trial. But she never paid that one-hundred-dollar fine. Susan B. Anthony was a woman of her word as well as a woman of courage. ❖

---

12. **stock in trade:** resources available in a given situation.
13. **in lieu (lōō) of:** in place of.
14. **writ of habeas corpus** (hā′bē-əs kôr′pəs): a legal document requesting that a person appear in court—the document is used to gain the release of a person being held illegally.
15. **appeal:** transfer a case to a higher court for rehearing.

302   UNIT TWO   PART 2: AGAINST THE ODDS

Assessment Option

INFORMAL ASSESSMENT Ask students to draw K-W-L charts. In the K column, have them jot down what they knew about Susan B. Anthony or women's suffrage before reading the essay. In the W column, they should jot down questions that arise in their minds before and during their reading. In the L column, they should jot down significant facts and ideas they learned from reading the essay.

Rubric

3 Full Accomplishment Contents of K column will vary. W and L columns contain insightful, relevant questions and solid evidence of learning.

2 Substantial Accomplishment W and L columns contain some relevant questions and partial evidence of learning.

1 Little or Partial Accomplishment Contents of W and L columns are skimpy and sometimes inaccurate.

RESPONDING OPTIONS

FROM PERSONAL RESPONSE TO CRITICAL ANALYSIS

REFLECT
1. What did you think of the way Susan B. Anthony behaved before, during, and after her trial? In your notebook, list words and phrases that describe her behavior and share your thoughts in class.

RETHINK
2. What do you think was wrong about this trial? Explain your reasoning.

Close Textual Reading

Consider
- what the 14th Amendment says
- how the verdict was arrived at
- how Anthony was treated in the courtroom

Thematic Link
3. What do you think was the biggest obstacle that Anthony faced—male attitudes in general, specific men in power, or laws of the day? Support your answer.

4. Reread the first two paragraphs of this selection. What do you think caused Truman's opinion of Anthony to change?

RELATE
5. Review your list of reasons for why the right to vote is so important. If you had lived in Anthony's time, would you have joined her struggle? Why or why not?

6. How far should equality for women go? Is there anything that a woman should not be allowed to do? Debate this issue in class.

LITERARY LINKS
Both *The Devil and Daniel Webster* and this true-life account describe trials and the tribulations that accompany them. Use a Venn diagram to compare the situations of the trials. Is it more difficult to find similarities or differences between them?

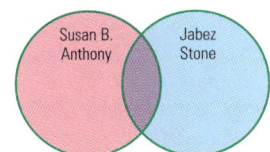

Multimodal Learning
ANOTHER PATHWAY
Cooperative Learning
Newspapers of Anthony's day ran political cartoons for and against women voting. Check a current newspaper's editorial page for examples of political cartoons. Then, in a small group, create two cartoons about Anthony's cause—one in favor and one opposed. Present them to the class.

QUICKWRITES

1. Create a small **pamphlet** that Susan B. Anthony might have distributed to promote women's voting rights. If you have access to computer software that can create different sizes and styles of type, you can use it for the text.

2. If women were denied the right to vote in the 1800s, what does that imply about people's attitudes toward women at the time? What did you learn about public attitudes from Truman's essay? Write a brief **commentary** on the subject.

3. What right do you think U.S. citizens should have today that they do not have? Write a draft of a proposed **amendment** to the Constitution stating this right.

📁 **PORTFOLIO** Save your writing. You may want to use it later as a springboard to a piece for your portfolio.

THE UNITED STATES VS. SUSAN B. ANTHONY 303

From Personal Response to Critical Analysis

1. Accept all reasonable responses. Possible responses: strong-willed, courageous, principled, eloquent
2. Most students will say that the directed verdict and the prejudice of the judge made the trial unfair.
3. All three possibilities are valid, but many students will feel that men's attitudes in general were the worst problem.
4. Possible responses: Some students will say that discovering Anthony's humor made the author change her mind. Support may include Anthony's amused reaction to the editorial and her teasing of the marshal sent to arrest her. Other students may say it was Anthony's courage in the face of official intimidation and the risk of prison.
5. Answers will vary.
6. Accept all reasonable responses. Make sure students present well-reasoned arguments.

Another Pathway
Cooperative Learning Suggest that students work in groups of six or seven to brainstorm cartoon ideas, including captions and visuals. A recorder should jot down notes, and an extender should invent details to add. A presenter should explain the cartoons to the class.

Rubric
3 Full Accomplishment The students create two recognizable and entertaining cartoons that express opposing views.
2 Substantial Accomplishment The students' cartoons are weak in one or two of the qualities required.
1 Little or Partial Accomplishment Students produce unintelligible cartoons.

Literary Links
Possible similarities: Both accounts describe legal battles for freedom with judges set against the defendant. Possible differences: Jabez Stone wins his case; Anthony loses her case but is ultimately victorious.

QuickWrites
1. Students might work in pairs to create pamphlets that have graphic as well as textual content.
2. Suggest that students think of themselves as writing within a specific role, such as newspaper commentator, magazine editor, or historian. Encourage them to make an attempt to adopt the literary style of that type of writer.
3. Invite students to brainstorm in groups to decide on a right. Urge them to reread the Bill of Rights to emulate its eloquent, concise style.

📘 **The Writer's Craft**
Supporting Opinions, pp. 208–221

Literary Concepts

Susan B. Anthony had a strong and determined character as the author shows us. Objective statements might include descriptions of Susan seeking legal advice before attempting to vote, her refusing to post bail, and her paying the legal expenses of the three inspectors. Subjective statements might include direct expressions of the author's opinion in the opening paragraphs of the essay, as well as loaded words such as "buckled under" her resistance to vote and her "cowing" of the U.S. marshal sent to arrest her. See Annotations A, C, D, E, G, K, O, Q, and T.

Characterization Possible responses: Anthony's actions and words during her trial; the narrator's direct comments in the third paragraph; the actions and feelings of Anthony's supporters toward her

Words to Know

1. oratory
2. adamant
3. tirade
4. denunciation
5. competent
6. blatant
7. fortitude
8. concur
9. retrospect
10. inadvertently

Reteaching/Reinforcement
• *Unit Two Resource Book*, p. 46

ART GALLERY
Politics and Equality Throughout history, cartoonists have used politics as a target for their humor. These images show students some political cartoons dealing with women's equal rights.

Side A, Frame 49308

LITERARY CONCEPTS

A **biography** is the true story of a person's life told by someone else. The writer, or biographer, interviews the subject if possible and researches the person's life. Biographers often focus on remarkable or admirable aspects of their subjects. Although biographers often present their subject in a favorable way, they also strive for a balance between fact and interpretation. In your opinion, how objective is Truman's portrayal of Susan B. Anthony? Identify three objective statements and three subjective ones in the selection.

CONCEPT REVIEW:
Characterization Review the four methods of characterization detailed in the Literary Concepts for *The Devil and Daniel Webster* on page 280. Give an example of each method that Truman uses to characterize Susan B. Anthony.

WORDS TO KNOW

Review the Words to Know at the bottom of the selection pages. Write the word that each rhyme illustrates.

1. I have words at my command that give my speech the upper hand.
2. The stubborn lawyer stood his ground, certain that his case was sound.
3. With fists waving and nostrils flaring, I state my case with rage and daring.
4. The judge expressed his condemnation of the lawyer's lack of preparation.
5. The defendant was quite sane and able as she calmly sat at her lawyer's table.
6. The judge's bias was open and clear; he gave the defendant good reason to fear.
7. This defendant shows the inner strength, to survive the trial, regardless of length.
8. The trial showed for all to see that the defendant is innocent— so we agree.
9. A look to the past can help us see that some old laws weren't meant to be.
10. The witness proclaimed 'twas an accident: "Don't send her to jail for what was not meant."

MARGARET TRUMAN

When Franklin Delano Roosevelt died suddenly on April 12, 1945, Harry S. Truman became President of the United States. He moved into the White House with his wife, Bess, and his 21-year-old daughter, Margaret. The Trumans were a close, devoted family with a strong sense of privacy. In her autobiography, Margaret Truman comments on that time: "As a family, we had a code, which was to do the right thing, do it the best we could, never complain and never take advantage. When my father became President, our code did not change."

After graduating from George Washington University in 1946, Truman sang professionally in operas, acted, and worked in radio and television. For seven years, as a President's daughter, Truman had a tough time. She was sometimes the object of ridicule and harsh reviews from critics—particularly over her singing. She gave up her performing career in 1954 and two years later published her first book—an autobiographical work called *Souvenir*. She later wrote biographies of her parents and a collection of biographies, *Women of Courage*, from which this selection comes.

1924–

Truman has also written 12 murder mysteries, all of which center around famous sites in Washington, D.C. Her biographies and mysteries have been bestsellers.
OTHER WORKS *Harry S. Truman*, *Bess W. Truman*, *Murder in the White House*, *Murder on the Potomac*

Extended Reading

• ART GALLERY

304 UNIT TWO PART 2: AGAINST THE ODDS

Alternative Activities

1. Set up your classroom for a retrial of the case—a fair one. Students can play the roles of Anthony, her lawyer, the judge, the district attorney, and the clerk. The rest of the class can be the jury.
2. Invite volunteers to present impersonations of Susan B. Anthony to the class, based on what they learned from the selection.

MARGARET TRUMAN

Truman's experiences as an entertainer included several concert tours, a stint as cohost of a weekly radio program with Mike Wallace, and a job as host of a television program. She turned to mystery writing in the 1980s, with titles including *Murder on Capitol Hill*, *Murder in the Supreme Court*, and *Murder in the Smithsonian*.

PREVIEWING

FICTION

Beauty Is Truth
Anna Guest

Activating Prior Knowledge
PERSONAL CONNECTION

As the title of this selection suggests, the idea of beauty is an important element in the story you are about to read. What does the word *beauty* mean to you? What other words and contexts come to mind? Use a diagram modeled on the one below to organize your ideas.

Building Background
LITERARY CONNECTION

Jeanie, the main character in this story, wonders how her English teacher can be "so stirred up" by a poem written about an old Greek urn, or vase. The poem, "Ode on a Grecian Urn," was written in 1819 by John Keats, one of England's most famous poets of the Romantic movement. It describes the picture that appears on a Grecian urn—a forest scene in which young men and women chase each other while someone nearby plays music on pipes, a type of flute. The speaker in the poem contrasts the never-changing beauty and joy of the scene to the short-lived beauty in everyday life. The speaker ends by expressing Keats' own philosophy:

"Beauty is truth, truth beauty,—that is all
Ye know on earth, and all ye need to know."

Setting a Purpose
WRITING CONNECTION

What is beautiful in your life? Would *beautiful* describe a person, a relationship, a place, or something else in your life? In your notebook, describe this beauty. Then, as you read, compare your idea of beauty with what Jeanie sees in her everyday life.

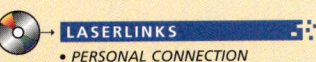
- PERSONAL CONNECTION

BEAUTY IS TRUTH **305**

OVERVIEW

Objectives
- To appreciate and understand a short story that explores a girl's discovery of beauty in an unlikely setting
- To identify and understand third-person limited point of view
- To express understanding of a selection through a choice of writing forms, including a composition and a personal narrative
- To extend understanding of the selection through a variety of multimodal and cross-curricular activities

Skills

LITERARY CONCEPTS
- Third-person limited point of view
- Setting

THE WRITER'S STYLE
- Using sentence fragments to reveal character

GENRE STUDY
- Fiction: short story

GRAMMAR
- *There/their/they're*

SPEAKING, LISTENING, AND VIEWING
- Role-playing
- Group discussion
- Oral presentation

ALTERNATIVE

Previewing
Students can choose partners and use the following prompts to preview "Beauty Is Truth" orally.

Writing Connection
Discussion Prompts Share your recollections about beauty with your partner. Use the following questions as prompts.
- Is beauty always visible, or can it be hidden?
- Is truth always beautiful?

As you read "Beauty Is Truth," watch for the beauty that Jeanie discovers in her life.

 PERSONAL CONNECTION
Beauty and Truth If we keep our eyes open, we can see around us both beauty and truth. These images will help students define for themselves the idea of beauty.

Side A, Frame 49317

PRINT AND MEDIA RESOURCES

UNIT TWO RESOURCE BOOK
Strategic Reading: Literature, p. 49
Vocabulary SkillBuilder, p. 50

WRITING MINI-LESSONS
Transparencies, p. 52

ACCESS FOR STUDENTS ACQUIRING ENGLISH
Selection Summaries
Reading Support

FORMAL ASSESSMENT
Selection Test, pp. 51–52
 Test Generator

LASERLINKS
Personal Connection

THE LANGUAGE OF LITERATURE TEACHER'S EDITION **305**

Beauty Is

SUMMARY

Jeanie is sensitive and bright, but she is a poor student. She lives with her mother and little brother, Billy, in a small apartment. On her way home from school, she sees Billy pitching pennies, which he has been forbidden to do. She says nothing but begins studying, trying to understand John Keats's poem "Ode on a Grecian Urn" and the words "Beauty is truth, truth beauty." Her mother arrives home and learns that Billy has been gambling. She beats him and sends him to bed without supper. After their meal, Jeanie's mother sends Billy a plate of food, dessert, and a quarter. Jeanie writes about this incident in an English essay. A few days later, Jeanie's teacher praises Jeanie's story. "It's literature. It's life. It's pain and truth and beauty," her teacher says.

Thematic Link: *Against the Odds* A teenage girl turns her family's life of struggle in a sooty, urban neighborhood into something beautiful by writing about both the pain and love that exist in it.

CUSTOMIZING FOR
Students Acquiring English
- Use **ACCESS FOR STUDENTS ACQUIRING ENGLISH**, *Reading Support*.
- The descriptions of a girl in an urban high school should hold interest.

STRATEGIC READING FOR
Less-Proficient Readers

Ask students to read the first paragraph, visualizing the teenagers.

Set a Purpose Have students read on to learn about Jeanie's home life.

Use **UNIT TWO RESOURCE BOOK**, p. 49, for guidance in reading.

Literary Concept: Setting

A Ask students what they learn about the story's setting from the first paragraph. *(Harlem, today)*

CUSTOMIZING FOR
Multiple Learning Styles

B **Bodily/Kinesthetic Learners** To give students a sense of Jeanie's withdrawn character, ask a volunteer to act out Jeanie's reactions to Norman.

A At 125th Street, they all got off—Jeanie and her friend, Barbara, and a crowd of other boys and girls coming home from the same downtown high school. Through the train window, Jeanie thought she saw the remaining passengers look at them with relief and <u>disdain</u>. Around her, the boys and girls pressed forward with noisy gaiety. They were all friends now. They were home again in Harlem. A tall boy detached himself from a group, bowed low and swept his cap before him in a courtly salute.

"Greetings, Lady Jeanie. Greetings, Barbara."

Jeanie bit her lip. Frowning, she pulled her coat closer and shrugged. Barbara smiled and dimpled, pleased for her friend.

"I told you he likes you," she whispered. "Look, he's waiting. Want me to go on ahead?"

B Jeanie really was wasting an opportunity, Barbara thought. Norman was keen. She saw Jeanie's head, slightly bowed and thrust forward. It was no use. She was an odd girl, but Barbara liked her anyway. The boy swung gracefully back to his group.

"Coming to the show tonight?" Barbara asked.

Jeanie still frowned.

"No, I can't," she said. "I'm so far behind in my homework, I'd better try to do some before they decide to throw me out."

"Want a cola or something?" asked Barbara as they passed the big ice-cream-parlor window, cluttered with candy boxes and ornate with curly lettering. They could see the jukebox near the door and some boys and girls sitting down at a table. It looked warm and friendly.

Jeanie shook her head, one brief shake. "I think I'll stop in. I'm awful thirsty," said Barbara.

Jeanie shrugged.

"So long, then."

"So long."

Jeanie walked along the busy street, aimlessly **C**

WORDS TO KNOW

disdain (dĭs-dān′) *n.* scorn; contempt

WORDS TO KNOW

constricted (kən-strĭk′tĭd) *adj.* small and narrow (p. 309)
dank (dăngk) *adj.* unpleasantly damp (p. 308)
disdain (dĭs-dān′) *n.* scorn; contempt (p. 306)
intensity (ĭn-tĕn′sĭ-tē) *n.* great power or force (p. 307)
irresolute (ĭ-rĕz′ə-lōōt′) *adj.* unsure of how to act or proceed; undecided (p. 308)

jeer (jîr) *n.* a rude, ridiculing remark; taunt (p. 307)
reproach (rĭ-prōch′) *n.* blame (p. 310)
repugnance (rĭ-pŭg′nəns) *n.* extreme dislike or distaste (p. 307)
tremulous (trĕm′yə-ləs) *adj.* quivering; shaking (p. 310)
unconventional (ŭn′kən-vĕn′shə-nəl) *adj.* not conforming to customary or accepted rules (p. 311)

ANNA GUEST

looking in the store windows. She turned the corner and walked the few blocks to her house. Though it was chilly, each brownstone or gray stoop¹ had its cluster of people clinging to the iron railings. Some children on skates played a desperate game of hockey with sticks that were not hockey sticks. When a car approached, they did not interrupt their game until it was almost too late. Amid shouts from the driver and wild <u>jeers</u> from the children, the car passed, and the game was resumed in all its concentrated <u>intensity</u>.

Her little brother Billy was playing in front of the stoop with three or four other kids. They were bending over something on the sidewalk, in a closed circle. Pitching pennies again, she thought with <u>repugnance</u>. She was going to pass them and started up the three stone steps to the doorway. A window on the ground floor opened, and Fat Mary leaned out, dressed only in a slip and a worn, brown sweater.

---

1. **stoop:** a small porch or staircase in front of an entrance to a house or an apartment building.

| WORDS TO KNOW | **jeer** (jîr) *n.* a rude, ridiculing remark; taunt **intensity** (ĭn-tĕnʹsĭ-tē) *n.* great power or force **repugnance** (rĭ-pŭgʹnəns) *n.* extreme dislike or distaste |

CUSTOMIZING FOR
Gifted and Talented Students

Invite students to read Keats's "Ode on a Grecian Urn" and to respond orally or in writing to the famous couplet quoted on page 309. Have them link the couplet thematically to the story as they read. *(Possible responses: The couplet means that our understanding of our lives is limited, but the ability to perceive beauty gives us a handhold; it means that things that appear to be ugly may actually be beautiful; Jeanie expresses the truth of pain and love in her life and in turn realizes its beauty.)*

Literary Concept: Setting

C Ask students to visualize Jeanie's walk through her neighborhood as if it were the opening scene in a movie. Ask them what feelings or sensations they get from the details in the description. *(Possible responses: cold, bleak, congested)*

CUSTOMIZING FOR
Students Acquiring English

I Tell students that pitching pennies is a game that was once popular among kids. Pennies are thrown at a crack in a sidewalk or at a wall, with the person whose penny lands closest to the line or wall winning all the pennies thrown.

Literary Concept: CHARACTERIZATION

D Ask students what they learn about Jeanie from her reaction to pitching pennies. *(Possible response: She has strong feelings of right and wrong.)*

Mini-Lesson Literary Concepts

REVIEWING SETTING Remind students that the setting of a story is the time and place in which the action occurs. A story may be set in the past, the present, or the future; during the day or at night; during a particular time of year or in a certain historic period. The place may be real or imaginary. Sometimes the setting is left to the reader's imagination.

Application Ask a volunteer to help fill out a chalkboard chart. In the left-hand column, list the places the story is set. In the middle column, put the times the story is set in each of those places. In a right-hand column, labeled "Description," have a student give his or her view as to whether the setting or parts of it are clearly or vaguely described.

Place	Time
128th Street	after 3:00 on a warm school day
Harlem borough	
J's apartment	afternoon/ evening
school	next day (Friday) and Monday

Art Note

Portrait of a Girl by Ian Sidaway This full-face portrait is notable for its contrast of dark and light tones, of earth tones and primary colors. Contrasting shadings and subtle details, such as the ridges of braided hair, work together to create a vivid impression of the subject.

Reading the Art What do you imagine this girl is like as a person? How do the details convey her character?

CUSTOMIZING FOR
Students Acquiring English

② Ask students to figure out the meaning of "catch it" from context clues. *(be scolded or punished)*

Literary Concept: SETTING

E Invite students to describe the setting of Jeanie's apartment in their own words. *(Possible responses: It is cramped and smelly; mother and teenage daughter share a room.)*

Literary Concept: POINT OF VIEW

F Remind students that if the story's narrator tells what only one character sees, thinks, and feels, the story is told from the third-person limited point of view. Invite students to identify words and phrases in the description of Jeanie's actions that are consistent with this point of view. *(Possible responses: "unwillingly attracted," "She thought of," "It was hardly worth trying")*

Portrait of a Girl (about 1987), Ian Sidaway. Copyright © Quarto Publishing.

② "Now you're going to catch it, Billy Boy. Your sister's going to tell your mama you been pitching pennies again."

Jeanie did not pause.

Billy sprang up. "Hi, Jeanie. Jeanie, gimme a nickel. I need a nickel. A nickel, a nickel. I gotta have a nickel."

The other little boys took up the chant. "A nickel, a nickel. Billy needs a nickel."

She threw them a furious glance and went in.

Two little girls sat on the second landing, playing house. They had a set of toy dishes spread out on the top stair, and each held a doll in her lap. Jeanie stepped over them, careful not to disturb their arrangements.

The kitchen smelled <u>dank</u> and unused, and the opening of the door dislodged a flake of green-painted plaster. It fell into the sink with a dry powdering. A black dress someone had given her mother lay over the chair before the sewing machine. It reminded her that her own dress sleeve had torn half out, dressing after gym. She really should sew it, but the sight of the black dress waiting to be made over made her dislike the thought of sewing. She would just have to wear her coat in school tomorrow. Lots of other kids had to do that, too.

She hung her coat on a hook in the room she shared with her mother and stood <u>irresolute</u>. Her mother would be coming in soon and would expect to find the potatoes peeled and the table laid. She caught sight of a comic book and, unwillingly attracted by the garish colors, read one side. "Ah!" she thought in disgust. "Billy!" She thought of her homework. She was so far behind in social studies, she could probably never make it up. It was hardly worth trying. Mercantilism. The rise of the merchant class. She would probably fail. And gym, all those cuts in gym. Miss Fisher, her grade adviser, had called her down yesterday and warned her. "Ah!" she said again. Miss Fisher was all right. She had even been encouraging. "I know you can do it," Miss Fisher had said.

She sat down on the bed and opened her loose-leaf notebook at random. A page fell out. She was about to jam it back in, when the freshly inked writing caught her eye. Today's English. Some poem about a vase and youths and maidens. Miss Lowy had brought in some pictures of vases with people on them, dressed

| WORDS TO KNOW | **dank** (dăngk) *adj.* unpleasantly damp |
| | **irresolute** (ĭ-rĕz′ə-lōōt′) *adj.* unsure of how to act or proceed; undecided |

308

Mini-Lesson — Genre Study

FICTION A **short story** is a work of fiction that can be read in one sitting. It usually tells about one or two major characters and one main conflict. The basic elements of a short story are character, plot, setting, and theme.

Application Invite volunteers to supply specific details for the basic short-story elements in "Beauty Is Truth." If you wish, use a chart such as the one shown.

Character	Jeanie (major character), Billy, mother, Miss Lowy
Plot	A troubling incident at home leads to a school essay that is "beautiful for its honest portrayal."
Setting	a Harlem neighborhood; a high-school classroom
Theme	Beauty can be whatever is truthful.

Why did everybody get so excited about the Greeks? It was so long ago.

in togas or whatever they were, spinning and reading from scrolls. Why did everybody get so excited about the Greeks? It was so long ago. "Wonderful! Wonderful!" Miss Lowy had exclaimed. How could anybody get so stirred up over a poem? She meant it, too. You could tell from her expression.

"Listen, boys and girls. Listen." A lifted arm enjoined them.

"*Beauty is truth, truth beauty,—that is all
Ye know on earth, and all ye need to know.*"

There it was, copied into her notebook. Caught by something in the lines, she tried to find the poem in her tattered anthology, not bothering about the index, but riffling the pages to and fro. John Keats, at last—*On First Looking into Chapman's Homer.* More Greeks. Here it was—*Ode on a Grecian Urn.* The poem, all squeezed together in the middle of the page, looked dry and dusty, withered and far away, at the bottom of a dry well. She saw, not so much words, as an uninteresting, meandering pattern. The big *thou* at the opening repelled her. She turned the page to find that the poem went on. Recognizing the last lines, she heard them again, falling so roundly, so perfectly, from the lips of Miss Lowy. She turned back to the beginning. Why "Grecian," why not "Greek"? With an effort, she began to dig the poem out of its <u>constricted</u> print.

Thou foster child of silence and slow time, its soft susurrus[2] carried her on. She read the poem through to the end, trying to remember her teacher's cadences.[3]

"Write about beauty and truth. About life," Miss Lowy had said.

Jeanie tore a page out of her notebook and opened her pen. Pulling over a chair, she rested her book on the sooty windowsill. She stared out at the dusk falling sadly, sadly, thickening into darkness over the coal yards.

A crash of the kitchen door caused a reverberation in the windowsill. The notebook slipped out of her hands.

"Where'd you get that bottle of pop?" she heard her mother's voice, hard and sounding more Southern than usual.

A high-pitched, wordless sniveling came in reply.

"I asked you. Where'd you get that pop? You better tell me."

"A lady gave me a nickel. A lady came down the street and ask' me . . ."

"You' lying. I know where you got that money. Gambling, that's what you was doing."

"I was only pitching pennies, Ma. It's only a game, Ma."

"Gambling and stealing and associating with bad friends. I told you to stay away from them boys. Didn't I? Didn't I?" Her mother's voice rose. "I'm going to give you a beating you ain't going to forget."

---

2. **susurrus** (sŏŏ-sûr′əs): a soft, whispering sound.
3. **cadences** (kād′n-səz): inflections or variations in stress or pitch when speaking.

WORDS TO KNOW
constricted (kən-strĭk′tĭd) *adj.* small and narrow

309

Linking to History

G If possible, bring in photographs of ancient Greek pottery or illustrations of life in ancient Athens. Invite students to answer Jeanie's question, "Why did everybody get so excited about the Greeks?" *(Possible responses: because of their mythology, literature, arts, philosophy, science, and democratic government)*

CUSTOMIZING FOR
Students Acquiring English

3 You may wish to write these lines on the board and discuss what they might mean. What is implied by the words *on earth*? *(Possible response: that people might know more after they die than they do while living on earth)*

Literary Note

H John Keats (1795–1821) was born in London, the son of a stable keeper. His family was plagued by tuberculosis; his mother and brother Tom died of it, as did Keats himself at the age of 26. As a teenager he became a surgical apprentice, but later he decided to give up medicine for poetry. In an incredibly short career he created some of the greatest poems in the English language, including "Ode to a Nightingale," "To Autumn," and "La Belle Dame Sans Merci."

Critical Thinking:
COMPARING/CONTRASTING

I Invite students to compare and contrast Jeanie's feelings about reading the "dry and dusty" poem for school with their own experiences. Ask them how Jeanie ultimately finds pleasure and meaning in the experience. *(Possible response: by rereading the poem and paying attention to the sound of the words when read aloud)*

Mini-Lesson Study Skills

TAKING ESSAY TESTS: PLANNING YOUR ANSWERS To do well on essay tests, students should analyze the writing prompt to determine the type of question. After determining the type, they should plan by jotting down notes, which they might organize by numbering or by making a rough outline. A thesis statement containing the student's main idea can help keep the answer on track.

Application Ask students to plan an essay answer interpreting the lines, "Beauty is truth, truth beauty,—that is all / Ye know on earth, and all ye need to know." Specify that students include a thesis statement that presents their central idea. You might allow students to discuss their interpretations with one or more partners beforehand to help them evaluate their ideas.

Types of Essay Questions

explanation	identification
comparison/contrast	interpretation
definition	analysis
description	summarization

THE LANGUAGE OF LITERATURE **TEACHER'S EDITION** 309

Critical Thinking: MAKING JUDGMENTS

J Ask students to discuss their responses to the way Billy's mother disciplines him. *(Possible responses: Most students will be opposed to corporal punishment; others may find it forgivable if it is for a good reason.)*

Critical Thinking: ANALYZING

K Ask students how they can tell that Jeanie is upset by her brother's beating. *(During the beating, she clutches her pen so hard her fingers ache.)*

Literary Concept: CHARACTERIZATION

L Ask students why Billy's mother prepares a plate of food for Billy with the best of the tarts and a quarter. *(Possible responses: She is trying to make up for the beating; it shows that the beating, although harsh, is an expression of her love for her son.)*

STRATEGIC READING FOR
Less-Proficient Readers

M Ask a volunteer to describe Jeanie's home life.

- Ask students to identify the stresses that Jeanie and her family are under. *(lack of money; crowded living quarters; negative peer pressure)* **Noting Relevant Details**

- Ask them how Jeanie responds to her environment. *(She withdraws.)* **Drawing Conclusions**

- Ask them what Jeanie writes about for her English assignment. *(the beating Billy receives)* **Noting Relevant Details**

Set a Purpose Have students read to find out about Jeanie's life at school. How does her life at home affect her life at school?

J Billy wailed on a long descending note. Jeanie could hear each impact of the strap and her mother's heavy breathing.

"I want you to grow up good, not lying and gambling and stealing," her mother gasped, "and I'm going to make you good. You ain't never going to forget this." When it had been going on forever, it stopped. A final slap of the strap. "And you ain't going to get any supper either. You can go now. You can go to bed and reflect on what I told you."

Letting her pen dig into the paper, she began to write.

He stumbled past her, whimpering, fists grinding into eyes, and into the dark little alcove which was his room. Jeanie heard the groan of the bed as he threw himself on it. She felt the pain in her fingers and saw them still **K** pressed tightly around the pen.

Her mother appeared in the doorway. She wore her hat and coat.

"Come and help me get supper, Jeanie. You should have got things started." Her voice was tired and <u>tremulous</u> and held no <u>reproach</u>.

"I don't want any supper, Ma."

Her mother came in and sat down heavily on the bed, taking off her hat and letting her coat fall open.

"I had a hard day. I worked hard every minute," she said. "I brought you something extra nice for dessert. I stood on line to get some of them tarts from Sutter's."

Jeanie rose and silently put her mother's hat on the shelf. She held out her hand for her mother's coat and hung it up.

Together they opened the paper bags on the kitchen table. She set the water to boil.

As they ate in silence, the three tarts shone like subtle jewels on a plate, at one end of the chipped porcelain table. Her mother looked tired and stern.

"You' better fix your brother up a plate," her mother said, still stern. "Put it on a tray. Here, take this." And she put on the tray the most luscious, the most perfect of the tarts. "Wait." **L** She went heavily over to her swollen black handbag, took out a small clasp purse, opened it, and carefully, seriously, deliberately, picked out a coin, rejected it, and took out another. "Give him this." It was a quarter.

After the dishes were washed, Jeanie brought her books into the kitchen and spread them out under the glaring overhead light. Billy had been asleep, huddled in his clothes. Tears had left dusty streaks on his face.

Her mother sat in the armchair, ripping out the sides of the black dress. Her spectacles made her look strange. *Beauty is truth,* Jeanie read in her notebook. Hastily, carelessly, defiantly disregarding margins and doubtful spellings, letting her pen dig into the paper, she began to write: *Last night my brother Billy got a terrible beating....* **M**

Scramble to borrow the social studies homework from a girl in her homeroom, say hello to

| WORDS TO KNOW | **tremulous** (trĕm′yə-ləs) *adj.* quivering; shaking
 reproach (rĭ-prōch′) *n.* blame |

310

Mini-Lesson: Speaking, Listening, and Viewing

ROLE-PLAYING One very effective way for students to understand a work of fiction is to interact while playing the characters' roles. When role-playing, students may speak lines of dialogue directly from a story, transform narrative passages into dialogue, and offer elaborations and explanations of events and character motivations.

Application Invite partners to play the roles of Jeanie and her mother in the scene after the beating. Suggest that pairs meet to discuss the scene beforehand and rehearse at least once in private. In addition to playing out the scene, role players should be prepared to answer questions about their interpretations.

Barbara, undress for gym, dress again, the torn sleeve, bookkeeping—a blot, get another piece of ledger paper. "This is the third I've given you. You might say thank you." Get to English early. Slip her composition in under the others, sit in the last seat. Don't bother me. I am in a bad mood. Rows and rows of seats. Rows and rows of windows opposite. She could even read the writing on some of the blackboards, but who cared? A boy leaned far out of the window before closing it. Other heads turning. Would he fall? No, he was safe. Heads turned back. A poem about a skylark.[4] From where she sat, she could see about a square foot of sky, drained of all color by the looming school walls.

Miss Lowy read clearly, standing all alone at the front of the room in her clean white blouse, her blonde hair smoothed down.

Miss Lowy, maybe you see skylarks. Me, I'd be glad to see some sky, Jeanie thought and nearly uttered it. Around her, students were writing in their notebooks. Miss Lowy was about to speak to her. Better start writing something. Sullen, Mr. MacIver had called her last week. She felt about for her notebook and pen. It had been a mistake to write as she had done about her brother's beating. They would laugh if they knew. Shirley, who was the class secretary, and Saul, with the prominent forehead. No, he would not laugh. He was always writing about spaceships and the end of the world. No danger, though, that her story would be read. Only the best manuscripts were read. She remembered keenly the blotched appearance of the paper, the lines crossed out and the words whose spelling she could never be sure of. Oh, well, she didn't care. Only one more period and then the weekend. "Lady Jeanie's too proud to come to our party. Jeanie, what are you waiting for? Jeanie's waiting for a Prince Charming with a red Cadillac to come and take her away." If Barbara asked her again, she would go with her, maybe. There was going to be a party at Norman's Saturday night, with Cokes and sandwiches and records and dancing, everybody chipping in. Jeanie, I need a nickel. Mama, I need a dollar. I need, I need.

The bell rang, and the pens dropped; the books were closed with a clatter. She slipped out ahead of the pushing, jostling boys and girls.

Monday, Miss Lowy had on still another perfect white blouse. She stood facing the class, holding a sheaf of papers in her hand. Most of the students looked at her expectantly. Marion, who nearly always got 90, whispered to her neighbor. Michael, who had but recently come from Greece—ah, but that was a different Greece—grumbled and shifted in his seat. He would have to do his composition over. He always did.

"I spent a very enjoyable time this weekend, reading your work," said Miss Lowy, waiting for the class to smile.

"Seriously, though, many of your pieces were most interesting, even though they were a trifle <u>unconventional</u> about spelling and punctuation." A smile was obviously indicated here too, and the class obeyed. She paused. "Sometimes, however, a piece of writing is so honest and human that you have to forgive the technical weaknesses. Not that they aren't important," she said hastily, "but what the writer has to say is more significant."

---

4. **poem about a skylark:** Percy Bysshe (bĭsh) Shelley, another English Romantic poet, wrote a famous poem called "To a Skylark."

WORDS TO KNOW	**unconventional** (ŭn′kən-vĕn′shə-nəl) *adj.* not conforming to customary or accepted rules

311

Mini-Lesson   The Writer's Style

USING SENTENCE FRAGMENTS TO REVEAL CHARACTER A sentence fragment is a group of words that is only part of a sentence. It may be missing either the subject or the verb or both. In writing, fragments are usually the result of haste or incorrect punctuation. However, writers sometimes consciously use fragments with the following purposes in mind:
- to create realistic dialogue
- to establish a certain mood
- to reveal a character's thoughts and feelings
- to achieve a particular rhythm in their prose

Application Have students work with partners to identify sentence fragments throughout the story and discuss what purpose the writer had in mind when she used each fragment. Then ask students to rewrite the fragments as complete sentences and discuss the altered effect.

Reteaching/Reinforcement
- *Writing Mini-Lessons* transparencies, p. 52

Fragments Used for Effect, p. 525

Literary Concept: SETTING

N Ask students how the setting has changed since the previous paragraph. *(It is the next morning and Jeanie is in school.)* Students may need help understanding that the ellipses after the previous paragraph indicate the passage of time.

Literary Concept: POINT OF VIEW

O This paragraph is a good example of the use of third-person limited point of view. Invite students to pick out passages that show Jeanie's thoughts, *("Me, I'd be glad to see some sky . . ."),* description through Jeanie's eyes *("It was going to be a party at Norman's Saturday night. . . ."),* Jeanie's view of other characters *("Saul, with the prominent forehead . . ."),* and Jeanie's view of herself *("Sullen, Mr. MacIver had called her last week. . . .").*

CUSTOMIZING FOR
Students Acquiring English

4 Students may not be familiar with the colloquial idiom "chipping in." Explain that it means "to contribute money or labor to something," in this case sharing the expenses of the party.

Critical Thinking: MAKING INFERENCES

P Ask students to infer why Miss Lowy waited for the class to smile. *(Possible response: She believes that most of her students will take her comment about her weekend ironically, assuming that she actually means that she found the pieces poor and had a disappointing weekend reading them.)*

CUSTOMIZING FOR
Students Acquiring English

5 Help students see that *technical weakness* refers to errors in spelling, grammar, and punctuation and that these errors might be overlooked in a strong, honest piece of writing.

Critical Thinking:
MAKING INFERENCES

 Invite students to infer why these top students were "confused." *(Possible response: They assumed that the "honest and human" piece about to be read would be one of theirs, but the teacher's mention that the piece had "technical weaknesses" confused them because none of their writing would have such flaws.)*

Literary Concept:
POINT OF VIEW

 Ask students to explain how the author uses third-person limited point of view to reveal the impact on Jeanie of realizing that her piece had been chosen. *(Possible response: Jeanie's nervous embarrassment is shown through her heartbeat, nervous fingers, and paranoia-like feeling that everyone everywhere is going to listen to her piece.)*

Literary Concept: **THEME**

 Ask students what central idea, or theme, of the story is expressed in Miss Lowy's comment. *(Possible responses: To understand truth is to discover beauty; life is beautiful; even the pain of life can be seen as beautiful.)*

 The three best students in the class looked confused. It was their pride not to have technical errors.

"When you hear this," Miss Lowy continued, "I think you'll agree with me. I know it brought tears to my eyes."

The class looked incredulous.

"It's called 'Evening Comes to 128th Street.'" Her face took on that rapt look.

 Jeanie's heart beat painfully. She picked up a pencil but dropped it, so unsteady were her fingers. Even the back of Shirley's head was listening. Even the classes in the other wing of the building, across the courtyard, seemed fixed, row on row, in an attitude of listening. Miss Lowy read on. It was all there, the coal yards and Fat Mary, the stoop and the tarts from Sutter's, Billy asleep with the tears dried on his face, the clasp purse and the quarter.

"The funny part of it was, when I woke him, Billy wasn't mad. He was glad about the quarter and ate his supper, dessert and all, but Mama never did eat her tart, so I put it away." Miss Lowy stopped reading.

A poignancy of remembrance swept over Jeanie, the shame and regret. It was no business of theirs, these strange white people.

No one spoke. The silence was unbearable. Finally, Marion, the incomparable Marion, raised her hand.

"It was so real," she said, "you felt you were right in that kitchen."

"You didn't know who to feel sorry for," said another student. "You wanted to cry with the mother, and you wanted to cry with Billy."

"With the girl, too," said another.

Several heads nodded.

 "You see," said Miss Lowy. "It's literature. It's life. It's pain and truth and beauty."

Jeanie's heart beat so, it made a mist come before her eyes. Through the blur she heard Miss Lowy say it was good enough to be sent in to *Scholastic*.[5] It showed talent; it showed promise. She heard her name called and shrank from the eyes turned upon her.

After school, she hurried out and caught

---

5. ***Scholastic:*** a magazine that is distributed in schools and that publishes student writing.

312   UNIT TWO   PART 2: AGAINST THE ODDS

THERE/THEIR/THEY'RE Point out that among these homophones, *there* is an adverb that indicates a location or place.

"It is all *there* [in the story], the coal yards and Fat Mary, . . ."

Their is the possessive form of the pronoun *they* and shows ownership.

"It was *their* pride [belonging to them] . . ."

They're is a contraction of the pronoun and verb *they* and *are*.

They're [They are] studying "Ode on a Grecian Urn."

Application Choose the correct word to fill in the blanks in the following sentences.
1. There/Their/They're is silence in the class as they read their/there/they're papers. *(There/their)*
2. There/Their/They're all listening. *(They're)*

📘 The Writer's Craft

Possessive Pronouns and Contractions, pp. 572–573

---

312   THE LANGUAGE OF LITERATURE   **TEACHER'S EDITION**

Pep's Car with an Assist from Clyde, Snake, and Peabody (1975), Colleen Browning. Oil on canvas, 36" × 60¼".

the first train, the one you could catch only if you left immediately and did not stroll or stop the least little bit to talk to someone. She did not want to meet anyone, not even Barbara.

Was that Billy among the kids on the stoop?

"Billy," she called. "Billy."

What would she say to him? *Beauty is truth, truth beauty?*

"Billy," she called again urgently.

Billy lifted his head and, seeing who it was, tore himself reluctantly away from his friends and took a step toward her. ❖

BEAUTY IS TRUTH 313

Art Note

***Pep's Car, with an Assist from Clyde, Snake, and Peabody* by Colleen Browning** Colleen Browning (1929–) was born in County Cork, Ireland. She moved to the United States in the early 1950s and became a U.S. citizen. Her 3-foot-by-5-foot oil painting shows a graffiti-covered subway car from outside.

Reading the Art *Who might Pep, Clyde, Snake, and Peabody be, and how do you know?*

Critical Thinking:
COMPARING/CONTRASTING

 Have students compare Jeanie's reaction to Billy and his friends here to her reaction at the beginning of the story. (Possible response: She calls out to him instead of passing the boys "with repugnance"; Jeanie reaches out to him in an attempt to help guide him.)

STRATEGIC READING FOR
Less-Proficient Readers

 Help students connect the lessons Jeanie learned at school with those she learned at home.

- Ask students how Jeanie used her home life to succeed at school. (She wrote about it.) **Clarifying**

- Ask them what she learned at school that can help her in life. (Possible responses: Truth and beauty are linked; being truthful in writing can lead to artistic beauty.) **Making Judgments**

COMPREHENSION CHECK

1. Where does Jeanie live? *(Harlem)* Whom does she live with? *(mother, brother Billy)*
2. What happens to Billy when his mother comes home? *(He gets a beating from her for pitching pennies.)*
3. What is the subject of Jeanie's writing assignment? *(her brother's beating at the hands of her mother, which is shown not to affect their love for each other)*
4. What does the English teacher think of Jeanie's work? *(By honestly depicting this incident in her family's life, it reveals a beauty born of truth and pain.)*

Assessment Option

INFORMAL ASSESSMENT Divide students into pairs and ask partners to choose two characters from "Beauty Is Truth" and imagine themselves in their shoes. How might the incidents have appeared to these two characters? Then have students each write a letter from one character to another discussing the major events of the story. The letter should express the character's thoughts and feelings about events that the character experienced or witnessed. It may also contain comments about aspects of the characters' lives that the student infers but that are not explicitly shown.

Rubric

3 Full Accomplishment The letters convincingly express the appropriate characters' viewpoints, thoughts, and feelings as portrayed in the story.

2 Substantial Accomplishment The letters express partial understanding of the events and characters in the story.

1 Little or Partial Accomplishment The letters reflect little understanding of the story content.

THE LANGUAGE OF LITERATURE **TEACHER'S EDITION** 313

From Personal Response to Critical Analysis

1. Accept all reasonable responses.
2. Some students will say that Jeanie will feel better about her life, because she calls out to her brother at the end. Others may say she will feel even more uncomfortable, because she hurries away from school after her work is read.
3. Some students may find beauty in the family's love for one another that survives the mother's harsh punishment of the boy; others may have negative feelings because of the beating.
4. Some students may say that she loves her children and worries about them; she is a tough disciplinarian and hard working. Other students may say she is unkind and is not beautiful.
5. Possible responses: Beating a child is never justified; it is, however, an understandable reaction given the temptations on the street.
6. Responses will vary.
7. Accept all convincing portrayals.
8. Accept all reasonable responses.

Another Pathway

Cooperative Learning Encourage students to brainstorm and then show preliminary sketches within the group. Students can review the story illustrations for possible inspiration. In the planning stage, a recorder should note suggestions, a generator should propose additional ideas, and a summarizer should restate the possibilities before the group chooses a medium. In the execution stage, students should select roles based on individual skills.

Rubric

3 Full Accomplishment Students create an imaginative, original artwork that portrays Jeanie's life.

2 Substantial Accomplishment Students create an interesting artwork that falls short of fully portraying Jeanie's life.

1 Little or Partial Accomplishment Students have difficulty creating a story-inspired artwork.

RESPONDING OPTIONS

FROM PERSONAL RESPONSE TO CRITICAL ANALYSIS

REFLECT
1. What thoughts did you have after reading this story? Describe your thoughts in your notebook and share it in class.

RETHINK
2. In your opinion, will Jeanie's feelings about herself and her life change as a result of this episode? Give reasons to support your point of view.

3. The teacher finds beauty in a truthful account of Jeanie's life. Do you agree with that observation? Explain.

4. What do the mother's actions and words reveal about her character? Is there anything beautiful about her? Explain.

Thematic Link
5. Each member of Jeanie's family struggles against the odds in a number of ways. Considering those odds, do you think the reaction of Jeanie's mother to Billy's misbehavior is justified? Why or why not?

Close Textual Reading
Consider
- the pressures on the mother as a single working parent
- the environment in which the children are growing up
- the mother's values and her goals for her children

6. Whom do you identify with more in this story—Jeanie or Billy? Why?

RELATE
7. Imagine that the story continues. What do you think Jeanie will say to Billy? With a partner, act out the scene in class.

8. Many students face problems similar to Jeanie's. If you were Jeanie's friend, how would you help her?

Multimodal Learning
ANOTHER PATHWAY

Cooperative Learning
Think about the places, people, sights, and colors that make up Jeanie's world. Then, with a small group of classmates, choose an art form that can represent the various aspects of Jeanie's life and create a collage, a montage, a mobile, or a painting. Display your finished artwork to the rest of the class and ask for their comments.

QUICKWRITES

1. This story contains a description of Jeanie's writing and one quotation from it. Using the details given in the story, write a draft of the **composition** you think Jeanie wrote.

2. Did this story expand your idea of beauty? Look back at what you wrote for the Writing Connection on page 305 and think again about what you find beautiful. Draft a **personal narrative** that completes Miss Lowy's assignment: "Write about beauty and truth. About life."

📁 **PORTFOLIO** Save your writing. You may want to use it later as a springboard to a piece for your portfolio.

314   UNIT TWO   PART 2: AGAINST THE ODDS

QuickWrites

1. Student compositions should contain many specific details from the scene in which Billy gets a beating and should be written in Jeanie's first-person point of view. Encourage students to include a mix of literary techniques (description, dialogue, and narrative) and to create a vivid setting.
2. Emphasize that this is to be a personal narrative rather than an abstract discussion of beauty and truth. Remind students to write from the first-person point of view by using *I, me,* and *my.*

 The Writer's Craft

Personal Narrative, pp. 86–100
Point of View, 250–254 and 430–433

LITERARY CONCEPTS

"Beauty Is Truth" is told from a **third-person point of view**—that is, the narrator is someone outside the action, not a character within the story. The characters are referred to by name or by the pronouns *he, she,* or *they.* For the most part, this story is told in a **third-person limited point of view,** meaning that the narrator tells what only one character—Jeanie—sees, thinks, and feels.

Think about the events at Jeanie's home and answer these questions:

1. How does the point of view influence your understanding of the events?
2. How might the story have been different if the events had been told from Billy's point of view?
3. How might the mother's viewpoint differ from that of Jeanie and Billy?

LITERARY LINKS

What similarities do you see between the situation of Jeanie in "Beauty Is Truth" and that of Marguerite in *I Know Why the Caged Bird Sings*?

ART CONNECTION

Artist Colleen Browning paints "realism"—images based on what she sees and feels. Her paintings also cover a wide variety of subjects, since, as she says, "people and fruit and subways and skies all make insistent demands to be creatively resolved." Look at her artwork on pages 312–313. Who do you think the Pep, Clyde, Snake, and Peabody of the title are? What "realism" is reflected? What connections do you see between Browning's painting and "Beauty Is Truth"?

Detail of *Pep's Car with an Assist from Clyde, Snake and Peabody* (1975), Colleen Browning. Oil on canvas, 36" × 60¼".

Multimodal Learning

ALTERNATIVE ACTIVITIES

1. Select a poem that you think reflects Jeanie's life more closely than "Ode on a Grecian Urn" does. Give a **dramatic reading** of the poem to the class.
2. Writing as a social worker consulted by Jeanie's mother, draft a **recommendation** for a way of disciplining her children that would omit physical punishment.

ACROSS THE CURRICULUM

Fine Art In books or magazines, look for artwork that you feel reflects both beauty and truth. For each piece that you find, briefly discuss how the two elements coexist in the painting.

WORDS TO KNOW

Review the Words to Know at the bottom of the selection pages. Then, following the model below, create a diagram for each of the words.

```
        Poignant
          |
    Definition: emotionally painful
          
    Synonyms: distressing, aching, smarting
          
    Example sentence: Losing to a lesser team can be poignant.
```

BEAUTY IS TRUTH **315**

Literary Links

Possible response: In both selections, an African-American girl discovers the value of literature or creative writing through the influence of a concerned role model.

Art Connection

Possible response: kids who spray painted graffiti on the subway car; the need for personal expression in a congested urban setting; the artist creates beauty in truthfully depicting a slice of city life in all its colorful and sometimes crude details.

Across the Curriculum

Fine Art If time permits, send students to the school library to search for magazines and art books. Art magazines, nature magazines, science magazines, sports magazines, travel magazines, and newsmagazines can provide a variety of images that contain both painful truth and beauty.

Words to Know

Accept all responses that follow the diagram form and contain correct definitions, synonyms, and usages. You might have students work in groups, each member selecting one or two words to diagram. Alternatively, in a group of three, one member can specialize in definitions, another in synonyms, and another in example sentences.

Reteaching/Reinforcement
• *Unit Two Resource Book*, p. 50

Literary Concepts

Possible responses:

1. The point of view shows how Jeanie perceives and responds to events such as Billy's beating and the reading of her composition.
2. From Billy's point of view, the beating might have seemed either harsher or less harsh. His view of Jeanie would be that of a younger child who did not understand Jeanie's complicated emotions and did not know much about her life in school.
3. The mother probably would have been most concerned with how to raise her children in a difficult environment.

Alternative Activities

1. To find poems, you might recommend the works of Maya Angelou, Gwendolyn Brooks, Langston Hughes, Countee Cullen, Claude McKay, Nikki Giovanni, and Rita Dove.
2. Remind students to use the social worker's first-person point of view. Recommendations might include reasoning, time-outs, prohibitions and "groundings," and family conferences.

OVERVIEW

Objectives

- To understand and appreciate a short story that explores the creative process of a factory worker/poet
- To identify and understand personification
- To appreciate imagery
- To express understanding of a selection through a choice of writing forms, including a journal entry and a poem
- To extend understanding of the story through a variety of multimodal and cross-curricular activities

Skills

LITERARY CONCEPTS
- Personification
- Tone

THE WRITER'S STYLE
- Personification

GRAMMAR
- Pronouns in the nominative case

SPEAKING, LISTENING, AND VIEWING
- Group discussion
- Oral presentation

 SOCIOLOGICAL CONNECTION

Factory Workers Throughout history, men and women have toiled in factories. These images of blue-collar workers over the years will help students understand the environment in which the author of the story worked.

Side A, Frame 49321

ALTERNATIVE
Previewing

Instead of writing down their feelings about work, students can discuss their feelings with partners.

Writing Connection

Discussion Prompts Recall a job you have held or imagine working at a factory on the night shift. Use the following questions to share your feelings with a partner:

- What images come into your mind?
- How do you feel at the end of a shift or a workday?
- What do you like and dislike about the job?

As you read "The Cultural Worker," notice the images the author uses.

316 THE LANGUAGE OF LITERATURE TEACHER'S EDITION

PREVIEWING

FICTION

The Cultural Worker
Sue Doro

Activating Prior Knowledge
PERSONAL CONNECTION

The main character in this story is a factory worker. People often have ideas about what factory work is like without having experienced it themselves. What images come to you when you think of factory work? Explore your ideas by making a word web like the one shown.

Building Background
SOCIOLOGICAL CONNECTION

The factory worker in this story is a *machinist,* a skilled craftworker who uses power-driven tools to shape machine parts. She works in a *machine shop,* a factory where parts are machined to size and assembled. Factory workers and others who do manual labor are often called blue-collar workers or referred to as the working class. Blue-collar workers make up a fourth of the labor force in the United States.

Setting a Purpose
WRITING CONNECTION

Imagine yourself as a factory worker, perhaps as a machinist in a railway parts plant, working on train wheels as the worker in this story does. You work the second shift, from 4 p.m. to midnight. You have just returned home from your eight-hour shift. Write a brief diary entry, describing how you feel at the end of the workday. Or, if you have a job, write about how you feel at the end of your workday. As you read, compare your diary entry with the poem that the character in this story writes.

Woman welder.
H.A.R., B. Paulson /
H. Armstrong Roberts

316 UNIT TWO PART 2: AGAINST THE ODDS

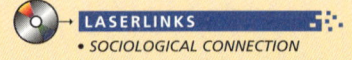 LASERLINKS
• SOCIOLOGICAL CONNECTION

PRINT AND MEDIA RESOURCES

UNIT TWO RESOURCE BOOK
Strategic Reading: Literature, p. 53

GRAMMAR MINI-LESSONS
Transparencies, p. 14
Copymasters, p. 16

WRITING MINI-LESSONS
Transparencies, p. 47

ACCESS FOR STUDENTS ACQUIRING ENGLISH
Selection Summaries
Reading Support

FORMAL ASSESSMENT
Selection Test, p. 53
Test Generator

 AUDIO LIBRARY
See Reference Card

 LASERLINKS
Sociological Connection
Art Gallery

Illustration by Gary Kelley.

THE CULTURAL WORKER

SUE DORO

The poem waited for her outside the wheel-shop door. Waited, as if it were one of the leaning train wheels stacked against each other, like round brown five-hundred-pound dominoes. Train wheels waiting to be hauled inside the factory, machined to order, then mounted on shiny steel axles and rolled out the door into the Menomonee Valley[1] train yard.

So too, the poem waited. It had been waiting for her to finish work since 3:30 that afternoon. Now it was midnight. Soon she would step out of second shift into the dark of the going-home night.

Hours ago in the early evening, the summer sun hung low and rosy over old freight cars in the yard. The poem had gone to the window nearest the machine the woman was operating

---
1. **Menomonee** (mə-nŏm′ə-nē) **Valley:** a river valley in the vicinity of Milwaukee, Wisconsin.

CUSTOMIZING FOR
Gifted and Talented Students

Invite students to write a personal profile of the machinist based on a careful reading of the story. Comment on her work habits, her relations with co-workers, her attitude toward management, and other characteristics.

Critical Thinking: MAKING GENERALIZATIONS

A Ask students what they think the author means by "poem words." *(Possible response: words that are descriptive, full of imagery, lyrical, and evocative)*

CUSTOMIZING FOR
Multiple Learning Styles

B **Linguistic Learners** Ask students to reconstruct and role-play the conversation that the woman might have had with the man in the hardhat, starting with the fragments given here.

C Remind students that the tone of a work of literature reflects the writer's attitude toward his or her subject. Ask students to identify the tones in the passage describing the eight o'clock break. *(Possible response: lyrical, pensive, and poignant and then anxious, angry, and frightened)*

CUSTOMIZING FOR
Multiple Learning Styles

D **Musical Learners** The factory whistle is one example of the sound imagery that fills the story, culminating in the song-poem. Ask students whether the references to factory sounds create a "soundtrack" that they can "hear" as they read.

A that night. The poem thought that the sunset would surely get her attention. But not tonight. She was measuring a train axle with a micrometer,[2] straining on her tiptoes to reach around its diameter. The poem could see she was too busy to be thinking poem words, so it did what it knew how to do.

It waited. Measuring minutes against the sun's shadows on the dirty cream-colored brick wall. It waited, as 5 o'clock break time came. It waited and watched through a different window as the woman ate half of her sandwich sitting at the lunch table by the men's locker room, sharing a newspaper and talking with some of the guys. She was the only woman in the shop. There used to be two others, but they got laid off. Now she was the only one of her kind left, and sometimes she was lonely. But tonight the poem saw that she was having a good time, joking with her "buddies."

B It was an hour and a half later when the poem looked in again. The woman was standing with the micrometer in her hand, listening to a short elderly man with gray-brown whiskers. He wore a work-worn green hardhat, low over his eyes. His hands glistened with dark brown dirty train-bearing grease. In one, he held a red-handled putty scraper. In the other, by their cuffs, a pair of oily rubber gloves. The ring finger was missing on that hand. A cigarette bobbed up and down from his mouth as he talked. Its ashes dusting the man's brown shirt every so often. The poem could catch only a few of the man's words . . . "wife . . . divorce . . . still love her . . . the kids don't . . ." The woman was intent on listening to the man. The poem went back to wait at the door until dinner break.

In summer it was still light at 8 in the evening, and the poem knew that the woman would come outside to sit on the long bench against the building. Most of the men would go out for dinner to the tavern up the hill, so she would usually be alone. Sometimes she would take a walk by the railroad tracks, heading under the freeway. There was a river to watch and listen to, and wild flowers to pick. In the early spring, there were little green onions and asparagus hidden in the tall grasses. Sometimes she would read or write in her journal. But tonight she had no pad of paper, no pencil or pen. She was sitting on the bench, but she was leaning forward a bit, holding a book. A union agreement. And she was not alone. She and some other workers were talking words like "lost jobs . . . bankruptcy . . . layoffs beginning in July . . . the company can't . . . illegal . . . they'll try . . . four guys fired . . ." The poem saw it was useless to try to get into her head. Then the factory whistle blew, and a foreman appeared in the doorway, motioning the woman and the men back to work. **C**

The poem stayed outside. **D**

At 10 o'clock the poem went to look in the window by the woman again. She was staring out into the blackness of the night, but she didn't notice the poem. Her eyes were taking in the silhouettes of axles and wheels and oil drums. Watching black birds fly in front of the huge pink streetlights on tall poles that illuminated the train yard. Her face was feeling a good west wind blowing in. She was thinking of going home and wishing the night would hurry so she could get there. "A few more axles," is what she was thinking, as she turned away from the warm starry night. A night smelling of Menomonee Valley city wilderness, and NOT the stockyards, thanks to the west wind. Away from the window she turned. Away from

---
2. **micrometer** (mī-krŏm′ĭ-tər): a device for measuring very small distances, objects, or angles.

318 UNIT TWO PART 2: AGAINST THE ODDS

Mini-Lesson ✎ Grammar

PRONOUNS IN THE NOMINATIVE CASE
Point out that pronouns, like nouns, can function as both subjects and predicate nominatives. A pronoun that follows a linking verb such as *be* or *become* is a predicate pronoun and takes the nominative case, sometimes called the subject form. Read the following sentence aloud. *It was she who measured the axle.* Ask students to name the subject. *(she)*

Application Have a volunteer name the subject of the sentence on page 318. *(she)* Then ask pairs of students to compose three sentences based on the story by using predicate pronouns in the form *It was she.*

Reteaching/Reinforcement
- *Grammar Handbook,* anthology pp. 911–912
- *Grammar Mini-Lessons* copymasters p. 16, transparencies, p. 14

📓 **The Writer's Craft**

The Nominative Case p. 552

the poem looking in the window, and back to her job.

And finally it was midnight. The moon was high over the factory roof. The yard was a watercolored wash of moonlight and pink from the lights in the valley. The moon was a white ball with a golden ring. The poem waited with the moon, holding its breath. The pink lights shone down over the top of the building, casting shadows on the path next to the tracks.

The woman would be the first ready to leave. Usually she waited for the guys by the little gray door at the far end of the shop. But tonight she had told them she was in a hurry. She stepped alone into the night as the midnight whistle blew. She was short, but her shadow was ten feet tall. She carried a paper sack of dirty work clothes in her arms. The poem was with her like her shadow, walking quickly. The farther away from the building, the taller her shadow grew, from the pink lights and the moon on her shoulders. Little rocks and pebbles at her feet crunched under her shoes. Each pebble had its own shadow, like pink moon rocks under her feet. She smiled to herself, enjoying the moment.

A cat meowed and scampered under a parked freight car. Night birds called. Now her shadow split in two, growing taller, taller, taller. Catching pink lights on more poles in the train yard. She stepped carefully across one, two, three sets of tracks. Past stacks of unmachined main axles and rows of wheels. Past lines of mounted wheels and axles waiting to be shipped out. A lone black bird cawed at her from a telephone wire. Something stirred in her brain. Some disjointed words seemed to come together. She laughed aloud, and the crow cawed again, leaving its perch to fly over her head into the blackness beyond the realm of pink lights. Then suddenly the woman threw her head back and yelled up into the pink and black sky. "HEY . . . I'm a midnight rider. A cat's eye glider. I'm a second shift lady goin' home!"

She laughed again. And surprised and delighted, the poem jumped INSIDE HER like a fetus kicking in the ninth month. She hurried along, faster now, almost running the last few yards past the guard shanty.

She was at her car in the parking lot now. She unlocked its door, opened it and flung her sack of dirty clothes in the back seat. Getting in, she started the car up and aimed it out of the lot, waving to other workers that were now crossing the tracks behind her. Finally she would have time for herself. She felt the uneasy urgency she'd had all night go from her in a deep earth-moving sigh, as she drove past the guard shanty and turned up the road to the ramp leading from the valley.

And a poem was born, comfortable as a well-fitting work shoe, and satisfying as the end of the workday. The poem. The woman. The machinist. All became one. And she sang to the hum of her car:

I'm a midnight rider
A cat's eye glider
I'm a second shift woman goin' home

I'm a moon rock walker
A night bird stalker
I'm a short tall shadow headin' home

I'm a cool old river
A seasoned survivor
I'm a factory workin' poet goin' home

Critic's Corner

"I liked the personification of the poem but especially the ending. Throughout the story, the job had been in conflict with the woman's creativity, but they finally merged into a work of art. An intriguing definition of poetry."

W. Caleb McDaniel,
Ninth-Grade Member,
Student Advisory Board

INSIGHT

1. Which work spoke more strongly to you, "The Cultural Worker" or "My Poetry"? Why? *(Some students may say "My Poetry" because it is simpler, because it is a poem, and because of the first-person point of view. Others may say the "The Cultural Worker" because of the complex imagery and personification and because of the merging of the poem and the woman.)*

2. Based on the poem, what do you think the speaker's life is like? *(Possible responses: Her life is very busy, filled with household chores that need to be done, taking care of her children and husband, and somehow trying to find time to write the poems that so desperately need to be expressed.)*

María Herrera-Sobek

Educated at the University of California at Los Angeles, María Herrera-Sobek is the author of two works of critical prose, one of them on Chicana literature and the other on *braceros*, Latin American folk musicians. She works in the Mexico/Chicano Program of the University of California at Irvine.

INSIGHT

MY POETRY
María Herrera-Sobek

My poetry
follows me
between tin cans
between chiles and tomatoes
5 apples and peaches
brooms and garbage
that on another day
were my only song.

My poetry
10 bursts out between cries
of children
and husbands hurt
by the explosion
of a pen
15 that bleeds
and leaves
gutted worms
on the pages.

My poetry
20 assaults me
among the rivers of embraces
I receive
from impatient lovers
in desperate competition
25 with my pen.

MI POESÍA

Mi poesía
me persigue
entre botes de hojalata,
entre chiles y tomates,
5 manzanas y duraznos,
escobas y basura
que otro día
eran mi única canción.

Mi poesía
10 surge entre chillidos
de niños
y esposos lastimados
por la explosión
de pluma
15 que sangra
y deja
gusanos destripados
en las páginas.

Mi poesía
20 me asalta
entre ríos de caricias
que recibo
de impacientes amantes
en desesperada competencia
25 con mi pluma.

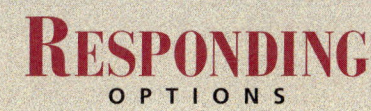

RESPONDING OPTIONS

FROM PERSONAL RESPONSE TO CRITICAL ANALYSIS

REFLECT 1. What do you think of the poem that the factory worker composed? Write your opinion in your notebook and share it in class.

RETHINK 2. How does the woman seem to feel about herself and her job?

Close Textual Reading

Consider
- the feeling you get from the poem
- her thoughts during her work shift
- her relationship with her coworkers

Thematic Link 3. What purpose do you think writing serves in the woman's life?

4. Why do you think the author called this story "The Cultural Worker"?

5. Based on your impressions of the woman, draw a portrait of her during a significant moment on the shift, and list some adjectives that describe her. Explain your portrait to the class.

6. Look at the word web and the diary entry you created for the activities on page 316. Does the story support your images of factory work? If so, how? If not, how is the portrayal of factory work different from what you imagined?

RELATE 7. Compare "The Cultural Worker" and the Insight poem, "My Poetry." Consider the poets' lives, the relationships between the poet and her poem, and the characterizations of the poems.

Multimodal Learning
ANOTHER PATHWAY

Cooperative Learning
With a small group, look closely at each line of the poem on page 319 to see how specific words and images relate to the woman's thoughts, feelings, and actions. Share your group's analysis with other groups, and discuss similarities and differences in interpretation.

LITERARY CONCEPTS

Personification is a figure of speech in which human qualities are attributed to an object, animal, or idea. "The Cultural Worker" is based on personification. The poem is not only depicted as a living thing, it is actually a main character in the story. Skim the story and list what the poem does, thinks, and feels. Why do you think the author personified the poem in this way?

CONCEPT REVIEW: Tone Identify words or phrases that express the tone of this story—that is, the writer's attitude toward the trials and tribulations of factory work.

QUICKWRITES

1. The narrator indicates that the factory worker often writes in a journal. Write a **journal entry** that you think the woman might compose.

2. Using the factory worker's **poem** as a model, write a short poem that describes you. You might try stringing together images from your day that occur to you at certain moments in time.

📁 **PORTFOLIO** Save your writing. You may want to use it later as a springboard to a piece for your portfolio.

THE CULTURAL WORKER 321

From Personal Response to Critical Analysis

1. Accept all responses.
2. Possible responses: She feels good about the job she does. She listens attentively to her co-workers and seems to relate well to them, although she is the only woman working among the men. She is waiting for her shift to end so that she can return to the poem that is ready to be written.
3. Possible responses: It makes her feel better about herself and her job; it gives her a means of expressing herself.
4. Some students will say that it unites her factory work and her poetic work. Others may say that the title stresses her creative side.
5. Accept all drawings. Possible adjectives include *strong, creative, smart, poetic, hardworking, sad, happy*.
6. Many students will say the story bears out their image of factory work. Some might say the story glamorizes factory work by making it seem poetic.
7. Possible responses: Both works show a strong psychological relationship between a poet and her poetry. However, in "The Cultural Worker" the relationship is a loving one, while in "My Poetry," it is adversarial, tempestuous.

Another Pathway
Cooperative Learning Group members might take turns reading lines aloud for discussion, with one member serving as turn-taking monitor. After each member introduces his or her line, other members can offer interpretations, and a paraphraser can clarify students' ideas.

Rubric
3 Full Accomplishment Students insightfully relate the poem's language to the woman's life.
2 Substantial Accomplishment Students relate some of the poem's language to aspects of the woman's life.
1 Little or Partial Accomplishment Students are not able to connect the poem with the woman's life.

Literary Concepts
The poem stays outside the factory, waiting for the woman and watching the events on her shift by looking in the window. When she emerges after the shift, it jumps inside her, becoming a fetus, and is born. The author personifies the poem this way because it expresses her perception of the creative process.

Concept Review: Tone The elliptical conversations of co-workers on page 318 are sources of words and phrases indicating tone, as is the poem at the end.

QuickWrites
1. Suggest that students use their clusters from Personal Connection and their diary entries from Writing Connection as bases for their journal entries.
2. Encourage students to say the poem aloud to hear its songlike rhythms. Point out the short, rhyming nature of the first two lines in each stanza and the refrain in the third line of each stanza.

The Writer's Craft
Keep a Journal, p. 31
Literal and Figurative Language, pp. 413–415

THE LANGUAGE OF LITERATURE TEACHER'S EDITION **321**

Critic's Corner

Possible responses: Everyday work and writing poetry can merge in a person's life; even mundane things can inspire poetry.

Across the Curriculum

Music Point out that the poem at the end of "The Cultural Worker" seems obviously influenced by popular music. Encourage students to bring in recordings of songs about factory work; or, if time and resources are limited, ask them to name song titles and quote lyrics. Encourage students to compare and contrast views of factory work found in songs with the view presented in "The Cultural Worker." Folk music, country and western, blues, and rock are four American musical genres that will provide good examples. You might also bring in a recording of Aaron Copland's stirring, well-known classical piece, "Fanfare for the Common Man." Invite students to share their responses to the music.

ART GALLERY
A Tribute to Workers Many artists have depicted working people in their artwork. Show these images to help students understand how the lives of blue collar workers have inspired artists.

Side A, Frame 49330

Multimodal Learning

ALTERNATIVE ACTIVITIES

1. Imagine the poem that the woman composes as the lyrics for a work song. Set the lyrics to **music** and perform the song for the class.
2. Make a **mobile** that reflects the woman's interests and personality, a mobile that she might hang in her home. Display the mobile in class.

Red and White on Post (1950), Alexander Calder. Private collection. Copyright © 1996 Artists Rights Society (ARS), New York/ ADAGP, Paris.

CRITIC'S CORNER

Angie Lang, a member of our student board, liked the way this story is told from the point of view of "the poem." She wrote, "It showed how things looked from the outside. Stories are sometimes told better from this point of view." Explain whether you agree that seeing the woman from the outside makes the story better. Notice the place in the story where the viewpoints of both the poem and the woman become one. What does this blending of viewpoints suggest to you?

THE WRITER'S STYLE

In describing the woman's experiences during her day, Doro uses images that appeal to a variety of senses. For example, there is rich visual **imagery** in the portrait of the fellow worker in the fifth paragraph. What other interesting visual images do you find? Point out passages that involve sound, smell, and touch. Is there any reference to taste?

SUE DORO

Sue Doro has been living a busy life, with impressive credentials both as a writer and a tradeswoman. She started writing in her late twenties, choosing labor and feminist topics. Meanwhile, she worked as a railway machinist in Milwaukee, Wisconsin, for thirteen years—and raised five children. A social activist, Doro aims to bring "worker writing"—literature written by and about blue-collar workers—into the mainstream of American culture. Her book *Blue Collar Goodbyes* is based on her experiences at the railway factory around the time of its closing. The selections in the book cap-

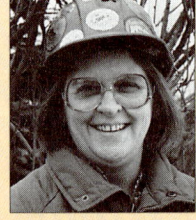

1936–

ture "the hearts of survivors/that corporate minds will never know."

After the railway plant closed down, Doro moved to Oakland, California. For two and a half years, she served as the Executive Director of Tradeswomen, Inc., a national organization for women in blue-collar jobs. She currently works as an affirmative-action compliance officer for the U.S. Department of Labor. She is also poetry editor for *Tradeswomen Magazine*.

OTHER WORKS *Of Birds and Factories; Heart, Home, and Hard Hats*

Extended Reading

• ART GALLERY

322 UNIT TWO PART 2: AGAINST THE ODDS

The Writer's Style

You might make a chart listing the five senses and recording images from the story for each sense. Possible examples:
Visual: description of elderly man, p. 318
Sound: cat meowing, bird cawing, p. 319
Touch: carrying a sack of dirty clothes, p. 319
Smell: a night smelling of Menomonee Valley city wilderness, p. 318
Taste: eating a sandwich; green onions and asparagus by the river, p. 318

 The Writer's Craft

Sensory Language, pp. 62, 65

Alternative Activities

1. Students may wish to do the activity individually or in groups, depending on their musical skills. Make an audiotape of their performances.
2. Direct student attention to the Calder mobile on this page, and tell them that a mobile may be abstract or representational. In small groups, some students may plan and design the mobile, and others may construct it.

ON YOUR OWN

Fish Cheeks

Amy Tan

I fell in love with the minister's son the winter I turned fourteen. He was not Chinese, but as white as Mary in the manger. For Christmas I prayed for this blond-haired boy, Robert, and a slim new American nose.

When I found out that my parents had invited the minister's family over for Christmas Eve dinner, I cried. What would Robert think of our shabby *Chinese* Christmas? What would he think of our noisy *Chinese* relatives who lacked proper American manners? What terrible disappointment would he feel upon seeing not a roasted turkey and sweet potatoes but *Chinese* food?

On Christmas Eve I saw that my mother had outdone herself in creating a strange menu. She was pulling black veins out of the backs of fleshy prawns. The kitchen was littered with appalling mounds of raw food: A slimy rock cod with bulging fish eyes that pleaded not to be thrown into a pan of hot oil. Tofu, which looked like stacked wedges of rubbery white sponges. A bowl soaking dried fungus back to life. A plate of squid, their backs crisscrossed with knife markings so they resembled bicycle tires.

And then they arrived—the minister's family and all my relatives in a clamor of doorbells and rumpled Christmas packages. Robert grunted hello, and I pretended he was not worthy of existence.

FISH CHEEKS **323**

Objectives

- To promote independent, active reading
- To practice and apply skills learned in previous selections
- To provide an opportunity to assess students' performance through an alternative assessment instrument

SUMMARY

Amy, a 14-year-old Chinese-American girl, has fallen in love with the minister's son, a blond-haired boy named Robert. At Christmas she prays for this boy and also for a slim new American nose. But she is dismayed when she learns that her parents have invited the minister's family for Christmas Eve dinner. She knows that the boy and his parents will now be exposed to her "shabby Chinese Christmas" and her "noisy Chinese relatives" with their table manners, which are different from American manners. At the dinner Amy becomes even more dismayed, because her mother has "outdone herself in preparing a strange menu," including the fish cheek, a tender morsel that her father offers her, saying: "Amy, your favorite." The Chinese custom of belching after dinner somewhat embarrasses the guests and stuns Amy into silence. Afterward, her mother says she understands that Amy wants to be American on the outside. "But inside you must always be Chinese. You must be proud you are different. The only shame is to have shame." Years later, Amy appreciates this lesson.

Reading Pathways

- Invite students to keep a dialogue journal of their responses to the narrative. Then invite them to trade journals with partners and offer responses to each other's entries.

- Invite a small group of students to take turns reading the narrative aloud, one paragraph at a time. Suggest that they pause after each paragraph to offer any comments and discuss any questions they have.

- Evaluate how well students can read, interpret, discuss, and write about the selection on their own by using the Integrated Assessment for Unit Two, located in the Alternative Assessment booklet. Set aside two class periods, or about two hours, to administer the assessment after students have completed the final writing assignment for the unit.

PRINT AND MEDIA RESOURCES

UNIT TWO RESOURCE BOOK
Strategic Reading: Literature, p. 57

FORMAL ASSESSMENT
Selection Test, p. 55
Part Test, pp. 57–58
 Test Generator

ALTERNATIVE ASSESSMENT
Unit Two Integrated Assessment, pp. 7–12

ACCESS FOR STUDENTS ACQUIRING ENGLISH
Selection Summaries

AUDIO LIBRARY
See Reference Card

THE LANGUAGE OF LITERATURE **TEACHER'S EDITION** **323**

OPTION 1

Cooperative Learning
ROLE-PLAYING

Invite small groups to practice and perform the narrative as a skit consisting of three scenes: before dinner, during dinner, and after dinner. Groups of six may represent all six characters. Approaches to the skit may vary depending on the composition of your class: Chinese-American students might give the most knowing performances, while students from other cultures may interpret the setting differently based on personal experience.

Teacher's Role Serve as drama consultant during rehearsals, answering questions about groups' ideas and asking probing questions about aspects of performance that need extra support. Then serve as audience for the role-playing. Offer constructive comments afterward while serving as moderator for the class's comments.

Rubric

3 Full Accomplishment Students present an enthusiastic and well-rehearsed performance that entertains and provides insight into character and culture.

2 Substantial Accomplishment Skit is diligently prepared and sincerely performed, reflecting insight into character and culture.

1 Little or Partial Accomplishment Skit is ill-prepared and lacking in character insight or cultural awareness.

Um den Fisch [Around the fish] (1926), Paul Klee. Oil on canvas, 18 ⅜″ × 25 ⅛″, The Museum of Modern Art, New York, Abby Aldrich Rockefeller Fund, photo Copyright © 1995 The Museum of Modern Art, New York.

Dinner threw me deeper into despair. My relatives licked the ends of their chopsticks and reached across the table, dipping them into the dozen or so plates of food. Robert and his family waited patiently for platters to be passed to them. My relatives murmured with pleasure when my mother brought out the whole steamed fish. Robert grimaced. Then my father poked his chopsticks just below the fish eye and plucked out the soft meat. "Amy, your favorite," he said, offering me the tender fish cheek. I wanted to disappear.

At the end of the meal my father leaned back and belched loudly, thanking my mother for her fine cooking. "It's a polite Chinese custom to show you are satisfied," explained my father to our astonished guests. Robert was looking down at his plate with a reddened face. The minister managed to muster up a quiet burp. I was stunned into silence for the rest of the night.

After everyone had gone, my mother said to me, "You want to be the same as American girls on the outside." She handed me an early gift. It

324 UNIT TWO PART 2: AGAINST THE ODDS

Art Note

Around the Fish by Paul Klee Born in Bern, Switzerland, to a German father and Swiss mother who were both musicians, Paul Klee (1879–1940) showed artistic talent at an early age. He eventually developed many techniques, and *Around the Fish* is representative of his deliberately playful, pictorial style in which cryptic, symbolic elements combine with everyday objects and beings such as houses, trees, birds, and fish.

Reading the Art What do you think the title *Around the Fish* means? What relationship, if any, do you see between Klee's painting and Tan's narrative?

was a miniskirt in beige tweed. "But inside you must always be Chinese. You must be proud you are different. Your only shame is to have shame."

And even though I didn't agree with her then, I knew that she understood how much I had suffered during the evening's dinner. It wasn't until many years later—long after I had gotten over my crush on Robert—that I was able to fully appreciate her lesson and the true purpose behind our particular menu. For Christmas Eve that year, she had chosen all my favorite foods. ❖

1952–

AMY TAN

Amy Tan was not always the proud Chinese American that she is now. She recalls dreaming when she was young of making her features look more Western by having plastic surgery. It was not until she made her first trip to China in 1987 that Tan could truly accept both the Chinese and American cultures as her own.

Though Tan won a writing contest at the age of eight, her identity as a writer was slow in coming, too. In fact, she did not plan on a literary career. After two years of postgraduate study at the University of California in Berkeley, Tan worked for several years as a consultant to programs for children with disabilities. She then became a reporter for a medical publication and eventually a freelance technical writer. Later, Tan started playing jazz piano and writing fiction instead.

After getting some of her stories published in magazines, Tan combined the stories with others to form a novel called *The Joy Luck Club*. The book became a bestseller and was made into a movie. It portrays the cultural and generational gaps between four young Chinese-American women and their mothers.

OTHER WORKS *The Kitchen God's Wife*

FISH CHEEKS **325**

AMY TAN

Amy Tan was born in Oakland, California, two and a half years after her parents moved there from China. In the early 1990s, a successful movie was made of her first adult novel, *The Joy Luck Club*. After writing two childrens books, she had a third adult novel, *The Hundred Secret Senses*, published in 1995.

Thematic Link: *Against the Odds*
Many years after a disastrous "Chinese" Christmas dinner, the narrator has come to understand and cherish the lesson in self-esteem her mother taught her.

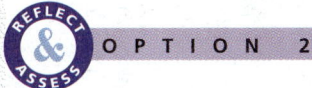

OPTION 2

Individual Activity
WRITING LETTERS

Invite students to imagine Amy Tan during two phases of her life: at the time of the dinner and at the time of writing the narrative. Ask them to write a letter from one Amy to the other, discussing her thoughts and feelings about the dinner and possibly about larger, related issues and to write a response to it. Students may choose whether the first letter comes from Amy's younger or older self.

Teacher's Role Allow students to work independently on drafts of both letters. Read their drafts or listen as students read them aloud. Offer criticism and suggestions for revision.

Rubric

3 Full Accomplishment Letters distinguish between the voices of two phases of the author's life and show keen insight into the issue of cultural self-esteem.

2 Substantial Accomplishment Letters show understanding of the issue of cultural self-esteem but are not written in two convincing voices.

1 Little or Partial Accomplishment Letters do not convincingly reflect the author's voice or views at either phase of her life.

OPTION 3

Class Discussion
SHARING IDEAS

Teacher's Role Ask questions to spark whole-class discussion and invite responses from volunteers while you serve as clarifier, elaborator, extender, and prober.

1. What did the narrator understand years later that she didn't understand at the time of the dinner? *(Possible responses: that her mother planned the menu deliberately with her in mind to please her and to teach her a valuable lesson; that she had no reason to be ashamed of who she was)*

2. How do you think you would have acted if you were Amy or Robert? *(Possible responses: Some students will say that they would have acted with more sophistication and awareness; others will say that they would have acted with pride in their cultural backgrounds.)*

THE LANGUAGE OF LITERATURE **TEACHER'S EDITION 325**

OVERVIEW

To gain a deeper understanding of the selections they have read in this unit, students will explore the characteristics of a persuasive essay and then create a well-developed example in this lesson.

Objectives

- To plan a persuasive essay by considering elements such as research, supporting evidence, format, and method of organization
- To draft a persuasive essay and solicit response
- To revise, edit, and publish a persuasive essay

Skills

LITERATURE
- Identifying essay elements

WRITING AND LANGUAGE
- Writing a thesis statement
- Using active voice

MEDIA LITERACY
- Evaluating news articles and photos
- Analyzing controversial issues
- Using on-line forums
- Composing a letter to the editor

SPEAKING, LISTENING, AND VIEWING
- Conducting interviews

- Conferring
- Conducting a survey
- Role-playing

CRITICAL THINKING
- Comparing/contrasting
- Analyzing
- Making inferences
- Avoiding circular reasoning

RESEARCH SKILLS
- Researching articles
- Using databases
- Conducting interviews
- Using the computer

Teaching Strategy: MODELING

 To demonstrate how students can generate essay ideas from a variety of sources, ask them to examine the news article titled "Cheering Unlimited." Call on volunteers to come up with essay topics based on this article. (*Possible responses: Is a no-cut policy a good idea? Should all 72 cheerleaders have been allowed into the game for free?*)

B Possible responses: the policy is positive because it fosters inclusiveness and students' feelings of achievement; the policy might lead to mediocre performances by the groups.

WRITING FROM EXPERIENCE

WRITING TO PERSUADE

If you've ever wanted to change a difficult or unjust situation, like the ones described in Unit Two, "Trials and Tribulations," you're not alone. One way you can make changes is by persuading others to agree with your position and to join you in taking action.

GUIDED ASSIGNMENT

Write a Persuasive Essay Write an essay that persuades others to agree with your position on an issue.

1 Examine Some Issues

The news articles and the photo on these pages spotlight some issues that teenagers may see as problems or hardships. What other issues and situations concern you?

Evaluating the Ideas Look for the main ideas in the news articles and photo. Are the ideas communicated clearly? Do you think the ideas for the policies are valid? Why? Compare your reactions with the comments a student wrote on self-stick notes. How are they alike and different?

Digging for Ideas In a small group, brainstorm situations about which you have definite opinions. Think of stories you've heard in the news, new policies at school, and community issues. What arguments can you make in favor of each opinion? against?

B What benefit do you see to the no-cut policy? what drawback?

326 UNIT TWO: TRIALS AND TRIBULATIONS

Magazine Article

Cheering Unlimited

In an Indiana school, pom-pom democracy

THE PLAINFIELD (IND.) COMMUNITY Middle School's football team was psyched for the game at Cascade Junior High in Clayton. There was just one snag: Cascade didn't want to let Plainfield's cheerleaders on the field. Cheerleaders are admitted free—and Plainfield had brought along 72.

Lucky for the Cascade Cadets, they weren't asked to invite Plainfield's top-rated band—the 140-member band, that is—or the 229-member choir. In fact, half of Plainfield's 800 students belong to some team, band, choir etc. (compared with a 20 percent extracurricular average in public schools nationwide) because of one simple rule: Anyone who wants to be on a team is on the team. Says cheerleader Allison Kern, 12: "Usually it's only the popular people that made cheerleading—and I'm just medium popular." (The cheerleaders were welcomed at the Cascade game when someone pointed out the amount of sodas and hot dogs they and their parents would buy.)

Plainfield's no-cut policy was instituted in 1990 by Principal Jerry Goldsberry, who remembers being cut from his college baseball team. That sort of thing won't happen at his school.

from People

PRINT AND MEDIA RESOURCES

UNIT TWO RESOURCE BOOK
Prewriting, p. 61
Elaboration, p. 62
Peer Response Guide, pp. 63–64
Revising and Proofreading, p. 65
Student Model, pp. 66–67
Rubric, p. 68

WRITING MINI-LESSONS
Transparencies, p. 38

FORMAL ASSESSMENT
Guidelines for Writing Assessment

 WRITING COACH

 LASERLINKS
Writing Springboard

 The Writer's Craft
Persuasion, pp. 207–232

Critical Thinking: ANALYZING

C Have students compare and contrast the self-stick notes on either side of the photo on this page. What do these notes suggest about the writer's reactions to the issue so far? *(Possible response: The note on the left indicates a negative reaction to the curfew policy; the note on the right suggests that the writer wants more information about the legal status of curfews, perhaps to support his or her feelings that curfews are unjust.)*

CUSTOMIZING FOR
Students Acquiring English

D Certain phrases in the photo caption may be difficult for some students. Explain the following words:

cruisers: young people roaming the streets with no specific purpose

nineties thing: phenomenon or trend seemingly characteristic of the 1990s

teens: teenagers

Critical Thinking: ANALYZING

E According to the final paragraph, what may be a positive result of the "zero tolerance" policy? What may be a negative result? *(Possible responses: The policy may cut down on fights, but it may be unfair to students by imposing harsh punishments on them for rather minor infractions.)*

CUSTOMIZING FOR
Less-Proficient Writers

F Remind students to let their ideas and reactions flow. Reassure them that spelling, grammar, and mechanical skills such as punctuation are not crucial at this stage. Students may find that their notes flow more easily if they use a computer for freewriting. Remind them that they should avoid erasing or crossing out; instead, they should feel free to rebut themselves or to announce that they have changed their minds.

News Photograph

What right do police have to pick on teens?

Are curfews really illegal?

D A California police officer sends young cruisers home. It's a nineties thing: dozens of cities across the nation have imposed strict curfews to keep teens off the streets at night and to battle crime. Opponents claim that curfews are illegal.

Newspaper Article

High School Brawlers Will Go Directly to Police Station

LAKE ZURICH, IL—Bathroom brawls and cafeteria scrapes won't be taken lightly anymore at Lake Zurich High School. Instead of a trip to the counselor's office, the school will begin Tuesday to send the aggressors directly to the police station.

Once in the hands of police, the students are to be charged or sent home with their parents, depending on the severity of the injuries in the fight and whether weapons were used, police say.

The new policy—dubbed "zero tolerance"—is part of an effort to crack down after the number of fights rose to 27 so far this year from 20 last year.

E Some students said the policy may cut down on fights, but they worry that it's too draconian, and some fear they could get a police record just for getting into a shoving match.

from Chicago Tribune

❷ Take a Stand

F Choose an issue or a topic that you would like to explore. Do you agree or disagree with the situation? Why? Spend about ten minutes freewriting what you know about different sides of the topic. Don't worry yet about what you don't know. Just record your initial thoughts and reactions. You'll have an opportunity later to gather information that might change your opinion.

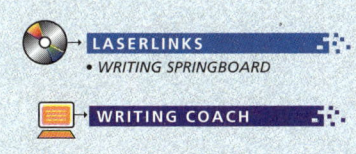

- LASERLINKS
  • WRITING SPRINGBOARD
- WRITING COACH

WRITING FROM EXPERIENCE **327**

WRITING SPRINGBOARD

Nobody Gets Cut Teens discuss their opinions about the policy at their school that opens school teams and clubs to anyone who wishes to join

Writing Prompt
Write a letter to the principal of your school explaining why you think a school policy is fair or unfair. Persuade him or her to support a change in the policy.

Side B, Frame 4968

Teaching Strategy: MODELING

G Have students look at the research questions displayed on page 328. Point out to students that the questions cover a broad field of inquiry, including support for curfews, possible implications and consequences of the policy, opposition to curfews, and an open-ended search for opinions. Remind students that an argument for one point of view on a controversial issue is effective only to the extent that it reflects an understanding of opposing points of view.

Teaching Strategy: STUMBLING BLOCK

H Share the following suggestions about designing and implementing opinion surveys with students who need guidance:
- Plan to query enough respondents to make the survey statistically valid.
- Formulate direct, easy-to-answer questions.
- Fill out the survey yourself to ensure that it does not impose on respondents' time or patience.
- Assure respondents that their answers will be kept confidential.
- Ask respondents to return the survey within a specified time period.

PREWRITING

Gathering Information

Researching Your Position Now you're ready to explore your topic and decide what the goal of your persuasive writing should be. Don't be surprised if your opinions change as you learn more about your topic!

❶ List Your Questions

G You probably generated a lot of ideas during freewriting. Where are the gaps in your knowledge? If your topic is curfews, for example, what questions do you still have about them? Where might you find the answers? Jot down the questions you'd like to research, as one student did below.

Student's Research Questions

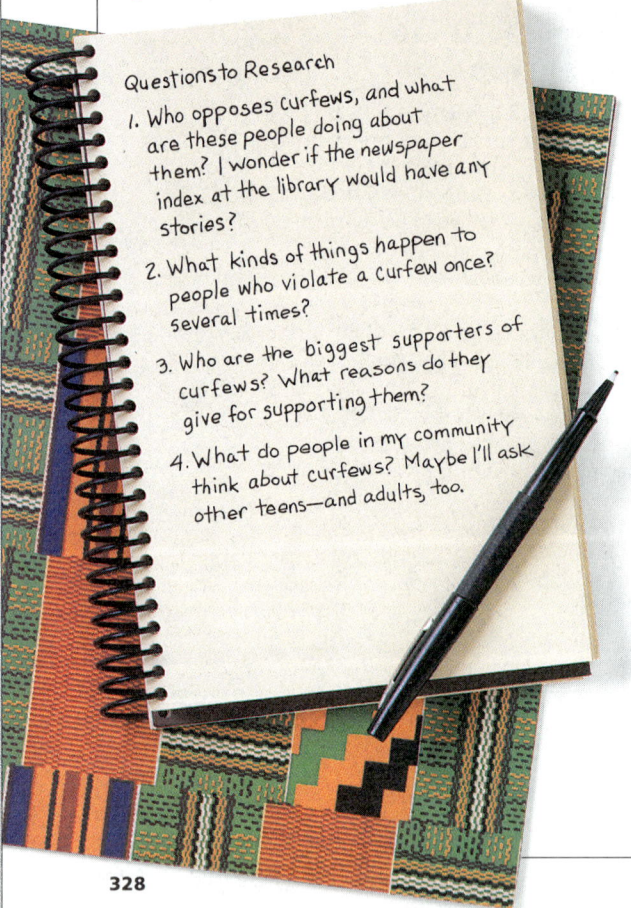

Questions to Research
1. Who opposes curfews, and what are these people doing about them? I wonder if the newspaper index at the library would have any stories?
2. What kinds of things happen to people who violate a curfew once? several times?
3. Who are the biggest supporters of curfews? What reasons do they give for supporting them?
4. What do people in my community think about curfews? Maybe I'll ask other teens—and adults, too.

❷ Access Print Media

Your librarian can direct you to reference materials with information about your topic. You also might check magazine and newspaper indexes for articles, graphs, surveys, editorials, and letters to the editor. It's a good idea to take notes as you find answers to your questions. In addition to your questions, be on the lookout for the following:

- background information on the topic
- reasons for adopting your position
- evidence to support your view

❸ Gather Other Opinions

Students, school personnel, and community leaders can help you see different sides of an issue. Here are some ideas for tapping their knowledge and ideas:

Interview a Public Official Ask your principal, a school board member, or a police official for an interview. Find out the person's opinion on your topic and reasons for the opinion.

H **Survey Students** Find out how your peers feel about the issue you are researching. What reasons do they give for their views?

328

 SkillBuilder RESEARCH SKILLS

PERIODICAL INDEXES Some students may need guidance in using newspaper and magazine indexes. Point out that indexes for leading newspapers are published yearly in bound form and are arranged alphabetically by subject. Entries often contain cross-references to related information in the same volume. Many periodicals are indexed yearly in the *Reader's Guide to Periodical Literature*. Students can often supplement their research by using key words to search databases on CD-ROM, which contain entries on a broad range of fields and topics. Though these listings are helpful because they often include summaries, they are frequently limited to material from the past three to five years.

Application Students can prepare lists of index entries and key words to be used in carrying out research on their topic.

Additional Suggestions Lists of key words can be refined by using supplementary terms, such as CURFEW–TEENS or SCHOOLS–CURFEW REGULATIONS, to limit broad topics.

328 THE LANGUAGE OF LITERATURE TEACHER'S EDITION

Role-Play Invite a friend to take the role of someone who opposes your position. Present your ideas and try to satisfy your partner's objections. Then look back at your arguments. Which ones did your partner think were effective? Which need work?

Go On-line If you have access to a computer with a modem, visit a student on-line chat room. Many on-line services allow subscribers to chat with people all over the country.

J Doe: Hi. I'm doing a survey. Is there a curfew for teenagers in your community? If so, what do you know about it?

Ginny Z: Orlando has one. Kids can't hang out downtown after midnight.

Soccer star: I'm from Harvard, Illinois. We have a nighttime curfew too. And during the school year, it's illegal to be on the streets during school hours.

J Doe: Soccer star, why does Harvard have a daytime curfew? And what happens to kids who get caught?

4 Focus on Purpose and Audience

What do you hope your essay will accomplish? Your purpose may be to change your readers' minds, help them see another point of view, or encourage them to act on an issue. Think of a person or a group of people who could help you achieve your goal. Then write your essay with that audience in mind.

SkillBuilder

 WRITER'S CRAFT

Writing a Thesis Statement

Good writers often write a thesis statement after they've completed their research. A thesis statement is one or two sentences describing the main idea of a piece of writing. The statement may reflect your tone and point of view. What point of view does the example below show?

A teen curfew is a bad idea. It goes against certain constitutional rights and suggests that teens are to blame for crime.

APPLYING WHAT YOU'VE LEARNED
You might want to draft a thesis statement for your persuasive essay. The statement can guide you in organizing the ideas you want to include. It also can help you stay on track when you write your draft.

THINK & PLAN

Checking Your Progress

1. How has the research changed your first impressions of the issue?
2. Do you have enough support for your ideas? If not, where can you find more information?
3. Do you understand both sides of your issue? If not, how can you broaden your understanding?

WRITING FROM EXPERIENCE **329**

Speaking and Listening: COLLABORATIVE OPPORTUNITY

I Two or more pairs of students may want to pool their ideas on an issue of general interest and stage a debate for the class as a whole. Help them set the ground rules for a debate, including the order and time limitations of speakers.

Research Skill: USING THE COMPUTER

J Offer students these additional tips on using an on-line chat room or forum:
- *Prepare questions in advance. Lead off with your most important or broad-based question.*
- *Be prepared to discard some irrelevant information. Focus on one or two responses for follow-up questions.*
- *Make follow-up questions as specific as possible. Request facts, quotations, and other evidence that you can cite in your essay.*

Critical Thinking: MAKING INFERENCES

K As students prepare to write a draft, they should make inferences about what their audience may already know and think about the issue. Remind them how advertising is a good example of persuasion, and that just as effective advertising is deliberately tailored for specific groups, good persuasive argument contains well-chosen appeals delivered in an appropriate tone.

SkillBuilder WRITER'S CRAFT

WRITING A THESIS STATEMENT

Guide students to recognize that a thesis statement at the start of a persuasive essay accomplishes three important goals: It introduces the issue, it states the writer's position, and it establishes a certain tone or attitude toward the topic. The thesis statement shown above signals that the writer is opposed to a teen curfew. Ask students to discuss what kind of tone this statement sets for the essay. *(Possible responses: serious, urgent, relatively formal.)*

Application Point out that an effective thesis statement takes a firm stance on its issue.

Additional Suggestions Encourage students to reconsider their thesis statements in light of their intended audiences and purposes. They should be sure that the arguments they intend to make will effectively capture their audiences' interest.

Reteaching/Reinforcement
- *Writing Handbook,* anthology pp. 867, 874
- *Writing Mini-Lessons* transparencies, p. 38

Writing Thesis Statements, pp. 300, 343

THE LANGUAGE OF LITERATURE **TEACHER'S EDITION 329**

Teaching Strategy: USING THE SKILLBUILDER

L You may wish to teach the SkillBuilder on Avoiding Circular Reasoning at this time. Circular reasoning, by its nature, makes it difficult to integrate supporting details into an argument. Students will find it easier to draft, even in the earliest stages, if their organizational skills are sharp.

Research Skill: USING THE COMPUTER

M If students compose their drafts on computers, remind them to save all drafts separately so that nothing will be lost or written over. Remind them, too, that it is wise to save frequently in order to avoid losing an evening's work with a single system failure.

DRAFTING

Mapping Out Your Ideas

L **Shaping Your Argument** How do you turn your research into a powerful persuasive essay? You can start by putting your ideas in writing.

1 Write a Discovery Draft

M Throw yourself into the issue by writing the main points you want to get across to your audience. (If you have access to it, use the Writing Coach software for your draft.) What specific evidence can you cite to support each of your points? Let your thoughts flow onto the page. You can polish your writing later.

Student's Discovery Draft

Not Crazy About Curfews

My Discovery Draft	My Comments — My Discovery Draft
I found out that <u>lots of cities have set juvenile curfews</u> in the past few years to keep teens off the streets at night. And now my town is thinking about starting one up. Seems like these policies have some positive effects in fighting crime, but that doesn't make them a good idea. And they might not even be legal!	Maybe I should just focus on my town in the introduction. I could use facts from other cities to support my points later.
<u>My main problem with curfews</u> is that they go against the constitutional rights to free assembly and free speech. I've heard of a group called the American Civil Liberties Union that opposes curfews. My research says that the ACLU is actually suing cities that pass curfews for teenagers!	Which reasons should I put first? The ones I feel most strongly about?
Another problem is that curfews unfairly single out teenagers under the age of 17. I found out that crime in my town is spread out over all age groups and in all areas of the city. So why punish just teens?	Need to address opposing views. Additional comments: Maybe I'll make this a letter to the editor of my local paper. It could stir up some support!

---

330 UNIT TWO: TRIALS AND TRIBULATIONS

WRITING SPRINGBOARD
Against the Odds Patricia, a teenager dedicated to her high school studies, is unfairly prevented by a teacher from taking an advanced placement Spanish class. Patricia talks about how she worked through this problem.

Writing Prompt
Write a letter to your school adviser about a situation you feel is unjust. Try to persuade him or her to take some action to correct the situation.

Side B, Frame 8311

330 THE LANGUAGE OF LITERATURE TEACHER'S EDITION

❷ Analyze Your Discovery Draft

As you drafted, did you uncover any new arguments? Did any points seem clearer or stronger than others? You might record your ideas for revision, as one student did in the essay at the left. Be on the lookout for reasons or evidence that you should highlight.

❸ Rework Your Draft

These tips can help you shape your discovery draft.

Choose a Format Your writing doesn't have to look like an essay. How about a speech for a rally or a letter to a local official? For more ideas, see Showcase Your Work on page 333.

Address Opposing Views To be persuasive, you'll need to think about more than your own opinion. You'll also need to state the opposing view and give reasons not to support it.

Organize Your Ideas How will you organize your arguments? Below are two approaches that writers often use. For more information on organizing persuasive writing, see page 885 of the Writing Handbook.

- **State the issue.** Explain your position and support it with evidence. Conclude by restating the issue and your position.
- **Introduce the issue.** Explain both sides. Describe the pros of each side and then the cons. Finish with a recommendation and support it with reasons.

Write Your Introduction and Conclusion To make your position clear, you should state your point of view in the introduction. At the end of your piece, you can write a conclusion that reinforces your position and your purpose.

PEER RESPONSE

A peer reviewer can give you helpful feedback on your draft. Ask your reviewer questions like the following:

- How would you summarize the issue and my position?
- What part of my argument seems strongest?
- What do you want to know more about?
- What don't you understand about my position?

SkillBuilder

CRITICAL THINKING

Avoiding Circular Reasoning

As you sort through your reasons and evidence, you may find the same argument repeated in different words. Avoid the temptation to prove a point by restating it differently. This kind of circular reasoning doesn't tell the reader why your point is important. Which example below uses circular reasoning?

We should protect teenagers' constitutional right to free assembly because teens have rights under our system of government.

Taking away the right to free assembly is the same as telling teens that society doesn't trust or respect them, and it may make teenagers lose their self-respect.

APPLYING WHAT YOU'VE LEARNED
You may want to reread your draft and weed out any examples of circular reasoning.

RETHINK & EVALUATE

Reviewing Your Draft
1. What evidence best helped you state your position?
2. Which of your arguments need strengthening?
3. What comments from your peers were most helpful?

WRITING FROM EXPERIENCE **331**

Critical Thinking: ANALYZING

Have students get together in small groups to analyze the writer's revision ideas for the draft on page 330. Make sure that they understand that these ideas cover several areas, including the essay's focus, the method of organizing ideas, and the publication format. Then suggest that students first share and then list ideas for revising their own writing.

Teaching Strategy: PEER REVIEW

Have reviewers read the entire essay before they make any comments. During the second reading, they should jot down comments and suggestions. Remind students to include specific ideas for revision, such as "Why not emphasize your strongest argument?"

SkillBuilder CRITICAL THINKING

AVOIDING CIRCULAR REASONING

Tell students that although circular reasoning is often hidden in a different wording of the same statement, the repetition of a key word or phrase sometimes offers a clue that the writer's reasoning is circular. Be sure that students recognize that the first statement of the pair in the text uses circular reasoning and that they notice the repetition of *right* and *rights*. In contrast to the first statement, the second statement supports an assertion by citing possible negative consequences.

Application Have students rewrite the following sentence to avoid circular reasoning: *Everyone should be allowed free entrance to our national and state parks because the land should be freely accessible to all of us.* (Possible response: Free entry to our national and state parks would remove the barrier of compulsory fees, making a valuable resource more accessible and boosting popular support for the parks.)

THE LANGUAGE OF LITERATURE TEACHER'S EDITION **331**

Teaching Strategy: USING THE SKILLBUILDER

P You may wish to teach the SkillBuilder on the active voice as students begin the final revision process. Students will find that using the active voice will clarify their language and point out areas that require further revision.

Writing Skill: REVISING

Q As students revise and edit their reports, they will work to improve their drafts by
1. adding new material
2. cutting repetitive or unnecessary material
3. substituting more appropriate or relevant words, sentences, and paragraphs for deleted material
4. rearranging parts of the text to provide better coherence and unity

Teaching Strategy: MODELING

R Discuss how the model presented below meets the standards for evaluation on page 333. For example, the opening paragraph sets a serious tone for the essay and presents the writer's thesis statement in the final sentence of the paragraph.

S The writer's approach to opposing views is also in keeping with the standards for evaluation. At the beginning of the third paragraph, the writer acknowledges an opposing view—curfews may result in reducing crime—but addresses it with a counterargument regarding the statistically low percentage of crime committed by teenagers.

PORTFOLIO

Invite students to compare their finished persuasive essay to other essays that they have previously written. Then ask students to write a brief description of what they have learned about writing persuasive essays as a result of this assignment. They may wish to include their description and their finished essay in their portfolio.

REVISING AND PUBLISHING

Completing Your Essay

P **Polishing Your Arguments** Your essay may need some finishing touches before you are ready to share it. The guidelines on these two pages can help you examine your reasoning and fix any problems that you identify.

Q **Revise and Edit**

Try these tips for improving your draft.

- Invite a peer to read your draft and consider acting on the issue. If the student isn't moved to take action, you may need more evidence to support your stand.
- Read the excerpts on the right from one student's revision. What has changed since the discovery draft on page 330?
- Look at the Standards for Evaluation, the Editing Checklist, and the SkillBuilder on the right-hand page. How well have you satisfied these guidelines? Which do you need to work on?

S How does the writer address opposing arguments?

Student's Final Letter to the Editor

 R How does the introduction present the topic and set the tone for the letter?

To the Editor of the Sun Gazette:

How would you feel if you were thrown into jail for eating an ice cream cone on the street at night or bicycling home from a late movie? That penalty could become a reality for teenagers under 17 if the town council approves a juvenile curfew it is studying. I'm a teen, and I'm writing to explain why a curfew is a bad idea for our town.

The curfew our town council is considering would require teenagers to stay at home from 10 p.m. to 6 a.m. At first glance, the rule might seem like a good idea. However, the policy would break an existing law—the constitutional right to free assembly. Our country is a democracy, and the dictionary defines democracy as a place that practices "the principle of equality of rights, opportunity, and treatment."

The bottom line is that a curfew in Salter Heights could create legal problems for the town and also leave psychological scars on the teenagers and parents of our community.

I'd like to encourage your readers to come to the public hearing at the town hall next Tuesday and speak out against the teen curfew. Remember, teenagers have rights, too.

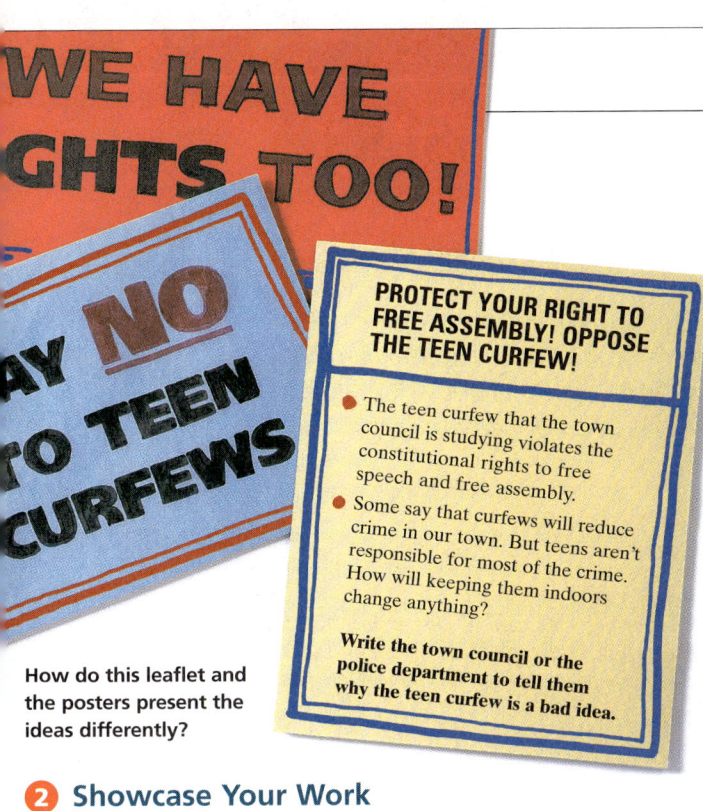

How do this leaflet and the posters present the ideas differently?

2 Showcase Your Work

You've written your persuasive essay and now want to share your ideas with a wider audience. The example above shows how a group of students shared their ideas by marching at the town hall and circulating leaflets. Below are more format options. Which ideas appeal to you most, and why?

PUBLISHING IDEAS

- Send your essay to a teen magazine.
- Create a poster to display at school.
- Write a letter to your congressional representative.

Standards for Evaluation

A persuasive essay
- clearly states the topic in the introduction
- gives opinions and supports them with facts or reasons
- has a reasonable and respectful tone
- takes into account and answers opposing views
- uses sound logic and effective language
- concludes by summing up reasons or calling for action

SkillBuilder

 GRAMMAR FROM WRITING

Using Active Voice

Good writers use the active voice as much as possible to keep readers involved. Active voice places the emphasis on the person or object that acts. Passive voice emphasizes the action instead. Consider the examples below.

Active: *Curfews violate our constitutional rights.*

Passive: *Our constitutional rights are violated by curfews.*

Editing Checklist

- Did you proofread your essay for spelling and punctuation?
- Did you use active voice whenever possible?
- Did you use words that say precisely what you mean?

REFLECT & ASSESS

Checking Your Persuasive Power

1. What was the most difficult part of writing your essay? Why?
2. Advertisements use persuasive writing. How does this lesson help you look at ads differently?

 PORTFOLIO Write yourself a note about your essay's strong and weak points. Add the essay and note to your portfolio.

WRITING FROM EXPERIENCE   **333**

Critical Thinking: COMPARING/CONTRASTING

T Invite volunteers to comment on how the same ideas can be presented in different ways depending on the format: poster, leaflet, or essay. Guide students to understand that posters can make a powerful, persuasive appeal by using large lettering, slogans, or visual cues and that leaflets can present major points in a condensed, easily understandable form. On the other hand, they should recognize that the essay offers the most comprehensive format for the thoughtful consideration of an issue.

Teaching Strategy: MANAGING THE PAPER LOAD

U Whenever possible, phrase your written comments as questions that will encourage students to reflect on and assess their work. For example, instead of writing "unsupported," try "Why not use a fact or a reason to support this claim?"

Standards for Evaluation

Have students review their essays for the following:

Ideas and Content
- clearly states the issue and the writer's opinion in the introduction
- supports opinions and ideas with observations, facts, and expert opinions
- takes into account and answers opposing views
- uses sound logic and effective language
- concludes with a strong argument, summary, or call to action

Structure and Form
- uses well-organized paragraphs and a clear organization
- includes transitional words and phrases to show relationships among ideas

Grammar, Usage, and Mechanics
- contains no more than two or three minor errors in grammar and usage
- contains no more than two or three minor errors in spelling, capitalization, and punctuation

---

SkillBuilder GRAMMAR FROM WRITING

USING ACTIVE VOICE

Remind students that verbs in the passive voice often give writing a listless, impersonal quality. As a test, have students experiment with the draft on page 332. Ask them to turn as many verbs as they can into the passive voice. Then call on volunteers to read the new sentences aloud.

Application Students can work in pairs to check each other's essays for the use of strong, active-voice verbs.

Additional Suggestions Have students read a newspaper or magazine article and make a list of all the passive-voice verbs that they find. Then invite them to discuss ways to revise the article by using stronger verbs in the active voice.

Reteaching/Reinforcement

The Writer's Craft
Active and Passive Voice, pp. 590–591

UNIT REVIEW

This feature allows students to reflect on what they have learned in Unit Two and to assess how well they have understood it. This feature provides students with multiple opportunities for self-assessment. You may also wish to use some of the activities to assess specific skills, such as speaking, listening, or cooperative learning.

Objectives

- To allow students to reflect on and assess their understanding of theme
- To allow students to reflect on and assess their understanding of literary concepts, such as point of view and characterization
- To provides students with the opportunity to assess and build their portfolios

REFLECTING ON THEME

OPTION 1

Begin this task with a brief discussion. What is a friend? What is a foe? How do you interpret the expression "The enemy of your enemy is your friend"? Can there be friendly enemies or hostile friends? If so, what might explain such a situation? Encourage students to explore and discover their feelings as they make their choices of friends and foes from the characters in the selections.

OPTION 2

Review the concept of struggle, making connections to characters in Unit One as well as Unit Two. Have students skim the selections and jot down the struggles, arranging them in a hierarchy from most inspiring to least inspiring. Suggest that a friendly, conversational tone may be appropriate for these expressions of admiration and support.

OPTION 3

Remind students to share the connections they made between the quotation and the selections and also to discuss its application to their own lives.

Self–Assessment

Encourage students to make a rough outline of the various characters and their struggles. When they write their profiles, the notes in the outline should be helpful. Students need not choose a character about whom to write, but they should use details from the selections to support their ideas about valuable qualities in times of stress.

REFLECT & ASSESS

UNIT TWO: TRIALS AND TRIBULATIONS

Has reading the selections in this unit given you any new insights about friendship or about dealing with obstacles? Choose one or more of the options in each of the following sections to help you demonstrate the insights you have gained.

REFLECTING ON THEME

OPTION 1 **Assigning Labels** As you found out in Part 1 of this unit, determining whether someone is a friend or a foe can be tricky. Of the characters in this unit, whom would you probably be friends with? Who would be your enemy? In a few paragraphs, explain your choice of friends and foes from the characters in the unit.

OPTION 2 **Appreciating the Effort** Think about whom or what each of the main characters in Part 2 of the unit is up against. Then decide which three or four of the characters' and authors' struggles you find the most inspiring. Write a brief personal letter of support to each of those characters or authors, expressing your feelings about their accomplishments and explaining why you are so impressed.

OPTION 3 **Discussing the Quotation** With a small group of classmates, discuss the meaning of the quotation from Frederick Douglass at the beginning of the unit. Cite some of the moral and physical struggles in the selections to support your interpretation, but also be prepared to include examples from your own experience or the experiences of people you know.

Self-Assessment: Using examples of behavior and character from the selections in this unit, write a short profile of the kind of person you now believe stands the best chance of triumphing in times of stress and conflict.

REVIEWING LITERARY CONCEPTS

OPTION 1 **Evaluating Point of View** Some of the stories and poems in this unit are written from the first-person point of view; others are written from the third-person point of view. To survey the different points of view in the selections, make two lists. First list the titles of all the selections told from the first-person point of view, then list the titles of all the selections told from the third-person point of view. Circle the titles of the selections in which you think the choice of point of view had a major influence on your understanding and enjoyment.

334 UNIT TWO: TRIALS AND TRIBULATIONS

OPTION 2 **Analyzing Characterization** As you know, a writer can develop a character through (1) physical description, (2) the character's speech, thoughts, feelings, and actions, (3) the speech, thoughts, feelings, and actions of other characters, and (4) direct comments about the character's nature. From the selections you've read in this unit, choose five or six main characters that you find most interesting. Then, in a chart like the one shown, identify an important trait of each character and the method of characterization that was used to convey that trait. After you've filled in your chart, ask yourself, Did I respond more to one method of characterization than to the others?

Character/ Selection	Character Trait	Method of Characterization
Narrator/"The Day the Cisco Kid Shot John Wayne"	tough and smart	his own speech, thoughts, and actions

PORTFOLIO BUILDING

- **QuickWrites** For some of the QuickWrites in this unit, you wrote about how you would handle trials and tribulations of life. Choose one or two of the responses that you think best convey your thoughts on the subject, and write a cover note explaining your choice. Attach the note to your writing and add both to your portfolio.
- **Writing About Literature** When you explored your responses to one of the selections in this unit after several readings, did you find that your opinion changed, or did each reading strengthen your first impression? Write a note summarizing your response and attach it to your essay.
- **Writing from Experience** You have now written an essay to persuade others to agree with your position on an important issue. Show your essay to several people, keeping a record of how many it influences to support your position. Attach a note to your essay, describing the level of your success.
- **Personal Choice** Look back through your records and evaluations of the activities you completed for

Self-Assessment: Did you find that you are comfortable enough with the concepts of point of view and characterization to be able to complete Options 1 and 2? On a sheet of paper, copy the following literary terms introduced in this unit, but list them in order of difficulty. Write down what you think are the easiest concepts first, and put at the bottom of the list the concepts that you're still not quite sure of.

imagery   flashback
metaphor   biography
pun   personification
theme

this unit and through the writing you completed for the unit and on your own. Which work were you most satisfied with? Write a note explaining your thoughts, attach it to the writing or activity record, and add both to your portfolio.

Self-Assessment: Now that you have some pieces in your portfolio, notice which kinds of writing contain your strongest work. What other kinds of writing would you like to try as the year goes on?

SETTING GOALS

Look back through your portfolio, worksheets, and notebook. What did you learn that might help you in your own life? Create a short list of ideas—such as friendship or conflict resolution—that you are interested in learning more about as you complete the next unit.

REVIEWING LITERARY CONCEPTS

OPTION 1
Once students have made their lists, you might have a whole-class discussion, so that they can share their ideas about the importance of a specific point of view to a particular selection. You might spark discussion by asking students for their ideas about how the selections might have been changed if written from another point of view.

OPTION 2
Encourage students to work with partners to develop their charts. If they responded to one method of characterization rather than to another, does that preference relate to their preference for a particular point of view? For example, students who prefer learning about characters from the characters' own words and thoughts may enjoy first-person narratives. See also Unit Two Resource Book, p. 71.

Self-Assessment Have students define each term for themselves, without looking in the dictionary. Then have them check their definitions to see how well they comprehend each term. Students can then identify one instance of each element in the selections in this unit.

PORTFOLIO BUILDING

You may wish to help students choose or modify options, to suit the needs you have established for the class. Encourage students to incorporate drafts, not just final products, into their portfolios, so that they can reflect on and assess their development and progress.

Self-Assessment Encourage students to consider the rewards of focusing on writing that seems difficult or problematic. Invite them to reflect on and assess their strengths as writers and to apply their particular skills to all writing assignments. Tell them that especially good and strong writing probably results from strong interest in particular topics; when reviewing their writing, they should consider what stimulated them to make their best efforts.

SETTING GOALS
Suggest that developing a friendship or resolving a conflict is like the process of developing one's strengths as a writer. Underlying all three processes is the notion of building confidence, which all people need to overcome the trials and tribulations of life.

UNIT THREE

UNIT THREE

UNIT THEMES

Unit Three

All in the Family In this unit, students will read selections that explore the pain and the joy involved in family relationships. The unit contains two parts: Part 1, "Mixed Blessings," and Part 2, "On Your Own Terms." Selections in both parts contribute to the unit theme by recounting the close family relationships, both supportive and restrictive, of a variety of characters.

Part 1

Mixed Blessings Selections in Part 1 highlight tensions among family members. For example, in "Marine Corps Issue," a boy comes to an understanding of his withdrawn father by attempting to learn the truth about his father's never-discussed Vietnam War experiences.

Part 2

On Your Own Terms Selections in Part 2 explore characters' attempts to establish identities of their own, beyond their family roles. For example, in "Only Daughter," a girl becomes a professional writer rather than the wife and mother her father expected her to become.

All in the Family

Call it a clan,

call it a network,

call it a tribe,

call it a family.

Whatever you call it,

whoever you are,

you need one.

Jane Howard
Journalist and lecturer

Family (1992), Varnette P. Honeywood. Collage, Copyright © 1992 Varnette P. Honeywood.

Exploring Theme

To help students explore the connections between the art, the quotation, and the unit theme, have them consider the following questions:

1. Do you think family relationships constitute a theme worth exploring? Why or why not? *(Possible response: yes, because we are all members of families and can apply this theme to our own lives)*

2. How would you define the word *one* at the end of Jane Howard's statement? *(Possible response: The word refers to a group—whatever it's called—that gives an individual moral guidance, education, love, and security.)*

3. What does the collage suggest about family relationships? *(Possible response: that family members provide one another with love and support)*

4. What kinds of stories might you expect to read in this unit? *(Possible response: stories about families; stories that detail characters' experiences in coping with family members; stories about the importance of families)*

5. Discuss a particular experience of your own that taught you something about the impact that family members can have on a person's life. *(Responses will vary.)*

Art Note

Family by Varnette P. Honeywood
Varnette Honeywood, the grandniece of stonemason and sculptor Ozzie Allen, was born in California in 1950. Her interest in collage art began when she was designing posters, in junior high school, for the after-school and summer playground activities taught by her father. In her work, she turns again and again to the theme of family and community life. During the 1980s, Honeywood lectured at Spelman College in Atlanta and held a one-woman show there. At about this time, Honeywood met comedian Bill Cosby, and throughout the episodes of *The Cosby Show,* a reproduction of her painting *Birthday* hung in the Huxtables' living-room set.

Reading the Art *What can you infer about the relationships between these four people? What details support your opinion?*

UNIT THREE
Part 1 Skills Trace

(ML) DENOTES MINI-LESSON IN TEACHER'S EDITION

Selections	Reading Skills and Strategies	Literary Concepts	Writing Opportunities	Speaking, Listening, and Viewing
FICTION **Marine Corps Issue** David McLean	Understanding cause and effect, PE p. 339	Flashback, PE p. 356 Suspense, PE p. 356 Reviewing first-person point of view, (ML) TE p. 349	Write copy for a follow-up field manual, PE p. 356 Write a personal letter, PE p. 356 Write a eulogy or tribute, PE p. 356 Purpose, (ML) TE p. 342	Deliver a eulogy, PE p. 356 Present a short oral report, PE p. 357 Dramatic performance, (ML) TE p. 347
POETRY **Lineage** Margaret Walker **The Courage That My Mother Had** Edna St. Vincent Millay		Alliteration, PE p. 362 Repetition, PE p. 362 Poetry, (ML) TE p. 360 Reviewing imagery and figurative language, (ML) TE p. 361	Write about a special ancestor, PE p. 359 Write a will, PE p. 362 Write a poem, PE p. 362 Write a brief reply, PE p. 362	Small group discussion, PE p. 362
FICTION **The Warriors** Anna Lee Walters	Making inferences about characters, PE p. 365 Using a reading log, PE p. 365	External conflict, PE p. 378 Internal conflict, PE p. 378 Tone, PE p. 378 Fiction, (ML) TE p. 370 Reviewing characterization, (ML) TE p. 371	Make a list, PE p. 378 Write a different ending, PE p. 378 Write a eulogy, PE p. 378 Brainstorm ten commandments "Live Beautifully," PE p. 378	Choose film music for listening, (ML) TE p. 373 Oral presentation, TE p. 379
POETRY **My Papa's Waltz** Theodore Roethke **Touch Football** Jack Driscoll	Recognizing imagery, PE p. 380	Simile, PE p. 383 Rhyme, PE p. 383	Write a detective's report, PE p. 383 Write a description, PE p. 383 Compile a list, PE p. 383 Write a dialogue between two characters, TE p. 384 Description of setting and stage, TE p. 384	Compare lists, PE p. 383 Oral interpretation, (ML) TE p. 382 Oral presentation, TE p. 384
DRAMA **A Marriage Proposal** Anton Chekhov		Foreshadowing, PE p. 399 Mood, PE p. 399 Drama, (ML) TE p. 387 Reviewing rising action, (ML) TE p. 390	Create a recipe for proposal of marriage, PE p. 385 Using dialogue in plays and skits, (ML) TE p. 394 Prepare a list of reasons, (ML) TE p. 400	Perform readers theater, PE p. 399 Pantomime, (ML) TE p. 395
NONFICTION ON YOUR OWN **Father's Day** Michael Dorris				Paired and grouped reading, TE p. 401 Debate, TE p. 402

Writing	Reading Skills and Strategies	Literary Concepts	Writing Opportunities	Speaking, Listening, and Viewing
WRITING ABOUT LITERATURE **Interpretation**	Understanding main idea, PE pp. 404–405 Responding to literature, PE pp. 406–409	Understanding main idea, PE pp. 404–405 Theme, PE pp. 406–407	Write a topic sentence, PE p. 405 Make the main idea clear, PE p. 405 Share an idea, PE p. 405 Interpretive essay, PE pp. 406–409 Writing introductions, PE p. 407	Viewing an object, PE p. 411 Interpreting an object, PE p. 411 Discussion, PE p. 411 Discussing experiences, PE p. 411

Grammar, Usage, Mechanics, and Spelling	Multimodal Learning	Research and Study Skills	Vocabulary
Participles, ML TE p. 344	Eulogy, PE p. 356 Sketch or painting of two images, PE p. 357 Design and write a message for a greeting card, PE p. 357 Present short oral report, PE p. 357	Investigate the regulations governing international prisoners of war, PE p. 357 Skimming, ML TE p. 357 Research Hague Convention/Geneva Convention, TE p. 357	agitated disjunction animosity grotesque demeanor intrigue deprivation trepidation devoid vulnerability
	Set two poems to music or dramatic readings, PE p. 363 Create a work of art, PE p. 365 Tape-record or write a family record, of an interview, PE p. 363		
Combining sentences with *who*, *which*, or *that*, ML TE p. 374 Clauses, ML TE p. 375	Design a warrior shield, PE p. 379 Create a design on computer, PE p. 379 Read a book by a Native American, PE p. 379 Create visual aids, TE p. 379 Encyclopedia, PE p. 379 Teaching others, ML TE p. 366 Choose film music, ML TE p. 373	Encyclopedia: Research alcoholism, PE p. 379	fantasize haggard obsessively ravage retort
	Chart, TE p. 383 Oral presentation, TE p. 384 Develop comparative rule books for each sport, TE p. 384 Choose music as background for "Touch Football," TE p. 384	Research history of the waltz, TE p. 384 Research origins and regulations of American football, rugby, and soccer, TE p. 384	
Possessive pronouns, ML TE p. 392	Create a program for performance, PE p. 400 Cast play with TV or movie actors, PE p. 400 Negotiating, ML TE p. 393 Choose music by 19th-century Russian composers, TE p.400 Locate copy of playbill, TE p. 400	Research social structure in Russia during late 1880s, TE p. 400	appropriate contrary dumbfounded palpitation usurper
	Creating a greeting card, TE p. 402		

Grammar, Usage, Mechanics, and Spelling	Multimodal Learning	Research and Study Skills	Media Literacy
Varying sentence beginnings, PE p. 405 Achieving verb agreement with compound subjects, PE p. 409	Viewing an object or situation, PE p. 411 Interpreting an object or situation, PE p. 411 Discussion, PE p. 411 Discussing experiences, PE p. 411	Interpreting literature, PE pp. 406–409 Interpreting experiences, PE p. 411	Interpreting an object or situation, PE p. 411

UNIT THREE
Part 2 Skills Trace

ML DENOTES MINI-LESSON IN TEACHER'S EDITION

Selections	Reading Skills and Strategies	Literary Concepts	Writing Opportunities	Speaking, Listening, and Viewing
FICTION **The Scarlet Ibis** James Hurst	Understanding exposition, PE p. 413 Using a reading log, PE p. 413	Symbol, PE p. 427 Foreshadowing, PE p. 427 Reviewing mood, **ML** TE p. 419 Fiction, **ML** TE p. 420	Create a diary entry, PE p. 426 Write analysis as interview, PE p. 426 Write an interpretation, PE p. 426 Using repeated words to build coherence, **ML** TE p. 422	Stage a trial, PE p. 426 Present a soliloquy, PE p. 427
NONFICTION **from Black Boy** Richard Wright		Dialogue, PE p. 435 Metaphor, PE p. 435 Reviewing author's purpose, **ML** TE p. 432	Comment on other people's reactions to your aspirations, PE p. 429 Write a letter of recommendation, PE p. 435 Write thoughts, PE p. 435 Write a brief story, PE p. 435 List events and influences, PE p. 435 Compose blues or rap song, PE p. 436	Compare lists, PE p. 435 Present an oral report, PE p. 436
NONFICTION **Only Daughter** Sandra Cisneros	Understanding generalizations, PE p. 437	Theme, PE p. 441	Write a dialogue, PE p. 441 Write your own biographical sketch, PE p. 441 Write a proverb, PE p. 441 Make notes for an essay, PE p. 441	Compare ideas, PE p. 441
POETRY **Theme for English B** Langston Hughes **The Writer** Richard Wilbur	Movies of the mind, PE p. 444 Using a reading log, PE p. 444	Stanza, PE p. 449 Reviewing free verse, **ML** TE p. 445	Give a grade and comments, PE p. 449 Write a page of poetry or prose, PE p. 449	Class discussion, PE p. 449 Reading of "Movie of the Mind," PE p. 449 Present poll results, TE p. 450
FICTION **Lakshmi** Vasanthi Victor		Description, PE p. 460 Reviewing tone, **ML** TE p. 459	Write about someone you like/others misunderstand, PE p. 452 Write a brief character sketch, PE p. 460 Write a letter, PE p. 460 List of character traits, PE p. 460 Use chronological transitions, **ML** TE p. 456	Share choices, PE p. 460 Present oral report, PE p. 461 Storytelling, **ML** TE p. 455
NONFICTION ON YOUR OWN **Fish Eyes** David Brenner			Dialogue journal, TE p. 462	Reading aloud, TE p. 462 Performing a stand-up comedy act, TE p. 465
Writing	**Reading Skills and Strategies**	**Literary Concepts**	**Writing Opportunities**	**Speaking, Listening, and Viewing**
WRITING FROM EXPERIENCE **Firsthand and Expressive Writing**			Writing about a personal experience, PE pp. 468–475 Drafting, PE pp. 472–473 Using transitions to show time order, PE p. 473 Revising and publishing, PE pp. 474–475	Audiotape, PE p. 475 Interviewing, PE p. 471 Oral history, **ML** TE p. 470

Grammar, Usage, Mechanics, and Spelling	Multimodal Learning	Research and Study Skills	Vocabulary
Infinitives, ML TE p. 416	Create a map, PE p. 427	Research ibises, PE p. 428 Using a Venn diagram, ML TE p. 423	careen infallibility doggedness invalid exotic iridescent heresy precariously imminent reiterate
Vary sentence length and structure, ML TE p. 431	Oral report, PE p. 436	Research Jim Crow laws, PE p. 436 Writing press releases, ML TE p. 434	alien relent articulate mode hedge naive heedless speculate intuitively stifle
Using *who* and *whom*, ML TE p. 439	Interview for ideas about gender roles, PE p. 442	Research gender roles, PE p. 442 Research a different culture, TE p. 442 Research childhood of favorite author, TE p. 442	anthology embroider fulfilled nostalgia trauma
Using vivid verbs, ML TE p. 448	Create a drawing, painting, or sculpture, PE p. 450 Conduct a poll, PE p. 450 Make a graph, TE p. 450		
Subject/verb agreement with *here* and *there*, ML TE p. 454	Create a mandala, PE p. 461 Oral report, PE p. 461 Encyclopedias of mythology, TE p. 461	Research the goddess Lakshmi, PE p. 461	afflicted insipid congregate murky diligence pliant eccentricity prudent escapade skeptical
	Designing a practical joke invention, TE p. 464		

Grammar, Usage, Mechanics, and Spelling	Multimodal Learning	Research and Study Skills	Media Literacy
Using transitions to show time order, PE p. 473 Avoiding shifts in tenses, PE p. 475	Analyzing data and graphs, PE pp. 468–469 Interpreting a comic strip, PE p. 468 Interpreting a poem, PE p. 469		Analyzing data and graphs, PE pp. 468–469 Interpreting a comic strip, PE p. 468 Interpreting a poem, PE p. 469

UNIT THREE
Recommended Resources

ENRICHMENT   RESEARCH

✓ Recommended Novels

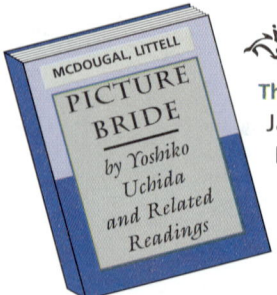

LITERATURE CONNECTIONS WITH SOURCEBOOK FOR TEACHERS

Thematic Link In this novel, a young Japanese woman emigrates to San Francisco to join the fiancé who chose her from a photograph. Once the arranged marriage takes place, the "picture bride" adapts to America on her own terms as her expectations change.

About the Author Yoshiko Uchida (1921–1992) was a novelist and short story writer whose work reflects her deep concern for Japanese and Japanese-American people.

Other Works by Yoshiko Uchida *The Dancing Kettle, The Magic Listening Cap, Takao and Grandfather's Sword, Sumi's Prize, A Jar of Dreams, Desert Exile*

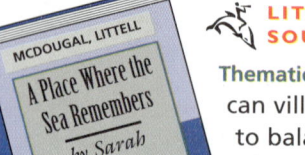

LITERATURE CONNECTIONS WITH SOURCEBOOK FOR TEACHERS

Thematic Link In this novel about a Mexican village, several characters are forced to balance their own desires and family demands as they try to determine what really matters.

About the Author Raised in Mexico, El Salvador, and the Midwest, Sandra Benitez is a versatile writer who, besides publishing both fiction and essays, also teaches creative writing.

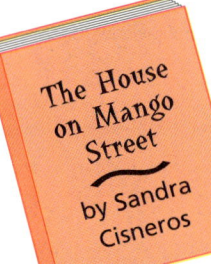

Thematic Link This popular novel follows the trials and tribulations of a young girl growing up in a traditional Latino family in Chicago.

About the Author (born 1954) In addition to being a writer, Sandra Cisneros has worked as a college recruiter and an arts administrator. Her writing is especially popular for its liveliness and color.

Other Work by Sandra Cisneros *My Wicked Ways*

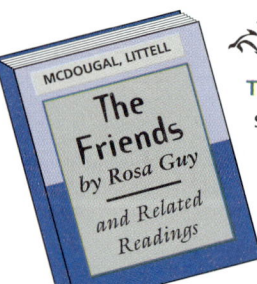

LITERATURE CONNECTIONS WITH SOURCEBOOK FOR TEACHERS

Thematic Link This novel deals with three sets of complicated and painful relationships. As the main character, Phyllisa, struggles toward a true friendship with a classmate, she must cope with an overbearing father and a dying mother.

About the Author Rosa Guy (born 1928) often writes about African-American teenagers, and her books appeal to readers of all ages. She has traveled extensively throughout Africa and the West Indies to study African history and culture.

Other Works by Rosa Guy *Edith Jackson, The Disappearance, Mirror of Her Own, A Measure of Time, New Guys Around the Block, My Love, My Love: or The Peasant Girl*

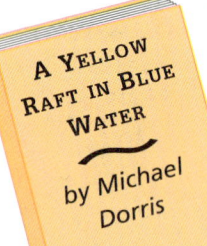

Thematic Link A young man comes into his own as he begins to understand his true family ties.

About the Author A member of the Modoc tribe, Michael Dorris (born 1945) has fought all his life for Native American rights. Native American traditions are the foundation of his work.

Other Works by Michael Dorris *The Broken Cord, The Crown of Columbus* (with Louise Erdrich)

Professional Development — TEACHING THE NOVEL

Brown, Joseph Epes. *The Spiritual Legacy of the American Indian.* NY: Crossroad, 1995.

Dorris, Michael. *Paper Trail: Essays.* NY: Harper Perennial, 1979.

Dwyer, Augusta. *On the Line—Life on the U.S.-Mexican Border.* Nottingham, England: LAB, Russel Press, 1994.

Gates, Henry Louis, Jr., ed. *Black Literature and Literary Theory.* NY: Routledge, 1990.

Lesley, Craig. "Characteristics of Contemporary Native American Literature," *Emerging Voices.* NY: Harcourt Brace Jovanovich, 1993.

Turkov, Andrei. *Anton Chekhov and His Times.* Fayetteville, AK: University of Arkansas Press, 1995.

CROSS-CURRICULAR TEACHING   PROFESSIONAL DEVELOPMENT

Recommended Readings in Cross-Curricular Areas

SOCIAL STUDIES

Passing Time: Memoir of a Vietnam Veteran Against the War by W.D. Ehrhart (1986) Generally considered one of the most moving portraits of personal experience in Vietnam. Links to David McLean's "Marine Corps Issue."

Native American Traditions by Arthur Versluis (1994) A powerful pictorial journey through variations on Native American traditions and beliefs. Links to Anna Lee Walters's "The Warriors" and Michael Dorris's "Father's Day."

Mexico: A History by Robert Ryal Miller (1985) Offers a solid foundation for understanding the context of Mexican thought and life. Links to Sandra Cisneros's "Only Daughter."

Professional Development — CROSS-CURRICULAR INSTRUCTION

Davis, Vivian I. "Working Toward Language-Centered Writing and Literature Courses," *English Journal* 84:1 (January 1995) 35.

Hobbs, Tony, ed. *Experiential Training.* NY: Routledge, 1992.

Lightfoot, Sara Lawrence. *The Good High School.* NY: HarperCollins, 1983.

Noskin, David, and Marshalek, Angela. "Applying Multiculturalism to a High School American Literature Course: Changing Lenses," *English Journal* 84:6 (October 1995).

Recommended Media Resources

THE LANGUAGE OF LITERATURE

ELECTRONIC LIBRARY
CD-ROM
Additional literature selections for Unit Three can be found on the Electronic Library CD-ROM.

LASERLINKS
Videodisc, Gr. 9
See *LaserLinks Teacher's Source Book*, pages 26–27, for overview of Unit Three.

AUDIO LIBRARY
Tapes
Unit Three: All in the Family
Gr. 9, Tapes 8–10, Sides A & B

WRITING COACH
Writing Coach Software: Writing About Literature—Interpretive Response, Personal Narrative

OUTSIDE RESOURCES

Films/Videos/Film Strips/Audiocassettes
Anton Chekhov: A Writer's Life, video, Films for the Humanities & Sciences, 1974. (37 minutes)
Richard Wright: Black Boy, video, California Newsreel, 1995.
Margaret Walker Reads, audiocassette, American Audio Prose Library.
Sandra Cisneros Reads, 2 audiocassettes, Random House. (3 hours)

Internet Resources
McDougal Littell Literature Center at http://www.hmco.com/mcdougal/lit

Professional Development — TEACHING WITH TECHNOLOGY

Kinnaman, Daniel E., and Dyrli, Odvard Egil. "Gaining Access to Technology: First Step in Making a Difference for Your Students," *Technology & Learning* 14:16 (January 1994) 7.

Mageau, Therese, and Chion-Kenney, Linda. "Facing the Future," *Electronic Learning* 14 (October 1994) 37–40.

Technology and Learning. Peter Li Educational Group. 300 Progress Road, Dayton, OH 45449.

RECOMMENDED RESOURCES TEACHER'S EDITION **337f**

UNIT THREE
Professional Enrichment

The Reader as Problem-Maker: Responding to a Poem with Questions
Carl Leggo

> This intriguing idea can be used in the study of poetry found in Unit 3 and other units.

FOUR KINDS OF READERS

One of the most prevalent weaknesses of students' responses to poetry is the persistent tendency to closure. Patrick Dias describes four kinds of readers: paraphrasers, thematizers, allegorizers, and problem-solvers (1986, "Making Sense of Poetry: Patterns of Response among Canadian and British Secondary School Pupils," *English in Education* 20.2 [Sum.]: 44-52.) Paraphrasers seldom push "beyond the literal meaning of the poem." Thematizers seek to "crack the code" of the poem and conceptualize a general theme about "Life, Nature, Man, Animals, Landscapes, or Loneliness." Allegorizers are intent on exercising ingenuity "to work out the equivalences between the poem and life," even if their ingenuity requires twisting "the text to fit the meaning they are creating." Paraphrasers, thematizers, and allegorizers are all motivated by the desire to consume the poem, to close off the encounter with the text. Problem-solvers, on the other hand, refuse "to settle immediately on meaning" and are "tentative in their formulations of meaning" because "for them, a poem is never ever fully understood."

I not only endorse Dias's conclusions, but I am also concerned that students frequently reflect their teachers' reading orientations. In other words, students learn to read poetry from experiencing the ways teachers read poetry, and teachers are often paraphrasers, thematizers, and allegorizers intent on revealing the meaning (perhaps hidden or purposely obscure or needlessly obfuscated but nonetheless decipherable) and closing down the transaction with the text.

Needed are reading strategies that defer closure and promote openness in the encounter with poems. Therefore, while I applaud Dias's research and insights, I question his term "problem-solvers" because it still suggests that a poem is a puzzle that can be solved and closed. I prefer the label "problem-makers" because it implies a refusal to invite closure. I recommend an approach to reading a poem which treats the poem as an expansive space to romp and play in, to explore and travel in. The responsive reader is a problem-maker. In order to help readers become more responsive, more willing to engage in a performance of the poem, they must be encouraged to spend time with the poem. One way to foster reading as problem-making is to invite readers to pose their initial responses in the form of questions, lists, and lists of questions which do not need to be ordered or categorized. Instead of expressing their interaction with a poem in declarative sentences which posit statements and conclusions (however inconclusive), readers can compile a lengthy and wide-ranging list of questions generated by reading and rereading the poem.

AN ILLUSTRATION OF PROBLEM-MAKING

During the school year 1989 to 1990 I taught English at Herdman Collegiate in Corner Brook, Newfoundland. For several lessons I invited my students to respond with questions to several of my poems. One lesson was focused on the following poem:

I Still Hear the Bell Ringing
*On long walks from Crescent Pond
in cool/warm Mays on the keen edge
of promised summer (our creels
heavy with a dozen trout more
than the law permitted) my father
offered the only advice I remember:*

*Take your garbage home,
and in my knapsack, then and now,
empty Vienna sausage cans,
wax paper, pop bottles*

*If you don't know a word,
look it up in a dictionary,
strong advice, for now I know
many words and in words I am known*

*Never hate anybody,
wisdom like an iron bell ringing
from a gray sky, its echoes
heard through the years*

*Never hate anybody
    Never hate anybody
My one wish (who needs three?):
on long walks from Crescent Pond
through the dense spruce, across the bog
on a trail only my father could see,
I wish he had taught me how*

After I read the poem to the students, I asked them to respond to it with questions. I advised them to ask questions about *anything*. I explained that the purpose of the exercise was to generate questions as paths into the poem, as ways to explore the significance of the poem. There was some initial confusion and hesitation: "Just ask questions? About anything? Are you sure?" But my students accepted the invitation and produced lists of questions that clearly indicated they were responding to the poem from many different perspectives....

1. What does the bell ringing have to do with the poem?
2. How come you named the poem "I

Still Hear the Bell Ringing" when it only refers to it once?
3. Where is Crescent Pond?
4. What does "our creels heavy with a dozen trout" mean?
5. How come at one point you're talking about fish and garbage and then turn around and start talking about words in dictionaries?
6. What does "in words I am known" mean?
7. How come you say "never hate anybody" twice together?
8. Was this poem really about your father taking you on fishing trips?
9. What do you wish your father had taught you?
10. Is your father dead, or did you just put the poem in the past tense?
11. What do you mean when you say "take your garbage home, then and now"?
12. How come you wrote the poem in the way it's written?
13. Was Crescent Pond far from civilization?
14. What does "wisdom like an iron bell ringing" mean?
15. Why did you divide cool and warm with a "/"?
16. Why would your father let you take more fish than the law permitted?
17. Was that the only advice your father gave you?
18. Was Crescent Pond surrounded by a forest or just some trees?
19. Was it only you that your father took fishing?
20. How does a dictionary give "strong advice"?
21. Is it legal to trout that early in the year?
22. What does "on the keen edge" mean?
23. Would the bell act as a guide to people (or you) further in life?
24. Why would your father tell you to take home garbage? Wouldn't you have enough sense to do it anyway?
25. Why is this poem one long sentence?
26. Why does he refer to the father's wisdom as a ringing iron bell?
27. What does wisdom have to do with an iron bell?
28. Why did you use brackets in this poem?
29. Why is the poem written in this shape and with this arrangement?
30. What bell is the writer hearing ring?
31. How can you walk on the keen edge of promised summer?
32. How old is the writer in the poem?
33. What are creels?
34. What is the setting of the poem?
35. Who is the speaker?
36. How do the stanzas relate to one another?
37. Is this a true story?
38. What are "cool/warm Mays"?
39. Does the son receive all the advice at once?
40. Why don't you have a period at the end?
41. Why did you indent the first two lines in the third paragraph?
42. How come his father was the only one who could see the trail?
43. Why did you exceed the trout limit?
44. What does the author wish his father had taught him how to do?
45. What is the father like?
46. How much time has passed since the words of advice were given?
47. Why did you use colons?
48. Who is the "I" in the poem?
49. Does the trail symbolize something? Does the trail have a meaning?
50. Why did the poet ask only one wish and not three?
51. What is the theme of the poem?
52. Why is the sky gray and not blue?
53. Where did the author get the similes (like an iron bell)?
54. Why did you write this poem?
55. Why doesn't this poem rhyme?

RESPONDING BY QUESTIONING

In discussing with students their experiences of this strategy for responding to a poem as questioners, as problem-makers, there was a consensus of opinion that the approach was nonthreatening, even fun. Many of them expressed surprise at how many questions they asked. I was especially pleased with the wide range of questions. Semantic, syntactic, and prosodic questions were intermingled with personal and reflective questions. There was no neat pattern to the questions. Some students spoke about the sense of freedom that they enjoyed during the process of questioning. They did not feel any pressure to produce the correct answers. One student observed, "With each new question I felt like I was opening up another window on the poem."

After compiling the list of questions, my students and I confronted the issue of what to do with the questions. We decided to do nothing. We agreed that students are required to answer too many questions. Too many students grow up with the mistaken notion that all questions have answers, that questions are meant to be answered. The advantages of doing nothing with the questions are multiple: the poem remains open, the questions hint at tantalizing ideas and experiences and people and places to pursue, and the questioner remains open.

By suggesting that the questions do not need to be answered, I am not proposing that students will not eventually engage in other kinds of more definitive responses. But as an initial strategy for encouraging an active participation with a text, I think the exercise of asking questions without seeking conclusions can motivate more readers to be problem-makers. And schools need to celebrate problem-makers.

Copyrighted material reprinted with permission.

UNIT THREE
Starting Points for Unit Projects

The following suggestions will help you initiate individual and group projects during the course of this unit.

Creating a Photo Album

ART PROJECT Ask students to make a photo album or scrapbook that shows the diverse relationships between members of their family. Students may want to include old family photographs, photographs they have taken themselves, cards, drawings, and small mementos such as scraps of fabric or ribbons. Students should include labels that indicate the special significance of each item in their scrapbooks.

Cooking a Meal

HOME ECONOMICS PROJECT Have students take turns cooking and sharing family recipes or their favorite dishes with the rest of the class, or have them organize a potluck lunch. Students may contribute ideas, then work in groups to concoct one of the suggested recipe ideas. If students wish, they may write down their favorite recipes on cards to share with classmates.

Painting a Mural

GROUP ART PROJECT Have students work together in groups to design a colorful mural representing the family relationships depicted in this unit and in their own lives. Each group may want to plan out part of a class mural, or each group may create a separate mural.

Researching Family Characteristics

RESEARCH PROJECT Have students research the characteristics of families worldwide. What are their differing structures and the varied roles assumed by their members? What family traditions are most prevalent? How does family size vary? In groups, have students make comparative charts illustrating the differences between families around the world. For example, in one column they might have "Native American Families," in another "Japanese Families," and so on. In each column, they may want to affix photographs or images from magazines.

Writing an Illustrated Report

GROUP RESEARCH PROJECT Have small groups of students explore the concept of family in the animal kingdom. Ask students to consider the following questions in their research: Are there any species that live in what could be considered "families"? What advantages could there be in maintaining a family structure in the wild? Why do students think that humans are different from animals in their approach to family? What are the most significant differences (for example, in child-rearing, group unity, loyalty, and so on)? Have students present some of their findings in a creative illustrated report.

Making an Audiotape

MUSIC PROJECT Have students collect ideas from friends and family members and compile a music tape. Have them ask each person to contribute a favorite song to the tape. Using recording materials available to them, students should put together a "Best of Friends and Family" tape to play for the class. Along with the tape, have them put together a brief booklet that explains why the song each person chose is his or her favorite.

Family and Community Involvement

✓ Family

The selections in Unit Three portray a variety of families and important events that bring them closer or pull them apart. The following activities will help students and their families explore the impact of families on individual lives.

OPTION 1: CONDUCT A CONFERENCE
- **Connection** The selections in Unit Three explore how family members relate to one another.
- **Activity** *Copymaster 1* Students can plan a conference with family members to discuss ways in which conflicts, especially between siblings, can be resolved.

OPTION 2: WRITE AN ANECDOTE
- **Connection** Some of the selections in Unit Three describe touching, emotional, and sometimes funny episodes from family life.
- **Activity** *Copymaster 2* Students and family members should recall anecdotes about memorable family episodes, especially those that were funny. The anecdotes can be written or tape recorded by the student or another family member.

OPTION 3: WATCH A VIDEO
- **Connection** "Fish Eyes" and "The Scarlet Ibis" explore the relationships among family members.
- **Activity** *Copymaster 3* Students and family members should watch a movie such as *Parenthood* or *Avalon* that portrays the relationships among family members. They can discuss what arguments the family members had and what memorable experiences they shared.

✓ Community

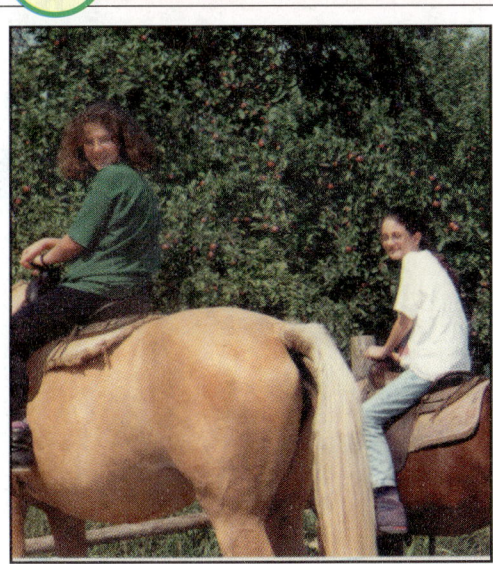

OPTION 1
- **Connection** The selections in Unit Three examine relationships between generations within families.
- **Activity** Invite a member of a Native American group, or any other ethnic group, to talk about the importance of passing traditions, lore, and cultural knowledge from generation to generation. Discuss the importance of family and cultural identity.

OPTION 2
- **Connection** Some of the selections in Unit Three explore how families handle difficult or painful memories.
- **Activity** Invite a war veteran, preferably from the Vietnam War, to speak to the class about his or her experiences. Discuss why some war experiences are difficult to share and are also difficult for family members to understand.

OPTION 3
- **Connection** Some of the selections in Unit Three explore the difficulties some family members have in going their own way, apart from the rest of the family.
- **Activity** Arrange to visit a small, family-owned business in the community. Have students talk with the owner and other family members about the rewards and difficulties of running a family business.

UNIT THREE
Part 1 Lesson Planner

TIME ALLOTMENTS SHOWN ARE APPROXIMATE. DEPENDING ON YOUR GOALS AND THE NEEDS OF YOUR STUDENTS, YOU MAY WISH TO ALLOW MORE OR LESS TIME FOR CERTAIN PORTIONS OF THE LESSON.

Table of Contents	Discussion	Previewing the Selection	Reading the Selection
PART OPENER **Mixed Blessings** page 336	**20 MINUTES** • Reflect on the part theme		
SELECTION **Marine Corps Issue** page 340 AVERAGE		**20 MINUTES** • PERSONAL CONNECTION • HISTORICAL CONNECTION • READING CONNECTION: Understanding cause and effect	**60 MINUTES** • Introduce vocabulary • Read pp. 340–355 (16 pp.)
SELECTIONS **Lineage/The Courage That My Mother Had** page 360 AVERAGE		**20 MINUTES** • PERSONAL CONNECTION • BIOGRAPHICAL CONNECTION • WRITING CONNECTION	**10 MINUTES** • Read pp. 360–361 (2 pp.)
SELECTION **The Warriors** page 366 EASY		**20 MINUTES** • PERSONAL CONNECTION • HISTORICAL CONNECTION • READING CONNECTION: Making inferences about characters	**50 MINUTES** • Introduce vocabulary • Read pp. 366–377 (12 pp.)
SELECTIONS **My Papa's Waltz/ Touch Football** page 381 AVERAGE		**20 MINUTES** • PERSONAL CONNECTION • BIOGRAPHICAL CONNECTION • READING CONNECTION: Recognizing imagery	**10 MINUTES** • Read pp. 381–382 (2 pp.)
SELECTION **A Marriage Proposal** page 386 AVERAGE		**20 MINUTES** • PERSONAL CONNECTION • LITERARY CONNECTION • WRITING CONNECTION	**50 MINUTES** • Introduce vocabulary • Read pp. 386–397 (12 pp.)
NONFICTION ON YOUR OWN **Father's Day** page 401 AVERAGE			**15 MINUTES** • Read pp. 401–403 (3 pp.)
Writing **WRITING ABOUT LITERATURE** **Interpretation**	**15 MINUTES**	**15 MINUTES**	**55 MINUTES**

Time estimates assume in-class work. You may wish to assign some of these stages as homework.

Responding to the Selection

	FROM PERSONAL RESPONSE TO CRITICAL ANALYSIS	OR	ANOTHER PATHWAY	LITERARY CONCEPTS	QUICKWRITES
	60 MINUTES				
	• Discussion questions	OR	• Eulogy	• Flashback • Suspense	• Field manual • Personal letter
	30 MINUTES				
	• Discussion questions	OR	• Character replies	• Alliteration • Repetition	• Will • Poem
	60 MINUTES				
	• Discussion questions	OR	• Cooperative learning (commandments)	• Internal/External conflict • Tone	• List • Ending • Eulogy • Short story
	50 MINUTES				
	• Discussion questions	OR	• Cooperative learning (compare characters)	• Simile • Rhyme	• Detective's report • Description
	60 MINUTES				
	• Discussion questions	OR	• Cooperative learning (readers theater presentation)	• Foreshadowing • Mood	• Poem • Report

Extension Activities

	ALTERNATIVE ACTIVITIES	LITERARY LINKS	CRITIC'S CORNER	THE WRITER'S STYLE	ACROSS THE CURRICULUM	ART CONNECTION	WORDS TO KNOW	BIOGRAPHY
60 MINUTES	✓		✓	✓	POLITICAL SCIENCE	✓	✓	✓
30 MINUTES	✓	✓						✓
40 MINUTES	✓	✓			SOCIAL STUDIES HEALTH	✓	✓	
20 MINUTES	✓		✓	✓				✓
30 MINUTES	✓	✓					✓	✓

Publishing and Reflecting	Grammar in Context	Reading the World
15 MINUTES	10 MINUTES	25 MINUTES

PART 1

REFLECTING ON THEME

Write the quotation "There is nothing either good or bad but thinking makes it so" (from Act II of *Hamlet*) on the chalkboard. In a whole-class discussion, ask students to paraphrase this statement. Then have them consider how what might seem a bad experience can seem good from another point of view.

What Do You Think?

You may ask students to think of a hypothetical mixed blessing rather than one they have experienced. Give them examples to get them started, such as winning the lottery, being accepted to a prestigious college across the country, or getting a summer job. Students will return to this activity on page 358.

UNIT THREE **PART 1**

MIXED BLESSINGS

REFLECTING ON THEME

Has your happiness about something ever been tinged with regret? For example, you've finally made the team, but now you don't have enough time to spend with your friends. Such an experience is known as a mixed blessing. Families can be a source of mixed blessings: anyone who has a sibling understands the complicated feelings of love and annoyance one can inspire. As you read this part of Unit Three, you'll learn that you're not alone in sometimes feeling the mixed blessings of family life.

What Do You Think? Think of a mixed blessing that you have experienced. In your notebook, create a two-column chart. In the left-hand column, list the advantages of the mixed blessing; in the right-hand column, the disadvantages. Discuss with your classmates whether the advantages outweigh the disadvantages.

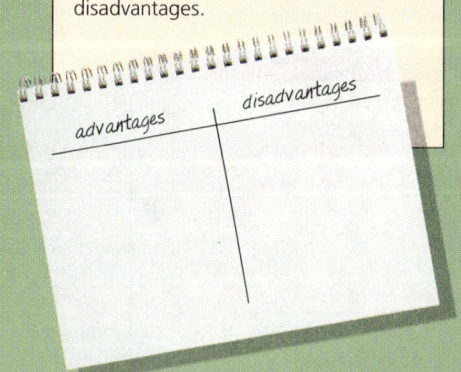

David McLean	**Marine Corps Issue** *The locked boxes in his father's tool shed hold the key to his father's behavior.*	339
David McLean	**On Writing "Marine Corps Issue"**/INSIGHT *One writer's idea for his story*	355
Margaret Walker	**Lineage** *Why does this grandchild not measure up?*	359
Edna St. Vincent Millay	**The Courage That My Mother Had** *A mother does not leave behind what is needed most.*	359
Anna Lee Walters	**The Warriors** *To live beautifully from day to day becomes a battle for Uncle Ralph.*	364
Theodore Roethke	**My Papa's Waltz** *An unusual bedtime ritual*	380
Jack Driscoll	**Touch Football** *A father is surprised by his son's rough play.*	380
Anton Chekhov	**A Marriage Proposal** *Lomov and Natalia may get married—if they can ever stop arguing.*	385
Ogden Nash	**The Strange Case of Mr. Ormantude's Bride**/INSIGHT *Can too much kindness ruin a marriage?*	398
Michael Dorris	**Father's Day** *To the author, Aunt Marion becomes a father—a hilarious irony.*	401

PREVIEWING

FICTION

Marine Corps Issue
David McLean

Activating Prior Knowledge
PERSONAL CONNECTION

The impact of war often extends far beyond the battlefield. In this story, the lingering effects of the Vietnam War on one U.S. soldier are dramatically portrayed. From books, movies, newspapers, magazines, and perhaps personal experience, you will have impressions about the aftermath of war. How do you think war affects those who fight—and relatives who stay at home? In a small group, brainstorm a list of the effects of war on returning soldiers and their families. Then, in your notebook, record your list in a diagram like the one shown.

Building Background
HISTORICAL CONNECTION

The war between North Vietnam and South Vietnam lasted from 1957 to 1975, though U.S. troops fought in it (alongside South Vietnamese troops) only from 1965 to 1973. This war is particularly notable for being the first one in which the United States ever failed in its mission—in this case, to prevent a Communist takeover of South Vietnam. The effects of this war were devastating for many soldiers and their families. The fighting took the lives of about 58,000 Americans and left another 365,000 wounded.

Wounded American soldiers in Vietnam

Many U.S. servicemen, especially the wounded and the hundreds who had been held prisoner by the North Vietnamese, returned from the war with both physical and psychological scars.

Active Reading/Setting a Purpose
READING CONNECTION

Understanding Cause and Effect
Sometimes two events are related as cause and effect—that is, one event brings about the other. The first event in time is the cause; the second event is the effect. For example, in this story, the father, a Vietnam veteran, has disabled hands (cause), which force him to retire from the Marines (effect). His son, not knowing the causes, is puzzled by the lingering effects of the war on his father. As you read, look for cause-and-effect relationships to help you solve the mystery of the father's life.

 LASERLINKS
• HISTORICAL CONNECTION

OVERVIEW
Objectives

- To understand and appreciate a short story that recounts a boy's discovery of the terrible truth that explains his father's elusive behavior
- To identify and understand flashback and suspense
- To appreciate physical descriptions
- To express understanding of the story through a choice of writing forms, including a field manual and a personal letter
- To extend understanding of the story through a variety of multimodal and cross-curricular activities

Skills

LITERARY CONCEPTS
- Flashback
- Suspense
- Point of view
- Irony

READING SKILLS/STRATEGIES
- Understanding cause and effect

THE WRITER'S STYLE
- Purpose

GRAMMAR
- Participles

SPEAKING, LISTENING, AND VIEWING
- Dramatic performance

HISTORICAL CONNECTION
U.S. Soldiers in Vietnam The Vietnam War was a military conflict that began in 1957 and ended in 1975. By viewing this brief film, students will learn about the causes of the conflict and will get a sense of what it was like to be a soldier in Vietnam.

Side A, Frame 20006

PRINT AND MEDIA RESOURCES

UNIT THREE RESOURCE BOOK
Strategic Reading: Literature, p. 4
Vocabulary SkillBuilder, p. 5

GRAMMAR MINI-LESSONS
Transparencies, pp. 29–32
Copymasters, pp. 31–32

WRITING MINI-LESSONS
Transparencies, p. 34

ACCESS FOR STUDENTS ACQUIRING ENGLISH
Selection Summaries
Reading Support

TEACHER'S GUIDE TO ASSESSMENT AND PORTFOLIO USE

FORMAL ASSESSMENT
Selection Test, pp. 59–60
 Test Generator

 AUDIO LIBRARY
See Reference Card

LASERLINKS
Historical Connection
Art Gallery

INTERNET RESOURCES
McDougall Littell Literature Center at http://www.hmco.com/mcdougal/lit

MARINE CORPS ISSUE

David McLean

SUMMARY

Johnny was born while his father was serving as a Marine in Vietnam. He saw his father only once during his first five years. His father returned from the war but never spoke of it. The only clue to this part of his father's life was locked in three wooden boxes stacked in a tool shed. When Johnny was 16, he saw the movie *Apocalypse Now* and suddenly became interested in Vietnam and in his father's past. He read books about the war, always hiding them from his father. Finally, Johnny takes keys to the lockers from his father's key ring. Taking just one key at a time, it takes him three days to go through the boxes. He learns that his father was a prisoner of war and was tortured. As Johnny is looking through the third box, his father catches him. His father is angry but says nothing. During the following four years, the last years of his life, Johnny's father tells Johnny about the war. These are the moments with his father Johnny remembers and loves most.

Thematic Link: *Mixed Blessings* The blessings of a closer relationship between father and son are offset by the pain released when Johnny unlocks the secrets of his father's war experiences.

CUSTOMIZING FOR
Students Acquiring English

- Use **ACCESS FOR STUDENTS ACQUIRING ENGLISH**, *Reading Support*.
- Students should have little difficulty with the vocabulary of this selection. However, you may wish to check their understanding of the Historical Connection on page 339 to make sure they have a sufficient background for understanding the story's subject matter.

STRATEGIC READING FOR
Less-Proficient Readers

Set a Purpose To help students become involved in the selection, have them think of great fictional detectives and list the attributes they share. After students read the first paragraph, ask them to identify what they think the mystery in this story might be. Then have them read to find out which character plays detective in the story and why.

Use **UNIT THREE RESOURCE BOOK**, p. 4, for guidance in reading the selection.

My father used to keep three wooden locker boxes stacked in the tool shed behind our garage. This was at our house in southern Illinois, where I grew up. The boxes, big heavy chests with an iron handle on each end, were fatigue green but had splintered in places. Chips of paint and wood had broken off during the miles of travel, and a shiny splayed pine showed underneath. Each box was padlocked with an oily bronze lock, the keys to which my father kept on his key ring, along with his house keys and car keys. I knew that because I saw him open the top box once, when a friend of his came to visit. My father lifted the lid of the top chest and then a tray within and pulled out an album or a

WORDS TO KNOW

agitated (ăj′ĭ-tā′tĭd) *adj.* emotionally excited or disturbed **agitate** *v.* (p. 344)

animosity (ăn′ə-mŏs′ĭ-tē) *n.* a feeling of strong dislike or hatred (p. 344)

demeanor (dĭ-mē′nər) *n.* outward behavior; conduct (p. 344)

deprivation (dĕp′rə-vā′shən) *n.* a state of being forced to do without (p. 353)

devoid (dĭ-void′) *adj.* completely without; empty (p. 344)

disjunction (dĭs-jŭngk′shən) *n.* a dividing or disjoining; separation (p. 342)

grotesque (grō-tĕsk′) *adj.* odd, twisted, or bizarre (p. 341)

intrigue (ĭn-trēg′) *v.* to stir up the interest or curiosity of; fascinate (p. 343)

trepidation (trĕp′ĭ-dā′shən) *n.* fearful uncertainty or worry (p. 350)

vulnerability (vŭl′nər-ə-bĭl′ĭ-tē) *n.* a state of being easily hurt (p. 349) yearbook of some kind, something to do with the war. The visitor was an old Marine Corps buddy, still active and in uniform. They laughed over photographs and drank whiskey, a whole bottle. I crouched in the hallway around the corner from the kitchen and listened as long as I dared. I don't remember much of the talk, names and places I had never heard of, but I do recall the man's calling my father "gunny,"[1] and commenting on his hands. My father had damaged hands. "Look at your hands, gunny—Damn it, look at them!" And I think they cried, or maybe it was just drunken giggles. I don't know. That was the only time I ever saw my father drink. That was 1974. I was ten years old.

My original name was Charles Michael, and for the first ten months of my life, my mother tells me, I was called Charlie. I had no father then—that is, he had never seen me. But when he returned from Vietnam the first time, in early 1965, within a week he began the legal proceedings to change my name. Soon after, I was Jonathan Allen; I still am. I learned all this from my mother when I was twenty and needed my birth certificate for a passport application. My father was three months dead then, when my mother explained to me about Charlie[2] and how I had been renamed for a dead corporal from a small town in Georgia.

I see my father most often in two ways: playing handball or, years later, sitting on the edge of our elevated garden, black ashes from a distant fire falling lightly like snow around him. As I said, my father had damaged hands—a degenerative arthritis,[3] we were told. They were large, leprous[4] hands, thick with scar tissue and slightly curled. He could neither make a fist nor straighten them completely. Normally they hung limp at his sides or were stashed in his pockets. To grip things he had to use a lot of wrist movement, giving him a <u>grotesque</u> bird-on-a-perch

---

1. **gunny:** a nickname for a gunnery sergeant in the U.S. Marine Corps.
2. **Charlie:** a slang term for the Vietcong—Communist-trained South Vietnamese soldiers against whom the United States fought.
3. **degenerative arthritis:** a condition in which the cartilage in joints breaks down, so that bones rub together painfully.
4. **leprous:** having an appearance like that caused by the disease leprosy.

WORDS TO KNOW

grotesque (grō-tĕsk') *adj.* odd, twisted, or bizarre

341

Multicultural Perspectives

VIETNAM WAR Vietnam, a French colony during World War II, resisted the Japanese, and after the war, Ho Chi Minh, a communist leader, declared Vietnam an independent country. In order to restore colonial rule, France attacked Ho Chi Minh's nationalist forces in 1947. The war continued until 1954, when France suffered a devastating defeat. The Geneva Accord, which officially ended the war, divided Vietnam into communist North Vietnam and noncommunist South Vietnam. Soon civil war broke out, and the United States, opposed to a unified communist government in Vietnam, sent military advisors to assist the South Vietnamese. The number of advisors increased year by year until the United States became an active combatant. Eventually more than 500,000 U.S. troops were involved in the fighting.

Literary Concept: DESCRIPTION

B Ask students what impression the description of the father in this paragraph and the following one makes on them. *(Possible response: He seems, in some vague way, possessed with a rage or inner demon that drives him to exhaustion on the handball court.)*

Literary Concept: FLASHBACK

C Point out that Johnny is looking back at his first memory of his father. Ask students what that meeting reveals about the beginning of the relationship. *(Possible response: They are like strangers to each other, with no emotional bonds.)*

Literary Concept: IRONY

D Have students explain what is unusual about the narrator's being a noisy child out of necessity? *(Possible response: Normally children are encouraged to behave as quietly as possible by parents, who are usually annoyed and upset by noisy children.)*

Critical Thinking: MAKE INFERENCES

E Ask students what happens in this paragraph. *(Possible responses: Johnny receives his "well-deserved blow"; frightened by Johnny, his ex-soldier father instinctively swings his arm in self-defense, hitting Johnny and sending him flying through the air.)*

---

appearance. He rarely touched anyone with them, though he did hit me once, a well-deserved blow I know now and knew even then in the vague way of an innocent.

y older brother, Joe, and I would watch him from the walkway above and behind the handball courts while our mother waited outside. I was six years old but can still see him clearly, playing alone, as always. He wears olive-green shorts, plain white canvas shoes and long white socks, a gray sweatshirt, the neck ripped loose down the front, and a fatigue-green headband wrapped tightly around his bony forehead. Black thinning hair dipped in gray rises up like tufts of crabgrass around the headband. He wears dirty white leather gloves. He swings at the hard black ball forcefully, as though he held paddles of thick oak. I hear the amplified slap of his hand and then a huge explosion booming through the court as the ball ricochets back. He runs after it, catches up to it, and slaps it again, driving it powerfully into the corner. His tall, thin figure jerks across the court and off the wall, his slaps alternating with the hollow explosions, his shoes squeaking, his controlled breaths bursting out of him as he tries, it seems to me, to break the ball or maybe rid himself of it forever.

But it always returns, somehow, even dribbling, to the center of the court. Exhausted, he sits against the wall, breathing heavily, his court gone suddenly quiet, though the booming echoes from nearby courts can still be heard. He watches the ball bounce off its final wall and then slowly roll to a stop. I watch it with him, until it again becomes an inert black ball on the wooden floor.

I said that my father had hit me once; it was at our second meeting. The first had been on that six-month home leave when he changed my name. I remember nothing of that, of course. I do remember his second return home, though, when I was five years old. To my new consciousness, Daddy was simply a figure in a photograph, a steely, strong-looking man in dress blues.[5] I remember the <u>disjunction</u> I felt upon seeing him for the first time, how I had trouble believing that this man was the same man as in the photograph. He was thin and gaunt and silent, with deeper eyes and a higher forehead than I had expected to see. He looked at me strangely. He hadn't seen me grow up. I could have been any child, an adopted son, were it not for my resemblance to him.

What I learned shortly after that first real meeting was the necessity of being a noisy child. Noise alerted him to my presence and prevented his being surprised and reacting on instinct. I began to knock on the walls or shuffle my feet or sing to myself as I walked through the house.

I discovered this survival technique one Saturday morning shortly after his return. I had awakened early and had rolled off the lower bunk, my blanket under my arms, a sleepy animal child going to look for his mother. I walked down the hall and into the living room, where my father sat reading. He had not heard me come in. I wanted to play a game. I crept around an end table near his chair, suppressing a giggle, and watched him for a minute. I looked at the back of his head, smelled his sharp after-shave smell, stared freely, for the first time, at his gnarled left hand holding the book in that rolled-wrist way, and then I leaped out from the table and shouted *Boo!*

I saw a white flash—I was airborne, backwards, on my shoulders and over my head. I

---

5. **dress blues:** the dress uniform of the Marine Corps.

WORDS TO KNOW

disjunction (dĭs-jŭngk′shən) *n.* a dividing or disjoining; separation

342

Mini-Lesson — The Writer's Style

AUTHOR'S PURPOSE Point out that every writer has a purpose in writing a particular work. Writers of fiction strive to entertain their readers while they explore issues of universal interest. In "Marine Corps Issue," the author shows how the parent-child relationship can be an unemotional, fragile one. For example, the writer lets the reader know something about the distance between Johnny and his father through descriptions of the latter's actions and altered appearance in the passage <u>highlighted</u> above.

Application Ask students to illustrate author's purpose by describing individuals that the class knows. Have them write their descriptions without naming the subjects. Then ask them to trade papers to see whether their descriptions helped their classmates identify their subjects. The class should also make suggestions about how to improve the descriptions.

Reteaching/Reinforcement
- *Writing Handbook*, anthology p. 850
- *Writing Mini-Lessons* transparencies, p. 34

 The Writer's Craft

Purpose, pp. 312–313

landed hard on my face and knees, bleeding from the nose and mouth. I looked up and saw him crouched and rigid, eyes on fire, palms flat, fingers as stiff as he could make them.

Then he melted, right there before me, his body slumping down like warm wax, and he began shouting, and crying, "Damn it, Diane! come and get this damned child away from me!" He wouldn't look at me. His hands were in his pockets. He walked out of the house and into the back yard. I didn't see him again until breakfast the following morning. My mother arrived and swooped me into her arms. Only then did I begin to cry.

My mother's life intrigues me. Her strength, well hidden when I was younger, becomes obvious upon reflection. I spend a lot of time reading about the Marine Corps and Vietnam; it is a way of knowing my father. And yet I often find my mother in the books. I cannot read of Khe Sanh or Da Nang[6] without imagining my mother at home with two children under the age of seven and a husband across the world fighting in a war, what I think of as a stupid war at that. She has never spoken about that time, not even about the four continuous years of my father's absence, when, my grandmother told me, she would spend at least two hours every night weeping alone, the children already asleep, and when she could hardly sleep herself. Even after my father's return tension and distance continued for some time. Our family was different from others. I can best describe it as being composed of opposing camps—not camps at war with each other but survival camps: my

---

6. **Khe Sanh** (kā sän′) . . . **Da Nang** (də năng′): South Vietnamese towns near the North Vietnamese border—sites of U.S. military bases during the Vietnam War.

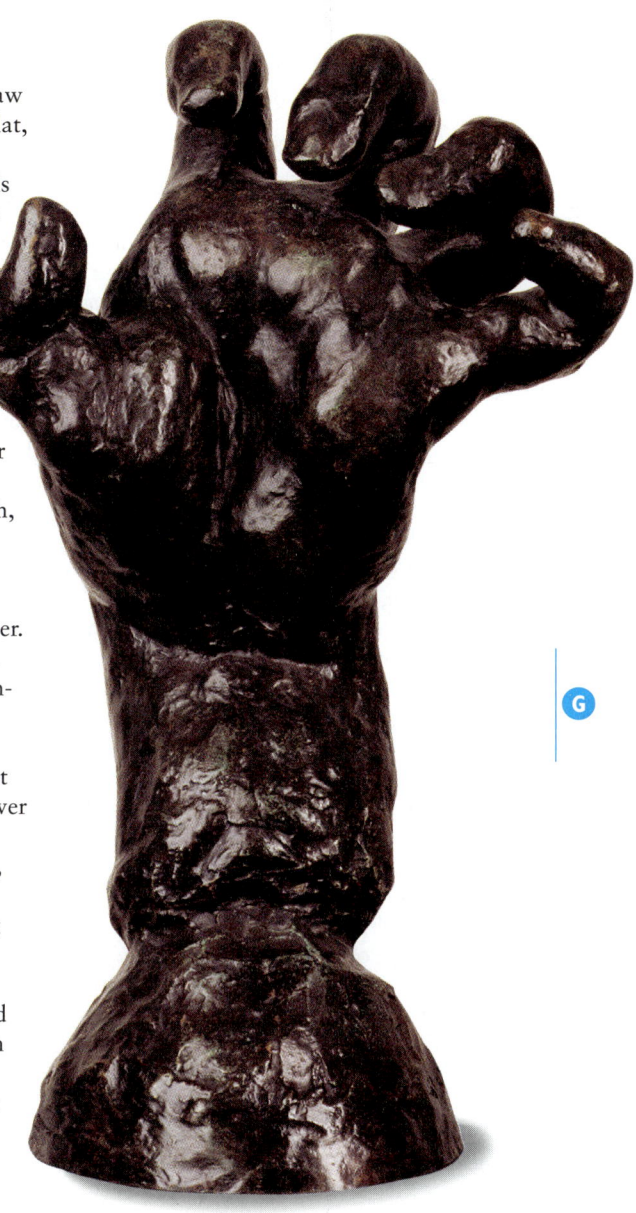

The Mighty Hand (1885), Auguste Rodin. Bronze, 18″ × 11½″ × 7½″, collection of the First National Bank of Chicago.

WORDS TO KNOW

intrigue (ĭn-trēg′) *v.* to stir up the interest or curiosity of; fascinate

343

Art Note

The Mighty Hand **by Auguste Rodin** (rō-dăn′) A master at recreating the human body, French sculptor Auguste Rodin (1840–1917) is world famous for *The Thinker,* his bronze of a seated man, chin in hand. His bronze work on this page presents a dramatic pose of the human hand.

Reading the Art *What about the sculpture suggests emotional intensity?*

CUSTOMIZING FOR
Students Acquiring English

② Ask students to explain how a person can "melt." If necessary, explain that this is a form of figurative speech to describe the father's slumping after realizing that he was under attack only from his young son.

Literary Concept:
POINT OF VIEW

Ⓕ Ask students what feelings and attitudes of the narrator are revealed through the first-person point of view. *(His mother had strength of character; the Vietnam War was a stupid war; there was tension and distance between family members.)*

CUSTOMIZING FOR
Multiple Learning Styles

Ⓖ **Spatial or Graphic Learners** Have students compare the art on this page with the description of the father's hands on page 341. Ask them to discuss in what way the sculpture would have to be altered in order to faithfully depict the father's hands.

Linking to Government

H Tell students that the United States Marine Corps is a separate service within the Navy Department.

Literary Concept:
CHARACTERIZATION

I Ask students what further aspects of the father's character are revealed in these two sentences. *(Possible responses: Possibly because of shame or hurt, he does not want visitors to his house to know of his military background; it is apparent only to someone who can recognize the certain walk and attitude—serious and cautious—that he has.)*

CUSTOMIZING FOR
Multiple Learning Styles

J **Spatial or Graphic Learners**
Show students some examples of Norman Rockwell's illustrations. Ask their impressions of Rockwell's work and why these illustrations would be chosen to decorate Johnny's household. *(Possible response: The pictures are pleasant, even slightly humorous; they may indicate that the mother is careful to maintain a calm atmosphere.)*

Literary Concept:
POINT OF VIEW

K Ask students to describe Johnny's "epiphany." *(Johnny suddenly understands what it means that his father is a Vietnam veteran.)*

Critical Thinking: ANALYZE

L Have students discuss why the narrator lies about what movie he saw. *(Possible response: Because his father had never discussed his war experiences, Johnny would have felt uncomfortable if he had disclosed that he had seen a movie about the Vietnam War.)*

---

mother and I in one, my father and Joe in the other. We had no open <u>animosity</u> toward each other, only distance.

My father was in the Marine Corps for seventeen years before beginning his second career in the offices of the Stone City Steel Mill. He was a decorated soldier, a career man forced to retire disabled because of his hands. He had been a drill instructor, a fact that always widens the eyes of those I tell. I can see them reassessing me as soon as I say it—Marine Corps drill instructor—and they look at me in a shifted way that is hard to define. A pity, perhaps, sometimes a fear. I do have a temper comparable to my father's, which usually shows itself in short, explosive bursts of expletives that roll out of my mouth naturally, as if I were a polyglot[7] switching tongues. The violence is verbal only, though I can still see my father, if I make the effort, at my brother's throat. Joe has been caught smoking in the garage a second time. He is fourteen and has been warned. He is pinned to the wall of the garage by my father's crooked paw, his feet dangling, toes groping for solid ground as though he will fall upward and off the earth if he can't find a grip. His eyes are wide and swollen with tears. My father's voice is a slow burn, his nostrils wide. He finishes speaking, drops Joe onto the concrete floor, and strides quickly away.

Despite my father's years of service, our house was <u>devoid</u> of memorabilia.[8] A visitor would have no idea about my father's military career were it not evident in his walk and <u>demeanor</u>. Civilians might miss even these clues. Our house was not a family museum like other houses. We had few family photographs; the decor consisted chiefly of landscape paintings and small ceramic collectibles, dolls and Norman Rockwell scenes and wooden elephants from around the world.

At sixteen I saw the movie *Apocalypse Now*.[9] I had no interest in Vietnam then; I knew nothing of it. The film left me enthralled and fascinated, even a little horrified in an abstract way. I came home <u>agitated</u> but still had not made any connection. The epiphany[10] came when I walked in the front door. My father was sitting quietly in his recliner, sipping coffee and watching the Cardinals play the Reds on television. My mother sat on the couch crocheting under a lamp, humming a hymn to herself, our Labrador, Casey, resting on the floor at her feet. I stared at them for a long twenty seconds before my father snapped the spell. "Hey, Johnny," he said, "come in here and watch the game. Redbirds are up five to three in the seventh."

"Yeah?" I moved into the room and turned to face the television.

"What'd you go see, hon?" my mother asked.
"What?"
"What movie'd you see?"

I lied. I quickly named some comedy that was showing in the same complex. "It was awful," I added, to cut off the questioning.

I saw the movie again a few days later, and I saw it anew. My father was in there somewhere, dug into a bunker, behind a wall of foliage, there amid the ragged poor and the dripping trees and the sounds of gunfire and explosions. And when I returned home from the movie that night, he was

---

7. **polyglot:** a person who speaks or writes many languages.
8. **memorabilia:** objects valued for their connection with important events; souvenirs.
9. *Apocalypse Now:* a 1979 film about the Vietnam War in which battles are dramatically re-created.
10. **epiphany:** a sudden insight into the meaning of something.

WORDS TO KNOW
animosity (ăn′ə-mŏs′ĭ-tē) *n.* a feeling of strong dislike or hatred
devoid (dĭ-void′) *adj.* completely without; empty
demeanor (dĭ-mē′nər) *n.* outward behavior; conduct
agitated (ăj′ĭ-tā′tĭd) *adj.* emotionally excited or disturbed **agitate** *v.*

344

Mini-Lesson Grammar

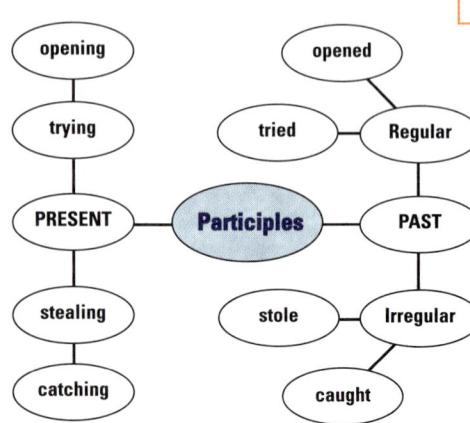

PARTICIPLES Remind students that a participle is a verb form that functions as an adjective. Explain that participles, like adjectives, modify nouns and pronouns.
1. The *patrol, lost* for an hour, suddenly reappeared out of the jungle.
2. *Shaking,* I left the movie quickly.

Application Draw the web shown at the left on the chalkboard and go over its examples. Ask students to identify the many participles in the paragraph on page 344 and to tell whether each one modifies a noun or a pronoun. Then ask them to use at least five participles in a written description of a movie they have seen.

Reteaching/Reinforcement
- *Grammar Handbook,* anthology p. 943
- *Grammar Mini-Lessons* copymasters pp. 31–32, transparencies pp. 29–32

📁 The Writer's Craft
Participles, pp. 683–684

reading a John Le Carré novel, sipping coffee, the silky voice of Jack Buck in the background describing the Cardinals game in Atlanta. The evening was hot and dry. It would be a hard summer of drought in southern Illinois.

The next day I walked to the library and borrowed three books about the Vietnam War. My summer project would be to learn about the war and my father's place there. Under a hot midmorning sun I skimmed the thinnest of the three on the way home, anxious, as though poised to turn the knob of a mysterious door. At home I hid two of the books in my safest place, above the loose tiles of the lowered ceiling in my bedroom, and took the third book and my copy of *The Pickwick Papers*[11] into the back yard.

> **I SAW THE MOVIE AGAIN A FEW DAYS LATER, AND I SAW IT ANEW. MY FATHER WAS IN THERE SOMEWHERE.**

We had a large yard behind the house, enclosed by a fence of pointed wooden slats five feet high. Against the back fence stood a terraced flower garden, built long before by a previous owner. It ran the length of the fence and was fronted by a red brick wall about two feet high. The three levels were separated by stacked railroad ties. My parents loved the garden and would labor all summer to keep it lush. Even that summer of drought, as the grass was browning under a merciless sun, my parents kept the garden well watered. From April to September we had cut flowers on the dinner table every night.

I kept a private place in the upper left corner of the garden. It was known to everyone; if I was nowhere to be found, my family would always check to see if I was there reading. Before watering, my parents would always shout a warning lest I be rained on. Although known, it was still quiet and just isolated enough. I would lie down on the ground behind a thick wall of day lilies, my back against the fence, and read or think while staring up at the sky.

That is where I learned about the Vietnam War. I lay on my side and read for at least three hours every day, softly repeating the names of places and operations, marking pages with thin weeds. If called or found, I would rise from the flowers with *The Pickwick Papers* in hand, leaving the history book in a plastic bag among the day lilies, to be collected later. In the evenings, while listening to baseball games, I transferred notes from the weed-marked pages into a notebook that I kept hidden in my sock-and-underwear drawer.

Within two weeks I had finished those first three books. Upon completion of the third I emerged from the day lilies feeling expert. My knowledge of the war—dates, places, names—had zoomed up from zero. I was ready to ask my mother some questions. I approached her one afternoon before my father had returned from work. She was peeling potatoes over the kitchen sink when I padded in nervously. "Mom?"

"Yes, Johnny?"

"Mom, where was Dad stationed in Vietnam?" My throat was dry. I had never before uttered the word to my parents. My mother stopped working and turned to face me, potato peeler held upright in her hand. She looked puzzled.

"I don't remember, Johnny. Lord, that was

---
11. *The Pickwick Papers*: a classic 19th-century novel by Charles Dickens.

MARINE CORPS ISSUE **345**

Mini-Lesson Study Skills

SKIMMING In learning about the Vietnam War, Johnny probably read some sources closely and skimmed others. Point out to students that skimming involves reading material very rapidly to get an overall impression of its content. Before skimming an entire book, students should glance at its title, table of contents, and index to get a general idea of the material inside. When skimming a chapter or selection, they should follow the specific steps listed on the chalkboard.

Application Ask students to skim a chapter in a textbook that they have not read. Give them a set amount of time, about ten minutes, to do this. Then ask them to discuss what they learned.

1. Look at the title, headings, and subheadings.
2. Glance at pictures and captions.
3. Read any definitions highlighted in bold or italic print.
4. Look for main ideas, often stated in the first or last sentence of a paragraph.

Linking to Science

M Drought is a condition that results from a long period of dry weather. Drought can have a devastating effect on farming and other sectors of the economy. A terrible drought occurred during the early 1930s in the Great Plains. Large areas of dry topsoil were blown away, ruining countless farms and spurring a migration to California.

STRATEGIC READING FOR
Less-Proficient Readers

N Pose the following questions to make sure that students understand who is telling the story and what he plans to do.

- Who is telling the story? *(Johnny)* **Drawing Conclusions**
- What mystery does he want to investigate? *(He wants to know what the Vietnam War was all about and how his father might have fit into it.)* **Noting Relevant Details**
- What first investigative step does Johnny take? *(He acquires books about the Vietnam War.)* **Noting Sequence of Events**

Set a Purpose Have students read on to discover Johnny's next step.

Literary Concept:
CHARACTERIZATION

O Ask students to discuss what this passage implies about Johnny's character. *(Johnny is basically a private and contemplative person.)*

Critical Thinking: SPECULATE

P Have students predict Johnny's mother's reaction to his question. *(Possible responses: She will be upset; she will welcome the question; she will discourage him.)*

THE LANGUAGE OF LITERATURE TEACHER'S EDITION **345**

Art Note

Art and Artie by Connie Hayes Tell students that because Connie Hayes (1952–) loves to paint landscapes, she usually sets her compositions outdoors, as she did this painting. She says there are two "veins" in her work: subjects directly observed, like the landscapes, and, dating mainly from 1985 to 1990, "more orchestrated, planned work" based mostly on photographs of family.

Reading the Art *What suggests that this painting might have been done from a photograph? In what way is it very different from a photograph?*

Literary Concept: PARADOX

Q Remind students that a paradox is a statement that seems contradictory but is nevertheless true. Ask them in what way the mother could have "laughed an unhumorous laugh." *(if the laugh reflected nervousness, not amusement)*

Literary Concept: FLASHBACK

R Ask students what the flashback reveals about Johnny's mother. *(Possible response: She fears the resumption of pain experienced by the family when her husband returned from Vietnam.)*

Art and Artie (1989), Connie Hayes. Oil on paper, 27″ × 27″, collection of the artist. Copyright © Connie Hayes.

over ten years ago. I don't remember those funny foreign names. He was stationed in more than one place anyway. Why?"

I felt ashamed, flushed. "Just curious. We learned a little about it at school, and I was just curious. That's all."

"I wish I could tell you, but I don't remember. You know me. I have trouble remembering what I did last week." She laughed an unhumorous laugh.

"Should I ask Dad?"

She suddenly looked very tired and thoughtful. "Oh, Johnny, please don't," she whispered. "Don't bring it up with him. It took him so long to forget all of that. Don't ask him to start remembering again." Then she looked directly at me, and I could see that she was pleading with me, and I thought that she was going to cry. But she turned back to the sink and ran her hands and a potato under the tap. She began working again.

"Okay, Momma. I won't. I'm sorry."

"Don't be sorry, honey. You've a right to be curious."

The next day I was with Joe. We were returning from the shopping mall in Fairview Heights, twenty miles away. We were in the old pickup truck he used on construction jobs, trying to cool ourselves with wide-open windows, though even the rushing air was warm and uncomfortable. Joe was eighteen then and worked nearly every day. I was enjoying the trip all the more because he allowed himself so few days off.

We were speeding down an empty two-lane road through the farmland south of Stone City. It was sickening to see. The corn, usually head high by the end of June, was barely up to my waist. The ground was cracked and broken in places. Some farmers had recently given up. You could see by the dry brown stalks, standing packed closely together, that they had stopped watering.

"Look at it," Joe said, shaking his head and poking his thumb out the window. He had to shout to be heard over the sound of rushing air. "I've never seen anything like this before. Even Grandma says it's the worst she's seen." I nodded and looked around at the dying fields.

"What'd you buy?" he shouted, pointing at my bag. I pulled out *Great Expectations*[12] and showed it to him. He gave it only half a look and a nod. Then he shouted, "What's the other?" pointing again at the bag. I hesitated but pulled out *Dispatches,* by Michael Herr.[13] Joe grabbed it and began reading the back cover, completely ignoring the road. We began to drift across the center line into the oncoming lane. I reached over and gave the wheel a slight pull to the right. Joe looked up and grinned. He continued reading, now flicking his eyes up every few seconds.

"Vietnam?" he shouted. "What'd you buy this for?" I shrugged. Joe rolled up his window and motioned for me to do the same. The cab was suddenly very quiet. I looked over and watched a red-winged blackbird light upon a fence post. Joe nearly whispered, "What'd you buy this for?"

"Just curious. I've been reading some history of the war."

"Does Dad know?"

"No."

"Mom?"

"Only a little. Not about my reading." Joe looked down the road. We were already baking in the closed, quiet cabin.

"Just watch out. Keep it to yourself." He threw the book into my lap.

"What do you remember about the war?"

"Hell, not much. I remember Dad coming home, hands all screwed up. Quiet, but I hadn't seen him in so long that I don't remember him being different or anything. Maybe quieter. I don't know. I was only seven. And I remember the POW-MIA sticker.[14] Never understood that until I was in high school. We had a bumper sticker on the old green Impala. Remember?"

"No."

"Well, that's all I remember, really. I never took too much interest. I figured he'd tell us if he wanted to."

"Weren't you ever curious?"

"No, not too much. It seemed all bad and ancient history. Water under the bridge and all that. I got to roll this window down!"

I considered asking Joe what he thought about my plan but didn't. I had decided after talking to my mother that I was going to get into the locker boxes, though I had yet to figure out how. My father was in the garden nearly every day after work and saw the boxes while getting tools or the hose. Obviously, I needed the keys.

---

12. *Great Expectations*: another classic novel by Charles Dickens.
13. *Dispatches,* by Michael Herr: a book consisting of impressions of the Vietnam War by an on-the-scene reporter—considered by many to be the best account of the war.
14. POW-MIA sticker: a bumper sticker directing public attention to the U.S. servicemen who were prisoners of war (POW's) or missing in action (MIA) in Vietnam and whose deaths were unaccounted for at the time.

MARINE CORPS ISSUE **347**

Mini-Lesson: Speaking, Listening, and Viewing

DRAMATIC PERFORMANCE Tell students that they can use the conversation between Johnny and Joe on page 347 as dialogue for a dramatic performance of a scene. Students should decide whether they will use the dialogue as it appears in the story or develop their own script. Ask them to consider whether a narrator should set the scene and to practice using their voices, faces, and gestures to express emotion.

Application Have pairs of students take turns performing the scene while their classmates listen and offer constructive criticism.

Linking to Math

S Ask students to calculate how long it would have taken Joe and Johnny to complete the 20-mile trip from the mall to home if the truck traveled 45 miles an hour ($60/45 \times 20/20$ = about 27 minutes), 55 miles an hour ($60/55 \times 20/20$ = about 22 minutes), or 65 miles an hour. ($60/65 \times 20/20$ = about 18 minutes)

Critical Thinking: SPECULATE

T Invite students to speculate about why Joe rolls up the window. (Possible response: The subject of the Vietnam War and their father's experiences in it has always been so mysterious and off-limits that Joe goes out of his way to make sure that nothing can distract from their discussion.)

Literary Concept: DIALOGUE

U Remind students that dialogue is written conversation between two or more characters. Ask what the dialogue reveals about the differences between Johnny and Joe. (Possible response: Johnny is curious and eager for knowledge; Joe is cautious and tries to take things at face value.)

Critical Thinking: ANALYZE

V Challenge students to analyze why Johnny does not tell Joe about his plan. (Possible responses: Johnny may suspect that Joe would try to talk him out of pursuing his plan; Johnny feels guilty about invading his father's privacy and doesn't want his brother to judge him or to share his guilt.)

STRATEGIC READING FOR
Less-Proficient Readers

W Pose the following questions to make sure that students understand Johnny's plan for getting into the boxes and the dangers involved in carrying out his plan.

- What is Johnny's plan for unlocking the boxes? *(He plans to switch an old key for each of three keys on his father's key ring so that he will be able to open and examine one box a day.)* **Noting Relevant Details**

- What dangers are involved in carrying out his plan? *(His father could discover the useless key at any time, and Johnny could get caught opening the chest.)* **Making Inferences**

Set a Purpose Ask students to read to learn the outcome of Johnny's plan of action.

Literary Concept: SUSPENSE

X Ask how the writer builds suspense as he describes Johnny's act of unlocking the first box. *(The narrator describes Johnny's back and hands as shivering and shaky despite the heat.)*

Literary Concept: DESCRIPTION

Y Ask students to discuss how the style used to describe the items in the box mirrors Johnny's actions. *(Possible response: The short, incomplete sentences dramatize the frantic actions of someone who feels nervous about what he is doing but is eager to find something meaningful.)*

---

examined the boxes the next morning. They were stacked in a corner next to a small worktable. Coffee cans full of paintbrushes and nails and loose nuts and bolts stood on top of them. As far as I knew, they hadn't been opened in six years. Spider webs were constructed with a confident permanence between the sides of the boxes and the shed walls. I gave a cursory tug at the three locks, each of which had been scratched with a number.

The locks were the common hardware-store variety that always come with two keys. I began searching for the extras in the drawers in the tool shed. In the days that followed, I rummaged through boxes and cleaned the attic over the garage. I carefully went through my father's dresser, with no luck. I did find one loose key at the bottom of a toolbox and raced out to the shed to try it, but it wouldn't even slide into the core of the locks. I would have to take the risky route for the operation. The useless old key would help.

I spent three scorching days in the garden reading *Dispatches* and an oral history of the war while I looked for the courage necessary to put the plan into effect. The plan was simple, but I wasn't certain it was safe. I would switch the old key I'd found for one from the key ring, rummage a box and switch the key for a second the following day, and then switch the one after that, for a three-day operation.

The next morning I rose as early as my father, much to his and my mother's surprise. My mother was in the kitchen scrambling eggs, and my father was in the shower, as I'd hoped. I slipped into their bedroom and with nervous, fumbling fingers forced the key numbered one off the key ring, replacing it with my found key. The key ring was tight, and I slipped in my haste, gouging my index finger in doing so. I left the bedroom with my slightly bleeding finger in my mouth, jamming it into my pocket as I passed my mother in the kitchen.

Later, quietly, with an archaeologist's caution, I moved the coffee cans from the top box and set them on the worktable. I then slipped in the key and flicked open the lock. Despite the heat, I felt a shiver through my back and shoulders, my body reminding me that I was crossing some line of knowledge, transgressing some boundary of my father's. My hands shook and I held my breath as I lifted the lid.

The first thing I saw was a yellowed newspaper clipping: the death of James Dean,[15] carefully cut to keep the date intact. I read the whole article with interest. I knew nothing of his death. Then I saw my mother's high school diploma, class of 1955. Stacks of old photographs. Family snapshots, black and white with wavy white borders. I found my old report cards from early grade school and all of my brother's report cards up to the sixth grade. I found a baked-clay saucer with a tiny handprint pressed into it and "Johnny 1968" scratched on the back. It was all interesting but not my reason for the risk, so I lifted out the tray full of family memorabilia and set it to one side.

Underneath I found uniforms. Dress blues neatly pressed and folded. A shoeshine kit. A drill instructor's Smokey the Bear hat. Little plastic bags full of Marine Corps emblem pins like the one on the hat. A tan uniform. And the yearbook my father had pulled out six years before for his visitor. It was a thin platoon book dated 1964, San Diego. I flipped slowly through the black-and-white photos, looking for pictures of my father. The photos were mostly head shots of similar-looking boys in dress blues and white hats. I found action shots of boot training, of the mess hall, of track-and-field competitions. I saw my father here and there, leading a parade, demonstrating a hand-to-hand hold. He was still youthful and very muscular, stern-looking but not weary. The picture of him in his dress blues was the same I'd learned to call Daddy before I'd met

---

15. **James Dean:** young American movie star who died in an automobile accident in 1955, at the age of 24.

him. His hands looked normal in the photographs, the vulnerability gone, his arms strong and well shaped, like solid tree limbs. Upon looking through again, I noticed small notations next to a few of the photos: "KIA,"[16] followed by a date. I was looking at dead men. I didn't know it then, but I would go back years later and find a picture of my namesake, Jonathan Allen Whitney, of Hinesville, Georgia, in that book.

But that was all, and it amounted to little. I replaced the tray and closed the lid, reconstructing the tool shed as well as I could.

That night at dinner I waited for the explosion, the accusation, my father holding up the key ring, his tight voice burning through me. I saw it all, but it never came. Later, in my room, I sorted through what I'd seen and made notes in my journal. I hadn't learned much, except that my mother loved James Dean and was a curator[17] of her young sons' lives. As for my father, I'd found little new except the images of a younger, stronger man.

---

16. **KIA:** military shorthand for *killed in action*.
17. **curator:** one who manages or has care over something, often a museum or library.

© Donald J. Weber

WORDS TO KNOW
vulnerability (vŭl′nər-ə-bĭl′ĭ-tē) *n.* a state of being easily hurt

---

Mini-Lesson — Literary Concepts

REVIEWING FIRST-PERSON POINT OF VIEW A story told from the first-person point of view has a narrator who is a character in the story and tells everything in his or her own words. Readers know what the narrator is feeling and thinking, but they have to infer from the narrator's descriptions what other characters are feeling or thinking.

Application Have students find examples in the story of the narrator's telling them his own thoughts or feelings. What do these examples reveal to them about Johnny and the other characters? In what way do students think the story would be different if another character were the narrator?

I opened the second box with less trepidation, half expecting to see my mother's junior-prom dress folded neatly inside, a dry corsage still pinned to the front. Instead, I found the memorabilia that probably should have been hanging on the walls inside the house. In the top tray were three wooden plaques commemorating different things my father had done, all before the war. They were homely little plaques given to him by platoons or friends. His dog tags[18] lay wrapped in a green handkerchief underneath the plaques, "Joseph D Bowen" pressed into the thin aluminum. The tags read "Methodist," which surprised me, since he never went to church. I found a pile of old letters written by my mother which had been mailed to an address in San Francisco. I couldn't bring myself to read them. I did, however, find three letters dated shortly after my birthday and opened them. One contained the expected photograph, the usual hideous newborn, with the words "Hi, Daddy! Love, Charlie" written on the back. There was another photo, of my mother with Joe and me. Joe was two, and I was just weeks old. The picture was taken at my grandmother's house and dated June 30, 1964.

Beneath the tray I found more uniforms. Khakis this time, combat-style fatigues with "Bowen" stenciled onto them. There was also a pair of worn black boots, a canteen, two thick belts, and a cigar box full of uniform ribbons and their matching medals. Vietnam service, the crossed rifles for marksmanship, and others. There was an unexpected find: a Purple Heart.[19] He'd been wounded. I wondered where. His hands, perhaps, or the fairly large scar on his left thigh—a childhood farming accident, he'd told us. I was staring at the medal, trying to open my imagination, when I heard the back door of the house swing out and bang against the siding. I threw the medal back into the box, and the box into the locker, and hurriedly shoved everything else inside. I pushed on the lock as the footsteps left the patio, and heaved the first box back on top. I was arranging the coffee cans when Joe walked in.

"Hey, what are you doing?" he said. I was sweating but felt a twitching relief that it was only Joe.

"Looking for a nut. I need one for my bicycle." I dumped one can over and began sifting through the dirty nuts and bolts. Joe walked around me, glanced down at the wall, and began sifting through the pile with me. "I need one for the seat," I told him. He quickly handed me a nut.

"That'll do it," he said and then added, "Hear what happened?"

"What?"

"Some old farmer set his fields on fire this morning. Acres and acres are burning like hell."

"Where?"

"Just east of town, off one-eleven. You can see smoke from the front yard. I thought we could drive out and see it."

"Why'd he do it?"

"I don't know. Just mad, probably. Wasn't doing him any good, dying there in front of him."

It wasn't much to see, really. The flames

---

18. **dog tags:** metal identification tags worn on a neck chain by members of the armed forces.
19. **Purple Heart:** a U.S. military decoration showing George Washington in profile, awarded to personnel who have been wounded in action.

WORDS TO KNOW

trepidation (trĕp′ĭ-dā′shən) *n.* fearful uncertainty or worry weren't huge, just crawling slowly across the field of dry stalks, crackling softly. Large glowing leaves swirled into the sky and became flocks of black birds in erratic flight. A few other people had pulled over to watch from the highway before a patrolman came slowly by and moved them along. Joe asked him if the fire department would put it out, and he said no, that it was no real danger, though the farmer would be fined or something. He said it would burn itself out in a day or so. We saw a man near the farmhouse, about a hundred yards from the road. He was old, wearing a red baseball cap, sitting on a tractor watching the wall of black smoke rise from the field. "Probably him," Joe said.

hat night my father came home with two tickets to a Cardinals game against the Mets. "Box seats," he said, dropping them onto the table. He was as excited as we ever saw him, shining eyes and a slight smile, nothing showy or too expressive. "Let's go, Johnny."

From the car I watched the thin sheet of black smoke rising harmlessly like a veil on the horizon, not the ominous black plume that comes from a single house burning. I told my father about Joe and me driving out to see the fire and about the old man on the tractor. My father just shook his head. We were driving by his office at the steel mill, a different kind of fire and smoke shooting from the stacks. "Poor old man" was all he said.

I kept looking at the keys hanging from the steering column, expecting a wave of recognition to light up his face any second. I couldn't imagine how he would react, though I considered anger to be the best guess. What I was doing was wrong; I knew that and felt bad about it, especially since he was in such a good mood. His face was relaxed and peaceful, and he was smiling. He'd fought in a war; he'd been wounded in some unknown place; his hands gripped the steering wheel like arthritic talons; his friends had been killed, and his sons had grown without him. I imagined him weathering bitter nights; he was driving us to a baseball game, sliding easily through traffic. I kept glancing at his profile, the thinning hair touched with gray, the deep circles under his eyes, the rounded nose—my nose. We were crossing the Mississippi River on the Poplar Street Bridge. The Arch was a bright filament in the afternoon sun. The river was remarkably low, looking as though you could simply wade across the once unswimmable, strong-currented distance. I considered telling my father everything right then. I was consumed by guilt, tapping my fingers on my leg. "What happened to your finger?" he asked.

"Nothing. Caught it on a nail in the tool shed. I was looking for a key to my old bike lock." I'd had that excuse saved for two days. I couldn't look at him. I watched people in the streets. He began talking baseball. It had always been the bridge between us. There had always been the gap and one bridge, a love of the game.

The game that night was exciting, a pitchers' duel with outstanding defensive plays. We had never sat together in box seats before, and we marveled at seeing everything so close up, how quickly the game really moves. We talked baseball all night. I kept score; I marked every pitch on the card, like a memory. The game went into extra innings. I didn't want it to end. I knew even then that this was the first time I had ever felt really close to my father. We shared a soul that night, and then, in the bottom of the twelfth, the game ended suddenly with one swing by Ted Simmons, a crack, and a long home run disappearing over the left-field wall. We drove home happy, though quiet from fatigue.

Strangely, he passed our exit and continued around town to the east. "You missed our exit," I said.

"I didn't miss it" was all he said. He was

MARINE CORPS ISSUE **351**

pensive. I was puzzled, but only for a few minutes. We turned onto Route 111 and headed south on the dark highway. Suddenly the land to our left was a glowing pile of embers. We could see little smoke, but the field was alive with orange fires, flickering and rising like fireflies. My father clicked on his hazard lights and pulled onto the shoulder. He stepped out of the car and walked across the still road, with me trailing behind. The unseen smoke was too thick. I coughed and my eyes burned. "I just wanted to see it," he said quietly, and we stood in silence watching for ten minutes before driving home.

didn't notice the ashes falling until after I'd changed the second key for the third. I was walking back through the kitchen when I saw, out of the corner of my eye, a leaf fall against the window screen, break into pieces, and then disappear. I looked up and out the window. The wind had shifted in the night, and the ashes from the corn field were swirling above like elm leaves in autumn, some falling gently to earth like a light November flurry, except that the flakes were black. In the back yard I held out my hand to catch one, and it disintegrated in my grasp. The temperature was already over ninety degrees. It was a wonderful and hellish sight. Ashes blew across the patio and collected in the corner against the house.

After my father left for work, I went into the garden to read. Ashes drifted down, breaking between the pages of my book and landing in the day lilies and roses along the fence. I felt strangely uninterested in the third box. The previous night had left me content with my knowledge of my father's past. A new understanding had come to our relationship. I felt guilty opening the third box, as though I were breaking some new agreement between us.

The top tray contained nothing of interest. I found shoe polish, dried and cracked, two more plaques, socks, two dungaree hats. I sifted through these things mechanically and quickly, wanting to be done with it all. The compartment beneath was only half full. A musty smell rose out of the box. It came from the clothing—an old khaki uniform tattered and worn, filthy but neatly folded—that lay on top of the items inside. Also within sight was an old pair of combat boots, unpolished and ragged. They, too, smelled musty. I lifted out the uniform and found a small box made of dried palm fronds. It was poorly woven around narrow sticks with an ill-fitting lid on top. Inside it were yellow newspaper clippings folded up into squares and a small paper ring box. I unfolded one of the clippings carefully, so as not to tear its tightly creased edges. The headline read "LOCAL PRISONER OF WAR TO COME HOME," and was accompanied by that same photograph of my father in his dress blues. The clipping was dated July 13, 1969. I read the article slowly, trying not to miss any details. It explained that my father had been a prisoner for just over three years, that he was to be released July 30, and that he would be returning to the base in San Diego within days. He was being held in a prison camp in the North, just above the DMZ,[20] and had been captured while on patrol near Khe Sanh in 1966. It gave details about the family in Stone City.

I set the clipping aside and quickly unfolded the others. They all told the same story. One was from the Stone City paper, dated the day of his release. I read them all twice, almost uncomprehendingly, before carefully folding them and returning them to the homemade box. I was a little afraid to go further, but I picked up the small paperboard box, felt it rattle, and opened it. Inside were teeth, all molars, yellowed and with black spots in places. I picked one up. On closer inspection the black blemishes became legible: painted on the side of the molar in tiny

---

20. **DMZ:** military shorthand for *demilitarized zone*—a term used to describe a buffer area between opposing armies, in which military forces and operations are prohibited.

352   UNIT THREE   PART 1: MIXED BLESSINGS

letters was "N.V. 3.3.66." I picked up a second. It read "N.V. 5.12.66." All six of them had dates, three from March third, one each from three other days. I was breathing through my nose in a deep, mechanical way, sweating heavily in the hot late morning. I put the teeth back in the box and set the box aside. I was shaking and didn't want to continue. There was more to see, a few letters, some folders, a small book.

The book was a paperback, a Marine Corps field manual bound with a manila cover. It was titled *Escape and Torture*. I began flicking through the pages. There were some small, meaningless diagrams, a dull text about techniques for escaping from some generalized prison camp. Then there was a section on Vietnamese torture techniques. I began reading the clinical, distant descriptions of various forms of torture. Naked men in small, cold concrete cells, sleep <u>deprivation</u>, swelling legs, tied hands, beatings. A few pages into the text the notations began. They were written in black ink, always the single word "this" in the margin next to an underlined passage. The first, as I recall, described something with the feet. Then beating on the legs, "this." Then the hands. "This" was bamboo splinters under the nails. "This" was a beating of the knuckles. "This" was being strung up by the wrists. I felt my stomach go hollow and my comprehension numb as I stared at that awkward, childlike scrawl in the margin of each page.

Illustration by Jim Dietz.

WORDS TO KNOW

deprivation (dĕp′rə-vā′shən) *n.* a state of being forced to do without

353

Art Note

Solitary Confinement: Insects Witness My Agony by Theodore Gostas Theodore Gostas dramatically depicts a bleeding prisoner held in a small box, handcuffed and in stocks, whose ordeal is seen only by five cockroaches.

Reading the Art Why do you think the artist used such a crude style to portray the subject matter? What feelings does the painting evoke?

Critical Thinking:
MAKE JUDGMENTS

 Point out that the father experiences many emotions after discovering that his son knows about his past. Ask students to rank these emotions in order of intensity, beginning with the most intense. *(Possible response: anger, frustration, panic, hurt; some students may interpret the "weary" eyes as conveying relief that everything is finally out in the open.)*

CUSTOMIZING FOR
Gifted and Talented Students

After speculating about the kinds of events that stay with us no matter what we do to get over them, students should decide whether the beneficial effects of Johnny's discovery outweigh the harmful effects.

Solitary Confinement: Insects Witness My Agony (1982), Theodore Gostas. Collection of the U.S. Air Force, Washington, D.C.

I didn't hear my father walk into the tool shed. He appeared suddenly, as though he'd sprung from the ground. I felt a presence and turned to see him standing there in the doorway of the shed, holding his key ring in his right hand and my useless bronze key in his left. I have never seen such confusion on a man's face. He was startlingly angry, I could see, his body stiff, his nostrils flared, his breathing heavy, his jaw muscles rolling beneath his skin. But his eyes were weary, even desperate. We stared at each other while he decided what to do. I didn't move. I said nothing, only watching him. His eyes welled, and bright molten tears ran down his cheeks. Then he dropped the single key and walked away.

I rose and walked out of the dark shed into the hot sun and falling ashes. He was sitting on

354   UNIT THREE   PART 1: MIXED BLESSINGS

Assessment ✓ Option

INFORMAL ASSESSMENT You can assess students' understanding of the story by having them retell it from the point of view of Johnny's father. Have them consider in what ways this would change the story. For example, the father would now be talking through personal experiences and providing a firsthand account of his reactions to events. Have students provide written versions.

Rubric

3 Full Accomplishment Students accurately describe the story events from the father's point of view and include reactions appropriate to his character.

2 Substantial Accomplishment Students describe the events of the story but show less awareness of the father's likely responses.

1 Little or Partial Accomplishment Students have difficulty describing the story events and are unable to express the father's likely reactions to them.

the edge of the garden with his head down and his eyes closed as if in prayer, his hands lying loose and unattached in his lap. He then moved them to his sides and began clawing at the dry dirt in the garden until he had dug two holes and half buried each hand under the loose dirt. He sat as still as a memorial statue, and I realized that I didn't belong there. I left him with his head down and eyes closed and walked into the house. I see him there every day.

In the four years that he lived beyond that moment he told me a little about the war. It was a topic I could never raise. On occasion, if we were alone, he would begin talking about some aspect of the war or of his service. These were heavily guarded moments, slow monologues as he groped for the correct words to tell me. It is another way I remember him, speaking the things that he knew he wasn't capable of saying. This is how I love him the most, this great man. Semper Fi.[21] ❖

---

21. **Semper Fi** (sĕm′pər fī′): a shortened version of *Semper Fidelis* (*Latin* for "Always Faithful"), the Marine Corps motto.

INSIGHT

ON WRITING "MARINE CORPS ISSUE"
David McLean

The origin of "Marine Corps Issue" is in the book mentioned at the end of the story. My father was a Marine. While I was growing up, this field manual, *Escape and Torture,* was sitting on a dusty bookshelf. Unlike the house in the story, our house contained a lot of Marine Corps memorabilia on display. I had always been interested in my father's career, but only after I had moved away did I think it strange to have had this kind of book on my shelves as a teenager. I grew up very near the Vietnam War—my father had been there twice and afterwards, from 1969 to 1972, was a drill instructor training men for the war. My brothers and sisters and I used to watch him parade his recruits as each platoon graduated, never realizing that they were young men on their way to war. So, despite this nearness to the war, I was completely unaware of it. I knew nothing about it until I was in college.

These elements—a war, a book, a father, and a son—caused me to think of a story. I thought of what a son might learn about his father if he found *Escape and Torture* locked away in a box. The idea began there. The rest of the story grew from that little picture of a boy secretly reading the book. The story was difficult to write at first, getting the voice and the details right, but at one point—the scene with the two brothers driving in the truck—something magical happened and the story began to tell itself, as though I had reached the top of a hill and could coast down the other side. These little moments of magic are what keep writers at their desks.

From Personal Response to Critical Analysis

1. Accept all reasonable responses.
2. Possible response: The pain caused by being tortured was so great as to make the father wish to bury the experience both literally and figuratively.
3. Possible responses: He does not want to discuss painful memories; he wants to shield them from the horrors he endured.
4. Possible responses: Yes, any family with secrets breeds suspicion and distrust; no, people have the right to privacy even within a family, and if Johnny felt it was so important to know about his father's past, he should have had the nerve—and respect—to simply ask for the truth.
5. Possible responses: Yes, because he has gained new insight into his father; no, because now he must live with the knowledge of his father's horrendous experience
6. Possible response: Knowing the author's background as the son of a military man increases the reader's feeling that the emotions and motivations in the story are true to life and have a near-autobiographical honesty.
7. Accept all reasonable, well-supported responses.

Another Pathway
Cooperative Learning Students should work in small groups to plan, write, and deliver the eulogy. One student can record points to include in the eulogy. Another might formulate the points into a written eulogy. A third student can deliver the eulogy to the class.

Rubric
3 Full Accomplishment The eulogy presents all key characteristics of the father, including the son's feelings for him.

2 Substantial Accomplishment The eulogy presents most key characteristics of the father. There is partial indication of the son's feelings.

1 Little or Partial Accomplishment The eulogy presents only some of the key characteristics of the father. There is little or no indication of the son's feelings.

RESPONDING OPTIONS

FROM PERSONAL RESPONSE TO CRITICAL ANALYSIS

REFLECT
1. What were your thoughts at the end of this story? Write your response in your notebook.

RETHINK
2. How does the secret that Johnny learns about his father help explain the way his father has behaved?

Close Textual Reading

Consider
- the cause of his father's injuries
- the effects of his father's experience as a prisoner of war

3. Why do you think the father has kept his war experience a secret from his sons?

4. Does Johnny have a right to know everything about his father's war experience—and to use any method to learn about it? Explain your reasoning.

5. Do you think Johnny is better off for having learned the truth about his father? Explain why or why not.

RELATE
6. How does the Insight selection "On Writing 'Marine Corps Issue'" add to your understanding of the story? Explain your answer.

7. In general, do you think it is better to talk about a terrible experience or to remain silent about it, as the father in this story mostly does? Explain.

Multimodal Learning
ANOTHER PATHWAY
Imagine that you are Johnny. Using what you have learned about your father, write a **eulogy**, or tribute, to him, to be read at his funeral. Deliver this eulogy to your classmates as if they were in attendance at the funeral and did not know the man well. Be sure to make it clear how you came to love "this great man."

LITERARY CONCEPTS

A **flashback** is an account of a conversation, an episode, or an event that happened before the beginning of a story. At the beginning of "Marine Corps Issue," the narrator is a grown man. He tells the story in a series of flashbacks to different times in his life. Go back through the story, identify these flashbacks, and discuss with your classmates why the author chose to tell his story in this way.

The gradual unfolding of the story in flashbacks helps build **suspense**, the excitement or tension that readers feel as they become involved in a story and eager to know the outcome. What places in the story do you think are suspenseful? Discuss these places with your classmates.

QUICKWRITES

1. The field manual *Escape and Torture* prepared military personnel for prison camp. Write copy for a follow-up **field manual**, called *Return and Adjustment*, to help former POW's take up civilian life again. Offer the kinds of tips you think Johnny's father could have used.

2. Imagine that you are Johnny's mother. Using information in the story as your guide, write a **personal letter** to Johnny, explaining what your life was like as you raised two young sons while your husband was away at war.

 PORTFOLIO Save your writing. You may want to use it later as a springboard to a piece for your portfolio.

356   UNIT THREE   PART 1: MIXED BLESSINGS

Literary Concepts
Have students form small groups to identify flashbacks and suspenseful moments in the story. For example, students may point to the narrator's recollection of the impact of viewing *Apocalypse Now* as a key flashback in the story. The drawn-out description of the narrator's opening of his father's boxes is a particularly suspenseful moment. When students have finished, have them compare their interpretations with those of at least one other group. Then have the whole class discuss them together.

QuickWrites
1. Suggest that students list the problems Johnny's father had adjusting to civilian life. They should then jot down some words of advice that might have helped him with each problem. As they draft their copy, they should use an informational style appropriate for a field manual.
2. Encourage students to examine the story for information about Johnny's mother. Inform them that they will have to use their imaginations to fill in details. Suggest that they keep the mother's character in mind as they draft the letter.

The Writer's Craft
Personal Letters, pp. 44–46

Multimodal Learning

ALTERNATIVE ACTIVITIES

1. The narrator describes two vivid images he has of his father—one of his father on the handball court and the other of his father sitting like a statue at the edge of the garden. In a **sketch** or **painting,** capture the two images of the father that you found most vivid in this story.

2. Design and write a message for a Father's Day **greeting card** that Johnny might choose in one of the last four years of his father's life. If you have access to a computer with a graphics program, here's a chance to use it.

THE WRITER'S STYLE

One of the ways in which writers create and develop characters is through **physical description.** In this story, the writer's detailed descriptions help create a vivid image of the father in the reader's mind. For example, the father's hands are described as "large, leprous hands, thick with scar tissue and slightly curled," and his grip is described as "giving him a grotesque bird-on-a-perch appearance." Notice the similes in the following descriptions of the father: "Black thinning hair dipped in gray rises up like tufts of crabgrass" and "He sat as still as a memorial statue." Find at least three other examples of physical descriptions that create a vivid image of the father.

CRITIC'S CORNER

Peter Lum and Michael Little, members of our student advisory board, had different reactions to the way the story ended. Peter was disappointed that the story "did not have a very happy ending." Michael, however, felt the ending "had a nice touch." What do you think about the ending? Were you disappointed? Did you find it true to life? Discuss your reaction to the story's final two paragraphs.

Multimodal Learning

ACROSS THE CURRICULUM

Political Science *Cooperative Learning* With a small group of classmates, investigate the regulations governing international prisoners of war that were established in The Hague Convention and the Geneva Convention. Were these international rules violated in the treatment of the father in this story? Present your findings in a short oral report to the class. If you have access to an encyclopedia program or an on-line service, you might use a computer to start your research.

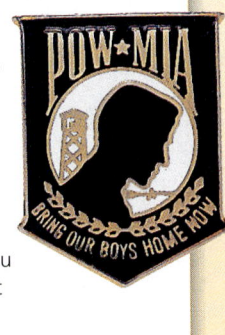

ART CONNECTION

Look again at the painting on page 354. Solitary confinement is an especially agonizing form of imprisonment in which a prisoner is shut off from contact with other prisoners. What aspects of the story can you find in the painting? From what you see in the painting, would it surprise you to learn that from 1968 to 1973 the artist, Theodore Gostas, was himself a prisoner of war in North Vietnam?

Detail of *Solitary Confinement: Insects Witness My Agony* (1982), Theodore Gostas.

MARINE CORPS ISSUE **357**

Critic's Corner

Some students might feel disappointed because the father and son never really discussed what was on their minds; there was still a part of the father's world to which the son could never belong. Other students might feel that the ending was satisfying because the son came to understand his father, love him, and respect him. The father, in turn, showed love for his son by "speaking the things that he knew he wasn't capable of saying."

Across the Curriculum

Political Science *Cooperative Learning* Students should collaborate on their research. One student can gather the needed materials for the group's research on the Hague Convention and the Geneva Convention. Another student might summarize the international rules so other members of the group can decide if they were violated in the treatment of Johnny's father. A third student might record the group's findings, while yet another group member can present these findings in the oral report.

Art Connection

Students might suggest that both the physical torture the father endured while a POW and the mental agony that followed are reflected in the torment of the prisoner in the painting. Because of the graphic intensity of the painting, they should not be surprised to learn that the artist himself is a former Vietnam POW.

The Writer's Style

Encourage students to look for descriptions of the father that help the reader visualize what the man looks like. Point out that these descriptions will make use of figurative language such as similes and metaphors and will appeal to the senses, especially the sense of sight. For more practice in developing characters through physical description, see The Writer's Craft, p. 92.

Alternative Activities

1. Encourage students to find vivid descriptions of the father that would easily translate into a sketch or painting. It might be helpful for students to have models for their drawings. Encourage them to work in pairs, taking turns as artist and model.
2. Remind students that the message should reflect Johnny's attitude toward his father after discovering the truth about his past. Before writing, they should consider the main point that Johnny would want to convey to his father.

Words to Know

Exercise A
1. b
2. a
3. a
4. c
5. c
6. a
7. a
8. c
9. b
10. b

Exercise B
Encourage students to brainstorm with their partner as to how best to act out each word. Suggest that they draw a word web with the key word in the center and then fill in the other circles with associations the word holds for them.

Reteaching/Reinforcement
• *Unit Three Resource Book,* p. 5

ART GALLERY
Through the Eyes of Soldiers
During the Vietnam War, some soldiers documented their lives by painting scenes of the conflict. These images will give students a glimpse of the war through the eyes of the soldiers.

Side A, Frame 49340

WORDS TO KNOW

EXERCISE A Write the letter of the word that is a synonym of each boldfaced vocabulary word below.

1. **vulnerability:** (a) charm, (b) sensitivity, (c) immunity
2. **demeanor:** (a) behavior, (b) rudeness, (c) intelligence
3. **deprivation:** (a) hardship, (b) publicity, (c) bravery
4. **grotesque:** (a) huge, (b) mean, (c) deformed
5. **agitated:** (a) puzzled, (b) humble, (c) jumpy
6. **devoid:** (a) empty, (b) roomy, (c) scarce
7. **trepidation:** (a) anxiety, (b) loyalty, (c) shock
8. **animosity:** (a) cruelty (b) jealousy, (c) hostility
9. **disjunction:** (a) collision, (b) disconnection, (c) loneliness
10. **intrigue:** (a) worry, (b) fascinate, (c) affect

EXERCISE B Work with a partner to act out the meaning of *disjunction, agitated, animosity, vulnerability,* or *deprivation* while another pair of students tries to guess the word. Then switch, with you and your partner trying to guess which word the other pair is acting out. Keep playing this game of charades until all the words are used.

DAVID MCLEAN

1964–

David McLean was a 1994 winner of the O. Henry Award for outstanding American short stories. He currently lives in California, and he has provided the following information about his life:

"I was born and grew up in Granite City, Illinois, a town very much like the Stone City of 'Marine Corps Issue.' My father was a career Marine, and my brothers, sisters, and I moved a number of times. He retired when I was 11, and we settled permanently in Granite City.

"In 1987, I graduated from Bradley University in Peoria, Illinois, where I studied biology as well as English. I knew when I was in high school that I wanted to be a writer, but it was at Bradley that I first began to think seriously about it. I spent one year of college in London, England, and then attended graduate school at Boston University, where I obtained a master's degree in English.

"Not many people can make a living solely as a writer, especially during the years when you are learning your craft. After finishing graduate school, I worked in a bookstore in Boston for about 3½ years before traveling to Slovakia. The revolutions in Eastern Europe had occurred in 1989, and I was curious to see what life was like there. I love to travel and wanted to teach, so in January 1992 I went to Slovakia (then still part of Czechoslovakia) and spent seven months teaching English to high school students.

"I was in Slovakia when I wrote 'Marine Corps Issue.' I have found during my years of writing that I often write better about a place when I'm living somewhere else. I think the distance forces the imagination to work harder, to recall or invent details of a place that is a disorganized jumble of memories. As a result, Stone City in the story resembles my hometown but has taken on an existence all its own. I have a picture of it in my mind, and it is not exactly my hometown but is like a lot of similar towns in the Midwest. It is like an actual place for me. I visit there often and write stories about others who 'live' there."

358 UNIT THREE PART 1: MIXED BLESSINGS

• ART GALLERY

REFLECTING ON THEME
What Do You Think?

Have students think about the chart they created in their notebooks before they began reading the selections in Part One. Ask them how "Marine Corps Issue" illustrates the theme "Mixed Blessings" and whether the pain revealed seems worth the satisfaction in knowing the truth. Has "Marine Corps Issue" altered their judgment of what a mixed blessing is?

PREVIEWING

POETRY

Lineage
Margaret Walker

The Courage That My Mother Had
Edna St. Vincent Millay

Activating Prior Knowledge
PERSONAL CONNECTION
How much do you know about your ancestors—the people you are descended from? To explore your lineage, or ancestry, draw a family tree based on the model shown here. Fill in your family members' names where possible, and extend the tree, if you can, with great-grandparents. After completing the diagram, identify the qualities that made these ancestors special in the lives of those younger than they. Then share your thoughts with the rest of the class.

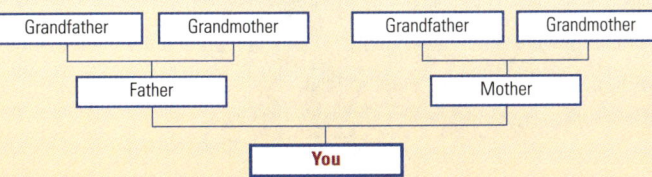

Building Background
BIOGRAPHICAL CONNECTION
In the poems you are about to read, the speakers describe their ancestors. Although the poets are from different backgrounds, both appreciated the admirable qualities of their own female ancestors. Margaret Walker, who was born in Alabama, grew up listening to stories her grandmother told about her family history during the years of slavery. Edna St. Vincent Millay grew up in Maine. Her mother was a singer and practical nurse who raised her three children alone after divorcing her husband.

Setting a Purpose
WRITING CONNECTION
An ancestor can often have a direct impact on someone your age. Write about a special ancestor of yours, telling why that person means so much to you. As you read these poems, compare the speakers' feelings about their ancestors with the way you feel about your own.

LINEAGE / THE COURAGE THAT MY MOTHER HAD   **359**

PRINT AND MEDIA RESOURCES

UNIT THREE RESOURCE BOOK
Strategic Reading: Literature, p. 9

ACCESS FOR STUDENTS ACQUIRING ENGLISH
Selection Summaries
Reading Support

FORMAL ASSESSMENT
Selection Test, pp. 61–62
Test Generator

AUDIO LIBRARY
"The Courage That My Mother Had"
See Reference Card

OVERVIEW

Objectives
- To understand and appreciate two poems that explore the legacy of mothers or grandmothers
- To identify and examine alliteration and repetition
- To express understanding of the poems through a choice of writing forms, including a will and a poem
- To extend understanding of the poems through a variety of multimodal and cross-curricular activities

Skills

LITERARY CONCEPTS
- Alliteration
- Repetition
- Imagery and figurative language

GENRE STUDY
- Poetry: lyric poetry

Thematic Link: *Mixed Blessings* The speakers in these two poems praise their mothers or grandmothers for strength and courage but lament their own lack of these qualities.

CUSTOMIZING FOR
Students Acquiring English

- Use **ACCESS FOR STUDENTS ACQUIRING ENGLISH,** *Reading Support.*
- Both poems contain some challenging diction, or word choice. Urge students to read the poems aloud slowly, watching phrasing and punctuation.

As you guide students through the selections, you may want to use the suggestions in these boxes as well as the suggestions under Strategic Reading for Less-Proficient Readers.

STRATEGIC READING FOR
Less-Proficient Readers

Set a Purpose Ask students to read the poems to discover what the speakers admire about their female ancestors.

Use **UNIT THREE RESOURCE BOOK,** p. 9, for guidance in reading the selection.

THE LANGUAGE OF LITERATURE TEACHER'S EDITION   **359**

Art Note

The Way They Live by Thomas Pollack Anshutz In this painting Thomas P. Anshutz (1851–1912) realistically portrays two members of an African-American family tending a cabbage patch.

Reading the Art In what way does the realism of the painting bring out the strength of its subjects?

CUSTOMIZING FOR
Gifted and Talented Students

As students read the poems, have them think about the different ways in which courage can be displayed. Have them notice the development of courage in the two poems and how it is built upon that of previous generations.

CUSTOMIZING FOR
Students Acquiring English

1 Explain that the speaker refers not only to her immediate grandmothers but also to the female ancestors who came before them.

Literary Concept: ALLITERATION

A Have students read these lines aloud, then ask students what series of words produces alliteration. (*s* sound in *sowing, seed*; *g* sound in *grain, grew*; *s* sound in *sturdiness, singing*) Have them explain the effect of the alliteration. (*Possible response: It makes each line powerful, reflecting the strength of the women.*)

Critical Thinking: SPECULATE

B Have students speculate about the specific qualities the speaker feels she lacks. (*Possible responses: physical strength; the ability to spark the growth of things; an optimistic outlook on life*)

From Personal Response to Critical Analysis

1. Sketches should depict whatever qualities students identify.
2. Possible response: Students may say that this means that the grandmothers, although they worked hard, had few complaints about their lives.
3. Accept all reasonable, well-supported responses.

Lineage
Margaret Walker

The Way They Live (1879), Thomas Pollock Anshutz. Oil on canvas, 24" × 17", The Metropolitan Museum of Art, Morris K. Jesup Fund, 1940 (40.40). Copyright © 1985 The Metropolitan Museum of Art.

1 My grandmothers were strong.
They followed plows and bent to toil.
They moved through fields sowing seed.
A They touched earth and grain grew.
5 They were full of sturdiness and singing.
My grandmothers were strong.

My grandmothers are full of memories
Smelling of soap and onions and wet clay
With veins rolling roughly over quick hands
10 They have many clean words to say.
My grandmothers were strong.
B Why am I not as they?

FROM PERSONAL RESPONSE TO CRITICAL ANALYSIS

REFLECT 1. What image do you have of the speaker's grandmothers? Sketch this image in your notebook.

RETHINK 2. What do you think the statement "They have many clean words to say" (line 10) means?
   Consider
   • the line "Smelling of soap and onions and wet clay"
   • other characteristics of the grandmothers

3. What effect does the last line have on your interpretation of the poem?

360 UNIT THREE PART 1: MIXED BLESSINGS

Mini-Lesson Genre Study

POETRY Remind students that a **lyric poem** usually expresses the personal thoughts or emotions of a single speaker. It is usually short, emphasizing sound and language and containing vivid imagery. The poet strives for a single, powerful effect.

Application Have students compare and contrast these two poems using a Venn diagram, like the one shown.

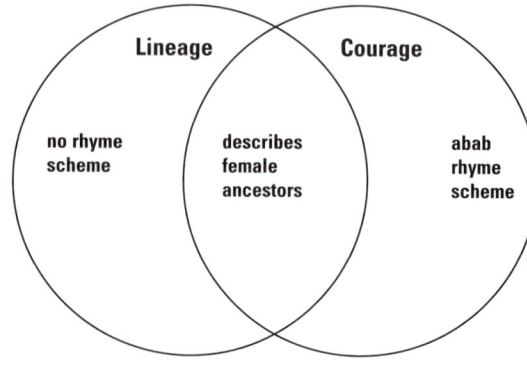

The Courage That My Mother Had
Edna St. Vincent Millay

The courage that my mother had
Went with her, and is with her still:
Rock from New England quarried;
Now granite in a granite hill.

5 The golden brooch my mother wore
She left behind for me to wear;
I have no thing I treasure more:
Yet, it is something I could spare.

Oh, if instead she'd left to me
10 The thing she took into the grave!—
That courage like a rock, which she
Has no more need of, and I have.

CUSTOMIZING FOR
Students Acquiring English

② Define the word *quarried* and use the photograph to show the properties of granite. Then elicit that the speaker's mother is buried in a New England hill. Emphasize that she uses the word *granite* to refer to her mother's strength.

③ Explain to students that *spare* in this line means "give up," or "give away."

Literary Concept: REPETITION

Ⓒ Have students identify the repeated word in this line. *(granite)* Ask why this repetition is used. *(Possible response: The repetition emphasizes a deep "bedrock" of courage.)*

Literary Concept: IMAGERY

Ⓓ Ask students what the image of a rock, repeated throughout the poem suggests about the speaker's mother. *(Possible responses: She had strength and endurance.)*

STRATEGIC READING FOR
Less-Proficient Readers

Ⓔ Ask students what the speakers of these poems admire about their female ancestors. *(their strength and courage)*
Summarizing

COMPREHENSION CHECK

1. In "Lineage," where did the grandmothers work? *(in the fields)*
2. What quality of her ancestors does the speaker feel she lacks? *(strength)*
3. In "The Courage That My Mother Had," what did the mother leave her daughter? *(a golden brooch)*
4. What does the daughter wish her mother had left her? *(courage)*

Mini-Lesson Literary Concepts

REVIEWING IMAGERY AND FIGURATIVE LANGUAGE Remind students that imagery consists of descriptive words and phrases that re-create sensory experiences for the reader. Imagery usually appeals to one or more of the five senses—sight, hearing, smell, taste, and touch. For instance, Walker appeals to the sense of smell in line 8, "Smelling of soap and onions and wet clay." Figurative language communicates ideas and feelings beyond the ordinary, literal meanings of the words. For example, Millay uses this metaphor to describe her mother: "Rock from New England quarried." The word *rock* suggests an outer and inner strength that Millay admired in her mother.

Application Have students work in groups of four or five to identify imagery in the two poems and the senses to which it appeals. Ask them what general feeling or mood is conveyed by the imagery in each poem.

From Personal Response to Critical Analysis

1. Possible responses: Students may suggest words and phrases such as *courageous, strong, realistic, persevering, loving, firm, determined.*
2. Possible response: She respects inner strength and places less value on material things.
3. Possible response: The daughter has the inspiring example of her mother's courage, but the daughter needs actual courage, not just a memory of it.
4. Accept all reasonable, well-supported responses.
5. Accept all, reasonable, well-supported responses.

Another Pathway

Cooperative Learning One or two students can identify which comments in the poems warrant a reply. A facilitator can ask all group members to give their opinions about how to reply to each comment. Then a recorder can write down the group's remarks and formulate its replies.

Rubric

3 Full Accomplishment The replies address the themes of the poems and reflect the characters of the grandmothers and the mother.

2 Substantial Accomplishment The replies address most of the themes and to some extent reflect the characters of the grandmothers and the mother.

1 Little or Partial Accomplishment Students show little understanding of the poems' themes and characterizations of grandmothers or mother.

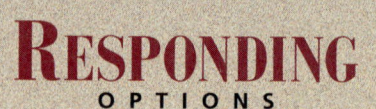

RESPONDING OPTIONS

FROM PERSONAL RESPONSE TO CRITICAL ANALYSIS

REFLECT 1. What image of the speaker's mother do you get from "The Courage That My Mother Had"? In your notebook, list words and phrases that come to mind, and then share them with your classmates.

RETHINK 2. What does the poem suggest to you about the speaker's values and priorities?

Thematic Link 3. In what way has the daughter received mixed blessings from her mother?

RELATE 4. Compare the feelings that the speakers of these poems have toward their ancestors with the feelings you wrote about for the Writing Connection on page 359.

5. Do you feel that your ancestors were more courageous or stronger than you are? Explain your opinion by giving examples, just as the poets did.

Multimodal Learning
ANOTHER PATHWAY
Cooperative Learning

If the speakers' ancestors could read these poems, what might they want to say to the speakers? What advice might they have? With a small group of classmates, write a brief reply to the speaker of each poem, in words that might be spoken by the grandmothers or the mother. Share your responses with the rest of the class.

LITERARY CONCEPTS

Alliteration is a repetition of consonant sounds at the beginnings of words. In "Lineage," the phrase "smelling of soap" is an example of alliteration because of the repeated *s* sound. What other examples can you find in the poem? What effect does the alliteration have on your understanding of the poem? Try substituting other words for the alliterating words, and notice the difference in the sound and feeling of the poem.

Repetition is a repeated use of words or phrases for effect or emphasis. In the poem "Lineage," the repetition of the word "They" emphasizes the difference the speaker feels between herself and her grandmothers. What phrase is repeated in the poem? What effect does the repetition have? What words are repeated in Millay's poem, and what is the effect of the repetition?

QUICKWRITES

1. Imagine that people could write wills in which they leave personal qualities to their descendants. Choose one of the ancestors from these poems—or one of your own ancestors—and write such a **will**.

2. Look over the family tree and the writing about an admired ancestor you completed for the Previewing activities. Write a **poem** about that ancestor. Use specific images to help readers see why the person commands your respect. Consider following the form of Walker's poem: "My _____ was _____. He/she . . ."

📁 **PORTFOLIO** Save your writing. You may want to use it later as a springboard to a piece for your portfolio.

362 UNIT THREE PART 1: MIXED BLESSINGS

Literary Concepts

Examples include *s* sound in *sowing, seed*; *g* sound in *grain, grew*; *s* sound in *sturdiness, singing*; *r* sound in *rolling roughly*. The language emphasizes the stamina and the strength of the grandmothers. Pairs of students should read each other's rewrites and discuss how the sound and feeling have been altered.

Repetition "My grandmothers were strong." Students may conclude that the repetition underscores the grandmothers' strength. Students should identify the repeated words in "Courage" (*rock, granite, courage*) and connect them to the rock metaphor.

QuickWrites

1. Have students research the format of wills before they begin the assignment. Then encourage them to think about what personal qualities should be bequeathed and what effect they may have on the recipients.
2. Suggest that students create a word web, listing the admirable characteristics of their chosen ancestors. Then encourage them to use their word webs for help in thinking of specific images to portray those characteristics in their poems.

Multimodal Learning

ALTERNATIVE ACTIVITIES

1. Set the two poems to music, either as **songs** or as **dramatic readings** with musical backgrounds, and present them to the class.
2. Create a **work of art** to accompany each poem. You might choose to make a collage, a mobile, a sculpture, a carving, a mural, or a painting.

Multimodal Learning

LITERARY LINKS

How do the feelings the speakers of these poems have about their ancestors compare with the way the boy feels about his father in "Marine Corps Issue"?

ACROSS THE CURRICULUM

Social Studies Interview your parents or grandparents and find out what they know about their parents. What were the parents' lives like? What qualities or values did they pass on? Make a tape-recorded or written family record of what you learn.

Alternative Activities

1. In preparation for presenting the song or dramatic reading, students should consider the feelings portrayed in each poem so that they can select appropriate musical background. Encourage them to think about ways to use their voices and gestures to express these feelings. It may be beneficial to have them work in small groups in which one volunteer can perform while the other group members listen and offer constructive criticism.
2. Recommend that students first decide on the aspect (or aspects) of the poem they wish to portray; that decision will help them choose the form the work will take. For example, if they wish to portray the various tasks that the grandmothers performed, they might consider a painting or a collage; if they wish to focus on the rocklike courage of the mother in Millay's poem, they might consider a sculpture.

Literary Links

Students may conclude that both speakers in the poems as well as the narrator of the short story admire their ancestors for their strength and courage but that the narrator in "Marine Corps Issue" does not express regret about not having his father's qualities.

Across the Curriculum

Social Studies Suggest that students use the following prompts when conducting their interviews:

- Where and when were your parents born?
- Where did they live when you were growing up?
- What did they do for a living?
- What words would you use to describe what their lives were like?
- What qualities or values did they pass on to you?
- In what ways have those qualities affected your life?

MARGARET WALKER

1915–

Margaret Walker grew up with books. Her father was a well-educated, scholarly Methodist minister, and her mother was a music teacher. Her father shared with her his great love of literature, and her mother played ragtime music and read poetry to her daughter.

Early in life, Walker decided to write poetry. She won the Yale University Younger Poets Award in 1942 for her first collection of poems, *For My People*. The title poem portrays the experiences of African Americans and is written in the rhythm of a preacher's sermon. One of Walker's most famous works is a novel, *Jubilee*. It tells the story of her great-grandmother, a slave in Georgia during the time of the Civil War. Walker used the traditional form of the slave narrative to create her historical novel. During the 30 years it took her to write this novel, she also raised four children, taught school, and earned a doctorate. Walker was a teacher for much of her career, most of the time as a professor of English at Jackson State College in Mississippi.

OTHER WORKS *Prophets for a New Day, How I Wrote Jubilee, This Is My Century: New and Collected Poems*
Extended Reading

EDNA ST. VINCENT MILLAY

1892–1950

Edna St. Vincent Millay was considered by many to be the voice of the rebellious youth of her time. A Pulitzer Prize–winning poet and a feminist, she stressed women's liberation in much of her poetry.

Encouraged by her mother, Millay began writing poetry as a child. At the age of 14, she published a poem in a children's magazine. At 20, she received national recognition after publishing her poem "Renascence." The recognition enabled her to win a scholarship to Vassar College.

After graduating, Millay became a part of New York City's controversial Greenwich Village scene. From the 1920s through the 1940s, this area's reputation as a center for artists and writers grew. Millay created some of her most successful writing while living there in the early 1920s. Her works often shocked the older generation while voicing the views of her liberated contemporaries during the decade that became known as the Roaring Twenties. In all, Millay wrote more than 20 volumes of poetry, plays, and essays, as well as an opera. She also directed and acted in plays.

OTHER WORKS *Renascence and Other Poems*
Extended Reading

MARGARET WALKER

"Lineage" appears in Margaret Walker's first collection of poems, *For My People*, which focuses on the strengths and trials of African Americans. The goal of her work, she says, is "to fashion a world that will hold all the people, all the faces, all the adams and eves and their countless generations."

EDNA ST. VINCENT MILLAY

According to her friend, the writer Floyd Dell, Edna St. Vincent Millay was "very much a revolutionary in all her sympathies, and a wholehearted Feminist."

OVERVIEW

Objectives

- To understand and appreciate a short story that explores the relationship between an uncle and his two nieces
- To enrich reading by using active reading strategies
- To identify and understand conflict
- To express understanding of the story through a choice of writing forms, including a list, a story ending, a eulogy, and a short story
- To extend understanding of the story through a variety of multimodal and cross-curricular activities

Skills

LITERARY CONCEPTS
- Conflict
- Tone
- Characterization

READING SKILLS/ STRATEGIES
- Making inferences about characters
- Clarifying

THE WRITER'S STYLE
- Combining sentences with *who, which,* or *that*

GENRE STUDY
- Fiction: short story

GRAMMAR
- Clauses

SPEAKING, LISTENING, AND VIEWING
- Film music

CUSTOMIZING FOR
Students Acquiring English

- Use **ACCESS FOR STUDENTS ACQUIRING ENGLISH,** *Reading Support.*
- Explain to students that this story is about a Native American child's uncle and how he influenced her life. Tell students that Native Americans lived in the United States before the arrival of European settlers. Ask students from other countries if there are any native peoples in their homelands. If so, how long have they lived there? And how do they live today?

PREVIEWING

FICTION

The Warriors
Anna Lee Walters

Activating Prior Knowledge
PERSONAL CONNECTION

In the following story, a contemporary Pawnee woman tells about a relative who was special to her and her sister when they were young. Is there a relative you are particularly fond of? An aunt who thinks the world of you, or a cousin who always makes you laugh? Think about the relative who has meant the most to you in your life. Then create a cluster diagram like the one shown, detailing the qualities that make this relative special to you.

Building Background
HISTORICAL CONNECTION

The special relative in "The Warriors" is an uncle who shares with his nieces his knowledge of traditional Pawnee songs, stories, and beliefs. The Pawnee are a group of Plains Indians who originally lived in what is now Texas and later migrated north to Oklahoma, Kansas, and Nebraska. In the past, the Pawnee lived in earth lodges in small villages, grew food crops, and hunted buffalo. Conflicts and raids among tribes on the Great Plains were common then, and the Pawnee often fought other tribes. Pawnee warriors formed a special society, and brave warriors were highly honored by their people.

The westward expansion of the United States drastically changed the Pawnee way of life. As more Indian tribes were pushed westward and crowded into the Great Plains, conflicts between tribes increased. In the late 1700s, the Pawnee numbered about 10,000. Warfare and disease reduced their number to about 4,500 during the 1800s, and by 1906 there were only about 650 Pawnee left. In treaties with the U.S. government, the Pawnee lost all their lands, and they were moved to a reservation in Oklahoma. Many Pawnee still live on or near the reservation today.

364 UNIT THREE PART 1: MIXED BLESSINGS

PRINT AND MEDIA RESOURCES

UNIT THREE RESOURCE BOOK
Strategic Reading: Literature, p. 13
Vocabulary SkillBuilder, p. 14

GRAMMAR MINI-LESSONS
Transparencies, p. 2
Copymasters, p. 3

WRITING MINI-LESSONS
Transparencies, p. 51

ACCESS FOR STUDENTS ACQUIRING ENGLISH
Selection Summaries
Reading Support

FORMAL ASSESSMENT
Selection Test, pp. 63–64
 Test Generator

 AUDIO LIBRARY
See Reference Card

INTERNET RESOURCES
McDougal Littell Literature Center at http://www.hmco.com/mcdougal/lit

364 THE LANGUAGE OF LITERATURE TEACHER'S EDITION

Active Reading/Setting a Purpose
READING CONNECTION

Making Inferences About Characters

You make an inference every time you figure something out on the basis of bits of evidence. You can't get through a single day without making some inferences. For example, your book isn't in your bag, so you must have left it at school; there's nobody standing at the bus stop, so the bus has probably already come and gone.

You make inferences when you read fiction too—that is, you come to certain conclusions about the characters and why they act or think as they do. Making inferences is like "reading between the lines." Usually you infer by combining clues in the text with what you already know from your experiences or other reading.

In "The Warriors," the author may not tell you everything that's going on in the characters' heads. However, there are plenty of clues that a careful reader can use to make inferences. Notice especially what the main character, Uncle Ralph, says and does. What you infer from his behavior will help you understand the kind of life he leads and the inner conflict he feels. Here is an example of the kind of inference you might make about Uncle Ralph, based on clues presented early in the story.

```
What the narrator says  →  What I know from experience or reading
                        ↓
                   What I can infer
```

What the narrator says	What I know from experience or reading	What I can infer
"He liked to pray. He prayed for Sister and me and for everyone and every tiny thing in the world, but we never heard him ask for anything for himself from Atius, the Father."	People often pray for help for their families. It seems weird, though, to pray for tiny things in the world but not for yourself.	Uncle Ralph is unselfish and spiritual. He has sympathy for all living things.

Using Your Reading Log Several questions have been inserted in the story to help you make inferences. As you read, take a moment to jot down in your reading log some brief answers to these questions and to list other thoughts that occur to you. Drawing on your own experience as well as details from the story, try to infer why Uncle Ralph thinks and acts as he does and what he is trying to teach his nieces.

THE WARRIORS   **365**

SUMMARY

When the narrator and her sister were children, they often watched hobos passing by their house. It did not occur to them that their Uncle Ralph would end his life as a hobo. Uncle Ralph is a Pawnee warrior who teaches them the old ways of the Pawnee warriors. He tells them they should live for beauty. As the years pass, Uncle Ralph begins drinking heavily. The narrator's mother tells him not to come around when he is drunk. He visits less often and his health declines. On his last visit, the narrator recalls for Uncle Ralph all that he has taught her. One day, years later, she wakes up gloomy, a feeling that lasts for days. She later learns that on that day Uncle Ralph died of exposure in a hobo camp. Both sisters still miss Uncle Ralph and thank him for teaching them to live beautifully as Pawnee warriors.

Thematic Link: *Mixed Blessings* The relationship between Uncle Ralph and his nieces becomes a mixed blessing for the girls when he succumbs to alcoholism.

ALTERNATIVE
Previewing

Students can choose partners and use the following prompts to discuss "The Warriors."

Personal Connection

Discussion Prompts
- *Which relative means the most to you?*
- *What qualities make that person special to you?*
- *What effect has your special relative had on your life?*

As you read "The Warriors," note the qualities that make Uncle Ralph special to his nieces.

WORDS TO KNOW

fantasize (făn'tə-sīz') *v.* to imagine, as if in a daydream (p. 368)

haggard (hăg'ərd) *adj.* having a worn, exhausted look, as from hunger or illness (p. 369)

obsessively (əb-sĕs'ĭv-lē) *adv.* in a way showing an excessive concern with a single idea or thought (p. 368)

ravage (răv'ĭj) *v.* to destroy violently (p. 368)

retort (rĭ-tôrt') *v.* to reply quickly, usually with an angry or witty response (p. 370)

STRATEGIC READING FOR
Less-Proficient Readers

Set a Purpose After students have read the first paragraph, discuss with them the conditions in which hobos live. Then ask them to read to find out why the narrator says that Uncle Ralph would end up like the hobos.

Use **UNIT THREE RESOURCE BOOK**, p. 13, for guidance in reading the selection.

CUSTOMIZING FOR
Students Acquiring English

1 Explain that at various times in the United States many people have not been able to find regular jobs. Some traveled from state to state, staying a few days or weeks in a town and doing odd jobs in exchange for food and a place to sleep. Wandering, homeless people used to be called hobos. They often carried their possessions in a bundle tied to a stick.

Literary Concept:
CHARACTERIZATION

A Ask students what Uncle Ralph's lack of interest in disciplining his nieces reveals about him. *(Possible response: He is a gentle man more interested in teaching than in correcting.)*

THE WARRIORS

ANNA LEE WALTERS

In our youth, we saw hobos come and go, sliding by our faded white house like wary cats who did not want us too close. Sister and I waved at the strange procession of passing men and women hobos. Just between ourselves, Sister and I talked of that hobo parade. We guessed at and imagined the places and towns we thought the hobos might have come from or had been. Mostly they were White or Black people. But there were Indian hobos too. It never occurred to Sister and me that this would be Uncle Ralph's end.

Sister and I were little and Uncle Ralph came to visit us. He lifted us over his head and shook us around him like gourd rattles. He was Momma's younger brother, and he could have disciplined us if he so desired. That was part of our custom. But he never did. Instead, he taught us Pawnee words. "*Pari'* is Pawnee and *pita* is man," he said. Between the words, he tapped out drumbeats with his fingers on the tabletop, ghost dance and round dance songs that he suddenly remembered and sang. His melodic voice lilted over us and hung around the corners of the house for days. His stories of life and death were fierce and gentle. Warriors dangled in delicate balance.

Detail of *Young Omaha, War Eagle, Little Missouri, and Pawnees* (1821), Charles Bird King.

Mini-Lesson — Workplace Literacy

SCANS Goal: Teaches Others

TEACHING OTHERS Emphasize that communicating well is an essential part of teaching and that workers frequently teach one another in the workplace. Introduce the idea that Uncle Ralph is a good teacher because he:

1. knows the subject matter well
2. organizes ideas and communicates oral messages appropriate to listeners
3. selects an appropriate medium for conveying a message
4. uses language appropriate in style, tone, and level of complexity to the audience
5. understands and responds to listener feedback
6. asks questions when needed

Application Working in small groups, students should take turns playing the part of a supervisor who teaches new employees—the other group members—how to perform a task. Employees will evaluate the supervisor by determining whether they have learned the task.

CUSTOMIZING FOR
Gifted and Talented Students

As students read the selection, they should look for specific events and passages that indicate how Uncle Ralph strives for beauty in his life. Ask them to state the significance of each passage.

Possible responses:

- Page 368—"He prayed for Sister and me and for everyone and every tiny thing in the world, but we never heard him ask for anything for himself." He is generous and spiritual.
- Page 369—"'Them hobos are kind of like us. We're not like other people in some ways and yet we are.'" He does not judge others harshly.
- Page 372—"They said that he was only one of a few who knew the old ways and the songs." He values the traditions and customs of his culture.
- Page 376—"He was moved by my recitation and clutched my hand tightly." He is a gentle, responsive teacher who inspires others.

CUSTOMIZING FOR
Multiple Learning Styles

B **Spatial or Graphic Learners** Ask students to compare the photograph on this page with the description of hobos in the first paragraph. Ask them to discuss whether they think the people depicted in the photograph look like the hobos who passed by the narrator's house.

Multicultural Perspectives

THE PAWNEE A spiritual people, the Pawnee were revered by other Native American groups for their rituals and their myths. The Pawnee believed that all things came from "The One Above," including the stars in the heavens. The Evening Star symbolized woman, and the Morning Star symbolized man. According to Pawnee religion, creation was achieved when the Morning Star met the Evening Star. Pawnee priests, also called shamans or medicine men, were viewed as messengers between the spirit world and earth. Pawnee shamans presided over ceremonies performed to protect the crops and used special rites to promote success in hunting. When the Pawnee shaman presided over the ghost dance, he expressed the people's desire to restore the traditional way of life.

Cultural Note

C A myth is a traditional story that explains how something came into existence. Greek, Roman, and Norse myths feature gods and goddesses. Native American myths recount the deeds of anthropomorphized (personified) animals.

Literary Concept: CONFLICT

D Ask students to speculate about what conflict the narrator is referring to when she states that "Uncle Ralph had a great battlefield of his own." (Possible responses: his struggle to hold fast to the old ways in modern times; his struggle against alcoholism)

Literary Concept: METAPHOR

E Remind students that a metaphor is a figure of speech that makes a comparison between two things that have something in common. Have students discuss what this metaphor reveals about the difference between the uncle and his nieces. (Possible response: Uncle Ralph was having a hard time adjusting to the modern world, whereas his nieces accepted the world as they found it.)

Critical Thinking: ANALYZE

F Ask students to analyze what the narrator means when she says that Uncle Ralph was a warrior when he died. (Possible response: Though he was troubled, he was still fighting to preserve the old ways.)

He told us his version of the story of *Pahukatawa*, a Skidi[1] Pawnee warrior. He was killed by the Sioux, but the animals, feeling compassion for him, brought *Pahukatawa* to life again. "The Evening Star and the Morning Star bore children and some people say that these offspring are who we are," he often said. At times he pointed to those stars and greeted them by their Pawnee names. He liked to pray. He prayed for Sister and me and for everyone and every tiny thing in the world, but we never heard him ask for anything for himself from *Atius*, the Father.

"For beauty is why we live," Uncle Ralph said when he talked of precious things only the Pawnees know. "We die for it too." He called himself an ancient Pawnee warrior when he was quite young. He told us that warriors must brave all storms and odds and stand their ground. He knew intimate details of every battle the Pawnees ever fought since Pawnee time began, and Sister and I knew even then that Uncle Ralph had a great battlefield of his own.

As a child I thought that Uncle Ralph had been born into the wrong time. The Pawnees had been <u>ravaged</u> so often by then. The tribe of several thousand at its peak over a century before were then a few hundred people who had been closely confined for over a century. The warrior life was gone. Uncle Ralph was trapped in a transparent bubble of new time. The bubble bound him tight as it blew around us.

Uncle Ralph talked <u>obsessively</u> of warriors, painted proud warriors who shrieked poignant battle cries at the top of their lungs and died with honor. Sister and I were very little then, lost from him in the world of children who saw everything with children's eyes. And though we saw with wide eyes the painted warriors that he <u>fantasized</u> and heard their fierce and haunting battle cries, we did not hear this. Now that we are old and Uncle Ralph has been gone for a long time, Sister and I know that when he died, he was tired and alone. But he was a warrior.

The hobos were always around in our youth. Sister and I were curious about them, and this curiosity claimed much of our time. They crept by the house at all hours of the day and night, dressed in rags and odd clothing. They wandered to us from the railroad tracks where they had leaped from slow-moving boxcars onto the flatland. They hid in high clumps of

---

1. **Skidi:** one of the four bands, or groups, of the Pawnee.

WORDS TO KNOW
ravage (răv′ĭj) *v.* to destroy violently
obsessively (əb-sĕs′ĭv-lē) *adv.* in a way showing an excessive concern with a single idea or thought
fantasize (făn′tə-sīz′) *v.* to imagine, as if in a daydream

Critic's Corner

"The story was too predictable. By the second page, I already knew what was going to happen."

Yanaira Ferreira,
Ninth-Grade Member,
Student Advisory Board

Ask students to discuss whether knowledge of Uncle Ralph's death ruined the story for them. Have them consider how they might have reacted if the reader had not found out Uncle Ralph's fate until the end of the story.

CONNECT

The hobos in this story are similar to the homeless of today. Have you ever wondered about the background and lives of homeless people?
Using a Reading Log

CLARIFY

Notice the difference between the way Uncle Ralph and the girl's parents view the hobos. What does Uncle Ralph think of the hobos?
Using a Reading Log

weeds and brush that ran along the fence near the tracks. The hobos usually travelled alone, but Sister and I saw them come together, like poor families, to share a tin of beans or sardines they ate with sticks or twigs. Uncle Ralph watched them from a distance too.

One early morning, Sister and I crossed the tracks on our way to school and collided with a tall, haggard whiteman. He wore a very old-fashioned pin-striped black jacket covered with lint and soot. There was fright in his eyes when they met ours. He scurried around us, quickening his pace. The pole over his shoulder where his possessions hung in a bundle at the end bounced as he nearly ran from us.

"Looks just like a scared jackrabbit," Sister said as she watched him dart away.

That evening we told Momma about the scared man. She warned us about the dangers of hobos as our father threw us a stern look. Uncle Ralph was visiting but he didn't say anything. He stayed the night and Sister asked him, "Hey, Uncle Ralph, why do you suppose they's hobos?"

Uncle Ralph was a large man. He took Sister and put her on one knee. "You see, Sister," he said, "hobos are a different kind. They see things in a different way. Them hobos are kind of like us. We're not like other people in some ways and yet we are. It has to do with what you see and feel when you look at this old world."

His answer satisfied Sister for awhile and he taught us some more Pawnee words that night.

Not long after Uncle Ralph's explanation, Sister and I surprised a Black man with white whiskers and fuzzy hair. He was climbing through the barbed wire fence that marked our property line. He wore faded blue overalls with pockets stuffed full of handkerchiefs. He wiped sweat from his face, and when it dried he looked up and saw us. I remember what Uncle Ralph had said and wondered what the Black man saw when he looked at us standing there.

"We might scare him," Sister said softly to me, remembering the whiteman who had scampered away.

Sister whispered, "Hi," to the Black man. Her voice was barely audible.

"Boy, it's shore hot," he said. His voice was big and he smiled.

"Where are you going?" Sister asked.

"Me? Nowheres, I guess," he muttered.

"Then what you doing here?" Sister went on. She was bold for a seven-year-old kid. I was a year older but I was also more quiet. "This here place is ours," she said.

He looked around and saw our house with its flowering mimosa trees and rich green, mowed lawn stretching out before him. Other houses sat around ours.

"I reckon I'm lost," he said.

Sister pointed to the weeds and brush further up the road. "That's where you want to go. That's where they all go, the hobos."

I tried to quiet Sister but she didn't hush. "The hobos stay up there," she said. "You a hobo?"

He ignored her question and asked his own. "Say, what is you all? You not Black, you not White. What is you all?"

Sister looked at me. She put one hand on her chest and the other hand on me. "We Indians!" Sister said.

He stared at us and smiled again. "Is that a fact," he said.

"Know what kind of Indians we are?" Sister asked him.

WORDS TO KNOW
haggard (hăg′ərd) *adj.* having a worn, exhausted look, as from hunger or illness

369

Literary Concept:
CHARACTERIZATION

J Ask students what Sister's response to the hobo's remark that "Indians is Indians" suggests about her. *(Possible responses: She is proud and bold; she knows that there are different groups of "Indians.")*

Critical Thinking:
MAKING INFERENCES

K Ask students why the girls tell Uncle Ralph about their conversation with the hobo. *(Possible response: They know he will understand.)* Ask why Uncle Ralph smiles. *(Possible response: He appreciates Sister's bragging about being a Pawnee warrior.)*

Literary Concept: DESCRIPTION

L Ask students what impression this description makes on them. *(Possible responses: The man seems alarming; poor; exhausted; angry.)*

Critical Thinking: HYPOTHESIZE

M Have students explain what the narrator means when she says, "a man's always got people." *(Possible response: that according to what she has been taught, there is always someone who will try to help you and take care of you)*

He shook his fuzzy head. "Indians is Indians, I guess," he said.

Sister wrinkled her forehead and <u>retorted</u>, "Not us! We not like others. We see things different. We're Pawnees. We're warriors!"

I pushed my elbow into Sister's side. She quieted.

The man was looking down the road and he shuffled his feet. "I'd best go," he said.

Sister pointed to the brush and weeds one more time. "That way," she said.

He climbed back through the fence and brush as Sister yelled, "Bye now!" She waved a damp handkerchief.

Sister and I didn't tell Momma and Dad about the Black man. But much later Sister told Uncle Ralph every word that had been exchanged with the Black man. Uncle Ralph listened and smiled.

Months later when the warm weather had cooled and Uncle Ralph came to stay with us for a couple of weeks, Sister and I went to the hobo place. We had planned it for a long time. That afternoon when we pushed away the weeds, not a hobo was in sight.

The ground was packed down tight in the clearing among the high weeds. We walked around the encircling brush and found folded cardboards stacked together. Burned cans in assorted sizes were stashed under the cardboards and there were remains of old fires. Rags were tied to the bush, snapping in the hard wind.

Sister said, "Maybe they're all in the boxcars now. It's starting to get cold."

She was right. The November wind had a bite to it, and the cold stung our hands and froze our breaths as we spoke.

"You want to go over to them boxcars?" she asked. We looked at the Railroad Crossing sign where the boxcars stood.

I was prepared to answer when a voice roared from somewhere behind us.

"Now, you young ones, you git on home! Go on! Git!"

A man crawled out of the weeds and looked angrily at us. His eyes were red and his face was unshaven. He wore a red plaid shirt with striped gray and black pants too large for him. His face was swollen and bruised. An old woolen pink scarf hid some of the bruise marks around his neck and his top coat was splattered with mud.

Sister looked at him. She stood close to me and told him defiantly, "You can't tell us what to do! You don't know us!"

He didn't answer Sister but tried to stand. He couldn't. Sister ran to him and took his arm and pulled on it. "You need help?" she questioned.

He frowned at her but let us help him. He was tall. He seemed to be embarrassed by our help.

"You Indian, ain't you?" I dared to ask him.

He didn't answer me but looked at his feet as if they could talk so he wouldn't have to. His feet were in big brown overshoes.

"Who's your people?" Sister asked. He looked to be about Uncle Ralph's age when he finally lifted his face and met mine. He didn't respond for a minute. Then he sighed. "I ain't got no people," he told us as he tenderly stroked his swollen jaw.

"Sure you got people. Our folks says a man's always got people," I said softly. The wind blew our clothes and covered the words.

But he heard. He exploded like a firecracker. "Well, I don't! I ain't got no people! I ain't got nobody!"

"What you doing out here anyway? Sister asked. "You hurt? You want to come over to our house?"

"Naw," he said. "Now you little ones, go on home. Don't be walking round out here. Didn't

---

WORDS TO KNOW **retort** (rĭ-tôrt′) *v.* to reply quickly, usually with an angry or witty response

370

Mini-Lesson — Genre Study

FICTION Remind students that a short story is much shorter than a novel and can usually be read in one sitting. Generally, a short story has one main conflict that involves the characters, keeps the story moving, and makes it interesting. Draw a word web on the chalkboard. Use it to explain the characteristics of a short story.

Application Have students copy the word web in their notebooks. Ask them to refer to it as they look for the characteristics of a short story in "The Warriors."

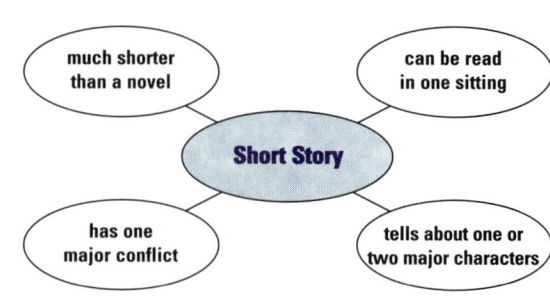

370 THE LANGUAGE OF LITERATURE TEACHER'S EDITION

nobody tell you little girls ain't supposed to be going round by themselves. You might git hurt."

"We just wanted to talk to hobos," Sister said.

"Naw, you don't. Just go on home. Your folks is probably looking for you and worrying 'bout you."

I took Sister's arm and told her we were going home. Then we said "Bye" to the man. But Sister couldn't resist a few last words, "You Indian, ain't you?"

He nodded his head like it was a painful thing to do. "Yeah, I'm Indian."

"You ought to go on home yourself," Sister said. "Your folks probably looking for you and worrying 'bout you."

His voice rose again as Sister and I walked away from him. "I told you kids, I don't have any people!" There was exasperation in his voice.

Sister would not be outdone. She turned and yelled, "Oh yeah? You Indian, ain't you? Ain't you?" she screamed, "We your people!"

His top-coat and pink scarf flapped in the wind as we turned away from him.

We went home to Momma and Dad and Uncle Ralph then. Uncle Ralph met us at the front door. "Where you all been?" he asked and looked toward the railroad tracks. Momma and Dad were talking in the kitchen.

"Just playing, Uncle," Sister and I said simultaneously.

Uncle Ralph grabbed both Sister and I by our hands and yanked us out the door. *"Awkuh!"*

he said, using the Pawnee expression to show his dissatisfaction.

Outside, we sat on the cement porch. Uncle Ralph was quiet for a long time, and neither Sister nor I knew what to expect.

"I want to tell you all a story," he finally said. "Once, there were these two rats who ran around everywhere and got into everything all the time. Everything they were told not to do, well, they went right out and did. They'd get into one mess and then another. It seems that they never could learn."

At that point Uncle Ralph cleared his throat. He looked at me and said, "Sister do you understand this story? Is it too hard for you? You're older."

I nodded my head up and down and said, "I understand."

Then Uncle Ralph looked at Sister. He said to her, "Sister, do I need to go on with this story?"

Sister shook her head from side to side. "Naw, Uncle Ralph," she said.

"So you both know how this story ends?" he said gruffly. Sister and I bobbed our heads up and down again.

We followed at his heels the rest of the day. When he tightened the loose hide on top of his drum, we watched him and held it in place as he laced the wet hide down. He got his drumsticks down from the

Brave Chief, A Skidi (Wolf) Pawnee (1832), George Catlin. Oil on canvas, 29″ × 24″, National Museum of American Art, gift of Mrs. Joseph Harrison, Jr. (1985.66.110), Smithsonian Institution, Washington, D.C./Art Resource, New York.

CLARIFY

What is Uncle Ralph telling the girls through his story? Why does he want them to get that message?
Using a Reading Log

THE WARRIORS 371

Art Note

Brave Chief, A Skidi (Wolf) Pawnee (1832) by George Catlin George Catlin (1796–1872) is perhaps the best-known painter of Native Americans. This portrait shows a painted Pawnee warrior who has been victorious in battle. The hands painted on his chest signify that he killed a foe in hand-to-hand combat.

Reading the Art *Compare this painting with the description of warriors on page 368. Do you think that this painting is a good representation of one of Uncle Ralph's warriors? Why or why not?*

Literary Concept: TONE

 Remind students that tone is the attitude a writer takes toward a subject. Ask them what tone Sister uses in her conversation with the Native-American hobo. (*Possible responses: compassionate; assertive*)

Active Reading: CLARIFY

Possible responses: He is telling them that going to the hobo place is not a safe thing for them to do. He tells them this because he is concerned about their welfare; He also knew that they were lying about where they had been. He uses a story to emphasize what he means.

CUSTOMIZING FOR
Students Acquiring English

③ Explain that the noun *hide* in this passage refers to animal skin, used here as the top of a drum. You may want to draw a simple graphic on the board to demonstrate how Uncle Ralph laced the wet hide on top of his drum.

Mini-Lesson · Literary Concepts

REVIEWING CHARACTERIZATION
Remind students that characterization is the methods that a writer uses to develop characters. Emphasize that writers use four basic methods of characterization: describing a character's physical appearance; revealing a character's speech, thoughts, feelings, or actions; providing others' speech, thoughts, or feelings about a character; and making direct comments about a character.

Application Have students work in groups to find examples of different techniques that the writer uses to characterize Uncle Ralph. For example, after students have read the passage on page 372 that describes Uncle Ralph's gift of food, have them note that the author uses this passage to reveal that Ralph is a generous man who practices what he preaches. Students can record their findings by completing a chart like the one on the right.

Linking to History

P Four months after the historic *Apollo 11* mission, *Apollo 12* landed on the moon. The *Apollo 13* flight, in April 1970, almost ended tragically after an explosion occurred in the service module. The Apollo flights ended with *Apollo 17* in December 1972.

STRATEGIC READING FOR
Less-Proficient Readers

Q To understand what Uncle Ralph has in common with the hobos, students should reread his thoughts about them on page 369.

- In what way does Uncle Ralph feel that hobos are like Native Americans? *(They see things differently.)* **Noting Relevant Details**

- What is most important to Uncle Ralph? *(preserving the old ways; beauty)* **Summarizing**

- In what different way does Uncle Ralph see things? *(He sees beauty in all things.)* **Compare and Contrast**

Set a Purpose Have students read to find out how Uncle Ralph becomes a hobo.

Active Reading: EVALUATE

R Students' opinions will vary.

Art Note

***Young Omaha, War Eagle, Little Missouri, and Pawnees* by Charles Bird King**
Charles Bird King (1785–1862), like George Catlin, painted portraits of Native Americans. These Pawnee warriors wear wampum ornaments hung from slits in their ear lobes. They have also ornamented the tufts of remaining hair on their shaved heads with crests of dyed deer's hair.

Reading the Art *The warriors are not interacting with one another or with the viewer. What feeling does that evoke?*

---

top shelf of the closet and began to pound the drum slowly.

"Where you going, Uncle Ralph?" I asked. Sister and I knew that when he took his drum out, he was always gone shortly after.

"I have to be a drummer at some doings tomorrow," he said.

"You a good singer, Uncle Ralph," Sister said. "You know all them old songs."

P "The young people nowadays, it seems they don't care bout nothing that's old. They just want to go to the Moon."² He was drumming low as he spoke.

"We care, Uncle Ralph," Sister said.

"Why?" Uncle Ralph asked in a hard challenging tone that he seldom used on us.

Sister thought for a minute and then said, "I guess because you care so much, Uncle Ralph."

His eyes softened and he said, "I'll sing you an *Eruska* song, a song for the warriors."

The song he sang was a war dance song. At first Sister and I listened attentively but then Sister began to dance the man's dance. She had never danced before and she tried to imitate what she had seen. Her chubby body whirled and jumped the way she'd seen the men dance. Her head tilted from side to side the way the men moved theirs. I laughed aloud at her clumsy effort and Uncle Ralph laughed heartily too.

Q Uncle Ralph went in and out of our lives after that. We heard that he sang at one place and then another, and people came to Momma to find him. They said that he was only one of a few who knew the old ways and the songs.

EVALUATE

R What do you think of Uncle Ralph, his views, and the life he leads? **Using a Reading Log**

When he came to visit us, he always brought something to eat. The Pawnee custom was that the man, the warrior, should bring food, preferably meat. Then whatever food was brought to the host was prepared and served to the man, the warrior, along with the host's family. Many times Momma and I, or Sister and I, came home to an empty house to find a sack of food on the table. I or Momma cooked it for the next meal, and Uncle Ralph showed up to eat.

"I'll sing you an *Eruska* song, a song for the warriors."

Young Omaha, War Eagle, Little Missouri, and Pawnees (1821), Charles Bird King. National Museum of American Art, Washington, D.C./Art Resource, New York.

As Sister and I grew older, our fascination with the hobos decreased. Other things took our time, and Uncle Ralph did not appear as frequently as he did before.

Once while I was home alone, I picked up Momma's old photo album. Inside was a gray photo of Uncle Ralph in an army uniform. Behind him were tents on a flat terrain. Other photos showed other poses but in only one picture did he smile. All the photos were written over in black ink in Momma's handwriting. "Ralphie in Korea,"³ the writing said.

2. **go to the Moon:** In 1961, President Kennedy committed the United States to the goal of landing men on the moon by the end of the decade. Astronauts first stepped onto the moon's surface on July 20, 1969.
3. **in Korea:** Around 480,000 American troops fought in the Korean War, a conflict between Communist and non-Communist forces lasting from 1950 to 1953.

Multicultural Perspectives

PAWNEE CUSTOMS War dances are most often performed during a powwow, or ceremony of hunting rituals. The *Iruska*, or *Eruska*, warriors of the Pawnee were among the originators of this dance. The ceremonies were organized around a group of four "officers" chosen to wear the feather bustles called crow belts. The officers symbolized crows flocking over a battlefield. The dancers would perform a set of ceremonial and ritual acts that evoked heroic deeds done during war. A feast was usually placed in the center of the dance arena and "stalked" by the dancers, who would take away pieces of meat with their bare hands.

Other photos in the album showed our Pawnee relatives. Dad was from another tribe. Momma's momma was in the album, a tiny gray-haired woman who no longer lived. And Momma's momma's Dad was in the album; he wore old Pawnee leggings and the long feathers of a dark bird sat upon his head. I closed the album when Momma, Dad, and Sister came home.

Momma went into the kitchen to cook. She called me and Sister to help. As she put on a bibbed apron, she said, "We just came from town, and we saw someone from home there." She meant someone from her tribal community.

"This man told me that Ralphie's been drinking hard," she said sadly. "He used to do that quite a bit a long time ago, but we thought that it had stopped. He seemed to be all right for a few years." We cooked and then ate in silence.

Washing the dishes, I asked Momma, "How come Uncle Ralph never did marry?"

Momma looked up at me but was not surprised by my question. She answered, "I don't know, Sister. It would have been better if he had. There was one woman who I thought he really loved. I think he still does. I think it had something to do with Mom. She wanted him to wait."

"Wait for what?" I asked.

"I don't know," Momma said and sank into a chair.

After that we heard unsettling rumors of Uncle Ralph drinking here and there.

He finally came to the house once when only I happened to be home. He was haggard and tired. His appearance was much like that of the whiteman that Sister and I met on the railroad tracks years before.

I opened the door when he tapped on it. Uncle Ralph looked years older than his age. He brought food in his arms. "*Nowa*, Sister," he said in greeting. "Where's the other one?" He meant Sister.

"She's gone now, Uncle Ralph. School in Kansas," I answered. "Where you been, Uncle Ralph? We been worrying about you."

He ignored my question and said, "I bring food. The warrior brings home food. To his family, to his people." His face was lined and had not been cleaned for days. He smelled of cheap wine.

I asked again, "Where you been, Uncle Ralph?"

He forced himself to smile. "Pumpkin Flower," he said, using the Pawnee name, "I've been out with my warriors all this time."

He put one arm around me as we went to the kitchen table with the food. "That's what your Pawnee name is. Now don't forget it."

"Did somebody bring you here, Uncle Ralph, or are you on foot?" I asked him.

"I'm on foot," he answered. "Where's your Momma?"

I told him that she and Dad would be back soon, I started to prepare the food he brought.

Then I heard Uncle Ralph say, "Life is sure hard sometimes. Sometimes it seems I just can't go on."

"What's wrong, Uncle Ralph?" I asked.

Uncle Ralph let out a bitter little laugh. "What's wrong?" he repeated. "What's wrong? All my life, I've tried to live what I've been taught but, Pumpkin Flower, some things are all wrong!"

He took a folded pack of cigarettes from his coat pocket. His hand shook as he pulled one from the pack and lit the end. "Too much drink," he said sadly. "That stuff is bad for us."

"What are you trying to do, Uncle Ralph?" I then asked.

"Live," he said.

He puffed on the shaking cigarette awhile and said, "The old people said to live beautifully with prayers and song. Some died for beauty too."

"How do we do that, Uncle Ralph, live for beauty?" I asked.

"It's simple, Pumpkin Flower," he said. "Believe!"

"Believe what?" I asked.

He looked at me hard. "*Aw-kuh!*" he said, "that's one of the things that is wrong.

THE WARRIORS 373

Active Reading: CLARIFY

W Have students discuss how Uncle Ralph wants people to live. Ask them to consider why living beautifully with prayers and song may not be practical in light of modern conditions.

Cultural Note

X The Pawnee family is matrilineal, which means that the mother's family is regarded as the family to which her children belong. In "The Warriors," the narrator's father is not a Pawnee, so he does not try to defuse the conflict between his wife and her brother.

Critical Thinking: SPECULATE

Y Ask students to speculate about what Uncle Ralph's "pleading look" to his niece signifies. *(Possible response: He feels vulnerable because of his obvious deterioration and begs for her respect and understanding.)*

Active Reading: CLARIFY

Z Ask students what inference the narrator's father makes. Invite them to discuss how he arrived at his conclusion. *(Possible response: Each time Ralph leaves the table, he comes back more talkative.)*

Everyone questions. Everyone doubts. No one believes in the old ways anymore. They want to believe when it's convenient, when it doesn't cost them anything and when they get something in return. There are no more believers. There are no more warriors. They are all gone. Those who are left only want to go to the Moon."

A car drove up outside. It was Momma and Dad. Uncle Ralph heard it too. He slumped in the chair, resigned to whatever Momma would say to him.

Momma came in first. Dad then greeted Uncle Ralph and disappeared into the back of the house. Custom and etiquette required that Dad, who was not a member of Momma's tribe, allow Momma to handle her brother's problems.

She hugged Uncle Ralph. Her eyes filled with tears when she saw how thin he was and how his hands shook.

> **CLARIFY**
> How do you think Uncle Ralph wants people to live? How does his views conflict with the way most people live?
> Using a Reading Log

"Ralphie," she said, "you look awful but I am glad to see you."

She then spoke to him of everyday things, how the car failed to start and the latest gossip. He was silent, tolerant of the passing of time in this way. His eyes sent me a pleading look while his hands shook and he tried to hold them still.

When supper was ready, Uncle Ralph went to wash himself for the meal. When he returned to the table, he was calm. His hands didn't shake so much.

At first he ate without many words, but in the course of the meal he left the table twice. Each time he came back, he was more talkative than before, answering Momma's questions in Pawnee. He left the table a third time and Dad rose.

Dad said to Momma, "He's drinking again. Can't you tell?" Dad left the table and went outside.

Momma frowned. A determined look grew on her face.

> **CLARIFY**
> Notice the inference that the girls' father makes.
> Using a Reading Log

374 UNIT THREE PART 1: MIXED BLESSINGS

Mini-Lesson The Writer's Style

COMBINING SENTENCES WITH WHO, WHICH, OR THAT Explain that the word *who* can be used to combine two related sentences about a person or a group of persons. For example, in the passage highlighted above, combining the sentences "Custom and etiquette required that Dad allow Momma to handle her brother's problems" and "Dad was not a member of Momma's tribe" with *who* produces a concise complex sentence. Point out that the words *that* and *which* can be used to combine related details about things. If the added details are necessary to the meaning of the sentence, *that* should be used; if they are not essential, *which* should be used.

Application Have students scan the story for at least five pairs of sentences that can be combined with the word *who, which,* or *that*. Then ask them to write five complex sentences.

Reteaching/Reinforcement
- *Writing Mini-Lessons* transparencies, p. 51

 The Writer's Craft

Combining with *Who, Which,* and *That*, p. 425

When Uncle Ralph sat down to the table once more, Momma told him, "Ralphie, you're my brother but I want you to leave now. Come back when you are sober."

He held a tarnished spoon in mid-air and he put it down slowly. He hadn't finished eating but he didn't seem to mind leaving. He stood, looked at me with his red eyes and went to the door. Momma followed him. In a low voice, she said, "Ralphie, you've got to stop drinking and wandering—or don't come to see us again."

He pulled himself to his full height then. His frame filled the doorway. He leaned over Momma and yelled, "Who are you? Are you God that you will say what will be or what will not be?"

Momma met his angry eyes. She stood firm and did not back down.

His eyes finally dropped from her face to the linoleum floor. A cough came from deep in his throat.

"I'll leave here," he said. "But I'll get all my warriors and come back! I have thousands of warriors and they'll ride with me. We'll get our bows and arrows. Then we'll come back!" He staggered out the door.

In the years that followed, Uncle Ralph saw us only when he was sober. He visited less and less. When he did show up, he did a tapping ritual on our front door. We welcomed the rare visits. Occasionally he stayed at our house for a few days at a time when he was not drinking. He slept on the floor.

He did odd jobs for minimum pay but never complained about the work or money. He'd acquired a vacant look in his eyes. It was the same look that Sister and I had seen in the hobos when we were children. He wore a similar careless array of clothing and carried no property with him at all.

The last time he came to the house, he called me by my English name and asked if I remembered anything of all that he'd taught me. His hair had turned pure white. He looked older than anyone I knew. I marveled at his appearance and said, "I remember everything." That night I pointed out his stars for him and

THE WARRIORS **375**

Mini-Lesson Grammar

CLAUSES Remind students that a clause is a group of words that contains a subject and a verb. If necessary, explain the two kinds of clauses: an independent, or main, clause, which can stand alone as a sentence; a subordinate, or dependent, clause, which cannot stand alone as a sentence. Write these examples on the chalkboard for the students to refer to.

1. Afraid of strangers, *the hobo ran away from us.* (independent)
2. *If you like to dance,* you will enjoy this song. (dependent)

Application Ask students to identify the independent and dependent clauses in the section. Then ask them to reword the passage to eliminate all the subordinate clauses. Have them discuss what effect the omission has on the paragraph.

Reteaching/Reinforcement
- *Grammar Handbook,* anthology p. 51
- *Grammar Mini-Lesson* copymasters p. 3 transparencies p. 2

The Writer's Craft
What Is a Clause? pp. 721–722

Literary Concept: CONFLICT

EE Ask students to explain how Uncle Ralph's internal conflict is resolved and to give evidence from the story to support their answers. *(He finally acknowledges that he cannot live in the modern world while holding fast to the old ways; this conclusion is supported by his admission, "I couldn't make it work. I tried to fit the pieces.")*

Literary Concept: TONE

FF Ask students what tone the narrator uses to convey her attitude toward Uncle Ralph in this section of the story. *(Possible responses: affectionate; sympathetic; respectful)*

Active Reading: QUESTION

GG Possible response: She wants Uncle Ralph to know that she respects him and what he taught her and her sister about Pawnee customs and culture and that she will remember and teach others what she has learned.

CUSTOMIZING FOR
Multiple Learning Styles

HH Musical Learners Ask students what musical pieces or songs they would choose to represent Uncle Ralph's life. Encourage them to explain their choices.

---

told him how *Pahukatawa* lived and died and lived again through another's dreams. I'd grown and Uncle Ralph could not hold me on his knee anymore. His arm circled my waist while we sat on the grass.

He was moved by my recitation and clutched my hand tightly. He said, "It's more than this. It's more than just repeating words. You know that, don't you?"

I nodded my head. "Yes, I know. The recitation is the easiest part but it's more than this, Uncle Ralph."

EE He was quiet but after a few minutes his hand touched my shoulder. He said, "I couldn't make it work. I tried to fit the pieces."

"I know," I said.

"Now before I go," he said, "do you know who you are?"

The question took me by surprise. I thought very hard. I cleared my throat and told him, "I know that I am fourteen. I know that it's too young."

"Do you know that you are a Pawnee?" he asked in a choked whisper.

"Yes, Uncle," I said.

"Good," he said with a long sigh that was swallowed by the night.

Then he stood and said, "Well, Sister, I have to go. Have to move on."

"Where are you going?" I asked. "Where all the warriors go?" I teased.

He managed a smile and a soft laugh. "Yeah, wherever the warriors are, I'll find them."

"Before you go," I asked, "Uncle Ralph, can women be warriors too?"

FF He laughed again and hugged me merrily. "Don't tell me you want to be one of the warriors too?"

QUESTION
Why do you think the narrator wants to be one of Uncle Ralph's warriors?
Using a Reading Log

GG "No, Uncle," I said, "Just one of yours." I hated to let him go because I knew that I would not see him again.

He pulled away. His last words were, "Don't forget what I've told you all these years. It's the only chance not to become what everyone else is. Do you understand?"

I nodded and he left. I never saw him again.

The years passed quickly. I moved away from Momma and Dad and married. Sister left them before I did.

> "Don't forget what I've told you all these years. It's the only chance not to become what everyone else is."

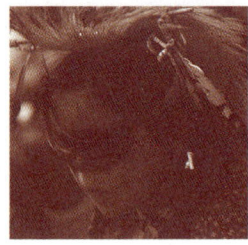

Years later in another town, hundreds of miles away, I awoke in a terrible gloom, a sense that something was gone from the world the Pawnees knew. The despair filled days, though the reason for the sense of loss went unexplained. Finally, the telephone rang. Momma was on the line. She said, "Sister came home for a few days not too long ago. While she was here and alone, someone came and tapped on the door, like Ralphie always does. Sister yelled, 'Is that you, Uncle Ralph? Come on in.' But no one entered."

Then I understood, Uncle Ralph was dead. **HH** Momma probably knew too. She wept softly into the phone.

Later Momma received an official call that confirmed Uncle Ralph's death. He had died

376   UNIT THREE PART 1: MIXED BLESSINGS

 Assessment Option

INFORMAL ASSESSMENT You can informally assess your students' understanding of the selection by setting up the following scenario:

Pretend that you are Uncle Ralph. Before you die, you write a letter to your nieces in which you explain the following: what living for beauty means to you; why you have had trouble living in the modern world; why you are a hobo; how you feel about your nieces; and what you expect from them.

Have students provide written versions of the letter. Remind them to use language appropriate for Uncle Ralph.

Rubric

3 Full Accomplishment Students accurately and specifically address all the points. They use language appropriate to Uncle Ralph.

2 Substantial Accomplishment Students accurately address most of the points. Some of their language, however, is not appropriate to Uncle Ralph.

1 Little or Partial Accomplishment Students have difficulty addressing the points and do not use language appropriate to Uncle Ralph.

376 THE LANGUAGE OF LITERATURE TEACHER'S EDITION

from exposure in a hobo shanty, near the railroad tracks outside a tiny Oklahoma town. He'd been dead for several days and nobody knew but Momma, Sister and me.

The funeral was well attended by the Pawnee people, Momma reported to me as I did not attend. Uncle Ralph and I had said our farewells years earlier. Momma told me that someone there had spoken well of Uncle Ralph before they put him in the ground. It was said that "Ralph came from a fine family, an old line of warriors."

Ten years later, Sister and I visited briefly at Momma's and Dad's home. We had been separated by hundreds of miles for all that time. As we sat under Momma's flowering mimosa trees, I made a confession to Sister. I said, "Sometimes I wish that Uncle Ralph were here. I'm a grown woman but I still miss him after all these years."

Sister nodded her head in agreement. I continued. "He knew so many things. He knew why the sun pours its liquid all over us and why it must do just that. He knew why babes and insects crawl. He knew that we must live beautifully or not live at all."

Sister's eyes were thoughtful but she waited to speak while I went on. "To live beautifully from day to day is a battle that warriors have to plot for as long as they can. It's a battle all the way. The things that he knew are so beautiful. And to feel and know that kind of beauty is the reason that we should live at all. Uncle Ralph said so. But now, there is no one who knows what that beauty is or any of the other things that he knew."

Sister pushed back smoky gray wisps of her dark hair. "You do," she pronounced. "And I do too."

"Why do you suppose he left us like that?" I asked.

Keokuk on Horseback (1834), George Catin. National Museum of American Art, Smithsonian Institution, Washington, D.C./Art Resource, New York

"It couldn't be helped," Sister said. "There was a battle on."

"I wanted to be one of his warriors," I said with an embarrassed half-smile.

She leaned over and patted my hand. "You are," she said. Then she stood and placed one hand on her bosom and one hand on my arm. "We'll carry on," she said.

I touched her hand resting on my arm. I said, "Sister, tell me again. What is the battle for?"

She looked down toward the fence where a hobo was coming through. We waved at him.

"Beauty," she said to me. "Our battle is for beauty. It's what Uncle Ralph fought for too. He often said that everyone else just wanted to go to the Moon. But remember, Sister, you and I done been there. Don't forget that, after all, we're children of the stars." ❖

THE WARRIORS **377**

From Personal Response to Critical Analysis

1. Accept all reasonable responses.
2. Possible responses: Some students may consider Uncle Ralph special because he enriches his relatives' lives. Others may not, pointing to his alcoholism and his inability to live in the present.
3. Possible response: Uncle Ralph holds fast to the past and cannot adjust to a changing world.
4. Accept all reasonable, well-supported responses.
5. Possible response: Uncle Ralph left his nieces the legacy of pride, but they had to watch his deterioration and death.
6. Accept all reasonable, well-supported responses.

Another Pathway

Cooperative Learning One student can be responsible for recording the groups' ideas. Another can summarize the thoughts of the group. A third student can check to make sure that the ideas reflect the characters' perceptions of how to "live beautifully."

Rubric

3 Full Accomplishment The commandments reflect the characters' ideas of how to live beautifully.

2 Substantial Accomplishment Most of the commandments reflect the characters' ideas of how to live beautifully.

1 Little or Partial Accomplishment The commandments do not reflect the characters' ideas of how to live beautifully.

RESPONDING OPTIONS

FROM PERSONAL RESPONSE TO CRITICAL ANALYSIS

REFLECT
1. What is your reaction to Uncle Ralph's life and death? Write down your thoughts in your notebook and share your reaction in class.

RETHINK
2. If you were a member of the narrator's family, would you consider Uncle Ralph a special relative? Why or why not?

3. Why does Uncle Ralph find living so hard?
   Consider
   Close Textual Reading
   - what he values and believes
   - the "transparent bubble of new time" that "bound him tight" (page 368)
   - what he means by "I couldn't make it work. I tried to fit the pieces." (page 376)

4. Think about Uncle Ralph's battle for beauty. How do you suppose his nieces will continue the battle in their adult lives?

Thematic Link
5. In what ways has Uncle Ralph been a mixed blessing for his nieces?

RELATE
6. Do you think that Uncle Ralph's message has meaning today for you or for people you know? Explain why or why not.

LITERARY CONCEPTS

A **conflict** is a struggle between opposing forces in a story. An **external conflict** is one in which a character struggles against some outside person or force. An **internal conflict** is one that occurs within a character. In a sentence or two, summarize the different kinds of conflicts in "The Warriors."

CONCEPT REVIEW: Tone A writer's tone is an expression of his or her attitude toward a subject. Consider the narrator's attitude toward her uncle in "The Warriors." Do you think the author, Anna Lee Walters, has the same attitude? Identify two passages that convey the tone of the story as you understand it.

378 UNIT THREE PART 1: MIXED BLESSINGS

Multimodal Learning
ANOTHER PATHWAY
Cooperative Learning

With a small group of classmates, brainstorm ten commandments for how to "live beautifully." Base the commandments on your inferences about Uncle Ralph's and his nieces' ideas of the beautiful life. Compare your commandments with those of other groups.

QUICKWRITES

1. Make a **list** of things you learned about Pawnee beliefs and customs in your reading of this story.

2. People do not always get what they deserve in life. Write a different **ending** to Uncle Ralph's life story—the ending you think he deserves.

3. Write a **eulogy**, or tribute, that might be delivered at Uncle Ralph's funeral. Be sure to describe his admirable qualities and his accomplishments.

4. Using the information in the cluster diagram you made for the Personal Connection on page 364, draft a **short story** about your special relative.

📁 **PORTFOLIO** Save your writing. You may want to use it later as a springboard to a piece for your portfolio.

Literary Concepts

Have students form small groups to consider Uncle Ralph's major conflicts. *(Possible response: Ralph's external conflict pits his dedication to the old ways against the attitudes characteristic of modern society; his internal conflict pits his realization that he has to adapt against his inability to do so.)*

Tone Possible response: affectionate/sympathetic; page 372, from "The young . . ." through ". . . for the warriors"; page 377, last five paragraphs.

QuickWrites

1. Students' lists should include specific information that Uncle Ralph gives his nieces as well as cultural knowledge that the narrator communicates.
2. Encourage students to maintain the narrator's style and tone.
3. As a prewriting activity, students should create a graphic organizer showing Ralph's admirable qualities.
4. Suggest that students outline their plot before they begin.

 The Writer's Craft

How Do I Write a Conclusion, pp. 371–373
Personal Narrative, pp. 86–99

Multimodal Learning

ALTERNATIVE ACTIVITIES

Plains Indian warriors often carried decorated buffalo-hide shields into battle for protection. Find out more about these shields and the symbols used on them, then design a **warrior shield** for Uncle Ralph to carry through life. You might create the design on your computer if you have an illustrator program.

Cheyenne shield

LITERARY LINKS

At the end of this story, the narrator's sister says, "Our battle is for beauty." How would you compare the search for beauty in this story with that in the story "Beauty is Truth" on page 305?

Multimodal Learning

ACROSS THE CURRICULUM

Social Studies To learn more about the traditional cultures of Native Americans, read a book written by a Native American, such as *Land of the Spotted Eagle* by Luther Standing Bear; the collection *We Rode the Wind*, edited by Jane Katz; or one of the books by Anna Lee Walters listed at the end of the biographical feature below. Share what you learn with the class.

Health Uncle Ralph's drinking problem suggests that he is an alcoholic. Do some encyclopedia research on the disease of alcoholism—its causes, effects, and treatment. Present your conclusions in an oral report.

WORDS TO KNOW

Review the Words to Know in the boxes at the bottom of the selection pages. Then write the vocabulary word that is suggested by each set of idioms below.

1. one-upmanship, have the last word, talk back
2. wipe out, lay waste, reduce to ashes
3. pie in the sky, castles in the air, in your mind's eye
4. burned out, out of steam, on your last legs, zonked
5. hung up on, one-track mind, really stuck on

ANNA LEE WALTERS

Part Pawnee and part Otoe, Anna Lee Walters is married to a Navajo artist and is a painter herself. Nevertheless, she finds the time to write every day— "because," she says, "of my need to write. It is my true love."

Walters was born in Pawnee, Oklahoma, in 1946, but moved to the Southwest—a region she calls "too much a part of me to ever leave behind"—when she was a teenager. She has held various jobs—as a library technician, a technical writer, and the director of a college press—and is now an English instructor at Navajo Community College in Tsaile, Arizona. She has written nonfiction texts about Native American culture as well as short stories, a novel, and poetry. In the children's book *The Two-Legged Creature: An Otoe Story,* she retells an Otoe folk tale. Walters' writing has appeared in numerous magazines and anthologies.

OTHER WORKS *The Sacred: Ways of Knowledge, Sources of Life; The Sun Is Not Merciful; Talking Indian: Reflections on Writing and Survival; Ghost Singer*

Extended Reading

THE WARRIORS 379

Across the Curriculum

Social Studies Suggest that students work with a partner to discuss the book, create visual aids, and draft an oral presentation to be given to the class. After all reports have been given, students should compare the traditions that they studied.

Health Divide students into small research groups. Ask each group to focus on an aspect of the disease. After all the reports have been given, students should discuss the warning signs of alcoholism and ways that have been devised to prevent and control the disease.

Words to Know

1. retort
2. ravage
3. fantasize
4. haggard
5. obsessively

Reteaching/ Reinforcement
- Unit Three Resource Book, p. 14

Literary Links

Possible responses:

Similarities

- In both stories, the search for beauty involves a degree of suffering.

Differences

- Uncle Ralph and his nieces understand the Pawnee concept of beauty and strive to achieve it.
- Jeanie achieves beauty by relating the truth about her everyday life.

Alternative Activities

After students read about the warrior shields and what the symbols on them represent, they should try to find photographs or illustrations of various shields to get an idea of how they were designed. Tell students their designs should include pictures and other symbols that represent Uncle Ralph's beliefs. If they can't create their design on a computer, they should draw it. As they share their designs with the class, students should explain the meaning of each symbol and how it relates to Uncle Ralph.

OVERVIEW

Objectives

- To understand and appreciate two lyric poems that explore the relationship between fathers and sons
- To identify and examine simile in a poem
- To appreciate rhythm in a poem
- To express understanding of the poems through a choice of writing forms, including a detective's report and a description
- To extend understanding of the poems through a variety of multimodal and cross-curricular activities

Skills

LITERARY CONCEPTS
- Simile
- Rhyme

SPEAKING, LISTENING AND VIEWING
- Oral interpretation

Thematic Link: *Mixed Blessings* The speakers of these poems reveal the mixed blessings of their relationships with their fathers.

CUSTOMIZING FOR
Students Acquiring English

- Use **ACCESS FOR STUDENTS ACQUIRING ENGLISH**, *Reading Support.*
- Explain that "My Papa's Waltz" contains concrete images that students can cite in paraphrasing each stanza. "Touch Football," in contrast, contains more abstract images.

STRATEGIC READING FOR
Less-Proficient Readers

Set a Purpose Tell students to read the poems to discover the difference between the two fathers.

Use **UNIT THREE RESOURCE BOOK**, p. 17, for guidance in reading the selection.

PREVIEWING

POETRY

My Papa's Waltz
Theodore Roethke (rĕt′kē)

Touch Football
Jack Driscoll

Activating Prior Knowledge/Setting a Purpose
PERSONAL CONNECTION

The two poems you are about to read are about fathers and their sons. Before you read them, think about your image of a typical father. In your notebook, jot down the words or phrases that come to mind when you think about a father's role in a family, his habits and activities, and the way his children see him. As you read, compare your image of a father with the father in these two poems.

Building Background
BIOGRAPHICAL CONNECTION

Father-son relationships appear frequently in the works of Theodore Roethke and Jack Driscoll. Roethke's father, Otto, who ran a floral business, was a stern man who demanded that his son work hard in the family greenhouse as he was growing up. The "life-giving" and "earthy" spirit of Roethke's father, however, was a side of the man that the poet valued, and he made his father the subject of several poems, including one titled simply "Otto."

Driscoll frequently writes about the unpredictable nature of father-son relationships. One critic, in reviewing a collection of Driscoll's short fiction, wrote that the author "explores what it is like to grow up male in a world that demands physical and mental testing almost beyond endurance." Driscoll's own father died just four years after the poem "Touch Football" was published.

Active Reading
READING CONNECTION

Recognizing Imagery Imagery consists of words and phrases that help a reader imagine physical experiences. An image can appeal to any of the five senses. For example, in "My Papa's Waltz," there is this description:

> We romped until the pans
> Slid from the kitchen shelf;

Pans sliding from a shelf would create a crash, right? This is a sound image that helps you imagine what it's like to be *in* the poem, hearing what the speaker hears.

In your notebook, create a chart like the one begun here, listing the five senses: sight, hearing, smell, taste, and touch. Then, after you have read each poem several times, fill in examples of as many kinds of images as you can find in each poem.

Senses	Images in "My Papa's Waltz"	Images in "Touch Football"
Sight	mother's frown	
Hearing	pans falling from shelf	

380   UNIT THREE   PART 1: MIXED BLESSINGS

PRINT AND MEDIA RESOURCES

UNIT THREE RESOURCE BOOK
Strategic Reading: Literature, p. 17

ACCESS FOR STUDENTS ACQUIRING ENGLISH
Selection Summaries
Reading Support

FORMAL ASSESSMENT
Selection Test, pp. 65–66
 Test Generator

AUDIO LIBRARY
See Reference Card

---

380   THE LANGUAGE OF LITERATURE   TEACHER'S EDITION

MY PAPA'S WALTZ

Theodore Roethke

The whiskey on your breath
Could make a small boy dizzy;
But I hung on like death:
Such waltzing was not easy.

5 We romped until the pans
Slid from the kitchen shelf;
My mother's countenance[1]
Could not unfrown itself.

The hand that held my wrist
10 Was battered on one knuckle;
At every step you missed
My right ear scraped a buckle.

You beat time on my head
With a palm caked hard by dirt,
15 Then waltzed me off to bed
Still clinging to your shirt.

---

1. **countenance:** face or facial expression.

FROM PERSONAL RESPONSE TO CRITICAL ANALYSIS

REFLECT 1. What is your impression of the boy's experience in this poem? Write your impression in your notebook.

RETHINK 2. How do you judge the father's behavior in this poem? Comment on specific lines that show his behavior.

3. Explain how the young boy feels about being waltzed by his father.
   Consider
   - phrases that re-create the boy's physical experiences
   - phrases that describe the way he holds on to his father
   - the title of the poem

CUSTOMIZING FOR
Gifted and Talented Students

As students read the poems, have them consider the flaw each son perceives in his father. *(Possible response: In "My Papa's Waltz," the father's drinking causes him to handle his son roughly; in "Touch Football," the father displays weakness.)* Have students discuss how these flaws affect the relationship between father and son. *(Accept all reasonable responses.)*

CUSTOMIZING FOR
Students Acquiring English

I Explain to students that the phrase *hung on like death* means "held on tightly."

Literary Concept: SIMILE

A Remind students that a simile is a comparison that uses the word *like* or *as*. Ask them to identify the simile in the first stanza. *("But I hung on like death.")* Ask what this reveals about the boy. *(Possible response: He is very frightened.)*

Literary Concept: RHYME

B Have students identify the end rhymes. *(wrist/missed; knuckle/buckle)* Ask them why the poet uses rhyme in this poem. *(Possible response: to emphasize the poem's musicality, suggesting a waltz)*

Critical Thinking: SPECULATE

C Have students speculate about why the son doesn't refuse to dance with his father. *(Possible response: He wants his father's attention.)*

From Personal Response to Critical Analysis

1. Accept all reasonable, well-supported responses.
2. Some students may suppose that the father handled the boy too roughly, citing these lines from the poem: "I hung on like death," "My right ear scraped a buckle," and "You beat time on my head."
3. Some students may think that the waltzing was generally positive for the boy, noting words and phrases that can have positive connotations, such as "romped," "waltzed me off to bed," and the affectionate term *Papa*.

Touch FOOTBALL

Jack Driscoll

I tackle my father so hard
he fumbles the light
from his frightened hands.
On his back
5 he looks like a man asleep,
his legs stiff and skinny
in those baggy pants.
                       Standing over him
I watch the evening disappear
10 into his open mouth.
He whispers, "It was only touch."[1]

In high grass I kneel,
touch the small hill behind his ear.
I touch his lips,
15 blue and dreaming towards the year of his death.
I put on his broken glasses,
stare at the first few stars
breathing above the house.
When the lights come on
20 I reach into the dark hood of his sweatshirt,
pull it like a dream over his bald head.

It was only touch,
and my father's crooked fingers feel like winter
twisting downriver in the first hush of snow.
25 I hold his hand tightly on the abandoned field
where this string of losses
still grips our empty hearts, awakened
and unable to forgive.

1. **touch:** touch football, a variety of backyard football in which a play is stopped when the ball carrier is touched (rather than tackled) by an opposing player.

382 UNIT THREE PART 1: MIXED BLESSINGS

Mini-Lesson: Speaking, Listening, and Viewing

Oral Interpretation
Imagine that you are the speaker of the poem.
Follow the phrasing indicated by the punctuation.
Be aware of rhyme and rhythm, but do not overemphasize them.
Use your knowledge of the poem's content to help you maintain the mood.

ORAL INTERPRETATION Explain that lyric poetry, which emphasizes sound and language, is highly musical and that therefore, reading a lyric poem aloud can make it come alive. Use the chalkboard shown to explain the guidelines for giving an oral interpretation. Suggest that students read the poems a number of times to become acquainted with their language and structure.

Application Have students work in small groups. Each member should take a turn reading one of the poems aloud, while the others listen and offer constructive criticism. Then have reviewers indicate how the presentations helped them understand the poem.

RESPONDING OPTIONS

FROM PERSONAL RESPONSE TO CRITICAL ANALYSIS

REFLECT 1. What words or images stayed with you after you read "Touch Football"? Write or sketch them in your notebook and share them with a classmate.

RETHINK 2. Why do you think the speaker tackles his father while playing touch football?

3. What feelings do you think the speaker has for his father?
   Consider
   Close Textual Reading
   - how the speaker describes his father's appearance after the tackle
   - how the speaker acts toward his father

4. What do you think the last four lines of the poem mean?
   Consider
   Close Textual Reading
   - what the "string of losses" is
   - what they both are "unable to forgive"

RELATE 5. How do the portraits of the fathers in these two poems compare with the image of a typical father that you described for the Personal Connection on page 380?

6. Compare the chart of images you made for the Reading Connection on page 380 with the charts made by others in your class. Discuss whether filling out the chart helped you gain a better understanding of the poems, and explain the reasons for your opinion.

Multimodal Learning
ANOTHER PATHWAY
Cooperative Learning
Working with a small group of classmates, compare the experiences of the sons in these two poems. (At one point, for example, both boys hold on to their fathers tightly, though for different reasons.) Then compare your list with the lists of other groups.

Similarities	Differences

LITERARY CONCEPTS

A **simile** is a figure of speech in which a comparison is made between two things by means of the word *like* or *as*. The speaker of "Touch Football" uses three similes to describe his father, in lines 5, 21, and 23. Look at those similes. What do you think the speaker means by connecting the ideas of sleep, dreams, and winter with his father? What do you imagine when you think of these things?

CONCEPT REVIEW: Rhyme In which of these poems is rhyme used? Identify the rhyme scheme of the poem.

QUICKWRITES

1. Choose one of the poems, and make a list of the sensory details that you think are clues to important things left unsaid about either the "waltz" or the football tackle. Then jot down what you think the clues indicate about the son's true feelings or attitude. Write a **detective's report** summarizing the conclusions you have drawn from your observations.

2. From the mother's point of view, write a **description** of the waltz between the father and son in "My Papa's Waltz"—one that might help explain what she feels about the waltz.

📁 **PORTFOLIO** Save your writing. You may want to use it later as a springboard to a piece for your portfolio.

MY PAPA'S WALTZ / TOUCH FOOTBALL   **383**

From Personal Response to Critical Analysis

1. Accept all reasonable, well-supported responses.
2. Possible responses: He is angry with his father; he is showing off; he has a strong desire to win.
3. Possible responses: anger; pity; love; regret; tenderness
4. Possible response: The father cannot forgive the hurt his son causes him, while the son cannot forgive his father's weakness.
5. Responses will vary.
6. Accept all reasonable, well-supported responses.

Another Pathway

Cooperative Learning After groups of four or five students set up the chart, one student can explain what happens to each son. Another student should act as the recorder. If the group has trouble finding comparisons, a third student can act as a generator of further ideas.

Rubric
3 Full Accomplishment Students create a detailed chart that lists similarities and differences between the sons' experiences.
2 Substantial Accomplishment Students create a less-detailed chart of the similarities or differences.
1 Little or Partial Accomplishment Students list only a few similarities and differences.

Literary Concepts

Have students work in small groups of four or five to examine the similes and discuss their meanings. *(Possible response: By connecting the ideas of sleep, dreams, and winter to his father, the speaker is expressing his belief that his father is near death.)*

Rhyme Have students reread the poems. They should identify "My Papa's Waltz" as the one that uses rhyme. Then have them indicate the rhyme scheme by assigning a letter to each new end rhyme. *(abab)*

QuickWrites

1. Encourage students to imagine that they are detectives trying to solve a mystery: What are the son's true feelings toward his father? Have them list sensory details that can be used as clues and indicate what each signifies. Suggest that the Reading Connection chart can provide clues.

2. Emphasize that students' descriptions should reflect the mother's point of view.

📁 **The Writer's Craft**
Observation and Description, pp. 58–65

Critic's Corner

Possible responses: Yes, though the father gets carried away, he does not really mistreat the boy; no, the father has been drinking and his behavior exposes his son to injury.

Across the Curriculum

Social Studies Theodore Roethke uses the image of a waltz to underscore a father's rough play with his son. With a small group of classmates, research the history of the waltz. Present your findings in an oral presentation to the class.

Physical Education *Cooperative Learning* Divide students into small groups to research the origins and regulations of American football, rugby, and soccer. Each group member can research one of these sports. Have students use their findings to develop comparative rule books for each sport.

JACK DRISCOLL

Many of Jack Driscoll's short stories have appeared in literary quarterlies, such as the *Gettysburg Review, Missouri Review,* and *Denver Quarterly.*

THEODORE ROETHKE

Theodore Roethke's father, Otto, died when the author was only 14. A stern German American, Otto was reluctant to show his sensitive side to his son. Theodore felt abandoned and angered by his father's early death, which greatly affected him and his writings.

CRITIC'S CORNER

In writing about "My Papa's Waltz," one critic remarked that Roethke "captures something of his own joy, and bafflement, as the victim of his father's exuberant energy." Do you consider *victim* too harsh a word to describe the boy's part in the evening waltz? Explain why or why not.

THE WRITER'S STYLE

The rhythm, or beat, of each line of "My Papa's Waltz" is meant to imitate the three-beats-to-the-measure rhythm of waltz music. Try to tap out the rhythm of each line of the poem as you read it aloud. Work with a partner to help you listen for the stressed and unstressed syllables in each line.

THEODORE ROETHKE

1908–1963

Born in Saginaw, Michigan, Theodore Roethke was the son of German immigrants who sold flowers for a living. The family's greenhouse came to be an important symbol in Roethke's poetry, much of which deals with nature.

After a half-hearted attempt to study law at the University of Michigan, Roethke switched to literature. In addition to publishing poetry, Roethke eventually taught at a number of universities, from Vermont to Washington State. He came to be recognized as a major American poet and won numerous awards, including the Pulitzer Prize. He was also a highly popular teacher, considered a natural inspiration to his students. A large man—standing over six feet tall and weighing more than 200 pounds—Roethke brought a unique intensity to the classroom. Once, to stimulate students' writing, he asked them to describe the action he was about to perform. Then he climbed through a classroom window and moved along the outside ledge, making faces at the class through the windows.

Despite his many accomplishments, Roethke suffered from alcoholism and mental illness throughout his life, occasionally needing to be hospitalized. Still, it is felt by many that if Roethke had lived to at least the age of 60, he would have realized his dream of winning a Nobel Prize.

OTHER WORKS *Words for the Wind: The Collected Verse of Theodore Roethke, The Far Field*
Extended Reading

JACK DRISCOLL

1946–

The state of Michigan forms a geographical link between Jack Driscoll and Theodore Roethke. The settings of much of Driscoll's work reflect the landscape of northern Michigan, where the author lives. Driscoll is writer-in-residence at the Interlochen Arts Academy, a high school of the arts near Traverse City. A winner of the PEN/Nelson Algren Fiction Award, Driscoll has published poetry, short stories, and a "bittersweet" novel for older teenagers, *Skylight,* that deals with first love and with a relationship between a father and a son.

OTHER WORKS *The Language of Bone, Fishing the Backwash, Building the Cold from Memory*
Extended Reading

384 UNIT THREE PART 1: MIXED BLESSINGS

The Writer's Style

You may wish to bring a recording of a waltz to play for the class before students begin this exercise. Have students work with a partner to listen for the stressed and unstressed syllables in each line of the poem. Encourage one student to tap out the rhythm of each line as the other student reads it aloud. Then have them switch places and repeat the exercise. Point out to them how the rhythm of the poem mimics the rhythm of the waltz.

Alternative Activities

1. Imagine that you have been hired as a playwright. Choose one of the poems and write a dialogue between the two characters from the point of view of the son. Include both a description of the setting and stage directions to help convey the meaning of the play.
2. Roethke uses a waltz for the rhythm of his poem. Choose a piece of music as a background for "Touch Football." Play your music for the class as you read the poem. Then explain why you chose that particular piece.

PREVIEWING

DRAMA

A Marriage Proposal
Anton Chekhov (chĕk'ôf)

Activating Prior Knowledge
PERSONAL CONNECTION

From the title, you can infer that a proposal of marriage will be an important ingredient in this play. By your age, young people have begun to develop ideas about why people marry and what makes an ideal marriage partner. With a small group of classmates, share your notions on the topic of marriage. Use these questions to guide the group's discussion: What are good reasons for wanting to marry? What are desirable characteristics in a marriage partner?

Building Background
LITERARY CONNECTION

Anton Chekhov, a Russian author of the late 1800s, is one of the world's major playwrights. Although he is known primarily for his longer, serious plays, Chekhov also wrote a number of short farces, such as the one-act *A Marriage Proposal*. A **farce** is a play that uses exaggeration to humorous effect. During Chekhov's time, farces that centered on obstacles to love affairs or marriages were highly popular. In Russia, one obstacle to loving marriages was the tendency of wealthy families to seek to increase their estates by encouraging marriages that made good economic sense.

Setting a Purpose
WRITING CONNECTION

In your notebook, create a "recipe" for the perfect way to make a proposal of marriage. Model your recipe card on the one shown here. List as many ingredients as you can think of, along with your instructions. Then, as you read *A Marriage Proposal*, compare your recipe with the elements of the proposal in the play.

```
                          Marriage Proposal
Ingredients    _____
               _____
               _____

Instructions   _____
               _____
               _____
```

OVERVIEW

Objectives

- To understand and appreciate a farce that explores the complications that arise when a man tries to propose marriage
- To identify and understand foreshadowing
- To express understanding of the selection through a choice of writing forms, including a poem and a report
- To extend understanding of the selection through a variety of multimodal and cross-curricular activities

Skills

LITERARY CONCEPTS
- Foreshadowing
- Rising action

THE WRITER'S STYLE
- Using dialogue in plays and skits

GENRE STUDY
- Drama: farce

GRAMMAR
- Possessive pronouns

SPEAKING, LISTENING, AND VIEWING
- Pantomime

ALTERNATIVE

Previewing

In lieu of listing "ingredients" of the perfect marriage proposal, students can discuss them with partners.

Writing Connection

Discussion Prompts

- When and where should the proposal take place?
- Who should do the proposing—the man or woman?
- How should the couple be dressed?
- What should the person proposing do and say?

As you read *A Marriage Proposal*, consider how closely the proposal in the play reflects your ideas of the perfect proposal.

A MARRIAGE PROPOSAL **385**

PRINT AND MEDIA RESOURCES

UNIT THREE RESOURCE BOOK
Strategic Reading: Literature, p. 21
Vocabulary SkillBuilder, p. 22

GRAMMAR MINI-LESSONS
Transparencies, pp. 12, 15
Copymasters, p. 18

WRITING MINI-LESSONS
Transparencies, p. 56

ACCESS FOR STUDENTS ACQUIRING ENGLISH
Selection Summaries
Reading Support

FORMAL ASSESSMENT
Selection Test, pp. 67–68
 Test Generator

 AUDIO LIBRARY
See Reference Card

LASERLINKS
Literary Connection

SUMMARY

Ivan Vassiliyitch Lomov visits his neighbor, Stepan Stepanovitch Tschubukov, to propose to Tschubukov's daughter, Natalia Stepanovna. While attempting to propose, Lomov mentions his family meadows. When Natalia retorts that the meadows belong to her family, an argument starts. Tschubukov joins the fight. Lomov storms out. When Natalia realizes that Lomov had been going to propose, she sends her father to pacify him, but the three are soon fighting again. Lomov faints. After Lomov regains consciousness, Tschubukov agrees to the marriage, and the argument resumes.

Thematic Link: *Mixed Blessings* A marriage proposal truly becomes a mixed blessing when the couple cannot stop arguing with each other.

CUSTOMIZING FOR
Students Acquiring English

- Use **ACCESS FOR STUDENTS ACQUIRING ENGLISH,** *Reading Support.*
- Help students pronounce the difficult names of the Russian characters.

STRATEGIC READING FOR
Less-Proficient Readers

Set a Purpose To help students get involved in the selection, have them list the different emotions one would feel when about to propose marriage. After they read the page, ask which of the listed feelings accurately reflect Lomov's emotions. Then ask them to read to find out how Lomov's emotions change as the play progresses.

Use **UNIT THREE RESOURCE BOOK,** p. 21, for guidance in reading the selection.

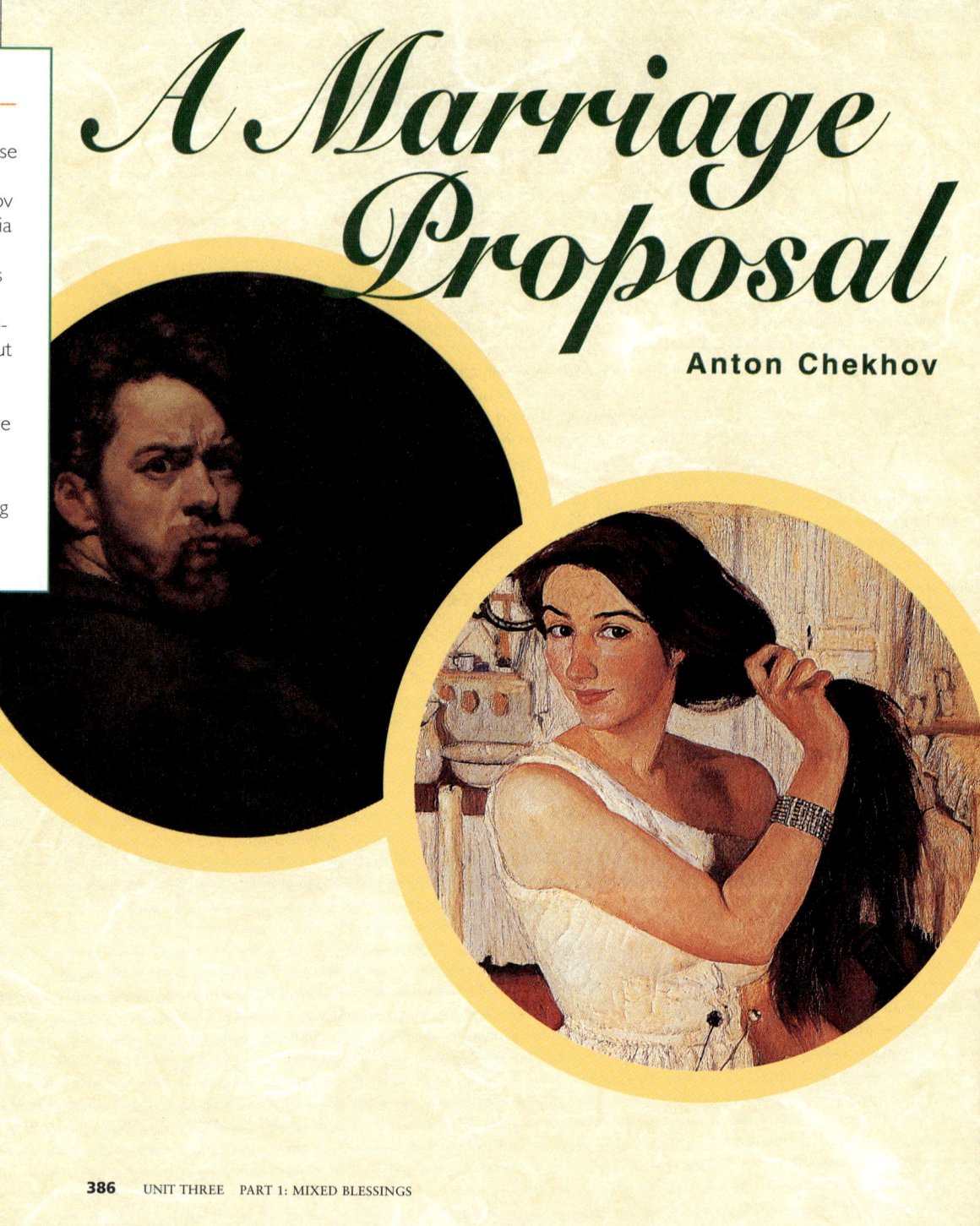

A Marriage Proposal
Anton Chekhov

386 UNIT THREE PART 1: MIXED BLESSINGS

WORDS TO KNOW

appropriate (ə-prō′prē-āt′) *v.* to take for one's own use, especially without permission (p. 391)
contrary (kŏn′trĕr′ē) *adj.* tending to stubbornly oppose or contradict (p. 395)
dumbfounded (dŭm′foun′dĭd) *adj.* filled with shock and amazement; astonished **dumbfound** *v.* (p. 388)

palpitation (păl′pĭ-tā′shən) *n.* a rapid, fluttering heartbeat, often caused by stress or nervousness (p. 388)
usurper (yōō-sûr′pər) *n.* one who takes possession of that which does not rightfully belong to him or her (p. 391)

CHARACTERS

Stepan Stepanovitch Tschubukov,[1]
a country farmer

Natalia Stepanovna,[2]
his daughter (aged 25)

Ivan Vassiliyitch Lomov,[3]
Tschubukov's neighbor

Time: The present [1890s]

Scene: *The reception room in Tschubukov's country home in Russia. Tschubukov discovered as the curtain rises. Enter Lomov, wearing a dress suit.*

Tschubukov (*going toward him and greeting him*). Who is this I see? My dear fellow! Ivan Vassiliyitch! I'm so glad to see you! (*Shakes hands.*) But this is a surprise! How are you?

Lomov. Thank you! And how are you?

Tschubukov. Oh, so-so, my friend. Please sit down. It isn't right to forget one's neighbor. But tell me, why all this ceremony? Dress clothes, white gloves, and all? Are you on your way to some engagement, my good fellow?

Lomov. No, I have no engagement except with you, Stepan Stepanovitch.

Tschubukov. But why in evening clothes, my friend? This isn't New Year's!

Lomov. You see, it's simply this, that—(*composing himself*) I have come to you, Stepan Stepanovitch, to trouble you with a request. It is not the first time I have had the honor of turning to you for assistance, and you have always, that is—I beg your pardon, I am a bit excited! I'll take a drink of water first, dear Stepan Stepanovitch. (*He drinks.*)

---

1. Stepan Stepanovitch Tschubukov (styĭ-pän′ styĭ-pän′əv-yĭch chü-bü′kəf).
2. Natalia Stepanovna (nə-täl′yə styĭ′pä-nôv′nə).
3. Ivan Vassiliyitch Lomov (ĭ-vän′ vəs-yēl′yĭch lô′məf).

387

Mini-Lesson — Genre Study

DRAMA Draw the web shown on the right on the chalkboard and use it to explain that a **farce** is a kind of drama with these characteristics.

Application Have students copy the web into their notebooks. Ask them to refer to it as they look for the characteristics of a farce in *A Marriage Proposal*.

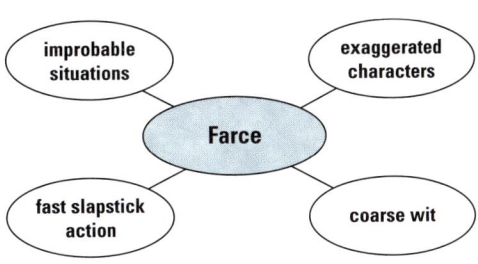

Literary Concept: ASIDE

C Remind students that an aside is meant to be heard by the audience but not by the other characters in the play. Ask what is revealed by Tschubukov's aside. (Possible response: He is suspicious of Lomov and not particularly fond of him.)

CUSTOMIZING FOR
Students Acquiring English

1. Explain that "beat about the bush" means "fail to get to the point."

2. Explain that "ask for the hand of" means "ask your permission to propose marriage to." It was customary in Chekhov's Russia for the man to approach a woman's father for his approval of marriage before proposing to the woman herself.

Literary Concept: FORESHADOWING

D Ask students what Lomov's admission about his interest in Natalia indicates about the nature of any marriage proposal he will be delivering. (Possible response: As he does not love Natalia, Lomov probably will not be delivering a romantic, heartfelt, passionate proposal.)

Critical Thinking: ANALYZE

E Ask students why Tschubukov referred to Lomov as "a dealer who'd come to buy something." (Possible response: Even though Tschubukov did not hear Lomov's revelation, he probably realizes that this neighbor he doesn't see often has shown up suddenly with a marriage proposal because he needs to have a wife—any wife.)

C **Tschubukov** (*aside*). He's come to borrow money! I won't give him any! (*To* Lomov) What is it, then, dear Lomov?

Lomov. You see—dear—Stepanovitch, pardon me, Stepan—Stepan—dearvitch—I mean—I am terribly nervous, as you will be so good as to see—! What I mean to say—you are the only one who can help me, though I don't deserve it, and—and I have no right whatever to make this request of you.

1 **Tschubukov.** Oh, don't beat about the bush, my dear fellow. Tell me!

2 **Lomov.** Immediately—in a moment. Here it is, then: I have come to ask for the hand of your daughter, Natalia Stepanovna.

Tschubukov (*joyfully*). Angel! Ivan Vassiliyitch! Say that once again! I didn't quite hear it!

Lomov. I have the honor to beg—

Tschubukov (*interrupting*). My dear, dear man! I am so happy that everything is so—everything! (*embraces and kisses him*) I have wanted this to happen for so long. It has been my dearest wish! (*He represses a tear.*) And I have always loved you, my dear fellow, as my own son! May God give you his blessings and his grace and—I always wanted it to happen. But why am I standing here like a blockhead? I am completely <u>dumbfounded</u> with pleasure, completely dumbfounded. My whole being—! I'll call Natalia—

Lomov. Dear Stepan Stepanovitch, what do you think? May I hope for Natalia Stepanovna's acceptance?

Tschubukov. Really! A fine boy like you—and you think she won't accept on the minute? Lovesick as a cat and all that—! (*He goes out, right.*)

Lomov. I'm cold. My whole body is trembling as though I was going to take my examination! But the chief thing is to settle matters! If a person meditates too much, or hesitates, or talks about it, waits for an ideal or for true love, he never gets it. Brrr! It's cold! Natalia is an excellent housekeeper, not at all bad looking, well educated—what more could I ask? I'm so excited my ears are roaring! (*He drinks water.*) And not to marry, that won't do! In the first place, I'm thirty-five—a critical age, you might say. In the second place, I must live a well-regulated life. I have a weak heart, continual <u>palpitation</u>, and I am very sensitive and always getting excited. My lips begin to tremble and the pulse in my right temple throbs terribly. But the worst of all is sleep! I hardly lie down and begin to doze before something in my left side begins to pull and tug, and something begins to hammer in my left shoulder—and in my head, too! I jump up like a madman, walk about a little, lie down again, but the moment I fall asleep I have a terrible cramp in the side. And so it is all night long! (*Enter* Natalia Stepanovna.)

Natalia. Ah! It's you. Papa said to go in: there was a dealer in there who'd come to buy something. Good afternoon, Ivan Vassiliyitch.

Lomov. Good day, my dear Natalia Stepanovna.

Natalia. You must pardon me for wearing my apron and this old dress: we are working today. Why haven't you come to see us oftener? You've not been here for so long! Sit down. (*They sit down.*) Won't you have something to eat?

Lomov. Thank you, I have just had lunch.

Natalia. Smoke, do, there are the matches. Today it is beautiful, and only yesterday it rained so hard that the workmen couldn't do a stroke of work. How many bricks have you cut? Think of it! I was so anxious that I had the whole field mowed, and now I'm sorry I did it, because I'm afraid the hay will rot. It would

---

WORDS TO KNOW
dumbfounded (dŭm'foun'dĭd) *adj.* filled with shock and amazement; astonished **dumbfound** *v.*
palpitation (păl'pĭ-tā'shən) *n.* a rapid, fluttering heartbeat, often caused by stress or nervousness

388

Multicultural Perspectives

MARRIAGE Arranged marriages were once the custom in our own society and were traditional among Native Americans long before the arrival of the European settlers. In parts of China, and elsewhere, parents still arrange marriages, and the betrothed couple may not meet until shortly before the wedding. An arranged marriage, like any other business proposition, involves an exchange of wealth. Grooms in some Asian and African societies purchase a spouse by paying her family a bride price. In one section of India, parents of daughters who cannot attract a prosperous husband save face by first "marrying" a daughter to a bouquet of flowers, which is then tossed down a well. This makes the girl a "widow," allowing her parents to accept a modest bride price for her without shame.

Portrait of the Poet N. A. Nekrasov (1877), Ivan Nikolaevich Kramskoi. Oil on canvas, 75 cm × 55 cm, The State Tretyakov Gallery, Moscow.

have been better if I had waited. But what on earth is this? You are in evening clothes! The latest cut! Are you on your way to a ball? And you seem to be looking better, too—really. Why are you dressed up so gorgeously?

Lomov (*excited*). You see, my dear Natalia Stepanovna—it's simply this: I have decided to ask you to listen to me—of course it will be a surprise, and indeed you'll be angry, but I—(*aside*) How fearfully cold it is!

Natalia. What is it? (*a pause*) Well?

Lomov. I'll try to be brief. My dear Natalia Stepanovna, as you know, for many years, since my childhood, I have had the honor to know your family. My poor aunt and her husband, from whom, as you know, I inherited the estate, always had the greatest respect for your father and your poor mother. The Lomovs and the Tschubukovs have been for decades on the friendliest, indeed the closest, terms with each

A MARRIAGE PROPOSAL **389**

Art Note

June by George Inness Landscape painter George Inness (1825–1894) believed that the goal of art is "to awaken an emotion." In this painting, he depicts a serene summer scene. *June* reflects the artist's late style and was painted at a time when his work was gaining both critical and popular acclaim.

Reading the Art What emotion is awakened by this painting? How does the artist accomplish this?

Literary Concept: FORESHADOWING

J Ask what this dispute over ownership of the meadows may foretell. *(Possible response: This dispute may evolve into a major obstacle to marriage.)*

Literary Concept: RISING ACTION

K Ask students what is happening to the conflict at this point. *(The argument over the meadow ownership has quickly become quite serious, with the odds growing against a successful marriage proposal.)*

June (1882), George Inness. Oil on canvas, 30¼″ × 45″, The Brooklyn (New York) Museum, bequest of Mrs. William A. Putnam (41.776).

other, and furthermore my property, as you know, adjoins your own. If you will be so good as to remember, my meadows touch your birch woods.

Natalia. Pardon the interruption. You said "my meadows"—but are they yours?

Lomov. Yes, they belong to me.

Natalia. What nonsense! The meadows belong to us—not to you!

Lomov. No, to me! Now, my dear Natalia Stepanovna!

Natalia. Well, that is certainly news to me. How do they belong to you?

Lomov. How? I am speaking of the meadows lying between your birch woods and my brick earth.[4]

Natalia. Yes, exactly. They belong to us.

Lomov. No, you are mistaken, my dear Natalia Stepanovna, they belong to me.

Natalia. Try to remember exactly, Ivan Vassiliyitch. Is it so long ago that you inherited them?

Lomov. Long ago! As far back as I can remember they have always belonged to us.

Natalia. But that isn't true! You'll pardon my saying so.

---

4. **brick earth:** earth or clay suitable for making bricks.

390   UNIT THREE   PART 1: MIXED BLESSINGS

Mini-Lesson Literary Concepts

REVIEWING RISING ACTION Remind students that rising action refers to the events that move the plot along by adding complications or expanding the conflict. Rising action ultimately builds suspense to a climax, or turning point.

Application Ask the class to identify the conflict of the play. Then have them work in small groups of three or four to find and list events that make up the rising action. Next to each listed event, they should then jot down a sentence describing how it adds complications or expands the conflict. After the groups agree among themselves, ask them to share their conclusions with the entire class. Then have the class discuss how the rising action builds suspense and leads to a climax.

Lomov. It is all a matter of record, my dear Natalia Stepanovna. It is true that at one time the title to the meadows was disputed, but now everyone knows they belong to me. There is no room for discussion. Be so good as to listen: my aunt's grandmother put these meadows, free from all costs, into the hands of your father's grandfather's peasants for a certain time while they were making bricks for my grandmother. These people used the meadows free of cost for about forty years, living there as they would on their own property. Later, however, when—

Natalia. There's not a word of truth in that! My grandfather, and my great grandfather, too, knew that their estate reached back to the swamp, so that the meadows belong to us. What further discussion can there be? I can't understand it. It is really most annoying.

Lomov. I'll show you the papers, Natalia Stepanovna.

Natalia. No, either you are joking or trying to lead me into a discussion. That's not at all nice! We have owned this property for nearly three hundred years, and now all at once we hear that it doesn't belong to us. Ivan Vassiliyitch, you will pardon me, but I really can't believe my ears. So far as I am concerned, the meadows are worth very little. In all they don't contain more than five acres, and they are worth only a few hundred roubles,[5] say three hundred, but the injustice of the thing is what affects me. Say what you will, I can't bear injustice.

Lomov. Only listen until I have finished, please! The peasants of your respected father's grandfather, as I have already had the honor to tell you, baked bricks for my grandmother. My aunt's grandmother wished to do them a favor—

Natalia. Grandfather! Grandmother! Aunt! I know nothing about them. All I know is that the meadows belong to us, and that ends the matter.

Lomov. No, they belong to me!

Natalia. And if you keep on explaining it for two days and put on five suits of evening clothes, the meadows are still ours, ours, ours! I don't want to take your property, but I refuse to give up what belongs to us!

Lomov. Natalia Stepanovna, I don't need the meadows, I am only concerned with the principle. If you are agreeable, I beg of you, accept them as a gift from me!

Natalia. But I can give them to you, because they belong to me! That is very peculiar, Ivan Vassiliyitch! Until now we have considered you as a good neighbor and a good friend; only last year we lent you our threshing machine so that we couldn't thresh until November, and now you treat us like thieves! You offer to give me my own land. Excuse me, but neighbors don't treat each other that way. In my opinion, it's a very low trick—to speak frankly—

Lomov. According to you I'm a <u>usurper</u>, then, am I? My dear lady, I have never <u>appropriated</u> other people's property, and I shall permit no one to accuse me of such a thing! (*He goes quickly to the bottle and drinks water.*) The meadows are mine!

Natalia. That's not the truth! They are mine!

Lomov. Mine!

Natalia. Eh? I'll prove it to you! This afternoon I'll send my reapers into the meadows.

Lomov. W—h—a—t?

Natalia. My reapers will be there today!

Lomov. And I'll chase them off!

Natalia. If you dare!

---

5. **roubles** (roo′bəlz): units of Russian money.

WORDS TO KNOW
usurper (yōō-sûr′pər) *n.* one who takes possession of that which does not rightfully belong to him or her
appropriate (ə-prō′prē-āt′) *v.* to take for one's own use, especially without permission

Art Note

Der Zornige (Selbstbildnis) [The angry one (self-portrait)] by Ferdinand Hodler Ferdinand Hodler (1853–1918) is regarded as one of the foremost modern Swiss painters. He painted many self-portraits, of which this is an example. In this case, he was angry, living a meager existence in an abandoned watch factory after being stung by adverse criticism of his most recent paintings.

Reading the Art What is the focus of this painting? How would you describe the artist's expression?

Literary Concept: FARCE

P Ask students to describe the mood created by Lomov's repeated references to his poor health. (*Possible responses: comic; melodramatic; silly*) Point out that Lomov uses his poor health as an excuse not to carry out his threats.

Critical Thinking: MAKING JUDGMENTS

Q Ask students to be the judge and decide to whom the meadows belong. Have them explain their decisions. (*Accept all reasonable responses.*)

Literary Concept: RISING ACTION

R Ask students what complication has been added to the plot. (*Possible response: Tschubukov has joined the argument on the side of Natalia and seems to have changed the tone from heated disagreement to one of real hatred.*)

Lomov. The meadows are mine, you understand? Mine!

Natalia. Really, you needn't scream so! If you want to scream and snort and rage you may do it at home, but here please keep yourself within the limits of common decency.

Lomov. My dear lady, if it weren't that I were suffering from palpitation of the heart and hammering of the arteries in my temples, I would deal with you very differently! (*In a loud voice*) The meadows belong to me!

Natalia. Us!

Lomov. Me! (*Enter Tschubukov, right*)

Tschubukov. What's going on here? What is he yelling about?

Natalia. Papa, please tell this gentleman to whom the meadows belong, to us or to him?

Tschubukov (*to Lomov*). My dear fellow, the meadows are ours.

Lomov. But, merciful heavens, Stepan Stepanovitch, how do you make that out? You at least might be reasonable. My aunt's grandmother gave the use of the meadows free of cost to your grandfather's peasants; the peasants lived on the land for forty years and used it as their own, but later when—

Tschubukov. Permit me, my dear friend. You forget that your grandmother's peasants never paid, because there had been a lawsuit over the meadows, and everyone knows that the meadows belong to us. You haven't looked at the map.

Lomov. I'll prove to you that they belong to me!

Tschubukov. Don't try to prove it, my dear fellow.

Lomov. I will!

Tschubukov. My good fellow, what are you shrieking about? You can't prove anything by yelling, you know. I don't ask for anything that belongs to you, nor do I intend to give up anything of my own. Why should I? If it has gone so far, my dear man, that you really intend to claim the meadows, I'd rather give them to the peasants than you, and I certainly shall!

Der Zornige (Selbstbildnis) [The angry one (self-portrait)] (1881), Ferdinand Hodler. Oil on canvas, 72.5 cm × 52.5 cm, Kunstmuseum Bern, Switzerland. Photo by Peter Lauri, 1992.

392 UNIT THREE PART 1: MIXED BLESSINGS

Mini-Lesson Grammar

Possessive Pronouns

Singular	Plural
my, mine	our, ours
your, yours	your, yours
his, her, hers, its	their, theirs

POSSESSIVE PRONOUNS Write the pronouns shown on the left on the chalkboard. Point out to students that possessive pronouns are special forms of personal pronouns that show ownership or belonging. Five such pronouns are found in the section above.

Ownership: The book is *hers*.
Belonging: *My* family likes to read.

Application Read the following sentences aloud. Have students fill in the correct pronoun forms.
1. To Lomov the meadows were ____. (*his*)
2. Natalia argued ____ side no less forcefully than Lomov did his. (*her*)
3. ____ meadows, as Natalia and Tschubukov saw them, would never be Lomov's. (*Their*)

Reteaching/Reinforcement
- *Grammar Handbook*, anthology p. 943
- *Grammar Mini-Lessons* copymasters p. 18, transparencies pp. 12, 15

📖 The Writer's Craft

The Possessive Case, pp. 553–554

392 THE LANGUAGE OF LITERATURE TEACHER'S EDITION

Lomov. I can't believe it! By what right can you give away property that doesn't belong to you?

Tschubukov. Really, you must allow me to decide what I am to do with my own land! I'm not accustomed, young man, to have people address me in that tone of voice. I, young man, am twice your age, and I beg you to address me respectfully.

Lomov. No! No! You think I'm a fool! You're making fun of me! You call my property yours and then expect me to stand quietly by and talk to you like a human being. That isn't the way a good neighbor behaves, Stepan Stepanovitch! You are no neighbor, you're no better than a land grabber. That's what you are!

Tschubukov. Wh—at? What did he say?

Natalia. Papa, send the reapers into the meadows this minute!

Tschubukov. (*to* Lomov). What was that you said, sir?

Natalia. The meadows belong to us, and I won't give them up! I won't give them up! I won't give them up!

Lomov. We'll see about that! I'll prove in court that they belong to me.

Tschubukov. In court! You may sue in court, sir, if you like! Oh, I know you, you are only waiting to find an excuse to go to law! You're an intriguer,[6] that's what you are! Your whole family were always looking for quarrels. The whole lot!

Lomov. Kindly refrain from insulting my family. The entire race of Lomov has always been honorable! And never has one been brought to trial for embezzlement, as your dear uncle was!

Tschubukov. And the whole Lomov family were insane!

Natalia. Every one of them!

Self-Portrait at the Dressing Table (1909), Zinaida Serebryakova. Oil on canvas, 75 cm × 65 cm, The State Tretyakov Gallery, Moscow.

---

6. **intriguer** (ĭn-trē′gər): one who plans secret, sly actions; schemer.

A MARRIAGE PROPOSAL **393**

Art Note

Self-Portrait at the Dressing Table by Zinaida Serebryakova Like Hodler, Russian-born artist Zinaida Serebryakova (1884–1967) excelled at self-portraiture. One critic declared that in her early paintings "the simple real-life atmosphere . . . is joyous and lovely."

Reading the Art *What is your impression of this painting? How would you compare it with Hodler's self-portrait?*

Critical Thinking: ANALYZE

Ask students why they think Tschubukov would escalate the argument and thus risk losing a son-in-law. *(Possible response: Tschubukov is so angry that he is not even thinking about the proposal.)*

CUSTOMIZING FOR Multiple Learning Styles

Bodily-Kinesthetic Learners Have students discuss subtle differences among characters' reactions. Ask how they would stage this scene. *(Possible responses: All the characters have lost their tempers, but Lomov seems the most rational, offering to provide proof for his claim and to go to court; Natalia seems the most defensive, retreating behind the integrity of her family's claim; Tschubukov wants a more civil argument, and his willingness to give the land to peasants and his low opinion of going to the law hint that he fears the meadows may not be his.)*

Literary Concept: MOOD

Have students describe how mood is affected by these lines between Tschubukov and Lomov. *(Possible responses: The comic aspect is increased, because the argument escalates to the point where they insult each other's families, when earlier they were ready to join the families.)*

Mini-Lesson Workplace Literacy

SCANS Goal: Negotiates

NEGOTIATING Point out to the class that the characters in this play could use a good negotiator. Indicate to students that negotiating means working toward an agreement that may involve resolving conflicting interests. Explain that a good negotiator will
- listen carefully
- organize ideas and communicate effectively
- recognize problems and devise possible solutions
- exhibit understanding, adaptability, empathy, and politeness to others

Application Divide students into groups of four and have them enact the roles of the characters in the play and a negotiator, who will attempt to resolve the conflict over the meadows. A successful negotiator should be able to come up with a compromise and convince the parties to agree to it.

THE LANGUAGE OF LITERATURE TEACHER'S EDITION **393**

Linking to Science

Lomov suffers from hypochondria, a morbidly extreme anxiety about one's health accompanied by imagined symptoms of illness. Noted hypochondriacs include the evolutionist Charles Darwin, the lexicographer Samuel Johnson, and the poet Sara Teasdale.

CUSTOMIZING FOR
Students Acquiring English

Explain that the expression "May you never darken my door again" means "I hope you never return to my house." The image is literally that of a guest's shadow on the door as he or she waits outside to be admitted to the house.

STRATEGIC READING FOR
Less-Proficient Readers

To make sure that students are following the action of the play, have them respond to the following questions.

- What happens when Tschubukov joins the argument? *(The fight escalates and Lomov leaves in a huff.)* **Summarizing**

- Why does Tschubukov ask Lomov to come back? *(Natalia goes into hysterics when she realizes that Lomov was going to propose.)* **Noting Relevant Details**

Set a Purpose Have students read to find out if the couple will be reconciled.

Tschubukov. Your grandmother was a dipsomaniac,[7] and the younger aunt, Nastasia Michailovna, ran off with an architect.

Lomov. And your mother limped. *(He puts his hand over his heart.)* Oh, my side pains! My temples are bursting! Lord in heaven! Water!

Tschubukov. And your dear father was a gambler—and a glutton!

Natalia. And your aunt was a gossip like few others!

Lomov. And you are an intriguer. Oh, my heart! And it's an open secret that you cheated at the elections—my eyes are blurred! Where is my hat?

Natalia. Oh, how low! Liar! Disgusting thing!

Lomov. Where's the hat? My heart! Where shall I go? Where is the door? Oh—it seems—as though I were dying! I can't—my legs won't hold me—*(Goes to the door.)*

Tschubukov *(following him).* May you never darken my door again!

Natalia. Bring your suit to court! We'll see! *(Lomov staggers out, center.)*

Tschubukov *(angrily).* The devil!

Natalia. Such a good-for-nothing! And then they talk about being good neighbors!

Tschubukov. Loafer! Scarecrow! Monster!

Natalia. A swindler like that takes over a piece of property that doesn't belong to him and then dares to argue about it!

Tschubukov. And to think that this fool dares to make a proposal of marriage!

Natalia. What? A proposal of marriage?

Tschubukov. Why, yes! He came here to make you a proposal of marriage.

Natalia. Why didn't you tell me that before?

Tschubukov. That's why he had on his evening clothes! The poor fool!

Natalia. Proposal for me? Oh! *(Falls into an armchair and groans.)* Bring him back! Bring him back!

Tschubukov. Bring whom back?

Natalia. Faster, faster, I'm sinking! Bring him back! *(She becomes hysterical.)*

Tschubukov. What is it? What's wrong with you? *(his hands to his head)* I'm cursed with bad luck! I'll shoot myself! I'll hang myself!

Natalia. I'm dying! Bring him back!

Tschubukov. Bah! In a minute! Don't bawl! *(He rushes out, center.)*

Natalia *(groaning).* What have they done to me? Bring him back! Bring him back!

Tschubukov *(comes running in).* He's coming at once! The devil take him! Ugh! Talk to him yourself, I can't.

Natalia *(groaning).* Bring him back!

Tschubukov. He's coming, I tell you! "Oh, Lord! What a task it is to be the father of a grown daughter!" I'll cut my throat! I really will cut my throat! We've argued with the fellow, insulted him, and now we've thrown him out!—and you did it all, you!

Natalia. No, you! You haven't any manners, you are brutal! If it weren't for you, he wouldn't have gone!

Tschubukov. Oh, yes, I'm to blame! If I shoot or hang myself, remember *you'll* be to blame. You forced me to it! You! *(Lomov appears in the doorway.)* There, talk to him yourself! *(He goes out.)*

Lomov. Terrible palpitation! My leg is lamed! My side hurts me—

Natalia. Pardon us, we were angry, Ivan Vassiliyitch. I remember now—the meadows really belong to you.

Lomov. My heart is beating terribly! My meadows—my eyelids tremble—*(They sit down.)* We were wrong. It was only the principle of the thing—the property isn't worth much to me, but the principle is worth a great deal.

---

7. **dipsomaniac** (dĭp′sə-mā′nē-ăk′): drunkard.

394 UNIT THREE PART 1: MIXED BLESSINGS

Mini-Lesson The Writer's Style

USING DIALOGUE IN PLAYS AND SKITS
Explain to students that plays and skits consist almost entirely of dialogue, which must effectively reveal both characters and events. Have students study the highlighted section of page 394 to note how the dialogue reveals the following about Natalia and Tschubukov:

- Natalia is not too fussy about whom she marries.
- Natalia can make Tschubukov do as she wishes.
- Father and daughter are quarrelsome even with each other.

Application Remind students that they do not really know what dialogue takes place when Tschubukov rushes out to retrieve Lomov for Natalia. Have students write the dialogue they imagine takes place between the two men.

Reteaching/Reinforcement
- *Writing Handbook*, anthology, p. 877
- *Writing Mini-Lessons* transparencies, p. 56

 The Writer's Craft

Using Dialogue in Plays and Skits, p. 436

Natalia. Exactly, the principle! Let us talk about something else.

Lomov. Because I have proofs that my aunt's grandmother had, with the peasants of your good father—

Natalia. Enough, enough. (*aside*) I don't know how to begin. (To Lomov.) Are you going hunting soon?

Lomov. Yes, heath cock shooting, respected Natalia Stepanovna. I expect to begin after the harvest. Oh, did you hear? My dog, Ugadi, you know him—limps!

Natalia. What a shame! How did that happen?

Lomov. I don't know. Perhaps it's a dislocation, or maybe he was bitten by some other dog. (*He sighs.*) The best dog I ever had—to say nothing of his price! I paid Mironov a hundred and twenty-five roubles for him.

Natalia. That was too much to pay, Ivan Vassiliyitch.

Lomov. In my opinion it was very cheap. A wonderful dog!

Natalia. Papa paid eighty-five roubles for his Otkatai, and Otkatai is much better than your Ugadi!

Lomov. Really? Otkatai is better than Ugadi? What an idea! (*He laughs.*) Otkatai better then Ugadi!

Natalia. Of course he is better. It is true Otkatai is still young; he isn't full grown yet, but in the pack or on the leash with two or three, there is no better than he, even—

Lomov. I really beg your pardon, Natalia Stepanovna, but you quite overlooked the fact that he has a short lower jaw, and a dog with a short lower jaw can't snap.

Natalia. Short lower jaw? That's the first time I ever heard that!

Lomov. I assure you, his lower jaw is shorter than the upper.

Natalia. Have you measured it?

Lomov. I have measured it. He is good at running, though.

Natalia. In the first place, our Otkatai is pure-bred, a full-blooded son of Sapragavas and Stameskis, and as for your mongrel, nobody could ever figure out his pedigree; he's old and ugly and as skinny as an old hag.

Lomov. Old, certainly! I wouldn't take five of your Otkatais for him! Ugadi is a dog, and Otkatai is—it is laughable to argue about it! Dogs like your Otkatai can be found by the dozens at any dog dealer's, a whole pound full!

Natalia. Ivan Vassiliyitch, you are very contrary today. First our meadows belong to you, and then Ugadi is better than Otkatai. I don't like it when a person doesn't say what he really thinks. You know perfectly well that Otkatai is a hundred times better than your silly Ugadi. What makes you keep on saying he isn't?

Lomov. I can see, Natalia Stepanovna, that you consider me either a blind man or a fool. But at least you may as well admit that Otkatai has a short lower jaw!

Natalia. It isn't so!

Lomov. Yes, a short lower jaw!

Natalia (*loudly*). It's not so!

Lomov. What makes you scream, my dear lady?

Natalia. What makes you talk such nonsense? It's disgusting! It is high time that Ugadi was shot, and yet you compare him with Otkatai!

Lomov. Pardon me, but I can't carry on this argument any longer. I have palpitation of the heart!

Natalia. I have always noticed that the hunters who do the most talking know the least about hunting.

Lomov. My dear lady, I beg of you to be still. My heart is bursting! (*He shouts.*) Be still!

WORDS TO KNOW
contrary (kŏn′trĕr′ē) *adj.* tending to stubbornly oppose or contradict

---

Mini-Lesson: Speaking, Listening, and Viewing

PANTOMIME Explain to students that a pantomime is a play without words, in which the actors express themselves in gestures. Tell them that a farce is a perfect vehicle for a pantomime because of the exaggerated characters and actions. In preparation for doing a pantomime of a scene from *A Marriage Proposal*, students should consider the exaggerated aspects of each character as well as the slapstick action of the scene. Also have them consider how to use their faces and gestures rather than their voices to express emotion and events.

Application Have students work in groups of three to plan a pantomime of one scene from *A Marriage Proposal*. Ask each group to present the pantomime for the entire class. As the class reviews the success of each, they should consider how well the actors portrayed the characters' emotions, exaggerated qualities, and slapstick action.

Art Note

Drei Windhunde [Three greyhounds] by Frans Snyders Frans Snyders (1579–1657) was born in Belgium and is best known for his paintings of animals fighting among themselves and of hunting scenes.

Reading the Art *What effect does Snyders achieve here by portraying the animals looking away from each other?*

Critical Thinking:
MAKING JUDGMENTS

BB Have students judge Tschubukov's response to Lomov. Would they have responded in the same way? Why or why not? *(Possible responses: Yes, because Tschubukov does make an effort to pacify Lomov; no, because the response only serves to aggravate the situation. Students might suggest that Tschubukov might have done better to say that the dogs are equal.)*

Linking to History

CC *Count* is a title indicating hereditary nobility. Some Russian noblemen were landowners or professionals, while others served in the military or in government. Titles of nobility existed in Russia until the 1917 revolution, when they were abolished.

Literary Concept:
STAGE DIRECTIONS

DD Point out that the stage direction indicates how Tschubukov utters the first sentence. Ask why the playwright does this rather than leaving the interpretation to the actor or the reader. *(Possible response: It needs to be clear that this sentence is spoken in mimicry or else it doesn't make sense at first.)*

Natalia. I won't be still until you admit that Otkatai is better! (*Enter Tschubukov.*)

Tschubukov. Well, has it begun again?

Natalia. Papa, say frankly, on your honor, which dog is better: Otkatai or Ugadi?

Lomov. Stepan Stepanovitch, I beg of you, just answer this: has your dog a short lower jaw or not? Yes or no?

Tschubukov. And what if he has? Is it of such importance? There is no better dog in the whole country.

Lomov. My Ugadi is better. Tell the truth, now!

Tschubukov. Don't get so excited, my dear fellow! Permit me. Your Ugadi certainly has his good points. He is from a good breed, has a good stride, strong haunches, and so forth. But the dog, if you really want to know it, has two faults; he is old and he has a short lower jaw.

Lomov. Pardon me, I have palpitation of the heart!—Let us keep to facts—just remember in Maruskins's meadows, my Ugadi kept ear to ear with the Count Rasvachai and your dog.

Tschubukov. He was behind, because the count struck him with his whip.

Lomov. Quite right. All the other dogs were on the fox's scent, but Otkatai found it necessary to bite a sheep.

Tschubukov. That isn't so!—I am sensitive about that and beg you to stop this argument. He struck him because everybody looks on a strange dog of good blood with envy. Even you, sir, aren't free from the sin. No sooner do you find a dog better than Ugadi than you begin to—this, that—his, mine—and so forth! I remember distinctly.

Lomov. I remember something, too!

Drei Windhunde [Three greyhounds], Frans Snyders. Herzog Anton Ulrich-Museum, Braunschweig, Germany. Photo by B. P. Keiser.

Tschubukov (*mimicking him*). I remember something, too! What do you remember?

Lomov. Palpitation! My leg is lame—I can't—

Natalia. Palpitation! What kind of hunter are you? You ought to stay in the kitchen by the stove and wrestle with the potato peelings and not go fox hunting! Palpitation!

Tschubukov. And what kind of hunter are you? A man with your diseases ought to stay at home and not jolt around in the saddle. If you were a hunter! But you only ride round in order to find out about other people's dogs and make trouble for everyone. I am sensitive! Let's drop the subject. Besides, you're no hunter.

Lomov. You only ride around to flatter the count! My heart! You intriguer! Swindler!

Tschubukov. And what of it? (*shouting*) Be still!

Lomov. Intriguer!

Tschubukov. Baby! Puppy! Walking drugstore!

Lomov. Old rat! Jesuit![8] Oh, I know you!

Tschubukov. Be still! Or I'll shoot you—with my worst gun, like a partridge! Fool! Loafer!

Lomov. Everyone knows that—oh, my heart!—that your poor late wife beat you. My leg—my temples—heavens—I'm dying—I—

Tschubukov. And your housekeeper wears the trousers in your house!

Lomov. Here—here—there—there—my heart has burst! My shoulder is torn apart. Where is my shoulder? I'm dying! (*He falls into a chair.*) The doctor! (*faints*)

Tschubukov. Baby! Half-baked clam! Fool!

Natalia. Nice sort of hunter you are! You can't even sit on a horse. (*To Tschubukov.*) Papa, what's the matter with him? (*She screams.*) Ivan Vassiliyitch! He is dead!

Lomov. I'm ill! I can't breathe! Air!

Natalia. He is dead! (*She shakes Lomov in the chair.*) Ivan Vassiliyitch! What have we done! He is dead! (*She sinks into a chair.*) The doctor—doctor! (*She goes into hysterics.*)

Tschubukov. Ahh! What is it? What's the matter with you?

Natalia (*groaning*). He's dead! Dead!

Tschubukov. Who is dead? Who? (*Looking at Lomov*) Yes, he is dead! Good God! Water! The doctor! (*Holding the glass to Lomov's lips*) Drink! No, he won't drink! He's dead!

What a terrible situation! Why didn't I shoot myself? Why have I never cut my throat? What am I waiting for now? Only give me a knife! Give me a pistol! (*Lomov moves.*) He's coming to! Drink some water—there!

Lomov. Sparks! Mists! Where am I?

Tschubukov. Get married! Quick, and then go to the devil! She's willing! (*He joins the hands of Lomov and Natalia.*) She's agreed! Only leave me in peace!

Lomov. Wh—what? (*getting up*) Whom?

Tschubukov. She's willing! Well? Kiss each other and—the devil take you both!

Natalia (*groans*). He lives! Yes, yes, I'm willing!

Tschubukov. Kiss each other!

Lomov. Eh? Whom? (*Natalia and Lomov kiss.*) Very nice! Pardon me, but what is this for? Oh, yes, I understand! My heart—sparks—I am happy. Natalia Stepanovna. (*He kisses her hand.*) My leg is lame!

Natalia. I'm happy, too!

Tschubukov. Ahh! A load off my shoulders! Ahh!

Natalia. And now at least you'll admit that Ugadi is worse than Otkatai!

Lomov. Better!

Natalia. Worse!

Tschubukov. Now the domestic joys have begun. Champagne!

Lomov. Better!

Natalia. Worse, worse, worse!

Tschubukov (*trying to drown them out*). Champagne, champagne!

Translated from the Russian by Hilmar Baukhage and Barrett H. Clark

---

8. **Jesuit** (jĕzh′ōō-ĭt): schemer. The Jesuits—members of the Society of Jesus, a Roman Catholic order of men—long had a reputation for subtle thought and political meddling.

INSIGHT

The Strange Case of Mr. Ormantude's Bride

OGDEN NASH

Man and Woman, Provincetown (1934), Charles Demuth. Watercolor and pencil on paper, private collection.

Once there was a bridegroom named Mr. Ormantude
    whose intentions were hard to disparage,[1]
Because he intended to make his a happy marriage,
And he succeeded for going on fifty years,
During which he was in marital bliss up to his ears.
5 His wife's days and nights were enjoyable
Because he catered to every foible;[2]
He went around humming her favorite hymns
And anticipating her whims.
Many a fine bit of repartee[3] died on his lips
10 Lest it throw her anecdotes into eclipse;
He was always silent when his cause was
    meritorious,[4]
And he never engaged in argument unless sure he was
    so obviously wrong that she couldn't help emerg-
    ing victorious,
And always when in her vicinity
He was careful to make allowances for her femininity;
15 Were she snappish, he was sweetish,
And of understanding her he made a fetish.[5]
Everybody said his chances of celebrating his golden
    wedding looked good,
But on his golden wedding eve he was competently
    poisoned by his wife who could no longer stand
    being perpetually understood.

---

1. **disparage:** speak badly of.
2. **foible** (foi′bəl): a small weakness in a person's character.
3. **repartee** (rĕp′ər-tē′): a quick, witty reply or series of such replies.
4. **meritorious:** deserving praise.
5. **fetish:** an object or activity to which a person is unreasonably devoted.

OGDEN NASH

Born in Rye, New York, Ogden Nash (1902–1971) was probably the best-known writer of light verse in the United States during his lifetime. Nash characterized his whimsical verses (or "worses," as he called them) as "slightly goofy and cheerfully sour" and once said, "There have been many truly bad poets, and I've read a lot of them and learned from them." He became a free-lance writer, published thousands of verses, wrote screenplays, appeared in radio and television shows, and gave lectures.

RESPONDING OPTIONS

FROM PERSONAL RESPONSE TO CRITICAL ANALYSIS

REFLECT
1. What, if anything, did you find amusing in this play? Share your reactions with a classmate.

RETHINK
Thematic Link

2. Think about your earlier discussion of marriage and the ideal marriage partner. Do you think Lomov is a good candidate for marriage? Explain why or why not.
   Consider
   - his reasons for wanting to marry
   - what his speeches reveal about him
   - his physical and emotional condition

Close Textual Reading

3. Why do you think Lomov and Natalia want to marry each other?

4. How happy do you think Lomov and Natalia will be in their marriage? Cite evidence to support your opinion.

5. Review the recipe that you created for the Writing Connection on page 385. Did your creation of the recipe influence your reaction to the play in any way? Explain.

6. What do you think was Chekhov's purpose in writing this play?

RELATE
Literary Link

7. Think about the Insight poem "The Strange Case of Mr. Ormantude's Bride." Do you think that Lomov will ever act the way Mr. Ormantude did for 50 years? Explain.

8. Are the dating rituals of teenagers today humorous? Create a comic strip of four panels, showing two young people who are interested in each other but who have disagreements. You may include parents.

Multimodal Learning
ANOTHER PATHWAY
Cooperative Learning

Work with a small group of classmates to prepare a Readers Theater presentation of part of this play and to perform it for the class. After watching all the performances, your class could give awards for excellence in acting, directing, and other aspects of the productions.

LITERARY CONCEPTS

Foreshadowing is a writer's use of hints or clues to indicate events and situations that will occur later in a plot. When does Chekhov first hint that love may not be the motivating factor in Lomov's proposal?

CONCEPT REVIEW: Mood Mood is a feeling or atmosphere that a writer creates for the reader. Foreshadowing, figurative language, imagery, descriptive words, setting, and dialogue all contribute to a work's mood. How would you describe the mood of *A Marriage Proposal*? Find words, phrases, and passages that help create this mood. Share your ideas with a classmate.

QUICKWRITES

1. Using "The Strange Case of Mr. Ormantude's Bride" as a model, write a lighthearted **poem** about the marriage of Lomov and Natalia.

2. Imagine that you are a marriage counselor and that Lomov and Natalia, now married, have come to you seeking help. Write a **report** of their first session with you.

📁 **PORTFOLIO** Save your writing. You may want to use it later as a springboard to a piece for your portfolio.

A MARRIAGE PROPOSAL 399

From Personal Response to Critical Analysis

1. Accept all reasonable responses.
2. Possible response: Yes—when you consider his time, he probably offers what the average Russian woman could expect from marriage, and care and companionship may even tame his insecurity and hypochondria; no, he just wants a wife to take care of him and is a nervous hypochondriac who gets upset easily
3. Possible responses: They have no other prospects; they would rather marry any reasonably suitable person than remain single; they want to join their estates.
4. Some students may say that they will not be happy, citing their arguments as evidence. Others may think that they are a good match because they enjoy arguing and uniting their property should lessen tensions.
5. Accept all reasonable responses.
6. Possible responses: to make fun of the pettiness of the upper class; to amuse his audience; to criticize the foibles of humans in general
7. Most students will suggest that Lomov is too argumentative to behave like Mr. Ormantude. Some might suggest that Natalia will browbeat him into submission.
8. Presentations will vary.

Another Pathway

Cooperative Learning Students should collaborate in groups of five or six to make sure that their presentation is a success. One student should direct the performance. Another might coach, correcting misread lines or interpretations during rehearsals. A third might act as a critic, providing constructive viewpoints.

Rubric
- **3 Full Accomplishment** The presentation convincingly portrays the comic mood of the play through strong characterizations.
- **2 Substantial Accomplishment** The presentation has comic moments, but some of the actors do not adequately convey the comic mood.
- **1 Little or Partial Accomplishment** The presentation is disjointed, actors do not show an understanding of their lines, and characterizations are weak.

Literary Concepts

Students can work in pairs to find the first hint that love is not Lomov's motivation. They should discuss the play together and collaborate on a list of examples of foreshadowing.

Mood Students might describe the mood as comic, lighthearted, or silly. Many words, phrases, and passages help create this mood: Lomov's frequent health complaints, the escalating arguments, Natalia's hysteria, and Tschubukov's laments.

QuickWrites

1. Encourage students to think about what Lomov and Natalia's marriage would be like. Then suggest they consider the construction of the poem. How will they use figurative language, rhythm, and rhyme?

2. Encourage students to consider the following organization for their reports: an introduction describing the couple and their complaint; a body dealing with what took place at the session; a conclusion focusing on suggestions for solving the problem.

📓 **The Writer's Craft**

paraphrases and summaries in reports, pp. 464–465

Words to Know

1. a pirate
2. a brat [A flirt is also acceptable.]
3. her chest
4. stare wide-eyed
5. to take it and wear it

Reteaching/Reinforcement
- *Unit Three Resource Book*, p. 22

Critic's Corner

Some students might suggest that Chekhov did have sympathy for Lomov and Natalia, since he felt that the institution of marriage was faulty. Others might believe that even if Chekhov found fault with the institution of marriage, the characters are too exaggerated to reflect any sympathy on his part.

Across the Curriculum

History Research the social structure that existed in Russia during the 1890s, when this play was written. Create a chart showing the structure of Russian society at that time.

Sociology What reasons do sociologists cite for the increase in the divorce rate in the 20th century? Prepare a list of reasons and share them with the class.

Music Ask students to find music by 19th-century Russian composers (such as Tchaikovsky, Mussorgsky, Rimsky-Korsakov, Borodin) and to select a piece that they feel captures the play's mood.

LITERARY CONNECTION
Scenes from *A Marriage Proposal* In a play, mood is created both by the language the writer uses and by the actors' vocal and physical expressiveness. These images show a number of ways in which actors can convey mood through body language.

Side A, Frame 49351

Multimodal Learning

ALTERNATIVE ACTIVITIES

Cooperative Learning Work with a small group to create a **program** for a performance of *A Marriage Proposal*, complete with a cover design, a list of the cast, a substantial plot summary, and ads. Cast the play with television or movie actors who you think are suited to the roles.

CRITIC'S CORNER

The writer Ruth Davies characterized Chekhov's view of marriage this way: "To Chekhov marriage was not an idyllic relationship, but usually an unavailing struggle between two people to achieve compatibility." In other words, Chekhov viewed marriage more as two people's constant struggle to get along than as a relationship characterized by happiness and love. With this in mind, do you think Chekhov had any sympathy for the characters in this play?

WORDS TO KNOW

Answer the following questions on a sheet of paper.

1. Which Halloween costume represents a **usurper**—one of a pirate, one of a ghost, or one of a superhero?
2. Who is most likely to behave in a **contrary** fashion—a flirt, a banker, or a brat?
3. Would a person having a **palpitation** be most likely to clutch at her head, her chest, or her stomach?
4. Is a person who is **dumbfounded** by an event most likely to shriek hysterically, stare wide-eyed, or criticize harshly?
5. If you were worried that someone was going to **appropriate** an outfit of yours, would you fear that the person intended to make fun of it, to ruin it, or to take it and wear it?

ANTON CHEKHOV

1860–1904

Although Anton Chekhov was one of the world's greatest playwrights and a writer who helped create the modern short story, he was by training a doctor. To study medicine, he moved to Moscow at the age of 19. There he began writing for satirical magazines to help support his family, which had fallen into debt. Chekhov published stories for the next five years under a pen name, keeping his real name to use in future medical writing. However, because his success as a writer was immediate and because he suffered from slowly advancing, incurable tuberculosis, he practiced medicine only occasionally during the rest of his life. He never got around to medical writing.

In 1887 Chekhov's first play was produced, and by 1888 he was considered among the best young Russian writers. In 1889–1890, four of his one-act plays—including *A Marriage Proposal*—were produced to a favorable reception by both critics and the public. Although humor remained important in his work, Chekhov's later writing became more serious. His realistic stories and dramas tend to focus on the drabness and hardship in life.

In 1901 Chekhov married the Russian actress Olga Knipper. Unfortunately, because of his poor health and his dislike of the theater scene, he was often separated from his wife, who stayed in Moscow. Chekhov spent many of his later years in the warmer climates of southern Russia and Europe. His relatively brief writing career of 25 years ended with his death at a German health resort in 1904. His works were not fully appreciated in English-speaking countries until later.

OTHER WORKS "Ward Number Six," "The Bet," "A Slander," "A Chameleon," *Uncle Vanya*, *The Cherry Orchard*

Extended Reading
- LITERARY CONNECTOIN

400 UNIT THREE PART 1: MIXED BLESSINGS

Alternative Activities

Encourage students to locate a copy of a playbill to see how the different sections fit together. Suggest that tasks be assigned to different members of the group according to ability and interest. For example, some students might work on the cover design. Remind students that this design should reflect an important aspect of the play. The entire group can make suggestions on how to cast the play. Some students can work on the plot summary, and others can design and write copy for advertisements.

ON YOUR OWN

Father's Day

MICHAEL DORRIS

OBJECTIVES

- To promote independent active reading
- To practice and apply skills learned in previous selections
- To provide an opportunity to assess student's performance through an alternative assessment instrument

SUMMARY

In this short essay, the author tells about the fathers in his life. His biological father was killed in World War II at the age of 27. The author never knew his biological father and finds out what his father was like only through stories told by other people. His real father was his Aunt Marion, who played catch with the author, nursed him when he was sick, and bought him his first typewriter. When she needed a man's help for father-son banquets or for teaching the author how to shave, she enlisted the aid of friends. Otherwise, it was Aunt Marion who taught the author about life and gave him every opportunity to learn and grow. He sends her a Father's Day card each June.

Thematic Link: Mixed Blessings Michael Dorris's loss of his father at an early age is compensated for by the loving care and attention that his Aunt Marion gives him. In playing the vital role of a male parent, she becomes his "father."

Reading Pathways

- Have students read the essay on their own and complete a KWL chart.
- Invite students to do a paired reading and complete a character cluster centered on Aunt Marion.
- Encourage students to do a group reading followed by a discussion comparing Aunt Marion to their notion of the perfect father.
- Evaluate how well students can read, interpret, discuss, and write about the selection on their own by using the Integrated Assessment for Unit Three, located in the Alternative Assessment booklet. Administer the assessment at the end of the unit after students have read all the selections and completed all the writing they have been assigned.

PRINT AND MEDIA RESOURCES

UNIT THREE RESOURCE BOOK
Strategic Reading: Literature, p. 25

FORMAL ASSESSMENT
Selection Test, p. 69
Part Test, pp. 71–72
 Test Generator

ALTERNATIVE ASSESSMENT
Unit Three Integrated Assessment pp. 13–18

ACCESS FOR STUDENTS ACQUIRING ENGLISH
Selection Summaries

AUDIO LIBRARY
See Reference Card

Individual Activity
CREATING A GREETING CARD

Have students design and write a message for a Father's Day greeting card that the author might send to Aunt Marion.

Teacher's Role Encourage students to look at several greeting cards to note the variety of messages and tones. Then ask them to consider what message and tone would suit a card from the author to Aunt Marion. As they create their card, students should recall the author's attitude toward his aunt.

Rubric

3 Full Accomplishment Students create a card whose design and message accurately reflect the author's attitude toward his aunt.

2 Substantial Accomplishment Students create a card that essentially reflects the author's attitude toward his aunt.

1 Little or Partial Accomplishment Students have difficulty creating a card that accurately reflects the author's attitude toward his aunt.

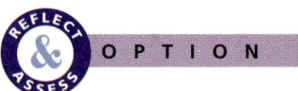

Cooperative Learning
DEBATE

Have groups of students debate whether or not, as dedicated as she was, Aunt Marion was an adequate father substitute for the author. Before they begin, students should check their knowledge of the rules and procedures for debating by consulting *Robert's Rules of Order* or other resources in the library.

Teacher's Role Act as a moderator for the debate. Suggest that each team choose a director to lead the group, a researcher to locate support material, and a prober to make sure that the group's arguments are logical and defensible.

Rubric

3 Full Accomplishment Students present logical and cogent arguments to support their point of view.

2 Substantial Accomplishment Students present many logical arguments, but a part of their presentation may be somewhat disjointed.

1 Little or Partial Accomplishment Students have difficulty presenting any logical arguments to support their point of view.

402 THE LANGUAGE OF LITERATURE TEACHER'S EDITION

My father, a career army officer, was twenty-seven when he was killed, and as a result, I can't help but take war personally. Over the years his image has coalesced for me as an amalgam of familiar anecdotes:[1] a dashing mixed-blood man from the Northwest who, improbably, could do the rumba; a soldier who regularly had his uniform altered by a tailor so that it would fit better; a date, according to my mother, who "knew how to order" in a restaurant; the person whom, in certain lights and to some people, I resemble. He is a compromise of his quirkier[2] qualities, indistinct, better remembered for his death—my grandmother still wears a gold star on her best coat—than for his brief life.

From the perspective of the present, my father was a bit player on the edges of the movie frame, the one who didn't make it back, whose fatality added anonymous atmosphere and a sense of mayhem[3] to the plot. His grave, in a military cemetery near Tacoma, is located by graph paper like a small town on a map: E-9. He's frozen in age, a kid in a T-shirt, a pair of dog tags stored in a box in my closet. His willingness to die for his country may have contributed in some small part to the fall of the Nazis but more in the way of a pawn exchanged for its counterpart, a pair of lives eliminated with the result that there were two fewer people to engage in combat. I was a few months old the last time he saw me, and a single photograph of me in his arms is the only hard evidence that we ever met.

The fact of my father's death exempted me, under the classification "sole surviving son" (A-IV),[4] from being drafted during the Vietnam War, but it also obliged me to empathize with the child of every serviceperson killed in an armed engagement. "Glory" is an inadequate substitute, a pale abstraction, compared to the enduring, baffling blankness of a missing parent.

There was a children's book in the 1950s—perhaps it still exists—titled *The Happy Family,*

402   UNIT THREE   PART 1: MIXED BLESSINGS

---

and it was a piece of work. Dad toiled at the office, Mom baked in the kitchen, and brother and sister always had neighborhood friends sleeping over. The prototype of "Leave It to Beaver" and "Father Knows Best," this little text reflects a midcentury standard, a brightly illustrated reproach to my own unorthodox household, but luckily that wasn't the way I heard it. As read to me by my Aunt Marion—her acid delivery was laced with sarcasm and punctuated with many a sidelong glance—it turned into hilarious irony.

My aunt was the one who pitched a baseball with me in the early summer evenings.

Compassionate and generous, irreverent, simultaneously opinionated and open-minded, iron willed and ever optimistic, my aunt was the one who pitched a baseball with me in the early summer evenings, who took me horseback riding, who sat by my bed when I was ill. A fierce, lifelong Democrat—a precinct captain even—she helped me find my first jobs and arranged among her friends at work for my escorts to the father–son dinners that closed each sports season. When the time came, she prevailed upon the elderly man next door to teach me how to shave.

---

1. **has coalesced** (kō´ə-lĕst´) . . . **anecdotes** (ăn´ĭk-dōts´): has come together as a merging of familiar stories.
2. **quirkier:** stranger; more peculiar.
3. **mayhem:** great disorder or confusion.
4. **exempted . . . (A-IV):** The author was excused from military service because he was the only living son of a serviceman who had been killed in action. A-IV is the official designation of this exemption.

"Daddy" Tingle, as he was known to his own children and grandchildren, was a man of many talents. He could spit tobacco juice over the low roof of his garage, gum a sharpened mumbly-peg twig from the ground even without his false teeth, and produce, from the Bourbon Stockyards where he worked, the jewel-like cornea of a cow's eye—but he wasn't much of a shaver. After his instruction, neither am I.

Aunt Marion, on the other hand, was a font of information and influence. When I was fifteen, on a series of tempestuous Sunday mornings at a deserted River Road park, she gave me lessons in how to drive a stick shift. A great believer in the efficacy[5] of the *World Book Encyclopedia*—the major literary purchase of my childhood—she insisted that I confirm any vague belief by looking it up. To the then-popular tune of "You, You, You," she counted my laps in the Crescent Hill pool while I practiced for a lifesaving certificate. Operating on the assumption that anything out of the ordinary was probably good for me, she once offered to mortgage the house so that I could afford to go to Mali as a volunteer participant in Operation Crossroads Africa. She paid for my first Smith-Corona typewriter in thirty-six $4-a-week installments.

For over sixty years Aunt Marion was never without steady employment: telegraph operator for Western Union, budget officer for the City of Louisville, "new girl" at a small savings and loan (when, after twenty-five years in a patronage job,[6] the Democrats lost the mayor's race), executive secretary for a nationally renowned attorney.

Being Aunt Marion, she didn't and doesn't give herself much credit. Unless dragged to center stage, she stands at the periphery[7] in snapshots, minimizes her contributions. Every June for forty years I've sent her a Father's Day card. ❖

---

5. **efficacy** (ĕf´ĭ-kə-sē): effectiveness.
6. **patronage job:** a job given to someone as a reward for political support.
7. **periphery** (pə-rĭf´ə-rē): outer edge.

MICHAEL DORRIS

Although he grew up without a father, Michael Dorris (born 1945) knows a great deal about *being* a father. As a single parent, Dorris adopted three children; later, after marrying the writer Louise Erdrich, he became the father of three more. In his 1989 book *The Broken Cord: A Family's Ongoing Struggle with Fetal Alcohol Syndrome,* Dorris tells the traumatic story of his first adopted child, Abel, who had fetal alcohol syndrome. This incurable disorder, which results from excess alcohol consumption by a mother during pregnancy, causes serious physical and mental defects. Dorris wrote the book to alert people to this tragic condition and to educate them about its prevention. Unfortunately, further tragedy lay ahead for Abel (called Adam in the book). In 1991, just as plans for a television movie of his life were being made, Abel, then 23 years old, was hit by a car and killed. The movie, first broadcast in 1992, became his memorial.

A member of the Native American Modoc tribe, Dorris is chairman of the Department of Native American Studies at Dartmouth College. He earned his bachelor's degree in English and his master's in the history of theater before specializing in cultural anthropology. He has displayed a similar range and versatility in his writing, producing poetry, short stories, novels, songs, essays, and reviews. Dorris sometimes collaborates with his wife in writing, and the two produced the novel *The Crown of Columbus.* He has also written two children's books with Native American themes, *Morning Girl* and *Guests.*

OTHER WORKS *Native Americans: Five Hundred Years After, A Yellow Raft in Blue Water, Rooms in the House of Stone, Working Men, Paper Trail: Collected Essays 1967–1992*

Extended Reading

FATHER'S DAY **403**

Class Discussion
SHARING IDEAS

Teacher's Role After students have read the selection, engage them in a whole-class discussion based on the following questions.

1. The author mentions a book entitled *The Happy Family.* What do you think constitutes a happy family? *(Possible response: people who care for one another)*
2. Would you like to have a relative like Aunt Marion? Why or why not? *(Possible responses: yes, because she took care of her nephew and entered into his concerns; yes, because she was very independent and always supported herself)*
3. If you had to sum up Aunt Marion in one word, what would that word be? Explain your choice. *(Possible responses: independent; loving; resourceful)*
4. What might the author have missed by not having a real father? What do you think he has gained by having Aunt Marion as a "father"? *(Accept all reasonable responses.)*

MICHAEL DORRIS

Perhaps growing up without a father made Michael Dorris acutely sensitive to the needs of children, for he has been involved in children's causes for many years. He is a member of the National Indian Education Association, the National Indian Youth Council, and the Society for Values in Higher Education. He has also been a consultant to television stations, including Los Angeles Educational Television and the Toledo Public Broadcast Center.

OVERVIEW

In the Guided Assignment for this section, students will write an essay interpreting the theme of a work of literature. By identifying its main idea or message, students will gain a deeper appreciation of the literary work. As preparation for this assignment, the Writer's Style will help them understand how writers present main ideas in paragraphs. In Reading the World, students will interpret a real-life experience by examining the meaning they get from coming across a fatigue cap at the Vietnam Veterans Memorial.

Objectives

- To recognize how writers present main ideas in unified paragraphs
- To develop main ideas for paragraphs
- To write an effective introduction to an essay
- To write an essay that interprets the theme of a literary work
- To analyze a real-world image

Skills

LITERATURE
- Identifying stated and implied main ideas

GRAMMAR AND USAGE
- Varying sentence beginnings
- Achieving verb agreement with compound subjects

MEDIA LITERACY
- Analyzing a situation image

SPEAKING, LISTENING, AND VIEWING
- Sharing interpretation of a situation
- Group conferencing

CRITICAL THINKING
- Analyzing
- Making inferences
- Making generalizations
- Observing
- Interpreting experience

Teaching Strategy: MODELING

In the following literature models, the first excerpt states the main idea in a topic sentence. In the second excerpt, the main idea can be inferred from the details.

A **Walters** *Answer: The first sentence states the main idea—Uncle Ralph was born in the wrong time. Supporting ideas—The Pawnees had declined in numbers, their warrior way of life was gone, and Uncle Ralph was trapped by his nostalgia for the past.*

B **Walters** *Possible response: The details of the weeds, the folded cardboards, the burned cans, the remains of old fires, and the rags snapping in the hard wind combine to suggest that the life of people living out of doors, on the move, can be harsh and lonely.*

WRITING ABOUT LITERATURE

Making Sense

Have you ever read a story, seen a movie, or studied a painting that had a special meaning for you? Which selections in this unit were most compelling? How can you find the meaning they had for you? What lessons might you learn for everyday life? In the following pages you will

- learn how writers present main ideas in paragraphs
- interpret a piece of literature to find its central meaning for you
- apply interpretation skills to everyday situations

The Writer's Style: Unity in Paragraphs Finding the main ideas in paragraphs will help you understand the message a writer wants to communicate.

Read the Literature

Note how the writer of these excerpts presents main ideas. The first excerpt contains a topic sentence. In the second excerpt, the main idea is implied but not stated.

Literature Models

Main Idea Stated in a Topic Sentence
A Which sentence states the main idea? Analyzing the details in the paragraph will lead you to the topic sentence.

> As a child I thought that Uncle Ralph had been born into the wrong time. The Pawnees had been ravaged so often by then. The tribe of several thousand at its peak over a century before were then a few hundred people who had been closely confined for over a century. The warrior life was gone. Uncle Ralph was trapped in a transparent bubble of new time. The bubble bound him tight as it blew around us.
>
> Anna Lee Walters, from "The Warriors"

Implied Main Idea
B These sentences all supply details. What idea do they suggest?

> The ground was packed down tight in the clearing among the high weeds. We walked around the encircling brush and found folded cardboards stacked together. Burned cans in assorted sizes were stashed under the cardboards and there were remains of old fires. Rags were tied to the bush, snapping in the hard wind.
>
> Anna Lee Walters, from "The Warriors"

404 UNIT THREE: ALL IN THE FAMILY

PRINT AND MEDIA RESOURCES

UNIT THREE RESOURCE BOOK
Writer's Style, p. 29
Prewriting, p. 30
Elaboration, p. 31
Peer Response Guide, pp. 32–33
Revising and Proofreading, p. 34
Student Model, pp. 35–36
Rubric, p. 37

FORMAL ASSESSMENT
Guidelines for Writing Assessment

GRAMMAR MINI-LESSONS
Transparencies, p. 7
Copymasters, p. 5

WRITING MINI-LESSONS
Transparencies, p. 50

WRITING COACH

The Writer's Craft

Personal Response to Literature, pp. 238–249

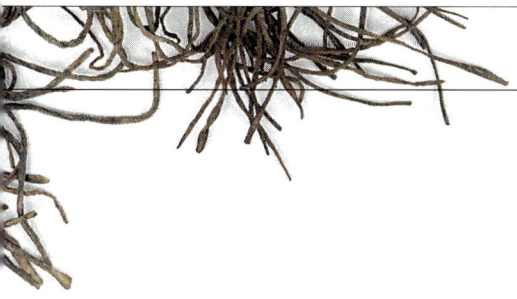

Connect to Life

This excerpt is from an article about an important writer. Note how the author uses examples to elaborate on the main idea.

Magazine Article

During his prodigiously productive career, [Langston] Hughes had created a number of outstanding works for children. *The Dream Keeper*, a book of poems, had appeared in 1932. His inspired series of nonfiction, offering pioneering excursions into African-American culture, included *The First Book of Jazz* and *The First Book of Africa*.

Kathleen Burke, from "A to Z: The Happy Rescue of a Poet's Antic Alphabet" *Smithsonian*, August 1994

Topic Sentence Supported by Examples
Find the sentence that states the main idea. Which examples support that topic sentence?

Try Your Hand: Developing a Main Idea

1. **State a Main Idea** Write topic sentences for paragraphs you could develop on two of the topics listed below.
   - a powerful friendship
   - a modern warrior
   - a disturbing change

2. **Make the Main Idea Clear** Select a piece of writing from your portfolio. Ask a partner to read it and to list the main ideas as he or she reads. Discuss main ideas that are missing or that were misinterpreted. Then revise your piece.

3. **Share an Idea** Look again at the topic sentence in the first excerpt from "The Warriors." Think of someone you know well, write a topic sentence for a paragraph about that person, and add details to support the main idea.

SkillBuilder

 WRITER'S CRAFT

Varying Sentence Beginnings

A series of sentences that all begin the same way can be dull. This is true whether they are topic sentences or supporting sentences. Notice how Anna Lee Walters begins sentences in different ways.

> At times he pointed to those stars and greeted them by their Pawnee names. (prepositional phrase)

> When he came to visit us, he always brought something to eat. (subordinate clause)

> Instead, he taught us Pawnee words. (adverb)

You can use these same parts of speech to vary the beginnings of your sentences. You can also use adjectives and verb forms.

APPLYING WHAT YOU'VE LEARNED
Rewrite these sentences using different beginnings. You may need to add words or phrases.

1. The girls were free and curious, and they roamed the woods around them.
2. The girls met a hobo while walking in the woods.
3. Ralph's relatives show their concern for him throughout the story.

 WRITING HANDBOOK

For more help with sentence beginnings, see pages 867–868 in the Writing Handbook.

WRITING ABOUT LITERATURE **405**

Teaching Strategy: MODELING

C **Burke** The first sentence is the topic sentence that states the main idea of the paragraph. Examples that support this idea are references to three children's books written by Langston Hughes: *The Dream Keeper*, *The First Book of Jazz*, and *The First Book of Africa*.

Try Your Hand

1. Responses will vary. Sample topic sentences are listed below.
   - A powerful friendship sometimes connects people who have very different personalities.
   - A modern warrior is as likely to have attended business school as he or she is to have graduated from boot camp.
   - The increasing number of hate crimes in our city signals a disturbing change in community relations.

2. Responses will vary. Encourage partners to continue their collaboration in the revision process.

3. Responses will vary. Suggest that students who are having difficulty begin by creating an outline briefly giving the main idea they wish to express and the details that support it.

SkillBuilder WRITER'S CRAFT

VARYING SENTENCE BEGINNINGS Point out that students can also vary sentence beginnings by occasionally using different kinds of sentences such as commands, questions, or exclamations.

Application Possible responses:
1. Free and curious, the girls roamed the woods around them.
2. While walking in the woods, the girls met a hobo.
3. Throughout the story, Ralph's relatives show their concern for him.

Additional Suggestions Point out that introductory elements such as clauses, appositive phrases, long prepositional phrases, and some adverbs need to be set off from the rest of the sentence by a comma.

Reteaching/Reinforcement
- *Writing Mini-Lessons* transparencies, p. 50

The Writer's Craft

Varying Sentence Beginnings, p. 417

Critical Thinking:
MAKING INFERENCES

D Be sure that students understand that the theme or main idea of a work is not the same as its subject. The subject of a poem or story is what it is "about." The theme is the underlying insight into life or behavior—one's interpretation of what the author wants to convey. Tell students that they can usually describe the subject of a work in a word or a brief phrase. A theme statement, however, usually requires a complete sentence. Because authors rarely state their themes directly, students must be prepared to make inferences to identify a work's main idea. In this process, readers use evidence from the work, such as prominent ideas, the behavior of characters, and specific lines or passages, as the basis for their inferences.

CUSTOMIZING FOR
Less-Proficient Writers

E Remind students that the title of a work is often a clue to its theme. Also, tell students that the way a principal character changes or develops in the course of a work can signal the theme.

Writing Skill: USING THE COMPUTER

F Freewriting on the computer may help students get their ideas down rapidly and efficiently. A useful freewriting technique is to have students cover or shut off the monitor while they type. This will force them to stay "in the moment," writing from a stream of consciousness rather than distracting themselves by rewriting a few sentences over and over.

WRITING ABOUT LITERATURE

Interpretation

D Have you ever talked with a friend about a book or movie that had an impact on you? Perhaps you've tried to make sense of the work by looking for its main idea or message. In a work of literature, that message is the theme. A theme gives readers insight into some truth about human life. For example, one theme of "The Strange Case of Mr. Ormantude's Bride" might be that good intentions alone won't make others happy.

GUIDED ASSIGNMENT
Interpreting a Theme Choose a selection in this unit and write an essay in which you explain how you interpreted all or part of the selection and identified a theme. The steps on these pages will help you with your essay.

1 Prewrite and Explore

List titles of several selections that were especially meaningful or interesting to you. You might list those that raised questions in your mind or those that made you wonder exactly what they meant. After considering your list, choose a selection you would find interesting to write about and interpret.

EXPLORING IDEAS

To better understand your selection and find a theme, ask yourself questions such as the following:

E
- What ideas does the writer seem to emphasize?
- Which passages caused me to react in some way?
- What line or passage seems most important to me?

GATHERING SUPPORT

F Choose one of the lines or passages you don't completely understand and freewrite about it. What new understanding results from freewriting?

Now gather details from the selection to support your ideas. You may use a cluster like the one on this page to organize details. This one shows how a writer connected ideas and noted details that support an interpretation of the poem "Lineage."

406 UNIT THREE: ALL IN THE FAMILY

Student's Prewriting Cluster

Assessment Option

SELF-ASSESSMENT After students have completed Gathering Support, have them assess their notes and details by answering the following questions:

- *Have I focused on the most important ideas in the work?*
- *Have I noted the ways I reacted to significant lines or passages?*
- *Can I use my notes to support an interpretation of the work's theme or message?*
- *Have I collected examples and quotes from the work that explain or support my interpretation?*

② Write and Analyze a Discovery Draft

If you are still not quite sure what your selection means, use your ideas and your freewriting to begin a discovery draft. When you complete your discovery draft, ask the following questions:

- Am I satisfied with the ideas I have developed so far?
- Have I found a meaning I am satisfied with?
- Do I need more examples to make my ideas clear?

Look at this student's draft on "Lineage."

Student's Discovery Draft

The first stanza tells how the speaker feels about her grandmothers. They worked hard on the land and were strong and sturdy. They seem happy in spite of their hard work, because the narrator says they were singing.

The second stanza uses images that show more about the grandmothers. They smell of soap and onions and clay. They have veins that show in their hands and say clean things.

The speaker in the poem is talking about women in her family who lived long ago. I think she's proud of them. When she compares herself with them, she doesn't seem to think she is as good as they were. Many people say our ancestors were stronger than we are. Maybe the narrator feels this way too.

Why does the writer say three times that her grandmothers were strong?

Is she saying that people in the past were stronger? I think Uncle Ralph had this idea too.

The poem "The Courage That My Mother Had" says this too. Maybe I'll end my essay with this comparison.

③ Draft and Share

Use what you learned from your discovery draft to write a more focused draft. The SkillBuilder at the right can help you with your introduction. When you've finished, share drafts within a small group.

PEER RESPONSE

- Summarize my interpretation in your own words.
- Why does or doesn't my interpretation make sense to you?
- What more do you want to know about my explanation?

SkillBuilder

WRITER'S CRAFT

Writing an Introduction

An effective introduction is important in an interpretive essay. Here are three functions of a good introduction.

Introduce the Selection Give basic information about the story or poem so a reader who isn't familiar with the selection can make sense of your essay.

Catch Your Reader's Attention Why should your reader pay attention to your interpretation? Make your introduction so interesting that readers will want to know what you think.

Give a Clue to Your Message Readers will find your essay easier to follow if they know what to expect. In the introduction, let them know the kind of information you plan to give them. Then, in the paragraphs that follow, explain your interpretation and support your ideas with details from the selection.

APPLYING WHAT YOU'VE LEARNED
Consider how you can include these three elements in your introduction as you move on to the next step and write a draft of your essay to share with others.

WRITING HANDBOOK

For more help with writing an introduction, see page 866 in the Writing Handbook.

WRITING ABOUT LITERATURE **407**

Critical Thinking: MAKING GENERALIZATIONS

The Discovery Draft provides an opportunity for students to sort through the ideas they have been forming and to further explore them. Remind students that for a generalization about a theme to be valid, it must be based on an adequate amount of evidence such as examples or details from the work. Students should be cautious about using overly broad generalizations to state the theme of a work because they are especially vulnerable to objections or counterexamples. You can model the distinction between a valid generalization and an overgeneralization by having students compare the following two theme statements for Margaret Walker's "Lineage": (1) We aren't as strong as our ancestors were; (2) Our ancestors were superior to us in every way.

Teaching Strategy: PEER REVIEW

Have peer reviewers read the essay before they make any comments. During the second reading, they should jot down brief reactions and suggestions. Remind students to include specific ideas for revision, such as "Why not quote lines 5–6? They seem to support your interpretation."

SkillBuilder WRITER'S CRAFT

WRITING AN INTRODUCTION Point out that students can often use a striking quotation from the work to capture readers' attention in the introduction. Another strategy is to tell a brief personal anecdote that relates to the theme. A third technique is to begin the introduction with unexpected syntax such as a question, a command, or an exclamation.

Application Students can work in pairs to draft their introductions. Partners should make sure that their drafts fulfill the three functions listed in the text.

Additional Suggestions Have students work in small groups to examine the introductory paragraphs of two or three book reviews. Tell students to focus on how the reviewers capture the attention of their audience.

Reteaching/Reinforcement

The Writer's Craft

Writing the Introduction, pp. 341–2

Critical Thinking: ANALYZING

I Point out to students that revising their drafts involves molding the text to fit their audience and purpose. To evaluate and revise their interpretive essays, students should
- check to see that they have clearly stated a main idea about theme
- make sure that the details that they have included support their main idea
- check that they have used a logical and effective order for the supporting details in their interpretation

Teaching Strategy: USING THE SKILLBUILDER

J You can help students avoid grammatical errors in their writing by teaching the SkillBuilder on Achieving Verb Agreement with Compound Subjects.

Teaching Tip: MODELING

K Discuss how the writer's final draft meets the Standards for Evaluation on this page. Point out that the writer uses contrast in the third sentence of the second paragraph, juxtaposing images that emphasize strength with images of perfume and pretty clothes. This contrast bolsters the main idea of the paragraph, which is the speaker's emphasis on her grandmothers' sturdiness and capacity for endurance.

Teaching Strategy: MODELING

L The writer supports the idea of similar themes in the three selections by quoting a simile from "The Courage That My Mother Had" and by referring to Uncle Ralph's characterization in "The Warriors." The writer draws on personal experience to elaborate on the main idea by mentioning that he or she recently read another poem that presented a similar theme.

PORTFOLIO

Ask students to write a brief description of what they have learned about writing themes as a result of this assignment. They may wish to include their description and their finished theme in their portfolio.

WRITING ABOUT LITERATURE

4 Revise and Edit

I J As you revise and edit your draft, be sure to include a clear statement of what the selection you chose means to you. Also be sure that you use examples from the literature to support your interpretation. After you finish revising, reflect on how well you presented your ideas.

Student's Final Draft

Interpreting "Lineage"

The speaker in "Lineage" by Margaret Walker is looking at the past. She thinks about the women in her family who worked hard in fields and in kitchens. They were strong women, the speaker says.

The speaker uses the word <u>strong</u> three times and the word <u>sturdy</u> once. Also, the images she uses emphasize the grandmothers' strength. She doesn't describe perfume and pretty clothes. She tells about the smell of soap, onions, and wet clay. She describes hard-working, quick hands with veins that show. Only one line in the poem isn't about the grandmothers. In the last line the speaker wonders why she isn't as they were.

How does the second paragraph use contrast to make a point? K

How does the writer support the idea that there are similar themes in the three selections? How does the writer use personal experience to elaborate on the idea? L

I think a theme in this poem is that we aren't as strong as our ancestors were. I just read another poem with the same message. The speaker in "The Courage That My Mother Had" is sorry she didn't inherit her mother's courage that was "like a rock." Also, "The Warriors" shows a character whose life is affected by respect for his brave ancestors, and I think Uncle Ralph knew he wasn't living up to them. The two poets seem to say that our generation isn't as strong as people were in the past. The writer of "The Warriors" seems to say that too.

Standards for Evaluation

An interpretive essay
- identifies the work to be interpreted
- makes clear the purpose of the essay
- uses details that support the interpretation
- leads to a theme
- includes an evaluation of or reaction to the theme

408 UNIT THREE: ALL IN THE FAMILY

Assessment Option

SELF-ASSESSMENT To help students assess their own writing, they should answer the following questions:
- *Does my introduction capture the audience's attention?*
- *Have I identified the work I am writing about?*
- *What is the main idea of my essay?*
- *Have I used specific details from the work to support my interpretation of its theme?*
- *Have I organized my essay so that it is clear and easy to follow?*
- *Have I included my own response to the work and my evaluation of the theme?*

Grammar in Context

Compound Subjects You can often avoid short, choppy sentences in your writing by combining two subjects to create a more graceful sentence with a compound subject. Reread the last two sentences of the writing sample on page 408. See how they could be combined to make a smoother sentence.

Original sentences: *The two poets seem to say that our generation isn't as strong as people were in the past. The writer of "The Warriors" seems to say that too.*

Rewritten sentence: *The two poets and the writer of "The Warriors" seem to say that our generation isn't as strong as people were in the past.*

Combining these sentences results in one sentence with a compound subject—that is, two subjects joined by a conjunction and having the same predicate. The most common conjunctions that connect parts of a compound subject are *and*, *or*, and *nor*. You usually use *either* with *or* and *neither* with *nor*.

- The poems and the stories are about ancestors.
- Neither the narrator nor her sister attended the funeral.
- Either their uncle or their mother told the girls to be careful when the hobos were around.

Try Your Hand: Using Compound Subjects

On a sheet of paper, combine each pair of sentences to make one sentence with a compound subject. Use the conjunction shown in parentheses.

1. My grandmother showed courage when she came to America to find work. So did my grandfather. (and)
2. Anna never moved from the house in which she was born. Her brother stayed in the same house all his life. (neither/nor)
3. Leaving familiar places requires courage. Separating from family and friends requires courage too. (and)

SkillBuilder

GRAMMAR FROM WRITING

Achieving Verb Agreement with Compound Subjects

When your sentence has a compound subject, choosing the correct verb form can be difficult. Study these examples.

Margaret Walker and *Edna St. Vincent Millay write* about similar themes.

Either the grandmothers or Uncle Ralph *makes* me think of my ancestors.

The first compound subject is joined by the conjunction *and*, so the writer uses a plural verb. The compound subject in the second sentence is joined by the conjunction *or*. When *or* or *nor* is used in a compound subject, the verb must agree with the subject nearest it. Since *Uncle Ralph* is singular, the verb is singular.

APPLYING WHAT YOU'VE LEARNED
From the following sentences, create a single sentence with a compound subject. Be sure the verb agrees with the subject.

Their aunts do not visit often. Their uncle does not visit often, either.

 GRAMMAR HANDBOOK

For more information on the agreement of subjects and verbs, see page 903 of the Grammar Handbook.

WRITING ABOUT LITERATURE **409**

CUSTOMIZING FOR
Students Acquiring English

Before you begin this page, be sure that students understand the definition of a compound subject: a subject made up of two or more key words joined by a conjunction such as *and* or *or*. Point out that mistakes in agreement are likely to occur when a compound subject is separated from the verb by an intervening prepositional phrase. Offer students an example like the following: *The two novelists and the writer of the essay emphasize the same theme.*

Try Your Hand

Possible responses:
1. My grandmother and my grandfather showed courage when they came to America to find work.
2. Neither Anna nor her brother ever moved from the house in which they were born.
3. Separating from family and friends and leaving familiar places require courage.

Standards for Evaluation

Have students review their themes for the following:

Ideas and Content
- gives the author, title, and brief summary of the literature
- explains what the writer thinks a passage or selection means
- is supported by quotes, reasons, and other evidence
- shows why the writer thinks the passage, selection, or theme is important

Structure and Form
- uses well-organized paragraphs and a clear organization
- includes transitional words and phrases to show relationships among ideas
- uses a variety of sentence structures

Grammar, Usage, and Mechanics
- contains no more than two or three minor errors in grammar and usage
- contains no more than two or

SkillBuilder — GRAMMAR FROM WRITING

ACHIEVING VERB AGREEMENT WITH COMPOUND SUBJECTS Point out that there are two important exceptions to the grammar rule explained in the text. When a compound subject joined by *and* refers to a single thing, the subject takes a singular verb: for example, *Ham and cheese is a favorite sandwich combination.* A compound subject preceded by *each*, *every*, or *many a* also takes a singular verb: *Every teacher and student in the auditorium was listening intently.*

Application Possible answer: Neither their aunts nor their uncle visits often.

Additional Suggestions Point out also that using compound subjects to combine sentences sometimes requires changing some words to make pronouns or other sentence parts consistent.

Reteaching/Reinforcement
- *Grammar Mini-Lessons* copymasters p. 5, transparencies p. 7

The Writer's Craft

Compound Subjects, p. 703

READING THE WORLD

On pages 406–409, students wrote an interpretation of a theme in a literary work. They should be aware that they can interpret situations in everyday life by using observation and drawing on experience. In this lesson, students will explore the meanings that a pictorial image has for them.

Critical Thinking: OBSERVING

N Possible response: A fatigue cap with a purple heart medal and a note pinned to it.

Critical Thinking: MAKING INFERENCES

O Possible response: the cap and medal may have belonged to a soldier killed in the war; the note suggests that the dead soldier is still remembered by those who survived. The wall is also a memorial to the dead made by the living.

Speaking and Listening: GROUP DISCUSSION

P Have students work in small groups to compare their interpretations. Encourage them to speculate about how they can apply the skills of observation and interpretation to other real-world images and situations.

410 UNIT THREE: ALL IN THE FAMILY

READING THE WORLD

FINDING MEANING

You use facts and experience to interpret literature and discover its meaning. You interpret situations in everyday life, too, examining the meaning they have for you and others.

View Imagine that you came across this fatigue cap during a visit to the Vietnam Veterans Memorial wall. Describe what you see.

Interpret What is the significance of the objects in the picture? What do the wall and the cap represent? What does the note mean?

Discuss With a group, share your interpretation of the fatigue cap and the situation. How do others in your group respond? What have you gained by discussing your various interpretations? The SkillBuilder on this page will help you with your interpretations.

SkillBuilder

CRITICAL THINKING

Interpreting Experience
Whether you are interpreting a work of literature or an experience of your own, you have skills that can help you. To discover the meaning in any experience, take time to do the following:

- Look and listen carefully.
- Ask yourself what is clear about the meaning of the experience and what is not clear.
- Identify information you may already know that can help you understand the experience.
- Share your questions and your interpretation, and listen to those of others.
- Evaluate other interpretations and possibly rethink your own.

APPLYING WHAT YOU'VE LEARNED
With a small group, discuss the photograph. Name several other experiences that members of the group have had involving memorials and public events such as parades and assemblies. Interpret the meaning of one or two of these experiences, and discuss details that lead to your interpretation.

READING THE WORLD 411

SkillBuilder — CRITICAL THINKING

INTERPRETING EXPERIENCE Emphasize that one of the most important guidelines to follow in shaping an interpretation of an experience is to avoid jumping to conclusions about it. Most real-life experiences are complex, for they involve a multitude of impressions that very often conflict with one another.

Application Suggest that students begin by visualizing their experiences and then note as many concrete sensory details as they can about each experience.

UNIT THREE
Part 2 Lesson Planner

TIME ALLOTMENTS SHOWN ARE APPROXIMATE. DEPENDING ON YOUR GOALS AND THE NEEDS OF YOUR STUDENTS, YOU MAY WISH TO ALLOW MORE OR LESS TIME FOR CERTAIN PORTIONS OF THE LESSON.

Table of Contents	Discussion	Previewing the Selection	Reading the Selection
PART OPENER **On Your Own Terms** page 412	**20 MINUTES** • Reflect on the part theme		
SELECTION **The Scarlet Ibis** page 414 CHALLENGING		**20 MINUTES** • PERSONAL CONNECTION • GEOGRAPHICAL CONNECTION • READING CONNECTION: Understanding exposition	**50 MINUTES** • Introduce vocabulary • Read pp. 414–425 (12 pp.)
SELECTION *from* **Black Boy** page 430 CHALLENGING		**20 MINUTES** • PERSONAL CONNECTION • HISTORICAL CONNECTION • WRITING CONNECTION	**30 MINUTES** • Introduce vocabulary • Read pp. 430–434 (5 pp.)
SELECTION **Only Daughter** page 438 AVERAGE		**20 MINUTES** • PERSONAL CONNECTION • CULTURAL CONNECTION • READING CONNECTION: Understanding generalizations	**15 MINUTES** • Introduce vocabulary • Read pp. 438–440 (3 pp.)
SELECTIONS **Theme for English B/ The Writer** page 445 CHALLENGING		**20 MINUTES** • PERSONAL CONNECTION • PROFESSIONAL CONNECTION • READING CONNECTION: Movies of the mind/Using a reading log	**15 MINUTES** • Read pp. 445–448 (4 pp.)
SELECTION **Lakshmi** page 453 EASY		**20 MINUTES** • PERSONAL CONNECTION • GEOGRAPHICAL CONNECTION • WRITING CONNECTION	**40 MINUTES** • Introduce vocabulary • Read pp. 453–459 (7 pp.)
NONFICTION ON YOUR OWN **Fish Eyes** page 462 AVERAGE			**30 MINUTES** • Read pp. 462–467 (6 pp.)

Writing	Exploring Topics	Prewriting	Drafting and Revising
WRITING FROM EXPERIENCE **Firsthand and Expressive Writing**	**20 MINUTES**	**20 MINUTES**	**50 MINUTES**

Time estimates assume in-class work. You may wish to assign some of these stages as homework.

Responding to the Selection

FROM PERSONAL RESPONSE TO CRITICAL ANALYSIS	OR	ANOTHER PATHWAY	LITERARY CONCEPTS	QUICKWRITES
\multicolumn{5}{c}{**60 MINUTES**}
• Discussion questions	OR	• Cooperative learning (trial)	• Symbol • Foreshadowing	• Diary entry • Interview • Interpretation
\multicolumn{5}{c}{**30 MINUTES**}
• Discussion questions	OR	• Cooperative learning (ranking character traits)	• Dialogue • Metaphor	• Letters of recommendation • Thoughts • Story
\multicolumn{5}{c}{**60 MINUTES**}
• Discussion questions	OR	• Retelling	• Theme	• Dialogue • Biographical sketch • Proverb
\multicolumn{5}{c}{**50 MINUTES**}
• Discussion questions	OR	• Literary discussion	• Stanza	• Grade comments • Page
\multicolumn{5}{c}{**60 MINUTES**}
• Discussion questions	OR	• Cooperative learning (character traits)	• Description	• Letter • Personal essay

Extension Activities

	ALTERNATIVE ACTIVITIES	LITERARY LINKS	CRITIC'S CORNER	THE WRITER'S STYLE	ACROSS THE CURRICULUM	ART CONNECTION	WORDS TO KNOW	BIOGRAPHY
60 MINUTES	✓	✓		✓	SCIENCE	✓	✓	✓
30 MINUTES	✓				HISTORY		✓	✓
30 MINUTES		✓			HISTORY SOCIAL STUDIES		✓	✓
20 MINUTES	✓	✓	✓	✓		✓		✓
30 MINUTES	✓				SOCIAL STUDIES		✓	✓

Publishing and Reflecting

25 MINUTES

PART 2

REFLECTING ON THEME

Read this paragraph aloud to students. Remind them that being true to ourselves is one of the most difficult challenges we face in a world where everyone is pressured to conform. Geniuses throughout history have had to contend with public disapproval. Ask students to freewrite briefly on ways in which *they* conform. Then ask them to write one or two sentences about something that makes them stand out: for example, an unusual way of dressing, unconventional opinions, or the ability to perform a particular skill. Invite them to include how these personal "statements" make them feel.

What Do You Think?

Encourage group members to take turns with this activity, so that each student will have a chance to resist peer pressure. You might suggest that students within each group make a list of scenarios and then draw lots so that each student can resist a different issue. Encourage a whole-class discussion of student's feelings as they held out against pressure. Students will return to this ativity on pages 428 and 451.

UNIT THREE PART 2

ON YOUR OWN TERMS

REFLECTING ON THEME

When an older brother or sister wants you to do something one way and you want to do it another, what do you do? If your friends decide to go to a movie that you've already seen, do you go anyway? Sometimes you have to do things your way—on your own terms—even if doing so may make you unpopular. As you read this part of Unit Three, see how the characters in the selections try to act on their own terms within their families.

What Do You Think? With a small group of classmates, role-play a situation in which a person has to resist pressure from others in order to act on his or her own terms. For example, a person's friends might try to convince him or her to ostracize someone, stay out past curfew, or go to a party instead of studying for a test. Choose a member of the group to try to resist the persuasions of the others. Share the results of your group's experience with the rest of the class, performing your role-playing for them if you like.

James Hurst	**The Scarlet Ibis** *How would you treat a brother like Doodle?*	413
Naomi Long Madgett	**Woman with Flower**/INSIGHT *What do flowers and children have in common?*	425
Richard Wright	**from Black Boy** *They blamed the whole thing on his upbringing.*	429
Sandra Cisneros	**Only Daughter** *The author's father laughed in all the right places.*	437
Langston Hughes	**Theme for English B** *You are part of me; I am part of you.*	443
Richard Wilbur	**The Writer** *Can writing that story really be a matter of life or death?*	443
Isabelle C. Chang	**The Artist**/INSIGHT *Perfection takes time.*	448
Vasanthi Victor	**Lakshmi** *Only the narrator accepted Grandfather's third wife.*	452
David Brenner	**Fish Eyes** *The War of the Socks and other family matters*	462

PREVIEWING

FICTION

The Scarlet Ibis
James Hurst

Activating Prior Knowledge
PERSONAL CONNECTION

Expectations are ideas about what a person is capable of doing or becoming. The narrator of this story has high expectations of his younger brother. Think about the expectations that others have of you. Do some people expect great things of you? Do you expect great things of yourself? Make a bar graph similar to the sample shown, drawing bars to show how high are the expectations that people have of you. (A bar reaching to 10 indicates the highest expectations.)

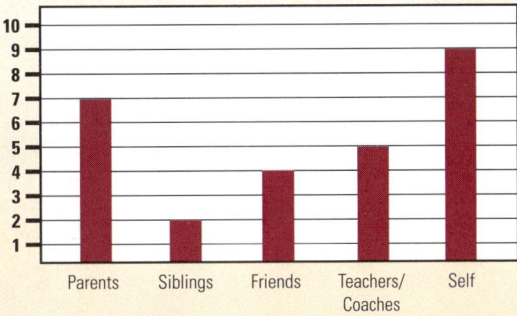

Building Background
GEOGRAPHICAL CONNECTION

The events in "The Scarlet Ibis" span several years, with the climax occurring in late August of 1918, near the end of World War I. The story is set on a cotton farm in the South, a setting much like the one in which the author, James Hurst, grew up. Hurst refers to a number of trees and flowers by the local names that he learned as a boy. For example, the "bleeding tree" is a type of pine from which white sap runs like blood when the bark is cut. "Graveyard flowers" are sweet-smelling gardenias, which, because they bloom year after year, are often planted in cemeteries. The frayed twigs of the "toothbrush tree" were once used by people to pick their teeth clean after eating.

Active Reading/Setting a Purpose
READING CONNECTION

Understanding Exposition A story's exposition is the part of the story—usually a few paragraphs at the beginning—that establishes the mood, presents the setting, introduces the main characters, and gives the reader important background information. This story begins with a memory: the narrator recalls his childhood with his younger brother, Doodle. As you read, pay attention to the detailed description of the setting in the first two paragraphs—the flowers, trees, and birds—and try to identify the mood that is established by the narrator's remembrance. As the characters are introduced, notice the expectations each has of Doodle.

Using Your Reading Log Use your reading log to record your responses to the questions inserted throughout the selection. Also jot down other thoughts and feelings that come to you as you read.

- *HISTORICAL CONNECTION*
- *VISUAL VOCABULARY*

OVERVIEW

Objectives

- To understand and appreciate a classic short story that explores a boy's expectations that his sickly brother can make it on his own
- To identify and understand a symbol
- To appreciate and write examples of images, similes, and metaphors
- To express understanding of the selection through a choice of writing forms, including a diary entry, an interview, and an interpretation
- To extend understanding of the selection through a variety of multimodal and cross-curricular activities

Skills

LITERARY CONCEPTS
- Symbol
- Foreshadowing
- Mood

THE WRITER'S STYLE
- Using repeated words to build coherence

GENRE STUDY
- Fiction: short story

GRAMMAR
- Infinitives

SPEAKING, LISTENING, AND VIEWING
- Group discussion
- Oral presentation

HISTORICAL CONNECTION
Southern Life The setting of the story comes alive in this group of historical images depicting life on a Southern plantation. You may wish to use the images to generate discussion about Southern culture and its influence on the actions of the characters in the story.

Side A, Frame 49359

ALTERNATIVE
Previewing

Instead of filling out the graph, students can choose partners to preview the story orally using these prompts:

Personal Connection

Discussion Prompts *What are some expectations that people, including yourself, have of you? In as much detail as possible, describe these expectations to a partner. Then listen as your partner describes the expectations that people have of him or her. The following questions might help you start.*

- *Who expects things of me?*
- *What kinds of things do they expect?*
- *What do I expect of myself?*

As you read "The Scarlet Ibis," watch to see what individual members of Doodle's family do or do not expect of him.

PRINT AND MEDIA RESOURCES

UNIT THREE RESOURCE BOOK
Strategic Reading: Literature, p. 41
Vocabulary SkillBuilder, p. 42

GRAMMAR MINI-LESSONS
Transparencies, p. 2
Copymasters, p. 2

WRITING MINI-LESSONS
Transparencies, p. 39

ACCESS FOR STUDENTS ACQUIRING ENGLISH
Selection Summaries
Reading Support

FORMAL ASSESSMENT
Selection Test, pp. 73–74
 Test Generator

AUDIO LIBRARY
See Reference Card

LASERLINKS
Historical Connection
Science Connection
Visual Vocabulary

SUMMARY

The narrator remembers his brother, Doodle, who was born with a tiny, weak body. Doodle isn't expected to live past infancy, but he surprises people by surviving and then by talking and crawling. No one expects him to walk. He and the narrator become good friends. The narrator takes him everywhere. Their favorite place is Old Woman Swamp, where they pick flowers. When Doodle is five, the narrator secretly teaches Doodle to walk. Then they set a new goal of getting Doodle to run, swim, and row a boat. They work hard but make little progress. In the fall, just before Doodle is to begin school, the family is having lunch when they hear an odd croaking noise. They rush outside and see a scarlet ibis. The ibis falls to the ground dead. Doodle buries the bird. After lunch, the narrator and Doodle go rowing. As they step out of the boat, a thunderstorm overtakes them. The narrator, feeling bitter and cruel, runs ahead, leaving Doodle behind. When he goes back to try to find Doodle, he finds Doodle slumped under a bush, dead.

Thematic Link: *On Your Own Terms* A boy's expectations that his fragile younger brother can face life by himself, on his own terms, grow to an unrealistic level, with tragic consequences.

DESIGN NOTE

This illustration shows the bird referred to in the title, a vibrantly colored scarlet ibis.

Reading the Art What emotions or events do you associate with the color red?

WORDS TO KNOW

careen (kə-rēn′) *v.* to rush carelessly (p. 417)
doggedness (dô′gĭd-nĭs) *n.* persistence; stubbornness (p. 422)
exotic (ĭg-zŏt′ĭk) *adj.* excitingly strange (p. 423)
heresy (hĕr′ĭ-sē) *n.* something that contradicts what is generally thought of as right (p. 425)
imminent (ĭm′ə-nənt) *adj.* about to occur (p. 419)
infallibility (ĭn-făl′ə-bĭl′ĭ-tē) *n.* the condition of being unable to make an error (p. 420)
invalid (ĭn′və-lĭd) *adj.* too ill to live a normal life (p. 416)
iridescent (ĭr′ĭ-dĕs′ənt) *adj.* having shifting changes of color or colors like a rainbow (p. 420)
precariously (prĭ-kâr′ē-əs-lē) *adv.* insecurely; in an unsafe manner (p. 423)
reiterate (rē-ĭt′ə-rāt′) *v.* to repeat (p. 423)

 VISUAL VOCABULARY
• **nettles** (nĕt′lz)   • **palmetto fronds**
• **piazza** (pē-ăz′ə)   (păl-mĕt′ō frŏndz′)

Side A, Frame 49365

The Scarlet Ibis

James Hurst

It was in the clove[1] of seasons, summer was dead but autumn had not yet been born, that the ibis lit in the bleeding tree. The flower garden was stained with rotting brown magnolia petals and ironweeds grew rank[2] amid the purple phlox. The five o'clocks by the chimney still marked time, but the oriole nest in the elm was untenanted and rocked back and forth like an empty cradle.

---

1. **clove:** a separation or split.
2. **rank:** growing wildly and vigorously.

Literary Concept: MOOD

A Ask students what kind of mood or feeling the author creates in this passage. *(Possible responses: sadness, poignancy, nostalgia, dread)*

Literary Concept: FLASHBACK

B Ask when the events the narrator will describe took place. *(years ago, when the narrator was just a boy)*

Literary Concept: SIMILE

C Have students analyze this comparison, explaining how the name is like "a big tail on a small kite." *(The brother is small and weak, while his name is long and, ironically, suggests strength and vigor.)*

CUSTOMIZING FOR
Students Acquiring English

I Explain that when people say someone is not "all there" they mean that the person has an incomplete, underdeveloped mental capacity.

A The last graveyard flowers were blooming, and their smell drifted across the cotton field and through every room of our house, speaking softly the names of our dead.

It's strange that all this is still so clear to me, now that summer has long since fled and time has had its way. A grindstone stands where the bleeding tree stood, just outside the kitchen door, and now if an oriole sings in the elm, its song seems to die up in the leaves, a silvery dust. The flower garden is prim, the house a gleaming white, and the pale fence across the yard stands straight and spruce. But sometimes (like right now), as I sit in the cool, green-draped parlor, the grindstone begins to turn, and time with all its changes is ground away— and I remember Doodle.

B

Doodle was just about the craziest brother a boy ever had. Of course, he wasn't a crazy crazy like old Miss Leedie, who was in love with President Wilson and wrote him a letter every day, but was a nice crazy, like someone you meet in your dreams. He was born when I was six and was, from the outset, a disappointment. He seemed all head, with a tiny body which was red and shriveled like an old man's. Everybody thought he was going to die—everybody except Aunt Nicey, who had delivered him. She said he would live because he was born in a caul,³ and cauls were made from Jesus' nightgown. Daddy had Mr. Heath, the carpenter, build a little mahogany coffin for him. But he didn't die, and when he was three months old, Mama and Daddy decided they might as well name him. They named him William Armstrong, which was like tying a big tail on a small kite. Such a name sounds good only on a tombstone.

C

I thought myself pretty smart at many things, like holding my breath, running, jumping, or climbing the vines in Old Woman Swamp, and I wanted more than anything else someone to race to Horsehead Landing, someone to box with, and someone to perch with in the top fork of the great pine behind the barn, where across the fields and swamps you could see the sea. I wanted a brother. But Mama, crying, told me that even if William Armstrong lived, he would never do these things with me. He might not, she sobbed, even be "all there." He might, as long as he lived, lie on the rubber sheet in the center of the bed in the front bedroom where the white marquisette curtains billowed out in the afternoon sea breeze, rustling like palmetto fronds.⁴

I

It was bad enough having an <u>invalid</u> brother, but having one who possibly was not all there was unbearable, so I began to make plans to kill him by smothering him with a pillow. However, one afternoon as I watched him, my head poked between the iron posts of the foot of the bed, he looked straight at me and grinned. I skipped through the rooms, down the echoing halls, shouting, "Mama, he smiled. He's all there! He's all there!" and he was.

When he was two, if you laid him on his stomach, he began to move himself, straining terribly. The doctor said that with his weak heart this strain would probably kill him, but it didn't. Trembling, he'd push himself up, turning first red, then a soft purple, and finally collapse back onto the bed like an old worn-out doll. I can still see Mama watching him, her hand pressed tight across her mouth, her eyes wide and unblinking. But he learned to crawl (it was his third winter), and we brought him out of the front bedroom, putting him on the rug

---

3. **caul** (kôl): a thin membrane that covers the head of some babies at birth.
4. **palmetto fronds:** the fanlike leaves of a kind of palm tree.

WORDS TO KNOW
invalid (ĭn′və-lĭd) *adj.* too ill to live a normal life

416

INFINITIVES Tell students that an infinitive is a verb form that usually begins with *to* and functions as a noun, an adjective, or an adverb. Point out that in the first highlighted passage on page 416, the infinitives *to race*, *to box*, and *to perch* are all adjectives modifying the pronoun *someone*. In the second highlighted passage, the infinitive *to crawl* functions as a noun. It is a direct object telling what Doodle learned.

Application Have students write sentences about the story using the following infinitives or infinitive phrases: *to walk, to play, to row the boat, to be cruel, to leave Doodle behind.*

Reteaching/Reinforcement
- *Grammar Handbook*, anthology pp. 942, 943, 945
- *Grammar Mini-Lessons* copymasters p. 2, transparencies p. 2

Infinitives, pp. 686–687

before the fireplace. For the first time he became one of us.

As long as he lay all the time in bed, we called him William Armstrong, even though it was formal and sounded as if we were referring to one of our ancestors, but with his creeping around on the deerskin rug and beginning to talk, something had to be done about his name. It was I who renamed him. When he crawled, he crawled backward, as if he were in reverse and couldn't change gears. If you called him, he'd turn around as if he were going in the other direction, then he'd back right up to you to be picked up. Crawling backward made him look like a doodlebug, so I began to call him Doodle, and in time even Mama and Daddy thought it was a better name than William Armstrong. Only Aunt Nicey disagreed. She said caul babies should be treated with special respect since they might turn out to be saints. Renaming my brother was perhaps the kindest thing I ever did for him, because nobody expects much from someone called Doodle.

Although Doodle learned to crawl, he showed no signs of walking, but he wasn't idle. He talked so much that we all quit listening to what he said. It was about this time that Daddy built him a go-cart and I had to pull him around. At first I just paraded him up and down the piazza,⁵ but then he started crying to be taken out into the yard, and it ended up by my having to lug him wherever I went. If I so much as picked up my cap, he'd start crying to go with me, and Mama would call from wherever she was, "Take Doodle with you."

He was a burden in many ways. The doctor had said that he mustn't get too excited, too hot, too cold, or too tired and that he must always be treated gently. A long list of don'ts went with him, all of which I ignored once we got out of the house. To discourage his coming with me, I'd run with him across the ends of the cotton rows and careen him around corners on two wheels. Sometimes I accidentally turned him over, but he never told Mama. His skin was very sensitive, and he had to wear a big straw hat whenever he went out. When the going got rough and he had to cling to the sides of the go-cart, the hat slipped all the way down over his ears. He was a sight.

Finally, I could see I was licked. Doodle was my brother and he was going to cling to me forever, no matter what I did, so I dragged him across the burning cotton field to share with him the only beauty I knew, Old Woman Swamp. I pulled the go-cart through the sawtooth fern, down into the green dimness where the palmetto fronds whispered by the stream. I lifted him out and set him down in the soft rubber grass beside a tall pine. His eyes were round with wonder as he gazed about him, and his little hands began to stroke the rubber grass. Then he began to cry.

"For heaven's sake, what's the matter?" I asked, annoyed.

> Nobody expects much from someone called Doodle.

CONNECT

As a child, how would you have felt about having to take a brother like Doodle with you everywhere?
Using a Reading Log

---
5. **piazza** (pē-ăz′ə): a large covered porch.

WORDS TO KNOW
careen (kə-rēn′) *v.* to rush carelessly

Art Note

***Richard at Age Five* by Alice Neel.** Alice Neel (1900–1984) is known especially for her portraits of family, neighbors, and friends. She claimed she was a "collector of souls." To more honestly capture a person's character, she refused to deliberately pose those who sat for her paintings.

Reading the Art *What gives this painting a fresh, unposed look?*

Literary Concept: MOOD

G Ask students what mood this description of Old Woman Swamp evokes. *(Possible responses: otherworldliness; beauty; languid peace; the two boys seem to be in a safe, secret paradise.)*

Literary Concept: FIGURATIVE LANGUAGE

H Ask students to interpret the central metaphor—the knot of cruelty—of this thematic statement. *(Possible response: A "stream of love" can carry within it a cruelty of its own making—a knot or blockage—that brings it to a halt, just as a person's bloodstream can create a clot that will destroy that person by stopping the flow of blood.)*

Literary Concept: FORESHADOWING

I Ask students what event Doodle's leaning toward his own coffin might portend. *(his own death)*

STRATEGIC READING FOR
Less-Proficient Readers

J Make sure students understand that Doodle was born with a frail, sickly body.

- Ask students how the narrator responded to orders to treat Doodle gently. *(He ignored them.)* **Summarizing**
- Ask them why the narrator took Doodle to Old Woman Swamp. *(He wanted to share something beautiful with his brother.)* **Making Inferences**

Set a Purpose Have students read to find other things the narrator decided to do with Doodle.

Richard at Age Five (1944), Alice Neel. Oil on canvas, 26″ × 14″, courtesy of Robert Miller Gallery, New York. Copyright © Estate of Alice Neel.

"It's so pretty," he said. "So pretty, pretty, pretty."

After that day Doodle and I often went down into Old Woman Swamp. I would gather wildflowers, wild violets, honeysuckle, yellow jasmine, snakeflowers, and water lilies, and with wire grass we'd weave them into necklaces and crowns. We'd bedeck ourselves with our handiwork and loll about thus beautified, beyond the touch of the everyday world. Then when the slanted rays of the sun burned orange in the tops of the pines, we'd drop our jewels into the stream and watch them float away toward the sea.

There is within me (and with sadness I have watched it in others) a knot of cruelty borne by the stream of love, much as our blood sometimes bears the seed of our destruction, and at times I was mean to Doodle. One day I took him up to the barn loft and showed him his casket, telling him how we all had believed he would die. It was covered with a film of Paris green[6] sprinkled to kill the rats, and screech owls had built a nest inside it.

Doodle studied the mahogany box for a long time, then said, "It's not mine."

"It is," I said. "And before I'll help you down from the loft, you're going to have to touch it."

"I won't touch it," he said sullenly.

"Then I'll leave you here by yourself," I threatened, and made as if I were going down.

Doodle was frightened of being left. "Don't go leave me, Brother," he cried, and he leaned toward the coffin. His hand, trembling, reached out, and when he touched the casket he screamed. A screech owl flapped out of the box into our faces, scaring us and covering us with Paris green. Doodle was paralyzed, so I put him on my shoulder and carried him down the ladder, and even when we were outside in the bright sunshine, he clung to me, crying, "Don't leave me. Don't leave me."

When Doodle was five years old, I was embarrassed at having a brother of that age who couldn't walk, so I set out to teach him. We were down in Old Woman Swamp and it was spring and the sick-sweet smell of bay flowers hung everywhere like a mournful song. "I'm going to teach you to walk, Doodle," I said.

---

6. **Paris green:** a poisonous green powder used to kill pests.

418 UNIT THREE PART 2: ON YOUR OWN TERMS

Multicultural Perspectives

BIRD SYMBOLISM Bird symbolism is central to this selection. For instance, the ibis is a symbol of Doodle within the story. Students might be interested to know, however, that Egyptians believed the ibis symbolized perseverance, aspiration, and the soul. The screech owl that flies out of Doodle's coffin symbolizes death in both Egyptian and Chinese cultures; more commonly today, however, the owl is seen as a symbol of wisdom—a carryover from the Greek goddess Athena. Other modern bird symbolism includes the dove, which is united with peace, and the eagle, which is associated with military strength. One particular eagle, the bald eagle, has come to symbolize the United States.

He was sitting comfortably on the soft grass, leaning back against the pine. "Why?" he asked.

I hadn't expected such an answer. "So I won't have to haul you around all the time."

"I can't walk, Brother," he said.

"Who says so?" I demanded.

"Mama, the doctor—everybody."

"Oh, you can walk," I said, and I took him by the arms and stood him up. He collapsed onto the grass like a half-empty flour sack. It was as if he had no bones in his little legs.

"Don't hurt me, Brother," he warned.

"Shut up. I'm not going to hurt you. I'm going to teach you to walk." I heaved him up again, and again he collapsed.

This time he did not lift his face up out of the rubber grass. "I just can't do it. Let's make honeysuckle wreaths."

"Oh yes you can, Doodle," I said. "All you got to do is try. Now come on," and I hauled him up once more.

It seemed so hopeless from the beginning that it's a miracle I didn't give up. But all of us must have something or someone to be proud of, and Doodle had become mine. I did not know then that pride is a wonderful, terrible thing, a seed that bears two vines, life and death. Every day that summer we went to the pine beside the stream of Old Woman Swamp, and I put him on his feet at least a hundred times each afternoon. Occasionally I too became discouraged because it didn't seem as if he was trying, and I would say, "Doodle, don't you *want* to learn to walk?"

He'd nod his head, and I'd say, "Well, if you don't keep trying, you'll never learn." Then I'd paint for him a picture of us as old men, white-haired, him with a long white beard and me still pulling him around in the go-cart. This never failed to make him try again.

Finally one day, after many weeks of practicing, he stood alone for a few seconds. When he fell, I grabbed him in my arms and hugged him, our laughter pealing through the swamp like a ringing bell. Now we knew it could be done. Hope no longer hid in the dark palmetto thicket but perched like a cardinal in the lacy toothbrush tree, brilliantly visible.

"Yes, yes," I cried, and he cried it too, and the grass beneath us was soft and the smell of the swamp was sweet.

With success so <u>imminent</u>, we decided not to tell anyone until he could actually walk. Each day, barring rain, we sneaked into Old Woman Swamp, and by cotton-picking time Doodle was ready to show what he could do. He still wasn't able to walk far, but we could wait no longer. Keeping a nice secret is very hard to do, like holding your breath. We chose to reveal all on October eighth, Doodle's sixth birthday, and for weeks ahead we mooned around the house, promising everybody a most spectacular surprise. Aunt Nicey said that, after so much talk, if we produced anything less tremendous than the Resurrection,[7] she was going to be disappointed.

At breakfast on our chosen day, when Mama, Daddy, and Aunt Nicey were in the dining room, I brought Doodle to the door in the go-cart just as usual and had them turn their backs, making them cross their hearts and hope to die if they peeked. I helped Doodle up, and when he was standing alone I let them look. There wasn't a sound as Doodle walked slowly across the room and sat down at his place at the table. Then Mama began to cry and ran over to him, hugging him and kissing him. Daddy hugged him too, so I went to Aunt Nicey, who was thanks

---

7. **the Resurrection:** the rising of Jesus Christ from the dead after his burial.

WORDS TO KNOW

imminent (ĭm′ə-nənt) *adj.* about to occur

PREDICT

Do you think Doodle will be able to walk?
Using a Reading Log

Active Reading: EVALUATE

N Some students may judge the narrator as being very selfish, because he really helped Doodle for his own sake to try to remove the "shame" of having a crippled brother. Other students may feel that the narrator is too harsh on himself, because regardless of how the narrator benefited, if he did not truly love Doodle, he probably would not have put all this time and effort into getting Doodle to walk.

Critical Thinking: MAKING INFERENCES

O Ask students what they think Doodle's "lies" reveal about him. *(Possible responses: He is acutely aware of his frailty; he wishes he had magic powers that would make his life easier; he wishes everyone would admire him; he wishes he had a magnificent protector.)*

Linking to Science

P Old Woman Swamp's ecosystem includes pines, palmetto trees, bald cypress, and wildflowers such as violets, honeysuckle, jasmine, water lilies, and wire or marsh grass. Tell students that since 1918 much of this ecosystem has been destroyed by urban and industrial development.

Literary Concept: SIMILE

Q Ask students to what the narrator compares Doodle's success. *(a pot of gold at the end of the rainbow)* Ask them what this simile hints about the narrator's hopes. *(Possible response: They are an illusion.)*

---

praying in the doorway, and began to waltz her around. We danced together quite well until she came down on my big toe with her brogans,[8] hurting me so badly I thought I was crippled for life.

Doodle told them it was I who had taught him to walk, so everyone wanted to hug me, and I began to cry.

"What are you crying for?" asked Daddy, but I couldn't answer. They did not know that I did it for myself; that pride, whose slave I was, spoke to me louder than all their voices, and that Doodle walked only because I was ashamed of having a crippled brother.

EVALUATE

Notice how the narrator's expectations of Doodle are tied to his own feelings. Do you judge the narrator for his pride as much as he judges himself?

Using a Reading Log

Within a few months Doodle had learned to walk well and his go-cart was put up in the barn loft (it's still there) beside his little mahogany coffin. Now, when we roamed off together, resting often, we never turned back until our destination had been reached, and to help pass the time, we took up lying.[9] From the beginning Doodle was a terrible liar and he got me in the habit. Had anyone stopped to listen to us, we would have been sent off to Dix Hill.

My lies were scary, involved, and usually pointless, but Doodle's were twice as crazy. People in his stories all had wings and flew wherever they wanted to go. His favorite lie was about a boy named Peter who had a pet peacock with a ten-foot tail. Peter wore a golden robe that glittered so brightly that when he walked through the sunflowers they turned away from the sun to face him. When Peter was ready to go to sleep, the peacock spread his magnificent tail, enfolding the boy gently like a closing go-to-sleep flower, burying him in the gloriously <u>iridescent</u>, rustling vortex.[10] Yes, I must admit it. Doodle could beat me lying.

Doodle and I spent lots of time thinking about our future. We decided that when we were grown we'd live in Old Woman Swamp and pick dog-tongue for a living. Beside the stream, he planned, we'd build us a house of whispering leaves and the swamp birds would be our chickens. All day long (when we weren't gathering dog-tongue) we'd swing through the cypresses on the rope vines, and if it rained we'd huddle beneath an umbrella tree and play stickfrog. Mama and Daddy could come and live with us if they wanted to. He even came up with the idea that he could marry Mama and I could marry Daddy. Of course, I was old enough to know this wouldn't work out, but the picture he painted was so beautiful and serene that all I could do was whisper Yes, yes.

nce I had succeeded in teaching Doodle to walk, I began to believe in my own <u>infallibility</u>, and I prepared a terrific development program for him, unknown to Mama and Daddy, of course. I would teach him to run, to swim, to climb trees, and to fight. He, too, now believed in my infallibility, so we set the deadline for these accomplishments less than a year away, when, it had been decided, Doodle could start to school.

That winter we didn't make much progress, for I was in school and Doodle suffered from one bad cold after another. But when spring came, rich and warm, we raised our sights again. Success lay at the end of summer like a pot of gold, and our campaign got off to a good start. On hot days, Doodle and I went down to Horsehead Landing, and I gave him swimming

---

8. **brogans** (brō´gənz): heavy, ankle-high work shoes.
9. **lying:** here used to refer to the telling of tall tales, not untruths intended to deceive.
10. **vortex:** a whirlpool or whirlwind; here, a reference to the funnel-shaped covering of feathers.

WORDS TO KNOW
iridescent (ĭr´ĭ-dĕs´ənt) *adj.* shining with shifting rainbow colors
infallibility (ĭn-făl´ə-bĭl´ĭ-tē) *n.* an inability to make errors

420

Mini-Lesson — Genre Study

FICTION Explain that in an effective **short story**, plot, setting, characters, and theme often work together to create an overall effect that has an impact on the reader. Each element must do its part or the story will seem disjointed.

Application Have students copy the chalkboard into their notebooks. After they read the selection, have them discuss in small groups how well they think the selection succeeds as a short story.

> How effectively does the author bring the characters and setting to life?
>
> How well are the characters' conflicts built into a suspenseful plot?
>
> Does the theme of the story arise naturally from the plot, or does it seem imposed?

lessons or showed him how to row a boat. Sometimes we descended into the cool greenness of Old Woman Swamp and climbed the rope vines or boxed scientifically beneath the pine where he had learned to walk. Promise hung about us like the leaves, and wherever we looked, ferns unfurled and birds broke into song.

That summer, the summer of 1918, was blighted. In May and June there was no rain and the crops withered, curled up, then died under the thirsty sun. One morning in July a hurricane came out of the east, tipping over the oaks in the yard and splitting the limbs of the elm trees. That afternoon it roared back out of the west, blew the fallen oaks around, snapping their roots and tearing them out of the earth like a hawk at the entrails[11] of a chicken. Cotton bolls were wrenched from the stalks and lay like green walnuts in the valleys between the rows, while the cornfield leaned over uniformly so that the tassels touched the ground. Doodle and I followed Daddy out into the cotton field, where he stood, shoulders sagging, surveying the ruin. When his chin sank down onto his chest, we were frightened, and Doodle slipped his hand into mine. Suddenly Daddy straightened his shoulders, raised a giant knuckly fist, and with a voice that seemed to rumble out of the earth itself began cursing heaven, hell, the weather, and the Republican Party.[12] Doodle and I, prodding each other and giggling, went back to the house, knowing that everything would be all right.

And during that summer, strange names were heard through the house: Château-Thierry, Amiens, Soissons, and in her blessing at the supper table, Mama once said, "And bless the Pearsons,

---

11. **entrails:** internal organs.
12. **Republican Party:** In 1918, most Southerners were Democrats.

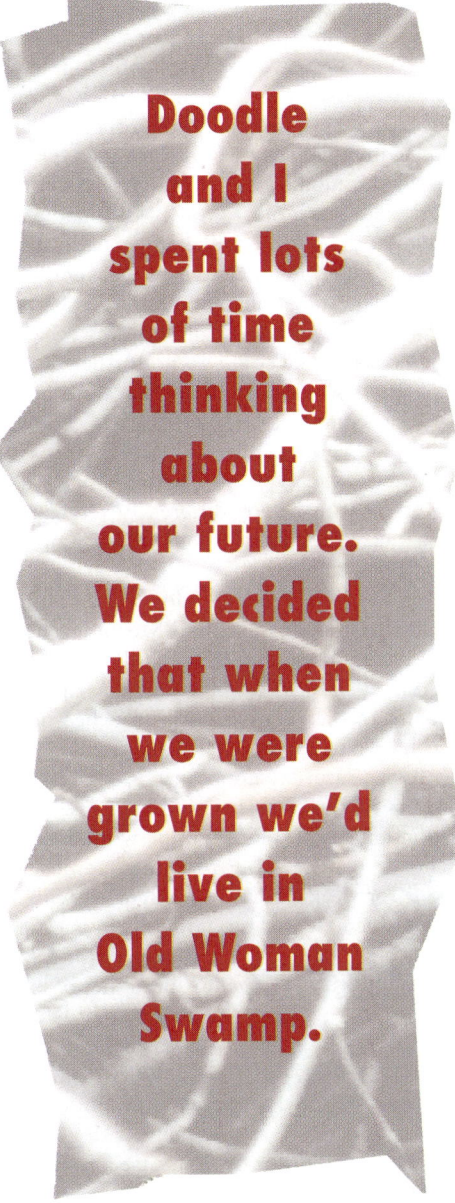

Doodle and I spent lots of time thinking about our future. We decided that when we were grown we'd live in Old Woman Swamp.

Literary Concept:
FORESHADOWING

U Ask students to analyze the significance of Doodle's collapse. *(Possible responses: He has probably reached his limit; he is weakening and cannot withstand the narrator's plans for him; such workouts may kill him.)*

Critical Thinking: ANALYZING

V Ask students which brother cares about the impression Doodle will make in school and which brother does not. *(Doodle himself does not care; the narrator does.)*

Active Reading: CLARIFY

W In discussing with students the reasons the boys can't give up their program, you may want to lead them through the "net" metaphor as well as the "crumbs" allusion. *(Possible response: The narrator's pride and their shared high expectations of success have caught them in an emotional "net" that won't let them give up. Because they made no plans for the possibility of defeat—dropped no crumbs on the ground, as in "Hansel and Gretel"—they remain trapped and cannot retreat from their dark woods, their continuation of a hopeless program.)*

---

whose boy Joe was lost at Belleau Wood."[13]

So we came to that clove of seasons. School was only a few weeks away, and Doodle was far behind schedule. He could barely clear the ground when climbing up the rope vines, and his swimming was certainly not passable. We decided to double our efforts, to make that last drive and reach our pot of gold. I made him swim until he turned blue and row until he couldn't lift an oar. Wherever we went, I purposely walked fast, and although he kept up, his face turned red and his eyes became glazed. Once, he could go no further, so he collapsed on the ground and began to cry.

"Aw, come on, Doodle," I urged. "You can do it. Do you want to be different from everybody else when you start school?"

"Does it make any difference?"

"It certainly does," I said. "Now, come on," and I helped him up.

As we slipped through dog days,[14] Doodle began to look feverish, and Mama felt his forehead, asking him if he felt ill. At night he didn't sleep well, and sometimes he had nightmares, crying out until I touched him and said, "Wake up, Doodle. Wake up."

It was Saturday noon, just a few days before school was to start. I should have already admitted defeat, but my pride wouldn't let me. The excitement of our program had now been gone for weeks, but still we kept on with a tired doggedness. It was too late to turn back, for we had both wandered too far into a net of expectations and had left no crumbs behind.

Daddy, Mama, Doodle, and I were seated at the dining-room table having lunch. It was a hot day, with all the windows and doors open in case a breeze should come. In the kitchen Aunt Nicey was humming softly. After a long silence, Daddy spoke. "It's so calm, I wouldn't be surprised if we had a storm this afternoon."

"I haven't heard a rain frog," said Mama, who believed in signs, as she served the bread around the table.

CLARIFY

W Why can't the two boys give up their program?
Using a Reading Log

---

13. **Château-Thierry** (shä-tō-tyĕ-rē′), **Amiens** (ä-myăN′), **Soissons** (swä-sôN′) . . . **Belleau** (bĕ-lō′) **Wood:** places in France where famous battles were fought near the end of World War I.
14. **dog days:** the hot, uncomfortable days between early July and early September (named after the Dog Star, Sirius, which rises and sets with the sun at that time).

WORDS TO KNOW
doggedness (dô′gĭd-nĭs) *n.* persistence; stubbornness

Mini-Lesson — The Writer's Style

USING REPEATED WORDS TO BUILD COHERENCE Tell students that a good way to unify their writing and to help readers see the connections among their ideas is to repeat key words from earlier sentences or paragraphs of their work. Point out the highlighted section above and ask if they remember where the phrase "clove of seasons" appeared earlier in the story *(on p. 415, in the first line of the story)*. Have students reread the entire first paragraph and note that it refers to the scarlet ibis. Repeating the phrase signals that the scarlet ibis is about to appear.

Application Have students write a brief essay about the consequences of pride. Encourage them to repeat the words *pride* and *proud* occasionally to give their essay coherence. If they wish, students can write about another topic, choosing a word or words that will help build coherence in their writing.

Reteaching/Reinforcement
• *Writing Handbook,* anthology p. 869
• *Writing Mini-Lessons* transparencies, p. 39

Coherence in Compositions, pp. 368–369

Down Home (1992), Tony Couch. Watercolor, 22″ × 30″, private collection. Copyright © Tony Couch, from *Tony Couch's Keys to Successful Painting*, published by North Light Books, 1992.

"I did," declared Doodle. "Down in the swamp."

"He didn't," I said contrarily.

"You did, eh?" said Daddy, ignoring my denial.

"I certainly did," Doodle <u>reiterated</u>, scowling at me over the top of his iced-tea glass, and we were quiet again.

Suddenly, from out in the yard, came a strange croaking noise. Doodle stopped eating, with a piece of bread poised ready for his mouth, his eyes popped round like two blue buttons. "What's that?" he whispered.

I jumped up, knocking over my chair, and had reached the door when Mama called, "Pick up the chair, sit down again, and say excuse me."

By the time I had done this, Doodle had excused himself and had slipped out into the yard. He was looking up into the bleeding tree. "It's a great big red bird!" he called.

The bird croaked loudly again, and Mama and Daddy came out into the yard. We shaded our eyes with our hands against the hazy glare of the sun and peered up through the still leaves. On the topmost branch a bird the size of a chicken, with scarlet feathers and long legs, was perched <u>precariously</u>. Its wings hung down loosely, and as we watched, a feather dropped away and floated slowly down through the green leaves.

"It's not even frightened of us," Mama said.

"It looks tired," Daddy added. "Or maybe sick."

Doodle's hands were clasped at his throat, and I had never seen him stand still so long. "What is it?" he asked.

Daddy shook his head. "I don't know, maybe it's—"

At that moment the bird began to flutter, but the wings were uncoordinated, and amid much flapping and a spray of flying feathers, it tumbled down, bumping through the limbs of the bleeding tree and landing at our feet with a thud. Its long, graceful neck jerked twice into an S, then straightened out, and the bird was still. A white veil came over the eyes and the long white beak unhinged. Its legs were crossed and its clawlike feet were delicately curved at rest. Even death did not mar its grace, for it lay on the earth like a broken vase of red flowers, and we stood around it, awed by its <u>exotic</u> beauty.

WORDS TO KNOW	
reiterate (rē-ĭt′ə-rāt′) *v.* to repeat	
precariously (prĭ-kâr′ē-əs-lē) *adv.* insecurely; in a dangerous way	
exotic (ĭg-zŏt′ĭk) *adj.* excitingly strange	

423

Art Note

Down Home by Tony Couch. In this work a white house and an old tree draped with hairlike Spanish moss dominate the scene with a mixture of glowing light and dim shades of gray and green.

Reading the Art *What aspects of the Deep South is the artist trying to capture?*

Critical Thinking: MAKING INFERENCES

X Ask students why they think the narrator is so quick to deny that Doodle heard a rain frog in the swamp. *(Possible response: He doesn't want the rest of the family to start asking questions about what they do in the swamp.)*

Literary Concept: SUSPENSE

Y Ask what details here create suspense. *(Possible responses: the strange noise, Doodle's suddenly ceasing to eat, Doodle's whisper)* Ask students whether they suspected what the sound was. *(Responses will vary. Some may remember that the ibis's appearance was foreshadowed at the beginning of the story.)*

Literary Concept: SYMBOL

Z Ask students in what ways the ibis is like Doodle. *(Possible responses: It looks tired and sick; it is uncoordinated; it is very fragile; it has beauty even in its dying awkwardness.)*

Mini-Lesson Study Skills

USING A VENN DIAGRAM Tell students that a Venn diagram (two overlapping circles) can be a useful graphic organizer for analyzing two categories that overlap. For example, some of the narrator's actions are cruel and others are helpful, and still others are somewhat cruel and somewhat helpful at the same time.

Application Have students use the Venn diagram to analyze the narrator's behavior toward Doodle. Which of his actions were cruel? Which were helpful? Which were both cruel and helpful? Invite students to share their completed diagrams and evaluate as a group the narrator's actions.

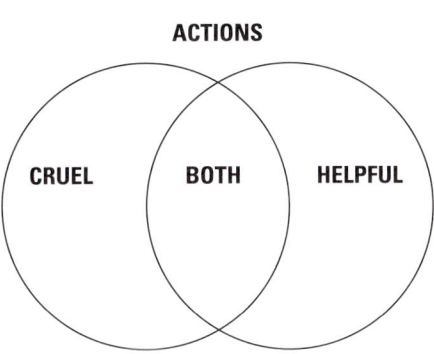

Literary Concept:
FORESHADOWING

AA Ask students if they think the mention of a storm may hint at other dangers to come. *(Possible response: It may hint that Doodle and the narrator will encounter either a real or emotional storm.)*

Critical Thinking: INFERENCE

BB Ask students what they think caused the scarlet ibis to die in the family's backyard. *(Possible response: It was apparently gravely battered and bruised after being caught in a storm that blew it many miles from its home.)*

Active Reading: QUESTION

CC You may wish to use the following model to help students organize their thoughts about the question.
Think-Aloud Model *I can see the similarity between Doodle and the scarlet ibis. He obviously is aware of it too; that must be why he feels such compassion for the bird's suffering and weakness. The bird's death also may have given Doodle a premonition about events to come.*

CUSTOMIZING FOR
Gifted and Talented Students

Have students discuss the ambiguous nature of the relationship between the two brothers. Ask them what difficulties each presented to the other and what rewards each gained from the relationship. Ask them how this relationship seems similar to and different from sibling relationships they have known.

"It's dead," Mama said.

"What is it?" Doodle repeated.

"Go bring me the bird book," said Daddy.

AA I ran into the house and brought back the bird book. As we watched, Daddy thumbed through its pages. "It's a scarlet ibis," he said, pointing to a picture. "It lives in the tropics— South America to Florida. A storm must have brought it here."

BB Sadly, we all looked back at the bird. A scarlet ibis! How many miles it had traveled to die like this, in *our* yard, beneath the bleeding tree.

"Let's finish lunch," Mama said, nudging us back toward the dining room.

"I'm not hungry," said Doodle, and he knelt down beside the ibis.

"We've got peach cobbler for dessert," Mama tempted from the doorway.

Doodle remained kneeling. "I'm going to bury him."

"Don't you dare touch him," Mama warned. "There's no telling what disease he might have had."

"All right," said Doodle. "I won't."

Daddy, Mama, and I went back to the dining-room table, but we watched Doodle through the open door. He took out a piece of string from his pocket and, without touching the ibis, looped one end around its neck. Slowly, while singing softly "Shall We Gather at the River," he carried the bird around to the front yard and dug a hole in the flower garden, next to the petunia bed. Now we were watching him through the front window, but he didn't know it. His awkwardness at digging the hole with a shovel whose handle was twice as long as he was made us laugh, and we covered our mouths with our hands so he wouldn't hear.

When Doodle came into the dining room, he found us seriously eating our cobbler. He was pale and lingered just inside the screen door. "Did you get the scarlet ibis buried?" asked Daddy.

Doodle didn't speak but nodded his head.

"Go wash your hands, and then you can have some peach cobbler," said Mama.

"I'm not hungry," he said.

"Dead birds is bad luck," said Aunt Nicey, poking her head from the kitchen door. "Specially *red* dead birds!"

As soon as I had finished eating, Doodle and I hurried off to Horsehead Landing. Time was short, and Doodle still had a long way to go if he was going to keep up with the other boys when he started school. The sun, gilded with the yellow cast of autumn, still burned fiercely, but the dark green woods through which we passed were shady and cool. When we reached the landing, Doodle said he was too tired to swim, so we got into a skiff and floated down the creek with the tide. Far off in the marsh a rail was scolding, and over on the beach locusts were singing in the myrtle trees. Doodle did not speak and kept his head turned away, letting one hand trail limply in the water.

fter we had drifted a long way, I put the oars in place and made Doodle row back against the tide. Black clouds began to gather in the southwest, and he kept watching them, trying to pull the oars a little faster. When we reached Horsehead Landing, lightning was playing across half the sky and thunder roared out, hiding even the sound of the sea. The sun disappeared and darkness descended, almost like night. Flocks of marsh crows flew by, heading inland to their roosting trees; and two egrets, squawking, arose from the oyster-rock shallows and careened away.

Doodle was both tired and frightened, and when he stepped from the skiff he collapsed onto the mud, sending an armada of fiddler crabs rustling off into the marsh grass. I helped him up, and as he wiped the mud off his

> **QUESTION**
> **CC** Why do you think Doodle is so moved by the scarlet ibis?
> Using a Reading Log

424   UNIT THREE   PART 2: ON YOUR OWN TERMS

Assessment ✓ Option

Have two students imagine that they are the hosts of a TV show that reviews popular literary works. Their topic for the week is "The Scarlet Ibis." Have the pair briefly summarize the plot and then offer a "thumbs up" and/or "thumbs down" critique of the story. If students wish, they can ask another student to videotape their show and play it for the class.

Rubric

3 Full Accomplishment Students' summaries and critiques reflect full and sensitive understanding of the selection content.

2 Substantial Accomplishment Students' summaries and critiques reflect partial understanding of the selection content.

1 Little or Partial Accomplishment Students have difficulty summarizing the story events, and their critiques lack analysis and insight.

trousers, he smiled at me ashamedly. He had failed and we both knew it, so we started back home, racing the storm. We never spoke (What are the words that can solder[15] cracked pride?), but I knew he was watching me, watching for a sign of mercy. The lightning was near now, and from fear he walked so close behind me he kept stepping on my heels. The faster I walked, the faster he walked, so I began to run. The rain was coming, roaring through the pines, and then, like a bursting Roman candle, a gum tree ahead of us was shattered by a bolt of lightning. When the deafening peal of thunder had died, and in the moment before the rain arrived, I heard Doodle, who had fallen behind, cry out, "Brother, Brother, don't leave me! Don't leave me!"

The knowledge that Doodle's and my plans had come to naught[16] was bitter, and that streak of cruelty within me awakened. I ran as fast as I could, leaving him far behind with a wall of rain dividing us. The drops stung my face like nettles,[17] and the wind flared the wet glistening leaves of the bordering trees. Soon I could hear his voice no more.

I hadn't run too far before I became tired, and the flood of childish spite evanesced[18] as well. I stopped and waited for Doodle. The sound of rain was everywhere, but the wind had died and it fell straight down in parallel paths like ropes hanging from the sky. As I waited, I peered through the downpour, but no one came. Finally I went back and found him huddled beneath a red nightshade bush beside the road. He was sitting on the ground, his face buried in his arms, which were resting on his drawn-up knees. "Let's go, Doodle," I said.

He didn't answer, so I placed my hand on his forehead and lifted his head. Limply, he fell backward onto the earth. He had been bleeding from the mouth, and his neck and the front of his shirt were stained a brilliant red.

"Doodle! Doodle!" I cried, shaking him, but there was no answer but the ropy rain. He lay very awkwardly, with his head thrown far back, making his vermilion[19] neck appear unusually long and slim. His little legs, bent sharply at the knees, had never before seemed so fragile, so thin.

I began to weep, and the tear-blurred vision in red before me looked very familiar. "Doodle!" I screamed above the pounding storm and threw my body to the earth above his. For a long long time, it seemed forever, I lay there crying, sheltering my fallen scarlet ibis from the heresy of rain. ❖

---

15. **solder** (sŏd′ər): to join or bond together.
16. **naught:** nothing.
17. **nettles:** weeds covered with stinging hairs.
18. **evanesced** (ĕv′ə-nĕst′): disappeared; vanished.
19. **vermilion** (vər-mĭl′yən): bright red or scarlet.

INSIGHT

WOMAN WITH FLOWER
Naomi Long Madgett

I wouldn't coax the plant if I were you.
Such watchful nurturing may do it harm.
Let the soil rest from so much digging
And wait until it's dry before you water it.
5   The leaf's inclined to find its own direction;
Give it a chance to seek the sunlight
   for itself.

Much growth is stunted by too careful
   prodding,
Too eager tenderness.
The things we love we have to learn to
   leave alone.

WORDS TO KNOW

heresy (hĕr′ĭ-sē) *n.* an action or opinion contrary to what is generally thought of as right

425

INSIGHT

1. According to the poem, how do plants respond to too much attention and "prodding"? *(They can be damaged and have their growth stunted.)*
2. How was Doodle like a plant that gets too much attention? *(At first he flourished; then he died.)*
3. Should you try to change the people you love? Explain. *(Possible responses: Yes, you should coax and nurture people to improve themselves. No, you should let people develop in their own way.)*

NAOMI LONG MADGETT

Naomi Long Madgett was born in 1923 in Norfolk, Virginia. In 1955, while teaching high school, Madgett established the first African American literature classes in Detroit. In 1988, Madgett wrote and published *Octavia and Other Poems*, which represents a lifetime commitment to the craft of writing poetry.

Critical Thinking: EVALUATING

DD Have students evaluate the narrator's state of mind at this point and whether he still loves his brother. *(Possible responses: His "knot of cruelty" reemerged in this time of great frustration and has taken over for the moment, but there is still an overriding feeling that deep down, the narrator loves Doodle.)*

Literary Concept: SYMBOL

EE Have students find similarities between the description of Doodle in death and the description of the dead ibis on page 423. *(Possible responses: The ibis rests below a bleeding tree; Doodle rests below a red nightshade bush. The ibis has bright red feathers; Doodle's shirt is stained a brilliant red from blood. Doodle's neck is red and looks long and slim like the ibis's. Doodle's legs look fragile and delicate like the ibis's.)*

STRATEGIC READING FOR Less-Proficient Readers

FF Ask students to explain what happened to the two brothers. *(Possible responses: The narrator pushes Doodle to swim and row; Doodle collapses and dies after being left behind while trying to outrun a storm.)* Summarizing

- Ask students to describe the emotions that the narrator experiences at Doodle's death. *(Possible responses: grief, guilt, shame)* Making Inferences

COMPREHENSION CHECK

1. How is Doodle different from other children? *(He is born weak and sickly; he doesn't walk until age five.)*
2. How does the narrator try to help Doodle? *(by pushing him to do physical things and not accept limitations)*
3. What are the narrator's motives for working with Doodle? *(pride that he could affect Doodle's life; shame that Doodle wasn't like other children; natural love for a sibling)*
4. What does the stranded ibis symbolize? *(It symbolizes Doodle, who was also fragile and out of his element and who also died as the result of a storm.)*

From Personal Response to Critical Analysis

1. Accept all reasonable responses.
2. Accept all reasonable responses.
3. Students should indicate that the narrator's expectations of Doodle are much higher than his parents' expectations.
4. Possible responses: The brother is to blame because he pushed Doodle too hard; the parents are to blame for not keeping a close eye on the boys; no one is to blame because Doodle was too fragile to have lived much longer regardless of his treatment.
5. Possible responses: The narrator only helped Doodle to gratify his own pride; the narrator truly loved Doodle and wanted him to be accepted by other boys, but he didn't understand Doodle's limitations.
6. Possible response: Doodle is caring and imaginative but easily led by those he loves. He craves attention and protection and wishes he could move with skill and grace.
7. Accept all reasonable responses.
8. Possible responses: Leave your brother alone; let your brother go at his own pace. Opinions will vary as to whether this is good advice.

Another Pathway

Cooperative Learning The prosecuting attorney should gather evidence against the narrator, and the defense attorney should collect evidence in his favor. Story characters should discuss their views of the narrator. The judge should explain the meaning of "guilty beyond a reasonable doubt" to the jury.

Rubric

3 Full Accomplishment Students present a convincing criminal trial with accurate evidence.

2 Substantial Accomplishment Students do not present entirely accurate evidence at their trial.

1 Little or Partial Accomplishment Students have difficulty finding relevant evidence for and against the narrator.

RESPONDING OPTIONS

FROM PERSONAL RESPONSE TO CRITICAL ANALYSIS

REFLECT 1. What was your reaction to the end of the story? Jot down your thoughts in your notebook and share them in class.

RETHINK 2. Draw or sketch the most vivid image left in your mind by this story. Then explain your drawing to the class.

3. Look at the bar graph of expectations that you created for the Personal Connection on page 413. On that scale, how would you rate the narrator's and his parents' expectations of Doodle?

4. Whom, if anyone, do you blame for Doodle's death? Explain your opinion.

5. What is your judgment of the narrator's treatment of Doodle?
Consider
- which of his actions seem cruel
- the reasons he gives for his actions
- the effect of his actions on Doodle

Close Textual Reading

6. What is your opinion of Doodle's character?
Consider
- his strengths and weaknesses
- why his brother has such a powerful influence on him
- what his "lies" may reveal about him

Close Textual Reading

RELATE 7. The narrator says, "There is within me . . . a knot of cruelty borne by the stream of love." Think about your relationships with people you love, especially in your family. Can love and cruelty coexist? Why or why not?

Thematic Link

8. What advice does the Insight poem "Woman with Flower" seem to offer the narrator of "The Scarlet Ibis"? Do you agree with the message of this poem?

Literary Link

Multimodal Learning
ANOTHER PATHWAY

Cooperative Learning

To what extent do you hold the narrator responsible for Doodle's death? Stage a trial, using passages from the story as evidence both for and against him. Include witnesses—family members and the doctor—as well as the narrator, attorneys, and a judge. The rest of the class may serve as the jury.

QUICKWRITES

1. Create a **diary entry** in which the narrator describes his feelings on the night of Doodle's death. The entry should reflect the ways in which the narrator's viewpoint at that time may have differed from his perspective in looking back on the events many years later.

2. Analyze the narrator's relationship with Doodle from another character's point of view. Write up your analysis as an **interview** between your character and a police officer investigating the case.

3. Write an **interpretation** of Doodle's favorite lie, the one about the boy named Peter. Explain what you think it means.

 PORTFOLIO Save your writing. You may want to use it later as a springboard to a piece for your portfolio.

426 UNIT THREE PART 2: ON YOUR OWN TERMS

QuickWrites

1. Have students discuss how the narrator might have felt on the night of Doodle's death: grief-stricken, guilty, regretful.
2. Remind students of how Doodle's parents and Aunt Nicey reacted when they found out that the narrator had taught Doodle to walk.
3. Read the passage on page 420 aloud and have students list the most important elements on the board. Then have them interpret each element.

The Writer's Craft

Journal Writing, pp. 28–33
Interviewing Skills, pp. 481–482
Personal Response to Literature, pp. 238–248

LITERARY CONCEPTS

A **symbol** is a person, an animal, a place, an activity, or an object that stands for something beyond itself. In this story, the scarlet ibis, with its vulnerability and strange beauty, symbolizes Doodle, and its death foreshadows Doodle's own death. In order to explore the richness and depth that this symbolic connection adds to the story, create a diagram like the one started below. With a small group of classmates, identify as many connections between the scarlet ibis and Doodle as you can. Then share your findings with the rest of the class and discuss how recognizing these connections adds to your understanding of the story.

CONCEPT REVIEW: Foreshadowing This story contains many examples of foreshadowing—hints or clues that point to events that will occur later. Numerous passages foreshadow Doodle's eventual death. For example, the opening paragraph details the death of summer, in which "graveyard flowers" are "speaking softly" the names of the family's dead. Identify at least three other passages, sentences, or events that foreshadow the story's conclusion.

Multimodal Learning
ALTERNATIVE ACTIVITIES

1. Imagine that Doodle is only unconscious at the end of the story and that he later recovers. How might this affect the narrator, and what might he think to do next? Present his thoughts in a **soliloquy,** a speech in which a character reveals his or her thoughts when alone.

2. Use the descriptions in the story to create a **map** of Doodle's small world, with the house in the center and roads and paths leading away from it. Show where you imagine Horsehead Landing and the creek, Old Woman Swamp, the garden, the corn and cotton fields, the barn, and the bleeding tree to be located. Compare your map with those of your classmates.

THE WRITER'S STYLE

In "The Scarlet Ibis," Hurst displays a lush style of writing. The opening paragraphs, for example, describe the setting in language that is full of rich imagery and figurative language. Skim the story for passages that contain striking **images, similes,** and **metaphors,** and read your favorite examples aloud to the rest of the class.

ART CONNECTION

The portrait of a five-year-old boy on page 418 is one of several portraits Alice Neel (1900–1984) made of children. This boy, Richard, is posed naturally. What qualities of Doodle do you find reflected in Neel's painting?

Detail of *Richard at Age Five* (1944) Alice Neel. Courtesy, Robert Miller Gallery, New York. Copyright © Estate of Alice Neel.

THE SCARLET IBIS **427**

Alternative Activities

1. Tell students that in a soliloquy a character is thinking aloud. Ask what thoughts would be going through the narrator's mind as he learned about Doodle's recovery.
2. Encourage students to skim the story for details about where items on the map are located. For example, p. 416: "A grindstone stands where the bleeding tree stood, just outside the kitchen door."

The Writer's Style

Annotations C, H, Q, and S identify passages with vivid imagery and figurative language. Students might also choose descriptions of the scarlet ibis on page 423 and of the storm at the top of page 425.

The Writer's Craft

Literal and Figurative Language, pp. 413–414

Literary Concepts

To help students complete their diagrams, review the passages on symbol on pages 423 and 425, which identify several similarities between the scarlet ibis and Doodle. Ask whether Doodle's burying of the ibis intensified students' feelings about the connections between the two. Finally, have students note the identification of Doodle and the scarlet ibis ("my fallen scarlet ibis") in the narrator's mind at the end of the story.

Foreshadowing Annotations I, L, S, U, and AA identify and help students analyze examples of foreshadowing.

Art Connection

Possible responses: simplicity; innocence; gentleness; wide-eyed wonder

Literary Links

Possible response: Jerry's pride drives him into physical training to perform a dangerous underwater stunt. Afterward, he emerges as a more courageous, confident person. The narrator's pride drives him to make his sickly brother undergo physical training that at first makes him more competent but ultimately helps bring about his death. Both boys are partly motivated by what other boys think about them.

Across the Curriculum

Science If students cannot access computer research facilities, any library's encyclopedias or field guides to birds contain the information. Ibises are large wading birds that live in warm climates, breed in large colonies, and feed on fish in shallow waterways. Types include the glossy ibis, white-faced ibis, white ibis, and scarlet ibis. They differ in color and live in different territories.

Words to Know

Exercise A
1. a
2. a
3. b
4. a
5. a
6. c
7. b
8. b
9. c
10. a

Exercise B
Good choices of words to act out include *precariously, doggedness, invalid, careen,* and *exotic.*

Reteaching/Reinforcement
• *Unit Three Resource Book,* p. 42

SCIENCE CONNECTION
The Ibis The basic characteristics of ibises can be seen in this group of images. You may wish to refer students to the images as they investigate these birds.

Side A, Frame 49369

LITERARY LINKS

Compare and contrast the narrator's pride with that of another boy about his age—Jerry in "Through the Tunnel" (page 91). How do the two characters' experiences illustrate the narrator's belief that "pride is a wonderful, terrible thing, a seed that bears two vines, life and death"?

ACROSS THE CURRICULUM

Science Research ibises, which are little known in the United States outside of Florida. What are the basic characteristics of these birds? What kinds of ibises are there? How do they differ from one another? If you have access to a computer encyclopedia program or to an on-line service, you might use it to start your research.

WORDS TO KNOW

EXERCISE A For each group of words below, write the letter of the word that is an antonym of the boldfaced word.

1. **exotic:** (a) ordinary, (b) frightening, (c) indirect
2. **careen:** (a) crawl, (b) hide, (c) race
3. **heresy:** (a) conflict, (b) conformity, (c) distance
4. **reiterate:** (a) cease, (b) lose, (c) originate
5. **precariously:** (a) firmly, (b) cleverly, (c) thoughtlessly
6. **doggedness:** (a) intelligence, (b) kindness, (c) casualness
7. **invalid:** (a) large, (b) healthy, (c) probable
8. **infallibility:** (a) respectability, (b) inaccuracy, (c) absence
9. **iridescent:** (a) obvious, (b) charming, (c) dull
10. **imminent:** (a) distant, (b) native, (c) unknown

EXERCISE B With a small group of classmates, act out five of the vocabulary words, having the rest of the class try to guess the words.

1922–

James Hurst grew up in North Carolina on a farm near the sea. Today, he lives not far from the place where he was born. In his garden grow many of the flowers mentioned in "The Scarlet Ibis."

After attending North Carolina State College and serving in the United States Army during World War II, Hurst studied singing at the famous Juilliard School of Music in New York. Hoping for an operatic career, Hurst went to Italy for additional study, but he soon abandoned his musical ambitions. In 1951, he began a 34-year career in the international department of a large New York bank.

During his early years at the bank, he wrote and published short stories and a play, mostly in small literary magazines. "The Scarlet Ibis" was first published in *The Atlantic Monthly* in July 1960 and won the "Atlantic First" award that year. Quickly recognized as a classic, the story has appeared in virtually every high-school literature textbook series published since the late 1960s.

Hurst says that there are three "characters" in the story—Doodle, the narrator, and the setting, which comments on the inner action. When asked about the meaning of the story, Hurst once replied, "I hesitate to respond, since authors seldom understand what they write. That is why we have critics. I venture to say, however, that it comments on the tenacity and the splendor of the human spirit."

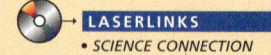
• SCIENCE CONNECTION

REFLECTING ON THEME
What Do You Think?

Have students think about Doodle's inability to act—to face life—on his own terms. As an extension of the role-playing they conducted before reading this first selection in Part 1, ask students to express their thoughts on the unique circumstances that Doodle struggled against. (First, there is his physical condition that denies him the ability to naturally participate in the character-building, rough-and-tumble aspects of day-to-day life. Then, there is the embarrassment an older brother experiences that drives the brother to deny Doodle even the ability to be a calm observer of life; he forces Doodle into a program of strenuous activity that may not have been in Doodle's best interests.)

PREVIEWING

NONFICTION

from Black Boy
Richard Wright

Activating Prior Knowledge
PERSONAL CONNECTION

The selection you are about to read is an excerpt from the autobiography of Richard Wright, a well-known African-American writer. In the excerpt, Wright tells about an aspiration—a strong desire to achieve something—that he had when he was 15 years old, trying to succeed on his own terms. Think about your own aspirations. What do you dream of achieving in your life? Share one of your aspirations with a classmate.

Building Background
HISTORICAL CONNECTION

In *Black Boy,* Wright tells about his life between the ages of 4 and 19. At the time described in this excerpt, Wright was living in Jackson, Mississippi, with his mother, his grandmother, and other relatives. In the South during the early 1900s, when Wright was growing up, discrimination against African Americans was legally enforced through what were called Jim Crow laws. In many parts of the southern United States, laws required separate public facilities, including schools, for blacks and whites. Through these discriminatory practices, whites attempted to restrict the lives and aspirations of African Americans. Blacks received less schooling than whites or were given only vocational education. Blacks who fought such discrimination were often beaten or killed.

Segregated drinking fountains

Setting a Purpose
WRITING CONNECTION

What you expect of yourself may depend partly on what other people expect of you. How do you think your aspirations are influenced by your family, teachers, and friends? Do they support your ambitions? Do your own hopes differ from what they expect? In your notebook, comment on other people's reactions to your aspirations. Describe how their reactions affect you. As you read this selection, compare your experiences with Richard Wright's.

OVERVIEW

Objectives
- To understand an autobiographical excerpt that tells of a teenage boy's aspirations to become a writer
- To identify and understand dialogue
- To express understanding of the selection through a choice of writing forms, including a letter of recommendation, an internal monologue, and a short story
- To extend understanding of the selection through a variety of multimodal and cross-curricular activities

Skills

LITERARY CONCEPTS
- Dialogue
- Metaphor
- Author's purpose

SPEAKING, LISTENING, AND VIEWING
- Group discussion
- Oral presentation

THE WRITER'S STYLE
- Varying sentence length and structure

HISTORICAL CONNECTION
Segregation Discrimination against African Americans was legal in the South when Richard Wright was growing up. These historical photographs show scenes of 20th-century segregation.

Side A, Frame 49376

LASERLINKS
- HISTORICAL CONNECTION

PRINT AND MEDIA RESOURCES

UNIT THREE RESOURCE BOOK
Strategic Reading: Literature, p. 45
Vocabulary SkillBuilder, p. 46

WRITING MINI–LESSONS
Transparencies, p. 50

ACCESS FOR STUDENTS ACQUIRING ENGLISH
Selection Summaries
Reading Support

FORMAL ASSESSMENT
Selection Test, pp. 75–76
 Test Generator

AUDIO LIBRARY
See Reference Card

 LASERLINKS
Historical Connection
Art Gallery

 INTERNET RESOURCES
McDougal Littell Literature Center at http://www.hmco.com/mcdougal/lit

SUMMARY

One day in eighth grade, the author became bored and wrote a story called "The Voodoo of Hell's Half-Acre." He took it to the editor of a local African-American newspaper, and it was published. None of Wright's relatives or friends could understand why he had written the story or what he hoped to accomplish. His grandmother called it a lie because it was fiction. His mother believed that people would think him weak-minded. Wright himself didn't know exactly why he had written the story either, but he began to dream of going north and becoming a writer. Looking back, he realizes that he had unknowingly started off in a direction that society did not approve of, a direction that would lead to great hardships for him.

Thematic Link: *On Your Own Terms* With no support from others and with active discouragement from everyone around him, a teenage African-American boy takes the first steps toward a career as a writer.

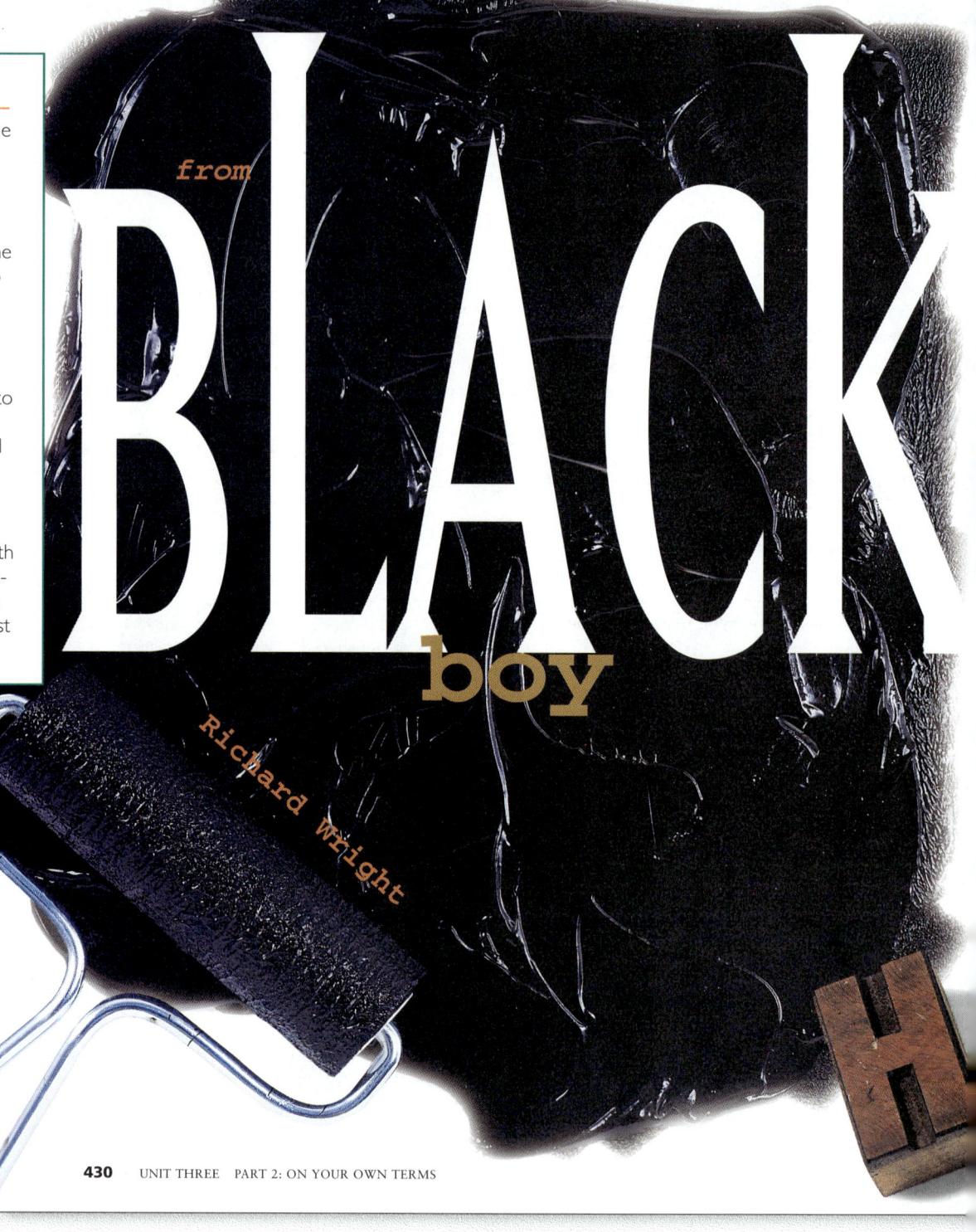

from **BLACK** *boy*

Richard Wright

WORDS TO KNOW

alien (ā′lē-ən) *adj.* foreign; strange; unfamiliar (p. 432)

articulate (är-tĭk′yə-lĭt) *adj.* clear and effective in speech (p. 434)

hedge (hĕj) *v.* to avoid giving direct answers (p. 433)

heedless (hēd′lĭs) *adj.* unmindful; careless; unaware (p. 434)

intuitively (ĭn-tōō′ĭ-tĭv-lē) *adv.* in a way that involves knowing something without having consciously learned it (p. 431)

mode (mōd) *n.* a manner or way (p. 434)

naive (nä-ēv′) *adj.* simple in a natural and sometimes foolish way; unsophisticated (p. 434)

relent (rĭ-lĕnt′) *v.* to become less harsh, strict, or stubborn (p. 431)

speculate (spĕk′yə-lāt′) *v.* to guess (p. 434)

stifle (stī′fəl) *v.* to smother; hold back (p. 434)

The eighth grade days flowed in their hungry path, and I grew more conscious of myself; I sat in classes, bored, wondering, dreaming. One long dry afternoon I took out my composition book and told myself that I would write a story; it was sheer idleness that led me to it. What would the story be about? It resolved itself into a plot about a villain who wanted a widow's home, and I called it *The Voodoo of Hell's Half-Acre*. It was crudely atmospheric, emotional, <u>intuitively</u> psychological, and stemmed from pure feeling. I finished it in three days and then wondered what to do with it.

The local Negro newspaper! That's it . . . I sailed into the office and shoved my ragged composition book under the nose of the man who called himself the editor.

"What's that?" he asked.

"A story," I said.

"A news story?"

"No, fiction."

"All right. I'll read it," he said.

He pushed my composition book back on his desk and looked at me curiously, sucking at his pipe.

"But I want you to read it *now*," I said.

He blinked. I had no idea how newspapers were run. I thought that one took a story to an editor, and he sat down then and there and read it and said yes or no.

"I'll read this and let you know about it tomorrow," he said.

I was disappointed; I had taken time to write it, and he seemed distant and uninterested.

"Give me the story," I said, reaching for it.

He turned from me, took up the book, and read ten pages or more.

Brown Boy, (1935), Lois Mailou Jones. Watercolor, private collection.

"Won't you come in tomorrow?" he asked. "I'll have it finished then."

I honestly <u>relented</u>.

"All right," I said. "I'll stop in tomorrow."

I left with the conviction that he would not read it. Now, where else could I take it after he had turned it down? The next afternoon, en route to my job, I stepped into the newspaper office.

"Where's my story?" I asked.

"It's in galleys," he said.

"What's that?" I asked; I did not know what galleys were.

"It's set up in type," he said. "We're publishing it."

WORDS TO KNOW	**intuitively** (ĭn-tōō′ĭ-tĭv-lē) *adv.* in a way that involves knowing something without having consciously learned it
	relent (rĭ-lĕnt′) *v.* to become less harsh, strict, or stubborn

431

Mini-Lesson The Writer's Style

VARYING SENTENCE LENGTH AND STRUCTURE Write the following paragraph on the board, and have students evaluate how interesting it is to read:

> I was bored. I wrote a story. It was very emotional. I called it The Voodoo of Hell's Half-Acre. I finished it in three days. I wondered what to do with it.

Then have students compare the paragraph you wrote on the board with the first paragraph of the selection. Point out how Wright made his writing interesting by using a variety of sentence patterns.

Application Ask students to work in small groups to locate other passages in the selection in which Wright uses a variety of sentence patterns. Then have students write a paragraph about young Richard. Encourage them to use a variety of sentence lengths and structures.

Reteaching/Reinforcement
- Writing Handbook, anthology p. 864
- *Writing Mini-Lessons* transparencies, p. 50

 The Writer's Craft

How Can I Vary My Sentences? p. 416–418

CUSTOMIZING FOR
Students Acquiring English

- Use **ACCESS FOR STUDENTS ACQUIRING ENGLISH**, *Reading Support*.
- Review the Historical Connection with students, and help them understand the extent of overt racial discrimination that existed in the United States at the time in which this autobiographical excerpt is set. Tell students that because of the threat of violence, many blacks were often extremely cautious not to seem aggressive or ambitious. Ask students if they have ever been the victims of discrimination.

STRATEGIC READING FOR
Less Proficient Readers

To help students become involved in the selection, have them act out the short scene that Wright describes in the first paragraph.

Set a Purpose Ask students to read to find out what happens to the narrator and his story.

Use **UNIT THREE RESOURCE BOOK**, p. 45, for guidance in reading the selection.

CUSTOMIZING FOR
Gifted and Talented Students

Have students analyze the conversation between Wright and the newspaper editor, then have them write a conversation the two might have had about Wright's plans for his future as a writer.

Art Note

Brown Boy by **Lois Mailou Jones.** Lois Mailou Jones was born in Boston in 1905. She taught art in North Carolina before becoming a professor of watercolor painting at Howard University in Washington, D.C., (1930–1977). She is considered the first major African-American woman artist, and in 1990 an important retrospective, "The World of Lois Mailou Jones," began a two-year tour across the U.S. This portrait was painted in 1935.

Reading the Art *What is your impression of the subject of the painting?*

THE LANGUAGE OF LITERATURE TEACHER'S EDITION **431**

Critical Thinking:
MAKING INFERENCES

A Ask students what this dialogue shows about Wright's character. *(Possible responses: He is very persistent; he is not easily taken advantage of; he has a gift for logical argument and is very articulate.)*

CUSTOMIZING FOR
Multiple Learning Styles

B **Mathematical Learners** Ask students to assume that Wright worked two hours in the morning and two at night, Monday through Friday, and made three dollars per week. What was Wright's hourly wage? *($0.15)* What would a teenager working for the same hours at a wage of $4.25 per hour make? *($85/week)*

Literary Concept: DIALOGUE

C Have students summarize the tone of voice they think Wright's classmates are using in this conversation. *(Possible responses: accusing, disbelieving, hostile, confused)*

Critical Thinking: SPECULATING

D Have students speculate as to why Wright's classmates were not convinced that he wrote the story that appeared in the newspaper. *(Possible responses: Since neither he nor his classmates had been instructed in literary matters, they found it hard to believe that a person could just make up a story. Given their limited background, they seemed to think that making up stories was something someone told you to do.)*

CUSTOMIZING FOR
Students Acquiring English

I Explain that *voodoo* is a religion practiced by some African Americans in the New Orleans area. It is based on African folk magic practices brought over by African slaves and is most commonly found in Haiti.

A "How much money will I get?" I asked, excited.

"We can't pay for manuscript," he said.

"But you sell your papers for money," I said with logic.

"Yes, but we're young in business," he explained.

"But you're asking me to *give* you my story, but you don't *give* your papers away," I said.

He laughed.

"Look, you're just starting. This story will put your name before our readers. Now, that's something," he said.

"But if the story is good enough to sell to your readers, then you ought to give me some of the money you get from it," I insisted.

He laughed again, and I sensed that I was amusing him.

"I'm going to offer you something more valuable than money," he said. "I'll give you a chance to learn to write."

I was pleased, but I still thought he was taking advantage of me.

"When will you publish my story?"

"I'm dividing it into three installments," he said. "The first installment appears this week. But the main thing is this: Will you get news for me on a space rate basis?"[1]

B "I work mornings and evenings for three dollars a week," I said.

"Oh," he said. "Then you better keep that. But what are you doing this summer?"

"Nothing."

"Then come to see me before you take another job," he said. "And write some more stories."

A few days later my classmates came to me with baffled eyes, holding copies of the *Southern Register* in their hands.

"Did you really write that story?" they asked me.

"Yes."

"Why?"

"Because I wanted to."

"Where did you get it from?"

"I made it up."

"You didn't. You copied it out of a book."

"If I had, no one would publish it."

"But what are they publishing it for?"

"So people can read it."

"Who told you to do that?"

"Nobody."

"Then why did you do it?"

"Because I wanted to," I said again.

They were convinced that I had not told them the truth. We had never had any instruction in literary matters at school; the literature of the nation or the Negro had never been mentioned. My schoolmates could not understand why anyone would want to write a story; and, above all, they could not understand why I had called it *The Voodoo of Hell's Half-Acre*. The mood out of which a story was written was the most <u>alien</u> thing conceivable to them. They looked at me with new eyes, and a distance, a suspiciousness, came between us. If I had thought anything in writing the story, I had thought that perhaps it would make me more acceptable to them, and now it was cutting me off from them more completely than ever.

At home the effects were no less disturbing. Granny came into my room early one morning and sat on the edge of my bed.

"Richard, what is this you're putting in the papers?" she asked.

"A story," I said.

"About what?"

"It's just a story, Granny."

"But they tell me it's been in three times."

"It's the same story. It's in three parts."

"But what is it about?" she insisted.

---

1. **space rate basis:** a system of payment based on the length of the articles.

WORDS TO KNOW

alien (āʹlē-ən) *adj.* foreign; strange; unfamiliar

Mini-Lesson — Literary Concepts

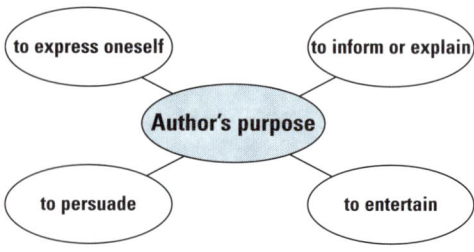

REVIEWING AUTHOR'S PURPOSE On the chalkboard draw the web shown on the left and use it to remind students that authors write for four main purposes: to express themselves, to inform or explain, to persuade, and to entertain. Writers may combine two or three purposes in one piece, but one purpose is usually the most important.

Application Ask students to copy the web into their notebooks. Then have them use it to discuss Richard Wright's purpose in writing this autobiography. Ask them which purpose they think was most important to him and have them explain their answers. *(Possible responses: Wright wrote this excerpt to inform readers of the discouragement and narrow-minded thinking he encountered during his youth in Mississippi; he wrote it to explain how discriminatory laws kept blacks from receiving better schooling, which led to their limited thinking. Students may think that his most important purpose was to inspire and persuade others not to give up their aspirations.)*

Portrait of My Father (about 1921), Archibald J. Motley, Jr. Collection of Archie Motley and Valerie Gerrand Browne, Chicago Historical Society.

I hedged, fearful of getting into a religious argument.

"It's just a story I made up," I said.

"Then it's a lie," she said.

"Oh, Christ," I said.

"You must get out of this house if you take the name of the Lord in vain," she said.

"Granny, please . . . I'm sorry," I pleaded. "But it's hard to tell you about the story. You see, Granny, everybody knows that the story isn't true, but . . ."

"Then why write it?" she asked.

"Because people might want to read it."

"That's the Devil's work," she said and left.

My mother also was worried.

"Son, you ought to be more serious," she said. "You're growing up now, and you won't be able to get jobs if you let people think that you're weak-minded. Suppose the superintendent of schools would ask you to teach here in Jackson, and he found out that you had been writing stories?"

I could not answer her.

"I'll be all right, Mama," I said.

Uncle Tom, though surprised, was highly critical and contemptuous. The story had no point, he said. And whoever heard of a story by the title of *The Voodoo of Hell's Half-Acre?* Aunt Addie said that it was a sin for anyone to use the word "hell" and that what was wrong with me was that I had nobody to guide me. She blamed the whole thing upon my upbringing.

In the end I was so angry that I refused to talk about the story. From no quarter,[2] with the exception of the Negro newspaper editor, had there come a single encouraging word. It was rumored that the principal wanted to know why I had used the word "hell." I felt that I had committed a crime. Had I been conscious of the full extent to which I was pushing against the current of my environment, I would have been frightened altogether out of my attempts at writing. But my reactions were limited to the attitude of the people

2. **quarter:** direction.

WORDS TO KNOW

hedge (hĕj) *v.* to avoid giving a direct answer

Linking to History

G Between 1920 and 1930, over half a million African Americans migrated from the South to the North. Many settled in large cities such as New York, Chicago, Detroit, and Cleveland, where jobs were plentiful. Richard Wright also migrated north, settling first in Chicago and then in New York.

Literary Concept:
AUTHOR'S PURPOSE

H Ask students to speculate about Wright's purpose in including details about Jim Crow laws in this incident about the short story in his autobiography. *(Possible response: Students may say that he wanted to express his views on how Jim Crow laws kept blacks from getting a good education, how the laws limited their aspirations. He wanted to show that in spite of what the laws were designed to do, he still had "dreams" that he wanted to pursue, and being a writer was his greatest dream.)*

STRATEGIC READING FOR
Less-Proficient Readers

I Help students summarize the importance of this episode in Wright's life. *(Possible response: It confirmed for him that he wanted to be a writer and that he could write.)* Summarizing

---

COMPREHENSION CHECK

1. When did Wright write his first story, and where was it published? *(in eighth grade; in the local African-American newspaper)*
2. How did his friends and family respond to his story? *(critically, suspiciously)*
3. How did Wright respond to everyone's criticism? *(It made him angry and more determined than ever to be a writer.)*

---

about me, and I did not <u>speculate</u> or generalize.

G I dreamed of going north and writing books, novels. The North symbolized to me all that I had not felt and seen; it had no relation whatever to what actually existed. Yet, by imagining a place where everything was possible, I kept hope alive in me. But where had I got this notion of doing something in the future, of going away from home and accomplishing something that would be recognized by others? I had, of course, read my Horatio Alger stories, my pulp stories, and I knew my Get-Rich-Quick Wallingford series³ from cover to cover, though I had sense enough not to hope to get rich; even to my <u>naive</u> imagination that possibility was too remote. I knew that I lived in a country in which the aspirations of black people were limited, marked off. Yet I felt that I had to go somewhere and do something to redeem my being alive.

I was building up in me a dream which the entire educational system of the South had been rigged to <u>stifle</u>. I was feeling the very thing that the state of Mississippi had spent millions of dollars to make sure that I would never feel;

H I was becoming aware of the thing that the Jim Crow laws had been drafted and passed to keep out of my consciousness; I was acting on impulses that southern senators in the nation's capital had striven to keep out of Negro life; I was beginning to dream the dreams that the state had said were wrong, that the schools had said were taboo.⁴

Had I been <u>articulate</u> about my ultimate aspirations, no doubt someone would have told me what I was bargaining for; but nobody seemed to know, and least of all did I. My classmates felt that I was doing something that was vaguely wrong, but they did not know how to express it. As the outside world grew more meaningful, I became more concerned, tense; and my classmates and my teachers would say: "Why do you ask so many questions?" Or: "Keep quiet."

I was in my fifteenth year; in terms of schooling I was far behind the average youth of the nation, but I did not know that. In me was shaping a yearning for a kind of consciousness, a <u>mode</u> of being that the way of life about me had said could not be, must not be, and upon which the penalty of death had been placed. Somewhere in the dead of the southern night my life had switched onto the wrong track, and, without my knowing it, the locomotive of my heart was rushing down a dangerously steep slope, heading for a collision, <u>heedless</u> of the warning red lights that blinked all about me, the sirens and the bells and the screams that filled the air. ❖

---

3. **Horatio Alger stories ... Wallingford series:** works of popular fiction about achieving wealth through hard work or cleverness.
4. **taboo:** forbidden.

WORDS TO KNOW
speculate (spĕk′yə-lāt′) *v.* to guess
naive (nä-ēv′) *adj.* simple in a natural and perhaps foolish way; unsophisticated
stifle (stī′fəl) *v.* to smother; hold back
articulate (är-tĭk′yə-lĭt) *adj.* clear and effective in speech
mode (mōd) *n.* a manner or way
heedless (hēd′lĭs) *adj.* unmindful; careless; unaware

434

Mini-Lesson Workplace Literacy

SCANS Goal: Communicates Information

WRITING PRESS RELEASES Point out that Wright's story was published in the local newspaper, the *Southern Register*. The editor who published his story offered Wright a job writing news copy. Wright would likely have had to gather all his information himself. Today, however, reporters can get some of their information from press releases, which are articles containing information that a group or business wishes to publicize. An effective press release generally:

- explains how its topic is of interest to the community
- begins by telling *who, what, where, when, why,* and *how*
- adds details in order of importance
- limits details to be as brief as possible
- is written in clear, simple sentences

Application Ask students to write a press release detailing a recent or upcoming event in their class, family, or other organization with which they are involved.

RESPONDING OPTIONS

FROM PERSONAL RESPONSE TO CRITICAL ANALYSIS

REFLECT 1. What do you think of the ways in which people reacted to Wright's writing? Jot down your thoughts in your notebook.

RETHINK 2. Why do you think Wright's family and classmates reacted as they did?
Consider
Close Textual Reading
- their unfamiliarity with teenagers who wrote stories
- their attitudes about fiction and imaginative writing
- the limitations imposed upon African Americans at the time

Thematic Link 3. Why do you think Wright clung to his aspirations despite the lack of support from people around him?

RELATE 4. Look over what you wrote about your aspirations and others' reactions to them for the Writing Connection on page 429. What do you think you would you do if you met with the kind of resistance Wright encountered?

5. Do you think the aspirations of African Americans and other minorities are still limited by society? Give evidence to support your answer.

ANOTHER PATHWAY
Cooperative Learning
With a small group, make a list of events and influences in Wright's life that might have kept him from fulfilling his aspirations. Then make a list of items that might have helped him. Rank the items on each list, including character traits, in order of importance. Compare your rankings with those of other groups.

QUICKWRITES

1. Write a **letter of recommendation** for Wright to the college of his choice. The letter could come from you or from a character in the selection.

2. Write the **thoughts** that might have gone through the newspaper editor's mind as he talked to Wright and read his story.

3. Imagine that you have had a piece of writing published in a local newspaper. How might the people close to you react to your accomplishment? Write a brief **story**, describing those reactions as you imagine them.

 PORTFOLIO Save your writing. You may want to use it later as a springboard to a piece for your portfolio.

LITERARY CONCEPTS

Dialogue is conversation between two or more characters. Well-written dialogue not only moves a story forward but reveals the personalities of the speakers. Dialogue is a way to "show, not tell," because it presents a scene directly instead of simply summarizing it. In this excerpt from *Black Boy*, look for a passage of dialogue that you think is particularly effective. Explain what the passage tells you about one or both of the characters.

 CONCEPT REVIEW: Metaphor At the end of this excerpt, Wright compares his life to a train in several ways, creating an extended metaphor. Examine the details of this metaphor. Why does it seem appropriate? In what ways does Wright's life resemble a train?

BLACK BOY **435**

From Personal Response to Critical Analysis

1. Accept all reasonable responses.
2. Possible responses: Since nobody else in Wright's world wrote fiction or even read it, his classmates reacted negatively. Wright's family members, on the other hand, had religious reasons for being suspicious of fiction. His mother thought writing fiction might ruin his chances to get a good job; nobody expected an African-American boy to have such high aspirations.
3. Possible responses: He was a very determined person; he was imaginative and had a strong calling to be a writer.
4. Accept all reasonable responses.
5. Accept all reasonable, well-supported responses.

Another Pathway

Cooperative Learning One student can make sure that each item on the lists can be justified with facts from the selection. Have each student rank the items independently. Members can then compare rankings. One student can probe differences in opinion and ask others to justify their rankings. Another can integrate the ideas into a final ranking that everyone can agree on.

Rubric
3 Full Accomplishment Students classify positive and negative influences, agree on a ranking of the items, and give reasons to justify the ranking.
2 Substantial Accomplishment Students compile and rank their lists but have some difficulty supporting their ideas.
1 Little or Partial Accomplishment Students have difficulty classifying and ranking listed items or have difficulty forming lists at all.

Literary Concepts

Use TE annotations A, B, and C to help students analyze how dialogue is used to reveal character.

Metaphor Like a train, he is speeding toward a collision with cultural expectations. The warning lights and sirens are all the negative responses to his writing.

QuickWrites

1. Explain that a letter of recommendation should identify the writer's relationship to Wright and identify aspects of Wright's character and ability that would make him a successful college student.
2. Have students consider what aspects of Wright's personality and writing the editor might have found surprising or intriguing.
3. Have students identify three relatives or friends to include in their story. Tell them to make sure each person's dialogue reflects the way that person talks.

The Writer's Craft

Supporting Opinions, pp. 208–221
Personal Narrative, pp. 86–101

Alternative Activities

1. Tell students that the script for a skit should include only dialogue and stage directions. Remind students that the setting and each character's gestures and facial expressions are written in parentheses.
2. Students are probably well acquainted with rap but may not be as familiar with the blues. Popular artists who have recently recorded blues songs include Buddy Guy, Eric Clapton, B. B. King, and Robert Cray.

Words to Know

1. heedless
2. intuitively
3. alien
4. relent
5. naive
6. stifle
7. hedge
8. speculate
9. articulate
10. mode

Reteaching/Reinforcement
- *Unit Three Resource Book*, p. 46

Across the Curriculum

History Suggest that students use the topics *Jim Crow, segregation, racial discrimination,* and *civil rights movement* to research this topic in encyclopedias, library books, and online information searches. Historical figures to include in their searches include Rosa Parks, Martin Luther King, Jr., Thurgood Marshall, and Jackie Robinson.

ART GALLERY
Life in the South Many artists have used their experiences of living in the South as themes in their works. You may wish to use these images to generate discussion about the subjects their creators chose to depict.

Side A, Frame 49383

Multimodal Learning

ALTERNATIVE ACTIVITIES

1. In a small group, rewrite this excerpt as a **skit** and present it to the rest of the class.
2. Find or compose a blues or rap **song** that expresses Wright's feelings. Play your song for the class.

Multimodal Learning

ACROSS THE CURRICULUM

History Research Jim Crow laws and make a list of what facilities and activities the laws covered. Identify historical people who defied the laws and helped bring about their repeal. Present your findings in class as an oral report.

WORDS TO KNOW

Review the Words to Know at the bottom of the selection pages. Then write the vocabulary word that best completes each of the following sentences.

1. When Wright took his story to the newspaper, he was _____ of the difficulties he might face.
2. Although the newspaper editor laughed at him, Wright somehow knew _____ that the man was amused, not scornful.
3. Wright did not know what galleys were, because the world of publishing was _____ to him.
4. Even though Wright argued with him, the editor did not _____ and agree to pay Wright for the story.
5. Wright knew that it would have been _____ of him to believe that his writing would gain him quick wealth.
6. It seemed, at least at first, that more people wanted to _____ Wright's creativity than wanted to encourage it.
7. It was not completely truthful of Wright to _____ when his grandmother asked him questions about his story.
8. Some of Wright's relatives were upset by words he used in his writing and began to _____ about what was wrong with him.
9. Wright's classmates were not _____ enough to express clearly what they thought was wrong with what he was doing.
10. Wright thought that if he moved to the North, he might find a _____ of existence that was more to his liking.

436 UNIT THREE PART 2: ON YOUR OWN TERMS

RICHARD WRIGHT

1908–1960

The son of a sharecropper and a teacher, Richard Wright grew up in poverty in the South; *Black Boy* contains frequent references to the hunger that he had to endure while he was growing up. Wright's father deserted the family when Wright was young, and his mother worked as a cook to support her two sons. Because the family moved often and his mother became ill, Wright attended school irregularly.

After he left school, Wright worked at menial jobs, reading widely in his spare time. While living in Chicago and New York City, he began to get his stories and articles published in magazines. Recognition came to him with his first published book, *Uncle Tom's Children,* which consists of four long short stories. He then won a Guggenheim Fellowship and completed the novel *Native Son.* Considered by many a classic work of American literature, *Native Son* was a great success, and in 1941 Wright received the Spingarn Medal from the NAACP for his achievement. Later, in *American Hunger,* Wright continued the autobiography he had begun with *Black Boy.*

In 1947, Wright and his family moved to Paris, where he felt greater acceptance and freedom than in the United States. Wright became a French citizen, and though he traveled widely, France remained his home until his death.

OTHER WORKS *Twelve Million Black Voices; The Outsider; Black Power; White Man, Listen!*

Extended Reading

- ART GALLERY

RICHARD WRIGHT

Ironically, it was the Depression that led to Richard Wright's first important chance to write professionally. Through the Federal Writers' Project, Wright and other unemployed writers were hired to produce books that would give the country "a detailed portrait of itself." Soon afterward, Wright began receiving critical acclaim for his stories. Wright's novel *Native Son* sold a quarter of a million hardcover copies in its first month of publication in March of 1940. It was that month's Book-of-the-Month-Club selection—the first time a black writer's novel was featured—and headed the best seller list for several weeks.

436 THE LANGUAGE OF LITERATURE TEACHER'S EDITION

PREVIEWING

NONFICTION

Only Daughter
Sandra Cisneros (sĭz-nĕ´rôs)

Activating Prior Knowledge
PERSONAL CONNECTION

In recent decades, ideas about the proper roles of males and females have changed dramatically. No longer, for example, do many people think it odd for girls to be athletic and interested in sports. In a class discussion, share your thoughts about the roles of males and females today. Discuss gender roles at school, at home, and in the community.

Building Background
CULTURAL CONNECTION

In "Only Daughter," the Chicago-born writer Sandra Cisneros describes her father's ideas about the proper role of females. Coming from the culture of old Mexico, Cisneros's father holds the patriarchal beliefs of many traditional cultures—that is, he considers men the heads of families and the leaders of society. For him a woman needs only to "become someone's wife" and devote herself to her home and family.

Active Reading/Setting a Purpose
READING CONNECTION

Understanding Generalizations A generalization is a broad statement about a whole group. Valid generalizations are based on a wide range of evidence. "Edgar Allan Poe's short stories rarely contain humor," for instance, is a valid generalization when made by someone who has read many of Poe's stories. Notice, moreover, that the word *rarely* qualifies the statement, so that it is not claiming to be universally true.

Generalizations can be faulty if they are either overgeneralized (unsupported by backup evidence and, often, containing the word *all*) or stereotyped (based on fixed, unfair ideas about all members of ethnic, racial, or other groups). "Dogs are better pets than cats" and "Women can't repair cars" are examples of such faulty generalizations. As you read this selection, use a chart like the one shown here to judge the accuracy of the generalizations you find about females and their roles. Write each generalization in the first column, then put a check in one of the other columns to classify it.

Generalization	Valid	Over-generalized	Stereo-typed

ONLY DAUGHTER **437**

OVERVIEW

Objectives
- To understand and appreciate an essay that shows how a man's perception of his daughter changes
- To identify and understand theme
- To express understanding of the selection through a variety of writing forms, including a dialogue, a biographical sketch, and a proverb
- To extend understanding of the selection through a variety of multimodal and cross-curricular activities

Skills

LITERARY CONCEPTS
- Theme

GRAMMAR
- Using *who* and *whom*

SPEAKING, LISTENING, AND VIEWING
- Group discussion
- Oral presentation

PRINT AND MEDIA RESOURCES

UNIT THREE RESOURCE BOOK
Strategic Reading: Literature, p. 49
Vocabulary SkillBuilder, p. 50

GRAMMAR MINI-LESSONS
Transparencies, p. 19
Copymasters, p. 21

ACCESS FOR STUDENTS ACQUIRING ENGLISH
Selection Summaries
Reading Support

FORMAL ASSESSMENT
Selection Test, pp. 77–78
 Test Generator

 AUDIO LIBRARY
See Reference Card

 LASERLINKS
Author Background

INTERNET RESOURCES
McDougal Littell Literature Center at http://www.hmco.com/mcdougal/lit

THE LANGUAGE OF LITERATURE TEACHER'S EDITION **437**

Only Daughter

Sandra Cisneros

Student with Guitar (1975), Simon Samsonian. Oil on canvas, 52″ × 37″, private collection, New York.

Once, several years ago, when I was just starting out my writing career, I was asked to write my own contributor's note for an anthology I was part of. I wrote: "I am the only daughter in a family of six sons. *That* explains everything."

Well, I've thought about that ever since, and yes, it explains a lot to me, but for the reader's sake I should have written: "I am the only daughter in a *Mexican* family of six sons." Or even: "I am the only daughter of a Mexican farmer and a Mexican-American mother." Or: "I am the only daughter of a working-class family of nine." All of these had everything to do with who I am today.

I was/am the only daughter and *only* a daughter. Being an only daughter in a family of six sons forced me by circumstance to spend a lot of time by myself because my brothers felt it beneath them to play with a *girl* in public. But that aloneness, that loneliness, was good for a would-be writer— it allowed me time to think and think, to imagine, to read and prepare myself.

Being only a daughter for my father meant my destiny would

WORDS TO KNOW
anthology (ăn-thŏl′ə-jē) *n.* a collection of writings

lead me to become someone's wife. That's what he believed. But when I was in the fifth grade and shared my plans for college with him, I was sure he understood. I remember my father saying, "Que bueno, mi'ja,¹ that's good." That meant a lot to me, especially since my brothers thought the idea hilarious. What I didn't realize was that my father thought college was good for girls—good for finding a husband. After four years in college and two more in graduate school and still no husband, my father shakes his head even now and says I wasted all that education.

In retrospect, I'm lucky my father believed daughters were meant for husbands. It meant it didn't matter if I majored in something silly like English. After all, I'd find a nice professional eventually, right? This allowed me the liberty to putter about <u>embroidering</u> my little poems and stories without my father interrupting with so much as a "What's that you're writing?"

But the truth is, I wanted him to interrupt. I wanted my father to understand what it was I was scribbling, to introduce me as "My only daughter, the writer." Not as "This is only my daughter. She teaches." *Es maestra*²—teacher. Not even *profesora.*³

In a sense, everything I have ever written has been for him, to win his approval even though I know my father can't read English words, even though my father's only reading includes the brown-ink *Esto* sports magazines from Mexico City and the bloody *¡Alarma!* magazines that feature yet another sighting of *La Virgen de Guadalupe*⁴ on a tortilla or a wife's revenge on her philandering⁵ husband by bashing his skull in with a *molcajete*⁶ (a kitchen mortar⁷ made of volcanic rock). Or the *fotonovelas,*⁸ the little picture paperbacks with tragedy and <u>trauma</u> erupting from the characters' mouths in bubbles.

My father represents, then, the public majority. A public who is disinterested in reading, and yet one whom I am writing about and for and privately trying to woo.

When we were growing up in Chicago, we moved a lot because of my father. He suffered bouts of <u>nostalgia</u>. Then we'd have to let go our flat, store the furniture with mother's relatives, load the station wagon with baggage and bologna sandwiches, and head south. To Mexico City.

We came back, of course. To yet another Chicago flat, another Chicago neighborhood, another Catholic school. Each time, my father would seek out the parish priest in order to get a tuition break and complain or boast: "I have seven sons."

He meant *siete hijos,*⁹ seven children, but he translated it as "sons." "I have seven sons." To anyone who would listen. The Sears Roebuck employee who sold us the washing machine. The short-order cook where my father ate his ham-and-eggs breakfasts. "I have seven sons." As if he deserved a medal from the state.

My papa. He didn't mean anything by that mistranslation, I'm sure. But somehow I could feel myself being erased. I'd tug my father's sleeve and whisper: "Not seven sons. Six! and *one daughter.*"

---

1. *Que bueno, mi'ja* (kĕ bwĕ′nô mē′hä) *Spanish:* That's good, my daughter. (*Mi'ja* is a shortened form of *mi hija*.)
2. *Es maestra* (ĕs mä-ĕs′trä) *Spanish:* She is a teacher.
3. *profesora* (prô-fĕ-sô′rä) *Spanish:* professor.
4. *La Virgen de Guadalupe* (lä vēr′hĕn dĕ gwä-dä-lōō′pĕ) *Spanish:* the Virgin of Guadalupe. According to legend, a vision of Mary, the virgin mother of Jesus, appeared on a hill outside Mexico City in 1531.
5. **philandering:** engaging in many casual love affairs.
6. *molcajete* (môl-kä-hĕ′tĕ) *Spanish.*
7. **mortar:** a bowl for grinding up grain.
8. *fotonovelas* (fô-tô-nô-vĕ′läs) *Spanish.*
9. *siete hijos* (syĕ′tĕ ē′hôs) *Spanish.* (*Hijos* can mean either "children" or "sons.")

WORDS TO KNOW

embroider (ĕm-broi′dər) *v.* to add imaginative details to; ornament
trauma (trou′mə) *n.* a serious physical or emotional shock or injury
nostalgia (nŏ-stăl′jə) *n.* a bittersweet longing for something or someone in the past

439

Mini-Lesson Grammar

USING WHO AND WHOM Tell students that the words *who* and *whom* can be used to introduce clauses. *Who* is in the nominative case, and it is used as a subject. *Whom* is in the objective case and must be used when the sentence requires an object. Use the information on the chalkboard at the right to help students differentiate between these pronouns.

Application Have students choose the correct pronoun for each sentence.
1. Sandra Cisneros is a writer (who/whom) describes growing up in a Latino family. *(who)*
2. She is a writer (who/whom) I admire. *(whom)*
3. Her family, of (who/whom) she writes fondly, is a large, closely knit one. *(whom)*

Reteaching/Reinforcement
- Grammar Handbook, anthology pp. 915–916
- Grammar Mini-Lessons copymasters p. 21, transparencies p. 19

 The Writer's Craft

Who and Whom, p. 573

Critical Thinking:
MAKING INFERENCES

D Ask students to infer how Cisneros's emotions have changed from the beginning of this passage to the end. *(Possible responses: She was probably nervous at first, then excited that her father was willing to read her story; she was worried about how he would react, then happy with his response.)*

Literary Concept: THEME

E Ask students why a parent's response to a child's success can matter more than winning prizes. *(Possible response: We want the people we love and respect to feel the same way about us.)*

STRATEGIC READING FOR
Less-Proficient Readers

F Have students explain why, after her father reads her story, she says that it was the most wonderful thing that happened to her that year. *(She finally has her father's approval for her writing.)*
Making Inferences/Summarizing

COMPREHENSION CHECK
Have students indicate whether the statement is true or false.
1. Cisneros's father had high career aspirations for her. *(F)*
2. Her writing was motivated by her anger at her father. *(F)*
3. She finally won her father's approval of her writing. *(T)*

When my oldest brother graduated from medical school, he <u>fulfilled</u> my father's dream that we study hard and use this—our heads, instead of this—our hands. Even now my father's hands are thick and yellow, stubbed by a history of hammer and nails and twine and coils and springs. "Use this," my father said, tapping his head, "and not this," showing us those hands. He always looked tired when he said it.

Wasn't college an investment? And hadn't I spent all those years in college? And if I didn't marry, what was it all for? Why would anyone go to college and then choose to be poor? Especially someone who had always been poor.

Last year, after ten years of writing professionally, the financial rewards started to trickle in. My second National Endowment for the Arts Fellowship.[10] A guest professorship at the University of California, Berkeley. My book, which sold to a major New York publishing house.

At Christmas, I flew home to Chicago. The house was throbbing, same as always; hot *tamales*[11] and sweet *tamales* hissing in my mother's pressure cooker, and everybody—my mother, six brothers, wives, babies, aunts, cousins—talking too loud and at the same time, like in a Fellini[12] film, because that's just how we are.

I went upstairs to my father's room. One of my stories had just been translated into Spanish and published in an anthology of Chicano[13] writing, and I wanted to show it to him. Ever since he recovered from a stroke two years ago, my father likes to spend his leisure hours horizontally. And that's how I found him, watching a Pedro Infante[14] movie on Galavisión[15] and eating rice pudding.

There was a glass filmed with milk on the bedside table. There were several vials of pills and balled Kleenex. And on the floor, one black sock and a plastic urinal that I didn't want to look at but looked at anyway. Pedro Infante was about to burst into song, and my father was laughing.

I'm not sure if it was because my story was translated into Spanish or because it was published in Mexico or perhaps because the story dealt with Tepeyac,[16] the *colonia* my father was raised in and the house he grew up in, but at any rate, my father punched the mute button on his remote control and read my story.

I sat on the bed next to my father and waited. He read it very slowly. As if he were reading each line over and over. He laughed at all the right places and read lines he liked out loud. He pointed and asked questions: "Is this So-and-so?"

"Yes," I said. He kept reading.

When he was finally finished, after what seemed like hours, my father looked up and asked: "Where can we get more copies of this for the relatives?"

Of all the wonderful things that happened to me last year, that was the most wonderful. ❖

---

10. **National Endowment for the Arts Fellowship:** The National Endowment for the Arts (NEA)—a U.S. government agency—awards money in the form of fellowships to artists and writers.
11. *tamales* (tä-mä′lĕs) *Spanish:* rolls of cornmeal dough filled with meat and peppers and steamed in cornhusk wrappings.
12. **Fellini:** the Italian movie director Federico Fellini (1920–1994), famous for his noisy, energetic films.
13. **Chicano:** Mexican-American.
14. **Pedro Infante:** a popular Mexican film star.
15. **Galavisión:** a cable TV network that features movies and programs in Spanish.
16. **Tepeyac** (tĕ-pĕ-yäk′): a district of Mexico City.

WORDS TO KNOW
fulfill (fŏŏl-fĭl′) *v.* to achieve; make a reality

Critic's Corner

"sensitive, alert, nuanceful . . . rich with music and picture."

Gwendolyn Brooks,
describing the writing of Sandra Cisneros

Ask students what nuances they notice in the author's description of the father's response to Cisneros's story.

RESPONDING OPTIONS

FROM PERSONAL RESPONSE TO CRITICAL ANALYSIS

REFLECT 1. How did this selection affect you? Jot down your thoughts in your notebook and share them with a classmate.

RETHINK 2. Look over the chart of generalizations that you made for the Reading Connection on page 437. How might those generalizations have affected Sandra Cisneros as she was growing up?

3. Why do you think Cisneros says that everything she has ever written has been written to win her father's approval?
Consider
Close Textual Reading
- her role in her home as she was growing up
- her father's attitude toward her and her writing

Thematic Link 4. In what ways has Cisneros lived her life on her own terms?

RELATE 5. How important is your own need for approval from your parents?

6. Think back to the class discussion about the roles of males and females for the Personal Connection on page 437. What, if any, generalizations about gender roles are still common?

ANOTHER PATHWAY

What if Cisneros's father were to write his own "Only Daughter" essay, on the subject of his daughter's upbringing? How might his viewpoint differ from his daughter's? Make notes on what you think his feelings toward his only daughter might be, his reasons for raising her as he did, and his opinion of her accomplishments. Then compare your ideas with those of your classmates.

QUICKWRITES

1. Imagine that you are the young Cisneros and your father has just bragged to a salesclerk that he has seven sons. Write a **dialogue** between you and your father, in which you politely but forcefully correct him.

2. Based on the information in this selection, write your own **biographical sketch** of Sandra Cisneros.

3. Write a **proverb**—a short, wise saying that expresses a basic truth—about a kind of approval that children seek from their parents.

📁 **PORTFOLIO** Save your writing. You may want to use it later as a springboard to a piece for your portfolio.

LITERARY CONCEPTS

As you may recall, a story's **theme** is an idea about life or human nature that the story conveys. Even though "Only Daughter" is nonfiction, it is still a story that Sandra Cisneros tells. What idea about life do you think she wants the reader to understand? In one or two sentences, state what you feel the theme of "Only Daughter" is.

ONLY DAUGHTER **441**

From Personal Response to Critical Analysis

1. Accept all reasonable responses.
2. Possible response: Students may say that the father's opinion—that a girl's only destiny is to become a wife—may have caused her to feel less important than her brothers and may have made her want to prove something to her father.
3. Possible response: Because of her father's attitude about girls, she wanted to do something to show him she was not just a daughter but rather was someone capable of doing something other than finding a husband. She became a writer.
4. Possible response: Despite her father's expectations for her, Cisneros achieved her dream.
5. Accept all reasonable responses.
6. Accept all reasonable, well-supported responses.

Another Pathway

Have students look in the selection for clues to the father's feelings, viewpoint, and opinions.

Rubric

3 Full Accomplishment Students make reasonable inferences about the father's viewpoint and use evidence from the selection to support their ideas.

2 Substantial Accomplishment Students make inferences but have difficulty finding evidence from the selection to support them.

1 Little or Partial Accomplishment Students have difficulty inferring the father's viewpoint.

Literary Concepts

Use annotations B and D to help students analyze theme. Theme statements should focus on how parents' expectations influence their children. Possible responses: Trying to win a parent's approval can be a strong motivating force in life. Parents need to recognize all of their children's achievements.

QuickWrites

1. Pairs of students might act out this situation and improvise dialogue together.
2. Sketches should include such information as Cisneros's family history, childhood years, and later accomplishments.
3. Refer students to the theme statements they generated in the Literary Concept activity before having them draft proverbs. Then have them consider examples such as "Don't count your chickens before they are hatched" and "A stitch in time saves nine."

Using Dialogue Effectively, pp. 434–436

Literary Links

Possible response: Cisneros's father had few aspirations for her, so she was allowed to pursue her education and her dream of writing. On the other hand, Wright's family actively criticized him and discouraged him from writing.

Words to Know

1. embroider
2. fulfilled
3. trauma
4. anthology
5. nostalgia

Reteaching/Reinforcement
- *Unit Three Resource Book,* p. 50

Across the Curriculum

History Help students brainstorm a list of specific questions to ask, such as *Were boys and girls expected to participate in sports? Were boys and girls expected to get an education or a job?* Review note-taking techniques and suggest that students consider tape-recording their interviews.

Social Studies *Cooperative Learning* Students can each research a different culture and then compare their results in a group discussion. One student can make sure that generalizations are supported with evidence. Another student can point out areas where additional research is needed. A third can summarize and record similarities and differences among the cultures.

AUTHOR BACKGROUND
Sandra Cisneros The author speaks about her life and her use of Hispanic characters and settings in her works.

Side A, Frame 22282

Multimodal Learning

ACROSS THE CURRICULUM

History Interview any older relatives to find out the ideas about gender roles that were common when they were growing up. Share with your classmates how ideas have changed in one or two generations.

Social Studies *Cooperative Learning* With a small group of classmates, investigate differences in gender roles in different cultures of the world. For example, you might consider Japan, India, and Saudi Arabia.

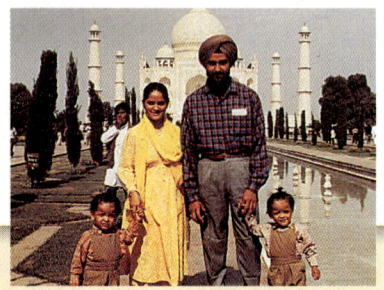

Indian family in front of the Taj Mahal

LITERARY LINKS

Compare Cisneros's father's reactions to her aspirations with the ways in which Richard Wright's family reacts to his aspirations in the excerpt from *Black Boy.*

WORDS TO KNOW

Review the Words to Know at the bottom of the selection pages. Then read each book title below and write the vocabulary word that you would expect to find in that book.

1. *Tall Tales and How to Tell Them*
2. *You Can Make Your Dreams Come True*
3. *First Aid on the Battlefield*
4. *The Best Short Stories of the Nineties*
5. *The Good Old Days and Why We Miss Them*

SANDRA CISNEROS

1954–

Books and writing define Sandra Cisneros's life. As a shy child she escaped into her reading. One biographer learned that the young Cisneros "viewed her life as a story in which she was the main character manipulated by a romantic narrator."

Cisneros wrote secretly at home, openly expressing her creativity only in high school. She later graduated from college and in the late 1970s enrolled in the Iowa Writers' Workshop, where she found herself an outsider. "My classmates . . . had been bred as fine hothouse flowers," she has said. "I was a yellow weed among the city's cracks." This realization about being different from others in her writing classes lead to Cisneros' finding her own literary voice: "I knew I was a Mexican woman. . . . My race, my gender, my class! That's when I decided I would write about something my classmates couldn't write about."

What she wrote first was *The House on Mango Street,* a series of 44 related stories told by Esperanza Cordero, a young girl growing up in a Latino neighborhood of Chicago. The book, considered by some a novel and by others a collection of prose poems, has been read by students in classes ranging from Chicano studies to psychology. Since then, Cisneros has worked as a teacher and a poet-in-residence at schools. She remains "nobody's mother and nobody's wife."

OTHER WORKS "My Lucy Friend Who Smells Like Corn," "Three Wise Guys," "Bums in the Attic"

Extended Reading

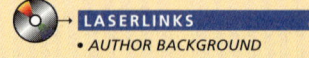
• AUTHOR BACKGROUND

Alternative Activities

Have each student research the childhood of a favorite author. Have them answer the following questions about the authors: *When did he or she decide to become a writer? What encouragement or discouragement did the writer receive from his or her family?* If students have difficulty deciding on an author, you might suggest Louisa May Alcott, Charles Dickens, Mark Twain, Alice Walker, or any author in the first three units of this book whose work students especially enjoyed. Have students present their findings to the class in informal speeches, which should include biographical information as well as the students' opinions of the writers' work.

PREVIEWING

POETRY

Theme for English B
Langston Hughes

The Writer
Richard Wilbur

Activating Prior Knowledge/Setting a Purpose
PERSONAL CONNECTION

Each of the two poems you are about to read focuses on the struggle of a young writer. Since you are a young writer too, think about your own experiences with the writing process—both its difficulties and its pleasures. In your notebook, briefly describe these experiences and your reactions to them. Then share some of your ideas with your classmates. As you read, compare your experiences with writing with the experiences described in the poems.

Building Background
PROFESSIONAL CONNECTION

The activity of writing has its own joys and frustrations. Even famous writers often struggle painfully with their craft. Richard Wilbur, for example, has said that he sometimes spends years writing one poem. All writers really face the same challenge—finding something to say and the right words to say it. Part of this challenge is to develop a distinct voice, an individual manner of expression. Listen for the personal voice in each of these two poems.

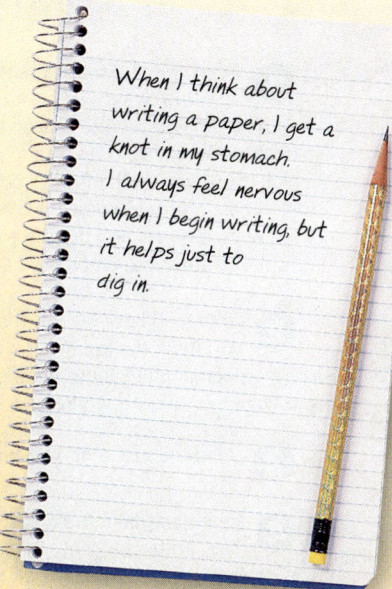

OVERVIEW

Objectives

- To understand and appreciate two poems that reveal the artistic struggles of two young writers
- To examine stanza form and compare it to other kinds of poetic structure
- To compare the diction of two poets
- To express understanding of the poems through a choice of writing forms, including an evaluation, a poem, and a personal narrative
- To extend understanding of the selection through a variety of multimodal and cross-curricular activities

Skills

LITERARY CONCEPTS
- Stanza form
- Free verse

THE WRITER'S STYLE
- Diction
- Vivid verbs

READING SKILLS/ STRATEGIES
- Movies of the mind

SPEAKING, LISTENING, AND VIEWING
- Group discussion
- Oral interpretation

Thematic Link: *On Your Own Terms*
Two young writers struggle in their own ways to write something that expresses their true selves.

ALTERNATIVE
Previewing

Students can choose partners and use the following discussion prompts to preview the two poems orally instead of writing in their notebooks.

Personal Connection

Discussion Prompts

- *Describe a time when you had trouble getting started on a writing project. What strategies did you use to solve the problem?*
- *How did your writing turn out in the end?*

As students read the poems have them compare their struggles to create with those of the young writers in the poems.

PRINT AND MEDIA RESOURCES

UNIT THREE RESOURCE BOOK
Strategic Reading: Literature, p. 53

WRITING MINI-LESSONS
Transparencies, p. 46

ACCESS FOR STUDENTS ACQUIRING ENGLISH
Selection Summaries
Reading Support

FORMAL ASSESSMENT
Selection Test, pp. 79–80
 Test Generator

 AUDIO LIBRARY
See Reference Card

 LASERLINKS
Author Background

INTERNET RESOURCES
McDougal Littell Literature Center at http://www.hmco.com/mcdougal/lit

Reading Connection

Discussion Prompts Read each section of the poem aloud, instead of having students read the poem on their own. Then ask students to share their responses to the questions in steps 1–3 orally. For step 4, have students read the poem silently and then freewrite their final responses to the poem.

CUSTOMIZING FOR
Gifted and Talented Students

Invite students to find examples of vivid verbs in the two poems. Have them discuss the ways in which these verbs contribute to the imagery in the poems.

CUSTOMIZING FOR
Less-Proficient Readers

Explain to students that each poem presents the story of a young writer struggling to find his or her own voice.

Set a Purpose Have students read to find out who the writers are and what they are writing.

Use **UNIT THREE RESOURCE BOOK,** p. 53, for guidance in reading the selection.

Active Reading
READING CONNECTION

Movies of the Mind

Reading is an active process in which your mind is constantly making sense of what you "take in" from the printed page. However, what you read last can change your impression of what you had read earlier. For example, you may like a character better at the end of a story than you did at the beginning. A surprise ending can even make you rethink your reaction to a whole story. Many times, you're not aware of how much you change your mind.

One way to understand the process of reading is to think of your mind as a video camera with a personality—yours. In this exercise you will turn the video camera down to slow motion and look at what's going on in your mind as you read. Just as athletes improve their moves by watching videos of themselves in action, you can improve your reading skills by becoming aware of how your mind works when you read a poem.

STEP 1 Read lines 1–15 of "Theme for English B." Then stop. Take a few minutes to freewrite what was going on in your mind as you were reading the lines and afterward, when you tried to make sense of the words. What does the poem mean to you so far? What ideas, sounds, and pictures stand out in your mind? What did the lines make you feel, think of, or remember?

Sometimes, your mind draws a blank during a first reading. If this happens, read the lines a few more times and then freewrite your response. Write down any words or phrases that stump you, and record any frustration or impatience you feel.

STEP 2 Now read lines 16–24, then stop. Freewrite your response again. What do you think the poem is saying? Has there been anything that you particularly like in the poem so far? Try to be as specific and as honest as you can. Your goal is to record how your mind is working.

STEP 3 Read the rest of the poem (lines 25–41) and freewrite your response.

STEP 4 Read the poem from start to finish at least two more times. You may have new insights when you read the poem as a whole, or you may just feel more certain of what you thought before. In any case, be sure to freewrite your response.

By reading over your responses to the poem, you will be able to examine your own personal process of reading. Did you change your mind about the poem's meaning at any point during the exercise? When did your understanding of the poem become clear? What did you learn about yourself by studying the process of your own mind?

Using Your Reading Log Do all your freewriting for this exercise in your reading log so that you can compare your experience of reading poetry with the experiences of reading fiction that you have been recording. Then, as you read the poem "The Writer," stop after line 9, after line 15, and at the end to freewrite your responses.

444 UNIT THREE PART 2: ON YOUR OWN TERMS

Theme for English B

Langston Hughes

Portrait of Langston Hughes (about 1925), Winold Reiss. National Portrait Gallery, Smithsonian Institution/Art Resource. Copyright © National Portrait Gallery, Washington, D.C.

The instructor said,

    Go home and write
    a page tonight.
    And let that page come out of you—
5   Then, it will be true.

    I wonder if it's that simple?

    I am twenty-two, colored, born in Winston-Salem.
    I went to school there, then Durham,[1] then here
    to this college on the hill above Harlem.[2]
10   I am the only colored student in my class.

---
1. **Winston-Salem . . . Durham:** cities in North Carolina.
2. **this college on the hill above Harlem:** Columbia University in New York City. Harlem, a district in upper Manhattan, is home to an important African-American community.

Art Note

Langston Hughes by Winold Reiss Reiss (1886–1953) was a German painter who immigrated to the United States in 1913. In the 1920s he began painting portraits of African-American leaders of the Harlem Renaissance.

Reading the Art Do the decorative designs in the background add to your enjoyment of the picture or distract you from the subject? How do they relate to the subject?

CUSTOMIZING FOR
Students Acquiring English

- Use **ACCESS FOR STUDENTS ACQUIRING ENGLISH**, *Reading Support*.
- "Theme for English B" is written in simple, everyday English and should not be difficult for students. "The Writer" contains extended metaphors that may require explanation.

Literary Concept: FREE VERSE

A Point out to students that lines 2–5 have a regular pattern of rhythm and rhyme, but the rest of the poem does not. Then help them analyze the meter and the *aabb* rhyme scheme of lines 2–5. Ask them to look for a similar pattern elsewhere in the poem. *(There is none.)* Finally, have students find other rhyming lines in the poem. *(lines 18 and 20, 27 and 28, 35, 36, 37, and 41)*

Linking to History

B Tell students that the word *colored* was the term used to identify African Americans in the early decades of the 20th century.

Mini-Lesson   Literary Concepts

REVIEWING FREE VERSE Remind students that free verse is poetry without regular patterns of rhyme and meter—poetry that sounds like everyday conversation. Have students read lines 1–6 of "Theme for English B" and help them analyze the rhythm and rhyme. Help students conclude that the poem is written in free verse.

Application Have students read "The Writer" aloud. Then have them tell whether or not it is written in free verse *(yes)*. Then ask students what elements make the poem free verse. *(Even though it is in stanza form, it has no regular pattern of rhythm and rhyme. It also has a conversational tone.)*

Literary Concept: RHYME

C Point out to students that in addition to the rhymes at the ends of the lines in this section, there are also internal rhymes—that is, rhymes within the lines. Have students identify these internal rhymes and discuss what effect they have on the poem. *(Possible response: The internal rhymes create a bouncing, lilting rhythm.)*

CUSTOMIZING FOR
Students Acquiring English

I Students may have difficulty comprehending this complicated sentence. Help them paraphrase it in simpler terms. *(Possible response: African Americans like me often like the same things that people of other races like.)*

From Personal Response to Critical Analysis

1. Accept all reasonable responses.
2. Possible responses: The speaker is honest (lines 21 and 35), introspective (line 16 on), open-minded about music and racial differences (lines 24–26), and optimistic (lines 37–38).
3. Possible responses: Some students might say yes, because the speaker told about his life and what he enjoyed and examined a deeply personal issue about his racial identity. Others might say no, because the speaker should have focused more deeply on one or two things instead of listing so many.
4. Possible responses: Some students might conclude that black culture and white culture influence each other in many ways. Others might not agree saying that people of different races and ethnic groups have isolated themselves so that they don't have to interact.

The steps from the hill lead down into Harlem,
through a park, then I cross St. Nicholas,
Eighth Avenue, Seventh, and I come to the Y,
the Harlem Branch Y, where I take the elevator
15 up to my room, sit down, and write this page:

It's not easy to know what is true for you or me
at twenty-two, my age. But I guess I'm what
I feel and see and hear. Harlem, I hear you:
hear you, hear me—we two—you, me talk on this page.
20 (I hear New York, too.) Me—who?

Well, I like to eat, sleep, drink, and be in love.
I like to work, read, learn, and understand life.
I like a pipe for a Christmas present,
or records—Bessie, bop, or Bach.³

---
3. **Bessie, bop, or Bach:** Bessie Smith was a leading jazz and blues singer of the 1920s and early 1930s. Bop is a style of jazz that became popular in the 1940s. Johann Sebastian Bach was an 18th-century German composer of classical music.

25 I guess being colored doesn't make me not like
the same things other folks like who are other races.
So will my page be colored that I write?
Being me, it will not be white.
But it will be
30 a part of you, instructor.
You are white—
yet a part of me, as I am a part of you.
That's American.
Sometimes perhaps you don't want to be a part of me.
35 Nor do I often want to be a part of you.
But we are, that's true!
As I learn from you,
I guess you learn from me—
although you're older—and white—
40 and somewhat more free.

This is my page for English B.

FROM PERSONAL RESPONSE TO CRITICAL ANALYSIS

REFLECT 1. What did you like most about this poem? Share your reaction with your classmates.

RETHINK 2. What is your impression of the poem's speaker? Point to lines in the poem that support your ideas.

Thematic Link 3. Do you think the poem is "true" in the sense that the instructor meant? Why or why not?
   Consider
   Close Textual Reading
   • the instructions "And let that page come out of you" (line 4)
   • the personal information that the speaker reveals

4. Do you agree that the speaker and the instructor are part of each other, whether they want to be or not? Explain the reasons for your opinion.

446 UNIT THREE PART 2: ON YOUR OWN TERMS

Multicultural Perspectives

JAZZ Langston Hughes sought to capture the rhythms of jazz in his poetry. Jazz is a style of music noted for its syncopated beat, "blue" or flatted notes, and its tradition of improvisation. Jazz music is an important contribution to the culture of the United States by African Americans. Its roots are in the early spiritual and gospel songs dating back to the era of slavery. Several early musical styles contributed to the development of jazz—ragtime, a syncopated, energetic kind of music, and the blues, music known for its mournful scale and simple, repeated harmonies. It was during the 1920s that musicians like Benny Goodman, Bix Beiderbecke, and Fletcher Henderson helped popularize jazz music. In the 1940s musicians such as Dizzy Gillespie, Charlie Parker, Bud Powell, and Thelonius Monk began experimenting with more complicated melodies and chord patterns. They pioneered the bebop, or bop, style of jazz. In the late 1940s came the cool style of jazz, which had a more even beat. Recently, musicians have blended the electronic rhythms of rock with jazz to create the new style called fusion jazz.

The Writer

Richard Wilbur

Painted pottery typewriter, Adrián Luis González. Photo by David Lavender.

In her room at the prow[1] of the house
Where light breaks, and the windows are tossed with linden,[2]
My daughter is writing a story.

I pause in the stairwell, hearing
From her shut door a commotion of typewriter-keys
Like a chain hauled over a gunwale.[3]

Young as she is, the stuff
Of her life is a great cargo, and some of it heavy:
I wish her a lucky passage.

But now it is she who pauses,
As if to reject my thought and its easy figure.[4]
A stillness greatens, in which

The whole house seems to be thinking,
And then she is at it again with a bunched clamor
Of strokes, and again is silent.

---

1. **prow:** the forward part of a ship.
2. **linden:** a shade tree with heart-shaped leaves.
3. **gunwale** (gŭn′əl): the upper edge of the side of a ship.
4. **figure:** figure of speech (such as a simile or metaphor).

Critic's Corner

"What a poem like 'The Writer' stresses, finally . . . is how tentative any poetic position must be if the poet wishes to remain truly open to the mystery and wonders of life."

Robert Richman
New York Times Book Review, May 29, 1988

Ask students how they think Wilbur's metaphors explore the mystery and wonders of life.

CUSTOMIZING FOR
Students Acquiring English

2 Explain that a *sash* in this context is part of a window.

Literary Concept: IMAGERY

G Ask students what sensory words the poet uses to help readers visualize the starling. *(sleek, wild, dark, iridescent, humped, bloody)*

STRATEGIC READING FOR
Less-Proficient Readers

H Ask students what wish the father makes for his daughter at the beginning of the poem. *(He wishes her a safe passage.)* Noting Relevant Details

---

COMPREHENSION CHECK

1. In "The Writer" what is the extended metaphor? *(The writer's comparison of his daughter's writing to a ship preparing for a journey.)*
2. In "Theme for English B" what are some of the things the speaker likes? *(He likes to sleep, eat, drink, be in love. He also likes music and New York.)*
3. In "The Writer" what is the speaker's daughter trying to write? *(a story)*

INSIGHT

1. Do you think trying to write is as hard a creative struggle as trying to draw? Explain your answer. *(Answers will vary.)*
2. How do you think the maxim "Life is short, art is long" applies to "Theme for English B" and "The Writer"? *(Creating art is hard work, requiring time and dedication.)*

ISABELLE C. CHANG

Isabelle Chang was born in Boston in 1924. She is a librarian and writer who has traveled around the world. Her books include *Chinese Fairy Tales*, *Tales of the Far East*, and *Tales from Old China*.

I remember the dazed starling
Which was trapped in that very room, two years ago;
2 How we stole in, lifted a sash

And retreated, not to affright[5] it;
20 And how for a helpless hour, through the crack of the door,
We watched the sleek, wild, dark

G And iridescent creature
Batter against the brilliance, drop like a glove
To the hard floor, or the desk-top,

25 And wait then, humped and bloody,
For the wits to try it again; and how our spirits
Rose when, suddenly sure,

It lifted off from a chair-back,
Beating a smooth course for the right window
30 And clearing the sill of the world.

It is always a matter, my darling,
Of life or death, as I had forgotten. I wish
H What I wished you before, but harder.

---

5. **affright:** scare.

INSIGHT

The Artist A Chinese Fable
Isabelle C. Chang

There was once a king who loved the graceful curves of the rooster. He asked the court artist to paint a picture of a rooster for him. For one year he waited, and still this order was not fulfilled. In a rage, he stomped into the artist's studio and demanded to see the artist.

Quickly the artist brought out paper, paint, and brush. In five minutes a perfect picture of a rooster emerged from his skillful brush. The king turned purple with anger, saying, "If you can paint a perfect picture of a rooster in five minutes, why did you keep me waiting for over a year?"

"Come with me," begged the artist. He led the king to his storage room. Paper was piled from the floor to the ceiling. On every sheet was a painting of a rooster.

"Your Majesty," explained the artist, "it took me more than a year to learn how to paint a perfect rooster in five minutes."

Life is short, art is long.

---

448 UNIT THREE PART 2: ON YOUR OWN TERMS

Mini-Lesson The Writer's Style

USING VIVID VERBS Point out to students the verbs *stole* in Line 18 and *retreated* in Line 19 in the poem. Ask students why the writer used these verbs instead of the verb *went*. *(Possible responses: The verbs he used are more vivid; stole suggests sneaking in and retreated suggests trying to get out before the bird sees them and panics.)* Tell students that vivid verbs help readers picture in their minds the actions being described.

Application In each sentence, have students replace the verb *went* with a more vivid verb.

1. The little boy went happily down the sidewalk. *(skipped)*
2. The snake went slowly over the sand. *(slithered)*
3. An old dilapidated car went past our house. *(clanked)*

Reteaching/Reinforcement
- *Writing Handbook,* anthology p. 945
- *Writing Mini-Lessons* transparencies p. 46

Using Vivid Action Verbs, p. 585

RESPONDING OPTIONS

FROM PERSONAL RESPONSE TO CRITICAL ANALYSIS

REFLECT
1. How did you react to "The Writer"? Share your reaction with your classmates.

RETHINK
Close Textual Reading
2. Think about the similarities between the speaker's daughter and the bird described in lines 16–30. How are the daughter's efforts to write like the trapped starling's efforts to escape the room?

Close Textual Reading
3. In the first three stanzas, the poet develops an extended metaphor involving a ship. Explain how the daughter's act of writing a story is like a ship's beginning a voyage.

4. Reread what you wrote for the Personal Connection on page 443. Does the ship metaphor or the speaker's recollection of the starling more closely reflect your own experiences with writing? Explain your response.

RELATE
5. Discuss the similarities and the differences between the situations of the daughter in "The Writer" and the student in "Theme for English B." Which situation do you more often find yourself in?

Thematic Link
6. What similar ideas about the creative struggle do you find in "Theme for English B," "The Writer," and the Insight selection "The Artist"?

Multimodal Learning
ANOTHER PATHWAY

With your classmates, discuss the exercise you completed for the Reading Connection on page 444. Volunteer to read part or all of what you recorded as your "movie of the mind," and compare your reading process with those of your classmates. Discuss specifically what you learned about the poems and about yourself from the exercise. Did you enjoy the exercise?

QUICKWRITES

1. Imagine you are the instructor in "Theme for English B." Give a **grade** for and **comments** about the speaker's theme.

2. Follow the instructor's directions in "Theme for English B," writing a **page**—poetry or prose—that comes out of you. If you are writing poetry on a computer, you can easily experiment with line lengths and stanza formats.

📁 **PORTFOLIO** Save your writing. You may want to use it later as a springboard to a piece for your portfolio.

LITERARY CONCEPTS

A **stanza** is a grouping of two or more lines in a pattern that is repeated throughout a poem. Often, the stanzas of a poem share a rhythm and rhyme scheme. In some poems, stanzas function the way paragraphs do in prose. "The Writer" is written in stanzas, whereas "Theme for English B" is not. Read the two poems aloud, paying attention to the ways in which they differ in sound and feeling. Then discuss these differences in class. Explain which kind of structure you prefer to read and which you prefer to write.

THEME FOR ENGLISH B/THE WRITER   **449**

From Personal Response to Critical Analysis

1. Accept all reasonable responses.
2. Possible responses: Students may answer that the daughter's pause in writing suggests that she is trapped like the starling, not knowing how to reach what she wants to attain.
3. Possible responses: Students may say the sound of the typewriter keys is reminiscent of a ship pulling up its chain before it begins its voyage. Others may say that she is like the captain sitting at the prow looking out the window of her room anticipating her journey.
4. Accept all reasonable responses.
5. Possible response: The student in "Theme for English B" says he's not sure what to write, but his poem flows freely; the daughter in "The Writer" suffers from more stops and starts.
6. Possible response: Creating something worthwhile can be hard work and takes lots of patience and perseverance.

Another Pathway

Cooperative Learning One student can review the instructions and purpose of the assignment and suggest ways to keep the discussion on track. A second can clarify each speaker's ideas, while a third student differentiates between ideas so that everyone can compare them.

Rubric

3 Full Accomplishment Students cover each point in the instructions and offer reactions to the poem and the exercise.

2 Substantial Accomplishment Students cover each point in the instructions, but their responses are somewhat sketchy.

1 Little or Partial Accomplishment Students have difficulty covering all the points in the instructions.

Literary Concepts

Use annotation F (p. 447) to help students analyze the stanzas of "The Writer." Since both poems are in free verse, the differences are not great, but the ideas and feelings in "Theme for English B" tend to flow more freely, while those in "The Writer" shift from stanza to stanza.

QuickWrites

1. Have students review the directions that were given by the instructor in the first five lines of the poem. Ask students to evaluate the poem based on how well it fits the instructor's directions.
2. If students need help getting started, have them use Hughes's first five lines as the beginning of their own poem. Then have them consider what puzzles, fascinates, or troubles them the most in their lives.

📁 **The Writer's Craft**

Personal Response to Literature, pp. 238–249

THE LANGUAGE OF LITERATURE TEACHER'S EDITION **449**

Critic's Corner

Possible response: Students may say that Wilbur was very concerned about his daughter, that he very much wanted her to succeed as a writer, and that he identified with her struggle. All of these feelings come across very powerfully in the poem.

Literary Links

Possible response: The story Wright wrote as a child was fiction and was written more for fun. Hughes, on the other hand, wrote his poem for a writing class and struggled to make it reflect his true self.

Art Connection

Possible response: She might treasure it if it was a gift from her father because she is struggling to be a writer just as he is. Or, if her writing failed, she might hate being reminded of it.

Across the Curriculum

Music Suggest that interested students go to the public library to locate and listen to recordings of music by the artists or in the styles mentioned in Hughes's poem: the blues singer Bessie Smith, the baroque composer Johann Sebastian Bach, and jazz artists such as Charlie Parker, Dizzy Gillespie, and Thelonius Monk. Students can then discuss which artist or style they prefer and why.

Multimodal Learning

ALTERNATIVE ACTIVITIES

1. Create a **drawing, painting,** or **sculpture** inspired by your reading of these poems. Entitle it "The Struggling Writer."

2. **Cooperative Learning** With two or three other classmates, conduct a **poll** of your classmates to find out what kind of writing environment they like best. Would they rather write in a quiet room or have music playing? Do they like to write at the library or in their bedroom, at a desk or in bed? Present your results in a chart or graph.

CRITIC'S CORNER

Writing in the *Dictionary of Literary Biography*, the critic Richard J. Calhoun noted that although Richard Wilbur seldom reveals personal information in his poetry, he found the subject of this poem in his own family. According to Calhoun, "'The Writer' is one of Wilbur's most personal poems, and, even more important, perhaps one of his best." In what way do you think the personal connection helps to make this poem effective?

THE WRITER'S STYLE

Richard Wilbur has generally written traditional poetry, using established forms of stanzas, meter, and rhyme. Langston Hughes's poetry was more experimental, often based on jazz and blues rhythms. You have already looked at the differences in stanza structure in these two poems. Now compare the poets' choice of words, or **diction.** Which poem sounds more like conversation? Which is closer to what you usually expect a poem to be? Choose a few lines from the poems that clearly demonstrate their differences.

LITERARY LINKS

Like "Theme for English B," the excerpt from Richard Wright's *Black Boy* on page 429 deals with the struggles of a young African-American writer. How does Wright's experience differ from that of the speaker of "Theme for English B"?

ART CONNECTION

The work on page 447 is a painted clay typewriter by Mexican pottery-maker Adrían Luis González. The typewriter is small —less than five inches wide—and was a gift for his young daughter. How do you think the daughter in "The Writer" would react to getting such a gift?

Painted pottery typewriter, Adrían Luis González. Photo by David Lavender.

450 UNIT THREE PART 2: ON YOUR OWN TERMS

Alternative Activities

1. Students may want to use one of Richard Wilbur's metaphors as inspiration for their artwork: a ship setting out on a voyage or a trapped bird trying to escape out a window.

2. One or two students can conduct the poll. Another student can add up the results and make the graph. A third can present the results of the poll to the class.

The Writer's Style

Hughes's poem is more conversational, Wilbur's uses more "poetic" language. Students may choose almost any lines from the poems as examples of this difference. For more on diction and personal voice and style, see The Writer's Craft.

 The Writer's Craft

What Is Voice? pp. 405–407.

LANGSTON HUGHES

1902–1967

In his lifetime, Langston Hughes became both famous and well loved. He was known as a generous man who helped many young African-American writers get published. In the 1920s he became associated with the black arts movement known as the Harlem Renaissance, and he sought to capture the rhythms of folk speech and jazz music in his poetry. In his stories, novels, and plays as well as in his poems, he gave voice to the sorrows, struggles, and triumphs of African Americans.

Hughes was born in Joplin, Missouri. His parents separated shortly after he was born, and Hughes moved often as his mother sought work in different cities. At Central High School in Cleveland, Hughes wrote poems for a student magazine, was a member of the school's winning track team, and made the monthly honor roll. After briefly attending Columbia University in New York City, he worked at odd jobs while writing poetry and absorbing the music and nightlife of Harlem. As more and more of his poetry was published, he gradually became well-known. While completing college at Lincoln University in Pennsylvania, Hughes wrote his first novel, *Not Without Laughter*.

For the rest of his life, Hughes traveled widely and wrote prolifically. He gave readings of his poetry to overflowing audiences and founded theaters in New York, Los Angeles, and Chicago. He also wrote a weekly newspaper column, which featured stories about a black laborer and folk philosopher. These highly popular stories became known as the Simple stories, after the last name of the main character.

OTHER WORKS *The Weary Blues, The Dream Keeper and Other Poems, The Big Sea: An Autobiography, The Best of Simple* Extended Reading

RICHARD WILBUR

1921–

Richard Wilbur's accomplishments have not gone unrecognized. In his distinguished career as a poet, professor of English, and literary critic, he has won two Pulitzer Prizes, a National Book Award, and a Bollingen Prize. Named the second poet laureate of the United States, he served a term as the nation's official poet. Moreover, his highly acclaimed translations of French poetry and plays have won him many additional awards.

Born in New York City, Wilbur had an early interest in painting. His decision to take up writing as a career was sparked by his mother's father and grandfather, both of whom were newspaper editors. In high school Wilbur began writing for his school newspaper, and he wrote stories and poems for the student magazine while attending Amherst College. After graduation, Wilbur served with the U.S. forces in Europe during World War II. Around this time he became serious about writing poetry as a way of coping with the wartime disorder and confusion.

Unlike many other contemporary poets, Wilbur is known for his lack of experimentation and his optimistic viewpoint. His poetry displays a wide and varied vocabulary, which is not surprising for a man who describes himself as "crazy about words." Wilbur now makes his home in Cummington, Massachusetts, and in Key West, Florida.

OTHER WORKS *Things of This World, New and Collected Poems* Extended Reading

OVERVIEW

Objectives

- To understand and appreciate a short story that explores a woman's memories of a step-grandmother who made her own way in life
- To identify and understand description
- To express understanding of the selection through a choice of writing forms, including a letter and a personal essay
- To extend understanding of the selection through a variety of multimodal and cross-curricular activities

Skills

LITERARY CONCEPTS
- Description
- Tone

THE WRITER'S STYLE
- Chronological transitions

GRAMMAR
- Subject/verb agreement with *here/there*

SPEAKING, LISTENING, AND VIEWING
- Storytelling
- Group discussion
- Oral presentation

CULTURAL CONNECTION
The Culture of India As students read the story, they may conclude that life in India is very different from life in the United States. These images can be used to generate a discussion about differences between the two countries' cultures.

Side A, Frame 49396

ALTERNATIVE
Previewing

In lieu of writing, students can choose partners and discuss their subjects.

Personal Connection

Discussion Prompts *Think of someone you like whom many, if not most, others misunderstand and avoid contact with. In as much detail as possible, describe the person to your partner. If you need help getting started, the following questions might help:*

- Is this person avoided because of his or her personality or physical traits?
- How does this person seem to react to being misunderstood and avoided?
- What do you see in this person that others miss seeing?

As you read "Lakshmi," see if the qualities that endear the step-grandmother to the narrator happen to match any of the qualities of your unique friend or relative.

PREVIEWING

FICTION

Lakshmi

Vasanthi (və-sän'thē) Victor

Activating Prior Knowledge
PERSONAL CONNECTION

In this story the narrator relives vivid memories of her grandparents. She especially remembers her step-grandmother, a person whom most of her relatives avoided because of her unusual behavior. Do any of your traits, habits, or behaviors seem strange to other people? Maybe you collect bird feathers or never sit with your back to a door. Perhaps you once did something so unexpected that your friends were totally puzzled. Create a chart like the one shown, listing two or three of your "strange" traits or actions and recording your friends' reactions to them.

Trait or Action	Friends' Reactions

Building Background
GEOGRAPHICAL CONNECTION

The action of "Lakshmi" takes place in India, where the author was born. The narrator tells about her grandparents, who lived a ten-minute walk from the ocean in the state of Kerala (kĕr'ə-lə). Kerala extends along the southwestern coast of India, on the shore of the Arabian Sea. Although it is a densely populated state of more than 25 million people, many of its inhabitants live in small villages like the one described in this story.

Setting a Purpose
WRITING CONNECTION

The narrator of this story is probably the only member of her family who remembers her step-grandmother with affection. In your notebook, write about someone you like whom many, if not most, others misunderstand and avoid. Then, as you read the story, see if the qualities that endear the step-grandmother to the narrator happen to match any of the qualities of your unique friend or relative.

452 UNIT THREE PART 2: ON YOUR OWN TERMS

- CULTURAL CONNECTION

PRINT AND MEDIA RESOURCES

UNIT THREE RESOURCE BOOK
Strategic Reading: Literature, p. 57
Vocabulary SkillBuilder, p. 58

GRAMMAR MINI-LESSONS
Transparencies, p. 7
Copymasters, p. 9

WRITING MINI-LESSONS
Transparencies, pp. 40, 41

ACCESS FOR STUDENTS ACQUIRING ENGLISH
Selection Summaries
Reading Support

FORMAL ASSESSMENT
Selection Test, pp. 81–82
Test Generator

 AUDIO LIBRARY
See Reference Card

 LASERLINKS
Cultural Connection
Art Gallery

452 THE LANGUAGE OF LITERATURE TEACHER'S EDITION

Lakshmi

Vasanthi Victor

SUMMARY

The narrator remembers visiting her grandparents as a child. She recalls her grandfather's house, especially the main room where her grandfather told stories to her. Her grandfather was married three times. Her own grandmother was the first wife. She died young, leaving small children. Her grandfather then married his first wife's sister. Grandmother number two was a strong woman who raised a large family and saw that they were all well educated. When she died, the narrator's grandfather married once more. This last grandmother was an outsider and was never accepted by the family. She was not pretty but was a shrewd businessperson who ran the family's store and looked after the cows. The narrator was her favorite grandchild, and they spent much time together. The narrator thinks that the third grandmother chose her as her favorite because both of them were outsiders, kindred spirits. This grandmother died shortly before Grandfather, who lived until he was about 100 years old.

Thematic Link: *On Your Own Terms* A woman recalls her relationship with her grandfather's third wife, who forges her own identity in the family.

CUSTOMIZING FOR
Gifted and Talented Students

Have students note the similarities and differences between this large, extended family and their own extended families. Have them analyze what forces draw families together and what forces pull them apart.

WORDS TO KNOW

afflict (ə-flĭkt′) *v.* to produce distress and suffering in (p. 457)
congregate (kŏng′grĭ-gāt′) *v.* to come together in a group; gather (p. 454)
diligence (dĭl′ə-jəns) *n.* careful, patient, and steady effort (p. 455)
eccentricity (ĕk′sĕn-trĭs′ĭ-tē) *n.* an example of odd or unconventional behavior (p. 457)
escapade (ĕs′kə-pād′) *n.* an unusual adventure (p. 455)

insipid (ĭn-sĭp′ĭd) *adj.* dull and lifeless (p. 457)
murky (mûr′kē) *adj.* dark or cloudy; not clear (p. 454)
pliant (plī′ənt) *adj.* easily influenced or dominated (p. 459)
prudent (prōōd′nt) *adj.* wise in handling practical matters; showing good judgment (p. 458)
skeptical (skĕp′tĭ-kəl) *adj.* inclined to doubt or disbelieve (p. 454)

CUSTOMIZING FOR
Students Acquiring English

- Use **ACCESS FOR STUDENTS ACQUIRING ENGLISH**, *Reading Support*.
- Invite students whose families are from India to share facts about the climate and vegetation of the country, as well as about marriage customs and the importance of extended families. Students can note the similarities and differences between Indian culture and their home culture.

STRATEGIC READING FOR
Less-Proficient Readers

In the first two pages of the selection, the narrator describes the village where her grandfather lived and recalls a story the grandfather used to tell. Encourage students to visualize the setting and the people as you read these pages aloud.

Set a Purpose Tell students that much of the rest of the selection describes the narrator's three grandmothers. Have them read on to find out why the narrator's grandfather married three different times and what each wife was like.

Use **UNIT THREE RESOURCE BOOK**, p. 57, for guidance in reading the selection.

Literary Concept: DESCRIPTION

A Help students identify descriptive details in these two paragraphs that bring the setting to life. *(Possible responses: no electricity or running water, the "murky waters" of the pond, "freshly swept" sand, the sound of the ocean, "huts made of woven palm leaves . . . dried and tied together," nets spread out of long canoes, "gleaming, slithering fish," "baskets balanced on their heads," "coconuts hanging on the palms")*

My grandfather had passed away. It said so in this letter from home, in black and white. It was written by Mother who matter-of-factly moved on to other news about the rest of the family in India. This unexpected jolt took me back into the past—his death had triggered some old memory long since wiped out by the conscious present. My parents had come from the state of Kerala, and I remembered visiting there in my childhood. On these occasions I visited my grandfather and step-grandmother as well as innumerable uncles, aunts and cousins.

A It was a great change for us those days to go from our house in the city to a remote village in Kerala. There was no electricity or running water in the homes. But almost every household had its pond which supplied water for washing and bathing. Some of those ponds were used to breed fish. We children enjoyed playing at the pond's edge since none of us dared to swim in its <u>murky</u> waters. Or we played in the sand that covered the front yard. It was freshly swept in the early hours of the morning by a woman who came in each day to do the chores.

The sound of the ocean could be heard in the distance, and a ten-minute walk brought one to the beach. Here fishermen still lived in huts made of woven palm leaves that were dried and tied together. Their floor was nothing but sand on which they spread mats to sit and sleep. Their livelihood depended on the catch of the day. These sturdy men left in their long canoes to spread their nets in the predawn hours and returned at midmorning with gleaming, slithering fish which their wives carried in baskets balanced on their heads to the gates of surrounding homes. Sometimes their children ran ahead to announce the catch of the day. I remember old women saying, "Twenty years ago there were more fish than you could eat in a week on any single day. Now you can count the fish on your fingers, just like those coconuts hanging on the palms."

Coconut was used for everything—as oil for frying or as hair oil on our heads. Nothing like fish curry done in coconut milk or meat fried with coconut slivers. My aunts grated it to mix with vegetable dishes. Some men carried out the task of climbing palms to gather the nut. Grandfather usually had them climbing for tender young coconuts as a special treat for us. We delighted in feasting on the big bananas, the jackfruit and mangoes that grew nearby.

In Grandfather's house the main room where visitors were received also contained his bed. This is where he was to be found when he was not out working or tending to business. At night, after the evening meal, we <u>congregated</u> around his bed and listened to stories in the semidarkness of the oil lamps. The glow of the lamps attracted bugs and mosquitoes so that we could never sit still but kept slapping our bodies to kill the insects. One of our favorite stories was about the man returning home at nightfall, on foot, by way of the beach. There was no transportation so most people walked ten to fifteen miles a day while they went about their business. At the time there was a tale going around about a crooked lawyer who had met a violent death. His ghost was supposed to frequent this particular stretch of oceanfront. He waylaid unsuspecting travelers and scared them out of their wits. Some said he wore his lawyer's robe; others, that he appeared headless or with a walking stick. Whatever his attire, they swore they had seen him and came back frightened and panting from running.

This man was more <u>skeptical</u> than others and, refusing to be scared by such tales, set out as usual. On his journey home he carried a sack

WORDS TO KNOW	**murky** (mûr′kē) *adj.* dark or cloudy; not clear
	congregate (kŏng′grĭ-gāt′) *v.* to come together in a group; gather
	skeptical (skĕp′tĭ-kəl) *adj.* inclined to doubt or disbelieve

454

Mini-Lesson Grammar

SUBJECT/VERB AGREEMENT WITH HERE AND THERE Tell students that *here* and *there* are never subjects. Sentences and clauses beginning with them are inverted: the subject follows the verb. Students must find the subject and make the verb agree in number. Point out the highlighted examples:

- There <u>was</u> no <u>electricity</u> or running <u>water</u>.
- Twenty years ago there <u>were</u> more <u>fish</u>.

Application Have students choose the correct verb for each sentence.
1. There (was/were) many relatives living in Grandfather's house. *(were)*
2. There (is/are) little privacy or personal space in large, extended families. *(is)*
3. There (was/were) several reasons the family disliked the step-grandmother. *(were)*

Reteaching/Reinforcement
- *Grammar Handbook*, anthology pp. 907, 942
- *Grammar Mini-Lessons* copymasters p. 9, transparencies p. 7

 The Writer's Craft

Subjects in Unusual Positions, p. 508

of dried peppers on his back. As he made his way in the falling twilight, alone with no soul in sight, he was reminded of the lawyer's ghost. Except for the sea there was no other sound, maybe a solitary gull or two. In the growing stillness he suddenly heard a rustling sound; the faster he walked, the louder it grew. He began to think it was the swish of a cape behind him and turned a few times to see who was following. He saw nothing. All the same, as he approached the spot of the last sighting, he hurried even quicker. Louder and louder was the swish behind his back, until he was running, sure that the ghost was chasing him. He reached home in a state of anxiety and fear and ran a high fever during the night. It was only later—after he had recovered and in the light of bright day—that it dawned on him: he had been scared witless by the sound of the dried peppers on his back. He told his wife and children about what had really happened, and soon the whole village came to know about his escapade. He could never walk among them without it being recalled by one or the other, and the village children laughed behind his back.

The children heard many stories from Grandfather but none as funny as this one. Sometimes in the afternoon when the household was napping, they got into his wall-side shelves and went through his books and personal belongings. It was rumored among the family that he hid money in the pages of his books and forgot about it. On one visit, my brother found forty rupees[1] in a book that he had casually opened. He was too honest to keep the money and gave it to Grandfather. However, my other relatives didn't think twice about deceiving him, and as he grew older, his sons stole most of the property and wealth that he had acquired through hard work and diligence. He never walked without his cane now, and his feet were flat, knobby and twisted from all the walking he had done in his lifetime.

He had been married three times. His first wife had been our grandmother. She died when their children were still young, the last a toddler. It was while traveling to attend the

A Maulvi meditating (about 1630), Mughal School. Copyright © British Museum.

---

1. **rupees** (rōō-pēz′): Indian units of money.

WORDS TO KNOW
escapade (ĕs′kə-pād′) *n.* an unusual adventure
diligence (dĭl′ə-jəns) *n.* careful, patient, and steady effort

Art Note

***Dipak Raga* by Nisaradi.** This painting is by Nisaradi, an early 17th-century Muslim artist living in the Mewar region of northern India. It is taken from a *Ragamala,* a set of miniature paintings symbolically depicting the various modes of raga, the traditional Hindu musical form. The Dipak Raga (*dipak* meaning "fire") is sung to brighten and enliven one's spirit.

Reading the Art *What details of traditional Indian life did the artist capture in this painting?*

Critical Thinking:
MAKING JUDGMENTS

D Ask students if they consider the grandfather's second marriage a good one. Why or why not? *(Possible response: The second marriage seems a good one because the new wife kept the family organized and motivated and had a strong sense of priorities for the children.)*

Linking to Social Studies

E Even today, many children in rural India receive little formal education. Girls are often kept at home to watch their younger siblings. Paper, pens, and books are scarce outside of large cities.

Linking to Science

F Smallpox was once a deadly disease spread by a virus, but vaccinations eventually conquered it. A smallpox vaccine was developed by Edward Jenner in 1796—the first vaccine ever made. Early vaccines often did not work, but by the 1940s improved vaccines had eliminated smallpox from Europe and North America. In 1967 the United Nations began a campaign to rid the rest of the world of smallpox, and by 1980 this had been accomplished.

---

funeral of a relative on another island that death had snatched her. I had been told she was a kind and charitable person and people remembered her good deeds. She had gone by canoe, accompanied by a relative and two servants, when a sudden storm struck and they capsized in the raging water. When news of the tragedy reached my grandfather, he cried and wailed in sorrow. For months he could not be consoled, but some of the elders eventually persuaded him to marry again for the sake of his little children. The woman he wed was his wife's younger sister.

Perhaps it was because she resembled his former wife, or his wife's family had reasoned their daughter's children could best be looked after by their aunt rather than a stranger. Whatever the reason, the marriage was a success, and she bore him ten children in the course of twenty years. Though all the children did not survive, it was a large family.

Grandmother number two was a strong and capable woman who ruled her family with discipline and will. She was ambitious for their futures and realized the value of education. As her children grew, she made plans for each of them. One was to be a doctor, the other a lawyer, one an accountant and so on. Under her urging and influence Grandfather was persuaded to donate funds to erect a schoolhouse where all of the children could attend. Among them were children from neighboring villages who did not have such a facility. It was a grand schoolhouse, one made of stone and brick. Grandmother could hear the lesson recital from where she stood inside the compound[2] walls. At that time, the teachers believed the louder the students recited, the better they learnt their lessons. A few years after it was built, she died of smallpox.

In a place where vaccinations were unheard of, smallpox was a mysterious and fatal disease. People believed it was a curse wrought[3] by a cruel goddess, and in her fury she went home to home wreaking havoc[4] until entire villages were afflicted. They cowered in their homes not knowing when she might descend on them and prayed feverishly, burning

Dipak Raga (1605), Nisaradi. From a Ragamala, Mewar School, F. K. Kanoria Collection, Calcutta, India.

---

2. **compound:** belonging to a large fenced or walled-in area.
3. **wrought** (rôt): produced; brought about.
4. **wreaking havoc** (rē′kĭng hăv′ək): causing great destruction or disorder.

WORDS TO KNOW
afflict (ə-flĭkt′) *v.* to produce distress and suffering in

456

Mini-Lesson The Writer's Style

USING CHRONOLOGICAL TRANSITIONS
Point out to students that transitions are words and phrases that help connect ideas and achieve coherence in writing. Chronological transitions help clarify the time sequences in a narrative. Point out the highlighted words and phrases in the first column on this page. The narrator used them to keep clear the sequence of events from the death of grandfather's first wife to the death of his second wife.

Application Have students write a brief personal narrative about recent events in their life. Tell them to use chronological transitions to help readers follow the sequence of events.

Reteaching/Reinforcement
- *Writing Handbook,* anthology p. 869
- *Writing Mini-Lessons* transparencies, pp. 40, 41

 The Writer's Craft

Transitions That Show Time, pp. 364–365

---

456 THE LANGUAGE OF LITERATURE **TEACHER'S EDITION**

incense to keep her away. When struck, they still prayed in their misery to be spared, and some miraculously survived, their flesh scarred for life. One of our uncles carried the pox marks; they said he was lucky to be alive. None of her children died, and Grandfather was a widower again with many young children.

The third time he married he must have been in his fifties, though he couldn't remember and no one was sure of his age. There were no birth or marriage certificates. His wife was much younger and from a distant town. She had given up on any man marrying her and was considered an old spinster at age thirty-eight. She was tall and gawky. Her protruding teeth gave her a seemingly <u>insipid</u> look, but this was not really the case. She had seized the offer to marry an aging widower with ten children and travel far from her family to live in comparative ease and luxury. It rescued her from being a poor woman who was only tolerated because of her usefulness in doing chores around the house. At home she was nothing more than a servant; here she was its main keeper.

Everyone hated her for invading their territory. Grandfather's sons and daughters, some of whom were grown, could not bear to see their mother replaced by this ugly and stupid creature. They did not want her turning their father's attention away from them. They did not understand what he saw in her and why he felt he had to marry again. Certainly she was not going to bear him any children, nor did he want any. Some of his friends and family snickered he was too randy for his age and that's why he had taken another wife. He himself thought she would be the comfort of his old age and, when none of his children would care, he would have a wife to take care of his needs.

Later, he doubted himself in taking such a step. It was too late; Grandmother number three was here to stay.

I was one of the few who did get along with step-Grandmother. She tolerated my presence and allowed me to tag along on her daily rounds. Each morning she was up before the rest of the household to supervise the milking of the cows she kept. These cows were regarded as one of her <u>eccentricities</u> by her stepchildren. She had named each of the cows and spoke to them like they were her own children. It may or may not be true that she took better care of them than her spouse. Later, she could be found tending the store that supplied essentials to the laborers who were employed by Grandfather. Here she kept a strict eye on the debit and credit ledger[5] as most of our customers had very little cash to pay for goods. I was especially favored because Grandmother gave me goodies to eat, as well as coins to add to my growing collection of small change which I kept in a can. The can was locked up in the store at closing time because she didn't want my cousins to find its treasure.

My cousins envied my favored status since they were not so lucky. At the evening meal when all the members gathered around the table in the large kitchen, they teased me for growing rich at such an early age. They hinted that one day soon it would be found. Then where would I be? In fact, among my uncles and aunts, one trusted the other so little that each kept their belongings under lock and key in old wooden almirahs.[6] These almirahs were brought by the daughters-in-law as part of their dowry,[7] and each took special pride in her piece of furniture.

---

5. **debit and credit ledger:** a book in which records of money owed by and to a business are kept.
6. **almirahs** (ăl-mī′rəz): storage chests.
7. **dowry:** the money and goods that a woman brings to her husband when she marries.

WORDS TO KNOW
insipid (ĭn-sĭp′ĭd) *adj.* dull and lifeless
eccentricity (ĕk′sĕn-trĭs′ĭ-tē) *n.* an example of odd or unconventional behavior

---

Multicultural Perspectives

NAMES FOR SIBLINGS AND RELATIVES
In India and many other traditional cultures, family relationships are much more defined and complex than those many Americans are accustomed to. For example, whereas English has one word for uncles, Indians distinguish between their mother's brother and their father's brother. There is a different term used for each relative, and each is treated in a different way. In Chinese and Korean families, there is a hierarchy of power and respect based on age. Sisters and brothers are addressed as "first eldest sister," "second eldest brother," and so on, rather than by name. In these cultures one's position in the family is of paramount importance and is reinforced on a daily basis.

Literary Concept: DESCRIPTION

K The sense memories the narrator describes here help her recall a conversation she had with her grandmother many years ago. Ask what senses are included in the description. *(hearing: the whistling sound of coconut palms in the breeze; sight: the image of the grandmother's face; touch: the soft feel of her earlobes)*

Literary Concept: DIALOGUE/CHARACTERIZATION

L Point out to students that this short exchange is the only dialogue in the story. Ask why they think the author included it. *(Possible responses: Having her speak adds a flesh-and-blood reality to the grandmother; it adds variety to the way the reader learns more about her character, her relationship with Lakshmi, and her relationship with her cows.)*

Everyone examined the wood and kind of workmanship displayed and pronounced it good or bad accordingly. Grandmother had brought her own, and its contents were still a mystery because she took great care to open it when no one else was around. Some of her stepchildren grew so curious that they began spying on her at all times of the day and night. It was on one of these occasions, much later in their lives, that one of my uncles came on her exercising in the nude, her body glistening with oil in the light of the moon coming through a window.

When this report spread among the family, they were stunned. It was strange even for someone as eccentric as her. Women were never known to exercise in those parts, let alone in the nude by moonlight. Among us grandchildren, it conjured up visions of an old lady dancing eerily in the pale moon, to some hidden god in a forgotten ancient ritual. This vision still danced in my eyes as I reached back into the past.

When Grandfather became ill and had to remain in a hospital for weeks, the enormity of the bill so struck his wife's <u>prudent</u> nature that she never recovered from the shock and hastily preceded him in death, or so it was related by her enemies. He died a few months later, his back covered with bedsores from being confined so long with no one to care for him but a young compassionate grandson. He might have been in his late nineties or past one hundred; no one could be sure. In his days he had walked tall and proud, built a thriving business from scratch, and raised enough children to create a future generation that spread to many corners of the world.

In my distant home, I can almost hear the whistling of coconut palms in the breeze. And if I closed my eyes and was absolutely still, there is Grandmother smiling her bucktoothed grin—her hair grey and tightly wound, big gold hoops dangling from the top of her ears, her ear lobes stretched and torn from heavy jewelry, empty and gaping holes. Those same lobes I had pulled and felt as a child because they were soft to the touch and curious. I remember asking, "How come they are so big?" But Grandmother only laughed and said, "Go mind your own business, child. I have things to do."

"Will you be bringing the cows again tonight?"

"Yes, Lakshmi."

"Can I come with you?"

"No, it will be dark, and I can't watch out for those stupid cows and you at the same time."

"I promise I will be good and walk right behind you."

"And step into their dung and come crying home. No. It's better you go in; they will be beginning their evening prayers soon."

"But Grandma . . ."

"Shush, child. Go, go on in, before someone comes looking for you. I think I hear your mother calling."

Pressing on with youthful optimism, "Okay, but tomorrow will you teach me to milk the cows?"

I never did learn how to milk those cows but watched from a safe distance their swollen udders being pulled and stretched to give a steady stream of milk—by Grandmother's strong and capable hands, while she soothed and coaxed those animals with talk. From the way they stood, yielding and <u>pliant</u>, it was easy to believe her. They were like great big children, letting her do as she willed, trusting her closeness, her love.

| WORDS TO KNOW | **prudent** (prōō'dnt) *adj.* wise in handling practical matters; showing good judgment |
| | **pliant** (plī'ənt) *adj.* easily influenced or dominated |

458

Assessment Option

SELF-ASSESSMENT To help students assess their understanding of the selection, have pairs of students discuss and compile a list of the advantages and disadvantages Lakshmi faced by growing up in a large, extended family surrounded by cousins, aunts, uncles, parents, and grandparents. Have them base their ideas on Lakshmi's memories of growing up.

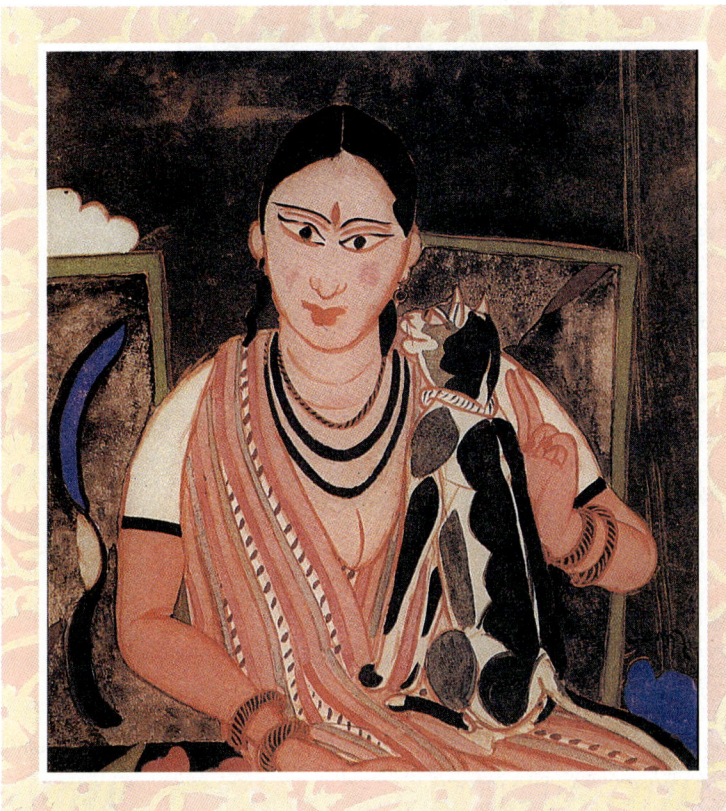

Sundari (1980), K. G. Subramanyan. Watercolor and oil on glass, backed with gold paper, collection of Vivan Sundaram, New Delhi, India.

Yes, Grandmother had been a loving soul. The others couldn't see it and never gave her the chance to belong. So she turned her attention to the cows and, when I came visiting, thought I was special. A kindred spirit,[8] trying to belong and not belonging. Apart and a little withdrawn—she could see, from the way I watched. I had nothing to do, and time heavy on my hands. So Grandmother had picked me to be her favorite. I reminded her of herself, when she was a little girl. Grandmother had found me, so to speak. Now I would have to find myself. ❖

---

8. **kindred spirit:** a person to whom one feels close because of a perceived likeness in nature or character.

LAKSHMI   459

Art Note

Sundari by K. G. Subramanyan. Contemporary Indian artist K. G. Subramanyan (1924–) paints in watercolors and oil on glass. He has created many portraits of women.

Reading the Art *What attitude do you think the painter has toward his subject? What details support your idea?*

Literary Concept: TONE

M Ask students what tone the narrator takes toward the grandmother in the last paragraph. *(Possible responses: grieving, longing, loving, wistful, sad)*

STRATEGIC READING FOR
Less-Proficient Readers

N Make sure students understand the relationship between the grandmother and the narrator.

- Ask students in what way they think the narrator reminded the grandmother of herself as a young girl. *(Possible responses: Because she hadn't grown up in her grandfather's household, the narrator did not possess the envy, hatred, and distrust of the other children and showed instead a sensitive, independent, caring nature, which apparently matched that of Grandmother in her youth.)* **Clarifying**

COMPREHENSION CHECK

1. What news causes Lakshmi to remember her past? *(the news of her grandfather's death)*
2. How many wives did Grandfather have during his life? *(three)*
3. Why did the relatives dislike his third wife? *(She was poor, eccentric, unattractive, and too independent.)*
4. What are the bonds that seemingly united the narrator with the third grandmother? *(Both appear to be sensitive people with loving natures, not fitting in with the intolerant, self-serving behavior of the others in the extended family.)*

Mini-Lesson   Literary Concepts

REVIEWING TONE Remind students that the tone of a piece of writing is the attitude the writer takes toward the subject. In a piece of fiction, the writer or narrator may assume different tones when describing different characters.

Application Use annotations C and M to help students analyze what tone the narrator uses to describe different story characters. Suggest that students read these passages aloud, and notice how their tone of voice changes as they read what the narrator has to say about different characters.

THE LANGUAGE OF LITERATURE **TEACHER'S EDITION** 459

From Personal Response to Critical Analysis

1. Accept all reasonable responses.
2. Possible response: Grandmother noticed her and nurtured her; now she must nurture herself and discover who she really is.
3. Possible response: Since no one else likes Grandmother, she chooses Lakshmi, a loner who loves her in return, for special treatment.
4. Possible response: Grandfather seems like a caring father and family man but too trusting and not mindful enough of the family squabbles swirling around his household. His second wife brought a valuable discipline to the household. He seems somewhat selfish in marrying a third wife mainly to take care of him in his old age.
5. Accept all reasonable, well-supported responses. (Because more is learned about the third grandmother than the narrator, students may find that they have their strongest feelings for the grandmother.)
6. Possible responses: Social life is easier if people know what to expect from others; people don't want to associate with those who don't conform.

Another Pathway

Cooperative Learning One student can make sure traits are justified with evidence from the selection. Another can extend superficial ideas into deeper analyses of character. A third student can integrate ideas into a choice everyone can accept.

Rubric

3 Full Accomplishment Students compile an accurate list of traits, agree on their most admired character, and give reasons for their choice.

2 Substantial Accomplishment Students compile an accurate list and reach a consensus on the admired character but cannot defend their choice.

1 Little or Partial Accomplishment Students' lists are incomplete or inaccurate, and they are unable to reach a consensus.

RESPONDING OPTIONS

FROM PERSONAL RESPONSE TO CRITICAL ANALYSIS

REFLECT 1. What were you thinking about when you finished reading this story? Jot down your thoughts in your notebook and share them in class.

RETHINK
Thematic Link 2. What do you think Lakshmi, the narrator, means when she concludes, "Grandmother had found me. . . . Now I would have to find myself"?

3. Why do you think the step-grandmother chooses Lakshmi for favored treatment?

Consider
Close Textual Reading
• Lakshmi's status among her relatives
• how the step-grandmother is thought of by most others

4. What do you think about the grandfather and the way he lives his life?

5. For which character in this story do you have the strongest feeling? Explain your choice.

RELATE
Thematic Link 6. Think about the behavior of Lakshmi's relatives, as well as the reactions you noted in your chart for the Personal Connection on page 452. Why do you think many people seem to have little tolerance for those who try to live on their own terms?

Multimodal Learning
ANOTHER PATHWAY

Cooperative Learning

With a small group of classmates, make a list of the character traits of the grandfather and his three wives. Then vote on which of these characters you admire the most. Share your choice with other groups, giving reasons for it.

LITERARY CONCEPTS

Description helps readers understand exactly what a scene, an event, or a character is like. Readers of "Lakshmi" are given a good sense of the coastal region of southwestern India by description that involves sensory images. What descriptions help you picture the setting and daily life of the area?

QUICKWRITES

1. Put yourself in the place of the step-grandmother. Imagine that you are still alive and that the narrator is now a grown woman. Write a **letter** to the narrator, telling her why she was special to you when she was a child.

2. Draft a **personal essay** comparing the person you wrote about for the Writing Connection (page 452) with the step-grandmother in this story.

 PORTFOLIO Save your writing. You may want to use it later as a springboard to a piece for your portfolio.

460 UNIT THREE PART 2: ON YOUR OWN TERMS

Literary Concepts

Use annotations A and K to help students analyze descriptive details. Other details also appear in the description of the main room with the oil lamps that "attracted bugs and mosquitoes" (p. 454) and the description of the step-grandmother milking the cows (p. 459).

QuickWrites

1. Letters should focus on how the grandmother felt about her place in the family and on identifying character traits that made Lakshmi special.
2. Students can make a list of character traits of the person they wrote about for the Writing Connection and compare it to the list they compiled for the step-grandmother in the Another Pathway activity.

The Writer's Craft

Personal Letter, pp. 42–46
Comparison and Contrast, pp. 138–142

Multimodal Learning

ALTERNATIVE ACTIVITIES

1. A mandala is a circular design used in the Hindu and Buddhist religions (both of which originated in India) as a symbol of the universe. Today a mandala also refers to any circular design including images that symbolize a person, idea, or place. Create a **mandala** that represents the personality of one of the grandparents in this story.
2. Using descriptive details from the story, make a **model** of the Indian village in which the grandparents live. You might use such materials as clay, sand, construction paper, and tissue paper.

WORDS TO KNOW

EXERCISE A Review the Words to Know at the bottom of the selection pages. Then write the vocabulary word described by each sentence below.

1. This word describes muddy water and foggy weather.
2. People must do this before they can be a mob, a horde, a throng, or a pack.
3. This word might be used to describe a person who gives in easily to peer pressure or to a bully.
4. Ideal housekeepers and trustworthy bankers can be described with this word.
5. This word describes a person who is by nature doubtful and therefore not likely to fall for get-rich-quick schemes.
6. Tyrants, plagues, and severe poverty do this to their victims.
7. The activity named by this word appeals both to bold adventurers and to mere thrill seekers.
8. This quality is lacking in a lazy and irresponsible person.
9. We tend to expect this in geniuses, artists, and anyone who's "a real character."
10. A person whom this word describes will never be very popular or even an interesting companion.

EXERCISE B Team up with a partner to write a sentence that contains as many of the vocabulary words as possible. Describing a humorous or unlikely situation is fine, as long as the words are used accurately.

LASERLINKS
• ART GALLERY

ACROSS THE CURRICULUM

Social Studies This story is named for its narrator, Lakshmi, whose name comes, in turn, from the name of a Hindu goddess. Research this goddess (her name sometimes appears as Laksmi, and she is also called Sri). What qualities might a Hindu family hope to encourage in a daughter by naming her Lakshmi? Present your findings in an oral report.

VASANTHI VICTOR

Vasanthi Victor was born in 1953, near Bombay, India, and raised in that city. After studying English literature and journalism at Bombay University, she worked as a freelance writer, arriving in the United States in 1978. The next year she married an Indian systems engineer (in a marriage arranged by her parents) and has since raised two children in California. She writes newspaper articles, poems, and short stories.

The setting of "Lakshmi," reflects Victor's roots in southern India. Originally intended to celebrate the grandfather, the story is woven out of memories and stories that she heard while growing up.

LAKSHMI **461**

Words to Know

Exercise A
1. murky
2. congregate
3. pliant
4. prudent
5. skeptical
6. afflict
7. escapade
8. diligence
9. eccentricity
10. insipid

Exercise B
Encourage students to identify nouns, verbs, and adjectives. They may be able to build a sentence around one of the two verbs *congregate* or *afflict*.

Reteaching/Reinforcement
• *Unit Three Resource Book*, p. 58

Across the Curriculum

Social Studies Students can use general encyclopedias or special encyclopedias of mythology to research this topic. Lakshmi is the wife of Vishnu, one of the most important Hindu gods. She is considered the epitome of female beauty, as well as the goddess of fortune and prosperity.

ART GALLERY
The Art of India Religious scenes form the subject of much Indian art. These images show some striking representations of religious figures.

Side A, Frame 49404

Alternative Activities

1. Point out to students that mandalas usually contain smaller concentric circles inside a larger circle. In addition, the designs are usually symmetrical. That is, the design on one half of the circle is the mirror image of the design on the other half.
2. Tell students that they should consider the relatively close ocean as part of the village neighborhood and include the water and beach environment, as described on page 454, in their models.

OBJECTIVES

- To promote independent, active reading
- To practice and apply skills learned in previous selections

Reading Pathways

- Invite small groups of students to take turns reading aloud from this humorous personal narrative.
- Have students read independently and write their responses to the selection in a dialogue journal.
- Suggest to students that they read the selection twice, once for enjoyment and a second time to analyze relationships among the members of the Brenner family.

ON YOUR OWN

fish.

PRINT AND MEDIA RESOURCES

UNIT THREE RESOURCE BOOK
Strategic Reading: Literature, p. 61

FORMAL ASSESSMENT
Selection Test, p. 83
Part Test, pp. 85–86
 Test Generator

ACCESS FOR STUDENTS ACQUIRING ENGLISH
Selection Summaries

 AUDIO LIBRARY
See Reference Card

Ladies and Gentlemen and Children of all ages (drum roll, please), I am proud to bring to you, from its very beginning to its very ending, the very true and hopefully very funny story of little David Brenner and his fish eyes.

Let's have a brief background of the Louis and Estelle Brenner offsprings. The oldest, Mel "Moby Dick"; the middle, Blanche "Bib"; and the itsy-bitsy little baby, David "Kingy." Very close and very much in love with one another in spite of great differences in age and life-style. Whatever sibling rivalry existed was expressed lovingly in the wildest, weirdest, most bizarre practical jokes and most disturbingly creative attacks. The oldest was the most devious.[1] For example:

My brother offered me a delicious new drink, and I discovered—pure carrot juice. He pretended to join me in drinking some. I didn't pretend, taking the biggest gulp of all time of the most rancid-tasting[2] liquid of all time, almost causing me to throw up on the spot. The oldest rolled on the floor bursting with laughter as I charged upstairs to brush my teeth and gargle. The youngest strikes back. Every night I poured just a few drops of the awful carrot juice into my brother's milk. Every night he complained that his milk tasted rather peculiar but continued to drink it until all the juice was consumed. As the last glass was finished I announced what I had been doing. His turn to brush and gargle.

The oldest also had the sickest sense of humor. His idea of fun was to sneak up on me while I was reading or sleeping and place a dirty sock of his on my shoulder or over my face. Now remember that this is a man tormenting a boy, a full-grown man with a Ph.D. degree, a college professor, a brilliant intellect. I'd be watching TV, and all of a sudden I'm smothered with a dirty gym sock, or I'd be doing my homework and suddenly would smell something rotten, only to see the sock my brother was dangling in front of my forehead. I was never safe in my own house, not even when I went to sleep in the bedroom I shared with my big, demented[3] brother. When he would return home after a date, he would sneak up to the bed and lay a dirty sock over my sleeping face. Sometimes, he would pile as many as a half-dozen socks on my face. Of course, I struck back as best I could. For these sock wars, we wouldn't put our dirty socks in the clothing hamper to be washed. My mother was always complaining about the missing socks. So as not to aggravate Mother and in order to better aggravate each other, we both began wearing the same socks for a week or so while throwing clean socks into the hamper. My mother was happy, and we developed more deadly sock bombs.

My best attack ended the war forever. While my brother was out on a date, I rigged a series of clothesline pulleys across the ceiling of my

---

1. **devious** (dē′vē-əs): sneaky; underhanded.
2. **rancid-tasting** (răn′sĭd-tā′stĭng): spoiled or rotten to the taste.
3. **demented** (dĭ-měn′tĭd): insane; mad.

OPTION 1

Cooperative Learning

DESIGNING A PRACTICAL JOKE INVENTION

Have students read the description of Brenner's invention for terrorizing his brother with dirty socks. Then have students collaborate on designing their own invention for playing a practical joke. First, they can brainstorm ideas for what the machine should do. Then they can take turns suggesting creative steps to achieving the final result. Finally, the most artistically gifted student can draw the final design, and another student can explain the machine to the class.

Teacher's Role Encourage students to be as creative as possible in their inventions. Suggest that a good machine should carry out a chain of causes and effects. If possible, display the cartoons of Rube Goldberg, who drew outrageously complicated machines to achieve simple ends.

Rubric

3 Full Accomplishment Students plan a series of logical and creative steps to achieve a humorous end. Their final drawing makes sense and is easy to follow.

2 Substantial Accomplishment Students have humorous ideas and break the workings of their machine down into logical steps but have some difficulty explaining exactly how it works.

1 Little or Partial Accomplishment Students have difficulty imagining a series of logical steps that would lead to a humorous result.

---

bedroom, through which I put a string, on the end of which was a rancid sock. When lowered, this foul article of clothing would come to rest directly above my brother's pillow. A second dreadful sock was rigged so that it could be pulled across his pillow. I then tied the string to my hand and forced myself to stay awake until my brother returned from his date.

In the middle of the night he came home. I faked deep breathing as I heard him climb into our bed. I waited until I heard the familiar sound of his sleeping breathing, then I ever so slowly pulled the string that released the sock so that it hung a few inches above his nose. As he sniffed, twisted, and turned onto his side, I pulled the string that brought the other sock slowly sliding up onto and across his pillow, coming to rest directly at his nose. He sniffed, coughed, and opened his watering eyes and stared at the moldy cloth object perched at the tip of his nose. I then released the pulley string so that the first sock came pummeling from the ceiling. A direct hit—right over his face. My brother gagged and shot up. I rolled around the bed in hysterics. Moby Dick, on the merits of originality and ingenuity,[4] conceded victory and called a truce. So ended the War of the Socks.

Warfare with sister Bib was of an entirely different nature. She had a proof-perfect aim. She could hit just about any target, from any distance, with just about any weapon, her favorite being a rubber band with a semi-straightened paper clip or a V-shaped wad made from tightly rolled paper. Then, too, she could throw anything, from a sofa pillow to a stale end of a rye bread, with the same deadly skill. I would tease her, she'd pick up something, I'd run as quickly as I could, she'd haul off and throw, I'd get smacked with it. I never learned my lesson. What I should have done was tease her from behind a protective shield or from another city.

Now for the fish eye incident. One day I challenged a friend of mine to a game of stickball.

The fellow I challenged to a game was the best, or second best, according to me, stickball player in the neighborhood. We were to play longways on my street. Kids from all over the neighborhood came to see the playoff.

We flipped a coin and he won. I would bat first. I got myself positioned at home plate, a small pothole in the street. The first pitch was a big mistake on his part. It was low and on the outside, just where I liked it. I knew it was going to be a home run as soon as the bat left my shoulder, and it would've been, if I didn't get hit in the back of the head with a small red brick.

I collapsed to the street. I didn't know what or who had hit me. I saw who as soon as I rolled over onto my back. There she was, my sister, running across the roofs.

The game was called off. I got to my feet dizzily and staggered toward my house. A huge lump was already coming out on the back of my head. It looked like a person was following me. When I got into the house I didn't say anything to my mother, because there was an unwritten rule in the streets that one never squeals. It was a sacred law.

I weaved into the kitchen, where my mother was preparing fish for dinner. The lump on my head reflected a large shadow on the wall.

Now, preparing fish for dinner was different

---

4. **ingenuity** (ĭn′jə-nōō′ĭ-tē): cleverness.

Multicultural Perspectives

STICKBALL Stickball is a form of baseball, adapted to fit a "playing field" of streets, sidewalks, and buildings. Many poor children in cramped city neighborhoods did not have the money for bats or gloves or the convenience of a nearby open field in which to play baseball. So they made use of the materials at hand: old broom handles served as bats, and bases were manhole covers, sewer grates, or sidewalk corners. Stickball was an especially popular pastime in New York City and Brooklyn.

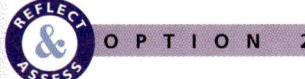

in those days. Nowadays you go to a supermarket and there's a fish counter, and inside are all the fish already prepared for you. You reach in, you take a white thing wrapped in cellophane paper marked "Fish." It could be anything—a gym sock, anything. When I was a kid, it was a lot different, especially if you were poor. Your mother either went to the local fish market or she bought the fish off a pushcart.[5] No matter where you bought it, you had to prepare the fish yourself. It wasn't cleaned. You bought the whole fish, with the head and the tail, a little hat, eyeglasses, sneakers, the works. Then the fish man would wrap it up in a newspaper. I still feel a little squeamish when I open a newspaper, because as a kid, sometimes you'd open a paper and under the headlines there'd be this open-mouthed carp staring at you.

Next, your mother had to prepare the fish herself. She had to cut off the head and the tail and put in her own mercury.[6] It was entirely different then, and it was difficult.

While my mother was preparing the fish for dinner, I was standing there wobbling, thinking of how I could get revenge on my sister. I glanced down on the drain board of the sink and saw a pair of fish eyes staring at me. I scooped them up

---

5. **off a pushcart:** from a peddler pushing through the streets a cart filled with his goods.
6. **put in her own mercury:** a joking reference to the high levels of the poisonous chemical mercury found in many fish today as a result of water pollution.

FISH EYES **465**

OPTION 2

Individual Activity

PERFORMING A STAND-UP COMEDY ACT

Comedian David Brenner based this essay on material he uses in his stand-up comedy act. Have individual students write and perform their own stand-up comedy routine in which they tell about the funniest thing that ever happened in their family.

Teacher's Role Tell students that timing, tone of voice, and facial expression are very important in a comedy routine. Suggest that students observe several stand-up comedians on television before deciding how to deliver their funny story.

Rubric

3 Full Accomplishment Students choose a humorous episode from their own experience, write a coherent personal narrative, and give an effective oral performance.

2 Substantial Accomplishment Students write a humorous, coherent personal narrative, but their performance is not completely effective.

1 Little or Partial Accomplishment Students have difficulty transforming their experience into a humorous, coherent personal narrative.

Literary Note

Often critics distinguish between high comedy—highly verbal, intellectual humor—and low comedy—"gags" or physical, clownish actions. Low comedy, a key element of farce, can make very entertaining theater—such as in several comic scenes from Shakespeare's *Taming of the Shrew*.

and put them in my pocket. I got some Krazy Glue and glued them to my forehead and then climbed into the dirty clothing hamper in the hallway with a flashlight in my mouth, the light flashing inward. I waited until my sister opened the hamper to throw in some of her delicacies,[7] then I turned on the flashlight. When my sister saw my red cheeks and the four eyes, she fainted, but as she fell, she slammed the lid of the hamper against the end of my flashlight, lodging it in my throat. Immediately, I climbed out of the hamper and started running down the hall. My mother saw me, thought I had jammed a pipe in my throat and my eyes were coming out of my head. She collapsed on the spot. I charged downstairs. My father glanced up. Nothing ever bothered my father. He just looked at me and said, "How ya doin', four eyes?"

My father followed me into the kitchen, where I was removing the fish eyes from my forehead, after having successfully extracted the flashlight from my throat. Lou took a long puff on his cigar and slowly blew the smoke up to the kitchen ceiling. He removed the cigar from his mouth and looked at me. Then in his soft Godfather-type[8] whisper, he spoke: "Kingy, I want you to take those fish eyes into the backyard and throw them into the garbage can or else I'm going to see that you eat them for dinner."

I didn't need more convincing. I ran out into the backyard, opened the garbage can lid and . . . well, I looked into the eyes of the eyes. It was as if we had become friends. I just couldn't throw my newfound friends into the garbage just like that. They were pleading with me to save them, silently promising that they could offer me more fun. I opened the lid and rattled the can noisily, as though I were throwing away the eyes, which was really dumb because there was no way two

"Nobody gets away alive from Morris the bug killer."

eyes could make that much noise. You could throw away an entire cow more quietly.

I then carefully put the fish eyes into my pocket and went into the house. I apologized to my sister and mother for the incident. Then I casually walked into the dining room and as silently as possible slid open the top drawer of the dresser where the glue was kept. I took the glue and ducked out into the back alley. I then re-glued the fish eyes to my forehead and walked up to 60th Street, the bustling shopping area for the neighborhood.

I would walk up to a store whose front window was painted halfway up in order to use the space for advertising, and then I would tap on the window lightly but loudly enough to be heard while simultaneously raising my head so that the fish eyes would appear first and then my own wide-open eyes. Women shoppers would scream. I did it to about six stores. The rumor was flying that a monster was loose on 60th Street. The neighborhood was terrorized. I was very happy.

I returned to my house and placed the two fish eyes in the center drawer of my bedroom dresser, a hand-me-down from my brother, who had as a child put a big ball of roofing tar in the center drawer. I think he was trying to corner the black-tar market.

Well, you know the attention span and memory span of young children. It isn't very long. The world is all new and all exciting, and there is so much to enjoy and remember that

---

7. **delicacies:** here, a humorous reference to underwear.
8. **Godfather-type:** hoarse and quiet, like the threatening voice of the title character (played by Marlon Brando) in the 1972 gangster movie *The Godfather*.

one forgets so much, such as a pair of fish eyes casually placed in a drawer.

The summer rolled along. July came and with it a horrific heat spell. The second floor of our house began to stink. Then the first floor. The whole housed reeked of a strange and horrible odor. Although we really could not afford to call an exterminator, we were forced to, because we would gag upon entering the house, and my father's search for the dead animal had failed. We had no choice—Morris the Exterminator Man.

He arrived in his exterminator truck, which had a huge water bug on the roof almost as big as the truck itself. The water bug was on its back with its legs up in the air, and Morris's slogan was painted across the side paneling: "Nobody Gets Away Alive From Morris the Bug Killer."

Morris came into the house and sniffed around. He went up the stairs to the second floor. I could hear him open the door to my bedroom and enter. I think I even remember hearing him sniffing around in there. I know I do remember hearing him scream and seeing him charge down the stairs.

"What is it, Morris? Have you found it?"

"Yes, it's a dead animal."

"What kind of animal?"

"I don't really know, Mrs. Brenner. I've never seen anything like it in my life. It's in the center drawer of David's dresser. It's this real small, soft, black animal, and from the look of its eyes, I'd say it's been dead at least two years."

My father, mother, sister, and brother snapped their heads in my direction. I leaped to my feet and ran out of the house. There was no way I was going to have fish eyes and tar for dinner.

That's the truth, the whole truth, nothing but the truth about the pair of fish eyes as it all happened during one of those glorious summers so long ago in the days of my wild, woolly, disturbed—and fun-filled—youth. Would I do it all over again if I could? You're damn right I would. ❖

DAVID BRENNER

1945–

In the foreword to his 1983 autobiography, *Soft Pretzels with Mustard*, David Brenner lists his five proudest school achievements. They include always making the honor roll, never being late for class, being elected class president for nine years, never letting the "system" beat him—and being voted class comedian.

Brenner grew up in Philadelphia, in a neighborhood that he describes as "poor" and "tough" but also as having "stockpiles of laughter." Later, he majored in mass communications at Temple University, then found success as a producer, director, and writer of serious documentary films. At the age of 24, however, he suddenly thought the world needed more laughter, so he quit his job and headed for the comedy stages of New York. He never looked back.

Since 1969 Brenner has performed standup comedy in nightclubs, in concert halls, and at colleges and has been a frequent game-show panelist and guest host on TV. In 1986 he published an autobiographical sequel, *Nobody Ever Sees You Eat Tuna Fish,* from which "Fish Eyes" is taken. Turning to radio in 1994, he became the host of a talk-show that he hopes will be "the David Letterman of radio, with fun people."

OTHER WORKS *Revenge Is the Best Exercise, If God Wanted Us to Travel . . .*

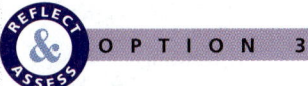

OPTION 3

Class Discussion
SHARING IDEAS

Teacher's Role After students have read the selection, engage the class in a discussion with the following questions:
1. What might be some positive and negative effects of sibling rivalry? *(Possible responses: positive effects—competition stimulates siblings to make their best efforts to achieve; negative effects—children can develop deep resentment at siblings' success)*
2. How effective is humor in relieving tensions between friends or family members? *(Possible responses: It's very effective, because it's very hard to maintain anger in the face of laughter; it's not effective, because once the humor of a gag has faded, tension may still exist.)*
3. Do you think all the childhood incidents Brenner describes seemed funny to him at the time they happened? *(Possible response: Yes, he seems to have thoroughly enjoyed the sock battles and thinking up ways to retaliate against his brother and sister when they got the best of him with a practical joke.)*

EDITOR'S NOTE *With the permission of the author or copyright holder, material has been deleted to shorten and focus the selection, and potentially offensive material has been deleted.*

DAVID BRENNER

Brenner was working as a producer for a television station when he decided that he needed a career change—not because he had "a burning desire to be an entertainer" but because he wanted to get away from what he was doing. While on vacation in the West Indies, he listened for three days to news reports that he found very depressing. He thought, as he says, "If you don't laugh, you'll never get through the day with that news . . . so . . . let me be a comedian for a year." After Brenner returned from his vacation, he made his first unpaid public appearance in New York City's Greenwich Village. He bombed, but he kept performing. Then in 1971, his big break came when he was booked as a guest performer on *The Tonight Show.*

OVERVIEW

To gain a deeper appreciation of the selections they have read in this unit, students will explore the characteristics of a firsthand narrative and then create a well-developed example in this lesson.

Objectives

- To plan a firsthand narrative by considering elements such as a meaningful personal experience, character, setting, and plot
- To draft a firsthand narrative and solicit response
- To revise, edit, and publish a firsthand narrative

Skills

LITERATURE
- Identifying elements of a firsthand narrative

WRITING AND LANGUAGE
- Using dialogue
- Using transitions to show time order

GRAMMAR AND USAGE
- Avoiding shifts in tense

MEDIA LITERACY
- Reading and interpreting graphs and charts
- Interpreting a comic strip
- Interpreting a poem

SPEAKING, LISTENING, AND VIEWING
- Conducting interviews
- Oral history
- Peer review

CRITICAL THINKING
- Analyzing
- Visualizing an experience

RESEARCH SKILLS
- Using databases
- Conducting interviews
- Using the computer

Media Literacy:
INTERPRETING A GRAPH

A Have students look at the graph on page 468. Tell them that the graph reflects the percentage of change in the number of children who lived with both parents from 1960 to 1990. Ask them what the graph indicates about the percentage of children who live with their mother only. *(The graph shows that the percentage rose from 8.0 in 1960 to 21.6 in 1990.)*

CUSTOMIZING FOR
Less-Proficient Writers

B Students still having problems thinking of possible topics might try studying photographs of important people in their lives, as well as pictures of special occasions like holidays, birthdays, weddings, and family reunions.

WRITING FROM EXPERIENCE

Writing a Firsthand Narrative

Have you ever been surprised or puzzled by someone you are close to? Were you pleased? disappointed? What did you learn from that experience? In Unit Three, "All in the Family," you've read stories about the natural pleasures and disappointments shared by people who live together. What firsthand experiences can you explore through writing?

GUIDED ASSIGNMENT
Write About a Personal Experience Writing about yourself can give you insight into something that happened to you, such as a significant family event. It also may be a way for you to share with others an important lesson you've learned.

Census Data

1 Look for Ideas

You can find ideas for your true story in many places, but you might start with the items on these two pages. They suggest some of the joys and problems families experience. Do the sources trigger memories of events you could write about? Note your reactions as you read.

A **Read the Graphs** According to the census data, how have families changed from 1960 to 1990? Based on the poll, what seems to be the greatest need of families today?

B **Tap Your Memories** Having trouble thinking of ideas? Try leafing through your journal. Studying objects at home—toys, children's artwork, clothes, and gifts to or from relatives—can also yield ideas for writing. You might even construct a time line of the meaningful events in your life.

C

Comic Strip

468 UNIT THREE: ALL IN THE FAMILY

PRINT AND MEDIA RESOURCES

UNIT THREE RESOURCE BOOK
Prewriting, p. 65
Elaboration, p. 66
Peer Response Guide, pp. 67–68
Revising and Proofreading, p. 69
Student Model, pp. 70–71
Rubric, p. 72

GRAMMAR MINI-LESSONS
Transparencies, p. 31
Copymasters, p. 29

WRITING MINI-LESSONS
Transparencies, pp. 41–42

FORMAL ASSESSMENT
Guidelines for Writing Assessment

 WRITING COACH

 LASERLINKS
Writing Springboard

 The Writer's Craft

Personal Narrative, pp. 86–101

Public Opinion Poll

D Q. If you could change any one of the following about your family, which would it be?

1993 survey of 1,000 adults
Roper Center for Public Opinion Research

- Not sure (5%)
- Have nicer things at home (3%)
- Have people get along better (15%)
- Go on more family vacations (17%)
- Spend more time together (28%)
- Communicate with one another better (32%)

Poem

E
For there is no friend like a sister
In calm or stormy weather;
To cheer one on the tedious way,
To fetch one if one goes astray,
To lift one if one totters down,
To strengthen whilst one stands.

Christina Rossetti
from "Goblin Market"

I can't say that I agree with this poem. My little sister drives me crazy sometimes!

F *However, this poem does remind me of a time my sister helped me out.*

Like a snapshot, a poll shows opinions from one moment in time. How would you answer this survey question now? How would you have answered it a few years ago?

2 Try a QuickWrite

Spend about ten minutes freewriting about the memories and feelings you've generated. If you want to focus your writing, try completing some of the following sentences:

- I'll never forget how I felt the day that my brother/sister/friend . . .
- The most important lesson another person taught me was . .

LASERLINKS
• WRITING SPRINGBOARD

WRITING COACH

WRITING FROM EXPERIENCE   469

Teaching Strategy: MODELING

C Students might use childhood-centered comic strips like *Peanuts* to reminisce about their own lives. For example, the strip shown may prompt some students to consider their own roles in brother-sister relationships.

Teaching Strategy: MODELING

D Demonstrate how the chart can serve as a springboard for a narrative by suggesting that students think about incidents involving a misunderstanding between family members or the separation of family members on a special occasion.

CUSTOMIZING FOR
Students Acquiring English

E Some of the vocabulary in the poem may cause problems for readers. Define the following:

tedious: weary
fetch: find
astray: in the wrong direction
totters: stumbles

Teaching Strategy:
STUMBLING BLOCK

F If students claim that their experiences seem too insignificant to write about, tell them that most personal narratives do not deal with major issues but with quiet yet telling moments that reveal some important truth about a person, time, or place. Remind students that among the things they can use as springboards for their own writing are events from stories, novels, poems, or nonfiction that they have read.

WRITING SPRINGBOARD

Family Experiences This film deals with family life and some of the stages of growing up.

Side B, Frame 11631

Writing Prompt
After viewing this film, think about some of your own experiences that you might want to write about. What experiences have been particularly important or special to you?

THE LANGUAGE OF LITERATURE **Teacher's Edition**   469

Critical Thinking: ANALYZING

G Point out that the purpose of sharing a personal narrative is usually to bring out the significance or overall meaning of the experience. Suggest that students analyze their prewriting ideas, select the most promising ones, and then try to state in a sentence or two the meaning of each. Such a "theme statement" can serve as the main idea or overall focus for their narrative.

CUSTOMIZING FOR
Students Acquiring English

H Some students may be from cultures or families in which sharing personal experiences is discouraged. Guide students who are uncomfortable with this aspect of the assignment to choose topics based on events outside the home, such as those associated with school.

PREWRITING

Selecting Your True Story

Sorting Through Your Ideas Experiences that have an impact on you are usually the best ones to write about. You've been thinking about important moments in your life. Now you'll choose one of those experiences and plan how you'll retell it.

G

1 Identify a Meaningful Event

To help you decide what to write about, try looking back at your notes and any objects that remind you of experiences that were important to you. You might also ask yourself the following questions:

H
- Which experience affected me most?
- Which event would I change if I could?
- Which incident taught me a lesson?

One student wrote her ideas on the index cards at the right.

Telecommunication Device for the Deaf (TDD)

I have one little sister, Amalia. She's in fifth grade at a special boarding school for the deaf. I call her once a week on a TDD.

Amalia's tenth birthday was last week. Mom and I picked her up and took her to dinner.

In the summer, Amalia is home with me, and follows me everywhere. "Madeline, I want to go with you!" she always signs to me.

She's pretty smart. She definitely has a better sense of direction than I do. I remember one time I got us lost. Amalia came to the rescue.

One Student's Idea Cards

Mini-Lesson: Speaking, Listening, and Viewing

ORAL HISTORY Discuss with students how every person has a rich store of unique memories. Explore how these memories tell not only about the person but also about his or her time and place. Invite volunteers to share some of the stories their older relatives have told them about their childhood. Explain to the class that when we tape-record or write these memories, we are creating a document called an oral history. These historical texts provide a rich source for personal narratives.

Application Invite students to interview each other to construct oral histories. Before the interview, have students write a list of questions. Examples might include the following:

- What events from your life are especially important? Why?
- What do you remember about these experiences?

Have students tape-record their oral histories and refer to them as springboards for planning their narratives.

② Tell It to Others

Do other people think your experience will make a good story? Try telling your story to family members or friends.

Decision Point After telling your story, do you still like it enough to write about it?

③ Gather Details

Now you're ready to focus on details that will help you tell the story. You might try one of these activities to find details.

- Freewrite about what you and others were like at the time. What did you look like? What clothes did you wear? What hobbies were you really into? What was the weather like?
- If you've thought of an incident but don't remember it well, draft a list of questions to ask a friend or relative who is familiar with the event. Be sure to ask for details and bits of dialogue so that you can re-create the story.

SkillBuilder

 CRITICAL THINKING

Visualizing an Experience
When writers tell personal stories, they often begin by reliving the experience in their minds. Creating a mental picture of an event helps writers remember important details and dialogue that can give their narrative an authentic flavor. These are some of the questions writers ask themselves:

- Who was there, and what did these people do?
- What did people say?
- What did the place look like?
- How did I feel physically? emotionally?
- What did I smell? hear? touch? taste?

APPLYING WHAT YOU'VE LEARNED
When you try to visualize your own experience, record details that you remember about the people, places, and events. These notes will be helpful as you begin drafting.

THINK & PLAN

Evaluating Your Ideas

1. How is the incident you've chosen meaningful to you? How might it be meaningful to others?
2. Do you remember enough about your experience to write a coherent story? If not, where can you get more information?

WRITING FROM EXPERIENCE **471**

Speaking and Listening:
COLLABORATIVE OPPORTUNITY

I Point out that narrating their incidents orally will give students practice in putting the events in chronological order. It will also give them a chance to gain valuable feedback or additional information, especially if the listener is someone who also witnessed or was a party to the incident.

Writing Skill:
USING DIALOGUE

J Remind students that using dialogue, or the exact words of the people involved in the incident, is an effective way to *show* events rather than merely *telling* about them. In addition to presenting events, dialogue can reveal character and contribute to the atmosphere or mood of a narrative. Students should not use dialogue in an offhand way, however. They should make sure that the speaker's words reveal something about his or her personality.

SkillBuilder CRITICAL THINKING

VISUALIZING AN EXPERIENCE Go over the tips for visualizing. Suggest that students practice this technique by closing their eyes for a few minutes at a time and imagining that the action of their narrative is unfolding on a huge movie screen. Challenge them to see the action in slow motion, taking in as many specific details as they can.

Application Students may want to create a chart with a column for each of the five senses and record their details in tabular form.

THE LANGUAGE OF LITERATURE TEACHER'S EDITION **471**

Teaching Strategy:
STUMBLING BLOCK

K Remind students that they can use fictional short stories they have read as springboards for planning their own true narrative. If students have difficulty, have them work with partners to review how the elements of character, setting, and plot are revealed in some of their favorite short stories.

Teaching Strategy: USING THE SKILLBUILDER

L You may wish to teach the SkillBuilder on transitional words at this time. Knowing how to create chronological transitions will help students focus, as they write, on the order in which events occurred.

DRAFTING

Putting the Story on Paper

Getting Started A firsthand narrative is inside your head. It's time to put it in writing so that you and others can enjoy it! What follows are strategies for exploring, drafting, and organizing the ideas in your true story.

❶ Explore Your Story

Character, setting, and plot are elements of a story, whether true or made-up. Before starting your draft, you may want to give some thought to these story elements.

Characters Who are the people in your true story? Have you included details about them, such as their age, appearance, and behavior at the time?

Setting When and where did your story take place? If the setting is important to the story, you'll want to describe it. (A story about getting lost in a city should include details about the streets, buildings, and signs. Such details will show readers that the city can be a confusing place.)

Plot What happens in your story? You know the sequence of events because you were there. Remember, however, that many narratives throw the speaker into a conflict. If your story has a conflict, how is it resolved?

❷ Write a Rough Draft

Put your ideas onto paper. Use your notes to help you remember details. Don't try to make your writing perfect. You can clean it up later. As you write, try to address the questions below.

- What audience will you write for?
- What format will you use—a column in a family newsletter, a story in a magazine, or something else?

Student's Index Cards

Characters
Amalia—nine years old, smart, quiet, short curly hair, likes to draw, wears purple clothes
Me—fourteen, impatient

Setting
Downtown on a July afternoon. Sidewalk is hot as a griddle. Heat first makes you dizzy, then makes you sweat. Buildings don't offer much shade.

Plot
Amalia and I take the bus to run errands, but we miss the stop. We wander around in the heat. Amalia shows me the map she has drawn. It helps us get home.

472 UNIT THREE: ALL IN THE FAMILY

 WRITING SPRINGBOARD
Living in Two Cultures An Armenian-American teenager talks about her enjoyment of life in the United States and about the pressure her parents put on her to adhere to the traditional practices of the Armenian culture.

Writing Prompt
Think of a time when you or someone you know experienced a clash of ideas with parents. Write a personal-experience essay in which you explore the situation.

Side B, Frame 13582

Teaching Strategy: STUMBLING BLOCK

 Remind students that the introduction in a narrative, essay, or report should grab the reader's attention. Therefore, long and rambling introductions should be avoided. In a personal narrative, one good strategy is to plunge the reader into an exciting phase of the action and then use a flashback to provide necessary background information.

Teaching Strategy: PEER REVIEW

 Have reviewers read the narrative before they make any comments. During the second reading, they should jot down brief comments and suggestions. Remind students to include specific ideas for revision, such as "Can you revise this passage to make the order of events clear?"

Student's Rough Draft

> I remember one day when Mom asked me to run some errands downtown. She made me take my kid sister Amalia with me. That made me mad because she always followed me around. Amalia isn't a brat or anything like that. She is deaf, and so she depends on me more than most little sisters do. Last summer, Amalia wasn't the best lip reader in the world and she was just learning sign language. So whenever anyone said anything, I had to face her and repeat very slowly what was said or she wouldn't understand. On this one day, though, I ended up depending on Amalia.

My introduction seems long and unfocused. Should I begin with the problem (being lost)?

This story is for a family newsletter, so I don't have to say who everyone is. My family knows Amalia.

SkillBuilder — WRITER'S CRAFT

Using Transitions to Show Time Order

Firsthand narratives usually include a sequence of events over time. Good writers use transition words or phrases to connect ideas and make a story coherent. Some words that show time are *first, after, next, during,* and *every time.* Which words in the example help you see the order of events?

First, Amalia and I took the bus downtown. Then we missed our stop and got lost. Finally, we used Amalia's map to get home.

APPLYING WHAT YOU'VE LEARNED
Examine the sequence of events in your draft. Add transitions where necessary so that readers are aware of changes in time.

WRITING HANDBOOK
For more information on transitions, see page 869 of the Writing Handbook.

3 Organize Your Draft

Try one of these methods for organizing your draft.

- Tell your story in chronological order (first event to the last).
- Begin with an exciting event or dialogue and then continue in chronological order.
- Start in the middle of the story and refer to earlier events with a flashback. Tell the rest of the events in sequence.

PEER RESPONSE

Invite a friend to read your draft and answer these questions.

- How did you react to the experience I wrote about?
- What parts helped you really understand my narrative?
- What people or events were most vivid to you and why?
- What would you like to know more about?

RETHINK & EVALUATE

Checking Your Progress

1. How well does the draft match the story in your head?
2. Have you found a focus for your story? If not, how can you shape a focus and stick to it?
3. Why is the story important to you? Does this meaning come through in your writing?

WRITING FROM EXPERIENCE   473

SkillBuilder — WRITER'S CRAFT

USING TRANSITIONS TO SHOW TIME ORDER Encourage students to use these additional transitions to show time order: *at once, before, early, eventually, finally, immediately, lately, later, meanwhile, recently, soon, suddenly, then, until, when,* and *while.* Make sure that students can identify the transition words in the sample passage: *first, then, finally.*

Application Students can work with partners to check that they have incorporated appropriate transitions in their drafts.

Additional Suggestions Suggest that students insert consecutive superscript numbers before each event described in their drafts. The numbers should indicate good places to use transitions.

Reteaching/Reinforcement
- *Writing Mini-Lessons* transparencies, pp. 41–42

The Writer's Craft
Transitional Devices, pp. 364-367

Writing Skill: REVISING

🔵 As students revise and edit their narratives, they will work to improve their drafts by
1. adding needed words, sentences, and paragraphs
2. cutting unnecessary material by focusing on repetitive or unrelated details
3. substituting words, sentences, and paragraphs for deleted material if necessary
4. rearranging parts of the text to create coherence and unity

Teaching Strategy: MODELING

🅿 Discuss how this model meets the Standards for Evaluation given on page 475. Words and phrases giving clues about the narrator's attitude include the following: "bug me," "tagged along," "practically saved my life," "Thank goodness for Amalia. . . ."

🆀 Guide students to identify the meaning of the experience: The narrator learned to value her little sister's company and her abilities. The event was important because it marked a turning point in the writer's relationship with Amalia.

REVISING AND PUBLISHING

Refining Your Story

Problem Solving and Polishing Now you're ready to put the finishing touches on your story. The activities on these pages will assist you in making any final changes.

1 Revise and Edit

Before revising your narrative, you might want to think about your peer reviewer's comments. Use your judgment and the pointers below to decide which comments you'll address.

🔵
- Have you shaped your writing for a specific audience? Have you included enough details to make the story clear?
- On the right are one student's introduction and conclusion. What ideas do they give you for making your beginning and ending clearer?
- For additional tips on improving your story, consult the SkillBuilder, the Standards for Evaluation, and the Editing Checklist on the next page.

🆀 What does the narrator learn from this experience? Why do you think this event was important to the writer?

474   UNIT THREE: ALL IN THE FAMILY

How does the beginning set the scene for the story? What words or phrases give clues about the narrator's attitude?

Student's Revised Draft

Amalia, My Little Hero

It used to bug me that Amalia tagged along with me wherever I went. However, that changed one scorching day last summer when my kid sister practically saved my life.

Mom had asked me to run some errands downtown. Of course, Amalia had to go too. We were going to take the bus to the usual stop and then walk from there. I never thought that we'd miss our stop and get terribly lost. Thank goodness for Amalia and her little notebook.

When we arrived home red-faced and worn out two hours late, Mom had never been happier to see us. Of course, she wanted to know why we took so long to run her errands. I explained how I got us lost and how my smart sister saved the day. "Amalia found the way back!" I sputtered between gulps of iced tea. We showed Mom the map that Amalia was sketching in her notebook all along. Mom was so proud of her! I smiled as we both gave my little sister a hug. I was proud of her too.

Another student produced a puppet show about herself and her younger brother. What audience do you think she had in mind?

② Share Your Work

How will you present your narrative? The format you've chosen will determine your options. The student whose work is shown above wrote her narrative as a puppet show. She and some friends performed the show at an after-school program for third graders. Some other publishing ideas are below.

- Record your story on a cassette for your family and friends.
- Send your narrative to a student literary magazine.

Standards for Evaluation

A firsthand narrative
- uses descriptive details and dialogue to develop the characters, setting, and plot
- develops a clear beginning, middle, and end
- maintains a consistent tone and first-person point of view
- uses appropriate language for the selected audience
- shows readers how the event is important to the writer

SkillBuilder

 GRAMMAR FROM WRITING

Avoiding Shifts in Tense
Your narrative will be confusing if you change verb tense between sentences or within paragraphs. When two actions occur at the same time, use the same tense for both actions.

*My head **swam** with anxiety when I realized we were lost, but Amalia **seemed** calm and sure of her way.*

 GRAMMAR HANDBOOK

For more information on avoiding shifts in tense, see page 923 of the Grammar Handbook.

Editing Checklist Use these questions to revise and edit your true story.

- Did you use transition words to show the order of events?
- Did you avoid unnecessary shifts in verb tense?

REFLECT & ASSESS

Look at Your Experiences

1. What did you learn about yourself as you wrote your narrative?
2. Did you find the peer comments helpful? Why or why not?

 PORTFOLIO Jot down your answers to these questions. Attach the answers to your narrative when it goes in your portfolio.

WRITING FROM EXPERIENCE 475

Teaching Strategy: MODELING

R Elicit from students that the student probably had an audience of younger viewers in mind. Remind the class that students can work together to implement many publishing and sharing ideas.

Teaching Strategy: MANAGING THE PAPER LOAD

S Whenever possible, phrase your written comments as questions that will encourage students to reflect on and assess their work. For example, instead of writing "lacks a good conclusion," try "How would you sum up the meaning that this experience had for you?"

Standards for Evaluation

Have students review their narratives for the following:

Ideas and Content
- recounts a personal experience vividly
- draws readers in with an interesting introduction
- gives a sense of time, place, and characters through use of sensory details and dialogue
- shows why the event is important to the writer

Structure and Form
- displays a clear order of events
- presents a single focus in each paragraph
- uses a variety of sentence structures

Grammar, Usage, and Mechanics
- contains no more than two or three minor errors in grammar, usage, spelling, capitalization, and punctuation

PORTFOLIO

Ask students to jot down what they like best about their personal-experience narratives. Then invite them to make a brief list of the weaknesses or trouble spots in their narratives. Students may wish to include their informal evaluations along with their narratives in their portfolio.

SkillBuilder GRAMMAR FROM WRITING

AVOIDING SHIFTS IN TENSE Make sure that students can identify all the past-tense verbs in the sample sentence: *swam, realized, were, seemed.* Then have students work with partners to go over their narratives to identify any errors in tense usage.

Application You may wish to reinforce the SkillBuilder by writing these sentences on the chalkboard and asking students to correct any errors.

1. Mom wanted to know why we take so long to run her errands. (*wants* or *took*)
2. I told her that Amalia come to the rescue when she pulls out her notebook with a map. (*came, pulled*)
3. I smiled and we both give Amalia a hug. (*gave*)

Reteaching/Reinforcement
- *Grammar Mini-Lessons* copymasters p. 29, transparencies, p. 31

The Writer's Craft
Avoiding Shifts in Tense, pp. 608–609

UNIT REVIEW

This feature allows students to reflect on what they have learned in Unit Three and to assess how well they have understood it. This feature provides students with multiple opportunities for self-assessment. You may also wish to use some of the activities to assess specific skills, such as speaking, listening, or cooperative learning.

Objectives

- To allow students to reflect on and assess their understanding of theme
- To allow students to reflect on and assess their understanding of literary concepts, such as symbol, dialogue, and description
- To provide students with the opportunity to assess and build their portfolios

REFLECTING ON THEME

OPTION 1

Spark a class discussion of what kinds of conflicts can and cannot be resolved. Suggest that two or more people can resolve a conflict in which they are involved but that no one can resolve another person's internal conflicts. Once students have discussed the issue in groups, you might have a whole-class discussion so that they can share their ideas.

OPTION 2

Have students consider whether the character they admire most and the character they would like to have as a brother or sister are the same character. Why or why not?

OPTION 3

After students jot down selections for their anthology, challenge them to choose some organizing hierarchy. The introduction should explain the rationale for that arrangement.

 Self–Assessment
Encourage students to go beyond the "one thing I've learned" format by writing about a series of lessons they have learned. Encourage them to link these lessons to sum up what they have learned.

REFLECT & ASSESS

UNIT THREE: ALL IN THE FAMILY

The selections in this unit deal with a variety of family relationships and situations. To explore the new understanding of family that you may have gained, complete one or more of the options in each of the following sections.

REFLECTING ON THEME

OPTION 1 **Taking Stock** In many of the selections in this unit, family conflicts don't get fully resolved. For example, even though the narrator of "Marine Corps Issue" finds out about his father's injury, the two of them still cannot really talk about the war. With a small group of classmates, discuss some of the unresolved family conflicts in the selections. Decide which conflicts you think should—or even *can*—be resolved, then propose ways to resolve them or otherwise ease the tensions in the situations.

OPTION 2 **Choosing a Favorite** Which of the spirited young characters in this unit do you admire the most? Make a list of the main characters, noting a couple of the positive traits of each one. Then decide on one that you would like to have for a brother or sister, and write your reasons for choosing that person.

OPTION 3 **Becoming an Editor** Imagine that you have been asked to compile an anthology—a collection of writings—about the family for teenage readers. What selections from this unit would you include? What title would you give the anthology? Pick four or five selections and create a table of contents, listing their titles in the order you want the works to be read. Then write an introduction to your anthology, explaining why you chose the selections.

Self-Assessment: Complete the following two statements:

- *One thing I've learned about families from reading this unit is _____.*
- *One thing I've learned about myself as part of a family is _____.*

REVIEWING LITERARY CONCEPTS

OPTION 1 **Thinking About Symbols** Writers often add depth and meaning to their works through the use of symbolism. Working with a partner, look back through this unit's selections for things that seem to be symbols. For each selection that you've read, try to list one thing—an object, an action, a person, or a place—that might stand for something beyond itself. Then explain what you think the symbol might mean.

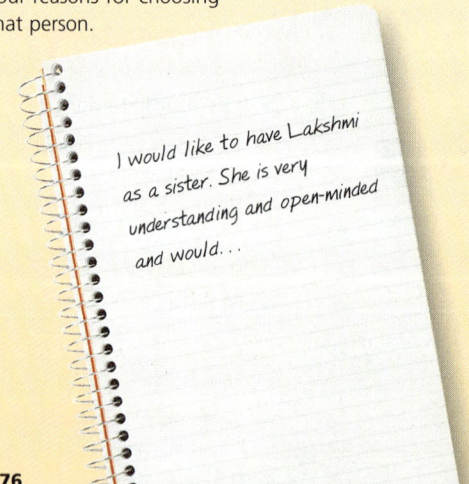

476

OPTION 2 Recognizing the Impact of Dialogue and Description Most writers use a combination of dialogue and description in telling their stories or expressing themselves. To recognize how these two elements influence your reading experience, make a chart like the one shown, listing in the first column the titles of the fiction, nonfiction, and drama selections that you've read. In the second column, record the image or scene that you remember most vividly from each selection. In the last column, indicate whether each image or scene was expressed through dialogue, description, or a combination of both. If you need to, look back at the selections to jog your memory.

Selection	Strong Memory from Selection	Description, Dialogue, or Both?
"Marine Corps Issue"	when the father catches his son looking in the locker box	Description

Self-Assessment: The following literary terms that relate to poetry were either introduced or reviewed in this unit: alliteration, repetition, imagery, simile, rhyme, metaphor, and stanza. With a partner, go back through all the poetry you've read and find examples to illustrate each term.

PORTFOLIO BUILDING

- **QuickWrites** Many of the QuickWrites in this unit asked you to express opinions about family life. Choose the piece of writing in which you feel you expressed an opinion most clearly. In a cover note, explain why you do or do not still hold the same opinion. Include the piece of writing and the cover note in your portfolio.

- **Writing About Literature** As you wrote an essay exploring the theme of a literary work, how did you go about reaching a deeper understanding of the writer's purpose? Did your own understanding of human life change? Write a note describing how you explored the theme of the work and what you learned from the experience. Include your note with your essay if you choose to place the essay in your portfolio.

- **Writing from Experience** Writing about an experience often gives a writer new insight into the experience. What were your reasons for choosing the particular personal experience you just wrote about? What did you learn as you wrote? Were there details of the experience that you left out? If so, why? Attach a note to your personal-experience essay, describing the lessons you learned as you wrote about an important personal experience.

- **Personal Choice** Think about the activities and writing that you have done for this unit and on your own. Which one did you learn the most from? Write a note that explains your choice, attach it to the piece of writing or record of the activity, and include both in your portfolio.

Self-Assessment: Check to see whether your portfolio contains enough variety. Have you included a story, a poem, or another kind of creative writing? Is there a record of an activity? Throughout the year, look for opportunities to add diversity to your portfolio.

SETTING GOALS

As you work through the next unit, think of ways you'd like to challenge yourself—perhaps by volunteering to be part of a performance, giving an oral reading of a selection, or doing research to find out more about a subject and sharing your findings with the class.

REVIEWING LITERARY CONCEPTS

OPTION 1

Review traditional symbols, such as a flag, a heart, biblical names, a no-parking sign. Tell students that literary symbols work in much the same way as these conventional symbols, except that they have been created by an author to stand for something in a specific text. As students work in pairs to identify symbols in the various selections, caution them against seeing every object as a symbol.

OPTION 2

When students have completed their charts, challenge them to look for patterns. Are particular types of scenes usually described? Are other types of scenes usually revealed through dialogue? You might have a whole-class discussion in which students share ideas about such patterns and possible reasons for them. See also Unit Three Resource Book, p. 75.

 Self-Assessment Have students define each term for themselves, without looking in the dictionary. Then have them check their definitions to see how well they comprehend each term. Students can then identify one instance of each element in the selections in this unit.

PORTFOLIO BUILDING

You may wish to help students choose or modify options, to suit the needs you have established for the class. Encourage students to incorporate drafts, not just final products, into their portfolios, so that they can reflect on and assess their development and progress. Suggest that students periodically examine their portfolios, ranking each piece as satisfactory and worth keeping, or needing improvement. This process will help them identify any problems that recur in their writing.

Self-Assessment Suggest that though diversity is encouraged, multiple examples in some genres are acceptable.

SETTING GOALS

Reassure students that the skills they have developed as readers and writers will help them to become skilled speakers, performers, and researchers. Tell them that self-confidence, determination, trial and error, and practice are stepping stones to acquiring all kinds of skills.

UNIT FOUR

UNIT THEMES

Unit Four

Portrait of a Hero In this unit, students will read selections from Homer's epic poem the *Odyssey* and two 20th-century poems based on it. The unit contains two parts: Part 1, "The Wanderings of Odysseus," and Part 2, "The Homecoming." Selections in both parts contribute to the unit theme by examining the heroic aspects of Odysseus' character as they are revealed in the course of his adventures and his struggle to get home.

Part 1

The Wanderings of Odysseus Part 1 features excerpts from Books 9, 10, and 12 of the *Odyssey*, in which Odysseus describes the many adventures he has as he and his men make their way back to Ithaca after the Trojan War. Also included is Margaret Atwood's poem "Siren Song."

Part 2

The Homecoming Part 2 tells of Odysseus' arrival in Ithaca after a 20-year absence; his battle with the suitors, who have taken over his home; and his reunion with his wife, Penelope. Part 2 concludes with a Dorothy Parker poem about Penelope.

OF A HERO

HEROISM HURTS AND NO ONE EASILY CONSENTS TO BE UNDER ITS RULE.

ELIZABETH HARDWICK
Writer and literary critic

Battle with Cicones, Romare Bearden (1914–1988). Courtesy of the Estate of Romare Bearden.

Exploring Theme

To help students explore the connections between the art, the quotation, and the unit theme, have them consider the following questions:

1. If you had to paint a portrait of a hero, what would your hero look like? Would your hero be real or fictional? *(Responses will vary.)*

2. Ask students whether they agree with Elizabeth Hardwick's idea that "heroism hurts." *(Possible responses: yes, because heroes face physical dangers; yes, because heroes have to make difficult decisions and be responsible for those they lead; no, because heroes are admired, respected, and treated well by society)*

3. How does the collage suggest that heroism hurts? *(Possible response: The collage conveys the physical pain involved in being a hero in battle; it implies that the hero, or the leader, is ultimately responsible for everyone's suffering.)*

4. What kinds of experiences might you expect to read about in this unit? *(Possible response: experiences that show the heroic aspects of the characters, especially Odysseus)*

5. Discuss a particular experience of your own from which you learned the meaning of what it is to be a hero. *(Responses will vary.)*

Art Note

Battle with Cicones by Romare Bearden
Romare Bearden (1914–1988) was born in North Carolina, and he spent much of his adult life in New York City. In his work, Bearden tried to realistically depict the urban and the rural lives of African Americans; in doing so, he focused on many aspects of African-American culture, including music, religion, and family life. In the latter part of his life, Bearden spent a great deal of time on the Caribbean island of St. Martin; the colors and forms of his new surroundings influenced much of his work during this period. This collage is one in a series he created based on the adventures of Odysseus.

Reading the Art *How do the colors in this collage affect the mood of the scene? How do you think the effect would change if the figures were not silhouettes but portraits with faces?*

UNIT FOUR
Part 1 Skills Trace

 DENOTES MINI-LESSON IN TEACHER'S EDITION

Selections	Reading Skills and Strategies	Literary Concepts	Writing Opportunities	Speaking, Listening, and Viewing
EPIC POETRY *from the* **Odyssey** Homer, translated by Robert Fitzgerald Book 9: **New Coasts and Poseidon's Son**	Defining the epic, PE p. 482 Examining the Homeric epics, PE p. 482 Reading the epic, PE p. 484	Epic hero, PE p. 507 Reviewing foreshadowing, ML TE p. 491 Poetry, ML TE p. 503	Create your own epithets, PE p. 506 Draft an episode, PE p. 506 Vivid description, ML TE p. 495	Act out scenes from Book 9, PE p. 506 Devise an escape plan, PE p. 507 Share with the class, PE p. 507 Storytelling, ML TE p. 492
Book 10: **The Grace of the Witch**		Description, PE p. 519 Conflict, PE p. 519 Reviewing characterization, ML TE p. 513	Try writing the lyrics, PE p. 518 Write a news story, PE p. 518 Write one or two diary entries, PE p. 518	Prepare an oral reading, PE p. 519 Analyzing a speech, ML TE p. 579 Review storytelling, TE p. 519
Book 12: **Sea Perils and Defeat**		Theme, PE p. 531 Reviewing imagery, ML TE p. 526	Write short encyclopedia entries, PE p. 530 Draft a character sketch, PE p. 530 Write a plot outline, PE p. 530	Compose/perform a song, PE p. 531
POETRY ON YOUR OWN **Siren Song** Margaret Atwood			Writing descriptions, TE p. 532 Describing a situation, TE p. 533	Paired reading, TE p. 532

Writing	Reading Skills and Strategies	Literary Concepts	Writing Opportunities	Speaking, Listening, and Viewing
WRITING ABOUT LITERATURE **Creative Response**	Understanding levels of language, PE pp. 534–535 Responding to literature, PE pp. 536–539	Understanding levels of language, PE pp. 534–535 Style, PE pp. 536–537	Making a choice, PE p. 535 Looking back, PE p. 535 Trying it out, PE p. 535 Parody, PE pp. 536–539	Telling a story, PE p. 537 Viewing a parody, PE p. 541 Interpreting a parody, PE p. 541 Discussion, PE p. 541 Discussing elements of parody, PE p. 541

Grammar, Usage, Mechanics, and Spelling	Multimodal Learning	Research and Study Skills	Vocabulary	
Capitalization: Religious terms ML TE p. 498	Allocating human resources, ML TE p. 500	Research ancient Greek civilization, ML TE p. 507	adversary appalled avenge disdain entreat	formidable guile indifferent ponderous whim
Capitalization: Titles, ML TE p. 517	Create a painting or diorama, PE p. 519 Oral reading, PE p. 519 Make a model of Odysseus' ship, PE p. 519	Research kinds of ships used by Greeks in Homeric times, PE p. 519 Indexes, ML TE p. 514 Research varying positions on the concept of "afterlife," TE p. 519	beguile chide contender disconsolate enticing	regaled snare stealth succumb vile
Capitalization: Geographical names, ML TE p. 524		Consult an atlas or encyclopedia for map's modern names, PE p. 531 Research geography of *Odyssey*, TE p. 531	abominably anguish chaos dire dwindle	lurk peril questing travail scourge

Grammar, Usage, Mechanics, and Spelling	Multimodal Learning	Research and Study Skills	Media Literacy
Understanding informal language, PE p. 535 Using conjunctions, PE p. 539 Compound-complex sentences, PE p. 539	Telling a story, PE p. 537 Viewing a parody, PE p. 541 Interpreting a parody, PE p. 541 Discussion, PE p. 541 Discussing elements of parody, PE p. 541	Creatively responding to literature, PE pp. 536 Analyzing parody, PE p. 541	Analyzing parody, PE pp. 540–541

SKILLS TRACE TEACHER'S EDITION **479b**

UNIT FOUR
Part 2 Skills Trace

 DENOTES MINI-LESSON IN TEACHER'S EDITION

Selections	Reading Skills and Strategies	Literary Concepts	Writing Opportunities	Speaking, Listening, and Viewing
EPIC POETRY *from the Odyssey* **(continued)** Homer, translated by Robert Fitzgerald Book 21: **The Test of the Bow** Book 22: **Death in the Great Hall** Book 23: **The Trunk of the Olive Tree**	Predicting, PE p. 543	Characterization, PE p. 568 Reviewing irony, ML TE p. 560	Create a plot outline for a story, PE p. 567 Identify examples of human and heroic qualities, PE p. 567 Dialogue, ML TE p. 557	Plan and stage a TV talk show interview, PE p. 568 Report, PE p. 568 Choreographing a dance, ML TE p. 551
POETRY ON YOUR OWN **Penelope** Dorothy Parker			Writing impressions, TE p. 570	Choral reading, TE p. 570 Hold a debate, TE p. 571
Writing				
WRITING FROM EXPERIENCE **Informative Exposition**			Writing an extended definition, PE pp. 572–579 Drafting, PE pp. 576–577 Revising and publishing, PE pp. 578–579	Group discussion, PE pp. 573–574 Videotape with a voice-over narrative, PE p. 579 Conducting a survey, PE p. 579

Grammar, Usage, Mechanics, and Spelling	Multimodal Learning	Research and Study Skills	Vocabulary
Troublesome verbs, ML TE p. 548	Interview for TV talk show, PE p. 568 Create a storyboard, PE p. 568 Report, PE p. 568 Choreographing a dance, ML TE p. 551 Computers, TE p. 554 Recreate the battle, TE p. 568 Sketching interpretations, TE p. 570	Research paintings depicting adventures of Odysseus, PE p. 568 Reference: Using electronic media, ML TE p. 554	aloof　　　justification commander　omen contemptible　plunder desolation　restitution dithering　revelry frenzy　　throng gall　　　wiliest implacable

Grammar, Usage, Mechanics, and Spelling	Multimodal Learning	Research and Study Skills	Media Literacy
Avoiding illogical comparisons, PE p. 141	Analyzing a cartoon, PE p. 572 Interpreting a graph, PE p. 572 Interpreting memorabilia, PE p. 573	Reference books, TE p. 574 Using a thesaurus, PE p. 577	Analyzing a cartoon, PE p. 572 Interpreting a graph, PE p. 572 Interpreting memorabilia, PE p. 573 Using a thesaurus, PE p. 577

UNIT FOUR
Recommended Resources

ENRICHMENT RESEARCH

✓ Recommended Novels and Play

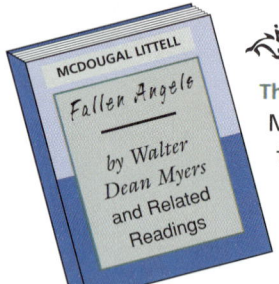

LITERATURE CONNECTIONS WITH SOURCEBOOK FOR TEACHERS

Thematic Link In brutally realistic terms, Myers presents the experiences—terrifying, numbly routine, and heartbreaking—of a small group of young men who come of age as soldiers during the Vietnam War. The novel's protagonist finds himself in the middle of a war more confusing and traumatic than the life he fled.

About the Author Writing is the pleasure and passion of Walter Dean Myers (born 1937). He says, "There is always one more story to tell, one more person whose life needs to be held up to the sun."

Other Works by Walter Dean Myers *Hoops, The Outside Shot, Scorpions, The Legend of Tarik, Now Is Your Time! The African-American Struggle for Freedom*

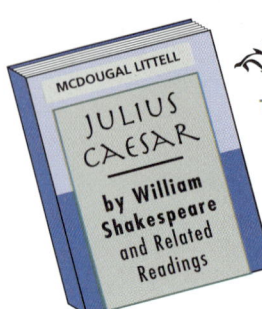

LITERATURE CONNECTIONS WITH SOURCEBOOK FOR TEACHERS

Thematic Link In ancient Rome, tragic heroes—good and noble characters—make fatal errors in judgment that lead to their downfalls.

About the Author William Shakespeare (1564–1616), the gifted playwright and poet, probed the mysteries of human nature, creating memorable characters whose experiences transcend time and place.

Other Works by William Shakespeare *Hamlet, Macbeth, A Midsummer Night's Dream, The Tragedy of Romeo and Juliet, Antony and Cleopatra*

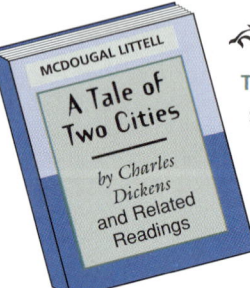

LITERATURE CONNECTIONS WITH SOURCEBOOK FOR TEACHERS

Thematic Link In this Victorian novel, set against the raging upheaval of the French Revolution, love and self-sacrifice prove to be the virtues of a true hero.

About the Author A shrewd observer of 19th-century London and an influential social critic, Charles Dickens (1812–1870) created striking and compassionate portrayals of the troubled society of his time.

Other Works by Charles Dickens *Oliver Twist, Great Expectations, David Copperfield, Hard Times, Little Dorritt*

Thematic Link This tale of a simple fisherman's battle to land an enormous catch is one of Hemingway's finest achievements. His spare prose beautifully underscores the elemental struggle between man and nature.

About the Author Hemingway (1899–1961) fought in the first World War and afterwards lived much of his life in Europe. Many of his novels are set there. Like Dickens, Hemingway has had tremendous popular success, and many of his novels and stories have been filmed.

Other Works by Ernest Hemingway *The Sun Also Rises, To Have and Have Not, A Farewell to Arms*

Professional Development — TEACHING THE NOVEL

Easterling, P.E., and Knox, B.M.W., eds. *The Cambridge History of Classical Literature, Volume I Part III: Philosophy, History and Oratory.* Cambridge, England: Cambridge University Press, 1989.

Easterling, P.E., and Knox, B.M.W., eds. *The Cambridge History of Classical Literature, Volume I Part IV: The Hellenistic Period and the Empire.* Cambridge, England: Cambridge University Press, 1989.

Meade, Marion. *Dorothy Parker: What Fresh Hell Is This?* NY: Penguin, 1987.

Pucci, Pietro. "The Song of the Sirens," *Reading the Odyssey.* Princeton, NJ: Princeton University Press, 1996.

Vernant, Jean-Pierre. "The Refusal of Odysseus," *Reading the Odyssey.* Princeton, NJ: Princeton University Press, 1996.

CROSS-CURRICULAR TEACHING   PROFESSIONAL DEVELOPMENT

Recommended Readings in Cross-Curricular Areas

LITERATURE/HISTORY

Bullfinch's Mythology by Thomas Bullfinch (1995) Indispensable guide through the world of classical mythology. Links to Homer's *Odyssey*.

Greek Myths by Lucilla Burn (1990) Finely illustrated and concise approach that makes classical mythology accessible. Links to Homer's *Odyssey*.

The Cambridge History of Classical Literature, Volume I Part I: Early Greek Poetry Offers a broad, inclusive context for Homer's work. Links to Homer's *Odyssey*.

The Power of Myth by Joseph Campbell (1988) Insightful presentation of the power of myth and its effects on modern society. Links to Homer's *Odyssey*.

Professional Development — CROSS-CURRICULAR INSTRUCTION

Beane, James A., ed. *Toward a Coherent Curriculum.* Alexandria, VA: ASCD, 1995.

Glasser, William. *The Quality School Teacher.* NY: Harper Perennial, 1993.

Hern, Matt, ed. *Deschooling Our Lives.* Philadelphia, PA: New Society Publishers, 1996.

Reissman, Rose. "Hero Rites: An Exercise in Defining Ourselves and Others," *Notes Plus.* NCTE, January 1996.

Recommended Media Resources

THE LANGUAGE OF LITERATURE

ELECTRONIC LIBRARY
CD-ROM
Additional literature selections for Unit Four can be found on the Electronic Library CD-ROM.

LASERLINKS
Videodisc, Gr.9
See *LaserLinks Teacher's Source Book,* page 37, for overview of Unit Four.

AUDIO LIBRARY
Tapes
Gr. 9, Tape 11: Sides A & B
Novel in Spanish
Historia de dos ciudades (A Tale of Two Cities)

WRITING COACH
Writing Coach Software: Writing about Literature—Interpretive Response, Explanation of an Idea

OUTSIDE RESOURCES

Films/Videos/Film Strips/Audiocassettes
The Odyssey, 3 videos, Britannica Films, 1965, (90 minutes).
The Odyssey: An Epic Telling, 4 audiocassettes or 4 CDs, Rivertree Productions, 1995, (4:10 hours).
Homer's Mythology: Tracing a Tradition, 3 sound filmstrips, Guidance Associates.
The Voyages of Ulysses and Aeneas, CD-ROM, Society for Visual Education, 1995.
Margaret Atwood Reads, audiocassette, American Audio Prose Library.

Internet Resources
McDougal Littell Literature Center at http://www.hmco.com/mcdougal/lit

Professional Development — TEACHING WITH TECHNOLOGY

Cuban, Larry. "Dejá Vu All Over Again: A History of Technology in the American Schools," *Electronic Learning.* 15:2 (October 1995) 34.

Means, Barbara et. al. *Using Technology to Support Education Reform.* Newton, MA: Education Development Center, Inc., Menlo Park, CA: SRT International.

Interface: The Computer Education Quarterly. Mitchell Publishing, Inc., 55 Penny Lane, Ste. 103, Watsonville, CA 95076.

UNIT FOUR
Professional Enrichment

Finding Ithaca: The Odyssey Personalized
Jane Ellen Glasser

In *The Power of Myth,* Joseph Campbell (with Bill Moyers, 1988, ed. Betty Sue Flowers, New York: Anchor) speaks of the hero's adventure as an archetype for our times. It is this connecting thread between universal models and the hero lurking within each of us that I throw out to my students, inviting them into the world of Homer's *Odyssey.*

Even before my introduction to Campbell's works, in those semesters when teaching the epic was limited to impersonal literary analysis, I began to feel ties that could reach across continents and nearly three millennia to speak to my students. Metaphorically, human life is an odyssey, a series of wanderings, even if, as with most of my pupils, the hero's path does not extend beyond one's neighborhood. And despite their few years, they have experienced trials. The lure of the lotus, the seduction of the Sirens' song, the brutish realm of the Cyclopes resonated as tropes for the tests and ordeals inner-city youth confront almost daily.

My new understanding changed my teaching. Before they begin the epic, I now let my students know that I expect them to identify with Odysseus, to use his hero's journey as a paradigm for exploring and experiencing the meaning of their own lives. I explain that the culmination of the unit will be a composition, a creation of their own personal odyssey laced with allusions to Homer's work, and a project based on their personal narrative to present to the class. Although at this point the assignments seem inchoate and abstract, students enter Homer's world with an expectation of relevance and the kind of ego-energy that sends them regularly to mirrors.

I focus the reading of *The Odyssey* around two themes: the role of the hero (that which is within his control), and the role of divine intervention (that which is beyond his control). I have them freewrite in response to the word "hero": What are the essential characteristics of a hero?

Who are the heroes in history, literature, movies? Do we have living heroes? We collaborate to list traits; later we try them on Odysseus, discuss whether the hero role has evolved, try to determine if Luke Skywalker or Batman or Mahatma Gandhi or Martin Luther King bear resemblance to the Greek model. In discussing the concept of divine intervention, if students cannot identify with the polytheism in which the gods whimsically dictate man's destiny, many of them do believe in transcendent power, or that fortune and misfortune are providential. Each student is given two graphic organizers. The hero chart is sectioned into four parts, each to be labeled according to a dominant heroic trait with supporting examples listed beneath. The chart on the role of the Olympians is two-columned: gods that help, gods that harm. The class is divided into collaborative-learning groups; each group is made responsible for teaching one theme for an assigned section. At the conclusion of these presentations, each student's two charts are filled in with details from the entire work. Predictably, I find that students love to swap roles with the teacher, that group work paired with peer teaching results in high energy, high involvement, constructive fun, and increased learning. My only delivery during this process is a mini-lesson at the beginning of each period, teaching such relevant literary terms as epithet, dramatic irony, and Homeric simile, and assisting students in scouting examples.

Up to this point my methodology is unchanged from the way I have taught *The Odyssey* for the past few years, when the unit would terminate with a standard third-person paper analyzing the charted themes. This year, however, I defied a curriculum that spurns the "I-paper" by having the students write personal odysseys in response to Homer's work. Instead of turning in stilted essays like the ones I used to get, all emptily saying the same thing, students turned in narratives that were imaginative and profound, demonstrating their grasp of the epic's themes and their ability to apply them to their own lives.

As a warm-up for writing the compositions, students created a third chart. In the center of large blank sheets I had them draw an island, their metaphoric Ithaca—a variation on Joseph Campbell's "bliss station" (115)—and asked them, "As Odysseus was striving toward his homeland, what are you striving toward, and where do you hope finally to arrive?" Once students had filled in their goal, they drew a thick vertical line, a barrier, and listed behind it all the people and forces that had delayed or blocked them from reaching their Ithaca. Around these deterrents they clustered allusions— vengeful Poseidon, distracting Calypso, uncivilized Polyphemus. Then they listed the people and forces that have helped. Again they drew parallels with the epic, identifying their Circes and Athenas.

The day I collected the papers, I knew, by the weight of the stack in my hand, that my students had no trouble responding to the assignment. I have found in the past that most students end compositions not when they have said what they have to say, but when the word count matches the minimum requirement for the assignment, sort of like the air compressor I recently bought for my bike. Set it on seventy and it automatically shuts off when the tire pressure hits seventy pounds. I had given them a minimal "page setting" of two; the average length was six pages. As I read the opening of Tuwanna's, the first paper in the stack, I could feel the gods smiling.

So like Odysseus's journey is the story of my life, a never ending odyssey that shall continue through all my days. The birth of a new soul is the beginning of a new odyssey; and so begins my journey.

I read their stories in one sitting, enjoying their individuality and echoing threads. Many students identified their Ithaca in terms of external values, today's twin gods of success and money. Ayonna's goal is to have her own business. Like Homer, she divided her odyssey into labeled sections: Introduction, New Beginnings, The Island of Trouble, The Stream of Doubt, Unfortunate Accidents, and Guidance for Success. Her continually thwarted plans for starting a company fueled the naysayers, her chief antagonists:

Many people laughed, said I told you so. I felt like one of the six men that were eaten by Scylla in Odysseus's journey . . . like some monster had chewed me up and spat me out. But even though I was hurt, as Odysseus was hurt after his men were devoured, that didn't stop me, nor Odysseus.

Charles dreams of finishing high school to "go to college and become a wealthy engineer," but he realizes that "for the short time I've been on this Earth, my life has been set off course." His distractions and temptations are clear to him.

My neighborhood is a land of Lotus-Eaters; drugs have buried my friends and family members. . . . Another diversion on my way to Ithaca is gangs in my neighborhood who like a giant cyclops try to intimidate with their guns and weapons.

Unfortunately for many of my students, courage is tested in the battlefields of their back yards. In plotting revenge on a gang for a wrong done to his sister, Michael relates a transforming experience.

Before my confrontation with the Wong Brothers, a strange concept entered my psyche. It was as if someone were piloting my thoughts, like Athena who worked through Odysseus. She made him invulnerable to attack, gave him a new body. Something was new in my spirit.

The temptation of the lotus was a pervasive motif. Lionel's odyssey, conceived as a parable, shows the hero's mission to be the rescue of youth from the "pleasure palace" (crack house). His narrator invokes a night journey, down through the layers of the Earth, in search of Costumus, who, like Athena, can grant the hero disguises. In this modern tale, however, those who assist, gods and men, expect to be paid for their services. Costumus asks, "Why are you here, and how will I profit from it?" The bum who agrees to direct him to the pleasure palace stipulates, "I could tell you where it is but you have to give me pleasure as well." The characters are assigned Latin-like names: Policius, one of Lawnimus's workers (an undercover cop); Renewvemus, the god of new lives (a drug counselor). All don disguises; even the palace itself is a "huge, nice house to stand as a trick to Lawnimus and his men," as if, in this netherworld, nothing is as it seems.

Several students identified their Ithaca as an emotional state. Lance's journey, a quest for love, utilized the imagery of myth and fairy tale. Held by a Circean sorceress on the Island of the Lost, the hero escapes, loses his boat at sea, is rescued by a female serpent and delivered to the Temple Island where love waits to be awakened. The primeval forest, the island that defies the finding of its sea borders, the cursed boat whose leak is unstoppable, the serpent goddess who ferries the dark waters, the wakening at the end of the hero quest—where do these mythic elements come from? I like to think the archetypes in Homer's work "awakened" universal images in his own subconscious.

For some the odyssey takes place within, as Rumi states in his poem, "That Journeys Are Good": "And you, if you have no feet to leave your country, go / Into yourself, become a ruby mine, open to the gifts of the sun." Alicia's spiritual quest has an eastern ring.

Many perils have beset me and I have faltered in my path, but through it all, I still concentrate on attaining a level of contentment, a level of satisfaction. That is my home, my resting place, my Ithaca.

Tuwanna is assisted on her journey for self-acceptance by an Athena-like mother.

She helped me to discover hidden talents within myself that I never thought to look for, to overcome my troubles, allowing the other half of me to come forth.

Her chief antagonist, she says, was "a nightmare that took the form of my father." She compares him to the cyclops Polyphemus, "a one-minded monster, a violent drunk whose habit could kill." The close of her paper suggests the determination and hopefulness of "the other half," the newly emerging hero-self.

*Though the sea is wide and strong
my boat is fast and strong
that I may reach my Ithaca
and Zeus be on my side*
. . .

I knew by the quality of the papers and projects that my decision to personalize *The Odyssey* had been enjoyable and meaningful for my students. The sense of success was confirmed when I asked them for written responses to the unit. Adam liked the fact that the assignment gave students "a chance to learn about themselves and each other." Almost all of them commented on the personal discovery that resulted, clarifying their goals or revealing new possibilities. As Marlana said, "I saw many great things I could achieve right before my eyes that I had not seen before.". . . And Lisa experienced the universality of great literature: how we are connected to these works and through them, to each other: "The assignment taught me that good literature is timeless and all of our lives are connected by trials, tests, happiness, and sadness."

To repeat Joseph Campbell's words, "where we had thought to be alone, we will be with all the world" (1988, 151).

Copyrighted material reprinted with permission.

UNIT FOUR
Starting Points for Unit Projects

The following suggestions will help you initiate individual and group projects during the course of this unit.

Nominating a Hero

GROUP DEBATE PROJECT Have students get together in small groups to nominate at least ten people who should be considered for a newly created "International Hero of Our Times" award. Have each group draw up an agreed-upon set of standards for the award, discuss the qualities of the people nominated, and vote on the person they feel best meets the standards. Have groups compare their winners and explain to the class why each winner was chosen. Then have the class vote on one overall winner. If you wish, ask students to do further research on this person's life.

Researching a War Hero

HISTORY PROJECT Tell students that it is often said that "war makes heroes of ordinary people." Have them research wars with American involvement and find out who became the heroes and heroines of these particular wars. What made them heroes? Did they strive for peace? Were they honored in any way? You might divide students into groups, each of which can choose a different war to research. Groups can present their findings to the class.

Visualizing a Hero

ART PROJECT Have students create a visual impression—by drawing, painting, or sculpting—of what a hero should look like. Have students decide on the physical features that they feel best embody the heroic spirit. Remind them that a hero need not be physically strong and all-powerful.

Designing a Map

GROUP ART PROJECT Have students work in small groups to design a map of the journey Odysseus takes in Books 9–12 of the *Odyssey*. Have them illustrate their maps and draw a key to explain any symbols they use. Ask them to display their finished maps in the classroom.

Writing an Epic

WRITING PROJECT Have students write a mini-epic or a chapter of an epic about a character they invent, a figure from literature, or a famous figure from current events. Ask them to include features found in traditional epics: travel, a quest, dangerous encounters, riddles. They can make their epic humorous or serious. Some students may wish to do a modern parody of the epic of Odysseus.

Creating a Dramatization

GROUP DRAMA PROJECT Have students work in small groups to prepare a dramatic interpretation of one of the scenes from the *Odyssey*. One student might serve as director; other students can take on various roles, from actors to set designers. Give students a week to rehearse and to prepare minimal costumes, sets, and lighting. Groups should then take turns performing their scenes for the class.

Family and Community Involvement

Family

Heroes come in many shapes and sizes and can be found in unlikely places and walks of life. Some heroes are real people, while others are known only through exaggerated tales and grand epics. The selections in Unit Four follow the adventures of Odysseus, one of the most well-known heroes in classical Western literature. The following activities will help students, their families, and other community members to explore heroic tales and identify what traits make someone a hero.

OPTION 1: CREATE A LIST
- **Connection** The selections in Unit Four relate the adventures of an epic hero.
- **Activity** *Copymaster 1* Students and family members can work together on creating a list of their favorite stories containing heroic main characters. They can discuss why the stories are memorable and why they find the characters heroic.

OPTION 2: WATCH A VIDEO
- **Connection** The selections in Unit Four tell tales of heroic adventures that have been told in one form or another for hundreds of years.
- **Activity** *Copymaster 2* Students and family members should watch a movie based on heroic themes such as *Clash of the Titans*. After viewing the movie, they can discuss why the main character is a hero.

OPTION 3: DISCUSS FAMILY HEROES
- **Connection** The selections in Unit Four portray a heroic figure familiar to many people.
- **Activity** *Copymaster 3* Students can interview different family members to find out who their heroes are, both past and present. Students should ask why these people are heroes.

Community

OPTION 1
- **Connection** The selections in Unit Four relate the tale of a famous Greek hero from ancient times.
- **Activity** Arrange a visit to a museum that exhibits art from ancient Greece. Discuss the items, such as sculpture or pottery, that include scenes of mythical heroic figures.

OPTION 2
- **Connection** The selections in Unit Four represent one of the most famous works in classical Western literature.
- **Activity** Invite someone who speaks Greek to read passages from *The Odyssey* in Greek. Then have your visitor or a student read some of the same passages in English. Have students compare the sounds and rhythms of both languages.

OPTION 3
- **Connection** The selections in Unit Four include themes that have long been a part of heroic stories.
- **Activity** Invite a professional storyteller to visit your class and tell a heroic tale. Afterwards, talk about the differences in listening to a story versus reading one.

UNIT FOUR
Part 1 Lesson Planner

TIME ALLOTMENTS SHOWN ARE APPROXIMATE. DEPENDING ON YOUR GOALS AND THE NEEDS OF YOUR STUDENTS, YOU MAY WISH TO ALLOW MORE OR LESS TIME FOR CERTAIN PORTIONS OF THE LESSON.

Table of Contents	Discussion	Previewing the Selection	Reading the Selection
PART OPENER **The Wanderings of Odysseus** page 478	**20 MINUTES** • Reflect on the part theme		
SELECTIONS *from the* **Odyssey:** **Book 9: New Coasts and Poseidon's Son** page 486 CHALLENGING		**40 MINUTES** • PERSONAL CONNECTION • HISTORICAL CONNECTION • READING CONNECTION: Defining the epic/Examining Homeric epics/Reading the epic	**90 MINUTES** • Introduce vocabulary • Read pp. 486–505 (20 pp.)
Book 10: The Grace of the Witch page 508 CHALLENGING			**50 MINUTES** • Introduce vocabulary • Read pp. 508–517 (10 pp.)
Book 12: Sea Perils and Defeat page 520 CHALLENGING			**50 MINUTES** • Introduce vocabulary • Read pp. 520–529 (10 pp.)
POETRY ON YOUR OWN **Siren Song** page 532 AVERAGE			**15 MINUTES** • Read pp. 532–533 (2 pp.)

Writing	Writer's Style	Prewriting	Drafting and Revising
WRITING ABOUT LITERATURE **Creative Response**	**20 MINUTES**	**25 MINUTES**	**70 MINUTES**

Time estimates assume in-class work. You may wish to assign some of these stages as homework.

Responding to the Selection

FROM PERSONAL RESPONSE TO CRITICAL ANALYSIS	OR	ANOTHER PATHWAY	LITERARY CONCEPTS	QUICKWRITES
60 MINUTES				
• Discussion questions	OR	• Cooperative learning (drama)	• Epic hero	• Epithets • Episode
60 MINUTES				
• Discussion questions	OR	• Epithets	• Description • Conflict	• Lyrics • News story • Diary entries
60 MINUTES				
• Discussion questions	OR	• Cooperative learning (debate)	• Theme	• Encyclopedia entries • Character sketch • Plot outline

Extension Activities

ALTERNATIVE ACTIVITIES	LITERARY LINKS	CRITIC'S CORNER	THE WRITER'S STYLE	ACROSS THE CURRICULUM	ART CONNECTION	WORDS TO KNOW	BIOGRAPHY
20 MINUTES							
✔			✔			✔	
30 MINUTES							
✔			✔			✔	
30 MINUTES							
✔	✔			MATH GEO- GRAPHY		✔	

Publishing and Reflecting	Grammar in Context	Reading the World
20 MINUTES	**15 MINUTES**	**30 MINUTES**

PART 1

REFLECTING ON THEME

Ask students to write a five-line poem about their own personal heroes. Heroes might include family members, friends, or famous people. Poems can be in any format—rhymed, free verse, or even limericks. Encourage students to read their efforts aloud to the class.

What Do You Think?

Encourage students to consider the qualities of their own heroes as they make their lists. You may want to list some responses to this activity on the board for class discussion before students begin reading from the *Odyssey*.

UNIT FOUR PART 1

THE WANDERINGS OF ODYSSEUS

REFLECTING ON THEME

Have you met any heroes lately? Forget about superheroes for a moment—the comic-book characters and action figures you're familiar with. Can someone be heroic and human too, with human flaws and weaknesses? You're about to meet Odysseus, one of the most famous heroes of all time. You'll follow him on a legendary journey as he battles monsters, explores the unknown, and overcomes incredible hazards. Through it all, he never stops being human. Hey, nobody's perfect—and Odysseus' imperfections make him even more interesting to the rest of us.

What Do You Think? Get together with a partner to brainstorm two lists. First list qualities that you think a hero should have—perhaps physical strength is one. Then list qualities—like forgetfulness or allergies—that you think might interfere with a person's being an effective hero. List the qualities in order of their importance, and compare your lists with those of the rest of the class. Keep your lists in mind as you read this part of the *Odyssey*.

Homer Translated by Robert Fitzgerald	**from the Odyssey**	481
	Book 9: **New Coasts and** **Poseidon's Son** *Odysseus introduces himself and battles the giant Cyclops.*	486
	Book 10: **The Grace of the Witch** *Odysseus is trapped by Circe's magic and romance.*	508
	Book 12: **Sea Perils and Defeat** *Who can resist the bewitching song of the Sirens?*	520
Margaret Atwood	**Siren Song** *It works evey time.*	532

480 UNIT FOUR PART 1: THE WANDERINGS OF ODYSSEUS

PREVIEWING

EPIC POETRY

from the Odyssey
Homer
Translated by Robert Fitzgerald

Activating Prior Knowledge/Setting a Purpose
PERSONAL CONNECTION

Who is your favorite monster? What science fiction or horror creature do you think is the most unusual or frightening? In your notebook, make a chart similar to the one shown, listing the characteristics of your favorite monster. Then briefly explain why your choice qualifies as the best monster ever created.

In Books 9–12 of the *Odyssey*, the poem's hero, Odysseus (ō-dĭs′ē-əs), tells of his encounters with several types of monsters. The ways in which he deals with these monsters are part of what makes him a hero. After you finish reading each episode, make other charts to list the characteristics of any monsters Odysseus encounters. Think about the heroic qualities that Odysseus reveals as he battles each of them.

Building Background
HISTORICAL CONNECTION

The *Iliad* and its sequel, the *Odyssey*, are epic poems that were composed in Greece around 800 B.C. They contain timeless portraits of several heroes and present plots, characters, and themes that have echoed throughout all subsequent Western literature. An artful blending of mythology and legend, the poems are based on an event that may be factual—a war waged by the combined forces of a number of Greek city-states against the walled city of Troy. For centuries Troy was thought to be imaginary. In 1871, however, an archaeologist began unearthing the remains of nine ancient cities—each built on the ruins of the last—in northwestern Turkey, near where the *Iliad* places Troy. One of those cities may have been the legendary city of the Trojan War.

The *Iliad* and the *Odyssey* were first told orally, perhaps even sung. It may not have been until several generations later that they were recorded in writing. Partly because of this delay, scholars disagree over the authorship of the epics. A blind poet named Homer usually gets the credit, but many think that the epics are actually the combined work of several poets. Although there have been many translations of these poems into English, Robert Fitzgerald's verse renderings are considered among the best at capturing the high drama and intense emotions of the epics.

• HISTORICAL CONNECTION

481

OVERVIEW

Objectives

- To understand and appreciate a classic epic poem that relates the dramatic adventures of a hero returning home from war
- To identify and understand the traits of an epic hero (Book 9)
- To identify and appreciate description (Book 10)
- To identify and understand theme (Book 12)
- To appreciate and understand epic similes
- To express understanding of the selection through a choice of writing forms, including epithets, an episode, song lyrics, a news story, diary entries, encyclopedia entries, a character sketch, and a plot outline
- To extend understanding of the selection through a variety of multimodal and cross-curricular activities

Skills

LITERARY CONCEPTS
Book 9:
- Epic hero
- Foreshadowing

Book 10:
- Description
- Characterization

Book 12:
- Theme
- Imagery

READING SKILLS/STRATEGIES
- Reading an epic

THE WRITER'S STYLE
Book 9:
- Vivid description

GENRE STUDY
Book 9:
- Poetry: epic poem

GRAMMAR
Book 9:
- Capitalization of religious terms

Book 10:
- Capitalization of personal titles

Book 12:
- Capitalization of geographical names

HISTORICAL CONNECTION
The Ruins of Troy German archaeologist Heinrich Schliemann discovered the remains of the ancient city of Troy in 1871. In these images students will be able to see the land surrounding the city and part of the ancient walls that can be found there today.

Side A, Frame 49412

PRINT AND MEDIA RESOURCES

UNIT FOUR RESOURCE BOOK
Strategic Reading: Literature, pp. 4, 9, 13
Vocabulary SkillBuilder, pp. 5, 10, 14

GRAMMAR MINI-LESSONS
Transparencies, p. 37
Copymasters, pp. 37, 38

WRITING MINI-LESSONS
Transparencies, pp. 46, 47

ACCESS FOR SAE
Selection Summaries
Reading Support

TEACHER'S GUIDE TO ASSESSMENT

FORMAL ASSESSMENT
Selection Tests
(Book 9) pp. 87–88
(Book 10) pp. 89–90
(Book 12) pp. 91–92
 Test Generator

AUDIO LIBRARY
See Reference Card

LASERLINKS
Historical Connection (Book 9)
Art Gallery (Book 9)
Art Gallery (Book 10)
Art Gallery (Book 12)

INTERNET RESOURCES
McDougal Littell Literature Center at http://www.hmco.com/mcdougal/lit

THE LANGUAGE OF LITERATURE **TEACHER'S EDITION** 481

ALTERNATIVE

Previewing

Students can choose partners and use the following prompts to preview the excerpt from the *Odyssey* orally.

Personal Connection

Discussion Prompts *Think of your favorite monsters. What science fiction or horror creature do you think is the most unusual or frightening? In as much detail as possible, describe the characteristics of the monster to your partner. Then listen as your partner describes a monster. If you have trouble getting started, the following questions might help:*

- *Do you remember a monster from a movie, television show, or book that frightened you when you were younger?*
- *Why were you frightened of the monster?*
- *What is the physical appearance of the monster?*
- *What are the special characteristics of the monster?*

As you read each episode, think about the characteristics of each monster Odysseus encounters and how he deals with each one.

Active Reading
READING CONNECTION

The Epic

DEFINING THE EPIC

An epic is a long narrative poem about the adventures of a hero whose actions reflect the ideals and values of a nation or race. The complete *Odyssey* has more than 12,000 lines and is divided into 24 books. Epics address universal concerns, such as good and evil, life and death, and sin and redemption. The chart at the right shows some other characteristics that distinguish much epic poetry.

Characteristics of an Epic
- The story is set in many locations, real or imaginary, across a wide area.
- The hero is an important historical or legendary character of high social position—a king or a prince, for example.
- The hero is usually pitted against overwhelming odds and must be strong and courageous.
- Supernatural events and beings play an important role in the plot.
- The story is told in language that is formal and grand but also simple and clear.

EXAMINING THE HOMERIC EPICS

Homer's two related epics—the *Iliad* and the *Odyssey*—are perhaps the greatest masterpieces of the epic form. Three important elements of their plots are the Trojan War, the heroism of Odysseus, and the interference of the gods.

The Trojan War The *Iliad* presents an episode of the Trojan War, which may have occurred around 1200 B.C. According to legend, this war began after Paris, a prince of Troy, kidnapped Helen—the most beautiful woman in the world—from her husband, Menelaus (měn'ə-lā'əs), the king of Sparta. Menelaus then recruited kings and soldiers from all over Greece to help him avenge his honor and recover his wife. Odysseus, the king of the island of Ithaca (ĭth'ə-kə), was one of many Greeks who sailed to Troy and besieged the walled city. For ten long years the Greeks battled the Trojans without succeeding in conquering them. To break the stalemate, Odysseus, "the master strategist," thought of a plan to deceive the Trojans into thinking that the Greeks had abandoned the struggle. He ordered a giant wooden horse built and left at the gates of Troy at night. The Trojans, waking to find it there—and not a Greek in sight—assumed that their enemy had fled and left them a peace offering. They took the horse inside the city, only to discover, too late, that it was filled with Greek soldiers and Troy was doomed.

Replica of the Trojan horse. Copyright © Hunter / H. Armstrong Roberts.

482   UNIT FOUR   PART 1: THE WANDERINGS OF ODYSSEUS

WORDS TO KNOW (BOOK 9)

adversary (ăd'vər-sĕr'ē) *n.* an opponent; enemy (p. 502)

appalled (ə-pôld') *adj.* filled with dismay; horrified **appall** *v.*(p. 495)

avenge (ə-vĕnj') *v.* to take revenge on behalf of (p. 494)

disdain (dĭs-dān') *v.* to refuse or reject scornfully (p. 504)

entreat (ĕn-trēt') *v.* to ask earnestly; beg (p. 494)

formidable (fôr'mĭ-də-bəl) *adj.* inspiring admiration, awe, or fear (p. 488)

guile (gīl) *n.* skillful slyness; craftiness (p. 488)

indifferent (ĭn-dĭf'ər-ənt) *adj.* having no interest in or concern for (p. 490)

ponderous (pŏn'dər-əs) *adj.* heavy in a clumsy way; bulky (p. 495)

whim (hwĭm) *n.* a sudden impulse or notion; fancy (p. 494)

Large bowl depicting Odysseus receiving wine as a parting gift, unknown artist. Museo Eoliano, Lipani, Italy, Scala / Art Resource, New York.

The Story of Odysseus The *Odyssey* deals with Odysseus' adventures as he makes his way home from Troy and with events that take place on Ithaca just before and after his return. The excerpts included in this part of the unit depict some of the wanderings of Odysseus after his departure from Troy with a fleet of 12 ships carrying about 720 men. Instead of military opponents, Odysseus most often encounters monsters who try to devour him and enchanting women who try to keep him from his wife, Penelope (pə-nĕl′ə-pē). In addition to his great strength and courage, what sets Odysseus apart from others is the ingenious tricks he uses to get himself out of many difficult situations.

The Olympian Gods and Goddesses Adding another dimension to the human struggles recounted in Homer's epics are the conflicts among the gods and goddesses on Mount Olympus (ə-lĭm′pəs). In Homer's time, most Greeks believed that the gods not only took an active interest in human affairs but also behaved in recognizably human ways, often engaging in their own trivial quarrels and petty jealousies. For example, Athena (ə-thē′nə), the goddess of war and practical wisdom, supported the Greek cause in the Trojan War and championed Odysseus, while Aphrodite (ăf′rə-dī′tē), the goddess of love, sided with Paris and his fellow Trojans. The story of Odysseus' return from Troy contains some notable instances of divine interference. Because Odysseus has angered the gods who were on the side of Troy and, as you will see, angers another god during one of his first adventures, he is forced to suffer many hardships before he manages to return home.

To Homer's audience, the *Odyssey*, with its interfering gods and goddesses, its strange lands and creatures, must have seemed as full of mystery and danger as science fiction and fantasy adventures seem to people today. Just as we can imagine aliens in the next galaxy or creatures created in a laboratory, the ancient Greeks could imagine monsters living just beyond the boundaries of their known world. It was not necessary for them to believe that a one-eyed giant *did* exist, only that it *could* exist.

Statue of Athena from the 4th century B.C. Photo by Erich Lessing / Art Resource, New York.

SUMMARY

In Books 9–12, Odysseus is telling King Alcinous the story of his adventures up to that time. After leaving Troy, Odysseus leads his crew to the land of the Cicones, allies of the Trojans. Odysseus steals from the Cicones until their army drives him back to sea. Gales then blow Odysseus' fleet to the land of the Lotus Eaters, a peaceful people who live by eating lotus blossoms. A few crew members eat the blossoms, which makes them want to stay there forever. Odysseus forces the men back to their ships. Next they explore the land of the Cyclopes—giant one-eyed monsters. Odysseus and his men are trapped in a cave by the Cyclops Polyphemus, who eats two men at every meal. Odysseus and his men make a stake from an olive tree. When Polyphemus returns, Odysseus offers him brandy. The Cyclops falls asleep, and the men blind him with the stake. Odysseus had given his name as "Nohbdy," so when Polyphemus roars, "Nohbdy's ruined me!" the other Cyclopes ignore him. Odysseus and his men escape by hanging on to the bellies of Polyphemus' sheep. When the Cyclops lets his flock out to graze, the men ride to safety. Once aboard his ship, Odysseus taunts Polyphemus and tells his true name. The Cyclops prays to his father, Poseidon, for revenge on Odysseus.

Thematic Link: *The Wanderings of Odysseus* A hero's voyage home leads him and his crew to many unfamiliar lands and dangerous encounters.

Literary Note

Go over the phonetic pronunciations of each character's name with students. Point out that each syllable in each name is pronounced. Vowels and diphthongs—for example, long and short e and the combinations *eu* and *ae*—are likely to pose the most problems.

READING AN EPIC

As you read these excerpts from the *Odyssey*, bear in mind that an epic is primarily an adventure story. The ancient Greeks flocked to public recitations of these exciting tales of heroism, danger, and romance just as we stand in line for tickets to action movies today. Here are some tips to keep in mind as you read:

- Don't be put off by the poetry; just read the lines as you would read any other story. The more you read, the more you'll get used to the poetic language.
- Read parts of the poem aloud. Remember that the ancient Greeks were accustomed to *hear* epic poetry. Make the language as well as the situations come alive by reciting dialogue the way the characters might say it. Books 9–12 of the *Odyssey* are actually spoken by Odysseus as he relates his adventures to his host. Get to know him through his own words as well as through his adventures.
- Use the Guide for Reading notes. They provide pronunciations of names, meanings of difficult terms, background information, hints to alert you to what's important, and questions to help you follow the action.
- Reread sections you don't understand at first.
- To keep track of all the characters and events, try drawing pictures of the action and labeling them with the names of the characters as you read each episode. You may end up with a personal comic-book version of the *Odyssey* that you can share.

Important Characters in the *Odyssey* (in order of mention)

PART 1: The Wanderings of Odysseus

Book 9

Calypso (kə-lĭp′sō)—a sea goddess who lives on the island of **Ogygia** (ō-gĭj′yə)

Alcinous (ăl-sĭn′ō-əs)—the king of the **Phaeacians** (fē-ā′shənz)

Laertes (lā-ûr′tēz)—Odysseus' father

Circe (sûr′sē)—a goddess and enchantress who lives on the island of **Aeaea** (ē-ē′ə)

Zeus (zōōs)—the chief of the Greek gods and goddesses; father of Athena and Apollo

Cicones (sĭ-kō′nēz)—allies of the Trojans, who live at **Ismarus** (ĭs-măr′əs)

Lotus Eaters (lō′təs-ē′tərz)—inhabitants of a land Odysseus visits

Cyclopes (sī-klō′pēz)—a race of one-eyed giants; an individual member of the race is a **Cyclops** (sī′klŏps)

Apollo (ə-pŏl′ō)—the god of music, poetry, prophecy, and medicine

Poseidon (pō-sīd′n)—the god of the sea, earthquakes, and horses; father of the Cyclops who battles Odysseus

Book 10

Aeolus (ē′ə-ləs)—the guardian of the winds

Laestrygones (lĕs′trĭ-gō′nēz)—cannibal inhabitants of a distant land

Eurylochus (yŏŏ-rĭl′ə-kəs)—a trusted officer of Odysseus

Hermes (hûr′mēz)—the god of invention, commerce, and cunning; messenger of the gods

Persephone (pər-sĕf′ə-nē)—the wife of the ruler of the underworld

Tiresias (tī-rēs′yəs) of **Thebes** (thēbz)—a blind prophet whose spirit Odysseus visits in the underworld

Book 12

Sirens (sī′rənz)—creatures, part woman and part bird, whose songs lure sailors to their death

Scylla (sĭl′ə)—a six-headed sea monster who devours sailors

Charybdis (kə-rĭb′dĭs)—a dangerous whirlpool personified as a female sea monster

Helios (hē′lē-ŏs′)—the sun god, who pastures his cattle on the island of **Thrinacia** (thrĭ-nā′shə)

You will find it helpful to become familiar with important people and places in the *Odyssey* before you begin reading. The chart on the previous page identifies important characters and places and tells you how to pronounce their names. The map below identifies real places mentioned in the poem—such as Troy, Sparta, and Ithaca. It also shows where later readers have thought that some of the imaginary lands visited by Odysseus—such as Aeaea, Ogygia, and the islands of Aeolus and the Sirens—could have been located, after applying actual Mediterranean area geography to Homer's descriptions.

Real and Imaginary Places in the *Odyssey*

CUSTOMIZING FOR

Students Acquiring English

- Use **ACCESS FOR STUDENTS ACQUIRING ENGLISH**, *Reading Support*.
- Review with students the reading tips and map on pages 484 and 485 and help them figure out how to make use of them. Ask students to pay particular attention to the list of important characters. Tell them not to be concerned about the pronunciation of names but to focus instead on the events that take place.
- As you guide students through the selection, you may want to use the suggestions in these boxes as well as the suggestions under Strategic Reading for Less-Proficient Readers.

Cultural Note

Have students compare the map in the text with a modern map of the eastern half of the Mediterranean Sea. Help them identify major geographical places, such as the countries of Turkey, Libya, Tunisia, France, Italy, and Greece; the islands of Crete, Sicily, Sardinia, and Corsica; the Strait of Messina, which separates Sicily from the Italian mainland; and the Adriatic and Aegean seas.

CUSTOMIZING FOR
Gifted and Talented Students

Explain to students that Homer's two epics, the *Iliad* and the *Odyssey*, are considered ancestors of the whole of Western literature. Encourage students to look in the selection for situations, characters, or aspects of the plot or theme that are familiar to them from present-day works. Have them brainstorm a list of stories, books, or movies that have one or more aspects in common with the *Odyssey*. Students should share their lists and discuss the familiar elements they have found.

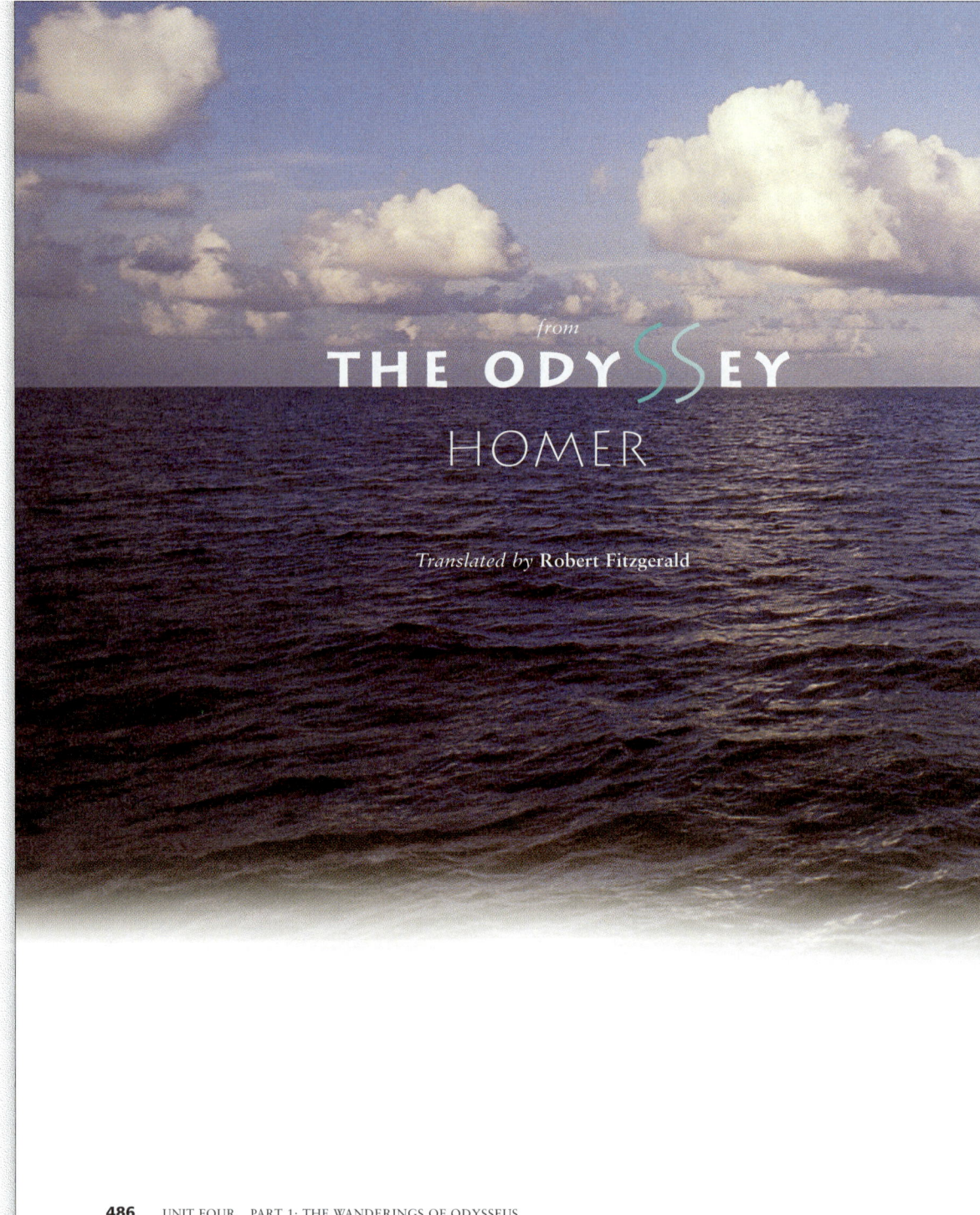

from THE ODYSSEY
HOMER

Translated by Robert Fitzgerald

During seven of Odysseus' ten years on the Mediterranean Sea, he is held captive by the goddess Calypso. Odysseus finally persuades Calypso to let him go, and she helps him build a raft to leave her island. After Odysseus sails away, his raft is destroyed by storms.

Alone and exhausted, Odysseus is washed up on the land of the Phaeacians, where Alcinous is king. Alcinous gives a banquet in honor of Odysseus and asks him to reveal who he is and where he came from. Odysseus relates to the king his adventures up to that time. His account makes up Books 9–12 of the Odyssey.

STRATEGIC READING FOR
Less-Proficient Readers

Help prepare students for the selection by reviewing what they learned about the *Odyssey* and Odysseus at the beginning of the selection. Then ask students if they have ever been away from home for an extended period. How would they have felt if their voyage back had been filled with uncertainty and danger?

Set a Purpose Have students read Odysseus' description of his encounter with the Lotus Eaters and how he and his men escape from the land of the Cyclopes.

Use **UNIT FOUR RESOURCE BOOK,** p. 4, for guidance in reading the selection.

Literary Concept: CONFLICT

A Ask students what type of conflict is introduced in Odysseus' initial statements at the banquet. What do these statements indicate about the kind of journey he has had? *(Possible responses: He has been in prolonged conflict with the gods; they have made his journey home very difficult.)*

Literary Concept: EPIC HERO

B Invite students to discuss how Odysseus' comments about himself during his speech at Alcinous' banquet are appropriate for a classical epic hero. *(Possible response: Although Odysseus may seem to be boasting, a reference by a hero to his worldwide fame was expected in ancient times.)*

Cultural Note

C Odysseus alludes to his boyhood here and hints that the harsh environment of Ithaca was a factor in his youthful training to become a strong warrior. Greek boys took pride in training for athletic contests in such sports as boxing, wrestling, foot racing, and horsemanship.

NEW COASTS AND POSEIDON'S SON

A   "What shall I
say first? What shall I keep until the end?
The gods have tried me in a thousand ways.
But first my name: let that be known to you,
5 and if I pull away from pitiless death,
friendship will bind us, though my land lies far.

I am Laertes' son, Odysseus.
                             Men hold me
B formidable for guile in peace and war:
this fame has gone abroad to the sky's rim.
10 My home is on the peaked sea-mark of Ithaca
under Mount Neion's wind-blown robe of leaves,
in sight of other islands—Dulichium,
Same, wooded Zacynthus—Ithaca
being most lofty in that coastal sea,
15 and northwest, while the rest lie east and south.
C A rocky isle, but good for a boy's training;
I shall not see on earth a place more dear,
though I have been detained long by Calypso,

Guide for Reading

3 tried: tested.

7 hold: regard.

11–13 Mount Neion's (nē'ŏnz') . . . **Dulichium** (dōō-lĭk'ē-əm) . . . **Same** (sā'mē) . . . **Zacynthus** (zə-sĭn'thəs).

WORDS TO KNOW

formidable (fôr'mĭ-də-bəl) *adj.* inspiring admiration, awe, or fear
guile (gīl) *n.* skillful slyness; craftiness

loveliest among goddesses, who held me
in her smooth caves, to be her heart's delight,
as Circe of Aeaea, the enchantress,
desired me, and detained me in her hall.
But in my heart I never gave consent.
Where shall a man find sweetness to surpass
his own home and his parents? In far lands
he shall not, though he find a house of gold.

What of my sailing, then, from Troy?
                    What of those years
of rough adventure, weathered under Zeus?"

SOON AFTER LEAVING TROY, *Odysseus and his crew land near Ismarus, the city of the Cicones. The Cicones are allies of the Trojans and therefore enemies of Odysseus. Odysseus and his crew raid the Cicones, robbing and killing people, until the Ciconian army kills 72 of Odysseus' men and drives the rest out to sea. Delayed by a storm for two days, Odysseus and his remaining companions continue their journey.*

"I might have made it safely home, that time,
but as I came round Malea the current
took me out to sea, and from the north
a fresh gale drove me on, past Cythera.
Nine days I drifted on the teeming sea
before dangerous high winds. Upon the tenth
we came to the coastline of the Lotus Eaters,
who live upon that flower. We landed there
to take on water. All ships' companies
mustered alongside for the mid-day meal.
Then I sent out two picked men and a runner
to learn what race of men that land sustained.
They fell in, soon enough, with Lotus Eaters,
who showed no will to do us harm, only
offering the sweet Lotus to our friends—
but those who ate this honeyed plant, the Lotus,
never cared to report, nor to return:
they longed to stay forever, browsing on
that native bloom, forgetful of their homeland.

I drove them, all three wailing, to the ships,
tied them down under their rowing benches,
50 called the rest: 'All hands aboard;
come, clear the beach and no one taste
the Lotus, or you lose your hope of home.'
Filing in to their places by the rowlocks
my oarsmen dipped their long oars in the surf,
55 and we moved out again on our sea faring.

In the next land we found were Cyclopes,
giants, louts, without a law to bless them.
In ignorance leaving the fruitage of the earth in mystery
to the immortal gods, they neither plow
60 nor sow by hand, nor till the ground, though grain—
wild wheat and barley—grows untended, and
wine-grapes, in clusters, ripen in heaven's rain.
Cyclopes have no muster and no meeting,
no consultation or old tribal ways,
65 but each one dwells in his own mountain cave
dealing out rough justice to wife and child,
<u>indifferent</u> to what the others do."

57 louts: clumsy, stupid people.

58–67 Why doesn't Odysseus respect the Cyclopes?

Cross the bay *from the land of the Cyclopes is a lush, deserted island. Odysseus and his crew land on the island in a dense fog and spend several days feasting on wine and wild goats and observing the mainland, where the Cyclopes live. On the third day, Odysseus and his company of men set out to learn if the Cyclopes are friends or foes.*

"When the young Dawn with fingertips of rose
came in the east, I called my men together
70 and made a speech to them:

          'Old shipmates, friends,
the rest of you stand by; I'll make the crossing
in my own ship, with my own company,
and find out what the mainland natives are—
for they may be wild savages, and lawless,
75 or hospitable and god-fearing men.'

68 This use of "with fingertips of rose" to describe the personified Dawn is a famous epithet—a descriptive phrase that presents a trait of a person or thing. Watch for reappearances of this epithet in the poem, and be on the lookout for other epithets.

WORDS TO KNOW

indifferent (ĭn-dĭf′ər-ənt) *adj.* having no interest in or concern for

At this I went aboard, and gave the word
to cast off by the stern. My oarsmen followed,
filing in to their benches by the rowlocks,
and all in line dipped oars in the gray sea.

80 As we rowed on, and nearer to the mainland,
at one end of the bay, we saw a cavern
yawning above the water, screened with laurel,
and many rams and goats about the place
inside a sheepfold—made from slabs of stone
85 earthfast between tall trunks of pine and rugged
towering oak trees.
                                A prodigious man
slept in this cave alone, and took his flocks
to graze afield—remote from all companions,
knowing none but savage ways, a brute
90 so huge, he seemed no man at all of those
who eat good wheaten bread; but he seemed rather
a shaggy mountain reared in solitude.
We beached there, and I told the crew
to stand by and keep watch over the ship;
95 as for myself I took my twelve best fighters
and went ahead. I had a goatskin full
of that sweet liquor that Euanthes' son,
Maron, had given me. He kept Apollo's
holy grove at Ismarus; for kindness
100 we showed him there, and showed his wife and child,
he gave me seven shining golden talents
perfectly formed, a solid silver winebowl,
and then this liquor—twelve two-handled jars
of brandy, pure and fiery. Not a slave
105 in Maron's household knew this drink; only
he, his wife and the storeroom mistress knew;
and they would put one cupful—ruby-colored,
honey-smooth—in twenty more of water,
but still the sweet scent hovered like a fume
110 over the winebowl. No man turned away
when cups of this came round.
                                A wineskin full
I brought along, and victuals in a bag,
for in my bones I knew some towering brute
would be upon us soon—all outward power,

77 **stern:** the rear end of a ship.

82 **screened with laurel:** partially hidden by laurel trees.
84 **sheepfold:** a pen for sheep.

86 **prodigious** (prə-dĭj′əs): enormous, huge.

91–92 What does Odysseus' metaphor imply about the Cyclops?

97–98 **Euanthes'** (yōō-ăn′thēz) . . . **Maron** (mâr′ŏn).

101 **talents:** bars of gold or silver of a specified weight, used as money in ancient Greece.

112 **victuals** (vĭt′lz): food.

ODYSSEY **491**

CUSTOMIZING FOR
Students Acquiring English

③ Define the word *flocks* as "groups of sheep" and *graze* as "eat."

Linking to Government

K Odysseus' disdain for the Cyclopes' solitary ways probably stems from the civic orientation of the Greeks. Ancient Greece was not a nation but an area divided into many small city-states. Each city-state, called a *polis*, had an individual identity, with its own symbols, religious beliefs, social structures, and systems of government. The *polis* had a town at its center—the focus of civic life—but usually encompassed the neighboring countryside as well. To people with such a background, the Cyclopes' lack of communal culture would have seemed uncivilized and backward.

Guide for Reading

L *Possible response: The metaphor implies that the Cyclops is a huge, hairy, and unsocialized beast.*

Literary Concept:
FORESHADOWING

M Ask students why they think the author interrupts his telling of the exploration of the land of the Cyclopes to describe in detail a goatskin of wine. *(Possible response: It is a clue that the wine will play an important role later in the story, making it a kind of foreshadowing.)*

Mini-Lesson   Literary Concepts

REVIEWING FORESHADOWING Remind students that foreshadowing is a writer's use of hints or clues to indicate events and situations that will occur later in a plot. The use of this technique creates suspense while at the same time preparing the reader for what is to come.

Application Review with students the ways in which Homer hints at or indicates events and situations that will come later in the story. For example, there are subtle clues by the author (the inclusion of a lengthy description of the wine), the statements of Odysseus (his words previewing the difficulty of his journey, his statements that foretell the outcomes of situations before he relates them), and hints about the story revealed through prophecies or curses. Then ask them to work in small groups to locate specific passages that illustrate these techniques of foreshadowing.

Literary Concept: SETTING

N Ask students why they think Homer describes the interior of the cave in such detail. *(Possible responses: The details help make the setting realistic and believable; the sheep may later play an important role in the plot. The details show the Cyclops to be prosperous, a good shepherd, and careful with his animals.)*

Guide for Reading

O *Possible response: Odysseus refuses the request because he wants to satisfy his curiosity about the inhabitant of the cave.*

Literary Concept: FORESHADOWING

P Ask students what they think Odysseus means when he says, "no pretty sight, it turned out, for my friends." *(Possible response: He is hinting that his friends will be harmed when the Cyclops arrives.)*

Literary Concept: DICTION

Q Remind students that the language of an epic is relatively formal. Here the word *ushered* is used to mean "lead" or "guided." *Ewes* are the female sheep; *rams* are the males.

---

115 a wild man, ignorant of civility.

We climbed, then, briskly to the cave. But Cyclops
had gone afield, to pasture his fat sheep,
so we looked round at everything inside:
a drying rack that sagged with cheeses, pens
120 crowded with lambs and kids, each in its class:
firstlings apart from middlings, and the 'dewdrops,'
or newborn lambkins, penned apart from both.
And vessels full of whey were brimming there—
bowls of earthenware and pails for milking.
125 My men came pressing round me, pleading:

'Why not
Take these cheeses, get them stowed, come back,
throw open all the pens, and make a run for it?
We'll drive the kids and lambs aboard. We say
put out again on good salt water!'

Ah,
130 how sound that was! Yet I refused. I wished
to see the caveman, what he had to offer—
no pretty sight, it turned out, for my friends.
We lit a fire, burnt an offering,
and took some cheese to eat; then sat in silence
135 around the embers, waiting. When he came
he had a load of dry boughs on his shoulder
to stoke his fire at suppertime. He dumped it
with a great crash into that hollow cave,
and we all scattered fast to the far wall.
140 Then over the broad cavern floor he ushered
the ewes he meant to milk. He left his rams
and he-goats in the yard outside, and swung
high overhead a slab of solid rock
to close the cave. Two dozen four-wheeled wagons,
145 with heaving wagon teams, could not have stirred
the tonnage of that rock from where he wedged it
over the doorsill. Next he took his seat
and milked his bleating ewes. A practiced job
he made of it, giving each ewe her suckling;
150 thickened his milk, then, into curds and whey,
sieved out the curds to drip in withy baskets,
and poured the whey to stand in bowls
cooling until he drank it for his supper.

115 civility: polite behavior.

120 kids: young goats.

121–122 The Cyclops has separated his lambs into three age groups.

123 whey: the watery part of milk, which separates from the curds, or solid part, during the making of cheese.

129 good salt water: the open sea. (The men want to rob the Cyclops and quickly sail away.)

130–132 Why does Odysseus refuse his men's "sound" request?

133 burnt an offering: burned a portion of the food as an offering to secure the gods' goodwill. (Such offerings were frequently performed by Greek sailors during difficult journeys.)

137 stoke: build up; feed.

144–147 Notice the size of the rock that closes the entrance of the Cyclops' cave.

492 UNIT FOUR PART 1: THE WANDERINGS OF ODYSSEUS

Mini-Lesson: Speaking, Listening, and Viewing

STORYTELLING Remind students that the *Odyssey* was first told orally and that storytelling is an old form of entertainment. Families and friends keep oral traditions by telling and retelling stories about past events that have never been written down. Often, one person may be asked to tell the story because he or she tells it best. Storytelling is a skill that can be practiced and improved. Discuss the tips below with students.

Practice: Rehearse the story by telling it to yourself over and over.

Pause: Occasional pauses allow the audience to reflect on what's been told and anticipate what's to come.

Pace: Adjust your tone and pace as appropriate to the events being recounted.

Application Ask students to choose a story that is frequently retold by their family or friends. Have them rehearse the story and then tell it to the class. Students should use the tips above to hone their storytelling skills.

492 THE LANGUAGE OF LITERATURE TEACHER'S EDITION

Linking to Geography

A glance at a map provides insight into why a Greek epic might focus on seafaring and nautical exploration. The coastline of mainland Greece comprises 2,500 miles and no part of it is more than 85 miles from the sea. About 20 percent of Greece's territory is made up of islands—2,000 in number. Many of them extend deep into the Mediterranean, close to the Turkish coast—a source of tension between Greece and Turkey that at times threatens to escalate into active conflict.

Literary Concept: THEME

R Point out to students that an important element of the Homeric epics is the theme of heroes acquiring immortal fame. Ask students why Odysseus describes Agamemnon and the Trojan War to the Cyclops. *(Possible response: He wants to impress upon the Cyclops that he is a fighter; the Cyclops may hesitate to attack a man famous for achievements in battle.)*

Critical Thinking: MAKING INFERENCES

S Ask students why Odysseus emphasizes the social custom of giving hospitality to strangers and invokes the possible wrath of Zeus if such hospitality is not extended. *(Possible response: Odysseus already realizes that the Cyclops may mistreat his guests and is trying to dissuade him from doing so.)*

Guide for Reading

T Possible response: The Cyclops declares that he is without fear or respect for any of the gods, including the mightiest, Zeus.

CUSTOMIZING FOR
Students Acquiring English

4 Explain to students that Odysseus' statement "I saw through this" means that he understood that the Cyclops was trying to trick him.

Guide for Reading

U Possible responses: He's hoping to gain sympathy by describing himself and his crew as shipwreck victims; he fears the Cyclops may destroy the ship if he learns its location.

       When all these chores were done, he poked the fire,
155   heaping on brushwood. In the glare he saw us.

       'Strangers,' he said, 'who are you? And where from?
       What brings you here by sea ways—a fair traffic?
       Or are you wandering rogues, who cast your lives
       like dice, and ravage other folk by sea?'

160   We felt a pressure on our hearts, in dread
       of that deep rumble and that mighty man.
       But all the same I spoke up in reply:

       'We are from Troy, Achaeans, blown off course
       by shifting gales on the Great South Sea;
165   homeward bound, but taking routes and ways
       uncommon; so the will of Zeus would have it.
       We served under Agamemnon, son of Atreus—
       the whole world knows what city
       he laid waste, what armies he destroyed.
170   It was our luck to come here; here we stand,
       beholden for your help, or any gifts
       you give—as custom is to honor strangers.
       We would <u>entreat</u> you, great Sir, have a care
       for the gods' courtesy; Zeus will <u>avenge</u>
175   the unoffending guest.'

                       He answered this
       from his brute chest, unmoved:

                       'You are a ninny,
       or else you come from the other end of nowhere,
       telling me, mind the gods! We Cyclopes
       care not a whistle for your thundering Zeus
180   or all the gods in bliss; we have more force by far.
       I would not let you go for fear of Zeus—
       you or your friends—unless I had a <u>whim</u> to.
       Tell me, where was it, now, you left your ship—
       around the point, or down the shore, I wonder?'

185   He thought he'd find out, but I saw through this,
       and answered with a ready lie:

157–159 The Cyclops asks whether the seafaring men are here for honest trading ("fair traffic") or are dishonest people ("rogues") who steal from ("ravage") those they meet.

163 Achaeans (ə-kē´ənz): Greeks.

167 Agamemnon (ăg´ə-měm´nŏn´): the Greek king (Menelaus' brother) who led the war against the Trojans; Atreus (ā´trē-əs).

172–175 It was a sacred Greek custom to honor strangers with food and gifts. Odysseus is warning the Cyclops that Zeus will punish anyone who mistreats a guest.

176 ninny: fool.

178–182 What is the Cyclops' attitude toward the gods?

185–190 Why do you think Odysseus lies about his ship?

WORDS TO KNOW
entreat (ĕn-trēt´) *v.* to ask earnestly; beg
avenge (ə-vĕnj´) *v.* to take revenge on behalf of
whim (hwĭm) *n.* a sudden impulse or notion; fancy

494

Multicultural Perspectives

HOSPITALITY The extending of hospitality to visitors and guests manifests itself in a variety of traditions. In Hawaii a garland of flowers called a *lei* is hung around the necks of visitors to the islands.

Not only members of the Zoroastrian religion in Iran but also Hindus in India continue to perform an ancient ritual called *yazna*, in which a visitor's arrival is met with the offering of special food and drink. Afterwards, a song is performed that celebrates the visitor's attributes and accomplishments.

Hospitality is particularly valued in places where harsh terrain makes travel difficult or dangerous. On the outskirts of the Kalahari desert in Botswana, the Tswana people are particularly known for their hospitable reception of visitors. The name of the town of Mochudi refers to this tradition: in the Setswana language, it means "a person who dishes out food from a pot."

'My ship?
Poseidon Lord, who sets the earth a-tremble,
broke it up on the rocks at your land's end.
A wind from seaward served him, drove us there.
190 We are survivors, these good men and I.'

Neither reply nor pity came from him,
but in one stride he clutched at my companions
and caught two in his hands like squirming puppies
to beat their brains out, spattering the floor.
195 Then he dismembered them and made his meal,
gaping and crunching like a mountain lion—
everything: innards, flesh, and marrow bones.
We cried aloud, lifting our hands to Zeus,
powerless, looking on at this, <u>appalled</u>;
200 but Cyclops went on filling up his belly
with manflesh and great gulps of whey,
then lay down like a mast among his sheep.
My heart beat high now at the chance of action,
and drawing the sharp sword from my hip I went
205 along his flank to stab him where the midriff
holds the liver. I had touched the spot
when sudden fear stayed me: if I killed him
we perished there as well, for we could never
move his <u>ponderous</u> doorway slab aside.
210 So we were left to groan and wait for morning.

When the young Dawn with fingertips of rose
lit up the world, the Cyclops built a fire
and milked his handsome ewes, all in due order,
putting the sucklings to the mothers. Then,
215 his chores being all dispatched, he caught
another brace of men to make his breakfast,
and whisked away his great door slab
to let his sheep go through—but he, behind,
reset the stone as one would cap a quiver.
220 There was a din of whistling as the Cyclops
rounded his flock to higher ground, then stillness.
And now I pondered how to hurt him worst,
if but Athena granted what I prayed for.
Here are the means I thought would serve my turn:

193–196 The two similes in this passage emphasize the helplessness of the men ("like squirming puppies") and the savagery of the Cyclops ("gaping and crunching like a mountain lion").

203–210 Why doesn't Odysseus kill the Cyclops at this time?

215 dispatched: completed.
216 brace: pair.

218–219 The Cyclops reseals the cave with the massive rock as easily as an ordinary human places the cap on a container of arrows.

223 Odysseus calls on his protector, the goddess Athena, for help as he forms a plan.

> **WORDS TO KNOW**
> **appalled** (ə-pôld′) *adj.* filled with dismay; horrified **appall** *v.*
> **ponderous** (pŏn′dər-əs) *adj.* heavy in a clumsy way; bulky

Art Note

In this bronze statuette from the second century B.C., the sea god Poseidon stands holding his trident in his outstretched left hand.

Reading the Art Does this figure match your image of Poseidon? Why or why not?

Guide for Reading

Possible response: If Odysseus kills the Cyclops, there will be no one able to dislodge the stone doorway slab, and the men will be trapped.

Literary Concept: EPIC HERO

Invite students to discuss how this passage reflects both the physical and mental abilities of Odysseus. What traits does he reveal that students might consider heroic? (*Possible response: Although Odysseus is not afraid to attack the Cyclops, he realizes that if he killed the monster, he and his men would be trapped inside the cave.*)

STRATEGIC READING FOR
Less-Proficient Readers

Ask students to summarize what has happened so far to Odysseus and his men in the land of the Cyclopes. (*Possible response: Odysseus takes 12 men to explore a cave; they wait for the inhabitant, who seals the cave with a stone slab, trapping them inside, and eats two of the men.*) **Noting Sequence of Events**

Set a Purpose Have students read to find out how Odysseus tricks the Cyclops.

| Mini-Lesson The Writer's Style |

VIVID DESCRIPTION Ask students to look at the <u>highlighted</u> passage above and note the author's use of vivid, detailed description. Have students discuss the details that help the reader imagine the scene being described. Point out that writers and storytellers often use imagery and figurative language when creating descriptions to help the audience visualize the action.

Application Invite students to write a short description of an event or scene they have witnessed, using vivid descriptive details. Encourage them to use imagery and figurative language in their descriptions to help the reader picture the scene.

Reteaching/Reinforcement
• *Writing Handbook*, anthology p. 866
• *Writing Mini-Lessons* transparencies, pp. 46, 47

 The Writer's Craft

Observation and Description, pp. 57–80

Literary Concept: EPIC SIMILE

Y Ask students to explain the comparison being made in this epic simile. *(Possible response: Odysseus says that the olive tree used by the Cyclops as a club or staff is as big as a mast for a 20-oared ship.)* Ask students what qualities this simile conveys. *(Possible response: power, awe-inspiring size, skill)*

Guide for Reading

Z *Possible response: Odysseus plans to blind the Cyclops by grinding a stake into his eye.*

Critical Thinking: SUMMARIZE

AA Have students use details in the passage to describe the main points of Odysseus' plan. *(Possible response: He plans to shape the pole into a pointed stake, toughen the end by holding it in the fire, hide the stake, and then pick a small group of men to help him catch the Cyclops off guard and blind the monster.)*

Guide for Reading

BB *Possible response: Odysseus wants to get him drunk so it will be easier to carry out his plan.*

Critical Thinking: HYPOTHESIZE

CC Have students discuss why Odysseus might insult the Cyclops, calling him "a bloody monster" even as he tries to get him to drink the wine. *(Possible responses: Odysseus has witnessed his crew members killed; the Cyclops might suspect a trick if Odysseus didn't display anger at him.)*

---

225 a club, or staff, lay there along the fold—
an olive tree, felled green and left to season
for Cyclops' hand. And it was like a mast
a lugger of twenty oars, broad in the beam—
a deep-sea-going craft—might carry:
230 so long, so big around, it seemed. Now I
chopped out a six-foot section of this pole
and set it down before my men, who scraped it;
and when they had it smooth, I hewed again
to make a stake with pointed end. I held this
235 in the fire's heart and turned it, toughening it,
then hid it, well back in the cavern, under
one of the dung piles in profusion there.
Now came the time to toss for it: who ventured
along with me? whose hand could bear to thrust
240 and grind that spike in Cyclops' eye, when mild
sleep had mastered him? As luck would have it,
the men I would have chosen won the toss—
four strong men, and I made five as captain.

At evening came the shepherd with his flock,
245 his woolly flock. The rams as well, this time,
entered the cave: by some sheep-herding whim—
or a god's bidding—none were left outside.
He hefted his great boulder into place
and sat him down to milk the bleating ewes
250 in proper order, put the lambs to suck,
and swiftly ran through all his evening chores.
Then he caught two more men and feasted on them.
My moment was at hand, and I went forward
holding an ivy bowl of my dark drink,
255 looking up, saying:

'Cyclops, try some wine.
Here's liquor to wash down your scraps of men.
Taste it, and see the kind of drink we carried
under our planks. I meant it for an offering
if you would help us home. But you are mad,
260 unbearable, a bloody monster! After this,
will any other traveler come to see you?'

He seized and drained the bowl, and it went down
so fiery and smooth he called for more:

228 lugger: a small, wide sailing ship.

233 hewed: chopped.

237 profusion: abundance.

238–243 What does Odysseus plan to do to the Cyclops? **Z**

255–261 Why does Odysseus offer the Cyclops the liquor he brought from the ship? **BB**

Cultural Note

The ancient Greeks always drank their wine mixed with water, never undiluted (note the reference to the dilution of wine in lines 107–108). That the Cyclops drinks the wine at full strength, thereby hastening his inebriation and serving Odysseus' purposes, would have been viewed by an audience of Homer's era as further evidence of the Cyclopes' barbarism.

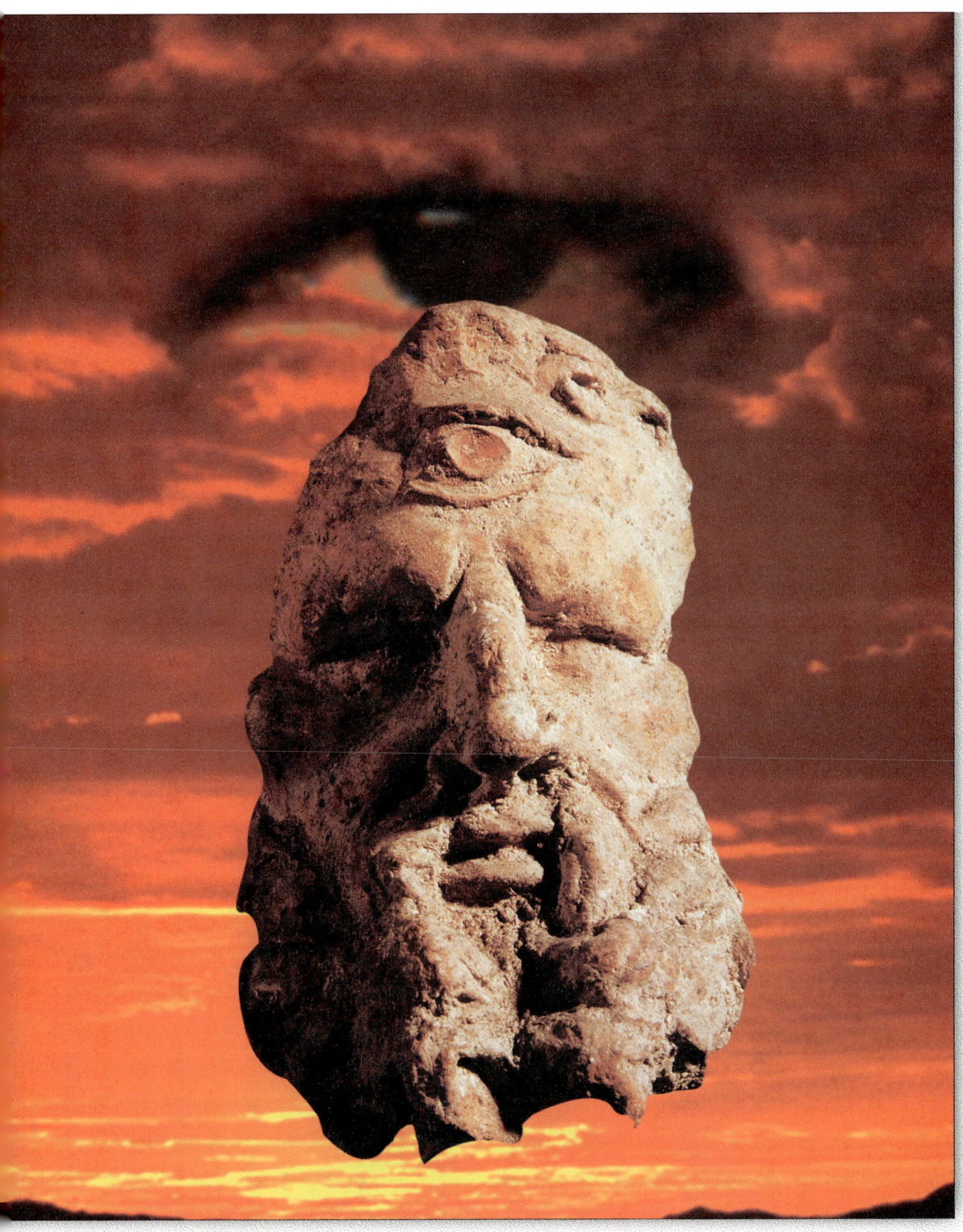

DESIGN NOTE

The designer has set a stone-carved depiction of the Cyclops' head against a background of the sky. The carving depicts him as having three eyes: two apparently useless ones on the left and right and one larger, seeing eye centered in his forehead. Homer's description of the creature allows the audience to use their imagination to create a mental picture of the monster. This has also allowed artists to depict the Cyclops in many different ways.

Reading the Art *How does this rendering of the Cyclops compare with your mental image of him?*

Art Note

This scene from a seventh-century-B.C. Greek jar portrays the blinding of the Cyclops by Odysseus and a crew member. The expression of the Cyclops reveals his pain and surprise. His attackers look calm, almost pleased.

Reading the Art *Which do you think better conveys the action of the scene: the artwork or Homer's description?*

Cultural Note

DD The ancient Greeks believed that knowing other people's names gave one power over them. Here the Cyclops pretends that he is eager to know Odysseus' name so that he can make him a special present. The ancient Greek audience of the epic would have realized that the Cyclops meant no good by his request. Odysseus, however, tricks the Cyclops here. (Later the Cyclops will learn Odysseus' real name and use it to call down the wrath of his father, Poseidon, to punish Odysseus.)

CUSTOMIZING FOR
Students Acquiring English

5 Ask students to use knowledge acquired from health class or elsewhere to describe what happens to people when they drink too much. List the responses on the board. Then use the list to illustrate the meaning of the terms *fuddle,* "to become confused," and *flush,* "to turn red in the face."

Guide for Reading

EE *Possible response: He is planning on somehow using the name Nohbdy to trick the Cyclops.*

Literary Concept: EPIC HERO

FF Have students discuss how these lines illustrate the heroic qualities of Odysseus. *(Possible response: He acts like a general at the battlefront, unafraid, cheering on his men to keep their courage up.)*

'Give me another, thank you kindly. Tell me,
how are you called? I'll make a gift will please you.
Even Cyclopes know the wine-grapes grow
out of grassland and loam in heaven's rain,
but here's a bit of nectar and ambrosia!'

Three bowls I brought him, and he poured them down.
I saw the fuddle and flush come over him,
then I sang out in cordial tones:

                'Cyclops,
you ask my honorable name? Remember
the gift you promised me, and I shall tell you.
My name is Nohbdy: mother, father, and friends,
everyone calls me Nohbdy.'

                 And he said:
'Nohbdy's my meat, then, after I eat his friends.
Others come first. There's a noble gift, now.'

Even as he spoke, he reeled and tumbled backward,
his great head lolling to one side: and sleep
took him like any creature. Drunk, hiccupping,
he dribbled streams of liquor and bits of men.

Now, by the gods, I drove my big hand spike
deep in the embers, charring it again,
and cheered my men along with battle talk
to keep their courage up: no quitting now.
The pike of olive, green though it had been,
reddened and glowed as if about to catch.
I drew it from the coals and my four fellows
gave me a hand, lugging it near the Cyclops
as more than natural force nerved them; straight
forward they sprinted, lifted it, and rammed it
deep in his crater eye, and I leaned on it
turning it as a shipwright turns a drill
in planking, having men below to swing
the two-handled strap that spins it in the groove.
So with our brand we bored that great eye socket
while blood ran out around the red hot bar.
Eyelid and lash were seared; the pierced ball
hissed broiling, and the roots popped.

268 nectar (nĕk'tər) **and ambrosia** (ăm-brō'zhə): the drink and food of the gods.

270 fuddle and flush: the state of confusion and redness of the face caused by drinking alcohol.

274–275 Say the name Nohbdy out loud and listen to what it sounds like. *What might Odysseus be planning?* **EE**

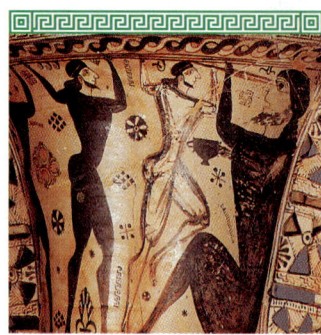

286 the pike: the pointed stake.

292–295 Odysseus compares the way he stabs the Cyclops in the eye to the way a shipbuilder drills a hole in a board.

498 UNIT FOUR PART 1: THE WANDERINGS OF ODYSSEUS

Mini-Lesson Grammar

CAPITALIZATION: Religious Terms Explain that words referring to God, the Holy Family, and religious scriptures are proper nouns and must be capitalized. Personal pronouns referring to God are usually not capitalized.

    the **V**irgin **M**ary   the **L**ord   **A**llah
    the **N**ew **T**estament   our **G**od   the **T**orah

However, the words *god* and *goddess,* when referring to mythical deities, should not be capitalized. Point out the example in the highlighted lines above.

Application Write the following sentences on the board. Have students decide if the underlined word in each sentence has correct capitalization.
1. He broadcast passages from the bible. *(no)*
2. Who is the Greek Goddess of war? *(no)*

Reteaching/Reinforcement
- *Grammar Handbook,* anthology p. 928
- *Grammar Mini-Lessons* copymasters p. 37, transparencies p. 37

 The Writer's Craft

Proper Nouns and Proper Adjectives, pp. 749–750

	In a smithy
300	one sees a white-hot axehead or an adze
	plunged and wrung in a cold tub, screeching steam—
	the way they make soft iron hale and hard—:
	just so that eyeball hissed around the spike.
	The Cyclops bellowed and the rock roared round him,
305	and we fell back in fear. Clawing his face
	he tugged the bloody spike out of his eye,
	threw it away, and his wild hands went groping;
	then he set up a howl for Cyclopes
	who lived in caves on windy peaks nearby.
310	Some heard him; and they came by divers ways
	to clump around outside and call:

        'What ails you,
Polyphemus? Why do you cry so sore
in the starry night? You will not let us sleep.
Sure no man's driving off your flock? No man
315 has tricked you, ruined you?'

        Out of the cave
the mammoth Polyphemus roared in answer:

'Nohbdy, Nohbdy's tricked me, Nohbdy's ruined me!'

To this rough shout they made a sage reply:

'Ah well, if nobody has played you foul
320 there in your lonely bed, we are no use in pain
given by great Zeus. Let it be your father,
Poseidon Lord, to whom you pray.'

        So saying
they trailed away. And I was filled with laughter
to see how like a charm the name deceived them.
325 Now Cyclops, wheezing as the pain came on him,
fumbled to wrench away the great doorstone
and squatted in the breach with arms thrown wide
for any silly beast or man who bolted—
hoping somehow I might be such a fool.
330 But I kept thinking how to win the game:
death sat there huge; how could we slip away?
I drew on all my wits, and ran through tactics,
reasoning as a man will for dear life,

299 smithy: blacksmith's shop.

300 adze (ădz): an axlike tool with a curved blade.

310 divers: various.

312 Polyphemus (pŏl´ə-fē´məs): the name of the Cyclops.

318 sage: wise.

319–322 Odysseus' lie about his name has paid off. What do the other Cyclopes assume to be the source of Polyphemus' pain?

327 breach: opening.

330–334 Notice Odysseus' great mental struggle and, as you read on, the clever plan he has managed to come up with on the spot.

STRATEGIC READING FOR
Less-Proficient Readers

JJ Have students summarize how Odysseus tricks Polyphemus. *(He gets the Cyclops drunk and tells him that his own name is Nohbdy. After the monster has passed out from the wine, he and his men blind Polyphemus with a sharpened log; other Cyclopes don't come to Polyphemus' aid because when he calls for help, he says "Nohbdy" has injured him.)*
Clarifying

Set a Purpose Have students read to find out how Odysseus and his men escape from the cave. Ask them to pay special attention to Odysseus' reaction to his victory.

Literary Concept: SUSPENSE

KK Ask students how Polyphemus' speech to the ram beneath which Odysseus hides adds to the suspense of the passage. *(Possible response: It creates the expectation that Odysseus might be discovered because of the ram's unusual behavior; the audience knows that Polyphemus will kill Odysseus if he discovers him.)*

Literary Concept: TONE

LL Have students discuss how the tone changes at the end of the Cyclops' speech. *(Possible response: At the beginning of the speech, the Cyclops seems tender, almost pitiable. At the end of the speech, he reasserts his hostility and his desire for revenge.)*

---

until a trick came—and it pleased me well.
335   The Cyclops' rams were handsome, fat, with heavy
fleeces, a dark violet.

                             Three abreast
I tied them silently together, twining
cords of willow from the ogre's bed;
then slung a man under each middle one
340   to ride there safely, shielded left and right.
So three sheep could convey each man. I took
the woolliest ram, the choicest of the flock,
and hung myself under his kinky belly,
pulled up tight, with fingers twisted deep
345   in sheepskin ringlets for an iron grip.
So, breathing hard, we waited until morning.

When Dawn spread out her fingertips of rose
the rams began to stir, moving for pasture,
and peals of bleating echoed round the pens
350   where dams with udders full called for a milking.
Blinded, and sick with pain from his head wound,
the master stroked each ram, then let it pass,
but my men riding on the pectoral fleece
the giant's blind hands blundering never found.
355   Last of them all my ram, the leader, came,
weighted by wool and me with my meditations.
The Cyclops patted him, and then he said:

'Sweet cousin ram, why lag behind the rest
in the night cave? You never linger so,
360   but graze before them all, and go afar
to crop sweet grass, and take your stately way
leading along the streams, until at evening
you run to be the first one in the fold.
Why, now, so far behind? Can you be grieving
365   over your Master's eye? That carrion rogue
and his accurst companions burnt it out
when he had conquered all my wits with wine.
Nohbdy will not get out alive, I swear.
Oh, had you brain and voice to tell
370   where he may be now, dodging all my fury!
Bashed by this hand and bashed on this rock wall

353 pectoral fleece: the wool covering a sheep's chest.

500   UNIT FOUR   PART 1: THE WANDERINGS OF ODYSSEUS

Mini-Lesson   Workplace Literacy

SCANS Goal: Resources

ALLOCATING HUMAN RESOURCES
Utilizing human resources well is an important component of any group project. A workplace leader assesses the skills of team members and distributes work accordingly. Ask students to note the way Odysseus manages his crew in order to minimize risk and achieve maximum results:
- He takes only one company to the land of the Cyclopes, leaving the rest at the island.
- He utilizes a group of four—the strongest men—to attack Polyphemus.

Application Have students choose a small business they would like to manage, such as an ice-cream parlor, a delivery service, a baby-sitting agency, or a bike-repair shop. Then have the students form groups of four. Explain that they should each imagine that the other three are their employees. Next, each student should describe his or her talents and job skills to the group. Finally, students should decide how best to allocate their three employees in their business. Ask students to write a paragraph detailing their decisions.

DESIGN NOTE

The designer created a backdrop for this sculpture by taking the image of a landscape and bending it so that its horizon formed an oval, its eastern and western ends joined. This backdrop could be interpreted as the vengeful eye of Zeus, as the mouth of Polyphemus' cave, as a representation of the blinded Polyphemus' attempts to remember his surroundings, or in any number of other ways. The sculpture itself is a marble relief from a sarcophus in the Vatican Museum. It represents a scene from *Oedipus Rex* in which the young Oedipus is abandoned on a mountain by a shepherd. The similarity between this image and the way in which Odysseus escapes from Polyphemus is intended to suggest the common heritage of the Greek classics.

Reading the Art *What does the image behind the sculpture suggest to you?*

his brains would strew the floor, and I should have
rest from the outrage Nohbdy worked upon me.'

He sent us into the open, then. Close by,
375 I dropped and rolled clear of the ram's belly,
going this way and that to untie the men.
With many glances back, we rounded up
his fat, stiff-legged sheep to take aboard,
and drove them down to where the good ship lay.
380 We saw, as we came near, our fellows' faces
shining; then we saw them turn to grief
tallying those who had not fled from death.
I hushed them, jerking head and eyebrows up,
and in a low voice told them: 'Load this herd;
385 move fast, and put the ship's head toward the breakers.'
They all pitched in at loading, then embarked
and struck their oars into the sea. Far out,
as far off shore as shouted words would carry,
I sent a few back to the **adversary**:

390 'O Cyclops! Would you feast on my companions?
Puny, am I, in a Caveman's hands?
How do you like the beating that we gave you,
you damned cannibal? Eater of guests
under your roof! Zeus and the gods have paid you!'

395 The blind thing in his doubled fury broke
a hilltop in his hands and heaved it after us.
Ahead of our black prow it struck and sank
whelmed in a spuming geyser, a giant wave
that washed the ship stern foremost back to shore.
400 I got the longest boathook out and stood
fending us off, with furious nods to all
to put their backs into a racing stroke—
row, row, or perish. So the long oars bent
kicking the foam sternward, making head
405 until we drew away, and twice as far.
Now when I cupped my hands I heard the crew
in low voices protesting:

'Godsake, Captain!

385 put . . . the breakers: turn the ship around so that it is heading toward the open sea.

390–394 Notice that Odysseus assumes that the gods are on his side.

395–403 The hilltop thrown by Polyphemus lands in front of the ship, causing a huge wave that carries the ship back to the shore. Odysseus uses a long pole to push the boat away from the land.

> WORDS TO KNOW
> **adversary** (ăd'vər-sĕr'ē) *n.* an opponent; enemy

Literary Concept: CHARACTERIZATION

OO Invite students to compare the crew's plea to their advice given earlier in the episode, in lines 126–130. *(Possible response: In both cases, the advice is prudent and sensible.)* How does Odysseus react to the advice in each case? *(He ignores it.)* Ask students what this tells us about the characters. *(Possible responses: The crew is sensible and Odysseus is foolhardy; the crew is cowardly and Odysseus is brave; Odysseus should listen to the crew's advice, since his curiosity has already endangered their lives.)*

Guide for Reading

PP Possible responses: Odysseus is proud of his victory; he wants to taunt the Cyclops by showing he is not afraid to reveal information about himself.

Critical Thinking: SPECULATE

QQ Ask students whether they think it is a mistake for Odysseus to reveal his true name to Polyphemus. Will the revelation have negative consequences later? You might share with students the information in the Literary Note on page 504 to help them formulate their response.

Literary Note

RR Prophecies are important plot elements in the ancient epic. Here the revelation of Odysseus' true name triggers in Polyphemus the memory of a prediction made long ago. Epic prophecies are often ironic, since characters usually realize too late how a prophecy has come to be fulfilled.

OO Why bait the beast again? Let him alone!'

'That tidal wave he made on the first throw
410　all but beached us.'

　　　　　　　　'All but stove us in!'

'Give him our bearing with your trumpeting,
he'll get the range and lob a boulder.'

　　　　　　　　'Aye
he'll smash our timbers and our heads together!'

I would not heed them in my glorying spirit,
415　but let my anger flare and yelled:

　　　　　　　　'Cyclops,
if ever mortal man inquire
QQ　how you were put to shame and blinded, tell him
Odysseus, raider of cities, took your eye:
Laertes' son, whose home's on Ithaca!'

420　At this he gave a mighty sob and rumbled:

'Now comes the weird upon me, spoken of old.
A wizard, grand and wondrous, lived here—Telemus,
RR　a son of Eurymus; great length of days
he had in wizardry among the Cyclopes,
425　and these things he foretold for time to come:
my great eye lost, and at Odysseus' hands.
Always I had in mind some giant, armed
in giant force, would come against me here.
But this, but you—small, pitiful and twiggy—
430　you put me down with wine, you blinded me.
Come back, Odysseus, and I'll treat you well,
praying the god of earthquake to befriend you—
his son I am, for he by his avowal
fathered me, and, if he will, he may
435　heal me of this black wound—he and no other
of all the happy gods or mortal men.'

Few words I shouted in reply to him:

407–413 The near disaster of Odysseus' boast has frightened the crew. As earlier, in the cave, the men make reasonable appeals.

415–419 Odysseus uses the warlike epithet "raider of cities" in his second boast to the Cyclops. Why do you think he reveals so much about himself?

421 Now comes . . . of old: Now I recall the destiny predicted long ago.

422 Telemus (tĕl'ə-məs): a magician who could predict the future for the Cyclopes.

427–430 Polyphemus is not blind to the irony of being beaten by someone only about one-eighth his size.

432 the god of earthquake: Poseidon.

433 avowal: honest admission.

ODYSSEY　**503**

Mini-Lesson Genre Study

POETRY On the chalkboard, draw the word web on the right and use it to review the characteristics of an **epic** with students:
- It is a long narrative poem.
- It reflects the ideals of a nation or race.
- It addresses universal concerns.
- It focuses on the adventures of a historical or legendary hero.
- The supernatural plays an important role.

Application Ask students to copy the web into their notebooks. Then ask them to refer to it as they look for each characteristic in the *Odyssey*.

Literary Note

SS Ritual curses, like prophecies, play an important role in epic poems. Notice how Polyphemus mentions in his curse the same details that Odysseus had revealed in lines 418–419. The ancient Greeks believed that the more thoroughly a person could identify the target of a curse, the more effective the curse was likely to be.

Literary Concept:
FORESHADOWING

TT Ask students to discuss what the statement "and the god heard him" may foreshadow for Odysseus and his men. *(Possible responses: Poseidon will grant Polyphemus' wish; Odysseus will not return to Ithaca with his companions.)*

CUSTOMIZING FOR
Gifted and Talented Students

After students have read the selection, ask them whether Odysseus' curiosity is a mark of his intelligence, inseparable from his cunning and ability to escape from dangerous situations, or a character flaw that leads him and his crew into trouble. Is it possible to have the benefits of curiosity without the risks? Are there ways that curious people can learn caution and overly cautious people can sharpen their curiosity? Encourage students to discuss these questions as they relate both to their own lives and to other current situations where curiosity may be both an asset and a liability.

'If I could take your life I would and take
your time away, and hurl you down to hell!
440 The god of earthquake could not heal you there!'

At this he stretched his hands out in his darkness
toward the sky of stars, and prayed Poseidon:

'O hear me, lord, blue girdler of the islands,
if I am thine indeed, and thou art father:
445 grant that Odysseus, raider of cities, never
see his home: Laertes' son, I mean,
who kept his hall on Ithaca. Should destiny
intend that he shall see his roof again
among his family in his father land,
450 far be that day, and dark the years between.
Let him lose all companions, and return
under strange sail to bitter days at home.'

In these words he prayed, and the god heard him.
Now he laid hands upon a bigger stone
455 and wheeled around, titanic for the cast,
to let it fly in the black-prowed vessel's track.
But it fell short, just aft the steering oar,
and whelming seas rose giant above the stone
to bear us onward toward the island.
                                         There
460 as we ran in we saw the squadron waiting,
the trim ships drawn up side by side, and all
our troubled friends who waited, looking seaward.
We beached her, grinding keel in the soft sand,
and waded in, ourselves, on the sandy beach.
465 Then we unloaded all the Cyclops' flock
to make division, share and share alike,
only my fighters voted that my ram,
the prize of all, should go to me. I slew him
by the seaside and burnt his long thighbones
470 to Zeus beyond the stormcloud, Cronus' son,
who rules the world. But Zeus **disdained** my offering;
destruction for my ships he had in store
and death for those who sailed them, my companions.
Now all day long until the sun went down

443–452 Note the details of Polyphemus' curse on Odysseus. As you read on, you'll find out whether the curse comes true.

455 titanic for the cast: drawing on all his enormous strength in preparing to throw.
457 aft: behind.
459 the island: the deserted island where most of Odysseus' men had stayed behind.

> **WORDS TO KNOW**
> **disdain** (dĭs-dān') *v.* to refuse or reject scornfully

475 we made our feast on mutton and sweet wine,
     till after sunset in the gathering dark
     we went to sleep above the wash of ripples.

     When the young Dawn with fingertips of rose
     touched the world, I roused the men, gave orders
480 to man the ships, cast off the mooring lines;
     and filing in to sit beside the rowlocks
     oarsmen in line dipped oars in the gray sea.
     So we moved out, sad in the vast offing,
     having our precious lives, but not our friends."

483 in the vast offing: toward the open sea.

STRATEGIC READING FOR
Less-Proficient Readers

Make sure students understand the events after Polyphemus is blinded. Ask these questions:

- How do Odysseus and his men escape from the cave? *(by hanging underneath Polyphemus' sheep as he lets the flock out to graze)* **Summarizing**

- How does Odysseus act after his escape? *(He taunts the blinded Cyclops.)* **Noting Relevant Details**

- Why are Odysseus' men upset about this action? *(because they are worried that the blinded Cyclops will be able to follow the sound of Odysseus' voice and sink the ship by throwing a boulder)* **Making Inferences**

- Where do Odysseus and his men go after they leave the land of the Cyclopes? *(They go back to the deserted island where their shipmates await them.)* **Noting Sequence of Events**

EDITOR'S NOTE With the permission of the copyright holder, material has been deleted to shorten and focus the selection.

COMPREHENSION CHECK

1. What is Odysseus' ultimate destination? *(his home in Ithaca)*
2. What does Odysseus think of the way the Cyclopes live? *(He believes they are brutish and uncivilized.)*
3. How does the Cyclops respond to Odysseus' request for hospitality? *(He scoffs at it and eats two of Odysseus' crew members.)*
4. How does Odysseus injure Polyphemus? *(by putting out his eye with a sharpened wooden stake)*
5. Why does Odysseus tie his men underneath the Cyclops' sheep? *(so they can escape from the cave)*

Assessment Option

INFORMAL ASSESSMENT To assess your students' understanding of the selection, ask them to create a problem-solution log. Have students draw a two-column chart in their notebooks. In the left column, students should list the major problems encountered by Odysseus and his crew in the episode. In the right column, they should list the means by which Odysseus and his crew overcame each problem.

Rubric

3 Full Accomplishment Students accurately list the problems encountered by Odysseus and his crew and the solutions to each problem.

2 Substantial Accomplishment Students accurately list most of the problems and solutions.

1 Little or Partial Accomplishment Students either are unable to list the problems or have difficulty matching the problems with solutions.

From Personal Response to Critical Analysis

1. Accept all reasonable responses.
2. Possible responses: He is brave, cunning, and a great leader; he is foolhardy and stubborn, as is shown by his decision to wait for Polyphemus and his taunting of him from the boat; his curiosity invites trouble.
3. Accept all reasonable, well-supported responses.
4. Accept all reasonable, well-supported responses.
5. Possible response: The Greeks viewed cannibalism and the absence of such traits as social organization, laws, agricultural achievement, and respect for the gods and social customs as evidence of barbarism.
6. Accept all reasonable, well-supported responses.
7. Accept all reasonable responses.

Another Pathway

Cooperative Learning Students can work in groups of five to eight. After choosing a scene to enact, students should review the scene, paying special attention to the qualities displayed by Odysseus. One student should then direct the group during rehearsals and presentation. Another can make sure that Odysseus' character is accurately portrayed.

Rubric
- **3 Full Accomplishment** Performances accurately portray Odysseus' character.
- **2 Substantial Accomplishment** Performances demonstrate partial understanding of Odysseus' character.
- **1 Little or Partial Accomplishment** Performances demonstrate little understanding of Odysseus' character.

RESPONDING OPTIONS

FROM PERSONAL RESPONSE TO CRITICAL ANALYSIS

REFLECT 1. What is your impression of Odysseus? Describe or draw your image of him in your notebook, and then discuss it.

RETHINK 2. What positive and negative qualities of Odysseus' character are revealed by his behavior in the land of the Cyclopes?
Consider
Close Textual Reading
- why he insists on seeing the Cyclops in the first place
- how he defeats Polyphemus
- why he taunts Polyphemus and reveals his real name as he sails away

3. When Odysseus tells Alcinous who he is, he says that he is famous for his guile. From what you have learned about Odysseus, do you think his reputation is deserved? Support your opinion.

4. Do you consider Polyphemus a villain? Do Odysseus' actions toward him seem justified? Explain.

Close Textual Reading 5. From the characterization of Polyphemus, what conclusions can you draw about the qualities that ancient Greek society considered barbaric or monstrous? Use specific examples from the excerpt to support your ideas.

RELATE 6. What qualities do people in today's society consider barbaric or monstrous? What qualities do we think of as civilized?

7. Look over the characteristics of your favorite monster that you recorded for the Personal Connection on page 481. How does Polyphemus compare with your favorite monster?

Multimodal Learning
ANOTHER PATHWAY

Cooperative Learning

With the class divided into small groups, act out scenes from Book 9 of the *Odyssey*. (Scenes could include Odysseus and his crew in the land of the Lotus Eaters, the attack on the Cyclops, the escape from the Cyclops' cave, and the departure from the land of the Cyclopes.) Focus on portraying the character of Odysseus.

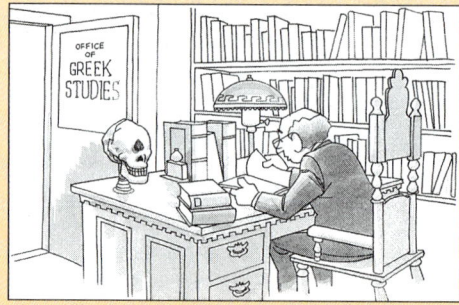

Reprinted courtesy of Bunny Hoest and *Parade Magazine*. Copyright © 1995.

506

QUICKWRITES

1. Look again at the explanation of the term *epithet* in the Guide for Reading note to line 68. In the style of "raider of cities" (line 418), create your own **epithets** for Odysseus, the members of his crew, and Polyphemus.

2. How might the Cyclops have viewed the events? Experiment with writing a draft of the **episode** as Polyphemus might tell it.

📁 **PORTFOLIO** Save your writing. You may want to use it later as a springboard to a piece for your portfolio.

QuickWrites

1. Write sample epithets from the selection on the chalkboard and have students discuss how they aid characterization. Students can also practice creating epithets for modern political or entertainment figures.
2. Encourage students to use elements of epic style in their retelling of the episode from Polyphemus' point of view.

The Writer's Craft

Point of View, pp. 431–433

LITERARY CONCEPTS

An **epic hero** is a larger-than-life figure who embodies the ideals of a nation or race. Epic heroes take part in long, dangerous adventures and accomplish great deeds, requiring great courage and superhuman strength. Odysseus is an epic hero who displays some of the qualities that were honored in Greek society. Yet because he is human, Odysseus also displays human faults.

With a partner, create a two-column chart to evaluate the extent to which Odysseus acts like an epic hero in Book 9. In the first column, list the larger-than-life qualities and actions that show Odysseus to be an epic hero. In the second column, list Odysseus' human weaknesses and unwise actions that do not seem to fit the ideal of an epic hero. After you complete your chart, jot down ways in which you think Odysseus' character needs improvement. As you read more of the *Odyssey*, you'll be able to decide whether Odysseus changes for the better.

Multimodal Learning

ALTERNATIVE ACTIVITIES

If Polyphemus had not brought the rams into the cave, how might Odysseus and his men have escaped? With a partner, devise an **escape plan** and share it with your classmates.

THE WRITER'S STYLE

One distinguishing feature of Homer's epics is the use of epic similes. An **epic simile** (also called a Homeric simile) is a more involved version of a regular simile. Epic similes contain words such as *like, as, so,* or *just as,* and may extend for a number of lines. Study the epic similes in lines 293–295 and lines 299–303. Explain what is being compared in each. What do the similes add to the description of the action?

WORDS TO KNOW

EXERCISE A For each group of words below, write the letter of the word that is an antonym of the boldfaced word.

1. **ponderous:** (a) dainty, (b) careless, (c) intelligent
2. **adversary:** (a) partner, (b) guarantee, (c) obstacle
3. **avenge:** (a) dare, (b) resist, (c) forgive
4. **disdain:** (a) stop, (b) accept, (c) scorn
5. **formidable:** (a) shapeless, (b) unimpressive, (c) likely

EXERCISE B Write the letter of the word pair that expresses the relationship most similar to that expressed by the capitalized pair.

1. GUILE : FOX ::
   (a) loyalty : squirrel
   (b) wisdom : sparrow
   (c) timidity : mouse
   (d) courage : sheep
2. WHIM : NOTION ::
   (a) request : plea
   (b) idea : emotion
   (c) letter : invitation
   (d) separation : link
3. ENTREAT : RESPOND ::
   (a) speak : shout
   (b) throw : catch
   (c) reject : refuse
   (d) suggest : recommend
4. APPALLED : AWFUL ::
   (a) bored : amusing
   (b) surprised : predicted
   (c) tortured : helpful
   (d) interested : fascinating
5. INDIFFERENT : SHRUG ::
   (a) rebellious : nod
   (b) sleepy : yawn
   (c) enthusiastic : sigh
   (d) startled : groan

READING ON

As you read the next adventure, pay attention to Odysseus' weaknesses as well as his strengths. Compare him with his loyal but cautious officer Eurylochus.

LASERLINKS
• ART GALLERY

ODYSSEY 507

Alternative Activities

Have students review the description of Polyphemus' cave and make a list of the physical details as well as the articles contained in it. Students and their partners can use the list to develop alternative ways of escape. Suggest that students sketch a diagram of the cave to help generate ideas. They can also use the sketch to demonstrate their escape plan to the class.

The Writer's Style

Make sure students understand that in lines 293–295, Odysseus is comparing the action of blinding the Cyclops with a stake to the action a ship's carpenter makes turning a drill into a ship's plank. Students should understand that the simile in lines 299–303 compares the hissing noise of the Cyclops' blinded eye to the hissing made when white-hot metal is plunged by a blacksmith into a tub of cold water. Both similes help to make the action more graphic and vivid.

Words to Know

Exercise A
1. a
2. a
3. c
4. b
5. b

Exercise B
1. c
2. a
3. b
4. d
5. b

Reteaching/Reinforcement
• *Unit Four Resource Book,* p. 5

Across the Curriculum

History Cooperative Learning The influence of classical Greek culture extends beyond literature. Encourage students to form small groups to find out more about ancient Greek civilization and its impact upon later cultures of the world. Each group member may want to research a different aspect of the subject, such as religion, the arts, government, or technology.

Literary Concepts

Students' lists of Odysseus' heroic qualities may include his recitations of accomplishment, desirability as a companion by goddesses, readiness to battle, bravery, cunning, and ability to escape difficult situations. Lists of his human failings may include his curiosity, unwillingness to heed the warnings of his crew, and his boastfulness at the end of the episode. When students are finished, have them compare their charts with that of at least one other pair.

ART GALLERY
The Adventures of Odysseus

Throughout history, artists have depicted the adventures of Odysseus in paintings, mosaics, and other art forms. Students will be able to see some of these artworks in this set of images. You may wish to use them to discuss the aspects of the *Odyssey* that have been most fascinating to artists.

Side A, Frame 49417

THE LANGUAGE OF LITERATURE TEACHER'S EDITION 507

SUMMARY

After several more adventures, Odysseus and one remaining ship arrive at Aeaea, home of the goddess Circe. Some of Odysseus' men visit Circe's house. She pretends to entertain them, but instead turns them into pigs and imprisons them in a pigsty. One man, Eurylochus, does not trust Circe and runs to tell Odysseus. On his way to rescue his men, Odysseus meets Hermes, who gives Odysseus a flower to protect him from Circe's power. So armed, Odysseus meets Circe. When her powers fail against him, she realizes he is Odysseus and tries to seduce him. She succeeds, but only after releasing his men and returning them to human form. Odysseus and his men feast at Circe's table and linger for a year until the men begin longing for home. Odysseus asks Circe to help him prepare for his return voyage. She agrees but warns him that his journey will not lead directly home. He must first visit the underworld and hear the prophecy of Tiresias.

Thematic Link: *The Wanderings of Odysseus* Prolonging their voyage by their own greed, Odysseus and his crew make an extended visit to the island of the goddess Circe.

BOOK

THE GRACE OF THE WITCH

TEN

ODYSSEUS AND HIS MEN next land on the island of Aeolus, the wind king, and stay with him a month. To extend his hospitality, Aeolus gives Odysseus two parting gifts, a fair west wind blowing the ships toward Ithaca and a great bag holding all the unfavorable, stormy winds. Within sight of home, and while Odysseus is sleeping, the men open the bag, thinking it contains gold and silver. The bad winds thus escape and blow the ships back to Aeolus' island. The king refuses to help them again, believing now that their voyage has been cursed by the gods.

The discouraged mariners next stop briefly in the land of the Laestrygones, fierce cannibals, who bombard their ships with boulders. Only Odysseus, his ship, and its crew of 45 survive the shower of boulders. The lone ship then sails to Aeaea, home of the goddess Circe, considered by many to be a witch. There, Odysseus divides his men into two groups. Eurylochus leads one platoon to explore the island, while Odysseus stays behind on the ship with the remaining crew.

WORDS TO KNOW (BOOK 10)

beguiling (bĭ-gī'lĭng) *adj.* charming; pleasing **beguile** *v.* (p. 510)
chide (chīd) *v.* to scold mildly (p. 513)
contender (kən-tĕn'dər) *n.* a fighter (p. 513)
disconsolate (dĭs-kŏn'sə-lĭt) *adj.* extremely sad (p. 513)
enticing (ĕn-tī'sĭng) *adj.* luring; tempting **entice** *v.* (p. 513)

regaled (rĭ-gāld') *adj.* entertained or amused **regale** *v.* (p. 515)
snare (snâr) *n.* a trap (p. 510)
stealth (stĕlth) *n.* quiet, secret, or sneaky behavior (p. 510)
succumb (sə-kŭm') *v.* to be overpowered; surrender (p. 513)
vile (vīl) *adj.* evil; disgusting (p. 510)

STRATEGIC READING FOR
Less-Proficient Readers

Set a Purpose Have students read the introductory passage on page 508. Then ask students if they've ever made plans to go somewhere with a group and decided not to go at the last minute, perhaps due to a premonition of danger. Have students read to find out what happens to Odysseus' men when they encounter Circe.

Use **UNIT FOUR RESOURCE BOOK,** p. 9, for guidance in reading the selection.

CUSTOMIZING FOR
Gifted and Talented Students

In this epic, Circe is portrayed as a woman who is capable of both great good and great harm, a common portrayal of women in Greek myths. Ask students to write a paragraph analyzing the stereotype of the dangerous yet enchanting woman. Does this stereotype appear in the myths of other cultures? Do students feel that this stereotype is present in today's society? Has the stereotype changed over the years? If so, how?

Linking to History

Improvements in the technology of shipbuilding greatly enhanced the ability of the ancient Greeks to explore, trade, and wage battle throughout the Mediterranean. Early Greek ships were single-banked galleys, so called because they had one bank, or level, of oarsmen on each side of the ship. By 500 B.C., two- and three-banked galleys—called biremes and triremes—had been constructed, featuring multiple levels of oarsmen for greater speed. These ships could contain over 150 oarsmen.

Guide for Reading

A *Possible response: It is surrounded by wild animals that do not attack the men, but fawn on them instead.*

Literary Concept: CHARACTERIZATION

B Ask students to compare and contrast the characters of Polites and Eurylochus. What techniques does the author use to develop each character? *(Possible responses: Polites is friendly and guileless; Eurylochus is more suspicious. The author uses direct comments ["most faithful and likable"] and the character's words ["Dear friends, no need for stealth"] to develop Polites; Eurylochus' suspicious nature is illustrated by his actions—he doesn't follow the others into Circe's house.)*

Guide for Reading

C *Possible response: Answers will vary.*

D *Possible response: They are turned into pigs and forget their desire to go home.*

Literary Concept: DESCRIPTION

E Ask students how the author makes it easy for the audience to visualize the scene. *(Possible response: By using sensory images like "squealing" and the list of body parts that are now "swinish"; by giving details of the food and drink the men are served)*

CUSTOMIZING FOR
Students Acquiring English

I Explain that *all swinish now* means that the men had been turned into swine, or pigs. Ask what the line "though minds were still unchanged" means. *(They could still think like human beings.)*

"In the wild wood they found an open glade,
around a smooth stone house—the hall of Circe—
and wolves and mountain lions lay there, mild
in her soft spell, fed on her drug of evil.
5 None would attack—oh, it was strange, I tell you—
but switching their long tails they faced our men
like hounds, who look up when their master comes
with tidbits for them—as he will—from table.
Humbly those wolves and lions with mighty paws
10 fawned on our men—who met their yellow eyes
and feared them.
                        In the entrance way they stayed
to listen there: inside her quiet house
they heard the goddess Circe.
                                Low she sang
in her <u>beguiling</u> voice, while on her loom
15 she wove ambrosial fabric sheer and bright,
by that craft known to the goddesses of heaven.
No one would speak, until Polites—most
faithful and likable of my officers, said:

'Dear friends, no need for <u>stealth</u>: here's a young weaver
20 singing a pretty song to set the air
a-tingle on these lawns and paven courts.
Goddess she is, or lady. Shall we greet her?'

So reassured, they all cried out together,
and she came swiftly to the shining doors
25 to call them in. All but Eurylochus—
who feared a <u>snare</u>—the innocents went after her.
On thrones she seated them, and lounging chairs,
while she prepared a meal of cheese and barley
and amber honey mixed with Pramnian wine,
30 adding her own <u>vile</u> pinch, to make them lose
desire or thought of our dear father land.
Scarce had they drunk when she flew after them
with her long stick and shut them in a pigsty—
bodies, voices, heads, and bristles, all
35 swinish now, though minds were still unchanged.
So, squealing, in they went. And Circe tossed them

WORDS TO KNOW	**beguiling** (bĭ-gī′lĭng) *adj.* charming; pleasing **beguile** *v.* **stealth** (stĕlth) *n.* quiet, secret, or sneaky behavior **snare** (snâr) *n.* a trap **vile** (vīl) *adj.* evil; disgusting

Guide for Reading

1–11 What is unusual about Circe's hall? **A**

10 fawned on: showed affection for

15 ambrosial: fit for the gods.

17 Polites (pə-lī′tēz).

23–26 If you were among this group, whom would you follow—Polites or Eurylochus? Why? **C**

27–36 What happens to the men after they drink Circe's magic potion? **D**

DESIGN NOTE

To convey the sly and mystical nature of the goddess Circe, the designer placed the photograph of a statue at an angle and merged it into a photograph of jungle ferns and leaves. The blurred background adds a sense of mystery to the figure, as if Circe could magically appear or disappear.

Reading the Art Why do you think the artist placed the statue at an angle? What kind of feeling does the composition evoke in you?

Literary Concept: CONFLICT

F Ask students to explain Eurylochus' internal conflict in this passage. *(Possible response: He wants desperately to tell his story, but fear and shock temporarily silence him.)*

STRATEGIC READING FOR
Less-Proficient Readers

G Ask students to summarize what happens to the men and how Eurylochus escapes. *(Circe serves the men a meal, turns them into pigs, and locks them in a sty. Being wary of the situation, Eurylochus had not followed the men into Circe's house.)* **Summarizing**

Set a Purpose Ask students to read on, paying close attention to Odysseus' relationship with Circe.

Critical Thinking:
COMPARE AND CONTRAST

H Ask students how Eurylochus contrasts with Odysseus as a leader. *(Contrary to what Odysseus might have done, he did not take charge and stop the men from going into Circe's house. Also like Odysseus, he makes no attempt to rescue the men.)*

Cultural Note

I In ancient Greece, to grasp the knees of another was a classic gesture of an inferior or conquered person.

Art Note

This painting, from the fifth century B.C., portrays two of Odysseus' men transformed into swine. These creatures have pigs' heads and human bodies.

Reading the Art Why do you think the artist represented the creatures as part man and part swine?

---

acorns, mast, and cornel berries—fodder
for hogs who rut and slumber on the earth.

Down to the ship Eurylochus came running
40 to cry alarm, foul magic doomed his men!
F But working with dry lips to speak a word
he could not, being so shaken; blinding tears
welled in his eyes; foreboding filled his heart.
When we were frantic questioning him, at last
G 45 we heard the tale: our friends were gone."

EURYLOCHUS TELLS ODYSSEUS *what has happened and begs his captain to sail away from Circe's island. Against Eurylochus' advice, however, Odysseus rushes to save his men from the enchantress. On the way, he meets the god Hermes, who gives him a magical plant—called moly—to protect him from Circe's power. Still, Hermes warns, Odysseus must make the goddess swear that she will play* **H** *no "witches' tricks." Armed with the moly and Hermes' warning, Odysseus arrives at Circe's palace. Circe welcomes him and leads him to a magnificent silver-studded chair.*

43 **foreboding:** a sense of approaching evil.

"The lady Circe
mixed me a golden cup of honeyed wine,
adding in mischief her unholy drug.
I drank, and the drink failed. But she came forward
50 aiming a stroke with her long stick, and whispered:

'Down in the sty and snore among the rest!'

Without a word, I drew my sharpened sword
and in one bound held it against her throat.
I She cried out, then slid under to take my knees,
55 catching her breath to say, in her distress:

'What champion, of what country, can you be?
Where are your kinsmen and your city?
Are you not sluggish with my wine? Ah, wonder!
Never a mortal man that drank this cup

60 but when it passed his lips he had succumbed.
Hale must your heart be and your tempered will.
Odysseus then you are, O great contender,
of whom the glittering god with golden wand
spoke to me ever, and foretold
65 the black swift ship would carry you from Troy.
Put up your weapon in the sheath. We two
shall mingle and make love upon our bed.
So mutual trust may come of play and love.'

To this I said:

      'Circe, am I a boy,
70 that you should make me soft and doting now?
Here in this house you turned my men to swine;
now it is I myself you hold, enticing
into your chamber, to your dangerous bed,
to take my manhood when you have me stripped.
75 I mount no bed of love with you upon it.
Or swear me first a great oath, if I do,
you'll work no more enchantment to my harm.'

She swore at once, outright, as I demanded,
and after she had sworn, and bound herself,
80 I entered Circe's flawless bed of love."

 CIRCE'S MAIDENS BATHE ODYSSEUS *and offer him a tempting meal, yet his mind remains on his captive men.*

"Circe regarded me, as there I sat
disconsolate, and never touched a crust.
Then she stood over me and chided me:

'Why sit at table mute, Odysseus?
85 Are you mistrustful of my bread and drink?
Can it be treachery that you fear again,
after the gods' great oath I swore for you?'

I turned to her at once, and said:

61 tempered: strengthened and hardened, like steel.

63 The "glittering god with golden wand" is Hermes.

70 doting: fond; loving.

75–78 How does Odysseus protect himself from Circe?

81–106 Why does Circe free Odysseus' men from her spell?

WORDS TO KNOW
succumb (sə-kŭm′) *v.* to be overpowered; surrender
contender (kən-tĕn′dər) *n.* a fighter
enticing (ĕn-tī′sĭng) *adj.* luring; tempting **entice** *v.*
disconsolate (dĭs-kŏn′sə-lĭt) *adj.* extremely sad
chide (chīd) *v.* to scold mildly

513

Literary Note

J Explain to students that the phrase "the glittering god with golden wand" is an allusion to Hermes. In Greek myth, the wand was a sign of Hermes' role as one of the principal messengers and representatives of the gods. In ancient Greece, messengers and heralds carried a wand or staff as a symbol of their office.

Guide for Reading

K *Possible responses: Odysseus makes Circe promise not to harm him.*

Cultural Note

L In ancient Greece, the sanctity of oaths was guaranteed by Zeus. The king of the gods himself is often portrayed as irrevocably bound by the oaths he takes. Thus it would be unthinkable for the goddess Circe to break her oath. Odysseus can now trust her.

Guide for Reading

M *Possible response: Circe realizes that Odysseus will be unhappy until his men are free.*

Mini-Lesson — Literary Concepts

REVIEWING CHARACTERIZATION
On the chalkboard draw the web shown on the right and use it to remind students that writers use four different means of developing characters:
- physical description
- a character's speech, thoughts, feelings, and actions
- the speech, thoughts, feelings, and actions of other characters
- direct comments about a character

Application Ask students to search the selection for examples of the different techniques Homer uses to develop the character of Circe. Students can copy the web into their notebooks and refer to it as they review the selection for characterization techniques.

Literary Concept:
CHARACTERIZATION

N Invite students to discuss what this stanza and the preceding two, on page 513, illustrate about Odysseus' character. *(Possible response: He is a man who, despite being surrounded by comforts, does not lose sight of his responsibility for his crew.)* How does the author depict Odysseus' concern? *(Possible responses: through Odysseus' words and behavior)*

Guide for Reading

O *Possible responses:* Odysseus may mean that being a mortal, he has to obey the goddess Circe. He may also mean that being male, he cannot resist Circe's beauty and charms.

P *Possible responses:* The simile compares the reaction of Odysseus' men upon their leader's reappearance to the commotion calves make when trying to get near their mothers. It suggests how much the men depend on Odysseus for their protection.

CUSTOMIZING FOR
Students Acquiring English

② Define *crags* as "rugged rocks or cliffs."

'Circe,
where is the captain who could bear to touch
90 this banquet, in my place? A decent man
N would see his company before him first.
Put heart in me to eat and drink—you may,
by freeing my companions. I must see them.'

But Circe had already turned away.
95 Her long staff in her hand, she left the hall
and opened up the sty. I saw her enter,
driving those men turned swine to stand before me.
She stroked them, each in turn, with some new chrism;
and then, behold! their bristles fell away,
100 the coarse pelt grown upon them by her drug
melted away, and they were men again,
younger, more handsome, taller than before.
Their eyes upon me, each one took my hands,
and wild regret and longing pierced them through,
105 so the room rang with sobs, and even Circe
pitied that transformation. Exquisite
the goddess looked as she stood near me, saying:

'Son of Laertes and the gods of old,
Odysseus, master mariner and soldier,
110 go to the sea beach and sea-breasting ship;
drag it ashore, full length upon the land;
stow gear and stores in rock-holes under cover;
return; be quick; bring all your dear companions.'

Now, being a man, I could not help consenting.
115 So I went down to the sea beach and the ship,
where I found all my other men on board,
weeping, in despair along the benches.
Sometimes in farmyards when the cows return
well-fed from pasture to the barn, one sees
120 the pens give way before the calves in tumult,
breaking through to cluster about their mothers,
bumping together, bawling. Just that way
my crew poured round me when they saw me come—
their faces wet with tears as if they saw
② 125 their homeland, and the crags of Ithaca,
even the very town where they were born.
And weeping still they all cried out in greeting:

98 chrism (krĭz′əm): ointment.

108–110 Notice these epithets, which Circe will use repeatedly in addressing Odysseus.

114 Odysseus says that "being a man," he had to go along with Circe's request. What do you think he means by this statement? **O**

118–126 What two things are compared in this epic simile? How does the simile help you picture the scene that Odysseus is describing? **P**

514 UNIT FOUR PART 1: THE WANDERINGS OF ODYSSEUS

Mini-Lesson Study Skills

INDEXES Explain to students that the index of a book can be a good reference source. Remind students that this section of a book alphabetically lists all people, places, and significant topics covered within the book. They can use a book's index to locate the page numbers of specific information.

Application Have students work with partners to create their own indexes for Book 9 and Book 10 of the *Odyssey*. Have pairs choose from the subjects listed below.

Polites	Troy	prophecy
Circe	wine	Poseidon
Zeus	Eurylochus	Ithaca

Each pair should then review the selections to find mention in the text of the subjects chosen. They should list a page reference in their indexes for each mention found. Then have pairs trade indexes and use them to find the subjects listed.

DESIGN NOTE

This ancient frieze depicts the victims of Circe's magic as creatures with the heads of animals and the bodies of men. Four wolves in the background regard the characters in the frieze.

Reading the Art *Does this image evoke the feeling of being trapped inside the body of a beast? Why or why not?*

Critical Thinking: SYNTHESIZE

Q Ask students to explain this emphasis on Ithaca. *(Possible responses: The men seeing Odysseus are very conscious of their home; Odysseus represents for them the way back home.)*

Q

'Prince, what joy this is, your safe return!
Now Ithaca seems here, and we in Ithaca!
130 But tell us now, what death befell our friends?'

And, speaking gently, I replied:

'First we must get the ship high on the shingle,
and stow our gear and stores in clefts of rock
for cover. Then come follow me, to see
135 your shipmates in the magic house of Circe
eating and drinking, endlessly regaled.'

They turned back, as commanded, to this work;
only one lagged, and tried to hold the others:
Eurylochus it was, who blurted out:

140 'Where now, poor remnants? Is it devil's work

132 **shingle:** pebbly beach.
133 **clefts:** openings; cracks.

140 **remnants:** a small group of survivors.

WORDS TO KNOW
regaled (rĭ-gāld′) *adj.* entertained or amused **regale** *v.*

Mini-Lesson: Speaking, Listening, and Viewing

ANALYZING A SPEECH When Eurylochus urges the men not to follow Odysseus, they do not appear to find the speech or the speaker persuasive. When listening to a speaker make a persuasive appeal, use critical listening skills to analyze the speaker's words—and decide whether or not to follow the advice:

- Take notes during the speech and record the main points. Do they still seem valid when examined afterwards?
- Decide if the speaker is using logic or emotion to make his or her appeal.
- Analyze the speaker's credibility. Does the speaker have the qualifications to speak on the topic? What is the speaker's purpose for making this appeal?

Application Have students use the skills listed above to listen to and analyze a recorded persuasive speech. Then have them analyze the content of the speech and discuss their reactions. Can the speech be improved? If so, how?

Guide for Reading

R *Possible responses: Some will say that given the history of Odysseus with the Cyclops, Eurylochus' words are well warranted. Others might say that Odysseus is the captain and Eurylochus shouldn't criticize him.*

Literary Concept: CONFLICT

S *Ask students to identify how the conflict has changed over the course of this episode. (Possible response: First Eurylochus was in conflict with his own men; then the men were in conflict with Circe, who turned them into pigs; then Circe was in conflict with Odysseus; now Eurylochus is in conflict with Odysseus.)*

Art Note

This painting portrays Circe as she is being pursued by Odysseus.

Reading the Art *How does this representation of Circe differ from the image on page 511?*

CUSTOMIZING FOR
Gifted and Talented Students

Encourage students to find details that illustrate changes in the relationship between Circe and Odysseus. *(Possible response: Odysseus' grasping of her knees illustrates how the balance of power in the relationship has changed; earlier it was Circe who grasped Odysseus' knees in supplication.)*

---

you long for? Will you go to Circe's hall?
Swine, wolves, and lions she will make us all,
beasts of her courtyard, bound by her enchantment.
Remember those the Cyclops held, remember
145　shipmates who made that visit with Odysseus!
The daring man! They died for his foolishness!'

140–146 Do you think Eurylochus is right in his harsh criticism of Odysseus? Why or why not? **R**

When I heard this I had a mind to draw
the blade that swung against my side and chop him,
bowling his head upon the ground—kinsman
150　or no kinsman, close to me though he was.
But others came between, saying, to stop me,

'Prince, we can leave him, if you say the word;
let him stay here on guard. As for ourselves,
show us the way to Circe's magic hall.'

155　So all turned inland, leaving shore and ship,
and Eurylochus—he, too, came on behind,
fearing the rough edge of my tongue. Meanwhile
at Circe's hands the rest were gently bathed,
anointed with sweet oil, and dressed afresh
160　in tunics and new cloaks with fleecy linings.
We found them all at supper when we came.
But greeting their old friends once more, the crew
could not hold back their tears; and now again
the rooms rang with sobs. Then Circe, loveliest
165　of all immortals, came to counsel me:

'Son of Laertes and the gods of old,
Odysseus, master mariner and soldier,
enough of weeping fits. I know—I, too—
what you endured upon the inhuman sea,
170　what odds you met on land from hostile men.
Remain with me, and share my meat and wine;
restore behind your ribs those gallant hearts
that served you in the old days, when you sailed
from stony Ithaca. Now parched and spent,
175　your cruel wandering is all you think of,
never of joy, after so many blows.'

174 parched and spent: thirsty and worn out.

As we were men we could not help consenting.
So day by day we lingered, feasting long

516　UNIT FOUR PART 1: THE WANDERINGS OF ODYSSEUS

Assessment Option

SELF-ASSESSMENT You can help students assess their understanding of the selection by having them write a dialogue between Odysseus and Eurylochus in which each criticizes the leadership skills of the other. Before they begin to write, students should review the speeches and actions of each character, focusing on the points of conflict between them.

To help students assess their own work, have them respond to the following questions:
- Are the contents of the dialogue consistent with the events depicted in the selection?
- Are the contents of the dialogue consistent with the description of each character?

on roasts and wine, until a year grew fat.
180 But when the passing months and wheeling seasons
brought the long summery days, the pause of summer,
my shipmates one day summoned me and said:

'Captain, shake off this trance, and think of home—
if home indeed awaits us,
                                    if we shall ever see
185 your own well-timbered hall on Ithaca.'

They made me feel a pang, and I agreed.
That day, and all day long, from dawn to sundown,
we feasted on roast meat and ruddy wine,
and after sunset when the dusk came on
190 my men slept in the shadowy hall, but I
went through the dark to Circe's flawless bed
and took the goddess' knees in supplication,
urging, as she bent to hear:

                                    'O Circe,
now you must keep your promise; it is time.
195 Help me make sail for home. Day after day
(3) my longing quickens, and my company
give me no peace, but wear my heart away
pleading when you are not at hand to hear.'

The loveliest of goddesses replied:

200 'Son of Laertes and the gods of old,
Odysseus, master mariner and soldier,
you shall not stay here longer against your will;
but home you may not go
unless you take a strange way round and come
205 to the cold homes of Death and pale Persephone.
You shall hear prophecy from the rapt shade
of blind Tiresias of Thebes, forever
charged with reason even among the dead;
to him alone, of all the flitting ghosts,
210 Persephone has given a mind undarkened.'

At this I felt a weight like stone within me,
and, moaning, pressed my length against the bed,
with no desire to see the daylight more."

180–185 Notice that Odysseus' men have to remind him of home.

185 well-timbered: well-constructed.

186 pang: a sharp feeling of emotional distress. What emotion do you think Odysseus is feeling?

192 supplication: humble request or prayer.

200–213 Circe tells Odysseus that he must go to the underworld, the land of the dead. The god of the underworld is Hades (hā′dēz), referred to here as Death; Persephone is his wife. One of the spirits—or "shades"—in the underworld is that of Tiresias, a blind prophet who has been allowed to keep his mental powers. He will give Odysseus instructions about returning home. What is Odysseus' reaction upon hearing all of this?

ODYSSEY **517**

Guide for Reading

T Possible responses: Odysseus is homesick for Ithaca and feeling guilty over his long delay on Circe's island.

CUSTOMIZING FOR
Students Acquiring English

3 Write the expressions "my longing quickens" and "they wear my heart away" on the board. Ask students to use context clues to rephrase these expressions. (Possible responses: my longing grows; they upset me)

Guide for Reading

U Possible response: Odysseus is in despair. He is frightened at the prospect of what is to come.

STRATEGIC READING FOR
Less-Proficient Readers

V Ask students to summarize Odysseus' relationship with Circe at the end of the episode. (Possible response: Circe has become a friend and companion to Odysseus and no longer poses a threat to him and his crew.)
Drawing Conclusions

COMPREHENSION CHECK

1. What happens to Eurylochus' men after they drink Circe's wine? (They are changed into pigs.)
2. How is Odysseus able to withstand Circe's magic? (The god Hermes has given him a magic plant and specific instructions that protect him.)
3. How does Odysseus react when Eurylochus urges the men not to obey him? (He becomes angry and almost kills Eurylochus.)
4. After a year of Circe's hospitality, who convinces Odysseus that it is time to depart? (his crew)
5. Where does Circe tell Odysseus he must go before he can return home? (to the land of the dead)

Mini-Lesson   Grammar

CAPITALIZATION: Personal Titles
Remind students that personal titles used before people's names or in direct address are capitalized. Such titles are not capitalized when they do not precede the name, with a few exceptions such as *President* when it refers to the current president of the United States.

Application Point out the word *Captain* in the highlighted section above. Tell students that when used in this way, the word *captain* would be capitalized even if it did not begin a sentence, because it is used in direct address. Then write the words at the right on the board. Have students write two sentences for each word: one in which the word is capitalized, one in which it is not.

Reteaching/Reinforcement
- *Grammar Handbook,* anthology p. 927
- *Grammar Mini-Lessons* copymasters p. 37, transparencies p. 37

The Writer's Craft

Names of People and Personal Titles, pp. 749–750

THE LANGUAGE OF LITERATURE TEACHER'S EDITION **517**

From Personal Response to Critical Analysis

1. Accept all reasonable responses.
2. Possible responses: Students may note that Circe poses a physical danger, the risk of being transformed into pigs. Circe poses a psychological danger because her beauty and hospitality cause Odysseus to lose the desire to continue his journey. Some will say that Circe, who kills no one, is less dangerous than Polyphemus; others will point out that she has the power to delay or obstruct the voyage.
3. Possible responses: Eurylochus is more cautious, distrusting Circe even after she restores the men and lavishes them with hospitality; Odysseus is braver, not afraid to challenge Circe; Eurylochus, who senses danger, wants to flee; Odysseus' reaction to Eurylochus' criticism is evidence of his temper and impulsiveness.
4. Possible responses: courage; leadership; strength
5. Accept all reasonable, well-supported responses.
6. Accept all reasonable, well-supported responses.

Another Pathway

Use examples to discuss epithets (lines 108–109, 164–165) and remind students that epic similes (lines 6–8, 118–126) are complex, often extending for a number of lines.

Rubric
3 Full Accomplishment Students' similes and epithets accurately convey the threat as well as the appeal of Circe.
2 Substantial Accomplishment Students' similes and epithets convey some of the qualities of Circe.
1 Little or Partial Accomplishment Students have difficulty creating similes and epithets.

FROM PERSONAL RESPONSE TO CRITICAL ANALYSIS

REFLECT 1. What new impressions of Odysseus did you get from this part of the story? Add your new ideas in your notebook.

RETHINK 2. In what ways is Circe a danger to Odysseus and his men? Is she more dangerous or less dangerous than the Cyclops? Support your opinion with evidence from the epic.

3. Eurylochus' character contrasts sharply with Odysseus' in this episode. What aspects of Odysseus' character are revealed through this contrast?
   Consider
   Close Textual Reading
   - how each feels about Circe
   - what each wants to do after Circe has transformed the first group of men
   - how Eurylochus criticizes Odysseus
   - how Odysseus reacts to Eurylochus' criticism

Thematic Link 4. What heroic qualities does Odysseus reveal in this episode?

5. Do you think that it is wise of Odysseus to linger so long with Circe? Give reasons for your opinion.

RELATE 6. In what ways can sexual or romantic appeal be a trap today? Give several examples.

THE WRITER'S STYLE

The **epithets** in the *Odyssey* often serve as quick aids to characterization. For example, Circe calls Odysseus "great contender" and "master mariner and soldier." What epithet does Odysseus use to describe Circe? What does the epithet say about her—and perhaps about his feelings for her?

ANOTHER PATHWAY

With a partner, compose two epic similes about Circe. In the first, convey the appeal that she has for Odysseus and his men and the way she helps them. In the second, convey the threat that she poses to them. Then make up two epithets that describe Circe—one to fit with each of your epic similes. Share your epithets and epic similes with your classmates.

1. Try writing the **lyrics** of the beguiling song that Circe sings, described by Polites as "a pretty song to set the air a-tingle."

2. Describe Circe's capturing of Odysseus' men in a **news story** that might appear in a tabloid newspaper.

3. Write one or two **diary entries** in which Eurylochus describes the events of this episode from his point of view.

📁 **PORTFOLIO** Save your writing. You may want to use it later as a springboard to a piece for your portfolio.

518 UNIT FOUR PART 1: THE WANDERINGS OF ODYSSEUS

The Writer's Style

Odysseus uses the epithets "loveliest of all immortals" (lines 164–165) and "loveliest of goddesses" (line 199) to describe Circe. Students may say that these epithets illustrate Circe's great beauty or that they reveal Odysseus' desire for the goddess.

QuickWrites

1. Suggest that students review details about Circe to help them imagine the lyrics that she might be singing.
2. Have students examine the writing style of tabloid newspaper articles. Suggest they list the details of the event from the selection before they begin writing.
3. Encourage students to imagine themselves in Eurylochus' position. Would they trust Odysseus' judgment? How would it feel to be threatened by Odysseus?

LITERARY CONCEPTS

Good **description** can bring a scene to life for readers and create a particular mood or atmosphere. Writers can produce effective descriptions by means of sharp details, lively sensory images, and figurative language. Note, for example, the opening scene of this episode, in which Eurylochus and his men approach Circe's stone house in the forest clearing. They come upon wild animals—wolves and lions with mighty paws, yellow eyes, and switching tails—but the beasts are strangely quiet, as if drugged or enchanted. The animals are compared to hounds expecting treats from their master. All this gives the reader an ominous feeling of something strange and dangerous. Point out details in another descriptive passage, and describe the effect they create.

CONCEPT REVIEW: Conflict As you know, the basis of a plot is conflict. What are the main external and internal conflicts that Odysseus faces in his encounter with Circe?

Multimodal Learning

ALTERNATIVE ACTIVITIES

1. *Cooperative Learning* Work with a small group of classmates to skim this adventure, looking for descriptive details about Circe's "magic house." Then create a **painting** or **diorama** of her hall and its surroundings.

2. Imagine that you are Odysseus, describing your adventures to King Alcinous. Prepare an **oral reading** of this episode. Practice reading with appropriate feelings, pauses, and changes in pitch and volume. Make a recording of your reading and play it for your class.

3. Notice the references to ships in the parts of the *Odyssey* you have read. Do some research to find out about the kinds of ships used by the Greeks in Homeric times. (You might investigate the work of the navigator Tim Severin.) Use your findings to make a **model** of Odysseus' ship.

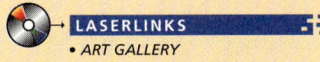
• ART GALLERY

WORDS TO KNOW

EXERCISE A Answer the following questions.

1. Whom would you expect to act with **stealth**—a spy, a surgeon, or a firefighter?
2. If you're feeling **disconsolate,** are you happy, sad, or angry?
3. Is a **vile** deed a wicked deed, a brave deed, or an impractical deed?
4. Would a **beguiling** person disgust other people, attract other people, or bore other people?
5. Which is meant to be **enticing** to a fish—a hook, a worm, or a net?
6. Who is most likely to use a **snare** at work—a beautician, a doctor, or a dogcatcher?
7. Would you be most likely to **chide** someone for being cruel, for being mischievous, or for being heroic?
8. Does someone ready to **succumb** in a struggle say "Charge," "Take that," or "I give up"?
9. If you were **regaled** with a performance, would you applaud, yawn, or stomp out?
10. Would you expect someone known as a **contender** to compete, to surrender, or to cooperate?

EXERCISE B Construct a crossword puzzle (see model below), using five of the vocabulary words, such as *snare, chide, stealth, succumb,* and *regaled.* (When writing the clues, avoid using the definitions and synonyms given in this book.) Then trade puzzles with a classmate.

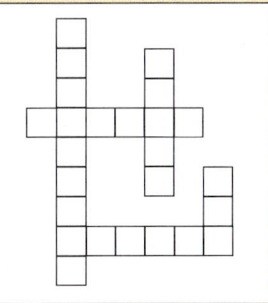

READING ON

In his next adventures, Odysseus faces more challenges. As you read, evaluate his handling of each new situation.

ODYSSEY **519**

Alternative Activities

1. Students may remember relevant descriptive details from the Literary Concepts activity. Have one student act as a recorder of descriptive details found. Another can act as encourager of participation to make sure everyone contributes.
2. Remind students that the Odyssey was originally told as an oral tale. Suggest they review the storytelling skills they practiced in the mini-lesson on speaking on page 492.
3. Have students present their models and research findings to the class.

Literary Concepts

Make sure students can identify the techniques used to create effective description, such as imagery, simile, and descriptive details. Students can work in small groups to discuss how they were affected by each of the descriptive passages.

Conflict Students may point to Odysseus' effort to defeat Circe as external conflict; they may cite Odysseus' struggle between his longing to return home and his desire to stay with Circe as internal conflict.

Words to Know

Exercise A

1. a spy
2. sad
3. wicked
4. attract other people
5. a worm
6. a dogcatcher
7. mischievous
8. "I give up"
9. applaud
10. compete

Exercise B
Student puzzles will vary. If students have trouble getting started, begin a grid on the chalkboard and practice as a group creating a class crossword puzzle.

Reteaching/Reinforcement
• *Unit Four Resource Book,* p. 10

Across the Curriculum

Religion *Cooperative Learning* Circe tells Odysseus that he must first go to the underworld, the land of the dead, before he is allowed to return home. Beliefs about the existence and location of human spirits after death vary from culture to culture and among different religions. Have students form small groups to research varying positions on the concept of an afterlife. You may wish to assign each group member a different topic; for example, the underworld, heaven, hell, ancestor worship, or reincarnation.

ART GALLERY
Circe, the Enchantress These images will show students examples of how artists have depicted Circe, the enchantress. You may wish to use the images to generate a discussion about the various ways artists can represent compelling stories.

Side A, Frame 49430

THE LANGUAGE OF LITERATURE TEACHER'S EDITION **519**

SUMMARY

After their visit to the underworld, Odysseus and his men return to Circe. She warns Odysseus of dangers awaiting him: the Sirens, monsters who sing so beautifully that people are lured to their death; Scylla, a monster with twelve legs and six heads, who takes from every passing ship a man to feed each head; Charybdis, who lurks below the sea and can swallow whole ships; the island of Thrinacia, where the sun god Helios' cattle graze. Circe gives good advice for escaping these dangers. To escape the Sirens, Odysseus fills his crew's ears with beeswax so they cannot hear the cries and has them bind him to the mast of his ship. When they sail past the Sirens, Odysseus longs to go to them, but his men ignore his commands and so escape. Then, to avoid Charybdis, they pass near Scylla. The monster swoops and takes six crew members. The ship and remaining crew escape. Then Odysseus tries to persuade his crew to bypass the island of Thrinacia, but they land and eat Helios' cattle. Zeus appeases the angry Helios by destroying the ship. Only Odysseus survives.

Thematic Link: *The Wanderings of Odysseus* Heading toward Ithaca, Odysseus must navigate between two equally formidable dangers.

BOOK TWELVE

SEA PERILS AND DEFEAT

IN BOOK 11, *Odysseus and his men visit the underworld, where the shades, or spirits of the dead, reside. During Odysseus' visit there, the spirit of the prophet Tiresias warns him that death and destruction will follow unless he and his crew act with restraint and control. Tiresias then reveals what Odysseus must do on his return to Ithaca. Odysseus also speaks with the spirit of his mother, who died of grief because Odysseus was away for so long.*

Odysseus and his men then leave the underworld and return to Circe's island. While his men sleep, Circe takes Odysseus aside to hear about the underworld and to offer advice.

"Then said the Lady Circe:
'So: all those trials are over.
                    Listen with care
to this, now, and a god will arm your mind.
Square in your ship's path are Sirens, crying

Guide for Reading

2–3 In Circe, Odysseus has found a valuable ally. In the next hundred lines, she describes in detail each danger that he and his men will meet on their way home.

WORDS TO KNOW (BOOK 12)

abominably (ə-bŏm′ə-nə-blē) *adv.* in a hateful way; horribly (p. 522)
anguish (ăng′gwĭsh) *n.* great physical or mental suffering; agony (p. 528)
chaos (kā′ŏs′) *n.* great disorder or confusion (p. 524)
dire (dīr) *adj.* dreadful; terrible (p. 528)
dwindle (dwĭn′dl) *v.* to become gradually less; diminish (p. 525)

lurk (lûrk) *v.* to lie hidden, ready to ambush (p. 522)
peril (pĕr′əl) *n.* danger; risk (p. 526)
questing (kwĕs′tĭng) *adj.* journeying over; exploring **quest** *v.* (p. 529)
scourge (skûrj) *n.* a cause of great suffering or destruction (p. 524)
travail (trə-vāl′) *n.* painful effort (p. 528)

5 beauty to bewitch men coasting by;
   woe to the innocent who hears that sound!
   He will not see his lady nor his children
   in joy, crowding about him, home from sea;
   the Sirens will sing his mind away
10 on their sweet meadow lolling. There are bones
   of dead men rotting in a pile beside them
   and flayed skins shrivel around the spot.
                                            Steer wide;
   keep well to seaward; plug your oarsmen's ears
   with beeswax kneaded soft; none of the rest
15 should hear that song.
                          But if you wish to listen,
   let the men tie you in the lugger, hand
   and foot, back to the mast, lashed to the mast,
   so you may hear those harpies' thrilling voices;
   shout as you will, begging to be untied,
20 your crew must only twist more line around you
   and keep their stroke up, till the singers fade.
   What then? One of two courses you may take,
   and you yourself must weigh them. I shall not
   plan the whole action for you now, but only
25 tell you of both.
                   Ahead are beetling rocks
   and dark blue glancing Amphitrite, surging,
   roars around them. Prowling Rocks, or Drifters,
   the gods in bliss have named them—named them well.
   Not even birds can pass them by.

30   A second course
   lies between headlands. One is a sharp mountain
   piercing the sky, with stormcloud round the peak
   dissolving never, not in the brightest summer,
   to show heaven's azure there, nor in the fall.
35 No mortal man could scale it, nor so much
   as land there, not with twenty hands and feet,
   so sheer the cliffs are—as of polished stone.
   Midway that height, a cavern full of mist
   opens toward Erebus and evening. Skirting
40 this in the lugger, great Odysseus,
   your master bowman, shooting from the deck,
   would come short of the cavemouth with his shaft;

12 flayed: torn off; stripped.

14 kneaded (nē′dĭd): squeezed and pressed.

15–21 Circe suggests a way for Odysseus to hear the Sirens safely. Do you think he will follow her suggestion?

18 those harpies' thrilling voices: the delightful voices of those evil females.

25 beetling: jutting or overhanging.

26 glancing Amphitrite (ăm′fĭ-trī′tē): sparkling seawater. (Amphitrite is the goddess of the sea and the wife of Poseidon. Here, Circe uses the name to refer to the sea itself.)

31 headlands: points of land jutting out into the sea; promontories.

34 heaven's azure (ăzh′ər): the blue sky.

39 Erebus (ĕr′ə-bəs): a land of darkness beneath the earth.

Literary Concept: IMAGERY

B To help students more easily visualize the monster, have them tell what animals' bodies the different parts of Scylla's body are compared to. *(Possible response: Her legs are compared to an octopus's; her necks are compared to snakes; her rows of teeth may remind one of a shark.)*

Literary Note

C The word *maelstrom* originally referred to the Moskenstraumen, a dangerous sea passage in the Arctic Ocean off the west coast of Norway, subject to treacherous tidal currents. The word was popularized in the English language through exaggerations in the writings of Jules Verne and Edgar Allan Poe, the latter using it especially to describe the fictional phenomenon of giant whirlpools capable of sinking entire ships.

Guide for Reading

D *Possible response: Odysseus must avoid Charybdis entirely by steering close to the cliff of Scylla—even though this will result in the loss of six men.*

E *Possible response: Circe warns Odysseus not to try to defend his crew against Scylla because it would be futile and would result in even greater losses.*

---

but that is the den of Scylla, where she yaps
abominably, a newborn whelp's cry,
though she is huge and monstrous. God or man,
no one could look on her in joy. Her legs—
and there are twelve—are like great tentacles,
unjointed, and upon her serpent necks
are borne six heads like nightmares of ferocity,
with triple serried rows of fangs and deep
gullets of black death. Half her length, she sways
her head in air, outside her horrid cleft,
hunting the sea around that promontory
for dolphins, dogfish, or what bigger game
thundering Amphitrite feeds in thousands.
And no ship's company can claim
to have passed her without loss and grief; she takes,
from every ship, one man for every gullet.

The opposite point seems more a tongue of land
you'd touch with a good bowshot, at the narrows.
A great wild fig, a shaggy mass of leaves,
grows on it, and Charybdis lurks below
to swallow down the dark sea tide. Three times
from dawn to dusk she spews it up
and sucks it down again three times, a whirling
maelstrom; if you come upon her then
the god who makes earth tremble could not save you.
No, hug the cliff of Scylla, take your ship
through on a racing stroke. Better to mourn
six men than lose them all, and the ship, too.'

So her advice ran; but I faced her, saying:

'Only instruct me, goddess, if you will,
how, if possible, can I pass Charybdis,
or fight off Scylla when she raids my crew?'

Swiftly that loveliest goddess answered me:

'Must you have battle in your heart forever?
The bloody toil of combat? Old contender,
will you not yield to the immortal gods?

43–55 Circe presents a very unpleasant image of Scylla. To get a better idea of what Odysseus and his crew will be up against, try using this detailed description to draw a picture of Scylla.

66 maelstrom (māl′strəm): a large, violent whirlpool.

68–70 What is Circe's advice for dealing with Charybdis? **D**

72–85 Notice this exchange between Odysseus and Circe. What does Circe caution Odysseus against doing, and why? **E**

WORDS TO KNOW
abominably (ə-bŏm′ə-nə-blē) *adv.* in a hateful way; horribly
lurk (lûrk) *v.* to lie hidden, ready to ambush

DESIGN NOTE

Through the centuries, Sirens have been portrayed by artists in many different forms. Sometimes they are depicted as mermaids; at other times as a combination of woman, fish, and bird. This illustration of a Siren shows a creature with a woman's torso and a bird's feet and wings. Of course, the main characteristic of the Siren is her beguiling song; here, the Siren is holding the remains of an instrument, perhaps a lyre, in her hands.

Reading the Art *How does this image compare with the picture you have of a Siren? Explain what is similar or different about this image.*

Linking to History

F The ancient Greeks believed that Helios, the god of the sun, left his palace in the East every morning and traveled across the sky in a golden chariot. Helios was revered in the city of Rhodes, where a towering bronze statue—120 feet high—was built at the entrance to the harbor to honor him. The Colossus of Rhodes, one of the Seven Wonders of the Ancient World, was destroyed by an earthquake in 224 B.C.

STRATEGIC READING FOR
Less-Proficient Readers

G Have students summarize the dangers that lie ahead for Odysseus. *(the Sirens, who lure seafarers with their beguiling voices; the raging waters of the Drifters; the monster Scylla, who plucks men from passing ships; Charybdis, who creates huge whirlpools that swallow entire vessels; the temptation of the cattle and sheep of Helios on the island of Thrinacia, the raiding of which would result in destruction for everyone but Odysseus)* **Summarizing**

Set a Purpose Have students read to find out whether Odysseus will come safely through these trials.

That nightmare cannot die, being eternal
80 evil itself—horror, and pain, and <u>chaos</u>;
there is no fighting her, no power can fight her,
all that avails is flight.

82 all . . . flight: all you can do is flee.

    Lose headway there
along that rockface while you break out arms,
and she'll swoop over you, I fear, once more,
85 taking one man again for every gullet.
No, no, put all your backs into it, row on;
invoke Blind Force, that bore this <u>scourge</u> of men,
to keep her from a second strike against you.

87 invoke . . . men: pray to the goddess of blind force, who gave birth to Scylla.

Then you will coast Thrinacia, the island
90 where Helios' cattle graze, fine herds, and flocks
of goodly sheep. The herds and flocks are seven,
with fifty beasts in each.

89 coast: sail along the coast of.

    No lambs are dropped,
or calves, and these fat cattle never die.
Immortal, too, their cowherds are—their shepherds—
95 Phaethusa and Lampetia, sweetly braided
nymphs that divine Neaera bore

95–96 Phaethusa (fā′ə-thōō′sə) . . . **Lampetia** (lăm-pē′shə) . . . **Neaera** (nē-ē′rə).

 to the overlord of high noon, Helios.
These nymphs their gentle mother bred and placed
upon Thrinacia, the distant land,
100 in care of flocks and cattle for their father.

Now give those kine a wide berth, keep your thoughts
intent upon your course for home,
and hard seafaring brings you all to Ithaca.
But if you raid the beeves, I see destruction
105 for ship and crew.

101–105 Circe warns Odysseus not to steal Helios' fine cattle (also called kine and beeves) because Helios will take revenge.

    Rough years then lie between
you and your homecoming, alone and old,
 the one survivor, all companions lost.'"

 AT DAWN, *Odysseus and his men continue their journey. Odysseus decides to tell the men only of Circe's warnings about the Sirens, whom they will soon encounter. He is fairly sure that they can survive this peril if he keeps their spirits up. Suddenly, the wind stops.*

> **WORDS TO KNOW**
> **chaos** (kā′ŏs′) *n.* great disorder or confusion
> **scourge** (skûrj) *n.* a cause of great suffering or destruction

524

CAPITALIZATION: Geographical Names
Remind students that geographical names, nationalities, languages, races, and any adjectives formed from these words must be capitalized. For example:

    Ithaca, French, Asian Americans

Capitalize the word modified by a geographical adjective only if it and the adjective together form a geographical name, event, or time period. For example:

    Trojan horse, Trojan War, Greek epic

Proper Noun	Proper Adjective
Mediterranean	Mediterranean fruit fly
	Mediterranean Sea
Rome	Roman calendar
	Roman Empire

Application Have students decide whether the following words are correctly capitalized.
1. thrinacian Cattle *(Thrinacian cattle)*
2. the Greek language *(correct)*
3. Circe's Island *(Circe's island)*

Reteaching/Reinforcement
- *Grammar Handbook*, anthology p. 929
- *Grammar Mini-Lessons* copymasters p. 38

The Writer's Craft
Capitalization, pp. 621 and 749–754

524 THE LANGUAGE OF LITERATURE **TEACHER'S EDITION**

"The crew were on their feet
briskly, to furl the sail, and stow it; then,
110 each in place, they poised the smooth oar blades
and sent the white foam scudding by. I carved
a massive cake of beeswax into bits
and rolled them in my hands until they softened—
no long task, for a burning heat came down
115 from Helios, lord of high noon. Going forward
I carried wax along the line, and laid it
thick on their ears. They tied me up, then, plumb
amidships, back to the mast, lashed to the mast,
and took themselves again to rowing. Soon,
120 as we came smartly within hailing distance,
the two Sirens, noting our fast ship
off their point, made ready, and they sang.

The lovely voices in ardor appealing over the water
made me crave to listen, and I tried to say
125 'Untie me!' to the crew, jerking my brows;
but they bent steady to the oars. Then Perimedes
got to his feet, he and Eurylochus,
and passed more line about, to hold me still.
So all rowed on, until the Sirens
130 dropped under the sea rim, and their singing
dwindled away.
              My faithful company
rested on their oars now, peeling off
the wax that I had laid thick on their ears;
then set me free.
                But scarcely had that island
135 faded in blue air than I saw smoke
and white water, with sound of waves in tumult—
a sound the men heard, and it terrified them.
Oars flew from their hands; the blades went knocking
wild alongside till the ship lost way,
140 with no oarblades to drive her through the water.

Well, I walked up and down from bow to stern,
trying to put heart into them, standing over
every oarsman, saying gently,

117–118 plumb amidships: exactly in the center of the ship.

123 ardor: passion.

126 Perimedes (pĕr′ĭ-mē′dēz).

134–159 The men panic when they hear the thundering surf. How does Odysseus help them overcome their fear and thus regain control of the ship?

WORDS TO KNOW
dwindle (dwĭn′dl) *v.* to become gradually less; diminish

DESIGN NOTE

Unlike the Sirens, who are enchanting singers as well as dangerous, Scylla has no appealing qualities. The designer here transformed a photo of a sculpture of Scylla into an image that emphasizes the monster's mean and threatening nature. The six heads of Scylla become like writhing snakes, with burning eyes that pierce through the darkness.

Reading the Art *Do you think this image successfully conveys the horrible threat of Scylla? Why or why not?*

Literary Concept: THEME

K Have students discuss how Odysseus' speech relates to the theme of a character's growth to maturity as he passes through adventures and dangers. *(Possible response: It suggests that he has learned that protecting his men in dangerous situations is more important than satisfying his own curiosity and lust for battle.)*

CUSTOMIZING FOR
Students Acquiring English

2 Ask students to paraphrase the idiom "by hook or crook" using context clues. Ask them to share idioms in other languages that mean the same thing.

              'Friends,
have we never been in danger before this?
145 More fearsome, is it now, than when the Cyclops
penned us in his cave? What power he had!
Did I not keep my nerve, and use my wits
to find a way out for us?
              Now I say
by hook or crook this <u>peril</u> too shall be
150 something that we remember.

> WORDS TO KNOW
> **peril** (pĕr′əl) *n.* danger; risk

526

Mini-Lesson Literary Concepts

REVIEWING IMAGERY Copy the word web at left onto the chalkboard. Use it to remind students that imagery consists of descriptive words and phrases that re-create sensory experiences for the reader.

Application Ask students to work with a partner to review the selection for examples of imagery. Then have students choose one of the events of the episode and rewrite it in their own words, using descriptive words and phrases. Encourage them to try to use imagery that appeals to at least three of the five senses.

CUSTOMIZING FOR
Multiple Learning Styles

L **Interpersonal Learners** Have students discuss what techniques of good leadership Odysseus applies in this situation. *(Possible responses: addresses men with affection; insists on obedience to orders; reminds men that he's protected them in past adventures)*

Literary Concept:
CHARACTERIZATION

M Ask students to sum up Odysseus' character as revealed in his speech on these two pages, and to support their answers. *(Possible responses: brave, because he shows no fear; responsible, because he tries to lessen the fear of the crew; paternal, because he treats the crew with affection while insisting on obedience)*

Heads up, lads!
We must obey the orders as I give them.
Get the oarshafts in your hands, and lay back
hard on your benches; hit these breaking seas.
Zeus help us pull away before we founder.
155 You at the tiller, listen, and take in
all that I say—the rudders are your duty;
keep her out of the combers and the smoke;
steer for that headland; watch the drift, or we
fetch up in the smother, and you drown us.'

154 **founder:** sink.

157 **combers:** breaking waves.
158–159 **watch . . . smother:** keep the ship on course, or it will be crushed in the rough water.

ODYSSEY **527**

Multicultural Perspectives

THE EPIC Epic poetry exists in many cultures. The *Ramayana* and *Mahabharata* are two Indian epics dating from between 400 B.C. and A.D. 200. The *Mahabharata* is the longest poem ever written—seven times the length of the *Iliad* and the *Odyssey* combined. The poem focuses on a fight for power between two families and includes the *Bhagavad-Gita*, the most important text of the Hindu religion. The *Ramayana* concerns Prince Rama's attempts to rescue his wife, Sita, from the demon king Ravana. The *Ramayana* is immensely popular in present-day India, and the story is reenacted in annual pageants across the country.

The *Kalevala* is the national epic of Finland and is composed of a series of folk songs. These songs were passed down orally from generation to generation until they were recorded and combined by a Finnish doctor in the 1830s. The *Kalevala*, which means "land of heroes," contains stories that feature adventurers, warriors, a powerful female king, and the Sampo, a magic mill that creates riches for its owner.

Critical Thinking: ANALYZE

N Have students discuss Odysseus' decision to conceal part of Circe's prophecy. Was he right not to tell the men that some of them would be killed? *(Possible responses: Yes—since the deaths are inevitable, why cause panic?; no—the men have a right to know.)*

Guide for Reading

O *Possible response: Odysseus will attack Scylla and will suffer great losses after ignoring Circe's advice.*

Linking to Geography

P The two neighboring monsters described by Homer in this episode may have been inspired by the Straight of Messina, a 20-mile-long channel named for a city in present-day Sicily. The channel separates Sicily, founded by the ancient Greeks in the eighth century B.C., from the Italian mainland. On the mainland side of the passage lies a long promontory, possibly represented by Scylla in Greek myth. The whirlpools and perilous currents of the Sicilian side could well have provided the inspiration for the ship-swallowing Charybdis.

Literary Concept: IMAGERY

Q Have students describe the two phases of Charybdis' action in their own words. *(Possible responses: Charybdis causes the water, as in a hot kettle, to rise and violently roll and tumble until erupting—shooting into the air as from a geyser, then falling like rain; then she sucks water down to the sea bottom, like a whirlpool or maelstrom.)*

---

160 That was all, and it brought them round to action.
N But as I sent them on toward Scylla, I
told them nothing, as they could do nothing.
They would have dropped their oars again, in panic,
to roll for cover under the decking. Circe's
165 bidding against arms had slipped my mind,
so I tied on my cuirass and took up
two heavy spears, then made my way along
to the foredeck—thinking to see her first from there,
the monster of the gray rock, harboring
170 torment for my friends. I strained my eyes
upon that cliffside veiled in cloud, but nowhere
could I catch sight of her.
　　　　　　　　　　And all this time,
in <u>travail</u>, sobbing, gaining on the current,
we rowed into the strait—Scylla to port
P 175 and on our starboard beam Charybdis, <u>dire</u>
Q gorge of the salt sea tide. By heaven! when she
vomited, all the sea was like a cauldron
seething over intense fire, when the mixture
suddenly heaves and rises.
　　　　　　　　　　The shot spume
180 soared to the landside heights, and fell like rain.

But when she swallowed the sea water down
we saw the funnel of the maelstrom, heard
the rock bellowing all around, and dark
sand raged on the bottom far below.
185 My men all blanched against the gloom, our eyes
were fixed upon that yawning mouth in fear
of being devoured.
　　　　　　　　　Then Scylla made her strike,
whisking six of my best men from the ship.
I happened to glance aft at ship and oarsmen
190 and caught sight of their arms and legs, dangling
high overhead. Voices came down to me
in <u>anguish</u>, calling my name for the last time.

A man surfcasting on a point of rock
for bass or mackerel, whipping his long rod

161–168 Odysseus doesn't tell his men that several of them will be killed. Moreover, forgetting Circe's warning against trying to fight Scylla, he takes up his body armor (cuirass) and spears. What do you think will happen? **O**

176 gorge: throat; gullet.

179 shot spume: flying foam.

185 blanched: became pale.

189 aft: toward the rear of the ship.

WORDS TO KNOW	**travail** (trə-vāl′) *n.* painful effort
	dire (dīr) *adj.* dreadful; terrible
	anguish (ăng′gwĭsh) *n.* great physical or mental suffering; agony

195 to drop the sinker and the bait far out,
will hook a fish and rip it from the surface
to dangle wriggling through the air:
                              so these
were borne aloft in spasms toward the cliff.

198 borne aloft in spasms: lifted high while struggling violently.

She ate them as they shrieked there, in her den,
200 in the dire grapple, reaching still for me—
and deathly pity ran me through
at that sight—far the worst I ever suffered,
questing the passes of the strange sea.
                              We rowed on.
The Rocks were now behind; Charybdis, too,
205 and Scylla dropped astern."

200 grapple: grasp.

ODYSSEUS TRIES TO PERSUADE *his men to bypass Thrinacia, the island of the sun god Helios, but they insist on landing. Driven by hunger, they ignore Odysseus' warning not to feast on Helios' cattle. This disobedience angers the sun god, who threatens to stop shining if payment is not made for the loss of his cattle. To appease Helios, Zeus sends down a thunderbolt to sink Odysseus' ship. Odysseus alone survives. He eventually drifts to Ogygia, the home of Calypso, who keeps him on her island for seven years. With this episode, Odysseus ends the telling of his tale to King Alcinous.*

WORDS TO KNOW **questing** (kwĕs´tĭng) *adj.* journeying over; exploring **quest** *v.*

Literary Element: EPIC SIMILE

R For this epic simile beginning at line 193, have students explain who is compared to the fisherman and who is compared to the wriggling fish. *(Scylla is like the fisherman, and the oarsmen she catches and eats are like the fish.)*

Literary Concept: THEME

S What continuing major concerns presented in the epic does Odysseus' restrained behavior in this sequence illustrate? *(Possible responses: the need for humans to respect the will of the gods; the importance of avoiding arrogance and overconfidence; the struggle to maintain self-control)*

STRATEGIC READING FOR Less-Proficient Readers

T Make sure students understand the cost of Odysseus' escape from Scylla.
- What sight does Odysseus call "far the worst I ever suffered"? *(Scylla eating his men)* **Analyzing**

COMPREHENSION CHECK
Ask students whether the following statements are true or false.
1. Circe refuses to give Odysseus information about the voyage ahead. *(F)*
2. Odysseus ties his shipmates to the mast so they won't be lured by the Sirens. *(F)*
3. Circe predicts that only Odysseus will survive the voyage to Ithaca. *(T)*
4. Odysseus doesn't reveal everything he knows about Scylla to his men. *(T)*
5. Odysseus is deeply disturbed by the loss of his men to Scylla. *(T)*

Critic's Corner

"The virtues of Odysseus are not those of a warrior, but those of a merchant-adventurer who has wandered the ancient seas from Gibraltar to the Crimea and the Caucasus and has survived and profited: agility, inventiveness, courage, prudence, and persistence."

Kenneth Rexroth

Have students consider Odysseus' actions in Books 9, 10, and 12. Do they agree or disagree with Rexroth's statement? How would their own list of Odysseus' virtues differ?

From Personal Response to Critical Analysis

1. Accept all reasonable responses.
2. Possible responses: It is unfair of Odysseus not to share the information with his crew; it was a wise decision because the crew might have panicked or mutinied had they been told about the dangers ahead or of Circe's prediction that only Odysseus would survive the entire journey.
3. Possible responses: Yes, because he obeys Tiresias' warning, controls his hasty temper, and no longer endangers crew members with his desire to explore; no, he has always been concerned for the crew, and his recklessness is unchanged—he ignores Circe's instructions and raises arms against Scylla.
4. Opinions will vary. Accept all reasonable, well-supported responses.
5. In framing their responses, students may acknowledge that our society presents dangers just as strange and unlikely as those encountered by Odysseus. Students might be inclined to consider Odysseus best suited to a military job and view him as a citizen of a country that borders one of the oceans or the Mediterranean.

Another Pathway

Cooperative Learning Encourage students to prepare their arguments by making lists of Odysseus' decisions thus far and evaluating each decision.

Rubric

3 Full Accomplishment Teams support their positions with valid arguments and details from the selections.

2 Substantial Accomplishment Teams present valid arguments but have some difficulty supporting them with details from the selections.

1 Little or Partial Accomplishment Teams fail to support their positions with valid arguments and details.

FROM PERSONAL RESPONSE TO CRITICAL ANALYSIS

REFLECT 1. What did you think of Odysseus' adventures in this section? Share your thoughts with your classmates.

RETHINK 2. Odysseus chooses to tell his crew only part of what Circe reveals about the dangers ahead. Do you think this is a wise decision? Why or why not?

Thematic Link 3. Do you think Odysseus has improved as a leader and a hero over the course of his adventures? Why or why not?

Consider

Close Textual Reading
- the chart that you completed for the Literary Concepts feature for Book 9 on page 507
- Tiresias' warning to Odysseus about acting with restraint and control
- Odysseus' power over and later obedience to Circe
- Odysseus' treatment of his crew

4. Of all the monsters and perils that Odysseus and his crew face during their wanderings, which do you think is the most terrifying? Why? Refer to the chart on monsters that you made for the Personal Connection on page 481.

RELATE 5. Imagine Odysseus in our society today—as a guest in your home, for example. How would you treat him? What would you tell him about the dangers and the pleasures of our world? Suggest some jobs you think he might be suited for and a place you think he might want to live.

Multimodal Learning
ANOTHER PATHWAY
Cooperative Learning

If you had been a member of Odysseus' crew, would you have followed his leadership? With the class divided into opposing teams, debate Odysseus' worthiness as a leader. Cite examples of his decisions and actions in Books 9–12. If your team declares Odysseus unworthy, explain how you think he should have acted.

QUICKWRITES

1. Write short **encyclopedia entries** about two of the creatures Odysseus and his crew encounter. Begin with a definition, and then provide additional information from the *Odyssey* and your own imagination.

2. Draft a **character sketch** of Odysseus, based on the episodes you have read. Include details about his appearance, attitudes, and heroic acts.

3. Write a **plot outline** of another adventure that Odysseus and his crew might have. It should feature Odysseus in the role of epic hero.

📁 **PORTFOLIO** *Save your writing. You may want to use it later as a springboard to a piece for your portfolio.*

LITERARY LINKS

Think about the heroic qualities of the father in the story "Marine Corps Issue" (page 339). What similarities do you see between his experiences and those of Odysseus? How do the two characters differ in the ways they look back on their experiences?

530 UNIT FOUR PART 1: THE WANDERINGS OF ODYSSEUS

Literary Links

Students may point to the father's battle experience, extended stay far from home and family, and great physical suffering as similar to the experiences of Odysseus. They may contrast the father's secrecy about his experience—refusing to speak about it with his son and hiding away his memorabilia—with Odysseus' love for sharing his experiences.

QuickWrites

1. Encourage students to create drawings to enhance their written entries.
2. Suggest that students refer to the mini-lesson on characterization (p. 513) for help.
3. Suggest that students review the charts they made evaluating Odysseus' qualities as an epic hero before creating their plot outlines.

Descriptive Writing, pp. 60–64
Outline Form, pp. 816–817

LITERARY CONCEPTS

Recall that a story's **theme** is an important idea that the story conveys to the reader. In his epics, Homer passed on lessons about life and human nature that were important to the Greeks of his time and that have remained important down to our own time. A long narrative like the *Odyssey* usually has several themes. One of the *Odyssey*'s themes involves what it means to be a hero—an idea you've already been discussing. Think about other meaningful ideas or lessons about life that you found in these episodes. For example, what do Odysseus' experiences tell you about pride, about power and self-control, about the importance of home and family, and about responsibility to others?

Cooperative Learning Discuss these ideas with a small group of classmates. Then work with your group to write a statement explaining a theme that you've identified. If possible, use a quotation from the poem to support your choice of a theme. Share your statement with the rest of the class.

Multimodal Learning

ALTERNATIVE ACTIVITIES

1. Create a **board game** based on the travels and adventures of Odysseus. To get ideas, review each adventure and study the map on page 485. Read the rules of a familiar game to get tips on writing the rules for your game. Decide whether players' moves will be determined by choosing cards, spinning a wheel, or rolling dice. A computer can help you design the game.

2. The Sirens' song was so beautiful and alluring that mortals found it impossible to resist. Sailors hearing the Sirens would be enchanted and lured to their death. Compose and perform a **song** that the Sirens might have sung.

Multimodal Learning

ACROSS THE CURRICULUM

Mathematics/Geography Trace or redraw the map on page 485. Then, on the basis of the episodes you have read, draw lines on the map to represent Odysseus' wanderings from Troy to the imaginary land of the Phaeacians—where he tells of his adventures—and then home to Ithaca. (Leave out the voyage to Hades.) Estimate, in miles or kilometers, the distance he travels. Finally, consult an atlas or encyclopedia and label the places on your map with their modern names.

WORDS TO KNOW

EXERCISE A Review the Words to Know at the bottom of the selection pages. Then, for each phrase in the first column, write the letter of the rhyming phrase in the second column that has a similar meaning.

1. lurk on the left
2. traveling in one's dreams
3. designed to dwindle
4. a terrifying blaze
5. mental anguish

a. a dire fire
b. made to fade
c. questing while resting
d. brain pain
e. hide on one side

EXERCISE B Write the vocabulary word, not used in Exercise A, described by each sentence below.

1. People wear seat belts, hardhats, and safety goggles to protect themselves against this.
2. Odysseus goes through a lot of this on his homeward journey, and the truth is, it isn't easy.
3. An example of this might be the Black Death of the Middle Ages, Scylla in Odysseus' day, or war in any time or place.
4. How terrible is unbearable? It's how Scylla expresses herself and how the men she captures die.
5. When Scylla is yapping, Charybdis is spewing up the sea, and Odysseus' men are losing their oars, this pretty accurately describes the scene.

 LASERLINKS
• ART GALLERY

531

Across the Curriculum

Mathematics/Geography *Cooperative Learning* Encourage students to form small groups to research the geography of the Odyssey. Each group can assign one member to research each chosen location, such as Ithaca, Troy, and the Strait of Messina (Scylla and Charybdis). Point out that debate and research continues about whether the places described by Homer in the Iliad and the Odyssey correspond to actual locations; the limited knowledge of the world in Homer's day likely means that most of Odysseus' "ports" are merely Homer's inventions.

Words to Know

Exercise A
1. e
2. c
3. b
4. a
5. d

Exercise B
1. peril
2. travail
3. scourge
4. abominably
5. chaos

Reteaching/Reinforcement
• *Unit Four Resource Book*, p. 14

 ART GALLERY
Perils at Sea Odysseus traveled for nearly 20 years before his return to Ithaca. These images illustrate some of the perils that he and his men encountered along the way. You may wish to use the images as examples to help students create their own imagery about events that took place in this epic poem.

Side A, Frame 49435

Literary Concepts

Responses will vary. Students may point to several continuing themes illustrated by the experiences of Odysseus. These include the ongoing concern of Odysseus for his men, the longing to return to home and family, the relationship between mortals and gods, the importance of self-control, and the consequences of a lack of restraint, citing the Sirens, the bag of Aeolus', the delay at Circe's, and Helios' cattle as examples.

Alternative Activities

1. Encourage students to include characters, locations, and dangers from the Odyssey in the games that they create. They may also brainstorm ways to include, as facets of the play, aspects of the poem such as the interaction between mortals and the gods and the pitfalls of giving in to temptation.

2. Suggest that students begin by thinking about the kinds of music that they find create an alluring or beguiling mood. They can use this as a starting point for creating their own Sirens' song.

OBJECTIVES

- To promote independent active reading
- To practice and apply skills learned in previous lessons

Reading Pathways

- Invite students to choose partners and take turns reading the poem aloud. After each student has read the poem once, both should take a few moments to discuss the persona of the poem. Ask, Who is the character that is speaking? What do students know about her from reading the selections from the *Odyssey*? Then each student should reread the poem, trying to interpret the characteristics of this particular speaker. After the second readings, students can discuss whether their first or second reading was more enjoyable.

- Have students read the poem twice. After the first reading, they should make a list of any questions they have about the poem. As they reread the poem, they should try to answer the questions generated by their first reading.

- Ask students to write brief descriptions of the Sirens based on Book 12 of the *Odyssey*. Then have them read "Siren Song." Finally, have them look back at their descriptions and discuss any new impressions they have gained from the poem.

Thematic Link: *The Wanderings of Odysseus* A Siren reveals her own perspective on the unfortunate travelers who happen to pass in her direction.

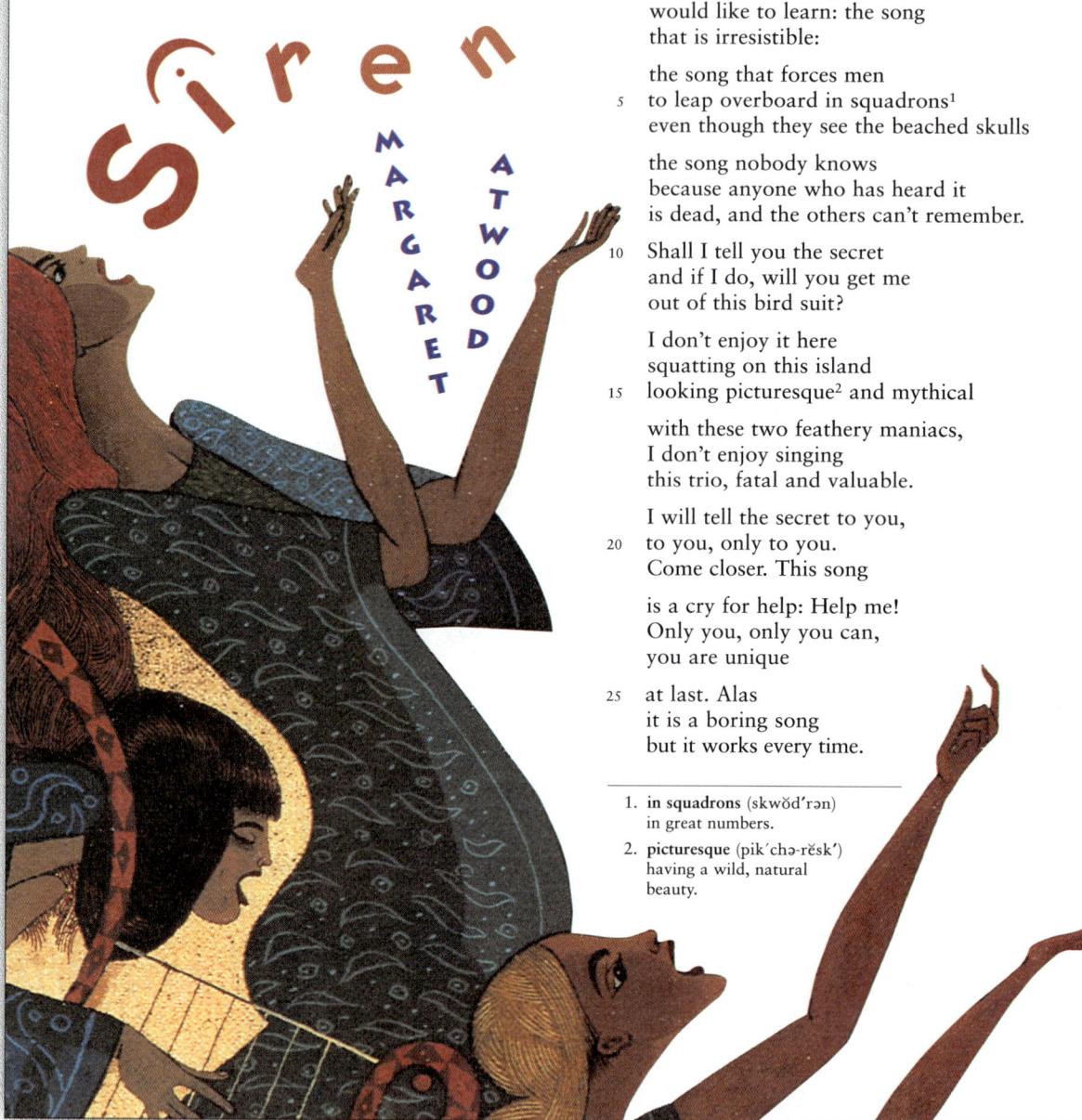

ON YOUR OWN — REFLECT & ASSESS

Siren Song

MARGARET ATWOOD

This is the one song everyone
would like to learn: the song
that is irresistible:

5 the song that forces men
to leap overboard in squadrons[1]
even though they see the beached skulls

the song nobody knows
because anyone who has heard it
is dead, and the others can't remember.

10 Shall I tell you the secret
and if I do, will you get me
out of this bird suit?

I don't enjoy it here
squatting on this island
15 looking picturesque[2] and mythical

with these two feathery maniacs,
I don't enjoy singing
this trio, fatal and valuable.

I will tell the secret to you,
20 to you, only to you.
Come closer. This song

is a cry for help: Help me!
Only you, only you can,
you are unique

25 at last. Alas
it is a boring song
but it works every time.

---

1. **in squadrons** (skwŏd´rən) in great numbers.
2. **picturesque** (pĭk´chə-rĕsk´) having a wild, natural beauty.

PRINT AND MEDIA RESOURCES

UNIT FOUR RESOURCE BOOK
Strategic Reading: Literature, p. 17

FORMAL ASSESSMENT
Selection Test, p. 93
Part Test, pp. 95–96
■ Test Generator

ACCESS FOR STUDENTS ACQUIRING ENGLISH
Selection Summaries

AUDIO LIBRARY
See Reference Card

INTERNET RESOURCES
McDougal Littell Literature Center at http://www.hmco.com/mcdougal/lit

The Sirens (1990), Shlomo Katz, Courtesy of Strictly Limited Editions, San Francisco.

MARGARET ATWOOD

1939–

The Canadian poet and novelist Margaret Atwood is unusual among writers. She never finished a year of school until she was 11, but she went on to become a favorite both with the reading public and with critics. In fact, her second book of poetry, *The Circle Game*, won Canada's highest literary honor, the Governor General's Award. Her novels *The Handmaid's Tale* and *Cat's Eye* were bestsellers. She is also known for her short stories, television plays, children's books, and critical works. Her interests range from the position of women and the search for identity to the role of Canadian literature in the world.

The daughter of a scientist and a dietician, Atwood was born in Ottawa, Ontario. Her father's research took him into remote areas of Quebec for part of every year, so Atwood grew up moving in and out of the wilderness. She finds it a "definite advantage" that the eighth grade was her first full year of school. Even as a very young girl she showed a strong interest in both writing and reading.

In an interview in the *New York Times Book Review*, Atwood said she is frequently asked why she writes. She replied, "I think the real question is, 'Why doesn't everyone?'" In the same interview, Atwood said that in poetry the texture of sound "is at least as important to me as the 'argument.'" It bothers her when students ask what a poet is "trying to say." To her, such a question implies "that the poet is some kind of verbal cripple who can't quite 'say' what he 'means' and has to resort to a lot of round-the-mulberrybush, thereby putting the student to a great deal of trouble extracting his 'meaning.'"

OTHER WORKS *Selected Poems II, The Edible Woman, Surfacing, Life Before Man, Bodily Harm, For the Birds, The Robber Bride* Extended Reading

SIREN SONG **533**

MARGARET ATWOOD

In her native Canada, Margaret Atwood has used her literary success to champion Canadian literature and to argue that its unifying theme is one of survival. Atwood's own work returns to this theme again and again. Her novels feature characters who are trapped in abusive relationships of all sorts but who struggle to endure and to triumph, rather than giving up.

Art Note

The Sirens by Shlomo Katz. Israeli artist Shlomo Katz (1937–1992) is known for his technique of painting with oil upon gilded metal surfaces. His paintings recall medieval works but are infused with a modern sense of humor.

Reading the Art How does the artist convey the allure of the Sirens and their song? What details illustrate this allure?

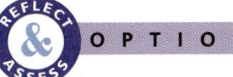

OPTION 1

Individual Activity

DESCRIBE A SIREN SITUATION

The Siren reveals some of the ways she uses to compel "men to leap overboard." How can people be endangered by someone who lets them in on a secret, or begs them for their help saying they are uniquely suited to do the job? Write a paragraph describing a situation in which someone is lured into dangerous behavior by one of these techniques.

Teacher's Role Prepare students by asking them to think about ways in which people are lured into dangerous situations.

Rubric

3 Full Accomplishment Paragraphs describe techniques that are effective in luring people into dangerous situations.

2 Substantial Accomplishment Paragraphs demonstrate some understanding of the techniques.

1 Little or Partial Accomplishment Students have difficulty describing dangerous situations or the techniques.

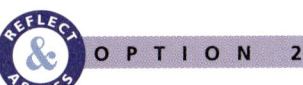

OPTION 2

Class Discussion

SHARING IDEAS

Teacher's Role After students have read the selection, engage them in a whole-class discussion using the following questions.

1. Do you think the Siren song is "the one song everyone would like to learn"? Why or why not? *(Possible responses: Yes, everyone wants to be irresistible; yes, everyone wants to learn unknowable secrets.)*

2. What did you find surprising about the poem? Why? *(Possible responses: that the poem itself was a demonstration of the Sirens' call; the speaker's description of the other Sirens as "feathery maniacs"; the idea that the Sirens don't enjoy what they do)*

3. Why do you think cries for help or appeals to uniqueness might effectively lure people? *(Possible responses: Most people want to believe that they are the only person in the world who can save someone.)*

THE LANGUAGE OF LITERATURE **TEACHER'S EDITION** **533**

OVERVIEW

In the Guided Assignment for this section, students will write a parody of Homer's epic, the *Odyssey*. As preparation for this assignment, they will use the Writer's Style to help themselves understand how writers or storytellers choose levels of language carefully. In Reading the World, students will analyze elements of parody in a visual image.

Objectives

- To recognize how writers and storytellers use appropriate levels of language
- To use formal and informal language in appropriate contexts
- To write a parody of a passage in the *Odyssey*
- To analyze elements of a visual parody

Skills

LITERATURE
- Identifying and analyzing formal and informal language

GRAMMAR AND USAGE
- Using conjunctions

MEDIA LITERACY
- Analyzing a parody

SPEAKING, LISTENING, AND VIEWING
- Peer review

- Telling a story
- Discuss the message of a parody

CRITICAL THINKING
- Analyzing a parody
- Comparing/contrasting
- Making inferences

Teaching Strategy: MODELING

A **Homer** Possible response: Odysseus impresses the king by alluding to his own courage in surviving a thousand trials, boasting about his guile, and offering his friendship, even though he and the king are strangers. Odysseus' formal, dignified language invites us to respond to him with admiration and respect.

WRITING ABOUT LITERATURE

THE HERO'S TALE

How did you feel about Odysseus as you read about his fantastic adventures? Did you wish you were with him? Or were you glad to be far away from that long, dangerous voyage? On the following pages you will

- consider the kinds of language used in epic poetry
- respond to the *Odyssey* by writing a humorous imitation
- analyze a parody of a well-known piece of art

Writer's Style: Levels of Language A writer or storyteller chooses language carefully. Epic poems use language that is formal and elaborate to give weight to their message.

Read the Literature

Formal language has a serious tone and often includes long sentences. Informal language is more casual in tone, often with shorter sentences.

Literature Model

Formal Language
The language Odysseus uses here is meant to impress his audience, King Alcinous. Notice the long sentences and serious tone. What else does Odysseus do to impress the king as he introduces himself? How does his language affect your response to him as a hero?

> "What shall I say first? What shall I keep until the end? The gods have tried me in a thousand ways. But first my name: let that be known to you, and if I pull away from pitiless death, friendship will bind us, though my land lies far.
>
> I am Laertes' son, Odysseus.
>
> Men hold me formidable for guile in peace and war: this fame has gone abroad to the sky's rim."
>
> Homer
> from the *Odyssey*
> translated by Robert Fitzgerald

534 UNIT FOUR: PORTRAIT OF A HERO

PRINT AND MEDIA RESOURCES

UNIT FOUR RESOURCE BOOK
Writer's Style, p. 21
Prewriting, p. 22
Elaboration, p. 23
Peer Response Guide, pp. 24–25
Revising and Proofreading, p. 26
Student Model, p. 27
Rubric, p. 28

GRAMMAR MINI-LESSONS
Transparencies, pp. 39–40
Copymasters, p. 41

WRITING MINI-LESSONS
Transparencies, p. 44

FORMAL ASSESSMENT
Guidelines for Writing Assessment

 WRITING COACH

 The Writer's Craft
Varieties of Language, pp. 409–410

Connect to Life

The writer of this news article uses informal language to introduce a modern adventurer, a man who has traveled the world searching for Bigfoot.

Newspaper Feature Article

He [Peter Byrne] says, "It's like we're trying to find a needle in a haystack and the needle is moving and it doesn't want to be found."

Byrne pauses, so again you look into those eyes—those piercing blue eyes that have seen the slopes of Mt. Everest, the roiling waters of the Indian Ocean, the charge of the tiger....

After a while, the phone rings. Some guy has heard weird screams in the woods. Byrne has said, earlier in the day, that 98 percent of the reports he gets turn out to be "rubbish." But still you start hoping.... Maybe this time.

Bill Donahue
from "On the Trail of Bigfoot"
Chicago Tribune

Using Informal Tone

How would you describe the tone of this article? How do the sentences and words compare to those in the first model?

Try Your Hand: Using Levels of Language

1. **Making a Choice** For which of these kinds of writing would you use formal language? Explain why.
   - A story about yourself
   - A biographical sketch of a person you admire
   - A letter to a person from whom you are requesting funds for computers for your school

2. **Looking Back** Select one piece of writing from your folder or portfolio that would be more effective if the language were less or more formal. Rewrite one paragraph. With a partner, evaluate both versions. Which works better?

3. **Trying It Out** Write three sentences introducing an adventure. Use informal language. Then rewrite the sentences, using very formal language. Share your writing with a partner and discuss the effect.

SkillBuilder

WRITER'S CRAFT

Understanding Informal Language

Whether you use formal or informal language, you must choose appropriate words. In informal writing, you may use colloquial language. Two types of colloquial language are slang and idioms.

Slang is nonstandard language, used by a particular group, and often popular only briefly.

"You nerd," my sister said.

Idioms are phrases in which the words have a meaning different from the literal meaning.

"Hold your tongue," I warned.

Notice how the newspaper writer uses informal language.

Some guy has heard weird screams in the woods.

"It's like we're trying to find a needle in a haystack and the needle is moving and it doesn't want to be found."

APPLYING WHAT YOU'VE LEARNED

Write a statement about a hero. Select words appropriate to formal language. Rewrite your statement, using informal language and appropriate words. Compare the effects of your statements.

WRITING ABOUT LITERATURE 535

Teaching Strategy: MODELING

B **Donahue** Possible response: The tone is lighter and more informal. The sentences are shorter than in the first model. Word choices that help establish the informal tone include the following: *guy, weird*. The writer also quotes a clichéd simile, "like we're trying to find a needle in a haystack." Finally, the use of the second-person pronoun *you* reinforces the light conversational tone by appealing directly to the reader.

Try Your Hand

1. Responses may vary, but most students will answer that they would use formal language for the latter two.

2. You may wish to have students preview the SkillBuilder on this page for information about elements of informal language before they begin this activity.

3. Responses will vary. Sample sentences using informal language follow:

   Baxter cast an eye on his list one last time. When you're climbing Mount Kilimanjaro with only your shadow, forgetting something could prove unhealthy. It's the mother of all African mountains, and one mistake could be the ultimate bad career move.

   A rewritten, more formal version follows:

   Thinking methodically, Baxter checked the items on his list one last time. He was acutely aware that climbing Mount Kilimanjaro solo would be a great contrast from spending a week's holiday on a guided safari. Kilimanjaro is the tallest mountain in Africa, and a single misstep could result in serious, even fatal consequences.

SkillBuilder — WRITER'S CRAFT

UNDERSTANDING INFORMAL LANGUAGE

Point out that slang and idioms are especially appropriate for dialogue, since everyone tends to use informal language in conversation. Additional techniques that help to create an informal tone include the use of contractions, elements of dialect, simplified sentence structure, sentence fragments, and second-person pronouns that address the reader directly.

Application Possible responses:

Formal: Despite his misfortunes at the hands of the gods, Odysseus' innate resilience never deserts him.

Informal: The gods give Odysseus a pretty bad time, but he always manages to bounce back.

Additional Suggestions You may wish to have students work with partners on this activity. Students could exchange papers and "informalize" one another's sentences.

Reteaching/Reinforcement
- *Writing Mini-Lessons* transparencies, p. 44

Varieties of Language, pp. 409–410

Critical Thinking: ANALYZING

C Help students break down a parody into its parts. After mentioning the elements of informal tone and satire, for example, you might have students focus on the element of distortion. Parody almost always pokes fun at the original by singling out one or two features and distorting them using exaggeration. Point out that artists use the same technique in cartoon caricatures when they intentionally exaggerate one feature of a person's face. Furthermore, mimics use the same technique in impressions or comic take–offs on people's speech mannerisms.

Speaking and Listening: COLLABORATIVE OPPORTUNITY

D Invite students to work in small groups. After group members devote some time to identifying likely passages, urge them to take turns reading each passage aloud. Then ask them to pause so that they can discuss features of epic style that might be good candidates for parody: for example, noun-epithet formulas or extended similes.

Critical Thinking: COMPARING/ CONTRASTING

E As students study the prewriting notes, they should come to understand that a successful parody must contain certain elements in common with the original as well as certain crucial changes. Suggest that students use Venn diagrams to compare and contrast all the elements on each line of the prewriting chart.

WRITING ABOUT LITERATURE

Creative Response

You've looked at the language and words used in the story of Odysseus and have watched the hero as he led his crew into dangerous adventures. The *Odyssey*, like other epic poems, is meant to impress listeners with the importance of the hero and his role.

GUIDED ASSIGNMENT

Write a Parody One way to show your understanding of a work of literature is to write a parody, or humorous imitation. After all, you can't imitate a work without understanding how it was put together. Writing a parody can be fun for you and for your readers and listeners.

1 Prewrite and Explore

A parody can imitate any elements of a work. A parody of an epic, for example, might have fun with a hero's adventures in dangerous places. Choose a passage from the *Odyssey* that represents the style of the whole epic. The passage should have elements easy to imitate, such as strange action, unusual language, or an unusual form.

2 Analyze and Plan

Read again the excerpt that you want to parody and identify the characteristics you want to keep in your parody. You might use several of the following elements:

- a bragging hero
- unusual names
- formal language
- monsters of some kind

Begin to translate the characteristics you selected into parody elements. Use the student's notebook on this page for ideas.

Student's Notebook

Odyssey	My Parody
Odysseus	Arnold Schwarzenegger (Arnoldeus)
monsters	movie critics
gale winds	bad reviews
several days the boat drifted at sea	two weeks the movie drifted through theaters

536 UNIT FOUR: PORTRAIT OF A HERO

Assessment Option

SELF-ASSESSMENT After students have completed Analyze and Plan, they should assess their notes by answering the following questions:

- Did I select specific features of the original work that I can imitate humorously in my parody?
- Have I designed my parody so that its comic relationship to the original work will be clear to the reader?
- Have I generated ideas about how to use a suitable level of language in my parody?

3 Write and Analyze a Discovery Draft

Now have fun with the excerpt you chose. Make sure you keep the characteristics of the original as you write. Imitate the hero's adventures. Exaggerate, brag, do whatever works, but be sure readers will recognize your parody as an imitation of the *Odyssey*. Look at the student writing sample for ideas.

Original Passage

"I might have made it safely home, that time, but as I came round Malea the current took me out to sea, and from the north a fresh gale drove me on, past Cythera. Nine days I drifted on the teeming sea before dangerous high winds."

Homer
from the *Odyssey*
translated by Robert Fitzgerald

Student's Discovery Draft

I might have gone to the Academy Awards.
But the critics gave my movie bad reviews.
Even magazines sneered at it.
For two weeks that movie drifted through empty theaters.
It ended up on the shelf in video stores.

Name the "monsters" or critics. I'll try to make the lines match the original better.

4 Draft and Share

Share the results of your discovery draft with a partner or a small group and ask for ideas and criticisms. Then use the responses to help you draft. When you've finished, ask for additional responses.

 PEER RESPONSE

- What did you like most about my parody?
- Tell which elements of the *Odyssey* I imitated.
- Compare my hero with Odysseus.

SkillBuilder

 SPEAKING & LISTENING

Telling a Story
Remember that the original epics were often passed along orally. You might want to share your parody in a storytelling session. If so, here are some skills you'll want to review.

Preparing the material
- Highlight ideas or images you want to emphasize.
- Mark places where gestures are appropriate.
- If you want to introduce your story, be brief and excite the interest of your audience.

Presenting the story
- Telling a story is better than reading it. If you have time, memorize your parody.
- Speak at a comfortable level. Your voice should reach everyone but shouldn't be too loud.
- Try to look at members of your audience.
- Use facial expressions and gestures for emphasis.

APPLYING WHAT YOU'VE LEARNED
Tell your story to a partner or a small group. Then use the suggestions in this column to evaluate how well you presented your parody. Discuss what else you can do before telling your story to a larger audience.

WRITING ABOUT LITERATURE 537

Writing Skill: USING HYPERBOLE

The Discovery Draft provides an opportunity for students to do some writing in a light vein. However, the expectations of wit and humor that accompany this type of writing might intimidate some students unaccustomed to writing for fun. Remind these students of the type of writing found in "Grover Dill and the Tasmanian Devil," where images built on exaggeration provide much of the humor. Thinking along the lines of hyperbole may help these students to imagine something "fun."

Teaching Strategy: MANAGING THE PAPER LOAD

As you read the drafts, concentrate on the single element that each student finds most troublesome, such as pairing distinctive elements of the original with humorous counterparts in the parody or using a proper level of language. Reassure students that they can work out less serious problems in a peer review setting.

SkillBuilder SPEAKING & LISTENING

TELLING A STORY Remind students that even though storytelling (especially of comic material) is more effective when it appears to be spontaneous, most people consider rehearsal and preparation to be essential to an effective presentation.

Application You may wish to suggest that students take written notes on their discussion.

Additional Suggestions Remind students of the importance of good timing in comic storytelling. Suggest that they watch a live or videotaped performance by a skilled comedian, focusing on how he or she paces his or her material and the points at which he or she pauses.

Critical Thinking: ANALYZING

H Point out to students that revising their drafts involves molding the text to fit their audience and purpose. To evaluate and revise their plays, students should

- check to see that they have exaggerated recognizable features of the original work
- verify that they have organized the parody so that it is easy to read
- make sure they have used levels of language effectively

Teaching Strategy: MODELING

I Discuss how the writer's final draft meets the Standards for Evaluation on this page. Point out that the outlandish proper names, takeoffs on the famous reviewers Gene Siskel and Roger Ebert, have been altered by the "suffixes" of *kill it* and *thumb*. Thus the sense of the passage is reinforced: These movie-critic monsters "killed" the movie by giving it "two deadly thumbs down"—their trademark signal for a bad movie. Guide students to recognize that the writer used more complex sentence structure in the final draft of the parody to poke fun at the dignified tone and formality of the epic form. You may also want to point out two additional comic touches: the allusion to Odysseus' voyages in the phrase "sailed into theaters" as well as the archaic flavor of the emphatic verb form "did sneer."

Standards for Evaluation

Have students review their parodies for the following:

Ideas and Content
- uses humor as it imitates and exaggerates features of the original work
- shows clearly its relationship to the original work
- makes effective use of word choice

Structure and Form
- has a clear organization that is appropriate for the parodied work
- uses sentence structures that are appropriate for the parodied work

Grammar, Usage, and Mechanics
- contains no more than two or three minor errors in grammar and usage
- contains no more than two or three minor errors in spelling, capitalization, and punctuation

---

WRITING ABOUT LITERATURE

5 Revise and Edit

Now examine the draft of your parody.

- Be sure it is clear which elements you are imitating.
- Share your parody with a partner and ask him or her to evaluate the humor.
- Read the Standards for Evaluation below.
- Use the Grammar in Context activity on the following page as you work with sentence structure.

Student's Final Draft

The Adventures of Arnoldeus

I might have gone to the Academy Awards that time,
but, as my movie sailed into theaters, Siskillit and Eberthumb,
from their lofty chairs, gave it two deadly thumbs down.
And from the east, the mighty
Timeweek magazine did sneer beyond all reason.
Two weeks the movie drifted through the empty shells
of theaters, moving slowly toward death
on the shelves of Chartbuster Video.

How does the writer's naming of the "monsters" improve the parody?

How do the changes in sentence structure make the parody work better?

Standards for Evaluation

A parody
- uses humor as it imitates and exaggerates features of the original work
- shows its relationship to an original work
- has a clear organization
- makes effective use of the levels of language and word choice

538 UNIT FOUR: PORTRAIT OF A HERO

Assessment Option

SELF-ASSESSMENT To help students assess their own writing, they should answer the following questions:

- Can I make my parody funnier by adding and poking fun at any other elements of the original?
- Have I used appropriate sentence structure and language level in the parody?
- Have I chosen names and words that add to the effectiveness of the parody?

Grammar in Context

Compound-Complex Sentences You may have been trying to work with sentence length in your parody. You'll find that a compound-complex sentence is a natural way to create a long sentence that's clear and organized. A compound-complex sentence contains two or more independent clauses and one or more subordinate clauses. The writer of the sample parody, for example, reorganized three short sentences to create a compound-complex sentence.

> I might have gone to the Academy Awards.
> My movie sailed into theaters.
> Siskillit and Eberthumb gave it thumbs down.
>
> I might have gone to the Academy Awards that time, but, as my movie sailed into theaters, Siskillit and Eberthumb gave it two deadly thumbs down.

Combined, these sentences make a compound-complex sentence with one subordinate clause ("as my movie sailed into theaters") and two independent clauses.

Try Your Hand: Writing Compound-Complex Sentences

1. Identify the independent and subordinate clauses in the following compound-complex sentence.

   Three critics I then found who admired my work, and these critics wrote praising words while I thanked them all.

2. Reorganize the following sentences into a compound-complex sentence.

   An audience had assembled. I, Arnoldeus, was nowhere to be found. They looked for me throughout the city.

SkillBuilder

 GRAMMAR FROM WRITING

Using Conjunctions

When you write a compound-complex sentence, choose a conjunction that clearly shows how the parts of your sentence are related. When you connect independent clauses, use a coordinating conjunction—*and, but, for, nor, or, so,* or *yet.*

Calypso was a sorceress, yet *Odysseus escaped from her.*

Join a subordinate clause to an independent clause with a subordinating conjunction, such as *after, before, although,* or *where.*

After *he left Troy, Odysseus traveled for ten long years.*

APPLYING WHAT YOU'VE LEARNED
Write a compound-complex sentence from these sentences.

Odysseus guarded the ship.

His men explored Circe's island.

They soon found themselves transformed.

Now try rewriting lines from your draft to create a long sentence. Work with conjunctions. Share the results with a partner and discuss what works best for the level of language you have chosen.

 GRAMMAR HANDBOOK

For more information on coordinating and subordinating conjunctions, see page 931 of the Grammar Handbook.

WRITING ABOUT LITERATURE   **539**

Teaching Strategy: USING THE SKILLBUILDER

J You can help students create effective compound-complex sentences by teaching the SkillBuilder on Using Conjunctions on page 539 at this time. Be certain that students do not confuse a prepositional phrase with a clause; they should understand that the presence of a prepositional phrase has no bearing on a sentence's category.

CUSTOMIZING FOR
Students Acquiring English

K Be sure that students understand the major categories of sentence structure in English: simple sentence, compound sentence, complex sentence, and compound-complex sentence.

Try Your Hand

1. Independent clauses: *Three critics I then found; these critics wrote praising words.* Subordinate clauses: *who admired my work; while I thanked them all.*

2. Possible response: After an audience had assembled, I, Arnoldeus, was nowhere to be found, so they looked for me throughout the city.

PORTFOLIO

Ask students to write a brief description of what they have learned about writing parodies as a result of this assignment. They may wish to include their description and their finished parody in their portfolio.

SkillBuilder   GRAMMAR FROM WRITING

USING CONJUNCTIONS Remind students that they should use a comma before a conjunction that joins two independent clauses in a compound sentence unless the two clauses are very brief. When a subordinate clause serves as an introductory element in a sentence—as in the sample sentence given in the text—it is followed by a comma.

Application Possible response: As Odysseus guarded the ship, his men explored Circe's island, and they soon found themselves transformed.

Additional Suggestions Remind students that long sentences featuring intricate syntax are generally associated with a formal level of language.

Reteaching/Reinforcement
- *Grammar Mini-Lessons* copymasters p. 41, transparencies pp. 39–40

 The Writer's Craft

Conjunctions, pp. 664–667

READING THE WORLD

On pages 536–539, students wrote a parody of a literary work in which they used exaggeration, word choice, sentence structure, and language level. They should be aware that real-world images sometimes use visual parodies to make a point. In this lesson, students will analyze the elements of a visual parody.

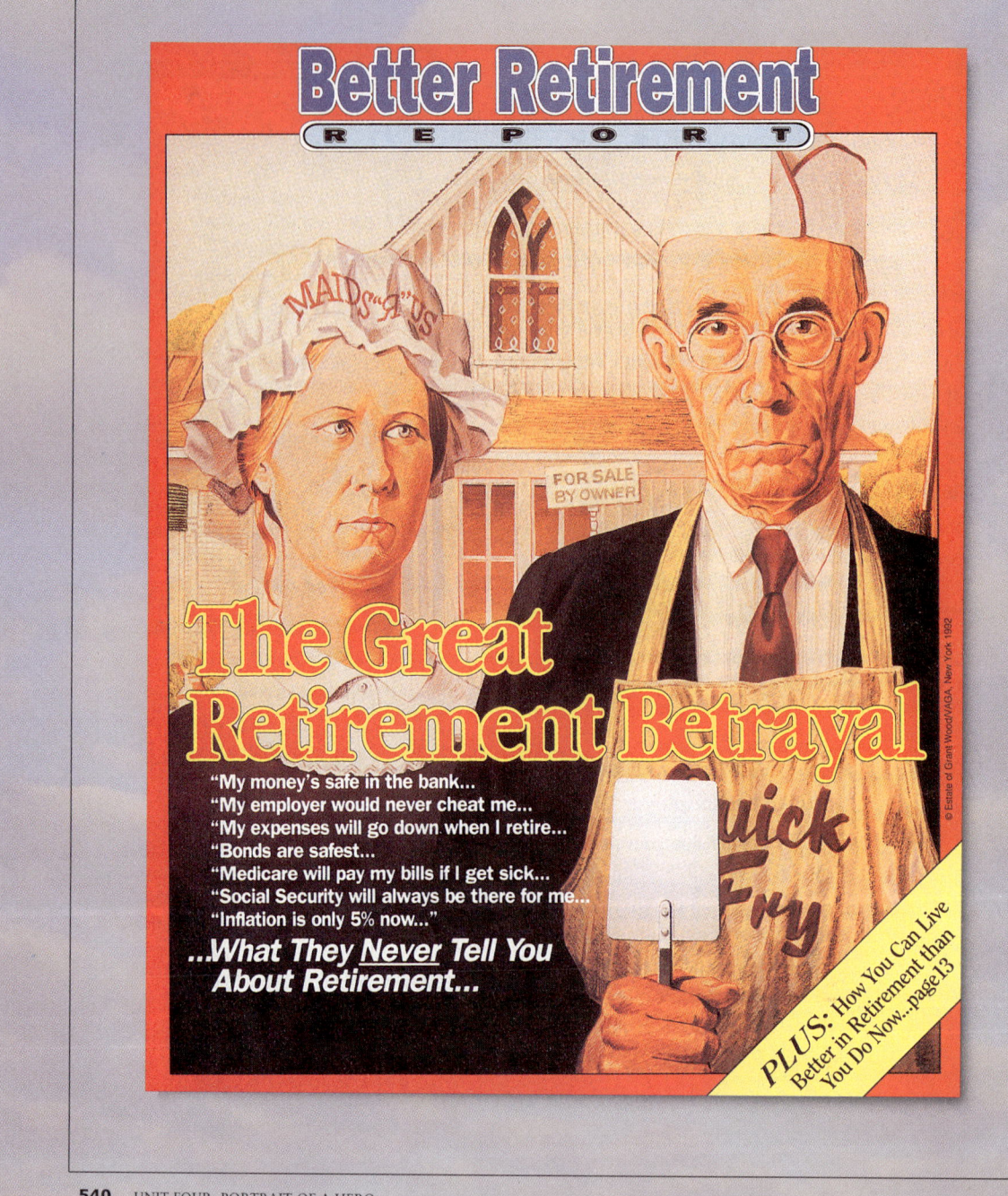

READING THE WORLD

VISUAL PARODIES

You've probably seen visual parodies in ads or cartoons. In a visual parody an artist imitates a well-known work, just as you imitated a passage from a well-known epic. Why would an artist create a parody?

View Note the details in the pictures on these pages. Which details are alike? Which have been changed?

Interpret What message do you think Grant Wood's *American Gothic* sends? What is the message of the parody?

Discuss Talk about the messages you and other members of your group receive from the original painting and from the parody. Then, using the SkillBuilder on the right, think further about how parody works.

American Gothic (1930) Grant Wood

SkillBuilder

CRITICAL THINKING

Analyzing the Elements of Parody

To understand a parody, look first for the components, or individual parts, that make up the whole work. When you know the components, think about the characteristics or meanings that belong to each one.

Identify the components of the original art on this page:

- people
- expressions
- clothing
- surroundings

Think about each component. What do the surroundings suggest? What does the man's expression seem to mean? What does the pitchfork tell you? Then compare components of the original art with those of the parody. Why do you think *American Gothic* was chosen as the source of this parody? How did changing details change the message?

APPLYING WHAT YOU'VE LEARNED

With a partner or a small group, discuss a message you'd like to share through a visual parody. Find a picture or symbol you think would work well. How would you change the components of the original to fit your message?

READING THE WORLD **541**

Critical Thinking: OBSERVING

L Students' answers will vary. In general, they should point out that the man, the woman, and the house in the background are the same in both images. The building in the magazine cover image, however, contains a "For Sale" sign, and the man's and woman's costumes are different. The man is holding a spatula rather than a pitchfork.

Critical Thinking: MAKING INFERENCES

M Students' answers will vary. The original painting conveys an image of somber and sober simplicity, suggesting that they are hard-working, simple folk who lead a plain, rigorous life. The parody on the magazine cover amounts to a biting indictment, summed up by the word *betrayal* in the headline. The visual parody sends the message that these older citizens have been deprived of benefits to which they thought they were entitled and that they must sell their house and return to work in their old age—at low-paying, menial jobs.

Speaking and Listening: GROUP DISCUSSION

N Ask students to work in small groups to compare their interpretations. Encourage them to speculate about some of the specific ways that the parody reinforces the original in order to establish a different mood and message.

SkillBuilder — CRITICAL THINKING

ANALYZING THE ELEMENTS OF PARODY
Be sure that students can identify the elements listed in the text and can explain how each element of the original has been altered in the parody.

Application Suggest that partners or groups consider well-known portraits such as the *Mona Lisa* or portraits of the American founding fathers as subjects for parody. They might also find promising material by looking at advertisements for cars, clothing, or luxury items.

UNIT FOUR
Part 2 Lesson Planner

TIME ALLOTMENTS SHOWN ARE APPROXIMATE. DEPENDING ON YOUR GOALS AND THE NEEDS OF YOUR STUDENTS, YOU MAY WISH TO ALLOW MORE OR LESS TIME FOR CERTAIN PORTIONS OF THE LESSON.

Table of Contents	Discussion	Previewing the Selection	Reading the Selection
PART OPENER **The Homecoming** page 542	**20 MINUTES** • Reflect on the part theme		
SELECTIONS *from the* **Odyssey:** **Book 21: The Test of the Bow** page 544 CHALLENGING		**20 MINUTES** • PERSONAL CONNECTION • CULTURAL CONNECTION • READING CONNECTION: Predicting	**50 MINUTES** • Introduce vocabulary • Read pp. 544–556 (13 pp.)
Book 22: Death in the Great Hall page 557 CHALLENGING			**30 MINUTES** • Read pp. 557–62 (6 pp.)
Book 23: The Trunk of the Olive Tree page 563 CHALLENGING			**15 MINUTES** • Read pp. 563–566 (4 pp.)
POETRY ON YOUR OWN **Penelope** page 570 AVERAGE			**20 MINUTES** • Read pp. 570–571 (2 pp.)
Writing WRITING FROM EXPERIENCE **Informative Exposition**	**Exploring Topics** **20 MINUTES**	**Prewriting** **25 MINUTES**	**Drafting and Revising** **60 MINUTES**

Time estimates assume in-class work. You may wish to assign some of these stages as homework.

Responding to the Selection

FROM PERSONAL RESPONSE TO CRITICAL ANALYSIS	OR	ANOTHER PATHWAY	LITERARY CONCEPTS	QUICKWRITES
60 MINUTES				
• Discussion questions	OR	• Identify heroism and humanity (character sketch)	• Characterization	• Story

Extension Activities

ALTERNATIVE ACTIVITIES	LITERARY LINKS	CRITIC'S CORNER	THE WRITER'S STYLE	ACROSS THE CURRICULUM	ART CONNECTION	WORDS TO KNOW	BIOGRAPHY
60 MINUTES							
✔		✔	✔	ART		✔	✔

Publishing and Reflecting

25 MINUTES

PART 2

REFLECTING ON THEME

Ask students to make a list of homes they have had. (Where were they born? Where do they live now? Have any of them had homes in another country?) Next to each place they list, students can write one or two sentences that sum up what that home means to them. Students can include temporary homes, such as a campsite they have stayed at or a relative's house that they visit during vacation time.

What Do You Think?

To facilitate group discussion, you may want to assign some of the following cooperative learning roles to members of each group:
- An encourager of participation ensures that all members of the group participate.
- A recorder writes down ideas submitted by the group and edits the final product. (The recorder might also be the one to draw the final version of the group's ideal home.)
- A support giver reinforces and praises others' ideas and conclusions.

Students will return to this activity on page 569.

UNIT FOUR PART 2

THE HOMECOMING

REFLECTING ON THEME

What do you call home, and what makes it seem like home? In a Robert Frost poem, home is "the place where, when you have to go there, they have to take you in." Do you agree? Is home a place to get away from? Is it a place to come back to? Maybe both? For Odysseus, home is the place he's been trying to get back to for a long time. In this part of the unit, you'll see whether they want to take him in.

What Do You Think? With a small group of classmates, imagine a perfect home. What qualities would make it comfortable and appealing—a place you'd gladly come back to after being away. Who and what would be there? You might also want to imagine your home's surroundings. Then draw (or write a description of) the group's image of the perfect home, complete with all the details you've created in your discussion. Share your drawing or description with the rest of the class and, as you read these excerpts from the *Odyssey,* think of the emotions you might feel on returning to your perfect home after a long absence.

Homer Translated by Robert Fitzgerald	**from the *Odyssey*** (continued)	543
	Book 21: The Test of the Bow	544
	Book 22: Death in the Great Hall	557
	Book 23: The Trunk of the Olive Tree	563
	A hero returns home, but his battles are not yet over.	
Dorothy Parker	**Penelope** *Gracefully enduring a long wait*	570

PREVIEWING

EPIC POETRY

from the Odyssey (continued)
Homer
Translated by Robert Fitzgerald

Activating Prior Knowledge
PERSONAL CONNECTION

These excerpts from the *Odyssey* present the hero's homecoming: Odysseus returns to Ithaca and is reunited with his son and wife after an absence of nearly 20 years. If you had not seen a close relative—a grandparent, a parent, or a sibling—for a long time, how would you react when you were reunited with him or her? What thoughts, feelings, and problems do you think you might have? Imagine such a reunion and, in your notebook, make a chart like the one shown to explore your reactions.

Reunion with Relative After Long Absence		
Thoughts	Feelings	Problems
Is it really you?		

Building background
CULTURAL CONNECTION

In ancient Greece, rules of hospitality governed the behavior of hosts and guests. The Greek social code required people to take strangers in and feed them without question. Remember that King Alcinous, a model king, hosted a banquet for Odysseus without knowing who he was, whereas the barbaric Cyclops not only refused to give Odysseus and his men food and drink but started to eat them instead. After allowing a stranger to stay as long as he wished, a host also had to give him a gift when he left. These obligations were enforced by Zeus, the king of the gods and also the god of hospitality.

Guests as well as hosts could violate the code of hospitality. In this part of the *Odyssey*, you'll meet the suitors who, believing that Odysseus is dead, want to marry his wife, Penelope, and take over his lands and fortune. Because Penelope still hopes for a reunion with her husband, she delays making a choice—but the suitors remain.

Important Characters in the *Odyssey*
PART 2: The Homecoming
Books 21–23
Antinous (ăn-tĭn′ō-əs)—a suitor of Penelope
Eurymachus (yŏō-rĭm′ə-kəs)—a suitor of Penelope
Telemachus (tə-lĕm′ə-kəs)—Odysseus' son
Eumaeus (yŏō-mē′əs)—a servant in Odysseus' household
Philoetius (fĭ-lē′shəs)—a servant in Odysseus' household
Eurycleia (yŏōr′ĭ-klē′ə)—an old female servant, still loyal to Odysseus

Active Reading/Setting a Purpose
READING CONNECTION

Predicting When Odysseus arrives home, he encounters a band of inhospitable guests—more than 100 men eating his food, drinking his wine, and courting his wife. How do you think Odysseus will deal with these suitors, most of whom are young, strong, armed, and dangerous? Jot down your prediction in your notebook. Then, as you read about the reunion of Odysseus and Penelope, see how accurate your prediction was. The chart on the left shows some of the characters introduced in this part of the *Odyssey*.

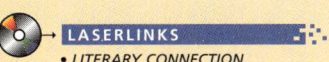
- LITERARY CONNECTION

ODYSSEY **543**

OVERVIEW
Objectives

- To understand and appreciate an epic poem that explores a hero's homecoming after a long absence
- To identify and understand characterization
- To appreciate and understand translation
- To express understanding of the selection through a choice of writing forms, including a plot outline for a story
- To extend understanding of the selection through a variety of multimodal and cross-curricular activities

Skills

LITERARY CONCEPTS
- Characterization
- Irony

READING SKILLS/ STRATEGIES
- Predicting

THE WRITER'S STYLE
- Dialogue

GRAMMAR
- Troublesome verbs: *lie/lay*

SPEAKING, LISTENING, AND VIEWING
- Choreographing a dance

 LITERARY CONNECTION
Odysseus Returns to Ithaca When Odysseus returns to Ithaca, he discovers greedy and unruly suitors courting his wife and coveting his kingdom. These images depict Odysseus's efforts to control the suitors and to reclaim his lands and his family. You may wish to use the images to generate discussion about the heroic efforts he makes to accomplish this.

Side A, Frame 49444

ALTERNATIVE
Previewing

Students can choose partners and use the following prompts to preview the *Odyssey* orally.

Personal Connection

Discussion Prompts *If you had not seen a favorite relative for a long time, how would you react if you were reunited? If you need help getting started, the following question might help:*

- *What thoughts, feelings, and problems might you have?*

As you read, think about the difficulties Odysseus encounters when he and Penelope meet again.

PRINT AND MEDIA RESOURCES

UNIT FOUR RESOURCE BOOK
Strategic Reading: Literature, p. 31
Vocabulary SkillBuilder, p. 32

GRAMMAR MINI-LESSONS
Transparencies, p. 33
Copymasters, p. 33

WRITING MINI-LESSONS
Transparencies, p. 56

ACCESS FOR STUDENTS ACQUIRING ENGLISH
Selection Summaries
Reading Support

FORMAL ASSESSMENT
Selection Test, pp. 97–98
 Test Generator

AUDIO LIBRARY
See Reference Card

LASERLINKS
Literary Connection

 INTERNET RESOURCES
McDougal Littell Literature Center at http://www.hmco.com/mcdougal/lit

THE LANGUAGE OF LITERATURE TEACHER'S EDITION **543**

SUMMARY

Books 21, 22, 23 In Book 21, Penelope, Odysseus' wife, is bothered by suitors who want to marry her and take Odysseus' wealth. Penelope holds a contest to see which suitor can string Odysseus' bow and shoot an arrow through the sockets of twelve axe heads; the winner will marry her. One after another, the suitors try and fail to string the bow. Odysseus, who is disguised as a beggar, asks if he may try. Penelope ignores the suitors' objections, and Odysseus effortlessly strings the bow and sends an arrow through every axe socket. Then he calls on his son, Telemachus, to help him slay the suitors. In Book 22, Odysseus kills Antinous, the leader of the suitors. Another suitor, Eurymachus, tries to appease Odysseus, but Odysseus is not merciful. With the help of Telemachus and the goddess Athena, Odysseus continues fighting until all the suitors are dead. In Book 23, Odysseus must convince Penelope that he is truly Odysseus. She tests him by ordering her servant to have his bed placed outside his bedchamber. In a rage, Odysseus asks who dared to move his bed, which he had carved from an olive tree rooted to the spot. Odysseus alone knew the secret of the bed, and Penelope knows he is her husband. After 20 years, they are reunited.

Thematic Link: *The Homecoming* Odysseus returns home after 20 years but must continue to battle before reclaiming his place.

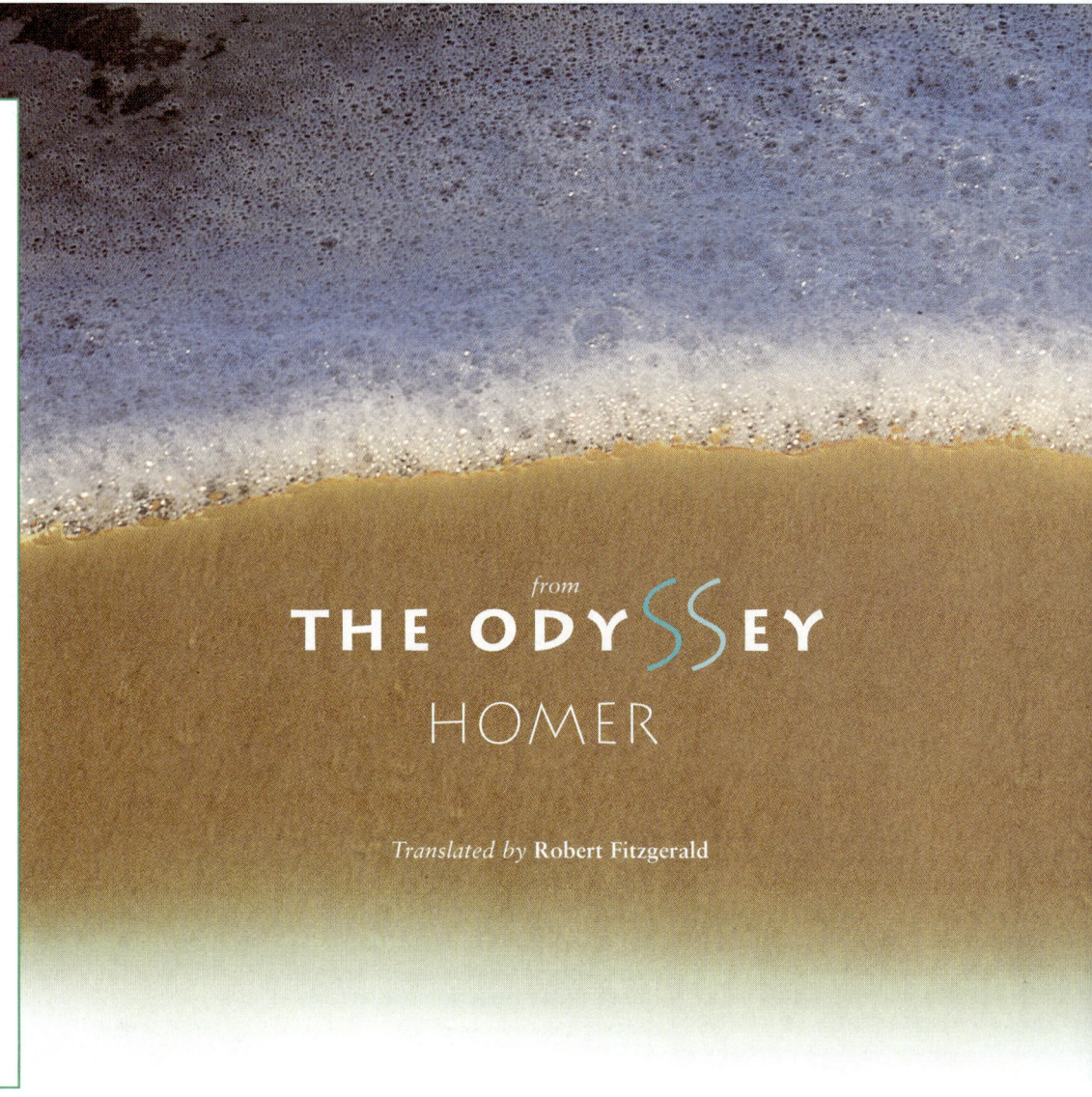

from THE ODYSSEY

HOMER

Translated by Robert Fitzgerald

544   UNIT FOUR   PART 2: THE HOMECOMING

WORDS TO KNOW

aloof (ə-lōōf') *adj.* distant; remote; standoffish (p. 563)

commandeer (kŏm'ən-dîr') *v.* to take control of by force (p. 546)

contemptible (kən-tĕmp'tə-bəl) *adj.* deserving of scorn or disdain; worthless (p. 556)

desolation (dĕs'ə-lā'shən) *n.* lonely grief; misery (p. 566)

dithering (dĭth'ər-ĭng) *n.* acting in a nervous or uncertain way **dither** *v.* (p. 554)

frenzy (frĕn'zē) *n.* a wildly excited state of mind (p. 554)

gall (gôl) *n.* scornful boldness (p. 552)

implacable (ĭm-plăk'ə-bəl) *adj.* impossible to soothe; unforgiving (p. 560)

justification (jŭs'tə-fĭ-kā'shən) *n.* an explanation or excuse for an action (p. 546)

omen (ō'mən) *n.* an event thought to foretell good or evil; sign (p. 556)

plunder (plŭn'dər) *v.* to rob of property by force; steal from (p. 548)

restitution (rĕs'tĭ-tōō'shən) *n.* a making good for loss or damage; repayment (p. 560)

revelry (rĕv'əl-rē) *n.* noisy merrymaking; festivity (p. 557)

throng (thrông) *n.* a large gathering; crowd (p. 557)

wiliest (wī'lē-ĭst) *adj.* most crafty or sly; trickiest (p. 557)

WITH THE HELP of King Alcinous, Odysseus finally returns home to the shores of Ithaca, where he is met by the goddess Athena. She warns him that his palace is overrun by more than 100 suitors who, believing Odysseus is dead, want to marry Penelope and take over his fortune. Following her advice, Odysseus disguises himself as a beggar and visits the palace. There he sees that two suitors in particular, Antinous and Eurymachus, are rude and demanding. Odysseus has a tearful reunion with his son, Telemachus, and together they discuss how to avenge their family honor. In the meantime, Penelope—who knows nothing of this and has given up hope for Odysseus' return—proposes an archery contest to the suitors, with marriage to her as the prize. She enters the storeroom and takes down the heavy bow that Odysseus left behind.

CUSTOMIZING FOR
Students Acquiring English

- Use **ACCESS FOR STUDENTS ACQUIRING ENGLISH**, *Reading Support*.
- Use the information in the Cultural Connection to help prepare students for the rest of the story of Odysseus. Explain the meaning of the term *suitor* and review the list of important characters in the *Odyssey*.

1 To help students understand what the verb *overrun* means, divide the verb into two parts—*run* and *over*. The suitors are running over—overflowing—the palace the way water overflows a glass.

STRATEGIC READING FOR
Less-Proficient Readers

Set a Purpose To help immerse students in the selection, ask them how it would feel to arrive home after a long journey to find a house filled with enemies. Then ask them to read to find out who Odysseus calls upon for assistance in order to deal with the suitors.

Use **UNIT FOUR RESOURCE BOOK**, p. 31, for guidance in reading the selection.

Literary Concept:
CHARACTERIZATION

A Ask students how the author illustrates Penelope's continued sadness over the absence of Odysseus. *(Possible response: by describing how the sight of her husband's bow moves her to tears)*

Linking to Science

B The bow and arrow has been used since prehistoric times as a weapon and hunting tool. The bow is a curved strip, usually wooden, with its two ends connected by a thick string of various fibers, including animal sinew. When the string is drawn, or pulled back, with an arrow inserted, the bow bends and tension is created. When the archer releases the string, the bow snaps back; the arrow is propelled forward, and the arrow's feathers help to stabilize its flight. The bow lost importance as a weapon with the development of firearms, but archery has grown in popularity as a recreational and competitive pursuit. The Ancient Scorton Arrow tournament in Yorkshire, England, has been held annually since 1673. The National Archery Association of the United States was founded in Boston in 1879.

Guide for Reading

C *Possible Response:* The author is referring to the arrows, sticking out of the quiver, that deliver a "coughing death"— the fate suffered by someone shot with an arrow and choking to death on his or her own blood.

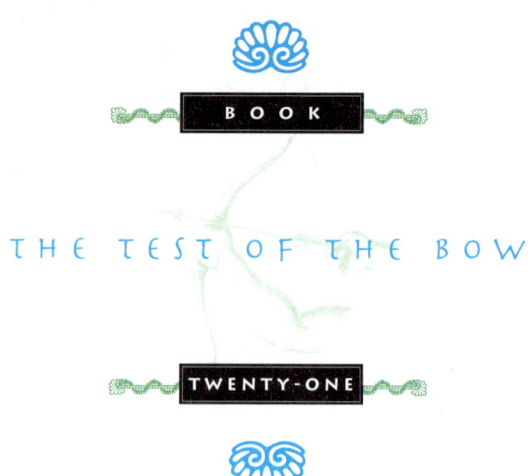

BOOK TWENTY-ONE
THE TEST OF THE BOW

                            Now Penelope
A sank down, holding the weapon on her knees,
and drew her husband's great bow out, and sobbed
and bit her lip and let the salt tears flow.
5 Then back she went to face the crowded hall,
tremendous bow in hand, and on her shoulder hung
B the quiver spiked with coughing death. Behind her
maids bore a basket full of axeheads, bronze
and iron implements for the master's game.
10 Thus in her beauty she approached the suitors,
and near a pillar of the solid roof
she paused, her shining veil across her cheeks,
her maids on either hand and still,
then spoke to the banqueters:

                        "My lords, hear me:
15 suitors indeed, you <u>commandeered</u> this house
to feast and drink in, day and night, my husband
being long gone, long out of mind. You found
no <u>justification</u> for yourselves—none
except your lust to marry me. Stand up, then:

Guide for Reading

1–4 Notice that Penelope still grieves for Odysseus, even after 20 years.

7 quiver (kwĭv′ər): a case in which arrows are carried. What do you think is meant by "the quiver spiked with coughing death"?

8–9 axeheads . . . game: metal heads of axes (without handles) that Odysseus used to employ in a display of archery skill.

> **WORDS TO KNOW**
> **commandeer** (kŏm′ən-dîr′) *v.* to take control of by force
> **justification** (jŭs′tə-fĭ-kā′shən) *n.* an explanation or excuse for an action

546

Multicultural Perspectives

CONTESTS AND GAMES Competitive events such as archery have been popular around the world for thousands of years. For example, among Native American groups, especially the Plains Indians, archery contests were an important part of a young child's training for both hunting and war. In addition, Native Americans from the Midwest, Northeast, and Canada played a competitive game known as baggataway, the forerunner of the modern game of lacrosse. Players used long sticks tipped with nets made from animal skin to carry a ball, pass it to teammates, and finally hurl it into the opposing team's goal. Matches often featured hundreds of players on each team, and the distance between each goal could be several miles. Like the contest in the *Odyssey*, competition among Native Americans was often more than mere recreation and sport: games between tribes could be used to settle ongoing disputes.

CUSTOMIZING FOR
Gifted and Talented Students

Remind students of Athena's suggestion—in the summary of intervening chapters on page 545—that Odysseus disguise himself as an old beggar. Then have them point to examples in the selection that illustrate how this particular disguise is both a help to Odysseus and a useful way for the author to make observations.

Possible responses:

- lines 41–43—It makes it more unlikely that Odysseus will be discovered since the disguise contrasts highly with the memory of Odysseus held by the suitors.

- lines 55–60—The disguise makes it easier for Odysseus to test the loyalty of his servants; they have no fear of a beggar and no reason to lie.

- lines 134–39, 153–157, 192–196—The way in which the suitors treat the beggar—a member of the lowest level of society, even as they themselves act as freeloaders and abuse the hospitality of the house—helps to highlight their abhorrent behavior.

CUSTOMIZING FOR
Students Acquiring English

2 Ask students to describe in their own words what the successful suitor must do. Invite a student to accompany his or her explanation with a simple sketch on the board. *(Possible response: The successful suitor has to string the bow—bend the bow enough to slide the loose string into notches and make it taut—and then shoot an arrow through the lined-up, empty handle holes, or sockets, in 12 axe heads.)*

Critical Thinking: SPECULATING

D Ask students why they think Penelope has devised the contest of the bow. *(Possible responses: She has given up hope of Odysseus' return and, believing she can no longer hold off the suitors, wants to hurry the process of choosing one; she thinks that none will succeed and believes that their failure will provide a reason to get rid of them; she is stalling for time and still hopes for the return of her husband.)*

Literary Concept: CHARACTERIZATION

E Ask students for their impression of Antinous as revealed in his dialogue here. *(Possible responses: Based on his words to the servants, Antinous is rude and insensitive; he seems insincere, based on his unconvincing words about Penelope's pain and Odysseus' loss; he appears to be a realist, based on his acknowledgment that maybe no one can handle a bow like Odysseus could.)*

Literary Concept: FORESHADOWING

F Ask students what the effect is of learning Antinous' fate so soon. *(Possible response: There is no longer any suspense about whether Antinous—or any other suitor—will win Penelope's hand. Attention now shifts to learning exactly how Odysseus will accomplish the task of defeating them.)*

---

20 we now declare a contest for that prize.
    Here is my lord Odysseus' hunting bow.
    Bend and string it if you can. Who sends an arrow
    through iron axe-helve sockets, twelve in line?
    I join my life with his, and leave this place, my home,
25 my rich and beautiful bridal house, forever
    to be remembered, though I dream it only."

    Then to Eumaeus:
                            "Carry the bow forward.
    Carry the blades."
                            Tears came to the swineherd's eyes
    as he reached out for the big bow. He laid it
30 down at the suitors' feet. Across the room
    the cowherd sobbed, knowing the master's weapon.
    Antinous growled, with a glance at both:

                            "Clods.
    They go to pieces over nothing.
                            You two, there,
    why are you sniveling? To upset the woman
35 even more? Has she not pain enough
    over her lost husband? *Sit down.*
    Get on with dinner quietly, or cry about it
    outside, if you must. Leave us the bow.
    A clean-cut game, it looks to me.
40 Nobody bends that bowstave easily
    in this company. Is there a man here
    made like Odysseus? I remember him
    from childhood: I can see him even now."

    That was the way he played it, hoping inwardly
45 to span the great horn bow with corded gut
    and drill the iron with his shot—he, Antinous,
    destined to be the first of all to savor
    blood from a biting arrow at his throat,
    a shaft drawn by the fingers of Odysseus
50 whom he had mocked and <u>plundered</u>, leading on
    the rest, his boon companions.

21–23 Note that the contest has two parts: first the suitor must bend the heavy bow and string it—a task that requires immense strength and skill—then he must shoot an arrow straight through the holes in 12 ax heads set up in a row.

28–38 Notice the emotion expressed by the swineherd Eumaeus and the cowherd Philoetius when they are reminded of their master. Then notice how Antinous treats Odysseus' servants.

44–51 Antinous imagines himself winning Penelope's contest. Notice, however, that his death is foreshadowed here.

51 boon companions: jolly friends.

WORDS TO KNOW
plunder (plŭn′dər) *v.* to rob of property by force; steal from

548

Mini-Lesson Grammar

TROUBLESOME VERBS Remind students that the verbs *lie* and *lay* are commonly confused. *Lie* means "to rest" or "to be in a certain place"; it never has a direct object. *Lay* means "to place"; it always has a direct object, unless it is in the passive voice.

lie: present and past
The spear always *lies* next to the table.
The spear *lay* next to the fallen soldier.

lay: present and past
The servants *lay* the sheets on the bed.
The warrior was *laid* in the grave.

Present	Pres. Part.	Past	Past Part.
lie	(is) lying	lay	(have) lain
lay	(is) laying	laid	(have) laid

Application Point out the use of the verbs (lines 29, 253, 343, 401, 435) as they occur in the selection. Then ask students to write four sentences using each verb—one each for the present, present participle, past, and past participle forms.

Reteaching/Reinforcement
- *Grammar Handbook*, anthology p. 925
- *Grammar Mini-Lessons* copymasters p. 33, transparencies p. 33

 The Writer's Craft
Lie and *Lay*, p. 613

548 THE LANGUAGE OF LITERATURE TEACHER'S EDITION

Despite heating and greasing the bow, the lesser suitors prove unable to string it. The most able suitors, Antinous and Eurymachus, hold off. While the suitors are busy with the bow, Odysseus—still disguised as an old beggar—goes to enlist the aid of two of his trusted servants, Eumaeus the swineherd and Philoetius the cowherd.

Two men had meanwhile left the hall:
swineherd and cowherd, in companionship,
one downcast as the other. But Odysseus
55 followed them outdoors, outside the court,
and coming up said gently:

                  "You, herdsman,
and you, too, swineherd, I could say a thing to you,
or should I keep it dark?

                          No, no; speak,
my heart tells me. Would you be men enough
60 to stand by Odysseus if he came back?
Suppose he dropped out of a clear sky, as I did?
Suppose some god should bring him?
Would you bear arms for him, or for the suitors?"

The cowherd said:

                    "Ah, let the master come!
65 Father Zeus, grant our old wish! Some courier
guide him back! Then judge what stuff is in me
and how I manage arms!"

                        Likewise Eumaeus
fell to praying all heaven for his return,
so that Odysseus, sure at least of these,
70 told them:

            "I am at home, for I am he.
I bore adversities, but in the twentieth year
I am ashore in my own land. I find
the two of you, alone among my people,
longed for my coming. Prayers I never heard
75 except your own that I might come again.
So now what is in store for you I'll tell you:

72–75 What is the quality that Odysseus values so highly in these two servants?

ODYSSEY   **549**

Guide for Reading

Possible Responses: Because he requests that the bow be brought to him, the outer gate locked, and the women told to stay away, and because he warns of battle noises, Odysseus is probably planning to attack the suitors; Odysseus may be planning to attempt the challenge of the axeheads himself.

If Zeus brings down the suitors by my hand
I promise marriages to both, and cattle,
and houses built near mine. And you shall be
80 brothers-in-arms of my Telemachus.
Here, let me show you something else, a sign
that I am he, that you can trust me, look:
this old scar from the tusk wound that I got
boar hunting on Parnassus—
85 Autolycus' sons and I."

                                    Shifting his rags
he bared the long gash. Both men looked, and knew,
and threw their arms around the old soldier, weeping,
kissing his head and shoulders. He as well
took each man's head and hands to kiss, then said—
90 to cut it short, else they might weep till dark—

"Break off, no more of this.
Anyone at the door could see and tell them.
Drift back in, but separately at intervals
after me.
                    Now listen to your orders:
95 when the time comes, those gentlemen, to a man,
will be dead against giving me bow or quiver.
Defy them. Eumaeus, bring the bow
and put it in my hands there at the door.
Tell the women to lock their own door tight.
100 Tell them if someone hears the shock of arms
or groans of men, in hall or court, not one
must show her face, but keep still at her weaving.
Philoetius, run to the outer gate and lock it.
Throw the cross bar and lash it."

                                    He turned back
105 into the courtyard and the beautiful house
and took the stool he had before. They followed
one by one, the two hands loyal to him.

Eurymachus had now picked up the bow.
He turned it round, and turned it round
110 before the licking flame to warm it up,
but could not, even so, put stress upon it

---

84 Parnassus (pär-năs′əs): a mountain in central Greece.

85 Autolycus' (ô-tŏl′ĭ-kəs) **sons:** Odysseus' uncles. (Autolycus was Odysseus' grandfather on his mother's side.)

94–104 Odysseus has a plan but reveals to the servants only the details they must take care of. On the basis of the orders he gives, what do you think Odysseus is planning?

to jam the loop over the tip
          though his heart groaned to bursting.
Then he said grimly:

                    "Curse this day.
What gloom I feel, not for myself alone,
115 and not only because we lose that bride.
Women are not lacking in Achaea,
in other towns, or on Ithaca. No, the worst
is humiliation—to be shown up for children
measured against Odysseus—we who cannot
120 even hitch the string over his bow.
What shame to be repeated of us, after us!"

113–121 Since most of the suitors have already tried the challenge and failed, Eurymachus here speaks for all of them when he expresses his shame and embarrassment. Is the suitors' concern about their reputation for physical strength similar to attitudes men have today?

116 Achaea (ə-kē′ə): the Greek mainland.

Guide for Reading

J *Possible Responses: Responses will vary, but many students may feel that such attitudes are still common today.*

STRATEGIC READING FOR
Less-Proficient Readers

K Make sure students understand the assistance Odysseus has asked for in order to deal with the suitors.

- Why does Odysseus reveal his identity to his two servants? *(because he is certain of their loyalty and needs their help)* **Making Inferences**
- How does Odysseus plan to get the bow? *(He asks his servant Eumaeus to defy the suitors and bring him the bow when the time comes.)* **Noting Relevant Details**

Set a Purpose Have students read to find out why Odysseus wants the bow and who will win the contest.

Mini-Lesson: Speaking, Listening, and Viewing

CHOREOGRAPHING A DANCE Explain to students that dance is an art form in which meaning or beauty is expressed through movement. A choreographer chooses movements that create a desired effect upon a viewer. Dances can be created to interpret an event, tell a story, express themes and ideas, or simply illustrate the beauty of form and movement. Lighting, costumes, stage setting, and the music to which a dance piece is set can all contribute to a viewer's impression of a piece.

Application Have students form small groups to choreograph a dance that interprets a scene from the *Odyssey*. Students may want to watch videotapes of ballets, jazz or modern dances to come up with ideas about movement and staging. Students should try to illustrate both the scene's events and its underlying emotions. If they like, students can create costumes to wear while performing the dance piece. After the dance is performed, have students discuss the ways in which dance can be effective in interpreting a dramatic scene.

Literary Concept: IRONY

L Remind students that irony is the contrast between appearance and reality and that verbal irony occurs when someone knowingly exaggerates or says one thing and means another. Why might Odysseus' words in this passage be considered verbal irony? *(Possible responses: because he is acting out a careful plan of misrepresenting himself; because he actually despises Antinous; because he is not at all out of practice of performing feats of strength; because during many of his voyages he was well fed and well received)*

Guide for Reading

M *Possible Responses: Antinous is insulting to the beggar. Antinous claims that the beggar is talking nonsense and charges that the man shows no respect for the privileges he has already received.*

Literary Concept: IRONY

N Have students discuss how Penelope's speech is an example of dramatic irony—a situation where the reader or viewer knows something that a character does not know. *(Possible response: There is a conflict between what Penelope believes—that the beggar cannot draw the bow and that he has no interest in her anyway—and what the reader knows to be true.)*

Then spoke Odysseus, all craft and <u>gall</u>:

"My lords, contenders for the queen, permit me:
a passion in me moves me to speak out.
125 I put it to Eurymachus above all
and to that brilliant prince, Antinous. . . .
But let me try my hand at the smooth bow!
Let me test my fingers and my pull
to see if any of the oldtime kick is there,
130 or if thin fare and roving took it out of me."

Now irritation beyond reason swept them all,
since they were nagged by fear that he could string it.
Antinous answered, coldly and at length:

"You bleary vagabond, no rag of sense is left you.
135 Are you not coddled here enough, at table
taking meat with gentlemen, your betters,
denied nothing, and listening to our talk?
When have we let a tramp hear all our talk?
The sweet goad of wine has made you rave!"

140 At this the watchful queen Penelope
interposed:

                    "Antinous, discourtesy
to a guest of Telemachus—whatever guest—
that is not handsome. What are you afraid of?
Suppose this exile put his back into it
145 and drew the great bow of Odysseus—
could he then take me home to be his bride?
You know he does not imagine that! No one
need let that prospect weigh upon his dinner!
How very, very improbable it seems."

 AT TELEMACHUS' REQUEST, *Penelope leaves the men to settle the question of the bow among themselves.*

122–130 Remember that Odysseus is disguised as an old beggar. Think about the effect of an old beggar's request to try the challenge just after the finest princes in the land have failed so miserably.

130 thin fare and roving: poor food and hard travel.

134–139 How does Antinous react to the beggar's request?

140–149 The epithet "watchful queen" characterizes Penelope as patient and observant. Here she scolds the suitors for their lack of courtesy and hospitality—values they consistently ignore—and urges them to give the stranger a chance.

WORDS TO KNOW
gall (gôl) *n.* scornful boldness

DESIGN NOTE

The terra-cotta frieze (a classical building's decorated, horizontal upper section, resting on columns) that this image comes from is in particularly bad condition. In fact, the bow and arrow that Odysseus is so obviously aiming have been completely eroded through time. This gave the designer the idea to replace the bow and arrow with contemporary neon colors, to further highlight the incredible nature of this feat. Men half his age could not string the bow, yet Odysseus does this effortlessly on page 555, as though by magic, to the amazement of all the suitors. Then on page 556 Odysseus will send an arrow through the 12 axe-head sockets "clean as a whistle." The designer imagined that this further magic must have made the bow and arrow appear to glow unnaturally to all those present.

Critic's ★ Corner

"The artist is of no importance. Only what he creates is important, since there is nothing new to be said. Shakespeare, Balzac, Homer have all written about the same things, and if they had lived one thousand or two thousand years longer, the publishers wouldn't have needed anyone since."

William Faulkner (1897–1962)

Ask students to discuss Faulkner's statement. Do they agree or disagree? What does he imply about the content of Homer's work?

Guide for Reading

O *Possible Response: The suitors continue to show the old beggar no respect, calling him names and making fun of him.*

Literary Concept:
CHARACTERIZATION

P Ask students what impressions they have of Eumaeus in light of his reaction to the suitors' harassment. *(Possible responses: He wants badly to help Odysseus but is unnerved by the suitors; he is determined enough to regain his composure, deliver the bow, and give necessary orders to Eurycleia.)*

CUSTOMIZING FOR
Students Acquiring English

4 Ask students what the narrator is telling the reader or listener about the coming events in the poem. Lead them to understand that the "shock of arms" and "groans of men" refer to sounds of fighting and injury that will soon take place.

Guide for Reading

Q *Possible response: because Eurycleia does not yet know that Odysseus has returned and Eumaeus doesn't want to give away the secret*

---

150 The swineherd had the horned bow in his hands
moving toward Odysseus, when the crowd
in the banquet hall broke into an ugly din,
shouts rising from the flushed young men:

> "Ho! Where
do you think you are taking that, you smutty slave?"

155 "What is this <u>dithering</u>?"

> "We'll toss you back alone
among the pigs, for your own dogs to eat,
if bright Apollo nods and the gods are kind!"

He faltered, all at once put down the bow, and stood
in panic, buffeted by waves of cries,
160 hearing Telemachus from another quarter
shout:

> "Go on, take him the bow!
Do you obey this pack?
You will be stoned back to your hills! Young as I am
my power is over you! I wish to God
165 I had as much the upper hand of these!
There would be suitors pitched like dead rats
through our gate, for the evil plotted here!"

Telemachus' <u>frenzy</u> struck someone as funny,
and soon the whole room roared with laughter at him,
170 so that all tension passed. Eumaeus picked up
bow and quiver, making for the door,
and there he placed them in Odysseus' hands.
Calling Eurycleia to his side he said:

> "Telemachus
trusts you to take care of the women's doorway.
175 Lock it tight. If anyone inside
should hear the shock of arms or groans of men
in hall or court, not one must show her face,
but go on with her weaving."

> The old woman
nodded and kept still. She disappeared

153–157 *How would you describe the way the suitors treat the old swineherd?*

162–172 As Penelope did earlier, Telemachus stands up to the suitors. He wishes that he had as much power over them as he has, despite his youth, over the servant Eumaeus. The suitors just laugh at Telemachus, but as they do, Eumaeus is able to deliver the bow safely to Odysseus.

173–178 Eumaeus orders Eurycleia to lock the women's room. *Why does he say that the orders came from Telemachus rather than from Odysseus?*

WORDS TO KNOW	**dithering** (dĭth′ər-ĭng) *n.* acting in a nervous or uncertain way **dither** *v.* **frenzy** (frĕn′zē) *n.* a wildly excited state of mind

554

Mini-Lesson — Study Skills

REFERENCE: USING ELECTRONIC MEDIA
Explain that electronic media can be a valuable supplement to print reference sources. Some resources, such as CD-ROM encyclopedias (electronic editions of books), offer the advantages of computerized search capabilities and audio and video information. Other CD-ROM resources include databases of government statistics, magazine indexes and abstracts, and collections of newspaper articles. Online resources make information available to those with access to a computer and a modem. These resources include the World Wide Web, a large collection of electronic documents viewable using special browsers; the FTP, or file transfer protocol, that allows people to retrieve files from computers linked to the Internet; and commercial online services for subscribers.

Application Encourage students to use one electronic resource to research an aspect of ancient Greece. They can use home or school computers or ask at a local library about the electronic media available there.

554 THE LANGUAGE OF LITERATURE TEACHER'S EDITION

180 into the women's hall, bolting the door behind her.
Philoetius left the house now at one bound,
catlike, running to bolt the courtyard gate.
A coil of deck-rope of papyrus fiber
lay in the gateway; this he used for lashing,
185 and ran back to the same stool as before,
fastening his eyes upon Odysseus.
                    And Odysseus took his time,
turning the bow, tapping it, every inch,
for borings that termites might have made
while the master of the weapon was abroad.
190 The suitors were now watching him, and some
jested among themselves:

                    "A bow lover!"

"Dealer in old bows!"

                    "Maybe he has one like it
at home!"

        "Or has an itch to make one for himself."

"See how he handles it, the sly old buzzard!"

195 And one disdainful suitor added this:

"May his fortune grow an inch for every inch he bends it!"

But the man skilled in all ways of contending,
satisfied by the great bow's look and heft,
like a musician, like a harper, when
200 with quiet hand upon his instrument
he draws between his thumb and forefinger
a sweet new string upon a peg: so effortlessly
Odysseus in one motion strung the bow.
Then slid his right hand down the cord and plucked it,
205 so the taut gut vibrating hummed and sang
a swallow's note.
                    In the hushed hall it smote the suitors
and all their faces changed. Then Zeus thundered
overhead, one loud crack for a sign.
And Odysseus laughed within him that the son

198 heft: weight.

199–203 In this epic simile Odysseus' stringing of the bow is compared to the stringing of a harp. What qualities of Odysseus does this comparison emphasize?

206 smote: struck; affected sharply.

207–208 The thunder, a sign from Zeus, indicates that the gods are on Odysseus' side.

ODYSSEY **555**

Critical Thinking:
MAKING INFERENCES

T Discuss Odysseus' intent in making the statement "neither did I take all day stringing the bow." *(Possible responses: He is taunting the suitors for their weakness; he is comparing himself favorably to the suitors, none of whom was able to string the bow.)*

Literary Concept: IRONY

U Ask students to explain the irony in these lines. *(Possible responses: Odysseus has no intention of providing a meal and entertainment for the suitors; in fact the time of their feasting has come to an end; the literal meaning of his statements could not be further removed from the truth, for he intends to take revenge against them.)*

STRATEGIC READING FOR
Less-Proficient Readers

V Make sure students understand the events of the contest.

- Why does none of the suitors actually attempt to send the arrow through the axeheads? *(because none is able to complete the preliminary step of stringing the bow)* **Analyzing**

- What event stuns the suitors and makes them cease to jeer at the old beggar? *(He is able to string the bow.)* **Noting Relevant Details**

Set a Purpose Have students read to find out how Odysseus and Telemachus rid the house of the suitors.

---

210 of crooked-minded Cronus had flung that <u>omen</u> down.
He picked one ready arrow from his table
where it lay bare: the rest were waiting still
in the quiver for the young men's turn to come.
He nocked it, let it rest across the handgrip,
215 and drew the string and grooved butt of the arrow,
aiming from where he sat upon the stool.
                                    Now flashed
arrow from twanging bow clean as a whistle
through every socket ring, and grazed not one,
to thud with heavy brazen head beyond.
                                    Then quietly
220 Odysseus said:
                    "Telemachus, the stranger
you welcomed in your hall has not disgraced you.
I did not miss, neither did I take all day
stringing the bow. My hand and eye are sound,
not so <u>contemptible</u> as the young men say.
225 The hour has come to cook their lordships' mutton—
supper by daylight. Other amusements later,
with song and harping that adorn a feast."

He dropped his eyes and nodded, and the prince
Telemachus, true son of King Odysseus,
230 belted his sword on, clapped hand to his spear,
and with a clink and glitter of keen bronze
stood by his chair, in the forefront near his father.

210 Cronus (krō′nəs): Zeus' father.

214 nocked it: placed the arrow's feathered end against the bowstring.

219 brazen: made of brass.

228–232 Book 21 ends with the image of father and son standing side by side facing more than 100 enemies.

WORDS TO KNOW
omen (ō′mən) *n.* an event thought to foretell good or evil; sign
contemptible (kən-tĕmp′tə-bəl) *adj.* deserving of scorn or disdain; worthless

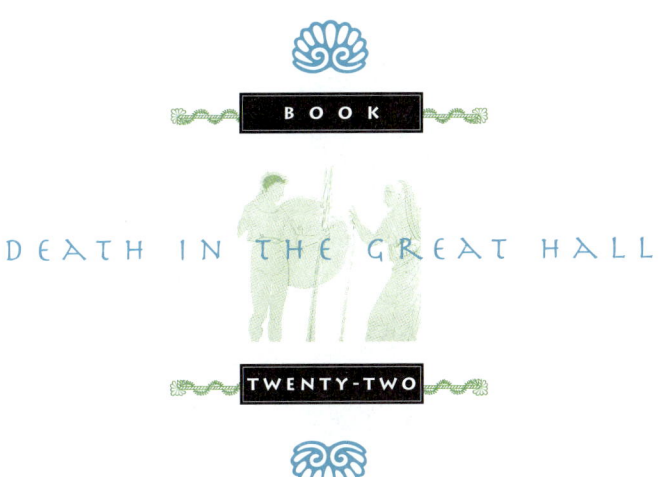

BOOK TWENTY-TWO
DEATH IN THE GREAT HALL

Literary Concept: DESCRIPTION

W Ask students to discuss the why they think Homer describes Antinous' golden cup in such detail. *(Possible responses: The details of Antinous drinking from the beautiful cup help to create a contrast with the moment of his terrible death; it helps the reader to imagine the shock Antinous must have felt at the moment he is struck; it highlights Antinous' sudden transition from feasting to dying.)*

Guide for Reading

X *Possible responses:* Odysseus kills Antinous first because he is the leader of the suitors; after watching the sudden and awful death of their leader, the other suitors may become discouraged and less dangerous foes to Odysseus.

Now shrugging off his rags the <u>wiliest</u> fighter of the islands
leapt and stood on the broad door sill, his own bow in his
   hand.
235 He poured out at his feet a rain of arrows from the quiver
and spoke to the crowd:

      "So much for that. Your clean-cut game is over.
Now watch me hit a target that no man has hit before,
if I can make this shot. Help me, Apollo."

W 240 He drew to his fist the cruel head of an arrow for Antinous
just as the young man leaned to lift his beautiful drinking
   cup,
embossed, two-handled, golden: the cup was in his fingers:
the wine was even at his lips: and did he dream of death?
How could he? In that <u>revelry</u> amid his <u>throng</u> of friends
who would imagine a single foe—though a strong foe
   indeed—
245 could dare to bring death's pain on him and darkness on
   his eyes?
Odysseus' arrow hit him under the chin
and punched up to the feathers through his throat.

233 The epithet "wiliest fighter of the islands" emphasizes Odysseus' cleverness and skill at this important point in the story.

238 The god Apollo was, among other things, the supporter and protector of archers. The bow was his sacred weapon.

239–252 Why does Odysseus kill Antinous first? Why does he do it in such a sudden, terrible way? **X**

> **WORDS TO KNOW**
> **wiliest** (wī′lē-ĭst) *adj.* most crafty or sly; trickiest
> **revelry** (rĕv′əl-rē) *n.* noisy merrymaking; festivity
> **throng** (thrông) *n.* a large gathering; crowd

557

Mini-Lesson The Writer's Style

DIALOGUE Remind students that dialogue can be a more vivid way of showing what a character is doing and feeling than if the author states the actions or feelings. For example, in several passages (lines 153–57, 190–196, 259–262), the author includes sets of remarks, mainly jeers and insults, by anonymous suitors. In these passages, the author uses few speaker's tags such as *he said*. Notice how the omission of these tags helps to evoke a mob-like quality.

Application Have students imagine a group situation such as people attending a sporting event, walking in a parade, or waiting in line for a bus. Then ask them to write a dialogue that helps re-create the scene's mood and illustrates the emotions of the people involved.

Reteaching/Reinforcement
- Writing Handbook, anthology p. 877
- *Writing Mini-Lessons* transparencies, p. 56

📁 The Writer's Craft
Using Dialogue Effectively, p. 434

THE LANGUAGE OF LITERATURE **TEACHER'S EDITION** 557

DESIGN NOTE

Unable to find surviving depictions of Odysseus' battle with the suitors, the designer has created his own representation, appropriating characters from different ancient Greek battle scenes sculpted in marble and framing them beneath a series of arches.

Reading the Art *Who might the designer be trying to represent with the two figures in the first arch? in the remaining three arches?*

Literary Concept: SIMILE

 Ask students to explain the comparison this simile makes and why the author might use it. *(Possible response: It compares the nostrils of Antinous to great pipes pouring out blood; it helps the reader visualize Antinous' awful death.)*

 Backward and down he went, letting the winecup fall
from his shocked hand. Like pipes his nostrils jetted
250   crimson runnels, a river of mortal red,
and one last kick upset his table
knocking the bread and meat to soak in dusty blood.

Now as they craned to see their champion where he lay
the suitors jostled in uproar down the hall,
255   everyone on his feet. Wildly they turned and scanned
the walls in the long room for arms; but not a shield,
not a good ashen spear was there for a man to take and
      throw.
All they could do was yell in outrage at Odysseus:

"Foul! to shoot at a man! That was your last shot!"

260   "Your own throat will be slit for this!"

                              "Our finest lad is down!
You killed the best on Ithaca."

250 runnels: streams.

255–257 Earlier, in preparation for this confrontation, Odysseus and Telemachus removed all the weapons and shields that were hanging on the walls.

"Buzzards will tear your eyes out!"

For they imagined as they wished—that it was a wild shot,
an unintended killing—fools, not to comprehend
they were already in the grip of death.
265 But glaring under his brows Odysseus answered:

"You yellow dogs, you thought I'd never make it
home from the land of Troy. You took my house to plunder,
twisted my maids to serve your beds. You dared
bid for my wife while I was still alive.
270 Contempt was all you had for the gods who rule wide heaven,
contempt for what men say of you hereafter.
Your last hour has come. You die in blood."

As they all took this in, sickly green fear
pulled at their entrails, and their eyes flickered
275 looking for some hatch or hideaway from death.

266–272 At last Odysseus reveals his true identity and announces that he plans to kill all the suitors. What reasons does he give for killing them?

274 entrails: internal organs.

Guide for Reading

AA Eurymachus reminds Odysseus that Antinous bore the greatest share of guilt, and promises that he and the other suitors will pay for all supplies consumed by them.

Critical Thinking: MAKING JUDGMENTS/PREDICTING

BB Have students discuss the offer that Eurymachus makes to Odysseus. Ask whether they feel it is a fair offer and have them predict whether Odysseus will accept it. *(Responses will vary. However, many students should doubt that he will accept it.)*

Guide for Reading

CC *Possible Responses:* Odysseus is so enraged by the scene he has arrived to find in Ithaca that nothing less than the death of all the suitors can placate him; Odysseus is more concerned with honor than with money.

Eurymachus alone could speak. He said:

"If you are Odysseus of Ithaca come back,
all that you say these men have done is true.
Rash actions, many here, more in the countryside.
280 But here he lies, the man who caused them all.
Antinous was the ringleader; he whipped us on
to do these things. He cared less for a marriage
than for the power Cronion has denied him
as king of Ithaca. For that
285 he tried to trap your son and would have killed him.
He is dead now and has his portion. Spare
your own people. As for ourselves, we'll make
<u>restitution</u> of wine and meat consumed,
and add, each one, a tithe of twenty oxen
290 with gifts of bronze and gold to warm your heart.
Meanwhile we cannot blame you for your anger."

Odysseus glowered under his black brows
and said:

      "Not for the whole treasure of your fathers,
all you enjoy, lands, flocks, or any gold
295 put up by others, would I hold my hand.
There will be killing till the score is paid.
You forced yourselves upon this house. Fight your way
    out,
or run for it, if you think you'll escape death.
I doubt one man of you skins by."

300 They felt their knees fail, and their hearts—but heard
Eurymachus for the last time rallying them.

"Friends," he said, "the man is <u>implacable</u>.
Now that he's got his hands on bow and quiver
he'll shoot from the big door stone there
305 until he kills us to the last man.
                              Fight, I say,
let's remember the joy of it. Swords out!
Hold up your tables to deflect his arrows.
After me, everyone: rush him where he stands.
If we can budge him from the door, if we can pass

276–291 What is Eurymachus' strategy here? How does he hope to save himself and the remaining suitors?

279 rash: foolish; thoughtless.

283 Cronion (krō′nē-ŏn′): Zeus, the son of Cronus.

289 tithe: payment.

293–299 Why do you think Odysseus rejects Eurymachus' explanation and offer of restitution?

299 skins by: sneaks away.

> **WORDS TO KNOW**
> **restitution** (rĕs′tĭ-tōō′shən) *n.* a making good for loss or damage; repayment
> **implacable** (ĭm-plăk′ə-bəl) *adj.* impossible to soothe; unforgiving

560

Mini-Lesson Literary Concepts

Example	Type of Irony	Reason It Is Ironic
lines 144–49: How very, very improbable it seems!	dramatic	The reader knows the "exile" is Odysseus.

REVIEWING IRONY Three major types of irony are situational, dramatic, and verbal. Situational irony is the contrast between what a reader or character expects and what actually happens. Dramatic irony is when the reader or viewer knows something that a character does not know. Verbal irony occurs when a character knowingly exaggerates or says one thing and means another.

Application Ask students to work in groups to identify instances of irony in Books 21–23. Have them copy the chart at the left and use it to record each example, the type of irony it represents, and the reasons they find the situation ironic. To help get them started, point out some of the numerous instances of dramatic irony in which Homer reveals beforehand a character's fate, a fate the character himself does not yet know.

310 into the town, we'll call out men to chase him.
    This fellow with his bow will shoot no more."

He drew his own sword as he spoke, a broadsword of fine bronze,
honed like a razor on either edge. Then crying hoarse and loud
he hurled himself at Odysseus. But the kingly man let fly
315 an arrow at that instant, and the quivering feathered butt
sprang to the nipple of his breast as the barb stuck in his liver.
The bright broadsword clanged down. He lurched and fell aside,
pitching across his table. His cup, his bread and meat,
were spilt and scattered far and wide, and his head slammed on the ground.
320 Revulsion, anguish in his heart, with both feet kicking out,
he downed his chair, while the shrouding wave of mist closed on his eyes.

Amphinomus now came running at Odysseus,
broadsword naked in his hand. He thought to make
the great soldier give way at the door.
325 But with a spear throw from behind Telemachus hit him
between the shoulders, and the lancehead drove
clear through his chest. He left his feet and fell
forward, thudding, forehead against the ground.
Telemachus swerved around him, leaving the long dark spear
330 planted in Amphinomus. If he paused to yank it out
someone might jump him from behind or cut him down with a sword
at the moment he bent over. So he ran—ran from the tables
to his father's side and halted, panting, saying:

"Father let me bring you a shield and spear,
335 a pair of spears, a helmet.
I can arm on the run myself; I'll give
outfits to Eumaeus and this cowherd.
Better to have equipment."

           Said Odysseus:

"Run then, while I hold them off with arrows

320 revulsion (rĭ-vŭl′shən): a sudden feeling of disgust.

320–321 Eurymachus' death is physically painful, but he also has "revulsion, anguish in his heart." What do you think causes this emotional pain?

322 Amphinomus (ăm-fĭn′ə-məs): one of the suitors.

325–332 Telemachus proves to be a valuable help to his father.

STRATEGIC READING FOR
Less-Proficient Readers

FF Have students discuss the details of the battle with the suitors.

- Why is it difficult for the suitors to defend themselves? *(Odysseus has had all the weapons and shields removed from the room.)* **Noting Relevant Details**

- Who are Odysseus' first two victims? *(Antinous and Eurymachus)* **Noting Sequence of Events**

- Why does Eurymachus blame the situation on Antinous and offer to make restitution? *(in the hope of saving his own life and those of the other suitors)* **Drawing Conclusions**

- How does Telemachus aid Odysseus? *(He kills Amphinomus, obtains weapons, and outfits and arms the servants.)* **Summarizing**

Set a Purpose Have students read to see how Penelope reacts to Odysseus.

---

340 as long as the arrows last. When all are gone
if I'm alone they can dislodge me."

　　　　　　　　　　　　　　　　　Quick
upon his father's word Telemachus
ran to the room where spears and armor lay.
He caught up four light shields, four pairs of spears,
345 four helms of war high-plumed with flowing manes,
and ran back, loaded down, to his father's side.
He was the first to pull a helmet on
and slide his bare arm in a buckler strap.
The servants armed themselves, and all three took their stand
350 beside the master of battle.

　　　　　　　　　　　　　While he had arrows
he aimed and shot, and every shot brought down
one of his huddling enemies.
But when all barbs had flown from the bowman's fist,
he leaned his bow in the bright entry way
355 beside the door, and armed: a four-ply shield
hard on his shoulder, and a crested helm,
horsetailed, nodding stormy upon his head,
then took his tough and bronze-shod spears.

345 helms: helmets.

353–358 Notice this depiction of Odysseus as a warrior. Try drawing a sketch of him armed for battle to get the full impact.

The suitors make various unsuccessful attempts to expel Odysseus from his post at the door. Athena urges Odysseus on to battle, yet holds back her fullest aid, waiting for Odysseus and Telemachus to prove themselves. Six of the suitors attempt an attack on Odysseus, but Athena deflects their arrows. Odysseus and his men seize this opportunity to launch their own attack, and the suitors begin to fall. At last Athena's presence becomes known to all, as the shape of her shield becomes visible above the hall. The suitors, recognizing the intervention of the gods on Odysseus' behalf, are frantic to escape but to no avail. Odysseus and his men are compared to falcons who show no mercy to the flocks of birds they pursue and capture. Soon the room is reeking with blood. Thus the battle with the suitors comes to an end, and Odysseus prepares himself to meet Penelope.

562　UNIT FOUR　PART 2: THE HOMECOMING

THE TRUNK OF THE OLIVE TREE

BOOK TWENTY-THREE

    Greathearted Odysseus, home at last,
360 was being bathed now by Eurynome
    and rubbed with golden oil, and clothed again
    in a fresh tunic and a cloak. Athena
    lent him beauty, head to foot. She made him
    taller, and massive, too, with crisping hair
365 in curls like petals of wild hyacinth
    but all red-golden. Think of gold infused
    on silver by a craftsman, whose fine art
    Hephaestus taught him, or Athena: one
    whose work moves to delight: just so she lavished
370 beauty over Odysseus' head and shoulders.
    He sat then in the same chair by the pillar,
    facing his silent wife, and said:

              "Strange woman,
    the immortals of Olympus made you hard,
    harder than any. Who else in the world
375 would keep <u>aloof</u> as you do from her husband
    if he returned to her from years of trouble,
    cast on his own land in the twentieth year?

360 Eurynome (yŏŏ-rĭn′ə-mē): a female servant.

368 Hephaestus (hĭ-fĕs′təs): the god of metalworking.
369 lavished: showered.

373 immortals of Olympus: the gods, who live on Mount Olympus.

WORDS TO KNOW
aloof (ə-lōōf′) *adj.* distant; remote; standoffish

CUSTOMIZING FOR
Students Acquiring English

6 Ask students to describe in their own words how the goddess Athena has changed Odysseus' appearance.

Linking to Geography

GG The goddess Athena was considered the protector of the city of Athens, the city named in her honor. Occupying about 165 square miles on the Greek mainland, the city is crossed by two rivers, the Kifisos and the Ilisos, and surrounded by mountains. The influence of the ancient Greek culture centered there upon later European cultures has been so great that the city is often referred to as the birthplace of Western civilization. Today, Athens is the capital and commercial center of modern Greece with a population of over three million. Several ancient monuments survive including the Parthenon, a 5th-century B.C. temple to Athena, considered among the finest examples of classical Greek architecture.

Guide for Reading

HH *Possible Response: Penelope may not believe that this person is really Odysseus; in fact, she expresses doubt that he is man at all, believing that perhaps he is a ghost or a god.*

II *Possible Response: Penelope realizes that if this man is really Odysseus, he will know that the bed cannot be moved.*

CUSTOMIZING FOR
Students Acquiring English

7 Ask a volunteer to read this passage aloud as the rest of the group listens. Then have students take turns describing in their own words as many aspects of the bedroom as they can. Then fill in the missing details. Be sure they understand that one of the bedposts was a living olive tree rooted in the ground and that for that reason, the bed could never be moved.

Nurse, make up a bed for me to sleep on.
Her heart is iron in her breast."

                                                 Penelope
380 spoke to Odysseus now. She said:

                                  "Strange man,
if man you are . . . This is no pride on my part
nor scorn for you—not even wonder, merely.
I know so well how you—how he—appeared
boarding the ship for Troy. But all the same . . .

385 Make up his bed for him, Eurycleia.
Place it outside the bedchamber my lord
built with his own hands. Pile the big bed
with fleeces, rugs, and sheets of purest linen."

With this she tried him to the breaking point,
390 and he turned on her in a flash raging:

"Woman, by heaven you've stung me now!
Who dared to move my bed?
No builder had the skill for that—unless
a god came down to turn the trick. No mortal
395 in his best days could budge it with a crowbar.
There is our pact and pledge, our secret sign,
built into that bed—my handiwork
and no one else's!

                                An old trunk of olive
grew like a pillar on the building plot,
400 and I laid out our bedroom round that tree,
lined up the stone walls, built the walls and roof,
gave it a doorway and smooth-fitting doors.
Then I lopped off the silvery leaves and branches,
hewed and shaped that stump from the roots up
405 into a bedpost, drilled it, let it serve
as model for the rest. I planed them all,
inlaid them all with silver, gold and ivory,
and stretched a bed between—a pliant web
of oxhide thongs dyed crimson.
                                     There's our sign!
410 I know no more. Could someone else's hand
have sawn that trunk and dragged the frame away?"

564   UNIT FOUR   PART 2: THE HOMECOMING

380–384 Think about why Penelope might hold herself aloof from a man who claims to be the husband she hasn't seen in 20 years and who has just killed more than 100 men in her banquet hall. Note the doubt she expresses in "if man you are."

385–411 The bed symbolizes the lasting love between Odysseus and Penelope, and the way it was built is a secret only they know. Because one of the bedposts is the trunk of an olive tree still rooted in the ground, the bed is unmovable. *Why do you think Penelope asks the servant to move a bed that she knows cannot be moved?*

408–409 a pliant web . . . crimson: a network of ox-hide straps, dyed red, stretched between the sides of the bed to form a springy base for the bedding.

Critic's Corner

"Why care about an old work in a dead language that no one reads. . . ? If the world was given to us to explore and master, here is a tale, a play, a song about that endeavor long ago, by no means neglecting self-mastery, which in a sense is the whole point. Electronic brains may help us to use our heads but will not excuse us from that duty, and as to our hearts—cardiograms cannot diagnose what may be most ill about them, or confirm what may be best. The faithful woman and the versatile brave man, these are still exemplary for our kind, as they always were and always will be. Nor do I suppose that the pleasure of hearing a story in words has quite gone out. Even movies and TV make use of words. The Odyssey *at all events was made for your pleasure, in Homer's words and in mine."*

                                      Robert Fitzgerald (in his *Odyssey* Postscript)

Ask students to rephrase what the translator of the *Odyssey* feels is the value of this old epic poem.

Art Note

This portion of a terra-cotta relief from the fifth-century B.C. shows Odysseus and Penelope finally together again. The poses of both characters tells volumes about what they are feeling and the people have become. Legs regally folded and eyes cast thoughtfully down, Penelope is patient, strong, and still a bit hesitant to allow herself to believe that Odysseus has finally returned. Odysseus, his frame racked and bent with wear and age, hardly resembles the powerful warrior who left Ithaca twenty years before. He looks upon the face of his wife with care and concern. The sculptor has left just enough room to allow the designer to simply add a background olive tree as a bridge between them, which perfectly symbolizes their union and emphasizes the fact that all nature of beasts and perils, and the gods themselves, could not keep these two apart.

CUSTOMIZING FOR
Gifted and Talented Students

Encourage students to read other books of the *Odyssey*, particularly Books 15–20. Students can write a paragraph detailing further insight gained into the characters and events through their extended reading. Students may also choose to examine the other translations of the *Odyssey* identified on page 568. Students should write a paragraph comparing and contrasting the differences between the translations and explaining whether they prefer one over another and why.

THE LANGUAGE OF LITERATURE TEACHER'S EDITION **565**

Critical Thinking: ANALYZING

JJ Ask students to discuss what Penelope means in lines 416–420. *(Possible responses: She is appealing to Odysseus not to be angry, pointing out that he would have been just as suspicious as she; she had to be certain this was not another trick played by the gods.)*

CUSTOMIZING FOR
Students Acquiring English

8 Ask students to repeat in their own words the explanation Penelope gives for not being more excited by Odysseus's return. *(Possible response: She has been careful to stop liars from getting close to her for a long time. Now she has a hard time believing that this man is really telling the truth.)*

STRATEGIC READING FOR
Less-Proficient Readers

KK Have students explain the way Odysseus finally gains Penelope's trust. *(Penelope tests Odysseus by ordering that his bed be placed outside the bed chamber. The bed had been made by Odysseus himself, carved from an olive tree, and cannot be moved. Odysseus alone knows this secret and his rage at Penelope's request proves his identity.)*
Clarifying

COMPREHENSION CHECK

1. What does Penelope set up for the suitors who want to marry her? *(an archery contest)*
2. Why isn't Odysseus recognized when he first arrives? *(He disguises himself as an old beggar.)*
3. Who is able to string the bow and shoot an arrow through the open axeheads? *(Odysseus)*
4. Why does Odysseus kill Antinous first? *(He is the leader of the invading suitors.)*
5. Who helps Odysseus fight the suitors? *(his son and his servants)*
6. Why does Penelope test Odysseus? *(She needs proof of his identity.)*

EDITOR'S NOTE *With the permission of the translator's estate or copyright holder, material was deleted to focus this long selection.*

Their secret! as she heard it told, her knees
grew tremulous and weak, her heart failed her.
With eyes brimming tears she ran to him,
415 throwing her arms around his neck and kissed him,
murmuring:

       "Do not rage at me, Odysseus!
No one ever matched your caution! Think
what difficulty the gods gave: they denied us
life together in our prime and flowering years,
420 kept us from crossing into age together.
Forgive me, don't be angry. I could not
welcome you with love on sight! I armed myself
long ago against the frauds of men,
impostors who might come—and all those many
425 whose underhanded ways bring evil on!
Helen of Argos, daughter of Zeus and Leda,
would she have joined the stranger, lain with him,
if she had known her destiny? known the Achaeans
in arms would bring her back to her own country?
430 Surely a goddess moved her to adultery,
her blood unchilled by war and evil coming,
the years, the desolation; ours, too.
But here and now, what sign could be so clear
as this of our own bed?
435 No other man has ever laid eyes on it—
only my own slave, Actoris, that my father
sent with me as a gift—she kept our door.
You make my stiff heart know that I am yours."

Now from his breast into his eyes the ache
440 of longing mounted, and he wept at last,
his dear wife, clear and faithful, in his arms,
longed for
      as the sunwarmed earth is longed for by a swimmer
spent in rough water where his ship went down
under Poseidon's blows, gale winds and tons of sea.
445 Few men can keep alive through a big surf
to crawl, clotted with brine, on kindly beaches
in joy, in joy, knowing the abyss behind:
and so she too rejoiced, her gaze upon her husband,
her white arms round him pressed as though forever.

413 tremulous: trembling; quivering.

421–425 Like Odysseus, Penelope proves to be an able trickster. Her explanation here gives insight into the troubles that she's had to endure during Odysseus' long absence.

426 Argos (är′gŏs) . . . **Leda** (lē′də).

426–432 Penelope contrasts her faithfulness with Helen's adultery, which caused the Trojan War and therefore the long separation between Penelope and Odysseus.

436 Actoris (ăk-tôr′ĭs).

442–449 In this epic simile, Odysseus is compared to a person who has suffered a shipwreck, swum through rough seas, and finally crawled ashore, covered with sea salt ("clotted with brine") but rejoicing to have survived the ordeal.

WORDS TO KNOW
desolation (dĕs′ə-lā′shən) *n.* lonely grief; misery

566

Assessment Option

SELF-ASSESSMENT You can help students assess their understanding of the selection and the characters by having them write a dialogue between Odysseus and Penelope as it might occur after she accepts him. Students should have each character ask the other any questions they might have and have the characters discuss their feelings for each other and the events that occurred during their long separation. To help students assess their own work, have them respond to the following questions:

- Is my dialogue consistent with the characters as they are described in the selections?
- Are the details mentioned in my dialogue consistent with the events of the selections?
- Do the details accurately reflect the sequence of events?

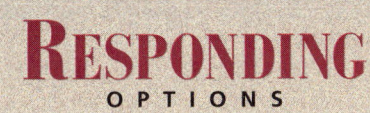

RESPONDING OPTIONS

FROM PERSONAL RESPONSE TO CRITICAL ANALYSIS

REFLECT
Thematic Link

1. What was your reaction to the reunion of Odysseus and Penelope? Jot down your impressions in your notebook and share them in class.

RETHINK

2. Whose pain and suffering do you think has been greater—Odysseus' or Penelope's? Defend your choice.

Close Textual Reading **Consider**
- the obstacles that Odysseus has faced during his 20-year absence
- the uncertainty that Penelope has lived with, as expressed in lines 416–425

3. Do you think Odysseus is right to kill all the suitors? Why or why not?

4. Why do you think Penelope devises the contest with the bow? What does this contest reveal about her?

5. Look back at the chart you made for the Personal Connection and the prediction you made for the Reading Connection on page 543. What, if anything, surprised you about the way things turned out in the *Odyssey*?

Thematic Link

6. Do Odysseus' actions in these excerpts seem consistent with what you have come to expect of him as an epic hero? Explain your opinion.

RELATE

7. Assume that Odysseus represents the ancient Greeks' ideal of a man and that Penelope represents their ideal of a woman. In what ways are the characters similar to and different from the ideal man and woman of today?

Multimodal Learning
ANOTHER PATHWAY

Think about Odysseus' human qualities and his heroic qualities. Identify an example of each kind of quality, and explain to your classmates which aspect of Odysseus you like more—his heroism or his humanity. As an alternative, draw two sketches of Odysseus, emphasizing his heroic side in one and his human side in the other.

CRITIC'S CORNER

In his book *The Art of the Odyssey*, Howard Clarke downplays Odysseus' feelings for Penelope: "One can hardly characterize Odysseus' love for Penelope as romantic or sentimental. Odysseus wants to get back to his wife because she is part of his home and hearth, part of his very being. There can be no doubt that he loves Penelope very much, but it . . . is his father and his land that give Odysseus status and substance . . . and these are his overt reasons for wanting to return home." Think about the parts of the *Odyssey* you have read, especially the reunion in Book 23. Do you agree or disagree with Clarke's assessment? State your reasons.

QUICKWRITES

Think of a modern-day equivalent of the suitors—a serious one, such as a group of terrorists or a street gang, or a humorous one, such as a carload of unwelcome relatives. Then, working alone or with a partner, create a plot outline for a **story** of epic proportions, relating how you, as an epic hero or heroine, get rid of the intruders.

📁 **PORTFOLIO** Save your writing. You may want to use it later as a springboard to a piece for your portfolio.

ODYSSEY **567**

From Personal Response to Critical Analysis

1. Accept all reasonable responses.
2. Possible responses: Odysseus', because he encountered great physical dangers; Penelope's, because she was ignorant of his fate, she had no adventures to occupy her as Odysseus did, and she was surrounded by intruders.
3. Possible responses: no, deliberate murder is never justifiable; yes, because in the context of the time and place, the slaughter was necessary for Odysseus to regain his home and his honor.
4. Possible responses: because she is sure they will all fail and then finally give up and go home; it reveals her intelligence and courage.
5. Accept all reasonable responses.
6. Accept all reasonable, well-supported responses. Some students may have been surprised by Odysseus' ruthlessness in dealing with Penelope's suitors, though his occasional aggressive behavior earlier should have hinted at this capability on his part.
7. Accept all reasonable responses. Many students should feel that time-honored traits such as loyalty, courage, and faith are common to the ancient Greeks and modern people; however, the ancient Greeks' tolerance for and acceptance of personal revenge is a trait not condoned today.

Another Pathway

Students may point to Odysseus' emotional reaction to his reunion with wife, son, and servants as an example of his human side. His battle with the suitors provides many examples of his heroic nature.

Rubric

3 Full Accomplishment Students identify and provide examples of Odysseus' heroic and human qualities.

2 Substantial Accomplishment Students identify qualities but have some difficulty finding examples of or illustrating them.

1 Little or Partial Accomplishment Students are unable to identify or provide examples of his heroic and human qualities.

Critic's Corner

Students who agree may point to Odysseus' infidelities and his self-introduction in Book 9 in which he mentions Ithaca, his home, and parents, but not Penelope. Others may disagree, citing his anger at the suitors and his emotional response to his reunion with Penelope.

QuickWrites

Ask students to review the Previewing pages for Books 9–12 on epic poetry and the word webs they created for the genre study activity. As they write, students can refer to the webs to make sure a story created from their outlines would contain some of the characteristics of an epic.

📖 **The Writer's Craft**
Narrative and Literary Writing, pp. 85–112

Literary Concepts

As students look through the selection for examples, they can refer to the word webs they made for the mini-lesson on characterization in Book 10.

Possible examples for Penelope:
- skepticism revealed through her speech, lines 380–384
- love for Odysseus revealed through her actions, lines 412–415

Possible examples for Telemachus:
- valor revealed through his actions, lines 329–333
- intelligence revealed through his speech, lines 334–338

Across the Curriculum

Art Encourage students to work in small groups, each choosing the works of one artist to research. Have them make copies of the artwork they find. They can show these copies to the class while they give their reports. Students may also want to compare ancient Greek representations of the adventures of Odysseus with those of medieval and contemporary artists.

LITERARY CONCEPTS

Review the methods of **characterization** listed in the chart. The characters of Penelope and Telemachus are not as fully developed as Odysseus' character, but from a few details you can tell a lot about them. For example, when Penelope scolds Antinous for not letting the beggar try his hand at the bow contest, her speech reveals her respect for the values of hospitality and courtesy. Look through this selection to find two more passages in which Penelope's character is revealed and two passages in which Telemachus' character is revealed. Identify each method of characterization used.

Methods of Characterization
• Physical description
• Character's speech, thoughts, feelings, or actions
• Speech, thoughts, feelings, or actions of other characters
• Direct comments about the character

Multimodal Learning

ALTERNATIVE ACTIVITIES

1. **Cooperative Learning** Work with a small group of classmates to plan and stage a TV talk-show **interview** with Odysseus. Ask about his revenge on the suitors, his plans for his kingdom, and his feelings on finally being home. You might also interview Penelope or perhaps some relatives of the suitors.

2. In Book 22, when Odysseus and Telemachus face more than 100 opponents, the scene is almost like one in an adventure film. To plan such a scene, a filmmaker may create a **storyboard**—a series of rough sketches that shows the sequence of actions or camera shots. Create your own storyboard to show how you would film the defeat of the suitors. (This is a good opportunity to use a computer graphics program.)

568   UNIT FOUR PART 2: THE HOMECOMING

THE WRITER'S STYLE

The *Odyssey* has been translated, both in verse and in prose, by many writers throughout the ages. To appreciate how much a translation reflects the translator's personal style, compare the following words of Penelope in Fitzgerald's translation (lines 416–420) and in two other modern translations. Explain which one you like best.

> "Do not rage at me, Odysseus!
> No one ever matched your caution! Think
> what difficulty the gods gave: they denied us
> life together in our prime and flowering years,
> kept us from crossing into age together."
> —Robert Fitzgerald

> "Do not be angry with me, Odysseus, since, beyond other men, you have the most understanding. The gods granted us misery, in jealousy over the thought that we two, always together, should enjoy our youth, and then come to the threshold of old age."
> —Richmond Lattimore

> "Do not scowl at me, Odysseus, since in everything else You have been the wisest of men. The gods have given us woe Who begrudged it to us that, staying with one another, We should enjoy our vigor and reach the threshold of age."
> —Albert Cook

Multimodal Learning

ACROSS THE CURRICULUM

Art Research paintings depicting the adventures of Odysseus, such as those by Romare Bearden, N. C. Wyeth, Odilon Redon, Edward Burne-Jones, and Earl Staley. Report to the class on which adventures seem to have been the most popular with painters.

Alternative Activities

1. **Cooperative Learning** Groups can assign individual students to play each of the different characters who will appear on the show. These students should review the excerpts for insight into their characters. Others can prepare a list of questions they are interested in having answered.
2. Encourage students to experiment with the angles, points of view, and perspectives that will best re-create the battle. Students can also review their favorite movies on videotape for techniques that make action scenes exciting.

The Writer's Style

After students have discussed the three excerpts, tell them about Fitzgerald's own claim that the *Odyssey* "can no more be translated into English than rhododendron can be translated into dogwood." Ask: What might the translator mean by his statement? What are the challenges a translator faces?

WORDS TO KNOW

For each numbered word, write the letter of the best synonym.

1. wiliest
2. frenzy
3. commandeer
4. aloof
5. desolation
6. plunder
7. omen
8. contemptible
9. implacable
10. revelry
11. throng
12. gall
13. restitution
14. justification
15. dithering

a. seize
b. disgusting
c. nerve
d. raid
e. forewarning
f. fit
g. sadness
h. grounds

i. sneakiest
j. unsociable
k. repayment
l. bumbling
m. celebration
n. unforgiving
o. mob

HOMER

Although the ancient Greeks credited a man named Homer with composing the *Iliad* and the *Odyssey,* scholars have long debated whether Homer really existed. There are many theories about who Homer may have been and when and where he may have lived. According to ancient accounts, he lived sometime between 900 and 700 B.C., possibly on the island of Chios in the eastern Aegean Sea, and he was blind. Most modern scholars agree that the Homeric poems are the work of one or more exceptionally talented bards—singers who make up their verses as they sing.

Homer's epics are all that remains of a series of poems that told the whole story of the Trojan War. In later centuries, the *Iliad* and the *Odyssey* were memorized by professional reciters, who performed them at religious festivals throughout Greece. They were also the first works read by Greek schoolchildren. By 300 B.C. many slightly different versions of the poems existed, and scholars began to work at restoring them to their original form.

Homer's epics became models for many later writers, including the Roman poet Virgil and the English poet John Milton. Moreover, by helping to shape classical Greek culture, they have contributed to the development of all later Western ideas and values.

ROBERT FITZGERALD

1910–1985

Robert Fitzgerald spent six years in Italy translating the *Odyssey.* He once suggested that life included "moments that seem mysterious gifts from we know not where." He went on to describe one of these moments, which occurred when he visited Ithaca while translating the *Odyssey:*

"As I came abreast of the eucalyptus trees one old fellow got up and shuffled toward me. He stopped and spoke in perfect English. . . . He said: 'You know, *we* say that he never died. *We* say that he still turns up now and then, looking like a soldier or a sea captain . . . or . . . just a stranger.' He paused and looked serenely at me. And there in the burning sun I shivered from head to foot. I could not say a word. I bowed my head and walked on.

"Just a coincidence, of course—that an old Ithacan capable of saying that to me in my language, without any preamble, should have been there on that particular afternoon when for the only time in my life I came to that spot, and came from years of companionship, almost of identification with the hero whom he didn't have to name. . . . But isn't that how the gods used to appear to mortals out of the radiant Aegean air, or how the messengers of heaven appeared to men in another mythical landscape?"

OTHER WORKS *Iliad* (translation), *Spring Shade*

Extended Reading

ODYSSEY **569**

Words To Know

1. i
2. f
3. a
4. j
5. g
6. d
7. e
8. b
9. n
10. m
11. o
12. c
13. k
14. h
15. l

Reteaching/Reinforcement
- *Unit Four Resource Book,* p. 32.

HOMER

Whether or not Homer was one or a group of poets, it is clear that the author was responsible for numerous innovations. While prior poets and bards surely celebrated heroes and battles in their work, the sheer length of the Homeric epics sets them apart; their performances would have required several evenings. Some critics have used this fact to support their claim that Homer could not have been a single poet, arguing that no single performer could memorize and recite such a volume of verse. Others, however, note the use of formulaic devices (epithets and repeated passages) that would have made the length of the poems manageable for a single performer.

ROBERT FITZGERALD

Fitzgerald also translated another ancient epic, the *Aeneid* by the Roman poet Virgil.

REFLECTING ON THEME
What Do You Think?

Have students think about the perfect home and the emotions they might feel upon returning to it after a long absence. Ask them to compare their thoughts then to their thoughts now. Is the idea of home still as much one of a place or of people as they originally imagined? Do they see their emotions being any stronger for thinking of "home" as a place as opposed to a gathering of people?

OBJECTIVES

- To promote independent active reading
- To practice and apply skills learned in previous selections
- To provide an opportunity to assess students' performance through an alternative assessment instrument

Thematic Link: *The Homecoming* Penelope reveals her perspective on the long wait for Odysseus to return.

Reading Pathways

- Invite students to give a choral reading of the poem. First, have individual students read the poem to themselves. Then assign each line of the poem to a different student and have all the students read it aloud as a group.

- Ask students to write down their impressions of Penelope and her feelings from their reading of the *Odyssey*. After they have read "Penelope," have them look back at their notes and compare their previous impressions to any new ones they have gained from the poem.

- Have students use the imagery from the poem to sketch or draw their own interpretations of Penelope and Odysseus.

- Evaluate how well students can read, interpret, discuss, and write on their own by using the Integrated Assessment for Unit Four, located in the Alternative Assessment booklet. The assessment for this unit covers both On Your Own selections, the poems "Siren Song" and "Penelope." Administer the assessment at the end of the unit after students have finished reading, studying, and writing about the *Odyssey*.

Art Note

Penelope by Shlomo Katz In this painting of Penelope, Katz uses the same technique as he did for *The Sirens* shown on page 533.

Reading the Art What does the artist show Penelope doing? Who are figures lurking in the background?

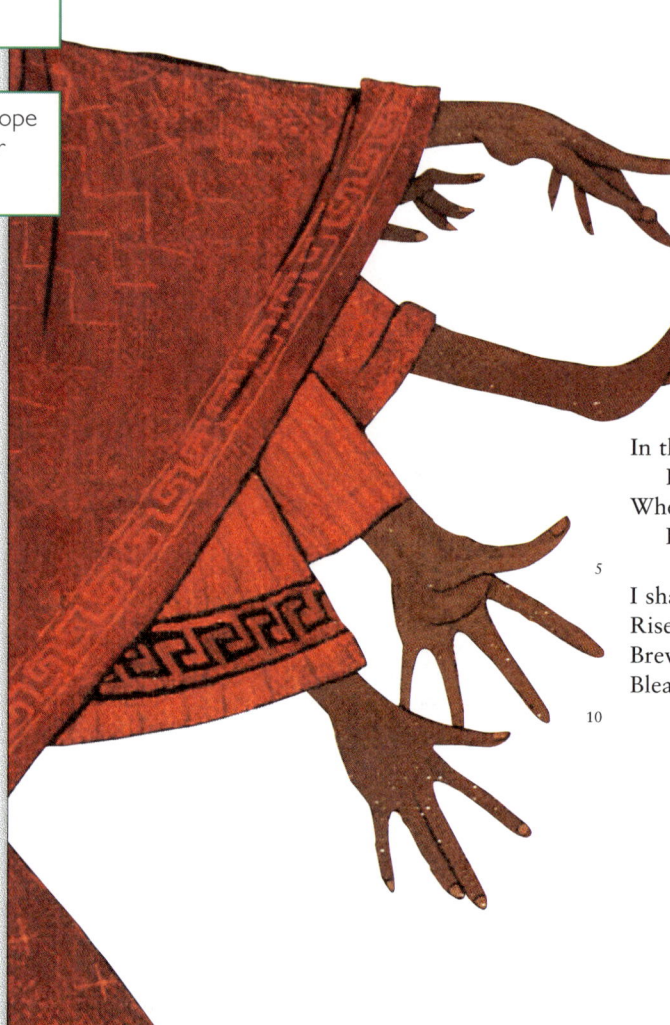

ON YOUR OWN

Penelope

DOROTHY PARKER

In the pathway of the sun,
  In the footsteps of the breeze,
Where the world and sky are one,
  He shall ride the silver seas,
5   He shall cut the glittering wave.
I shall sit at home, and rock;
Rise, to heed a neighbor's knock;
Brew my tea, and snip my thread;
Bleach the linen for my bed.
10   They will call him brave.

PRINT AND MEDIA RESOURCES

UNIT FOUR RESOURCE BOOK
Strategic Reading: Literature, p. 35

FORMAL ASSESSMENT
Selection Test, p. 99
Part Test, pp. 101–102
▪ Test Generator

ALTERNATIVE ASSESSMENT
Unit Four Integrated Assessment, pp. 19–24

ACCESS FOR STUDENTS ACQUIRING ENGLISH
Selection Summaries

AUDIO LIBRARY
See Reference Card

INTERNET RESOURCES
McDougal Littell Literature Center at http://www.hmco.com/mcdougal/lit

Penelope (1990) by Shlomo Katz. Courtesy of Strictly Limited Editions, San Francisco, CA.

DOROTHY PARKER

1893–1967

Considered one of the wittiest women in America, Dorothy Parker was regularly quoted by newspaper columnists during her lifetime. In 1933, upon hearing that former President Calvin Coolidge, a solemn man of few words, had died, Parker remarked "How could they tell?" Although her best known poetry is light verse on the subject of romantic love (she coined the often-quoted "Men seldom make passes/At girls who wear glasses"), she also wrote poems centering on lonely love. Many of them deal with women abandoned by their lovers—as one critic put it, "smarting from the sense of unworthiness and the pain of rejection, trying to cope with her dismay and despair."

Parker also achieved critical acclaim for her well-crafted short stories, portraying the shallow lives of wealthy women of the 1920s and early 1930s. For a time, Parker herself was a wealthy woman, living a lavish life among the rich and famous in New York during the Roaring Twenties. But in her later life, she was plagued by financial difficulties and alcoholism. After her death, a friend described her as being "at war with herself all her life."

OTHER WORKS *Enough Rope, Sunset Gun, Death and Taxes, Laments for the Living, After Such Pleasures*

Extended Reading

PENELOPE **571**

STORYTELLER

Laura Simms Tells "Penelope and the Suitors" The story of Penelope from the epic poem the *Odyssey*, is retold here by professional storyteller Laura Simms. She tells of Penelope's strategies for avoiding the unruly suitors, of her reaction to her husband's return, and of her test to identify Odysseus. Throughout history, singers in the oral tradition have developed the stories they tell. You may wish to generate discussion on this topic after viewing the telling of "Penelope and the Suitors."

Side A, Frame 49444

DOROTHY PARKER

Parker spent the 1930s and 1940s in Hollywood, where she wrote numerous screenplays and became heavily involved in political activity. During this period, she gave up writing poetry; her last published poem appeared in 1944. Always her own harshest critic, she refused to view her success as an affirmation of quality, stating pointedly, "My verses are no damn good. . . . anything once fashionable is dreadful now. I gave it up knowing it wasn't getting any better. . . ."

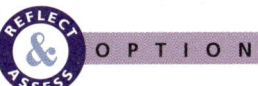

OPTION 1

Cooperative Learning
HOLD A DEBATE

Have students form teams and hold a debate on the question of who is braver, Odysseus or Penelope. One student can moderate the debate, making sure that teams have equal time to speak.

Teacher's Role Encourage all students to explore both sides of the issue in order to prepare a strong argument for their team's position.

Rubric

3 Full Accomplishment Each group presents convincing arguments and supporting evidence for its position.

2 Substantial Accomplishment Groups present clear arguments but may lack examples or details to support its position.

1 Little or Partial Accomplishment Groups are unable to present clear arguments for their positions.

OPTION 2

Class Discussion
SHARING IDEAS

Teacher's Role After students have read the poem, engage them in a whole-class discussion using the following questions:

1. How does Penelope contrast her own life to that of her husband? *(Possible responses: She points out his role as a glorious adventuring hero; in contrast, she describes her own existence as ordinary, domestic, and dull.)*

2. How does this image of Penelope compare with the one presented in the *Odyssey*? *(Possible responses: In the* Odyssey, *she is not purely passive in her wait, but uses her intelligence to fend off the suitors and to try to maintain order in her besieged home; in the poem, she has only ordinary household chores to occupy her.)*

3. What perspective on Penelope is conveyed by the final line of the poem? *(Possible responses: She seems to feel that people will not recognize her suffering and bravery.)*

THE LANGUAGE OF LITERATURE TEACHER'S EDITION **571**

OVERVIEW

To help students gain a deeper appreciation of the selections they have read in this unit, they will explore the definitions of abstract ideas and then create an extended definition of their own in this lesson.

Objectives

- To plan an extended definition by comparing ideas, listing terms, and looking at literary sources
- To draft an extended definition and solicit response
- To revise, edit, and publish an extended definition

Skills

LITERATURE
- Character

WRITING AND LANGUAGE
- Developing examples
- Identifying audience and purpose
- Exploring methods of organization

GRAMMAR AND USAGE
- Avoiding illogical comparisons

MEDIA LITERACY
- Interpreting a graph

SPEAKING, LISTENING, AND VIEWING
- Group discussion
- Conducting a survey
- Peer review

CRITICAL THINKING
- Classifying ideas
- Comparing/contrasting

RESEARCH SKILLS
- Using a thesaurus
- Using a dictionary

CUSTOMIZING FOR
Students Acquiring English

A Make sure students understand the concept of brand names and brand loyalty. Invite volunteers to suggest examples of brand names for each category.

Teaching Strategy: MODELING

B Have students explain which item on the graph the students surveyed are most likely to have a brand name loyalty for. *(sneakers)* Which item are they least likely to have a brand preference for? *(jeans)* Ask students to discuss their personal brand loyalties, if any, and whether they think such loyalties are based on an item's features or its image.

WRITING FROM EXPERIENCE

WRITING TO EXPLAIN

What words sum up your thoughts about Odysseus and Penelope in the *Odyssey*? Do terms like *bravery* and *loyalty* come to mind? We all use such words, but what do they really mean? Looking them up in a dictionary won't tell you all you need to know. That's why people write extended definitions—to clarify ideas that mean different things to different people.

GUIDED ASSIGNMENT
Write an Extended Definition In this lesson, you'll choose a term that represents an idea and write an extended definition to explain it clearly.

1 Explore Ideas

What word or idea will you define? The activities below can help you decide.

Comparing the Sources Take a look at the items on these pages. Can you find the idea they all have in common? What term do they all represent?

Listing Terms Group discussions often go off course when the participants define a key term differently. In a group, brainstorm a list of words or ideas that people talk about but that are hard to define. You might include words like *genius*, *foolishness*, and *loyalty*.

Looking at Literature What characters have you read about who possessed a special quality, such as bravery, talent, cleverness, or kindness? Think about how you might define that special quality in writing.

B What does this graph say about young people's shopping preferences? What brand-name products are you loyal to? Why?

Cartoon

"A few cattle are going to stray off in the morning, and tomorrow night a stampede is planned around midnight. Look, I gotta get back. . . . Remember, when we reach Santa Fe, I ain't slaughtered."

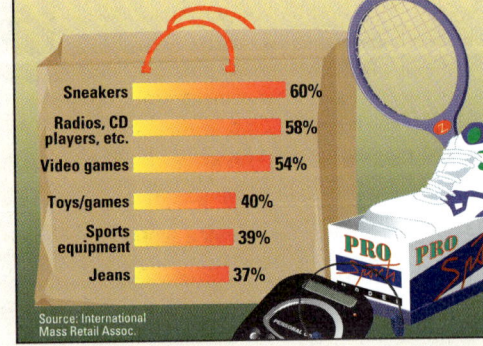

572 UNIT FOUR: PORTRAIT OF A HERO

PRINT AND MEDIA RESOURCES

UNIT FOUR RESOURCE BOOK
Prewriting, p. 39
Elaboration, p. 40
Peer Response Guide, pp. 41–42
Revising and Proofreading, p. 43
Student Model, pp. 44–45
Rubric, p. 46

GRAMMAR MINI-LESSONS
Transparencies, p. 25
Copymasters, p. 26

WRITING MINI-LESSONS
Transparencies, p. 61

FORMAL ASSESSMENT
Guidelines for Writing Assessment

 LASERLINKS
Writing Springboard

Extended Definition, pp. 120–128

Letter to an Advice Column

"Ask Adam"
Arrow Magazine
P.O. Box 2417Z
Los Angeles, CA

Dear Adam,
   My best buddy, Saul, and I were going to volunteer together this summer at a day camp for disabled kids. Now Saul has decided to go to basketball camp because he wants to make the varsity team next year. We had made plans a long time ago, and now I feel that he's leaving me in the lurch! This really messes up my summer. Is he being a lousy friend, or am I the bad guy for not understanding? Should I bother to try to work this out?

Signed,
Grant

My friends are important to me, too, but I wouldn't plan my whole summer around them.

Unlike Grant, I'm having a real problem with a friend of mine, and I don't know how to handle it.

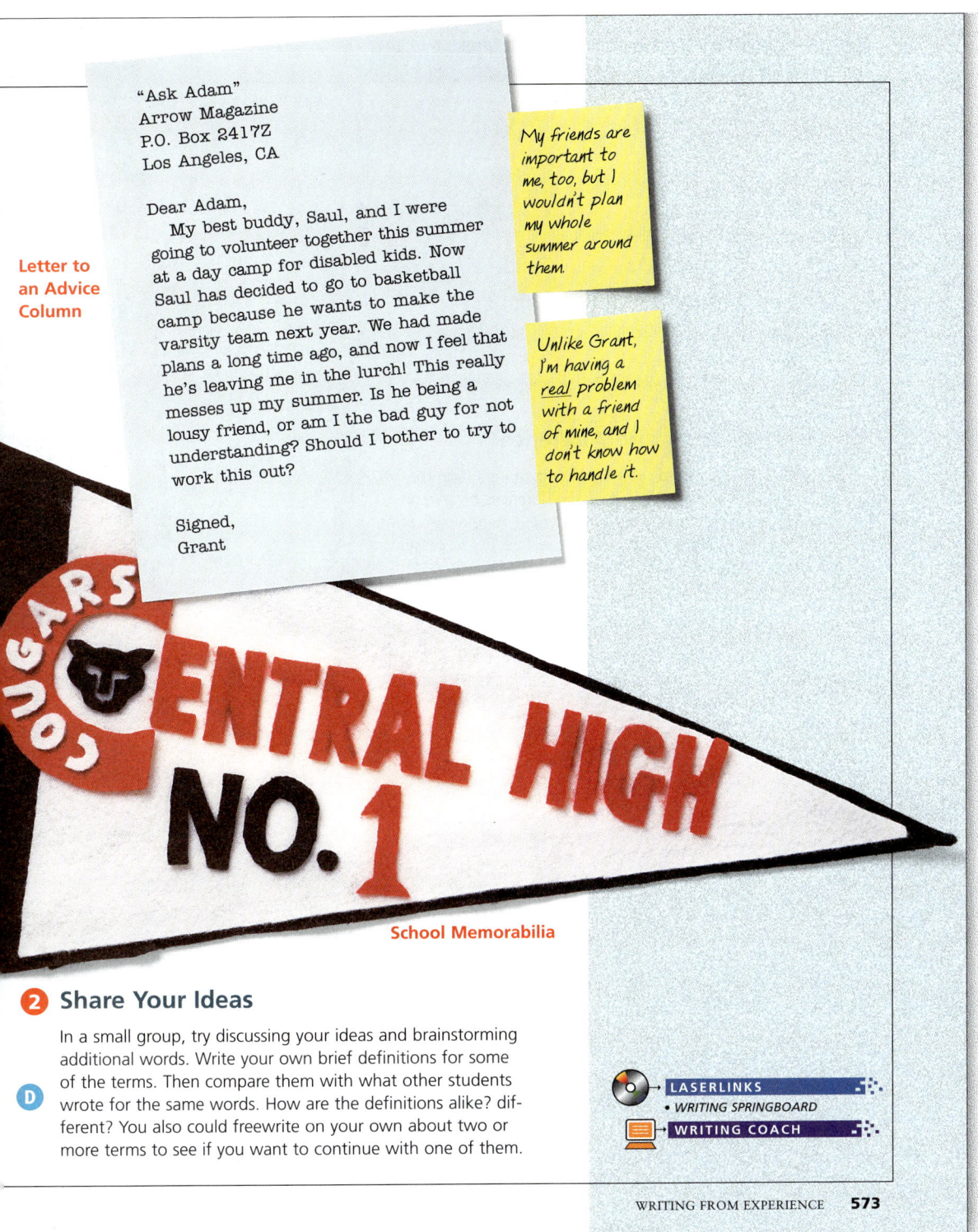

School Memorabilia

2 Share Your Ideas

In a small group, try discussing your ideas and brainstorming additional words. Write your own brief definitions for some of the terms. Then compare them with what other students wrote for the same words. How are the definitions alike? different? You also could freewrite on your own about two or more terms to see if you want to continue with one of them.

LASERLINKS
• WRITING SPRINGBOARD
WRITING COACH

WRITING FROM EXPERIENCE   **573**

Teaching Strategy: MODELING

C **Banner** Have students look at the banner and ask what qualities, in addition to loyalty, might this banner represent. Write their answers on the chalkboard. *(Possible responses: friendship, achievement, sportsmanship, success, school spirit)* Then have student volunteers take turns briefly defining each of the qualities listed. Discuss with students how the definitions differ.

Speaking and Listening: GROUP DISCUSSION

D Suggest that groups appoint a recorder to write down all the suggested words. Then have all the group members free-associate using these words, calling out ideas or examples that they associate with each, while the recorder writes them down. The recorder may then read back the ideas to the group for members to write down.

WRITING SPRINGBOARD
Amelia Earhart This courageous aviator was the first woman to fly solo across the Atlantic Ocean. While attempting a flight around the world in 1937, she disappeared over the Pacific Ocean. This documentary film will give students a glimpse into the life of this remarkable woman.

Side B, Frame 19142

Writing Prompt
Using this documentary footage to give you ideas about the concept of heroism, write an essay defining what it means to be a hero.

Writing Skill:
IDENTIFYING AUDIENCE

E To help students identify their audience, suggest that they ask themselves the following questions:

- Who will be reading this paper—my teacher? my classmates? Is it possible that it will be published in my school newspaper?
- Will the concept I have chosen be interesting to my audience? Will they be able to relate to it?
- What kinds of examples or anecdotes will appeal to my audience?

CUSTOMIZING FOR
Students Acquiring English

F Review dictionary style with students, helping them identify the pronunciation key, the part of speech, and the multiple definitions for each word.

PREWRITING

Exploring Your Idea

The Next Steps When your group compared definitions, did you all agree on the meanings of the terms? Before you can write a definition that is complete and clear, you'll need to do some research and more thinking.

1 Choose a Term to Define

It's time to pick a word that you think is worth exploring! Look over your brainstorming notes. Which word appeals to you most? Select one term to investigate and define.

2 Focus on Goals and Audience

Think about what you'd like your extended definition to accomplish. Do you want to resolve differences of opinion about a term? Is your goal to make people more aware of an idea? Also consider who your readers will be. Try to present your ideas in a way that will keep your audience interested.

3 Start with the Basics

Grab a dictionary and find the simple definition of your word. How does it compare with the definitions you and other students wrote earlier? Look for similarities and differences.

 SkillBuilder **RESEARCH SKILLS**

USING A DICTIONARY Remind students that when checking a word in the dictionary, it is important to read the entire entry, because many words have multiple meanings. For example, the dictionary entry on page 574 shows the first meaning of the word *lozenge* as "a four-sided figure." The second meaning is very different: "a lozenge-shaped medicated drop."

Application Have students write two sentences for each of the following words: check, ideal, mean. Each sentence should reflect a different definition of the word.

Reteaching/Reinforcement
- *Writing Mini-Lessons* transparencies, p. 61

The Writer's Craft
Dictionaries, pp. 122, 474

574 THE LANGUAGE OF LITERATURE **TEACHER'S EDITION**

One Student's Cluster

4 Gather Supporting Information

To learn more about your term, try some of these activities.

Find Examples What are some examples of the term you're defining? (Loyalty is standing by a friend in trouble.) To find examples, you could poll students. Ask, "What things are you loyal to?" You also might check books of quotations, the *Readers' Guide to Periodical Literature,* and poetry anthologies for information.

Classify the Types Make a cluster to help you think about the term you've chosen, as one student did above. Show all the different ways that you've discovered of looking at your idea. The SkillBuilder on the right can help you organize your ideas.

Make Comparisons Try comparing your subject with something more familiar. How are the two ideas similar? different? You also might compare examples of what the term is to what it isn't. (Loyalty is helping out a friend. Loyalty isn't helping that friend only when it's convenient.)

SkillBuilder

CRITICAL THINKING

Classifying Ideas

When writers explore different aspects of an idea, they often begin by grouping, or classifying, their information. They may group information by characteristics, such as style, size, color, or value. A student might chart different types of loyalty, such as blind loyalty and misplaced loyalty. Or a student might chart different objects that people are loyal to, as shown below.

Objects of Loyalty	
Ideas	recycling, buying American products, fighting world hunger
People	family, friends
Organizations	club, school, sports team, political party
Things	brand of cereal, television program

APPLYING WHAT YOU'VE LEARNED
Consider making a similar chart to help you sort through your ideas.

THINK & PLAN

Evaluating Your Topic

1. Do you have a clear understanding of what your term means? How would you state it in a couple of sentences?
2. Have you gathered enough examples and details to support your definition? If not, where can you find more information?

WRITING FROM EXPERIENCE 575

SkillBuilder — CRITICAL THINKING

CLASSIFYING IDEAS Remind students that they should have a purpose in mind when grouping ideas into categories. For example, by grouping Objects of Loyalty into categories such as those shown on the chart, the writer's purpose may be to show that there are many things to which people can be loyal. If a writer wishes to show that loyalty can sometimes be a virtue and sometimes a vice, he or she could chart different types of loyalty, such as blind loyalty or misplaced loyalty.

Application Encourage students to articulate the purpose of their classification as they chart their ideas. As practice, have them discuss at least two different ways the concept *courage* can be classified, and then have them explain the purpose for each method of classification.

CUSTOMIZING FOR
Less-Proficient Writers

G Have students work in small groups to brainstorm examples of the terms they wish to define. Suggest students share anecdotes or stories from literature that illustrate the term. For example, if the term to be defined is *brave*, students may recall a story about someone—either in real life or in literature—who acted bravely.

Critical Thinking: COMPARE AND CONTRAST

H In order to help students develop a better definition of their term, you may suggest that they look at the antonym of the term being defined. For example, if students are defining *bravery*, they might also look at *cowardice*, checking definitions and thinking about examples of *cowardice*.

Writing Skill:
USING THE COMPUTER

I Encourage students to use a computer first, making charts to classify their ideas, and then to draft their definitions. Explain that they can use the Writing Coach program to help organize their definitions by using the classification charts they have created. Remind students to save each draft of their definition as a separate document.

Teaching Strategies:
STUMBLING BLOCK

J Students may be inclined to quote directly a dictionary definition of the term they are defining. Encourage them to look at the dictionary definition, but then to define the term in their own words. Point out that if they do use a direct quotation, they must use quotation marks and cite the source (for example, "According to the *American Heritage Dictionary,* the word *courage* means '...'")

Teaching Strategies: MANAGING THE PAPER LOAD

K As students work on their drafts in class, you may wish to stop by each student's desk briefly to check the term being defined. If a student has misunderstood the assignment or chosen an unsuitable term, you can save time both for yourself and for the student by suggesting suitable changes before the student gets too far in his or her draft.

DRAFTING

Crafting Your Definition

A Time to Focus How much information do you want to include in your extended definition? Which examples will you focus on? One good way to answer questions like these is to start writing your ideas and then see where they lead you.

❶ Write a Discovery Draft

I Start writing out the ideas you have about your term. Jot down anything that strikes you as interesting, important, or even funny. Early in your draft, you may want to include a brief definition of your term or idea. Your examples and
J details can follow it.

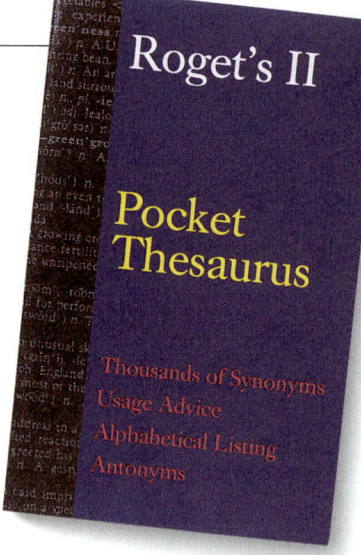

Using a thesaurus can make your writing more lively, as the SkillBuilder on the right explains.

Student's Discovery Draft

K I decided to write about loyalty because of something that happened the other day. I was taking a test in one of my morning classes, when I looked up from my multiple-choice questions and couldn't believe my eyes. A good friend of mine was holding a cheat sheet in his left hand. I was shocked that he would cheat, not just because it's wrong, but also because we have an honor system. Any student who sees someone cheating is supposed to turn that person in. I didn't want to be disloyal to the system, but I didn't want to be disloyal to my friend, either.
    The experience made me rethink what loyalty means to me. I know that I have loyal feelings toward many people and things. Mostly, I am loyal to my family and my close friends. Sometimes things happen that test my loyalty or abuse it, like seeing my friend cheat.

I'll show this essay to my friend. Maybe he'll realize that he let himself—and me—down.

I need to give a short definition of loyalty at the beginning.

576   UNIT FOUR: PORTRAIT OF A HERO

WRITING SPRINGBOARD
This Land Is Your Land... This film will show students imagery that is inspired by the patriotism we feel in the United States for our flag and our country.

Side B, Frame 22569

Writing Prompt
Using this brief film as a reference, write a definition of *patriotism*. Discuss the different ways in which people express patriotism. Include as many examples as you can of patriotism in the United States and in other countries.

② Analyze Your Draft

Take a look at your work. Do you have a clear definition and purpose? Are your details and examples appropriate for the audience you have in mind? Also think about the format your definition might take. It could be a report, a poem, a speech, or even a poster. For more publishing ideas, see page 579.

③ Rework Your Draft and Share

It's time to rework your draft into an extended definition. Below are some suggestions for doing that.

Develop Your Ideas Your definition will be more interesting if you illustrate it with examples and details. Show how various aspects of your term are alike or different. (At the age of four, I was as devoted to my brother as a dog is to its owner.) If you need help using description to highlight comparisons, see page 872 of the Writing Handbook.

Get Organized Do you need help organizing your ideas? After giving a brief definition in your introduction, you can describe different aspects of your concept or give examples of it, one per paragraph. You can conclude by summarizing the definition. For more organizational tips, see page 882 of the Writing Handbook.

PEER RESPONSE

Another student often can help you improve your draft. Try asking a peer questions like the following:

- After reading my draft, how would you define my subject in one or two sentences?
- Which parts of my writing are unclear?
- Which parts are especially interesting or amusing?
- What have you learned from my definition?

SkillBuilder

RESEARCH SKILLS

Using a Thesaurus

As you draft your definition, you may find that you're repeating the term over and over. To avoid that repetition, consult a thesaurus to find synonyms for your term. Sprinkling a few synonyms into your extended definition can make it more engaging, as the example below shows.

*Sports fans demonstrate their loyalty in different ways. Some prove their **faithfulness** by painting their faces with a team's colors. Others show their **allegiance** by wearing caps and T-shirts that display a team's emblem.*

APPLYING WHAT YOU'VE LEARNED

How many times do you repeat the term you're defining in your draft? You may want to find a few synonyms to use in place of your word some of the time.

RETHINK & EVALUATE

Reviewing Your Work

1. How did you decide to organize your draft? Is the organization clear and easy to follow?
2. Which examples and details do you think best illustrate different aspects of your term? Why?

WRITING FROM EXPERIENCE   577

Critical Thinking: ANALYZING

L To help students analyze their drafts, suggest that they write brief outlines of their main ideas and that they then analyze the outlines to see that all the important main ideas are covered and are presented in a logical order.

Teaching Strategy: USING THE SKILLBUILDER

M You may wish to teach the SkillBuilder on Using a Thesaurus at this time. Familiarity with a thesaurus will enable students to develop their definitions more fully, using more varied language.

Writing Skill: ELABORATION

N Encourage students to use specific language as they write and to support their points with examples. Tell students that for each main idea or classification—for instance, moral courage, physical courage, and so on—they should have at least one specific example of someone displaying that sort of courage.

SkillBuilder   RESEARCH SKILLS

USING A THESAURUS Remind students that few synonyms carry *exactly* the same meaning. For example, the thesaurus lists synonyms of the verb *praise* as *compliment, flatter,* and *glorify*. However, these words have slightly different meanings and are used in different ways. Tell students to use care in selecting synonyms for the concept they are defining. If they are unsure of the exact meaning of a synonym, they should always consult a dictionary.

Application Have students check the thesaurus for lists of synonyms of the terms they are defining, and then check the dictionary for the definitions of each term. Have them tell which synonym is closest in meaning and connotation to the terms they are defining.

Additional Suggestions Have students write a sentence using each of the following words: *annoyance, honesty, silence, patriotism, appreciate*. Then have them use a thesaurus to find synonyms that are closest in meaning to each of the words as they are used in their sentences.

THE LANGUAGE OF LITERATURE TEACHER'S EDITION   577

Writing Skill: REVISING

O Students should ask themselves the following questions as they begin their revisions:

- *Does the opening catch the reader's interest? Is the language meaningful, or is there an interesting anecdote?*
- *Do I use concrete, concise language?*
- *Are there specific examples that support my definition?*
- *Who is the audience? Is the language and tone appropriate for them?*
- *Are there any awkward or confusing sentences?*

Critical Thinking: ANALYZING

P Have students compare this final essay with the discovery draft on page 576 and explain the changes. *(The final draft begins with the anecdote; some of the sentences are revised and condensed.)* Explain that the goal of the writer is to explain his personal definition of loyalty, and discuss how the writer's revisions have advanced that purpose.

Teaching Strategy: MODELING

Q Discuss with students how this model meets the Standards for Evaluation on page 579. Elicit that the opening anecdote catches readers' interest and makes them want to read further. The somewhat informal language ("just plain wrong" and "really believe in") and tone indicate that the audience is the student's peers, and possibly his teacher.

REVISING AND PUBLISHING

Finalizing Your Definition

The Finishing Touches Nobody's writing is perfect the first time around. With an extended definition, it's especially important to review your writing several times so you can make sure other people will understand it.

1 Revise and Edit

Look again at the comments your peer reviewer made about your draft. Now is the time to incorporate the changes that will make your definition clearer or more interesting. You also might consider the following:

- How has the final essay shown here changed from the discovery draft?
- What might be the goal of the essay shown here? What is your goal in writing your definition?
- Use the SkillBuilder and the Editing Checklist at the right to help you improve any comparisons you made.

Student's Final Essay

Can Loyalty Be Wrong?

I was taking a test not long ago, when I looked up from my multiple-choice questions and couldn't believe my eyes. A good friend of mine had a cheat sheet in the palm of his left hand. I looked away, barely able to concentrate. Not only is cheating wrong, but we have an honor code at school. Any student who sees someone cheating is supposed to turn that person in. I felt torn between my loyalty to a friend and my respect for the code.

The experience made me rethink what loyalty really means. In general, loyalty is faithfulness to a person, organization, idea, or thing. Feelings of loyalty can be strong, such as a dog's blind loyalty to its owner or a soldier saluting a flag. They can also be somewhat obligatory. But what if they're misguided, such as my feelings toward a friend who had cheated our honor system?

I feel very loyal to my family and friends. That's why seeing my friend breaking an important rule bothered me so much. But I've also learned that loyalty does not mean ignoring what's right.

The writer introduces his term by way of an incident. Why is this an effective way to begin his extended definition?

This student wrote an essay. Who do you think his audience is?

Writing Skill: USING THE COMPUTER

 Students who have taken surveys may wish to use the computer to print a graph or chart showing the results. If the class decides to combine their work in a portfolio, the computer can be used to design a cover for the portfolio.

Teaching Strategy: MANAGING THE PAPER LOAD

Have students exchange papers and read them critically, marking errors in grammar, usage, and spelling, and writing any stylistic comments they may have. Students are usually conscientious about grading their peers' papers, and they often learn nearly as much from the editorial process as they do from writing.

Standards for Evaluation

Have students review their definitions for the following:

Ideas and Content
- clearly states the subject to be defined
- elaborates on the subject with detailed examples
- compares and contrasts different aspects of the subject
- has a strong introduction and satisfying ending

Structure and Form
- uses well-organized paragraphs and a clear organization
- includes transitional words and phrases to show relationships among ideas
- uses a variety of sentence structure

Grammar, Usage, and Mechanics
- contains no more than two or three minor errors in grammar, usage, spelling, capitalization, and punctuation

PORTFOLIO

Ask students to jot down what they like best about their extended definitions. Then invite them to make a brief list of the weaknesses or trouble spots in their definitions. Students may wish to include their informal evaluations along with their definitions in their portfolio.

Survey Questionnaire
Student Survey on Loyalty
1. Do you loyally watch any television programs? If so, what programs?
2. What would you do if someone you admire criticized a friend of yours?

Survey Results
Student Survey on Loyalty (continued)
2. Asked what they would do if someone they admire criticized a friend of theirs, students responded:
- Stay quiet, but don't speak to the critical person again (5%)
- Laugh, but don't say anything (5%)
- Gave other responses (40%)
- Speak up and defend the friend (50%)

Student's Survey Results

❷ Share Your Definition

 A student conducted the survey shown above during the prewriting stage and then included the results with his paper. The following are some additional ideas for publishing.

- Combine your definition with those of your peers to create a class portfolio.
- Create a videotape with a voice-over narrative to explain what the concept means to you.

Standards for Evaluation

An extended definition
- clearly states the subject to be defined
- elaborates on the subject with detailed examples
- compares and contrasts different aspects of the subject
- has a well-developed introduction, body, and conclusion
- targets a specific audience through the choice of language and details

---

SkillBuilder

GRAMMAR FROM WRITING

Avoiding Illogical Comparisons

Missing words or illogical construction can make a comparison unclear, as this example shows.

Unclear
I'm more loyal to the softball team than my friends.

Clear
I'm more loyal to the softball team than my friends are.

Is the speaker more loyal to the team than to her friends? The first comparison is unclear.

GRAMMAR HANDBOOK

For more information about illogical comparisons, see page 919 of the Grammar Handbook.

Editing Checklist
- Are your comparisons worded clearly? Do they make sense?
- Do you use synonyms for your term where appropriate?

REFLECT & ASSESS

Looking at What You Learned
1. Compare your definition with other students' pieces. What do you like about the others? yours?
2. What did you learn that you can use in other kinds of writing?

 PORTFOLIO Write a note comparing your definition with others. Slip it into your portfolio.

WRITING FROM EXPERIENCE   579

SkillBuilder GRAMMAR FROM WRITING

AVOIDING ILLOGICAL COMPARISONS

Give students the following additional rules for keeping comparisons logical and clear:

- Always use *other* or *else* when comparing one thing to all other things of the same kind.
- State both parts of a comparison completely.

UNCLEAR: *The Nile is longer than any river.* (This implies that the Nile is not a river.)

CLEAR: *The Nile is longer than any other river.*

UNCLEAR: *Joanne likes music better than Fred.* (The implication is that Joanne likes music better than she likes Fred.)

CLEAR: *Joanne likes music better than Fred does.*

Application Have students correct the following incomplete comparisons:
1. Janet likes the book better than Liz.
2. Jim scored more goals than any member of the team.
3. Roy's computer is newer than Nathan.

Reteaching/Reinforcement
- *Grammar Mini-Lessons* copymasters p. 26, transparencies, p. 21

Illogical Comparisons, p. 635

THE LANGUAGE OF LITERATURE **TEACHER'S EDITION** 579

UNIT REVIEW

This feature allows students to reflect on what they have learned in Unit Four and to assess how well they have understood it. This feature provides students with multiple opportunities for self-assessment. You may also wish to use some of the activities to assess specific skills, such as speaking, listening, or cooperative learning.

Objectives

- To allow students to reflect on and assess their understanding of theme
- To allow students to reflect on and assess their understanding of literary concepts, such as theme and epic hero
- To provide students with the opportunity to assess and build their portfolios

REFLECTING ON THEME

OPTION 1

Set aside time for students to reread passages and to find examples of the difficulties of being a hero. Have them jot down in their notebooks ideas to use as springboards for a group discussion.

OPTION 2

Preview the creative and cooperative process of writing a script. Remind students that effective dialogue is based on characterization. Have students write dialogue based on their understanding of Homer's characterization of this heroic couple.

OPINION 3

Discuss with the students what they know about reporting the news, both print and broadcast news. Do reporters mold or reflect public opinion, or do their reports illustrate the effects of both kinds of influence? Have students form cooperative discussion groups and choose roles (direction giver, recorder, summarizer, integrator) that will facilitate the exchange of opinions about how a reporter would present the story of Odysseus' homecoming.

 Self-Assessment Ask students to record a list of Odysseus' heroic traits as well as a definition of "hero" in their notebooks.

REFLECT & ASSESS

UNIT FOUR: PORTRAIT OF A HERO

*Is Odysseus the kind of hero you expected?
To explore what you have learned about Odysseus' heroism,
choose one or more of the options in each
of the following sections.*

REFLECTING ON THEME

OPTION 1 **Heroism Isn't Easy** The quotation that opens this unit—"Heroism hurts and no one easily consents to be under its rule"—acknowledges the difficulties of being a hero. Review Odysseus' adventures in this unit to find examples of his being hurt by what he has to do and examples of his reluctance to act heroically sometimes.

OPTION 2 **How Do You Explain?** How do you think Odysseus would describe his adventures to his wife, Penelope? Would he tell her everything? Do you think Penelope would want to know everything? With a partner, role-play a conversation in which Odysseus and Penelope discuss where he's been since the Trojan War.

OPTION 3 **Odysseus on the News** Imagine that a reporter for the Ithaca News Service (INS) has managed to hide in Odysseus' house and see everything that happens when Odysseus returns. How might that reporter present Odysseus' homecoming to the general public? With a small group of classmates, discuss how the reporter might explain what happened. Whose side would the reporter be on—the suitors' or Odysseus'? How might the reporter's account of Odysseus' actions differ from Odysseus' own account?

Self-Assessment: Now that you have considered the complexity of Odysseus' heroism, write a definition of the term hero, *focusing on qualities that you think make Odysseus a prime example of a hero.*

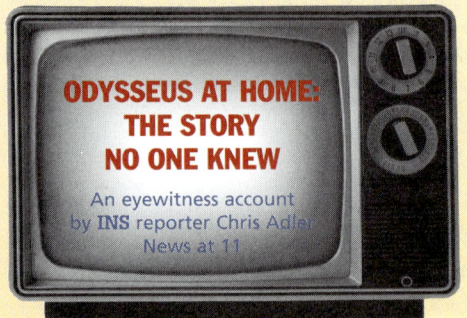

REVIEWING LITERARY CONCEPTS

OPTION 1 **Identifying Themes** One reason the Odyssey has appealed to so many people for such a long time is that it's more than just a good adventure story. It also contains universal themes—insights and lessons about human life. Most themes are not stated directly but only implied. Write down several themes that you can find in this unit's excerpts from the *Odyssey,* expressing each theme as a statement.

580 UNIT FOUR: PORTRAIT OF A HERO

OPTION 2 **Evaluating an Epic Hero** Review the definition of epic hero on page 507. Does Odysseus measure up to your idea of what the hero of an epic should be? On a graph like the one shown, rate his heroism in each of the episodes you have read from 1 (not heroic) to 10 (very heroic). Then plot a line showing the rises and falls of his heroism during his adventures.

 Self-Assessment: Three of the literary terms introduced in this unit are epic hero, epic simile, and epithet. Ask yourself how each of them relates to epic poetry. How does each element contribute to the effect an epic should have? Review the definition of epic on page 482.

PORTFOLIO BUILDING

- **QuickWrites** Some of the QuickWrites in this unit asked you to write about events and episodes from various characters' points of view. Choose one of your responses for your portfolio. In your cover note, tell what new ideas or insights you gained from such a writing assignment.

- **Writing About Literature** Writing a parody may have given you new insights into the joys and difficulties of writing to make others laugh. It may also have given you a new understanding of the work you were imitating. Write a short piece in which you describe the challenges of writing a parody. What did you learn about the structure of the *Odyssey* as you wrote? Add your brief essay, along with the parody, to your portfolio.

- **Writing from Experience** You have now written an extended definition in which you explained an idea that may mean different things to different people. Ask at least two people what the term you defined means to them. Then show those people your definition and ask them whether they agree with your explanation. Write a brief note describing how they responded and what you learned from sharing your definition. If you have chosen to place your definition in your portfolio, include your reflections with it.

- **Personal Choice** Some of the activities in this unit asked for the creation of products; others suggested performances. Choose an activity that you think gave you extra insight into the *Odyssey*. (If you prefer, choose a piece of writing in which you discovered something special about the epic—something you didn't learn from the questions or from the class discussion.) Write a cover note explaining what special insight you gained.

Self-Assessment: Now that you have some writing pieces and records of activities in your portfolio, look them over. Do you see any improvement in your work? Would you like to replace any of your earlier choices?

SETTING GOALS

Now that you are more than halfway through this book, what expectations do you have for the remaining lessons? Do you think you'll polish your writing skills? Do you expect to improve your skill in interpreting literary works and explaining your interpretations to others?

REFLECT & ASSESS **581**

PORTFOLIO BUILDING

Remind students that their purpose in writing from various points of view, writing a parody, and writing an extended definition is the same as a professional writer's purpose: to convey a message about a lesson learned. Like Odysseus, a writer who dares to experiment and take chances in his or her writing is striving to learn the lessons of effective creative writing.

Self-Assessment Suggest that students' experience in writing from the third-person point of view will help them make an objective evaluation of the work in their portfolio. Ask them to draw on that experience to review and assess their writing at this time, which marks the halfway point in the text. Mention that it is a natural point for analyzing the growth and development of their skills as readers and writers.

REVIEWING LITERARY CONCEPTS

OPTION 1

Remind students that a writer's theme consists of the lessons and generalizations about life that he or she wishes to convey. Take time to talk about how genres such as fables or parables (e.g., "The Grasshopper and the Ant") present simple lessons.

OPTION 2

Form the class into small groups to decide what standards to use to determine whether Odysseus measures up to students' ideas of an epic hero. Do they think that the daring, verve, and courage that Odysseus demonstrated in surviving his perilous journey earn him the title of epic hero? Lead students to realize that all evaluations involve the application of both quantitative and qualitative measures. See also Unit Four Resource Book, p. 49.

Self-Assessment Guide students to see that using an epithet such as "Son of Laertes and the gods of old" to address Odysseus conveys the message that he is a superhuman epic hero. Similarly, the use of an epic simile testifies to his extraordinary courage and superhuman strength in navigating the turbulent sea and further reinforces the image of Odysseus as an epic hero. In essence, the use of epic simile and epithet lends credibility to the image of Odysseus as an epic hero.

SETTING GOALS

Tell students that you won't take no for an answer to any one of the questions. Inform them that you expect them to polish their writing skills, learn new techniques, improve their skill in interpreting literary works, and explain their interpretations to others. Encourage them to add other goals to this list and to refer to the list after they reflect on and assess what they have learned in Unit Five.

UNIT FIVE

UNIT THEMES

Unit Five

Mysteries and Deceptions In Unit Five, students will read selections that reveal lies, puzzles, contradictions, and hidden meanings encountered by a variety of characters. This unit contains two parts: Part 1, "False Pretenses," and Part 2, "Jumping to Conclusions." Selections in both parts contribute to the unit theme by recounting experiences in which characters learn that things are not always what they appear.

Part 1

False Pretenses Selections in Part 1 reveal what lies beneath the surface of situations. For example, in *Trifles*, two women discover the motive for a murder by examining items that appear insignificant at first.

Part 2

Jumping to Conclusions Part 2 explores the consequences of judging situations by their appearances. For example, in "The Necklace," a woman's assumption that a necklace is genuine leads her and her husband to great hardship and toil.

UNIT FIVE

Mysteries & Deceptions

A lie hides the truth.

A story tries to find it.

Paula Fox
Writer and professor

Voice I (1963), George Tooker. Egg tempera on gesso panel, 19½" × 17½", courtesy of Marisa Del Re Gallery, New York.

583

Exploring Theme

To help students explore the connections among the art, the quotation, and the unit theme, have them consider the following questions:

1. When you think about mysteries and deceptions, what is the first thing that comes to your mind? *(Accept all reasonable responses.)*

2. What do you think Paula Fox means when says that "a story tries to find truth?" *(Possible responses: A story is a writer's attempt to express something he or she feels is true. The writer tries hard to go beneath the surface of its characters to show what the characters' true motives might or might not be.)*

3. What atmosphere or mood does the painting evoke? *(Possible response: mystery, fear, anxiety, deception, futility, ambiguity)* What do you think the images of the two men convey? *(Possible responses: One man is trying to communicate with another man, but the door seems to be a barrier to what the man is saying; one man seems trapped behind the door and is pleading for help; one man seems to be trying to reveal something important to the waiting listener.)*

4. What kinds of stories and experiences might you expect to read about in this unit? *(Possible responses: mystery stories; detective stories; lies and misunderstandings; puzzles that characters will try to solve)*

5. Discuss a time in your own life when you came up against a mysterious or puzzling situation. *(Responses will vary.)*

Art Note

Voice I by George Tooker
Voice I is the first in a series of paintings American artist George Tooker (1920–) executed between 1962 and 1972. At that time, Tooker was greatly concerned with the breakdown in communication he saw in American society, and this series of paintings reflects his absorption with this theme. He has pointed out in interviews that the two figures on either side of the door are identical.

Reading the Art Why do you think the two men try to talk through an open door, rather than walking around it? Do you think the listener can hear and understand what the speaker is saying? Why?

THE LANGUAGE OF LITERATURE TEACHER'S EDITION **583**

UNIT FIVE
Part 1 Skills Trace

ML DENOTES MINI-LESSON IN TEACHER'S EDITION

Selections	Reading Skills and Strategies	Literary Concepts	Writing Opportunities	Speaking, Listening, and Viewing
FICTION **One Ordinary Day, with Peanuts** Shirley Jackson		Irony, PE p. 596 Situational irony, PE p. 596 Mood, PE p. 596 Fiction, ML TE p. 587 Reviewing third-person limited point of view, ML TE p. 591	Write about a time when you were surprised to learn something new, PE p. 585 Create a cast list, PE p. 596 Write a program teaser, PE p. 596 Combining sentences, ML TE p. 590	Act out interviews, ML TE p. 593 Report, TE p. 597
FICTION **The Last Boast** Dorothy M. Johnson		Extended metaphor, PE p. 603 Dramatic irony, PE p. 602 Reviewing conflict, ML TE p. 602	Write a paragraph, PE p. 598 Compose a note, PE p. 603 Write a character sketch, PE p. 603 Outline a short story, PE p. 603 Draft two summary statements, PE p. 603 Show, don't tell, ML TE p. 600	Discuss outlaws, PE p. 604 Tall tale, PE p. 604 Debate issue, PE p. 603 Group discussion, TE p. 603 Dramatic presentation, TE p. 604
FICTION **Full Circle** Sue Grafton	Understanding the detective story, PE p. 606 What is a detective story? PE p. 606 Predicting the solution to the crime, PE p. 606 Using a reading log, PE p. 606	Plot, PE p. 620 Rising action, PE p. 620 Exposition, PE p. 620 Climax, PE p. 620 Falling action, PE p. 620 Fiction, ML TE p. 607 Reviewing description, ML TE p. 608	Draft a different ending, PE p. 620 Write a plot outline, PE p. 620 List the clues, PE p. 620 Using similes, ML TE p. 609 Write an accident report, TE p. 621	Speeches, ML TE p. 619 Solve the mystery, TE p. 620 Role-play, TE p. 621
POETRY **O What Is That Sound** W. H. Auden	Interpreting dialogue, PE p. 622 Ballad, PE p. 622	Ballad, PE p. 622 Rhythm, PE p. 625 Suspense, PE p. 625 Poetry, ML TE p. 623 Reviewing stanza, ML TE p. 624	Write a letter, PE p. 625 Write a dialogue, PE p. 625 Draft a ballad, PE p. 625	Discuss conclusions, PE p. 625 Listen to music, PE p. 626 Listen to discuss a ballad, PE p. 626
DRAMA **Trifles** Susan Glaspell	Making inferences, PE p. 627	Dramatic irony, PE p. 641 Symbol, PE p. 641 Drama, ML TE p. 629 One-act play, PE p. 641 Reviewing dialogue, ML TE p. 633	List main facts on a crime report, PE p. 641 Write a news account, PE p. 641 Create a list of props and costumes, PE p. 642 Informal English, ML TE p. 639	Stage a trial, PE p. 641 Demonstrate knotting, PE p. 642 Present a musical score, PE p. 642 Read clues and solve a crime, PE p. 642 Scientific observation, ML TE p. 631
FICTION ON YOUR OWN **The Chaser** John Collier			Double-entry journal, TE p. 644 Writing a sequel, TE p. 645 Creating an advertisement, TE p. 646	Paired and choral reading, TE p. 644

Writing	Reading Skills and Strategies	Literary Concepts	Writing Opportunities	Speaking, Listening, and Viewing
WRITING ABOUT LITERATURE **Criticism**	Analyzing point of view, PE pp. 648–649 Responding to literature, PE pp. 650–653	Analyzing point of view, PE pp. 648–649 Plot, PE pp. 650–651	Write a paragraph, PE p. 649 Write two different accounts, PE p. 649 Using a different point of view, PE p. 649	Viewing a newscast, PE p. 654 Interpreting a news story, PE p. 654 Discussion, PE p. 654 Discussing issues, PE p. 655

Grammar, Usage, Mechanics, and Spelling	Multimodal Learning	Research and Study Skills	Vocabulary
Adjective and adverb phrases, ML TE p. 589	Interview, ML TE p. 597 Report, TE p. 597	Research George Washington Carver, TE p. 597	ambiguously genial impertinent insatiable repress
Compound-complex sentences, ML TE p. 601	Paint a scene, PE p. 604 Make up a tall tale, PE p. 604 Design a wanted poster, PE p. 604 Different fonts on the computer, PE p. 604 Choose song/music for presentation, TE p. 604 Paint a scene, TE p. 604	Investigate the life of a legendary outlaw, PE p. 604	
Using *sit* and *set*, ML TE p. 610	Create a brochure, PE p. 621 Use desktop publishing program on computer, PE p. 621 Draw a sketch, TE p. 621 Role-play, TE p. 621	Research the field of forensic science, PE p. 621 Notetaking, ML TE p. 614	brevity harass despondently inexplicable dispel skewed egotistical sullen enigmatic wary
	Sketch a picture, PE p. 626 Choose/compose a piece of music, PE p. 626 Find a ballad, PE p. 626 Suspenseful music, TE p. 626	Research which armies have worn scarlet, TE p. 626 Research when use of cavalry horses was discontinued, TE p. 626 Research clothing, hair styles, and furniture of story's time, TE p. 626	
Dash in dialogue, ML TE p. 637	Create two diagrams, PE p. 642 Graphics program, PE p. 642 Prepare a musical score, PE p. 642 Make up a mystery game, PE p. 642 Make a model of a set, PE p. 642 Telephone communication skills, ML TE p. 630 Period paintings/photos, TE p. 642 Mood music, TE p. 642	Investigate knotting, PE p. 642	abashed comprehension covert facetiously preoccupied
	Creating an advertisement, TE p. 646		

Grammar, Usage, Mechanics, and Spelling	Multimodal Learning	Research and Study Skills	Media Literacy
Correcting vague pronoun references, PE p. 649 Using past participles correctly, PE p. 653 Active and passive, PE p. 653	Viewing a newscast, PE p. 654 Interpreting a news story, PE p. 654 Discussion, PE p. 654 Discussing issues, PE p. 655	Criticizing literature, PE pp. 650–653 Formulating questions, PE p. 655	Analyzing an issue, PE pp. 654–655

UNIT FIVE
Part 2 Skills Trace

 DENOTES MINI-LESSON IN TEACHER'S EDITION

Selections	Reading Skills and Strategies	Literary Concepts	Writing Opportunities	Speaking, Listening, and Viewing
FICTION **The Necklace** Guy de Maupassant		Main character, PE p. 667 Minor characters, PE p. 667 Symbol, PE p. 667 Reviewing plot, ML TE p. 660	Description of what you value, PE p. 657 Draft an epilogue, PE p. 666 Notes for a speech, PE p. 666 Write a theme, PE p. 666 Specific examples, ML TE p. 662 List symbols of status and wealth, TE p. 666	Small group discussion, PE p. 666 Prepare/present a skit, PE p. 667 Pantomime, ML TE p. 661
NONFICTION **The Great Taos Bank Robbery** Tony Hillerman	Visualizing, PE p. 669	Verbal irony, PE p. 678 Author's purpose, PE p. 678 Reviewing setting, ML TE p. 672 Nonfiction, ML TE p. 674	List of questions, PE p. 678 Draft a confession, PE p. 678 Create a dialogue, PE p. 678 Address the reader, ML TE p. 675	Present a skit, PE p. 678 Discuss verbal irony, TE p. 678 Attend court session, TE p. 679
FICTION **The Mountain** Martin J. Hamer		Theme, PE p. 687 Metaphor, PE p. 687 Reviewing conflict, ML TE p. 684	Write about stereotyped assumptions, PE p. 680 Compare incident to story, PE p. 680 Write a proverb, PE p. 686 Draft a personal narrative, PE p. 686 Write a rap or folk song, PE p. 687 Use sentence fragments for effect, ML TE p. 683	Present a reading, PE p. 687 Debate, TE p. 686 Listen to tapes, TE p. 687
FICTION **Everybody Knows Tobie** Daniel Garza	Denotation, PE p. 688 Connotation, PE p. 688	Setting, PE p. 696 Reviewing dialogue, ML TE p. 694	Create a character sketch, PE p. 696 Draft an essay, PE p. 696 First-person point of view, ML TE p. 695	Small group discussion, PE p. 686 Debate teams, PE p. 687 Act out an interview, PE p. 697 Oral history, ML TE p. 693 Watch TV news programs for insight, TE p. 693
POETRY ON YOUR OWN **Hanging Fire** Audre Lorde				

Writing	Reading Skills and Strategies	Literary Concepts	Writing Opportunities	Speaking, Listening, and Viewing
WRITING FROM EXPERIENCE **Report**			Writing a research paper, PE pp. 700–707 Drafting, PE pp. 704–705 Crediting source, PE p. 705 Revising and publishing, PE pp. 706–707	

583c UNIT FIVE MYSTERIES AND DECEPTIONS

Grammar, Usage, Mechanics, and Spelling	Multimodal Learning	Research and Study Skills	Vocabulary
Elliptical clauses, ML TE p. 659	Encyclopedia program or on-line service on computer, PE p. 667 Math question, PE p. 667 Skit, PE p. 667 Budgeting funds, ML TE p. 664 Graphic aids, TE p. 666	Research materials used to make artificial jewels, PE p. 667	adulation gamut aghast pauper askew prospect clad ruinous exorbitant vexation
Subject-verb agreement, ML TE p. 671	Contact local district attorney's office, TE p. 679 Attend a court session, TE p. 679	Research procedures by which a case is brought to trial, TE p. 679	authenticity impeccable conformity influx depreciate irreverence disoriented litany fiasco tolerant
Appositives, ML TE p. 682	Computer/personal narrative, PE p. 686 Write a rap or folk song, PE p. 687 Sketch a map, PE p. 687 Debate, TE p. 686		
Troublesome modifiers: *Good* and *well*, ML TE p. 690	Contact local AFL–CIO or VFW offices, TE p. 697	Research labor leader Cesar Chavez and how he improved working conditions for migrant workers, PE p. 697 Taking objective tests: Antonyms, ML TE p. 691	
	Conduct a poll, TE p. 699		

Grammar, Usage, Mechanics, and Spelling	Multimodal Learning	Research and Study Skills	Media Literacy
Punctuating a works cited list, PE p. 707	Analyzing a science illustration, PE p. 700 Analyzing different articles, PE p. 701	On-line resources, PE p. 703 Taking notes, PE p. 703	Analyzing a science illustration, PE p. 700 Analyzing different articles, PE p. 701 On-line resources, PE p. 703

UNIT FIVE
Recommended Resources

ENRICHMENT   RESEARCH

✓ Recommended Novels and Play

LITERATURE CONNECTIONS WITH SOURCEBOOK FOR TEACHERS

A Midsummer Night's Dream by William Shakespeare and Related Readings

Thematic Link This play tells of the hilarious effects of enchantment on four lovers, a fairy queen, and a weaver.
About the Author William Shakespeare (1564–1616) is one of the greatest of all poets and playwrights. He excelled equally at tragedy, comedy, and historical writing.
Other Works by William Shakespeare *Hamlet, Prince of Denmark; Julius Caesar; Macbeth; The Tragedy of Romeo and Juliet; Antony and Cleopatra*

A Christmas Carol by Charles Dickens

Thematic Link This classic "ghost story of Christmas" portrays the redemption of a miser, whose recollections of his long-forgotten past show him the error of his ways. It is a superb example of Dickens's vivid and dramatic prose.
About the Author Since the publication of his first novel, Charles Dickens (1812–1870) has continued to have an enormous popular and critical following. Because of this, he accomplished a great deal towards social reform by making the public aware of the plight of the Victorian poor and dispossessed.
Other Works by Charles Dickens *The Pickwick Papers, Oliver Twist, Nicholas Nickleby, Bleak House, Hard Times, A Tale of Two Cities, Great Expectations*

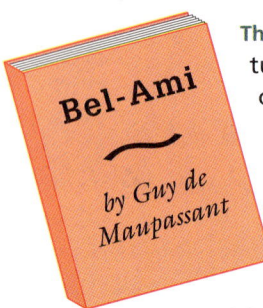

Bel-Ami by Guy de Maupassant

Thematic Link This novel chronicles the fortunes of a young Parisian journalist, caught up in the deceptions of French society.
About the Author Gustave Flaubert encouraged the young de Maupassant (1850–1893) in his career. In the short time span of 11 years, de Maupassant published six novels, dozens of articles, and 300 short stories.
Other Works by Guy de Maupassant *Scenes de la vie Parisienne, Pierre et Jean*

The Haunting of Hill House by Shirley Jackson

Thematic Link This book reveals Jackson's fascination with the supernatural.
About the Author Shirley Jackson (born 1919), one of America's most popular storytellers, achieved unexpectedly wide notoriety when her short story "The Lottery" appeared in the *New Yorker* magazine.
Other Works by Shirley Jackson *Hangsaman, Raising Demons*

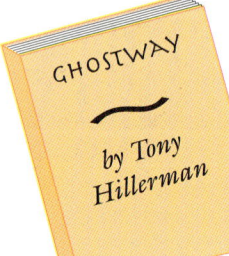

Ghostway by Tony Hillerman

Thematic Link Jim Chee, an officer in the Navajo Tribal Police, follows the trail of a mysterious killer.
About the Author Tony Hillerman writes detective mysteries set mostly in the Navajo reservation in New Mexico.
Other Works by Tony Hillerman *Talking God, Scared Clowns, Finding Moon*

Professional Development   TEACHING THE NOVEL

Auden, W.H. "The I Without a Self," *The Dyer's Hand*. NY: Vintage, 1989.

Lorde, Audre. *Sister Outsider*. Trumansburg, NY: Crossing Press, 1984.

Oppenheimer, Judy. *Private Demons: The Life of Shirley Jackson*. NY: G.P. Putnam's Sons, 1989.

Osborne, Charles. *W.H. Auden: The Life of a Poet*. NY: M. Evans and Company, 1975.

Tolstoy, Leo. *Guy de Maupassant*. Brooklyn, NY: Hashell Booksellers, Inc., 1974.

CROSS-CURRICULAR TEACHING   PROFESSIONAL DEVELOPMENT

Recommended Readings in Cross-Curricular Areas

SOCIAL STUDIES

The Yellow Emperor's Classic Book of Medicine by Maoshing Ni (1995) An informative perspective on an alternative to Western medicine. Links to John Collier's "The Chaser."

Western Badmen by Dorothy Johnson (1970) A historical sampling of outlaws from the Old West. Links to Dorothy Johnson's "The Last Boast."

"Does Bilingual Teaching Work?" *U.S. News* (September 25, 1995) p. 44. Useful information on what bilingual programs in American schools accomplish. Links to Daniel Garza's "Everybody Knows Tobie."

The Black Americans: A History in Their Own Words 1619–1983 by Milton Meltzer, ed. (1983) This book conveys the agonies of slavery and the struggle for freedom through the voices of African Americans. Links to "The Mountain" and "The Pocketbook Game."

Professional Development — CROSS-CURRICULAR INSTRUCTION

Dilg, Mary A. "The Opening of the American Mind: Challenges in the Cross-Curricular Teaching of Literature," *English Journal.* 84:3 (March 1995) 18–25.

Gutmann, Amy. *Democratic Education.* Princeton, NJ: Princeton University Press, 1987.

Tollefson, James W., ed. *Power and Inequality in Language Education.* Cambridge, England: Cambridge University Press, 1995.

Recommended Media Resources

THE LANGUAGE OF LITERATURE

ELECTRONIC LIBRARY
CD-ROM
Additional literature selections for Unit Five can be found on the Electronic Library CD-ROM.

LASERLINKS
Videodisc, Gr. 9
See *LaserLinks Teacher's Source Book,* page 42, for overview of Unit Five.

AUDIO LIBRARY
Tapes
Unit Five: Mysteries and Deceptions Gr. 9, Tapes 12–14: Sides A & B

WRITING COACH
Writing Coach Software: Writing About Literature— Critical Response, Research Paper

OUTSIDE RESOURCES

Films/Videos/Film Strips/Audiocassettes
The Necklace, video, Knowledge Unlimited/Britannica Films, 1981, (20 minutes).
Come Along with Me (by Shirley Jackson) video, Coronet/MTI, 1986.
The Lottery and Other Stories, audiocassette, Caedmon.
Tony Hillerman Reads Coyote Waits, audiocassette, New Letters, 1993, (30 minutes).

Internet Resources
McDougal Littell Literature Center at http://www.hmco.com/mcdougal/lit

Professional Development — TEACHING WITH TECHNOLOGY

Holland, Holly. "A Strong Heart at a Technology-Rich Georgia School," *Electronic Learning* 14:8 (May/June 1995) 36.

Marcus, Stephen. "The Only Technology You Really Need," *Quarterly of the National Writing Project and The Center for the Study of Writing and Literacy.* 15:2 (Spring 1993) 19–21.

Electronic Learning: The Magazine for Technology and School Change. Scholastic Inc., 555 Broadway, NY, NY 10003.

UNIT FIVE
Professional Enrichment

Motivating Students through Reading Aloud

Catherine Ann Ecroyd

> The author of this article discusses a fundamental activity for use in any English classroom.

Motivating students to read—the bane of many an English teacher's existence. How many of us have coveted the elementary teacher's students? Those eager faces streaming into school every morning, enjoying school, loving learning, wanting to read. . . . How many secondary English students have retained that enjoyment of school, that love of learning, that desire to read? The study of literature has value and should not be neglected, but unless we somehow instill (or reinstate, as the case may be) the motivation to learn through reading, our students will be learners and readers in school only, not lifelong learners and lifelong readers. And, as their teachers, we will have failed them.

While elementary reading teachers have long known the value of reading aloud to their students, secondary English teachers have often seen this as a "babyish" time-waster or have interpreted oral reading as *students'* reading orally. While this type of oral reading has been found to raise reading test scores, teachers' reading aloud to students who listen without following along also has value.

Jim Trelease, perhaps the United States' best known advocate of reading aloud to children, says that reading aloud is motivational, that "desire is the 'lead role.'" He calls reading aloud "advertising"—a commercial for the joy of reading. Unfortunately, it is an advertisement sorely needed in most of today's high schools.

One of the biggest shocks I experienced as a new English teacher was the antagonism toward reading which many of my students displayed. Perhaps because reading is so vital a part of my life and well-being, the shock is still there even after 16 years of teaching. . . . Joyce Carol Oates calls reading a "phenomenon . . . by which we slip, involuntarily, often helplessly, into another's skin; another's voice; another's soul." I am saddened by the numbers of people who do not know these pleasures—44 percent of all United States adults do not read even one book during an entire year—and, at the same time, challenged by these statistics. In response to this challenge, I give my students as many choices and as much control over their reading as possible . . . and I read aloud.

In *Voices of Readers,* an NCTE publication devoted to giving us "hints of how to go about developing and encouraging readers within our educational and societal framework," G. Robert Carlsen and Anne Sherrill devote a section to oral reading by the secondary English teacher. Occasionally, the reactions to these readings are negative, but the majority are positive, using descriptions such as "unforgettable" and "incredible."

My own experience is similar. When I am reading a book aloud to my class, often the first question of the day is, "Are you reading today?" Other frequent comments are "Let's read first" and "Don't stop now—read more." In addition, students are often motivated to choose other books by the same author to read on their own. This fall, one of my students read every book by M. E. Kerr in our school library after I read *Gentlehands* (1978) to her class. Last year, a student who knew that I had cut the narrative between the grandfather and grandson, wanted to read all of William Goldman's *Princess Bride* (1973). Similarly, when I read John Gunther's *Death Be Not Proud* (1949), several students checked out the book so they could read the letters and Francis' entry at the end—which I had edited out in my oral reading. Thus, reading aloud can successfully motivate students to read on their own.

For years I have read to all my English classes except honors English. I rationalized this omission, saying we had "too much to do," as if reading to honors students were a waste of time. Last year, however, my honors class begged me to read *The Princess Bride* to them, for I had already read it to my other classes. It's a long novel, and I truly did not have time. Last year, however, I "found" Gunther's *Death Be Not Proud* over Thanksgiving vacation. On January 2, I began reading it aloud. Although not all of my 46 honors students cared for the book, few did not enjoy being read to. Unfortunately, many of these same honors students profess not to enjoy reading. . . . Reading aloud to them, however, was an enjoyable experience, as the following excerpts from response journals indicate:

At first I did [not] feel like listening to your reading, because of Julie [a friend who died only a few weeks before]. But [now that] you [have] started the book, it kind of makes me feel good because Julie was kind of like Johnny. She always seemed to put a smile on everyone's face when she was around.

         Atanya

I don't know if I was a teacher that I would read Death Be Not Proud. *It is a pretty emotional story and a few people may not be able to deal with it. However, reading a book, in general, gives the students time to relax during a hectic day . . . I did like the time just to sit in a desk and not be thinking about doing schoolwork or anything.*

         Hayden

High school students are under a lot of stress; they don't have much time for pleasurable reading, even if they enjoy reading. Reading aloud can motivate students to make time to read on their own.

Students see teachers as their reading role models. When students listen to a teacher read, they are receiving a message that reading is important; conversely, students may [decide that reading isn't important if no time is made for it.] Students who are "at risk in reading" are quick to pick up on this value system, misguided as it may be. These are the students who avoid reading whenever possible. . . . Thus, even honors students may be "at risk readers," or readers whose reading is motivated not by pleasure but by academic success achieved by "getting through" the coursework. Students at risk in reading will not value reading per se unless they believe their teachers value reading. One way for teachers to "practice what they preach" is to read aloud books they have read and enjoyed themselves.

Atwell and Trelease have developed lists of the do's and don'ts of reading aloud. I however, have only a few suggestions.

1. Read aloud only literature that you have enjoyed yourself.
2. Read "dramatically." Be a storyteller in the traditional sense.
3. Read at the beginning of the hour for no more than fifteen minutes. This ensures that you, not the dismissal bell, have control over how long you read.
4. Make sure students are listening—no note taking or other work allowed.

Trelease suggests that as teachers, we need not tie everything we read aloud into the curriculum. To a certain extent, I believe this to be true. However, at the secondary level, when we see our students often less than one hour per day, we may feel guilty about spending what can add up to a considerable amount of time on a work which we have not tied to our curriculum. I, personally, tie everything into my curriculum—sometimes loosely, sometimes with more structure. For example, I have built entire units around *Go Ask Alice* and Charles Dickens' *Christmas Carol.* Reader-response journals were the primary means of writing about Paul Zindel's *Pigman's Legacy* (1980) and short stories from Robert Cormier's *Eight Plus One* (1980) and Donald R. Gallo's *Sixteen* (1985). Students wrote in response journals through the reading of Kerr's *Gentlehands,* then wrote a paper personalizing one of the maxims stated by Grandpa Trenker in the book. After reading Goldman's *Princess Bride,* students viewed the video (1981) and wrote a comparison-contrast paper. As students listened to Gunther's *Death Be Not Proud,* they wrote in their journals; after the book was completed, these same students interpreted John Donne's "Death Be Not Proud" and discussed its relevance to Gunther's memoirs. Acrostic poems were written after reading Lord Dunsany's "Two Bottles of Relish" (1947); found poems were written after hearing Edgar Allan Poe's "The Black Cat." Related assignments should be as varied as the works themselves. Activities depend upon the difficulty of the work and the limitations of the class—as with any piece of literature. . . .

Copyrighted material reprinted with permission.

UNIT FIVE
Starting Points for Unit Projects

The following suggestions will help you initiate individual and group projects during the course of this unit.

Creating a Magazine

GROUP LITERATURE PROJECT Ask small groups of students to select a real-life mystery that has not yet been solved and to work on it as armchair investigators. The mystery might be an unexplained disappearance or phenomenon, or an act by an unknown perpetrator. It might come from science, history, current events, or students' communities. Have students compile mysteries into an illustrated class magazine of the strange and unknown.

Designing a Game

GROUP DESIGN PROJECT Ask groups of three to five students to invent a game that involves solving an unanswered question. Possible game types include board games, word games, question games, and role-playing games. The game might involve tasks such as identifying a criminal, guessing a word, or using clues to locate a hidden object. Ask students to create a game package, and allow time for the groups to play each other's games.

Displaying an Art Exhibit

GROUP ART PROJECT Have students prepare a bulletin board display of art that intentionally tries to deceive the viewer. This might include *trompe l'oeil* paintings that try to copy objects so minutely that the viewer believes them to be real rather than painted, surrealistic art by painters such as Salvador Dalí, the graphic designs of M. C. Escher, and three-dimensional "magic eye" paintings (which do retain their 3-D properties when photocopied).

Keeping a Log of Observations

WRITING PROJECT Ask students to keep a log in which they record, as completely as they can from memory, lists of details of objects and environments around them, such as room furnishings, landscapes, individuals' clothing and appearance, and the contents of store shelves or desks. During the course of a week, each student should make at least one entry per day, each on a different subject. At the end of the week, have students discuss whether they see any improvement in their powers of observation.

Performing a Magic Trick

PERFORMANCE PROJECT Invite each student to learn one magic trick and perform it for the class. Students can go to the school or public library to consult books on magic tricks, or they can visit a magic shop to find tricks. Give students a specific amount of time—perhaps a week—to learn their tricks. Students may perform individually or with a partner. Give students the option of revealing how the trick was done or of keeping it a secret.

Presenting an Oral Report

RESEARCH/HISTORY PROJECT Encourage pairs or groups of students to find out about people who have gained fame or affected history through deception. Subjects might include real-life spies, magicians, and individuals who have falsely claimed professional qualifications. Students should ask the school or public librarian for help in locating sources. Places to look for inspiration might include the film *The Great Impostor* (1960; starring Tony Curtis as real-life impostor Ferdinand Demara) and the book *The Duke of Deception* by Geoffrey Wolff, a memoir of the author's father. Invite students to give oral reports, using photographs and other visual aids.

Family and Community Involvement

Family

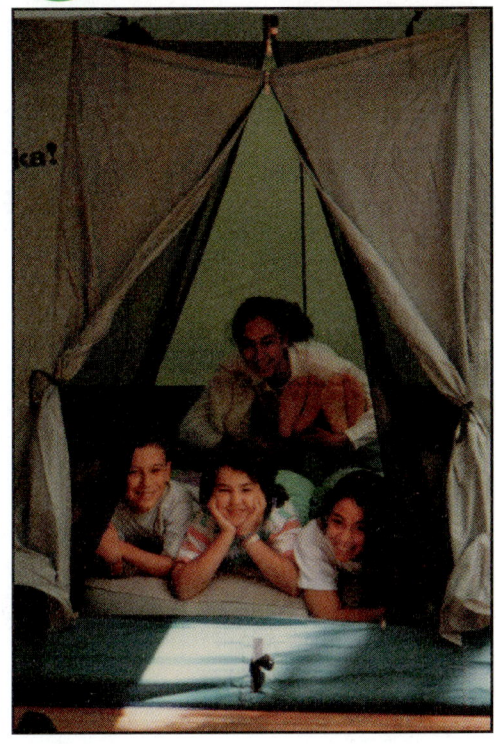

The following Copymasters provide activities that students can take home and complete with a parent or other family member.

OPTION 1: WRITE A MYSTERY

- **Connection** All of the selections in Unit Five relate a mystery or the results of a deception.
- **Activity** *Copymaster 1* Students and family members can work together to write or tell a mystery story. They might create their own idea, or they might use a newspaper or television report on an unsolved bank robbery or other mystery as their starting point.

OPTION 2: WATCH A VIDEO

- **Connection** Some of the selections in Unit Five deal with the importance of collecting information to solve a mystery or reveal a deception.
- **Activity** *Copymaster 2* Students and family members should watch a movie that portrays the collection of evidence to solve a crime, such as a Sherlock Holmes mystery. After the film, they can discuss the need to look beyond first impressions and the importance of the most seemingly important clues.

OPTION 3: TAKE A WALK

- **Connection** Many of the selections in Unit Five explore the importance of observation and solving mysteries.
- **Activity** *Copymaster 3* Students and family members can plan to take a walk around the neighborhood or some other familiar place, each writing observations about people, things, and events seen. After the walk, they should compare their observations to see who noticed what and note the differences between or among observations.

Community

OPTION 1

- **Connection** The selections in Unit Five deal with people searching for answers.
- **Activity** Invite a member of the local police department to explain how crimes are investigated. Encourage your visitor to demonstrate evidence-gathering techniques such as collecting fingerprints or examining footprints.

OPTION 2

- **Connection** Many of the selections in Unit Five examine the problem of identifying what is real and what is not real.
- **Activity** Invite a local jeweler to explain and demonstrate the differences between real and synthetic gems. Have students find out how Madame Loisel would have been able to tell if the necklace she borrowed contained real or fake gems.

OPTION 3

- **Connection** One of the selections in Unit Five examines how mistaken identity results in discrimination.
- **Activity** Invite a spokesperson for a civil rights agency to discuss what the law guarantees, including freedom from service, housing, and employment discrimination. Encourage students to share any experiences they have had with discrimination.

UNIT FIVE
Part 1 Lesson Planner

TIME ALLOTMENTS SHOWN ARE APPROXIMATE. DEPENDING ON YOUR GOALS AND THE NEEDS OF YOUR STUDENTS, YOU MAY WISH TO ALLOW MORE OR LESS TIME FOR CERTAIN PORTIONS OF THE LESSON.

Table of Contents	Discussion	Previewing the Selection	Reading the Selection
PART OPENER **False Pretenses** page 582	**20 MINUTES** • Reflect on the part theme		
SELECTION **One Ordinary Day, with Peanuts** page 586 EASY		**20 MINUTES** • PERSONAL CONNECTION • LITERARY CONNECTION • WRITING CONNECTION	**40 MINUTES** • Introduce vocabulary • Read pp. 586–594 (9 pp.)
SELECTION **The Last Boast** page 599 AVERAGE		**20 MINUTES** • PERSONAL CONNECTION • HISTORICAL CONNECTION • WRITING CONNECTION	**20 MINUTES** • Introduce vocabulary • Read pp. 599–602 (4 pp.)
SELECTION **Full Circle** page 607 CHALLENGING		**20 MINUTES** • PERSONAL CONNECTION • GEOGRAPHICAL CONNECTION • READING CONNECTION: Understanding the detective story	**50 MINUTES** • Introduce vocabulary • Read pp. 607–618 (12 pp.)
SELECTION **O What Is That Sound** page 623 AVERAGE		**20 MINUTES** • PERSONAL CONNECTION • HISTORICAL CONNECTION • READING CONNECTION: Interpreting dialogue	**10 MINUTES** • Read pp. 623–624 (2 pp.)
SELECTION **Trifles** page 628 CHALLENGING		**20 MINUTES** • PERSONAL CONNECTION • HISTORICAL CONNECTION • READING CONNECTION: Making inferences	**60 MINUTES** • Introduce vocabulary • Read pp. 628–640 (13 pp.)
FICTION ON YOUR OWN **The Chaser** page 644 AVERAGE			**20 MINUTES** • Read pp. 644–647 (4 pp.)

Writing	Writer's Style	Prewriting	Drafting and Revising
WRITING ABOUT LITERATURE **Criticism**	**20 MINUTES**	**25 MINUTES**	**60 MINUTES**

Time estimates assume in-class work. You may wish to assign some of these stages as homework.

Responding to the Selection

FROM PERSONAL RESPONSE TO CRITICAL ANALYSIS	OR	ANOTHER PATHWAY	LITERARY CONCEPTS	QUICKWRITES
60 MINUTES				
• Discussion questions	OR	• Cooperative learning (theme)	• Situational irony • Mood	• Cast list • Program teaser
30 MINUTES				
• Discussion questions	OR	• Cooperative learning (summary statements)	• Extended metaphor • Dramatic irony	• Note • Character sketch • Short story
60 MINUTES				
• Discussion questions	OR	• Cooperative learning (solving the case)	• Plot • Exposition • Climax • Rising action • Falling action	• Ending • Plot
50 MINUTES				
• Discussion questions	OR	• Cooperative learning (poem)	• Rhythm	• Letter • Dialogue • Ballad
60 MINUTES				
• Discussion questions	OR	• Cooperative learning (trial)	• Dramatic irony • Symbol	• Crime report • News account

Extension Activities

ALTERNATIVE ACTIVITIES	LITERARY LINKS	CRITIC'S CORNER	THE WRITER'S STYLE	ACROSS THE CURRICULUM	ART CONNECTION	WORDS TO KNOW	BIOGRAPHY
60 MINUTES							
✔	✔				✔	✔	
20 MINUTES							
✔				HISTORY FOLKLORE	✔	✔	
20 MINUTES							
			✔	SCIENCE	✔	✔	
20 MINUTES							
✔	✔		✔				✔
60 MINUTES							
✔	✔	✔	✔	THEATER ARTS	✔	✔	✔

Publishing and Reflecting

25 MINUTES

Grammar in Context

15 MINUTES

Reading the World

35 MINUTES

PART 1

REFLECTING ON THEME

Read this paragraph aloud to the class. Then invite volunteers to role-play scenes showing how sometimes people pretend to be what they are not. After each skit, encourage the rest of the class to explore the advantages and disadvantages of putting up a false front to hide your true nature. When might false pretenses be a good thing? When might they cause harm? Invite students to consider these questions as they read each of the following selections.

What Do You Think?

Before students begin this activity, tell them to work independently to brainstorm a list of questions they can ask their partner about the new event or possession. Guide students to generate at least ten questions. Explain that these questions will give them a jumping-off point for the interview. During the interview, students should take turns serving as Recorder to take notes. Students will return to this activity on page 643.

UNIT FIVE **PART 1**

FALSE PRETENSES

REFLECTING ON THEME

Do you ever run into folks who pretend to be what they are not? Do some people put up a false front that hides their true nature? Or, have you ever found yourself playing a role you weren't really comfortable with? One of the common mysteries of life is whether people are what they seem to be—or whether they are operating under false pretenses. This part of Unit Five focuses on a number of variations on that theme.

What Do You Think? Can you tell if someone is acting under false pretenses? Find out by doing this activity. First, interview a classmate about something new in his or her life. For example, your classmate might begin by saying, "My family just bought a new car," "My sister's getting married," or "I got a new CD." Next, ask your classmate questions about this new event or possession to figure out whether he or she is telling the truth. Then switch places so that you are the one being interviewed and your classmate has to guess whether you're being honest. Share your experience with the rest of the class and explain how you knew or didn't know whether your partner was lying.

Author	Title	Page
Shirley Jackson	**One Ordinary Day, with Peanuts** *But what an "ordinary" day it is!*	585
Bai Xiao-Yi	**The Explosion in the Parlor**/INSIGHT *Would you ever willingly take the blame for something you didn't do?*	595
Dorothy M. Johnson	**The Last Boast** *The one good thing in Wolfer Joe's entire life*	598
Sue Grafton	**Full Circle** *A traffic accident becomes a case for detective Kinsey Millhone.*	605
Maria Simson	**"Who Killed My Daughter?": Lois Duncan Searches for an Answer**/INSIGHT *A writer's real-life tragedy imitates one of her novels.*	618
W. H. Auden	**O What Is That Sound** *Who could those soldiers be after?*	622
Susan Glaspell	**Trifles** *Two women become unlikely detectives.*	627
John Collier	**The Chaser** *Cleaning Fluid. Spot Remover. Whatever.*	644

PREVIEWING

FICTION

One Ordinary Day, with Peanuts
Shirley Jackson

Activating Prior Knowledge
PERSONAL CONNECTION

The main character in this story is about to experience another ordinary day in his life. In terms of how you interact with people, what is a typical day in your life like? Think about your behavior yesterday or the day before. Did you say or do anything that you think made someone else's life more pleasant? On the other hand, do you think you said or did anything that hurt another person's feelings or caused a problem for someone? In your notebook, make a chart like the one shown. Describe a few positive and negative experiences that seem to take place on typical days.

A Typical Day	
Positive Experiences	**Negative Experiences**
Helped two friends resolve an argument	Made some people mad by cutting in line

Building Background
LITERARY CONNECTION

Shirley Jackson has a very distinctive literary style, and readers unfamiliar with it can benefit by knowing ahead of time what may lie in store. Jackson's writing is matter-of-fact and unemotional. Her plots often consist of apparently normal events that, the reader comes to discover, conceal an evil or twisted reality. Many of her characters are people isolated from others—people who lack feeling, display contradictory personalities, and are capable of seemingly unmotivated actions. Thus, Jackson's reputation has become that of a writer of eerie, "catch-you-by-surprise" tales that explore the private world of odd behavior.

Setting a Purpose
WRITING CONNECTION

On any given day, most of us are capable of surprising our friends with unexpected behavior. In your notebook, write about a time when you were surprised to learn something new—positive or negative—about a person you felt you already knew well. As you read "One Ordinary Day, with Peanuts," compare this reaction to the reaction you have as you learn more about the story's main characters.

Drawing by Charles Addams. Copyright 1946, © 1974 The New Yorker Magazine, Inc.

OVERVIEW

Objectives
- To understand and appreciate a short story that describes an ordinary day in a man's life
- To identify and understand situational irony
- To express understanding of the story through a choice of writing forms, including a cast list and a program teaser
- To extend understanding of the story through a variety of multimodal and cross-curricular activities

Skills

LITERARY CONCEPTS
- Situational irony
- Point of view: limited third-person

THE WRITER'S STYLE
- Combining sentences

GENRE STUDY
- Fiction: fantasy

GRAMMAR
- Adjective and adverb phrases as modifiers

SPEAKING, LISTENING, AND VIEWING
- Interviews

ALTERNATIVE
Previewing

In lieu of writing their reactions to something they learned about someone, students can choose partners and discuss their reactions to what they learned.

Writing Connection

Discussion Prompts *Describe in detail what you learned and your reaction to your partner. Then listen as your partner describes what he or she learned and his or her reaction. The following questions might help you get started:*
- *What did you learn?*
- *How did you react to this discovery?*
- *Did what you learned change your impressions of the person?*

As you read "One Ordinary Day, with Peanuts" take note of the main character's actions throughout the story.

PRINT AND MEDIA RESOURCES

UNIT FIVE RESOURCE BOOK
Strategic Reading: Literature, p. 4
Vocabulary SkillBuilder, p. 5

WRITING MINI-LESSONS
Transparencies, pp. 48–49

ACCESS FOR STUDENTS ACQUIRING ENGLISH
Selection Summaries
Reading Support

TEACHER'S GUIDE TO ASSESSMENT AND PORTFOLIO USE

FORMAL ASSESSMENT
Selection Test, pp. 103–104
 Test Generator

 AUDIO LIBRARY
See Reference Card

INTERNET RESOURCES
McDougal Littell Literature Center at http://www.hmco.com/mcdougal/lit

One Ordinary Day, with Peanuts

Shirley Jackson

84 Madison (1982), Philip Reisman. Oil on canvas, 48 ¼″ × 22″, Edwin A. Ulrich Museum of Art, Wichita (Kansas) State University, Endowment Association Art Collection (84.7.3).

Mr. John Philip Johnson shut his front door behind him and came down his front steps into the bright morning with a feeling that all was well with the world on this best of all days, and wasn't the sun warm and good, and didn't his shoes feel comfortable after the resoling, and he knew that he had undoubtedly chosen the precise very tie which belonged with the day and the sun and his comfortable feet, and, after all, wasn't the world just a wonderful place? In spite of the fact that he was a small man, and the tie was perhaps a shade vivid, Mr. Johnson irradiated this feeling of well-being as he came down the steps and onto the dirty sidewalk, and he smiled at people who passed him, and some of them even smiled back. He stopped at the newsstand on the corner and bought his paper, saying "*Good* morning" with real conviction to the man who sold him the paper and the two or three other people who were lucky enough to

---

SUMMARY

Mr. Johnson leaves his house on a bright morning feeling that all is well with the world. He smiles and wishes everyone who will listen a good day. He purchases a newspaper, candy, and peanuts and walks leisurely uptown, stopping often to help people and give them peanuts and candy. He watches a young child so the child's mother can pack her household belongings for a move to Vermont. He introduces two young people who were rushing to work and gives them money to enjoy the day together. He gives money to a beggar. He spends the day spreading goodwill and friendliness. At the end of the day, he returns home and greets his wife. She has spent her day quarreling with people, trying to get them arrested or fired from their jobs, and generally creating trouble for everyone around her. Because she is tired, her husband suggests that they change roles the following day.

Thematic Link: *False Pretenses* A man's motives for doing good deeds are not what they seem.

CUSTOMIZING FOR
Students Acquiring English

- Use **ACCESS FOR STUDENTS ACQUIRING ENGLISH,** *Reading Support.*
- As you guide students through the selection, you may want to use the suggestions in these boxes as well as those under Strategic Reading for Less-Proficient Readers.

STRATEGIC READING FOR
Less-Proficient Readers

Set a Purpose Have students read to see how Mr. Johnson's good mood affects others.

Use **UNIT FIVE RESOURCE BOOK,** p. 4, for guidance in reading the selection.

WORDS TO KNOW

ambiguously (ăm-bĭg′yōō-əs-lē) *adv.* in a way that is open to more than one interpretation; unclearly (p. 592)

genial (jēn′yəl) *adj.* sympathetically cheerful; pleasant (p. 587)

impertinent (ĭm-pûr′tn-ənt) *adj.* going beyond the limit of good manners; improperly bold (p. 594)

insatiable (ĭn-sā′shə-bəl) *adj.* impossible to satisfy (p. 592)

repress (rĭ-prĕs′) *v.* to retrain something struggling to find an outlet; hold back (p. 590) be buying papers when Mr. Johnson skipped up. He remembered to fill his pockets with candy and peanuts, and then he set out to get himself uptown. He stopped in a flower shop and bought a carnation for his buttonhole, and stopped almost immediately afterward to give the carnation to a small child in a carriage, who looked at him dumbly, and then smiled, and Mr. Johnson smiled, and the child's mother looked at Mr. Johnson for a minute and then smiled too.

When he had gone several blocks uptown, Mr. Johnson cut across the avenue and went along a side street, chosen at random; he did not follow the same route every morning, but preferred to pursue his eventful way in wide detours, more like a puppy than a man intent upon business. It happened this morning that halfway down the block a moving van was parked, and the furniture from an upstairs apartment stood half on the sidewalk, half on the steps, while an amused group of people loitered, examining the scratches on the tables and the worn spots on the chairs, and a harassed woman, trying to watch a young child and the movers and the furniture all at the same time, gave the clear impression of endeavoring to shelter her private life from the people staring at her belongings. Mr. Johnson stopped, and for a moment joined the crowd, and then he came forward and, touching his hat civilly, said, "Perhaps I can keep an eye on your little boy for you?"

The woman turned and glared at him distrustfully, and Mr. Johnson added hastily, "We'll sit right here on the steps." He beckoned to the little boy, who hesitated and then responded agreeably to Mr. Johnson's <u>genial</u> smile. Mr. Johnson brought out a handful of peanuts from his pocket and sat on the steps with the boy, who at first refused the peanuts on the grounds that his mother did not allow him to accept food from strangers; Mr. Johnson said that probably his mother had not intended peanuts to be included, since elephants at the circus ate them, and the boy considered, and then agreed solemnly. They sat on the steps cracking peanuts in a comradely fashion, and Mr. Johnson said, "So you're moving?"

"Yep," said the boy.

"Where you going?"

"Vermont."

"Nice place. Plenty of snow there. Maple sugar, too; you like maple sugar?"

"Sure."

"Plenty of maple sugar in Vermont. You going to live on a farm?"

"Going to live with Grandpa."

"Grandpa like peanuts?"

"Sure."

"Ought to take him some," said Mr. Johnson, reaching into his pocket. "Just you and Mommy going?"

"Yep."

"Tell you what," Mr. Johnson said. "You take some peanuts to eat on the train."

The boy's mother, after glancing at them frequently, had seemingly decided that Mr. Johnson was trustworthy, because she had devoted herself wholeheartedly to seeing that the movers did not—what movers rarely do, but every housewife believes they will—crack a leg from her good table, or set a kitchen chair down on a lamp. Most of the furniture was loaded by now, and she was deep in that

WORDS TO KNOW

genial (jēn´yəl) *adj.* warmly cheerful; pleasant

587

Mini-Lesson Genre Study

FANTASY On the chalkboard draw the web shown on the right, and use it to focus on the characteristics of **fantasy**.

Application Have students copy the word web into their notebooks. Ask them to refer to it to help them identify the characteristics of a fantasy in "One Ordinary Day, with Peanuts."

Critical Thinking: ANALYZING

C Ask students to analyze why the mother is unwilling to tell Mr. Johnson where she is moving. *(Possible response: He is a stranger; his unexpected offer arouses her suspicions.)*

STRATEGIC READING FOR
Less-Proficient Readers

D Make sure that students understand the episode involving Mr. Johnson and the woman who is moving. Ask these questions:

- How does Mr. Johnson help the woman who is moving? *(He watches over her little boy.)* **Noting Relevant Details**

- How successful is he at putting both the mother and the little boy at ease? *(Possible response: Quite successful, for the boy becomes talkative and relaxed; the mother relaxes too and turns her attention to supervising the movers.)* **Making Judgments**

Set a Purpose Have students continue reading to find out how Mr. Johnson spreads more goodwill by helping others.

Literary Concept:
CHARACTERIZATION

E Ask students what is revealed about the young woman who crashes into Mr. Johnson. *(Her impatience can be detected in her frown; her appearance shows that she dressed in a hurry; she is suspicious of and annoyed with Mr. Johnson.)*

Critical Thinking: SPECULATING

F Ask students to speculate about whether Mr. Johnson will be able to win over the young woman. *(Possible responses: Some may say that he won't be able to win her over because she is in a hurry and very hostile. Others might say that he will win her over because he is a very persuasive individual.)*

---

nervous stage when she knew there was something she had forgotten to pack—hidden away in the back of a closet somewhere, or left at a neighbor's and forgotten, or on the clothesline—and was trying to remember under stress what it was.

"This all, lady?" the chief mover said, completing her dismay.

Uncertainly, she nodded.

"Want to go on the truck with the furniture, sonny?" the mover asked the boy, and laughed. The boy laughed too and said to Mr. Johnson, "I guess I'll have a good time at Vermont."

"Fine time," said Mr. Johnson, and stood up. "Have one more peanut before you go," he said to the boy.

The boy's mother said to Mr. Johnson, "Thank you so much; it was a great help to me."

"Nothing at all," said Mr. Johnson gallantly. "Where in Vermont are you going?"

The mother looked at the little boy accusingly, as though he had given away a secret of some importance, and said unwillingly, "Greenwich."

"Lovely town," said Mr. Johnson. He took out a card, and wrote a name on the back. "Very good friend of mine lives in Greenwich," he said. "Call on him for anything you need. His wife makes the best doughnuts in town," he added soberly to the little boy.

"Swell," said the little boy.

"Goodbye," said Mr. Johnson.

He went on, stepping happily with his new-shod[1] feet, feeling the warm sun on his back and on the top of his head. Halfway down the block he met a stray dog and fed him a peanut.

At the corner, where another wide avenue faced him, Mr. Johnson decided to go on uptown again. Moving with comparative laziness, he was passed on either side by people hurrying and frowning, and people brushed past him going the other way, clattering along to get somewhere quickly. Mr. Johnson stopped on every corner and waited patiently for the light to change, and he stepped out of the way of anyone who seemed to be in any particular hurry, but one young lady came too fast for him, and crashed wildly into him when he stooped to pat a kitten which had run out onto the sidewalk from an apartment house and was now unable to get back through the rushing feet.

"Excuse me," said the young lady, trying frantically to pick up Mr. Johnson and hurry on at the same time, "terribly sorry."

The kitten, regardless now of danger, raced back to its home. "Perfectly all right," said Mr. Johnson, adjusting himself carefully. "You seem to be in a hurry."

"Of course I'm in a hurry," said the young lady. "I'm late."

She was extremely cross and the frown between her eyes seemed well on its way to becoming permanent. She had obviously awakened late, because she had not spent any extra time in making herself look pretty, and her dress was plain and unadorned with collar or brooch, and her lipstick was noticeably crooked. She tried to brush past Mr. Johnson, but, risking her suspicious displeasure, he took her arm and said, "Please wait."

"Look," she said ominously, "I ran into you and your lawyer can see my lawyer and I will gladly pay all damages and all inconveniences suffered therefrom but please this minute let me go because *I am late.*"

"Late for what?" said Mr. Johnson; he tried his winning smile on her but it did no more than keep her, he suspected, from knocking him down again.

"Late for work," she said between her teeth. "Late for my employment. I have a job and if I am late I lose exactly so much an hour and I

---

[1] **new-shod:** wearing new shoes.

588   UNIT FIVE   PART 1: FALSE PRETENSES

Critic's ⭐ Corner

"I found it unrealistic that the woman who was moving trusted a total stranger with watching her son. I guess it's not necessarily unrealistic, at least it wouldn't have been so many years ago. It's obvious that this story does not take place in the present."

Nancy Beirne
Ninth-Grade Member
Student Advisory Board

Have students identify passages that suggest that the story takes place in the past. Do they agree with Nancy that certain events make more sense once the reader realizes they are set in the past?

cannot really afford what your pleasant conversation is costing me, be it *ever* so pleasant."

"I'll pay for it," said Mr. Johnson. Now these were magic words, not necessarily because they were true, or because she seriously expected Mr. Johnson to pay for anything, but because Mr. Johnson's flat statement, obviously innocent of irony, could not be, coming from Mr. Johnson, anything but the statement of a responsible and truthful and respectable man.

"What *do* you mean?" she asked.

"I said that since I am obviously responsible for your being late I shall certainly pay for it."

"Don't be silly," she said, and for the first time the frown disappeared. "*I* wouldn't expect you to pay for anything—a few minutes ago I was offering to pay *you*. Anyway," she added, almost smiling, "it *was* my fault."

"What happens if you don't go to work?"

She stared. "I don't get paid."

"Precisely," said Mr. Johnson.

"What do you mean, precisely? If I don't show up at the office exactly twenty minutes ago I lose a dollar and twenty cents an hour, or two cents a minute or . . ." She thought. ". . . Almost a dime for the time I've spent talking to you."

Mr. Johnson laughed, and finally she laughed, too. "You're late already," he pointed out. "Will you give me another four cents worth?"

"I don't understand why."

"You'll see," Mr. Johnson promised. He led her over to the side of the walk, next to the buildings, and said, "Stand here," and went out into the rush of people going both ways. Selecting and considering, as one who must make a choice involving perhaps whole years of lives, he estimated the people going by. Once he almost moved, and then at the last minute thought better of it and drew back. Finally, from half a block away, he saw what he wanted, and moved out into the center of the traffic to intercept a young man, who was hurrying, and dressed as though he had awakened late, and frowning.

"Oof," said the young man, because Mr.

Critical Thinking: SUMMARIZING

I Ask students to explain how Mr. Johnson intercepts the young man. *(Possible response: Mr. Johnson brushes into the young man, knocking him to the sidewalk.)* What is the young man's reaction to Mr. Johnson? *(Possible response: He is nervous and suspicious of Mr. Johnson.)*

CUSTOMIZING FOR
Multiple Learning Styles

J **Bodily-Kinesthetic Learners** Ask students to think about how the young woman views Mr. Johnson's successful attempt to engage the young man in a conversation. Have pairs of students pantomime the episode from the young woman's perspective. What understanding of the characters have they gained from the pantomime?

Critical Thinking: CLASSIFYING

K Ask students to describe Mr. Johnson's attitude toward the young couple. *(Possible response: kind and benevolent)*

Johnson had thought of no better way to intercept anyone than the one the young woman had unwittingly used upon him. "Where do you think you're going?" the young man demanded from the sidewalk.

"I want to speak to you," said Mr. Johnson ominously.

The young man got up nervously, dusting himself and eyeing Mr. Johnson. "What for?" he said. "What'd *I* do?"

"That's what bothers me most about people nowadays," Mr. Johnson complained broadly to the people passing. "No matter whether they've done anything or not, they always figure someone's after them. About what you're going to do," he told the young man.

"Listen," said the young man, trying to brush past him, "I'm late, and I don't have any time to listen. Here's a dime, now get going."

"Thank you," said Mr. Johnson, pocketing the dime. "Look," he said, "what happens if you stop running?"

"I'm late," said the young man, still trying to get past Mr. Johnson, who was unexpectedly clinging.

"How much you make an hour?" Mr. Johnson demanded.

"A communist,[2] are you?" said the young man. "Now will you please let me—"

"No," said Mr. Johnson insistently, "*how* much?"

"Dollar fifty," said the young man. "And *now* will you—"

"You like adventure?"

The young man stared, and staring, found himself caught and held by Mr. Johnson's genial smile; he almost smiled back and then repressed it and made an effort to tear away. "I got to *hurry*," he said.

"Mystery? Like surprises? Unusual and exciting events?"

"You selling something?"

"Sure," said Mr. Johnson. "You want to take a chance?"

The young man hesitated, looked longingly up the avenue toward what might have been his destination and then, when Mr. Johnson said "I'll pay for it" with his own peculiar convincing emphasis, turned and said, "Well, okay. But I got to *see* it first, what I'm buying."

Mr. Johnson, breathing hard, led the young man over to the side where the girl was standing; she had been watching with interest Mr. Johnson's capture of the young man and now, smiling timidly, she looked at Mr. Johnson as though prepared to be surprised at nothing.

Mr. Johnson reached into his pocket and took out his wallet. "Here," he said, and handed a bill to the girl. "This about equals your day's pay."

"But no," she said, surprised in spite of herself. "I mean, I *couldn't.*"

"Please do not interrupt," Mr. Johnson told her. "And *here,*" he said to the young man, "this will take care of *you.*" The young man accepted the bill dazedly, but said, "Probably counterfeit" to the young woman out of the side of his mouth. "Now," Mr. Johnson went on, disregarding the young man, "what is your name, miss?"

"Kent," she said helplessly. "Mildred Kent."

"Fine," said Mr. Johnson. "And you, sir?"

"Arthur Adams," said the young man stiffly.

"Splendid," said Mr. Johnson. "Now, Miss Kent, I would like you to meet Mr. Adams. Mr. Adams, Miss Kent."

Miss Kent stared, wet her lips nervously,

---

2. **communist:** At the time the story was written (1951), communists—people who believed in worker ownership of all businesses—were thought to be everywhere, trying to undermine the United States by convincing workers that they were underpaid and oppressed and should seize control of the government.

> **WORDS TO KNOW**
> **repress** (rĭ-prĕs′) *v.* to restrain something struggling to find an outlet; hold back

590

Mini-Lesson — The Writer's Style

COMBINING SENTENCES Tell students that good writers combine sentences by transferring a key word from one sentence to another. Sometimes writers can combine sentences without changing the form of the word. However, occasionally they need to add endings such as *-y, -ed, -ing,* or *-ly.*

Application On the chalkboard, write the following sentences. Have students combine each pair of sentences.
1. The young man got up dusting himself and eyeing Mr. Johnson. The young man was nervous. *(The young man got up nervously, dusting himself and eyeing Mr. Johnson.)*
2. The young woman smiled timidly. She looked at Mr. Johnson. *(The young woman smiled timidly, looking at Mr. Johnson.)*

Reteaching/Reinforcement
- *Writing Handbook,* anthology, p. 864
- *Writing Mini-Lessons* transparencies, p.p 48–49

Adding Words to Sentences, pp. 421–422

made a gesture as though she might run, and said, "How do you do?"

Mr. Adams straightened his shoulders, scowled at Mr. Johnson, made a gesture as though he might run, and said, "How do you do?"

"Now this," said Mr. Johnson, taking several bills from his wallet, "should be enough for the day for both of you. I would suggest, perhaps, Coney Island—although I personally am not fond of the place—or perhaps a nice lunch somewhere, and dancing, or a matinee, or even a movie, although take care to choose a really *good* one; there are *so* many bad movies these days. You might," he said, struck with an inspiration, "visit the Bronx Zoo, or the Planetarium. Anywhere, as a matter of fact," he concluded, "that you would like to go. Have a nice time."

As he started to move away Arthur Adams, breaking from his dumbfounded stare, said, "But see here, mister, you *can't* do this. Why—how do you know—I mean, *we* don't even know—I mean, how do you know we won't just take the money and not do what you said?"

"You've taken the money," Mr. Johnson said. "You don't have to follow any of my suggestions. You may know something you prefer to do—perhaps a museum, or something."

"But suppose I just run away with it and leave her here?"

"I know you won't," said Mr. Johnson gently, "because you remembered to ask *me* that. Goodbye," he added, and went on.

As he stepped up the street, conscious of the sun on his head and his good shoes, he heard from somewhere behind him the young man saying, "Look, you know you don't *have* to if you don't want to," and the girl saying, "But unless *you* don't want to . . ." Mr. Johnson smiled to himself and then thought that he had better hurry along; when he wanted to he could move very quickly, and before the young woman had gotten around to saying, "Well, *I* will if *you* will," Mr. Johnson was several blocks away and had already stopped twice, once to help a lady lift several large packages into a taxi and once to hand a peanut to a seagull. By this time he was in an area of large stores and many more people and he was buffeted constantly from either side by people hurrying and cross and late and sullen. Once he offered a peanut to a man who asked him for a dime, and once he offered a peanut to a bus driver who had stopped his bus at an intersection and had opened the window next to his seat and put out his head as though longing for fresh air and the comparative quiet of the traffic. The man wanting a dime took the peanut because Mr. Johnson had wrapped a dollar bill around it, but the bus driver took the peanut and asked ironically, "You want a transfer, Jack?"

On a busy corner Mr. Johnson encountered two young people—for one minute he thought they might be Mildred Kent and Arthur Adams—who were eagerly scanning a newspaper, their backs pressed against a storefront to avoid the people passing, their heads bent together. Mr. Johnson, whose curiosity was <u>insatiable</u>, leaned onto the

once he offered a peanut to a man who asked him for a dime.

WORDS TO KNOW

insatiable (ĭn-sā′shə-bəl) *adj.* impossible to satisfy

591

Literary Concept: MOOD

O Ask students in what way the use of description in this passage helps to set the mood. *(Possible response: Descriptions such as "pleasant restaurant," "excellent digestion," "wonderful sunlight," and "comfortable and fresh" help to set a cheerful mood.)*

STRATEGIC READING FOR
Less-Proficient Readers

P Ask students to summarize how Mr. Johnson spends the rest of his day after leaving the young woman and the young man. *(Possible response: He hands out peanuts, suggests that a couple looking for an apartment check out the one vacated by the woman and boy who are moving to Vermont, gives a beggar money for lunch, and helps various people in the park.)* **Summarizing**

Set a Purpose Have students read to find out the nature of Mr. Johnson's kindness.

Literary Concept: MOOD

Q Ask students what mood is accentuated by this passage. *(Possible response: A hint of fantasy is introduced by the way in which the cab is irresistibly drawn toward Mr. Johnson.)*

---

storefront next to them and peeked over the man's shoulder; they were scanning the "Apartments Vacant" columns.

Mr. Johnson remembered the street where the woman and her little boy were going to Vermont and he tapped the man on the shoulder and said amiably, "Try down on West Seventeen. About the middle of the block, people moved out this morning."

"Say, what do you—" said the man, and then, seeing Mr. Johnson clearly, "Well, thanks. Where did you say?"

"West Seventeen," said Mr. Johnson. "About the middle of the block." He smiled again and said, "Good luck."

"Thanks," said the man.

"Thanks," said the girl, as they moved off.

"Goodbye," said Mr. Johnson.

He lunched alone in a pleasant restaurant, where the food was rich, and only Mr. Johnson's excellent digestion could encompass two of their whipped-cream-and-chocolate-and-rum-cake pastries for dessert. He had three cups of coffee, tipped the waiter largely, and went out into the street again into the wonderful sunlight, his shoes still comfortable and fresh on his feet. Outside he found a beggar staring into the windows of the restaurant he had left and, carefully looking through the money in his pocket, Mr. Johnson approached the beggar and pressed some coins and a couple of bills into his hand. "It's the price of the veal cutlet lunch plus tip," said Mr. Johnson. "Goodbye."

After his lunch he rested; he walked into the nearest park and fed peanuts to the pigeons. It was late afternoon by the time he was ready to start back downtown, and he had refereed two checker games and watched a small boy and girl whose mother had fallen asleep and awakened with surprise and fear which turned to amusement when she saw Mr. Johnson. He had given away almost all of his candy, and had fed all the rest of his peanuts to the pigeons, and it was time to go home. Although the late afternoon sun was pleasant, and his shoes were still entirely comfortable, he decided to take a taxi downtown.

He had a difficult time catching a taxi, because he gave up the first three or four empty ones to people who seemed to need them more; finally, however, he stood alone on the corner and—almost like netting a frisky fish—he hailed desperately until he succeeded in catching a cab which had been proceeding with haste uptown and seemed to draw in toward Mr. Johnson against its own will.

"Mister," the cab driver said as Mr. Johnson climbed in, "I figured you was an omen, like. I wasn't going to pick you up at all."

"Kind of you," said Mr. Johnson ambiguously.

"If I'd of let you go it would of cost me ten bucks," said the driver.

"Really?" said Mr. Johnson.

"Yeah," said the driver. "Guy just got out of the cab, he turned around and give me ten bucks, said take this and bet it in a hurry on a horse named Vulcan,[3] right away."

"Vulcan?" said Mr. Johnson, horrified. "A fire sign on a Wednesday?"

"What?" said the driver. "Anyway, I said to myself if I got no fare between here and there I'd bet the ten, but if anyone looked like they needed the cab I'd take it as a omen and I'd take the ten home to the wife."

"You were very right," said Mr. Johnson heartily. "This is Wednesday, you would have lost your money. Monday, yes, or even Saturday.

---

3. **Vulcan:** the god of fire in Roman mythology.

WORDS TO KNOW
ambiguously (ăm-bĭg′yōō-əs-lē) *adv.* in a way that is open to more than one interpretation; unclearly

But never never never a fire sign on a Wednesday. Sunday would have been good, now."

"Vulcan don't run on Sunday," said the driver.

"You wait till another day," said Mr. Johnson. "Down this street, please, driver. I'll get off on the next corner."

"He *told* me Vulcan, though," said the driver.

"I'll tell you," said Mr. Johnson, hesitating with the door of the cab half open. "You take that ten dollars and I'll give you another ten dollars to go with it, and you go right ahead and bet that money on any Thursday on any horse that has a name indicating . . . let me see, Thursday . . . well, grain. Or any growing food."

"Grain?" said the driver. "You mean a horse named, like, Wheat or something?"

"Certainly," said Mr. Johnson. "Or, as a matter of fact, to make it even easier, any horse whose name includes the letters C, R, L. Perfectly simple."

"Tall corn?" said the driver, a light in his eye. "You mean a horse named, like, Tall Corn?"

"Absolutely," said Mr. Johnson. "Here's your money."

"Tall Corn," said the driver. "Thank *you*, mister."

"Goodbye," said Mr. Johnson.

He was on his own corner and went straight up to his apartment. He let himself in and called "Hello?" and Mrs. Johnson answered from the kitchen, "Hello, dear, aren't you early?"

"Took a taxi home," Mr. Johnson said. "I remembered the cheesecake, too. What's for dinner?"

Mrs. Johnson came out of the kitchen and kissed him; she was a comfortable woman, and smiling as Mr. Johnson smiled. "Hard day?" she asked.

"Not very," said Mr. Johnson, hanging his coat in the closet. "How about you?"

"So-so," she said. She stood in the kitchen doorway while he settled into his easy chair and

Critical Thinking: SPECULATING

R Ask students to speculate about whether the cab driver would make money by following Mr. Johnson's advice. *(Possible response: Probably, because Mr. Johnson seems to have a magical ability to make things turn out his way.)*

Literary Concept: DIALOGUE

S Ask students what the dialogue between the cab driver and Mr. Johnson reveals about the driver. *(Possible response: He is gullible and eager to take chances.)*

Literary Concept: CHARACTERIZATION

T Ask students what they can infer about Mrs. Johnson's character based on the narrator's description of her. *(Possible response: She will probably be as helpful and considerate as her husband, because the narrator says that they have the same way of smiling.)*

CUSTOMIZING FOR
Multiple Learning Styles

U **Spatial or Graphic Learners** Invite students to compare the woman depicted in the art on this page to the description of Mrs. Johnson. Is this how they picture her? Why or why not?

Mini-Lesson: Speaking, Listening, and Viewing

INTERVIEWS Remind students that an interview is an effective way of gathering information. Both the subject and the interviewer must be well prepared. For example, the subject will probably want to anticipate questions and prepare responses. The interviewer should focus on asking questions that will elicit the information sought. Both parties should make eye contact and speak clearly and audibly. Questions should be clear and appropriate and should be answered as thoughtfully and as completely as possible.

Application Have students select partners and prepare to present an interview. The subject should be one of the characters whom Mr. Johnson encountered. The interviewer should prepare a list of questions to ask the character about his or her sense of the encounter and his or her impressions of Mr. Johnson. Have each pair conduct its interview in class.

Art Note

Autobiographical by Moses Soyer The Russian-American painter Moses Soyer (1899–1974) etched the inner life of an individual on the person's face, making his or her thoughts, feelings, and mood appear to be transparent. The theme that always engaged this artist is the nobility of the common person, and so Soyer's subjects are ordinary people struggling to survive their personal dramas.

Reading the Art How would you describe the couple's facial expressions? What do you think has occurred between them?

STRATEGIC READING FOR
Less-Proficient Readers

V Have students summarize how Mr. and Mrs. Johnson spend their days. *(Possible response: They take turns being mean and kind to people.)* **Summarizing**

- Why was Mr. Johnson kind to the people he met? *(He was playing the perverse role of a peculiarly kind person.)* **Drawing Conclusions**

Literary Concept: IRONY

W Ask students what is ironic about the good deeds that Mr. Johnson did for people all day? *(Possible responses: Mr. Johnson did not do the good deeds because he cares about people and their welfare. He did them because it was his day to be good.)*

COMPREHENSION CHECK
True or false
1. Mr. Johnson radiates goodwill. *(True)*
2. He helps a woman by supervising her movers. *(False)*
3. He introduces two impatient young people and gives them money to take the day off from work and enjoy it together. *(True)*
4. He and his wife take turns being kind and mean. *(True)*

Autobiographical (1954), Moses Soyer. Courtesy of ACA Galleries, New York.

took off his good shoes and took out the paper he had bought that morning. "Here and there," she said.

"I didn't do so badly," Mr. Johnson said. "Couple young people."

"Fine," she said. "I had a little nap this afternoon, took it easy most of the day. Went into a department store this morning and accused the woman next to me of shoplifting, and had the store detective pick her up. Sent three dogs to the pound—*you* know, the usual thing. Oh, and listen," she added, remembering.

"What?" asked Mr. Johnson.

"Well," she said, "I got onto a bus and asked the driver for a transfer, and when he helped someone else first I said that he was <u>impertinent</u>, and quarreled with him. And then I said why wasn't he in the army,[4] and I said it loud enough for everyone to hear, and I took his number and I turned in a complaint. Probably got him fired."

"Fine," said Mr. Johnson. "But you do look tired. Want to change over tomorrow?"

"I *would* like to," she said. "I could do with a change."

"Right," said Mr. Johnson. "What's for dinner?"

"Veal cutlet."

"Had it for lunch," said Mr. Johnson. ❖

---

4. **why wasn't he in the army:** In 1951 the United States was in the middle of the Korean War, and thousands of males were being drafted into or volunteering for army duty.

WORDS TO KNOW

impertinent (ĭm-pûr′tn-ənt) *adj.* going beyond the limit of good manners; improperly bold

---

Assessment Option

INFORMAL ASSESSMENT You can informally assess students' understanding of the selection by having them summarize the events in the story. Ask students to imagine that they are Mr. Johnson retelling in detail the events of the day to his wife.

Rubric

3 Full Accomplishment Students accurately describe in detail the events of Mr. Johnson's day.

2 Substantial Accomplishment Students describe only partially in detail the events of Mr. Johnson's day.

1 Little or Partial Accomplishment Students have difficulty describing the events of the Mr. Johnson's day.

INSIGHT

the explosion in the parlor

BAI XIAO-YI

The host poured tea into the cup and placed it on the small table in front of his guests, who were a father and daughter, and put the lid on the cup with a clink. Apparently thinking of something, he hurried into the inner room, leaving the Thermos on the table. His two guests heard a chest of drawers opening and a rustling.

They remained sitting in the parlor, the ten-year-old daughter looking at the flowers outside the window, the father just about to take his cup, when the crash came, right there in the parlor. Something was hopelessly broken.

It was the Thermos, which had fallen to the floor. The girl looked over her shoulder abruptly, startled, staring. It was mysterious. Neither of them had touched it, not even a little bit. True, it hadn't stood steadily when their host placed it on the table, but it hadn't fallen then.

The crash of the Thermos caused the host, with a box of sugar cubes in his hand, to rush back from the inner room. He gawked at the steaming floor and blurted out, "It doesn't matter! It doesn't matter!"

The father started to say something. Then he muttered, "Sorry, I touched it and it fell."

"It doesn't matter," the host said.

Later, when they left the house, the daughter said, "Daddy, *did* you touch it?"

"No. But it stood so close to me."

"But you *didn't* touch it. I saw your reflection in the windowpane. You were sitting perfectly still."

The father laughed. "What then would you give as the cause of its fall?"

"The Thermos fell by itself. The floor is uneven. It wasn't steady when Mr. Li put it there. Daddy, *why* did you say that you . . ."

"That won't do, girl. It sounds more acceptable when I say I knocked it down. There are things which people accept less the more you defend them. The truer the story you tell, the less true it sounds."

The daughter was lost in silence for a while. Then she said, "Can you explain it only this way?"

"Only this way," her father said.

From Personal Response to Critical Analysis

1. Accept all reasonable responses.
2. Responses will vary. Students may indicate that they thought the story was about human kindness until they read his exchange with Mrs. Johnson.
3. Possible response: The Johnsons are motivated by the enjoyment they get from manipulating people.
4. Accept all reasonable responses.
5. Possible response: They are similar to the extent that they focus on blame; they are different in apportioning blame: Mrs. Johnson blames innocent people; in contrast, the house guest takes the blame for something he didn't do.
6. Accept all reasonable responses.

Another Pathway

Cooperative Learning Be sure that all students participate in discussion, contributing ideas and opinions to help the group arrive at a statement of the main theme. One student can take notes during discussion; notes can be revised into a brief essay on theme.

Rubric

3 Full Accomplishment The group identifies the theme of the story through an in-depth consideration of the topics suggested in the assignment.

2 Substantial Accomplishment The group identifies the theme but has not considered all the topics suggested in the assignment.

1 Little or Partial Accomplishment The group has difficulty identifying the theme and has not considered the suggested topics.

RESPONDING OPTIONS

FROM PERSONAL RESPONSE TO CRITICAL ANALYSIS

REFLECT
1. What was your reaction to the ending of the story? Write your response in your notebook and share it in class.

RETHINK
2. How did the ending alter your interpretation of the story up to that point?
3. Explain what you think motivates the Johnsons to behave as they do.
   Consider
   - the mood each is in at the end
   - what values you think they have
   - what they may gain from their false pretenses

Thematic Link
4. How do you judge the Johnsons' behavior? Think about what you would do if you found out that people like the Johnsons existed.

RELATE
Literary Link
5. Mrs. Johnson and the house guest in the Insight selection, "The Explosion in the Parlor," both get involved in the issue of blame. How are the situations similar? What makes them different?

6. Think about how most people spend their days and the typical day that you described in the chart for the Personal Connection activity on page 585. What similarities and differences do you see between how the Johnsons behave and how most people behave on an ordinary day?

Multimodal Learning
ANOTHER PATHWAY

Cooperative Learning

In a small group, discuss what you think is the theme, or main idea, of this story. Consider whether you think the story is primarily humorous or serious, what the Johnsons represent, and what the author wanted the reader to think about the Johnsons. Compare your interpretations with the rest of the class.

LITERARY CONCEPTS

Irony is a contrast between appearance and reality. One type of irony is **situational irony,** the contrast between what a reader or character expects and what actually exists or happens. For example, situational irony might occur in a story in which a criminal proves to be trustworthy. What situational irony do you see in Jackson's story? How would the story be different if it did not have this element of irony?

CONCEPT REVIEW: Mood In this story the mood, or feeling that the writer creates, contributes to the irony. How would you describe the mood? What makes it ironic?

QUICKWRITES

1. Imagine that you are a casting director for a televised series of classic short stories. Your challenge is to find actors for the roles of Mr. and Mrs. Johnson. The actors must be able to fool the audience until the characters' strange behavior is revealed. Create a **cast list,** with well-known actors playing the Johnsons, and defend your choices.

2. You are now publicity director for the same television presentation. Write a **program teaser** for the story, a short plot description to be sent to weekly television guides. Be sure that your teaser doesn't give away the surprise.

PORTFOLIO Save your writing. You may want to use it later as a springboard to a piece for your portfolio.

596   UNIT FIVE   PART 1: FALSE PRETENSES

Literary Concepts

Possible responses: Readers believe that Mr. Johnson is kind until the end of the story when they discover that he is a dishonest manipulator; without the ironic twist at the end, the story would have been a study of the positive effects of human kindness.

Mood Possible responses: The mood is upbeat, humorous, and fanciful; It is ironic because the Johnsons are playing an ugly game using people as their pawns.

QuickWrites

1. Encourage students to make a list of actors they think might be right for the roles. Then they can narrow their list by discussing similar roles that those actors played in the past.
2. Suggest that students read program teasers in a few television guides and observe their length and format. Challenge them to develop a teaser that describes the plot but does not give away the ending.

Multimodal Learning

ALTERNATIVE ACTIVITIES

It is now the end of the next day, a day during which Mr. and Mrs. Johnson have switched their behaviors. With a partner, **act out** the two of them talking about their day—what they did and how they felt about what they did.

CRITIC'S CORNER

W. Caleb McDaniel, one of the members of our student advisory board, wrote that the story "seemed like a fairy tale until almost the end. Then I thought the irony was great." Do you agree or disagree with this observation? Explain your reasoning.

WORDS TO KNOW

Answer the following questions.

1. Is a **genial** person one who is more likely to have friends, excuses, or good grades?
2. Would someone who spoke **ambiguously** be most likely to cause admiration, confusion, or offense?
3. Is an **impertinent** person sleepy, rude, or tired?
4. If someone has an **insatiable** appetite, does that mean the person eats only certain foods, a wide range of foods, or a lot of food?
5. Which is something a person might **repress** at a play—applause, a smile, or a cough?

SHIRLEY JACKSON

1916–1965

Shirley Jackson possessed as complex a personality as any character she ever created. She was a woman of keen intelligence, a believer in magic and psychic phenomena, and a busy homemaker raising children in a small Vermont town.

Throughout the 1940s Jackson published short stories in various magazines and did so rather quietly—until the summer of 1948. In that year an idea for a story came to her on a sunny June morning as she pushed her daughter and some groceries home in a stroller; after putting the child in her playpen and the frozen food in the freezer, she wrote "The Lottery," quickly and without hesitation. Just three weeks later this chilling tale of a bizarre, deadly ritual in a small, seemingly innocent New England town was published in *The New Yorker*. Neither Jackson nor the magazine was prepared for what would happen next. That summer Jackson received about 300 letters, nearly all negative and some she was "downright scared to open." *The New Yorker* got more mail over this story than any other in its history, and subscriptions were canceled "right and left."

Jackson would become forever known for this one story, even though many of her other stories were singled out for attention. "One Ordinary Day, with Peanuts," for example, appeared in the 1956 volume of *The Best American Short Stories*.

Jackson almost never gave interviews—she refused to comment about the meaning of "The Lottery"—but she did enjoy teaching and sharing insights about her craft at writing conferences. In advising young writers how to turn experience into writing, she said, "The only way to turn something that really happened into something that happens on paper is to attack it in the beginning the way a puppy attacks an old shoe. Shake it, snarl at it, sneak up on it from various angles."

Jackson coped with stress by using a combination of pills and alcohol, which may have contributed to the anxieties and physical decline of her later life. She was only 48 when she died suddenly in her sleep of heart failure.

OTHER WORKS *The Haunting of Hill House, We Have Always Lived in the Castle, The Magic of Shirley Jackson*

Extended Reading

ONE ORDINARY DAY, WITH PEANUTS **597**

Words to Know

1. friends
2. confusion
3. rude
4. a lot of food
5. a cough

Reteaching/Reinforcement
- *Unit Five Resource Book*, p. 5

Critic's Corner

Accept all reasonable responses. Most students will concur that the story has an unreal quality that makes the story seem like a fairy tale without a happy ending.

Across the Curriculum

Science Remind students that peanuts are nutritious. Not only are they good for people and animals, but they are also good for the soil. After his experiments established that fact, George Washington Carver (1863-1943), an African-American botanist, developed more than 300 products derived from peanuts while he was the director of agricultural research at Tuskegee Institute. Ask volunteers to prepare a research report on Carver's work with peanuts and to present it to the class.

Alternative Activities

Remind students that Mr. and Mrs. Johnson have switched roles so that he acts in a mean way and she pretends to be kind. Before they act out the dialogue, students who will be playing Mr. Johnson should list the mean things that he might do and those playing Mrs. Johnson should list the kind things that she might do. Suggest that students use their lists as the basis for the conversation. Remind them to stay in character as they act out their roles.

SHIRLEY JACKSON

"Madame of Mystery," "Queen of the Macabre," and "The Virginia Werewolf of Séance Fiction" are all labels Shirley Jackson's friends and critics used to describe the reclusive writer. With tongue in cheek, her friends claimed that she wrote with a broomstick. For many of her stories, she drew on her own fears, which eventually began to take control of her life.

OVERVIEW

Objectives

- To understand and appreciate a short story that explores the mystery of how a man's betrayal of a woman could be considered the one good thing in his life
- To identify and understand an extended metaphor
- To express understanding of the story through a choice of writing forms including a note, a character sketch, and a short story
- To extend understanding of the story through a variety of multimodal and cross-curricular activities

Skills

LITERARY CONCEPTS
- Conflict
- Extended metaphor

THE WRITER'S STYLE
- Show, Don't Tell

GRAMMAR
- Compound-complex sentences

SPEAKING, LISTENING, AND VIEWING
- Group discussion
- Oral presentation

ALTERNATIVE
Previewing

Students can choose partners and use the following prompts to preview "The Last Boast" orally.

Writing Connection

Discussion Prompts *Think of a good deed you have done or one from which you have benefited. Describe it to your partner and then listen as your partner describes his or her own good deed. If you need help getting started, the following questions might help:*

- Who was involved?
- What was the good deed?
- What was the effect of the deed?

As you read "The Last Boast," compare the good deed that you described with the one featured in the story.

HISTORICAL CONNECTION

The Wild West Lured by the prospect of robbing miners of their gold, outlaws traveled to the West in the 1800s. These historical images depict how wild the West really was during that time. You may wish to generate discussion about the well-known outlaws of the time.

Side A, Frame 49455

PREVIEWING

FICTION

The Last Boast
Dorothy M. Johnson

Activating Prior Knowledge/Setting a Purpose

PERSONAL CONNECTION

The concept of a good deed plays a major part in the story you are about to read. What kind of action do you think of as a good deed? What kind of action would be a bad deed? In your notebook, list some good and bad deeds in a chart like the one shown. As you read this story, decide whether the main character's boast is a good deed or a bad deed.

Good Deeds	Bad Deeds
Giving to the needy	Lying to a friend

Building Background

HISTORICAL CONNECTION

"The Last Boast" is a Western, an adventure story set in the frontier days of the American West. Most Westerns are set in the period of 1850–1890. At the time, discoveries of gold and silver drew swarms of miners to the mountains of the West—but attracted outlaws as well, whose good and bad deeds have often been sensationalized in popular books and movies. With the great distance between settlements or mining camps, law enforcement was often difficult. Sometimes citizens formed groups of vigilantes (vĭj'ə-lăn'tēz), who hunted down and punished outlaws, without legal authority, sometimes killing innocent people by mistake.

WRITING CONNECTION

After looking over the good and bad deeds you listed on your chart, think for a few minutes about a good deed you have done or one from which you have benefited. Then write a paragraph in your notebook describing this good deed.

On the left, miners panning for gold. Copyright © Underwood Photo Archives.

On the right, the notorious outlaw, Billy the Kid. The Bettman Archive.

- HISTORICAL CONNECTION

598 UNIT FIVE PART 1: FALSE PRETENSES

PRINT AND MEDIA RESOURCES

UNIT FIVE RESOURCE BOOK
Strategic Reading: Literature, p. 9
Vocabulary SkillBuilder, p. 10

GRAMMAR MINI-LESSONS
Transparencies, pp. 52–53
Copymasters, p. 41

WRITING MINI-LESSONS
Transparencies, p. 54

ACCESS FOR STUDENTS ACQUIRING ENGLISH
Selection Summaries
Reading and Writing Support

FORMAL ASSESSMENT
Selection Test, pp. 105–106
Test Generator

 AUDIO LIBRARY
See Reference Card

 LASERLINKS
Historical Connection

INTERNET RESOURCES
McDougal Littell Literature Center at http://www.hmco.com/mcdougal/lit

598 THE LANGUAGE OF LITERATURE TEACHER'S EDITION

☞ When the time came for them to die, Pete Gossard cursed and Knife Hilton cried, but Wolfer Joe Kennedy yawned in the face of the hangman.

What he wanted to do was spit, to show he was not afraid, because he knew men would talk about him later and describe the end he made. But even Wolfer Joe could

THE LAST BOAST

Dorothy M. Johnson

SUMMARY

Three men stand on boxes in a mining camp. Each has a noose around his neck and is preparing to be executed. One cries and one curses, but Wolfer Joe Kennedy yawns. He intends to die bravely. He has been a criminal for most of his life. Just before the boxes are pulled away, the marshal asks Wolfer Joe if he has ever done anything good in his life. "Yeah. Once." Wolfer Joe boasts, "I betrayed a woman." Years before, Wolfer Joe loved, and betrayed, Annie. She loved him and wanted to run away with him. She arrived at the meeting place and waited. Dark came, and she built a fire and waited. All the time, Wolfer Joe lay on a rock and watched, wondering at her love and faith. Finally, not wanting to witness a time when her love might end, he left her. After Wolfer Joe finishes the story about Annie, he is hanged.

Thematic Link: *False Pretenses* An outlaw, having hidden his true nature from the young woman who has come to love him and trust him, abandons the girl rather than taking her with him and risking the sight of it all coming to an end someday.

CUSTOMIZING FOR
Students Acquiring English

- Use **ACCESS FOR STUDENTS ACQUIRING ENGLISH**, *Reading Support*.

Some students acquiring English have trouble discerning changes in time. Help them by pointing out that the story is broken in two: the first part describes the hanging of Wolfer Joe and his partners; the second explains the boast that Wolfer Joe made just before he was hung.

STRATEGIC READING FOR
Less-Proficient Readers

Set a Purpose Have students brainstorm a list of reactions that a person about to be executed might have. After they read the first two paragraphs, they should compare the reactions of the three condemned men to those on their list. Then ask them to read to find out how Wolfer Joe views his imminent death and the life that has led him to the gallows.

Use **UNIT FIVE RESOURCE BOOK**, p. 9, for guidance in reading the selection.

WORDS TO KNOW

abiding (ə-bī'dĭng) *adj.* continuing without change; lasting (p. 602)

acquittal (ə-kwĭt'l) *n.* a declaration not guilty by a judge or jury (p. 600)

constitute (kŏn'stĭ-tōōt') *v.* to form; be part of (p. 600)

farce (färs) *n.* an action or situation that is ridiculous or unbelievable (p. 600)

reflectively (rĭ-flĕk'tĭv-lē) *adv.* thoughtfully (p. 600)

CUSTOMIZING FOR
Gifted and Talented Students

Have students discuss the choices Wolfer Joe makes throughout the story and whether they agree or disagree with his decisions.

Literary Concept: MOOD

A Ask students what mood the banter between Wolfer Joe and Gallagher establishes. *(Possible response: Their sarcasm brings a lighter mood to a normally grim hanging scene.)*

Critical Thinking: MAKING INFERENCES

B Ask students how Wolfer Joe foresaw "the hour of his death." *(Possible response: Wolfer Joe imagined that he would die when he was about this age.)* What is meant by the reference to the bullet, the arrow, and the grizzly's claws? *(Because of his lifestyle, Wolfer Joe imagined his death would come from something like a gunshot, an arrow, or a bear's attack.)*

Literary Concept: CONFLICT

C Ask students to identify the story's external conflict. *(Possible response: Wolfer Joe and either established law or any group acting to enforce justice.)*

STRATEGIC READING FOR
Less-Proficient Readers

D Make sure that students understand how Wolfer Joe views his execution and his life of crime.

- How would you summarize Wolfer Joe's feelings about his execution? *(Possible response: He is resigned to it, having expected to die at about this age, but he is surprised that it isn't the romantic ending he imagined.)* **Summarizing**

- How would you sum up his feelings about his life? *(Possible response: He believes that he was born bad and that he has lived his life naturally as an outlaw.)* **Summarizing**

- What does he boast was his only good deed? *(once betraying a woman)* **Noting Relevant Details**

Set a Purpose Have students read on to find out how and why Wolfer Joe betrayed a woman.

---

not raise enough saliva for spitting when he had a noose around his neck. The yawn was the next best thing.

Barney Gallagher, the United States deputy marshal, finished adjusting the rope and asked half-admiringly, "Are we keeping you up?"

A "Hanging me up, they told me," Wolfer Joe answered.

On a packing box between his companions, he stood glaring out at the crowd of miners, with his lips pulled back from his teeth in the grin that was his trademark. He had foreseen the hour of his death, but not the way of it. He had felt the jar of the bullet, heard the Cheyenne arrow whir, gone down screaming under a grizzly's claws—all these were probabilities for a man who had lived as he had lived, and a man had to die sometime.

But he had always seen himself fighting to the end. He had not dreamed of an end by hanging, helpless, with his hands tied behind him. He would not give his executioners the satisfaction of knowing he was astonished. They were going to get satisfaction enough without that.

Knife Hilton stopped crying and stood drooping on his packing box, snuffling like a baby. Pete Gossard stopped yelling curses, and thinking he had figured out a way to delay the performance, shouted earnestly, "I want a preacher! You wouldn't deny a man a preacher, would you?"

The Vigilanters had thought of that, too, and had a preacher there. They knew, by this time, about all the tricks a man could think of to make delay. Pete Gossard had nothing to say to the preacher, after all, except the frantic plea: "Tell 'em to give me a good drop."

"They will, Pete," the preacher promised. He shivered and added, "They always have. May God have mercy!"

There was still a lot of noise from the crowd of miners—the seven or eight hundred of them who had <u>constituted</u> the jury and had filed solemnly between two wagons to vote. Fourteen men had voted for <u>acquittal</u>, and after four hundred voted "guilty," the Vigilanters had stopped the <u>farce</u> of tallying. The noise was far out on the edge of the crowd, where those who could not see clearly were milling around, but in the center, at the hanging place, there was hardly any sound. Here death was, and the men who would beckon to it had nothing much to say.

The three packing boxes were sturdy; each had a rope tied to it by which it would be pulled away at the signal; the nooses were soundly wound. The Vigilanters, Wolfer Joe recollected, had had plenty of practice.

He felt a shudder coming over him, and to disguise it, he threw back his head and laughed.

He had few illusions about himself. Once he had said, grinning, "Reckon I was born bad." More accurately, he might have said, "I was born outside the law, and mostly I've stayed outside it." He had kept moving westward to places where the law was not. And what caught up with him at last was not law but anger. The angry men at the diggings could not wait for the law to catch up; they set up the Vigilance Committee to enforce ruthless justice.

Barney Gallagher frowned at that laugh. He stepped down from the box, wiping his hands on his pants, and said <u>reflectively</u>, "I was wondering—did you ever do one good thing in your life?"

Wolfer Joe looked into his eyes and answered with his lips pulled back from his teeth, "Yeah. Once. I betrayed a woman."

At the hangman's signal, men pulled the ropes on the packing box.

WORDS TO KNOW
constitute (kŏn'stĭ-tōōt') *v.* to form; be part of
acquittal (ə-kwĭt'l) *n.* a declaration not guilty by a judge or jury
farce (färs) *n.* an action or situation that is ridiculous or unbelievable
reflectively (rĭ-flĕk'tĭv-lē) *adv.* thoughtfully

600

Mini-Lesson ✒ The Writer's Style

SHOW, DON'T TELL Explain that throughout the selection, Johnson uses precise and vivid verbs, nouns, and adjectives to give her readers a colorful picture of Wolfer Joe and his life as an outlaw. In doing so, she shows, rather than tells, the story of Wolfer Joe's life. In the highlighted passage, rather than tell readers that "Everything was ready for the hangings," the writer shows the preparations.

Application Invite students to imagine that Annie happens to enter the hanging field just before the executions are to take place. Ask them to use precise and vivid verbs, nouns, and adjectives to write a description that shows her reaction.

Reteaching/Reinforcement
- *Writing Handbook*, anthology p. 873
- *Writing Mini-Lessons* transparencies p. 54

The Writer's Craft
Showing Rather Than Telling, p. 388

---

600 THE LANGUAGE OF LITERATURE TEACHER'S EDITION

he word love was in the language he used with women, but its meaning was not in his understanding when he met Annie. Even when he left her, he was not sure he knew the meaning, and after that he never had much chance to find out.

She stood with her arms outspread, her hands touching the barn wall, trembling, withdrawing not so much from Wolfer Joe as from life itself pressing toward her.

"You don't really like me," he insisted. "Bet you don't."

"Maybe I do," Annie answered, breathless. "I got to go in now." She could have ducked under his arm, but she only glanced up at him with a scared smile. She was seventeen years old. Wolfer Joe was twenty-nine.

"You go in now," he said, "and I'll know you don't love me." He said the word lightly; he had said it before. The shape of it was easy in his mouth.

She looked away desperately, and the color rose on her neck. "I do so l-love you," she said. "You could just as well stay here, instead of going on."

Oh, no, not at twenty-nine. He could not stay in the settlements for long at a time. The law was creeping westward too fast. He was not sure what the law was, but he knew that he and his like had better keep ahead of it.

"Nothing here to keep me," he said. The words hurt her as he had meant them to hurt, and she drew back. "I got to go on," he said. He added boldly, suddenly seeing a dream, "Going to move on and settle down somewheres. Where I'm going, a girl like you wouldn't go. You wouldn't go with me."

She was pressed tight against the barn wall. "Maybe I would, if I wanted to."

"Your pa wouldn't let you," he scoffed.

"Pa couldn't stop me. Now let me be—let me go!" She struggled against him, but his arms were an iron cage, and his heart pounded against hers.

"Tonight at the fork of the trail," he said when he let her go, when he loosed her arms from their clinging. "Wait for me there.—But you won't come."

"I will!" she said. "Because I l-love you."

That was the last thing she ever said to him.

"I believe you mean it," he answered, and found his voice was hushed with wonder. "I guess you really do," he said, trying to laugh.

The wonder was still on him when he waited where the trail forked. But Doubt hovered there too, and roosting on his shoulder, Suspicion watched the trail with cold, yellow eyes.

If she came, he could take her west and build a soddy,[1] get a bunch of cattle started—he knew how to swing a long loop on someone else's beef. He had done it before, for pay.

"What makes you think she'll come?" hooted Doubt, circling over him.

"What reason would she have if she did?" croaked Suspicion, with claws sharp in his shoulder.

"There's no reward out for me around here," argued Wolfer Joe. "Supposing she does come, her reason's her own business. It's her I want, not her reasons. I'll settle down somewheres. If she comes."

He watched the trail from up above, belly-down on a flat rock. He jerked when he saw her ride to the meeting place and look anxiously around. She had a little bundle of clothing tied to the saddle. He saw her dismount and look around again. But she didn't call out or say a word. She simply sat down to wait.

He was furious, with an unreasoning anger. "Damn little fool!" he whispered. "Running off with a man she don't hardly know! What she'll get is no more'n she's got coming."

He remembered that he himself was the man, and he lay there grinning at his own nonsense.

He would wait a while. When she gave up, he would appear and accuse her: "I knowed it

---

1. **soddy:** a sod house.

THE LAST BOAST **601**

Mini-Lesson Grammar

COMPOUND-COMPLEX SENTENCES
Remind students that a clause has a subject and a predicate and that a compound-complex sentence has one or more subordinate clauses and two or more independent clauses. Write this sample on the board, using a double underscore for the subordinate clause.

Soon after the storm hit, the wind toppled trees, and snow blocked the canyons.

Application Have students identify the independent and subordinate clauses in the compound-complex sentence above. (*Independent:* *The word love was in the language; its meaning was not in his understanding.* **Dependent:** *[that] he used with women; when he met Annie*) After calling their attention to the words at the right, have students write two compound-complex sentences based on the story.

Reteaching/Reinforcement
- *Grammar Handbook,* anthology p. 944
- *Grammar Mini-Lessons* copymasters p. 41, transparencies pp. 52–53

The Writer's Craft
Compound-Complex Sentences, p. 739

Literary Concept: CONFLICT

E Ask students what Annie's internal conflict is. (*Possible response: She apparently loves Wolfer Joe but seems unsure what to do about it.*)

Literary Concept: VERBAL IRONY

F Have students reread Wolfer Joe's dialogue. Ask what it means. (*Possible responses: Wolfer Joe is playing a mind game with the young girl, falsely claiming that any action of leaving on Annie's part is proof that she doesn't love him; he is pressing her to confirm her love for him openly and on the spot.*)

Literary Concept: EXTENDED METAPHOR

G Ask students what metaphor is used to characterize Wolfer Joe's doubt and suspicion about Annie's commitment to him. (*His doubt and suspicion are depicted as birds.*) Ask students if they think the imagery is appropriate. (*Possible responses: No—The imagery of talking birds seems too cartoonish; Yes—The notion of cold, pestering, and annoying birds is common and gives the dialogue between Wolfer Joe and his nagging inner voices a strong visual image.*)

CUSTOMIZING FOR
Multiple Learning Styles

H **Spatial or Graphic Learners** Invite students to draw pictures of Doubt and Suspicion. Then ask them to discuss how their pictures portray these feelings.

Critical Thinking: ANALYZING

I Ask students to what man Wolfer Joe refers. (*Wolfer Joe himself*) Have students consider why Wolfer Joe becomes so furious with Annie. (*Possible responses: Wolfer Joe feels she knows too little about himself to run off with him, and because of this, if she finds only grief, it's her own fault; he hopes that she won't show up so he won't have to face his feelings for her and can blame her for ending their relationship.*)

Words that Introduce Subordinate Clauses

after	when
because	where
if	which
that	who

THE LANGUAGE OF LITERATURE TEACHER'S EDITION **601**

Art Note

***Apprehension of the Stage Robbers* by Harvey Johnson** Considered one of the premier artists of the West, Harvey Johnson (1921–) combines his love of the region with his fascination with detail to portray his scenes realistically.

Reading the Art How is the artist's eye for detail reflected in this painting? On the basis of your reading of the painting, explain how you think the sheriff got so close to the robbers before they noticed him.

STRATEGIC READING FOR
Less-Proficient Readers

J Have students tell how and why Wolfer Joe betrayed Annie. *(Possible responses: By staying hidden on the rock, Wolfer Joe broke his promise to Annie that if she'd show up at the fork of the trail, he'd take her with him as he "moved on and settled down." He did this because he feared seeing her faith in him someday end and her love for him possibly turn into betrayal on her part.)*
Summarizing/Drawing Conclusions

- In what way might his betrayal have benefited Annie? *(Possible response: She was freed from living the dangerous, uncertain, probably unhappy life of the wife of an outlaw.)* Making Inferences

CUSTOMIZING FOR
Students Acquiring English

I Explain that gunslingers traditionally marked or notched their gun for each person they killed.

CUSTOMIZING FOR
Gifted and Talented Students

Have students debate whether either Wolfer Joe or Annie was really in love with the other.

COMPREHENSION CHECK
1. How does Wolfer Joe act before he is hanged? *(cocky)*
2. Of what does he boast? *(betraying a woman)*
3. How did he betray Annie? *(He hid, refusing to join up with her after she had come to meet him.)*
4. What caused him to desert her? *(fear that he might see her love for him end and be replaced possibly by betrayal of its own)*

Apprehension of the Stage Robbers (1992), Harvey W. Johnson, C. A. Oil, 24″ × 36″.

was just a notion. You never meant what you said. You start but you can't finish."

Then he would let her go home weeping—or on with him, to do her crying later, when she knew what a fool she was.

But she did not give up. When darkness came, she built a little fire to keep the night away. With his heart pounding, with his lips pulled back from his teeth, Wolfer Joe lay on the flat rock, watching her. She had come so far; she had been so faithful. How long would she wait there for him? How far could he trust her?

Suspicion whispered, "There'll come a day when she'll go crying to the law and say, 'I know where Wolfer Joe is if you want him.'"

He answered, "You don't know my Annie."

He watched her head bend forward on her knees as she waited and dozed. He saw it snap up again when a night sound scared her. After a while the fire burned low, and he knew she was sleeping. She awoke and fed it, and it blazed.

Then he knew he wasn't going down there. He saw not the girl but her patience. He saw not the red glow of the fire but faith <u>abiding</u>.

He saw love by the fire, and he could not endure looking for fear he might see it end, during that night or some year to come.

He crept back off the rock and slid silently into the darkness to where his horse was waiting.

He lived for fourteen years after that. He was said to have seventeen notches on his gun, but that wasn't true. He never notched his gun butt for anything he did.

He was justly sentenced to hang for helping to murder two miners whom he and Pete Gossard and Knife Hilton had dry-gulched[2] when the miners tried to take their gold out.

Wolfer Joe made an ending that earned him grim respect, and he left Barney Gallagher puzzling about how betraying a woman could be a thing a man might boast of with the last words he ever had a chance to speak. ❖

---

2. **dry-gulched:** killed from ambush.

WORDS TO KNOW
abiding (ə-bī′dĭng) *adj.* continuing without change; lasting

---

Mini-Lesson Literary Concepts

REVIEWING CONFLICT Remind students that the plot of a story always involves conflict, or struggle, between opposing forces. Summarize the two kinds of conflict: An external conflict involves a character pitted against an outside force such as nature, a physical obstacle, or another character; an internal conflict occurs within a character, such as trying to make a decision.

Application Have students work in small groups to write brief descriptions of the story's various external and internal conflicts. Be sure they consider whether Wolfer Joe's conflicts are all external and Annie's are all internal. Ask the groups to state whether each conflict they identify is resolved and, if so, how.

RESPONDING OPTIONS

FROM PERSONAL RESPONSE TO CRITICAL ANALYSIS

REFLECT
1. Did you enjoy this story? Why or why not? Jot down your response in your notebook.

RETHINK
2. Review the chart you made of good and bad deeds. In which column would you record the deed that Wolfer Joe boasted about? Explain why.

3. Why do you think Wolfer Joe decided to leave without Annie?
   Consider
   - his argument with himself as he watched her waiting
   - what he saw in her
   - what he feared

Close Textual Reading

4. If Annie had gone with Wolfer Joe, do you think he might have become a better person? Explain your reasoning.

Thematic Link

5. The narrator says that Wolfer Joe knew nothing about love when he met Annie. What does that suggest about his past?

RELATE
6. Do you think the U.S. justice system should try to rehabilitate criminals like Wolfer Joe or simply punish them? Explain.

LITERARY CONCEPTS

An **extended metaphor** is a figure of speech that compares two unlike things at some length and in several ways. Notice that the feelings of doubt and suspicion that Wolfer Joe experiences as he waits for Annie are compared to things that are not actually named. Explain this extended metaphor and point out its details. What is the effect created?

As you know, irony often results when appearance and reality are opposites. For example, it is ironic that Wolfer Joe considered his betrayal of Annie a good deed. One type of irony is **dramatic irony,** where the reader or viewer knows something that a character does not. Identify the dramatic irony in "The Last Boast."

Multimodal Learning

ANOTHER PATHWAY
Cooperative Learning
Imagine a sentencing hearing to determine if Wolfer Joe should be sent to prison or executed. In a small group, draft two summary statements: one asking for mercy and the other arguing for death. Then debate the issue in class and vote on which sentence Joe should get.

QUICKWRITES

1. Imagine that before he died, Wolfer Joe came out from behind his false pretense and sent a message to Annie. Compose the **note** that you think he might have written.

2. Write a **character sketch** of Wolfer Joe, describing the kind of man he was and explaining why he chose an outlaw's life.

3. Using the good deed you described earlier in the Writing Connection, create an outline of a **short story** in which this deed plays a major role.

📁 **PORTFOLIO** Save your writing. You may want to use it later as a springboard to a piece for your portfolio.

The Writer's Craft
Point of View, pp. 250–254
Storyboard, pp. 108–112

From Personal Response to Critical Analysis

1. Accept all reasonable responses.
2. Possible responses: good, because he saved Annie from a life she would probably live to regret; bad, because by not telling Annie the reason he didn't take her with him, she probably spent her whole life tormented by wondering why Wolfer Joe never showed up.
3. Possible responses: He was afraid of commitment and the possibility of her eventual betrayal of him once she tired of living his kind of life; he cared too much for her to make her miserable.
4. Accept all reasonable, well-supported responses. Some students may feel that because Wolfer Joe appeared to have genuine feelings for a woman for the first time, Annie might have been able to make him a better person.
5. Accept all reasonable, well-supported responses. Many students might imagine that Wolfer Joe's past life was one of constant struggle to survive and may have been caused by either growing up in an uncaring or abusive home or suffering the general hardships of life in that part of the country in those days.
6. Accept all reasonable, well-supported responses. Some students may feel that Wolfer Joe's feelings for Annie are evidence that people such as he can be rehabilitated if they are worked with. Others may feel that Wolfer Joe was basically beyond reform—that he would have eventually turned cruel and heartless toward Annie—and that simple punishment is all that is called for.

Another Pathway

Cooperative Learning Students should work together to ensure that their summary statements are convincing. Be sure that all students contribute ideas and opinions to discussion.

Rubric
3 Full Accomplishment The summary statements contain cogent and concise arguments that reflect the information given about Wolfer Joe in "The Last Boast."
2 Substantial Accomplishment The summary statements are adequate but either ramble a bit or contain minor inaccuracies.
1 Little or Partial Accomplishment The summary statements are not persuasive and contain inaccurate information.

Literary Concepts

Have students work in pairs to examine the extended metaphor. *(Possible responses: The extended metaphor compares doubt and suspicion to birds; the metaphor is implied through word pictures such as "hovered there," "roosting on his shoulder," "cold, yellow eyes," "hooted," "circling," and "claws sharp;" the effect is to make doubt and suspicion vulturelike in their destructive preying on Wolfer Joe's mind.)*

Dramatic Irony Students can continue to work in pairs to identify the substance of dramatic irony. *(Possible response: There is dramatic irony both in Annie's never knowing why Wolfer Joe failed to show up and in Barney Gallagher's failure to understand Wolfer Joe's final boast.)*

QuickWrites

1. Remind students to stay in the character of Wolfer Joe.
2. Encourage students to search the text for clues to Wolfer Joe's character.
3. Suggest that students make a story map that addresses important elements of the story, such as title, setting, characters, and conflicts.

Words to Know

1. constituted
2. abiding
3. farce
4. acquittal
5. reflectively

Reteaching/Reinforcement
- Unit Five Resource Book, p. 10

Across the Curriculum

History and Folklore Suggest that students work in pairs to do their research and make their presentation. If they present an episode or a tale, they may wish to make a dramatic presentation. If they present a song, one student may choose to provide musical accompaniment while the other sings.

Literary Links

Have students compare Wolfer Joe's good deed with those of Mr. Johnson in "One Ordinary Day, with Peanuts." Suggest that they consider motivation, behaviors, and effect. You may suggest that they consider whether they feel that Wolfer Joe had the equal capability for either good or evil.

DOROTHY M. JOHNSON

In his review of one of Dorothy M. Johnson's works, Frederick J. Stefon states that she "has provided the reader with a sensitive portrayal of the period of American history often distorted by historians and sensationalized by novelists...." Accuracy of detail and subjects commonly involving the courage and faults of ordinary people mark her writings. Popular throughout the world as well as United States, Johnson's stories have been translated into Spanish, German, Urdu, Indonesian, Russian, and Polish.

Multimodal Learning

ALTERNATIVE ACTIVITIES

1. From what you know about the settings of old Westerns, paint the **scene** of Wolfer Joe's hanging.
2. Make up a **tall tale** of how Wolfer Joe got his name, and tell it to the class.
3. Design a "Wanted" **poster** for Wolfer Joe that might have been posted in a frontier town. If you're working on a computer, try experimenting with different type fonts.

Multimodal Learning

ACROSS THE CURRICULUM

History and Folklore Investigate the life of one of the legendary outlaws of the Old West, such as Jesse James, Billy the Kid, Sam Bass, or Belle Starr. Share with the class an episode from this person's life or a tale or song about the outlaw.

WORDS TO KNOW

Review the Words to Know in the boxes at the bottom of the selection pages. Then write the vocabulary word that best completes each sentence.

1. If what you see in movies and on TV _____ all that you know about the Old West, your knowledge may be somewhat inaccurate.
2. You may think, for example, that the pony express was an _____ part of western life, but the truth is that it ran for less than two years.
3. For people who know the facts, a film showing cowboys having regular barroom fist fights is a _____ because, in reality, cowboys were very careful not to injure their hands.
4. Now you may decide that a moviemaker accused of deliberate inaccuracy deserves an _____ because the intent is to entertain rather than educate.
5. Still, sometimes a Western comes along that deals _____ with the realities of life in the Old West and still manages to be both interesting and accurate.

DOROTHY M. JOHNSON

Dorothy M. Johnson was not just another Western writer. Her award-winning fiction has become known for the way it portrays the real American West, not just the legends and stereotypes. Moreover, Johnson demonstrated an insight into the lives of Native Americans, with books such as *Warrior for a Lost Nation: A Biography of Sitting Bull* and *Buffalo Woman*. As a result, she was made an honorary member of Montana's Blackfoot tribe and given the Native American name Kills-Both-Places. Meanwhile, three of her stories became popular movies: *The Hanging Tree*, *The Man Who Shot Liberty Valance*, and *A Man Called Horse*.

1905–1984

Johnson was born in McGregor, Iowa, but moved to Montana with her family as a young girl. After working as an editor for New York City publishers for 15 years, she returned to the state where she had grown up. She became a newspaper editor and later a professor of journalism at the University of Montana.

Johnson asked that the inscription "Paid" be placed on her grave marker. "God and I know what it means," she said, "and nobody else needs to know."

OTHER WORKS *All the Buffalo Returning*, *Flame on the Frontier*, *The Bloody Bozeman* Extended Reading

604 UNIT FIVE PART 1: FALSE PRETENSES

Alternative Activities

1. Suggest that students think about television programs and movies that they have seen about the Old West. Have them draw on those images as well as the descriptions in the selection to paint the scene.
2. Remind students that a tall tale is a story of unbelievable events told in an apparently serious voice. Point out that a tall tale makes use of exaggeration by stretching the truth.
3. Encourage students to locate photos of Old West "wanted" posters in the library. Suggest that they think about such details as the crimes Wolfer Joe committed and how much money his capture would be worth before they design their posters.

PREVIEWING

FICTION

Full Circle
Sue Grafton

Activating Prior Knowledge

PERSONAL CONNECTION

Think about the mystery stories you have read or seen. What do you think causes readers to enjoy stories of mystery and deception? In your notebook, create a cluster diagram in which you explore what draws people to mystery stories.

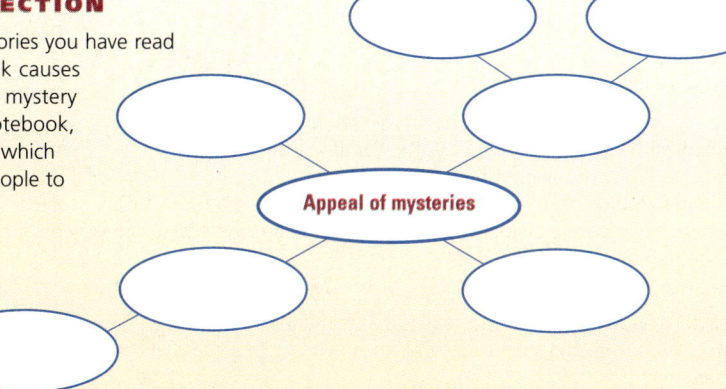

Building Background

GEOGRAPHICAL CONNECTION

Like other Sue Grafton mystery stories, this one features a private investigator named Kinsey Millhone and is set in a fictional California town called Santa Teresa. Santa Teresa is based on the actual town of Santa Barbara, where Grafton lives. Santa Barbara is a little more than an hour's drive northwest of Los Angeles. Along with two nearby cities, it forms a metropolitan area with a population of about 370,000. The University of California has a large campus about ten miles northwest of Santa Barbara. Appropriately enough for a city near Los Angeles, much of the action in this mystery occurs on a freeway.

OVERVIEW

Objectives

- To understand and appreciate a detective story that describes the investigative techniques that a detective uses to solve a crime
- To identify and understand the elements of plot
- To express understanding of the story through a choice of writing forms, including a story ending and a plot outline
- To extend understanding of the story through a variety of multimodal and cross-curricular activities

Skills

LITERARY CONCEPTS
- Plot
- Description

READING SKILLS/ STRATEGIES
- Understanding the detective story

THE WRITER'S STYLE
- Using similes

GENRE STUDY
- Fiction: detective story

GRAMMAR
- Using *sit* and *set*

SPEAKING, LISTENING, AND VIEWING
- Speeches
- Group discussion
- Oral presentation

ALTERNATIVE
Previewing

Choose partners and use the following prompts to preview "Full Circle" orally.

Personal Connection

Discussion Prompts

- What mystery stories have you read or seen on TV or in films?
- List five common elements that made the stories enjoyable.
- Which element was most important to you? Why?

As you read "Full Circle," notice the clues that Kinsey Millhone uses to solve the crime.

PRINT AND MEDIA RESOURCES

UNIT FIVE RESOURCE BOOK
Strategic Reading: Literature, p. 13
Vocabulary SkillBuilder, p. 14

GRAMMAR MINI-LESSONS
Transparencies, p. 33
Copymasters, p. 33

WRITING MINI-LESSONS
Transparencies, p. 47

ACCESS FOR STUDENTS ACQUIRING ENGLISH
Selection Summaries
Reading Support

FORMAL ASSESSMENT
Selection Test, pp. 107–108
 Test Generator

AUDIO LIBRARY
See Reference Card

INTERNET RESOURCES
McDougal Littell Literature Center at http://www.hmco.com/mcdougal/lit

SUMMARY

The narrator, a private detective, witnesses a traffic accident in which a young woman is killed. The next week the mother of the dead driver hires the narrator to find out who killed her daughter. The driver, it turns out, had been shot. The detective interviews witnesses and people who knew the dead woman, including the woman's roommate. She learns little except that the woman was being stalked by a boyfriend whose identity is unknown. She is unable to locate one witness, a young man driving a pickup who gave the police a false name. The narrator goes to talk to the roommate a second time. No one is home, but on a hunch, she looks in the garage and sees the pickup. As she goes to call the police, she observes the missing witness driving up. She realizes he is the roommate's brother, the dead woman's boyfriend, and the killer. When he sees her, a high-speed chase ensues that ends in an accident and the death of the young man. The accident takes place at precisely the same spot where the first accident occurred.

Thematic Link: *False Pretenses* A detective sees through false pretenses to solve the murder of a young woman.

Active Reading

READING CONNECTION

Understanding the Detective Story

What Is a Detective Story?
A detective story is a specific type of mystery story. Detective stories in general share these traits:

- an actual detective, either a police investigator or a private detective (private eye) hired by an ordinary citizen
- a crime, usually a murder, committed by an unknown person
- a set of clues

Many people feel that if any one of these three basics is altered—if there is no detective, if the identity of the murderer is known early on, or if the solution does not come from a logical reasoning based on clues—then a story is a mystery story, not a detective story.

Besides having these elements in common, traditional detective stories generally play by these rules to varying degrees:

- the crime is significant (if the crime is not murder, then the crime must be serious enough to warrant the reader's attention)
- the reader gets the same clues that the detective gets—and at the same time
- the character who is unmasked as the murderer must be someone who has been known of, if not shown, throughout much of the story

These rules give the reader a fair chance to solve the crime by the time the detective does, or even before. Piecing together the solution—often involving first figuring out how and why—means eventually answering the basic question *who*: Whodunit? Who committed the crime?

Predicting the Solution to the Crime
Much of the appeal of reading detective stories comes from the sense of solving the puzzle right along with the investigator. As you read "Full Circle," look for clues that answer the questions how, why, and who. To add to your involvement in and enjoyment of the story, try to predict possible solutions to the crime at different points. Imagine yourself as the private eye, Kinsey Millhone, and in your mind assemble the how, the why, and the who of the mystery as it unfolds. Then use what you know to guess the solution to the crime.

Using Your Reading Log Use the questions inserted throughout the selection to help you make predictions about the solution to the crime. Write your responses in your reading log.

606   UNIT FIVE   PART 1: FALSE PRETENSES

WORDS TO KNOW

brevity (brĕv′ĭ-tē) *n.* the quality of being brief in time; shortness (p. 617)
despondently (dĭ-spŏn′dənt-lē) *adv.* in a very discouraged or depressed manner (p. 613)
dispel (dĭ-spĕl′) *v.* to scatter; drive away (p. 609)
egotistical (ē′gə-tĭs′tĭ-kəl) *adj.* conceited; proud (p. 615)
enigmatic (ĕn′ĭg-măt′ĭk) *adj.* mysterious; puzzling (p. 614)

harass (hăr′əs) *v.* to irritate or torment in a determined or continual way (p. 611)
inexplicable (ĭn-ĕk′splĭ-kə-bəl) *adj.* difficult or impossible to explain (p. 617)
skewed (skyo͞od) *adj.* distorted or slanted in a particular direction; unbalanced **skew** *v.* (p. 617)
sullen (sŭl′ən) *adj.* showing irritation or unhappiness by a gloomy silence; moody (p. 614)
wary (wâr′ē) *adj.* cautious; watchful (p. 612)

Full Circle

SUE GRAFTON

DESIGN NOTE

Reading the Art Ask students to discuss the effect of the shattered glass. What mood does it help convey? In what way is it appropriate for a detective story? *(Possible responses: The shattered glass creates a suspenseful, anxious mood; it is appropriate for a detective story, for it suggests violence.)*

CUSTOMIZING FOR
Students Acquiring English

- Use **ACCESS FOR STUDENTS ACQUIRING ENGLISH,** *Reading Support.*

- Tell students that in many detective stories, the characters often use slang, using *dude* for *gut* and *bugging* for *bothering.* Point out to them that the narrator and Lieutenant Dolan occasionally use police jargon when speaking. Encourage students to ask questions if they cannot figure out these terms.

Mini-Lesson Genre Study

FICTION On the chalkboard draw the web shown at the right and use it to point out the characteristics of a detective story.

Application Ask students to copy the web into their notebooks. Then have them use it as they look for the traits of a detective story in "Full Circle."

STRATEGIC READING FOR
Less-Proficient Readers

To help students understand the chain reaction described in the first three paragraphs, ask them to draw a simple diagram showing the movement of the cars.

Set a Purpose Ask students to read on to find out how a tragic accident turns into a detective story.

Use **UNIT FIVE RESOURCE BOOK**, p. 13, for guidance in reading the selection.

CUSTOMIZING FOR
Gifted and Talented Students

As students read, they should identify passages that reveal the qualities that make Kinsey Millhone a good detective.

Possible responses:

- *Page 612—"he grumbled so I pressed for specifics." / She is assertive.*

- *Page 614—"suddenly remembered John Birkett at the scene" / She has good recall.*

- *Page 589—"Doggedly I went through the list of witnesses" / She is thorough and persistent.*

- *Page 617—"I peeled after him, flooring it." / She is daring.*

Literary Concept: EXPOSITION

A Ask students what they learned about the narrator and the setting of the story from the opening paragraph of the selection. (*Possible response: The narrator is a female private eye. The setting is a freeway in Santa Teresa.*)

Active Reading: QUESTION

B Discuss with students what you think could have made the popping sound using the following model.

Think-aloud Model *I think the popping sound could have been a gun shot. I'll have to continue reading to find out if my suspicion is correct.*

A The accident seemed to happen in slow motion . . . one of those stop-action sequences that seem to go on forever though in truth no more than a few seconds have elapsed. It was Friday afternoon, rush hour, Santa Teresa traffic moving at a lively pace, my little VW holding its own despite the fact that it's fifteen years out of date. I was feeling good. I'd just wrapped up a case and I had a check in my handbag for four thousand bucks, not bad considering that I'm a female private eye, self-employed, and subject to the feast-or-famine vagaries[1] of any other free-lance work.

I glanced to my left as a young woman, driving a white compact, appeared in my side view mirror. A bright red Porsche was bearing down on her in the fast lane. I adjusted my speed, making room for her, sensing that she meant to cut in front of me. A navy blue pickup truck was coming up on my right, each of us jockeying for position as the late afternoon sun washed down out of a cloudless California spring sky. I had glanced in my rearview mirror, checking traffic behind me, when I heard a loud popping noise. I snapped my attention back to the road in front of me. The white compact veered abruptly back into the fast lane, clipped the rear of the red Porsche, then hit the center divider and careened directly into my path. I slammed on my brakes, adrenaline shooting through me as I fought to control the VW's fishtailing rear end.

B > **QUESTION**
> What might the loud popping noise be?
> *Using a Reading Log*

Suddenly a dark green Mercedes appeared from out of nowhere and caught the girl's car broadside, flipping the vehicle with all the expertise[2] of a movie stunt. Brakes squealed all around me like a chorus of squawking birds and I could hear the successive thumps of colliding cars piling up behind me in a drum roll of destruction. It was over in an instant, a cloud of dust roiling up from the shoulder where the girl's car had finally come to rest, right side up, half-buried in the shrubbery. She had sheared off one of the support posts for the exit sign that now leaned crazily across her car roof. The ensuing silence was profound.

I pulled over and was out of my car like a shot, the fellow from the navy blue pickup truck right behind me. There must have been five of us running toward the wreckage, spurred by the possibility of exploding gasoline, which mercifully did not ignite. The white car was accordion-folded, the door on the driver's side jammed shut. Steam billowed out from under the hood with an alarming hiss. The impact had rammed the girl headfirst into the windshield, which had cracked in a starburst effect. She was unconscious, her face bathed in blood. I willed myself to move toward her though my instinct was to turn away in horror.

The guy from the pickup truck nearly wrenched the car door off its hinges in one of those emergency-generated bursts of strength that can't be duplicated under ordinary circumstances. As he reached for her, I caught his arm.

"Don't move her," I said. "Let the paramedics handle this."

He gave me a startled look but drew back as he was told. I shed my windbreaker and we used it to form a compress, stanching the flow of blood from the worst of her cuts. The guy was in his twenties, with dark curly hair and dark eyes filled with anxiety.

Over my shoulder, someone was asking me if I knew first aid, and I realized that others had been hurt in the accident as well. The driver from the green Mercedes was already using the roadside emergency phone, presumably calling

---

1. **vagaries** (vā′gə-rēz): odd or erratic ideas or actions; whims.
2. **expertise** (ĕk′spûr-tēz′): special skill or knowledge.

608 UNIT FIVE PART 1: FALSE PRETENSES

Mini-Lesson Literary Concepts

REVIEWING DESCRIPTION Remind students that description helps the reader to picture scenes, events, and characters. Tell them that description usually includes imagery—words and phrases that appeal to the senses—and figurative language.

Application Ask students to review the description of the accident on page 608 and to find details that appeal to the senses of sight and hearing. What other details does the author use to help create scenes, events, and characters?

police and ambulance. I looked back at the guy from the pickup truck, who was pressing the girl's neck, looking for a pulse.

"Is she alive?" I asked.

"Looks like it."

I jerked my head at the people on the berm[3] behind me. "Let me see what I can do down there until the ambulance comes," I said. "Holler if you need me."

He nodded in reply.

I left him with the girl and moved along the shoulder toward a writhing man whose leg was visibly broken. A woman was sobbing hysterically somewhere close by and her cries added an eerie counterpoint to the moans of those in pain. The fellow from the red Porsche simply stood there numb, immobilized by shock.

Meanwhile, traffic had slowed to a crawl and commuters were rubbernecking as if freeway accidents were some sort of spectator sport and this was the main event. Sirens approached. The next hour was a blur of police and emergency vehicles. I spotted my friend John Birkett, a photographer from the local paper, who'd reached the scene moments behind the paramedics. I remember marveling at the speed with which news of the pileup had spread. I watched as the girl was loaded into the ambulance. While flashbulbs went off, several of us gave our accounts of the accident to the highway patrol officer, conferring with one another compulsively as if repetition might relieve us of tension and distress. I didn't get home until nearly seven and my hands were still shaking. The jumble of images made sleep a torment of sudden awakenings, my foot jerking in a dream sequence as I slammed on my brakes again and again.

When I read in the morning paper that the girl had died, I felt sick with regret. The article was brief. Caroline Spurrier was twenty-two, a senior psychology major at the University of California, Santa Teresa. She was a native of Denver, Colorado, just two months short of graduation at the time of her death. The photograph showed shoulder-length blond hair, bright eyes, and an impish grin.

A WOMAN WAS SOBBING HYSTERICALLY.

According to the paper, six other people had suffered injuries, none fatal. The weight of the young woman's death settled in my chest like a cold I couldn't shake.

My office in town was being repainted, so I worked at home that next week, catching up on reports. On Thursday, when the knock came, I'd just broken for lunch. I opened the door. At first glance, I thought the dead girl was miraculously alive, restored to health, and standing on my doorstep with all the solemnity of a ghost. The illusion was dispelled. A close look showed a blond woman in her midforties, her face etched with weariness.

"I'm Michelle Spurrier," she said. "I understand you were a witness to my daughter's accident."

I stepped back. "Please come in. I'm sorry for your loss, Mrs. Spurrier. That was terrible."

She moved past me like a sleepwalker as I closed the door.

---

3. **berm:** the edge or shoulder of a road.

WORDS TO KNOW
dispel (dĭ-spĕl´) *v.* to scatter; drive away

Mini-Lesson The Writer's Style

USING SIMILES Point out to students that Sue Grafton makes use of both literal and figurative language. Literal language is straightforward and to the point. The meaning is evident. In contrast, figures of speech such as similes are imaginative. A sentence or phrase that contains a simile reveals similarities in things that appear to be very different. In the highlighted sentence on this page, Michelle Spurrier is compared to a sleepwalker. Ask students why they think Sue Grafton used this simile.

Application Invite students to find a paragraph in the story that uses literal language and then to rewrite it to include at least two similes. Ask them to tell which version they prefer and why.

Reteaching/Reinforcement
- *Writing Handbook,* anthology p. 874
- *Writing Mini-Lesson* transparencies, p. 47

 The Writer's Craft

Literal and Figurative Language, p. 413

Art Note

Untitled by Don Eddy Don Eddy is a Photo-Realist. He creates paintings featuring amazingly lifelike images. Born in Long Beach, California, in 1944, Eddy's career began in high school as custom paint jobs on cars and motorcycles. He was attending college in Santa Barbara in 1969 when, then working on canvas, he began panting automobiles, capturing the reflective qualities of the cars' color and chrome surfaces; in 1971 he concentrated specifically on Volkswagens. Working from black-and-white photographs, Eddy airbrushes vibrant color onto his canvas, creating details that would be apparent in a photograph and showing images that could not be captured by a camera.

Reading the Art In what way is this painting like a photograph? In what way is it different from a photograph? Do you think that realistic artwork style is appropriate to illustrate a detective story? Why or why not?

Literary Concept: EXPOSITION

F Ask students what important piece of information was revealed in this section. (*Caroline was shot.*) Invite them to discuss how they think this disclosure advances the plot. (*Kinsey will use her detective skills to find out who killed Caroline and why.*)

Active Reading: CLARIFY

G Students should conclude that the loud popping noise was a gun shot.

Untitled (Green Volkswagen) (1971), Don Eddy. Acrylic on canvas, 66″ × 95″, courtesy of Nancy Hoffman Gallery, New York.

"Please sit down. Can I get you anything?"

She shook her head, looking around with bewilderment as if she couldn't quite remember what had brought her here. She set her purse aside and sank down on my couch, placing her cupped hands across her nose and mouth like an oxygen mask.

I sat down beside her, watching as she breathed deeply, struggling to speak. "Take your time," I said.

When the words came, her voice was so low I had to lean closely to hear her. "The police examined Caroline's car at the impound lot and found a bullet hole in the window on the passenger side. My daughter was shot." She burst into tears.

CLARIFY
What was the loud popping noise?
Using a Reading Log

I sat beside her while she poured out a grief tinged with rage and frustration. I brought her a glass of water and a fistful of tissues, small comfort, but all I could think to do. "What are the police telling you?" I asked when she'd composed herself.

She blew her nose and then took another deep breath. "The case has been transferred from traffic detail to homicide. The officer I talked to this morning says it looks like a random freeway shooting, but I don't believe it."

"God knows they've had enough of those down in Los Angeles," I remarked.

"Well, I can't accept that. For one thing,

610 UNIT FIVE PART 1: FALSE PRETENSES

Mini-Lesson Grammar

Present	Present Participle	Past	Past Participle
sit	(is) sitting	sat	(have) sat
set	(is) setting	set	(have) set

USING *SIT* AND *SET* Explain that *sit* is an intransitive verb that means "to occupy a seat." It does not take a direct object. *Set* is a transitive verb that means "to place." In the active voice, *set* requires a direct object. Write the principal parts of the verbs *sit* and *set* on the chalkboard for the students' reference.

Application Have students use the information from the chalkboard to identify the forms of *sit* and *set* in the highlighted passage on page 610. Then read the following sentences aloud, and ask students to choose the correct verb forms.

1. Mrs. Spurrier (sat, set) on the couch. (*sat*)
2. Where did she (sit, set) her purse? (*set*)
3. Kinsey is (sitting, setting) next to her. (*sitting*)

Reteaching/Reinforcement
- Grammar Handbook, anthology p. 925
- *Grammar Mini-Lessons* transparencies p. 33, copymasters p. 33

 The Writer's Craft

Sit and *Set*, pp. 614, 826

610 THE LANGUAGE OF LITERATURE TEACHER'S EDITION

what was she doing speeding down the highway at that hour of the day? She was supposed to be at work, but they tell me she left abruptly without a word to anyone."

"Where was she employed?"

"A restaurant out in Colgate. She'd been waiting tables there for a year. The shift manager told me a man had been harassing her. He thinks she might have left to try to get away from him."

"Did he know who the guy was?"

She shook her head. "He wasn't sure. Some fellow she'd been dating. Apparently, he kept stopping by the restaurant, calling her at all hours, making a terrible pest of himself. Lieutenant Dolan tells me you're a private detective, which is why I'm here. I want you to find out who's responsible for this."

"Mrs. Spurrier, the police here are very competent. I'm sure they're doing everything possible."

"Skip the public relations message," she said with bitterness. "I have to fly back to Denver. Caroline's stepfather is very ill and I need to get home, but I can't go unless I know someone here is looking into this. Please."

I thought about it briefly, but it didn't take much to persuade me. As a witness to the accident, I felt more than a professional interest in the case. "I'll need the names of her friends," I said.

I made a note of Mrs. Spurrier's address and phone number, along with the name of Caroline's roommate and the restaurant where she'd worked. I drew up a standard contract, waiving the advance. I'd bill her later for whatever time I put in. Ordinarily I bypass police business in an attempt to stay out of Lieutenant Dolan's way. As the officer in charge of homicide, he's not crazy about private eyes. Though he's fairly tolerant of me, I couldn't imagine what she'd had to threaten to warrant the referral.[4]

As soon as she left, I grabbed a jacket and my handbag and drove over to the police station, where I paid six dollars for a copy of the police report. Lieutenant Dolan wasn't in, but I spent a few minutes chatting with Emerald, the clerk in Identification and Records. She's a heavy black woman in her fifties, usually wary of my questions but a sucker for gossip.

"I hear Jasper's wife caught him with Rowena Hairston," I said, throwing out some bait. Jasper Sax is one of Emerald's interdepartmental foes.

---

4. **warrant the referral:** be a good reason for sending Mrs. Spurrier to the narrator for help.

WORDS TO KNOW
harass (hăr′əs) *v.* to persistently bother or torment
wary (wâr′ē) *adj.* cautious; watchful

611

**Literary Concept:
CHARACTERIZATION**

J Ask what is revealed about Kinsey through her interaction with Emerald. *(Possible response: She is adept at manipulating people.)*

Literary Concept: FIRST-PERSON POINT OF VIEW

K Ask students why first-person point of view is appropriate for a detective story. *(Possible response: It gives the reader the chance to follow the detective's thought processes.)*

Critical Thinking: CLASSIFYING

L Have students describe the interaction between the narrator and Emerald. *(Possible response: They seem to be playing a well practiced cat-and-mouse game.)*

Critical Thinking: SPECULATING

M Point out to students that Emerald speculates that the driver of the pickup gave a fake name because a warrant might be outstanding against him. Invite students to come up with other reasons why he would conceal his identity. *(Possible responses: He doesn't want to get involved in a lawsuit; he is the killer; he is afraid someone will blame him for the "accident.")*

"Why tell me?" she said. She was pretending disinterest, but I could tell the rumor cheered her. Jasper, from the crime lab, is forever lifting files from Emerald's desk, which only gets her in trouble when Lieutenant Dolan comes around.

"I was hoping you'd fill me in on the Spurrier accident. I know you've memorized all the paperwork."

She grumbled something about flattery that implied she felt flattered, so I pressed for specifics. "Anybody see where the shot was fired from?" I asked.

"No ma'am."

I thought about the fellow in the red Porsche. He'd been in the lane to my left, just a few yards ahead of me when the accident occurred. The man in the pickup might be a help as well. "What about the other witnesses? There must have been half a dozen of us at the scene. Who's been interviewed?"

Emerald gave me an indignant look. "What's the matter with you? You know I'm not allowed to give out information like that!"

"Worth a try," I said equably.⁵ "What about the girl's professors from the university? Has Dolan talked to them?"

"Check it out yourself if you're so interested," she snapped.

"Come on, Emerald. Dolan knows I'm doing this. He was the one who told Mrs. Spurrier about me in the first place. I'll make it easy for you. Just one name."

She squinted at me suspiciously. "Which one's that?"

I took a flier,⁶ describing the guy in the pickup, figuring she could identify him from the list by age. Grudgingly, she checked the list and her expression changed.

"Uh-oh," she said. "I might know you'd zero in on this one. Fellow in the pickup gave a phony name and address. Benny Seco was the name, but he must have made that up. Telephone was a fake, too. Looks like he took off and nobody's seen him since. Might have been a warrant out against him he was trying to duck."

"How about the guy in the Porsche?"

I heard a voice behind me. "Well, well, well. Kinsey Millhone. Hard at work, I see."

Emerald faded into the background with all the practice of a spy. I turned to find Lieutenant Dolan standing in the hallway in his habitual pose: hands shoved down in his pants pockets, rocking on his heels. He'd recently celebrated a birthday, his baggy face reflecting every one of his sixty years.

I folded the police report and tucked it in my bag. "Mrs. Spurrier got in touch with me and asked me to follow up on this business of her daughter's death. I feel bad about the girl."

His manner shifted. "I do, too," he said.

"What's the story on the missing witness?"

Dolan shrugged. "He must have had some reason to give out a phony name. Did you talk to him at the scene?"

"Just briefly, but I'd know him if I saw him again. Do you think he could be of help?"

Dolan ran a hand across his balding pate.⁷ "I'd sure like to hear what the fellow has to say. Nobody else was aware that the girl was shot. I gather

> "ANYBODY SEE WHERE THE SHOT WAS FIRED FROM?"

---

5. **equably** (ĕk′wə-blē): calmly.
6. **took a flier:** took a chance; did something risky.
7. **pate** (pāt): the top of the head.

612 UNIT FIVE PART 1: FALSE PRETENSES

he was close enough to have done it himself."

"There's gotta be a way to track him down, don't you think?"

"Maybe," he said. "No one remembers much about the man except the truck he drove. Toyota, dark blue, maybe four or five years old from what they say."

"Would you object if I checked back with the other witnesses? I might get more out of them since I was there."

> **PREDICT**
> Do you think the guy in the blue pickup is a suspect?
> Using a Reading Log

He studied me for a moment, then reached over to the file and removed the list of witnesses, which he handed to me without a word.

"Don't you need this?" I said, surprised.

"I have a copy."

"Thanks. This is great. I'll let you know what I find out."

Dolan pointed a finger. "Keep in touch with the department. I don't want you going off half-cocked."

I drove out to the campus area to the restaurant where Caroline Spurrier had worked. The place had changed hands recently, the decor downgraded from real plants to fake as the nationality of the food changed from Mexican to Thai. The shift manager, David Cole, was just a kid himself, barely twenty-two, tall, skinny, with a nose that belonged on a much larger face.

I introduced myself and told him I was looking into Caroline's death.

"Oh, yeah, that was awful. I talked to her mom."

"She says you mentioned some guy who'd been bugging her. What else can you tell me?"

"That's about all I know. I mean, I never saw the guy myself. She was working nights for the last couple months and just switched back to days to see if she could get away from him."

"She ever mention his name?"

"Terry something, I think. She said he used to follow her around in this green van he drove. She really thought the dude was bent."

"Bent?"

"You know . . . twisted." He twiddled an index finger beside his head to indicate his craziness.

"Why'd she go out with him?"

"She said he seemed like a real nice guy at first, but then he got real possessive, all jealous and like that. In the end, I guess he was totally nuts. He must have showed up on Friday, which is why she took off."

> **PREDICT**
> This guy has a motive. Could he be the guy in the blue pickup?
> Using a Reading Log

I quizzed him, but couldn't glean much more from his account. I thanked him and drove over to the block of university housing where Caroline had lived. The apartment was typical of student digs;[8] faintly shabby, furnished with mismatched items that had probably been languishing in someone's garage. Her roommate was a young woman named Judy Layton, who chatted <u>despondently</u> as she emptied kitchen cabinets and packed assorted cardboard boxes. I kept the questions light at first, asking her about herself as she wrapped some dinner plates in newspaper, shoving each in a box. She was twenty-two, a senior English major with family living in town.

"How long did you know Caroline?"

"About a year," she said. "I had another roommate, but Alice graduated last year. Caroline and I connected up through one of those roommate referral services."

"How come you're moving out?"

She shrugged. "Going back to my folks'. It's too late in the school year to find someone else and I can't afford this place on my own. My brother's on his way over to help me move."

---
8. **digs:** a slang term for apartment or lodgings.

> WORDS TO KNOW
> **despondently** (dĭ-spŏn′dənt-lē) *adv.* in a very discouraged or depressed manner

613

Active Reading: EVALUATE

(R) Ask students how does Judy Layton act that makes them think that she might be lying. *(Possible response: She is sullen, unresponsive, evasive, and defensive.)*

STRATEGIC READING FOR
Less-Proficient Readers

(S) Make sure that students are aware of important clues. Use these questions:

- Why are the police eager to find the man from the pickup truck? *(He gave a false name and then disappeared.)* **Noting Relevant Details**

- Who might have had a reason for killing Caroline? *(the man who was harassing her)* **Drawing Conclusions**

- How would you describe Judy Layton's behavior? *(Possible response: suspicious, as if she has something to hide)* **Classifying/Categorizing**

Set a Purpose Have students read on to find out how Kinsey's good detective work leads her to the killer.

Linking to Science

(T) Photography is the science of using light to produce permanent pictures. The process begins when the camera lens collects light from the subject and focuses on a light-sensitive material, causing a chemical reaction which produces an invisible image. This image is made into a visible negative by treating it with a developer. The negative is then used as a template to print the photograph.

According to her, Caroline was a "party-hearty" who somehow managed to keep her grades up and still have a good time.

"Did she have a boyfriend?"

"She dated lots of guys."

"But no one in particular?"

She shook her head, intent on her work.

I tried again. "She told her mom about some guy harassing her at work. Apparently she'd dated him and they'd just broken up. Do you have any idea who she might have been talking about?"

"Not really. I didn't keep track of the guys in her life."

"She must have mentioned this guy if he was causing such a fuss."

"Look. She and I were not close. We were roommates and that was it. She went her way and I went mine. If some guy was bugging her, she didn't say a word to me."

"She wasn't in any trouble that you knew about?"

"No."

Her manner seemed <u>sullen</u> and it was getting on my nerves. I stared at her. "Judy, I could use a little help. People get murdered for a reason. It might seem stupid or insignificant to the rest of us, but there was *something* going on. What gives?"

EVALUATE

(R) Do you think Judy Layton is telling the truth?
Using a Reading Log

"You don't know it was murder. The policeman I talked to said it might have been some bozo in a passing car."

"Her mother disagrees."

"Well, I can't help you. I already told you everything I know."

I nailed her with a look and let a silence fall, hoping her discomfort would generate further comment. No such luck. If she knew more, she was determined to keep it to herself. I left a business card, asking her to phone me if she remembered anything.

I spent the next two days talking to Caroline Spurrier's professors and friends. From the portrait that emerged, she seemed like a likable kid, funny, good-natured, popular, and sweet. She'd complained of the harassment to a couple of classmates without giving any indication who the fellow was. I went back to the list of witnesses at the scene of the accident, talking to each in turn. I was still tantalized[9] by the guy in the pickup. What reason could he have to falsify his identity?

I'd clipped out the news account of Caroline Spurrier's death, pinning her picture on the bulletin board above my desk. She looked down at me with a smile that seemed more <u>enigmatic</u> with the passing days. I couldn't bear the idea of having to tell her mother my investigation was at an impasse,[10] but I knew I owed her a report.

I was sitting at my typewriter when an idea came to me, quite literally, in a flash. I was staring at the newspaper picture of the wreckage when I spotted the photo credit. I suddenly remembered John Birkett at the scene, his flash going off as he shot pictures of the wreck. If he'd inadvertently snapped one of the guy in the pickup, at least I'd have something to show the cops. Maybe we could get a lead on the fellow that way. I gave Birkett a call. Twenty minutes later, I was in his cubbyhole at the Santa Teresa *Dispatch*, our heads bent together while we scanned the contact sheets.

"No good," John said. "This one's not bad, but the focus is off. Damn. I never really got a clear shot of him."

"What about the truck?"

John pulled out another contact sheet that showed various views of the wrecked compact, the pickup visible on the berm behind. "Well,

---

9. **tantalized:** tempted; enticed; provoked.
10. **impasse** (ĭm′păs′): a difficulty without a solution; a standstill.

WORDS TO KNOW
sullen (sŭl′ən) *adj.* showing irritation or unhappiness by a gloomy silence; moody
enigmatic (ĕn′ĭg-măt′ĭk) *adj.* mysterious; puzzling

614

Mini-Lesson • Study Skills

NOTETAKING Explain that good note taking is important whether you are a student trying to learn or a detective trying to solve a crime. Effective note taking involves paying careful attention and recording major thoughts and main points. Remind students to organize their notes so that the main ideas stand out clearly, and to list important facts and details under the main ideas. On the chalkboard, write examples showing how some students organized their notes.

Application Have students pretend that they are Kinsey Millhone as she interviews one of the witnesses. Ask them to take notes.

Main Idea
I. Important Fact
II. Important Fact
III. Important Fact
   A. Detail
   B. Detail

614 THE LANGUAGE OF LITERATURE TEACHER'S EDITION

you can see it in the background, if that's any help."

"Can we get an enlargement?"

"You looking for anything in particular?"

"The license plate," I said.

The California plate bore a seven-place combination of numbers and letters that we finally discerned[11] in the grainy haze of the two blowups. I should have called Lieutenant Dolan and had him run the license number, but I confess to an egotistical streak that sometimes overrides common sense. I didn't want to give the lead back to him just yet. I called a pal of mine at the Department of Motor Vehicles and asked him to check it out instead.

The license plate was registered to a 1984 Toyota pickup, navy blue, the owner listed as Ron Cagle with an address on McClatchy Way.

The house was stucco, dark gray, with the trim done in white. My heart was pounding as I rang the bell. The fellow's face was printed so indelibly in my memory that when the door was finally opened, I just stood there and stared. Wrong man. This guy was probably six foot seven, over two hundred pounds, with a strong chin, ruddy complexion, blue eyes, auburn hair, red moustache. "Yes?"

"I'm looking for Ron Cagle."

"I'm Ron Cagle."

"You are?" My voice broke in astonishment like a kid reaching puberty. "You're the owner of a navy blue Toyota pickup?" I read off the number of the license plate.

He looked at me quizzically. "Yes. Is something wrong?"

"Well, I don't know. Has someone else been driving it?"

"Not for the last six months."

"Are you sure?"

He half laughed. "See for yourself. It's sitting on the parking pad just behind the house."

He pulled the door shut behind him, leading

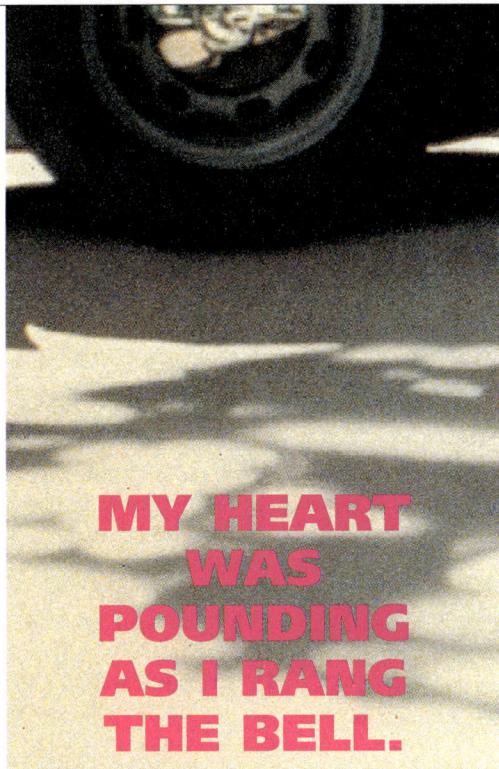

MY HEART WAS POUNDING AS I RANG THE BELL.

the way as the two of us moved off the porch and down the driveway to the rear. There sat the navy blue Toyota pickup, without wheels, up on blocks. The hood was open and there was empty space where the engine should have been. "What's going on?" he asked.

"That's what I'm about to ask you. This truck was at the scene of a recent accident where a girl was killed."

"Not this one," he said. "This has been right here."

Without another word, I pulled out the photographs. "Isn't that your license plate?"

He studied the photos with a frown. "Well, yes, but the truck isn't mine. It couldn't be." He

---

11. **discerned** (dĭ-sûrnd′): perceived; recognized.

WORDS TO KNOW

egotistical (ē′gə-tĭs′tĭ-kəl) *adj.* conceited; proud

Critic's Corner

One critic applauds Sue Grafton for not including the macho attitude and bloodshed found so often in detective stories written by and about men. He states that, "she has successfully replaced the raw, masculine-fantasy brutality and gore . . . with heart-pounding, totally mesmerizing suspense."

Have students discuss how the element of suspense in "Full Circle" keeps the reader engaged in the story. Invite them to consider how the story might have been different if it had been written by a man and featured a male detective.

Active Reading: PREDICT

Y Have students predict whether the guy in the blue pickup will turn out to be the murderer.

Literary Concept: MOOD

Z Ask students to describe the feeling or atmosphere the writer creates in this passage. *(Possible responses: frustrating; anxious; disheartening)*

Literary Concept: DESCRIPTION

AA Invite students to discuss why Kinsey describes the house and the neighborhood. *(Possible response: A good detective notes details that may prove to be important in solving a crime.)* Ask students which detail turns out to be important. *(the three-car garage)*

Literary Concept: SUSPENSE

BB Remind students that suspense is the heightened sense of excitement or tension that readers feel as they read a story and anticipate the outcome. Ask them how the author builds suspense in this passage. *(Possible response: The narrator suddenly follows a hunch and goes into the garage, where she sees a pickup that has been stripped of its paint; the reader wants to know if this is the pickup that was at the scene of the crime and, if so, to whom it belongs.)*

---

glanced back at his pickup, spotting the discrepancy.¹² "There's the problem . . ." He pointed to the license. The plate on the truck was an altogether different set of numbers.

It took me about thirty seconds before the light finally dawned. "Somebody must have lifted your plates and substituted these."

"What would be the point?"

I shrugged. "Maybe someone stole a navy blue Toyota truck and wanted plates that would clear a license check if he was stopped by the cops. Can I use your telephone?"

I called Lieutenant Dolan and told him what I'd found. He ran a check on the plates for the pickup sitting in the drive that turned out to match the numbers on a vehicle reported stolen two weeks before. An APB¹³ was issued for the truck with Cagle's plates. Dolan's guess was that the guy had left the state, or abandoned the pickup shortly after the accident. It was also possible that even if we found the guy, he might not have any real connection with the shooting death. Somehow I doubted it.

PREDICT

What do you think? Will the guy in the blue pickup turn out to be the murderer?
Using a Reading Log

A week passed with no results. The silence was discouraging. I was right back where I started from with no appreciable progress. If a case is going to break, it usually happens fast, and the chances of cracking this one were diminishing with every passing day. Caroline Spurrier's photograph was still pinned to the bulletin board above my desk, her smile nearly mocking as the days went by. In situations like this, all I know to do is go back to the beginning and start again.

Doggedly¹⁴ I went through the list of witnesses, calling everybody on the list. Most tried to be helpful, but there was really nothing new to add. I drove back to the campus to look for Caroline's roommate. Judy Layton had to know something more than she'd told me at first. Maybe I could find a way to worm some information out of her.

The apartment was locked, and a quick peek in the front window showed that all the furniture was gone. I picked up her forwarding address from the manager on the premises and headed over to her parents' house in Colgate, the little suburb to the north.

The house was pleasant, a story and a half of stucco and frame, an attached three-car garage visible at the right. I rang the bell and waited, idly scanning the neighborhood from my vantage point on the porch. It was a nice street, wide and tree-lined, with a grassy divider down the center planted with pink and white flowering shrubs. I rang the bell again. Apparently no one was home.

I went down the porch steps and paused in the driveway, intending to return to my car, which was parked at the curb. I hesitated where I stood. There are times in this business when a hunch is a hunch . . . when a little voice in your gut tells you something's amiss. I turned with curiosity toward the three-car garage at the rear. I cupped my hands, shading my eyes so I could peer through the side window. In the shadowy interior, I saw a pickup, stripped of paint.

I tried the garage's side entrance. The door was unlocked and I pushed my way in. The space smelled of dust, motor oil, and primer. The pickup's license plates were gone. This had to be the same truck, though I couldn't think why it hadn't been dumped. Maybe it was too perilous¹⁵ to attempt at this point. Heart thumping, I did a quick search of the cab's

---

12. **discrepancy** (dĭ-skrĕp′ən-sē): difference or disagreement between facts.
13. **APB:** all points bulletin: a radio message for all police officers.
14. **doggedly:** with stubborn determination.
15. **perilous:** dangerous; risky.

interior. Under the front seat, on the driver's side, I saw a handgun, a .45. I left it where it was, eased the cab door shut, and backed away from the truck. Clearly, someone in the Layton household had been at the murder scene.

PREDICT
What do you think now? Who's the murderer?
Using a Reading Log

I left the garage at a quick clip, trotting toward the street. I had to find a telephone and call the cops. I had just started my car, shoving it into gear, when I saw a dark green VW van pass on the far side of the divider and circle back in my direction, headed toward the Layton's drive. The fellow driving was the man I'd seen at the accident. Judy's brother? The similarities were obvious, now that I thought of it. No wonder she'd been unwilling to tell me what was going on! He slowed for the turn, and that's when he spotted me.

If I'd had any doubts about his guilt, they vanished the minute he and I locked eyes. His surprise was replaced by panic, and he gunned his engine, taking off. I peeled after him, flooring it. At the corner he skidded sideways and recovered, speeding out of sight. I went after him, zigzagging crazily through a residential area that was laid out like a maze. I could almost chart his course ahead of me by the whine of his transmission. He was heading toward the freeway.

At the overpass, I caught a glimpse of him in the southbound lane. He wasn't hard to track, the boxy shape of the van clearly visible as we tore toward town. The traffic began to slow, massing in one of those <u>inexplicable</u> logjams on the road. I couldn't tell if the problem was a fender-bender in the northbound lane, or a bottleneck in ours, but it gave me the advantage I needed. I was catching him.

As I eased up on his left, I saw him lean on the accelerator, cutting to his right. He hit the shoulder of the road, his tires spewing out gravel as he widened the gap between us. He was bypassing stalled cars, hugging the shrubbery as he flew down the berm. I was right behind him, keeping as close to him as I dared. My car wasn't very swift, but then neither was his van. I jammed my accelerator to the floor and pinned myself to his tail. He was watching me steadily in his rearview mirror, our eyes meeting in a deadlock of determination and grit.

I spotted the maintenance crew just seconds before he did; guys in bright orange vests working with a crane that was parked squarely in his path. There was no way for him to slow in time and no place else to go. His van plowed into the rear of the crane with a crash that made my blood freeze as I slammed on my brakes. I was luckier than he. My VW came to a stop just a kiss away from death.

Like a nightmare, we repeated all the horror of the first wreck. Police and paramedics, the wailing of the ambulance. When I finally stopped shaking, I realized where I was. The road crew was replacing the big green highway sign sheared in half when Caroline Spurrier's car had smashed into it. Terry Layton died at the very spot where he killed her.

Caroline's smile has shifted back to impishness in the photograph above my desk. I keep it there as a reminder, but of what I couldn't say. The <u>brevity</u> of life, perhaps, the finality of death . . . the irony of events that sometimes connect the two. We live in a world in which justice is <u>skewed</u>. ❖

> WORDS TO KNOW
> **inexplicable** (ĭn-ĕk′splĭ-kə-bəl) *adj.* difficult or impossible to explain
> **brevity** (brĕv′ĭ-tē) *n.* the quality of being brief in time; shortness
> **skewed** (skyōōd) *adj.* distorted or slanted in a particular direction; unbalanced
> **skew** *v.*

617

Active Reading: PREDICT

CC Have students predict who in the Layton household may have killed Caroline—Judy or her brother.

Literary Concept: SUSPENSE

DD Ask students how the writer builds suspense in this section. *(Possible response: The reader wants Kinsey to catch the killer but fears that she will be injured or killed in a car crash.)*

STRATEGIC READING FOR Less-Proficient Readers

EE Have students explain how Kinsey finds out that the pickup was stolen. *(She reads the plate numbers in a blown-up photo and tracks the registration to a disabled pickup, whose plates had been stolen and switched for those of a stolen truck of the same make and color.)* Summarizing

- Who stole the pickup? *(Judy Layton's brother, the killer)* Drawing Conclusions
- What happens to Judy's brother? *(He is killed in a car crash while trying to escape.)* Summarizing

CUSTOMIZING FOR Gifted and Talented Students

Most murders of young women in their twenties are committed by jealous boyfriends or husbands. Ask students to discuss what can be done to deter such violent "domestic" crimes.

COMPREHENSION CHECK

1. How does Caroline Spurrier die? *(She is shot while driving on the freeway.)*
2. Why are the police looking for the man in the pickup? *(He gave a false name, address, and phone number.)*
3. How does Kinsey find out that Terry Layton is the killer? *(She finds a pickup containing a handgun in the Laytons' garage; she recognizes him as the man in the pickup; he speeds off after spotting her.)*
4. What is ironic about his end? *(He dies in the exact spot where the dying Caroline's car crashed.)*

A s s e s s m e n t O p t i o n

INFORMAL ASSESSMENT You can informally assess students' understanding of the story and their ability to summarize the events in the story accurately and suspensefully.

Rubric

3 Full Accomplishment Students recount the events in the story accurately, concisely, and suspensefully.

2 Substantial Accomplishment Students recount most events in the story accurately. They are not concise or suspenseful, however.

1 Little or Partial Accomplishment Students have difficulty recounting the events in the story, overlooking some that are important and focusing on others that are irrelevant to the solution of the crime.

INSIGHT

"Who Killed My Daughter?":
Lois Duncan Searches for an Answer

MARIA SIMSON

When her 18-year-old daughter was murdered in 1989, Lois Duncan, a popular author of young adult (YA) mystery and crime novels, suffered the tragedy of having one of her plots become reality. The following article was written for the "Book News" section of Publisher's Weekly *magazine just prior to the release of Duncan's 1992 book* Who Killed My Daughter?, *published by Delacorte.*

"*Don't Look Behind You* was a book about a teenage girl who was chased by a hitman in a Camaro," says Lois Duncan of her 1989 YA novel. "Later that year, my eldest daughter, who was the model for the girl, was chased by a hitman driving a Camaro." The difference is that in real life, 18-year-old Kaitlyn Arquette was shot and killed. Since then, Duncan, who has 39 novels to her credit, has written only one book—*Who Killed My Daughter?: The True Story of a Mother's Search for Her Daughter's Murderer.*

Had Kaitlyn's death been the random killing that the police labeled it, there would have been no need for a search. But while settling her daughter's affairs, Duncan discovered from a telephone bill that calls had been made from Kaitlyn's apartment to an unlisted California number minutes *after* her death. Other discrepancies, too, led Duncan to suspect that her daughter's death was no accident.

"Soon after the murder I began having memory blackouts," says Duncan. "As I didn't want to misremember anything, I began taking daily notes"—notes that quickly began developing into a book. "It helped keep me sane. I would sit down and write a chapter in real time, but I never knew what was going to happen next."

Duncan, who used to teach journalism at the University of New Mexico, spent the next two years following up leads. When these cooled, she turned, with some skepticism, to psychic investigators who helped her pick up the trail. But these leads, too, petered out. Duncan decided that "the only way to find out the missing information was to make the story public."

This January, on what would have been Kaitlyn's 21st birthday, she mailed the manuscript to her agent, Claire Smith, who in turn sent it on to both Dell/Delacorte publisher Carole Baron and Books for Young

Readers division publisher George Nicholson. "We had done a lot of business with Lois through the Books for Young Readers department, so it was natural we would see it," says Baron. Even though she did not know Duncan personally, she was well aware of her daughter's death, having been in Albuquerque at the time of the killing.

Baron hopes that the book will travel beyond the normal true-crime audience to interest any parent who is concerned about the increasing violence against children: "It doesn't matter who you are—all kids can get hurt," she says. According to associate publicity director Judy Westerman, the mainstream media, including major talk shows, have already expressed considerable interest in the book, which will no doubt bolster[1] Duncan on her first-ever author tour.

But Delacorte sees yet another audience as well, among Duncan's original readers—young adults. "Booksellers who know her from her novels are very interested in this project, and our sales force is tapping into that," says Baron. "Young adults will have no difficulty reading the book." Everyone

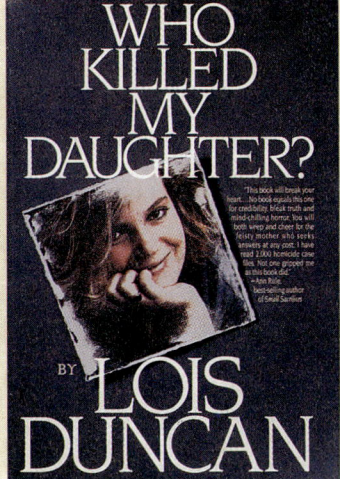

connected with the book remarks upon its similarities to Duncan's YA stories of murder and mystery. And when Duncan visits the American Library Association and the Canadian Library Association this year, she will be participating both as an adult author and as a YA author.

There is, however, one other audience and that is the one Duncan is most desperate to reach. "We've found out so much [about Kaitlyn's death] but there are still holes. We're hoping that someone out there will be able to help fill a few of those holes." With that in mind, *Who Killed My Daughter?* opens with a list of possible scenarios[2] and unanswered questions, along with addresses for Duncan and for the New Mexico attorney general, in the hope that some reader will come forward with information that answers the question in Duncan's title.

---

1. **bolster:** support or strengthen.
2. **scenarios:** outlines or models of a supposed sequence of events.

INSIGHT CONT.

3. Lois Duncan used her writing ability to publicize her quest to bring her daughter's murderer to justice. How might a parent who does not have her particular talent go about doing the same thing? *(Possible responses: He or she could tell the story to newspaper or television reporters.)*

4. How successful do you think Duncan's book will be in convincing people to turn in the murderer? *(Student responses will vary.)* What other beneficial effects might the book produce? *(Possible responses: It might be a catharsis for the author; it might provide comfort to other parents whose children have met the similar violent fates.)*

Mini-Lesson: Speaking, Listening, and Viewing

SPEECHES Explain that a speech usually contains an introduction, a thesis statement supported by facts and details, and a conclusion. Tell students that delivering a speech can be challenging, even for a professional lecturer. As a result, even experienced speakers use certain techniques to prepare for giving a speech.

Write the steps shown at right on the chalkboard and discuss their advice with the class.

Application Ask students to prepare and deliver a talk that Lois Duncan might give at your school, your local library, or your local bookstore. Students can research or invent details of the crime as time allows; remind them that Duncan is intent on finding someone who can help solve the mystery.

> 1. Prewriting—Choose a topic, identify the audience, and do research.
> 2. Drafting—Write a thesis statement and outline the speech on index cards.
> 3. Revising—Review the organization and add necessary transitions.
> 4. Practicing—Time the speech as you read it aloud.
> 5. Presenting—Maintain eye contact; speak clearly, audibly, expressively, and at a moderate pace.

From Personal Response to Critical Analysis

1. Accept all reasonable responses.
2. Accept all reasonable responses. Encourage students to indicate how they arrived at the solution.
3. Possible response: Justice does not only occur in the courtroom; instead of being brought to trial, Terry receives a just sentence by experiencing the same end that he inflicted on Caroline.
4. Possible responses: Some might say it is an appropriate title because the story ends where it began. Others might say that the title doesn't matter because Caroline is still dead.
5. Possible responses: Students might suggest that he wanted to make sure she was dead; he regretted what he had done; he wanted to see her one last time.
6. Accept all reasonably well-supported responses.

Another Pathway

Cooperative Learning Students should collaborate to make sure that they list all the clues for each card and can solve the mystery without the missing cards. One student should be responsible for encouraging all members to participate. Another should record the clues on the cards. Another should check to make sure that the mystery can be solved without the missing cards.

Rubric

3 Full Accomplishment Each card provides a comprehensive list of clues for that person. The mystery can be solved without the missing cards.

2 Substantial Accomplishment Most of the important clues appear on the remaining cards, but minor ones are missing. The mystery can be solved without the missing cards.

1 Little or Partial Accomplishment Important clues are missing from the cards. The mystery cannot be solved without the missing cards.

RESPONDING OPTIONS

FROM PERSONAL RESPONSE TO CRITICAL ANALYSIS

REFLECT
1. Did you find this story interesting? Why or why not? Share your reaction with your classmates.

RETHINK
2. At what point in the story did you predict the solution to the crime?

Thematic Link
3. This story ends with the narrator's statement, "We live in a world in which justice is skewed." Explain what you think this means and how the story illustrates it.

4. Do you think "Full Circle" is an appropriate title for this story? Explain why or why not.

5. Think about the beginning of the story. Why do you think Terry Layton stopped at the accident scene and went to Caroline Spurrier's car? Explain your interpretation.

RELATE
6. Do you think justice in this world is "skewed"? Give examples that support your opinion.

Close Textual Reading

Consider
- the Insight article about Lois Duncan's daughter
- examples within the legal or judicial system
- examples from your own experience

Multimodal Learning
ANOTHER PATHWAY

Cooperative Learning
With a small group, write these names on separate index cards: Michelle Spurrier, Emerald, Lt. Dolan, D. Cole, Judy Layton, J. Birkett, R. Cagle. On each card, list the clues that person provides. Then, taking away a card at a time, try to solve the case with the remaining clues. Are any clues unimportant?

LITERARY CONCEPTS

As you know, the **plot** of a story includes exposition, rising action, climax, and falling action. Note that while the **rising action** starts at the very beginning of this story, the first paragraph also includes **exposition** identifying the setting and character. The **climax**, or turning point, comes at a story's highest point of interest or suspense. The **falling action**, or resolution, occurs at the conclusion of the story and ties up the story's loose ends. Now think about the main interest of a detective story and the questions it answers. What point in "Full Circle" would you identify as the climax? What do you find out in the falling action?

620   UNIT FIVE   PART 1: FALSE PRETENSES

QUICKWRITES

1. A common device in detective stories is to include one or more misleading clues, or red herrings, to divert readers from the identity of the real killer. Imagine that Terry Layton did not kill Caroline Spurrier, even though he was pursuing her down the freeway. Draft a different **ending** to the story, explaining why he stole the truck, changed the license plates, carried a gun, and later stripped the truck's paint. Provide clues leading to the identify of the real killer.

2. Many mystery writers plan their stories by starting with the ending—that is, they first decide on the who, what, why, and how. Then they build a story that will intrigue readers and lead them up to the ending. Try this method to write a **plot** outline for a mystery story.

📁 **PORTFOLIO** Save your writing. You may want to use it later as a springboard to a piece for your portfolio.

Literary Concepts

Suggest that students work in small groups to trace the plot of the story. Encourage them to list developments under the following headings: "Exposition," "Rising Action," "Climax," and "Falling Action." Students should identify the climax as the point at which the narrator discovers the stripped pickup in the garage. They should also indicate that the falling action reveals that Terry Layton is the murderer.

QuickWrites

1. Encourage students to plot their new ending by answering the following questions: If Terry is not the killer, who is? What is the motive for the murder? What clues lead to the identity of the real killer? Why did Terry steal the truck, change the license plates, carry a gun, and strip the paint from the truck after the accident?

2. Suggest that students answer who, what, why, and how before they write a summary of the ending of their mystery. Then they should fill in the other parts of their plot outline such as setting, characters, rising action, climax, and falling action.

Outlines, pp. 816–817

CRITIC'S CORNER

Detective stories have traditionally been written by men, such as Raymond Chandler, and have featured male heroes. One critic says the reason for Kinsey Millhone's popularity is that she really is a traditional hero. "Chandler's concept of a detective hero was that 'he must be the best man in his world, and a good enough man for any world.' Gender aside, Kinsey fills that prescription perfectly." Compare and contrast Kinsey Millhone with male detectives you may be familiar with from books, films, or TV.

Multimodal Learning

ACROSS THE CURRICULUM

Science Investigate the field of forensic science, which applies scientific methods to the analysis of evidence in crimes. Find out what the word *forensic* means, what the specialties within the field are, what training is required to become a forensic scientist, and what kinds of evidence are collected and analyzed. Create a brochure explaining the field as a career option. You might use a desktop publishing program on a computer to create your brochure.

WORDS TO KNOW

EXERCISE A For each group of words below, write the letter of the word that is the best antonym for the boldfaced word.

1. **egotistical** (a) secure, (b) modest, (c) dull
2. **harass** (a) protect, (b) discourage, (c) scorn
3. **brevity** (a) sadness, (b) courage, (c) permanence
4. **enigmatic** (a) common, (b) important, (c) understandable
5. **skewed** (a) balanced, (b) loyal, (c) fortunate

EXERCISE B For each phrase in the first column, write the letter of the synonymous phrase from the second column.

1. a sullen visitor
2. despondently separated
3. an inexplicable increase
4. get rid of the odor
5. distrustful of Lawrence

a. wary of Larry
b. dispel the smell
c. a depressed guest
d. downheartedly parted
e. an unexplainable gain

SUE GRAFTON

Someone once asked the award-winning mystery writer Sue Grafton (born 1940) what themes are in her books. Her answer was that she is interested in why people do what they do. "Why do we kill each other?" she said. "Why can't we be happy? I'm looking for answers, trying to figure it out."

Grafton's novels feature the California private investigator Kinsey Millhone, a tough, independent, sassy heroine. With the popular Millhone, Grafton has firmly established a female hero as a detective, a role that has traditionally been male. Grafton, who was born in 1940, and is the mother of three grown children, compared herself to Kinsey Millhone in an interview in *Armchair Detective:* "She's the person I would have been had I not married young and had children. She'll always be thinner and younger and braver, the lucky so-and-so. Her biography is different, but our sensibilities are identical. At the core, we're the same. . . . Because of Kinsey, I get to lead two lives—hers and mine. Sometimes I'm not sure which I prefer."

Besides mysteries, Grafton has written screenplays and television scripts, sometimes collaborating with her husband.

OTHER WORKS *"A" Is for Alibi, "B" Is for Burglar, "C" Is for Corpse* through *"L" Is for Lawless*

Extended Reading

FULL CIRCLE **621**

Critic's Corner

Accept all reasonable responses. Although students may indicate that Kinsey Millhone has many qualities in common with male detectives, they may identify some differences associated with gender.

Words to Know

Exercise A
1. b
2. a
3. c
4. c
5. a

Exercise B
1. c
2. d
3. e
4. b
5. a

Reteaching/Reinforcement
- *Unit Five Resource Book*, p. 14

Across the Curriculum

Science Suggest that students work in small groups to research the field of forensic science. Some group members can do the research, while others collaborate to create the brochure.

SUE GRAFTON

As a child, Sue Grafton showed an interest in detective stories, and was drawn to the hard-boiled mysteries of writer Mickey Spillane. As an adult, she researched the genre by taking courses in marksmanship and self-defense, visiting morgues, and compiling and reading works on forensic medicine and fingerprinting.

Alternative Activities

1. The witnesses to the "accident" give their accounts to a highway patrol officer. Write the accident report that the officer might have turned in.
2. Imagine that you are a police artist. Based on Kinsey Millhone's description, draw a sketch of the man in the blue pickup.
3. With another classmate, role-play the conversation that takes place when Kinsey Millhone calls Michelle Spurrier to report the conclusion of her investigation.

OVERVIEW

Objectives

- To understand and appreciate a ballad that explores two people's reactions to the approach of soldiers and reveals a relationship built on false pretenses
- To identify and examine rhythm in a ballad
- To appreciate rhyme scheme and repetition
- To express understanding of the ballad through a choice of writing forms, including a letter, a dialogue, and a ballad
- To extend understanding of the ballad through a variety of multimodal and cross-curricular activities

Skills

LITERARY CONCEPTS
- Rhythm
- Stanza

GENRE STUDY
- Poetry: ballad

Thematic Link: *False Pretenses* A speaker makes reassuring comments to a lover to conceal the speaker's own fear and lack of commitment to that partner.

CUSTOMIZING FOR
Students Acquiring English

- Use **ACCESS FOR STUDENTS ACQUIRING ENGLISH,** *Reading Support*.
- Students may have difficulty understanding which character speaks which lines. Suggest that they choose partners and read aloud to one another to determine who speaks when.

PREVIEWING

POETRY

O What Is That Sound
W. H. Auden

Activating Prior Knowledge
PERSONAL CONNECTION

Think of words that indicate a feeling of fear—words such as *terror, fright, dread, panic, alarm, anxiety.* Emotions like these are familiar to all human beings. They are felt also by the two characters in the poem you are about to read. With your classmates, brainstorm some common fears—things that most people are afraid of—and list them in your notebook.

Building Background
HISTORICAL CONNECTION

Many details in the poem you are about to read—the references to drums, horses, and the red uniforms of soldiers—suggest a faraway time, perhaps around the time of the American Revolution. However, the poem was written in the 1930s—a time that its author, W. H. Auden, called "the age of anxiety." It was a period that saw an economic depression and the beginnings of a terrible world war that devastated Europe. Even after these events were over, ordinary citizens were afraid of again being swept away by events they could not control.

Active Reading/Setting a Purpose
READING CONNECTION

Interpreting Dialogue "O What Is That Sound" is a **ballad,** a poem that tells a story and is meant to be sung or recited. Like many traditional ballads, this poem tells its story entirely in dialogue, and this gives it a mysterious quality. There are two speakers. In each stanza except the last, one person speaks the first two lines, and the other replies in the next two lines. As you read this poem, use the reactions of the speakers to try to imagine what is happening. Look for changes in either speaker's attitude as the action takes place. Then in your notebook, fill out a chart like the one shown, using information that you have inferred about the speakers in the poem. Indicate who the two people might be and how they react to the soldiers—at first and then later in the poem.

	Identity	First Reaction to Sound	Later Reaction to Sound
First speaker			
Second speaker			

622 UNIT FIVE PART 1: FALSE PRETENSES

PRINT AND MEDIA RESOURCES

UNIT FIVE RESOURCE BOOK
Strategic Reading: Literature, p. 17

ACCESS FOR STUDENTS ACQUIRING ENGLISH
Selection Summaries
Reading Support

FORMAL ASSESSMENT
Selection Test, p. 109
 Test Generator

AUDIO LIBRARY
See Reference Card

O What Is That Sound

W. H. Auden

A
O what is that sound which so thrills the ear
    Down in the valley drumming, drumming?
Only the scarlet soldiers,[1] dear,
    The soldiers coming.

5 O what is that light I see flashing so clear
    Over the distance brightly, brightly?
Only the sun on their weapons, dear,
    As they step lightly.

O what are they doing with all that gear,
10   What are they doing this morning, this morning?
Only their usual maneuvers,[2] dear,
B
    Or perhaps a warning.

---

1. **scarlet soldiers:** British soldiers, who wore bright red coats.
2. **maneuvers:** training exercises carried out by troops.

STRATEGIC READING FOR
Less-Proficient Readers

Set a Purpose Ask students to read the ballad to find out what the sound referred to in the title is and what situation grows out of it.

Use **UNIT FIVE RESOURCE BOOK**, p. 17, for guidance in reading the selection.

CUSTOMIZING FOR
Gifted and Talented Students

Have students discuss why they think Auden chose to include so few details—the characters are not named, the time and place are not defined, the future of the two speakers is uncertain.

Literary Concept: STANZA

A Ask students to characterize the way the dialogue is set up in the first stanza. *(Possible response: A question is posed by the first speaker, and an answer is given by the second.)*

Critical Thinking: SPECULATING

B Ask students what effect the breaks between stanzas have. *(Possible response: They allow momentarily for the tension to build before the next observation.)*

Mini-Lesson Genre Study

POETRY Draw the word web on the chalkboard, and use it to discuss the characteristics of a **ballad**.

Application Ask students to copy the web into their notebooks so that they can refer to it as they look for the characteristics of a ballad in "O What Is That Sound."

CUSTOMIZING FOR
Students Acquiring English

I Encourage students to try to figure out what the word *wheeling* means in this context. Help them discover the meaning by asking what a wheel does (*turns*), and then ask them to substitute the word *turning*.

Literary Concept: SUSPENSE

C Ask students to discuss how tension builds in these two stanzas. (*Possible response: The soldiers pass by other houses as they near the speaker's house, and their sudden running signals that they are coming for at least one of the speakers.*)

Literary Concept: RHYTHM

D Ask students to describe the rhythm of this poem. (*regular, strongly marked, same in each stanza*) Ask how this type of rhythm relates to the ballad's plot. (*Possible response: drives the reader forward, just as the soldiers are marching forward; stresses the danger and suspense*)

STRATEGIC READING FOR
Less-Proficient Readers

E Ask students where the soldiers are headed and for whom they are coming. (*They are headed for the speakers' home and are coming for the second speaker.*) Summarizing/Making Inferences

COMPREHENSION CHECK

1. Whom do the speakers observe in the distance? (*soldiers*)
2. Which speaker seems calm? (*the second speaker*)
3. Why does the first speaker feel deceived? (*The second speaker leaves when the soldiers begin to run.*)
4. What do the soldiers do? (*break into the house*)

O why have they left the road down there,
    Why are they suddenly wheeling, wheeling?
15 Perhaps a change in their orders, dear.
    Why are you kneeling?

O haven't they stopped for the doctor's care,
    Haven't they reined their horses, their horses?
Why, they are none of them wounded, dear.
20   None of these forces.

O is it the parson they want, with white hair,
    Is it the parson, is it, is it?
No, they are passing his gateway, dear,
    Without a visit.

25 O it must be the farmer who lives so near.
    It must be the farmer so cunning, so cunning?
They have passed the farmyard already, dear,
    And now they are running.

O where are you going? Stay with me here!
30   Were the vows you swore deceiving, deceiving?
No, I promised to love you, dear,
    But I must be leaving.

O it's broken the lock and splintered the door,
    O it's the gate where they're turning, turning;
35 Their boots are heavy on the floor
    And their eyes are burning.

624   UNIT FIVE   PART 1: FALSE PRETENSES

Mini-Lesson Literary Concepts

REVIEWING STANZA Remind students that a stanza is a grouping of two or more lines in a pattern that is repeated throughout a poem. A stanza is comparable to a paragraph in a work of prose. It indicates a change in subject, focus, time, or tone. Each stanza may have the same number of lines, or the number of lines may vary.

Application Have students work in small groups to examine the stanzas in the ballad by considering the following questions: How many stanzas make up the poem? How many lines are in each stanza? What similarities are there in the stanzas? What is the effect of these similarities? If this were a prose piece, would the selection work if it were broken into paragraphs of the same length? Why or why not?

RESPONDING OPTIONS

FROM PERSONAL RESPONSE TO CRITICAL ANALYSIS

REFLECT 1. What emotion did you feel most strongly by the end of this poem? Record your response in your notebook and compare it with those of others in the class.

RETHINK
Thematic Link

Close Textual Reading

2. Referring to the Reading Connection activity on page 622, describe what you think is happening in the poem.
    Consider
    • who the two speakers could be
    • what one of them is afraid of
    • the actions that are taking place
    • the possible reasons for these actions

3. How do the two people react to the soldiers and to each other as the situation changes? Demonstrate this change with a partner by acting out in pantomime the three scenes described in stanza one, stanza four, and stanzas eight and nine.

RELATE 4. Under what kinds of circumstances might the action in this poem take place today?

Multimodal Learning
ANOTHER PATHWAY
Cooperative Learning

In a group of five classmates, have two read the poem aloud, each taking the part of one speaker. Then have the rest of the group ask the readers questions about the situation described in the poem and the feelings of the two speakers. Share with the class your conclusion about what is going on in the poem.

LITERARY CONCEPTS

Rhythm in poetry is like the beat in music. It is a pattern created by the arrangement of stressed and unstressed syllables. The symbol used to show an accented, or stressed, syllable is (´), and the symbol for an unstressed syllable is (˘). Examples from the poem are *drúmmĭng* and *mănéuvĕrs*. Copy the first two stanzas in your notebook and mark the stressed and unstressed syllables in each line. Then, while tapping your foot to a regular beat, read the stanzas aloud, listening to the rhythm. In what way does this rhythmic effect seem appropriate for this poem?

CONCEPT REVIEW: Suspense In this ballad, the rhythm also contributes to the suspense—the excitement or tension that readers feel as they become involved in a story and eager to know the outcome. What elements in the poem, besides rhythm, contribute to the feeling of suspense? At what point do you think the suspense reaches its peak?

QUICKWRITES

1. Suppose that the first speaker in the poem ends up in prison. Write a **letter** that the second speaker might send to this person in prison.

2. Imagine how this story might continue. Write a **dialogue** showing what happens next, such as a soldier questioning the first speaker. If you're using a computer, the copy feature can save you from having to type characters' names more than once.

3. Refer to the list of fears that you brainstormed for the Personal Connection activity. Draft a **ballad** modeled on "O What Is That Sound" about a situation that conjures up one of the fears.

 PORTFOLIO Save your writing. You may want to use it later as a springboard to a piece for your portfolio.

O WHAT IS THAT SOUND 625

From Personal Response to Critical Analysis

1. Accept all reasonable responses.
2. Possible response: The two speakers might be a husband and wife, or a pair of lovers; the one who leaves may be the man and may be a deserter or spy that the soldiers are coming to arrest, or the one who leaves may be the woman and may be a spy or simply the one of the two who more quickly anticipates the threat that the soldiers pose to them.
3. Possible response: The first speaker is at first thrilled and then nervously disbelieving as the soldiers get closer and closer; the second speaker is calm, and then panics and runs away.
4. Accept all reasonable, well-supported responses. Many students may cite any number of situations where people have hidden themselves from civil or military authority for some reason, have just been discovered, and are the object of an attempted capture.

Another Pathway

Cooperative Learning The groups should form two subgroups of questioners and speakers. The questioners should collaborate to formulate the questions, which will be recorded by a member of the group. The speakers should prepare to answer the questions by taking turns explaining the poem's meaning—a process that will enable them to agree on a common interpretation. One student should be chosen to ensure that the questioners take turns.

3 Full Accomplishment The questioners ask intelligent and incisive questions. The speakers answer by developing a common and logical interpretation.

2 Substantial Accomplishment The questioners ask intelligent questions. The speakers' answers reflect a common interpretation but reveal confusion about some minor details.

1 Little or Partial Accomplishment Both questioners and speakers show little or no understanding of the ballad.

Literary Concepts

Students should indicate that the rhythm reflects the beat of drumming and marching and reinforces the menacing image of soldiers out to get someone.

Suspense Students should indicate that the advance of the soldiers, the first speaker's increasing terror, and the growing realization that the speakers are the soldiers' targets heightens the reader's sense of suspense, which peaks when the soldiers begin to run toward the house.

QuickWrites

1. Encourage students to consider how the second speaker feels about leaving the first speaker to face the soldiers alone. What feeling would he or she want to emphasize in his letter?
2. Suggest that students first discuss why they think the soldiers have come.
3. Encourage students to use the same rhyme scheme and rhythm used in the ballad.

The Writer's Craft

Writing a Personal Letter, pp. 44–46
Using Dialogue Effectively, pp. 434–435

Literary Links

Students should indicate that although the other poems tell a story, they do not build suspense by focusing on the emotions of fear and terror that are obvious in "O What Is That Sound."

Across the Curriculum

Social Studies Point out the ballad's clues as to its time and place—scarlet uniforms and soldiers on horseback. Have students do some research to find out what armies have worn scarlet and when the use of cavalry horses was discontinued. Have them share their findings with the class.

Music The ballad was written to be sung. Some famous American ballads are "Springfield Mountain," "Lovewell's Fight," "Casey Jones," and "John Henry." Locate recordings of these or other American ballads and play them for the class. Ask students to discuss their similarities and their differences.

W. H. AUDEN

In writing about W. H. Auden, one critic commented, "The influence of music on Auden's verse . . . has always been salient: even his worst lines often 'sound' impressive." As he continued to write his rhythmic works, Auden developed an idiosyncratic, terse language. His linguistic innovations were celebrated in the coining of a definitive adjective—*Audenesque*.

Multimodal Learning

ALTERNATIVE ACTIVITIES

1. Sketch a **picture** to illustrate this poem. What do you imagine the two speakers look like? What are they doing as they speak? Show and explain your sketch to the class.
2. Choose or compose a piece of **music** that captures the suspense and tension in this poem and play it for the class.

THE WRITER'S STYLE

In addition to the rhythm, the **rhyme scheme** *(abab)* serves to unify "O What Is That Sound" by setting up a pattern that is the same in each stanza. Furthermore, the first and third lines in every stanza (except the last) all rhyme with *ear*. Another unifying device is **repetition,** that is, the repeated use of some word or phrase, usually for emphasis. Notice the repetition in the second line of each stanza. Also, what word is repeated in every stanza? What do you think this repetition reveals about the speaker who uses it?

LITERARY LINKS

In earlier units you read several poems with narrative elements—poems that have a story to tell. Think of "My Papa's Waltz," "Touch Football," "Theme for English B," and "The Writer." Auden's poem also has a story to tell, but it tells it in the manner of the traditional English folk ballads. Look again at one or more of the four poems named above and compare it or them with "O What Is That Sound." Notice the differences in the way they tell their stories. What do you think gives this ballad its special quality as a narrative—a story that you might hear around a campfire? On the other hand, what kind of information do the other poems provide that is left out of the ballad? Which kind of poem do you prefer?

W. H. AUDEN

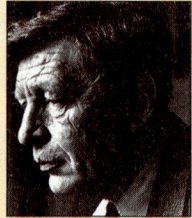

1907–1973

W. H. Auden, one of the major poets of the twentieth century, was a prolific writer whose works explored political, personal, and religious values. Known and respected for his lyrical, inventive, and thoughtful poetry, Auden won the Pulitzer Prize and the National Book Award.

Wystan Hugh Auden was born in York, England, the third son of a doctor and a nurse, and received a traditional English boarding school education. He first majored in biology at Christ Church College, Oxford, but changed his field of study to English. By then he had decided to become a "great poet." In his first years after graduating, Auden quickly established his reputation with the publication of a book of poetry, *The Orators*. Soon he became the best known of a group of young British writers of the 1930s.

Just before the outbreak of World War II, Auden immigrated to the United States. He wanted to live "deliberately without roots" by breaking away from English literary and political life and from his family. "America may break one completely," he wrote to a friend, "but the best of which one is capable is more likely to be drawn out of one here than anywhere else." As an American citizen he became a part of New York City's intellectual and artistic community, writing, teaching, and lecturing.

OTHER WORKS *Another Time, The Age of Anxiety, The Shield of Achilles, The English Auden, Collected Poems*

Extended Reading

626 UNIT FIVE PART 1: FALSE PRETENSES

The Writer's Style

Students should indicate that "O" is repeated in every stanza. They may conclude that this interjection indicates that the speaker is very anxious and upset. Invite students to examine the rhyme scheme and repetition in the ballad they wrote for QuickWrite 3.

Alternative Activities

1. Tell students to decide when they think the story takes place and to research clothing, hair styles, and furnishings of that period.
2. Suggest that students give some thought to what kind of music would reflect the suspense in the poem. They might also wish to consider a piece of music that is funereal in tone or punctuated by the roll of drums.

PREVIEWING

DRAMA

Trifles
Susan Glaspell

Activating Prior Knowledge
PERSONAL CONNECTION

Trifles is a short play about a murder in an isolated farmhouse. The word *trifle* means something of little importance or significance. Think about murder investigations that you have read or heard about and the kinds of rules or procedures that police follow when examining a crime scene. What kind of evidence do you think is considered major and what evidence might be considered of little importance? In your notebook, write examples of each and share them with your classmates.

Building Background
HISTORICAL CONNECTION

This play has an unusual setting for a murder—a Midwestern farm in the early 1900s. Farm life at that time was very different from today. Few farmers owned cars or tractors. Some farmers had telephones, but many—probably most—did not. Neither television nor radio had been invented yet. In fact, some farmhouses did not have electricity for many years. These conditions often created a sense of isolation, especially among farm women. Local church organizations, such as the Ladies' Aid, sponsored occasional social events that brought people together; still, relief from the isolation and the loneliness of farm life was temporary at best.

Active Reading/Setting a Purpose
READING CONNECTION

Making Inferences In *Trifles,* shrewd observations from a set of clues reconstruct the crime and reveal the killer. The clues—often isolated and seemingly unimportant—are put together to make inferences about the circumstances surrounding the murder. In your notebook, draw a chart like the one shown. Then, as you read *Trifles,* fill out the chart with your inferences from two or three additional clues.

Clues	Possible Inference
1. a half-wiped table	Some interruption caused Mrs. Wright to stop cleaning.
2.	

TRIFLES **627**

OVERVIEW
Objectives

- To understand and appreciate a one-act play that explores a woman's motives for murder
- To identify and understand dramatic irony
- To appreciate the technique of keeping a drama's central character offstage
- To express understanding of the play through a choice of writing forms including a crime report and a news account
- To extend understanding of the selection through a variety of cross-curricular and multimodal activities

Skills

LITERARY CONCEPTS
- Dramatic irony
- Dialogue

THE WRITER'S STYLE
- Informal English

GENRE STUDY
- Drama: one-act play

GRAMMAR
- Dash in dialogue

SPEAKING, LISTENING, AND VIEWING
- Scientific observation

ALTERNATIVE
Previewing

Students can choose partners to discuss what they know about the collection of evidence at a crime scene.

Personal Connection

Discussion Prompts

- *What procedures do police follow when examining a murder scene?*
- *What kinds of evidence do they look for?*
- *Of the items you mentioned above, which would you consider major evidence?*
- *Which would you consider evidence of little importance?*

As you read *Trifles,* consider which evidence is major and which is of little importance.

PRINT AND MEDIA RESOURCES

UNIT FIVE RESOURCE BOOK
Strategic Reading: Literature, p. 21
Vocabulary SkillBuilder, p. 22

ACCESS FOR STUDENTS ACQUIRING ENGLISH
Selection Summaries
Reading Support

FORMAL ASSESSMENT
Selection Test, pp. 111–112
 Test Generator

 AUDIO LIBRARY
See Reference Card

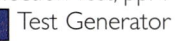 **LASERLINKS**
Literary Connection

THE LANGUAGE OF LITERATURE TEACHER'S EDITION **627**

SUMMARY

The county attorney, the sheriff, Mr. Hale, Mrs. Hale, and the sheriff's wife, Mrs. Peters, arrive at a farmhouse. The men have come to investigate a murder. The women are there to pick up a few things for Mrs. Wright, the wife of the dead farmer and the suspected murderer. The farmer, John Wright, had been strangled in his sleep. The men talk about what happened, study the crime scene, and look for evidence. The women talk to pass the time. Intent on their serious business, the men laugh at the trifles that occupy the women. The women, however, find evidence of a motive for the murder—information that would help the attorney with his case against the suspect, Mrs. Wright. Mrs. Wright was a lonely woman, they decide. She didn't have any children, and Mr. Wright was not a cheerful man to live with. Mrs. Wright had a canary to keep her company. The women find the dead canary, carefully wrapped up in a fancy box, its neck broken. Mr. Wright, they suspect, had killed it. Perhaps this action was Mrs. Wright's motive for killing her husband. The women hide the canary from the men.

Thematic Link: *False Pretenses* Under the pretenses of taking care of trifles, two women are able to learn and then cover up the motive for a murder.

CUSTOMIZING FOR
Students Acquiring English

- Use **ACCESS FOR STUDENTS ACQUIRING ENGLISH,** *Reading Support.*
- Review with students the formal conventions used for plays when they appear in print and ask them locate examples of each in the selection. For example, background material is given in italics, each speakers' name is printed in bold type followed by a period, stage directions are in italics within parentheses, and references to the play's characters by name are in regular type even within passages in italics.

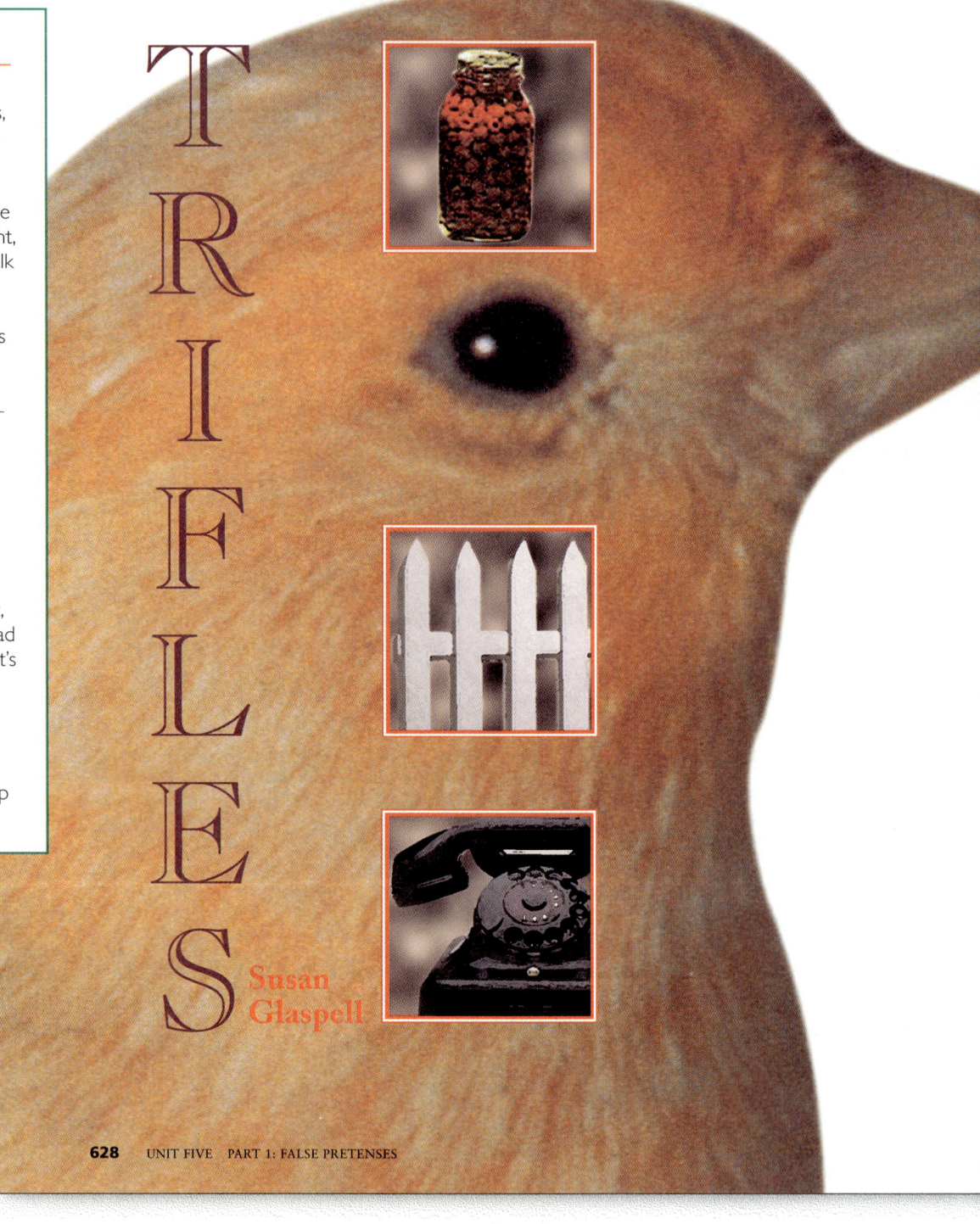

TRIFLES
Susan Glaspell

WORDS TO KNOW

abashed [ə-băshd] *adj.* embarrassed or ashamed **abash** *v.* (p. 636)
comprehension [kŏm′prĭ-hĕn′shən] *n.* awareness and understanding (p. 638)
covert [kō′vərt] *adj.* concealed; secretive (p. 638)

facetiously [fə-sē′shəs-lē] *adv.* in a manner not meant to be taken seriously; humorously (p. 640)
preoccupied [prē-ŏk′yə-pīd′] *adj.* absorbed in other thoughts (p. 638)

CAST OF CHARACTERS

George Henderson, **County Attorney**
Henry Peters, **Sheriff**
Lewis **Hale,** a neighboring farmer
Mrs. Peters
Mrs. Hale

SCENE: *The kitchen in the now abandoned farmhouse of* John Wright, *a gloomy kitchen, and left without having been put in order—the walls covered with a faded wallpaper. Downstage right is a door leading to the parlor. On the right wall above this door is a built-in kitchen cupboard with shelves in the upper portion and drawers below. In the rear wall at right, up two steps, is a door opening onto stairs leading to the second floor. In the rear wall at left is a door to the shed and from there to the outside. Between these two doors is an old-fashioned black iron stove. Running along the left wall from the shed door is an old iron sink and sink shelf, in which is set a hand pump. Downstage of the sink is an uncurtained window. Near the window is an old wooden rocker. Center stage is an unpainted wooden kitchen table with* *straight chairs on either side. There is a small chair downstage right. Unwashed pans under the sink, a loaf of bread outside the breadbox, a dish towel on the table—other signs of incompleted work. At the rear the shed door opens and the* Sheriff *comes in followed by the* County Attorney *and* Hale. *The* Sheriff *and* Hale *are men in middle life, the* County Attorney *is a young man; all are much bundled up and go at once to the stove. They are followed by the two women—the* Sheriff's *wife,* Mrs. Peters, *first; she is a slight wiry woman, a thin nervous face.* Mrs. Hale *is larger and would ordinarily be called more comfortable-looking, but she is disturbed now and looks fearfully about as she enters. The women have come in slowly, and stand close together near the door.*

TRIFLES **629**

Mini-Lesson Genre Study

DRAMA Draw the web shown on the right on the chalkboard, and use it to explain that a **one-act play** brings a script to life in the theater through scenery, lighting, costumes, and acting, just like a multi-act drama with several scenes. Because they are shorter, one-act plays usually are limited to a single scene; however, *The Devil and Daniel Webster*, though having only one act, establishes a second scene by blacking out the stage and then having the courtroom action played out with reduced lighting.

Application Have students copy the web into their notebooks. Ask them to refer to it as they compare the stage directions of *Trifles* to the traditional one-act play.

CUSTOMIZING FOR
Students Acquiring English

1 Write the terms *sheriff* and *county attorney* on the board and explain the role of each one in the investigation of a murder: the sheriff makes an arrest and the county attorney is in charge of prosecuting the case in court. The fact that the county attorney is accompanying the sheriff is evidence of the unusual nature of the crime.

Critical Thinking: CLARIFYING

B Have students explain what the county attorney means by this line. *(Possible response: He implies that someone should have been present in the house to insure that nothing was disturbed or altered.)*

Critical Thinking: SPECULATING

C Ask students why the county attorney interrupts Mr. Hale at this moment. *(Possible response: He does not want Hale to give personal opinions and theories; he wants him to stick to the facts.)*

CUSTOMIZING FOR
Students Acquiring English

2 Explain that to *pleat* something means to fold and crease it (usually cloth material) by doubling the material upon itself in an accordion style.

Literary Concept:
CHARACTERIZATION

D Ask students to evaluate Mrs. Wright's behavior as it is described by Mr. Hale. *(Possible response: Her lack of attention to Mr. Hale is peculiar, as are her laugh and curt replies to his questions; she seems to be either very upset or very preoccupied.)*

County Attorney (*at stove rubbing his hands*). This feels good. Come up to the fire, ladies.

Mrs. Peters (*after taking a step forward*). I'm not—cold.

Sheriff (*unbuttoning his overcoat and stepping away from the stove to right of table as if to mark the beginning of official business*). Now, Mr. Hale, before we move things about, you explain to Mr. Henderson just what you saw when you came here yesterday morning.

County Attorney (*crossing down to left of the table*). By the way, has anything been moved? Are things just as you left them yesterday?

Sheriff (*looking about*). It's just the same. When it dropped below zero last night, I thought I'd better send Frank out this morning to make a fire for us—(*sits right of center table*) no use getting pneumonia with a big case on, but I told him not to touch anything except the stove—and you know Frank.

County Attorney. Somebody should have been left here yesterday.

Sheriff. Oh—yesterday. When I had to send Frank to Morris Center for that man who went crazy—I want you to know I had my hands full yesterday. I knew you could get back from Omaha by today and as long as I went over everything here myself—

County Attorney. Well, Mr. Hale, tell just what happened when you came here yesterday morning.

Hale (*crossing down to above table*). Harry and I had started to town with a load of potatoes. We came along the road from my place and as I got here I said, "I'm going to see if I can't get John Wright to go in with me on a party telephone."[1] I spoke to Wright about it once before and he put me off, saying folks talked too much anyway, and all he asked was peace and quiet—I guess you know about how much he talked himself; but I thought maybe if I went to the house and talked about it before his wife, though I said to Harry that I didn't know as what his wife wanted made much difference to John—

County Attorney. Let's talk about that later, Mr. Hale. I do want to talk about that, but tell now just what happened when you got to the house.

Hale. I didn't hear or see anything; I knocked at the door, and still it was all quiet inside. I knew they must be up, it was past eight o'clock. So I knocked again, and I thought I heard somebody say, "Come in." I wasn't sure, I'm not sure yet, but I opened the door—this door (*indicating the door by which the two women are still standing*) and there in that rocker—(*pointing to it*) sat Mrs. Wright. (*They all look at the rocker downstage left.*)

County Attorney. What—was she doing?

Hale. She was rockin' back and forth. She had her apron in her hand and was kind of—pleating it.

County Attorney. And how did she—look?

Hale. Well, she looked queer.

County Attorney. How do you mean—queer?

Hale. Well, as if she didn't know what she was going to do next. And kind of done up.

County Attorney (*takes out notebook and pencil and sits left of center table*). How did she seem to feel about your coming?

Hale. Why, I don't think she minded—one way or other. She didn't pay much attention. I said, "How do, Mrs. Wright, it's cold, ain't it?" And she said, "Is it?"—and went on kind of pleating at her apron. Well, I was surprised; she didn't ask me to come up to the stove, or to set down, but just sat there, not even looking at me, so I said, "I want to see John." And then she—laughed. I guess you would call it a laugh. I thought of Harry and the team outside, so I said a little sharp: "Can't I see John?" "No,"

---

1. **party telephone:** A form of telephone circuit in which the telephone users—referred to as parties by the telephone company—within a particular community had to share the same phone line.

630 UNIT FIVE PART 1: FALSE PRETENSES

Mini-Lesson Workplace Literacy

TELEPHONE COMMUNICATIONS SKILLS

Point out that it is probably just as well that John Wright never got a telephone because he seldom spoke and was not interested in what others had to say. To communicate competently over the telephone, one must listen and speak effectively. Write this list on the chalkboard, and use it to explain the characteristics of a good telephone communicator in the workplace.

1. is knowledgeable about the subject at hand
2. organizes ideas and communicates effectively
3. speaks clearly
4. exhibits understanding, friendliness, and politeness to others

Application Have students choose partners and portray a telephone conversation between the county attorney's assistant and a reporter who has called Mr. Henderson's office to find out information about the case against Mrs. Wright.

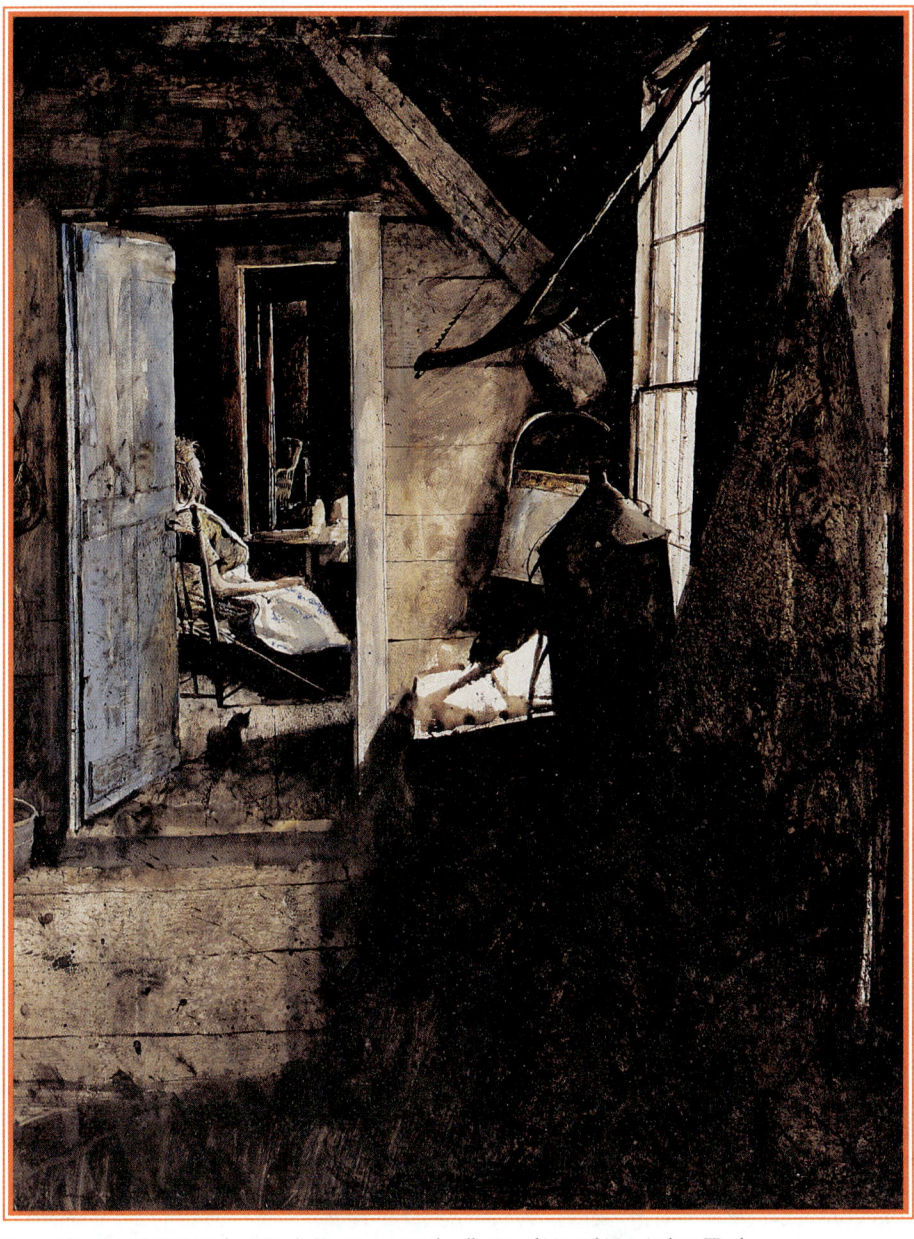

Room After Room (1967), Andrew Wyeth. Tempera on panel, collection of Mr. and Mrs. Andrew Wyeth. Copyright © 1995 Andrew Wyeth.

TRIFLES **631**

Art Note

***Room After Room* by Andrew Wyeth**
Andrew Wyeth, one of the most popular painters in modern American art, was born July 12, 1917, in Chadds Ford, Pennsylvania. Wyeth's subjects are the landmarks, countryside, and people of Maine and Pennsylvania. Often in warm tones of brown and gray, his paintings highlight details of texture and light. While paying attention to detail, Wyeth strives for an expression of mood rather than an accurate reproduction of nature.

Reading the Art *What is the mood of this painting? What do you think the woman in the chair is thinking about?*

CUSTOMIZING FOR
Multiple Learning Styles

E **Spatial or Graphic Learners** Have students compare the art on this page with the description of how Mr. Hale found Mrs. Wright the prior morning. Ask them to discuss how accurate the art is in depicting the scene.

Mini-Lesson: Speaking, Listening, and Viewing

SCIENTIFIC OBSERVATION Explain to students the importance of careful observation. Point out that because Mrs. Hale and Mrs. Peters carefully observe the small details at the crime scene, they are able to solve the mystery of Mr. Wright's murder. Often, by putting small details together, we can better see the whole picture.

Application Ask students to take a close look at the painting above. Then have them list as many details as possible about it. Tell students to compare their lists with those of other classmates. Have them discuss what the details reveal about the painting as a whole.

THE LANGUAGE OF LITERATURE TEACHER'S EDITION **631**

Critical Thinking:
MAKING INFERENCES

F Have students complete Hale's sentence that begins "It looked" by considering what Hale felt and what Harry said aloud. *(Possible answer: Hale might have been about to say it looked "as if he were only sleeping," because Harry answered with the words, "No, he's dead all right.")*

Critical Thinking:
MAKING JUDGMENTS

G Have students discuss whether or not they think Mrs. Wright's summary of events is plausible. *(Possible responses: Yes, a person could sleep deeply enough so as not to be awakened by a strangulation, a method of murder which would prevent the victim from crying out; no, she would certainly have been awakened by the murder.)*

Literary Concept:
CHARACTERIZATION

H Ask students what Mrs. Wright's laughter at different points reveals about her feelings for her husband. *(Possible response: Mrs. Wright's laughter might indicate that she is disturbed and upset, as well as being somewhat relieved that her husband is dead.)*

CUSTOMIZING FOR
Students Acquiring English

3 Point out this only appearance of the word *trifles* in the dialogue. Be certain students remember that *Trifles* is the title of the play and that the word means "things of little importance or value."

---

she says, kind o' dull like. "Ain't he home?" says I. "Yes," says she, "he's home." "Then why can't I see him?" I asked her, out of patience. "'Cause he's dead," says she. "Dead?" says I. She just nodded her head, not getting a bit excited, but rockin' back and forth. "Why—where is he?" says I, not knowing what to say. She just pointed upstairs—like that (*himself pointing to the room above*). I started for the stairs, with the idea of going up there. I walked from there to here—then I says, "Why, what did he die of?" "He died of a rope round his neck," says she, and just went on pleatin' at her apron. Well, I went out and called Harry. I thought I might—need help. We went upstairs and there he was lyin'—

County Attorney. I think I'd rather have you go into that upstairs, where you can point it all out. Just go on now with the rest of the story.

Hale. Well, my first thought was to get that rope off. It looked . . . (*Stops. His face twitches.*) . . . but Harry, he went up to him, and he said, "No, he's dead all right, and we'd better not touch anything." So we went back downstairs. She was still sitting that same way. "Has anybody been notified?" I asked. "No," says she, unconcerned. "Who did this, Mrs. Wright?" said Harry. He said it businesslike—and she stopped pleatin' of her apron. "I don't know," she says. "You don't *know?*" says Harry. "No," says she. "Weren't you sleepin' in the bed with him?" says Harry. "Yes," says she, "but I was on the inside." "Somebody slipped a rope round his neck and strangled him and you didn't wake up?" says Harry. "I didn't wake up," she said after him. We must 'a' looked as if we didn't see how that could be, for after a minute she said, "I sleep sound." Harry was going to ask her more questions but I said maybe we ought to let her tell her story first to the coroner, or the sheriff, so Harry went fast as he could to Rivers' place, where there's a telephone.

County Attorney. And what did Mrs. Wright do when she knew that you had gone for the coroner?

Hale. She moved from the rocker to that chair over there (*pointing to a small chair in the downstage right corner*) and just sat there with her hands held together and looking down. I got a feeling that I ought to make some conversation, so I said I had come in to see if John wanted to put in a telephone, and at that she started to laugh, and then she stopped and looked at me—scared. (*The County Attorney, who has had his notebook out, makes a note.*) I dunno, maybe it wasn't scared. I wouldn't like to say it was. Soon Harry got back, and then Dr. Lloyd came, and you, Mr. Peters, and so I guess that's all I know that you don't.

County Attorney (*rising and looking around*). I guess we'll go upstairs first—and then out to the barn and around there. (*To the* Sheriff) You're convinced that there was nothing important here—nothing that would point to any motive?

Sheriff. Nothing here but kitchen things. (*The County Attorney, after again looking around the kitchen, opens the door of a cupboard closet in right wall. He brings a small chair from right—gets up on it and looks on a shelf. Pulls his hand away, sticky.*)

County Attorney. Here's a nice mess. (*The women draw nearer upstage center.*)

Mrs. Peters (*to the other woman*). Oh, her fruit; it did freeze. (*To the* Lawyer) She worried about that when it turned so cold. She said the fire'd go out and her jars would break.

Sheriff (*rises*). Well, can you beat the women! Held for murder and worryin' about her preserves.

County Attorney (*getting down from chair*). I guess before we're through she may have something more serious than preserves to worry about. (*crosses down right center*)

Hale. Well, women are used to worrying over trifles.

(*The two women move a little closer together.*)

County Attorney (*with the gallantry of a young politician*). And yet, for all their worries, what would we do without the ladies? (*The women do not unbend. He goes below the center table to the sink, takes a dipperful of water from the pail and, pouring it into a basin, washes his hands. While he is doing this, the* Sheriff *and* Hale *cross to cupboard, which they inspect. The* County Attorney *starts to wipe his hands on the roller towel, turns it for a cleaner place.*) Dirty towels! (*Kicks his foot against the pans under the sink.*) Not much of a housekeeper, would you say, ladies?

Mrs. Hale (*stiffly*). There's a great deal of work to be done on a farm.

County Attorney. To be sure. And yet (*with a little bow to her*) I know there are some Dickson County farmhouses which do not have such roller towels. (*He gives it a pull to expose its full length again.*)

Mrs. Hale. Those towels get dirty awful quick. Men's hands aren't always as clean as they might be.

County Attorney. Ah, loyal to your sex, I see. But you and Mrs. Wright were neighbors. I suppose you were friends, too.

Mrs. Hale (*shaking her head*). I've not seen much of her of late years. I've not been in this house—it's more than a year.

County Attorney (*crossing to women upstage center*). And why was that? You didn't like her?

Mrs. Hale. I liked her all well enough. Farmers' wives have their hands full, Mr. Henderson. And then—

County Attorney. Yes—?

Mrs. Hale (*looking about*). It never seemed a very cheerful place.

County Attorney. No—it's not cheerful. I shouldn't say she had the homemaking instinct.

Mrs. Hale. Well, I don't know as Wright had, either.

County Attorney. You mean that they didn't get on very well?

Mrs. Hale. No, I don't mean anything. But I don't think a place'd be any cheerfuller for John Wright's being in it.

County Attorney. I'd like to talk more of that a little later. I want to get the lay of things upstairs now. (*He goes past the women to upstage right where steps lead to a stair door.*)

Sheriff. I suppose anything Mrs. Peters does'll be all right. She was to take in some clothes for her, you know, and a few little things. We left in such a hurry yesterday.

County Attorney. Yes, but I would like to see what you take, Mrs. Peters, and keep an eye out for anything that might be of use to us.

Mrs. Peters. Yes, Mr. Henderson. (*The men leave by upstage right door to stairs. The women listen to the men's steps on the stairs, then look about the kitchen.*)

Mrs. Hale (*crossing left to sink*). I'd hate to have men coming into my kitchen, snooping around and criticizing. (*She arranges the pans under sink which the lawyer had shoved out of place.*)

Mrs. Peters. Of course it's no more than their duty. (*crosses to cupboard upstage right*)

Mrs. Hale. Duty's all right, but I guess that deputy sheriff that came out to make the fire might have got a little of this on. (*Gives the roller towel a pull.*) Wish I'd thought of that sooner. Seems mean to talk about her for not having things slicked up when she had to come away in such a hurry. (*Crosses right to* Mrs. Peters *at cupboard.*)

Mrs. Peters (*who has been looking through cupboard, lifts one end of a towel that covers a pan*). She had bread set. (*Stands still.*)

Mrs. Hale (*eyes fixed on a loaf of bread beside the breadbox, which is on a low shelf of the cupboard*). She was going to put this in there. (*Picks up loaf, then abruptly drops it. In a manner of returning to familiar things.*) It's a

Art Note

The Pantry by Art Gore Art Gore (1926–) developed a love for photography while growing up in North Carolina. Gore is fascinated by "old things" and spends time browsing through antique shops looking for objects to photograph. Gore says that he wonders "about the faces and personalities of the people who owned these treasures that I collect today for still lifes." However, before he can take a picture of something, he claims, he "must be able to see it for the beauty of its form or texture" and provide viewers a new insight into the richness of their heritage.

Reading the Art What do you think attracted Art Gore to this scene? What feelings does the photograph evoke?

Literary Concept: SYMBOL

L Ask students what the rocking chair might represent to Mrs. Hale. (*Possible responses: despair; tragedy; loss; Mrs. Wright*)

Literary Concept: MOOD

M Have students describe the mood that the empty rocking chair evoked. (*Possible response: The mood is somewhat eerie, as the women seem to imagine Mrs. Wright in the room the previous day.*)

The Pantry, Art Gore.

shame about her fruit. I wonder if it's all gone. (*Gets up on the chair and looks.*) I think there's some here that's all right, Mrs. Peters. Yes—here; (*holding it toward the window*) this is cherries, too. (*looking again*) I declare I believe that's the only one. (*Gets down, jar in her hand. Goes to the sink and wipes it off on the outside.*) She'll feel awful bad after all her hard work in the hot weather. I remember the afternoon I put up my cherries last summer. (*She puts the jar on the big kitchen table, center of the room. With a sigh, is about to sit down in the rocking chair. Before she is seated realizes what chair it is; with a slow look at it, steps back. The chair which she has touched rocks back and forth. Mrs. Peters moves to center table and they both watch the chair rock for a moment or two.*)

634 UNIT FIVE PART 1: FALSE PRETENSES

Mrs. Peters (*shaking off the mood which the empty rocking chair has evoked; now in a businesslike manner she speaks*). Well, I must get those things from the front room closet. (*She goes to the door at the right, but, after looking into the other room, steps back*). You coming with me, Mrs. Hale? You could help me carry them. (*They go in the other room; reappear,* Mrs. Peters *carrying a dress, petticoat and skirt,* Mrs. Hale *following with a pair of shoes.*) My, it's cold in there. (*She puts the clothes on the big table, and hurries to the stove.*)

Mrs. Hale (*right of center table examining the skirt*). Wright was close.[2] I think maybe that's why she kept so much to herself. She didn't even belong to the Ladies' Aid. I suppose she felt she couldn't do her part, and then you don't enjoy things when you feel shabby. I heard she used to wear pretty clothes and be lively, when she was Minnie Foster, one of the town girls singing in the choir. But that—oh, that was thirty years ago. This all you was to take in?

Mrs. Peters. She said she wanted an apron. Funny thing to want, for there isn't much to get you dirty in jail, goodness knows. But I suppose just to make her feel more natural. (*crosses to cupboard.*) She said they was in the top drawer in this cupboard. Yes, here. And then her little shawl that always hung behind the door. (*Opens stair door and looks.*) Yes, here it is. (*Quickly shuts door leading upstairs.*)

Mrs. Hale (*abruptly moving toward her*). Mrs. Peters?

Mrs. Peters. Yes, Mrs. Hale? (*At upstage right door.*)

Mrs. Hale. Do you think she did it?

Mrs. Peters (*in a frightened voice*). Oh, I don't know.

Mrs. Hale. Well, I don't think she did. Asking for an apron and her little shawl. Worrying about her fruit.

Mrs. Peters (*Starts to speak, glances up, where footsteps are heard in the room above. In a low voice*). Mr. Peters says it looks bad for her. Mr. Henderson is awful sarcastic in a speech and he'll make fun of her sayin' she didn't wake up.

Mrs. Hale. Well, I guess John Wright didn't wake when they was slipping that rope under his neck.

Mrs. Peters (*crossing slowly to table and placing shawl and apron on table with other clothing*). No, it's strange. It must have been done awful crafty and still. They say it was such a—funny way to kill a man, rigging it all up like that.

Mrs. Hale (*crossing to left of* Mrs. Peters *at table*). That's just what Mr. Hale said. There was a gun in the house. He says that's what he can't understand.

Mrs. Peters. Mr. Henderson said coming out that what was needed for the case was a motive; something to show anger, or—sudden feeling.

Mrs. Hale (*who is standing by the table*). Well, I don't see any signs of anger around here. (*She puts her hand on the dishtowel which lies on the table, stands looking down at table, one-half of which is clean, the other half messy.*) It's wiped to here. (*Makes a move as if to finish work, then turns and looks at loaf of bread outside the breadbox. Drops towel. In that voice of coming back to familiar things.*) Wonder how they are finding things upstairs. (*Crossing below table to downstage right*) I hope she had it a little more readied-up[3] up there. You know, it seems kind of sneaking. Locking her up in town and then coming out here and trying to get her own house to turn against her!

Mrs. Peters. But, Mrs. Hale, the law is the law.

Mrs. Hale. I s'pose 'tis. (*unbuttoning her coat*) Better loosen up your things, Mrs. Peters. You won't feel them when you go out. (Mrs. Peters *takes off her fur tippet,[4] goes to hang it on chair back left of table, stands looking at the work basket on floor near downstage left window.*)

---

2. **close:** secretive; not open or friendly.
3. **readied-up:** *dialect,* made ready; straightened up.
4. **tippet:** a scarflike or shawllike garment.

Multicultural Perspectives

Students may be interested to know that a new art form developed in Japan after a famous collection of American quilts toured major Japanese cities in 1976. The Japanese traditionally sleep on a futon, a pad on the floor, and pull another pad over themselves. In fact, a type of futon was probably the forerunner of our modern quilt. In the past, futons were beautifully and elaborately decorated. Today, the Japanese have borrowed our passion for quilt making but have developed their own distinctive style. Using their own form of quilting, called *sashiko,* they make ornate and exquisite quilts from old textiles: futon covers, kimonos, scraps, and ornamental wrapping cloths.

Literary Note

Q This seemingly unimportant question about a technical distinction of quiltmaking comes to take on more meaning as it is repeated throughout the play. Glaspell uses the terms in the play's last line—the "curtain line." The two terms refer to securing the three layers of cloth by the usual, painstaking method ("quilting") or by a quicker method ("knotting" or "typing"). However, by the curtain line, the term *knot it* carries a second meaning, referring to the way the noose was knotted.

STRATEGIC READING FOR
Less-Proficient Readers

R Make sure students have the facts to begin to link Mrs. Wright's unhappy marriage to a motive for murder.

- What was Minnie's life like before and after marrying John Wright? *(She was lively and wore pretty clothes before; she kept to herself and dressed shabbily after.)* **Comparing/Contrasting**
- What did Mr. Henderson say was needed for the case? *(a motive)* **Noting Relevant Details**

Set a Purpose Have students read to find out how attention to "trifles" uncover a motive for murder.

Critical Thinking: SPECULATING

S Ask students why Mrs. Hale resews the block of quilt. *(Possible response: to cover up evidence of "sudden feeling"—the evidence of anger that Mr. Henderson feels is needed to find a motive)*

Literary Concept: SYMBOL

T Ask students to identify what two things Mrs. Hale compares in this passage. *(a canary and Mrs. Wright)* What does this comparison imply? *(Possible response: that John Wright kept his wife "caged up" in their home)* Encourage students to look for other passages where this identification between Mrs. Wright and a bird is repeated.

Mrs. Peters. She was piecing a quilt. (*She brings the large sewing basket to the center table and they look at the bright pieces,* Mrs. Hale *above the table and* Mrs. Peters *left of it.*)

Mrs. Hale. It's a log cabin pattern.[5] Pretty, isn't it? I wonder if she was goin' to quilt it or just knot it?[6] (*Footsteps have been heard coming down the stairs. The* Sheriff *enters followed by* Hale *and the* County Attorney.)

Sheriff. They wonder if she was going to quilt it or just knot it! (*The men laugh, the women look* abashed.)

County Attorney (*rubbing his hands over the stove*). Frank's fire didn't do much up there, did it? Well, let's go out to the barn and get that cleared up. (*The men go outside by upstage left door.*)

Mrs. Hale (*resentfully*). I don't know as there's anything so strange, our takin' up our time with little things while we're waiting for them to get the evidence. (*She sits in chair right of table smoothing out a block with decision.*) I don't see as it's anything to laugh about.

Mrs. Peters (*apologetically*). Of course they've got awful important things on their minds. (*Pulls up a chair and joins* Mrs. Hale *at the left of the table.*)

Mrs. Hale (*examining another block*). Mrs. Peters, look at this one. Here, this is the one she was working on, and look at the sewing! All the rest of it has been so nice and even. And look at this! It's all over the place! Why, it looks as if she didn't know what she was about! (*After she has said this they look at each other, then start to glance back at the door. After an instant* Mrs. Hale *has pulled at a knot and ripped the sewing.*)

Mrs. Peters. Oh, what are you doing, Mrs. Hale?

Mrs. Hale (*mildly*). Just pulling out a stitch or two that's not sewed very good. (*threading a needle*) Bad sewing always made me fidgety.

Mrs. Peters (*with a glance at door, nervously*). I don't think we ought to touch things.

Mrs. Hale. I'll just finish up this end. (*suddenly stopping and leaning forward*) Mrs. Peters?

Mrs. Peters. Yes, Mrs. Hale?

Mrs. Hale. What do you suppose she was so nervous about?

Mrs. Peters. Oh—I don't know, I don't know as she was nervous. I sometimes sew awful queer when I'm just tired. (Mrs. Hale *starts to say something, looks at* Mrs. Peters, *then goes on sewing.*) Well, I must get these things wrapped up. They may be through sooner than we think. (*Putting apron and other things together*) I wonder where I can find a piece of paper, and string. (*Rises.*)

Mrs. Hale. In that cupboard, maybe.

Mrs. Peters (*crosses right looking in cupboard*). Why, here's a birdcage. (*Holds it up.*) Did she have a bird, Mrs. Hale?

Mrs. Hale. Why, I don't know whether she did or not—I've not been here for so long. There was a man around last year selling canaries cheap, but I don't know as she took one; maybe she did. She used to sing real pretty herself.

Mrs. Peters (*glancing around*). Seems funny to think of a bird here. But she must have had one, or why would she have a cage? I wonder what happened to it?

Mrs. Hale. I s'pose maybe the cat got it.

Mrs. Peters. No, she didn't have a cat. She's got that feeling some people have about cats—being afraid of them. My cat got in her room and she was real upset and asked me to take it out.

---

5. **log cabin pattern:** a common pattern for a quilt.
6. **quilt it or just knot it:** the bottom and top layers of a quilt are either quilted—sewn together—or knotted—held together with yarn tied into knots. Knotting is a much simpler and faster method.

WORDS TO KNOW
abashed (ə-băshd′) *adj.* embarrassed or ashamed **abash** *v.*

Mrs. Hale. My sister Bessie was like that. Queer, ain't it?

Mrs. Peters (*examining the cage*). Why, look at this door. It's broke. One hinge is pulled apart. (*Takes a step down to* Mrs. Hale's *right.*)

Mrs. Hale (*looking too*). Looks as if someone must have been rough with it.

Mrs. Peters. Why, yes. (*She brings the cage forward and puts it on the table.*)

Mrs. Hale (*glancing toward upstage left door*). I wish if they're going to find any evidence they'd be about it. I don't like this place.

Mrs. Peters. But I'm awful glad you came with me, Mrs. Hale. It would be lonesome for me sitting here alone.

Mrs. Hale. It would, wouldn't it? (*dropping her sewing*) But I tell you what I do wish, Mrs. Peters. I wish I had come over sometimes when she was here. I—(*looking around the room*)—wish I had.

Mrs. Peters. But of course you were awful busy, Mrs. Hale—your house and your children.

Mrs. Hale (*rises and crosses left*). I could've come. I stayed away because it weren't cheerful—and that's why I ought to have come. I—(*looking out left window*)—I've never liked this place. Maybe because it's down in a hollow and you don't see the road. I dunno what it is, but it's a lonesome place and always was. I wish I had come over to see Minnie Foster sometimes. I can see now—(*shakes her head*)

Mrs. Peters (*left of table and above it*). Well, you mustn't reproach yourself, Mrs. Hale. Somehow we just don't see how it is with other folks until—something turns up.

Mrs. Hale. Not having children makes less work—but it makes a quiet house, and Wright out to work all day, and no company when he did come in. (*turning from window*) Did you know John Wright, Mrs. Peters?

Mrs. Peters. Not to know him; I've seen him in town. They say he was a good man.

Mrs. Hale. Yes—good; he didn't drink, and kept his word as well as most, I guess, and paid his debts. But he was a hard man, Mrs. Peters. Just to pass the time of day with him—(*shivers*) Like a raw wind that gets to the bone. (*pauses, her eye falling on the cage*) I should think she would 'a' wanted a bird. But what do you suppose went with it?

Mrs. Peters. I don't know, unless it got sick and died. (*She reaches over and swings the broken door, swings it again, both women watch it.*)

Mrs. Hale. You weren't raised round here, were you? (Mrs. Peters *shakes her head.*) You didn't know—her?

Mrs. Peters. Not till they brought her yesterday.

Mrs. Hale. She—come to think of it, she was kind of like a bird herself—real sweet and pretty, but kind of timid and—fluttery. How—she—did—change. (*Silence; then as if struck by a happy thought and relieved to get back to everyday things, crosses right above* Mrs. Peters *to cupboard, replaces small chair used to stand on to its original place downstage right.*) Tell you what, Mrs. Peters, why don't you take the quilt in with you? It might take up her mind.

Mrs. Peters. Why, I think that's a real nice idea, Mrs. Hale. There couldn't possibly be any objection to it, could there? Now, just what would I take? I wonder if her patches are in here—and her things. (*They look in the sewing basket.*)

Mrs. Hale (*crosses to right of table*). Here's some red. I expect this has got sewing things in it. (*Brings out a fancy box.*) What a pretty box. Looks like something somebody would give you. Maybe her scissors are in here. (*Opens box. Suddenly puts her hand to her nose.*) Why— (Mrs. Peters *bends nearer, then turns her face away.*) There's something wrapped up in this piece of silk.

Mrs. Peters. Why, this isn't her scissors.

Mrs. Hale (*lifting the silk*). Oh, Mrs. Peters—it's— (Mrs. Peters *bends closer.*)

TRIFLES 637

Literary Concept:
CHARACTERIZATION

U Ask students what this speech reveals about Mrs. Hale's personality. (*Possible response: She is a kind person who identifies with other people; her regret for not having visited Mrs. Wright shows her ability to feel compassion.*)

Critical Thinking:
MAKING JUDGMENTS

V Ask students if they would consider Mr. Wright a "good man." (*Possible responses: yes, because he did not drink, was truthful, and paid his debts; no, because he was a hard man who did not treat his wife well.*)

CUSTOMIZING FOR
Students Acquiring English

5 Tell students that the expression "what do you suppose went with it?" means "what do you suppose happened to it?"

Linking to History

W The play takes place in the early 1900s. By that time Elias Howe had invented the first practical sewing machine, but few people owned them. Most sewing, especially in rural areas, was still done completely by hand.

Mini-Lesson Grammar

DASH IN DIALOGUE Explain that in dialogue a dash shows an abrupt break in thought, often caused by uncertainty or hesitancy. Have students note how the dashes used in the highlighted passage above help evoke the character's emotional state as she attempts to recall the past. The dash can also add a casual, conversational tone to dialogue since people often change their thoughts in midsentence.

Application Ask students to identify at least five other passages in which dashes are used in the dialogue of the play. Then have them rewrite these passages to eliminate the dashes and discuss the effect this has on each passage.

Reteaching/Reinforcement
- Grammar Handbook, anthology p. 934

The Writer's Craft
The Dash, p. 789

THE LANGUAGE OF LITERATURE TEACHER'S EDITION 637

Literary Concept: CLIMAX

X Have students explain the "growing comprehension" the women experience. *(Possible response: They are realizing that it was John Wright who tore open the bird cage and killed the canary, and that Mrs. Wright is guilty.)*

Literary Concept: DRAMATIC IRONY

Y Explain that dramatic irony occurs when the audience knows more than do certain characters. Have students explain the dramatic irony in this passage. *(Possible response: The men have no idea what happened, while the audience knows that the women they treat contemptuously have found the sought-for evidence.)*

Literary Concept: FLASHBACK

Z Invite students to draw the connection between Mrs. Peter's experience when she was a girl and how John Wright met his death. *(Possible response: Mrs. Peter's memory illustrates Mrs. Wright's "sudden feeling" and motive for killing her husband.)*

STRATEGIC READING FOR Less-Proficient Readers

AA Have students describe the evidence found by the women that might indicate a motive. *(Possible response: The irregular sewing shows "strong feeling"; the dead bird and its broken cage show Mr. Wright's cruelty and may have been the catalyst to cause Minnie to kill John.)*
Summarizing/Drawing Conclusions

Set a Purpose Have students read to find out whether the women ever tell the men what they have learned.

Mrs. Peters. It's the bird.
Mrs. Hale. But, Mrs. Peters—look at it! Its neck! Look at its neck! It's all—other side *to*.[7]
Mrs. Peters. Somebody—wrung—its—neck. (*Their eyes meet. A look of growing* comprehension, *of horror. Steps are heard outside,* Mrs. Hale *slips box under quilt pieces, and sinks into her chair. Enter* Sheriff *and* County Attorney. Mrs. Peters *steps downstage left and stands looking out of window.*)
County Attorney (*as one turning from serious things to little pleasantries*). Well, ladies, have you decided whether she was going to quilt it or knot it? (*Crosses to center above table.*)
Mrs. Peters. We think she was going to—knot it. (Sheriff *crosses to right of stove, lifts stove lid and glances at fire, then stands warming hands at stove.*)
County Attorney. Well, that's interesting, I'm sure. (*Seeing the birdcage.*) Has the bird flown?
Mrs. Hale (*putting more quilt pieces over the box*). We think the—cat got it.
County Attorney (preoccupied). Is there a cat? (Mrs. Hale *glances in a quick* covert *way at* Mrs. Peters.)
Mrs. Peters (*turning from window takes a step in*). Well, not now. They're superstitious, you know. They leave.
County Attorney (*to* Sheriff Peters, *continuing an interrupted conversation*). No sign at all of anyone having come from the outside. Their own rope. Now let's go up again and go over it piece by piece. (*They start upstairs.*) It would have to have been someone who knew just the— (Mrs. Peters *sits down left of table. The two women sit there not looking at one another, but as if peering into something and at the same time holding back. When they talk now it is in the manner of feeling their way over strange ground, as if afraid of what they are saying, but as if they cannot help saying it.*)
Mrs. Hale (*hesitantly and in hushed voice*). She liked the bird. She was going to bury it in that pretty box.
Mrs. Peters (*in a whisper*). When I was a girl—my kitten—there was a boy took a hatchet, and before my eyes—and before I could get there— (*covers her face an instant*) If they hadn't held me back I would have—(*catches herself, looks upstairs where steps are heard, falters weakly*)—hurt him.
Mrs. Hale (*with a slow look around her*). I wonder how it would seem never to have had any children around. (*pause*) No, Wright wouldn't like the bird—a thing that sang. She used to sing. He killed that, too.
Mrs. Peters (*moving uneasily*). We don't know who killed the bird.
Mrs. Hale. I knew John Wright.
Mrs. Peters. It was an awful thing was done in this house that night, Mrs. Hale. Killing a man while he slept, slipping a rope around his neck that choked the life out of him.
Mrs. Hale. His neck. Choked the life out of him. (*Her hand goes out and rests on the birdcage.*)
Mrs. Peters (*with rising voice*). We don't know who killed him. We don't *know*.
Mrs. Hale (*her own feeling not interrupted*). If there'd been years and years of nothing, then a bird to sing to you, it would be awful—still, after the bird was still.
Mrs. Peters (*something within her speaking*). I know what stillness is. When we homesteaded[8]

---

7. **other side *to*:** back side forward. The bird's head was facing the wrong way.
8. **homesteaded:** settled and farmed on land that was given to settlers by the U.S. government following the 1862 Homestead Act; ownership was granted after the settler had lived on the land for five years.

| WORDS TO KNOW | **comprehension** (kŏm'prĭ-hĕn'shən) *n.* awareness and understanding. **preoccupied** (prē-ŏk'yə-pīd') *adj.* absorbed in other thoughts. **covert** (kō'vərt) *adj.* concealed; secretive. |

The Gilded Cage, Art Gore.

in Dakota, and my first baby died—after he was two years old, and me with no other then—

Mrs. Hale (*moving*). How soon do you suppose they'll be through looking for the evidence?

Mrs. Peters. I know what stillness is. (*pulling herself back*) The law has got to punish crime, Mrs. Hale.

Mrs. Hale (*not as if answering that*). I wish you'd seen Minnie Foster when she wore a white dress with blue ribbons and stood up there in the choir and sang. (*a look around the room*) Oh, I *wish* I'd come over here once in a while! That was a crime! That was a crime! Who's going to punish that?

Mrs. Peters (*looking upstairs*). We mustn't—take on.

Mrs. Hale. I might have known she needed help! I know how things can be—for women. I tell you, it's queer, Mrs. Peters. We live close

---

Critic's Corner

"*Trifles* is different from [Glaspell's] other one-acts in that it is neither satiric nor overtly idealistic. With its precise realism, exact details, accurate dialogue, and conscious awareness of certain Midwestern ingredients, it is local color on stage. We expect men like John Wright to live on the prairie, women like Minnie Foster to marry him; and the sudden violence after twenty years of repression seems inevitable in that bleak Iowan homestead."

Arthur Waterman
Susan Glaspell

Literary Concept: SYMBOL

CC Ask students what the unbroken jar of fruit preserves might represent. *(Possible responses: hope, comfort, support)*

Critical Thinking: ANALYZING

DD Have students explain how the halted sewing and the dead canary fit this description of "something to make a story about." *(Possible response: The knotted sewing suggests what Mrs. Wright did with the noose. The canary suggests John Wright's cruelty, the motive for Mrs. Wright, and it echoes the death—Wright's neck was "wrung.")*

Literary Concept: DRAMATIC IRONY

EE Have students explain the dramatic irony in this passage. *(Possible response: The county attorney and the sheriff agree that Mrs. Peters does not need supervision since she is "married to the law" only a moment after she has hidden evidence, and thus abetted a criminal.)*

STRATEGIC READING FOR
Less-Proficient Readers

FF Have students tell what the women do with the information they've learned about the murder. *(They keep the facts to themselves, allowing the men to continue to make fun of their attention to "trifles.")* Summarizing/Drawing Conclusions

CUSTOMIZING FOR
Gifted and Talented Students

GG Have students debate whether or not there is ever a justification for murder. Challenge them to debate whether Mrs. Wright was justified in killing her husband.

COMPREHENSION CHECK
True or false
1. Mrs. Wright is accused of shooting her husband. *(false)*
2. The men tease the women for their concern over small matters. *(true)*
3. Mrs. Hale resews some erratic sewing on a piece of Mrs. Wright's quilt. *(true)*
4. Finding a dead canary convinces the women that Mrs. Wright killed her husband. *(true)*
5. The women plan to tell the men about the dead canary at a later time. *(false)*

---

together and we live far apart. We all go through the same things—it's all just a different kind of the same thing. (*Brushes her eyes. Noticing the jar of fruit, reaches out for it.*) If I was you I wouldn't tell her her fruit was gone. Tell her it *ain't*. Tell her it's all right. Take this in to prove it to her. She—she may never know whether it was broke or not.

Mrs. Peters (*takes the jar, looks about for something to wrap it in; takes petticoat from the clothes brought from the other room, very nervously begins winding this around the jar; in a false voice*). My, it's a good thing the men couldn't hear us. Wouldn't they just laugh! Getting all stirred up over a little thing like a—dead canary. As if that could have anything to do with—with—wouldn't they *laugh*! (*The men are heard coming downstairs.*)

Mrs. Hale (*under her breath*). Maybe they would—maybe they wouldn't.

County Attorney. No, Peters, it's all perfectly clear except a reason for doing it. But you know juries when it comes to women. If there was some definite thing. (*Crosses slowly to above table. Sheriff crosses downstage right. Mrs. Hale and Mrs. Peters remain seated at either side of table.*) Something to show—something to make a story about—a thing that would connect up with this strange way of doing it— (*The women's eyes meet for an instant. Enter Hale from outer door.*)

Hale (*remaining upstage left by door*). Well, I've got the team around. Pretty cold out there.

County Attorney. I'm going to stay awhile by myself. (*To the Sheriff*) You can send Frank out for me, can't you? I want to go over everything. I'm not satisfied that we can't do better.

Sheriff. Do you want to see what Mrs. Peters is going to take in? (*The Lawyer picks up the apron, laughs.*)

County Attorney. Oh, I guess they're not very dangerous things the ladies have picked out. (*Moves a few things about, disturbing the quilt pieces which cover the box. Steps back.*) No, Mrs. Peters doesn't need supervising. For that matter a sheriff's wife is married to the law. Ever think of it that way, Mrs. Peters?

Mrs. Peters. Not—just that way.

Sheriff (*chuckling*). Married to the law. (*Moves to downstage right door to the other room.*) I just want you to come in here a minute, George. We ought to take a look at these windows.

County Attorney (*scoffingly*). Oh, windows!

Sheriff. We'll be right out, Mr. Hale. (*Hale goes outside. The Sheriff follows the County Attorney into the other room. Then Mrs. Hale rises, hands tight together, looking intensely at Mrs. Peters, whose eyes make a slow turn, finally meeting Mrs. Hale's. A moment Mrs. Hale holds her, then her own eyes point the way to where the box is concealed. Suddenly Mrs. Peters throws back quilt pieces and tries to put the box in the bag she is carrying. It is too big. She opens box, starts to take bird out, cannot touch it, goes to pieces, stands there helpless. Sound of a knob turning in the other room, Mrs. Hale snatches the box and puts it in the pocket of her big coat. Enter County Attorney and Sheriff, who remains downstage right.*)

County Attorney (*crosses to upstage left door facetiously*). Well, Henry, at least we found out that she was not going to quilt it. She was going to—what is it you call it, ladies?

Mrs. Hale (*standing center below table facing front, her hand against her pocket*). We call it—knot it, Mr. Henderson.

Curtain

WORDS TO KNOW
facetiously (fə-sē′shəs-lē) *adv.* in a manner not meant to be taken seriously; humorously.

640

Assessment Option

INFORMAL ASSESSMENT You can informally assess your students' understanding of the selection by setting up the following scenario: *Pretend that Mrs. Wright is acquitted of the murder of her husband, and she finds out how Mrs. Hale and Mrs. Peters have helped her. Years later, as she lies dying, she leaves a letter that explains what is was like for her living with John Wright; she relates the incident leading to the murder and what happened afterward, and expresses her gratitude to the women.*

Have students provide written versions of the letter that reflect the character of Mrs. Wright.

Rubric

3 Full Accomplishment The letter accurately and specifically describes the events in the play and reflects the character of Mrs. Wright.

2 Substantial Accomplishment The letter accurately describes most of the important events in the play, but might not always reflect the character of Mrs. Wright.

1 Little or Partial Accomplishment Students have difficulty describing the events in the play. The letter does not reflect the character of Mrs. Wright.

FROM PERSONAL RESPONSE TO CRITICAL ANALYSIS

REFLECT 1. What is your reaction to the ending of the story? Jot down your thoughts in your notebook and share them with your classmates.

RETHINK 2. Review the chart you created for the Reading Connection on page 627. Reconstruct the crime as you think it happened. With a partner, dramatize the events leading up to and following the murder.

3. The county attorney feels he needs a clear "reason," or motive, for the murder because "you know juries when it comes to women." What do you think he means by this remark?

4. Why do you think Mrs. Hale and Mrs. Peters are sympathetic toward the murder suspect, Mrs. Wright, and deceive the men about their discoveries?

Close Textual Reading

Consider
- the life that Mrs. Hale leads
- their view of the Wrights' married life
- the men's attitude toward the women

Thematic Link

5. Do you think Mrs. Hale and Mrs. Peters do the right thing? Explain your opinion.

RELATE 6. Do you think women are generally more observant and intuitive than men? Explain.

LITERARY CONCEPTS

Dramatic irony occurs when the reader or viewer is aware of information of which a character is unaware. In *Trifles*, the reader is aware of the clues that the women have uncovered, while the men are unaware of this evidence. How does this dramatic irony affect a reader's interpretation of Mrs. Hale's final statement?

CONCEPT REVIEW: Symbol The bird cage and the dead canary in this play are important images that stand for something beyond themselves. Think about the characters in the play and explain what these symbols suggest.

Multimodal Learning
ANOTHER PATHWAY

Cooperative Learning

As a class, stage the trial of Minnie Wright. One group can prepare the county attorney's case, which will try to prove guilt. Another can act as the defense attorney, trying for a verdict of not guilty based on lack of evidence. Other groups can act as the judge, the jury, and the play's characters who are witnesses.

QUICKWRITES

1. List the main facts you think that Sheriff Peters will have on his **crime report**. The facts should be those that he has gathered from his observations and from Mr. Hale.

2. Imagine that you are a local reporter covering the Wright murder. Write a **news account** of the murder and the investigation. Include characters in the play through interviews that hint at concealed evidence.

📁 **PORTFOLIO** *Save your writing. You may want to use it later as a springboard to a piece for your portfolio.*

From Personal Response to Critical Analysis

1. Accept all reasonable responses.
2. The dramatization should include all important events surrounding the murder.
3. Possible response: A jury is likely to be more lenient towards a woman accused of murder, so it is very important to establish a clear motive to prove her guilt.
4. Possible responses: empathize with Mrs. Wright, having had similar experiences; they pity her for the suffering in her marriage; they resent the County Attorney's condescending attitude
5. Possible responses: Yes—all the men in this play are conceited and condescending to the women and deserve to be excluded; no—there is no excusing murder, nor is there an excuse for withholding information that denies legal justice.
6. Encourage students to validate their answers with real-life examples that show men and women's powers of observation and intuition.

Another Pathway

Cooperative Learning Students in each group should collaborate on a plan for their presentation. Within each group, one student can be responsible for directing the group's activities. A second can explain ideas and procedures, while a third might summarize important points.

Rubric

3 Full Accomplishment The trial reflects thorough preparation, and accurately and effectively presents the case.

2 Substantial Accomplishment The trial is basically effective in presenting the case, but some groups might not be adequately prepared.

1 Little or Partial Accomplishment The groups have difficulty playing their roles and presenting the case.

Literary Concepts

Suggest that students consider the men's impression of the women's activity with their own. Possible response: The reader is aware that the mystery has been solved by the women's attention to details—considered "trifles" by the men; the last line, which hints at the way the noose was knotted, indicates that the women are the investigators who know what clues to look for and how to use them.

Symbol Students might indicate that the bird cage symbolizes the isolated and restricted life led by Minnie Wright, while the dead canary represents the death of her spirit.

QuickWrites

1. Remind students that Sheriff Peters is not aware of the evidence that the women have discovered. Remind them that a crime report should be objective, and should not reflect the sheriff's personality.

2. Encourage students to read some news accounts in local newspapers to see the content and form. For the interviews, have them consider what questions they would ask and how the characters might respond.

Literary Links

Possible responses: They are similar in that they both have a set of clues that the reader gets as they are discovered, the crime is significant, and the murderer is someone who is known; they are different in that *Trifles* has no actual detective and the identity of the murderer is known early on, making it a dramatized version of a mystery story rather than a detective story.

Critic's Corner

Possible response: The phrase means that Glaspell writes about a woman's uniqueness and individuality; this play is a good example because it shows how the women's unique view of the world allows them to perceive things that the men cannot.

Art Connection

Possible responses: isolation, simplicity, hardship

Across the Curriculum

Theater Arts Cooperative Learning Have students work in groups of four or five. Encourage them to find paintings or photos depicting the time and place of the play to help with their model. One student might do the necessary research, another might record the list of props and costumes, and another might direct students in making the model.

Multimodal Learning

ALTERNATIVE ACTIVITIES

1. Create two **diagrams,** one of the Wrights' kitchen—the setting for *Trifles*—and one of the crime scene, with X marking the spot where the body was found. Include the clues from the play in your diagram. If you have a computer with a graphics program, here's a chance to use the program.

2. Investigate how knotting is used in quilting, and demonstrate the kind of **knot** Mrs. Wright might have made to strangle her husband. If you have access to an encyclopedia program or an on-line service, you might use your computer to start your research.

3. Prepare a **musical score** for a production of *Trifles*. Collect music to use to dramatize scenes, or provide written descriptions of original music and its functions. Present your music or description to the class.

4. Demonstrate your understanding of the mystery genre by making up a **mystery game** that includes a detective, a murder victim, a crime scene, suspects, and clues. On note cards, write about twenty pieces of information regarding the murder, including both helpful clues and not-so-relevant information. Give one card to each of your classmates. Have class members take turns reading aloud their clues and trying to solve the crime.

CRITIC'S CORNER

Writing in *The Dictionary of Literary Biography*, critic Rachel France comments that six years after the first staging of *Trifles*, people began proclaiming Glaspell as "the playwright of woman's selfhood." What do you think that phrase means? Do you think *Trifles* is a good example? Explain.

THE WRITER'S STYLE

Trifles is the first play by Susan Glaspell to display what was to become her unique trademark: the nonappearance on stage of a drama's central character—in this case Minnie Wright. Nevertheless, though she is never presented directly, Mrs. Wright's presence is felt throughout the play. Explain the way that Glaspell makes this unseen woman the play's central character.

LITERARY LINKS

A murder is central to both *Trifles* and "Full Circle." Beyond that, how are the two selections similar? How are they different? Refer to the Reading Connection activity on detective stories on page 606. Would you call *Trifles* a dramatized version of a mystery story or detective story? Defend your choice.

ART CONNECTION

The painting on page 631 is by the American artist Andrew Wyeth. One critic has noted that Wyeth, at his best, captures "the essence of a particular moment in a specific place," such as in finding "the simple dignity of an aging farmhouse." About *Room After Room* the artist himself has written that "it's the succession of rooms that makes the impact." What elements of *Trifles* do you feel are found in Wyeth's painting?

ACROSS THE CURRICULUM

Theater Arts In a group, make a model of the set for *Trifles* and create a list of props and costumes that might be required in a production of the play. You will need to find out where you can acquire some of the period pieces. If time permits, join with other groups to stage the play.

Alternative Activities

1. Encourage students to use information in the stage directions, as well as characters' descriptions, to be as precise and factual as possible.
2. Suggest that students consider the speed with which Mrs. Wright would have had to work and the strength necessary.
3. Have students consider the mood of various scenes to select appropriate music.
4. Encourage students to carefully plan out the murder mystery. Who was murdered? Who are the suspects? Where and when did the murder take place? Who is the detective? What evidence was found at the crime scene? Who is the murderer? How and why was the murder committed?

The Writer's Style

Possible responses: Mrs. Wright is responsible for bringing the play's characters together; characters' comments give a clear picture of her personality, both before and during her marriage; she is responsible for the appearance of the room in which the play takes place; the major props (quilt, birdcage, etc.) are her personal property.

WORDS TO KNOW

EXERCISE A Review the Words to Know in the boxes at the bottom of the selection pages. Then on a separate sheet of paper write the vocabulary word that best completes each sentence.

1. Trifles are those small details that we tend not to notice when we're _____ with more important things.
2. However, what seems at first to be trifles may be clues that reveal _____ problems and tensions.
3. The women take what they discover quite seriously, although the men speak _____ about it.
4. Because they cannot see the importance of small details, the men lack any real _____ of Minnie Wright's motives.
5. Can you imagine the men's _____ reaction if they had discovered that there were important clues in the kitchen?

EXERCISE B Create a crossword puzzle from the vocabulary words in *Trifles*. (When writing clues, avoid using the definitions and synonyms given in this book.) Then trade puzzles with a classmate.

SUSAN GLASPELL

1882?–1948

A year after Susan Glaspell and her husband, George Cook, founded an experimental Massachusetts theater group, The Provincetown Players, in 1915, they found themselves in need of new scripts. Cook told his wife, "Now, Susan, I have announced a play of yours for the next bill." A shocked Glaspell protested that she had no play, to which Cook responded that she would have to write one.

As Glaspell sat down in front of the theater group's stage the next day, she reflected on her days as a newspaper reporter in her home state of Iowa. Glaspell had once covered a murder trial and had never forgotten how she felt in the kitchen of the woman who sat in jail, accused of murdering her husband. Glaspell had wanted to turn the event into a short story one day, but after a time, sitting there, the bare stage became a kitchen. As Glaspell put it, the stage took the story "for its own," and ten days later *Trifles* was born, becoming Glaspell's most popular play. One critic said that "*Trifles* is not simply a play of detection, in which two women discover the missing motive for a murder and decide to suppress the evidence . . . it is a play about compassion." For the Provincetown Players, Glaspell wrote, directed, and sometimes acted in nine more plays between 1917 and 1922. Then, following the sudden death of George Cook in Greece in 1924, Glaspell wrote *The Road to the Temple*, a moving memorial to her husband. Later she wrote her most acclaimed play, *Alison's House*, which is loosely based on the life of Emily Dickinson. *Alison's House* won the 1931 Pulitzer Prize, but Glaspell wrote only one play afterward, instead concentrating on writing novels.

Most of Glaspell's writing features strong women characters dealing with psychological conflicts often caused by roles they are expected to play in society.

OTHER WORKS *Suppressed Desires, The Outside, Bernice, Lifted Masks*

Extended Reading

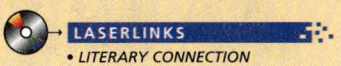
• LITERARY CONNECTION

TRIFLES **643**

Words to Know

Exercise A
1. preoccupied
2. covert
3. facetiously
4. comprehension
5. abashed

Exercise B
Responses will vary.

Reteaching/Reinforcement
• *Unit Five Resource Book*, p. 22

SUSAN GLASPELL

Susan Glaspell began her writing career with short stories and novels, but later turned to plays. The Provincetown Players were an experimental group of actors, directors, and writers (including Eugene O'Neill) who invigorated American theater after World War I.

 LITERARY CONNECTION
A Jury Of Her Peers: The Movie
Symbolism is an important part of this short play. In this excerpt from the movie, students can see the moment when the bird cage and the dead canary are found.

Side A, Frame 27713

REFLECTING ON THEME
What Do You Think?

Have students think again about the activity demonstrating the difficulty in determining the truth, which they did before reading the selections in Part 1. Ask them to consider the extra difficulty in determining the truth of a situation when they have a preconceived, but erroneous, notion of something and another person simply allows them to keep that belief. Invite students to offer ideas on how such "passive" lying can ever be detected.

OBJECTIVES

- To promote independent active reading
- To practice and apply skills learned in previous selections
- To provide an opportunity to assess students' performance through an alternative assessment instrument

SUMMARY

A young man, Alan Austen, visits an old man who sells potions. The old man sells several kinds of potions and tells Alan about one that sells for five thousand dollars. The potion is a tasteless poison that can't be detected in an autopsy. The old man calls his poison a spot remover. Alan is horrified. He doesn't want a poison; he wants a love potion. The old man has just the thing. It will make the woman that Alan loves fall completely and permanently in love with him. The potion costs only one dollar. It is cheap, the old man says, because satisfied customers will come back later when they are wealthier and want something more expensive.

Thematic Link: *False Pretenses* She will love him—but under false pretenses.

Reading Pathways

- Have students read independently and write in a double-entry journal.
- Invite students to choose partners and do a paired reading.
- Encourage students to do a choral reading, choosing parts for each individual to read.
- Evaluate how well students can read, interpret, discuss, and write about the selection on their own by using the Integrated Assessment for Unit Five, located in the Alternative Assessment booklet. Administer the assessment at the end of the unit after students have read all the selections and completed all the writing that they have been assigned.

Art Note

The Alchemist's Dilemma by Chuck Wood Wood's painting has great textural variety—metal and glass objects on a rough wood surface. In addition, the shapes of the objects, though interesting in their own right, have a curious chemistry when collected.

Reading the Art *What atmosphere is created by the featureless background, top lighting, dust, and discoloration?*

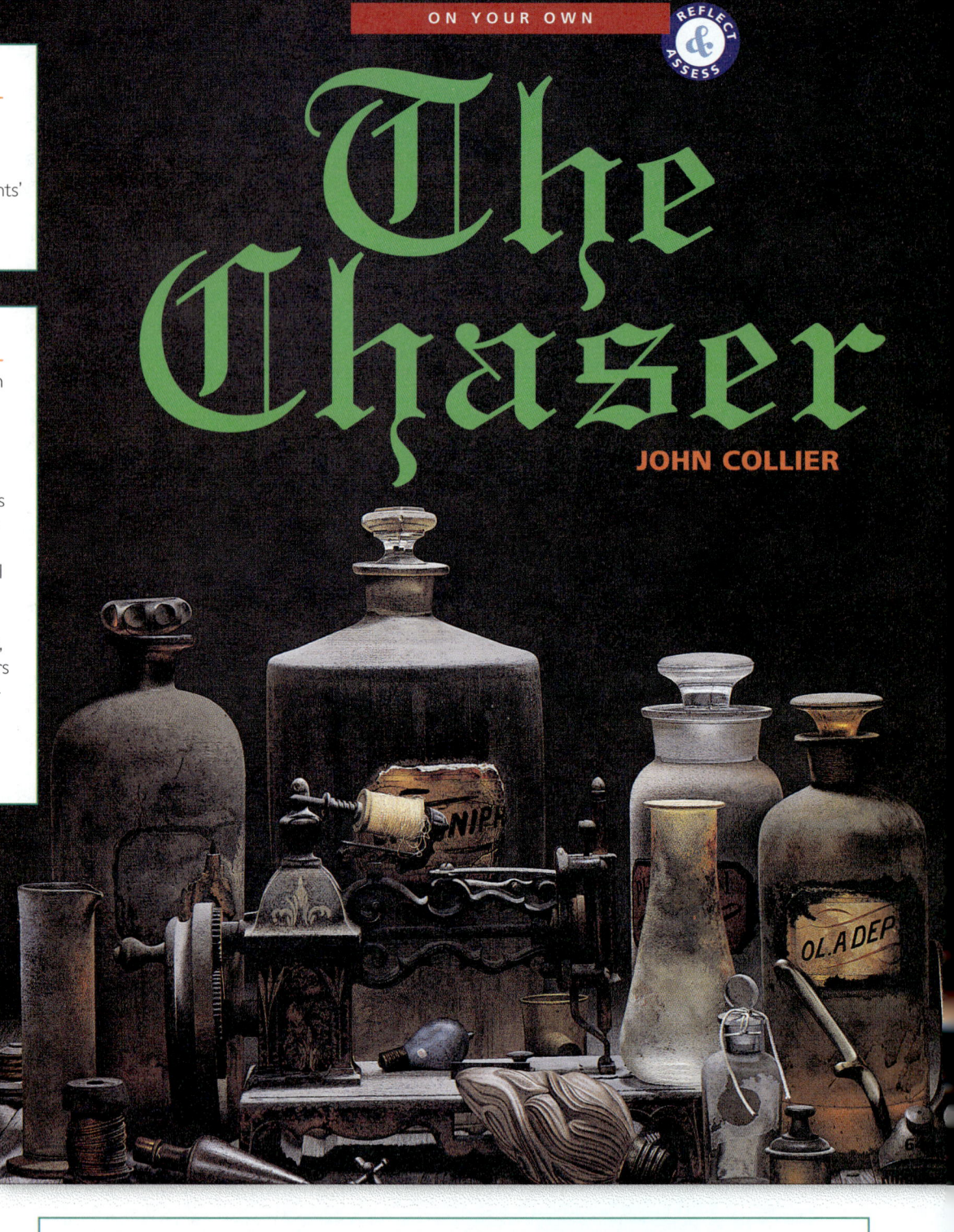

ON YOUR OWN

The Chaser
JOHN COLLIER

PRINT AND MEDIA RESOURCES

UNIT FIVE RESOURCE BOOK
Strategic Reading: Literature, p. 25

FORMAL ASSESSMENT
Selection Test, p. 113
Part Test, pp. 115–116
Test Generator

ALTERNATIVE ASSESSMENT
Unit Five Integrated Assessment, pp. 25–30

ACCESS FOR STUDENTS ACQUIRING ENGLISH
Selection Summaries

Alan Austen, as nervous as a kitten, went up certain dark and creaky stairs in the neighborhood of Pell Street, and peered about for a long time on the dim landing before he found the name he wanted written obscurely on one of the doors.

He pushed open this door, as he had been told to do, and found himself in a tiny room, which contained no furniture but a plain kitchen table, a rocking chair, and an ordinary chair. On one of the dirty buff-colored walls were a couple of shelves, containing in all perhaps a dozen bottles and jars.

An old man sat in the rocking chair, reading a newspaper. Alan, without a word, handed him the card he had been given. "Sit down, Mr. Austen," said the old man very politely. "I am glad to make your acquaintance."

"Is it true," asked Alan, "that you have a certain mixture that has—er—quite extraordinary effects?"

"My dear sir," replied the old man, "my stock in trade is not very large—I don't deal in laxatives and teething mixtures—but, such as it is, it is varied. I think nothing I sell has effects which could be precisely described as ordinary."

"Well, the fact is—" began Alan.

"Here, for example," interrupted the old man, reaching for a bottle from the shelf. "Here is a liquid as colorless as water, almost tasteless, quite imperceptible[1] in coffee, milk, wine, or any other beverage. It is also quite imperceptible to any known method of autopsy."

"Do you mean it is a poison?" cried Alan, very much horrified.

"Call it cleaning fluid if you like," said the old man indifferently. "Lives need cleaning. Call it a spot remover. 'Out, damned spot!' Eh? 'Out, brief candle!'"[2]

"I want nothing of that sort," said Alan.

"Probably it is just as well," said the old man. "Do you know the price of this? For one teaspoonful, which is sufficient, I ask five thousand dollars. Never less. Not a penny less."

"I hope all your mixtures are not as expensive," said Alan apprehensively.

"Oh, dear, no," said the old man. "It would be no good charging that sort of price for a love potion, for example. Young people who need a love potion very seldom have five thousand dollars. If they had they would not need a love potion."

"I'm glad to hear you say so," said Alan.

"I look at it like this," said the old man. "Please a customer with one article, and he will come back when he needs another. Even if it is more costly. He will save up for it, if necessary."

"So," said Alan, "you really do sell love potions?"

"If I did not sell love potions," said the old man, reaching for another bottle, "I should not have mentioned the other matter to you. It is only when one is in a position to oblige that one can afford to be so confidential."

"And these potions," said Alan. "They are not just—just—er—"

"Oh, no," said the old man. "Their effects are permanent and extend far beyond the mere carnal[3]

---

1. **imperceptible:** not noticeable.
2. **"Out, damned . . . brief candle!":** references to lines from Shakespeare's play *Macbeth*. "Out, damned spot!" is spoken by Lady Macbeth as she tries to remove imagined blood from her hands. "Out, out, brief candle!" is Macbeth's comment about the shortness of life when he learns that Lady Macbeth has died.
3. **carnal:** having to do with physical desire.

The Alchemist's Dilemma (1992), Chuck Wood. Oil on canvas, 39" × 48", collection of the artist.

"Call it cleaning fluid if you like."

OPTION 1

Individual Activity
WRITING A SEQUEL

Have students pretend that it is 20 years later. Alan has returned to the old man to purchase the "spot remover" for Diana. Ask students to write a short sequel, describing what happens.

Teacher's Role Encourage students to consider what kind of wife Diana must now be and how this might have affected Alan. You might suggest that they create a story map as a prewriting activity.

Rubric

3 Full Accomplishment Students write a sequel which logically builds on the details given in the story. The writing is concise, correct in grammar and usage, and effective.

2 Substantial Accomplishment Students write an essentially logical sequel, but some parts may not be grammatically correct or may be somewhat confusing.

1 Little or Partial Accomplishment Students have difficulty writing any kind of logical, cohesive sequel.

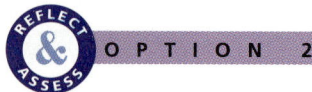

OPTION 2

Cooperative Learning
CREATING AN ADVERTISEMENT

Have groups of students write and present television advertisements for the love potion and the "spot remover."

Teacher's Role Suggest that each group assign the roles of script writers, performers, prop people, etc. One student might write the final scripts. Another might direct the production. Students can videotape their ads for viewing by the entire class, or they can perform them live.

Rubric

3 Full Accomplishment The ads accurately, effectively, and convincingly portray the selling points of each potion.

2 Substantial Accomplishment The ads basically relate the selling points of each potion, but may not be totally effective.

1 Little or Partial Accomplishment Students have difficulty creating accurate and effective ads.

Art Note

Portrait of Max Hermann-Neisse by Ludwig Meidner A poet and theater critic well known in Berlin in the 1920s, Max Hermann was born in 1886 in the town of Neisse, now part of Poland. Hermann—a hunchback with a large bald head, protruding teeth, and giant, bony hands—was a popular subject of German Expressionist artists such as Ludwig Meidner (1884–1966). Expressionists communicated emotion rather than realism, portraying their own subjective visions of reality. (Hermann died in exile in England in 1941.)

Reading the Art What emotion is communicated by this portrait? What details add to this emotion?

---

impulse. But they include it. Oh, yes, they include it. Bountifully. Insistently. Everlastingly."

"Dear me!" said Alan, attempting a look of scientific detachment. "How very interesting!"

"But consider the spiritual side," said the old man.

"I do, indeed," said Alan.

"For indifference," said the old man, "they substitute devotion. For scorn, adoration. Give one tiny measure of this to the young lady—its flavor is imperceptible in orange juice, soup, or cocktails—and however gay and giddy she is, she will change altogether. She'll want nothing but solitude, and you."

"I can hardly believe it," said Alan. "She is so fond of parties."

"She will not like them anymore," said the old man. "She'll be afraid of the pretty girls you may meet."

"She'll actually be jealous?" cried Alan in a rapture. "Of me?"

"Yes, she will want to be everything to you."

"She is, already. Only she doesn't care about it."

"She will, when she has taken this. She will care intensely. You'll be her sole nterest in life."

"Wonderful!" cried Alan.

"She'll want to know all you do," said the old man. "All that has happened to you during the day. Every word of it. She'll want to know

Portrait of Max Hermann-Neisse (1913), Ludwig Meidner. Oil on canvas, 89.2 cm × 74.9 cm, The Art Institute of Chicago, gift of Mr. and Mrs. Harold Weinstein (1959.215). Photo Copyright © 1994, The Art Institute of Chicago, all rights reserved.

what you are thinking about, why you smile suddenly, why you are looking sad."

"That is love!" cried Alan.

"Yes," said the old man. "How carefully she'll look after you! She'll never allow you to be tired, to sit in a draft, to neglect your food. If you are

646 UNIT FIVE PART 1: FALSE PRETENSES

Critic's Corner

A critic for the New Republic *once wrote of John Collier's works, "He persuades us not of the reality of his tale[s], but of the probability that real men and women might feel and do such evil things."*

Ask students to discuss this statement as it relates to "The Chaser."

an hour late, she'll be terrified. She'll think you are killed, or that some siren has caught you."

"I can hardly imagine Diana like that!" cried Alan, overwhelmed with joy.

"You will not have to use your imagination," said the old man. "And, by the way, since there are always sirens, if by any chance you *should*, later on, slip a little, you need not worry. She will forgive you, in the end. She'll be terribly hurt, of course, but she'll forgive you—in the end."

"That will not happen," said Alan fervently.

"Of course not," said the old man. "But, if it does, you need not worry. She'll never divorce you. Oh, no! And, of course, she herself will never give you the least, the very least, grounds for—not divorce, of course—but even uneasiness."

"And how much," said Alan, "how much is this wonderful mixture?"

"It is not so dear," said the old man, "as the spot remover, as I think we agreed to call it. No. That is five thousand dollars; never a penny less. One has to be older than you are to indulge in that sort of thing. One has to save up for it."

"But the love potion?" said Alan.

"Oh, that," said the old man, opening the drawer in the kitchen table and taking out a tiny, rather dirty-looking phial. "That is just a dollar."

"I can't tell you how grateful I am," said Alan, watching him fill it.

"I like to oblige," said the old man. "Then customers come back, later in life, when they are rather better-off, and want more expensive things. Here you are. You will find it very effective."

"Thank you again," said Alan. "Good-bye."

"*Au revoir*,"[4] said the old man. ❖

---

4. *Au revoir* (ō′ rə-vwär′): a French phrase for goodbye; its literal meaning is "Until we meet again."

JOHN COLLIER

1901–1980

John Collier grew roses, enjoyed cooking, and had a passion for boats. He once was so taken with a fishing boat that he went to Hollywood to write a script so that he could earn the money to buy the boat, even though he "had seen scarcely a dozen films" in his life.

Born in London, England, Collier was taught to read at age three by his mother, a teacher, and was thereafter tutored by his uncle. He never went to school except for kindergarten, but he read an average of a book a day for the rest of his life.

Although he wrote poetry, reviews, and movie scripts, Collier is best known for his imaginative fantasies and suspenseful mysteries. Some critics regard his novel *His Monkey Wife; or, Married to a Chimp* as a masterpiece. In this fantasy, a man marries a chimpanzee who is more civilized than the people and who represents a kind of innocence that the human race has lost.

Three of Collier's most famous suspense stories are "De Mortuis," "Back for Christmas," and "Another American Tragedy." The critic Paul Theroux called Collier "one of the great literary unclassifiables—it is another synonym for genius."

OTHER WORKS *Fancies and Goodnights, The John Collier Reader*

Extended Reading

THE CHASER **647**

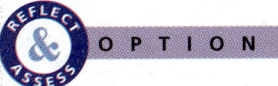

OPTION 3

Class Discussion
SHARING IDEAS

Teacher's Role After students have read the selection, act as a moderator to engage them in a whole-class discussion, using the following questions:

- What qualities do you think are desirable in a mate? How do your qualities compare with those induced by the love potion? *(Accept all reasonable responses.)*

- Do you think Alan Austen or anyone should use a love potion to make someone love them? Explain. *(Some might say that to get someone to love you under false pretenses is wrong. Others might say that when you love someone, you might do anything—even get a love potion to win their love.)*

- What do you think the old man means when he says "customers come back, later in life, when they are rather better-off, and want more expensive things"? *(Possible response: He implies that the excessive devotion induced by the love potion will motivate its purchaser to buy the poison and murder the beloved.)*

- Do you think that Alan will return one day to purchase the "spot remover"? Why or why not? *(Possible responses: Yes—Diana's obsession with him, as described by the old man, will drive him to the point of murder; no—he'll find a cheaper method.)*

- Does the old man sell Alan the love potion under false pretenses? Explain. *(Possible responses: No—he describes its effects in great detail; yes—he takes advantage of Austen's poor judgment.)*

- What do you think the author's purpose was in writing this story? *(Accept all reasonable, well-supported responses.)*

JOHN COLLIER

John Collier's ability to create tales of psychological evil with wit and style gained him popularity as a writer of fantastic fiction of the macabre. However, like many writers in this genre, Collier has not received great recognition by scholars. A versatile author, Collier also wrote many screenplays, including those for the films *The Story of Three Loves, I Am a Camera*, and *The War Lord*.

OVERVIEW

In the Guided Assignment for this section, students will write a critical essay analyzing a writer's use of events and details to develop the plot. The Writer's Style will help students evaluate the importance of perspective and contrast the difference between the first-person point of view and the third-person point of view. In Reading the World, students will examine the ways in which opinions demonstrate differing perspectives on an issue.

Objectives

- To recognize the difference between the first-person and third-person points of view
- To clarify the antecedents of pronouns
- To develop standards for critical judgment
- To write a critical essay evaluating the development of the plot
- To analyze conflicting perspectives in the real world

Skills

LITERATURE
- Analyzing the use of first- and third-person points of view

GRAMMAR AND USAGE
- Making pronoun antecedents clear
- Using active and passive voice
- Using past participles

MEDIA LITERACY
- Analyzing opinions

SPEAKING, LISTENING, AND VIEWING
- Discussing differences of opinion
- Group analysis

CRITICAL THINKING
- Formulating questions
- Clarifying standards for critical judgment

Teaching Strategy: MODELING

The following models show how perspective affects a story. Participants use the first-person point of view, whereas observers use the third-person point of view.

Ⓐ Jackson Possible response: The narrator is able to reveal to the reader each character's thoughts to explain his or her behavior. (Be certain that students understand that this is the all-knowing, or omniscient, form of third-person point of view. There is also a limited third-person point of view, in which the narrator lets the reader know what only one character thinks and feels. Both of these versions of third person occur commonly in fiction.)

Ⓑ Grafton Possible response: The first-person point of view allows the reader to read the detective's mind and empathize with her reactions. Readers can imagine reading the paper and feeling regret.

WRITING ABOUT LITERATURE

What a Story!

Two people's versions of an experience often differ. The point of view—the perspective, or angle, from which a story is told—is as important as what happens. In this lesson, you will

- study the point of view in a story and how it affects plot
- evaluate the plot of a story
- analyze a real-life event from different points of view

Writer's Style: Point of View In the first-person point of view, the story is told by a character in the story. In the third-person point of view, the story is told by a narrative voice outside the action, not one of the characters.

Literature Selection

Notice how the point of view used in each model affects the kind of information you get as a reader.

Literature Model

Ⓐ Third-Person Point of View
The narrative voice in this story can tell you not only what Mr. Johnson is thinking and feeling, but what other characters think and feel too. What is one advantage of using this point of view?

> Mr. John Philip Johnson shut his front door behind him and came down his front steps into the bright morning with a feeling that all was well with the world on this best of all days, and wasn't the sun warm and good, and didn't his shoes feel comfortable after the resoling, and he knew that he had undoubtedly chosen the precise very tie which belonged with the day and the sun and his comfortable feet, and, after all, wasn't the world just a wonderful place?
>
> Shirley Jackson, from "One Ordinary Day, with Peanuts"

Ⓑ First-Person Point of View
The detective who must solve a mystery in this story is the narrator. Why might the author have made this choice?

> I didn't get home until nearly seven and my hands were still shaking. The jumble of images made sleep a torment of sudden awakenings, my foot jerking in a dream sequence as I slammed on my brakes again and again.
> When I read in the morning paper that the girl had died, I felt sick with regret.
>
> Sue Grafton, from "Full Circle"

UNIT FIVE: MYSTERIES AND DECEPTIONS

PRINT AND MEDIA RESOURCES

UNIT FIVE RESOURCE BOOK
Writer's Style, p. 29
Prewriting, p. 30
Peer Response Guide, pp. 32–33
Revising and Proofreading, p. 34
Student Model, pp. 35–36
Rubric, p. 37

GRAMMAR MINI-LESSONS
Transparencies, pp. 20, 30
Copymasters, p. 18

FORMAL ASSESSMENT
Guidelines for Writing Assessment

 WRITING COACH

 The Writer's Craft
Personal Response to Literature, pp. 238–249

Teaching Strategy: MODELING

C Randles Possible response: The writer simply reports what the youth claims to have seen. Her account contains no descriptive embellishment, nor does it express her reaction to the claim.

Try Your Hand

1. Possible response: Horrified, he watched the speeding car hit the gravel and overturn. He steered around the scene and stopped. Fire terrified him, but he ran to the car and pulled out the unconscious young driver.

2. Answers will vary. Sample responses should demonstrate the reactions of the athlete as he or she resumes playing the game and those of a spectator such as a sports announcer or a fan as the player enters the gym.

3. Encourage students to analyze the differences between the two accounts. Some students may feel that the first-person point of view, in a sense, allows the reader to become the character by feeling what he feels, whereas the third-person point of view requires the reader to infer the emotional state of the character.

Connect to Life

Writers of nonfiction often use third-person point of view when reporting facts. Why do you think they usually avoid first person?

Magazine Article

The first recorded close encounter of the third kind (or alien contact) occurred at Bournbrook, West Midlands, England, when an object like a 'hut' was seen in a garden by a youth. It contained two small men, under 4 feet tall, wearing khaki suits and helmets, one of whom approached the witness before returning inside. The object created an electrical glow around its base and took off skyward with a whooshing noise.

Jenny Randles
"1901 June: An Early Close Encounter" from *Strange and Unexplained Mysteries of the 20th Century*

Third-Person Point of View

This writer reports a nonfiction mystery. How do you know she is trying to be objective, giving only facts and making no judgments?

SkillBuilder

 GRAMMAR FROM WRITING

Correcting Vague Pronoun References

Juan told his father he should work on his pitching.

The situation above is described from a third-person point of view, but the sentence is unclear. Whose pitching needs practice? When a pronoun has no antecedent or when the antecedent is unclear, the pronoun reference is vague. Study these vague pronoun references.

Unclear antecedent: *The investigator notified the police officer of the man's injury when he got home.* (Who got home—the investigator, the police officer, or the man?)

No antecedent: *Don't go skating. They say skating can cause injuries.* (Who says it?)

APPLYING WHAT YOU'VE LEARNED

Rewrite to correct each sentence that has a vague pronoun reference. You may add words.

1. In that TV show it said that some people believe in UFOs.
2. Since teachers give frequent tests to students, they have to be ready every day.
3. As the home-team players faced the opposition players, they knew they were in trouble.

GRAMMAR HANDBOOK

For more help with pronouns and antecedents, see pages 913–915 of the Grammar Handbook.

Try Your Hand: Using Point of View

1. Rewrite the following paragraph, using the third-person point of view.

   Horrified, I watched the speeding car hit the gravel and overturn. I steered around him and stopped. Fire terrifies me, but I ran to the car and pulled out the unconscious young driver.

2. A star player in your favorite sport is returning after an injury. Write a first-person and a third-person account describing the first game.

3. Select a narrative you have written that could be told from another point of view. Rewrite a paragraph and evaluate the two examples. Explain why one point of view is more effective.

WRITING ABOUT LITERATURE **649**

SkillBuilder GRAMMAR FROM WRITING

CORRECTING VAGUE PRONOUN REFERENCES Remind students that murky pronoun references will confuse readers. In order to write clear prose that their readers will understand, students must connect pronouns to their antecedents. Ask them to review the examples of vague pronoun references and missing antecedents.

Application Possible responses:

1. That TV show said that some people believe in UFOs.
2. Students have to be ready every day since teachers give them frequent tests.
3. The home-team players knew they were in trouble as they faced their opposition.

Additional Suggestions Have each student write five sentences in which the pronoun has no antecedent or the antecedent is unclear. Then have students exchange papers for corrections.

Reteaching/Reinforcement

- *Grammar Mini-Lessons* copymasters p. 18, transparencies p. 20

The Writer's Craft

Pronoun Reference, p. 158

Critical Thinking:
MAKING JUDGMENTS

D Encourage students to explore why they like or don't like the writers' styles in the models. After students assess the strengths and weaknesses of the literature samples, discuss the criteria that they used to make their judgments, and list them on the chalkboard.

Speaking and Listening:
GROUP DISCUSSION

E Ask students to summarize the plots that they found especially exciting or especially boring. Emphasize the common points, such as a fast-paced plot, that they judge to be interesting aspects of a narrative.

Teaching Strategy:
STUMBLING BLOCK

F Students often need help in developing the ability to provide concrete details to support their opinions. Use the sample chart on this page to illustrate the effective use of specific details.

WRITING ABOUT LITERATURE

Criticism

D Did the plot of "Full Circle" keep you in suspense? Did the situation in "One Ordinary Day, with Peanuts" intrigue you? You may finish a story and want to share it with a friend. Or you may say, "Who cares?" Everyone's a critic!

GUIDED ASSIGNMENT
Write a Critical Essay Consider how the writer used events and details to develop the plot of a story you've read. Evaluate how well the story keeps you interested.

1 Prewrite and Explore

E Choose a story—one with a plot you liked or one you found dull, one you would recommend or one you think no one else should ever have to read. What are the reasons for your response to the story?

2 Review the Main Points

Note how the plot developed in the story you selected. What made it interesting or dull?

- Did the writer present a problem or question that the characters had to solve?
- Did the writer use suspense?
- How did the point of view used by the writer help you understand what was going on?
- Was there a twist to the plot that surprised you?
- How did the writer's choice of words and details affect your response to the story?

F You might find it helpful to list important plot events, using a chart like the one on the right. You can make notes to help you as you write your critical essay.

Student's Notes

650

 Assessment Option

SELF-ASSESSMENT After students have completed the Prewrite and Explore discussion, they should assess their own tastes in literature. Ask them to consider the following questions:

- What type of story do I like to read? Science fiction? Romance? Mystery? What attracts me to this genre?
- Which writing techniques appeal to me? Descriptive writing? A lot of dialogue? Fast action?

3 Write and Analyze a Discovery Draft

When you have chosen a story and gathered ideas about how the plot unfolded, you are ready to write a discovery draft. As you write, ask yourself some questions.

- What helped me understand why the story did or didn't interest me?
- Where can I use details to support my statements?

Examine this discovery draft of a critical essay on "One Ordinary Day, with Peanuts." The SkillBuilder can help you set standards for evaluating a story.

Student's Discovery Draft

I think that the author of "One Ordinary Day, with Peanuts" left out an important element: suspense. At first, I thought the story was just a list of examples showing how kind Mr. Johnson was. I wondered what the author's reason was for listing these pretty dull acts.

At the very end of the story, I got a surprise, but it seems that the story would have been more interesting if the writer built up suspense by hinting that a surprise was coming.

This needs an interesting introduction and some quotations.

I should check. Maybe I missed a clue telling me this surprise was coming.

4 Draft and Share

 What did you learn from analyzing your discovery draft? Use this knowledge to write a draft of your critical essay. Introduce your ideas, give examples to support them, and draw conclusions at the end that your reader will understand.

PEER RESPONSE

- What part of the introduction made you want to read my essay? What will make the introduction stronger?
- Put my evaluation of the story into your own words.

SkillBuilder

 CRITICAL THINKING

Using Criteria for Evaluation

A critical review of a fiction selection involves an opinion or a judgment. How do you make a critical judgment? You can't just say, "That was a great story." You need standards for your criticism. Ask yourself questions such as the following to clarify your standards for criticizing a story.

- What was the writer's purpose? Was that purpose fulfilled?
- Was the story believable?
- Did the plot develop in a reasonable way?
- If the plot had a surprise twist, did it make sense or was it just a trick?
- Did the story keep me feeling challenged or entertained?
- Would the story challenge or entertain other readers? Why or why not?

APPLYING WHAT YOU'VE LEARNED

As you begin to revise and edit your draft, ask yourself questions that will help you establish standards.

WRITING ABOUT LITERATURE **651**

SkillBuilder CRITICAL THINKING

USING CRITERIA FOR EVALUATION

Read aloud a very short story and then conduct a discussion in which you help the students clarify standards for criticizing the story. Use the questions in this SkillBuilder to guide the discussion. Suggest to students who feel that the plot of Jackson's story is boring that perhaps the author intended the too-good-to-be-true, commonplace adventures of a person to lull the reader, thus setting him or her up for a shocking ending. You might also tell students that readers of Jackson's writing are usually suspicious that something unusual is going on, and this keeps fans of Jackson's stories reading through seemingly "ordinary" plots.

Application Remind students to refer to the questions on this page as they develop criteria for evaluation. Responses will vary, but the following sample shows how framing and answering a question can help a student revise his or her essay during the editing process. The initial reaction "this is a neat story" might give rise to the question "What is so neat about it?" Students can then restate their assertion more concretely: "The story is neat because it is completely believable and surprising at the same time. I was astonished by the ending."

CUSTOMIZING FOR
Less-Proficient Writers

G Remind students that when they are writing a critical essay about a work of literature, they should always include the title of the story and the author's name in the introduction.

Critical Thinking: ANALYZING

H Tell students to analyze the point of view as they critique the stories. Remind them that perspective sets the tone of the narrative and draws the reader into the plot. When editing their drafts students should

- check to make sure that all their pronoun references are clear
- evaluate their drafts based on the criteria they generated during class discussions
- proofread their drafts to verify that they have cited a number of specific examples to support their ideas.

Teaching Strategy: MODELING

I Discuss with students how the model meets with the Standards for Evaluation. You might note, for instance, that it provides enough information to engage the reader but does not give away the plot. The writer states his or her opinion clearly and supports the opinion through the use of examples. In the paragraphs that follow the introduction, the writer will probably explain why the story was a disappointment. In the conclusion, the writer refers to specific qualities in various sections of the story to provide a comprehensive evaluation. The writer does not simply give the story a negative review, because it meets some of the evaluative criteria for a good story.

PORTFOLIO

Ask students to jot down what they like best about their critical essays. Then invite them to make a brief list of the weaknesses or trouble spots in their essays. Students may wish to include their informal evaluations along with their essays in their portfolio.

WRITING ABOUT LITERATURE

5 Revise and Edit

When you begin to revise and edit your draft, be sure that your opinion of the story you selected is clear and that it measures up to the standards you have for evaluating a story.

H Think about ways to present your final work. Perhaps several students who have chosen the same story could present their critical essays to the class and then hold a class discussion of the areas of agreement and disagreement.

Student's Final Draft

I
A Criticism of "One Ordinary Day, with Peanuts"

The story "One Ordinary Day, with Peanuts" begins with an ordinary man doing ordinary things. Mr. Johnson is happy as he begins his walk "with a feeling that all was well with the world on this best of all days." But by the end of the story, I felt I had been fooled. Usually I like that, but something didn't work for me this time.

Notice how the introduction ends with a critical opinion of the story. What would you expect the writer to include in the paragraphs that follow?

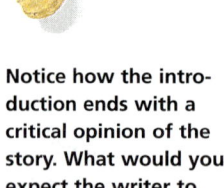

How does the last paragraph of this critical essay bring the writer's thoughts together? Why did the writer not just give the story a negative review?

As I go back over this story, I think my problem is with the middle part. The beginning introduces the character in a nice way. The end is a real surprise. But all of the rest is just repetition and there are no clues to the kind of person Mr. Johnson really is. I think that the story should have hinted that something is odd. Maybe it could have built up gradually to the surprise, or used foreshadowing. As it is, if I recommend the story, I'll tell my friend to keep reading to find the surprise.

Standards for Evaluation

An effective critical essay
- includes a summary to help the reader understand the story but does not give away the plot
- includes a clear statement of the writer's opinion
- includes examples, quotations, and details that support that opinion
- indicates the standards on which opinions are based

652 UNIT FIVE: MYSTERIES AND DECEPTIONS

Assessment Option

SELF-ASSESSMENT To assess their own critical essays, students should ask themselves the following questions:

- *Did I clearly state my opinion of this story?*
- *Did I identify what I liked and didn't like about the story?*
- *Did I get carried away in my criticism—negative or positive—of the story?*
- *Did I reveal too much of the plot and spoil the story for prospective readers?*

Grammar in Context

Active and Passive Voice Keep in mind that one of the elements that affects your reaction to a story is the author's choice of sentence style. One way writers vary their style is through grammatical voice. The voice of a verb tells whether the subject performs or receives the action of the verb. There are two voices, active and passive.

In **active voice,** the subject of the verb is the doer of the action. Notice how Shirley Jackson's use of active verbs emphasizes that Mrs. Johnson is the doer of the actions in this scene from "One Ordinary Day, with Peanuts."

> I had a little nap this afternoon, took it easy most of the day. Went into a department store this morning and accused the woman next to me of shoplifting, and had the store detective pick her up.

In **passive voice,** the subject is the receiver of the action. You might use passive voice to emphasize the receiver of an action.

> The woman was accused of shoplifting. She was arrested.

In general, it is best to use active voice. Active voice is stronger, livelier, and more direct because it emphasizes the doer of an action. You may choose passive voice if you want to stress the receiver of an action or if you don't want your reader to know who performed an action.

> Mrs. Johnson tricked the police. The police were tricked by Mrs. Johnson. The police were tricked.

Try Your Hand:
Using Active and Passive Voice

On a sheet of paper, rewrite these sentences, changing the verbs from active to passive or from passive to active.

1. I was confused by the surprise ending.
2. My favorite story of deception was written by Shirley Jackson.
3. Police captured the burglar at last.
4. Surprise endings are enjoyed by most readers.
5. Why are mysteries enjoyed by readers?

SkillBuilder
GRAMMAR FROM WRITING

Using Past Participles Correctly

Both active and passive voice can use a helping verb with the past participle of a main verb.

For regular verbs, the past participle is formed by adding *-ed*.

The river has moved tons of soil.

The past participles of irregular verbs differ. You must learn them or use a dictionary. Be careful to use the past participle form, not the past form, of the verb when you use a helping verb.

Present	Past	Past Participle
write	wrote	(has) written
wear	wore	(has) worn

Jackson has written many stories.

Trench coats were worn by both detectives.

APPLYING WHAT YOU'VE LEARNED
Write each sentence, using the past participle of the verb in parentheses.

- All of the seats had been (take) when we got to the theater.
- Luckily, the usher had (set) aside two seats for us.
- We had (choose) a horror film.

GRAMMAR HANDBOOK

For more information on verb forms, see pages 923–924 of the Grammar Handbook.

WRITING ABOUT LITERATURE **653**

Teaching Strategy:
COLLABORATIVE OPPORTUNITY

Review the information on the difference between active and passive voice. Have students work in small groups to write two descriptions of a person performing an activity such as eating popcorn, playing soccer, or watching a horror film. One description should be in the active voice and the other should be in the passive voice. Have students share their work with the class.

Try Your Hand

Possible responses:
1. The surprise ending confused me.
2. Shirley Jackson wrote my favorite story of deception.
3. The burglar was captured by the police at last.
4. Most readers enjoy surprise endings.
5. Why do most readers enjoy mysteries?

Standards for Evaluation

Have students review their essays for the following:

Ideas and Content
- gives title, author, and a brief summary of the literature
- gives supported evaluation of an element of the selection
- includes examples, quotations, and details that support the evaluation
- has a conclusion that clearly summarizes the evaluation

Structure and Form
- uses well-organized paragraphs and a clear organization
- include transitional words and phrases to show relationships among ideas

Grammar, Usage, and Mechanics
- contains no more than two or three minor errors in grammar and usage
- correctly integrates quotations into the text
- contains no more than two or three minor errors in spelling, capitalization, and punctuation

---

SkillBuilder GRAMMAR FROM WRITING

USING PAST PARTICIPLES CORRECTLY

Remind students that they can commit to memory irregular verbs or they can identify their forms by looking up each verb in a dictionary. List several of the more troublesome irregular verbs on the chalkboard and invite students to contribute more.

| begin | began | (has) begun |
| fight | fought | (has) fought |

Application Answers:
- All of the seats had been taken when we got to the theater.
- Luckily, the usher had set aside seats for us.
- We had chosen a horror film.

Additional Suggestions After referring to the list of irregular verbs, students can use their past participle forms to write a short story about a victim of a practical joke. Present the first sentence of the story:

> John was *astonished* by the events of the morning.

Reteaching/Reinforcement
- *Grammar Mini-Lessons* transparencies, p. 30

The Writer's Craft
Participles, p. 683

READING THE WORLD

Remind students that different points of view reflect different priorities that people have developed. People's viewpoints reflect their knowledge and understanding of certain issues as well as their values and beliefs.

Critical Thinking:
SPECULATING

K The environmental activist opposes the storage of radioactive waste even in deserts because she believes it would cause damage to plants and animals. She will make a strong case that waste spilling into the water supply will result in contaminated water, which would harm people as well as animals. The advocate for the disposal site argues that modern technology ensures the safe storage of this material and that the work will help people and boost the economy by providing jobs.

Media Literacy:
GATHERING FACTS

L Students will probably discuss familiar information about the dangers of radioactive waste, such as birth defects, cancer and the harm to the ecosystem. Sparsely populated areas are selected as sites for nuclear waste disposal because their low density minimizes the number of people at risk in the event of an accident.

Speaking and Listening:
GROUP DISCUSSION

M Have students discuss the two divergent viewpoints presented on this controversial issue. Encourage them to express their own points of view, but remind them to be open-minded as they listen to perspectives that differ from their own.

READING THE WORLD

WHERE DO YOU STAND?

You've seen how different points of view can affect literature. How can they affect your opinions on important issues? Several years ago, decisions were made to store radioactive waste in sparsely populated areas such as deserts. Do you feel this is a good policy or a poor one? How can you make an informed decision?

View Imagine you were watching a newscast about this issue. The two people pictured on the page were among the people interviewed. What is each one's view on this policy?

Interpret Why is storing radioactive waste a problem? Why were sparsely populated areas selected?

Discuss In a group, discuss how opinions on this issue demonstrate different points of view. Use the SkillBuilder at the right to formulate questions that can help you understand different points of view.

Environmental Activist: "Threatened species of plants and animals, as well as underground waters, can be contaminated by leaks. We can't afford the risk."

Advocate for Disposal Site: "Modern techniques make storage safe. In addition, construction on this site will provide jobs for people in the area."

654

SkillBuilder

 CRITICAL THINKING

Formulating Questions

How can you understand points of view on issues like the one discussed on these pages? How can you be sure you have all of the right information? Formulating questions will help you.

- Begin by writing the headings *who, what, when, why,* and *how*—each on a separate sheet of paper.
- Under each heading, jot down facts that you already know about the topic.
- List ideas you don't understand. Write questions concerning parts of the issue you wonder about.
- Talk to interested and informed people. Think about the ideas held by people with different points of view.
- Use your questions to help you with research.
- Decide what you think, but keep listening to others.

APPLYING WHAT YOU'VE LEARNED

With a small group, choose an interesting topic that people see from different perspectives, such as censoring library books available to students, making all school sports coed, or using tax money to support public radio and television. List what you know about the topic. Then brainstorm questions you need to answer in order to understand the different points of view.

READING THE WORLD   655

SkillBuilder CRITICAL THINKING

FORMULATING QUESTIONS To avoid accepting uninformed opinions on important issues, students should learn how to ask open-ended questions that will help them acquire unbiased information. Students can use the guidelines on this page to help them develop questions and identify and rectify gaps in knowledge.

Application Assist students in choosing an interesting topic. List on the chalkboard what the group knows about the topic. Help students identify the questions that need to be answered, and discuss how they can go about getting answers. For example, engage students in a discussion of whether to make all sports coed and to ask them to generate a list of arguments for and against such a policy. Questions such as "Who decided that girls can't be on the football team?" could be addressed to the school coach or principal.

UNIT FIVE
Part 2 Lesson Planner

TIME ALLOTMENTS SHOWN ARE APPROXIMATE. DEPENDING ON YOUR GOALS AND THE NEEDS OF YOUR STUDENTS, YOU MAY WISH TO ALLOW MORE OR LESS TIME FOR CERTAIN PORTIONS OF THE LESSON.

Table of Contents	Discussion	Previewing the Selection	Reading the Selection
PART OPENER **Jumping to Conclusions** page 656	**20 MINUTES** • Reflect on the part theme		
SELECTION **The Necklace** page 658 AVERAGE		**20 MINUTES** • PERSONAL CONNECTION • HISTORICAL CONNECTION • WRITING CONNECTION	**40 MINUTES** • Introduce vocabulary • Read pp. 658–665 (8 pp.)
SELECTION **The Great Taos Bank Robbery** page 670 AVERAGE		**20 MINUTES** • PERSONAL CONNECTION • GEOGRAPHICAL CONNECTION • READING CONNECTION: Visualizing	**40 MINUTES** • Introduce vocabulary • Read pp. 670–677 (8 pp.)
SELECTION **The Mountain** page 681 AVERAGE		**20 MINUTES** • PERSONAL CONNECTION • GEOGRAPHICAL CONNECTION • WRITING CONNECTION	**20 MINUTES** • Read pp. 681–684 (4 pp.)
SELECTION **Everybody Knows Tobie** page 689 EASY		**20 MINUTES** • PERSONAL CONNECTION • CULTURAL CONNECTION • READING CONNECTION: Recognizing connotations of words	**30 MINUTES** • Read pp. 689–695 (7 pp.)
POETRY ON YOUR OWN **Hanging Fire** page 698 CHALLENGING			**15 MINUTES** • Read pp. 698–699 (2 pp.)
Writing	**Exploring Topics**	**Prewriting**	**Drafting and Revising**
WRITING FROM EXPERIENCE **Report**	**25 MINUTES**	**30 MINUTES**	**70 MINUTES**

Time estimates assume in-class work. You may wish to assign some of these stages as homework.

Responding to the Selection

FROM PERSONAL RESPONSE TO CRITICAL ANALYSIS	OR	ANOTHER PATHWAY	LITERARY CONCEPTS	QUICKWRITES
		60 MINUTES		
• Discussion questions	OR	• Cooperative learning (theme)	• Major/minor characters • Symbol	• Epilogue • Speech
		40 MINUTES		
• Discussion questions	OR	• Cooperative learning (dialogue)	• Verbal irony • Author's purpose	• List of questions • Confession
		60 MINUTES		
• Discussion questions	OR	• Cooperative learning (debate)	• Theme • Metaphor	• Proverb • Personal narrative
		50 MINUTES		
• Discussion questions	OR	• Cooperative learning (course of action)	• Setting	• Character sketch • Essay

Extension Activities

	ALTERNATIVE ACTIVITIES	LITERARY LINKS	CRITIC'S CORNER	THE WRITER'S STYLE	ACROSS THE CURRICULUM	ART CONNECTION	WORDS TO KNOW	BIOGRAPHY
60 MINUTES	✔	✔	✔		MATH		✔	✔
20 MINUTES				✔			✔	✔
20 MINUTES	✔		✔	✔	GEO-GRAPHY			✔
30 MINUTES	✔	✔		✔	SOCIAL STUDIES			✔

Publishing and Reflecting

20 MINUTES

PART 2

REFLECTING ON THEME

Ask a volunteer to read this paragraph aloud to the class. Then have students share instances when they have jumped to conclusions. Discuss with the class how everyone makes hasty assumptions at one time or another. Suggest that as students read, they see how the characters react to their hasty assumptions and what this reveals about their personalities.

What Do You Think?

Allow students sufficient time to rehearse their description before each get together with another group. Lead the class to see that people often make hasty assumptions as a result of incomplete information and preconceived ideas. Remind students to keep this in mind as they read the selections in this subunit. Students will return to this activity on page 668.

UNIT FIVE PART 2

JUMPING TO CONCLUSIONS

REFLECTING ON THEME

Your teacher wants to see you after class, and you think, "I knew it—I must have flunked that test!" It turns out, though, he only wanted you to deliver an assignment to an absent friend. Perhaps a letter tells you you've won a prize, and you're excited—until the prize turns out to be a key chain, some advertising gimmick. We all tend to jump to conclusions at times, perhaps expecting something better or something worse. Sometimes the results are sad, sometimes funny—as you'll discover as you read this part of Unit Five.

What Do You Think? In a small group, think of an incident that could cause someone to make a hasty assumption. It might be a phone call in the middle of the night, somebody laughing at the wrong moment, an unexpected look from a member of the opposite sex. Then describe this situation to another group in the class, and see what conclusions they come to from the facts you give them—what quick assumptions they make. In turn, react to the incident that the other group has thought of. In class discussion, consider some of the reasons why people sometimes jump to conclusions.

Guy de Maupassant	**The Necklace** *Life can change in an instant.*	657
Tony Hillerman	**The Great Taos Bank Robbery** *Mrs. Fish calls the police to predict a robbery.*	669
Martin J. Hamer	**The Mountain** *Would things have been different if the boys had been dressed up?*	680
Alice Childress	**The Pocketbook Game** / INSIGHT *Turnabout is fair play.*	685
Daniel Garza	**Everybody Knows Tobie** *How could a haircut be so important?*	688
Audre Lorde	**Hanging Fire** *It's not easy being 14.*	698

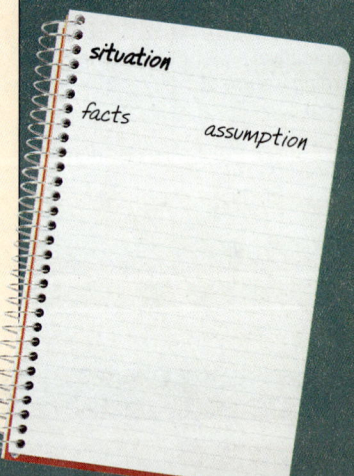

656 UNIT FIVE PART 2: JUMPING TO CONCLUSIONS

PREVIEWING

FICTION

The Necklace
Guy de Maupassant (gē′ də mō-pă-säN′)

Activating Prior Knowledge
PERSONAL CONNECTION

Status and social class play a major role in the short story you are about to read. The societies of most countries of the world can be divided into upper, middle, and lower classes. In your notebook, create a chart that includes what you know about these three social classes. For each class, identify typical sources of income and describe typical kinds of living conditions.

Class	Sources of Income	Living Conditions
Upper		
Middle		
Lower		

Building Background
HISTORICAL CONNECTION

"The Necklace" takes place in Paris in the second half of the 19th century. At that time, the life of a typical French woman was dictated by the income and social class of her father or her husband. A wealthy woman of the upper class could look forward to a life of luxury. A middle-class woman was expected to find happiness in taking care of her family and modest home. A woman of the lower class could expect a life of poverty and hard work. The only way a woman could move up in class was by marrying someone of higher status. A major obstacle to such a marriage, however, was the tradition of the dowry— money or property that the bride's family was expected to give her new husband. Upper-class parents sought to match their sons with mates who had large dowries. Few women could come up with a large enough dowry to marry into the upper classes.

Setting a Purpose
WRITING CONNECTION

What kinds of things and experiences do you value most? For example, do you enjoy having many material things, or are you satisfied with just a few? Do you dream of wealth, status, fame, power, or love? Would you rather be smart, popular, or cool? In your notebook, describe what you value most. Then, as you read "The Necklace," compare your values with those of the main character.

Using Your Reading Log Use your reading log to record your responses to the questions inserted throughout the selection. Also jot down other thoughts and feelings that come to you as you read.

- HISTORICAL CONNECTION

OVERVIEW
Objectives

- To understand and appreciate a classic in the short story genre that details the grave consequences of making an incorrect assumption
- To enrich reading by using active reading strategies
- To understand the concept of major and minor characters
- To express understanding of the selection through a choice of writing forms, including an epilogue and notes for a speech
- To extend understanding of the selection through a variety of multimodal and cross-curricular activities

Skills

LITERARY CONCEPTS
- Major and minor characters
- Plot

READING SKILLS/ STRATEGIES
- Active reading: To enrich reading by using active reading strategies

THE WRITER'S STYLE
- Specific examples

GRAMMAR
- Elliptical clauses

SPEAKING, LISTENING, AND VIEWING
- Pantomime
- Group discussion
- Oral presentation

HISTORICAL CONNECTION
Life in 19th Century Paris These images will help students imagine the lifestyles of middle- and upper-class members of French society in the 1800s.

Side A, Frames 49465

PRINT AND MEDIA RESOURCES

UNIT FIVE RESOURCE BOOK
Strategic Reading: Literature, p. 41
Vocabulary SkillBuilder, p. 42

GRAMMAR MINI-LESSONS
Transparencies, p. 2
Copymasters, pp. 1–3

WRITING MINI-LESSONS
Transparencies, p. 54

ACCESS FOR STUDENTS ACQUIRING ENGLISH
Selection Summaries
Reading Support

FORMAL ASSESSMENT
Selection Test, pp. 117–118
Test Generator

 AUDIO LIBRARY
See Reference Card

 LASERLINKS
Historical Connection

 INTERNET RESOURCES
McDougal Littell Literature Center at http://www.hmco.com/mcdougal/lit

The Necklace
Guy de Maupassant

SUMMARY

Madame Loisel, the pretty wife of a clerk, yearns for a life of elegance. When the Loisels are invited to a fancy ball, they use their savings to buy Madame Loisel a grand dress. She also borrows a necklace from a wealthy friend. On the way home from the ball, Madame Loisel loses the necklace. Ashamed to tell the friend what has happened, the Loisels borrow a huge sum of money to buy a diamond necklace identical to the one they lost. The Loisels work long and exhausting hours for ten years to repay the debt. One day, her youth and beauty spent, Madame Loisel encounters her friend and tells her the story, only to be told that the original necklace was not made of real diamonds and was worth very little money.

Thematic Link: *Jumping to Conclusions*
A Parisian woman's tragic misjudgment of a borrowed necklace's value leads to misfortune.

CUSTOMIZING FOR
Students Acquiring English

- Use **ACCESS FOR STUDENTS ACQUIRING ENGLISH,** *Reading Support.*
- This story's syntax is characteristic of translations of French literature of the late 1800s. Help students break down long sentences into manageable "chunks."

STRATEGIC READING FOR
Less-Proficient Readers

Set a Purpose Ask students to read to discover Mme. Loisel's reaction when she receives an invitation to a high-society ball.

Use **UNIT FIVE RESOURCE BOOK,** p. 41, for guidance in reading the selection.

WORDS TO KNOW

adulation (ăj′ə-lā′shən) *n.* excessive praise or flattery (p. 662)
aghast (ə-găst′) *adj.* filled with shock or horror (p. 662)
askew (ə-skyo͞o′) *adj.* crooked; on one side (p. 665)
exorbitant (ĭg-zôr′bĭ-tənt) *adj.* much too high; excessive (p. 665)
gamut (găm′ət) *n.* the entire range or series of something (p. 663)

pauper (pô′pər) *n.* a poor person, especially one who depends on public charity (p. 661)
privation (prī-vā′shən) *n.* lack of basic necessities or comforts of life (p. 663)
prospects (prŏs′pĕkts′) *n.* chances or possibilities, especially for success or profit (p. 659)
ruinous (ro͞o′ə-nəs) *adj.* bringing ruin or downfall; disastrous (p. 663)
vexation (věk-sā′shən) *n.* anger or annoyance (p. 660)

She was one of those pretty and charming girls, born, as if by an accident of fate, into a family of clerks. With no dowry, no prospects, no way of any kind of being met, understood, loved, and married by a man both prosperous and famous, she was finally married to a minor clerk[1] in the Ministry of Education. She dressed plainly because she could not afford fine clothes, but was as unhappy as a woman who has come down in the world; for women have no family rank or social class. With them, beauty, grace, and charm take the place of birth and breeding. Their natural poise, their instinctive good taste, and their mental cleverness are the sole guiding principles which make daughters of the common people the equals of ladies in high society.

She grieved incessantly, feeling that she had been born for all the little niceties and luxuries of living. She grieved over the shabbiness of her apartment, the dinginess of the walls, the worn-out appearance of the chairs, the ugliness of the draperies. All these things, which another woman of her class would not even have noticed, gnawed at her and made her furious.

The sight of the little Breton[2] girl who did her humble housework roused in her disconsolate[3] regrets and wild daydreams. She would dream of silent chambers, draped with Oriental tapestries and lighted by tall bronze floor lamps, and of two handsome butlers in knee breeches, who, drowsy from the heavy warmth cast by the central stove, dozed in large overstuffed armchairs.

She would dream of great reception halls hung with old silks, of fine furniture filled with priceless curios,[4] and of small, stylish, scented sitting rooms just right for the four o'clock chat with intimate friends, with distinguished and sought-after men whose attention every woman envies and longs to attract.

When dining at the round table, covered for the third day with the same cloth, opposite her husband, who would raise the cover of the soup tureen, declaring delightedly, "Ah! A good stew! There's nothing I like better . . . ," she would dream of fashionable dinner parties, of gleaming silverware, of tapestries making the

---

1. **clerk:** office worker who handles routine tasks such as letter writing and record keeping.
2. **Breton** (brĕt′n): of or relating to the province of Brittany in northwestern France.
3. **disconsolate:** very unhappy; beyond cheering up.
4. **curios:** rare or unusual ornamental objects.

WORDS TO KNOW **prospects** (prŏs′pĕkts′) *n.* chances or possibilities, especially for success or profit

---

Art Note

Mademoiselle Suzanne Poirson by John Singer Sargent

The portrait on page 658 of Mademoiselle Poirson was done in 1884 by John Singer Sargent (1856–1925). The portrait depicts the poise and elegance of a lady of the late 19th century. For 30 years Sargent painted portraits of the British and American upper classes, becoming known for his ability to reveal the personalities of his aristocratic subjects.

Reading the Art How does this woman compare with your image of Mme. Loisel? How does she compare with your image of the person Mme. Loisel yearns to be?

CUSTOMIZING FOR
Gifted and Talented Students

Ask students to bear in mind any details they find in the story that involve the difference between appearance and reality. After they have read the story, have them discuss what difference there is between a genuine and a fake if no one can tell them apart.

CUSTOMIZING FOR
Students Acquiring English

I These phrases may be difficult for some students: *natural poise, instinctive good taste,* and *mental cleverness.* Have volunteers paraphrase them.

Literary Concept: CHARACTER

A Have students describe the emotions that Madame Loisel feels and cite details that reveal them. (*Possible response:* anger, frustration, self-pity; details: "grieved incessantly"; "feeling . . . born for luxuries"; "things . . . gnawed at her . . . made her furious")

Mini-Lesson Grammar

ELLIPTICAL CLAUSES Explain to students that elliptical clauses are adverb clauses from which a word or words have been omitted. Direct students' attention to the highlighted sentence above that begins "When dining at the round table . . ." Point out that in the opening adverbial clause, the words *she was* have been omitted: ("When [*she was*] dining at the round table . . .") Stress that it is important to avoid ambiguity when using elliptical clauses. Elliptical clauses at the beginning of a sentence must be followed by a comma.

Application Ask students to look at the following sentences and identify the words being omitted in the elliptical clauses.
1. If unable to find the necklace, the couple would have to buy a replacement. (*they were*)
2. While strolling on the Champs Élysées, she saw her old friend. (*she was*)

Reteaching/Reinforcement
- *Grammar Handbook*, anthology p. 941
- *Grammar Mini-Lessons* copymasters pp. 1–3, transparencies p. 2

Adverb Clauses p. 729

Active Reading: CLARIFY

B Students should conclude that Madame Loisel is unhappy because she feels deprived of luxuries she thinks she deserves; she envies her rich friend. Discuss with students whether they think that Madame Loisel is being unreasonable about her present life.

CUSTOMIZING FOR
Students Acquiring English

2 Help students differentiate among the terms *vexation, regret, despair,* and *anguish*. Point out ways in which the terms are alike. *(they all describe negative feelings)* Then discuss how each one is different from the others by giving an example of a situation that would cause a person involved to experience the feeling.

3 Give students an idea of the amounts of money mentioned in the story by explaining that an item costing 400 francs at that time would be approximately $400 today.

Active Reading: CONNECT

C Invite students to discuss occasions when they think that having the "right" clothes can be important. If they need help, share the following model with them.

Think-Aloud Model: *I think that you should wear the appropriate clothes for a job interview or maybe for a special occasion like a wedding. I don't think you should wear blue jeans. What other occasions can you think of when you might need to wear the "right" clothes?*

---

walls alive with characters out of history and strange birds in a fairyland forest; she would dream of delicious dishes served on wonderful china, of gallant compliments whispered and listened to with a sphinxlike[5] smile as one eats the rosy flesh of a trout or nibbles at the wings of a grouse.

She had no evening clothes, no jewels, nothing. But those were the things she wanted; she felt that was the kind of life for her. She so much longed to please, be envied, be fascinating and sought after.

She had a well-to-do friend, a classmate of convent-school days whom she would no longer go to see, simply because she would feel so distressed on returning home. And she would weep for days on end from vexation, regret, despair, and anguish.

CLARIFY

B Why is Mme. Loisel so unhappy?
Using a Reading Log

Then one evening, her husband came home proudly holding out a large envelope.

"Look," he said, "I've got something for you."

She excitedly tore open the envelope and pulled out a printed card bearing these words:

"The Minister of Education and Mme. Georges Ramponneau[6] beg M. and Mme. Loisel[7] to do them the honor of attending an evening reception at the Ministerial Mansion on Friday, January 18."

Instead of being delighted, as her husband had hoped, she scornfully tossed the invitation on the table, murmuring, "What good is that to me?"

"But, my dear, I thought you'd be thrilled to death. You never get a chance to go out, and this is a real affair, a wonderful one! I had an awful time getting a card. Everybody wants one; it's much sought after, and not many clerks have a chance at one. You'll see all the most important people there."

She gave him an irritated glance and burst out impatiently, "What do you think I have to go in?"

He hadn't given that a thought. He stammered, "Why, the dress you wear when we go to the theater. That looks quite nice, I think."

He stopped talking, dazed and distracted to see his wife burst out weeping. Two large tears slowly rolled from the corners of her eyes to the corners of her mouth; he gasped, "Why, what's the matter? What's the trouble?"

By sheer willpower she overcame her outburst and answered in a calm voice while wiping the tears from her wet cheeks:

"Oh, nothing. Only I don't have an evening dress and therefore I can't go to that affair. Give the card to some friend at the office whose wife can dress better than I can."

CONNECT

In social situations, is having the "right" clothes still that important today?
Using a Reading Log

He was stunned. He resumed. "Let's see, Mathilde.[8] How much would a suitable outfit cost—one you could wear for other affairs too—something very simple?"

She thought it over for several seconds, going over her allowance and thinking also of the amount she could ask for without bringing an immediate refusal and an exclamation of dismay from the thrifty clerk.

Finally, she answered hesitatingly, "I'm not sure exactly, but I think with four hundred francs[9] I could manage it."

---

5. **sphinxlike:** mysterious; from the Greek myth of the sphinx, a winged creature that killed those who could not answer its riddle.
6. **Mme. Georges Ramponneau** (zhôrzh′ rän-pô-nō′): *Mme.* is an abbreviation for *Madame* (mə-däm′), a title of courtesy for a married French woman.
7. **M. and Mme. Loisel** (lwä-zĕl′): *M.* is an abbreviation for *Monsieur* (mə-syœ′), a title of courtesy for a French man.
8. **Mathilde** (mä′tĕld).
9. **francs** (frăngks): the franc is the basic monetary unit of France.

WORDS TO KNOW
vexation (vĕk-sā′shən) *n.* anger or annoyance

660

Mini-Lesson · Literary Concepts

REVIEWING PLOT Remind students that the sequence of events in a story is called the plot. The plot is usually centered around a conflict, and it tells what happens and when and to whom it happens. A story's plot usually includes four stages: exposition, rising action, climax, and falling action.

Application A long series of events leads up to the surprising conclusion in "The Necklace." Ask students to review the selection and make a list of the conflicts and problems faced by the Loisels that make up the story's plot. Then, ask them to discuss how the solution of each problem leads to new complications. Suggest students use a chart similar to the one below in which the first problem and solution have been identified to track the story's plot.

660 THE LANGUAGE OF LITERATURE TEACHER'S EDITION

Too Early (1873), Jacques-Joseph Tissot. Guildhall Gallery, London/Art Resource, New York.

He turned a bit pale, for he had set aside just that amount to buy a rifle so that, the following summer, he could join some friends who were getting up a group to shoot larks on the plain near Nanterre.

However, he said, "All right. I'll give you four hundred francs. But try to get a nice dress."

As the day of the party approached, Mme. Loisel seemed sad, moody, and ill at ease. Her outfit was ready, however. Her husband said to her one evening, "What's the matter? You've been all out of sorts for three days."

And she answered, "It's embarrassing not to have a jewel or a gem—nothing to wear on my dress. I'll look like a pauper: I'd almost rather not go to that party."

He answered, "Why not wear some flowers? They're very fashionable this season. For ten francs you can get two or three gorgeous roses."

She wasn't at all convinced. "No.... There's nothing more humiliating than to look poor among a lot of rich women."

But her husband exclaimed, "My, but you're silly! Go see your friend Mme. Forestier[10] and

---

10. **Forestier** (fô-rĕs-tyā′).

WORDS TO KNOW

pauper (pô′pər) *n.* a poor person, especially one who depends on public charity

661

Cultural Note

F Maupassant and his readers were undoubtedly familiar with "The Affair of the Diamond Necklace," a real-life political scandal that would affect the course of French history 100 years later. This fateful necklace was a string of 500 diamonds worth about $40,000. Cardinal de Rohan, a member of the French aristocracy, attempted to obtain the necklace in order to curry favor with the luxury-loving French queen, Marie Antoinette, whose extravagances pointed up the contrast between the wealth of the nobility and the poverty of the common people. When the gossip spread about the diamond necklace, the affair so fueled the rage French citizens felt toward royalty that the affair is considered one of the events which helped bring about the downfall of royalty in the French Revolution of 1789.

Active Reading: QUESTION

G Possible response: It represented for Madame Loisel her fantasy of being rich.

CUSTOMIZING FOR
Students Acquiring English

4 Explain that *wrap* is another word for *coat*.

Literary Concept:
FORESHADOWING

H Explain to students that martyrs are those who suffer on account of others or their own beliefs. Ask students why the author uses the street name Rue des Martyrs. *(Possible response: It foreshadows tragedy and suffering for the Loisels.)*

---

ask her to lend you some jewelry. You and she know each other well enough for you to do that."

She gave a cry of joy, "Why, that's so! I hadn't thought of it."

The next day she paid her friend a visit and told her of her predicament.

Mme. Forestier went toward a large closet with mirrored doors, took out a large jewel box, brought it over, opened it, and said to Mme. Loisel, "Pick something out, my dear."

At first her eyes noted some bracelets, then a pearl necklace, then a Venetian cross, gold and gems, of marvelous workmanship. She tried on these adornments in front of the mirror, but hesitated, unable to decide which to part with and put back. She kept on asking, "Haven't you something else?"

"Oh, yes, keep on looking. I don't know just what you'd like."

F All at once she found, in a black satin box, a superb diamond necklace; and her pulse beat faster with longing. Her hands trembled as she took it up. Clasping it around her throat, outside her high-necked dress, she stood in ecstasy looking at her reflection.

Then she asked, hesitatingly, pleading, "Could I borrow that, just that and nothing else?"

G QUESTION
Why do you think Mme. Loisel finally chooses only the diamond necklace?
Using a Reading Log

"Why, of course."
She threw her arms around her friend, kissed her warmly, and fled with her treasure.

The day of the party arrived. Mme. Loisel was a sensation. She was the prettiest one there, fashionable, gracious, smiling, and wild with joy. All the men turned to look at her, asked who she was, begged to be introduced. All the Cabinet officials wanted to waltz with her. The minister took notice of her.

She danced madly, wildly, drunk with pleasure, giving no thought to anything in the triumph of her beauty, the pride of her success, in a kind of happy cloud composed of all the <u>adulation</u>, of all the admiring glances, of all the awakened longings, of a sense of complete victory that is so sweet to a woman's heart.

She left around four o'clock in the morning. Her husband, since midnight, had been dozing in a small empty sitting room with three other gentlemen whose wives were having too good a time.

He threw over her shoulders the wraps he had brought for going home, modest garments of everyday life whose shabbiness clashed with the stylishness of her evening clothes. She felt this and longed to escape, unseen by the other women who were draped in expensive furs.

Loisel held her back.

"Hold on! You'll catch cold outside. I'll call a cab."

But she wouldn't listen to him and went rapidly down the stairs. When they were on the street, they didn't find a carriage; and they set out to hunt for one, hailing drivers whom they saw going by at a distance.

They walked toward the Seine,[11] disconsolate and shivering. Finally on the docks they found one of those carriages that one sees in Paris only after nightfall, as if they were ashamed to show their drabness during daylight hours.

It dropped them at their door in the Rue des Martyrs,[12] and they climbed wearily up to their apartment. For her, it was all over. For him, there was the thought that he would have to be at the Ministry at ten o'clock.

Before the mirror, she let the wraps fall from her shoulders to see herself once again in all her

---
11. **Seine** (sĕn): the principal river of Paris.
12. **Rue des Martyrs** (rü′ dā mär-tēr′): a street in Paris.

WORDS TO KNOW

adulation (ăj′ə-lā′shən) *n.* excessive praise or flattery

662

Mini-Lesson The Writer's Style

USING SPECIFIC WORDS Have students note Maupassant's use of specific examples to illustrate important points in the story. For example, to illustrate Mme. Loisel's unhappiness with her shabby apartment, he lists the dingy walls, worn-out chairs, and ugly drapes (page 659). In the same paragraph, he contrasts this dissatisfaction with her dreams of affluence, specifically citing "Oriental tapestries," "bronze floor lamps," "handsome butlers," and "overstuffed armchairs" as examples of her desires.

Application Have students find other instances of the author's use of specific examples to make his events more graphic or illustrate the personalities of the characters involved. Then have them each write a paragraph about something they long for, using specific examples.

Reteaching/Reinforcement
- *Writing Handbook,* anthology p. 873
- *Writing Mini-Lessons* transparencies p. 54

Using Specific Words, pp. 383–384

glory. Suddenly she gave a cry. The necklace was gone.

Her husband, already half-undressed, said, "What's the trouble?"

She turned toward him despairingly, "I . . . I . . . I don't have Mme. Forestier's necklace."

"What! You can't mean it! It's impossible!"

They hunted everywhere, through the folds of the dress, through the folds of the coat, in the pockets. They found nothing.

He asked, "Are you sure you had it when leaving the dance?"

"Yes, I felt it when I was in the hall of the Ministry."

"But if you had lost it on the street, we'd have heard it drop. It must be in the cab."

"Yes. Quite likely. Did you get its number?"

"No. Didn't you notice it either?"

"No."

They looked at each other aghast. Finally Loisel got dressed again.

"I'll retrace our steps on foot," he said, "to see if I can find it."

And he went out. She remained in her evening clothes, without the strength to go to bed, slumped in a chair in the unheated room, her mind a blank.

Her husband came in about seven o'clock. He had had no luck.

He went to the police station, to the newspapers to post a reward, to the cab companies, everywhere the slightest hope drove him.

That evening Loisel returned, pale, his face lined; still he had learned nothing.

"We'll have to write your friend," he said, "to tell her you have broken the catch and are having it repaired. That will give us a little time to turn around."

She wrote to his dictation.

At the end of a week, they had given up all hope.

And Loisel, looking five years older, declared, "We must take steps to replace that piece of jewelry."

The next day they took the case to the jeweler whose name they found inside. He consulted his records. "I didn't sell that necklace, madame," he said. "I only supplied the case."

Then they went from one jeweler to another hunting for a similar necklace, going over their recollections, both sick with despair and anxiety.

They found, in a shop in Palais Royal, a string of diamonds which seemed exactly like the one they were seeking. It was priced at forty thousand francs. They could get it for thirty-six.

They asked the jeweler to hold it for them for three days. And they reached an agreement that he would take it back for thirty-four thousand if the lost one was found before the end of February.

Loisel had eighteen thousand francs he had inherited from his father. He would borrow the rest.

He went about raising the money, asking a thousand francs from one, four hundred from another, a hundred here, sixty there. He signed notes, made ruinous deals, did business with loan sharks, ran the whole gamut of money-

Suddenly she gave a cry. The necklace was gone.

WORDS TO KNOW	**aghast** (ə-găst′) *adj.* filled with shock or horror
	ruinous (rōō′ə-nəs) *adj.* bringing ruin or downfall; disastrous
	gamut (găm′ət) *n.* the entire range or series of something

663

Art Note

A Girl Sweeping (1912) by William McGregor Paxton William Paxton (1869–1941), known as "the court painter of Philadelphia," depicts a young woman in the act of sweeping an elegant, well-appointed room. The painting is unusual in that few artists of the day chose working women as their subject matter.

Reading the Art *Do you think the artist is more concerned with illustrating the effort of the woman or the beauty of the room? Why?*

Critical Thinking: ANALYZING

L Have students explain what is meant by the phrase "compromised the rest of his life." *(Possible response: He promises to repay a heavy debt that might take him a lifetime to accomplish.)*

Literary Concept: PLOT

M Have students discuss what problem the Loisels now face. *(Possible response: The Loisels now have to pay back the large sums of money that they borrowed to replace the lost necklace.)*

Critical Thinking: ANALYZING

N Have students explain how Madame Loisel's approach to her new problem differs from her previous behavior. *(She is accepting facts and taking action, not dreaming or grieving.)*

CUSTOMIZING FOR
Gifted and Talented Students

Have students debate whether, having learned what has happened to the Loisels, Mme. Forestier has any moral or financial obligation to them. Have them hypothesize: if she were to aid them, how much in the Loisels' lives would really change?

L lenders. He compromised[13] the rest of his life, risked his signature without knowing if he'd be able to honor it, and then, terrified by the outlook for the future, by the blackness of despair about to close around him, by the prospect of all the <u>privations</u> of the body and tortures of the spirit, he went to claim the new necklace with the thirty-six thousand francs which he placed on the counter of the shopkeeper.

When Mme. Loisel took the necklace back, Mme. Forestier said to her frostily, "You should have brought it back sooner; I might have needed it."

She didn't open the case, an action her friend was afraid of. If she had noticed the substitution, what would she have thought? What would she have said? Would **M** she have thought her a thief?

Girl Sweeping (1912), William McGregor Paxton. Oil on canvas, 40 ¼" × 30 ⅜", courtesy of the Museum of American Art of the Pennsylvania Academy of the Fine Arts, Philadelphia, Joseph E. Temple Fund (1912.4).

$\mathcal{M}$me. Loisel experienced the horrible life the needy live. She played her part, however, with sudden heroism. That frightful debt had to be paid. She would pay it. She dismissed her maid; they rented a garret[14] under the eaves.

N She learned to do the heavy housework, to perform the hateful duties of cooking. She washed dishes, wearing down her shell-pink nails scouring the grease from pots and pans; she scrubbed dirty linen, shirts, and cleaning rags, which she hung on a line to dry; she took the garbage down to the street each morning and brought up water, stopping on each landing to get her breath. And, clad like a peasant woman, basket on arm, guarding sou[15] by sou her scanty allowance, she bargained with the fruit dealers, the grocer, the butcher, and was insulted by them.

---
13. **compromised:** exposed to danger.
14. **garret:** room just below the sloping roof of a building; attic.
15. **sou** (sōō): a French coin of small value.

> WORDS TO KNOW
> **privation** (prī-vā′shən) *n.* lack of basic necessities or comforts of life

664

Mini-Lesson Workplace Literacy

SCANS Goal: Allocates Money

BUDGETING FUNDS Explain to students that a budget is a plan that forecasts income and expenses over a given period of time. Businesses and households both use budgets to help make decisions about how to allocate money. Although misfortune and misunderstanding force the Loisels to carefully budget their funds, keeping to a budget makes sense even if financial difficulty never occurs.

Application Ask students to plan a one-week budget for themselves. First, have them write down the amount of income they will have available during the week. Then have them list the expenses they expect to incur during the same period. Students should compare their total income with their total expenses for the week and decide how best to allocate the funds available to them. During the week, students should attempt to adhere to the budget they have prepared, recording their spending and then matching their actual spending against their budgetary projections.

664 THE LANGUAGE OF LITERATURE TEACHER'S EDITION

Each month notes had to be paid, and others renewed to give more time.

Her husband labored evenings to balance a tradesman's accounts, and at night, often, he copied documents at five sous a page.

And this went on for ten years.

Finally, all was paid back, everything including the exorbitant rates of the loan sharks and accumulated compound interest.

Mme. Loisel appeared an old woman, now. She became heavy, rough, harsh, like one of the poor. Her hair untended, her skirts askew, her hands red, her voice shrill, she even slopped water on her floors and scrubbed them herself. But, sometimes, while her husband was at work, she would sit near the window and think of that long-ago evening when, at the dance, she had been so beautiful and admired.

PREDICT

How do you think the story will end?

What would have happened if she had not lost that necklace? Who knows? Who can say? How strange and unpredictable life is! How little there is between happiness and misery!

Then one Sunday when she had gone for a walk on the Champs Élysées[16] to relax a bit from the week's labors, she suddenly noticed a woman strolling with a child. It was Mme. Forestier, still young-looking; still beautiful, still charming.

Mme. Loisel felt a rush of emotion. Should she speak to her? Of course. And now that everything was paid off, she would tell her the whole story. Why not?

She went toward her. "Hello, Jeanne."

The other, not recognizing her, showed astonishment at being spoken to so familiarly by this common person. She stammered. "But . . . madame . . . I don't recognize . . . You must be mistaken."

"No, I'm Mathilde Loisel."

Her friend gave a cry, "Oh, my poor Mathilde, how you've changed!"

"Yes, I've had a hard time since last seeing you. And plenty of misfortunes—and all on account of you!"

"Of me . . . How do you mean?"

"Do you remember that diamond necklace you loaned me to wear to the dance at the Ministry?"

"Yes, but what about it?"

"Well, I lost it."

"You lost it! But you returned it."

"I brought you another just like it. And we've been paying for it for ten years now. You can imagine that wasn't easy for us who had nothing. Well, it's over now, and I am glad of it."

Mme. Forestier stopped short, "You mean to say you bought a diamond necklace to replace mine?"

"Yes. You never noticed, then? They were quite alike."

And she smiled with proud and simple joy. Mme. Forestier, quite overcome, clasped her by the hands. "Oh, my poor Mathilde. But mine was only paste.[17] Why, at most it was worth only five hundred francs!" ❖

---

16. **Champs Élysées** (shäN zā-lē-zā'): a famous wide street in Paris.
17. **paste:** a hard, glassy material used in making imitations of precious stones.

WORDS TO KNOW
exorbitant (ĭg-zôr′bĭ-tənt) *adj.* much too high; excessive
askew (ə-skyōō′) *adj.* crooked; to one side

665

From Personal Response to Critical Analysis

1. Accept all reasonable responses.
2. Possible responses: The necklace, which represented affluence and the upper-class lifestyle to Mme. Loisel, turns out to be a fake; she and her husband struggle needlessly for ten years; the necklace she borrows in order to appear wealthy forces her into poverty.
3. Possible responses: At the beginning of the story Mme. Loisel is vain, selfish, proud, unrealistic, and spoiled. After she loses the necklace, she is forced to deal with reality. She develops character and becomes hard working, thrifty, and self-sacrificing.
4. Accept all reasonable responses.
5. Possible responses: She was destined for an unhappy existence regardless of the loss of the necklace; she is the better for the experience, despite the hardship incurred.
6. Accept all reasonable responses.
7. Accept all reasonable, well-supported responses.

Another Pathway

Cooperative Learning Assign one group member to be seeker of justification, encouraging others to support their ideas with examples from the text.

Rubric

3 Full Accomplishment Students work together and identify themes or messages learned from the story.

2 Substantial Accomplishment Students have some difficulty identifying themes or messages.

1 Little or Partial Accomplishment Students are unable to identify themes or messages.

RESPONDING
OPTIONS

FROM PERSONAL RESPONSE TO CRITICAL ANALYSIS

REFLECT
1. What was your reaction to the surprise ending? Jot down your thoughts in your notebook and share them in class.

RETHINK
2. What do you find ironic about the ending of this story?

3. How does Madame Loisel change as a result of her experiences?
   Consider
   - what she values in life
   - her positive and negative character traits
   - whether any of her values or traits change

   Close Textual Reading

4. Suppose that Madame Loisel had not lost the necklace. On the basis of her feelings and actions up to that point in the story, what do you predict her future would have been like?

Thematic Link
5. Madame Loisel pays dearly for jumping to a wrong conclusion. Do you think it ultimately ruins her life or saves her life? Explain your answer.

RELATE
6. Look over what you wrote for the Writing Connection on page 657. How do your values compare with Madame Loisel's?

7. Do people still chase after wealth and social status today? Do you think the effort is worthwhile? Explain your opinion.

Multimodal Learning
ANOTHER PATHWAY
Cooperative Learning
What theme, message, or moral do you find in this story? With a small group, discuss what you learned from this simple story of one woman's misfortune. Write down the theme as your group explains it—or the two or three themes, if you can't agree on one. Then share your ideas with the rest of the class.

QUICKWRITES

1. What do you think Madame Loisel's life will be like now that she has paid off her debt and found out the real value of the necklace? Draft an **epilogue** to the story that explains how she has come to terms with what's happened.

2. Apply the saying "Success is getting what you want, but happiness is wanting what you get" to the characters in "The Necklace." Explain your ideas in notes for a **speech**.

📁 **PORTFOLIO** Save your writing. You may want to use it later as a springboard to a piece for your portfolio.

666 UNIT FIVE PART 2: JUMPING TO CONCLUSIONS

QuickWrites

1. Encourage students to review the beginning and end of the story for insight into Mme. Loisel's character in order to get ideas about how she might react to Mme. Forestier's revelation.
2. Suggest that students incorporate specific details from the story into their speeches to support their interpretation of the saying.

LITERARY CONCEPTS

Because "The Necklace" focuses on the thoughts and feelings of Madame Loisel, she is the **main character** in the story. Monsieur Loisel and Madame Forestier are **minor characters,** who serve as important contrasts to Madame Loisel. Think about the kind of man and husband Monsieur Loisel is. How does his view of middle-class life contrast with his wife's? Think about the kind of woman and friend Madame Forestier is. Why do you think she first conceals the truth about the necklace but then reveals the truth ten years later? How do these minor characters help you understand Madame Loisel?

CONCEPT REVIEW: Symbol The necklace is a symbol that changes in meaning as the story progresses. Think about what the diamond necklace symbolizes to Madame Loisel when she first chooses it. When she loses the necklace, what has she lost? When the diamonds are revealed to be fake, how does that change the meaning of the symbol?

CRITIC'S CORNER

The literary critic Edward D. Sullivan declares that "The Necklace" was not written to force a reader to think that if Madame Loisel had just told the truth, none of the rest would have happened. Sullivan says "The Necklace" is *not* just a story pointing to a moral, such as "Honesty is the best policy," but a story showing that in people's lives "blind chance rules." Do you agree or disagree with Sullivan's argument? State your reasons.

LITERARY LINKS

Compare "The Necklace" with "The Bass, the River, and Sheila Mant," focusing on the similarities between what the main characters desire and what the characters learn.

ACROSS THE CURRICULUM

Mathematics Madame Loisel paid 36,000 francs for the diamond necklace. In 1884 the exchange rate was about 5.25 francs to one dollar. How much was the necklace worth in dollars in 1884? Find out how much the value of the dollar has changed since 1884 due to inflation, and calculate the value of the necklace in today's dollars.

Multimodal Learning

ALTERNATIVE ACTIVITIES

1. *Cooperative Learning* In a small group, make up a story about a modern-day teenage version of Madame Loisel. Use the story to prepare and present a short **skit** showing how a high school student today might get into a predicament similar to Madame Loisel's.

2. Do **research** to discover what materials are used to make artificial jewels and how jewelers can tell real jewels from fakes. You might look in books about costume jewelry or talk to a jeweler. If you have access to an encyclopedia program or an on-line service, you might use your computer to start your research. Share your findings with your class.

Alternative Activities

1. Suggest that groups brainstorm a list of the things that many modern-day teenagers long for as symbols of status or wealth. They can use these lists to help develop the story on which to base their skit.
2. Encourage students to use graphic aids (photos or samples of artificial jewelry) to demonstrate to the class how jewelers distinguish real gems from fakes.

Across the Curriculum

Mathematics Suggest that students use library reference sources to find the change in the value of the dollar due to inflation. At an exchange rate of 5.25 to 1, the necklace was worth $6,857 in 1884. The value of the dollar has roughly tripled since that time making the present-day worth of the necklace well over $20,000.

Literary Concepts

Students may say that the character of Monsieur Loisel provides contrast to that of his wife. His thrifty nature and contentment with their middle-class existence highlight the extravagance or unattainability of his wife's desires. Students may say that the character of Mme. Forestier is seen by Mme. Loisel as representative of the upper class, yet the fact that the diamonds lent by Mme. Forestier are actually valueless illustrates the gap between appearance and reality.

Symbol Students may say that the necklace initially symbolizes the affluent life of the upper class. When lost, it might represent the inability of Mme. Loisel to be a part of that life. When revealed to be a fake at the end of the story, it might symbolize the illusory value of wealth and status.

Critic's Corner

Some students may agree, saying that bad luck or "blind chance" in the form of losing the necklace was the determining factor in the couple's fate. Others may argue that there *are* moral lessons to be taken from the story, and they may maintain that although chance does play a role, it is Mme. Loisel's vanity that ultimately results in their downfall.

Literary Links

Students may point out that in both stories, the main characters are motivated by strong desires. In "The Necklace," Mme. Loisel yearns for the luxury and elegance of an upper-class existence. In "The Bass, the River, and Sheila Mant," the narrator, a young boy, seeks the attention of an older girl. Both desires have negative consequences for the characters—the young narrator must give up a huge fish he has caught and Mme. Loisel must face ten years of hard work and poverty. In both stories, the characters learn the dangers of desire.

Words to Know

Exercise A
1. pauper
2. privation
3. prospects
4. aghast
5. vexation
6. askew
7. adulation
8. gamut
9. exorbitant
10. ruinous

Exercise B
Student stories will vary.

Reteaching/Reinforcement
- *Unit Five Resource Book,* p. 42

GUY DE MAUPASSANT

Maupassant's parents had a very difficult and unhappy marriage, culminating in their separation when Maupassant was 11 years old. Although he sided with his mother in his parents' conflict, his father provided him with financial and employment assistance at numerous points in his life. Perhaps because of his family situation, the figure of the beleaguered or absent father is a common one in Maupassant's work. The writer Gustave Flaubert, a family friend, helped fill the void of fatherhood for the young Maupassant and served as an early and important mentor. Like the main character of "The Necklace," Maupassant was obsessed with the appearance of wealth. He achieved financial success late in his career, owning several boats, multiple residences, and traveling frequently.

WORDS TO KNOW

EXERCISE A Review the Words to Know in the boxes at the bottom of the selection pages. Then write the vocabulary word that best completes each of the following photo captions from a fashion magazine article.

1. What's *out*? The rags of last year's <u>pauper</u> look. What's *in*? Elegance like this!
2. In this classy, elegant outfit, any <u>privation</u> you feel will be quickly forgotten.
3. This beautiful suit is the perfect thing to wear in seeking new job <u>prospects</u>.
4. Although those with traditional taste may be <u>aghast</u> at this wedding gown in black and crimson, the gown is making its mark on the fashion scene.
5. This one-of-a-kind design by Tanto Denaro will save its wearer the <u>vexation</u> of running into three other women in the same dress.
6. Wearing this hat straight would be too dull for designer Baka Kyappu, so all of her carefree and oh-so-current headwear is worn <u>askew</u>.
7. With this fabulous creation, Modéliste Vaniteux proves that he deserved the <u>adulation</u> his talent received last season.
8. This sporty number, combining glittering rhinestones and sturdy denim, shows just one of the looks available in the broad <u>gamut</u> of Jaquette Atroce's new designs.
9. Although some may feel that the $87,000 price of this outfit is <u>exorbitant</u>, it was the most photographed design at the fashion show.
10. This lovely frock demonstrates how completely The House of Pelea has recovered from the nearly <u>ruinous</u> dispute between its two top designers.

EXERCISE B Tell a "round robin" story in which one person begins the story and must keep talking until he or she has used one of the vocabulary words. Then, another person continues the story, using another word. Continue the story until all ten vocabulary words are used.

GUY DE MAUPASSANT

1850–1893

Guy de Maupassant may be the best-known French writer outside France. Maupassant was born in northwestern France to an upper-middle-class family. When the family fortune ran out, he was forced into tiring work as a government clerk, which he pursued from 1872 to 1882, until he achieved success as a writer. Although his writing eventually brought him modest wealth, he led a tortured life. From 1877 until his death, he suffered from an incurable disease, experiencing occasional hallucinations. As the infection spread to his brain, Maupassant became insane and died in a Paris asylum at age 42.

Maupassant's hundreds of stories excel in portraying everyday life, and his subjects reflect his background. He wrote about peasants in the countryside near his home, government clerks, upper-class society—and madness. One critic has noted that his strength is not his subject matter but his style, which is clear and to the point: he had the "remarkable ability to suggest character with one deft stroke of the pen—a single phrase, a couple of well-chosen verbs." A biographer of Maupassant claims that it was the "brevity and brisk pace" of his writing that gave the short story genre "both a worthy literary form and a new popularity."

OTHER WORKS "A Piece of String," "The Umbrella"

Extended Reading

668 UNIT FIVE PART 2: JUMPING TO CONCLUSIONS

REFLECTING ON THEME
What Do You Think?

Have students think about the activity that they participated in before they began reading the selections in Part Two. Now that they have completed this selection, discuss with them ways in which the Loisels' could have avoided the fate they suffered because of their false assumptions about the necklace.

PREVIEWING

NONFICTION

The Great Taos Bank Robbery
Tony Hillerman

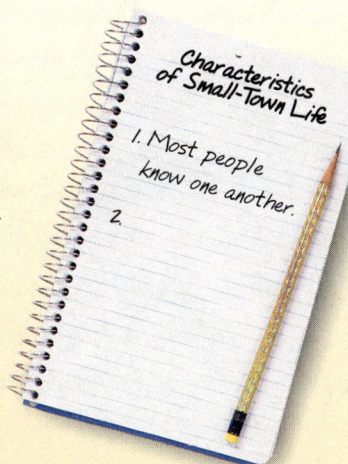

Activating Prior Knowledge/Setting a Purpose
PERSONAL CONNECTION
What is your image of life in a small town? How is the way of life different from that in large cities and suburbs? What are the people like? With a group of classmates, brainstorm a list of characteristics of small-town life. Record your list in your notebook. As you read this selection, compare your image of a small town to the one Tony Hillerman portrays.

Building Background
GEOGRAPHICAL CONNECTION
This selection tells about actual events that occurred in 1957 in Taos, New Mexico. Taos is a small town today, with a population of about 4,000, but at the time of this story it was even smaller—about 1,850. The town lies north of Santa Fe in north-central New Mexico. Situated on a high plateau amid the Sangre de Cristo Mountains, Taos has a unique beauty that has attracted many artists and writers to the area. The town also has an interesting mixture of three cultures: Native American, Mexican American, and Anglo-American.

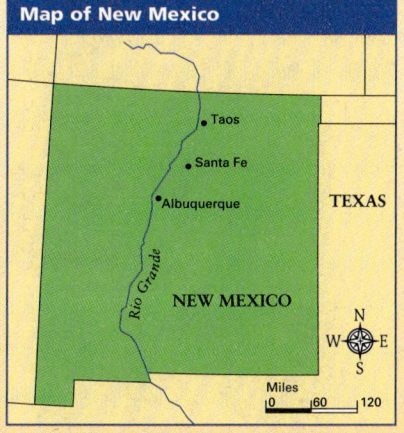

READING CONNECTION
Visualizing In this selection, the author presents details that create a picture of a small town—a picture that can be enlivened by a reader who visualizes the characters, setting, and action. To best visualize the characters, pay attention to what they do and to what the narrator says about them; write down key phrases in your notebook. To imagine the setting and action, follow what is happening as if it were in a movie. You may find it helpful to sketch in your notebook a map of the town of Taos as you imagine it from the description of the "robbery," "chase scene," and "manhunt" in the selection.

OVERVIEW

Objectives
- To understand and appreciate a narrative essay that explores the reaction of a small town to an apparent bank robbery attempt
- To appreciate and understand verbal irony
- To explore and understand the writer's use of humor and irony
- To express understanding of the essay through a choice of writing forms, including a list of questions and a confession
- To extend understanding of the selection through a variety of multimodal and cross-curricular activities

Skills

LITERARY CONCEPTS
- Verbal irony
- Setting

THE WRITER'S STYLE
- Addressing the reader

GENRE STUDY
- Nonfiction: narrative essay

GRAMMAR
- Subject-verb agreement

SPEAKING, LISTENING, AND VIEWING
- Group discussion
- Oral presentation

THE GREAT TAOS BANK ROBBERY **669**

PRINT AND MEDIA RESOURCES

UNIT FIVE RESOURCE BOOK
Strategic Reading: Literature, p. 45
Vocabulary SkillBuilder, p. 46

GRAMMAR MINI-LESSONS
Transparencies, p. 4
Copymasters, p. 5

WRITING MINI-LESSONS
Transparencies, p. 44

ACCESS FOR STUDENTS ACQUIRING ENGLISH
Selection Summaries
Reading Support

FORMAL ASSESSMENT
Selection Test, p. 119
 Test Generator

 AUDIO LIBRARY
See Reference Card

 LASERLINKS
Author Background
Art Gallery

 INTERNET RESOURCES
McDougal Littell Literature Center at http://www.hmco.com/mcdougal/lit

---

THE LANGUAGE OF LITERATURE TEACHER'S EDITION **669**

THE GREAT TAOS BANK ROBBERY

Taos Today (1934), Ward Lockwood. Oil on panel, Spencer Museum of Art, University of Kansas, gift of the Ward and Clyde Lockwood Collection.

WORDS TO KNOW

affront (ə-frŭnt′) *n.* an intentional insult (p. 675)
authenticity (ô′thĕn-tĭs′ĭ-tē) *n.* genuineness (p. 674)
conformity (kən-fôr′mĭ-tē) *n.* the state of being in agreement with rules, customs, or popular opinion (p. 673)
depreciate (dĭ-prē′shē-āt′) *v.* to make something seem unimportant; belittle (p. 674)
dissenting (dĭ-sĕn′tĭng) *adj.* disagreeing; having a different opinion **dissent** *v.* (p. 674)

fiasco (fē-ăs′kō) *n.* a complete failure; especially, a project whose great plans end in ridiculous failure (p. 674)
impeccable (ĭm-pĕk′ə-bəl) *adj.* flawless; perfect (p. 672)
influx (ĭn′flŭks′) *n.* a mass arrival or incoming (p. 675)
irreverence (ĭ-rĕv′ər-əns) *n.* lack of proper respect (p. 677)
tolerant (tŏl′ər-ənt) *adj.* having or showing understanding and respect for others' customs or beliefs (p. 673)

TONY HILLERMAN

The newsroom of *The New Mexican* first got word of the incident about ten minutes after nine the morning of November 12, 1957. Mrs. Ruth Fish, who had served for many years as manager of the Taos Chamber of Commerce and almost as many as Taos correspondent for the Santa Fe newspaper, called collect and asked for the city editor.

She told the city editor that the Taos bank would be robbed that morning. She said that she would walk over to the bank and watch this operation. She promised to call in an eyewitness account before the first edition deadline at 11:00 A.M.

The city editor asked how Mrs. Fish knew the bank was to be robbed. Mrs. Fish, in a hurry to get off the telephone and become an eyewitness, explained very briefly that one of her lady friends had stopped in her office and told her so. The lady was now waiting so that they could walk down together and watch.

But, the city editor insisted, how did the lady friend know the bank was to be robbed that morning?

Because, Mrs. Fish explained with patience, the two bank robbers were standing in line at this very moment waiting their turn at the teller's cage.

But, persisted the city editor, how was it possible to predict that these two persons intended to rob the bank?

This presumption seemed safe, Mrs. Fish said, because one of the two men was disguised as a woman and because he was holding a pistol under his purse. Whereupon she said good-bye and hung up.

While astonished by the foregoing, the city editor recalled later that he had no doubt at all that the bank would indeed be robbed in the fashion described. If the reader feels less

THE GREAT TAOS BANK ROBBERY **671**

STRATEGIC READING FOR
Less-Proficient Readers

Ask students how they would react if they heard that a bank robbery was about to occur. Would they want to get to the scene to watch it or would they stay as far away as possible?

Set a Purpose Ask students to pay attention, as they read, to the citizens' reactions to rumors of an impending crime.

Use **UNIT FIVE RESOURCE BOOK**, p. 45, for guidance in reading the selection.

CUSTOMIZING FOR
Gifted and Talented Students

Ask students to look for the narrator's statement about the residents of Taos—that "a certain amount of eccentricity is required for conformity." Have them discuss what the narrator means by this statement. In their experience, have they met people who, while trying to be different or unusual, are actually just trying to fit in? Can the "requirement" to be eccentric be a kind of conformity in itself?

CUSTOMIZING FOR
Students Acquiring English

Tell students that the "Taos correspondent for the Santa Fe newspaper" is the official source for news of Taos appearing in the newspaper of nearby Santa Fe. The city editor is the person who handles a newspaper's local news coverage—deciding what stories to highlight and giving assignments to reporters.

Mini-Lesson Grammar

SUBJECT-VERB AGREEMENT Remind students that subjects and verbs must agree in number. When a group of words, often a prepositional phrase, comes between the subject and the verb, the verb must still agree with the subject. Look at this example from the first subordinate clause in the highlighted sentence above:

. . . one of the two men was disguised as a woman. . . .

Application Have students decide which sentences are correct.

1. The cash in the bank machines were safe. *(incorrect)*

2. The chief, including all police officers, organizes the search. *(correct)*

Reteaching/Reinforcement
- Grammar Handbook, anthology p. 940
- *Grammar Mini-Lessons* copymasters p. 5, transparencies p. 4

 The Writer's Craft

Agreement in Number, p. 700

SUBJECT-VERB AGREEMENT

Pay Attention To	Ignore
1. subject number (singular or plural)	1. prepositional phrases
2. verb number (singular or plural)	2. other interrupting phrases

Linking to Geography

A Taos, New Mexico, located 55 miles north-northeast of Santa Fe, is the site of an ancient Indian village of multistoried adobe dwellings known as the Taos Pueblo. The area was originally settled by the Spanish in 1615. In 1680, the Spanish were driven out in a revolt by local Pueblo Indians, but they returned 16 years later. A second revolt in 1847 resulted in the death of the first governor of the New Mexico Territory, Charles Bent. An artists' colony since the late 19th century, the town continues to depend on art galleries and tourism for much of its income.

Literary Concept:
VERBAL IRONY

B Tell students to consider the information the author provides about the Great Flood of 1935—that there is no river in Taos and little available water—and ask them what conclusions they can draw about the author's choice of words "litany of notable events." *(Possible responses: The author is being sarcastic; the word* litany *implies that there has been a great number of notable events in Taos, yet if there can be a "great" flood with little water, it apparently doesn't take much for something to be counted as notable.)*

---

sure at this point, it is because the city editor had two advantages. First, he knew Mrs. Fish. An elderly woman of dignity, charm, and grandmotherly appearance, she possessed a flawless reputation for accuracy. Second, he knew Taos. While bank robbers probably wouldn't stand politely in line with the paying customers in Omaha or Atlanta, there was no reason to believe they wouldn't in this peculiar little town.

As a matter of fact they were doing exactly this, and their courtliness was about to cause them trouble. The chain of events that followed did not reach its semi-final anticlimax[1] until sixty hours later and was not officially ended until the following February, when the federal grand jury met sixty-five miles south in Santa Fe. By then the affair was being called The Great Taos Bank Robbery.

Lest the reader be misled by this title, he should be warned that Taos also lists in its litany[2] of notable events The Great Flood of 1935. If the reader can accept the fact that Taos managed a Great Flood without a river and with the very modest amount of water available in its arid climate, he is prepared to hear more about what happened on November 12, 1957.

After the city editor collected his wits, he placed a long-distance call to the bank. The secretary who answered didn't know anything about any bank robbery, but she referred the call to a higher ranking official. The city editor asked this gentleman if his bank had been robbed. Certainly not, said the banker. How in the world did such rumors get started?

A few minutes later Mrs. Fish called back, slightly breathless. She reported that she and her friend had walked through the alley behind the Safeway store and arrived at the bank just as two men with drawn pistols dashed from the front door. One of the men was dressed as a woman, as previously reported. He ran awkwardly in his high heels. The two jumped into a green pickup truck parked in the alley and drove away. From what she had learned from spectators fortunate enough to arrive earlier, the two men had not taken any money from the bank. She would investigate further and call back. Mrs. Fish, a woman of impeccable courtesy, hung up without a word of reproach to the city editor for causing her to be late for the event.

The city editor now placed another call to the banker. He asked the banker if he was sure his bank hadn't been robbed, or something. The bank official now was less confident. He was sure nobody had taken any money but he was also sure that something funny had been going on. He had been hearing something about a man dressed as a woman, and two men running wildly out of the bank lobby, and other confusing stories.

Meanwhile, the police reporter had called the Taos police department and said he was checking on a rumor that there had been a bank robbery. The policeman who answered said no, there hadn't been one and he guessed the police would be the first to hear about it if there was one, wouldn't they? The reporter said yes, he guessed that was true. Actually, the police would be approximately the last to hear about it, being informed only after the pastor of the local United Brethren Church entered the picture.

By then Mrs. Fish had made her third call and provided the city editor with a detailed account of what had happened in the bank lobby. The two men had arrived just as the bank opened its doors at 9:00 A.M. They found a crowd of Taos businessmen waiting to

---

1. **anticlimax:** something low-key or commonplace that concludes a series of exciting or significant events.
2. **litany:** in this case, something often referred to or repeated.

WORDS TO KNOW
impeccable (ĭm-pĕk'ə-bəl) *adj.* flawless; perfect

672

Mini-Lesson Literary Concepts

REVIEWING SETTING Remind students that setting includes not only the place but also the time of the action in a story. The time can be a specific time of day such as morning or evening, or a period in the past, present, or future. In some works, the setting is minimally defined and left largely up to the reader's imagination. In others, the setting is defined in detail and is an important contributor to the story's total effect.

Application Have students work in small groups to discuss the importance of the setting to "The Great Taos Bank Robbery." What aspects of the setting contribute to the humor in the narrative? Ask them to consider how the events might have differed if the incident had occurred in a large urban center rather than Taos, or in another small town, one with a more conservative population.

672 THE LANGUAGE OF LITERATURE **TEACHER'S EDITION**

check out funds to fuel their cash registers for the day. The suspects joined the rush to the tellers' cages but were outdistanced, perhaps because of the high heels, and were stuck well back in the line. Customers quickly noticed that the line-stander clad as a woman had a full day's growth of dark stubble bristling through his pancake makeup and that the nylons encased an unseemly growth of leg hair. They also noticed that this person's costume was remarkably chic for Taos, which is one of the few places where a man can still feel adequately dressed downtown in bib overalls. All this was enough to cause a modest amount of buzzing in the lobby, but probably not much. Taos is a <u>tolerant</u> village, well accustomed to whimsy. It has been said that if the late James Thurber had been raised here he would never have celebrated the antics of his family in print, since what seems outlandish in Columbus, Ohio, seems fairly normal in Taos. It is also said that if Sinclair Lewis had been a Taoseño, Babbitt would have had a common-law wife and worn sandals.³ In Taos a certain amount of eccentricity is required for <u>conformity</u>.

Interest among the spectators quickened, however, when some of them saw—or thought they saw—a pistol in the hand of the pseudo-⁴ woman. The fleet-footed ones, who had beaten the rush to the tellers' windows and therefore left early, spread the news of this unusual sight around Taos Plaza. Thus did Mrs. Fish receive the word, and thus were many curious townfolks drawn to the bank to watch the spectacle.

Several days later, one of the two suspects was to complain to federal agents that some among this growing crowd of spectators began giggling. Whether or not Taos residents were guilty of such churlishness,⁵ the two young men soon began suffering from stage fright. Embarrassed by the scrutiny of the crowd, they fled from the bank just as Mrs. Fish and her friend were arriving.

It was definitely established finally that both men were armed with loaded pistols. Although they were not to use these weapons until later, and then only when cruelly provoked, these revolvers are important because they lend an air of reality to The Great Taos Bank Robbery. It was much the same with The Great Flood of 1935. While it wasn't a flood in the usual definition, people actually did get wet and Taoseños defend this historic event from scoffers by pointing out that Governor Clyde Tingley declared an emergency and scores of families were evacuated to the National Guard Armory.

These facts seem persuasive unless one knows that this Great Flood was actually an epidemic of leaking roofs—the combined effect of a freakishly slow and persistent rain and the traditional Taos habit of roofing flat-topped adobe buildings with

---

3. **Sinclair Lewis . . . sandals:** In a novel by Lewis, Babbitt is a businessman who conforms blindly to his small town's conservative ethics and standards. The suggestion is that the people of Taos tend to have a freer and more permissive lifestyle.
4. **pseudo-** (sōō′dō): false; pretend.
5. **churlishness:** bad-tempered, rude behavior.

WORDS TO KNOW

tolerant (tŏl′ər-ənt) *adj.* having or showing understanding and respect for others' customs or beliefs
conformity (kən-fôr′mĭ-tē) *n.* the state of being in agreement with rules, customs, or popular opinion

673

Multicultural Perspectives

Adobe is the name for the sun-dried brick used in construction by Native Americans for thousands of years. Most commonly used in the American Southwest and Mexico, the bricks are made by mixing clay soil with straw, molding the mixture into bricks, and baking them in the sun for up to two weeks. The most impressive adobe structures date from the period between A.D. 1050–1300 when Pueblo Indians built the cliff houses at Mesa Verde and multilevel houses in various locations. In the 17th and 18th centuries, European settlers in the Southwest and California found adobe construction well-suited to the region. The Southwestern style that developed continues to display the strongest Native American influence of any American architectural style.

CUSTOMIZING FOR
Students Acquiring English

② Use the expression "to turn the other cheek" in several different sentences and explain its Biblical origin. Invite students to tell about similar idioms in their first languages. Then lead them to understand the humor in the expression "to turn the other fender."

Literary Concept: SETTING

G Ask students how the author's description of Taos' streets adds to the comic aspect of the car chase. *(Possible response: A car chase is supposed to be high-speed and dangerous, and so imagining one in this setting of narrow, crooked, and short streets is humorous.)*

---

hard-packed adobe clay. This roofing material is usually as effective as it is inexpensive, since Taos rainstorms are commonly brief, noisy, and productive of very little moisture. Taos learned in 1935 that when an Eastern-style three-day drizzle happens, such economical roofs tend to dissolve and pour through the ceilings. Residents, Taos-like, persist in using dirt roofs and profited from the experience only by the legends of bravery, charity, and outrageous discomfort that it created.

Today Taoseños rely on the two loaded pistols to lend <u>authenticity</u> to their Great Taos Bank Robbery just as they drag out the governor's unlocking of the armory when an outsider <u>depreciates</u> their flood. But before these pistols started going off, a couple of things had to happen.

As Mrs. Fish reported, the two suspects roared away from the scene of their <u>fiasco</u> in a pickup truck. Their rush may have been prompted by the erroneous notion that someone would call the police, or perhaps by sheer embarrassment. Whatever the cause, the two ran a stop sign and sideswiped a car driven by the United Brethren minister. The minister was not in the mood that morning to turn the other fender. He insisted that the accident be reported to the police and that neither vehicle be moved until an officer arrived. The suspects took a <u>dissenting</u> position and insisted on driving away. The reader is aware that they had good reason for this rudeness but the pastor at the moment was not. Neither could he know that the man in the pickup who wore lipstick and face powder had gotten himself up as a female for the relatively innocent purpose of misleading bank personnel. It is safe to guess that the minister suspected a darker purpose, since Taos has long been known as a place of confusion concerning gender. At any rate, when the two men drove away, the minister gave chase.

Taos is a small community and its streets are few, narrow, crooked, and short. It is a

WORDS TO KNOW
authenticity (ô′thĕn-tĭs′ĭ-tē) *n.* genuineness
depreciate (dĭ-prē′shē-āt′) *v.* to make something seem unimportant; belittle
fiasco (fē-ăs′kō) *n.* a complete failure; especially, a project whose great plans end in ridiculous failure
dissenting (dĭ-sĕn′tĭng) *adj.* disagreeing; having a different opinion **dissent** *v.*

674

Mini-Lesson Genre Study

NONFICTION Draw the web shown at left on the chalkboard. Use it to explain that a **narrative essay** is a type of nonfiction with the following characteristics:
- It is a relatively brief composition.
- It focuses on a particular incident or series of incidents.
- It tells a story.
- It presents the personal views of the author.

Application Have students copy the web into their notebooks. Then ask them to refer to it as they look for each characteristic in "The Great Taos Bank Robbery." Ask students to find several passages that they believe express the personal views of the author.

completely inappropriate setting for a high-speed automobile chase and offers limited opportunity for the chasees to elude the chaser. After two or three times around the village the two suspects must have faced the fact that there was no hope of shaking off their pursuer. They began firing their pistols at the minister's car. Thus discouraged, the minister stopped at a telephone and the police, at long last, learned that something was amiss in Taos. . . .

Once the police were belatedly informed of the doings of November 12, at the bank and elsewhere, they reacted with vigor. A search began immediately for the two suspects. The State Police were notified and the Federal Bureau of Investigation was told of the apparent affront to the Federal Banking Act. By noon, the population of Taos—normally about 1,850—had been swollen by the influx of various types of officers. In addition to the genuine gendarmes[6] representing federal, state, county, and village governments, volunteer organizations such as the Mounted Patrol and Sheriff's Posse were mobilized.

Authorities soon had the escape vehicle. It was driven into the midst of a swarm of lawmen by Jose T. Cardenas. Mr. Cardenas, when he collected himself from the shock of having guns pointed at him, explained that he had lent his truck to a friend the previous day and that it had been left at his house that morning bearing signs of collision damage. Mr. Cardenas was at that moment in search of this friend to demand an explanation.

The reader might well pause here and recollect that it is traditional among robbers to steal escape vehicles, not to borrow them from friends. Borrowing, while more polite, leads to speedy identification when the car is recovered. Mr. Cardenas was able to tell police that he had loaned his truck to a man I shall call Joe Gomez, a thirty-three-year-old Taos native, and

---

6. **gendarmes** (zhän'därmz') *French:* police officers.

WORDS TO KNOW
affront (ə-frŭnt') *n.* an intentional insult
influx (ĭn'flŭks') *n.* a mass arrival or incoming

675

Mini-Lesson The Writer's Style

ADDRESSING THE READER Point out that at several points in "The Great Taos Bank Robbery" the narrator pauses in his retelling of the events to address the reader directly. For example, he has the reader contrast his or her knowledge of the events with that of the pastor (page 674) and at other points encourages readers to use their own knowledge to evaluate aspects of the action (page 675).

Application Ask students to review the selection for examples of the narrator directly addressing the reader. Discuss with them why the writer might use this technique. Does it help to actively involve the reader in the story? Does it reinforce the humorous tone of the narrative? Then ask students to think of a humorous event they have witnessed. Have them write the first paragraph of a description of the event, addressing the reader directly.

Reteaching/Reinforcement
• *Writing Handbook*, anthology p. 867
• *Writing Mini-Lessons* transparencies, p. 44

Voice, p. 315

Literary Concept: SETTING

J Ask students to discuss how the small size of Taos becomes an important element of the humor in the narrative. *(Possible responses: The large presence of the authorities becomes comically out of proportion to the size of the town and the significance of the event; it makes the lawmen's inability to find the two fugitives even more ludicrous since they are using such extensive resources to search such a small area.)*

CUSTOMIZING FOR
Students Acquiring English

4 Explain that when a group of people follow traditional rules for democratically run meetings, at least two people must agree on a topic for the rest of the group to vote on. The first person "makes a motion," and the second person "seconds the motion."

CUSTOMIZING FOR
Multiple Learning Styles

Spatial or Graphic Learners Have students use information from the narrative to sketch a pictorial map of Taos as they imagine it. Ask them to include details such as the narrow, crooked streets, the location of the bank and plaza, and the mountains that surround the city. Then have them mark out the route of the two would-be bank robbers, illustrating the time and location of the major events in the story.

---

that Mr. Gomez was accompanied by Frederick Smith, a twenty-three-year-old resident of Maine who had been visiting in the village.

Police also quickly received a hint of why the two had borrowed the truck a day early. Witnesses were found who had seen them at the entrance of the bank the previous morning—the morning of November 11. The witnesses remembered this because they thought it odd to see a man dressed as a woman trying to get into the bank on Veterans' Day. If any doubts remained on the subject, this should have proved that the two were not professional bank bandits, since professionals presumably would know about national bank holidays.

At this point, the authorities appeared to be in an unusually happy position. They knew the identities of both men they sought. They had excellent descriptions of the suspects. They were confident both were afoot in Taos. The village is small, the lawmen were numerous, and there was every reason for confidence that the two culprits would be in custody in a very few minutes. The officers fanned out from the plaza to press their search.

This proved to be a mistake, because Gomez and Smith had decided to walk down to the plaza to try to borrow some money. While the federal, state, county, and city officers and their volunteer posses manned roadblocks and poked around in the outlying areas, the two fugitives were making a door-to-door canvass of downtown bars soliciting loans from the bartenders. Not unnaturally, the barkeeps considered the two as poor credit risks at the moment. By the time it occurred to someone to inform the law of this activity, Gomez and Smith had become discouraged and wandered off.

By the time the sun dipped behind the Conejos Mountains, the lawmen had found Gomez's female attire abandoned in an outdoor toilet but the fugitives were still at large. The hunt continued through the night, brightening the frosty November darkness with flashlights and electric lanterns. Considering the number of officers involved and the modest dimensions of Taos it is safe to guess that at least one policeman looked almost everywhere at least once, except in the deserted house where the two had chosen to sleep. When the sun rose over the Taos Mountains the morning of November 13, Gomez and Smith were still at large. There was some talk now of sending for Sam, the New Mexico bloodhound, but the motion apparently died for lack of a second. Perhaps this was because the only time Sam was used in Taos County he immediately became disoriented, strayed, and was lost for two days.

THE VILLAGE IS SMALL, THE LAWMEN WERE NUMEROUS.

November 13 passed with a methodical and fruitless combing of the village. There was a brief flurry of excitement when officers learned in some roundabout manner that Gomez and Smith had again appeared on the plaza, renewing their futile attempts to float a loan. Police now discovered, twelve hours too late to do them any good, where Gomez and Smith had spent the previous night. They discovered that a neighborhood householder had happened by their hideout, had seen the fugitives, had stopped to chat with them about the excitement they had caused and had then left to buy them some groceries. The reader by now will not be surprised to know that this good neighbor did not bother to notify the police. But he did play a little joke on the culprits when he returned with the food, telling them that they had critically wounded the minister and that officers had orders to get them dead or alive. This unnerving bit of misinformation drove the two to make their second return to the plaza the next morning to renew the attempt to borrow traveling money. While one can imagine that their pleas were eloquent, the bartenders remained adamant. Gomez told a reporter two days later that by now he and Smith were "feeling mighty blue."

If the fugitives were depressed by November 13, it is reasonable to bet that those involved in the search for them shared this feeling. Taos does not lend itself to extended manhunts, since the posse members soon run out of places to look. To make matters worse, the press had taken the matter lightly from the first and the newspaper <u>irreverence</u> increased as the search dragged. When November 14 wore on without a sign of the fugitives, those in charge of the hunt must have been casting about for a dignified excuse to call off the whole affair. Their ordeal, however, was almost over.

That night, a Taos resident named Nat Flores was lying on his bed reading the evening paper when he heard a tapping on his window. Outside he saw two young men whom he recognized as Gomez and Smith. The two inquired if he might provide them with a meal and Flores, with typical "my house is your house" Taos hospitality, invited his visitors in for supper. During the meal, Flores and Joe V. Montoya, a brother-in-law who had stopped in for a chat, found Gomez and Smith in a gloomy mood. The two said they had spent the previous night in frostbitten discomfort in Kit Carson Park, a small recreation area not far from Taos Plaza. One of the possemen, Smith complained, had almost stepped on his finger.

Flores and Montoya, after a lengthy argument in which Flores recalled quoting passages from the Bible, persuaded the two that they should accept a ride down to the sheriff's office after supper and turn themselves in.

The final footnote on The Great Taos Bank Robbery was not written until February 4, 1958. After the surrender, officers found the two refreshingly frank about their activities. In due course, Joe Gomez and Frederick Smith were accused by the U.S. District Attorney of conspiring to violate the provisions of the Federal Banking Act and their case was placed on the winter docket for consideration by the Federal Grand Jury. Unfortunately, grand jury proceedings are secret so we will never know exactly what happened when the case was presented. We do know that the jury returned a "no bill," which indicates—at the very least—that the jurors could not be convinced that Gomez and Smith took their pistols into the Taos bank with felonious[7] intentions. If the jurors were not familiar with Taos, they may have suspected the FBI imagined the whole unlikely episode.

Thus The Great Bank Robbery was denied the official federal imprimatur[8] of indictments and was left as the sort of thing Alice's Mad Hatter might call an Unfelonious Unrobbery.

Still, if you happen to be in Taos on Veterans' Day and the man on the next barstool happens to be an Old Taos Hand, you're likely to hear something like this:

"You know, tomorrow is the anniversary of our Big Bank Robbery."

Or maybe he'll tell you about The Great Flood of 1935. ❖

---

7. **felonious** (fə-lō′nē-əs): of or like a major crime; criminal.
8. **imprimatur** (ĭm′prə-mä′tŏŏr) **of indictments**: official approval of statements formally charging a person with a crime.

WORDS TO KNOW
irreverence (ĭ-rĕv′ər-əns) *n.* lack of proper respect

Linking to Social Studies

K A grand jury does not meet to determine whether the accused is innocent or guilty. Instead, it examines the accusations against the defendant and decides whether or not there is sufficient evidence to try him or her for the crime in question. If they do, an indictment is returned and the matter proceeds to trial. Grand jury proceedings are held in secret, and, unlike a trial, only a simple majority is necessary to produce an indictment.

STRATEGIC READING FOR Less-Proficient Readers

L Ask students why it might be considered strange that the authorities had so much difficulty apprehending the two men. (Possible response: There were many law enforcement agents and the identity of the two men was known; Taos is a very small town with few hiding places; the men didn't make much of an effort to conceal themselves, twice walking into the main plaza.) **Analyzing**

CUSTOMIZING FOR Gifted and Talented Students

Have interested students investigate the federal law that the two men were accused of breaking. Then have them summarize the case for and against the defendants. Students should be reminded that the letter of the law demands that they must be able to prove felonious intent—not just unusual, even suspicious, behavior.

COMPREHENSION CHECK
True or false
1. The bank robbers waited politely in line after they entered the bank. *(t)*
2. The robbery attempt was thwarted by the rapid arrival of the Taos police. *(f)*
3. During the manhunt, the two fugitives entered town in broad daylight, hoping to borrow money from local bartenders. *(t)*
4. The fugitives turned themselves in after having supper with a Taos resident. *(t)*
5. The Federal Grand Jury indicted the two men on the charge of bank robbery. *(f)*

EDITOR'S NOTE *With the permission of the author or copyright holder, this selection has been excerpted from a larger work. Material has been deleted to shorten and focus the selection.*

Assessment Option

SELF-ASSESSMENT You can help students assess their understanding of the narrative by having them create a timeline marking the activities of the two fugitives. The timeline should include all the events in the narrative in which the fugitives participated, and it should indicate any other people involved at each juncture.

To help students assess their own work, have them respond to the following questions:
- Does my timeline chronicle the events of the narrative in the order in which they occurred?
- Does my timeline indicate which people were involved in each event?
- Could someone who hadn't read the narrative understand the sequence of events by using my timeline?

From Personal Response to Critical Analysis

1. Accept all reasonable responses.
2. Possible responses: Since the two men never actually attempted to rob the bank and no one was harmed during the episode, the grand jury's decision was justified; the shots fired at the minister are evidence that the two men should have been prosecuted.
3. Accept all reasonable, well-supported responses.
4. Accept all reasonable, well-supported responses. Some students will find the incidents just too absurd to be believable; other students may have had enough experience with people's irrational behavior to find the selection quite believable.
5. Possible responses: The author's tone is tongue-in-cheek; he doesn't seem to take the events too seriously; he isn't laughing at the people of Taos but does point out their eccentricities and the humor inherent in the events.
6. Possible responses: Just as the Great Bank Robbery wasn't actually a robbery, the Great Flood wasn't actually a flood at all, it was merely a rainstorm; the use of the adjective *great* is hyperbole in both cases.
7. Accept all reasonable responses.

Another Pathway

Cooperative Learning Have each group hold a meeting to choose a scene from the narrative and brainstorm ideas about the characters. Assign one student in each group to act as encourager of participation, making sure that everyone gets involved in either writing dialogue or performing in character.

Rubric

3 Full Accomplishment Skit is entirely consistent with the characters as represented in the selection.

2 Substantial Accomplishment Students enact scene, but aspects of characterization or dialogue may be inconsistent with selection.

1 Little or Partial Accomplishment Students have difficulty writing dialogue and representing the characters in the skit.

RESPONDING OPTIONS

FROM PERSONAL RESPONSE TO CRITICAL ANALYSIS

REFLECT 1. What did you like most about this selection? Jot down your response in your notebook and share it with a partner.

RETHINK 2. Do you agree with the grand jury's decision? Would you have decided to indict the would-be robbers? Explain why or why not.

3. Compare the list that you created for the Personal Connection on page 669 with what you learned about Taos from this selection. How does Taos fit your idea of a small town? How is it different?

Close Textual Reading

Consider
- the way the robbers acted
- the way the witnesses and other townspeople acted
- what the author says about the eccentricities of Taoseños

4. Do you find this nonfiction selection believable? Why or why not?

5. Describe the author's tone—his attitude toward the events in Taos. Do you think the author is laughing at the residents of Taos? Explain your answer.

Thematic Link 6. In what ways is The Great Taos Bank Robbery similar to the town's Great Flood of 1935?

RELATE 7. Would you want to live in a small town like Taos? Why or why not?

Multimodal Learning
ANOTHER PATHWAY

Cooperative Learning

This selection has no dialogue, but one can imagine what the colorful characters might have said. In a small group, choose a scene from the selection, create dialogue for it, and dramatize it in a skit. Cast a narrator to briefly set up the scene. Then perform your skit for the class.

LITERARY CONCEPTS

Verbal irony is a type of irony that occurs when someone knowingly exaggerates or says one thing and means another. For example, if someone asked how you felt about your favorite team's nine-game losing streak, you might say "I couldn't be happier" but actually mean that you're disgusted. What examples of verbal irony do you see in this selection?

CONCEPT REVIEW: Author's Purpose Describe what you think was the author's purpose or purposes in writing this selection.

QUICKWRITES

1. Which person in this selection would you most like to interview about the events of The Great Taos Bank Robbery or about life in Taos in general? Imagine that you could interview this person. Write a **list of questions** you would ask him or her.

2. Draft the **confession** that Gomez or Smith might have given the authorities after they turned themselves in. Imagine the confession as a dialogue in which the suspect is interviewed by an FBI agent.

 PORTFOLIO Save your writing. You may want to use it later as a springboard to a piece for your portfolio.

678   UNIT FIVE PART 2: JUMPING TO CONCLUSIONS

Literary Concepts

Verbal Irony Explore the concept of verbal irony by having students discuss examples they use in their own conversation. There are numerous instances in the selection, including the title itself.

Author's Purpose Remind students of the four main purposes for which an author usually writes: to express oneself, to inform or explain, to persuade, and to entertain. Most will say that Hillerman's main purpose is to entertain; some may suggest that he is also trying to inform readers about life in a unique small town.

QuickWrites

1. Encourage students to create questions about aspects of the events that struck them as curious or strange.
2. Have students review the actions of Gomez and Smith as depicted in the narrative. Then, when writing the confessions, they should try to imagine what motivated the characters to act as they did.

Conducting the Interview, p. 104

THE WRITER'S STYLE

The **humor** and the **irony** in this selection come not only from comic situations but also from tongue-in-cheek language. Look at the choice of words (indicated in italic type) in the following passage:

> The minister was not in the mood that morning *to turn the other fender.* He insisted that the accident be reported to the police and that neither vehicle be moved until an officer arrived. The suspects took *a dissenting position* and insisted on driving away.

This passage is much more humorous than one written like this: "The minister was in a bad mood that morning. . . . The suspects disagreed and drove away." Find other passages in which Hillerman's choice of words emphasizes humor and irony.

ART CONNECTION

The painting on pages 670–671 is by Ward Lockwood, who lived most of his life in the vicinity of Taos. What aspects of the artwork hint at Taos's unique, easygoing lifestyle?

WORDS TO KNOW

For each group of words below, write the letter of the word that is the best antonym of the boldfaced word.

1. **irreverence** (a) honor, (b) connection, (c) wit
2. **fiasco** (a) control, (b) success, (c) honesty
3. **tolerant** (a) foolish, (b) unfriendly, (c) narrow-minded
4. **impeccable** (a) cheap, (b) faulty, (c) critical
5. **depreciate** (a) praise, (b) consider, (c) ignore
6. **affront** (a) decrease, (b) pleasantness, (c) outrage
7. **authenticity** (a) restlessness, (b) kindness, (c) falseness
8. **conformity** (a) pain, (b) creation, (c) opposition
9. **influx** (a) departure, (b) memory, (c) panic
10. **dissenting** (a) cooperative, (b) humble, (c) senseless

TONY HILLERMAN

1925–

A long-time resident of New Mexico, Tony Hillerman is noted for his detective novels featuring two Navajo police officers. One critic called him "one of the nation's most convincing and authentic interpreters of Navajo culture, as well as one of our best and most innovative mystery writers."

Hillerman grew up in Oklahoma but, at the time of The Great Taos Bank Robbery, he was working as a reporter for *The New Mexican.* Several years later, at age 38, he wanted a change. He quit his job, got a master's degree in English, and began teaching and writing books. Since 1970, he has published more than 25 titles, mostly novels.

Hillerman never outlines a plot ahead of time; he wants to be open to suggestions. In a 1995 interview, he said that "a writer is like a bag lady going through life with a sack and pointed stick collecting stuff"—that is, collecting ideas. With regard to setting, Hillerman says that he never starts a chapter without an "exact vision of the place it will happen . . . the temperature, direction of the breeze, the aromas it carries, time of day, the way the light falls, the cloud formations."

Like many writers who dread getting started, Hillerman has a daily routine that helps him avoid writing. He will get up at 7:30, read the paper, go to the office, look at unanswered mail, turn on his computer, reread what he wrote the day before and "maybe take out an adverb or something," and then take a walk.

OTHER WORKS *Leaphorn and Chee: Three Classic Mysteries, Indian Country: America's Sacred Land*

Extended Reading

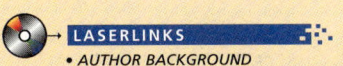
- AUTHOR BACKGROUND
- ART GALLERY

THE GREAT TAOS BANK ROBBERY 679

Alternative Activities

1. Choose a scene from this selection to present in the form of a cartoon or comic strip.
2. Imagine yourself as an "Old Taos Hand." In the style of Hillerman's work, make up and tell a story about another legendary event in the town's history, such as The Great Fire, The Great Earthquake, or The Great Winter Storm.

 ART GALLERY
Landscapes of the Southwest
The wonder and beauty of the Southwest has influenced the work of many artists. Painters who have used the landscape and culture of the Southwest are represented here.

Side A, Frame 34678

Words to Know

1. a	6. b
2. b	7. c
3. c	8. c
4. b	9. a
5. a	10. a

Reteaching/Reinforcement
• *Unit Five Resource Book*, p. 46

The Writer's Style

Students can review the examples of verbal irony they found in the Literary Concepts activity.

Across the Curriculum

Law *Cooperative Learning* Have students form small groups to research the procedures by which a case is brought to trial. Some students can research aspects of the law at the library. Others can contact their local district attorney's office to find out more about legal proceedings. Although grand jury proceedings are held in secret, most trials are open to the public. Students may wish to attend a court session to gain understanding of the workings of the legal system.

Art Connection

The people in the painting seem relaxed and unhurried, content to pass the day in quiet thought or friendly conversation.

TONY HILLERMAN

Contrasts such as the differing attitudes of the federal agents and the inhabitants of Taos are typical of Hillerman's writing. His detective novels are rich with illustrations of the differences and tensions between traditional Navajo values and those of contemporary Anglo culture. Hillerman has also addressed Southwestern topics in nonfiction; his *New Mexico, Rio Grande, and Other Essays* explores the geography, history, and politics of the region.

AUTHOR BACKGROUND
Tony Hillerman This famous mystery writer speaks about how life in the Southwest has influenced his writing. You may wish to discuss how the culture and setting of the Southwest are reflected in this story.

Side A, Frame 49475

OVERVIEW

Objectives

- To appreciate a short story that describes the painful consequences of stereotyped assumptions
- To appreciate and understand the concept of theme
- To appreciate and understand description
- To express understanding of the selection through a choice of writing forms, including a proverb and a personal narrative
- To extend understanding of the story through a variety of multimodal and cross-curricular activities

Skills

LITERARY CONCEPTS
- Theme
- Conflict

THE WRITER'S STYLE
- Using sentence fragments for effect

GRAMMAR
- Appositives

ALTERNATE
Previewing

Students can choose partners and use the following prompts to preview "The Mountain" orally.

Personal Connection

Discussion Prompts *Have you ever been in a situation in which someone acted on the basis of a stereotyped assumption? In as much detail as possible, describe the situation to your partner. Then listen as your partner describes his or her situation. If you need help getting started, use the following questions:*

- *What assumption was made?*
- *How did the person being stereotyped react?*

As you read "The Mountain," compare these situations to the experience of the boys in the story.

GEOGRAPHICAL CONNECTION
The Harlem Community and Columbia University Harlem today is a much more diverse community than in the 1940s. However, it still has one of the largest African-American communities in the United States. These images will give students a glimpse of the time and place of this story—Harlem and the Columbia University campus.

Side A, Frame 49486

PREVIEWING

FICTION

The Mountain
Martin J. Hamer

Activating Prior Knowledge

PERSONAL CONNECTION

Have you ever heard the expression "dumb blonds," "computer nerds," or "rowdy teenagers"? If you have, you have run into some stereotyped thinking. A stereotype is a fixed and oversimplified view of a group of people, a view that disregards individual differences. For example, if you are of a certain age, race, sex, religion, occupation, nationality, or even hair color, some people may jump to conclusions and assume that you have certain traits and will act in a certain way. Think of some stereotypes you have encountered or perhaps assumed to be true. In your notebook, make a two-column chart listing different groups of people and the stereotypes associated with them.

Group	Stereotypes Associated with the Group

Building Background

GEOGRAPHICAL CONNECTION

This story is set in 1943 in Harlem, a section of the borough of Manhattan in New York City. Harlem includes the largest African-American community in the United States. Just west of Harlem, high on a cliff along the Hudson River, stands Columbia University, which is featured in the story. One of the top universities in the United States, Columbia enjoys great social and academic prestige.

The Low Library of Columbia University.
Copyright © Superstock.

Setting a Purpose

WRITING CONNECTION

Look back at the chart of stereotypes that you created for the Personal Connection. Have you ever known someone to act on the basis of any of these stereotyped assumptions? Have you ever felt stereotyped yourself? Take a few moments to write in your notebook about an incident you observed or experienced in which someone spoke or acted on the basis of stereotyped assumptions. Then, as you read, compare this incident with the experience and feelings of the two boys in the story.

LASERLINKS
- GEOGRAPHICAL CONNECTION

680   UNIT FIVE   PART 2: JUMPING TO CONCLUSIONS

PRINT AND MEDIA RESOURCES

UNIT FIVE RESOURCE BOOK
Strategic Reading: Literature, p. 49

GRAMMAR MINI-LESSONS
Transparencies, pp. 2, 41
Copymasters, p. 3

ACCESS FOR STUDENTS ACQUIRING ENGLISH
Selection Summaries
Reading Support

FORMAL ASSESSMENT
Selection Test, p. 121
 Test Generator

 AUDIO LIBRARY
See Reference Card

 LASERLINKS
Geographical Connection

 INTERNET RESOURCES
McDougal Littell Literature Center at http://www.hmco.com/mcdougal/lit

Quenton and Andre, Stephen Scott Young. Watercolor on archies paper, 38" × 76", private collection. Copyright © Stephen Scott Young, photo courtesy John H. Surovek Gallery, Palm Beach, Florida.

THE MOUNTAIN
Martin J. Hamer

In the summer of 1943, Charlie was my best friend. We were in the same class in elementary school and we lived right next door to each other. He, in the first high stoop house from the corner and I in the second. By standing on our backyard fire escapes and reaching out, we could pass things to one another. My mother came home late in the evening and my father never until much later, so when I came in from school, and my sister wasn't there to tell on me, I would climb out on the fire escape and call to Charlie. To do this, we each had a long string with a stone wrapped in cloth tied to it, hanging from our fire escapes. Once, when Charlie had been mean to the lady under him, she cut his string. Anyway, to call to each other, we would swing the stones so that they tapped the window.

The day of graduation from elementary school, Charlie was so excited when he came home that he almost broke my window. When I climbed out on the fire escape, he was there all dressed up in his blue suit with a tragic look on his face.

"I thought you were dead," he said. "Why didn't you come to school?"

"I was sick," I answered.

"You don't look sick now . . ."

"How was it?" I interrupted.

"You didn't get left back, did you?"

"Of course I didn't."

"You know what somebody said?" he continued. "They said your Mama couldn't afford to buy you a new suit."

"They were right."

"You mean you missed graduation because you didn't have a new suit?"

"Would you have gone if you didn't have one?"

THE MOUNTAIN **681**

Art Note

Quenton and Andre by Stephen Scott Young Young's watercolors display a tightly drawn realism and careful use of light and shadow. The artist often depicts young people, frequently the inhabitants of Florida and the Bahamas, engaged in the normal setting of their everyday routines.

Reading the Art *Judging from their expressions, what might the two children in the painting be doing or thinking?*

SUMMARY

The narrator, an African American, graduates from elementary school. He doesn't attend the graduation, however, because his white principal requires that everyone wear a blue suit, and the narrator's mother won't buy him one. His Sunday suit should be good enough, she says, and she won't buy a new suit just to please this white man. It won't make any difference anyway. "To him you'll always be a little colored boy," she tells him. "That man is up on a mountain, . . . but remember, you're as good as he is, new suit or no new suit." The narrator doesn't talk about this to Charlie, his best friend, but one day he and Charlie walk to Columbia University and take the subway home. During the ride, a woman accuses the boys of stealing her wallet, and a man offers to search them. The woman finds her wallet in her purse, but the experience has shamed and frightened the boys. Afterward, Charlie says that it would have been different if they had been dressed up. But the narrator thinks about what his mother had told him. "It wouldn't have made any difference," he says.

Thematic Link: *Jumping to Conclusions*
A woman makes false assumptions about the narrator and his friend because they are African Americans.

CUSTOMIZING FOR
Students Acquiring English

- Use **ACCESS FOR STUDENTS ACQUIRING ENGLISH**, *Reading Support.*
- After discussing the definition of stereotyped thinking in the Personal Connection section, ask students if stereotypes are ever applied to people of their own culture. Urge the class to be very sensitive to these comments and to consider the feelings of others as they read and discuss this story.

STRATEGIC READING FOR
Less-Proficient Readers

Set a Purpose Have students read to find out how the two boys in "The Mountain" react when they are falsely accused.

Use **UNIT FIVE RESOURCE BOOK**, p. 49, for guidance in reading the selection.

CUSTOMIZING FOR
Gifted and Talented Students

Invite students to discuss the importance of clothing—for instance, a new blue suit—as a symbol of wealth or status.

CUSTOMIZING FOR
Students Acquiring English

I Explain that the word "colored" is used in this story to describe someone of African descent. Point out that this story is set in New York City in 1943 and that this term is no longer used. Today the term "African American" is generally preferred, and the term "black" is sometimes acceptable.

Literary Concept: THEME

A Ask students to discuss what the narrator's mother might mean when she says "That man . . . is up there on a mountain, and he'll probably be up there all your life. . . ." (*Possible responses: The principal lives in a different world than he does; there will always be white people in the narrator's life who are going to look down upon him because he is an African American.*)

Critical Thinking: ANALYZING

B Have students discuss why the narrator's mother refuses to buy him a new suit so he can attend the graduation. (*Possible responses: She doesn't believe clothing is important; she wants to teach the boy to respect himself and not worry about the views of others.*)

CUSTOMIZING FOR
Multiple Learning Styles

C **Spatial or Graphic Learners** To help students picture the setting, invite them to sketch their impressions of the scene that the narrator and Charlie view from atop Morningside Park.

"Yeah," he answered, "I guess you're right. I probably wouldn't have . . . It's all that stupid Principal's fault. If he hadn't announced that everybody had to wear blue suits and all that, this wouldn't have happened . . ."

Then as an afterthought he added, "Couldn't your Mama afford to buy you a new suit?"

"I don't know," I replied. "I guess not."

But I really didn't know. We weren't any poorer than Charlie's family, and from the way Mama had explained it when I had asked her, I had been unable to figure out whether we could afford it or not.

She had said that the Sunday suit I had was good enough for anybody's graduation, and that if any of the other kids were getting new ones, she hoped it was because they needed them. When I tried to explain that it wasn't the other kids that I was thinking of, but my teachers, she looked at me real hard and said, "I *know* you don't want a new suit because the white man says so!"

"My principal says we should all . . ."

"Your principal, huh? A hundred boys sitting up there in blue suits may be the most important thing in the world to him, but it's not to me. If how you look is all that counts then maybe you'd better stay home."

"But Mama, I can't stay home," I cried.

"Then go in what you got!"

I stared at her, unable to believe this lack of understanding, then turned and walked away.

I was sitting at the fire escape window indulging in a fantasy of how I would kill myself and she would have to buy the new suit to bury me in, when I felt her come up behind me.

"Look here," she said, "I want to talk to you." I dragged myself around, and saw her standing there, wiping her hands in her apron.

"Honey," she began softly, "a new suit isn't going to change you as far as the white man is concerned. To him you'll still be a little colored boy . . ."

682   UNIT FIVE   PART 2: JUMPING TO CONCLUSIONS

"That man," she continued looking off out of the window, "is up there on a mountain, and he'll probably be up there all your life . . . but remember, you're as good as he is, new suit or no new suit."

Tears began to run down my cheeks, but I gave no sign of even noticing them. She didn't understand me, my own mother. Here she was talking about mountains, and all I wanted was a new suit.

"Did you hear what I said?"

The tears came faster, and finally unable to ignore them, I wiped my shirtsleeve across my face, and blurted out, "All I want is a new suit!" Just then, the door opened and daddy came in. When Mama turned around, I ran off.

I didn't tell Charlie any of this that day on the fire escape, and it wasn't until August that I realized what she meant. In August, Charlie and I decided to visit Columbia University. We planned the trip one day in advance, and the following morning arose very early and set out through Morningside Park, which separated the valley where we lived, from the area where the University lay. The park, a two-block-wide strip of trees, grass, rocks, and sand, rose steeply from Morningside Avenue to Morningside Heights. Its many planned paths and beaten trails having long since given up their secrets to us, we crossed it rapidly, pausing only twice. Once to cautiously inspect a man who was lying in the bushes; we thought we had accidentally stumbled onto a murder, but it turned out he was a drunk. And the other time to throw stones at two dogs. . . .

At the top, we rested in an oval from where we could look out over the whole of Harlem. It was bunched up it seemed, between Central Park and the Yankee Stadium, its old buildings spilling almost into the East River with cars and people filling the remaining spaces like black lava. We tried to count all the parked cars we could see but, after reaching two hundred, we tired, turned, and headed toward the University.

Mini-Lesson Grammar

APPOSITIVES Point out to students that an appositive is a noun or pronoun that usually follows another noun and identifies or explains it. There are two kinds of appositives—essential and nonessential. A nonessential appositive adds extra meaning to a sentence that is already complete and is set off by commas. An essential appositive makes the main idea of a sentence complete. An appositive phrase consists of an appositive and its modifiers.

Application Point to the passage on page 682, and have students find the appositive phrase. (*a two-block-wide strip of trees, grass, rocks, and sand*) Then ask students to find the appositives below and label them as essential or nonessential.

1. Columbia University, *the college on the hill,* has an impressive campus. (*nonessential*)
2. My friend *Charlie* lives next door. (*essential*)

Reteaching/Reinforcement
- *Grammar Handbook,* anthology p. 940
- *Grammar Mini-Lessons* transparencies pp. 2, 41, copymasters p. 3

📖 **The Writer's Craft**
The Appositive Phrase pp. 693–695, 775–776

Subway Passengers (1966), Richard Estes. Copyright © Richard Estes/Marlborough Gallery.

We found ourselves in another world. The buildings were tall and immaculate,[1] their polished brass fronts opening onto glistening tile floors which beckoned towards cool dark opulent[2] depths. Awnings everywhere. And the streets were large and clean, the white granite faces of the buildings meeting the sidewalks in a line unbroken from corner to corner. After two blocks, we came to a sprawling group of buildings and Charlie said, "This must be it."

We stood, two small dark boys, before the Taj Mahal, before the Parthenon, and the Sphinx of Egypt.[3] We stood, two small dark boys, before the reality of our dreams. There were steps of stone that ran for almost a block, with lions, one at either end, from which a king might speak. And red bricks where girls in veils could dance before a great feast. And a pool. And tennis courts. And flagstone walks, that led through gardens with benches hewed from stone by slaves. We climbed the stairs, stood before the doors, and read the inscription carved there in the stone: "The Low Library, Columbia University."

Then we continued westward to the Hudson River and south along Riverside Drive, finding ourselves by four in the afternoon in Columbus Circle. With our last bit of change we paid our subway fare for the ride home. The trains were

---

1. **immaculate:** perfectly clean; spotless.
2. **opulent:** showing wealth and luxury.
3. **Taj Mahal ... Sphinx of Egypt:** well-known examples of magnificent and historically significant structures.

THE MOUNTAIN **683**

Art Note

Subway Passengers by Richard Estes
Many of Richard Estes's (1936–) works can be considered group portraits, in which the specific details of each figure help to convey his or her personality. In this work, the passengers on the train are revealed through their body postures, expressions, dress, and the belongings they hold.

Reading the Art *What do you think is the mood of this painting? Why?*

Linking to History

D Columbia University was founded in 1754 as King's College and in 1770 became the first institution in North America to offer a degree in medicine. Today it has more than 6,000 faculty members and 20,000 students. In 1968, Columbia became the site of large protests during which several buildings were seized by students and community activists. More than 700 people were arrested. Although Vietnam-era antimilitary issues were also involved, the immediate cause was Columbia's plan to build a gym on land in Morningside Park. Many Harlem residents opposed the gym, claiming that a neighborhood park should not be used for a facility that would primarily benefit Columbia students and faculty. Eventually, the university changed its plans and the new gymnasium was built on campus grounds instead.

Critical Thinking:
MAKING INFERENCES

E Ask students why the two boys might be so impressed by Columbia University. *(Possible response: The immaculate campus provided a striking contrast to the surrounding neighborhood, which was inhabited by unconscious drunks and wild dogs.)*

Mini-Lesson The Writer's Style

USING SENTENCE FRAGMENTS FOR EFFECT Remind students that a sentence fragment is a group of words that does not express a complete thought. The subject maybe left out or the verb omitted. Occasionally, however, a professional writer may consciously choose to use fragments to create realistic dialogue, establish a certain mood, or achieve a particular rhythm in their prose.

Application Have students look through the selection and note the author's purposeful use of sentence fragments. *(some examples: p. 683: "Awnings everywhere"; p. 684: "The surrounding bodies moving away from us.")* Have them discuss the effect these usages have on the story. Then ask them to write a paragraph in which they use one or two sentence fragments for effect.

Reteaching/Reinforcement

The Writer's Craft
What Is a Sentence Fragment? pp. 525–527

THE LANGUAGE OF LITERATURE **TEACHER'S EDITION 683**

Literary Concept: CONFLICT

F Ask students to describe what the narrator is feeling in this passage. *(Possible responses: The narrator is hurt and angry that he and his friend have been wrongly accused of stealing. He knows that they were accused because they are African Americans.)*

Literary Concept: THEME

G Ask students whether the woman on the train still would have thought the boys had robbed her if the boys had been wearing suits. *(Possible response: It wouldn't have made any difference, because the woman, as well as the man, already had preconceived notions about the boys because of their race.)*

STRATEGIC READING FOR
Less-Proficient Readers

H Have students describe the reaction of the two boys to the woman's accusation. *(At first they feel shame and humiliation; then the narrator becomes angry.)* **Clarifying**

COMPREHENSION CHECK

1. Why doesn't the narrator attend his graduation ceremony? *(The principal says everyone must wear a blue suit, and the narrator's mother won't buy him one.)*

2. Why won't the narrator's mother buy him a new suit? *(Possible response: He is just as good as the principal, regardless of what he is wearing.)*

3. What are the two boys accused of doing by the woman in the subway train? *(stealing her wallet)*

4. With what statement by Charlie does the narrator disagree after the subway incident? *(that they were accused of theft because of the way they were dressed)*

EDITOR'S NOTE With the permission of the author, potentially offensive material has been deleted from the selection.

---

crowded, and Charlie and I were pressed up against the doors hardly able to breathe as the express left 59th Street. We were grinning at each other, our day having been filled with wonders that only we two shared, when the lady in front of me suddenly looked down, saw that her purse was open, fumbled around inside it for a moment, then turned to me and said, "Little boy, give me back my wallet!" All noises ceased. All except the roar of the fans. "Little boy, *please* give me back my wallet!" All pressures ceased. The surrounding bodies moving away from us. All except the pressure of shame and humiliation that came with her words. I finally replied, "I haven't got your wallet, Miss."

The train rushed on towards 125th Street. A man pushed his way to the front of the crowd. The woman repeated her plea. And Charlie and I stood, our hands locked together, their perspiration forming a bond that was our only salvation.

It takes seven minutes for the express to travel between 59th Street and 125th Street. After five of those minutes, the man offered to search us. The woman, busily searching her purse, either did not hear him or did not care to commit herself. Seconds later, she found her wallet—in her purse.

She apologized. And the man, feeling perhaps even more ashamed, reached into his pocket, brought out a half dollar, and tried to press it into Charlie's hand. Water reached the crotch of Charlie's trousers, chose the left leg, coursed its way down his thigh, across his knee, into his socks, over his shoe, and puddled at its tip. And my shame gave way to anger as it grew in size. I raised my head, looking directly at no one, but into the crowd and said, "No thank you mister. No thank you."

That evening we met on the fire escape. We passed things to each other for a while and then Charlie said, "Some trip today, huh?" I was staring off towards the park and didn't answer. "Yeah," he continued, "that was some trip . . . You know what? I bet if we had been dressed up, I bet that woman wouldn't have thought we robbed her."

"Yes she would have, too," I replied. "It wouldn't have made any difference."

"How do you know it wouldn't have made any difference?" I almost told him what Mama had said, but changed my mind.

"I just do, that's all. I just do."

We stood looking at each other; I'm sure he knew what I meant. Then two cats began fighting in the backyard, we turned to watch, and night fell. ❖

684   UNIT FIVE   PART 2: JUMPING TO CONCLUSIONS

Mini-Lesson   Literary Concepts

REVIEWING CONFLICT Remind students that the plot of a story always involves some sort of conflict or struggle between opposing forces. An external conflict involves a character pitted against an outside force such as nature, a physical obstacle, or another character. An internal conflict is one that occurs within a character.

Application Draw the chart at right on the chalkboard and have students copy it into their notebooks. Then ask students to review the story to identify the different conflicts that occur in the selection. Have them identify the conflicts as external or internal and list them in the appropriate side of their charts. Students should then compare their lists and discuss the ways in which these conflicts form the basis of the story's plot.

Conflicts	
Internal	**External**

684   THE LANGUAGE OF LITERATURE   TEACHER'S EDITION

INSIGHT

THE POCKETBOOK GAME
ALICE CHILDRESS

Marge . . . day's work is an education! Well, I mean workin' in different homes you learn much more than if you was steady in one place. . . . I tell you, it really keeps your mind sharp tryin' to watch for what folks will put over on you.

What? . . . No, Marge, I do not want to help shell no beans, but I'd be more than glad to stay and have supper with you, and I'll wash the dishes after. Is that all right? . . .

Who put anything over on who? . . . Oh yes! It's like this. . . . I been working for Mrs. E . . . one day a week for several months, and I notice that she has some peculiar ways. Well, there was only one thing that really bothered me, and that was her pocketbook habit. . . . No, not those little novels. . . . I mean her purse—her handbag.

Marge, she's got a big old pocketbook with two long straps on it . . . and whenever I'd go there, she'd be propped up in a chair with her handbag double wrapped tight around her wrist, and from room to room she'd roam with that purse hugged to her bosom. . . . Yes, girl! This happens every time! No, there's *nobody* there but me and her. . . . Marge, I couldn't say nothin' to her! It's her purse, ain't it? She can hold onto it if she wants to!

I held my peace for months, tryin' to figure out how I'd make my point. . . . Well, bless Bess! *Today was the day!* . . . Please, Marge, keep shellin' the beans so we can eat! I know you're listenin', but you listen with your ears, not your hands. . . . Well, anyway, I was almost ready to go home when she steps in the room hangin' onto her bag as usual and says, "Mildred, will you ask the super¹ to come up and fix the kitchen faucet?" "Yes, Mrs. E . . . ," I says, "as soon as I leave." "Oh, no," she says, "he may be gone by then. Please go now." "All right," I says, and out the door I went, still wearin' my Hoover apron.²

I just went down the hall and stood there a few minutes . . . and then I rushed back to the door and knocked on it as hard and frantic as I could. She flung open the door sayin', "What's the matter? Did you see the super?" . . . "No," I says, gaspin' hard for breath, "I was almost downstairs when I remembered . . . *I left my pocketbook!*"

With that I dashed in, grabbed my purse and then went down to get the super! Later, when I was leavin', she says real timid-like, "Mildred, I hope that you don't think I distrust you because . . ." I cut her off real quick. . . . "That's all right, Mrs. E . . . , I understand. 'Cause if I paid anybody as little as you pay me, I'd hold my pocketbook too!"

Marge, you fool . . . look out! . . . You gonna drop the beans on the floor!

---
1. **super:** building superintendent, or janitor.
2. **Hoover apron:** a reversible apron.

Multicultural Perspectives

The area of New York City known as Harlem was established as the village of Nieuw Haarlem by the Dutch governor Peter Stuyvesant in 1658. By the 1880s it had become a popular residential center; after the turn of the century it was populated largely by African Americans. During the period between World Wars I and II, Harlem was home to the Harlem Renaissance. This literary and intellectual movement saw the creation of an extraordinary body of work by African-American artists, writers, and musicians. Writers associated with the Renaissance include the novelists James Weldon Johnson and Zora Neale Hurston and the poets Countee Cullen, Langston Hughes, and Claude McKay. The Renaissance was brought to an end by the Great Depression, when many writers and artists were forced to leave the area in search of employment.

From Personal Response to Critical Analysis

1. Accept all reasonable responses.
2. Possible response: Some students will say that it brought home the mother's message that African Americans can't change the stereotyped views some whites hold of them.
3. Possible responses: They are pessimistic because they portray white attitudes as immutable; they are optimistic because they encourage the boy to maintain a positive sense of his own self-worth.
4. Accept all reasonable, well-supported responses.
5. Possible responses: dreams of the future; the "mountain" inhabited by white people; education; a fantasy-like world of majestic buildings
6. Accept all reasonable responses.
7. Possible responses: anger, fear, sadness, outrage, shame

Another Pathway

Cooperative Learning Assign an encourager of participation to facilitate idea-sharing, a turn-taking monitor to maintain order during the debate, and two criticizers of ideas to examine the positions of the students representing the characters.

Rubric

3 Full Accomplishment Students present clear arguments for their positions presented from the point of view of the two characters.

2 Substantial Accomplishment Students present clear arguments but may have difficulty speaking from the point of view of the characters.

1 Little or Partial Accomplishment Students have difficulty presenting a clear argument or speaking from the points of view of the characters.

RESPONDING
OPTIONS

FROM PERSONAL RESPONSE TO CRITICAL ANALYSIS

REFLECT 1. What thoughts and feelings did this story stir in you? Describe your reaction in your notebook.

RETHINK 2. How did the incident on the train help the narrator understand what his mother was trying to tell him about a new suit?

3. Do you think the mother's words to the boy were pessimistic or optimistic? Explain.

Close Textual Reading
4. Is the mother right in not buying her son a new suit for graduation? Explain your response.

Consider
- the importance of the occasion and the boy's desire to fit in
- what the mother is trying to teach her son
- whether or not you think appearances matter

5. What do you think Columbia University represents to the two boys?

RELATE 6. On the chart of sterotypes that you created for the Personal Connection (page 680), did you list the stereotype exposed in both "The Mountain" and the Insight selection "The Pocketbook Game"? Explain whether you think this stereotype is still widespread today.

Thematic Link

7. Imagine yourself in the place of one of the boys on the train. How would you have felt when the woman accused you of taking her wallet? What would you have done? Act out the scene in pantomime.

CRITIC'S CORNER

Student board member Michael Little liked how the author "kept the story short and to the point," but he was bothered by the ending. "It just seemed to come to a halt. I think there should have been a better-defined end to the story." Do you agree? What happens at the end? What has changed? Why do you think that there is no dramatic event at the end?

686 UNIT FIVE PART 2: JUMPING TO CONCLUSIONS

Multimodal Learning

ANOTHER PATHWAY

Cooperative Learning

Get together in a small group to discuss why the principal wants the students to have new suits and why the mother refuses to buy one. Then stage a debate between the mother and the principal on this question. As part of her argument, the mother should describe her son's experience on the subway train.

QUICKWRITES

1. A proverb is a short saying that expresses some basic truth or practical wisdom. "The apple doesn't fall far from the tree" is a proverb. Write a **proverb** that expresses some basic truth about prejudice or stereotyping.

2. Review the incident you described in your notebook for the Writing Connection. Then draft a **personal narrative** about a time when you witnessed prejudice in action—perhaps when you first recognized its existence or its destructiveness. If you have access to a computer, use it to input your draft so that the draft will be easier to revise later on.

📁 **PORTFOLIO** *Save your writing. You may want to use it later as a springboard to a piece for your portfolio.*

Critic's Corner

Some students will agree saying that they would have preferred a more dramatic ending instead of the two boys discussing the day's events; others will disagree and maintain that the ending provides sufficient resolution—the discussion illustrates the insight the narrator has gained into the meaning of the words spoken earlier by his mother.

QuickWrites

1. Discuss the meanings of the sample proverbs below with students.
   A friend in need is a friend indeed.
   A bird in hand is worth two in the bush.
   Then, point out the use of internal rhyme, contrast, and metaphor in the proverbs and suggest that students experiment with these devices.

2. Encourage students to include the feelings they experienced at the time of the incident.

Personal Narrative, pp. 86–101

LITERARY CONCEPTS

As you recall, the **theme** of a story is the main idea the writer wishes to share with the reader. It may be a lesson about life or a belief about people and their actions. To identify the theme in this story, use these strategies:
- Think about the title of the selection. Does its meaning lead you to the main idea of the story?
- Review what happens to the narrator. How does he change during the story? What does he learn about life? State the theme of this story in one or two sentences.

CONCEPT REVIEW: Metaphor As you know, a metaphor compares two unlike things. The mother in this story says that the white man "is up there on a mountain." Since there is no actual mountain in the story, what does she mean? When the two boys reach Columbia University, the narrator says they stood "before the Taj Mahal, before the Parthenon, and the Sphinx of Egypt." What does he mean by these metaphors?

THE WRITER'S STYLE

Sometimes readers are impatient with descriptive passages, but in good writing, description appears only because it is needed. Look at the two paragraphs describing the Columbia University campus, where the boys find themselves "in another world." Note the descriptive details—and the contrast with what was described in the preceding two paragraphs. How does all this description strengthen the theme of the story?

ACROSS THE CURRICULUM

Geography Based on city maps you can find in the library, sketch a map of New York City and indicate the location of Manhattan, Harlem, Morningside Park, Morningside Heights, Columbia University, Central Park, Yankee Stadium, the East River, and the Hudson River.

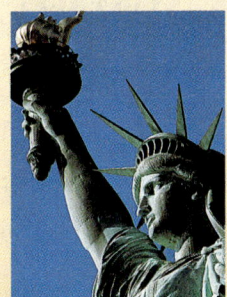

Multimodal Learning
ALTERNATIVE ACTIVITIES

1. Write a **rap song** or a **folk song** that expresses the theme of "The Mountain." Perform the song for your class.
2. With a partner, practice and present a **reading** of "The Pocketbook Game." Your partner can pantomime Marge's part.

MARTIN J. HAMER

1931–

Martin J. Hamer grew up in Harlem. While studying psychology at the City College of New York, he worked as an electro-mechanical designer. His short stories have appeared in *The Atlantic* and other magazines and in anthologies, including *Brothers and Sisters: Modern Stories by Black Americans*. Hamer's short story "Sarah" was published in *The Best Short Stories of 1965*, and his poetry has appeared in *Negro Digest*. Along with his wife, Hamer has been investigating African-American literary traditions—in particular, America's black women writers. **OTHER WORKS** Editor, with Judith A. Hamer, of *Centers of the Self: Stories by Black American Women, from the Nineteenth Century to the Present*

Extended Reading

THE MOUNTAIN **687**

Literary Concepts

Encourage students to brainstorm major thematic elements of the story in groups if they are unable to complete the task on their own. Some students may say that the theme of the story is the obstacle of white stereotyping, represented by the mountain, that African Americans must deal with. Others may say that the theme involves a young boy's growing understanding of important values and the difficulties of dealing with the white world.

Metaphor The mother may mean that white people consider themselves superior to African Americans or that they live in a very different world. In reference to Columbia University, the narrator may be implying that despite the institution's geographic proximity to Harlem, it symbolizes something distant, dreamlike, even mythical to the two boys.

Across the Curriculum

Geography *Cooperative Learning* Students can form a group to turn their maps into a gigantic mural of northern Manhattan.

ADDITIONAL SUGGESTIONS

Math In the story, it takes the express train seven minutes to travel from 59th street to 125th street. Ask students to calculate how long it would take the train to reach the 181st Street stop if it continued to travel at the same rate of speed per block.

Alternative Activities

1. Suggest that students consider including ways to overcome one's stereotypical attitudes in their songs.
2. Encourage students to tape their practice readings of "The Pocketbook Game." They can listen to the tapes to get ideas about how to improve their readings.

The Writer's Style

Some students may say that the details contrasting the opulent Columbia campus with the narrator's crowded and dilapidated neighborhood strengthen the theme of the separation between the narrator and the seemingly distant world of the university.

For more practice in descriptive detail, see

Focused Description, pp. 58–65

THE LANGUAGE OF LITERATURE TEACHER'S EDITION **687**

OVERVIEW

Objectives

- To understand and appreciate a short story that explores prejudice in its obvious and subtle forms
- To appreciate and understand setting
- To appreciate and understand characterization
- To express understanding of the selection through a choice of writing forms, including a character sketch and an essay
- To extend understanding of the selection through a variety of multimodal and cross-curricular activities

Skills

LITERARY CONCEPTS
- Setting
- Dialogue

THE WRITER'S STYLE
- Point of view: first person

GRAMMAR
- Troublesome modifiers: *good* and *well*

SPEAKING, LISTENING, AND VIEWING
- Oral history
- Group discussion
- Oral presentation

ALTERNATIVE

Previewing

Students can choose partners and use the following prompts to preview "Everybody Knows Tobie."

Personal Connection

Discussion Prompts *Think of ways that prejudice is evident in society, in your community, or in your school. In as much detail as possible, describe it to your partner. Then listen as your partner describes his or her examples of prejudice in those places. If you need help getting started, the following questions might help:*

- *Has the prejudice existed for a long time?*
- *Does the prejudice come as much from young people as from older people?*
- *Is this prejudice something everyone is aware of or do you feel you are the only one or one of the few who realize it?*

PREVIEWING

FICTION

Everybody Knows Tobie
Daniel Garza

Activating Prior Knowledge
PERSONAL CONNECTION

The story you are about to read focuses on the interactions between people of different cultural backgrounds. These interactions involve prejudice—some of it openly expressed and some so subtle that it is hard to identify. In your notebook, list ways prejudice is exhibited in society, in your community, or in your school. Then share your list with a partner. As you read, look for the different ways prejudice is shown in this story.

Building Background
CULTURAL CONNECTION

This story takes place in a small farming town in northern Texas. In this town, migrant workers—traveling laborers—are hired for a short time every fall to help harvest cotton. The use of migrant labor is common on large farms in the United States. Many migrant workers receive low wages and endure poor working and living conditions because they are not protected by federal labor laws. Since their work is seasonal, they often do not live in a place long enough to gain acceptance as part of the community.

Active Reading/Setting a Purpose
READING CONNECTION

Recognizing Connotations of Words
A word can have one or more exact meanings, or **denotations.** However, beyond its dictionary definition, a word can have a **connotation**—the feeling or idea that comes to be associated with the word over time. For example, for most people, the noun *smell* has a negative connotation, but *aroma* has a positive connotation. Connotations can reveal a great deal about people's attitudes and beliefs—especially their prejudices. As you read this story, watch for words that suggest positive or negative feelings toward a character or a group. In your notebook, jot down a few of these words on a chart similar to the one shown.

Words with Positive Connotations	Words with Negative Connotations

688   UNIT FIVE   PART 2: JUMPING TO CONCLUSIONS

PRINT AND MEDIA RESOURCES

UNIT FIVE RESOURCE BOOK
Strategic Reading: Literature, p. 53

GRAMMAR MINI-LESSONS
Copymasters, p. 27

WRITING MINI-LESSONS
Transparencies, p. 55

ACCESS FOR STUDENTS ACQUIRING ENGLISH
Selection Summaries
Reading Support

FORMAL ASSESSMENT
Selection Test, pp. 123–124
 Test Generator

AUDIO LIBRARY
See Reference Card

---

688   THE LANGUAGE OF LITERATURE   **TEACHER'S EDITION**

Everybody Knows Tobie

DANIEL GARZA

SUMMARY

Joey's older brother Tobie delivers newspapers to white people in town. Unlike most Chicanos in this north Texas town, Tobie is so popular with the whites that he can get a haircut from one of their barbers, Mr. Brewer. Joey, the narrator, admires his older brother and wants, like Tobie, to have the approval of the whites. Encouraged by Tobie, Joey goes to Mr. Brewer for a haircut. Before Joey has a chance to identify himself as Tobie's brother, however, Mr. Brewer sends him away, mistaking him for just another migrant Chicano from South Texas. Hurt and humiliated, Joey tries to get a haircut from the Chicano barber, but Mr. Lopez is too busy to take him. Joey goes away feeling rejected by the entire world. Outside the barber shop, he experiences yet another rejection: one of the migrant Chicanos starts a conversation but loses interest when he learns that Joey is a permanent town resident. Later, Joey takes over Tobie's route, and soon the white people accept him, too. Delivering newspapers to the businessmen has given him a place among them, "because of the fact that everybody in my town knew Tobie."

Thematic Link: *Jumping to Conclusions*
A young Chicano boy experiences pain after an encounter with the prejudicial assumptions of his small Texas town.

CUSTOMIZING FOR
Students Acquiring English

- Use **ACCESS FOR STUDENTS ACQUIRING ENGLISH,** *Reading Support.*
- If there are Spanish speakers in your class, ask them to explain the Spanish terms they use to refer to themselves and to those of other ethnic groups. Compare these with those mentioned in the story and explained in the footnotes.

STRATEGIC READING FOR
Less-Proficient Readers

To help immerse students in the selection, ask them if they have ever had an unfair, negative assumption made about them because of their race, sex, or appearance.

Set a Purpose Have students pay close attention to the selection's depiction of Joey's and the gringos' attitudes towards the migrant workers.

Use **UNIT FIVE RESOURCE BOOK**, p. 55, for guidance in reading the selection.

CUSTOMIZING FOR
Gifted and Talented Students

Interested students may wish to research the position of migrant farm workers in the Texan or Californian economies. Have them consider the question: If Chicanos were unwelcome in some communities, why were they still employed—even depended upon—in such tremendous numbers?

Literary Concept: SETTING

A Ask students where the story takes place and have them point out details that tell them. *(The story is set in a small town in rural north Texas. Details include references to the cotton harvest and the phrase "little town.")*

Critical Thinking: SUMMARIZING

B Have students tell what they have learned so far about characters, town attitudes, and possible conflicts in the story. *(Possible response: Tobie is well-liked by everyone; the narrator considers Tobie to be lucky insofar as his newspaper route goes; the gringo barbers are prejudiced against the Chicanos; conflicts may involve the gringos and the Chicanos.)*

CUSTOMIZING FOR
Students Acquiring English

Explain that a *flattop* is a kind of haircut that was popular in the 1950s. Use of this term provides a clue that the story takes place during that time.

When I was thirteen years old, my older brother, Tobie, had the town newspaper route. Everyone in the town knew him well because he had been delivering their papers for a year and a half. Tobie used to tell me that he had the best route of all because his customers would pay promptly each month, and sometimes, he used to brag that the nice people of the town would tip him a quarter or maybe fifty cents at the end of the month because he would trudge up many stairs to deliver the paper personally.

The other newspaper boys were not as lucky as Tobie because sometimes their customers would not be at home when they went by to collect payment for that month's newspaper, or maybe at the end of the month the customers would just try to avoid the paper boys to keep from paying.

Yes, Tobie had it good. The biggest advantage, I thought, that Tobie had over all the newspaper boys was that he knew the gringos[1] of the town so well that he could go into a gringo barbershop and get a haircut without having the barber tell him to go to the Mexican barber in our town or maybe just embarrassing him in front of all the gringo customers in the shop as they often did when Chicano[2] cotton pickers came into their places during the fall months.

The gringo barbers of my town were careful whom they allowed in their shops during the cotton harvest season in the fall. September and October and cotton brought Chicanos from the south to the north of Texas where I lived, and where the cotton was sometimes plentiful and sometimes scarce. Chicanos is what we say in our language, and it is slang among our people. It means the Mexicans of Texas. These Chicano cotton pickers came from the Rio Grande Valley in South Texas, and sometimes, even people from Mexico made the trip to the north of Texas. All these Chicanos came to my little town in which many gringos lived, and a few of us who spoke both English and Spanish.

When the Chicanos came to my town on Saturdays after working frightfully in the cotton fields all week, they would go to the town market for food, and the fathers would buy candy and ice cream for their flocks of little black-headed ones. The younger ones, the *jovenes*,[3] would go to the local movie house. And then maybe those who had never been to the north of Texas before would go to the gringos' barbershops for haircuts not knowing that they would be refused. The gringo barbers would be very careful not to let them come too close to their shops because the regular gringo customers would get mad, and sometimes they would curse the Chicanos.

"Hell, it's them damn pepper bellies again. Can't seem to get rid of 'em in the fall," the prejudiced gringos of my town would say. Some of the nicer people would only become uneasy at seeing so many Chicanos with long, black, greasy hair wanting haircuts.

The barbers of the town liked Tobie, and they invited him to their shops for haircuts. Tobie said that the barbers told him that they would cut his hair because he did not belong to that group of people who came from the south of Texas. Tobie understood. And he did not argue with the barbers because he knew how Chicanos from South Texas were, and how maybe gringo scissors would get all greasy from cutting their hair.

During that fall Tobie encouraged me to go to the gringo's place for a haircut. "Joey, when are you going to get rid of that mop of hair," he asked.

"I guess I'll get rid of it when Mr. Lopez learns how to cut flat-tops."

"Golly, Joey, Mr. Lopez is a good ole guy and all that, but if he doesn't know how to give flat-tops, then you should go to some other barber for flat-tops. Really, Kid-brother, that hair looks awful."

---

1. **gringos** (grĭng′gōs): an offensive slang word, used principally in Latin America, to refer to foreign or English-speaking persons.
2. **Chicano** (chĭ-kä′nō): Mexican-American.
3. **jovenes** (hô′vĕ-nĕs) *Spanish.*

690   UNIT FIVE   PART 2: JUMPING TO CONCLUSIONS

Mini-Lesson Grammar

TROUBLESOME MODIFIERS: GOOD AND WELL Remind students that the words *good* and *well* are commonly misused. *Good* is always an adjective ("a *good* haircut," "this haircut is *good*"). *Well* generally functions as an adverb ("his route is planned *well*"), but *good* often appears erroneously in its place.

Well can be a predicate adjective referring to good health ("he feels *well*"). When *good* is a predicate adjective with the verb *feel*, it refers solely to happiness or comfort, not to health ("Tobie's brother felt *good* when he was accepted").

Application Point out the use of *well* in the section on page 690. Then ask students to write sentences that correctly use *good* and *well* in the four ways just shown.

Reteaching/Reinforcement
• *Grammar Mini-Lessons* copymasters p. 27

The Writer's Craft

Good and *Well*, p. 640

690   THE LANGUAGE OF LITERATURE   TEACHER'S EDITION

"Yeah, but I'm afraid."

"Afraid of what?" Tobie asked.

"I'm afraid the barber will mistake me for one of those guys from South Texas and run me out of his shop."

"Oh, forget it," Tobie said. "Mr. Brewer . . . you know, the barber who cuts my hair . . . is a nice man, and he'll cut your hair. Just tell him you're my kid-brother."

I thought about this new adventure for several days, and then on a Saturday, when there was no school, I decided on the haircut at Mr. Brewer's. I hurriedly rode my bike to town and parked it in the alley close to the barbershop. As I walked into the shop, I noticed that all of a sudden the gringos inside stopped their conversation and looked at me. The shop was silent for a moment. I thought then that maybe this was not too good and that I should leave. I remembered what Tobie had told me about being his brother, and about Mr. Brewer being a nice man. I was convinced that I belonged in the gringo barbershop.

I found an empty chair and sat down to wait my turn for a haircut. One gringo customer sitting next to me rose and explained to the barber that he had to go to the courthouse for something. Another customer left without saying anything. And then one, who was dressed in dirty coveralls and a faded khaki shirt, got up from Mr. Brewer's chair and said to him, "Say, Tom, looks like you got yourself a little tamale to clip."

Mr. Brewer smiled only.

My turn was next, and I was afraid. But I remembered again that this was all right because I was Tobie's brother, and everybody liked Tobie. I went to Mr. Brewer's chair. As I started to sit down, he looked at me and smiled a nice smile.

He said, "I'm sorry, Sonny, but I can't cut your hair. You go to Mr. Lopez's. He'll cut your hair."

Mr. Brewer took me to the door and pointed the way to Lopez's barbershop. He pointed with his finger and said, "See, over there behind that service station. That's his place. You go there. He'll clip your hair."

Tears were welling in my eyes. I felt a lump in my throat. I was too choked up to tell him I was Tobie's brother, and that it was all right to cut my hair. I only looked at him as he finished giving directions. He smiled again and patted me on the back. As I left, Mr. Brewer said, "Say hello to Mr. Lopez for me, will you, Sonny?"

I did not turn back to look at Mr. Brewer. I kept my head bowed as I walked to Mr. Lopez's because tears filled my eyes, and these tears were tears of hurt to the pride and confidence which I had slowly gained in my gringo town.

Copyright © Claudia de Teresa.

EVERYBODY KNOWS TOBIE 691

Mini-Lesson Study Skills

TAKING OBJECTIVE TESTS: ANTONYMS

In the sections of a standardized test dealing with antonyms, students are given a word and asked to choose the answer that means the opposite of that word. If they don't immediately recognize the antonym among the answer choices, one technique students can use to find the answer is to make opposites for each option. They can then look to see which of the opposites they have created is closest to the definition of the original word. For example:

1. exhilarating
   a. diligent — lazy
   b. increasing — decreasing
   c. fatiguing — energy-giving
   d. impatient — patient
   e. intricate — simple

Because *energy-giving* is closest in meaning to *exhilarating*, *fatiguing* would be the correct antonym.

Application Ask students to make their own opposites for the following words from the selection: *experienced, astonishment, unconcerned, curious*.

Linking to Social Studies

F Migrant workers move from region to region, often across national borders, to find work on a temporary basis. Migrant work tends to be primarily agricultural, due to the great demand for labor during the harvest season. In the United States, however, the use of migrant labor has been on the decline due to the increasingly mechanized nature of modern agriculture. Almost 95 percent of the cotton in the United States, for example, is harvested mechanically. Today, fewer than 500,000 migrant workers are employed in the United States, down from more than 2 million in the 1920s.

Critical Thinking: DRAWING CONCLUSIONS

G Ask students how they think Joey feels at this point in the story. (Possible responses: He feels mixed up and confused because the gringos do not accept him; he thinks their ill will should be directed at other people rather than at him.)

Critical Thinking: HYPOTHESIZING

H Ask students why they think the Chicanos waiting in the barbershop begin to whisper to each other. (Possible responses: They realize that Joey has been sent away by Mr. Brewer; they can tell by Joey's statement that he is a town resident and not a fellow migrant worker.)

Literary Concept: DIALOGUE

I Ask students why they think the author wrote some dialogue here in Spanish. (Possible responses: It gives a sense of Joey moving back and forth between cultures; it helps contrast the desire of Joey to "belong to one race" with the multiethnic nature of his actual existence.)

I thought of many things as I walked slowly. Maybe this was a foolish thing which I had done. There were too many gringos in the town, and too few of us who lived there all the year long. This was a bad thing because the gringos had the right to say yes or no, and we could only follow what they said. It was useless to go against them. It was foolish. But I was different from the Chicanos who came from the south, much different. I did live in the town the ten months of the year when the other Chicanos were in the south or in Mexico. Then I remembered what the barber had told my brother about the South Texas people, and why the gringo customers had left while I was in Mr. Brewer's shop. I began to understand. But it was very hard for me to realize that even though I had lived among gringos all of my life that I still had to go to my own people for such things as haircuts. Why wouldn't gringos cut my hair? I was clean. My hair was not long and greasy.

I walked into Mr. Lopez's shop. There were many Chicanos sitting in the chairs and even on the floor waiting their turn for a haircut. Mr. Lopez paused from his work as he saw me enter and said, "Sorry, Joey, full up. Come back in a couple of hours."

I shrugged my shoulders and said O.K. As I started to leave I remembered what Mr. Brewer had told me to say to Mr. Lopez. "Mr. Lopez," I said, and all the Chicanos, the ones who were waiting, turned and looked at me with curious eyes. "Mr. Brewer told me to tell you hello."

Mr. Lopez shook his head approvingly, not digesting the content of my statement. The Chicanos looked at me again and began to whisper among themselves. I did not hear, but I understood.

I told Mr. Lopez that I would return later in the day, but I did not because there would be other Chicanos wanting haircuts on Saturday. I could come during the week when he had more time, and when all the Chicanos would be in the fields working.

I went away feeling rejected both by the gringos and even my people, the entire world I knew.

Back in the alley where my bike was parked I sat on the curb for a long while thinking how maybe I did not fit into this town. Maybe my place was in the south of Texas where there were many of my kind of people, and where there were more Chicano barbershops and less gringo barbers. Yes, I thought, I needed a land where I could belong to one race. I was so concerned with myself that I did not notice a Chicano, a middle-aged man dressed in a new chambray shirt and faded denim pants, studying me.

He asked, "*¿Qué pasó, Chamaco?*"⁴

"*Nada,*"⁵ I answered.

"Maybe the cotton has not been good for you this year."

"No, Señor. I live here in the town."

> I went away feeling rejected both by the gringos and even my people, the entire world I knew.

---

4. *¿Qué pasó, Chamaco?* (kĕ pä-sô′ chä-mäˊkô) Spanish: What happened, boy?
5. *Nada* (näˊdä) Spanish: Nothing.

692 UNIT FIVE PART 2: JUMPING TO CONCLUSIONS

Multicultural Perspectives

Cesar Chavez (1927–1993) organized the National Farm Workers Association in 1962 to combat prejudice and to improve the standard of living of his fellow migrant workers. Chavez knew the difficulties of migrant life firsthand, having himself worked in the fields from age ten and having attended more than 60 schools during the course of his childhood. Committed to nonviolence, Chavez organized strikes, pickets, fasts, and marches to call attention to the working conditions of the migrant laborers. Chavez's most effective blow for justice was struck when he organized national boycotts of table grapes and lettuce. In 1973, Chavez's new union, the United Farm Workers of America (UFW), became a member union of the AFL-CIO. It now has more than 100,000 members.

And then the Chicano said, "*Chico*, I mistook you for one of us."

Suddenly the Chicano became less interested in me and walked away unconcerned.

I could not have told him that I had tried for a haircut at the gringo's because he would have laughed at me, and called me *pocho*,[6] a Chicano who prefers gringo ways. These experienced Chicanos knew the ways of the gringos in the north of Texas.

After the Chicano had left me, I thought that maybe these things which were happening to me in the town would all pass in a short time. The entire cotton crop would soon be harvested, and the farmers around my town would have it baled and sold. Then the Chicanos would leave the north of Texas and journey back to their homes in the Valley in the south and to Mexico.

My town would be left alone for ten more months of the year, and in this time everything and everybody would be all right again. The gringo barbers would maybe think twice before sending me to Mr. Lopez's.

Early in November the last of the cotton around my town had been harvested. The people of South Texas climbed aboard their big trucks with tall sideboards and canvas on the top to shield the sun, and they began their long journey to their homes in the border country.

The streets of the little town were now empty on Saturday. A few farmers came to town on Saturday and brought their families to do their shopping, still the streets were quiet and empty.

In my home there was new excitement for me. Tobie considered leaving his newspaper route for another job, one that would pay more money. And I thought that maybe he would let me take over his route. This was something very good. By taking his route I would know all the gringos of the town, and maybe . . . maybe then the barbers would invite me to their shops as they had invited Tobie.

At supper that night I asked Tobie if he would take me on his delivery for a few days, and then let me deliver the newspaper on my own.

Tobie said, "No, Joey. You're too young to handle money. Besides, the newspaper bag would be too heavy for you to carry on your shoulder all over town. No, I think I'll turn the route over to Red."

My father was quiet during this time, but soon he spoke, "Tobie, you give the route to Joey. He knows about money. And he needs to put a little muscle on his shoulders."

The issue was settled.

The next day Tobie took me to the newspaper office. Tobie's boss, a nice elderly man wearing glasses, studied me carefully, scratched his white head, and then asked Tobie, "Well, what do you think?"

"Oh," Tobie said, "I told him he was too young to handle this job, but he says he can do it."

"Yes, sir," I butted in enthusiastically.

Tobie's boss looked at me and chuckled, "Well, he's got enough spunk."

He thought some more.

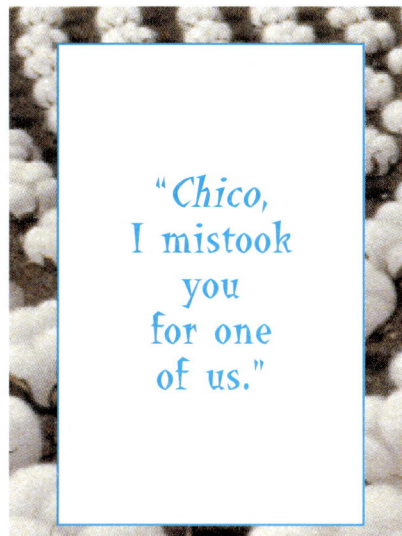

"*Chico, I mistook you for one of us.*"

---

6. *pocho* (pô'chô) *Spanish.*

ORAL HISTORY Explain to students that oral histories are spoken recollections by people about their past. These recollections can provide insight into a person's feelings and life experiences. Preserved on audio- or videotape, these recordings keep the stories of their subjects alive so that listeners can learn about them.

Application The migrant workers in "Everybody Knows Tobie" face especially trying conditions as they move from place to place in search of work. For many people, the experience of moving into a new town because of a new job or the search for work can be difficult. Ask students to each try to find a relative, neighbor, teacher, or community member who has made such a move in his or her lifetime. Have students ask these individuals if they would be willing to give oral histories. Before they begin, students should brainstorm a list of questions they would like to ask. Suggest that they focus on each person's experience of moving into a new area and on any difficulties he or she experienced. After recording the oral histories on tape, students can share them with the class.

Literary Concept: DIALOGUE

K Ask students to discuss the impressions they have of Tobie and Tobie's boss from the characters' own comments. *(Possible responses: Tobie seems to be a good brother and a responsible young man; others may say that Tobie seems to have little faith in his brother and seems to be playing up to the boss. Tobie's boss seems to be a fair person and treats Joey as an individual; he has confidence in Joey's abilities; he is willing to take chances.)*

CUSTOMIZING FOR
Students Acquiring English

3 Ask students to guess what the expression *Young'un* means. Explain that it is a contraction of "young one" and is equivalent to the Spanish *jovenes*.

Critical Thinking:
MAKING INFERENCES

L Ask students why they think Mr. Brewer has trouble remembering Tobie's name. *(Possible response: All Chicanos look alike to a prejudiced person like Mr. Brewer.)*

Literary Concept: SETTING

M Point out that Joey hopes that he will now be accepted. Ask students if they think this story's setting makes that more or less likely. *(Possible responses: more likely, because this is a town in which it is common for people of different ethnic backgrounds to live, and they may change their minds; less likely, because in this town he and Tobie are token minorities, and their "acceptance" will always be false)*

Tobie spoke, "I think he'll make you a good delivery boy, sir."

A short silence followed while Tobie's boss put his thoughts down on a scratch pad on his desk.

3 Finally, the boss said, "We'll give him a try, Tobie." He looked at me. "But, Young'un, you'd better be careful with that money. It's your responsibility."

K "Yes, sir," I gulped.

"O.K., that's settled," the boss said.

Tobie smiled and said, "Sir, I'm taking him on my delivery for a few days so he can get the hang of it, and then I'll let him take it over."

The boss agreed. I took his hand and shook it and promised him that I would do my extra best. Then Tobie left, and I followed behind.

In a few days I was delivering the *Daily News* to all the gringos of the town and also to Mr. Brewer.

Each afternoon, during my delivery, I was careful not to go into Mr. Brewer's with the newspaper. I would carefully open the door and drop the paper in. I did this because I thought that maybe Mr. Brewer would remember me, and this might cause an embarrassing incident. But I did this a very few times because one afternoon Mr. Brewer was standing at the door. He saw me. I opened the door and quickly handed him the newspaper, but before I could shut the door he said, "Say, Sonny, aren't you the one I sent to Mr. Lopez's a while back?"

"Yes, sir," I said.

"Why'd you stay around here? Didn't your people go back home last week? You do belong to 'em, don't you?"

"No, sir," I said. "I live here in the town."

"You mean to say you're not one of those . . . ?"

"No, sir."

L "Well, I'll be durned." He paused and thought. "You know, Sonny, I have a young Meskin[7] boy who lives here in town come to this here shop for haircuts every other Saturday. His name is . . . durn, can't think of his name to save my soul . . ."

"Tobie?"

"Yeah, yeah, that's his name. Fine boy. You know him?"

"Yes, sir. He's my older brother."

Then Mr. Brewer's eyes got bigger in astonishment, "Well, I'll be doubly durned." He paused and shook his head unbelievingly. "And I told you to go to Mr. Lopez's. Why didn't you speak up and tell me you was Tobie's brother? I woulda put you in that there chair and clipped you a pretty head of hair."

"Oh, I guess I forgot to tell you," I said.

"Well, from now on, Sonny, you come to this here shop, and I'll cut your hair."

"But what about your customers? Won't they get mad?"

"Naw. I'll tell 'em you're Tobie's brother, and everything will be all right. Everybody in town knows Tobie, and everybody likes him."

Then a customer walked into the barbershop. He looked at Mr. Brewer, and then at me, and then at my newspaper bag. And then the gringo customer smiled a nice smile at me.

"Well, excuse me, Sonny, got a customer waitin'. Remember now, come Saturday, and I'll clip your hair."

"O.K., Mr. Brewer. Bye."

Mr. Brewer turned and said goodbye.

As I continued my delivery I began to chuckle small bits of contentment to myself because Mr. Brewer had invited me to his shop for haircuts, and because the gringo customer had smiled at me, and because now all the gringos of the town would know me and maybe accept me.

Those incidents which had happened to me during the cotton harvest in my town: Mr. Brewer sending me to Mr. Lopez's for the

---

7. **Meskin:** mispronunciation of *Mexican*.

694 UNIT FIVE PART 2: JUMPING TO CONCLUSIONS

Mini-Lesson Literary Concepts

REVIEWING DIALOGUE Remind students that dialogue is written conversation between two or more characters. In a play, the story is told primarily through dialogue, which appears in lines next to the characters' names. In other kinds of writing, such as "Everybody Knows Tobie," the words each character speaks are usually set off by quotation marks. Dialogue in a story can help to advance the events of the plot and bring the reader close up to the characters who are speaking.

Application Have students work in small groups to review the instances of dialogue in the story. Ask them to discuss the effectiveness of having characters present themselves in their own words. How does the author use dialogue to illustrate the attitudes of the town residents and the relationship between Tobie and Joey? Why might the remark about "a little tamale" (p. 691) be a more vivid way of demonstrating the customer's attitude toward Mexican-Americans than a statement by the narrators?

Short Back & Sides (1977), Mike Dempsey. Acrylic on board, private collection.

haircut, and the Chicano cotton picker avoiding me after discovering that I was not one of his people, and the gringo customers leaving Mr. Brewer's barbershop because of me; all seemed so insignificant. And now I felt that delivering the *Daily News* to the businessmen had given me a place among them, and all because of the fact that everybody in my town knew Tobie. ❖

EVERYBODY KNOWS TOBIE **695**

Art Note

Short Back & Sides by Mike Dempsey Despite an early fascination with drawing, Mike Dempsey (1944–) never received any formal artistic training. In this work, the faces of the barbershop occupants barely indicate expression and almost disappear into the similarly colored wall in the background.

Reading the Art Describe the attitudes of the figures in the barbershop. Does it seem as if they are aware of being watched by the viewer?

STRATEGIC READING FOR
Less-Proficient Readers

N Ask students to summarize Mr. Brewer's reaction to the revelation that Joey is Tobie's brother. *(He is surprised, telling Joey that he should have brought the fact to his attention on his initial visit, and explains that he is welcome in the shop.)* Summarizing

CUSTOMIZING FOR
Gifted and Talented Students

O Have students look ahead and predict how Joey might feel about his job and about his place among the townspeople after a year or so on the job. *(Possible responses: Some students may feel that Joey's high hopes of acceptance have been realized and that he will be quite happy; others may feel that, apparently unlike Tobie, Joey will eventually become dissatisfied, realizing that there are greater and more complicated social barriers to overcome.)*

COMPREHENSION CHECK

1. What job does Tobie have at the beginning of the story? *(He delivers newspapers.)*
2. Why do groups of Chicanos come to the narrator's town every fall? *(to find work harvesting cotton)*
3. Why does Mr. Brewer send Joey away from his barbershop? *(because he thinks he is a migrant worker)*
4. What does Mr. Brewer learn about Joey that makes him decide to cut Joey's hair? *(that he is Tobie's brother)*

EDITOR'S NOTE *With the permission of the author, potentially offensive language has been deleted from the text.*

Mini-Lesson The Writer's Style

POINT OF VIEW: FIRST PERSON Remind students that the point of view in a piece of fiction is the perspective from which a story is told. Writing told by a narrator who refers to himself or herself as *I* or *me* is told from the first-person point of view. In the first-person point of view, the narrator is a character in the story who shares his or her own experiences, attitudes, and opinions with the reader. In "Everybody Knows Tobie," for example, the use of the first-person view helps the reader understand better what Joey does and does not understand about the prejudices he faces in a small town.

Application Ask students to rewrite a scene from the story in the first-person point of view from the perspective of another character, perhaps Tobie or Mr. Brewer. Then have them share their writing and discuss how the story changes when told from a different perspective.

Reteaching/Reinforcement
- *Writing Handbook*, anthology p. 876
- *Writing Mini-Lessons* transparencies p. 55

The Writer's Craft
Point of View, pp. 430–433

From Personal Response to Critical Analysis

1. Accept all reasonable responses.
2. Possible responses: Joey's acceptance by Mr. Brewer is a victory; since Mr. Brewer and other town residents are still prejudiced against Chicanos in general, he has not won a victory at all.
3. Possible responses: Since they treat the permanent Chicano population better than the transients, they are less prejudiced against them; the pejorative slang used and the barber's initial rejection of Joey are evidence that they are actually prejudiced against all Chicanos.
4. Possible responses: Some students may feel that Joey's resentment at being thought of as a migrant worker shows his prejudice; others may say that Joey wants to be considered "better" than the migrant workers, but he can also identify with them. As for Tobie, some students may feel his use of Mr. Brewer's barbershop shows his prejudice.
5. Possible responses: Some students may say *acceptance* because it appears that Joey won a small, personal victory by being taken into Mr. Brewer's barbershop. Others may say *tolerance* because Joey's "victory" amounts to merely being allowed to have his hair cut by Mr. Brewer's.
6. Accept all reasonable, well-supported responses.

Another Pathway

Cooperative Learning Assign one member of each group to be an encourager of participation and another to act as a clarifier or paraphraser. A third should act as recorder, documenting the group's conclusions and presenting them to the class. If students cannot agree on a course of action, have them identify the point of contention for their group.

Rubric

3 Full Accomplishment Students agree on an alternate course of action for Joey and present reasonable arguments to support their position or they clearly articulate the point on which they cannot agree.

2 Substantial Accomplishment Students agree on an alternate course of action but fail to provide support for their position.

1 Little or Partial Accomplishment Students have difficulty agreeing on an alternate course of action and cannot articulate the philosophical point on which they cannot agree.

RESPONDING OPTIONS

FROM PERSONAL RESPONSE TO CRITICAL ANALYSIS

REFLECT
1. In your notebook, jot down your thoughts about Joey, the narrator of this story. Then share your ideas with a partner.

RETHINK
2. At the end of the story, Joey feels he has won a small personal victory. Do you agree? Explain your answer.

3. Do you think Mr. Brewer and his customers are as prejudiced against the town's permanent Chicano population as they are against the migrant workers? Support your opinion.

Close Textual Reading
Consider
- their treatment of the migrant workers
- the connotations of the words they use in talking about the migrant workers
- why they let Tobie and Joey in the barbershop

4. In your opinion, do Tobie and Joey share the gringos' prejudice against migrant workers? Support your opinion with evidence from the story.

Thematic Link
5. Consider the connotations of the words *acceptance* and *tolerance*. Explain which one you would use to describe the gringos' attitude toward Tobie and Joey once they know who Joey is.

RELATE
6. Two kinds of prejudice are addressed in this story. Look over the list you made for the Personal Connection activity on page 688. Explain which you think is worse—open prejudice or the more subtle kind of prejudice.

LITERARY CONCEPTS

The importance of **setting**—the time and place of the action—varies from story to story. Explain the importance of setting in this story. Consider these points:
- How much does the writer tell you about the setting?
- Does the setting influence the events in the story?
- How are the characters influenced by the setting?

696   UNIT FIVE   PART 2: JUMPING TO CONCLUSIONS

Multimodal Learning
ANOTHER PATHWAY
Cooperative Learning
Mr. Brewer and his customers jump to a conclusion about Joey. In a small group, discuss how Joey might have handled the situation when he first entered the barbershop. Then discuss whether Joey should ever return. Agree on a course of action, and present your suggestion to the rest of the class.

QUICKWRITES

1. Skim the story for details that describe Tobie's appearance, behavior, opinions, and feelings. Note how others speak of him and react to him. Then summarize your notes to create a **character sketch** of Tobie. Input your notes into a computer to make them easier to organize.

2. Joey wants to be like Tobie. Think of a person you would like to emulate. Write a draft of an **essay** explaining why you wish to be like this person and how achieving this objective might change your life.

📁 **PORTFOLIO** Save your writing. You may want to use it later as a springboard to a piece for your portfolio.

Literary Concepts

Possible responses: The writer provides a great deal of information about setting, including the time of year, the town, and its inhabitants. Aspects of the setting such as the town's multiethnic nature and seasonal influx of Chicano migrants play a central role in the story's events and allow the author to explore the themes of prejudice and acceptance. If Joey and Tobie had grown up in a different town without a large white or Mexican-American population, the story would probably be very different.

QuickWrites

1. Have students share their character sketches and discuss any differences in the ways they view the character of Tobie.
2. Suggest that students create a character-trait map of the person they want to emulate before they do the drafting.

 The Writer's Craft
The Writing Variables, pp. 311–315

Multimodal Learning

ALTERNATIVE ACTIVITIES

1. **Cooperative Learning** Should Mr. Brewer be forced to accept anyone who has the money to pay for a haircut? Form **debate teams** to discuss this issue. Give reasons to support your position, including a consideration of the legal aspects of the question.

2. Imagine that you are a reporter whose assignment is to cover human-interest stories. You have just witnessed Joey leaving Mr. Brewer's barbershop in tears. With other students, act out an **interview** with Joey and follow-up interviews with Mr. Brewer and anyone else you wish to include in order to present a balanced report. Present your interviews as a special report for a radio or television news show.

Multimodal Learning

ACROSS THE CURRICULUM

Social Studies Research the attempts of the labor leader Cesar Chavez to improve working conditions for migrant laborers. In an oral report, describe what Chavez did, what he achieved, and what conditions are like today for migrant workers.

THE WRITER'S STYLE

The author demonstrates his skill at **characterization** by making Tobie's presence in the story strongly felt, although the boy appears only twice. Tobie's example and achievements hang over Joey and increase the pressure on the younger brother to succeed. What image of Tobie do you get from the way he is characterized?

LITERARY LINKS

Compare the main incident in this story with that in "The Mountain." Consider these points: How are the main incidents similar? Are the attitudes of the men in the barbershop the same as those of the people in the subway car? Do the boys view their experiences similarly? Are similar lessons learned?

DANIEL GARZA

Daniel Garza was born near Hillsboro, Texas, in 1938, several years after his family had emigrated from Mexico. Educated at Texas Christian University in Fort Worth, Garza later served as an officer in the U.S. Army. Garza's works focus primarily on the relationship between Mexican Americans and Anglos in the rural communities of the Southwest. He received the *Harper's Magazine* Southwest Literature Award in 1962 for his article "Saturday Belongs to the *Palomia*." Since then, his works have been widely reprinted.

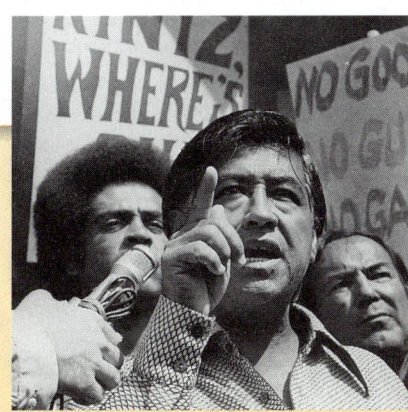

Cezar Chavez holding a news conference in 1975. AP/Wide World Photos.

Across the Curriculum

Social Studies Students may consult a librarian for suggestions about information sources on Cesar Chavez and the struggle to improve the conditions of migrant workers. They can also look for recent newspaper and magazine articles on present-day conditions of migrant workers or contact a local AFL-CIO or UFW office for more information about the struggle to unionize migrant labor. Interested students may want to research the conditions of migrant workers in other countries.

Literary Links

Students may say that the incidents are similar in that both Mr. Brewer and the people on the subway jump to conclusions based on race. Others may say that Mr. Brewer's actions may be mitigated by a wariness of outsiders, and in any case, he doesn't accuse Joey of a crime. Some may point out that while Joey is happy when he is finally accepted by Mr. Brewer, the narrator of "The Mountain" isn't interested in the apologies and money offered by the subway passengers.

EVERYBODY KNOWS TOBIE 697

Alternative Activities

1. **Cooperative Learning** Assign a turn-taking monitor to maintain order and a panel of criticizers of ideas to act as judges. Before the debate starts, have two or three interested students research the legal aspects of the question and share their findings with the class.
2. Students may wish to watch television news programs to gain insight into interviewing techniques.

The Writer's Style

Remind students of the four ways writers develop characterization. Have them point to examples of these methods in the story as they discuss their images of Tobie. Students may say that despite his infrequent appearances in the story, Tobie is a constant presence because Joey feels the pressure to live up to the example of his popular and successful brother.

OBJECTIVES

- To promote independent, active reading
- To practice and apply skills learned in previous selections

Thematic Link: *Jumping to Conclusions* A teenage girl fears dealing with her problems alone and perceives them as insurmountable.

Reading Pathways

- Before students read, ask them to think about the poem's title and write down any connotations that come to mind. Then, after reading the poem, have them review their lists. Have them discuss whether these items relate to what they have read and why they think the poet chose the title.

- Have students read the poem twice. After the first reading, they should brainstorm a list of any questions they may have about the speaker. As they reread the poem they should try to answer the questions generated by their first reading.

- As they read, students can make a list of the problems to which they think the speaker of the poem is referring. Then have students share their lists and see whether they came to the same conclusions about what is troubling the speaker.

ON YOUR OWN

Hanging FIRE

AUDRE LORDE

I am fourteen
and my skin has betrayed me
the boy I cannot live without
still sucks his thumb
5 in secret
how come my knees are
always so ashy
what if I die
before morning
10 and momma's in the bedroom
with the door closed.

I have to learn how to dance
in time for the next party
my room is too small for me
15 suppose I die before graduation
they will sing sad melodies
but finally
tell the truth about me
There is nothing I want to do
20 and too much
that has to be done
and momma's in the bedroom
with the door closed.

Nobody even stops to think
25 about my side of it
I should have been on Math Team
my marks were better than his
why do I have to be
the one
30 wearing braces
I have nothing to wear tomorrow
will I live long enough
to grow up
and momma's in the bedroom
35 with the door closed.

PRINT AND MEDIA RESOURCES

UNIT FIVE RESOURCE BOOK
Strategic Reading: Literature, p. 57

FORMAL ASSESSMENT
Selection Test, pp. 125–126
Part Test, pp. 127–128
Test Generator

ACCESS FOR STUDENTS ACQUIRING ENGLISH
Selection Summaries

AUDIO LIBRARY
See Reference Card

By the Gate (1953), Ernest Crichlov. Oil on board, 10½" × 14½", The Harmon and Harriet Kelley Collection.

AUDRE LORDE

One could almost say that Audre Lorde (1934–1992) had no choice but to become a poet. The young, insecure Lorde, who had been born with severe speech and sight problems, developed a habit of responding to questions by reciting poetry she had memorized. She once explained to an interviewer what this meant: "When someone said to me, 'How do you feel?' or 'What do you think?' or asked another direct question, I would recite a poem, and somewhere in that poem would be the feeling, the vital piece of information. It might be a line. It might be an image. The poem was my response." However, as she grew older, she could not find poems to express her increasingly complex emotions, and so she was forced to write her own.

In her autobiography, *Zami: A New Spelling of My Name,* Lorde reveals that at the time she learned to write, around the age of four, she didn't like the tail of the *y* hanging down below the line in her first name, Audrey. So she dropped the *y* and became Audre. A biographer, Ann Trapasso, suggests that this anecdote indicates the importance of "naming and self-definition to Lorde, themes that she develops in her later writings." The poem reprinted here reflects the self-definition theme: a teenage speaker wrestles with some mysteries of life, but she is unable to figure out who she is, she gets no help from her mother, and she finds her situation unsettled and unresolved—hanging fire, as the title tells us.

During the 1960s, Lorde published her poetry in various magazines and became active in the civil rights, antiwar, and feminist movements. She went on to publish essays, speeches, and journal entries as well as poetry. In *The Cancer Journals,* she relates her experiences with cancer, which she was first diagnosed as having in 1978 and which eventually caused her death.

OTHER WORKS *The Black Unicorn*

HANGING FIRE **699**

Art Note

By the Gate by Ernest Crichlow Ernest Crichlow (1914–) first showed his paintings publicly in 1941 at a New York gallery as part of what is believed to be the earliest exhibition of African American artists ever held. Crichlow's special talent is the sensitive portrayal of youths. Here, a young girl seems entrapped by a gate and heavy post in the foreground and a dark brick wall behind.

Reading the Art *Do you think the girl might be experiencing worries similar to those of the speaker of "Hanging Fire"? Why or why not?*

AUDRE LORDE

Of West Indian heritage, Lorde was born in New York City and for many years lived in the Virgin Islands. Joan Martin, writing in *Black Women Writers,* points out that a key to understanding Lorde's poems is knowing Lorde's feelings about her mother. "In many of Lorde's poems, the figure of her mother is one of a woman who resents her daughter, tries to repress her child's unique personality . . . and withholds the emotional nourishment of parental love."

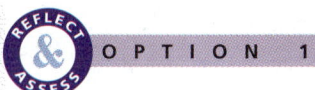

OPTION 1

Cooperative Learning
CONDUCT A POLL

Have students form groups to conduct a poll of the fears and problems that people in different age groups have. Groups should write survey questions and have each member poll 15–20 respondents from different age groups. Groups should calculate their results and report all findings.

Teacher's Role Facilitate surveying by helping groups prepare their questions.

Rubric
3 Full Accomplishment Students complete surveys and insightfully interpret the results.
2 Substantial Accomplishment Students complete surveys but have difficulty interpreting the results.
1 Little or Partial Accomplishment Students have difficulty preparing surveys.

OPTION 2

Class Discussion
SHARING IDEAS

Teacher's Role After students have read the selection, engage them in a whole-class discussion with the following questions.

1. How common are the anxieties voiced by the speaker in the poem? *(Possible responses: They are universal, especially among teenagers; although common, the anxieties experienced by the speaker seem more pronounced.)*

2. What impression do you get from the repeated lines "and momma's in the bedroom/with the door closed"? Do you think that the mother is purposely ignoring her daughter? *(Possible responses: Yes, she is not there for her daughter, who needs her advice and reassurance; no, the daughter may be keeping her problems inside, leaving her mother unaware.)*

THE LANGUAGE OF LITERATURE **TEACHER'S EDITION 699**

OVERVIEW

To gain a deeper appreciation of the selections that they read in this unit, students will explore the characteristics of a research paper and then create a well-developed research report.

Objectives

- To plan a report by considering elements such as topic, focus, research sources, and organization
- To draft a research paper and solicit a response
- To revise, edit, and publish a report

Skills

LITERATURE
- Transforming an interest into a research topic

WRITING AND LANGUAGE
- Crediting sources
- Quoting and paraphrasing
- Developing ideas clearly and logically
- Editing drafts

GRAMMAR AND USAGE
- Punctuating a list of citations

MEDIA LITERACY
- Reading news articles

SPEAKING, LISTENING, AND VIEWING
- Conferencing
- Giving and receiving constructive criticism

RESEARCH SKILLS
- Finding sources
- Taking notes
- Making an outline
- Avoiding plagiarism

CRITICAL THINKING
- Evaluating research sources
- Generating information

Teaching Strategy: COLLABORATIVE OPPORTUNITY

A To demonstrate how students can turn their curiosity into research topics, have them name and briefly describe unsolved mysteries that they have heard of—for example, UFOs.

Form the class into groups, and assign one mystery to each group. Invite each group to talk about what they would like to know about the mystery and to generate a list of questions. Some examples:

- Are UFO's alien spaceships?
- What makes people think that the Bermuda Triangle is dangerous?
- Is the Loch Ness monster a hoax?

Finally, have the group turn their questions into statements that can be researched. Some possibilities:

- UFOs are a hoax.
- Many strange things have happened in the Bermuda Triangle.
- People claim that the monster has been sighted in Loch Ness.

WRITING FROM EXPERIENCE

WRITING A REPORT

In Unit Five, "Mysteries and Deceptions," you sampled stories about misleading appearances and unexplainable events. The world is full of such stories. Some of them are actually true, at least in part. Reporting on them requires gathering data from several sources, analyzing it, and then presenting the findings.

GUIDED ASSIGNMENT
Write a Research Paper The next few pages will give you information to help you write a short paper about a mystery, a practical joke, or a hoax.

❶ What Do You Wonder About?

The articles and photos on these pages describe famous mysteries. What are the unanswered questions in each case? What other mysteries and hoaxes do you know of?

Ⓐ Hunt for Mysteries If you look carefully, you can find a mystery almost anywhere. The TV listings are one place to check for programs about mysteries like the ones shown here. Magazines and books are rich resources too.

Be a Critical Reader Would you believe a tabloid headline that said, "Aliens record top-selling rock CD!"? Some mysterious events are just too bizarre to be true. If a story seems unreasonable, question it. Some additional research may tell you whether it is real or a hoax.

Freewrite Jot down your thoughts or questions about any of the mysteries or hoaxes that interest you.

Ⓑ What are your impressions of Bigfoot after comparing the two photos at the right?

Science Illustration

A cast of a footprint believed to be Bigfoot's, with bone structure sketched in, makes a skeleton of a human foot look tiny. Believers insist that Bigfoot exists, although many sightings of the legendary primate are hoaxes.

How much do people really know about Bigfoot?

I wonder why some people believe in Bigfoot.

700 UNIT FIVE: MYSTERIES AND DECEPTIONS

PRINT AND MEDIA RESOURCES

UNIT FIVE RESOURCE BOOK
Prewriting, p. 61
Elaboration, p. 62
Peer Response Guide, pp. 63–64
Revising and Proofreading, p. 65
Student Model, pp. 66–69
Rubric, p. 70

WRITING MINI-LESSONS
Transparencies, p. 68

FORMAL ASSESSMENT
Guidelines for Writing Assessment

  WRITING COACH

  LASERLINKS
Writing Springboard

  The Writer's Craft
The Short Research Paper, pp. 266–86

Going in Circles

For 15 years those strange flying saucer-size rings pressed into the corn and wheat fields of southern England have had folks running—and thinking—in circles. How they got there was anyone's guess. Meteorologists spun theories of whirling air masses, and farmers speculated about crazed hedgehogs. Scientists from as far away as Japan spent millions searching for evidence that extraterrestrials were at work.

Then editors at the London tabloid *Today* trumpeted a solution to the

magic-circle mystery: The creations were a down-to-earth scam, perpetrated by a mischievous pair of Englishmen.

from *People*

News Story

Puzzling Pyramids

Probably no monuments of lost worlds have been the object of so much awe—and so much pseudo-scientific and near-mystical nonsense—as the three pyramids and the Great Sphinx on the Giza Plateau across the Nile from modern Cairo.

In a spurt of energy unmatched before or since, the pharaohs of the Fourth Dynasty managed, from roughly 2700 to 2550 B.C., to quarry and transport 11 million cubic yards of stone and fashion them into pyramids, temples, causeways, without the aid of either beasts of burden or the wheel.

Dora Jane Hamblin
from "A unique approach to unraveling the secrets of the great pyramids"
Smithsonian

Magazine Article

❷ Choose a Topic You're Curious About

Look over your freewriting. Which mysteries or hoaxes interest you most? For each topic, list the things you know and what you'd like to find out. Then choose the topic that intrigues you most as your writing topic.

WRITING FROM EXPERIENCE

WRITING SPRINGBOARD
It's a Mystery to Me! Mysterious looking designs began to appear suddenly in the wheat fields of England in 1989. This short film discusses some possible answers to these mysterious crop circles.

Side B, Frame 40361

Writing Prompt Research an event in history that is shrouded in mystery. Write a research paper discussing the information you have found.

Teaching Strategy:
STUMBLING BLOCK

E If students are hesitant to test their library skills, arrange with the librarian for a tour focused on reference materials.

Research Skills: KEEPING GOOD RECORDS

F Remind students of the importance of writing things down, including the title and the author of everything they read and collect before they narrow their focus. Urge them to make their notes neat, concise, and accessible. Remind them that it is frustrating to recall having read something but not to remember the details or the source. If they have good notes, though, they can always find and retrieve material.

PREWRITING

Brushing Up on a Topic

On the Research Trail When you write a paper, you can't rely just on what you already know about a subject. You need to do some research. Then you can combine your new knowledge with the information that's already in your head.

❶ Read All About It!

Is your topic the best one for you? To find out, get a quick overview of it in an encyclopedia. Do you think the topic will hold your interest over time? Also, will you be able to find enough sources about your topic to write a paper?

❷ Narrow Your Focus

What if your topic has many parts? You can zero in on one aspect of it. To break a broad topic into smaller parts, gather some books on your subject, skim the tables of contents, and read some introductory materials. The ideas below also can help you get focused.

- Draft a list of questions about your topic that you would like your research to answer.
- Think about your reason for writing. Do you want to solve a mystery? Having a purpose will help you find an aspect of your topic to focus on.
- Write a statement of controlling purpose that tells what your report will be about. It can keep you focused as you research.

❸ Gather Your Information

You're ready to research! These suggestions will help you look for information about your topic.

Visit the Library Not sure where to start? The library's card catalog or computer catalog can lead
E you to books about your topic. For recent articles, try newspaper and magazine indexes. Other helpful materials, such as almanacs and encyclopedias, are in the library's reference section.

Source Cards
F One student made cards for a book, an encyclopedia article, and an on-line newsletter.

1
Krantz, Grover S. *Big Footprints.*
Boulder: Johnson Books, 1992.

Public Library   QL 892.S2
K73
1992

2
"Bigfoot." *The World Book Encyclopedia.*
1995 ed.

Public Library

3
The Bigfoot Research Project.
(1 Aug. 1995): 3 pp. On-line. Internet.
29 Aug. 1995.

Web site http://www.teleport.com/~tbrp

702 UNIT FIVE: MYSTERIES AND DECEPTIONS

SkillBuilder — **RESEARCH SKILLS**

ACCESSING INFORMATION Making research into a game is a good way to help students overcome their fear of the unknown or their impression that research is boring. Remind them that good researchers often think of themselves as detectives on a case or treasure hunters on an expedition. Adopting those perspectives will enable students to think of the library as a source of clues and will encourage them to develop the skills that will allow them to find those clues.

Application Tell students you are sending them on a treasure hunt to satisfy their curiosity about something they have already heard of or read about. Ask them to find two articles on the subject, each from a different database. If your library has both computerized and bound databases, tell students to use both. They should summarize each article in one paragraph of fewer than fifty words. In addition, ask students to compile bibliographical information about three other references on the subject.

Go On-line If you have access to a computer with a modem, you may be able to search on-line databases. For help with these resources, see page 890 of the Multimedia Handbook.

Evaluate Your Sources As you look over a source, ask yourself these questions: Is the author an expert? Is the source up-to-date? Is the source respected? If a source doesn't seem credible, you shouldn't use it.

Create Source Cards Make source cards like the ones on the left page to keep track of your research materials. Number each card. If you need help, see page 887 of the Writing Handbook.

Make Note Cards Taking notes on index cards is a good way to record answers to your research questions. For each card, write the number of the source and only one piece of information. For more help, see the SkillBuilder at the right.

Student's Note Cards

1. Evaluating Evidence
"Science requires solid evidence for the existence of a new species—footprints and sightings by local people are never enough." 3
(quotation)

2. Number of Sightings
Hundreds of people have reported seeing Bigfoot or his footprints.
(general knowledge)

3. Behavior/Habits
Bigfoot tends to come out only at night but, if disturbed, will appear in daytime. 1
(paraphrase)

SkillBuilder

RESEARCH SKILLS

Taking Notes
Taking notes on four-by-six-inch index cards will help you keep track of your data. After each note, add the page number of the source. You also can color-code your note cards and source cards. Here are three types of notes:

Quotation Copy the original text word-for-word. Use quotation marks at the beginning and the end of the quotation.

Paraphrase Rewrite material from a source in your own words.

General Knowledge Rewrite a fact that appears in several sources.

APPLYING WHAT YOU'VE LEARNED
Try using note cards to record the information you've uncovered.

WRITING HANDBOOK

For more help with note cards, see page 887 of the Writing Handbook.

THINK & PLAN

Looking at What You've Found

1. Did you find several good sources of information? If not, where can you find more?
2. Now that you know more about your topic, do you need to change your statement of controlling purpose? If so, how?

WRITING FROM EXPERIENCE 703

Critical Thinking: CLASSIFYING

I Students may find it difficult to group their notecards based on similarities in main headings because the main headings may not seem to have much in common. Remind them that classifying their notes is an important part of the research process. Suggest that they routinely ask themselves why they are taking notes on a particular passage. Encourage them to look for patterns in the material that they have gathered and to write headings that reflect those patterns. If they do that while they are taking notes, they will be ready to group their cards and create a working outline when they finish the process of taking notes.

Writing Skill: THESIS STATEMENT

J Point out to students that the thesis statement in the outline comprises two sentences. The first sentence tells what the topic is, and the second one tells how it will be treated. Ask them what they can expect a paper written from this thesis statement to accomplish. Possible responses:

- To show that Bigfoot has intrigued many people
- To show that no one really knows whether Bigfoot exists

 WRITING SPRINGBOARD
Stonehenge: An Ancient Mystery
Who built Stonehenge? Why? Rising from a green field in the southwestern England, these huge, mysterious stones date from 2000–1800 B.C. Even today, scholars do not completely understand their purpose.

Side B, Frame 43366

Writing Prompt Research a prehistoric place or event and write a research paper discussing what is now known about it. Include in your paper a discussion of the processes scholars use to uncover information about ancient places or events.

704 THE LANGUAGE OF LITERATURE TEACHER'S EDITION

using any method that makes sense to you. The main ideas in your note cards can be headings in your outline; the supporting details can be subheadings. If it's available to you, use the Writing Coach at this stage.

③ Begin Your Draft

Using your outline as a guide, start your draft. Feel free to adjust your outline as your draft takes shape, but do write at least one paragraph for each heading in your outline. The following strategies may also help you present your ideas.

Definition and Description Use details and examples to present the basic facts about your topic.

Comparison Compare your subject with other, similar subjects. For example, Bigfoot could be compared with the *Yeti* of Nepal and the *Almas* of Mongolia and China.

Cause and Effect Explore the effects of different events on your topic over time. How has your subject changed?

④ Rework Your Draft and Share

When you're ready to look over your draft, consider the following suggestions for improving it.

Include Your Own Ideas Drawing your own conclusions about a topic is an important part of writing a research paper. Just back up those ideas with facts, examples, and evidence.

Avoid Plagiarism Where did you get the information in your report? If it is common knowledge, you don't need to credit the source. However, most sources should be credited to avoid plagiarism, the presentation of someone else's ideas as your own. For help with crediting sources, see the SkillBuilder on the right.

PEER RESPONSE

Exchange drafts with a classmate and ask these questions:

- How well does my report match my thesis statement?
- Which parts of my report do you think I could leave out?
- Did the introduction make you want to keep reading?
- How well does my conclusion sum up the report?

SkillBuilder

WRITER'S CRAFT

Crediting Sources

Writers usually credit their sources in the body of a report. After a quotation or a paraphrase, add a brief note in parentheses that refers readers to a list of sources at the end of the report. The examples below are followed by the authors' last names—or the title of the work, if no author is given—and the page number of the source.

"According to those witnesses, the animal was, in a word, smelly" (Stein and MacNee 9).

Many scientists doubt that Bigfoot exists, because so-called evidence, such as footprints and photographs, has proved to be fake ("Bigfoot" 286).

WRITING HANDBOOK

For more information on crediting sources, see page 889 of the Writing Handbook.

RETHINK & EVALUATE

Reflecting on Your Draft

1. Did you change your outline as you drafted? If so, how did you change it, and why?
2. Did you develop your ideas clearly and logically? If not, how can you reshape them?
3. What information and ideas do you need to credit in your report?

Teaching Strategy: STUMBLING BLOCK

K Remind students that writing is a process and that sometimes getting started is the hardest part. Suggest that this is so because they can't know precisely what they are going to say in the paper until it they have written it. Remind them that their ideas will change as they write, and during this process much learning will take place. Encourage them to take the plunge by starting to write and then letting their first thoughts lead them to make connections and develop ideas and insights.

Speaking and Listening: GROUP DISCUSSION

L To help students understand which material needs to be credited, form the class into small groups whose members will read two or three paragraphs from their drafts to one another. Listeners will tell the reader which material is new information for them and which is information that they know. If the group agrees that something is common knowledge, then it does not need to be credited. There should be citations for all other information in the draft.

SkillBuilder — WRITER'S CRAFT

CREDITING SOURCES Point out that citations have two purposes: to give credit for ideas that are not theirs and to tell readers where they can find more material for their own purposes. Suggest that citations involve acting ethically and responsibly and showing courtesy toward the person who wrote the work cited and their readers. Researchers accept and discharge responsibility when they provide all the information that readers need to find the cited source.

Application Form the class into pairs, and ask them to exchange rough drafts. Tell them to record the first three citations in the other students' papers. Then direct them to go to the library to find the works cited and to photocopy the first page of each source. This exercise will underscore the importance of providing accurate information for all sources cited.

Reteaching/Reinforcement

- *Writing Mini-Lessons* transparencies, p. 68

The Writer's Craft

Documenting Sources, p. 278

Teaching Strategy:
STUMBLING BLOCKS

M Remind students that everyone has trouble accepting criticism, but that responding to evaluations of their work will help them improve their work. Suggest that they try to see their work from the peer reviewer's point of view and to bear in mind that their classmate is trying to help them. Remind them that although they need not change anything, responding to others' questions is the best way to strengthen their work.

Teaching Strategy: MODELING

N Possible answers:
- by using humor
- by referring to names for Bigfoot that many readers already know
- by using vivid descriptions

O Possible answers:
- It is possible to fake pictures of Bigfoot.
- Bigfoot takes a human form.

Teaching Strategy: MODELING

P Discuss how this excerpt meets the Standards for Evaluation on page 707.
- The excerpt presents detailed factual information about Bigfoot.
- It contains a citation.
- Ideas flow logically: Each sentence follows from the preceding one.

REVISING AND PUBLISHING

Finishing It Up

A Chance to Polish Your Work Set your draft aside for a day or two, and then take a look at it again. Now you can read it—and your peer responses—objectively before you identify any changes you want to make.

Student's Revised Report

1 Revise and Edit

The questions below will help you put the finishing touches on your report.

- Which of your peer comments will you address? How will making those changes improve your report?
- **M** The model at the right begins by engaging the reader and telling what the report is about. How well does your introduction do these things?

2 Prepare Your Final Copy

Use the Standards for Evaluation and the Editing Checklist on the next page to assess how well you documented your sources. For more help, see page 889 of the Writing Handbook. This handbook page, along with the SkillBuilder on page 707, will help you create a Works Cited list like the one on the far right.

N How does the writer capture readers' interest?

O What information do you get from the photograph in the report?

Vanderhouse 1

Cedric Vanderhouse
Ms. Bramanti
Freshman English
27 March 1996

Tracking Bigfoot

The legendary creature has many names: Bigfoot, the Abominable Snowman, Sasquatch, Alma, the Yeti, and the Wildman. Yet it doesn't seem to have many friends. In fact, few people have ever gotten close to a Bigfoot. There are plenty of Bigfoot enthusiasts, however. These people spend their lives looking for evidence that the tall, hairy primate exists.

What does Bigfoot look like? In the United States, descriptions are pretty much the same. People remember seeing a seven- or eight-foot-tall animal walking upright on two feet and having fur that is tan, brownish red, or black (Stein and MacNee 9).

706 UNIT FIVE: MYSTERIES AND DECEPTIONS

This image of Bigfoot is from a 1967 film that turned out to be a hoax.

Vanderhouse 7

Works Cited

"Bigfoot." <u>The World Book Encyclopedia</u> 1995 ed.

<u>The Bigfoot Research Project.</u> (1 Aug. 1995): 3 pp. On-line. Web site http://www.teleport.com/~tbrp. 29 Aug. 1995.

Donahue, Bill. "On the trail of Bigfoot." <u>Chicago Tribune</u> 2 July 1995, sec. 5: 1.

Krantz, Grover S. <u>Big Footprints.</u> Boulder: Johnson Books, 1992.

Stein, Gordon, and Marie J. MacNee. <u>Hoaxes! Dupes, Dodges & Other Dastardly Deceptions</u>. Detroit: Visible Ink, 1995.

Standards for Evaluation

An effective research report
- includes a thesis statement in the introduction that explains the topic and purpose of the report
- contains accurate, relevant facts
- documents sources correctly
- presents ideas in a logical sequence
- develops the topic fully with details and examples
- includes a properly formatted Works Cited list

SkillBuilder

GRAMMAR FROM WRITING

Punctuating a Works Cited List
A list of works cited shows that the data in your report are real. To make a list, gather the source cards you actually used and alphabetize them by the author's last name. Then use the publication information from each card to prepare a list like the one at the left. Notice that a period follows a main section and a comma separates parts of a section.

GRAMMAR HANDBOOK

For more information on punctuating titles, see page 930 of the Grammar Handbook.

Editing Checklist
1. Did you format the sources on your Works Cited list correctly?
2. Did you list only the sources that you used in your report?

REFLECT & ASSESS

Evaluating Your New Knowledge
1. How is writing a report different from other kinds of writing?
2. What jobs might use research skills like the ones you learned in this assignment?

PORTFOLIO What unanswered questions do you still have about your topic? Write a note for your portfolio.

WRITING FROM EXPERIENCE 707

Research Skills: CROSS-REFERENCING

Students should make certain that all works cited appear in this list and that all works in this list are cited in the body of the paper. Suggest that they go through their reports and make a list of all citations. Then they should check off each citation on the Works Cited list.

Writing Skill: USING THE COMPUTER

Some computers have programs for alphabetizing. Encourage students to use them to draw up their Works Cited list. For example, they can make entries on the list in the order in which they appear in the paper and then alphabetize the list.

PORTFOLIO

Encourage students to make copies of interesting articles that they have read or of provocative pictures that they have come across. They might give these copies to interested friends or family members or use them again in their work.

Standards for Evaluation

Have students review their reports for the following:

Ideas and Content
- includes a thesis statement in the introduction that explains the topic and purpose of the report
- develops the idea fully with details and examples
- contains accurate and relevant facts
- sums up the writer's ideas in an effective conclusion

Structure and Form
- presents information and ideas in a logical sequence
- gives credit for ideas and statements of others
- includes a properly formatted Works Cited list

Grammar, Usage, and Mechanics
- contains no more than two or three minor errors in grammar and usage
- contains no more than two or three minor errors in spelling, capitalization, and punctuation

---

SkillBuilder — GRAMMAR FROM WRITING

PUNCTUATING A WORKS CITED LIST
Inform students that there are a number of styles for incorporating citations in the body of their work and for naming them in a Works Cited list. For instance, the Modern Languages Association has one style; the American Psychological Association has another. Point out that there is no one correct method but that they should choose one style and use it consistently. Tell students that each style has its own guidebook that is usually available in the reference section of a library.

Application Have students go to the library and obtain two style manuals. Ask them to select two paragraphs in their papers and to format the citations in both styles. Then have them make two Works Cited lists based on both styles.

Reteaching/Reinforcement

The Writer's Craft
Prepare a Bibliography, pp. 281–82

UNIT REVIEW

This feature allows students to reflect on what they have learned in Unit Five and to assess how well they have understood it. This feature provides students with multiple opportunities for self-assessment. You may also wish to use some of the activities to assess specific skills, such as speaking, listening, or cooperative learning.

Objectives

- To allow students to reflect on and assess their understanding of theme
- To allow students to reflect on and assess their understanding of literary concepts, such as climax and irony
- To give students the opportunity to assess and build their portfolios

REFLECTING ON THEME

OPTION 1

After students complete their lists, you may want to initiate a class discussion in which students who have listed the same characters pool their notes. Before each character is discussed, appoint a summarizer to restate students' perceptions.

OPTION 2

Suggest that students consider whether their insights have generated greater self-awareness or greater understanding of others' behavior.

OPINION 3

Consider appointing a monitor to facilitate this activity. This student could ensure that each member of the group has a chance to present a character and that other members justify their identifications.

REFLECT & ASSESS

UNIT FIVE: MYSTERIES AND DECEPTIONS

Has reading these selections about mysteries and deceptions given you any new ideas that you can apply in your everyday life? Complete one or more of the following options to help you explore this question.

REFLECTING ON THEME

OPTION 1 Getting to Know You Several characters in Part 1 of this unit are not what they at first appear to be. Review the selections, making a list of characters who aren't what they seem. After each name, briefly describe the nature of that character's deceptions. Which of the characters' false pretenses fooled you the most? Circle the names of those characters in your list.

OPTION 2 Insights Gained As you read the selections in Part 2 of this unit, did you learn anything important about the hazards of jumping to conclusions? Review the characters' experiences, and then pick at least two that gave you meaningful insights. In a few paragraphs, explain what lesson or lessons you learned from the plight of each character.

OPTION 3 Mysterious Characters To survey the range of interesting and unusual characters in this unit, get together with a small group of classmates and play a mystery game. Take turns acting out characters for the other members of the group to identify.

To add interest to the game, don't give away the identity of your character with obvious statements, such as "I lost a diamond necklace!" Be a bit mysterious, perhaps saying, "I used to be so spoiled, until I realized what I had to lose." You might also use distinctive gestures or pantomime emotions to reveal aspects of the character. Continue playing the game until your group has acted out all the characters.

Self-Assessment: List the titles of the selections that you learned the most from in this unit. Next to each title, briefly describe what you learned from the selection.

Deceptive Characters
1. Mr. Johnson in "One Ordinary Day, with Peanuts"—His kindness is fake; he'll be doing nasty things the next day.

REVIEWING LITERARY CONCEPTS

OPTION 1 Understanding Climax The climax, or turning point, of a story is the key event that the earlier events build up to. Choose about six stories from this unit. In a chart, identify the climax of each story, and explain how a character or situation is changed by the climax.

Story	Climax	What Changes?
"The Last Boast"	Wolfer Joe decides not to take Annie with him.	Wolfer Joe saves Annie but loses his chance of ever leading a regular, law-abiding life.

708 UNIT FIVE: MYSTERIES AND DECEPTIONS

Self-Assessment Encourage students to skim the unit, reconsidering each selection before making their choices. Ask students to be as specific as possible in their learning statements.

OPTION 2 **Appreciating Irony** A situation turns out to be the exact opposite of what you'd expected; an audience knows something that a character doesn't; someone makes a point by stating its opposite. These are the three kinds of irony—situational, dramatic, and verbal. What ironies have you noticed in this unit's selections? With a small group of classmates, try to identify examples of all three kinds of irony in the selections you have read.

Self-Assessment: In addition to climax, the following literary terms reviewed in this unit are also used in analyzing the plot of a story: exposition, rising action, and falling action. Working with a partner, choose one story from this unit and use it to identify examples of each of these plot elements.

PORTFOLIO BUILDING

- **QuickWrites** Several of the QuickWrites in this unit asked you to share your insights and opinions about the literature and characters in it. From your responses, choose the one that you feel was your best work. Write a note explaining why the piece is good, attach it to the piece, and include both in your portfolio.

- **Writing About Literature** When you wrote a critical essay evaluating one of the literary works in this unit, did you recommend the work, or did you warn readers away? How did you arrive at the criteria you used in making your positive or negative evaluation? Write a note outlining the way you went about establishing criteria, and then evaluate your own process. What might you have done differently? Include your note with your critical essay.

- **Writing from Experience** What were your reasons for choosing the particular mystery, practical joke, or hoax you researched and wrote about in this unit? Did you learn anything unexpected or surprising about your topic? Write a description of your research process, identifying the most useful sources and noting the most surprising things you learned. Attach your description to your research paper if you choose to place it in your portfolio.

- **Personal Choice** Think about all the activities and short writing assignments that you completed for this unit or on your own. Which do you think best illustrates the unit theme, "Mysteries and Deceptions"? Write a note that explains your choice, attach it to your writing or activity record, and include both in your portfolio.

Self-Assessment: Now that you have some pieces of writing in your portfolio, look back over them. Which ones reflect improvements in your writing skills? Are you gaining more confidence in your ability to organize and express your thoughts?

SETTING GOALS

Have the mystery stories in this unit sharpened your skills of observation, analysis, and inference? Use your detective skills as you read the selections in the next unit—or the next time you encounter a mystery.

REFLECT & ASSESS **709**

SETTING GOALS

Have students define each of the skills mentioned; observation, analysis, and inference. Then encourage them to cite examples of stories in the unit that helped them sharpen each of the skills and of life stituations, real or hypothetical, to which those skills can be applied.

REVIEWING LITERARY CONCEPTS

OPTION 1

Some students may note that the climax, especially in a story that has a surprise ending, often comes in the final moments; in these cases what changes is the reader's perception of all that has gone before. In "The Chaser," for example, when the old man reveals that customers come back, readers grasp the logic of his unusual pricing structure and begin to reevaluate the love potion that he dispenses. See also Unit Five Resource Book, p. 73.

OPTION 2

Remind students to consider the poems, drama, and nonfiction as well as the short stories in the unit. Note, for example, the dramatic irony that sets off one speaker from the other in "O What Is That Sound": the calm speaker rather than the terrified one may be the soldiers' target.

 Self-Assessment Suggest that students first review the three kinds of irony in the Handbook and then write a definition of each in their own words.

PORTFOLIO BUILDING

Review the main elements in the portfolio system that students are using. Ask them to choose from the options suggested in the book or help them work out an alternative that meets the needs of the class. Encourage students to be as specific as possible in their notes; doing so will give them valuable insight into their own learning process.

 Self-Assessment You may wish to suggest that students identify the strengths in the pieces that they think reflect improvement. They might cite, for example, their use of specific examples, or they may sight the organizational structure of a piece or their mastery of a particular grammatical concept. Ask students to articulate why they feel confident about a particular piece.

THE LANGUAGE OF LITERATURE TEACHER'S EDITION **709**

UNIT SIX

UNIT THEMES

Unit Six

A Matter of Life and Death In Unit Six, students will read selections that portray the difficulties and dangers that threaten one's survival. This unit contains two parts: Part 1, "Uncharted Territory," and Part 2, "Fateful Encounters." Selections in both parts contribute to the unit theme by recounting a variety of characters' struggles for survival.

Part 1

Uncharted Territory Selections in Part 1 examine the fear of death and the universal human effort to avoid it. For example, in "A Trip to the Edge of Survival," five men cling to life despite being lost at sea in a leaky boat for many days.

Part 2

Fateful Encounters Part 2 highlights the endeavors characters take to escape certain death. For example, in "The Most Dangerous Game," a man is hunted like a wild animal but refuses to accept the possibility of capture despite heavy odds against survival.

UNIT SIX

A MATTER OF LIFE AND DEATH

Living on earth has always been a dangerous way to spend your time.

ANNE LAMOTT
Novelist and critic

Paricutín (1949), Alfredo Zalce. Collection of Andrés Blaisten. Photo by Gilberto Chen.

Exploring Theme

To help students explore the connections among the art, the quotation, and the unit theme, have them consider the following questions:

1. From her quotation, what do you think Anne Lamott is implying about living on earth? *(Possible response: Anyone who lives on earth is likely at anytime to face potentially dangerous situations. There are no guarantees in life.)*

2. What details in the painting help to create a atmosphere of danger? *(Possible response: The background of towering, dark mountains and sunless sky lend an eerie, ominous mood to the painting. The splash of red signifies the threat of the more immediate danger of the volcano about to erupt.)*

3. What kinds of stories and experiences might you expect to read about in this unit? *(Possible response: stories about characters who confront death; characters who have to make important decisions; urgent matters)*

4. Discuss a particular experience of your own in which you were confronted with a serious risk or grave danger. *(Responses will vary.)*

Art Note

Paricutín by Alfredo Zalce

About two hundred miles west of Mexico City is Paricutín, the more recent of the only two new volcanoes born in North America in historic times. It burst up dramatically from a crack in a farmer's cornfield between mountainous ridges in early 1943, and eruptions continued until March of 1952. Paricutín's nine-square-mile lava flow eventually destroyed two villages and damaged nine others before the volcano became dormant, topping off at 1,345 feet (410 meters) above the original surface of land. The artist, Alfredo Zalce (1908–), was born about fifty miles southeast of where the volcano was formed, and his painting captures a still-dangerous Paricutín six years after its birth.

Reading the Art *What attitude do the men seem to have about the volcano erupting? What details in the painting make you think so?*

THE LANGUAGE OF LITERATURE TEACHER'S EDITION **711**

UNIT SIX
Part 1 Skills Trace

ML DENOTES MINI-LESSON IN TEACHER'S EDITION

Selections	Reading Skills and Strategies	Literary Concepts	Writing Opportunities	Speaking, Listening, and Viewing
NONFICTION **Unfinished Business** Elisabeth Kübler-Ross, interviewed by Lynn Gilbert and Gaylen Moore	Understanding an interview format, PE p. 713	Paradox, PE p. 722 Theme, PE p. 722 Reviewing figurative language, **ML** TE p. 719	Write a list of interview questions, PE p. 721 Paragraph, PE p. 721 Write a brief character sketch, PE p. 721 Write a short poem, PE p. 721 List lessons of life, PE p. 721	Group discussion, PE p. 721 Interviews, PE p. 722 Brief oral report, PE p. 722 Critical viewing, **ML** TE p. 718
POETRY **Annabel Lee** Edgar Allen Poe **Incident in a Rose Garden** Donald Justice	Appreciating narrative poetry, PE p. 725 Identifying narrative elements, PE p. 725 Identifying poetic elements, PE p. 725	Meter, PE p. 731 Feet, PE p. 731 Personification, PE p. 731 Reviewing rhyme, **ML** TE p. 727	Write a description, PE p. 730 Draft a psychological examination, PE p. 730 Write an explanation of your opinion, PE p. 730 Repetition, **ML** TE p. 729 Brainstorm a list of characters, TE p. 730	Partner discussion, PE p. 730 Class/panel discussion, PE p. 731 Perform a skit, PE p. 730
POETRY **Traveling Through the Dark** William Stafford **The Sharks** Denise Levertov		Imagery, PE p. 735	Write words and phrases associated with deer and shark, PE p. 732 Prepare a letter of argument, PE p. 735 Rewrite "The Sharks" as a first-person narrative, PE p. 735 Write a short poem, PE p. 735 Brainstorm a list of ideas unique to poems, PE p. 735	Small group discussion, PE p. 735 Viewing art, **ML** TE p. 734
DRAMA **Sorry, Right Number** Stephen King	Visualizing, PE p. 737	Suspense, PE p. 754 Falling action, PE p. 754 Drama, **ML** TE p. 743 Reviewing foreshadowing, **ML** TE p. 751	Write an outline, PE p. 754 Make up a "scientific" explanation, PE p. 754 Irony and humor, **ML** TE p. 747	Class discussion, PE p. 754 Dramatization, PE p. 754 Small group discussion, PE p. 755 Present a scene, PE p. 755 View video *Sorry, Right Number*, PE p. 755 Oral report, PE p. 755 Watching a TV drama, **ML** TE p. 746
NONFICTION ON YOUR OWN **A Trip to the Edge of Survival** Ron Arias			Keeping a captain's log, TE p. 756	Dramatic reading, TE p. 756

Writing	Reading Skills and Strategies	Literary Concepts	Writing Opportunities	Speaking, Listening, and Viewing
WRITING ABOUT LITERATURE **Creative Response**	Understanding mood, PE pp. 766–767 Responding to literature, PE pp. 768–771	Understanding mood, PE pp. 766–767 Story elements, PE pp. 768–769	Changing a mood, PE p. 767 Describing a mood, PE p. 767 Creating a mood, PE p. 767 Playwriting, PE pp. 768–771 Using foreshadowing, PE p. 767	Viewing a scene, PE p. 773 Interpreting a mood, PE p. 773 Discussion, PE p. 773 Discussing a setting, PE p. 773

Grammar, Usage, Mechanics, and Spelling	Multimodal Learning	Research and Study Skills	Vocabulary
	Sketch or painting, PE p. 722 Videotape interviews, PE p. 722 Brief oral report, PE p. 722	Research the five stages of dying, PE p. 722 Goal: Teaches others new skills, ML TE p. 716	bland procrastinating concretely punitive contaminated spontaneous convey transcend devastated uniqueness
	Class/panel discussion, PE p. 731 Create a comparison/contrast chart, TE p. 730 Create a collage of pictures and words, TE p. 730	Research various geographical areas, time periods, myths, and legends on personification of death, PE p. 731	
	Cause and effect chart, PE p. 736 Contact local or national environmental organizations, TE p. 736 Create a shark fact poster, TE p. 736 Conduct a poll, TE p. 736 Create a perception/reality chart, TE p. 736	Research the impact of waste and littering on the environment, TE p. 736	
Capitalization of titles, ML TE p. 741	Design a magazine cover, PE p. 755 Computer graphics program, PE p. 755 View Sorry, Right Number, PE p. 755 Oral report, PE p. 755 Create an effective stage adaptation, TE p. 755	Memorizing, ML TE p. 749	bleakly chasm interim intuition prone
Sketch a storyboard, TE p. 763 Pack a survival kit, TE p. 764			

Grammar, Usage, Mechanics, and Spelling	Multimodal Learning	Research and Study Skills	Media Literacy
Choosing the correct modifier, PE p. 771 Using adjectives and adverbs, PE p. 771	Viewing a scene, PE p. 773 Interpreting a mood, PE p. 773 Discussion, PE p. 773 Discussing a setting, PE p. 773	Creatively responding to literature, PE pp. 768–771 Analyzing setting, PE p. 773	Interpreting mood, PE p. 773

UNIT SIX
Part 2 Skills Trace

ML DENOTES MINI-LESSON IN TEACHER'S EDITION

Selections	Reading Skills and Strategies	Literary Concepts	Writing Opportunities	Speaking, Listening, and Viewing
FICTION **The Cask of Amontillado** Edgar Allan Poe	Evaluating the narrator, PE p. 775	Verbal irony, PE p. 785 Mood, PE p. 785 Reviewing point of view, **ML** TE p. 777 Fiction, **ML** TE p. 779	Write director's notes, PE p. 784 Write a final scene, PE p. 784 Using specific modifiers, **ML** TE p. 780	Small group discussion, PE p. 784 Dramatic reading, PE p. 785 Oral report, PE p. 785 Class discussion, TE p. 784
FICTION **The Most Dangerous Game** Richard Connell	Making inferences, PE p. 787	Suspense, PE p. 807 Reviewing setting, **ML** TE p. 794 Figurative language, TE p. 802 Irony, TE p. 806	Write a diary entry, PE p. 807 Write an article for sensational tabloid, PE p. 807 Venn diagram, PE p. 807 Specific examples, **ML** TE p. 797	Class discussion, PE p. 807 Sportscast: Play-by-play, **ML** TE p. 799
NONFICTION **Not to Go With the Others** John Hersey	Inferring motivation, PE p. 809 Using a reading log, PE p. 809	Tone, PE p. 815 Author's purpose, PE p. 815 Reviewing author's purpose, **ML** TE p. 813	Expository paragraph, PE p. 815 Write a reflection, PE p. 815 Create a flow chart, PE p. 815 Sentence variety: Using short sentences to build suspense, **ML** TE p. 811	Group discussion, PE p. 815 Oral report, PE p. 816
FICTION **My Wonder Horse/Mi Caballo Mago** Sabine R. Ulibarrí		Imagery, PE p. 828 Reviewing symbol, **ML** TE p. 821	Write several sentences, PE p. 817 Write a description, PE p. 828 Write an outline, PE p. 828 Make a list, PE p. 828 Using repeated words to build coherence, **ML** TE p. 820	Class discussion, PE p. 828 Oral report, PE p. 829 Storyboarding, **ML** TE p. 825 Oral report, TE p. 829
FICTION ON YOUR OWN **The Wife's Story** Ursula K. LeGuin			Dialogue journal, TE p. 830 Writing a story, TE p. 832	Paired reading, TE p. 830 Panel discussion, TE p. 831

Writing	Reading Skills and Strategies	Literary Concepts	Writing Opportunities	Speaking, Listening, and Viewing
WRITING FROM EXPERIENCE **Narrative and Literary Writing**		Story elements, PE pp. 836–839	Writing a short story, PE pp. 834–841 Drafting, PE pp. 838–839 Creating paragraphs, PE p. 839 Revising and publishing, PE pp. 840–841	Audiotape, PE p. 841

Grammar, Usage, Mechanics, and Spelling	Multimodal Learning	Research and Study Skills	Vocabulary	
Subject-verb agreement: Inverted sentences, ML TE p. 778	Tape-record using sound effects, PE p. 785 Draw a picture, PE p. 785 Create a set design, PE p. 785 Oral report, PE p. 785 Managing an inventory, ML TE p. 781	Research the history of catacombs, PE p. 785 Research the origin and history of carnival celebrations, PE p. 785	accost destined fetter implore impunity	preclude repose subside termination virtuoso
Demonstrative adjectives, ML TE p. 790	Create an illustrated map, PE p. 808 Computer graphics program, PE p. 808	Research the Cape buffalo, PE p. 808 Reference: Other sources, ML TE p. 801 Research cartography, TE p. 808	affable amenity condone deplorable disarming droll elude	imperative quarry scruple solicitously stamina tangible uncanny
Using the past perfect tense, ML TE p. 812	Computer, PE p. 816 Oral report, PE p. 816 Timelines, graphs, or charts, TE p. 816	Research a concentration camp in Poland, PE p. 816	dispatch ensue immersed pretense prostrate	
Using commas between coordinate adjectives, ML TE p. 824	Choreograph a short dance, PE p. 829 Oral report, PE p. 829 Giving a persuasive speech, ML TE p. 826 Oral report, TE p. 829 Consult Reader's Guide to Periodical Literature or an on-line guide, TE p. 829	Research importance of ranching and cowboys to New Mexico's economy, TE p. 829 Researching stories from folklore, literature, and film, TE p. 831	evoke indignity indomitable lethargy mandate	mystic transcendent ultimate vigil wane

Grammar, Usage, Mechanics, and Spelling	Multimodal Learning	Research and Study Skills	Media Literacy
Using commas in dialogue, PE p. 841	Analyzing magazine photographs, PE pp. 834–835 Analyzing newspaper articles, PE p. 835	Researching details, PE p. 837 Researching details, ML TE p. 837	Analyzing magazine photographs, PE pp. 834–835 Analyzing newspaper articles, PE p. 835

UNIT SIX
Recommended Resources

ENRICHMENT   RESEARCH

Recommended Novels and Play

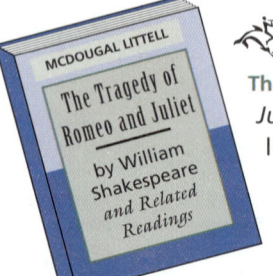

LITERATURE CONNECTIONS WITH SOURCEBOOK FOR TEACHERS

Thematic Link *The Tragedy of Romeo and Juliet* is a classic drama of love, hate, life, death, revenge, and realization set in Renaissance Italy. Fateful encounters lead to a tragic conclusion.

About the Author William Shakespeare (1564–1616) was an actor, poet, and playwright whose work was popular among the working class and the educated upper classes. He is considered by many to be the greatest playwright of all time.

Other Works by William Shakespeare *Julius Caesar; Hamlet, Prince of Denmark; Othello, the Moor of Venice; King Lear; Macbeth; Antony and Cleopatra*

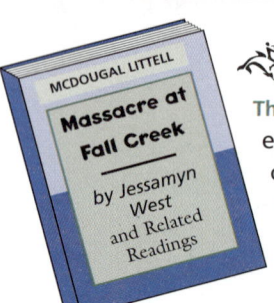

LITERATURE CONNECTIONS WITH SOURCEBOOK FOR TEACHERS

Thematic Link This novel dramatizes an event in the early 1800s—five men charged with the murder of several Native Americans. It chronicles the allegations and subsequent courtroom encounters as it addresses a rarely discussed point in American history.

About the Author Jessamyn West (1907–1984), an American Quaker from Indiana, won critical praise for this historical novel. She has also written about everyday Quaker life in the United States.

Other Works by Jessamyn West *The Friendly Persuasion; A Mirror for the Sky; The Witch Diggers; Cress Delahanty; Love, Death, and the Ladies' Drill Team*

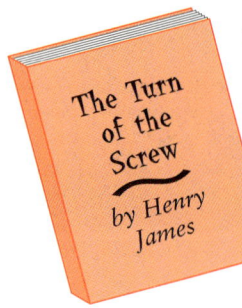

Thematic Link This multi-layered ghost story tells of a governess and her two enigmatic charges. It leads readers into uncharted territory.

About the Author Born to a prominent New York family, Henry James (1843–1916) spent most of his adult life in England. He was perhaps the greatest master of the short novel and the long short story.

Other Works by Henry James *Washington Square, The Portrait of a Lady, The Golden Bowl, The Ambassadors, The Wings of the Dove*

Professional Development — TEACHING THE NOVEL

Collins, Patricia Hill. *Black Feminist Thought.* NY: Routledge, 1991.

du Plessis, Rachel Blau. "The Critique of Consciousness and Myth in Levertov, Rich, and Rukeyser," *Writing Beyond the Ending.* Bloomington, IN: Indiana University Press, 1985.

Justice, Donald. "The Prose Sublime," *A Donald Justice Reader.* Hanover, NH: Press of New England, 1991.

Kübler-Ross, Elisabeth. *Death Is of Vital Importance.* Tarrytown, NY: Station Hill Press, 1991.

Walker, Alice. *Living by the Word.* NY: Harcourt Brace Jovanovich, 1981.

CROSS-CURRICULAR TEACHING   PROFESSIONAL DEVELOPMENT

Recommended Readings in Cross-Curricular Areas

SOCIAL STUDIES

Death Be Not Proud by John Gunther (1971) A popular book about a young man's courageous struggle against a fatal brain tumor. Links to Kübler-Ross's "Unfinished Business."

The Oxford Book of Death (1983) This comprehensive anthology contains a marvelous collection of passages and quotes on the subject of death. Links to most selections in this unit.

Admitting the Holocaust by Laurence Langor, ed. (1995) A rich combination of essays that ask about this tragedy's portrayal in literature. Links to John Hersey's "Not to Go with the Others."

Professional Development — CROSS-CURRICULAR INSTRUCTION

Fagan, Edward R. "Interdisciplinary English: Science, Technology, and Society," *English Journal* 76 (September 1987) 81–83.

Gulyas, Carol. "Reflections on Telling Stories," *English Education*. 26:3 (October 1994) 189.

Heuser, Linda. "Death Education: A Model for Student-Participatory Learning," *Death Studies*. 19:6 (November/December 1995).

Recommended Media Resources

THE LANGUAGE OF LITERATURE

ELECTRONIC LIBRARY
CD-ROM
Additional literature selections for Unit Six can be found on the Electronic Library CD-ROM.

LASERLINKS
Videodisc, Gr. 9
See *LaserLinks Teacher's Source Book*, page 48, for overview of Unit Six.

AUDIO LIBRARY
Tapes
Unit Six: A Matter of Life and Death Gr. 9, Tapes 15–17: Sides A & B

WRITING COACH
Writing Coach Software: Writing About Literature—Interpretive Response, Short Story

OUTSIDE RESOURCES

Films/Videos/Film Strips/Audiocassettes
The Cask of Amontillado, video, Knowledge Unlimited, 1965, (29 minutes).
Annabel Lee, video, Aims Media, 1971, (10 minutes).
Poetry of Edgar Allan Poe, audiocassette or CD, Dove Audio, 1995, (60 minutes).
Alice Walker Reads, audiocassette, American Audio Prose Library, (36 minutes).
John Hersey Reads, audiocassette, American Audio Prose Library, (55 minutes).

Internet Resources
McDougal Littell Literature Center at http://www.hmco.com/mcdougal/lit

Professional Development — TEACHING WITH TECHNOLOGY

Banson, Robert K., and Buckner, Terrelle. "Quality Applications to the Classroom of Tomorrow," *Educational Technologies*. 35:3 (May/June 1995) 19.

Bruder, Isabelle. "Alternative Assessment: Putting Technology to the Test," *Electronic Learning*. 12:4 (January 1993) 23–29.

Education Technology. Business Publishers, Inc., 951 Pershing Drive, Silver Springs, MD 20910.

RECOMMENDED RESOURCES   TEACHER'S EDITION   **711f**

UNIT SIX
Professional Enrichment

F.A.L.L. into Literature: A First- and Last-Line Approach to Reading and Writing
Rose Reissman

> The following article provides a unique strategy for literature study that has wide-reaching application.

As a lover of literature and a lifelong writer, I always try to find ways to draw my students into reading and writing.

Recently, while going through the bargain-book shelves at a local bookstore, I found an intriguing title: *In the Beginning—Great First Lines from Your Favorite Books* (collected by Hans Baven, San Francisco: Chronicle Books, 1991).

As I leafed through the volume, picking out the first lines of many of my favorite works of literature, I realized that many of the first lines were evocative in and of themselves. Reading the first lines of unfamiliar works, I found myself thinking about what sorts of plots might be developed from these opening lines. Intending to satisfy my curiosity at the library, I pulled out my notebook and copied down the unfamiliar lines I was particularly intrigued with, noting also the titles of the books these lines were taken from.

Then it hit me. If first lines were so intriguing to me, why not use the same interest to motivate my students to do some reading and writing?

I selected seven first lines from works I felt confident the students hadn't read, but which I felt would be accessible and age-appropriate reading:

1. "Serene was a word you could put to Brooklyn, New York."
2. "Early in the summer of 1750, in the village of Juffure, four days upriver from the coast of The Gambia, West Africa, a man-child was born to Omoro and Binta Kinte."
3. "Somewhere a child began to cry."
4. "Now she sits alone and remembers."
5. "The law, as quoted, lays down a fair conduct of life, and one not easy to follow."
6. "I look at myself in the mirror."
7. "José Palacios, his oldest servant, found him floating naked with his eyes open in the purifying waters of his bath and thought he had drowned."

I reproduced these quotes on a worksheet and distributed copies to the class. The students were given a chance to read through the quotes and decide which particularly intrigued them or raised questions for them. When they had a chance to review the first lines on their own, they shared their initial reactions. Among their comments were:

"That quote about Brooklyn must be from some really-out-of-date book. 'Serene'—are you kidding?"
"Is Juffure a real place in Africa? I'm going to look it up."
"'She sits alone and remembers'... that's my grandma. She's always talking about what happened long ago."
"That José quote could be the opening of a detective story."
"'A child began to cry.' Is that a book about Bosnia?"

As they talked, the students "sparked" writing ideas from one another's comments. They discussed which quotes were suggestive of mystery (#7) and/or horror (#6 and #7). Also they speculated that quotes #1 and #2 were from stories in which geography played an important role.

After the students had shared their initial responses to these first lines, I invited them each to choose a first line they found most inspiring and to follow it up by writing a first paragraph for that book. Students had about 15 minutes to develop paragraphs that followed logically from their chosen lines.

First Lines

NAME _____
DATE _____

Instructions: The following are the first lines from seven famous books. Read them through first and list any questions or reactions you have to them.

1. "Serene was a word you could put to Brooklyn, New York."
Questions/Reaction _____
_____

2. "Early in the summer of 1750, in the village of Juffure, four days upriver from the coast of The Gambia, West Africa, a man-child was born to Omoro and Binta Kinte."
Questions/Reaction _____
_____

3. "Somewhere a child began to cry."
Questions/Reaction _____
_____

4. "Now she sits alone and remembers."
Questions/Reaction _____
_____

5. "The law, as quoted, lays down a fair conduct of life, and one not easy to follow."
Questions/Reaction _____
_____

6. "I look at myself in the mirror."
Questions/Reaction _____
_____

7. "José Palacios, his oldest servant, found him floating naked with his eyes open in the purifying waters of his bath and thought he had drowned."
Questions/Reaction _____
_____

Now select the one that touches you the most and follow it up by writing the rest of the first paragraph for this book.

When the students finished writing, I encouraged them to respond to one another's writings. Many students expressed support and admiration for one another's writing. Because only seven quotations had been offered, many students had written first paragraphs for the same quotations, and students were fascinated by the variety of paragraphs that had been written for the same first line.

The session ended with students asking me to reveal who the authors were and what books the first lines were from, which I did:

1. Betty Smith, *A Tree Grows in Brooklyn*, 1943
2. Alex Haley, *Roots*, 1976
3. Elie Wiesel, *Dawn*, 1960
4. Carlos Fuentes, *The Old Gringo*, 1985
5. Rudyard Kipling, *The Man Who Would Be King*, 1888
6. James Baldwin, *If Beale Street Could Talk*, 1974
7. Gabriel García Márquez, *The General in his Labyrinth*, 1989

My reward was watching students copy down the sources of their favorite first lines and hearing them say they wanted to read the books.

As a result of this initial success, I decided that since the students had enjoyed working "forward" from the first lines so much, they might also respond to the challenge of "falling back" into literature by working backward in plot from the last lines of literary works. But this time, rather than create my own worksheet of last lines from literary works for them, I asked each of my students to select the last line from a favorite book and write it on a piece of paper. They were given two days and asked to select books whose last lines would not be easily identified by their peers (in other words, not a recent class assignment or a book that "everybody" had just been talking about).

When the students came to class with their selections on slips of paper, I distributed a small envelope to each student. I asked students to write their names on the front of the envelopes and place the slips inside. Then I had the students seal the envelopes. One student collected them and redistributed them so no student received his or her own envelope back.

Next, the students opened the envelopes and proceeded to "fall back" from the enclosed last lines into the plots that had preceded them. Once the students had written their last paragraphs, they shared them with the student whose name was on the envelope. The student who had chosen the book then revealed how close the invented ending was to the actual last paragraph. (Since many students are curious to compare their endings to the original, you might want to ask each student to photocopy or write down the actual last paragraph of the book they selected and to bring it to class at the same time they bring their slips of paper.) The students shared the titles and authors of their last lines with one another. Again they were eager to exchange works so they could read each other's authors.

These strategies were also used by my students as peer teaching and parent-child workshop strategies. The envelope approach proved particularly popular since every student was both a preparer and a participant.

As a consequence of this "collaboration," with the actual writer of a particular piece, students become accustomed to the roles of reader and author—good roles to F.A.L.L. into.

Copyrighted material reprinted with permission.

UNIT SIX

Starting Points for Unit Projects

The following suggestions will help you initiate individual and group projects during the course of this unit.

Creating a Set Of Drawings

ART PROJECT Invite students, either individually or in small groups, to create a set of drawings that represent danger. You might ask students to preview the titles and illustrations in Unit Six in order to get ideas for subject matter. Allow students to draw in media of their choice, such as pencil, colored pencil, pen and ink, or charcoal. Display students' work in the classroom.

Creating a Time Line

RESEARCH PROJECT Ask students to make time lines of the major events of their own lives, from birth to the present. Choice of events to include should be up to the individual student, but suggest that students highlight encounters that changed their lives in some way. Encourage students to share their time lines with their classmates by displaying them on a bulletin board or summarizing them orally.

Investigating Dangerous Occupations

GROUP RESEARCH PROJECT Divide students into groups of three or four and ask them to list about ten occupations that they think might be especially dangerous. Then have them go to the library and, with the librarian's assistance, locate U.S. labor statistics showing the most dangerous occupations. After students have done their research, have a whole-class discussion in which they can compare results and share opinions about the appeal of dangerous jobs.

Writing a Short Story

WRITING PROJECT Ask students to imagine that they have been invited to contribute a short story to a student-written textbook, in a unit called "A Matter of Life and Death." They have a one-week deadline to invent a plot summary and begin a draft. Students may plan and write their stories individually, in pairs, or in groups of three or four. Allow students to preview the title pages of the subunits and the opening pages of the selections in Unit Six for inspiration. Encourage volunteers to read their stories or story plans aloud, or to distribute printed copies.

Packing a Survival Kit

PHYSICAL EDUCATION PROJECT Invite groups of three or four students to imagine that they are embarking on a rigorous survival training expedition. They are allowed to take as much food, clothing, and equipment as they can carry in backpacks. (You might want to specify a weight limit, such as 30, 40, or 50 pounds.) Ask students to list what they would take. If possible, you might also ask them to bring in the items and explain why they chose to include them in their survival kits.

Holding a Panel Discussion

GROUP DISCUSSION PROJECT Ask students to hold panel discussions on the death, violence, and danger that they see in television shows, movies, or other entertainment during the course of the week. Have one member of each group serve as moderator. Questions the moderator might ask include
- What was the most realistic depiction of death and danger you encountered?
- What was the most offensive or unbelievable depiction?
- What effect do you think the constant depiction of death and danger in entertainment has on young people?

Invite the groups to share their ideas with one another.

Family and Community Involvement

Family

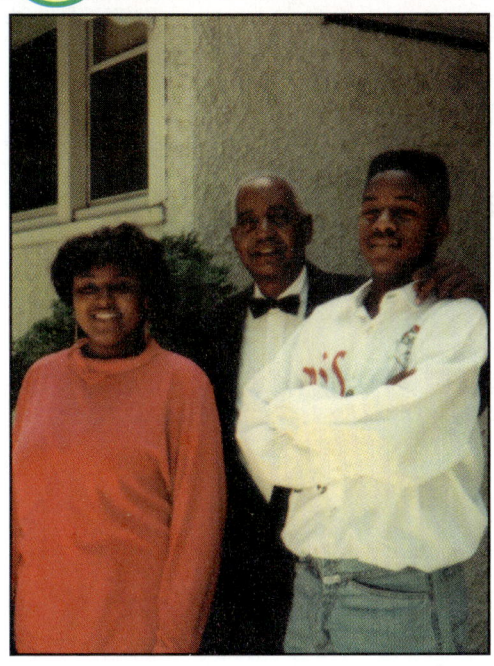

The selections in Unit Six offer unusual encounters and escapes from death—fateful encounters that often lead to philosophical examinations of the nature of life and death. The following activities will help students, their families, and other community members to share their ideas and reflections about death.

OPTION 1: WATCH A VIDEO

- **Connection** The selections in Unit Six portray individuals trying to save their own lives or the lives of others.
- **Activity** *Copymaster 1* Students and family members can watch a movie that presents rescues, such as *The Princess Bride* or *Schindler's List*. After viewing the film, they can talk about how people choose whether or not to help those in need.

OPTION 2 CREATE A SAFETY PLAN

- **Connection** Some of the selections in Unit Six explore the will to survive when faced with life-threatening danger.
- **Activity** *Copymaster 2* Students and family members can survey their home and create a safety plan to follow in case of a fire or other danger. They can gather the necessary equipment, explain the plan to other family members, and conduct a drill to make sure everyone knows what to do.

OPTION 3 WRITE AN ANECDOTE

- **Connection** Two selections in Unit Six portray recollections of choices that made the difference between life and death.
- **Activity** *Copymaster 3* Students and family members can recall memories of times they made choices that led them away from possible danger, though they may not have known at the time how their decision would affect their future.

Community

OPTION 1

- **Connection** The selections in Unit Six explore how some people face the thought of death.
- **Activity** Invite a hospice worker to class to explain the program and the services offered to terminally ill patients and their families.

OPTION 2

- **Connection** Some of the selections in Unit Six relate escapes from almost certain death.
- **Activity** Invite a boating expert or representative of the coast guard to discuss safety at sea and boating laws. Have your visitor relate stories of rescues at sea.

OPTION 3

- **Connection** "My Wonder Horse" examines the survival and freedom of animals in the wild.
- **Activity** Arrange to visit a veterinary hospital or humane society to learn about the care and rescue of animals. Also, encourage students to find out what to do in case they ever encounter an injured animal.

UNIT SIX
Part 1 Lesson Planner

TIME ALLOTMENTS SHOWN ARE APPROXIMATE. DEPENDING ON YOUR GOALS AND THE NEEDS OF YOUR STUDENTS, YOU MAY WISH TO ALLOW MORE OR LESS TIME FOR CERTAIN PORTIONS OF THE LESSON.

Table of Contents	Discussion	Previewing the Selection	Reading the Selection
PART OPENER **Uncharted Territory** page 710	**20 MINUTES** • Reflect on the part theme		
SELECTION **Unfinished Business** page 714 AVERAGE		**20 MINUTES** • PERSONAL CONNECTION • ART THERAPY CONNECTION • READING CONNECTION: Understanding an interview format	**40 MINUTES** • Introduce vocabulary • Read pp. 714–720 (7 pp.)
SELECTIONS **Annabel Lee** **Incident in a Rose Garden** page 726 CHALLENGING		**20 MINUTES** • PERSONAL CONNECTION • LITERARY CONNECTION • READING CONNECTION: Appreciating narrative poetry	**20 MINUTES** • Read pp. 726–729 (4 pp.)
SELECTIONS **Traveling Through the Dark** **The Sharks** page 733 AVERAGE		**20 MINUTES** • PERSONAL CONNECTION • CULTURAL CONNECTION • WRITING CONNECTION	**15 MINUTES** • Read pp. 733–734 (2 pp.)
SELECTION **Sorry, Right Number** page 738 CHALLENGING		**20 MINUTES** • PERSONAL CONNECTION • LITERARY CONNECTION • READING CONNECTION: Visualizing	**60 MINUTES** • Introduce vocabulary • Read pp. 738–753 (16 pp.)
NONFICTION ON YOUR OWN **A Trip to the Edge of Survival** page 756 AVERAGE			**40 MINUTES** • Read pp. 756–765 (10 pp.)
Writing	**Writer's Style**	**Prewriting**	**Drafting and Revising**
WRITING ABOUT LITERATURE **Creative Response**	**15 MINUTES**	**25 MINUTES**	**55 MINUTES**

Time estimates assume in-class work. You may wish to assign some of these stages as homework.

Responding to the Selection

FROM PERSONAL RESPONSE TO CRITICAL ANALYSIS	OR	ANOTHER PATHWAY	LITERARY CONCEPTS	QUICKWRITES
		60 MINUTES		
• Discussion questions	OR	• Cooperative learning (lessons)	• Paradox • Theme	• Interview questions • Paragraph • Character sketch • Poem
		40 MINUTES		
• Discussion questions	OR	• Character attitudes	• Meter • Personification	• Description • Psychological examination
		40 MINUTES		
• Discussion questions	OR	• Cooperative learning (brainstorm)	• Imagery	• Letter • First-person narrative • Poem
		50 MINUTES		
• Discussion questions	OR	• Dramatization	• Suspense • Falling action	• Outline • Explanation

Extension Activities

	ALTERNATIVE ACTIVITIES	LITERARY LINKS	CRITIC'S CORNER	THE WRITER'S STYLE	ACROSS THE CURRICULUM	ART CONNECTION	WORDS TO KNOW	BIOGRAPHY
40 MINUTES								
	✔		✔		PSYCHOLOGY	✔	✔	✔
15 MINUTES								
		✔			WORLD CULTURES			✔
15 MINUTES								
				✔	ECOLOGY		✔	
30 MINUTES								
	✔				MEDIA		✔	✔

Publishing and Reflecting	Grammar in Context	Reading the World
20 MINUTES	**20 MINUTES**	**25 MINUTES**

PART 1

REFLECTING ON THEME

Have students imagine that they were going alone to explore uncharted territory, such as the ocean in "A Trip to the Edge of Survival." First have students select an uncharted place to explore. Then ask students to list five things they would take with them on their exploration. Finally, have volunteers share their "survival kits" with the class. As students read these selections, have them see what literal and figurative "survival kits" each character has packed to explore uncharted territory.

What Do You Think?

Before students begin their interviews, invite them to create a "risk scale" from 1 to 10, ranking events from least to most risky. For example, selecting clothing or food might rank at least risky; learning a new skill or performing in front of others as most risky. Have students mark their risk's "comfort zone" to compare with their partner's as they assess risk and its affects on life choices and attitude. Students will return to this activity on page 723.

UNIT SIX **PART 1**

UNCHARTED TERRITORY

REFLECTING ON THEME

Have you ever ventured into the unknown—into uncharted territory? Actually, every minute of your life is a step into the unknown. Each day outward on the voyage from your birth, you are carried into unexplored regions, through dangers and uncertainties, and sometimes past narrow escapes. The daily human journey is often a matter of life and death, as you will see in reading the selections in this part of Unit Six.

What Do You Think? Interview a classmate about an event or a decision that seemed like a move into uncharted territory—something never done before, something that took courage. Record the results of your interview in your notebook, then have the same classmate interview you. Afterward, share with the class what both of you learned. In discussion, consider how experiences of risk and uncertainty can affect one's attitudes toward life.

interview
Kate told me about the time she got lost on a camping trip.

Author	Title	Page
Elisabeth Kübler-Ross Interview by Lynn Gilbert and Gaylen Moore	**Unfinished Business** *Challenging the taboo of silence surrounding death*	713
Alice Walker	**"Good Night, Willie Lee, I'll See You in the Morning"** / INSIGHT *A lesson in forgiveness*	720
Edgar Allan Poe	**Annabel Lee** *A young man mourns his bride.*	724
Donald Justice	**Incident in a Rose Garden** *The stranger's hand was a little cage of bone.*	724
William Stafford	**Traveling Through the Dark** *A life-and-death decision by the side of a road.*	732
Denise Levertov	**The Sharks** *Their dark fins announce their presence.*	732
Stephen King	**Sorry, Right Number** *Who made that telephone call?*	737
Ron Arias	**A Trip to the Edge of Survival** *Five fishermen lost at sea for five months*	756

PREVIEWING

NONFICTION

Unfinished Business
Elisabeth Kübler-Ross
Interview by Lynn Gilbert and Gaylen Moore

Activating Prior Knowledge
PERSONAL CONNECTION

In this selection, a psychiatrist tells about her work with a dying child and the child's family. Think about how you might react if you or a loved one were dying from an incurable illness. Copy into your notebook the chart shown here, and check the phrases that describe what you think your reaction would be. If you wish, put numbers in the boxes to show how you might react at first and then at later stages. Add any other reactions you think you might have.

Reactions to Dying	
accept it	get angry
avoid thinking about it	learn from it
become depressed	make the most of time left
deny it	try to make a bargain with God
face it	view it as a horrible thing
fear it	view it as a natural process
fight it	

Building Background
ART THERAPY CONNECTION

Adults often think children are too young to understand what dying is. But even though young children may not be able to express in words their understanding of death, there is a way that they can share their inner awareness and their deepest feelings. Think of the times you've seen a child draw a picture and then explain it. In this selection, you will read how Elisabeth Kübler-Ross helped three children use drawing as a kind of "symbolic language" to describe their feelings about their dying sister. As you read, notice the drawings accompanying the selection. They were not made by the children Kübler-Ross describes but by the children from another family after their nine-month-old brother Kevin died as the result of a heart defect. The drawings by Sean, Mary Kate, and Kerry Cullen provide an example of the kind of "symbolic language" by which, Kübler-Ross says, even the very young can teach us about life and death.

Active Reading/Setting a Purpose
READING CONNECTION

Understanding an Interview Format What you are about to read is an interview with Kübler-Ross conducted by Lynn Gilbert and Gaylen Moore. In an interview, the subject answers questions that the interviewer asks. The interviewer usually comes away with notes and often with a tape recording. He or she may then shape the information into a biographical essay, known as a profile. Another approach—the one used here by Gilbert and Moore—is to edit a taped interview, focusing on the best parts of the conversation and allowing the subject to speak directly to the reader. This format allows the subject's personality to emerge clearly. As you read "Unfinished Business," pay attention to the impressions you get of Kübler-Ross as well as to her message about dying.

UNFINISHED BUSINESS **713**

OVERVIEW

Objectives
- To understand and appreciate an interview that explores how a family confronts a child's death
- To identify and understand paradox
- To express understanding of the interview through a choice of writing forms, including interview questions, a paragraph, a character sketch, and a poem
- To extend understanding of the interview through a variety of multimodal and cross-curricular activities

Skills

LITERARY CONCEPTS
- Paradox
- Figurative language

READING SKILLS/ STRATEGIES
- Understanding an interview format

SPEAKING, LISTENING, AND VIEWING
- Critical viewing

PRINT AND MEDIA RESOURCES

UNIT SIX RESOURCE BOOK
Strategic Reading: Literature, p. 4
Vocabulary SkillBuilder, p. 5

ACCESS FOR STUDENTS ACQUIRING ENGLISH
Selection Summaries
Reading Support

TEACHER'S GUIDE TO ASSESSMENT AND PORTFOLIO USE

FORMAL ASSESSMENT
Selection Test, pp. 129–130
 Test Generator

 AUDIO LIBRARY
See Reference Card

 LASERLINKS
Psychology Connection

INTERNET RESOURCES
McDougal Littell Literature Center at http://www.hmco.com /mcdougal/lit

THE LANGUAGE OF LITERATURE TEACHER'S EDITION **713**

SUMMARY

Elisabeth Kübler-Ross, an expert on issues related to death and dying, talks about her experiences with dying children, who she says have taught her about life. She tells about a 12-year-old girl who went home to die. Kübler-Ross asked the other children in the household to draw pictures. The girl's 6-year-old brother depicted his sister dying. When Kübler-Ross asked him what he would like to say to his sister, he told her that he wished his sister would die and get it over with. She urged him to tell his sister how he felt. When he did, he and his sister discovered how much they loved each other. For days thereafter, the girl suffered but was unable to die. She said it was because she loved her parents more than God, and she knew this was wrong. Kübler-Ross helped the girl understand that God is a teacher and that if her death was difficult, it was because God especially loved her. Shortly before the girl's death, Kübler-Ross visited her once more. Unable to speak, she looked at Kübler-Ross and then looked down at her deformed body, communicating her certainty that God loved her. Soon after, she died.

Thematic Link: *Uncharted Territory* A psychiatrist speaks about her experiences with the dying and about the lessons to be learned from those facing the unknowable experience of death.

CUSTOMIZING FOR
Students Acquiring English

- Use **ACCESS FOR STUDENTS ACQUIRING ENGLISH**, *Reading Support*.
- After introducing the selection using some of the elements on page 713, ask students to share any special attitudes or customs concerning death that they find in their own culture.

Literary Concept: PARADOX

A Point out to students the paradox in the opening sentences, and explain how it captures the readers' interest. Tell students that a paradox is a statement that seems self-contradictory or opposed to common sense but that may nevertheless be true. Point out that most people would not "love" to work with dying children, nor would they find them "beautiful."

UNFINISHED BUSINESS

ELISABETH KÜBLER-ROSS

INTERVIEW BY LYNN GILBERT AND GAYLEN MOORE

A *I love to work with dying children. They're just so beautiful.*

Nobody knows what pearls they are. They have all the wisdom in

the world. They know that they are dying. They know how and

when they are dying. They teach you all about life if you can hear,

if you can listen to them. They use an incredible symbolic language

714 UNIT SIX PART 1: UNCHARTED TERRITORY

WORDS TO KNOW

bland (blănd) *adj.* smooth and untroubled but also ordinary or dull (p. 720)
concretely (kŏn-krēt'lē) *adv.* in a real, solid, material way (p. 718)
contaminated (kən-tăm'ə-nā-tĭd) *adj.* dirtied, polluted, or spoiled by contact with or addition of something **contaminate** *v.* (p. 717)
convey (kən-vā') *v.* to make known; communicate (p. 715)
devastated (dĕv'ə-stā'tĭd) *adj.* destroyed; stunned and overwhelmed **devastate** *v.* (p. 718)

procrastinating (prō-krăs'tə-nā'tĭng) *n.* putting off doing something until later; delaying **procrastinate** *v.* (p. 717)
punitive (pyōō'nĭ-tĭv) *adj.* punishing or having to do with punishment (p. 718)
spontaneous (spŏn-tā'nē-əs) *adj.* happening in a free, natural way, without effort or much thought (p. 716)
transcend (trăn-sĕnd') *v.* to pass beyond the limits of; be greater than (p. 716)
uniqueness (yōō-nēk'nĭs) *n.* the quality or condition of being like no other (p. 720)

Kerry, age 5, drew this picture of herself with Kevin in the bathtub.

to convey to you how much they know. If people would only understand their symbolic language.

One of my girls, I took her home to die, but she couldn't die. She was just lying there week after week after week. And the father couldn't communicate with her. He was a very non-verbal man. The mother was very verbal and a practicing Catholic. Every family member was at a different stage and used his own coping mechanism.[1] That's the time when you have to help always the ones who limp behind because they're going to hurt the most and they're going to have the most unfinished business. We try to help them finish the unfinished business *before* somebody dies, otherwise they have all the grief work afterward.

Grief is the most God-given gift to get in touch with your losses. You shed your tears and then stand up and start again like a child who falls and hurts his knees, cries for fifteen seconds

---

1. **coping mechanism:** way of thinking or behaving that helps one deal with problems, troubles, or sorrows.

WORDS TO KNOW

convey (kən-vā′) *v.* to make known; communicate

Linking to Science

B Dr. Carl Jung (1875–1961) performed some of the first psychiatric research on aspects of the mind that are "beyond speech"—the unconscious. It is in this part of the mind that the emotions that influence conscious behavior are thought to reside. Since cultural conditioning is sometimes an obstacle to honest expression, Jungian psychiatrists encourage patients to use nonverbal techniques of communication, such as drawing, in order to bypass these obstacles.

Critical Thinking: SUMMARIZING

C Ask students why the doctor has the children draw pictures. *(Possible response: She feels that people are more open and spontaneous and less deceptive in their drawings.)* Then ask what each child's picture reveals. *(The children know that their sister is dying.)*

---

and then jumps up and plays ball again. That's a natural thing. My work is preventive psychiatry, it's to finish as much as possible before death, like we bring flowers to our patients before they die so we don't have to pile them up on the casket afterward. If I love somebody, I tell them "I love you" now, so I can skip the schmaltzy eulogies[2] afterward.

> They know they are going to die, and they share their concepts of life and death and unfinished business in their pictures.

One day I asked the father of this twelve-year-old girl if he would give me permission to talk to the other children, six, ten and eleven years old. He said, "They don't know about it." I said, "Come, your child's arms and legs are like pieces of chalk, and her belly is like she's nine months pregnant, and she's lying there slowly dying in the living room. How can a six-, ten- and eleven-year-old not know?" I said, "All I want is for you to give your permission for me to sit with them without grownups, and I'll ask them to draw me a picture." We used the Susan Bach method. She's a Jungian analyst[3] from London who worked in Zurich in my hospital there with children who had brain tumors. She saw that children who had brain tumors, little children, show in their pictures that they know they are going to die, and they share their concepts of life and death and unfinished business in their pictures.

I use this technique daily. In a few minutes I can evaluate the whole family and know who needs the most help and who's O.K. and who's in pain. You don't need hours and hours of psychiatric evaluation, which is just talking and just touches the surface. This is all preconscious[4] material. It's the same material that you would get if you had ten consecutive dreams, but I can get it at a morgue, at a wake, in a church, in a school, in a motel, in a shack in Alaska in an Eskimo family, with Aborigines in Australia; it costs nothing, it takes five minutes, it <u>transcends</u> language, it's human. All human beings are the same anyway.

So the father finally gave me permission, and I went there at three-thirty when school was out so that the father wouldn't be back, you know, and have second thoughts and give in to his own anxiety. The children were absolutely gorgeous. I locked the dining room with a key so no grownup could interfere, and I said, "Let's have a competition. We're going to draw a picture and we have ten minutes." I limit the time so they don't start thinking, so it's as genuine and authentic and <u>spontaneous</u> as possible. In every picture these children revealed they knew that their sister was dying. I just said, "Use any color and draw a picture."

Anyway, the six-year-old was just gorgeous. His picture was so clear. I talked with him about it in the presence of the others. I said to him, "What your picture is telling is that your sister is dying." He said, "Yes." I said, "Well, if she's going to die tomorrow, is there anything you haven't done, because this is your last chance to say or do anything you want to

---

2. **schmaltzy eulogies** (shmält′sē yōō′lə-jēz): overly sentimental talk in praise of a dead person.
3. **Jungian** (yōōng′ē-ən) **analyst**: psychiatrist who follows the teachings of Carl Jung (1875–1961), a Swiss psychiatrist.
4. **preconscious:** having to do with memories or feelings that are not part of one's immediate awareness but that can be recalled through conscious effort.

WORDS TO KNOW
transcend (trăn-sĕnd′) *v.* to pass beyond the limits of; be greater than
spontaneous (spŏn-tā′nē-əs) *adj.* happening in a free, natural way, without effort or much thought

---

Mini-Lesson Workplace Literacy

SCANS Goal: Teaches Others New Skills

TEACHING OTHERS Have students note the way Kübler-Ross helps the children she works with learn to express their emotions and come to a greater understanding of their own feelings. Point out that by using verbal prompts, encouragement, and specific examples (such as the teacher who gives tough assignments), Kübler-Ross is able to help the children communicate better and achieve a greater understanding. Then tell students that the ability to help others learn, rather than simply telling them to do something, is an important workplace skill.

Application Have students work in pairs. Ask each student to think of something he or she knows how to do that the partner doesn't and to teach that skill to the partner, using encouragement and example. Afterwards, students should discuss which teaching techniques were most beneficial in helping them to acquire their partner's skill.

do, so that you don't have to worry about it afterwards when it's too late. That's what grownups do, but you don't have to do that." That challenged him. He said, "Yeah, I guess I'm supposed to tell her I love her." I said, "You're already a phoney-baloney at six years old." Children shouldn't be that contaminated. I said, "I've never seen a six-year-old who goes to a twelve-year-old and says, 'I love you.' There must have been a lot of things that she did that drove you up the wall, that she was unfair, you know, negative stuff." I said, "You can only really love her when you get rid of all the negative stuff, all the fights that you had, and when you get rid of that, then you love her so much that you don't need to say it, because she'll know it anyway and you'll know it."

He was fidgeting around at the table, and I said, "Come on, you're the youngest"—and the younger, the more honest they are—"get it out, what bugs you?" And he said, "Well, I really would like to tell her to get it over with already. I would like her to drop dead already." And I said, "Yes, naturally," as carefully as I could. And I said, "Why does it bug you that it takes so long?" He said, "I can't slam the doors ever, I can't bring my friends home, and I can't watch television anymore, and it's sickening how long it takes." You know, very natural, honest answers for a six-year-old.

I'm sitting there putting fuel on the fire and encouraging him to talk. The ten- and eleven-year-olds just sat there and stared at him. I said, "I wonder if you're honest enough and have the courage to share that with your sister." He said, "One ought not to do that." I said, "Who says? Do you think it's better to swallow this down, and then after she dies you have all these guilt

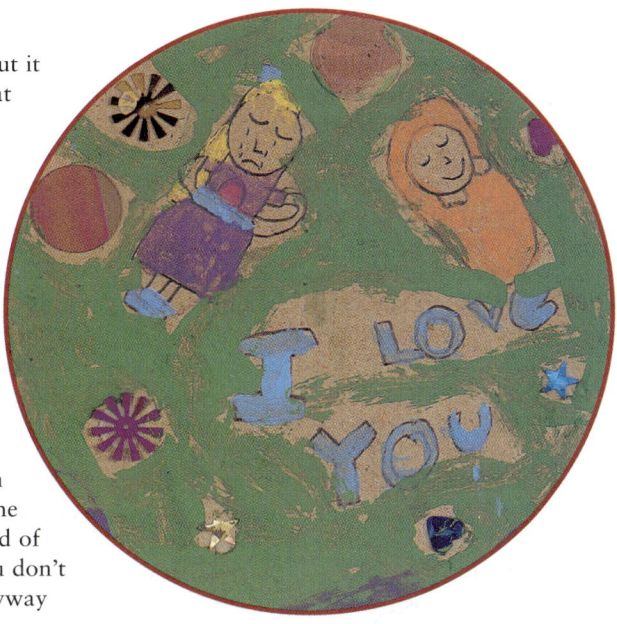

Mary Kate, age 7, shows her sorrow and her love in this collage done on a round lid.

trips and later on need counseling, or is it better to share it with your sister now and then you can love each other or forgive each other, whatever is necessary? And then you'll really feel super-duper. You will still miss her." They will have grief, you understand, but not grief *work*. He said, "Oh, I would love to be able to do that."

So you have to visualize . . . we go out into this living room where she lies there. And the six-year-old sits next to her, and I'm behind him, then the ten-year-old is behind me and the eleven-year-old behind her, then the mother came in and at the very end, the father behind her. And the arrangement was very symbolically beautiful. They came in the right chronological order in the courage they had to do that. Then the six-year-old starts procrastinating a little,

WORDS TO KNOW
contaminated (kən-tăm′ə-nā-tĭd) *adj.* dirtied, polluted, or spoiled by contact with or addition of something **contaminate** *v.*
procrastinating (prō-krăs′tə-nā′tĭng) *n.* putting off doing something until later; delaying **procrastinate** *v.*

717

Literary Concept:
FIGURATIVE LANGUAGE

G Ask students why they think the "floodgates" simile is appropriate for describing this scene. (*Possible response: The girl and her brother begin crying, releasing a reservoir of held-back emotions; the water image is particularly appropriate, considering their tears.*)

H Have students identify the use of hyperbole to describe the boy's reaction. Ask how it helps them visualize the scene. (*The description "he was the proudest man in the world" helps to illustrate the child's pleasure at what has taken place.*)

Critical Thinking:
SYNTHESIZING

I Ask students why the girl feels she can't "die." (*Possible response: She is afraid that she won't go to heaven; she has been taught that only those who love God more than anyone else go to heaven, and she loves her parents more than God.*) Ask students to discuss the doctor's method of dealing with the girl's belief. (*She avoids attacking the religious training the girl has had.*)

---

and I gave him a little nudge in the pants with my foot. Then he blurted it out and said to her, "You know, sometimes it takes so long, sometimes I pray to get it over with."

He was just ready to explain, and something very beautiful happened with that symbolic language. His sister lifted her arms up with her last strength and fell over his shoulders, and hanging on to him she started to sob and sob and cry, not painful crying but tremendous relief. It was just like floodgates opening. In her sobbing she kept repeating, "Thank God, thank God, thank God. I prayed for the last three days for God to take me already because it really is getting too much now. And every time I finish my prayer, Mom comes in and stands in the doorway and said she spent the whole night sitting up, praying to God to keep me." And she said, "If you help me, then together we can outdo Mom."

Children take everything very <u>concretely</u>.

> **His sister lifted her arms up with her last strength and fell over his shoulders, and hanging on to him she started to sob and sob.**

And he was the proudest man in the world, he was just beaming, and they were holding onto each other, crying and laughing. It was one of the most moving moments of house calls, and I've made lots of them. The other siblings naturally were envious that they weren't the ones who had the courage to do that.

About three days later I went back to see not just how she was doing, but how the six-year-old was doing, if he had any second thoughts about it. He was in super shape, he was high. But the girl couldn't die and so I asked the mother, I said, "If you don't mind, I'm just going to ask her straightforward, not in symbolic language, why she can't die, if that's O.K. with you. And I want you to come in and see how I'm doing that so you're never worried that I'm hurting anybody." She had great faith in me.

So I walked into the living room, and I looked at her and I said, "You just can't die, can you?" She said, "No." I said, "Why?" She said, "Because I can't get to heaven." I said, "Who told you that?" She said she was always taught for twelve years that nobody gets to heaven unless you have loved God more than anybody else in the whole world. Then she lifted her arms up and whispered in my ear as if she would try to prevent God from hearing her. She whispered very quietly, "You understand that I love my mommy and daddy better than anybody in the whole world."

That made me very sad that children have to apologize for that. What you then have to do is to set aside your own anger at the people who teach this kind of <u>punitive</u> approach. I said, "We're not going to get into an argument about who is right and who is wrong, because each one believes what they need to believe. I can only work with you and talk with you the way I always have. You and I always talked about school, and the biggest dream of your life was to be a schoolteacher. The only time I ever saw you <u>devastated</u> was in September when the school buses rolled up and school started after the summer vacation, and your brothers and sisters boarded the school bus, and you looked through this window and you really looked devastated." I said, "I think what happened was that at that moment it began to dawn on you that you will never again go back to your beloved school and you will never become a

WORDS TO KNOW	**concretely** (kŏn-krēt′lē) *adv.* in a real, solid, material way
	punitive (pyōō′nĭ-tĭv) *adj.* punishing or having to do with punishment
	devastated (dĕv′ə-stā′tĭd) *adj.* destroyed; stunned and overwhelmed **devastate** *v.*

Mini-Lesson: Speaking, Listening, and Viewing

CRITICAL VIEWING Point out to students Kübler-Ross's discussion of symbolic language throughout the selection. Have students talk about the ways in which a person can communicate meaning without the use of words, both consciously and unconsciously, through gestures, movements, and mannerisms. Explain that by paying close attention to a person's body language through critical viewing, people can infer information that they might otherwise miss.

Application Have students form small groups in which to practice critical viewing skills. Suggest that they videotape a newscast and watch it several times, at least once with the sound off. Have them take notes on the gestures, movements, and mannerisms of the different people they see on screen, including anchors, interview subjects, and public figures. Then ask them to discuss what they learned through the symbolic language of the people they viewed and whether they believe the body language was conscious or unconscious.

In this picture, Sean, age 9, imagines playing football with Kevin as an older boy. Sean praises Kevin with the words "nice throw."

Art Note

Sean's Drawing This picture was drawn by Kevin's older brother, Sean. Sean imagines what it might have been like for him if Kevin had lived.

Reading the Art What elements in the picture show how Sean feels about Kevin? Why do you think that Sean chose to draw his brother as an older boy?

STRATEGIC READING FOR
Less-Proficient Students

J Have students explain how the doctor helped the girl overcome her inability to die. *(The doctor compared the girl's terminal illness to a tough assignment given by a teacher to only the best students. God has therefore chosen her to accomplish this tough assignment.)*
Analyzing

Critical Thinking: SUMMARIZING

K Ask students how this scene demonstrates what the doctor means by symbolic language. *(Possible response: The girl uses her eyes and a smirk to express what she could not say.)*

teacher." I said, "I want to ask only one question. Sometimes your teacher gives very tough assignments to some students." It was in the back of my mind that she was an honor student. I said, "Does she give these assignments to her lousy students? Does she give it to everybody in the class without discrimination, or does she give it to a very few of her hand-picked, chosen students?" Then her face lit up and she said, "Oh, she gives it to very few of us." I said, "Since God is also a teacher, do you think He gave you a tough assignment? Or an assignment he could give to any child?"

What she did then was symbolic language. At first she didn't answer me in words. Ever so slowly she looked down at her belly and her arms which were not thicker than my thumb, and her belly full of cancer. She very slowly looked down her body, and then she looked at me and said, "I don't think God could give a tougher assignment to any child."

She died about two and a half or three days later. My last communication with her was totally nonverbal and to me very beautiful because I knew that it helped her. I thought at that time she was in a coma, and I came then so as not to disturb the family in the last day or two. I stood in the doorway and took another look at her, and she suddenly opened her eyes. She couldn't speak anymore at that time. And she looked down at her belly and her legs, and she had a big smirk on her face. And I nodded. She knew what I talked about and I knew what she talked about. It was totally nonverbal. It was very beautiful.

I learn always from dying patients. Instead

UNFINISHED BUSINESS **719**

Mini-Lesson Literary Concepts

REVIEWING FIGURATIVE LANGUAGE
Remind students that figurative language is language that conveys meaning beyond the literal meaning of the words. Tell them that figurative language is commonly used in everyday speech, not just in writing. Point out that at times during the interview, Kübler-Ross uses metaphor, simile, and hyperbole to help describe a scene, convey ideas, and illustrate actions. Then tell students that certain figurative comparisons are so common in speech and writing that they have become clichés—expressions that have been used so many times that they serve as a kind of shorthand for expressing an idea.

Application Ask students to review the selection for examples of figurative language used by Kübler-Ross. *(page 715, "limp behind"; page 717, "fuel on the fire"; page 718, "floodgates opening" and "proudest man in the world"; page 720, "throw overboard")* Then have students discuss whether they have ever heard or used any of these expressions, and if so, in what context.

COMPREHENSION CHECK
1. Who is Dr. Kübler-Ross, and what is her work? *(She is a counselor for dying patients and their families. She encourages them to express their feelings before the death occurs, to prevent problems later.)*
2. Give one or more examples of how she encourages honesty in the terminally ill and their families. *(She tells a boy not to be a "phoney-baloney" and to tell his sister how he feels; she helps a dying girl understand that it is OK to let go.)*
3. What lessons does Kübler-Ross say can be learned from people who are dying? *(how to communicate; how to look at the positive aspects of people, by seeing that every individual is unique and strong; how to be honest before it is too late)*

EDITOR'S NOTE With the permission of the author or copyright holder, potentially offensive material has been deleted from the selection.

INSIGHT

1. What impression do you have of the speaker's mother? of her reaction to her husband's death? *(Possible response: She is resigned to her husband's death; she takes it calmly because she has accepted the situation.)*
2. Do you agree or disagree with the speaker's statement about healing? Why or why not? *(Responses will vary.)*

ALICE WALKER

The eighth and youngest child of sharecropper parents in Georgia, Alice Walker (1944–) entered first grade at the age of four because her mother could no longer carry her while working in the fields. She began writing after a childhood accident that damaged one of her eyes. Walker was active in the civil rights movement during the 1960s, during which time she also taught at a number of universities. Besides poetry, Walker has written short stories, essays, and novels, including *The Color Purple*, which won the Pulitzer Prize in 1982. The characters in her fiction are often black women facing the challenges of racism, sexism, and alienation.

---

of always looking at the negative, what you see is the <u>uniqueness</u> and strength in every single human being. I have patients who never share, never communicate. They live a very <u>bland</u> life, and anybody who looked at them would say, Is this all there is to it? and then you really get to know those people. There is a beauty in them that very few see. And all you have to do is look.

Dying patients look back at their lives, and they review and evaluate what they would do over again if they had a second chance, and that's very instructive because dying patients throw overboard all the following: they don't have to impress you anymore, they do not have to pretend. They're not interested in material things. They have no secondary gains except to honestly share what life is all about and what lessons they have learned too late. And they pass it on to you, and I pass it on to others so they don't have to wait until they're on their deathbed and say the same thing. Dying patients literally teach you about life. ❖

INSIGHT

"Good Night, Willie Lee, I'll See You in the Morning"

Alice Walker

Looking down into my father's
dead face
for the last time
my mother said without
5   tears, without smiles
without regrets
but with *civility*[1]
"Good night, Willie Lee, I'll see you
in the morning."

10   And it was then I knew that the healing
of all our wounds
is forgiveness
that permits a promise
of our return
at the end.

---
1. **civility:** politeness, especially of a merely formal kind.

WORDS TO KNOW
uniqueness (yōō-nēk′nĭs) *n.* the quality or condition of being like no other
bland (blănd) *adj.* smooth and untroubled but also ordinary or dull

RESPONDING OPTIONS

FROM PERSONAL RESPONSE TO CRITICAL ANALYSIS

REFLECT
1. In your notebook, jot down words and phrases that describe your reactions to this selection. Share some of your reactions with a classmate.

RETHINK
Thematic Link

2. Consider the title. What unfinished business is described in this interview?

Close Textual Reading

3. What do you think of the approach that Kübler-Ross uses in trying to help the dying girl and her family?
   Consider
   - "You're already a phoney-baloney at six years old."
   - "You can only really love her when you get rid of all the negative stuff."
   - "I'm just going to ask her straightforward . . . why she can't die."

4. What impressions of Kübler-Ross do you get from reading this interview?

5. What do you think people can learn from those who are dying?

RELATE
6. How honest should people be with a dying person? Should the terminally ill be told they are dying, or should they always be offered hope? Should a patient's age affect this decision?

7. Look over the chart you completed for the Personal Connection activity on page 713. Now that you have read the selection, would you change any of the marks you made? Explain.

8. Why do you think people in our society tend to fear death so much and to avoid talking about it?

Multimodal Learning
ANOTHER PATHWAY
Cooperative Learning

Kübler-Ross says that "dying patients literally teach you about life." Skim this selection and make a list of all the lessons about life that it contains. Then, working in a small group, rank these lessons in the order of their importance as you see it. Share and discuss your rankings with the entire class.

QUICKWRITES

1. Imagine that you have been asked to do a follow-up interview of Kübler-Ross. Write a list of **interview questions** that you would ask her.

2. Do you think the mother in the Insight poem "Good Night, Willie Lee, I'll See You in the Morning" had any "unfinished business" to resolve? In a **paragraph**, explain your answer. If you're using a computer, don't forget to use the spelling checker.

3. Write a brief **character sketch** of Kübler-Ross, drawing upon the impressions you gained from reading this interview.

4. Write a short **poem** about an experience you have had concerning death and dying.

📁 **PORTFOLIO** *Save your writing. You may want to use it later as a springboard to a piece for your portfolio.*

UNFINISHED BUSINESS **721**

QuickWrites

1. Encourage students to view their interview questions as opportunities to clarify or explore aspects of her work they disagree with, find intriguing, or find unclear.
2. Ask students whether they believe that the description of the mother as "without tears, without smiles" implies that she has no "unfinished business" or that she is hiding emotions she will have to deal with later.
3. Students should share their work and discuss their impressions of the doctor.
4. Suggest that students read their poems aloud to themselves while they write.

📁 The Writer's Craft
Conducting the Interview, pp. 104–106
Character, p. 92
Personal Narrative, pp. 86–101

From Personal Response to Critical Analysis

1. Accept all reasonable responses.
2. Possible responses: the unexpressed feelings of the dying patients and their families and friends; the coming to terms with one's own death, which the dying girl does before she dies; the difficult business of dying, which may be "unfinished" for some time.
3. Responses will vary. Some students may find her approach blunt or even intrusive and may object to her statements and actions, such as locking the dining room door. Others may "forgive" her methods in view of the results. Some may find her work and frank approach inspiring.
4. Possible responses: Some students will note that she seems perceptive, honest, practical, and intelligent. Others may feel that she is too abrasive in encouraging people to say things they should not say.
5. Accept all reasonable, well-supported responses.
6. Accept all reasonable, well-supported responses.
7. Responses will vary.
8. Responses will vary.

Another Pathway

Cooperative Learning Groups need not reach unanimous conclusions. Differences of opinion within each group can be part of the class discussion.

Rubric
3 Full Accomplishment Students list lessons, discuss their relative importance, and rank them accordingly.
2 Substantial Accomplishment Students list lessons but have difficulty reaching conclusions about their relative importance.
1 Little or Partial Accomplishment Students have difficulty identifying the lessons that are contained in the selection.

Across the Curriculum

Psychology Students can ask a librarian for help in finding information about the five stages identified by Kübler-Ross. Another research option might be to learn more about hospices or to identify local programs aimed at helping terminally ill children and their families. Interested students can contact a hospice or children's organization in their area.

Art Connection

Some students may conclude that the dark shapes in Kerry's drawing represent death waiting to take Kevin away. They might say that the colorful figures in Mary Kate's drawing represent heaven. Students may feel that Sean's picture represents the loss he feels of not having had the chance to know Kevin before he died.

Critic's Corner

While some students may be bothered by the choppiness, others will point out that in an interview, a person's words are presented just as they were spoken. No matter how carefully the subject speaks, the result will always be "jumpier" than a polished piece of edited writing.

LITERARY CONCEPTS

A **paradox** is a statement that seems to contradict itself or to be contrary to common sense but may still be true. An example is "Standing is more tiring than walking." Kübler-Ross says: "I love to work with dying children. They're just so beautiful." This statement seems to run counter to common sense, since most people would think that working with dying children would be sad and depressing. They would not expect such children to be "beautiful." Explain the paradox in each of the following statements:

"But the [dying] girl couldn't die . . ."
"Dying patients literally teach you about life."

CONCEPT REVIEW: Theme Summarize the theme—the main idea—of this selection.

ALTERNATIVE ACTIVITIES

1. For most people, death is the ultimate uncharted territory. In a **sketch** or a **painting,** communicate the impressions of the experience of dying that you gained from reading this selection.

2. Interview ten people you know well about their attitudes toward dying. Videotape the **interviews** and share them in class. Discuss the different reactions that people have to the subject.

ACROSS THE CURRICULUM

Psychology Elisabeth Kübler-Ross has written that dying people go through five stages as they deal with their impending death. Research these stages and describe them to your classmates in a brief oral report.

722   UNIT SIX   PART 1: UNCHARTED TERRITORY

CRITIC'S CORNER

Most members of our student board responded favorably to this selection, some saying they had never read anything like it before. Many said they learned something important and appreciated being able to view life and death from a child's viewpoint. There was an occasional complaint about the language—sentences that seemed "choppy" or "jumpy." What might account for this style? Do you think it adds to or detracts from the effect of the interview?

ART CONNECTION

Sean, Mary Kate, and Kerry Cullen drew their pictures during a 12-week art-therapy program run by Rose Richardson, a licensed clinical social worker. According to Richardson, children in the program express their feelings in a safe environment with others their own age who have experienced similar losses. The children learn to accept the range of strong emotions—from sadness to anger—and to hold on to their good memories. In Kerry's drawing (p. 715), you'll notice that both Kerry and Kevin are smiling, but dark geometric shapes cover the top part of the picture. How do you interpret this picture? Mary Kate's colorful collage (p. 717) includes stars, hearts, and other shiny decorations. What feelings does this picture communicate to you? In Sean's drawing (p. 719), why do you think Kevin is depicted as an older boy?

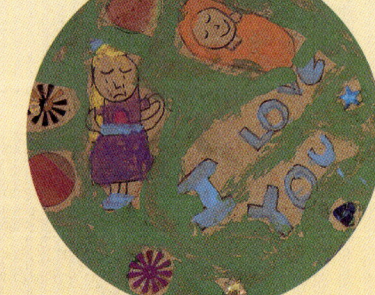

Literary Concepts

Students may point out that in the first statement, the fact that the girl couldn't die contradicts the description of her as dying. Students may say that in the second statement, it is strange that those who are about to die know more about life than those who will continue to live it.

Concept Review: Theme Possible responses: It is important to take an open and honest approach to death; things about life can be learned from the dying.

Alternative Activities

1. Have students experiment with the method described by Kübler-Ross by limiting the time they spend thinking about the subject. Ask them to try to paint spontaneously, using whatever impressions and images are immediately conjured up by the subject.

2. Remind students that some people may find the subject painful to talk about, particularly if they have experienced the loss of someone close.

WORDS TO KNOW

EXERCISE A Review the Words to Know in the boxes at the bottom of the selection pages. Then write the vocabulary word that goes with each clue below.

1. This word describes rivers that industries dump waste products into.
2. Charities need to be supported in this way, as well as with kind thoughts.
3. You don't have to speak or write to do this; body language can do it.
4. Both fines and jail sentences can be described with this word.
5. If this word describes your life, you might feel you need to spice your life up a bit.
6. If you wanted to advise someone against doing this, you might say, "A stitch in time saves nine."
7. Things made on an assembly line or with a cookie cutter do not have this quality.
8. People who have suffered a terrible tragedy may describe their lives with this word.
9. A great work of art will often do this to any verbal attempt to describe the work.
10. If you suddenly want to have a picnic and you throw some sandwiches in a bag and go, your decision is this kind.

EXERCISE B Working with a partner, see how quickly you can communicate each of the vocabulary words by saying things that call that word to mind—but without using synonyms. For example, for *bland,* you might say, "Mashed potatoes, the color beige, boring movies, baby food . . . ," continuing until the correct word is guessed. Note that anything that could help your partner guess the word is allowed—a phrase, a description, an example—anything but a synonym. You might be the clue giver for half of the list and the guesser for the other half.

ELISABETH KÜBLER-ROSS

1926–

Elisabeth Kübler-Ross is one of the great humanitarians of our time. Raised in an upper-middle-class Swiss family, she decided early in life to become a doctor. Her father opposed this idea, however, so she had to postpone her medical education and took a position as a domestic servant. At the age of 18, she volunteered to help with war relief. While visiting the concentration camp of Majdanek in Poland, she was struck by pictures of butterflies scratched on the prison walls. She realized that the doomed inmates, nearing their deaths in the gas chamber, must have viewed their spirits as butterflies leaving the cocoons of their bodies. This image of hope amid despair made a deep impression on her.

Always determined, Kübler-Ross eventually gained her medical degree and worked as a country doctor in Switzerland. After immigrating to New York, she worked in a state mental hospital and achieved remarkable success in helping mentally ill patients who had been labeled hopeless.

As a psychiatrist at Billings Hospital of the University of Chicago, Kübler-Ross began a series of seminars in which she interviewed dying patients. These seminars attracted national attention and publicity—but upset some of her colleagues. One doctor complained: "We have tried for years to make this hospital famous for our excellent cancer care. Now this woman comes along and makes us famous for our dying patients!" Meanwhile, Kübler-Ross continued to help countless people view life and death as "a challenge and not a threat." She left the University of Chicago in 1969 and began giving workshops all over the world. Her work has inspired the establishment of hospice programs, which support terminally ill patients and their families.

OTHER WORKS *On Death and Dying, Death: The Final Stage of Growth, On Children and Death*
Extended Reading

• PSYCHOLOGY CONNECTION

UNFINISHED BUSINESS   723

Words to Know

Exercise A
1. contaminated
2. concretely
3. convey
4. punitive
5. bland
6. procrastinating
7. uniqueness
8. devastated
9. transcend
10. spontaneous

Exercise B
Responses will vary.

Reteaching/Reinforcement
• *Unit Six Resource Book,* p. 5

PSYCHOLOGY CONNECTION
Make a Wish The organization known as the Make a Wish Foundation grants the wishes of dying children. This brief film shows the work of this organization and some of the children whose wishes have been granted. You may wish to use this film to discuss how these children have reacted to their illnesses. How do the children in the film affirm or contradict Kübler-Ross's beliefs?

Side A, Frame 36476

ELISABETH KÜBLER-ROSS
Kubler-Ross is credited with discovering that dying people go through five stages: denial and isolation, anger, bargaining, depression and acceptance. In 1979, based on readers' poll, *Ladies' Home Journal* named her one of its Ten Women of the Decade.

REFLECTING ON THEME
What Do You Think?

Before students began reading Part One, they shared with a partner how they thought risks and uncertainties could affect one's attitude toward life. Now that they have finished this selection, ask them how an individual's impending death would affect his or her attitude toward life.

OVERVIEW

Objectives
- To understand and appreciate two poems that explore people's reactions to death
- To identify and understand meter
- To express understanding of the poems through a choice of writing forms, including a description and a psychological examination
- To extend understanding of the poems through a variety of multimodal and cross-curricular activities

Skills

LITERARY CONCEPTS
- Meter
- Rhyme

THE WRITER'S STYLE
- Repetition

Thematic Link: *Uncharted Territory* In each poem, the speaker faces death—the ultimate unknown.

ALTERNATIVE
Previewing

Instead of drawing a picture of their image of death, students can use the following prompts to discuss their image with a partner.

Personal Connection

Discussion Prompts In as much detail as possible, describe to your partner the qualities and appearance of your image of death. Then listen as your partner describes his or her image. If you need help getting started, the following questions might help:

- What does death look like?
- What does death wear or carry?
- How does death act?
- What human qualities does death have?

As you read, compare these images with those in the two poems.

PREVIEWING

POETRY

Annabel Lee
Edgar Allan Poe

Incident in a Rose Garden
Donald Justice

Activating Prior Knowledge/Setting a Purpose
PERSONAL CONNECTION

Down through the ages, the different cultures of the world have **personified**, or given human qualities to, the concept of death. In Western cultures, the standard image of death is that of a fearsome destroyer. A hooded figure dressed in black, this personification of death often carries a scythe (sīth), an implement with a long, curved blade attached to a long handle, used for cutting down tall grasses for harvest. Thus, death is imagined as someone who comes to "harvest" human beings. Throughout the ages, writers and artists have created different variations of this standard image. What image of death do you have? Draw the picture you imagine and share your sketch with a classmate. Discuss the qualities of death that your image emphasizes. As you read each of these poems, compare your sketch with the image presented by the poet.

Building Background
LITERARY CONNECTION

Although Edgar Allan Poe and Donald Justice lived in different centuries, their work displays similarities in both theme and attention to technique. Images of death or loss recur in the poetry of both men, and both are known for their controlled and masterful use of poetic devices.

By the time that Poe was 39 years old, three important women in his life had died—his mother, the woman who took care of him after his mother died, and his young wife. This may explain why Poe often associated beauty with tragedy and loss and why some of his most famous poems, including "Annabel Lee," focus on the death of a beautiful woman. In an essay written one year before his wife died, Poe commented that "[the] death . . . of a beautiful woman is, unquestionably, the most poetical topic in the world." Themes of death and loss also can be found in some of the poetry of Donald Justice. Such themes possibly stem from his youth and the death from rheumatic fever of a close nine-year-old friend. In fact, one of Justice's poems is titled "On the Death of Friends in Childhood."

In composing poems, Poe paid close attention not only to rhythm but to rhyme, repetition, and alliteration. These sound devices in Poe's "Annabel Lee" give it a musical, almost singsong quality. A close attention to poetic techniques can also be seen in the poetry of Donald Justice. Although "Incident in a Rose Garden" lacks the rhyme and regular meter of "Annabel Lee"—displaying, instead, the less flowing rhythm of everyday speech—it includes such poetic elements as alliteration, vivid imagery, and personification.

724   UNIT SIX   PART 1: UNCHARTED TERRITORY

Poe's portrait of his wife, Virginia.

PRINT AND MEDIA RESOURCES

UNIT SIX RESOURCE BOOK
Strategic Reading: Literature, p. 9

ACCESS FOR STUDENTS ACQUIRING ENGLISH
Reading Support

FORMAL ASSESSMENT
Selection Test, p. 131
 Test Generator

 AUDIO LIBRARY
See Reference Card

 LASERLINKS
Author Background
Art Gallery

INTERNET RESOURCES
"Annabel Lee"
McDougal Littell Literature Center at http://www.hmco.com/mcdougal/lit

Active Reading
READING CONNECTION

Appreciating Narrative Poetry

Poetry can do more than touch your mind and heart with movement, sound, and figurative meaning. It can also tell a story, and such poetry is called **narrative poetry**, a unique combination of two forms of writing. The story told in a narrative poem can be fictional or nonfictional. In addition, narrative poems can vary greatly in length. They can be book-length sagas of thousands of lines, like the Homeric epics the *Iliad* and the *Odyssey,* or they can be just a few stanzas long.

Identifying Narrative Elements
In a narrative poem, you will find a narrator or main speaker, as you would in a story. You will also probably encounter characters involved in a conflict, and a plot that may build with suspenseful rising action, reach a climax, and then end with falling action. The poem may contain dialogue, set off either with quotation marks, as in a story, or with some other stylistic device, such as indenting or italics. Look at the beginning of one of the most famous of all narrative poems:

> Listen, my children, and you shall hear
> Of the midnight ride of Paul Revere,
> On the eighteenth of April, in Seventy-five;
> Hardly a man is now alive
> Who remembers that famous day and year.
>
> He said to his friend, "If the British march
> By land or sea from the town to-night,
> Hang a lantern aloft in the belfry arch
> Of the North Church tower as a signal light, . . ."
>
> from "Paul Revere's Ride"
> by Henry Wadsworth Longfellow

Discuss the questions at the right with your classmates.

Narrative poems can also have themes, or main ideas. Some themes will be stated directly, whereas others must be inferred from the characters and situations in the story. To discover the theme in a narrative poem, summarize the plot and look for any message about life or human nature.

Identifying Poetic Elements
A narrative poem is meant to be appreciated for its poetic elements as well as for its story. Refer to the section "Focus on Poetry" on pages 120–121 and review the definitions of terms. Then read aloud the excerpt from "Paul Revere's Ride" and discuss the questions at the right with your classmates.

- Is the poem told in first person or third person?
- Who is the narrator, and who is a character in this poem?
- Is the story fiction or nonfiction?
- What will be a source of suspense?
- Who is being quoted directly?

- What is the rhyme scheme of the first stanza? the second stanza?
- Which line contains alliteration?
- What are two lines that have consonance?
- What vowel sound is heard three times in lines 1 and 2?

Reading Connection

Identifying Narrative Elements
Discussion of the questions about the beginning of "Paul Revere's Ride" should lead to these responses: The poem is told in the first person; the speaker is a storyteller; Paul Revere is a character in the poem; the story is nonfiction; whether the British leave the town by land or by sea is the source of immediate suspense; Paul Revere is quoted directly.

Identifying Poetic Elements Discussion of the questions concerning poetic elements in the excerpt from the poem should lead to these responses: The rhyme scheme of the first stanza is a-a-b-b-a and of the second, a-b-a-b; line 7 contains alliteration; almost every line has an example of consonance; the short *i* sound appears three times in lines 1 and 2.

CUSTOMIZING FOR
Students Acquiring English

- Use **ACCESS FOR STUDENTS ACQUIRING ENGLISH,** *Reading Support.*

- As you guide students through the Poe poem on the next two pages, you may want to use the suggestions in these boxes and the suggestions under Strategic Reading for Less-Proficient Readers.

Annabel Lee

Edgar Allan Poe

Study of a Head for "The Mill," Sir Edward Coley Burne Jones (1833–1898). Graphite and wash, 7¼" × 6½", Bankside Gallery, London.

It was many and many a year ago,
   In a kingdom by the sea,
That a maiden there lived whom you may know
   By the name of Annabel Lee;
5 And this maiden she lived with no other thought
   Than to love and be loved by me.

I was a child and *she* was a child,
   In this kingdom by the sea:
But we loved with a love that was more than love—
10   I and my Annabel Lee;
With a love that the winged seraphs of heaven
   Coveted her and me.

And this was the reason that, long ago,
   In this kingdom by the sea,
15 A wind blew out of a cloud, chilling
   My beautiful Annabel Lee;

11 seraphs (sĕr′əfs): any of the highest order of angels.
12 coveted: envied.

	So that her high-born kinsmen came
	And bore her away from me,
	To shut her up in a sepulcher
20	In this kingdom by the sea.

19 **sepulcher** (sĕp′əl-kər): a place for burial; tomb.

	The angels, not half so happy in heaven,
	Went envying her and me—
	Yes!—that was the reason (as all men know,
	In this kingdom by the sea)
25	That the wind came out of the cloud by night,
	Chilling and killing my Annabel Lee.

	But our love it was stronger by far than the love
	Of those who were older than we—
	Of many far wiser than we—
30	And neither the angels in heaven above,
	Nor the demons down under the sea,
	Can ever dissever my soul from the soul
	Of the beautiful Annabel Lee,

32 **dissever**: disunite; separate.

	For the moon never beams, without bringing me dreams
35	Of the beautiful Annabel Lee;
	And the stars never rise, but I feel the bright eyes
	Of the beautiful Annabel Lee;
	And so, all the night-tide, I lie down by the side
	Of my darling—my darling—my life and my bride,
40	In the sepulcher there by the sea,
	In her tomb by the sounding sea.

FROM PERSONAL RESPONSE TO CRITICAL ANALYSIS

REFLECT 1. What is your reaction to the speaker and his story? Describe your reaction in your notebook, and share your ideas with a partner.

RETHINK 2. In your own words, summarize the plot and the theme of "Annabel Lee."

3. What do you think caused Annabel Lee's death? Do you think the speaker would agree with your view? Why or why not?

4. How well is the speaker dealing with his bride's death? Explain your response.
   Consider
   - the speaker's description of his relationship with Annabel Lee
   - the sentiments described in lines 34–37
   - the speaker's nightly habit, described in lines 38–41

Close Textual Reading

ANNABEL LEE 727

Mini-Lesson   Literary Concepts

REVIEWING RHYME Remind students that rhyme is the occurrence of a similar or identical sound at the ends of two or more words in a poem. Tell them that internal rhyme occurs within a line of poetry, whereas end rhyme occurs at the ends of lines.

Application Ask students to identify the internal rhyme used in line 32 of "Annabel Lee" (*ever, dissever*). Then have students point out other examples of internal rhyme in the poem. (*line 26—chilling, killing; line 34—beams, dreams; line 36—rise, eyes; line 38—night-tide, side*) Discuss how having both internal and end rhyme affects the poem.

CUSTOMIZING FOR
Students Acquiring English

Ⓘ Explain to students that the "high-born kinsmen" are upper-class male relatives of Annabel Lee who come to bury her.

Literary Concept: REPETITION

Ⓑ Have students point out instances of repetition in the poem. ("*kingdom by the sea,*" "*wind. . . out of a cloud,*" "*chilling. . . my Annabel Lee*") Then ask them why they think Poe might have used this device. (*Possible responses: to emphasize the speaker's great love for the departed; to add to the poem's musical nature*)

Literary Concept: METER

Ⓒ Point out that the first and last stanzas of the poem have similar metrical patterns in which anapests predominate. Explain that an anapest is a metrical foot in which two short syllables are followed by one long syllable. Ask what effect this metrical pattern has. (*Possible response: It creates a steady rhythm, similar to that of waves from the sea washing ashore.*)

STRATEGIC READING FOR
Less-Proficient Readers

Ⓓ How did death affect the speaker? (*Possible responses: It caused him to create a fantasy of his lost love; it left him obsessed with the love he once shared and drove him to strange behavior.*)

Set a Purpose Have students read the next poem to see for whom death comes.

From Personal Response to Critical Analysis

1. Accept all reasonable responses.
2. Accept all reasonable, well-supported responses. Some students may say that the theme is that death need not mean the total separation of two people.
3. Possible responses: sickness caused by the chilling wind; the wrath of the jealous angels
4. Some students may feel that, at best, the speaker has never accepted her death. Others may say that the speaker is crazy and is living in a world of sick illusions.

Art Note

Death with an Hourglass, anonymous
This 16th-century sculpture by a member of the Strasbourg school shows Death with one of his traditional props, an hourglass. Explain to students that an hourglass is a device used to measure time.

Reading the Art Why might the figure of death be holding an hourglass? What connections are there between the idea of death and the idea of time?

Literary Concept: PERSONIFICATION

E Have students list some human qualities that these lines of the poem give to Death. *(Possible responses: well-dressed, cool, confident)*

Literary Concept: METER

F Pause at this point and ask a volunteer to read the first stanza aloud. Have students discuss the meter. *(It's irregular, but for the most part, each line has three stressed syllables.)*

Incident in a Rose Garden

Donald Justice

The gardener came running.
An old man, out of breath.
Fear had given him legs.
  Sir, I encountered Death
5 Just now among the roses.
  Thin as a scythe he stood there.
  I knew him by his pictures.
  He had his black coat on,
  Black gloves, a broad black hat.
10 I think he would have spoken,
  Seeing his mouth stood open.
  Big it was, with white teeth.
  As soon as he beckoned, I ran.
  I ran until I found you.
15 Sir, I am quitting my job.
  I want to see my sons
  Once more before I die.
  I want to see California.
We shook hands; he was off.

20 And there stood Death in the garden.
Dressed like a Spanish waiter.
He had the air of someone
Who because he likes arriving
At all appointments early
25 Learns to think himself patient.

Death with an Hourglass (1500s), unknown sculptor. Musées de Strasbourg, France.

Multicultural Perspectives

EL DÍA DE LOS MUERTOS For centuries, the holiday of *el día de los muertos*, or the Day of the Dead, has been celebrated every November 1–2 in Mexico. On this day, Mexicans celebrate the continuity of life by honoring those who have passed away. Children play with skeleton puppets and make papier-mâché *calaveras*, or skulls. A special bread—*pan de muerto*—is prepared, often with toy skeletons baked inside, and the markets are filled with stacks of sugar candies—*calaveras de azucar*—shaped into skulls. Musical and dance performances are held. In the evening, cemeteries are illuminated by hundreds of candles as families come to welcome the spirits of departed loved ones—said to return for the holiday. Gravesites are decorated with flowers, food, and skeleton figures, and altars are built to welcome back the departed spirits. The origins of the festival lie in the Christian holiday of All Hallows Eve and in traditional Aztec festivals that honored children and the dead.

I watched him pinch one bloom off
And hold it to his nose—
A connoisseur of roses—
One bloom and then another.
30 They strewed the earth around him.
   Sir, you must be that stranger
   Who threatened my gardener.
   This is my property, sir.
   I welcome only friends here.
35 Death grinned, and his eyes lit up
With the pale glow of those lanterns
That workmen carry sometimes
To light their way through the dusk.
Now with great care he slid
40 The glove from his right hand
And held that out in greeting,
A little cage of bone.
   Sir, I knew your father,
   And we were friends at the end.
45 As for your gardener,
   I did not threaten him.
   Old men mistake my gestures.
   I only meant to ask him
   To show me to his master.
50 I take it you are he?

for Mark Strand

28 connoisseur (kŏn′ə-sûr′): an expert or authority in some field, especially in the fine arts or in matters of taste.

INCIDENT IN A ROSE GARDEN   729

Literary Concept: RHYME

G Have students notice the near-rhyme in lines 27–28. Discuss the effect of this near-rhyming couplet in an otherwise-unrhymed stanza.

Literary Concept: RHYTHM

H Have a volunteer read the second stanza aloud. Ask students to discuss the effect of the short, end-stopped lines. *(Accept all reasonable responses.)*

Literary Concept: MOOD

I Ask students to share their opinions about the mood of the poem and to support their ideas with details from the poem. *(Possible responses: somber, wry, ironic)*

Critical Thinking: MAKING INFERENCES

J Ask students why they think the speaker's father and Death were friends. *(Possible response: The speaker's father welcomed Death and probably died peacefully.)*

STRATEGIC READING FOR
Less-Proficient Learners

K Direct students' attention to the final line of the poem. Ask them why the poem ends with this question. *(Possible response: Surprisingly, Death has come for the master of the estate, not for the old gardener, and Death asks this question to make sure he is addressing the correct person.)*

CUSTOMIZING FOR
Gifted and Talented Students

Suggest that students read other poems by Poe and discuss them as a group. Ask them to make inferences and draw conclusions about Poe's treatment of the theme of death.

COMPREHENSION CHECK

1. In Poe's poem, who is jealous of the speaker and Annabel Lee? *(angels)*
2. What is the cause of this jealousy? *(their love for each other)*
3. In Justice's poem, how does the gardener recognize Death? *(He has seen pictures of him.)*
4. For whom has Death come? *(the speaker)*

Mini-Lesson   The Writer's Style

REPETITION Remind students that writers sometimes repeat words or phrases for effect or emphasis in their poetry or prose and that this literary technique is called repetition. Point out lines 4, 15, 31, and 43 in "Incident in a Rose Garden," all of which contain short sentences that address a character as "Sir."

Application Have students write a brief essay in which they discuss the use of repetition in either "Annabel Lee" or "Incident in a Rose Garden." Suggest that they consider these questions before they begin writing:

- Is the repetition appropriate to the character of the speaker?
- What effect does the repetition have on the mood of the poem?

Reteaching/Reinforcement

Repeated Words, p. 368

THE LANGUAGE OF LITERATURE **TEACHER'S EDITION**   **729**

From Personal Response to Critical Analysis

1. Accept all reasonable responses.
2. Possible response: The person who fears that Death has come for him is safe, whereas the man who appears to have no reason to fear Death is the one that Death seeks. The gardener, because he is old, has reason to fear Death, whereas the master, presumably a much younger man, does not. Nevertheless, it is the master whom Death seeks.
3. Possible responses: The gardener, an old man, appears fearful and panicky at the arrival of Death, while the master, presumably a much younger man with no reason to fear Death, is calm and controlled; the gardener is respectful and realistic, while the master treats Death with too little respect.
4. Accept all reasonable responses.
5. Accept all reasonable, well-supported responses.

Another Pathway

Suggest that students create a comparison-and-contrast chart of the characters' attitudes toward death.

Rubric

3 Full Accomplishment Students support their opinions with details.
2 Substantial Accomplishment Students do not fully support their opinions with details.
1 Little or Partial Accomplishment Students have difficulty forming an opinion.

Literary Links

Both poems tell of the approach of something ominous—an army and death. A character in each poem runs off, afraid that he or she is the one being sought. In each poem, it is the person left behind, however, who either may have been the intended target of the approaching force ("O What Is That Sound") or definitely was the target ("Incident in a Rose Garden"). Both poems stress one's inability to correctly gauge the true meaning of a situation or an event. Both poems are rather ambiguous as to the setting—one is set in a house and one in a garden, but neither poem specifies a time or place.

RESPONDING OPTIONS

FROM PERSONAL RESPONSE TO CRITICAL ANALYSIS

REFLECT 1. What effect did the ending of "Incident in a Rose Garden" have on you? Jot down your response in your notebook, and share it with a partner.

RETHINK 2. Explain any ironies, or unexpected twists, that you see in this poem.

3. Contrast the gardener's and master's attitudes toward Death. Why do you think they have such different attitudes?

Close Textual Reading

Consider
- the description of the gardener in the first three lines
- the master's description of Death in lines 21–25
- the master's attitude when speaking to Death, in lines 31–34

RELATE 4. Sketch the images of death presented in "Annabel Lee" and "Incident in a Rose Garden." How do these images compare with the sketch you made for the Personal Connection activity on page 724?

Thematic Link 5. Discuss some different ways people react to death. What do you think causes reactions to vary?

Multimodal Learning
ANOTHER PATHWAY

Get together with a partner to discuss the attitudes toward death expressed in the poems. Who do you think has the best attitude—the speaker in "Annabel Lee" or the gardener or the master in "Incident in a Rose Garden"? Write a brief explanation of your opinion in your notebook, then share it with the rest of your classmates.

LITERARY LINKS

Compare and contrast the narrative elements of characters, setting, plot, and theme in "Incident in a Rose Garden" with those in W. H. Auden's "O What Is That Sound" (page 622), which is also a narrative poem.

The Garden, Reg Cartwright. Collection of the artist.

QUICKWRITES

1. Extend "Incident in a Rose Garden" by writing a **description** of how the master might respond to Death's question at the end.
2. Write a draft for a **psychological examination** of the speaker of "Annabel Lee," giving your idea of his state of mind.

📁 **PORTFOLIO** Save your writing. You may want to use it later as a springboard to a piece for your portfolio.

730 UNIT SIX PART 1: UNCHARTED TERRITORY

QuickWrites

1. Remind students that good description helps the reader picture the scene. Encourage students to include imagery that illustrates the reaction of the master to Death's question. Tell them that they are free to include dialogue.
2. Suggest that students list details of the speaker's personality and behavior. Students should try to analyze these details objectively and should refer to them in their conclusion about his state of mind.

 The Writer's Craft

Using Dialogue Effectively, pp. 85–112
Point of View, pp. 250–254

Alternative Activities

1. Ask students to create a collage of pictures and words inspired by the themes and images in "Annabel Lee."
2. Have students form groups of three to perform a skit based on "Incident in a Rose Garden." If they choose, students can create costumes or use props that are suggestive of the three characters.
3. Encourage students to brainstorm a list of famous characters—from books, movies, or other literary works—who, like the speaker of "Annabel Lee," have been separated by death from the one they love.

730 THE LANGUAGE OF LITERATURE TEACHER'S EDITION

LITERARY CONCEPTS

Meter is the rhythm created by the regular or almost regular pattern of stressed and unstressed syllables in a line of poetry. The syllables are grouped together in units called **feet**. Each foot commonly consists of one accented syllable and one or two unaccented syllables. The two lines below, from the beginning of "Annabel Lee," are divided into feet by a vertical line; the accented syllables are indicated by a diagonal line (´) and the unaccented syllables by a curved line (˘).

Ĭt wăs mán | ў ănd mán | ў ă yéar | ăgó, |

Ĭn ă kíng | dŏm bý | thĕ séa,

Copy into your notebook the last four lines of the first stanza of "Annabel Lee." Mark the accented and unaccented syllables in each line. Then look at the six lines of the stanza and say them aloud. What provides the feeling of a regular rhythm?

CONCEPT REVIEW: Personification What kind of a "person" is Death in "Incident in a Rose Garden"? List at least three personality traits of Death as imagined by Justice.

Multimodal Learning
ACROSS THE CURRICULUM

World Cultures Cooperative Learning Organize a class panel discussion on the personification of death in other cultures and times. In small groups, research various geographical areas, time periods, and myths and legends. These groups should then present their findings to the entire class, and an additional group should compare and contrast findings from the presentations and look for common trends.

Across the Curriculum

World Cultures *Cooperative Learning* Divide the class into groups of four or five. Encourage each group to divide up responsibilities for preparing its presentation. Different group members can research different aspects of the topic. Groups may want to look for the personification of death in the art, films, literature, myths, and religions of various cultures. Encourage students to make copies of the different artistic representations of death that they encounter and to share them with the class.

EDGAR ALLAN POE

For Edgar Allan Poe, poetry was a totally sensory experience. According to Poe, a poem should appeal only to the reader's sense of beauty and should not be informational, full of realistic details or "ideas," or even particularly truthful. Yet, Poe felt that poetry should be well planned out beforehand, with its effects deftly calculated.

EDGAR ALLAN POE

Though famous for his terrifying short stories, Poe (1809–1849) stated that his aim in writing poetry was to produce a sense of beauty. This artistic guideline is equally remarkable for having come from a person who experienced so much personal tragedy. By the time he was three years old, his father had deserted the family and his mother had died in poverty. Poe was then raised by the Allans. Although Poe was well loved by Mrs. Allan, his relationship with Mr. Allan was often strained.

After a dismissal from the U.S. Military Academy at West Point, Poe became a journalist and an editor. At the age of 27, he married his 13-year-old cousin, Virginia Clemm. After almost 11 years of marriage, Virginia died from tuberculosis, and a depressed Poe sought escape in alcohol. Although Poe continued to write, he died a tormented man less than three years later.

OTHER WORKS "The Raven," "To Helen," "The Bells"

DONALD JUSTICE

Donald Justice was born in 1925, in Miami, Florida, and grew up during the Great Depression in circumstances he describes as "near poor." He received a doctorate from the University of Iowa in 1954 and 26 years later won the Pulitzer Prize in poetry for *Selected Poems*. Justice has taught at a number of universities, including the University of Iowa and the University of Florida.

As one critic has noted, Justice has long been fascinated with "the ease with which [language] creates worlds." An example of his constant experimenting with poetic form, "Incident in a Rose Garden" exists in two versions—an original one using dialogue only and a revised one, appearing here, that includes descriptive passages.

OTHER WORKS *The Summer Anniversaries, Night Light, The Sunset Maker*

DONALD JUSTICE

Though the poetry of Donald Justice is similar to Poe's in that Justice also writes on the epic themes of madness, love, and death, Justice's approach is in marked contrast to Poe's. Once, when asked what he hoped readers would find in his poetry, Justice replied that he didn't think about it much but that "once asked the question, I would probably have to answer something large and grand like *the truth.*"

AUTHOR BACKGROUND
Edgar Allan Poe The life and times of this American author, as well as his fascination with the macabre, are presented in this short film.

Side A, Frame 41688

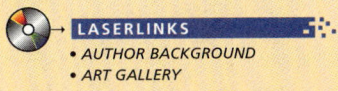
- AUTHOR BACKGROUND
- ART GALLERY

ANNABEL LEE/INCIDENT IN A ROSE GARDEN **731**

ART GALLERY
Heaven and Hell The concept of death has been given human qualities by artists throughout history. You may wish to use these examples to generate discussion about ways that death has been presented in art.

Side A, Frame 49433

Literary Concepts

Students should have marked the lines as follows:

Thăt ă máid | ĕn thĕre líved | whŏm yóu | măy knów

Bў thĕ náme | ŏf Án | năbĕl Lée;

Ănd thĭs máid | ĕn shĕ líved | wĭth nó | ŏthĕr thóught

Thăn tŏ lóve | ănd bĕ lóved | bў mé.

The nearly regular pattern of stressed and unstressed syllables provides the feeling of a regular rhythm.

Concept Review: Personification Students may point to Death's air of patience and punctuality, his politeness, and his apparent good humor as examples of personality traits.

OVERVIEW

Objectives

- To understand and appreciate two poems that explore the connections between humans and nature, life and death
- To identify and understand imagery
- To understand and appreciate tone
- To express understanding of the poems through a choice of writing forms, including a letter, a first-person narrative, and a poem
- To extend understanding of the poems through a variety of multimodal and cross-curricular activities

Skills

LITERARY CONCEPTS
- Imagery

SPEAKING, LISTENING, AND VIEWING
- Art

Thematic Link: *Uncharted Territory*
Chance encounters with nature propel the speakers of these two poems into its mystery.

CUSTOMIZING FOR
Students Acquiring English

- Use **ACCESS FOR STUDENTS ACQUIRING ENGLISH**, *Reading Support*.
- Students should have little difficulty with the vocabulary and events described in these two poems.

STRATEGIC READING FOR
Less-Proficient Readers

Set a Purpose Have students read to find out how the speaker in each poem reacts to animals in nature.

Use **UNIT SIX RESOURCE BOOK**, p 13, for guidance in reading the selection.

PREVIEWING

POETRY

Traveling Through the Dark
William Stafford

The Sharks
Denise Levertov

Activating Prior Knowledge
PERSONAL CONNECTION

Almost anything that's important has a positive side and a negative side. For example, it's wonderful to love someone, but being in love also means you can be hurt more easily. Now think about different ways of regarding the natural world we live in. What are some of the positive aspects people see in nature—its good side? What are some of the negative aspects? In your notebook, make a two-column chart like the one shown here. With a partner, brainstorm some common ways of looking at nature and record them on your chart.

Nature	
Positive Aspects	Negative Aspects

Building Background
CULTURAL CONNECTION

In each of these two poems, a speaker is reacting to an animal in nature, against a backdrop of life and death. In Western culture, people have long had various conflicting attitudes toward nature—embracing or ignoring it, fearing or exploiting it. Whatever one's attitude, the cycle of life and death in nature and the struggle to survive are inescapable facts. As you read the two poems, keep these facts in mind.

Setting a Purpose
WRITING CONNECTION

Different animals in nature evoke different responses from people. For example, think about the deer and the shark, and consider the different images that are associated with each of these animals. In your notebook, jot down all the words and phrases that immediately come to mind when you think of the deer. Expand these notes into a thumbnail sketch of the animal as you see it. Then do the same for the shark. Be aware of the images associated with these animals as you read the two poems.

732   UNIT SIX   PART 1: UNCHARTED TERRITORY

PRINT AND MEDIA RESOURCES

UNIT SIX RESOURCE BOOK
Strategic Reading: Literature, p. 13

ACCESS FOR STUDENTS ACQUIRING ENGLISH
Reading Support

FORMAL ASSESSMENT
Selection Test, p. 133
Test Generator

 AUDIO LIBRARY
See Reference Card

 LASERLINKS
Ecology Connection

TRAVELING Through THE Dark

William Stafford

Traveling through the dark I found a deer
dead on the edge of the Wilson River road.
It is usually best to roll them into the canyon:
that road is narrow; to swerve might make more dead.

5   By glow of the tail-light I stumbled back of the car
and stood by the heap, a doe, a recent killing;
she had stiffened already, almost cold.
I dragged her off; she was large in the belly.

My fingers touching her side brought me the reason—
10 her side was warm; her fawn lay there waiting,
alive, still, never to be born.
Beside that mountain road I hesitated.

The car aimed ahead its lowered parking lights;
under the hood purred the steady engine.
15 I stood in the glare of the warm exhaust turning red;
around our group I could hear the wilderness listen.

I thought hard for us all—my only swerving—,
then pushed her over the edge into the river.

FROM PERSONAL RESPONSE TO CRITICAL ANALYSIS

REFLECT   1. Do you like this poem? Share your response with your classmates.

RETHINK   2. The speaker hesitates and thinks about what to do with the dead deer. What choices does the speaker have, and what are the pros and cons of each choice?
Consider
- the value of the deer's life in nature
- what "swerve" and "swerving" mean in lines 4 and 17
- the wilderness that "listens"

Close Textual Reading

3. What would you do if you were in the speaker's place? Why?

4. Consider the title. What are the different things that "traveling through the dark" could mean?

TRAVELING THROUGH THE DARK   733

CUSTOMIZING FOR
Gifted and Talented Students

Have students discuss the title "Traveling Through the Dark." Have them consider possible figurative or symbolic meaning as well as the literal meaning.

Literary Concept: IMAGERY

A Ask students to discuss the effect of the imagery in these two stanzas. *(Possible responses: Vivid details help the reader picture the scene; the imagery makes the scene more real.)*

CUSTOMIZING FOR
Students Acquiring English

1 Explain that the idiom *large in the belly* means "pregnant."

Literary Concept: PERSONIFICATION

B Have students identify the instances of personification in this stanza. *("The car aimed," "purred the steady engine," "the wilderness listen")* Ask why the poet chose to personify the car and the wilderness. *(In the poem, cars are important—a car caused the deer's death, and the speaker's car is almost like a companion to him. The wilderness is also important to the speaker—it has a presence that the speaker feels.)*

Critical Thinking: ANALYZING

C Ask students why the speaker refers to his thinking as "my only swerving." *(Possible response: The word swerving recalls the first-stanza image of a car swerving to miss the dead deer; the speaker is swerving from his original path of action in order to consider alternatives.)*

From Personal Response to Critical Analysis

1. Accept all reasonable responses.
2. Students may say that the speaker can either roll the deer into the canyon or take the deer to a veterinarian, to try to save the fawn. Rolling the deer into the canyon would clear the road and eliminate the possibility of someone's having an accident; however, the fawn would die. Taking the deer to the veterinarian would be more difficult; the fawn might live, but if it did, it would be raised by humans.
3. Accept all reasonable responses.
4. Some students may say that the title refers to the physical situation the poem presents—a person who is traveling through the dark on a mountain road and who stops to save a deer. Others may say the title refers to the speaker's mental state—he is traveling through the dark, trying to find the right solution to an uncertain situation.

Literary Concept: IMAGERY

D Ask students to describe how the ocean looks when the sharks arrive. *(Possible responses: dark, threatening, sinister)* Then ask them what sensory details the poet uses to describe the sea. *("sheen of copper stills the sea," "clear enough to see them easily")*

Critical Thinking: COMPARE AND CONTRAST

E Ask students to compare the speakers of the two poems. *(Possible responses: The speaker in "Traveling Through the Dark" seems mature and responsible— concerned about others and careful to weigh consequences; the speaker in "The Sharks" seems younger—concerned about being able to play in the sea—and more excitable, using conversational asides such as "Well then" and "I tell you.")*

COMPREHENSION CHECK

1. What does the speaker in "Traveling Through the Dark" find by the edge of the road? *(a dead deer)*
2. Why does the speaker hesitate to decide what to do with the deer? *(Its unborn fawn is alive.)*
3. What does the speaker do in the end? *(pushes the body into the river)*
4. What happens to the speaker in "The Sharks" on the last day by the sea? *(She sees sharks appear in the water.)*
5. How does the speaker know there are sharks in the water? *(Their fins are visible.)*

The Sharks
Denise Levertov

Well then, the last day the sharks appeared.
Dark fins appear, innocent
as if in fair warning. The sea becomes
sinister, are they everywhere?
5   I tell you, they break six feet of water.
Isn't it the same sea, and won't we
play in it any more?
I liked it clear and not
too calm, enough waves
10 to fly in on. For the first time
I dared to swim out of my depth.
It was sundown when they came, the time
when a sheen of copper stills the sea,
not dark enough for moonlight, clear enough
15 to see them easily. Dark
the sharp lift of the fins.

4 sinister (sĭn′ĭ-stər): threatening harm, evil, or misfortune.

5 they break . . . water: The sharks can enter water as shallow as six feet, posing a danger to swimmers.

13 sheen: brightness; shininess.

Mini-Lesson: Speaking, Listening, and Viewing

ART Point out to students that in "The Sharks," the speaker describes the sea as becoming "sinister." Ask them to think about the ways in which a body of water could appear threatening or evil. Then discuss what techniques an artist might use to convey this aspect of nature.

Application Have students form groups to find artistic representations of the sea or other scenes from nature. Ask them to find works that they think depict nature as sinister or foreboding. Groups should prepare a selection of works to present to the class in the form of a slide show or by passing around books or reproductions of the art. Have students discuss the impression of nature created by the individual artists. Ask them to tell, aside from any obvious dangers depicted, such as the presence of sharks' fins, what techniques used by the artists help to create a sinister mood or elicit a feeling of danger.

RESPONDING OPTIONS

FROM PERSONAL RESPONSE TO CRITICAL ANALYSIS

REFLECT 1. In your notebook, jot down a few words that describe your impressions of "The Sharks."

RETHINK 2. Line 1 suggests this is the last day of the speaker's vacation at the seashore. How does the presence of the sharks change the way the speaker perceives the sea?
Consider
Close Textual Reading
- the description of the speaker's activities in lines 8–11
- the words used to describe the sea when the sharks are sighted

Thematic Link 3. Do you think the sharks in the poem are evil? Explain. Consider the cycle of life and death in nature.

RELATE 4. Look back at what you wrote about the deer and the shark for the Writing Connection activity. How do your descriptions compare with the way these two animals are portrayed in the poems?

5. Point out both the positive and the negative aspects of nature that you can see in each of the poems. Do you think each poem presents a generally positive or a generally negative view of nature?

Multimodal Learning
ANOTHER PATHWAY

Cooperative Learning
In a small group, discuss what each of these poems suggests to you about matters of life and death in the natural world. For each poem, brainstorm a list of ideas that are unique to each poem and then circle the ideas that are common to both poems. Share your list with other groups.

QUICKWRITES

1. Prepare an argument in support of the idea that the speaker of "Traveling Through the Dark" should have tried to save the fawn. Present your argument in a **letter** to the speaker.

2. Rewrite "The Sharks" as a **first-person narrative** that might appear in a teen magazine. Make up the details, but keep the story consistent with the feeling and the theme of the poem.

3. Review the chart you made on the positive and negative aspects of nature. Write a short **poem** that conveys one of the ideas on your chart. Your poem might relate a dramatic encounter you have had with nature.

📁 **PORTFOLIO** Save your writing. You may want to use it later as a springboard to a piece for your portfolio.

LITERARY CONCEPTS

Imagery consists of words and phrases that appeal to the five senses. As you know, poets use imagery to create pictures in readers' minds or to remind readers of familiar sensations. For example, Stafford and Levertov use contrasting images of light and dark to heighten the feelings expressed in the poems. Notice how the images in the fourth stanza of "Traveling Through the Dark" appeal to several senses. The imagery in "The Sharks" is largely visual, and both poems leave a strong impression in the reader's mind. For each poem, choose what you think is the central image—the one that best illustrates the poem. Then, either describe or draw this image in your notebook. Share the image with your classmates, and explain.

TRAVELING THROUGH THE DARK/THE SHARKS **735**

From Personal Response to Critical Analysis

1. Accept all reasonable responses.
2. Possible responses: The sea is no longer a welcoming or safe place to play; the sharks have introduced to the scene the element of threat.
3. Possible responses: The sharks are evil because they sometimes attack and kill people; the sharks are a part of nature, and moral concepts such as good and evil cannot be ascribed to animals; in nature, animals hunt other animals for food.
4. Accept all reasonable, well-supported responses.
5. Accept all reasonable, well-supported responses.

Another Pathway

Cooperative Learning Make sure that all students contribute to the discussion. One group member can record the lists on paper, and another can serve as spokesperson presenting the results to other groups. Groups may wish to use a Venn diagram to indicate common ideas.

Rubric

3 Full Accomplishment Students list ideas suggested by each poem and identify ideas that are common to both poems.

2 Substantial Accomplishment Students list ideas from each poem but have some difficulty comparing and contrasting those ideas.

1 Little or Partial Accomplishment Students have difficulty identifying ideas suggested by the poems.

Literary Concepts

Students' choices of images will vary. Make sure students can identify the images appealing to hearing (*"purred the steady engine"*), touch (*"warm exhaust"*), and sight (*"glare... turning red"*) in the fourth stanza of "Traveling Through the Dark."

QuickWrites

1. Suggest that students list possible reasons for saving the fawn. Then encourage them to use these ideas to create a persuasive argument.
2. Ask students to bring in some teen magazines and to discuss the tones and styles common to the first-person narratives they contain.
3. Encourage students to review the imagery used in the two poems and to try to incorporate imagery when writing their own poem.

📖 The Writer's Craft

Persuasion, pp. 207–232
First-Person Narrative, p. 353
Figurative Language, pp. 413–414

Across the Curriculum

Ecology In addition to using library resources, students may wish to contact local or national environmental organizations to find out more about the effects of various human actions on the natural world.

WILLIAM STAFFORD

William Stafford lived and taught in Oregon for many years. The land and the wildlife of the American West often feature prominently in his writings.

DENISE LEVERTOV

Although Denise Levertov was born in England, she is generally considered an American writer. Of the poems she wrote after moving to the United States and reading the work of American poets in the late 1940s, Levertov says, "They began to sound less 'literary,'... the rhythms come closer to speech." In addition to writing poetry, Levertov has translated the work of foreign poets into English and has written several collections of essays on poetry.

ECOLOGY CONNECTION
Preserving the Environment In recent decades there have been more and more people who feel it is important to preserve the environment. These images show examples of the negative impact modern societies have had on the environment and a few ways people have tried to help. You may wish to use these images to discuss various ways in which people can help preserve the environment in their communities.

Side A, Frame 49510

THE WRITER'S STYLE

You can usually get an idea of the **tone**, or the speaker's attitude, in a poem from the imagery and from the comments of the speaker. In Stafford's poem, for example, the line "I thought hard for us all" indicates that the speaker's decision was not an easy one. How would you describe the tone of "The Sharks"? What lines or images reveal the speaker's attitude toward the sharks?

Jaw bone of a shark

ACROSS THE CURRICULUM

Ecology In what ways do you think your own actions might affect the natural world and the other living creatures in it? Consider the following actions and the effects they might have: wasteful use of natural resources, littering, use of throwaway products and packages, reliance on forms of transportation that pollute. Choose one of these actions, or another that you think of, and research its impact on the environment. Then make a cause-and-effect chart displaying your findings, and share it with the class.

Multimodal Learning

WILLIAM STAFFORD

William Stafford referred to himself as "one of the quiet of the land." Born in Hutchinson, Kansas, he worked in U.S. Forest Service camps as a conscientious objector during World War II. There he began his lifelong habit of rising before dawn each morning to write. Following his impulses, he would write down whatever came to mind without judging it. Stafford compared writing to fishing—in each case, he said, one must be receptive and "willing to fail." He spent most of his career juggling his writing with college and university teaching.

1926–

Stafford's poetry often concerns the gap that seems to separate the modern world from nature. His poems suggest that people must be reawakened to the lessons that nature can teach; they must rely on intuition to find their way in life. In addition to focusing on nature, Stafford's poems often reveal an interest in Native Americans and in issues of home and family and the past. He won the National Book Award in 1963 for his volume of poetry *Traveling Through the Dark*.
OTHER WORKS *Learning to Live in the World: Earth Poems, Allegiances, A Glass Face in the Rain*

Extended Reading

DENISE LEVERTOV

Denise Levertov, born in 1923, grew up in England in an unusual atmosphere. Her father, a Russian Jew who converted to Christianity, became an Anglican minister who filled the house with thousands of books and dozens of temporary refugees, artists, and literary exiles. Her mother, a descendant of a Welsh preacher, read classics to the family and provided most of Levertov's education. When Levertov was 12 years old, she sent some poems she had written to the famous British poet T. S. Eliot, who thought them worthy enough to merit a long letter of advice.

During World War II, Levertov became a nurse and helped care for war veterans in a London hospital. She wrote poems in the evenings and published her first collection of poetry when she was 23. Her second volume did not appear until about 10 years later.

After moving to New York, Levertov became an antiwar activist during the Vietnam War, and social and political themes dominated her poetry. Since then she has published poetry on many topics.
OTHER WORKS *The Jacob's Ladder, Relearning the Alphabet, Footprints, Breathing the Water, Tesserae*

Extended Reading

• ECOLOGY CONNECTION

736 UNIT SIX PART 1: UNCHARTED TERRITORY

The Writer's Style

Students may say that the writer's tone is one of fear and respect for the animals and the way they transform the character of the sea. They may cite the line "I tell you . . ." as an example of the speaker's emphasizing the impression the sharks have made.

Tone, p. 407

Alternative Activities

1. Have interested students create a poster of facts about sharks. Students can combine information about sharks— including answers to common questions and perceptions—with photos and pictures of shark species.
2. Students can conduct a poll to find out which wild animals are most feared by the people they know. If they like, they can also research which animals are actually most dangerous to humans and then create a perception/reality chart that compares their findings with the poll results.

736 THE LANGUAGE OF LITERATURE TEACHER'S EDITION

PREVIEWING

DRAMA

Sorry, Right Number
Stephen King

Activating Prior Knowledge
PERSONAL CONNECTION

Because Stephen King is the author of the next selection, it should come as no surprise to you that the story will contain at least one supernatural event. Supernatural events play a part in many stories of fantasy, mystery, and horror. Think of as many supernatural occurrences as you can that come from stories and movies you are familiar with. Jot them down on a cluster diagram like the one shown. Then compare your diagram with those of your classmates.

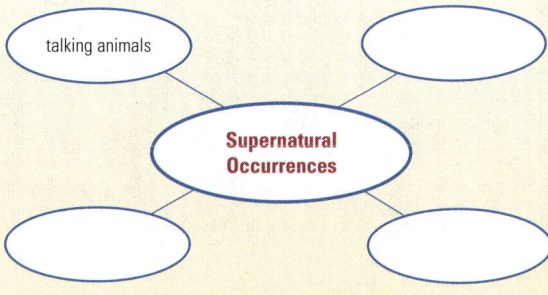

Building Background
LITERARY CONNECTION

The following selection is a screenplay, a script for a story to be filmed as a movie. To be more exact, *Sorry, Right Number* is a teleplay, since King wrote the script for a television series of supernatural stories. Stage directions, as found in regular plays, are replaced here by camera directions, which let the reader know exactly what is filling the screen. Mixed in with the camera directions, however, is King's own voice. He acts as both author and narrator of the story, frequently using the word *we.* He also points out things he wants his reader to know and comments on situations. For example, when the characters Dennis and Connie torment their younger brother, Jeff, and get him visibly upset, King's narration points out that the two of them are pleased, "in the grand tradition of older brothers and sisters." Further, King explains the abbreviations he uses in the teleplay in a unique personal note at the beginning.

Active Reading/Setting a Purpose
READING CONNECTION

Visualizing Reading a screenplay is different from reading a script for a stage play. Your mind's eye will be challenged to visualize what the camera is focusing on. For example, a camera can take you much closer to the action. In *Sorry, Right Number,* when a camera direction calls for an "extreme close-up" and then takes you inside a telephone receiver, you have to imagine not only what this looks like but also what visual effect it creates. In addition, in a screenplay, you don't have to wait for official scene changes to have changes in setting, as you do in a script for a stage play. You can be instantly thrown from one setting to the next, even from one time period to another, by a camera direction that reads "slam cut to." As you read King's teleplay, use your experience in watching TV and movies to help you visualize what the camera wants you to see. Notice how the camera gives you clues for interpreting the play's supernatural occurrence.

OVERVIEW

Objectives

- To understand and appreciate a television play that features a strange instance of time travel
- To understand and appreciate suspense
- To express understanding of the selection through a choice of writing forms, including an outline and an explanation
- To extend understanding of the selection through a variety of multimodal and cross-curricular activities

Skills

LITERARY CONCEPTS
- Suspense
- Foreshadowing

READING SKILLS/STRATEGIES
- Visualizing

GENRE STUDY
- Drama: television play

THE WRITER'S STYLE
- Irony and humor

GRAMMAR
- Capitalizing titles

SPEAKING, LISTENING, AND VIEWING
- Watching a TV drama

ALTERNATIVE
Previewing

Instead of making a diagram, students can use the following prompts for discussion with a partner:

Personal Connection

Discussion Prompts

- *What was the most frightening scene you have ever seen on TV? Did it contain an element of the supernatural?*
- *What movies have you seen with ghosts or demons?*
- *What movies or TV shows have you seen with characters who have extrasensory powers?*

PRINT AND MEDIA RESOURCES

UNIT SIX RESOURCE BOOK
Strategic Reading: Literature, p. 17
Vocabulary SkillBuilder, p. 18

GRAMMAR MINI–LESSONS
Transparencies, p. 38
Copymasters, p. 40

ACCESS FOR STUDENTS ACQUIRING ENGLISH
Selection Summaries
Reading Support

FORMAL ASSESSMENT
Selection Test, pp. 135–136
 Test Generator

INTERNET RESOURCES
McDougal Littell Literature Center at http://www.hmco.com/mcdougal/lit

SORRY, NUMBER

SUMMARY

Katie Weiderman is talking to her sister on the telephone. The other telephone line rings, and Katie answers it. Someone is sobbing and trying to say something. Then the line goes dead. Katie knows it was a family member. She calls everyone in her family, and then she and her husband, Bill, drive out to check on her other sister. Everyone is okay. Back at home, Katie goes to bed, but Bill sits up watching a movie that is based on a book he has written. In the middle of the night, Katie finds Bill in his chair, dead from a heart attack. Five years later, Katie's oldest daughter gets married. That evening, the fifth anniversary of Bill's death, Katie sits up. She turns on the television and finds that Bill's movie is being shown. She has an idea, picks up the phone, and dials her own phone number. Her own self, from five years before, answers. The older Katie, sobbing, tries to tell her younger self to take Bill to the hospital. She is sobbing too hard to make the message clear before the connection is broken.

Thematic Link: *Uncharted Territory* A mysterious phone call becomes a terrifying connection between the past and the present.

CUSTOMIZING FOR
Students Acquiring English

- Use **ACCESS FOR STUDENTS ACQUIRING ENGLISH**, *Reading Support*.
- The unusual format of this drama may prove challenging for students. Ask them to read key scenes aloud in class. Pause to explain the changing points of view and the interjected elements as they occur.
- As you guide students through the selection, you may want to use the suggestions in these boxes and the suggestions under Strategic Reading for Less-Proficient Readers.

CAST OF CHARACTERS

Katie Weiderman
Jeff Weiderman
Connie Weiderman
Dennis Weiderman
Bill Weiderman
Polly Weiderman
Operator
Dawn
Minister
Groundskeeper
Hank

WORDS TO KNOW

bleakly (blēk´lē) *adv.* gloomily; without hope (p. 745)

chasm (kăz´əm) *n.* a deep hole, as in the earth's surface (p. 751)

interim (ĭn´tər-ĭm) *n.* the period of time between one event and another (p. 749)

intuition (ĭn´tōō-ĭsh´ən) *n.* a piece of knowledge or a sense of something that is gained without the use of logical reasoning (p. 751)

prone (prōn) *adj.* having a tendency; inclined (p. 742)

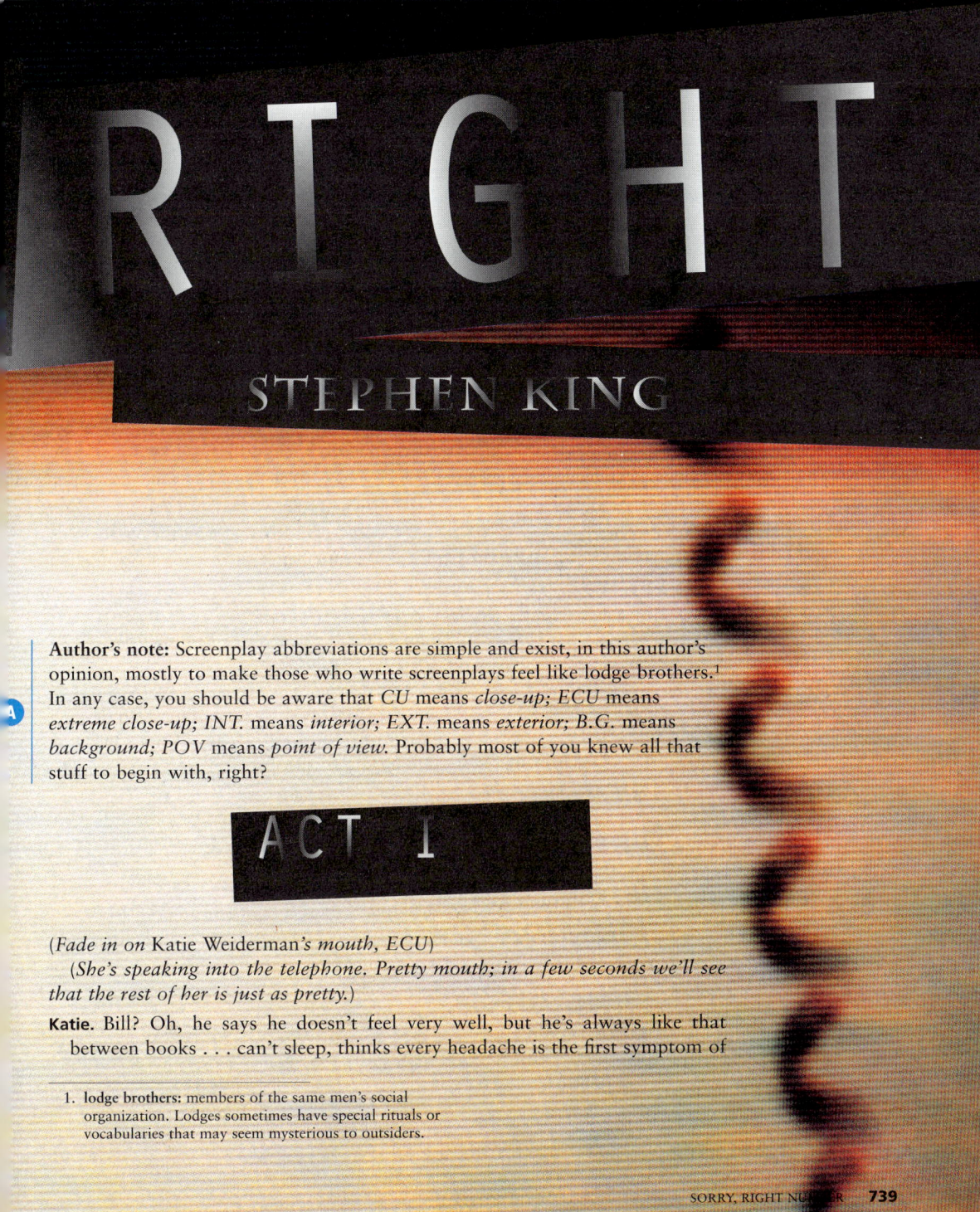

RIGHT
STEPHEN KING

Author's note: Screenplay abbreviations are simple and exist, in this author's opinion, mostly to make those who write screenplays feel like lodge brothers.[1] In any case, you should be aware that *CU* means *close-up*; *ECU* means *extreme close-up*; *INT.* means *interior*; *EXT.* means *exterior*; *B.G.* means *background*; *POV* means *point of view*. Probably most of you knew all that stuff to begin with, right?

ACT I

(*Fade in on* Katie Weiderman's *mouth, ECU*)
(*She's speaking into the telephone. Pretty mouth; in a few seconds we'll see that the rest of her is just as pretty.*)

Katie. Bill? Oh, he says he doesn't feel very well, but he's always like that between books . . . can't sleep, thinks every headache is the first symptom of

---

1. **lodge brothers:** members of the same men's social organization. Lodges sometimes have special rituals or vocabularies that may seem mysterious to outsiders.

Literary Concept:
FORESHADOWING

B Have students discuss the first camera shot called for in the directions and the first line of dialogue in the script. Ask them what the author might be hinting at. *(Possible response: The camera close-up may imply that the telephone will play an important role in the story; Katie's words may indicate that the story will focus on Bill's health.)*

Literary Concept: DIALOGUE

C Point out the ellipses in Katie's dialogue. Ask students to explain their presence. *(They indicate pauses as Katie listens to Lois talk.)*

Cultural Note

D From this point on, King's play includes several references to real current and past TV shows—such as *Wheel of Fortune*, *Cheers*, and *Wings*— and real TV and film personalities— such as Vanna White of *Wheel of Fortune* and Bela Lugosi of *Dracula* movies. This may predispose some students to believe that Bill Weiderman's books and movies— *Ghost Kiss*, *Spider Doom*, and *Night of the Beast*—are real, which they are not.

B a brain tumor . . . once he gets going on something new, he'll be fine.

(*Sound, B.G.: the television*)

(*The camera draws back.* Katie *is sitting in the kitchen phone nook, having a good gab with her sister while she idles through some catalogues. We should notice one not-quite-ordinary thing about the phone she's on: it's the sort with two lines. There are lighted buttons to show which ones are engaged. Right now only one—Katie's —is. As* Katie *continues her conversation, the camera swings away from her, tracks[2] across the kitchen, and through the arched doorway that leads into the family room.*)

C **Katie** (*voice, fading*). Oh, I saw Janie Charlton today . . . yes! Big as a *house!* . . .

D (*She fades. The TV gets louder. There are three kids:* Jeff, *eight,* Connie, *ten, and* Dennis, *thirteen.* Wheel of Fortune *is on, but they're not watching. Instead they're engaged in that great pastime, Fighting About What Comes On Later.*)

Jeff. Come *onnn!* It was his first *book!*

Connie. His first *gross* book.

Dennis. We're gonna watch *Cheers* and *Wings,* just like we do every week, Jeff.

(Dennis *speaks with the utter finality only a big brother can manage. "Wanna talk about it some more and see how much pain I can inflict on your scrawny body, Jeff?" his face says.*)

Jeff. Could we at least tape it?

Connie. We're taping CNN[3] for Mom. She said she might be on the phone with Aunt Lois for quite a while.

Jeff. How can you tape CNN, for God's sake? It *never* stops!

Dennis. That's what she likes about it.

Connie. And don't say God's sake, Jeffie—you're not old enough to talk about God except in church.

Jeff. Then don't call me Jeffie.

Connie. Jeffie, Jeffie, Jeffie.

(Jeff *gets up, walks to the window, and looks out into the dark. He's really upset.* Dennis *and* Connie, *in the grand tradition of older brothers and sisters, are delighted to see it.*)

Dennis. Poor Jeffie.

Connie. I think he's gonna commit suicide.

Jeff (*turns to them*). It was his *first* book! Don't you guys even *care*?

Connie. Rent it down at the Video Stop tomorrow, if you want to see it so bad.

Jeff. They don't rent R-rated pictures to little kids and you know it!

Connie (*dreamily*). Shut up, it's Vanna! I *love* Vanna!

Jeff. Dennis—

Dennis. Go ask Dad to tape it on the VCR in his office and quit being such a totally annoying little booger.

(Jeff *crosses the room, poking his tongue out at Vanna White as he goes. The camera follows as he goes into the kitchen.*)

Katie. . . . so when he asked me if *Polly* had tested strep[4] positive, I had to remind him she's away at prep school[5] . . . Lois, I miss her . . .

(Jeff *is just passing through, on his way to the stairs.*)

Katie. Will you kids *please* be quiet?

Jeff (*glum*). They'll be quiet. *Now.*

(*He goes up the stairs, a little dejected.* Katie *looks after him for a moment, loving and worried.*)

Katie. They're squabbling again. Polly used to keep them in line, but now that she's away at school

---

2. **tracks:** moves smoothly.
3. **CNN:** abbreviation for Cable News Network.
4. **strep:** strep throat, an infection caused by a bacteria called streptococcus.
5. **prep school:** a private high school that prepares students for entering college.

. . . I don't know . . . maybe sending her to Bolton wasn't such a hot idea. Sometimes when she calls home she sounds so unhappy . . .

(INT. Bela Lugosi[6] as Dracula, CU)

(*Drac's standing at the door of his Transylvanian castle. Someone has pasted a comic-balloon coming out of his mouth which reads:* "Listen! My children of the night! What music they make!" *The poster is on a door but we only see this as* Jeff *opens it and goes into his father's study.*)

(INT. *a photograph of* Katie, CU)

(*The camera holds, then pans[7] slowly right. We pass another photo, this one of* Polly, *the daughter away at school. She's a lovely girl of sixteen or so. Past Polly is* Dennis . . . *then* Connie . . . *then* Jeff.)

(*The camera continues to pan and also widens out so we can see* Bill Weiderman, *a man of about forty-four. He looks tired. He's peering into the word processor on his desk, but his mental crystal ball must be taking the night off, because the screen is blank. On the walls we see framed book covers. All of them are spooky. One of the titles is* Ghost Kiss.)

(Jeff *comes up quietly behind his dad. The carpet muffles his feet.* Bill *sighs and shuts off the word-cruncher. A moment later* Jeff *claps his hands on his father's shoulders.*)

Jeff. BOOGA-BOOGA!

Bill. Hi, Jeffie.

(*He turns in his chair to look at his son, who is disappointed.*)

Jeff. How come you didn't get scared?

---

6. **Bela Lugosi** (bĕl′ə lōō-gō′sē): American actor known for portraying monsters in a number of films of the 1930s and 1940s.
7. **pans:** moves horizontally to reveal a series of images representing a continuous scene.

SORRY, RIGHT NUMBER 741

Critical Thinking:
SYNTHESIZING

G Ask students to discuss what Bill Weiderman does for a living. *(He is a writer of horror novels.)* Have them point out the details that reveal this information. *(Katie refers to his writing, the kids to his books. The framed book covers on the walls have spooky titles, and he says "Scaring is my business.")*

STRATEGIC READING FOR
Less-Proficient Readers

H Have students describe the scene in the Weiderman household at this point. Ask these questions:

- What is each family member doing? *(Katie is talking on the telephone in the kitchen; Connie and Dennis are sitting in the family room, arguing about what to watch on television; Bill and Jeff are talking in Bill's office.)* **Visualizing**

- Does there seem to be anything strange or unusual going on? *(no)* **Making Judgments**

Set a Purpose Have students read on to see who is calling on the other line and how this will affect the plot.

CUSTOMIZING FOR
Students Acquiring English

3 Ask students to use context clues such as "Why I ever let you talk me into it" to figure out what "bumming her out" means. *(Possible responses: lowering her self-esteem; depressing her; making her feel bad)*

Literary Concept: SUSPENSE

I Ask students what elements of this scene help to build suspense. *(Possible responses: The scattering of the catalogues shows Katie's frantic state of mind, adding to the sense of urgency; the fact that she can't find her address book and that the dorm phone is often busy create the possibility that she won't be able to talk with her daughter, who may be in trouble.)*

G **Bill.** Scaring is my business. I'm case-hardened. Something wrong?

Jeff. Daddy, can I watch the first hour of *Ghost Kiss* and you tape the rest? Dennis and Connie are hogging *everything*.

(Bill *swivels to look at the bookjacket, bemused.*)

Bill. You sure you want to watch *that*, champ? It's pretty—

Jeff. Yes!

(INT. Katie, *in the phone nook*)

(*In this shot, we clearly see the stairs leading to her husband's study behind her.*)

H **Katie.** I *really* think Jeff needs the orthodontic work but you know Bill—

(*The other line rings. The other light stutters.*)

Katie. That's just the other line, Bill will—

(*But now we see Bill and Jeff coming downstairs behind her.*)

Bill. Honey, where're the blank videotapes? I can't find any in the study and—

Katie (*to Bill*). Wait!

(*to Lois*). Gonna put you on hold a sec, Lo.

(*She does. Now both lines are blinking. She pushes the top one, where the new call has just come in.*)

Katie. Hello, Weiderman residence.

(*Sound: desperate sobbing*)

Sobbing voice (*filter*).[8] Take . . . please take . . . t-t-

Katie. Polly? Is that you? What's wrong?

(*Sound: sobbing. It's awful, heartbreaking.*)

Sobbing voice (*filter*). Please—quick—

(*Sound: sobbing . . . Then, click! A broken connection.*)

Katie. Polly, calm down! Whatever it is can't be that b—

(*hum of an open line*)

(Jeff *has wandered toward the TV room, hoping to find a blank tape.*)

Bill. Who was that?

(*Without looking at her husband or answering him,* Katie *slams the lower button in again.*)

Katie. Lois? Listen, I'll call you back. That was Polly, and she sounded very upset. No . . . she hung up. Yes. I will. Thanks.

(*She hangs up.*)

Bill (*concerned*). It was Polly?

Katie. Crying her head off. It sounded like she was trying to say "Please take me home" . . . I knew that damn school was bumming her out . . . Why I ever let you talk me into it . . .

(*She's rummaging frantically on her little phone desk. Catalogues go slithering to the floor around her stool.*)

Katie. Connie did you take my address book?

Connie (*voice*). No, Mom.

(Bill *pulls a battered book out of his back pocket and pages through it.*)

Bill. I got it. Except—

Katie. I know, damn dorm phone is always busy. Give it to me.

Bill. Honey, calm down.

Katie. I'll calm down after I talk to her. She is sixteen, Bill. Sixteen-year-old girls are <u>prone</u> to depressive interludes. Sometimes they even k . . . just give me the damn number!

Bill. 617-555-8641.

(*As she punches the numbers, the camera slides in to CU.*)

Katie. Come on, come on . . . don't be busy . . . just this once . . .

---

8. **filter:** The caller's voice is processed through an electronic filter to make it sound as if it is coming over the telephone line.

WORDS TO KNOW
prone (prōn) *adj.* having a tendency; inclined

(*Sound: clicks. A pause. Then . . . the phone starts ringing.*)

Katie (*eyes closed*). Thank You, God.

Voice (*filter*). Hartshorn Hall, this is Frieda.

Katie. Could you call Polly to the phone? Polly Weiderman? This is Kate Weiderman. Her mother.

Voice (*filter*). Hang on, please, Mrs. Weiderman.

(*Sound: the phone clunks down.*)

Voice (*filter, and very faint*). Polly? Pol? . . . Phone call! . . . It's your mother!

(INT. *a wider angle on the phone nook, with* Bill)

Bill. Well?

Katie. Somebody's getting her. I hope.

(*Jeff comes back in with a tape.*)

Jeff. I found one, Dad. Dennis hid 'em. As usual.

Bill. In a minute, Jeff. Go watch the tube.

Jeff. But—

Bill. I won't forget. Now go *on*.

(*Jeff goes.*)

Katie. Come on, come on, come on . . .

Bill. Calm down, Katie.

Katie (*snaps*). If you'd heard her, you wouldn't tell me to calm down! She sounded—

Polly (*filter, cheery voice*). Hi, Mom!

Katie. Pol? Honey? Are you all right?

Polly (*happy, bubbling voice*). Am I *all right*? I aced my bio exam, got a B on my French Conversational Essay, and Ronnie Hansen asked me to the Harvest Ball. I'm so all right that if one more good thing happens to me today, I'll probably blow up like the Hindenburg.⁹

Katie. You didn't just call me up, crying your head off?

(*We see by* Kate's *face that she already knows the answer to this question.*)

Polly (*filter*). Heck no!

Katie. I'm glad about your test and your date, honey. I guess it was someone else. I'll call you back, okay?

Polly (*filter*). 'Kay. Say hi to Dad!

Katie. I will.

(INT. *the phone nook, wider*)

Bill. She okay?

Katie. Fine. I could have *sworn* it was Polly, but . . . *she's* walking on air.

Bill. So it was a prank. Or someone who was crying so hard she dialed a wrong number . . . "through a shimmering film of tears," as we veteran hacks¹⁰ like to say.

Katie. It was not a prank and it was not a wrong number! It was someone in *my family!*

Bill. Honey, you can't know that.

Katie. No? If Jeffie called up, just crying, would you know it was him?

Bill (*struck by this*). Yeah, maybe. I guess I might.

(*She's not listening. She's punching numbers, fast.*)

Bill. Who you calling?

(*She doesn't answer him. Sound: phone rings twice. Then:*)

Older Female Voice (*filter*). Hello?

Katie. Mom? Are you . . . (*She pauses.*) Did you call just a few seconds ago?

Voice (*filter*). No, dear . . . why?

Katie. Oh . . . you know these phones. I was talking to Lois and I lost the other call.

Voice (*filter*). Well, it wasn't me. Kate, I saw the *prettiest* dress in La Boutique today, and—

Katie. We'll talk about it later, Mom, okay?

Voice (*filter*). Kate, are you all right?

---

9. **Hindenburg:** an airship that exploded, crashed, and burned spectacularly in 1937.
10. **veteran hacks:** writers whose books sell well but are not great, or even good, literature. "Through a shimmering film of tears" is Bill's example of the sort of unimaginative, overused phrases such writers turn out.

SORRY, RIGHT NUMBER **743**

Mini-Lesson Genre Study

DRAMA Tell students that stage plays, radio plays, movies, and television plays, such as *Sorry, Right Number*, are types of drama. Point out that in a drama, plot and characters are developed through dialogue and action. Tell them that a **television play** is a drama written specifically for television. Explain that the action in a television play, as in a stage play, is usually divided into scenes, each indicating a particular time and place. In a stage play, the scenes usually provide a break in the play, giving the stage crew a chance to physically change the set on stage. A television play is not subject to this constraint; the action can easily switch from scene to scene with just a few seconds of blackout, and a writer can use this capability for dramatic effect. For example, point out King's transition, on page 749, from the somber shot of Bill's grave to the joyous scene at Polly's wedding five years later.

Application Draw on the chalkboard the chart shown on the right. Have students copy it into their notebooks. Then ask them to review the scene structure of the television play. For each scene, students should enter the place, time, and characters.

Scene	Place	Time	Characters
1	kitchen/ family room	evening	Katie/ family
2			

CUSTOMIZING FOR
Students Acquiring English

④ Explain that *tube* is slang for "television."

⑤ Some students may not know that to *ace* a school exam means "to get an A," or the highest grade possible, on it.

Linking to Social Studies

The United States has more telephones and telephone numbers than any other country in the world. In 1995, there was one telephone for every 1.3 persons in the United States, compared with one for every 6.1 persons in Russia, and one for every 20 in Ecuador. The demand for phone numbers is growing at a fast pace—mainly because of the growing popularity of pagers, fax machines, computer modems, and cellular phones. New area codes are continually added in order to create enough phone numbers to meet predicted demand.

CUSTOMIZING FOR
Multiple Learning Styles

J **Bodily-Kinesthetic Learners** You might invite students to act out this dialogue, making sure that gestures and tone of voice reflect the characters' emotions.

Cultural Note

K In the United States, the first three digits of a telephone number are called the exchange. Telephone numbers were once a combination of a two-letter exchange, one digit, and then four additional digits—for instance, PA6–5000. The two letters were an abbreviation for a district; in the example given, the district was the Pennsylvania Station area of New York City. During the mid-1960s, the system was changed to seven digits. The 555 exchange that Katie mentions does not function (except for 555-1212 for long-distance information) and is always used in films and on television to avoid inadvertently giving a real phone number.

Katie. I have . . . Mom, I think maybe I've got diarrhea. I have to go. 'Bye.

(*She hangs up.* Bill *hangs on until she does; then he bursts into wild donkey-brays of laughter.*)

Bill. Oh boy . . . diarrhea . . . I gotta remember that the next time my agent calls . . . oh Katie, that was so cool—

Katie (*almost screaming*). This is not funny!

(Bill *stops laughing.*)
   (INT. *the TV room*)
   (Jeff *and* Dennis *have been tussling. They stop. All three kids look toward the kitchen.*)
   (INT. *the phone nook, with* Bill *and* Katie)

J **Katie.** *I tell you it was someone in my family and she sounded*—oh, you don't understand. I *knew* that voice.

Bill. But if Polly's okay and your mom's okay . . .

Katie (*positive*). It's Dawn.

Bill. Come on, hon, a minute ago you were sure it was Polly.

Katie. It *had* to be Dawn. I was on the phone with Lois and Mom's okay, so Dawn's the only other one it *could* have been. She's the youngest . . . I could have mistaken her for Polly . . . and she's out there in that farmhouse alone with the baby!

Bill (*startled*). What do you mean, alone?

Katie. Jerry's in Burlington! It's Dawn! *Something's happened to Dawn!*

(Connie *comes into the kitchen, worried.*)

Connie. Mom? Is Aunt Dawn Okay?

Bill. So far as we know, she's fine. Take it easy, doll. Bad to buy trouble before you know it's on sale.

(Katie *punches numbers and listens. Sound: the dah-dah-dah of a busy signal.* Katie *hangs up.* Bill *looks a question at her with raised eyebrows.*)

Katie. Busy.

Bill. Katie, are you sure—

Katie. She's the only one left—it had to be her. Bill, I'm scared. Will you drive me out there?

(Bill *takes the phone from her.*)

Bill. What's her number?

Katie. 555-6169.

(Bill *dials. Gets a busy. Hangs up and punches 0.*)

K

Operator (*filter*). Operator.

Bill. I'm trying to reach my sister-in-law, operator. The line is busy. I suspect there may be a problem. Can you break into the call, please?

(INT. *the door to the TV room*)
   (*All three kids are standing there, silent and worried.*)
   (INT. *the phone nook, with* Bill *and* Katie)

Operator (*filter*). What is your name, sir?

Bill. William Weiderman. My number is—

Operator (*filter*). Not the William Weiderman that wrote *Spider Doom*?!

Bill. Yes, that was mine. If—

Operator (*filter*). Oh my God, I just *loved* that book! I love *all* your books! I—

744   UNIT SIX   PART 1: UNCHARTED TERRITORY

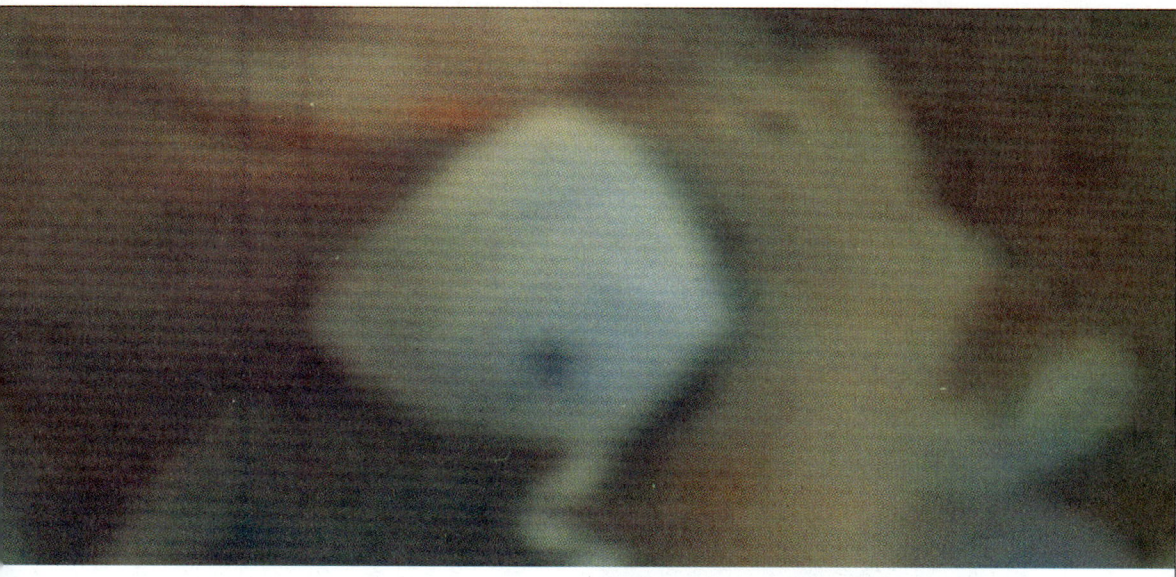

Bill. I'm delighted you do. But right now my wife is very worried about her sister. If it's possible for you to—

Operator (*filter*). Yes, I can do that. Please give me your number, Mr. Weiderman, for the records. (*She giggles.*) I *promise* not to give it out.

Bill. It's 555-4408.

Operator (*filter*). And the call number?

Bill (*looks at* Katie). Uh . . .

Katie. 555-6169.

Bill. 555-6169.

Operator (*filter*). Just a moment, Mr. Weiderman . . . *Night of the Beast* was also great, by the way. Hold on.

(*Sound: telephonic clicks and clacks.*)

Katie. Is she—

Bill. Yes. Just . . .

(*There's one final click.*)

Operator (*filter*). I'm sorry, Mr. Weiderman, but that line is not busy. It's off the hook. I wonder if I sent you my copy of *Spider Doom*—

(Bill *hangs up the phone.*)

Katie. Why did you hang up?

Bill. She can't break in. Phone's not busy. It's off the hook.

(*They stare at each other* bleakly.)
(*EXT. A low-slung sports car passes the camera. Night.*)
(*INT. the car, with* Katie *and* Bill)
(Katie's *scared.* Bill, *at the wheel, doesn't look exactly calm.*)

Katie. Hey, Bill—tell me she's all right.

Bill. She's all right.

Katie. Now tell me what you really think.

Bill. Jeff snuck up behind me tonight and put the old booga-booga on me. He was disappointed as hell when I didn't jump. I told him I was case-hardened. (*pause*) I lied.

Katie. Why did Jerry have to move out there when he's gone half the time? Just her and that little tiny baby? *Why?*

Bill. Shh, Kate. We're almost there.

> WORDS TO KNOW
> **bleakly** (blēk′lē) *adv.* gloomily; without hope

Critic's Corner

"Once again, as I edged myself nervously toward the climax of one of his thrillers, I found myself considering what wonders Stephen King could accomplish if he would only put his storytelling talents to serious use. And then I had to ask myself: if Mr. King's aim in writing . . . was not entirely serious by some standard that I was vaguely invoking, then why, somebody please tell me, was I holding on to his book so hard that my knuckles had begun to turn white?"

Christopher Lehmann-Haupt
The New York Times

Have students discuss Lehmann-Haupt's comments. Ask them why he, as well as others, might prefer to view King as less than a "serious" writer.

Literary Concept:
FORESHADOWING

M Have students note the image before the fade-out. Ask them why they think the camera focuses on the telephone once again. *(Possible responses: It may be a clue that there will be another phone call later in the story; it reminds the viewer that Dawn's phone is off the hook and adds to the suspense.)*

STRATEGIC READING FOR
Less-Proficient Readers

N Make sure students understand the phone call Katie receives and the action that follows.

- Ask students why Katie becomes upset by the phone call. *(because the caller is crying hysterically, as if in trouble, and Katie believes it is her daughter Polly)* Drawing Conclusions

- Describe the events that occur after Katie receives the phone call. *(Katie calls Polly and her mother, finding out that both are fine. She then tries to call her sister Dawn, but the line is busy. Bill checks with the operator and finds out that the phone is off the hook, so Katie and Bill drive out to the farmhouse where Dawn lives, to make sure she's all right.)* Noting Sequence of Events

Set a Purpose Have students read on to find out whether Dawn is all right and what happens after Bill and Katie return home.

Critical Thinking: ANALYZING

O Ask students how the sequence of camera shots might heighten the tension for the viewer. *(Possible response: By showing only a small section of the room at first, the impression is created that something sinister will be revealed when the camera pans out to the wider shot.)*

Katie. Go faster.
(*INT. the car*)
   (*He does. That car is smokin'.*)
(*INT. the Weiderman TV room*)
   (*The tube's still on and the kids are still there, but the horsing around has stopped.*)
Connie. Dennis, do you think Aunt Dawn's okay?
Dennis (*thinks she's dead, decapitated[11] by a maniac*). Yeah. Sure she is.
(*INT. the phone, POV from the TV room*)
   (*just sitting there on the wall in the phone nook, lights dark, looking like a snake ready to strike*)
   (*Fade out*)

(*EXT. an isolated farmhouse*)
   (*A long driveway leads up to it. There's one light on in the living room. Car lights sweep up the driveway. The Weiderman car pulls up close to the garage and stops.*)
(*INT. the car, with Bill and Katie*)
Katie. I'm scared.
(*Bill bends down, reaches under his seat, and brings out a pistol.*)
Bill (*solemnly*). Booga-booga.
Katie (*total surprise*). How long have you had that?
Bill. Since last year. I didn't want to scare you or the kids. I've got a license to carry. Come on.
(*EXT. Bill and Katie*)
   (*They get out. Katie stands by the front of the car while Bill goes to the garage and peers in.*)
Bill. Her car's here.
(*The camera tracks with them to the front door. Now we can hear the TV, playing loud. Bill pushes the doorbell. We hear it inside. They wait. Katie pushes it. Still no answer. She pushes it again and doesn't take her finger off. Bill looks down at:*)

(*EXT. the lock, Bill's POV*)
   (*Big scratches on it.*)
(*EXT. Bill and Katie*)
Bill (*low*). The lock's been tampered with.
(*Katie looks, and whimpers. Bill tries the door. It opens. The TV is louder.*)
Bill. Stay behind me. Be ready to run if something happens. God, I wish I'd left you home, Kate.
(*He starts in. Katie comes after him, terrified, near tears.*)
(*INT. Dawn and Jerry's living room*)
   (*From this angle we see only a small section of the room. The TV is much louder. Bill enters the room, gun up. He looks to the right . . . and suddenly all the tension goes out of him. He lowers the gun.*)
Katie (*draws up beside him*). Bill . . . what . . .
(*He points.*)
(*INT. the living room, wide, Bill and Katie's POV*)
   (*The place looks like a cyclone hit it . . . but it wasn't robbery and murder that caused this mess; only a healthy eighteen-month-old baby. After a strenuous day of trashing the living room, Baby got tired and Mommy got tired and they fell asleep on the couch together. The baby is in Dawn's lap. There is a pair of Walkman earphones on her head. There are toys—tough plastic Sesame Street and PlaySkool stuff, for the most part—scattered hell to breakfast. The baby has also pulled most of the books out of the bookcase. Had a good munch on one of them, too, by the look. Bill goes over and picks it up. It is Ghost Kiss.*)
Bill. I've had people say they just eat my books up, but this is ridiculous.
(*He's amused. Katie isn't. She walks over to her sister, ready to be mad . . . but she sees how really exhausted Dawn looks and softens.*)
(*INT. Dawn and the baby, Katie's POV*)

---
11. **decapitated:** beheaded.

746   UNIT SIX   PART 1: UNCHARTED TERRITORY

Mini-Lesson: Speaking, Listening, and Viewing

WATCHING A TV DRAMA Tell students that when watching a television play, an audience must use both listening and viewing skills. Point out that the camera provides clues for interpreting the characters and events in the drama. Also tell them that the dialogue often foreshadows events to come. Thus, the audience must notice the clues and "add them up" to fully appreciate the broadcast.

Application Ask students to watch a mystery show on TV and to list the clues to the solution under the heads "Dialog" and "Camera Shots." Then have students get together and compare and contrast their lists.

746   THE LANGUAGE OF LITERATURE TEACHER'S EDITION

(*Fast asleep and breathing easily, like a Raphael painting of Madonna and Child. The camera pans down to: the Walkman. We can hear the faint strains of Huey Lewis and the News. The camera pans a bit further to a Princess telephone on the table by the chair. It's off the cradle. Not much; just enough to break the connection and scare people to death.*)

(INT. Katie)

(*She sighs, bends down, and replaces the phone. Then she pushes the stop button on the Walkman.*)

(INT. Dawn, Bill, *and* Katie)

(Dawn *wakes up when the music stops. Looks at* Bill *and* Katie, *puzzled.*)

Dawn (*fuzzed out*). Well . . . hi.

(*She realizes she's got the Walkman phones on and removes them.*)

Bill. Hi, Dawn.

Dawn (*still half asleep*). Shoulda called, guys. Place is a mess.

(*She smiles. She's radiant when she smiles.*)

Katie. We *tried*. The operator told Bill the phone was off the hook. I thought something was wrong. How can you sleep with that music blasting?

Dawn. It's restful. (*Sees the gnawed book Bill's holding*) Oh . . . Bill, I'm sorry! Justin's teething and—

Bill. There are critics who'd say he picked just the right thing to teethe on. I don't want to scare you, beautiful, but somebody's been at your front door lock with a screwdriver or something. Whoever it was forced it.

Dawn. Gosh, no! That was Jerry, last week. I locked us out by mistake and he didn't have his key and the spare wasn't over the door like it's supposed to be. He was mad because he had to take a whiz real bad and so he took the screwdriver to it. It didn't work, either—that's one tough lock. (*pause*) By the time I found my key he'd already gone in the bushes.

Bill. If it wasn't forced, how come I could just open the door and walk in?

Dawn (*guiltily*). Well . . . sometimes I forget to lock it.

Katie. You didn't call me tonight, Dawn?

Dawn. Gee, no! I didn't call *anyone*! I was too busy chasing Justin around! He kept wanting to eat the fabric softener! Then he got sleepy and I sat down here and thought I'd listen to some tunes while I waited for your movie to come on, Bill, and I fell asleep—

(*At the mention of the movie* Bill *starts visibly and looks at the book. Then he glances at his watch.*)

Bill. I promised to tape it for Jeff. Come on, Katie, we've got time to get back.

Katie. Just a second.

(*She picks up the phone and dials.*)

Dawn. Gee, Bill, do you think Jeffie's old enough to watch something like that?

Bill. It's network. They take out the blood-bags.

Dawn (*confused but amiable*). Oh. That's good.

(INT. Katie, CU)

Dennis (*filter*). Hello?

Katie. Just thought you'd like to know your Aunt Dawn's fine.

Dennis (*filter*). Oh! Cool. Thanks, Mom.

(INT. *the phone nook, with* Dennis *and the others*)

(*He looks very relieved.*)

Dennis. Aunt Dawn's okay.

(INT. *the car, with* Bill *and* Katie)

(*They drive in silence for a while.*)

Katie. You think I'm a hysterical idiot, don't you?

Bill (*genuinely surprised*). No! I was scared, too.

Katie. You sure you're not mad?

Bill. I'm too relieved. (*laughs*) She's sort of a scatterbrain, old Dawn, but I love her.

SORRY, RIGHT NUMBER **747**

Linking to Art

King is referring to the painter Raffaello Sanzio, known as Raphael (1483–1520). This Renaissance painter studied in Florence with the masters Leonardo da Vinci and Michelangelo. During this Florentine period, he created his many famous portrayals of the Madonna and Child. He later moved to Rome at the call of Pope Julius II and painted frescoes for the walls of the Palace of the Vatican. Have students note that the reference is not aimed at viewers; instead, it indicates to the director the kind of serene appearance of Dawn and her child that the screenwriter desires.

Literary Concept: IRONY

Ask students what aspects of the scene Bill and Katie find at Dawn's house are different from what they anticipated. (*Possible response: They expected to discover that some tragedy had occurred, but the worst thing that has happened is that the baby has chewed up a copy of Bill's book.*)

Critical Thinking: ANALYZING

Ask students what Bill's comment about removing the "blood-bags" means. (*Possible response: Television networks normally censor excessively gory, bloody scenes; "blood-bags" is a reference to the special-effects use of bags filled with a bloodlike liquid to fake a great loss of blood in violent scenes.*)

Mini-Lesson The Writer's Style

IRONY AND HUMOR Remind students that irony is the contrast between appearance and reality. Tell them that one type of irony found in *Sorry, Right Number* is situational irony, the contrast between what the reader or character expects and what actually exists or happens. For example, Dawn's warning about a gory section of the movie is ironic because Jeff has already seen and enjoyed the gory decapitation. Then explain that another type of irony, called verbal irony, occurs when someone knowingly exaggerates or says one thing and means another. For example, the name of Jeff's dragon, Rambo, is ironic because Rambo is the name of a violent movie character, and the cute stuffed animal is anything but violent.

Application Have students review the television play, including the title, for instances of irony. Then ask them to write a paragraph discussing how the author uses irony to create a drama that is simultaneously funny and scary.

Reteaching/Reinforcement

Developing Your Writing Voice, p. 64

THE LANGUAGE OF LITERATURE TEACHER'S EDITION **747**

Linking to Science

A telephone transmits sound by translating the fluctuations of air pressure created by a speaker's voice into changes in the strength of an electric current. This current is relayed over wires to the receiver at the other end, where the electric current is converted back into sound waves by an electromagnet and a diaphragm. Alexander Graham Bell invented the telephone in 1876. Barely ten years after Bell received his patent, more than 150,000 telephones were in operation across the United States.

Literary Concept:
FORESHADOWING

S Have students note the emphasis placed on *"you know your own."* Ask them whether they agree with Bill that the caller was a "sound-alike" or whether they think this is a clue that Katie really does know the caller. *(Responses will vary.)*

Katie (*leans over and kisses him*). I love *you.* You're a sweet man.

Bill. I'm the *boogeyman!*

Katie. I am not fooled, sweetheart.

(*EXT. the car*)
  (*Passes the camera and we dissolve*[12] *to:*)
  (*INT. Jeff, in bed*)
  (*His room is dark. The covers are pulled up to his chin.*)

Jeff. You promise to tape the rest?

(*Camera widens out so we can see* Bill, *sitting on the bed.*)

Bill. I promise.

Jeff. I especially liked the part where the dead guy ripped off the punk rocker's head.

Bill. Well . . . they *used* to take out all the blood-bags.

Jeff. What, Dad?

Bill. Nothing. I love you, Jeffie.

Jeff. I love you, too. So does Rambo.

(*Jeff holds up a stuffed dragon of decidedly unmilitant aspect.*[13] *Bill kisses the dragon, then* Jeff.)

Bill. 'Night.

Jeff. 'Night. (*As Bill reaches his door*) Glad Aunt Dawn was okay.

Bill. Me too.

(*He goes out.*)
  (*INT. TV, CU*)
  (*A guy who looks like he died in a car crash about two weeks prior to filming [and has since been subjected to a lot of hot weather] is staggering out of a crypt.*[14] *The camera widens to show* Bill, *releasing the VCR pause button.*)

Katie (*voice*). Booga-booga.

(*Bill looks around companionably. The camera widens out more to show* Katie, *wearing a . . . nightgown.*)

Bill. Same to you. I missed the first forty seconds or so after the break. I had to kiss Rambo.

Katie. You sure you're not mad at me, Bill?

(*He goes to her and kisses her.*)

Bill. Not even a smidge.

Katie. It's just that I could have sworn it was one of mine. You know what I mean? One of mine?

Bill. Yes.

Katie. I can still hear those sobs. So lost . . . so heartbroken.

Bill. Kate, have you ever thought you recognized someone on the street, and called her, and when she finally turned around it was a total stranger?

Katie. Yes, once. In Seattle. I was in a mall and I thought I saw my old roommate. I . . . oh. I see what you're saying.

Bill. Sure. There are sound-alikes as well as look-alikes.

Katie. But . . . *you know your own.* At least I thought so until tonight.

(*She puts her cheek on his shoulder, looking troubled.*)

Katie. I was so *positive* it was Polly . . .

Bill. Because you've been worried about her getting her feet under her at the new school . . . but judging from the stuff she told you tonight, I'd say she's doing just fine in that department. Wouldn't you?

Katie. Yes . . . I guess I would.

Bill. Let it go, hon.

Katie (*looks at him closely*). I hate to see you looking so tired. Hurry up and have an idea, you.

Bill. Well, I'm trying.

Katie. You coming to bed?

Bill. Soon as I finish taping this for Jeff.

---

12. **dissolve:** This is a film technique for shifting scenes in which one scene fades out while the next appears and grows clearer.
13. **unmilitant aspect:** nonaggressive appearance.
14. **crypt:** underground burial chamber.

Katie (*amused*). Bill, that machine was made by Japanese technicians who think of damned near everything. It'll run on its own.

Bill. Yeah, but it's been a long time since I've seen this one, and . . .

Katie. Okay. Enjoy. I think I'll be awake for a little while. . . .

(*She starts out, . . . then turns in the doorway as something else strikes her.*)

Katie. If they show the part where the punk's head gets—

Bill (*guiltily*). I'll edit it.

Katie. 'Night. And thanks again. For everything.

(*She leaves. Bill sits in his chair.*)
(INT. TV, CU)
(*A couple is necking in a car. Suddenly the passenger door is ripped open by the dead guy and we dissolve to:*)
(INT. *Katie, in bed*)
(*It's dark. She's asleep. She wakes up . . . sort of.*)

Katie (*sleepy*). Hey, big guy—

(*She feels for him, but his side of the bed is empty, the coverlet still pulled up. She sits up. Looks at:*)
(INT. *A clock on the night table,* Katie's POV)
(*It says 2:03 a.m. Then it flashes to 2:04.*)
(INT. *Katie*)
(*Fully awake now. And concerned. She gets up, puts on her robe, and leaves the bedroom.*)
(INT. *The TV screen,* CU)
(*snow*)

Katie (*voice, approaching*). Bill? Honey? You okay? Bill? Bi—

(INT. *Katie, in* Bill's *study*)
(*She's frozen, wide-eyed with horror.*)
(INT. Bill, *in his chair*)
(*He's slumped to one side, eyes closed, hand inside his shirt.* Dawn *was sleeping.* Bill *is not.*)
(EXT. *A coffin, being lowered into a grave*)

Minister (*voice*). And so we commit the earthly remains of William Weiderman to the ground, confident of his spirit and soul. "Be ye not cast down, brethren . . ."

(EXT. *graveside*)
(*All the Weidermans are ranged here.* Katie *and* Polly *wear identical black dresses and veils.* Connie *wears a black skirt and white blouse.* Dennis *and* Jeff *wear black suits.* Jeff *is crying. He has Rambo the Dragon under his arm for a little extra comfort.*)
(*Camera moves in on* Katie. *Tears course slowly down her cheeks. She bends and gets a handful of earth. Tosses it into the grave.*)

Katie. Love you, big guy.

(EXT. Jeff)
(*weeping*)
(EXT. *looking down into the grave*)
(*scattered earth on top of the coffin*)
(*Dissolve to:*)
(EXT. *the grave*)
(*A groundskeeper pats the last sod into place.*)

Groundskeeper. My wife says she wishes you'd written a couple more before you had your heart attack, mister. (*pause*) I like Westerns, m'self.

(*The* groundskeeper *walks away, whistling.*)
(*Dissolve to:*)
(EXT. *A church. Day.*)
(*Title card: five years later*)
(*The Wedding March is playing.* Polly, *older and radiant with joy, emerges into a pelting shower of rice. She's in a wedding gown, her new husband by her side.*)
(*Celebrants throwing rice line either side of the path. From behind the bride and groom come others. Among them are* Katie, Dennis, Connie, *and* Jeff . . . *all five years older. With* Katie *is another man. This is* Hank. *In the* <u>interim</u>, Katie *has also taken a husband.*)

> **WORDS TO KNOW**
> **interim** (ĭn′tər-ĭm) *n.* the period of time between one event and another

749

Literary Concept: IRONY

Ask students why this passage about the decapitation is ironic. (*Possible response: The "guilty" Bill and viewers know that Jeff has already seen this gory scene, but Katie is in the dark.*)

Literary Concept: TELEVISION PLAY

Ask students to note how quickly scenes can be changed and time telescoped in a television play. Have students tell what is happening now and approximately how much time has elapsed since the last scene. (*The family is burying Bill; it has probably been three or four days since he died.*)

STRATEGIC READING FOR
Less-Proficient Readers

Make sure students understand what happens to Bill and Katie after the phone call. Ask them these questions:

- Why are Bill and Katie relieved by what they see at Dawn's house? (*They are relieved because Dawn is fine; she had just fallen asleep with the phone off the hook.*) **Summarizing**
- What does Katie discover in the middle of the night? (*that Bill hasn't returned to bed and that he has had a fatal heart attack in his study*) **Noting Relevant Details**

Set a Purpose Have students read on to find out how Katie finds out who made the mysterious phone call.

Mini-Lesson — Study Skills

MEMORIZING Point out to students that actors and actresses must remember their dialogue perfectly. Then say that memorizing is also an important skill for students to develop. Tell them that whether they are rehearsing a part or trying to remember the meaning of a vocabulary word, a scientific name, or a geometric formula, they can enhance their memorization through practice and by using the following techniques:

- Record yourself speaking the information you are trying to remember. Then play back the recording several times.
- Highlight difficult-to-remember lines or words so that you'll remember to give them extra attention.
- It's easier to remember small pieces of information. Break down long passages or pieces of information into parts. Then put them together as a whole.
- Memorize in a quiet place, where you won't be distracted by noise or conversation.

Application Have students work in pairs to memorize and perform a scene from the television play or a piece of their choosing. Then have them share their memorization techniques.

Critical Thinking:
MAKING INFERENCES

 Ask students why they think Polly apologizes to Hank. *(Possible responses: She was mean to him because she was upset over the death of her father; it took her a long time to accept her stepfather.)*

 Ask students what Hank does for a living and how they know this. *(Possible response: He is an architect or a contractor; the narration describes blueprints on the desk and photos of buildings on the wall.)*

(*Polly turns and her mother is there.*)

Polly. Thank you, Mom.

Katie (*crying*). Oh doll, you're so welcome.

(*They embrace. After a moment* Polly *draws away and looks at* Hank. *There is a brief moment of tension, and then* Polly *embraces* Hank, *too.*)

Polly. Thank you too, Hank. I'm sorry I was such a creep for so long . . .

Hank (*easily*). You were never a creep, Pol. A girl only has one father.

Connie. Throw it! Throw it!

(*After a moment,* Polly *throws her bouquet.*)
(*EXT. The bouquet, CU, slow motion.*)
(*turning and turning through the air*)

(*Dissolves to:*)
(*INT. The study, with* Katie. *Night.*)
(*The word processor has been replaced by a wide lamp looming over a stack of blueprints. The book jackets have been replaced by photos of buildings. Ones that have first been built in* Hank's *mind, presumably.*)
(Katie *is looking at the desk, thoughtful and a little sad.*)

Hank (*voice*). Coming to bed, Kate?

(*She turns and the camera widens out to give us* Hank. *He's wearing a robe over pajamas. She comes to him and gives him a little hug, smiling. Maybe we notice a few streaks of gray in her hair; her pretty pony has done its fair share of running since* Bill *died.*)

Katie. In a little while. A woman doesn't see her first one get married every day, you know.

Hank. I know.

(*The camera follows as they walk from the work area of the study to the more informal area. This is much the same as it was in the old days, with a coffee table, stereo, TV, couch, and Bill's old easy chair. She looks at this.*)

Hank. You still miss him, don't you?

Katie. Some days more than others. You didn't know, and Polly didn't remember.

Hank (*gently*). Remember what, doll?

Katie. Polly got married on the five-year anniversary of Bill's death.

Hank (*hugs her*). Come on to bed, why don't you?

Katie. In a little while.

Hank. Okay. Maybe I'll still be awake.

(*He kisses her, then leaves, closing the door behind him. Katie sits in Bill's old chair. Close by, on the coffee table, is a remote control for the TV and an extension phone. Katie looks at the blank TV, and the camera moves in on her face. One tear rims one eye, sparkling like a sapphire.*)

Katie. I *do* still miss you, big guy. Lots and lots. Every day. And you know what? It hurts.

(*The tear falls. She picks up the TV remote and pushes the on button.*)

(*INT. TV, Katie's POV*)

(*An ad for Ginsu Knives comes to an end and is replaced by a star logo.*)

Announcer (*voice*). Now back to Channel 63's Thursday night Star Time Movie . . . *Ghost Kiss*.

(*The logo dissolves into a guy who looks like he died in a car crash about two weeks ago and has since been subjected to a lot of hot weather. He comes staggering out of the same old crypt.*)

(*INT. Katie*)

(*Terribly startled—almost horrified. She hits the off button on the remote control. The TV blinks off.*)

(*Katie's face begins to work. She struggles against the impending emotional storm, but the coincidence of the movie is just one thing too many on what must have already been one of the most emotionally trying days of her life. The dam breaks and she begins to sob . . . terrible, heartbroken sobs. She reaches out for the little table by the chair, meaning to put the remote control on it, and knocks the phone onto the floor.*)

(*Sound: the hum of an open line*)

(*Her tear-stained face grows suddenly still as she looks at the telephone. Something begins to fill it . . . an idea? an <u>intuition</u>? Hard to tell. And maybe it doesn't matter.*)

(*INT. the telephone, Katie's POV*)

(*The camera moves in to ECU . . . moves in until the dots in the off-the-hook receiver look like <u>chasms</u>.*)

(*Sound of open-line buzz up to loud.*)

(*We go into the black . . . and hear*)

Bill (*voice*). Who are you calling? Who do you *want* to call? Who *would* you call, if it wasn't too late?

(*INT. Katie*)

(*There is now a strange hypnotized look on her face. She reaches down, scoops the telephone up, and punches in numbers, seemingly at random.*)

(*Sound: ringing phone*)

(*Katie continues to look hypnotized. The look holds until the phone is answered . . . and she hears herself on the other end of the line.*)

Katie (*voice; filter*). Hello, Weiderman residence.

(*Katie—our present-day Katie with the streaks of gray in her hair—goes on sobbing, yet an expression of desperate hope is trying to be born on her face. On some level she understands that the

WORDS TO KNOW
intuition (ĭn'to͞o-ĭsh'ən) *n.* a piece of knowledge or a sense of something that is gained without the use of logical reasoning
chasm (kăz'əm) *n.* a deep hole, as in the earth's surface

751

Critical Thinking: COMPARE AND CONTRAST

Y Ask students to find similarities between this scene and the one on pages 748–749. Then have students speculate on what might happen. (*Possible responses: In the earlier scene, Katie goes to bed, leaving Bill up alone; here, the new husband, Hank, goes to bed, leaving Katie up alone. Some students may say that Katie will die as Bill did; others may feel that Katie is about to find out who made the mysterious telephone call the night of Bill's death.*)

Literary Concept: CONFLICT

Z Ask students to describe the source of Katie's problems and to tell whether the conflict here is internal or external. (*Possible response: The conflict is internal; she is struggling with her own emotions—the accumulated stress of going through her daughter's wedding, realizing that it is the fifth anniversary of her first husband's death, and seeing a reminder of Bill on television.*)

Mini-Lesson Literary Concepts

REVIEWING FORESHADOWING Remind students that foreshadowing is the use of hints or clues by a writer to indicate events and situations that will occur later. Tell them that the use of this technique creates suspense and also prepares the reader for what is to come. Point out that in prose, a writer creates foreshadowing by incorporating hints and clues into the description of the events or the dialogue of the characters; in a television play, a writer has an additional means of foreshadowing—by calling for specific camera shots that will provide visual clues for the audience.

Application Have students work in small groups to review the selection in order to find examples of foreshadowing. Students should list each instance in which King seems to be hinting at events and situations to come. For each item on their list, students should indicate the means by which King provides the clue: through the dialogue of the characters, the voice of the narrator, or the directions for the camera.

DESIGN NOTE

In creating the photograph here, the designer followed King's instruction that *"the holes in the receiver once more look like huge dark chasms."*

CUSTOMIZING FOR
Multiple Learning Styles

AA Bodily-Kinesthetic Learners Ask students whether they think they would recognize their own voice if they heard it over the phone. Have students work with partners to make tape recordings of themselves, possibly pretending to laugh or cry. Then have them take turns with their partners calling each other and playing the recording of their own voice. Ask them whether their voice sounded the way they expected. Then, ask whether they think they could recognize their own voice over a bad connection in a one-second or two-second call such as the one in the television play.

CUSTOMIZING FOR
Gifted and Talented Students

Students may note that the entire premise of the television play is based upon a single telephone call. The questions generated by the call provide the suspense and motivation for the action that follows. Suggest that students brainstorm their own "telephone scenarios." Have them write a brief scenario—such as an overheard snippet of conversation on a cordless phone—that could provide the premise for a suspenseful drama.

---

depth of her grief has allowed a kind of telephonic time travel. She's trying to talk, to force the words out.)

Katie (*sobbing*). Take . . . please take . . . t-t-

(*INT.* Katie, *in the phone nook, reprise*)[15]

(*It's five years ago,* Bill *is standing beside her, looking concerned.* Jeff *is wandering off to look for a blank tape in the other room.*)

Katie. Polly? What's wrong?

(*INT.* Katie, *in the study*)

Katie (*sobbing*). Please—quick—

(*Sound: click of a broken connection*)

Katie (*screaming*). Take him to the hospital! If you want him to live, take him to the hospital! He's going to have a heart attack! He—

(*Sound: hum of an open line*)

(*Slowly, very slowly,* Katie *hangs up the telephone. Then, after a moment, she picks it up again. She speaks aloud with no self-consciousness whatever. Probably doesn't even know she's doing it.*)

Katie. I dialed the old number. I dialed—

(*Slam cut*[16] *to:*)

(*INT.* Bill, *in the phone nook with* Katie *beside him*)

(*He's just taken the phone from* Katie *and is speaking to the operator.*)

Operator (*filter,* giggles). I *promise* not to give it out.

Bill. It's 555-

(*Slam cut to:*)

(*INT.* Katie, *in* Bill's *old chair, CU*)

Katie (*finishes*) -4408.

(*INT. the phone, CU*)

(Katie's *trembling finger carefully picks out*

---

15. **reprise:** to repeat something that happened earlier.
16. **slam cut:** a sudden, sharp change of scene.

752

Assessment Option

INFORMAL ASSESSMENT You can assess your students' understanding of the selection by having them write a dialogue between the past Katie and the present Katie. Students should use their knowledge of the events and the characters to imagine what conversation the two Katies would have had if the telephone connection hadn't failed.

Rubric

3 Full Accomplishment The dialogues show a full understanding of the characters and the events in the selection.

2 Substantial Accomplishment The dialogues show general understanding of the selection but may be inconsistent in some details.

1 Little or Partial Accomplishment The dialogues show little understanding of the events and the characters in the selection.

the number, and we hear the corresponding tones: 555-4408.)

(*INT.* Katie, *in* Bill's *old chair,CU*)

(*She closes her eyes as the phone begins to ring. Her face is filled with an agonizing mixture of hope and fear. If only she can have one more chance to pass the vital message on, it says . . . just one more chance.*)

Katie (*low*). Please . . . please . . .

Recorded voice (*filter*). You have reached a non-working number. Please hang up and dial again. If you need assistance—

(Katie *hangs up again. Tears stream down her cheeks. The camera pans away and down to the telephone.*)

(*INT. The phone nook, with* Katie *and* Bill, *reprise*)

Bill. So it was a prank. Or someone who was crying so hard she dialed a wrong number . . . "through a shimmering film of tears," as we veteran hacks like to say.

Katie. It was not a prank and it was not a wrong number! It was someone in *my family!*

(*INT.* Katie *[present day] in* Bill's *study*)

Katie. Yes. Someone in *my family.* Someone very close. (*pause*) Me.

(*She suddenly throws the phone across the room. Then she begins to sob again and puts her hands over her face. The camera holds on her for a moment, then dollies[17] across to:*)

(*INT. the phone*)

(*It lies on the carpet, looking both bland and somehow ominous. Camera moves in to ECU—the holes in the receiver once more look like huge dark chasms. We hold, then*)

(*Fade to black.*)

---

17. **dollies:** moves smoothly.

STRATEGIC READING FOR
Less-Proficient Readers

BB Have students describe how Katie finally finds out who made the mysterious call the night Bill died. *(On the fifth anniversary of Bill's death, Katie finds his old movie on television and is struck with the idea of calling her old number. Katie hears her younger self from five years before. She tries to warn her younger self to take Bill to the hospital, but she is cut off and then realizes it was herself she had heard five years before.)* **Clarifying**

COMPREHENSION CHECK

1. When Katie receives a strange phone call from someone who is crying, whom does she believe the call is from? *(someone she knows—maybe her daughter Polly or her sister Dawn)*
2. Why do Katie and Bill drive out to check on Katie's sister Dawn? *(Dawn is alone in a farmhouse, and they are alarmed that her phone is off the hook.)*
3. Why doesn't Bill return to bed after watching the movie? *(He has a heart attack and dies in the chair.)*
4. What does Katie see when she turns on the television on the fifth anniversary of Bill's death? *(the movie version of one of Bill's books)*
5. What does Katie try to tell her younger self on the telephone before the connection breaks? *(to rush Bill to the hospital before he has the heart attack that she knows is coming)*

EDITOR'S NOTE With the permission of the author, potentially offensive material has been deleted from the selection.

From Personal Response to Critical Analysis

1. Accept all reasonable responses.
2. Responses will vary. Students should note that the supernatural occurrence was the younger Katie's receiving a phone call from her five-years-older self.
3. Possible responses: Katie realizes that it was herself who had called five years earlier; she may be hoping that this time she can change the events that occurred by getting the warning through.
4. Possible responses: yes, because she was unable to prevent the death of her husband; yes, because she may feel responsible for the heart attack her husband suffered five years earlier, thinking that it might have resulted from her frantic reaction to the phone call she received
5. Accept all reasonable, well-supported responses. Many students may think that King plays on the notion we all have that if we just had a hint that something negative was about to happen, we could probably have prevented it.
6. Accept all reasonable, well-supported responses. Some students may feel that many people read the types of stories that King writes because they enjoy imagining that the impossible can actually happen.

Another Pathway

Cooperative Learning After the class discusses the ending, be sure you assign someone to compare rehearsal performances and tapes with the directions given in the television play.

Rubric

3 Full Accomplishment The dramatizations show an understanding of the ending and an ability to follow the author's camera directions.

2 Substantial Accomplishment The dramatizations show an understanding of the ending, but students have some difficulty following the camera directions.

1 Little or Partial Accomplishment The dramatizations do not show an understanding of the ending or of the camera directions.

RESPONDING OPTIONS

FROM PERSONAL RESPONSE TO CRITICAL ANALYSIS

REFLECT
1. What did you think of the ending of this teleplay? Describe your reaction in your notebook, and share it with a partner.

RETHINK
Thematic Link
2. Give your interpretation of the story's supernatural occurrence. Did you have anything similar to it on the cluster diagram you created for the Personal Connection activity on page 737?

Close Textual Reading
3. How would you explain the vague understanding—the "desperate hope . . . trying to be born"—that comes to Katie after she hears her own voice on the phone (page 751)? If you'd like, act as Katie and show the expression on her face at that moment.

4. Do you have sympathy for Katie? Why or why not?
   Consider
Close Textual Reading
   • the interactions between Katie and her children
   • the relationship between Katie and Bill
   • the relationship between Katie and Hank

RELATE
5. What common fear or fears do you think this story plays on?

6. What do you think attracts readers to tales of the supernatural such as the kind that Stephen King writes?

Multimodal Learning
ANOTHER PATHWAY

As a class, discuss the teleplay's ending from the point where Hank leaves and Katie is left alone. Then demonstrate your understanding of the ending by dramatizing it. Use two sets of actors for the switches from present to past. Other students can create the settings, and one can videotape the dramatization, using the play's camera directions.

QUICKWRITES

1. What would you imagine as the outcome of King's story if Katie's phone call at the end had accomplished its purpose? Write an **outline** for a new ending for the teleplay based on this development.

2. Use your imagination and make up a "scientific" **explanation** of how telephonic time travel works.

📁 **PORTFOLIO** Save your writing. You may want to use it later as a springboard to a piece for your portfolio.

LITERARY CONCEPTS

Suspense—the excitement or tension that readers feel as they become involved in a story and are eager to know the outcome—is a crucial element in tales of horror and mystery. As evidenced by the popularity of his stories, Stephen King is a master at creating suspense. How does King build suspense in *Sorry, Right Number*?

CONCEPT REVIEW: Falling Action In the falling action, or resolution, of a story, loose ends are tied up and the suspense ends. What event or events form the falling action in this teleplay?

754 UNIT SIX PART 1: UNCHARTED TERRITORY

Literary Concepts

Suspense Students may say that unanswered questions such as "Who made the phone call?" "What was the caller trying to say?" and "Is Dawn all right?" create suspense as the viewer waits for the answers.

Concept Review: Falling Action The play's brief falling action amounts to Katie's repeating what the five-years-younger Katie had said about the phone call coming from "someone in my family" and then throwing the phone across the room after she and the reader or audience finally realize who made the mysterious phone call and why.

QuickWrites

1. Encourage students to experiment with different outcomes before they begin their outlines.
2. Point out to students that science fiction writers often use real scientific facts, theories, and phenomena as the basis for their plots.

 The Writer's Craft

Types of Outlines, pp. 816–817
Describing a Process, pp. 148–161

Multimodal Learning

ALTERNATIVE ACTIVITIES

1. **Cooperative Learning** In a small group, work out the ending of the teleplay, from the point where Katie turns on the TV set, as a straight stage production. Decide what elements of the teleplay you could not transfer to a stage production, and find a way to get that information to a live audience. When you are comfortable with your solution, present the **scene** to the rest of your class.

2. Suppose that *Sorry, Right Number* were being featured on the **cover** of a magazine that lists and describes TV shows. Design the art for this cover. If you have access to a computer with a graphics program, here's a chance to use it.

Multimodal Learning

ACROSS THE CURRICULUM

Media The title and certain other elements of King's teleplay are reminiscent of a classic 1948 movie in black and white titled *Sorry, Wrong Number*. Watch the video of that classic and take notes, comparing the plot of the movie to that of *Sorry, Right Number*. Present your findings in an oral report to the class.

WORDS TO KNOW

Answer the questions that follow.

1. What is another name for an **interim** between classes—a hallway, a break, or a competition?
2. Would a person who was **prone** to illness be sickly, healthy, or a good nurse?
3. Would a person who had an **intuition** about something have learned it, guessed it, or forgotten it?
4. Which is a famous **chasm**—the Washington Monument, Niagara Falls, or the Grand Canyon?
5. Would a child be most likely to look out the window **bleakly** at warm sunshine, dripping rain, or freshly fallen snow?

STEPHEN KING

1947–

Stephen King, a former English teacher, nearly threw away his writing career before it began. He originally dumped his manuscript for *Carrie* into the trash, but his wife retrieved it and urged him to continue working on it. Later, after *Carrie* became a hit movie, King went on to become a best-selling author and the first writer to have five titles on the *New York Times'* bestseller lists at the same time. Credited with reviving the market for both horror fiction and horror films, King has been called a "one-man entertainment industry."

Born in Portland, Maine, King began writing as a child and published his first story, "I Was a Teenage Grave Robber," in *Comics Review* when he was 18. A prolific and compulsive writer, King works every day except the Fourth of July, his birthday, and Christmas. Devoting his mornings to writing and his afternoons to rewriting, he produces six pages daily.

About *Sorry, Right Number*, King has written that the idea came to him "one night on my way home from buying a pair of shoes." He wrote the script in two sittings and about a week later submitted it to a friend who had a TV series called *Tales from the Darkside*. The friend bought the teleplay the day he read it, had it in production a week or two later, and a month after that telecast it—"one of the fastest turns from in-the-head to on-the-screen that I've ever heard of," King commented.

OTHER WORKS *The Shining, The Stand, The Dead Zone, Firestarter*

Extended Reading

Words to Know

1. a break
2. sickly
3. guessed it
4. the Grand Canyon
5. dripping rain

Reteaching/Reinforcement
• *Unit Six Resource Book,* p. 18

Across the Curriculum

Media Students can consult a video guide to find other films *(Dial M for Murder, When a Stranger Calls)* in which telephones and telephone references figure prominently in the title or the story. Encourage students to view several of these films, compare them with *Sorry, Right Number,* and discuss why a telephone might be commonly used as an element of the plot in suspense and horror films.

STEPHEN KING

Stephen King worked as a janitor, a laundry man, a high-school teacher, and a knitting-mill employee before finally achieving tremendous success as a writer. Today, more than 100 million copies of his works have been sold. Many of the characters in King's works are writers—and some are horror writers, such as Bill in *Sorry, Right Number*—but King states that although he "dredges" his "memory for material," his fiction is rarely autobiographical.

Alternative Activities

1. Explain to students that when transferring a drama from one medium, such as television, to another, such as the stage, producers often make changes in the dialogue or the setting. Ensure that all group members contribute their ideas to creating an effective stage adaptation of the scene from the television play.

2. Suggest that students review the television play for scenes or objects that are important to the story and that would be effective if used as visual images to generate viewer interest.

OBJECTIVES

- To promote independent active reading
- To practice and apply skills learned in previous selections
- To provide an opportunity to assess students' performance through an alternative assessment instrument

Reading Pathways

- Invite students to form small groups and give a dramatic reading of the selection. One student can read the third-person narration; other students can read the excerpts from Joel's letter to Edith and the dialogue of the crew members.

- Suggest that students think about what might be the greatest dangers facing the crew of a small boat lost at sea for several months. Then, have them make a list of the challenges they foresee. As they read, students should note the dangers faced by the crew of the *Cairo III* and should compare them with the items on their list. Ask students to note which challenges they had predicted and which problems they hadn't expected.

- Ask students to keep a "captain's log" as they read the selection. Students should write down entries noting important events, the physical state of the boat, and the physical and mental state of the crew at various points during the ordeal. After they have finished reading, they can use their log to create a time line of the voyage.

- Evaluate how well students can read, interpret, discuss, and write about the selection on their own by using the Integrated Assessment for Unit Six, located in the Alternative Assessment booklet. Administer the assessment at the end of the unit, after students have read all the selections and completed all the writing that they were assigned.

ON YOUR OWN

REFLECT & ASSESS

A TRIP TO THE

> To My Beloved Wife, I want to write you so bad but I don't know what to say. Only that I feel this great desire to live, which is all that gives me strength. But I don't think I can resist because God is making it very difficult for me. But what can I do? I love you and my four daughters so much. I only know that if I die, you won't have bad memories nor will you tell my daughters I was a bad man. My strength is ending, and if I die, I hope someone will be able to send you this.
>
> —Joel González[1]

On Jan. 24, as the dawn's first light brightened the cloudless sky 20 miles off the coast of Costa Rica, Joel González, 27, stood at the helm of the *Cairo III*, maneuvering the squat, 29½-foot fishing boat through light swells in the Pacific Ocean. Suddenly, Joel felt a squall[2] send the vessel shuddering and lurching to one side. Within minutes, the dreaded north wind, a 50- to-60-mph seasonal scourge of the coastal area, struck with full force, heaving up 30-foot swells that bashed in doors and windows, swamped the cabin and left the wooden craft bobbing wildly and close to foundering.[3]

"That was the beginning of our nightmare," says Joel, who was alone on deck until his four panicked crewmates scrambled from their bunks. "There was so much noise, I thought the boat was breaking up. The guys looked like monkeys, hanging on to anything they could grab. It's a miracle we didn't go down. The boat was half filled with water, and we bailed like madmen. We lost our net, the radio went out, and before long the engine overheated and gave out. All day the water poured in. We'd nail the doors shut, but the waves would just smash them open again. We fought and fought, bailing and working the pump. From that day we never saw the coast again."

Eventually, the five fishermen, who had left the port city of Puntarenas[4] Jan. 19 on a routine, week long trip near the coast, would remember the 22-day storm as one of the most terrifying chapters in the five months they were lost at sea. They would still have to face many desperate bouts of hunger and thirst, a badly leaking hull, the constant danger of shark attacks and the threat of mental collapse. But amazingly, they would battle on for a total of 144 days, to be rescued near the end of their endurance June 15 by a Japanese fishing ship about 700 miles from Honolulu and 4,000 miles from Costa Rica. Their odyssey would set a world record for survivors cast adrift, surpassing the 133 days a Chinese seaman spent

---

1. Joel González (jō'əl gôn-sä'lĕs).
2. **squall:** a sudden, brief, violent storm.
3. **foundering:** filling with water and sinking.
4. Puntarenas (pōōn-tä-rĕ'näs).

756 UNIT SIX PART 1: UNCHARTED TERRITORY

PRINT AND MEDIA RESOURCES

UNIT SIX RESOURCE BOOK
Strategic Reading: Literature, p. 21

FORMAL ASSESSMENT
Selection Test, pp. 137–138
Part Test, pp. 139–140
 Test Generator

ALTERNATIVE ASSESSMENT
- Unit Six Integrated Assessment, pp. 31–36

ACCESS FOR STUDENTS ACQUIRING ENGLISH
Selection Summaries

AUDIO LIBRARY
See Reference Card

---

756 THE LANGUAGE OF LITERATURE **TEACHER'S EDITION**

EDGE OF SURVIVAL
Ron Arias

alone in the Atlantic in 1942-43. Shaky but miraculously healthy after such an ordeal, they would return home as heroes. "I never thought I'd see my wife and kids again," says Joel. "That's why I started to write her a note explaining how we died. I kept it in a little bottle with my gold ring tied to the top. With my last strength, I was going to throw the bottle into the water, hoping someone would find it and send her the note."

The captain of the *Cairo III* on its epic voyage into maritime history was Gerardo Obregón,[5] 33, a quiet, affable[6] man with five years' experience as a skipper. Except for Pastor López,[7] 27, the small, talkative fisherman who joined the group in December and who would become its spiritual leader in the crisis, the crew had sailed together for a year. The veterans included Joel, the poet of the group; Jorge Hernández,[8] 26, a tall, sober-faced young man; and Juan Bolívar,[9] the crew's elder at 47, with more than 30 years of seagoing experience.

> I only know one thing—that if it's possible to love after life, I will love you. This is the last I'll write you, since I see things are so difficult that I no longer have the illusion or the strength to go on. We're out here two months now and nothing has happened to lift our spirits.

The day the *Cairo III* put out to sea, Joel's wife, Edith, 26, awoke with a strange feeling. Though her husband had gone on many fishing tours with Captain Obregón, on this morning she feared unreasonably for Joel's safety. She was worried about the condition of the boat's wooden hull, about all the holes and cracks they had tried to fix in a hurry. When Joel was leaving the house that he and the family shared with his parents in an impoverished barrio[10] near Puntarenas, he kissed his four daughters—ages 2 months to 5 years—and turned to go.

"Hey, what's this?" Edith protested when her husband forgot to kiss her.

"What are you so worried about?" Joel said, picking up on his wife's anxiety. "I'm not going as far as Panama."

"Well, you never know," Edith said. And with that, Joel gave her a kiss and departed.

Eight days later, Edith and Gerardo's wife, Lydia, 27, knew something had happened to their husbands; all the fishing-fleet boats except the *Cairo III* had fled into port to escape the rough seas and winds that had been pounding the coast for several days. Alarmed, the women asked the local coast guard office to begin an air-and-sea search for the boat. Officials assured them that they would scour the adjacent Gulf of Nicoya and the ocean beyond.

---

5. **Gerardo Obregón** (hĕ-rär′dô ô-brĕ-gôn′).
6. **affable:** friendly, pleasant, and easy to talk to.
7. **Pastor López** (päs-tôr′ lô′pĕs).
8. **Jorge Hernández** (hôr′hĕ hĕr-nän′dĕs).
9. **Juan Bolívar** (hwän bô-lē′vär).
10. **barrio:** in Spanish-speaking countries or areas, a section or suburb of a city.

SUMMARY

On a day in January, a storm caught five fishermen 20 miles off the coast of Costa Rica in their fishing boat. The boat became half-filled with water, the radio stopped working, and the engine overheated and failed. For 22 days, the storm battered the boat and blew it far out into the Pacific Ocean. The sailors feared that every day might be their last. When the sea finally calmed, the men were lost. They survived by catching turtles and sharks and collecting rainwater. They had to bail water continuously because the boat was leaking so badly. They tore down the cabin so that they would have wood for cooking. On some days, they had nothing to eat and no water. Twice they saw ships far off, but the ships did not notice them. One fisherman wrote an ongoing letter to his wife, telling about the ordeal and how much he loved her. He kept the letter in a bottle, which he planned to throw into the sea if he found himself near death. Five months after being lost at sea, the five men were rescued 700 miles from Honolulu—and 4,000 miles from home—by a Japanese fishing boat.

Thematic Link: **Uncharted Territory** Five Costa Rican fishermen struggle to survive after a storm batters their boat and sends them far out into the Pacific.

Linking to Economics

Commercial fishing is a huge industry throughout the world, including the United States. In 1992, U.S. commercial fishermen earned $3.7 billion in revenue on almost 5 million metric tons of fish and shellfish. The U.S. fleet brings in almost 6 percent of the world's commercial landings and is the sixth largest producer of seafood in the world. About 80 percent of this catch goes to human consumption. On average, one American consumes about 15 pounds of seafood each year.

Linking to Science

The trade winds are strong winds that blow in the direction of the equator from the northeast to the southwest. Early sailors found the paths of these winds so predictable and regular that they named them *trade winds,* meaning "course or track winds." Like the men in the selection, early sailors depended on the trade winds to carry their sailing ships where they wanted to go. The winds are caused by the difference in temperature between low latitudes (that is, near the equator) and northern regions. The warm air of the low latitudes rises, creating an area of low pressure near the surface. This causes the cooler and heavier air of the polar regions to move in to fill the area of low pressure. The polar winds blow from the northeast and from the southeast because of the eastward whirling motion of the earth.

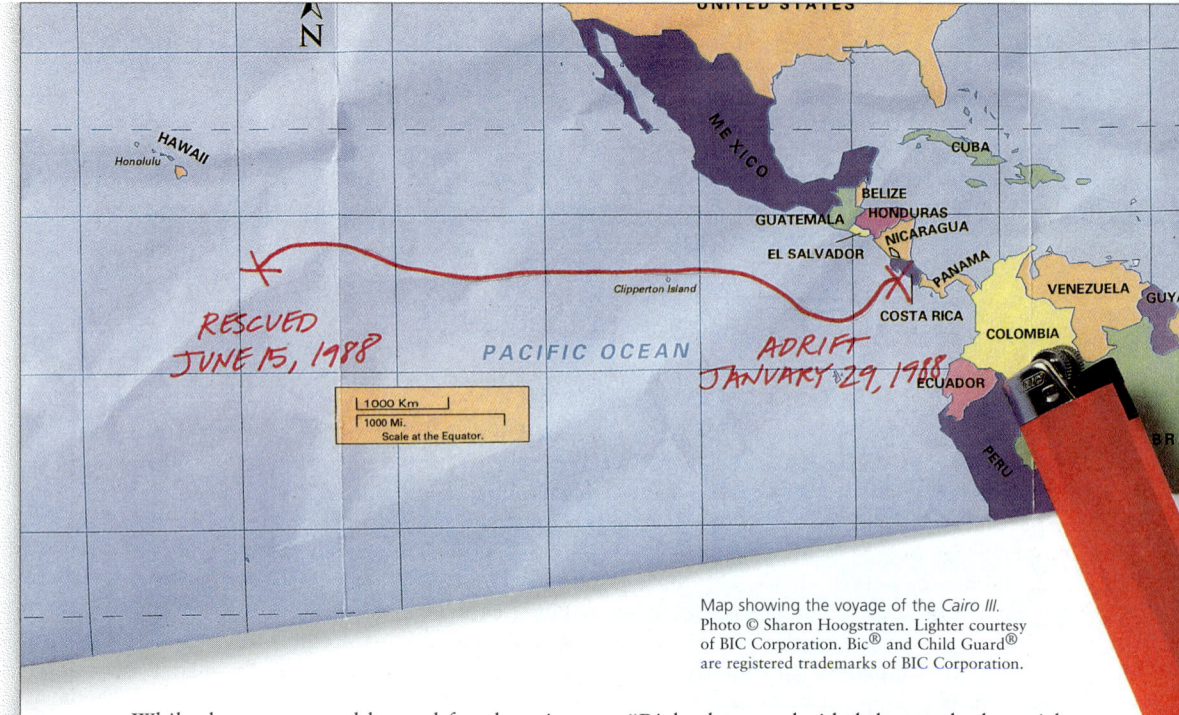

Map showing the voyage of the *Cairo III*. Photo © Sharon Hoogstraten. Lighter courtesy of BIC Corporation. Bic® and Child Guard® are registered trademarks of BIC Corporation.

While the coast guard hunted for them in vain, Joel, Gerardo, Jorge, Juan and Pastor were battling crashing waves and their own exhaustion, bailing continuously, eating or resting when they could, crawling about on all fours to keep their balance on the dizzily pitching deck of their five-ton vessel. "We were desperate, terrified that at any minute we would sink," says Joel. "Until the end of the storm all we did was bail, crawl into our bunks for a few hours' sleep and bail some more." The provisions—rice, flour, beans, crackers, sugar and some meat—ran out on the third day of the storm. The men had to make do on the few fish they had caught before the storm hit.

After three weeks of fierce winds and high seas, the storm calmed, leaving the crew of the *Cairo III* free to consider their predicament; they were alone in the ocean with no way of getting back to shore and no hope of a swift rescue. "We realized we had to depend on our own resources and couldn't expect help," Joel recalls.

"Right then we decided that we had to stick together. We made rules to ration food and water and agreed to bail in four-hour shifts, day and night." They began dismantling the wooden cabin and its four sleeping berths to provide fuel for their cooking fire. With the bunks gone, the crew found that the most protected niche[11] on board was the hatch-covered icebox set under the rear deck. No longer used to store their catch, the icebox was barely large enough to accommodate four men in a crouch or lying down. All but the captain, who would lie down in a sheltered spot in the bow, would sleep here.

A daily struggle for food and survival had begun. All they had was a long, trailing fishing line with a lot of dangling hooks and no bait. As soon as the swells began to abate,[12] they decided to try and catch some of the turtles they had seen inquisitively approaching the boat. Though a half-dozen 12-foot sharks

---

11. **niche** (nĭch): recess or hollow; nook.
12. **abate:** lessen or decrease.

What the *Cairo III* looked like before its fateful voyage.

Gerardo showing the strain of the voyage.
Copyright © 1995 Peter Serling.

Linking to Science

Sea turtles are migratory animals found in warm ocean waters in various parts of the world. They use their long flippers to travel distances of hundreds of miles or more. Well-known sea turtles include the green turtle, the fastest sea turtle, which can swim at 20 miles per hour; the hawksbill, a small carnivorous turtle valued for the commercial uses of its shell; and the leatherback, the largest of all land or sea turtles, which can sometimes weigh over 1,200 pounds. Many sea turtles are endangered by overhunting (their meat is sought as the main ingredient for turtle soup, and their eggs are valued by some as a delicacy); accidental death, which occurs when they become caught in the drift nets of commercial fishing boats; and coastal development, which threatens their breeding grounds. Female turtles lay their eggs in shallow nests above the tide line, where their eggs are easily accessible.

were already circling nearby, catching them would require baited hooks. The turtles, some measuring up to three feet in width, could be gaffed[13] with a big hook tied to a pole.

"My job," Joel explains, "was to hide behind the side rail and, before they could see me and be scared away, I'd have to spring up and hook them. As soon as we pulled one onto the deck, Gerardo would kill it and open the bottom part with his knife. Then Jorge would clean the meat, Pastor would cook us something like a stew in seawater, and Juan would divide up the pieces. I guess we trusted Juan the most to be fair. This was very important because some days we wouldn't catch anything, and when we finally did, even if it was a fish no bigger than a man's hand, it was Juan who'd cut up and distribute the little pieces that would tease our stomachs for another day." Some days when their luck was running they would eat well, other days they caught nothing and went hungry. Their only source of fresh water being rain, they measured their chances of survival by the weather.

> *The rainwater that we had is about used up. We have no food. And all around us, the same thing, water and more water. We have suffered so much that I believe, with death, God will finally allow us to rest. I know you may never get this note, Edith, but anything is possible. And if I can't hang on, I hope you will find out exactly how and when it was that I died.*

After three weeks of waiting with no news from the coast guard, Edith and Lydia hitched a two-hour ride to the capital city of San José. There they spoke with a government official

---

13. **gaffed:** caught or hooked.

A TRIP TO THE EDGE OF SURVIVAL **759**

Linking to Geography

The Pacific Ocean was named by the Portuguese navigator Ferdinand Magellan (about 1480–1521), whose expedition circumnavigated the globe and proved that the earth was round. That he encountered a peaceful, or pacific, ocean was not unusual; neither is it unusual to encounter the wrathful ocean described in this selection. The vast Pacific breeds deadly typhoons that have sunk fleets of ships and inundated cities. Earthquakes and volcanic eruptions deep under this ocean can cause tidal waves 100 feet high that sweep over islands, washing out to sea everything in their path.

---

who told them that the coast guard had been unable to make a search beyond the gulf because their large patrol boat had broken down. "He made all these excuses," says Edith. "And when we suggested that the *Cairo III* might have drifted into Nicaraguan waters, he said it was out of his hands. He also said there were no clues about our husbands' whereabouts and that they couldn't invest a lot of money on a search when the chances of finding something were so small."

By late February, the men were drifting with the prevailing westerly winds and current. The boat's compass, the only navigational device on board, now showed their course was almost due west. On a day of relative calm, Juan, whom the others nicknamed "the old man," suggested they make a mast and sail. The only one among them who had worked on a sailboat, he volunteered to design and direct the project. "On our own, the way we were, we couldn't get anywhere," he recalls having told them. "Only God could take us there, but it wouldn't hurt if we helped Him a bit. The wind and current were too strong for us to get back home, but a sail would move us to the west faster." With a thick crossbeam wrenched out of the cabin roof, the men fashioned a 21-foot mast, tore away planks to make a boom[14] and sewed together blankets and pieces of vinyl cushion covers to create a crude, triangular sail. After the sail was fastened to the boom and mast with fishing line and wire, Juan had them make a rudder. While prying out nails for reuse in these tasks, the crew found themselves blessing the thoroughness of *Cairo III*'s original builders. "The boat turned into a floating hardware store," says Pastor. "We had so much wire and nails of all sizes." The makeshift rudder worked well at first, but, like the sail, it had to be constantly repaired.

Getting the boat back under way was a psychological boost and allowed the five to weather the storms and towering seas they encountered frequently. The men confess they had little idea of world geography or where they might wash ashore. By mid-March they must have crossed a couple of time zones because they knew from their watches that the sun was setting much later than it did in Costa Rica. The crew's two-date wristwatches also helped them keep track of their voyage. "The watches gave us an idea how far we had gone and how many days we'd been out," says Gerardo. "By keeping them set to Costa Rican time, they were also a reminder, or a way of tying us to our country." Gathering food—usually turtles, sometimes a shark they would snare with a baited hook and fishing line—had become almost an obsession.[15] And since the thought of eating raw flesh was repulsive to all five, they took extreme care in safeguarding and cleaning what became their most cherished possession—a plastic Bic lighter that Joel, a nonsmoker, absentmindedly threw in his suitcase before the trip. "I was chosen to cook," says Pastor, "because I was the most careful in lighting the wood. It's funny now, but during the trip that lighter seemed like life itself for us. Late in the trip, when we had torn down the cabin and the wood was running out, we could just barely warm up the meat. But it still made all the difference to our stomachs." The moment when Pastor flicked the lighter into flame became an important, hope-affirming ritual. With the other four watching intently, Pastor would start the fire with fragments of a sponge mattress and nurse it to glowing life

---

14. **boom:** long pole extending from a mast to hold the bottom of a sail.
15. **obsession:** an intense interest in a single idea or desire.

---

760   UNIT SIX   PART 1: UNCHARTED TERRITORY

Multicultural Perspectives

RAW FISH   While uncooked fish may not have been appetizing to the crew of the *Cairo III*, it is regarded as a delicacy in many cultures. Raw fish is a classic element of Japanese cuisine. Sashimi is slices or cubes of fresh raw fish—often tuna, mackerel, or salmon—served with soy sauce and horseradish mustard. The fish is prepared by special chefs who are trained in the cutting technique appropriate to the taste and texture of each particular fish. Sushi is sliced raw fish served on small rolls of rice. The origins of sushi lie in a traditional method of preserving fish. Raw fish was pressed with rice, stored, and fermented with vinegar. Eventually, some Japanese chefs decided to forgo the fermentation process and serve the fish-and-rice combination fresh.

An uncooked but marinated seafood dish called ceviche is popular in many Latin countries, including Peru and Ecuador. Raw ocean fish is cut into cubes and marinated with lime juice, avocado, onion, and spices.

with splinters of wood. Once, the Bic slipped from Pastor's grasp and fell to the bottom of the flooded engine well; without hesitating, he dived into the oily slop to retrieve it. "We were angry at him for being so clumsy," says Joel, "but I think he felt worse than we did."

> Edith, don't spend the rest of your life suffering and wondering what happened to me. Be courageous and try to overcome life's hardships, since from the time of our birth we know we're going to die sooner or later. And if God takes me first, what can I do? I fought till the end and did everything I could to return to you. But finally I was defeated. Yet even now, on the brink of death, there's still a little flame in me that refuses to go out.

Sometime in April Edith dreamed that she received letters from Joel, postmarked in Korea, instructing her to take care of the children. Desperate for news of Joel, she clung to her faith that he was still alive and hid her anxiety from the children. Emily, their 2-year-old daughter, who was especially close to her father, also had dreams that Joel was still alive. In one dream, she was stranded on a rock in the sea and he came to save her. In another, he returned home and, complaining of hunger, asked for a plate of rice, beans, and fried eggs.

By this time, most of the boat's cabin had been torn apart to be used as firewood in the small, cylindrical stove they had made out of a gas tank. All that remained above deck was a flat wooden awning held up by four posts. They used the awning for shade from the intense tropical sun

Photographs Copyright © 1995 Peter Serling.

The men haul a fish aboard ship.

Above: Pastor (left) and Joel cut up a fish.
Below: Joel's letter with the ring and bottle he had planned to throw overboard before he died.

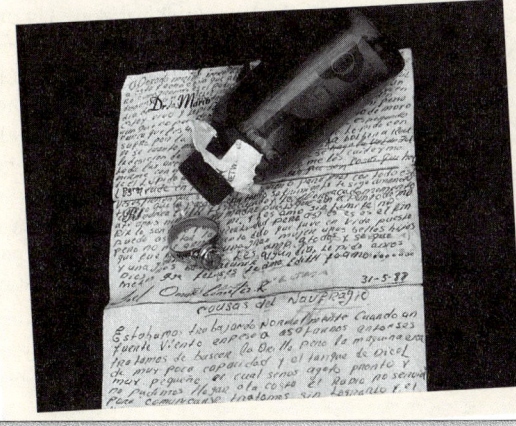

Linking to Geography

Costa Rica is a small Central American country. It is a democratic country, bordered by Nicaragua, the Caribbean Sea, Panama, and the Pacific Ocean. Spanish explorers arrived in Costa Rica in the 1500s. The Indians living there told the Spaniards stories about gold and other precious metals that could be mined from the land. After hearing these stories, the Spanish explorers named the land *Costa Rico*, which means "rich coast." The explorers eventually found out that the land had little mineral wealth.

and to catch rainwater, which they trapped in a gutter on one side by tilting the boat with their weight; the runoff spilled into a 40-gallon barrel.

Gradually the stress and punishing hardship of life aboard the *Cairo III* began to distort the crew's sense of reality. Food deprivation became a maddening fixation.[16] At first they had argued over choice pieces of turtle liver, but now, increasingly, the bickering was centering on their dreams of favorite meals. At night, ravenous[17] and unable to sleep, they lay under the stars, their thoughts plagued by tantalizing[18] visions of heavenly dishes. In a lunatic game, the men would find themselves haggling endlessly over an ideal plate of food, "buying" the fruits of their imagination with the little money each man carried on board. Upset that the others were only torturing themselves, Juan pleaded with them to stop, but they refused, finding some humor in taunting[19] the older man.

A ship came on the morning of April 15, as a few small birds flitted low over the foam-tipped swells. Jorge was brushing his teeth near the stern when he glimpsed a freighter about two miles away. "Look!" he shouted. "A ship! A ship!" For a long time the men shouted and waved their arms. "I dropped my toothbrush in the water, I was so happy," Jorge recalls. Alas, no one aboard the freighter spotted the tiny speck of the *Cairo III* in the vast ocean, and the ship disappeared over the horizon. The men fell silent and despondent, their disappointment all the more acute because it was the second time a distant ship had passed them by. "We thought it was another of God's tests for us," says Pastor. "After that, we just assumed that we'd be saved or hit land if God meant us to."

The day of that second boat sighting, Juan suffered a crippling attack of stomach pains. Although they all contended with constant diarrhea, the normally stoic[20] Juan finally asked Joel, the crew's designated "doctor," for some antacid pills. "I was the doctor only because I happened to bring along some aspirin and a handful of other pills," he says. "Poor Juan. He was hurting the most, but the pills helped. He also had to have a tooth pulled, which we yanked out with a piece of twine."

In mid May, Gerardo ordered the dismantling of the engine. It was dumped overboard, along with batteries and a gas tank, to reduce the boat's weight. They had been riding ever lower in the water, bailing around the clock to control the flooding below decks, and now Gerardo began going into the water to plug holes and cracks in the hull from the outside, tethered to *Cairo III* by a rope. Wary of the sharks that circled the boat with nerve-racking constancy, the others would keep a close lookout while the captain stuffed rags and pieces of plastic and mattress sponge into the vessel's leaking skin.

It was after completing this chore, after Gerardo had been pulled up and the men were sitting down to rest under the awning, when Pastor shouted: "My God, look at that!" The others started, then froze at the sight of a monstrous whale.

"It was about 20 feet away, so big it looked like a piece of land," Gerardo recalls. "The tail alone was as big as our boat. All we could do was hold on and watch. If it touched us, we would sink in a minute. There were other whales but never that big or that close. I was ready to poke it with a little harpoon we'd made, just to shoo it away. But as it came closer, it dove under

---

16. **fixation:** preoccupation; obsession.
17. **ravenous** (răv′ə-nəs): wildly hungry; famished.
18. **tantalizing:** fascinating and desirable but disappointingly out of reach.
19. **taunting:** mocking or insulting.
20. **stoic** (stō′ĭk): calm and unemotional, especially while in pain; uncomplaining.

us and stayed there for about 20 minutes. We held our breath and prayed, and then, thank God, it went away."

> May 10. My beloved. Incredibly I'm still alive, since by this date I thought I would have been rescued or dead. But so great is God's power that even from here I can wish you a happy birthday and my mother, a happy Mother's Day.

Not long after the day the whale appeared Jorge was on deck, about to clean the severed head of a 10-foot shark. As he stooped to pick it up, the jaws reflexively snapped shut on one of his fingers. Yelling in pain, he yanked his hand free and saw that a tooth had punctured a finger. "It shocked him so much his legs wouldn't stop trembling," Joel remembers. "You could bash a shark over and over with a club, cut his insides out, and he would still go flopping around and twitching for an hour. We all had cuts from those fights, but Jorge's wound was the worst."

On May 31, they once again rationed out the last dregs of water. "There were many days when we had no rain," says Joel. "By the end, we cherished the water we could drink more than food." Tormented by thirst, the men lay about on the deck in their tattered shorts, looking at the faraway, dark clouds that seemed to taunt them with the promise of rain. They had begun to eat their fish raw, something they had sworn they wouldn't do. "We had to," says Pastor, "because we'd used up all the wood to make a fire. If we ripped up any more of the boat, we'd probably sink, since there wasn't much left of it." But now their tongues and throats were so parched that they could hardly swallow. They had killed about 200 turtles so far, and the creature that had saved them from starving was no longer of use.

For four days they waited for rain. Some thought of suicide, and all five passed into a kind of delirious stupor.[21] But at their lowest ebb, Pastor gave a rousing talk to get the men moving again. "The sail was down and we had been drifting," Pastor remembers. "I told them that God was tempting us to die the way the devil tempted Jesus. 'Fight back, get up and let's raise the sail,' I said. And somehow we did and we started moving again."

Though Pastor's brave talk rallied his friends, he too was feeling almost overwhelmed by despair. "A lot of the time I thought of suicide, how wonderful it would be to find a way out of this situation," he says. "But I knew it was better to fight like a man than die like a coward."

> I don't know how much life remains in me, Edith. I pray with all my will to be reunited with you. You and my daughters are everything. I love you without limits. I can't accept reality, but that's the way the end is. I don't regret what I had in life, because it was the best — a great woman, beautiful children and a wonderful mother. I love you, Edith. I love you.

As death became increasingly likely, the crew of the *Cairo III* began to prepare for it. Joel scribbled the last entry in his letter to his wife—

---
21. **stupor:** dazed condition.

OPTION 2

Cooperative Learning
PACK A SURVIVAL KIT

Tell students that they are going on a dangerous ocean voyage. Tell them that other than clothing and a two-week supply of food, they are allowed to pack only 15 items in their survival kit and that they must decide what they will take. Have students form small groups, and ask each group to decide on the items for its kit, numbering the items in order of priority. Then have groups share their lists, explain how each item will help them survive the voyage, and give their reasons for ranking them the way they did.

Teacher's Role Encourage students to divide up aspects of planning among themselves. All students should contribute ideas and suggest a list of items for the kit.

Rubric

3 Full Accomplishment Students create a list of items for the kit, rank each item, and are able to explain why each item would be necessary.

2 Substantial Accomplishment Students create a list of items but have some difficulty explaining why one item is more important than another.

1 Little or Partial Accomplishment Students have difficulty creating a list of items.

---

something he had shown only to Pastor, thinking the others would find it overly sentimental—and Pastor carved a loving message to his family on a plank, weeping as he did so. The five men carefully put on their best clothes, the ones they had been saving for their rescue, which now seemed a futile hope. Then they lay down, closed their eyes and readied themselves for the end.

After a while, a light rain began to sprinkle their faces. Their hopes reborn, the men became nearly hysterical with joy, licking moisture from the surface of the awning roof. "We were afraid it would stop," says Joel, "but our prayers were answered, and it started to rain hard. At that point we were all crying."

Ten days later, on the afternoon of June 15, a crewman on the bridge of the *Kinei Maru*,[22] a Japanese fishing vessel, spotted the bobbing, sea-stained white hull of the *Cairo III*.

Joel saw the ship first: "I'd just caught a shark when I looked up and saw it," he says. "I remember saying, 'Hey a boat! A boat!' and screaming to them to wave to it. We were all leaping with joy. I cut loose the shark, and I remember thinking, 'Thank you, God, thank you, thank you.' Tears came to my eyes; I realized I wasn't going to die."

At home in Costa Rica, Edith was the first of the wives to receive the news from the boat's owner, Carlos Rohman, of their rescue. When she heard the words "alive" and "saved," she dropped the telephone receiver and collapsed on the sofa.

---

22. **Kinei Maru** (kē′nā′ mä′rōō′).

764   UNIT SIX   PART 1: UNCHARTED TERRITORY

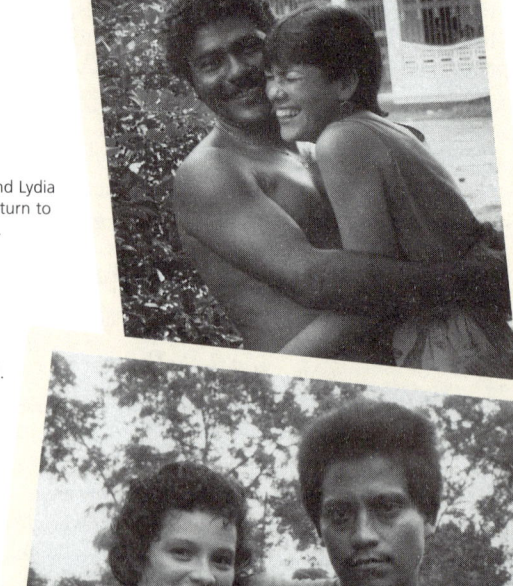

Gerardo and Lydia after his return to Costa Rica.

Edith and Joel.

The crew of the *Cairo III* after their ordeal. Back row from left: Gerardo Obregón and Joel González. Front row from left: Jorge Hernández, Juan Bolívar, and Pastor López. Photographs Copyright © Peter Serling.

The five survivors, who regretted leaving their boat behind—probably to sink in a matter of hours—were taken by the Japanese to Honolulu, where U.S. Army physician Dr. Fred Thaler examined them, proclaiming the Costa Ricans surprisingly fit. "There were no obvious signs of scurvy,[23] nor did they seem terribly emaciated,"[24] says Thaler. "For what they had been through, they were in superb shape."

After a flight back to their country by way of Los Angeles, the men were given a hero's welcome home, especially in the port of Puntarenas. There, after sharing tears and hugs with their families, hundreds of cheering fishermen and other townsfolk paraded them through the streets.

Joel and Edith clung to each other, in the grip of emotions they hardly dared to voice. Edith's eyes followed Joel wherever he went, as if she were afraid he might disappear again. Some days later he showed her the note from the bottle. She sat down and read it, crying softly, and telling him finally, "You touch my heart with your words."

Today, two days after the tumultuous homecoming, Joel sits on the deck of *Cairo III*'s sister boat, the *Cairo V*. He's just finished eating his third ham and cheese sandwich of the morning (like the other survivors, he eats often now, throughout the day). Fingering the bottle and the note to Edith, which is deeply creased from many foldings and unfoldings, he says he hasn't returned to work yet but he will. He likes how it feels to be on a boat again. He has decided to keep the bottle as a memento of the voyage that nearly cost him his life—but also as a symbol of what the experience taught him. "During those days," he says, "I realized how much I love my wife and children. And now I want to show them that without the family, there is no reason to live." ❖

---

23. **scurvy:** a disease caused by a shortage of vitamin C in the body and characterized by weakness, spongy gums, nosebleeds, and a decrease in red blood cells.
24. **emaciated** (ĭ-mā'shē-ā'tĭd): extremely thin, especially as a result of starvation.

RON ARIAS

1941–

Ron Arias first met the crew of the *Cairo III* when he interviewed them in Los Angeles on their return home to Costa Rica. "None of them spoke English, so when I walked in and introduced myself in Spanish, it was as if they were welcoming a brother." Arias believes that his close ties to his Latin heritage helped him understand the fishermen and their point of view. This article on their adventure first appeared in *People* magazine. Arias later expanded the account into a book, *Five Against the Sea*.

Born in Los Angeles, Arias traveled throughout the United States and Europe as he was growing up because his stepfather was in the army. He began writing at the age of nine, when he was hospitalized for a tonsillectomy and his mother gave him a notebook in which to keep a journal. Although he has a master's degree in journalism, he feels that his real education for a career in writing has come from his travels and his newspaper work.

Arias, who enjoys the adventure of changing places and jobs, has been a foreign newspaper reporter, a Peace Corps volunteer, a teacher, and a senior writer for *People* magazine. He has produced short stories, screenplays, teleplays, many types of nonfiction and a novel, *The Road to Tamazunchale*, which is considered a masterpiece of Chicano literature. As a member of the Peace Corps in Peru in the 1960s, he worked with the poor. This gave him "insight into the world of basic survival," the theme of much of his writing.

OTHER WORKS "The Castle," "Chinches"

OVERVIEW

In the Guided Assignment for this section, students will write a short play based on a dramatic incident. As preparation for this assignment, students will use the Writer's Style to help them understand how writers use word choice, details, action, and dialogue to create a mood. In Reading the World, students will analyze the setting of a special event in order to identify and interpret details that create its mood.

Objectives

- To recognize how writers use details, action, and dialogue to evoke a mood
- To use details, dialogue, and foreshadowing to create a mood
- To write a short play that engagingly evokes a mood
- To analyze a real-life image for details of setting that create a mood

Skills

LITERATURE
- Identifying dialogue and word choices that create a mood
- Using foreshadowing
- Writing dialogue

GRAMMAR AND USAGE
- Choosing the correct modifier

MEDIA LITERACY
- Analyzing a special event

SPEAKING, LISTENING, AND VIEWING
- Discussing how a setting's details influence mood
- Partner and peer conferring

CRITICAL THINKING
- Analyzing setting

Teaching Strategy: MODELING

In the first literary excerpt that follows, the writer uses dialogue to create a mood. In the second excerpt, the writer's choice of words creates a mood.

A **King** Possible response: King creates a suspenseful mood by having Katie repeatedly insist that something bad is going to happen to Dawn, who is alone with a baby in a farmhouse.

B **Poe** Possible response: Word choices that contribute to the mood of fright and near-hysteria include *shrill screams, bursting, chained form, thrust, violently, trembled.*

WRITING ABOUT LITERATURE

IN THE MOOD

Imagine an adventure story with no excitement. What about a horror tale that doesn't scare you? These aren't stories you would be eager to read. Writers create emotions through words and action. In these pages you will

- study how writers create mood
- write a mood-filled drama
- study ways real-life situations evoke moods

Writer's Style: Creating a Mood A good story can evoke fear or joy, excitement or dread. You can create a mood or feeling through the words you choose, the details you include, and the action and dialogue you use.

Literature Selection

Notice how these writers create different moods.

Literature Models

Creating Mood Through Dialogue

A What mood does King create in this scene? How does his use of dialogue help create that mood?

> Katie. *I tell you it was someone in my family and she sounded—* oh, you don't understand. I *knew* that voice.
> Bill. But if Polly's okay and your mom's okay . . .
> Katie (*positive*). It's Dawn.
> Bill. Come on, hon, a minute ago you were sure it was Polly.
> Katie. It *had* to be Dawn. I was on the phone with Lois and Mom's okay so Dawn's the only other one it *could* have been. She's the youngest . . . I could have mistaken her for Polly . . . and she's out there in that farmhouse alone with the baby!
>
> Stephen King, from *Sorry, Right Number*

Creating Mood Through Word Choice

B How does Poe's choice of words help you enter into the mood of this passage?

> A succession of loud and shrill screams, bursting suddenly from the throat of the chained form, seemed to thrust me violently back. For a brief moment I hesitated—I trembled.
>
> Edgar Allan Poe, from "The Cask of Amontillado"

766 UNIT SIX: A MATTER OF LIFE AND DEATH

PRINT AND MEDIA RESOURCES

UNIT SIX RESOURCE BOOK
Writer's Style, p. 25
Prewriting, p. 26
Elaboration, p. 27
Peer Response Guide, pp. 28–29
Revising and Proofreading, p. 30
Student Model, pp. 31–33
Rubric, p. 34

FORMAL ASSESSMENT
Guidelines for Writing Assessement

GRAMMAR MINI-LESSONS
Transparencies, p. 22
Copymasters, p. 24

WRITING MINI-LESSONS
Transparencies, p. 56

 WRITING COACH

 The Writer's Craft
Guidelines for Writing Dialogue, p. 436

766 THE LANGUAGE OF LITERATURE **TEACHER'S EDITION**

Connect to Life

Nonfiction writing can also create a mood. Note how the writer of this essay moves from one mood to another. What feelings does this excerpt evoke for you?

Magazine Article

My father was a man who could look at a skinny child wearing perpetually crooked wire eyeglasses and harboring a generally pessimistic outlook on life, and say to her, "You are the best there is!" Repeating it so convincingly that, for a little while, she would believe it. I cannot say of him, however, that he was a man who kept his promises to his family. He made, in fact, the same promise over and over, but he was unable to keep it.

Katharine Byrne
from "The promise of spring"
Chicago Tribune Magazine

Creating Mood Through Word Choice and Details C How does the essayist use words and details to create contrasting moods?

Try Your Hand: Creating Mood

1. **Changing a Mood** In a book or story you have read, find a short passage that creates a strong mood. Rewrite the passage, making changes in words and details to change the mood.

2. **Describing a Mood** Find a mood-filled photograph or illustration. Write a description of what you see, using words that convey the mood to a reader who has not seen the picture.

3. **Creating a Mood** With a group, brainstorm and list at least five moods experienced by most people. Write a brief dialogue that creates one of the moods on the list.

SkillBuilder

WRITER'S CRAFT

Using Foreshadowing

Foreshadowing, hints of events to come, can add to the mood of your writing. In *Sorry, Right Number,* Stephen King builds suspense by hinting that something dreadful is going to happen. Notice how a series of clues foreshadow Bill's death and add to the mood of suspense and dread.

- Katie reports that Bill "says he doesn't feel very well."
- The screenplay directions state that Bill "looks tired."
- A mysterious caller pleads for help.
- The caller and message are not explained.
- Katie wakes up at 2:03 A.M. and is concerned that Bill is not in bed.
- Katie finds Bill is in his chair "slumped to one side."

Only at the end of the drama does King show how the mysterious phone call is connected to Bill's death.

APPLYING WHAT YOU'VE LEARNED

You're planning a play about four teens who are friends. Write three sentences that foreshadow one of the following events for your play.

1. A fire will destroy a clubhouse.
2. One of the characters will know who set the fire.

WRITING ABOUT LITERATURE **767**

Teaching Strategy: MODELING

C **Byrne** Possible response: In the first part of the paragraph, the father's attempt to build up his daughter's self-esteem evokes an affectionate, optimistic mood. In the second part of the paragraph, the detail revealing that the father never kept his promises to his family produces a sad mood.

Try Your Hand

1. Responses will vary. Students' word choices should produce a consistent shift in the mood of the original passage.

2. Responses will vary. Students' descriptions should include sensory imagery and strong word choices that contribute to a single, overall impression of the mood.

3. Responses will vary. Sample moods that students may list include the following: joy, sadness, anxiety, pride, impatience, anger, wonder, laziness, surprise.

SkillBuilder WRITER'S CRAFT

USING FORESHADOWING Point out that foreshadowing provides clues to awaken the audience's curiosity and to stimulate predictions.

Application Possible responses:

1. The gang's new clubhouse was a rickety, three-room shack that had been abandoned by its owners. This was the guys' fourth clubhouse in the past three years. They had lost previous clubhouses to either wind or rain storms, though fire remained the most obvious danger to hanging around these old wooden buildings.

2. During the fall, Manuel had noticed that Scott seemed to crave constant attention, needing the others in the gang to look up to him, even fear him. Manuel was certain that Scott was capable of turning on his friends. So he feared that the clubhouse fire that was certain to come was likely to be an "inside" job.

Additional Suggestions Have students brainstorm about the uses of foreshadowing that they have noticed in movies or television dramas.

Critical Thinking: SPECULATING

D Tell students that speculating about "What if?" scenarios is a good way to generate ideas for a drama. For example, what if a ferocious tiger or bear escaped from a zoo? What if two young people were having a picnic nearby at the time?

CUSTOMIZING FOR
Less-Proficient Writers

E Tell students that dialogue can also serve as a springboard for developing a plot. Suggest that students close their eyes and visualize an argument, an exciting exchange at a sports contest, or another emotion-charged scene at school or at home. Then tell them to freewrite all the dialogue that belongs in that scene.

WRITING ABOUT LITERATURE

Creative Response

Why do some plays capture an audience and hold its attention? By writing a play, you can begin to understand the techniques and tools a writer uses to hold an audience.

GUIDED ASSIGNMENT
Write a Drama You can write a play about anything that interests you, using words, characters, and action to create a mood that will involve your audience.

❶ Prewrite and Explore

Think of a dramatic incident or some interesting characters on which to base your play. You might imitate a scene or borrow a character from a Stephen King story, or write a play based on an experience of your own. You can choose to create one scene or an entire play, to write a stage drama or a screenplay.

❷ Plan a Plot

These steps can help you get your play started.

- Create some characters and describe them for yourself so that you know them well.
- Plan a problem for the characters.
- Decide if your story can be dramatized on a stage or if you will write a screenplay like *Sorry, Right Number*. For example, a story with action that takes place on a lake would be difficult to show on a stage but would make a good screenplay.
- If you choose to write a screenplay, review the camera directions Stephen King explains in the introduction to his play on page 739.

You may find it helpful to jot down ideas in a notebook to get your play started. The student's prewriting notes on this page show how one writer began to develop a screenplay.

768 UNIT SIX: A MATTER OF LIFE AND DEATH

Student's Prewriting Notes

I'll write a screenplay with a mood of suspense. I'll use hints that something awful is going to happen.

Characters: Martin, Dina, James, and Joel. The first three are nice kids but noisy and kind of hyperactive. Joel likes them, but he's not sure he's part of the group.

Problem: Joel discovers his new friends are expert swimmers. Joel's scared of water, but will Martin, Dina, and James dump him if he doesn't do the things they like? He's afraid so.

Setting: lake with rocky, muddy edges

Start with a scene at the lake.

Assessment ✓ Option

SELF-ASSESSMENT After students have completed Plan a Plot, they should assess their notes by answering the following questions:

- *Have I planned to develop a stage play or a screenplay?*
- *Have I focused on at least two characters and a problem or conflict that involves them?*
- *Have I identified the setting for the action?*
- *Have I planned what mood I want to create in the opening scene?*

3 Write a Discovery Draft

Once you have notes to help you with your play, take a few minutes to review the form used by playwrights.

- Show the speaker's name at the beginning of each speech.
- Put directions for actors and cameras in parentheses. Underline directions or put them in italic type. Include important directions, but don't worry about details until you write your draft.

Examine this student's discovery draft of an important scene in a screenplay.

Student's Discovery Draft

(*Show* Joel *standing at the edge of the lake.*)

Dina. Oh, come on, Joel. You're worse than my little brother. The water isn't even deep!

(Joel *takes one step forward.* Martin *and* James *are dog-paddling in circles around* Dina, *grabbing at her legs. One of them pulls her down.*)

Martin (*laughing*). Joel, be careful. The Loch Ness monster is right here waiting to pull you under.

(Joel *shuts his eyes and walks into the lake. He is really scared.*)

Add details to my directions. For example, what can you see at first? Where is Dina?

Martin doesn't sound real. I'll use some slang.

4 Draft and Share

Read your discovery drafts aloud in a group. Work together to be sure your dialogue sounds natural. When you are ready, write a draft of your scene.

PEER RESPONSE

- Which character seems the most real? Why?
- What can I do to make the dialogue sound more realistic?
- What mood do you think my drama conveys?

SkillBuilder
WRITER'S CRAFT

Writing Dialogue

Dialogue in a play carries a very heavy load.

- It must provide information about the plot and about what is happening offscreen or offstage.
- It often describes or explains the play's action.
- It must tell what characters think and feel.
- Dialogue must sound natural and appropriate for the character who is speaking.

The following suggestions can help you write dialogue.

- Listen to how people talk—people like those in your play.
- Practice writing dialogue that is formal, informal, appropriate for a small child, for a teen, for an adult.
- Use run-on sentences, fragments, slang, contractions, and a vocabulary that sounds natural for your character.
- Always read dialogue aloud to yourself, then to a partner.

APPLYING WHAT YOU'VE LEARNED

Rewrite the following sentences as your friends might say them.

1. It was a lovely party.
2. I'm nervous about taking the driving test.
3. The movie was action-packed and held my interest.

WRITING ABOUT LITERATURE **769**

Writing Skill: USING THE COMPUTER

F A discovery draft gives students a chance to get their ideas down without worrying too much about spelling, grammar, or mechanics. Instead, students should focus on maintaining a steady stream of ideas. They can clean up the format easily once they have written everything down.

Teaching Strategy: STUMBLING BLOCK

G If students are having difficulty recognizing how dialogue and stage directions work together in a play, go over the function of each stage direction in the discovery draft, showing how the directions relate to physical action, the delivery of lines, and the overall mood.

Teaching Strategy: MANAGING THE PAPER LOAD

H You may wish to have students affix a single self-stick note to their drafts upon handing them in. On the notes, they could each write the main question or concern upon which they would like you to focus as you read.

Teaching Strategy: COLLABORATIVE OPPORTUNITY

I Have peer reviewers point out any passages of dialogue that they think need revision. Peer-review groups could read these passages aloud; hearing one's dialogue spoken aloud can reveal to the writer strengths and weaknesses not previously realized.

SkillBuilder WRITER'S CRAFT

WRITING DIALOGUE

Visualizing each character often helps a writer create suitable dialogue. Suggest that when students write a line of dialogue, they form a mental snapshot of the character who delivers it, including the character's height and weight, age, hair color and style, clothes, facial expression, movements, and so on.

Application Possible responses:
1. What a blast!
2. I'm seriously sweating the driving test.
3. Man, that flick really blew me away!

Additional Suggestions Remind students how often people interrupt one another in real life. Suggest that when they write dialogue, they have their characters do the same to one another, especially at highly emotional moments in a scene.

Reteaching/Reinforcing
- *Writing Mini-Lessons* transparencies, p. 56

The Writer's Craft
Using Dialogue in Plays and Skits, p. 436

THE LANGUAGE OF LITERATURE TEACHER'S EDITION **769**

Critical Thinking: ANALYZING

J Point out to students that revising their drafts involves molding the text to fit their audience and purpose. When evaluating and revising their plays, students should:

- include stage directions that help to create mood
- check to see that they have written realistic dialogue
- make sure that the dialogue and action move the plot forward and reveal character

Teaching Strategy: MODELING

K Details that suggest that something bad might happen include: Martin and James's act of pulling Dina down and Martin's reference to the Loch Ness Monster.

L The whooping and splashing show that Martin and James are carefree and possibly reckless. Martin and Dina's teasing of Joel shows that Joel's companions pick on him. The stage directions show that Joel is really frightened.

M The detail that works best to increase suspense is the stage direction calling for Joel to suddenly fall backward into the water, as if pulled from beneath.

N Discuss how the writer's final draft meets the Standards for Evaluation on this page. Point out that the writer uses informal language in the dialogue. The draft also employs stage directions to foreshadow an accident or some other crisis, thus creating a suspenseful mood.

Standards for Evaluation

Ideas and Content
- uses realistic dialogue that enhances and advances the plot
- presents central problem or conflict through plot
- includes stage directions that establish setting, describe action, and give clues to character
- reveals mood and character through dialogue and action

Structure and Form
- is formatted clearly and accurately according to guidelines
- organizes scene effectively so audience can follow story line

Grammar, Usage, and Mechanics
- contains no more than two or three minor errors in grammar and usage
- contains no more than two or three minor errors in spelling, capitalization, and punctuation

---

WRITING ABOUT LITERATURE

5 Revise and Edit

As you begin to revise and edit your draft, be sure that the dialogue and characters are realistic and that the audience can feel the mood. Think of ways the students in your class can share their plays with an audience. You might videotape the plays, hold a play fest and read the works aloud, or bind the finished play scripts together and add them to your classroom library.

Student's Final Draft

Sorry, Joel!

ACT TWO, SCENE 1

(*Camera shows* Joel *at the water's edge. Then it pans to* Dina *standing in the middle of a small pond. Water is up to her waist. We can't see the other boys, but we can hear them whooping and splashing.*)

Dina. Oh, come on, Joel. You're worse than my little brother.

(*Camera widens out to show pond and kids.* Joel *takes one step, still not in the water.* Martin *and* James *dog-paddle toward* Dina *and pull her down. She laughs and splashes water.*)

Martin (*deep, spooky voice*). Joel, watch your feet! The Loch Ness monster is here! (*in his own voice*) He'll sink you, man!

(Joel *shuts his eyes and walks into the pond. He looks terrified. CU*)

James. Here it comes, Joel!

(*POV* James. Joel *suddenly falls backward into water, as if pulled from beneath.*)

James. Joel! Hey, man, what's the matter? Joel! (*Camera on* James *as he runs toward* Joel, *awkwardly, in waist-deep water.*)

Which details hint that something bad might happen? What do they suggest?

How does the writer use dialogue and action to show what the characters are like?

Which detail works best to increase suspense?

Standards for Evaluation

A play
- uses realistic dialogue
- reveals mood and character through dialogue and action
- includes directions that help create mood
- uses techniques such as foreshadowing to interest the audience

---

Assessment Option

SELF-ASSESSMENT To help students assess their own writing, they should answer the following questions:

- *Do my stage directions clearly show how lines are to be delivered and how the characters are to move?*
- *Should I change any of the dialogue to make it sound more like the way people really speak?*
- *Have I used foreshadowing to hold the attention of the audience and build suspense?*

Grammar in Context

Using Adverbs and Adjectives All good writing makes use of precise adjectives and adverbs, but these are especially important in the directions for a play. Clear directions serve several purposes.

- They give the actors clues that help them portray a character.
- They tell readers how a character feels and looks.
- They direct the camera.
- They help to set the mood for a scene.

See how King uses precise adjectives in screenplay directions.

(*We should notice one not-quite-ordinary thing about the phone she's on.*)
The phone isn't rare or common. It's just "not-quite-ordinary."

(*He goes up the stairs, a little dejected.*)
Jeff is not crying and he isn't feeling great. His feelings are in between those two emotions, "a little dejected."

The screenplay directions in *Sorry, Right Number* also show King's precise use of adverbs that give readers and performers clues to characters' feelings, actions, or tone of voice.

After the phone call, Katie hunts for her address book.
(*She's rummaging frantically.*)

When Bill tells Dawn she left her door unlocked, she explains, but she knows it was a foolish thing to do. She answers Bill.
Dawn (*guiltily*).

Try Your Hand: Using Adjectives and Adverbs

On a sheet of paper, rewrite the following sentences. Add at least one precise adjective or adverb to make the directions clear.

1. The three friends greet Joel.
2. The water isn't clear.
3. Dina begins swimming toward Joel.
4. Martin stands in the water.

SkillBuilder

 GRAMMAR FROM WRITING

Choosing the Correct Modifier

As you select precise modifiers for your play directions or for setting a mood, be sure you choose them carefully.

An **adverb** tells *how, when, where,* or *to what extent,* and describes an action verb, an adjective, or an adverb. An **adjective** tells *which one, what kind,* or *how many* and describes a noun or pronoun.

Which modifier is correct in these pairs of sentences?

The dancers moved slowly.
The dancers moved slow.

Use an adverb. *Slowly* tells how and it modifies an action verb.

The storm grew loudly.
The storm grew loud.

Use an adjective. *Loud* tells what kind and modifies the noun *storm.*

APPLYING WHAT YOU'VE LEARNED
Look at the stage directions for your play. Find places where adding a modifier will help create a mood or give a clearer direction for the camera or actor.

 GRAMMAR HANDBOOK

For more information on using adjectives and adverbs, see page 918 of the Grammar Handbook.

WRITING ABOUT LITERATURE **771**

Teaching Strategy: USING THE SKILLBUILDER

You may wish to teach the SkillBuilder on modifiers at this time. This exercise requires a thorough understanding of adjectives and adverbs and their uses.

Try Your Hand

Possible responses:

1. The three friends greet Joel *playfully.*
2. The water is *muddy.*
3. Dina begins swimming *lazily* toward Joel.
4. Martin stands *timidly* in the water.

PORTFOLIO

Ask students to write a brief description of what they have learned about writing drama as a result of this assignment. They may wish to include their description and their finished play in their portfolio.

SkillBuilder GRAMMAR FROM WRITING

CHOOSING THE CORRECT MODIFIER Be sure that students understand that both adjectives and adverbs can be used with both transitive and intransitive verbs, depending on the context; for example, *grow, look, feel,* or *turn.*

Application Remind students that adjectives and adverbs are often used in stage directions to indicate how the actors are to deliver their lines.

Additional Suggestions Tell students that precise modifiers create clarity. For example, *whispering* is more exact than *soft,* and *frantically* has stronger connotations than *busily.*

Reteaching/Reinforcing
- *Grammar Mini-Lessons* copymasters p. 24, transparencies p. 22

 The Writer's Craft

Adjective or Adverb?, p. 628

THE LANGUAGE OF LITERATURE TEACHER'S EDITION **771**

READING THE WORLD

On pages 768–771, students wrote a drama, a dramatic scene, or a screenplay in which they used action, dialogue, and word choice to create a mood. They should be aware that real-world images use details of setting to create a mood. In this lesson, students will analyze details of setting in a photograph.

Critical Thinking: OBSERVING

P Students' answers will vary. In general, they should point out that the setting is night in a large stadium or arena. Performers or marchers are gathered around a large, torchlike focal point, where an event is being staged. Spectators in the stands are excitedly waving light sticks.

Critical Thinking: MAKING INFERENCES

Q Students' answers will vary. In general, the mood burns with excitement. Planners would want to create this mood in order to draw spectators into the scene and get them to participate in a major, memorable "event."

Speaking and Listening: GROUP DISCUSSION

R Have students work in small groups to compare their interpretations. Encourage them to speculate about some of the specific ways that the planners of this event mapped out details of the setting.

772 THE LANGUAGE OF LITERATURE TEACHER'S EDITION

READING THE WORLD

SETTING THE STAGE

Dramas are planned all the time in ordinary life. Think of times, for example, that you've decorated a place to create a special mood for a special occasion, just as a set designer decorates a stage to influence the mood of an audience.

View Imagine you have just walked into the scene in the photograph. What is happening?

Interpret What mood is suggested? Why would planners want to create this mood?

Discuss Talk about your interpretation of the event in the photograph and the way planners created a mood to draw people into the activity. The SkillBuilder suggests some ways you may use details to interpret the mood of an event.

SkillBuilder

CRITICAL THINKING

Analyzing Setting
You know how to analyze a literature selection by looking for parts that develop a mood—especially the dialogue, details, descriptions, and events. Also, you have written pieces that bring out a feeling or mood.

In the same way, you can analyze settings that create a mood, and you can use setting to create a mood for events you plan. What did the organizers of the celebration shown on these pages do to create a mood? What is that mood? How do colors add to the mood? What other details can you find that would affect the mood of the people in the arena?

APPLYING WHAT YOU'VE LEARNED
With a group, analyze some special events from your own experience. How did details of the setting create a mood to draw in the participants? You might consider such events as pep rallies, school dances, quiet ceremonies in memory of someone, celebrations of a success, or end-of-the-year school parties.

SkillBuilder — CRITICAL THINKING

ANALYZING SETTING Guide students to recognize that "happenings" or spectator events such as the one shown in the picture may look spontaneous but in fact are most often the result of careful planning by organizers. Have students identify as many details as they can that contribute to the overall mood.

Application Encourage student groups to consider a wide range of events and gatherings, including graduations, birthday parties, political rallies for candidates, and protests.

UNIT SIX
Part 2 Lesson Planner

TIME ALLOTMENTS SHOWN ARE APPROXIMATE. DEPENDING ON YOUR GOALS AND THE NEEDS OF YOUR STUDENTS, YOU MAY WISH TO ALLOW MORE OR LESS TIME FOR CERTAIN PORTIONS OF THE LESSON.

Table of Contents	Discussion	Previewing the Selection	Reading the Selection
PART OPENER **Fateful Encounters** page 774	**20 MINUTES** • Reflect on the part theme		
SELECTION **The Cask of Amontillado** page 776 CHALLENGING		**20 MINUTES** • PERSONAL CONNECTION • CULTURAL CONNECTION • READING CONNECTION: Evaluating the narrator	**40 MINUTES** • Introduce vocabulary • Read pp. 776–83 (8 pp.)
SELECTION **The Most Dangerous Game** page 788 CHALLENGING		**20 MINUTES** • PERSONAL CONNECTION • CULTURAL CONNECTION • READING CONNECTION: Making inferences	**90 MINUTES** • Introduce vocabulary • Read pp. 788–806 (19 pp.)
SELECTION **Not to Go With the Others** page 810 AVERAGE		**20 MINUTES** • PERSONAL CONNECTION • HISTORICAL CONNECTION • READING CONNECTION: Inferring motivation/Using your reading log	**30 MINUTES** • Introduce vocabulary • Read pp. 810–814 (5 pp.)
SELECTION **My Wonder Horse/ Mi Caballo Mago** page 818 CHALLENGING		**20 MINUTES** • PERSONAL CONNECTION • GEOGRAPHICAL CONNECTION • WRITING CONNECTION	**40 MINUTES** • Introduce vocabulary • Read pp. 818–827 (10 pp.)
FICTION ON YOUR OWN **The Wife's Story** page 830 CHALLENGING			**20 MINUTES** • Read pp. 830–833 (4 pp.)

Writing	Exploring Topics	Prewriting	Drafting and Revising
WRITING FROM EXPERIENCE **Narrative and Literary Writing**	**15 MINUTES**	**20 MINUTES**	**50 MINUTES**

Time estimates assume in-class work. You may wish to assign some of these stages as homework.

Responding to the Selection

FROM PERSONAL RESPONSE TO CRITICAL ANALYSIS	OR	ANOTHER PATHWAY	LITERARY CONCEPTS	QUICKWRITES
		40 MINUTES		
• Discussion questions	OR	• Cooperative learning (comparing evidence)	• Verbal irony • Mood	• Director's notes • Final scene
		40 MINUTES		
• Discussion questions	OR	• Cooperative learning (comparing characters)	• Suspense	• Diary entry • Article
		40 MINUTES		
• Discussion questions	OR	• Cooperative learning (flow chart)	• Author's purpose	• Expository paragraph • Reflection
		40 MINUTES		
• Discussion questions	OR	• Character maturity	• Imagery	• Description • Outline

Extension Activities

ALTERNATIVE ACTIVITIES	LITERARY LINKS	CRITIC'S CORNER	THE WRITER'S STYLE	ACROSS THE CURRICULUM	ART CONNECTION	WORDS TO KNOW	BIOGRAPHY
40 MINUTES							
✔	✔	✔	✔	HISTORY		✔	✔
40 MINUTES							
✔			✔	ZOOLOGY		✔	✔
30 MINUTES							
				HISTORY	✔	✔	✔
30 MINUTES							
✔			✔			✔	✔

Publishing and Reflecting

25 MINUTES

LESSON PLANNER TEACHER'S EDITION **773b**

PART 2

REFLECTING ON THEME

After students read the paragraph, explain that fateful encounters often lead to great *suspense*—the feeling of tension or anticipation an author creates in a work. Describe how authors create suspense by unexpected plot twists. As they read, challenge students to see how the authors in this subunit reverse their expectations to make these stories especially exciting.

What Do You Think?

Before the interview, suggest that partners create charts to help them trace how the experience changed the person's life. Present these words as column headings:

Before Event   *Event*   *Life Changes*

Students can use these charts during the interview to help their subjects more fully explain the changes that resulted from their fateful encounters. Students will return to this activity on pages 786 and 816.

UNIT SIX PART 2

FATEFUL ENCOUNTERS

REFLECTING ON THEME

Have you ever had an experience that changed your life? Let's say you have always wanted to star in the school play. At the audition, your main competitor gets stage fright, and fate is on your side—you get the lead part. How might this fateful event change you? Maybe it would help you gain courage and self-confidence. Maybe you would decide on a career in acting. As you read this part of Unit Six, you will meet characters who experience unexpected happenings—the twists and turns of fate that can sometimes be a matter of life and death.

What Do You Think? Interview a partner about a fateful encounter or unexpected event. Find out how the experience changed his or her life. Record the results of your interview on a sheet of paper, then let your partner interview you. Give each interview to your teacher to read aloud, with the class trying to guess whose fateful encounter is being described.

Edgar Allan Poe	**The Cask of Amontillado** *A grotesque tale of revenge*	775
Edward Rowe Snow	**The Story Behind "The Cask of Amontillado"** / INSIGHT *Could this story possibly be true?*	783
Richard Connell	**The Most Dangerous Game** *What is the most challenging animal to hunt?*	787
John Hersey	**Not to Go with the Others** *Survival in a Nazi concentration camp*	809
Faye Porter, Henry Abramowicz, and Anonymous	**Reflections on the Holocaust** / INSIGHT *Who can understand it?*	814
Sabine R. Ulibarrí	**My Wonder Horse / Mi Caballo Mago** *Freedom is at stake.*	817
Ursula K. Le Guin	**The Wife's Story** *For a while, he was such a good husband.*	830

This person was rescued from his burning house by the local fire department. After that, he decided he wanted to be a firefighter.

PREVIEWING

FICTION

The Cask of Amontillado
Edgar Allan Poe

Activating Prior Knowledge
PERSONAL CONNECTION

In this story, a man wants to redress—or set right—the wrongs that he feels have been done to him. In fact, he wants revenge. Think about a time when you have felt wronged or unfairly treated. Did you feel like getting even? How did you actually react? Why? In your notebook, describe two such incidents in a chart like the sample shown here.

Incident	What I Felt Like Doing	What I Actually Did	Why I Acted As I Did
My friend asked a girl I liked for a date.	Ripping up his jacket.	I acted as though I didn't care.	It would be wrong to destroy his jacket. I didn't want him to know I was hurt.

Building Background
CULTURAL CONNECTION

Edgar Allan Poe's horror tale of revenge "The Cask of Amontillado" takes place in a European country, perhaps Italy or France, during carnival. Mainly celebrated in predominantly Roman Catholic regions, carnival is a time of festival just before the 40-day period of fasting known as Lent. During carnival, people wear fanciful costumes and masks and participate in balls and colorful parades.

Most of this story takes place in the catacombs beneath the estate of Montresor (môn′trĕ-sôr′), the narrator of the story. Catacombs are underground passageways that once served as burial sites. They consist of extensive chambers and tunnels with recesses for graves. In this story, the catacombs are used as a storage cellar for wine.

Active Reading / Setting a Purpose
READING CONNECTION

Evaluating the Narrator Montresor, who tells this story, is also one of its two main characters. As you read, evaluate his approach to revenge. Look for insights into his motivation and state of mind. In the first paragraph, notice the conditions he sets for his revenge.

• VISUAL VOCABULARY

OVERVIEW

Objectives

- To understand and appreciate a classic horror story that explores a murderous vengeance
- To identify and appreciate verbal irony
- To appreciate and understand diction
- To express understanding of the story through a choice of writing forms, including director's notes and a scene with dialogue
- To extend understanding of the story through a variety of multimodal and cross-curricular activities

Skills

LITERARY CONCEPTS
- Verbal irony
- Mood
- First-person point of view

READING SKILLS/STRATEGIES
- Evaluating the narrator

THE WRITER'S STYLE
- Using specific modifiers

GRAMMAR
- Subject-verb agreement: inverted sentences

GENRE STUDY
- Fiction: horror story

SPEAKING, LISTENING, AND VIEWING
- Group discussion
- Oral presentation

ALTERNATIVE
Previewing

Students can choose partners and use the following prompts to preview "The Cask of Amontillado" orally.

Personal Connection

Discussion Prompts *Think about a time when you felt that you had been wronged or treated unfairly. Did you feel like getting even? How did you actually react? In as much detail as possible, describe this time to your partner. Then listen as your partner describes a time when he or she was treated unfairly. If you need help getting started, the following questions might help:*

- *How old were you at the time?*
- *Where were you?*
- *What was the incident?*
- *What did you feel like doing?*
- *What did you actually do?*
- *Why did you respond as you did?*

PRINT AND MEDIA RESOURCES

UNIT SIX RESOURCE BOOK
Strategic Reading: Literature, p. 37
Vocabulary SkillBuilder, p. 38

GRAMMAR MINI–LESSONS
Transparencies, p. 7
Copymasters, pp. 9–10

WRITING MINI–LESSONS
Transparencies, p. 42

ACCESS FOR STUDENTS ACQUIRING ENGLISH
Selection Summaries
Reading Support

FORMAL ASSESSMENT
Selection Test, pp. 141–142
 Test Generator

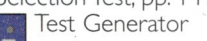 **AUDIO LIBRARY**
See Reference Card

 LASERLINKS
Visual Vocabulary

INTERNET RESOURCES
McDougal Littell Literature Center at http://www.hmco.com/mcdougal/lit

SUMMARY

Fortunato insulted Montresor, the narrator of this story, and the narrator vowed to get revenge. The narrator knew Fortunato prided himself on being a wine connoisseur and used this weakness to achieve his purpose. One night during a carnival festival, he told Fortunato he had bought some Amontillado wine, but he wondered if it was genuine. Fortunato insisted on going with him to taste the wine and give his verdict. The narrator guided Fortunato deep into the vaults beneath his home to a small, dark crypt. The Amontillado was in there, he said. Fortunato stepped forward, and the narrator quickly chained him to the wall. Fortunato, already drunk from wine, did not grasp what was happening until it was too late. The narrator walled up the entrance to the crypt with stone and mortar and left Fortunato to die.

Thematic Link: *Fateful Encounters*
Fortunato's vanity leads him into a fateful encounter with an enemy seeking retribution.

CUSTOMIZING FOR
Students Acquiring English

- Use **ACCESS FOR STUDENTS ACQUIRING ENGLISH,** *Reading Support.*
- This selection contains many vocabulary words and formal expressions that may challenge students. Have each SAE student read the story with a more fluent partner. Have them stop at the end of each paragraph to discuss the meaning of unfamiliar words and phrases.
- As you guide students through the selection, you may want to use the suggestions in these boxes and the suggestions under Strategic Reading for Less-Proficient Readers.

THE CASK OF AMONTILLADO
EDGAR ALLAN POE

WORDS TO KNOW

accost (ə-kôst′) *v.* to approach and speak to in an aggressive or hostile manner (p. 777)
destined (dĕs′tĭnd) *adj.* determined beforehand; fated **destine** *v.* (p. 782)
fetter (fĕt′ər) *v.* to restrain with chains or shackles (p. 780)
implore (ĭm-plôr′) *v.* to beg; earnestly ask for (p. 780)
impunity (ĭm-pyoo′nĭ-tē) *n.* freedom from punishment, penalty, or harm (p. 777)

preclude (prĭ-klood′) *v.* to make impossible, especially by taking action in advance; prevent (p. 777)
repose (rĭ-pōz′) *v.* to lie dead or at rest (p. 779)
subside (səb-sīd′) *v.* to become less agitated or active; decrease (p. 782)
termination (tûr′mə-nā′shən) *n.* the end of something; limit or edge (p. 780)
virtuoso (vûr′choo-ō′sō) *adj.* characteristic of a person with masterly knowledge or skill (p. 777)

VISUAL VOCABULARY
- **cask** (kăsk)
- **catacomb** (kăt′ə-kōm′)
- **coat of arms** (kōt ŭv ärmz)
- **crypt** (krĭpt)
- **palazzo** (pə-lät′sō)

Side A, Frame 49520

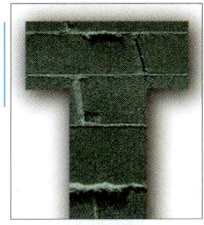

The thousand injuries of Fortunato[1] I had borne as I best could; but when he ventured upon insult, I vowed revenge. You, who so well know the nature of my soul, will not suppose, however, that I gave utterance to a threat. *At length* I would be avenged; this was a point definitively settled—but the very definitiveness with which it was resolved, <u>precluded</u> the idea of risk. I must not only punish, but punish with <u>impunity</u>. A wrong is unredressed when retribution overtakes its redresser. It is equally unredressed when the avenger fails to make himself felt as such to him who has done the wrong.

It must be understood, that neither by word nor deed had I given Fortunato cause to doubt my good-will. I continued, as was my wont, to smile in his face, and he did not perceive that my smile *now* was at the thought of his immolation.[2]

He had a weak point—this Fortunato—although in other regards he was a man to be respected and even feared. He prided himself on his connoisseurship[3] in wine. Few Italians have the true <u>virtuoso</u> spirit. For the most part their enthusiasm is adopted to suit the time and opportunity—to practice imposture[4] upon the British and Austrian *millionnaires*. In painting and gemmary[5] Fortunato, like his countrymen, was a quack—but in the matter of old wines he was sincere. In this respect I did not differ from him materially; I was skilful in the Italian vintages myself, and bought largely whenever I could.

It was about dusk, one evening during the supreme madness of the carnival season, that I encountered my friend. He <u>accosted</u> me with excessive warmth, for he had been drinking much. The man wore motley.[6] He had on a tight-fitting parti-striped dress, and his head was surmounted by the conical cap and bells. I was so pleased to see him, that I thought I should never have done wringing his hand.

---

1. **Fortunato** (fôr′too̅-nä′tō).
2. **immolation** (ĭm′ə-lā′shən): death or destruction.
3. **connoisseurship** (kŏn′ə-sûr′shĭp): expertise or authority, especially in the fine arts or in matters of taste.
4. **imposture:** deception.
5. **gemmary** (jĕm′ə-rē): knowledge of precious gems.
6. **motley:** the costume of a court jester or clown.

WORDS TO KNOW

preclude (prĭ-klood′) *v.* to make impossible, especially by taking action in advance; prevent
impunity (ĭm-pyoo̅′nĭ-tē) *n.* freedom from punishment, penalty, or harm
virtuoso (vûr′choo̅-ō′sō) *adj.* characteristic of a person with masterly knowledge or skill
accost (ə-kôst′) *v.* to approach and speak to in an aggressive or hostile manner

777

Mini-Lesson Literary Concepts

REVIEWING POINT OF VIEW Remind students that point of view refers to the perspective from which events in a story or novel are told. Tell them that in the first-person point of view, the narrator is a character in the story and tells everything in his or her own words. Point out that the reader knows what the narrator is feeling and thinking but must infer from the narrator's descriptions what other characters are feeling and thinking.

Application Tell students that in reading "The Cask of Amontillado," they learn about the events through Montresor's narration and are dependent upon the narrator to describe the actions, feelings, and character of Fortunato. Ask students to make a list of points in the story where they doubt the reliability of the narrator's interpretation. Have them share their lists in class and discuss how a third-person narration or a first-person narration by Fortunato might differ from Montresor's.

CUSTOMIZING FOR
Gifted and Talented Students

Encourage students to look, as they read, for elements of horror and suspense that are similar to elements they have encountered in present-day works of horror and suspense. Tell them to look for such elements in situations, character traits, aspects of the plot or setting, and techniques used to create moods. Students should make a list of familiar elements that they find and discuss them with classmates.

CUSTOMIZING FOR
Students Acquiring English

3 Explain that a person with "a critical turn" has a skill for judging the worth of something.

4 Explain that *abscond* means "to leave quickly and secretly."

Critical Thinking: ANALYZING

C Ask students why Montresor's ploy of saying he is headed to Luchesi's is effective in getting Fortunato to accompany him. *(Possible response: It appeals to Fortunato's vanity, to his need to appear superior to others.)*

STRATEGIC READING FOR
Less-Proficient Readers

D Make sure students understand Montresor's true feelings towards Fortunato. Ask these questions:

- What does Montresor intend to do to Fortunato? Why? *(He wants to punish him; he feels that Fortunato has insulted him.)* Drawing Conclusions

- Why does Montresor hide his feelings and act friendly to Fortunato? *(to trick him into accompanying him)* Making Inferences

Set a Purpose Have students pay close attention to the place where the narrator takes Fortunato.

Literary Concept:
POINT OF VIEW

E Ask students what aspect of Montresor's character is reinforced by his statement "I knew well." *(Possible response: In this follow-up to Montresor's handling of Fortunato, Montresor is seen, again, as a shrewd manipulator of others—one who can effectively use ploys with people because he understands how they think and react in various situations.)*

I said to him: "My dear Fortunato, you are luckily met. How remarkably well you are looking to-day! But I have received a pipe[7] of what passes for Amontillado,[8] and I have my doubts."

"How?" said he. "Amontillado? A pipe? Impossible! And in the middle of the carnival!"

"I have my doubts," I replied; "and I was silly enough to pay the full Amontillado price without consulting you in the matter. You were not to be found, and I was fearful of losing a bargain."

"Amontillado!"

"I have my doubts."

"Amontillado!"

"And I must satisfy them."

"Amontillado!"

"As you are engaged, I am on my way to Luchesi.[9] If anyone has a critical turn, it is he. He will tell me—"

"Luchesi cannot tell Amontillado from Sherry."

"And yet some fools will have it that his taste is a match for your own."

"Come, let us go."

"Whither?"

"To your vaults."

"My friend, no; I will not impose upon your good nature. I perceive you have an engagement. Luchesi—"

"I have no engagement;—come."

"My friend, no. It is not the engagement, but the severe cold with which I perceive you are afflicted. The vaults are insufferably damp. They are encrusted with niter."[10]

"Let us go, nevertheless. The cold is merely nothing. Amontillado! You have been imposed upon. And as for Luchesi, he cannot distinguish Sherry from Amontillado."

Thus speaking, Fortunato possessed himself of my arm. Putting on a mask of black silk, and drawing a *roquelaure*[11] closely about my person, I suffered him to hurry me to my palazzo.[12]

There were no attendants at home; they had absconded to make merry in honor of the time. I had told them that I should not return until the morning, and had given them explicit orders not to stir from the house. These orders were sufficient, I well knew, to insure their immediate disappearance, one and all, as soon as my back was turned.

I took from their sconces two flambeaux,[13] and giving one to Fortunato, bowed him through several suites of rooms to the archway that led into the vaults. I passed down a long and winding staircase, requesting him to be cautious as he followed. We came at length to the foot of the descent and stood together on the damp ground of the catacombs of the Montresors.

The gait of my friend was unsteady, and the bells upon his cap jingled as he strode.

"The pipe?" said he.

"It is farther on," said I; "but observe the white web-work which gleams from these cavern walls."

He turned toward me, and looked into my eyes with two filmy orbs that distilled the rheum of intoxication.[14]

"Niter?" he asked, at length.

---

7. **pipe:** a wine barrel with a capacity of 126 gallons.
8. **Amontillado** (ə-mŏn'tl-ä'dō): a pale dry sherry.
9. **Luchesi** (lōō-kā'sē).
10. **niter:** a white, gray, or colorless mineral, consisting of potassium nitrate.
11. ***roquelaure*** (rôk-lōr') *French:* a man's knee-length cloak, popular during the 18th century.
12. **palazzo** (pə-lät'sō): a palace or mansion.
13. **from ... flambeaux** (flăm'bōz'): from their wall brackets two lighted torches.
14. **filmy ... intoxication:** eyes clouded and watery from drunkenness.

778 UNIT SIX PART 2: FATEFUL ENCOUNTERS

Mini-Lesson Grammar

SUBJECT-VERB AGREEMENT: INVERTED SENTENCES Direct students' attention to the inverted sentence that is highlighted on this page. Remind them that in inverted sentences it is still the subject that determines whether the verb is singular or plural. Sentences beginning with *here* and *there* can be especially troublesome.

In the catacombs is [not *are*] found the Amontillado.

Here are [not *is*] the mossy vaults.

Application Write the following sentences on the chalkboard. Have students decide whether each shows correct subject-verb agreement.

1. In its surface was two iron staples. *(incorrect)*
2. But now, here come out of the depths a short laugh. *(incorrect)*
3. Finally, there are heard no sounds. *(correct)*

Reteaching/Reinforcement
- *Grammar Handbook,* anthology p. 907
- *Grammar Mini-Lessons* copymasters pp. 9–10, transparencies p. 7

 The Writer's Craft

Subjects in Unusual Positions, pp. 508–509

"Niter," I replied. "How long have you had that cough?"

"Ugh! ugh! ugh!—ugh! ugh! ugh!—ugh! ugh!—ugh! ugh!—ugh! ugh! ugh!"

My poor friend found it impossible to reply for many minutes.

"It is nothing," he said, at last.

"Come," I said, with decision, "we will go back; your health is precious. You are rich, respected, admired, beloved; you are happy, as once I was. You are a man to be missed. For me it is no matter. We will go back; you will be ill, and I cannot be responsible. Besides, there is Luchesi—"

"Enough," he said; "the cough is a mere nothing; it will not kill me. I shall not die of a cough."

"True—true," I replied; "and, indeed, I had no intention of alarming you unnecessarily; but you should use all proper caution. A draft of this Medoc[15] will defend us from the damps."

Here I knocked off the neck of a bottle that I drew from a long row of its fellows that lay upon the mold.

"Drink," I said, presenting him the wine.

He raised it to his lips with a leer. He paused and nodded to me familiarly, while his bells jingled.

"I drink," he said, "to the buried that repose around us."

"And I to your long life."

He again took my arm, and we proceeded.

"These vaults," he said, "are extensive."

"The Montresors," I replied, "were a great and numerous family."

"I forget your arms."[16]

"A huge human foot d'or,[17] in a field azure; the foot crushes a serpent rampant whose fangs are imbedded in the heel."

"And the motto?"

"*Nemo me impune lacessit.*"[18]

"Good!" he said.

The wine sparkled in his eyes and the bells jingled. My own fancy grew warm with the Medoc. We had passed through walls of piled bones, with casks and puncheons[19] intermingling, into the inmost recesses of the catacombs. I paused again, and this time I made bold to seize Fortunato by an arm above the elbow.

"The niter!" I said; "see, it increases. It hangs like moss upon the vaults. We are below the river's bed. The drops of moisture trickle among the bones. Come, we will go back ere it is too late. Your cough—"

"It is nothing," he said; "let us go on. But first, another draft of the Medoc."

I broke and reached him a flagon of De Grâve.[20] He emptied it at a breath. His eyes flashed with a fierce light. He laughed and threw the bottle upward with a gesticulation[21] I did not understand.

I looked at him in surprise. He repeated the movement—a grotesque one.

"You do not comprehend?" he said.

"Not I," I replied.

"Then you are not of the brotherhood."

"How?"

"You are not of the masons."[22]

"Yes, yes," I said; "yes, yes."

15. **Medoc** (mā-dôk′): a red Bordeaux wine.
16. **arms**: coat of arms—a design that represents one's ancestry and family heritage. (In the following paragraph, Montresor describes his family's coat of arms.)
17. **d'or** (dôr): gold-colored.
18. ***Nemo me impune lacessit*** (nā′mō mā ĭm-pōō′nĕ lä-kĕs′ĭt) *Latin:* Nobody provokes me with impunity.
19. **casks and puncheons**: large containers for storing wine.
20. **De Grâve** (də gräv′).
21. **gesticulation** (jə-stĭk′yə-lā′shən): a vigorous motion or gesture.
22. **of the masons**: a member of the Freemasons, a social organization with secret rituals and signs.

WORDS TO KNOW

repose (rĭ-pōz′) *v.* to lie dead or at rest

Literary Concept: MOOD

F Ask students to describe the feeling or mood that is established in this paragraph. *(Possible response: a mood of fear or dread, caused by wonder over what Montresor has planned for this trip to the catacombs beneath his mansion)*

Literary Concept: IRONY

G Ask students to explain the verbal irony in Fortunato's remark and Montresor's reply. *(Possible response: Montresor and Fortunato are both certain that Fortunato won't die of a cough—but for drastically different reasons.)*

H Have students discuss Fortunato's reaction to the motto of the Montresors. *(Possible response: The drunken Fortunato compliments Montresor on the motto, completely oblivious to the fact that Montresor is planning to live up to its meaning.)*

Linking to Economics

I The Masons were a secret society formed in the Middle Ages, when craftsmen's guilds were outlawed. Masons were traveling stoneworkers who organized themselves into lodges, and they and similar societies enabled people to establish themselves within social communities and business economies in places where outsiders were not always welcome. Members recognized one another through various secret rituals and signs. Through the centuries, with the decline in building with stone, masons' societies eventually became social organizations. Today, the Masons are a worldwide fraternal organization, with nearly 4 million members in the United States alone.

Mini-Lesson Genre Study

FICTION Draw on the chalkboard the word web shown on the right, and use it to explain that **horror fiction** is a type of fiction whose aim is to produce a feeling of great suspense and terror in the reader. Famous writers of horror fiction include Edgar Allan Poe, H. P. Lovecraft, Stephen King, and Clive Barker.

Application Have students create in their notebook a chart with the following four headings: Mysterious, Terrifying, Violent, and Supernatural. Along the left-hand side, students should write the titles "The Cask of Amontillado" and *Sorry, Right Number* (from the first part of this unit). Have students fill in the chart by providing as many examples as they can in each of the four categories for each of the two works. Ask students which categories did not apply to each work and why.

Critical Thinking: ANALYZING

I Ask students to discuss the humor in Montresor's gesture. *(Possible response: When asked if he is a member of the Masonic organization, Montresor produces a trowel used for masonry.)*

STRATEGIC READING FOR
Less-Proficient Readers

J Ask students where the narrator leads Fortunato. *(into his house, down a stairway, through an extensive series of damp vaults and catacombs, and finally into a dark, foul crypt)* Visualizing

Set a Purpose Have students read on to discover the punishment Montresor has planned for Fortunato.

Linking to History

K *Catacombs* is a term that was first applied to the underground cemeteries found in the vicinity of Rome. About 40 chambers, located a few miles from the modern city, have been discovered so far. Because of their complex layouts, hidden entrances, and secret passageways, catacombs became useful hiding places for early Christians suffering persecution.

Literary Concept: MOOD

L Ask students to comment on the mood at this point in the story. *(Possible response: The mood of horror has increased; the two men can walk no farther, and Fortunato's doom must be at hand.)*

CUSTOMIZING FOR
Students Acquiring English

5 Explain that an ignoramus is a stupid person.

6 Ask students to explain this key scene. Ask how Montresor was able to lock Fortunato up without his catching on to what was happening.

Literary Concept: IRONY

M Have students comment on the irony in Montresor's imploring. *(Earlier, Montresor warned Fortunato of the niter and urged him to leave, when he was free to do so. Now Fortunato is chained to the wall, and Montresor's pleas are a sadistic taunt.)*

I
"You? Impossible! A mason?"
"A mason," I replied.
"A sign," he said.
"It is this," I answered, producing a trowel from beneath the folds of my *roquelaure*.
"You jest," he exclaimed, recoiling a few paces. "But let us proceed to the Amontillado."
"Be it so," I said, replacing the tool beneath the cloak, and again offering him my arm. He leaned upon it heavily. We continued our route in search of the Amontillado. We passed through a range of low arches, descended, passed on, and descending again, arrived at a deep crypt,[23]

J in which the foulness of the air caused our flambeaux rather to glow than flame.

At the most remote end of the crypt there appeared another less spacious. Its walls had been lined with human remains, piled to the vault overhead, in the fashion of the great catacombs of Paris. Three sides of this interior crypt were still ornamented in this manner. From the fourth the bones had been thrown down, and lay promiscuously[24] upon the earth, forming at one point a mound of some size. Within the wall thus exposed by the displacing of the bones, we perceived a still interior recess, in depth about four feet, in width three, in height six or seven. It seemed to have been constructed for no especial use within itself, but formed merely the interval between two of the

K colossal supports of the roof of the catacombs, and was backed by one of their circumscribing

L walls of solid granite.

It was in vain that Fortunato, uplifting his dull torch, endeavored to pry into the depth of the recess. Its <u>termination</u> the feeble light did not enable us to see.

Copyright © 1995 Jay Maisel

"Proceed," I said; "herein is the Amontillado. As for Luchesi—"

"He is an ignoramus," interrupted my friend, **5** as he stepped unsteadily forward, while I followed immediately at his heels. In an instant he had reached the extremity of the niche, and finding his progress arrested by the rock, stood stupidly bewildered. A moment more and I had <u>fettered</u> him to the granite. In its surface were two iron staples, distant from each other about two feet, horizontally. From one of these depended a short chain, from the other a padlock. Throwing the links about his waist, it was but the work of a few seconds to secure it. He **6** was too much astounded to resist. Withdrawing the key I stepped back from the recess.

"Pass your hand," I said, "over the wall; you cannot help feeling the niter. Indeed it is *very* damp. Once more let me <u>implore</u> you to return. **M** No? Then I must positively leave you. But I must first render you all the little attentions in my power."

"The Amontillado!" ejaculated my friend, not yet recovered from his astonishment.

"True," I replied; "the Amontillado."

As I said these words I busied myself among the pile of bones of which I have before spoken. Throwing them aside, I soon uncovered a quantity of building stone and mortar. With these materials and with the aid of my trowel, I began vigorously to wall up the entrance of the niche.

I had scarcely laid the first tier of the masonry[25] when I discovered that the intoxication of Fortunato had in a great measure worn off. The

---

23. **crypt:** an underground chamber serving as a burial place.
24. **promiscuously** (prə-mĭs′kyōō-əs-lē): randomly.
25. **masonry:** stonework.

WORDS TO KNOW	**termination** (tûr′mə-nā′shən) *n.* the end of something; limit or edge
	fetter (fĕt′ər) *v.* to restrain with chains or shackles
	implore (ĭm-plôr′) *v.* to beg; earnestly ask for

780

Mini-Lesson — The Writer's Style

USING SPECIFIC MODIFIERS Discuss with students Poe's use of specific adjectives and adverbs to create vivid description and reinforce the mood in "The Cask of Amontillado." Point out, for example, that when Montresor prepares the last stone for placement in the wall (page 782), Poe uses the adjective *destined* to describe its soon-to-be final position, reinforcing the sense of inevitability regarding Fortunato's fate. Other notable examples of specific modifiers include Poe's capturing of Fortunato's intoxicated appearance by describing his eyes as "filmy orbs" and Poe's referring to the silence behind the wall as *obstinate*.

Application Ask students to write a paragraph describing the most frightening place they have ever been. Encourage them to use specific adjectives and adverbs in their writing to help the reader understand exactly what filled them with fear, and why.

Reteaching/Reinforcement
• *Writing Handbook*, anthology p. 866
• *Writing Mini-Lessons* transparencies, p. 42

 The Writer's Craft

Specific Modifiers, p. 384

PHOTOGRAPHY NOTE

Photograph by Jay Maisel Jay Maisel (1931–) was born in Brooklyn and studied painting at Yale University. Since 1954, he has made his living as a free-lance photographer, winning numerous awards. One critic has noted that Maisel's photographs have an "all-over" quality that is similar to painting.

Reading the Photograph *The untitled photograph on this page is of the interior of an Iranian mosque. What qualities of Maisel's photograph give it the impression of being a painting? How does the mood of the photo relate to Poe's story?*

CUSTOMIZING FOR
Multiple Learning Styles

Interpersonal Learners Point out that the specific way in which Fortunato insulted Montresor is never made clear in the story. Invite these students to lead a discussion of what Fortunato might have done, if anything, to incite Montresor to such violence.

Linking to Science

Wine is often stored in caverns or dark cellars because underground storage provides the constant cool temperature the liquid requires and prevents the deteriorating effects of light and vibration. Temperatures of between 54°F. and 61°F. are considered optimal. Bottles of wine are laid on their side during storage in order to keep the corks moist. Should the corks dry out, they may shrink or crack, allowing harmful oxygen into the bottle.

Mini-Lesson Workplace Literacy

SCANS GOAL: Organizes and Maintains Information

MANAGING AN INVENTORY Explain to students that an inventory is an itemized list of goods and materials at hand. Point out, for example, that a wine merchant with an extensive wine cellar would periodically take an inventory to find out exactly what wines of various ages and types he or she had on hand. By matching the inventory list against receipts of sales made since the last inventory was taken, the merchant could find out which wines are available to sell and which ones he or she needs to order more of.

Application Suggest that students take an inventory of some type of goods used in their home— for example, clothing, food, or school supplies. Their inventory should list each item and the quantity on hand. Then have them discuss what they can learn from the inventory they have taken— for example, what items they need to put on a shopping list and what items they could get rid of.

Critical Thinking: MAKING INFERENCES/SUMMARIZING

N Ask students to explain what happens in this paragraph. *(Fortunato suddenly screams loudly, surprising Montresor and briefly causing him to fear that the screams can be heard outside the catacombs; with his sword touching the solid walls, Montresor reassures himself that the catacombs are soundproof, and in a display of mocking self-confidence, he even shouts back, "re-echoing" and surpassing Fortunato's screams, until Fortunato "grows still.")*

Literary Concept: POINT OF VIEW

O Ask students what they think Montresor's self-admission that his "heart grew sick" reveals about his character. *(Possible response: Montresor actually feels remorse for what he's done—though he denies it by pretending that the dampness of the catacombs, which had not bothered him previously, is solely responsible for his heartsickness.)* Then ask them what might be different if this were revealed in third-person narration. *(Possible response: A third-person account might not communicate the man's brief remorse as sharply as hearing Montresor himself confess it.)*

STRATEGIC READING FOR
Less-Proficient Readers

P Ask students to describe Montresor's revenge. *(He chains up Fortunato in the recess, walls up the entrance, and leaves him buried alive in the crypt, where his body is yet to be found.)* Summarizing

COMPREHENSION CHECK

Have students indicate whether each of the following statements is true or false.
1. The narrator is seeking revenge because Fortunato physically injured him. *(false)*
2. Fortunato is a connoisseur of wine. *(true)*
3. Montresor lures Fortunato into his vaults by appealing to his pride and jealousy. *(true)*
4. Fortunato refuses Montresor's offerings of drink, preferring to wait to try the Amontillado. *(false)*
5. Montresor achieves revenge by burying Fortunato alive. *(true)*

---

earliest indication I had of this was a low moaning cry from the depth of the recess. It was *not* the cry of a drunken man. There was then a long and obstinate silence. I laid the second tier, and the third, and the fourth; and then I heard the furious vibrations of the chain. The noise lasted for several minutes, during which, that I might hearken to it with the more satisfaction, I ceased my labors and sat down upon the bones. When at last the clanking <u>subsided</u>, I resumed the trowel, and finished without interruption the fifth, the sixth, and the seventh tier. The wall was now nearly upon a level with my breast. I again paused, and holding the flambeaux over the mason-work, threw a few feeble rays upon the figure within.

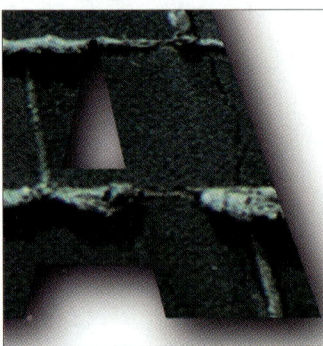

A succession of loud and shrill screams, bursting suddenly from the throat of the chained form, seemed to thrust me violently back. For a brief moment I hesitated—I trembled. Unsheathing my rapier,[26] I began to grope with it about the recess; but the thought of an instant reassured me. I placed my hand upon the solid fabric of the catacombs, and felt satisfied. I reapproached the wall. I replied to the yells of him who clamored. I re-echoed—I aided—I surpassed them in volume and in strength. I did this, and the clamorer grew still.

It was now midnight, and my task was drawing to a close. I had completed the eighth, the ninth, and the tenth tier. I had finished a portion of the last and the eleventh; there remained but a single stone to be fitted and plastered in. I struggled with its weight; I placed it partially in its <u>destined</u> position. But now there came from out the niche a low laugh that erected the hairs upon my head. It was succeeded by a sad voice, which I had difficulty in recognizing as that of the noble Fortunato. The voice said—

"Ha! ha! ha!—he! he!—a very good joke indeed—an excellent jest. We will have many a rich laugh about it at the palazzo—he! he! he! —over our wine—he! he! he!"

"The Amontillado!" I said.

"He! he! he!—he! he! he!—yes, the Amontillado. But is it not getting late? Will not they be awaiting us at the palazzo, the Lady Fortunato and the rest? Let us be gone."

"Yes," I said, "let us be gone."

"*For the love of God, Montresor!*"

"Yes," I said, "for the love of God!"

But to these words I hearkened in vain for a reply. I grew impatient. I called aloud, "Fortunato!"

No answer. I called again, "Fortunato!"

No answer still. I thrust a torch through the remaining aperture[27] and let it fall within. There came forth in return only a jingling of the bells. My heart grew sick—on account of the dampness of the catacombs. I hastened to make an end of my labor. I forced the last stone into its position; I plastered it up. Against the new masonry I re-erected the old rampart[28] of bones. For the half of a century no mortal has disturbed them. *In pace requiescat!*[29] ❖

---

26. **rapier** (rā′pē-ər): a long, slender sword.
27. **aperture** (ăp′ər-chər): an opening, such as a hole or a gap.
28. **rampart**: fortification; protective barrier.
29. *In pace requiescat* (ĭn pä′kĕ rĕ-kwē-ĕs′kät) *Latin*: May he rest in peace.

WORDS TO KNOW
subside (səb-sīd′) *v.* to become less agitated or active; decrease
destined (dĕs′tĭnd) *adj.* determined beforehand; fated **destine** *v.*

782

SELF-ASSESSMENT Students can informally assess their understanding of the selection by rewriting a portion of the story with Fortunato as the narrator rather than Montresor. Suggest that they try to maintain Poe's mood of suspense in their version. To help students assess their own work, have them respond to whichever of the following questions are applicable:

• Does my writing explain why Fortunato trusts Montresor?
• Does my writing explain what motivates Fortunato to follow Montresor?
• Do I convey Fortunato's shock and horror when he discovers Montresor's intent?
• How do I convey a mood of suspense and terror in my retelling?

INSIGHT

THE STORY BEHIND "THE CASK OF AMONTILLADO"
Edward Rowe Snow

While at Fort Independence, Poe [who was a private there in 1827] became fascinated with the inscriptions on a gravestone on a small monument outside the walls of the fort. . . .

Beneath this stone are deposited the remains of Lieut. ROBERT F. MASSIE, of the U. S. Regt. of Light Artillery. . . .

During the summer of 1817, Poe learned, twenty-year-old Lieutenant Robert F. Massie of Virginia had arrived at Fort Independence as a newly appointed officer. Most of the men at the post came to enjoy Massie's friendship, but one officer, Captain Green, took a violent dislike to him. Green was known at the fort as a bully and a dangerous swordsman.

When Christmas vacations were allotted, few of the officers were allowed to leave the fort, and Christmas Eve found them up in the old barracks hall, playing cards. Just before midnight, at the height of the card game, Captain Green sprang to his feet, reached across the table and slapped Lieutenant Massie squarely in the face. "You're a cheat," he roared, "and I demand immediate satisfaction!" . . .

The duel began. Captain Green, an expert swordsman, soon had Massie at a disadvantage and ran him through. Fatally wounded, the young Virginian was carried back to the fort, where he died that afternoon. His many friends mourned the passing of a gallant officer. . . .

Feeling against Captain Green ran high for many weeks, and then suddenly he completely vanished. Years went by without a sign of him, and Green was written off the army records as a deserter.

According to the story which Poe finally gathered together, Captain Green had been so detested by his fellow officers at the fort that they decided to take a terrible revenge on him for Massie's death. . . .

Visiting Captain Green one moonless night, they pretended to be friendly and plied him with wine until he was helplessly intoxicated. Then, carrying the captain down to one of the ancient dungeons, the officers forced his body through a tiny opening which led into the subterranean casemate. . . .[1]

By this time Green had awakened from his drunken stupor and demanded to know what was taking place. Without answering, his captors began to shackle him to the floor, using the heavy iron handcuffs and footcuffs fastened into the stone. Then they all left the dungeon and proceeded to seal the captain up alive inside the windowless casemate, using bricks and mortar. . . .

Captain Green shrieked in terror and begged for mercy, but his cries fell on deaf ears. The last brick was finally inserted, mortar applied, and the room sealed up, the officers believed, forever. Captain Green undoubtedly died a horrible death within a few days. . . .

[In 1905, workmen repairing the fort found the dungeon. To their amazement, they found a skeleton inside, shackled to the floor, with a few fragments of an old army uniform clinging to the bones.]

---

1. **subterranean casemate** (sŭb′tə-rā′nē-ən kās′māt′): a fortified underground or partly underground room with small windows for firing weapons.

INSIGHT

1. Which do you find more involving—fact or fiction? Does the fact that "The Cask of Amontillado" was based on an actual event make the story more or less chilling? *(Responses will vary.)*
2. Point out that Poe drastically altered the setting when he developed the Massie/Green incident into a story. What effect does this change have on the story? *(Possible responses: The story seems more fantastical because of the picturesque details Poe added; the carnival setting gives an overall impression that the story is entertainment rather than a real incident.)*
3. Given what you know about Edgar Allan Poe's life and work, why might this incident have captured his imagination? *(Possible response: because it showed Poe a dark side of human nature in ordinarily decent people)*

EDWARD ROWE SNOW

Edward Rowe Snow (1902–1982) gave up his career as a high school teacher to become a freelance writer and a newspaper columnist. The Massachusetts native wrote more than 90 books, including *Mysteries and Adventures Along the Atlantic Coast* and *True Tales of Buried Treasure*. Snow was an Air Force pilot during World War II. He later became known as the "Flying Santa" to the lighthouse keepers living along the New England coast because every year he would fly in to deliver them Christmas gifts in order to repay them for telling him the stories that became the basis for his tales of storms, pirates, buried treasure, and adventures at sea.

Multicultural Perspectives

CARNIVAL Poe set his story in a European country in the indefinite past, depicting the terrifying entombment of Fortunato during the joyous festivities of the carnival season. Carnival is a time of feasting and revelry that occurs mainly in Roman Catholic regions just before Lent, a time of fasting in preparation for Easter. This is a time when societal rules are relaxed and people are encouraged to briefly step outside rigid codes of behavior—although not to the degree that Montresor does. In centuries past, Rome was considered the preeminent site of carnival activity, with a richness of costuming, parades, and masked balls rarely equaled elsewhere. Mardi Gras, held annually in New Orleans, is the principal carnival activity in the United States.

From Personal Response to Critical Analysis

1. Accept all reasonable, well-supported responses.
2. Possible responses: He is cold, evil, and manipulative; he plans his revenge well and shows no emotion; he is supremely evil; one cannot evaluate the degree to which he is evil without knowing exactly what Fortunato did to him; he does not seem to be insane.
3. Possible response: Yes; Fortunato dies knowing who killed him, and Montresor gets away with the crime—he is looking back on the event after 50 years have passed.
4. Possible responses: Montresor tells Fortunato, "You are happy, as once I was"; Montresor displays the trowel.
5. Accept all reasonable, well-supported responses.

Another Pathway

Cooperative Learning Ensure that all students contribute their ideas to the group discussion. You might have a class discussion of the issue afterwards.

Rubric

3 Full Accomplishment Groups present reasonable arguments and evidence to support their position.

2 Substantial Accomplishment Groups present reasonable arguments but may fail to support them with evidence from the story.

1 Little or Partial Accomplishment Groups fail to support their position with arguments or details from the story.

RESPONDING OPTIONS

FROM PERSONAL RESPONSE TO CRITICAL ANALYSIS

REFLECT 1. What do you think about the events of this story? Describe your reaction in your notebook and share it with your classmates.

RETHINK 2. What is your evaluation of Montresor, his state of mind, and his actions? Is he evil? Is he insane? Support your opinion with evidence from the story.

Close Textual Reading

Consider
- Montresor's motives for revenge as stated in the first paragraph
- how he gets his servants and Fortunato to behave as he wishes
- his reaction to Fortunato's screams
- his final comments

3. Do you think Montresor achieves the kind of revenge he says he wants? Is his conflict with Fortunato resolved? Support your answer.

Thematic Link 4. What does Montresor say or do that might give Fortunato—if Fortunato would notice—a clue to his intentions?

RELATE 5. Look again at the chart you made for the Personal Connection on page 775. Do you think revenge is ever justified, or is it always better to learn from injustice and not hold a grudge? Explain your opinion.

Multimodal Learning
ANOTHER PATHWAY
Cooperative Learning
Some readers feel that Montresor has suffered for his crime—is haunted by guilt. Others see him as a criminal gloating about his evil act. With a small group, look for evidence in the story and decide which view you agree with. Then compare your conclusions with those of other groups.

LITERARY LINKS

1. How would you compare Montresor's state of mind with that of Doug Spaulding, the narrator of "The Utterly Perfect Murder" (page 17)? Compare the different ways they resolve their conflicts.
2. How does Poe's horror tale compare with others you have read and enjoyed? Is it more or less horrifying? Why?

QUICKWRITES

1. Write **director's notes** to be used by an actor preparing to play the role of Montresor in a dramatized version of the story. Include a personality profile of Montresor.
2. Reread the Insight selection on page 783. Then write the **final scene**, including dialogue, that might have taken place between the soldiers and Captain Green.

📁 **PORTFOLIO** Save your writing. You may want to use it later as a springboard to a piece for your portfolio.

Literary Links

1. Students may note that both Montresor and Doug Spaulding feel injured or slighted and hatch complicated plans to take revenge and eliminate the pain caused by their perceived adversaries. Doug, however, stops short of committing the murder he believed would resolve his problem and finds resolution within himself instead.
2. Accept all reasonable, well-supported responses

QuickWrites

1. Suggest that students list questions an actor might have about Montresor's character. Then create director's notes that answer these questions and help an actor focus on the attributes most important to the character's personality.
2. To help students imagine the dialogue that might have occurred between the soldiers and Captain Green, suggest that they focus on the soldiers' reasons for their actions.

Using Dialogue in Plays and Skits, p. 436

LITERARY CONCEPTS

Verbal irony occurs when a character says one thing but means another, as when Montresor greets his friend (whose name means "fortunate") with the words "My dear Fortunato, you are luckily met." Obviously, Fortunato's fateful encounter with Montresor is anything but lucky. Find three other examples of verbal irony in this story.

CONCEPT REVIEW: Mood The mood—the feeling or atmosphere—conveyed by this story might be described as creepy, eerie, foreboding, suspenseful, or horrifying. The descriptions of the catacombs, with their darkness, foul air, and damp walls, help create this mood. What other descriptive details contribute to the mood of the story?

Multimodal Learning

ALTERNATIVE ACTIVITIES

1. Do a **dramatic reading** of all or part of "The Cask of Amontillado" as a radio presentation. First rehearse the reading; then tape-record it, with appropriate sound effects. Play the recording for your class.
2. Reread what Montresor says about his family's coat of arms on page 779. In an encyclopedia, look at examples of other coats of arms. Then draw a **picture** of Montresor's, based on his description and on your research. Present your picture to the class and explain how Montresor lives up to the threat implied in the coat of arms.

3. Create a **set design** for a play version of this story. Show your design to the class, pointing out where Fortunato is walled in.

Multimodal Learning

ACROSS THE CURRICULUM

History Research the history of catacombs as burial and hiding places, or look into the origin and history of carnival celebrations. Prepare an oral report for the class.

THE WRITER'S STYLE

A writer's **diction** is his or her choice of words and ways of arranging the words. Poe's formal diction seems to heighten the abnormality and horror of the story. Compare the vocabulary and sentence structure of the opening sentence with a much less formal way of expressing the same idea:

> The thousand injuries of Fortunato I had borne as I best could; but when he ventured upon insult, I vowed revenge.

> I put up with Fortunato's many wrongs as well as I could; but when he insulted me, I swore to get even.

Now examine the following sentences and express them in everyday English:

> A wrong is unredressed when retribution overtakes its redresser.

> I continued, as was my wont, to smile in his face, and he did not perceive that my smile *now* was at the thought of his immolation.

What, if anything, do you think is lost in the translation of Poe's words?

CRITIC'S CORNER

In the first paragraph of this story, the narrator says, "You, who so well know the nature of my soul, will not suppose, however, that I gave utterance to a threat." Who is the "you" that the narrator is addressing, and why is the narrator confessing? The critic Charles E. May has suggested "that the listener is a priest and that Montresor is an old man who is dying and making a final confession." Do you find this explanation reasonable? Explain why or why not.

THE CASK OF AMONTILLADO **785**

The Writer's Style

Possible rephrasings:
- A wrong is not made right when the person righting the wrong faces punishment for his or her actions.
- I kept smiling at him, but he didn't realize that this smile was brought about solely by thoughts of his death.

Students may say that in the rephrased sentences, the sense of Montresor's extravagant wickedness and his extreme sense of purpose are lost.

 The Writer's Craft
Diction, pp. 406–407

Across the Curriculum

History Students who research carnival celebrations may wish to focus on the celebrations of a particular country or region. Suggest that students with access to the Internet utilize country-specific resources, such as soc.culture.[name of the country] news groups, to gather information about particular carnival celebrations. Encourage groups to supplement their oral reports with visual aids, such as pictures of carnival costumes and parades and/or audio recordings of the music played at specific celebrations.

Critic's Corner

Some students may find the explanation of Charles E. May plausible. Others, however, may note that Montresor conveys no sense of remorse or fear of heavenly punishment during his narration, making it unlikely that he is confessing to a priest. Some may suggest that the "you" may simply be a literary device to involve the reader.

Literary Concepts

Students may point to any of the numerous examples of verbal irony, including the following: Montresor's ordering his servants to stay in the house while he fully expects them to leave (page 778); Montresor's saying "your health is precious" and "I [drink] to your long life" to a man he plans to kill (page 779); and Montresor's imploring Fortunato to return after he has already fettered him (page 780). The name Fortunato means "good fortune" and is in itself verbal irony.

Concept Review: Mood Possible responses: "web-work which gleams" (page 778); "walls of piled bones" (page 779); "walls... lined with human remains" (page 780); "loud and shrill screams" (page 782)

Alternative Activities

1. To create sound effects for their readings, students can record common noises such as dripping taps, creaky doors, radio static, and silverware clanking against metal pots.
2. In addition to the encyclopedia, students can consult books on Italian coats of arms for inspiration for their own drawings.
3. Remind students that the sets must fit on a theater stage. Encourage them to experiment with different ways of re-creating the labyrinthine character of the underground vaults within the confines of a limited space.

THE LANGUAGE OF LITERATURE TEACHER'S EDITION **785**

Words to Know

Exercise A
1. b
2. a
3. a
4. c
5. b
6. c
7. c
8. a
9. b
10. c

Exercise B
Responses will vary.

Reteaching/Reinforcement
• Unit Six Resource Book, p. 38

EDGAR ALLAN POE

Although Edgar Allan Poe achieved international fame when "The Raven" was published, he was unsuccessful and in desperate financial circumstances throughout much of his career. Over the years, however, his literary reputation has improved far beyond the reputations of the successful writers of his day, such as Longfellow. Poe's stories have been translated into many languages, made into films, set to music by great composers, and read for popular entertainment.

WORDS TO KNOW

EXERCISE A For each group of words below, write the letter of the word that is the best antonym of the boldfaced word.

1. **fetter:** (a) cover, (b) free, (c) control
2. **destined:** (a) accidental, (b) cheerful, (c) historical
3. **repose:** (a) work, (b) duplicate, (c) answer
4. **termination:** (a) doubt, (b) excellence, (c) beginning
5. **preclude:** (a) omit, (b) assist, (c) finish
6. **implore:** (a) guess, (b) relieve, (c) demand
7. **virtuoso:** (a) lengthy, (b) hidden, (c) unskilled
8. **subside:** (a) intensify, (b) obey, (c) challenge
9. **accost:** (a) purchase, (b) avoid, (c) support
10. **impunity:** (a) tact, (b) luck, (c) risk

EXERCISE B Work with a partner to act out the meaning of *accost, repose, fetter, implore,* or *subside* while another pair of students tries to guess the word. Then switch, with you and your partner trying to guess which word the other pair of students is acting out.

EDGAR ALLAN POE

1809–1849

Edgar Allan Poe was an innovator of the modern short story. He is considered to have written the first detective story, "The Murders in the Rue Morgue," and his classic horror tales, such as "The Black Cat" and "The Tell-Tale Heart," established his reputation as a master of psychological terror.

In brilliantly portraying the mind of Montresor, a character who revels in murderous revenge, Poe may have been inspired by some of his own feelings. He was a man who made strong enemies in his life, as well as loyal friends. Some biographers believe that "The Cask of Amontillado" reflects Poe's bitter hatred of two New York literary figures of the early 1800s—the author Thomas Dunn English and the newspaper editor Hiram Fuller.

As a literary critic, Poe often wrote stinging criticisms of other writers' works, sometimes including personal attacks on his contemporaries. In 1846 he published a spiteful sketch of English in a popular magazine of the time. English then counterattacked in an article published in the *New York Evening Mirror*, describing Poe as mentally unstable and frequently drunk. Poe filed a libel suit against the newspaper's owners, one of whom was Fuller. Fuller responded by blasting Poe in an editorial and by publishing, on the front page of the newspaper, segments of a novel in which English satirized Poe as a pretentious drunkard. It was in this nasty climate of personal vendetta that Poe wrote and published "The Cask of Amontillado."

OTHER WORKS "Hop-Frog," "The Pit and the Pendulum," "The Purloined Letter" *Extended Reading*

REFLECTING ON THEME
What Do You Think?

Lead students to realize that fateful encounters need not always be accidental or unforeseen. At the beginning of the fourth paragraph of "The Cask of Amontillado," Montresor says he "encountered" his friend and claims that he was "so pleased to see him." Readers soon learn, however, that the two had anything but a chance meeting: Montresor had carefully planned the convergence. Students can discuss situations in which initiating an encounter could be right and necessary, as when "running into" someone who owes you money borrowed long ago gives you an excuse to bring up the subject of the overdue repayment in a friendly way.

PREVIEWING

FICTION

The Most Dangerous Game
Richard Connell

Activating Prior Knowledge
PERSONAL CONNECTION

This story is about hunting—a sport that in many cases is a game of life and death. The games you play are not as serious, but the combination of skill and luck involved is basically the same. Think about what it takes to be a winner in a physical contest. Then copy the chart on this page, adding other factors that you can think of. In the blank boxes, rate each factor's contribution to the winning of physical contests, on a scale of 1 (completely unimportant) to 10 (most important). Discuss your responses with a classmate.

Factors in Winning Physical Contests	
luck	
daring	
desire	
cleverness	
mental toughness	
physical condition	
quickness	

Building Background
CULTURAL CONNECTION

The thrill of the hunt! For those under its influence, hunting has a powerful appeal. "The Most Dangerous Game" is about big-game hunters, people with the desire—as well as the money and time—to travel the world, seeking big and challenging animals to hunt. For such people, big-game hunting may be either a sport or a career. In either case, the danger and excitement of the chase are the major part of the appeal.

Over the years big-game hunts increased to the point that some species as common as the tiger have become endangered in the wild. There are now laws protecting such animals, and modern hunters are encouraged to "shoot" their prey with cameras, not guns.

Active Reading / Setting a Purpose
READING CONNECTION

Making Inferences The narrator of this story does not always directly tell you what happens. You have to make logical guesses, or inferences, to figure out some events and understand the meaning of some conversations. Near the beginning of the story, for example, Rainsford (the main character) is on the deck of a ship when he grabs for his pipe and loses his balance. Next, the narrator says only that Rainsford feels warm sea water close over his head. You can infer that he has fallen overboard. As you read "The Most Dangerous Game," jot down two or three inferences that help explain how hunting for sport turns into a deadly game of survival.

• CULTURAL CONNECTION   **787**

OVERVIEW

Objectives
- To understand and appreciate a classic short story that explores a battle for survival
- To understand and appreciate suspense
- To identify and appreciate figurative language
- To express understanding of the story through a choice of writing forms, including a diary entry and an article
- To extend understanding of the story through a variety of multimodal and cross-curricular activities

Skills

LITERARY CONCEPTS
- Suspense
- Setting

READING SKILLS/ STRATEGIES
- Making inferences

THE WRITER'S STYLE
- Using specific examples

GRAMMAR
- Demonstrative adjectives

SPEAKING, LISTENING, AND VIEWING
- Sportscast: play-by-play
- Group discussion
- Oral presentation

CULTURAL CONNECTION
Big-Game Hunting The sport of hunting big game was once so popular that animals were killed at a rate high enough to threaten entire species with extinction. Today, big-game hunting is illegal in many countries. These historical images show hunters with their animal trophies. You may wish to generate discussion about how such hunters viewed nature.

Side A, Frame 49526

PRINT AND MEDIA RESOURCES

UNIT SIX RESOURCE BOOK
Strategic Reading: Literature, p. 41
Vocabulary SkillBuilder, p. 42

GRAMMAR MINI–LESSONS
Transparencies, p. 27
Copymasters, p. 27

WRITING MINI–LESSONS
Transparencies, pp. 42, 54

ACCESS FOR STUDENTS ACQUIRING ENGLISH
Selection Summaries
Reading Support

FORMAL ASSESSMENT
Selection Test, pp. 143–144
 Test Generator

 AUDIO LIBRARY
See Reference Card

 LASERLINKS
Cultural Connection
Contemporary Connection

THE LANGUAGE OF LITERATURE TEACHER'S EDITION **787**

SUMMARY

Sanger Rainsford, a famous big-game hunter, falls overboard while sailing past mysterious Ship-Trap Island, a place that sailors dread. Swimming to the island, Rainsford finds that it belongs to another hunter, General Zaroff. Zaroff explains that he retreated to his island when he became bored with hunting animals that no longer presented a challenge. He now hunts the most dangerous game: human beings. The people he hunts are shipwrecked sailors he has captured. When Rainsford declines Zaroff's invitation to join him in the hunt, Zaroff decides to hunt Rainsford instead. Rainsford must use all his hunter's skills to stay alive. With great cunning, he defeats Zaroff at Zaroff's own deadly contest.

Thematic Link: *Fateful Encounters*
A shipwrecked game hunter has a fateful encounter when he becomes the prey in the hunt of another.

CUSTOMIZING FOR
Students Acquiring English

- Use **ACCESS FOR STUDENTS ACQUIRING ENGLISH,** *Reading Support.*
- Explain the two meanings of the word *game:* (1) an enjoyable pastime or contest—like soccer or baseball—and (2) animals, such as deer and rabbits, that are hunted for food or sport. Ask students to discuss what the title might mean in light of these two different definitions.
- As you guide students through the selection, you may want to use the suggestions in these boxes and the suggestions under Strategic Reading for Less-Proficient Readers.

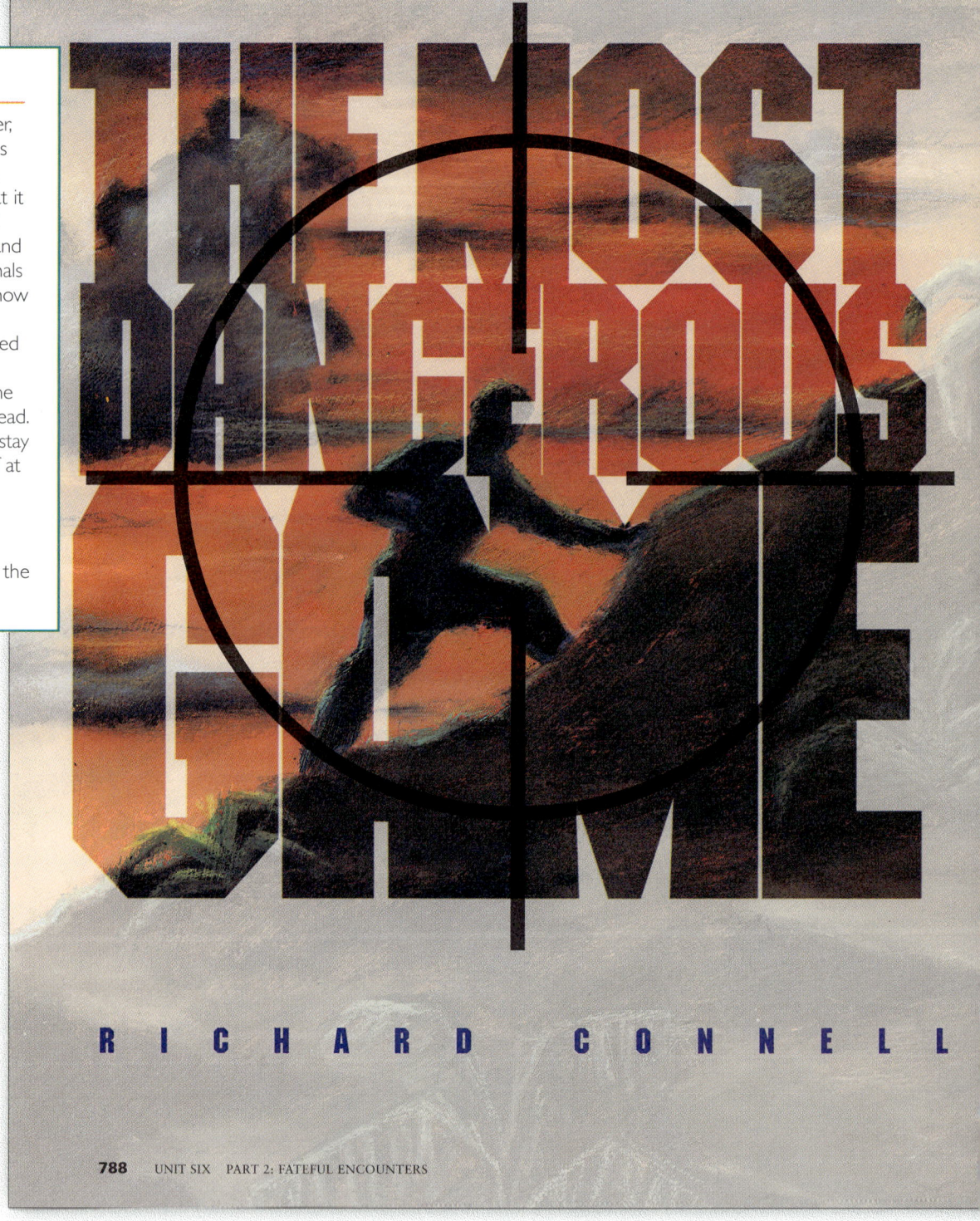

THE MOST DANGEROUS GAME

RICHARD CONNELL

788 UNIT SIX PART 2: FATEFUL ENCOUNTERS

WORDS TO KNOW

affable (ăf′ə-bəl) *adj.* friendly, pleasant, and easy to talk to (p. 795)

amenity (ə-mĕn′ĭ-tē) *n.* something that adds to one's comfort or convenience (p. 794)

condone (kən-dōn′) *v.* to overlook, forgive, or disregard (p. 798)

deplorable (dĭ-plôr′ə-bəl) *adj.* deeply regrettable; unfortunate (p. 801)

disarming (dĭs-är′mĭng) *adj.* removing or overcoming suspicion; inspiring confidence (p. 793)

droll (drōl) *adj.* amusingly odd or comical (p. 798)

elude (ĭ-lōōd′) *v.* to escape, especially by means of daring, cleverness, or skill (p. 799)

imperative (ĭm-pĕr′ə-tĭv) *adj.* absolutely necessary (p. 802)

quarry (kwôr′ē) *n.* the object of a hunt; prey (p. 792)

scruple (skrōō′pəl) *n.* an uneasy feeling arising from one's conscience or principles (p. 799)

solicitously (sə-lĭs′ĭ-təs-lē) *adv.* expressing care or concern (p. 800)

stamina (stăm′ə-nə) *n.* physical or moral strength; endurance (p. 801)

tangible (tăn′jə-bəl) *adj.* capable of being touched or felt; having actual form and substance (p. 790)

uncanny (ŭn-kăn′ē) *adj.* so remarkable as to seem supernatural (p. 803)

zealous (zĕl′əs) *adj.* intensely devoted and enthusiastic (p. 802)

"OFF THERE TO THE RIGHT—somewhere—is a large island," said Whitney. "It's rather a mystery—"

"What island is it?" Rainsford asked.

"The old charts call it 'Ship-Trap Island,'" Whitney replied. "A suggestive name, isn't it? Sailors have a curious dread of the place. I don't know why. Some superstition—"

"Can't see it," remarked Rainsford, trying to peer through the dank tropical night that was palpable as it pressed its thick warm blackness in upon the yacht.

"You've good eyes," said Whitney, with a laugh, "and I've seen you pick off a moose moving in the brown fall bush at four hundred yards, but even you can't see four miles or so through a moonless Caribbean night."

"Nor four yards," admitted Rainsford. "Ugh! It's like moist black velvet."

"It will be light enough in Rio," promised Whitney. "We should make it in a few days. I hope the jaguar guns have come from Purdey's. We should have some good hunting up the Amazon. Great sport, hunting."

"The best sport in the world," agreed Rainsford.

"For the hunter," amended Whitney. "Not for the jaguar."

"Don't talk rot, Whitney," said Rainsford. "You're a big-game hunter, not a philosopher. Who cares how a jaguar feels?"

"Perhaps the jaguar does," observed Whitney.

"Bah! They've no understanding."

"Even so, I rather think they understand one thing—fear. The fear of pain and the fear of death."

"Nonsense," laughed Rainsford. "This hot weather is making you soft, Whitney. Be a realist. The world is made up of two classes—the hunters and the huntees. Luckily, you and I are hunters. Do you think we've passed that island yet?"

"I can't tell in the dark. I hope so."

"Why?" asked Rainsford.

"The place has a reputation—a bad one."

"Cannibals?" suggested Rainsford.

"Hardly. Even cannibals wouldn't live in such a Godforsaken place. But it's gotten into sailor lore, somehow. Didn't you notice that the crew's nerves seemed a bit jumpy today?"

"They were a bit strange, now you mention it. Even Captain Nielsen—"

"Yes, even that tough-minded old Swede, who'd go up to the devil himself and ask him for a light. Those fishy blue eyes held a look I never saw there before. All I could get out of him was: 'This place has an evil name among seafaring men, sir.' Then he said to me, very gravely: 'Don't you feel anything?'—as if the air about us was actually poisonous. Now, you mustn't laugh when I tell you this—I did feel something like a sudden chill.

"There was no breeze. The sea was as flat as a plate-glass window. We were drawing near the island then. What I felt was a—a mental chill; a sort of sudden dread."

"Pure imagination," said Rainsford. "One superstitious sailor can taint the whole ship's company with his fear."

"Maybe. But sometimes I think sailors have an extra sense that tells them when they are in

STRATEGIC READING FOR
Less-Proficient Readers

C Invite students to discuss Rainsford's feelings about hunting. Use the following questions:
- How does Rainsford describe hunting? *(as the greatest sport in the world)* **Noting Relevant Details**
- Does he show any concern for the animals that he hunts? *(None—he dismisses Whitney's talk of a jaguar's having feelings as "rot.")* **Making Inferences**

Set a Purpose Have students read to find out how Rainsford ends up on Ship-Trap Island and what occurs afterward.

Literary Concept: SUSPENSE

D Ask students to identify details in the selection so far that help to contribute to the mood of suspense. *(Possible responses: the description of the sailors' fear; Whitney's comment about the air being poisonous and his mentioning a sudden chill; the sound of gunshots; the description of the waters as "blood-warm")*

---

danger. Sometimes I think evil is a <u>tangible</u> thing—with wavelengths, just as sound and light have. An evil place can, so to speak, broadcast vibrations of evil. Anyhow, I'm glad we're getting out of this zone. Well, I think I'll **C** turn in now, Rainsford."

"I'm not sleepy," said Rainsford. "I'm going to smoke another pipe up on the afterdeck."

"Good night, then, Rainsford. See you at breakfast."

"Right. Good night, Whitney."

There was no sound in the night as Rainsford sat there but the muffled throb of the engine that drove the yacht swiftly through the darkness, and the swish and ripple of the wash of the propeller.

Rainsford, reclining in a steamer chair, indolently puffed on his favorite brier.[1] The sensuous drowsiness of the night was on him. "It's so dark," he thought, "that I could sleep without closing my eyes; the night would be my eyelids—"

An abrupt sound startled him. Off to the right he heard it, and his ears, expert in such matters, could not be mistaken. Again he heard the sound, and again. Somewhere, off in the blackness, someone had fired a gun three times.

Rainsford sprang up and moved quickly to the rail, mystified. He strained his eyes in the direction from which the reports had come, but it was like trying to see through a blanket. He leaped upon the rail and balanced himself there, to get greater elevation; his pipe, striking a rope, was knocked from his mouth. He lunged for it; a short, hoarse cry came from his lips as he realized he had reached too far and had lost his balance. The cry was pinched off short as **D** the blood-warm waters of the Caribbean Sea closed over his head.

He struggled up to the surface and tried to cry out, but the wash from the speeding yacht slapped him in the face, and the salt water in his open mouth made him gag and strangle. Desperately he struck out with strong strokes after the receding lights of the yacht, but he stopped before he had swum fifty feet. A certain cool-headedness had come to him; it was not the first time he had been in a tight place. There was a chance that his cries could be heard by someone aboard the yacht, but that chance was slender and grew more slender as the yacht raced on. He wrestled himself out of his clothes and shouted with all his power. The lights of the yacht became faint and ever-vanishing

---

1. **brier** (brī′ər): a tobacco pipe.

| WORDS TO KNOW | **tangible** (tăn′jə-bəl) *adj.* capable of being touched or felt; having actual form and substance |

790

Mini-Lesson   Grammar

DEMONSTRATIVE ADJECTIVES Point out to students that the following words can function as adjectives: *this, these, that,* and *those.* Tell students that pronouns—as well as nouns—are used as adjectives when they answer one of the following questions: What kind? Which one or ones? How many? How much? Remind students that occasionally the pronoun *them* is misused in place of the pronoun *those.* Tell students that *them* never functions as an adjective. From page 789:

Correct: Those fishy blue eyes held a look I never saw there before.

Incorrect: Them fishy blue eyes held a look I never saw there before.

Application Have students write short paragraphs about the story, correctly using the demonstrative adjectives *this, that, these,* and *those.*

Reteaching/Reinforcement
- *Grammar Handbook,* anthology p. 921
- *Grammar Mini-Lessons* transparencies p. 27, copymasters p. 27

The Writer's Craft
Pronouns as Adjectives, p. 623

Untitled [Nyack] (1973), Julio Larraz. Private collection, courtesy of Nohra Haime Gallery, New York.

fireflies; then they were blotted out entirely by the night.

Rainsford remembered the shots. They had come from the right, and doggedly he swam in that direction, swimming with slow, deliberate strokes, conserving his strength. For a seemingly endless time he fought the sea. He began to count his strokes; he could do possibly a hundred more and then—

Rainsford heard a sound. It came out of the darkness, a high, screaming sound, the sound of an animal in an extremity of anguish and terror.

He did not recognize the animal that made the sound; he did not try to; with fresh vitality he swam toward the sound. He heard it again; then it was cut short by another noise, crisp, staccato.

"Pistol shot," muttered Rainsford, swimming on.

Ten minutes of determined effort brought another sound to his ears—the most welcome he had ever heard—the muttering and growling of the sea breaking on a rocky shore. He was almost on the rocks before he saw them; on a night less calm he would have been shattered against them. With his remaining strength he dragged himself from the swirling waters. Jagged crags appeared to jut up into the opaqueness; he forced himself upward, hand over hand. Gasping, his hands raw, he reached a flat place at the top. Dense jungle came down to the very edge of the cliffs. What perils that tangle of trees and underbrush might hold for him did

THE MOST DANGEROUS GAME **791**

not concern Rainsford just then. All he knew was that he was safe from his enemy, the sea, and that utter weariness was on him. He flung himself down at the jungle edge and tumbled headlong into the deepest sleep of his life.

 WHEN HE OPENED HIS EYES, he knew from the position of the sun that it was late in the afternoon. Sleep had given him new vigor; a sharp hunger was picking at him. He looked about him, almost cheerfully.

"Where there are pistol shots, there are men. Where there are men, there is food," he thought. But what kind of men, he wondered, in so forbidding a place? An unbroken front of snarled and ragged jungle fringed the shore.

He saw no sign of a trail through the closely knit web of weeds and trees; it was easier to go along the shore, and Rainsford floundered along by the water. Not far from where he had landed, he stopped.

Some wounded thing, by the evidence a large animal, had thrashed about in the underbrush; the jungle weeds were crushed down, and the moss was lacerated; one patch of weeds was stained crimson. A small, glittering object not far away caught Rainsford's eye, and he picked it up. It was an empty cartridge.

"A twenty-two," he remarked. "That's odd. It must have been a fairly large animal, too. The hunter had his nerve with him to tackle it with a light gun. It's clear that the brute put up a fight. I suppose the first three shots I heard was when the hunter flushed[2] his quarry and wounded it. The last shot was when he trailed it here and finished it."

He examined the ground closely and found what he had hoped to find—the print of hunting boots. They pointed along the cliff in the direction he had been going. Eagerly he hurried along, now slipping on a rotten log or a loose stone, but making headway; night was beginning to settle down on the island.

Bleak darkness was blacking out the sea and jungle when Rainsford sighted the lights. He came upon them as he turned a crook in the coastline, and his first thought was that he had come upon a village, for there were many lights. But as he forged along, he saw to his great astonishment that all the lights were in one enormous building—a lofty structure with pointed towers plunging upward into the gloom. His eyes made out the shadowy outlines of a palatial château;[3] it was set on a high bluff, and on three sides of it cliffs dived down to where the sea licked greedy lips in the shadows.

"Mirage," thought Rainsford. But it was no mirage, he found, when he opened the tall spiked iron gate. The stone steps were real enough; the massive door with a leering gargoyle[4] for a knocker was real enough; yet about it all hung an air of unreality.

He lifted the knocker, and it creaked up stiffly as if it had never before been used. He let it fall, and it startled him with its booming loudness. He thought he heard steps within; the door remained closed. Again Rainsford lifted the heavy knocker and let it fall. The door opened then, opened as suddenly as if it were on a spring, and Rainsford stood blinking in the river of glaring gold light that poured out. The first thing Rainsford's eyes discerned was the largest man Rainsford had ever seen—a gigantic creature, solidly made and black-bearded to the waist. In his hand the man held a long-barreled revolver, and he was pointing it straight at Rainsford's heart.

---

2. **flushed:** forced out of a hiding place.
3. **palatial château** (pə-lā′shəl shă-tō′): palacelike mansion.
4. **gargoyle** (gär′goil): an ornamental figure in the shape of a bizarre, monstrous creature.

WORDS TO KNOW

quarry (kwôr′ē) *n.* the object of a hunt; prey

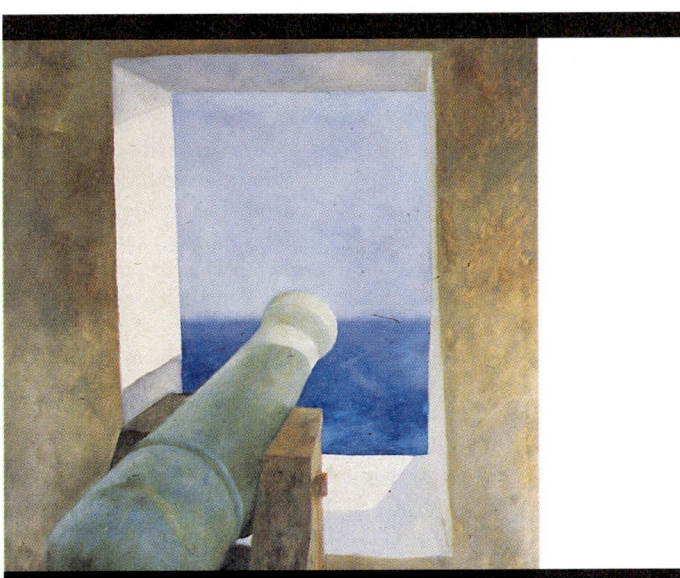

Waiting for Henry Morgan (1984), Julio Larraz. Oil on canvas, 49½" × 47", private collection, courtesy of Nohra Haime Gallery, New York.

Out of the snarl of beard two small eyes regarded Rainsford.

"Don't be alarmed," said Rainsford, with a smile which he hoped was <u>disarming</u>. "I'm no robber. I fell off a yacht. My name is Sanger Rainsford of New York City."

The menacing look in the eyes did not change. The revolver pointed as rigidly as if the giant were a statue. He gave no sign that he understood Rainsford's words, or that he had even heard them. He was dressed in uniform, a black uniform trimmed with gray astrakhan.[5]

"I'm Sanger Rainsford of New York," Rainsford began again. "I fell off a yacht. I am hungry."

The man's only answer was to raise with his thumb the hammer of his revolver. Then Rainsford saw the man's free hand go to his forehead in a military salute, and he saw him click his heels together and stand at attention. Another man was coming down the broad marble steps, an erect, slender man in evening clothes. He advanced to Rainsford and held out his hand.

In a cultivated[6] voice marked by a slight accent that gave it added precision and deliberateness, he said: "It is a very great pleasure and honor to welcome Mr. Sanger Rainsford, the celebrated hunter, to my home."

Automatically Rainsford shook the man's hand.

"I've read your book about hunting snow leopards in Tibet, you see," explained the man. "I am General Zaroff."

Rainsford's first impression was that the man

---

5. **astrakhan** (ăs′trə-kăn′): a fur made from skins of young lambs.
6. **cultivated**: educated and cultured.

WORDS TO KNOW

disarming (dĭs-är′mĭng) *adj.* removing or overcoming suspicion; inspiring confidence

Literary Concept:
CHARACTERIZATION

1 Ask students what insight this introduction provides into Zaroff's character. *(Possible responses: He seems dangerous and threatening; he seems a bit unpredictable.)*

CUSTOMIZING FOR
Students Acquiring English

3 Point out that *dumb* means "unable to speak," not "witless."

4 Explain that a refectory table is a long, narrow table with a trestle support at each end. A score is twenty, so "two-score" would be forty, which suggests the huge length of the table and the room.

STRATEGIC READING FOR
Less-Proficient Readers

J Make sure students understand the events that have occurred since Rainsford fell off the yacht. Use the following questions:
- How does Rainsford manage to find land after falling off the yacht? *(He swims in the direction from which he earlier heard shots.)* **Literal Recall**
- How would you describe the structure that Rainsford comes across? *(a huge mansion with towers and many lights, sitting high up on a bluff)* **Visualizing**
- How is Rainsford received at the house? *(First he is received at gunpoint by a huge man; then he is given a friendly, if formal, welcome by the giant's master, General Zaroff.)* **Summarizing**

Set a Purpose Have students read on to find out what Zaroff reveals that deeply disturbs Rainsford.

---

was singularly handsome; his second was that there was an original, almost bizarre quality about the general's face. He was a tall man past middle age, for his hair was a vivid white; but his thick eyebrows and pointed military moustache were as black as the night from which Rainsford had come. His eyes, too, were black and very bright. He had high cheekbones, a sharp-cut nose, a spare, dark face, the face of a man used to giving orders, the face of an aristocrat. Turning to the giant in uniform, the general made a sign. The giant put away his pistol, saluted, withdrew.

"Ivan is an incredibly strong fellow," remarked the general, "but he has the misfortune to be deaf and dumb. A simple fellow, but, I'm afraid, like all his race, a bit of a savage."

"Is he Russian?"

"He is a Cossack,"[7] said the general, and his smile showed red lips and pointed teeth. "So am I."

"Come," he said, "we shouldn't be chatting here. We can talk later. Now you want clothes, food, rest. You shall have them. This is a most restful spot."

Ivan had reappeared, and the general spoke to him with lips that moved but gave forth no sound.

"Follow Ivan, if you please, Mr. Rainsford," said the general. "I was about to have my dinner when you came. I'll wait for you. You'll find that my clothes will fit you, I think."

It was to a huge, beam-ceilinged bedroom with a canopied bed big enough for six men that Rainsford followed the silent giant. Ivan laid out an evening suit, and Rainsford, as he put it on, noticed that it came from a London tailor who ordinarily cut and sewed for none below the rank of duke.

The dining room to which Ivan conducted him was in many ways remarkable. There was a medieval magnificence about it; it suggested a baronial hall of feudal times[7] with its oaken panels, its high ceiling, its vast refectory table where two score men could sit down to eat. About the hall were the mounted heads of many animals—lions, tigers, elephants, moose, bears; larger or more perfect specimens Rainsford had never seen. At the great table the general was sitting, alone.

"You'll have a cocktail, Mr. Rainsford," he suggested. The cocktail was surpassingly good; and, Rainsford noted, the table appointments were of the finest—the linen, the crystal, the silver, the china.

They were eating *borsch*, the rich red soup with whipped cream so dear to Russian palates. Half apologetically General Zaroff said: "We do our best to preserve the <u>amenities</u> of civilization here. Please forgive any lapses. We are well off the beaten track, you know. Do you think the champagne has suffered from its long ocean trip?"

---

7. **Cossack** (kŏs′ăk): a member of a southern Russian people formerly famous as cavalrymen.

WORDS TO KNOW

amenity (ə-mĕn′ĭ-tē) *n.* something that adds to one's comfort or convenience

794

Mini-Lesson Literary Concepts

REVIEWING SETTING Remind students that setting is the time and place of the action in a story. Point out that the time can be a specific time of day, or a period in the past, present, or future. Then say that in some works, the setting is minimally defined and left largely up to the reader's imagination, whereas in other works, it is described in detail and makes an important contribution to the total effect of the story. Point out that most of the action in "The Most Dangerous Game" takes place in three defined locations: on board the yacht, in Zaroff's mansion, and in the island's dense jungle.

Application Have students work in groups to answer the following questions:
- How much detail does the author provide about the setting? Give examples.
- What aspects of the setting are major contributors to the plot?
- What aspects of the three major locations contribute to the feeling of suspense in the story?

794 THE LANGUAGE OF LITERATURE **TEACHER'S EDITION**

"Not in the least," declared Rainsford. He was finding the general a most thoughtful and affable host, a true cosmopolite.[8] But there was one small trait of the general's that made Rainsford uncomfortable. Whenever he looked up from his plate, he found the general studying him, appraising him narrowly.

"Perhaps," said General Zaroff, "you were surprised that I recognized your name. You see, I read all books on hunting published in English, French, and Russian. I have but one passion in my life, Mr. Rainsford, and it is the hunt."

"You have some wonderful heads here," said Rainsford as he ate a particularly well cooked filet mignon. "That Cape buffalo is the largest I ever saw."

"Oh, that fellow. Yes, he was a monster."

"Did he charge you?"

"Hurled me against a tree," said the general. "Fractured my skull. But I got the brute."

"I've always thought," said Rainsford, "that the Cape buffalo is the most dangerous of all big game."

For a moment the general did not reply; he was smiling his curious red-lipped smile. Then he said slowly: "No. You are wrong, sir. The Cape buffalo is not the most dangerous big game." He sipped his wine. "Here in my preserve on this island," he said, in the same slow tone, "I hunt more dangerous game."

Rainsford expressed his surprise. "Is there big game on this island?"

The general nodded. "The biggest."

"Really?"

"Oh, it isn't here naturally, of course. I have to stock the island."

"What have you imported, General?" Rainsford asked. "Tigers?"

The general smiled. "No," he said. "Hunting tigers ceased to interest me some years ago. I exhausted their possibilities, you see. No thrill left in tigers, no real danger. I live for danger, Mr. Rainsford."

The general took from his pocket a gold cigarette case and offered his guest a long black cigarette with a silver tip; it was perfumed and gave off a smell like incense.

"We will have some capital hunting, you and I," said the general. "I shall be most glad to have your society."

"But what game—" began Rainsford.

"I'll tell you," said the general. "You will be amused, I know. I think I may say, in all modesty, that I have done a rare thing. I have invented a new sensation. May I pour you another glass of port, Mr. Rainsford?"

"Thank you, General."

The general filled both glasses and said: "God makes some men poets. Some he makes kings, some beggars. Me he made a hunter. My hand was made for the trigger, my father said. He was a very rich man with a quarter of a million acres in the Crimea, and he was an ardent sportsman. When I was only five years old, he gave me a little gun, specially made in Moscow for me, to shoot sparrows with. When I shot some of his prize turkeys with it, he did not punish me; he complimented me on my marksmanship. I killed my first bear in the Caucasus[9] when I was ten. My whole life has been one prolonged hunt. I went into the army—it was expected of noblemen's sons—and for a time commanded a division of Cossack cavalry, but my real interest was always the hunt. I have hunted every kind of game in every land. It would be impossible for me to tell you how many animals I have killed."

---

8. **cosmopolite** (kŏz-mŏp′ə-līt′): a sophisticated person who can handle any situation well.
9. **Crimea** (krī-mē′ə) . . . **Caucasus** (kô′kə-səs): regions in the southern part of the former Russian Empire, near the Black Sea.

WORDS TO KNOW

affable (ăf′ə-bəl) *adj.* friendly, pleasant, and easy to talk to

Art Note

Casanova by Julio Larraz Tell students that a Casanova is a man whose behavior toward women is unscrupulous and that such a man is considered to be without a moral sense, and therefore dangerous. In this oil painting, Larraz depicts such a man in a sinister light and in a setting rife with the remains of creatures he has caught and killed.

Reading the Art *How would you characterize the subject of this painting? If the man in the painting were Zaroff, what might he be thinking?*

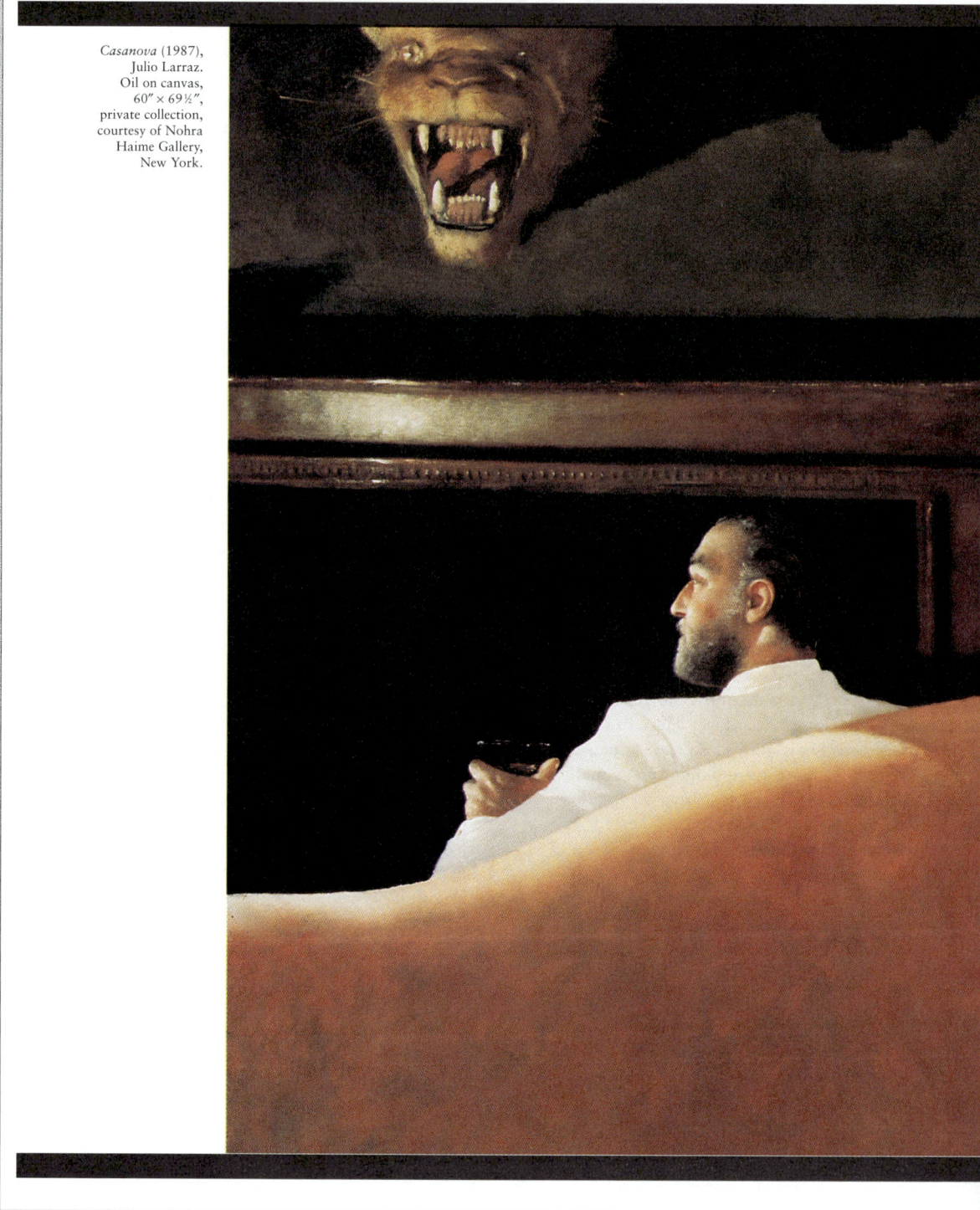

Casanova (1987), Julio Larraz. Oil on canvas, 60″ × 69½″, private collection, courtesy of Nohra Haime Gallery, New York.

The general puffed at his cigarette.

"After the debacle[10] in Russia I left the country, for it was imprudent[11] for an officer of the Tsar to stay there. Many noble Russians lost everything. I, luckily, had invested heavily in American securities, so I shall never have to open a tearoom in Monte Carlo or drive a taxi in Paris. Naturally, I continued to hunt— grizzlies in your Rockies, crocodiles in the Ganges,[12] rhinoceroses in East Africa. It was in Africa that the Cape buffalo hit me and laid me up for six months. As soon as I recovered, I started for the Amazon to hunt jaguars, for I had heard they were unusually cunning. They weren't." The Cossack sighed. "They were no match at all for a hunter with his wits about him, and a high-powered rifle. I was bitterly disappointed. I was lying in my tent with a splitting headache one night when a terrible thought pushed its way into my mind. Hunting was beginning to bore me! And hunting, remember, had been my life. I have heard that in America businessmen often go to pieces when they give up the business that has been their life."

"Yes, that's so," said Rainsford.

The general smiled. "I had no wish to go to pieces," he said. "I must do something. Now, mine is an analytical mind, Mr. Rainsford. Doubtless that is why I enjoy the problems of the chase."

"No doubt, General Zaroff."

"So," continued the general, "I asked myself why the hunt no longer fascinated me. You are much younger than I am, Mr. Rainsford, and have not hunted as much, but you perhaps can guess the answer."

"What was it?"

"Simply this: hunting had ceased to be what you call 'a sporting proposition.' It had become

---

10. **debacle** (dĭ-bä′kəl): a disastrous defeat; rout (a reference to the 1917 Russian Revolution that overthrew the czar).
11. **imprudent**: showing poor judgment; unwise.
12. **Ganges** (găn′jēz′): a river in northern India.

THE MOST DANGEROUS GAME **797**

Linking to Government

N The hunting of animals, particularly endangered species, is regulated at international, national, state, and local levels. International agreements—such as the Convention on International Trade in Endangered Species (CITES), which was signed by more than 120 nations—regulate the trade in endangered species. The U.S. federal government maintains prohibitions against the hunting of marine mammals, threatened species, bald eagles, and other animals. The U.S. Wildlife Service oversees 442 wildlife refuges and 150 wildlife production areas, and it sets regulations to protect migratory wildlife, including fish and birds. Each of the 50 states has its own hunting regulations. These prohibit the taking of certain species; specify hunting seasons and the age, sex, or size of the animal that may be hunted; and limit the number of animals taken and the types of weapons and ammunition used.

Critical Thinking: SUMMARIZING

O Have students summarize what Zaroff tells Rainsford about his life. *(Trained from childhood to hunt, Zaroff, as expected, entered the Russian czar's cavalry. After the Russian Revolution, he returned to hunting. However, hunting now bores him because he always outwits his prey.)*

Mini-Lesson The Writer's Style

USING SPECIFIC EXAMPLES Invite students to discuss the way in which Richard Connell uses specific examples throughout "The Most Dangerous Game" to emphasize the nature of the characters, aspects of the setting, and elements important to the plot. Tell them that to convey information about General Zaroff's luxurious lifestyle, veneer of civility, and hunting prowess, for example, Connell uses such specific examples as the wine Zaroff drinks (Veuve Cliquot), the opera he hums (*Madama Butterfly*), and the knowledge he has of the names of the traps used by Rainsford (Malay man-catcher, Burmese tiger pit).

Application Have students review the selection for other instances of the author's use of specific examples. Then have them write a brief paragraph describing how the author's use of specific examples is important to developing the plot, describing the setting, or creating rich characterization.

Reteaching/Reinforcement
- *Writing Handbook*, anthology pp. 872, 874
- *Writing Mini-Lessons* transparencies, pp. 42, 54

 The Writer's Craft

Elaboration, pp. 351–356

THE LANGUAGE OF LITERATURE TEACHER'S EDITION **797**

Critical Thinking:
MAKING INFERENCES

P Ask students to infer from this interchange what Zaroff actually hunts. *(He hunts humans.)* Then ask them how this relates to the double meaning in the title of the story. *(Possible response: "Game" is both prey and sport. The most dangerous game [prey] is a human, and the most dangerous game [sport] is the hunting of humans.)*

Critical Thinking:
COMPARISON/CONTRAST

Q Ask students to discuss the meaning of Zaroff's comparison. *(Possible response: A snuffbox is an old-fashioned object; Zaroff is emphasizing that he finds Rainsford's views about human life old-fashioned—and particularly surprising in a modern young man.)*

---

too easy. I always got my quarry. Always. There is no greater bore than perfection."

The general lit a fresh cigarette.

"No animal had a chance with me any more. That is no boast; it is a mathematical certainty. The animal had nothing but his legs and his instinct. Instinct is no match for reason. When I thought of this, it was a tragic moment for me, I can tell you."

Rainsford leaned across the table, absorbed in what his host was saying.

"It came to me as an inspiration what I must do," the general went on.

"And that was?"

The general smiled the quiet smile of one who has faced an obstacle and surmounted it with success. "I had to invent a new animal to hunt," he said.

"A new animal? You're joking."

"Not at all," said the general. "I never joke about hunting. I needed a new animal. I found one. So I bought this island, built this house, and here I do my hunting. The island is perfect for my purposes—there are jungles with a maze of trails in them, hills, swamps—"

"But the animal, General Zaroff?"

"Oh," said the general, "it supplies me with the most exciting hunting in the world. No other hunting compares with it for an instant. Every day I hunt, and I never grow bored now, for I have a quarry with which I can match my wits."

Rainsford's bewilderment showed in his face.

"I wanted the ideal animal to hunt," explained the general. "So I said: 'What are the attributes of an ideal quarry?' And the answer was, of course: 'It must have courage, cunning, and, above all, it must be able to reason.'"

"But no animal can reason," objected Rainsford.

"My dear fellow," said the general, "there is one that can."

"But you can't mean—" gasped Rainsford.

"And why not?"

"I can't believe you are serious, General Zaroff. This is a grisly[13] joke."

"Why should I not be serious? I am speaking of hunting."

"Hunting? Good God, General Zaroff, what you speak of is murder."

The general laughed with entire good nature. He regarded Rainsford quizzically. "I refuse to believe that so modern and civilized a young man as you seem to be harbors romantic ideas about the value of human life. Surely your experiences in the war—"

"Did not make me condone cold-blooded murder," finished Rainsford, stiffly.

Laughter shook the general. "How extraordinarily droll you are!" he said. "One does not expect nowadays to find a young man of the educated class, even in America, with such a naïve, and, if I may say so, mid-Victorian point of view. It's like finding a snuffbox in a limousine. Ah, well, doubtless

---

13. **grisly** (grĭz′lē): horrible; ghastly.

WORDS TO KNOW
condone (kən-dōn′) *v.* to overlook, forgive, or disregard
droll (drōl) *adj.* amusingly odd or comical

you had Puritan ancestors. So many Americans appear to have had. I'll wager you'll forget your notions when you go hunting with me. You've a genuine new thrill in store for you, Mr. Rainsford."

"Thank you, I'm a hunter, not a murderer."

"Dear me," said the general, quite unruffled, "again that unpleasant word. But I think I can show you that your scruples are quite ill-founded."

"Yes?"

"Life is for the strong, to be lived by the strong, and, if needs be, taken by the strong. The weak of the world were put here to give the strong pleasure. I am strong. Why should I not use my gift? If I wish to hunt, why should I not? I hunt the scum of the earth—sailors from tramp ships—lascars,[14] blacks, Chinese, whites, mongrels—a thoroughbred horse or hound is worth more than a score of them."

"But they are men," said Rainsford, hotly.

"Precisely," said the general. "That is why I use them. It gives me pleasure. They can reason, after a fashion. So they are dangerous."

"But where do you get them?"

The general's left eyelid fluttered down in a wink. "This island is called Ship Trap," he answered. "Sometimes an angry god of the high seas sends them to me. Sometimes, when Providence is not so kind, I help Providence a bit. Come to the window with me."

Rainsford went to the window and looked out toward the sea.

"Watch! Out there!" exclaimed the general, pointing into the night. Rainsford's eyes saw only blackness, and then, as the general pressed a button, far out to sea Rainsford saw the flash of lights.

The general chuckled. "They indicate a channel," he said, "where there's none: giant rocks with razor edges crouch like a sea monster with wide-open jaws. They can crush a ship as easily as I crush this nut." He dropped a walnut on the hardwood floor and brought his heel grinding down on it. "Oh, yes," he said, casually, as if in answer to a question, "I have electricity. We try to be civilized here."

"Civilized? And you shoot down men?"

A trace of anger was in the general's black eyes, but it was there for but a second, and he said, in his most pleasant manner: "Dear me, what a righteous young man you are! I assure you I do not do the thing you suggest. That would be barbarous. I treat these visitors with every consideration. They get plenty of good food and exercise. They get into splendid physical condition. You shall see for yourself tomorrow."

"What do you mean?"

"We'll visit my training school," smiled the general. "It's in the cellar. I have about a dozen pupils down there now. They're from the Spanish bark *Sanlúcar* that had the bad luck to go on the rocks out there. A very inferior lot, I regret to say. Poor specimens and more accustomed to the deck than to the jungle."

He raised his hand, and Ivan, who served as waiter, brought thick Turkish coffee. Rainsford, with an effort, held his tongue in check.

"It's a game, you see," pursued the general, blandly. "I suggest to one of them that we go hunting. I give him a supply of food and an excellent hunting knife. I give him three hours' start. I am to follow, armed only with a pistol of the smallest caliber and range. If my quarry eludes me for three whole days, he wins the game. If I find him"—the general smiled—"he loses."

"Suppose he refuses to be hunted?"

"Oh," said the general, "I give him his

---

14. **lascars** (lăs′kərz): sailors from India.

WORDS TO KNOW

scruple (skrōō′pəl) *n.* an uneasy feeling arising from one's conscience or principles
elude (ĭ-lōōd′) *v.* to escape, especially by means of daring, cleverness, or skill

---

Cultural Note

Zaroff's philosophy that "life is for the strong" echoes the ideas of the social Darwinists, who thrived in the late 19th and early 20th centuries.

The social Darwinists shaped Darwin's evolutionary theory to explain social behavior. They held that society should not be protected from competition, or "natural selection"—that people should compete with one another for resources, a process that would weed out the strong from the weak. Those who couldn't compete successfully would die out, leaving the human race more "fit."

These distortions of Darwin's original ideas were used to justify various barbarous acts, including the war crimes committed by Nazi Germany in the 1930s and 1940s.

Critical Thinking: MAKING INFERENCES

Ask students to infer the general's meaning in the passage. *(Possible response: He means that sometimes travelers suitable for use as prey do crash on the shores of his island. At other times, however, when his stock of prey runs low, he creates artificial traps to lure victims.)*

Critical Thinking: EVALUATING

Ask students whether they think Zaroff's "game" is fair. Have them explain their opinion. *(Possible response: The game is not fair, because the general is armed with a pistol, while his quarry carries only a knife. Further, the general knows the topography of the island, while his quarry does not.)*

Mini-Lesson: Speaking, Listening, and Viewing

SPORTSCAST: PLAY-BY-PLAY Ask students to discuss the typical elements of a radio or television broadcast of a live sports event. Point out that a typical sports-announcing team usually includes at least two sportscasters. One provides the play-by-play, or running description of the action as it occurs. The other sportscaster, known as a color commentator, backs up the play-by-play man by providing background on the athletes, interesting facts, and analysis of the action after it occurs.

Application Have students work in teams of two or three to provide a play-by-play reenactment of Zaroff's hunt for Rainsford. One student on each team can provide the play-by-play, describing the actions of Rainsford and Zaroff. The others can use facts from the story and their own imagination to provide the color commentary. Encourage the teams to include aspects typical of a live sports broadcast, including statistics and sports jargon. Student teams can take turns performing their sportscasts in front of the class.

option, of course. He need not play that game if he doesn't wish to. If he does not wish to hunt, I turn him over to Ivan. Ivan once had the honor of serving as official knouter[15] to the Great White Tsar, and he has his own ideas of sport. Invariably, Mr. Rainsford, invariably they choose the hunt."

"And if they win?"

The smile on the general's face widened. "To date I have not lost," he said.

Then he added, hastily: "I don't wish you to think me a braggart, Mr. Rainsford. Many of them afford only the most elementary sort of problem. Occasionally I strike a tartar.[16] One almost did win. I eventually had to use the dogs."

"The dogs?"

"This way, please. I'll show you."

The general steered Rainsford to a window. The lights from the windows sent a flickering illumination that made grotesque patterns on the courtyard below, and Rainsford could see moving about there a dozen or so huge black shapes; as they turned toward him, their eyes glittered greenly.

"A rather good lot, I think," observed the general. "They are let out at seven every night. If anyone should try to get into my house—or out of it—something extremely regrettable would occur to him." He hummed a snatch of song from the Folies Bergère.[17]

"And now," said the general, "I want to show you my new collection of heads. Will you come with me to the library?"

"I hope," said Rainsford, "that you will excuse me tonight, General Zaroff. I'm really not feeling at all well."

"Ah, indeed?" the general inquired, solicitously. "Well, I suppose that's only natural, after your long swim. You need a good, restful night's sleep. Tomorrow you'll feel like a new man, I'll wager. Then we'll hunt, eh? I've one rather promising prospect—"

Rainsford was hurrying from the room.

"Sorry you can't go with me tonight," called the general. "I expect rather fair sport—a big, strong black. He looks resourceful— Well, good night, Mr. Rainsford; I hope you have a good night's rest."

THE BED WAS GOOD, AND THE pajamas of the softest silk, and he was tired in every fiber of his being, but nevertheless Rainsford could not quiet his brain with the opiate of sleep. He lay, eyes wide open. Once he thought he heard stealthy steps in the corridor outside his room. He sought to throw open the door; it would not open. He went to the window and looked out. His room was high up in one of the towers. The lights of the château were out now, and it was dark and silent, but there was a fragment of sallow moon, and by its wan light he could see, dimly, the courtyard; there, weaving in and out in the pattern of shadow, were black, noiseless forms; the hounds heard him at the window and looked up, expectantly, with their green eyes. Rainsford went back to the bed and lay down. By many methods he tried to put himself to sleep. He had achieved a doze when, just as morning began to come, he heard, far off in the jungle, the faint report of a pistol.

General Zaroff did not appear until luncheon. He was dressed faultlessly in the tweeds of a country squire. He was solicitous

---

15. **knouter** (nout′ər): a person who whipped criminals in Russia.
16. **strike a tartar:** encounter a fierce opponent.
17. **Folies Bergère** (fô-lē′ běr-zhěr′): a music hall in Paris, famous for its variety shows.

WORDS TO KNOW
solicitously (sə-lĭs′ĭ-təs-lē) *adj.* expressing care or concern

800

about the state of Rainsford's health.

"As for me," sighed the general, "I do not feel so well. I am worried, Mr. Rainsford. Last night I detected traces of my old complaint."

To Rainsford's questioning glance the general said: "Ennui. Boredom."

Then, taking a second helping of crêpes suzettes, the general explained: "The hunting was not good last night. The fellow lost his head. He made a straight trail that offered no problems at all. That's the trouble with these sailors; they have dull brains to begin with, and they do not know how to get about in the woods. They do excessively stupid and obvious things. It's most annoying. Will you have another glass of Chablis,[18] Mr. Rainsford?"

"General," said Rainsford, firmly, "I wish to leave this island at once."

The general raised his thickets of eyebrows; he seemed hurt. "But, my dear fellow," the general protested, "you've only just come. You've had no hunting—"

"I wish to go today," said Rainsford. He saw the dead black eyes of the general on him, studying him. General Zaroff's face suddenly brightened.

He filled Rainsford's glass with venerable Chablis from a dusty bottle.

"Tonight," said the general, "we will hunt—you and I."

Rainsford shook his head. "No, General," he said. "I will not hunt."

The general shrugged his shoulders and delicately ate a hothouse grape. "As you wish, my friend," he said. "The choice rests entirely with you. But may I not venture to suggest that you will find my idea of sport more diverting than Ivan's?"

He nodded toward the corner to where the giant stood, scowling, his thick arms crossed on his hogshead of chest.

"You don't mean—" cried Rainsford.

"My dear fellow," said the general, "have I not told you I always mean what I say about hunting? This is really an inspiration. I drink to a foeman worthy of my steel—at last."

The general raised his glass, but Rainsford sat staring at him.

"You'll find this game worth playing," the general said, enthusiastically. "Your brain against mine. Your woodcraft against mine. Your strength and stamina against mine. Outdoor chess! And the stake is not without value, eh?"

"And if I win—" began Rainsford, huskily.

"I'll cheerfully acknowledge myself defeated if I do not find you by midnight of the third day," said General Zaroff. "My sloop will place you on the mainland near a town."

The general read what Rainsford was thinking.

"Oh, you can trust me," said the Cossack. "I will give you my word as a gentleman and a sportsman. Of course, you, in turn, must agree to say nothing of your visit here."

"I'll agree to nothing of the kind," said Rainsford.

"Oh," said the general, "in that case— But why discuss that now? Three days hence we can discuss it over a bottle of Veuve Cliquot, unless—"

The general sipped his wine.

Then a businesslike air animated him. "Ivan," he said to Rainsford, "will supply you with hunting clothes, food, a knife. I suggest you wear moccasins; they leave a poorer trail. I suggest, too, that you avoid the big swamp in the southeast corner of the island. We call it Death Swamp. There's quicksand there. One foolish fellow tried it. The deplorable part of it was that Lazarus followed him. You can imag-

---

18. **Chablis** (shă-blē′): a white wine.

WORDS TO KNOW
stamina (stăm′ə-nə) *n.* physical or moral strength; endurance
deplorable (dĭ-plôr′ə-bəl) *adj.* deeply regrettable; unfortunate

Literary Concept:
CHARACTERIZATION

 Ask students to explain what Zaroff's comment in this passage reveals about his character. *(Possible response: Zaroff's concern for his hunting dog reveals that he places little value on human life but deeply values his animals.)*

Literary Note

AA Point out to students that at this point, Connell omits details of Rainsford's preparation for the hunt, cutting, instead, directly to the hunt. Tell students that this serves to increase suspense by immediately plunging the reader into a more dramatic part of the story. Explain that by doing this, Connell shows the action rather than telling about it, one of the hallmarks of effective writing.

STRATEGIC READING FOR
Less-Proficient Readers

BB Have students explain why Rainsford agrees to allow Zaroff to hunt him as prey. *(Possible response: If Rainsford can elude the general for three days, then Rainsford will be free to leave the island.)* **Summarizing**

Set a Purpose Have students continue reading to find out what happens to Rainsford and Zaroff.

---

 ine my feelings, Mr. Rainsford. I loved Lazarus; he was the finest hound in my pack. Well, I must beg you to excuse me now. I always take a siesta after lunch. You'll hardly have time for a nap, I fear. You'll want to start, no doubt. I shall not follow till dusk. Hunting at night is so much more exciting than by day, don't you think? Au revoir,[19] Mr. Rainsford, au revoir."

General Zaroff, with a deep, courtly bow, strolled from the room.

From another door came Ivan. Under one arm he carried khaki hunting clothes, a haversack of food, a leather sheath containing a long-bladed hunting knife; his right hand rested on a cocked revolver thrust in the crimson sash about his waist. . . .

Rainsford had fought his way through the bush for two hours. "I must keep my nerve. I must keep my nerve," he said, through tight teeth.

He had not been entirely clear-headed when the château gates snapped shut behind him. His whole idea at first was to put distance between himself and General Zaroff, and, to this end, he had plunged along, spurred on by the sharp rowels of something very like panic. Now he had got a grip on himself, had stopped, and was taking stock of himself and the situation.

He saw that straight flight was futile; inevitably it would bring him face to face with the sea. He was in a picture with a frame of water, and his operations, clearly, must take place within that frame.

"I'll give him a trail to follow," muttered Rainsford, and he struck off from the rude path he had been following into the trackless wilderness. He executed a series of intricate loops; he doubled on his trail again and again, recalling all the lore of the fox hunt, and all the dodges of the fox. Night found him leg-weary, with hands and face lashed by the branches, on a thickly wooded ridge. He knew it would be insane to blunder on through the dark, even if he had the strength. His need for rest was <u>imperative</u>, and he thought, "I have played the fox; now I must play the cat of the fable." A big tree with a thick trunk and outspread branches was nearby, and, taking care to leave not the slightest mark, he climbed up into the crotch and, stretching out on one of the broad limbs, after a fashion, rested. Rest brought him new confidence and almost a feeling of security. Even so <u>zealous</u> a hunter as General Zaroff could not trace him there, he told himself; only the devil himself could follow that complicated trail through the jungle after dark. But perhaps the general was a devil—

AN APPREHENSIVE NIGHT crawled slowly by like a wounded snake, and sleep did not visit Rainsford, although the silence of a dead world was on the jungle. Toward morning, when a dingy gray was varnishing the sky, the cry of some startled bird focused Rainsford's attention in that direction. Something was coming through the bush, coming slowly, carefully, coming by the same winding way Rainsford had come. He flattened himself down on the limb, and through a screen of leaves almost as thick as tapestry, he watched. The thing that was approaching was a man.

It was General Zaroff. He made his way along with his eyes fixed in utmost concentration on the ground before him. He paused, almost beneath the tree, dropped to his knees, and studied the ground. Rainsford's impulse was to hurl himself down like a panther, but he saw

---

19. **au revoir** (ō′ rə-vwär′): goodbye; farewell until we meet again

---

WORDS TO KNOW	**imperative** (ĭm-pĕr′ə-tĭv) *adj.* absolutely necessary **zealous** (zĕl′əs) *adj.* intensely devoted and enthusiastic

that the general's right hand held something metallic—a small automatic pistol.

The hunter shook his head several times, as if he were puzzled. Then he straightened up and took from his case one of his black cigarettes; its pungent, incenselike smoke floated up to Rainsford's nostrils.

Rainsford held his breath. The general's eyes had left the ground and were traveling inch by inch up the tree. Rainsford froze there, every muscle tensed for a spring. But the sharp eyes of the hunter stopped before they reached the limb where Rainsford lay; a smile spread over his brown face. Very deliberately he blew a smoke ring into the air; then he turned his back on the tree and walked carelessly away, back along the trail he had come. The swish of the underbrush against his hunting boots grew fainter and fainter.

The pent-up air burst hotly from Rainsford's lungs. His first thought made him feel sick and numb. The general could follow a trail through the woods at night; he could follow an extremely difficult trail; he must have uncanny powers; only by the merest chance had the Cossack failed to see his quarry.

Rainsford's second thought was even more terrible. It sent a shudder of cold horror through his whole being. Why had the general smiled? Why had he turned back?

Rainsford did not want to believe what his reason told him was true, but the truth was as evident as the sun that had by now pushed through the morning mists. The general was playing with him! The general was saving him for another day's sport! The Cossack was the cat; he was the mouse. Then it was that Rainsford knew the full meaning of terror.

"I will not lose my nerve. I will not."

He slid down from the tree and struck off again into the woods. His face was set, and he

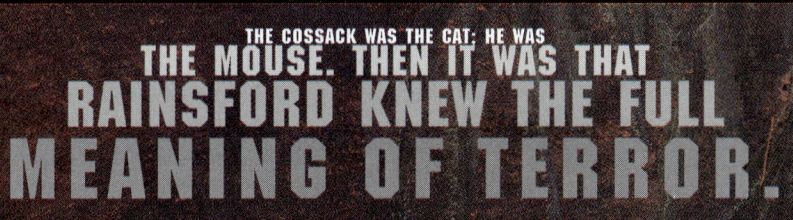

forced the machinery of his mind to function. Three hundred yards from his hiding place he stopped where a huge dead tree leaned precariously on a smaller, living one. Throwing off his sack of food, Rainsford took his knife from its sheath and began to work with all his energy.

The job was finished at last, and he threw himself down behind a fallen log a hundred feet away. He did not have to wait long. The cat was coming again to play with the mouse.

Following the trail with the sureness of a bloodhound came General Zaroff. Nothing escaped those searching black eyes, no crushed blade of grass, no bent twig, no mark, no matter how faint, in the moss. So intent was the Cossack on his stalking that he was upon the thing Rainsford had made before he saw it. His foot touched the protruding bough[20] that was

---

20. **protruding bough** (bou): a tree branch that extends or juts out.

WORDS TO KNOW

uncanny (ŭn-kăn'ē) *adj.* so remarkable as to seem supernatural

Art Note

The Voice of the Casuarina by Julio Larraz Like the scenes in many of Larraz's paintings, this scene conveys prior, and perhaps suspicious, activity. Here, a house is set before the sea and a dark, somber sky. A rope, or series of connected sheets, descends from a small window near the roof, hinting at a surreptitious escape in the middle of the night.

Reading the Art *How would you describe the mood of this painting? What aspects of the painting contribute to the mood?*

The Voice of the Casuarina (1985), Julio Larraz. Oil on canvas, 60½" × 60½", private collection, courtesy of Nohra Haime Gallery, New York.

the trigger. Even as he touched it, the general sensed his danger and leaped back with the agility of an ape. But he was not quite quick enough; the dead tree, delicately adjusted to rest on the cut living one, crashed down and struck the general a glancing blow on the shoulder as it fell; but for his alertness, he must have been smashed beneath it. He staggered, but he did not fall; nor did he drop his revolver. He stood there, rubbing his injured shoulder, and Rainsford, with fear again gripping his heart, heard the general's mocking laugh ring through the jungle.

"Rainsford," called the general, "if you are within sound of my voice, as I suppose you are, let me congratulate you. Not many men know how to make a Malay man-catcher. Luckily for me I, too, have hunted in Malacca.[21] You are proving interesting, Mr. Rainsford. I am going now to have my wound dressed; it's only a slight one. But I shall be back. I shall be back."

When the general, nursing his bruised

---

21. **Malay** (mə-lā′) . . . **Malacca** (mə-lăk′ə): The Malays are a people of southeast Asia. Malacca is a region they inhabit, just south of Thailand.

 Multicultural Perspectives

THE JAINS OF INDIA For the 4 million to 6 million followers of the Jain religion in India, hunting is strictly prohibited. Jainism, founded around 500 B.C., is one of the three oldest religions in India, the other two being Buddhism and Hinduism. The majority of Jains live in the northwestern Indian states of Gujarat, Maharashtra, and Rajasthan. There are five great vows in Jainism; the first vow, *ahimsa*, or nonviolence, is the cardinal principle of the religion. Ahimsa is a reverence for all forms of life, regardless of size or shape, including animals, insects, and even plants. The Jains classify all forms of life in a hierarchy, with humans, animals, and birds at the highest level, and plants at the lowest. It is impossible to live without killing any organism, so Jains subsist on the lowest form in the hierarchy—they are strict vegetarians.

shoulder, had gone, Rainsford took up his flight again. It was flight now, a desperate, hopeless flight, that carried him on for some hours. Dusk came, then darkness, and still he pressed on. The ground grew softer under his moccasins; the vegetation grew ranker, denser; insects bit him savagely. Then, as he stepped forward, his foot sank into the ooze. He tried to wrench it back, but the muck sucked viciously at his foot as if it were a giant leech. With a violent effort he tore his foot loose. He knew where he was now. Death Swamp and its quicksand.

His hands were tight closed as if his nerve were something tangible that someone in the darkness was trying to tear from his grip. The softness of the earth had given him an idea. He stepped back from the quicksand a dozen feet or so, and like some huge prehistoric beaver, he began to dig.

Rainsford had dug himself in in France when a second's delay meant death. That had been a placid pastime compared to his digging now. The pit grew deeper; when it was above his shoulders, he climbed out and from some hard saplings cut stakes and sharpened them to a fine point. These stakes he planted in the bottom of the pit with the points sticking up. With flying fingers he wove a rough carpet of weeds and branches, and with it he covered the mouth of the pit. Then, wet with sweat and aching with tiredness, he crouched behind the stump of a lightning-charred tree.

He knew his pursuer was coming; he heard the padding sound of feet on the soft earth, and the night breeze brought him the perfume of the general's cigarette. It seemed to Rainsford that the general was coming with unusual swiftness; he was not feeling his way along, foot by foot. Rainsford, crouching there, could not see the general, nor could he see the pit. He lived a year in a minute. Then he felt an impulse to cry aloud with joy, for he heard the sharp crackle of the breaking branches as the cover of the pit gave way; he heard the sharp scream of pain as the pointed stakes found their mark. He leaped up from his place of concealment. Then he cowered back. Three feet from the pit a man was standing, with an electric torch in his hand.

"You've done well, Rainsford," the voice of the general called. "Your Burmese tiger pit has claimed one of my best dogs. Again you score. I think, Mr. Rainsford, I'll see what you can do against my whole pack. I'm going home for a rest now. Thank you for a most amusing evening."

AT DAYBREAK RAINSFORD, lying near the swamp, was awakened by a sound that made him know that he had new things to learn about fear. It was a distant sound, faint and wavering, but he knew it. It was the baying of a pack of hounds.

Rainsford knew he could do one of two things. He could stay where he was and wait. That was suicide. He could flee. That was postponing the inevitable. For a moment he stood there, thinking. An idea that held a wild chance came to him, and, tightening his belt, he headed away from the swamp.

The baying of the hounds grew nearer, then still nearer, nearer, ever nearer. On a ridge Rainsford climbed a tree. Down a watercourse, not a quarter of a mile away, he could see the bush moving. Straining his eyes, he saw the lean figure of General Zaroff; just ahead of him, Rainsford made out another figure whose wide shoulders surged through the tall jungle weeds; it was the giant Ivan, and he seemed pulled forward by some unseen force; Rainsford knew that Ivan must be holding the pack in leash.

They would be on him any minute now. His mind worked frantically. He thought of a native

Literary Concept: THEME

HH Ask students to explain how Rainsford's feelings about animals have changed. *(Possible response: In the beginning of the story, Rainsford had no sympathy for his prey, even denying that they felt "the fear of pain and the fear of death." At this point, he understands how the quarry feel.)*

Literary Concept: IRONY

II Ask students to explain what is unexpected about Zaroff's thoughts. *(Possible response: He salves his ego by thinking that Rainsford has not played fairly when it is really he—armed with guns, dogs, and Ivan—who has cheated.)*

STRATEGIC READING FOR
Less-Proficient Readers

JJ Ask students to summarize what happens to Rainsford and Zaroff. *(Rainsford escapes from Zaroff by using old hunting tricks, and he eventually makes his way back to Zaroff's estate, where he kills the general.)* **Summarizing**

COMPREHENSION CHECK

1. How does Rainsford end up on "Ship-Trap Island"? *(He falls off the yacht on which he is sailing.)*
2. Who is Ivan? *(Zaroff's servant)*
3. Why has General Zaroff given up hunting animals? *(He is bored by the pursuit because it no longer presents a challenge.)*
4. Who becomes Zaroff's quarry when he refuses to participate in Zaroff's hunt? *(Rainsford)*
5. Who wins the game in the end? *(Rainsford)*

---

trick he had learned in Uganda. He slid down the tree. He caught hold of a springy young sapling, and to it he fastened his hunting knife, with the blade pointing down the trail; with a bit of wild grapevine he tied back the sapling. Then he ran for his life. The hounds raised their voices as they hit the fresh scent. Rainsford knew now how an animal at bay feels.

He had to stop to get his breath. The baying of the hounds stopped abruptly, and Rainsford's heart stopped, too. They must have reached the knife.

He shinned excitedly up a tree and looked back. His pursuers had stopped. But the hope that was in Rainsford's brain when he climbed died, for he saw in the shallow valley that General Zaroff was still on his feet. But Ivan was not. The knife, driven by the recoil of the springing tree, had not wholly failed.

Rainsford had hardly tumbled to the ground when the pack took up the cry again.

"Nerve, nerve, nerve!" he panted, as he dashed along. A blue gap showed between the trees dead ahead. Ever nearer drew the hounds. Rainsford forced himself on toward that gap. He reached it. It was the shore of the sea. Across a cove he could see the gloomy gray stone of the château. Twenty feet below him the sea rumbled and hissed. Rainsford hesitated. He heard the hounds. Then he leaped far out into the sea. . . .

When the general and his pack reached the place by the sea, the Cossack stopped. For some minutes he stood regarding the blue-green expanse of water. He shrugged his shoulders. Then he sat down, took a drink of brandy from a silver flask, lit a perfumed cigarette, and hummed a bit from *Madama Butterfly*.²²

General Zaroff had an exceedingly good dinner in his great paneled dining hall that evening. With it he had a bottle of Pol Roger and half a bottle of Chambertin. Two slight annoyances kept him from perfect enjoyment. One was the thought that it would be difficult to replace Ivan; the other was that his quarry had escaped him; of course the American hadn't played the game—so thought the general as he tasted his after-dinner liqueur. In his library he read, to soothe himself, from the works of Marcus Aurelius.²³ At ten he went up to his bedroom. He was deliciously tired, he said to himself, as he locked himself in. There was a little moonlight, so before turning on his light he went to the window and looked down at the courtyard. He could see the great hounds, and he called "Better luck another time" to them. Then he switched on the light.

A man, who had been hiding in the curtains of the bed, was standing there.

"Rainsford!" screamed the general. "How in God's name did you get here?"

"Swam," said Rainsford. "I found it quicker than walking through the jungle."

The general sucked in his breath and smiled. "I congratulate you," he said. "You have won the game."

Rainsford did not smile. "I am still a beast at bay," he said, in a low, hoarse voice. "Get ready, General Zaroff."

The general made one of his deepest bows. "I see," he said. "Splendid! One of us is to furnish a repast²⁴ for the hounds. The other will sleep in this very excellent bed. On guard, Rainsford. . . ."

He had never slept in a better bed, Rainsford decided. ❖

---

22. *Madama Butterfly:* a famous opera.
23. Marcus Aurelius (mär′kəs ô-rē′lē-əs): an ancient Roman emperor and philosopher.
24. **repast** (rĭ-păst′): meal.

806   UNIT SIX   PART 2: FATEFUL ENCOUNTERS

Assessment ✓ Option

INFORMAL ASSESSMENT You can informally assess students' understanding of the selection by having them imagine an alternative ending in which Zaroff is not killed but is captured by authorities and charged for his crimes. Students' writing could take the form of testimony by Zaroff telling what happened on the island from his point of view.

Rubric

3 Full Accomplishment Student writing reflects a full understanding of the events in the story and of the character of Zaroff.

2 Substantial Accomplishment Student writing shows a general understanding of the events but may not fully reflect the character of Zaroff.

1 Little or Partial Accomplishment Student writing displays little understanding of the events or of the character of Zaroff.

RESPONDING OPTIONS

FROM PERSONAL RESPONSE TO CRITICAL ANALYSIS

REFLECT
1. What do you think about the ending of this story? Jot down your thoughts in your notebook and share them in class.

RETHINK
2. How do you think Rainsford kills Zaroff? Explain what you based your inferences on.

3. Give Rainsford a rating, from 1 to 10, on each of the qualities listed in the chart you made for the Personal Connection on page 787. What other factors, if any, explain why he was able to beat Zaroff?

Thematic Link
4. Do you think that Rainsford's views on hunting have been permanently changed by his experience of being hunted? Why or why not?

Close Textual Reading
5. How do you judge Zaroff? Does he deserve to die?
Consider
- the first impression he makes
- his belief that "life is for the strong"
- his justification for hunting humans

6. How would you explain the meaning of the title of the story?

RELATE
Thematic Link
7. Early in the story Rainsford declares that "the world is made up of two classes—the hunters and the huntees." Do you agree? Why or why not?

Multimodal Learning
ANOTHER PATHWAY
Cooperative Learning

Work with a few classmates to compare the two hunters, Rainsford and Zaroff. Use a Venn diagram to record their similarities and differences. Note details such as morals, intelligence, and attitude toward hunting. In your group's opinion, do the two men have more similarities or more differences? Discuss your opinion with the rest of the class.

QUICKWRITES

1. Imagine that you are Rainsford and you have returned home. Write a **diary entry** in which you record what you learned from your experience with General Zaroff.

2. Describe the legend of Zaroff's island in an **article** for a sensationalistic tabloid.

📁 **PORTFOLIO** Save your writing. You may want to use it later as a springboard to a piece for your portfolio.

LITERARY CONCEPTS

Create a line graph to show the different amounts of tension—**suspense**—that you felt as you read the story. On the horizontal axis, list the major events of the plot, beginning with "Rainsford falls overboard." On the vertical axis at the left, make a suspense scale extending from 1 (least suspenseful) at the bottom to 10 (most suspenseful) at the top. Then place a dot on the graph above each event and across from the number that indicates your level of suspense at that point in the story. Finally, draw a line to connect the dots, and compare your graph with those of some of your classmates.

THE MOST DANGEROUS GAME **807**

From Personal Response to Critical Analysis

1. Accept all reasonable responses.
2. Accept all reasonable, well-supported responses.
3. Ratings will vary. Students will probably give him very high marks for cleverness, mental toughness, and physical condition. They may note that Zaroff's desire to extend the hunt helped Rainsford to survive longer.
4. Most students will say that Rainsford's views have been permanently changed, because he "felt the terror of death" that animals feel.
5. Some students may say that according to Zaroff's own rules, Rainsford is justified in killing him, or that Rainsford had no other choice because he couldn't trust the general. Others might say that despite Zaroff's behavior, Rainsford had no right to kill the general—that instead, he should have brought him to justice.
6. Most students will realize that the word *game* carries double a meaning: it refers to the game Zaroff is playing, and it refers to the quarry, or "big game," that Zaroff hunts.
7. Accept all reasonable, well-supported responses.

Another Pathway

Cooperative Learning Make sure all students are familiar with Venn diagrams.

Rubric
3 Full Accomplishment Students' diagrams indicate the similarities and the differences between the men.
2 Substantial Accomplishment Students create diagrams but omit some important characteristics.
1 Little or Partial Accomplishment Students have difficulty creating diagrams that compare the men's characteristics.

Literary Concepts

Events and levels of suspense noted on students' graphs will vary, depending on students' reactions to the story. Encourage them to discuss why they gave specific events the ratings they did, where in the story the suspense is at its peak, and whether they had expected Rainsford to survive in the end.

QuickWrites

1. Suggest that students have Rainsford address whether he will continue to hunt, how he feels about killing Zaroff, and what he has gained from the experience of being "the hunted."
2. Explain to students that tabloids present news and stories in a sensational way in order to grab the reader's attention. Suggest that students examine the reporting style of a particular tabloid. Interested students may also want to create a tabloid-style headline for their article.

Journal Writing, pp. 28–41

Words to Know

Exercise A
1. uncanny
2. droll
3. scruple
4. elude
5. condone

Exercise B
1. Antonyms
2. Antonyms
3. Synonyms
4. Antonyms
5. Synonyms
6. Antonyms
7. Synonyms
8. Synonyms
9. Antonyms
10. Synonyms

Reteaching/Reinforcement
- *Unit Six Resource Book*, p. 42

CONTEMPORARY CONNECTION
The Photo Safari Naturalists, photographers, and others—in the name of animal preservation and armed only with a camera—sometimes place themselves in dangerous situations because of their fascination with big-game animals. These images illustrate the photo safari.

Side A, Frame 49532

Across the Curriculum

Zoology Students may work with a partner to research the Cape buffalo, also known as the African buffalo. Partners can use such reference sources as encyclopedias, zoology books, and books on game hunting. Students may want to search for an Internet discussion group on hunting, to find out why the Cape buffalo is so feared by hunters.

Literary Links

Encourage students to compare "The Cask of Amontillado" and "The Most Dangerous Game" in terms of the main character and the level of suspense. Ask students these questions:

- Did they believe that either Fortunato or Rainsford would survive?
- With which character did they sympathize more—Rainsford being hunted by Zaroff or the drunken Fortunato being led to his doom? Why?

ALTERNATIVE ACTIVITIES
Create an **illustrated map** of Zaroff's island. Include the cliffs, the château, Death Swamp, and other features. Consider using a computer graphics program to help you prepare the map.

THE WRITER'S STYLE
"The Most Dangerous Game" is rich in **figurative language**. Find several examples of similes, metaphors, and personification involving animal imagery.

Multimodal Learning

ACROSS THE CURRICULUM
Zoology A Cape buffalo once nearly killed Zaroff, and Rainsford considers the species "the most dangerous of all big game." Research the Cape buffalo, explaining how it is similar to and different from other kinds of buffalo. Do you agree that it is the most dangerous animal to hunt?

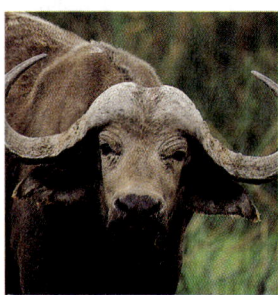

WORDS TO KNOW
EXERCISE A Review the Words to Know at the bottom of the selection pages. Then, on your paper, fill in each blank with the vocabulary word that best completes the sentence.

1. The children's nurse Mary Poppins could float in the air and talk to animals. She was quite the _____ nanny.
2. When trying to cast the _____ role, a director wanted an actor who could play a strange, funny character.
3. After you've misbehaved, if your conscience bothers you only about one-fourth of the time, you should quadruple your _____s.
4. My aunt's children bother me when they visit, so I hide in the cellar to _____ her brood.
5. "This is a quiet building," said the landlord, eyeing my large instrument case. "I will not _____ a trombone!"

EXERCISE B Identify the relationship between each pair of words by writing *Synonyms* or *Antonyms*.

1. solicitously—indifferently
2. affable—disagreeable
3. tangible—physical
4. quarry—trapper
5. imperative—required
6. disarming—offensive
7. zealous—passionate
8. stamina—vigor
9. amenity—crudeness
10. deplorable—distressing

RICHARD CONNELL

1893–1949

An author of a number of stories, Richard Connell is a prime example of a prolific writer remembered for just a single work. After graduating from Harvard University, Connell worked for newspapers and advertising agencies before becoming a fiction writer in 1919. His books—novels and short-story collections—appeared in the 1920s and 1930s and have now largely disappeared, even from library shelves. Only "The Most Dangerous Game" survives, both as a classic story in itself and as an inspiration for countless movie plots involving one-on-one, fateful encounters.

OTHER WORKS *Ironies* *Extended Reading*

LASERLINKS
• CONTEMPORARY CONNECTION

808 UNIT SIX PART 2: FATEFUL ENCOUNTERS

Alternative Activities
Students may want to obtain a book on cartography to learn about the techniques of mapmaking. Encourage students to include legends and symbols in their map and to experiment with different techniques for indicating the island's varied terrain.

The Writer's Style
Students may point to any of the numerous examples, including the following: "It's [the night's] like moist black velvet" *(simile)*; "sea . . . as flat as a plate-glass window" *(simile)*; "The lights of the yacht became faint and ever-vanishing fireflies" *(metaphor)*; "the sea licked greedy lips" *(personification)*; "An apprehensive night crawled slowly by like a wounded snake" *(personification/simile)*.

📄 **The Writer's Craft**
Types of Figurative Language, pp. 413–414

PREVIEWING

NONFICTION

Not to Go with the Others
John Hersey

Activating Prior Knowledge
PERSONAL CONNECTION
The following selection takes place in a small Nazi concentration camp near the end of World War II. People were being held in this camp temporarily, awaiting transfer to a larger camp. Think of what you know about concentration camps. With a small group of classmates, fill in a chart, like the one shown, with some information about such camps: what countries they were located in, some reasons for holding people there, and what activity went on inside the camps. Then discuss your ideas with the rest of the class.

Nazi Concentration Camps	
Locations	
Reasons for Holding People	
Camp Activities	

Building Background
HISTORICAL CONNECTION
In 1933, the Nazis—short for the National Socialist German Workers' Party—led by Adolf Hitler, came to power in Germany, with plans to control all of Europe. Finally in 1939, Germany invaded Poland, and the Second World War was underway.

One of the most tragic aspects of Nazi domination in Europe was the imprisonment in concentration camps of millions of civilians—mostly Jews, Gypsies, political opponents, and religious leaders. Prisoners were held in more than 30 such camps located in Germany and neighboring countries. More than 10 million people—6 million of them Jews—were killed in the camps by overwork, starvation, or outright murder.

By early 1945 the Russians and other Allied Forces were closing in on German troops in Poland and Germany itself. At this time, John Hersey was working in Moscow as a reporter for *Time* magazine. A few days after the Russians drove the Germans from the Polish city of Łódź (lōōj), Hersey toured the area and was told this story in a farmhouse by Frantizek Zaremski (frän'tĭ-zĕk' zä-rĕm'skē), the survivor who lived it.

Prisoners at Buchenwald concentration camp in Germany.

Active Reading / Setting a Purpose
READING CONNECTION

Inferring Motivation In this journalistic account of Zaremski's survival in a concentration camp during the last days of the war, Hersey gives very little information about Zaremski himself—his thoughts or feelings. As you read the selection, try to determine Zaremski's reasons for making the key decisions that mean the difference between life and death.

Using Your Reading Log Use your reading log to record your responses to the questions inserted throughout the selection. Also, jot down other thoughts and feelings that come to you as you read.

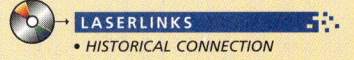
• HISTORICAL CONNECTION

OVERVIEW

Objectives
- To understand and appreciate a true-life story of one man's survival during the Nazi Holocaust
- To enrich reading by using active reading strategies
- To identify and understand tone
- To express understanding of the selection through a choice of writing forms, including an expository paragraph and a reflection
- To extend understanding of the selection through a variety of multimodal and cross-curricular activities

Skills

LITERARY CONCEPTS
- Tone
- Author's purpose

READING SKILLS/ STRATEGIES
- Inferring motivation
- Active reading: clarify

THE WRITER'S STYLE
- Using short sentences to build suspense

GRAMMAR
- Past perfect tense

HISTORICAL CONNECTION
A Soldier Remembers World War II
Many American soldiers aided in the liberation of the concentration camps in Germany after World War II. In this short film, students can hear the story of this effort as told by one of the soldiers who was there.

Side A, Frame 45521

PRINT AND MEDIA RESOURCES

UNIT SIX RESOURCE BOOK
Strategic Reading: Literature, p. 45
Vocabulary SkillBuilder, p. 46

GRAMMAR MINI-LESSONS
Transparencies, p. 30
Copymasters, p. 30

WRITING MINI-LESSONS
Transparencies, p. 50

ACCESS FOR STUDENTS ACQUIRING ENGLISH
Selection Summaries
Reading Support

FORMAL ASSESSMENT
Selection Test, pp. 145–146
 Test Generator

 AUDIO LIBRARY
See Reference Card

 LASERLINKS
Historical Connection

INTERNET RESOURCES
McDougal Littell Literature Center at http://www.hmco.com/mcdougal/lit

THE LANGUAGE OF LITERATURE **TEACHER'S EDITION** 809

NOT TO GO WITH

SUMMARY

During World War II, Frantizek Zaremski was arrested by the Nazis in Poland and forced to do slave labor as a carpenter. When the Russians broke through the German lines, the Nazis shipped Zaremski and other prisoners to a prison in Poland. One evening, the prisoners were marched in groups to a loft and told to run in pairs into the loft. When they did, SS men shot them. Zaremski pretended to fall dead. More prisoners fell dead on top of him. Later, the SS men searched among the bodies for survivors and shot them with pistols. Then they set fire to the building. Some prisoners who were still alive were shot trying to escape from the burning building. Zaremski survived the fire by hiding in a water tank. When the fire and shooting ended, Zaremski and six others left the building. The others tried to escape by climbing the wall; all were shot. Zaremski hid in a box in a shed. SS men inspected the shed three times but never found him. The Nazis eventually left, and Zaremski came out of hiding.

Thematic Link: *Fateful Encounters*
Zaremski's fateful encounter with SS men leads to a death-defying struggle.

CUSTOMIZING FOR
Students Acquiring English

- Use **ACCESS FOR STUDENTS ACQUIRING ENGLISH**, *Reading Support*.
- One or more students in the class may be immigrants who have experienced political violence or who know relatives who have. Be sensitive to this possibility.

STRATEGIC READING FOR
Less-Proficient Readers

Read aloud the first three paragraphs, and make sure students understand how and why Zaremski got into this situation.

Set a Purpose Have students read on to find out what threats Zaremski faces and how he handles each one.

Use **UNIT SIX RESOURCE BOOK**, p. 45, for guidance in reading the selection.

IN THE THIRD YEAR OF the war, Frantizek Zaremski was arrested by the invaders on a charge of spreading underground literature—specifically, for carrying about his person a poem a friend from Gdynia[1] had given him, which began:

Sleep, beloved Hitler, planes will come by night . . .

After he had spent six weeks of a three-year sentence for this crime in the Gestapo[2] prison at Inowroczon, Zaremski was sent to Kalice[3] to do carpentry. By bad luck, at the time when his term expired, the Russians had broken through at the Vistula,[4] and his captors, instead of releasing him, took him, in their general panic, to the transfer camp for Polish political prisoners at Rodogoszcz,[5] where he was placed in Hall Number Four with nine hundred men. Altogether there were between two and three thousand men and women—no Jews, only "Aryan"[6] Poles suspected or convicted of political activity—in the prison.

A Late in the evening of Wednesday, January 17, 1945, three days before Lódź[5] was to fall to the Russians, all the prisoners were gathered on the third and fourth floors of the main building, even those who were sick, and there they all lay down on wooden bunks and floors to try to sleep. At about two in the morning guards came and ordered the inmates to get up for roll call.

They divided the prisoners into groups of about twenty each and lined up the groups in pairs. Zaremski was in the second group. SS[7] men led it down concrete stairs in a brick-walled stairwell at one end of the building and halted it on a landing of the stairway, near a door opening into a large loft on the second floor. The first group had apparently been led down to the ground floor.

Someone gave an order that the prisoners should run in pairs into the loft as fast as they could. When the first pairs of Zaremski's group

---

1. **Gdynia** (gə-dĭn′ē-ə): a city on Poland's northern coast.
2. **Gestapo** (gə-stä′pō): the Nazi secret police force.
3. **Inowroczon** (ē-nəv-rô′zôn) . . . **Kalice** (kä′lĭsh): more commonly spelled *Inowroclaw* and *Kalisz*, cities in central Poland.
4. **Vistula** (vĭs′chə-lə): Vistula River, in central Poland.
5. **Rodogoszcz** (rô-dô-gôzh′): more commonly spelled *Radogoszcz*, a northern suburb of Lódź.
6. **"Aryan"** (âr′ē-ən): The Nazis glorified northern European peoples who were tall, light-skinned, and blond-haired. They called people who fit this description Aryans and claimed that non-Aryans—such as Jews, some eastern Europeans, and other minority groups—were inferior.
7. **SS:** an elite military guard unit of the Nazi party that ran the concentration camps; abbreviation of the German *Schutzstaffel*.

810 UNIT SIX PART 2: FATEFUL ENCOUNTERS

WORDS TO KNOW

dispatch (dĭ-spăch′) *v.* to put to death speedily and without ceremony; kill (p. 811)
ensue (ĕn-sōō′) *v.* to take place next; follow (p. 811)
immersed (ĭ-mûrst′) *adj.* covered completely in a liquid; submerged **immerse** *v.* (p. 812)
pretense (prē′tĕns′) *n.* the act of pretending; a false appearance or action intended to deceive (p. 811)
prostrate (prŏs′trāt′) *adj.* lying on the ground; overcome (p. 811)

THE OTHERS
John Hersey

ran in, SS men with their backs to the wall inside the room began to shoot at them from behind. Zaremski's turn came. He ran in terror. A bullet burned through his trouser leg. Another grazed his thigh. He fell down and feigned death.

CLARIFY

What might have happened if Zaremski had not pretended to be dead?
Using a Reading Log

Others, from Zaremski's and later groups, ran into the hall and were shot and fell dead or wounded on top of Zaremski and those who had gone first. At one time Zaremski heard the Polish national anthem being sung somewhere.

Finally the running and shooting ended, and there <u>ensued</u> some shooting on the upper floors, perhaps of people who had refused to run downstairs.

SS men with flashlights waded among the bodies, shining lights in the faces of the <u>prostrate</u> victims. Any wounded who moaned or moved, or any whose eyes reacted when the shafts of light hit their faces, were <u>dispatched</u> with pistol shots. Somehow Zaremski passed the test of <u>pretense</u>.

WORDS TO KNOW
ensue (ĕn-sōō′) v. to take place next; follow
prostrate (prŏs′trāt′) adj. lying on the ground; overcome
dispatch (dĭ-spăch′) v. to put to death speedily and without ceremony; kill
pretense (prē′tĕns′) n. the act of pretending; a false appearance or action intended to deceive

811

Literary Concept: AUTHOR'S PURPOSE

A Ask students what details suggest that the author wants to inform readers about what happened in the final days of World War II. *(He gives dates of historical events and traces causes and effects.)* Have students also look, as they read, for details showing that the author wanted to tell a suspenseful story.

Active Reading: CLARIFY

B If Zaremski hadn't pretended to be dead, the soldiers would have shot him again.

Linking to History

C In the late 1800s, Poland was a weak country surrounded by powerful neighbors: Austria and Prussia (both German states) and Russia. These governments divided up Polish lands among themselves, and there was no Polish nation again until World War I ended, in 1918. When Germany invaded Poland in the 1930s, the Germans claimed to be retaking land that was rightfully theirs. Having just regained their nation, Poles were fiercely patriotic.

Literary Concept: TONE

D Ask students to list some synonyms for *dispatched*. *(Possible responses: killed, murdered, slaughtered)* Ask them what tone, or feeling, the synonyms suggest. *(angry, outraged)* Then ask what tone the word *dispatched* conveys, and have them note the contrast. *(Possible response: cool, objective, dispassionate)*

Mini-Lesson The Writer's Style

SENTENCE VARIETY: USING SHORT SENTENCES TO BUILD SUSPENSE Point out to students that in many places in this selection, Hersey uses a series of short sentences. Tell them that by doing so, he helps to build suspense. Explain that short sentences force the reader to stop after each one and wonder "Then what happened?" Have a volunteer read aloud the sentences in the <u>highlighted</u> section on this page.

Application Have students choose their favorite suspenseful scene from a story. Then have them write a scene of their own based on it. Tell them to use a series of short sentences to build reader interest at the most suspenseful part of the scene. Have students share their work and discuss the effect of short, staccato sentences.

Reteaching/Reinforcement
• *Writing Mini-Lessons* transparencies, p. 50

 The Writer's Craft

How Can I Vary My Sentences? pp. 416–418

THE LANGUAGE OF LITERATURE **TEACHER'S EDITION** **811**

Critical Thinking:
MAKING INFERENCES

E Ask students what they can infer about Zaremski's character from the way he behaves during the fire. *(Possible responses: He is resourceful, clever, compassionate, determined to survive, and able to endure pain.)*

Active Reading: **CLARIFY**

F Discuss the comments students have at this point. You may wish to use the following model to give students an idea of what they might be thinking about.

Think-Aloud Model *When I got to this section, I thought, What can he possibly do now? If he leaves the building, he'll certainly be shot. But if he stays, he's likely to die in the fire.*

Literary Concept: TONE

G Ask students to imagine the horror Zaremski must have felt in this situation. Ask whether they feel the author's matter-of-fact tone adequately suggests that horror. *(Answers will vary.)*

Literary Concept:
AUTHOR'S PURPOSE

H Ask students to explain why the author tells of the first three men's attempted escape and then of the next three men's attempt, which leaves only Zaremski. *(Possible responses: to add suspense; to show how luck has so far been a factor in Zaremski's staying alive; to keep the reader guessing as to whether or not Zaremski will survive)*

Active Reading: **QUESTION**

I Possible responses: Students might conclude that Zaremski was afraid. Some may say that he acted intuitively after seeing the other men get killed—that maybe he wanted to wait and see if he would have a better chance for escape later.

As dawn began to break, Zaremski heard the iron doors of the main building being locked, and he heard some sort of grenades or bombs being thrown into the lowest hall and exploding there; they seemed to him to make only smoke, but they may have been incendiaries.[8] Later, in any case, the ground floor began to burn. Perhaps benzine or petrol[9] had been poured around. Zaremski was still lying among the bodies of others.

There were several who were still alive, and they began jumping out of the burning building, some from windows on the upper stories. A few broke through a skylight to the roof, tied blankets from the prisoners' bunks into long ropes and let themselves down outside. Zaremski, now scurrying about the building, held back to see what would happen. Those who jumped or climbed down were shot at leisure in the camp enclosure by SS men in the turrets on the walls, and Zaremski decided to try to stay inside.

On the fourth floor, at the top of the reinforced concrete staircase, in the bricked stairwell at the end of the building, Zaremski found the plant's water tank, and for a time he and others poured water over the wounded lying on the wooden floors in the main rooms. Later Zaremski took all his clothes off, soaked them in the tank, and put them back on. He lay down and kept pouring water over himself. He put a soaked blanket around his head.

CLARIFY
What is Zaremski's predicament at this point?
Using a Reading Log

The tank was a tall one, separated from the main room by the stairwell's brick wall, and when the fire began to eat through the wooden floor of the fourth story and the heat in the stairwell grew unbearable, Zaremski climbed up and got right into the water in the tank. He stayed immersed there all day long. Every few minutes he could hear shots from the wall turrets. He heard floors of the main halls fall and heard the side walls collapse. The staircase shell and the concrete stairs remained standing.

It was evening before the shooting and the fire died down. When he felt sure both had ended, Zaremski pulled himself out of the tank and lay awhile on the cement floor beside it. Then, his strength somewhat restored, he made his way down the stairs, and on the way he found six others who were wounded but could walk.

The seven went outside. Dusk. All quiet. They thought the Germans had left, and they wanted to climb the wall and escape. The first three climbed up and dropped away in apparent safety, but then the lights flashed on in the turrets and bursts of firing broke out. Three of the remaining four decided to take their chances at climbing out after total darkness; they did not know whether the first three had been killed or had escaped. Only Zaremski decided to stay.

QUESTION
Why do you think Zaremski held back?
Using a Reading Log

The three climbed, but this time the lights came sooner, and the guards killed all three while they were still scaling the wall.

Zaremski crept into the camp's storehouse in a separate building. Finding some damp blankets, he wrapped them around himself and climbed into a big box, where he stayed all night. Once during the night he heard steps outside the building, and in the early morning he heard walking again. This time the footsteps approached the storeroom door. The door opened. The steps entered. Through the cracks

---
8. **incendiaries** (ĭn-sĕn′dē-ĕr′ēz): chemical bombs that produce intensely hot fire when exploded.
9. **benzine** (bĕn′zēn′) . . . **petrol** (pĕt′rəl): highly flammable liquid fuels.

WORDS TO KNOW
immersed (ĭ-mûrsd′) *adj.* covered completely in a liquid; submerged **immerse** *v.*

812

Mini-Lesson — Grammar

USING THE PAST PERFECT TENSE Tell students that the past perfect tense is used to show an action that preceded another past action. Explain that the past perfect tense is formed by using the helping verb *had* with the past participle. Point out the highlighted sentence on this page as an example.

Application Have students fill in a past perfect verb to complete each sentence.

1. After he _____ six weeks at one concentration camp, Zaremski was sent to another one. *(had stayed)*
2. By the time his prison term expired, the Russians _____ through German lines. *(had crossed)*
3. Zaremski told John Hersey the true story of how he _____ a horrifying experience. *(had endured)*

Reteaching/Reinforcement
- *Grammar Handbook*, anthology p. 945
- *Grammar Mini-Lessons* transparencies p. 30, copymasters p. 30

Perfect Tenses, pp. 604–605

812 THE LANGUAGE OF LITERATURE TEACHER'S EDITION

Angstausbruch III [Outburst of fear] (1939), Paul Klee. Kunstmuseum Bern, Paul-Klee-Stiftung, Bern, Switzerland. (Inv. F 127). Copyright © 1996 Artists Rights Society (ARS), New York/VG Bild-Kunst, Bonn, Germany.

Art Note

Angstausbruch III [Outburst of Fear] by Paul Klee This is one of the paintings that Paul Klee (1879–1940) completed in the last year of his life, while he was very ill and living in exile in Switzerland. Many of his final paintings depict fragmented figures like this one. Notice how the parts of the body completely fill the space, adding a feeling of claustrophobia to the work.

Reading the Art *What emotions besides fear do you think this work conveys? Does it express sadness? tenderness? anger?*

CUSTOMIZING FOR
Multiple Learning Styles

Spatial or Graphic Learners Ask students what images stick in their mind as they read about Zaremski's horrifying experience. Then ask what images they might draw to represent those experiences or to represent the general emotion of fear.

Mini-Lesson Literary Concepts

REVIEWING AUTHOR'S PURPOSE Draw on the chalkboard the web shown on the right, and use it to remind students that there are four main purposes for writing: to express oneself, to inform or explain, to persuade, and to entertain. Point out that sometimes the author has more than one purpose in mind.

Application Ask students to copy the web into their notebook. Then have them work in pairs, using the information from the web, to discuss what purpose or purposes the author had in mind when writing this story.

Literary Concept: TONE

J Ask students whether they think the author's matter-of-fact tone adds to or detracts from the emotion of this moment. *(Answers will vary.)*

STRATEGIC READING FOR
Less-Proficient Readers

K Have students list in order all the decisions Zaremski made that helped to keep him alive. *(pretended to be dead when shot, stayed in the burning building and hid in the water tank, didn't climb over the wall with the others, hid in a box and held the lid shut)* Noting Sequence of Events

CUSTOMIZING FOR
Gifted and Talented Students

Tell students that Hersey based this account on an interview he had with Zaremski three days after the man escaped. Have students write a transcript of questions Hersey might have asked and the replies Zaremski might have given.

COMPREHENSION CHECK
Have students indicate whether each of the following statements are true or false.
1. When Zaremski was shot, he pretended to be dead. *(true)*
2. When the Nazis set fire to the building, he escaped. *(false)*
3. When he hid in a box, the Nazis found him. *(false)*

INSIGHT
1. How would you paraphrase each reflection? *(Accept all reasonable responses.)*
2. Which reflection do you think would make the best epigraph, or opening quotation, for this selection? *(Answers will vary.)*

---

of the box Zaremski sensed that the beam of a flashlight was probing the room. Zaremski could hear box tops opening and slamming and a foot kicking barrels. He held the lid of his box from the inside. Steps came near, a hand tried the lid, but Zaremski held tight, and the searcher must have decided the box was locked or nailed down. The footsteps went away.

Later two others came at different times and inspected the room, but neither tried Zaremski's box; the third hunter locked the door from the outside.

Much later Zaremski heard a car start and drive away.

Much later still—some time on the nineteenth of January in the year of victory—Zaremski heard the Polish language being spoken, even by the voices of women and children. He jumped out of the box and broke the window of the storehouse and climbed out to his countrymen. ❖

INSIGHT

REFLECTIONS ON THE HOLOCAUST

We weren't organized, you know. That was the trouble. No leaders, no place to go. The last minute, some people fled, but everyone, if he fled, he fled by himself, not knowing where you go, what you're going to do.

—Faye Porter
(A native of Poland, Faye Porter escaped a Nazi roundup in 1942 by hiding in a barn and crawling into a nearby forest that night.)

I don't talk to my family about the past. There's no point of talking. An American cannot understand it. The only person who can understand is one who was there. I try to tell my kids other things, like not to be cowards. My son, he's eighteen; he wouldn't let anybody beat him up.

—Henry Abramowicz
(A native of Lódź, 11-year-old Henry Abramowicz escaped into Russia in 1941 with his parents; he settled in the United States in 1954, married here, and had five children.)

I believe in the sun even when it is not shining.
I believe in love even when feeling it not.
I believe in God even when He is silent.

—inscription on the walls of a cellar in Cologne, Germany, where Jews hid from Nazis

FROM PERSONAL RESPONSE TO CRITICAL ANALYSIS

REFLECT
1. What impressions and thoughts did this selection leave you with? Jot down your reactions in your notebook and share some of them with a classmate.

RETHINK
2. How do you explain the key decisions that Zaremski made? In your opinion, was his survival due primarily to his judgment or to luck, or both? Explain.

3. What do you think motivated the SS men to kill the prisoners?
   Consider
   Close Textual Reading
   • the role of the SS men in the concentration camp
   • the status of the war at this point
   • what survivors might be able to do

Thematic Link
4. Which of Zaremski's close calls created the most lasting impression on you? Explain why the episode impressed you or draw a sketch from the description and share it with the class.

RELATE
5. Look again at the chart you filled out for the Personal Connection activity on page 809. What, if anything, did Zaremski's experience teach you about concentration camps?

Multimodal Learning
ANOTHER PATHWAY
Cooperative Learning

The right decision at the right time accounts for Zaremski's survival. With a small group, create a flow chart to analyze his decisions. For each danger, list the threat, the choices he has, and his decision. Could he have made another decision at any point and still survived? Discuss your opinions with the other groups.

QUICKWRITES

1. Think about the meaning of the title of this selection. In an **expository paragraph** or two, explain what the title suggests about the theme of the selection. Give examples from the selection to support your explanation.

2. Think about the quotations in the Insight selection. What do you think Zaremski would add to these comments? Write the **reflection** that you think Zaremski would pass on to his children.

📁 **PORTFOLIO** *Save your writing. You may want to use it later as a springboard to a piece for your portfolio.*

LITERARY CONCEPTS

Tone is the attitude a writer takes toward a subject. In this selection, Hersey tells a remarkable story in an unemotional, very matter-of-fact tone. In effect, he allows the story to speak for itself, without any commentary or buildup on his part. Do you think the tone is an effective one for this story? Explain your answer.

CONCEPT REVIEW: Author's Purpose In this article, Hersey gives no commentary that might reveal his purpose in writing. The reader must infer the author's purpose. What do you think was Hersey's purpose in writing this article?

NOT TO GO WITH THE OTHERS **815**

From Personal Response to Critical Analysis

1. Accept all reasonable responses.
2. Possible responses: Students who say his survival was due to luck may point to his having been lucky enough not to have died immediately when shot, to his having survived the fire, and to the fact that he was not found in his hiding place. Those who say his survival was due to sensible thinking may cite the following decisions he made: to feign death; not to jump out of the window during the fire, to hide in the water tank, not to go over the wall, and to hide until the Nazis left.
3. Possible response: Students may say that the SS men knew the war would soon be over and didn't want prisoners left to testify against them. Others might feel that the SS men were so used to murdering people that they killed from habit.
4. Accept all reasonable responses.
5. Accept all reasonable, well-supported responses.

Another Pathway

Cooperative Learning Suggest that students reread the selection together, listing each decision Zaremski made and deciding what other choices he had. Then have them share their opinions of each decision. One student can correct any mistaken impressions of Zaremski's situation. Another can list other courses of action Zaremski might have taken.

Rubric

3 Full Accomplishment Students accurately outline Zaremski's decisions in a flow chart and discuss realistic options.

2 Substantial Accomplishment Students outline Zaremski's decisions, but options they discuss may be unrealistic.

1 Little or Partial Accomplishment Students cannot analyze Zaremski's decisions or options.

Literary Concepts

Some students may say the matter-of-fact tone heightens the sense of horror and suspense. Some may wish the author had described Zaremski's emotions and inner conflicts. Others may say the objective tone makes the emotional impact of the story easier to take.

Concept Review: Author's Purpose Some students may say that Hersey intended to write a suspenseful story that would inform readers about the terrible atrocities that people confronted during the Nazis' rule. Others may say that he wanted to suspensefully relate how Zaremski was able to survive.

QuickWrites

1. Have students consider why the decisions were difficult for Zaremski and would also be difficult under ordinary circumstances.
2. Have students consider Zaremski's character traits (see annotation E before students respond). Have them give reasons for their selection.

Personal Response, pp. 238–249

Words to Know

1. c
2. c
3. a
4. b
5. a

Reteaching/Reinforcement
- *Unit Six Resource Book,* p. 46

Across the Curriculum

History Cooperative Learning To help students work cooperatively, suggest that one or two of them locate and obtain encyclopedia articles and books on this subject. (Be sure to urge them to contact the U.S. Holocaust Memorial Museum in Washington, D.C., for information.) Another student can make a chart listing all the information to be found. Students can share the reference books and write on the chart each fact they find. One or two students can prepare time lines, graphs, or charts, and another student can present the information orally to the class.

Art Connection

Possible responses: the horror of being surrounded by death; the claustrophobic feeling of being trapped in a tight space, such as the water tank

JOHN HERSEY

John Hersey's novel *A Bell for Adano,* based on his observations of the American occupation of Italy during World War II, was awarded a Pulitzer Prize in 1945.

Multimodal Learning
ACROSS THE CURRICULUM

History Cooperative Learning Research one of the major concentration camps in Poland, such as Auschwitz, Majdanek, or Treblinka. Find out where the camp was located, when it was established, what kinds of people were taken there, how many prisoners died, how many survived, and what conditions were like. Present your findings to the class. You might use your computer to create headings and text for a visual of time lines, graphs, or charts to accompany your oral report.

ART CONNECTION

The painting on page 813 is by Paul Klee, a Swiss-born artist who studied and lived most of his life in Germany. In 1933, because the Nazis condemned the "modernism" of his art, he was forced to flee Germany. What aspects of Zaremski's experience are foreshadowed in Klee's 1939 *Outbreak of Fear III*?

WORDS TO KNOW

For each boldfaced word, write the letter of the situation that best demonstrates its meaning.

1. **dispatch**
   a. a dog gnawing on a bone
   b. a judge hearing a case in traffic court
   c. a person whacking flies with a swatter

2. **immersed**
   a. a box of tea on a cupboard shelf
   b. a tea kettle whistling on the stove
   c. a tea bag soaking in a cup of hot water

3. **pretense**
   a. a spy working undercover
   b. a baseball player warming up
   c. a teacher reading a story aloud

4. **ensue**
   a. children and games
   b. sunset and darkness
   c. teachers and students

5. **prostrate**
   a. a person sleeping
   b. a person showering
   c. a person eating breakfast

JOHN HERSEY

1914–1993

For John Hersey, writing was a moral mission. He wrote to jar people from an unthinking acceptance of the horrors of the Holocaust, racism, nuclear weapons, and the lack of concern for individuals in a technological age. He strongly believed in the value of education and democracy, and he thought of writers as educators for social change. Hersey called literature "the only hope man has of rising above . . . his foul nest of murder, war, greed, madness, and cruelty."

Hersey's nonfiction book *Hiroshima* portrays the experiences of six survivors of the atomic bomb dropped on that city on August 6, 1945. At the time, the work so deeply impressed people that the Book-of-the-Month Club gave away copies, citing the importance of the story to the human race. In his novel *The Wall,* Hersey told of the Nazis' killing of 500,000 Jews in the Warsaw ghetto of Poland.

Hersey was born in Tientsin, China, the son of American missionaries. In 1924, his family returned to the United States. From 1937 until 1945, he was a correspondent for *Time* magazine, principally reporting war news in China, Japan, and Europe. When Hersey met Zaremski in Poland a few days after his escape, the man "was obviously suffering from shock. . . . The skin of his face was drawn tight over the bones and cartilage." At times during the interview, Hersey thought Zaremski would faint.

OTHER WORKS *A Bell for Adano, Here to Stay*

Extended Reading

816 UNIT SIX PART 2: FATEFUL ENCOUNTERS

REFLECTING ON THEME
What Do You Think?

Have students think about the experience they related before they began reading the selections in Part 2. Have them tell what they learned from Zaremski's behavior that they could have applied to the experience they related earlier.

PREVIEWING

FICTION

My Wonder Horse/Mi Caballo Mago

Sabine R. Ulibarrí (o͞o′lē-bä-rē′)

Activating Prior Knowledge
PERSONAL CONNECTION

What is your favorite wild animal? Perhaps it's the dolphin, the bear, the snow leopard—or maybe an animal you've seen in films or only heard about. In your notebook, make a sketch of this animal and share your sketch with a classmate.

Building Background
GEOGRAPHICAL CONNECTION

"My Wonder Horse" is set in the mountains of northern New Mexico. In this and other areas of the West, wild horses have lived for hundreds of years, and they survive to the present day. These horses live in bands consisting of a single stallion and his mares, which the stallion guards fiercely. Since the early 1800s, stories have been told in the West of a white stallion, sometimes known as the Pacing White Mustang, remarkable for his beauty, speed, grace, intelligence, and elusiveness. In Native American legends, the white stallion is considered a ghost horse. "My Wonder Horse" builds on this tradition of the legendary white stallion.

Setting a Purpose
WRITING CONNECTION

To accompany your sketch of a wild animal, write several sentences indicating why it appeals to your imagination. What traits do you find admirable or intriguing? Its intelligence or strength? Its beauty or grace? Its similarities to humans? As you read, compare your feelings for this wild animal to those that the narrator has for his "wonder horse."

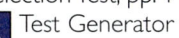

OVERVIEW

Objectives

- To understand and appreciate a short story that explores the relationship between a boy and a legendary white horse
- To identify and understand imagery
- To appreciate and use repeated words to build coherence in writing
- To express understanding of the story through a choice of writing forms, including a description and an outline
- To extend understanding of the selection through a variety of multimodal and cross-curricular activities

Skills

LITERARY CONCEPTS
- Imagery
- Symbol

THE WRITER'S STYLE
- Using repetition to build coherence

GRAMMAR
- Using commas between coordinate adjectives

SPEAKING, LISTENING, AND VIEWING
- Using storyboards
- Group discussion
- Oral presentation

ALTERNATIVE

Previewing

Have students use the following questions to talk about their favorite wild animal.

Writing Connection

Discussion Prompts
- *Where does this animal live?*
- *Why does this animal appeal to you?*
- *How much do you actually know about this animal?*

As you read "My Wonder Horse," see how the narrator feels about his special animal.

PRINT AND MEDIA RESOURCES

UNIT SIX RESOURCE BOOK
Strategic Reading: Literature, p. 49
Vocabulary SkillBuilder, p. 50

GRAMMAR MINI-LESSONS
Transparencies, p. 43
Copymasters, p. 44

ACCESS FOR STUDENTS ACQUIRING ENGLISH
Selection Summaries
Reading Support

FORMAL ASSESSMENT
Selection Test, pp. 147–148
Test Generator

AUDIO LIBRARY
See Reference Card

SUMMARY

A boy of 15 has heard, from his father and other ranch hands, tales of a great white horse, a mysterious, legendary animal that lives in the mountain valleys and the surrounding plains. No one has ever been able to catch him. For the boy this mystical creature symbolizes fantasy, freedom, and excitement. He dreams of someday capturing the animal and showing him off to the girls of the town. One summer day as the boy is sitting on his horse, watching the cattle, time seems to stop for a moment. The Wonder Horse appears briefly, then is gone. As the summer passes, the boy dreams of the horse constantly, looking for him everywhere. Then on a sunny winter day in open country, the boy again comes across the beautiful, noble animal, who stands still a moment, then takes off, breaking a trail through the snow. As the boy pursues, eventually the great horse tires and the boy is able to lasso him and, after a struggle, to lead him home, where his father praises his son's manly work. Respecting the courage and intelligence of the animal, the boy turns him loose in a fenced pasture for the night. But the next morning the horse has somehow disappeared. Following his tracks, the boy finds that the Wonder Horse has managed to scale the fence, leaving white hair on the wire and blood on the barbs. Hoof prints lead away in the snow. The boy weeps, but he also rejoices over the freedom of the Wonder Horse. He feels that his life has been enriched forever.

Thematic Link: *Fateful Encounters* A teenage boy's fateful encounter with a magnificent wild horse marks his entrance into manhood.

STRATEGIC READING FOR
Less-Proficient Readers

To help students become immersed in the story, have them discuss the photo of the wild horse on this spread. Ask them to share any experiences they have had with such a horse and to tell about any books they have read or movies they have seen on the subject.

Set a Purpose Tell students that the boy in this story wants to catch a wild horse. Then have them read to find out why.

Use **UNIT SIX RESOURCE BOOK,** p. 49, for guidance in reading the selection.

My Wonder Horse

Sabine R. Ulibarrí

Mi Caballo Mago

He was white. White as memories lost. He was free. Free as happiness is. He was fantasy, liberty, and excitement. He filled and dominated the mountain valleys and surrounding plains. He was a white horse that flooded my youth with dreams and poetry.

Era blanco. Blanco como el olvido. Era libre. Libre como la alegría. Era la ilusión, la libertad y la emoción. Poblaba y dominaba las serranías y las llanuras de las cercanías. Era un caballo blanco que llenó mi juventud de fantasía y poesía.

818 UNIT SIX PART 2: FATEFUL ENCOUNTERS

WORDS TO KNOW

evoke (ĭ-vōk′) *v.* to call to mind (p. 820)
indignity (ĭn-dĭg′nĭ-tē) *n.* something that insults or hurts one's dignity or pride (p. 826)
indomitable (ĭn-dŏm′ĭ-tə-bəl) *adj.* not easily discouraged or defeated (p. 826)
lethargy (lĕth′ər-jē) *n.* a state of drowsiness, inactivity, and lack of energy (p. 820)
mandate (măn′dāt) *n.* a command or instruction by someone in authority (p. 822)

mystic (mĭs′tĭk) *adj.* inspiring a sense of mystery and wonder (p. 820)
transcendent (trăn-sĕn′dənt) *adj.* far above or beyond the usual and ordinary; supreme (p. 826)
ultimate (ŭl′tə-mĭt) *n.* the greatest extreme; maximum (p. 824)
vigil (vĭj′əl) *n.* a watchful staying awake during normal sleeping hours (p. 822)
wane (wān) *v.* to decrease gradually (p. 824)

PHOTOGRAPHY NOTE

Photo of white horse by Robert Vavra Robert Vavra (1935–), who was born in California, has lived mostly in Europe since 1958. He is the author of more than 20 books and has provided photographs for illustrated books by other authors. Vavra has spent much of his career capturing on film the beauty and power of horses. He sees each horse as an individual with its own personality.

Reading the Photograph *What feeling do you think the photo conveys? How would the feeling differ if the horse had been photographed at rest or running through a pasture?*

CUSTOMIZING FOR
Gifted and Talented Students

Have students note the imagery and figurative language the narrator uses to describe the horse. Then have them choose their favorite descriptive words and phrases and use them to compose a poem about the horse.

CUSTOMIZING FOR
Students Acquiring English

- Use **ACCESS FOR STUDENTS ACQUIRING ENGLISH,** *Reading Support.*
- Students whose first language is Spanish can read the original Spanish version of the story aloud to one another in groups and try to translate it into English. They can compare their translation with the English version of the story.

Literary Concept: SYMBOL

A Have students note what qualities the horse represents to the boy. Then ask whether they think a wild horse is a good symbol for fantasy, liberty, and excitement. *(Responses will vary.)*

THE LANGUAGE OF LITERATURE **TEACHER'S EDITION** 819

CUSTOMIZING FOR
Students Acquiring English

I Tell students that *ranch hands* are workers who help out on a ranch. The term is synonymous with *cowboys*.

Literary Note
B Point out that the narrator compares the horse to three different types of literature: a myth, a poem, and a legend. Tell students that these three types of literature often have a symbolic meaning—a meaning that goes beyond the literal meaning of the beings that are described and the stories that are told.

Critical Thinking:
MAKING INFERENCES

C Ask students what feelings the horse seems to inspire in the boy as a result of its ability to escape from everyone. (*Possible responses: admiration, excitement, awe*)

STRATEGIC READING FOR
Less-Proficient Readers

D Make sure students understand why the narrator wants to catch the horse. (*to prove his manhood, to prove himself worthy of a great challenge, and to show off for the girls in town*) Clarifying

Set a Purpose Have students read on to find out whether the boy is able to catch the horse.

Linking to History
E The glory days of cowboys in the West extended only from the 1860s to the 1880s. At that time, there were huge stretches of unfenced land, called the open range, in which cattle could graze, and the animals had to be driven long distances to railroad stations for shipment to the East. Today, fewer cowboys are needed because there is no open range and because cattle no longer need to be driven long distances.

I Around the campfires of the country and in the sunny patios of the town, the ranch hands talked about him with enthusiasm and admiration. But gradually their eyes would become hazy and blurred with dreaming. The lively talk would die down. All thoughts fixed on the vision <u>evoked</u> by the horse. Myth of the animal kingdom. Poem of the world of men.

B White and mysterious, he paraded his harem through the summer forests with lordly rejoicing. Winter sent him to the plains and sheltered hillsides for the protection of his females. He spent the summer like an Oriental potentate¹ in his woodland gardens. The winter he passed like an illustrious warrior celebrating a well-earned victory.

He was a legend. The stories told of the Wonder Horse were endless. Some true, others fabricated. **C** So many traps, so many snares, so many searching parties, and all in vain. The horse always escaped, always mocked his pursuers, always rose above the control of man. Many a valiant cowboy swore to put his halter and his brand on the animal. But always he had to confess later that the <u>mystic</u> horse was more of a man than he.

D I was fifteen years old. Although I had never seen the Wonder Horse, he filled my imagination and fired my ambition. I used to listen open-mouthed as my father and the ranch hands talked about the phantom horse who turned into mist and air and nothingness when he was trapped. I joined in the universal obsession—like the hope of winning the lottery—of putting my lasso on him some day, of capturing him and showing him off on Sunday afternoons when the girls of the town strolled through the streets.

It was high summer. The forests were fresh, green, and gay. The cattle moved slowly, fat and sleek in the August sun and shadow. Listless and drowsy in the <u>lethargy</u> of late afternoon, I was dozing on my horse. It was time to round up the herd and go back to the good bread of the cowboy camp. Already my comrades would be sitting around the campfire, playing the guitar, telling stories of past or present, or surrendering to the languor² of the late afternoon. The sun was setting behind me in a riot of streaks and colors. Deep, harmonious silence. **E**

I sit drowsily still, forgetting the cattle in the glade. Suddenly the forest falls silent, a deafening quiet. The afternoon comes to a standstill. The breeze stops blowing, but it vibrates. The sun flares hotly. The planet, life, and time itself have stopped in an inexplicable way. For a moment, I don't understand what is happening.

Then my eyes focus. There he is! The Wonder Horse! At the end of the glade, on high ground surrounded by summer green. He is a statue. He is an engraving. Line and form and white stain on a green background. Pride, prestige, and art incarnate in animal flesh. A picture of burning beauty and virile³ freedom. An ideal, pure and invincible, rising from the eternal dreams of humanity. Even today my being thrills when I remember him. **F**

A sharp neigh. A far-reaching challenge that soars on high, ripping the virginal fabric of the rosy clouds. Ears at the point. Eyes flashing. Tail waving active defiance. Hoofs glossy and destructive. Arrogant ruler of the countryside. **G**

The moment is never-ending, a momentary eternity. It no longer exists, but it will always live. . . . There must have been mares. I did not see them. The cattle went on their indifferent way. My horse followed them, and I came slowly back from the land of dreams to the world of toil. But life could no longer be what it was before.

---

1. **Oriental potentate** (pōt′n-tāt′): Asian king.
2. **languor** (lăng′gər): a dreamy, lazy mood or quality.
3. **virile** (vîr′əl): masculine, strong, vigorous, and powerful.

| WORDS TO KNOW | **evoke** (ĭ-vōk′) *v.* to call to mind
mystic (mĭs′tĭk) *adj.* inspiring a sense of mystery and wonder
lethargy (lĕth′ər-jē) *n.* a state of drowsiness, inactivity, and lack of energy |

820

Mini-Lesson The Writer's Style

USING REPEATED WORDS TO BUILD COHERENCE Tell students that repeating key words and phrases is one way of creating coherence and adding dramatic emphasis to their writing. Provide an example by reading aloud the highlighted paragraph on this page. Have students listen for the effect of the repeated words *so many* and *always*.

Application Have students write their own paragraphs about a personal experience, repeating words of their choice to build coherence and create a dramatic effect.

Reteaching/Reinforcement
- Writing Handbook, anthology p. 869

Coherence in Composition, pp. 368–369

Alrededor de las fogatas del campo y en las resolanas del pueblo los vaqueros de esas tierras hablaban de él con entusiasmo y admiración. Y la mirada se volvía turbia y borrosa de ensueño. La animada charla se apagaba. Todos atentos a la visión evocada. Mito del reino animal. Poema del mundo viril.

Blanco y arcano. Paseaba su harén por el bosque de verano en regocijo imperial. El invierno decretaba el llano y la ladera para sus hembras. Veraneaba como rey de oriente en su jardín silvestre. Invernaba como guerrero ilustre que celebra la victoria ganada.

Era leyenda. Eran sin fin las historias que se contaban del caballo brujo. Unas verdad, otras invención. Tantas trampas, tantas redes, tantas expediciones. Todas venidas a menos. El caballo siempre se escapaba, siempre se burlaba, siempre se alzaba por encima del dominio de los hombres. ¡Cuánto valedor no juró ponerle su jáquima y su marca para confesar después que el brujo había sido más hombre que él!

Yo tenía quince años. Y sin haberlo visto nunca el brujo me llenaba ya la imaginación y la esperanza. Escuchaba embobado a mi padre y a sus vaqueros hablar del caballo fantasma que al atraparlo se volvía espuma y aire y nada. Participaba de la obsesión de todos, ambición de lotería, de algún día ponerle yo mi lazo, de hacerlo mío, y lucirlo los domingos por a la tarde cuando las muchachas salen a paseo por la calle.

Pleno el verano. Los bosques verdes, frescos y alegres. Las reses lentas, gordas y luminosas en la sombra y en el sol de agosto. Dormitaba yo en un caballo brioso, lánguido y sutil en el sopor del atardecer. Era hora ya de acercarse a la majada, al buen pan y al rancho del rodeo. Ya los compañeros estarían alrededor de la

MY WONDER HORSE / MI CABALLO MAGO   821

Literary Concept: SYMBOL

F Remind students that the narrator has already said that the horse represents freedom, fantasy, liberty, and excitement. Ask them what other qualities he now says the horse represents. *(pride, prestige, art, beauty, virility, a pure and invincible ideal)*

Literary Concept: IMAGERY

G Ask students what sensory details in this paragraph help them imagine how a wild horse looks and sounds when it is challenged. *(Possible responses: "soars on high," "ears at the point," "eyes flashing," "tail waving," "hoofs glossy and destructive")*

Mini-Lesson Literary Concepts

REVIEWING SYMBOL Draw on the chalkboard the web shown on the right. Use it to remind students of the things that can be symbols—things that can stand for something beyond themselves. Provide an example by pointing out the passage analyzed in annotation F.

Application Ask students what one word in the passage they think best sums up what the horse represents to the boy. *(Answers will vary.)* Then have students form small groups to discuss symbols they have found in works of literature they have read recently or in TV films or movies they have seen. Students will have an opportunity to write about the symbol of the horse in the QuickWrite on page 828.

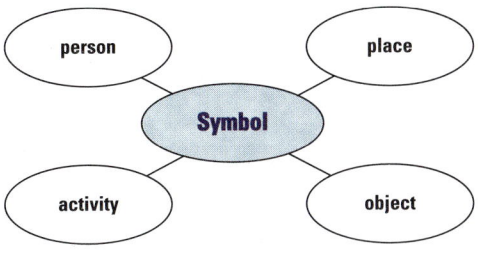

THE LANGUAGE OF LITERATURE TEACHER'S EDITION   821

Linking to Geography

H In New Mexico, where this story is set, it is generally very warm and dry. The northern, mountainous areas, however, receive more than 20 inches of precipitation a year. In the winter, snow can fall anywhere in the state, and the high mountains of the northern region can receive up to 300 inches of snow per year.

Literary Concept: IMAGERY

I Ask which sensory details in this paragraph and the next best help students imagine the sights, sounds, and feel of a cold, snowy day. (*Possible responses: "My breath was a white cloud"; "trembling with cold"; "a silence, deep, white, and sparkling"; "an unending wake, an open rift, in the white sea"*)

CUSTOMIZING FOR
Students Acquiring English

2 Tell students that the word *wake* usually refers to the path a boat makes as it cuts through the water. Then say that in this case, it refers to the path of a horse through the snow. Ask students what the comparable word for *wake* is in their first language. Spanish-speaking students can point out the Spanish word the author used.

Literary Concept:
RISING ACTION

J Ask students what new complication or conflict begins to move the plot along here. (*Possible response: The boy encounters the horse again, on a snowy day. The horse seems to challenge the boy but then begins to run away. The boy follows, hoping to catch it.*)

That night under the stars I didn't sleep. I dreamed. How much I dreamed awake and how much I dreamed asleep, I do not know. I only know that a white horse occupied my dreams and filled them with vibrant sound, and light, and turmoil.

H Summer passed and winter came. Green grass gave place to white snow. The herds descended from the mountains to the valleys and the hollows. And in the town they kept saying that the Wonder Horse was roaming through this or that secluded area. I inquired everywhere for his whereabouts. Every day he became for me more of an ideal, more of an idol, more of a mystery.

> EVERY DAY HE BECAME FOR ME MORE OF AN IDEAL, MORE OF AN IDOL, MORE OF A MYSTERY.

I It was Sunday. The sun had barely risen above the snowy mountains. My breath was a white cloud. My horse was trembling with cold and fear like me. I left without going to mass. Without any breakfast. Without the usual bread and sardines in my saddlebags. I had slept badly but had kept the <u>vigil</u> well. I was going in search of the white light that galloped through my dreams.

On leaving the town for the open country, the roads disappear. There are no tracks, human or animal. Only a silence, deep, white, and sparkling. My horse breaks trail with his chest and leaves an unending wake, an open rift, in the white sea. My trained, concentrated gaze covers the landscape from horizon to horizon, searching for the noble silhouette of the talismanic[4] horse.

It must have been midday. I don't know. Time had lost its meaning. I found him! On a slope stained with sunlight. We saw one another at the same time. Together, we turned to stone. Motionless, absorbed, and panting, I gazed at his beauty, his pride, his nobility. As still as sculptured marble, he allowed himself to be admired.

A sudden, violent scream breaks the silence. A glove hurled into my face.[5] A challenge and a <u>mandate</u>. Then something surprising happens. The horse that in summer takes his stand between any threat and his herd, swinging back and forth from left to right, now plunges into the snow. Stronger than they, he is breaking trail for his mares. They follow him. His flight is slow in order to conserve his strength.

I follow. Slowly. Quivering. Thinking about his intelligence. Admiring his courage. Understanding his courtesy. The afternoon advances. My horse is taking it easy.

One by one the mares become weary. One by one, they drop out of the trail. Alone! He and I. My inner ferment[6] bubbles to my lips. I speak to him. He listens and is quiet.

---

4. **talismanic** (tăl'ĭs-măn'ĭk): possessing or believed to possess magic power.
5. **A glove . . . face:** a defiant challenge. Historically, one man challenged another to a duel by throwing down a glove, or gauntlet.
6. **ferment:** agitation or excitement.

WORDS TO KNOW
vigil (vĭj'əl) *n.* a watchful staying awake during normal sleeping hours
mandate (măn'dāt) *n.* a command or instruction by someone in authority

822

 Multicultural Perspectives

THE VISION QUEST Tell students that the dream about a wild animal that the narrator has in the wilderness and his subsequent meeting with that animal call to mind the tradition of the vision quest that was common to several Native American peoples of the Eastern woodlands and the Great Plains. Tell them that the vision quest marked a young boy's (and sometimes a girl's) initiation into manhood (womanhood). Say that the boy would be sent alone into the wilderness and be told to fast and pray until he had a dream about a special animal. Point out that the animal he encountered was called his guardian spirit and that it would teach him something he needed to know in order to gain his maturity.

hoguera agitando la guitarra, contando cuentos del pasado o de hoy o entregándose al cansancio de la tarde. El sol se ponía ya, detrás de mí, en escándalos de rayo y color. Silencio orgánico y denso.

Sigo insensible a las reses al abra. De pronto el bosque se calla. El silencio enmudece. La tarde se detiene. La brisa deja de respirar, pero tiembla. El sol se excita. El planeta, la vida y el tiempo se han detenido de una manera inexplicable. Por un instante no sé lo que pasa.

Luego mis ojos aciertan. ¡Allí está! ¡El caballo mago! Al extremo del abra, en un promontorio, rodeado de verde. Hecho estatua, hecho estampa. Línea y forma y mancha blanca en fondo verde. Orgullo, fama y arte en carne animal. Cuadro de belleza encendida y libertad varonil. Ideal invicto y limpio de la eterna ilusión humana. Hoy palpito todo aún al recordarlo.

Silbido. Reto trascendental que sube y rompe la tela virginal de las nubes rojas. Orejas lanzas. Ojos rayos. Cola viva y ondulante, desafío movedizo. Pezuña tersa y destructiva. Arrogante majestad de los campos.

El momento es eterno. La eternidad momentanea. Ya no está, pero siempre estará. Debió de haber yeguas. Yo no las vi. Las reses siguen indiferentes. Mi caballo las sigue y yo vuelvo lentamente del mundo del sueño a la tierra del sudor. Pero ya la vida no volverá a ser lo que antes fue.

Aquella noche bajo las estrellas no dormí. Soñé. Cuánto soñé despierto y cuánto soñé dormido yo no sé. Sólo sé que un caballo blanco pobló mis sueños y los llenó de resonancia y de luz y de violencia.

Pasó el verano y entró el invierno. El verde pasto dió lugar a la blanca nieve. Las manadas bajaron de las sierras a los valles y cañadas. Y en el pueblo se comentaba que el brujo andaba por este o aquel rincón. Yo indagaba por todas partes su paradero. Cada día se me hacía más ideal, más imagen, más misterio.

Domingo. Apenas rayaba el sol de la sierra nevada. Aliento vaporoso. Caballo tembloroso de frío y de ansias. Como yo. Salí sin ir a misa. Sin desayunarme siquiera. Sin pan y sardinas en las alforjas. Había dormido mal y velado bien. Iba en busca de la blanca luz que galopaba en mis sueños.

Al salir del pueblo al campo libre desaparecen los caminos. No hay rastro humano o animal. Silencio blanco, hondo y rutilante. Mi caballo corta el camino con el pecho y deja estela eterna, grieta abierta, en la mar cana. La mirada diestra y atenta puebla el paisaje hasta cada horizonte buscando el noble perfil del caballo místico.

Sería medio día. No sé. El tiempo había perdido su rigor. Di con él. En una ladera contaminada de sol. Nos vimos al mismo tiempo. Juntos nos hicimos piedra. Inmóvil, absorto y jadeante contemplé su belleza, su arrogancia, su nobleza. Esculpido en mármol, se dejó admirar.

Literary Concept: IMAGERY

K Ask students what impression of the horse is conveyed here and what sensory details paint that picture. *(Possible responses: The horse suddenly appears vulnerable and desperate; sweat and wet snow have combined to "stain" his legendary white coat; the use of the words and phrases "sweat," "snorting breath, turned to steam," and "white spume" show him to be laboring.)*

Critical Thinking: SYNTHESIZING

L Ask students why they think the boy feels like an executioner. *(Possible response: The horse represents freedom to the boy; if he succeeds in catching the horse, he will end its life as a free animal.)*

Literary Concept: IMAGERY/SUSPENSE

M Ask how the author uses sensory details to build excitement and tension at this point in the story. *(Possible response: Instead of telling exactly what is happening, he describes what the boy sees, hears, and feels: for example, the horse frantically kicking up fans of snow, a rope that whistles in the air as it is being jerked and pulled, which burns both the anchoring saddle and the boy's gloved hands. The reader isn't exactly sure what is happening and has to use the details to build a mental picture of the scene.)*

STRATEGIC READING FOR
Less-Proficient Readers

N Have students summarize how the boy manages to capture the horse. *(He lassos the horse, which then struggles to break free.)* Summarizing

Set a Purpose Have students read on to find out whether the boy is able to keep the horse.

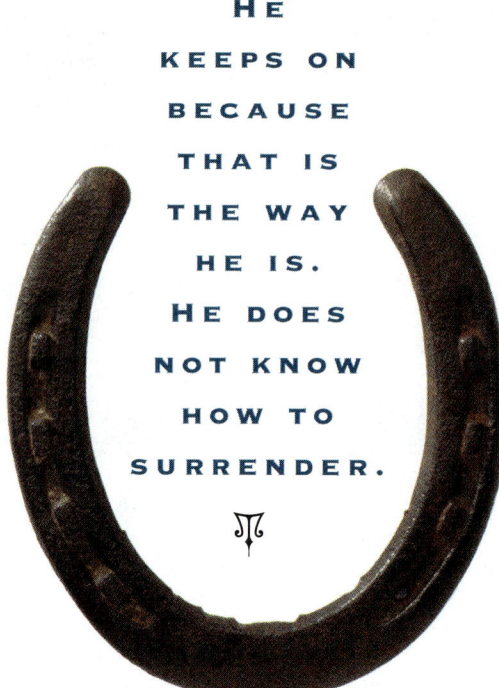

HE KEEPS ON BECAUSE THAT IS THE WAY HE IS. HE DOES NOT KNOW HOW TO SURRENDER.

He still opens the way, and I follow in the path he leaves me. Behind us a long, deep trench crosses the white plain. My horse, which has eaten grain and good hay, is still strong. Undernourished as the Wonder Horse is, his strength is waning. But he keeps on because that is the way he is. He does not know how to surrender.

I now see black stains over his body. Sweat and the wet snow have revealed the black skin beneath the white hair. Snorting breath, turned to steam, tears the air. White spume[7] above white snow. Sweat, spume, and steam. Uneasiness.

I felt like an executioner. But there was no turning back. The distance between us was growing relentlessly shorter. God and Nature watched indifferently.

I feel sure of myself at last. I untie the rope. I open the lasso and pull the reins tight. Every nerve, every muscle is tense. My heart is in my mouth. Spurs pressed against trembling flanks. The horse leaps. I whirl the rope and throw the obedient lasso.

A frenzy of fury and rage. Whirlpools of light and fans of transparent snow. A rope that whistles and burns the saddletree. Smoking, fighting gloves. Eyes burning in their sockets. Mouth parched. Fevered forehead. The whole earth shakes and shudders. The long, white trench ends in a wide, white pool.

Deep, gasping quiet. The Wonder Horse is mine! Both still trembling, we look at one another squarely for a long time. Intelligent and realistic, he stops struggling and even takes a hesitant step toward me. I speak to him. As I talk, I approach him. At first, he flinches and recoils. Then he waits for me. The two horses greet one another in their own way. Finally, I succeed in stroking his mane. I tell him many things, and he seems to understand.

Ahead of me, along the trail already made, I drove him toward the town. Triumphant. Exultant. Childish laughter gathered in my throat. With my newfound manliness, I controlled it. I wanted to sing, but I fought down the desire. I wanted to shout, but I kept quiet. It was the ultimate in happiness. It was the pride of the male adolescent. I felt myself a conqueror.

Occasionally the Wonder Horse made a try for his liberty, snatching me abruptly from my thoughts. For a few moments, the struggle was renewed. Then we went on.

---

7. **spume** (spyōōm): foam or froth.

WORDS TO KNOW
wane (wān) *v.* to decrease gradually
ultimate (ŭl′tə-mĭt) *n.* the greatest extreme; maximum

824

Mini-Lesson Grammar

USING COMMAS BETWEEN ADJECTIVES OF EQUAL RANK Tell students that when two adjectives of equal rank modify the same noun, a comma is placed between them. The four commas in the highlighted section on this page are examples of commas that separate equal adjectives. To demonstrate this, have students place the word *and* between each pair of adjectives or reverse the order of the adjectives. If everything still makes sense, a comma is needed.

Application Have students decide whether to add a comma between these paired adjectives:

1. The boy had two special encounters with the horse. *(no)*
2. The horse was a beautiful majestic symbol of freedom. *(yes)*
3. The narrator is an idealistic teenage boy. *(no)*

Reteaching/Reinforcement
- *Grammar Handbook,* anthology p. 936
- *Grammar Mini-Lessons* transparencies p. 43, copymasters p. 44

 The Writer's Craft

Adjectives of Equal Rank, p. 773

Testing Adjectives for Rank

Original	Add "and"	Finding
old dirty stable	old and dirty stable	equal: add comma
old horse stable	old and horse stable	unequal: no comma

Silbido violento que rompe el silencio. Guante arrojado a la cara. Desafío y decreto a la vez. Asombro nuevo. El caballo que en verano se coloca entre la amenaza y la manada, oscilando a distancia de diestra a siniestra, ahora se lanza a la nieve. Más fuerte que ellas, abre la vereda a las yeguas. Y ellas lo siguen. Su fuga es lenta para conservar sus fuerzas.

Sigo. Despacio. Palpitante. Pensando en su inteligencia. Admirando su valentía. Apreciando su cortesía. La tarde se alarga. Mi caballo cebado a sus anchas.

Una a una las yeguas se van cansando. Una a una se van quedando a un lado. ¡Solos! El y yo. La agitación interna reboza a los labios. Le hablo. Me escucha y calla.

El abre el camino y yo sigo por la vereda que me deja. Detrás de nosotros una larga y honda zanja blanca que cruza la llanura. El caballo que ha comido grano y buen pasto sigue fuerte. A él, mal nutrido, se la han agotado las fuerzas. Pero sigue porque es él y porque no sabe ceder.

Encuentro negro y manchas negras por el cuerpo. La nieve y el sudor han revelado la piel negra bajo el pelo. Mecheros violentos de vapor rompen el aire. Espumparajos blancos sobre la blanca nieve. Sudor, espuma y vapor. Ansia.

Me sentí verdugo. Pero ya no había retorno. La distancia entre nosotros se acortaba implacablemente. Dios y la naturaleza indiferentes.

Me siento seguro. Desato el cabestro. Abro el lazo. Las riendas tirantes. Cada nervio, cada músculo alerta y el alma en la boca. Espuelas tensas en ijares temblorosos. Arranca el caballo. Remolineo el cabestro y lanzo el lazo obediente.

Vértigo de furia y rabia. Remolinos de luz y abanicos de transparente nieve. Cabestro que silba y quema en la teja de la silla. Guantes violentos que humean. Ojos ardientes en sus pozos. Boca seca. Frente caliente. Y el mundo se sacude y se estremece. Y se acaba la larga zanja blanca en un ancho charco blanco.

Sosiego jadeante y denso. El caballo mago es mío. Temblorosos ambos, nos miramos de hito en hito por un largo rato. Inteligente y realista, deja de forcejear y hasta toma un paso hacia mí. Yo le hablo. Hablándole me acerco. Primero recula. Luego me espera. Hasta que los dos caballos se saludan a la manera suya. Y por fin llego a alisarle la crin. Le digo muchas cosas, y parece que me entiende.

Por delante y por las huellas de antes lo dirigí hacia el pueblo. Triunfante. Exaltado. Una risa infantil me brotaba. Yo, varonil, la dominaba. Quería cantar y pronto me olvidaba. Quería gritar pero callaba. Era un manojo de alegría. Era el orgullo del hombre adolescente. Me sentí conquistador.

El Mago ensayaba la libertad una y otra vez, arrancándome de mis meditaciones abruptamente. Por unos instantes se armaba la lucha otra vez. Luego seguíamos.

Fue necesario pasar por el pueblo. No había remedio. Sol poniente. Calles de hielo y gente en los portales. El Mago lleno de terror y pánico por primera vez. Huía y mi caballo herrado lo detenía. Se resbalaba y caía de costalazo. Yo lloré por él. La indignidad. La humillación. La alteza venida a menos. Le rogaba que no forcejeara, que se dejara llevar. ¡Cómo me dolió que lo vieran así los otros!

Por fin llegamos a la casa. "¿Qué hacer contigo, Mago? Si te meto en el establo o en el corral, de seguro te haces daño. Además sería un insulto. No eres esclavo. No eres criado. Ni siquiera eres animal." Decidí soltarlo en el potrero. Allí podría el Mago irse acostumbrando poco a poco a mi amistad y compañía. De ese potrero no se había escapado nunca un animal.

Mi padre me vió llegar y me esperó sin hablar. En la cara le jugaba una sonrisa y en los ojos le bailaba una chispa. Me vió quitarle el cabestro al Mago y los dos lo vimos alejarse, pensativos. Me estrechó la mano un poco más fuerte que de ordinario y me dijo: "Esos son

---

Mini-Lesson: Speaking, Listening, and Viewing

USING STORYBOARDS Tell students that filmmakers often use storyboards to plan their movies before filming them. That is, they draw pictures of each important scene, showing not only what happens but also from whose or what point of view the scene will be shot.

Application Have students work with a partner to storyboard the events on pages 822–824—in which the boy sights and captures the Wonder Horse—as if they were going to shoot the scene for a movie. Before they begin, have them decide whether they would show the events from the boy's point of view or the horse's point of view, or would switch back and forth between the two points of view.

Critical Thinking:
MAKING JUDGMENTS

P Ask students whether they found it believable that the boy suffered for the horse as it struggled and fell in front of the townspeople. *(Answers will vary. Some students will understand the boy's intense identification with the horse as a symbol of freedom and majestic power, and others will not.)*

CUSTOMIZING FOR
Multiple Learning Styles

Q **Logical-Mathematical Learners** Ask students to give logical reasons for and against keeping the horse in a fenced pasture. Then have them draw conclusions as to whether the boy made the right decision.

Critical Thinking:
SYNTHESIZING

R Ask students why the boy is pleased, rather than disappointed, by his father's unemotional response to his capturing the horse. *(Possible response: Such a response is a recognition that the boy has achieved manhood; the boy appreciates this recognition from his father.)*

Linking to History

S It was the invention of barbed wire in 1874 that marked the beginning of the end of the open range in the West. This wire allowed farmers to fence in land formerly used as pasture, to form small homesteads. Cattle ranchers were opposed to this practice because it made acres of open pasture land unavailable to them.

It was necessary to go through the town. There was no other way. The sun was setting. Icy streets and people on the porches. The Wonder Horse full of terror and panic for the first time. He ran, and my well-shod horse stopped him. He slipped and fell on his side. I suffered for him. The <u>indignity</u>. The humiliation. Majesty degraded. I begged him not to struggle, to let himself be led. How it hurt me that other people should see him like that!

Finally we reached home.

"What shall I do with you, Mago?"[8] If I put you into the stable or the corral, you are sure to hurt yourself. Besides, it would be an insult. You aren't a slave. You aren't a servant. You aren't even an animal."

I decided to turn him loose in the fenced pasture. There, little by little, Mago would become accustomed to my friendship and my company. No animal had ever escaped from that pasture.

My father saw me coming and waited for me without a word. A smile played over his face, and a spark danced in his eyes. He watched me take the rope from Mago, and the two of us thoughtfully observed him move away. My father clasped my hand a little more firmly than usual and said, "That was a man's job." That was all. Nothing more was needed. We understood one another very well. I was playing the role of a real man, but the childish laughter and shouting that bubbled up inside me almost destroyed the impression I wanted to create.

That night I slept little, and when I slept, I did not know that I was asleep. For dreaming is the same when one really dreams, asleep or awake. I was up at dawn. I had to go to see my Wonder Horse. As soon as it was light, I went out into the cold to look for him.

The pasture was large. It contained a grove of trees and a small gully. The Wonder Horse was not visible anywhere, but I was not worried. I walked slowly, my head full of the events of yesterday and my plans for the future. Suddenly I realized that I had walked a long way. I quicken my steps. I look apprehensively around me. I begin to be afraid. Without knowing it, I begin to run. Faster and faster.

He is not there. The Wonder Horse has escaped. I search every corner where he could be hidden. I follow his tracks. I see that during the night he walked incessantly, sniffing, searching for a way out. He did not find one. He made one for himself.

I followed the track that led straight to the fence. And I saw that the trail did not stop but continued on the other side. It was a barbed-wire fence. There was white hair on the wire. There was blood on the barbs. There were red stains on the snow and little red drops in the hoofprints on the other side of the fence.

I stopped there. I did not go any farther. The rays of the morning sun on my face. Eyes clouded and yet filled with light. Childish tears on the cheeks of a man. A cry stifled in my throat. Slow, silent sobs.

Standing there, I forgot myself and the world and time. I cannot explain it, but my sorrow was mixed with pleasure. I was weeping with happiness. No matter how much it hurt me, I was rejoicing over the flight and the freedom of the Wonder Horse, the dimensions of his <u>indomitable</u> spirit. Now he would always be fantasy, freedom, and excitement. The Wonder Horse was <u>transcendent</u>. He had enriched my life forever.

My father found me there. He came close without a word and laid his arm across my shoulders. We stood looking at the white trench with its flecks of red that led into the rising sun.

Translated by Thelma Campbell Nason

---

8. **Mago** (mä′gô) *Spanish:* magician; wizard.

WORDS TO KNOW
indignity (ĭn-dĭg′nĭ-tē) *n.* something that insults or hurts one's dignity or pride
indomitable (ĭn-dŏm′ĭ-tə-bəl) *adj.* not easily discouraged or defeated
transcendent (trăn-sĕn′dənt) *adj.* far above or beyond the usual and ordinary; supreme

---

Mini-Lesson Workplace Literacy

SCANS GOAL: Exercises Leadership

GIVING A PERSUASIVE SPEECH Tell students that in many jobs, employees have to persuade others to take a certain course of action. Point out that in order to do so, such workers must collect facts that support their point of view and must use those facts to articulate reasons that will persuade others to act in a certain way.

Application Have students imagine that they are lobbyists working for an environmental organization. Have them prepare a speech they would deliver in order to persuade members of Congress to pass a law protecting the habitat of New Mexico's wild horses from commercial development. Remind students to collect facts and articulate reasons to support their arguments. (You may want to use this activity as a follow-up to the Alternative Activity, on page 829, in which students research wild horses.)

hombres." Nada más. Ni hacía falta. Nos entendíamos mi padre y yo muy bien. Yo hacía el papel de *muy hombre* pero aquella risa infantil y aquel grito que me andaban por dentro por poco estropean la impresión que yo quería dar.

Aquella noche casi no dormí y cuando dormí no supe que dormía. Pues el soñar es igual, cuando se sueña de veras, dormido o despierto. Al amanecer yo ya estaba de pie. Tenía que ir a ver al Mago. En cuanto aclaró salí al frío a buscarlo.

El potrero era grande. Tenía un bosque y una cañada. No se veía el Mago en ninguna parte pero yo me sentía seguro. Caminaba despacio, la cabeza toda llena de los acontecimientos de ayer y de los proyectos de mañana. De pronto me di cuenta que había andado mucho. Aprieto el paso. Miro aprensivo a todos lados. Empieza a entrarme el miedo. Sin saber voy corriendo. Cada vez más rápido.

No está. El Mago se ha escapado. Recorro cada rincón donde pudiera haberse agazapado. Sigo la huella. Veo que durante toda la noche el Mago anduvo sin cesar buscando, olfateando, una salida. No la encontró. La inventó.

Seguí la huella que se dirigía directamente a la cerca. Y vi como el rastro no se detenía sino continuaba del otro lado. El alambre era de púa. Y había pelos blancos en el alambre. Había sangre en las púas. Había manchas rojas en la nieve y gotitas rojas en las huellas del otro lado de la cerca.

Allí me detuve. No fui más allá. Sol rayante en la cara. Ojos nublados y llenos de luz. Lágrimas infantiles en mejillas varoniles. Grito hecho nudo en la garganta. Sollozos despaciosos y silenciosos.

Allí me quedé y me olvidé de mí y del mundo y del tiempo. No sé cómo estuvo, pero mi tristeza era gusto. Lloraba de alegría. Estaba celebrando, por mucho que me dolía, la fuga y la libertad del Mago, la transcendencia de ese espíritu indomable. Ahora seguiría siendo el ideal, la ilusión y la emoción. El Mago era un absoluto. A mí me había enriquecido la vida para siempre.

Allí me halló mi padre. Se acercó sin decir nada y me puso el brazo sobre el hombro. Nos quedamos mirando la zanja blanca con flecos de rojo que se dirigía al sol rayante. ❖

From Personal Response to Critical Analysis

1. Accept all reasonable, well-supported responses.
2. Possible responses: a powerful symbol of freedom and wildness; his sense of an "impossible dream" to strive for
3. Possible responses: that becoming a man means more than conquering things; that he can share in the joy of another creature's freedom and identify with that creature
4. Accept all reasonable, well-supported responses.
5. Accept all reasonable, well-supported responses.

Another Pathway

Cooperative Learning One student can make sure ideas are backed up with evidence from the selection. Another can extend superficial ideas into a deeper analysis of character change. A third can synthesize all the ideas into a few conclusions that everyone can accept.

Rubric

3 Full Accomplishment Students list, and support with evidence from the text, ways the narrator has matured.

2 Substantial Accomplishment Students list ways the narrator has matured but may have difficulty supporting their ideas with evidence.

1 Little or Partial Accomplishment Students have difficulty drawing conclusions about the narrator.

RESPONDING OPTIONS

FROM PERSONAL RESPONSE TO CRITICAL ANALYSIS

REFLECT 1. How did you react to the ending of the story? Describe your reaction in your notebook.

RETHINK 2. What if the horse had not escaped? What would the narrator have lost in owning him?
Thematic Link

3. What do you think the boy learns through his experience with the wonder horse?
Close Textual Reading

Consider
- his age and stage in life
- what the horse represents for him
- what he hopes to achieve by capturing and owning the horse
- why he weeps with happiness at the end

4. Explain whether you would like to capture and own the wild animal you described for the Previewing activities on page 817. How do your feelings compare with the narrator's feelings about his wonder horse?

RELATE 5. Do you think it is acceptable to capture wild animals and raise them as pets? Explain your reasoning.

> **Multimodal Learning**
> **ANOTHER PATHWAY**
> **Cooperative Learning**
> How has the narrator's fateful encounter with his wonder horse changed his life? With a small group of classmates, list the ways that the narrator matures in this story. Look especially at references to his being a man and a child. Share your conclusions with the rest of the class.

LITERARY CONCEPTS

The strong, simple **imagery** of this story helps the reader imagine the setting and feel close to the action. At the same time, these sensory details heighten the drama and echo the various emotions that the boy is feeling. Notice that paragraph six, just before the boy sees the horse, paints a picture of a lazy late afternoon in high summer, a deep quiet moment captured through images of both sight and sound. Now look back at a descriptive passage or scene in this story that stands out strongly in your mind. How do various images come together in the passage to heighten the intensity of the moment? Try capturing your impression of the scene in a drawing, using as many sensory details as you can. Then describe your impression in words to the class, showing your drawing as an illustration.

QUICKWRITES

1. Write a **description** of what the wonder horse symbolizes, or represents, for the narrator.
2. Use this story as a model for one of your own about your favorite wild animal. Write an **outline** of the story.

📁 **PORTFOLIO** Save your writing. You may want to use it later as a springboard to a piece for your portfolio.

828 UNIT SIX PART 2: FATEFUL ENCOUNTERS

Literary Concepts

TE annotations G, I, K, M, and T highlight examples of vivid imagery in the selection. If students have difficulty choosing a passage to illustrate, help them analyze these passages and then ask them to choose the one they like best.

QuickWrites

1. Use TE annotations A and F to help students analyze the symbolism of the Wonder Horse.
2. Remind students that the plot for their story should have an exposition, a conflict, rising action, a climax, and falling action.

Focused Description, pp. 58–71
Outline Form, pp. 816–817

THE WRITER'S STYLE

Most of the time this story is told in the past tense, but sometimes the narrator shifts to the present tense. Find the passages written in present tense. What is the effect of this shift in verb tense?

WORDS TO KNOW

EXERCISE A Review the Words to Know in the boxes at the bottom of the selection pages. Then write the vocabulary word that best completes each sentence.

1. The story "My Wonder Horse" will _____, in some readers, memories about other remarkable animals.
2. A horse named Clever Hans that could solve math problems was, perhaps, the _____ "wonder horse" of all time.
3. Since Clever Hans's behavior was not the result of trickery, people were amazed by his strange, _____ performances.
4. An _____ psychologist, O. Pfungst, refused to accept this and eventually discovered that Clever Hans responded to clues from members of the audience.
5. As this news spread, the public's intense interest in Clever Hans began to _____.

EXERCISE B Answer the following questions.

1. Would a person show **lethargy** by yawning, sobbing, or shuddering?
2. Does someone who gives a **mandate** have wealth, wit, or power?
3. Does a person who is keeping a **vigil** most need to be alert, sympathetic, or relaxed?
4. Would you expect a person with **transcendent** ability to win a first-place ribbon, honorable mention, or a booby prize?
5. Would a proud person be most likely to respond to an **indignity** by saying "Thank you!" "How dare you!" or "I deserved that"?

Multimodal Learning

ALTERNATIVE ACTIVITIES

1. Find out more about the wild horses of the West, also called mustangs. In an **oral report** to the class, give details about their numbers, their location, and threats to their continued existence.
2. Choreograph a short **dance** that captures what the wonder horse symbolizes to the boy, or a dance that conveys the story of the boy's capture and loss of the wonder horse.

SABINE R. ULIBARRÍ

1919–

There is a strong autobiographical element in the setting and events of "My Wonder Horse." Sabine Ulibarrí's family is part of an established Hispanic heritage in northern New Mexico that pre-dates by three centuries the formation of the United States. Ulibarrí was born in a town in the mountain foothills of the region, rode the range on his father's cattle ranch there, and as a child listened to stories of a legendary white horse.

Ulibarrí was a constant reader even before reaching school age. While still an adolescent, he organized a literary club among students his age and led debates on various topics. After finishing his schooling, he taught Spanish for many years at the University of New Mexico. However, Ulibarrí was 42 years old before he published his first writings. "This business of publishing is frightening because . . . one is confessing whether one has talent or not," he once said in an interview.

Documenting the history of Hispanics of northern New Mexico is the focus of Ulibarrí's short stories. He feels that the Hispanic world of his childhood is becoming lost, and so his stories "attempt to document the *historia sentimental,* the essence of that culture before it completely disappears." In the United States, most of his writings appear in bilingual editions, because he writes entirely in Spanish.

OTHER WORKS *Tierra Amarilla: Stories of New Mexico*

Extended Reading

MY WONDER HORSE / MI CABALLO MAGO **829**

Words to Know

Exercise A
1. evoke
2. ultimate
3. mystic
4. indomitable
5. wane

Exercise B
1. yawning
2. power
3. alert
4. first-place ribbon
5. "How dare you!"

Reteaching/Reinforcement
- *Unit Six Resource Book,* p. 50

The Writer's Style

Possible response: The shift to present tense creates a sense of immediacy in scenes in which something important is happening, making the reader feel as if events are occurring as he or she reads.

Across the Curriculum

Geography Have students research the importance of ranching and cowboys to New Mexico's economy today. Urge them to answer these questions: How does ranching rank as a source of income for the state? How many people are employed on ranches? How has the work of cowboys and ranch hands changed in recent years? Have students present their findings in an oral report.

SABINE R. ULIBARRÍ

That Sabine Ulibarrí writes entirely in Spanish even though he was born in the United States can be attributed to his strong feeling for Hispanic tradition. He has written that Hispanic "culture is based on the soil." He goes on to say: "We have a running and ancient dialogue going with the mountains and the mesas, the sunsets and the deserts, the paisano [peasant] and the ponderosa."

Alternative Activities

1. Point out to students that for this activity, they need up-to-date information. Suggest they consult the *Readers' Guide to Periodical Literature* or an on-line guide to periodicals, using the topic "mustang" or "horse."
2. Students can work cooperatively to choreograph and perform their dance. They may either choose one group member as the choreographer or work together to improvise a dance.

OBJECTIVES

- To promote independent active reading
- To practice and apply skills learned in previous selections

Reading Pathways

- Invite students to choose a partner and take turns reading the story aloud. After each partner reads, the two should stop to discuss clues about who the characters are and what is happening to the "good husband."
- Have students read independently and then write their impressions of the characters in their notebook.
- Encourage students to read the story twice, once for enjoyment and a second time to trace the clues that help them identify who the narrator is.

SUMMARY

A wife remembers that her husband was kind, hard-working, and a good father. She recalls how she met him and how he was when he first moved in with her. Then the curse came over him. The dark of the moon brought it out in him. Unable to sleep, he would go out into the glaring sun to be with those like himself. When he returned, he was tired and he smelled strange. One day, she saw the change for herself. She had been sleeping, but she woke up and discovered her husband standing outside. Right before her eyes he changed into something horrible. His hair disappeared, his feet became long, white, and fleshy, and he stood up on two legs. She couldn't help herself; she growled and howled. Her husband, now a man, grabbed a tree branch and shoved it into their house. As she moved forward to protect her children, her sister wolf was already attacking. Soon the entire pack was there. They chased down the man and killed him.

Thematic Link: *Fateful Encounters* A wolf is transformed into a man and has a fateful—and deadly—encounter with his former family and friends.

ON YOUR OWN

He was a good husband, a good father. I don't understand it. I don't believe in it. I don't believe that it happened. I saw it happen but it isn't true. It can't be. He was always gentle. If you'd have seen him playing with the children, anybody who saw him with the children would have known that there wasn't any bad in him, not one mean bone. When I first met him he was still living with his mother, over near Spring Lake, and I used to see them together, the mother and the sons, and think that any young fellow that was that nice with his family must be one worth knowing. Then one time when I was walking in the woods I met him by himself coming back from a hunting trip. He hadn't got any game at all, not so much as a field mouse, but he wasn't cast down about it. He was just larking along enjoying the morning air. That's one of the things I first loved about him. He didn't take things hard, he didn't grouch and whine when things didn't go his way. So we got to talking that day. And I guess things moved right along after that, because pretty soon he was over here pretty near all the time. And my sister said—see, my parents had moved out the year before and gone south, leaving us the place—my sister said, kind of teasing but serious, "Well! If he's going to be here every day and half the night, I guess there isn't room for me!" And she moved out—just

830 UNIT SIX PART 2: FATEFUL ENCOUNTERS

PRINT AND MEDIA RESOURCES

UNIT SIX RESOURCE BOOK
Strategic Reading: Literature, p. 53

FORMAL ASSESSMENT
Selection Test, p. 149
Part Test, pp. 151–152
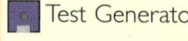 Test Generator

ALTERNATIVE ASSESSMENT
End-of-Year Integrated Assessment
- Reader, pp. 37–44
- Student Response Booklet, pp. 45–57

ACCESS FOR STUDENTS ACQUIRING ENGLISH
Selection Summaries

 AUDIO LIBRARY
See Reference Card

 INTERNET RESOURCES
McDougal Littell
Literature Center at
http://www.com/mcdougal/lit

THE WIFE'S STORY

URSULA K. LE GUIN

down the way. We've always been real close, her and me. That's the sort of thing doesn't ever change. I couldn't ever have got through this bad time without my sis.

Well, so he come to live here. And all I can say is, it was the happy year of my life. He was just purely good to me. A hard worker and never lazy, and so big and fine-looking. Everybody looked up to him, you know, young as he was. Lodge[1] Meeting nights, more and more often they had him to lead the singing. He had such a beautiful voice, and he'd lead off strong, and the others following and joining in, high voices and low. It brings the shivers on me now to think of it, hearing it, nights when I'd stayed home from meeting when the children was babies—the singing coming up through the trees there, and the moonlight, summer nights, the full moon shining. I'll never hear anything so beautiful. I'll never know a joy like that again.

It was the moon, that's what they say. It's the moon's fault, and the blood. It was in his father's blood. I never knew his father, and now I wonder what become of him. He was from up Whitewater way and had no kin around here. I always thought he went back there, but now I don't know. There was some talk about him, tales, that come out after what happened to my

---

1. **Lodge:** a social organization.

OPTION 2

Individual Activity
WRITING A STORY

Tell students that this selection takes the conventions of a werewolf story—a full moon and human-into-wolf metamorphosis—and reverses them—dark of the moon and wolf-into-human metamorphosis. Also tell them that the story is told sympathetically from a wolf's point of view and that the human-being creation is considered the "monster." Have students rewrite the story from the husband's point of view, changing the ending to one in which he escapes.

Teacher's Role Before students write, have them discuss the events the wife describes and imagine what the husband might be thinking and feeling during those events. After they finish writing, have two or three volunteers read their stories aloud and discuss which point of view they think makes a better story, the husband's or the wife's.

Rubric

3 Full Accomplishment Students write imaginative stories that capture the newly human husband's conflicting feelings, such as fear, excitement, guilt, and superiority.

2 Substantial Accomplishment Students accurately describe events from the husband's point of view, but their understanding of his feelings may be somewhat superficial.

1 Little or Partial Accomplishment Students have difficulty imagining or expressing how the husband would have viewed the events in the story.

---

husband. It's something runs in the blood, they say, and it may never come out, but if it does, it's the change of the moon that does it. Always it happens in the dark of the moon. When everybody's home and asleep. Something comes over the one that's got the curse in his blood, they say, and he gets up because he can't sleep, and goes out into the glaring sun, and goes off all alone—drawn to find those like him.

And it may be so, because my husband would do that. I'd half rouse and say, "Where you going to?" and he'd say, "Oh, hunting, be back this evening," and it wasn't like him, even his voice was different. But I'd be so sleepy, and not wanting to wake the kids, and he was so good and responsible, it was no call of mine to go asking "Why?" and "Where?" and all like that.

So it happened that way maybe three times or four. He'd come back late, and worn out, and pretty near cross for one so sweet-tempered—not wanting to talk about it. I figured everybody got to bust out now and then, and nagging never helped anything. But it did begin to worry me. Not so much that he went, but that he come back so tired and strange. Even, he smelled strange. It made my hair stand up on end. I could not endure it and I said, "What is that—those smells on you? All over you!" And he said, "I don't know," real short, and made like he was sleeping. But he went down when he thought I wasn't noticing, and washed and washed himself. But those smells stayed in his hair, and in our bed, for days.

And then the awful thing. I don't find it easy to tell about this. I want to cry when I have to bring it to my mind. Our youngest, the little one, my baby, she turned from her father. Just overnight. He come in and she got scared-looking, stiff, with her eyes wide, and then she begun to cry and try to hide behind me. She didn't yet talk plain but she was saying over and over, "Make it go away! Make it go away!"

The look in his eyes, just for one moment, when he heard that. That's what I don't want ever to remember. That's what I can't forget. The look in his eyes looking at his own child.

I said to the child, "Shame on you, what's got into you!"—scolding, but keeping her right up close to me at the same time, because I was frightened too. Frightened to shaking.

He looked away then and said something like, "Guess she just waked up dreaming," and passed it off that way. Or tried to. And so did I. And I got real mad with my baby when she kept on acting crazy scared of her own dad. But she couldn't help it and I couldn't change it.

He kept away that whole day. Because he knew, I guess. It was just beginning dark of the moon.

It was hot and close inside, and dark, and we'd all been asleep some while, when something woke me up. He wasn't there beside me. I heard a little stir in the passage, when I listened. So I got up, because I could bear it no longer. I went out into the passage, and it was light there, hard sunlight coming in from the door. And I saw him standing just outside, in the tall grass by the entrance. His head was hanging. Presently he sat down, like he felt weary, and looked down at his feet. I held still, inside, and watched—I didn't know what for.

And I saw what he saw. I saw the changing. In his feet, it was, first. They got long, each foot got longer, stretching out, the toes stretching out and the foot getting long, and fleshy, and white. And no hair on them.

The hair begun to come away all over his body. It was like his hair fried away in the sunlight and was gone. He was white all over, then, like a worm's skin. And he turned his face. It was changing while I looked. It got flatter and flatter, the mouth flat and wide, and the teeth grinning flat and dull, and the nose just a knob of flesh with nostril holes, and the ears gone, and the eyes gone blue—blue, with white rims around the blue—staring at me out of that flat, soft, white face.

832   UNIT SIX   PART 2: FATEFUL ENCOUNTERS

He stood up then on two legs.

I saw him, I had to see him, my own dear love, turned into the hateful one.

I couldn't move, but as I crouched there in the passage staring out into the day, I was trembling and shaking with a growl that burst out into a crazy, awful howling. A grief howl and a terror howl and a calling howl. And the others heard it, even sleeping, and woke up.

It stared and peered, that thing my husband had turned into, and shoved its face up to the entrance of our house. I was still bound by mortal fear, but behind me the children had waked up, and the baby was whimpering. The mother anger come into me then, and I snarled and crept forward.

The man thing looked around. It had no gun, like the ones from the man places do. But it picked up a heavy fallen tree branch in its long white foot, and shoved the end of that down into our house, at me. I snapped the end of it in my teeth and started to force my way out, because I knew the man would kill our children if it could. But my sister was already coming. I saw her running at the man with her head low and her mane high and her eyes yellow as the winter sun. It turned on her and raised up that branch to hit her. But I come out of the doorway, mad with the mother anger, and the others all were coming answering my call, the whole pack gathering, there in that blind glare and heat of the sun at noon.

The man looked round at us and yelled out loud, and brandished[2] the branch it held. Then it broke and ran, heading for the cleared fields and plowlands, down the mountainside. It ran, on two legs, leaping and weaving, and we followed it.

I was last, because love still bound the anger and the fear in me. I was running when I saw them pull it down. My sister's teeth were in its throat. I got there and it was dead. The others were drawing back from the kill, because of the taste of the blood, and the smell. The younger ones were cowering[3] and some crying, and my sister rubbed her mouth against her forelegs over and over to get rid of the taste. I went up close because I thought if the thing was dead, the spell, the curse, must be done, and my husband could come back—alive, or even dead, if I could only see him, my true love, in his true form, beautiful. But only the dead man lay there white and bloody. We drew back and back from it, and turned and ran, back up into the hills, back to the woods of the shadows and the twilight and the blessed dark. ❖

---

2. **brandished:** waved in warning or as a threat.
3. **cowering:** crouching or shrinking down in fear.

URSULA K. LE GUIN

1929–

Science fiction/fantasy writer Ursula K. Le Guin is famous for her unusual stories and is best known for her four novels, beginning with *The Wizard of Earthsea,* that are set in the imaginary land of Earthsea.

Le Guin was born in Berkeley, California. Growing up in a stimulating home filled with books and visited by scientists and writers, Le Guin absorbed her parents' interest in the study of different cultures. "My father studied real cultures and I make them up—in a way, it's the same thing," she notes.

Le Guin keeps extending her work. Her futuristic novel *Always Coming Home* includes both poetry and prose, and the book comes with a tape of music.

It has been noted that Le Guin brings to science fiction and fantasy a "new sensitivity" and "a number of striking and sympathetic characters." One critic even claims that she "examines, attacks, unbuttons, takes down, and exposes our notions of reality" and does so "in almost unearthly terms."

OTHER WORKS *The Beginning Place*

OVERVIEW

To gain a deeper appreciation of the selections they have read in this unit, students will explore the characteristics of a short story and then create a well-developed example in this lesson.

Objectives

- To plan a short story by considering elements such as plot, conflict, characters, setting, point of view, mood, dialogue, figurative language, and suspense
- To draft a short story and solicit a response
- To revise, edit, and publish a short story

Skills

LITERATURE
- Identifying elements of a short story

WRITING AND LANGUAGE
- Creating a storyboard
- Creating paragraphs
- Using commas in dialogue

MEDIA LITERACY
- Interpreting magazine photographs

- Using news articles as story springboards

SPEAKING, LISTENING, AND VIEWING
- Conferencing
- Conducting interviews

RESEARCH SKILLS
- Researching details
- Using the computer

Teaching Strategy: STUMBLING BLOCK

A Some students may develop so many springboards that they will have trouble focusing their story ideas. Encourage them to make a list of five story ideas and then generate at least three specific details about each idea. Students should eliminate the story ideas for which they can provide no details. If one idea provokes a host of details, then that may be the best choice for a story topic.

Teaching Strategy: COLLABORATIVE OPPORTUNITY

B As a variation on this prewriting technique, a single "What if?" statement should be developed by each group. Tell each member of the group to expand the statement by adding one specific detail.

WRITING FROM EXPERIENCE

WRITING A NARRATIVE

Sometimes when you least expect it, something will happen that disrupts your daily routine. It may be annoying, exciting, or even dangerous. Most of the selections in Unit Six, "A Matter of Life and Death," focus on events such as these. Some are about struggles for survival. Others are about surprising and sad events.

GUIDED ASSIGNMENT

Write a Short Story You may not have faced the kinds of danger described in this unit, but your experiences and imagination can yield many story ideas. In this lesson, you will write a short story.

❶ Explore Some Ideas

What story ideas are inside your head? These activities will help you discover them.

Visualizing Experiences Think of interesting, funny, scary, or sad experiences you've had or read about. Relive one or two of them in your mind. Jot down the events and what you see, hear, smell, taste, and feel.

Finding Springboards The clippings on these pages can help you imagine some stories.
A (After reading the hurricane article, you might think of a story about a person your age who survives a similar storm.)

Brainstorming "What if" Questions In a small group, create a list of questions that begin with "What if," such as, "What
B if I could travel 20 years into the future?" or "What if I could communicate with sharks?" These questions might lead to story ideas.

Magazine Photograph

A gray reef shark took a bite out of photographer Bill Curtsinger's shoulder one day in 1973. Curtsinger (above) writes in *National Geographic* that he now believes gray reef sharks attack humans only if the sharks feel threatened.

834 UNIT SIX: A MATTER OF LIFE AND DEATH

PRINT AND MEDIA RESOURCES

UNIT SIX RESOURCE BOOK
Prewriting, p. 57
Elaboration, p. 58
Peer Response Guide, pp. 59–60
Revising and Proofreading, p. 61
Student Model, pp. 62–63
Rubric, p. 64

GRAMMAR MINI-LESSONS
Transparencies, p. 44
Copymasters, pp. 45–46

WRITING MINI-LESSONS
Transparencies, p. 37

FORMAL ASSESSMENT
Guidelines for Writing Assessment

 LASERLINKS
Writing Springboard

 WRITING COACH

 The Writer's Craft
Point of View in Fiction, p. 431

834 THE LANGUAGE OF LITERATURE TEACHER'S EDITION

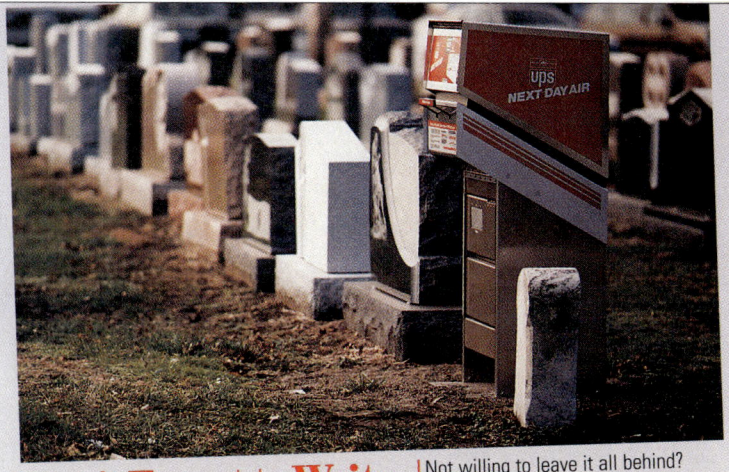

Magazine Photograph
What strange stories does this image suggest?

Don't Forget to Write
Not willing to leave it all behind? No problem at this monument company in Berwick, Pa.: Just because you can't take it with you doesn't mean you can't send it on ahead.

What if I lost my home in a hurricane?

What would it be like to live through a storm like this one?

What Andrew Left Behind

by Peter Slevin and Dexter Filkins
Herald Staff Writers

A new accounting of Hurricane Andrew's fury put the number of homes destroyed at 63,000 and the homeless population at 175,000 or more. The death toll rose Wednesday to at least 22 in Dade County.

As the great storm slammed ashore one last time in Louisiana, Florida's scarred landscape offered little but the prospect of an arduous climb toward normality.

Two days of shock are yielding to a fresh and delicate phase that will test the already frayed nerves of Andrew's victims. Operating on little sleep and much uncertainty about the future, many survivors are adding frustration to their catalog of post-storm emotions.

Pain and doubt grew, along with the casualty totals.

"The first day, residents were pretty stoic. They were just happy to be alive," said Florida City Manager Dick Anderson. "Now, people are increasingly worrying about where their next meal is coming from, how they are going to feed the kids, where can they find [diapers], those kinds of things."

from the Miami Herald

Newspaper Article

❷ Freewrite About Your Favorite Ideas

Choose two or three of your most promising story ideas. Think about who the characters might be and how the story could end. Freewrite about how you might develop each of these ideas into a story.

- WRITING SPRINGBOARD
- WRITING COACH

WRITING FROM EXPERIENCE **835**

Critical Thinking: SPECULATING

C Encourage students to use the offbeat photograph and caption here as springboards for their imagination. Remind them that in ancient Egypt, for example, the dead were provided with food and clothing for their journey to the afterlife, and similar beliefs are current in some cultures today.

CUSTOMIZING FOR
Students Acquiring English

D Some of the vocabulary in the newspaper article may cause problems for readers. You may wish to define the following terms:

accounting: detailed summary or analysis
post-storm: after the storm
stoic: calm under pressure, determined to endure

Writing Skill: USING THE COMPUTER

E Students may find that their thoughts flow more freely when they use a computer for freewriting. Suggest that they try shutting off or covering the monitor as they write. This will help them concentrate on their ideas, writing constantly, rather than being distracted by what they have already written.

WRITING SPRINGBOARD
Kids and Guns Life in the inner city can sometimes be a life and death situation. In this brief film a young man explains why some kids in his neighborhood carry guns.

Writing Prompt Using this short film as an example, write a short story about a dangerous situation you know about in your community.

Side B, Frame 47203

CUSTOMIZING FOR
Students Acquiring English

F Some students may be thrown off by the negative overtones of the word *conflict*. Help these students understand the literary meaning of this word by supplying additional examples of real-life conflicts, such as deciding between joining a school athletic team or taking on a part-time job in after-school hours.

Teaching Strategy: MODELING

G Remind students that besides serving as links to action and character, aspects of setting (indoors versus outdoors, time of day or night, time of year) can be extremely important to the mood or atmosphere of a story. Call on volunteers to give specific examples of how the setting was an important part of their favorite stories, novels, plays, or films.

PREWRITING

Shaping an Idea

A Topic to Explore You've generated plenty of story ideas. On these two pages, you'll begin to develop one of them into a story.

1 Choose an Idea to Write About

Which story ideas jump out at you from your brainstorming and freewriting? Choose the one you would most enjoy writing about. Don't worry if you don't know how your story will end. You can figure that out as you develop your ideas.

2 Explore Story Elements

A story is only as good as its characters, setting, plot, and conflict. The questions below will help you develop these elements in your story. You might use sketches or a flow chart to explore various story options, as shown on the right.

Plot What happens in your story? Most stories have events that build to a climax, or a high point, and then end with the solution to a problem.

Conflict What is the conflict, or main problem, in the story? Is it a conflict between characters, or is it something else, such as a natural disaster the characters must deal with? When is the conflict introduced and developed? What happens at the end?

Characters Who are the characters in your story? What do they look like? How do they act? What do they think about and believe? You might role-play one of your characters to help you gather details.

Setting Where and when does your story take place? How important is the setting to the action and the characters in the story?

Student's Sketches

836 UNIT SIX: A MATTER OF LIFE AND DEATH

 Mini-Lesson — The Writer's Style

CREATING REALISM Remind students that realism in a story is the quality of its appearing to be true or factual. To create realism, writers rely on specific details that contribute to the believability of a setting, a character, or dialogue. For example, geographical details like proper names help to create authenticity in a setting or description, whereas professional jargon or slang makes a character's dialogue seem natural and real.

Application Have students discuss how scientific knowledge would help to create realism for a story set in the desert or on the ocean floor.

Additional Suggestions Suggest that students consult at least one seemingly peripheral source for their short stories. Brief digressions regarding incidental events or details can often lend realism to a work. For instance, if students wish to write about desert naturalists, they might also consult a catalogue of the latest camping equipment suitable for desert use.

Reteaching/Reinforcement

 The Writer's Craft

Using Dialogue Effectively, pp. 434–35

836 THE LANGUAGE OF LITERATURE TEACHER'S EDITION

③ Plan Your Story

Your story may be entirely made up or based on your experience. If it is a true story, let your imagination fill in any memory gaps. Don't just limit yourself to what you remember. Here are a few other things to think about before you write.

Point of View You can tell your story from the first-person point of view, in which the narrator is a character in the story. Or you may prefer to tell it from the third-person point of view. A third-person narrator is outside the story and may be aware of the characters' thoughts.

Mood Your story can be spooky, funny, nostalgic, dramatic, or suspenseful. It depends on the mood, or atmosphere, you create. To help choose a mood, think about what happens in your story and about how you want your readers to react.

Goals and Audience Most short stories are for entertainment. However, you might have other goals, such as raising awareness about how dangerous a hurricane can be. Before you write, also think about your audience. Will you write for your friends, a magazine, your family, or someone else?

Student's Exploratory Chart

SkillBuilder

RESEARCH SKILLS

Researching Details
Your story will be more realistic if you provide details about the setting, characters, and other elements. If you aren't familiar with certain aspects of your story, you can do some research. For example, a student writing about a hurricane might look in books and magazine indexes for information on hurricanes. News articles, videos, and pictures are also helpful sources. They can show how hurricanes behave and what kind of damage they can cause.

APPLYING WHAT YOU'VE LEARNED
Look over the notes you took for each story element. If you need more details, consider doing some research at the library or interviewing people who are familiar with your topic.

THINK & PLAN

Reviewing Your Story Idea

1. Is your story idea believable? If not, how can you make the plot more realistic?
2. What mood would be most appealing to the audience you have in mind?
3. Did you generate plenty of details for each story element? If not, how will you find more?

WRITING FROM EXPERIENCE 837

Writing Skill: POINT OF VIEW

H Point out the benefits and drawbacks of using first-person point of view. Telling the narrative from the vantage point of a major character who uses the pronouns *I, me, we,* and *our* can create sympathy for and an intimate insight into that character's personality. Nevertheless, first-person point of view is limited because the narrator can reveal only those events and statements that he or she witnesses directly.

Writing Skill: MOOD

I Remind students that word connotations are extremely important in establishing and maintaining the mood or atmosphere in a story. Call on volunteers to offer some nouns, verbs, adjectives, and adverbs whose connotations suggest each of the moods listed in the text. For example, for "nostalgic" students might suggest word choices such as these: *era, memory, recollection, pined, rambled, bygone, wistful, softly.*

CUSTOMIZING FOR
Less-Proficient Writers

J Visual learners will find it especially helpful to use story maps, timelines, outlines, sketches, lists, tree diagrams, or other graphic aids to organize their thoughts before they begin to write. Auditory learners may benefit from using a tape recorder to brainstorm and to tell their stories in rough outline from before they write them.

SkillBuilder   RESEARCH SKILLS

RESEARCHING DETAILS Emphasize that research is an important part of prewriting for many skilled fiction writers, poets, and dramatists. Some writers travel to the places where they plan to set their material in order to soak up local atmosphere and to acquire specialized knowledge about the inhabitants and their environment.

Application Students may want to work with partners to carry out their library research or conduct their interviews.

Additional Suggestions Remind students that computerized databases may be extremely helpful in locating newspaper and magazine articles on recent events or current trends.

Teaching Strategy: USING THE SKILLBUILDER

K You may wish to teach the SkillBuilder on Creating Paragraphs at this time. An initial understanding of how and when to create paragraphs will make the draft easier for students to read and revise later.

Teaching Strategy: MODELING

L This is a good opportunity to review figures of speech. Make sure that students understand that a simile is a figure of speech that makes a comparison between two things using the words *like* or *as*. Call on volunteers to suggest similes for a hurricane. Then review the definition of metaphor: a figure of speech that makes a comparison between two things that have something in common. Ask students to suggest metaphors for a hurricane.

Teaching Strategy: MANAGING THE PAPER LOAD

M You may wish to have students affix a single self-stick note to their drafts bearing their major question or concern. You could then focus upon that issue as you read, relegating more general concerns to peer-review sessions.

DRAFTING

Getting Your Story Down

A First Draft Are you ready to write your story? These pages will give you strategies for putting your ideas on paper and then crafting them into a memorable story.

1 Write a Rough Draft

Begin writing any part of your story you feel comfortable with. Don't worry about the order—you can organize the sections later. As you write, think about how you can include these elements:

Dialogue How do your characters talk? If there are teenagers in your story, remember to have them speak like teens, not like children or like businesspeople.

Description Include details that will help readers "see" your characters, their actions, and the setting. For example, the photo on the right could help a student writing about a hurricane include these details: bent palms, twisted metal gutters, and strewn concrete blocks.

Figurative Language You might want to include metaphors, similes, or other figures of speech in your story. For example, you could compare the sound of a hurricane to the sound of a freight train.

Suspense Consider using dialogue, details, or narration in your story to build suspense—a growing interest in the conflict and its resolution.

I need to make this opening moment seem real. Maybe more details would help.

Student's Rough Draft

I could add some suspense here, like hinting at the problems to come.

Bryan stared at the TV. The anchorwoman was talking about a hurricane that was headed for the Florida coast. Straight for his town!

What could he do? Dad was already on the phone with the local police to find out whether people were leaving town. Evacuating, he called it.

When his dad got off the phone, Bryan went right over to him and told him what the guys were talking about at school. They put masking tape on their windows at home and locked the shutters to keep the wind out. They said the storm wouldn't be strong. Their families weren't leaving, or evacuating, or whatever you call it.

838

WRITING SPRINGBOARD
Earthquake in Kobe, Japan Nature can sometimes present us with a life and death situation. This brief documentary film shows the devastation of a recent earthquake in Japan.

Side B, Frame 47203

Writing Prompt After viewing this short film, write a short story about a life and death situation that resulted from an act of nature.

838 THE LANGUAGE OF LITERATURE TEACHER'S EDITION

2 Analyze Your Draft

Asking yourself questions like the ones below can help you evaluate how well you've developed your story.

- What point of view do I use? Is it consistent throughout?
- Will my readers understand how the action moves from one point to the next? Will more details make the plot clearer?
- Does the ending fit the story? Is the ending realistic?

3 Rework Your Draft and Share

You can organize the events in your story in many ways. Just be sure to give your story a beginning, middle, and end. Below are some organizational strategies you might consider using.

Chronological Order Once your plot is in place, you can tell your story in chronological order, from the first event to the last.

Flashback You might start in the middle with a dramatic event. Later on, you'll need to fill in the events that happened earlier. This technique is called flashback.

PEER RESPONSE

A student reviewer can help you strengthen your story. Ask your reviewer questions such as these:

- Can you picture the time and place in your mind? What details or bits of dialogue help you create that picture?
- Are my characters believable? What dialogue seems real? What dialogue doesn't?
- What are your feelings at different points in the story? How can I make the story more interesting for the reader?

SkillBuilder
WRITER'S CRAFT

Creating Paragraphs

Knowing when to create a new paragraph is a key to good story writing. It also helps readers follow the conversation and events. You should begin a new paragraph when each character begins speaking, when the action changes, or when the scene changes. Note the example.

> We heard a crash, the sound of splintering window glass in my bedroom. I leapt to my closed bedroom door, wanting to do something.
> "Just stay in the living room," Dad said. "We need to be calm."
> I crawled back onto the couch and hugged a pillow, wondering when the storm would end.

APPLYING WHAT YOU'VE LEARNED

You might want to look over your draft to make sure you've met the guidelines described above for creating new paragraphs.

RETHINK & EVALUATE

Thinking About Your Draft

1. What details can you add to make your characters more realistic? How can you make their voices distinct?
2. What would happen if you changed the point of view?
3. If your story needs suspense, how will you build it in? Could you use flashback?

WRITING FROM EXPERIENCE 839

Teaching Strategy:
STUMBLING BLOCK

N Remind students that a good short story captures and holds the reader's interest in the first paragraph. Students who are having trouble writing their introductions can consider starting with a striking exchange of dialogue that plunges the reader directly into the action. They can then use flashback to fill readers in on any important background information about the characters or the setting.

Teaching Strategy:
PEER REVIEW

O Have reviewers read the story before they make any comments. During the second reading, they should jot down brief comments and suggestions. Remind reviewers to include specific ideas for revision, such as "Why not tell us how the beach looked and smelled after the hurricane passed over?"

SkillBuilder WRITER'S CRAFT

CREATING PARAGRAPHS Emphasize that good paragraphing in stories helps readers in much the same way that transition words help them: by providing cues that give structure to the events, ideas, and dialogue. Like all stylistic techniques, paragraphing should be flexible and appropriate to the content. For example, scenes that feature rapid action and animated dialogue usually require short paragraphs. For sustained descriptions or passages of interior monologue, writers often use much longer paragraphs.

Application Invite students to work with partners or in other small groups to apply to their drafts what they have learned about paragraphing.

Additional Suggestions Have students work with partners to examine the paragraphing in two or three of their favorite stories.

Reteaching/Reinforcing
- *Writing Mini-Lessons* transparencies, p. 37

The Writer's Craft
Paragraphing, pp. 388–389

THE LANGUAGE OF LITERATURE TEACHER'S EDITION 839

Writing Skill: REVISING

P As students revise and edit their stories, they will work to improve their drafts by

1. adding needed words, sentences, and paragraphs
2. cutting unnecessary material by focusing on repetitive or unrelated details
3. substituting words, sentences, and paragraphs for deleted material if necessary
4. rearranging parts of the text to create coherence and unity

Teaching Strategy: MODELING

Q Discuss how this model meets the standards for evaluation on page 841. Details on the first page that build suspense include the science teacher's comments on hurricanes, the fact that the storm is headed straight for Miami, the conversation with the police about evacuating, and Bryan's ignorance of the storm's severity.

REVISING AND PUBLISHING

Finishing Your Story

Another Look at Your Draft Are you satisfied with the way your story is developing? On these pages, you'll have a chance to make additional changes before you publish it.

1 Revise and Edit

The following tips may help you improve your short story.

P
- In the excerpts at the right, how does the plot develop from the beginning to the middle? Are the events in your plot clearly organized?
- How does the narrator in this student model feel early in the story? later? In your story, how do you use description and dialogue to make your characters seem real?
- Use the Standards for Evaluation on the lower right to make sure that your plot is realistic and presents events and characters clearly. The Editing Checklist and the SkillBuilder on the far right can help you make it clear who is speaking.

Student's Final Draft

How do the details on the first page build suspense?

A Stormy Nightmare

Bryan stared at the TV, his eyes fixed on the picture above the anchorwoman's head. It looked harmless enough, like a whirlpool of soap suds in a dish drain. Yet he'd heard from his ninth-grade science teacher just how dangerous the condition shown on TV could be. It was a hurricane, and it was headed straight for the Florida coast. Straight for Miami!

Bryan's dad was on the phone with the local police station to find out whether they should leave town. Evacuating, he called it. If Bryan's family stayed, it would be their first hurricane since moving to Miami. Bryan was curious, and the idea of actually experiencing a hurricane made him tingle with excitement. He had no idea it would be the worst storm in Florida history.

The wind pounded the sides of his house and roared in his ears like a freight train. Bryan heard a crash, the sound of splintering window glass in his bedroom. He leapt up from the couch and started toward his closed bedroom door, wanting to do something.

"Just stay in the living room with the rest of us," Dad said. "We have to stay calm."

Bryan crawled back onto the couch and hugged a pillow, wondering when the storm would end.

840 UNIT SIX: A MATTER OF LIFE AND DEATH

Student's Storyboard and Script

② Share Your Work

It's time to publish your story! One student created a movie based on the storyboard and text shown above. Other publishing ideas are listed below.

- Record your story on a cassette tape and send it to friends or relatives who live out of town.
- Send your story to a magazine that publishes the work of young writers. If you wish, include your own illustrations.

Standards for Evaluation

An effective short story
- includes believable characters, a setting that readers can picture in their minds, and a plot that is realistic
- introduces, develops, and resolves a conflict
- presents events in a clear sequence
- includes description, dialogue, figurative language, and suspense to liven up the story elements
- uses language that is suitable for the audience

SkillBuilder

 GRAMMAR FROM WRITING

Using Commas in Dialogue

To add interest to their dialogue, writers often vary the placement of a speaker's tag. A comma follows the speaker's tag before or in the middle of a quotation. A period follows the tag after a quotation.

> Mom asked, *"How do you feel about weathering out the storm?"*
> *"I don't mind,"* I replied, *"because my friends say it won't be bad."*
> *"Then it's settled,"* Dad said.

GRAMMAR HANDBOOK

For more help with punctuating dialogue, see page 938 of the Grammar Handbook.

Editing Checklist

1. Did you punctuate the dialogue correctly?
2. Did you create new paragraphs at the appropriate places?

REFLECT & ASSESS

Evaluate Your New Knowledge

1. How is your story different from your initial idea? What does this say about the writing process?
2. What one piece of advice would you give to other story writers?

 PORTFOLIO Write a note telling what you learned about developing a plot.

WRITING FROM EXPERIENCE   **841**

Writing Skill: SHARING

In addition to the sharing options listed in the text, suggest the following possibilities:
- staging stories in class in a Reader's Theater
- reading stories to a class of younger students
- publishing stories on a computer web site
- adapting a story to create a ballad

Teaching Strategy: MANAGING THE PAPER LOAD

Whenever possible, phrase your written comments as questions that will encourage students to reflect on and assess their own work. For example, instead of writing "lacks depth," try "Couldn't you flesh out Matt's character by referring to his career training and one or two specific hobbies?"

Standards for Evaluation

Ideas and Content
- creates believable characters who use natural-sounding dialogue
- introduces, develops, and resolves conflict through a realistic plot
- uses sensory details and description to create a setting readers can picture in their minds
- uses description and suspense to liven up story elements

Structure and Form
- demonstrates proper and effective paragraphing
- includes transitional words and phrases to show relationships among ideas
- uses variety of sentence structures

Grammar, Usage, and Mechanics
- contains no more than two or three minor errors in grammar usage
- contains no more than two or three minor errors in spelling, capitalization, and punctuation

PORTFOLIO

Ask students to write a brief description of what they have learned about writing short stories as a result of this assignment. They may wish to include their description and their finished stories in their portfolio.

SkillBuilder GRAMMAR FROM WRITING

USING COMMAS IN DIALOGUE In addition to going over the punctuation rules discussed in the text, you may want to remind students that a comma at the end of quoted material is always placed inside the quotation marks. Semicolons and colons, however, are always placed outside quotation marks. Question marks and exclamation points are placed inside the quotation marks if they are part of the quoted material; otherwise, they are placed outside.

Application You may wish to have students work with partners to check the punctuation of dialogue in their drafts.

Additional Suggestions Remind students that the first word of the second part of a divided quotation is capitalized only if it begins a new sentence, as this re-written second paragraph shows:

> "I don't mind," I replied. "My friends say it won't be bad."

Reteaching/Reinforcing
- *Grammar Mini-Lessons* copymasters pp. 45–46, transparencies p. 44

The Writer's Craft

Punctuating Dialogue, pp. 798–799

THE LANGUAGE OF LITERATURE   TEACHER'S EDITION   **841**

UNIT REVIEW

This feature allows students to reflect on what they have learned in Unit Six and to assess how well they have understood it. This feature provides students with multiple opportunities for self-assessment. You may also wish to use some of the activities to assess specific skills, such as speaking, listening, or cooperative learning.

Objectives

- To allow students to reflect on and assess their understanding of theme
- To allow students to reflect on and assess their understanding of literary concepts, such as imagery and suspense
- To provide students with the opportunity to assess and build their portfolios

REFLECTING ON THEME

OPTION 1

You may first want to challenge students to explain the quotation. When they have completed their webs, engage the class in discussion by asking them to defend their placement of various characters and people. (See Unit Resource Book for additional information on creating webs.)

OPTION 2

You may want to appoint one member of each group as an encourager to elicit responses from all members. Then, because students will be discussing momentous decisions, consider appointing a clarifier in each group to help other members articulate their thoughts.

OPTION 3

Suggest that students skim the selections to identify the key traits of the characters and people. Then they should select traits from the list to create their "composite person." A lively discussion will ensue if you ask a number of students to defend their final choices.

 Self-Assessment Suggest that students focus on the specific attitudes or actions that make both of the chosen characters or people impressive as they explore their reasons for admiring them.

REFLECT & ASSESS

UNIT SIX: A MATTER OF LIFE AND DEATH

What impact did the selections in this unit have on you? Did any selection make you think about something in a new way? Did you enjoy the mysteries and the adventure stories? Explore these questions by completing one or more of the options in each of the following sections.

REFLECTING ON THEME

OPTION 1 Is Life Dangerous? Consider the quotation on the opening page of this unit: "Living on earth has always been a dangerous way to spend your time." Which characters and people in this unit might agree with that statement? Create a web to identify those who would agree. Then identify the characters and people who might disagree, explaining the possible reasons for their disagreement.

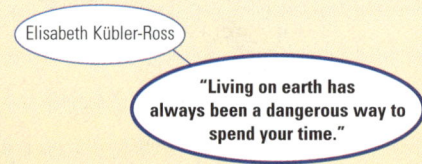

OPTION 2 Decisions, Decisions In many of the selections in this unit, people make decisions about issues of life and death. With a small group of classmates, discuss the life-and-death decisions faced by the characters and people in the selections you've read. Consider what options each has and whether any of them seem to value anything more than life.

OPTION 3 Building on Strengths In terms of the most desirable traits of the characters and people in this unit, describe the kind of person that you think is best suited to face a life-and-death struggle. For example, you might say that the person should have the quick-thinking ability of Sanger Rainsford and the compassion of Elisabeth Kübler-Ross. Complete your composite person with traits from at least three other characters.

Self-Assessment: Make two lists—one of the characters and people in this unit who face death, the other of those who confront the death of another person or thing. Which character or person in each list impressed you the most? In a paragraph, explain your choices.

REVIEWING LITERARY CONCEPTS

OPTION 1 Examining Imagery Many of the selections in Unit Six are rich in imagery—language that appeals to one or more of the five senses. In a chart like the one shown, compile a list of effective images from the selections in this unit, identifying the sense or senses (sight, hearing, smell, taste, touch) that each image appeals to. Compare your findings with those of your classmates, and discuss why you think those particular images are effective.

Selection	Image	Sense
"The Most Dangerous Game"	"Twenty feet below him the sea rumbled and hissed."	sight, hearing

842 UNIT SIX: A MATTER OF LIFE AND DEATH

OPTION 2 Considering Suspense In most stories of life-and-death struggles, readers are carried along by a feeling of tension or anticipation as they wonder what will happen next. In some writing, such suspense becomes a main ingredient. Think of the selections you have read in this unit. Which ones do you think would register the highest on a "suspense thermometer"? In a paragraph, explain your choices and describe what exactly contributes to the suspense in the selections.

The most suspenseful selections I read in this unit are

Self-Assessment: On a sheet of paper, copy this list of literary terms introduced or reviewed in this unit. Next to each term, write W (for "well"), S (for "somewhat"), or N (for "not at all") to indicate how well you feel you now understand it. If you need to, you can look terms up in the Handbook of Literary Terms on page 850.

paradox   personification
theme   verbal irony
meter   mood

PORTFOLIO BUILDING

- **QuickWrites** Some of the QuickWrites in this unit asked you to write something creative, such as a poem, a narrative, a new ending, or an outline for a story. Choose one piece that you feel showcases your creative talents, and explain in a cover note why it does.

- **Writing About Literature** Writing a scene from a drama may have given you new insight into the challenges of writing for television, film, or the stage. What did you learn about the nature of drama as you wrote? Write a brief essay in which you describe what problems you encountered in writing the scene and how you tried to solve the problems. Attach your essay to your dramatic scene.

- **Writing from Experience** You have now written a short story—creating characters, deciding on a setting, developing a plot, and creating a conflict. Was this process a challenge for you, or did some of the elements come together easily? What parts of the process were especially challenging? What made them challenging? Write a brief description of what you liked about writing a short story and what you

learned from the process. If you add your story for your portfolio, include your description with it.

- **Personal Choice** Look over your records of the activities that you completed for this unit or on your own. Which kind of activity do you think you especially excel in? Drawing? Dramatization? Oral presentation? Write an assessment of your ability in a cover note, attach it to your record of one such activity, and add both to your portfolio.

Self-Assessment: Look through your portfolio for examples of writing or activities that you think are particularly well done. Then pat yourself on the back for all you've accomplished during this year.

SETTING GOALS

Think about important learning experiences you've had during this year. What key strategies and processes have helped you improve as a reader and as a writer? Jot them down so that you can remember to use them again.

REFLECT & ASSESS   **843**

SETTING GOALS

Suggest that students consider the various reading and writing strategies that they have focused on in this book, reviewing them by skimming through the book or their own portfolios. This exercise will help students think about their learning process in a concrete way.

REVIEWING LITERARY CONCEPTS

OPTION 1

As a variation, you might ask small groups to list from five to ten images from a particular selection. Encourage students to find at least one that appeals to each sense. Post the groups' charts around the classroom. See also Unit Six Resource Book, p. 67.

OPTION 2

You may wish to use the following rubric for evaluating paragraphs.

3 Full Accomplishment Student identifies the title and author of a selection, provides concrete details from the selection, and explains the importance of those details.

2 Substantial Accomplishment Student identifies the selection and focuses on either a summary or on response without linking it to the text.

1 Little or Partial Accomplishment Student fails to identify the selection or relies primarily on a summary of action or on generalizations such as "I found everything very exciting."

Self-Assessment Suggest that students, perhaps in pairs, find in the selections examples of the concepts they labeled S or N.

PORTFOLIO BUILDING

Review the main elements in the portfolio system that students are using. Ask them to choose from the options suggested in the book or help them work out an alternative that meets the needs of the class. Encourage students to be as specific as possible in their notes; doing so will give them valuable insight into their own learning process. If a number of budding playwrights choose the Writing about Literature option, encourage them to share their problems and solutions in a brainstorming group.

Self-Assessment Suggest that students share an example of a well-done piece with a larger audience, perhaps reading it aloud in class, submitting it to the school literary journal, and so on.

THE LANGUAGE OF LITERATURE TEACHER'S EDITION **843**

Student Resource Bank

Words to Know: Access Guide 846

Handbook of Literary Terms 850

Writing Handbook
1 The Writing Process 860
2 Building Blocks of Good Writing 866
3 Narrative Writing 876
4 Explanatory Writing 878
5 Persuasive Writing 884
6 Research Report Writing 886

Multimedia Handbook
1 Getting Information Electronically 890
2 Word Processing 892
3 Using Visuals 895
4 Creating a Multimedia Presentation 897

Grammar Handbook
1 Writing Complete Sentences 900
2 Making Subjects and Verbs Agree 903
3 Using Nouns and Pronouns 910
4 Using Modifiers Effectively 918
5 Using Verbs Correctly 923
6 Correcting Capitalization 927
7 Correcting Punctuation 931
8 Grammar Glossary 940

Index of Fine Art 946

Index of Skills 949

Index of Titles and Authors 961

Words to Know: Access Guide

A
abashed, 636
abiding, 602
abominably, 522
abusive, 30
accosted, 777
acquittal, 600
adamant, 301
adulation, 662
adversary, 502
adversity, 228
affable, 795
afflict, 456
affront, 675
aghast, 663
agitated, 344
agnostic, 288
alien, 432
aloof, 563
ambiguously, 592
amenity, 794
anguish, 528
animosity, 344
antagonism, 20
anthology, 438
antipathy, 44
apathetically, 224
appalled, 495
apprehensive, 179
appropriate, 391
aristocrat, 53
articulate, 434
askew, 665
assuage, 285
audacity, 180
aura, 59
authenticity, 674
avenge, 494

B
beguiling, 510
bereaved, 136
beseeching, 97
bias, 274
bland, 720
blatant, 301
bleakly, 745
bravado, 111
brevity, 617

C
careen, 417
cascading, 59
cavort, 74
chaos, 524
chasm, 751
chide, 513
commandeer, 546
compassion, 116
competent, 298
comprehension, 638
concretely, 718
concur, 296
concussion, 23
condone, 798
conformity, 673
conglomeration, 204
congregate, 454
conspicuous, 45
conspiracy, 67
constitute, 600
constricted, 309
contaminated, 717
contemptible, 556
contemptuously, 270
contender, 513
contrary, 395
contrition, 93
convalescence, 151
convey, 715
covert, 638

D
dank, 308
debilitate, 290
defiant, 97
definitive, 150
degradation, 115
demeanor, 344
denunciation, 301
deplorable, 801
depreciates, 674
deprivation, 353
desolation, 566
despondently, 613
destined, 782
devastated, 718
devoid, 344
dexterity, 149
dilapidated, 35
diligence, 455
dire, 528
disarming, 793
disconsolate, 513
discordant, 260
disdain, 306, 504
disjunction, 342
disoriented, 676
dispatch, 811
dispel, 609
dissenting, 674
distended, 151
distraught, 34
dithering, 554
doggedness, 422
droll, 798
dubious, 43
dumbfounded, 388
duress, 202
dwindle, 525

E
eccentricity, 457
egotistical, 615
elation, 34
elicit, 151
elude, 799
emblem, 20
embroider, 439
enamored, 285
enigmatic, 614
ensue, 811
enticing, 513
entreat, 494
epitome, 42
equanimity, 146
escapade, 455
essence, 59
evoke, 820
exasperation, 179
exhilarate, 65
exorbitant, 665
exotic, 423
exploitation, 228

F
facetiously, 640
familiarity, 53
fanaticism, 264
fantasize, 368
farce, 600
feigned, 261
ferocity, 198

fetter, 780
fiasco, 674
foreboding, 189
formidable, 488
fortitude, 298
frenzy, 554
fulfill, 440
futile, 108

G
gall, 552
gamut, 663
garish, 68
genial, 587
goad, 71
grotesque, 341
guile, 488

H
haggard, 369
harass, 611
hedge, 433
heedless, 434
heresy, 425
hierarchy, 30
homage, 260

I
illiteracy, 58
immersed, 812
imminent, 419
impeccable, 672
imperative, 802
impertinent, 594
implacable, 560
implore, 780
impotent, 113
impoverished, 108
impunity, 777
inadvertently, 296

inaugurate, 65
incarnation, 42
incessantly, 55
incorrigible, 290
incredulous, 99
indifferent, 490
indignity, 826
indomitable, 826
inept, 287
inexplicable, 617
infallibility, 420
infatuated, 32
infernal, 131
infinitesimal, 149
influx, 675
infuse, 57
insatiable, 591
insinuatingly, 260
insipid, 457
insurgent, 199
intensity, 307
interim, 749
intimidation, 274
intrigue, 343
intuition, 751
intuitively, 431
invalid, 416
invincible, 219
iridescent, 420
irresolute, 308
irreverence, 677

J
jeer, 307
justification, 546

K
kin, 140

L
laggard, 187
latent, 202
lethargy, 820
lurk, 522

M
malevolent, 199
maliciously, 191
mandate, 822
maneuvering, 32
maniacal, 198
martyrs, 30
maudlin, 219
mode, 434
monopoly, 220
murky, 454
mystic, 820

N
naive, 434
noncommittal, 71
nonentity, 182
nostalgia, 439

O
oblivion, 224
obsessively, 368
omen, 556
ominous, 180
oppressor, 277
oratory, 295
overcompensate, 46

P
palpitation, 388
patronizing, 288
pauper, 661
pensive, 42
peril, 526

perverse, 111
placidly, 268
pliant, 458
plunder, 548
poignantly, 108
ponderous, 495
precariously, 423
preclude, 777
precocious, 284
premonition, 182
preoccupied, 638
presumptuous, 284
pretense, 811
privation, 664
procrastinate, 717
proficiency, 149
prone, 742
prosaic, 68
prospects, 659
prostrate, 811
prudent, 458
punitive, 718

Q
quarry, 792
quell, 199
query, 21
questing, 529

R
ravage, 368
recoil, 24
reflectively, 600
regaled, 515
reiterate, 423
relent, 431
remorse, 134
repose, 779
repress, 590

reproach, 310
repugnance, 307
resigned, 35
restitution, 560
retort, 370
retribution, 204
retrospect, 298
revelry, 557
ruinous, 663

S
sacrilegious, 55
sardonically, 290
scourge, 524
scruples, 799
scrutinize, 191
sever, 75
sham, 198
skeptical, 454
skewed, 617
snare, 510
solace, 36
solicitous, 800
sophistication, 59
speculate, 434
spontaneous, 716
squalor, 116
squander, 67

stamina, 801
stealth, 510
stifle, 434
stoicism, 111
suave, 42
subside, 782
succumb, 513
sullen, 614
superficial, 150
supplication, 95
surreptitiously, 45
synthetic, 218

T
tangible, 790
termination, 780
throes, 132
throng, 557
tirade, 301
tolerant, 673
transcend, 716
transcendent, 826
trauma, 439
travail, 528
tremulous, 310
trepidation, 350
tribute, 45

U
ultimate, 824
uncanny, 803
unconventional, 311
uniqueness, 720
unscrupulous, 229
usurper, 391

V
venture, 146
vexation, 660
vigil, 822
vile, 510
virtuoso, 777
void, 218
vulnerability, 349

W
wane, 824
wary, 612
whim, 494
wiliest, 557

Z
zealous, 802

Pronunciation Key

Symbol	Examples	Symbol	Examples	Symbol	Examples
ă	at, gas	m	man, seem	v	van, save
ā	ape, day	n	night, mitten	w	web, twice
ä	father, barn	ng	sing, anger	y	yard, lawyer
âr	fair, dare	ŏ	odd, not	z	zoo, reason
b	bell, table	ō	open, road, grow	zh	treasure, garage
ch	chin, lunch	ô	awful, bought, horse	ə	awake, even, pencil,
d	dig, bored	oi	coin, boy		pilot, focus
ĕ	egg, ten	ŏŏ	look, full	ər	perform, letter
ē	evil, see, meal	ōō	root, glue, through		
f	fall, laugh, phrase	ou	out, cow		**Sounds in Foreign Words**
g	gold, big	p	pig, cap	KH	German ich, auch;
h	hit, inhale	r	rose, star		Scottish loch
hw	white, everywhere	s	sit, face	N	French entre, bon, fin
ĭ	inch, fit	sh	she, mash	œ	French feu, cœur;
ī	idle, my, tried	t	tap, hopped		German schön
îr	dear, here	th	thing, with	ü	French utile, rue;
j	jar, gem, badge	*th*	then, other		German grün
k	keep, cat, luck	ŭ	up, nut		
l	load, rattle	ûr	fur, earn, bird, worm		

Stress Marks

′ This mark indicates that the preceding syllable receives the primary stress. For example, in the word *language,* the first syllable is stressed: lăng′gwĭj.

′ This mark is used only in words in which more than one syllable is stressed. It indicates that the preceding syllable is stressed, but somewhat more weakly than the syllable receiving the primary stress. In the word *literature,* for example, the first syllable receives the primary stress, and the last syllable receives a weaker stress: lĭt′ər-ə-chŏŏr′.

Adapted from *The American Heritage Dictionary of the English Language, Third Edition;* Copyright © 1992 by Houghton Mifflin Company. Used with the permission of Houghton Mifflin Company.

Handbook of Literary Terms

Act An act is a major unit of action in a play, similar to a chapter in a book. Depending on their lengths, plays can have as many as five acts. *A Marriage Proposal* is a one-act play.

Alliteration Alliteration is the repetition of consonant sounds at the beginnings of words. Note this example of repetition of the l sounds in these lines from E. E. Cummings's poem "since feeling is first."

> laugh, leaning back in my arms
> for life's not a paragraph.

Allusion An allusion is an indirect reference to another literary work or to a famous person, place, or event. The title *I Know Why the Caged Bird Sings* is an allusion to the poem "Sympathy" by Paul Laurence Dunbar.

Antagonist An antagonist is usually the principal character in opposition to the **protagonist,** or hero of a narrative or drama. In *The Devil and Daniel Webster,* Mr. Scratch is the antagonist. Sometimes the antagonist is not a character, but something else, like force of nature.

See **Protagonist.**

Aside An aside is a dramatic device in which a character speaks his or her thoughts aloud, in words meant to be heard by the audience but not by the other characters.

See **Soliloquy.**

Assonance Assonance is the repetition of vowel sounds within non-rhyming words as in this line from "since feeling is first": "the best gesture of my brain is less than."

Author's Purpose A writer usually writes for one or more of these purposes: to express himself or herself, to inform or explain, to persuade, and to entertain.

Autobiography An autobiography is an account of a person's life written by that person and usually told from the first-person point of view. It is usually book length because it covers a long span of time. Other forms of autobiographical writing include personal narratives, journals, diaries, and letters.

See **Personal Narrative.**

Ballad A ballad is a poem that tells a story and is meant to be sung or recited. "O What Is That Sound" is an example of a ballad.

Biography Biography is a true account of a person's life told by someone else. "The United States vs. Susan B. Anthony" by Margaret Truman is an example of a biography.

Character Characters are the people who take part in the action of a story or a novel. Sometimes characters can be animals or imaginary creatures, such as monsters from other space. Events in a story center on the lives of one or more characters, referred to as **main characters.** The other characters in a story, called **minor characters,** interact with the main characters and help move the story along. In "The Last Boast," Wolfer Joe Kennedy is the main character; Barney Gallagher, the marshal, is a minor character.

Characterization Characterization refers to the methods that a writer uses to develop characters. Four basic methods of characterization are through (1) description of a character's physical appearance, (2) a character's speech, thoughts, feelings, or actions, (3) the speech thoughts, feelings, or actions of other characters, and (4) direct comments about a character.

Climax Often called the **turning point,** the climax is the moment when the reader's interest and emotional intensity reach the highest point. The climax usually occurs toward the end of a story, after the reader has understood the conflict and gotten emotionally involved with the characters. The climax sometimes, but not always, points to the resolution of the conflict.

See **Plot.**

Conflict The plot of a story always involves some sort of conflict, or struggle between opposing forces. An **external conflict** involves a character pitted against an outside force, such as nature, a physical obstacle, or another character. An **internal conflict** is one that occurs within a character.

See **Plot.**

Description Description is writing that helps a reader to picture scenes, events, and characters. To create description, writers often use imagery—words and phrases that appeal to the reader's senses—and figurative language.

See **Imagery, Figurative Language.**

Diction A writer's or speaker's choice of words and way of arranging the words in sentences is called diction. In "The Cask of Amontillado," Edgar Allan Poe uses very formal diction, whereas most contemporary stories, such as Kurt Vonnegut's "The Euphio Question," use informal diction.

Dialogue Dialogue is written conversation between two or more characters. Dialogue is used in all forms of literature but is most important in drama. In a play, the story is told primarily through dialogue, which appears in lines next to the characters' names. Here is an example of dialogue from *The Devil and Daniel Webster*:

> **Jabez.** Are you happy, Mary?
> **Mary.** Yes. So happy, I'm afraid.

In other kinds of writing, the words each character speaks are commonly set off by quotation marks.

Drama Drama is literature in which plot and characters are developed through dialogue and action; in other words, drama is literature in play form. Stage plays, radio plays, movies, and television programs are all types of drama.

See **Act, Scene.**

Dramatic Irony

See **Irony.**

Epic An epic is a long narrative poem about adventures of a hero whose actions reflect the ideals and values of a nation or race. Epics address universal concerns, such as good and evil, life and death, and sin and redemption. The *Odyssey* is an epic.

Epic Hero An epic hero is a larger-than-life figure who embodies the ideals of a nation or race. Epic heroes take part in dangerous adventures and accomplish great deeds. Many undertake long, difficult journeys, displaying great courage and superhuman strength. Odysseus is an epic hero.

Epic Simile An epic simile (also called a Homeric simile) is an elaborate, more involved version of regular simile. Epic similes contain words such as *like, as, so, just as,* or *just so* and may extend for a number of lines.

Epilogue An epilogue is a short addition at the end of a literary work, often dealing with the future of characters.

Epithet An epithet is a brief descriptive phrase that points out traits associated with a particular person or thing. An epithet is often an aid to characterization. In the *Odyssey*, Odysseus is often called "the master strategist."

Essay An essay is a brief composition on a single subject that usually presents the personal views of the author. Essays are often found in newspapers and magazines. Generally, an **expository essay** seeks to explain something and therefore fosters readers' understanding, such as David Raymond's essay "On Being Seventeen, Bright, and Unable to Read." A **narrative essay** tells a story, such as Tony Hillerman's "The Great Taos Bank Robbery." A **persuasive essay** attempts

852 Literary Handbook

to convince readers to adopt a certain point of view or to take a particular action.

Exposition In fiction, the structure of the plot normally begins with exposition. In the early part of the story, the exposition sets the tone, establishes the setting, introduces the characters, and gives the reader important background information.

See **Plot.**

Expository Essay

See **Essay.**

Extended Metaphor An extended metaphor is a figure of speech that compares two things at some length and in several ways. For example, in the poem "Battle Report," an extended metaphor compares the arrival of jazz music to the invasion of an army.

See **Figurative Language.**

External Conflict

See **Conflict.**

Falling Action In a plot structure, the falling action is sometimes called the **resolution** and occurs at the end of the story. The conflict is usually resolved at this time, and any loose ends of the story are tied up.

See **Plot.**

Fantasy Fantasy is a type of fiction that is highly imaginative and could not really happen. In a fantasy the setting might be a nonexistent and unrealistic world, the plot might involve magic, or characters might employ extra human powers. "The Wife's Story" is an example of a fantasy.

Fiction Fiction refers to works of prose that have imaginary elements, such as the novel and the short story. Although fiction is sometimes based on actual events and real people, it primarily comes from the imagination of the writer.

Figurative Language Figurative language is language that communicates ideas beyond the ordinary, literal meanings of words. Special types of figurative language called **figures of speech** include personification, simile, and metaphor.

See **Hyperbole, Metaphor, Onomatopoeia, Personification, Simile.**

First-Person Point of View A story told in the first-person point of view has a narrator who is a character in the story and tells everything in his or her own words. "The Day the Cisco Kid Shot John Wayne" is told from the first-person point of view. You know what the narrator is feeling and thinking, but you have to infer from the narrator's descriptions what other characters are feeling or thinking.

See **Point of View.**

Flashback A flashback is a conversation, an episode, or an event that happened before the beginning of a story. Often a flashback interrupts the chronological flow of a story to give the reader information to help in understanding a character's present situation.

Foreshadowing Foreshadowing is a writer's use of hints or clues to indicate events and situations that will occur in a later plot. The use of this technique creates suspense while at the same time preparing the reader for what is to come.

Form Form refers to the way a poem is laid out on the page. Poems are usually printed in individual lines, which may or may not be sentences. In some poems, lines are grouped into stanzas.

See **Stanza**.

Free Verse Free verse is poetry that does not contain a regular pattern of rhyme and meter. "Fable for When There's No Way Out" is an example of free verse.

Historical Fiction Historical fiction is contemporary fiction that takes place in the past. It may contain references to actual people and events of the past. "Plainswoman" and "The Last Boast" are examples of historical fiction.

Horror Fiction Horror fiction contains strange, mysterious, violent, and often supernatural events that create suspense and terror in the reader. Edgar Allan Poe and Stephen King are famous authors of horror fiction.

Hyperbole Hyperbole is a figure of speech in which the truth is exaggerated for emphasis or for humorous effect. In "Grover Dill and the Tasmanian Devil," Jean Shepherd uses hyperbole when he states that "We'd go to school in a sandstorm and come home before a tornado."

Idiom An idiom is an expression that has meaning different from the meaning of its individual words. For example, "go to the dogs" is an idiom meaning "go to ruin."

Imagery Imagery consists of descriptive words and phrases that re-create sensory experiences for the reader. Imagery usually appeals to one or more of the five senses—sight, hearing, smell, taste, and touch—to help the reader imagine exactly what is being described.

Informative Article An informative article gives facts about a specific subject. This type of writing is found primarily in newspapers, magazines, pamphlets, textbooks, anthologies, encyclopedias, and reference books. "'Who Killed My Daughter?': Lois Duncan Searches for an Answer" is an example of an informative article.

Internal Conflict

See *Conflict*.

Irony Irony is a special kind of contrast between appearance and reality—usually one in which reality is the opposite from what it seems. One type of irony is **situational irony,** the contrast between what a reader or character expects and what actually exists or happens. The unexpected twist at the end of "One Ordinary Day, with Peanuts," in which Mr. Johnson turns out to be just the opposite from what he seems, is an example of situational irony. Another type of irony is **dramatic irony,** where the reader or viewer knows something that a character does not know. For example, in "The Last Boast," Barney Gallagher is puzzled by Wolfer Joe's last comment about betraying a woman, but readers of the story know what Wolfer Joe means by his boast. **Verbal irony** occurs when someone knowingly exaggerates or says one things and means another.

Metaphor A metaphor is a figure of speech that makes a comparison between two things that have something in common. Unlike similes, metaphors do not use the word *like* or *as*. In these lines from "Training" the sea is compared to a boxer.

> The sea —quick pugilist—
> uses for a pun
>   ching
>   ball
> the restless little boats.

See **Figurative Language, Simile.**

Meter Meter is the regular pattern of accented and unaccented syllables in a line of poetry. The accented, or stressed, syllables are marked with ´, while unaccented, or unstressed, syllables are marked with ˘. Although all poems have rhythm, not all of them have regular meter. Each unit of meter is known as a **foot,** which consists of one accented syllable and one or two unaccented syllables. The feet and the meter are marked on these lines from Emily Dickinson's poem "Surgeons must be very careful."

> Súrgeŏns | múst bĕ | vérў | cáreful
> Whén theў | táke thĕ | knífe!
> Úndĕr | neáth theĭr | fíne ĭn | císiŏns
> Stírs thĕ | Cúlprĭt— | Lífe!

See **Rhythm.**

Mood In a literary work, the feeling or atmosphere that the writer creates for the reader is called mood. Descriptive words, the setting, and figurative language contribute to the mood of a work, as do the sound and rhythm of the language used.

Narrative Essay

See **Essay.**

Narrator The narrator is the character or voice from whose point of view events are told.

See **Point of View, Speaker.**

Nonfiction Nonfiction is prose writing that deals with real people, events, and places. The major types of nonfiction are autobiography, biography, and the essay. Other examples of nonfiction include newspapers, informative articles, true-life adventures, personal diaries, and letters.

See **Autobiography, Biography, Essay.**

Novel A novel is a long work that takes the average reader several days, or even weeks, to finish. Typically, a novel tells a complex story that unfolds through the actions, speech, and thoughts of the characters.

Onomatopoeia Onomatopoeia is the use of words such as *pow, buzz,* and *crunch* whose pronunciations suggest their meanings.

Paradox A paradox is a statement that seems to contradict itself but is, nevertheless, true. The statement "Standing is more tiring than walking" is a paradox.

Personal Narrative A personal narrative is a short form of autobiographical writing in which the writer focuses on a significant experience in his or her life. Both Truman Capote's "A Christmas Memory" and William Nolen's "The First Appendectomy" are personal narratives.

See **Autobiography.**

Personification Personification is a figure of speech in which human qualities are attributed to an object, animal, or idea. A poem is personified in the story "The Cultural Worker."

Persuasive Essay

See **Essay.**

Plot The sequence of events in a story is called the plot. Generally built around a conflict, the plot tells what happens, when, and to whom. A story's plot usually includes four stages: exposition, rising action, climax, falling action.

See **Conflict, Exposition, Rising Action, Climax, Falling Action.**

Poetry Poetry is a type of literature in which words are chosen and arranged to create a certain effect. Poets use a variety of sound devices, imagery, and figurative language to express emotions and ideas.

See **Rhyme, Rhythm, Alliteration, Assonance.**

Point of View The point of view refers to the perspective from which events in a story or novel are told. Point of view is usually either first person or third person. In **first-person** point of view, the narrator is a character in the story and tells everything in his or her own words. In **third-person** point view, a story is told by a narrative voice outside the action, not by one of the characters. If a story is told from a **third-person omniscient,** or all-knowing, point of view, the narrator sees into the minds of more than one character. If events are related from a **third-person limited** point of view, the narrator tells only what one character thinks, feels, and observes.

Protagonist The protagonist is the central character or hero in a narrative or drama, usually the one with whom the audience tends to identify. In Ortiz Cofer's "American History," Elena is the protagonist as well as the narrator.

See **Antagonist.**

Pun A pun is a joke that comes from a play on words. Puns can make use of a word's multiple meanings or of a word's rhyme. In "Battle Report," the phrase "Drops a note" (line 15) plays on the two meanings of *note* as a message and as a musical note.

Realistic Fiction Realistic fiction is a type of fiction that creates a truthful imitation of ordinary life. "Through the Tunnel" by Doris Lessing is an example of realistic fiction.

Repetition Repetition is a repeated use of words or phrases for effect or emphasis. The word *They* is repeated for emphasis in the poem "Lineage."

Resolution

See **Falling Action.**

Rhyme Rhyme is the occurrence of a similar or identical sound at the ends of two or more words, such as *suite, heat,* and *complete.* **Internal rhyme** occurs within a line; **end rhyme** occurs at the ends of lines.

Rhyme Scheme The pattern of end rhyme in a poem is called a rhyme scheme. The pattern is charted by assigning a letter of the alphabet, beginning with the letter *a,* to each line. Lines that rhyme are given the same letter. Notice the rhyme scheme for the first stanza of Robert Frost's "The Road Not Taken."

Two roads diverged in a yellow wood,	a
And sorry I could not travel both	b
And be one traveler, long I stood	a
And looked down one as far as I could	a
To where it bent in the undergrowth;	b

Rhythm Rhythm refers to the pattern or flow of sound created by the arrangement of stressed and unstressed syllables in a line of poetry. The accented, or stressed, syllables are marked with ´, while unaccented, or unstressed, syllables are marked with ˘. A regular pattern of rhythm is called **meter.**

See **Meter.**

Rising Action The rising action refers to the events in a story that move the plot along by adding complications or expanding the conflict. Rising action usually builds suspense to a climax, or turning point.

See **Plot.**

Satire Satire is a literary technique in which ideas or customs are ridiculed for the purpose of improving society. Satire may be gently witty, mildly abrasive, or bitterly critical. "The Euphio Question" satirizes people's desire to escape from reality.

Scene In drama, the action is often divided into acts and scenes. Each new scene in a play indicates a different time and place. For example, *The Devil and Daniel Webster* is a one-act play, with two scene changes. In long plays, scenes are grouped into acts.

See **Act.**

Science Fiction Science fiction is prose writing in which a writer explores unexpected possibilities of the past or the future, using known scientific data and theories as well as his or her creative imagination. Most science fiction writers create a believable world, although some create a fantasy world that has familiar elements. "The Euphio Question" is an example of science fiction.

See **Fantasy.**

Setting Setting is the time and place of action of a story. Some stories, such as "The Utterly Perfect Murder," have only a minimal description of setting. In other literary works, such as "Through the Tunnel" and "Marigolds," setting is described in detail and becomes a major contributor to the story's total effect.

Short Story A short story is a much shorter than a novel and can usually be read in one sitting. Generally, a short story has one main conflict that involves the characters, keeps the story moving, and makes it interesting.

Simile A simile is a figure of speech that makes a comparison between two things using the words *like* or *as*. In "Incident in a Rose Garden," the line "Dressed like a Spanish waiter" contains a simile.

See **Figurative Language.**

Soliloquy In drama a soliloquy is a speech in which a character speaks thoughts aloud. Generally, the character is on the stage alone, not speaking to other characters and perhaps not even consciously addressing the audience.

Speaker In poetry the speaker in the poem is the voice that talks to the reader, similar to the narrator in fiction. The speaker is not necessarily the poet.

Stage Directions A play normally includes a set of instructions called stage directions which are often printed in italic type and separated from the dialogue by parentheses. Stage directions give important information to the reader and to the performers. They are most often used to explain how actors should move and speak, but they also describe the scenery and the props, or those objects that actors need during the play.

Stanza A stanza is a grouping of two or more lines in a pattern that is repeated throughout a poem. A stanza is comparable to a paragraph in prose. Each stanza may have the same number of lines, or the number of lines may vary. "The Road Not Taken" is divided into four stanzas.

Suspense Suspense is the excitement or tension that readers feel as they become involved in a story and eager to know the outcome.

858 Literary Handbook

Symbol A symbol is a person, place, an activity, or an object that stands for something beyond itself. For example, a dove is a common symbol for peace.

Theme Theme is the main idea in a work of fiction. It is a perception about life or human nature that the writer shares with the reader. In most cases, the theme is not stated directly but must be inferred from the characters and situations in a story.

Third-Person Point of View In the third-person point of view, the narrator is someone outside of the action, not a character writing the story. The characters are referred to by name or by the pronouns *he, she, they.* "Beauty Is Truth" is told from a third-person point of view.

See **Point of View.**

Tone Tone is the attitude a writer takes toward a subject. For example, *The Devil and Daniel Webster* has a light, humorous tone.

True-Life Adventure A true-life adventure is a type of nonfiction found in popular magazines and books. "A Trip to the Edge of Survival" is a true-life adventure.

Turning Point

See **Climax.**

Verbal Irony

See **Irony.**

1 The Writing Process

The writing process consists of four stages: prewriting, drafting, revising and editing, and publishing and reflecting. As the graphic to the right shows, these stages are not steps that you must complete in a set order. Rather, you may return to any one at any time in your writing process, using feedback from your readers along the way.

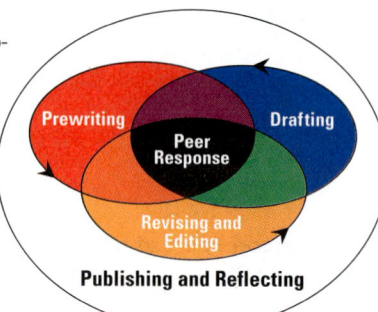

1.1 Prewriting

In the prewriting stage, you explore your ideas and discover what you want to write about.

Finding Ideas for Writing

Ideas for writing can come from just about anywhere: experiences, memories, conversations, dreams, or imaginings. Try one or more of the following techniques to help you find and explore a writing topic.

Personal Techniques
Practice imaging, or trying to remember mainly sensory details about a subject—its look, sound, feel, taste, and smell.
Complete a knowledge inventory to discover what you already know about a subject.
Browse through magazines, newspapers, and on-line bulletin boards for ideas.
Start a clip file of articles that you want to save for future reference. Be sure to label each clip with source information.

Sharing Techniques
With a group, brainstorm a topic by trying to come up with as many ideas as you can without stopping to critique or examine them.
Interview someone who knows a great deal about your topic.

Writing Techniques
After freewriting on a topic, try looping, or choosing your best idea for more freewriting. Repeat the loop at least once.
Make a list to help you organize ideas, examine them, or identify areas for further research.

Graphic Techniques
Create a pro-and-con chart to compare the positive and negative aspects of an idea or a course of action.
Use a cluster map or tree diagram to explore subordinate ideas that relate to your general topic or central idea.

Determining Your Purpose

At some time during your writing process, you need to consider your purpose, or general reason, for writing. For example, your purpose may be one of the following: to express yourself, to entertain, to explain, to describe, to analyze, or to persuade. To clarify your purpose, ask yourself questions like these:

- Why did I choose to write about my topic?
- What aspects of the topic mean the most to me?
- What do I want others to think or feel after they read my writing?

Identifying Your Audience

Knowing who will read your writing can help you clarify your purpose, focus your topic, and choose the details and tone that will best communicate your ideas. As you think about your readers, ask yourself questions like these:

- What does my audience already know about my topic?
- What will they be most interested in?
- What language is most appropriate for this audience?

1.2 Drafting

In the drafting stage, you put your ideas on paper and allow them to develop and change as you write.

There's no right or wrong way to draft. Sometimes you might be adventuresome and dive right into your writing. At other times, you might draft slowly, planning carefully beforehand. You can combine aspects of these approaches to suit yourself and your writing projects.

 LINK TO LITERATURE

Job experiences can be a good source of writing ideas. The author Kurt Vonnegut, Jr., drew on his experience working in the public-relations department of a large corporation to write some of his works of science fiction, such as "The Euphio Question," page 215.

WRITING HANDBOOK **861**

LINK TO LITERATURE

Ray Bradbury, author of "The Utterly Perfect Murder," page 17, says that when he begins to write a new work, he gets everything down on paper before thinking about it carefully. He advises, "Get it done, and after the action, when you have finished a thing or you've worked on it for a number of hours or days, then is where your intellect comes into play."

Discovery drafting is a good approach when you've gathered some information on your topic or have a rough idea for writing but are not quite sure how you feel about your subject or what exactly you want to say. You just plunge into your draft and let your ideas lead you where they will. After finishing a discovery draft, you may decide to start another draft, do more prewriting, or revise your first draft.

Planned drafting may work better for research reports, critical reviews, and other kinds of formal writing. Try thinking through a writing plan or making an outline before you begin drafting. Then, as you write, you can develop your ideas and fill in the details.

1.3 Using Peer Response

The suggestions and comments your peers or classmates make about your writing are called peer response.

Talking with peers about your writing can help you discover what you want to say or how well you have communicated your ideas. You can ask a peer reader for help at any point in the writing process. For example, your peers can help you develop a topic, narrow your focus, discover confusing passages, or organize your writing.

Questions for Your Peer Readers

You can help your peer readers provide you with the most useful kinds of feedback by following these guidelines:

- Tell readers where you are in the writing process. Are you still trying out ideas, or have you completed a draft?
- Ask questions that will help you get specific information about your writing. Open-ended questions that require more than a simple yes-or-no answer are more likely to give you information you can use as you revise.
- Give your readers plenty of time to respond thoughtfully to your writing.
- Encourage your readers to be honest when they respond to your work. It's OK if you don't agree with them—you always get to decide which changes to make.

The chart on the following page explains different peer-response techniques you might use when you're ready to share your work with others.

862 WRITING HANDBOOK

Technique	When to Use It	Questions to Ask
Sharing	Use this when you are just exploring ideas or when you want to celebrate the completion of a piece of writing.	Will you please read or listen to my writing without criticizing or making suggestions afterward?
Summarizing	Use this when you want to know if your main idea or goals are clear.	What do you think I'm saying? What's my main idea or message?
Replying	Use this strategy when you want to make your writing richer by adding new ideas.	What are your ideas about my topic? What do you think about what I have said in my piece?
Responding to Specific Features	Use this when you want a quick overview of the strengths and weaknesses of your writing.	Are the ideas supported with enough examples? Did I persuade you? Is the organization clear enough so you could follow the ideas?
Telling	Use this to find out which parts of your writing are affecting readers the way you want and which parts are confusing.	What did you think or feel as you read my words? Would you show me which passage you were reading when you had that response?

Tips for Being a Peer Reader

Follow these guidelines when you respond to someone else's work:

- Respect the writer's feelings.
- Make sure you understand what kind of feedback the writer is looking for, and then respond accordingly.
- Use "I" statements, such as "I like . . . ," "I think . . . ," or "It would help me if. . . ." Remember that your impressions and opinions may not be the same as someone else's.

1.4 Revising and Editing

In the revising and editing stage, you improve your draft, choose the words that best express your ideas, and proofread for mistakes in spelling, grammar, usage, and punctuation.

The changes you make in your writing during this stage usually fall into three categories: revising for content, revising for structure, and editing to correct mistakes in mechanics. Use the questions and suggestions that follow to help you assess problems in your draft and determine what kinds of changes would improve it.

> **WRITING TIP**
>
> Writers are more likely to accept criticism of their work if they first receive positive feedback. When you act as a peer reader, try to start your review by telling something you like about the piece.

WRITING TIP

Be sure to consider the needs of your audience as you answer the questions under Revising for Content. For example, before you can determine whether any of your material is unnecessary or irrelevant, you need to identify what your audience already knows.

 WRITING TIP

For help identifying and correcting problems that are listed in the Proofreading Checklist, see the Grammar Handbook, pages 900–939.

Revising for Content
- Does my writing have a main idea or central focus? Is my thesis clear?
- Have I incorporated adequate detail? Where might I include a telling detail, revealing statistic, or vivid example?
- Is any material unnecessary, irrelevant, or confusing?

Revising for Structure
- Is my writing unified? Do all ideas and supporting details pertain to my main idea or advance my thesis?
- Is my writing clear and coherent? Is the flow of sentences and paragraphs smooth and logical?
- Do I need to add transitional words, phrases, or sentences to make the relationships among ideas clearer?
- Are my sentences well constructed? What sentences might I combine to improve the grace and rhythm of my writing?

Editing to Correct Mistakes in Mechanics

When you are satisfied with your draft, proofread and edit it, correcting any mistakes you might have made in spelling, grammar, usage, and punctuation. You may want to proofread your writing several times, looking for different types of mistakes each time. The following checklist may help you proofread your work.

Proofreading Checklist	
Sentence Structure and Agreement	Are there any run-on sentences or sentence fragments? Do all verbs agree with their subjects? Do all pronouns agree with their antecedents? Are verb tenses correct and consistent?
Forms of Words	Do adverbs and adjectives modify the appropriate words? Are all forms of *be* and other irregular verbs used correctly? Are pronouns used correctly? Are comparative and superlative forms of adjectives correct?
Capitalization, Punctuation, and Spelling	Is any punctuation mark missing or not needed? Are all words spelled correctly? Are all proper nouns and all proper adjectives capitalized?

If you have a printout of your draft or a handwritten copy, mark changes on it by using the proofreading symbols shown in the chart on the next page. The Grammar Handbook, starting on page 900, includes models for using these symbols.

864 WRITING HANDBOOK

Proofreading Symbols	
∧ Add letters or words.	/ Make a capital letter lowercase.
⊙ Add a period.	¶ Begin a new paragraph.
≡ Capitalize a letter.	— or ℘ Delete letters or words.
◡ Close up space.	∽ Switch the positions of letters, words, or punctuation marks.
∧ Add a comma.	

1.5 Publishing and Reflecting

After you've completed a writing project, consider sharing it with a wider audience—even when you've produced it for a class assignment. Reflecting on your writing process is another good way to bring closure to a writing project.

Creative Publishing Ideas

Following are some ideas for publishing and sharing your writing.

- Post your writing on an electronic bulletin board or send it to others via e-mail.
- Create a multimedia presentation and share it with classmates.
- Publish your writing in a school newspaper or literary magazine.
- Present your work orally in a report, a speech, a reading, or a dramatic performance.
- Submit your writing to a local newspaper or a magazine that publishes student writing.
- Form a writing exchange group with other students.

Reflecting on Your Writing

Think about your writing process and consider whether you'd like to add your writing to your portfolio. You might attach to your work a note in which you answer questions like these:

- What did I learn about myself and my subject through this writing project?
- Which parts of the writing process did I most and least enjoy?
- As I wrote, what was my biggest problem? How did I solve it?
- What did I learn that I can use the next time I write?

WRITING TIP

You might work with other students to publish an anthology of class writing. Then exchange your anthology with another class or another school. Reading the work of other student writers will help you get ideas for new writing projects and for ways to improve your work.

WRITING HANDBOOK 865

Building Blocks of Good Writing

2.1 Introductions

A good introduction catches your reader's interest and often presents the main idea of your writing. To introduce your writing effectively, try one of the following methods.

Make a Surprising Statement

Beginning with a startling or an interesting fact can capture your reader's curiosity about the subject, as in the example below.

> A normal cough explodes from the mouth at about 60 miles per hour. With germs traveling nearly as fast as the speed limit on an interstate, you should learn how to "head them off at the pass" and protect yourself from cold germs.

Provide a Description

A vivid description sets a mood and brings a scene to life for your reader. The following introduces a narrative about a former prisoner's visit to the site of his labor camp.

> The midnight summer sun sheds a ghostly light on the solitary figure slowly making his way among the broken grave markers and bones of the dead protruding through the mossy Siberian tundra.

Pose a Question

Beginning with a question can make your reader want to read on to find out the answer. The following introduction asks a question to get the reader interested in the topic of industrial recycling.

LINK TO LITERATURE

A vivid description is a good way to introduce readers to the characters or setting of a narrative. Beryl Markham paints a colorful picture of the Masai at the start of "Brothers Are the Same," page 233.

What happens to the caffeine when coffee companies decaffeinate the coffee? Actually, it's often sold to soft drink companies to add to their products. Many manufacturers have adopted similar by-product recycling programs.

Relate an Anecdote

Beginning with a brief anecdote, or story, can hook readers and help you make a point in a dramatic way. The following anecdote sets the scene for a discussion of safety measures on public transportation.

Two tough-looking men swaggered onto the platform and stopped cold when they spied the canine patrol. The dog's jaws looked strong enough to snap its muzzle. As the men boarded the train, the conductor's voice crackled over the speaker, "Welcome to the safest form of transportation."

 WRITING TIP

Dialogue can enhance an introduction. The conductor's comment makes the anecdote at the left more vivid and realistic.

Address the Reader Directly

Speaking directly to readers in your introduction establishes a friendly, informal tone and involves them in your topic.

Like many others, you may welcome autumn into your home with the long-awaited season premieres of TV series. Unfortunately, you'll have to do a lot of channel surfing to find a good program in this fall's lineup.

Begin with a Thesis Statement

A thesis statement expressing a paper's main idea may be woven into both the beginning and the end of nonfiction writing. The following is a thesis statement that introduces a literary analysis.

Susan Glaspell's play *Trifles* illustrates that men in the first part of the 20th century stereotyped women as trifling creatures incapable of doing anything of consequence.

WRITING HANDBOOK 867

2.2 Paragraphs

A paragraph is made up of sentences that work together to develop an idea or accomplish a purpose. Whether or not it contains a topic sentence stating the main idea, a good paragraph must have both unity and coherence.

Unity

A paragraph has unity when all the sentences support and develop one stated or implied idea. Use the following techniques to create unity in your paragraphs.

Write a Topic Sentence A topic sentence states the main idea of the paragraph; all the other sentences in the paragraph provide supporting details. A topic sentence is often the first sentence in a paragraph, as shown in the model below. However, it may also appear later in the paragraph or at the end, to summarize or reinforce the main idea.

> *Shoppers should feel confident that the organic produce they buy is truly chemical-free.* Before a farm can be certified as organic, its crops and soil must not be treated with chemical pesticides and herbicides for a period of 36 months. The farm's soil is then tested by the National Organic Standards Board for traces of these chemicals. If the soil is deemed pure, a certificate is issued to the grower, and organic fruits and vegetables may then be sold in the marketplace.

Relate All Sentences to an Implied Main Idea A paragraph can be unified without a topic sentence as long as every sentence supports the implied, or unstated, main idea. In the example below, all the sentences work together to create a unified impression of a cold autumn morning.

> Under the early-morning glow of street lamps, commuters leaned into the wind with hunched shoulders, crunching dry leaves underfoot. Cold gusts plucked hats from their heads and tossed leaves into somersaults and cartwheels down the streets. Jack wove his bicycle among the bent figures, tossing papers on porches and front steps that glistened with hints of frost.

> **WRITING TIP**
>
> You can use the same techniques to create unity in an entire paper that you use to write unified paragraphs. Be sure that all of your paragraphs support the thesis statement or the implied main idea of your paper. If a paragraph includes information irrelevant to the main idea, you should delete it or revise it to establish a clear connection.

868 WRITING HANDBOOK

Coherence

A paragraph is coherent when all its sentences are related to one another and flow logically from one to the next. The following techniques will help you achieve coherence in paragraphs.

- Present your ideas in the most logical order.
- Use pronouns, synonyms, and repeated words to connect ideas.
- Use transitional devices to show the relationships among ideas.

In the example below, the italicized words show how the writer used some of these techniques to create a unified paragraph.

> Cadets in the United States Coast Guard Academy receive *their* training on a 295-foot sailing ship much like *the ones* used in the time before motor-driven ships were built. The old-fashioned way of sailing requires *cadets* to work well together. *For example*, it takes at least 20 of *them* to hoist by hand the thousands of pounds of sails on *the ship*. *This cooperation* is particularly important in bad weather, when *they* depend on *one another* to ensure the safety of *the ship* and *crew*.

WRITING TIP

You can use the techniques at the left to create coherence in an entire paper. Be sure that paragraphs flow logically from one to the next.

2.3 Transitions

Transitions are words and phrases that show the connections between details, such as relationships in time and space, order of importance, causes and effects, and similarities or differences.

Time or Sequence

Some transitions help to clarify the sequence of events over time. When you are telling a story or describing a process, you can connect ideas with such transitional words as *first, second, always, then, next, later, soon, before, finally, after, earlier, afterward,* and *tomorrow*.

> *Before* Dr. Crawford Long successfully used ether as an anesthetic in 1842, doctors used practices such as having their patients drink alcohol. *After* further studies with anesthetics, physicians were able to perform surgeries more effectively.

LINK TO LITERATURE

Look at the third section of "Through the Tunnel," page 98. Notice how Doris Lessing uses transitions at the beginning of each paragraph to indicate the sequential order of Jerry's experience.

Spatial Relationships

Transition words and phrases such as *in front, behind, next to, along, nearest, lowest, above, below, underneath, on the left,* and *in the middle* can help readers visualize a scene.

> Covered with more than 58,000 names, the black walls of the Vietnam Veterans Memorial stretch *along* a walkway on the National Mall. *In front* of the walls, friends and family have left thousands of mementos.

Degree

Transitions of degree, such as *mainly, strongest, weakest, first, second, most important, least important, worst,* and *best,* may be used to rank ideas or to show degree of importance, as in the model below.

> Nathan has several qualifications that make him a good candidate for class representative; his *greatest* strength is his tolerance of more than one point of view.

Compare and Contrast

Words and phrases such as *similarly, likewise, also, like, as, neither . . . nor,* and *either . . . or* show similarity between details. *However, by contrast, yet, but, unlike, instead, whereas,* and *while* show difference. Note the use of both types of transitions in the model below.

> *Like* newspaper editorials, editorial cartoons can effectively address controversial topics and persuade readers; *however,* cartoons influence our opinions by appealing to our sense of humor as well as to our intellect.

Cause and Effect

When you are writing about a cause-and-effect relationship, use transitional words and phrases such as *since, because, therefore, thus, so, due to, for this reason,* and *as a result* to help clarify that relationship and to make your writing coherent.

WRITING TIP

Both *but* and *however* may be used to join two independent clauses. When *but* is used as a coordinating conjunction, it is preceded by a comma. When *however* is used as a conjunctive adverb, it is preceded by a semicolon and followed by a comma, as shown in the example at the right.

Because high humidity makes it harder for our bodies to cool off, the temperature may feel like 102 degrees Fahrenheit when it is actually 90 degrees. *For this reason*, meteorologists give the actual temperature and the heat index—the combined effect of humidity and temperature.

2.4 Elaboration

Elaboration is the process of developing a writing idea by providing specific supporting details that are appropriate for the purpose and form of your writing.

Facts and Statistics

A fact is a statement that can be verified, while a statistic is a fact stated in numbers. As in the model below, the facts and statistics you use should strongly support the statements you make.

Although South Africa's apartheid laws were repealed in 1991, living conditions there suggest that change is happening slowly. In 1995, for example, approximately 200,000 residents in Johannesburg's black neighborhoods did not have running water.

WRITING TIP

Facts and statistics can be used to explain opposing points of view, depending on how you interpret the information for the reader. Be certain that you clearly and logically establish how the facts you have chosen support your writing.

Sensory Details

Details that show how something looks, sounds, smells, tastes, or feels can enliven a description. Which senses does the writer appeal to in the following paragraph?

At the last football game, it was so cold that clouds of breath rose from the huddled players like smoke from a campfire. In the stands the thick scent of hot cocoa blended with the stale smell of blankets pulled from the trunks of cars.

Incidents

One way to illustrate a point is to relate an incident or tell a story, as in the example on the following page.

People's concern for personal safety often prevents them from accepting help. Recently, while walking by the library, I offered to help someone with an armful of books. Although we were going in the same direction, she declined. I could have helped, but I understood why she had refused my offer.

Examples

An example can help make an abstract or a complex idea concrete for the reader.

In 19th-century England, the rules for proper forms of address were very rigid, even among members of a family. For example, girls were expected to call their parents *papa* and *mama*; boys called them *father* and *mother*.

Quotations

Choose quotations that clearly support your points and be sure that you copy each quotation word for word. Always remember to credit the source.

In his essay "On Being Seventeen, Bright, and Unable to Read," David Raymond explains that people's misunderstandings about dyslexia lead to hurtful, unfair treatment. Recalling how classmates reacted, he states, "They'd make fun of me every chance they got, asking me to spell 'cat' or something like that."

2.5 Description

A good description contains carefully chosen details that create a unified impression for the reader.

Description is an important part of most writing genres—essays, stories, biography, and poetry, for example. Effective description can help readers to recognize the significance of an issue, to visualize a scene, or to understand a character.

LINK TO LITERATURE

In the essay "Father's Day," page 403, Michael Dorris uses four examples to support the idea that his Aunt Marion was "a font of information and influence."

Use a Variety of Details

If you include plenty of sensory details, the reader can better imagine the scene you are describing. In the example below, the sensory details help capture the character's nervousness.

> Amy thought she would enjoy the evening alone. As soon as her family left, however, the house seemed to come alive, sighing and creaking in corners. Amy wandered around, flipping on lights and peeking in closets. She tried to watch TV but thought she smelled burnt toast. Finally, when Amy sat on the front porch under a fuzzy afghan and drank a cup of warm milk, the house seemed to drift back to sleep.

LINK TO LITERATURE

Look at the first description of the character Sheila in "The Bass, the River, and Sheila Mant," page 41. Notice how W. D. Wetherell describes the character by using details about how Sheila sat and lay down.

Show, Don't Tell

Simply telling your readers about an event or idea in a general way does not give them a clear impression. Showing your readers the specific details, however, helps them develop a better sense of your subject. The following example just tells how the writer felt.

> I was so nervous the opening night of the play, I didn't think I could go on stage.

The paragraph below uses descriptive details to show how nervous he was.

> I finished putting on my makeup two hours before the eight o'clock curtain, long before anyone else had arrived on the set. Pacing back and forth among prop tables and braces that held up the scenery, I repeated my lines over and over. When my co-star said, "Break a leg," I mumbled my thanks and forced a smile.

Use Figurative Language

Figurative language is descriptive writing that evokes associations beyond the literal meaning of words. The following types of figurative language can make your descriptions clear and fresh.

WRITING HANDBOOK **873**

WRITING TIP

Be careful not to mix metaphors or use two or more comparisons that create a confusing image. *Barking orders right and left, the drill sergeant thundered through the barracks.*

WRITING TIP

You can clarify your descriptive writing by choosing precise words. For example, replace general nouns (*tool*) with more specific nouns (*lug wrench*).

- A **simile** is a figure of speech comparing two essentially unlike things, signaling the comparison with a word such as *like* or *as*.
- A **metaphor** is a figure of speech describing something by speaking of it as if it were something else, without using a word such as *like* or *as* to signal the comparison.

In the example below, the description of a gardener is made vivid and concrete with the use of a simile.

> Mrs. Tyler drifted among her rows of snow peas, kohlrabi, kale, and sweet corn *like* a dancer in slow motion.

Organize Your Details

Organize descriptions carefully to create a clear image for your reader. Descriptive details may be organized chronologically, spatially, by order of importance, or by order of impression.

> Entering London's Heathrow Airport, I was overwhelmed by the hush. No children ran about. No travelers shouted into cellular phones, and people waited quietly in customs lines.

2.6 Conclusions

A conclusion should leave readers with a strong final impression. Try any of these approaches for concluding your writing.

Restate Your Thesis

A good way to conclude an essay is by restating your thesis, or main idea, in different words. Notice how the conclusion below summarizes the central idea in a literary analysis and restates the thesis introduced in an example on page 867.

> Had the men in *Trifles* believed that the women in the house were capable of contributing anything to the investigation, the men would have found the information they were looking for. They missed the opportunity to uncover a motive for Mr. Wright's murder because of their stereotypic views of women.

Ask a Question

Try asking a question that sums up what you have said and gives readers something new to think about. The question below concludes a persuasive appeal against building a new highway.

> A commuter train can transport as many people as 270 automobiles can, so wouldn't the money spent to build bigger highways be better used to improve public transportation systems?

Make a Recommendation

When you are persuading your audience to take a position on an issue, you can conclude by recommending a specific course of action.

> In order for the school's new recycling program to work, you need to do your part by disposing of recyclable products in the appropriate containers around the school.

Make a Prediction

Readers are concerned about matters that may affect them and therefore are moved by a conclusion that predicts the future.

> The students who take advantage of the new After-Hours Study Hour will be able to get the specific help they need from teachers and will see improvements in their grades.

Summarize Your Information

Summarizing reinforces the writer's main ideas, leaving a strong, lasting impression. The model below concludes with a statement that summarizes the relationship described in a personal essay.

> Ultimately, my sister and I have become best friends. Even though we resented being stuck with each other as kids, we now choose to spend time together as often as we can.

LINK TO LITERATURE

Note the conclusion of Sucheng Chan's "You're Short, Besides!" on page 290. To conclude her essay about people's perceptions of her, she asks, "So, has being physically handicapped been a handicap?"

WRITING HANDBOOK **875**

Narrative Writing

Narrative writing tells a story. If you write a story from your imagination, it is called a fictional narrative. A true story about actual events is called a nonfictional narrative.

Key Techniques of Narrative Writing

Writing Standards

Good narrative writing

- includes descriptive details and dialogue to develop the characters, setting, and plot
- has a clear beginning, middle, and end
- has a logical organization with clues and transitions to help the reader understand the order of events
- maintains a consistent tone and point of view
- uses language that is appropriate for the audience
- demonstrates the significance of events or ideas

Describe the Setting

The setting is the time and place of a narrative. It is clear from the example below that the story takes place in a school.

Example
The day after the coaches made cuts for the track team, I wandered through the crowded halls as if I were the only one there.

Clearly Organize the Events

Choose the important events and explain them in an order that is easy to understand. In a fictional narrative, this series of events is the story's plot.

Example
- Tyler was a good friend, but we were competitive in everything we did.
- When he made the track team and I was cut, I didn't want to talk to him afterward.
- Tyler stopped me in the corridor and asked me to help him with his math homework. I realized that we had different strengths.
- I went to cheer him on at the next track meet.

Depict Characters Vividly

Use vivid details to show your readers what your characters look like, what they say, and what they think.

Example
Tyler walked toward me with his proud, confident stride. "Hey, Simon," he said, "I've been trying to find you all day."

876 WRITING HANDBOOK

Organizing Narrative Writing

One way to organize a piece of narrative writing is to arrange the events in chronological order, as shown in Option 1 below.

Option 1

Focus on Events	Example
• Introduce characters and setting	Tyler's name was at the top of the track team list posted outside the gym, but I couldn't find mine anywhere.
• Show event 1	Even though Tyler was my best friend, I avoided him the whole day because I was so jealous and embarrassed.
• Show event 2	At the end of day, he finally cornered me and asked me to help him study for his math exam.
• End, perhaps showing the significance of the events	I appreciated Tyler's confidence in me, and at the first track meet, no one cheered him on more enthusiastically than I did.

WRITING TIP

Story Elements A fictional narrative has a central conflict (a problem), characters (people involved in the conflict), a setting (the time and place where the conflict occurs), and a plot (a series of events that lead to the conflict's resolution).

When the telling of a fictional narrative focuses on a central conflict, the story's plot may follow the model shown in Option 2. It is also possible in narrative writing to arrange the order of events by starting *in medias res,* or in the middle of things (Option 3).

Option 2

Focus on Conflict
- Describe the main characters and setting
- Present the conflict
- Relate the events that make the conflict complex and cause the characters to change
- Present the resolution, or outcome of the conflict

Option 3

Flashback
- Begin with the conflict
- Present the events leading up to the conflict
- Present the resolution, or outcome of the conflict

WRITING TIP

Dialogue Dialogue is an effective way of depicting characters in a narrative. As you write dialogue, choose words that express your characters' personalities and show how they feel about one another.

WRITING HANDBOOK **877**

Explanatory Writing

LINK TO LITERATURE

Explanatory writing provides many opportunities to explore issues in literature. The examples on the following pages use explanatory writing techniques to examine W. D. Wetherell's story, "The Bass, the River, and Sheila Mant," page 40.

Explanatory writing informs and explains. For example, you can use it to evaluate the effects of a new law, to compare two movie reviews, or to analyze a piece of literature.

Types of Explanatory Writing

Compare and Contrast
Compare-and-contrast writing explores the similarities and differences between two or more subjects.

Example
Sheila Mant and the narrator have very different interests, personalities, and social lives.

Cause and Effect
Cause-and-effect writing explains why something happened, why certain conditions exist, or what resulted from an action or a condition.

Example
Because the narrator wanted to impress Sheila Mant, he at first made a point of demonstrating his knowledge of bass fishing.

Analysis
Analysis explains how something works, how it is defined, or what its parts are.

Example
The term *anglers* refers to people who fish for fun and sport and enjoy the challenge of trying to catch certain kinds of fish, such as bass.

Problem-Solution
Problem-solution writing states a problem, analyzes the problem, and proposes a solution to the problem.

Example
The narrator of "The Bass, the River, and Sheila Mant" faced the problem of liking someone with whom he had nothing in common.

878 WRITING HANDBOOK

4.1 Compare and Contrast

Compare-and-contrast writing explores the similarities and differences between two or more subjects.

Organizing Compare-and-Contrast Writing

Compare-and-contrast writing can be organized in different ways. The examples below demonstrate feature-by-feature organization and subject-by-subject organization.

Option 1

Feature by Feature
- Feature 1
  - Subject A
  - Subject B
- Feature 2
  - Subject A
  - Subject B

Example
- The narrator and Sheila Mant have very different interests.
- Sheila is interested in getting a tan, meeting college boys, and skiing.
- The narrator likes swimming, canoeing, and bass fishing.
- The narrator and Sheila also have very different personalities.

Option 2

Subject by Subject
- Subject A
  - Feature 1
  - Feature 2
  - Feature 3
- Subject B
  - Feature 1
  - Feature 2
  - Feature 3

Example
- Sheila Mant has shallow interests and a vain personality yet is very popular.
- She is interested in getting a tan, meeting college boys, and skiing.
- She only talks about herself.
- Many people admire her.
- The narrator's interests, personality, and popularity are very different from Sheila's.

Remember: The purpose of comparing and contrasting two subjects is to come to a better understanding of each.

Writing Standards

Good compare-and-contrast writing
- clearly identifies the subjects that are being compared and contrasted
- includes specific, relevant details
- follows a clear plan of organization dealing with the same features of both subjects under discussion
- uses language and details appropriate to the audience
- uses transitional words and phrases to clarify similarities and differences

WRITING TIP

Remember your purpose for comparing the items you are writing about and support your purpose with expressive language and specific details.

Writing Standards
Good cause-and-effect writing
► clearly states the cause-and-effect relationship being examined
► shows clear connections between causes and effects
► presents causes and effects in a logical order and uses transitions effectively
► uses facts, examples, and other details to illustrate each cause and effect
► uses language and details appropriate to the audience

WRITING TIP

Possible topics for cause-and-effect writing are important historical events that had an impact on society. For example, what caused the California gold rush? What were the results? You can explore current events and their potential outcomes as well.

4.2 Cause and Effect

Cause-and-effect writing explains why something happened, why certain conditions exist, or what resulted from an action or a condition.

Organizing Cause-and-Effect Writing

Your organization will depend on your topic and purpose for writing. If your focus is on explaining the effects of an event, such as the passage of a law, you might first state the cause and then explain the effects (Option 1). If you want to explain the causes of an event such as the closing of a factory, you might first state the effect and then examine its causes (Option 2). Sometimes you'll want to describe a chain of cause-and-effect relationships (Option 3) to explore a topic such as the disappearance of tropical rain forests or the development of home computers.

Option 1 — **Example**

Cause to Effect	
Cause	The narrator wanted to win Sheila's affection.
• Effect 1	He got up the nerve to ask her out.
• Effect 2	He hid his love of bass fishing from her after he discovered she thought fishing was stupid.
• Effect 3	He chose Sheila over fishing.

Option 2

Effect to Cause
Effect
• Cause 1
• Cause 2
• Cause 3

Option 3

Cause-and-Effect Chain
Cause
↓
effect (cause)
↓
effect (cause)
↓
effect (cause)

Remember: You cannot assume that a cause-and-effect relationship exists simply because one event follows another. Be sure your facts indicate that the effect could not have happened without the cause.

4.3 Problem-Solution

Problem-solution writing clearly states a problem, analyzes the problem, and proposes a solution to the problem.

Organizing Problem-Solution Writing

Your organization will depend on the goal of your problem-solution piece, your intended audience, and the specific problem you choose to address. The organizational methods outlined below are effective for different kinds of problem-solution writing.

Option 1

Simple Problem-Solution
- Description of problem and why it needs to be solved
- Recommended solution
- Explanation of solution
- Conclusion

Example
- In "The Bass, the River, and Sheila Mant," the narrator liked someone who didn't share his interests. What would you do if the person you liked had interests that were different from your own?
- I think you should be honest about your own interests.
- If you can't talk about your interests, it may not be easy to have an open and sharing friendship.
- It is important to be true to yourself and your interests to make friends worth having.

Option 2

Deciding Between Solutions
- Description of problem
- Solution A
  - Pros
  - Cons
- Solution B
  - Pros
  - Cons

Example
- The person you like has different interests from your own.
- You can pretend that you have interests in common.
- The person might like you more than they would if you were honest.
- It might be boring to be friends with someone with whom you couldn't share your interests.
- You can be honest with the person about your interests.

Writing Standards

Good problem-solution writing
- identifies the problem and helps the reader understand the issues involved
- analyzes the causes and effects of the problem
- integrates quotes, facts, and statistics into the text
- explores potential solutions to the problem and recommends the best one(s)
- uses language, tone, and details appropriate to the audience

WRITING TIP

Ask a classmate to read and respond to your writing in the problem-solution form. Here are some questions for your peer reader to respond to: Is my language clear? Is the writing organized in a way that is easy to follow? Do the proposed solutions seem logical?

4.4 Analysis

In an analysis you try to help your readers understand a subject by explaining how it works, how it is defined, or what its parts are.

The details you include will depend upon the kind of analysis you're writing.

- A **process analysis** should provide background information—such as definitions of terms and a list of needed equipment—and then explain each important step or stage in the process. For example, you might explain the steps to program a VCR or the stages in a plant's growth cycle.
- A **definition** should include the most important characteristics of the subject. To define a quality, such as honesty, you might include the characteristic of telling the truth.
- A **parts analysis** should describe each of the parts, groups, or types that make up the subject. For example, you might analyze the human brain by looking at its parts, analyze a new law by looking at how different groups are affected by it, or analyze jazz music by describing the different styles of jazz.

Organizing Your Analysis

Organize your details in a logical order appropriate for the kind of analysis you're writing. A process analysis is usually organized chronologically, with steps or stages in the order they occur.

Option 1 Process Analysis	Example
Introduce topic	Casting is a popular method of bass fishing.
Background information	Bass is a kind of fish known for its ability to fight when hooked on a line.
Explain steps	
• Step 1	First, the angler casts a lure, a kind of artificial bait, into the water.
• Step 2	Then, the angler slowly reels in the fishing line to attract the fish to the lure.
• Step 3	When a bass is hooked, it will fight to free itself, but the angler must fight back, pulling hard on the line to reel in the fish.

Writing Standards

A good analysis

- hooks the reader's attention with a strong introduction
- clearly states the subject and its individual parts
- uses a specific organizing structure to provide a logical flow of information
- shows connections among facts and ideas through subordinate clauses and transitional words and phrases
- uses language and details appropriate for the audience

WRITING TIP

Introductions You may want to begin your analysis with a vivid description of the subject to capture the reader's attention. For example, a description of reeling in a huge bass could introduce this process analysis.

You can organize the details in a definition or parts analysis in order of importance or impression.

Option 2

Definition	Example
Introduce term	The narrator of "The Bass, the River, and Sheila Mant" is infatuated with Sheila.
General definition	*Infatuation* means "being carried away with an attraction for someone."
Explain qualities	
• Quality 1	An infatuation is usually based on an idealized impression of someone. The narrator thought Sheila was the "epitome of sophistication."
• Quality 2	An infatuation creates the desire to impress someone, as when the narrator uses the scientific name for largemouth bass.
• Quality 3	An infatuation is often short-lived. After the narrator witnesses Sheila's self-centered personality, his infatuation ends.

In the following parts analysis, the character of Sheila Mant is broken down into examples of her personality and behavior.

Option 3

Parts Analysis	Example
Introduce subject	As the narrator describes why he was infatuated with Sheila Mant, he also reveals negative aspects of her personality.
Explain parts	
• Part 1	Sheila is self-centered. When the narrator takes her to a fair, she talks only about herself.
• Part 2	Sheila is lazy. She doesn't make any effort during the softball game and doesn't help the narrator paddle the canoe.
• Part 3	Sheila is fickle. At the fair, she announces that she is going home in another boy's car.

WRITING TIP

Conclusions An effective way to conclude an analysis is to return to your thesis and restate it in different words.

5 Persuasive Writing

Persuasive writing allows you to use the power of language to inform and influence others.

Key Techniques of Persuasive Writing

Writing Standards

Good persuasive writing
- clearly states the issue and the writer's position
- gives opinions and supports them with facts or reasons
- has a reasonable and respectful tone
- takes into account and answers opposing views
- uses sound logic and effective language
- concludes by summing up reasons or calling for action

State Your Opinion
Taking a stand on an issue and clearly stating your opinion are essential to every piece of persuasive writing you do.

Example
Businesses should hire teenagers for part-time work.

Know Your Audience
Knowing who will read your writing will help you decide what information you need to share and what tone you should use to communicate your message. A formal tone appropriate for a letter to a community leader or for a newspaper editorial is modeled below.

Example
Many businesses in our community have part-time job openings; however, they seem to be biased against hiring teenagers.

Support Your Opinion
Using reasons, examples, facts, statistics, and anecdotes to support your opinion will show your audience why you feel the way you do.

Example
Studies show that teenagers who work part-time have higher self-esteem and do better in school than those who do not work.

884 WRITING HANDBOOK

Organizing Persuasive Writing

In persuasive writing, you need to gather information to support your opinions. Here are some ways you can organize that material to convince your audience.

Option 1 — Example

Reasons for Your Opinion	Example
Your opinion	Businesses should hire teenagers for part-time work.
• Reason 1	Teenagers are energetic and learn new tasks quickly.
• Reason 2	Teenagers gain new skills and self-esteem when they take on the responsibility of a part-time job.
• Reason 3	Teenagers need their own money and independence.

Depending on the purpose and form of your writing, you may want to show the weaknesses of other opinions as you explain the strengths of your own. Two options for organizing persuasive writing that include opposing viewpoints are shown below.

Option 2

Why Your Opinion Is Stronger

Your opinion
- your reasons

Other opinion
- evidence refuting reasons for other opinion and showing strengths of your opinion

Option 3

Why Another Opinion Is Weaker

Other opinion
- reasons

Your opinion
- reasons supporting your opinion and pointing out the weaknesses of the other side

Remember: Persuasive writing can take many forms, including literary analyses, speeches, newspaper editorials, and advertisements. Choose your form according to the audience you want to reach.

WRITING TIP

Introductions Capture your readers' attention in the introduction to your piece. Try opening with a quote, a statistic, or an anecdote that shows the importance of your topic.

WRITING TIP

Conclusions Writing persuasively means convincing the reader to feel the way you do about something. Your conclusion in a persuasive essay might summarize your opinion, make a final appeal, or urge the reader to take action.

6 Research Report Writing

A research report explores a topic in depth, incorporating information from a variety of sources.

Writing Standards

Good research report writing

- clearly states the purpose of the report in a thesis statement
- uses evidence and details from a variety of sources to support the thesis
- contains only accurate and relevant information
- documents sources correctly
- develops the topic logically and includes appropriate transitions
- includes a properly formatted Works Cited list

Key Techniques of Research Report Writing

Clarify Your Thesis
A thesis statement is one or two sentences clearly stating the main idea that you will develop in your report. A thesis may also indicate the organizational pattern you will follow and reflect your tone and point of view.

Example
Greek mythology—the religious beliefs and practices of the ancient Greeks—directly shaped the development of the art, literature, and values of Greek society.

Support Your Ideas
You should support your ideas with relevant evidence—facts, anecdotes, and statistics—from reliable sources. In the example below, the writer supports a claim about the influence of religion on architectural design.

Example
To accommodate different religious cults, the Erechtheum temple was designed with three distinct porches, including one with columns carved in the form of women (Boardman and Watkin 907).

Document Your Sources
You need to document, or credit, the sources you use in your writing. In the example below, the writer uses a quotation as a supporting detail and documents the source.

Example
The Greeks would seek guidance at oracles where priests offered "often deceptive answers to questions ranging from military strategy to personal problems" (Eliade, Couliano, and Wiesner 123).

886 WRITING HANDBOOK

Evaluating Sources

To help you determine whether your sources are reliable and contain useful and accurate information, use the following checklist.

Checklist for Evaluating Your Sources	
Authoritative	Someone who has written several books or articles on your subject or whose work has been published in a well-respected newspaper or journal may be considered an authority.
Up-to-date	Check the publication dates to see if the source contains the most current research on your subject.
Respected	In general, tabloid newspapers and popular-interest magazines are not reliable sources. If you have questions about whether you are using a respected source, ask your librarian.

WRITING TIP

For additional help, see the research report about Bigfoot on page 706 or McDougal Littell's *Writing Research Papers*.

Making Source Cards

For each source you find, record the bibliographic information on a separate index card. You will need this information to give credit to the sources you use in your paper. The samples at the right show how to make source cards for magazine articles, on-line articles, and books. You will use the source number on each card to identify the notes you take during your research.

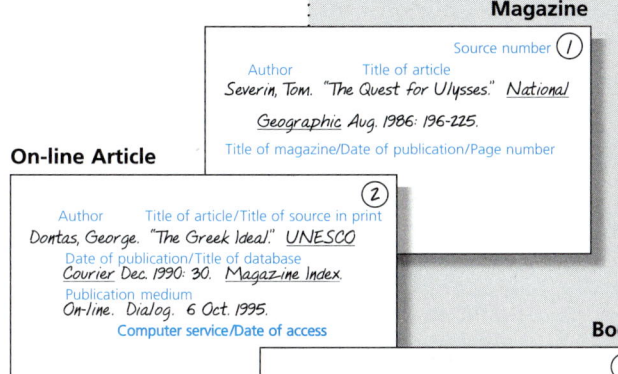

Taking Notes

As you read your sources, record on note cards information that is relevant to the purpose of your research. You will probably use all three of the following note-taking methods.

- **Paraphrase,** or restate in your own words, the main ideas and supporting details from a passage.
- **Summarize,** or rephrase the original material in fewer words, trying to capture the key ideas.
- **Quote,** or copy the original text word for word, if you think the author's own words best clarify a particular point. Use quotation marks to signal the beginning and the end of the quotation.

WRITING HANDBOOK **887**

Organizing Your Research Report

Making an outline can help guide the drafting process. Begin by reading over your note cards and sorting them into groups. The main-idea headings may help you find connections among the notes. Then arrange the groups of related note cards so that the ideas flow logically from one group to the next.

Note the format for a topic outline shown below. Remember that in a topic outline, items of the same degree of importance should be parallel in form. For instance, if A is a noun, then B and C should also be nouns. Subtopics need not be parallel with main topics.

> Mythology and the Daily Lives of the Ancient Greeks
> Introduction—Mythology shaped art, literature, and values of Greeks
> I. Mythology's influence on art
>   A. Sculpture
>   1. Decoration of religious temples
>   2. Idealized human figures
>   B. Architecture
> II. Mythology's influence on literature

Documenting Your Sources

When you quote, paraphrase, or summarize information from one of your sources, you need to credit that source using parenthetical documentation.

Guidelines for Parenthetical Documentation	
Work by One Author	Put the author's last name and the page reference in parentheses: (Severin 206). If you mention the author's name in the sentence, put only the page reference in parentheses: (206).
Work by Two or Three Authors	Put the authors' last names and the page reference in parentheses: (Eliade, Couliano, and Wiesner 122).
Work by More than Three Authors	Give the first author's last name followed by *et al.*, and the page reference: (Ellis et al. 59).
Work with No Author Given	Give the title or a shortened version and the page reference: ("Erechtheum" 537).
One of Two or More Works by Same Author	Give the author's last name, the title or a shortened version, and the page reference: (Starr, Ancient Greeks 41).

> **WRITING TIP**
>
> **Plagiarism** Presenting someone else's writing or ideas as your own is plagiarism. To avoid plagiarism, you need to credit sources as noted at the right. However, if a piece of information is common knowledge—available in several sources—you do not need to credit a source. To see an example of parenthetical documentation, see the essay on page 706.

WRITING HANDBOOK

Following MLA Manuscript Guidelines

The final copy of your report should follow the Modern Language Association guidelines for manuscript preparation.

- The heading in the upper left-hand corner of the first page should include your name, your teacher's name, the course name, and the date, each on a separate line.
- Below the heading, center the title on the page.
- Number all the pages consecutively in the upper right-hand corner, one-half inch from the top. Also, include your last name before the page number.
- Double-space the entire paper.
- Except for the margins above the page numbers, leave one-inch margins on all sides of every page.

The Works Cited list at the end of your paper is an alphabetized list of the sources you have used and documented in your report. The additional line or lines of each entry are indented one-half inch.

WRITING TIP

When your report includes a quotation that is longer than four lines, set it off from the rest of the text by indenting the entire quotation one inch from the left margin. In this case, you should not use quotation marks.

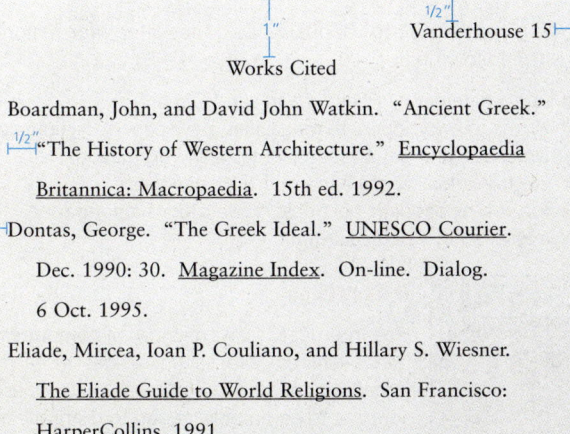

Models for Works Cited Entries

— Encyclopedia article section with two authors (Boardman, John, and David John Watkin. "Ancient Greek.")

— On-line article (Dontas, George. "The Greek Ideal." *UNESCO Courier*. Dec. 1990: 30. *Magazine Index*. On-line. Dialog. 6 Oct. 1995.)

— Book with three authors (Eliade, Mircea, Ioan P. Couliano, and Hillary S. Wiesner. *The Eliade Guide to World Religions*. San Francisco: HarperCollins, 1991.)

— Encyclopedia article with no author given ("Erechtheum." *Encyclopedia Britannica: Micropaedia*. 15th ed. 1992.)

— Book with editor but no single author (Scarre, Chris, ed. *Smithsonian Timelines of the Ancient World*. New York: Dorling Kindersley, 1993.)

— Magazine article (Severin, Tim. "The Quest for Ulysses." *National Geographic* Aug. 1986: 196–225.)

— Book with one author (Starr, Chester G. *The Ancient Greeks*. New York: Oxford UP, 1971.)

1 Getting Information Electronically

Electronic resources provide you with a convenient and efficient way to gather information.

1.1 On-line Resources

When you use your computer to communicate with another computer or with another person using a computer, you are working "on-line." On-line resources include commercial information services and information available on the Internet.

Commercial Information Services

You can subscribe to various services that offer information such as the following:

- up-to-date news, weather, and sports reports
- access to encyclopedias, magazines, newspapers, dictionaries, almanacs, and databases (collections of information)
- electronic mail (e-mail) to and from other users
- forums, or ongoing electronic conversations among users interested in a particular topic

Internet

The Internet is a vast network of computers. News services, libraries, universities, researchers, organizations, and government agencies use the Internet to communicate and to distribute information. The Internet includes two key features:

- **World Wide Web,** which provides you with information on particular subjects and links you to related topics and resources (such as the Web pages shown at the left)
- **Electronic mail** (e-mail), which allows you to communicate with other e-mail users worldwide

890 MULTIMEDIA HANDBOOK

1.2 CD-ROM

A CD-ROM (compact disc–read-only memory) stores data, which may include text, sound, photographs, and video.

Almost any kind of information can be found on CD-ROMs, which you can use at the library or purchase, including

- encyclopedias, almanacs, and indexes
- other reference books on a variety of subjects
- news reports from newspapers, magazines, television, or radio
- museum art collections
- back issues of magazines
- literature collections

WHAT YOU'LL NEED

- To access on-line resources, you need a computer with a modem linked to a telephone line. Your school computer lab or resource center may be linked to the Internet or to a commercial information service.
- To use CD-ROMs, you need a computer system with a CD-ROM player.

1.3 Library Computer Services

Many libraries offer computerized catalogs and a variety of other electronic resources.

Computerized Catalogs

You may search for a book in a library by typing the title, author, subject, or key words into a computer terminal. If you enter the title of a book, the screen will display the bibliographic information and the current availability of the book. When a particular work is not available, you may be able to search the catalogs of other libraries.

Other Electronic Resources

In addition to computerized catalogs, many libraries offer electronic versions of books or other reference materials. They may also have a variety of indexes on CD-ROM, which allow you to search for magazine or newspaper articles on any topic you choose. When you have found an article on the topic you want, the screen will display the kind of information shown at the right.

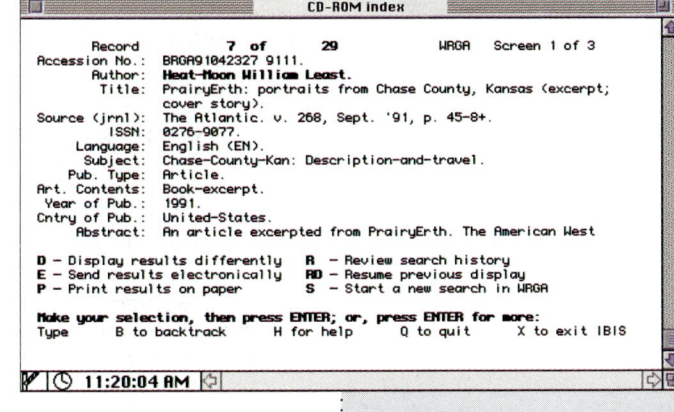

MULTIMEDIA HANDBOOK **891**

2 Word Processing

WHAT YOU'LL NEED

- Computer
- Word-processing program
- Printer

Word-processing programs allow you to draft, revise, edit, and format your writing and to produce neat, professional-looking papers. They also allow you to share your writing with others.

2.1 Revising and Editing

Improving the quality of your writing becomes easier when you use a word-processing program to revise and edit.

Revising a Document

Most word-processing programs allow you to make the following kinds of changes:

- add or delete words
- move text from one location in your document to another
- undo a change you have made in the text
- save a document with a new name, allowing you to keep old drafts for reference
- view more than one document at a time, so you can copy text from one document and add it to another

Editing a Document

Many word-processing programs have the following features to help you catch errors and polish your writing:

- The **spell checker** automatically finds misspelled words and suggests possible corrections.
- The **grammar checker** spots possible grammatical errors and suggests ways you might correct them.
- The **thesaurus** suggests synonyms for a word you want to replace.
- The **dictionary** will give you the definitions of words so you can be sure you have used words correctly.
- The **search and replace** feature searches your whole document and corrects every occurrence of something you want to change, such as a misspelled name.

WRITING TIP

Spell checkers and grammar checkers offer suggestions for corrections, but you must carefully assess these suggestions before picking the right one. This will involve looking at the suggested change in the context of your writing.

2.2 Formatting Your Work

Format is the layout and appearance of your writing on the page. You may choose your formatting options before or after you write.

Formatting Type

You may want to make changes in the typeface, type size, and type style of the words in your document. For each of these, your word-processing program will most likely have several options to choose from. These options allow you to

- change the typeface to create a different look for the words in your document
- change the type size of the entire document or of just the headings of sections in the paper
- change the type style when necessary; for example, use italics or underline for the titles of books and magazines

Typeface	Size	Style
Geneva	7-point Times	*Italic*
Times	10-point Times	**Bold**
Chicago	12-point Times	Underline
Courier	14-point Times	

Formatting Pages

Not only can you change the way individual words look; you can also change the way they are arranged on the page. Some of the formatting decisions you make will depend on how you plan to use a printout of a draft or on the guidelines of an assignment.

- Set the line spacing, or the amount of space you need between lines of text. Double spacing is commonly used for final drafts.
- Set the margins, or the amount of white space around the edges of your text. A one-inch margin on all sides is commonly used for final drafts.
- Create a header for the top of the page or a footer for the bottom if you want to include such information as your name, the date, or the page number on every page.
- Determine the alignment of your text. The screen at the left shows your options.

TECHNOLOGY TIP

Some word-processing programs or other software packages provide preset templates, or patterns, for writing outlines, memos, letters, newsletters, or invitations. If you use one of these templates, you will not need to adjust the formatting.

2.3 Working Collaboratively

Computers allow you to share your writing electronically. Send a copy of your work to someone via e-mail or put it in someone's drop box if your computer is linked to other computers on a network. Then use the feedback of your peers to help you improve the quality of your writing.

Peer Editing on a Computer

The writer and the reader can both benefit from the convenience of peer editing "on screen," or at the computer.

- Be sure to save your current draft and then make a copy of it for each of your peer readers.
- You might have each peer reader use a different typeface or type style for making comments, as shown in the example below.
- Ask each of your readers to include his or her initials in the file name.

TECHNOLOGY TIP

Some word-processing programs, such as the Writing Coach software referred to in this book, allow you to leave notes for your peer readers in the side column or in a separate text box. If you wish, leave those areas blank so your readers can write comments or questions.

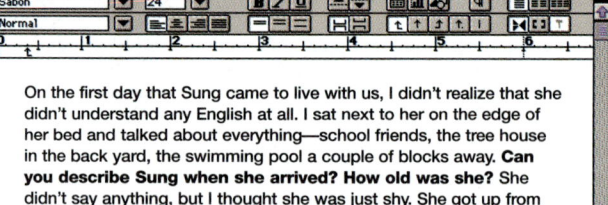

- If your computer allows you to open more than one file at a time, open each reviewer's file and refer to the files as you revise your draft.

Peer Editing on a Printout

Some peer readers prefer to respond to a draft on paper rather than on the computer.

- Double-space or triple-space your document so that your peer editor can make suggestions between the lines.
- Leave extra-wide margins to give your readers room to note their reactions and questions as they read.
- Print out your draft and photocopy it if you want to share it with more than one reader.

Using Visuals 3

Tables, charts, graphs, diagrams, and pictures often communicate information more effectively than words alone do. Many computer programs allow you to create visuals to use with your written text.

3.1 When to Use Visuals

Use visuals in your work to illustrate complex concepts and processes or to make a page look more interesting.

Although you should not expect a visual to do all the work of written text, combining words and pictures or graphics can increase the understanding and enjoyment of your writing. Many computer programs allow you to create and insert graphs, tables, time lines, diagrams, and flow charts into your document. An art program allows you to create border designs for a title page or to draw an unusual character or setting for narrative or descriptive writing. You may also be able to add clip art, or premade pictures, to your document. Clip art can be used to illustrate an idea or concept in your writing or to make your writing more appealing for young readers.

WHAT YOU'LL NEED

- A graphics program to create visuals
- Access to clip-art files from a CD-ROM, a computer disk, or an on-line service

3.2 Kinds of Visuals

The visuals you choose will depend on the type of information you want to present to your readers.

Tables

Tables allow you to arrange facts or numbers into rows and columns so that your reader can compare information more easily. In many word-processing programs, you can create a table by choosing the number of vertical columns and horizontal rows you need and then entering information in each box, as the illustration shows.

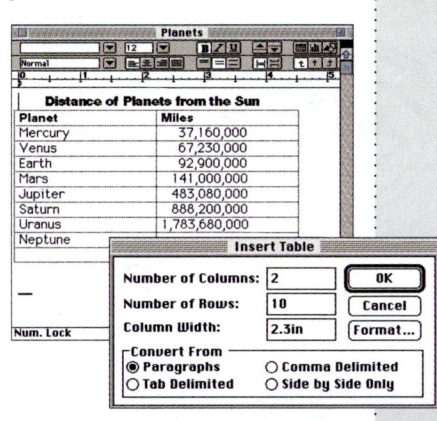

TECHNOLOGY TIP

A spreadsheet program provides you with a preset table for your statistics and performs any necessary calculations.

MULTIMEDIA HANDBOOK

> **WRITING TIP**
>
> Be sure that you have effectively integrated your written text and visuals. The body of your text should refer to the information in your visuals and explain the relevance of the information. Also, captions, headings, and labels in your visuals should clearly identify each component.

Graphs and Charts

You can sometimes use a graph or chart to help communicate complex information in a clear visual image. For example, you could use a line graph to show how a trend changes over time, a bar graph such as the one at the right to compare statistics, or a pie chart to compare percentages. You might want to explore ways of displaying data in more than one visual format before deciding which will work best for you.

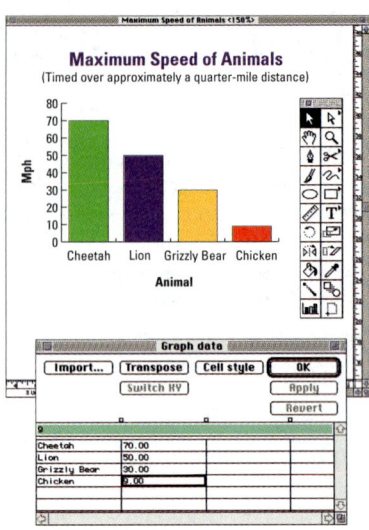

Other Visuals

Art and design programs allow you to create visuals for your writing. Many programs include the following features:

- drawing tools that allow you to draw, color, and shade pictures, such as the one shown below
- clip art, that you can copy or change with drawing tools
- page borders that you can use to decorate title pages, invitations, or brochures
- text options that allow you to combine words with your illustrations
- tools for making geometric shapes in flow charts, time lines, and diagrams that show a process or sequence of events

896 MULTIMEDIA HANDBOOK

Creating a Multimedia Presentation

A multimedia presentation is a combination of text, sound, and visuals such as photographs, videos, and animation. Your audience reads, hears, and sees your presentation at a computer, following different "paths" you create to lead the user through the information you have gathered.

4.1 Features of Multimedia Programs

To start planning your multimedia presentation, you need to know what options are available to you. You can combine sound, photos, videos, and animation to enhance any text you write about your topic.

Sound

Including sound in your presentation can help your audience understand information in your written text. For example, the user may be able to listen and learn from

- the pronunciation of an unfamiliar or foreign word
- a speech
- a recorded news interview
- a musical selection
- a dramatic reading of a work of literature

Photos and Videos

Photographs and live-action videos can make your subject come alive for the user. Here are some examples:

- videotaped news coverage of a historical event
- videos of music, dance, or theater performances
- charts and diagrams
- photos of an artist's work
- photos or video of a geographical setting that is important to the written text

WHAT YOU'LL NEED

- Individual programs to create and edit the text, graphics, sound, and videos you will use
- A multimedia authoring program that allows you to combine these elements and create links between the screens

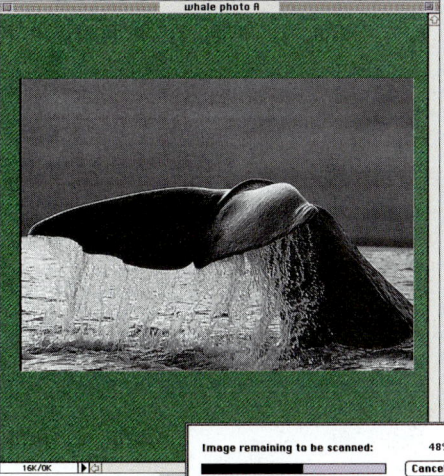

MULTIMEDIA HANDBOOK **897**

Animation

Many graphics programs allow you to add animation, or movement, to the visuals in your presentation. Animated figures add to the user's enjoyment and understanding of what you present. You can use animation to illustrate

- what happens in a story
- the steps in a process
- changes in a chart, graph, or diagram
- how your user can explore information in your presentation

4.2 Planning Your Presentation

To create a multimedia presentation, first choose your topic and decide what you want to include. Then plan how you want your user to move through your presentation.

Imagine you are creating a multimedia presentation about musical compositions written to incorporate the songs of humpback whales. You know you want to include the following items:

- text about humpback-whale songs
- a photo of a humpback whale
- a video of humpback whales
- a recording of whale songs and organ music written to accompany it
- a radio interview with Linda Guinee, who has studied whale songs
- texts of transcribed musical scores of whale songs

You can choose one of the following ways to organize your presentation:

- step by step with only one path, or order, in which the user can see and hear the information
- a branching path that allows users to make some choices about what they will see and hear, and in what order

A flow chart can help you figure out the path a user can take through your presentation. Each box in the flow chart on the following page represents something about humpback-whale songs for the audience to read, see, or hear. The arrows on the flow chart show a branching path the user can follow.

 TECHNOLOGY TIP

You can download photos, sound, and video from Internet sources onto your computer. This process allows you to add elements to your multimedia presentation that would usually require complex editing equipment.

 TECHNOLOGY TIP

You can now find CD-ROMs with videos of things like wildlife, weather, street scenes, and events, and other CD-ROMs with recordings of famous speeches, musical selections, and dramatic readings.

Whenever boxes branch in more than one direction, it means that the user can choose which item to see or hear first.

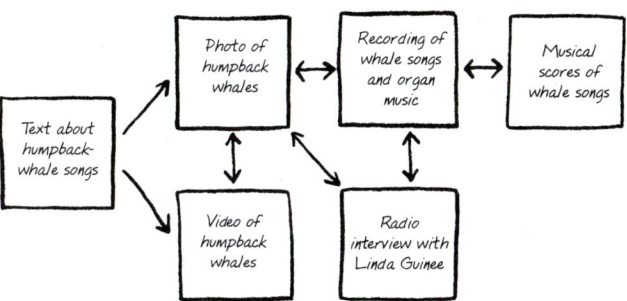

4.3 Guiding Your User

Your user will need directions to follow the path you have planned for your multimedia presentation.

Most multimedia authoring programs allow you to create screens that include text or audio directions that guide the user from one part of your presentation to the next. In the example below, the user can choose between several paths, and directions on the screen explain how to make the choice.

If you need help creating your multimedia presentation, ask your school's technology adviser. You may also be able to get help from your classmates or your software manual.

WRITING TIP

You usually need permission from the person or organization that owns the copyright on materials if you want to copy them. You do not need permission, however, if you are not making money from your presentation, if you use it only for educational purposes, and if you use only a small percentage of the original material.

The user clicks on a button to select any of these options.

Navigational buttons take the user back and forth, one screen at a time.

This screen shows a photo of humpback whales.

MULTIMEDIA HANDBOOK **899**

1 Writing Complete Sentences

1.1 Sentence Fragments

A sentence fragment is a group of words that does not express a complete thought. Sentence fragments may be missing a subject, a predicate, or both.

Completing an Incomplete Thought

You can correct a sentence fragment by adding the missing subject, predicate, or both to complete the thought.

> ~~I enjoyed~~ The story "Grover Dill and the Tasmanian Devil." ^ Ralph Feels rage when the local bully attacks him once too often.

When the fragment is a subordinate clause, you can join the fragment to an existing sentence or rewrite the clause so it can stand alone.

> ~~Because~~ the risk involved in fighting back was so great. Ordinarily, Ralph wouldn't have done anything. ~~But~~ run from Grover Dill.

Correcting Punctuation

A sentence fragment may be a clause or a phrase that can be connected to a complete sentence. To correct it, you may simply change the punctuation.

> But this time. Everything was different because Ralph didn't have a chance to think—only to act.

APPLY WHAT YOU'VE LEARNED

Rewrite this paragraph, correcting the sentence fragments.

¹"Grover Dill and the Tasmanian Devil" looks at explosive retaliation. ²And compares it to the outrageously combative behavior of a marsupial called the Tasmanian devil. ³These creatures able to open their mouths very wide, the better to scavenge dead cows or sheep. ⁴Bones, hooves, and all. ⁵A Tasmanian devil in good health has as many as 46 teeth. ⁶Also drools a lot. ⁷This animal has an inherently foul odor. ⁸Perhaps because of the way it gets its dinner. ⁹The Tasmanian devil has no known social organization or protective instincts. ¹⁰Even for others of its own species. ¹¹The young of Tasmanian devils are raised. ¹²In the mother's pouch. ¹³Sometimes they fall out and may be devoured by the mother. ¹⁴Or another devil.

1.2 Run-on Sentences

A run-on sentence consists of two or more sentences incorrectly written as one. It is unclear where one idea ends and the next begins.

Forming Separate Sentences

One way to correct a run-on sentence is to form two separate sentences. Use a period or other end punctuation after the first complete thought and capitalize the first letter of the next sentence.

> In "Sea Perils and Defeat" from the *Odyssey*, a grim task confronted Odysseus he had to lead his men into great danger.

Sometimes a writer mistakenly uses a comma instead of a period to separate two complete thoughts. You can correct this kind of mistake, called a comma splice, by changing the comma to a period and capitalizing the first letter of the second sentence.

> Odysseus was aware of the danger, some of his crew would die.

REVISING TIP

To correct a run-on sentence, read it to yourself, noticing where you naturally pause between ideas. The pause usually indicates where you should place end punctuation.

1.1 Sentence Fragments

Answers will vary. See typical answers below.

"Grover Dill and the Tasmanian Devil" looks at explosive retaliation and compares it to the outrageously combative behavior of a marsupial called the Tasmanian devil. These creatures are able to open their mouths very wide, the better to scavenge dead cows or sheep. They eat the dead animals bones, hooves, and all. A Tasmanian devil in good health has as many as 46 teeth. It also drools a lot. This animal has an inherently foul odor, perhaps because of the way it gets its dinner. The Tasmanian devil has no known social organization or protective instincts, even for others of its own species. The young of Tasmanian devils are raised in the mother's pouch. Sometimes they fall out and may be devoured by the mother or another devil.

Joining Sentences

If the ideas expressed in a run-on sentence are closely related, you may wish to join them to form a compound sentence. One way to do this is to use a comma and a coordinating conjunction to join the main clauses.

> Odysseus plugged his men's ears with wax ^*and* then the men lashed him to the mast.

Use a semicolon alone, or with a conjunctive adverb, to join main clauses having closely related ideas.

Some commonly used conjunctive adverbs are *however, therefore, nevertheless,* and *besides.*

> The monster Scylla raged on the port side of the ship^; Charybdis seethed on the starboard side. Scylla killed six men^*however,* the rest of the crew survived.

APPLY WHAT YOU'VE LEARNED

Rewrite this paragraph, correcting the run-on sentences.

¹In "Sea Perils and Defeat" from the *Odyssey,* readers learn about seafaring in antiquity it could be hazardous. ²In those days trading ships were large, these slowpokes were moved only by the wind. ³They had no oarsmen pirates found them easy to attack. ⁴Pirate ships and warships were as small as 40 feet long each ship had at least 20 oarsmen. ⁵Bronze axes were used to cut aspen, alder, or pine wood for these fast ships, masts had linen sails made of patches sewn together. ⁶Pitch protected the wood from saltwater damage leather straps attached oars to a boat's wooden frame. ⁷All Mediterranean sea travel back then was limited it took place only from April to October. ⁸Warship captains set courses that hugged the shorelines they traveled during the day. ⁹Crossing the open sea was dangerous few captains tried it.

902 GRAMMAR HANDBOOK

1.2 Run-on Sentences

Answers will vary. See typical answers below.

1 In "Sea Perils and Defeat" from the Odyssey, readers learn about seafaring. In antiquity it could be hazardous. 2 In those days trading ships were large, but these slowpokes were moved only by the wind. 3 They had no oarsmen; therefore, pirates found them easy to attack. 4 Pirate ships and warships were as small as 40 feet long, but each ship had at least 20 oarsmen. 5 Bronze axes were used to cut aspen, alder, or pine wood for these fast ships. Masts had linen sails made of patches sewn together. 6 Pitch protected the wood from saltwater damage, and leather straps attached oars to a boat's wooden frame. 7 All Mediterranean sea travel back then was limited; it took place only from April to October. 8 Warship captains set courses that hugged the shorelines, and they traveled during the day. 9 Crossing the open sea was dangerous; therefore, few captains tried it.

Making Subjects and Verbs Agree 2

2.1 Simple and Compound Subjects

A verb must agree in number with its subject. The word *number* refers to whether a word is singular or plural. When a word refers to one thing, it is singular. When it refers to more than one thing, it is plural.

Agreement with Simple Subjects

Use a singular verb with a singular subject.

When the subject is a singular noun, you use the singular form of the verb. The present-tense third-person singular form of a regular verb usually ends in *-s* or *-es*.

> The story "Fish Eyes" open^s with a call to attention that is straight out of vaudeville.

Use a plural verb with a plural subject.

> The author's goals includes entertaining and delighting the reader with a true story of dirty socks and dead fish.

Agreement with Compound Subjects

Use a plural verb with a compound subject whose parts are joined by *and*, regardless of the number of each part.

> The author's brother, Mel, and sister, Blanche, exercises great ingenuity in tormenting David, also known as Kingy.

LINK TO LITERATURE

Notice the shifts in verb tense throughout David Brenner's "Fish Eyes." This author shifts frequently from past tense to present tense, giving a sense of immediacy and childlike quirkiness to his story about practical jokes in his family. In spite of these shifts, Brenner maintains the necessary subject-verb agreement.

REVISING TIP

To find the subject of a sentence, first find the verb. Then ask *who* or *what* performs the action of the verb. Say the subject and the verb together to see whether they agree.

GRAMMAR HANDBOOK 903

When the parts of a compound subject are joined by *or* or *nor*, make the verb agree in number with the part that is closer to it.

Neither the parents nor any child ~~have~~ *has* an idea about what's causing the hideous fishy smell.

APPLY WHAT YOU'VE LEARNED

Write the correct form of the verbs.

[1] In writing "Fish Eyes," David Brenner use many devices of humor. [2] Humor are a form of play. [3] Unexpected combinations creates humor. [4] Humor put together things with no obvious or logical relation to one another. [5] Either a humorous event or an amusing story evoke laughter. [6] The laughter provide a release from tension. [7] Aggressive impulses or fear are handled safely through humor. [8] Sometimes a person laugh in response to mere exaggeration. [9] Practical jokes is thought to be a rather primitive form of humor. [10] Children usually indulges in them more frequently than adults does. [11] Some scholars and philosophers thinks wit is a more sophisticated form of humor because it is primarily verbal. [12] Children prefers cruder forms of humor. [13] They finds wit hard to understand. [14] Neither laughter nor giggling are easy to stop once it starts within a close-knit group. [15] A group member laugh long and hard for very little reason.

2.1 Simple and Compound Subjects

1. uses
2. is
3. create
4. puts
5. evokes
6. provides
7. is
8. laughs
9. are
10. indulge; do
11. think
12. prefer
13. find
14. is
15. laughs

2.2 Pronoun Subjects

When a pronoun is used as a subject, the verb must agree with it in number.

Agreement with Personal Pronouns

When the subject is a singular personal pronoun, use a singular verb. When the subject is plural, use a plural verb.

Singular pronouns are *I, you, he, she,* and *it*. Plural pronouns are *we, you,* and *they*. Although *I* and *you* are singular, they take plural verbs.

After discussing *The Devil and Daniel Webster*, we concludes that the play is powerful. It show the main character dealing with the devil.

904 GRAMMAR HANDBOOK

When *he, she,* or *it* is the part of a compound subject that is closer to the verb and the parts are joined by *or* or *nor,* use a singular verb. When a pronoun is part of a compound subject joined by *and,* use a plural verb.

> Mary Stone and he proves to be Jabez's truest friends.
> Neither Webster nor she abandon Jabez to his fate.

Agreement with Indefinite Pronouns

When the subject is a singular indefinite pronoun, use the singular form of the verb.

The following are singular indefinite pronouns: *another, either, nobody, anybody, everybody, no one, anyone, everyone, someone, one, anything, everything, each,* and *neither*.

> On Jabez's old farm everything go bad. Nobody want to marry him when he has such poor land and poor luck. Anyone become frustrated and discouraged when faced with such troubles.

When the subject is a plural indefinite pronoun use the plural form of the verb.

The following are plural indefinite pronouns: *both, few, many,* and *several*.

> Many expresses fear when they discover the bargain Jabez made to get his farm and his political power. Few reacts calmly to the human weakness that led to his trouble.

2.2 Pronoun Subjects

1. has
2. were
3. is
4. was
5. raise
6. was
7. were; were
8. was
9. were
10. was; has

> **REVISING TIP**
>
> In many sentences these indefinite pronouns will be followed by a prepositional phrase that might help you determine whether the subject is singular or plural. Remember, however, that the object of the preposition is not the subject of the sentence.

The indefinite pronouns *some, all, any, none,* and *most* can be either singular or plural. When the pronoun refers to one thing, use a singular verb. When the pronoun refers to several things, use a plural verb.

> All of Jabez's sorrow converge$_\wedge^s$ on him that night, even though he admits his mistake and wishes he hadn't made it. However, none of his regrets stops̸ Scratch.

APPLY WHAT YOU'VE LEARNED

In each sentence write the correct form of the verb(s).

¹*The Devil and Daniel Webster* shows the root of Jabez Stone's troubles: he have an unproductive New Hampshire farm. ²Of the farms in New England in his day, many was rocky and hard to farm. ³New Hampshire is called the Granite State, and it are well named. ⁴Of all the land in the state, none were suited for small family farms. ⁵Today, most of the New England farms raises dairy cows. ⁶Gravity caused Jabez's problems: he were farming on a hill. ⁷Of the soils few was rich; usually they was thin, sandy, and full of gravel. ⁸Just 10,000 years ago, a mile-thick glacier covered the state; it were successful in scouring away the soil. ⁹Some of the New Englanders was so discouraged by the harsh land that they left for the Midwest. ¹⁰Of the New England land that were cleared for farming, much have reverted to forest.

2.3 Common Agreement Problems

Several other situations can cause problems in subject-verb agreement.

Interrupting Words and Phrases

Be sure the verb agrees with its subject when words or phrases come between them.

The subject of a verb is never found in a prepositional phrase or an appositive, which may follow the subject and come before the verb. Other phrases—such as those beginning with *including, as well as, along with, such as,* and *in addition to*—can also separate the subject and verb.

Johnny, the narrator in "Marine Corps Issue," look^s in his father's boxes to learn more about his father's past. These boxes containing his father's keepsakes from Vietnam remains/locked at all times.

 REVISING TIP

The forms of *do, be,* and *have* can be main verbs or helping verbs. They can also be part of contractions with *not* (*doesn't/don't, isn't/aren't, hasn't/haven't*). In every case, the verb should agree in number with its subject.

When phrases—such as those beginning with *including, as well as, along with, such as,* and *in addition to*—separate subjects and verbs, be sure that the verb agrees with the subject.

Johnny, as well as his brother, know^s little about Vietnam. Books, including *Dispatches* by Michael Herr, teaches/ Johnny some basic facts about the war.

Inverted Sentences

When the simple subject comes after the verb, be sure the verb agrees with the subject in number.

A sentence in which the subject follows the verb is called an inverted sentence. Questions are usually in inverted form, as are sentences beginning with *Here* and *There*. (*Where **are** the **children**? Here **stands** a great **monument**.*)

 REVISING TIP

To check subject-verb agreement in inverted sentences, place the subject before the verb. For example, change *Here is my family* to *My family is here*.

Inside his father's boxes, there is^are medals, teeth, and uniforms. Here lies/ the keys to understanding Johnny's father.

GRAMMAR HANDBOOK 907

> **REVISING TIP**
>
> Look carefully at words that come before the verb to find the subject. Remember that the subject may not be the noun or pronoun closest to the verb.

Singular Nouns with Plural Forms

Be sure to use a singular verb when the subject is a noun that is singular in meaning but appears to be plural.

Words such as *mumps, news,* and *molasses* appear to be plural because they end in *-s*. However, these words are singular in meaning. Words ending in *-ics* that refer to a science or branch of study (*physics, mathematics, genetics, ethics*) are also singular.

> The dismal politics of war wrench*es* Joseph from his home and family. Eventually the news come*s* that Joseph has been captured and imprisoned.

Collective Nouns

Use a singular verb when the subject is a collective noun—such as *class, team, crowd,* and *flock*—that refers to the group acting as a unit. Use a plural verb when the collective noun refers to members of the group acting individually.

> Joseph's marine unit ~~are~~ *is* stationed in Vietnam. The majority of soldiers probably want~~s~~ to go home.

Nouns of Time, Weight, Measure, Number

Use a singular verb with a subject that identifies a period of time, a weight, a measure, or a number.

> Three years of captivity totally change*s* Joseph's life. A million dollars ~~are~~ *is* not enough payment for his suffering at this time.

908 GRAMMAR HANDBOOK

Titles

Use a singular verb when the subject is the title of a work of art, literature, or music, even though the title may contain plural words.

"Marigolds" remind**s** me of "Marine Corps Issue" because both stories keep you in suspense.

> **REVISING TIP**
>
> The fact that a title is set off by quotation marks, italics, or an underscore helps to remind you that it is singular and takes a singular verb.

Predicate Nominatives

Use a verb that agrees with the subject, not with the predicate nominative, when the subject is different in number from the predicate nominative.

Joseph's well-kept secrets ~~was~~ *were* a stumbling block to communication with his family. His flashbacks ~~was~~ *were* a consequence of his years in prison.

APPLY WHAT YOU'VE LEARNED

Write the following paragraph, correcting the form of the verbs.

¹"Marine Corps Issue" tell the story of Joseph Bowen, an American Marine captured in South Vietnam in 1966. ²Khe Sanh, a Marine base in the jungles of Vietnam, were near the Demilitarized Zone. ³The aim of North Vietnamese military leaders were the destruction of Khe Sanh. ⁴There was 20,000 enemy soldiers sent to cut off the base's land supply routes. ⁵A majority of historians believes that the siege was intended to distract U.S. military bombers from more critical tasks. ⁶In all, 77 days were the duration of the siege. ⁷The U.S. response were airlifts of supplies for the defenders. ⁸Thirteen hundred tons of explosive were dropped around Khe Sanh each day. ⁹The news of the bombings were quickly communicated to the enemy's ground forces. ¹⁰The Vietcong's loss of men, as well as their losses in equipment, were too great for them to stay.

GRAMMAR HANDBOOK **909**

3 Using Nouns and Pronouns

3.1 Plural and Possessive Nouns

Nouns refer to people, places, things, and ideas. A noun is plural when it refers to more than one person, place, thing, or idea. A possessive noun shows who or what owns something.

Plural Nouns

Follow these guidelines to form noun plurals.

- For most nouns, add -s (ballot—ballots, poll—polls).
- For nouns ending in s, sh, ch, x, or z, add -es (speech—speeches, process—processes).
- For nouns ending in a consonant and y, change y to i and add -es (party—parties, jury—juries).
- For most nouns that end in a consonant and o, add -es (hero—heroes, potato—potatoes).
- For many nouns that end in f or fe, change f to v and add -s or -es (life—lives, wife—wives).

Some nouns have the same spelling in both the singular and the plural: *series, trout, sheep*. Some noun plurals have irregular forms that don't follow any rule: *children, women*.

> "The United States vs. Susan B. Anthony" shows some crucial moment for Anthony. Echos of her speechs still resound when civil rights are abused.

(edits: "moments"; "Echoes"; "speeches")

Possessive Nouns

Follow these guidelines to form possessive nouns.

- Add an apostrophe and -s to form the possessive of a singular noun or a plural noun that does not end in -s (freedom—freedom's, men—men's).
- Add only an apostrophe to plural nouns that end in -s (elections—elections', citizens—citizens').

REVISING TIP

The dictionary usually lists the plural form of a noun if it is formed irregularly or if it might be formed in more than one way. For example, the plural of *phenomenon* is *phenomena*. Dictionary listings are especially helpful for nouns that end in *o, f,* and *fe*.

Anthony stood up grandly to the judges' intimidation. The judge underestimated her speeches' effects, not realizing how they would help in the fight for women's rights.

APPLY WHAT YOU'VE LEARNED
Write the correct plural or possessive.

¹"The United States v. Susan B. Anthony" details Anthony first voter registration drive. ²However, woman suffrage drew on two feminist dynamos strength. ³Anthony and Elizabeth Cady Stanton had both dedicated their lifes to helping U.S. women attain full citizenship. ⁴As she watched her fathers law practice, Stanton became aware of many injustices suffered by wifes. ⁵She later financed her seven childrens college educations with her earnings as a feminist speaker. ⁶Stanton gave women more than the vote—she got woman to think and question their lot. ⁷This beloved public figure saw 6,000 well-wisher at her 80th birthday party in New York City.

3.1 Plural and Possessive Nouns
1. Anthony's
2. dynamos'
3. lives
4. father's; wives
5. children's
6. women
7. well-wishers

3.2 Pronoun Forms

A personal pronoun is a pronoun that can be used in the first, second, or third person. A personal pronoun has three forms: the subject form, the object form, and the possessive form.

Subject Pronouns

Use the subject form of a pronoun when it is the subject of a sentence or the subject of a clause. *I, you, he, she, it, we,* and *they* are subject pronouns.

Problems usually arise when a noun and a pronoun, or two pronouns, are used in a compound subject or compound object. To see whether you are using the correct form, read the sentence with just one pronoun.

LINK TO LITERATURE

Notice how Ron Arias uses pronouns to avoid repetition of the nouns and to link ideas between sentences throughout "A Trip to the Edge of Survival," beginning on page 756.

"A Trip to the Edge of Survival" tells of some men who, with their captain, drifted on the Pacific. The captain and ~~them~~ *they* ate many fish and sea turtles during the journey.

GRAMMAR HANDBOOK **911**

Use the subject form of a pronoun when it is a predicate pronoun following a linking verb.

You often hear the object form used for a predicate pronoun in casual conversation. (*It is her.*) However, the subject form is preferred for more formal writing.

 REVISING TIP

To check the form of a predicate pronoun, see if the sentence still makes sense when the subject and the predicate pronoun are reversed. (*It was she. She was it.*)

> Toward the voyage's end one crewman, Joel, wrote many goodbye letters to his wife. It was ~~him~~ *he* who provided most of the quotations used in Arias's account.

Object Pronouns

Use the object form of a pronoun when it is the object of a verb or a preposition. *Me, you, him, her, it, us,* and *them* are object pronouns.

> Gerardo went into the water to repair the boat's leaky hull. This work was risky—the sharks made the crew and ~~he~~ *him* very nervous.

Possessive Pronouns

Never use an apostrophe with a possessive pronoun. *My, mine, your, yours, his, her, hers, its, our, ours, their,* and *theirs* are possessive pronouns.

> Just two weeks before ~~they're~~ *their* rescue, the crew had been without fresh water for many days. When rain came, ~~it's~~ *its* touch rekindled their will to live.

912 GRAMMAR HANDBOOK

APPLY WHAT YOU'VE LEARNED

Write the correct pronoun forms.

¹In "A Trip to the Edge of Survival," after the fishermen's boat encountered a major ocean current, it's westward course became inevitable. ²Juan saved the day; it was him who really made use of the current. ³He showed Joel and they how to make a sail. ⁴Surface ocean currents are strong; their's is a strength many times greater than the combined current of all rivers. ⁵On the whole, them are created by prevailing winds. ⁶As close as 100 meters below the surface, deeper currents usually flow in the opposite direction from they. ⁷Because sound carries so well underwater, researchers are using it's properties to chart the force and duration of deepwater currents.

3.2 Pronoun Forms

1. its
2. he
3. them
4. theirs
5. they
6. them
7. its

3.3 Pronoun Antecedents

An antecedent is the noun or pronoun to which a personal pronoun refers. The antecedent usually precedes the pronoun.

Pronoun and Antecedent Agreement

A pronoun must agree with its antecedent in number, person, and gender.

Use a singular pronoun to refer to a singular antecedent; use a plural pronoun to refer to a plural antecedent.

Do not allow interrupters to determine the number of the personal pronoun.

> If Elena in "American History" had put aside her private issues during a time of public grief, she might have resolved it *them* more successfully.

 LINK TO LITERATURE

Notice the care Judith Ortiz Cofer takes to ensure that pronouns agree with their antecedents throughout "American History." Readers have no trouble understanding the events and relationships described in her story, which is a modern version of *Romeo and Juliet*.

If the antecedent is a noun that could be either male or female, use *he or she* (*him or her, his or her*) or reword the sentence to avoid the singular pronoun.

> Almost every person Elena meets is distraught about the tragedy in Dallas, and ~~they are~~ *he or she is* unable to respond to Elena's concerns.

 REVISING TIP

You also could revise the second example, at the left, like this: *Most of the people Elena meets are distraught about the tragedy in Dallas, and they are unable to respond to Elena's concerns.*

REVISING TIP

To avoid vague pronoun reference, do not use *this* or *that* alone to start a clause. Instead, include a word stating the thing or idea to which *this* or *that* refers—*this method, this grouping, that idea.*

Be sure that the antecedent of a pronoun is clear.

In most cases do not use a pronoun to refer to an entire idea or clause. Writing is much clearer if you repeat the idea.

> Elena's fascination with Eugene drew her mother's nagging attention. This ^*vigilance* was mildly irritating to Elena.

Unclear Antecedents

Make sure that each personal pronoun has a clear reference.

Clarify unidentified references.

The words *it, they, this, which,* and *that* can create problems when there is no clear antecedent to which they refer.

> *Readers*
> ~~They~~ say that "American History" could be a true story.

Clarify ambiguous references.

Ambiguous means "having two or more possible meanings." A pronoun reference is ambiguous if the pronoun may refer to more than one word.

> Elena's encounter with Eugene's mother was especially awkward for ~~her~~ *Elena*.

Compound Antecedents Using *Or* or *Nor*

When two or more singular antecedents are joined by *or* or *nor,* use a singular pronoun. When two or more plural antecedents are joined by *or* or *nor,* use a plural pronoun.

> Neither Elena nor Eugene knew what ~~they~~ *she or he* would do.
>
> Neither Elena's nor Eugene's family members wanted ~~his or her~~ *their* children to be close friends.

914 GRAMMAR HANDBOOK

When one singular and one plural antecedent are joined by *or* or *nor,* use the noun or pronoun nearer the verb to determine whether the pronoun should be singular or plural.

> Neither Elena nor her parents liked living in the city, and ~~she~~ *they* hoped to be able to move someday.

Indefinite Pronouns as Antecedents

When a singular indefinite pronoun is the antecedent, use *he or she (him or her, his or her),* or rewrite the sentence.

> ~~Everyone was~~ *Their classmates were* used to seeing "Skinny Bones" with "The Hick," but they still teased Eugene about his accent.

REVISING TIP

Avoid the indefinite use of *you* and *they.*

> Through foreshadowing, ~~you~~ *the reader* could tell that Elena was going to be disappointed. ~~They~~ *The mothers* weren't being fair to Elena when they tried to separate her from Eugene.

APPLY WHAT YOU'VE LEARNED

Correct the pronouns to clarify antecedents.

¹"American History" describes the impact of assassination; William McKinley was one of their victims. ²He was shot by the anarchist Leon Czolgosz in 1901 at Buffalo, and he later admitted that he had no personal grievance against him. ³On one of the many occasions when McKinley shook hands and spoke briefly with ordinary citizens, it happened. ⁴This was probably his best-loved activity as president. ⁵Neither his wife nor his advisers wanted him to be so vulnerable; she kept after him about security. ⁶Everyone was shocked when they heard about McKinley's assassination. ⁷Neither family members nor other citizens could hide his or her grief as the funeral train carried the president's body to Ohio for burial.

3.4 Pronoun Usage

The form that a pronoun takes is always determined by its function within its own clause.

Who and Whom

Use *who* or *whoever* as the subject of a clause or a sentence.

> The writer of "The Euphio Question" asks, ~~whom~~ *who* would want to be constantly happy?

REVISING TIP

In the example at the left, "who" is the subject of the clause "who would want to be constantly happy."

Use *whom* as the direct or indirect object of a verb or verbal and as the object of a preposition.

People often use *who* for *whom* when speaking informally. However, in written English the pronouns should be used correctly.

> To ~~who~~ **whom** does continual bliss make sense? ~~Whoever~~ **Whomever** I ask, I get the same answer: to no one.

 REVISING TIP

Whom should replace *who* in each sentence of the example at the right:
To whom—object of the preposition *to*
Whomever (I ask)—direct object of the verb *ask*

In trying to determine the correct pronoun form, ignore interrupters that come between the subject and the verb.

In the example that follows, *who* should replace *whom* because the pronoun is the subject of the verb *can question*.

> ~~Whom~~ **Who**, I might ask, can question Kurt Vonnegut's message in this story?

Pronouns in Contractions

Do not confuse these contractions—*it's, they're, who's,* and *you're*—with possessive pronouns that sound the same—*its, their, whose,* and *your*.

> People ~~who's~~ **whose** happiness is synthetic often become oblivious to ~~they're~~ **their** surroundings. Anyone ~~whose~~ **who's** thought about it knows ~~its~~ **it's** dangerous to lose touch with reality.

Pronouns with Nouns

Determine the correct pronoun form in phrases such as *we girls* and *us boys* by imagining what the sentence would look like if the pronoun appeared without the noun.

> Consciousness is amazing. ~~Us~~ **We** human beings are most alive when we are most aware.

916 GRAMMAR HANDBOOK

Pronouns in Comparisons

Be sure you use the correct form of a pronoun in a comparison.

Than or *as* often begins an elliptical clause, one in which some words have been left out. To decide which form of the pronoun to use, fill in the missing words.

> No one is as happy as me. [I (am)] Vonnegut's message affected Joan more than I. [(it affected) me]

Avoiding Shifts in Person

Be sure that a pronoun agrees with its antecedent in person.

One, everyone, and *everybody* are in the third person. They should be referred to by the third-person pronouns.

> One should try to be sure that you are [he or she is] always in touch with reality.

APPLY WHAT YOU'VE LEARNED

Write the following paragraph, correcting errors in pronouns and contractions.

¹"The Euphio Question" mentions that radio waves are emitted in certain parts of space and their received on Earth. ²Whom hasn't wondered how radio waves travel? ³Its a fact that only a small number of radio waves reach Earth's surface. ⁴Whom, I wonder, realizes that short radio waves are absorbed in the atmosphere? ⁵Most long radio waves are reflected away from Earth, so its impossible to receive them. ⁶Astronomers know better than you or me the size and location of the sources of radio waves. ⁷Among these scientists, whomever is asked can also tell what molecular structures are involved. ⁸One marvels at the information you can get from these men and women of science.

4 Using Modifiers Effectively

4.1 Adjective or Adverb?

Use an adjective to modify a noun or a pronoun. Use an adverb to modify a verb, an adjective, or another adverb.

REVISING TIP

Always determine first which word is being modified. In the second sentence of the first example, *attention* is the word being modified; since *attention* is a noun, the modifier must be an adjective.

> In "The Bass, the River, and Sheila Mant" the narrator gradual~ly~ realizes that he chose wrong~ly~. He should have given his completely~∅~ attention to catching the bass.

Use an adjective after a linking verb to describe the subject.

In addition to forms of the verb *be*, the following are linking verbs: *become*, *seem*, *appear*, *look*, *sound*, *feel*, *taste*, *grow*, and *smell*.

> To the narrator, Sheila looked perfectly~∅~ when he was 14, but later his impression of her grows dimly~∅~.

APPLY WHAT YOU'VE LEARNED

Rewrite this paragraph, selecting the correct modifier in each pair.

¹The narrator of "The Bass, the River, and Sheila Mant" feels (enthusiastic, enthusiastically) about bass fishing in the summer. ²Because of the hot weather, bass swim (lazily, lazy) in cool, shady water. ³Since the food is (plentiful, plentifully), they don't (active, actively) go after your bait. ⁴Therefore, you have to select and use your tackle (careful, carefully). ⁵The best lure for summertime bass fishing is a plastic worm because it looks (helplessly, helpless) and (easily, easy) to catch. ⁶If you are fishing in the early morning or late evening, when it is not (usual, usually) hot outside, you can use surface lures. ⁷When it is cool or shady, the bass don't need to swim in the (deeply, deep) water. ⁸If you practice with different lures, your fishing will be (enjoyably, enjoyable).

4.1 Adjective or Adverb?

1. enthusiastic
2. lazily
3. plentiful; actively
4. carefully
5. helpless; easy
6. usually
7. deep
8. enjoyable

4.2 Comparisons and Negatives

Comparative and Superlative Modifiers

Use the comparative form of an adjective or adverb to compare two things or actions. Use the superlative form to compare more than two things or actions.

Form the comparative by adding *-er* to short modifiers or by using the word *more* with longer modifiers. Form the superlative by adding *-est* or by using the word *most*.

> In "Brothers Are the Same" Temas faces a ~~powerfuler~~ *more powerful* enemy than a lion; he learns that the ~~most~~ bravest warrior can admit to a fear of failure. The lion pounces ~~quicklier~~ *more quickly* than Temas expects; but of all the Masai warriors, Temas fights ~~most~~ hardest.

Illogical Comparisons

Avoid comparisons that don't make sense because of missing words or illogical construction.

> Medoto seems more courageous than any *other* Masai warrior, and Medoto reacts to the lion's charge faster than Temas *does*. However, Temas's blow is more deadly than Medoto*'s*.

REVISING TIP

Without the added words, the comparisons in the example are hard to understand. Since Medoto is himself a Masai warrior, he can only be more courageous than any *other* warrior. Medoto does not react to the lion faster than to Temas; Medoto reacted faster than Temas *does*. The comparison in the last sentence is between Temas's blow and *Medoto's* blow, not between Temas's blow and Medoto.

Double Negatives

To avoid double negatives in comparisons, use only one negative word in a clause.

Besides *not* and *no*, the following are negative words: *never, nobody, none, no one, nothing, nowhere, hardly,* and *scarcely*.

> Temas ~~doesn't~~ tremble*s* no more than Medoto had.

GRAMMAR HANDBOOK 919

4.2 Comparisons and Negatives

Answers will vary. See typical answers below.

1 "Brothers Are the Same" is set in the most beautiful territory of the Masai. **2** In the Masai culture a laibon is a spiritual leader who is more important than other tribal leaders. **3** A laibon passes on his position to the son of his most honored wife. **4** In the late 1800s, when the two sons of the laibon Batiany fought over the position, the British colonial government did nothing to stop the rivalry. **5** When Batiany was old and losing his sight, he decided to give his blessing and powers to his elder son, Senteu. **6** The younger son, Lenana, knew of the plan and schemed to get the blessing sooner than his brother. **7** Because of his father's poor sight, Lenana deceived his father, and Senteu never received the blessing. **8** When the rivalry between the two brothers divided the Masai, the colonial government took advantage of the conflict and seized the most fertile Masai land.

APPLY WHAT YOU'VE LEARNED

Rewrite this paragraph, correcting mistakes in modifiers.

1 "Brothers Are the Same" is set in the beautifulest territory of the Masai. **2** In the Masai culture a *laibon* is a spiritual leader who is importanter than any tribal leaders. **3** A *laibon* passes on his position to the son of his honoredest wife. **4** In the late 1800s, when the two sons of the *laibon* Batiany fought over this position, the British colonial government in East Africa didn't do nothing to stop the rivalry. **5** When Batiany was old and losing his sight, he decided to give his blessing and powers to his most eldest son, Senteu. **6** The younger son, Lenana, knew of the plan and schemed to get the blessing more sooner than his brother. **7** Because of his father's poor sight, Lenana deceived his father, and Senteu didn't never receive the blessing. **8** When the rivalry between the two brothers divided the Masai, the colonial government took advantage of the conflict and seized the fertilest Masai land.

> **REVISING TIP**
>
> Misplaced modifiers can change the meaning of a sentence. Without the change shown in the example, the reader could assume that the murder was committed by the women.

4.3 Misplaced or Dangling Modifiers

A misplaced modifier is separated from the word it modifies. It may appear to modify the wrong word and can confuse the reader. A dangling modifier seems unrelated to any word in the sentence. Misplaced and dangling modifiers are usually phrases or clauses.

Misplaced Modifier

Place a modifier near the word it modifies.

In *Trifles* a motive [is discovered] [for a murder] by some women.

Dangling Modifier

Be sure a modifier describes a particular word in the sentence.

Feeling sorry for the murderer, ^*the women hide* evidence about the crime. ~~gets hidden.~~

APPLY WHAT YOU'VE LEARNED

Rewrite this paragraph, correcting misplaced and dangling modifiers.

¹Like urban women in the 19th century, married life made huge domestic demands on the women in rural areas. ²Though they were expected to help their husbands on the farm, few farmers shared household chores with their wives. ³In the 1860s, fed up with this inequality, the right to hold office and to vote in a farm organization called the Grange was won by rural women. ⁴Although worried mostly about domestic and health issues, the right to vote in government elections became another important battle to win. ⁵Dissatisfied with their lack of real power in the Grange, the woman suffrage movement attracted many rural women.

4.4 Special Problems with Modifiers

The following terms are frequently misused in spoken English. Be careful to use them correctly in written English.

Bad and *Badly*

Always use *bad* as an adjective, whether before a noun or after a linking verb. *Badly* should generally be used to modify an action verb.

> In "Not to Go with the Others" a Nazi soldier aimed bad*ly* and failed to kill his prisoner Zaremski.

This, That, These, Those, and *Them*

Whether used as adjectives or pronouns, *this* and *these* refer to people and things that are nearby, and *that* and *those* refer to people and things that are farther away.

Them is a pronoun; it never modifies a noun. *Those* may be a pronoun or an adjective.

> Reading about Holocaust survivors like Zaremski, I realize that them *these* people could not control their fate any more than could these *those* people who died.

REVISING TIP

Avoid the use of *here* with *this* and *these*; also, do not use *there* with *that* and *those*.

I found this ~~here~~ story about Zaremski's escape very difficult to read because of the brutal killings.

4.3 Misplaced or Dangling Modifiers

Answers will vary. See typical answers below.

1 In the 19th century, women in rural areas, like urban women, found that married life made huge domestic demands. **2** Though wives were expected to help their husbands on the farm, few farmers shared household chores with their wives. **3** In the 1860s rural women, fed up with this inequality, won the right to hold office and to vote in a farm organization called the Grange. **4** Although the women were worried mostly about domestic and health issues, the right to vote in government elections became another important battle for them to win. **5** Dissatisfied with their lack of real power in the Grange, many rural women were attracted to the woman suffrage movement.

Few, Fewer, Fewest and Little, Less, Least

Few, fewer, and fewest refer to numbers of things that can be counted. Little, less, and least refer to amounts or quantities.

> Because the Nazis wanted the least [fewest] survivors possible, they tried to kill all their prisoners. Zaremski knew he had few [little] chance of surviving if he tried to escape.

Misplacement of Only

For clarity, only should be positioned before the word or words it modifies.

The misplacement of only can alter, and sometimes confuse, the meaning of a sentence. Notice in the example below the difference in meaning when only is moved.

> Zaremski's [crime was possessing] only an anti-Nazi poem.

APPLY WHAT YOU'VE LEARNED

Rewrite this paragraph, correcting the errors in modifiers.

¹Like Frantizek Zaremski in "Not to Go with the Others," Aung San Suu Kyi of Burma was treated bad and arrested in 1989 by a brutal government. ²Those prisoners of conscience remind me of these in the Bible who suffered for their beliefs. ³The Burmese government had few tolerance for Suu Kyi's campaign to restore democratic and human rights in her country. ⁴When Suu Kyi received the Nobel Peace Prize in 1991, while she was still a captive, her award made the Burmese government look badly. ⁵Her angry captors allowed her family to visit only her. ⁶Them tyrants received less votes than the captive Suu Kyi in the 1993 election, but they refused to give up control. ⁷Though Suu Kyi was released in 1995, her captors still allow the people little rights and few freedom.

4.4 Special Problems with Modifiers

1 Like Frantizek Zaremski in "Not to Go with the Others," Aung San Suu Kyi of Burma was treated badly and arrested in 1989 by a brutal government. **2** These prisoners of conscience remind me of those in the Bible who suffered for their beliefs. **3** The Burmese government had little tolerance for Suu Kyi's campaign to restore democratic and human rights in her country. **4** When Suu Kyi received the Nobel Peace Prize in 1991, while she was still a captive, her award made the Burmese government look bad. **5** Her angry captors allowed only her family to visit her. **6** Those tyrants received fewer votes than the captive Suu Kyi in the 1993 election, but they refused to give up control. **7** Though Suu Kyi was released in 1995, her captors still allow the people few rights and little freedom.

Using Verbs Correctly — 5

5.1 Verb Tenses and Forms

Verb tense shows the time of an action or a condition. Writers sometimes cause confusion when they use different verb tenses in describing actions that occur at the same time.

Consistent Use of Tenses

When two or more actions occur at the same time or in sequence, use the same verb tense to describe the actions.

> The author of *I Know Why the Caged Bird Sings* admired the refined Mrs. Flowers, ~~becomes~~ *became* a friend of the kind woman, and ~~will be~~ *was* inspired by her.

A shift in tense is necessary when two events occur at different times or out of sequence. The tenses of the verbs should clearly indicate that one action precedes the other.

> An event in her past *had* robbed young Marguerite of the ability to speak. That is why saying only "Yes, ma'am" seemed both the least and the most that she could do.

Tense	Verb Form
Present	walk/walks
Past	walked
Future	will walk
Present perfect	have/has walked
Past perfect	had walked
Future perfect	will/shall have walked

REVISING TIP

In telling a story, be careful not to shift tenses so often that the reader finds the sequence of events unclear.

LINK TO LITERATURE

In *I Know Why the Caged Bird Sings* Maya Angelou most often uses the past tense to tell her story. However, notice on page 59 how she switches to the present tense when she writes about the impact that reading and Mrs. Flowers have on her life. In so doing, she creates a sense of immediacy, a "you are there" feeling.

REVISING TIP

The past tense and past participle of regular verbs have the same spelling. Both forms end in -ed. However, you usually double the final consonant before adding -ed when a short-vowel sound precedes the consonant (*slip/slipped, knit/knitted, rot/rotted, pat/patted, stub/stubbed*).

Past Tense and Past Participle

The simple past form of a verb can always stand alone. The past participle of the following irregular verbs should always be used with a helping verb.

Present Tense	Past Tense	Past Participle
am/is/are	was/were	(have, had) been
begin	began	(have, had) begun
break	broke	(have, had) broken
choose	chose	(have, had) chosen
come	came	(have, had) come
do	did	(have, had) done
drink	drank	(have, had) drunk
eat	ate	(have, had) eaten
fall	fell	(have, had) fallen
freeze	froze	(have, had) frozen
give	gave	(have, had) given
go	went	(have, had) gone
know	knew	(have, had) known
speak	spoke	(have, had) spoken
wear	worn	(have, had) worn

Her mother's misuse of verbs ^had^ been an embarrassment to Marguerite. Mrs. Henderson always either chosen the wrong verb form or left out the verb entirely.

APPLY WHAT YOU'VE LEARNED

Write the correct verb tense in the parentheses.

¹When Maya Angelou wrote *I Know Why the Caged Bird Sings* as an autobiography, she (describes, described) only the first 16 years of her life. ²The traumas she (experiences, experienced) then could (make, have made) her fearful; instead, they (will teach, have taught) her to hope and love. ³Marguerite, as Angelou (is, was) called in childhood, had not (spoke, spoken) a word for almost a year when she first (visits, visited) Mrs. Flowers. ⁴With the help of this kind and cultured lady, Marguerite (began, begun) to gain the self-confidence to speak. ⁵Mrs. Flowers (inspires, inspired) her, and since then Angelou (gave, has given) the same inspiration to others. ⁶Although Angelou is best (knew, known) as a writer and poet, she also (enjoys, enjoyed) singing, dancing, and acting.

924 GRAMMAR HANDBOOK

5.1 Verb Tenses and Forms

1. described
2. experienced; have made; have taught
3. was; spoken; visited
4. began
5. inspired; has given
6. known; enjoys

5.2 Commonly Confused Verbs

The following verb pairs are often confused.

Affect and Effect

Affect means "to influence." **Effect** means "to cause."

> Moving to a town full of Anglos greatly ~~effected~~ *affected* the attitudes of a Chicano boy named Junior in "The Day the Cisco Kid Shot John Wayne."

Lie and Lay, Sit and Set

Lie means "to rest in a flat position" or "to be in a certain place"; *lay* means "to put or place." **Sit** means "to be in a seated position"; *set* means "to put or place."

> Junior's friends would all ~~lay~~ *lie* in wait at the movie-theater exit until Junior let them in. Then they ~~set~~ *sat* in the front row.

 REVISING TIP

If you're uncertain about which verb to use, check to see whether the verb has an object. The verbs *lie* and *sit* never have objects—and they both refer to position. The verbs *lay* and *set* both have objects—and they have the same meaning.

Rise and Raise

Rise means "to move upward." **Raise** means "to move something upward."

> One day Junior and his friends knocked down his neighbor Denver, who ~~raised~~ *rose* to escape at the first opportunity.

Learn and Teach

Learn means "to gain knowledge or skill." **Teach** means "to help someone learn."

> Junior's gang wanted to ~~learn~~ *teach* Anglo enemies like Denver to fear them.

Bring and Take

Bring refers to movement toward or with the speaker. **Take** refers to movement away from the speaker.

> Junior's mother insisted that he ~~bring~~ ^take^ Denver with him to the movie theater.

> **REVISING TIP**
> When no movement is implied, *bring* may be used to mean "produce a result."

Here are the principal parts of these troublesome verb pairs.

Present Tense	Past Tense	Past Participle
affect	affected	(have, had) affected
effect	effected	(have, had) effected
lie	lay	(have, had) lain
lay	laid	(have, had) laid
sit	sat	(have, had) sat
set	set	(have, had) set
rise	rose	(have, had) risen
raise	raised	(have, had) raised
learn	learned	(have, had) learned
teach	taught	(have, had) taught
bring	brought	(have, had) brought
take	took	(have, had) taken

APPLY WHAT YOU'VE LEARNED

Choose the correct verb from each pair in parentheses.

[1] "The Day the Cisco Kid Shot John Wayne" (rises, raises) the issue of albinism when Junior claims Denver is an albino Indian. [2] No one had ever (taught, learned) the boys in the gang that true albinos have no pigmentation, or color, in their eyes, skin, and hair. [3] Lacking the protection from ultraviolet rays that the pigments provide, albinos dare not (sit, set) out in the sun. [4] The condition also (affects, effects) vision. [5] The gene that carries the trait of albinism (brings, takes) with it an extraordinary sensitivity to light. [6] Only one in 20,000 people is born with albinism because the gene that (effects, affects) it is recessive, causing albinism to (lie, lay) dormant in most carriers.

5.2 Commonly Confused Verbs

1. raises
2. taught
3. sit
4. affects
5. brings
6. effects; lie

Correcting Capitalization

6.1 Proper Nouns and Adjectives

A common noun is the name of a class of persons, places, things, or ideas. A proper noun is the name of a particular person, place, thing, or idea. A proper adjective is an adjective formed from a proper noun. Capitalize all proper nouns and proper adjectives.

Names and Titles

Capitalize the name of a person and the initials that stand for the name of a person.

> In "The Great Taos Bank Robbery" r. fish telephoned and reported that a bank robbery was about to occur.

Capitalize a title used before a name or an abbreviation for the title. In general, do not capitalize either a title that follows a name or a title that stands alone.

> The citizens remind those who scoff at the flood that governor clyde tingley declared an emergency.

Capitalize a title indicating a family relationship when it is used before or as someone's name (Uncle Al, Granny) **but not when used simply to identify a person** (Jill's uncle).

> The editor of the newspaper thought Mrs. Fish's appearance was much like that of his Grandmother.

REVISING TIP

Prefixes and suffixes such as *ex-* and *-elect* are not capitalized when used with a title. (*President-**elect** Clinton announced his cabinet appointments in December 1992.*)

GRAMMAR HANDBOOK 927

Languages, Nationalities, Religious Terms

Capitalize languages and nationalities, as well as religious names and terms. Do not capitalize the words *god* and *goddess* when they refer to mythological deities.

Capitalize languages and nationalities, such as *Hindi, Sanskrit, Afrikaans, Korean, German,* and *Nigerian*. Capitalize religious names and terms, such as *God, Buddha, the Bible,* and *the Koran*.

> REVISING TIP
>
> Do not capitalize pronouns that refer to a deity. (*Allah in **his** mercy will protect you.*)

Several taoseños had seen and talked to the robbers, but no one reported them to the police.

School Subjects

Capitalize the name of a specific school course (*Biology I, World History*). Do not capitalize a general reference to a school subject (*mathematics, history, music*).

The press's irreverent treatment of the robbery would be a good discussion topic for journalism 101.

Organizations, Institutions

Capitalize the important words in the official names of organizations and institutions (*Congress, Duke University*).

Do not capitalize words that represent kinds of organizations or institutions (*school, church, university*) or words that refer to a specific organization when they are not part of its official name (*at the university*).

> REVISING TIP
>
> Do not capitalize minor words in a proper noun that is made up of several words. (***the** Federal Bureau **of** Investigation*)

When trying to make their escape, the robbers sideswiped the car of the united brethren church minister.

Geographical Names, Events, Time Periods

Capitalize geographical names—as well as the names of events, historical periods and documents, holidays, and months and days—but not the names of seasons.

Names	Examples
Continents	North America, Asia
Bodies of water	Atlantic Ocean, Ohio River, Lake Louise
Political units	China, Kentucky, Moscow
Areas of a country	New England, the Midwest
Public areas	Central Park, Fort McHenry
Roads and structures	Main Street, Aswan Dam, Acme Building
Events	Battle of Shiloh, Super Bowl
Documents	the Constitution, the Treaty of Ghent
Periods of history	Reconstruction, the Renaissance
Holidays	Christmas, Presidents' Day, Fourth of July
Months and days	June, Tuesday
Seasons	winter, spring
Directions	east, west

 REVISING TIP

Do not capitalize a reference that does not use the full name of a place, an event, or a period. (*The fugitives begged for money in Taos Plaza, but no one in the* **plaza** *reported them to the authorities.*)

The great taos bank robbery brought the city of taos, new mexico, to life on a november Morning in 1957. The citizens of taos recall its memory as fondly as they do the great flood of 1935.

APPLY WHAT YOU'VE LEARNED

Rewrite the following paragraph, correcting the errors in capitalization.

¹"The Great Taos Bank Robbery" tells the story of a highly unsuccessful robbery in taos, new mexico. ²Similar botched crimes have happened elsewhere, such as the attempted robbery of the lafayette cooperative bank in swanee, massachusetts, by a man who fainted during the attempt. ³When a man tried to rob a New Haven Bank in connecticut, he did not get away because someone stole his parked car. ⁴In harrieta, michigan, a man held the congregation of a methodist church hostage on a sunday morning. ⁵The Police arrested him after he sold the gun to the Congregation, who took up a collection in the offering plates. ⁶An escaped convict in washington, d.c., was arrested after his girlfriend had him paged over a public address system. ⁷Attempts at crime prevention, however, can be almost as strange; in philadelphia, councilman john f. street introduced a bill to ban carrying snakes in public because he was tired of seeing this occur so often.

6.2 Titles of Created Works

The titles of published material follow certain capitalization rules.

Books, Plays, Magazines, Newspapers, Films

Capitalize the first word, last word, and all other important words in the title of a book, play, periodical, newspaper, or film. Underline or italicize the title to set it off.

Within a title, do not capitalize articles, conjunctions, and prepositions of fewer than five letters.

> In his first volume of poetry, <u>the weary blues</u>, Langston Hughes featured a poem about a Harlem piano player.

Poems, Stories, Articles

Capitalize the first word, last word, and all other important words in the title of a poem, a short story, or an article. Enclose the title in quotation marks.

> In 1920 Hughes wrote his well-known poem "the negro speaks of rivers" after crossing the Mississippi River on a train.

APPLY WHAT YOU'VE LEARNED

Rewrite the paragraph. Correct the punctuation and capitalization of the titles.

¹Langston Hughes wrote poems for his high school magazine, belfry owl. ²An early poem, mulatto, appeared in the saturday review of literature. ³Hughes used dialect with dignity in poems such as mother to son, included in his book the weary blues. ⁴His work was praised by the new york times and other newspapers. ⁵He began work on his first novel, not without laughter, and a play called mule bone. ⁶Esquire published his story called Home, while another story, blues I'm playing, appeared in scribner's. ⁷Meanwhile he wrote the script for a Hollywood film, way down south, and worked on his autobiography, the big sea. ⁸For the Chicago defender, a black newspaper, he wrote tales about Jesse B. Simple. ⁹Some of these stories, such as there ought to be a law, were collected in the book the best of simple.

6.2 Titles of Created Works

1 Langston Hughes wrote poems for his high school magazine, *Belfry Owl*. **2** An early poem, "Mulatto," appeared in *The Saturday Review of Literature*. **3** Hughes used dialect with dignity in poems such as "Mother to Son," included in his book *The Weary Blues*. **4** His work was praised by the *New York Times* and other newspapers. **5** He began work on his first novel, *Not Without Laughter*, and a play called *Mule Bone*. **6** Esquire published his story called "Home," while another story, "Blues I'm Playing," appeared in *Scribner's*. **7** Meanwhile he wrote the script for a Hollywood film, *Way Down South*, and worked on his autobiography, *The Big Sea*. **8** For the *Chicago Defender*, a black newspaper, he wrote tales about Jesse B. Semple. **9** Some of these stories, such as "There Ought to Be a Law," were collected in the book *The Best of Simple*.

Correcting Punctuation   7

7.1 Punctuating Compound Sentences

Punctuation helps organize sentences that have more than one clause.

Commas in Compound Sentences

Use a comma before the conjunction that joins the clauses of a compound sentence.

Do not use a comma before the conjunction that joins a compound subject or a compound predicate.

> In "Unfinished Business" Elisabeth Kübler-Ross describes her work with dying children ˌbut she emphasizes what they can teach us about how to live.

Semicolons in Compound Sentences

Use a semicolon between the clauses of a compound sentence when no conjunction is used. Use a semicolon before a conjunctive adverb that joins the clauses of a compound sentence.

Conjunctive adverbs include *therefore, however, consequently, nevertheless,* and *besides*. You should place a comma after a conjunctive adverb in a compound sentence.

> Adults often do not share their thoughts honestly with a dying person ˌhowever ˌdying children will use pictures to show their thoughts about life and death.

 REVISING TIP

Even when clauses are connected by a coordinating conjunction, you should use a semicolon between them if one or both clauses contain a comma. (*Kübler-Ross, the parents, and the three children met with the dying sister;* **but** *the youngest boy, who was six years old, was able to help all of them accept her illness.*)

GRAMMAR HANDBOOK **931**

7.1 Punctuating Compound Sentences

Answers will vary. See typical answers below.

¹The Make-a-Wish Foundation grants the last wishes of dying children; the organization works with some of the same children Elisabeth Kübler-Ross describes in "Unfinished Business." ²Make-a-Wish began with a single act of kindness by a man named Tommy Austin, and his idea of helping dying children spread all over the country. ³Austin wanted to help a four-year-old boy with leukemia; the boy's dying wish was to become a police officer. ⁴Austin contacted the Arizona Highway Patrol; and the organization made the boy an honorary member, gave him a regulation uniform, and let him ride in a helicopter. ⁵The boy was admitted to the hospital a few days later; but it cheered him up to see his police uniform hanging in his hospital room. ⁶Austin and others who granted the boy's last wish decided to help more children in the same way; that's how Make-a-Wish Foundation started.

APPLY WHAT YOU'VE LEARNED

Rewrite this paragraph, correcting problems with commas or semicolons.

¹The Make-a-Wish Foundation grants the last wishes of dying children, the organization works with some of the same children Elisabeth Kübler-Ross describes in "Unfinished Business." ²Make-a-Wish began with a single act of kindness by a man named Tommy Austin and his idea of helping dying children spread all over the country. ³Austin wanted to help a four-year-old boy with leukemia, the boy's dying wish was to become a police officer. ⁴Austin contacted the Arizona Highway Patrol, and the organization made the boy an honorary member, gave him a regulation uniform, and let him ride in a helicopter. ⁵The boy was admitted to the hospital a few days later; but it cheered him up to see his police uniform hanging in his hospital room. ⁶Austin and others who granted the boy's last wish decided to help more children in the same way, that's how Make-a-Wish Foundation started.

7.2 Setting Off Elements in a Sentence

Most elements that are not essential to a sentence are set off by commas or by other punctuation marks to highlight the main idea of the sentence. A nonessential element merely adds information to an already complete sentence. An essential element is necessary to convey the accurate meaning of the sentence; without it, the meaning is unclear.

Commas

You should often use a comma to separate an introductory word or phrase from the rest of the sentence.

An introductory prepositional phrase usually need not be set off with a comma. You should use a comma, however, for two or more prepositional phrases or for a phrase that includes a verb or a verbal.

> In the play *A Marriage Proposal* by Anton Chekhov˄ a young man named Lomov tries to propose to his neighbor Natalia. However˄ this proves difficult. With each attempt, Lomov starts an argument.

932 GRAMMAR HANDBOOK

In a complex sentence, set off an introductory subordinate clause with a comma.

> When Lomov and Natalia begin their conversation‸they argue about ownership of a tract of land.

Use commas to set off a word or group of words that interrupt the flow of a sentence. When a subordinate clause interrupts the main clause, set off the subordinate clause with commas only if it is not essential.

> Natalia‸when she changes the subject to hunting‸starts another rousing argument. Everything‚that they discuss‚provides them with an excuse to fight.

The words shown in the chart below are commonly used to begin a subordinate clause. When such words appear with introductory or interrupting clauses, they usually signal the need for a comma.

Words Often Used to Introduce Subordinate Clauses				
Subordinating Conjunctions	after although as as if as long as as though as much as	because before even if even though if in order that provided	since so that than though till unless until	whatever when whenever where wherever while
Relative Pronouns	which	who	whom	whose

Parentheses

Use parentheses to set off material that is only incidentally connected to the main idea of a sentence.

> Tschubukov(he is Natalia's father)doesn't help matters when he supports his daughter's arguments.

> **REVISING TIP**
> Try saying the sentence without the interrupter; if the basic meaning doesn't change, you should use punctuation (commas, dashes, or parentheses) to set off the interrupter.

Dashes

Use dashes to set off a word, or a group of words, that abruptly interrupts the flow of a sentence.

> Natalia—amazingly—wants to accept the proposal anyway. Apparently—although Lomov's suit, one might think, seems doomed—all three characters thrive on conflict.

Colons

Use a colon to introduce a list of items or a long quotation. Never use a colon after a preposition or after a verb when the items listed are essential to the clause.

> Unrelated issues continue to threaten Lomov's proposal: land ownership, family reputations, and dogs' pedigrees. The characters are: contentious, fractious, and ridiculous.

> **REVISING TIP**
> A colon often follows a word or phrase such as *these* or *the following items*. (We purchased the following supplies: pencils, paper, folders, and erasers.)

Use a colon between two sentences when the second explains or summarizes the first.

> All ends well: Natalia and Lomov kiss and pledge to marry.

934 GRAMMAR HANDBOOK

For Clarity

Use a comma to prevent misreading or misunderstanding.

> The couple continues their arguments put on hold just long enough for them to get engaged.

REVISING TIP

Sometimes when a comma is missing, parts of a sentence can be grouped in more than one way by a reader. A comma separates the parts so they can be read in only one way.

APPLY WHAT YOU'VE LEARNED

Rewrite these sentences. Add commas, parentheses, dashes, and colons where necessary.

¹In the early 19th century Russia still used serfs who were attached to the land much as America's slaves of the period were. ²By the middle of the century Russian landowners were becoming more enlightened. ³The selling or mortgaging of privately owned serfs which many deplored did not affect those owned by the state or the czar. ⁴Because Alexander II was hoping to win favor with the intellectuals he decreed emancipation for the serfs in 1861. ⁵They were not however truly free although many were granted ownership of farmland. ⁶Peasants were heavily taxed and when they could not bear the burden often had to forfeit their land or become part of forced labor teams. ⁷Writers Anton Chekhov was one criticized the landed aristocracy and merchant class. ⁸They implied that the landowners didn't deserve the land the peasants who worked it had more right to it.

7.3 Elements in a Series

Use commas to separate three or more elements in a series and to separate multiple adjectives preceding a noun.

Subjects, Verbs, Objects, and Other Elements

Use a comma after every item except the last in a series of three or more items.

The three or more items can be nouns, verbs, adjectives, adverbs, phrases, independent clauses, or other parts of a sentence.

> Before Jerry attempts his dive in "Through the Tunnel," he practices studies and goes shopping.

REVISING TIP

Note in the example that a comma followed by a conjunction precedes the last element in the series. That comma is always used.

7.2 Setting Off Elements in a Sentence

Answers will vary. See typical answers below.

1 In the early 19th century Russia still used serfs, who were attached to the land much as America's slaves of the period were. **2** By the middle of the century, Russian landowners were becoming more enlightened. **3** The selling or mortgaging of privately owned serfs—which many deplored—did not affect those owned by the state or the czar. **4** Because Alexander II was hoping to win favor with the intellectuals, he decreed emancipation for the serfs in 1861. **5** They were not, however, truly free, although many were granted ownership of farmland. **6** Peasants were heavily taxed and, when they could not bear the burden, often had to forfeit their land or become part of forced labor teams. **7** Writers (Anton Chekhov was one) criticized the landed aristocracy and merchant class. **8** They implied that the landowners didn't deserve the land: the peasants who worked it had more right to it.

Two or More Adjectives

When more than one adjective precedes a noun, in most cases, use a comma after each adjective except the last one.

If you can't reverse the order of adjectives without changing the meaning or if you can't use the word *and* between them, do not separate them with a comma.

> When Jerry reached the light⁀green surface of the water on the other side, he released a frantic‸desperate breath.

APPLY WHAT YOU'VE LEARNED

Rewrite the paragraph, correcting the comma errors.

¹In "Through the Tunnel" Jerry and the other boys dive from high rocky cliffs into the bay. ²Off one cliff in Mexico, divers plunge 130 feet into the roaring dangerous surf. ³The diving at La Quebrada, meaning "the break in the rocks," is a tourist attraction, with daily performances at 12:45 P.M. 7:30 P.M. 8:30 P.M. 9:30 P.M. and 10:30 P.M. ⁴At the late show, performers dive holding large, burning torches in their hands. ⁵Before they dive, they say a prayer at a small, religious shrine on the cliff. ⁶The tourists always applaud them for their amazing hardiness courage and skill.

7.4 Dates, Addresses, and Letters

Punctuation in addresses, dates, and letters makes information easy to understand.

Dates

Use a comma after the day and the year to set off the date from the rest of the sentence.

> Michael Dorris, author of "Father's Day," was born on January 30‸1945‸shortly before his father died fighting in Europe.

REVISING TIP

In dates that include only the month and the year, do not use a comma after the month. (*Michael Dorris was born in January 1945 during World War II.*)

7.3 Elements in a Series

1 In "Through the Tunnel" Jerry and the other boys dive from high, rocky cliffs into the bay. **2** Off one cliff in Mexico, divers plunge 130 feet into the roaring, dangerous surf. **3** The diving at La Quebrada, meaning "the break in the rocks," is a tourist attraction, with daily performances at 12:45 p.m., 7:30 p.m., 8:30 p.m., 9:30 p.m., and 10:30 p.m. **4** At the late show, performers dive holding large burning torches in their hands. **5** Before they dive, they say a prayer at a small religious shrine on the cliff. **6** The tourists always applaud them for their amazing hardiness, courage, and skill.

Addresses

In an address with more than one part, use a comma after each part to set it off from the rest of the sentence.

> Every year Dorris sends a card to his Aunt Marion in Louisville⋀Kentucky⋀for Father's Day.

REVISING TIP

In an address that includes the ZIP code, do not use a comma between the state abbreviation and the ZIP code.

Parts of a Letter

Use a comma after the greeting and after the closing of a letter.

> Dear Aunt Marion⋀
> Thanks always for everything you've taught me. Happy Father's Day!
>
>   Love⋀
>   Michael

APPLY WHAT YOU'VE LEARNED

Rewrite the following paragraph, correcting the comma errors.

¹The ship *Liberty* left Newport Virginia in 1944 with servicemen destined for Europe, like Michael Dorris's father in "Father's Day." ²Of the many letters the men wrote while on board, 235 were lost, only to be rediscovered in 1986 in the attic of a house in Raleigh North Carolina. ³One of the letters, recently returned to the writer, Raul Alvarez, began as follows:

My dearest sweet
[I] think of you and picture ourselves together again.

⁴Although his sweetheart did not get the letter, Alvarez and she are married and living in Los Angeles California. ⁵Another serviceman, Robert Kirsch of North Huntingdon Pennsylvania, who was a radioman on his way to Foggia Italy, wrote seven of the undelivered letters. ⁶He received his letters in August, 1986, at a ceremony in Washington D.C.

GRAMMAR HANDBOOK 937

7.4 Dates, Addresses, and Letters

1 The ship Liberty left Newport, Virginia, in 1944 with servicemen destined for Europe, like Michael Dorris's father in "Father's Day." **2** Of the many letters the men wrote while on board, 235 were lost, only to be rediscovered in 1986 in the attic of a house in Raleigh, North Carolina. **3** One of the letters, recently returned to the writer, Raul Alvarez, began as follows:

My dearest sweet,

[I] think of you and picture ourselves together again.

4 Although his sweetheart did not get the letter, Alvarez and she are married and living in Los Angeles, California. **5** Another serviceman, Robert Kirsch of North Huntingdon, Pennsylvania, who was a radioman on his way to Foggia, Italy, wrote seven of the undelivered letters. **6** He received his letters in August 1986 at a ceremony in Washington, D.C.

7.5 Quotations

Quotation marks tell readers who said what. Incorrectly placed or missing quotation marks lead to misunderstanding.

Direct Quotation from a Source

Use quotation marks at the beginning and the end of a direct quotation from source material and to set off the title of a short work. Do not use quotation marks to set off an indirect quotation.

> Truman Capote, in ˅A Christmas Memory˅, speaks of the smells of the ingredients for 31 fruitcakes. He says that he remembers ˄"his childhood when it's fruitcake weather."

Introducing a Quotation

Introduce a short direct quotation with a comma. Use a colon for a long quotation. Capitalize the first word in a direct quotation but not in an indirect one.

> The boy Truman says that according to his calculations, we had exactly $13. His cousin replies˄ "I do hope you're wrong, Buddy. We can't mess around with 13."

End Punctuation

Place periods inside quotation marks. Place question marks and exclamation points inside quotation marks if they belong to the quotation; place them outside if they do not belong to the quotation. Place semicolons outside quotation marks.

> "What do you want with Haha˄"˄? Mr. Haha Jones asks. The cousin answers, "A quart of your finest whiskey˄;˄" and Buddy explains, "It's for making fruitcakes˄"˄!

REVISING TIP

If quoted words are from a written source and are not complete sentences, begin the quote with a lowercase letter. (Jefferson said that all people have a right to "life, liberty, and the pursuit of happiness.")

REVISING TIP

Use a colon to introduce a long quotation. (*The Preamble to the Constitution* makes this statement: "We the people of the United States, in order to form a more perfect union . . .)

Use a comma to end a quotation that is a complete sentence followed by explanatory words.

"Queenie [the dog] tries to eat an angel˄" says the author.

Divided Quotations

Capitalize the first word of the second part of a direct quotation if it begins a new sentence.

"Don't cry˄" Buddy says. "you're too old for that."

Do not capitalize the first word of the second part of a divided quotation if it does not begin a new sentence.

"My memories take me back to my childhood," the author tells the reader, "W̶henever it feels like fruitcake weather."

 REVISING TIP

Should the first word of the second part of a divided quotation be capitalized? Imagine the quotation without the explanatory words. If a capital letter would not be used, then do not use one in the divided quotation.

APPLY WHAT YOU'VE LEARNED

Rewrite the paragraph, inserting quotation marks and other appropriate punctuation.

¹During the Great Depression my father said people were lucky just to have jobs. ²When was that? I asked. ³The hard times began in 1929 and continued for about ten years he replied some people called that period the dirty thirties! ⁴Interested, I questioned what was life like? I know that it must have been terrible for your family! ⁵Well, he said, it was difficult, but we children didn't know how hard it really was. We just made do. ⁶I said that I had read in an article The Crash that money was in short supply when investments failed. ⁷That's so Dad admitted but many things we take for granted today we didn't really need. We ate at home; my mother made and remade our clothes, linens, and curtains; appliances such as refrigerators and vacuum cleaners were luxuries. ⁸Finally, Mom said "she remembered most how people helped one another."

GRAMMAR HANDBOOK **939**

7.5 Quotations

1 "During the Great Depression," my father said, "people were lucky just to have jobs." 2 "When was that?" I asked. 3 "The hard times began in 1929 and continued for about ten years," he replied. "Some people called that period the dirty thirties!" 4 Interested, I questioned, "What was life like? I know that it must have been terrible for your family!" 5 "Well," he said, "it was difficult, but we children didn't know how hard it really was. We just made do." 6 I said that I had read in an article, "The Crash," that money was in short supply when investments failed. 7 "That's so," Dad admitted," but many things we take for granted today we didn't really need. We ate at home; my mother made and remade our clothes, linens, and curtains; appliances such as refrigerators and vacuum cleaners were luxuries." 8 Finally, Mom said she remembered most how people helped one another.

Grammar Glossary

This glossary contains various terms you need to understand when you use the Grammar Handbook. Used as a reference source, this glossary will help you explore grammar concepts and the ways they relate to one another.

Abbreviation An abbreviation is a shortened form of a word or word group; it is often made up of initials. (*A.D., P.M., Capt., YMCA*)

Active voice. See **Voice.**

Adjective An adjective modifies, or describes, a noun or pronoun. (*beautiful* day, *poor* me)

A **predicate adjective** follows a linking verb and describes the subject. (The air smelled *sweet*.)

A **proper adjective** is formed from a proper noun. (*Christian* services, *Iberian* peninsula)

The **comparative** form of an adjective compares two things. (*more elegant*, *stronger*)

The **superlative** form of an adjective compares more than two things. (*most important*, *clearest*)

What Adjectives Tell	Examples
How many	*few* friends *many* painters
What kind	*new* techniques *older* people
Which one(s)	*this* basket *those* students

Adjective phrase. See **Phrase.**

Adverb An adverb modifies a verb, an adjective, or another adverb. (Mieko jumped *quickly*.)

The **comparative** form of an adverb compares two actions. (*sooner, more cheerfully*)

The **superlative** form of an adverb compares more than two actions. (*nearest, most gently*)

What Adverbs Tell	Examples
How	walk *carefully* skate *smoothly*
When	*Now* I see. *once* upon a time
Where	She went *out*. *here* in the forest
To what extent	I am *very* pleased. This is *quite* fine.

Adverb, conjunctive. See **Conjunctive adverb.**

Adverb phrase. See **Phrase.**

Agreement Sentence parts that correspond with one another are said to be in agreement.

In **pronoun-antecedent agreement,** a pronoun and the word it refers to are the same in number, gender, and person. (The *girl* lost *her* key. The *girls* lost *their* key.)

In **subject-verb agreement,** the subject and the verb in a sentence are the same in number. (Anita *flies* home. They *fly* often.)

Ambiguous reference An ambiguous reference occurs when a pronoun may refer to more than one word. (Irene told Carmela that *she* had to go home early.)

Antecedent An antecedent is the noun or pronoun to which a pronoun refers. (Because *Dan* practiced *his* backstroke, *he* improved. I lost *my* pen.)

Appositive An appositive is a noun or phrase that explains one or more words in a sentence. (Julie, *my friend,* enjoys algebra.)

An **essential appositive** is needed to make the sense of a sentence complete. (The aviator *Beryl Markham* wrote about her life in Africa.)

A **nonessential appositive** is one that adds information to a sentence but is not necessary to its sense. (Nevil Norway, *a British pilot,* wrote novels.)

Article Articles are the special adjectives *a, an,* and *the.* (*the* car, *a* bug)

A **definite article** (the word *the*) is used with a noun that refers to a particular thing. (*the* boat)

An **indefinite article** is used with a noun that does not refer to a particular example of a kind. (*a* plate, *an* apple)

Auxiliary verb. See **Verb.**

940 GRAMMAR HANDBOOK

Clause A clause is a group of words that contains a verb and its subject. (*I wondered*)

An **adjective clause** is a subordinate clause that modifies a noun or pronoun. (He found a bird *that sings well.*)

An **adverb clause** is a subordinate clause used as an adverb to modify a verb, an adjective, or an adverb. (I put the package *where you could find it.*)

A **noun clause** is a subordinate clause that is used as a noun. (*Where my keys are* is my immediate concern.)

An **elliptical clause** is a clause from which a word or words have been omitted. (You seem happier *than I.*)

A **main (independent) clause** can stand by itself as a sentence. (*the dog barked loudly*)

A **subordinate (dependent) clause** does not express a complete thought and cannot stand by itself. (*when a stranger appeared at the door*)

Clause	Example
Main (independent)	The robot began operating
Subordinate (dependent)	before we were out of bed.

Collective noun. *See* **Noun.**

Comma splice A comma splice is an error caused when two sentences are separated with a comma instead of a correct end mark. (*Why is the street blocked off, is there going to be a parade?*)

Common noun. *See* **Noun.**

Comparative. *See* **Adjective; Adverb.**

Complement A complement is a word or group of words that completes the meaning of a verb. (Friction produces *heat.*) *See also* **Direct object; Indirect object.**

An **objective complement** is a word or a group of words that follows a direct object and renames or describes that object. (Fans consider Steffi Graf a unique *player.*)

A **subject complement** follows a linking verb and renames or describes the subject. (We all felt *confident.*) *See also* **Noun, predicate; Adjective, predicate.**

Complete predicate The complete predicate of a sentence consists of the main verb plus any words that modify or complete the verb's meaning. (The lake *shimmered in the heat.*)

Complete subject The complete subject of a sentence consists of the simple subject plus any words that modify or describe the simple subject. (*The vast mountains in the distance* blocked the sunlight.)

Sentence Part	Example
Complete subject	The old clock on the wall
Complete predicate	marked time with loud ticktocks.

Compound sentence part A sentence element that consists of two or more subjects, predicates, objects, or other parts is compound. (*Jim* and *Janette* moved. Diane *makes* and *sells* jewelry. Jan plays *soccer* and *tennis.*)

Conjunction A conjunction is a word that links other words or groups of words.

A **coordinating conjunction** connects related words, groups of words, or sentences. (*and, but, or*)

A **correlative conjunction** is one of a pair of conjunctions that work together to connect sentence parts. (*either . . . or, neither . . . nor, not only . . . but also, both . . . and*)

A **subordinating conjunction** introduces a subordinate clause. (*after, although, as, as if, as long as, as though, because, before, if, in order that, since, so that, than, though, till, unless, until, whatever, when, where, while*)

Conjunctive adverb A conjunctive adverb joins the clauses of a compound sentence. (*however, therefore, yet*)

Contraction A contraction is formed by joining two words and substituting an apostrophe for letters left out of one of the words. (*hasn't, you'll*)

Coordinating conjunction. *See* **Conjunction.**

Correlative conjunction. *See* **Conjunction.**

Dangling modifier A dangling modifier is one that does not clearly modify any word in the sentence. (*Running down the street,* Ted's red hair drew the shopkeeper's notice.)

Demonstrative pronoun. *See* **Pronoun.**

Dependent clause. *See* **Clause.**

Direct object A direct object receives the action of a verb. Direct objects follow transitive verbs. (Stanley hit the *ball.*)

Direct quotation. *See* **Quotation.**

Divided quotation. *See* **Quotation.**

Double negative A double negative is an incorrect use of two negative words when only one is needed. (I *can't hardly* see you.)

End mark An end mark is one of several punctuation marks that can end a sentence. See the punctuation chart on page 944.

Fragment. See **Sentence fragment.**

Future tense. See **Verb tense.**

Gender The gender of a personal pronoun indicates whether the person or thing referred to is male, female, or neuter. (My dog Penny is lively; *she* zooms across the yard and almost bounces off walls.)

Gerund A gerund is a verbal ending in *-ing* that functions as a noun. (*Hitting* a home run is easy.)

Helping verb. See **Verb, auxiliary verb.**

Illogical comparison An illogical comparison is a comparison that does not make sense because words are missing or illogical. (Mai loves cats *more than any animal*.)

Indefinite pronoun. See **Pronoun.**

Indefinite reference Indefinite reference occurs when a pronoun refers to an idea that is vaguely expressed. (Maria plays the flute, and *it* is more important to her than anything else.)

Independent clause. See **Clause.**

Indirect object An indirect object tells to whom or for whom (sometimes to what or for what) something is done. (She told *Beth* a joke.)

Indirect question An indirect question tells what someone asked without using the person's exact words. (*Stan was wondering when you could talk to him.*)

Indirect quotation. See **Quotation.**

Infinitive An infinitive is a verbal that begins with the word *to*; the two words create a phrase. (*to see*)

Intensive pronoun. See **Pronoun.**

Interjection An interjection is a word or phrase used to express strong feeling. (*Oh! Heavens!*)

Interrogative pronoun. See **Pronoun.**

Intransitive verb. See **Verb.**

Inverted sentence An inverted sentence is one in which the subject comes after the verb. (*Where are my shoes? There stood the captain.*)

Irregular verb. See **Verb.**

Linking verb. See **Verb.**

Main clause. See **Clause.**

Main verb. See **Verb.**

Modifier A modifier makes another word more precise. Modifiers most often are adjectives or adverbs; they may also be phrases, verbals, or clauses that function as adjectives or adverbs. (*sunny* day, scowled *grimly*, tower *of granite*, woman *frowning fiercely*)

An **essential modifier** is one that is necessary to the meaning of a sentence. (Anybody *who has not registered for this class* must leave immediately. Every driver *in the car pool* must park in a special place.)

A **nonessential modifier** is one that merely adds more information to a sentence that is clear without the addition. (The bashful child, *hiding behind his older brother,* finally came into the room.)

Noun A noun names a person, a place, a thing, or an idea. (*Don, home, plant, honor*)

An **abstract noun** names an idea, a quality, or a feeling. (*truth*)

A **collective noun** names a group of things. (*herd*)

A **common noun** is the general name of a person, a place, a thing, or an idea. (*girl, mountain, snow, honesty*)

A **compound noun** contains two or more words. (*folklore, spark plug, one-tenth*)

A **noun of direct address** is the name of a person being directly spoken to. (*Sam,* will you do the dishes? Remember, *Rachel,* what you promised.)

A **possessive noun** shows who or what owns something. (*Carl's* jacket, the *sun's* light)

A **predicate noun** follows a linking verb and renames the subject. (She is a good *friend*.)

A **proper noun** names a particular person, place, or thing. (*Drew Smith, London, Eiffel Tower, Buckingham Palace*)

Number A noun, pronoun, or verb is **singular** in number if it refers to just one person, place, thing, or idea; it is **plural** in number if it refers to more than one.

Object of a preposition The object of a preposition is the noun or pronoun that follows the preposition. (We climbed over the *fence*. I sent the package to *him*.)

Object of a verb The object of a verb receives the action of the verb. (They moved *mountains*.)

Participle A participle is often used as part of a verb phrase. (had *danced*) It can also be used as a verbal that functions as an adjective. (the *shining* star, the letter *stolen* from my purse)

The **present participle** is formed by adding *-ing* to the present tense of a verb. (*Skating* rapidly, we traveled miles up the river.)

The **past participle** of a regular verb is formed by adding *-d* or *-ed* to the present tense. The past participles of irregular verbs do not follow this pattern. (*Astonished,* they opened the gift. The *lost* kitten finally came home. A tree had *fallen* across my driveway.)

Passive voice. *See* **Voice.**

Past tense. *See* **Verb tense.**

Perfect tenses. *See* **Verb tense.**

Person The person of pronouns is a means of classifying them.

A **first-person** pronoun refers to the person speaking. (*I* jumped.)

A **second-person** pronoun refers to the person spoken to. (*You* sat.)

A **third-person** pronoun refers to some other person(s) or thing(s) being spoken of. (*They* sang.)

Personal pronoun. *See* **Pronoun.**

Phrase A phrase is a group of related words that does not contain a verb and its subject. (*gracefully leaping, over the rainbow*)

An **adjective phrase** modifies a noun or a pronoun. (The shutter *on my camera* is broken.)

An **adverb phrase** modifies a verb, an adjective, or an adverb. (Milk spilled *on the floor.*)

An **appositive phrase** explains one or more words in a sentence. (Anne Morrow Lindbergh, *a noted pilot,* was also a skilled writer.)

A **gerund phrase** consists of a gerund and its modifiers and complements. (*Running away* won't solve this problem.)

An **infinitive phrase** consists of an infinitive, its modifiers, and its complements. (We brought food *to eat on the train.*)

A **participial phrase** consists of a participle and its modifiers and complements. (*Completely exhausted,* I struggled on.)

A **prepositional phrase** consists of a preposition, its object, and the object's modifiers. (The catbird imitates the calls *of other birds.*)

A **verb phrase** consists of a main verb and one or more helping verbs. (*should have been working*)

Possessive A noun or pronoun that is possessive shows ownership. (*Dean's* job, *her* sister)

Possessive noun. *See* **Noun.**

Possessive pronoun. *See* **Pronoun.**

Predicate The predicate of a sentence tells what the subject is or does. (The camel *runs across the desert.* The children *appear tired.*) *See also* **Complete predicate; Simple predicate.**

Predicate adjective. *See* **Adjective.**

Predicate nominative A predicate nominative is a noun or pronoun that follows a linking verb and renames or explains the subject. (Alice is my favorite *cousin.* The girl on the phone was *she.*)

Predicate pronoun. *See* **Pronoun.**

Preposition A preposition is a word that relates its object to another part of the sentence or to the sentence as a whole. (Jason ran *around* the corner.)

Prepositional phrase. *See* **Phrase.**

Present tense. *See* **Verb tense.**

Progressive form. *See* **Verb.**

Pronoun A pronoun replaces a noun or another pronoun. (Donna and I agreed that *we* would help.) Some pronouns allow a writer or speaker to avoid repeating a noun. Other pronouns refer to unknown persons, places, or things.

A **demonstrative pronoun** singles out one or more persons or things. (*This* is a leaky boat.)

An **indefinite pronoun** refers to an unidentified person or thing. (*Someone* walked here. Have you seen *anybody?*)

An **intensive pronoun** emphasizes a noun or pronoun. (The doctor *herself* operated on the elderly patient.)

An **interrogative pronoun** asks a question. (*Who* took my wrench?)

A **personal pronoun** replaces a noun or another pronoun. (*They* swam.)

A **possessive pronoun** shows ownership. (*Your* story is in the class magazine. Is the blue notebook *his?*)

A **predicate pronoun** follows a linking verb and renames the subject. (The midnight caller was *he.*)

A **reflexive pronoun** reflects an action back on the subject of the sentence. (Ed treated *himself* to a soda.)

A **relative pronoun** relates a subordinate clause to the word it modifies in the main clause. (Our reasons, *which* had made sense at the time, suddenly seemed ridiculous.)

Pronoun-antecedent agreement. *See* **Agreement.**

Pronoun forms

The ***subject form of a pronoun*** is used when the pronoun is the subject of a sentence or follows a linking verb as a predicate pronoun. (*He* subtracted. The new secretary is *she*.)

The ***object form of a pronoun*** is used when a personal pronoun is the direct or indirect object of a verb or the object of a preposition or a verbal. (I gave *her* a clue. We will carpool with *them*.)

Proper adjective. *See* **Adjective.**

Proper noun. *See* **Noun.**

Punctuation Punctuation clarifies the structure of sentences. See the punctuation chart below.

Quotation A quotation consists of words from another speaker or writer.

A ***direct quotation*** is the exact words of a speaker or writer. (Jean said, "I'll be home at eight.")

A ***divided quotation*** is a quotation separated by words that identify the speaker. ("I think," Jean said, "that I will be home at eight.")

An ***indirect quotation*** repeats what a person said without using the exact words. (I remember Jean said she would be home at eight.)

Reflexive pronoun. *See* **Pronoun.**

Regular verb. *See* **Verb.**

Relative pronoun. *See* **Pronoun.**

Run-on sentence A run-on sentence consists of two or more sentences written incorrectly as one. (Verdell said he would go home Jim said he wouldn't.)

Sentence A sentence expresses a complete thought. The chart on the next page shows the four kinds of sentences.

A ***complex sentence*** contains one main clause and one or more subordinate clauses. (*When you leave, shut the door. If Donna fails to study, she will regret it later on.*)

A ***compound sentence*** is made up of two or more simple sentences combined with a comma and a conjunction or with a semicolon. (*Everyone stopped work, and the noise ceased.*)

A ***simple sentence*** consists of only a main clause. (*The candidate is confident. Anna's ferret escaped from its cage last week.*)

Punctuation	Uses	Examples
Apostrophe (')	Shows possession Forms a contraction	John's bike Sara's mitt We'll leave right away. The train's here.
Colon (:)	Introduces a list or quotation Joins some compound sentences	these games: tennis, golf, and soccer He had this plan: we would swim and then jog.
Comma (,)	Separates ideas Separates modifiers Separates items in series	I went home, and I fed my iguana. The bored, restless children yawned. She brought apples, pears, and grapes.
Exclamation point (!)	Ends an exclamatory sentence	It's the cutest puppy!
Hyphen (-)	Joins words in some compound nouns	sister-in-law, great-grandfather
Period (.)	Ends a declarative sentence Indicates most abbreviations	We saw white-tailed deer and crows. lb. oz. St. Mr. Sept.
Question mark (?)	Ends an interrogative sentence	How are you?
Semicolon (;)	Joins some compound sentences Separates items in series that contain commas	Andrei left a week ago; have you heard from him? Cara served steaming, delicious soup; fresh, crispy bread; and sweet, fluffy pudding.

Kind of Sentence	Example
Declarative (statement)	They went home.
Exclamatory (strong feeling)	We won!
Imperative (request, command)	Let the dog out.
Interrogative (question)	Where is Ronnie?

Sentence fragment A sentence fragment is a group of words that is only part of a sentence. (*As I walked. Cheerfully wandering.*)

Simple predicate A simple predicate is the verb in the predicate. (Joseph always *chooses* the software.)

Simple subject A simple subject is the key noun or pronoun in the subject. (The fast *horse* won.)

Split infinitive A split infinitive occurs when a modifier is placed between the word *to* and the verb in an infinitive. (*to boldly go*)

Subject The subject is the part of a sentence that tells whom or what the sentence is about. (*Gary* drove.) See **Complete subject; Simple subject.**

Subject-verb agreement. See **Agreement.**

Subordinate clause. See **Clause.**

Superlative. See **Adjective; Adverb.**

Transitive verb. See **Verb.**

Unidentified reference An unidentified reference often occurs when the word *it, they, this, which,* or *that* is used. (In New Mexico *they* have beautiful sunsets every evening.)

Verb A verb expresses an action, a condition, or a state of being.

An **action verb** tells what the subject does, has done, or will do. The action may be physical or mental. (Danielle *soared.*)

An **auxiliary verb** is added to a main verb to express tense, add emphasis, or otherwise affect the meaning of the verb. Together the auxiliary and main verbs make up a verb phrase. (*does* intend, *have* gone, *shall* remember)

A **linking verb** expresses a state of being or connects the subject with a word or words that describe the subject. (The ice *feels* cold.) Linking verbs include *appear, be (am, are, is, was, were, been, being), become, feel, grow, look, remain, seem, smell, sound,* and *taste.*

A **main verb** describes action or state of being; it may have one or more auxiliaries. (has *searched*)

The **progressive form** of a verb shows continuing action. (They *are hiking.*)

The past tense and past participle of a **regular verb** are formed by adding -d or -ed. (*sail, sailed*) An **irregular verb** does not follow this pattern. (*grow, grown; drink, drank; bring, brought; lose, lost*)

The action of a **transitive verb** is directed toward someone or something, called the object of the verb. (Nerve cells *transmit* impulses.) An **intransitive verb** has no object. (The child *sang.*)

Verbal A verbal is formed from a verb and acts as another part of speech, such as a noun, an adjective, or an adverb.

Verb phrase. See **Phrase.**

Verb tense Verb tense shows the time of an action or the time of a state of being.

The **present tense** places an action or condition in the present. (We *walk* down the street.)

The **past tense** places an action or condition in the past. (They *left.*)

The **future tense** places an action or condition in the future. (They *will go.*)

The **present perfect tense** describes an action in an indefinite past time or an action that began in the past and continues in the present. (*has looked, have seen*)

The **past perfect tense** describes one action that happened before another action in the past. (*had wondered, had promised*)

The **future perfect tense** describes an event that will be finished before another future action begins. (*will have fallen, shall have finished*)

Verbal	Example
Gerund (used as a noun)	*Canoeing* across the lake is risky.
Infinitive (used as an adjective, an adverb, or a noun)	It's grand *to see* the midnight sun.
Participle (acts as an adjective)	The roads, *covered* with ice, were dangerous.

Voice The voice of a verb depends on whether the subject performs or receives the action of the verb.

In the **active voice** the subject of the sentence performs the action. (The principal *made* an appeal. We *heard* the news.)

In the **passive voice** the subject of the sentence receives the action of the verb. (The ball *was thrown* out of bounds. The story *had been written* by a famous author.)

Index of Fine Art

xi, 137	*Isabella and Lois* (1968), Warren Brandt.
xiii, 312-313	*Pep's Car with an Assist from Clyde, Snake and Peabody* (1975), Colleen Browning.
xv, 418	*Richard at Age Five* (1944), Alice Neel.
xix, 658	*Suzanne Poirson* (1884), John Singer Sargent.
xxi, 796-797	*Casanova* (1987), Julio Larraz.
12-13	*Geography* (1984), Janet Fish.
18	Drawing of a Face from the *Rilke Portfolio* (1968), Ben Shahn.
22	*Bolton Junction, Eccleshill* (1956), David Hockney.
31	*In the Province* (1920), Charles Demuth.
35	*Little Girl Reading* (1973), Simon Samsonian.
44	*Early Evening* (1978), Ken Danby.
54	*Portrait of Dorothy Porter, Librarian* (1952), James Porter.
57	*Back Street*, (1983), LaVere Hutchings.
64	*Cookstove* (1986), Hubert Shuptrine.
73	*Anna Kuerner* (1971), Andrew Wyeth.
94-95	*Balston Beach, Cape Cod* (1989), Charles Sovek.
98-99	*Ice Blue* (1981), Susan Shatter.
102	*Reflections* (1970), Ken Danby.
109	*Two Figures, Still Pond* (1990), W. Joe Innis.
112	*Maudell Sleet's Magic Garden* (1978), Romare Bearden.
132	*Katie on Sofa* (1959), Fairfield Porter.
139	*Boy and Car* (1955), David Park.
155	*Shadows of the Past* (1989), Al Stine.
156	*Ringside* (1994), William Matthews.
159	*Fresh Eggs* (1874), Winslow Homer.
174-175	*East Twelfth Street* (1946), Ben Shahn.
211	*In E Sharp* (1981), Romare Bearden.
212	*Lullaby* (1942), Fletcher Martin.
221	*Upward* (1925), Wassily Kandinsky.
225	*Auf Grau* [On gray] (1923), Wassily Kandinsky.
265	*My Night Visage* (1913), Ludwig Meidner.
269	*Daniel Webster (Black Dan)* (1835), Francis Alexander.
275	*Trial Scene* (1860–1863), David Gilmour Blythe.
283	*Leg* (1984), Elizabeth Murray.
305	Red-figured hydria
308	*Portrait of a Girl* (about 1987), Ian Sidaway.
322	*Red and White on Post* (1950), Alexander Calder.
324	*Um den Fisch* [Around the fish] (1926), Paul Klee.
336-337	*Family* (1992), Varnette P. Honeywood.
343	*The Mighty Hand* (1885), Auguste Rodin.
346	*Art and Artie* (1989), Connie Hayes.

354	*Solitary Confinement: Insects Witness My Agony* (1982), Theodore Gostas.
360	*The Way They Live* (1879), Thomas Pollock Anshutz.
371	*Brave Chief, a Skidi (Wolf) Pawnee* (1832), George Catlin.
372	*Young Omaha, War Eagle, Little Missouri, and Pawnees* (1821), Charles Bird King.
377	*Keokuk on Horseback* (1834), George Catlin.
389	*Portrait of the Poet N. A. Nekrasov* (1877), Ivan Nikolaevich Kramskoi.
390	*June* (1822), George Inness.
392	*Der Zornige (Selbstbildnis)* [The angry one (self-portrait)] (1881), Ferdinand Hodler.
393	*Self-Portrait at the Dressing Table* (1909), Zinaida Serebryakova.
396	*Drei Windhunde* [Three greyhounds], Frans Snyders.
398	*Man and Woman, Provincetown* (1934), Charles Demuth.
422-423	*Down Home* (1992), Tony Couch.
431	*Brown Boy* (1935), Lois Mailou Jones.
433	*Portrait of My Father* (about 1921), Archibald J. Motley, Jr.
438	*Student with Guitar* (1975), Simon Samsonian.
445	*Portrait of Langston Hughes* (about 1925), Winold Reiss.
455	*A Maulvi Meditating* (about 1630), Mughal School.
456	*Dipak Raga* (1605), Nisaradi.
459	*Sundari* (1980), K.G. Subramanyan.
478-9	*Battle with Cicones*, Romare Bearden.
483, *top*	*Odysseus receiving wine*
483, *bottom*	*Athena* (4th century B.C.), Cephisodotos.
490	Greek merchant ships from a vase painting (540 B.C.)
495	Poseidon with his trident (about 100 B.C.).
497	Polyphemus (6th century B.C.)
498	Detail of *The Blinding of Polyphemus* (about 600 B.C.),
501	Oedipus, (3rd century)
502	Detail of *Ulysses Espcaping from Polyphemus* (510 B.C.)
512	Vase Painting from Euboea, (about 400 B.C.),
515	Ulyssses threatening Circe (about 500 B.C.)
516	Circe pursued by Ulysses, unknown artist.
523	Siren, Greek sculpture from the Dipylon tomb (300 B.C.),
525	Odysseus' barge passing the Sirens' island south of Capri
526-527	Scylla (about 4th Century B.C.)
532, 533	*The Sirens* (1990) Shlomo Katz.
534	Ulysses' Barge (1st to 3rd century)
541	*American Gothic* (1930), Grant Wood.
548	Penelope mourning (abour A.D. 10)
549	Return of Odysseus (about 400 B.C.)
553	Penelope's suitors slain by Ulysses and Telemachos (380 B.C.)

555	Ulysses with his arch competing with the suitors (about 400 B.C.)
558	Agamemnon's Ghost, marble relief from a sarcophagus
559, right	Orestes killing Clytemnestra
559, left	Penelope's suitors slain by Ulysses and Telemachos (380 B.C.)
561	Nestor and Telemachos (about 300 B.C.)
565	Ulysses and Penelope (460-450 B.C.)
571	*Penelope* (1990), Shlomo Katz.
582-583	*Voice I* (1963), George Tooker.
586	*84 Madison* (1982), Philip Reisman.
594	*Autobiographical* (1954), Moses Soyer.
602	*Apprehension of Stage Robbers* (1992), Harvey W. Johnson.
610-611	*Untitled (Green Volkswagen)* (1971), Don Eddy.
634	*The Pantry*, Art Gore.
631	*Room After Room* (1967), Andrew Wyeth.
639	*The Gilded Cage*, Art Gore.
644	*The Alchemist's Dilemma* (1992), Chuck Wood.
646	*Portrait of Max Hermann-Neisse* (1913), Ludwig Meidner.
661	*Too Early* (1873), Jame Jacques Joseph Tissot.
664	*Girl Sweeping* (1912), William McGregor Paxton.
670	*Taos Today* (1934), Ward Lockwood.
681	*Quenton and Andre*, Stephen Scott Young.
683	*Subway Passengers* (1966), Richard Estes.
695	*Short Back & Sides* (1977), Mike Dempsey.
699	*By the Gate* (1953), Ernest Crichlov.
710-711	*Paricutín* (1949), Alfredo Zalce.
724	*Sissy [Virginia Clem]* (date unknown), Edgar Allan Poe.
726-727	*Study of a Head for "The Mill"*, Sir Edward Coley Burne Jones.
728	*Death with an Hourglass* (about 1500), Unknown Artist.
730	*The Garden*, Reg Cartwright.
790-791	*Untitled [Nyack]* (1973), Julio Larraz.
793	*Waiting for Henry Morgan* (1984), Julio Larraz.
804	*The Voice of the Casuarina* (1985), Julio Larraz.
813	*Angstausbruch III, [Outburst of fear]* (1939), Paul Klee.

Index of Skills

Literary Terms

Act, 850
Action
    falling, 16, 48, 620, 754
    rising, 16, 37, 620
Alliteration, 120, 362, 850
Allusion, 60, 850
Antagonist, 850
Aside, 850
Assonance, 120, 850
Audience, 837
Author's purpose, 152, 815, 850
Autobiography, 50, 850
Ballad, 622, 851
Biography, 50, 304, 851
Characterization, 83, 280, 304, 335, 568, 697, 851
Characters, 15, 82–83, 84, 85, 88, 103, 282, 472, 836, 851
    in drama, 253
    epic hero, 507, 581
    as first-person narrator, 127
    main, 143, 667, 851
    making inferences about, 365
    minor, 143, 667, 851
Character study, 86
Chronological order, 839
Climax, 16, 37, 48, 580, 620, 708, 851
Conflict, 172, 193, 196, 206, 378, 836, 851
    external, 25, 172, 378, 519, 851
    internal, 25, 48, 172, 378, 519, 851
Confidant, 254
Connotation, 696
Consonance, 120
Description, 118, 460, 477, 519, 838, 851
    physical, 357
Detective story, 606
Dialogue, 83, 435, 477, 766, 769, 838, 852, 867, 877
    in drama, 253–254
    in poetry, 622
Diction, 450, 785
Drama, 253–254, 852
Dramatic reading, 315
Elaboration, 244, 245
Epic, 482–484, 852
Epic hero, 507, 581, 852
Epic simile, 507, 852
Epilogue, 230, 852
Epithets, 506, 518, 852
Essay, 50–51, 852
Exaggeration, 385
Exposition, 16, 39, 413, 620, 853

Extended metaphor, 213, 214, 853
External conflict, 25, 172, 378, 519
Fables, 125
Falling action, 16, 48, 620, 754, 853
Fantasy, 853
Farce, 385
Feet, 731
Fiction, 15–16, 853
Figurative language, 121, 209, 838, 853, 873–874
    hyperbole, 207
    metaphor, 121, 209, 427, 435, 838, 874
        extended, 213, 214
    personification, 121, 209, 321, 724, 731
    simile, 121, 209, 383, 427, 838, 874
        epic, 507
First-person narrative, 127
First-person point of view, 194, 334, 648, 649, 853
Flashback, 118, 231, 356, 839, 854, 877
Foreshadowing, 399, 427, 767, 854
Form, 854
Formal language, 534
Free verse, 125, 854
Generalization, 251
Goals, 837
Historical fiction, 854
Homeric simile, 507
Horror fiction, 854
Hyperbole, 207, 854
Idioms, 280, 535, 854
Imagery, 121, 206, 322, 380, 427, 735, 828, 854
Informal language, 535
Informative article, 854
Internal conflict, 25, 48, 172, 378, 519, 854
Interpretation
    oral, 61
Irony, 581, 603, 641, 666, 709, 854
    dramatic, 855
    situational, 855
    verbal, 785
Language
    formal, 534
    informal, 535
Metaphors, 209, 427, 435, 838, 855
    extended, 213, 214, 603
Meter, 121, 731, 855
Monologues, 61
Mood, 118, 399, 766, 767, 785, 837, 855
Narrative poetry, 725
Narrators, 177, 193, 194, 452, 855. *See also* Point of view.
    first-person, 127
Nonfiction, 50–51, 855
Novel, 15, 856

Onomatopoeia, 120, 856
Oral interpretation, 61
Oral presentation, 77
Oral reading, 519
Oral tale, 104
Paradox, 722, 856
Parody, 536, 538, 541
Personal narrative, 856
Personification, 209, 321, 724, 731, 856
Physical description, 357
Play. *See* Drama.
Plot, 15, 472, 620, 768, 836, 856
    character in, 143
    conflict in, 25
    in drama, 253
    exposition in, 39
    falling action in, 48, 754
    flashback in, 231, 356, 839
    foreshadowing in, 399, 427, 767
    rising action in, 37
Poetry, 120–121, 856
    meter in, 121, 731
    narrative, 725
    rhyme in, 120, 125, 383, 724
    rhythm in, 120–121, 384, 724
Point of view, 194, 334, 648, 649, 837, 856. *See also* Narrator
    first-person, 194, 334, 648, 856
    third-person, 315, 334, 648, 649, 856
Protagonist, 856
Pun, 213, 857
Realistic fiction, 857
Repetition, 362, 626, 857, 911
Resolution, 48, 857
Rhyme, 120, 125, 383, 724, 857
    end, 120, 857
    external, 120
    internal, 120, 857
Rhyme scheme, 120, 125, 626, 857
Rhythm, 118, 384, 620, 724, 857
Rising action, 16, 37, 620, 857
Satire, 215, 231, 857
Scene, 857
Science fiction, 215, 858
Setting, 15, 104, 118, 173, 472, 696, 773, 836, 858
Short story, 15, 858
Similes, 209, 383, 427, 838, 858
    epic, 507
Slang, 535
Soliloquy, 427, 858
Speaker, in poetry, 121, 858
Stage directions, 858
Stanza, 858
Stereotypes, 89
Suspense, 104, 356, 620, 754, 807, 838, 858
Symbols, 76, 104, 118, 427, 476, 641, 667, 859
Theme, 16, 231, 441, 476, 531, 580, 722, 859
Third-person point of view, 315, 334, 648, 649, 859
    limited, 315, 648

Tone, 51, 291, 321, 378, 535, 736, 815, 859
    exposition in setting, 39
True-life adventure, 859
Venn diagram, 303
Verbal irony, 785
Voice, 443
Word choice, 766
Writer's purpose, 291

Reading and Critical Thinking Skills

Active reading, strategies for, 17
Analysis, 25, 37, 48, 60, 76, 103, 117, 123, 125, 143, 152, 167, 193, 206, 209, 210, 213, 230, 279, 291, 303, 314, 321, 331, 335, 356, 360, 362, 378, 381, 383, 399, 411, 426, 435, 441, 446, 460, 506, 518, 530, 541, 567, 625, 666, 708, 721, 730, 735, 754, 773, 784, 807, 815, 828
Applying what you've learned, 167, 209, 249, 251, 471, 473, 575, 577, 603, 625, 769, 771, 773, 837, 839
Assessing, 333, 475, 579, 707, 841
Brainstorming, 213, 252, 480, 622, 669, 735, 834, 860
Cause and effect relationships, 339
Chart. *See* Graphic organizer.
Clarifying, 5, 8, 9, 10, 11, 16, 70, 116, 218, 222, 369, 371, 374, 422, 610, 660
Classifying, 193, 575
Cluster diagrams, 27, 177, 364, 861
Comparing and contrasting, 125, 193, 206, 291, 303, 321, 362, 383, 426, 428, 506, 518, 621, 642, 666, 667, 697, 730
Connecting, 5, 9, 11, 73, 74, 108, 228, 288, 369, 452, 660
    art, 26, 118, 214, 231, 315, 357, 427, 450, 642, 722, 816
    art therapy, 713
    biographical, 17, 62, 359, 380
    cultural, 127, 177, 208, 437, 543, 732, 775, 787
    geographical, 39, 91, 413, 452, 669, 817
    historical, 27, 106, 255, 293, 339, 364, 429, 481, 622, 809
    literary, 305, 385, 724, 737
    medical, 145, 282
    personal, 17, 27, 39, 62, 91, 106, 122, 127, 145, 177, 196, 208, 215, 255, 282, 293, 305, 316, 339, 359, 364, 380, 385, 413, 429, 437, 443, 450, 481, 543, 713, 724, 732, 737, 775, 787, 809, 817
    professional, 443
    psychological, 122
    reading, 17, 39, 62, 91, 106, 127, 145, 196, 209, 215, 255, 282, 293, 339, 365, 380, 413, 437, 444, 482–485, 543, 606, 713, 725, 737, 787, 809
    science, 196, 215
    sociological, 316
    writing, 27, 122, 177, 305, 316, 359, 385, 429, 452, 732, 817

Cooperative learning. *See* the Speaking, Listening, and Viewing Index.
Cutaway diagrams, 104
Debating, 303
Describing, 25, 69, 76, 77, 103, 152, 206, 213, 230, 291, 303, 314, 321, 362, 383, 426, 435, 441, 443, 460, 625, 721, 730, 735, 754, 784, 807, 828
Diagrams, 193
    cluster, 27, 177, 255, 364, 861
    cutaway, 104
    tree, 359, 861
    Venn, 303, 807
    See also Graphic organizers.
Discussing, 103, 123, 172, 334, 654, 730
Drama, strategies for reading, 253–254
Drawing conclusions, 91
Evaluating, 5, 8, 9, 10, 11, 16, 72, 171, 193, 220, 223, 286, 290, 326, 331, 372, 420, 471, 473, 575, 577, 581, 603, 614, 620, 665, 696, 705, 707, 733, 784, 839, 841
Explaining, 76, 103, 152, 230, 303, 314, 356, 362, 399, 426, 435, 446, 460, 506, 518, 530, 567, 580, 620, 730, 754, 784, 807, 815
Fact and opinion, 51
Feedback, 863
Fiction, strategies for reading, 16
Freewriting, 85, 444, 700, 701, 835, 861
Generalizing, 437, 441
Goal setting, 173, 335, 477, 581
Graphic organizers, 17, 39, 77, 91, 103, 104, 118, 122, 127, 145, 172, 177, 193, 196, 215, 280, 316, 321, 335, 338, 365, 380, 383, 437, 452, 477, 481, 536, 543, 605, 622, 708, 713, 732, 736, 775, 787, 807, 815, 837, 861
Inferring, 365, 603, 627, 696, 787, 807, 809
Interpreting, 620, 654
Judging, 17, 172, 381, 426, 641, 666, 696
KWL strategy, 165, 166
Labeling, 213, 334
Listing, 123, 383, 480, 861
Making inferences. *See* Inferring.
Making judgments. *See* Judging.
Nonfiction, strategies for reading, 51
Pantomiming, 625
Personal response, 17, 25, 37, 48, 60, 76, 103, 117, 123, 125, 143, 152, 193, 206, 209, 210, 213, 230, 279, 291, 303, 314, 321, 356, 360, 362, 378, 381, 383, 399, 426, 435, 441, 446, 460, 506, 518, 530, 567, 624, 721, 730, 735, 754, 784, 807, 815, 828
Poetry, strategies for reading, 121
Predicting, 5, 16, 17, 25, 111, 115, 419, 567, 603, 613, 616, 617, 666
Previewing, 16, 51
Questioning, 7, 8, 9, 10, 11, 16, 67, 109, 143, 226, 376, 424, 608, 655, 662, 700
Reacting, 25, 117, 125, 143
Reading log, 5, 62, 106, 215, 246, 282, 365, 413, 444, 809
Recalling prior experiences, 17
Reflecting, 14, 16, 25, 37, 48, 60, 76, 90, 103, 117, 123, 125, 143, 152, 167, 172, 176, 193, 206, 210, 213, 230, 252, 279, 291, 303, 314, 321, 333, 334, 356, 360, 362, 378, 381, 383, 399, 412, 426, 435, 441, 446, 460, 475, 476, 480, 506, 518, 530, 542, 567, 579, 580, 584, 624, 641, 656, 705, 707, 712, 721, 730, 735, 754, 774, 784, 807, 815, 828, 841
Relating, 25, 37, 76, 103, 125, 143, 152, 193, 206, 213, 230, 279, 291, 303, 314, 321, 356, 362, 378, 383, 399, 426, 435, 441, 460, 506, 518, 530, 567, 624, 721, 730, 733, 735, 754, 784, 807, 815, 828
Rethinking, 25, 37, 48, 60, 76, 103, 117, 123, 125, 143, 152, 193, 206, 210, 213, 230, 279, 291, 303, 314, 321, 331, 356, 360, 378, 381, 383, 399, 426, 435, 441, 446, 460, 473, 506, 518, 530, 567, 577, 624, 705, 721, 730, 735, 754, 784, 807, 815, 828, 839
Reviewing, 303, 837
Rising action parallelogram, 37
Self-assessment, 172, 173, 334, 335, 476, 477, 580, 581, 708, 709
Setting a purpose, 51, 709
Sharing, 193, 213, 230, 279, 321, 378, 399, 426, 441, 446, 460, 530, 624, 721, 730, 735, 754, 784, 807
Strategies for reading, 5–6
Summarizing, 51
Synthesizing, 193
Tree diagrams, 359, 861
Understanding specialized vocabulary, 145, 293
Venn diagram, 303, 807
Visualizing, 196, 206, 213, 230, 255, 314, 321, 356, 360, 381, 383, 399, 435, 446, 471, 506, 518, 530, 567, 669, 721, 730, 754, 815
Word web, 316, 321, 605

Grammar, Usage, and Mechanics

Abbreviations, 940
Active voice, 333, 653, 942, 945
Addresses, commas in, 937
Adjective clause, 941
Adjective phrase, 943
Adjectives, 940. *See also* Modifiers
    versus adverbs, 771, 918
    commas with, 936
    comparative form of, 919, 940
    effective placement of, 249
    predicate, 940
    proper, 927–929, 940
    superlative form of, 919, 940
    using specific, 25, 26, 771
Adverb clause, 941
Adverb phrase, 943
Adverbs, 918, 940. *See also* Modifiers
    versus adjectives, 771, 918
    comparative form of, 919, 940
    conjunctive, 870, 902, 931, 941

precise, 771
superlative form of, 919, 940
Affect and *effect*, 925
Agreement
    pronoun-antecedent, 913–915, 917, 940
    subject-verb, 409, 903–909, 940
Ambiguous references, 914, 940
Antecedents, 913, 940. *See also* Pronoun-antecedent agreement
    compound using *or* or *nor,* 914–915
    correcting missing, 649
    correcting unclear, 649, 914
    indefinite pronouns as, 915
Antonyms, 26, 428
Apostrophe, 944
    in forming possessive nouns, 910–911
Appositive, 940
    essential, 940
    nonessential, 940
Appositive phrase, 83, 943
Articles (*a, an, the*), 940
Articles, capitalizing titles of, 930
Auxiliary verb, 945
Bad and *badly,* 921
Book titles, capitalization of, 930
Bring and *take,* 926
But, as coordinating conjunction, 870
Capitalization
    of events, 929
    of first words, 901, 938
    of geographical names, 929
    of institutions, 928
    of languages, 928
    of nationalities, 928
    of organizations, 928
    of personal titles, 927
    of proper nouns and adjectives, 927–929
    of religious terms, 928
    of school subjects, 928
    of time periods, 929
    of titles of created works, 930
Clarity, use of commas for, 935
Clauses, 941
    adjective, 941
    adverb, 941
    effective placement of, 249
    elliptical, 941
    main (independent), 941
    noun, 941
    subordinate, 900, 933, 941
Collective nouns, 908, 942
Colons, 944
    to introduce lists of items, 914
    to introduce quotations, 914, 938
    to separate sentences, 914
Commas, 944
    in addresses, 937
    in combining sentences, 870
    in compound sentences, 931
    with conjunctive adverbs, 931
    with coordinating conjunctions, 870
    in dates, 936
    in dialogue, 841
    for items in a series, 935–936
    in joining sentences, 902
    in letters, 937
    in quotations, 938, 939
    in a series, 171
    to set off elements in sentences, 932–933
    use of, for clarity, 935
Comma splice, 901, 941
Common noun, 942
Comparative form of adjective, 919, 940
Comparative form of adverb, 919, 940
Comparisons
    avoiding double negatives in, 919
    cooperative, 919, 940
    illogical, 579, 919, 942
    pronouns in, 917
    superlative, 919, 940
Complement, 941
    objective, 941
    subject, 941
Complete predicate, 941
Complete subject, 941
Complex sentence, 933, 944
Compound antecedents using *or* or *nor,* 914–915
Compound-complex sentence, 539
Compound noun, 942
Compound sentences, 902, 941, 944
    punctuating, 931
Compound subjects, 409, 903–904
Conjunctions, 539, 941
    coordinate, 539, 870, 902, 931, 941
    correlative, 941
    subordinate, 539, 941
Conjunctive adverbs, 870, 902, 941
    comma with, 931
Contractions, 907, 941
    pronouns in, 916
Coordinate conjunctions, 539, 870, 931, 941
    in joining sentences, 902
Correlative conjunction, 941
Dangling modifiers, 920, 941
Dashes, 934
Dates, commas in, 936
Declarative sentence, 945
Definite articles, 940
Demonstrative pronoun, 943
Dialogue, commas in, 841
Direct address, noun of, 942
Direct object, 941
Direct quotation, 944
Double negatives, 919, 941

Effect and *affect,* 925
Elliptical clause, 941
End mark, 942
End punctuation. *See also* specific
    quotation marks with, 938–939
Essential appositive, 940
Essential modifier, 942
Events, capitalization of, 929
Exclamation points, 944
    quotation marks with, 938
Exclamatory sentence, 945
Few, fewer, fewest, 923
Film titles, capitalization of, 930
First person, 943
Future perfect tense, 945
Future tense, 945
Gender, 942
Geographical names, capitalization of, 929
Gerund, 942
Gerund phase, 943
However, as conjunctive adverb, 870
Hyphen, 944
Illogical comparisons, 579, 942
Imperative sentence, 945
Indefinite articles, 940
Indefinite pronouns, 943
    agreement with verb, 905–906
    use of, as antecedents, 915
Indefinite reference, 942
Indirect object, 942
Indirect question, 942
Indirect quotation, 944
Infinitive, 942
    split, 945
Infinitive phase, 943
Initials, capitalization of, 927
Institutions, capitalization of, 928
Intensive pronoun, 943
Interjection, 942
Interrogative pronoun, 943
Interrogative sentence, 945
Interrupting words and phrases, 906–907
Intransitive verb, 945
Inverted sentences, 907, 942
I statements, 863
Italics, for titles of created works, 909, 930
Languages, capitalization of, 928
Lay and *lie,* 925
Learn and *teach,* 925
Least, 923
Less, 923
Letters, commas in, 937
Lie and *lay,* 925
Linking verbs, 945
    using adjectives after, 918
Little, 923
Magazine titles, capitalization of, 930

Main clause, 941
Main verb, 945
Measure, nouns of, 908
Misplaced modifiers, 920, 923
Modifiers, 942. *See also* Adjectives; Adverbs
    bad and *badly,* 921
    dangling, 920, 941
    essential, 942
    few, fewer, and *fewest,* 923
    little, less, and *least,* 923
    misplaced, 920, 923
    nonessential, 942
    this, that, these, those, and *them,* 921
Names, capitalization of personal, 927
Nationalities, capitalization of, 928
Negative, double, 919, 941
Newspaper titles, capitalization of, 930
Nominatives, predicate, 909, 943
Nonessential appositive, 940
Nonessential modifier, 942
Nor, compound antecedents using, 914–915
Noun clause, 941
Nouns, 910, 942
    abstract, 942
    collective, 908, 942
    common, 942
    compound, 942
    of direct address, 942
    plural, 910
    possessive, 910–911, 942
    predicate, 942
    pronouns with, 917
    proper, 927–929, 942
    singular, 908
    specific, 245, 874
    of time, weight, measure, number, 908
Number, 942
    nouns of, 908
Object
    direct, 941
    indirect, 942
    of a preposition, 942
    of pronoun, 944
    of a verb, 942
Objective complement, 941
Object pronouns, 912
Only, misplacement of, 923
Or, compound antecedents using, 914–915
Organizations, capitalization of, 928
Parentheses, 934
Participial phase, 943
Participles, 943
    past, 87, 653, 924, 943
    present, 87, 943
Passive voice, 333, 653, 945
Past participles, 87, 653, 924, 943
Past perfect tense, 945

Past tense, 924, 945
Periods, 944
    as end punctuation, 901
    quotation marks with, 938
Person
    first, 943
    second, 943
    third, 943
Personal pronouns, 943
    agreement with verb, 904–905
Personal titles, capitalization of, 927
Phrases
    adjective, 943
    adverb, 943
    appositive, 83, 943
    effective placement of, 249
    gerund, 943
    infinitive, 943
    interrupting, 906–907
    participial, 943
    prepositional, 932, 943
    verb, 943
Play titles, capitalization of, 930
Plural nouns, 910
Poems, capitalization of titles, 930
Possessive nouns, 910–911, 942, 943
Possessive pronouns, 912, 943
Predicate, 943
    complete, 941
    simple, 945
Predicate adjective, 940
Predicate nominatives, 909, 943
Predicate noun, 942
Predicate pronoun, 943
Preposition, object of, 942
Prepositional phrases, 943
    commas to set off, 932
Prepositions, 943
Present participle, 87, 943
Present perfect tense, 945
Present tense, 945
Progressive form of verb, 945
Pronoun-antecedent agreement, 913–915, 917, 940
Pronouns, 247, 943
    avoiding shifts in person, 917
    in comparisons, 917
    in contractions, 916
    correcting vague reference, 649
    demonstrative, 943
    indefinite, 905–906, 915, 943
    intensive, 943
    interrogative, 943
    with nouns, 916
    object, 912, 944
    personal, 904–905, 943
    possessive, 912, 943
    predicate, 943
    reflexive, 943
    relative, 943
    subject, 911–912, 944
    and subject-verb agreement, 904–906
    who and *whom,* 915–916
Proper adjectives, 927–929, 940
Proper nouns, 927–929, 942
Punctuation, 944. *See also* specific
    for works cited list, 707
Question marks, 944
    quotation marks with, 938
Questions, indirect, 942
Quotation marks, 889
    end punctuation with, 938–939
    for titles of created works, 909, 930
Quotations, 944
    block, 889
    direct, 944
    direct, from a source, 938
    divided, 939
    indirect, 944
    introducing, 914, 938
Raise and *rise,* 925
Reflexive pronoun, 943
Relative pronoun, 943
Religious terms, capitalization of, 928
Rise and *raise,* 925
Run-on sentences, 901, 944
Sat and *sit,* 925
School subjects, capitalization of, 928
Second person, 943
Semicolons, 944
    in compound sentences, 931
    with conjunctive adverb, 870
    in joining sentences, 902
    quotation marks with, 938
Sentence fragments, 945
    correcting, 900–901
Sentences, 944
    commas to set off elements in, 932–933
    complex, 933, 944
    compound, 902, 931, 941, 944
    compound-complex, 539
    declarative, 945
    exclamatory, 945
    imperative, 945
    interrogative, 945
    inverted, 907, 942
    joining, 902
    run-on, 901, 944
    setting off elements in, 932–935
    simple, 944
    varying beginnings of, 405
Series, commas in, 171, 935–936
Sexist language, revising, 913
Simple predicate, 945
Simple sentence, 944

Simple subjects, 903, 945
Singular nouns, with plural forms, 908
Sit and *sat*, 925
Split infinitive, 945
Stories, capitalization of titles, 930
Subject complement, 941
Subject pronouns, 911–912, 944
Subjects, 945
    complete, 941
    compound, 409, 903–904
    simple, 903, 945
Subject-verb agreement, 409, 940
    with collective nouns, 908
    with compound subjects, 903–904
    with interrupting words and phrases, 906–907
    in inverted sentences, 907
    with nouns or time, weight, measure, and number, 908
    with predicate nominates, 909
    with pronoun subjects, 903–906
    with simple subjects, 903
    for singular nouns with plural forms, 908
    with titles, 909
Subordinate clauses, 900, 933, 941
Subordinate conjunction, 539, 941
Superlative form of adjective, 919, 940
Superlative form of adverb, 919, 940
Synonyms, 26, 247, 358
Take and *bring*, 926
Teach and *learn*, 925
Tense. *See* under Verbs
That, 921
Them, 921
These, 921
Third person, 943
This, 921
Those, 921
Time, nouns of, 908
Time periods, capitalization of, 929
Titles, personal. *See also* Personal titles
Titles of created works
    capitalization of, 930
    italics for, 909, 930
    quotation marks for, 909, 930
    subject-verb agreement with, 909
Transitions, 473, 869, 870
Transitive verb, 945
Unidentified references, 914, 945
Verbals, 945
Verb phase, 943
Verbs, 945. *See also* Subject-verb agreement
    action, 945
    affect and *effect*, 925
    auxiliary, 945
    avoiding shifts in, 828, 903
    bring and *take*, 926
    intransitive, 945
    irregular, 87
    learn and *teach*, 925
    lie and *lay*, 925
    linking, 918, 945
    main, 945
    object of, 942
    progressive form of, 945
    rise and *raise*, 925
    sit and *set*, 925
    tense, 87, 945
        avoiding shifts in, 475
        consistent use of, 923–924
        future, 945
        future perfect, 945
        past, 945
        past perfect, 945
        present, 945
        present perfect, 945
    transitive, 945
Voice, 945
    active, 333, 653, 942, 945
    passive, 333, 653, 945
Weight, nouns of, 908
Who and *whom*, 915–916
Words, interrupting, 906–907
ZIP code, 937

Writing Skills, Modes, and Formats

Alternative ending, 620
Anecdotes, 867
Anthologies, 865
Articles, 807
Audience
    addressing directly, 867
    identifying, 861, 884
Ballad, 625
Biographical sketch, 441
Brainstorming, 213, 252, 480, 735, 834, 860
Character study/sketch, 60, 82–86, 88–89, 103, 280, 282, 291, 335, 530, 603, 696, 721
Charts, 17, 77, 91, 103, 104, 118, 122, 127, 145, 172, 177, 193, 196, 215, 280, 335, 365, 380, 383, 452, 477, 481, 536, 543, 713, 732, 736, 775, 787, 807, 815, 837, 861
Cluster diagrams, 208, 255, 279, 364, 378, 406, 737
Coherence of paragraph, 869
Commentary, 303
Compare/contrast, 103, 193, 730, 784
Composition, 314
Conclusions, 874–875, 885
    in analysis, 883
    asking questions in, 875
    making predictions in, 875
    making recommendations in, 875
    in persuasive writing, 885
    restating thesis in, 874
    summarizing information in, 875

Constitution amendment, 303
Content, revising for, 864
Crime report, 641
Critical essays, 648–652
Crossword puzzles, 213
Definitions, 882
Description, 25, 77, 117, 383, 730, 828, 872–874
    characterization through, 82
    figurative language in, 873–874
    organizing details in, 874
    show, don't tell technique in, 82–83, 873
    using variety of details in, 873
    vividness in, 866
Details, 77, 117, 169
    in descriptive writing, 873
    in elaboration, 871
    organizing, 874
Detective's report, 383
Diagrams, 305, 339, 359, 365, 427
    cluster, 208, 255, 279, 364, 378, 406, 737, 861
    tree, 359, 861
    Venn, 303, 807
Dialogue, 60, 441, 625, 784
    in characterization, 82, 83
    in introductions, 867
    in narrative writing, 877
Diary entries, 316, 426, 518, 807
Director's notes, 784
Discovery drafts, 85, 168–169, 247, 330, 407, 472–473, 537, 576, 651, 696, 705, 769, 838, 862
Drafts, 48, 60, 125, 143, 291, 303, 314, 861–862
    discovery, 85, 168–169, 247, 330, 407, 472–473, 537, 576, 651, 705, 769, 838, 862
    focused, 85
    formalizing, 169, 247, 331, 407, 473, 537, 577, 651, 705, 769, 839
    peer response in, 862–863
Dramas, 766–770
Editing. *See* Revising and editing
Elaboration, 244–245
    examples in, 872
    facts and statistics in, 871
    incidents in, 871–872
    quotations in, 872
    sensory details in, 871
Encyclopedia entries, 530
Epilogues, 230, 666
Episodes, 206, 506
Epitaphs, 76
Epithets, 506
Essays, 37, 117, 143
    critical, 648–651
    interpretative, 404–409, 426
    personal, 460
Eulogies, 378
Examples in elaboration, 244, 245, 872

Explanatory writing, 754, 878–883
    analysis in, 878, 882–883
    cause and effect in, 878, 880
    compare and contrast in, 878, 879
    drafting, 165, 168–169
    prewriting, 164–165, 166–167
    problem-solution in, 878, 881
    publishing, 171
    revising, 170–171
Expository paragraphs, 815
Extended definitions, 572–579
Facts in elaboration, 245, 871
Field manuals, 356
First-person narratives, 143, 735
Freewriting, 85, 444, 700, 701, 835, 861
Humorous accounts, 152
Ideas for writing. *See* Prewriting
Idea tree, 167
Incidents in elaboration, 871–872
Interpretative essays, 404–409, 426
Interviews, 167, 426, 712, 713, 721
Introductions, 866–869, 885
    addressing reader directly in, 867
    in analysis, 882
    in persuasive writing, 885
    posing questions in, 866–867
    providing description in, 866
    relating anecdotes in, 867
    surprising statements in, 866
    thesis statement in, 867
Investigative reports, 164–171
Job description, 152
Journal, writing in, 5, 17, 27, 37, 48, 62, 77, 91, 106, 117, 122, 123, 145, 173, 282, 293, 303, 305, 314, 321, 338, 339, 356, 380, 381, 383, 385, 426, 429, 435, 441, 443, 506, 518, 543, 567, 624, 713, 721, 730, 732, 754, 775, 784, 807
Legal briefs, 279
Letters, 25, 76, 356, 435, 460, 625, 735
Link to literature, 861, 862, 866, 869, 872, 873, 875, 878
Listing, 176, 177, 213, 279, 291, 303, 378, 435
Lyrics, 518
Main idea, relating sentences to, 868
Mechanics, revising for, 864
Memos, 291
MLA manuscript guidelines, 889
Movie reviews, 193
Narrative writing, 876–877
    depicting characters in, 876
    describing setting in, 876
    dialogue in, 877
    flashbacks in, 877
    focusing on conflict in, 877
    focusing on events in, 877
    organizing events in, 876, 877
    personal, 27, 76, 193, 314, 452, 468–475, 817
    story elements in, 877
    writing standards for, 876

News story, 518, 641
Notebook. *See* Journal, writing in.
Note-taking, 291, 703, 887
Outlining, 25, 168, 206, 567, 603, 620, 704, 754, 828
Pamphlets, 303
Paragraphs, 117, 721
    coherence in, 869
    unity in, 404–409, 868
Paraphrasing, 887
Parodies, 534–541
Parts analysis, 882
Peer response, 38, 85, 104, 169, 194, 232, 247, 280, 322, 331, 357, 400, 407, 450, 473, 537, 577, 651, 705, 722, 769, 839, 862–863, 881
Performance evaluation, 152
Personal essay, 460
Personal narratives, 27, 76, 193, 314, 452, 468–475, 817
Persuasive writing, 326–333, 884–885, 884–889
    conclusions in, 885
    introduction in, 885
    knowing audience in, 884
    organizing, 885
    stating opinion in, 884
    supporting opinion in, 884
    writing standards for, 884
Plagiarism, 888
Planned drafting, 862
Plot outlines, 530, 567
Poems, 37, 125, 143, 213, 321, 359, 362, 399, 721, 735
Portfolio building, 4, 25, 37, 48, 60, 76, 103, 117, 125, 143, 152, 173, 193, 206, 213, 230, 279, 291, 314, 321, 335, 356, 362, 378, 383, 399, 426, 435, 441, 460, 477, 506, 518, 530, 567, 581, 603, 625, 666, 696, 709, 721, 730, 735, 754, 807, 815, 828
Prediction, making, in conclusion, 875
Prewriting, 860–861
    brainstorming in, 213, 252, 480, 622, 669, 735, 834, 860
    graphic organizers in, 17, 62, 77, 91, 103, 104, 118, 122, 127, 145, 172, 177, 193, 196, 215, 246, 280, 335, 365, 380, 383, 452, 477, 481, 536, 543, 622, 713, 732, 736, 775, 787, 807, 815, 837, 861
    choosing topic in, 701
    cluster diagrams in, 208, 255, 279, 364, 378, 406, 737, 861
    conducting interviews in, 167, 426, 713, 721
    determining purpose in, 861
    examining character in, 84
    exploring ideas in, 164, 165, 326–327, 406, 468–471, 572–574, 702, 768, 834–835, 836, 860–861
    focusing on purpose and audience in, 329
    freewriting in, 85, 444, 700, 701, 835
    gathering information in, 84, 166–167, 328–329, 702–703
    gathering support in, 406, 575
    idea tree in, 167
    identifying your audience in, 861, 884

    listing in, 176, 177, 213, 279, 291, 328, 378, 861
    narrowing focus in, 702
    note taking in, 291, 703, 887
    outlining in, 25, 168, 206, 567, 704, 754, 828
    personal techniques in, 860
    planning in, 768, 837
    reviewing main points in, 650
    sharing techniques in, 860
    taking stand in, 327
    tree diagram in, 359, 861
    Venn diagram in, 303, 807
Process analysis, 882
Process response, 246–249
Proofreading symbols, 865
Proverb, 441
Psychological examination, 730
Public-service announcement, 231
Publishing and reflecting, 171, 333, 475, 579, 706–707, 815, 841, 865
    creative ideas in, 865
    reflecting on writing, 865
Purpose, determining, 861
Questioning, 291
    in conclusion, 875
    in introductions, 866–867
Quotations, 887
    in elaboration, 244, 245, 872
    indenting, 889
Radio commercials, 230
Rap songs, 436
Recommendation, making, in conclusion, 875
Reflecting. *See* Publishing and reflecting
Reports, 399
Research reports, 700–705, 886–889
    clarifying thesis in, 886
    documenting sources in, 886, 888
    evaluating sources in, 887
    following MLA manuscript guidelines in, 889
    making source cards in, 887
    note taking in, 887
    organizing, 888
    supporting ideas in, 886
    writing standards for, 886
Revising and editing, 86, 170, 248, 332, 408, 474–475, 538, 578, 652, 706, 770, 840, 863–865
    for content, 864
    for mechanics, 864
    proofreading symbols for, 865
    for structure, 864
    tips for, 901, 903, 906, 907, 908, 909, 910, 912, 913, 914, 915, 916, 918, 919, 920, 921, 923, 924, 925, 926, 927, 928, 929, 931, 934, 935, 936, 937, 938, 939
Science notes, 230
Scripts, 103, 117, 784
Self-help guides, 206
Set of instructions, 125

Skits, 48, 60
Speech notes, 666
Statistics, in elaboration, 245, 871
Stories, 378, 435, 567, 834–841
    endings in, 48, 103
Story elements, in narrative writing, 877
Structure, revising for, 864
Summations, 103, 169, 279, 887
    in conclusion, 875
Tall tale, 604
Thesis statement
    beginning introduction with, 867
    in research report writing, 886
    restating in conclusion, 874
Thoughts, 435
Time lines, 90
Topic sentence, 868
Transitions, 869–872
    cause and effect in, 870–871
    compare and contrast in, 870
    degree in, 870
    spatial relationships in, 870
    time or sequence in, 869
Tree diagram, 359, 861
Unity, of paragraphs, 404–409, 868
Venn diagrams, 303, 807
Wills, 362
Word webs, 316
Writing about literature, 173, 335, 477, 581
    characterization, 82–87
    critical essays, 648–652
    dramas, 766–770
    elaboration, 244–245
    interpretative essays, 404–409
    parodies, 534–541
    process response, 246–249
Writing from experience, 164–171, 171, 173, 335, 477, 581
    extended definitions, 572–579
    personal narratives, 468–475
    persuasive writing, 326–333
    research papers, 700–705
    short stories, 834–841
Writing standards
    for analysis, 882
    for cause-and-effect writing, 880
    for character studies, 86
    for compare-and-contrast writing, 879
    for critical essays, 652
    for dramas, 770
    for extended definition, 579
    for interpretative essays, 408
    for narrative writing, 876
    for parodies, 538
    for personal narratives, 475
    for personal response essay, 248
    for persuasive essay, 333, 884
    for problem-solution writing, 881
    for research reports, 707, 886
    short stories, 841

Vocabulary

Analogies, 61, 507
Antonyms, 26, 195, 207, 428, 507, 621, 786
Context clues, 38, 119, 144, 153, 281, 304, 436, 531
Definitions, 173, 195, 208, 315, 572–579, 581
Etymology, 195
Idioms, 379
Informal language, 535
LaserLinks visual vocabulary, 27, 39, 49, 62, 145, 413, 775
Pawnee words, 366
Root words, 145
Round-robin story, 668
Specialized, 145, 293
Syllables, 153
Synonyms, 26, 207, 232, 292, 315, 358, 569, 621, 723
Words to know exercises, 26, 38, 49, 78, 105, 119, 144, 153, 207, 232, 281, 292, 304, 315, 400, 436, 442, 461, 519, 531, 604, 621, 643, 668, 723, 755, 808, 816, 829
Words to know access guide, 848–849

Research and Study Skills

Almanacs, 702
Atlas, 531
Biographies, 304
Card catalog, 702
CD-ROM, 891, 898
Charts, 896
Commercial information services, 890
Computerized catalog, 702, 891
Cross-curricular research
    action heroes, 177
    affirmative action, 292
    alcoholism, 379
    Anthony, Susan B., 293, 303
    Bearden, Romare, 568
    big-game hunting, 787, 808
    Blackbeard, 281
    blue-collar workers, 316
    boxing, 208, 214
    Burne-Jones, Edward, 568
    Butler, Walter, 281
    cape buffalo, 785, 808
    catacombs, 785
    Cesar Chavez, 697
    Christian traditions, 127
    concentration camps, 809, 816
    death, 713, 721, 722, 731
    deep-sea diving, 104
    diabetes, 144

disabilities, 282, 291
discrimination, 429
diverse societies, 37
drugs, 232
ecology, 736
ethnic conflicts, 26
factory workers, 316
Federal Communications Commission, 230, 232
forensic science, 621
Fourteenth Amendment, 293
funeral customs, 127
gender roles, 442
genetic engineering, 232
Geneva Convention, 357
Girdy, Simon, 281
Great Depression, 106, 118
Greek gods/goddesses, 483
Greek social code, 543
Hague Convention, 357
Hathorne, Judge, 281
Hinduism, 461
holidays, 62, 77
hurricanes, 837
ibises, 428
India, 452, 461
jazz, 208, 213
jewelry, artificial, 667
Jim Crow laws, 429, 436
Kandinsky, Wassily, 231
Kennedy assassination, 27
Lake Michigan, 207
malpractice, 152
mathematics, 667
medical training, 145, 153
modernism, 816
native plants, 413
Nazi Germany, 809
Outlaws of the Old West, 604
Pawnee Indians, 364, 379
polio, 282, 292
postpolio syndrome, 292
prisoners of war, 339, 357
quilting, 642
radioactive wastes, 654
radio telescopes, 215, 231
realism, 315
Redon, Odilon, 568
shanty towns, 118
soccer, 208
sound, 231
Stanley, Earl, 568
suffrage movement, 293, 303
Tasmanian devil, 196
Trojan War, 481, 482
Vietnam War, 339
warrior shield, 379
Webster, Daniel, 255

wild horses, 817, 829
women's rights, 293, 303
Wyeth, N. C., 568
Electronic mail, 890
Encyclopedias, 531, 702
Graphs, 896
Indexes, 328, 702
Internet, 890
Interviewing, 77, 166, 167, 194, 328, 363, 584, 713, 721, 722, 860
Library
using, 166, 328, 702
Multimedia, 897–899
Note-taking, 291, 328, 703, 887
On-line research, 166, 232, 328, 329, 357, 428, 703, 816, 890–891
Outlining, 25, 168, 206, 567, 704, 754, 828
Surveys, 328
Thesaurus, 576, 577
Visuals, 896
World Wide Web, 890

Speaking, Listening, and Viewing

Class discussions, 37, 48, 62, 172, 193, 437, 721, 731, 735, 784, 787, 809, 815, 828
Cooperative learning. *See* Working in groups.
Creative responses
abstract paintings, 118
advertisements, 49
board games, 531
cartoons, 153, 303
carvings, 362
charts, 481, 575
collages, 118, 314
comic strips, 153
crossword puzzles, 213, 519
dance choreography, 829
diagrams, 104, 171
diary entries, 518, 807
dioramas, 519
drawings, 26, 357, 450, 542, 713, 722, 730, 785, 817, 828
escape plan, 507
field manuals, 356
game, 642, 708
greeting cards, 76, 357
illustrations, 38
letters, 172, 356
magazine covers, 755
mandalas, 461
maps, 427, 531, 808
mobiles, 314, 322, 363
models, 461, 519
montages, 314

murals, 362
  music, 626, 643
  obstacle courses, 14
  paintings, 314, 362, 450, 604, 722
  polls, 450
  posters, 125, 171, 194, 280, 604
  programs, 400
  sculpture, 362, 450
  set designs, 785
  sketches, 626, 722
  skit, 667
  soliloquy, 427
  songs, 531
  storyboards, 171, 568
  warrior shield, 379
Debating, 152, 231, 530, 697
Dramatic presentations, 117, 118, 279, 641, 754, 755, 784
Dramatic readings, 214, 315, 399, 506, 755, 785

Interviewing, 77, 166, 167, 194, 328, 363, 584, 713, 721, 722, 860
LaserLinks videodisc, 17, 26, 27, 38, 39, 49, 62, 78, 119, 145, 153, 165, 177, 196, 208, 214, 215, 232, 281, 282, 292, 293, 304, 316, 322, 327, 339, 358, 400, 413, 428, 429, 436, 442, 451, 452, 461, 469, 481, 519, 531, 543, 573, 643, 697, 701, 721, 722, 723, 724, 731, 735, 737, 754, 755, 775, 787, 808, 809, 816, 829, 834, 835, 895–896, 897–899
Role playing, 696
Speech notes, 666
Working in groups, 25, 27, 37, 60, 76, 103, 125, 127, 172, 196, 206, 213, 230, 280, 292, 303, 321, 339, 362, 378, 412, 542, 603, 620, 625, 641, 642, 666, 667, 696, 697, 708, 709, 784
  Partners, 48, 193, 213, 252, 282, 383, 480, 641, 696, 709, 712

Index of Titles and Authors

Page numbers that appear in italics refer to biographical information.

A
American History, 27
Angelou, Maya, 52, *61*
Annabel Lee, 724
Arias, Ron, 756, *765*
Artist, The, 448
Atwood, Margaret, 532, *533*
Auden, W. H., 622, *626*

B
Bass, the River, and Sheila Mant, The, 39
Battle Report, 208
Beauty Is Truth, 305
Beginning of Something, The, 127
Benét, Stephen Vincent, 255, *281*
Black Boy, from, 429
Blake, William, 192
Bradbury, Ray, 17, *26*
Brenner, David, 462, *467*
Bridgers, Sue Ellen, 127, *144*
Brothers Are the Same, 233

C
Candelaria, Nash, 177, *195*
Capote, Truman, 62, *78*
Cask of Amontillado, The, 775
Chan, Sucheng, 282, *292*
Chang, Isabelle C., 448
Chaser, The, 644
Chekhov, Anton, 385, *400*
Childress, Alice, 685
Christmas Memory, A, 62
Cisneros, Sandra, 437, *442*
Cofer, Judith Ortiz, 27, *38*
Collier, Eugenia, 106, *119*
Collier, John, 644, *647*
Connell, Richard, 787, *808*
Courage That My Mother Had, The, 359
Cultural Worker, The, 316
Cummings, E. E., 47

D
Day the Cisco Kid Shot John Wayne, The, 177
Devil and Daniel Webster, The, 255
Dickinson, Emily, 151
Doro, Sue, 316, *322*
Dorris, Michael, 401, *403*
Driscoll, Jack, 380, *384*

E
Euphio Question, The, 215
Everybody Knows Tobie, 688
Explosion in the Parlor, The, 595

F
Fable for When There's No Way Out, 122
Father's Day, 401
Fireworks, 205
First Appendectomy, The, 145
Fish Cheeks, 323
Fish Eyes, 462
Fitzgerald, Robert, from the *Odyssey*, Translated by, 481, *569*
Forrest, Williams, 154, *163*
Frost, Robert, 122, *126*
Full Circle, 605

G
Garza, Daniel, 688, *697*
Glaspell, Susan, 627, *643*
"*Good Night, Willie Lee, I'll See You in the Morning,*" 720
Grafton, Sue, 605, *621*
Great Taos Bank Robbery, The, 669

Grover Dill and the Tasmanian Devil, 196
Guest, Anna, 305

H
Hamer, Martin J., 680, *687*
Hanging Fire, 698
Herrera, Demetrio, 208, *214*
Herrera-Sobek, María, 320
Hersey, John, 809, *816*
Hillerman, Tony, 669, *679*
Homer, 481, *569*
Hughes, Langston, 443, *451*
Hurst, James, 413, *428*

I
I Know Why the Caged Bird Sings, from, 52
Incident in a Rose Garden, 724

J
Jackson, Shirley, 585, *597*
Johnson, Dorothy M., 598, *604*
Justice, Donald, 724, *731*

K
Kaufman, Bob, 208, *214*
King, Stephen, 737, *755*
Kübler-Ross, Elisabeth, 713, *723*

L
Lakshmi, 452
Last Boast, The, 598
Le Guin, Ursula K., 830, *833*
Lessing, Doris, 91, *105*
Levertov, Denise, 732, *736*
Lineage, 359
Lorde, Audre, 698, *699*
Lowell, Amy, 205

M
Madgett, Naomi Long, 425
Marigolds, 106
Marine Corps Issue, 339
Markham, Beryl, 233, *243*
Marriage Proposal, A, 385
Maupassant, Guy de, 657, *668*
McLean, David, 339, *357*

Merriam, Eve, 59
Metaphor, 59
Millay, Edna St. Vincent, 359, *363*
Most Dangerous Game, The, 787
Mountain, The, 680
My Papa's Waltz, 380
My Poetry/Mi Poesía, 320
My Wonder Horse/Mi Caballo Mago, 817

N
Nash, Ogden, 398
Necklace, The, 657
Nolen, William A., 145, *153*
Not to Go with the Others, 809

O
O What Is That Sound, 622
Odyssey, the, from, 481
On Being Seventeen, Bright, and Unable to Read, 79
On Writing "Marine Corps Issue," 355
One Ordinary Day, with Peanuts, 585
Only Daughter, 437
Oranges, 142

P
Parker, Dorothy, 570, *571*
Penelope, 570
Plainswoman, 154
Pocketbook Game, The, 685
Poe, Edgar Allan, 724, *731*, 775, *786*
Poison Tree, A, 192

R
Raymond, David, 79, *81*
Reflections on the Holocaust, 814
Road Not Taken, The, 122
Roethke, Theodore, 380, *384*

S
Scarlet Ibis, The, 413
Secret Life of Walter Mitty, The, 6
Sharks, The, 732
Shepherd, Jean, 196, *207*
Simson, Maria, 618
since feeling is first, 47
Siren Song, 532

Snow, Edward Rowe, 783
Sorry, Right Number, 737
Soto, Gary, 142
Stafford, William, 732, 736
Story Behind "The Cask of Amontillado," The, 783
Strange Case of Mr. Ormantude's Bride, The, 398
Surgeons must be very careful, 151
Swenson, May, 122, *126*

T
Tan, Amy, 323, *325*
Theme for English B, 443
Through the Tunnel, 91
Thurber, James, 6
Touch Football, 380
Training/Entrenamiento, 208
Traveling Through the Dark, 732
Trifles, 627
Trip to the Edge of Survival, A, 756
Truman, Margaret, 293, *304*

U
Ulibarrí, Sabine R., 817, *829*
Unfinished Business, 713
United States vs. Susan B. Anthony, The, 293
Utterly Perfect Murder, The, 17

V
Victor, Vasanthi, 452, *461*
Vonnegut, Kurt, Jr., 215, *232*

W
Walker, Alice, 720
Walker, Margaret, 359, *363*
Walters, Anna Lee, 364, *379*
Warriors, The, 364
Wetherell, W. D., 39, *49*
"Who Killed My Daughter?": Lois Duncan Searches for an Answer, 618
Wife's Story, The, 830
Wilbur, Richard, 443, *451*
Woman with Flower, 425
Wright, Richard, 429, *436*
Writer, The, 443

X
Xiao-Yi, Bai, 595

Y
You're Short, Besides!, 282

Acknowledgments (continued)

Random House, Inc.: Excerpt from *I Know Why the Caged Bird Sings* by Maya Angelou; Copyright © 1969 by Maya Angelou.

"A Christmas Memory," from *Breakfast at Tiffany's* by Truman Capote; Copyright 1956 by Truman Capote. Reprinted by permission of Random House, Inc.

Marian Reiner, Literary Agent: "Metaphor," from *A Sky Full of Poems* by Eve Merriam; Copyright © 1964, 1970, 1973 by Eve Merriam. Reprinted by permission of Marian Reiner.

The New York Times: "On Being 17, Bright—and Unable to Read" by David Raymond from *The New York Times,* April 25, 1976; Copyright © 1976 by The New York Times Company. Reprinted by permission.

HarperCollins Publishers, Inc., and Jonathon Clowes Limited: "Through the Tunnel" from *The Habit of Loving* by Doris Lessing; Copyright 1955 by Doris Lessing. Originally appeared in The New Yorker. Copyright renewed. Reprinted by permission of HarperCollins Publishers, Inc., and Jonathon Clowes Limited, London.

Eugenia Collier and Johnson Publishing Company, Inc.: "Marigolds" by Eugenia Collier, from *Negro Digest,* November 1969; Copyright © 1969 by Negro Digest. Reprinted by permission of Eugenia Collier and Johnson Publishing Company, Inc.

Houghton Mifflin Company: "Fable for When There's No Way Out," from *Nature* by May Swenson; Copyright © 1994 by The Literary Estate of May Swenson. Reprinted by permission of Houghton Mifflin Company. All rights reserved.

Dell Books: "The Beginning of Something" by Sue Ellen Bridgers, from *Visions,* edited by Donald R. Gallo; Copyright © 1987 by Sue Ellen Bridgers. Used by permission of Dell Books, a division of Bantam Doubleday Dell Publishing Group, Inc.

Chronicle Books and Gary Soto: "Oranges," from *Gary Soto: New and Selected Poems* by Gary Soto, Copyright © 1995 by Gary Soto, published by Chronicle Books.

Estate of William A. Nolen: "The First Appendectomy" by William A. Nolen. Reprinted by permission of Eleanor Wood, agent for the Estate of William A. Nolen.

Estate of Williams Forrest: "Plainswoman" by Williams Forrest, from *The Saturday Evening Post,* September 24, 1960. By permission of Mrs. Elaine Forrest.

Unit Two

Arte Publico Press: "The Day the Cisco Kid Shot John Wayne" by Nash Candelaria, from *The Americas Review,* Vol. XI, No. 2, 1983. Reprinted with permission from the publisher of The Americas Review, Arte Publico Press—University of Houston.

Doubleday: "Grover Dill and the Tasmanian Devil," from *In God We Trust: All Others Pay Cash* by Jean Shepherd; Copyright © 1966 by Jean Shepherd. Used by permission of Doubleday, a division of Bantam Doubleday Dell Publishing Group, Inc.

Harcourt Brace & Company: Excerpt from "Fog," from *Chicago Poems* by Carl Sandburg; Copyright 1926 by Holt, Rinehart and Winston, Inc., and renewed 1944 by Carl Sandburg, reprinted by permission of Harcourt Brace & Company.

New Directions Publishing Corporation: "Battle Report," from *Solitudes Crowded with Loneliness* by Bob Kaufman; Copyright © 1965 by Bob Kaufman.

"Training" by Demetrio Herrera, from *An Anthology of Contemporary Latin American Poetry,* edited by Dudley Fitts; Copyright © 1970 by New Directions Publishing Corporation. Reprinted by permission of New Directions Publishing Corporation.

Delacorte Press/Seymour Lawrence: "The Euphio Question," from *Welcome to the Monkey House* by Kurt Vonnegut, Jr.; Copyright 1951 by Kurt Vonnegut, Jr. Used by permission of Delacorte Press/Seymour Lawrence, a division of Bantam Doubleday Dell Publishing Group, Inc.

Laurence Pollinger Limited: "Brothers Are the Same" from *The Splendid Outcast* by Beryl Markham; Copyright © 1987 by Beryl Markham. Reprinted by permission of the Estate of Beryl Markham.

Brandt & Brandt Literary Agents, Inc.: "The Devil and Daniel Webster" by Stephen Vincent Benét; Copyright 1936 by Stephen Vincent Benét, Copyright renewed © 1964 by Thomas C. Benét, Stephanie B. Mahin, Rachel Benét Lewis. Reprinted by permission of Brandt & Brandt Literary Agents, Inc.

Sucheng Chan: "You're Short, Besides" by Sucheng Chan; Copyright © 1989 by Sucheng Chan. Originally published in *Making Waves: An Anthology of Writings By and About Asian American Women,* edited by Asian Women United of California (Boston: Beacon Press, 1989).

William Morrow & Company, Inc.: "The United States vs. Susan B. Anthony," from *Women of Courage* by Margaret Truman; Copyright © 1976 by Margaret Truman Daniel. Reprinted by permission of William Morrow & Company, Inc.

Sue Doro: "The Cultural Worker," from *Blue Collar Goodbyes* by Sue Doro, published by Papier-Mache Press.

María Herrera-Sobek: "Mi poesía/My Poetry" by María Herrera-Sobek, from *Chasqui,* February-May 1980. Reprinted by permission of María Herrera-Sobek.

Sandra Dijkstra Literary Agency: "Fish Cheeks" by Amy Tan, from *Seventeen Magazine,* December 1987; Copyright © 1987 by Amy Tan. Reprinted by permission of the author and the Sandra Dijkstra Literary Agency.

People Weekly: Excerpt from "Cheering Unlimited," from *People Weekly,* February, 1992; Copyright © 1992 by Time, Inc. Reprinted by permission of People Weekly.

Chicago Tribune: Excerpt from "High School Brawlers Will Go Directly to Police Station" by Stephen Price, from *Chicago Tribune,* April 5, 1994. Copyrighted © Chicago Tribune Company. All rights reserved. Used with permission.

Unit Three

David McLean: "Marine Corps Issue" by David McLean, as first published in *The Atlantic Monthly,* May 1993; Copyright © 1993 by David McLean.

Margaret Walker Alexander: "Lineage," from *For My People* by Margeret Walker, Yale University Press, 1942. Reprinted by permission of the author.

Elizabeth Barnett: "The Courage That My Mother Had," from *Collected Poems* by Edna St. Vincent Millay, published by HarperCollins. Copyright © 1954, 1982 by Edna St. Vincent Millay Ellis. Reprinted by permission of Elizabeth Barnett, literary executor.

Firebrand Books: "The Warriors," from *The Sun Is Not Merciful* by Anna Lee Walters; Copyright © 1985 by Anna Lee Walters. Reprinted by permission of Firebrand Books, Ithaca, New York.

Doubleday: "My Papa's Waltz," Copyright 1942 by Hearst Magazines, Inc., from *The Collected Poems of Theodore Roethke* by Theodore Roethke; Used by permission of Doubleday, a division of Bantam Doubleday Dell Publishing Group, Inc.

Jack Driscoll: "Touch Football" by Jack Driscoll from *Fishing the Backwash*. Reprinted by permission of the author.

Samuel French, Inc.: *The Marriage Proposal* by Anton Chekhov, English version by Hilmar Baukhage and Barrett H. Clark; Copyright 1914 by Barrett H. Clark, Copyright 1942, in renewal, by Barrett H. Clark. CAUTION: Professionals and amateurs are hereby warned that *The Marriage Proposal* being fully protected under the copyright laws of the United States of America, the British Commonwealth countries, including Canada, and the other countries of the Copyright Union, is subject to a royalty. All rights, including professional, amateur, motion picture, recitation, public reading, radio, television and cable broadcasting, and the rights of translation into foreign languages, are strictly reserved. Any inquiry regarding the availability of performance rights, or the purchase of individual copies of the authorized acting edition, must be directed to Samuel French Inc., 45 West 25 Street, NY, NY 10010, with other locations in Hollywood, CA, and Toronto, Canada.

Little, Brown and Company: "The Strange Case of Mr. Ormantude's Bride," from *Verses from 1929* On by Ogden Nash; Copyright 1942 by Ogden Nash. Reprinted by permission of Little, Brown and Company.

HarperCollins Publishers, Inc.: "Father's Day," from *Paper Trail* by Michael Dorris; Copyright © 1994 by Michael Dorris. By permission of HarperCollins Publishers, Inc.

James Hurst: "The Scarlet Ibis" by James Hurst; Copyright © 1960 by *The Atlantic Monthly* and renewed 1988 by James Hurst. Reprinted by permission of James Hurst.

Naomi Long Madgett: "Woman with Flower," from *Star by Star* by Naomi Long Madgett (Harlo, 1965). By permission of the author.

HarperCollins Publishers, Inc.: Excerpt from *Black Boy* by Richard Wright; Copyright 1937, 1942, 1944, 1945 by Richard Wright. Copyright renewed © 1973 by Ellen Wright. Reprinted by permission of HarperCollins Publishers, Inc.

Susan Bergholz Literary Services: "Only Daughter" by Sandra Cisneros; Copyright © 1990 by Sandra Cisneros. First published by *Glamour Magazine*, November 1990. Reprinted by permission of Susan Bergholz Literary Services, New York.

Harold Ober Associates: "Theme for English B," from *The Langston Hughes Reader* by Langston Hughes; Copyright 1951 by Langston Hughes, renewed © 1979 by George Houston Bass. Reprinted by permission of Harold Ober Associates.

Harcourt Brace & Company: "The Writer," from *The Mind-Reader* by Richard Wilbur; Copyright © 1971 by Richard Wilbur. Reprinted by permission of Harcourt Brace & Company.

Random House, Inc.: "The Artist," from *Tales of Old China* by Isabelle C. Chang; Copyright © 1969 by Isabelle C. Chang. Reprinted by permission of Random House, Inc.

Aunt Lute Books: "Lakshmi," from *Our Feet Walk the Sky: Women of the South Asian Diaspora* by Vasanthi Victor; Copyright © 1993 by The Women of South Asian Descent Collective. Reprinted with permission from Aunt Lute Books.

Arbor House: "Fish Eyes," from *Nobody Ever Sees You Eat Tunafish* by David Brenner; Copyright © 1986 by David Brenner. Reprinted by permission of Arbor House, a division of William Morrow & Company, Inc.

Smithsonian Magazine: From "A to Z: the happy rescue of a poet's antic alphabet" by Kathleen Burke, from *Smithsonian Magazine,* August 1995. Reprinted by permission of Smithsonian Magazine.

Roper Center: Survey Question by Yankelovich from *Women's Day Magazine,* August 12–18, 1993. Reprinted with permission of The Roper Center for Public Opinion Research, University of Connecticut, Storrs.

Unit Four

Vintage Books: Excerpts from *The Odyssey* by Homer, translated by Robert Fitzgerald; Copyright © 1961, 1963 by Robert Fitzgerald and renewed 1989 by Benedict R. C. Fitzgerald. Reprinted by permission of Vintage Books, a division of Random House, Inc.

Houghton Mifflin Company and Oxford University Press Canada: "Siren Song," from *You Are Happy: Selected Poems 1965–1975* by Margaret Atwood; Copyright © 1976 by Margaret Atwood. Reprinted by permission of Houghton Mifflin Company and Oxford University Press Canada. All Rights Reserved.

Viking Penguin: "Penelope," from *The Portable Dorothy Parker* by Dorothy Parker; Copyright 1928, renewed 1956 by Dorothy Parker. Used by permission of Viking Penguin, a division of Penguin Books, USA Inc.

Unit Five

Linda Allen, Literary Agent: "One Ordinary Day, with Peanuts" by Shirley Jackson, from *The Magazine of Fantasy and Science Fiction,* 1954. Reprinted by permission of the heirs of Shirley Jackson.

Zuxin Ding: "The Explosion in the Parlor" by Bai Xiao-Yi; Copyright © 1989 by Bai Xiao-Yi, English language translation © 1989 by Zuxin Ding. By permission of Zuxin Ding.

Ballantine Books: Excerpt from *The Hanging Tree* by Dorothy M. Johnson; Copyright 1950 and renewed © 1978 by Dorothy M. Johnson. Reprinted by permission of Ballantine Books, a division of Random House, Inc.

Aaron Priest Agency: "Full Circle" by Sue Grafton; Copyright © 1991 by Sue Grafton. Reprinted by permission of the Aaron Priest Agency.

Publishers Weekly: "Who Killed My Daughter?: Lois Duncan Searches for an Answer" by Maria Simson. Reprinted from the April 20, 1992 issue of *Publishers Weekly,* published by Cahners Publishing Company, a division of Reed Publishing USA; Copyright © 1992 by Reed Publishing USA

Random House, Inc.: "O What Is That Sound," from *W. H. Auden: Collected Poems* by W. H. Auden, edited and Preface by Edward Mendelson; Copyright 1937 and renewed © 1965 by W. H. Auden. Reprinted by permission of Random House, Inc.

Harold Matson Company, Inc.: "The Chaser," from *The John Collier Reader* by John Collier; Copyright 1940, renewed © 1968 by John Collier. Reprinted by permission of Harold Matson Company, Inc.

Harcourt Brace & Company: "The Necklace" by Guy de Maupassant from *Adventures in Reading,* Laureate Edition, by Evan Lodge, Marjorie Braymer, Mary R. Bowman, and Herbert Potell; Copyright © 1963 by Harcourt Brace & Company and renewed 1991 by Deborah Jean Lodge, Alice Lodge, Jeanne M. Shutes, Jessica Sand, Lydia Winderman, Florence F. Potell and Mary R. Bowman, reprinted by permission of the publisher.

University of New Mexico Press: "The Great Taos Bank Robbery," from *The Great Taos Bank Robbery and Other Indian Country Affairs* by Tony Hillerman; © 1973 by Anthony G. Hillerman. Reprinted by permission of the University of New Mexico Press.

Martin J. Hamer: "The Mountain" by Martin J. Hamer; Copyright © 1962 by Martin J. Hamer, Copyright renewed 1990 by Martin J. Hamer. First published in *Negro Digest,* June 1962. Reprinted by permission of the author.

Flora Roberts, Inc.: "The Pocketbook Game," from *Like One of the Family* by Alice Childress; Copyright 1956, renewed © 1984 by Alice Childress. Used by permission of Flora Roberts, Inc.

Texas Christian University: "Everybody Knows Tobie" by Daniel Garza, first published in *Descant, The Literary Magazine* of Texas Christian University, Spring 1963.

W. W. Norton & Company, Inc., and Charlotte Sheedy Literary Agency: "Hanging Fire," from *The Black Unicorn: Poems* by Audre Lorde; Copyright © 1978 by Audre Lorde. Reprinted by permission of W. W. Norton & Company, Inc., and Charlotte Sheedy Literary Agency.

Bigfoot Research Project: Excerpt from *The Bigfoot Research Project World Wide Web Site* by Peter Byrne; Copyright © 1995 by The Bigfoot Research Project. Reprinted by permission of The Bigfoot Research Project. 1-800-BIG-FOOT.

People Weekly: Excerpt from "Going in Circles," from *People Weekly,* September 23, 1991; Copyright © 1991 by Time Inc. Reprinted by permission of *People Weekly.*

Unit 6

Lynn Gilbert: Excerpt from "Elisabeth Kübler-Ross," from *Particular Passions: Talks with Women Who Have Shaped Our Times* by Lynn Gilbert and Gaylen Moore; Copyright © 1981 by Lynn Gilbert.

Doubleday: "Goodnight Willie Lee, I'll See You in the Morning," from *Goodnight Willie Lee, I'll See You in the Morning* by Alice Walker; Copyright © 1975 by Alice Walker. Used by permission of Doubleday, a division of Bantam Doubleday Dell Publishing Group, Inc.

Donald Justice: "Incident in a Rose Garden," from *Night Light* by Donald Justice; Copyright © 1981 by Donald Justice. Reprinted by permission of the author.

The Estate of William Stafford: "Traveling Through the Dark," from *Stories That Could Be True: New and Collected Poems* by William Stafford. Reprinted by permission of the Estate of William Stafford.

New Directions Publishing Corporation: "The Sharks," Copyright © 1958 by Denise Levertov, from *Collected Earlier Poems, 1940–1960* by Denise Levertov. Reprinted by permisson of New Directions Publishing Corporation.

Jay D. Kramer, Attorney at Law: "Sorry, Right Number" by Stephen King; Copyright © 1993 by Stephen King. All Rights Reserved. Reprinted by permission of the author.

Time Inc.: "A Trip to the Edge of Survival" by Ron Arias, from *People Weekly,* July 11, 1988; Copyright © 1988 Time Inc.

Anna Myrle Snow: Excerpt from "The Roving Skeleton of Boston Bay" by Edward R. Snow from *Yankee Magazine.* By permission of Mrs. Anna Myrle Snow.

Brandt & Brandt Literary Agents, Inc.: "The Most Dangerous Game" by Richard Connell; Copyright 1924 by Richard Connell, Copyright renewed 1952 by Louise Fox Connell. Reprinted by permisson of Brandt & Brandt Literary Agents, Inc.

Brook Hersey, literary executor for the Estate of John Hersey: "Not to Go with the Others" by John Hersey; Copyright © 1962, 1987 by John Hersey, originally appeared in *Here to Stay*, published by Alfred A. Knopf., Inc.

Twayne Publishers: Excerpt from *Witnesses to the Holocaust: An Oral History*, edited by Rhoda G. Lewin. Reprinted with the permission of Twayne Publishers, an imprint of Simon & Schuster Macmillan. Copyright © 1990 by the Jewish Community Relations Council/Anti Defamation League of Minnesota and the Dakotas.

Sabine R. Ulibarrí: "My Wonder Horse/Mi caballo mago," from *Tierra Amarilla: Stories of New Mexico* by Sabine R. Ulibarrí, translated from the Spanish by Thelma Campbell Nason. By permission of the author.

Virginia Kidd, Literary Agent: "The Wife's Story" by Ursula K. Le Guin, first appeared in *The Compass Rose*; Copyright © 1982 by Ursula K. Le Guin. Reprinted by permission of the author and the author's agent, Virginia Kidd.

Art Credits

Author Photographs and Portraits
26 Jay Kay Klein. **38** Courtesy of Arte Publico Press. **49** Greg Tousignant. **61** UPI/Bettmann. **78** Copyright © Henri Cartier-Bresson/Magnum Photos. **105** Globe Photos. **126** *top* The Granger Collection, New York. **126** *bottom*, **232**, **243**, **304**, **325**, **569** *right*, **571**, **597**, **679**, **723**, **755**, **816** AP/Wide World Photos, Inc. **281** National Archives. **363** *left* Handy Photo Studios; *right* The Bettmann Archive. **384** *top* UPI/Bettmann Newsphotos; *bottom* Courtesy of the University of Massachusetts Press, Amherst, Massachusetts. **400** Sovfoto. **436** National Archives. **442** Rubén Guzmán. **451** *left* National Portrait Gallery/Art Resource, New York; *right* Smith College, Northampton, Massachusetts. **569** *left* The Bettmann Archive. **604** Mansfield Library, University of Montana. **626** The Granger Collection, New York. **643** The State Historical Society of Iowa. **668** Culver Pictures. **765** Copyright © Peter Serling. **786** Stock Montage. **808** Schlesinger Library, Radcliffe College. **829** Courtesy of Arte Publico Press. **833** M. Berkley/Camera Press/Globe Photos.

Commissioned Art and Photography
2 *top*, **4**, **5**, **43**, **45**, **47**, **62**, **82–86**, **110**, **113–116**, **124**, **128–129**, **147**, **164–168**, **177–179**, **184–185**, **246** *bottom*, **262**, **265**, **269**, **275**, **300**, **320**, **326**, **327**, **328**, **332**, **340**, **342**, **344**, **347–348**, **350–352**, **357**, **368–369**, **371**, **377**, **401**, **406** *bottom*, **413**, **430**, **432–434**, **444–448**, **465**, **468–472**, **534–538**, **572–575**, **576** *top*, **578**, **579**, **595**, **599**, **648**, **649**, **650** *top*, **652**, **685**, **700**, **701**, **704**, **705**, **738–739**, **741**, **744–745**, **750**, **752–753**, **766**, **767**, **836**, **837**, **840**, **841** Sharon Hoogstraten.
66, **70**, **75** Rebecca McClellan.
170, **171**, **244–249**, **330**, **333**, **470–471** *top insets*, **474**, **475**, **574** *bottom*, **576**,

577 *bottom*, 650 *bottom*, 702, 703, 706, 707, 768–770, 834, 835, 838, 839 Allan Landau.
228–229, 738–739, 741, 744–745, 750, 752–753 Craig Niedermaier.
453–459 Lori Nelson Field/Koralik Associates. 674–675 Claudia de Teresa.
788–789, 794, 798, 803 Tinan Valk.

Miscellaneous Art Credits

xi *Isabella and Lois* (1968), Warren Brandt. Oil on canvas, 50″ × 60″, private collection. **xiii** *Pep's Car with an Assist from Clyde, Snake and Peabody* (1975), Colleen Browning. Oil on canvas, 36″ × 60 1/4″. **xv** *Richard at Age Five* (1944), Alice Neel. Oil on canvas, 26″ × 14″, courtesy of Robert Miller Gallery, New York. Copyright © Estate of Alice Neel. **xvii, 493, 547, 551** Copyright © Winfield Parks/National Geographic Society Image Collection. **xix** *Suzanne Poirson* (1884), John Singer Sargent. Oil on canvas 24 13/16″ × 18 7/8″, private collection, photo courtesy of Adelson Galleries, Inc., New York. **xxi** *Casanova* (1987), Julio Larraz. Private collection, courtesy of Nohra Haime Gallery, New York. **xxvi–1** *Magic Eye.* Copyright © N. E. Thing Enterprises, Inc. Reprinted with permission of Andrews & McMeel, all rights reserved. **2** *bottom left* Copyright © Walt Disney Productions, photo by Photofest; *bottom right* Copyright © Paul Clancy/Graphicstock. **3** *top* Yoav Levy/Phototake NYC; *top center* Harrod Blank; *center* Copyright © David M. Davis/FPG International; *bottom left* Copyright © Yvette Cardozo/Tony Stone Images; *bottom right* Copyright © Hugh Sitton/Tony Stone Images. **40–42, 46** Cy DeCosse, Inc. **52** Courtesy of Steven Hicks/Stamps Arkansas. **63, 67–68, 71, 74** Copyright © 1992–1994 Aridi Computer Graphics, Inc. All Rights Reserved. **77** Copyright © Michael Newman/PhotoEdit. **88–89** UPI/Bettmann. **91** Copyright © Eugene Zefa/H. Armstrong Roberts. **104** Copyright © Grove Zuckerman/ProFiles West. **127** Copyright © James Shaffer/PhotoEdit. **148** M. Howell/Camerique/H. Armstrong Roberts. **164** *top, Babe Ruth Monument,* Susan Luery. Photo Copyright © Brian D. Dziuba; *bottom* Editorial cartoon by Mike Keefe. Copyright © 1990, 1992, *U.S. News & World Report; center left, The World Almanac and Book of Facts 1993,* reproduced courtesy of Funk and Wagnalls Corporation; *center right* Copyright © 1995 Time Inc. **178–179, 194** Photofest. **188** Copyright © Dixie Knight. **197** Jean-Paul Ferrero. **199** Copyright © 1992 Chip Simons/FPG Internatioal Corp. **201** Copyright © Superstock, Inc. **203** *boy,* Copyright © Superstock, Inc.; *Tasmanian devil* Jean-Paul Ferrero. **230** Camerique/H. Armstrong Roberts. **233** Copyright © Richard J. Green/Photo Researchers, Inc.; *border* Copyright © 1995 PhotoDisc, Inc. **234, 237, 238, 242, 243** Copyright © 1995 PhotoDisc, Inc. **235** Copyright © Nigel J. Dennis/Photo Researchers, Inc. **236, 241** Copyright © Don Carl Steffen/Photo Researchers, Inc. **250–251** Copyright © 1982 Eve Arnold/Magnum Photos Inc. **284, 287** Detail of *Leg* (1984), Elizabeth Murray. Oil on canvas (two canvases), 117″ × 82″, collection of Mr. and Mrs. Graham Gund, courtesy of Paula Cooper Gallery, New York. Photo by Geoffrey Clements, **311** Detail of *Pep's Car with an Assist from Clyde, Snake and Peabody* (1975), Colleen Browning. Oil on canvas, 36″ × 60 1/4″. **316** B. Paulson/H. Armstrong Roberts. **327** *inset* Copyright © Douglas Burrows/Gamma Liaison. **339** UPI/Bettmann. **359** Courtesy of Donna Antkowiak. **361** John Heseltine/Science Photo Library/Photo Researchers, Inc. **366–367, 374–375** Detail of photo from *Riding the Rails* by Michael Mathers, published by The Harvard Common Press, publishers of Gambit

Books, 1973. **368** Copyright © 1995 John Running. **376** Photo by South Dakota Tourism. **379** Cheyenne Shield. Copyright © The Granger Collection, New York. **380** *left* Copyright © SuperStock; *right* Copyright © Myrleen Ferguson Cate/PhotoEdit. **381** Copyright © 1993, FPG International Corp. **382** *glasses* Copyright © Aaron Jones Studios/Tony Stone Images; *stars* Copyright © Doug Armand/Tony Stone Images. *Grass*: Copyright © James Ranoklev/Tony Stone Images. **404** *inset* Copyright © The Field Museum, Chicago (Neg. #1126). **404–405** Copyright © The Field Museum, Chicago (Neg. # A112803c). Photo by Diane Alexander White. **406** *top* Copyright © The Field Museum, Chicago (Neg. # A112804c). Photo by Diane Alexander White. **408–409** Copyright © The Field Museum, Chicago (Neg. # A112805c). Photo by Diane Alexander White. **410** *center* Copyright © 1994 Claudio Vazquez, courtesy of Turner Publishing. **410–411** Copyright © Colburn/Photoreporters. **414–415** *ibis* Copyright © L. L. T. Rhodes/Animals Animals; *grassy background* H. Armstrong Roberts. **417, 421, 442** H. Armstrong Roberts. **437** Copyright © Tom McCarthy/PhotoEdit. **443** Copyright © Mark Richards/PhotoEdit. **461** A Hindu mandala showing Vishnu seated on the snake Shesha and surrounded by deities. Copyright © The Granger Collection, New York. **462–463** S. Westmorland/Stock Imagery, Denver. **482** Copyright © Hunter/H. Armstrong Roberts. **486–487** Copyright © 1994 Bill Pogue/Sense Interactive Multimedia. **490** Greek merchant ships (540 B.C.), vase painting by an unknown artist. The Granger Collection, New York. **495** Poseidon with his trident (about 100 B.C.), bronze statuette by an unknown Greek artist. Loeb Collection 15, Antikensammlung, Munich, Germany. Photo Copyright © Erich Lessing/Art Resource, New York. **497** Polyphemus (fourth century B.C.), unknown artist. Terra cotta, Département des Antiquités Grecques/Romaines, Musée du Louvre, Paris. Photo Copyright © Erich Lessing/Art Resource, New York. **498** Detail of the blinding of Polyphemus (about 600 B.C.), black-figured early Attic amphora by an unknown artist. Archaeological Museum, Eleusis, Greece. Photo Copyright © Erich Lessing/Art Resource, New York. **501** Oedipus abandoned on Mount Cithaeron by the shepherd. Marble relief from a sarcophagus, Museo Vaticano, Vatican City. Photo Copyright © Erich Lessing/Art Resource. **502** Detail of Odysseus escaping from Polyphemus (510 B.C.), krater by an unknown Greek artist. Badisches Landesmuseum, Karlsruhe, Germany. **505, 509** Copyright © Kevin Fleming/National Geographic Society Image Collection. **506** Reprinted courtesy of Bunny Hoest and *Parade* Magazine. Copyright © 1995. **511** *classical head* Copyright © Steven Edson/Photonica; *evergreen abstract* Copyright © Vera Storman/Tony Stone Images. **512** Odysseus' men turned into swine (fifth century B.C.), vase painting by an unknown Euboean artist. National Archaeological Museum, Athens, Greece. **515** *background* Copyright © Art Wolfe/Tony Stone Images; *foreground* Odysseus threatening Circe (fourth century B.C.), relief on the side panel of a sarcophagus by an unknown Greek artist. Museo dell' Opera del Duomo, Orvieto, Italy. Photo Copyright © Erich Lessing/Art Resource. **516** Circe pursued by Odysseus, pitcher by an unknown artist. Musée du Louvre, Paris, Giraudon/Art Resource, New York. **523** Siren (300 B.C.), Greek sculpture from the Dipylon tomb by an unknown artist. National Archaeological Museum, Athens, Greece, Alinari/Art Resource, New York. **525, 534** *top right* Odysseus' ship passing the Sirens' island south of Capri, Italy (about 150 A.D.), unknown artist. Terra-cotta bas-relief, Campana Collection,

Département des Antiquités Grecques/Romaines, Musée du Louvre, Paris. Photo Copyright © Erich Lessing/Art Resource, New York. **526–527** Scylla (about 300 B.C.) unknown artist. Département des Antiquités Grecques/Romaines, Musée du Louvre, Paris. Photo Copyright © Erich Lessing/Art Resource. **532** Detail of *The Sirens* (1990), Shlomo Katz. Courtesy of Strictly Limited Editions, San Francisco. **540** Parody of *American Gothic* featured on the cover of *Better Retirement Report,* May 1992, published by Phillips Publishing, Inc.; Courtesy of the Davenport (Iowa) Museum of Art. *American Gothic* by Grant Wood, Copyright © 1996 by The Art Institute of Chicago and VAGA, New York, NY. Friends of the American Art Collection. **541** frame Copyright © PhotoDisc, Inc.; *inset, American Gothic* (1930), Grant Wood. Oil on beaver board, 74.3 × 62.4 cm. Friends of American Art Collection, Copyright © 1996 The Art Institute of Chicago and VAGA, New York, NY, 1930.934. Photo Copyright © 1995 by The Art Institute of Chicago, all rights reserved. **544–545** Copyright © Jeff DeBevec/Sense Interactive Multimedia. **545** Illustration Copyright © J. M. Dent and Sons, Ltd., all rights reserved. **548** Penelope mourning (about A.D. 10), terra-cotta plaque by an unknown Roman artist. British Museum, London. Photo Copyright © Erich Lessing/Art Resource, New York. **549** Return of Odysseus (about 470 B.C.) terra-cotta relief by an unknown Greek artist, 7 3/8″ × 10 15/16″, The Metropolitan Museum of Art, Fletcher Fund, 1930 (30.11.9). Copyright © 1982 The Metropolitan Museum of Art. **553** Odysseus slaying Penelope's suitors (380 B.C.), unknown artist. Frieze on the tomb of a Lycian prince, limestone relief from the inner south wall of the Heroon of Goelbasi-Trysa in Lycia, Turkey, 110 cm × 750 cm, Kunsthistorisches Museum, Antikensammlung, Vienna, Austria. Photo Copyright © Erich Lessing/Art Resource. **555** Odysseus with his bow, competing with the suitors (fifth century B.C.) red-figured Attic scyphus by an unknown artist. Staatliche Museen, Antikensammlung, Berlin. Photo Copyright © Erich Lessing/Art Resource, New York. **557** Detail of Nestor and Telemachus (about 300 B.C.), red-figured bowl by an unknown artist. Stiftung Preussischer Kulturbesitz, Berlin. Photo Copyright © Erich Lessing/Art Resource, New York. **558** Agamemnon's ghost with Orestes and Pylades (third century A.D.), unknown Roman artist. Marble relief from a sarcophagus. Museo Vaticano, Vatican City. Copyright © Erich Lessing/Art Resource. **559** Orestes killing Clytemnestra, unknown Roman artist. Marble relief from a sarcophagus. Museo Vaticano, Vatican City. Copyright © Erich Lessing/Art Resource. **561** Nestor and Telemachus (about 300 B.C.), red-figured bowl by an unknown artist. Stiftung Preussischer Kulturbesitz, Berlin. Photo Copyright © Erich Lessing/Art Resource, New York. **565** *tree* Copyright © Eric Wessman/Photonica; *sculpture* Odysseus and Penelope (450 B.C.), unknown artist. Terra-cotta relief, 18.2 × 15.5 cm, Département des Antiquités Grecques/Romaines, Musée du Louvre, Paris. Copyright © Erich Lessing/Art Resource. **570** Detail of *Penelope* (1990), Shlomo Katz. Courtesy of Strictly Limited Editions, San Francisco. **575** *top* Copyright © 1995 PhotoDisc, Inc.; *center* Courtesy of Kwok Chan. **576** *top* Courtesy of Houghton Mifflin Company. **589, 593** Detail of *Autobiographical* (1954), Moses Soyer. Courtesy of ACA Galleries, New York. **604** The Bettmann Archive. **615** Courtesy of Nancy Hoffman Gallery, New York. **622** Copyright © Richard Hutchings/PhotoEdit. **624** P. Degginger/H. Armstrong Roberts. **627** Copyright © Four By Five. **628–629** Copyright © Dr. William J. Jahoda/Photo Researchers, Inc. **644** Detail of *The*

Alchemist's Dilemma (1992), Chuck Wood. Oil on canvas, 39″ × 48″, collection of the artist. **654** *left* Copyright © Don Smetzer/Tony Stone Images; *right* Copyright © Chip Henderson/Tony Stone Images. **654–655** Copyright © 1994 Michael Melford. **658–659, 662, 667** Copyright © Buenos Dias Bildagenturt/Liaison International. **666** Reuters/Bettmann. **680, 687** Copyright © Superstock. **688** Copyright © Craig J. Brown/Gamma Liaison. **692** Detail of *Short Back & Sides* (1977), Mike Dempsey. Acrylic on board, private collection. **700** *center* AP/Wide World Photos, Inc. **701** *inset* Terence Meaden/SIPA. **702** *center* Courtesy of Johnson Books. **707** *inset* AP/Wide World Photos. **721** Copyright © 1991 Ed Wheeler/The Stock Market. **732** Superstock. **734** Copyright © David Fritts/Tony Stone Images. **736** Copyright © Thomas R. Taylor. **754, 775** SuperStock. **759** Directions International, Inc., Los Angeles. **772–773** Copyright © Benali/Olympic Games photo pool/Gamma Liaison. **777** Venice Carnival Mask. The Image Bank, Inc. **781** Copyright © 1995 Jay Maisel. **785** The Bettman Archive. **787** Culver Pictures, Inc. **808** Superstock. **811** Sovfoto/Eastfoto, New York. **818–9** Photo by Robert Vavra, reprinted by permission of the author and the Watkins/Loomis Agency. **821** Copyright © Jose Carrillo. **823** Detail of Photo by Robert Vavra, reprinted by permission of the author and the Watkins/Loomis Agency. **832** Copyright © Art Wolfe/Tony Stone Images. **834** *center* Eric Hiner/National Geographic Image Collection. **835** *top* Press Enterprise/David J. Maialetti. **839** *inset* Copyright © Edward Slater/Southern Stock Photo Agency. **876** Copyright © Robert E. Daemmrich/Tony Stone Images. **878** Copyright © Vince Streano/Tony Stone Images. **884** Copyright © David Young-Wolff/PhotoEdit. **886** Boltin Picture Library. **890** Netscape, Netscape Navigator and the Netscape Communications Corporation Logo are trademarks of Netscape Communications Corporation; *top inset* Courtesy of Los Angeles County Museum of Art; *bottom inset* Courtesy of Smithsonian Institute. **893–895** Screen shots reprinted with permission from Microsoft Corporation. **896** Used with express permission. Adobe and Adobe Illustrator are trademarks of Adobe Systems Incorporated. **897** Copyright © Kim Westerskov/Tony Stone Images. **899** Copyright © Darryl Torckler/Tony Stone Images.

Teacher Review Panels (continued)

Eileen Jones, English Department Chairperson, Spanish River High School, Palm Beach County School District

Jan McClure, Winter Park High School Orange County School District

Wanza Murray, English Department Chairperson (retired), Vero Beach Senior High School, Indian River City School District

Shirley Nichols, Language Arts Curriculum Specialist Supervisor, Marion County School District

Debbie Nostro, Ocoee Middle School, Orange County School District

Barbara Quinaz, Assistant Principal, Horace Mann Middle School, Dade County School District

OHIO

Joseph Bako, English Department Chairperson, Carl Shuler Middle School, Cleveland City School District

Deb Delisle, Language Arts Department Chairperson, Ballard Brady Middle School, Orange School District

Ellen Geisler, English/Language Arts Department Chairperson, Mentor Senior High School, Mentor School District

Dr. Mary Gove, English Department Chairperson, Shaw High School, East Cleveland School District

Loraine Hammack, Executive Teacher of the English Department, Beachwood High School, Beachwood City School District

Sue Nelson, Shaw High School, East Cleveland School District

Mary Jane Reed, English Department Chairperson, Solon High School, Solon City School District

Nancy Strauch, English Department Chairperson, Nordonia High School, Nordonia Hills City School Dictrict

Ruth Vukovich, Hubbard High School, Hubbard Exempted Village School District

TEXAS

Anita Arnold, English Department Chairperson, Thomas Jefferson High School, San Antonio Independent School District

Gilbert Barraza, J.M. Hanks High School, Ysleta School District

Sandi Capps, Dwight D. Eisenhower High School, Alding Independent School District

Judy Chapman, English Department Chairperson, Lawrence D. Bell High School, Hurst-Euless-Bedford School District

Pat Fox, Grapevine High School, Grapevine-Colley School District

LaVerne Johnson, McAllen Memorial High School, McAllen Independent School District

Donna Matsumura, W.H. Adamson High School, Dallas Independent School District

Ruby Mayes, Waltrip High School, Houston Independent School District

Mary McFarland, Amarillo High School, Amarillo Independent School District

Adrienne Thrasher, A.N. McCallum High School, Austin Independent School Distric

CALIFORNIA

Steve Bass, 8th Grade Team Leader, Meadowbrook Middle School, Ponway Unified School District

Cynthia Brickey, 8th Grade Academic Block Teacher, Kastner Intermediate School, Clovis Unified School District

Karen Buxton, English Department Chairperson, Winston Churchill Middle School, San Juan School District

Bonnie Garrett, Davis Middle School, Compton School District

Sally Jackson, Madrona Middle School, Torrance Unified School District

Sharon Kerson, Los Angeles Center for Enriched Studies, Los Angeles Unified School District

Gail Kidd, Center Middle School, Azusa School District

Corey Lay, ESL Department Chairperson, Chester Nimitz Middle School, Los Angeles Unified School District

Myra LeBendig, Forshay Learning Center, Los Angeles Unified School District

Dan Manske, Elmhurst Middle School, Oakland Unified School District

Joe Olague, Language Arts Department Chairperson, Alder Middle School, Fontana School District

Pat Salo, 6th Grade Village Leader, Hidden Valley Middle School, Escondido Elementary School District

Manuscript Reviewers *(continued)*

Beverly Ann Barge, Wasilla High School, Wasilla, Alaska

Louann Bohman, Wilbur Cross High School, New Haven, Connecticut

Rose Mary Bolden, J. F. Kimball High School, Dallas, Texas

Angela Boyd, Andrews High School, Andrews, Texas

Judith H. Briant, Armwood High School, Seffner, Florida

Hugh Delle Broadway, McCullough High School, The Woodlands, Texas

Stephan P. Clarke, Spencerport High School, Spencerport, New York

Dr. Shawn Eric DeNight, Miami Edison Senior High School, Miami, Florida

JoAnna R. Exacoustas, La Serna High School, Whittier, California

Linda Ferguson, English Department Head, Tyee High School, Seattle, Washington

Ellen Geisler, Mentor Senior High School, Mentor, Ohio

Ricardo Godoy, English Department Chairman, Moody High School, Corpus Christi, Texas

Robert Henderson, West Muskingum High School, Zanesville, Ohio

Martha Watt Hosenfeld, English Department Chairperson, Churchville-Chili High School, Churchville, New York

Janice M. Johnson, Assistant Principal, Union High School, Grand Rapids, Michigan

Eileen S. Jones, English Department Chair, Spanish River Community High School, Boca Raton, Florida

Paula S. L'Homme, West Orange High School, Winter Garden, Florida

Bonnie J. Mansell, Downey Adult School, Downey, California

Ruth McClain, Paint Valley High School, Bainbridge, Ohio

Rebecca Miller, Taft High School, San Antonio, Texas

Deborah Lynn Moeller, Western High School, Fort Lauderdale High School

Bobbi Darrell Montgomery, Batavia High School, Batavia, Ohio

Wanza Murray, Vero Beach High School, Vero Beach, Florida

Marjorie M. Nolan, Language Arts Department Head, William M. Raines Sr. High School, Jacksonville, Florida

Julia Pferdehirt, free-lance writer, former Special Education teacher, Middleton, Wisconsin

Pauline Sahakian, English Department Chairperson, San Marcos High School, San Marcos, Texas

Jacqueline Y. Schmidt, Department Chairperson and Coordinator of English, San Marcos High School, San Marcos, Texas

Milinda Schwab, Judson High School, Converse, Texas

John Sferro, Butler High School, Vandalia, Ohio

Faye S. Spangler, Versailles High School, Versailles, Ohio

Rita Stecich, Evergreen Park Community High School, Evergreen Park, Illinois

GayleAnn Turnage, Abeline High School, Abeline, Texas

Ruth Vukovich, Hubbard High School, Hubbard, Ohio

Charlotte Washington, Westwood Middle School, Grand Rapids, Michigan

Tom Watson, Westbridge Academy, Grand Rapids, Michigan

Description for the Discuss activity on page 88 of the student text: The woman pictured on page 89 is Grandma Moses (1860–1961), an American folk artist who started painting when she was in her 70s. Critics praised her simple, colorful paintings, which were based on memories of her own life in the late 1800s. Even though Grandma Moses never had an art lesson, her paintings were displayed in shows and museums throughout the country and are still treasured today.